WRITING SAMPLES

Writing samples in this book show you representative types of writing about literature—from initial notes to a revised, final research paper. Reading these samples along with their commentary should help you understand what is expected when your instructor asks you to write about the literature you are reading.

CRITICAL APPROACHES

This short guide to important critical approaches briefly explains the tools that professional critics and theorists employ when they write about literature.

*new to this edition

THE NORTON INTRODUCTION TO

Literature

SHORTER FOURTEENTH EDITION

Kelly J. Mays

UNIVERSITY OF NEVADA, LAS VEGAS

W. W. NORTON & COMPANY
Independent Publishers Since 1923

W. W. Norton & Company has been independent since its founding in 1923, when William Warder Norton and Mary D. Herter Norton first published lectures delivered at the People's Institute, the adult education division of New York City's Cooper Union. The firm soon expanded its program beyond the Institute, publishing books by celebrated academics from America and abroad. By midcentury, the two major pillars of Norton's publishing program—trade books and college texts—were firmly established. In the 1950s, the Norton family transferred control of the company to its employees, and today—with a staff of five hundred and hundreds of trade, college, and professional titles published each year—W. W. Norton & Company stands as the largest and oldest publishing house owned wholly by its employees.

Editor: Sarah Touborg
Project Editor: Thea Goodrich
Assistant Editor: Emma Peters
Managing Editor, College: Marian Johnson
Managing Editor, College Digital Media: Kim Yi
Production Manager: Stephen Sajdak
Media Editor: Sarah Rose Aquilina
Media Assistant Editor: Jessica Awad
Ebook Production Manager: Kate Barnes
Marketing Research and Strategy Manager: Megan Zwilling
Media Project Editors: Cooper Wilhelm, Diane Cipollone
Design Director: Lissi Sigillo
Book Designer: Pamela Schnitter
Photo Editor: Ted Szczepanski
Photo Research: Julie Tesser
Director of College Permissions: Megan Schindel
Permissions Manager: Bethany Salminen
Permissions Clearer: Josh Garvin
Composition: Westchester Publishing Services
Manufacturing: Lakeside Book Company, Crawfordsville

Permission to use copyrighted material is included in the permissions acknowledgments section of this book, which begins on page A27.

Library of Congress Cataloging-in-Publication Data

Names: Mays, Kelly J., editor.
Title: The Norton introduction to literature / [edited by] Kelly J. Mays.
Description: Shorter fourteenth edition. | New York : W.W. Norton &
    Company, [2022] | Includes bibliographical references and index.
Identifiers: LCCN 2021032429 | **ISBN 9780393870916** (paperback) |
    ISBN 9780393886214 (epub)
Subjects: LCSH: Literature—Collections.
Classification: LCC PN6014 .N67 2022 | DDC 808.8—dc23
LC record available at https://lccn.loc.gov/2021032429

ISBN: 978-0-393-87091-6 (pbk.)

W. W. Norton & Company, Inc., 500 Fifth Avenue, New York, N.Y. 10110
        www.wwnorton.com
W. W. Norton & Company Ltd., 15 Carlisle Street, London W1D 3BS

3 4 5 6 7 8 9 0

Brief Table of Contents

Contents

* new to this edition

* new to this edition

* new to this edition

* new to this edition

* new to this edition

PART TWO Poetry

* new to this edition

* new to this edition

* new to this edition

* new to this edition

* new to this edition

* new to this edition

* new to this edition

* new to this edition

* new to this edition

* new to this edition

* new to this edition

READING MORE POETRY   1187

PART THREE Drama

UNDERSTANDING THE TEXT 1277

EXPLORING CONTEXTS 1390

* new to this edition

* new to this edition

PART FOUR Writing about Literature

* new to this edition

Contents by Topic

For additional suggestions, refer to the Norton Teaching Tools.

EDUCATION & SCHOOLING

ETHNICITY, RACE & CLASS

FAMILY

GENDER

INITIATION & GROWING UP

LANGUAGE

LITERATURE & OTHER ARTS

NATURE & THE NATURAL ENVIRONMENT

POWER

ROMANTIC LOVE & RELATIONSHIPS

SCIENCE, TECHNOLOGY & THE VIRTUAL WORLD

WAR & ITS AFTERMATH

Preface for Instructors

L ike its predecessors, this Fourteenth Edition of *The Norton Introduction to Literature* offers in a single volume a complete course in reading literature and writing about it. A teaching anthology focused on the actual tasks, challenges, and questions typically faced by students and instructors, *The Norton Introduction to Literature* offers practical advice to help students transform their first impressions of literary works into fruitful discussions and meaningful critical essays, and it helps students and instructors together tackle the complex questions at the heart of literary study.

The *Norton Introduction to Literature* has been revised with an eye to providing a book that is as flexible, inclusive, and useful as possible—adaptable to many different teaching styles and individual preferences—and that also conveys the excitement at the heart of literature itself.

NEW TO THE FOURTEENTH EDITION

Fifty-nine new selections, forty-six by contemporary writers

Featuring ten new stories, over forty-five new poems, and two new plays, as well as a new section on the prose poem, the Fourteenth Edition of *The Norton Introduction to Literature* is the most inclusive anthology of its kind. Here, you will find exciting, highly teachable new selections by long-familiar, deservedly beloved writers—including Edgar Allan Poe's "The Black Cat," William Shakespeare's *Othello*, "mouse poems" by Robert Burns and Anna Laetitia Barbauld, and greatly expanded coverage of Gwendolyn Brooks and Louise Erdrich. But you will find, too, inspiring, vibrant, thought-provoking work by a diverse array of (mostly contemporary) authors utterly new to the anthology—including Chimamanda Ngozi Adichie, Isabel Allende, Sandra Cisneros, Haruki Murakami, Lynn Nottage, Zadie Smith, and Yiyun Li in Fiction and Drama, and Reginald Dwayne Betts, Richard Blanco, Lorna Dee Cervantes, Ada Limón, Campbell McGrath, Octavio Paz, Evie Shockley, Danez Smith, and Pulitzer Prize winners Natalie Diaz and Claudia Rankine in Poetry. Thanks to these and other additions we have greatly increased, broadened, and deepened representation of Indigenous, Latina/o, Black, and both Asian and Asian American voices and perspectives.

Many of our new selections speak to issues of immediate relevance and concern, from (social) media, gaming, and googling to quarantines (past and present), animal rights, and immigration, to de-industrialization, political polarization, and systemic racism. But in choosing new selections, we have, more than ever, sought to balance—and to help students appreciate—the simultaneously timeless and timely aspects of both classic and contemporary literature and its capacity to humanize and even transform us by encouraging us to consider diverse perspectives and experiences, states of mind, and feeling.

For ease of reference, all new selections are indicated with an asterisk in the table of contents.

New and updated albums

One of the most innovative and popular features of *The Norton Introduction to Literature* are albums inviting students to explore in more depth specific formal elements and contextual reading/writing strategies by comparing works linked by author, subgenre, topic, setting, and so on. The Fourteenth Edition offers eighteen such albums. These include albums of proven value in the classroom now enriched with new works by Louise Erdrich (Telling Stories), Zadie Smith (The Future), Sandra Cisneros (Cross-Cultural Encounters), Octavio Paz (The Art of [Reading] Poetry; Haiku), and Alice Dunbar-Nelson and Saeed Jones (Exploring Gender). But we are also excited to offer three entirely new albums:

- In keeping with our tradition of offering deep representation of select authors, the Fourteenth Edition now includes three stories by Louise Erdrich. A new album devoted to this acclaimed writer's work and career pairs classroom favorite "Love Medicine" with the more recent "The Years of My Birth," while inviting students to also consider Erdrich's "The Plague of Doves," newly added to the Telling Stories album.
- The first of two new albums devoted to enhancing students' experience and appreciation of poetry as a living, ever-evolving, multifaceted act and art, The Golden Shovel complements and expands upon the Sonnet and Haiku albums it follows by introducing a fixed form invented merely a decade rather than centuries ago. Originally created by Terrance Hayes in homage to Gwendolyn Brooks, the golden shovel is simultaneously a reverse acrostic and an act of poetic remixing or sampling of sorts, in which a line from an extant poem supplies the end words of an entirely new one. The album thus pairs golden shovels by Hayes, Julia Alvarez, and other contemporary poets with the Brooks poems that inspired them. (To complement this album, our "External Form" chapter also now includes abecedarians by Natalie Diaz and Evie Shockley, as well as a concrete poem from Justin Phillip Reed's National Book Award–winning *Indecency*.)
- The second of our new Poetry albums, #BlackLivesMatter samples some of the very best of the many poems and essays spawned by the largest protest movement in U.S. history, including work by Reginald Dwayne Betts, Danez Smith, Patricia Smith, Claudia Rankine, Kevin Young, and Tracy K. Smith. Following our chapter on the Harlem Renaissance, the album provides students with a framework for considering both how the two movements and bodies of poetry compare and how #BlackLivesMatter poetry reworks and reinvigorates the conventions of both protest poetry and elegy.

New sample writing, writing pedagogy, and critical approaches

Recent editions of *The Norton Introduction to Literature* greatly expanded and improved resources for student writers, including a "Quotation, Citation, and Documentation" chapter that, in keeping with the latest MLA guidelines (9th ed., 2021), explains the elements that comprise the work-cited entry and the principles by which any entry is assembled, rather than presenting a dizzying menu of entry types for student writers to pore through and copy. Here, as throughout "Writing about Literature," we demonstrate with brief examples drawn from the work of both student and professional writers.

In the Fourteenth Edition, new student writing on Isabel Allende's "And of Clay Are We Created" and on Robert Burns's "To a Mouse" and Anna Laetitia Barbauld's "The Mouse's Petition" bring the total of complete samples of student writing to nineteen, including notes, response papers, essays analyzing one work or comparing several, and research essays exploring critical and/or historical contexts.

As important and as always, by including more and more lengthy extracts from published literary criticism than any other textbook of its kind, *The Norton Introduction to Literature* offers student writers both a trove of sources to draw on in articulating their own responses to particular works and models of the sorts of questions, strategies, and "moves" that power effective reading and writing about literature. New to the Fourteenth Edition, a stimulating excerpt from Helen Morales's award-winning *Antigone Rising* (2020) gives students new insights into this ancient play's contemporary relevance by effectively modeling presentist, as well as historicist, reading and writing strategies.

In the same spirit, our Critical Approaches appendix now includes brief discussions of two newly relevant topics—intersectionality and critical race theory.

NEW AND EXPANDED RESOURCES FOR STUDENTS AND INSTRUCTORS

InQuizitive for *The Norton Introduction to Literature*

Brand-new to the Fourteenth Edition is InQuizitive, an adaptive, easy-to-use learning tool with a game-like twist that motivates students to complete the reading. Questions progress from comprehension to analysis and are accompanied by answer-specific feedback that models close reading skills. With modules on frequently taught works, the three major genres, and writing about literature, InQuizitive gives students the practice and tools they need to make the most of class discussion and assignments. Easily integrated with any learning management system, InQuizitive allows scores to flow right to your LMS gradebook, making it a snap to assign.

As with all of the resources accompanying the text, instructors played a crucial role in developing and authoring InQuizitive. Authors include Jeannine Morgan (St. Johns River State College), Jeff Grieneisen (State College of Florida), and Ben Cooper (Lindenwood University).

Close Reading Workshops

Based on an innovative and proven approach to close reading developed at the University of Texas at Austin, these workshops help students to paraphrase, observe, contextualize, analyze, and create an argument based on their close reading of a short excerpt. Each of the more than twenty workshops focuses on a passage from an often-taught work in the text and includes a series of guided writing prompts. Auto-graded at 100% for completion, with the ability for instructors to change students' scores if you so choose (all scores flow back to the LMS gradebook), the workshops provide students with valuable low-stakes writing practice.

The Norton Teaching Tools

The Norton Teaching Tools site for *The Norton Introduction to Literature* is your first stop when looking for creative and engaging resources to refresh your syllabus or design a new one. Dynamic and experienced instructors have created the content, which is organized and easily sortable by genre and type. Content includes teaching notes, discussion questions, writing prompts, lecture PowerPoints, videos, images, and audio links. The site also features tips and best practices for assigning Norton's digital learning tools, including sample syllabi and recommendations for how to get the most out of assigning InQuizitive. Jason Snart (College of DuPage) contributed to the site.

HALLMARK FEATURES OF *THE NORTON INTRODUCTION TO LITERATURE*

Although this Fourteenth Edition contains much that is new or refashioned, the essential features of the text have remained consistent over many editions:

Diverse selections with broad appeal

Because readings are the central component of any literature class, my most important task has been to select a rich array of appealing and challenging literary works. Among the 65 stories, 300 poems, and 12 plays in *The Norton Introduction to Literature*, readers will find selections by well-established and emerging voices alike, representing a broad range of times, places, cultural perspectives, and styles. The readings are excitingly diverse in terms of subject and style as well as authorship and national origin. In selecting and presenting literary texts, my top priorities continue to be quality as well as pedagogical relevance and usefulness. I have integrated the new with the old and the experimental with the canonical, believing that contrast and variety help students recognize and respond to the unique features of any literary work. In this way, I aim to help students and instructors alike approach the unfamiliar by way of the familiar (and vice versa).

Helpful and unobtrusive editorial matter

As always, the instructional material before and after each selection avoids dictating any particular interpretation or response, instead highlighting essential terms and concepts in order to make the literature that follows more accessible to student readers. Questions and writing suggestions help readers apply general concepts to specific readings in order to develop, articulate, refine, and defend their own responses. As in all Norton anthologies, works are here annotated with a light hand, with the goal of providing information, not interpretation.

An introduction to the study of literature

To introduce students to fiction, poetry, and drama is to open up a complex field of study with a long history. The Introduction addresses many of the questions that students may have about the nature of literature as well as the practice of literary criticism. By exploring some of the most compelling reasons for reading and writing about literature, we aim to dispel much of the mystery about matters of method and to provide students with a sense of the issues and opportunities that lie ahead as they study literature. As in earlier editions, I encourage student engagement with individual authors and their perspectives by way of "Authors on Their Work" features as well as single-author chapters and albums.

Thoughtful guidance for writing about literature

The Fourteenth Edition integrates opportunities for student writing at each step of the course, highlighting the mastery of skills for students at every level. "Reading, Responding, Writing" chapters at the beginning of each genre unit offer students concrete advice about how to transform careful reading into productive and insightful writing. Sample questions for each work or about each element (e.g., "Questions about Character") provide exercises for answering these questions or for applying new concepts to particular works, and examples of student writing demonstrate how a student's notes on a story or poem may be developed into a response paper or essay.

The constructive, step-by-step approach to the writing process is thoroughly demonstrated in the "Writing about Literature" section. As in the chapters introducing concepts and literary selections, the first steps presented in the writing section are simple and straightforward, outlining the basic formal elements common to essays—thesis, structure, and so on. Following these steps encourages students to approach the essay both as a distinctive genre with its own elements and as an accessible form of writing with a clear purpose. From here, I walk students through the writing process: how to choose a topic, gather evidence, and develop an argument; the methods of writing a research essay; and the mechanics of effective quotation and responsible citation and documentation. Also featured is a sample research essay annotated to call attention to important features of effective student writing.

A comprehensive approach to literature's contexts

The Fourteenth Edition not only offers expanded resources for interpreting and writing about literature but also extends the perspectives from which students can view particular authors and works. One of the greatest strengths of *The Norton Introduction to Literature* has been its exploration of the relation between literary texts and a variety of contexts. "Author's Work as Context," "Cultural and Historical Contexts," and "Critical Contexts" chapters, as well as supplementary albums, serve as mini-casebooks containing a wealth of material for in-depth, context-focused reading and writing assignments.

The "Critical Approaches" section provides an overview of contemporary critical theory and its terminology and is useful as an introduction, a refresher, or a preparation for further exploration.

A sensible and teachable organization

The accessible format of *The Norton Introduction to Literature*, which has worked so well for teachers and students for many editions, remains the same. Each genre is approached in three logical steps. Fiction, for example, is introduced by the chapter "Fiction: Reading, Responding, Writing," which treats the purpose and nature of fiction, the reading experience, and the steps one takes to begin writing about fiction. This feature is followed by the six-chapter section called "Understanding the Text," which concentrates on the genre's key elements. Appearing throughout are albums that build on the chapters they follow, inviting students to compare stories narrated by protagonists whom others deem monsters, featuring initiation plots or futuristic settings, and so on. The third section, "Exploring Contexts" suggests ways to embrace a work of literature by considering various literary, temporal, and cultural contexts. "Reading More Fiction," the final component in the Fiction section, is a reservoir of additional readings for independent study or a different approach. The Poetry and Drama sections, in turn, follow exactly the same organizational format as Fiction.

The book's arrangement allows movement from narrower to broader frameworks, from simpler to more complex questions and issues, and mirrors the way people read—wanting to learn more as they experience more. At the same time, I have worked hard to ensure that no section, chapter, album, or literary selection depends on any other, allowing individual teachers to pick and choose which to assign and in what order.

Deep representation of select authors

The Norton Introduction to Literature offers a range of opportunities for in-depth study of noted authors. "Author's Work" chapters and albums—on Flannery O'Connor, Louise Erdrich, Adrienne Rich, Emily Dickinson, Pat Mora, W. B. Yeats, and William Shakespeare—encourage students to make substantive connections among works from different phases of a writer's career, guiding them to ask both what binds such works together into a distinctive oeuvre and how a writer's approach and outlook evolves in and over time. But throughout the volume, students will encounter, too, at least two works each by a diverse array of other authors including William Faulkner, Tim O'Brien, Julia Alvarez, Lorna Dee Cervantes, Joy Harjo, Langston Hughes, Judith Ortiz Cofer, Danez Smith, Tracy K. Smith, and the fifty-six other poets whose biographies appear at the end of the Poetry section. "Critical Contexts" chapters on "The Things They Carried" (and *The Things They Carried*), on "Daddy," and on *Antigone* encourage students to delve deeper into specific works by Tim O'Brien, Sylvia Plath, and Sophocles by considering the rich and varied commentary, even controversy, those authors' works have inspired. "Cultural and Historical Context" chapters and albums—featuring stories by Susan Glaspell, Charlotte Perkins Gilman, and Kate Chopin; poetry and prose of the Harlem Renaissance and #BlackLivesMatter; and Lorraine Hansberry's *A Raisin in the Sun*—remind students that authors and their works also both emerge out of and shape the contours and controversies of particular moments and milieus.

ACKNOWLEDGMENTS

In working on this book, I have been guided by teachers and students in my own and other English departments who have used this textbook and responded with comments and suggestions. Thanks to such capable help, I am hopeful that this book will continue to offer a solid and stimulating introduction to the experience of literature.

This project continually reminds me why I follow the vocation of teaching literature, which after all is a communal rather than a solitary calling. Since its inception, *The Norton Introduction to Literature* has been very much a collaborative effort. I am grateful for the opportunity to carry on the work begun by the late Carl Bain and Jerome Beaty, as well as brilliant former co-editors Paul Hunter and Alison Booth and former in-house editors Pete Simon and Spencer Richardson-Jones. Their wisdom and intelligence have had a profound effect on me, and their stamp will endure on this and all future editions of this book.

This edition, like the last, I am thankful—as I think all users will be—for the perspective and insight editor Sarah Touborg brings to this project. With admirable skill and great energy, assistant editor Emma Peters managed myriad manuscript details. I am grateful to project editor Thea Goodrich and copyeditor Alice Gribbin, photo editor Ted Szczepanski and researcher Julie Tesser, production manager Stephen Sajdak, and media editor Sarah Rose Aquilina, who brought together the innovative array of web resources and other pedagogical tools. Huge, heartfelt thanks, too, to Kimberly Bowers, the very best, brightest, and most tireless of marketing managers, and to Megan Zwilling, who takes the reins on this Fourteenth Edition.

In putting together the Fourteenth Edition, I have accrued debts to many friends and colleagues, including Jonathan D. Andersen, of Quinebaug Valley Community College; Ralph Hayward, of Ocean County College; and other users of the Thirteenth Edition who generously reached out to point out its errors, as well as successes. Special thanks to Philip Gabriel, of the University of Arizona, for generously helping us secure permission to use his wonderful translation of Haruki Murakami's "Barn Burning"; to UNLV graduates Zoeie Neal and Renee Maalouf for allowing us to reprint their thoughtful work on Allende, Burns, and Barbauld; to Todd Martinez for both (re)introducing me to Isabel Allende's "And of Clay Are We Created" and Lorna Dee Cervantes's *Emplumada* and allowing me to draw, in so many other ways, on his expertise and patience; to my nephew Noah Jernigan, Northern Michigan University fine arts major and voracious reader, for inspiring more than one apt (and funny) example here; to the gifted Sin á Tes Souhaits, current Poet Laureate of Clark County, Nevada; to my colleagues Megan Becker, Kaitlin Clinnin, and Gary Totten, for sage advice on literary selections and much else; and to my UNLV students, whose strong-mindedness, perseverance, and passion inspire and challenge me every day. Finally, I am peculiarly aware this edition of other debts more enduring, enormous, and personal: to my father, Bill Mays (1930–2020), one of my first and best teachers; to my inspirations, my rocks, my family, through everything, Nelda Mays, Hugh Jackson, and Mary Jean Corbett; and to Ellis Lloyd, the (AP®) English teacher extraordinaire and extraordinary human being who long ago first launched me on this path and made me believe I could walk it.

Reviewers

The Norton Introduction to Literature continues to thrive because so many teachers and students generously take the time to provide valuable feedback and suggestions. Thank you to all who have done so. This book is equally your making. The authors and editors at W. W. Norton are grateful to the many instructors across the country whose astute feedback helped shape this new edition of *The Norton Introduction to Literature* and its digital resources: Savanna Andrasian (Bakersfield College), Richard Barakat (El Paso Community College), Amber Barnes (Trinity Valley Community College), Darlene Beaman (Lone Star College), Mary Bernal (San Antonio College), Kathleen Anne Bombach (El Paso Community College), Robin Bonner (Montgomery County Community College), David Bordelon (Ocean

County College), Douglas Branch (Southwest Tennessee Community College), Sandra Burr (Northern Michigan University), Brandy Chambless (University of West Georgia), Jessica Chapman (Caldwell Community College and Technical Institute), Annaliese Chaudhuri (Stephen F. Austin State University), Monica Chiu (University of New Hampshire), Ed Coursey (Hillsborough Community College–Dale Mabry Campus), Jennifer Dellner (Ocean County College), Amber Durfield (Citrus College), Catherine Edelmann (Santa Monica College), Karen Feldman (Seminole State College), Africa Fine (Palm Beach State College), Colleen Flanagan (Seminole State College), Sara Forti (Northern Marianas College), Kimberly George (Temple College), Jeff Gibbons (United States Military Academy West Point), Ronnie Gladden (Cincinnati State), Jeff Grieneisen (State College of Florida), Emily Grigg (Spartanburg Community College), Tracie Grimes (Bakersfield College), Richard Hartnett (Trident Technical College), Dallas Hulsey (New Mexico Junior College), Gregory Iannarella (Seton Hall University), Avery Johnson (Texas Southern University), Wesley Johnson (Pasco-Hernando State College), Lisa Jones (Pasco-Hernando State College), Mawusi Kambui (Georgia Military College), Scott Keim (Lehigh Carbon Community College), Keri Lamb (Chattanooga State Community College), Lynn Brown Lamere (Wallace Community College), Virve Lane (Ocean County College), Minerva Laveaga (El Paso Community College), Leslie Leinbach (Albright College), Jillian Linster (University of South Dakota), Christina Loucks (Columbia State Community College), Robert Machado (Lebanon Valley College), Leonard Macias (Paradise Valley Community College), Terri Mann (El Paso Community College), Kara Manning (SUNY Schenectady), Michael Mendoza (Seminole State College–Oviedo), Jeannine Morgan (St. Johns River State College), Roxanne Morgan (American River College), Michael O'Connor (Onondaga Community College), Clair Juenell Owens (Vincennes University), Marilyn Painter (Florida State College at Jacksonville), Sharon Pajka (Gallaudet University), Sioux Patashnik (Seton Hall University), Mary Payne (Wallace Community College), T. Madison Peschock (Ocean County College), Jessica Pingitore (Ocean County College), Tammy Powley (Indian River State College), Yasmin Ramirez (El Paso Community College), Paula Rash (Caldwell Community College and Technical Institute), Dana Resente (Montgomery County Community College), Jim Richey (Tyler Junior College), Aline Rogalski (Ocean County College), Jeffrey Rubinstein (Hillsborough Community College–Dale Mabry Campus), Courtney Ruffner (State College of Florida–Bradenton Campus), Kelly Shea (Seton Hall University), Jason Shrontz (Gogebic Community College), Carmen Simpson (St. Petersburg College), Jason Snart (College of DuPage), Catherine Stephens (State College of Florida–Bradenton Campus), Kristyn Stout (Ocean County College), S. Asher Sund (Ventura College), Jayanti Tamm (Ocean County College), Edwin Turner (St. Johns River State College), Richard Turner (Ozarks Technical Community College), Arturo Valdespino (El Paso Community College), Tondalaya VanLear (Dabney S. Lancaster Community College), Adriana Varga (Indiana University–Purdue University Indianapolis), Gail Vignola (Seton Hall University), Adam Walsh (Northern Marianas College), Rachael Warmington (Seton Hall University), Keith Wilhite (Siena College).

Introduction

In the opening chapters of Charles Dickens's novel *Hard Times* (1854), the aptly named Thomas Gradgrind warns the teachers and pupils at his "model" school to avoid using their imaginations. "Teach these boys and girls nothing but Facts. Facts alone are wanted in life," exclaims Mr. Gradgrind. To press his point, Mr. Gradgrind asks "girl number twenty," Sissy Jupe, the daughter of a circus performer, to define a horse. When she cannot, Gradgrind turns to Bitzer, a pale, spiritless boy who "looked as though, if he were cut, he would bleed white." A "model" student of this "model" school, Bitzer gives exactly the kind of definition to satisfy Mr. Gradgrind:

> Quadruped. Graminivorous. Forty teeth, namely, twenty-four grinders, four eye-teeth, and twelve incisive. Sheds coat in spring; in marshy countries, sheds hoofs.

Anyone who has any sense of what a horse is rebels against Bitzer's lifeless picture of that animal and against the "Gradgrind" view of reality. As these first **scenes** of *Hard Times* lead us to expect, in the course of the novel the fact-grinding Mr. Gradgrind learns that human beings cannot live on facts alone; that it is dangerous to stunt the faculties of imagination and feeling; that, in the words of one of the novel's more lovable characters, "People must be amused." Through the downfall of an exaggerated enemy of the imagination, Dickens reminds us why we like and even *need* to read literature.

What Is Literature?

But what is literature? Before you opened this book, you probably could guess that it would contain the sorts of short stories, poems, and plays you have encountered in English classes or in the literature section of a library or bookstore. But why are some written works called *literature* whereas others are not? And who gets to decide? *The American Heritage Dictionary of the English Language* offers a number of definitions for the word *literature*, one of which is "imaginative or creative writing, especially of recognized artistic value." In this book, we adopt a version of that definition by focusing on fiction, poetry, and drama—the three major kinds (or **genres**)[1] of "imaginative or creative writing" that form the heart of literature as it has been taught in schools and universities for over a century. Many of the works we have chosen to include are already ones "of recognized artistic value" and thus belong to what scholars call the **canon**, a select, if much-debated and ever-evolving, list of the most highly and widely esteemed works. Though quite a few of the literary texts we include are too new to have earned that status, they, too, have already drawn praise, and some have even generated controversy.

Certainly it helps to bear in mind what others have thought of a literary work. Yet one of this book's primary goals is to get you to think for yourself, as well as

1. Throughout this book, terms included in the glossary appear in bold font.

1

communicate with others, about what "imaginative writing" and "artistic value" are or might be and thus about what counts as literature. What makes a story or poem different from an essay, a newspaper editorial, or a technical manual? For that matter, what makes a published, canonical story like James Baldwin's SONNY'S BLUES[2] both like and unlike the sorts of stories we tell each other every day? What about so-called *oral literature*, such as the **fables** and **folktales** that circulated by word of mouth for hundreds of years before they were ever written down? or published works such as comic strips and graphic novels that rely little, if at all, on the written word? or Harlequin romances, television shows, and the stories you collaborate in making when you play a video game? Likewise, how is Shakespeare's poem MY MISTRESS' EYES ARE NOTHING LIKE THE SUN both like and unlike a verse you might find in a Hallmark card?

Today, literature departments offer courses in many of these forms of expression, expanding the realm of literature far beyond the limits of the dictionary definition. An essay, a song lyric, a screenplay, a supermarket romance, a novel by Toni Morrison or William Faulkner, and a poem by Langston Hughes or Emily Dickinson—each may be read and interpreted in *literary ways* that yield insight and pleasure. What makes the literary way of reading different from pragmatic reading is, as scholar Louise Rosenblatt explains, that it does not focus "on what

2. Titles of poems, stories, and other literary selections included in this book are formatted in small caps when those titles first appear in the body of any chapter and whenever they appear in a question or writing suggestion. Otherwise, all titles are formatted in accordance with MLA 2021 guidelines.

will remain [. . .] *after* the reading—the information to be acquired, the logical solution to a problem, the actions to be carried out," but rather on "what happens *during* [. . .] reading." The difference between pragmatic and literary reading, in other words, resembles the difference between a journey that is only about reaching a destination and one that is just as much about fully experiencing the ride.

In the pages of this book, you will find cartoons, song lyrics, folktales, and stories and plays that have spawned movies. Through this inclusiveness, we do not intend to suggest that there are no distinctions among these various forms of expression or between a good story, poem, or play and a bad one; rather, we want to get you thinking, talking, and writing both about what the key differences and similarities among these forms are and what makes one work a better example of its genre than another. Sharpening your skills at these peculiarly intensive and responsive sorts of reading and interpretation is a primary purpose of this book and of most literature courses.

Another goal of inclusiveness is to remind you that literature doesn't just belong in a textbook or a classroom, even if textbooks and classrooms are essential means for expanding your knowledge of the literary terrain and of the concepts and techniques essential to thoroughly enjoying and analyzing a broad range of literary forms. You may or may not be the kind of person who always takes a novel when you go to the beach or writes a poem about your experience when you get back home. You may or may not have taken literature courses before. Yet you already have a good deal of literary experience and expertise, as well as much more to discover about literature. A major aim of this book is to make you more conscious of how and to what end you might use the tools you already possess and to add many new ones to your tool belt.

What Does Literature Do?

One quality that may well differentiate stories, poems, and plays from other kinds of writing is that they help us move beyond and probe beneath abstractions by giving us concrete, vivid particulars. Rather than talking *about* things, they bring them to life for us by *representing* experience, and so they *become* an experience for us—one that engages our emotions, our imagination, and all of our senses, as well as our intellects. As the British poet Matthew Arnold put it more than a century ago, "The interpretations of science do not give us this intimate sense of objects as the interpretations of poetry give it; they appeal to a limited faculty, and not to the whole man. It is not Linnaeus [. . .] who gives us the true sense of animals, or water, or plants, who seizes their secret for us, who makes us participate in their life; it is Shakespeare [. . .] Wordsworth [. . .] Keats."

To test Arnold's theory, compare the *American Heritage Dictionary*'s rather dry definition of *literature* with the following poem, in which John Keats describes his first encounter with a specific literary work—George Chapman's translation of the *Iliad* and the *Odyssey*, two **epics** by the ancient Greek poet Homer.

JOHN KEATS
On First Looking into Chapman's Homer[3]

Much have I traveled in the realms of gold,
And many goodly states and kingdoms seen;
Round many western islands have I been
Which bards in fealty to Apollo[4] hold.
5 Oft of one wide expanse had I been told
That deep-browed Homer ruled as his demesne;
Yet did I never breathe its pure serene[5]
Till I heard Chapman speak out loud and bold:
Then felt I like some watcher of the skies
10 When a new planet swims into his ken;[6]
Or like stout Cortez[7] when with eagle eyes
He stared at the Pacific—and all his men
Looked at each other with a wild surmise—
Silent, upon a peak in Darien.

1816

Keats makes us *see* literature as a "wide expanse" by greatly developing this **metaphor** and complementing it with **similes** likening reading to the sighting of a "new planet" and the first glimpse of an undiscovered ocean. More important, he shows us what literature means and why it matters by allowing us to share with him the subjective experience of reading and the complex sensations it inspires—the dizzying exhilaration of discovery; the sense of power, accomplishment, and pride that comes of achieving something difficult; the wonder we feel in those rare moments when a much-anticipated experience turns out to be even better than we had imagined it would be.

It isn't the definitions of words alone that bring this experience to life for us as we read Keats's poem, but also their sensual qualities—the way the words look, sound, and even feel in our mouths because of the particular way they are put together on the page. The sensation of excitement—of a racing heart and mind—is reproduced *in* us as we read the poem. For example, notice how the **lines** in the middle run into each other, but then Keats forces us to slow down at the poem's end—stopped short by that dash and comma in the poem's final lines, just as Cortez and his men are when they reach the edge of the known world and peer into the vastness that lies beyond.

What Are the Genres of Literature?

The conversation that is literature, like the conversation about literature, invites all comers, requiring neither a visa nor a special license of any kind. Yet literary studies, like all disciplines, has developed its own terminology and its own sys-

3. George Chapman's were among the most famous Renaissance translations of Homer; he completed his *Iliad* in 1611, his *Odyssey* in 1616. Keats wrote the sonnet after being led to Chapman by a former teacher and reading the *Iliad* all night long.
4. Greek god of poetry and music. *Fealty*: literally, the loyalty owed by a vassal to his feudal lord.
5. Atmosphere.
6. Range of vision; awareness.
7. Actually, Balboa; he first viewed the Pacific from Darien, in Panama.

tems of classification. Helping you understand and effectively use both is a major purpose of this book.

Some essential literary terms are common, everyday words used in a special way in the conversation about literature. A case in point, perhaps, is the term *literary criticism*, as well as the closely related term *literary critic*. Despite the usual connotations of the word *criticism*, **literary criticism** is called *criticism* not because it is negative or corrective but rather because those who write criticism ask searching, analytical, "critical" questions about the works they read. Literary criticism is both the process of interpreting and commenting on literature and the result of that process. If you write an essay on the play FENCES, the poetry of John Keats, or the development of the short story in the 1990s, you engage in literary criticism. By writing the essay, you've become a literary critic.

Similarly, when we classify works of literature, we use terms that may be familiar to you but have specific meanings in a literary context. All academic disciplines have systems of classification, or taxonomies, as well as jargon. Biologists, for example, classify all organisms into a series of ever-smaller, more specific categories: *kingdom*, *phylum* or *division*, *class*, *order*, *family*, *genus*, and *species*. Classification and comparison are just as essential in the study of literature. We expect a poem to work in a certain way, for example, when we know from the outset that it *is* a poem and not, say, a factual news report or a short story. And—whether consciously or not—we compare it, as we read, to other poems we've read. If we know, further, that the poem was first published in eighteenth-century Japan, we expect it to work differently from one that appeared in the latest *New Yorker*. Indeed, we often choose what to read, just as we choose what movie to see, based on the "class" or "order" of book or movie we like or what we are in the mood for that day—horror or comedy, action or science fiction.

As these examples suggest, we generally tend to categorize literary works in two ways: (1) on the basis of contextual factors, especially historical and cultural context—that is, when, by whom, and where it was produced (as in *nineteenth-century literature*, *the literature of the Harlem Renaissance*, *American literature*, or *Asian American literature*)—and (2) on the basis of formal textual features. For the latter type of classification, the one we focus on in this book, the key term is *genre*, which simply means, as the *Oxford English Dictionary* tells us, "A particular style or category of works of art; esp. a type of literary work characterized by a particular form, style, or purpose."

Applied rigorously, *genre* refers to the largest categories around which this book is organized—**fiction**, **poetry**, and **drama** (as well as **nonfiction** prose). The word *subgenre* applies to smaller divisions within a genre, and the word *kind* to divisions within a subgenre. *Subgenres* of fiction include the **novel**, the **novella**, and the **short story**. *Kinds* of novels, in turn, include the **bildungsroman** and the epistolary novel. Similarly, important subgenres of nonfiction include the essay, as well as **biography** and autobiography; a memoir is a particular kind of autobiography, and so on.

However, the terms of literary criticism are not so fixed or so consistently, rigorously used as biologists' are. You will often see the word *genre* applied both much more narrowly—referring to the novel, for example, or even to a kind of novel such as the historical novel.

The way we classify a work depends on which aspects of its form or style we concentrate on, and categories may overlap. When we divide fiction, for example, into the subgenres novel, novella, and short story, we take the length of the works as the salient aspect. (Novels are much longer than short stories.) But other fictional subgenres—detective fiction, **gothic fiction**, **historical fiction**, science fiction, and even **romance**—are based on the types of **plots**, **characters**, **settings**, and so on that are customarily featured in these works. These latter categories may include works from all the other, length-based categories. There are, after all, gothic novels (think Stephenie Meyer), as well as gothic short stories (think Edgar Allan Poe).

A few genres or modes even cut across the boundaries dividing poetry, fiction, drama, and nonfiction. A prime example is **satire**—any literary work (whether poem, play, fiction, or nonfiction) "in which prevailing vices and follies are held up to ridicule" (*Oxford English Dictionary*). Examples of satire include poems such as Alexander Pope's *Dunciad* (1728); plays, movies, and television shows, from Molière's *Tartuffe* (1664) to Stanley Kubrick's *Dr. Strangelove* (1964) to *South Park*, *The Office*, and Jordan Peele's *Get Out* (2017); works of fiction like Jonathan Swift's *Gulliver's Travels* (1726) and Voltaire's *Candide* (1759); and works of nonfiction such as Swift's "A Modest Proposal" (1729). Three other major genres that cross the borders between fiction, poetry, drama, and nonfiction are **parody**, **pastoral**, and romance.

Individual works can thus belong simultaneously to multiple generic categories or observe some **conventions** of a genre without being an example of that genre in any simple or straightforward way. The Old English poem *Beowulf* is an **epic** and, because it's written in verse, a poem. Yet because (like all epics) it narrates a story, it is also a work of fiction in the more general sense of that term.

Given this complexity, the system of literary genres can be puzzling, especially to the uninitiated. Used well, however, classification schemes are among the most essential and effective tools we use to understand and enjoy just about everything, including literature.

Why Read Literature?

Because there has never been and never will be absolute agreement about where exactly the boundaries between one literary genre and another should be drawn or even about what counts as literature at all, it might be more useful from the outset to focus on *why* we look at particular forms of expression.

Over the ages, people have sometimes dismissed *all* literature or at least certain genres as a luxury, a frivolous pastime, even a sinful indulgence. Plato famously banned poetry from his ideal republic on the grounds that it tells beautiful lies that "feed and water our passions" rather than our reason. Thousands of years later, the influential eighteenth-century philosopher Jeremy Bentham decried the "magic art" of literature as doing a good deal of "mischief" by "stimulating our passions" and "exciting our prejudices." One of Bentham's contemporaries—a minister—blamed the rise of immorality, irreligion, and even prostitution on the increasing popularity of that particular brand of literature called the novel.

Today, many Americans express their sense of literature's insignificance by simply not reading it: According to a 2016 National Endowment for the Arts (NEA) report, only 43 percent of U.S. adults read at least one work of imaginative literature in the previous year, the lowest percentage since NEA began its annual surveys in 1982. Though the report also demonstrates that women are significantly more likely to read literature than men, as are college graduates, the drops in the literary reading rate occurred across the board, among people of all ages, races, and educational levels. Even if they very much enjoy reading on their own, many contemporary U.S. college students nonetheless hesitate to study or major in literature for fear that their degree won't provide them with marketable credentials, knowledge, or skills.

Yet that is far from the whole story. As a 2018 NEA report affirmed, poetry reading actually increased 76 percent among U.S. adults between 2012 and 2017, with the largest increase—an astonishing 100 percent—occurring among eighteen- to twenty-four-year-olds. Like respondents to that survey, millions of people around America and the globe find both reading literature and discussing it with others to be enjoyable, meaningful, even essential activities. English thrives as a major at most colleges and universities, almost all of which require undergraduates majoring in other areas to take at least one course in literature. (Perhaps that's why you are reading this book!) Schools of medicine, law, and business are today *more* likely to require their students to take literature courses than they were in past decades, and they continue to welcome literature majors as applicants, as do many corporations. (As former *Google* and *Twitter* executive Santosh Jayaram told the *Wall Street Journal*, "English majors are exactly the people I'm looking for.") So why do so many people read and study literature, and why do schools encourage and even require students to do so? Even if we know what literature is, what does it *do* for us? What is its value?

There are, of course, as many answers to such questions as there are readers. For centuries, a standard answer has been that imaginative literature provides a unique kind of "instruction and delight." John Keats's ON FIRST LOOKING INTO CHAPMAN'S HOMER illustrates some of the many forms such delight can take. Some kinds of imaginative writing offer us the delight of immediate escape, but imaginative writing that is more difficult to read and understand than a Harry Potter or Brandon Sanderson novel offers escape of a different, potentially more instructive sort, liberating us from the confines of our own time, place, and social milieu, as well as our habitual ways of thinking, feeling, and looking at the world. In this way, a story, poem, or play can satisfy our desire for broader experience—including the sorts of experience we might be unable or unwilling to endure in real life. We can learn what it might be like to grow up on a Canadian fox farm or to party-hop with a supermodel. We can travel back into the past, experiencing war from the perspective of a soldier watching his comrade die or of prisoners suffering in a Nazi labor camp. We can journey into the future or into universes governed by entirely different rules than our own. Perhaps we yearn for such knowledge because we can best come to understand our own identities and outlooks by leaping over the boundaries that separate us from other selves and worlds.

Keats's friend and fellow poet Percy Bysshe Shelley argued that literature increases a person's ability to make such leaps, to "imagine intensely and comprehensively" and "put himself in the place of another and of many othe[r]" people as one has to in order "to be greatly good." Shelley meant "good" in a moral sense, reasoning that the ability both to accurately imagine and to truly *feel* the human consequences of our actions is the key to ethical behavior. Numerous recent studies by cognitive psychologists and neuroscientists endorse and expand on Shelley's argument, demonstrating that while we read our brains respond to fictional events and characters precisely as they would to real ones. Perhaps as a result, readers—particularly of literary, as opposed to popular, fiction or nonfiction—perform better on tests measuring their ability to infer or even predict, to understand, and to empathize with others' thoughts and emotions. Reading a poem, as opposed to a prose translation, sparks more activity in more areas of the brain, including those associated with personal memory and emotion, as well as language. As a result, scientists posit, poetry triggers "reappraisal mechanisms," making us reflect and rethink our own experiences. Reading literature of various genres thus, as one review of a decade's worth of research concludes, "enables us to better understand people, better cooperate with them."

Such abilities have great pragmatic and economic, as well as personal, moral, even political value. In virtually any career you choose, you will need to interact positively and productively with both coworkers and clients, and in today's increasingly globalized world, you will need to learn to deal effectively and empathetically with people vastly different from yourself. At the very least, literature written by people from various backgrounds and depicting various places, times, experiences, and feelings will give you some understanding of how others' lives and worldviews may differ from your own—and how very much the same they may be. Such understanding is ever more in demand in an age when business success—according to many a venture capitalist, marketing consultant, and Silicon Valley entrepreneur—often depends less on technical know-how than on both a grasp of the whys and hows of human behavior within and across cultures (markets), and the ability to tell compelling stories to potential funders and consumers alike.

Similarly, our rapidly changing world and economy require intellectual flexibility, adaptability, and ingenuity, making ever more essential the human knowledge, general skills, and habits of mind developed through the study of literature. Literature explores issues and questions relevant in any walk of life. Yet rather than offering us neat or comforting solutions and answers, literature enables us to experience difficult situations and human conundrums in all their complexity and to consider them from various points of view. In so doing, it invites us sometimes to question conventional thinking and sometimes to see the wisdom of such thinking, even as it helps us imagine altogether new possibilities.

Finally, literature awakens us to the richness and complexity of language—our primary tool for engaging with, understanding, and shaping the world around us. As we read more and more, seeing how different writers use language to help us feel others' joy, pain, love, rage, or laughter, we begin to recognize the vast range of possibilities for expression. Writing and discussion in turn give us invaluable practice in discovering, expressing, and defending our own nuanced, often contradictory thoughts about both literature and life. The study of literature enhances our command of language and our sensitivity to its effects and meanings in every form or medium, providing interpretation and communication skills especially crucial in our information age. By learning to appreciate and articulate what the language of a story, a poem, a play, or an essay does to us and by considering how it affects others, we also learn much about what we can do with language.

What We Do with Literature: Three Tips

1. *Take a literary work on its own terms.* Adjust to the work; don't make the work adjust to you. Be prepared to hear things you do not want to hear. Not all works are about your ideas, nor will they always present emotions you want to feel. But be tolerant and listen to the work first; later you can explore the ways you do or don't agree with it.
2. *Assume there is a reason for everything.* Writers do make mistakes, but when a work shows some degree of verbal control it is usually safest to assume that the writer chose each word carefully; if the choice seems peculiar, you may be missing something. Try to account for everything in a work, see what kind of sense you can make of it, and figure out a coherent pattern that explains the text as it stands.

3. *Remember that literary texts exist in time and that times change.* Not only the meanings of words, but whole ways of looking at the universe vary in different ages. Consciousness of time works two ways: Your knowledge of history provides a context for reading the work, even as the work may modify your notion of past and present.

Why Study Literature?

You may already feel the power and pleasure to be gained from a sustained encounter with challenging reading. Then why not simply enjoy it in solitude, on your own time? Why take a course in literature? Literary study, like all disciplines, has developed its own terminology and its own techniques. Some knowledge and understanding of both can greatly enhance our personal appreciation of literature and our conversations with others about it. Literature also has a context and a history, and learning something about these can make all the difference in the amount and kind of pleasure and insight you derive from literature. By reading and discussing different genres of literature, as well as works from varied times and places, you may well come to appreciate and even love works that you might never have discovered or chosen to read on your own or that you might have disliked or misunderstood if you did.

Most important, writing about works of literature and discussing them with others will give you practice in analyzing literature in greater depth and in considering alternative views of both the works themselves and the situations and problems the works explore. A clear understanding of the aims and designs of a story, poem, or play never falls like a bolt from the blue. Instead, it emerges from a process that involves trying to put into words *how* and *why* this work had such an effect on you and, just as important, responding to what others say or write about it. Literature itself is a vast, ongoing, ever-evolving conversation in which we most fully participate when we enter into actual conversation with others.

As you engage in this conversation, you will notice that interpretation is always variable, always open to discussion. A great diversity of interpretations might suggest that the discussion is pointless. On the contrary, that's when the discussion gets most interesting. Because there is no single, straight, paved road to an understanding of a literary text, you can explore a variety of blazed trails and less traveled paths. In sharing your own interpretations, tested against your peers' responses and guided by your instructor's or other critics' expertise, you will hone your skills at both interpretation and communication. After the intricate and interactive process of interpretation, you will find that the work has changed when you read it again. What we do with literature alters what it does to us.

To help you think further about how literature operates as a vast, never-ending, ever-expanding conversation that outlives—even as it invites and potentially works through and on—all of us, we close this chapter with two poems, Hai-Dang Phan's MY FATHER'S "NORTON INTRODUCTION TO LITERATURE," THIRD EDITION (1981) and BELLS FOR JOHN WHITESIDE'S DAUGHTER, by another American poet, John Crowe Ransom. Phan's 2015 poem responds in a wonderfully personal way to an array of literary texts published decades, even centuries, before his own birth (in 1980), including Ransom's **elegy** and a Shakespeare play that elegy echoes. But as his title suggests, Phan responds to these texts by means of another one—the traces of his own still-living father's responses to them, as recorded many years ago on the pages of his father's copy of an earlier edition of the very book *you* are now reading and, we hope, literally leaving your own distinctive marks on. What answers might these poems offer to the questions *Why read literature? Why study it?*

HAI-DANG PHAN

My Father's "Norton Introduction to Literature," Third Edition (1981)

Certain words give him trouble: *cannibals, puzzles, sob,*
bosom, martyr, deteriorate, shake, astonishes, vexed, ode . . .
These he looks up and studiously annotates in Vietnamese.
Ravish means *cướp đoạt; shits* is like when you have to *đi ỉa;*
5   *mourners* are those whom we say are full of *buồn rầu.*
For "even the like precurse of feared events"[8] think *báo trước.*

Its thin translucent pages are webbed with his marginalia,
graphite ghosts of a living hand, and the notes often sound
just like him: "All depend on how look at thing," he pencils
10 after "I first surmised the Horses' Heads / Were toward Eternity—"[9]
His slanted handwriting is generally small, but firm and clear.
His pencil is a No. 2, his preferred Hi-Liter, arctic blue.

I can see my father trying out the tools of literary analysis.
He identifies the "turning point" of "The Short and Happy Life
15 of Francis Macomber"; underlines the simile in "Both the old man
and the child stared ahead <u>as if</u> they were awaiting an apparition."[1]
My father, as he reads, continues to notice relevant passages
and to register significant reactions, but increasingly sorts out

his ideas in English, shaking off those Vietnamese glosses.
20 1981 was the same year we *vượt biển*[2] and came to America,
where my father took Intro Lit ("for fun"), Comp Sci ("for job").
"Stopping by Woods on a Snowy Evening,"[3] he murmurs
something about the "dark side of life how awful it can be"
as I begin to track silence and signal to a cold source.

25 Reading Ransom's "Bells for John Whiteside's Daughter,"
a poem about a "young girl's death," as my father notes,
how could he not have been "<u>vexed</u> at her brown study /
Lying so primly propped," since he never properly observed
(I realize this just now) his own daughter's wake.
30 *Lấy làm ngạc nhiên về* is what it means to be astonished.

---

8. *Hamlet* 1.1.121; the line (spoken by Horatio) immediately precedes the second appearance of Hamlet's father's ghost.
9. Final lines (23–24) of Emily Dickinson's "Because I could not stop for Death—" (p. 901).
1. From Flannery O'Connor's short story "The Artificial Nigger" (1955). *"The Short and Happy Life of Francis Macomber"*: short story (1936) by Ernest Hemingway. *Turning point*: see chapter 1.
2. Crossed the border (Vietnamese).
3. Poem (1923) by Robert Frost (p. 1194).

Experiencing Poetry 545

The lazy geese, like a snow cloud
Dripping their snow on the green grass,   10
Tricking and stopping, sleepy and proud,
Who cried in goose, Alas,

For the tireless heart within the little
Lady with rod that made them rise
From their noon apple-dreams and scuttle   15
Goose-fashion under the skies!

But now go the bells, and we are ready,
In one house we are sternly stopped
To say we are vexed at her brown study,
Lying so primly propped.   20

1924

After an opening stanza that introduces the basic contrast between
activity and stillness and between life and death, the center of the
poem concentrates on one vivid scene in the dead girl's life, a moment
when she played Mother Goose to her world and created a colorful,

Hai-Dang Phan's father's annotations in his *Norton Introduction to Literature*

Her name was Đông Xưa, Ancient Winter, but at home she's Bebe.
"There was such speed in her <u>little body</u>, / And such lightness
in her footfall, / It is no wonder her brown study / Astonishes
us all." In the photo of her that hangs in my parents' house
35   she is always fourteen months old and staring into the future.
In "reeducation camp"[4] he had to believe she was alive

because my mother on visits "took arms against her shadow."
Did the memory of those days sweep over him like a leaf storm
from the pages of a forgotten autumn? Lost in the margins,
40   I'm reading the way I discourage my students from reading.
But this is "how we deal with death," his black pen replies.
Assume there is a reason for everything, instructs a green asterisk.[5]

Then between pp. 896–97, opened to Stevens' "Sunday Morning,"[6]
I pick out a newspaper clipping, small as a stamp, an old listing
45   from the 404-Employment Opps State of Minnesota, and read:
For current job opportunities dial (612) 297-3180. Answered 24 hrs.
When I dial, the automated female voice on the other end
tells me I have reached a non-working number.

2015

4. Prison camp used for the indoctrination or ideological retraining of political dissidents; such
camps were common in Communist-ruled postwar Vietnam (1975–86).
5. See above, "What We Do with Literature: Three Tips."
6. Poem (1915, 1923) by Wallace Stevens.

• What does Phan's poem suggest about what his father gained from reading and studying literature? about how his father's practices as a reader shaped what literature did for him? What does the **speaker** seem to gain from reading the traces of his own father's reading experiences?

AUTHORS ON THEIR WORK

HAI-DANG PHAN (b. 1980)

From *The Best American Poetry 2016* (2016)*

["My Father's 'Norton Introduction to Literature,' Third Edition (1981)" i]s a found poem, artifice meets accident, sourced from the literary works and reader's notes of my father's textbook. I wanted to convey the uniquely tactile, sensuous, and material experience of reading and responding to a printed book, alongside the intimate thrill of handwriting. It's a poem-quilt made of well-worn texts [. . .]. It's a capsule biography, a portrait of my father (who served during the war as an officer in the South Vietnamese Navy, mostly on a small patrol boat unit in the Mekong Delta); as an immigrant trying to learn the language and literature of his adopted country; as a father trying to come to terms with the loss of his first child, whom he only ever saw alive once, and while he was in reeducation camp. I feel compelled to note that it's my mother's grief, briefly acknowledged and secreted inside a borrowed metaphor, which haunts the margins of the poem when I return to it now. After all, she was the one who had to deal with the death of her daughter while her husband was imprisoned, her private sorrow its own prison house. It's also a self-portrait because my life is bound up with this family trauma, and the historical trauma surrounding it. Insofar as I grapple with these legacies, as a writer I'm interested in the formal problems and possibilities they pose. Given the intense emotional response my father's marginalia provoked in me and what became the concerns of the poem, I needed a distancing strategy to combat the threat of cheap sentiment, false immediacy, and unknowing appropriation. Hence, the professorial persona and voice of the detached academic. In October 2012, when I came across my father's *Norton* while visiting my parents in Wisconsin, I had just started teaching at Grinnell College and entered a period of uncertainty about the course of my writing life. It's a reconciliation between two selves, the poet and the professor, that I, too, often see as conflictual, not to mention the age-old wars between fathers and sons, the present and the past. It's my marginalia on his marginalia, a double-annotation and translation, of what words, memories, people, and events mean as they change contexts, of the unknowable. It's a record and reenactment of reading, between the lines, behind the words, for the lives we've missed, others' and our own.

*The Best American Poetry 2016. Edited by Edward Hirsch, Scribner Poetry, 2016, pp. 186–87. The Best American Poetry Series, edited by Dennis Lehman.

JOHN CROWE RANSOM
Bells for John Whiteside's Daughter

There was such speed in her little body,
And such lightness in her footfall,
It is no wonder her brown study[7]
Astonishes us all.

5   Her wars were bruited[8] in our high window.
We looked among orchard trees and beyond
Where she took arms against her shadow,[9]
Or harried unto the pond

The lazy geese, like a snow cloud
10   Dripping their snow on the green grass,
Tricking and stopping, sleepy and proud,
Who cried in goose, Alas,

For the tireless heart within the little
Lady with rod that made them rise
15   From their noon apple-dreams and scuttle
Goose-fashion under the skies!

But now go the bells,[1] and we are ready,
In one house we are sternly stopped
To say we are vexed at her brown study,
20   Lying so primly propped.

1924

- What can you surmise from the poem about the speaker's relationship to the dead girl? Why might it matter that the poem uses the first-person plural (*we*), not the singular (*I*)? that it never explicitly mentions death? Why exactly are "we [. . .] vexed" and "[a]stonishe[d]" (lines 19, 4)?

7. State of intense contemplation or reverie.
8. Heard, but also suggesting "noise," "clamor."
9. Compare *Hamlet* 3.1.56–60, in which Hamlet asks, "Whether 'tis nobler in the mind to suffer / The slings and arrows of outrageous fortune, / Or to take arms against a sea of troubles."
1. Perhaps alluding to John Donne's *Devotions upon Emergent Occasions*, Meditation 17 (1624): "Any Mans *death* diminishes *me*, because I am involved in *Mankinde*, And therefore never send to know for whom the *bell* tolls; It tolls for *thee*" (spelling original).

PART ONE Fiction

James Baldwin

1 | FICTION: READING, RESPONDING, WRITING

Stories are a part of daily life in every culture. Stories are what we tell when we return from vacation or survive an accident or illness. They help us make sense of growing up or growing old, of a hurricane or a war, of the country and world we live in. In conversations, a story may be invited by the listener ("What did you do last night?") or initiated by the teller ("Guess what I saw when I was driving home!"). We assume such stories are true, or at least that they are meant to describe an experience honestly. Of course, many of the stories we encounter daily, from jokes to online games to television sitcoms to novels and films, are intended to be **fiction**— that is, stories or narratives about imaginary persons and events. The difference between fact and fiction is obviously crucial. But every story, whether a news story, sworn testimony, idle gossip, or a fairy tale, is a version of events told from a particular perspective (or several) and is inevitably incomplete. As we listen to others' stories, we keep alert to the details, which make the stories rich and entertaining. But we also need to spend considerable time and energy making sure that we accurately interpret what we hear: We ask ourselves who is telling the story, why the story is being told, and whether we have all the information we need to understand it fully.

Even newspaper articles that tell true stories—the facts of what actually happened—are open to such interpretation. Take as an example the following article, which appeared in the *New York Times* on January 1, 1920:

ACCUSED WIFE KILLS HER ALLEGED LOVER

Cumberland (Md.) Woman Becomes Desperate When Her Husband Orders Her from Home.

Special to The New York Times.

CUMBERLAND, Md., Dec. 31.—Accused by her husband of unfaithfulness, Mrs. Kate Uhl, aged 25, this morning stabbed to death Bryan Pownall, who she alleged was the cause of the estrangement with her husband, Mervin Uhl.

Mrs. Uhl, who is the mother of three children, denies her husband's charge of misconduct with Pownall, asserting that the latter forced his attentions on her by main physical strength against her will.

The stabbing this morning came as a dramatic sequel to the woman's dilemma after she had been ordered to leave her home. Mrs. Uhl summoned Pownall after her husband had gone to work this morning, and according to her story begged him to tell her husband that she, Mrs. Uhl, was not to blame. This Pownall refused to do, but again tried to make love to her, Mrs. Uhl said. When Pownall sought to kiss her Mrs. Uhl seized a thin-bladed butcher knife and stabbed the man to the heart, she admitted.

The report's appearance in a reliable newspaper; its identification of date, location, and other information; and the legalistic adjectives "accused" and "alleged" suggest that it strives to be accurate and objective. And it fundamentally is. But this news story is still a *story*. Note that certain points of view are better represented than others, and certain details are highlighted, just as in a work of fiction. The news item is based almost entirely on what Kate Uhl asserts, and even the subtitle, "Woman Becomes Desperate," plays up the "dramatic sequel to the woman's dilemma." We don't know what Mervin Uhl said when he allegedly accused his wife and turned her out of the house, and Bryan Pownall, the murdered man, obviously has no chance to speak in his own defense. Judging from both internal and external evidence, the article reports accurately the husband's accusation of adultery and the wife's accusation of rape, but we have no way of knowing, based on the article alone, whose accusations are true.

Our everyday interpretation of the stories we hear from various sources—including other people, the Internet, television, newspapers, and ads—has much in common with the interpretation of short stories such as those in this anthology. The processes of carefully and critically reading, responding to, and writing about stories are already somewhat familiar to you. Most readers already know, for instance, that they should pay close attention to seemingly trivial details; they should ask questions and find out more about any matters of fact that seem mysterious, odd, or unclear. Most readers are well aware that words can have several meanings and that there are alternative ways to tell a story. How would someone else have told the story? What are the storyteller's perspective and motives? What is the context of the tale—for instance, when is it supposed to have taken place and what was the occasion of its telling? These and other questions from our experience of everyday storytelling are equally relevant in reading fiction. Similarly, we can usually tell in reading a story or hearing it whether it is supposed to make us laugh, shock us, or provoke some other response.

TELLING STORIES: INTERPRETATION

Everyone has a unique story to tell. In fact, many stories are about this difference or divergence among people's interpretations of reality. Consider a well-known example, "The Blind Men and the Elephant," a Buddhist story over two thousand years old. Like other **tales** that have been transmitted orally, this one exists in many versions. Here's one way of telling it:

The Elephant in the Village of the Blind

Once there was a village high in the mountains in which everyone was born blind. One day a traveler arrived from far away with many fine things to sell and many tales to tell. The villagers asked, "How did you travel so far and so high carrying so much?" The traveler said, "On my elephant." "What is an elephant?" the villagers asked, having never even heard of such an animal in their remote mountain village. "See for yourself," the traveler replied.

The elders of the village were a little afraid of the strange-smelling creature that took up so much space in the middle of the village square. They could hear it breathing and munching on hay, and feel its slow, swaying movements disturbing the air around them. First one elder reached out and felt its flapping ear. "An elephant is soft but tough, and flexible, like a leather fan." Another grasped its back leg. "An elephant is a rough, hairy pillar." An old woman took hold of a tusk and gasped, "An elephant is a cool, smooth staff." A young girl seized the tail and declared, "An elephant is a fringed rope." A boy took hold of the trunk and announced, "An elephant is a water pipe." Soon others were stroking its sides, which were furrowed like a dry plowed field, and others determined that its head was an overturned washing tub attached to the water pipe.

At first each villager argued with the others on the definition of the elephant, as the traveler watched in silence. Two elders were about to come to blows about a fan that could not possibly be a pillar. Meanwhile the elephant patiently enjoyed the investigations as the cries of curiosity and angry debate mixed in the afternoon sun. Soon someone suggested that a list could be made of all the parts: the elephant had four pillars, one tub, two fans, a water pipe, and two staffs, and was covered in tough, hairy leather or dried mud. Four young mothers, sitting on a bench and comparing impressions, realized that the elephant was in fact an enormous, gentle ox with a stretched nose. The traveler agreed, adding only that it was also a powerful draft horse and that if they bought some of his wares for a good price he would be sure to come that way again in the new year.

The different versions of such a tale, like the different descriptions of the elephant, alter its meaning. Changing any aspect of the story will inevitably change how it works and what it means to the listener or reader. For example, most versions of this tale feature not an entire village of blind people (as this version does), but a small group of blind men who claim to be wiser than their sighted neighbors. These blind men quarrel endlessly because none of them can see; none can put together all the evidence of all their senses or all the elephant's various parts to create a whole. Such traditional versions of the story criticize people who are too proud of what they think they know; these versions imply that sighted people would know better what an elephant is. However, other versions of the tale, like the one above, are set in an imaginary "country" of the blind. This setting changes the emphasis of the story from the errors of a few blind wise men to the value and the insufficiency of *any* one person's perspective. For though it's clear that the various members of the community in this version will never agree entirely on one interpretation of (or story about) the elephant, they do not let themselves get bogged down in endless dispute. Instead they compare and combine their various stories and "readings" in order to form a more satisfying, holistic understanding of the wonder in their midst. Similarly, listening to others' different interpretations of a story or any other literary work can enhance your experience of it and your skill in responding to new works.

Just as stories vary depending on who is telling them, so their meanings vary depending on who is responding to them. In the elephant story, the villagers pay attention to what the tail or the ear feels like; then they draw on comparisons to what they already know. But ultimately, the individual interpretations of the elephant depend on what previous experiences each villager brings to bear (of pillars, water pipes, oxen, and dried mud, for example), and also on where (quite literally) he or she stands in relation to the elephant. In the same way, readers participate in re-creating a story as they interpret it. When you read a story for the first time, your response will be informed by other stories you have heard and read and by your expectations for this kind of story. To grapple with what is new in any story, start by observing one part at a time and gradually trying to understand how those parts work together to form a whole. As you make sense of each new piece of the picture, you adjust your expectations about what is yet to come. When you have read and grasped it as fully as possible, you may share your interpretation with other readers, discussing different ways of seeing the story. Finally, you might express your understanding in writing—in a sense, telling *your* story about the work.

Questions about the Elements of Fiction

- Expectations: What do you expect?
  - from the title? from the first sentence or paragraph?
  - after the first events or interactions of characters?
  - as the **conflict** is resolved?
- What happens in the story? (See ch. 2.)
  - Do the characters or the situation change from the beginning to the end?
  - Can you summarize the **plot**? Is it a recognizable kind or **genre** of story?
- How is the story narrated? (See ch. 3.)
  - Is the **narrator** identified as a character?
  - Is it narrated in the past or present tense?
  - Is it narrated in the first, second, or third person?
  - Do you know what every character is thinking, or only some characters, or none?
- Who are the **characters**? (See ch. 4.)
  - Who is (or are) the **protagonist**(s)?
  - Who is (or are) the **antagonist**(s)?
  - Who are the other characters? What is their role in the story?
  - Do your expectations change with those of the characters, or do you know more or less than each of the characters?
- What is the **setting** of the story? (See ch. 5.)
  - When does the story take place?
  - Where does it take place?
  - Does the story move from one setting to another? Does it move in one direction only or back and forth in time and place?
- What do you notice about how the story is written?
  - What is the **style** of the prose? Are the sentences and the vocabulary simple or complex?
  - Are there any **images, figures of speech**, or **symbols**? (See ch. 6.)
  - What is the **tone** or mood? Does the reader feel sad, amused, worried, curious?
- What does the story mean? Can you express its **theme** or themes? (See ch. 7.)
  - Answers to these big questions may be found in many instances in your answers to the previous questions. The story's meaning or theme depends on all its features.

READING AND RESPONDING TO FICTION

When imaginary events are acted out onstage or onscreen, our experience of those events is that of being a witness to them. In contrast, prose fiction, whether oral or written, is relayed to us by someone. Reading it is more like hearing what happened after the fact than witnessing it with our very eyes. The teller, or **narrator**, of fiction addresses a listener or reader, often referred to as the audience. How much or how little we know about the characters and what they say or do depends on what a narrator tells us.

You should read a story attentively, just as you would listen attentively to someone telling a story out loud. This means limiting distractions and interruptions; you should take a break from social media and obtrusive music. Literary prose, like poetry, works with the sounds as well as meanings of words, just as film works with music and sound as well as images. Be prepared to mark up the text and to make notes.

While reading and writing, you should always have a good college-level dictionary on hand or on screen so that you can look up any unfamiliar terms. One excellent resource is the *Oxford English Dictionary*, available through most academic library websites, which reveals the wide range of meanings words have had over time. Words in English always have a long story to tell because over the centuries so many languages have contributed to ours. It's not uncommon for meanings to overlap or even reverse themselves.

The following short short story is a contemporary work. As in THE ELEPHANT IN THE VILLAGE OF THE BLIND, this narrator gives us a minimal amount of information, merely observing the characters' different perceptions and interpretations of things they see during a cross-country car trip. As you read the story, pay attention to your expectations, drawing on your personal experience and such clues as the title; the characters' statements and behavior; specifics of setting (time and place); and any repetitions or changes. When and how does the story begin to challenge and change your initial expectations? You can use the questions above to guide your reading of any story and help you focus on some of its important features.

LINDA BREWER

20/20

By the time they reached Indiana, Bill realized that Ruthie, his driving companion, was incapable of theoretical debate. She drove okay, she went halves on gas, etc., but she refused to argue. She didn't seem to know how. Bill was used to East Coast women who disputed everything he said, every step of the way. Ruthie stuck to simple observation, like "Look, cows." He chalked it up to the fact that she was from rural Ohio and thrilled to death to be anywhere else.

She didn't mind driving into the setting sun. The third evening out, Bill rested his eyes while she cruised along making the occasional announcement.

"Indian paintbrush. A golden eagle."

Miles later he frowned. There was no Indian paintbrush, that he knew of, near Chicago.

The next evening, driving, Ruthie said, "I never thought I'd see a Bigfoot in   5
real life." Bill turned and looked at the side of the road streaming innocently
out behind them. Two red spots winked back—reflectors nailed to a tree
stump.

"Ruthie, I'll drive," he said. She stopped the car and they changed places in
the light of the evening star.

"I'm so glad I got to come with you," Ruthie said. Her eyes were big, blue, and
capable of seeing wonderful sights. A white buffalo near Fargo. A UFO above
Twin Falls. A handsome genius in the person of Bill himself. This last vision
came to her in Spokane and Bill decided to let it ride.

1996

· · ·

SAMPLE WRITING: ANNOTATION AND NOTES ON "20/20"

Now re-read the story, along with the brief notes one reader made in the margins,
based on the "Questions about the Elements of Fiction" that appear on page 19. The
reader then expanded these annotations into longer, more detailed notes. These
notes could be organized and expanded into a response paper on the story. Some of
your insights might even form the basis for a longer essay on one of the elements
of the story.

Like "20/20 hind-sight" or perfect vision? Also like the way Bill and Ruthie go 50/50 on the trip, and see things in two different ways.

20/20

By the time they reached Indiana, Bill realized that Ruthie, his driv-ing companion, was incapable of theoretical debate. She drove okay, she went halves on gas, etc., but she refused to argue. She didn't seem to know how. Bill was used to East Coast women who disputed every-thing he said, every step of the way. Ruthie stuck to simple observa-tion, like "Look, cows." He chalked it up to the fact that she was from rural Ohio and thrilled to death to be anywhere else.

Bill's doubts about Ruthie. Is he reliable? Does she "refuse" or not "know how" to argue? What's her view of him?

Bill's keeping score; maybe Ruthie's nicer, or has better eyesight. She notices things.

She didn't mind driving into the setting sun. The third evening out, Bill rested his eyes while she cruised along making the occasional announcement.

"Indian paintbrush. A golden eagle."

Miles later he frowned. There was no Indian paintbrush, that he knew of, near Chicago.

Repetition, like a folktale: 2nd sun-set drive, 3rd time she speaks. Not much dialogue in story.

The next evening, driving, Ruthie said, "I never thought I'd see a Bigfoot in real life." Bill turned and looked at the side of the road streaming innocently out behind them. Two red spots winked back—reflectors nailed to a tree stump.

"Ruthie, I'll drive," he said. She stopped the car and they changed places in the light of the evening star.

"I'm so glad I got to come with you," Ruthie said. Her eyes were big, blue, and capable of seeing wonderful sights. A white buffalo near Fargo. A UFO above Twin Falls. A handsome genius in the person of Bill himself. This last vision came to her in Spokane and Bill decided to let it ride.

Bill's only speech. Turning point: Bill sees something he doesn't already know.

Repetition, like a joke, in 3 things Ruthie sees.

Story begins and ends in the middle of things: "By the time," "let it ride."

Initial Impressions

Plot: begins in the middle of action, on a journey. *Narration*: past tense, third person. *Setting*: Indiana is a middling, unromantic place.

Paragraph 1

Narration and Character: Bill's judgments of Ruthie show that he prides himself on arguing about abstract ideas; that he thinks Ruthie must be stupid; that they didn't know each other well and aren't suited for a long trip together. Bill is from the unfriendly East Coast; Ruthie, from easygoing, dull "rural Ohio." *Style*: The casual language—"okay" and "etc."—sounds like Bill's voice, but he's not the narrator. The vague "etc." hints that Bill isn't really curious about her. The observation of cows sounds funny, childlike, even stupid. But why does he have to "chalk it up" or keep score?

Paragraph 2

Plot and Character: This is the first specific time given in the story, the "third evening": Ruthie surprises the reader and Bill with more than dull "observation."

Paragraph 4

Style, Character, Setting, and Tone: Dozing in the speeding car, Bill is too late to check out what she says. He frowns (he doesn't argue) because the plant and the bird can't be seen in the Midwest. Brewer uses a series of place names to indicate the route of the car. There's humor in Ruthie's habit of pointing out bizarre sights.

Paragraph 5

Character and Setting: Bigfoot is a legendary creature living in Western forests. Is Ruthie's imagination getting the better of Bill's logic? "Innocently" personifies the road, and the reflectors on the stump wink like the monster; Bill is finally looking (though in hindsight). The scenery seems to be playing a joke on him.

Paragraph 6

Plot and Character: Here the characters change places. He wants to drive (is she hallucinating?), but it's as if she has won. The narration (which has been relying on Bill's voice and perspective) for the first time notices a romantic detail of scenery that Ruthie doesn't point out (the evening star).

Paragraph 7

Character and Theme: Bill begins to see Ruthie and what she is capable of. What they see *is* the journey these characters take toward falling in love, in the West where things become unreal. *Style*: The long "o" sounds and images in "A white buffalo near Fargo. A UFO above Twin Falls" (along with the words "Ohio," "Chicago," and "Spokane") give a feeling for the wildness (notice the Native American place names). The outcome of the story is that they *go far* to Fargo, see double and fall in love at Twin Falls—see and imagine wonderful things in each other. They end up with perfectly matched vision.

READING AND RESPONDING TO GRAPHIC FICTION

You may approach any narrative with the same questions that have been applied to 20/20. Try it on the following piece by Jules Feiffer. Originally published in the *Village Voice*, SUPERMAN made legendary *Maus* creator Art Spiegelman's 2016 list of eleven shorts whose "subject matter" or "resonance" earned them the right to be considered "one-page graphic novels." As you read "Superman," carefully consider the interplay between word and image and the role each plays, especially in characterization and plot. How would the strip mean differently if it depended wholly on words? on images? How, if at all, might graphic fiction change the way we ask or answer the "Questions about the Elements of Fiction" on page 19?

JULES FEIFFER

(b. 1929)

Superman

New Yorker Jules Feiffer got his professional start at age sixteen, assisting revered cartoonist Will Eisner, who reportedly thought little of Feiffer's drawing skills but came to respect his talent as a writer with a special gift for characterization and dialogue. After a stint in the army during the Korean War, Feiffer landed a job (initially unpaid) at the *Village Voice*, the nation's first alternative newspaper. Here his nationally syndicated, Pulitzer Prize–winning satirical strip appeared weekly for four decades, from 1956 to 1997, when the *New York Times* hired Feiffer as its first op-ed cartoonist. Also a playwright, screenwriter, children's book author, and book illustrator, whose credits include *The Phantom Tollbooth* (1961), Feiffer penned the first history of comic-book superheroes in 1965. Sometimes credited with helping to invent "graphic novels" with his "novel-in-pictures" *Tantrum* (1979), Feiffer himself reserves the label "graphic novels" for the noir trilogy he launched at age 85: *Kill My Mother* (2014), *Cousin Joseph* (2016), and *The Ghost Script* (2018). An illustrated memoir, *Backing into Forward*, appeared in 2010.

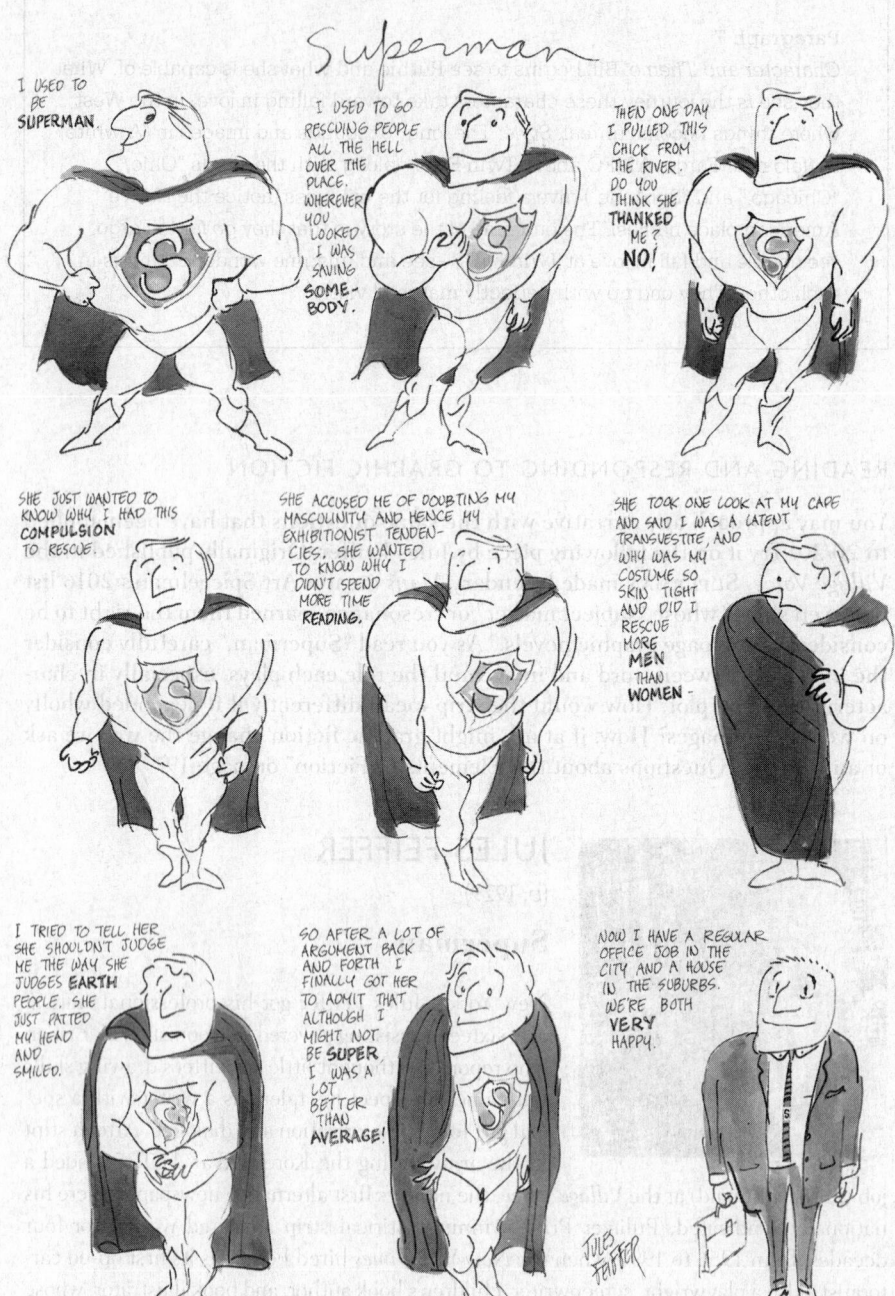

1960

KEY CONCEPTS

As you read, respond to, and write about fiction, some key terms and concepts will be useful in comparing or distinguishing different kinds of stories. Stories may be oral rather than written down, and they may be of different lengths. They may be based on true stories or completely invented. They may be written in verse rather than prose, or they may be created in media other than the printed page.

STORY AND NARRATIVE

Generally speaking, a *story* is a short account of an incident or series of incidents, whether actual or invented. The word is often used to refer to an entertaining tale of imaginary people and events, but it is also used in phrases like "the *story* of my life"—suggesting a true account. The term **narrative** is especially useful as a general concept for the substance rather than the form of what is told about persons and their actions. A story or a tale is usually short, whereas a narrative may be of any length.

Narratives in Daily Life

Narrative plays an important role in our lives beyond the telling of fictional stories. Consider the following:

- Today, sociologists and historians may collect *personal narratives* to present an account of society and everyday life in a certain time or place.
- Since the 1990s, the practice of *narrative medicine* has spread as an improved technique of diagnosis and treatment that takes into account the patient's point of view.
- There is a movement to encourage *mediation* rather than litigation in divorce cases. A mediator may collaborate with the couple in arriving at a shared perspective on the divorce; in a sense, they try to agree on the story of their marriage and how it ended.
- Some countries have attempted to recover from the trauma of genocidal ethnic conflict through *official hearings of testimony* by victims as well as defendants. South Africa's Truth and Reconciliation Commission is an example of this use of stories.

ORAL NARRATIVE AND TALES

We tend to think of stories in their written form, but many of the stories that we now regard as among the world's greatest, such as Homer's *Iliad* and the Old English epic *Beowulf*, were sung or recited by generations of storytellers before being written down. Just as rumors change shape as they circulate, oral stories tend to be more fluid than printed ones. Traditionally oral **tales** such as fairy tales or folktales may endure for a very long time yet take different forms in various countries and eras. And it's often difficult or impossible to trace such a story back to a single **author** or creator. In a sense, then, an oral story is the creation of a whole community or communities, just as oral storytelling tends to be a more communal event than reading.

Certain recognizable signals set a story or tale apart from common speech and encourage us to pay a different kind of attention. Children know that a story is beginning when they hear or read "Once upon a time . . . ," and traditional oral storytellers have formal ways to set up a tale, such as *Su-num-twee* ("Listen to me"), as Spokane storytellers say. "And they lived happily ever after," or simply "The End," may similarly indicate when the story is over.

FICTION AND NONFICTION

The word *fiction* comes from the Latin root *fingere*, "to fashion or form." The earliest definitions concern the act of making something artificial to imitate something else. In the past two centuries, *fiction* has become more narrowly defined as "prose narrative about imaginary people and events," the main meaning of the word as we use it in this anthology.

Genres of Prose Fiction by Length

A **novel** is a work of prose fiction of about forty thousand words or more. The form arose in the seventeenth and early eighteenth centuries as prose romances and adventure tales began to adopt techniques of history and travel narrative as well as memoir, letters, and biography.

A **novella** is a work of prose fiction of about seventeen thousand to forty thousand words. The novella form was especially favored between about 1850 and 1950, largely because it can be more tightly controlled and concentrated than a long novel, while focusing on the inner workings of a character.

A **short story** is broadly defined as anywhere between one thousand and twenty thousand words. One expectation of a short story is that it may be read in a single sitting. The modern short story developed in the mid- to late nineteenth century, in part because of the growing popularity of magazines.

A **short short story**, sometimes called "flash fiction" or "micro-fiction," is generally not much longer than one thousand words and sometimes much shorter. There have always been very short fictions, including **parables** and fables, but the short short story is an invention of recent decades.

In contrast with *fiction*, **nonfiction** usually refers to *factual* prose narrative. Some major nonfiction genres are history, **biography**, and autobiography. In film, documentaries and "biopics," or biographical feature films, similarly attempt to represent real people, places, and events. The boundary between fiction and creative nonfiction is porous. So-called true crime novels such as Truman Capote's *In*

Cold Blood (1966) and Marlon James's award-winning *A Brief History of Seven Killings* (2014), about the attempted assassination of musician Bob Marley, use the techniques of fiction writing to narrate actual events. Graphic novels, with a format derived from comic books, have become an increasingly popular medium for memoirs. (Famous examples include Marjane Satrapi's *Persepolis* [2003], Alison Bechdel's *Fun Home* [2006], and the late congressman John Lewis's *March* [2013–16].) Some Hollywood movies and TV shows dramatize real people in everyday situations or contexts, or real events such as the nuclear disaster at Chernobyl. In contrast, **historical fiction**, developed by Sir Walter Scott around 1815, comprises prose narratives that present history in imaginative ways. Such works of prose fiction adhere closely to the facts of history and actual lives, just as many "true"-life stories are more or less fictionalized.

The fiction chapters in this volume present a collection of prose works—mostly short stories. Even as you read the short prose fiction in this book, bear in mind the many ways we encounter stories or narrative in everyday life, and consider the almost limitless variety of forms that fiction may take.

WRITING ABOUT FICTION

During your first reading of any story, you may want to read without stopping to address each of the questions on page 19. After you have read the whole piece once, re-read it carefully, using the questions as a guide. It's always interesting to compare your initial reactions with your later ones. In fact, a paper may focus on comparing the expectations of readers (and characters) at the beginning of a story to their later conclusions. Responses to fiction may come in unpredictable order, so feel free to address the questions as they arise. Looking at how the story is told and what happens to which characters may lead to observations on expectations or setting. Consideration of setting and style can help explain the personalities, actions, mood, and effect of the story, which can lead to well-informed ideas about the meaning of the whole. But any one of the questions, pursued further, can serve as the focus of more formal writing.

Following this chapter are three written responses to Isabel Allende's short story AND OF CLAY ARE WE CREATED. First, read the story and make notes on any features that you find interesting, important, or confusing. Then look at the notes, response paper, and essay by Renee Maalouf, which illustrate different ways of writing about Allende's story.

ISABEL ALLENDE
(b. 1942)

And of Clay Are We Created[1]

Hailed by the *Latin American Herald Tribune* as "the world's most widely read Spanish-language author," Isabel Allende is the first woman writer to win the sort of international acclaim earlier afforded Gabriel García Márquez and other writers of the Latin American literary "boom" generation. Allende, for her part, sometimes describes her life as cleaved in two by a single traumatic historical event. Though born in Peru, where her father served with the Chilean diplomatic corps, Allende spent most of her early years in Santiago, Chile—from age three, when her father abandoned the family, into her early thirties, by which point she was herself a married mother of two, a television personality, and a magazine columnist and editor. In 1973, however, three years into his first term as Chile's president, Allende's second cousin, Salvador Allende, was assassinated as part of a right-wing coup culminating in the military dictatorship of General Augusto Pinochet. Forced to flee with her husband and children, Allende first found her voice as a writer during a thirteen-year exile in Venezuela. Allende has produced a body of work both abundant and diverse, including acclaimed memoirs such as *The Sum of Our Days* (2007) and at least fourteen novels ranging widely in setting, subject, and audience. Her most famous remains her first, *The House of Spirits* (1982). Offering a distinctly feminist, pointedly political take on magic realism, the novel traces the history of both the fictional Trueba family and an unnamed country resembling Chile, from the early twentieth century through the literally torturous aftermath of a violent coup. Allende, who regards the short story as among the most challenging of literary forms, has produced only one collection: Titled *The Stories of Eva Luna* (1989), it gathers tales ostensibly told by the eponymous heroine of Allende's third novel (1987) to her lover, Rolf Carlé. A resident of California since 1987 and a U.S. citizen since 1993, Allende was in 2014 awarded the nation's highest civilian honor, the Presidential Medal of Freedom.

THEY discovered the girl's head protruding from the mudpit, eyes wide open, calling soundlessly. She had a First Communion name, Azucena. Lily. In that vast cemetery where the odor of death was already attracting vultures from far away, and where the weeping of orphans and wails of the injured filled the air, the little girl obstinately clinging to life became the symbol of the tragedy. The television cameras transmitted so often the unbearable image of the head budding like a black squash from the clay that there was no one who did not recognize her and know her name. And every time we saw her on the screen, right behind her was Rolf Carlé, who had gone there on assignment, never suspecting that he would find a fragment of his past, lost thirty years before.

---

1. Translated from the Spanish by Margaret Sayers Peden.

First a subterranean sob rocked the cotton fields, curling them like waves of foam. Geologists had set up their seismographs[2] weeks before and knew that the mountain had awakened again. For some time they had predicted that the heat of the eruption could detach the eternal ice from the slopes of the volcano, but no one heeded their warnings; they sounded like the tales of frightened old women. The towns in the valley went about their daily life, deaf to the moaning of the earth, until that fateful Wednesday night in November when a prolonged roar announced the end of the world, and walls of snow broke loose, rolling in an avalanche of clay, stones, and water that descended on the villages and buried them beneath unfathomable meters of telluric[3] vomit. As soon as the survivors emerged from the paralysis of that first awful terror, they could see that houses, plazas, churches, white cotton plantations, dark coffee forests, cattle pastures—all had disappeared. Much later, after soldiers and volunteers had arrived to rescue the living and try to assess the magnitude of the cataclysm, it was calculated that beneath the mud lay more than twenty thousand human beings and an indefinite number of animals putrefying in a viscous soup. Forests and rivers had also been swept away, and there was nothing to be seen but an immense desert of mire.

When the station called before dawn, Rolf Carlé and I were together. I crawled out of bed, dazed with sleep, and went to prepare coffee while he hurriedly dressed. He stuffed his gear in the green canvas backpack he always carried, and we said goodbye, as we had so many times before. I had no presentiments. I sat in the kitchen, sipping my coffee and planning the long hours without him, sure that he would be back the next day.

He was one of the first to reach the scene, because while other reporters were fighting their way to the edges of that morass in jeeps, bicycles, or on foot, each getting there however he could, Rolf Carlé had the advantage of the television helicopter, which flew him over the avalanche. We watched on our screens the footage captured by his assistant's camera, in which he was up to his knees in muck, a microphone in his hand, in the midst of a bedlam of lost children, wounded survivors, corpses, and devastation. The story came to us in his calm voice. For years he had been a familiar figure in newscasts, reporting live at the scene of battles and catastrophes with awesome tenacity. Nothing could stop him, and I was always amazed at his equanimity in the face of danger and suffering; it seemed as if nothing could shake his fortitude or deter his curiosity. Fear seemed never to touch him, although he had confessed to me that he was not a courageous man, far from it. I believe that the lens of the camera had a strange effect on him; it was as if it transported him to a different time from which he could watch events without actually participating in them. When I knew him better, I came to realize that this fictive distance seemed to protect him from his own emotions.

Rolf Carlé was in on the story of Azucena from the beginning. He filmed the [5] volunteers who discovered her, and the first persons who tried to reach her; his

2. Instrument measuring and recording details of an earthquake such as its force and duration. Though Allende's story is fictional and deliberately references no specific event or country, its details recall the November 1985 eruption of Colombia's Nevado del Ruiz volcano and the experience of thirteen-year-old Omayra Sánchez Garzón.
3. Of the soil.

camera zoomed in on the girl, her dark face, her large desolate eyes, the plastered-down tangle of her hair. The mud was like quicksand around her, and anyone attempting to reach her was in danger of sinking. They threw a rope to her that she made no effort to grasp until they shouted to her to catch it; then she pulled a hand from the mire and tried to move, but immediately sank a little deeper. Rolf threw down his knapsack and the rest of his equipment and waded into the quagmire, commenting for his assistant's microphone that it was cold and that one could begin to smell the stench of corpses.

"What's your name?" he asked the girl, and she told him her flower name. "Don't move, Azucena," Rolf Carlé directed, and kept talking to her, without a thought for what he was saying, just to distract her, while slowly he worked his way forward in mud up to his waist. The air around him seemed as murky as the mud.

It was impossible to reach her from the approach he was attempting, so he retreated and circled around where there seemed to be firmer footing. When finally he was close enough, he took the rope and tied it beneath her arms, so they could pull her out. He smiled at her with that smile that crinkles his eyes and makes him look like a little boy; he told her that everything was fine, that he was here with her now, that soon they would have her out. He signaled the others to pull, but as soon as the cord tensed, the girl screamed. They tried again, and her shoulders and arms appeared, but they could move her no farther; she was trapped. Someone suggested that her legs might be caught in the collapsed walls of her house, but she said it was not just rubble, that she was also held by the bodies of her brothers and sisters clinging to her legs.

"Don't worry, we'll get you out of here," Rolf promised. Despite the quality of the transmission, I could hear his voice break, and I loved him more than ever. Azucena looked at him, but said nothing.

During those first hours Rolf Carlé exhausted all the resources of his ingenuity to rescue her. He struggled with poles and ropes, but every tug was an intolerable torture for the imprisoned girl. It occurred to him to use one of the poles as a lever but got no result and had to abandon the idea. He talked a couple of soldiers into working with him for a while, but they had to leave because so many other victims were calling for help. The girl could not move, she barely could breathe, but she did not seem desperate, as if an ancestral resignation allowed her to accept her fate. The reporter, on the other hand, was determined to snatch her from death. Someone brought him a tire, which he placed beneath her arms like a life buoy, and then laid a plank near the hole to hold his weight and allow him to stay closer to her. As it was impossible to remove the rubble blindly, he tried once or twice to dive toward her feet, but emerged frustrated, covered with mud, and spitting gravel. He concluded that he would have to have a pump to drain the water, and radioed a request for one, but received in return a message that there was no available transport and it could not be sent until the next morning.

10   "We can't wait that long!" Rolf Carlé shouted, but in the pandemonium no one stopped to commiserate. Many more hours would go by before he accepted that time had stagnated and reality had been irreparably distorted.

A military doctor came to examine the girl, and observed that her heart was functioning well and that if she did not get too cold she could survive the night.

"Hang on, Azucena, we'll have the pump tomorrow," Rolf Carlé tried to console her.

"Don't leave me alone," she begged.

"No, of course I won't leave you."

Someone brought him coffee, and he helped the girl drink it, sip by sip. The warm liquid revived her and she began telling him about her small life, about her family and her school, about how things were in that little bit of world before the volcano had erupted. She was thirteen, and she had never been outside her village. Rolf Carlé, buoyed by a premature optimism, was convinced that everything would end well: the pump would arrive, they would drain the water, move the rubble, and Azucena would be transported by helicopter to a hospital where she would recover rapidly and where he could visit her and bring her gifts. He thought, She's already too old for dolls, and I don't know what would please her, maybe a dress. I don't know much about women, he concluded, amused, reflecting that although he had known many women in his lifetime, none had taught him these details. To pass the hours he began to tell Azucena about his travels and adventures as a newshound, and when he exhausted his memory, he called upon imagination, inventing things he thought might entertain her. From time to time she dozed, but he kept talking in the darkness, to assure her that he was still there and to overcome the menace of uncertainty.

That was a long night.

Many miles away, I watched Rolf Carlé and the girl on a television screen. I could not bear the wait at home, so I went to National Television, where I often spent entire nights with Rolf editing programs. There, I was near his world, and I could at least get a feeling of what he lived through during those three decisive days. I called all the important people in the city, senators, commanders of the armed forces, the North American ambassador, and the president of National Petroleum, begging them for a pump to remove the silt, but obtained only vague promises. I began to ask for urgent help on radio and television, to see if there wasn't *someone* who could help us. Between calls I would run to the newsroom to monitor the satellite transmissions that periodically brought new details of the catastrophe. While reporters selected scenes with most impact for the news report, I searched for footage that featured Azucena's mudpit. The screen reduced the disaster to a single plane and accentuated the tremendous distance that separated me from Rolf Carlé; nonetheless, I was there with him. The child's every suffering hurt me as it did him; I felt his frustration, his impotence. Faced with the impossibility of communicating with him, the fantastic idea came to me that if I tried, I could reach him by force of mind and in that way give him encouragement. I concentrated until I was dizzy—a frenzied and futile activity. At times I would be overcome with compassion and burst out crying; at other times, I was so drained I felt as if I were staring through a telescope at the light of a star dead for a million years.

I watched that hell on the first morning broadcast, cadavers of people and animals awash in the current of new rivers formed overnight from the melted snow. Above the mud rose the tops of trees and the bell towers of a church where several people had taken refuge and were patiently awaiting rescue

teams. Hundreds of soldiers and volunteers from the Civil Defense[4] were clawing through rubble searching for survivors, while long rows of ragged specters
awaited their turn for a cup of hot broth. Radio networks announced that their
phones were jammed with calls from families offering shelter to orphaned
children. Drinking water was in scarce supply, along with gasoline and food.
Doctors, resigned to amputating arms and legs without anesthesia, pled that at
least they be sent serum and painkillers and antibiotics; most of the roads, however, were impassable, and worse were the bureaucratic obstacles that stood in
the way. To top it all, the clay contaminated by decomposing bodies threatened
the living with an outbreak of epidemics.

Azucena was shivering inside the tire that held her above the surface. Immo-
bility and tension had greatly weakened her, but she was conscious and could
still be heard when a microphone was held out to her. Her tone was humble, as
if apologizing for all the fuss. Rolf Carlé had a growth of beard, and dark circles
beneath his eyes; he looked near exhaustion. Even from that enormous distance
I could sense the quality of his weariness, so different from the fatigue of other
adventures. He had completely forgotten the camera; he could not look at the
girl through a lens any longer. The pictures we were receiving were not his assistant's but those of other reporters who had appropriated Azucena, bestowing on
her the pathetic responsibility of embodying the horror of what had happened
in that place. With the first light Rolf tried again to dislodge the obstacles that
held the girl in her tomb, but he had only his hands to work with; he did not
dare use a tool for fear of injuring her. He fed Azucena a cup of the cornmeal
mush and bananas the Army was distributing, but she immediately vomited it
up. A doctor stated that she had a fever, but added that there was little he could
do: antibiotics were being reserved for cases of gangrene.[5] A priest also passed by
and blessed her, hanging a medal of the Virgin[6] around her neck. By evening a
gentle, persistent drizzle began to fall.

20   "The sky is weeping," Azucena murmured, and she, too, began to cry.

"Don't be afraid," Rolf begged. "You have to keep your strength up and be
calm. Everything will be fine. I'm with you, and I'll get you out somehow."

Reporters returned to photograph Azucena and ask her the same questions,
which she no longer tried to answer. In the meanwhile, more television and
movie teams arrived with spools of cable, tapes, film, videos, precision lenses,
recorders, sound consoles, lights, reflecting screens, auxiliary motors, cartons of
supplies, electricians, sound technicians, and cameramen: Azucena's face was
beamed to millions of screens around the world. And all the while Rolf Carlé
kept pleading for a pump. The improved technical facilities bore results, and
National Television began receiving sharper pictures and clearer sound; the distance seemed suddenly compressed, and I had the horrible sensation that Azucena and Rolf were by my side, separated from me by impenetrable glass. I was
able to follow events hour by hour; I knew everything my love did to wrest the
girl from her prison and help her endure her suffering; I overheard fragments of

---

4. Organization(s) charged with the effort to protect citizens from, and to provide aid to them after, a
military attack or disaster.
5. Death of body tissue due to lack of blood flow or severe bacterial infection.
6. Mary or Maryam, mother of Jesus or Isa, in Christian and Islamic traditions, respectively.

what they said to one another and could guess the rest; I was present when she taught Rolf to pray, and when he distracted her with the stories I had told him in a thousand and one nights[7] beneath the white mosquito netting of our bed.

When darkness came on the second day, Rolf tried to sing Azucena to sleep with old Austrian folk songs he had learned from his mother, but she was far beyond sleep. They spent most of the night talking, each in a stupor of exhaustion and hunger, and shaking with cold. That night, imperceptibly, the unyielding floodgates that had contained Rolf Carlé's past for so many years began to open, and the torrent of all that had lain hidden in the deepest and most secret layers of memory poured out, leveling before it the obstacles that had blocked his consciousness for so long. He could not tell it all to Azucena; she perhaps did not know there was a world beyond the sea or time previous to her own; she was not capable of imagining Europe in the years of the war.[8] So he could not tell her of defeat, nor of the afternoon the Russians had led them to the concentration camp to bury prisoners dead from starvation. Why should he describe to her how the naked bodies piled like a mountain of firewood resembled fragile china? How could he tell this dying child about ovens[9] and gallows? Nor did he mention the night that he had seen his mother naked, shod in stiletto-heeled red boots, sobbing with humiliation. There was much he did not tell, but in those hours he relived for the first time all the things his mind had tried to erase. Azucena had surrendered her fear to him and so, without wishing it, had obliged Rolf to confront his own. There, beside that hellhole of mud, it was impossible for Rolf to flee from himself any longer, and the visceral terror he had lived as a boy suddenly invaded him. He reverted to the years when he was the age of Azucena, and younger, and, like her, found himself trapped in a pit without escape, buried in life, his head barely above ground; he saw before his eyes the boots and legs of his father, who had removed his belt and was whipping it in the air with the never-forgotten hiss of a viper coiled to strike. Sorrow flooded through him, intact and precise, as if it had lain always in his mind, waiting. He was once again in the armoire where his father locked him to punish him for imagined misbehavior, there where for eternal hours he had crouched with his eyes closed, not to see the darkness, with his hands over his ears, to shut out the beating of his heart, trembling, huddled like a cornered animal. Wandering in the mist of his memories he found his sister Katharina, a sweet, retarded child who spent her life hiding, with the hope that her father would forget the disgrace of her having been born. With Katharina, Rolf crawled beneath the dining room table, and with her hid there under the long white tablecloth, two children forever embraced, alert to footsteps and voices. Katharina's scent melded with his own sweat, with aromas of cooking, garlic, soup, freshly baked bread, and the unexpected odor of putrescent clay. His sister's hand in his, her frightened breathing, her silk hair against his cheek, the candid

7. *One Thousand and One Nights* is a collection of Persian, Indian, and Arabic folktales; in its frame narrative, Scheherazade avoids becoming the latest victim of a king who daily marries and kills a new wife by telling him a story each night and promising to finish it the following one.

8. World War II (1939–45), between the Allied powers (including the United States, Britain, and the Soviet Union) and the Axis powers led by the German Third Reich.

9. Cremation ovens or chambers; the corpses of many of the 2.7 million Jews and others killed in Nazi concentration camps were burned in on-site crematoria.

gaze of her eyes. Katharina . . . Katharina materialized before him, floating on the air like a flag, clothed in the white tablecloth, now a winding sheet,[1] and at last he could weep for her death and for the guilt of having abandoned her. He understood then that all his exploits as a reporter, the feats that had won him such recognition and fame, were merely an attempt to keep his most ancient fears at bay, a stratagem for taking refuge behind a lens to test whether reality was more tolerable from that perspective. He took excessive risks as an exercise of courage, training by day to conquer the monsters that tormented him by night. But he had come face to face with the moment of truth; he could not continue to escape his past. He *was* Azucena; he was buried in the clayey mud; his terror was not the distant emotion of an almost forgotten childhood, it was a claw sunk in his throat. In the flush of his tears he saw his mother, dressed in black and clutching her imitation-crocodile[2] pocketbook to her bosom, just as he had last seen her on the dock when she had come to put him on the boat to South America. She had not come to dry his tears, but to tell him to pick up a shovel: the war was over and now they must bury the dead.

"Don't cry. I don't hurt anymore. I'm fine," Azucena said when dawn came.

25   "I'm not crying for you," Rolf Carlé smiled. "I'm crying for myself. I hurt all over."

The third day in the valley of the cataclysm began with a pale light filtering through storm clouds. The President of the Republic visited the area in his tailored safari jacket to confirm that this was the worst catastrophe of the century; the country was in mourning; sister nations had offered aid; he had ordered a state of siege; the Armed Forces would be merciless, anyone caught stealing or committing other offenses would be shot on sight. He added that it was impossible to remove all the corpses or count the thousands who had disappeared; the entire valley would be declared holy ground, and bishops would come to celebrate a solemn mass for the souls of the victims. He went to the Army field tents to offer relief in the form of vague promises to crowds of the rescued, then to the improvised hospital to offer a word of encouragement to doctors and nurses worn down from so many hours of tribulations. Then he asked to be taken to see Azucena, the little girl the whole world had seen. He waved to her with a limp statesman's hand, and microphones recorded his emotional voice and paternal tone as he told her that her courage had served as an example to the nation. Rolf Carlé interrupted to ask for a pump, and the President assured him that he personally would attend to the matter. I caught a glimpse of Rolf for a few seconds kneeling beside the mudpit. On the evening news broadcast, he was still in the same position; and I, glued to the screen like a fortuneteller to her crystal ball, could tell that something fundamental had changed in him. I knew somehow that during the night his defenses had crumbled and he had given in to grief; finally he was vulnerable. The girl had touched a part of him that he himself had no access to, a part he had never shared with me. Rolf had wanted to console her, but it was Azucena who had given him consolation.

---

1. Cloth in which a body is wrapped for burial.
2. Material imitating leather and made from crocodile hides.

I recognized the precise moment at which Rolf gave up the fight and surrendered to the torture of watching the girl die. I was with them, three days and two nights, spying on them from the other side of life. I was there when she told him that in all her thirteen years no boy had ever loved her and that it was a pity to leave this world without knowing love. Rolf assured her that he loved her more than he could ever love anyone, more than he loved his mother, more than his sister, more than all the women who had slept in his arms, more than he loved me, his life companion, who would have given anything to be trapped in that well in her place, who would have exchanged her life for Azucena's, and I watched as he leaned down to kiss her poor forehead, consumed by a sweet, sad emotion he could not name. I felt how in that instant both were saved from despair, how they were freed from the clay, how they rose above the vultures and helicopters, how together they flew above the vast swamp of corruption and laments. How, finally, they were able to accept death. Rolf Carlé prayed in silence that she would die quickly, because such pain cannot be borne.

By then I had obtained a pump and was in touch with a general who had agreed to ship it the next morning on a military cargo plane. But on the night of that third day, beneath the unblinking focus of quartz lamps[3] and the lens of a hundred cameras, Azucena gave up, her eyes locked with those of the friend who had sustained her to the end. Rolf Carlé removed the life buoy, closed her eyelids, held her to his chest for a few moments, and then let her go. She sank slowly, a flower in the mud.

You are back with me, but you are not the same man. I often accompany you to the station and we watch the videos of Azucena again; you study them intently, looking for something you could have done to save her, something you did not think of in time. Or maybe you study them to see yourself as if in a mirror, naked. Your cameras lie forgotten in a closet; you do not write or sing; you sit long hours before the window, staring at the mountains. Beside you, I wait for you to complete the voyage into yourself, for the old wounds to heal. I know that when you return from your nightmares, we shall again walk hand in hand, as before.

1989

AUTHORS ON THEIR WORK

ISABEL ALLENDE (b. 1942)

From "An Interview with Isabel Allende" (1997)*

The last story in this collection, which is the most elaborate [. . .], is called "And of Clay Are We Created"; and it is based on a real story. In 1985, there was a volcano eruption in Colombia and a little girl was trapped in the mud, and she died there after four days of terrible agony. I saw her on television in Venezuela, and I wrote this story. When I finished the story, I realized that I had tried to tell the story from an intellectual point of view, very passionate but it was my mind working. And then I realized that it wasn't the story of the little girl; it was

---

3. Mercury-vapor lamps in tubes of quartz glass.

the story of the man who was holding the little girl. So I rewrote the story once more, and when it was finished, I realized that there was something phony about it too. It wasn't the story of the man who was holding the girl; it was the story of the woman who is watching through a screen the man who holds the girl. This filter of the screen creates an artificial distance but also a terrible proximity because you see details that you would not see if you were actually there.

I would much rather write a thousand pages of a long novel than a short story. The shorter, the more difficult it is. [. . .] In a novel, you can have a lot of knots and bad stitches [. . .]. [A] short story has very brief time, very condensed concentrated plot [. . .]. The subtleties are important; the suggestion is very important. You work with the reader's imagination, and your only tool is language, and there is no space or time for anything else. Everything shows. This is how I compare these genres: the novel being a very elaborate tapestry that has a lot of details, and you embroider it with threads of many colors without even knowing what the finished design is. A short story is like an arrow; you have only one shot, and you need the precision, the direction, the speed, the firm wrist of the archer to get it right.

* * *

[E]very time that I read aloud in English my own stories, I feel very uncomfortable. I think the translation is great; sometimes it sounds much better than in Spanish, but it's another story. I can only be myself in my own language. [. . .] When I play with my grandchildren, it's always in Spanish. There is something that is playful and sensuous; it happens at a gut level, a very organic level that can only happen in your own language; it's like dreams.

* * *

Journalists are in the streets hand in hand with people, talking, participating, and sharing. Writers are very isolated people. [. . .] They [. . .] forget that there is the world out there. So, my background as a journalist helps me in that way. And there is something else that helps enormously. As a journalist, you know you have a few sentences with which to grab your reader, and you are competing with other media [. . .]. So you have to be very efficient with language, and you have to remember that the first important thing is to have a reader. Without a reader, there is no text.

*"An Interview with Isabel Allende." Interview by Farhat Iftekharuddin. *Speaking of the Short Story: Interviews with Contemporary Writers*, edited by Farhat Iftekharuddin et al., UP of Mississippi, 1997, pp. 3–14.

SAMPLE WRITING: READING NOTES

Student Renee Maalouf wrote the notes below with the "Questions about the Elements of Fiction" in mind (p. 19). As you read these notes, compare them to the notes you took as you read AND OF CLAY ARE WE CREATED. Do Maalouf's notes reveal anything to you that you didn't notice while reading the story? Did you notice anything she did not, or do you disagree with any of her interpretations?

Notes on Isabel Allende's "And of Clay Are We Created"

What do you expect?

- The title is almost in the phrase of a question and makes me wonder if I am about to read a myth/story about how humans were created.
- The first paragraph, however, reveals that a tragedy occurred and that Azucena and Rolf Carlé seem to be at the center of that tragedy as the media reports it. The detail that Rolf Carlé "never suspect[ed] that he would find a fragment of his past" makes me expect Rolf will confront his past while saving Azucena (par. 1).
- Azucena's name ("lily") and the narrator's reference to her as "the symbol of the tragedy" (par. 1) make me think that she should eventually blossom and become a symbol of hope in the midst of destruction.

What happens in the story?

- A lot happens in this story that takes place over three days. Before the story starts, a volcano erupts, and a girl gets trapped in a mudpit. During the story, a reporter stays with her and tries to reassure her that she'll be okay, but because the necessary equipment doesn't get through in time, she dies.
- A lot also happens in between those major plot points. Rolf's partner (the narrator) monitors the situation, trying to get the pump to him. Meanwhile other media outlets report what is happening to Azucena without helping her get out.
- Rolf finally faces his past, the horrors he endured during WWII, his father's abuse, and the death of his sister. His reflection allows him to see himself as "buried in the clayey mud" (par. 23).

How is the story narrated?

- The narrator is Rolf's partner. Little details reveal the identity of the narrator as the story goes on, but there's confirmation when the narrator is described as "his life companion" (par. 27).

- The story is told in past tense and first person. There are four breaks within the story (after pars. 16, 25, and 28) that reflect the passage of time. The first three parts each focus on one day. The last break in the story stands out because the last paragraph has the narrator refer directly to the effects of all this on Rolf after he is "back with" her (par. 29).
- Because the narrator is so close to Rolf, we seem to gain access to a lot of Rolf's thoughts. There are moments where it is unclear whether the narrator knows/assumes what Rolf is thinking and how much gets revealed because the narrator is watching footage of Rolf. For example, she says she "overheard fragments of what [Rolf and Azucena] said to one another and could guess the rest" (par. 22).

Who are the characters?

- There are three main characters: the narrator, Azucena, and Rolf. The narrator is Rolf's partner and knows a lot about his past, so she understands the change that takes place in him. We never learn the narrator's name. Azucena is thirteen years old and has never been anywhere except her village (par. 15). She is trapped in the mudpit after the volcanic eruption and unfortunately dies at the end of the story. Rolf is a reporter with a past he has not confronted until he meets Azucena.
- He and the narrator seem to be the only people who care about Azucena, which is especially clear because of minor characters like the President of the Republic who arrives in "his tailored safari jacket" with "vague promises" and waves at her with "a limp statesman's hand" (par. 26). The presence of him and the media doesn't save her. Instead it's the narrator who manages to get the pump to her, albeit too late.
- There is not necessarily one person who serves as an antagonist or villain in this story. The characters instead face natural and personal disasters. As a result of this disaster, Rolf sees himself in Azucena, as someone trapped in the clay of their past.
- Katharina is Rolf's sister and the only other named character.

What is the setting of the story?

- The eruption takes place on a Wednesday in November, but the year is unclear. Rolf's memories of World War II and the reference to "thirty years" in the first paragraph let me know the story must take place in the 1970s. The technology that is available like tapes, precision lenses, recorders, etc. also means that the story can't take place too far in the past.
- The story is more unclear about place. We do not learn the name of the village or "the Republic," but obviously it is somewhere with a volcano, somewhere that people speak Spanish ("Azecuna" is Spanish for "lily") and where at least some of them are Catholic (this is her "First Communion name," par. 1). Why not name the country?
- Three days pass in the story. But we also go back and forth in time as Rolf remembers the memories he has been trying to repress.
- In terms of physical setting, we're either with Rolf and Azucena at the scene of the eruption, or we're with the narrator as she does what she can to help Azucena and monitor the situation.

What do you notice about how the story is written?

- The narrator mostly uses complex sentences and vocabulary to tell this story. I think this style is important because these longer sentences carry some of the emotional turmoil of the story.
- The narrator makes it very clear that three days pass with Azucena in the clay. This makes me wonder if this is a Biblical allusion to the three days until Jesus was resurrected. The rain could also be a sign of baptism or cleansing that takes place. The clay is also symbolic. One thing it might symbolize is the weight of Rolf's past.
- The narrator is very sympathetic to and worried about Rolf and Azucena. This is most likely due to the narrator's relationship with the former and concern for a girl in such a terrible situation. What makes the narrator's narration interesting is that at times she reveals just enough to hint at what happens without explicitly saying it, or there are hints along the way until she reveals the full picture. For example, when first introducing Rolf, the narrator says she "came to realize that this fictive distance seemed to protect him from his own emotions" (par. 4). This foreshadows Rolf facing his emotions later on in the story.

What does the story mean? Can you express its theme or themes?

- There are two main themes that stood out to me as I read this story. The first is about how the media reports a tragedy. Millions of people manage to see Azucena's face on their screens because of cameras that made their way through the rubble, but the pump that Rolf keeps asking for does not come through. Even though millions see Azucena as a symbol of this tragedy, no one except Rolf and the narrator seem to actively try to save her.
- The second is about Rolf's past. He suffered a great deal of trauma that he managed to bury in his role as a reporter. He manages to rid himself of the clay that held him down while Azucena submerges. This makes me think back to the title. Are we created from the moments of our past?

SAMPLE WRITING: RESPONSE PAPER

A response paper may use a less formal organization and style than a longer, more formal essay, but it should not just be a summary or description of the work. Indeed, a response paper could be a step on the way to a longer essay. You need not form a single thesis or argument, but you should try to develop your ideas and feelings about the story by making reference to some specifies. The point is to get your thoughts in writing without worrying too much about form and style.

Almost everything in the following response paper comes directly from the notes above, but notice how the writer has combined and developed observations, adding more direct quotations or details from the text. (For ease of reference, we have altered the citations in this paper to refer to paragraph numbers. Unless your instructor indicates otherwise, you should always follow convention by instead citing page numbers when writing about fiction.)

Maalouf 1

Renee Maalouf
Dr. Mays
ENG 298
10 April 2021

Response Paper on Isabel Allende's "And of Clay
Are We Created"

Allende's story begins and almost ends with the same detail. We learn in the second sentence that the girl's name is Azucena, lily in Spanish. At the end, the narrator refers to her again as a "flower in the mud" when she sinks into the clay (par. 28). Azucena's introduction to Rolf is also with the acknowledgement of "her flower name" (par. 6). Other than the use of her name, there are no other flowers in the story whether physically present in the scene around her or figuratively present as Azucena and Rolf Carlé do their best to make it through each day waiting for a pump. As she becomes a "symbol of the tragedy," Azucena and her floral name suggest that she should eventually flourish, blossom, and stand for a symbol of hope in the midst of all the destruction (par. 1). The text unfortunately does not have this happy ending because the attention Azucena receives does not help her survive, calling into question the media's empathy for her and making me wonder why Allende gives a hopeful name to a tragic character. In this regard it is also ironic that to keep Azucena alive, Rolf needs "a pump to drain the water" that keeps her down (par. 9). This runs counter to what a flower typically needs to survive, perhaps foreshadowing Azucena's ill fate. She even weeps when it starts to rain, the water only bringing more sorrow.

Also Azucena's claim that "the bodies of her brothers and sisters [cling] to her legs" and hold her in the mud is significant in relation to her name because they almost act as roots that keep her in place (par. 7). Azucena's roots are her family, memories, and past. Due to the volcanic eruption, the only remnants of those roots cling to her legs. I do not think, however, that Azucena succumbing to the mud is due to her roots pulling her down. Ultimately, what ends Azucena's life is the inability of anyone to get a pump to her in time. Figures who could have tended to this flower, such as the President of the Republic with his "emotional voice and paternal tone as he told her that her courage had served as an example to the nation," do not fulfill their role or responsibility to save her (par. 26). A symbol of hope in the wake of a tragedy does not garner empathy that leads to survival. Rolf and the narrator are the only characters who show affection for Azucena, the former staying by her side while the latter manages to get the pump to them, albeit too late.

Work Cited

Allende, Isabel. "And of Clay Are We Created." *The Norton Introduction to Literature*, edited by Kelly J. Mays, shorter 14th ed., W. W. Norton, 2021, pp. 28-35.

SAMPLE WRITING: ESSAY

Because it focuses on both character and theme in Isabel Allende's AND OF CLAY ARE WE CREATED, the following essay would be an appropriate response to essay assignments involving either of these elements. More specifically, Renee Maalouf here tackles a series of interesting, interlinked questions: How does the story's central character develop over its course? How do other characters, as well as narration, enhance our sense of this development? What theme might emerge from it?

Read this essay as you would one of your peers' drafts, looking for opportunities for the writer to improve her argument and presentation in revision. How effectively does the draft answer the questions it poses? Are there claims that might be developed further? other evidence that should be considered? How might the conclusion be strengthened?

For ease of reference, we have altered the citations in this essay to refer to paragraph numbers. Unless your instructor indicates otherwise, you should always follow convention by instead citing page numbers when writing about fiction. For more on citation, see chapter 33.

Renee Maalouf
Dr. Mays
ENG 298
20 April 2021

A Moment of Connection in Isabel Allende's "And of Clay Are We Created"

In the wake of tragedy, empathy and sincerity run rampant toward those afflicted, or at least we hope they do, as we now have technology that allows us to watch disasters happen in real time through our various devices. Such is the case in Isabel Allende's "And of Clay Are We Created," as the media gathers to cover a volcanic eruption that leaves more than twenty thousand people buried in clay and to record the last hours of one victim—a thirteen-year-old girl named Azucena. Thanks to the narrator, readers observe one of these reporters, Rolf Carlé, as he makes his way to the scene. He immediately stands out in the crowd, and not just because he means a great deal to the narrator. In the three days that pass in Allende's short story, Rolf, with the help of Azucena, teaches readers that to free themselves from the clay keeping them down they must first confront the past that weighs on them so heavily. He accomplishes this by empathizing with Azucena in a way that the cameras surrounding them cannot. Rolf's character development illuminates the theme that people cannot disconnect from others and, more importantly, they cannot disconnect from themselves.

On the first day, the narrator divulges how Rolf normally conducts his reports, how he maintains composure in the face of "battles and catastrophes." The narrator describes "his equanimity in the face of danger and suffering" as an advantage in his profession, as a quality that "always amaze[s]" her. This gives him a leg up in his career and almost literally places him above others, as Rolf also has "the advantage of the television helicopter" and arrives among "the first to reach the scene" because he soars above those traveling on foot or wheels (par. 4). It is important that the narrator establishes Rolf's conduct prior to meeting Azucena because these details allow readers to see that he disconnects from himself and the world as a means of self-preservation, but in doing so he does not realize that his body is stuck in the clay like Azucena's. The narrator informs the audience from the start of the story that Rolf "never suspect[ed] that he would find a fragment of his past" on this assignment (par. 1). This is presumably because he has had no one to challenge his former aloofness. His ability to perform professionally may have placed him miles ahead of other reporters, but all this does is make him sink feet further into the mud.

Azucena, by the nature of her situation and their talking, draws the truth and a connection out of him. On the second day, we see Rolf and Azucena's bond continue to grow, and as a result of this new friendship, Rolf connects with his past. He now has the ability to do so because he no longer detaches himself from his surroundings or himself. The narrator can see the change in Rolf, that he has "completely forgotten the camera; he could not look at the girl through a lens any longer" (par. 19). This comes after he promises that he will buy Azucena gifts once she is in the hospital (par. 15), after learning about her life, and after realizing that the pump to save her life would not come right away (par. 9). Time spent together as "[t]he sky is weeping" (par. 20), as Azucena puts it, opens "the unyielding floodgates that had contained Rolf Carlé's past for so many years," as he lays bare his deepest and most secret and painful memories (par. 23). In this moment, we realize that Azucena is not the only one with family "clinging to her legs" (par. 7). This is Rolf's own tragedy to bear, a tragedy that the narrator describes all in one large, almost stream-of-consciousness paragraph, as Rolf tries to process in one short night years of hurt from his father, his sister, and the war until he finally realizes that "[h]e *was* Azucena; he was buried in clayey mud" (par. 23). He could only achieve this emotional release after forming a bond with Azucena, a person Rolf could not hide behind "the lens of the camera" to see or keep at a "fictive distance" (par. 4). To connect with her is to connect with his own troubles.

To fully acknowledge Rolf's sincerity toward Azucena and the growth it affords him, readers merely have to compare his experience to that of the others at the scene. The media reports the tragedy from the beginning, but they do not heavily engage with Azucena until the second day, parading her as "the symbol of the tragedy" for viewers at home (par. 1). For them, however, the main concern is getting whatever footage has the "most impact for the news report" (par. 17). The reason why they do not bother reporting about Azucena from the first day is because they do not see her value until later on. That value has nothing to do with empathy toward the young girl. They do not extend a hand the way Rolf does. Readers can see the sharp contrast between others' apathy and Rolf's empathy and the irony of the situation when the narrator reports,

> more television and movie teams arrived with spools of cable, tapes, film, videos, precision lenses, recorders, sound consoles, lights, reflecting screens, auxiliary motors, cartons of supplies, electricians, sound technicians, and cameramen: Azucena's face was beamed to millions of screens around the world. And all the while Rolf Carlé kept pleading for a pump. (par. 22)

This is the second time Rolf asks for a pump, and the narrator highlights the importance of the pump and the irony of the circumstances by placing Rolf's plea after a sentence that lists more than ten pieces of equipment that make it through the rubble when the one piece of equipment that could save Azucena does not. Rolf's intentions are clear. He only wants "to snatch her from death" (par. 9), while the other reporters do not share this concern. Again, he cannot separate himself from her the way he normally would have before this assignment. Readers see this one more time on the third day when the President of the Republic arrives to display himself in front of the cameras. Rolf asks for a pump for the third and final time, only to "still [be] in the same position" on the evening broadcast (par. 26). Others maintain their distance, and as a result, lack the growth that Rolf develops throughout the story.

By the third day, the narrator gathers that Rolf has irrevocably changed and that Azucena was the one to accomplish this change. She sees "that something fundamental ha[s] changed in him" and that "finally he [is] vulnerable" (par. 26). More importantly, the narrator reveals that Rolf has never shared this vulnerability with her. This is significant for two reasons. First, Rolf calls the narrator "his life companion," meaning they must share a particularly close bond, but even this bond does not give Rolf the space to share such a fragile piece of himself (par. 27). Second and as mentioned previously, the narrator knows who Rolf was before he met Azucena, and it seems she knows him best. For the narrator to so explicitly tie Rolf's growth to Azucena demonstrates how important the girl is for Rolf because Azucena accomplishes in three days what the narrator could not in however long she has known Rolf. By bonding with Azucena, he ultimately learns how to look inward and connect with himself.

Rolf Carlé is initially just another reporter among many sent to cover the news of the tragic volcanic eruption. His refusal to form attachments on assignment, however, ultimately gets shattered by the attention he pays to Azucena because her tragic reality and the bond they form forces him to confront his own past trauma. The empathy he feels toward her can now be extended to himself. This touches on the overall theme of Allende's short story— that the past can drag us down if we do not learn to connect with others and reflect on past hurt. Tragedy can bring out the worst in people, but it can also provide a moment to heal, and the narrator hopes Rolf will.

Maalouf 4

Work Cited

Allende, Isabel. "And of Clay Are We Created." *The Norton Introduction to Literature,* edited by Kelly J. Mays, shorter 14th ed., W. W. Norton, 2021, pp. 28-35.

Telling Stories

AN ALBUM

I s it human nature or human culture? Is it hardwired in our brains or inspired by our need to live with others in a community? Whatever the cause, people tell stories in every known society. Professional and amateur storytellers, as well as scholars in the humanities and sciences, have been paying more attention to the phenomenon of stories or narrative in recent decades. Online forums and organizations around the world are dedicated to a revival of oral storytelling. Educators, religious leaders, therapists, doctors, and organizers of programs for the young or the needy have turned to various publications and programs for guidance on how the techniques of storytelling might benefit their clients.

Stories are part of our everyday lives, and everyone has stories to tell. Perhaps you have heard the life stories broadcast every week on National Public Radio's *Morning Edition* in conjunction with the StoryCorps project, which allows ordinary Americans to record their own interviews with friends or family (often in a traveling "studio" van) and have their recordings archived in the Library of Congress. Most likely you are familiar with blogs, *Facebook*, *Twitter*, *YouTube* videos, and other means of producing or sharing some version of yourself, some aspect of your experience or your life.

Authors of short fiction have often reflected on the irresistible appeal of stories by making storytelling part of the plot or action *within* their fiction. We include here three stories that do just that. As you read the stories, think about what each implies about how stories and storytelling work and what they can do for us. When and why do we both tell stories and listen to those of others? What do we derive from the act of telling or listening, as well as from the story itself? What makes a story compelling, worth listening to or even writing down, according to the characters in these stories? How might the sorts of choices we make in telling a story resemble those a fiction writer makes in writing one? As listeners or readers, how are our expectations of a story and our responses to it shaped by our knowledge of or assumptions about its teller? In what different ways might stories, whether oral or written, be "true"? When and why does (or doesn't) the facticity of a story matter?

ANTON CHEKHOV

(1860–1904)

Gooseberries[1]

The grandson of a serf who purchased his family's freedom, Anton Pavlovich Chekhov was born in the Russian port city of Taganrog, where he apparently learned from his mother how to read, write, and spin a good yarn. In 1875, his devoutly religious and somewhat tyrannical father, a grocer facing imprisonment for debt, fled to Moscow; shortly thereafter, the family lost its house to a former friend, a misfortune that Chekhov would revisit in his last play, *The Cherry Orchard* (1904). Chekhov would not begin writing for the stage until 1887, three years after earning his MD from Moscow University. Throughout the 1880s, he supported his family, financed his studies, and began to make a name for himself by instead writing short stories and sketches for newspapers and magazines. His debut collection appeared in 1884, the same year he experienced the first symptoms of the tuberculosis that would eventually kill him. Declaring, "If I'm a doctor, I need patients and a hospital; if I'm a *littérateur*, I need to live among the folk," Chekhov in 1892 moved his family into a newly purchased estate near Moscow; here he would live for the next seven years, becoming both an industrious landowner and an unpaid doctor to the peasants of his own and surrounding districts. Though theater was Chekhov's primary focus after 1895, he continued until the end of his life to write fiction, including the 1898 trilogy of which "Gooseberries" forms a part. Each of the three stories in this, Chekhov's only, sequence or cycle (the others are "Man in a Case" and "About Love") features a story told either by or to the veterinarian Ivan Ivanych and his friend, the schoolteacher Burkin, during their trip into the countryside.

The sky had been overcast with rain clouds since early morning. The weather was mild, and not hot and oppressive as it can be on dull grey days when storm clouds lie over the fields for ages and you wait for rain which never comes. Ivan Ivanych, the vet, and Burkin, a teacher at the high school, were tired of walking and thought they would never come to the end of the fields. They could just make out the windmills at the village of Mironositskoye in the far distance—a range of hills stretched away to the right and disappeared far beyond it. They both knew that the river was there, with meadows, green willows and farmsteads, and that if they climbed one of the hills they would see yet another vast expanse of fields, telegraph wires and a train resembling a caterpillar in the distance. In fine weather they could see even as far as the town. And now, in calm weather, when the whole of nature had become gentle and dreamy, Ivan Ivanych and Burkin were filled with love for those open spaces and they both thought what a vast and beautiful country it was.

---

1. Translated from the Russian by Ronald Wilks.

"Last time we were in Elder Prokofy's barn, you were going to tell me a story," Burkin said.

"Yes, I wanted to tell you about my brother."

Ivan Ivanych heaved a long sigh and lit his pipe before beginning his narrative; but at that moment down came the rain. Five minutes later it was simply teeming. Ivan Ivanych and Burkin were in two minds as to what they should do. The dogs were already soaked through and stood with their tails drooping, looking at them affectionately.

"We must take shelter," Burkin said. "Let's go to Alyokhin's, it's not very far." 5

"All right, let's go there."

They changed direction and went across mown fields, walking straight on at first, and then bearing right until they came out on the high road. Before long, poplars, a garden, then the red roofs of barns came into view. The river glinted, and then they caught sight of a wide stretch of water and a white bathing-hut. This was Sofino, where Alyokhin lived.

The mill was turning and drowned the noise of the rain. The wall of the dam shook. Wet horses with downcast heads were standing by some carts and peasants went around with sacks on their heads. Everything was damp, muddy and bleak, and the water had a cold, malevolent look. Ivan Ivanych and Burkin felt wet, dirty and terribly uncomfortable. Their feet were weighed down by mud and when they crossed the dam and walked up to the barns near the manor house they did not say a word and seemed to be angry with each other.

A winnowing fan was droning away in one of the barns and dust poured out of the open door. On the threshold stood the master himself, Alyokhin, a man of about forty, tall, stout, with long hair, and he looked more like a professor or an artist than a landowner. He wore a white shirt that hadn't been washed for a very long time, and it was tied round with a piece of rope as a belt. Instead of trousers he was wearing underpants; mud and straw clung to his boots. His nose and eyes were black with dust. He immediately recognized Ivan Ivanych and Burkin, and was clearly delighted to see them.

"Please come into the house, gentlemen," he said, smiling, "I'll be with you in 10 a jiffy."

It was a large house, with two storeys. Alyokhin lived on the ground floor in the two rooms with vaulted ceilings and small windows where his estate managers used to live. They were simply furnished and smelled of rye bread, cheap vodka and harness. He seldom used the main rooms upstairs, reserving them for guests. Ivan Ivanych and Burkin were welcomed by the maid, who was such a beautiful young woman that they both stopped and stared at each other.

"You can't imagine how glad I am to see you, gentlemen," Alyokhin said as he followed them into the hall. "A real surprise!" Then he turned to the maid and said, "Pelageya, bring some dry clothes for the gentlemen. I suppose I'd better change too. But I must have a wash first, or you'll think I haven't had one since spring. Would you like to come to the bathing-hut while they get things ready in the house?"

The beautiful Pelageya, who had such a dainty look and gentle face, brought soap and towels, and Alyokhin went off with his guests to the bathing-hut.

"Yes, it's ages since I had a good wash," he said as he undressed. "As you can see, it's a nice hut. My father built it, but I never find time these days for a swim."

15   He sat on one of the steps and smothered his long hair and neck with soap; the water turned brown.

"Yes, I must confess . . ." Ivan Ivanych muttered, with a meaningful look at his head.

"Haven't had a wash for ages," Alyokhin repeated in his embarrassment and soaped himself again; the water turned a dark inky blue.

Ivan Ivanych came out of the cabin, dived in with a loud splash and swam in the rain, making broad sweeps with his arms and sending out waves with white lilies bobbing about on them. He swam right out to the middle of the reach and dived. A moment later he popped up somewhere else and swam on, continually trying to dive right to the bottom.

"Oh, good God," he kept saying with great relish. "Good God . . ."

20   He reached the mill, said a few words to the peasants, then he turned and floated on his back in the middle with his face under the rain. Burkin and Alyokhin were already dressed and ready to leave, but he kept on swimming and diving.

"Oh, dear God," he said. "Oh, God!"

"Now that's enough," Burkin shouted.

They went back to the house. Only when the lamp in the large upstairs drawing-room was alight and Burkin and Ivan Ivanych, wearing silk dressing-gowns and warm slippers, were sitting in armchairs and Alyokhin, washed and combed now and with a new frock-coat on, was walking up and down, obviously savouring the warmth, cleanliness, dry clothes and light shoes, while his beautiful Pelageya glided silently over the carpet and gently smiled as she served tea and jam on a tray—only then did Ivan Ivanych begin his story. It seemed that Burkin and Alyokhin were not the only ones who were listening, but also the ladies (young and old) and the officers, who were looking down calmly and solemnly from their gilt frames on the walls.

"There are two of us brothers," he began, "myself—Ivan Ivanych—and Niko-lay Ivanych, who's two years younger. I studied to be a vet, while Nikolay worked in the district tax office from the time he was nineteen. Chimsha-Gimalaysky, our father, had served as a private, but when he was promoted to officer we became hereditary gentlemen and owners of a small estate. After he died, this estate was sequestrated to pay off his debts, but despite this we spent our boyhood in the country free to do what we wanted. Just like any other village children, we stayed out in the fields and woods for days and nights, minded horses, stripped bark, went fishing, and so on . . . As you know very well, anyone who has ever caught a ruff[2] or watched migrating thrushes swarming over his native village on cool clear autumn days can never live in a town afterwards and he'll always hanker after the free and open life until his dying day. My brother was miserable in the tax office. The years passed, but there he stayed, always at the same old desk, copying out the same old documents and obsessed with this longing for the country. And gradually this longing took the form of a definite wish, a dream of buying a nice little estate somewhere in the country, beside a river or a lake.

2. Medium-sized wading bird common to northern European wetlands.

"He was a kind, gentle man and I was very fond of him, but I could never feel 25
any sympathy for him in this longing to lock himself away in a country house for
the rest of his life. They say a man needs only six feet of earth,[3] but surely they
must mean a corpse—not a *man*! These days they seem to think that it's very
good if our educated classes want to go back to the land and set their hearts on
a country estate. But in reality these estates are only that same six feet all over
again. To leave the town and all its noise and hubbub, to go and shut yourself
away on your little estate—that's no life! It's selfishness, laziness, a peculiar
brand of monasticism that achieves nothing. A man needs more than six feet of
earth and a little place in the country, he needs the whole wide world, the
whole of nature, where there's room for him to display his potential, all the
manifold attributes of his free spirit.

"As he sat there in his office, my brother Nikolay dreamt of soup made from
his own home-grown cabbages, soup that would fill the whole house with a delicious smell; eating meals on the green grass; sleeping in the sun; sitting on a
bench outside the main gates for hours on end and looking at the fields and
woods. Booklets on agriculture and words of wisdom from calendars were his
joy, his favourite spiritual nourishment. He liked newspapers as well, but he
only read property adverts[4]—for so many acres of arable land and meadows,
with 'house, river, garden, mill, and ponds fed by running springs.' And he had
visions of garden paths, flowers, fruit, nesting-boxes for starlings, ponds teeming with carp—you know the kind of thing. These visions varied according to
the adverts he happened to see, but for some reason, in every single one, there
had to be gooseberry bushes. 'Life in the country has its comforts,' he used to
say. 'You can sit drinking tea on your balcony, while your ducks are swimming
in the pond . . . it all smells so good and um . . . there's your gooseberries growing away!'

"He drew up a plan for his estate and it turned out exactly the same every
time: (a) manor house; (b) servants' quarters; (c) kitchen garden; (d) gooseberry
bushes. He lived a frugal life, economizing on food and drink, dressing any-old-
how—just like a beggar—and putting every penny he saved straight into the
bank. He was terribly mean.[5] It was really painful to look at him, so I used to
send him a little money on special occasions. But he would put that in the
bank too. Once a man has his mind firmly made up there's nothing you can do
about it.

"Years passed and he was transferred to another province. He was now in his
forties, still reading newspaper adverts and still saving up. Then I heard that
he'd got married. So that he could buy a country estate with gooseberry bushes,
he married an ugly old widow, for whom he felt nothing and only because she
had a little money tucked away. He made her life miserable too, half-starved her
and banked her money into his own account. She'd been married to a postmas-
ter and was used to pies and fruit liqueurs, but with her second husband she
didn't even have enough black bread. This kind of life made her wither away,

3. In Russian novelist Leo Tolstoy's story "How Much Land Does a Man Need?" (1886), the answer
turns out to be the six feet required for a grave.
4. Advertisements.
5. Mainly in the sense of "stingy."

and within three years she'd gone to join her maker. Of course, my brother didn't think that *he* was to blame—not for one minute! Like vodka, money can make a man do the most peculiar things. There was once a merchant living in our town who was on his deathbed. Just before he died, he asked for some honey, stirred it up with all his money and winning lottery tickets, and swallowed the lot to stop anyone else from laying their hands on it. And another time, when I was inspecting cattle at some railway station, a dealer fell under a train and had his leg cut off. We took him to the local casualty department.[6] The blood simply gushed out, a terrible sight, but all he did was ask for his leg back and was only bothered about the twenty roubles he had tucked away in the boot. Scared he might lose them, I dare say!"

"But that's neither here nor there," Burkin said.

30   "When his wife died," Ivan continued, after a pause for thought, "my brother started looking for an estate. Of course, you can look around for five years and still make the wrong choice and you finish up with something you never even dreamt of. So brother Nikolay bought about three hundred acres, with manor house, servants' quarters and a park, on a mortgage through an estate agent. But there wasn't any orchard, gooseberries or duck pond. There *was* a river, but the water was always the colour of coffee because of the brickworks on one side of the estate and a bone-ash[7] factory on the other. But my dear Nikolay didn't seem to care. He ordered twenty gooseberry bushes, planted them out and settled down to a landowner's life.

"Last year I visited him, as I wanted to see what was going on. In his letter my brother had called his estate 'Chumbaroklov Patch' or 'Gimalaysky's.' One afternoon I turned up at 'Gimalaysky's.' It was a hot day. Everywhere there were ditches, fences, hedges, rows of small fir trees and there seemed no way into the yard or anywhere to leave my horse. I went up to the house, only to be welcomed by a fat ginger dog that looked rather like a pig. It wanted to bark, but it was too lazy. Then a barefooted, plump cook—she resembled a pig as well—came out of the kitchen and told me the master was having his after-lunch nap. So I went to my brother's room and there he was sitting up in bed with a blanket over his knees. He'd aged, put on weight and looked very flabby. His cheeks, nose and lips stuck out and I thought any moment he was going to grunt into his blanket, like a pig.

"We embraced and wept for joy, and at the sad thought that once we were young and now both of us were grey, and that our lives were nearly over. He got dressed and led me on a tour of the estate.

"'Well, how's it going?' I asked.

"'All right, thank God. It's a good life.'

35   "No longer was he the poor, timid little clerk of before, but a real squire, a *gentleman*. He felt quite at home, being used to country life by then and he was enjoying himself. He ate a great deal, took proper baths, and he was putting on weight. Already he was suing the district council and both factories, and he got very peeved when the villagers didn't call him 'sir.' He paid great attention to his spiritual wellbeing (as a gentleman should) and he couldn't dispense charity

---

6. Equivalent to the modern ER or emergency room.
7. Ash, made from animal bones, used in pottery and glassmaking.

nice and quietly, but had to make a great show of it. And what did it all add up to? He doled out bicarbonate of soda or castor oil to his villagers—regardless of what they were suffering from—and on his name-day held a thanksgiving service in the village, supplying vodka in plenty, as he thought this was the right thing to do. Oh, those horrid pints of vodka! Nowadays your fat squire drags his villagers off to court for letting their cattle stray on his land and the very next day (if it's a high holiday) stands them all a few pints of vodka. They'll drink it, shout hurray and fall at his feet in a drunken stupor. Better standards of living, plenty to eat, idleness—all this makes us Russians terribly smug. Back in his office, Nikolay had been too scared even to voice any opinions of his own, but now he was expounding the eternal verities in true ministerial style: 'Education is essential, but premature as far as the common people are concerned' or 'Corporal punishment, generally speaking, is harmful, but in certain cases it can be useful and irreplaceable.' And he'd say, 'I know the working classes and how to handle them. They *like* me, I only have to lift my little finger and they'll do *anything* for me.'

"And he said all this, mark you, with a clever, good-natured smile. Time after time he'd say 'we *gentlemen*' or 'speaking as *one of the gentry*.' He'd evidently forgotten that our grandfather had been a peasant and our father a common soldier. Even our absolutely ridiculous surname, Chimsha-Gimalaysky, was melodious, distinguished and highly agreeable to his ears now.

"But it's myself I'm concerned with, not him. I'd like to tell you about the change that came over me during the few hours I spent on his estate. Later, when we were having tea, his cook brought us a plateful of gooseberries. They weren't shop gooseberries, but home-grown, the first fruits of the bushes he'd planted. Nikolay laughed and stared at them for a whole minute, with tears in his eyes. He was too deeply moved for words. Then he popped one in his mouth, looked at me like an enraptured child that has finally been given a long-awaited toy and said, 'Absolutely delicious!' He ate some greedily and kept repeating, 'So tasty, you *must* try one!'

"They were hard and sour, but as Pushkin says: 'Uplifting illusion is dearer to us than a host of truths.'[8] This was a happy man whose cherished dreams had clearly come true, who had achieved his life's purpose, had got what he wanted and was happy with his lot—and himself. My thoughts about human happiness, for some peculiar reason, had always been tinged with a certain sadness. But now, seeing this happy man, I was overwhelmed by a feeling of despondency that was close to utter despair. I felt particularly low that night. They made up a bed for me in the room next to my brother's. He was wide awake and I could hear him getting up, going over to the plate and helping himself to one gooseberry at a time. And I thought how many satisfied, happy people really do exist in this world! And what a powerful force they are! Just take a look at this life of ours and you will see the arrogance and idleness of the strong, the ignorance and bestiality of the weak. Everywhere there's unspeakable poverty, overcrowding, degeneracy, drunkenness, hypocrisy and stupid lies . . . And yet peace and quiet reign in every house and street. Out of fifty thousand people you won't find one who is prepared to shout out loud and make a strong protest. We see

8. Slightly misquoted line from Alexander Pushkin's poem "The Hero" (1830).

people buying food in the market, eating during the day, sleeping at night-time, talking nonsense, marrying, growing old and then contentedly carting their dead off to the cemetery. But we don't hear or see those who suffer: the real tragedies of life are enacted somewhere behind the scenes. Everything is calm and peaceful and the only protest comes from statistics—and they can't talk. Figures show that so many went mad, so many bottles of vodka were emptied, so many children died from malnutrition. And clearly this kind of system is what people need. It's obvious that the happy man feels contented only because the unhappy ones bear their burden without saying a word: if it weren't for their silence, happiness would be quite impossible. It's a kind of mass hypnosis. Someone ought to stand with a hammer at the door of every happy contented man, continually banging on it to remind him that there are unhappy people around and that however happy *he* may be at the time, sooner or later life will show him its claws and disaster will overtake him in the form of illness, poverty, bereavement and there will be no one to hear or see him. But there isn't anyone holding a hammer, so our happy man goes his own sweet way and is only gently ruffled by life's trivial cares, as an aspen is ruffled by the breeze. All's well as far as *he's* concerned.

"That night I realized that I too was happy and contented," Ivan Ivanych went on, getting to his feet. "I too had lectured people over dinner—or out hunting—on how to live, on what to believe, on how to handle the common people. And I too had told them that knowledge is a shining lamp, that education is essential, and that plain reading and writing is good enough for the masses, for the moment. Freedom is a blessing, I told them, and we need it like the air we breathe, but we must wait for it patiently."

40   Ivan Ivanych turned to Burkin and said angrily, "Yes, that's what I used to say and now I'd like to know *what* is it we're waiting for? I'm asking you, *what*? What is it we're trying to prove? I'm told that nothing can be achieved in five minutes, that it takes time for any kind of idea to be realized; it's a gradual process. But who says so? And what is there to prove he's right? You refer to the natural order of things, to the law of cause and effect. But *is* there any law or order in a state of affairs where a lively, thinking person like myself should have to stand by a ditch and wait until it's choked with weeds, or silted up, when I could quite easily, perhaps, leap across it or bridge it? I ask you again, what are we waiting for? Until we have no more strength to live, although we long to and *need* to go on living?

"I left my brother early next morning and ever since then I've found town life unbearable. I'm depressed by peace and quiet, I'm scared of peering through windows, nothing makes me more dejected than the sight of a happy family sitting round the table drinking tea. But I'm old now, no longer fit for the fray, I'm even incapable of hating. I only feel sick at heart, irritable and exasperated. At night my head seems to be on fire with so many thoughts crowding in and I can't get any sleep . . . Oh, if only I were young again!"

Ivan Ivanych paced the room excitedly, repeating, "If only I were young again!"

Suddenly he went up to Alyokhin and squeezed one hand, then the other. "Pavel Konstantinych,"[9] he pleaded, "don't go to sleep or be lulled into complacency! While

---

9. Ivanych here addresses his friend by his formal name rather than his nickname (Alyokhin).

you're still young, strong and healthy, never stop doing good! Happiness doesn't exist, we don't need any such thing. If life has any meaning or purpose, you won't find it in happiness, but in something more rational, in something greater. Doing good!"

Ivan Ivanych said all this with a pitiful, imploring smile, as though pleading for himself.

Afterwards all three of them sat in armchairs in different parts of the room and said nothing. Ivan Ivanych's story satisfied neither Burkin nor Alyokhin. It was boring listening to that story about some poor devil of a clerk who ate gooseberries, while those generals and ladies, who seemed to have come to life in the gathering gloom, peered out of their gilt frames. For some reason they would have preferred discussing and hearing about refined people, about ladies. The fact that they were all sitting in a drawing-room where everything—the draped chandeliers, the armchairs, the carpets underfoot—indicated that those same people who were now looking out of their frames had once walked around, sat down and drunk their tea there . . . and with beautiful Pelageya moving about here without a sound—all this was better than any story.

Alyokhin was dying to get to bed. That morning he had been up and about very early (before three) working on the farm, and he could hardly keep his eyes open. However, he was frightened he might miss some interesting story if he left now, so he stayed. He didn't even try to fathom if everything that Ivan Ivanych had just been saying was clever, or even true: he was only too glad that his guests did not discuss oats or hay or tar, but things that had nothing to do with his way of life, and he wanted them to continue . . .

"But it's time we got some sleep," Burkin said, standing up. "May I wish you all a very good night!"

Alyokhin bade them good night and went down to his room, while his guests stayed upstairs. They had been given the large room with two old, elaborately carved beds and an ivory crucifix in one corner. These wide, cool beds had been made by the beautiful Pelageya and the linen had a pleasant fresh smell.

Ivan Ivanych undressed without a word and got into bed. Then he muttered, "Lord have mercy on us sinners!" and pulled the blankets over his head. His pipe, which was lying on a table, smelt strongly of stale tobacco and Burkin was so puzzled as to where the terrible smell was coming from that it was a long time before he fell asleep.

All night long the rain beat against the windows.

QUESTIONS

1. What does Ivanych see as the central theme or lesson of the story he tells? How might the rest of Chekhov's story reinforce and/or complicate Ivanych's interpretation?
2. Why exactly do Burkin and Alyokhin find Ivanych's story unsatisfying? What is their idea of a satisfying story? Do you think they would find GOOSEBERRIES itself satisfying? Why or why not?
3. What might be the significance of the final three paragraphs of GOOSEBERRIES, especially the details regarding the bedroom, the pipe, and the weather?

TIM O'BRIEN

(b. 1946)

The Lives of the Dead

The son of an insurance salesman who fought in World War II and of an elementary-school teacher who had served, during the war, as a WAVE (navy speak for Women Accepted for Volunteer Emergency Service), William Timothy (Tim) O'Brien grew up in Worthington, Minnesota, a place he has suggested one might find a sketch of "[i]f you look in a dictionary under the word 'boring.'" After a childhood spent playing Little League and "reading books like [. . .] *Huckleberry Finn* and *Tom Sawyer*," as well as "crap [. . .] like *The Hardy Boys*," O'Brien headed to college in 1964, just as the Vietnam War was escalating. In 1968, he was welcomed home, political science degree in hand, by a draft notice. Opposed to the war, O'Brien seriously considered evading service by heading to nearby Canada, only to decide that he simply "couldn't do it." Four months later he was an infantryman in Vietnam on a thirteen-month tour of duty. Returning home, in 1970, with a Bronze Star and a Purple Heart, O'Brien began work on a Harvard PhD (in government) that he would never finish and, with his hybrid memoir/novel *If I Die in a Combat Zone, Box Me Up and Ship Me Home* (1973), launched his career. Though he has published several other novels, O'Brien is primarily known for three books—*If I Die . . .*, the National Book Award–winning novel *Going after Cacciato* (1978), and the short-story collection *The Things They Carried* (1990). A finalist for both the Pulitzer Prize and the National Book Critics Circle Award, the latter book opens with "The Things They Carried" and closes with "The Lives of the Dead."

But this too is true: stories can save us. I'm forty-three years old, and a writer now, and even still, right here, I keep dreaming Linda alive. And Ted Lavender, too, and Kiowa, and Curt Lemon, and a slim young man I killed, and an old man sprawled beside a pigpen, and several others whose bodies I once lifted and dumped into a truck. They're all dead. But in a story, which is a kind of dreaming, the dead sometimes smile and sit up and return to the world.

Start here: a body without a name. On an afternoon in 1969 the platoon took sniper fire from a filthy little village along the South China Sea.[1] It lasted only a minute or two, and nobody was hurt, but even so Lieutenant Jimmy Cross got on the radio and ordered up an air strike. For the next half hour we watched the place burn. It was a cool bright morning, like early autumn, and the jets were glossy black against the sky. When it ended, we formed into a loose line and swept east through the village. It was all wreckage. I remember the smell of burnt straw; I remember broken fences and torn-up trees and heaps of stone and brick and pottery. The place was deserted—no people, no animals—and the only con-

1. Part of the Pacific Ocean enclosed by China and Taiwan (to the north), the Philippines (to the east), and Vietnam (to the west). The setting here is Vietnam during the Vietnam War (c. 1955–75).

firmed kill was an old man who lay face-up near a pigpen at the center of the village. His right arm was gone. At his face there were already many flies and gnats.

Dave Jensen went over and shook the old man's hand. "How-dee-doo," he said.

One by one the others did it too. They didn't disturb the body, they just grabbed the old man's hand and offered a few words and moved away.

Rat Kiley bent over the corpse. "Gimme five," he said. "A real honor." 5

"Pleased as punch," said Henry Dobbins.

I was brand-new to the war. It was my fourth day; I hadn't yet developed a sense of humor. Right away, as if I'd swallowed something, I felt a moist sickness rise up in my throat. I sat down beside the pigpen, closed my eyes, put my head between my knees.

After a moment Dave Jensen touched my shoulder.

"Be polite now," he said. "Go introduce yourself. Nothing to be afraid about, just a nice old man. Show a little respect for your elders."

"No way." 10

"Maybe it's too real for you?"

"That's right," I said. "Way too real."

Jensen kept after me, but I didn't go near the body. I didn't even look at it except by accident. For the rest of the day there was still that sickness inside me, but it wasn't the old man's corpse so much, it was that awesome act of greeting the dead. At one point, I remember, they sat the body up against a fence. They crossed his legs and talked to him. "The guest of honor," Mitchell Sanders said, and he placed a can of orange slices in the old man's lap. "Vitamin C," he said gently. "A guy's health, that's the most important thing."

They proposed toasts. They lifted their canteens and drank to the old man's family and ancestors, his many grandchildren, his newfound life after death. It was more than mockery. There was a formality to it, like a funeral without the sadness.

Dave Jensen flicked his eyes at me. 15

"Hey, O'Brien," he said, "you got a toast in mind? Never too late for manners."

I found things to do with my hands. I looked away and tried not to think.

Late in the afternoon, just before dusk, Kiowa came up and asked if he could sit at my foxhole for a minute. He offered me a Christmas cookie from a batch his father had sent him. It was February now, but the cookies tasted fine.

For a few moments Kiowa watched the sky.

"You did a good thing today," he said. "That shaking hands crap, it isn't 20 decent. The guys'll hassle you for a while—especially Jensen—but just keep saying no. Should've done it myself. Takes guts, I know that."

"It wasn't guts. I was scared."

Kiowa shrugged. "Same difference."

"No. I couldn't do it. A mental block or something . . . I don't know, just creepy."

"Well, you're new here. You'll get used to it." He paused for a second, studying the green and red sprinkles on a cookie. "Today—I guess this was your first look at a real body?"

I shook my head. All day long I'd been picturing Linda's face, the way she 25 smiled.

"It sounds funny," I said, "but that poor old man, he reminds me of . . . I mean, there's this girl I used to know. I took her to the movies once. My first date."

Kiowa looked at me for a long while. Then he leaned back and smiled. "Man," he said, "that's a bad date."

Linda was nine then, as I was, but we were in love. And it was real. When I write about her now, three decades later, it's tempting to dismiss it as a crush, an infatuation of childhood, but I know for a fact that what we felt for each other was as deep and rich as love can ever get. It had all the shadings and complexities of mature adult love, and maybe more, because there were not yet words for it, and because it was not yet fixed to comparisons or chronologies or the ways by which adults measure such things.

30   I just loved her.

She had poise and great dignity. Her eyes, I remember, were deep brown like her hair, and she was slender and very quiet and fragile-looking.

Even then, at nine years old, I wanted to live inside her body. I wanted to melt into her bones—*that* kind of love.

And so in the spring of 1956, when we were in the fourth grade, I took her out on the first real date of my life—a double date, actually, with my mother and father. Though I can't remember the exact sequence, my mother had somehow arranged it with Linda's parents, and on that damp spring night my dad did the driving while Linda and I sat in the back seat and stared out opposite windows, both of us trying to pretend it was nothing special. For me, though, it was very special. Down inside I had important things to tell her, big profound things, but I couldn't make any words come out. I had trouble breathing. Now and then I'd glance over at her, thinking how beautiful she was: her white skin and those dark brown eyes and the way she always smiled at the world—always, it seemed—as if her face had been designed that way. The smile never went away. That night, I remember, she wore a new red cap, which seemed to me very stylish and sophisticated, very unusual. It was a stocking cap, basically, except the tapered part at the top seemed extra long, almost too long, like a tail growing out of the back of her head. It made me think of the caps that Santa's elves wear, the same shape and color, the same fuzzy white tassel at the tip.

Sitting there in the back seat, I wanted to find some way to let her know how I felt, a compliment of some sort, but all I could manage was a stupid comment about the cap. "Jeez," I must've said, "what a *cap.*"

35   Linda smiled at the window—she knew what I meant—but my mother turned and gave me a hard look. It surprised me. It was as if I'd brought up some horrible secret.

For the rest of the ride I kept my mouth shut. We parked in front of the Ben Franklin store[2] and walked up Main Street toward the State Theater. My parents went first, side by side, and then Linda in her new red cap, and then me tailing along ten or twenty steps behind. I was nine years old; I didn't yet have the gift for small talk. Now and then my mother glanced back, making little motions with her hand to speed me up.

At the ticket booth, I remember, Linda stood off to one side. I moved over to the concession area, studying the candy, and both of us were very careful to avoid the awkwardness of eye contact. Which was how we knew about being in

2. Discount store common in small towns throughout the United States since the 1920s.

love. It was pure knowing. Neither of us, I suppose, would've thought to use that word, love, but by the fact of not looking at each other, and not talking, we understood with a clarity beyond language that we were sharing something huge and permanent.

Behind me, in the theater, I heard cartoon music.

"Hey, step it up," I said. I almost had the courage to look at her. "You want popcorn or *what*?"

The thing about a story is that you dream it as you tell it, hoping that others   40
might then dream along with you, and in this way memory and imagination and language combine to make spirits in the head. There is the illusion of aliveness. In Vietnam, for instance, Ted Lavender had a habit of popping four or five tran-quilizers every morning. It was his way of coping, just dealing with the realities, and the drugs helped to ease him through the days. I remember how peaceful his eyes were. Even in bad situations he had a soft, dreamy expression on his face, which was what he wanted, a kind of escape. "How's the war today?" somebody would ask, and Ted Lavender would give a little smile to the sky and say, "Mellow—a nice smooth war today." And then in April he was shot in the head outside the village of Than Khe. Kiowa and I and a couple of others were ordered to prepare his body for the dustoff.[3] I remember squatting down, not wanting to look but then looking. Lavender's left cheekbone was gone. There was a swollen blackness around his eye. Quickly, trying not to feel anything, we went through the kid's pockets. I remember wishing I had gloves. It wasn't the blood I hated; it was the deadness. We put his personal effects in a plastic bag and tied the bag to his arm. We stripped off the canteens and ammo, all the heavy stuff, and wrapped him up in his own poncho and carried him out to a dry paddy and laid him down.

For a while nobody said much. Then Mitchell Sanders laughed and looked over at the green plastic poncho.

"Hey, Lavender," he said, "how's the war today?"

There was a short quiet.

"Mellow," somebody said.

"Well, that's good," Sanders murmured, "that's real, real good. Stay cool now."   45

"Hey, no sweat, I'm mellow."

"Just ease on back, then. Don't need no pills. We got this incredible chopper on call, this once in a lifetime mind-trip."

"Oh, yeah—mellow!"

Mitchell Sanders smiled. "There it is, my man, this chopper gonna take you up high and cool. Gonna relax you. Gonna alter your whole perspective on this sorry, sorry shit."

We could almost see Ted Lavender's dreamy blue eyes. We could almost   50
hear him.

"Roger that," somebody said. "I'm ready to fly."

There was the sound of the wind, the sound of birds and the quiet afternoon, which was the world we were in.

3. Medical evacuation helicopter, perhaps an acronym for Dedicated Unhesitating Service To Our Fighting Forces.

That's what a story does. The bodies are animated. You make the dead talk. They sometimes say things like, "Roger that." Or they say, "Timmy, stop crying," which is what Linda said to me after she was dead.

Even now I can see her walking down the aisle of the old State Theater in Worthington, Minnesota.[4] I can see her face in profile beside me, the cheeks softly lighted by coming attractions.

55   The movie that night was *The Man Who Never Was.*[5] I remember the plot clearly, or at least the premise, because the main character was a corpse. That fact alone, I know, deeply impressed me. It was a World War Two film: the Allies[6] devise a scheme to mislead Germany about the site of the upcoming landings in Europe. They get their hands on a body—a British soldier, I believe; they dress him up in an officer's uniform, plant fake documents in his pockets, then dump him in the sea and let the currents wash him onto a Nazi beach. The Germans find the documents; the deception wins the war. Even now, I can remember the awful splash as that corpse fell into the sea. I remember glancing over at Linda, thinking it might be too much for her, but in the dim gray light she seemed to be smiling at the screen. There were little crinkles at her eyes, her lips open and gently curving at the corners. I couldn't understand it. There was nothing to smile at. Once or twice, in fact, I had to close my eyes, but it didn't help much. Even then I kept seeing the soldier's body tumbling toward the water, splashing down hard, how inert and heavy it was, how completely dead.

It was a relief when the movie finally ended.

Afterward, we drove out to the Dairy Queen at the edge of town. The night had a quilted, weighted-down quality, as if somehow burdened, and all around us the Minnesota prairies reached out in long repetitive waves of corn and soybeans, everything flat, everything the same. I remember eating ice cream in the back seat of the Buick, and a long blank drive in the dark, and then pulling up in front of Linda's house. Things must've been said, but it's all gone now except for a few last images. I remember walking her to the front door. I remember the brass porch light with its fierce yellow glow, my own feet, the juniper bushes along the front steps, the wet grass, Linda close beside me. We were in love. Nine years old, yes, but it was real love, and now we were alone on those front steps. Finally we looked at each other.

"Bye," I said.

Linda nodded and said, "Bye."

60   Over the next few weeks Linda wore her new red cap to school every day. She never took it off, not even in the classroom, and so it was inevitable that she took some teasing about it. Most of it came from a kid named Nick Veenhof. Out on the playground, during recess, Nick would creep up behind her and make a grab for the cap, almost yanking it off, then scampering away. It went on like that for weeks: the girls giggling, the guys egging him on. Naturally I wanted to do something about it, but it just wasn't possible. I had my reputation to think about. I had my pride. And there was also the problem of Nick Veenhof. So I stood off to

4. Small town near the South Dakota border where author Tim O'Brien grew up.
5. Film (1956) based on real events that occurred during World War II.
6. Coalition of nations including France, Great Britain, and the United States.

the side, just a spectator, wishing I could do things I couldn't do. I watched Linda clamp down the cap with the palm of her hand, holding it there, smiling over in Nick's direction as if none of it really mattered.

For me, though, it did matter. It still does. I should've stepped in; fourth grade is no excuse. Besides, it doesn't get easier with time, and twelve years later, when Vietnam presented much harder choices, some practice at being brave might've helped a little.

Also, too, I might've stopped what happened next. Maybe not, but at least it's possible.

Most of the details I've forgotten, or maybe blocked out, but I know it was an afternoon in late spring, and we were taking a spelling test, and halfway into the test Nick Veenhof held up his hand and asked to use the pencil sharpener. Right away a couple of kids laughed. No doubt he'd broken the pencil on purpose, but it wasn't something you could prove, and so the teacher nodded and told him to hustle it up. Which was a mistake. Out of nowhere Nick developed a terrible limp. He moved in slow motion, dragging himself up to the pencil sharpener and carefully slipping in his pencil and then grinding away forever. At the time, I suppose, it was funny. But on the way back to his seat Nick took a short detour. He squeezed between two desks, turned sharply right, and moved up the aisle toward Linda.

I saw him grin at one of his pals. In a way, I already knew what was coming.

As he passed Linda's desk, he dropped the pencil and squatted down to get 65 it. When he came up, his left hand slipped behind her back. There was a half-second hesitation. Maybe he was trying to stop himself; maybe then, just briefly, he felt some small approximation of guilt. But it wasn't enough. He took hold of the white tassel, stood up, and gently lifted off her cap.

Somebody must've laughed. I remember a short, tinny echo. I remember Nick Veenhof trying to smile. Somewhere behind me, a girl said, "Uh," or a sound like that.

Linda didn't move.

Even now, when I think back on it, I can still see the glossy whiteness of her scalp. She wasn't bald. Not quite. Not completely. There were some tufts of hair, little patches of grayish brown fuzz. But what I saw then, and keep seeing now, is all that whiteness. A smooth, pale, translucent white. I could see the bones and veins; I could see the exact structure of her skull. There was a large Band-Aid at the back of her head, a row of black stitches, a piece of gauze taped above her left ear.

Nick Veenhof took a step backward. He was still smiling, but the smile was doing strange things.

The whole time Linda stared straight ahead, her eyes locked on the black- 70 board, her hands loosely folded at her lap. She didn't say anything. After a time, though, she turned and looked at me across the room. It lasted only a moment, but I had the feeling that a whole conversation was happening between us. *Well?* she was saying, and I was saying, *Sure, okay.*

Later on, she cried for a while. The teacher helped her put the cap back on, then we finished the spelling test and did some fingerpainting, and after school that day Nick Veenhof and I walked her home.

It's now 1990. I'm forty-three years old, which would've seemed impossible to a fourth grader, and yet when I look at photographs of myself as I was in 1956,

I realize that in the important ways I haven't changed at all. I was Timmy then; now I'm Tim. But the essence remains the same. I'm not fooled by the baggy pants or the crew cut or the happy smile—I know my own eyes—and there is no doubt that the Timmy smiling at the camera is the Tim I am now. Inside the body, or beyond the body, there is something absolute and unchanging. The human life is all one thing, like a blade tracing loops on ice: a little kid, a twenty-three-year-old infantry sergeant, a middle-aged writer knowing guilt and sorrow.

And as a writer now, I want to save Linda's life. Not her body—her life.

She died, of course. Nine years old and she died. It was a brain tumor. She lived through the summer and into the first part of September, and then she was dead.

75   But in a story I can steal her soul. I can revive, at least briefly, that which is absolute and unchanging. In a story, miracles can happen. Linda can smile and sit up. She can reach out, touch my wrist, and say, "Timmy, stop crying."

I needed that kind of miracle. At some point I had come to understand that Linda was sick, maybe even dying, but I loved her and just couldn't accept it. In the middle of the summer, I remember, my mother tried to explain to me about brain tumors. Now and then, she said, bad things start growing inside us. Sometimes you can cut them out and other times you can't, and for Linda it was one of the times when you can't.

I thought about it for several days. "All right," I finally said. "So will she get better now?"

"Well, no," my mother said, "I don't think so." She stared at a spot behind my shoulder. "Sometimes people don't ever get better. They die sometimes."

I shook my head.

80   "Not Linda," I said.

But on a September afternoon, during noon recess, Nick Veenhof came up to me on the school playground. "Your girlfriend," he said, "she kicked the bucket."

At first I didn't understand.

"She's dead," he said. "My mom told me at lunch-time. No lie, she actually kicked the goddang *bucket*."

All I could do was nod. Somehow it didn't quite register. I turned away, glanced down at my hands for a second, then walked home without telling anyone.

85   It was a little after one o'clock, I remember, and the house was empty.

I drank some chocolate milk and then lay down on the sofa in the living room, not really sad, just floating, trying to imagine what it was to be dead. Nothing much came to me. I remember closing my eyes and whispering her name, almost begging, trying to make her come back. "Linda," I said, "please." And then I concentrated. I willed her alive. It was a dream, I suppose, or a daydream, but I made it happen. I saw her coming down the middle of Main Street, all alone. It was nearly dark and the street was deserted, no cars or people, and Linda wore a pink dress and shiny black shoes. I remember sitting down on the curb to watch. All her hair had grown back. The scars and stitches were gone. In the dream, if that's what it was, she was playing a game of some sort, laughing and running up the empty street, kicking a big aluminum water bucket.

Right then I started to cry. After a moment Linda stopped and carried her water bucket over to the curb and asked why I was so sad.

"Well, God," I said, "you're dead."

Linda nodded at me. She was standing under a yellow streetlight. A nine-year-old girl, just a kid, and yet there was something ageless in her eyes—not a child, not an adult—just a bright ongoing everness, that same pinprick of absolute lasting light that I see today in my own eyes as Timmy smiles at Tim from the graying photographs of that time.

"Dead," I said.

Linda smiled. It was a secret smile, as if she knew things nobody could ever know, and she reached out and touched my wrist and said, "Timmy, stop crying. It doesn't *matter*."

In Vietnam, too, we had ways of making the dead seem not quite so dead. Shaking hands, that was one way. By slighting death, by acting, we pretended it was not the terrible thing it was. By our language, which was both hard and wistful, we transformed the bodies into piles of waste. Thus, when someone got killed, as Curt Lemon did, his body was not really a body, but rather one small bit of waste in the midst of a much wider wastage. I learned that words make a difference. It's easier to cope with a kicked bucket than a corpse; if it isn't human, it doesn't matter much if it's dead. And so a VC nurse, fried by napalm,[7] was a crispy critter. A Vietnamese baby, which lay nearby, was a roasted peanut. "Just a crunchie munchie," Rat Kiley said as he stepped over the body.

We kept the dead alive with stories. When Ted Lavender was shot in the head, the men talked about how they'd never seen him so mellow, how tranquil he was, how it wasn't the bullet but the tranquilizers that blew his mind. He wasn't dead, just laid-back. There were Christians among us, like Kiowa, who believed in the New Testament stories of life after death. Other stories were passed down like legends from old-timer to newcomer. Mostly, though, we had to make up our own. Often they were exaggerated, or blatant lies, but it was a way of bringing body and soul back together, or a way of making new bodies for the souls to inhabit. There was a story, for instance, about how Curt Lemon had gone trick-or-treating on Halloween. A dark, spooky night, and so Lemon put on a ghost mask and painted up his body all different colors and crept across a paddy to a sleeping village—almost stark naked, the story went, just boots and balls and an M-16—and in the dark Lemon went from hootch to hootch[8]—ringing doorbells, he called it—and a few hours later, when he slipped back into the perimeter, he had a whole sackful of goodies to share with his pals: candles and joss[9] sticks and a pair of black pajamas and statuettes of the smiling Buddha. That was the story, anyway. Other versions were much more elaborate, full of descriptions and scraps of dialogue. Rat Kiley liked to spice it up with extra details: "See, what happens is, it's like four in the morning, and Lemon sneaks into a hootch with that weird ghost mask on. Everybody's asleep, right? So he wakes up this cute little mama-san.[1] Tickles her foot. 'Hey,

7. Flammable jelly used in incendiary bombs. *VC*: Viet Cong (military acronym/slang), short for *Viet Nam Cong San*, meaning "Vietnamese Communists," the guerrilla force that fought, with the support of the North Vietnamese Army, against both South Vietnam and the United States during the Vietnam War.
8. Hut or small dwelling (slang).
9. Incense.
1. In East Asia, a woman in authority; in Japanese, *san* is an honorific suffix, a title (not unlike "Mr." or "Mrs.") added to names and proper nouns to indicate respect.

Mama-san,' he goes, real soft like. Hey, Mama-san—trick or treat!' Should've seen her face. About freaks. I mean, there's this buck naked ghost standing there, and he's got this M-16 up against her ear and he whispers, 'Hey, Mama-san, trick or fuckin' treat!' Then he takes off her pj's. Strips her right down. Sticks the pajamas in his sack and tucks her into bed and heads for the next hootch."

Pausing a moment, Rat Kiley would grin and shake his head. "Honest to God," he'd murmur. "Trick or treat. Lemon—there's one class act."

95   To listen to the story, especially as Rat Kiley told it, you'd never know that Curt Lemon was dead. He was still out there in the dark, naked and painted up, trick-or-treating, sliding from hootch to hootch in that crazy white ghost mask. But he was dead.

In September, the day after Linda died, I asked my father to take me down to Benson's Funeral Home to view the body. I was a fifth grader then; I was curious. On the drive downtown my father kept his eyes straight ahead. At one point, I remember, he made a scratchy sound in his throat. It took him a long time to light up a cigarette.

"Timmy," he said, "you're sure about this?"

I nodded at him. Down inside, of course, I wasn't sure, and yet I had to see her one more time. What I needed, I suppose, was some sort of final confirmation, something to carry with me after she was gone.

When we parked in front of the funeral home, my father turned and looked at me. "If this bothers you," he said, "just say the word. We'll make a quick getaway. Fair enough?"

100   "Okay," I said.

"Or if you start to feel sick or anything—"

"I *won't*," I told him.

Inside, the first thing I noticed was the smell, thick and sweet, like something sprayed out of a can. The viewing room was empty except for Linda and my father and me. I felt a rush of panic as we walked up the aisle. The smell made me dizzy. I tried to fight it off, slowing down a little, taking short, shallow breaths through my mouth. But at the same time I felt a funny excitement. Anticipation, in a way—that same awkward feeling as when I'd walked up the sidewalk to ring her doorbell on our first date. I wanted to impress her. I wanted something to happen between us, a secret signal of some sort. The room was dimly lighted, almost dark, but at the far end of the aisle Linda's white casket was illuminated by a row of spotlights up in the ceiling. Everything was quiet. My father put his hand on my shoulder, whispered something, and backed off. After a moment I edged forward a few steps, pushing up on my toes for a better look.

It didn't seem real. A mistake, I thought. The girl lying in the white casket wasn't Linda. There was a resemblance, maybe, but where Linda had always been very slender and fragile-looking, almost skinny, the body in that casket was fat and swollen. For a second I wondered if somebody had made a terrible blunder. A technical mistake: pumped her too full of formaldehyde or embalming fluid or whatever they used. Her arms and face were bloated. The skin at her cheeks was stretched out tight like the rubber skin on a balloon just before it pops open. Even her fingers seemed puffy. I turned and glanced behind me, where my father stood, thinking that maybe it was a joke—hoping it was a joke—almost believing that Linda would jump out from behind one of the curtains and laugh and yell out my name.

But she didn't. The room was silent. When I looked back at the casket, I felt dizzy again. In my heart, I'm sure, I knew this was Linda, but even so I couldn't find much to recognize. I tried to pretend she was taking a nap, her hands folded at her stomach, just sleeping away the afternoon. Except she didn't *look* asleep. She looked dead. She looked heavy and totally dead.

I remember closing my eyes. After a while my father stepped up beside me.

"Come on now," he said. "Let's go get some ice cream."

In the months after Ted Lavender died, there were many other bodies. I never shook hands—not that—but one afternoon I climbed a tree and threw down what was left of Curt Lemon. I watched my friend Kiowa sink into the muck along the Song²Tra Bong. And in early July, after a battle in the mountains, I was assigned to a six-man detail to police up the enemy KIAs.³ There were twenty-seven bodies altogether, and parts of several others. The dead were everywhere. Some lay in piles. Some lay alone. One, I remember, seemed to kneel. Another was bent from the waist over a small boulder, the top of his head on the ground, his arms rigid, the eyes squinting in concentration as if he were about to perform a handstand or somersault. It was my worst day at the war. For three hours we carried the bodies down the mountain to a clearing alongside a narrow dirt road. We had lunch there, then a truck pulled up, and we worked in two-man teams to load the truck. I remember swinging the bodies up. Mitchell Sanders took a man's feet, I took the arms, and we counted to three, working up momentum, and then we tossed the body high and watched it bounce and come to rest among the other bodies. The dead had been dead for more than a day. They were all badly bloated. Their clothing was stretched tight like sausage skins, and when we picked them up, some made sharp burping sounds as the gases were released. They were heavy. Their feet were bluish green and cold. The smell was terrible. At one point Mitchell Sanders looked at me and said, "Hey, man, I just realized something."

"What?"

He wiped his eyes and spoke very quietly, as if awed by his own wisdom. "Death sucks," he said.

Lying in bed at night, I made up elaborate stories to bring Linda alive in my sleep. I invented my own dreams. It sounds impossible, I know, but I did it. I'd picture somebody's birthday party—a crowded room, I'd think, and a big chocolate cake with pink candles—and then soon I'd be dreaming it, and after a while Linda would show up, as I knew she would, and in the dream we'd look at each other and not talk much, because we were shy, but then later I'd walk her home and we'd sit on her front steps and stare at the dark and just be together. She'd say amazing things sometimes. "Once you're alive," she'd say, "you can't ever be dead."

Or she'd say: "Do I *look* dead?"

2. River (Vietnamese).
3. Killed in action (military acronym/slang).

It was a kind of self-hypnosis. Partly willpower, partly faith, which is how stories arrive.

But back then it felt like a miracle. My dreams had become a secret meeting place, and in the weeks after she died I couldn't wait to fall asleep at night. I began going to bed earlier and earlier, sometimes even in bright daylight. My mother, I remember, finally asked about it at breakfast one morning. "Timmy, what's *wrong*?" she said, but all I could do was shrug and say, "Nothing, I just need sleep, that's all." I didn't dare tell the truth. It was embarrassing, I suppose, but it was also a precious secret, like a magic trick, where if I tried to explain it, or even talk about it, the thrill and mystery would be gone. I didn't want to lose Linda.

She was dead. I understood that. After all, I'd seen her body. And yet even as a nine-year-old I had begun to practice the magic of stories. Some I just dreamed up. Others I wrote down—the scenes and dialogue. And at nighttime I'd slide into sleep knowing that Linda would be there waiting for me. Once, I remember, we went ice skating late at night, tracing loops and circles under yellow floodlights. Later we sat by a wood stove in the warming house, all alone, and after a while I asked her what it was like to be dead. Apparently Linda thought it was a silly question. She smiled and said, "Do I *look* dead?"

I told her no, she looked terrific. I waited a moment, then asked again, and Linda made a soft little sigh. I could smell our wool mittens drying on the stove.

For a few seconds she was quiet.

"Well, right now," she said, "I'm *not* dead. But when I am, it's like . . . I don't know. I guess it's like being inside a book that nobody's reading."

"A book?" I said.

"An old one. It's up on a library shelf, so you're safe and everything, but the book hasn't been checked out for a long, long time. All you can do is wait. Just hope somebody'll pick it up and start reading."

Linda smiled at me.

"Anyhow, it's not so bad," she said. "I mean, when you're dead, you just have to be yourself." She stood up and put on her red stocking cap. "This is stupid. Let's go skate some more."

So I followed her down to the frozen pond. It was late, and nobody else was there, and we held hands and skated almost all night under the yellow lights.

And then it becomes 1990. I'm forty-three years old, and a writer now, still dreaming Linda alive in exactly the same way. She's not the embodied Linda; she's mostly made up, with a new identity and a new name, like the man who never was. Her real name doesn't matter. She was nine years old. I loved her and then she died. And yet right here, in the spell of memory and imagination, I can still see her as if through ice, as if I'm gazing into some other world, a place where there are no brain tumors and no funeral homes, where there are no bodies at all. I can see Kiowa, too, and Ted Lavender and Curt Lemon, and sometimes I can even see Timmy skating with Linda under the yellow flood-lights. I'm young and happy. I'll never die. I'm skimming across the surface of my own history, moving fast, riding the melt beneath the blades, doing loops and spins, and when I take a high leap into the dark and come down thirty years later, I realize it is as Tim trying to save Timmy's life with a story.

1989, 1990

QUESTIONS

1. This story begins, "But this too is true: stories can save us" (par. 1). In what different ways does that prove true in this story? Why "but"?
2. In terms of the story's exploration of the relationship between fact and fiction, life and stories, how might it matter that the story's narrator is called Tim O'Brien? that the movie Linda and Timmy see is *The Man Who Never Was*?
3. What do Nick Veenhof and the incident with Linda's red cap contribute to the story? How would the story work differently, and how might its meaning change, without this character or incident?

LOUISE ERDRICH

(b. 1954)

The Plague of Doves

Having already collected more than one prestigious lifetime achievement award, Louise Erdrich is widely considered a strong contender to become the first Native American winner of the Nobel Prize in Literature. An enrolled member of the Turtle Mountain Band of Chippewa Indians, Erdrich grew up as part of a large family in Wahpeton, North Dakota, where her French-Chippewa (or Ojibwe) mother and German-American father taught at the local Bureau of Indian Affairs boarding school. She earned her BA in English at Dartmouth College (1976), as part of its first co-ed entering class, and an MA in creative writing at Johns Hopkins (1979). Having also, along the way, worked a series of "crazy jobs" including cucumber-picking and waitressing, Erdrich burst onto the literary scene in 1984 with both *Love Medicine* and *Jacklight*, a poetry collection including her Pushcart Prize–winning "Indian Boarding School: The Runaways." Simultaneously a novel and a collection of interlinked short stories, *Love Medicine* won the National Book Critics Circle Award, among other major prizes, and became the first of a series of novels chronicling the lives of three families in the fictional town of Argus, North Dakota. In the decades since, Erdrich has built among the most impressive oeuvres of any living American writer, including not only novels but also two additional poetry collections, a fiction series for young readers, and numerous short stories, some of which are collected in *The Red Convertible: Selected and New Stories, 1978–2008*. Each of the prize-winning novels in her Justice trilogy—*The Plague of Doves* (2008), *The Round House* (2012), and *LaRose* (2016)—focuses on the rippling effects of a particular tragic crime, while Erdrich makes her first foray into future fiction with *Future Home of the Living God* (2017). Her seventeenth novel, *The Night Watchman* (2020), was awarded the 2021 Pulitzer Prize in Fiction. In honoring her with its coveted Prize for American Fiction in 2015, the Library of Congress hailed Erdrich as "an American original" who "has portrayed her fellow Native Americans as no contemporary American novelist ever has, exploring—in intimate and fearless ways—the myriad cultural changes that indigenous and mixed-race Americans face," "[c]onnecting a dreamworld of Ojibwe legend to stark realities of the modern-day." Founder-owner of Birchbark Books & Native Arts, a mother, an avid animal lover, and a visual artist, Erdrich lives and works in Minneapolis, Minnesota.

Some years before the turn of the last century, my great-uncle, one of the first Catholic priests of aboriginal blood, put the call out to his congregation, telling everyone to gather at St. Gabriel's, wearing scapulars and holding missals.[1] From that place, they would proceed to walk the fields in a long, sweeping row, and with each step loudly pray away the doves. My great-uncle's human flock had taken up the plow and farmed among Norwegian settlers. Unlike the French, who mingled with my ancestors, the Norwegians took little interest in the women native to the land and did not intermarry. In fact, they disregarded everybody but themselves and were quite clannish. But the doves ate their crops just the same. They ate the wheat seedlings and the rye and started on the corn. They ate the sprouts of new flowers and the buds of apples and the tough leaves of oak trees and even last year's chaff.[2] The doves were plump, and delicious smoked, but one could wring the necks of hundreds or even thousands and effect no visible diminishment of their number. The pole-and-mud houses of the mixed-bloods and the skin tents of the blanket Indians[3] were crushed by the weight of the birds. When they descended, both Indians and whites set up great bonfires and tried to drive them into nets. The birds were burned, roasted, baked in pies, stewed, salted down in barrels, or clubbed to death with sticks and left to rot. But the dead only fed the living, and each morning when the people woke it was to the scraping and beating of wings, the murmurous susurration,[4] the awful cooing babble, and the sight of the curious and gentle faces of those creatures.

My great-uncle had hastily constructed crisscrossed racks of sticks to protect the rare glass windows of what was grandly called the rectory. In a corner of that one-room cabin, his twelve-year-old brother, whom he had saved from a life of excessive freedom, slept on a pallet of cottonwood branches and a mattress stuffed with grass. This was the softest bed the boy had ever had, and he did not want to leave it, but my great-uncle thrust a choirboy surplice[5] at him and ordered him to polish up the candelabra that he would carry in the procession.

This boy would be my grandfather's father, my Mooshum,[6] and since he lived to be over a hundred I was able to hear him tell and retell the story of the most momentous day of his life—which began with this attempt to vanquish the plague of doves. Sitting on a hard chair, between our first television and the small alcove of bookshelves set into the wall of our government-owned house

1. Book containing texts used in celebrating Roman Catholic Mass throughout the year. *Scapulars*: literally, "shoulders" (Latin); devotional garment consisting of two pieces of cloth, often bearing sacred images or symbols, joined by another piece across the shoulders so as to hang down the chest and back.
2. Husks separated from corn or grain by winnowing or threshing; waste.
3. Those adhering to traditional Native American lifeways, often by wearing traditional dress and/or living in "skin tents" made of animal hides.
4. Whispering, murmuring, rustling.
5. Loose white linen vestment worn by Christian clergy and choristers.
6. Grandfather (Michif or Métif, endangered language of the Métis peoples of the Northwest, including what is now North Dakota and Montana; a combination of Cree, French, and other indigenous languages such as Ojibwe).

on the Bureau of Indian Affairs[7] school campus, he told us how he'd heard the scratching of the doves' feet as they climbed all over the screens of sticks that his brother had made. He dreaded going to the outhouse, because some of the birds had got mired in the filth beneath the hole and set up a screeching clamor of despair that caused others of their kind to throw themselves against the hut in rescue attempts. But he did not dare relieve himself anywhere else. So through a flurry of wings, shuffling so as not to step on the birds, he made his way to the outhouse and completed the necessary actions with his eyes shut. Leaving, he tied the door closed so that no other doves would be trapped.

The outhouse drama, always the first scene in Mooshum's story of that momentous day, was filled with the sort of details that my brother and I found interesting; the outhouse—which was an exotic but not unfamiliar feature— and the horror of the birds' death by excrement gripped our attention. Mooshum was our second-favorite indoor entertainment. Television was the first. But our father had removed the television's knobs and hidden them. Despite constant efforts, we couldn't find the knobs, and we came to believe that he carried them on his person at all times. So instead we listened to our Mooshum. While he talked, we sat on kitchen chairs and twisted our hair. Our mother had given him a red Folgers coffee can for spitting snoose.[8] He wore soft, worn green Sears work clothes, a pair of battered brown lace-up boots, and a twill cap, even in the house. His eyes shone from slits cut deep into his face. He was hunched and dried-out, with random wisps of white hair falling over his ears and neck. From time to time, as he spoke, we glimpsed the murky scraggle of his teeth. Still, such was his conviction in the telling of this story that it wasn't hard at all to imagine him at twelve.

My great-uncle put on his vestments, hand-me-downs from a Minneapolis par- 5 ish. Since real incense was impossible to obtain, he stuffed the censer with dry sage rolled up in balls. Then he wet a comb at the cabin's iron hand pump and slicked back his hair and his little brother's hair. The church cabin was just across the yard, and wagons had been pulling up for the past hour or so, each with a dog or two tied in the box to keep the birds and their droppings off the piled hay where people would sit. The constant movement of the birds made some of the horses skittish. Many wore blinders and had bouquets of calming chamomile tied to their harnesses. As our Mooshum walked across the yard, he saw that the roof of the church was covered with birds that repeatedly—in play, it seemed—flew up and knocked one another off the holy cross that marked the cabin as a church. Great-Uncle was more than six feet tall, an imposing man, whose melodious voice carried over the confusion of sounds as he organized his parishioners into a line. The two brothers stood at the center, and with the faithful congregants spread out on either side they made their way slowly down the hill toward the first of the fields they hoped to clear.

7. Federal agency (founded 1824) responsible for working with recognized American Indian tribes and Alaska Natives, administrating lands held in trust by the United States and providing support for education, courts, law enforcement, and social services.
8. Chewing tobacco.

The sun was dull that day, thickly clouded over, and the air was oppressively still, so that pungent clouds of sage smoke hung all around the metal basket on its chain as it swung in each direction. In the first field, the doves were packed so tightly on the ground that there was a sudden agitation among the women, who could not move forward without sweeping the birds into their skirts. In panic, the birds tangled themselves in the cloth. The line halted suddenly as the women erupted in a raging dance, each twirling, stamping, beating, and flapping her skirts. So vehement was the dance that the birds all around them popped into flight, frightening other birds, and within moments the entire field was a storm of birds that roared and blasted down upon the people, who nonetheless stood firm with splayed missals on their heads. To move forward, the women forsook their modesty. They knotted their skirts up around their thighs, held out their rosaries or scapulars, and chanted the Hail Mary[9] into the wind of beating wings. Mooshum, who had rarely seen a woman's lower limbs, dropped behind, delighted. As he watched the women's naked round brown legs thrash through the field, he lowered the candelabra that his brother had given him to protect his face. Instantly, he was struck on the forehead by a bird that hurtled from the sky with such force that it seemed to have been flung directly by God, to smite and blind him before he carried his sin of appreciation any further.

At this point in the story, Mooshum often became so agitated that he acted out the smiting and, to our pleasure, mimed his collapse, throwing himself upon the floor. Then he opened his eyes and lifted his head and stared into space, clearly seeing, even now, the vision of the Holy Spirit, which appeared to him not in the form of a white bird among the brown doves but as the earthly body of a girl.

Our family has something of a historical reputation for romantic encounters. My aunt Philomena, struck by the smile of a man on a passenger train, raised her hand from the ditch where she stood picking berries, and was unable to see his hand wave in return. But something made her stay there until nightfall and then camp there overnight, and wait quietly for another whole day until the man came walking back to her from the next stop, sixty miles ahead. My oldest cousin, Curtis, dated the Haskell[1] Indian Princess, who cut her braids off and gave them to him the night she died of tuberculosis. He remained a bachelor, in her memory, until his fifties. My aunt Agathe left the convent for a priest. My cousin Eugene reformed a small-town stripper. Even my sedate-looking father was swept through the Second World War by one promising glance from my mother. And so on.

These tales of extravagant encounter contrasted with the modesty of the subsequent marriages and occupations of my relatives. We are a tribe of office workers, bank tellers, booksellers, and bureaucrats. The wildest of us (Eugene) owns a restaurant, and the most heroic of us (my father) teaches seventh grade. Yet this current of drama holds together the generations, I think, and my brother and I listened to Mooshum not only to find out what had happened but also

---

9. Roman Catholic prayer to the Virgin Mary including pleas for her intercession—here, to help solve the problem of the doves.

1. Haskell Indian Nations University in Lawrence, Kansas, founded 1884.

because we hoped for instructions on how to behave when our own moment of recognition, or romantic trial, should arrive.

In truth, I thought that mine had probably already come, for even as I sat there listening to Mooshum my fingers obsessively spelled out the name of my beloved on my arm or in my hand or on my knee. I believed that if I wrote his name on my body a million times he would kiss me. I knew that he loved me, and he was safe in the knowledge that I loved him, but we attended a Roman Catholic grade school in the early nineteen-sixties, when boys and girls who were known to be in love hardly talked to each other and certainly never touched. We played softball and kickball together, and acted and spoke through other children who were eager to deliver messages. I had copied a series of these secondhand love statements into my tiny leopard-print diary, which had a golden lock. The key was hidden in the hollow knob of my bedstead. Also, I had written the name of my beloved, in blood from a scratched mosquito bite, along the inner wall of my closet. His name held for me the sacred resonance of those Old Testament words written in fire by an invisible hand. *Mene, mene, tekel, upharsin.*[2] I could not say his name aloud. I could only write it with my fingers on my skin, until my mother feared I'd got lice and coated my hair with mayonnaise, covered my head with a shower cap, and told me to sit in a bath that was as hot as I could stand until my condition should satisfy her.

I locked the bathroom door, controlled the hot water with my toe, and, since I had nothing else to do, decided to advance my name-writing total by several thousand. As I wrote, I found places on myself that changed and warmed in response to the repetition of those letters, and without an idea in the world what I was doing I gave myself successive alphabetical orgasms so shocking in their intensity and delicacy that the mayonnaise must have melted off my head. I then stopped writing on myself. I believed that I had reached the million mark, and didn't dare try the same thing again.

Ash Wednesday passed, and I was reminded that I was made of dust only and would return to dust as soon as life was done with me.[3] My body, inscribed everywhere with the holy name Merlin Koppin (I can say it now), was only a temporary surface, soon to crumble like a leaf. As always, we entered the Lenten season aware that our hunger for sweets or salted pretzels or whatever we had given up was only a phantom craving. The hunger of the spirit alone was real. It was my good fortune not to understand that writing my boyfriend's name on myself had been an impure act, so I felt that I had nothing worse to atone for than my collaboration with my brother's discovery that pliers from the toolbox worked as well as knobs on the television. As soon as my parents were gone, we could watch "The Three Stooges"[4]—our and Mooshum's favorite, and a show

2. In chapter 5 of the book of Daniel, words appearing mysteriously on the wall of the Babylonian king Belshazzar's palace, which Daniel interprets to mean that God is displeased with the kingdom and will destroy it.
3. See Ecclesiastes 3.20: "All go unto one place; all are of the dust, and all turn to dust again." *Ash Wednesday:* first of the forty days of Lent, a period in Christian tradition of reflection, prayer, and fasting in preparation for Easter and ending with Holy Week, to which the story later refers.
4. Short slapstick films, repackaged for television, featuring actors Larry Fine, Moe Howard, and, usually, either Shemp or Curly Howard, as the proverbial "stooge." Moe's "bowl" haircut (to which the story later refers) was a trademark.

that my parents thought abominable. It was Palm Sunday before my father happened to come home from an errand and rest his hand on the hot surface of the television and then fix us with the foxlike suspicion that his students surely dreaded. He got the truth out of us quickly. The pliers were hidden, along with the knobs, and Mooshum's story resumed.

The girl who would become my great-grandmother had fallen behind the other women in the field, because she was too shy to knot up her skirts. Her name was Junesse, and she, too, was twelve years old. The trick, she found, was to walk very slowly so that the birds had time to move politely aside instead of starting upward. Junesse wore a long white Communion[5] dress made of layers of filmy muslin. She had insisted on wearing this dress, and the aunt who cared for her had given in but had promised to beat her if she returned with a rip or a stain. This threat, too, had deterred Junesse from joining in the other women's wild dance. But now, finding herself alone with the felled candelabra-bearer, she perhaps forced their fate in the world by kneeling in a patch of bird slime to revive him, and then sealed it by using her sash to blot away the wash of blood from his forehead, where the bird had wounded him.

And there she was! Mooshum paused in his story. His hands opened and the hundreds of wrinkles in his face folded into a mask of unsurpassable happiness. Her black hair was tied with a white ribbon. Her white dress had a bodice embroidered with white flower petals and white leaves. And she had the pale, heavy skin and slanting black eyes of the Métis[6] women in whose honor a bishop of that diocese had written a warning to his priests, advising them to pray hard and to remember that although women's forms could be inordinately fair, they were also savage and permeable. The Devil came and went in them at will. Of course, Junesse Malaterre was innocent, but she was also sharp of mind. Her last name, which came down to us from some French *voyageur*,[7] refers to the cleft furrows of godless rock, the barren valleys, striped outcrops, and mazelike configurations of rose, gray, tan, and purple stone that characterize the Badlands[8] of North Dakota. To this place Mooshum and Junesse eventually made their way.

15   "We seen into each udder's dept'" was how my Mooshum put it, in his gentle reservation accent. There was always a moment of silence among the three of us as the scene played out. Mooshum saw what he described. I don't know what my brother saw—perhaps another boy. (He eventually came out to everyone at my parents' silver-anniversary dinner party.) Or perhaps he saw that, after a whirl of experience and a minor car accident, he, too, would settle into the dull happiness of routine with his insurance-claims adjuster. As for me, I saw two beings—the boy shaken, frowning, the girl in white kneeling over him pressing

5. Service of Christian worship at which bread and wine are consecrated and shared; First Communion is an especially important sacrament in Roman Catholicism, typically involving the wearing of special garments, often white to symbolize purity.
6. Peoples of mixed European and indigenous ancestry originating in the region lying between the Great Lakes and Rocky Mountains, across what is now Canada and the United States.
7. Voyager; traveler (French).
8. Plateau region of the Western United States, mainly in southwestern South Dakota and northwestern Nebraska, noted for its harsh terrain.

the sash of her dress to the wound on his head, stanching the flow of blood. Most important, I saw their dark, mutual gaze. The Holy Spirit hovered between them. Her sash reddened. His blood defied gravity and flowed up her arm. Then her mouth opened. Did they kiss? I couldn't ask Mooshum. She hadn't had time to write his name on her body even once, and, besides, she didn't know his name. They had seen into each other's being, therefore names were irrelevant. They ran away together, Mooshum said, before either had thought to ask what the other was called. And then they decided not to have names for a while— all that mattered was that they had escaped, slipped their knots, cut the harnesses that their relatives had tightened. Junesse fled her aunt's beating and the endless drudgery of caring for six younger cousins, who would all die the following winter of a choking cough. Mooshum fled the sanctified future that his brother had picked out for him.

The two children in white clothes melted into the wall of birds. Their robes soon became as dark as the soil, and so they blended into the earth as they made their way along the edges of fields, through open country, to where the farmable land stopped and the ground split open and the beautifully abraded knobs and canyons of the Badlands began. Although it took them several years to physically consummate their feelings (Mooshum hinted at this but never came right out and said it), they were in love. And they were survivors. They knew how to make a fire from scratch, and for the first few days they were able to live on the roasted meat of doves. It was too early in the year for there to be much else to gather in the way of food, but they stole birds' eggs and dug up weeds. They snared rabbits, and begged what they could from isolated homesteads.

On the Monday that we braided our blessed palms in school,[9] braces were put on my teeth. Unlike now, when every other child undergoes some sort of orthodonture, braces were rare then. It is really extraordinary that my parents, in such modest circumstances, decided to correct my teeth at all. Our dentist was old-fashioned, and believed that to protect the enamel of my front teeth from the wires he should cap them in gold. So one day I appeared in school with two long, resplendent front teeth and a mouth full of hardware. It hadn't occurred to me that I'd be teased, but then somebody whispered, "Easter Bunny!" By noon recess, boys swirled around me, poking, trying to get me to smile. Suddenly, as if a great wind had blown everyone else off the bare gravel yard, there was Merlin Koppin. He shoved me and laughed right in my face. Then the other boys swept him away. I took refuge in the only sheltered spot on the playground, an alcove in the brick on the southern side facing the littered hulks of cars behind a gas station. I stood in a silent bubble, rubbing my collarbone where his hands had pushed, wondering. What had happened to our love? It was in danger, maybe finished. Because of golden teeth. Even then, such a radical change in feeling seemed impossible to bear. Remembering our family history, though, I rallied myself to the challenge. Included in the romantic tales were episodes of reversals. I had justice on my side, and, besides, when my

9. In celebration of Palm Sunday; the Sunday before Easter begins Holy Week and commemorates Jesus's entry into Jerusalem.

braces came off I would be beautiful. Of this I had been assured by my parents. So as we were entering the classroom in our usual parallel lines, me in the girls' line, he in the boys', I maneuvered myself across from Merlin, punched him in the arm, hard, and said, "Love me or leave me." Then I marched away. My knees were weak, my heart pounded. My act had been wild and unprecedented. Soon everyone had heard about it, and I was famous, even among the eighth-grade girls, one of whom, Tenny McElwayne, offered to beat Merlin up for me. Power was mine, and it was Holy Week.

The statues were shrouded in purple except for our church's exceptionally graphic Stations of the Cross.[1] Nowadays, the Stations of the Cross are carved in tasteful wood or otherwise abstracted. But our church's version was molded of plaster and painted with bloody relish. Eyes rolled to the whites. Mouths contorted. Limbs flailed. It was all there. The side aisles of the church were wide, and there was plenty of room for schoolchildren to kneel on the aggregate stone floor and contemplate the hard truths of torture. The most sensitive of the girls, and one boy, destined not for the priesthood but for a spectacular musical career, wept openly and luxuriantly. The rest of us, soaked in guilt or secretly admiring the gore, tried to sit back unobtrusively on our bottoms and spare our kneecaps. At some point, we were allowed into the pews, where, during the three holiest hours of the afternoon on Good Friday, with Christ slowly dying underneath his purple cape, we were supposed to maintain silence. During that time, I decided to begin erasing Merlin's name from my body by writing it backward a million times: Nippok Nilrem. I began my task in the palm of my hand, then moved to my knee. I'd managed only a hundred when I was thrilled to realize that Merlin was trying frantically to catch my eye, a thing that had never happened before. As I've said, our love affair had been carried out by intermediaries. But my fierce punch seemed to have hot-wired his emotions. That he should be so impetuous, so desperate, as to seek me out directly! I was overcome with a wash of shyness and terror. I wanted to acknowledge Merlin, but I couldn't now. I stayed frozen in place until we were dismissed.

Easter Sunday. I am dressed in blue dotted nylon swiss.[2] The seams prickle and the neck itches, but the over-all effect, I think, is glorious. I own a hat that has fake lilies of the valley on it and a stretchy band that digs into my chin. At the last moment, I beg to wear my mother's lace mantilla instead, the one like Jackie Kennedy's,[3] headgear that only the most fashionable older girls wear. Nevertheless, I am completely unprepared for what happens when I return from taking Holy Communion. I am kneeling at the end of the pew. We are instructed to remain silent and to allow Christ's presence to diffuse in us. I do my best. But then I see Merlin in the line for Communion on my side of the church, which means that on the way back to his seat he will pass only inches from me. I can keep my head demurely down, or I can look up. The choice dizzies me. And I do look up. He rounds the first pew. I hold my gaze steady. He sees that I am looking at him—freckles, dark slicked-back hair, narrow brown eyes—and

1. Series of images or statues depicting the chief scenes of Christ's final suffering and death.
2. Sheer light muslin, usually cotton, decorated with raised dots.
3. Jacqueline Kennedy Onassis (1929–94), a renowned fashion icon; First Lady of the United States during the presidency of John F. Kennedy (1961–63). *Mantilla*: lace or silk scarf typically worn over the hair and shoulders.

he does not look away. With the Host of the Resurrection in his mouth, my first love gives me a glare of anguished passion that suddenly ignites the million invisible names.

For one whole summer, my great-grandparents lived off a bag of contraband 20 pinto beans. They killed the rattlesnakes that came down to the streambed to hunt, roasted them, used salt from a little mineral wash to season the meat. They managed to find some berry bushes and to snare a few gophers and rabbits. But the taste of freedom was eclipsed now by their longing for a good, hot dinner. Though desolate, the Badlands were far from empty; they were peopled in Mooshum's time by unpurposed miscreants and outlaws as well as by honest ranchers. One day, Mooshum and Junesse heard an inhuman shrieking from some bushes deep in a draw where they'd set snares. Upon cautiously investigating, they found that they had snared a pig by its hind leg. While they were debating how to kill it, there appeared on a rise the silhouette of an immense person wearing a wide fedora and seated on a horse. They could have run, but as the rider approached them they were too amazed to move, or didn't want to, for the light now caught the features of a giant woman dressed in the clothing of a man. Her eyes were small and shrewd, her nose and cheeks pudgy, her lip a narrow curl of flesh. One long braid hung down beside a large and motherly breast. She wore twill trousers, boots, chaps, leather gauntlets, and a cowhide belt with silver conchas.[4] Her wide-brimmed hat was banded with the skin of a snake. Her brown bloodstock[5] horse stopped short, polite and obedient. The woman spat a stream of tobacco juice at a quiet lizard, laughed when it jumped and skittered, then ordered the two children to stand still while she roped her hog. With swift and expert motions, she dismounted and tied the pig to the pommel of her saddle, then released its hind leg.

"Climb on," she commanded, gesturing at the horse, and when the children did she grasped the halter and started walking. The roped pig trotted along behind. By the time they reached the woman's ranch, which was miles off, the two had fallen asleep. The woman had a ranch hand take them down, still sleeping, and lay them in a bedroom in her house, which was large and ramshackle, partly sod and partly framed. There were two little beds in the room, plus a trundle where she herself sometimes slept, snoring like an engine, when she was angry with her husband, the notorious Ott Black. In this place my Mooshum and his bride-to-be would live until they turned sixteen.

In Erling Nicolai Rolfsrud's compendium of memorable women and men from North Dakota,[6] "Mustache" Maude Black is described as not unwomanly, though she smoked, drank, was a crack shot and a hard-assed camp boss. These things, my Mooshum said, were all true, as was the mention of both her kind ways and her habit of casual rustling.[7] The last was just a sport to her, Mooshum

4. Decorative disks of American Indian origin, traditionally made of hammered silver and featuring a shell or flower design.
5. Thoroughbred.
6. Probably *Extraordinary North Dakotans* (1954); Rolfsrud (1912–94) was a teacher and writer whose parents immigrated to North Dakota from Norway.
7. Theft of livestock, especially cattle.

said; she never meant any harm by it. Mustache Maude sometimes had a mustache, and sometimes, when she plucked it out, she didn't. She kept a neat hen-house and a tidy kitchen. She grew very fond of Mooshum and Junesse, taught them to rope, ride, shoot, and make an unbeatable chicken-and-dumpling stew. Divining their love, she quickly banished Mooshum to the men's bunkhouse, where he soon learned the many ways in which he could make children in the future with Junesse. He practiced in his mind, and could hardly wait. But Maude forbade their marriage until both were sixteen. When that day came, she threw a wedding supper that was talked about for years, featuring several delectably roasted animals that seemed to be the same size and type as those which had gone missing from the farms of the dinner guests. This caused a stir, but Maude kept the liquor flowing, and most of the ranchers shrugged it off.

What was not shrugged off, what was truly resented, was the fact that Maude had thrown an elaborate shindig for a couple of Indians. Or half-breeds. It didn't matter which. These were uncertain times in North Dakota. People's nerves were still shot over what had happened to Custer,[8] and every few years there occurred a lynching. Just a few years before, the remains of five men had been found, still strung from trees, supposedly the victims of a vigilante party led by Flopping Bill Cantrell.[9] Some time later, an entire family was murdered and three Indians were caught by a mob and hanged for maybe doing it, including a boy named Paul Holy Track,[1] who was only thirteen.

The foul murder of a woman on a farm just to the west of Maude's place caused the neighbors to disregard, in their need for immediate revenge, the sudden absence of that woman's husband and to turn their thoughts to the nearest available Indian. There I was, Mooshum said. One night, the yard of pounded dirt between the bunkhouse and Maude's sleeping quarters filled with men hoisting torches of flaring pitch.[2] Their howls rousted Maude from her bed. As a precaution, she had sent Mooshum down to her kitchen cellar to sleep the night. So he knew what happened only through the memory of his wife, for he heard nothing and dreamed his way through the danger.

25   "Send him out to us," they bawled, "or we will take him ourselves."

Maude stood in the doorway in her nightgown, her holster belted on, a cocked pistol in either hand. She never liked to be woken from sleep.

"I'll shoot the first two of youse that climbs down off his horse," she said, then gestured to the sleepy man beside her, "and Ott Black will plug the next!"

The men were very drunk and could hardly control their horses. One fell off, and Maude shot him in the leg. He started screaming worse than the snared pig.

"Which one of you boys is next?" Maude roared.

8. U.S. Army officer George Armstrong Custer (1839–76) died at the Battle of the Little Bighorn (a.k.a. the Battle of the Greasy Grass or, proverbially, "Custer's Last Stand"); a major defeat for the U.S. Army, the battle was part of a military campaign aimed at forcing Lakota and Cheyenne peoples from their ancestral lands onto the Great Sioux Reservation.

9. In September and October 1885, northern Montana vigilantes led by Cantrell (1848–1900) reportedly lynched some thirty suspected rustlers, many of whom contemporaneous newspaper accounts describe as "breeds" or "half-breeds."

1. One of three American Indians hanged, November 13, 1897, by a lynch mob in Williamsport, North Dakota; all three were in jail, awaiting trial for the murder of a local White family.

2. Sticky, flammable resin derived from tar or petroleum.

"Send out the goddam Indian!" they called. But the yell had less conviction, 30
punctuated, as it was, by the shot man's hoarse shrieks.

"What Indian?"

"That boy!"

"He ain't no Indian," Maude said. "He's a Jew from the land of Galilee! One
of the lost tribe of Israel!"

Ott Black nearly choked at his wife's wit.

The men laughed nervously, and called for the boy again. 35

"I was just having fun with you," Maude said. "Fact is, he's Ott Black's true-
born son."

This threw the men back in their saddles. Ott blinked, then caught on and
bellowed, "You men never knowed a woman till you knowed Maude Black!"

The men fell back into the night and left their fallen would-be lyncher kicking in the dirt and pleading to God for mercy. Maybe Maude's bullet had hit a
nerve or a bone, for the man seemed to be in an unusual amount of pain for just
a gunshot wound to the leg. He began to rave and foam at the mouth, so Maude
tied him to his saddle and set out for the doctor's. He died on the way from loss
of blood. Before dawn, Maude came back, gave my great-grandparents her two
best horses, and told them to ride hard back the way they had come. Which was
how they ended up on their home reservation in time to receive their allotments,[3]
where they farmed using government-issue seed and plows and reared their six
children, one of whom was my grandfather, and where my parents took us every
summer just after the wood ticks had settled down.

The story may have been true, for, as I have said, there really was a Mustache
Maude Black who had a husband named Ott. Only the story changed. Sometimes Maude was the one to claim Mooshum as her son in the story and sometimes she went on to claim that she'd had an affair with Chief Gall.[4] And
sometimes she plugged the man in the gut. But if there was embellishment it
had to do only with facts. St. Gabriel's Church was named for God's messenger,
the archangel who currently serves as the patron saint of telecommunications
workers. Those doves were surely the passenger pigeons[5] of legend and truth,
whose numbers were such that nobody thought they could ever be wiped from
the earth.

As Mooshum grew frailer and had trouble getting out of his chair, our par- 40
ents relaxed their television boycott. More often now, our father fixed the magic
circles of plastic onto their metal posts and twiddled them until the picture
cleared. We sometimes all watched "The Three Stooges" together. The black-
haired one looked a lot like the woman who had saved his life, Mooshum said,
nodding and pointing at the set. I remember imagining his gnarled brown finger
as the hand of a strong young man gripping the candelabra, which, by the way,

3. The 1887 General Allotment, or Dawes, Act provided for the subdivision of tribal landholdings into
80- and 160-acre parcels and their allotment to Native American individuals and heads of family,
respectively, whom the U.S. government deemed eligible.

4. Hunkpapa Sioux war chief (c. 1840–94), one of the major field commanders at the Battle of the
Little Bighorn (1876).

5. Extinct species as of 1914; a close relative of the mourning dove and once among the most common
birds in North America.

my great-grandparents had lugged all the way down to the Badlands, where it had come in handy for killing snakes and gophers. They had given their only possession to Maude as a gesture of their gratitude. She had thrust it back at them the night they escaped.

That tall, seven-branched silver-plated instrument, with its finish worn down to tin in some spots, now stood in a place of honor in the center of our dining-room table. It held beeswax tapers, which had been lit during Easter dinner. A month later, in the little alcove on the school playground, I kissed Merlin Koppin. Our kiss was hard, passionate, strangely mature. Afterward, I walked home alone. I walked very slowly. Halfway there, I stopped and stared at a piece of the sidewalk that I'd crossed a thousand times and knew intimately. There was a crack in it—deep, long, jagged, and dark. It was the day when the huge old cottonwood trees shed cotton. Their heart-shaped leaves ticked and hissed high above me. The air was filled with falling down, and the gutters were plump with a snow of light. I had expected to feel joy, but instead I felt a confusion of sorrow, or maybe fear, for it suddenly seemed that my life was a hungry story and I its source and with this kiss I had begun to deliver myself to the words.

2004

QUESTIONS

1. Early in THE PLAGUE OF DOVES, its narrator describes her great-grandfather as her and her brother's "second-favorite indoor entertainment," after television (par. 4). What might the rest of Erdrich's story suggest about how the narrator is affected, even helped, by her interactions with Mooshum, by the story he tells, and by the other stories apparently shared within the family? In addition to "entertainment," what are stories and storytelling also depicted here as providing or doing for us?

2. Toward the end of THE PLAGUE OF DOVES, the narrator wonders whether her Mooshum's story is "true," concluding that "if there was embellishment it had to do only with facts" (par. 39). What do you think she means? How is she defining "facts" and "truth" and their relation to each other? How might the story as a whole thematize this issue, in part by alluding to actual people and events even as it focuses primarily on fictional ones?

3. Why might the narrator experience such mixed emotions at the story's end? What might she mean when she concludes, in the last sentence, "it suddenly seemed that my life was a hungry story and I its source and with this kiss I had begun to deliver myself to the words"? What is the realization she seems to come to here?

SUGGESTIONS FOR WRITING

1. Citing examples from one or more of the stories in this album, write an essay discussing the effects of storytelling on the actions, attitudes, and/or relationships of the characters.

2. Write an essay exploring what THE LIVES OF THE DEAD suggests about the relationship between death and stories. Might different views be expressed in the story? If so, which view, if any, does the story seem to embrace?

3. Write a response paper or essay comparing an experience you've had either telling or hearing a personally revealing story to the experience of a character or characters in one story in this album. What might the depiction of this character's experience now help you see or understand about your own? Conversely, how might your experience shape your response to theirs?

Understanding the Text

2 | PLOT

At its most basic, every story is an attempt to answer the question *What happened?* In some cases, this question is easy to answer. J. R. R. Tolkien's *The Lord of the Rings* trilogy (1954–55) is full of battles, chases, and other heart-stopping dramatic action; Nobel Laureate Toni Morrison's *Song of Solomon* (1977) begins with an insurance agent outfitted with blue silk wings leaping from a hospital roof. Yet if we ask what happens in other works of fiction, our initial answer might well be "Not much." In one of the most pivotal **scenes** in Henry James's novel *The Portrait of a Lady* (1881), for example, a woman enters a room, sees a man sitting down and a woman standing up, and beats a hasty retreat. Not terribly exciting stuff, it would seem. Yet this event ends up radically transforming the lives of everyone in the novel. "On very tiny pivots do human lives turn" would thus seem to be one common message—or **theme**—of fiction.

All fiction, regardless of its subject matter, should make us ask, *What will happen next?* and *How will all this turn out?* And responsive readers of fiction will often pause to consider those questions, trying to articulate what their expectations are and how the story has shaped them. But great fiction and responsive readers are often just as interested in questions about *why* things happen and about *how* the characters' lives are affected as a result. These *how* and *why* questions are likely to be answered very differently by different readers of the same fictional work; as a result, such questions will often generate powerful essays, whereas mainly factual questions about what happens in the work usually won't.

PLOT VERSUS ACTION, SEQUENCE, AND SUBPLOT

The term **plot** is sometimes used to refer to the events recounted in a fictional work. But in this book we instead use the term **action** in this way, reserving the term *plot* for the way the author sequences and paces events so as to shape our response and interpretation.

The difference between action and plot resembles the difference between ancient chronicles that merely list the events of a king's reign in chronological order and more modern histories that make a meaningful sequence out of those events. As the British novelist E. M. Forster puts it, "The king died and then the queen died" is not a plot, for it has not been "tampered with." "The queen died after the king died" describes the same events, but the order in which they are reported has been changed. The reader of the first sentence focuses on the king first, the reader of the second on the queen. The second sentence, moreover, subtly encourages us to speculate about *why* things happened, not just *what* happened and *when*: Did the queen die *because* her husband did? If so, was her death the result of her grief? Or was she murdered by a rival who saw the king's death as the perfect opportunity to get rid of her, too? Though our two sentences describe the same action, each has quite a different focus, emphasis, effect, and meaning thanks to its *sequencing*—the precise order in which events are related.

Like chronicles, many fictional works relate events in chronological order, starting with the earliest and ending with the latest. Folktales, for example, have this sort of plot. But fiction writers have other choices; events need not be recounted in the order in which they happened. Quite often, then, a writer will choose to mix things up, perhaps opening a story with the most recent event and then moving backward to show us all that led up to it. Still other stories begin somewhere in the middle of the action or, to use the Latin term, *in medias res* (literally, "in the middle of things"). In such plots, events that occurred before the story's opening are sometimes presented in **flashbacks**. Conversely, a story might jump forward in time to recount a later **episode** or event in a **flashforward**. **Foreshadowing** occurs when an author merely gives the reader subtle clues or hints about what will happen later in the story.

Though we often talk about *the* plot of a fictional work, however, keep in mind that some works, especially longer ones, have two or more. A plot that receives significantly less time and attention than another is called a **subplot**.

PACE

In life, we sometimes have little choice about how long a particular event lasts. If you want a driver's license, you may have to spend a boring hour or two at the motor vehicle office. And much as you might prefer a leisurely lunch, occasionally you have to scarf it down during your drive to campus.

One of the pleasures of turning experiences into a story, however, is that doing so gives a writer more power over them. In addition to choosing the order in which to recount events, the writer can also decide how much time and attention to devote to each. *Pacing*, or the duration of particular episodes—especially relative to each other and to the time they would take in real life—is a vital tool of storytellers and another important factor to consider in analyzing plots. In all fiction, pace as much as sequence determines focus and emphasis, effect and meaning. And though it can be very helpful to differentiate between "fast-paced" and "slow-paced" fiction, all effective stories contain both faster and slower bits. When an author slows down to home in on a particular moment and scene, often introduced by a phrase such as "Later that evening" or "The day before Maggie fell down," we call this a **discriminated occasion**. For example, the first paragraph of Linda Brewer's 20/20 quickly and generally refers to events that occur over three days. Then Brewer suddenly slows down, pinpointing an incident that takes place on "[t]he third evening out." That episode or discriminated occasion consumes four paragraphs of the story, even though the action described in those paragraphs accounts for only a few minutes of the characters' time. Next the story devotes two more paragraphs to an incident that occurs "[t]he next evening." In the last paragraph, Brewer speeds up again, telling us about the series of "wonderful sights" Ruthie sees between Indiana and Spokane, Washington.

CONFLICTS

Whatever their sequence and pace, all plots hinge on at least one **conflict**—some sort of struggle—and its resolution. Conflicts may be *external* or *internal*. External conflicts arise between characters and something or someone outside themselves.

Adventure stories and action films often present this sort of conflict in its purest form, keeping us poised on the edge of our seats as James Bond or the Black Panther struggles to outwit and outfight an archvillain intent on dominating or destroying his world. Yet external conflicts can also be much subtler, pitting an individual against nature or fate, against a social force such as racism or poverty, or against another person or group of people with a different way of looking at things (as in "20/20"). The cartoon below presents an external conflict of the latter type and one you may well see quite differently than the cartoonist does. How would you articulate that conflict?

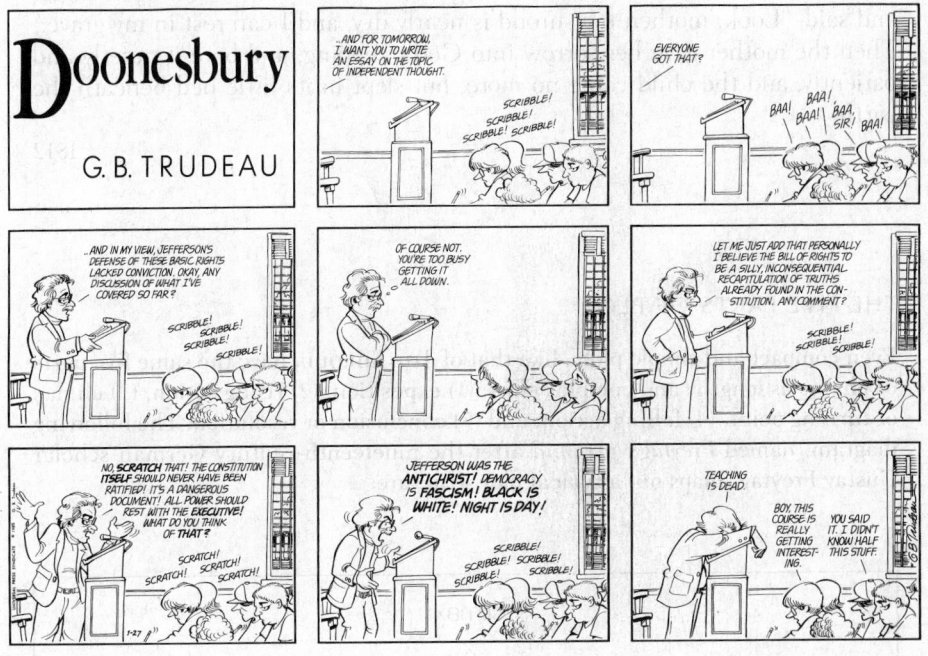

Internal conflicts occur when a character struggles to reconcile two competing desires, needs, or duties, or two parts or aspects of himself: His head, for instance, might tell him to do one thing, his heart another.

Often, a conflict is simultaneously external and internal, as in the following brief folktale, in which a woman seems to struggle simultaneously with nature, with mortality, with God, and with her desire to hold on to someone she loves versus her need to let go.

JACOB AND WILHELM GRIMM
The Shroud

There was once a mother who had a little boy of seven years old, who was so handsome and lovable that no one could look at him without liking him, and she herself worshipped him above everything in the world. Now it so happened that he suddenly became ill, and God took him to himself; and for this the mother could not be comforted, and wept both day and night. But soon afterwards, when the child had been buried, it appeared by night in the places where it had sat and played during its life, and if the mother wept, it wept also, and, when morning came, it disappeared. As, however, the mother would not stop crying, it came one night, in the little white shroud in which it had been laid in its coffin, and with its wreath of flowers round its head, and stood on the bed at her feet, and said, "Oh, mother, do stop crying, or I shall never fall asleep in my coffin, for my shroud will not dry because of all thy tears which fall upon it." The mother was afraid when she heard that, and wept no more. The next night the child came again, and held a little light in its hand, and said, "Look, mother, my shroud is nearly dry, and I can rest in my grave." Then the mother gave her sorrow into God's keeping, and bore it quietly and patiently, and the child came no more, but slept in its little bed beneath the earth.

1812

*   *   *

THE FIVE PARTS OF PLOT

Even compact and simple plots, like that of THE SHROUD, have the same five parts or phases as lengthy and complex plots: (1) exposition, (2) rising action, (3) climax or turning point, (4) falling action, and (5) conclusion or resolution. The following diagram, named *Freytag's pyramid* after the nineteenth-century German scholar Gustav Freytag, maps out a typical plot structure:

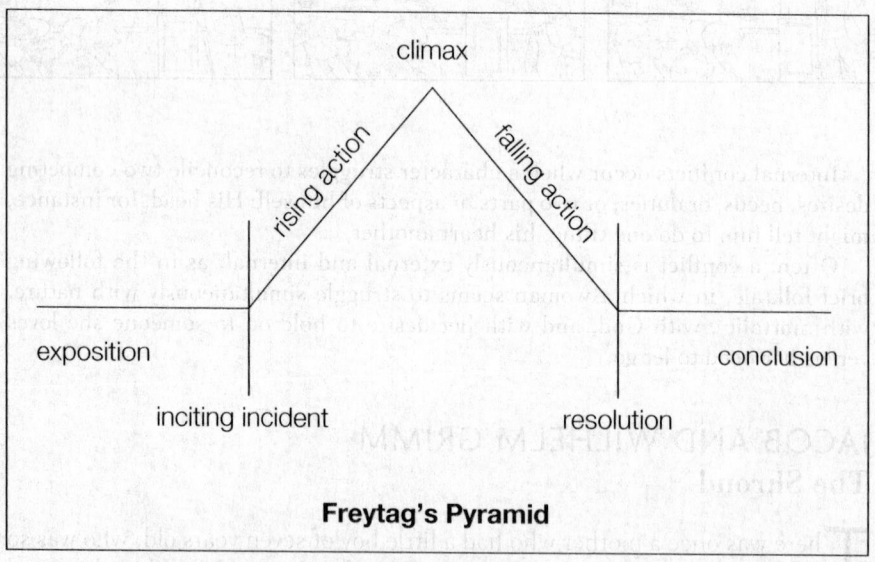

Freytag's Pyramid

Exposition

The first part of the plot, called the **exposition**, introduces the characters, their situations, and, usually, a time and place, giving us all the basic background information we need to understand what is to come. In longer works of fiction, exposition may go on for paragraphs or even pages, and some exposition may well be deferred until later phases of the plot. But in our examples, the exposition is all up-front and brief: Trudeau's first panel shows us a teacher (or at least his words), a group of students, and a classroom; the Grimms' first sentence introduces a mother, her young son, and the powerful love she feels for him.

Exposition usually reveals some source or seed of potential conflict in the initial situation, of which the characters may be as yet unaware. In Trudeau's cartoon, the contrast between the talkative teacher, who expects "independent thought" from those in his class, and the silent, scribbling students suggests a conflict in the making. So, too, does the Grimms' statement that the mother "worshipped" her boy "above everything" else in a world in which nothing and no one lasts forever.

Rising Action

By suggesting a conflict, exposition may blend into the second phase of the plot, the **rising action**, which begins with an **inciting incident** or *destabilizing event*— that is, some action that destabilizes the initial situation and incites open conflict, as does the death of the little boy in the second sentence of "The Shroud." Typically, what keeps the action rising is a **complication**, an event that introduces a new conflict or intensifies an existing one. This happens in the third sentence of "The Shroud," when the mother begins to see her little boy every night, although he is dead and buried.

Climax or Turning Point

The plot's **climax** or **turning point** is the moment of greatest emotional intensity. (Notice the way boldface lettering appears and exclamation points replace question marks in the second-to-last panel of the DOONESBURY strip.) The climax is also the moment when the outcome of the plot and the fate of the characters are decided. (A climax thus tends to be a literally *pivotal* incident that "turns things around," or involves, in Aristotle's words, "the change from one state of things [. . .] to its opposite.") "The Shroud" reaches its climax when the mother stops crying after her little boy tells her that her grief is what keeps him from sleeping and that peaceful sleep is what he craves.

Here, as in many plots, the turning point involves a discovery or new insight or even an **epiphany**, a sudden revelation of truth inspired by a seemingly trivial event. As a result, turning points often involve internal or psychological events, even if they are prompted by, and lead to, external action. In "The Shroud," for instance, the mother's new insight results in different behavior: She "wept no more."

Sometimes, though, critics differentiate between the story's climax and the **crisis** that precedes and precipitates it. In "The Shroud," for example, these critics would describe the crisis as the moment when the son confronts the mother with information that implicitly requires her to make a choice, the climax as the moment when she makes it. This distinction might be especially helpful when you grapple with longer works of fiction in which much more time and action intervenes between crisis and climax.

Falling Action

The **falling action** brings a release of emotional tension and moves us toward the resolution of the conflict(s). This release occurs in "The Shroud" when the boy speaks for the second and last time, assuring his mother that her more peaceful demeanor is giving him peace as well.

In some works of fiction, resolution is achieved through an utterly unexpected twist, as in "Meanwhile, unknown to our hero, the marines were just on the other side of the hill," or "Susan rolled over in bed and realized the whole thing had been just a dream." Such a device is sometimes called a **deus ex machina**. (This Latin term literally means "god out of the machine" and derives from the ancient theatrical practice of using a machine to lower onto the stage a god who solves the problems of the human characters.)

Conclusion

Finally, just as a plot begins with a situation that is later destabilized, so its **conclusion** presents us with a new and at least somewhat stable situation—one that gives a sense of closure because the conflicts have been resolved, if only temporarily and not necessarily in the way we or the characters expected. In "The Shroud," that resolution comes in the last sentence, in which the mother bears her grief "quietly and patiently" and the child peacefully sleeps his last sleep. The final *Doonesbury* panel presents us with a situation that is essentially the reverse of the one with which the strip begins—with the teacher silently slumped over his podium, his students suddenly talking to each other instead of scribbling down his words. Many plots instead end with a situation that outwardly looks almost identical to the one with which they began. But thanks to all that has happened between the story's beginning and its end, the final "steady state" at which the characters arrive can never be exactly the same as the one in which they started. A key question to ask at the end of a work of fiction is precisely why, as well as how, things are different.

Some fictional works may also include a final section called an **epilogue**, which ties up loose ends left dangling in the conclusion proper, updates us on what has happened to the characters since their conflicts were resolved, and/or provides some sort of commentary on the story's larger significance. (An epilogue is thus a little like this paragraph, which comes after we have concluded our discussion of the five phases of plot but still feel that there is one more term to deal with.)

A Note on *Dénouement*

In discussions of plot, you will often encounter the French word **dénouement** (literally, "untying," as of a knot). In this anthology, however, we generally try to avoid using *dénouement* because it tends to be used in three different, potentially contradictory ways—as a synonym for *falling action*; as a synonym for *conclusion* or *resolution*; and even as a label for a certain kind of epilogue.

Plot Summary: An Example and an Exercise

Although any good **plot summary** should be a relatively brief recounting (or *synopsis*) of what happens in a work of fiction, it need not necessarily tell what happens in the same order that the work itself does. As a result, many a plot summary is in fact more like an action summary in the sense that we define the terms *action* and *plot* in this book. But unless you have a good reason for reordering events, it is generally a good idea to follow the plot, as does the following plot summary of Isabel Allende's AND OF CLAY ARE WE CREATED:

> When a thirteen-year-old girl is trapped in a mudslide that consumes her village, journalist Rolf Carlé is helicoptered in to report on her rescue, becoming the first reporter on the scene. Unable to maintain his objectivity, he joins in the desperate attempt to rescue her. Talking with the girl over a period of days, Rolf recalls long-repressed memories and feelings. Meanwhile, Rolf's lover, a fellow journalist, watches all these events unfold on television, experiencing the developing intimacy between Rolf and the girl and their suffering at once up-close and at a distance.

Now try this yourself: Choose any of the stories in this anthology and write a one-paragraph plot summary. Then, in a paragraph or two, reflect on your choices about which details to include, which to omit, and how to order them (especially if you've deviated from the plot). What does your summary imply about the story's focus, meaning, and significance? Now repeat the exercise, summarizing the story in a different way and then reflecting on the significance and effect of the changes you've made.

Alternatively, try the same exercise with a friend who has also read the story: Each of you should write your own summary; then exchange them and (separately or together) write a few paragraphs comparing your summaries and reflecting on the significance of the similarities and differences.

COMMON PLOT TYPES

If most plots are essentially variations on the same five-part pattern, some plots have even more features in common. As you think back over the fiction you have read, the movies you have seen, and the role-playing games you have played, you might be surprised to discover just how many of their plots involve a quest—the journey of one or more characters to find something or someone of seemingly great material or spiritual value. Traditionally, that requires a literal journey, the challenge being both to find and acquire the object and to return home with it. Such quests occur often in folktales and are a **convention** of chivalric **romance** and **epic**, in which the questing heroes are often men of high rank sent on their quests by someone with even greater power—a god, a wizard, a prophet, a king. And many works of modern fiction—from James Joyce's ARABY to contemporary fantasy and science fiction—depend for their full effect on our knowledge of the conventions of traditional quest plots.

Many fictional works both ancient and modern also (or instead) follow patterns derived from the two most important and ancient forms (or subgenres) of drama— **tragedy** and **comedy**. Tragic plots, on the one hand, trace a downward movement centering on a character's fall from fortune into misfortune and isolation; they end unhappily, often with death. Comedic plots, on the other hand, tend to end happily, often with marriage or some other act of social integration and celebration.

As you read the stories in this chapter, or any other work of fiction, think about what sets each one apart when it comes to plot; how each uses variations on common plot conventions; how each generates, fulfills, and often frustrates our expectations about the action to come; and how each uses sequence, pace, and other techniques to endow action with both emotional charge and meaning. When it comes to action and plot, every good story holds its own surprises and offers a unique answer to the nagging question *What happened?*

Questions about Plot

- Read the first few paragraphs and then stop. What potential for conflict do you see here? What do you expect to happen in the rest of the story?
- What is the inciting incident or destabilizing event? How and why does this event destabilize the initial situation?
- How would you describe the conflict that ultimately develops? To what extent is it external, internal, or both? What, if any, complications or secondary conflicts arise?
- Where, when, how, and why does the story defy your expectations about what will happen next? What in this story—and in your experience of other stories—created these expectations?
- What is the climax or turning point? Why and how so?
- How is the conflict resolved? How and why might this resolution fulfill or defy your expectations? How and why is the situation at the end of the story different from what it was at the beginning?
- Looking back at the story as a whole, what seems especially significant and effective about its plot, especially in terms of the sequence and pace of the action?
- Does this plot follow any common plot pattern? Is there, for example, a quest of any kind? Or does this plot follow a tragic or comedic pattern?

RALPH ELLISON

(1914–94)

King of the Bingo Game

Named after nineteenth-century poet-essayist Ralph Waldo Emerson, Ralph Ellison lost his beloved father, a deliveryman and voracious reader, when he was only three. Ellison's mother thus had to raise her two sons by doing janitorial and domestic work, ensuring that the family endured "years of shabby rented rooms, hand-me-down clothing, second-rate meals, [and] sneers and slights from people better off," to quote biographer Arnold Rampersad. Oklahoma City nonetheless afforded Ellison opportunities he might not have had in the Jim Crow South, where his grandparents had once been slaves: He attended good schools; found mentors, both White and Black; and learned to play the cornet. A jazz lover, Ellison studied classical music at Alabama's Tuskegee Institute, where he enrolled in 1933 in hopes of becoming a composer. When he headed to New York three years later, he meant to stay only long enough to make the money necessary to complete his studies. But with the encouragement of poet Langston Hughes and novelist Richard Wright, Ellison stayed put, publishing short stories, essays, book reviews, and then, in 1952, *Invisible Man*. This best-selling, National Book Award–winning novel is widely regarded as among the greatest of the twentieth century; it aims to reveal, said Ellison, "the human universals hidden within the plight of one who was both black and American." Thereafter, Ellison lectured and taught at various institutions, including New York University, and published *Shadow and Act* (1964), a collection of critical essays on the novelist's art. Upon his death from cancer in 1994, the literary world learned that he had been working steadily on a second major novel, begun in 1952, seemingly lost in a fire in 1967. The nearly completed manuscript was edited by Ellison's friend John F. Callahan and published as *Juneteenth* (1999).

The woman in front of him was eating roasted peanuts that smelled so good that he could barely contain his hunger. He could not even sleep and wished they'd hurry and begin the bingo game. There, on his right, two fellows were drinking wine out of a bottle wrapped in a paper bag, and he could hear soft gurgling in the dark. His stomach gave a low, gnawing growl. "If this was down South," he thought, "all I'd have to do is lean over and say, 'Lady, gimme a few of those peanuts, please ma'am,' and she'd pass me the bag and never think nothing of it." Or he could ask the fellows for a drink in the same way. Folks down South stuck together that way; they didn't even have to know you. But up here it was different. Ask somebody for something, and they'd think you were crazy. Well, I ain't crazy. I'm just broke, 'cause I got no birth certificate to get a job, and Laura 'bout to die 'cause we got no money for a doctor. But I ain't crazy. And yet a pinpoint of doubt was focused in his mind as he glanced toward the screen and saw the hero stealthily entering a dark room and sending the beam of a flashlight along a wall of bookcases. This is where he finds the trapdoor, he remembered. The man would pass abruptly through the wall and find the girl tied to a bed, her legs and arms spread wide, and her clothing torn to rags. He laughed softly to himself. He had seen the picture three times, and this was one of the best scenes.

On his right the fellow whispered wide-eyed to his companion, "Man, look ayonder!"

"Damn!"

"Wouldn't I like to have her tied up like that . . ."

5 "Hey! That fool's letting her loose!"

"Aw, man, he loves her."

"Love or no love!"

The man moved impatiently beside him, and he tried to involve himself in the scene. But Laura was on his mind. Tiring quickly of watching the picture he looked back to where the white beam filtered from the projection room above the balcony. It started small and grew large, specks of dust dancing in its whiteness as it reached the screen. It was strange how the beam always landed right on the screen and didn't mess up and fall somewhere else. But they had it all fixed. Everything was fixed. Now suppose when they showed that girl with her dress torn the girl started taking off the rest of her clothes, and when the guy came in he didn't untie her but kept her there and went to taking off his own clothes? *That* would be something to see. If a picture got out of hand like that those guys up there would go nuts. Yeah, and there'd be so many folks in here you couldn't find a seat for nine months! A strange sensation played over his skin. He shuddered. Yesterday he'd seen a bedbug on a woman's neck as they walked out into the bright street. But exploring his thigh through a hole in his pocket he found only goose pimples and old scars.

The bottle gurgled again. He closed his eyes. Now a dreamy music was accompanying the film and train whistles were sounding in the distance, and he was a boy again walking along a railroad trestle down South, and seeing the train coming, and running back as fast as he could go, and hearing the whistle blowing, and getting off the trestle to solid ground just in time, with the earth trembling beneath his feet, and feeling relieved as he ran down the cinder-strewn embankment onto the highway, and looking back and seeing with terror that the train had left the track and was following him right down the middle of the street, and all the white people laughing as he ran screaming. . . .

10 "Wake up there, buddy! What the hell do you mean hollering like that? Can't you see we trying to enjoy this here picture?"

He stared at the man with gratitude.

"I'm sorry, old man," he said. "I musta been dreaming."

"Well, here, have a drink. And don't be making no noise like that, damn!"

His hands trembled as he tilted his head. It was not wine, but whiskey. Cold rye whiskey. He took a deep swoller, decided it was better not to take another, and handed the bottle back to its owner.

15 "Thanks, old man," he said.

Now he felt the cold whiskey breaking a warm path straight through the middle of him, growing hotter and sharper as it moved. He had not eaten all day, and it made him light-headed. The smell of the peanuts stabbed him like a knife, and he got up and found a seat in the middle aisle. But no sooner did he sit than he saw a row of intense-faced young girls, and got up again, thinking, "You chicks musta been Lindy-hopping[1] somewhere." He found a seat several rows ahead as the lights came on, and he saw the screen disappear behind a heavy red and gold curtain; then the curtain rising, and the man with the microphone and a uniformed attendant coming on the stage.

He felt for his bingo cards, smiling. The guy at the door wouldn't like it if he knew about his having *five* cards. Well, not everyone played the bingo game; and even with five cards he didn't have much of a chance. For Laura, though, he had to have faith. He studied the cards, each with its different numerals, punching the free center hole in each and spreading them neatly across his lap; and when the lights faded he sat slouched in his seat so that he could look from his cards to the bingo wheel with but a quick shifting of his eyes.

Ahead, at the end of the darkness, the man with the microphone was pressing a button attached to a long cord and spinning the bingo wheel and calling out the number each time the wheel came to rest. And each time the voice rang out his finger raced over the cards for the number. With five cards he had to move fast. He became nervous; there were too many cards, and the man went too fast with his grating voice. Perhaps he should just select one and throw the others away. But he was afraid. He became warm. Wonder how much Laura's doctor would cost? Damn that, watch the cards! And with despair he heard the man call three in a row which he missed on all five cards. This way he'd never win. . . .

When he saw the row of holes punched across the third card, he sat paralyzed and heard the man call three more numbers before he stumbled forward, screaming,

"Bingo! Bingo!"   20

"Let that fool up there," someone called.

"Get up there, man!"

He stumbled down the aisle and up the steps to the stage into a light so sharp and bright that for a moment it blinded him, and he felt that he had moved into the spell of some strange, mysterious power. Yet it was as familiar as the sun, and he knew it was the perfectly familiar bingo.

The man with the microphone was saying something to the audience as he held out his card. A cold light flashed from the man's finger as the card left his hand. His knees trembled. The man stepped closer, checking the card against the numbers chalked on the board. Suppose he had made a mistake? The pomade on the man's hair made him feel faint, and he backed away. But the man was checking the card over the microphone now, and he had to stay. He stood tense, listening.

"Under the O, forty-four," the man chanted. "Under the I, seven. Under the   25
G, three. Under the B, ninety-six. Under the N, thirteen!"

His breath came easier as the man smiled at the audience.

"Yes sir, ladies and gentlemen, he's one of the chosen people!"

The audience rippled with laughter and applause.

"Step right up to the front of the stage."

He moved slowly forward, wishing that the light was not so bright.   30

1. Dancing the "Lindy" or "Lindy Hop," a popular form of the jitterbug that originated in Harlem.

"To win tonight's jackpot of $36.90 the wheel must stop between the double zero, understand?"

He nodded, knowing the ritual from the many days and nights he had watched the winners march across the stage to press the button that controlled the spinning wheel and receive the prizes. And now he followed the instructions as though he'd crossed the slippery stage a million prize-winning times.

The man was making some kind of joke, and he nodded vacantly. So tense had he become that he felt a sudden desire to cry and shook it away. He felt vaguely that his whole life was determined by the bingo wheel; not only that which would happen now that he was at last before it, but all that had gone before, since his birth, and his mother's birth and the birth of his father. It had always been there, even though he had not been aware of it, handing out the unlucky cards and numbers of his days. The feeling persisted, and he started quickly away. I better get down from here before I make a fool of myself, he thought.

"Here, boy," the man called. "You haven't started yet."

35   Someone laughed as he went hesitantly back.

"Are you all reet?"

He grinned at the man's jive talk, but no words would come, and he knew it was not a convincing grin. For suddenly he knew that he stood on the slippery brink of some terrible embarrassment.

"Where are you from, boy?" the man asked.

"Down South."

40   "He's from down South, ladies and gentlemen," the man said. "Where from? Speak right into the mike."

"Rocky Mont," he said. "Rock' Mont, North Car'lina."

"So you decided to come down off that mountain to the U.S.," the man laughed. He felt that the man was making a fool of him, but then something cold was placed in his hand, and the lights were no longer behind him.

Standing before the wheel he felt alone, but that was somehow right, and he remembered his plan. He would give the wheel a short quick twirl. Just a touch of the button. He had watched it many times, and always it came close to double zero when it was short and quick. He steeled himself; the fear had left, and he felt a profound sense of promise, as though he were about to be repaid for all the things he'd suffered all his life. Trembling, he pressed the button. There was a whirl of lights, and in a second he realized with finality that though he wanted to, he could not stop. It was as though he held a high-powered line in his naked hand. His nerves tightened. As the wheel increased its speed it seemed to draw him more and more into its power, as though it held his fate; and with it came a deep need to submit, to whirl, to lose himself in its swirl of color. He could not stop it now. So let it be.

The button rested snugly in his palm where the man had placed it. And now he became aware of the man beside him, advising him through the microphone, while behind the shadowy audience hummed with noisy voices. He shifted his feet. There was still that feeling of helplessness within him, making part of him desire to turn back, even now that the jackpot was right in his hand. He squeezed the button until his fist ached. Then, like the sudden shriek of a subway whistle, a doubt tore through his head. Suppose he did not spin the wheel long enough? What could he do, and how could he tell? And then he knew, even as he wondered, that as long as he pressed the button, he could control the jackpot. He and only he could determine whether or not it was to be his. Not even the man with the microphone could do anything about it now. He felt drunk. Then, as though he had come down from a high hill into a valley of people, he heard the audience yelling.

"Come down from there, you jerk!" 45

"Let somebody else have a chance. . . ."

"Ole Jack thinks he done found the end of the rainbow. . . ."

The last voice was not unfriendly, and he turned and smiled dreamily into the yelling mouths. Then he turned his back squarely on them.

"Don't take too long, boy," a voice said.

He nodded. They were yelling behind him. Those folks did not understand 50 what had happened to him. They had been playing the bingo game day in and night out for years, trying to win rent money or hamburger change. But not one of those wise guys had discovered this wonderful thing. He watched the wheel whirling past the numbers and experienced a burst of exaltation: This is God! This is the really truly God! He said it aloud, "This is God!"

He said it with such absolute conviction that he feared he would fall fainting into the footlights. But the crowd yelled so loud that they could not hear. These fools, he thought. I'm here trying to tell them the most wonderful secret in the world, and they're yelling like they gone crazy. A hand fell upon his shoulder.

"You'll have to make a choice now, boy. You've taken too long."

He brushed the hand violently away.

"Leave me alone, man. I know what I'm doing!"

The man looked surprised and held on to the microphone for support. And 55 because he did not wish to hurt the man's feelings he smiled, realizing with a sudden pang that there was no way of explaining to the man just why he had to stand there pressing the button forever.

"Come here," he called tiredly.

The man approached, rolling the heavy microphone across the stage.

"Anybody can play this bingo game, right?" he said.

"Sure, but . . ."

He smiled, feeling inclined to be patient with this slick looking white man 60 with his blue shirt and his sharp gabardine suit.

"That's what I thought," he said. "Anybody can win the jackpot as long as they get the lucky number, right?"

"That's the rule, but after all . . ."

"That's what I thought," he said. "And the big prize goes to the man who knows how to win it?"

The man nodded speechlessly.

"Well then, go on over there and watch me win like I want to. I ain't going to 65 hurt nobody," he said, "and I'll show you how to win. I mean to show the whole world how it's got to be done."

And because he understood, he smiled again to let the man know that he held nothing against him for being white and impatient. Then he refused to see the man any longer and stood pressing the button, the voices of the crowd reaching him like sounds in distant streets. Let them yell. All the Negroes down there

were just ashamed because he was black like them. He smiled inwardly, knowing how it was. Most of the time he was ashamed of what Negroes did himself.
Well, let them be ashamed for something this time. Like him. He was like a
long thin black wire that was being stretched and wound upon the bingo wheel;
wound until he wanted to scream; wound, but this time himself controlling the
winding and the sadness and the shame, and because he did, Laura would be
all right. Suddenly the lights flickered. He staggered backwards. Had something gone wrong? All this noise. Didn't they know that although he controlled
the wheel, it also controlled him, and unless he pressed the button forever and
forever and ever it would stop, leaving him high and dry, dry and high on this
hard high slippery hill and Laura dead? There was only one chance; he had to
do whatever the wheel demanded. And gripping the button in despair, he discovered with surprise that it imparted a nervous energy. His spine tingled. He
felt a certain power.

Now he faced the raging crowd with defiance, its screams penetrating his
eardrums like trumpets shrieking from a juke-box. The vague faces glowing
in the bingo lights gave him a sense of himself that he had never known before.
He was running the show, by God! They had to react to him, for he was their
luck. This is *me*, he thought. Let the bastards yell. Then someone was laughing inside him, and he realized that somehow he had forgotten his own name.
It was a sad, lost feeling to lose your name, and a crazy thing to do. That name
had been given him by the white man who had owned his grandfather a long
lost time ago down South. But maybe those wise guys knew his name.

"Who am I?" he screamed.

"Hurry up and bingo, you jerk!"

70   They didn't know either, he thought sadly. They didn't even know their own
names, they were all poor nameless bastards. Well, he didn't need that old
name; he was reborn. For as long as he pressed the button he was The-man-
who-pressed-the-button-who-held-the-prize-who-was-the-King-of-Bingo.   That
was the way it was, and he'd have to press the button even if nobody understood, even though Laura did not understand.

"Live!" he shouted.

The audience quieted like the dying of a huge fan.

"Live, Laura, baby. I got holt of it now, sugar. Live!"

He screamed it, tears streaming down his face. "I got nobody but YOU!"

75   The screams tore from his very guts. He felt as though the rush of blood to
his head would burst out in baseball seams of small red droplets, like a head
beaten by police clubs. Bending over he saw a trickle of blood splashing the toe
of his shoe. With his free hand he searched his head. It was his nose. God, suppose something has gone wrong? He felt that the whole audience had somehow
entered him and was stamping its feet in his stomach and he was unable to
throw them out. They wanted the prize, that was it. They wanted the secret for
themselves. But they'd never get it; he would keep the bingo wheel whirling
forever, and Laura would be safe in the wheel. But would she? It had to be,
because if she were not safe the wheel would cease to turn; it could not go on.
He had to get away, *vomit* all, and his mind formed an image of himself running
with Laura in his arms down the tracks of the subway just ahead of an A train,
running desperately *vomit* with people screaming for him to come out but

knowing no way of leaving the tracks because to stop would bring the train crushing down upon him and to attempt to leave across the other tracks would mean to run into a hot third rail as high as his waist which threw blue sparks that blinded his eyes until he could hardly see.

He heard singing and the audience was clapping its hands.

> Shoot the liquor to him, Jim, boy!
> Clap-clap-clap
> Well a-calla the cop
> He's blowing his top!
> Shoot the liquor to him, Jim, boy!

Bitter anger grew within him at the singing. They think I'm crazy. Well let 'em laugh. I'll do what I got to do.

He was standing in an attitude of intense listening when he saw that they were watching something on the stage behind him. He felt weak. But when he turned he saw no one. If only his thumb did not ache so. Now they were applauding. And for a moment he thought that the wheel had stopped. But that was impossible, his thumb still pressed the button. Then he saw them. Two men in uniform beckoned from the end of the stage. They were coming toward him, walking in step, slowly, like a tap-dance team returning for a third encore. But their shoulders shot forward, and he backed away, looking wildly about. There was nothing to fight them with. He had only the long black cord which led to a plug somewhere back stage, and he couldn't use that because it operated the bingo wheel. He backed slowly, fixing the men with his eyes as his lips stretched over his teeth in a tight, fixed grin; moved toward the end of the stage and realizing that he couldn't go much further, for suddenly the cord became taut and he couldn't afford to break the cord. But he had to do something. The audience was howling. Suddenly he stopped dead, seeing the men halt, their legs lifted as in an interrupted step of a slow-motion dance. There was nothing to do but run in the other direction and he dashed forward, slipping and sliding. The men fell back, surprised. He struck out violently going past.

"Grab him!"

He ran, but all too quickly the cord tightened, resistingly, and he turned and 80
ran back again. This time he slipped them, and discovered by running in a circle before the wheel he could keep the cord from tightening. But this way he had to flail his arms to keep the men away. Why couldn't they leave a man alone? He ran, circling.

"Ring down the curtain," someone yelled. But they couldn't do that. If they did the wheel flashing from the projection room would be cut off. But they had him before he could tell them so, trying to pry open his fist, and he was wrestling and trying to bring his knees into the fight and holding on to the button, for it was his life. And now he was down, seeing a foot coming down, crushing his wrist cruelly, down, as he saw the wheel whirling serenely above.

"I can't give it up," he screamed. Then quietly, in a confidential tone, "Boys, I really can't give it up."

It landed hard against his head. And in the blank moment they had it away from him, completely now. He fought them trying to pull him up from the stage as he watched the wheel spin slowly to a stop. Without surprise he saw it rest at double-zero.

"You see," he pointed bitterly.

85   "Sure, boy, sure, it's O.K.," one of the men said smiling.

And seeing the man bow his head to someone he could not see, he felt very, very happy; he would receive what all the winners received.

But as he warmed in the justice of the man's tight smile he did not see the man's slow wink, nor see the bow-legged man behind him step clear of the swiftly descending curtain and set himself for a blow. He only felt the dull pain exploding in his skull, and he knew even as it slipped out of him that his luck had run out on the stage.

                                                                                        1944

QUESTIONS

1. Re-read the first paragraph of the story: What facts do we learn here about the pro-tagonist, his background, and his situation? Why has he come to the theater, espe-cially if he has already "seen the picture three times"? Does the paragraph introduce an actual or potential conflict?

2. What "wonderful thing" does the protagonist think he has "discovered" once he is onstage (par. 50)? Why can't or won't he let go of the button, even when the police arrive?

3. What is the effect of Ellison's choice not to give his protagonist a name? How might his namelessness shape your sense of what the story's central conflict is? What role does race play in that conflict?

JOYCE CAROL OATES
(b. 1938)

Where Are You Going, Where Have You Been?

A remarkably prolific writer of short stories, poems, novels, and nonfiction, Joyce Carol Oates was born in Lockport, New York. Daughter of a tool-and-die designer and his wife, she submitted her first novel to a publisher at fifteen and a few years later became the first person in her family to graduate from high school, later earning a BA from Syracuse University (1960) and an MA from the University of Wisconsin (1961). The recipient of countless awards, including a National Book Award for the novel *them* (1969), an O. Henry Special Award for Continuing Achievement (1970, 1986), a Pushcart Prize (1976), and at least four lifetime achievement awards, Oates taught for over thirty-five years at Prince-ton University, retiring in 2014. In addition to novels, Oates's recent work includes the collections *Night-Gaunts and Other Tales of Suspense* (2018), *The (Other) You: Stories* (2021), and *American Melancholy: Poems* (2021), as well as the memoirs *A Widow's Story* (2011) and *The Lost Landscape: A Writer's Coming of Age* (2015).

For Bob Dylan

Her name was Connie. She was fifteen and she had a quick, nervous gig-gling habit of craning her neck to glance into mirrors or checking other people's faces to make sure her own was all right. Her mother, who noticed everything and knew everything and who hadn't much reason any longer to look at her own face, always scolded Connie about it. "Stop gawking at your-self. Who are you? You think you're so pretty?" she would say. Connie would raise her eyebrows at these familiar old complaints and look right through her mother, into a shadowy vision of herself as she was right at that moment: she knew she was pretty and that was everything. Her mother had been pretty once too, if you could believe those old snapshots in the album, but now her looks were gone and that was why she was always after Connie.

"Why don't you keep your room clean like your sister? How've you got your hair fixed—what the hell stinks? Hair spray? You don't see your sister using that junk."

Her sister, June, was twenty-four and still lived at home. She was a secretary in the high school Connie attended, and if that wasn't bad enough—with her in the same building—she was so plain and chunky and steady that Connie had to hear her praised all the time by her mother and her mother's sisters. June did this, June did that, she saved money and helped clean the house and cooked and Connie couldn't do a thing, her mind was all filled with trashy daydreams. Their father was away at work most of the time and when he came home he wanted supper and he read the newspaper at supper and after supper he went to bed. He didn't bother talking much to them, but around his bent head Connie's mother kept picking at her until Connie wished her mother was dead and she herself was dead and it was all over. "She makes me want to throw up sometimes," she complained to her friends. She had a high, breathless, amused voice that made everything she said sound a little forced, whether it was sincere or not.

There was one good thing: June went places with girl friends of hers, girls who were just as plain and steady as she, and so when Connie wanted to do that her mother had no objections. The father of Connie's best girl friend drove the girls the three miles to town and left them at a shopping plaza so they could walk through the stores or go to a movie, and when he came to pick them up again at eleven he never bothered to ask what they had done.

They must have been familiar sights, walking around the shopping plaza in 5 their shorts and flat ballerina slippers that always scuffed on the sidewalk, with charm bracelets jingling on their thin wrists; they would lean together to whis-per and laugh secretly if someone passed who amused or interested them. Con-nie had long dark blond hair that drew anyone's eye to it, and she wore part of it pulled up on her head and puffed out and the rest of it she let fall down her back. She wore a pullover jersey top that looked one way when she was at home and another way when she was away from home. Everything about her had two sides to it, one for home and one for anywhere that was not home: her walk, which could be childlike and bobbing, or languid enough to make anyone think she was hearing music in her head; her mouth, which was pale and smirking most of the time, but bright and pink on these evenings out; her laugh, which was cynical and drawling at home—"Ha, ha, very funny,"—but high-pitched and nervous anywhere else, like the jingling of the charms on her bracelet.

Sometimes they did go shopping or to a movie, but sometimes they went across the highway, ducking fast across the busy road, to a drive-in restaurant where older kids hung out. The restaurant was shaped like a big bottle, though squatter than a real bottle, and on its cap was a revolving figure of a grinning boy holding a hamburger aloft. One night in midsummer they ran across, breathless with daring, and right away someone leaned out a car window and invited them over, but it was just a boy from high school they didn't like. It made them feel good to be able to ignore him. They went up through the maze of parked and cruising cars to the bright-lit, fly-infested restaurant, their faces pleased and expectant as if they were entering a sacred building that loomed up out of the night to give them what haven and blessing they yearned for. They sat at the counter and crossed their legs at the ankles, their thin shoulders rigid with excitement, and listened to the music that made everything so good: the music was always in the background, like music at a church service; it was something to depend upon.

A boy named Eddie came in to talk with them. He sat backward on his stool, turning himself jerkily around in semicircles and then stopping and turning back again, and after a while he asked Connie if she would like something to eat. She said she would so she tapped her friend's arm on her way out—her friend pulled her face up into a brave, droll look—and Connie said she would meet her at eleven across the way. "I just hate to leave her like that," Connie said earnestly, but the boy said that she wouldn't be alone for long. So they went out to his car, and on the way Connie couldn't help but let her eyes wander over the windshields and faces all around her, her face gleaming with a joy that had nothing to do with Eddie or even this place; it might have been the music. She drew her shoulders up and sucked in her breath with the pure pleasure of being alive, and just at that moment she happened to glance at a face just a few feet away from hers. It was a boy with shaggy black hair, in a convertible jalopy[1] painted gold. He stared at her and then his lips widened into a grin. Connie slit her eyes at him and turned away, but she couldn't help glancing back and there he was, still watching her. He wagged a finger and laughed and said, "Gonna get you, baby," and Connie turned away again without Eddie noticing anything.

She spent three hours with him, at the restaurant where they ate hamburgers and drank Cokes in wax cups that were always sweating, and then down an alley a mile or so away, and when he left her off at five to eleven only the movie house was still open at the plaza. Her girl friend was there, talking with a boy. When Connie came up, the two girls smiled at each other and Connie said, "How was the movie?" and the girl said, "*You* should know." They rode off with the girl's father, sleepy and pleased, and Connie couldn't help but look back at the darkened shopping plaza with its big empty parking lot and its signs that were faded and ghostly now, and over at the drive-in restaurant where cars were still circling tirelessly. She couldn't hear the music at this distance.

Next morning June asked her how the movie was and Connie said, "So-so."

10   She and that girl and occasionally another girl went out several times a week, and the rest of the time Connie spent around the house—it was summer vacation—getting in her mother's way and thinking, dreaming about the boys

1. Older car, often in poor condition.

she met. But all the boys fell back and dissolved into a single face that was not even a face but an idea, a feeling, mixed up with the urgent insistent pounding of the music and the humid night air of July. Connie's mother kept dragging her back to the daylight by finding things for her to do or saying suddenly, "What's this about the Pettinger girl?"

And Connie would say nervously, "Oh, her. That dope." She always drew thick clear lines between herself and such girls, and her mother was simple and kind enough to believe it. Her mother was so simple, Connie thought, that it was maybe cruel to fool her so much. Her mother went scuffling around the house in old bedroom slippers and complained over the telephone to one sister about the other, then the other called up and the two of them complained about the third one. If June's name was mentioned her mother's tone was approving, and if Connie's name was mentioned it was disapproving. This did not really mean she disliked Connie, and actually Connie thought that her mother preferred her to June just because she was prettier, but the two of them kept up a pretense of exasperation, a sense that they were tugging and struggling over something of little value to either of them. Sometimes, over coffee, they were almost friends, but something would come up—some vexation that was like a fly buzzing suddenly around their heads—and their faces went hard with contempt.

One Sunday Connie got up at eleven—none of them bothered with church—and washed her hair so that it could dry all day long in the sun. Her parents and sister were going to a barbecue at an aunt's house and Connie said no, she wasn't interested, rolling her eyes to let her mother know just what she thought of it. "Stay home alone then," her mother said sharply. Connie sat out back in a lawn chair and watched them drive away, her father quiet and bald, hunched around so that he could back the car out, her mother with a look that was still angry and not at all softened through the windshield, and in the backseat poor old June, all dressed up as if she didn't know what a barbecue was, with all the running yelling kids and the flies. Connie sat with her eyes closed in the sun, dreaming and dazed with the warmth about her as if this were a kind of love, the caresses of love, and her mind slipped over onto thoughts of the boy she had been with the night before and how nice he had been, how sweet it always was, not the way someone like June would suppose but sweet, gentle, the way it was in movies and promised in songs; and when she opened her eyes she hardly knew where she was, the backyard ran off into weeds and a fencelike line of trees and behind it the sky was perfectly blue and still. The asbestos "ranch house"[2] that was now three years old startled her—it looked small. She shook her head as if to get awake.

It was too hot. She went inside the house and turned on the radio to drown out the quiet. She sat on the edge of her bed, barefoot, and listened for an hour and a half to a program called XYZ Sunday Jamboree, record after record of hard, fast, shrieking songs she sang along with, interspersed by exclamations from "Bobby King": "An' look here, you girls at Napoleon's—Son and Charley want you to pay real close attention to this song coming up!"

2. Style of long, one-story houses common in suburban neighborhoods built between the 1940s and 1980s. Asbestos: fireproof building material once used in roofs and siding, but now known to be toxic.

And Connie paid close attention herself, bathed in a glow of slow-pulsed joy that seemed to rise mysteriously out of the music itself and lay languidly about the airless little room, breathed in and breathed out with each gentle rise and fall of her chest.

15   After a while she heard a car coming up the drive. She sat up at once, startled, because it couldn't be her father so soon. The gravel kept crunching all the way in from the road—the driveway was long—and Connie ran to the window. It was a car she didn't know. It was an open jalopy, painted a bright gold that caught the sunlight opaquely. Her heart began to pound and her fingers snatched at her hair, checking it, and she whispered, "Christ, Christ," wondering how she looked. The car came to a stop at the side door and the horn sounded four short taps, as if this were a signal Connie knew.

She went into the kitchen and approached the door slowly, then hung out the screen door, her bare toes curling down off the step. There were two boys in the car and now she recognized the driver: he had shaggy, shabby black hair that looked crazy as a wig and he was grinning at her.

"I ain't late, am I?" he said.

"Who the hell do you think you are?" Connie said.

"Toldja I'd be out, didn't I?"

20   "I don't even know who you are."

She spoke sullenly, careful to show no interest or pleasure, and he spoke in a fast, bright monotone. Connie looked past him to the other boy, taking her time. He had fair brown hair, with a lock that fell onto his forehead. His sideburns gave him a fierce, embarrassed look, but so far he hadn't even bothered to glance at her. Both boys wore sunglasses. The driver's glasses were metallic and mirrored everything in miniature.

"You wanta come for a ride?" he said.

Connie smirked and let her hair fall loose over one shoulder.

"Don'tcha like my car? New paint job," he said. "Hey."

25   "What?"

"You're cute."

She pretended to fidget, chasing flies away from the door.

"Don'tcha believe me, or what?" he said.

"Look, I don't even know who you are," Connie said in disgust.

30   "Hey, Ellie's got a radio, see. Mine broke down." He lifted his friend's arm and showed her the little transistor radio the boy was holding, and now Connie began to hear the music. It was the same program that was playing inside the house.

"Bobby King?" she said.

"I listen to him all the time. I think he's great."

"He's kind of great," Connie said reluctantly.

"Listen, that guy's *great*. He knows where the action is."

35   Connie blushed a little, because the glasses made it impossible for her to see just what this boy was looking at. She couldn't decide if she liked him or if he was a jerk, and so she dawdled in the doorway and wouldn't come down or go back inside. She said, "What's all that stuff painted on your car?"

"Can'tcha read it?" He opened the door very carefully, as if he were afraid it might fall off. He slid out just as carefully, planting his feet firmly on the ground, the tiny metallic world in his glasses slowing down like gelatine hardening, and in the midst of it Connie's bright-green blouse. "This here is my name, to begin with," he said. ARNOLD FRIEND was written in tarlike black letters on the side, with a drawing of a round, grinning face that reminded Connie of a pumpkin, except it wore sunglasses. "I wanta introduce myself. I'm Arnold Friend and that's my real name and I'm gonna be your friend, honey, and inside the car's Ellie Oscar, he's kinda shy." Ellie brought his transistor radio up to his shoulder and balanced it there. "Now, these numbers are a secret code, honey," Arnold Friend explained. He read off the numbers 33, 19, 17 and raised his eyebrows at her to see what she thought of that, but she didn't think much of it. The left rear fender had been smashed and around it was written, on the gleaming gold background: DONE BY CRAZY WOMAN DRIVER. Connie had to laugh at that. Arnold Friend was pleased at her laughter and looked up at her. "Around the other side's a lot more—you wanta come and see them?"

"No."

"Why not?"

"Why should I?"

"Don'tcha wanta see what's on the car? Don'tcha wanta go for a ride?"   40

"I don't know."

"Why not?"

"I got things to do."

"Like what?"

"Things."   45

He laughed as if she had said something funny. He slapped his thighs. He was standing in a strange way, leaning back against the car as if he were balancing himself. He wasn't tall, only an inch or so taller than she would be if she came down to him. Connie liked the way he was dressed, which was the way all of them dressed: tight faded jeans stuffed into black, scuffed boots, a belt that pulled his waist in and showed how lean he was, and a white pullover shirt that was a little soiled and showed the hard small muscles of his arms and shoulders. He looked as if he probably did hard work, lifting and carrying things. Even his neck looked muscular. And his face was a familiar face, somehow; the jaw and chin and cheeks slightly darkened because he hadn't shaved for a day or two, and the nose long and hawklike, sniffing as if she was a treat he was going to gobble up and it was all a joke.

"Connie, you ain't telling the truth. This is your day set aside for a ride with me and you know it," he said, still laughing. The way he straightened and recovered from his fit of laughing showed that it had been all fake.

"How do you know what my name is?" she said suspiciously.

"It's Connie."

"Maybe and maybe not."   50

"I know my Connie," he said, wagging his finger. Now she remembered him even better, back at the restaurant, and her cheeks warmed at the thought of how she had sucked in her breath just at the moment she passed him—how she must have looked to him. And he had remembered her. "Ellie and I come out here especially for you," he said. "Ellie can sit in back. How about it?"

"Where?"

"Where what?"

"Where're we going?"

He looked at her. He took off the sunglasses and she saw how pale the skin around his eyes was, like holes that were not in shadow but instead in light. His eyes were like chips of broken glass that catch the light in an amiable way. He smiled. It was as if the idea of going for a ride somewhere, to someplace, was a new idea to him.

"Just for a ride, Connie sweetheart."

"I never said my name was Connie," she said.

"But I know what it is. I know your name and all about you, lots of things," Arnold Friend said. He had not moved yet but stood still leaning back against the side of his jalopy. "I took a special interest in you, such a pretty girl, and found out all about you—like I know your parents and sister are gone some-wheres and I know where and how long they're going to be gone, and I know who you were with last night, and your best girl friend's name is Betty. Right?"

He spoke in a simple lilting voice, exactly as if he was reciting the words to a song. His smile assured her that everything was fine. In the car Ellie turned up the volume on his radio and did not bother to look around at them.

"Ellie can sit in the backseat," Arnold Friend said. He indicated his friend with a casual jerk of his chin, as if Ellie did not count and she should not bother with him.

"How'd you find out all that stuff?" Connie said.

"Listen: Betty Schultz and Tony Fitch and Jimmy Pettinger and Nancy Pet-tinger," he said in a chant. "Raymond Stanley and Bob Hutter—"

"Do you know all those kids?"

"I know everybody."

"Look, you're kidding. You're not from around here."

"Sure."

"But—how come we never saw you before?"

"Sure you saw me before," he said. He looked down at his boots, as if he was a little offended. "You just don't remember."

"I guess I'd remember you," Connie said.

"Yeah?" He looked up at this, beaming. He was pleased. He began to mark time with the music from Ellie's radio, tapping his fists lightly together. Connie looked away from his smile to the car, which was painted so bright it almost hurt her eyes to look at it. She looked at that name, ARNOLD FRIEND. And up at the front fender was an expression that was familiar—MAN THE FLY-ING SAUCERS. It was an expression kids had used the year before but didn't use this year. She looked at it for a while as if the words meant something to her that she did not yet know.

"What're you thinking about? Huh?" Arnold Friend demanded. "Not worried about your hair blowing around in the car, are you?"

"No."

"Think I maybe can't drive good?"

"How do I know?"

"You're a hard girl to handle. How come?" he said. "Don't you know I'm your friend? Didn't you see me put my sign in the air when you walked by?"

"What sign?"

"My sign." And he drew an X in the air, leaning out toward her. They were maybe ten feet apart. After his hand fell back to his side the X was still in the air, almost visible. Connie let the screen door close and stood perfectly still inside it, listening to the music from her radio and the boy's blend together. She stared at Arnold Friend. He stood there so stiffly relaxed, pretending to be relaxed, with one hand idly on the door handle as if he was keeping himself up that way and had no intention of ever moving again. She recognized most things about him, the tight jeans that showed his thighs and buttocks and the greasy leather boots and the tight shirt, and even that slippery friendly smile of his, that sleepy dreamy smile that all the boys used to get across ideas they didn't want to put into words. She recognized all this and also the singsong way he talked, slightly mocking, kidding, but serious and a little melancholy, and she recognized the way he tapped one fist against the other in homage to the perpetual music behind him. But all these things did not come together.

She said suddenly, "Hey, how old are you?"

His smile faded. She could see then that he wasn't a kid, he was much older—thirty, maybe more. At this knowledge her heart began to pound faster.

"That's a crazy thing to ask. Can'tcha see I'm your own age?" 80

"Like hell you are."

"Or maybe a coupla years older. I'm eighteen."

"Eighteen?" she said doubtfully.

He grinned to reassure her and lines appeared at the corners of his mouth. His teeth were big and white. He grinned so broadly his eyes became slits and she saw how thick the lashes were, thick and black as if painted with a black tarlike material. Then, abruptly, he seemed to become embarrassed and looked over his shoulder at Ellie. "*Him,* he's crazy," he said. "Ain't he a riot? He's a nut, a real character." Ellie was still listening to the music. His sunglasses told nothing about what he was thinking. He wore a bright-orange shirt unbuttoned halfway to show his chest, which was a pale, bluish chest and not muscular like Arnold Friend's. His shirt collar was turned up all around and the very tips of the collar pointed out past his chin as if they were protecting him. He was pressing the transistor radio up against his ear and sat there in a kind of daze, right in the sun.

"He's kinda strange," Connie said. 85

"Hey, she says you're kinda strange! Kinda strange!" Arnold Friend cried. He pounded on the car to get Ellie's attention. Ellie turned for the first time and Connie saw with shock that he wasn't a kid either—he had a fair, hairless face, cheeks reddened slightly as if the veins grew too close to the surface of his skin, the face of a forty-year-old baby. Connie felt a wave of dizziness rise in her at this sight and she stared at him as if waiting for something to change the shock of the moment, make it all right again. Ellie's lips kept shaping words, mumbling along with the words blasting in his ear.

"Maybe you two better go away," Connie said faintly.

"What? How come?" Arnold Friend cried. "We come out here to take you for a ride. It's Sunday." He had the voice of the man on the radio now. It was the same voice, Connie thought. "Don'tcha know it's Sunday all day? And honey, no matter who you were with last night, today you're with Arnold Friend and don't you forget it! Maybe you better step out here," he said, and this last was in a different voice. It was a little flatter, as if the heat was finally getting to him.

"No. I got things to do."

90   "Hey."

"You two better leave."

"We ain't leaving until you come with us."

"Like hell I am—"

"Connie, don't fool around with me. I mean—I mean, don't fool *around*," he said, shaking his head. He laughed incredulously. He placed his sunglasses on top of his head, carefully, as if he was indeed wearing a wig, and brought the stems down behind his ears. Connie stared at him, another wave of dizziness and fear rising in her so that for a moment he wasn't even in focus but was just a blur standing there against his gold car, and she had the idea that he had driven up the driveway all right but had come from nowhere before that and belonged nowhere and that everything about him and even about the music that was so familiar to her was only half real.

95   "If my father comes and sees you—"

"He ain't coming. He's at a barbecue."

"How do you know that?"

"Aunt Tillie's. Right now they're—uh—they're drinking. Sitting around," he said vaguely, squinting as if he was staring all the way to town and over to Aunt Tillie's backyard. Then the vision seemed to get clear and he nodded energetically. "Yeah. Sitting around. There's your sister in a blue dress, huh? And high heels, the poor sad bitch—nothing like you, sweetheart! And your mother's helping some fat woman with the corn, they're cleaning the corn—husking the corn—"

"What fat woman?" Connie cried.

100   "How do I know what fat woman, I don't know every goddamn fat woman in the world!" Arnold Friend laughed.

"Oh, that's Mrs. Hornsby. . . . Who invited her?" Connie said. She felt a little light-headed. Her breath was coming quickly.

"She's too fat. I don't like them fat. I like them the way you are, honey," he said, smiling sleepily at her. They stared at each other for a while through the screen door. He said softly, "Now, what you're going to do is this: you're going to come out that door. You're going to sit up front with me and Ellie's going to sit in the back, the hell with Ellie, right? This isn't Ellie's date. You're my date. I'm your lover, honey."

"What? You're crazy—"

"Yes. I'm your lover. You don't know what that is but you will," he said. "I know that too. I know all about you. But look: it's real nice and you couldn't ask for nobody better than me, or more polite. I always keep my word. I'll tell you how it is, I'm always nice at first, the first time. I'll hold you so tight you won't think you have to try to get away or pretend anything because you'll know you can't. And I'll come inside you where it's all secret and you'll give in to me and you'll love me—"

105   "Shut up! You're crazy!" Connie said. She backed away from the door. She put her hands up against her ears as if she'd heard something terrible, something not meant for her. "People don't talk like that, you're crazy," she muttered. Her heart was almost too big now for her chest and its pumping made sweat

break out all over her. She looked out to see Arnold Friend pause and then take a step toward the porch, lurching. He almost fell. But, like a clever drunken man, he managed to catch his balance. He wobbled in his high boots and grabbed hold of one of the porch posts.

"Honey?" he said. "You still listening?"

"Get the hell out of here!"

"Be nice, honey. Listen."

"I'm going to call the police—"

He wobbled again and out of the side of his mouth came a fast spat curse, an 110
aside not meant for her to hear. But even this "Christ!" sounded forced. Then he began to smile again. She watched this smile come, awkward as if he was smiling from inside a mask. His whole face was a mask, she thought wildly, tanned down to his throat but then running out as if he had plastered makeup on his face but had forgotten about his throat.

"Honey—? Listen, here's how it is. I always tell the truth and I promise you this: I ain't coming in that house after you."

"You better not! I'm going to call the police if you—if you don't—"

"Honey," he said, talking right through her voice, "honey. I'm not coming in there but you are coming out here. You know why?"

She was panting. The kitchen looked like a place she had never seen before, some room she had run inside but that wasn't good enough, wasn't going to help her. The kitchen window had never had a curtain, after three years, and there were dishes in the sink for her to do—probably—and if you ran your hand across the table you'd probably feel something sticky there.

"You listening, honey? Hey?" 115

"—going to call the police—"

"Soon as you touch the phone I don't need to keep my promise and can come inside. You won't want that."

She rushed forward and tried to lock the door. Her fingers were shaking. "But why lock it," Arnold Friend said gently, talking right into her face. "It's just a screen door. It's just nothing." One of his boots was at a strange angle, as if his foot wasn't in it. It pointed out to the left, bent at the ankle. "I mean, anybody can break through a screen door and glass and wood and iron or anything else if he needs to, anybody at all, and specially Arnold Friend. If the place got lit up with a fire, honey, you'd come runnin' out into my arms, right into my arms an' safe at home—like you knew I was your lover and'd stopped fooling around. I don't mind a nice shy girl but I don't like no fooling around." Part of those words were spoken with a slight rhythmic lilt, and Connie somehow recognized them—the echo of a song from last year, about a girl rushing into her boyfriend's arms and coming home again—

Connie stood barefoot on the linoleum floor, staring at him. "What do you want?" she whispered.

"I want you," he said. 120

"What?"

"Seen you that night and thought, that's the one, yes sir. I never needed to look anymore."

"But my father's coming back. He's coming to get me. I had to wash my hair first—" She spoke in a dry, rapid voice, hardly raising it for him to hear.

"No, your daddy is not coming and yes, you had to wash your hair and you washed it for me. It's nice and shining and all for me. I thank you, sweetheart," he said with a mock bow, but again he almost lost his balance. He had to bend and adjust his boots. Evidently his feet did not go all the way down; the boots must have been stuffed with something so that he would seem taller. Connie stared out at him and behind him at Ellie in the car, who seemed to be looking off toward Connie's right, into nothing. Then Ellie said, pulling the words out of the air one after another as if he were just discovering them, "You want me to pull out the phone?"

125   "Shut your mouth and keep it shut," Arnold Friend said, his face red from bending over or maybe from embarrassment because Connie had seen his boots. "This ain't none of your business."

"What—what are you doing? What do you want?" Connie said. "If I call the police they'll get you, they'll arrest you—"

"Promise was not to come in unless you touch that phone, and I'll keep that promise," he said. He resumed his erect position and tried to force his shoulders back. He sounded like a hero in a movie, declaring something important. But he spoke too loudly and it was as if he was speaking to someone behind Connie. "I ain't made plans for coming in that house where I don't belong but just for you to come out to me, the way you should. Don't you know who I am?"

"You're crazy," she whispered. She backed away from the door but did not want to go into another part of the house, as if this would give him permission to come through the door. "What do you . . . you're crazy, you . . ."

"Huh? What're you saying, honey?"

130   Her eyes darted everywhere in the kitchen. She could not remember what it was, this room.

"This is how it is, honey: you come out and we'll drive away, have a nice ride. But if you don't come out we're gonna wait till your people come home and then they're all going to get it."

"You want that telephone pulled out?" Ellie said. He held the radio away from his ear and grimaced, as if without the radio the air was too much for him.

"I toldja shut up, Ellie," Arnold Friend said, "you're deaf, get a hearing aid, right? Fix yourself up. This little girl's no trouble and's gonna be nice to me, so Ellie keep to yourself, this ain't your date—right? Don't hem in on me, don't hog, don't crush, don't bird dog, don't trail me," he said in a rapid, meaningless voice, as if he were running through all the expressions he'd learned but was no longer sure which of them was in style, then rushing on to new ones, making them up with his eyes closed. "Don't crawl under my fence, don't squeeze in my chipmunk hole, don't sniff my glue, suck my Popsicle, keep your own greasy fingers on yourself!" He shaded his eyes and peered in at Connie, who was backed against the kitchen table. "Don't mind him, honey, he's just a creep. He's a dope. Right? I'm the boy for you and like I said, you come out here nice like a lady and give me your hand, and nobody else gets hurt, I mean, your nice old bald-headed daddy and your mummy and your sister in her high heels. Because listen: why bring them in this?"

"Leave me alone," Connie whispered.

135   "Hey, you know that old woman down the road, the one with the chickens and stuff—you know her?"

"She's dead!"

"Dead? What? You know her?" Arnold Friend said.

"She's dead—"

"Don't you like her?"

"She's dead—she's—she isn't here anymore—" 140

"But don't you like her, I mean, you got something against her? Some grudge or something?" Then his voice dipped as if he was conscious of a rudeness. He touched the sunglasses perched up on top of his head as if to make sure they were still there. "Now, you be a good girl."

"What are you going to do?"

"Just two things, or maybe three," Arnold Friend said. "But I promise it won't last long and you'll like me the way you get to like people you're close to. You will. It's all over for you here, so come on out. You don't want your people in any trouble, do you?"

She turned and bumped against a chair or something, hurting her leg, but she ran into the back room and picked up the telephone. Something roared in her ear, a tiny roaring, and she was so sick with fear that she could do nothing but listen to it—the telephone was clammy and very heavy and her fingers groped down to the dial but were too weak to touch it. She began to scream into the phone, into the roaring. She cried out, she cried for her mother, she felt her breath start jerking back and forth in her lungs as if it was something Arnold Friend was stabbing her with again and again with no tenderness. A noisy sorrowful wailing rose all about her and she was locked inside it the way she was locked inside this house.

After a while she could hear again. She was sitting on the floor with her wet back against the wall. 145

Arnold Friend was saying from the door, "That's a good girl. Put the phone back."

She kicked the phone away from her.

"No, honey. Pick it up. Put it back right."

She picked it up and put it back. The dial tone stopped.

"That's a good girl. Now, you come outside." 150

She was hollow with what had been fear but what was now just an emptiness. All that screaming had blasted it out of her. She sat, one leg cramped under her, and deep inside her brain was something like a pin-point of light that kept going and would not let her relax. She thought, I'm not going to see my mother again. She thought, I'm not going to sleep in my bed again. Her bright-green blouse was all wet.

Arnold Friend said, in a gentle-loud voice that was like a stage voice, "The place where you came from ain't there anymore, and where you had in mind to go is canceled out. This place you are now—inside your daddy's house—is nothing but a cardboard box I can knock down anytime. You know that and always did know it. You hear me?"

She thought, I have got to think. I have got to know what to do.

"We'll go out to a nice field, out in the country here where it smells so nice and it's sunny," Arnold Friend said. "I'll have my arms tight around you so you won't need to try to get away and I'll show you what love is like, what it does. The hell with this house! It looks solid all right," he said. He ran his fingernail down the screen and the noise did not make Connie shiver, as it would have the day before. "Now, put your hand on your heart, honey. Feel that? That feels solid too but we know better. Be nice to me, be sweet like you can because what else is there for a girl like you but to be sweet and pretty and give in?—and get away before her people get back?"

155   She felt her pounding heart. Her hand seemed to enclose it. She thought for the first time in her life that it was nothing that was hers, that belonged to her, but just a pounding, living thing inside this body that wasn't really hers either.

"You don't want them to get hurt," Arnold Friend went on. "Now, get up, honey. Get up all by yourself."

She stood.

"Now, turn this way. That's right. Come over here to me.—Ellie, put that away, didn't I tell you? You dope. You miserable creepy dope," Arnold Friend said. His words were not angry but only part of an incantation. The incantation was kindly. "Now, come out through the kitchen to me, honey, and let's see a smile, try it, you're a brave, sweet little girl and now they're eating corn and hot dogs cooked to bursting over an outdoor fire, and they don't know one thing about you and never did and honey, you're better than them because not a one of them would have done this for you."

Connie felt the linoleum under her feet; it was cool. She brushed her hair back out of her eyes. Arnold Friend let go of the post tentatively and opened his arms for her, his elbows pointing in toward each other and his wrists limp, to show that this was an embarrassed embrace and a little mocking, he didn't want to make her self-conscious.

160   She put out her hand against the screen. She watched herself push the door slowly open as if she was back safe somewhere in the other doorway, watching this body and this head of long hair moving out into the sunlight where Arnold Friend waited.

"My sweet little blue-eyed girl," he said in a half-sung sigh that had nothing to do with her brown eyes but was taken up just the same by the vast sunlit reaches of the land behind him and on all sides of him—so much land that Connie had never seen before and did not recognize except to know that she was going to it.

1966

QUESTIONS

1. At what specific points in the story do your expectations about "where you are going" change? Why and how so? How might these shifts in your expectations relate to Connie's?

2. To what extent is the major conflict in Oates's story external (between Connie and Arnold, Connie and her family, Connie and her milieu)? To what extent is it internal (within Connie herself)? Why might she act as she does at the story's end? What happens next, or does it matter?

3. Both Connie and Arnold Friend more than once suggest that he is, or should be, familiar to her. Aside from the fact that she has seen him at least once before, why and how does he seem familiar? Why might that familiarity be significant, or how might it shape your sense of who Arnold is or what he might represent in the story?

AUTHORS ON THEIR WORK

JOYCE CAROL OATES (b. 1938)

From "'Where Are You Going, Where Have You Been?' and *Smooth Talk*: Short Story into Film" (1986)*

Some years ago in the American Southwest there surfaced a tabloid psychopath known as "The Pied Piper of Tucson." I have forgotten his name, but his specialty was the seduction and occasional murder of teen-aged girls. He may or may not have had actual accomplices, but his bizarre activities were known among a circle of teenagers in the Tucson area; for some reason they kept his secret, deliberately did not inform parents or police.

It was not after all the mass murderer himself who intrigued me, but the disturbing fact that a number of teenagers—from "good" families—aided and abetted his crimes. This is the sort of thing authorities and responsible citizens invariably call "inexplicable" because they can't find explanations for it. *They* would not have fallen under this maniac's spell, after all.

An early draft [. . .] had the rather too explicit title "Death and the Maiden." It was cast in a mode of fiction to which I am still partial—indeed, every third or fourth story of mine is probably in this mode—"realistic allegory," it might be called. It is Hawthornean, romantic, shading into parable. Like the medieval German engraving from which my title was taken, the story was minutely detailed yet clearly an allegory of the fatal attractions of death (or the devil). An innocent young girl is seduced by way of her own vanity; she mistakes death for erotic romance of a particularly American/trashy sort.

In subsequent drafts the story changed its tone, its focus, its language, its title. It became "Where Are You Going, Where Have You Been?" Written at a time when the author was intrigued by the music of Bob Dylan, particularly the hauntingly elegiac song "It's All Over Now, Baby Blue," it was dedicated to Bob Dylan. The charismatic mass murderer drops into the background and his innocent victim, a fifteen-year-old, moves into the foreground. She becomes the true protagonist of the tale [. . .].

*"Where Are You Going, Where Have You Been?' and *Smooth Talk*: Short Story into Film." *(Woman) Writer: Occasions and Opportunities*, Dutton, 1988, pp. 316–21.

VIET THANH NGUYEN
(b. 1971)

I'd Love You to Want Me

A graduate of the University of California, Berkeley (BA, 1992; PhD, 1997); a married father of two; and a professor of English, comparative literature, and American and ethnic studies at the University of Southern California, Viet Thanh Nguyen cannot remember a time before he became the refugee he has, in his words, "never stopped being." His first memories begin with the boat on which, when he was only four years old, he and his family fled South Vietnam and with the refugee camp, in Pennsylvania, where they found temporary refuge. After a stint in nearby Harrisburg, the family moved in 1978 to San Jose, California, where Nguyen's parents opened a small grocery store catering to the refugee community. With his brother leaving for college and his parents working twelve- to fourteen-hour days, Nguyen found "refuge in the library," devouring everything from science fiction to books on the Vietnam War, which fed his "fascination with" all that "had happened to my family" that they couldn't or wouldn't speak about. In the years since, that fascination has borne rich and varied fruit. The darkly comic confessions of a North Vietnamese double-agent posing as a South Vietnamese soldier-refugee, Nguyen's best-selling debut novel, *The Sympathizer* (2015), garnered six major prizes, including the Pulitzer; a sequel, *The Committed*, followed in 2021. Hailed as "a powerful reflection on how we choose to remember and forget," *Nothing Ever Dies: Vietnam and the Memory of War* (2016) was a finalist for both the National Book and the National Book Critics Circle awards for nonfiction. Originally titled "I'd Love You to Want Me," *The Refugees* (2017) collects stories written between 1997 and 2014. Since its publication, Nguyen has also become a *New York Times* opinion writer.

The first time the professor called Mrs. Khanh by the wrong name was at a wedding banquet, the kind of crowded affair they attended often, usually out of obligation. As the bride and groom approached their table, Mrs. Khanh noticed the professor reading his palms, where he'd jotted down his toast and the names of the newlyweds, whom they had never met. Leaning close to be heard over the chatter of four hundred guests and the din of the band, she found her husband redolent of well-worn paperbacks and threadbare carpet. It was a comforting mustiness, one that she associated with secondhand bookstores.

"Don't worry," she said. "You've done this a thousand times."

"Have I?" The professor rubbed his hands on his pants. "I can't seem to recall." His fair skin was thin as paper and lined with blue veins. From the precise part of his silver hair to the gleam on his brown oxfords, he appeared to be the same man who'd taught so many students he could no longer count them. During the two minutes the newlyweds visited their table, he didn't miss a beat, calling the couple by their correct names and bestowing the good wishes expected of him as the eldest among the ten guests. But while the groom tugged at the collar of his Nehru jacket[1] and the bride plucked at the skirt of her empire-waist gown, Mrs. Khanh could think only of the night of the diagnosis, when the professor had frightened her by weeping for the first time in their four decades together. Only after the young couple left could she relax, sighing as deeply as she could in the strict confines of her velvet *ao dai*.[2]

"The girl's mother tells me they're honeymooning for the first week in Paris." She spooned a lobster claw onto the professor's plate. "The second week they'll be on the French Riviera."

"Is that so?" Cracked lobster in tamarind sauce was Professor Khanh's favor- 5
ite, but tonight he stared with doubt at the claw pointing toward him. "What did the French call Vung Tau?"

"Cap Saint Jacques."[3]

"We had a very good time there. Didn't we?"

"That's when you finally started talking to me."

"Who wouldn't be shy around you," the professor murmured. Forty years ago, when she was nineteen and he was thirty-three, they had honeymooned at a beachside hotel on the cape. It was on their balcony, under a full, bright moon, listening to the French singing and shouting on their side of the beach, that the professor had suddenly started talking. "Imagine!" he said, voice filled with wonder as he began speaking about how the volume of the Pacific equaled the moon's. When he was finished, he went on to talk about the strange fish of deep sea canyons and then the inexplicability of rogue waves. If after a while she lost track of what he said, it hardly mattered, for by then the sound of his voice had seduced her, as reassuring in its measured tones as the first time she'd heard it, eavesdropping from her family's kitchen as he explained to her father his dissertation on the Kuroshio current's[4] thermodynamics.

Now the professor's memories were gradually stealing away from him, and 10
along with them the long sentences he once favored. When the band swung into "I'd Love You to Want Me,"[5] he loosened the fat Windsor knot of his tie and said, "Remember this song?"

"What about it?"

"We listened to it all the time. Before the children were born."

The song hadn't been released yet during her first pregnancy, but Mrs. Khanh said, "That's right."

"Let's dance." The professor leaned closer, draping one arm over the back of her chair. A fingerprint smudged one lens of his glasses. "You always insisted we dance when you heard this song, Yen."

1. Tailored coat with a mandarin collar resembling those worn by Jawaharlal Nehru, India's prime minister from 1947 to 1964.

2. Traditional Vietnamese garment consisting of a long tunic with side slits, worn over pants.

3. Coastal city in South Vietnam. From 1887 to 1954, Vietnam was a French colony.

4. North-flowing current in the North Pacific Ocean, beginning off the east coast of the Philippines and analogous to the Gulf Stream in the Atlantic Ocean.

5. Popular song (1972) by Lobo (a.k.a. Roland Kent LaVoie); its refrain begins, "Baby, I'd love to want me / The way that I want you / The way that it should be."

15   "Oh?" Mrs. Khanh took a slow sip from her glass of water, hiding her surprise at being called by someone else's name. "When did we ever dance?"

The professor didn't answer, for the swelling chorus of the song had brought him to his feet. As he stepped toward the parquet dance floor, Mrs. Khanh seized the tail of his gray pinstripe jacket. "Stop it!" she said, pulling hard. "Sit down!"

Giving her a wounded look, the professor obeyed. Mrs. Khanh was aware of the other guests at their table staring at them. She held herself very still, unable to account for any woman named Yen. Perhaps Yen was an old acquaintance whom the professor never saw fit to mention, or the maternal grandmother whom Mrs. Khanh had never met and whose name she couldn't now recall, or a grade school teacher with whom he'd once been infatuated. Mrs. Khanh had begun preparing for many things, but she wasn't prepared for unknown people emerging from the professor's mind.

"The song's almost over," the professor said.

"We'll dance when we get home. I promise."

20   Despite his condition, or perhaps because of it, the professor insisted on driving them back. Mrs. Khanh was tense as she watched him handling the car, but he drove in his usual slow and cautious manner. He was quiet until he took a left at Golden West instead of a right, his wrong turn taking them by the community college from where he'd retired last spring. After coming to America, he'd been unable to find work in oceanography, and had settled for teaching Vietnamese. For the last twenty years, he'd lectured under fluorescent lighting to bored students. When Mrs. Khanh wondered if one of those students might be Yen, she felt a jab of pain that she mistook at first for heartburn. Only upon second thought did she recognize it as jealousy.

The professor suddenly braked to a stop. Mrs. Khanh braced herself with one hand against the dashboard and waited to be called by that name again, but the professor made no mention of Yen. He swung the car into a U-turn instead, and as they headed toward home, he asked in a tone of great reproach, "Why didn't you tell me we were going in the wrong direction?" Watching all the traffic lights on the street ahead of them turn green as if on cue, Mrs. Khanh realized that his was a question for which she had no good answer.

The next morning, Mrs. Khanh was standing at the stove preparing brunch for their eldest son's visit when the professor came into the kitchen, freshly bathed and shaved. He took a seat at the kitchen counter, unfolded the newspaper, and began reading to her from the headlines. Only after he'd finished did she begin telling him about last night's events. He'd asked her to inform him of those moments when he no longer acted like himself, and she had gotten as far as his lunge for the dance floor when the sag of his shoulders stopped her.

"It's all right," she said, alarmed. "It's not your fault."

"But can you see me on the dance floor at my age?" The professor rolled up the newspaper and rapped it against the counter for emphasis. "And in my condition?"

25   Taking out a small blue notebook from his shirt pocket, the professor retreated to the patio, where he was writing down his errors when Vinh arrived. Fresh from his graveyard shift at the county hospital, their son wore a nurse's green scrubs, which, shapeless as they were, did little to hide his physique. If

only he visited his parents as much as he did the gym, Mrs. Khanh thought. The edge of her hand could have fitted into the deep cleft of her son's chest, and her thighs weren't quite as thick as his biceps. Under one arm, he was carrying a bulky package wrapped in brown paper, which he propped against the trellis behind his father.

The professor slipped the notebook into his pocket and pointed his pen at the package. "What's the surprise?" he asked. While Mrs. Khanh brought out the eggs Benedict, Vinh stripped off the wrapping to reveal a painting in a heavy gilded frame evocative of nineteenth-century Europe. "It cost me a hundred dollars on Dong Khoi,"[6] he said. He had gone to Saigon on vacation last month. "The galleries there can knock off anything, but it was easier to frame it here."

The professor leaned forward to squint at the painting. "There was a time when that street was called Tu Do," he remarked wistfully. "And before that, Rue Catinat."

"I hoped you'd remember," Vinh said, sitting down next to his mother at the patio table. Mrs. Khanh could tell that the subject of the painting was a woman, but one whose left eye was green and whose right eye was red, which was nowhere near as odd as the way the artist had flattened her arms and torso, leaving her to look less like a real person and more like a child's paper doll, cut out and pasted to a three-dimensional chair. "There's a new study that shows how Picasso's paintings can stimulate people like Ba."[7]

"Is that so?" The professor wiped his glasses with his napkin. Behind him was the scene to which Mrs. Khanh was now accustomed, an entrance ramp rising over their backyard and merging onto the freeway that Vinh would take home to Los Angeles, an hour north of their Westminster neighborhood. Her boys used to pass their afternoons spotting the makes and models of the passing cars, as if they were ornithologists distinguishing between juncos and sparrows. But that was a very long time ago, she thought, and Vinh was now a messenger dispatched by the rest of their six children.

"We think you should retire from the library, Ma," he said, knife and fork in hand. "We can send home enough money every month to cover all the bills. You can have a housekeeper to help you out. And a gardener, too."

Mrs. Khanh had never needed help with the garden, which was entirely of her own design. A horseshoe of green lawn divided a perimeter of persimmon trees from the center of the garden, where pale green cilantro, arrow-leafed basil, and Thai chilies grew abundantly in the beds she'd made for them. She seasoned her eggs Benedict with three dashes of pepper, and when she was certain that she could speak without betraying her irritation, she said, "I like to garden."

"Mexican gardeners come cheap, Ma. Besides, you'll want all the help you can get. You've got to be ready for the worst."

30

6. Literally, "total revolution" (Vietnamese), a major street in South Vietnam's most populous city, Ho Chi Minh. Prior to the 1975 North Vietnamese takeover, the street and city were named Tu Do ("Liberty") and Saigon respectively. Under French rule (1887–1954), the same street was "Rue Catinat." (In French, *rue* means "street.")

7. Dad or father (Vietnamese). *Picasso*: Pablo Picasso (1881–1973), Spanish painter and sculptor.

"We've seen much worse than you," the professor snapped. "We're ready for anything."

"And I'm not old enough for retirement," Mrs. Khanh added.

35   "Be reasonable." Vinh sounded nothing like the boy who, upon reaching his teenage years, had turned into someone his parents no longer knew, sneaking out of the house at night to be with his girlfriend, an American who painted her nails black and dyed her hair purple. The professor remedied the situation by nailing the windows shut, a problem Vinh solved by eloping soon after his graduation from Bolsa Grande High. "I'm in love," Vinh had screamed to his mother over the phone from Las Vegas. "But you wouldn't know anything about that, would you?" Sometimes Mrs. Khanh regretted ever telling him that her father had arranged her marriage.

"You don't need the money from that job," Vinh said. "But Ba needs you at home."

Mrs. Khanh pushed away her plate, the eggs barely touched. She wouldn't take advice from someone whose marriage hadn't lasted more than three years. "It's not about the money, Kevin."

Vinh sighed, for his mother used his American name only when she was upset with him. "Maybe you should help Ba," he said, pointing to the front of his father's polo shirt, marred by a splash of hollandaise sauce.

"Look at this," the professor said, brushing at the stain with his fingers. "It's only because you've upset me." Vinh sighed once more, but Mrs. Khanh refused to look at him as she dabbed a napkin in her glass of water. She wondered if he remembered their escape from Vung Tau on a rickety fishing trawler, overloaded with his five siblings and sixty strangers, three years after the war's end.[8] After the fourth day at sea, he and the rest of the children, bleached by the sun, were crying for water, even though there was none to offer but the sea's. Nevertheless, she had washed their faces and combed their hair every morning, using salt water and spit. She was teaching them that decorum mattered even now, and that their mother's fear wasn't so strong that it could prevent her from loving them.

40   "Don't worry," she said. "The stain will come out." As she leaned forward to scrub the professor's shirt, Mrs. Khanh had a clear view of the painting. She liked neither the painting nor its gilded frame. It was too ornate for her taste, and seemed too old-fashioned for the painting. The disjuncture between the frame and the painting only exaggerated the painting's most disturbing feature, the way the woman's eyes looked forth from one side of her face. The sight of those eyes made Mrs. Khanh so uneasy that later that day, after Vinh went home, she moved the painting to the professor's library, where she left it facing a wall.

It wasn't long after their son's visit that the professor stopped attending Sunday mass. Mrs. Khanh stayed home as well, and gradually they began seeing less and less of their friends. The only times she left the house were to go shopping or to the Garden Grove library, where her fellow librarians knew nothing of the professor's illness. She enjoyed her part-time job, ordering and sorting the sizable collection of Vietnamese books and movies purchased for the residents of

8. What Americans call the Vietnam War ended in 1975 with the defeat of South Vietnamese and U.S. forces by the North Vietnamese.

nearby Little Saigon, who, if they came to the library with a question, were directed to her perch behind the circulation desk. Answering those questions, Mrs. Khanh always felt the gratification that made her job worthwhile, the pleasure of being needed, if only for a brief amount of time.

When her shift ended at noon and she gathered her things to go home, she always did so with a sense of dread that shamed her. She made up for her shame by bidding goodbye to the other librarians with extra cheer, and by preparing the house for emergencies with great energy, as if she could forestall the inevitable through hard work. She marked a path from bed to bathroom with fluorescent yellow tape, so the professor wouldn't get lost at night, and on the wall across from the toilet, she taped a sign at eye level that said FLUSH. She composed a series of lists which, posted strategically around the house, reminded the professor in what order to put his clothes on, what to put in his pockets before he left home, and what times of the day he should eat. But it was the professor who hired a handyman to install iron bars on the windows. "You wouldn't want me sneaking out at night," the professor said with resignation, leaning his forehead against the bars. "And neither would I."

For Mrs. Khanh, the more urgent problem was the professor coming home as a stranger. Whereas her husband was never one to be romantic, this stranger returned from one of the afternoon walks he insisted on taking by himself with a red rose in a plastic tube. He'd never before bought flowers of any sort, preferring to surprise her with more enduring presents, like the books he gave her every now and again, on topics like how to make friends and influence people, or income tax preparation. Once he had surprised her by giving her fiction, a collection of short stories by an author she had never heard of before. Even this effort was slightly off the mark, for she preferred novels. She never read past the title pages of his gifts, satisfied at seeing her name penned in his elegant hand beneath those of the authors. But if the professor had spent his life practicing calligraphy, he'd never given a thought to presenting roses, and when he bowed while offering her the flower, he appeared to be suffering from a stomach cramp.

"Who's this for?" she asked.

"Is there anyone else here?" The professor shook the rose for emphasis, and   45 one of its petals, browning at the edges, fell off. "It's for you."

"It's very pretty." She took the rose reluctantly. "Where did you get it?"

"Mr. Esteban. He tried selling me oranges also, but I said we had our own."

"And who am I?" she demanded. "What's my name?"

He squinted at her. "Yen, of course."

"Of course." Biting her lip, she fought the urge to snap the head off the rose.   50 She displayed the flower in a vase on the dining table for the professor's sake, but by the time she brought out dinner an hour later, he had forgotten he bought it. As he nibbled on blackened tiger shrimp, grilled on skewers, and tofu shimmering in black bean sauce, he talked animatedly instead about the postcard they'd received that afternoon from their eldest daughter, working for American Express in Munich. Mrs. Khanh examined the picture of the Marienplatz[9]

9. Literally, "Mary's Square" (German), major square in Munich, Germany, so-named because of the column, dedicated to the Virgin Mary, erected at its center in 1638 to celebrate the end of Swedish occupation.

before turning over the postcard to read aloud the note, which remarked on the curious absence of pigeons.

"Little things stay with you when you travel," observed the professor, sniffing at the third course, a soup of bitter melon.[1] Their children had never acquired the taste for it, but it reminded the professor and Mrs. Khanh of their own childhood.

"Such as?"

"The price of cigarettes," the professor said. "When I returned to Saigon after finishing my studies, I couldn't buy my daily Gauloises[2] any longer. The imported price was too much."

She leaned the postcard against the vase, where it would serve as a memento of the plans they'd once made for traveling to all of the world's great cities after their retirement. The only form of transport Mrs. Khanh had ruled out was the ocean cruise. Open expanses of water prompted fears of drowning, a phobia so strong that she no longer took baths, and even when showering kept her back to the spray.

55   "Now why did you buy that?" the professor asked.

"The postcard?"

"No, the rose."

"I didn't buy it." Mrs. Khanh chose her words carefully, not wanting to disturb the professor too much, and yet wanting him to know what he had done. "You did."

"Me?" The professor was astonished. "Are you certain?"

60   "I am absolutely certain," she said, surprised to hear the gratification in her voice.

The professor didn't notice. He only sighed and took out the blue notebook from the pocket of his shirt. "Let's hope that won't happen again," he muttered.

"I don't suppose it will." Mrs. Khanh stood to gather the dishes. She hoped her face didn't show her anger, convinced as she was that the professor had intended the rose for this other woman. She was carrying four plates, the tureen, and both their glasses when, at the kitchen's threshold, the wobbling weight of her load became too much. The sound of silverware clattering on the tiled floor and the smash of porcelain breaking made the professor cry out from the dining room. "What's that?" he shouted.

Mrs. Khanh stared at the remains of the tureen at her feet. Three uneaten green coins of bitter melon, stuffed with pork, lay sodden on the floor among the shards. "It's nothing," she said. "I'll take care of it."

After he'd fallen asleep later that evening, she went to his library, where the painting she had propped by his desk was now turned face forward. She sighed. If he kept turning the painting this way, she would at least have to reframe it in something more modern and suitable. She sat down at his desk, flanked on either side by bookshelves that held several hundred volumes in Vietnamese, French, and English. His ambition was to own more books than he could ever possibly read, a desire fueled by having left behind all his books when they had fled Vietnam. Dozens of paperbacks cluttered his desk, and she had to shove

---

1. Rough-skinned, green-colored unripe fruit used in Asian cooking.
2. Famous brand of French cigarette.

them aside to find the notebooks where he'd been tracking his mistakes over the past months. He had poured salt into his coffee and sprinkled sugar into his soup; when a telemarketer had called, he'd agreed to five-year subscriptions to *Guns & Ammo* and *Cosmopolitan*; and one day he'd tucked his wallet in the freezer, giving new meaning to the phrase cold, hard cash, or so he'd joked with her when she discovered it. But there was no mention of Yen, and after a moment's hesitation, underneath his most recent entry, Mrs. Khanh composed the following: "Today I called my wife by the name of Yen," she wrote. She imitated the flourishes of the professor's penmanship with great care, pretending that what she was doing was for the professor's own good. "This mistake must not be repeated."

The following morning, the professor held forth his coffee cup and said, "Please 65 pass me the sugar, Yen." The next day, as she trimmed his hair in the bathroom, he asked, "What's on television tonight, Yen?" As he called her by the other woman's name again and again over the following weeks, the question of who this woman was consumed her days. Perhaps Yen was a childhood crush, or a fellow student of his graduate school years in Marseille,[3] or even a second wife in Saigon, someone he'd visited on the way home from the university, during those long early evening hours when he told her he was sitting in his office on campus, correcting student exams. She recorded every incident of mistaken identity in his notebooks, but the next morning he would read her forgeries without reaction, and not long afterward would call her Yen once more, until she thought she might burst into tears if she heard that name again.

The woman was most likely a fantasy found by the professor's wandering mind, or so she told herself after catching him naked from the waist down, kneeling over the bathtub and scrubbing furiously at his pants and underwear under a jet of hot water. Glaring over his shoulder, the professor had screamed, "Get out!" She jumped back, slamming the bathroom door in her haste. Never before had the professor lost such control of himself, or yelled at her, not even in those first days after coming to southern California, when they'd eaten from food stamps, gotten housing assistance, and worn secondhand clothes donated by the parishioners of St. Albans. That was true love, she thought, not giving roses but going to work every day and never once complaining about teaching Vietnamese to so-called heritage learners,[4] immigrant and refugee students who already knew the language but merely wanted an easy grade.

Not even during the most frightening time of her life, when they were lost on the great azure plain of the sea, rolling unbroken to the horizon, did the professor raise his voice. By the fifth evening, the only sounds besides the waves slapping at the hull were children whimpering and adults praying to God, Buddha, and their ancestors. The professor hadn't prayed. Instead, he had stood at the ship's bow as if he were at his lectern, the children huddled together at his knees for protection against the evening wind, and told them lies. "You can't see it even in daylight," he'd said, "but the current we're traveling on is going straight

3. France's second-largest city, home to Aix-Marseille Université (founded 1409).
4. Those studying a language of which their family's cultural heritage gives them some prior knowledge.

to the Philippines, the way it's done since the dawn of time." He repeated his story so often even she allowed herself to believe it, until the afternoon of the seventh day, when they saw, in the distance, the rocky landing strip of a foreign coast. Nesting upon it were the huts of a fishing village, seemingly composed of twigs and grass, brooded over by a fringe of mangroves. At the sight of land, she had thrown herself into the professor's arms, knocking his glasses askew, and sobbed openly for the first time in front of her startled children. She was so seized by the ecstasy of knowing that they would all live that she had blurted out "I love you." It was something she had never said in public and hardly ever in private, and the professor, embarrassed by their children's giggles, had only smiled and adjusted his glasses. His embarrassment only deepened once they reached land, which the locals informed them was the north shore of eastern Malaysia.[5]

For some reason, the professor never spoke of this time at sea, although he referred to so many other things they had done in the past together, including events of which she had no recollection. The more she listened to him, the more she feared her own memory was faltering. Perhaps they really had eaten ice cream flavored with durian[6] on the veranda of a tea plantation in the central highlands, reclining on rattan chairs. And was it possible they'd fed bamboo shoots to the tame deer in the Saigon zoo? Or together had beaten off a pick-pocket, a scabby refugee from the bombed-out countryside who'd sneaked up on them in the Ben Thanh market?[7]

As the days of spring lengthened into summer, she answered the phone less and less, eventually turning off the ringer so the professor wouldn't answer calls either. She was afraid that if someone asked for her, he would say, "Who?" Even more worrying was the prospect of him speaking to their friends or children of Yen. When her daughter phoned from Munich, she said, "Your father's not doing so well," but left the details vague. She was more forthcoming with Vinh, knowing that whatever she told him he would e-mail to the other children. Whenever he left a message, she could hear the hiss of grease in a pan, or the chatter of a news channel, or the beeping of horns. He called her on his cell phone only as he did something else. She admitted that as much as she loved her son, she liked him very little, a confession that made her unhappy with herself until the day she called him back and he asked, "Have you decided? Are you going to quit?"

70 "Don't make me tell you one more time." She wrapped the telephone cord tightly around her index finger. "I'm never going to quit."

After she hung up the phone, she returned to the task of changing the sheets the professor had bed-wet the previous evening. Her head was aching from lack of sleep, her back was sore from the chores, and her neck was tight with worry. When bedtime came, she was unable to sleep, listening to the professor talk about how gusts of the mistral blew him from one side to the other of the

5. Since Malaysia lies southwest of Vietnam, across the Gulf of Thailand, while the Philippines are on the South China Sea, to Vietnam's east, the family has traveled in the opposite direction and much less far than predicted.
6. Large, tasty fruit with a prickly rind.
7. Large, popular market in central Ho Chi Minh City.

winding narrow streets of Le Panier,[8] where he'd lived in a basement apartment during his Marseille years, or about the hypnotic sound made by the scratch of a hundred pens on paper as students took their exams. As he talked, she studied the dim light in their bedroom, cast off from the streetlamps outside, and remembered how the moon over the South China Sea was so bright that even at midnight she could see the fearful expressions on her children's faces. She was counting the cars passing by outside, listening for the sounds of their engines and hoping for sleep, when the professor touched her hand in the dark. "If you close your eyes," he said gently, "you might hear the ocean."

Mrs. Khanh closed her eyes.

September came and went. October passed and the Santa Ana winds came, rushing from the mountains to the east with the force of freeway traffic, breaking the stalks of the Egyptian papyruses she'd planted in ceramic pots next to the trellis. She no longer allowed the professor to walk by himself in the afternoons, but instead followed him discreetly at a distance of ten or twenty feet, clutching her hat against the winds. If the Santa Ana had subsided, they read together on the patio. Over the past few months, the professor had taken to reading out loud, and slowly. Each day he seemed to read even more loudly, and more slowly, until the afternoon in November when he stopped in mid-sentence for so long that the silence shook Mrs. Khanh from the grip of Quynh Dao's[9] latest romance.

"What's the matter?" she asked, closing her book.

"I've been trying to read this sentence for five minutes," the professor said,   75 staring at the page. When he looked up, she saw tears in his eyes. "I'm losing my mind, aren't I?"

From then on, she read to him whenever she was free, from books on academic topics she had no interest in whatsoever. She stopped whenever he began reciting a memory—the anxiety he felt on meeting her father for the first time, while she waited in the kitchen to be introduced; the day of their wedding, when he nearly fainted from the heat and the tightness of his cravat; or the day they returned to Saigon three years ago and visited their old house on Phan Than Gian, which they could not find at first because the street had been renamed Dien Bien Phu. Saigon had also changed names after it changed hands, but they couldn't bring themselves to call it Ho Chi Minh City. Neither could the taxi driver who ferried them from their hotel to the house, even though he was too young to remember a time when the city was officially Saigon.

They parked two houses down from their old house, and stayed in the taxi to avoid the revolutionary cadres from the north who had moved in after the Communist takeover. She and the professor were nearly overwhelmed by sadness and rage, fuming as they wondered who these strangers were who had taken such poor care of their house. The solitary alley lamp illuminated tears of rust

8. Literally, "the basket" (French), one of Marseille's oldest, most historic neighborhoods. *Mistral*: strong, cold, dry northerly wind of southern France.
9. Or Chiung Yao (Chinese), pseudonym of the Taiwanese writer (b. 1938) widely regarded as the most popular romance writer in the Chinese-speaking world; her works have been translated into many languages, including Vietnamese.

streaking the walls, washed down from the iron grill of the terrace by the monsoon rain. As the taxi's wipers squeaked against the windshield, a late-night masseur biked past, announcing his calling with the shake of a glass bottle filled with pebbles.

"You told me it was the loneliest sound in the world," said the professor.

Before he started talking, she'd been reading to him from a biography of de Gaulle,[1] and her finger was still on the last word she'd read. She didn't like to think about their lost home, and she didn't remember having said any such thing. "The wipers or the glass bottle?" she asked.

80   "The bottle."

"It seemed so at the time," she lied. "I hadn't heard that sound in years."

"We heard it often. In Dalat."[2] The professor took off his glasses and wiped them with his handkerchief. He had gone once to a resort in the mountains of Dalat for a conference while she stayed in Saigon, pregnant. "You always wanted to eat your ice cream outside in the evenings," the professor continued. "But it's hard to eat ice cream in the tropics, Yen. One has no time to savor it. Unless one is indoors, with air conditioning."

"Dairy products give you indigestion."

"If one eats ice cream in a bowl, it rapidly becomes soup. If one eats it in a cone, it melts all over one's hand." When he turned to her and smiled, she saw gumdrops of mucus in the corners of his eyes. "You loved those brown sugar cones, Yen. You insisted that I hold yours for you so your hand wouldn't get sticky."

85   A breeze rattled the bougainvillea, the first hint, perhaps, of the Santa Ana returning. The sound of her own voice shocked her as well as the professor, who stared at her with his mouth agape when she said, "That's not my name. I am not that woman, whoever she is, if she even exists."

"Oh?" The professor slowly closed his mouth and put his glasses back on. "Your name isn't Yen?"

"No," she said.

"Then what is it?"

She wasn't prepared for the question, having been worried only about her husband calling her by the wrong name. They rarely used each other's proper names, preferring endearments like *Anh*, for him, or *Em*,[3] for her, and when they spoke to each other in front of the children, they called themselves Ba and Ma. Usually she heard her first name spoken only by friends, relatives, or bureaucrats, or when she introduced herself to someone new, as she was, in a sense, doing now.

90   "My name is Sa," she said. "I am your wife."

"Right." The professor licked his lips and took out his notebook.

That evening, after they had gone to bed and she heard him breathing evenly, she switched on her lamp and reached across his body for the notebook, propped on the alarm clock. His writing had faded into such a scribble that she was

---

1. Charles de Gaulle (1890–1970), French military leader and France's president from 1959 to 1969.
2. City in the Central Highlands of South Vietnam, a popular tourist destination thanks in part to its relatively cool weather.
3. Vietnamese pet name meaning something like "little sibling," often used to refer to the woman in a romantic relationship, just as *anh* ("big brother") refers to the man.

forced to read what he wrote twice, following the jags and peaks of his letters down a dog-eared page until she reached the bottom, where she deciphered the following: *Matters worsening. Today she insisted I call her by another name. Must keep closer eye on her*—here she licked her finger and used it to turn the page—*for she may not know who she is anymore.* She closed the book abruptly, with a slap of the pages, but the professor, curled up on his side, remained still. A scent of sweat and sulfur emanated from underneath the sheets. If it wasn't for his quiet breathing and the heat of his body, he might have been dead, and for a moment as fleeting as déjà vu, she wished he really were.

In the end there was no choice. On her last day at work, her fellow librarians threw her a surprise farewell party, complete with cake and a wrapped gift box that held a set of travel guides for the vacations they knew she'd always wanted to take. She fondled the guides for a while, riffling through their pages, and when she almost wept, her fellow librarians thought she was being sentimental. Driving home with the box of guides in the backseat, next to a package of adult diapers she'd picked up from Sav-On's that morning, she fought to control the sense that ever so slowly the book of her life was being closed.

When she opened the door to their house and called out his name, she heard only bubbling from the fish tank. After not finding him in any of the bedrooms or bathrooms, she left the diapers and box of books in his library. An open copy of *Sports Illustrated* was on his recliner in the living room, a half-eaten jar of applesauce sat on the kitchen counter, and in the backyard, the chenille throw he wore around his lap in cool weather lay on the ground. Floating in his teacup on the patio table was a curled petal from the bougainvillea, shuttling back and forth.

Panic almost made her call the police. But they wouldn't do anything so soon; they'd tell her to call back when he was missing for a day or two. As for Vinh, she ruled him out, not wanting to hear him say, "I told you so." Regret swept over her then, a wave of feeling born from her guilt over being so selfish. Her librarian's instinct for problem solving and orderly research kept her standing under the weight of that regret, and she returned to her car determined to find the professor. She drove around her block first before expanding in ever-widening circles, the windows rolled down on both sides. The neighborhood park, where she and the professor often strolled, was abandoned except for squirrels chasing each other through the branches of an oak tree. The sidewalks were empty of pedestrians or joggers, except for a withered man in a plaid shirt standing on a corner, selling roses from plastic buckets and oranges from crates, his eyes shaded by a grimy baseball cap. When she called him Mr. Esteban, his eyes widened; when she asked him if he'd seen the professor, he smiled apologetically and said, "No hablo inglés. Lo siento."[4]

Doubling back on her tracks, she drove each street and lane and cul-de-sac a second time. Leaning out the window, she called his name, first in a low voice, shy about making a scene, and then in a shout. "Anh Khanh!" she cried. "Anh Khanh!" A few window curtains twitched, and a couple of passing cars slowed

95

4. I do not speak English. I'm sorry (Spanish).

down, their drivers glancing at her curiously. But he didn't spring forth from behind anyone's hedges, or emerge from a stranger's door.

Only after it was dark did she return. The moment she walked through the front door, she smelled the gas. A kettle was on the stove, but the burner hadn't been lit. Both her pace and her pulse quickened from a walk to a sprint. After shutting off the gas, she saw that the glass doors leading to the patio, which she'd closed before her departure, were slightly ajar. There was a heavy, long flashlight in one of the kitchen drawers, and the heft of the aluminum barrel in her hand was comforting as she slowly approached the glass doors. But when she shone the light over the patio and onto the garden, she saw only her persimmon trees and the red glint of the chilies.

She was in the hallway when she saw the light spilling out of the professor's library. When she peeked around the door frame, she saw the professor with his back to the door. At his feet was her box of books, and he stood facing the bookshelf that was reserved for her. Here, she kept her magazines and the books he'd given her over the years. The professor knelt, picked a book from the box, and stood up to shelve it. He repeated the same motion, one book at a time. *Hidden Tahiti and French Polynesia*. Frommer's *Hawaii*. *National Geographic Traveler: The Caribbean*. With each book, he mumbled something she couldn't hear, as if he might be trying to read the titles on the spines. *Essential Greek Islands. Jerusalem and the Holy Land. World Cultures: Japan. A Romantic's Guide to Italy.* He touched the cover of each book with great care, tenderly, and she knew, not for the first time, that it wasn't she who was the love of his life.

The professor shelved the last book and turned around. The expression on his face when he saw her was the one he'd worn forty years ago at their first meeting, when she'd entered the living room of her father's house and seen him pale with anxiety, eyes blinking in anticipation. "Who are you?" he cried, raising his hand as if to ward off a blow. Her heart was beating fast and her breathing was heavy. When she swallowed, her mouth was dry, but she could feel a sheen of dampness on her palms. It struck her then that these were the same sensations she'd felt that first time, seeing him in a white linen suit wrinkled by high humidity, straw fedora pinned between hand and thigh.

100   "It's just me," she said. "It's Yen."

"Oh," the professor said, lowering his hand. He sat down heavily in his armchair, and she saw that his oxfords were encrusted in mud. As she crossed the carpet to the bookshelf, he followed her with a hooded gaze, his look one of exhaustion. She was about to take *Les Petites Rues de Paris*[5] from the bookshelf for the evening's reading, but when she saw him close his eyes and lean back in his armchair, it was clear that he wouldn't be traveling anywhere. Neither would she. Having ruled out the travel guides, she decided against the self-help books and the how-to manuals as well. Then she saw the thin and uncracked spine of the book of short stories.

A short story, she thought, would be just long enough.

Sitting beside him on the carpet, she found herself next to the painting. She turned her back to the woman with the two eyes on one side of her face, and

5. The Small Streets of Paris (French).

she promised herself that tomorrow she would have the painting reframed. When she opened the book, she could feel the woman looking over her shoulder at her name, written in his precise hand under that of the author. She wondered what, if anything, she knew about love. Not much, perhaps, but enough to know that what she would do for him now she would do again tomorrow, and the next day, and the day after that. She would read out loud, from the beginning. She would read with measured breath, to the very end. She would read as if every letter counted, page by page and word by word.

2008, 2017

QUESTIONS

1. What is the significance of the episode (or discriminated occasion) with which the story opens? Why and how is this a destabilizing event? What conflict does it establish? In these terms, what might be meaningful about the setting and other details?
2. How does your sense of the conflict and of Mr. and Mrs.'s Khanh's relationship develop over subsequent episodes? In these terms, what does Nguyen gain by introducing the Khanh's son, Vinh, into the story, as well as glimpses into the Khanh family's past? How might and might not it matter that they are refugees? that they are Vietnamese?
3. Who is or was Yen, or was she a real person at all? What clues does the story offer? What is the significance of the fact that neither Mrs. Khanh nor the reader ever knows for sure?
4. Why, in the end, does Mrs. Khanh allow her husband to call her Yen? Why and how might this be a satisfactory resolution?

ADAM JOHNSON
(b. 1967)

Interesting Facts

Aptly described by the *Los Angeles Times* as a "gregarious, linebacker-sized guy of mixed Northern European and Native American extraction," Adam Johnson was born in South Dakota but grew up in the Arizona suburbs. "[A]n only child and latchkey kid, raised mostly by his clinical psychologist mother after his parents divorced" (to again quote the *Times*), Johnson reports nurturing his "imaginary life" both by biking "the neighborhoods and alleys," "open[ing] the trash dumpsters and [. . .] try[ing] to figure out who lived in those houses," and by visiting the Phoenix Zoo, after hours, with his father, then a night watchman: "I developed a sense really early on that there was a behind-the-scenes to everything," "that just behind the veil of anything was a richer, truer [. . .] story," he says. For Johnson—who has a BA in journalism, as well as an MFA, and a PhD in English—piercing that veil requires equal parts imagination and research, storytelling's "transformative power" residing in its ability to give us perspective on our own lives and minds by taking us into the most different of others', especially "those who might otherwise go unheard." Based on years of research, Johnson's second, Pulitzer Prize–winning novel, *The Orphan Master's Son*

(2012), offers a searing portrait of life in totalitarian North Korea; his first, *Parasites Like Us* (2003), imagines an apocalyptic pandemic. Johnson's darkly funny collections *Emporium* (2002) and *Fortune Smiles* (2015), which nabbed the National Book Award, offer the perspectives of characters including a fifteen-year-old employed to kill disgruntled corporate employees; a former East German prison warden; and Mr. Roses, a potential pedophile. Apparently written over the objections of his wife, fellow writer and breast-cancer survivor Stephanie Harrell, "Interesting Facts" is unusual only in being the most autobiographical and metafictional of these tales. Now a Stanford professor, Johnson lives in San Francisco with Harrell and their three children—James Geronimo, Jupiter, and Justice.

---

nteresting fact: Toucan cereal bedspread to my plunge and deliver.

It's okay if you can't make sense of that. I've tried and tried, but I can't grasp it, either. The most vital things we hide even from ourselves.

The topic of dead wives actually came up not too long ago. My husband and I talked about it while walking home from a literary reading. It was San Francisco, which means winter rains, and we'd just attended a reading from a local writer's short-story collection. The local writer was twentysomething and sexy. Her arms were taut, her black hair shimmered. And just so you're clear, I'm going to discuss the breasts of every woman who crosses my path. Neither hidden nor flaunted behind white satin, her breasts were utterly, excruciatingly normal, and I hated her for that. The story she read was about a man who decides to date again after losing his wife. It's always an aneurysm, a car accident or the long battle with cancer. Cancer is the worst way for a fictional wife to die. Anyway, the man in the story waits an appropriate amount of time after his wife's loss—sixteen months!—before deciding to date again. After so much grief, he is exuberant and endearing in his pursuit of a woman. The first chick he talks to is totally game. The man, after all this waiting, is positively frisky, and the sex is, like, wow. The fortysomething widower nails the twentysomething gal on the upturned hull of his fiberglass kayak. And there's even a moral, subtle and implied: when love blossoms, it's all the richer when a man has discovered, firsthand, the painful fragility of life. Well, secondhand.

Applause, Q&A, more applause.

5   Like I said, it was raining. We had just left the Booksmith on Haight Street. The sidewalk was littered with wet panhandlers. Bastards that we were, we never gave.

"What'd you think of the story?" my husband asked.

I could tell he liked it. He likes all stories.

I said, "I sympathized with the dead wife."

To which my husband, the biggest lunkhead ever to win a Pulitzer Prize, said: "But . . . she wasn't even a character."

10   This was a year after my diagnosis, surgery, chemo and the various interventions, injections, indignities and treatments. When I got sick, our youngest child turned herself into a horse: silent and untamable, our Horse-child now only whinnies and neighs. Before that, though, she went through a phase we called Interesting Facts. "Interesting fact," she would announce, and then share

a wonder with us: A killer whale has never killed a person in the wild. Insects are high in protein. Hummingbirds have feelings and are often sad.

So here are some of my interesting facts. Lupron,[1] aside from ceasing ovulation, is used to chemically castrate sexual predators. Vinblastine interrupts cell division. It is a poisonous alkaloid made from the purple blossoms of the periwinkle plant. Tamoxifen makes your hips creak. My eyebrows fell out a year after finishing chemo. And long after your tits are taken, their phantoms remain. They get cold, they ache when you exercise, they feel wet after you shower, and you can towel like a crazy woman, but still they drip.

Before my husband won a Pulitzer, we had a kind of deal. I would adore him, even though he packed on a few pounds. And he would adore me, even though I had a double mastectomy. Who else would want us? Who else, indeed. Now his readings are packed with young Dorothy Parkers[2] who crowd around my man. The worst part is that the novel he wrote is set in North Korea, so he gets invited to all these functions filled with Korean socialites and Korean donors and Korean activists and Korean writers and various pillars of the Korean community.

Did I leave out the words *beautiful* and *female*?

You're so sensitive to the Korean experience, the beautiful female Korean socialite says to my husband.

Oh, he's good about it. He always says, *And this is my lovely wife.*

Ignoring me, the beautiful female Korean socialite adds, *You must visit our book club.*

If I could simply press a button every time one of them said that.

But I'm just tired. These are the places my mind goes when I'm tired. We're four blocks from home, where our children are just old enough not to need a sitter. On these nights our eleven-year-old son draws comics of Mongolian invasions and the Civil Rights Movement—his history teacher allows him to write his reports graphically. (San Francisco!) Our daughter, at nine, is a master baker. Hair pulled into a ponytail, she is flour-dusted and kneading away. The Horse-child, who is only seven, does dressage.[3] She is the horse who needs no rider.

But talk of my children is for another story. I can barely gaze upon them now. Their little outlines, cut like black cameos, are too much to consider.

My husband and I walk in the rain. We don't hold hands. I still feel the itch of vinblastine in my nail beds, one of the places, it turns out, that the body stores toxins. Have you ever had the urge to peel back your fingernails and scratch underneath, to just wrench until the nails snap back so you can go scratch, scratch, scratch?

I flex my fingers, rub my nails against the studs on my leather belt.

I knew better, but still I asked him: "How long would you wait?"

"Wait for what?"

"Until after I was gone. How many months before you went and got some of that twentysomething kayak sex?"

1. Chemotherapy drug, like others mentioned in this paragraph.
2. That is, women resembling the famously witty American poet, satirist, and raconteur (1893–1967).
3. Equestrian sport (as practiced at horse shows) involving precision movements.

25   I shouldn't say shit like this, I know. He doesn't know a teaspoon of the crazy in my head.

He thought a moment. "Legally," he said, "I'd probably need to have a death certificate. Otherwise it would be like bigamy or something. So I'd have to wait for the autopsy and a burial and the slow wheels of bureaucracy to issue the paperwork. I bet we're talking twelve to sixteen weeks."

"Getting a death certificate," I say. "That has got to be a hassle. But wait— you know a guy at city hall. Keith Whatshisname."

"Yeah, Keith," he says. "I bet Keith could get me proof of death in no time. The dude owes me. A guy like Keith could walk that death certificate around by hand, getting everyone to sign off in, I don't know, seven to fourteen days."

"That's your answer, seven to fourteen days?"

30   "Give or take, of course. There are variables. Things that would be out of Keith's control. If he moved too fast or pushed too hard—a guy could get in trouble. He could even get fired."

"Poor Keith. Now I feel for *him*, at the mercy of the universe and all. And all he wanted to do was help a grieving buddy get laid."

My husband eyes me with concern.

We turn in to Frank's Liquors to buy some condoms, even though our house is overflowing with them. It's his subtle way of saying, *For the love of God, give up some sex.*

My husband hates all condoms, but there's a brand he hates less than others. I cannot take birth-control pills because my cancer was estrogen-receptive.[4] My husband does not believe what the doctors say: that even though Tamoxifen mimics menopause, you can still get pregnant. My husband is forty-six. I am forty-five. He does not think that, in my forties, after cancer, chemotherapy and chemically induced menopause, I can get pregnant again, but sisters, I know my womb. It's proven.

35   "You think there'd be an autopsy?" I ask as he scans the display case. "I can't stand the thought of being cut up like that."

He looks at me. "We're just joking, right? Processing your anxiety with humor and whimsical talk therapy?"

"Of course."

He nods. "Sure, I suppose. You're young and healthy. They'd want to open you up and determine what struck you down."

A small, citrusy *ha* escapes. I know better than to let these out.

40   He says, "Plus, if I'm dating again in seven to fourteen days—"

"Give or take."

"Yes, give or take. Then people would want to rule out foul play."

"You deserve a clean slate," I say. "No one would want the death taint of a first wife to foul a new relationship. That's not fair to the new girl."

"I don't think this game is therapeutic anymore," he says, and selects his condoms.

45   Interesting fact: Tamoxifen carries a dreaded class-D birth-defect risk.[5]

---

4. That is, triggered by the presence of estrogen, a hormone in birth-control pills.
5. Until 1979, the Federal Drug Administration (FDA) used a five-letter system to indicate the risk drugs posed to fetuses; "Category D" drugs were those for which there is "positive evidence of [. . .] risk."

Interesting fact: My husband refuses to get a vasectomy.

He makes his purchase from an old woman. Her saggy old-lady breasts flop around under her dress. The cash register drawer rolls out to bump them.

My friends say that one day I'll feel lucky. That I will have been spared this saggy fate. After my bilateral,[6] I chose not to reconstruct. So I have nothing, just two diagonal zipper lines where my boobs should be.

We turn south and head down Cole Street.

The condoms are wishful thinking. We both know I will go to sleep when we get home.

Interesting fact: I sleep twelve to thirteen hours a night.

Interesting fact: Taxotere turns your urine pink.

Interesting fact: Cytoxan is a blister agent related to mustard gas.[7] When filtered from the blood, it scars the bladder, which is why I wake, hour after hour, night in and night out, to pee.

Can you see why it would be hard for me to tell wake from sleep, how the two could feel reversed? Do you hear me trying to tell you that I have trouble telling the difference?

"What about your Native American obligations?" I ask my husband. "Wouldn't you have to wait a bunch of moons or something?"

He is silent, and I cringe to think of what I just said.

"I'm sorry," I say. "I don't know what's wrong with me."

"You're just tired," he says.

The rain is more mistlike now. I hated the woman who read tonight. I hated the people who attended. I hated the failed wannabe writers in the crowd. I loathe all failed wannabe writers, especially me.

I ask, "Have you thought of never?"

"Never what?"

"That there's never another woman."

"Why are you talking like this?" he asks. "You haven't talked like this in a long time."

"You could just go without," I say. "You know, just soldier on."

"I really feel bad for what's going through your head," he said.

Interesting fact: Charles Manson[8] used to live in our neighborhood at 636 Cole Street.

Manson's house looms ahead. I always stop and give it my attention. It's beige now, but long ago, when Manson used this place to recruit his murderous young girls, it was painted blue. I used this house as a location in my last novel, a book no one would publish. Where did all those years of writing go? Where does that book even reside? I gaze at the Manson house. I feel alive right now, though looking through the gauze of curtains into darkened inner rooms, I can't be sure. In researching my novel, I came across crime-scene photos of Sharon Tate, the most famous Manson stabbing victim. Her breasts are heavy and round, milk-laden since she is pregnant, with nipples that are wide and dark.

---

6. Mastectomy in which both breasts are removed.
7. Toxic gas used in chemical warfare.
8. California cult leader (1934–2017) whose "Family" in 1969 murdered nine people during a five-week killing spree.

I look up at my husband. He is big and tall, built like a football player. Not the svelte receivers they put on booster calendars. But the clunky linebackers whose bellies hang below their jerseys.

"I need to know," I said. "Just tell me how long you'd wait?"

70   He puts his hand on my shoulder and holds my gaze. It is impossible to look away.

"You're not going anywhere," he says. "I won't let you leave without us. We do everything together, so if someone has to go, we go together. Our 777 will lose cabin pressure. Better yet, we'll be in the minivan when it happens. We're headed to Pacifica,[9] hugging the turns on Devil's Slide, and then we go through the guardrail, all of us, you, me, the kids, the dog, even. There's no time for fear. There's no dwelling. We careen. We barrel down. We rocket toward the jagged shore." He squeezed my shoulder hard, almost too hard. "That's how it happens, understand? When it comes, it's all of us. We go together."

Something inside me melts. This kind of talk, it's what I live on.

My husband and kids came with me to the hospital for the first chemo dose. Was that a year ago? Three? What is time to you—a plucking harp string, the fucking *do-re-mi* of tuning forks? There are twelve IV bays, and our little one doesn't like any of the interesting facts on the chemo ward. This is the day she stops speaking and turns into Horse-child, galloping around the nursing station, expressing her desires with taps of her hooves. Our son recognized a boy from his middle school. I recognized him, too, from the talent show assembly. The boy had performed an old-timey joke routine, complete with some soft-shoe.[1] Those days were gone. Here he was with his mother, a hagged-out and battered woman beneath her own IV tree. She must have been deep into her treatments, but even I could tell she wasn't going to make it. I didn't talk to her. Who would greet a dead woman, who would make small talk with death itself? I didn't let my eyes drift to her, even as our identical bags of Taxotere dripped angry into our veins.

That's how people would later treat me; it's exactly the way I'm treated today when I come home to find my husband sitting on the couch with Megumi, a mom from the girls' grade school. My husband and Megumi are talking in the fog-dampened bay-window light. On the coffee table is chicken katsu in a Pyrex dish. Megumi wears a top that's trampoline-tight. She has a hand on my husband's shoulder. Even though she's a mother of two, her breasts are positively teenybopper. They pop. Her tits do everything but chew bubble gum and make Hello Kitty hearts.

75   "Just what's going on here?" I ask them.

They brazenly, brazenly ignore me.

I got to know Megumi on playground benches, where we struck up conversations while watching our daughters swing. I loved her Shinjuku[2] style, and she loved all things American vintage. We bonded over Tokidoki and Patsy Cline.[3]

9. Town just south of San Francisco, on coast-hugging Highway 1.

1. Tap dance performed in soft-soled shoes.

2. Famously fashionable district of Tokyo.

3. American country music star (1932–63). *Tokidoki*: Japanese-inspired line of clothes, shoes, and accessories featuring cartoon characters.

"I love your dress" is the first thing she said to me.

It was a rose-patterned myrtle[4] with a halter neck.

"Interesting fact," I told her. "I'm from Florida, and Florida is ground zero for 80 vintage wardrobe. Rich women retire there from New York and New Jersey. They bring along a lifetime of fabulous dresses, and then they die."

"This is something I like," she said in that slightly formal way she spoke. "No one in Tokyo would wear a dead woman's dress." Then she apologized, worried that she might have accidentally insulted me. "I have been saying the strangest things since moving to America," she admitted.

Our family was actually headed to Tokyo for the launch of my husband's book in Japanese. Over the weeks, Megumi used sticks in the sandbox to teach me kanji[5] that would help me navigate the Narita airport, the Shinkansen and Marunouchi subway lines. She asked about my husband and his book. "Writers are quite revered in Japan," she told me.

"I'm a writer, too," I said.

She turned from the kanji to regard me anew.

"But no one will publish my books," I added. 85

Perhaps because of this admission, she later confided something in me. It was a cold and foggy afternoon. We were watching a father push his daughter high on a swing, admiring how he savored her delighted squeals in that weightless moment at the top of the arc.

"If my life was a novel," Megumi suddenly said, "I would have to leave my husband. This is a rule in literature, isn't it? That you must act on your heart. My husband is distant and unemotional," she declared. "I didn't know that until I came here. America has taught me this."

I was supposed to reassure her. I was supposed to remind her that her husband was logging long hours and that things would get better.

Instead, I asked, "But what about your kids?"

Megumi said nothing. 90

And now here I find her, sitting on my couch, hand on my husband's shoulder!

I'm the one who introduced them. Can you believe that? I'm the one who got her a copy of his novel in Japanese. I watch Megumi open her large dark eyes to take him in. And I know when my husband gives someone his full attention.

I can't make out what they are saying, but they are discussing more than fiction, I can tell you that.

Something else catches my eye—arrows. There are quivers of arrows everywhere—red feathers, yellow feathers, white.

In the kitchen is a casserole dish wrapped in aluminum foil. No, two casse- 95 role dishes.

I discover a hospital band on my wrist. Have I left it on as a badge of honor? Or a darkly ironic accessory? Is the bracelet some kind of message to myself?

Interesting fact: The kanji for *irrational*, I learned, is a combination of the elements *woman* and *death*.

4. Fifties or fifties-inspired dress with a cowl or halter neckline and high waist.
5. Characters comprising written Japanese.

There was an episode not long ago that must be placed in the waking-and-sleeping-reversed column. I was in the hospital. Nothing unusual there. The beautiful thing was the presence of my family—they were all around me as we stood beside some patient's bed. The room was filled with Starbucks cups, and there were my brother, my sisters and my parents, and so on, all of us chatting away like old times. The topic was war stories. My great-uncle talked about playing football in the dunes of North Africa after a tank battle with Rommel.[6] My father told a sad story about trying to deliver a Vietcong[7] baby near Cu Chi.

Then my brother looked stricken. He said, "I think it's happening."

100   We all turned toward the bed, and that's when I saw the dying woman. There was a wheeze as her breathing slowed. She seemed to get lighter before our eyes. I'll admit I bore a resemblance to her. But only a little—that woman was all emaciated and droop-eyed and bald.

My sister asked, "Should we call the nurse?"

I pictured the crash cart bursting in, with its needles and paddles and intubation sleeve. It was none of my business, but: *Leave the poor woman be*, I thought. *Just let her go.*

We all looked to my father, a doctor who has seen death many times.

He is from Georgia. His eyes are old and wet, permanently pearlescent.

105   He turned to my mother, who was weeping. She shook her head.

Maybe you've heard of an out-of-body experience. Well, standing in that hospital room, I had an *in-the-body* experience, a profound sensation that I was leaving the real world and entering that strange woman, just as her eyes lost focus and her lips went slack. Right away, I felt the morphine inside her, the way it traced everything with halos of neon-tetra[8] light. I entered the dark tunnel of morphine time, where the past, the present and the future became simultaneously visible. I was a girl again, riding a yellow bicycle. I will soon be in Golden Gate Park, watching archers shoot arrows through the fog. I see that all week long, my parents have been visiting this woman and reading her my favorite Nancy Drew books.[9] Their yellow covers fill my vision. *The Hidden Staircase. The Whispering Statue. The Clue in the Diary.*

You know that between-pulse pause when, for a fraction, your heart is stopped? I feel the resonating bass note of this nothingness. Vision is just a black vibration, and your mind is only that bottom-of-the-pool feeling when your air is spent. I suddenly see the insides of this woman's body, something cancer teaches you to do. Here is a lumpy chain of dye-blue lymph nodes, there are the endometrial[1] tendrils of a thirsty tumor. Everywhere are the calcified Pop Rocks[2] of scatter-growth. Your best friend, Kitty, silently appears. She took leave of this world from cancer twelve years earlier. She lifts a finger to her lips.

6. Legendary World War II German commander, Field Marshal Erwin Rommel (1891–1944), a.k.a. "The Desert Fox."

7. Short for *Viet Nam Cong San*, meaning "Vietnamese Communists," the guerilla force that fought against South Vietnamese and U.S. forces during the Vietnam War (c. 1955–75).

8. Brightly colored South American fish common in aquariums.

9. Popular, oft-revised mysteries, published beginning in 1930, featuring an amateur teenage detective; *The Hidden Staircase* (1930) is a typical title.

1. The endometrium lines the uterus.

2. Fizzy, carbonated candy introduced in 1975.

Shh, she says. Then it really hits you that you're trapped inside a dying woman. You're being buried alive. *Will be* turns to *is* turns to *was*. You can no longer make out the Republican red of your mother's St. John[3] jacket. You can no longer hear the tremors of your sister's breathing. Then there's nothing but the *still*, the gathering, surrounding still of this woman you're in.

Then pop!—somehow, luckily, you make it out. You're free again, back in the land of Starbucks cups and pay-by-the-hour parking.

It was some serious brain-bending business, the illusion of being in that dead woman. But that's how powerful cancer is, that's how bad it can mess with your head. Even now you cannot shake that sense of time—how will you ever know again the difference between what's past and what's to come, let alone what is?

My husband and kids missed the entire nightmare. They are downstairs eat- 110
ing soup.

Interesting facts: The Geary Street Kaiser Permanente Hospital is where breasts are removed. The egg noodle wonton soup in their cafeteria is divine. The wontons are handmade, filled with steamed cabbage and white pepper. The Kaiser on Turk Street is chemo central. This basement cafeteria specializes in huge bowls of Vietnamese pho, made with beef ankles and topped with purple basil. Don't forget Sriracha. The Kaiser on Divisadero is for when the end is near. Their shio ramen with pork cheeks is simply heaven. Open all night.

My Vulcan mind-meld with death has strange effects on our family. Strangest of all is how I find it hard to look at my children. The thought of them moving forward in life without me, the person whose sole mission is to guide them—it's not tolerable. My arms tremble at how close they came to having their little spirits snuffed out. The idea of them making their way alone in this world makes me want to turn things into sticks, to wield a hatchet and make kindling of everything I see. I've never chopped a thing in my life, I'm not a competent person in general, so I would lift the blade in full knowledge that my aim would stray, that the evil and the innocent will fall together.

Interesting fact: My best friend, Kitty, died of cancer. Over the years, the doctors took her left leg, her breasts, her throat and her ovaries. In return, they gave her two free helpings of bone marrow. As the end came, I became afraid to go see her. What would I say? What does *goodbye* even mean? Finally, when she had only a few days left, I mustered the courage for a visit. To save money, I flew to Atlanta and then took a bus. But I got on the wrong one! I didn't realize this until I got to North Carolina. Kitty died in Florida.

My husband soldiers up. He gives me space and starts getting up early to make the kids' lunches and trek them off to school. The kids are rattled, too. They take to sleeping with their father in the big bed. With all those arms and legs, there's no room for yours truly. They're a pretty glum bunch, but I understand: it's not easy to almost lose someone.

I spend a lot of time in Golden Gate Park, where my senses are newly height- 115
ened. I can see a gull soaring past and know exactly where it will land. I develop

---

3. Upscale fashion brand specializing in women's knitwear.

an uncanny sense of what the weather will be. Just by gazing at a plant, I can tell its effects upon the human body.

Interesting fact: The blue cohosh plant grows in the botanical gardens just a short stroll into the park. Its berries are easily ground into a poultice, and from this can be extracted a violet oil that causes the uterus to contract. Coastal Miwok tribes used it to induce abortions.

All this is hard on my husband, but he does not start drinking again. I'm proud of him for that, though I would understand if he did. It would be a sign of how wounding it was to nearly lose me. If he hit the bourbon, I'd know how much he needed me. What he does instead is buy a set of kettle bells.[4] When the kids are asleep, he descends into the basement and swings these things around for hours, listening to podcasts about bow hunting, Brazilian jiujitsu and Native American folklore.

He sheds some weight, which troubles me. The pounds really start to fall off.

He gets the kids to music lessons, martial arts, dental appointments. The problem is school, where a cavalcade of chatty moms loiter away their mornings. There's the Thursday-morning coffee klatsch, the post-drop-off beignets[5] at Café Reverie, the book club at Zazie's. These moms are single, or single enough. Meet Liddi, mother of twins, famous in Cole Valley[6] for inventing and marketing the dual-mat yoga backpack. She's without an ounce of fat, but placed upon her A-cup chest is a pair of perfectly pronounced, fully articulated nipples. There's rocker mom Sabina, heavy into ink and steampunk chic. Octopus tentacles beckon from Sabina's cleavage. And don't forget Salima, a UCSF prof who's fooling nobody by cloaking her D's under layers of fabric. Salima will not speak of the husband—alive or dead—whom she left in Lahore.[7]

120   *How are you getting by?* they ask my husband.

Let us know if you need anything, they offer.

They give our kids lifts to birthday parties and away games.

Their ovens are on perpetual preheat. But it's Megumi who's always knocking. It's Megumi who gets inside the door.

Interesting facts: Chuck Norris tackles seventeen bad guys at once in *Missing in Action III*. Clint Eastwood takes up the gun again in *Unforgiven*. George Clooney is hauntingly vulnerable in *The Descendants*.[8] Do you know why? Dead wives.

125   Interesting fact: One wife who didn't die was Lady Mary Wortley Montagu.[9] My MFA thesis was a collection of linked stories on Lady Montagu's struggles

---

4. Large round cast-iron weights.
5. Sugar-coated doughnut-like pastries.
6. San Francisco neighborhood, near both the Haight-Ashbury district and Golden Gate Park, full of coffee shops and restaurants such as Zazie's.
7. Capital of Pakistan's Punjab province. UCSF: University of California, San Francisco.
8. Film (2011) featuring a man coping with a comatose wife and two troubled daughters. *Missing in Action III*: 1988 action-adventure film. *Unforgiven*: revisionist Western (1992).
9. British protofeminist, woman of letters, and mother of two (1689–1762), who first introduced the smallpox vaccine into England; her husband served as British ambassador to the Ottoman (Turkish) Empire.

to succeed as a writer despite her demanding children, famous husband and painful illness. I didn't have much to say about the subject. I just thought she was pretty amazing. Not a single person bothered to read my thesis, not even the female professor who directed it. "Write what you know," that's what my professor kept telling me. I never listened.

One afternoon, I wander deep into Golden Gate Park, beyond the pot dealers on Hippie Hill and the rust-colored conning tower of the de Young Museum. I pass even the buffalo pens. In the wide meadows near the Pacific Ocean, I discover, by chance, my husband and children at the archery range. What are they doing here? How long have they been coming? They have bows drawn and, without speaking, are solemnly shooting arrows, one after another, downrange into heavy bales. The Horse-child draws a recurve, while my daughter shoots Olympic and my son pulls a longbow with his lean and beautiful arms. My husband strains behind a compound,[1] its pulleys and cams creaking under the weight. He has purchased hundreds of arrows, so they rarely pause to retrieve. When the sunset fog rolls in, they fire on faith into a blanket of white. When darkness falls, they place balloons on the targets so they can hear the pop of a well-placed arrow. I have acquired a keen sense of dark trajectory. I stand beside my husband, the power of a full draw bound in his shoulders. I whisper *release* when his aim is perfect. He obeys. I don't need to walk through the dark with him to see the arrows stacked up yellow in the bull's-eye.

Later, he doesn't read books to the children before bed. Instead, on our California king, they gather to hear him repeat a story he has heard podcast by Lakota Sioux[2] storytellers. My husband never speaks of his Sioux blood. He has never even visited the reservation. All the people who would have connected him to that place were long ago taken by liquor, accidents, time-released mayhem and self-imposed exile.

The story he tells is of a ghost horse that was prized by braves riding into battle because the pony, already being dead, could not be shot from under them. This pony, afraid of nothing, reared high and counted its own coup.[3] Only at the end of the clashes do the braves realize a ghost warrior had been riding bareback with them, guiding the horse's every move. In this way the braves learn the gallop of death without having to leave this life.

The Horse-child asks, "Why didn't the ghost horse just go to heaven?"

I realize it's the first time I've heard the Horse-child speak in—how long?

My daughter answers her. "The story's really about the ghost warrior."

The Horse-child asks, "Why doesn't the ghost warrior go to heaven, then?"

My daughter says, "Because ghosts have unfinished business. Everybody knows that."

My son asks, "Did Mom leave unfinished business?"

My husband tells them, "A mom's work is never done."

A health issue can be hard on a family. And it breaks my heart to hear them talk like I no longer exist. If I'm so dead, where's my grave, why isn't there an

---

1. Modern bow using a pulley system.
2. Native peoples now occupying lands in North and South Dakota.
3. Acts of valor, recorded by Native American warriors on "coup sticks."

urn full of ashes on the mantel? No, this is just a sign that I've drifted too far from my family, that I need to pull my act together. If I want them to stop treating me like a ghost, I need to stop acting like one.

Interesting fact: In the TV movies, a ghost mom's job is to help her husband find a suitable replacement. It's an ancient trope—see Herodotus, Euripides and Virgil.[4] For recent examples, consult CBS's *A Gifted Man*, NBC's *Awake*, and *Safe Haven*, now in heavy rotation on TCM.[5] The TV ghost mom can see through the gold diggers and wicked stepmoms to find that heart-of-gold gal who can help those kiddos heal, who will clap at the piano recitals, provide much-needed cupcake pick-me-ups and say things like "Your mom would be proud."

I assure you that no such confectionary female exists. No new wife cares about the old wife's kids. They're just an unavoidable complication to the new wife's own family-to-be. That's what vasectomy reversals and Swiss boarding schools are for. If I were a ghost mom, my job would be to stab these rivals in the eyes, to dagger them all. Dagger, dagger, dagger.

The truth is, though, that you don't need to die to know what it's like to be a ghost. On the day my doctor called and gave me the diagnosis, we were at a party in New York. Our mission was to meet a young producer for *The Daily Show* who was considering a segment on my husband. She was tall and willowy in a too-tight black dress, and while her breasts may once have been perfect, she had dieted them down to nothing. Right away she greeted my husband with euro kisses,[6] laughed at nothing, then showed him her throat. I was standing right there! Talk about invisible. Then my phone rang—Kaiser Permanente with the biopsy results. I tried to talk, but words didn't come out. I walked through things. I found myself in a bathroom, washing my face. Then I was twenty floors below, on Fifty-seventh Street. I swear I didn't take the elevator. I just appeared. Then I was on a bus in North Carolina, letting a hard-drinking preacher massage my shoulders while my friend was dying in Florida. Then it was my turn. I saw my own memorial: My parents' lawn is covered with cars. They must buy a freezer to store all the HoneyBaked hams that arrive. My family and friends gather next to the river that slowly makes its way past my parents' home. Here, people take turns telling stories.

4. When the eponymous hero of his Latin-language epic, the *Aeneid* (c. 29–19 BCE), searches the fallen city of Troy for his wife, he instead encounters her ghost, who tells him that he is destined to find a new home, remarry, and rule a great kingdom. *Herodotus*: The ancient Greek author's *Histories* (440 BCE) include what classicist James Romm calls an especially "lurid episode, in which" a tyrant (Periander) "has intercourse with the body of his dead wife, Melissa, and is then tormented by her ghost." *Euripides*: In this ancient Greek playwright's *Alcestis* (438 BCE), Alcestis volunteers to die in her husband's stead after making him promise not to remarry and allow a stepmother to raise her children; later, he agrees to marry a veiled woman ultimately revealed to be Alcestis, returned from the dead by Heracles (a.k.a. Hercules).
5. Turner Classic Movies, a cable-television channel. *A Gifted Man*: 2011–12 drama series about a surgeon visited by the ghost of his dead wife. *Awake*: detective series (2012) whose protagonist oscillates between two lives, in one of which he is newly widowed. *Safe Haven*: 2013 film, based on a Nicholas Sparks novel, in which a mysterious young woman's relationship with a widowed father of two turns out to be the result of the dead wife's machinations.
6. Traditionally, kisses on one or both cheeks, a form of greeting.

My great-uncle tells a story about me as a little girl and my decision to wed 140
the boy next door. My folks got a cake and flowers and had the judge down the
street preside in robes over the ceremony. The whole neighborhood turned up,
and everyone got a kick out of it. The next day brought the sobering moment
when my folks had to tell me the marriage wasn't real.

My brother tells a story about my first Christmas home from college and how
I brought a stack of canvases to show everyone the nudes I'd been letting the
art-major boys paint of me.

My mother tries to tell a story. I can tell it will be the one about the Christmas poodle. But she is overcome. It scares the children, the way she slow-
motion folds up, dropping to the ground like a garment bag. To distract them,
my father decides on a canoe ride—that always was a treat for the kids. Tears
run from their eyes as they don orange vests and shove off. Right away, the
Horse-child screams that she is afraid of the water. She strikes notes of terror
we didn't know existed. My son, in the bow, tries to hide his clutched breathing,
and then I see the shuddering shoulders of my daughter. She swivels her head,
looking everywhere, desperately, and I know she is looking for me. My father,
stunned and bereft, is too inconsolable to lift the paddle. My father who performed more than fifteen hundred field surgeries near Da Nang, my father who
didn't flinch when the power went out at Charity Hospital in New Orleans,[7] my
father—he slowly closes his pearl-grey eyes. They float there, not twenty feet
from us, the boat too unsteady for them to comfort one another, and we onshore
can only wrench at the impossibility of reaching them.

Back inside the New York party, I realized time had ceased to flow: my husband and the producer were laughing the exact same laugh, the lime zest of
their breath still acrid in the air, and I saw this was in the future, too, all these
chilly women with their iron-filing eyes and rice-paper hearts. They wanted
something genuine, something real. They wanted what I had: a man who was
willing to go off the cliff with you. They would come after him when he was
weak, I suddenly understood, when I was no longer there to fend them off. This
wasn't hysteria. It wasn't imagination. I was in the room with one of them. Here
she was, perfect teeth forming a brittle smile, hips hollow as sake[8] boxes.

"That story is too funny," the producer said. "Stop it right there. Save it for
the segment!"

In a shrug of false modesty, my husband accidentally sloshed his soda water. 145
"Well," he said. "Only if you think it would be good for the show."

I put my hand on the producer's arm. She turned, startled, discovering me.

I used my grip to assess her soul—I felt the want of it, I calculated its lack,
in the same way Lady Montagu mapped the microscopic world of smallpox pus-
tules and Voltaire[9] learned to weigh vapor.

You tell me who the fucking ghost is.

There is a knock at the door. It's Megumi! 150

7. Presumably during Hurricane Katrina (2005), which so damaged the hospital that it has never
reopened. *Da Nang*: Vietnam's third-largest city.
8. Japanese alcohol made from rice and sometimes served in small wooden boxes called *masu*.
9. French philosopher-historian (1694–1778).

My husband answers, and the two of them regard each other, almost sadly, for a moment.

They are clearly acknowledging the wrongness of whatever it is they're up to.

They head upstairs together, where I realize there are Costco-size boxes of condoms everywhere—under the sink, in the medicine cabinet, taped under the bedside table, hidden in the battery flap of a full-size talking Tigger doll!

Megumi and my husband enter our bedroom. Right away, the worst possible thing happens—they move right past these birth-control depots. They do not collect any condoms at all.

155   My kind of ghost mom would make it her job to stop hussies like Megumi from fucking grieving men, and if I were too late, it would be my job to go to Megumi late at night, to approach her as she slept on her shabby single-mom futon and, with my eyedropper, dribble one, two, three purple drops upon her lips, just enough to abort the baby he put inside her. In her belly, the fetus would clutch and clench and double up dead.

Megumi and my husband do not approach the bed. They move instead toward the armoire, beside which is a rolling rack of all the vintage dresses I could no longer wear once I lost my bustline. I moved them onto the rack but couldn't bear to roll them out of the room.

Megumi runs her fingers along these dresses.

She pauses only to eye a stack of my training bras on the dresser.

Interesting fact: While you can get used to being titless, the naked feeling of not wearing a bra is harder to shake. You just become accustomed to the hug of one. I recommend the A-cup bras from Target's teen section. Mine are decorated with multicolor peace signs.

160   Megumi selects a dress from the rack and studies it—it's an earthy pink Hepburn[1] with a boat collar, white trim and pleated petticoat. At the Florida university where I met my husband, I was in his presence three different times before he finally noticed me. I was wearing that dress when he did. I wonder if he remembers it.

Megumi holds the dress to her body, studying herself in the mirror. Then she turns to my husband, draping the dress against her figure for his approval.

Interesting fact: The kanji for *figure* is a combination of the elements *next* and *woman*.

I study my own figure in the mirror.

Interesting fact: The loss of breasts doesn't flatten your chest—it leaves you concave and hollowed-looking. And something about the surgery pooches your tummy. My surgeon warned me of this. But who could picture it? Who would voluntarily conjure herself that way?

165   Megumi waits, my dress held against her. Then my husband reaches out. He has a faraway look in his eyes. With his fingertips, he tugs here and tapers there, adjusting the fall of fabric to the shape of her body. Finally, he nods. She accepts the dress, folding it in her arms.

I do not dagger her. I stand there and do nothing.

---

1. Fifties or fifties-inspired dress reminiscent of those worn by actress Audrey Hepburn (1929–93).

Interesting fact: My first novel that no one would publish was about Scottsdale[2] trophy wives who form a vigilante group to patrol their gated community. It contains, among other things, a bobcat killing, a night-golfing tragedy, the illegal use of a golf ball–collecting machine and a sex scene involving a man and a woman wearing backpack-mounted soda pistols. It was called *The Beige Berets*.[3]

Interesting fact: My second novel that no one would publish concerns two young girls who have rare powers of perception. One can read auras, while the other sees ghosts. To work the ghost angle, I had their father live in Charles Manson's old apartment. To make the girls more vulnerable, I decided to kill off their mother, so I gave her cancer. To ratchet up the tension, I had a sexual predator live next door named Mr. Roses. My husband came up with the name. In fact, my husband became quite enamored with this character. He was really helpful in developing Mr. Roses' backstory and generating his dialog. Then my husband stole this character and wrote a story from Mr. Roses' perspective called "Dark Meadow." I can't even say the name of this novel without getting angry.

My husband does not return to the novel he was working on before my cancer. After the kids are asleep, he instead calls up the website bigboobsalert. He regards this on slide-show mode, so ladies with monstrous chests appear and fade, one into the next. My husband has his hand lotion ready, but he doesn't masturbate. He stares at a nebulous place just past the computer screen. I contemplate these women. All I see in their saucerous nipples and pendulous breasts is the superpower of motherhood. Instead of offering come-hither looks to lonely men, these women should be feeding hungry babies, calling upon foundling wards and nursing the legion orphaned of the world. We should airdrop these bra-busters into tsunami zones, earthquake epicenters and the remote provinces of North Korea!

I kneel beside my husband, slouched in his ergonomic office chair. I align my vision with his, but I can't tell what he's looking at. Our faces are almost touching, and though he is lost and sad, I still feel his sweet energy. "Come to bed," I whisper, and he sort of wakes up. But he doesn't rise to face our bedroom. Instead, he opens a blank Word document and stares at it. Eventually, he types, "Toucan cereal."

"No!" I shout at him. "I'm the one who got cancer, I'm the one who was struck. That's my story. It belongs to me!"

Interesting fact: Cancer teaches you to see the insides of things. Do you see the *can* in *uncanny* or the *cer* in *concern*? When people want to make chitchat with you—even though, if they took the time, they could see that under your bandanna you have no hair—it's easier to just say to them, "Sorry, I have some uncanny concerns right now." If you're feeling feisty, try "I feel arcane and acerbic." Who hasn't felt that?

2. City just east of Phoenix, Arizona.
3. *The Green Berets* (1968) is a famous action-adventure movie set in Vietnam.

But sometimes you've got chemo brain and your balance is all woo-woo and your nails are itching like crazy and you don't want to talk to anybody. Be prepared for that.

Person 1: "Gosh, I haven't seen you in forever. How's it going?"

175   You: "Toucan cereal."

Person 2: "Hey, what's new? I'm so behind. I probably owe you like ten messages."

You: "Vulcan silencer." Smile blankly. Hold it.

Arrows boat-tail through the night. Raccoons rear, yellow-eyed, to watch them fly. In spring the surf sorrel,[4] considered an aphrodisiac by the Miwok peoples, open their gate-folding leaves. I can't look at my children head-on. From afar I study them. I watch my husband shuttle them to school from a distance great enough that I almost can't tell my kids from other ones.

Even worse than cancer glommers are widower clingers. They approach my husband with their big sympathetic eyes and force him to say things like "We're managing" and "Keeping our heads above water." But he's no fool. He returns their casserole dishes to be refilled.

180   Our daughter takes on my voice. I study her as she admonishes her brother and the Horse-child to take their asthma medicine and do their silent reading before bed. When lice outbreaks arrive, she is the one who meticulously combs through their hair after my husband succumbs to frustration and salty talk.

I keep a hairy eyeball wide for Megumi. She doesn't come around, which makes me all the more suspicious. I wonder if my husband took some of that Pulitzer money and bought a "studio" in the neighborhood. You know, a place to hide your book royalties from the IRS and "get some serious work done." I flip through his key chain, but there is nothing new, just keys to the house, his Stanford office, the Honda Odyssey, five Kryptonite bike locks.

I use my powers of perception to scan the neighborhood for signs of this so-called writer's studio. I try to detect the effervescence of my husband's ever-present sparkling water, the shimmer of his condom wrappers or the snap of Megumi's bra strap. My feelers feel only the fog rolling in, extinguishing the waking world block by block, starting with the outer avenues.

Interesting fact: The Miwok believed the advancing fog could draw one into the next world.

Interesting fact: Accidentally slipping into the afterlife was a grave concern for them. To locate one another in the fog, they darkened their skin with pigment made from the ashes of poison oak fires. They marked their chests with the scent of Brewer's angelica. They developed signature calls by which they alone would be known.

185   For some reason, my family skips archery tonight. And there is no Native American story when the kids are put to bed. Even bigboobsalert has to wait. In his office, my husband calls up his document and continues stealing my story. I don't shout at him this time. He is a slow and expressive writer. Word choices play across his face. He drinks sparkling water, urinating into the plastic bottles when they're empty, and writes most of the night. I miss talking with him. I

---

4. Plant native to the California coast, just as "Brewer's angelica" (par. 184) is to the mountains.

miss how nothing seemed like it really happened unless we told each other about it.

Interesting fact: My third, unfinished novel is about Buffalo Calf Road Woman, the Cheyenne warrior who struck the felling blow to Custer[5] at Little Bighorn. I wrote about her life only because it amazed me.

My husband has my research spread before him: atlases of Native American tribes and field guides for botanicals and customs and mythology. I think this is good for him.

I'm there when he hits one last Command-S for the night.

I follow him upstairs. The children are sleeping in the big bed. He climbs in among their flopped limbs, and I want to join, but there is no room. My husband's head comes to rest upon the pillow. Yet his eyes remain open, growing large, adjusting focus, like he is trying to follow something as it disappears into the dark.

Interesting fact: My husband doesn't believe that dreams carry higher meanings.

Interesting fact: I had a dream once. In the dream, I stood naked in the darkness. A woman approached me. When she neared, I could see she was me. She said to me, or I guess I said to myself, "It's happening." Then she reached out and touched my left breast. I woke to find my breast warm and buzzing. I felt a lump in a position I would later learn was the superior lateral quadrant. In the morning, I stood in front of the mirror, but the lump was nowhere to be found. I told my husband about the dream. He said, "Spooky." I told him I was going to the doctor right away. "I wouldn't worry," he said. "It's probably nothing."

Eventually, my husband sleeps. An arm passes over one child and secures another. All the pillows have been stolen, then half-stolen back. The children thrum to his deep, slow breathing. I have something to tell him.

Interesting fact: My husband has a secret name, a Sioux name.

He's embarrassed by it. He doesn't like anyone to say it, as he feels he doesn't deserve it. But when I utter the Lakota words, he wakes from his sleep. He sees me, I can tell, his eyes slowly dial me in. He doesn't smile, but on his face is a kind of recognition.

Through the bay windows, troughs of fog surge down Frederick Street.

"I think it's happening," I say to him.

He nods, then he drifts off again. Later, this will only have been a dream.

I near the bed and regard my children. Here is my son, back grown strong from pulling the bow. Still I see his little-boy cheeks and long eyelashes. Still I see the boy who nursed all night, who loved to hug fire hydrants, who ran long-haired and shirtless along a slow-moving river in Florida. His hair is buzzed now, like his father's, and his pupils behind closed eyes track slowly, like he is dreaming of a life that unfolds at a less jolting pace.

My daughter's hair is the gravest shade of black. If anyone got the Native blood, it is her. Dark-skinned and fast afoot, she also has fierce, far-seeing eyes. She is the one who would enter the battle to save her brother, as Buffalo Calf

5. U.S. Army General George Armstrong Custer (1839–76). In 2005, Northern Cheyenne storytellers publicly credited Buffalo Calf Road Woman (c. 1844–79) with killing Custer at the Battle of the Little Bighorn.

Road Woman famously did. Tonight she sleeps clutching my iPhone, alarm set for dawn, and in the set of her jaw, I can feel the list of things she'll have to accomplish to get her siblings up and fed and off to school.

200   And then there is the Horse-child.

Interesting fact: My youngest's love of interesting facts was just a stage. When my illness turned her into a horse, she never said interesting facts again.

Interesting fact: Horses cannot utter human words or feel human emotions. They are resilient beasts, immune from the sadness of the human cargo they carry.

She is once again a little human, a member of a weak and vulnerable breed. Who will explain what she missed while she was a horse? Who will hold her and tell her who I was and what I went through? If only she had never been a horse, if only she could remain one a little longer. What I wouldn't give to hear her whinny and neigh her desires again, to see how delicately she tapped her hoof to receive a carrot or sugar cube. But it is over. She'll never again gallop on all fours or give herself a mane by drawing with markers down her back. It will just have been a stage she went through, preserved only in a story. And that, I suppose, is all I will have been, a story from when they were little.

2015

QUESTIONS

1. INTERESTING FACTS begins **in medias res**, relating events out of chronological order. What is the effect of the way the story opens? of when and how it doles out background information (or **exposition**) and describes events that occurred earlier?
2. How would you describe the narrator's internal and external conflicts? those of her family members? How are they resolved?
3. After reading the whole story, how might you differently understand the meaning and significance of its first two paragraphs?

SUGGESTIONS FOR WRITING

1. Write an essay comparing the way any two of the stories in this chapter handle the traditional elements of plot: exposition, rising action, climax, falling action, conclusion. Consider especially how plot elements contribute to the overall artistic effect.
2. Like INTERESTING FACTS, many stories depict events out of chronological order. Select any story from this anthology, and write an essay discussing the significance of sequence.
3. Ralph Ellison described his novel *Invisible Man* as exploring "the human universals hidden within the plight of one who was both black and American." Write an essay exploring how this statement might apply to KING OF THE BINGO GAME. How does being "both black and American" shape the conflict experienced by the story's protagonist and its resolution? On the other hand, what might be universal about that conflict?
4. Write an essay comparing Connie's encounter with Arnold Friend in Oates's WHERE ARE YOU GOING, WHERE HAVE YOU BEEN? to that between the Grandmother and the Misfit in Flannery O'Connor's A GOOD MAN IS HARD TO FIND.
5. Write a response paper or essay comparing the conflicts experienced by the protagonists of THE SHROUD and INTERESTING FACTS and the way these conflicts are ultimately resolved. In terms of conflict and resolution, what are the key similarities and differences between these two mothers grappling with mortality?

6. Write an essay that explores the central conflict in any one of the stories in this chapter. What is the nature of the conflict? When, where, and how does it develop or become more complicated as the story unfolds? How is it resolved at the end of the story? Why and how is that resolution satisfying? If you write about Oates's story, consider how your interpretation of the conflict compares to her comments about it (as excerpted in this chapter).

SAMPLE WRITING: ESSAY

The following essay on Ralph Ellison's KING OF THE BINGO GAME responds to a writing suggestion in the last chapter:

> Write an essay that explores the central conflict in any one of the stories in this chapter. What is the nature of the conflict? When, where, and how does it develop or become more complicated as the story unfolds? How is it resolved at the end of the story? Why and how is that resolution satisfying?

As you read the essay, remember to approach it critically, much as you would a draft by one of your classmates. What are the essay's three strongest moments and elements? What are one or two weaknesses?

As you will notice, for example, Francis Moi Moi argues that Ellison's story explores a universal conflict—one related to the human condition generally. Yet the story from the beginning presents its protagonist as specifically "poor, hungry, and Black," as Moi Moi himself wrote in an earlier draft of his essay. Might the story's conflict thus also or instead be race and/or class specific? How might you suggest revising the essay to allow for this possibility or counterargument? Alternatively, how might you craft an essay either defending or rebutting Moi Moi's argument?

Moi Moi 1

Francis Moi Moi
Dr. Kelly Mays
ENG 298
24 September 2021

The Button and the Wheel in Ralph Ellison's "King of the Bingo Game"

In Ralph Ellison's short story "King of the Bingo Game," the unnamed protagonist presses down on a button, "watche[s] the wheel whirling . . . and experience[s] a burst of exaltation: This is God! This is the really truly God!" (par. 50). In popular culture, having a finger on the button has come to represent godlike power, calling up images of men with unchecked authority determining the fate of thousands with a touch. Fortune's wheel, on the other hand, is a more traditional symbol, representing a fate or chance beyond human control. Since medieval times, it has assumed the shape of celestial spheres and carnival wheels alike (Ross). Its influence has loomed over the destinies of countless unwitting literary characters, making beggars of kings and kings of bingo

---

players. The plot of "King of the Bingo Game" pits the drive for control against the reality of chance or fate, such that the protagonist's schemes are constantly trumped by some power outside himself. The namelessness of the protagonist suggests that he could be any man who "felt vaguely that his whole life was determined by the bingo wheel" (par. 33). The wheel confronts readers with the helplessness that underlies the human condition. Thus, "King of the Bingo Game" is about humans' attempt to take control of their lives only to realize they have no control.

Ellison's protagonist may have no name, but the expository, opening paragraphs present him as a "have-not" in a theater audience of "haves." In front of him is a woman with peanuts. Nearby two men share whiskey. But the protagonist, "light-headed" with hunger (par. 16), can find "through a hole in his pocket" only "goose pimples and old scars" (par. 8). He reassures himself, "I ain't crazy. I'm just broke, 'cause I got no birth certificate to get a job, and Laura 'bout to die 'cause we got no money for a doctor" (par. 1). The inability to present proof of his own identity, which remains a mystery even to the story's readers, prevents him from applying for employment, without which he cannot afford doctors for Laura. And while we do not know how the protagonist and Laura are related, we are compelled to empathize with the only character who has a name. The stakes are high for the protagonist. He nods off in the theater, having seen the picture three times already, while he waits for what he really came for. He is driven by the desire to keep Laura alive by the only means available to him—the bingo wheel. Existence is here reduced to a kind of game show in which the difference between life and death is just some winning numbers on the wheel.

Underlying the protagonist's drive is the greater conflict between control and chance or fate suggested by both his dream and his thoughts about the movie. He dreams he is a boy again who narrowly escapes an oncoming train, only to look over his shoulder and "se[e] with terror that the train had left the track and was following him right down the middle of the street" (par. 9). The tracks represent control and order, while the derailed train, which runs upon wheels, represents chance or chaos. The bad dream is suggestive of the protagonist's anxieties and circumstances, which, like the runaway train, have leapt their tracks and are bearing down on him. His thoughts about the movie are similar. He fantasizes about how it might turn out differently this time, getting "out of hand" like the train in his dream (par. 8). "*That* would be something to see," he thinks. But "[i]f a picture got out of hand like that," the projectionists "would go nuts," he realizes. "Everything was fixed," its outcome already determined by someone or something behind the scenes.

The rest of the story plays out this scenario, as the protagonist's efforts to "have faith" and exert control over his circumstances (in a way movie characters cannot) repeatedly come up against a chance or fate that sweeps him along regardless (par. 17). Like many classical heroes who try to cheat fate or death, he first tries to gain an edge over improbable odds by playing "*five* cards" at once, despite knowing that he's breaking the rules, that "[t]he guy at the door wouldn't like it if he knew." But this system immediately descends into chaos. His cards become unmanageable, as he tries and fails to keep up with the quick-paced announcer. After missing several numbers on all five cards, the narrator admits, "This way he'd never win" (par. 18).

Just then, however, fate or chance steps in. Despite the failure of his system, the protagonist realizes by chance that he has a bingo on his third card. The bingo is the turning point of the plot. The protagonist steps up onstage with the bingo wheel, feeling "that he had moved into the spell of some strange, mysterious power" (par. 23). The "mysterious power" is fortune or fate. He directly confronts what might be the antagonist of the story, foiling the protagonist while driving him as well. For the first time, he consciously realizes that "[i]t had always been there, even though he had not been aware of it, handing out the unlucky cards and numbers of his days" (par. 33), maybe even deciding who has birth certificates and who does not.

Once again, he has a plan to beat the odds. He tells himself to "give the wheel a short quick twirl. Just a touch of the button. He had watched it many times, and always it came close to double zero when it was short and quick" (par. 43). His confidence in his strategy makes him feel in control of the situation. But his plan, just like before, immediately goes south. As soon as he presses the button, he finds himself unable to break free of it, and he holds on to it. He admits that "[t]here [is] still that feeling of helplessness within him . . . even now that the jackpot [is] right in his hand" (par. 44). He derives his sense of power over the jackpot as he holds the button; as long as he keeps the wheel spinning, he maintains every possibility of winning. However, this sense of power is not power at all but a powerlessness that paralyzes him. He is aware "that although he control[s] the wheel, it also control[s] him" (par. 66). It always has.

The situation quickly spins more and more out of control, winding the growing tension with it. Because his showdown with the wheel is keeping others from trying their luck, they become impatient and angry. But it makes no difference to him because he is in control of "the winding and the sadness and the shame," and "[h]e [is] running the show" (pars. 66, 67). Whatever power he thinks he has begins to change him, dizzyingly altering his identity. He goes from asserting, "This is *me*" (par. 67), to desperately asking, "Who am I?" (par. 68), to believing that, because he is "The-man-who-pressed-the-button-who-held-the-prize-who-was-the-King-of-Bingo," he does not "need" his "old name" because he is "reborn" (par. 70). One gets a sense of him sitting on a chair fixed to Fortune's wheel, becoming the "King of Bingo" at the summit of its revolution, and yet, he is not transforming anything at all.

The tension and the irony culminate in the police arriving. The protagonist evades them by running around in circles; it is all he can do because he does not want to break the cord that connects the button to the wheel. He essentially becomes a part of a wheel, fixed to it, running with the cord like a radial spoke of a much larger wheel. It is all he can do to maintain control, which is the illusion of his power. For the protagonist, this illusory power is keeping Laura alive, as he suggests by crying out, "Live, Laura, baby. I got holt of it now, sugar. Live!" (par. 73). So convinced or so desperate is he that, even after the police subdue him and stop the wheel, when it lands on the winning numbers, he is "very happy" (par. 86), but not "surprise[d]" (par. 83), believing "he would receive what all the winners received" (par. 86).

In an ironic way, maybe he does. The king of bingo receives a violent blow to his head instead of a crown, the pain of which echoes the pangs of hunger with

Moi Moi 4

which he started. For all his faith and all his efforts, he is right back where he was to begin with, a "have-not," having no control or power. The story's plot comes full circle, turning into a wheel itself. Ultimately, chance and fate expose the ineffectiveness of the protagonist's schemes. Ellison contradicts the popular image of man exerting power through the button with one of man's paralyzing powerlessness. The button, according to Ellison, is only a gimmick.

Moi Moi 5

Works Cited

Ellison, Ralph. "King of the Bingo Game." *The Norton Introduction to Literature*, edited by Kelly J. Mays, shorter 14th ed., W. W. Norton, 2021, pp. 87-94.

Ross, Leslie. "Wheel of Fortune." *Medieval Art: A Topical Dictionary*, e-book ed., Greenwood, 1996, pp. 264-65.

Initiation Stories

AN ALBUM

I t may be true that most people's lives mainly consist of the "middle"—a long, stable passage of adult years—instead of the promising start, the turning point or crisis, the eventual catastrophe or triumph. Nevertheless, a great deal of fiction (as well as movies, television, and other media) focuses on the more momentous changes that we associate with youth. This album features a common kind of short fiction, the **initiation story**, also known as the coming-of-age story—the story of what happens as we define ourselves and set our own course toward the future. The short story, which often focuses on a brief, momentous occasion, is a form well suited to telling this sort of story.

Across cultures, social groups have various initiation rites to mark the *coming of age* of their youths—from "sweet sixteen" parties, bar and bat mitzvahs, debutante balls, and *quinceañeras*, to the laws that permit twenty-one-year-olds to inherit property and buy alcohol. These practices may feature prominently in stories that explore the transformation from childhood to adulthood, but such fiction doesn't have to include an obvious initiation rite like a fraternity hazing or a birthday party.

Initiation stories usually have common characteristics related to the "plot" of growing up. They always feature at least one young person, a child, an adolescent, or a young adult, who undergoes some sort of transformation. This character learns a significant truth about the world, society, people, or himself or herself. The nature of this knowledge differs widely in such stories, as does the character's response, but the plot of the story must culminate in a change of status or awareness that is depicted as more adult. The protagonist may struggle to find a place in society, but more often the challenge is to adjust his or her ideals to actual circumstances. Initiation stories may zoom in on such moments as when a child loses the protection of adults, a teenager sees a fellow creature die, or a young person faced with rejection or disappointment is suddenly made aware of a separate, lonely identity and an unknown future. Sometimes newfound freedom can lead to a joyful, if frightening, sense of possibility. At other times, the response of the young protagonist may be disbelief, denial, or retreat from the truth. Often the reader can only guess how the character will adapt to the hard-won, still-confusing knowledge gained in the experience.

Naturally there are countless such stories to tell, from the tragic to the euphoric and everything in between. Innumerable novels, films, and television shows—J. D. Salinger's *The Catcher in the Rye* (1951) and the Harry Potter series, to name a few—center on the trials and adventures of teens, often with pain, whimsy, humor, embarrassment, nostalgia, sympathy, and insight. Here we offer a variety of initiation stories that have some common features as well as very different visions of initiation. Which characters undergo initiation in each of these stories? What general or specific social conditions is each character initiated into, and how does each respond? Is there something about the passage of time and growing up that is both necessary and cruel? Can you recognize common elements in this selection of stories? in your own experience?

WILLIAM FAULKNER
(1897–1962)

Barn Burning

A native of Oxford, Mississippi, William Faulkner left high school without graduating, joined the Royal Canadian Air Force in 1918, and in the mid-1920s lived briefly in New Orleans, where he was encouraged as a writer by Sherwood Anderson. He then spent a few miserable months as a clerk in a New York bookstore; published a collection of poems, *The Marble Faun* (1924); and took a long walking tour of Europe (1925) before returning to Mississippi. With the publication of *Sartoris* in 1929, Faulkner began a cycle of works, featuring recurrent characters and set in fictional Yoknapatawpha County, including *The Sound and the Fury* (1929), *As I Lay Dying* (1930), *Light in August* (1932), *Absalom, Absalom!* (1936), *The Hamlet* (1940), and *Go Down, Moses* (1942). He spent time in Hollywood, writing screenplays for *The Big Sleep* and other films, and lived his last years in Charlottesville, Virginia. Faulkner received the 1949 Nobel Prize in Literature.

The store in which the Justice of the Peace's court was sitting smelled of cheese. The boy, crouched on his nail keg at the back of the crowded room, knew he smelled cheese, and more: from where he sat he could see the ranked shelves close-packed with the solid, squat, dynamic shapes of tin cans whose labels his stomach read, not from the lettering which meant nothing to his mind but from the scarlet devils and the silver curve of fish—this, the cheese which he knew he smelled and the hermetic meat which his intestines believed he smelled coming in intermittent gusts momentary and brief between the other constant one, the smell and sense just a little of fear because mostly of despair and grief, the old fierce pull of blood. He could not see the table where the Justice sat and before which his father and his father's enemy (*our enemy* he thought in that despair; *ourn! mine and hisn both! He's my father!*) stood, but he could hear them, the two of them that is, because his father had said no word yet:

"But what proof have you, Mr. Harris?"

"I told you. The hog got into my corn. I caught it up and sent it back to him. He had no fence that would hold it. I told him so, warned him. The next time I put the hog in my pen. When he came to get it I gave him enough wire to patch up his pen. The next time I put the hog up and kept it. I rode down to his house and saw the wire I gave him still rolled on to the spool in his yard. I told him he could have the hog when he paid me a dollar pound fee. That evening a nigger came with the dollar and got the hog. He was a strange nigger. He said, 'He say to tell you wood and hay kin burn.' I said, 'What?' 'That whut he say to tell you,' the nigger said. 'Wood and hay kin burn.' That night my barn burned. I got the stock out but I lost the barn."

"Where is the nigger? Have you got him?"

"He was a strange nigger, I tell you. I don't know what became of him." 5

"But that's not proof. Don't you see that's not proof?"

"Get that boy up here. He knows." For a moment the boy thought too that the man meant his older brother until Harris said, "Not him. The little one. The boy," and, crouching, small for his age, small and wiry like his father, in patched and faded jeans even too small for him, with straight, uncombed, brown hair and eyes gray and wild as storm scud, he saw the men between himself and the table part and become a lane of grim faces, at the end of which he saw the Justice, a shabby, collarless, graying man in spectacles, beckoning him. He felt no floor under his bare feet; he seemed to walk beneath the palpable weight of the grim turning faces. His father, stiff in his black Sunday coat donned not for the trial but for the moving, did not even look at him. *He aims for me to lie,* he thought, again with that frantic grief and despair. *And I will have to do hit.*

"What's your name, boy?" the Justice said.

"Colonel Sartoris Snopes," the boy whispered.

"Hey?" the Justice said. "Talk louder. Colonel Sartoris? I reckon anybody 10 named for Colonel Sartoris in this country can't help but tell the truth, can they?" The boy said nothing. *Enemy! Enemy!* he thought; for a moment he could not even see, could not see that the Justice's face was kindly nor discern that his voice was troubled when he spoke to the man named Harris: "Do you want me to question this boy?" But he could hear, and during those subsequent long seconds while there was absolutely no sound in the crowded little room save that of quiet and intent breathing it was as if he had swung outward at the end of a grape vine, over a ravine, and at the top of the swing had been caught in a prolonged instant of mesmerized gravity, weightless in time.

"No!" Harris said violently, explosively. "Damnation! Send him out of here!" Now time, the fluid world, rushed beneath him again, the voices coming to him again through the smell of cheese and sealed meat, the fear and despair and the old grief of blood:

"This case is closed. I can't find against you, Snopes, but I can give you advice. Leave this country and don't come back to it."

His father spoke for the first time, his voice cold and harsh, level, without emphasis: "I aim to. I don't figure to stay in a country among people who . . ." he said something unprintable and vile, addressed to no one.

"That'll do," the Justice said. "Take your wagon and get out of this country before dark. Case dismissed."

His father turned, and he followed the stiff black coat, the wiry figure walk- 15 ing a little stiffly from where a Confederate provost's man's[1] musket ball had taken him in the heel on a stolen horse thirty years ago, followed the two backs now, since his older brother had appeared from somewhere in the crowd, no taller than the father but thicker, chewing tobacco steadily, between the two lines of grim-faced men and out of the store and across the worn gallery and down the sagging steps and among the dogs and half-grown boys in the mild May dust, where as he passed a voice hissed:

1. Military policeman's.

"Barn burner!"

Again he could not see, whirling; there was a face in a red haze, moonlike, bigger than the full moon, the owner of it half again his size, he leaping in the red haze toward the face, feeling no blow, feeling no shock when his head struck the earth, scrabbling up and leaping again, feeling no blow this time either and tasting no blood, scrabbling up to see the other boy in full flight and himself already leaping into pursuit as his father's hand jerked him back, the harsh, cold voice speaking above him: "Go get in the wagon."

It stood in a grove of locusts and mulberries across the road. His two hulking sisters in their Sunday dresses and his mother and her sister in calico and sun-bonnets were already in it, sitting on and among the sorry residue of the dozen and more movings which even the boy could remember—the battered stove, the broken beds and chairs, the clock inlaid with mother-of-pearl, which would not run, stopped at some fourteen minutes past two o'clock of a dead and for-gotten day and time, which had been his mother's dowry. She was crying, though when she saw him she drew her sleeve across her face and began to descend from the wagon. "Get back," the father said.

"He's hurt. I got to get some water and wash his . . ."

20   "Get back in the wagon," his father said. He got in too, over the tail-gate. His father mounted to the seat where the older brother already sat and struck the gaunt mules two savage blows with the peeled willow, but without heat. It was not even sadistic; it was exactly that same quality which in later years would cause his descendants to overrun the engine before putting a motor car into motion, striking and reining back in the same movement. The wagon went on, the store with its quiet crowd of grimly watching men dropped behind; a curve in the road hid it. *Forever* he thought. *Maybe he's done satisfied now, now that he has* . . . stopping himself, not to say it aloud even to himself. His mother's hand touched his shoulder.

"Does hit hurt?" she said.

"Naw," he said. "Hit don't hurt. Lemme be."

"Can't you wipe some of the blood off before hit dries?"

"I'll wash to-night," he said. "Lemme be, I tell you."

25   The wagon went on. He did not know where they were going. None of them ever did or ever asked, because it was always somewhere, always a house of sorts waiting for them a day or two days or even three days away. Likely his father had already arranged to make a crop on another farm before he . . . Again he had to stop himself. He (the father) always did. There was something about his wolf-like independence and even courage when the advantage was at least neutral which impressed strangers, as if they got from his latent ravening feroc-ity not so much a sense of dependability as a feeling that his ferocious convic-tion in the rightness of his own actions would be of advantage to all whose interest lay with his.

That night they camped, in a grove of oaks and beeches where a spring ran. The nights were still cool and they had a fire against it, of a rail lifted from a nearby fence and cut into lengths—a small fire, neat, niggard almost, a shrewd fire; such fires were his father's habit and custom always, even in freezing weather. Older, the boy might have remarked this and wondered why not a big one; why should not a man who had not only seen the waste and extravagance of war, but who had in his blood an inherent voracious prodigality with material not his own, have burned everything in sight? Then he might have gone a step farther and thought that that was the reason: that niggard blaze was the living fruit of nights passed during those four years in the woods hiding from all men, blue or gray,[2] with his strings of horses (captured horses, he called them). And older still, he might have divined the true reason: that the element of fire spoke to some deep mainspring of his father's being, as the element of steel or of powder spoke to other men, as the one weapon for the preservation of integrity, else breath were not worth the breathing, and hence to be regarded with respect and used with discretion.

But he did not think this now and he had seen those same niggard blazes all his life. He merely ate his supper beside it and was already half asleep over his iron plate when his father called him, and once more he followed the stiff back, the stiff and ruthless limp, up the slope and on to the starlit road where, turning, he could see his father against the stars but without face or depth—a shape black, flat, and bloodless as though cut from tin in the iron folds of the frockcoat which had not been made for him, the voice harsh like tin and without heat like tin:

"You were fixing to tell them. You would have told him." He didn't answer. His father struck him with the flat of his hand on the side of the head, hard but without heat, exactly as he had struck the two mules at the store, exactly as he would strike either of them with any stick in order to kill a horse fly, his voice still without heat or anger: "You're getting to be a man. You got to learn. You got to learn to stick to your own blood or you ain't going to have any blood to stick to you. Do you think either of them, any man there this morning, would? Don't you know all they wanted was a chance to get at me because they knew I had them beat? Eh?" Later, twenty years later, he was to tell himself, "If I had said they wanted only truth, justice, he would have hit me again." But now he said nothing. He was not crying. He just stood there. "Answer me," his father said.

"Yes," he whispered. His father turned.

"Get on to bed. We'll be there tomorrow."

Tomorrow they were there. In the early afternoon the wagon stopped before a paintless two-room house identical almost with the dozen others it had stopped before even in the boy's ten years, and again, as on the other dozen occasions, his mother and aunt got down and began to unload the wagon, although his two sisters and his father and brother had not moved.

"Likely hit ain't fitten for hawgs," one of the sisters said.

"Nevertheless, fit it will and you'll hog it and like it," his father said. "Get out of them chairs and help your Ma unload."

The two sisters got down, big, bovine, in a flutter of cheap ribbons; one of them drew from the jumbled wagon bed a battered lantern, the other a worn broom. His father handed the reins to the older son and began to climb stiffly over the wheel. "When they get unloaded, take the team to the barn and feed them." Then he said, and at first the boy thought he was still speaking to his brother: "Come with me."

30

---

35   "Me?" he said.

"Yes," his father said. "You."

"Abner," his mother said. His father paused and looked back—the harsh level stare beneath the shaggy, graying, irascible brows.

"I reckon I'll have a word with the man that aims to begin to-morrow owning me body and soul for the next eight months."

They went back up the road. A week ago—or before last night, that is—he would have asked where they were going, but not now. His father had struck him before last night but never before had he paused afterward to explain why; it was as if the blow and the following calm, outrageous voice still rang, repercussed, divulging nothing to him save the terrible handicap of being young, the light weight of his few years, just heavy enough to prevent his soaring free of the world as it seemed to be ordered but not heavy enough to keep him footed solid in it, to resist it and try to change the course of its events.

40   Presently he could see the grove of oaks and cedars and the other flowering trees and shrubs, where the house would be, though not the house yet. They walked beside a fence massed with honeysuckle and Cherokee roses and came to a gate swinging open between two brick pillars, and now, beyond a sweep of drive, he saw the house for the first time and at that instant he forgot his father and the terror and despair both, and even when he remembered his father again (who had not stopped) the terror and despair did not return. Because, for all the twelve movings, they had sojourned until now in a poor country, a land of small farms and fields and houses, and he had never seen a house like this before. *Hit's big as a courthouse* he thought quietly, with a surge of peace and joy whose reason he could not have thought into words, being too young for that: *They are safe from him. People whose lives are a part of this peace and dignity are beyond his touch, he no more to them than a buzzing wasp: capable of stinging for a little moment but that's all; the spell of this peace and dignity rendering even the barns and stable and cribs which belong to it impervious to the puny flames he might contrive . . .* this, the peace and joy, ebbing for an instant as he looked again at the stiff black back, the stiff and implacable limp of the figure which was not dwarfed by the house, for the reason that it had never looked big anywhere and which now, against the serene columned backdrop, had more than ever that impervious quality of something cut ruthlessly from tin, depthless, as though, sidewise to the sun, it would cast no shadow. Watching him, the boy remarked the absolutely undeviating course which his father held and saw the stiff foot come squarely down in a pile of fresh droppings where a horse had stood in the drive and which his father could have avoided by a simple change of stride. But it ebbed only for a moment, though he could not have thought this into words either, walking on in the spell of the house, which he could even want but without envy, without sorrow, certainly never with that ravening and jealous rage which unknown to him walked in the ironlike black coat before him: *Maybe he will feel it too. Maybe it will even change him now from what maybe he couldn't help but be.*

They crossed the portico. Now he could hear his father's stiff foot as it came down on the boards with clocklike finality, a sound out of all proportion to the displacement of the body it bore and which was not dwarfed either by the white

door before it, as though it had attained to a sort of vicious and ravening minimum not to be dwarfed by anything—the flat, wide, black hat, the formal coat
of broadcloth which had once been black but which had now that friction-
glazed greenish cast of the bodies of old house flies, the lifted sleeve which was
too large, the lifted hand like a curled claw. The door opened so promptly that
the boy knew the Negro must have been watching them all the time, an old
man with neat grizzled hair, in a linen jacket, who stood barring the door with
his body, saying, "Wipe yo foots, white man, fo you come in here. Major ain't
home nohow."

"Get out of my way, nigger," his father said, without heat too, flinging the
door back and the Negro also and entering, his hat still on his head. And now
the boy saw the prints of the stiff foot on the doorjamb and saw them appear on
the pale rug behind the machinelike deliberation of the foot which seemed to
bear (or transmit) twice the weight which the body compassed. The Negro was
shouting "Miss Lula! Miss Lula!" somewhere behind them, then the boy, del-
uged as though by a warm wave by a suave turn of carpeted stair and a pendant
glitter of chandeliers and a mute gleam of gold frames, heard the swift feet and
saw her too, a lady—perhaps he had never seen her like before either—in a
gray, smooth gown with lace at the throat and an apron tied at the waist and the
sleeves turned back, wiping cake or biscuit dough from her hands with a towel
as she came up the hall, looking not at his father at all but at the tracks on the
blond rug with an expression of incredulous amazement.

"I tried," the Negro cried. "I tole him to . . ."

"Will you please go away?" she said in a shaking voice. "Major de Spain is not
at home. Will you please go away?"

His father had not spoken again. He did not speak again. He did not even 45
look at her. He just stood stiff in the center of the rug, in his hat, the shaggy
iron-gray brows twitching slightly above the pebble-colored eyes as he appeared
to examine the house with brief deliberation. Then with the same deliberation
he turned; the boy watched him pivot on the good leg and saw the stiff foot drag
round the arc of the turning, leaving a final long and fading smear. His father
never looked at it, he never once looked down at the rug. The Negro held the
door. It closed behind them, upon the hysteric and indistinguishable woman-
wail. His father stopped at the top of the steps and scraped his boot clean on
the edge of it. At the gate he stopped again. He stood for a moment, planted
stiffly on the stiff foot, looking back at the house. "Pretty and white, ain't it?" he
said. "That's sweat. Nigger sweat. Maybe it ain't white enough yet to suit him.
Maybe he wants to mix some white sweat with it."

Two hours later the boy was chopping wood behind the house within which
his mother and aunt and the two sisters (the mother and aunt, not the two girls,
he knew that; even at this distance and muffled by walls the flat loud voices of
the two girls emanated an incorrigible idle inertia) were setting up the stove to
prepare a meal, when he heard the hooves and saw the linen-clad man on a fine
sorrel mare, whom he recognized even before he saw the rolled rug in front of
the Negro youth following on a fat bay carriage horse—a suffused, angry face
vanishing, still at full gallop, beyond the corner of the house where his father
and brother were sitting in the two tilted chairs; and a moment later, almost

before he could have put the axe down, he heard the hooves again and watched the sorrel mare go back out of the yard, already galloping again. Then his father began to shout one of the sisters' names, who presently emerged backward from the kitchen door dragging the rolled rug along the ground by one end while the other sister walked behind it.

"If you ain't going to tote, go on and set up the wash pot," the first said.

"You, Sarty!" the second shouted. "Set up the wash pot!" His father appeared at the door, framed against that shabbiness, as he had been against that other bland perfection, impervious to either, the mother's anxious face at his shoulder.

"Go on," the father said. "Pick it up." The two sisters stooped, broad, lethargic; stooping, they presented an incredible expanse of pale cloth and a flutter of tawdry ribbons.

50   "If I thought enough of a rug to have to git hit all the way from France I wouldn't keep hit where folks coming in would have to tromp on hit," the first said. They raised the rug.

"Abner," the mother said. "Let me do it."

"You go back and git dinner," his father said. "I'll tend to this."

From the woodpile through the rest of the afternoon the boy watched them, the rug spread flat in the dust beside the bubbling wash-pot, the two sisters stooping over it with that profound and lethargic reluctance, while the father stood over them in turn, implacable and grim, driving them though never raising his voice again. He could smell the harsh homemade lye they were using; he saw his mother come to the door once and look toward them with an expression not anxious now but very like despair; he saw his father turn, and he fell to with the axe and saw from the corner of his eye his father raise from the ground a flattish fragment of field stone and examine it and return to the pot, and this time his mother actually spoke: "Abner. Abner. Please don't. Please, Abner."

Then he was done too. It was dusk; the whippoorwills had already begun. He could smell coffee from the room where they would presently eat the cold food remaining from the mid-afternoon meal, though when he entered the house he realized they were having coffee again probably because there was a fire on the hearth, before which the rug now lay spread over the backs of the two chairs. The tracks of his father's foot were gone. Where they had been were now long, water-cloudy scoriations resembling the sporadic course of a Lilliputian mowing machine.

55   It still hung there while they ate the cold food and then went to bed, scattered without order or claim up and down the two rooms, his mother in one bed, where his father would later lie, the older brother in the other, himself, the aunt, and the two sisters on pallets on the floor. But his father was not in bed yet. The last thing the boy remembered was the depthless, harsh silhouette of the hat and coat bending over the rug and it seemed to him that he had not even closed his eyes when the silhouette was standing over him, the fire almost dead behind it, the stiff foot prodding him awake. "Catch up the mule," his father said.

When he returned with the mule his father was standing in the black door, the rolled rug over his shoulder. "Ain't you going to ride?" he said.

"No. Give me your foot."

He bent his knee into his father's hand, the wiry, surprising power flowed smoothly, rising, he rising with it, on to the mule's bare back (they had owned a saddle once; the boy could remember it though not when or where) and with the same effortlessness his father swung the rug up in front of him. Now in the starlight they retraced the afternoon's path, up the dusty road rife with honeysuckle, through the gate and up the black tunnel of the drive to the lightless house, where he sat on the mule and felt the rough warp of the rug drag across his thighs and vanish.

"Don't you want me to help?" he whispered. His father did not answer and now he heard again that stiff foot striking the hollow portico with that wooden and clocklike deliberation, that outrageous overstatement of the weight it carried. The rug, hunched, not flung (the boy could tell that even in the darkness) from his father's shoulder struck the angle of wall and floor with a sound unbelievably loud, thunderous, then the foot again, unhurried and enormous; a light came on in the house and the boy sat, tense, breathing steadily and quietly and just a little fast, though the foot itself did not increase its beat at all, descending the steps now; now the boy could see him.

"Don't you want to ride now?" he whispered. "We kin both ride now," the light within the house altering now, flaring up and sinking. *He's coming down the stairs now,* he thought. He had already ridden the mule up beside the horse block; presently his father was up behind him and he doubled the reins over and slashed the mule across the neck, but before the animal could begin to trot the hard, thin arm came round him, the hard, knotted hand jerking the mule back to a walk.

In the first red rays of the sun they were in the lot, putting plow gear on the mules. This time the sorrel mare was in the lot before he heard it at all, the rider collarless and even bareheaded, trembling, speaking in a shaking voice as the woman in the house had done, his father merely looking up once before stooping again to the hame he was buckling, so that the man on the mare spoke to his stooping back:

"You must realize you have ruined that rug. Wasn't there anybody here, any of your women . . ." he ceased, shaking, the boy watching him, the older brother leaning now in the stable door, chewing, blinking slowly and steadily at nothing apparently. "It cost a hundred dollars. But you never had a hundred dollars. You never will. So I'm going to charge you twenty bushels of corn against your crop. I'll add it in your contract and when you come to the commissary you can sign it. That won't keep Mrs. de Spain quiet but maybe it will teach you to wipe your feet off before you enter her house again."

Then he was gone. The boy looked at his father, who still had not spoken or even looked up again, who was now adjusting the logger-head in the hame.

"Pap," he said. His father looked at him—the inscrutable face, the shaggy brows beneath which the gray eyes glinted coldly. Suddenly the boy went toward him, fast, stopping as suddenly. "You done the best you could!" he cried. "If he wanted hit done different why didn't he wait and tell you how? He won't git no twenty bushels! He won't git none! We'll gether hit and hide hit! I kin watch . . ."

"Did you put the cutter back in that straight stock like I told you?"

"No, sir," he said.

"Then go do it."

60

65

That was Wednesday. During the rest of that week he worked steadily, at what was within his scope and some which was beyond it, with an industry that did not need to be driven nor even commanded twice; he had this from his mother, with the difference that some at least of what he did he liked to do, such as splitting wood with the half-size axe which his mother and aunt had earned, or saved money somehow, to present him with at Christmas. In company with the two older women (and on one afternoon, even one of the sisters), he built pens for the shoat and the cow which were a part of his father's contract with the landlord, and one afternoon, his father being absent, gone somewhere on one of the mules, he went to the field.

They were running a middle buster[3] now, his brother holding the plow straight while he handled the reins, and walking beside the straining mule, the rich black soil shearing cool and damp against his bare ankles, he thought *Maybe this is the end of it. Maybe even that twenty bushels that seems hard to have to pay for just a rug will be a cheap price for him to stop forever and always from being what he used to be*; thinking, dreaming now, so that his brother had to speak sharply to him to mind the mule: *Maybe he even won't collect the twenty bushels. Maybe it will all add up and balance and vanish—corn, rug, fire; the terror and grief, the being pulled two ways like between two teams of horses—gone, done with for ever and ever.*

70   Then it was Saturday; he looked up from beneath the mule he was harnessing and saw his father in the black coat and hat. "Not that," his father said. "The wagon gear." And then, two hours later, sitting in the wagon bed behind his father and brother on the seat, the wagon accomplished a final curve, and he saw the weathered paintless store with its tattered tobacco- and patent-medicine posters and the tethered wagons and saddle animals below the gallery. He mounted the gnawed steps behind his father and brother, and there again was the lane of quiet, watching faces for the three of them to walk through. He saw the man in spectacles sitting at the plank table and he did not need to be told this was a Justice of the Peace; he sent one glare of fierce, exultant, partisan defiance at the man in collar and cravat now, whom he had seen but twice before in his life, and that on a galloping horse, who now wore on his face an expression not of rage but of amazed unbelief which the boy could not have known was at the incredible circumstance of being sued by one of his own tenants, and came and stood against his father and cried at the Justice: "He ain't done it! He ain't burnt . . ."

"Go back to the wagon," his father said.

"Burnt?" the Justice said. "Do I understand this rug was burned too?"

"Does anybody here claim it was?" his father said. "Go back to the wagon." But he did not, he merely retreated to the rear of the room, crowded as that other had been, but not to sit down this time, instead, to stand pressing among the motionless bodies, listening to the voices:

"And you claim twenty bushels of corn is too high for the damage you did to the rug?"

75   "He brought the rug to me and said he wanted the tracks washed out of it. I washed the tracks out and took the rug back to him."

3. Double moldboard plow that throws a ridge of earth both ways.

"But you didn't carry the rug back to him in the same condition it was in before you made the tracks on it."

His father did not answer, and now for perhaps half a minute there was no sound at all save that of breathing, the faint, steady suspiration of complete and intent listening.

"You decline to answer that, Mr. Snopes?" Again his father did not answer. "I'm going to find against you, Mr. Snopes. I'm going to find that you were responsible for the injury to Major de Spain's rug and hold you liable for it. But twenty bushels of corn seems a little high for a man in your circumstances to have to pay. Major de Spain claims it cost a hundred dollars. October corn will be worth about fifty cents. I figure that if Major de Spain can stand a ninety-five dollar loss on something he paid cash for, you can stand a five-dollar loss you haven't earned yet. I hold you in damages to Major de Spain to the amount of ten bushels of corn over and above your contract with him, to be paid to him out of your crop at gathering time. Court adjourned."

It had taken no time hardly, the morning was but half begun. He thought they would return home and perhaps back to the field, since they were late, far behind all other farmers. But instead his father passed on behind the wagon, merely indicating with his hand for the older brother to follow with it, and crossed the road toward the blacksmith shop opposite, pressing on after his father, overtaking him, speaking, whispering up at the harsh, calm face beneath the weathered hat: "He won't git no ten bushels neither. He won't git one. We'll . . ." until his father glanced for an instant down at him, the face absolutely calm, the grizzled eyebrows tangled above the cold eyes, the voice almost pleasant, almost gentle:

"You think so? Well, we'll wait till October anyway." 80

The matter of the wagon—the setting of a spoke or two and the tightening of the tires—did not take long either, the business of the tires accomplished by driving the wagon into the spring branch behind the shop and letting it stand there, the mules nuzzling into the water from time to time, and the boy on the seat with the idle reins, looking up the slope and through the sooty tunnel of the shed where the slow hammer rang and where his father sat on an upended cypress bolt, easily, either talking or listening, still sitting there when the boy brought the dripping wagon up out of the branch and halted it before the door.

"Take them on to the shade and hitch," his father said. He did so and returned. His father and the smith and a third man squatting on his heels inside the door were talking, about crops and animals; the boy, squatting too in the ammoniac dust and hoof-parings and scales of rust, heard his father tell a long and unhurried story out of the time before the birth of the older brother even when he had been a professional horsetrader. And then his father came up beside him where he stood before a tattered last year's circus poster on the other side of the store, gazing rapt and quiet at the scarlet horses, the incredible poisings and convolutions of tulle and tights and the painted leers of comedians, and said, "It's time to eat."

But not at home. Squatting beside his brother against the front wall, he watched his father emerge from the store and produce from a paper sack a segment of cheese and divide it carefully and deliberately into three with his pocket knife and produce crackers from the same sack. They all three squatted on the gallery and ate, slowly, without talking; then in the store again, they drank from a tin dipper tepid water smelling of the cedar bucket and of living beech trees. And still they did not go home. It was a horse lot this time, a tall rail fence upon and along which men stood and sat and out of which one by one horses were led, to be walked and trotted and then cantered back and forth along the road while the slow swapping and buying went on and the sun began to slant westward, they—the three of them—watching and listening, the older brother with his muddy eyes and his steady, inevitable tobacco, the father commenting now and then on certain of the animals, to no one in particular.

It was after sundown when they reached home. They ate supper by lamplight, then, sitting on the doorstep, the boy watched the night fully accomplish, listening to the whippoorwills and the frogs, when he heard his mother's voice: "Abner! No! No! Oh, God. Oh, God. Abner!" and he rose, whirled, and saw the altered light through the door where a candle stub now burned in a bottle neck on the table and his father, still in the hat and coat, at once formal and burlesque as though dressed carefully for some shabby and ceremonial violence, emptying the reservoir of the lamp back into the five-gallon kerosene can from which it had been filled, while the mother tugged at his arm until he shifted the lamp to the other hand and flung her back, not savagely or viciously, just hard, into the wall, her hands flung out against the wall for balance, her mouth open and in her face the same quality of hopeless despair as had been in her voice. Then his father saw him standing in the door.

85   "Go to the barn and get that can of oil we were oiling the wagon with," he said. The boy did not move. Then he could speak.

"What . . ." he cried. "What are you . . ."

"Go get that oil," his father said. "Go."

Then he was moving, running, outside the house, toward the stable: this the old habit, the old blood which he had not been permitted to choose for himself, which had been bequeathed him willy nilly and which had run for so long (and who knew where, battening on what of outrage and savagery and lust) before it came to him. *I could keep on,* he thought. *I could run on and on and never look back, never need to see his face again. Only I can't. I can't,* the rusted can in his hand now, the liquid sploshing in it as he ran back to the house and into it, into the sound of his mother's weeping in the next room, and handed the can to his father.

"Ain't you going to even send a nigger?" he cried. "At least you sent a nigger before!"

90   This time his father didn't strike him. The hand came even faster than the blow had, the same hand which had set the can on the table with almost excruciating care flashing from the can toward him too quick for him to follow it, gripping him by the back of his shirt and on to tiptoe before he had seen it quit the can, the face stooping at him in breathless and frozen ferocity, the cold, dead voice speaking over him to the older brother, who leaned against the table, chewing with that steady, curious, sidewise motion of cows:

"Empty the can into the big one and go on. I'll catch up with you."

"Better tie him up to the bedpost," the brother said.

"Do like I told you," the father said. Then the boy was moving, his bunched shirt and the hard, bony hand between his shoulder-blades, his toes just touching the floor, across the room and into the other one, past the sisters sitting with spread heavy thighs in the two chairs over the cold hearth, and to where his mother and aunt sat side by side on the bed, the aunt's arms about his mother's shoulders.

"Hold him," the father said. The aunt made a startled movement. "Not you," the father said. "Lennie. Take hold of him. I want to see you do it." His mother took him by the wrist. "You'll hold him better than that. If he gets loose don't you know what he is going to do? He will go up yonder." He jerked his head toward the road. "Maybe I'd better tie him."

"I'll hold him," his mother whispered.   95

"See you do then." Then his father was gone, the stiff foot heavy and measured upon the boards, ceasing at last.

Then he began to struggle. His mother caught him in both arms, he jerking and wrenching at them. He would be stronger in the end, he knew that. But he had no time to wait for it. "Lemme go!" he cried. "I don't want to have to hit you!"

"Let him go!" the aunt said. "If he don't go, before God, I am going up there myself!"

"Don't you see I can't?" his mother cried. "Sarty! Sarty! No! No! Help me, Lizzie!"

Then he was free. His aunt grasped at him but it was too late. He whirled,   100
running, his mother stumbled forward on to her knees behind him, crying to the nearer sister: "Catch him, Net! Catch him!" But that was too late too, the sister (the sisters were twins, born at the same time, yet either of them now gave the impression of being, encompassing as much living meat and volume and weight as any other two of the family) not yet having begun to rise from the chair, her head, face, alone merely turned, presenting to him in the flying instant an astonishing expanse of young female features untroubled by any surprise even, wearing only an expression of bovine interest. Then he was out of the room, out of the house, in the mild dust of the starlit road and the heavy rifeness of honeysuckle, the pale ribbon unspooling with terrific slowness under his running feet, reaching the gate at last and turning in, running, his heart and lungs drumming, on up the drive toward the lighted house, the lighted door. He did not knock, he burst in, sobbing for breath, incapable for the moment of speech; he saw the astonished face of the Negro in the linen jacket without knowing when the Negro had appeared.

"De Spain!" he cried, panted. "Where's . . ." then he saw the white man too emerging from a white door down the hall. "Barn!" he cried. "Barn!"

"What?" the white man said. "Barn?"

"Yes!" the boy cried. "Barn!"

"Catch him!" the white man shouted.

But it was too late this time too. The Negro grasped his shirt, but the entire   105
sleeve, rotten with washing, carried away, and he was out that door too and in the drive again, and had actually never ceased to run even while he was screaming into the white man's face.

Behind him the white man was shouting, "My horse! Fetch my horse!" and he thought for an instant of cutting across the park and climbing the fence into the road, but he did not know the park nor how high the vine-massed fence might be and he dared not risk it. So he ran on down the drive, blood and breath roaring; presently he was in the road again though he could not see it. He could not hear either: the galloping mare was almost upon him before he heard her, and even then he held his course, as if the very urgency of his wild grief and need must in a moment more find his wings, waiting until the ultimate instant to hurl himself aside and into the weed-choked roadside ditch as the horse thundered past and on, for an instant in furious silhouette against the stars, the tranquil early summer night sky which, even before the shape of the horse and rider vanished, stained abruptly and violently upward: a long, swirling roar incredible and soundless, blotting the stars, and he springing up and into the road again, running again, knowing it was too late yet still running even after he heard the shot and, an instant later, two shots, pausing now without knowing he had ceased to run, crying "Pap! Pap!", running again before he knew he had begun to run, stumbling, tripping over something and scrabbling up again without ceasing to run, looking backward over his shoulder at the glare as he got up, running on among the invisible trees, panting, sobbing, "Father! Father!"

At midnight he was sitting on the crest of a hill. He did not know it was midnight and he did not know how far he had come. But there was no glare behind him now and he sat now, his back toward what he had called home for four days anyhow, his face toward the dark woods which he would enter when breath was strong again, small, shaking steadily in the chill darkness, hugging himself into the remainder of his thin, rotten shirt, the grief and despair now no longer terror and fear but just grief and despair. *Father. My father*, he thought. "He was brave!" he cried suddenly, aloud but not loud, no more than a whisper: "He was! He was in the war! He was in Colonel Sartoris' cav'ry!" not knowing that his father had gone to that war a private in the fine old European sense, wearing no uniform, admitting the authority of and giving fidelity to no man or army or flag, going to war as Malbrouck[4] himself did: for booty—it meant nothing and less than nothing to him if it were enemy booty or his own.

The slow constellations wheeled on. It would be dawn and then sun-up after a while and he would be hungry. But that would be to-morrow and now he was only cold, and walking would cure that. His breathing was easier now and he decided to get up and go on, and then he found that he had been asleep because he knew it was almost dawn, the night almost over. He could tell that from the whippoorwills. They were everywhere now among the dark trees below him, constant and inflectioned and ceaseless, so that, as the instant for giving over to the day birds drew nearer and nearer, there was no interval at all between them. He got up. He was a little stiff, but walking would cure that too as it would the cold, and soon there would be the sun. He went on down the hill, toward the dark woods within which the liquid silver voices of the birds called unceasing— the rapid and urgent beating of the urgent and quiring heart of the late spring night. He did not look back.

1939

---

4. John Churchill, the first duke of Marlborough (1650–1722), an English general whose name became distorted as Malbrough and Malbrouck in English and French popular songs celebrating his exploits.

QUESTIONS

1. Barn Burning opens with a trial scene. Consider the details of the scene and the ways here, as later, Sarty's thoughts are indicated. What conflicts are established in the scene? In what ways might Sarty's conflicts be both internal and external?
2. Why does Sarty make the choice he does at the end of the story? What does the story suggest he is choosing by acting as he does?
3. Barn Burning makes Sarty's story inseparable from his father's story, one that—thanks to the third-person narrator—we know a bit more about than Sarty himself does. How does the story encourage us to see and understand Abner Snopes? What desires, motives, values, and views—especially of justice—seem to drive and explain him? What might be admirable, as well as abhorrent, about him?

TONI CADE BAMBARA

(1939–95)

The Lesson

Born in New York City, Toni Cade Bambara grew up in Harlem and Bedford-Stuyvesant, two of New York's poorest neighborhoods. She began writing as a child and took her last name from a signature on a sketchbook she found in a trunk belonging to her great-grandmother. (The Bambara are a people of northwest Africa.) After graduating from Queens College, she wrote fiction in "the predawn in-betweens" while studying for her MA at the City College of New York and working at a variety of jobs: dancer, social worker, recreation director, psychiatric counselor, college English teacher, literary critic, and film producer. Bambara began to publish her stories in 1962. Her fiction includes two collections of stories, *Gorilla, My Love* (1972) and *The Sea Birds Are Still Alive* (1977), as well as two novels, *The Salt Eaters* (1980) and *If Blessing Comes*, published posthumously as *Those Bones Are Not My Child* (1999). Bambara also edited two anthologies, *The Black Woman* (1970) and *Tales and Stories for Black Folks* (1971).

B ack in the days when everyone was old and stupid or young and foolish and me and Sugar were the only ones just right, this lady moved on our block with nappy[1] hair and proper speech and no makeup. And quite naturally we laughed at her, laughed the way we did at the junk man who went about his business like he was some big-time president and his sorry-ass horse his secretary. And we kinda hated her too, hated the way we did the winos who cluttered up our parks and pissed on our handball walls and stank up our hallways and stairs so you couldn't halfway play hide-and-seek without a goddamn gas mask. Miss Moore was her name. The only woman on the block with no first name. And she was black as hell, cept for her feet, which were fish-white and spooky. And she was always planning these boring-ass things for us to do, us being my cousin, mostly, who lived on the block cause we all moved North the

---

1. Untreated and unstraightened, naturally curly or coiled.

same time and to the same apartment then spread out gradual to breathe. And our parents would yank our heads into some kinda shape and crisp up our clothes so we'd be presentable for travel with Miss Moore, who always looked like she was going to church, though she never did. Which is just one of the things the grown-ups talked about when they talked behind her back like a dog. But when she came calling with some sachet she'd sewed up or some gingerbread she'd made or some book, why then they'd all be too embarrassed to turn her down and we'd get handed over all spruced up. She'd been to college and said it was only right that she should take responsibility for the young ones' education, and she not even related by marriage or blood. So they'd go for it. Specially Aunt Gretchen. She was the main gofer in the family. You got some ole dumb shit foolishness you want somebody to go for, you send for Aunt Gretchen. She been screwed into the go-along for so long, it's a blood-deep natural thing with her. Which is how she got saddled with me and Sugar and Junior in the first place while our mothers were in a la-de-da apartment up the block having a good ole time.

So this one day Miss Moore rounds us all up at the mailbox and it's puredee hot and she's knockin herself out about arithmetic. And school suppose to let up in summer I heard, but she don't never let up. And the starch in my pinafore scratching the shit outta me and I'm really hating this nappy-head bitch and her goddamn college degree. I'd much rather go to the pool or to the show where it's cool. So me and Sugar leaning on the mailbox being surly, which is a Miss Moore word. And Flyboy checking out what everybody brought for lunch. And Fat Butt already wasting his peanut-butter-and-jelly sandwich like the pig he is. And Junebug punchin on Q.T.'s arm for potato chips. And Rosie Giraffe shifting from one hip to the other waiting for somebody to step on her foot or ask her if she from Georgia so she can kick ass, preferably Mercedes'. And Miss Moore asking us do we know what money is, like we a bunch of retards. I mean real money, she say, like it's only poker chips or monopoly papers we lay on the grocer. So right away I'm tired of this and say so. And would much rather snatch Sugar and go to the Sunset and terrorize the West Indian kids and take their hair ribbons and their money too. And Miss Moore files that remark away for next week's lesson on brotherhood, I can tell. And finally I say we oughta get to the subway cause it's cooler and besides we might meet some cute boys. Sugar done swiped her mama's lipstick, so we ready.

So we heading down the street and she's boring us silly about what things cost and what our parents make and how much goes for rent and how money ain't divided up right in this country. And then she gets to the part about we all poor and live in the slums, which I don't feature. And I'm ready to speak on that, but she steps out in the street and hails two cabs just like that. Then she hustles half the crew in with her and hands me a five-dollar bill and tells me to calculate 10 percent tip for the driver. And we're off. Me and Sugar and Junebug and Flyboy hangin out the window and hollering to everybody, putting lipstick on each other cause Flyboy a faggot anyway, and making farts with our sweaty armpits. But I'm mostly trying to figure how to spend this money. But they all fascinated with the meter ticking and Junebug starts laying bets as to how much it'll read when Flyboy can't hold his breath no more. Then Sugar lays bets as to how much it'll be when we get there. So I'm stuck. Don't nobody want to go for my plan, which is to jump out at the next light and run off to the first bar-b-que we can find. Then the driver tells us to get the hell out cause we there already. And the meter reads eighty-five cents. And I'm stalling to figure out the tip and Sugar say give him a dime. And I decide he don't need it bad as I do, so later for him. But then he tries to take off with Junebug foot still in the door so we talk about his mama something ferocious. Then we check out that we on Fifth Avenue[2] and everybody dressed up in stockings. One lady in a fur coat, hot as it is. White folks crazy.

"This is the place," Miss Moore say, presenting it to us in the voice she uses at the museum. "Let's look in the windows before we go in."

"Can we steal?" Sugar asks very serious like she's getting the ground rules 5 squared away before she plays. "I beg your pardon," say Miss Moore, and we fall out. So she leads us around the windows of the toy store and me and Sugar screamin, "This is mine, that's mine, I gotta have that, that was made for me, I was born for that," till Big Butt drowns us out.

"Hey, I'm goin to buy that there."

"That there? You don't even know what it is, stupid."

"I do so," he say punchin on Rosie Giraffe. "It's a microscope."

"Whatcha gonna do with a microscope, fool?"

"Look at things." 10

"Like what, Ronald?" ask Miss Moore. And Big Butt ain't got the first notion. So here go Miss Moore gabbing about the thousands of bacteria in a drop of water and the somethinorother in a speck of blood and the million and one living things in the air around us is invisible to the naked eye. And what she say that for? Junebug go to town on that "naked" and we rolling. Then Miss Moore ask what it cost. So we all jam into the window smudgin it up and the price tag say $300. So then she ask how long'd take for Big Butt and Junebug to save up their allowances. "Too long," I say. "Yeh," adds Sugar, "outgrown it by that time." And Miss Moore say no, you never outgrow learning instruments. "Why, even medical students and interns and," blah, blah, blah. And we ready to choke Big Butt for bringing it up in the first damn place.

"This here costs four hundred eighty dollars," say Rosie Giraffe. So we pile up all over her to see what she pointin out. My eyes tell me it's a chunk of glass cracked with something heavy, and different-color inks dripped into the splits, then the whole thing put into a oven or something. But for $480 it don't make sense.

"That's a paperweight made of semi-precious stones fused together under tremendous pressure," she explains slowly, with her hands doing the mining and all the factory work.

"So what's a paperweight?" asks Rosie Giraffe.

"To weigh paper with, dumbbell," say Flyboy, the wise man from the East.[3] 15

"Not exactly," say Miss Moore, which is what she say when you warm or way off too. "It's to weigh paper down so it won't scatter and make your desk untidy." So right away me and Sugar curtsy to each other and then to Mercedes who is more the tidy type.

---

2. Major Manhattan street famous for its expensive, exclusive shops.
3. In the Bible three wise men travel from the East to visit the newborn Christ.

"We don't keep paper on top of the desk in my class," say Junebug, figuring Miss Moore crazy or lyin one.

"At home, then," she say. "Don't you have a calendar and a pencil case and a blotter[4] and a letter-opener on your desk at home where you do your homework?" And she know damn well what our homes look like cause she nosys around in them every chance she gets.

"I don't even have a desk," say Junebug. "Do we?"

20   "No. And I don't get no homework neither," say Big Butt.

"And I don't even have a home," say Flyboy like he do at school to keep the white folks off his back and sorry for him. Send this poor kid to camp posters, is his specialty.

"I do," says Mercedes. "I have a box of stationery on my desk and a picture of my cat. My godmother bought the stationery and the desk. There's a big rose on each sheet and the envelopes smell like roses."

"Who wants to know about your smelly-ass stationery," say Rosie Giraffe fore I can get my two cents in.

"It's important to have a work area all your own so that . . . ."

25   "Will you look at this sailboat, please," say Flyboy, cuttin her off and pointin to the thing like it was his. So once again we tumble all over each other to gaze at this magnificent thing in the toy store which is just big enough to maybe sail two kittens across the pond if you strap them to the posts tight. We all start reciting the price tag like we in assembly. "Handcrafted sailboat of fiberglass at one thousand one hundred ninety-five dollars."

"Unbelievable," I hear myself say and am really stunned. I read it again for myself just in case the group recitation put me in a trance. Same thing. For some reason this pisses me off. We look at Miss Moore and she lookin at us, waiting for I dunno what.

Who'd pay all that when you can buy a sailboat set for a quarter at Pop's, a tube of glue for a dime, and a ball of string for eight cents? "It must have a motor and a whole lot else besides," I say. "My sailboat cost me about fifty cents."

"But will it take water?" say Mercedes with her smart ass.

"Took mine to Alley Pond Park once," say Flyboy. "String broke. Lost it. Pity."

30   "Sailed mine in Central Park and it keeled over and sank. Had to ask my father for another dollar."

"And you got the strap," laugh Big Butt. "The jerk didn't even have a string on it. My old man wailed on his behind."

Little Q.T. was staring hard at the sailboat and you could see he wanted it bad. But he too little and somebody'd just take it from him. So what the hell. "This boat for kids, Miss Moore?"

"Parents silly to buy something like that just to get all broke up," say Rosie Giraffe.

"That much money it should last forever," I figure.

35   "My father'd buy it for me if I wanted it."

"Your father, my ass," say Rosie Giraffe getting a chance to finally push Mercedes.

"Must be rich people shop here," say Q.T.

---

4. Framed sheet or pad of paper designed to protect a desktop from excess ink.

"You are a very bright boy," say Flyboy. "What was your first clue?" And he rap him on the head with the back of his knuckles, since Q.T. the only one he could get away with. Though Q.T. liable to come up behind you years later and get his licks in when you half expect it.

"What I want to know is," I says to Miss Moore though I never talk to her, I wouldn't give the bitch that satisfaction, "is how much a real boat costs? I figure a thousand'd get you a yacht any day."

"Why don't you check that out," she says, "and report back to the group?" 40 Which really pains my ass. If you gonna mess up a perfectly good swim day least you could do is have some answers. "Let's go in," she say like she got something up her sleeve. Only she don't lead the way. So me and Sugar turn the corner to where the entrance is, but when we get there I kinda hang back. Not that I'm scared, what's there to be afraid of, just a toy store. But I feel funny, shame. But what I got to be shamed about? Got as much right to go in as anybody. But somehow I can't seem to get hold of the door, so I step away for Sugar to lead. But she hangs back too. And I look at her and she looks at me and this is ridiculous. I mean, damn, I have never ever been shy about doing nothing or going nowhere. But then Mercedes steps up and then Rosie Giraffe and Big Butt crowd in behind and shove, and next thing we all stuffed into the doorway with only Mercedes squeezing past us, smoothing out her jumper and walking right down the aisle. Then the rest of us tumble in like a glued-together jigsaw done all wrong. And people lookin at us. And it's like the time me and Sugar crashed into the Catholic church on a dare. But once we got in there and everything so hushed and holy and the candles and the bowin and the handkerchiefs on all the drooping heads, I just couldn't go through with the plan. Which was for me to run up to the altar and do a tap dance while Sugar played the nose flute and messed around in the holy water. And Sugar kept givin me the elbow. Then later teased me so bad I tied her up in the shower and turned it on and locked her in. And she'd be there till this day if Aunt Gretchen hadn't finally figured I was lyin about the boarder[5] takin a shower.

Same thing in the store. We all walkin on tiptoe and hardly touchin the games and puzzles and things. And I watched Miss Moore who is steady watchin us like she waitin for a sign. Like Mama Drewery watches the sky and sniffs the air and takes note of just how much slant is in the bird formation. Then me and Sugar bump smack into each other, so busy gazing at the toys, 'specially the sailboat. But we don't laugh and go into our fat-lady bump-stomach routine. We just stare at that price tag. Then Sugar run a finger over the whole boat. And I'm jealous and want to hit her. Maybe not her, but I sure want to punch somebody in the mouth.

"Watcha bring us here for, Miss Moore?"

"You sound angry, Sylvia. Are you mad about something?" Givin me one of them grins like she tellin a grown-up joke that never turns out to be funny. And she's lookin very closely at me like maybe she plannin to do my portrait from memory. I'm mad, but I won't give her that satisfaction. So I slouch around the store bein very bored and say, "Let's go."

---

5. Tenant in another person's house.

Me and Sugar at the back of the train watchin the tracks whizzin by large then small then gettin gobbled up in the dark. I'm thinkin about this tricky toy I saw in the store. A clown that somersaults on a bar then does chin-ups just cause you yank lightly at his leg. Cost $35. I could see me askin my mother for a $35 birthday clown. "You wanna who that costs what?" she'd say, cocking her head to the side to get a better view of the hole in my head. Thirty-five dollars could buy new bunk beds for Junior and Gretchen's boy. Thirty-five dollars and the whole household could go visit Granddaddy Nelson in the country. Thirty-five dollars would pay for the rent and the piano bill too. Who are these people that spend that much for performing clowns and $1,000 for toy sailboats? What kinda work they do and how they live and how come we ain't in on it? Where we are is who we are, Miss Moore always pointin out. But it don't necessarily have to be that way, she always adds then waits for somebody to say that poor people have to wake up and demand their share of the pie and don't none of us know what kind of pie she talkin about in the first damn place. But she ain't so smart cause I still got her four dollars from the taxi and she sure ain't gettin it. Messin up my day with this shit. Sugar nudges me in my pocket and winks.

45   Miss Moore lines us up in front of the mailbox where we started from, seem like years ago, and I got a headache for thinkin so hard. And we lean all over each other so we can hold up under the draggy-ass lecture she always finishes us off with at the end before we thank her for borin us to tears. But she just looks at us like she readin tea leaves. Finally she say, "Well, what did you think of F.A.O. Schwarz?"[6]

Rosie Giraffe mumbles, "White folks crazy."

"I'd like to go there again when I get my birthday money," says Mercedes, and we shove her out the pack so she has to lean on the mailbox by herself.

"I'd like a shower. Tiring day," say Flyboy.

Then Sugar surprises me by sayin, "You know, Miss Moore, I don't think all of us here put together eat in a year what that sailboat costs." And Miss Moore lights up like somebody goosed her. "And?" she say, urging Sugar on. Only I'm standin on her foot so she don't continue.

50   "Imagine for a minute what kind of society it is in which some people can spend on a toy what it would cost to feed a family of six or seven. What do you think?"

"I think," say Sugar pushing me off her feet like she never done before, cause I whip her ass in a minute, "that this is not much of a democracy if you ask me. Equal chance to pursue happiness means an equal crack at the dough, don't it?" Miss Moore is besides herself and I am disgusted with Sugar's treachery. So I stand on her foot one more time to see if she'll shove me. She shuts up, and Miss Moore looks at me, sorrowfully I'm thinkin. And somethin weird is goin on, I can feel it in my chest.

"Anybody else learn anything today?" lookin dead at me.

I walk away and Sugar has to run to catch up and don't even seem to notice when I shrug her arm off my shoulder.

"Well, we got four dollars anyway," she says.

---

6. Manhattan toy store (founded 1862), one of the world's largest and oldest, known for its expensive, one-of-a-kind offerings.

"Uh hunh."

"We could go to Hascombs and get half a chocolate layer and then go to the Sunset and still have plenty money for potato chips and ice-cream sodas."

"Uh hunh."

"Race you to Hascombs," she say.

We start down the block and she gets ahead which is O.K. by me cause I'm goin to the West End and then over to the Drive to think this day through. She can run if she want to and even run faster. But ain't nobody gonna beat me at nuthin.

1972

QUESTIONS

1. How does Sylvia feel about Miss Moore, and why? How do you know? Do her feelings change over the course of the story?
2. What lesson does Miss Moore seem to want the children to learn? What lesson does Sylvia seem to learn?
3. In terms of these lessons and THE LESSON as a whole, what might be interesting and significant about the fact that the children visit a toy store? about each of the three items they encounter there?

AUTHORS ON THEIR WORK

TONI CADE BAMBARA (1939–95)

From "How She Came by Her Name" (1996)*

I went to the library and read a bunch of [short-story] collections and noticed that the voice was consistent, but it was a boring and monotonous voice. Oh, your voice is supposed to be consistent in a collection, I figured. Then I pulled out a lot of stories that had a young protagonist-narrator because that voice is kind of consistent—a young, tough, compassionate girl. [. . .]

[. . .] The book [Gorilla, My Love] came out, and I never dreamed that such a big fuss would be made. "Oh, Gorilla, My Love, what a radical use of dialect! What a bold, political angle on linguistics!" At first I felt like a fraud. It didn't have anything to do with a political stance. I just thought people lived and moved around in this particular language system. It is also the language system I tend to remember childhood in. This is the language many of us speak. It just seemed polite to handle the characters in this mode.

*"How She Came by Her Name: An Interview with Louis Massiah." *Deep Sightings and Rescue Missions: Fiction, Essays, and Conversations*, edited by Toni Morrison, Pantheon Books, 1996, pp. 201–45.

ALICE MUNRO
(b. 1931)

Boys and Girls

Described by novelist Jonathan Franzen as having "a strong claim to being the best fiction writer now working in North America" and by the committee that awarded her the 2013 Nobel Prize in Literature as a "master of the contemporary short story," Alice Munro today enjoys an enviably high reputation. That was long in coming and unexpected for a girl raised during the Great Depression and World War II, on a farm in southwestern Ontario—that unglamorous terrain she has since so vividly memorialized in her fiction. She began publishing stories while attending the University of Western Ontario. But when her two-year scholarship ran out, she left the university, married James Munro, and moved first to Vancouver and then to Victoria, where the couple raised three daughters. Though her stories appeared sporadically during the 1950s, it was not until 1968 that then-thirty-eight-year-old Munro published her first book and won the first of multiple Governor General's Awards, Canada's highest literary prize. Divorced and remarried, Munro returned to Ontario and began regularly publishing collections including *Something I've Been Meaning to Tell You* (1974), *The Progress of Love* (1986), *Open Secrets* (1994), the Booker Prize–winning *View from Castle Rock* (2006), and *Dear Life* (2012). One reason Munro has not achieved the wide fame many believe she merits is her focus on short fiction: The one work she published as a novel, *Lives of Girls and Women* (1971), is in fact a series of interlinked stories.

M y father was a fox farmer. That is, he raised silver foxes, in pens; and in the fall and early winter, when their fur was prime, he killed them and skinned them and sold their pelts to the Hudson's Bay Company or the Montreal Fur Traders. These companies supplied us with heroic calendars to hang, one on each side of the kitchen door. Against a background of cold blue sky and black pine forests and treacherous northern rivers, plumed adventurers planted the flags of England or of France; magnificent savages bent their backs to the portage.

For several weeks before Christmas, my father worked after supper in the cellar of our house. The cellar was white-washed, and lit by a hundred-watt bulb over the worktable. My brother Laird and I sat on the top step and watched. My father removed the pelt inside-out from the body of the fox, which looked surprisingly small, mean and rat-like, deprived of its arrogant weight of fur. The naked, slippery bodies were collected in a sack and buried at the dump. One time the hired man, Henry Bailey, had taken a swipe at me with this sack, saying, "Christmas present!" My mother thought that was not funny. In fact she disliked the whole pelting operation—that was what the killing, skinning, and preparation of the furs was called—and wished it did not have to take place in the house. There was the smell. After the pelt had been stretched inside-out on a long board my father scraped away delicately, removing the little clotted webs of blood vessels, the bubbles of fat; the smell of blood and animal fat, with the strong primitive odour of the fox itself, penetrated all parts of the house. I found it reassuringly seasonal, like the smell of oranges and pine needles.

Henry Bailey suffered from bronchial troubles. He would cough and cough until his narrow face turned scarlet, and his light blue, derisive eyes filled up with tears; then he took the lid off the stove, and, standing well back, shot out a great clot of phlegm—hsss—straight into the heart of the flames. We admired him for this performance and for his ability to make his stomach growl at will, and for his laughter, which was full of high whistlings and gurglings and involved the whole faulty machinery of his chest. It was sometimes hard to tell what he was laughing at, and always possible that it might be us.

After we had been sent to bed we could still smell fox and still hear Henry's laugh, but these things, reminders of the warm, safe, brightly lit downstairs world, seemed lost and diminished, floating on the stale cold air upstairs. We were afraid at night in the winter. We were not afraid of *outside* though this was the time of year when snowdrifts curled around our house like sleeping whales and the wind harassed us all night, coming up from the buried fields, the frozen swamp, with its old bugbear chorus of threats and misery. We were afraid of *inside*, the room where we slept. At this time the upstairs of our house was not finished. A brick chimney went up one wall. In the middle of the floor was a square hole, with a wooden railing around it; that was where the stairs came up. On the other side of the stairwell were the things that nobody had any use for any more—a soldiery roll of linoleum, standing on end, a wicker baby carriage, a fern basket, china jugs and basins with cracks in them, a picture of the Battle of Balaclava,[1] very sad to look at. I had told Laird, as soon as he was old enough to understand such things, that bats and skeletons lived over there; whenever a man escaped from the county jail, twenty miles away, I imagined that he had somehow let himself in the window and was hiding behind the linoleum. But we had rules to keep us safe. When the light was on, we were safe as long as we did not step off the square of worn carpet which defined our bedroom-space; when the light was off no place was safe but the beds themselves. I had to turn out the light kneeling on the end of my bed, and stretching as far as I could to reach the cord.

In the dark we lay on our beds, our narrow life rafts, and fixed our eyes on the faint light coming up the stairwell, and sang songs. Laird sang "Jingle Bells," which he would sing any time, whether it was Christmas or not, and I sang "Danny Boy." I loved the sound of my own voice, frail and supplicating, rising in the dark. We could make out the tall frosted shapes of the windows now, gloomy and white. When I came to the part, *When I am dead, as dead I well may be*— a fit of shivering caused not by the cold sheets but by pleasurable emotion almost silenced me. *You'll kneel and say, an Ave there above me*—What was an Ave? Every day I forgot to find out.

Laird went straight from singing to sleep. I could hear his long, satisfied, bubbly breaths. Now for the time that remained to me, the most perfectly

---

1. Indecisive Crimean War battle fought on October 25, 1854, famous for the Charge of the Light Brigade.

private and perhaps the best time of the whole day, I arranged myself tightly under the covers and went on with one of the stories I was telling myself from night to night. These stories were about myself, when I had grown a little older; they took place in a world that was recognizably mine, yet one that presented opportunities for courage, boldness and self-sacrifice, as mine never did. I rescued people from a bombed building (it discouraged me that the real war[2] had gone on so far away from Jubilee). I shot two rabid wolves who were menacing the schoolyard (the teachers cowered terrified at my back). I rode a fine horse spiritedly down the main street of Jubilee, acknowledging the townspeople's gratitude for some yet-to-be-worked-out piece of heroism (nobody ever rode a horse there, except King Billy in the Orangemen's Day[3] parade). There was always riding and shooting in these stories, though I had only been on a horse twice—bareback because we did not own a saddle—and the second time I had slid right around and dropped under the horse's feet; it had stepped placidly over me. I really was learning to shoot, but I could not hit anything yet, not even tin cans on fence posts.

Alive, the foxes inhabited a world my father made for them. It was surrounded by a high guard fence, like a medieval town, with a gate that was padlocked at night. Along the streets of this town were ranged large, sturdy pens. Each of them had a real door that a man could go through, a wooden ramp along the wire, for the foxes to run up and down on, and a kennel—something like a clothes chest with airholes—where they slept and stayed in winter and had their young. There were feeding and watering dishes attached to the wire in such a way that they could be emptied and cleaned from the outside. The dishes were made of old tin cans, and the ramps and kennels of odds and ends of old lumber. Everything was tidy and ingenious; my father was tirelessly inventive and his favourite book in the world was *Robinson Crusoe*.[4] He had fitted a tin drum on a wheelbarrow, for bringing water down to the pens. This was my job in summer, when the foxes had to have water twice a day. Between nine and ten o'clock in the morning, and again after supper, I filled the drum at the pump and trundled it down through the barnyard to the pens, where I parked it, and filled my watering can and went along the streets. Laird came too, with his little cream and green gardening can, filled too full and knocking against his legs and slopping water on his canvas shoes. I had the real watering can, my father's, though I could only carry it three-quarters full.

The foxes all had names, which were printed on a tin plate and hung beside their doors. They were not named when they were born, but when they survived the first year's pelting and were added to the breeding stock. Those my father had named were called names like Prince, Bob, Wally and Betty. Those I had named were called Star or Turk, or Maureen or Diana. Laird named one Maud

2. World War II (1939–45).
3. The Orange Society is an Irish Protestant group named after William of Orange, who, as King William III of England, defeated the Catholic James II. The society sponsors an annual procession on July 12 to commemorate the victory of William III at the Battle of the Boyne (1690).
4. Novel (1719) by Daniel Defoe about a man shipwrecked on a desert island; it goes into great detail about the ingenious contraptions he fashions from simple materials.

after a hired girl we had when he was little, one Harold after a boy at school, and one Mexico, he did not say why.

Naming them did not make pets out of them, or anything like it. Nobody but my father ever went into the pens, and he had twice had blood-poisoning from bites. When I was bringing them their water they prowled up and down on the paths they had made inside their pens, barking seldom—they saved that for nighttime, when they might get up a chorus of community frenzy—but always watching me, their eyes burning, clear gold, in their pointed, malevolent faces. They were beautiful for their delicate legs and heavy, aristocratic tails and the bright fur sprinkled on dark down their backs—which gave them their name—but especially for their faces, drawn exquisitely sharp in pure hostility, and their golden eyes.

Besides carrying water I helped my father when he cut the long grass, and the lamb's quarter and flowering money-musk, that grew between the pens. He cut with the scythe and I raked into piles. Then he took a pitchfork and threw freshcut grass all over the top of the pens, to keep the foxes cooler and shade their coats, which were browned by too much sun. My father did not talk to me unless it was about the job we were doing. In this he was quite different from my mother, who, if she was feeling cheerful, would tell me all sorts of things—the name of a dog she had had when she was a little girl, the names of boys she had gone out with later on when she was grown up, and what certain dresses of hers had looked like—she could not imagine now what had become of them. Whatever thoughts and stories my father had were private, and I was shy of him and would never ask him questions. Nevertheless I worked willingly under his eyes, and with a feeling of pride. One time a feed salesman came down into the pens to talk to him and my father said, "Like to have you meet my new hired man." I turned away and raked furiously, red in the face with pleasure.

"Could of fooled me," said the salesman. "I thought it was only a girl."

After the grass was cut, it seemed suddenly much later in the year. I walked on stubble in the earlier evening, aware of the reddening skies, the entering silences, of fall. When I wheeled the tank out of the gate and put the padlock on, it was almost dark. One night at this time I saw my mother and father standing talking on the little rise of ground we called the gangway, in front of the barn. My father had just come from the meathouse; he had his stiff bloody apron on, and a pail of cut-up meat in his hand.

It was an odd thing to see my mother down at the barn. She did not often come out of the house unless it was to do something—hang out the wash or dig potatoes in the garden. She looked out of place, with her bare lumpy legs, not touched by the sun, her apron still on and damp across the stomach from the supper dishes. Her hair was tied up in a kerchief, wisps of it falling out. She would tie her hair up like this in the morning, saying she did not have time to do it properly, and it would stay tied up all day. It was true, too; she really did not have time. These days our back porch was piled with baskets of peaches and grapes and pears, bought in town, and onions and tomatoes and cucumbers grown at home, all waiting to be made into jelly and jam and preserves, pickles and chili sauce. In the kitchen there was a fire in the stove all day, jars clinked in boiling water, sometimes a cheesecloth bag was strung on a pole between two chairs, straining blue-black grape pulp for jelly. I was given jobs to do and I would sit at the table peeling peaches that had been soaked in the hot water, or cutting up onions, my eyes smarting and streaming. As soon as I was done I ran out of the house, trying to get out of earshot before my mother thought of what she wanted me to do next. I hated the hot dark kitchen in summer, the green blinds and the flypapers, the same old oilcloth table and wavy mirror and bumpy linoleum. My mother was too tired and preoccupied to talk to me, she had no heart to tell about the Normal School Graduation Dance; sweat trickled over her face and she was always counting under her breath, pointing at jars, dumping cups of sugar. It seemed to me that work in the house was endless, dreary and peculiarly depressing; work done out of doors, and in my father's service, was ritualistically important.

I wheeled the tank up to the barn, where it was kept, and I heard my mother saying, "Wait till Laird gets a little bigger, then you'll have a real help."

15   What my father said I did not hear. I was pleased by the way he stood listening, politely as he would to a salesman or a stranger, but with an air of wanting to get on with his real work. I felt my mother had no business down here and I wanted him to feel the same way. What did she mean about Laird? He was no help to anybody. Where was he now? Swinging himself sick on the swing, going around in circles, or trying to catch caterpillars. He never once stayed with me till I was finished.

"And then I can use her more in the house," I heard my mother say. She had a dead-quiet, regretful way of talking about me that always made me uneasy. "I just get my back turned and she runs off. It's not like I had a girl in the family at all."

I went and sat on a feed bag in the corner of the barn, not wanting to appear when this conversation was going on. My mother, I felt, was not to be trusted. She was kinder than my father and more easily fooled, but you could not depend on her, and the real reasons for the things she said and did were not to be known. She loved me, and she sat up late at night making a dress of the difficult style I wanted, for me to wear when school started, but she was also my enemy. She was always plotting. She was plotting now to get me to stay in the house more, although she knew I hated it (*because* she knew I hated it) and keep me from working for my father. It seemed to me she would do this simply out of perversity, and to try her power. It did not occur to me that she could be lonely, or jealous. No grown-up could be; they were too fortunate. I sat and kicked my heels monotonously against a feed bag, raising dust, and did not come out till she was gone.

At any rate, I did not expect my father to pay any attention to what she said. Who could imagine Laird doing my work—Laird remembering the padlock and cleaning out the watering-dishes with a leaf on the end of a stick, or even wheeling the tank without it tumbling over? It showed how little my mother knew about the way things really were.

I have forgotten to say what the foxes were fed. My father's bloody apron reminded me. They were fed horsemeat. At this time most farmers still kept horses, and when a horse got too old to work, or broke a leg or got down and would not get up, as they sometimes did, the owner would call my father, and he and Henry went out to the farm in the truck. Usually they shot and butchered the horse there, paying the farmer from five to twelve dollars. If they had already too much meat on hand, they would bring the horse back alive, and keep it for a few days or weeks in our stable, until the meat was needed. After the war the farmers were buying tractors and gradually getting rid of horses altogether, so it sometimes happened that we got a good healthy horse, that there was just no use for any more. If this happened in the winter we might keep the horse in our stable till spring, for we had plenty of hay and if there was a lot of snow—and the plow did not always get our road cleared—it was convenient to be able to go to town with a horse and cutter.[5]

The winter I was eleven years old we had two horses in the stable. We did not know what names they had had before, so we called them Mack and Flora. Mack was an old black workhorse, sooty and indifferent. Flora was a sorrel mare, a driver. We took them both out in the cutter. Mack was slow and easy to handle. Flora was given to fits of violent alarm, veering at cars and even at other horses, but we loved her speed and high-stepping, her general air of gallantry and abandon. On Saturdays we went down to the stable and as soon as we opened the door on its cosy, animal-smelling darkness Flora threw up her head, rolled her eyes, whinnied despairingly and pulled herself through a crisis of nerves on the spot. It was not safe to go into her stall; she would kick.

This winter also I began to hear a great deal more on the theme my mother had sounded when she had been talking in front of the barn. I no longer felt safe. It seemed that in the minds of the people around me there was a steady undercurrent of thought, not to be deflected, on this one subject. The word *girl* had formerly seemed to me innocent and unburdened, like the world *child*; now it appeared that it was no such thing. A girl was not, as I had supposed, simply what I was; it was what I had to become. It was a definition, always touched with emphasis, with reproach and disappointment. Also it was a joke on me. Once Laird and I were fighting, and for the first time ever I had to use all my strength against him; even so, he caught and pinned my arm for a moment, really hurting me. Henry saw this, and laughed, saying, "Oh, that there Laird's gonna show you, one of these days!" Laird was getting a lot bigger. But I was getting bigger too.

My grandmother came to stay with us for a few weeks and I heard other things. "Girls don't slam doors like that." "Girls keep their knees together when they sit down." And worse still, when I asked some questions, "That's none of girls' business." I continued to slam the doors and sit as awkwardly as possible, thinking that by such measures I kept myself free.

When spring came, the horses were let out in the barnyard. Mack stood against the barn wall trying to scratch his neck and haunches, but Flora trotted up and down and reared at the fences, clattering her hooves against the rails. Snow drifts dwindled quickly, revealing the hard grey and brown earth, the familiar rise and fall of the ground, plain and bare after the fantastic landscape of winter. There was a great feeling of opening-out, of release. We just wore rubbers now, over our shoes; our feet felt ridiculously light. One Saturday we went out to the stable and found all the doors open, letting in the unaccustomed sunlight and fresh air. Henry was there, just idling around looking at his collection of calendars which were tacked up behind the stalls in a part of the stable my mother had probably never seen.

5. Small, light sleigh.

"Come to say goodbye to your old friend Mack?" Henry said. "Here, you give him a taste of oats." He poured some oats into Laird's cupped hands and Laird went to feed Mack. Mack's teeth were in bad shape. He ate very slowly, patiently shifting the oats around in his mouth, trying to find a stump of a molar to grind it on. "Poor old Mack," said Henry mournfully. "When a horse's teeth's gone, he's gone. That's about the way."

25   "Are you going to shoot him today?" I said. Mack and Flora had been in the stable so long I had almost forgotten they were going to be shot.

Henry didn't answer me. Instead he started to sing in a high, trembly, mocking-sorrowful voice, *Oh, there's no more work, for poor Uncle Ned, he's gone where the good darkies go.*[6] Mack's thick, blackish tongue worked diligently at Laird's hand. I went out before the song was ended and sat down on the gangway.

I had never seen them shoot a horse, but I knew where it was done. Last summer Laird and I had come upon a horse's entrails before they were buried. We had thought it was a big black snake, coiled up in the sun. That was around in the field that ran up beside the barn. I thought that if we went inside the barn, and found a wide crack or knothole to look through we would be able to see them do it. It was not something I wanted to see; just the same, if a thing really happened, it was better to see it, and know.

My father came down from the house, carrying the gun.

"What are you doing here?" he said.

30   "Nothing."

"Go on up and play around the house."

He sent Laird out of the stable. I said to Laird, "Do you want to see them shoot Mack?" and without waiting for an answer led him around to the front door of the barn, opened it carefully, and went in. "Be quiet or they'll hear us," I said. We could hear Henry and my father talking in the stable, then the heavy, shuffling steps of Mack being backed out of his stall.

In the loft it was cold and dark. Thin, crisscrossed beams of sunlight fell through the cracks. The hay was low. It was a rolling country, hills and hollows, slipping under our feet. About four feet up was a beam going around the walls. We piled hay up in one corner and I boosted Laird up and hoisted myself. The beam was not very wide; we crept along it with our hands flat on the barn walls. There were plenty of knotholes, and I found one that gave me the view I wanted—a corner of the barnyard, the gate, part of the field. Laird did not have a knothole and began to complain.

I showed him a widened crack between two boards. "Be quiet and wait. If they hear you you'll get us in trouble."

35   My father came in sight carrying the gun. Henry was leading Mack by the halter. He dropped it and took out his cigarette papers and tobacco; he rolled cigarettes for my father and himself. While this was going on Mack nosed around in the old, dead grass along the fence. Then my father opened the gate and they took Mack through. Henry led Mack away from the path to a patch of ground and they talked together, not loud enough for us to hear. Mack again began searching for a mouthful of fresh grass, which was not to be found. My

6. Lines from the Stephen Foster (1826–64) song "Old Uncle Ned."

father walked away in a straight line, and stopped short at a distance which seemed to suit him. Henry was walking away from Mack too, but sideways, still negligently holding on to the halter. My father raised the gun and Mack looked up as if he had noticed something and my father shot him.

Mack did not collapse at once but swayed, lurched sideways and fell, first on his side; then he rolled over on his back and, amazingly, kicked his legs for a few seconds in the air. At this Henry laughed, as if Mack had done a trick for him. Laird, who had drawn a long, groaning breath of surprise when the shot was fired, said out loud, "He's not dead." And it seemed to me it might be true. But his legs stopped, he rolled on his side again, his muscles quivered and sank. The two men walked over and looked at him in a businesslike way; they bent down and examined his forehead where the bullet had gone in, and now I saw his blood on the brown grass.

"Now they just skin him and cut him up," I said. "Let's go." My legs were a little shaky and I jumped gratefully down into the hay. "Now you've seen how they shoot a horse," I said in a congratulatory way, as if I had seen it many times before. "Let's see if any barn cat's had kittens in the hay." Laird jumped. He seemed young and obedient again. Suddenly I remembered how, when he was little, I had brought him into the barn and told him to climb the ladder to the top beam. That was in the spring, too, when the hay was low. I had done it out of a need for excitement, a desire for something to happen so that I could tell about it. He was wearing a little bulky brown and white checked coat, made down from one of mine. He went all the way up, just as I told him, and sat down on the top beam with the hay far below him on one side, and the barn floor and some old machinery on the other. Then I ran screaming to my father, "Laird's up on the top beam!" My father came, my mother came, my father went up the ladder talking very quietly and brought Laird down under his arm, at which my mother leaned against the ladder and began to cry. They said to me, "Why weren't you watching him?" but nobody ever knew the truth. Laird did not know enough to tell. But whenever I saw the brown and white checked coat hanging in the closet, or at the bottom of the rag bag, which was where it ended up, I felt a weight in my stomach, the sadness of unexorcized guilt.

I looked at Laird who did not even remember this, and I did not like the look on this thin, winter-pale face. His expression was not frightened or upset, but remote, concentrating. "Listen," I said, in an unusually bright and friendly voice, "you aren't going to tell, are you?"

"No," he said absently.

"Promise."

"Promise," he said. I grabbed the hand behind his back to make sure he was not crossing his fingers. Even so, he might have a nightmare; it might come out that way. I decided I had better work hard to get all thoughts of what he had seen out of his mind—which, it seemed to me, could not hold very many things at a time. I got some money I had saved and that afternoon we went into Jubilee and saw a show, with Judy Canova,[7] at which we both laughed a great deal. After that I thought it would be all right.

40

7. American comedian (1913–83) best known for her yodeling in hillbilly movies of the 1940s.

Two weeks later I knew they were going to shoot Flora. I knew from the night before, when I heard my mother ask if the hay was holding out all right, and my father said, "Well, after to-morrow there'll just be the cow, and we should be able to put her out to grass in another week." So I knew it was Flora's turn in the morning.

This time I didn't think of watching it. That was something to see just one time. I had not thought about it very often since, but sometimes when I was busy, working at school, or standing in front of the mirror combing my hair and wondering if I would be pretty when I grew up, the whole scene would flash into my mind: I would see the easy, practised way my father raised the gun, and hear Henry laughing when Mack kicked his legs in the air. I did not have any great feeling of horror and opposition, such as a city child might have had; I was too used to seeing the death of animals as a necessity by which we lived. Yet I felt a little ashamed, and there was a new wariness, a sense of holding-off, in my attitude to my father and his work.

It was a fine day, and we were going around the yard picking up tree branches that had been torn off in winter storms. This was something we had been told to do, and also we wanted to use them to make a teepee. We heard Flora whinny, and then my father's voice and Henry's shouting, and we ran down to the barnyard to see what was going on.

45   The stable door was open. Henry had just brought Flora out, and she had broken away from him. She was running free in the barnyard, from one end to the other. We climbed up on the fence. It was exciting to see her running, whinnying, going up on her hind legs, prancing and threatening like a horse in a Western movie, an unbroken ranch horse, though she was just an old driver, an old sorrel mare. My father and Henry ran after her and tried to grab the dangling halter. They tried to work her into a corner, and they had almost succeeded when she made a run between them, wild-eyed, and disappeared around the corner of the barn. We heard the rails clatter down as she got over the fence, and Henry yelled, "She's into the field now!"

That meant she was in the long L-shaped field that ran up by the house. If she got around the center, heading towards the lane, the gate was open; the truck had been driven into the field this morning. My father shouted to me, because I was on the other side of the fence, nearest the lane, "Go shut the gate!"

I could run very fast. I ran across the garden, past the tree where our swing was hung, and jumped across a ditch into the lane. There was the open gate. She had not got out, I could not see her up on the road; she must have run to the other end of the field. The gate was heavy. I lifted it out of the gravel and carried it across the roadway. I had it half-way across when she came in sight, galloping straight towards me. There was just time to get the chain on. Laird came scrambling through the ditch to help me.

Instead of shutting the gate, I opened it as wide as I could. I did not make any decision to do this, it was just what I did. Flora never slowed down; she galloped straight past me, and Laird jumped up and down, yelling, "Shut it, shut it!" even after it was too late. My father and Henry appeared in the field a moment too late to see what I had done. They only saw Flora heading for the township road. They would think I had not got there in time.

They did not waste any time asking about it. They went back to the barn and got the gun and the knives they used, and put these in the truck; then they turned the truck around and came bouncing up the field toward us. Laird called to them, "Let me go too, let me go too!" and Henry stopped the truck and they took him in. I shut the gate after they were all gone.

I supposed Laird would tell. I wondered what would happen to me. I had never disobeyed my father before, and I could not understand why I had done it. Flora would not really get away. They would catch up with her in the truck. Or if they did not catch her this morning somebody would see her and telephone us this afternoon or tomorrow. There was no wild country here for her to run to, only farms. What was more, my father had paid for her, we needed the meat to feed the foxes, we needed the foxes to make our living. All I had done was make more work for my father who worked hard enough already. And when my father found out about it he was not going to trust me any more, he would know that I was not entirely on his side. I was on Flora's side, and that made me no use to anybody, not even to her. Just the same, I did not regret it; when she came running at me and I held the gate open, that was the only thing I could do.

I went back to the house, and my mother said, "What's all the commotion?" I told her that Flora had kicked down the fence and got away. "Your poor father," she said, "now he'll have to go chasing over the countryside. Well, there isn't any use planning dinner before one." She put up the ironing board. I wanted to tell her, but thought better of it and went upstairs and sat on my bed.

Lately I had been trying to make my part of the room fancy, spreading the bed with old lace curtains, and fixing myself a dressing-table with some leftovers of cretonne for a skirt. I planned to put up some kind of barricade between my bed and Laird's, to keep my section separate from his. In the sunlight, the lace curtains were just dusty rags. We did not sing at night any more. One night when I was singing Laird said, "You sound silly," and I went right on but the next night I did not start. There was not so much need to anyway, we were no longer afraid. We knew it was just old furniture over there, old jumble and confusion. We did not keep to the rules. I still stayed awake after Laird was asleep and told myself stories, but even in these stories something different was happening, mysterious alterations took place. A story might start off in the old way, with a spectacular danger, a fire or wild animals, and for a while I might rescue people; then things would change around, and instead, somebody would be rescuing me. It might be a boy from our class at school, or even Mr. Campbell, our teacher, who tickled girls under the arms. And at this point the story concerned itself at great length with what I looked like—how long my hair was, and what kind of dress I had on; by the time I had these details worked out the real excitement of the story was lost.

It was later than one o'clock when the truck came back. The tarpaulin was over the back, which meant there was meat in it. My mother had to heat dinner up all over again. Henry and my father had changed from their bloody overalls into ordinary working overalls in the barn, and they washed their arms and necks and faces at the sink, and splashed water on their hair and combed it. Laird lifted his arm to show off a streak of blood. "We shot old Flora," he said, "and cut her up in fifty pieces."

"Well I don't want to hear about it," my mother said. "And don't come to my table like that."

My father made him go and wash the blood off.

We sat down and my father said grace and Henry pasted his chewing-gum on the end of his fork, the way he always did; when he took it off he would have us admire the pattern. We began to pass the bowls of steaming, overcooked vegetables. Laird looked across the table at me and said proudly, distinctly, "Anyway it was her fault Flora got away."

"What?" my father said.

"She could of shut the gate and she didn't. She just open' it up and Flora run out."

"Is that right?" my father said.

60   Everybody at the table was looking at me. I nodded, swallowing food with great difficulty. To my shame, tears flooded my eyes.

My father made a curt sound of disgust. "What did you do that for?"

I did not answer. I put down my fork and waited to be sent from the table, still not looking up.

But this did not happen. For some time nobody said anything, then Laird said matter-of-factly, "She's crying."

"Never mind," my father said. He spoke with resignation, even good humour, the words which absolved and dismissed me for good. "She's only a girl," he said.

65   I didn't protest that, even in my heart. Maybe it was true.

1964, 1968

QUESTIONS

1. Since there is only one girl character and one boy character in Boys and Girls, why do you think Alice Munro uses plural words in the title?
2. Find the two occurrences of the phrase "only a girl." Why and how does the meaning of the phrase change?
3. Why does the narrator choose not to shut the gate on Flora? What role does this act play in her initiation?

SUGGESTIONS FOR WRITING

1. Initiation stories often concern a choice to abandon or join a family, group, or community. Write an essay in which you examine the choices made by one or more of the main characters in these stories. How do such choices shape the plot of each story or either propel or demonstrate the changes characters go through?
2. A child, teenager, or adult will have different perspectives on the same situations, and initiation stories often dramatically reveal such differences in the way characters and narrators respond. Write an essay on the way the narrator's age or other aspects of narration affect your understanding of the "initiation" in one of the stories in this album.
3. Traditional cultures like that of the Masai people of East Africa have highly ritualized methods of inducting young people into adulthood. Might developed Western societies also be said to have ritual forms of initiation? Drawing evidence from at least two stories in this album, write an essay exploring how young people in modern Western societies are initiated into adulthood.
4. Choose a story from any other chapter or album in this book and write an essay explaining why it should be considered an initiation story.
5. Using any story in this album as a model, write a first-person narrative of an actual or fictional initiation into adulthood.

3 | NARRATION AND POINT OF VIEW

When we read fiction, our sense of who is telling us the story is as important as what happens. Unlike drama, in which events are acted out in front of us, fiction is always mediated or represented to us by someone else, a **narrator**. Often a reader is very aware of the **voice** of a narrator telling the story, as if the words are being spoken aloud. Commonly, stories also reveal a distinct angle of vision or perspective from which the characters, events, and other aspects are viewed. Just as the verbal quality of narration is called the voice, the visual angle is called the **focus**. Focus acts much as a camera does, choosing the direction of our gaze, the framework in which we see things. Both voice and focus are generally considered together in the term **point of view**. To understand how a story is narrated, you need to recognize both voice and focus. These shape what we know and care about as the plot unfolds, and they determine how close we feel to each character.

A story is said to be from a character's point of view, or a character is said to be a focal or focalizing character, if for the most part the action centers on that character, as if we see with that character's eyes or we watch that character closely. But the effects of narration certainly involve more than attaching a video camera to a character's head or tracking wherever the character moves. What about the spoken and unspoken words? In some stories, the narrator is a character, and we may feel as if we are overhearing his or her thoughts, whereas in other stories the narrator takes a very distant or critical view of the characters. At times a narrator seems more like a disembodied, unidentified voice. Prose fiction has many ways to convey speech and thought, so it is important to consider voice as well as focus when we try to understand the narration of a story.

Besides focus and voice, point of view encompasses more general matters of value. A story's narrator may explicitly endorse or subtly support whatever a certain character values, knows, or seeks, even when the character is absent or silent or unaware. Other narrators may treat characters and their interests with far more detachment. At the same time, the **style** and **tone** of the narrator's voice—from echoing the characters' feelings to mocking their pretentious speech or thoughts to stating their actions in formal diction—may convey clues that a character or a narrator's perspective is limited. Such discrepancies or gaps between vision and voice, intentions and understandings, or expectations and outcomes generate **irony**.

Sometimes the point of view shifts over the course of a narrative. Or the style of narration itself may change dramatically from one section to another. Bram Stoker's novel *Dracula* (1897), for example, is variously narrated through characters' journals and letters, as well as newspaper articles, ship logs, and other documents.

The point of view varies according to the narrator's position in the story and the grammatical person (for example, first or third) the narrative voice assumes.

These elements determine who is telling the story, whom it is about, and what information the reader has access to.

TYPES OF NARRATION

Third-Person Narration

A *third-person narrator* tells an unidentified listener or reader what happened, referring to all characters using the pronouns *he*, *she*, or *they*. Third-person narration is virtually always external, meaning that the narrator is not a character in the story and does not participate in its action. Even so, different types of third-person narration—omniscient, limited, and objective—provide the reader with various amounts and kinds of information about the characters.

An *omniscient* or *unlimited narrator* has access to the thoughts, perceptions, and experiences of more than one character (often of several), though such narrators usually focus selectively on a few important characters. A *limited narrator* is an external, third-person narrator who tells the story from a distinct point of view, usually that of a single character, revealing that character's thoughts and relating the action exclusively from his or her perspective. This focal character is also known as a **central consciousness**. Sometimes a limited narrator will reveal the thoughts and feelings of a small number of the characters in order to enhance the story told about the central consciousness. (Jane Austen's novel *Emma* [1815] includes a few episodes from Mr. Knightley's point of view to show what he thinks about Emma Woodhouse, the focal character, and her relationships.) Finally, an *objective narrator* does not explicitly report the characters' thoughts and feelings but may obliquely suggest them through the characters' speech and actions. Stories with objective narrators consist mostly of **dialogue** interspersed with minimal description.

First-Person Narration

Instead of using third-person narration, an author might choose to tell a story from the point of view of a *first-person narrator*. Most common is first-person singular narration, in which the narrator uses the pronoun *I*. The narrator may be a major or minor character within the story and therefore is an *internal narrator*. Notice that the first-person narrator may be telling a story mainly about someone else or about his or her own experience. Sometimes the first-person narrator addresses an **auditor**, a listener within the fiction whose possible reaction is part of the story.

One kind of narrator that is especially effective at producing irony is the *unreliable narrator*. First-person narrators may unintentionally reveal their flaws as they try to impress. Or narrators may make claims that other characters or the audience knows to be false or distorted. Some fictions are narrated by villains, insane people, fools, liars, or hypocrites. When we resist a narrator's point of view and judge his or her flaws or misperceptions, we call that narrator unreliable. This does not mean that you should dismiss everything such a narrator says, but you should be on the alert for ironies.

Less common is the first-person plural, where the narrator uses the pronoun *we*. The plural may be used effectively to express the shared perspective of a community, particularly one that is isolated, unusually close-knit, and/or highly regulated.

Nobel Laureate Kazuo Ishiguro's dystopian novel *Never Let Me Go* (2005) is a good example. Its narrator often refers to herself as "I" or addresses the reader as "you." But especially in recalling her past at a strict boarding school, she speaks in the plural, as when another student, Polly, suddenly questions one of the rules: "*We* all went silent. Miss Lucy [the teacher] didn't often get cross, but when she did, *you* certainly knew about it, and we thought for a second Polly was for it [would be punished]. But then *we* saw Miss Lucy wasn't angry, just deep in thought. *I* remember feeling furious at Polly for so stupidly breaking the unwritten rule, but at the same time, being terribly excited about what answer Miss Lucy might give" (emphasis added). Ishiguro's narrator resorts to different narrative perspectives and voices to represent the experience of both an entire community and one individual within it.

Second-Person Narration

Like narrators who refer to themselves as "we" throughout a work of fiction, *second-person narrators* who consistently speak to *you* are unusual. This technique has the effect of turning the reader into a character in the story. Jay McInerney, for example, in his novel *Bright Lights, Big City* (1984) employs the second-person voice, creating an effect similar to conversational anecdotes. But second-person narratives can instead sound much like instructional manuals or "how-to" books or like parents or other elders speaking to children.

TENSE

Along with the grammatical "person," the verb tense used has an effect on the narration of a story. Since narrative is so wrapped up in memory, most stories rely on the past tense. In contemporary fiction, however, the present tense is also frequently used. The present tense can lend an impression of immediacy, of frequent repetition, or of a dreamlike or magical state in which time seems suspended. An author might also use the present tense to create a conversational tone. Rarely, for a strange prophetic outlook, a narrator may even use the future tense, predicting what *will* happen.

NARRATOR VERSUS IMPLIED AUTHOR

As you consider how a story is being narrated, by whom, and from what point of view, how should you respond to the shifting points of view, tones of voice, and hints of critical distance or irony toward characters? Who is really shaping the story, and how do you know what is intended? Readers may answer the question "Who is telling this story?" with the name of the author. It is more accurate and practical, however, to distinguish between the narrator who presents the story and the flesh-and-blood author who wrote it, even when the two are hard to tell apart. If you are writing an essay about a short story, you do not need to research the biography of the author or find letters or interviews in which the author comments on the work. This sort of biographical information may enrich your study of the story (it can be a good critical approach), but it is not *necessary* to an understanding of the text. And yet if you only consider the narrator when you interpret a story, you may find it difficult to account for the effects of distance and irony that come from a narrator's or a character's limitations. Many critics rely on the concept of the *implied author*, not to be confused with either the flesh-and-blood person who wrote the work or the narrator who relates the words to us. Most of the time, when we ask questions about the "author" of a work, we are asking about its implied author, the perspective and values that govern the whole work, including the narrator.

Reading a story, we know that it consists of words on a page, but we imagine the narrator speaking to us, giving shape, focus, and voice to a particular history. At the same time, we recognize that the reader should not take the narrator's words as absolute truth, but rather as effects shaped by an implied author. The concept of the implied author helps keep the particulars of the real author's (naturally imperfect) personality and life out of the picture. But it also reminds us to distinguish between the act of writing the work and the imaginary utterance of "telling" the story: The narrator is *neither* the real nor the implied author.

Questions about Narration and Point of View

- Does the narrator speak in the first, second, or third person?
- Is the story narrated in the past or present tense? Does the verb tense affect your reading of it in any way?
- Does the narrator use a distinctive vocabulary, style, and tone, or is the language more standard and neutral?
- Is the narrator identified as a character, and if so, how much does he or she participate in the action?
- Does the narrator ever seem to speak to the reader directly (addressing "you") or explicitly state opinions or values?
- Do you know what every character is thinking, or only some characters, or none?
- Does the narrative voice or focus shift during the story or remain consistent?
- Do the narrator, the characters, and the reader all perceive matters in the same way, or are there differences in levels of understanding?

Because our responses to a work of fiction are largely guided by the designs and values implied in a certain way of telling the story, questions about narration and point of view can often lead to good essay topics. You might start by considering any other choices the implied author might have made and how these would change your reading of the story. As you read the stories in this chapter, imagine different voices and visions, different narrative techniques, in order to assess the specific effects of the particular types of narration and point of view. How would each story's meaning and effects change if its narrative voice or focus were different? Can you show the reader of your essay how the specific narration and point of view of a story contribute to its significant effects?

EDGAR ALLAN POE

(1809–49)

The Black Cat

Orphaned before he was three, Edgar Poe was adopted by John Allan, a wealthy businessman in Richmond, Virginia. Poe received his early schooling in Richmond and in England before a brief, unsuccessful stint at the University of Virginia. After serving for two years in the army, he was appointed to West Point in 1830 but expelled within the year for cutting classes. Living in Baltimore, Maryland, with his grandmother, aunt, and cousin Virginia (whom he married in 1835, when she was thirteen), Poe eked out a precarious living as an editor; his keen-edged reviews earned him numerous literary enemies. His two-volume *Tales of the Grotesque and Arabesque* received little critical attention when published in 1839, but his poem "The Raven" (1845) made him a literary celebrity. After his wife's death of tuberculosis in 1847, Poe, already an alcoholic, became increasingly erratic; two years later he died mysteriously in Baltimore.

For the most wild yet most homely narrative which I am about to pen, I neither expect nor solicit belief. Mad indeed would I be to expect it, in a case where my very senses reject their own evidence. Yet, mad am I not—and very surely do I not dream. But to-morrow I die, and to-day I would unburthen my soul. My immediate purpose is to place before the world, plainly, succinctly, and without comment, a series of mere household events. In their consequences, these events have terrified—have tortured—have destroyed me. Yet I will not attempt to expound them. To me, they have presented little but horror—to many they will seem less terrible than *baroques*.[1] Hereafter, perhaps, some intellect may be found which will reduce my phantasm to the commonplace—some intellect more calm, more logical, and far less excitable than my own, which will perceive, in the circumstances I detail with awe, nothing more than an ordinary succession of very natural causes and effects.

From my infancy I was noted for the docility and humanity of my disposition. My tenderness of heart was even so conspicuous as to make me the jest of my companions. I was especially fond of animals, and was indulged by my parents with a great variety of pets. With these I spent most of my time, and never was so happy as when feeding and caressing them. This peculiarity of character grew with my growth, and, in my manhood, I derived from it one of my principal sources of pleasure. To those who have cherished an affection for a faithful and sagacious dog, I need hardly be at the trouble of explaining the nature or the intensity of the gratification thus derivable. There is something in the unselfish and self-sacrificing love of a brute, which goes directly to the heart of

1. (French); characterized by grotesqueness, extravagance, flamboyance, of a kind seen in some seventeenth-century art.

him who has had frequent occasion to test the paltry friendship and gossamer fidelity of mere *Man*.

I married early, and was happy to find in my wife a disposition not uncongenial with my own. Observing my partiality for domestic pets, she lost no opportunity of procuring those of the most agreeable kind. We had birds, gold-fish, a fine dog, rabbits, a small monkey, and a *cat*.

This latter was a remarkably large and beautiful animal, entirely black, and sagacious to an astonishing degree. In speaking of his intelligence, my wife, who at heart was not a little tinctured with superstition, made frequent allusions to the ancient popular notion, which regarded all black cats as witches in disguise. Not that she was ever *serious* upon this point—and I mention the matter at all for no better reason than that it happens, just now, to be remembered.

5   Pluto[2]—this was the cat's name—was my favorite pet and playmate. I alone fed him, and he attended me wherever I went about the house. It was even with difficulty that I could prevent him from following me through the streets.

Our friendship lasted, in this manner, for several years, during which my general temperament and character—through the instrumentality of the Fiend Intemperance[3]—had (I blush to confess it) experienced a radical alteration for the worse. I grew, day by day, more moody, more irritable, more regardless of the feelings of others. I suffered myself to use intemperate language to my wife. At length, I even offered her personal violence. My pets, of course, were made to feel the change in my disposition. I not only neglected, but ill-used them. For Pluto, however, I still retained sufficient regard to restrain me from maltreating him, as I made no scruple of maltreating the rabbits, the monkey, or even the dog, when, by accident, or through affection, they came in my way. But my disease grew upon me—for what disease is like Alcohol!—and at length even Pluto, who was now becoming old, and consequently somewhat peevish—even Pluto began to experience the effects of my ill temper.

One night, returning home, much intoxicated, from one of my haunts about town, I fancied that the cat avoided my presence. I seized him; when, in his fright at my violence, he inflicted a slight wound upon my hand with his teeth. The fury of a demon instantly possessed me. I knew myself no longer. My original soul seemed, at once, to take its flight from my body; and a more than fiendish malevolence, gin-nurtured, thrilled every fibre of my frame. I took from my waistcoat-pocket a penknife, opened it, grasped the poor beast by the throat, and deliberately cut one of its eyes from the socket! I blush, I burn, I shudder, while I pen the damnable atrocity.

When reason returned with the morning—when I had slept off the fumes of the night's debauch—I experienced a sentiment half of horror, half of remorse, for the crime of which I had been guilty; but it was, at best, a feeble and equivo-

2. Name of the Greek god of the underworld. (The planet Pluto was not discovered until the twentieth century.)

3. Here meaning especially indulgence in alcoholic drink. By 1833, there were six thousand temperance societies across the United States, and so-called temperance tales detailing alcohol's evil effects were widely distributed.

cal feeling, and the soul remained untouched. I again plunged into excess, and soon drowned in wine all memory of the deed.

In the meantime the cat slowly recovered. The socket of the lost eye presented, it is true, a frightful appearance, but he no longer appeared to suffer any pain. He went about the house as usual, but, as might be expected, fled in extreme terror at my approach. I had so much of my old heart left, as to be at first grieved by this evident dislike on the part of a creature which had once so loved me. But this feeling soon gave place to irritation. And then came, as if to my final and irrevocable overthrow, the spirit of PERVERSENESS. Of this spirit philosophy takes no account. Yet I am not more sure that my soul lives, than I am that perverseness is one of the primitive impulses of the human heart—one of the indivisible primary faculties, or sentiments, which give direction to the character of Man. Who has not, a hundred times, found himself committing a vile or a silly action, for no other reason than because he knows he should *not*? Have we not a perpetual inclination, in the teeth of our best judgment, to violate that which is *Law*, merely because we understand it to be such? This spirit of perverseness, I say, came to my final overthrow. It was this unfathomable longing of the soul to *vex itself*—to offer violence to its own nature—to do wrong for the wrong's sake only—that urged me to continue and finally to consummate the injury I had inflicted upon the unoffending brute. One morning, in cool blood, I slipped a noose around its neck and hung it to the limb of a tree—hung it with the tears streaming from my eyes, and with the bitterest remorse at my heart—hung it *because* I knew that it had loved me, and *because* I felt it had given me no reason of offence;—hung it *because* I knew that in so doing I was committing a sin—a deadly sin that would so jeopardize my immortal soul as to place it—if such a thing were possible—even beyond the reach of the infinite mercy of the Most Merciful and Most Terrible God.

On the night of the day on which this cruel deed was done, I was aroused 10 from sleep by the cry of fire. The curtains of my bed were in flames. The whole house was blazing. It was with great difficulty that my wife, a servant, and myself, made our escape from the conflagration. The destruction was complete. My entire worldly wealth was swallowed up, and I resigned myself thenceforward to despair.

I am above the weakness of seeking to establish a sequence of cause and effect, between the disaster and the atrocity. But I am detailing a chain of facts—and wish not to leave even a possible link imperfect. On the day succeeding the fire, I visited the ruins. The walls, with one exception, had fallen in. This exception was found in a compartment wall, not very thick, which stood about the middle of the house, and against which had rested the head of my bed. The plastering had here, in great measure, resisted the action of the fire—a fact which I attributed to its having been recently spread. About this wall a dense crowd were collected, and many persons seemed to be examining a particular portion of it with very minute and eager attention. The words "strange!" "singular!" and other similar expressions, excited my curiosity. I approached and saw, as if graven in *bas-relief*[4] upon the white surface, the figure of a gigantic *cat*.

4. Sculpture or sculptural technique in which shapes are cut from surrounding stone so as to stand out slightly.

The impression was given with an accuracy truly marvelous. There was a rope about the animal's neck.

When I first beheld this apparition—for I could scarcely regard it as less—my wonder and my terror were extreme. But at length reflection came to my aid. The cat, I remembered, had been hung in a garden adjacent to the house. Upon the alarm of fire, this garden had been immediately filled by the crowd—by some one of whom the animal must have been cut from the tree and thrown, through an open window, into my chamber. This had probably been done with the view of arousing me from sleep. The falling of other walls had compressed the victim of my cruelty into the substance of the freshly-spread plaster; the lime[5] of which, with the flames, and the *ammonia* from the carcass, had then accomplished the portraiture as I saw it.

Although I thus readily accounted to my reason, if not altogether to my conscience, for the startling fact just detailed, it did not the less fail to make a deep impression upon my fancy. For months I could not rid myself of the phantasm of the cat; and, during this period, there came back into my spirit a half-sentiment that seemed, but was not, remorse. I went so far as to regret the loss of the animal, and to look about me, among the vile haunts which I now habitually frequented, for another pet of the same species, and of somewhat similar appearance, with which to supply its place.

One night as I sat, half stupefied, in a den of more than infamy, my attention was suddenly drawn to some black object, reposing upon the head of one of the immense hogsheads[6] of Gin, or of Rum, which constituted the chief furniture of the apartment. I had been looking steadily at the top of this hogshead for some minutes, and what now caused me surprise was the fact that I had not sooner perceived the object thereupon. I approached it, and touched it with my hand. It was a black cat—a very large one—fully as large as Pluto, and closely resembling him in every respect but one. Pluto had not a white hair upon any portion of his body; but this cat had a large, although indefinite splotch of white, covering nearly the whole region of the breast.

15   Upon my touching him, he immediately arose, purred loudly, rubbed against my hand, and appeared delighted with my notice. This, then, was the very creature of which I was in search. I at once offered to purchase it of the landlord; but this person made no claim to it—knew nothing of it—had never seen it before.

I continued my caresses, and when I prepared to go home, the animal evinced a disposition to accompany me. I permitted it to do so, occasionally stooping and patting it as I proceeded. When it reached the house it domesticated itself at once, and became immediately a great favorite with my wife.

For my own part, I soon found a dislike to it arising within me. This was just the reverse of what I had anticipated; but—I know not how or why it was—its evident fondness for myself rather disgusted and annoyed. By slow degrees these feelings of disgust and annoyance rose into the bitterness of hatred. I avoided the creature; a certain sense of shame, and the remembrance of my former deed of cruelty, prevented me from physically abusing it. I did not, for

---

5. Caustic substance made from calcium oxide, often used in mortar and plaster.
6. Large cask or barrel.

some weeks, strike, or otherwise violently ill use it; but gradually—very gradu-ally—I came to look upon it with unutterable loathing, and to flee silently from its odious presence, as from the breath of a pestilence.

What added, no doubt, to my hatred of the beast, was the discovery, on the morning after I brought it home, that, like Pluto, it also had been deprived of one of its eyes. This circumstance, however, only endeared it to my wife, who, as I have already said, possessed, in a high degree, that humanity of feeling which had once been my distinguishing trait, and the source of many of my simplest and purest pleasures.

With my aversion to this cat, however, its partiality for myself seemed to increase. It followed my footsteps with a pertinacity which it would be difficult to make the reader comprehend. Wherever I sat, it would crouch beneath my chair, or spring upon my knees, covering me with its loathsome caresses. If I arose to walk it would get between my feet and thus nearly throw me down, or, fastening its long and sharp claws in my dress, clamber, in this manner, to my breast. At such times, although I longed to destroy it with a blow, I was yet withheld from so doing, partly by a memory of my former crime, but chiefly—let me confess it at once—by absolute *dread* of the beast.

This dread was not exactly a dread of physical evil—and yet I should be at a loss how otherwise to define it. I am almost ashamed to own—yes, even in this felon's cell, I am almost ashamed to own—that the terror and horror with which the animal inspired me, had been heightened by one of the merest chimeras it would be possible to conceive. My wife had called my attention, more than once, to the character of the mark of white hair, of which I have spoken, and which constituted the sole visible difference between the strange beast and the one I had destroyed. The reader will remember that this mark, although large, had been originally very indefinite; but, by slow degrees—degrees nearly imper-ceptible, and which for a long time my reason struggled to reject as fanciful—it had, at length, assumed a rigorous distinctness of outline. It was now the repre-sentation of an object that I shudder to name—and for this, above all, I loathed, and dreaded, and would have rid myself of the monster *had I dared*—it was now, I say, the image of a hideous—of a ghastly thing—of the GALLOWS!—oh, mournful and terrible engine of Horror and of Crime—of Agony and of Death!

And now I was indeed wretched beyond the wretchedness of mere Human-ity. And *a brute beast*—whose fellow I had contemptuously destroyed—*a brute beast* to work out for *me*—for me, a man fashioned in the image of the High God—so much of insufferable woe! Alas! neither by day nor by night knew I the blessing of Rest any more! During the former the creature left me no moment alone, and in the latter I started hourly from dreams of unutterable fear to find the hot breath of *the thing* upon my face, and its vast weight—an incarnate Night-Mare that I had no power to shake off—incumbent eternally upon my *heart!*

Beneath the pressure of torments such as these the feeble remnant of the good within me succumbed. Evil thoughts became my sole intimates—the darkest and most evil of thoughts. The moodiness of my usual temper increased to hatred of all things and of all mankind: while from the sudden, frequent, and ungovern-able outbursts of a fury to which I now blindly abandoned myself, my uncom-plaining wife, alas! was the most usual and the most patient of sufferers.

One day she accompanied me, upon some household errand, into the cellar of the old building which our poverty compelled us to inhabit. The cat followed me down the steep stairs, and nearly throwing me headlong, exasperated me to madness. Uplifting an axe, and forgetting in my wrath the childish dread which had hitherto stayed my hand, I aimed a blow at the animal, which, of course, would have proved instantly fatal had it descended as I wished. But this blow was arrested by the hand of my wife. Goaded by the interference into a rage more than demoniacal, I withdrew my arm from her grasp and buried the axe in her brain. She fell dead upon the spot without a groan.

This hideous murder accomplished, I set myself forthwith, and with entire deliberation, to the task of concealing the body. I knew that I could not remove it from the house, either by day or night, without the risk of being observed by the neighbors. Many projects entered my mind. At one period I thought of cutting the corpse into minute fragments, and destroying them by fire. At another, I resolved to dig a grave for it in the floor of the cellar. Again, I deliberated about casting it in the well in the yard—about packing it in a box, as if merchandise, with the usual arrangements, and so getting a porter to take it from the house. Finally I hit upon what I considered a far better expedient than either of these. I determined to wall it up in the cellar—as the monks of the Middle Ages are recorded to have walled up their victims.

25   For a purpose such as this the cellar was well adapted. Its walls were loosely constructed, and had lately been plastered throughout with a rough plaster, which the dampness of the atmosphere had prevented from hardening. Moreover, in one of the walls was a projection, caused by a false chimney, or fireplace, that had been filled up and made to resemble the rest of the cellar. I made no doubt that I could readily displace the bricks at this point, insert the corpse, and wall the whole up as before, so that no eye could detect any thing suspicious.

And in this calculation I was not deceived. By means of a crow-bar I easily dislodged the bricks, and, having carefully deposited the body against the inner wall, I propped it in that position, while with little trouble I relaid the whole structure as it originally stood. Having procured mortar, sand, and hair, with every possible precaution, I prepared a plaster which could not be distinguished from the old, and with this I very carefully went over the new brick-work. When I had finished, I felt satisfied that all was right. The wall did not present the slightest appearance of having been disturbed. The rubbish on the floor was picked up with the minutest care. I looked around triumphantly, and said to myself—"Here at least, then, my labor has not been in vain."

My next step was to look for the beast which had been the cause of so much wickedness; for I had, at length, firmly resolved to put it to death. Had I been able to meet with it at the moment, there could have been no doubt of its fate; but it appeared that the crafty animal had been alarmed at the violence of my previous anger, and forbore to present itself in my present mood. It is impossible to describe or to imagine the deep, the blissful sense of relief which the absence of the detested creature occasioned in my bosom. It did not make its appearance during the night—and thus for one night, at least, since its introduction into the house, I soundly and tranquilly slept; aye, *slept* even with the burden of murder upon my soul.

The second and the third day passed, and still my tormentor came not. Once again I breathed as a free man. The monster, in terror, had fled the premises for ever! I should behold it no more! My happiness was supreme! The guilt of my dark deed disturbed me but little. Some few inquiries had been made, but these had been readily answered. Even a search had been instituted—but of course nothing was to be discovered. I looked upon my future felicity as secured.

Upon the fourth day of the assassination, a party of the police came, very unexpectedly, into the house, and proceeded again to make rigorous investigation of the premises. Secure, however, in the inscrutability of my place of concealment, I felt no embarrassment whatever. The officers bade me accompany them in their search. They left no nook or corner unexplored. At length, for the third or fourth time, they descended into the cellar. I quivered not in a muscle. My heart beat calmly as that of one who slumbers in innocence. I walked the cellar from end to end. I folded my arms upon my bosom, and roamed easily to and fro. The police were thoroughly satisfied and prepared to depart. The glee at my heart was too strong to be restrained. I burned to say if but one word, by way of triumph, and to render doubly sure their assurance of my guiltlessness.

"Gentlemen," I said at last, as the party ascended the steps, "I delight to have 30 allayed your suspicions. I wish you all health and a little more courtesy. By the bye, gentlemen, this—this is a very well-constructed house," (in the rabid desire to say something easily, I scarcely knew what I uttered at all),—"I may say an *excellently* well-constructed house. These walls—are you going, gentlemen?—these walls are solidly put together"; and here, through the mere frenzy of bravado, I rapped heavily with a cane which I held in my hand, upon that very portion of the brickwork behind which stood the corpse of the wife of my bosom.

But may God shield and deliver me from the fangs of the Arch-Fiend! No sooner had the reverberation of my blows sunk into silence, than I was answered by a voice from within the tomb!—by a cry, at first muffled and broken, like the sobbing of a child, and then quickly swelling into one long, loud and continuous scream, utterly anomalous and inhuman—a howl—a wailing shriek, half of horror and half of triumph, such as might have arisen only out of hell, conjointly from the throats of the damned in their agony and of the demons that exult in the damnation.

Of my own thoughts it is folly to speak. Swooning, I staggered to the opposite wall. For one instant the party on the stairs remained motionless through extremity of terror and awe. In the next a dozen stout arms were toiling at the wall. It fell bodily. The corpse, already greatly decayed and clotted with gore, stood erect before the eyes of the spectators. Upon its head, with red extended mouth and solitary eye of fire, sat the hideous beast whose craft had seduced me into murder, and whose informing voice had consigned me to the hangman. I had walled the monster up within the tomb.

1843

QUESTIONS

1. What cues in THE BLACK CAT might encourage you to see its narrator as unreliable? About what specifically does he seem unreliable? reliable?
2. In the essay-like opening of Poe's short story "The Imp of the Perverse" (1845), the narrator argues that in considering human "faculties and impulses," we have failed to acknowledge the power of one "innate and primitive principle of human action," a sometimes "overwhelming tendency to do wrong for the wrong's sake," "which we may call *perverseness*." To what extent and how might THE BLACK CAT demonstrate the workings of this "primitive principle"?
3. Why might it be significant that the narrator's darkest thoughts, feelings, and actions involve his pets and his wife generally? a black cat (or cats) specifically?

GEORGE SAUNDERS

(b. 1958)

Puppy

When he described early-twentieth-century American novelist Thomas Wolfe as "broken-hearted [. . .] emotional, and in love with the world," George Saunders might have been talking about himself. A MacArthur "genius grant" recipient, Saunders is often compared to Kurt Vonnegut for his extraordinary ability to capture life's tragedy while simultaneously making readers laugh. Saunders's fiction includes intricately plotted social satires set in bizarre worlds. *The Brief and Frightening Reign of Phil* (2005), for instance, takes place in Inner and Outer Horner, the former a place "so small that only one Inner Hornerite at a time could fit inside." For all its fantastical, humorous elements, however, his work often concerns a very down-to-earth issue: compassion and the lack thereof.

Born in Amarillo, Texas, Saunders recalls that his first story, written when he was in third grade, depicted "a third-grade kid [. . .] who, in the face of an extreme manpower shortage, gets drafted by the Marines and goes to fight in WWII." Despite such precocious beginnings, Saunders took a circuitous path to his career as a writer, earning a degree in geophysical engineering from the Colorado School of Mines (1981) and working as everything from a slaughterhouse knuckle-puller in Texas to an oil-exploration crewman in Sumatra before entering the creative-writing program at Syracuse University (MA, 1988), where he now teaches. This diverse experience informs the short stories, novellas, and essays collected in *CivilWarLand in Bad Decline* (1996), *Pastoralia* (2000), *In Persuasion Nation* (2006), *The Braindead Megaphone* (2007), *Tenth of December* (2013), and *A Swim in a Pond in the Rain: In Which Four Russians Give a Master Class on Writing, Reading, and Life* (2021). His first novel, *Lincoln in the Bardo* (2017), won the Man Booker Prize.

Twice already Marie had pointed out the brilliance of the autumnal sun on the perfect field of corn, because the brilliance of the autumnal sun on the perfect field of corn put her in mind of a haunted house—not a haunted house she had ever actually seen but the mythical one that sometimes appeared in her mind (with adjacent graveyard and cat on a fence) whenever she saw the brilliance of the autumnal sun on the perfect etc. etc., and she wanted to make sure that, if the kids had a corresponding mythical haunted house that appeared in their minds whenever they saw the brilliance of the etc. etc., it would come up now, so that they could all experience it together, like friends, like college friends on a road trip, sans pot, ha ha ha!

But no. When she, a third time, said, "Wow, guys, check that out," Abbie said, "O.K., Mom, we get it, it's corn," and Josh said, "Not now, Mom, I'm Leavening my Loaves," which was fine with her; she had no problem with that, Noble Baker being preferable to Bra Stuffer, the game he'd asked for.

Well, who could say? Maybe they didn't even have any mythical vignettes in their heads. Or maybe the mythical vignettes they had in their heads were totally different from the ones she had in her head. Which was the beauty of it, because, after all, they were their own little people! You were just a caretaker. They didn't have to feel what *you* felt; they just had to be supported in feeling what *they* felt.

Still, wow, that cornfield was such a classic.

"Whenever I see a field like that, guys?" she said. "I somehow think of a haunted house!"

"Slicing Knife! Slicing Knife!" Josh shouted. "You nimrod machine! I chose that!"

Speaking of Halloween, she remembered last year, when their cornstalk column had tipped their shopping cart over. Gosh, how they'd laughed at that! Oh, family laughter was golden; she'd had none of that in her childhood, Dad being so dour and Mom so ashamed. If Mom and Dad's cart had tipped, Dad would have given the cart a despairing kick and Mom would have stridden purposefully away to reapply her lipstick, distancing herself from Dad, while she, Marie, would have nervously taken that horrid plastic Army man she'd named Brady into her mouth.

Well, in this family laughter was encouraged! Last night, when Josh had goosed her with his GameBoy, she'd shot a spray of toothpaste across the mirror and they'd all cracked up, rolling around on the floor with Goochie, and Josh had said, such nostalgia in his voice, "Mom, remember when Goochie was a puppy?" Which was when Abbie had burst into tears, because, being only five, she had no memory of Goochie as a puppy.

Hence this Family Mission. And as far as Robert? Oh, God bless Robert! There was a man. He would have no problem whatsoever with this Family Mission. She loved the way he had of saying "Ho HO!" whenever she brought home something new and unexpected.

"Ho HO!" Robert had said, coming home to find the iguana. "Ho HO!" he had said, coming home to find the ferret trying to get into the iguana cage. "We appear to be the happy operators of a menagerie!"

She loved him for his playfulness—you could bring home a hippo you'd put on a credit card (both the ferret and the iguana had gone on credit cards) and he'd just say "Ho HO!" and ask what the creature ate and what hours it slept and what the heck they were going to name the little bugger.

In the back seat, Josh made the *git-git-git* sound he always made when his Baker was in Baking Mode, trying to get his Loaves into the oven while fighting off various Hungry Denizens, such as a Fox with a distended stomach; such as a fey Robin that would improbably carry the Loaf away, speared on its beak, whenever it had succeeded in dropping a Clonking Rock on your Baker—all of which Marie had learned over the summer by studying the Noble Baker manual while Josh was asleep.

And it had helped, it really had. Josh was less withdrawn lately, and when she came up behind him now while he was playing and said, like, "Wow, honey, I didn't know you could do Pumpernickel," or "Sweetie, try Serrated Blade, it cuts quicker. Try it while doing Latch the Window," he would reach back with his non-controlling hand and swat at her affectionately, and yesterday they'd shared a good laugh when he'd accidentally knocked off her glasses.

So her mother could go right ahead and claim that she was spoiling the kids. These were not spoiled kids. These were *well-loved* kids. At least she'd never left one of them standing in a blizzard for two hours after a junior-high dance. At least she'd never drunkenly snapped at one of them, "I hardly consider you college material." At least she'd never locked one of them in a closet (a closet!) while entertaining a literal ditchdigger in the parlor.

15   Oh, God, what a beautiful world! The autumn colors, that glinting river, that lead-colored cloud pointing down like a rounded arrow at that half-remodelled McDonald's standing above I-90 like a castle.

This time would be different, she was sure of it. The kids would care for this pet themselves, since a puppy wasn't scaly and didn't bite. ("Ho HO!" Robert had said the first time the iguana bit him. "I see you have an opinion on the matter!")

Thank you, Lord, she thought, as the Lexus flew through the cornfield. You have given me so much: struggles and the strength to overcome them; grace, and new chances every day to spread that grace around. And in her mind she sang out, as she sometimes did when feeling that the world was good and she had at last found her place in it, "Ho HO, ho HO!"

Callie pulled back the blind.

Yes. Awesome. It was still solved so *perfect*.

20   There was plenty for him to do back there. A yard could be a whole world, like her yard when she was a kid had been a whole world. From the three holes in her wood fence she'd been able to see Exxon (Hole One) and Accident Corner (Hole Two), and Hole Three was actually two holes that if you lined them up right your eyes would do this weird crossing thing and you could play Oh My God I Am So High by staggering away with your eyes crossed, going "Peace, man, peace."

When Bo got older, it would be different. Then he'd need his freedom. But now he just needed not to get killed. Once they found him way over on Testament. And that was across I-90. How had he crossed I-90? She knew how. Darted. That's how he crossed streets. Once a total stranger called them from Hightown Plaza. Even Dr. Brile had said it: "Callie, this boy is going to end up dead if you don't get this under control. Is he taking the medication?"

Well, sometimes he was and sometimes he wasn't. The meds made him grind his teeth and his fist would suddenly pound down. He'd broken plates that way, and once a glass tabletop and got four stitches in his wrist.

Today he didn't need the medication because he was safe in the yard, because she'd fixed it so *perfect*.

He was out there practicing pitching by filling his Yankees helmet with pebbles and winging them at the tree.

He looked up and saw her and did the thing where he blew a kiss.   25

Sweet little man.

Now all she had to worry about was the pup. She hoped the lady who'd called would actually show up. It was a nice pup. White, with brown around one eye. Cute. If the lady showed up, she'd definitely want it. And if she took it Jimmy was off the hook. He'd hated doing it that time with the kittens. But if no one took the pup he'd do it. He'd have to. Because his feeling was, when you said you were going to do a thing and didn't do it, that was how kids got into drugs. Plus, he'd been raised on a farm, or near a farm anyways, and anybody raised on a farm knew that you had to do what you had to do in terms of sick animals or extra animals—the pup being not sick, just extra.

That time with the kittens, Jessi and Mollie had called him a murderer, getting Bo all worked up, and Jimmy had yelled, "Look, you kids, I was raised on a farm and you got to do what you got to do!" Then he'd cried in bed, saying how the kittens had mewed in the bag all the way to the pond, and how he wished he'd never been raised on a farm, and she'd almost said, "You mean near a farm" (his dad had run a car wash outside Cortland[1]), but sometimes when she got too smart-assed he would do this hard pinching thing on her arm while waltzing her around the bedroom, as if the place where he was pinching were like her handle, going, "I'm not sure I totally heard what you just said to me."

So, that time after the kittens, she'd only said, "Oh, honey, you did what you had to do."

And he'd said, "I guess I did, but it's sure not easy raising kids the right way."   30

And then, because she hadn't made his life harder by being a smart-ass, they had lain there making plans, like why not sell this place and move to Arizona and buy a car wash, why not buy the kids "Hooked on Phonics," why not plant tomatoes, and then they'd got to wrestling around and (she had no idea why she remembered this) he had done this thing of, while holding her close, bursting this sudden laugh/despair snort into her hair, like a sneeze, or like he was about to start crying.

Which had made her feel special, him trusting her with that.

So what she would love, for tonight? Was getting the pup sold, putting the kids to bed early, and then, Jimmy seeing her as all organized in terms of the pup, they could mess around and afterward lie there making plans, and he could do that laugh/snort thing in her hair again.

Why that laugh/snort meant so much to her she had no freaking idea. It was just one of the weird things about the Wonder That Was Her, ha ha ha.

Outside, Bo hopped to his feet, suddenly curious, because (here we go) the   35 lady who'd called had just pulled up?

---

1. City in upstate New York, between Binghamton and Syracuse.

Yep, and in a nice car, too, which meant too bad she'd put "Cheap" in the ad.

Abbie squealed, "I love it, Mommy, I want it!," as the puppy looked up dimly from its shoebox and the lady of the house went trudging away and one-two-three-four plucked up four *dog turds* from the rug.

Well, wow, what a super field trip for the kids, Marie thought, ha ha (the filth, the mildew smell, the dry aquarium holding the single encyclopedia volume, the pasta pot on the bookshelf with an inflatable candy cane inexplicably sticking out of it), and although some might have been disgusted (by the spare tire *on the dining-room table*, by the way the glum mother dog, the presumed in-house pooper, was dragging its rear over the pile of clothing in the corner, in a sitting position, splay-legged, a moronic look of pleasure on her face), Marie realized (resisting the urge to rush to the sink and wash her hands, in part because the sink had *a basketball in it*) that what this really was was deeply sad.

Please do not touch anything, please do not touch, she said to Josh and Abbie, but just in her head, wanting to give the children a chance to observe her being democratic and accepting, and afterward they could all wash up at the half-remodelled McDonald's, as long as they just please please kept their hands out of their mouths, and God forbid they should rub their eyes.

40　　The phone rang, and the lady of the house plodded into the kitchen, placing the daintily held, paper-towel-wrapped turds *on the counter*.

"Mommy, I want it," Abbie said.

"I will definitely walk him like twice a day," Josh said.

"Don't say 'like,'" Marie said.

"I will definitely walk him twice a day," Josh said.

45　　O.K., then, all right, they would adopt a white-trash dog. Ha ha. They could name it Zeke, buy it a little corncob pipe and a straw hat. She imagined the puppy, having crapped on the rug, looking up at her, going, *Cain't hep it*. But no. Had she come from a perfect place? Everything was transmutable. She imagined the puppy grown up, entertaining some friends, speaking to them in a British accent: *My family of origin was, um, rather not, shall we say, of the most respectable* . . .

Ha ha, wow, the mind was amazing, always cranking out these—

Marie stepped to the window and, anthropologically pulling the blind aside, was shocked, so shocked that she dropped the blind and shook her head, as if trying to wake herself, shocked to see a young boy, just a few years younger than Josh, harnessed and chained to a tree, via some sort of doohickey by which—she pulled the blind back again, sure she could not have seen what she thought she had—

When the boy ran, the chain spooled out. He was running now, looking back at her, showing off. When he reached the end of the chain, it jerked and he dropped as if shot.

He rose to a sitting position, railed against the chain, whipped it back and forth, crawled to a bowl of water, and, lifting it to his lips, took a drink: a drink *from a dog's bowl*.

50　　Josh joined her at the window. She let him look. He should know that the world was not all lessons and iguanas and Nintendo. It was also this muddy simple boy tethered like an animal.

She remembered coming out of the closet to find her mother's scattered lingerie and the ditchdigger's metal hanger full of orange flags. She remembered waiting outside the junior high in the bitter cold, the snow falling harder, as she counted over and over to two hundred, promising herself each time that when she reached two hundred she would begin the long walk back—

God, she would have killed for just one righteous adult to confront her mother, shake her, and say, "You idiot, this is your child, your child you're—"

"So what were you guys thinking of naming him?" the woman said, coming out of the kitchen.

The cruelty and ignorance just radiated from her fat face, with its little smear of lipstick.

"I'm afraid we won't be taking him after all," Marie said coldly.   55

Such an uproar from Abbie! But Josh—she would have to praise him later, maybe buy him the Italian Loaves Expansion Pak—hissed something to Abbie, and then they were moving out through the trashed kitchen (past some kind of *crankshaft* on a cookie sheet, past a partial red pepper afloat *in a can of green paint*) while the lady of the house scuttled after them, saying, wait, wait, they could have it for free, please take it—she really wanted them to have it.

No, Marie said, it would not be possible for them to take it at this time, her feeling being that one really shouldn't possess something if one wasn't up to properly caring for it.

"Oh," the woman said, slumping in the doorway, the scrambling pup on one shoulder.

Out in the Lexus, Abbie began to cry softly, saying, "Really, that was the perfect pup for me."

And it was a nice pup, but Marie was not going to contribute to a situation 60
like this in even the smallest way.

Simply was not going to do it.

The boy came to the fence. If only she could have said to him, with a single look, *Life will not necessarily always be like this. Your life could suddenly blossom into something wonderful. It can happen. It happened to me.*

But secret looks, looks that conveyed a world of meaning with their subtle blah blah blah—that was all bullshit. What was not bullshit was a call to Child Welfare, where she knew Linda Berling, a very no-nonsense lady who would snatch this poor kid away so fast it would make that fat mother's thick head spin.

Callie shouted, "Bo, back in a sec!," and, swiping the corn out of the way with her non-pup arm, walked until there was nothing but corn and sky.

It was so small it didn't move when she set it down, just sniffed and tumped 65
over.

Well, what did it matter, drowned in a bag or starved in the corn? This way Jimmy wouldn't have to do it. He had enough to worry about. The boy she'd first met with hair to his waist was now this old man shrunk with worry. As far as the money, she had sixty hidden away. She'd give him twenty of that and go, "The people who bought the pup were super-nice."

Don't look back, don't look back, she said in her head as she raced away through the corn.

Then she was walking along Teallback Road like a sportwalker, like some lady who walked every night to get slim, except that she was nowhere near slim, she knew that, and she also knew that when sportwalking you did not wear jeans and unlaced hiking boots. Ha ha! She wasn't stupid. She just made bad choices. She remembered Sister Carol saying, "Callie, you are bright enough but you incline toward that which does not benefit you." *Yep, well, Sister, you got that right,* she said to the nun in her mind. But what the hell. What the heck. When things got easier moneywise, she'd get some decent tennis shoes and start walking and get slim. And start night school. Slimmer. Maybe medical technology. She was never going to be really slim. But Jimmy liked her the way she was, and she liked him the way he was, which maybe that's what love was, liking someone how he was and doing things to help him get even better.

Like right now she was helping Jimmy by making his life easier by killing something so he—no. All she was doing was walking, walking away from—

70 Pushing the words *killing puppy* out of her head, she put in her head the words *beautiful sunny day wow I'm loving this beautiful sunny day so much*—

What had she just said? That had been good. *Love was liking someone how he was and doing things to help him get better.*

Like Bo wasn't perfect, but she loved him how he was and tried to help him get better. If they could keep him safe, maybe he'd mellow out as he got older. If he mellowed out, maybe he could someday have a family. Like there he was now in the yard, sitting quietly, looking at flowers. Tapping with his bat, happy enough. He looked up, waved the bat at her, gave her that smile. Yesterday he'd been stuck in the house, all miserable. He'd ended the day screaming in bed, so frustrated. Today he was looking at flowers. Who was it that thought up that idea, the idea that had made today better than yesterday? Who loved him enough to think that up? Who loved him more than anyone else in the world loved him?

Her.

She did.

2007

QUESTIONS

1. At what point in Puppy do you begin to realize that Saunders's third-person narrator might be speaking *like* or using the voice of his two main characters—first Marie, then Callie, and so on? How is your initial response and attitude to the characters different than it would be if one or both of these characters actually narrated the story (in the first person) or if the third-person narrator's voice were consistent throughout the story? What are the most distinctive features of each voice, and what do they tell us about the characters?

2. How does each of the subsequent shifts in both focus and voice affect the way you interpret and feel about the characters and their situations? What is the effect of Saunders's choice to end the story with Callie's point of view?

3. What is the effect of the way the narrator refers to real consumer products by using their brand names (Game Boy) and discusses (in some detail) entirely fictional products like the games "Noble Baker" and "Bra Stuffer"? What do these details contribute to the story, especially in terms of our attitudes toward the various characters and their world (or our own)?

AUTHORS ON THEIR WORK

GEORGE SAUNDERS (b. 1958)

From "'Knowable in the Smallest Fragment': An Interview with George Saunders" (2003)*

MV: While your short stories always have interesting plots [. . .] it's the voices of these stories [. . .] that make them so memorable. In fact, when I remember your stories, I remember the voices: the rhythms, the repetition, the idiosyncratic logic, the corporate-babble, the exuberance, the wisecracks. Can you talk a bit about the importance of voice in your fiction, and how you come to discover the voices of your characters?

GS: Basically, I work at voice through constant anal-retentive revising. The criteria is basically ear-driven—I keep changing it until it sounds right and it surprises me in some way. I think it has something to do with a thing we did in Chicago back when I was a kid, this constant mimicking of other people, invented people, famous people. [. . .] And then of course voice and plot get all tangled up—a certain plot point is interesting, or attainable, or believable, in and only in a certain voice. The belief of the reader is engaged with the voice [. . .]. So it's all tied up together somehow. A character whose voice expresses limited intelligence, for example, we are more likely to believe him getting duped by somebody. That sort of thing.

*"'Knowable in the Smallest Fragment': An Interview with George Saunders." Interview by Matthew Vollmer. *GutCult*, vol. 1, no. 2, 2003, www.gutcult.com/litjourn2/html/GS1.html.

VIRGINIA WOOLF

(1882–1941)

The Mark on the Wall

One of the twentieth century's most revered novelists, Adeline Virginia Stephen was educated at home by her mother and father, a critic and historian best remembered today as founding editor of the *Dictionary of National Biography*. After their parents' deaths, she and her siblings moved across London to Bloomsbury—a neighborhood then known mainly for its affordable housing but one they and the "Bloomsbury Group" of writers, artists, and intellectuals that gathered around them would soon make famous. In 1912, Virginia married another member of that circle—political theorist Leonard Woolf. Together, they created the Hogarth Press, which quickly emerged as a foremost publisher of experimental, cutting-edge work by writers ranging from T. S. Eliot to Sigmund Freud. Meanwhile, in 1915, Woolf published *The Voyage Out*, the first of eight novels including *To the Lighthouse* (1927) and *Mrs. Dalloway* (1925), the stream-of-consciousness tale of one day in the lives of a society hostess and a traumatized World War I veteran. Woolf's work as critic and essayist has proven just as enduring: The oft-taught *A Room of One's Own* (1929), for example—which famously avows that "a woman must have money and a room of her own if she is to write [great] fiction"—arguably pioneered what we now call feminist literary criticism. Though Woolf's short fiction is less well-known, it was here that she honed her own version of the radically modern fictional approach and style also championed in essays such as "Modern Fiction" (1921) and "Mr. Bennett and Mrs. Brown" (1924).

Perhaps it was the middle of January in the present year that I first looked up and saw the mark on the wall. In order to fix a date it is necessary to remember what one saw. So now I think of the fire; the steady film of yellow light upon the page of my book; the three chrysanthemums in the round glass bowl on the mantelpiece. Yes, it must have been the winter time, and we had just finished our tea, for I remember that I was smoking a cigarette when I looked up and saw the mark on the wall for the first time. I looked up through the smoke of my cigarette and my eye lodged for a moment upon the burning coals, and that old fancy of the crimson flag flapping from the castle tower came into my mind, and I thought of the cavalcade of red knights riding up the side of the black rock. Rather to my relief the sight of the mark interrupted the fancy, for it is an old fancy, an automatic fancy, made as a child perhaps. The mark was a small round mark, black upon the white wall, about six or seven inches above the mantelpiece.

How readily our thoughts swarm upon a new object, lifting it a little way, as ants carry a blade of straw so feverishly, and then leave it. . . . If that mark was made by a nail, it can't have been for a picture, it must have been for a miniature—the miniature of a lady with white powdered curls, powder-dusted cheeks, and lips like red carnations. A fraud of course, for the people who had this house before us would have chosen pictures in that way—an old picture for an old room. That is the sort of people they were—very interesting people, and I think of them so often, in such queer places, because one will never see them again, never know what happened next. They wanted to leave this house because they wanted to change their style of furniture, so he said, and he was in process of saying that in his opinion art should have ideas behind it when we were torn asunder, as one is torn from the old lady about to pour out tea and the young man about to hit the tennis ball in the back garden of the suburban villa as one rushes past in the train.

But as for that mark, I'm not sure about it; I don't believe it was made by a nail after all; it's too big, too round, for that. I might get up, but if I got up and looked at it, ten to one I shouldn't be able to say for certain; because once a thing's done, no one ever knows how it happened. Oh! dear me, the mystery of life! The inaccuracy of thought! The ignorance of humanity! To show how very little control of our possessions we have—what an accidental affair this living is after all our civilisation—let me just count over a few of the things lost in our lifetime, beginning, for that seems always the most mysterious of losses—what cat would gnaw, what rat would nibble—three pale blue canisters of bookbinding tools? Then there were the bird cages, the iron hoops, the steel skates, the Queen Anne coal-scuttle, the bagatelle board, the hand organ[1]—all gone, and jewels too. Opals and emeralds, they lie about the roots of turnips. What a scraping paring affair it is to be sure! The wonder is that I've any clothes on my back, that I sit surrounded by solid furniture at this moment. Why, if one wants to compare life to anything, one must liken it to being blown through the Tube[2] at fifty miles an hour—landing at the other end without a single hairpin in one's hair! Shot out at the feet of God entirely naked! Tumbling head over heels in the asphodel meadows[3] like brown paper parcels pitched down a shoot in the post office! With one's hair flying back like the tail of a racehorse. Yes, that seems to express the rapidity of life, the perpetual waste and repair; all so casual, all so haphazard. . . .

But after life. The slow pulling down of thick green stalks so that the cup of the flower, as it turns over, deluges one with purple and red light. Why, after all, should one not be born there as one is born here, helpless, speechless, unable to focus one's eyesight, groping at the roots of the grass, at the toes of the Giants? As for saying which are trees, and which are men and women, or whether there are such things, that one won't be in a condition to do for fifty years or so. There will be nothing but spaces of light and dark, intersected by thick stalks, and rather higher up perhaps, rose-shaped blots of an indistinct colour—dim pinks and blues—which will, as time goes on, become more definite, become—I don't know what. . . .

And yet the mark on the wall is not a hole at all. It may even be caused by some round black substance, such as a small rose leaf, left over from the summer, and I, not being a very vigilant housekeeper—look at the dust on the mantelpiece, for example, the dust which, so they say, buried Troy[4] three times over, only fragments of pots utterly refusing annihilation, as one can believe.

The tree outside the window taps very gently on the pane. . . . I want to think quietly, calmly, spaciously, never to be interrupted, never to have to rise from my chair, to slip easily from one thing to another, without any sense of hostility, or obstacle. I want to sink deeper and deeper, away from the surface, with its hard separate facts. To steady myself, let me catch hold of the first idea that passes. . . . Shakespeare. . . . Well, he will do as well as another. A man who sat himself solidly in an arm-chair, and looked into the fire, so—A shower of ideas fell perpetually from some very high Heaven down through his mind. He leant his forehead on his hand, and people, looking in through the open door—for this scene is supposed to take place on a summer's evening—But how dull this is, this historical fiction! It doesn't interest me at all. I wish I could hit upon a pleasant track of thought, a track indirectly reflecting credit upon myself, for those are the pleasantest thoughts, and very frequent even in the minds of modest mouse-coloured people, who believe genuinely that they dislike to hear their own praises. They are not thoughts directly praising oneself; that is the beauty of them; they are thoughts like this:

1. Barrel organ worked by hand crank. *Bagatelle*: game in which players roll balls into holes in a sloping board. *Queen Anne coal-scuttle*: pail for carrying coal, in this case designed in the so-called "Queen Anne" style of the late nineteenth century.
2. London Underground or subway system; its first deep-level line opened in 1890.
3. That is, heaven or the afterworld, especially the flower-strewn Elysian fields of Greek mythology.
4. Ancient city-state destroyed by the Greeks in the war chronicled in Homer's epic *The Iliad*.

"And then I came into the room. They were discussing botany. I said how I'd seen a flower growing on a dust heap on the site of an old house in Kingsway.[5] The seed, I said, must have been sown in the reign of Charles the First.[6] What flowers grew in the reign of Charles the First?" I asked—(but I don't remember the answer). Tall flowers with purple tassels to them perhaps. And so it goes on. All the time I'm dressing up the figure of myself in my own mind, lovingly, stealthily, not openly adoring it, for if I did that, I should catch myself out, and stretch my hand at once for a book in self-protection. Indeed, it is curious how instinctively one protects the image of oneself from idolatry or any other handling that could make it ridiculous, or too unlike the original to be believed in any longer. Or is it not so very curious after all? It is a matter of great importance. Suppose the looking-glass smashes, the image disappears, and the romantic figure with the green of forest depths all about it is there no longer, but only that shell of a person which is seen by other people—what an airless, shallow, bald, prominent world it becomes! A world not to be lived in. As we face each other in omnibuses and underground railways we are looking into the mirror; that accounts for the vagueness, the gleam of glassiness, in our eyes. And the novelists in future will realise more and more the importance of these reflections, for of course there is not one reflection but an almost infinite number; those are the depths they will explore, those the phantoms they will pursue, leaving the description of reality more and more out of their stories, taking a knowledge of it for granted, as the Greeks did and Shakespeare perhaps—but these generalisations are very worthless. The military sound of the word is enough. It recalls leading articles, cabinet ministers—a whole class of things indeed which as a child one thought the thing itself, the standard thing, the real thing, from which one could not depart save at the risk of nameless damnation. Generalisations bring back somehow Sunday in London, Sunday afternoon walks, Sunday luncheons, and also ways of speaking of the dead, clothes, and habits—like the habit of sitting all together in one room until a certain hour, although nobody liked it. There was a rule for everything. The rule for tablecloths at that particular period was that they should be made of tapestry with little yellow compartments marked upon them, such as you may see in photographs of the carpets in the corridors of the royal palaces. Tablecloths of a different kind were not real tablecloths. How shocking, and yet how wonderful it was to discover that these real things, Sunday luncheons, Sunday walks, country houses, and tablecloths were not entirely real, were indeed half phantoms, and the damnation which visited the disbeliever in them was only a sense of illegitimate freedom. What now takes the place of those things I wonder, those real standard things? Men perhaps, should you be a woman; the masculine point of view which governs our lives, which sets the standard, which establishes Whitaker's Table of Precedency, which has become, I suppose, since the war[7] half a phantom to many men and women, which soon, one may hope, will

5. Major road in central London.
6. King of England, Scotland, and Ireland from 1625 until his execution, by Oliver Cromwell's New Model Army, in 1649.
7. World War I (1914–18). *Whitaker's Table of Precedency*: the annual *Whitaker's Almanack* includes a "Table of Precedency" indicating the order in which various political and social ranks proceed on formal occasions—that is, who ranks below and thus follows whom (see par. 11).

be laughed into the dustbin where the phantoms go, the mahogany sideboards and the Landseer prints,[8] Gods and Devils, Hell and so forth, leaving us all with an intoxicating sense of illegitimate freedom—if freedom exists. . . .

In certain lights that mark on the wall seems actually to project from the wall. Nor is it entirely circular. I cannot be sure, but it seems to cast a perceptible shadow, suggesting that if I ran my finger down that strip of the wall it would, at a certain point, mount and descend a small tumulus, a smooth tumulus like those barrows on the South Downs[9] which are, they say, either tombs or camps. Of the two I should prefer them to be tombs, desiring melancholy like most English people, and finding it natural at the end of a walk to think of the bones stretched beneath the turf. . . . There must be some book about it. Some antiquary must have dug up those bones and given them a name. . . . What sort of a man is an antiquary, I wonder? Retired Colonels for the most part, I daresay, leading parties of aged labourers to the top here, examining clods of earth and stone, and getting into correspondence with the neighbouring clergy, which, being opened at break-fast time, gives them a feeling of importance, and the comparison of arrowheads necessitates cross-country journeys to the country towns, an agreeable necessity both to them and to their elderly wives, who wish to make plum jam or to clean out the study, and have every reason for keeping that great question of the camp or the tomb in perpetual suspension, while the Colonel himself feels agreeably philosophic in accumulating evidence on both sides of the question. It is true that he does finally incline to believe in the camp; and, being opposed, indites a pamphlet which he is about to read at the quarterly meeting of the local society when a stroke lays him low, and his last conscious thoughts are not of wife or child, but of the camp and that arrowhead there, which is now in the case at the local museum, together with the foot of a Chinese murderess, a handful of Elizabethan nails, a great many Tudor clay pipes, a piece of Roman pottery, and the wine-glass that Nelson[1] drank out of—proving I really don't know what.

No, no, nothing is proved, nothing is known. And if I were to get up at this very moment and ascertain that the mark on the wall is really—what shall I say?—the head of a gigantic old nail, driven in two hundred years ago, which has now, owing to the patient attrition of many generations of housemaids, revealed its head above the coat of paint, and is taking its first view of modern life in the sight of a white-walled fire-lit room, what should I gain? Knowledge? Matter for further speculation? I can think sitting still as well as standing up. And what is knowledge? What are our learned men save the descendants of witches and hermits who crouched in caves and in woods brewing herbs, interrogating shrew-mice and writing down the language of the stars? And the less we honour them as our superstitions dwindle and our respect for beauty and health of mind increases . . . Yes, one could imagine a very pleasant world. A quiet spacious world, with the flowers so red and blue in the open fields. A world without professors or specialists or house-keepers with the profiles of policemen,

8. Cheap reproductions of animal paintings by Victorian painter Sir Edwin Henry Landseer (1802–73).
9. Range of hills in southeastern England. *Barrows*: earth or stone mounds erected by prehistoric peoples.
1. Much-revered war hero Admiral Horatio Nelson (1758–1805).

a world which one could slice with one's thought as a fish slices the water with his fin, grazing the stems of the water-lilies, hanging suspended over nests of white sea eggs. . . . How peaceful it is down here, rooted in the centre of the world and gazing up through the grey waters, with their sudden gleams of light, and their reflections—if it were not for Whitaker's Almanack—if it were not for the Table of Precedency!

10   I must jump up and see for myself what that mark on the wall really is—a nail, a rose-leaf, a crack in the wood?

Here is Nature once more at her old game of self-preservation. This train of thought, she perceives, is threatening mere waste of energy, even some collision with reality, for who will ever be able to lift a finger against Whitaker's Table of Precedency? The Archbishop of Canterbury is followed by the Lord High Chancellor; the Lord High Chancellor is followed by the Archbishop of York. Everybody follows somebody, such is the philosophy of Whitaker; and the great thing is to know who follows whom. Whitaker knows, and let that, so Nature counsels, comfort you, instead of enraging you; and if you can't be comforted, if you must shatter this hour of peace, think of the mark on the wall.

I understand Nature's game—her prompting to take action as a way of ending any thought that threatens to excite or to pain. Hence, I suppose, comes our slight contempt for men of action—men, we assume, who don't think. Still, there's no harm in putting a full stop to one's disagreeable thoughts by looking at a mark on the wall.

Indeed, now that I have fixed my eyes upon it, I feel that I have grasped a plank in the sea; I feel a satisfying sense of reality which at once turns the two Archbishops and the Lord High Chancellor to the shadows of shades. Here is something definite, something real. Thus, waking from a midnight dream of horror, one hastily turns on the light and lies quiescent, worshipping the chest of drawers, worshipping solidity, worshipping reality, worshipping the impersonal world which is proof of some existence other than ours. That is what one wants to be sure of. . . . Wood is a pleasant thing to think about. It comes from a tree; and trees grow, and we don't know how they grow. For years and years they grow, without paying any attention to us, in meadows, in forests, and by the side of rivers—all things one likes to think about. The cows swish their tails beneath them on hot afternoons; they paint rivers so green that when a moorhen dives one expects to see its feathers all green when it comes up again. I like to think of the fish balanced against the stream like flags blown out; and of water-beetles slowly raising domes of mud upon the bed of the river. I like to think of the tree itself: first the close dry sensation of being wood; then the grinding of the storm; then the slow, delicious ooze of sap. I like to think of it, too, on winter's nights standing in the empty field with all leaves close-furled, nothing tender exposed to the iron bullets of the moon, a naked mast upon an earth that goes tumbling, tumbling all night long. The song of birds must sound very loud and strange in June; and how cold the feet of insects must feel upon it, as they make laborious progresses up the creases of the bark, or sun themselves upon the thin green awning of the leaves, and look straight in front of them with diamond-cut red eyes. . . . One by one the fibres snap beneath the immense cold pressure of the earth, then the last storm comes and, falling, the highest branches drive deep into the ground again. Even so, life isn't done with; there are a million patient, watchful lives still for a tree, all over the world, in bedrooms, in ships, on the pavement, lining rooms, where men and women sit after tea, smoking cigarettes. It is full of peaceful thoughts, happy thoughts, this tree. I should like to take each one separately—but something is getting in the way. . . . Where was I? What has it all been about? A tree? A river? The Downs? Whitaker's Almanack? The fields of asphodel? I can't remember a thing. Everything's moving, falling, slipping, vanishing. . . . There is a vast upheaval of matter. Someone is standing over me and saying—

"I'm going out to buy a newspaper."

"Yes?"

"Though it's no good buying newspapers. . . . Nothing ever happens. Curse this war; God damn this war! . . . All the same, I don't see why we should have a snail on our wall."

Ah, the mark on the wall! It was a snail.

1917

QUESTIONS

1. Why does Woolf's narrator become fascinated with the mark on the wall? What does focusing on it seem to do for her? Why does she choose not to get up to investigate?
2. How does the narrator characterize life "since the war" began versus life before it (par. 7)? What role does "Whitaker's Table of Precedency" play in that contrast? How might this contrast relate to the style of narration?
3. THE MARK ON THE WALL consists almost entirely of *interior monologue*—the unin-terrupted thoughts of a character just as they occur in the mind and voice of that character. Yet near its end we get dialogue. What is the effect of Woolf's choice to introduce dialogue here? What seems significant about what is said? about who says it?

JAMIL JAN KOCHAI
(b. 1992)

Playing Metal Gear Solid V: The Phantom Pain

"[B]efore I journeyed to Hogwarts with Potter, before Ms. Lung re-taught me my alphabets and pretty much all of the English language in second grade," says Jamil Jan Kochai, "I lived the (spoken) Word": "The oral tale [. . .] was my entire galaxy." Those tales were told—in Pashtun—by an extended family of extraor-dinarily gifted storytellers with a wealth of stories to tell, including a father steeped in Pashtun poetry and a mother, grandmother, and aunts who regaled Kochai daily with "fables from the old country," "stories [. . .] memorized from the Quran," and tales of life in Logar, the rural area in Afghanistan that a series of wars had forced them to flee. Born in the wake of that flight, in a Pakistani refugee camp, Kochai grew up in Sacramento,

California, making only occasional but memorable family visits to Afghanistan. Having earned his BA from California State University, Sacramento (2015), and an MA in Creative Writing from the University of California, Davis (2017), Kochai was a Truman Capote Fellow at the Iowa Writers' Workshop when he turned the experiences of one Logar summer into the O'Henry Prize–winning story "Nights in Logar" (2017), then expanded it into 99 *Nights in Logar* (2019). A coming-of-age novel, its form, of nested stories within stories, pays homage both to the oral stories and storytelling of his family and to that (originally Arabic) collection of folktales known as *One Thousand and One Nights* (a.k.a. *The Arabian Nights*). Like "Playing Metal Gear Solid V," it also reflects Kochai's determination to "capture [. . .] different perceptions and points of view," particularly of his homeland, and to explore the "deeply personal" as well as "collective trauma" shaping his own and other families and their stories, the "reasons [. . .] people end up becoming the way they are."

F irst, you have to gather the cash to preorder the game at the local Game-Stop, where your cousin works, and, even though he hooks it up with the employee discount, the game is still a bit out of your price range because you've been using your Taco Bell paychecks to help your pops, who's been out of work since you were ten, and who makes you feel unbearably guilty about spending money on useless hobbies while kids in Kabul are destroying their bodies to build compounds for white businessmen and warlords—but, shit, it's Kojima,[1] it's Metal Gear, so, after scrimping and saving (like literal dimes you're picking up off the street), you've got the cash, which you give to your cousin, who purchases the game on your behalf, and then, on the day it's released, you just have to find a way to get to the store.

But, because your oldest brother has taken the Civic to Sac State,[2] you're hauling your two-hundred-and-sixty-pound ass on a bicycle you haven't touched since middle school, and thank Allah (if He's up there) that the bike is still rideable, because you're sure there'll be a line if you don't get to GameStop early, so, huffing and puffing, you're regretting all the Taco Bell you've eaten over the past two years, but you ride with such fervor that you end up being only third in line, and it's your cousin himself who hands you the game in a brown paper bag, as if it were something illegal or illicit, which it isn't, of course, it's Metal Gear, it's Kojima, it's the final game in a series so fundamentally a part of your childhood that often, when you hear the Irish Gaelic chorus from "The Best Is Yet to Come,"[3] you cannot help weeping softly into your keyboard.

For some reason, riding back home is easier.

---

1. Hideo Kojima (b. 1963), legendary Japanese designer, director, producer, and writer of video games including the Metal Gear action-adventure series, launched in 1987. Released in 2015 and set in Afghanistan in 1984, when Afghani insurgents were at war with their own communist government and its backers, the Soviet Union, *Metal Gear Solid V: The Phantom Pain* follows mercenary Punished "Venom" Snake as he seeks revenge against the people who destroyed his forces at the end of the previous game in the series. *Kabul*: Afghanistan's capital and largest city.

2. California State University, Sacramento.

3. Vocal song for *Metal Gear Solid*, written by Rika Muranaka, with Gaelic lyrics sung by Aoife Ní Fhearraigh; its chorus, in one translation, reads, "Can you still remember / When little things made you happy? / And can you still remember / When simple things made you smile?"

You leave the bike behind the trash cans at the side of the house and hop the wooden fence into the back yard and, if the door to the garage is open, you slip in, and if it's not, which it isn't, you've got to take a chance on the screen door in the back yard, but, lo and behold, your father is ankle deep in the dirt, hunched over, yanking at weeds with his bare hands the way he used to as a farmer in Logar,[4] before war and famine forced him to flee to the western coast of the American empire, where he labored for many years until it broke his body for good, and even though his doctor has forbidden him to work in the yard, owing to the torn nerves in his neck and spine—which, you know from your mother, were first damaged when he was tortured by Russians shortly after the murder of his younger brother, Watak, during the Soviet War—he is out here clawing at the earth and its spoils, as if he were digging for treasure or his own grave.

Spotting you only four feet away from the sliding glass door, he gestures for   5
you to come over, and though you are tired and sweaty, with your feet aching and the most important game of the decade hidden inside your underwear, you approach him.

He signals for you to crouch down beside him, then he runs his dirty fingers through his hair until flakes of his scalp fall onto his shoulders and his beard.

This isn't good.

When your father runs his hands through his hair, it is because he has forgotten his terrible, flaking dandruff, which he forgets only during times of severe emotional or physical distress, which means that he is about to tell you a story that is either upsetting or horrifying or both, which isn't fair, because you are a son and not a therapist.

Your father is a dark, sturdy man, and so unlike you that, as a child, you were sure that one day Hagrid would come to your door and inform you of your status as a Mudblood,[5] and then your true life—the life without the weight of your father's history, pain, guilt, hopelessness, helplessness, judgment, and shame— would begin.

Your father asks you where you were.   10

"The library."

"You have to study?"

You tell him you do, which isn't, technically, a lie.

"All right," he says in English, because he has given up on speaking to you in Pashto,[6] "but, after you finish, come back down. I have something I need to talk to you about."

Hurry.   15

4. Eastern province of Afghanistan, a major theater of war during the Soviet-Afghan war (c. 1980– c. 1988).

5. In J. K. Rowling's Harry Potter series (1997–2016), a derogatory name for wizards whose ancestry includes non-wizards, or Muggles. *Hagrid*: Rubeus Hagrid, half-giant wizard and gamekeeper at Hogwarts School, in the same series; it is Hagrid who first reveals to orphaned Harry that he is a wizard and liberates him from the Muggle relatives who raised him.

6. Language of the Pashtun people, one of Afghanistan's two official languages; the other (mentioned later) is Farsi.

When you get to your room, you lock the door and turn up MF Doom[7] on your portable speaker to ward off mothers, fathers, grandmothers, sisters, and brothers who want to harp at you about prayer, the Quran,[8] Pashto, Farsi, a new job, new classes, exercise, basketball, jogging, talking, guests, chores, home-work help, bathroom help, family time, time, because usually "Madvillainy" does the trick.

Open the brown paper bag and toss the kush[9] your cousin has stashed with your game because he needs a new smoking buddy since his best friend gave up the ganja for God again, and he sees you as a prime target, probably because he thinks you've got nothing better to do with your time or you're not as religious as your brothers or you're desperate to escape the unrelenting nature of a corporeal existence, and, God damn, the physical map of Afghanistan that comes with the game is fucking beautiful.

Not that you're a patriot or a nationalist or one of those Afghans who walk around in a pakol and kameez and play the table and claim that their favorite singer is Ahmad Zahir,[1] but the fact that nineteen-eighties Afghanistan is the final setting of the most legendary and artistically significant gaming franchise in the history of time made you all the more excited to get your hands on it, especially since you've been shooting at Afghans in your games (Call of Duty and Battlefield and Splinter Cell) for so long that you've become oddly immune to the self-loathing you felt when you were first massacring wave after wave of militant fighters who looked just like your father.

Now, finally, start the game.

20 After you escape from the hospital where Big Boss was recovering from the explosion he barely survived in the prequel to the Phantom Pain, you and Revolver Ocelot travel to the brutal scenes of northern Kabul Province—its rocky cliffs, its dirt roads, and its sunlight bleeding off into the dark mountains just the way you remember from all those years ago, when you visited Kabul as a child—and although your initial mission is to locate and extract Kazuhira Miller, the Phantom Pain is the first Metal Gear Solid game to be set in a radically open-world environment, and you decide to postpone the rescue of Kazuhira Miller until after you get some Soviet blood on your hands, a feat you accomplish promptly by locating and massacring an entire base of Russian combatants.

Your father, you know, didn't kill a single Russian during his years as a mujahi-deen in Logar, but there is something in the act of slaughtering these Soviet N.P.C.s[2] that makes you feel connected to him and his history of warfare.

7. Stage name of American rapper, songwriter, and record producer Daniel Dumile (b. 1971) whose albums include *Madvillainy* (2004).
8. Or Koran; the sacred book or bible of Islam.
9. Type of cannabis (a.k.a. marijuana or, in Hindi, ganja), originally from the Kush Mountains span-ning the Afghanistan-Pakistan border.
1. Afghani musician, songwriter, and composer (1946–79); Afghanistan's first and biggest pop super-star, he is sometimes called the "Afghan Elvis." *Pakol*: soft, usually wool, round-topped men's cap popular in Afghanistan. *Kameez*: long shirt or tunic with side seams open below the waist, a tradi-tional South Asian garment. *Tabla*: traditional South Asian percussion instrument of Indian origin.
2. Non-player characters (acronym); video game characters not controlled by the game-player. *Mujahi-deen*: guerilla fighters, especially Muslims fighting against non-Muslim forces; literally meaning something like "those engaged in *jihad*, or struggle" (Arabic).

Thinking of your father and his small village, you head south to explore the outer limits of the open world in the Phantom Pain, crossing trails and deserts and mountain passes, occasionally stopping at a checkpoint or a military barracks to slaughter more Russians, and you find yourself, incredibly, skirting the city of Kabul, still dominated by the Soviets, and continuing on to Logar, to Mohammad Agha, and when you get to Wagh Jan, the roadside-market village that abuts the Kabul-Logar highway, just the way you remember it, you hitch your horse and begin to sneak along the clay compounds and the shops, climbing walls and crawling atop roofs, and, whenever a local Afghan spots you, you knock him out with a tranquillizer, until you make it to the bridge that leads to the inner corridors of your parents' home village, Naw'e Kaleh, which looks so much like the photos and your own blurred memories from the trip when you were a kid that you begin to become uneasy, not yet afraid, but as if consumed by an overwhelming sense of déjà vu.

Sneaking along the dirt roads, past the golden fields and the apple orchards and the mazes of clay compounds, you come upon the house where your father used to reside, and it is there—on the road in front of your father's home—that you spot Watak, your father's sixteen-year-old brother, whom you recognize only because his picture (unsmiling, head shaved, handsome, and sixteen forever) hangs on the wall of the room in your home where your parents pray, but here he is, in your game, and you press Pause and you set down the controller, and now you are afraid.

Sweat is running down your legs in rivulets, in streams, your heart is thumping, and you are wondering if sniffing the kush as you did earlier has got you high.

You look out the window and see your brother walking toward the house in   25
the dark and you realize that you've been playing for too long.

You're blinking a lot.

Too much.

You notice that your room is a mess and that it smells like ass and that you've become so accustomed to its smell and its mess that from the space inside your head, behind your eyes, the space in which your first-person P.O.V.[3] is rooted, you—

Ignore the knock.

It's just your little sister.   30

Get back to the game.

There is a bearded, heavyset man beside Watak, who, you soon realize, is your father.

You pause the game again and put down the controller.

Doom spits, "His life is like a folklore legend. . . . Why you so stiff, you need to smoke more, bredrin[4]. . . . Instead of trying to riff with the broke war veteran."

It seems to you a sign.   35

You extract the kush from the trash, and, because you have no matches or lighter, you put hunks of it in your mouth and you chew and nearly vomit twice.

---

3. Point of view (acronym).
4. Friend(s) or comrade(s) (Rastafarian slang).

Return to the game.

Hiding in your grandfather's mulberry tree, you listen to your father and his brother discuss what they will eat for suhoor, thereby indicating that it is still Ramadan,[5] that this is just days before Watak's murder.

Then it hits you.

40   Here is what you're going to do: before your father is tortured and his brother murdered, you are going to tranquillize them both and you are going to carry them to your horse and cross Logar's terrain until you reach a safe spot where you can call a helicopter and fly them back to your offshore platform: Mother Base.

But just as you load your tranquillizers your brother bangs on your door and demands that you come out, and after ignoring him for a bit, which only makes him madder and louder, you shout that you are sick, but the voice that comes out of your mouth is not your own, it is the voice of a faraway man imitating your voice, and your brother can tell.

He leaves, and you return to the game.

From the cover of the mulberry tree, you aim your tranquillizer gun, but you forget that you've got the laser scope activated, and Watak sees the red light flashing on your father's forehead and they're off, running and firing back at your tree with rifles they had hidden underneath their patus,[6] and you are struck twice, so you need a few moments to recover your health and, by the time you do, they're gone.

Your brother is back, and this time he has brought along your oldest brother, who somehow is able to shout louder and bang harder than your second-oldest brother, and they're both asking what you're doing and why you won't come out and why you won't grow up and why you insist on worrying your mother and your father, who you know gets those terrible migraines triggered by stress, and now your oldest brother is banging so hard you're afraid the door will come off its hinges, so you lug your dresser in front of it as a barricade and then you go back to your spot in front of the TV, and you sit on the floor and press Play.

45   At night, under cover of darkness, you sneak toward your father's compound, and you scale the fifteen-foot-high walls of clay and crawl along the rooftops until you get to the highest point in the compound, where your father stands, on the lookout for incoming jets and firebombs, and you shoot him twice in the back with tranquillizers and, as he is falling, you catch him in your arms, your father, who, at this time, is around the same age that you are now, and in the dark, on the roof of the compound that he will lose to this war, you hold him, his body still strong and well, his heart unbroken, and you set him down gently on the clay so that the sky does not swallow him.

Climbing down into the courtyard, you go from chamber to chamber, spotting uncles and aunts and cousins you've never met in real life, and you find Watak near the cow's shed, sleeping just behind the doorway of a room filled with women, as if to protect them, and, after you aim your tranquillizer gun and

5. Sacred month in the Islamic calendar, a period of fasting, introspection, and prayer. *Sahoor:* predawn meal eaten during Ramadan, in preparation for the daily fast.
6. Large woolen blankets or shawls.

send Watak into a deeper sleep, your grandmother, a lifelong insomniac, rises from her toshak[7] and strikes you in the shoulder with a machete and calls for the men in the house, of whom there are many, to awaken and slaughter the Russian who has come to kill us all in our sleep.

The damage from the machete is significant.

Nonetheless, you still have the strength to tranquillize your grandmother, pick up Watak, and climb back onto the roof while all your uncles and cousins and even your grandfather are awakened and armed and begin to fire at your legs as you hustle along, bleeding and weary, to the spot where your father rests.

With your uncle on one shoulder and your father on the other, you leap off the roof into the shadows of an apple orchard.

The men are pouring out onto the roads and the fields, calling upon neighbors and allies, and, because the orchard is soon surrounded on all sides, it seems certain that you will be captured, but you are saved by, of all things, a squadron of Spetsnaz,[8] who begin to fire on the villagers, and in the confusion of the shoot-out, as the entire village is lit up by a hundred gunfights, each fight a microcosm of larger battles and wars and global conflicts strung together by the invisible wires of beloved men who will die peacefully in their sleep, you make your way out of the orchard, passing trails and streams and rivers and mulberry trees, until you reach your horse and ride out of Wagh Jan, toward an extraction point in the nearby Black Mountains. 50

But now, at the door, is your father.

"Zoya?" he is saying, very gently, the way he used to say it when you were a kid, when you were in Logar, when you got the flu, when the pills and the I.V. and the home remedies weren't working, when there was nothing to do but wait for the aching to ebb, and your father was there, maybe in the orchard, maybe on the veranda, and he was holding you in his lap, running his fingers through your hair, and saying your name, the way he is saying it now, as if it were almost a question.

"Zoya?" he says and, when you do not reply, nothing else.

Keep going.

Russians chase you on the ground and in the air, they fire and you are struck once, twice, three or four times, and there are so many Russians, but your horse is quick and nimble and manages the terrain better than their trucks can, and you make it to the extraction point, in a hollow of the Black Mountains, with enough time to summon the helicopter and to set up a perimeter of mines, and you hide your father and his brother at the mouth of a cave, behind a large boulder the shape of a believer in prostration, where you lie prone with a sniper rifle and begin to pick off Russian paratroopers in the distance, and you fire at the engines of the trucks and ignore the tanks, which will reach you last, and it is mere moments before your helicopter will arrive, and, just as you think you are going to make it, your horse is slaughtered in a flurry of gunfire and your pilot is struck by a single bullet from a lone rifleman, and the helicopter falls to the earth and bursts into flames, killing many Russians, and giving you just enough time to rush into the cave, into the heart of the Black Mountains. 55

7. Narrow mattress serving as chair or bed in Afghan homes.
8. Russian special forces.

With your father on one shoulder and your uncle on the other, and with the lights of the Soviet gunfire dying away at the outer edges of your vision, you trudge deeper into the darkness of the cave, and though you cannot be sure that your father and his brother are still alive, that they haven't been shot in the chaos, that they are not, now, corpses, you feel compelled to keep moving into a darkness so complete that your reflection becomes visible on the screen of the television in front of you, and it is as if the figures in the image were journeying inside you, delving into your flesh.

To be saved.

2020

QUESTIONS

1. Besides the use of second person, what other features of this story's narration and style seem especially distinctive? (What do you notice, for example, about sentences and paragraphs? about **diction**?) What are the significance and effect of these techniques, or why might they be peculiarly effective and appropriate for this story?
2. How would you describe Zoya's conflict or conflicts? In these terms, what might be the significance of the story/game's subtitle?
3. What do you make of the story's final image and sentence? Who or what might Zoya be trying to save?

AUTHORS ON THEIR WORK

JAMIL JAN KOCHAI (b. 1992)

From "Jamil Jan Kochai on the Intimate Alienation of Video Games" (2019)*

I've always found the second-person point of view to be oddly intimate *and* alienating. When I first read Jamaica Kincaid's "Girl," for example, I felt both assaulted and also personally engaged by the narration. It disrupts the very nature of the subject-object relationship. In the process of reading, the "I," the reader, becomes "you," the addressee. I've always had a similar feeling of intimate alienation while playing video games, especially first-person shooters, where, in certain moments of intense gameplay, like a fire fight or a raid, you become totally immersed and feel as if it were "you" in the game, shooting and running and being shot. For me this sense of *becoming* the shooter in first-person gameplay was often disrupted by the depiction of the enemies in video games like Call of Duty. There I am in the game, playing as a white soldier, and all of a sudden I'm murdering an Afghan man who looks just like my father. Or even like me. My status as the hero facing the enemy, as the subject facing the object, falls apart. "I shoot you" becomes "I shoot me." I wanted to capture that sort of alienating intimacy in my story. Second person seemed like the best way to go about it.

*"Jamil Jan Kochai on the Intimate Alienation of Video Games." Interview by Deborah Treisman. *The New Yorker*, 30 Dec. 2019, www.newyorker.com/books/this-week-in-fiction/jamil-jan-kochai-01-06-20.

SUGGESTIONS FOR WRITING

1. Write a response paper or essay exploring the potential gap between the way one of the focal characters in Puppy perceives herself and her family and the way the story as a whole encourages us to perceive them. What specific techniques or details create that gap?

2. Write an essay exploring the claim that The Mark on the Wall celebrates the power of the imagination. How might the story do so through the style, as well as the content, of its narration? To what is imagination opposed here?

3. Write an essay comparing the depiction of video games, gaming, and/or gamers in Playing Metal Gear Solid V: The Phantom Pain and Zadie Smith's Meet the President! How does each story portray the experience and effects of gaming? Which best captures your experience? Which might show you something new about the gaming experience and its potential effects? In these terms, what are the effect and significance of the stories' different modes of narration? Alternatively, write an essay comparing the use of second-person narration in Kochai's story and in one of its inspirations, Jamaica Kincaid's Girl.

4. Choose any story in this anthology and write a response paper exploring how its effect and meaning are shaped by its narration.

5. Write an abbreviated version of Interesting Facts or The Black Cat, or re-envision one or two of the story's key episodes using a different point of view. If you choose a first-person narrator, work to capture that person's unique voice, as well as his or her perspective on events.

4 | CHARACTER

Robert Buss, *Dickens' Dream* (1870)

In the unfinished watercolor *Dickens' Dream*, the novelist peacefully dozes while above and around him float ghostly images of the hundreds of characters that people his fiction and, apparently, his dreams. This image captures the undeniable fact that characters loom large in the experience of fiction, for both writers and readers. Speaking for the former, Elie Wiesel describes a novelist like himself as practically possessed by characters who "force the writer to tell their stories" because "they want to get out." As readers of fiction, we care about *what* happens and *how* mainly because it happens *to* someone. Indeed, without a "someone," it is unlikely that anything would happen at all.

It is also often a "someone," or the *who* of a story, that sticks with us long after we have forgotten the details of what, where, and how. In this way, characters sometimes seem to take on a life of their own, to float free of the texts where we first encounter them, and even to haunt us. You may know almost nothing about

Charles Dickens, but you probably have a vivid sense of his characters Ebenezer Scrooge and Tiny Tim from *A Christmas Carol* (1843).

A **character** is any personage in a literary work who acts, appears, or is referred to as playing a part. Though *personage* usually means a human being, it doesn't have to. Whole genres or subgenres of fiction are distinguished, in part, by the specific kinds of nonhuman characters they conventionally feature, whether alien species and intelligent machines (as in science fiction), animals (as in **fables**), or elves and monsters (as in traditional fairy tales and modern fantasy). All characters must have at least some human qualities, however, such as the ability to think, to feel pain, or to fall in love.

Evidence to Consider in Analyzing a Character: A Checklist

- the character's name
- the character's physical appearance
- objects and places associated with the character
- the character's actions
- the character's thoughts and speech, including
  - content (what he or she thinks or says)
  - timing (when he or she thinks or says it)
  - phrasing (how he or she thinks or says it)
- other characters' thoughts about the character
- other characters' comments to and about the character
- the narrator's comments about the character

HEROES AND VILLAINS VERSUS PROTAGONISTS AND ANTAGONISTS

A common term for the character with the leading male role is **hero**, the "good guy," who opposes the **villain**, or "bad guy." The leading female character is the **heroine**. Heroes and heroines are usually larger-than-life, stronger or better than most human beings, sometimes almost godlike. They are characters that a text encourages us to admire and even to emulate, so that the words *hero* and *heroine* can also be applied to especially admirable characters who do not play leading roles.

In most modern fiction, however, the leading character is much more ordinary, not so clearly or simply a "good guy." For that reason, it is usually more appropriate to use the older and more neutral terms **protagonist** and **antagonist** for the leading character and his or her opponent. These terms do not imply either the presence or the absence of outstanding virtue or vice.

The claim that a particular character either is or is not heroic might well make a good thesis for an essay, whereas the claim that he is or is not the protagonist generally won't. Like most rules, however, this one admits of exceptions. Some stories do leave open to debate the question of which character most deserves to be called the *protagonist*. In James Baldwin's SONNY'S BLUES, for example, Sonny and his brother seem equally central.

Controversial in a different way is a particular type of protagonist known as an **antihero**. Found mainly in fiction written since around 1850, an antihero, as the name implies, possesses traits that make him or her the opposite of a traditional hero. An antihero may be difficult to like or admire. One early and influential example of an antihero is the narrator-protagonist of Fyodor Dostoevsky's 1864 Russian-language novella *Notes from the Underground*—a man utterly paralyzed by his own hypersensitivity. More familiar and recent examples might include Homer and Bart Simpson or BoJack Horseman.

It would be a mistake to see the quality of a work of fiction as dependent on whether we find its characters likable or admirable, just as it would be wrong to assume that an author's outlook or values are the same as those of the protagonist. Often, the characters we initially find least likable or admirable may ultimately move and teach us the most.

MAJOR VERSUS MINOR CHARACTERS

The *major* or *main characters* are those we see more of over time; we learn more about them, and we think of them as more complex and, frequently, as more "realistic" than the *minor characters*, the figures who fill out the story.

Yet even though minor characters are less prominent and may seem less complex, they are ultimately just as indispensable to a story as major characters. Minor characters often play a key role in shaping our interpretations of, and attitudes toward, the major characters, and also in precipitating the changes that major characters undergo. For example, a minor character might function as a **foil**—a character that helps by way of contrast to reveal the unique qualities of another (especially main) character.

Questions about minor characters can lead to good essay topics precisely because such characters' significance to a story is not immediately apparent. Rather, we often have to probe the details of the story to formulate a persuasive interpretation of their roles.

FLAT VERSUS ROUND AND STATIC VERSUS DYNAMIC CHARACTERS

Characters that act from varied, often conflicting motives, impulses, and desires, and who seem to have psychological complexity, are said to be *round characters*; they can "surprise convincingly," as one critic puts it. Simple, one-dimensional characters that behave and speak in predictable or repetitive (if sometimes odd) ways are called *flat*. Sometimes characters seem round to us because our impression of them evolves as a story unfolds. Other times, the characters themselves— not just our impression of them—change as a result of events that occur in the story. A character that changes is *dynamic*; one that doesn't is *static*. Roundness and dynamism tend to go together. But the two qualities are distinct, and one does not require the other: Not all round characters are dynamic; not all dynamic characters are round.

Terms like *flat* and *round* or *dynamic* and *static* are useful so long as we do not let them harden into value judgments. Because flat characters are less complex than round ones, it is easy to assume they are artistically inferior; however, we need only think of the characters of Charles Dickens, many of whom are flat, to realize that this is not always the case. A truly original flat character with only one or two very distinctive traits or behavioral or verbal tics will often prove more memorable than a round one. Unrealistic as such characters might seem, in real life you probably know at least one or two people who can always be counted on to say or do pretty much the same thing every time you see them. Exaggeration can provide insight, as well as humor. Dickens's large gallery of lovable flat characters includes a middle-aged man who constantly pulls himself up by his own hair and an old one who must continually be "fluffed up" by others because he tends to slide right out of his chair. *South Park*'s Kenny is little more than a hooded orange snowsuit with a habit of dying in ever more outrageous ways only to come back to life over and over again.

STOCK CHARACTERS AND ARCHETYPES

Flat characters who represent a familiar, frequently recurring type—the dumb blond, the mad scientist, the inept sidekick, the plain yet ever-sympathetic best friend—are called *stock characters* because they seem to be pulled out of a stock-room of familiar, prefabricated figures. Characters that recur in the myths and literature of many different ages and cultures are instead called **archetypes**, though this term also applies to recurring elements other than characters (such as actions or symbols). One archetypal character is the trickster figure that appears in the guise of Brer Rabbit in the Uncle Remus stories, the spider Anansi in African and Afro-Caribbean folktales, the coyote in Native American folklore, and, perhaps, Bugs Bunny. Another such character is the **scapegoat**.

READING CHARACTER IN FICTION AND LIFE

On the one hand, we get to know characters in a work of fiction and try to understand them much as we do people in real life. We observe what they own and wear, what they look like and where they live, how they carry themselves and what expressions flit across their faces, how they behave in various situations, what they say and how they say it, what they don't say, what others say about them, and how others act in their presence. Drawing on all that evidence and on our own past experience of both literature and life, we try to deduce characters' motives and desires, their values and beliefs, their strengths and weaknesses—in short, to figure out what makes them tick and how they might react if circumstances changed. In our daily lives, being able to "read" other people in this way is a vital skill, one that, science suggests, we hone by reading fiction. The skills of observation and interpretation, the enlarged experience and capacity for empathy, that we develop in reading fiction can help us better navigate our real world.

On the other hand, however, fictional characters are not real people; they are imaginary personages crafted by authors. Fiction offers us a more orderly and expansive world than the one we inhabit every day—one in which each person, gesture, and word is a meaningful part of a coherent, purposeful design; one in which our responses to people are guided by a narrator and, ultimately, an author; one in which we can sometimes crawl inside other people's heads and know their thoughts; one in which we can get to know murderers and ministers, monsters and miracle workers—the sorts of people (or personages) we might be afraid, unwilling, or simply unable to meet or spend time with in real life.

In other words, fictional characters are the products not of nature, chance, or God, but of careful, deliberate **characterization**—the art and technique of representing fictional personages. In analyzing character, we thus need to consider not only who a character is and what his or her most important traits, motivations, and values are, but also precisely how the text shapes our interpretation of, and degree of sympathy or admiration for, the character; what function the character serves in the narrative; and what the character might represent.

This last issue is important because all characters, no matter how individualized and idiosyncratic, ultimately become meaningful to us only if they represent something beyond the story, something bigger than themselves—a type of person, a particular set of values or way of looking at the world, a human tendency, a demographic group. When you set out to write about a character, consider how the story would be different without the character and what the author says or shows us through the character.

Direct and Indirect Characterization:
An Example and an Exercise

The following conversation appears in the pages of a well-known nineteenth-century novel. Even without being familiar with this novel, you should be able to discern a great deal about the two characters that converse in this scene simply by carefully attending to what each says and how each says it. As you will see, one of the things that differentiates the two speakers is that they hold conflicting views of "character" itself:

> "In what order you keep these rooms, Mrs Fairfax!" said I. "No dust, no canvas coverings: except that the air feels chilly, one would think they were inhabited daily."
>
> "Why, Miss Eyre, though Mr Rochester's visits here are rare, they are always sudden and unexpected; and as I observed that it put him out to find everything swathed up, and to have a bustle of arrangement on his arrival, I thought it best to keep the rooms in readiness."
>
> "Is Mr Rochester an exacting, fastidious sort of man?"
>
> "Not particularly so; but he has a gentleman's tastes and habits, and he expects to have things managed in conformity to them."
>
> "Do you like him? Is he generally liked?"
>
> "O yes; the family have always been respected here. Almost all the land in this neighbourhood, as far as you can see, has belonged to the Rochesters time out of mind."
>
> "Well, but leaving his land out of the question, do you like him? Is he liked for himself?"
>
> "I have no cause to do otherwise than like him; and I believe he is considered a just and liberal landlord by his tenants: but he has never lived much amongst them."
>
> "But has he no peculiarities? What, in short, is his character?"

"Oh! his character is unimpeachable, I suppose. He is rather peculiar, perhaps: he has travelled a great deal, and seen a great deal of the
world, I should think. I daresay he is clever: but I never had much
conversation with him."

"In what way is he peculiar?"

"I don't know—it is not easy to describe—nothing striking, but you
feel it when he speaks to you: you cannot be always sure whether he is
in jest or earnest, whether he is pleased or the contrary; you don't
thoroughly understand him, in short—at least, I don't: but it is of no
consequence, he is a very good master."

- What facts about the two speakers can you glean from this conversation? What do you infer about their individual outlooks, personalities, and values?
- What different definitions of the word *character* emerge here? How
  would you describe each speaker's view of what matters most in the
  assessment of character?

This scene—from Charlotte Brontë's *Jane Eyre* (1847)—demonstrates the
first of the two major methods of presenting character—*indirect characterization* or showing (as opposed to *direct characterization* or telling). In this
passage Brontë simply *shows* us what Jane (the narrator) and Mrs. Fairfax
say and invites us to infer from their words who each character is (including
the absent Mr. Rochester), how each looks at the world, and what each cares
about.

Sometimes, however, authors present characters more directly, having
narrators *tell* us what makes a character tick and what we are to think of
him or her. Charlotte Brontë engages in both direct and indirect characterization in the paragraph of *Jane Eyre* that immediately follows the passage
above. Here, Jane (the narrator) tells the reader precisely what she thinks
this conversation reveals about Mrs. Fairfax, even as she reveals more about
herself in the process:

This was all the account I got from Mrs Fairfax of her employer and
mine. There are people who seem to have no notion of sketching a
character, or observing and describing salient points, either in persons
or things: the good lady evidently belonged to this class; my queries
puzzled, but did not draw her out. Mr Rochester was Mr Rochester in
her eyes; a gentleman, a landed proprietor—nothing more: she
inquired and searched no further, and evidently wondered at my wish
to gain a more definite notion of his identity.

- How does Jane's interpretation of Mrs. Fairfax compare to yours?
- How and why might this paragraph corroborate or complicate your
  view of Jane herself?

Characters, Conventions, and Beliefs

Just as fiction and the characters that inhabit it operate by somewhat different rules than do the real world and real people, so the rules that govern particular fictional worlds and their characters differ from one another. As the critic James Wood argues, "our hunger for the particular depth or reality level of a character is tutored by each writer, and adapts to the internal conventions of each book." Works of fiction in various subgenres differ widely in how they handle characterization. Were a folktale, for example, to depict more than a few, mainly flat, archetypal characters; to make us privy to its characters' thoughts; or to offer up detailed descriptions of their physiques and wardrobes, it would cease both to be a folktale and to yield the particular sorts of pleasures and insights that only a folktale can. By the same token, readers of a folktale miss out on its pleasures and insights if they expect the wrong things of its characters and modes of characterization.

But even within the same fictional subgenre, the treatment of character varies over time and across cultures. Such variations sometimes reflect profound differences in the way people understand human nature. Individuals and cultures hold conflicting views of what produces personality, whether innate factors such as genes, environmental factors such as upbringing, supernatural forces, unconscious impulses or drives, or some combination of these. Views differ as well as to whether character is simply an unchanging given or something that can change through experience, conversion, or an act of will. Some works of fiction tackle such issues head-on. But many others—especially from cultures or eras different from our own—may raise these questions for us simply because their modes of characterization imply an understanding of the self different from the one we take for granted.

We can thus learn a lot about our own values, prejudices, and beliefs by reading a wide array of fiction. Similarly, we learn from encountering a wide array of fictional characters, including those whose values, beliefs, and ways of life differ from our own.

* * *

The stories in this chapter vary widely in terms of the number and types of characters they depict and the techniques they use to depict them. In their pages, you will meet a range of diverse individuals—some complex and compelling, some utterly ordinary—struggling to make sense of the people around them just as you work to make sense of them and, in the process, yourself.

Questions about Character

- Who is the protagonist, or might there be more than one? Why and how so? Which other characters, if any, are main or major characters? Which are minor characters?
- What are the protagonist's most distinctive traits, and what is most distinctive about his or her outlook and values? What motivates the character? What is it about the character that creates internal and/or external conflict?

- Which textual details and moments reveal most about this character? Which are most surprising or might complicate your interpretation of this character? How is your view of the character affected by what you *don't* know about him or her?
- What are the roles of other characters? Which, if any, functions as an antagonist? Which, if any, serves as a foil? Why and how so? How would the story as a whole (not just its action or plot) be different if any of these characters disappeared? What points might the author be raising or illustrating through each character?
- Which of the characters, or which aspects of the characters, does the text encourage us to sympathize with or to admire? to view negatively? Why and how so?
- Does your view of any character change over the course of the story, or do any of the characters themselves change? If so, when, how, and why?
- Does characterization tend to be indirect or direct in the story? What kinds of information do and don't we get about the characters, and how does the story tend to give us that information?

TONI MORRISON

(1931–2019)

Recitatif[1]

Born in Lorain, Ohio, a steel town on the shores of Lake Erie, Chloe Anthony Wofford was the first member of her family to attend college, graduating from Howard University in 1953 and earning an MA from Cornell two years later. She taught at both Texas Southern University and at Howard before becoming an editor at Random House, where she worked for nearly twenty years. In such novels as *The Bluest Eye* (1970), *Sula* (1973), *Song of Solomon* (1977), *Beloved* (1987), *Paradise* (1997), *A Mercy* (2008), and *God Help the Child* (2015), Morrison traces the problems and possibilities faced by Black Americans struggling with slavery and its aftermath in the United States. Morrison was also a gifted and influential critic and essayist: Her oft-cited *Playing in the Dark: Whiteness and the Literary Imagination* appeared in 1992, and the next year she became the first African American author to win the Nobel Prize in Literature. Remarkably, Morrison published only two short stories in her storied career: "Recitatif" (1983) and "Sweetness" (2015).

M y mother danced all night and Roberta's was sick. That's why we were taken to St. Bonny's. People want to put their arms around you when you tell them you were in a shelter, but it really wasn't bad. No big long room with

---

1. In classical music such as opera, a vocal passage that is sung in a speechlike manner.

one hundred beds like Bellevue.[2] There were four to a room, and when Roberta and me came, there was a shortage of state kids, so we were the only ones assigned to 406 and could go from bed to bed if we wanted to. And we wanted to, too. We changed beds every night and for the whole four months we were there we never picked one out as our own permanent bed.

It didn't start out that way. The minute I walked in and the Big Bozo introduced us, I got sick to my stomach. It was one thing to be taken out of your own bed early in the morning—it was something else to be stuck in a strange place with a girl from a whole other race. And Mary, that's my mother, she was right. Every now and then she would stop dancing long enough to tell me something important and one of the things she said was that they never washed their hair and they smelled funny. Roberta sure did. Smell funny, I mean. So when the Big Bozo (nobody ever called her Mrs. Itkin, just like nobody ever said St. Bonaventure)—when she said, "Twyla, this is Roberta. Roberta, this is Twyla. Make each other welcome." I said, "My mother won't like you putting me in here."

"Good," said Bozo. "Maybe then she'll come and take you home."

How's that for mean? If Roberta had laughed I would have killed her, but she didn't. She just walked over to the window and stood with her back to us.

5   "Turn around," said the Bozo. "Don't be rude. Now Twyla. Roberta. When you hear a loud buzzer, that's the call for dinner. Come down to the first floor. Any fights and no movie." And then, just to make sure we knew what we would be missing, "The Wizard of Oz."

Roberta must have thought I meant that my mother would be mad about my being put in the shelter. Not about rooming with her, because as soon as Bozo left she came over to me and said, "Is your mother sick too?"

"No," I said. "She just likes to dance all night."

"Oh," she nodded her head and I liked the way she understood things so fast. So for the moment it didn't matter that we looked like salt and pepper standing there and that's what the other kids called us sometimes. We were eight years old and got F's all the time. Me because I couldn't remember what I read or what the teacher said. And Roberta because she couldn't read at all and didn't even listen to the teacher. She wasn't good at anything except jacks, at which she was a killer: pow scoop pow scoop pow scoop.

We didn't like each other all that much at first, but nobody else wanted to play with us because we weren't real orphans with beautiful dead parents in the sky. We were dumped. Even the New York City Puerto Ricans and the upstate Indians ignored us. All kinds of kids were in there, black ones, white ones, even two Koreans. The food was good, though. At least I thought so. Roberta hated it and left whole pieces of things on her plate: Spam, Salisbury steak—even jello with fruit cocktail in it, and she didn't care if I ate what she wouldn't. Mary's idea of supper was popcorn and a can of Yoo-Hoo. Hot mashed potatoes and two weenies was like Thanksgiving for me.

10   It really wasn't bad, St. Bonny's. The big girls on the second floor pushed us around now and then. But that was all. They wore lipstick and eyebrow pencil and wobbled their knees while they watched TV. Fifteen, sixteen, even, some of

2. Large New York City hospital best known for its psychiatric wards.

them were. They were put-out girls, scared runaways most of them. Poor little girls who fought their uncles off but looked tough to us, and mean. God did they look mean. The staff tried to keep them separate from the younger children, but sometimes they caught us watching them in the orchard where they played radios and danced with each other. They'd light out after us and pull our hair or twist our arms. We were scared of them, Roberta and me, but neither of us wanted the other one to know it. So we got a good list of dirty names we could shout back when we ran from them through the orchard. I used to dream a lot and almost always the orchard was there. Two acres, four maybe, of these little apple trees. Hundreds of them. Empty and crooked like beggar women when I first came to St. Bonny's but fat with flowers when I left. I don't know why I dreamt about that orchard so much. Nothing really happened there. Nothing all that important, I mean. Just the big girls dancing and playing the radio. Roberta and me watching. Maggie fell down there once. The kitchen woman with legs like parentheses. And the big girls laughed at her. We should have helped her up, I know, but we were scared of those girls with lipstick and eyebrow pencil. Maggie couldn't talk. The kids said she had her tongue cut out, but I think she was just born that way: mute. She was old and sandy-colored and she worked in the kitchen. I don't know if she was nice or not. I just remember her legs like parentheses and how she rocked when she walked. She worked from early in the morning till two o'clock, and if she was late, if she had too much cleaning and didn't get out till two-fifteen or so, she'd cut through the orchard so she wouldn't miss her bus and have to wait another hour. She wore this really stupid little hat—a kid's hat with ear flaps—and she wasn't much taller than we were. A really awful little hat. Even for a mute, it was dumb—dressing like a kid and never saying anything at all.

"But what about if somebody tries to kill her?" I used to wonder about that. "Or what if she wants to cry? Can she cry?"

"Sure," Roberta said. "But just tears. No sounds come out."

"She can't scream?"

"Nope. Nothing."

"Can she hear?"

"I guess."

"Let's call her," I said. And we did.

"Dummy! Dummy!" She never turned her head.

"Bow legs! Bow legs!" Nothing. She just rocked on, the chin straps of her baby-boy hat swaying from side to side. I think we were wrong. I think she could hear and didn't let on. And it shames me even now to think there was somebody in there after all who heard us call her those names and couldn't tell on us.

We got along all right, Roberta and me. Changed beds every night, got F's in civics and communication skills and gym. The Bozo was disappointed in us, she said. Out of 130 of us state cases, 90 were under twelve. Almost all were real orphans with beautiful dead parents in the sky. We were the only ones dumped and the only ones with F's in three classes including gym. So we got along—what with her leaving whole pieces of things on her plate and being nice about not asking questions.

I think it was the day before Maggie fell down that we found out our mothers were coming to visit us on the same Sunday. We had been at the shelter twenty-eight days (Roberta twenty-eight and a half) and this was their first visit with us. Our mothers would come at ten o'clock in time for chapel, then lunch with us in the teachers' lounge. I thought if my dancing mother met her sick mother it might be good for her. And Roberta thought her sick mother would get a big bang out of a dancing one. We got excited about it and curled each other's hair. After breakfast we sat on the bed watching the road from the window. Roberta's socks were still wet. She washed them the night before and put them on the radiator to dry. They hadn't, but she put them on anyway because their tops were so pretty—scalloped in pink. Each of us had a purple construction-paper basket that we had made in craft class. Mine had a yellow crayon rabbit on it. Roberta's had eggs with wiggly lines of color. Inside were cellophane grass and just the jelly beans because I'd eaten the two marshmallow eggs they gave us. The Big Bozo came herself to get us. Smiling she told us we looked very nice and to come downstairs. We were so surprised by the smile we'd never seen before, neither of us moved.

"Don't you want to see your mommies?"

I stood up first and spilled the jelly beans all over the floor. Bozo's smile disappeared while we scrambled to get the candy up off the floor and put it back in the grass.

She escorted us downstairs to the first floor, where the other girls were lining up to file into the chapel. A bunch of grown-ups stood to one side. Viewers mostly. The old biddies who wanted servants and the fags who wanted company looking for children they might want to adopt. Once in a while a grandmother. Almost never anybody young or anybody whose face wouldn't scare you in the night. Because if any of the real orphans had young relatives they wouldn't be real orphans. I saw Mary right away. She had on those green slacks I hated and hated even more now because didn't she know we were going to chapel? And that fur jacket with the pocket linings so ripped she had to pull to get her hands out of them. But her face was pretty—like always, and she smiled and waved like she was the little girl looking for her mother—not me.

25   I walked slowly, trying not to drop the jelly beans and hoping the paper handle would hold. I had to use my last Chiclet because by the time I finished cutting everything out, all the Elmer's was gone. I am left-handed and the scissors never worked for me. It didn't matter, though; I might just as well have chewed the gum. Mary dropped to her knees and grabbed me, mashing the basket, the jelly beans, and the grass into her ratty fur jacket.

"Twyla, baby. Twyla, baby!"

I could have killed her. Already I heard the big girls in the orchard the next time saying, "Twyyyyyla, baby!" But I couldn't stay mad at Mary while she was smiling and hugging me and smelling of Lady Esther dusting powder. I wanted to stay buried in her fur all day.

To tell the truth I forgot about Roberta. Mary and I got in line for the traipse into chapel and I was feeling proud because she looked so beautiful even in those ugly green slacks that made her behind stick out. A pretty mother on earth is better than a beautiful dead one in the sky even if she did leave you all alone to go dancing.

I felt a tap on my shoulder, turned, and saw Roberta smiling. I smiled back, but not too much lest somebody think this visit was the biggest thing that ever happened in my life. Then Roberta said, "Mother, I want you to meet my room-mate, Twyla. And that's Twyla's mother."

I looked up it seemed for miles. She was big. Bigger than any man and on her chest was the biggest cross I'd ever seen. I swear it was six inches long each way. And in the crook of her arm was the biggest Bible ever made.

Mary, simple-minded as ever, grinned and tried to yank her hand out of the pocket with the raggedy lining—to shake hands, I guess. Roberta's mother looked down at me and then looked down at Mary too. She didn't say anything, just grabbed Roberta with her Bible-free hand and stepped out of line, walking quickly to the rear of it. Mary was still grinning because she's not too swift when it comes to what's really going on. Then this light bulb goes off in her head and she says "That bitch!" really loud and us almost in the chapel now. Organ music whining; the Bonny Angels singing sweetly. Everybody in the world turned around to look. And Mary would have kept it up—kept calling names if I hadn't squeezed her hand as hard as I could. That helped a little, but she still twitched and crossed and uncrossed her legs all through service. Even groaned a couple of times. Why did I think she would come there and act right? Slacks. No hat like the grandmothers and viewers, and groaning all the while. When we stood for hymns she kept her mouth shut. Wouldn't even look at the words on the page. She actually reached in her purse for a mirror to check her lipstick. All I could think of was that she really needed to be killed. The sermon lasted a year, and I knew the real orphans were looking smug again.

We were supposed to have lunch in the teachers' lounge, but Mary didn't bring anything, so we picked fur and cellophane grass off the mashed jelly beans and ate them. I could have killed her. I sneaked a look at Roberta. Her mother had brought chicken legs and ham sandwiches and oranges and a whole box of chocolate-covered grahams. Roberta drank milk from a thermos while her mother read the Bible to her.

Things are not right. The wrong food is always with the wrong people. Maybe that's why I got into waitress work later—to match up the right people with the right food. Roberta just let those chicken legs sit there, but she did bring a stack of grahams up to me later when the visit was over. I think she was sorry that her mother would not shake my mother's hand. And I liked that and I liked the fact that she didn't say a word about Mary groaning all the way through the service and not bringing any lunch.

Roberta left in May when the apple trees were heavy and white. On her last day we went to the orchard to watch the big girls smoke and dance by the radio. It didn't matter that they said, "Twyyyyyla, baby." We sat on the ground and breathed. Lady Esther. Apple blossoms. I still go soft when I smell one or the other. Roberta was going home. The big cross and the big Bible was coming to get her and she seemed sort of glad and sort of not. I thought I would die in that room of four beds without her and I knew Bozo had plans to move some other dumped kid in there with me. Roberta promised to write every day, which was really sweet of her because she couldn't read a lick so how could she write any-body. I would have drawn pictures and sent them to her but she never gave me her address. Little by little she faded. Her wet socks with the pink scalloped tops and her big serious-looking eyes—that's all I could catch when I tried to bring her to mind.

35   I was working behind the counter at the Howard Johnson's on the Thruway just before the Kingston exit. Not a bad job. Kind of a long ride from Newburgh,[3] but okay once I got there. Mine was the second night shift—eleven to seven. Very light until a Greyhound checked in for breakfast around six-thirty. At that hour the sun was all the way clear of the hills behind the restaurant. The place looked better at night—more like shelter—but I loved it when the sun broke in, even if it did show all the cracks in the vinyl and the speckled floor looked dirty no matter what the mop boy did.

It was August and a bus crowd was just unloading. They would stand around a long while: going to the john, and looking at gifts and junk-for-sale machines, reluctant to sit down so soon. Even to eat. I was trying to fill the coffee pots and get them all situated on the electric burners when I saw her. She was sitting in a booth smoking a cigarette with two guys smothered in head and facial hair. Her own hair was so big and wild I could hardly see her face. But the eyes. I would know them anywhere. She had on a powder-blue halter and shorts outfit and earrings the size of bracelets. Talk about lipstick and eyebrow pencil. She made the big girls look like nuns. I couldn't get off the counter until seven o'clock, but I kept watching the booth in case they got up to leave before that. My replacement was on time for a change, so I counted and stacked my receipts as fast as I could and signed off. I walked over to the booth, smiling and wondering if she would remember me. Or even if she wanted to remember me. Maybe she didn't want to be reminded of St. Bonny's or to have anybody know she was ever there. I know I never talked about it to anybody.

I put my hands in my apron pockets and leaned against the back of the booth facing them.

"Roberta? Roberta Fisk?"

She looked up. "Yeah?"

40   "Twyla."

She squinted for a second and then said, "Wow."

"Remember me?"

"Sure. Hey. Wow."

"It's been a while," I said, and gave a smile to the two hairy guys.

45   "Yeah. Wow. You work here?"

"Yeah," I said. "I live in Newburgh."

"Newburgh? No kidding?" She laughed then a private laugh that included the guys but only the guys, and they laughed with her. What could I do but laugh too and wonder why I was standing there with my knees showing out from under that uniform. Without looking I could see the blue and white triangle on my head, my hair shapeless in a net, my ankles thick in white oxfords. Nothing could have been less sheer than my stockings. There was this silence that came down right after I laughed. A silence it was her turn to fill up. With introductions, maybe, to her boyfriends or an invitation to sit down and have a Coke. Instead she lit a cigarette off the one she'd just finished and said, "We're on our way to the Coast. He's got an appointment with Hendrix." She gestured casually toward the boy next to her.

"Hendrix? Fantastic," I said. "Really fantastic. What's she doing now?"

3. City on the Hudson River north of New York City.

Roberta coughed on her cigarette and the two guys rolled their eyes up at the ceiling.

"Hendrix. Jimi Hendrix, asshole. He's only the biggest—Oh, wow. Forget it." 50

I was dismissed without anyone saying goodbye, so I thought I would do it for her.

"How's your mother?" I asked. Her grin cracked her whole face. She swallowed. "Fine," she said. "How's yours?"

"Pretty as a picture," I said and turned away. The backs of my knees were damp. Howard Johnson's really was a dump in the sunlight.

James is as comfortable as a house slipper. He liked my cooking and I liked his big loud family. They have lived in Newburgh all of their lives and talk about it the way people do who have always known a home. His grandmother is a porch swing older than his father and when they talk about streets and avenues and buildings they call them names they no longer have. They still call the A & P[4] Rico's because it stands on property once a mom and pop store owned by Mr. Rico. And they call the new community college Town Hall because it once was. My mother-in-law puts up jelly and cucumbers and buys butter wrapped in cloth from a dairy. James and his father talk about fishing and baseball and I can see them all together on the Hudson in a raggedy skiff. Half the population of Newburgh is on welfare now, but to my husband's family it was still some upstate paradise of a time long past. A time of ice houses and vegetable wagons, coal furnaces and children weeding gardens. When our son was born my mother-in-law gave me the crib blanket that had been hers.

But the town they remembered had changed. Something quick was in the 55 air. Magnificent old houses, so ruined they had become shelter for squatters and rent risks, were bought and renovated. Smart IBM[5] people moved out of their suburbs back into the city and put shutters up and herb gardens in their backyards. A brochure came in the mail announcing the opening of a Food Emporium. Gourmet food it said—and listed items the rich IBM crowd would want. It was located in a new mall at the edge of town and I drove out to shop there one day—just to see. It was late in June. After the tulips were gone and the Queen Elizabeth roses were open everywhere. I trailed my cart along the aisle tossing in smoked oysters and Robert's sauce and things I knew would sit in my cupboard for years. Only when I found some Klondike ice cream bars did I feel less guilty about spending James's fireman's salary so foolishly. My father-in-law ate them with the same gusto little Joseph did.

Waiting in the check-out line I heard a voice say, "Twyla!"

The classical music piped over the aisles had affected me and the woman leaning toward me was dressed to kill. Diamonds on her hand, a smart white summer dress. "I'm Mrs. Benson," I said.

"Ho. Ho. The Big Bozo," she sang.

For a split second I didn't know what she was talking about. She had a bunch of asparagus and two cartons of fancy water.

4. Supermarket, part of a chain originally known as the Great Atlantic and Pacific Tea Company.
5. The International Business Machine Corporation, which had its executive headquarters in Poughkeepsie, New York.

60   "Roberta!"

"Right."

"For heaven's sake. Roberta."

"You look great," she said.

"So do you. Where are you? Here? In Newburgh?"

65   "Yes. Over in Annandale."

I was opening my mouth to say more when the cashier called my attention to her empty counter.

"Meet you outside." Roberta pointed her finger and went into the express line.

I placed the groceries and kept myself from glancing around to check Roberta's progress. I remembered Howard Johnson's and looking for a chance to speak only to be greeted with a stingy "wow." But she was waiting for me and her huge hair was sleek now, smooth around a small, nicely shaped head. Shoes, dress, everything lovely and summery and rich. I was dying to know what happened to her, how she got from Jimi Hendrix to Annandale, a neighborhood full of doctors and IBM executives. Easy, I thought. Everything is so easy for them. They think they own the world.

"How long," I asked her. "How long have you been here?"

70   "A year. I got married to a man who lives here. And you, you're married too, right? Benson, you said."

"Yeah. James Benson."

"And is he nice?"

"Oh, is he nice?"

"Well, is he?" Roberta's eyes were steady as though she really meant the question and wanted an answer.

75   "He's wonderful, Roberta. Wonderful."

"So you're happy."

"Very."

"That's good," she said and nodded her head. "I always hoped you'd be happy. Any kids? I know you have kids."

"One. A boy. How about you?"

80   "Four."

"Four?"

She laughed. "Step kids. He's a widower."

"Oh."

"Got a minute? Let's have a coffee."

85   I thought about the Klondikes melting and the inconvenience of going all the way to my car and putting the bags in the trunk. Served me right for buying all that stuff I didn't need. Roberta was ahead of me.

"Put them in my car. It's right here."

And then I saw the dark blue limousine.

"You married a Chinaman?"

"No," she laughed. "He's the driver."

90   "Oh, my. If the Big Bozo could see you now."

We both giggled. Really giggled. Suddenly, in just a pulse beat, twenty years disappeared and all of it came rushing back. The big girls (whom we called gar girls—Roberta's misheard word for the evil stone faces described in a civics class) there dancing in the orchard, the ploppy mashed potatoes, the double weenies, the Spam with pineapple. We went into the coffee shop holding on to one another and I tried to think why we were glad to see each other this time and not before. Once, twelve years ago, we passed like strangers. A black girl and a white girl meeting in a Howard Johnson's on the road and having nothing to say. One in a blue and white triangle waitress hat—the other on her way to see Hendrix. Now we were behaving like sisters separated for much too long. Those four short months were nothing in time. Maybe it was the thing itself. Just being there, together. Two little girls who knew what nobody else in the world knew—how not to ask questions. How to believe what had to be believed. There was politeness in that reluctance and generosity as well. Is your mother sick too? No, she dances all night. Oh—and an understanding nod.

We sat in a booth by the window and fell into recollection like veterans.

"Did you ever learn to read?"

"Watch." She picked up the menu. "Special of the day. Cream of corn soup. Entrées. Two dots and a wriggly line. Quiche. Chef salad, scallops . . ."

I was laughing and applauding when the waitress came up.　95

"Remember the Easter baskets?"

"And how we tried to *introduce* them?"

"Your mother with that cross like two telephone poles."

"And yours with those tight slacks."

We laughed so loudly heads turned and made the laughter harder to　100 suppress.

"What happened to the Jimi Hendrix date?"

Roberta made a blow-out sound with her lips.

"When he died I thought about you."

"Oh, you heard about him finally?"

"Finally. Come on, I was a small-town country waitress."　105

"And I was a small-town country dropout. God, were we wild. I still don't know how I got out of there alive."

"But you did."

"I did. I really did. Now I'm Mrs. Kenneth Norton."

"Sounds like a mouthful."

"It is."　110

"Servants and all?"

Roberta held up two fingers.

"Ow! What does he do?"

"Computers and stuff. What do I know?"

"I don't remember a hell of a lot from those days, but Lord, St. Bonny's is as　115 clear as daylight. Remember Maggie? The day she fell down and those gar girls laughed at her?"

Roberta looked up from her salad and stared at me. "Maggie didn't fall," she said.

"Yes, she did. You remember."

"No, Twyla. They knocked her down. Those girls pushed her down and tore her clothes. In the orchard."

"I don't—that's not what happened."

"Sure it is. In the orchard. Remember how scared we were?"　120

"Wait a minute. I don't remember any of that."

"And Bozo was fired."

"You're crazy. She was there when I left. You left before me."

"I went back. You weren't there when they fired Bozo."

125 "What?"

"Twice. Once for a year when I was about ten, another for two months when I was fourteen. That's when I ran away."

"You ran away from St. Bonny's?"

"I had to. What do you want? Me dancing in that orchard?"

"Are you sure about Maggie?"

130 "Of course I'm sure. You've blocked it, Twyla. It happened. Those girls had behavior problems, you know."

"Didn't they, though. But why can't I remember the Maggie thing?"

"Believe me. It happened. And we were there."

"Who did you room with when you went back?" I asked her as if I would know her. The Maggie thing was troubling me.

"Creeps. They tickled themselves in the night."

135 My ears were itching and I wanted to go home suddenly. This was all very well but she couldn't just comb her hair, wash her face and pretend everything was hunky-dory. After the Howard Johnson's snub. And no apology. Nothing.

"Were you on dope or what that time at Howard Johnson's?" I tried to make my voice sound friendlier than I felt.

"Maybe, a little. I never did drugs much. Why?"

"I don't know; you acted sort of like you didn't want to know me then."

"Oh, Twyla, you know how it was in those days: black—white. You know how everything was."

140 But I didn't know. I thought it was just the opposite. Busloads of blacks and whites came into Howard Johnson's together. They roamed together then: students, musicians, lovers, protesters. You got to see everything at Howard Johnson's and blacks were very friendly with whites in those days. But sitting there with nothing on my plate but two hard tomato wedges wondering about the melting Klondikes it seemed childish remembering the slight. We went to her car, and with the help of the driver, got my stuff into my station wagon.

"We'll keep in touch this time," she said.

"Sure," I said. "Sure. Give me a call."

"I will," she said, and then just as I was sliding behind the wheel, she leaned into the window. "By the way. Your mother. Did she ever stop dancing?"

I shook my head. "No. Never."

145 Roberta nodded.

"And yours? Did she ever get well?"

She smiled a tiny sad smile. "No. She never did. Look, call me, okay?"

"Okay," I said, but I knew I wouldn't. Roberta had messed up my past somehow with that business about Maggie. I wouldn't forget a thing like that. Would I?

Strife came to us that fall. At least that's what the paper called it. Strife. Racial strife. The word made me think of a bird—a big shrieking bird out of 1,000,000,000 B.C. Flapping its wings and cawing. Its eye with no lid always bearing down on you. All day it screeched and at night it slept on the rooftops.

It woke you in the morning and from the *Today* show to the eleven o'clock news it kept you an awful company. I couldn't figure it out from one day to the next. I knew I was supposed to feel something strong, but I didn't know what, and James wasn't any help. Joseph was on the list of kids to be transferred from the junior high school to another one at some far-out-of-the-way place and I thought it was a good thing until I heard it was a bad thing. I mean I didn't know. All the schools seemed dumps to me, and the fact that one was nicer looking didn't hold much weight. But the papers were full of it and then the kids began to get jumpy. In August, mind you. Schools weren't even open yet. I thought Joseph might be frightened to go over there, but he didn't seem scared so I forgot about it, until I found myself driving along Hudson Street out there by the school they were trying to integrate and saw a line of women marching. And who do you suppose was in line, big as life, holding a sign in front of her bigger than her mother's cross? MOTHERS HAVE RIGHTS TOO! it said.

I drove on, and then changed my mind. I circled the block, slowed down, and honked my horn. 150

Roberta looked over and when she saw me she waved. I didn't wave back, but I didn't move either. She handed her sign to another woman and came over to where I was parked.

"Hi."

"What are you doing?"

"Picketing. What's it look like?"

"What for?" 155

"What do you mean, 'What for?' They want to take my kids and send them out of the neighborhood. They don't want to go."

"So what if they go to another school? My boy's being bussed too, and I don't mind. Why should you?"

"It's not about us, Twyla. Me and you. It's about our kids."

"What's more *us* than that?"

"Well, it is a free country." 160

"Not yet, but it will be."

"What the hell does that mean? I'm not doing anything to you."

"You really think that?"

"I know it."

"I wonder what made me think you were different." 165

"I wonder what made me think you were different."

"Look at them," I said. "Just look. Who do they think they are? Swarming all over the place like they own it. And now they think they can decide where my child goes to school. Look at them, Roberta. They're Bozos."

Roberta turned around and looked at the women. Almost all of them were standing still now, waiting. Some were even edging toward us. Roberta looked at me out of some refrigerator behind her eyes. "No, they're not. They're just mothers."

"And what am I? Swiss cheese?"

"I used to curl your hair." 170

"I hated your hands in my hair."

The women were moving. Our faces looked mean to them of course and they looked as though they could not wait to throw themselves in front of a police

car, or better yet, into my car and drag me away by my ankles. Now they surrounded my car and gently, gently began to rock it. I swayed back and forth like
a sideways yo-yo. Automatically I reached for Roberta, like the old days in the
orchard when they saw us watching them and we had to get out of there, and if
one of us fell the other pulled her up and if one of us was caught the other
stayed to kick and scratch, and neither would leave the other behind. My arm
shot out of the car window but no receiving hand was there. Roberta was looking at me sway from side to side in the car and her face was still. My purse slid
from the car seat down under the dashboard. The four policemen who had been
drinking Tab in their car finally got the message and strolled over, forcing their
way through the women. Quietly, firmly they spoke. "Okay, ladies. Back in line
or off the streets."

Some of them went away willingly; others had to be urged away from the car
doors and the hood. Roberta didn't move. She was looking steadily at me. I was
fumbling to turn on the ignition, which wouldn't catch because the gearshift
was still in drive. The seats of the car were a mess because the swaying had
thrown my grocery coupons all over it and my purse was sprawled on the floor.

"Maybe I am different now, Twyla. But you're not. You're the same little state
kid who kicked a poor old black lady when she was down on the ground. You
kicked a black lady and you have the nerve to call me a bigot."

175   The coupons were everywhere and the guts of my purse were bunched under
the dashboard. What was she saying? Black? Maggie wasn't black.

"She wasn't black," I said.

"Like hell she wasn't, and you kicked her. We both did. You kicked a black
lady who couldn't even scream."

"Liar!"

"You're the liar! Why don't you just go on home and leave us alone, huh?"

180   She turned away and I skidded away from the curb.

The next morning I went into the garage and cut the side out of the carton
our portable TV had come in. It wasn't nearly big enough, but after a while I had
a decent sign: red spray-painted letters on a white background—AND SO DO
CHILDREN ****. I meant just to go down to the school and tack it up somewhere
so those cows on the picket line across the street could see it, but when I got
there, some ten or so others had already assembled—protesting the cows across
the street. Police permits and everything. I got in line and we strutted in time
on our side while Roberta's group strutted on theirs. That first day we were all
dignified, pretending the other side didn't exist. The second day there was name
calling and finger gestures. But that was about all. People changed signs from
time to time, but Roberta never did and neither did I. Actually my sign didn't
make sense without Roberta's. "And so do children what?" one of the women on
my side asked me. Have rights, I said, as though it was obvious.

Roberta didn't acknowledge my presence in any way and I got to thinking
maybe she didn't know I was there. I began to pace myself in the line, jostling
people one minute and lagging behind the next, so Roberta and I could reach
the end of our respective lines at the same time and there would be a moment
in our turn when we would face each other. Still, I couldn't tell whether she saw
me and knew my sign was for her. The next day I went early before we were
scheduled to assemble. I waited until she got there before I exposed my new

creation. As soon as she hoisted her MOTHERS HAVE RIGHTS TOO I began to wave my new one, which said, HOW WOULD YOU KNOW? I know she saw that one, but I had gotten addicted now. My signs got crazier each day, and the women on my side decided that I was a kook. They couldn't make heads or tails out of my brilliant screaming posters.

I brought a painted sign in queenly red with huge black letters that said, IS YOUR MOTHER WELL? Roberta took her lunch break and didn't come back for the rest of the day or any day after. Two days later I stopped going too and couldn't have been missed because nobody understood my signs anyway.

It was a nasty six weeks. Classes were suspended and Joseph didn't go to anybody's school until October. The children—everybody's children—soon got bored with that extended vacation they thought was going to be so great. They looked at TV until their eyes flattened. I spent a couple of mornings tutoring my son, as the other mothers said we should. Twice I opened a text from last year that he had never turned in. Twice he yawned in my face. Other mothers organized living room sessions so the kids would keep up. None of the kids could concentrate so they drifted back to *The Price Is Right* and *The Brady Bunch*.[6] When the school finally opened there were fights once or twice and some sirens roared through the streets every once in a while. There were a lot of photographers from Albany. And just when ABC was about to send up a news crew, the kids settled down like nothing in the world had happened. Joseph hung my HOW WOULD YOU KNOW? sign in his bedroom. I don't know what became of AND SO DO CHILDREN ****. I think my father-in-law cleaned some fish on it. He was always puttering around in our garage. Each of his five children lived in Newburgh and he acted as though he had five extra homes.

I couldn't help looking for Roberta when Joseph graduated from high school, but I didn't see her. It didn't trouble me much what she had said to me in the car. I mean the kicking part. I know I didn't do that, I couldn't do that. But I was puzzled by her telling me Maggie was black. When I thought about it I actually couldn't be certain. She wasn't pitch-black, I knew, or I would have remembered that. What I remember was the kiddie hat, and the semicircle legs. I tried to reassure myself about the race thing for a long time until it dawned on me that the truth was already there, and Roberta knew it. I didn't kick her; I didn't join in with the gar girls and kick that lady, but I sure did want to. We watched and never tried to help her and never called for help. Maggie was my dancing mother. Deaf, I thought, and dumb. Nobody inside. Nobody who would hear you if you cried in the night. Nobody who could tell you anything important that you could use. Rocking, dancing, swaying as she walked. And when the gar girls pushed her down, and started roughhousing, I knew she wouldn't scream, couldn't—just like me—and I was glad about that.

We decided not to have a tree, because Christmas would be at my mother-in-law's house, so why have a tree at both places? Joseph was at SUNY New Paltz and we had to economize, we said. But at the last minute, I changed my mind. Nothing could be that bad. So I rushed around town looking for a tree, something small but wide. By the time I found a place, it was snowing and very late.

6. Television sitcom popular in the 1970s, as was the game show *The Price Is Right*.

I dawdled like it was the most important purchase in the world and the tree man was fed up with me. Finally I chose one and had it tied onto the trunk of the car. I drove away slowly because the sand trucks were not out yet and the streets could be murder at the beginning of a snowfall. Downtown the streets were wide and rather empty except for a cluster of people coming out of the Newburgh Hotel. The one hotel in town that wasn't built out of cardboard and Plexiglas. A party, probably. The men huddled in the snow were dressed in tails and the women had on furs. Shiny things glittered from underneath their coats. It made me tired to look at them. Tired, tired, tired. On the next corner was a small diner with loops and loops of paper bells in the window. I stopped the car and went in. Just for a cup of coffee and twenty minutes of peace before I went home and tried to finish everything before Christmas Eve.

"Twyla?"

There she was. In a silvery evening gown and dark fur coat. A man and another woman were with her, the man fumbling for change to put in the cigarette machine. The woman was humming and tapping on the counter with her fingernails. They all looked a little bit drunk.

"Well. It's you."

190 "How are you?"

I shrugged. "Pretty good. Frazzled. Christmas and all."

"Regular?" called the woman from the counter.

"Fine," Roberta called back and then, "Wait for me in the car."

She slipped into the booth beside me. "I have to tell you something, Twyla. I made up my mind if I ever saw you again, I'd tell you."

195 "I'd just as soon not hear anything, Roberta. It doesn't matter now, anyway."

"No," she said. "Not about that."

"Don't be long," said the woman. She carried two regulars to go and the man peeled his cigarette pack as they left.

"It's about St. Bonny's and Maggie."

"Oh, please."

200 "Listen to me. I really did think she was black. I didn't make that up. I really thought so. But now I can't be sure. I just remember her as old, so old. And because she couldn't talk—well, you know, I thought she was crazy. She'd been brought up in an institution like my mother was and like I thought I would be too. And you were right. We didn't kick her. It was the gar girls. Only them. But, well, I wanted to. I really wanted them to hurt her. I said we did it, too. You and me, but that's not true. And I don't want you to carry that around. It was just that I wanted to do it so bad that day—wanting to is doing it."

Her eyes were watery from the drinks she'd had, I guess. I know it's that way with me. One glass of wine and I start bawling over the littlest thing.

"We were kids, Roberta."

"Yeah. Yeah. I know, just kids."

"Eight."

205 "Eight."

"And lonely."

"Scared, too."

She wiped her cheeks with the heel of her hand and smiled. "Well, that's all I wanted to say."

I nodded and couldn't think of any way to fill the silence that went from the diner past the paper bells on out into the snow. It was heavy now. I thought I'd better wait for the sand trucks before starting home.

"Thanks, Roberta."

"Sure."

"Did I tell you? My mother, she never did stop dancing."

"Yes. You told me. And mine, she never got well." Roberta lifted her hands from the tabletop and covered her face with her palms. When she took them away she really was crying. "Oh shit, Twyla. Shit, shit, shit. What the hell happened to Maggie?"

1983

210

QUESTIONS

1. At the end of RECITATIF, how do Twyla's and Roberta's explorations of the "truth" of what they had seen at St. Bonny's many years earlier affect your sense of the "truth" of later episodes in the story? Is either Twyla or Roberta more reliable than the other?

2. At what point in the story do you first begin to make assumptions about the race and class of the two main characters, Twyla and Roberta? Why? Do you change your mind later in the story? When and why so—or not? What is the significance of Morrison's choice both to withhold information about the characters' race and class and to have Twyla narrate the story?

3. How does the relationship between Twyla and Roberta evolve over the course of the story?

AUTHORS ON THEIR WORK

TONI MORRISON (1931–2019)

From "Toni Morrison: The Art of Fiction CXXXIV" (1993)*

MORRISON: Faulkner in *Absalom, Absalom!* spends the entire book tracing race, and you can't find it. No one can see it, even the character who *is* black can't see it. [. . .] Do you know how hard it is to withhold that kind of information but hinting, pointing all of the time? And then to reveal it in order to say that it is *not* the point anyway? It is technically just astonishing. As a reader you have been forced to hunt for a drop of black blood that means everything and nothing. The insanity of racism.

MORRISON: [. . .] I wrote a story entitled "Recitatif," in which there are two little girls in an orphanage, one white and one black. But the reader doesn't know which is white and which is black. I use class codes, but no racial codes.

INTERVIEWER: Is this meant to confuse the reader?

MORRISON: Well, yes. But to provoke and enlighten. I did that as a lark. What was exciting was to be forced as a writer not to be lazy and rely on obvious codes. Soon as I say, "Black woman . . ." I can rest on or provoke predictable responses, but if I leave it out then I have to talk about her in a complicated way—as a person.

*"Toni Morrison: The Art of Fiction CXXXIV." Interview by Elisa Schappell with Claudia Brodsky Lacour. *The Paris Review*, no. 128, fall 1993, www.theparisreview.org/interviews/ 1888/the-art-of-fiction-no-134-toni-morrison.

DAVID FOSTER WALLACE
(1962–2008)
Good People

Born in Ithaca, New York, to a philosophy professor and an English teacher, David Foster Wallace has been dubbed an "outrageously gifted novelist" and "the genius of his generation," as well as a "recovering smart aleck" and "a decent, decent man." A philosophy and English major at Amherst College, he contemplated a career in math before—at age twenty-four—earning an MFA from the University of Arizona and publishing his first novel, *The Broom of the System* (1987). His subsequent work includes short-story collections like *Brief Interviews with Hideous Men* (1999) and *Oblivion* (2004), as well as wide-ranging nonfiction, some of which appears in *A Supposedly Fun Thing I'll Never Do Again* (1997) and *Consider the Lobster and Other Essays* (2005). At over a thousand pages and with almost four hundred footnotes, his most famous novel, *Infinite Jest* (1996), intertwines several narratives set in a near future in which years are named by their corporate sponsors ("Year of the Whopper") and New England is a giant toxic-waste dump. Included on *Time*'s list of the hundred best novels published since 1923, it also helped earn Wallace a MacArthur "genius grant."

Wallace described his own goal as creating "morally passionate, passionately moral fiction" that might help readers "become less alone inside." Though admired as much for its humor as for its bulk and complexity, his fiction often dwells on what he called "an ineluctable part of being a human"—"suffering." Though Wallace long battled depression, his 2008 suicide shocked and saddened fans and fellow writers around the world. The story "Good People," first published in 2007, ultimately became part of *The Pale King* (2011), the unfinished novel he left behind.

They were up on a picnic table at that park by the lake, by the edge of the lake, with part of a downed tree in the shallows half hidden by the bank. Lane A. Dean, Jr., and his girlfriend, both in bluejeans and button-up shirts. They sat up on the table's top portion and had their shoes on the bench part that people sat on to picnic or fellowship together in carefree times. They'd gone to different high schools but the same junior college, where they had met in campus ministries. It was springtime, and the park's grass was very green and the air suffused with honeysuckle and lilacs both, which was almost too much. There were bees, and the angle of the sun made the water of the shallows look dark. There had been more storms that week, with some downed trees and the sound of chainsaws all up and down his parents' street. Their postures on the picnic table were both the same forward kind with their shoulders rounded and elbows on their knees. In this position the girl rocked slightly and once put her face in her hands, but she was not crying. Lane was very still and immobile and looking past the bank at the downed tree in the shallows and its ball of exposed roots going all directions and the tree's cloud of branches all half in the water. The only other individual nearby was a dozen spaced tables away, by himself, standing upright. Looking at the torn-up hole in the ground there where the tree had gone over. It was still early yet and all the shadows wheeling right and shortening. The girl wore a thin old checked cotton shirt with pearl-colored snaps with the long sleeves down and always smelled very good and clean, like someone you could trust and care about even if you weren't in love. Lane Dean had liked the smell of her right away. His mother called her *down to earth* and liked her, thought she was good people, you could tell—she made this evident in little ways. The shallows lapped from different directions at the tree as if almost teething on it. Sometimes when alone and thinking or struggling to turn a matter over to Jesus Christ in prayer, he would find himself putting his fist in his palm and turning it slightly as if still playing and pounding his glove to stay sharp and alert in center. He did not do this now; it would be cruel and indecent to do this now. The older individual stood beside his picnic table—he was at it but not sitting—and looked also out of place in a suit coat or jacket and the kind of men's hat Lane's grandfather wore in photos as a young insurance man. He appeared to be looking across the lake. If he moved, Lane didn't see it. He looked more like a picture than a man. There were not any ducks in view.

One thing Lane Dean did was reassure her again that he'd go with her and be there with her. It was one of the few safe or decent things he could really say. The second time he said it again now she shook her head and laughed in an unhappy way that was more just air out her nose. Her real laugh was different. Where he'd be was the waiting room, she said. That he'd be thinking about her and feeling bad for her, she knew, but he couldn't be in there with her. This was so obviously true that he felt like a ninny that he'd kept on about it and now knew what she had thought every time he went and said it—it hadn't brought her comfort or eased the burden at all. The worse he felt, the stiller he sat. The whole thing felt balanced on a knife or wire; if he moved to put his arm up or touch her the whole thing could tip over. He hated himself for sitting so frozen. He could almost visualize himself tiptoeing past something explosive. A big stupid-looking tiptoe, like in a cartoon. The whole last black week had been this way and it was wrong. He knew it was wrong, knew something was required of him that was not this terrible frozen care and caution, but he pretended to himself he did not know what it was that was required. He pretended it had no name. He pretended that not saying aloud what he knew to be right and true was for her sake, was for the sake of her needs and feelings. He also worked dock and routing at UPS, on top of school, but had traded to get the day off after they'd decided together. Two days before, he had awakened very early and tried to pray but could not. He was freezing more and more solid, he felt like, but he had not thought of his father or the blank frozenness of his father, even in church, which had once filled him with such pity. This was the truth. Lane Dean, Jr., felt sun on one arm as he pictured in his mind an image of himself on a train, waving mechanically to something that got smaller and smaller as the train pulled away. His father and his mother's father had the same birthday, a Cancer. Sheri's hair was colored an almost corn blond, very clean, the skin through her central part pink in the sunlight. They'd sat here long enough that only their right side was shaded now. He could look at her head, but not at her. Different parts of him felt unconnected to each other. She was smarter than him and they both knew it. It wasn't just school—Lane Dean was in accounting and business and did all right; he was hanging in there. She was a year older, twenty, but it was also more—she had always seemed to Lane to be on good terms with her life in a way that age could not account for. His mother had put it that she *knew what it is she wanted*, which was nursing and not an easy program at Peoria Junior College, and plus she worked hostessing at the Embers and had bought her own car. She was serious in a way Lane liked. She had a cousin that died when she was thirteen, fourteen, that she'd loved and been close with. She only talked about it that once. He liked her smell and her downy arms and the way she exclaimed when something made her laugh. He had liked just being with her and talking to her. She was serious in her faith and values in a way that Lane had liked and now, sitting here with her on the table, found himself afraid of. This was an awful thing. He was starting to believe that he might not be serious in his faith. He might be somewhat of a hypocrite, like the Assyrians in Isaiah,[1] which would be a far graver sin than the appointment—he had decided he believed this. He was desperate to be good people, to still be able to feel he was good. He rarely before now had thought of damnation and Hell—that part of it didn't speak to his spirit—and in worship services he more just tuned himself out and tolerated Hell when it came up, the same way you tolerate the job you've got to have to save up for what it is you want. Her tennis shoes had little things doodled on them from sitting in her class lectures. She stayed looking down like that. Little notes or reading assignments in Bic in her neat round hand on the rubber elements around the sneaker's rim. Lane A. Dean, looking now at her inclined head's side's barrettes in the shape of blue ladybugs. The appointment was for afternoon, but when the doorbell had rung so early and his mother'd called to him up the stairs, he had known, and a terrible kind of blankness had commenced falling through him.

He told her that he did not know what to do. That he knew if he was the salesman of it and forced it upon her that was awful and wrong. But he was trying to understand—they'd prayed on it and talked it through from every different angle. Lane said how sorry she knew he was, and that if he was wrong in believing they'd truly decided together when they decided to make the appointment she should please tell him, because he thought he knew how she must

1. Perhaps a reference to Isaiah 36, in which the Assyrians promise to save the kingdom of Judah if its king will trust and surrender to them rather than relying on God. Later chapters describe Assyria's fall as punishment for their hubris.

have felt as it got closer and closer and how she must be so scared, but that what he couldn't tell was if it was more than that. He was totally still except for moving his mouth, it felt like. She did not reply. That if they needed to pray on it more and talk it through, then he was here, he was ready, he said. The appointment could get moved back; if she just said the word they could call and push it back to take more time to be sure in the decision. It was still so early in it—they both knew that, he said. This was true, that he felt this way, and yet he also knew he was also trying to say things that would get her to open up and say enough back that he could see her and read her heart and know what to say to get her to go through with it. He knew this without admitting to himself that this was what he wanted, for it would make him a hypocrite and liar. He knew, in some locked-up little part of him, why it was that he'd gone to no one to open up and seek their life counsel, not Pastor Steve or the prayer partners at campus ministries, not his UPS friends or the spiritual counselling available through his parents' old church. But he did not know why Sheri herself had not gone to Pastor Steve—he could not read her heart. She was blank and hidden. He so fervently wished it never happened. He felt like he knew now why it was a true sin and not just a leftover rule from past society. He felt like he had been brought low by it and humbled and now did believe that the rules were there for a reason. That the rules were concerned with him personally, as an individual. He promised God he had learned his lesson. But what if that, too, was a hollow promise, from a hypocrite who repented only after, who promised submission but really only wanted a reprieve? He might not even know his own heart or be able to read and know himself. He kept thinking also of 1 Timothy and the hypocrite therein who *disputeth over words.*[2] He felt a terrible inner resistance but could not feel what it was that it resisted. This was the truth. All the different angles and ways they had come at the decision together did not ever include it—the word—for had he once said it, avowed that he did love her, loved Sheri Fisher, then it all would have been transformed. It would not be a different stance or angle, but a difference in the very thing they were praying and deciding on together. Sometimes they had prayed together over the phone, in a kind of half code in case anybody accidentally picked up the extension. She continued to sit as if thinking, in the pose of thinking, like that one statue. They were right up next to each other on the table. He was looking over past her at the tree in the water. But he could not say he did: it was not true.

But neither did he ever open up and tell her straight out he did not love her. This might be his *lie by omission.* This might be the frozen resistance—were he to look right at her and tell her he didn't, she would keep the appointment and go. He knew this. Something in him, though, some terrible weakness or lack of values, could not tell her. It felt like a muscle he did not have. He didn't know why; he just could not do it, or even pray to do it. She believed he was good, serious in his values. Part of him seemed willing to more or less just about lie to someone with that kind of faith and trust, and what did that make him? How

2. See 1 Timothy 6.3–4: "If any man teach otherwise, and consent not to wholesome words, *even* the words of our Lord Jesus Christ, and to the doctrine which is according to godliness; He is proud, knowing nothing, but doting about questions and strifes of words, whereof cometh envy, strife, railings, evil surmisings."

could such a type of individual even pray? What it really felt like was a taste of the reality of what might be meant by Hell. Lane Dean had never believed in Hell as a lake of fire or a loving God consigning folks to a burning lake of fire—he knew in his heart this was not true. What he believed in was a living God of compassion and love and the possibility of a personal relationship with Jesus Christ through whom this love was enacted in human time. But sitting here beside this girl as unknown to him now as outer space, waiting for whatever she might say to unfreeze him, now he felt like he could see the edge or outline of what a real vision of Hell might be. It was of two great and terrible armies within himself, opposed and facing each other, silent. There would be battle but no victor. Or never a battle—the armies would stay like that, motionless, looking across at each other, and seeing therein something so different and alien from themselves that they could not understand, could not hear each other's speech as even words or read anything from what their face looked like, frozen like that, opposed and uncomprehending, for all human time. Two-hearted, a hypocrite to yourself either way.

5   When he moved his head, a part of the lake further out flashed with sun—the water up close wasn't black now, and you could see into the shallows and see that all the water was moving but gently, this way and that—and in this same way he besought to return to himself as Sheri moved her leg and started to turn beside him. He could see the man in the suit and gray hat standing motionless now at the lake's rim, holding something under one arm and looking across at the opposite side where a row of little forms on camp chairs sat in a way that meant they had lines in the water for crappie—which mostly only your blacks from the East Side ever did—and the little white shape at the row's end a Styrofoam creel. In his moment or time at the lake now just to come, Lane Dean first felt he could take this all in whole: everything seemed distinctly lit, for the circle of the pin oak's shade had rotated off all the way, and they sat now in sun with their shadow a two-headed thing in the grass before them. He was looking or gazing again at where the downed tree's branches seemed to all bend so sharply just under the shallows' surface when he was given to know that through all this frozen silence he'd despised he had, in truth, been praying, or some little part of his heart he could not hear had, for he was answered now with a type of vision, what he would later call within his own mind a vision or *moment of grace*. He was not a hypocrite, just broken and split off like all men. Later on, he believed that what happened was he'd had a moment of almost seeing them both as Jesus saw them—as blind but groping, wanting to please God despite their inborn fallen nature. For in that same given moment he saw, quick as light, into Sheri's heart, and was made to know what would occur here as she finished turning to him and the man in the hat watched the fishing and the downed elm shed cells into the water. This down-to-earth girl that smelled good and wanted to be a nurse would take and hold one of his hands in both of hers to unfreeze him and make him look at her, and she would say that she cannot do it. That she is sorry she did not know this sooner, that she hadn't meant to lie—she agreed because she'd wanted to believe that she could, but she cannot. That she will carry this and have it; she has to. With her gaze clear and steady. That all night last night she prayed and searched inside herself and decided this is what love commands of her. That Lane should please please

sweetie let her finish. That listen—this is her own decision and obliges him to nothing. That she knows he does not love her, not that way, has known it all this time, and that it's all right. That it is as it is and it's all right. She will carry this, and have it, and love it and make no claim on Lane except his good wishes and respecting what she has to do. That she releases him, all claim, and hopes he finishes up at P.J.C. and does so good in his life and has all joy and good things. Her voice will be clear and steady, and she will be lying, for Lane has been given to read her heart. To see through her. One of the opposite side's blacks raises his arm in what may be greeting, or waving off a bee. There is a mower cutting grass someplace off behind them. It will be a terrible, last-ditch gamble born out of the desperation in Sheri Fisher's soul, the knowledge that she can neither do this thing today nor carry a child alone and shame her family. Her values blocked the way either way, Lane could see, and she has no other options or choice—this lie is not a sin. Galatians 4:16, *Have I then become your enemy?*[3] She is gambling that he is good. There on the table, neither frozen nor yet moving, Lane Dean, Jr., sees all this, and is moved with pity, and also with something more, something without any name he knows, that is given to him in the form of a question that never once in all the long week's thinking and division had even so much as occurred—why is he so sure he doesn't love her? Why is one kind of love any different? What if he has no earthly idea what love is? What would even Jesus do? For it was just now he felt her two small strong soft hands on his, to turn him. What if he was just afraid, if the truth was no more than this, and if what to pray for was not even love but simple courage, to meet both her eyes as she says it and trust his heart?

2007

QUESTIONS

1. How would you summarize or characterize Lane Dean, Jr.'s conflicts, both internal and external? How does his religious faith intensify or even create those conflicts and help him to resolve them?

2. How is your interpretation of Lane Dean, Jr.'s character and conflicts shaped by all that the story withholds from us, including dialogue; Sheri's point of view or thoughts; explicit information about the nature of Sheri's "appointment" or of the "it" he "wished [. . .] never happened" (par. 3); a description of what actually happens at the end rather than Lane Dean's "vision" of what would happen and/or his later "belie[f]" about what happened?

3. What different definitions of "good people" or of a "good person" are implied here, or how might Lane Dean, Jr.'s understanding of what it means to be "good people" change over the course of the story? What part does the idea of hypocrisy play in those definitions?

3. "Am I therefore become your enemy, because I tell you the truth?" (Gal. 4.16). Earlier in this letter, Paul exhorts the Galatians to understand that when they "knew not God," they inevitably served "them which by nature are no gods," but now that they know God such "bondage" is instead a choice. At the same time, he reminds them that he is, like them, fallible, and that despite that "temptation which was in my flesh ye despised [me] not, nor rejected."

ALISSA NUTTING

(b. 1981)

Model's Assistant

Born in rural Michigan, raised in Florida, and today an Assistant Professor of creative writing at Grinnell College, in Iowa, Alissa Nutting describes herself as, for better or worse, irresistibly drawn to writing, calling her chosen career "kind of like an insane asylum that I checked myself into voluntarily: I can choose to leave any time, but I never will." Nutting earned her MFA at the University of Alabama (2008) and her PhD at the University of Nevada, Las Vegas (2011). Even before graduation, however, Nutting won the 2010 Starcherone Prize for Innovative Fiction for *Unclean Jobs for Women and Girls*, a collection featuring stories ranging from "Model's Assistant" and "Knife Thrower" to "Corpse Smoker" and "Dinner." As these titles suggest, Nutting's work is marked by a darkly satirical edge and a dash of the provocative and even surreal. Her stories and essays have appeared in venues ranging from the modern fairy-tale anthology *My Mother She Killed Me, My Father He Ate Me* (2010) to the *New York Times* online Anxiety column, *O: The Oprah Magazine*, and *Buzzfeed*. Dubbed "Most Controversial Book of Summer 2013" by both *Cosmopolitan* and the *Guardian*, Nutting's first novel, *Tampa* (2013), shares with "Model's Assistant" a concern with our contemporary tendency to, in her words, "treat beauty as a currency." With both a second novel, *Made for Love* (2017), and an expanded and revised version of *Unclean Jobs for Girls and Women* (2018), in Ecco Press's Art of the Story series, under her belt, as well as an HBO adaptation of *Made for Love* in the works, Nutting's star is on the rise. As one reviewer remarks, if the job of fiction "is to bottle and exhibit the zeitgeist through character in a way that is [. . .] novel, Nutting [. . .] goes for it, all out."

My best friend, Garla, is a model from somewhere Swedishy; when people try to pin down where she just yells, "Vodka," or if she's in a better mood, "Vodka, you know?" which seems like she's maybe saying she's Russian, but really she just wants to drink. Wherever she's from, Garla now lives inside the bubble of model-land. I wish I lived in model-land, too, but the closest I can come is hanging out with Garla, which is like going on vacation to a model-land time-share.

We met at a party in Chelsea[1] that I pond-skipped to. I definitely wasn't invited. I'd gone with a real friend to a not-so-hot party, and then left with her friend to go to a better party where I met a stranger who took me to a quite hot party. It was there that I made out with the photographer who took me to the party of Garla. She wasn't hosting it but she was present, and anywhere Garla goes is Garla's party.

---

1. Name of fashionable neighborhoods in both New York City and London.

I think the only reason I ever saw Garla again was because I was drunk enough to tell her the truth. She was trying on bizarre clothes—there was a shroud that looked space-like yet medical, like a gown one might wear to get a pap smear on Mars. Then she put on a dress whose pleating created the suggestion of a displaced goiter somewhere to the left of her neck and she sashayed toward me. I was holding my head onto my body, carefully and by the window, so that its breeze might sober me up enough to walk to the end of the room, where I might then become sober enough to walk to the toilet and land on the floor. There, hopefully, the pressure from my cheek against my cell phone could call someone who knew me and liked me enough to get me a cab and make sure this night was not where my life's journey would end. But for all I knew it was, and when I saw Garla I held on to my head just a little bit tighter, because she appeared to be strutting over to rip it off.

"You," she said, and I straightened up grammar-school style. I puked in my mouth but absolutely did not open my lips and let it fall on the floor. "Do you like this?" She did a turn that looked so elegant and stylized and unteachable to everyone in the room but to Garla was just something that accidentally slipped out of her like a tiny fart.

"It makes you look like you're pregnant in the back," I said, using the nose of 5 my beer bottle to itch between my shoulder blades, where the seam of her dress inexplicably globed out. She scowled and pranced off. I assumed she was offended until she brought over a silver-plated bowl filled with the car keys of various guests.

"Use for vomit," she said, and then, "have phone," and slipped a crystal-encrusted device into my purse. I think at that point two large gray wolfhounds magically walked up to either side of her and the three of them then headed toward the kitchen. "You love dogs and have a tendency to hallucinate them," I told myself as I stumbled toward the bathroom. Various refined guests stared on in horror as I groped onto pieces of furniture and potted plants, trying to stabilize my journey into a small room housing cold linoleum and a sink. "Why am I always the nerd at the party?" I thought. "I am in my thirties and by now I should at least know how to pretend."

The thing about bathrooms in parties is they don't always stay bathrooms; they start out as such but then become make-out rooms or cocaine-snorting rooms or bubble-bath-orgy rooms. When I burst through the door holding my abdomen, a slight and waify couple seemed to be using it as a now-that-we've-agreed-the-night-will-end-with-mutual-oral-sex-let's-take-our-time-getting-buzzed-first room; they were drinking very red wine, sitting on the side of the bathtub and giggling, using fingertips of wine to draw simple pictures onto the shower's white tile. The "braap" sound I made while becoming sick intrigued them. They were in their early twenties, and I could feel them looking at me with something real and concentrated. I don't think it was pity as much as curiosity; they seemed to wonder very much what it might be like to be so uncomposed. "I don't get when people use puking in art," said the boy, and the girl said, "Well, it's not like that, when they do," meaning not like me but like Garla throwing up pink paint onto a teal ceramic raccoon.

"I need a cab," I mumbled, and the boy was sympathetic but firm.

"I won't touch you," he said.

10   "No," I agreed. "I'll get myself down to the door."

It took a great while to do this. At some point I wondered if I should try to find Garla and give her the phone back, but then I saw a burst of light across the living room and there she was, the camera's flash bouncing off her oiled thigh, her foot inside the host's tropical aquarium. Everyone wanted a shot of her leather bondage shoe surrounded by fake coral: people were holding up cell phones and professional equipment and thin digital cameras; "Tickle fish," Garla was saying to everyone, which continually prompted a laugh-track response from the entire crowd. There was no way I could deal with calling her name and having that amount of attention suddenly focus over to my own body. Plus I didn't really want to give it back. A supermodel's phone! I was like a turd inside someone who'd accidentally swallowed an engagement ring: though I was nothing myself, I now carried something uniquely special.

I fell easily down the stairs and by the time I was able to stand, to my great surprise, a cab had come. "Thank you," I called up to the couple in the bathroom, but it came out gurgled, and they were likely busy readying to use their youth and beauty to give one another endless reciprocal orgasms.

I kept the phone on my desk for several days wondering what to do about it. There was something wrong with the phone; it didn't ring. Garla's phone would ring, wouldn't it?

It didn't ring until the fourth day.

15   "Hi, Womun." It was Garla. I began explaining how I'd meant to give the phone back, how I certainly hadn't called various pawnshops to price it (had!), but she interrupted. "It your phone, for me. I call you with it," she said, to which I could've said a lot of things, like how I already have a phone, or that I was very afraid of getting killed for this jewel-phone, should someone see me talking on it in my neighborhood, because I don't have a lot of money and neither does anyone else who lives here, but oftentimes people badly need money, and desperate times/desperate measures.

"I get you for fashion show," she said, "tonight at the seven-thirty." Out of some type of pride I wanted to make sure she didn't mean that *I* would be in the fashion show, that it wasn't an ironic thing where Beautifuls each try to snag themselves an Ugly, and whoever snags the ugliest Ugly and dresses it up best is the winner. "You mean go watch one with you?" I asked, and she said, "Ha," then it sounded like she lit a cigarette or something and said, "Ha. Ha. I mean this," and told me where to meet her.

Since that night my life has changed in many ways. I'm still no one, unless I am with Garla, and then I become *with Garla*, a new, exciting identity that makes nearly everything possible, except being attractive myself. And except being important when I am not with Garla.

At the oxygen bar, Garla gives my face three firm slaps on the cheek. She is always taking grandmotherly liberties such as these. "Put you in special coffin," she says, which is a term of endearment on her part but I don't know what it means exactly. I like to think that it's a sort of Snow White reference, that I'm so dear to her that she wants to keep my body displayed in a glass box next to her couch, forever asleep.[2]

---

2. In most versions of the folktale, after Snow White eats an apple poisoned by the jealous queen and falls asleep, she is put in a glass box by the dwarves who have twice saved her life.

Though I guess it could also mean she wants to close me inside an iron maiden.[3]

Garla is sitting in front of a laptop with a solar charger plugged into it, although it is raining outside and we are in a darkened room. Garla doesn't have opinions on things; she's not really the pro or con type. Right now she is into being very anti–global warming because she knows that being very anti–global warming is chic. Either things are chic or they aren't, and if they're chic then they're for Garla. "The web won't come," Garla says.

"Solar charger," I point out. "No sun." 20

"Global warming," Garla says. She will often randomly say the media titles of topics and events, such as "Crisis in Darfur,"[4] then take a drink and be silent for a few more hours.

A waitress wearing a hemp robe enters with two tanks and two breathing masks, hooking Garla in first. With the mask on Garla appears to be a pilot from the future, possibly a computer-generated one. Her perfect skin looks like a plasma screen.

"Are you from Sweden?" the waitress asks.

"Vodka, you know?" says Garla, and the waitress's eyes frown; perhaps she has just Botoxed[5] because I can tell she wants to make an expression but instead she blinks a few times.

"Could she get a glass of vodka," I ask, and the woman mentions that alcohol 25 is not usually consumed during the treatment. She is already on the way to get it, though, and when she returns there's also a glass for me.

It gets a little overwhelming in the mask when the pure oxygen starts to hit us at the same time as the vodka. Garla takes my hand. I don't know if I'm attracted to her or if she's just beautiful. I think it's the latter because she doesn't say much, and what she does say doesn't make much sense to me. But people don't have to talk a lot or make sense for others to love them. Just look at dogs and babies.

"Cloud of vodka!" Garla screams. I decide she wants another glass because I want another glass, so I hold two fingers up at the woman in hemp while pointing down to our melted ice. My fingers stay in an upright "peace" position; with our masks I imagine that Garla and I are on some kind of extreme roller coaster that goes into the stratosphere, and we're passing the camera that takes a picture for us to buy at the end, and I am saying, "This is me and Garla. Peace."

She has made me the best-dressed party nerd of all time. Once, she put these chain-link pants on me and I couldn't move, not even like a robot. So Garla—wearing six-inch stiletto heels—actually picked me up, carried me up the stairs to the party, and planted me by yet another fish tank, either so I'd have something to watch or because she knew that at some point, a part of her body would be posing inside of it and she very much wanted for me to be there to say, "Now Garla has to go home" when it started to get boring for her.

3. Torture device consisting of a hollow statue or coffin shaped like a woman and lined with spikes that impale the enclosed victim.
4. Between 2003 and 2010, hundreds of thousands died and millions were displaced due to conflict in the Darfur region of southwest Sudan, in northern Africa, inspiring a Save Darfur campaign championed by actor George Clooney and other celebrities.
5. Injected with Botox, a chemical that reduces wrinkles by paralyzing facial muscles.

There was never a conversation where Garla hired me to be her assistant. I just started speaking up when it made sense to, like when a director asked if he could film himself cutting her arm a tiny bit with a designer katana sword and licking her blood off the blade, and she answered him with "Special coffin," in a very small voice. "We have to go, Garla," I used to say, but I soon learned that "Garla has to go" is a better way to phrase it, because then it seems like she doesn't have a choice.

30   Tonight we go to another fashion show. Garla's walking in it so I wait back-stage in the chair where her makeup was done, and at several points people inquire as to why I'm there. Very few actually want me to leave; they're just baffled.

Afterward we go to the home of a fellow model where I watch Garla drink herself into a deep sea. She is a metronomic[6] drinker. I can count the glasses she drinks per hour, like a time signature, and know exactly how drunk she is at any given moment. With me it's the opposite; the drunk is that mystery wedding guest who may show up early, late, or not at all.

By four A.M. Garla is lying on an island countertop in the kitchen. Some guy has dumped a miniature Buddhist sand garden[7] out on her abdomen, and he's swirling the sand around her belly button with a tiny bamboo rake. Her head is hanging off the counter; it's flipped back like a Pez dispenser, and I walk over and we have this intoxicated moment.

"I know you're more," my drunken eyes say. They say this in a breathy, hesitant manner that insists it has taken a lot of time for them to work up the courage to say such a thing, without words nonetheless.

"Yes," answer Garla's eyes, and like all of Garla's answers it is a mysterious pearl whose full value I begin to appraise immediately. I walk over to her and lift her head up with my hands so it is level with the counter, holding it. I look down at her like a surgeon.

35   "Some type of sausage," Garla says; she likes the cured meats.

For a second I have the urge to drop her head. I'm reminded of being a child on the beach, the shells I'd leap to pick up and then throw back. They always seemed of greater worth from a distance, beneath the water.

I keep wondering if Garla will ask me to quit my job copyediting and join her full-time in model-land. Her agency is very good to her, but I know she needs me, or at least could really use me, more than she does, which leads me to wonder two things: Does Garla have others like Me? If so, how many Mes are there? Does she really need Me at all? The thing about Garla is that it's always okay for Garla. No matter what happens, Garla will be okay. I just speed the okayness up a little bit for her so that okay is sure to happen in real time.

Although my life has many more great things in it now than before I met Garla, I'm still beginning to feel a bit used. And—how can I deny this—I want more of Garla. She is a rare substance, if only because of the role and power she

6. Like a metronome, a device that marks time by ticking at precise intervals, allowing musicians to keep the meter indicated by the notation known as a *time signature*.
7. Space decorated with sand, rocks, and other natural materials in lines or patterns to create the meditative environment prized by Zen Buddhists.

has in our society and not anything she holds innately. Rare substances make people feel selfish and greedy, and Garla is no exception. Neither am I.

I am also getting a little sick of my special Garla-phone, but it's really expensive and the only thing Garla will call me on. I got rid of my other phone and now have only the phone Garla gave me, perhaps because I know she intended it to only be used when she called me, and this is a small rebellion on my part. Garla doesn't pick up on rebellions, though, big or small. She has no need for them.

I decide to ask if I can be her paid assistant, because she probably will not say yes or no, and I can just interpret it as yes. If anything, by quitting my job and hanging out with her more I will get additional goodies I can sell online, and Garla's schwag pays several times more than my current employer.

I strike when we are in the back of a town car on the way to a designer's private shoot. Garla is stretched out on my lap with her muss of blond hair hanging down over my knees. Her hair is softer than my shaved legs.

"Garla," I say, "I'm going to quit my job and be your assistant. You don't have to pay me hardly anything. I don't make very much as it is." There's a pause and she hands up a tiny golden comb to me, I presume for me to begin brushing her hair with. I also presume this means "yes," is a quid pro quo gesture. I call my boss right then on the Garla-phone and quit as loudly as I can without seeming hostile, just to try to burn the event a little deeper into the ether of Garla's memory.

The shoot goes well. Afterward I take her glasses of chilled vodka that look like refreshing water and we have a look at the pictures, which are beautiful. We leave with giant bags of expensive clothing that we neither paid nor asked for.

I am feeling more visible by the second. Perhaps, I think, I should move into Garla's apartment. That way I'd always be right there to meet her needs and there wouldn't be all the Garla-phone calls in the middle of the night; she could just yell or do a special grunt. Though I've never heard Garla yell. Everyone is already paying attention.

Except the next morning, she doesn't answer my calls, and she doesn't call me. This goes on for a week and a half. I sulk like a real model. I don't eat and I drink lots of vodka and I cut my own hair in the bathroom with dull scissors and then regret it, and the next morning I think about going to a really expensive salon and having it fixed except I don't have the money for that, especially now that I have no job. For that, I need Garla.

This is the root of my pain. I had convinced myself that she needed me, specifically, when really, anyone could and would do what I did: follow around a gorgeous person and get gifts and call outrages by name for what they are. How did I lend any type of panache to that role? Looking in the mirror at my botched home haircut, I realize that my new expensive clothes still look nerdy because they don't fit me right. They never will.

When the Garla-phone finally lights up and makes its synthetic music, it's like an air-raid siren. I'm paralyzed with fear but angst-ridden from loneliness and desperation. "Where have you been?" I scream. "We agreed I'd be your assistant. I quit my job! I haven't seen you for like ten days!"

"Vodka head," Garla explains.

I want to pretend like nothing is wrong. "I'm not a bad assistant," I say. "I'm a good assistant, which means I need to be where you are, and help you with things."

50   "Later, a party," she says. I can hear happy screams in the background and their shrillness stabs into me. I know those screams belong to completely impractical people, and I hate that she chose them over me. "What time?" I ask, but she already hung up.

Eventually she does text me the party's address. I stop by a nearby bar to have a few drinks alone first. It feels good to sulk over a glass in public. How could I have let my guard down so badly? Before Garla, I had been all-guard. Before Garla, I would've seen Garla coming. My pre-Garla life suddenly seems like an amazing thing; I hadn't even known what I was missing. As I walk out of the bar and look up near the balcony I'm headed to, I can actually see Garla. It makes me feel creepy but I stand there and watch for a while anyway, until the two of us seem like strangers. Even at this distance and with the party's disco lights, it's clear she has dazzling bone structure.

Compared to her, I am like a sandwich. I am completely inhuman and benign. I try to remember a sandwich I ate in the fourth grade and cannot. I can't even really remember one I ate a month ago. We all must be like fourth-grade sandwiches to Garla.

It's not until I get inside the suite and look around that I realize it's the same residence where Garla and I first met. This makes my hands and feet sweat rapidly; the line is becoming a circle.

As the night moves on, it's like going back in time. When I enter, Garla gives me a soft embrace and kisses my cheek, but I want restitution. I quit my job and had the week from hell, and she isn't going to reenter my life with one quick, pouty smile. Maybe I'm replaceable, but I don't have to be happy about it.

55   I take my old seat by the window and start rapidly boozing. The lights change colors in ways that suggest I'm going too fast, and that is the speed I want to go. It's a rush, like skydiving. I keep giving Garla a scowl that says, "Hey, you. I'm not holding on. I'm in free fall."

She's rubbing pieces of chocolate over her lips like ChapStick and men are helplessly pulled to her side of the room. Garla's face is a centrifuge that separates the confident from the weak and the jealous, and I have been spun away.

Stumbling to the bathroom, I get out my jeweled Garla-phone. Part of me wants to put it into the toilet, or at least try to see if it will fit through the hole in the bottom of the bowl. I want to throw up on it but it is so shiny that with its sparkling crystals and my drunken compound fly-eye vision, I have no aim. Instead the puke falls into the water and the phone falls on the ground, and when I'm finished and my cheek hits the floor the phone looks like a store of riches behind the plunger. I grab the phone and open it, kind of bumping it around, hoping it will call a friend who will come pick me up.

But it's Garla's phone, so it calls Garla. I hang up but a few minutes later she's standing over me in an Amazonian[8] manner, one leg on either side of my body. "Put you in tiny coffin," she says, rolling out some toilet paper and batting it against my wet cheek.

8. In Greek mythology the Amazons were a group of powerful female warriors.

"I wish you would."

She doesn't appreciate my display of self-pity. I watch her toss her martini 60 glass out the window onto the patio, where it breaks. "You go home and rest doctor-television."

After she leaves, a bodyguard enters and picks me up with a disgusted look, like he's emptying a full bedpan. He helps me into the taxi. Motoring away, I watch the colored streaks of Garla on the patio upstairs.

In a panic I check my purse to make sure I still have it: the Garla-phone, the jewel. The cursed treasure that brought distress alongside fortune. Glistening in my lap, it is too beautiful to be trusted. The cab nears my apartment, and I have the urge to leave the phone behind on the seat for someone else to find and answer. But I won't. Instead I'll go home and wait for her to call me and turn me into something special for however long she wants, and this time I won't forget to be grateful.

2010

QUESTIONS

1. What might we learn about the narrator by the style, as well as content, of her narration?
2. What attracts the narrator to Garla and vice versa?
3. Is the narrator's conflict external, internal, or both? Why doesn't she abandon the phone at the story's end?

CHIMAMANDA NGOZI ADICHIE

(b. 1977)

Apollo

The only MacArthur Foundation "genius grant" winner ever to have her work sampled by Beyoncé ("Flawless," 2013), Chimamanda Ngozi Adichie has lived a life as international as the acclaim she now enjoys. Most of what she describes as her "very happy childhood, full of laughter and love" was spent in Nigeria, in a "very close-knit," "conventional" middle-class Igbo family of six children whose house once belonged to influential novelist Chinua Achebe. Yet from age eight, Adichie spent some summers in the United States, where her father—a University of Nigeria statistics professor—had visiting appointments. After a brief stint as a pharmacy student at the same university, Adichie returned to the States part-time on a scholarship, ultimately earning a BA in political science (Eastern Connecticut State University, 2001) and MAs in both creative writing (Johns Hopkins, 2003) and African Studies (Yale, 2008). The fame Adichie also earned along the way derives in part from two viral TED Talks: "The Danger of a Single Story" (2009) and "We Should All Be Feminists" (2012). But Adichie's literary stature rests on three prize-winning best sellers. Begun when she was still a college senior living with her physician-sister,

Purple Hibiscus (2003) is a coming-of-age novel about Kambili, a fifteen-year-old from a wealthy, zealously religious Nigerian family. Made into a film starring Chiwetel Ejiofor and Thandie Newton (2013), the novel *Half of a Yellow Sun* (2006) explores the devastation wreaked by the Nigerian Civil War (1967–70). *Americanah* (2013) features a Nigerian student, on fellowship at Princeton, who creates a successful blog about being Black in America. Also a frequent contributor to major newspapers and magazines and an award-winning short-story writer, Adichie continues to split her time between Nigeria and the United States, where her husband works as a physician.

Twice a month, like a dutiful son, I visited my parents in Enugu, in their small overfurnished flat[1] that grew dark in the afternoon. Retirement had changed them, shrunk them. They were in their late eighties, both small and mahogany-skinned, with a tendency to stoop. They seemed to look more and more alike, as though all the years together had made their features blend and bleed into one another. They even smelled alike—a menthol scent, from the green vial of Vicks VapoRub they passed to each other, carefully rubbing a little in their nostrils and on aching joints. When I arrived, I would find them either sitting out on the veranda overlooking the road or sunk into the living-room sofa, watching Animal Planet.[2] They had a new, simple sense of wonder. They marvelled at the wiliness of wolves, laughed at the cleverness of apes, and asked each other, "Ifukwa?[3] Did you see that?"

They had, too, a new, baffling patience for incredible stories. Once, my mother told me that a sick neighbor in Abba, our ancestral home town, had vomited a grasshopper—a living, writhing insect, which, she said, was proof that wicked relatives had poisoned him. "Somebody texted us a picture of the grasshopper," my father said. They always supported each other's stories. When my father told me that Chief Okeke's young house help had mysteriously died, and the story around town was that the chief had killed the teenager and used her liver for moneymaking rituals, my mother added, "They say he used the heart, too."

Fifteen years earlier, my parents would have scoffed at these stories. My mother, a professor of political science, would have said "Nonsense" in her crisp manner, and my father, a professor of education, would merely have snorted, the stories not worth the effort of speech. It puzzled me that they had shed those old selves, and become the kind of Nigerians who told anecdotes about diabetes cured by drinking holy water.

Still, I humored them and half listened to their stories. It was a kind of innocence, this new childhood of old age. They had grown slower with the passing years, and their faces lit up at the sight of me and even their prying questions— "When will you give us a grandchild? When will you bring a girl to introduce to

---

1. Apartment (British English). *Enugu*: capital of Enugu State in southeastern Nigeria.
2. American multinational subscription television channel (est. 1996) primarily featuring shows about wild and domestic animals.
3. See that? (Igbo). Here, as throughout the story, words in Igbo (a language spoken by the Igbo peoples of southeastern Nigeria) are followed by their English translations.

us?"—no longer made me as tense as before. Each time I drove away, on Sunday afternoons after a big lunch of rice and stew, I wondered if it would be the last time I would see them both alive, if before my next visit I would receive a phone call from one of them telling me to come right away. The thought filled me with a nostalgic sadness that stayed with me until I got back to Port Harcourt.[4] And yet I knew that if I had a family, if I could complain about rising school fees as the children of their friends did, then I would not visit them so regularly. I would have nothing for which to make amends.

During a visit in November, my parents talked about the increase in armed robberies all over the east. Thieves, too, had to prepare for Christmas. My mother told me how a vigilante mob in Onitsha had caught some thieves, beaten them, and torn off their clothes—how old tires had been thrown over their heads like necklaces, amid shouts for petrol[5] and matches, before the police arrived, fired shots in the air to disperse the crowd, and took the robbers away. My mother paused, and I waited for a supernatural detail that would embellish the story. Perhaps, just as they arrived at the police station, the thieves had turned into vultures and flown away.

"Do you know," she continued, "one of the armed robbers, in fact the ring leader, was Raphael? He was our houseboy[6] years ago. I don't think you'll remember him."

I stared at my mother. "Raphael?"

"It's not surprising he ended like this," my father said. "He didn't start well."

My mind had been submerged in the foggy lull of my parents' storytelling, and I struggled now with the sharp awakening of memory.

My mother said again, "You probably won't remember him. There were so many of those houseboys. You were young."

But I remembered. Of course I remembered Raphael.

Nothing changed when Raphael came to live with us, not at first. He seemed like all the others, an ordinary-looking teen from a nearby village. The houseboy before him, Hyginus, had been sent home for insulting my mother. Before Hyginus was John, whom I remembered because he had not been sent away; he had broken a plate while washing it and, fearing my mother's anger, had packed his things and fled before she came home from work. All the houseboys treated me with the contemptuous care of people who disliked my mother. Please come and eat your food, they would say—I don't want trouble from Madam. My mother regularly shouted at them, for being slow, stupid, hard of hearing; even her bell-ringing, her thumb resting on the red knob, the shrillness searing through the house, sounded like shouting. How difficult could it be to remember to fry the eggs differently, my father's plain and hers with onions, or to put the Russian dolls back on the same shelf after dusting, or to iron my school uniform properly?

4. Or Pitakwa, capital of Rivers State, in southern Nigeria, roughly 150 miles from Enugu.
5. Gasoline (British English). *Onitsha*: city on the eastern bank of the Niger river, a commercial and educational hub about seventy miles southwest of Enugu.
6. Boy or man employed to perform domestic tasks.

I was my parents' only child, born late in their lives. "When I got pregnant, I thought it was menopause," my mother told me once. I must have been around eight years old, and did not know what "menopause" meant. She had a brusque manner, as did my father; they had about them the air of people who were quick to dismiss others. They had met at the University of Ibadan,[7] married against their families' wishes—his thought her too educated, while hers preferred a wealthier suitor—and spent their lives in an intense and intimate competition over who published more, who won at badminton, who had the last word in an argument. They often read aloud to each other in the evening, from journals or newspapers, standing rather than sitting in the parlor, sometimes pacing, as though about to spring at a new idea. They drank Mateus rosé[8]—that dark, shapely bottle always seemed to be resting on a table near them—and left behind glasses faint with reddish dregs. Throughout my childhood, I worried about not being quick enough to respond when they spoke to me.

I worried, too, that I did not care for books. Reading did not do to me what it did to my parents, agitating them or turning them into vague beings lost to time, who did not quite notice when I came and went. I read books only enough to satisfy them, and to answer the kinds of unexpected questions that might come in the middle of a meal—What did I think of Pip? Had Ezeulu[9] done the right thing? I sometimes felt like an interloper in our house. My bedroom had book-shelves, stacked with the overflow books that did not fit in the study and the corridor, and they made my stay feel transient, as though I were not quite where I was supposed to be. I sensed my parents' disappointment in the way they glanced at each other when I spoke about a book, and I knew that what I had said was not incorrect but merely ordinary, uncharged with their brand of origi-nality. Going to the staff club[1] with them was an ordeal: I found badminton bor-ing, the shuttlecock seemed to me an unfinished thing, as though whoever had invented the game had stopped halfway.

15   What I loved was kung fu. I watched "Enter the Dragon" so often that I knew all the lines, and I longed to wake up and be Bruce Lee.[2] I would kick and strike at the air, at imaginary enemies who had killed my imaginary family. I would pull my mattress onto the floor, stand on two thick books—usually hardcover copies of "Black Beauty" and "The Water-Babies"[3]—and leap onto the mattress, screaming "Haaa!" like Bruce Lee. One day, in the middle of my practice, I looked up to see Raphael standing in the doorway, watching me. I expected a

7. Nigeria's oldest and most prestigious higher-education institution (founded 1948).
8. Brand of pinkish, medium-sweet wine made in Portugal and sold in a distinctive narrow-necked, flask-shaped bottle.
9. Protagonist of influential Nigerian novelist Chinua Achebe's *Arrow of God* (1964), an Igbo priest in 1920s Nigeria, when the country was still under British colonial rule. *Pip*: narrator-protagonist of Charles Dickens's *Great Expectations* (1861).
1. A.k.a. faculty club; recreational facility where faculty, staff, administrators, and their guests social-ize and hold special events.
2. Hong Kong–raised Chinese American martial artist (1940–73); star of many action-adventure films of the 1970s. His *Enter the Dragon* (1973) is widely regarded as the all-time greatest martial arts film.
3. *The Water-Babies, A Fairy Tale for a Land Baby* (1863), popular children's novel by English novelist Charles Kingsley (1819–75). *Black Beauty*: 1877 novel by English author Anna Sewell (1820–78), a children's classic whose eponymous narrator-protagonist is a horse.

mild reprimand. He had made my bed that morning, and now the room was in disarray. Instead, he smiled, touched his chest, and brought his finger to his tongue, as though tasting his own blood. My favorite scene. I stared at Raphael with the pure thrill of unexpected pleasure. "I watched the film in the other house where I worked," he said. "Look at this."

He pivoted slightly, leaped up, and kicked, his leg straight and high, his body all taut grace. I was twelve years old and had, until then, never felt that I recognized myself in another person.

Raphael and I practiced in the backyard, leaping from the raised concrete soakaway[4] and landing on the grass. Raphael told me to suck in my belly, to keep my legs straight and my fingers precise. He taught me to breathe. My previous attempts, in the enclosure of my room, had felt stillborn. Now, outside with Raphael, slicing the air with my arms, I could feel my practice become real, with soft grass below and high sky above, and the endless space mine to conquer. This was truly happening. I could become a black belt one day. Outside the kitchen door was a high open veranda, and I wanted to jump off its flight of six steps and try a flying kick. "No," Raphael said. "That veranda is too high."

On weekends, if my parents went to the staff club without me, Raphael and I watched Bruce Lee videotapes, Raphael saying, "Watch it! Watch it!" Through his eyes, I saw the films anew; some moves that I had thought merely competent became luminous when he said, "Watch it!" Raphael knew what really mattered; his wisdom lay easy on his skin. He rewound the sections in which Bruce Lee used a nunchaku,[5] and watched unblinking, gasping at the clean aggression of the metal-and-wood weapon.

"I wish I had a nunchaku," I said.

"It is very difficult to use," Raphael said firmly, and I felt almost sorry to have 20
wanted one.

Not long afterward, I came back from school one day and Raphael said, "See." From the cupboard he took out a nunchaku—two pieces of wood, cut from an old cleaning mop and sanded down, held together by a spiral of metal springs. He must have been making it for at least a week, in his free time after his housework. He showed me how to use it. His moves seemed clumsy, nothing like Bruce Lee's. I took the nunchaku and tried to swing it, but only ended up with a thump on my chest. Raphael laughed. "You think you can just start like that?" he said. "You have to practice for a long time."

At school, I sat through classes thinking of the wood's smoothness in the palm of my hand. It was after school, with Raphael, that my real life began. My parents did not notice how close Raphael and I had become. All they saw was that I now happened to play outside, and Raphael was, of course, part of the landscape of outside: weeding the garden, washing pots at the water tank. One afternoon, Raphael finished plucking a chicken and interrupted my solo practice on the lawn. "Fight!" he said. A duel began, his hands bare, mine swinging

4. Pit into which rain or waste water drains.
5. A.k.a. nunchucks; Japanese martial arts weapon consisting of two sticks connected by a short chain or rope; first popularized by Bruce Lee.

my new weapon. He pushed me hard. One end hit him on the arm, and he looked surprised and then impressed, as if he had not thought me capable. I swung again and again. He feinted and dodged and kicked. Time collapsed. In the end, we were both panting and laughing. I remember, even now, very clearly, the smallness of his shorts that afternoon, and how the muscles ran wiry like ropes down his legs.

On weekends, I ate lunch with my parents. I always ate quickly, dreaming of escape and hoping that they would not turn to me with one of their test questions. At one lunch, Raphael served white disks of boiled yam on a bed of greens, and then cubed pawpaw[6] and pineapple.

"The vegetable was too tough," my mother said. "Are we grass-eating goats?" She glanced at him. "What is wrong with your eyes?"

25   It took me a moment to realize that this was not her usual figurative lambasting—"What is that big object blocking your nose?" she would ask, if she noticed a smell in the kitchen that he had not. The whites of Raphael's eyes were red. A painful, unnatural red. He mumbled that an insect had flown into them.

"It looks like Apollo,"[7] my father said.

My mother pushed back her chair and examined Raphael's face. "Ah-ah! Yes, it is. Go to your room and stay there."

Raphael hesitated, as though wanting to finish clearing the plates.

"Go!" my father said. "Before you infect us all with this thing."

30   Raphael, looking confused, edged away from the table. My mother called him back. "Have you had this before?"

"No, Madam."

"It's an infection of your conjunctiva, the thing that covers your eyes," she said. In the midst of her Igbo words, "conjunctiva" sounded sharp and dangerous. "We're going to buy medicine for you. Use it three times a day and stay in your room. Don't cook until it clears." Turning to me, she said, "Okenwa, make sure you don't go near him. Apollo is very infectious." From her perfunctory tone, it was clear that she did not imagine I would have any reason to go near Raphael.

Later, my parents drove to the pharmacy in town and came back with a bottle of eye drops, which my father took to Raphael's room in the boys' quarters, at the back of the house, with the air of someone going reluctantly into battle. That evening, I went with my parents to Obollo Road to buy akara[8] for dinner; when we returned, it felt strange not to have Raphael open the front door, not to find him closing the living-room curtains and turning on the lights. In the quiet kitchen, our house seemed emptied of life. As soon as my parents were immersed in themselves, I went out to the boys' quarters and knocked on Raphael's door. It was ajar. He was lying on his back, his narrow bed pushed

6. Papaya.
7. West African nickname for conjunctivitis or "pink eye," an infection of the mucous membrane (conjunctiva) covering the front surface of the eye. The name purportedly derives from the fact that the first epidemic of a new form of conjunctivitis, in Ghana, coincided with the Apollo 11 moon landing (1969). In classical mythology, Apollo is the god of medicine and healing, among other things.
8. Bean fritters.

against the wall, and turned when I came in, surprised, making as if to get up. I had never been in his room before. The exposed light bulb dangling from the ceiling cast sombre shadows.

"What is it?" he asked.

"Nothing. I came to see how you are."

He shrugged and settled back down on the bed. "I don't know how I got this. Don't come close."

But I went close.

"I had Apollo in Primary 3," I said. "It will go quickly, don't worry. Have you used the eye drops this evening?"

He shrugged and said nothing. The bottle of eye drops sat unopened on the table.

"You haven't used them at all?" I asked.

"No."

"Why?"

He avoided looking at me. "I cannot do it."

Raphael, who could disembowel a turkey and lift a full bag of rice, could not drip liquid medicine into his eyes. At first, I was astonished, then amused, and then moved. I looked around his room and was struck by how bare it was—the bed pushed against the wall, a spindly table, a gray metal box in the corner, which I assumed contained all that he owned.

"I will put the drops in for you," I said. I took the bottle and twisted off the cap.

"Don't come close," he said again.

I was already close. I bent over him. He began a frantic blinking.

"Breathe like in kung fu," I said.

I touched his face, gently pulled down his lower left eyelid, and dropped the liquid into his eye. The other lid I pulled more firmly, because he had shut his eyes tight.

"Ndo," I said. "Sorry."

He opened his eyes and looked at me, and on his face shone something wondrous. I had never felt myself the subject of admiration. It made me think of science class, of a new maize shoot growing greenly toward light. He touched my arm. I turned to go.

"I'll come before I go to school," I said.

In the morning, I slipped into his room, put in his eye drops, and slipped out and into my father's car, to be dropped off at school.

By the third day, Raphael's room felt familiar to me, welcoming, uncluttered by objects. As I put in the drops, I discovered things about him that I guarded closely: the early darkening of hair above his upper lip, the ringworm[9] patch in the hollow between his jaw and his neck. I sat on the edge of his bed and we talked about "Snake in the Monkey's Shadow."[1] We had discussed the film many times, and we said things that we had said before, but in the quiet of his room they felt like secrets. Our voices were low, almost hushed. His body's warmth cast warmth over me.

35

40

45

50

9. Fungal infection of the skin.
1. 1979 Hong Kong martial arts film.

55   He got up to demonstrate the snake style, and afterward, both of us laughing, he grasped my hand in his. Then he let go and moved slightly away from me.

"This Apollo has gone," he said.

His eyes were clear. I wished he had not healed so quickly.

I dreamed of being with Raphael and Bruce Lee in an open field, practicing for a fight. When I woke up, my eyes refused to open. I pried my lids apart. My eyes burned and itched. Each time I blinked, they seemed to produce more pale ugly fluid that coated my lashes. It felt as if heated grains of sand were under my eyelids. I feared that something inside me was thawing that was not supposed to thaw.

My mother shouted at Raphael, "Why did you bring this thing to my house? Why?" It was as though by catching Apollo he had conspired to infect her son. Raphael did not respond. He never did when she shouted at him. She was standing at the top of the stairs, and Raphael was below her.

60   "How did he manage to give you Apollo from his room?" my father asked me.

"It wasn't Raphael. I think I got it from somebody in my class," I told my parents.

"Who?" I should have known my mother would ask. At that moment, my mind erased all my classmates' names.

"Who?" she asked again.

"Chidi Obi," I said finally, the first name that came to me. He sat in front of me and smelled like old clothes.

65   "Do you have a headache?" my mother asked.

"Yes."

My father brought me Panadol.[2] My mother telephoned Dr. Igbokwe. My parents were brisk. They stood by my door, watching me drink a cup of Milo[3] that my father had made. I drank quickly. I hoped that they would not drag an armchair into my room, as they did every time I was sick with malaria, when I would wake up with a bitter tongue to find one parent inches from me, silently reading a book, and I would will myself to get well quickly, to free them.

Dr. Igbokwe arrived and shined a torch[4] in my eyes. His cologne was strong; I could smell it long after he'd gone, a heady scent close to alcohol that I imagined would worsen nausea. After he left, my parents created a patient's altar by my bed—on a table covered with cloth, they put a bottle of orange Lucozade, a blue tin of glucose,[5] and freshly peeled oranges on a plastic tray. They did not bring the armchair, but one of them was home throughout the week that I had Apollo. They took turns putting in my eye drops, my father more clumsily than my mother, leaving sticky liquid running down my face. They did not know how well I could put in the drops myself. Each time they raised the bottle above my face, I remembered the look in Raphael's eyes that first evening in his room, and I felt haunted by happiness.

2. Brand of acetaminophen, a pain reliever.
3. Brand of powder mixed with hot water or milk to make what Nestlé describes as "the world's leading chocolate malt beverage."
4. Flashlight (British English).
5. Essentially, canned powder used to make a high-energy drink rich in simple sugars. *Lucozade*: sports drink also high in glucose.

My parents closed the curtains and kept my room dark. I was sick of lying down. I wanted to see Raphael, but my mother had banned him from my room, as though he could somehow make my condition worse. I wished that he would come and see me. Surely he could pretend to be putting away a bedsheet, or bringing a bucket to the bathroom. Why didn't he come? He had not even said sorry to me. I strained to hear his voice, but the kitchen was too far away and his voice, when he spoke to my mother, was too low.

Once, after going to the toilet, I tried to sneak downstairs to the kitchen, but 70 my father loomed at the bottom of the stairs.

"Kedu?" He asked. "Are you all right?"

"I want water," I said.

"I'll bring it. Go and lie down."

Finally, my parents went out together. I had been sleeping, and woke up to sense the emptiness of the house. I hurried downstairs and to the kitchen. It, too, was empty. I wondered if Raphael was in the boys' quarters; he was not supposed to go to his room during the day, but maybe he had, now that my parents were away. I went out to the open veranda. I heard Raphael's voice before I saw him, standing near the tank, digging his foot into the sand, talking to Josephine, Professor Nwosu's house help. Professor Nwosu sometimes sent eggs from his poultry, and never let my parents pay for them. Had Josephine brought eggs? She was tall and plump; now she had the air of someone who had already said goodbye but was lingering. With her, Raphael was different—the slouch in his back, the agitated foot. He was shy. She was talking to him with a kind of playful power, as though she could see through him to things that amused her. My reason blurred.

"Raphael!" I called out. 75

He turned. "Oh. Okenwa. Are you allowed to come downstairs?"

He spoke as though I were a child, as though we had not sat together in his dim room.

"I'm hungry! Where is my food?" It was the first thing that came to me, but in trying to be imperious I sounded shrill.

Josephine's face puckered, as though she were about to break into slow, long laughter. Raphael said something that I could not hear, but it had the sound of betrayal. My parents drove up just then, and suddenly Josephine and Raphael were roused. Josephine hurried out of the compound, and Raphael came toward me. His shirt was stained in the front, orangish, like palm oil from soup. Had my parents not come back, he would have stayed there mumbling by the tank; my presence had changed nothing.

"What do you want to eat?" he asked. 80

"You didn't come to see me."

"You know Madam said I should not go near you."

Why was he making it all so common and ordinary? I, too, had been asked not to go to his room, and yet I had gone, I had put in his eye drops every day.

"After all, you gave me the Apollo," I said.

"Sorry." He said it dully, his mind elsewhere. 85

I could hear my mother's voice. I was angry that they were back. My time with Raphael was shortened, and I felt the sensation of a widening crack.

"Do you want plantain[6] or yam?" Raphael asked, not to placate me but as if nothing serious had happened. My eyes were burning again. He came up the steps. I moved away from him, too quickly, to the edge of the veranda, and my rubber slippers shifted under me. Unbalanced, I fell. I landed on my hands and knees, startled by the force of my own weight, and I felt the tears coming before I could stop them. Stiff with humiliation, I did not move.

My parents appeared.

"Okenwa!" my father shouted.

90   I stayed on the ground, a stone sunk in my knee. "Raphael pushed me."

"What?" My parents said it at the same time, in English. "What?"

There was time. Before my father turned to Raphael, and before my mother lunged at him as if to slap him, and before she told him to go pack his things and leave immediately, there was time. I could have spoken. I could have cut into that silence. I could have said that it was an accident. I could have taken back my lie and left my parents merely to wonder.

2015

QUESTIONS

1. How is Okenwa, Apollo's narrator-protagonist, characterized in the story's first section (through par. 11)? What is your impression of him at this point in the story?

2. How might your impression of Okenwa develop over the course of the story, as he relates the story of his childhood relationship with Raphael? How is that relationship characterized, and why does it seem to become so meaningful (hence memorable) to the narrator?

3. Why does Okenwa act as he does at the very end of the story? Though the adult narrator never explicitly offers a judgment on these actions, might the story imply one? How so, or not? What, if anything, might the story ultimately suggest about how this series of events in their childhoods may have shaped the adult characters and lives of Okenwa and Raphael?

SUGGESTIONS FOR WRITING

1. Choose any story in this anthology in which a character changes because of the events that occur in the story. Write an essay exploring exactly how, when, and why the character changes.

2. Choose any story in this chapter and write an essay analyzing its handling of character and methods of characterization. Do the story's characters tend to be more flat or round, static or dynamic, highly individualized or nearly indistinguishable? Is indirect or direct characterization more important? How important is each type of evidence listed on the checklist that appears earlier in this chapter? Why and how is this treatment of character appropriate to the story?

3. Write an essay comparing how the adult lives and personalities of the two central characters in Recitatif are shaped by their experience in the orphanage. Why and how is this experience so traumatic? How does each character understand and cope with this experience over time? In these terms, how are Twyla and Roberta both

6. Variety of banana used in cooking, a staple in West and Central Africa, the Caribbean, and Central America.

similar and different, and what role does Maggie play in their efforts to come to terms with their past?

4. Write an essay exploring how plotting—especially sequence and pace—and narration—including focus, voice, tense, and (biblical) allusion—contribute to the characterization of Lane Dean, Jr., in GOOD PEOPLE.

5. In her TED Talk "The Danger of a Single Story" (available online), Chimamanda Adichie compares the simplistic view she had of (or the "single story" she believed about) her family's houseboy when she was a child, to the simplistic view her American college roommate had of all Africans. Write an essay exploring what APOLLO might demonstrate about the nature and effects of class-based biases *among* Nigerians and/or how the story as a whole might complicate a modern American reader's simplistic view of Nigerians or of Africa and Africans more generally.

Monsters

AN ALBUM

The world's oldest work of fiction is a story about monsters. Known as *The Epic of Gilgamesh*, it depicts the unlikely friendship between the wise but ruthless king of Uruk (in modern Iraq) and his opposite, Enkidu. A hairy (and, by some accounts, horned and hooved) creature of the forest who runs naked with the animals, knowing "nothing of land or peoples" until he is taught how to speak, eat, and clothe himself like a man, Enkidu clearly counts as a *monster* in the term's most literal sense—"a mythical creature which is part animal and part human, or combines elements of two or more animal forms, and is frequently of great size and ferocious appearance" (*Oxford English Dictionary*). Yet Enkidu ultimately accompanies Gilgamesh deep into the Cedar Forest in order to slay its far more monstrous guardian—the dreaded, fire-breathing giant Humbaba the Terrible. Even before that, Enkidu stops Gilgamesh from exercising his "right" to be the first to enjoy the sexual favors of every newly married bride in his kingdom—precisely the sort of behavior that makes the king seem, to his people, the real *monster* in that term's more figurative or moral sense—"A person [. . .] exhibiting such extreme cruelty or wickedness as to appear inhuman." Like many of the greatest "monster stories" to come, the world's oldest provokes us to ponder just who "the monster" truly is and whether it just might be us.

Though human beings and their stories have obviously changed enormously in the thousands of years since someone etched *Gilgamesh* onto clay tablets, one thing that hasn't changed is our fascination with creatures who straddle borders we like to consider stable and impermeable—between human and animal, civilized and savage, good and evil, even life and death. Strange as it may seem, Stephenie Meyer's Edward Cullen and Jacob Black, J. K. Rowling's Professor Lupin, and J. R. R. Tolkien's hobbits and dragon, even Disney's Beast, are as much Enkidu and Humbaba's descendants as are *Beowulf*'s Grendel, Bram Stoker's Dracula, and Robert Louis Stevenson's Mr. Hyde. If one of fiction's basic goals is simply to help us imagine what it is like either to be, or to cope with, someone who appears utterly different from ourselves, the "monster" may well be the ultimate fictional character. As outsiders, outcasts, and sometimes **scapegoats**, such characters have also, at least since Mary Shelley's *Frankenstein* (1818), served as a means through which authors explore a variety of specific social prejudices, norms, and forms of exclusion and oppression. Often, they do so by allowing us to perceive the world from the point of view of the monster itself—precisely that point of view with which conventional horror fiction and film often have little sympathy.

Though different, all of the stories in this album do precisely that, taking us into a deliberately fantastic world in order to give us new insight into our own. As you read them, think about how each story depicts its protagonist's peculiar character and situation. In what different senses is and is not each of these characters

257

a monster? To what real people and situations do the stories encourage us to compare their fantastical ones? Or how might they help us to better understand our own distinctly human way of experiencing the world, ourselves, even time itself, by imagining an utterly alien way?

MARGARET ATWOOD

(b. 1939)

Lusus Naturae[1]

Margaret Atwood spent her first eleven years in sparsely populated areas of northern Ontario and Quebec, Canada, where her father worked as an entomologist—an upbringing that may help explain her enduring concern with humanity's often destructive relationship with the natural world. Educated at the University of Toronto and Harvard, the woman now widely regarded as Canada's preeminent woman of letters published her first poem at nineteen and the first of numerous poetry collections, *Double Persephone*, three years later. An equally gifted short-story writer who counts Edgar Allan Poe among her early inspirations, Atwood is best known for her novels. Translated into over thirty languages and often, like her poetry, exploring the unique experiences and perspectives of women, past, present, and future, these novels include straightforwardly realistic narratives like *The Edible Woman* (1969) and *Bodily Harm* (1981), at least one modernized fairy tale (*The Robber Bride* [1993]), multilayered historical fictions such as *Alias Grace* (1996) and the Booker Prize–winning *The Blind Assassin* (2000), and the futuristic dystopias Atwood herself prefers to call "speculative" rather than "science fiction"—*Oryx and Crake* (2003), *The Year of the Flood* (2009), *MaddAddam* (2013), *The Heart Goes Last* (2015), and *The Handmaid's Tale* (1985), which has inspired a Danish opera, a Hollywood movie, and a *Hulu* miniseries. A sequel, *The Testaments*, appeared in 2019.

W hat could be done with me, what should be done with me? These were the same question. The possibilities were limited. The family discussed them all, lugubriously, endlessly, as they sat around the kitchen table at night, with the shutters closed, eating their dry whiskery sausages and their potato soup. If I was in one of my lucid phases I would sit with them, entering into the conversation as best I could while searching out the chunks of potato in my bowl. If not, I'd be off in the darkest corner, mewing to myself and listening to the twittering voices nobody else could hear.

"She was such a lovely baby," my mother would say. "There was nothing wrong with her." It saddened her to have given birth to an item such as myself: it was like a reproach, a judgment. What had she done wrong?

1. Freak of nature (Latin).

"Maybe it's a curse," said my grandmother. She was as dry and whiskery as the sausages, but in her it was natural because of her age.

"She was fine for years," said my father. "It was after that case of measles, when she was seven. After that."

"Who would curse us?" said my mother. 5

My grandmother scowled. She had a long list of candidates. Even so, there was no one she could single out. Our family had always been respected, and even liked, more or less. It still was. It still would be, if something could be done about me. Before I leaked out, so to say.

"The doctor says it's a disease," said my father. He liked to claim he was a rational man. He took the newspapers. It was he who insisted that I learn to read, and he'd persisted in his encouragement, despite everything. I no longer nestled into the crook of his arm, however. He sat me on the other side of the table. Though this enforced distance pained me, I could see his point.

"Then why didn't he give us some medicine?" said my mother. My grandmother snorted. She had her own ideas, which involved puffballs and stump water. Once she'd held my head under the water in which the dirty clothes were soaking, praying while she did it. That was to eject the demon she was convinced had flown in through my mouth and was lodged near my breastbone. My mother said she had the best of intentions, at heart.

Feed her bread, the doctor had said. *She'll want a lot of bread. That, and potatoes. She'll want to drink blood. Chicken blood will do, or the blood of a cow. Don't let her have too much.* He told us the name of the disease, which had some Ps and Rs in it and meant nothing to us.[2] He'd only seen a case like me once before, he'd said, looking at my yellow eyes, my pink teeth, my red fingernails, the long dark hair that was sprouting on my chest and arms. He wanted to take me away to the city, so other doctors could look at me, but my family refused. "She's a lusus naturae," he'd said.

"What does that mean?" said my grandmother. 10

"Freak of nature," the doctor said. He was from far away: we'd summoned him. Our own doctor would have spread rumors. "It's Latin. Like a monster." He thought I couldn't hear, because I was mewing. "It's nobody's fault."

"She's a human being," said my father. He paid the doctor a lot of money to go away to his foreign parts and never come back.

"Why did God do this to us?" said my mother.

"Curse or disease, it doesn't matter," said my older sister. "Either way, no one will marry me if they find out." I nodded my head: true enough. She was a pretty girl, and we weren't poor, we were almost gentry. Without me, her coast would be clear.

In the daytimes I stayed shut up in my darkened room: I was getting beyond 15 a joke. That was fine with me, because I couldn't stand sunlight. At night, sleepless, I would roam the house, listening to the snores of the others, their yelps of

2. Porphyria, a group of usually incurable genetic disorders disrupting the body's production of hemoglobin (the protein that makes blood red); symptoms of the disease's more acute forms include insomnia, hallucinations, light sensitivity, excess body hair, reddish teeth, painful skin conditions, even disfigurement. Such symptoms, as well as certain blood-related treatments, have led some to propose porphyria as an inspiration for vampire legends, though such theories have been repeatedly debunked.

nightmare. The cat kept me company. He was the only living creature who wanted to be close to me. I smelled of blood, old dried-up blood: perhaps that was why he shadowed me, why he would climb up onto me and start licking.

They'd told the neighbors I had a wasting illness, a fever, a delirium. The neighbors sent eggs and cabbages; from time to time they visited, to scrounge for news, but they weren't eager to see me: whatever it was might be catching.

It was decided that I should die. That way I would not stand in the way of my sister, I would not loom over her like a fate. "Better one happy than both miserable," said my grandmother, who had taken to sticking garlic cloves around my door frame. I agreed to this plan, as I wanted to be helpful.

The priest was bribed; in addition to that, we appealed to his sense of compassion. Everyone likes to think they are doing good while at the same time pocketing a bag of cash, and our priest was no exception. He told me God had chosen me as a special girl, a sort of bride, you might say. He said I was called on to make sacrifices. He said my sufferings would purify my soul. He said I was lucky, because I would stay innocent all my life, no man would want to pollute me, and then I would go straight to Heaven.

He told the neighbors I had died in a saintly manner. I was put on display in a very deep coffin in a very dark room, in a white dress with a lot of white veiling over me, fitting for a virgin and useful in concealing my whiskers. I lay there for two days, though of course I could walk around at night. I held my breath when anyone entered. They tiptoed, they spoke in whispers, they didn't come close, they were still afraid of my disease. To my mother they said I looked just like an angel.

20   My mother sat in the kitchen and cried as if I really had died; even my sister managed to look glum. My father wore his black suit. My grandmother baked. Everyone stuffed themselves. On the third day they filled the coffin with damp straw and carted it off to the cemetery and buried it, with prayers and a modest headstone, and three months later my sister got married. She was driven to the church in a coach, a first in our family. My coffin was a rung on her ladder.

Now that I was dead, I was freer. No one but my mother was allowed into my room, my former room as they called it. They told the neighbors they were keeping it as a shrine to my memory. They hung a picture of me on the door, a picture made when I still looked human. I didn't know what I looked like now. I avoided mirrors.

In the dimness I read Pushkin,[3] and Lord Byron, and the poetry of John Keats. I learned about blighted love, and defiance, and the sweetness of death. I found these thoughts comforting. My mother would bring me my potatoes and bread, and my cup of blood, and take away the chamber pot. Once she used to brush my hair, before it came out in handfuls; she'd been in the habit of hugging me and weeping; but she was past that now. She came and went as quickly as she could. However she tried to hide it, she resented me, of course. There's only

---

3. Russian poet (1799–1837) associated, like Lord Byron and John Keats, with the Romantic movement; his verse-novel *Eugene Onegin* (1825–32) describes the ill-fated romance of a young aristocrat who travels the world out of both boredom with high society and guilt over killing his friend in a duel.

so long you can feel sorry for a person before you come to feel that their affliction is an act of malice committed by them against you.

At night I had the run of the house, and then the run of the yard, and after
that the run of the forest. I no longer had to worry about getting in the way of
other people and their futures. As for me, I had no future. I had only a present,
a present that changed—it seemed to me—along with the moon. If it weren't
for the fits, and the hours of pain, and the twittering of the voices I couldn't
understand, I might have said I was happy.

My grandmother died, then my father. The cat became elderly. My mother sank
further into despair. "My poor girl," she would say, though I was no longer
exactly a girl. "Who will take care of you when I'm gone?"

There was only one answer to that: it would have to be me. I began to explore   25
the limits of my power. I found I had a great deal more of it when unseen than
when seen, and most of all when partly seen. I frightened two children in the
woods, on purpose: I showed them my pink teeth, my hairy face, my red fingernails, I mewed at them, and they ran away screaming. Soon people avoided our
end of the forest. I peered into a window at night, and caused hysterics in a
young woman. "A thing! I saw a thing!" she sobbed. I was a thing, then. I considered this. In what way is a thing not a person?

A stranger made an offer to buy our farm. My mother wanted to sell and
move in with my sister and her gentry husband and her healthy growing family,
whose portraits had just been painted; she could no longer manage; but how
could she leave me?

"Do it," I told her. By now my voice was a sort of growl. "I'll vacate my room.
There's a place I can stay." She was grateful, poor soul. She had an attachment
to me, as if to a hangnail, a wart: I was hers. But she was glad to be rid of me.
She'd done enough duty for a lifetime.

During the packing-up and the sale of our furniture I spent the days inside a
hayrick. It was sufficient, but it would not do for winter. Once the new people had
moved in, it was no trouble to get rid of them. I knew the house better than they
did, its entrances, its exits. I could make my way around it in the dark. I became
an apparition, then another one; I was a red-nailed hand touching a face in the
moonlight; I was the sound of a rusted hinge that I made despite myself. They
took to their heels, and branded our place as haunted. Then I had it to myself.

I lived on stolen potatoes dug by moonlight, on eggs filched from henhouses.
Once in a while I'd purloin a hen—I'd drink the blood first. There were guard
dogs, but though they howled at me, they never attacked: they didn't know what
I was. Inside our house, I tried a mirror. They say dead people can't see their
own reflections, and it was true; I could not see myself. I saw something, but
that something was not myself: it looked nothing like the innocent, pretty girl I
knew myself to be, at heart.

But now things are coming to an end. I've become too visible.   30

This is how it happened.

I was picking blackberries in the dusk, at the verge where the meadow
met the trees, and I saw two people approaching, from opposite sides. One

was a young man, the other a girl. His clothing was better than hers. He had shoes.

The two of them looked furtive. I knew that look—the glances over the shoulder, the stops and starts—as I was unusually furtive myself. I crouched in the brambles to watch. They met, they twined together, they fell to the ground. Mewing noises came from them, growls, little screams. Perhaps they were having fits, both of them at once. Perhaps they were—oh, at last!—beings like myself. I crept closer to see better. They did not look like me—they were not hairy, for instance, except on their heads, and I could tell this because they had shed most of their clothing—but then, it had taken me some time to grow into what I was. They must be in the preliminary stages, I thought. They know they are changing, they have sought out each other for the company, and to share their fits.

They appeared to derive pleasure from their flailings about, even if they occasionally bit each other. I knew how that could happen. What a consolation it would be to me if I, too, could join in! Through the years I had hardened myself to loneliness; now I found that hardness dissolving. Still, I was too timorous to approach them.

35   One evening the young man fell asleep. The girl covered him with his cast-off shirt and kissed him on the forehead. Then she walked carefully away.

I detached myself from the brambles and came softly toward him. There he was, asleep in an oval of crushed grass, as if laid out on a platter. I'm sorry to say I lost control. I laid my red-nailed hands on him. I bit him on the neck. Was it lust or hunger? How could I tell the difference? He woke up, he saw my pink teeth, my yellow eyes; he saw my black dress fluttering; he saw me running away. He saw where.

He told the others in the village, and they began to speculate. They dug up my coffin and found it empty, and feared the worst. Now they're marching toward this house, in the dusk, with long stakes, with torches. My sister is among them, and her husband, and the young man I kissed. I meant it to be a kiss.

What can I say to them, how can I explain myself? When demons are required someone will always be found to supply the part, and whether you step forward or are pushed is all the same in the end. "I am a human being," I could say. But what proof do I have of that? "I am a lusus naturae! Take me to the city! I should be studied!" No hope there. I'm afraid it's bad news for the cat. Whatever they do to me, they'll do to him as well.

I am of a forgiving temperament, I know they have the best of intentions at heart. I've put on my white burial dress, my white veil, as befits a virgin. One must have a sense of occasion. The twittering voices are very loud: it's time for me to take flight. I'll fall from the burning rooftop like a comet, I'll blaze like a bonfire. They'll have to say many charms over my ashes, to make sure I'm really dead this time. After a while I'll become an upside-down saint; my finger bones will be sold as dark relics. I'll be a legend, by then.

40   Perhaps in Heaven I'll look like an angel. Or perhaps the angels will look like me. What a surprise that will be, for everyone else! It's something to look forward to.

2004

QUESTIONS

1. How and why does the protagonist's attitude toward her situation change over the course of the story? How and why does she paradoxically become more alive and powerful after she "dies" and as she becomes more and more "invisible"?
2. Why does she nonetheless choose to make herself "visible" at the story's conclusion (par. 30)? What new insight might this episode provide into both her character and situation, on the one hand, and "normal" human behavior, on the other? How, for example, might the conclusion complicate the idea that the story is exclusively about illness or disability and our attitudes toward it?
3. What conflicts does the protagonist's condition create for the story's other characters? How do they each understand that condition? How might the story encourage us to view their attitudes and behaviors?

KAREN RUSSELL

(b. 1981)

St. Lucy's Home for Girls Raised by Wolves

Karen Russell's first novel, *Swamplandia!* (2011), details the lives of a family of alligator wrestlers in what she calls "the most bizarre place" on earth—her childhood home of South Florida. After leaving Florida, Russell attended Northwestern University and toyed with the idea of becoming a veterinarian. Deciding that "loving animals and removing deflated basketballs from the intestinal tracts of animals are two very different skill sets," she instead turned to writing, earning an MFA from Columbia University. Just twenty-six when she published her first short-story collection, *St. Lucy's Home for Girls Raised by Wolves* (2006), Russell was, early in her career, almost as renowned for her youth as for her remarkable fiction; both ensured her inclusion on *New York* magazine's list of twenty-seven impressive New Yorkers under the age of twenty-six (2005), *Granta*'s Best Young American Novelists (2007), the National Book Foundation's "5 Under 35" (2009), and the *New Yorker*'s "20 under 40" (2010). Since winning a 2013 MacArthur "genius grant," Russell has published *Vampires in the Lemon Grove: Stories* (2013), *Sleep Donation: A Novella* (2014), and *Orange World and Other Stories* (2019). Often blending realism with the totally outlandish, her work has been compared to "slipstream," a genre-bending form of fiction with roots in magic realism. Russell herself, however, often cites "George Saunders's sad/funny ratio" and his work's "deep humility" as her inspirations.

> Stage 1: The initial period is one in which everything is new, exciting, and interesting for your students. It is fun for your students to explore their new environment.
>
> —From *The Jesuit Handbook on Lycanthropic Culture Shock*

At first, our pack was all hair and snarl and floor-thumping joy. We forgot the barked cautions of our mothers and fathers, all the promises we'd made to be civilized and ladylike, couth and kempt. We tore through the austere rooms, overturning dresser drawers, pawing through the neat piles of the Stage 3 girls' starched underwear, smashing lightbulbs with our bare fists. Things felt less foreign in the dark. The dim bedroom was windowless and odorless. We remedied this by spraying exuberant yellow streams all over the bunks. We jumped from bunk to bunk, spraying. We nosed each other midair, our bodies buckling in kinetic laughter. The nuns watched us from the corner of the bedroom, their tiny faces pinched with displeasure.

"*Ay caramba,*" Sister Maria de la Guardia sighed. "*Que barbaridad!*"[1] She made the Sign of the Cross. Sister Maria came to St. Lucy's from a halfway home in Copacabana. In Copacabana, the girls are fat and languid and eat pink slivers of guava right out of your hand. Even at Stage 1, their pelts are silky, sun-bleached to near invisibility. Our pack was hirsute and sinewy and mostly brunette. We had terrible posture. We went knuckling along the wooden floor on the calloused pads of our fists, baring row after row of tiny, wood-rotted teeth. Sister Josephine sucked in her breath. She removed a yellow wheel of floss from under her robes, looping it like a miniature lasso.

"The girls at our facility are *backwoods,*'" Sister Josephine whispered to Sister Maria de la Guardia with a beatific smile. "You must be patient with them." I clamped down on her ankle, straining to close my jaws around the woolly XXL sock. Sister Josephine tasted like sweat and freckles. She smelled easy to kill.

We'd arrived at St. Lucy's that morning, part of a pack fifteen-strong. We were accompanied by a mousy, nervous-smelling social worker; the baby-faced deacon; Bartholomew, the blue wolfhound; and four burly woodsmen. The deacon handed out some stale cupcakes and said a quick prayer. Then he led us through the woods. We ran past the wild apiary, past the felled oaks, until we could see the white steeple of St. Lucy's rising out of the forest. We stopped short at the edge of a muddy lake. Then the deacon took our brothers. Bartholomew helped him to herd the boys up the ramp of a small ferry. We girls ran along the shore, tearing at our new jumpers in a plaid agitation. Our brothers stood on the deck, looking small and confused.

5   Our mothers and fathers were werewolves. They lived an outsider's existence in caves at the edge of the forest, threatened by frost and pitchforks. They had been ostracized by the local farmers for eating their silled fruit pies and terrorizing the heifers. They had ostracized the local wolves by having sometimes-thumbs, and regrets, and human children. (Their condition skips a generation.) Our pack grew up in a green purgatory. We couldn't keep up with the purebred wolves, but we never stopped crawling. We spoke a slab-tongued pidgin[2] in the

---

1. What barbarity (Spanish). *Ay caramba*: good grief (Spanish).
2. Simplified speech used for communication between speakers of different languages.

cave, inflected with frequent howls. Our parents wanted something better for us; they wanted us to get braces, use towels, be fully bilingual. When the nuns showed up, our parents couldn't refuse their offer. The nuns, they said, would make us naturalized citizens of human society. We would go to St. Lucy's to study a better culture. We didn't know at the time that our parents were sending us away for good. Neither did they.

That first afternoon, the nuns gave us free rein of the grounds. Everything was new, exciting, and interesting. A low granite wall surrounded St. Lucy's, the blue woods humming for miles behind it. There was a stone fountain full of delectable birds. There was a statue of St. Lucy.[3] Her marble skin was colder than our mother's nose, her pupil-less eyes rolled heavenward. Doomed squirrels gamboled around her stony toes. Our diminished pack threw back our heads in a celebratory howl—an exultant and terrible noise, even without a chorus of wolf brothers in the background. There were holes everywhere!

We supplemented these holes by digging some of our own. We interred sticks, and our itchy new jumpers, and the bones of the friendly, unfortunate squirrels. Our noses ached beneath an invisible assault. Everything was smudged with a human odor: baking bread, petrol, the nuns' faint woman-smell sweating out beneath a dark perfume of tallow and incense. We smelled one another, too, with the same astounded fascination. Our own scent had become foreign in this strange place.

We had just sprawled out in the sun for an afternoon nap, yawning into the warm dirt, when the nuns reappeared. They conferred in the shadow of the juniper tree, whispering and pointing. Then they started towards us. The oldest sister had spent the past hour twitching in her sleep, dreaming of fatty and infirm elk. (The pack used to dream the same dreams back then, as naturally as we drank the same water and slept on the same red scree.[4]) When our oldest sister saw the nuns approaching, she instinctively bristled. It was an improvised bristle, given her new, human limitations. She took clumps of her scraggly, nut-brown hair and held it straight out from her head.

Sister Maria gave her a brave smile.

"And what is your name?" she asked.

10

The oldest sister howled something awful and inarticulable, a distillate of hurt and panic, half-forgotten hunts and eclipsed moons. Sister Maria nodded and scribbled on a yellow legal pad. She slapped on a name tag: HELLO, MY NAME IS _____! "Jeanette it is."

The rest of the pack ran in a loose, uncertain circle, torn between our instinct to help her and our new fear. We sensed some subtler danger afoot, written in a language we didn't understand.

Our littlest sister had the quickest reflexes. She used her hands to flatten her ears to the side of her head. She backed towards the far corner of the garden, snarling in the most menacing register that an eight-year-old wolf-girl can muster. Then she ran. It took them two hours to pin her down and tag her: HELLO, MY NAME IS MIRABELLA!

3. Patron saint of the blind, St. Lucy (283–304) either took out her own eyes or was blinded by others, according to legend, defending her vow to remain a virgin and dedicate her life and fortune to God rather than marry a pagan.
4. Loose stones or rocky debris.

"Stage 1," Sister Maria sighed, taking careful aim with her tranquilizer dart. "It can be a little overstimulating."

> Stage 2: After a time, your students realize that they must work to adjust to the new culture. This work may be stressful and students may experience a strong sense of dislocation. They may miss certain foods. They may spend a lot of time daydreaming during this period. Many students feel isolated, irritated, bewildered, depressed, or generally uncomfortable.

15   Those were the days when we dreamed of rivers and meat. The full-moon nights were the worst! Worse than cold toilet seats and boiled tomatoes, worse than trying to will our tongues to curl around our false new names. We would snarl at one another for no reason. I remember how disorienting it was to look down and see two square-toed shoes instead of my own four feet. Keep your mouth shut, I repeated during our walking drills, staring straight ahead. Keep your shoes on your feet. Mouth shut, shoes on feet. Do not chew on your new penny loafers. Do not. I stumbled around in a daze, my mouth black with shoe polish. The whole pack was irritated, bewildered, depressed. We were all uncomfortable, and between languages. We had never wanted to run away so badly in our lives; but who did we have to run back to? Only the curled black grimace of the mother. Only the father, holding his tawny head between his paws. Could we betray our parents by going back to them? After they'd given us the choicest part of the woodchuck, loved us at our hairless worst, nosed us across the ice floes and abandoned us at St. Lucy's for our own betterment?

Physically, we were all easily capable of clearing the low stone walls. Sister Josephine left the wooden gates wide open. They unslatted the windows at night so that long fingers of moonlight beckoned us from the woods. But we knew we couldn't return to the woods; not till we were civilized, not if we didn't want to break the mother's heart. It all felt like a sly, human taunt.

It was impossible to make the blank, chilly bedroom feel like home. In the beginning, we drank gallons of bathwater as part of a collaborative effort to mark our territory. We puddled up the yellow carpet of old newspapers. But later, when we returned to the bedroom, we were dismayed to find all trace of the pack musk had vanished. Someone was coming in and erasing us. We sprayed and sprayed every morning; and every night, we returned to the same ammonia eradication. We couldn't make our scent stick here; it made us feel invisible. Eventually we gave up. Still, the pack seemed to be adjusting on the same timetable. The advanced girls could already alternate between two speeds: "slouch" and "amble." Almost everybody was fully bipedal.

Almost.

The pack was worried about Mirabella.

20   Mirabella would rip foamy chunks out of the church pews and replace them with ham bones and girl dander. She loved to roam the grounds wagging her invisible tail. (We all had a hard time giving that up. When we got excited, we would fall to the ground and start pumping our backsides. Back in those days we could pump at rabbity velocities. *Que horror!* Sister Maria frowned, looking more than a little jealous.) We'd give her scolding pinches. "Mirabella," we hissed, imitating the nuns. "No." Mirabella cocked her ears at us, hurt and confused.

Still, some things remained the same. The main commandment of wolf life is Know Your Place, and that translated perfectly. Being around other humans had awakened a slavish-dog affection in us. An abasing, belly-to-the-ground desire to please. As soon as we realized that someone higher up in the food chain was watching us, we wanted only to be pleasing in their sight. Mouth shut, I repeated, shoes on feet. But if Mirabella had this latent instinct, the nuns couldn't figure out how to activate it. She'd go bounding around, gleefully spraying on their gilded statue of St. Lucy, mad-scratching at the virulent fleas that survived all of their powders and baths. At Sister Maria's tearful insistence, she'd stand upright for roll call, her knobby, oddly muscled legs quivering from the effort. Then she'd collapse right back to the ground with an ecstatic *oomph!* She was still loping around on all fours (which the nuns had taught us to see looked unnatural and ridiculous—we could barely believe it now, the shame of it, that we used to locomote like that!), her fists blue-white from the strain. As if she were holding a secret tight to the ground. Sister Maria de la Guardia would sigh every time she saw her. *"Caramba!"* She'd sit down with Mirabella and pry her fingers apart. "You see?" she'd say softly, again and again. "What are you holding on to? Nothing, little one. Nothing."

Then she would sing out the standard chorus, "Why can't you be more like your sister Jeanette?"

The pack hated Jeanette. She was the most successful of us, the one furthest removed from her origins. Her real name was GWARR!, but she wouldn't respond to this anymore. Jeanette spiffed her penny loafers until her very shoes seemed to gloat. (Linguists have since traced the colloquial origins of "goody two-shoes" back to our facilities.) She could even growl out a demonic-sounding precursor to "Pleased to meet you." She'd delicately extend her former paws to visitors, wearing white kid gloves.

"Our little wolf, disguised in sheep's clothing!" Sister Ignatius liked to joke with the visiting deacons, and Jeanette would surprise everyone by laughing along with them, a harsh, inhuman, barking sound. Her hearing was still twig-snap sharp. Jeanette was the first among us to apologize; to drink apple juice out of a sippy cup; to quit eyeballing the cleric's jugular in a disconcerting fashion. She curled her lips back into a cousin of a smile as the traveling barber cut her pelt into bangs. Then she swept her coarse black curls under the rug. When we entered a room, our nostrils flared beneath the new odors: onion and bleach, candle wax, the turnipy smell of unwashed bodies. Not Jeanette. Jeanette smiled and pretended like she couldn't smell a thing.

I was one of the good girls. Not great and not terrible, solidly middle of the 25 pack. But I had an ear for languages, and I could read before I could adequately wash myself. I probably could have vied with Jeanette for the number-one spot, but I'd seen what happened if you gave in to your natural aptitudes. This wasn't like the woods, where you had to be your fastest and your strongest and your bravest self. Different sorts of calculations were required to survive at the home.

The pack hated Jeanette, but we hated Mirabella more. We began to avoid her, but sometimes she'd surprise us, curled up beneath the beds or gnawing on a scapula in the garden. It was scary to be ambushed by your sister. I'd bristle and growl, the way that I'd begun to snarl at my own reflection as if it were a stranger.

"Whatever will become of Mirabella?" we asked, gulping back our own fear. We'd heard rumors about former wolf-girls who never adapted to their new culture. It was assumed that they were returned to our native country, the vanishing woods. We liked to speculate about this before bedtime, scaring ourselves with stories of catastrophic bliss. It was the disgrace, the failure that we all guiltily hoped for in our hard beds. Twitching with the shadow question: *Whatever will become of me?*

We spent a lot of time daydreaming during this period. Even Jeanette. Sometimes I'd see her looking out at the woods in a vacant way. If you interrupted her in the midst of one of these reveries, she would lunge at you with an elder-sister ferocity, momentarily forgetting her human catechism. We liked her better then, startled back into being foamy old Jeanette.

In school, they showed us the St. Francis of Assisi[5] slide show, again and again. Then the nuns would give us bags of bread. They never announced these things as a test; it was only much later that I realized that we were under constant examination. "Go feed the ducks," they urged us. "Go practice compassion for all God's creatures." *Don't pair me with Mirabella,* I prayed, *anybody but Mirabella.* "Claudette"—Sister Josephine beamed—"why don't you and Mirabella take some pumpernickel down to the ducks?"

30   "Ohhkaaythankyou," I said. (It took me a long time to say anything; first I had to translate it in my head from the Wolf.) It wasn't fair. They knew Mirabella couldn't make bread balls yet. She couldn't even undo the twist tie of the bag. She was sure to eat the birds; Mirabella didn't even try to curb her desire to kill things—and then who would get blamed for the dark spots of duck blood on our Peter Pan collars? Who would get penalized with negative Skill Points? Exactly.

As soon as we were beyond the wooden gates, I snatched the bread away from Mirabella and ran off to the duck pond on my own. Mirabella gave chase, nipping at my heels. She thought it was a game. "Stop it," I growled. I ran faster, but it was Stage 2 and I was still unsteady on my two feet. I fell sideways into a leaf pile, and then all I could see was my sister's blurry form, bounding towards me. In a moment, she was on top of me, barking the old word for tug-of-war. When she tried to steal the bread out of my hands, I whirled around and snarled at her, pushing my ears back from my head. I bit her shoulder, once, twice, the only language she would respond to. I used my new motor skills. I threw dirt, I threw stones. "Get away!" I screamed, long after she had made a cringing retreat into the shadows of the purple saplings. "Get away, get away!"

Much later, they found Mirabella wading in the shallows of a distant river, trying to strangle a mallard with her rosary beads. I was at the lake; I'd been sitting there for hours. Hunched in the long cattails, my yellow eyes flashing, shoving ragged hunks of bread into my mouth.

I don't know what they did to Mirabella. Me they separated from my sisters. They made me watch another slide show. This one showed images of former wolf-girls, the ones who had failed to be rehabilitated. Long-haired, sad-eyed women, limping after their former wolf packs in white tennis shoes and pleated

5. In one of many legends illustrating his special relationship with animals, St. Francis (1181–1226) talks a village out of killing a wolf that has been attacking them and convinces the wolf to stop killing; the villagers then make a pet of the wolf.

culottes. A wolf-girl bank teller, her makeup smeared in oily rainbows, eating a raw steak on the deposit slips while her colleagues looked on in disgust. Our parents. The final slide was a bolded sentence in St. Lucy's prim script: DO YOU WANT TO END UP SHUNNED BY BOTH SPECIES?

After that, I spent less time with Mirabella. One night she came to me, holding her hand out. She was covered with splinters, keening a high, whining noise through her nostrils. Of course I understood what she wanted; I wasn't that far removed from our language (even though I was reading at a fifth-grade level, halfway into Jack London's *The Son of the Wolf*[6]).

"Lick your own wounds," I said, not unkindly. It was what the nuns had   35
instructed us to say; wound licking was not something you did in polite company. Etiquette was so confounding in this country. Still, looking at Mirabella—her fists balled together like small, white porcupines, her brows knitted in animal confusion—I felt a throb of compassion. *How can people live like they do?* I wondered. Then I congratulated myself. This was a Stage 3 thought.

> Stage 3: It is common that students who start living in a new and different culture come to a point where they reject the host culture and withdraw into themselves. During this period, they make generalizations about the host culture and wonder how the people can live like they do. Your students may feel that their own culture's lifestyle and customs are far superior to those of the host country.

The nuns were worried about Mirabella, too. To correct a failing, you must first be aware of it as a failing. And there was Mirabella, shucking her plaid jumper in full view of the visiting cardinal. Mirabella, battling a raccoon under the dinner table while the rest of us took dainty bites of peas and borscht. Mirabella, doing belly flops into compost.

"You have to pull your weight around here," we overheard Sister Josephine saying one night. We paused below the vestry window and peered inside.

"Does Mirabella try to earn Skill Points by shelling walnuts and polishing Saint-in-the-Box? No. Does Mirabella even know how to say the word *walnut*? Has she learned how to say anything besides a sinful 'HraaaHA!' as she commits frottage[7] against the organ pipes? No."

There was a long silence.

"Something must be done," Sister Ignatius said firmly. The other nuns nod-   40
ded, a sea of thin, colorless lips and kettle-black brows. "Something must be done," they intoned. That ominously passive construction; a something so awful that nobody wanted to assume responsibility for it.

I could have warned her. If we were back home, and Mirabella had come under attack by territorial beavers or snow-blind bears, I would have warned her. But the truth is that by Stage 3 I wanted her gone. Mirabella's inability to adapt was taking a visible toll. Her teeth were ground down to nubbins; her hair was falling out. She hated the spongy, long-dead foods we were served, and it showed—her ribs were poking through her uniform. Her bright eyes had dulled to a sour whiskey color. But you couldn't show Mirabella the slightest kindness

---

6. Short story (1900) about a White settler in the Yukon whose determination to marry an indigenous woman over the objections of her people results in the death of two tribesmen.
7. Rubbing against a person or object for sexual stimulation.

anymore—she'd never leave you alone! You'd have to sit across from her at meals, shoving her away as she begged for your scraps. I slept fitfully during that period, unable to forget that Mirabella was living under my bed, gnawing on my loafers.

It was during Stage 3 that we met our first purebred girls. These were girls raised in captivity, volunteers from St. Lucy's School for Girls. The apple-cheeked fourth-grade class came to tutor us in playing. They had long golden braids or short, severe bobs. They had frilly-duvet names like Felicity and Beu-lah; and pert, bunny noses; and terrified smiles. We grinned back at them with genuine ferocity. It made us nervous to meet new humans. There were so many things that we could do wrong! And the rules here were different depending on which humans we were with: dancing or no dancing, checkers playing or no checkers playing, pumping or no pumping.

The purebred girls played checkers with us.

"These girl-girls sure is dumb," my sister Lavash panted to me between games. "I win it again! Five to none."

She was right. The purebred girls were making mistakes on purpose, in order to give us an advantage. "King me," I growled, out of turn. *"I say king me!"* and Felicity meekly complied. Beulah pretended not to mind when we got frustrated with the oblique, fussy movement from square to square and shredded the board to ribbons. I felt sorry for them. I wondered what it would be like to be bred in captivity, and always homesick for a dimly sensed forest, the trees you've never seen.

Jeanette was learning how to dance. On Holy Thursday, she mastered a rudimentary form of the Charleston. *"Brava!"* The nuns clapped. *"Brava!"*

Every Friday, the girls who had learned how to ride a bicycle celebrated by going on chaperoned trips into town. The purebred girls sold seven hundred rolls of gift-wrap paper and used the proceeds to buy us a yellow fleet of bicycles built for two. We'd ride the bicycles uphill, a sanctioned pumping, a grim-faced nun pedaling behind each one of us. "Congratulations!" the nuns would huff. "Being human is like riding this bicycle. Once you've learned how, you'll never forget." Mirabella would run after the bicycles, growling out our old names. HWRAA! GWARR! TRRRRRRR! We pedaled faster.

At this point, we'd had six weeks of lessons, and still nobody could do the Sausalito but Jeanette. The nuns decided we needed an inducement to dance. They announced that we would celebrate our successful rehabilitations with a Debutante Ball. There would be brothers, ferried over from the Home for Man-Boys Raised by Wolves. There would be a photographer from the *Gazette Sophisticate*. There would be a three-piece jazz band from West Toowoomba, and root beer in tiny plastic cups. The brothers! We'd almost forgotten about them. Our invisible tails went limp. I should have been excited; instead, I felt a low mad anger at the nuns. They knew we weren't ready to dance with the brothers; we weren't even ready to talk to them. Things had been so much simpler in the woods. That night I waited until my sisters were asleep. Then I slunk into the closet and practiced the Sausalito two-step in secret, a private mass of twitch and foam. Mouth shut— shoes on feet! Mouth shut—shoes on feet! Mouthshutmouthshut . . .

One night I came back early from the closet and stumbled on Jeanette. She was sitting in a patch of moonlight on the windowsill, reading from one of her library books. (She was the first of us to sign for her library card, too.) Her cheeks looked dewy.

"Why you cry?" I asked her, instinctively reaching over to lick Jeanette's 50 cheek and catching myself in the nick of time.

Jeanette blew her nose into a nearby curtain. (Even her mistakes annoyed us— they were always so well intentioned.) She sniffled and pointed to a line in her book: "The lake-water was reinventing the forest and the white moon above it, and wolves lapped up the cold reflection of the sky." But none of the pack besides me could read yet, and I wasn't ready to claim a common language with Jeanette.

The following day, Jeanette golfed. The nuns set up a miniature putt-putt course in the garden. Sister Maria dug four sandtraps and got old Walter, the groundskeeper, to make a windmill out of a lawn mower engine. The eighteenth hole was what they called a "doozy," a minuscule crack in St. Lucy's marble dress. Jeanette got a hole in one.

On Sundays, the pretending felt almost as natural as nature. The chapel was our favorite place. Long before we could understand what the priest was saying, the music instructed us in how to feel. The choir director—aggressively per- fumed Mrs. Valuchi, gold necklaces like pineapple rings around her neck— taught us more than the nuns ever did. She showed us how to pattern the old hunger into arias. Clouds moved behind the frosted oculus of the nave, glass shadows that reminded me of my mother. The mother, I'd think, struggling to conjure up a picture. A black shadow, running behind the watery screen of pines.

We sang at the chapel annexed to the home every morning. We understood that this was the humans' moon, the place for howling beyond purpose. Not for mating, not for hunting, not for fighting, not for anything but the sound itself. And we'd howl along with the choir, hurling every pitted thing within us at the stained glass. "Sotto voce."[8] The nuns would frown. But you could tell that they were pleased.

> Stage 4: As a more thorough understanding of the host culture is acquired,
> your students will begin to feel more comfortable in their new environment.
> Your students feel more at home, and their self-confidence grows. Everything
> begins to make sense.

"Hey, Claudette," Jeanette growled to me on the day before the ball. "Have 55 you noticed that everything's beginning to make sense?"

Before I could answer, Mirabella sprang out of the hall closet and snapped through Jeanette's homework binder. Pages and pages of words swirled around the stone corridor, like dead leaves off trees.

"What about you, Mirabella?" Jeanette asked politely, stooping to pick up her erasers. She was the only one of us who would still talk to Mirabella; she was high enough in the rankings that she could afford to talk to the scruggliest wolf- girl. "Has everything begun to make more sense, Mirabella?"

Mirabella let out a whimper. She scratched at us and scratched at us, raking her nails along our shins so hard that she drew blood. Then she rolled belly-up on the cold stone floor, squirming on a bed of spelling-bee worksheets. Above us, small pearls of light dotted the high, tinted window.

8. In a low voice (Italian).

Jeanette frowned. "You are a late bloomer, Mirabella! Usually, everything's begun to make more sense by Month Twelve at the latest." I noticed that she stumbled on the word *bloomer*. HraaaHA! Jeanette could never fully shake our accent. She'd talk like that her whole life, I thought with a gloomy satisfaction, each word winced out like an apology for itself.

60 "Claudette, help me," she yelped. Mirabella had closed her jaws around Jeanette's bald ankle and was dragging her towards the closet. "Please. Help me to mop up Mirabella's mess."

I ignored her and continued down the hall. I had only four more hours to perfect the Sausalito. I was worried only about myself. By that stage, I was no longer certain of how the pack felt about anything.

At seven o'clock on the dot, Sister Ignatius blew her whistle and frog-marched us into the ball. The nuns had transformed the rectory into a very scary place. Purple and silver balloons started popping all around us. Black streamers swooped down from the eaves and got stuck in our hair like bats. A full yellow moon smirked outside the window. We were greeted by blasts of a saxophone, and fizzy pink drinks, and the brothers.

The brothers didn't smell like our brothers anymore. They smelled like pomade and cold, sterile sweat. They looked like little boys. Someone had washed behind their ears and made them wear suspendered dungarees. Kyle used to be a blustery alpha male, BTWWWR!, chewing through rattlesnakes, spooking badgers, snatching a live trout out of a grizzly's mouth. He stood by the punch bowl, looking pained and out of place.

"My stars!" I growled. "What lovely weather we've been having!"

65 "Yeees," Kyle growled back. "It is beginning to look a lot like Christmas." All around the room, boys and girls raised by wolves were having the same conversation. Actually, it had been an unseasonably warm and brown winter, and just that morning a freak hailstorm had sent Sister Josephina to an early grave. But we had only gotten up to Unit 7: Party Dialogue; we hadn't yet learned the vocabulary for Unit 12: How to Tactfully Acknowledge Disaster. Instead, we wore pink party hats and sucked olives on little sticks, inured to our own strangeness.

The nuns swept our hair back into high, bouffant hairstyles. This made us look more girlish and less inclined to eat people, the way that squirrels are saved from looking like rodents by their poofy tails. I was wearing a white organdy dress with orange polka dots. Jeanette was wearing a mauve organdy dress with blue polka dots. Linette was wearing a red organdy dress with white polka dots. Mirabella was in a dark corner, wearing a muzzle. Her party culottes were duct-taped to her knees. The nuns had tied little bows on the muzzle to make it more festive. Even so, the jazz band from West Toowoomba kept glancing nervously her way.

"You smell astooooounding!" Kyle was saying, accidentally stretching the diphthong into a howl and then blushing. "I mean—"

"Yes, I know what it is that you mean," I snapped. (That's probably a little narrative embellishment on my part; it must have been months before I could really "snap" out words.) I didn't smell astounding. I had rubbed a pumpkin muffin all over my body earlier that morning to mask my natural, feral scent. Now I smelled like a purebred girl, easy to kill. I narrowed my eyes at Kyle and flattened my ears, something I hadn't done for months. Kyle looked panicked, trying to remember the words that would make me act like a girl again. I felt hot, oily tears squeezing out of the red corners of my eyes. *Shoesonfeet!* I barked at myself. I tried again. "My! What lovely weather—"

The jazz band struck up a tune.

"The time has come to do the Sausalito," Sister Maria announced, beaming into the microphone. "Every sister grab a brother!" She switched on Walter's industrial flashlight, struggling beneath its weight, and aimed the beam in the center of the room.

Uh-oh. I tried to skulk off into Mirabella's corner, but Kyle pushed me into the spotlight. "No," I moaned through my teeth, "noooooo." All of a sudden the only thing my body could remember how to do was pump and pump. In a flash of white-hot light, my months at St. Lucy's had vanished, and I was just a terrified animal again. As if of their own accord, my feet started to wiggle out of my shoes. *Mouth shut,* I gasped, staring down at my naked toes, *mouthshutmouthshut.*

"Ahem. The time has come," Sister Maria coughed, "to do the Sausalito." She paused. "The Sausalito," she added helpfully, "does not in any way resemble the thing that you are doing."

Beads of sweat stood out on my forehead. I could feel my jaws gaping open, my tongue lolling out of the left side of my mouth. What were the steps? I looked frantically for Jeanette; she would help me, she would tell me what to do.

Jeanette was sitting in the corner, sipping punch through a long straw and watching me pant. I locked eyes with her, pleading with the mute intensity that I had used to beg her for weasel bones in the forest. "What are the steps?" I mouthed.

"The steps!"

"The steps?" Then Jeanette gave me a wide, true wolf smile. For an instant, she looked just like our mother. "Not for you," she mouthed back.

I threw my head back, a howl clawing its way up my throat. I was about to lose all my Skill Points, I was about to fail my Adaptive Dancing test. But before the air could burst from my lungs, the wind got knocked out of me. *Oomph!* I fell to the ground, my skirt falling softly over my head. Mirabella had intercepted my eye-cry for help. She'd chewed through her restraints and tackled me from behind, barking at unseen cougars, trying to shield me with her tiny body. *"Caramba!"* Sister Maria squealed, dropping the flashlight. The music ground to a halt. And I have never loved someone so much, before or since, as I loved my littlest sister at that moment. I wanted to roll over and lick her ears, I wanted to kill a dozen spotted fawns and let her eat first.

But everybody was watching; everybody was waiting to see what I would do. "I wasn't talking to you," I grunted from underneath her. "I didn't want your help. Now you have ruined the Sausalito! You have ruined the ball!" I said more loudly, hoping the nuns would hear how much my enunciation had improved.

"You have ruined it!" my sisters panted, circling around us, eager to close ranks. "Mirabella has ruined it!" Every girl was wild-eyed and itching under her polka dots, punch froth dribbling down her chin. The pack had been waiting for this moment for some time. "Mirabella cannot adapt! Back to the woods, back to the woods!"

The band from West Toowoomba had quietly packed their instruments into black suitcases and were sneaking out the back. The boys had fled back towards the lake, bow ties spinning, snapping suspenders in their haste. Mirabella was still snarling in the center of it all, trying to figure out where the danger was so that she could defend me against it. The nuns exchanged glances.

In the morning, Mirabella was gone. We checked under all the beds. I pretended to be surprised. I'd known she would have to be expelled the minute I felt her weight on my back. Walter came and told me this in secret after the ball, "So you can say yer good-byes." I didn't want to face Mirabella. Instead, I packed a tin lunch pail for her: two jelly sandwiches on saltine crackers, a chloroformed squirrel, a gilt-edged placard of St. Bolio. I left it for her with Sister Ignatius, with a little note: "Best wishes!" I told myself I'd done everything I could.

"Hooray!" the pack crowed. "Something has been done!"

We raced outside into the bright sunlight, knowing full well that our sister had been turned loose, that we'd never find her. A low roar rippled through us and surged up and up, disappearing into the trees. I listened for an answering howl from Mirabella, heart thumping—what if she heard us and came back? But there was nothing.

We graduated from St. Lucy's shortly thereafter. As far as I can recollect, that was our last communal howl.

> Stage 5: At this point your students are able to interact effectively in the new cultural environment. They find it easy to move between the two cultures.

85   One Sunday, near the end of my time at St. Lucy's, the sisters gave me a special pass to go visit the parents. The woodsman had to accompany me; I couldn't remember how to find the way back on my own. I wore my best dress and brought along some prosciutto and dill pickles in a picnic basket. We crunched through the fall leaves in silence, and every step made me sadder. "I'll wait out here," the woodsman said, leaning on a blue elm and lighting a cigarette.

The cave looked so much smaller than I remembered it. I had to duck my head to enter. Everybody was eating when I walked in. They all looked up from the bull moose at the same time, my aunts and uncles, my sloe-eyed, lolling cousins, the parents. My uncle dropped a thighbone from his mouth. My littlest brother, a cross-eyed wolf-boy who has since been successfully rehabilitated and is now a dour, balding children's book author, started whining in terror. My mother recoiled from me, as if I was a stranger. TRRR? She sniffed me for a long moment. Then she sank her teeth into my ankle, looking proud and sad. After all the tail wagging and perfunctory barking had died down, the parents sat back on their hind legs. They stared up at me expectantly, panting in the cool gray envelope of the cave, waiting for a display of what I had learned.

"So," I said, telling my first human lie. "I'm home."

2006

QUESTIONS

1. How and why does the protagonist change over the course of the story? How might those changes be reflected in the way she shifts, as a narrator, between first-person plural and singular?

2. At one point in the story, the narrator remarks, "This wasn't like the woods, where you had to be your fastest and your strongest and your bravest self. Different sorts of calculations were required to survive [. . .]" (par. 25). What do you think she

means? How might this comment help us to understand both her later behavior and the roles that Jeanette and Mirabella play in her life and in the story?

3. To what extent do you think this story is simply about growing up, making the transition from childhood to adulthood? about schooling or education? about the experience of those who are bilingual or bicultural? What might the story suggest about the difficulties of those experiences? their benefits and costs? In these terms, what role is played by the quotations from the (fictional) *Jesuit Handbook on Lycanthropic Culture Shock*?

JORGE LUIS BORGES
(1899–1986)
The House of Asterion[1]

Widely considered Latin America's foremost author, Jorge Luis Borges was born and raised in Buenos Aires, Argentina. The son of a lawyer and would-be writer who also taught in an English school, the young Borges reportedly learned to speak English before Spanish and read avidly and widely; his early favorites included *The Adventures of Huckleberry Finn*, *The Arabian Nights*, and the novels of H. G. Wells and Charles Dickens. While traveling in Europe, his family was trapped in Geneva, Switzerland, at the outbreak of World War I, and Borges attended the Collège de Genève, where he added French, German, and Latin to his linguistic arsenal. He then spent two years in Spain, where he wrote his first poems, before returning to Argentina in 1921. Despite his persistent, outspoken opposition to the military dictatorship of Juan Perón, Borges became the director of Argentina's national library in 1955. The very same year, Borges lost his long battle against encroaching blindness; ordered by doctors never to read or write again, he abandoned fiction for poetry for the last thirty years of his life, taking comfort in the example of the great blind poets Homer and Milton. Though he thus began and ended his writing life as a poet, Borges—who never wrote a novel—is best known as both a writer of short *ficciones* ("fictions"), a label he preferred to *cuentos* ("stories"), and as a pioneer of magic realism.

And the queen gave birth to a son named Asterion.
APOLLODORUS,[2] LIBRARY, III:I

I know that I am accused of arrogance and perhaps of misanthropy, and perhaps even of madness. These accusations (which I shall punish in due time) are ludicrous. It is true that I never leave my house, but it is also true that its

1. Translated from the Spanish by Andrew Hurley.
2. Greek scholar (d. after 120 BCE); a librarian at the renowned library in Alexandria, Egypt, and author of works on history, philosophy, mythology, and geography. Though long attributed to him, the influential compendium of Greek myths known as *The Library* was in fact composed long after his death.

doors (whose number is infinite[3]) stand open night and day to men and also to animals. Anyone who wishes to enter may do so. Here, no womanly splendors, no palatial ostentation shall be found, but only calm and solitude. Here shall be found a house like none other on the face of the earth. (Those who say there is a similar house in Egypt speak lies.) Even my detractors admit that *there is not a single piece of furniture in the house.* Another absurd tale is that I, Asterion, am a prisoner. Need I repeat that the door stands open? Need I add that there is no lock? Furthermore, one afternoon I did go out into the streets; if I returned before nightfall, I did so because of the terrible dread inspired in me by the faces of the people—colorless faces, as flat as the palm of one's hand. The sun had already gone down, but the helpless cry of a babe and the crude supplications of the masses were signs that I had been recognized. The people prayed, fled, fell prostrate before me; some climbed up onto the stylobate[4] of the temple of the Axes, others gathered stones. One, I believe, hid in the sea. Not for nothing was my mother a queen; I cannot mix with commoners, even if my modesty should wish it.

The fact is, I am unique. I am not interested in what a man can publish abroad to other men; like the philosopher, I think that nothing can be communicated by the art of writing. Vexatious and trivial minutiæ find no refuge in my spirit, which has been formed for greatness; I have never grasped for long the difference between one letter and another. A certain generous impatience has prevented me from learning to read. Sometimes I regret that, because the nights and the days are long.

Of course I do not lack for distractions. Sometimes I run like a charging ram through the halls of stone until I tumble dizzily to the ground; sometimes I crouch in the shadow of a wellhead or at a corner in one of the corridors and pretend I am being hunted. There are rooftops from which I can hurl myself until I am bloody. I can pretend anytime I like that I am asleep, and lie with my eyes closed and my breathing heavy. (Sometimes I actually fall asleep; sometimes by the time I open my eyes, the color of the day has changed.) But of all the games, the one I like best is pretending that there is another Asterion. I pretend that he has come to visit me, and I show him around the house. Bowing majestically, I say to him: *Now let us return to our previous intersection* or *Let us go this way, now, out into another courtyard* or *I knew that you would like this rain gutter* or *Now you will see a cistern that has filled with sand* or *Now you will see how the cellar forks.* Sometimes I make a mistake and the two of us have a good laugh over it.

5   It is not just these games I have thought up—I have also thought a great deal about the house. Each part of the house occurs many times; any particular place is another place. There is not one wellhead, one courtyard, one drinking trough, one manger; there are fourteen [an infinite number of] mangers, drinking troughs, courtyards, wellheads. The house is as big as the world—or rather, it *is* the world. Nevertheless, by making my way through every single courtyard with its wellhead and every single dusty gallery of gray stone, I have come out onto the street and seen the temple of the Axes and the sea. That sight, I did not

3. The original reads "fourteen," but there is more than enough cause to conclude that when spoken by Asterion that number stands for "infinite" [Borges's note].
4. In classical architecture, the base or pavement supporting a row of columns.

The Minotaur, as depicted on an ancient Greek cup, c. 515 BCE

understand until a night vision revealed to me that there are also fourteen [an infinite number of] seas and temples. Everything exists many times, fourteen times, but there are two things in the world that apparently exist but once—on high, the intricate sun, and below, Asterion. Perhaps I have created the stars and the sun and this huge house, and no longer remember it.

Every nine years, nine men come into the house so that I can free them from all evil.[5] I hear their footsteps or their voices far away in the galleries of stone, and I run joyously to find them. The ceremony lasts but a few minutes. One after another, they fall, without my ever having to bloody my hands. Where they fall, they remain, and their bodies help distinguish one gallery from the others. I do not know how many there have been, but I do know that one of them predicted as he died that someday my redeemer would come. Since then, there has been no pain for me in solitude, because I know that my redeemer lives, and in the end he will rise and stand above the dust.[6] If my ear could hear every sound in the world, I would hear his footsteps. I hope he takes me to a place with fewer galleries and fewer doors. What will my redeemer be like, I wonder. Will he be bull or man? Could he possibly be a bull with the face of a man? Or will he be like me?

The morning sun shimmered on the bronze sword. Now there was not a trace of blood left on it.

"Can you believe it, Ariadne?" said Theseus. "The Minotaur[7] scarcely defended itself."

For Maria Mosquera Eastman

1947, 1949

---

5. Possibly, an echo of the Lord's Prayer, which ends, "And lead us not into temptation, but deliver us from evil: For thine is the kingdom, and the power, and the glory, for ever. Amen" (Matt. 6.13).

6. Compare Job 19.25–26: "For I know that my redeemer liveth, and that he shall stand at the latter day upon the earth: / And though after my skin worms destroy this body, yet in my flesh shall I see God"; "But ye should say, Why persecute we him [. . .] / Be ye afraid of the sword: for wrath bringeth the punishments of the sword, that ye may know there is a judgment."

7. Literally, the bull of Minos, also called Asterion or Asterius, meaning "the starry one" (Greek); in classical mythology, the creature born of the union between Queen Pasiphae of Crete (wife of King Minos and daughter of the sun god and a sea nymph) and a white bull sent by the sea god, Poseidon. To quote *The Library* from which Borges takes his epigraph, "Asterius, who was called the Minotaur," "had the face of a bull, but the rest of him was human; and Minos, in compliance with certain oracles, shut him up and guarded him in the Labyrinth" made by the great Athenian artificer Daedalus. By Minos's order, every year or every nine years Athens had to send seven young men and seven young women to be devoured by the Minotaur. Eventually, however, the Athenian hero Theseus volunteers to go and—with the help of a thread given to him by Minos and Pasiphaë's daughter (and thus also Asterion's half sister) Ariadne—succeeds in killing Asterion and escaping the labyrinth.

QUESTIONS

1. In reading or re-reading THE HOUSE OF ASTERION, when and why might you start to suspect or know that its narrator is the mythical Minotaur and/or that its setting is a labyrinth or maze?
2. What is the effect and significance of point of view in the story? of the title and **epigraph**, especially the fact that both use the name Asterion rather than Minotaur?
3. What various things might the labyrinth and the Minotaur symbolize in the story? In these terms, what might be the significance of the biblical allusions? the narrator's insistence that he is not "a prisoner" (par. 1)?

AUTHORS ON THEIR WORK

JORGE LUIS BORGES (1899–1986)

From "An Interview with Jorge Luis Borges" (1970)*

A[NSWER:] [W]hen people tell me that they're down-to-earth and they tell me that I should be down-to-earth and think of reality, I wonder why a dream or an idea should be less real than this table for example, or why Macbeth should be less real than today's newspaper. I cannot quite understand this. [. . .] I'm not sure I have to define myself. I'd rather go on wondering and puzzling about things, for I find that very enjoyable.

Q[UESTION:] That reminds me of the image of the labyrinth that recurs throughout your work.

A[NSWER:] Yes, it keeps cropping up all the time. It's the most obvious symbol of feeling puzzled and baffled, isn't it? It came to me through an engraving when I was a boy, an engraving of the seven wonders of the world, and there was one of the labyrinth. [. . .] I thought that if I looked into it, if I peered into it very closely, perhaps I might make out the minotaur at the center. Somehow I was rather frightened of that engraving [. . .]. I was afraid of the minotaur coming out.

[G. K.] Chesterton said, "What a man is really afraid of is a maze without a center." I suppose he was thinking of a godless universe, but I was thinking of the labyrinth without a minotaur, I mean, if anything is terrible, it is terrible because it is meaningless.

[I]f there's no minotaur, then the whole thing's incredible. You have a monstrous building built round a monster, and that in a sense is logical. But if there is no monster, then the whole thing is senseless, and that would be the case for the universe, for all we know.

*"An Interview with Jorge Luis Borges." Interview by L. S. Dembo. *Contemporary Literature*, vol. 11, no. 3, summer 1970, pp. 315–23. JSTOR, www.jstor.org/stable/1207790.

SUGGESTIONS FOR WRITING

1. Which of the monsters in these stories do you identify with most? least? Write an informal paper reflecting on your responses to at least two of these characters and the way those responses are shaped both by specifics in the story and by your personal experience.

2. Write a response paper or essay reflecting on the use of humor in at least one of the stories in this album. What kinds of humor do you see in the story? How does humor shape your response to the story and its characters?

3. Write an essay comparing how any two characters in these stories understand and cope (or not) with their deviation from the human norm and considering what each gains or loses as a result.

4. Write an essay comparing the conflicts experienced by the families in Lusus Naturae and St. Lucy's Home for Girls Raised by Wolves. Though we might not approve of the way some of these characters ultimately choose to resolve those conflicts, how and why might the stories encourage us to view these characters at least somewhat sympathetically?

5. Like Maggie in Toni Morrison's Recitatif, both the protagonist of Atwood's Lusus Naturae and Mirabella, in St. Lucy's Home for Girls Raised by Wolves, could be described as **scapegoats**, which simply means a person or group of people whom a community harshly punishes, casts out, or even kills in the hope of preserving its own unity, purity, and strength. Why are these characters singled out? What do the other characters in each story hope to gain by treating the "monsters" as they do? Write an essay in which you explore what at least one of these stories suggests about whom we tend to treat as scapegoats, when and why we do so, and what the consequences tend to be.

6. In the library or on the Internet, research traditional representations (literary and/or visual) of the Minotaur myth, as well as some authoritative interpretations of it. Then write an essay in which you draw on these sources and on Borges's story to explore how it reworks and perhaps comments on these traditions.

5 | SETTING

If plot and action are the way fictional works answer the question *What happened?* and characters are the *who*, **setting** is the *where* and *when*. All action in fiction, as in the real world, takes place in a context or setting—a time and place and a social environment or milieu.

TEMPORAL AND PHYSICAL, GENERAL AND PARTICULAR SETTING

The **time**—a work's *temporal setting* or *plot time*—can be roughly the same as that in which the work was written (its *author time*); or it can be much later, as in most science fiction; or much earlier, as in **historical fiction**. Especially in short stories, which tend not to cover as much time or space as novels do, time may be very restricted, involving only a few hours or even minutes. Yet even in short stories, the action may span years or even decades.

Similarly, the place—a work's *geographical* or *physical setting*—might be limited to a single locale, or it might encompass several disparate ones. Those places might be common and ordinary, unique and extraordinary, or fantastic and even impossible according to the laws of our world (as in modern **fantasy** or **magic realism**).

Even when a story's action takes place in multiple times and places, we still sometimes refer to its *setting* (singular). By this, we indicate what we might call the entire story's *general setting*—the year(s) and the region, country, or even world in which the story unfolds and which often provides a historical and cultural context for the action. The general setting of Richard Wright's novel *Native Son* (1940), for instance, is 1930s Depression-era Chicago. But this novel, like many, has numerous *particular settings*; its famous opening scene begins with an alarm clock shattering the temporary peace of a rundown, rat-infested, one-room apartment shared by Bigger Thomas, his two siblings, and their widowed mother, a dramatic contrast to the scene Bigger will, later in the same chapter, see on a movie screen: "a stretch of sparkling water" and the "gleaming sands" of a sunny, palm tree-studded beach, where "smiling, dark-haired" rich "girls lol[l]." To fully appreciate the nature and role of setting, we thus need to consider the specific time of day and year as well as the specific locales in which the action unfolds.

FUNCTIONS OF SETTING

Some stories merely offer hints about setting; others describe setting in great sensory detail. Especially in the latter case, we might be tempted to skim through what seems like mere "scenery" or "background information" to find out what happens next or how things turn out. But in good fiction, setting always functions as an integral part of the whole.

Fiction often relies on setting to establish mood, situation, and character. The first sentence of Edgar Allan Poe's short story "The Fall of the House of Usher" (1839), for example, quickly sets the **tone**:

> During the whole of a dull, dark, and soundless day in the autumn of the year, when the clouds hung oppressively low in the heavens, I had been passing alone, on horseback, through a singularly dreary tract of country; and at length found myself, as the shades of the evening drew on, within view of the melancholy House of Usher.

This sentence aims to instill in the reader the same fear, "melancholy," and "sense of insufferable gloom" the narrator feels. With it, Poe prepares the reader for the sad and eerie tale about to unfold. He also generates suspense and certain expectations about just what might happen, as well as empathy with the narrator-protagonist.

Here, as in other fiction, specific details prove crucial to setting's emotional effect and meaning precisely because, as Poe's narrator himself observes,

> there *are* combinations of very simple natural objects which have the power of thus affecting us [. . .]. It was possible, I reflected, that a mere different arrangement of the particulars of the scene, of the details of the picture, would be sufficient to modify [. . .] its [. . .] impression.

In addition to creating such emotional impressions, setting can reveal and even shape a character's personality, outlook, and values; it can occasionally be an actor in the plot; and it often prompts characters' actions. (Who might you become and what might you do if you lived in the isolated, gloomy House of Usher?) Descriptions of setting may even suggest a key **conflict** or **theme**. To gloss over descriptions of setting would thus mean not only missing much of the pleasure fiction affords but also potentially misreading its meanings. Setting is one of the many ways we learn about characters and the chief means by which characters and plots take on a larger historical, social, or even universal significance.

VAGUE AND VIVID SETTINGS

Not all stories, of course, rely as heavily on setting as Poe's does. In some works and in some subgenres, the general time, place, or both may be so vague as to seem, at first glance, unimportant. Many folktales and fairy tales take place in **archetypal** settings: "A long time ago," in "the forest" or "a village" or "a cottage," "in a land far, far away." By offering little, if any, specific information about their settings—neither locating the "forest" or "village" or faraway land in a place we can find on a map or a time we can identify on a calendar or clock, nor describing it in any detail—these works implicitly urge us to see the conflicts and aspects of human experience they depict (death, grief, a mother's relationship to her child, the danger and incomprehensibility of the unknown) as timeless and universal. Here, the very lack of attention to setting paradoxically turns out to be all-important.

At the opposite extreme are works and subgenres of fiction in which setting generates the conflicts, defines the characters, and gives the story purpose and meaning—so much so that there would be little, if any, story left if all the details about setting were removed or the characters and plot were somehow transported to a different time, place, and social milieu. Without their settings, what would

remain of historical novels like Nathaniel Hawthorne's *The Scarlet Letter* (1850)?
An even more extreme example is Italo Calvino's fantasy novel *Invisible Cities*,
which consists almost entirely of a series of descriptions of impossible, yet often
hauntingly beautiful places like the following one.

ITALO CALVINO

From Invisible Cities

What makes Argia different from other cities is that it has earth instead
of air. The streets are completely filled with dirt, clay packs the rooms
to the ceiling, on every stair another stairway is set in negative, over the roofs
of the houses hang layers of rocky terrain like skies with clouds. We do not know
if the inhabitants can move about the city, widening the worm tunnels and the
crevices where roots twist: the dampness destroys people's bodies and they have
scant strength; everyone is better off remaining still, prone; anyway, it is dark.

From up here, nothing of Argia can be seen; some say, "It's down below there,"
and we can only believe them. The place is deserted. At night, putting your ear to
the ground, you can sometimes hear a door slam.

1972

.   .   .

Most fiction, of course, occupies a middle ground between the extremes of Calvino's novel or historical fiction (with their highly particularized settings) versus
folklore (with its generic, archetypal setting). Though all fiction may ultimately
deal with some types of people, aspects of human experience, and conflicts that
can crop up in some form or fashion anywhere or any time, much fiction also
draws our attention to the way people, their experience, and their conflicts are
twisted into a particular "form and fashion" by specific contexts.

TRADITIONAL EXPECTATIONS OF TIME AND PLACE

The effects and meanings evoked by setting depend on our traditional associations
with, and often unconscious assumptions about, particular times, places, and even
such factors as weather conditions—autumn, evening, a deserted country road, a
house grand enough to have a name, a sky full of low and lowering clouds (to refer
back to the Poe example).

Traditional associations derive, in part, from literature and myth, and some are
culturally specific. (To someone unfamiliar with the Old Testament, an apple
orchard would simply be an apple orchard, without any suggestion of evil or sin.)
These associations also come from our learning, our experience, our own specific
social and historical context, and even our primal instincts and physical condition
as human beings. Almost all of us are more vulnerable in the dark and in inclem-
ent weather. And people do behave differently and expect different things to happen in different times and places—on a Saturday versus a Sunday versus a
Monday, during spring break versus midsemester or midweek, at a posh beach
resort we are just visiting versus the grocery store in our own neighborhood, and
so on.

Often, however, authors draw on such associations precisely in order to reverse and question them. John Updike has said that he was initially inspired to write his initiation story "A & P" because a suburban grocery store seemed just the sort of mundane place no reader would expect either heroism or a story to take place. ("Why don't you ever read a story set in an A & P?" he reportedly asked his wife.) By reversing expectations in this way, stories not only deepen their emotional effect but also encourage us to rethink our assumptions about particular times and places and the people who inhabit them.

Setting is key to each of the stories gathered in this chapter. Their settings range from the Western United States to Dublin, Ireland; from the nineteeth to the twenty-first century; from tiny towns to crowded, cosmopolitan cities. The stories take place in just about every season and all kinds of weather, but regardless of the specific setting, each paints a revealing portrait of a time and place. Just as our own memories of important experiences include complex impressions of when and where they occurred—the weather, the shape of the room, the music that was playing, even the fashions or the events in the news back then—so stories rely on setting to evoke emotion and generate meaning.

Questions about Setting

General Setting

- What is the general temporal and geographical setting of this work of fiction? How do you know?
- How important does the general setting seem to be? In what ways is it important? What about the plot and characters would remain the same if they were transported to a different setting? What wouldn't? For example, how does the setting
  - create or shape conflict?
  - affect characters' personalities, outlooks, and actions?
  - shape our impressions of who the characters are and what they represent?
  - establish mood?

Particular Settings

- Does all the action occur in one time and place, or in more than one? If the latter, what are those times and places?
- What patterns do you notice regarding where and when things happen? Which characters are associated with each setting? How do different characters relate to the same setting? When, how, and why do characters move from one setting to another? Are there significant deviations from these patterns?
- Are particular settings described in detail, or merely sketched? If the former, what seems significant about the details? How might they establish mood, reveal character, and affect individual characters and their interactions with one another?

JAMES JOYCE
(1882–1941)

Araby

In 1902, after graduating from University College, Dublin, James Joyce left Ireland for Paris, returning a year later. In October 1904, he eloped with Nora Barnacle and settled in Trieste, Italy, where he taught English for the Berlitz school. Though he lived as an expatriate for the rest of his life, all of his fiction is set in his native Dublin. Joyce had more than his share of difficulties with publication and censorship. His short-story collection, *Dubliners*, completed in 1905, was not published until 1914. His novel *Portrait of the Artist as a Young Man*, dated "Dublin 1904, Trieste 1914," appeared first in America, in 1916. His great novel *Ulysses* (1922) was banned for a dozen years in the United States and as long or longer elsewhere. In addition, Joyce published a play, *Exiles* (1918); two collections of poetry, *Chamber Music* (1907) and *Pomes Penyeach* (1927); and the monumental, experimental, and puzzling novel *Finnegans Wake* (1939).

N orth Richmond Street, being blind,[1] was a quiet street except at the hour when the Christian Brothers' School set the boys free. An uninhabited house of two storeys stood at the blind end, detached from its neighbours in a square ground. The other houses of the street, conscious of decent lives within them, gazed at one another with brown imperturbable faces.

The former tenant of our house, a priest, had died in the back drawing-room. Air, musty from having been long enclosed, hung in all the rooms, and the waste room behind the kitchen was littered with old useless papers. Among these I found a few paper-covered books, the pages of which were curled and damp: *The Abbot*, by Walter Scott, *The Devout Communicant* and *The Memoirs of Vidocq*.[2] I liked the last best because its leaves were yellow. The wild garden behind the house contained a central apple-tree and a few straggling bushes under one of which I found the late tenant's rusty bicycle-pump. He had been a very charitable priest; in his will he had left all his money to institutions and the furniture of his house to his sister.

When the short days of winter came dusk fell before we had well eaten our dinners. When we met in the street the houses had grown sombre. The space of sky above us was the colour of ever-changing violet and towards it the lamps of

1. That is, a dead-end street.
2. The "memoirs" were probably *not* written by François Vidocq (1775–1857), a French criminal who became chief of detectives and died poor and disgraced for his part in a crime that he solved. *The Abbot*: The 1820 novel by Sir Walter Scott (1771–1834) is a romance about the Catholic Mary, Queen of Scots (1542–87), who was beheaded. *The Devout Communicant, or, Pious Meditations and Aspirations, for Three Days before and Three Days after Receiving the Holy Eucharist* (1813) is a Catholic religious tract.

the street lifted their feeble lanterns. The cold air stung us and we played till our bodies glowed. Our shouts echoed in the silent street. The career of our play brought us through the dark muddy lanes behind the houses where we ran the gantlet of the rough tribes from the cottages, to the back doors of the dark dripping gardens where odours arose from the ashpits,[3] to the dark odorous stables where a coachman smoothed and combed the horse or shook music from the buckled harness. When we returned to the street light from the kitchen windows had filled the areas. If my uncle was seen turning the corner we hid in the shadow until we had seen him safely housed. Or if Mangan's sister came out on the doorstep to call her brother in to his tea we watched her from our shadow peer up and down the street. We waited to see whether she would remain or go in and, if she remained, we left our shadow and walked up to Mangan's steps resignedly. She was waiting for us, her figure defined by the light from the half-opened door. Her brother always teased her before he obeyed and I stood by the railings looking at her. Her dress swung as she moved her body and the soft rope of her hair tossed from side to side.

Every morning I lay on the floor in the front parlour watching her door. The blind was pulled down to within an inch of the sash so that I could not be seen. When she came out on the doorstep my heart leaped. I ran to the hall, seized my books and followed her. I kept her brown figure always in my eye and, when we came near the point at which our ways diverged, I quickened my pace and passed her. This happened morning after morning. I had never spoken to her, except for a few casual words, and yet her name was like a summons to all my foolish blood.

Her image accompanied me even in places the most hostile to romance. On 5 Saturday evenings when my aunt went marketing I had to go to carry some of the parcels. We walked through the flaring streets, jostled by drunken men and bargaining women, amid the curses of labourers, the shrill litanies of shop-boys who stood on guard by the barrels of pigs' cheeks, the nasal chanting of street-singers, who sang a come-all-you about O'Donovan Rossa,[4] or a ballad about the troubles in our native land. These noises converged in a single sensation of life for me: I imagined that I bore my chalice safely through a throng of foes. Her name sprang to my lips at moments in strange prayers and praises which I myself did not understand. My eyes were often full of tears (I could not tell why) and at times a flood from my heart seemed to pour itself out into my bosom. I thought little of the future. I did not know whether I would ever speak to her or not or, if I spoke to her, how I could tell her of my confused adoration. But my body was like a harp and her words and gestures were like fingers running upon the wires.

One evening I went into the back drawing-room in which the priest had died. It was a dark rainy evening and there was no sound in the house. Through one of the broken panes I heard the rain impinge upon the earth, the fine incessant needles of water playing in the sodden beds. Some distant lamp or lighted

3. Where fireplace ashes and other household refuse were dumped.
4. Jeremiah O'Donovan (1831–1915) was a militant Irish nationalist who fought on despite prison terms and banishment. Come-all-you: a song, of which there were many, that began "Come, all you Irishmen."

window gleamed below me. I was thankful that I could see so little. All my senses seemed to desire to veil themselves and, feeling that I was about to slip from them, I pressed the palms of my hands together until they trembled, murmuring: *O love! O love!* many times.

At last she spoke to me. When she addressed the first words to me I was so confused that I did not know what to answer. She asked me was I going to *Araby*.[5] I forget whether I answered yes or no. It would be a splendid bazaar, she said; she would love to go.

—And why can't you? I asked.

While she spoke she turned a silver bracelet round and round her wrist. She could not go, she said, because there would be a retreat[6] that week in her convent. Her brother and two other boys were fighting for their caps and I was alone at the railings. She held one of the spikes, bowing her head towards me. The light from the lamp opposite our door caught the white curve of her neck, lit up her hair that rested there and, falling, lit up the hand upon the railing. It fell over one side of her dress and caught the white border of a petticoat, just visible as she stood at ease.

10   —It's well for you, she said.

—If I go, I said, I will bring you something.

What innumerable follies laid waste my waking and sleeping thoughts after that evening! I wished to annihilate the tedious intervening days. I chafed against the work of school. At night in my bedroom and by day in the classroom her image came between me and the page I strove to read. The syllables of the word *Araby* were called to me through the silence in which my soul luxuriated and cast an Eastern enchantment over me. I asked for leave to go to the bazaar on Saturday night. My aunt was surprised and hoped it was not some Freemason[7] affair. I answered few questions in class. I watched my master's face pass from amiability to sternness; he hoped I was not beginning to idle. I could not call my wandering thoughts together. I had hardly any patience with the serious work of life which, now that it stood between me and my desire, seemed to me child's play, ugly monotonous child's play.

On Saturday morning I reminded my uncle that I wished to go to the bazaar in the evening. He was fussing at the hallstand, looking for the hat-brush, and answered me curtly:

—Yes, boy, I know.

15   As he was in the hall I could not go into the front parlour and lie at the window. I left the house in bad humour and walked slowly towards the school. The air was pitilessly raw and already my heart misgave me.

When I came home to dinner my uncle had not yet been home. Still it was early. I sat staring at the clock for some time and, when its ticking began to irritate me, I left the room. I mounted the staircase and gained the upper part of the house. The high cold empty gloomy rooms liberated me and I went from room to room singing. From the front window I saw my companions playing

---

5. Charity bazaar billed as a "Grand Oriental Fete," Dublin, May 1894.
6. Period of withdrawal dedicated to prayer and religious study.
7. Freemasons—members of an influential, secretive, and highly ritualistic fraternal organization—were considered enemies of Catholics.

below in the street. Their cries reached me weakened and indistinct and, leaning my forehead against the cool glass, I looked over at the dark house where
she lived. I may have stood there for an hour, seeing nothing but the brown-clad
figure cast by my imagination, touched discreetly by the lamplight at the curved
neck, at the hand upon the railings and at the border below the dress.

When I came downstairs again I found Mrs. Mercer sitting at the fire. She
was an old garrulous woman, a pawnbroker's widow, who collected used stamps
for some pious purpose. I had to endure the gossip of the tea-table. The meal
was prolonged beyond an hour and still my uncle did not come. Mrs. Mercer
stood up to go: she was sorry she couldn't wait any longer, but it was after eight
o'clock and she did not like to be out late, as the night air was bad for her. When
she had gone I began to walk up and down the room, clenching my fists. My
aunt said:

—I'm afraid you may put off your bazaar for this night of Our Lord.

At nine o'clock I heard my uncle's latchkey in the halldoor. I heard him talking to himself and heard the hallstand rocking when it had received the weight
of his overcoat. I could interpret these signs. When he was midway through his
dinner I asked him to give me the money to go to the bazaar. He had
forgotten.

—The people are in bed and after their first sleep now, he said.   20

I did not smile. My aunt said to him energetically:

—Can't you give him the money and let him go? You've kept him late enough
as it is.

My uncle said he was very sorry he had forgotten. He said he believed in the
old saying: *All work and no play makes Jack a dull boy.* He asked me where I was
going and, when I had told him a second time he asked me did I know *The
Arab's Farewell to his Steed.*[8] When I left the kitchen he was about to recite the
opening lines of the piece to my aunt.

I held a florin[9] tightly in my hand as I strode down Buckingham Street
towards the station. The sight of the streets thronged with buyers and glaring
with gas recalled to me the purpose of my journey. I took my seat in a third-
class carriage of a deserted train. After an intolerable delay the train moved out
of the station slowly. It crept onward among ruinous houses and over the twin-
kling river. At Westland Row Station a crowd of people pressed to the carriage
doors; but the porters moved them back, saying that it was a special train for
the bazaar. I remained alone in the bare carriage. In a few minutes the train
drew up beside an improvised wooden platform. I passed out on to the road and
saw by the lighted dial of a clock that it was ten minutes to ten. In front of me
was a large building which displayed the magical name.

I could not find any sixpenny entrance and, fearing that the bazaar would be   25
closed, I passed in quickly through a turnstile, handing a shilling to a weary-
looking man. I found myself in a big hall girdled at half its height by a gallery.
Nearly all the stalls were closed and the greater part of the hall was in darkness.
I recognized a silence like that which pervades a church after a service. I walked

8. Or "The Arab's Farewell to His Horse," a sentimental nineteenth-century poem by Caroline Norton.
The speaker has sold the horse.
9. A two-shilling piece, thus four times the "sixpenny entrance" fee.

into the centre of the bazaar timidly. A few people were gathered about the stalls which were still open. Before a curtain, over which the words *Café Chantant*[1] were written in coloured lamps, two men were counting money on a salver. I listened to the fall of the coins.

Remembering with difficulty why I had come I went over to one of the stalls and examined porcelain vases and flowered tea-sets. At the door of the stall a young lady was talking and laughing with two young gentlemen. I remarked their English accents and listened vaguely to their conversation.

—O, I never said such a thing!

—O, but you did!

—O, but I didn't!

—Didn't she say that?

—Yes. I heard her.

—O, there's a . . . . fib!

Observing me the young lady came over and asked me did I wish to buy anything. The tone of her voice was not encouraging; she seemed to have spoken to me out of a sense of duty. I looked humbly at the great jars that stood like eastern guards at either side of the dark entrance to the stall and murmured:

—No, thank you.

The young lady changed the position of one of the vases and went back to the two young men. They began to talk of the same subject. Once or twice the young lady glanced at me over her shoulder.

I lingered before her stall, though I knew my stay was useless, to make my interest in her wares seem the more real. Then I turned away slowly and walked down the middle of the bazaar. I allowed the two pennies to fall against the sixpence in my pocket. I heard a voice call from one end of the gallery that the light was out. The upper part of the hall was now completely dark.

Gazing up into the darkness I saw myself as a creature driven and derided by vanity; and my eyes burned with anguish and anger.

1914

QUESTIONS

1. How do the first three paragraphs of ARABY characterize the environment in which the narrator lives? How might that environment inspire and shape his fascination with Mangan's sister? with Araby?

2. What kind of "vanity" does the narrator attribute to himself at the story's end? Why is he filled with "anguish and anger"?

3. How might ARABY work as a sort of quest narrative (see "Common Plot Types" in ch. 2)? In these terms, what is the significance of the narrator's reference to "romance," his vision of himself carrying a "chalice safely through a throng of foes" (par. 5), and Araby's "Eastern" theme (par. 12)?

1. Café with music (French).

JUDITH ORTIZ COFER

(1952–2016)

Volar[1]

Born in Hormigueros, Puerto Rico, Judith Ortiz Cofer just two years later moved with her family first to New Jersey and later to Georgia, experiences that would inspire much of her later fiction and poetry. "How can you inject passion and purpose into your work if it has no roots?" she once asked, avowing that her own roots included a long line of women storytellers who "infected" her at a very early age with the desire to tell stories both on and off the page. After earning an MA at Florida Atlantic University (1977), Cofer returned to Georgia, teaching at the University of Georgia for over 26 years. Among her numerous publications are the novels *The Line of the Sun* (1989), in which a young girl relates the history of her ne'er-do-well uncle's emigration from Puerto Rico, *The Meaning of Consuelo* (2003), and *Call Me Maria* (2004); the poetry collection *A Love Story Beginning in Spanish* (2005); and *The Latin Deli* (1993) and *The Year of Our Revolution* (1998), two collections that seamlessly interweave fiction, nonfiction, and poetry, thereby demonstrating, in Cofer's words, "the need to put things together in a holistic way."

At twelve I was an avid consumer of comic books—*Supergirl* being my favorite. I spent my allowance of a quarter a day on two twelve-cent comic books or a double issue for twenty-five. I had a stack of *Legion of Super Heroes* and *Supergirl* comic books in my bedroom closet that was as tall as I am. I had a recurring dream in those days: that I had long blond hair and could fly. In my dream I climbed the stairs to the top of our apartment building as myself, but as I went up each flight, changes would be taking place. Step by step I would fill out: My legs would grow long, my arms harden into steel, and my hair would magically go straight and turn a golden color. Of course I would add the bonus of breasts, but not too large; Supergirl had to be aerodynamic. Sleek and hard as a supersonic missile. Once on the roof, my parents safely asleep in their beds, I would get on tiptoe, arms outstretched in the position for flight, and jump out my fifty-story-high window into the black lake of the sky. From up there, over the rooftops, I could see everything, even beyond the few blocks of our barrio;[2] with my X-ray vision I could look inside the homes of people who interested me. Once I saw our landlord, whom I knew my parents feared, sitting in a treasure-room dressed in an ermine coat and a large gold crown. He sat on the floor counting his dollar bills. I played a trick on him. Going up to his building's chimney, I blew a little puff of my superbreath into his fireplace, scattering his stacks of money so that he had to start counting all over again. I

---

1. To fly (Spanish).
2. Spanish-speaking neighborhood or district in the United States or any district in a Spanish-speaking country.

could more or less program my Supergirl dreams in those days by focusing on the object of my current obsession. This way I "saw" into the private lives of my neighbors, my teachers, and in the last days of my childish fantasy and the beginning of adolescence, into the secret room of the boys I liked. In the mornings I'd wake up in my tiny bedroom with the incongruous—at least in our tiny apartment—white "princess" furniture my mother had chosen for me, and find myself back in my body: my tight curls still clinging to my head, skinny arms and legs and flat chest unchanged.

In the kitchen my mother and father would be talking softly over a café con leche.[3] She would come "wake me" exactly forty-five minutes after they had gotten up. It was their time together at the beginning of each day and even at an early age I could feel their disappointment if I interrupted them by getting up too early. So I would stay in my bed recalling my dreams of flight, perhaps planning my next flight. In the kitchen they would be discussing events in the barrio. Actually, he would be carrying that part of the conversation; when it was her turn to speak she would, more often than not, try shifting the topic toward her desire to see her *familia* on the Island: *How about a vacation in Puerto Rico together this year, Querido?*[4] *We could rent a car, go to the beach. We could . . .* And he would answer patiently, gently, *Mi amor,*[5] *do you know how much it would cost for all of us to fly there? It is not possible for me to take the time off . . . Mi vida,*[6] *please understand. . . .* And I knew that soon she would rise from the table. Not abruptly. She would light a cigarette and look out the kitchen window. The view was of a dismal alley that was littered with refuse thrown from windows. The space was too narrow for anyone larger than a skinny child to enter safely, so it was never cleaned. My mother would check the time on the clock over her sink, the one with a prayer for patience and grace written in Spanish. A birthday gift. She would see that it was time to wake me. She'd sigh deeply and say the same thing the view from her kitchen window always inspired her to say: *Ay, si yo pudiera volar.*[7]

1996, 1998

QUESTIONS

1. VOLAR seems simultaneously vague about its general setting and detailed about its particular setting, at least when it comes to place (versus time). How does this combination of vagueness and specificity shape your response to the story and your sense of whom and what it is about?
2. What does the story suggest about how the characters have been shaped by their environment? about how they feel about it, and why?
3. What is the effect of the way Spanish is used both in the title and throughout the story? What might these uses of Spanish add to our understanding of the setting, the characters, and their conflicts?

3. Coffee with milk (Spanish).
4. Beloved, dear (Spanish).
5. My love (Spanish).
6. My life (Spanish).
7. Oh, if only I could fly (Spanish).

ANNIE PROULX

(b. 1935)

Job History

Connecticut-born Annie Proulx earned a BA with honors at Colby College and an MA in history at the University of Vermont before launching her nineteen-year career as a freelance writer of articles on, in her words, "weather, apples, canoeing, mountain lions, mice, cuisine, libraries, African beadwork, cider, and lettuces," as well as books including *The Complete Dairy Foods Cookbook* (with Lew Nichols, 1982) and *The Fine Art of Salad Gardening* (1985). Proulx's public debut as a fiction writer came in 1988, with the publication of *Heart Songs and Other Stories*. In 1993, she won the prestigious PEN/Faulkner Award for Fiction for her first novel, *Postcards*. Proulx's second novel, *The Shipping News* (1993), which was inspired by a canoeing trip to Newfoundland and reflects her keen interest in place, garnered numerous awards, including a Pulitzer, before being made into a movie (2001). Proulx's three other novels are the picaresque *Accordion Crimes* (1996); *That Old Ace in the Hole* (2002), set in Texas; and the historical novel *Barkskins* (2016). "Job History" appears in Proulx's second collection, *Close Range: Wyoming Stories* (1999), alongside the prize-winning story that inspired the Academy Award–winning film *Brokeback Mountain* (2005). The thrice-divorced mother of four has also published *Bird Cloud: A Memoir* (2011), as well as two more collections inspired by the state she long called home—*Bad Dirt: Wyoming Stories 2* (2004) and *Fine Just the Way It Is: Wyoming Stories 3* (2008).

Leeland Lee is born at home in Cora, Wyoming, November 17, 1947, the youngest of six. In the 1950s his parents move to Unique when his mother inherits a small dog-bone ranch. The ranch lies a few miles outside town. They raise sheep, a few chickens, and some hogs. The father is irascible and, as soon as they can, the older children disperse. Leeland can sing "That Doggie in the Window"[1] all the way through. His father strikes him with a flyswatter and tells him to shut up. There is no news on the radio. A blizzard has knocked out the power.

Leeland's face shows heavy bone from his mother's side. His neck is thick and his red-gold hair plastered down in bangs. Even as a child his eyes are as pouchy as those of a middle-aged alcoholic, the brows rod-straight above wandering, out-of-line eyes. His nose lies broad and close to his face, his mouth seems to have been cut with a single chisel blow into easy flesh. In the fifth grade, horsing around with friends, he falls off the school's fire escape and breaks his pelvis. He is in a body cast for three months. On the news an announcer says that the average American eats 8.6 pounds of margarine a year but only 8.3 pounds of butter. He never forgets this statistic.

---

1. American pop singer Patti Page's rendition of this song topped the Billboard charts in 1953.

When Leeland is seventeen he marries Lori Bovee. They quit school. Lori is pregnant and Leeland is proud of this. His pelvis gives him no trouble. She is a year younger than he, with an undistinguished, oval face, hair of medium length. She is a little stout but looks a confection in pastel sweater sets. Leeland and his mother fight over this marriage and Leeland leaves the ranch. He takes a job pumping gas at Egge's Service Station. Ed Egge says, "You may fire when ready, Gridley,"[2] and laughs. The station stands at the junction of highway 16 and a county road. Highway 16 is the main tourist road to Yellowstone. Leeland buys Lori's father's old truck for fifty dollars and Ed rebuilds the engine. Vietnam and Selma, Alabama,[3] are on the news.

The federal highway program[4] puts through the new four-lane interstate forty miles south of highway 16 and parallel with it. Overnight the tourist business in Unique falls flat. One day a hundred cars stop for gas and oil, hamburgers, cold soda. The next day only two cars pull in, both driven by locals asking how business is. In a few months there is a FOR SALE sign on the inside window of the service station. Ed Egge gets drunk and, driving at speed, hits two steers on the county road.

5   Leeland joins the army, puts in for the motor pool. He is stationed in Germany for six years and never learns a word of the language. He comes back to Wyoming heavier, moodier. He works with a snow-fence[5] crew during spring and summer, then moves Lori and the children—the boy and a new baby girl— to Casper[6] where he drives oil trucks. They live in a house trailer on Poison Spider Road, jammed between two rioting neighbors. On the news they hear that an enormous diamond has been discovered somewhere. The second girl is born. Leeland can't seem to get along with the oil company dispatcher. After a year they move back to Unique. Leeland and his mother make up their differences.

Lori is good at saving money and she has put aside a small nest egg. They set up in business for themselves. Leeland believes people will be glad to trade at a local ranch supply store that saves a long drive into town. He rents the service station from Mrs. Egge who has not been able to sell it after Ed's death. They spruce it up, Leeland doing all the carpenter work, Lori painting the interior and exterior. On the side Leeland raises hogs with his father. His father was born and raised in Iowa and knows hogs.

It becomes clear that people relish the long drive to a bigger town where they can see something different, buy fancy groceries, clothing, bakery goods as well as ranch supplies. One intensely cold winter when everything freezes from God to gizzard, Leeland and his father lose 112 hogs. They sell out. Eighteen months

---

2. Phrase popularized by Bugs Bunny in the 1950s but originally spoken to U.S. Navy captain Charles Gridley on May 1, 1898, commanding him to initiate a battle in the Spanish-American War.

3. In March 1965, the Vietnam War began to escalate with the introduction of general conflict troops; in Selma, Alabama, police attacked civil rights demonstrators, causing a national outrage that helped inspire the Voting Rights Act of 1965.

4. The Federal Highway Act of 1956 authorized the modern interstate highway system. Construction on the Wyoming portion began in the 1960s.

5. Slatted fence designed to block blowing snow, especially to protect roads.

6. Wyoming's second-largest city, nicknamed "The Oil City" because of its role in various oil booms, one of which peaked in 1970.

later the ranch supply business goes under. The new color television set goes back to the store.

After the bankruptcy proceedings Leeland finds work on a road construction crew. He is always out of town, it seems, but back often enough for what he calls "a good ride" and so makes Lori pregnant again. Before the baby is born he quits the road crew. He can't seem to get along with the foreman. No one can, and turnover is high. On his truck radio he hears that hundreds of religious cult members have swallowed Kool-Aid and cyanide.[7]

Leeland takes a job at Tongue River Meat Locker and Processing. Old Man Brose owns the business. Leeland is the only employee. He has an aptitude for sizing up and cutting large animals. He likes wrapping the tidy packages, the smell of damp bone and chill. He can throw his cleaver unerringly and when mice run along the wall they do not run far if Leeland is there. After months of discussion with Old Man Brose, Leeland and Lori sign a ten-year lease on the meat locker operation. Their oldest boy graduates from high school, the first in the family to do so, and joins the army. He signs up for six years. There is something on the news about school lunches and ketchup is classed as a vegetable.[8] Old Man Brose moves to Albuquerque.

The economy takes a dive. The news is full of talk about recession and unemployment. Thrifty owners of small ranches go back to doing their own butchering, cutting, and freezing. The meat locker lease payments are high and electricity jumps up. Leeland and Lori have to give up the business. Old Man Brose returns from Albuquerque. There are bad feelings. It didn't work out, Leeland says, and that's the truth of it.

It seems like a good time to try another place. The family moves to Thermopolis where Leeland finds a temporary job at a local meat locker during hunting season. A hunter from Des Moines, not far from where Leeland's father was born, tips him $100 when he loads packages of frozen elk and the elk's head onto the man's single-engine plane. The man has been drinking. The plane goes down in the Medicine Bow range to the southeast.

During this long winter Leeland is out of work and stays home with the baby. Lori works in the school cafeteria. The baby is a real crier and Leeland quiets him down with spoonsful of beer.

In the spring they move back to Unique and Leeland tries truck driving again, this time in long-distance rigs on coast-to-coast journeys that take him away two and three months at a time. He travels all over the continent, to Texas, Alaska, Montreal, and Corpus Christi. He says every place is the same. Lori works now in the kitchen of the Hi-Lo Café in Unique. The ownership of the café changes three times in two years. West Klinker, an elderly rancher, eats three meals a day at the Hi-Lo. He is sweet on Lori. He reads her an article

7. On November 18, 1978, over nine hundred people died in the Jonestown massacre, a mass suicide in a religious community in Guyana led by American Jim Jones. Because of the way its victims were poisoned, the event inspired the phrase "drink the Kool-Aid"—i.e., go along with others unquestioningly.
8. In an effort to cut costs in federally subsidized school lunch programs but still comply with existing nutritional guidelines, the Reagan administration proposed reclassifying ketchup as a vegetable in 1982. The resulting public outcry scuttled the proposal.

from the newspaper—a strange hole has appeared in the ozone layer.[9] He confuses ozone with oxygen.

One night while Leeland is somewhere on the east coast the baby goes into convulsions following a week's illness of fever and cough. Lori makes a frightening drive over icy roads to the distant hospital. The baby survives but he is slow. Lori starts a medical emergency response group in Unique. Three women and two men sign up to take the first aid course. They drive a hundred miles to the first aid classes. Only two of them pass the test on the first try. Lori is one of the two. The other is Stuttering Bob, an old bachelor. One of the failed students says Stuttering Bob has nothing to do but study the first aid manual as he enjoys the leisured life that goes with a monthly social security check.

15   Leeland quits driving trucks and again tries raising hogs with his father on the old ranch. He becomes a volunteer fireman and is at the bad February fire that kills two children. It takes the fire truck three hours to get in to the ranch through the wind-drifted snow. The family is related to Lori. When something inside explodes, Leeland tells, an object flies out of the house and strikes the fire engine hood. It is a Nintendo player and not even charred.

Stuttering Bob has cousins in Muncie, Indiana. One of the cousins works at the Muncie Medical Center. The cousin arranges for the Medical Center to donate an old ambulance to the Unique Rescue Squad although they had intended to give it to a group in Mississippi. Bob's cousin, who has been to Unique, persuades them. Bob is afraid to drive through congested cities so Leeland and Lori take a series of buses to Muncie to pick up the vehicle. It is their first vacation. They take the youngest boy with them. On the return trip Lori leaves her purse on a chair in a restaurant. The gas money for the return trip is in the purse. They go back to the restaurant, wild with anxiety. The purse has been turned in and nothing is missing. Lori and Leeland talk about the goodness of people, even strangers. In their absence Stuttering Bob is elected president of the rescue squad.

A husband and wife from California move to Unique and open a taxidermy business. They say they are artists and arrange the animals in unusual poses. Lori gets work cleaning their workshop. The locals make jokes about the coyote in their window, posed lifting a leg against sagebrush where a trap is set. The taxidermists hold out for almost two years, then move to Oregon. Leeland's and Lori's oldest son telephones from overseas. He is making a career of the service.

Leeland's father dies and they discover the hog business is deeply in debt, the ranch twice-mortgaged. The ranch is sold to pay off debts. Leeland's mother moves in with them. Leeland continues long-distance truck driving. His mother watches television all day. Sometimes she sits in Lori's kitchen, saying almost nothing, picking small stones from dried beans.

The youngest daughter baby-sits. One night, on the way home, her employer feels her small breasts and asks her to squeeze his penis, because, he says, she ate the piece of chocolate cake he was saving. She does it but runs crying into

---

9. In 1985, scientists discovered a hole in the atmosphere's ozone layer, which protects the planet from harmful ultraviolet light and is damaged by pollution.

the house and tells Lori who advises her to keep quiet and stay home from now on. The man is Leeland's friend; they hunt elk and antelope together.

Leeland quits truck driving. Lori has saved a little money. Once more they 20 decide to go into business for themselves. They lease the old gas station where Leeland had his first job and where they tried the ranch supply store. Now it is a gas station again, but also a convenience store. They try surefire gimmicks: plastic come-on banners that pop and tear in the wind, free ice cream cones with every fill-up, prize drawings. Leeland has been thinking of the glory days when a hundred cars stopped. Now highway 16 seems the emptiest road in the country. They hold on for a year, then Leeland admits that it hasn't worked out and he is right. He is depressed for days when San Francisco beats Denver in the Super Bowl.[1]

Their oldest boy is discharged from the service and will not say why but Leeland knows it is chemical substances, drugs. Leeland is driving long-distance trucks again despite his back pain. The oldest son is home, working as a ranch hand in Pie. Leeland studies him, looking for signs of addiction. The son's eyes are always red and streaming.

The worst year comes. Leeland's mother dies, Leeland hurts his back, and, in the same week, Lori learns that she has breast cancer and is pregnant again. She is forty-six. Lori's doctor advises an abortion. Lori refuses.

The oldest son is discovered to have an allergy to horses and quits the ranch job. He tells Leeland he wants to try raising hogs. Pork prices are high. For a few days Leeland is excited. He can see it clearly: Leeland Lee & Son, Livestock. But the son changes his mind when a friend he knew in the service comes by on a motorcycle. The next morning both of them leave for Phoenix.

Lori spontaneously aborts in the fifth month of the pregnancy and then the cancer burns her up. Leeland is at the hospital with her every day. Lori dies. The daughters, both married now, curse Leeland. No one knows how to reach the oldest son and he misses the funeral. The youngest boy cries inconsolably. They decide he will live in Billings, Montana, with the oldest sister who is expecting her first child.

Two springs after Lori's death a middle-aged woman from Ohio buys the 25 café, paints it orange, renames it Unique Eats and hires Leeland to cook. He is good with meat, knows how to choose the best cuts and grill or do them chicken-fried style to perfection. He has never cooked anything at home and everyone is surprised at this long-hidden skill. The oldest son comes back and next year they plan to lease the old gas station and convert it to a motorcycle repair shop and steak house. Nobody has time to listen to the news.

1999

QUESTIONS

1. How would you describe the central conflict in JOB HISTORY? Might this story lack the sort of climax and resolution we expect of short stories? How and why so, or not?
2. Proulx's minimalist narration involves little direct description of setting, yet setting—time, place, and milieu—arguably plays a major role in the story. Why and how so? What might the story suggest about how its particular fictional family's "job

---

1. On January 28, 1990, the San Francisco 49ers defeated the Denver Broncos 55–10.

history" relates to "history" in the broader, more collective sense, the kind of "history" contained in textbooks, for example?

3. Does the story as a whole seem to endorse Leeland's statement that "every place is the same" (par. 13)? How might the story reinforce and/or challenge our assumptions about the American West? the American dream?

YIYUN LI
(b. 1972)

A Flawless Silence

A longtime resident of Northern California and now a professor at Princeton University, Yiyun Li grew up in Beijing, China, living—in an apartment complex housing Department of Nuclear Industry employees—with her father (a physicist) and mother (a teacher), as well as her siblings and grandfather (a former editor, poet, and staunch anti-Communist). A teenager during the government crackdown following the 1989 Tiananmen Square protests, Li was required, along with her classmates, to serve a year in the Chinese Army before she became a student of immunology, first at Peking University (BS, 1996), then at the University of Iowa. Lonely and wanting to improve her English, Li—a voracious reader, who credits English-language novels with helping her to survive her year in the army—enrolled in a community-college creative writing course. That proved a life-changing choice. Abandoning immunology, Li in 2005 both earned an MFA from the famed Iowa Writers' Workshop and published *A Thousand Years of Good Prayers,* a short-story collection that garnered four major prizes; inspired two films by famed director Wayne Wang; and established Li as among the most important fiction-writers of her generation. An author of novels including *The Vagrants* (2009), *Kinder than Solitude* (2014), and *Must I Go* (2020), as well as a moving memoir inspired by her 2012 hospitalization for depression (*Dear Friend, from My Life I Write to You in Your Life* [2017]), Li remains fiercely committed to the short-story form, often citing masters of that form (especially William Trevor) as major influences. This mother of two sons and MacArthur Fellow remains committed, too, to writing, just as she dreams and talks to herself, in English, even as she continues to trawl Chinese-language websites and to speak Chinese at home with her husband (a computer programmer). Describing her "abandonment of [her] first language" as a "deeply personal" choice, simultaneously "a kind of suicide" and a "private salvation," Li credits English with enabling her to "explore thoughts [. . .] that I can't in my native tongue." As a Chinese-American daughter explains to her Chinese father in Li's "A Thousand Years of Good Prayers," "if you grew up in a language that you never used to express your feelings, it would be easier to take up another language and talk more in the new language. It makes you a new person."

A few times a year, around major Chinese holidays, Min received an e-mail from a man whom she had met twice in her life. Every November—after the celebration of another birthday, on November 3rd, he never failed to remind her—he also attached a picture of himself, and begged for a picture of her. In the past twelve years, the number of his grandchildren had quadrupled. His oldest grandson had graduated from college and taken a good job in New York City. The next two grandchildren were in college. There were a few more, mostly on the West Coast. The youngest, a boy born with a noble look, the man had nicknamed J.C., for Julius Caesar.[1] In 2012, his wife had died, but he was healthy in general, minus some common conditions that plagued old people—high blood pressure and faulty short-term memory. There were other details in his e-mails: a week of vacation in Hawaii, a couple new to the farmers' market who worked as elementary-school teachers but sold blueberries on weekends, a favorite restaurant closing because of a rent hike. Most people would have written long ago with a stern reply, telling the sender to stop e-mailing; most people would have blocked him had he persisted.

"I turned eighty-four last week," the most recent message began. "I was born in the Year of the Monkey.[2] I'm attaching a family picture taken on the day of my birthday. If my memory is still good, you were born in the Year of the Rat, so you're forty-four. Can you send me a picture of you so I can see what you look like now?"

It had been 3 A.M. when the man, who lived in a suburb of Seattle, in a retirement facility five minutes from his eldest son's family, wrote Min, who lived just south of San Francisco. Min had chronic insomnia, and checking her phone when she couldn't sleep exacerbated the condition. It was bad enough that the man had filled the void of his night calculating Min's age. It was much worse that the message had ambushed her during her own wakefulness. She thought of telling the man to leave her alone. You're a nuisance, she rehearsed, and you should be ashamed of yourself.

But in the morning, as Min drove the twins to school, she was glad she had not responded. Perhaps the man would die between this month and the next, or between this year and the next. Min looked forward to the day his e-mails stopped coming: for once, she would win a battle through silence.

"Mommy, tell Emmie she's wrong," Deanna said.   5

"Mommy, tell Deanna she's wrong."

The previous day, the girls had reported the addition of two new chicks in the school garden, Pancake and Waffle, thus named because the gardening teacher could not tell them apart. Emmie was insisting that after cleaning the coop she could tell the difference between the two. Deanna was sensibly pointing out that the chick Emmie called Pancake might have been Waffle in the first place.

Min said that they were both right, adding "in a way"—a phrase she used often when the girls were in disagreement. They refuted her at once in a joint effort.

"Shall we change the subject?" Min said.

1. General and statesman (100–44 BCE) who played a central role in Rome's transformation from a republic to an empire; he was declared perpetual dictator shortly before his assassination.
2. Ninth in the twelve-year recurring cycle of the Chinese zodiac calendar; both 2016 and 1932 (when Min's correspondent was likely born) were years of the monkey. The Year of the Rat (mentioned later) is the first year in the cycle; 1972 was a year of the rat.

10   "Amelia said she used to think pepper spray[3] was a condiment," Deanna said.
"Amelia's middle name is some pasta's name," Emmie said.
"No, a cheese's name," Deanna said.
"It may be both," Min said. In a way, she thought, everything can be something else.
"Kevin is Republican," Emmie said.

15   Min must have missed something. "How do you know?"
"He wrote a letter to Trump,"[4] Emmie said.
"And said, 'Dear Mr. Trump, I'm your supporter, but could you be a better person so more people will like you?'" Deanna said. "Everyone else wrote to Hillary."
Min looked at the twins in the rearview mirror. They nodded back convincingly. It turned out, when she questioned further, that the day before, during an activity called "Understanding the Election Results," the third graders had all written a letter to either Mrs. Clinton or Mr. Trump.

Sandra, Kevin's mother, was in tears when Min ran into her in the school parking lot. Had she heard this talk about Kevin's being Republican, Sandra asked, and Min admitted that she had. "I told the teacher to take his letter down from the display," Sandra said. "She should have checked with me first. He has no idea what it means to be Republican."

20   "There's no real harm done," Min said.
"All the kids will tell their parents, if they haven't already," Sandra said, and then, before a group of parents reached them, "Let's go get coffee."
Sandra and Min had served on the school's hospitality committee for the past two years, and, before that, on the lice-buster team. They got along because Sandra could make the smallest encounter in a grocery store into a story with a beginning and a middle and an end, and Min liked to listen. Sandra reminded Min of her mother, who, though widowed young, had never lost her fondness for storytelling, and had always been quick to laugh.
Min had not inherited her mother's storytelling abilities. When the twins were in kindergarten, their teacher had chastised Min. "They're strong readers," the teacher had said, "but in this country we have a tradition of reading to our children even if they can read by themselves. It's a bonding experience."
"In this country" did not sound like something that someone in a progressive school in California would say, and Min decided not to heed the teacher's comment. When the girls read together, they acted out each page with more liveliness than Min could offer. If the teacher talked to her again, she'd say she was hoping to foster her daughters' creativity, "creativity" being a versatile password.

25   Now, over coffee, Sandra recounted Election Night. "Even before they started counting, I had this pit in my stomach. I went upstairs and worked on Kevin's Halloween costume. Something was wrong with it, I thought. One of

3. Aerosol spray containing oils derived from cayenne pepper; an eye irritant usually used as a defensive weapon.
4. Republican Donald J. Trump (b. 1946), who defeated former First Lady and Democratic New York Senator Hillary Rodham Clinton (b. 1947) in the 2016 U.S. presidential election.

Pikachu's[5] ears looked crooked. Kevin said, Mommy, it's already past Halloween, and I said I wanted to make the thing right so that we could donate it. But the more I worked on it the worse it looked. Then Chuck came in, and I heard him yelling. He's winning! he said. He's winning! Why isn't the TV on? Kevin went downstairs while Chuck kept on and on: Didn't I tell you he'd win? Didn't I say that? You didn't believe me, did you? I knew if I didn't go downstairs he would go on yelling like that all night, so I went down and told Kevin it was his bedtime. He said it was early and he wanted to watch TV with his dad. And Chuck said, For God's sake, what's wrong with you? Let him stay up and celebrate with me."

There had been no raised voices in Min's house. Neither she nor Rich, her husband, had discussed the election results; neither had lost a moment of composure. Min had never revealed to Sandra that Rich was a Trump supporter. Chuck owned a company that dealt in cleaning supplies, a business that had been in the family for three generations. Rich, who had grown up in a poor neighborhood in Beijing and who had long ago given up his Chinese name, worked at a tech startup.[6] Each man would think that the other deserved little respect. Was there any good in sharing with Sandra that both their husbands had been among the twenty per cent in their county who had voted for Trump? Humiliation would not bring people closer.

Sandra said that she had called Chuck a bigot to his face, and he had called her an equally bad name. Min had not called Rich anything denigrating. He had married her because she was not the kind of woman who would use strong words. They had talked about the election only once—these days, their conversation rarely ventured out of the safety zone of children and grocery lists and holiday plans. Rich had made a long, fervid speech in favor of Trump, and when Min had simply said she was going to vote for Clinton he had called her brainwashed. "The longer a woman's hair is, the shorter her sight is," he said, quoting his favorite Chinese saying, which had also been his father's favorite and, before that, his grandfather's.

"Don't you sometimes want someone's death so much that you almost believe the person could die just because of your wish?" Min said now.

"I'm sure you're not the only one who feels that way."

"Oh . . ." Min said. She wasn't thinking about Trump, she admitted.

"Who are you talking about? Not Rich, I hope."

"Oh, no."

"Then who?"

It was unkind of her to wish an old man a speedy death. Min quickly said something about a novel she was reading and how she wished she could strangle a character in it. That was a poor lie. Sandra would have pressed more if not for her own trouble. Too bad no other children would pronounce themselves Kevin's allies. Min had warned the twins never to mention that their father was

30

5. Fictional character/species in the famous Pokémon series of video games, animated television shows and movies, trading cards, and comic books.
6. Entrepreneurial company that first develops technology products and services for the market. *Beijing*: China's capital.

a Trump supporter, and they had replied that of course they wouldn't be so stupid.

35   The man who would not stop writing to Min had, in a way, been responsible for her marriage, but whenever this thought occurred to her she would remind herself that nobody had forced her into marrying Rich.

Min was nineteen when she first met the man, who had been introduced to her as a potential father-in-law. He was a linguistics professor at a prominent university in Beijing, and he had three sons in America. The eldest, according to the matchmaker, worked for Microsoft,[7] and he was the one the family had in mind for Min, but if that didn't work out there were two other sons.

Min hadn't shown much academic promise. She had attended a vocational school that trained girls to become secretaries. After graduation, she had worked in a department store. Why would any of those boys need to find a wife in China when they're already in America? she asked her mother. You're asking the blind for directions, her mother said, but I would say that they can't possibly find someone as good as you in America.

America, Min could see, was alluring to her mother. Min's father had died during her second year of middle school, in an accident at the steel plant where he had worked since he was eighteen. After his death, Min and her mother had lived frugally on the money her mother made running a newsstand. The compensation for her father's accident had been saved by her mother as Min's dowry.

Min had once had a brief schoolgirl crush, but she had never dated. She was good-looking—not in a striking way, but she had a classic look, like a figure in a Ming-dynasty[8] painting or a period movie, her shoulders narrowing compliantly, her neck long, her complexion clear, her eyes and nose and mouth arranged in a pleasing manner.

40   Min had grown up thinking she was born into a role as a flawless daughter, and someday she would become a flawless daughter-in-law, wife, and mother. It turned out that she was none of these, yet she couldn't see where she had fallen short. No one was perfect, she knew, but women in books and films often seemed flawed in a meaningful or attractive way. The other mothers at the school, when they were unhappy, had a sensible reason: a husband's affair, a child's diagnosis, a power shift on the school-auction committee.

Perhaps they all lived in giant doll houses. Some, like the dolls that belonged to Emmie and Deanna, had complicated life stories, with many plots and dramas and excitements. Others were like the only doll Min had had when she was young—a little creature made of hard plastic, with unbending arms and legs connected to a torso through ball sockets. Min had carried the doll around dutifully, but she had never made up a story for it. The only catastrophe that had befallen the doll had occurred on a winter night. Min had left it on a windowsill, and a power outage caused the temperature in the apartment to drop. For

7. Major American multinational technology company headquartered in Washington state, specializing in computer software, personal computers, and related products and services.
8. 1368–1644, a period of Chinese history renowned, among other things, for great achievement in the arts.

reasons that neither she nor her parents understood, one of the doll's legs had disconnected from its socket and could not be put back.

The one-legged doll remained in her possession. Min did not remember ever feeling sad about the severed limb. A doll was a doll. She had not been a sentimental child.

Min had agreed with her mother that it wouldn't hurt to meet the professor. At nineteen, she was the kind of girl some parents wanted for their sons: pretty, meek, experienced enough with hardship not to be dreamily naïve, yet not broody, either, even after losing her father.

Min and her mother met the man at the matchmaker's apartment on a Sunday. They had tea together until the matchmaker suggested that she and Min's mother take a walk in a nearby park. Left alone with the man, Min did not know what she was expected to do to earn his approval. He looked like a professor from a film, with his wire-rimmed glasses and impeccably parted silver hair. When he asked her questions, he used words her father would never have used. What's your outlook on the world? What do you do to maximize your potential? When she did not know what to say, he said that the process of enlightening and perfecting oneself was like rowing a boat up a river. He then brought out a set of textbooks, called "New Concept English,"[9] and asked which level Min thought she was. She had never heard of the textbooks, and the man, looking at her over his glasses, told her that if she wanted to go to America she should start studying English right away.

Min thought she had failed the interview. She didn't much care.   45

The man moved next to her on the sofa and opened the second book in the series. He asked her to repeat after him the first lesson, titled "A Private Conversation." Her body tensed at the closeness of their shoulders and thighs as they bent over the book.

Perhaps he had been acting only out of fatherliness, she tried to convince herself afterward. He had left the books with her and insisted that she call him the following weekend. He would arrange his schedule so that he could tutor her, he said, a plan he didn't bring up with the matchmaker or Min's mother. Instead, he told them that his son would come home for a summer visit, and then the two young people could properly meet.

Min never made the call. They did not have a telephone at home, and she hated to use public phones. Even when the professor expressed an urgent wish to talk with her through the matchmaker, she remained silent. The books he'd loaned to her she buried under old newspapers. After a few weeks, she was able to pretend that she had never met the man, whose fingers had lingered on her arm for a moment too long when he had said goodbye.

One day, Min's mother told her that the professor had decided that she wasn't a good choice. Not diligent or smart enough for his intellectual family. This verdict had been conveyed to her mother by the matchmaker.

"Did you see the photo he showed us?" Min's mother said. "His son is not yet 50 thirty and already going bald. If this professor worried that you would not give

9. Hugely popular English language curriculum and book series created by British teacher L. G. Alexander in 1967; a revised edition designed for "Chinese learners" appeared in 1997.

him intellectual grandchildren, I'd be equally concerned that his Microsoft son would give me ugly grandchildren."

Known as "the orphan and the widow" to friends and neighbors, Min and her mother had maintained the solemnness required by their titles, but when nobody was around they had had many things to laugh about together.

At dinner a few days later, Emmie brought up Kevin's reputation as a Republican, already cemented, it seemed, among their classmates. "Everyone feels bad for him," Emmie said.

"I don't," Deanna said. "You feel bad for him because you have a crush on him."

"I don't think you are old enough to talk about boys or politics," Rich said.

55   "You're so ageist," Emmie said.

Min could sense Rich's impatience, but he only gave Emmie a cold look before turning to Deanna and asking her about her day. He had mellowed over the years. Their eldest child, Max, had grown up with a more unforgiving and volatile father, and right after college Max had moved to Singapore.[1] Min did not feel his absence keenly, though she thought that as a mother she should have done better at missing him. She had had Max at twenty-one, and the motherhood that had come too early had turned into a blur over the years. She had loved her son, still loved him—of this much she was certain, though she didn't know if she liked him. Can you love a person without liking him? Max and Rich had a fraught relationship, but they viewed the world similarly. For both, failing to calculate the price of every move in life was a character flaw; not taking advantage of someone else was a sin.

Sometimes Min pitied her future daughter-in-law, whoever she was, and wished that the girl could have chosen more wisely.

Conceiving another child had been Rich's solution to a marriage on the cusp of dissolution ten years ago. Divorce would be a disaster for everyone, he'd argued coolly: Max, who would experience adolescence with unnecessary turmoil; Rich, who would face a financial setback; and Min, too—most definitely, as he would do anything to minimize his loss and maximize hers. Min knew that Rich meant everything he said. Assets would be transferred back to China, to avoid alimony; custody of Max would be fought for. But Rich didn't know that she wanted neither his money nor his son—for a short period, she had found a strange relief in this thought. She could manage a simple life on the part-time salary she earned as a bookkeeper at Max's former preschool.

But what kind of mother would so readily give up a child? If she didn't love her husband enough, at least she should try to love her child better. Perhaps it wasn't a bad idea to have another baby. Motherhood was like one of those contracts that were automatically renewed. As long as you did nothing, a charge would show up on your credit card. What's wrong, though, with letting the automatic take over one's life?

---

1. Island city-state south of Malaysia, in Southeast Asia; known for its thriving economy, Western-style government, and very strict laws and regulations, enforced partly through hefty fines and corporal punishments like caning.

"Explain to me some of the dangers if Clinton had been elected," Rich said to 60 the girls now. Min wouldn't mind a silent meal, but Rich believed in dinner conversations. A preparation for the children to excel in the real world. "If you can't imagine that, you don't have a right to talk about politics at this table."

Emmie stuck her tongue out. Deanna, Rich's favorite—a fact she knew, as he had told her she was smarter than her sister and her mother combined— folded her hands under her chin. "What are the dangers, Daddy?"

"For instance, any boy could have used the girls' bathroom at school if he wanted,"[2] Rich said. "How would you have liked that?"

"I thought we agreed not to talk about politics," Min said.

"Except when I need to instruct my children," Rich said.

Abruptly Min stood up and went to the kitchen, where she rummaged 65 through the refrigerator as though she had forgotten something. On the counter there was a bottle of wine that Rich had brought home earlier, reading the label to her and telling her the price; he wanted something special, he said, when a couple of friends came over on Saturday to celebrate the election. She thought of nudging the bottle off the counter. He would tell the girls to go to their bedroom if he wanted to yell at her. She would say it was an accident, and he would say no one believed that, and, even if it had been an accident, it was unforgivable. It's only a bottle of wine, she would say, and she didn't need his forgiveness for such trifles. He would say something else, but they would be cut short by Emmie, who was not as good as Deanna at waiting out a storm. Why are you guys arguing? Emmie would say, and Rich would try to soften his voice and say that they were having a grownup discussion. About what? Emmie would say. About the fundamental difference between us, Min would answer. Are you going to divorce? Emmie would ask. No, of course not, they would say together.

Yet this scenario, which Min had seen in films, would never happen in her family. She and Rich had both come into the marriage without any fantasy about the other. Could love find a place in a marriage if it had not started with some degree of fantasy? They were realistic people, and marriage was weather. They lived in it without any desire to control it or change it. They knew each other well enough to know the forecast.

A few weeks after Min had met the professor, her mother had told her that a young man, who was working in America and was home for a visit, was interested in meeting her. "And this time," her mother said, "I've asked about his parents. They're just like us, not intellectuals."

A mail-order bride,[3] Min thought of herself much later, even though she and Rich had dated long-distance through letters and phone calls for eight months. She did not dislike him, though she'd never reread his letters, which often

2. In May 2016, eleven mostly Republican-led states sued the Obama administration over guidelines for public schools allowing transgender students to use the bathroom or locker room that accords with their gender identity rather than the sex assigned them at birth, in accordance with the administration's interpretation of federal civil rights law. The ensuing debate became a major issue in the ongoing presidential race.
3. Pejorative term for a woman who marries a man whom she met through a marriage agency; today, such agencies tend to be international, specializing in introducing women from developing countries, especially in the Eastern bloc and Southeast Asia, to Western men.

included lists of instructions. "You are what you wear," he wrote in one letter, going on to explain the importance of dressing in brand-name clothes and shoes "to boost your status and confidence." "Anyone who does not set his heart on getting rich should be ashamed of himself," he wrote in another. "Especially in America." On the phone, he prompted Min to study English and refresh her math skills, as his plan was to enroll her in an accounting program at a community college. From there, she could either find a stable government job with a good pension or, if she was ambitious and smart, join a company or a firm that would pay better.

Rich came from a background similar to Min's. His father worked in the boiler room of a municipal bathhouse,[4] and his mother in a high-school cafeteria. Rich could have turned out like many of his childhood friends, apprenticing at a factory after middle school. What had stopped him from going down that path was his fifth-grade teacher. Rich first told Min the story during one of their long-distance phone calls, and had since enjoyed repeating it to her and their children.

70   In the story, Rich and some friends had played truant one afternoon. The next day, the teacher, instead of giving them the usual punishment of extra work, made the boys stand in front of the class, and then asked the other pupils to imagine what the boys would look like in twenty or thirty years.

When no one spoke, the teacher turned to the boys. "All of you will end up like those men sitting out in the alleyways on a summer evening," she said, "shirtless, stomachs folded over your belts, a beer or a cigarette in your hands, having nothing better to do than yell at your wives and children so that you can feel good about yourselves. If your parents aren't ashamed of you, I assure you, your children will be."

Rich always ended his story by quoting the teacher, but Min knew there was more to it. His father had been one of those men. Her own father would have been described similarly. She might have married a man like that had she stayed in Beijing. Perhaps it was wrong to say there had not been any fantasy. Rich had offered her a change of scenery. She had offered him the possibility of offspring, who would admire and worship him.

When Min and Rich agreed, in a phone call, to get married, her mother asked her if she was sure.

Min lied and said yes. What made her decision clear, even before Rich had brought up the subject of marriage, was a visit from the professor. Her mother had been at her newsstand, and when Min opened the door the professor came into the apartment as though she had been expecting him. He studied the old furniture and the twelve-inch black-and-white television before turning to her. "I've been waiting for your call," he said. "You didn't keep your promise."

75   All of a sudden, it felt childish to pretend she had never met the man. Childish, too, to think he would forget that she still had his books. Min pulled them out from under the newspapers and tried to come up with a sensible apology,

4. Facility for communal, though often gender-segregated, bathing, typically including other amenities such as saunas.

but he cut her off. "I've come to set up a regular time to meet so you can study English with me."

Min thanked him and said that there was no need.

"Why not? You can't lower your standards because of the way you were brought up."

"I thought you decided I wasn't a good match for your son," Min said.

"But I've had a change of heart. You're like jadeite.[5] Less sympathetic people would think of you as a common rock, but you are not. Someone like me, someone who understands your value, has to make you into a polished masterpiece."

Min stepped back, but the professor moved closer, his hand resting on her shoulder, his thumb touching her collarbone. "Do you understand?" he said. "I can do a lot for you." 80

"I'm sorry, but I don't need your help."

"Why? Even my graduate students don't get this kind of attention from me."

Min shook her head. His fingers clutched her shoulder more tightly. "But I'm dating someone now," she said.

"What do you mean you're dating someone? Only two months ago you agreed to marry my son."

"I didn't." 85

"Why else did you meet me? Who is this man you're dating? Remember, I can help you go to America."

"I'm dating someone in America," Min said. "I'll marry him."

The anger in the man's eyes was not the anger of a concerned father—even at nineteen, Min could tell that. The resentment was that of a betrayed lover. "So you were only using me, but now you found someone better you can use," he said. "I should've known that girls like you have no honor to speak of."

Another girl would have laughed in his face and called him a lunatic. Another girl would have shaken off his hand and shown him the door. "I'm sorry if I'm disappointing you," Min said. "I can't help it."

"Of course you can. I can still teach you English. You don't have to marry my son. Just come and visit me. Say yes." 90

It was the helplessness of his plea that made Min cringe with pity. She did not want the power he'd handed her. It was not really power but an obligation or, worse, a debt. The moment he'd laid his eyes on her she owed him something. Still, she could not help feeling bad for him. *You're making a fool of yourself,* she wanted to say. *I'm only a girl, without any status or importance. Why are you embarrassing yourself like this?*

Over the years, Min had tried hard not to think about that moment. But when the man's e-mails came she often had an urge to tell her younger self, *It's not he who made a fool of himself but you. It's you who hastened into a marriage because you thought it was better to marry a man who would not act with such folly. You thought that a man without a crazed look in his eyes would be the right husband, but perhaps a marriage should be more like an illness that the couple agrees to submit to so that they can recover together. Some succeed, others fail, yet two people can't remain in their separate afflictions and hope for the best.*

5. Most prized of the two forms of jade.

"Listen, I don't want you to discuss politics with the girls," Rich said to Min after the twins went to bed that night.

Min did not reply.

95   "I don't want my children to be exposed to this left-wing crap."

The same conversation would take place in Sandra's house, though it would be a more heated fight, with words of passion being thrown back and forth like grenades. Yet Sandra would stay married to Chuck, just as Min would stay married to Rich.

"And, for the record," Rich continued, "if they ask you how you voted, you should either say you voted for Trump or, if you don't want to say that, tell them you didn't vote."

For a moment, Min felt a vindictive joy that the girls already knew to keep the truth about him from the world. In a few years, they would be teen-agers. Emmie would be high-strung, unable to mask her moods. Deanna would be coyer, but when she was ready to sabotage her father's authority she would do so with more tact, and with more devastation, too. Perhaps Min could just be patient and wait for the twins to grow up. Her mother might have felt the same way after the death of Min's father: children grow up, and they will solve the problems we can't solve for them.

They would find new problems, too, those they could not solve. You could wait for a harmless man to die, but he would not let loose his grasp, as if you were part of his life.

100   Max had been in elementary school when the professor first sent Min an e-mail, "to reconnect," as he put it. The previous summer, he said, he had visited Beijing for the first time since moving to America more than a decade earlier, and on a whim had stopped at Min's old apartment building. Surprisingly, he wrote, the complex had not been demolished, and her mother still lived there. "All these signs convinced me that I should get in touch with you again," the professor wrote. "As a lost friend."

He had written out of loneliness or nostalgia, Min had told herself, trying to be kind in her dismissal. All she had to do was to remain silent. But a silence stoically maintained, she now understood, did not give her any dignity. The next month, the month after next, he would send another e-mail, reminding her that she was never far from the girl he remembered. In his imagination she would still be young, pretty, and malleable. Her silence would do nothing to stop his boundless imagination.

That night, when Min failed to fall asleep, she opened the man's e-mail from the night before. In a large font that she hoped would be easy for him to read, she typed, "Please stop writing me."

Then, on second thought, she erased that, and wrote, "Go to hell."

2018

QUESTIONS

1. How does A Flawless Silence characterize Min's internal and external conflicts? In what way might her husband and the professor serve as antagonists? How does she resolve those conflicts at the end of the story, or how and why exactly does Min change by the end?

2. How might the story's general setting—both the timeframe and the place in which events unfold—cause, exacerbate, or otherwise shape or affect the story's conflicts? That is, in what ways does it matter that the story takes place in the aftermath of the 2016 presidential election and in Northern California?

3. Though mainly set in contemporary California, the story also includes some of Min's past experiences, especially as a young adult, in her native China. Particularly in terms of Min's conflicts, how exactly does and doesn't it matter to the story that she is an immigrant to the United States? that she, like her husband and the professor, grew up in China?

SUGGESTIONS FOR WRITING

1. Write an essay in which you compare the use of setting in any two stories in this book. You might compare the re-creation of two similar settings, such as landscapes far from home, foreign cities, or stifling suburbs; or you might contrast the treatment of different kinds of settings. Be sure to consider not only the authors' descriptive techniques but also the way the authors use setting to shape plot, point of view, and character.

2. Choose any story in this chapter and write an essay that explores how the story both draws on and encourages us to rethink our ideas about a particular place and time and social milieu, perhaps (but not necessarily) by showing us characters who themselves either come to see a setting differently or refuse to do so.

3. Whereas Job History and A Flawless Silence both cover a relatively long period of time and take us to a variety of places, Araby and Volar have more circumscribed settings. Write a response paper or essay exploring how these factors enhance our sense of the characters' conflicts and even the story's theme.

4. Write a story in which a newcomer brings a fresh perspective to a familiar setting or in which a character is changed by an encounter with an unfamiliar setting.

SAMPLE WRITING: ANNOTATION AND CLOSE READING

Close reading, with an eye toward setting or any other element, demands careful attention to detail. That process often begins with annotation—underlining significant details in a text and making notes in the margins, which you can then draw on to formulate arguments.

Below, you will find an annotation of the first paragraph of James Joyce's ARABY, followed by a paragraph of analysis written in response to the following prompt:

> The first paragraph of Joyce's story focuses entirely on setting. What tone is established here? How do specific details of setting and the diction used to describe them create tone?

As you read and compare the annotation and the analysis, notice how the analytical paragraph both elaborates on certain aspects of the annotation and ignores others (especially the references to religion) in order to stay focused exclusively on the claim about tone with which it opens (its topic sentence).

Repetition
literally, "dead end"

like school is a prison?

North Richmond Street, being blind, was a quiet street except at the hour when the Christian Brothers' School set the boys free. An uninhabited house of two storeys stood at the blind end, detached from its neighbours in a square ground. The other houses of the street, conscious of decent lives within them, gazed at one another with brown imperturbable faces.

education, religion, respectability

personification

The first paragraph of James Joyce's story "Araby" is solemn and emotionless or even depressing in tone. The street is called "blind" twice, meaning that it is literally a dead-end street, a kind of prison from which there is no exit. It also seems a pretty lifeless, stifled and stifling place—"quiet" all but one "hour" of the day, when the boys are "set . . . free," implying that they are imprisoned the rest of the time, too. The only individual house described here is "uninhabited," without any life inside; "detached from its neighbours," disconnected and alone; and itself trapped "in a square ground." Though the other houses do have "lives within them," those are only "decent"—not joyful or even sad, just "decent" or respectable. All the houses are personified: the uninhabited one has "neighbours" (which at first suggests people rather than houses), and these have "faces," are "conscious," and "gaz[e] at one another." But the terms of the personification only make these houses seem more, not less, lifeless: their "imperturbable faces" lack emotion or movement, and they are "brown," the bland color of mud or dirt rather than of the things that live and grow in it. This street is a dead end in more ways than one, as living on it must feel a little like being dead or at least deadened.

CAPTAIN NATIVE AMERICAN

The Future

AN ALBUM

I don't try to describe the future. I try to prevent it.
—RAY BRADBURY

When we say that many fictional subgenres are defined partly or even primarily by the settings they conventionally feature, what we usually have in mind is *where* the action takes place—in a forest, cottage, or village (as in most **folktales**) or in a dark, decaying, and potentially haunted medieval castle or abbey (as in early **gothic fiction**). In a few cases, however, *where* turns out to be infinitely less important than *when*. The most obvious such case is **historical fiction**—by strict definition, fiction set in a time previous to its author's birth. If writers of such fiction might be said to comment on their present by revisiting a moment from the actual past, writers of what some literary scholars call *future fiction* do the opposite: They show us something important about our present by imagining one or more possible futures.

But what of that amorphous, much-debated thing called *science fiction* or, more familiarly, *SF*? Though definitions of SF are as abundant and varied as the planets visited in *Star Trek*, few of those definitions *require* a future setting. The *Oxford English Dictionary*, for example, describes SF as fiction "featur[ing] hypothetical scientific or technological advances, the existence of alien life, space or time travel, etc., especially"—but not exclusively—"such fictions set in the future, or an imagined alternative universe." Insisting even less on particularities of setting, one early (1958) essay on the genre defines it as "a form of literature which crosses the frontiers of knowledge using imagination, intuition or logic to guide it," but relying, when it "goes beyond known facts," on "deductions" that are "feasible or at least not in obvious conflict with accepted [scientific] theories." Though much future fiction falls into the category of SF and vice versa, in other words, the two aren't precisely the same. Mary Shelley's novels *Frankenstein* (1818) and *The Last Man* (1826), for instance, are today widely considered early examples of SF, despite the fact that only one depicts the future and that both appeared over a hundred years before "pulp" magazine editor Hugo Gernsback first popularized the term *science fiction*.

Either way, fictional futures are ultimately as numerous and varied as are the writers who imagine them. Yet they often work in interestingly similar ways. For one thing, many are based on the principle of extrapolation—essentially, an educated guess about the unknown (in this case, the future) based on observations of the known (the present). Such fiction, in other words, invites us into a world that reflects its author's sense of where we might be headed *if* we continue on the path we're already on. For another thing, fictional futures have, over time, tended to swing between one of two extremes: Either they are models of perfection or *utopias*, like the world imagined in the sixteenth-century book by Sir Thomas More from which that word derives, or they are the very opposite—*dystopias*. Whatever particular shape they take, however, "imaginary futures are necessarily," as SF author William Gibson puts it, "about the moment in which they are written," even if the very best of them continue to be meaningful long after that particular moment is past.

For much of its history, SF has reflected its times by also reflecting the experiences and outlooks of its mainly white, mainly male producers and consumers. When a woman took third prize in a 1927 *Amazing Stories* competition, Gernsback found this "one of the [great] surprises of the contest," "for, as a rule," he explained, "women do not make good scientification writers, because their education and general tendencies on scientific matters are usually limited." As of 2021, only eight of thirty-seven winners of the Science Fiction and Fantasy Writers of America's (SFWA) "Grand Master" lifetime achievement award are women; only two are Black. Yet thanks to pioneers including Ursula K. Le Guin (1929–2018), Octavia Butler, and SFWA's first Black Grand Master, Samuel R. Delany (b. 1942), as well as younger writers like N. K. Jemisin (b. 1972), the field of SF—and thus our visions of our past, our present, our future, of who "we" are, have been, and might be—have been slowly but surely expanding since at least the 1970s, even as the boundary between SF and conventional fiction has grown ever thinner. With the emergence of Afrofuturism and Indigenous Futurisms in the 1990s and 2000s respectively—those multi-faceted, multi-media movements behind Ryan Coogler's epoch-making, record-busting *Black Panther* (2018)—the future of our future, as it were, has never looked brighter.

In this album, you'll find four very different SF stories written by very different writers at very different historical moments, ranging from the 1950s to the 2010s. What are the key characteristics of the future each describes? What might each imply about how that future came to be? Which describe their particular future mainly or only, in Ray Bradbury's words, "to prevent it"?

WILLIAM GIBSON
(b. 1948)

The Gernsback Continuum[1]

Widely hailed as the father of "cyberpunk" science fiction, the inventor of the term *cyberspace*, and one of the first fiction writers to make the "hacker" a hero, William Gibson was born in South Carolina but raised (from age six) in a small town in southwestern Virginia, where he and his mother moved after his contractor father's untimely death. An only child, Gibson today credits this experience of "trauma" and "exile" with turning him both on to science fiction and into "the sort of introverted, hyper-bookish boy you'll find in the biographies of most American science fiction writers." Gibson rocketed to fame thanks to his novel *Neuromancer* (1984), the first work ever to win all three of science fiction's top prizes (the Nebula, Hugo, and Philip K. Dick awards). In addition to the two other novels in the "Sprawl" or "Cyberspace" trilogy—*Count Zero* (1986) and *Mona Lisa Overdrive* (1988)—Gibson's publications include *Burning Chrome* (1986); *The*

---

1. Like a spectrum, a whole characterized as a collection or sequence of slightly varying elements or states. *Gernsback*: Between the late 1920s and early 1950s, Hugo Gernsback (1884–1967) founded and edited a series of science-fiction magazines, starting with the world's first, *Amazing Stories*.

Difference Engine (1990), a novel coauthored with Bruce Sterling; the "Bridge," "Blue Ant," and "Jackpot" trilogies (1993–99, 2003–10, 2014–20); and *Distrust That Particular Flavor* (2012), a collection of essays and articles.

Mercifully, the whole thing is starting to fade, to become an episode. When I do still catch the odd glimpse, it's peripheral; mere fragments of mad-doctor chrome, confining themselves to the corner of the eye. There was that flying-wing liner[2] over San Francisco last week, but it was almost translucent. And the shark-fin roadsters[3] have gotten scarcer, and freeways discreetly avoid unfolding themselves into the gleaming eighty-lane monsters I was forced to drive last month in my rented Toyota. And I know that none of it will follow me to New York; my vision is narrowing to a single wavelength of probability. I've worked hard for that. Television helped a lot.

I suppose it started in London, in that bogus Greek taverna in Battersea Park Road, with lunch on Cohen's corporate tab. Dead steam-table food and it took them thirty minutes to find an ice bucket for the retsina.[4] Cohen works for Barris-Watford, who publish big, trendy "trade" paperbacks: illustrated histories of the neon sign, the pinball machine, the windup toys of Occupied Japan.[5] I'd gone over to shoot a series of shoe ads; California girls with tanned legs and frisky Day-Glo jogging shoes had capered for me down the escalators of St. John's Wood and across the platforms of Tooting Bec.[6] A lean and hungry young agency had decided that the mystery of London Transport would sell waffle-tread nylon runners.[7] They decide; I shoot. And Cohen, whom I knew vaguely from the old days in New York, had invited me to lunch the day before I was due out of Heathrow.[8] He brought along a very fashionably dressed young woman named Dialta Downes, who was virtually chinless and evidently a noted pop-art historian. In retrospect, I see her walking in beside Cohen under a floating neon sign that flashes **THIS WAY LIES MADNESS** in huge sans-serif[9] capitals.

Cohen introduced us and explained that Dialta was the prime mover behind the latest Barris-Watford project, an illustrated history of what she called "American Streamlined Moderne." Cohen called it "raygun Gothic." Their working title was *The Airstream Futuropolis: The Tomorrow That Never Was.*

2. Large tailless passenger aircraft with a flattened appearance created by the way the wings flow seamlessly into the body.
3. Open-top two-seater automobile with a sharklike tail fin, a futuristic design popular in the 1950s and 1960s.
4. Strong resin-flavored Greek wine.
5. After its defeat in World War II, Japan was occupied for almost ten years (1945–52) by the Allied powers, led by the United States and Great Britain.
6. Subway station in Tooting, South London. *St. John's Wood*: affluent neighborhood in northwest London.
7. Running shoes or sneakers (British). *London Transport*: government body overseeing all public transportation in London, including the subway, buses, etc.
8. Major London airport.
9. Plain typeface, often used for headlines, in which letters are not embellished with decorative line strokes.

There's a British obsession with the more baroque elements of American pop culture, something like the weird cowboys-and-Indians fetish of the West Germans or the aberrant French hunger for old Jerry Lewis[1] films. In Dialta Downes this manifested itself in a mania for a uniquely American form of architecture that most Americans are scarcely aware of. At first I wasn't sure what she was talking about, but gradually it began to dawn on me. I found myself remembering Sunday morning television in the Fifties.

5   Sometimes they'd run old eroded newsreels as filler on the local station. You'd sit there with a peanut butter sandwich and a glass of milk, and a static-ridden Hollywood baritone would tell you that there was A Flying Car in Your Future. And three Detroit engineers would putter around with this big old Nash[2] with wings, and you'd see it rumbling furiously down some deserted Michigan runway. You never actually saw it take off, but it flew away to Dialta Downes's never-never land, true home of a generation of completely uninhibited technophiles. She was talking about those odds and ends of "futuristic" Thirties and Forties architecture you pass daily in American cities without noticing; the movie marquees ribbed to radiate some mysterious energy, the dime stores faced with fluted aluminum, the chrome-tube chairs gathering dust in the lobbies of transient hotels. She saw these things as segments of a dreamworld, abandoned in the uncaring present; she wanted me to photograph them for her.

The Thirties had seen the first generation of American industrial designers; until the Thirties, all pencil sharpeners had looked like pencil sharpeners—your basic Victorian[3] mechanism, perhaps with a curlicue of decorative trim. After the advent of the designers, some pencil sharpeners looked as though they'd been put together in wind tunnels. For the most part, the change was only skin-deep; under the streamlined chrome shell, you'd find the same Victorian mechanism. Which made a certain kind of sense, because the most successful American designers had been recruited from the ranks of Broadway theater designers. It was all a stage set, a series of elaborate props for playing at living in the future.

1. American comedian (1926–2017) featured in many popular 1950s films.
2. Car produced in the United States between 1916 and 1957.
3. Dating from the reign of Queen Victoria of the United Kingdom (1837–1901).

Over coffee, Cohen produced a fat manila envelope full of glossies. I saw the winged statues that guard the Hoover Dam,[4] forty-foot concrete hood ornaments leaning steadfastly into an imaginary hurricane. I saw a dozen shots of Frank Lloyd Wright's Johnson's Wax Building, juxtaposed with the covers of old *Amazing Stories* pulps, by an artist named Frank R. Paul;[5] the employees of Johnson's Wax must have felt as though they were walking into one of Paul's spray-paint pulp utopias. Wright's building looked as though it had been designed for people who wore white togas and Lucite sandals. I hesitated over one sketch of a particularly grandiose prop-driven airliner, all wing, like a fat symmetrical boomerang with windows in unlikely places. Labeled arrows indicated the locations of the grand ballroom and two squash courts. It was dated 1936.

"This thing couldn't have flown . . . ?" I looked at Dialta Downes.

"Oh, no, quite impossible, even with those twelve giant props; but they loved the look, don't you see? New York to London in less than two days, first-class dining rooms, private cabins, sun decks, dancing to jazz in the evening . . . The designers were populists, you see; they were trying to give the public what it wanted. What the public wanted was the future."

I'd been in Burbank[6] for three days, trying to suffuse a really dull-looking rocker 10 with charisma, when I got the package from Cohen. It is possible to photograph what isn't there; it's damned hard to do, and consequently a very marketable talent. While I'm not bad at it, I'm not exactly the best, either, and this poor guy strained my Nikon's credibility. I got out, depressed because I do like to do a good job, but not totally depressed, because I did make sure I'd gotten the check for the job, and I decided to restore myself with the sublime artiness of the Barris-Watford assignment. Cohen had sent me some books on Thirties design, more photos of streamlined buildings, and a list of Dialta Downes's fifty favorite examples of the style in California.

Architectural photography can involve a lot of waiting; the building becomes a kind of sundial, while you wait for a shadow to crawl away from a detail you want, or for the mass and balance of the structure to reveal itself in a certain way. While I was waiting, I thought myself in Dialta Downes's America. When I isolated a few of the factory buildings on the ground glass of the Hasselblad,[7] they came across with a kind of sinister totalitarian dignity, like the stadiums

---

4. On the Nevada-Arizona border, completed 1936; according to their creator, the "Winged Figures of the Republic," the iconic (bronze, not concrete) statues alluded to here represent "the immutable calm of intellectual resolution, and the enormous power of trained physical strength, equally enthroned in placid triumph of scientific accomplishment."

5. American illustrator (1884–1963) renowned for his work for popular science-fiction magazines including *Amazing Stories* (founded by Hugo Gernsback in 1926); popular, sensational publications, of whatever genre, are sometimes referred to as *pulps* because of the cheap paper on which they were printed. *Frank Lloyd Wright's Johnson's Wax Building*: Wisconsin headquarters of the company (founded 1886) now known as S. C. Johnson & Son; designed by famed modern architect Frank Lloyd Wright (1867–1959).

6. City just north of Los Angeles, California; Walt Disney and Warner Brothers are two of many media companies headquartered there.

7. High-quality camera made by the Swedish Hasselblad company. *Ground glass*: viewer inserted in the back of a camera for help with focusing and composing.

Albert Speer[8] built for Hitler. But the rest of it was relentlessly tacky: ephemeral stuff extruded by the collective American subconscious of the Thirties, tending mostly to survive along depressing strips lined with dusty motels, mattress wholesalers, and small used-car lots. I went for the gas stations in a big way.

During the high point of the Downes Age, they put Ming the Merciless[9] in charge of designing California gas stations. Favoring the architecture of his native Mongo, he cruised up and down the coast erecting raygun emplacements in white stucco. Lots of them featured superfluous central towers ringed with those strange radiator flanges that were a signature motif of the style, and made them look as though they might generate potent bursts of raw technological enthusiasm, if you could only find the switch that turned them on. I shot one in San Jose an hour before the bulldozers arrived and drove right through the structural truth of plaster and lathing and cheap concrete.

"Think of it," Dialta Downes had said, "as a kind of alternate America: a 1980 that never happened. An architecture of broken dreams."

And that was my frame of mind as I made the stations of her convoluted socioarchitectural cross[1] in my red Toyota—as I gradually tuned in to her image of a shadowy America-that-wasn't, of Coca-Cola plants like beached submarines, and fifth-run movie houses like the temples of some lost sect that had worshiped blue mirrors and geometry. And as I moved among these secret ruins, I found myself wondering what the inhabitants of that lost future would think of the world I lived in. The Thirties dreamed white marble and slipstream chrome, immortal crystal and burnished bronze, but the rockets on the covers of the Gernsback pulps had fallen on London in the dead of night, screaming. After the war,[2] everyone had a car—no wings for it—and the promised superhighway to drive it down, so that the sky itself darkened, and the fumes ate the marble and pitted the miracle crystal. . . .

15   And one day, on the outskirts of Bolinas,[3] when I was setting up to shoot a particularly lavish example of Ming's martial architecture, I penetrated a fine membrane, a membrane of probability. . . .

Every so gently, I went over the Edge—

And looked up to see a twelve-engined thing like a bloated boomerang, all wing, thrumming its way east with an elephantine grace, so low that I could count the rivets in its dull silver skin, and hear—maybe—the echo of jazz.

I took it to Kihn.

Merv Kihn, freelance journalist with an extensive line in Texas pterodactyls, redneck UFO contactees, bush-league Loch Ness monsters, and the Top Ten conspiracy theories in the loonier reaches of the American mass mind.

8. Chief architect (1905–81) and minister of armaments and war production in Nazi Germany; one of his projects was a monumental 400,000-seat stadium begun in 1937 but never completed.

9. Evil tyrant, from the planet Mongo, featured in *Flash Gordon*, a science-fiction comic strip and film series of the 1930s.

1. The term *stations of the cross* refers both to a series of images or statues, especially in a church, depicting the chief scenes of Christ's final suffering and death and to an act of religious devotion that involves meditating or praying at each station.

2. World War II (1939–45); between September 1940 and May 1941, London was bombed some seventy-one times.

3. Coastal community in Northern California, just north of San Francisco.

"It's good," said Kihn, polishing his yellow Polaroid shooting glasses on the   20
hem of his Hawaiian shirt, "but it's not *mental*; lacks the true quill."

"But I saw it, Mervyn." We were seated poolside in brilliant Arizona sunlight.
He was in Tucson waiting for a group of retired Las Vegas civil servants whose
leader received messages from Them on her microwave oven. I'd driven all night
and was feeling it.

"Of course you did. Of course you saw it. You've read my stuff; haven't you
grasped my blanket solution to the UFO problem? It's simple, plain and country
simple: people"—he settled the glasses carefully on his long hawk nose and
fixed me with his best basilisk glare—"*see* . . . things. People see these things.
Nothing's there, but people *see* them anyway. Because they need to, probably.
You've read Jung,[4] you should know the score. . . . In your case, it's so obvious:
You admit you were thinking about this crackpot architecture, having fantasies. . . . Look, I'm sure you've taken your share of drugs, right? How many
people survived the Sixties in California without having the odd hallucination?
All those nights when you discovered that whole armies of Disney technicians
had been employed to weave animated holograms of Egyptian hieroglyphs into
the fabric of your jeans, say, or the times when—"

"But it wasn't like that."

"Of course not. It wasn't like that at all; it was 'in a setting of clear reality,'
right? Everything normal, and then there's the monster, the mandala,[5] the neon
cigar. In your case, a giant Tom Swift[6] airplane. It happens *all the time*. You
aren't even crazy. You know that, don't you?" He fished a beer out of the battered foam cooler beside his deck chair.

"Last week I was in Virginia. Grayson County. I interviewed a sixteen-year-   25
old girl who'd been assaulted by a *bar hade*."

"A what?"

"A bear head. The severed head of a bear. This *bar hade*, see, was floating
around on its own little flying saucer, looked kind of like the hubcaps on cousin
Wayne's vintage Caddy. Had red, glowing eyes like two cigar stubs and tele-
scoping chrome antennas poking up behind its ears." He burped.

"It assaulted her? How?"

"You don't want to know; you're obviously impressionable. 'It was cold'"—he
lapsed into his bad southern accent—"'and metallic.' It made electronic noises.
Now that is the real thing, the straight goods from the mass unconscious,
friend; that little girl is a witch. There's just no place for her to function in this
society. She'd have seen the devil, if she hadn't been brought up on *The Bionic
Man* and all those *Star Trek* reruns.[7] She is clued into the main vein. And she
knows that it happened to her. I got out ten minutes before the heavy UFO boys
showed up with the polygraph."

4. Carl Jung (1875–1961), Swiss psychiatrist who posited the concept of the *collective unconscious*, a
reservoir of memories, impulses, and images (or *archetypes*) that all humans or at least those of a
particular culture share in common without their being consciously aware.
5. Literally, "sacred circle" (Sanskrit); in Hinduism and Buddhism, as well as Jungian therapy, a circular figure representing the universe and used as an aid to meditation.
6. Protagonist of a series of young-adult science-fiction and adventure novels that debuted in 1910.
7. The original series aired from 1966 to 1969. *The Bionic Man*: actually, *The Six Million Dollar Man*,
a popular 1970s American television series about a former astronaut turned secret agent with bionic
implants.

30   I must have looked pained, because he set his beer down carefully beside the cooler and sat up.

"If you want a classier explanation, I'd say you saw a semiotic[8] ghost. All these contactee stories, for instance, are framed in a kind of sci-fi imagery that permeates our culture. I could buy aliens, but not aliens that look like Fifties' comic art. They're semiotic phantoms, bits of deep cultural imagery that have split off and taken on a life of their own, like the Jules Verne[9] airships that those old Kansas farmers were always seeing. But you saw a different kind of ghost, that's all. That plane was part of the mass unconscious, once. You picked up on that, somehow. The important thing is not to worry about it."

I did worry about it, though.

Kihn combed his thinning blond hair and went off to hear what They had had to say over the radar range lately, and I drew the curtains in my room and lay down in air-conditioned darkness to worry about it. I was still worrying about it when I woke up. Kihn had left a note on my door; he was flying up north in a chartered plane to check out a cattle-mutilation rumor ("muties," he called them; another of his journalistic specialties).

I had a meal, showered, took a crumbling diet pill that had been kicking around in the bottom of my shaving kit for three years, and headed back to Los Angeles.

35   The speed limited my vision to the tunnel of the Toyota's headlights. The body could drive, I told myself, while the mind maintained. Maintained and stayed away from the weird peripheral window dressing of amphetamine and exhaustion, the spectral, luminous vegetation that grows out of the corners of the mind's eye along late-night highways. But the mind had its own ideas, and Kihn's opinion of what I was already thinking of as my "sighting" rattled endlessly, through my head in a tight, lopsided orbit. Semiotic ghosts. Fragments of the Mass Dream, whirling past in the wind of my passage. Somehow this feedback-loop aggravated the diet pill, and the speed-vegetation along the road began to assume the colors of infrared satellite images, glowing shreds blown apart in the Toyota's slipstream.

I pulled over, then, and a half-dozen aluminum beer cans winked goodnight as I killed the headlights. I wondered what time it was in London, and tried to imagine Dialta Downes having breakfast in her Hampstead flat,[1] surrounded by streamlined chrome figurines and books on American culture.

Desert nights in that country are enormous; the moon is closer. I watched the moon for a long time and decided that Kihn was right. The main thing was not to worry. All across the continent, daily, people who were more normal than I'd ever aspired to be saw giant birds, Bigfeet, flying oil refineries; they kept Kihn busy and solvent. Why should I be upset by a glimpse of the 1930s pop imagination loose over Bolinas? I decided to go to sleep, with nothing worse to worry about than rattlesnakes and cannibal hippies, safe amid the friendly roadside garbage of my own familiar continuum. In the morning I'd drive down

8. Of or relating to signs and symbols; systems of meaning making.
9. French author (1828–1905) often hailed as a father of science fiction thanks to novels such as *Journey to the Center of the Earth* (1864) and *Twenty Thousand Leagues under the Sea* (1870).
1. Apartment (British). *Hampstead:* London neighborhood, now very exclusive, previously known for its artsy, intellectual atmosphere.

to Nogales[2] and photograph the old brothels, something I'd intended to do for years. The diet pill had given up.

The light woke me, and then the voices.

The light came from somewhere behind me and threw shifting shadows inside the car. The voices were calm, indistinct, male and female, engaged in conversation.

My neck was stiff and my eyeballs felt gritty in their sockets. My leg had gone to sleep, pressed against the steering wheel. I fumbled for my glasses in the pocket of my work shirt and finally got them on.

Then I looked behind me and saw the city.

The books on Thirties' design were in the trunk; one of them contained sketches of an idealized city that drew on *Metropolis* and *Things to Come*,[3] but squared everything, soaring up through an architect's perfect clouds to zeppelin docks and mad neon spires. That city was a scale model of the one that rose behind me. Spire stood on spire in gleaming ziggurat steps that climbed to a central golden temple tower ringed with the crazy radiator flanges of the Mongo gas stations. You could hide the Empire State Building[4] in the smallest of those towers. Roads of crystal soared between the spires, crossed and recrossed by smooth silver shapes like beads of running mercury. The air was thick with ships: giant wing-liners, little darting silver things (sometimes one of the quicksilver shapes from the sky bridges rose gracefully into the air and flew up to join the dance), mile-long blimps, hovering dragonfly things that were gyrocopters . . .

I closed my eyes tight and swung around in the seat. When I opened them, I willed myself to see the mileage meter, the pale road dust on the black plastic dashboard, the overflowing ashtray.

"Amphetamine psychosis," I said. I opened my eyes. The dash was still there, the dust, the crushed filtertips. Very carefully, without moving my head, I turned the headlights on.

And saw them.

They were blond. They were standing beside their car, an aluminum avocado with a central shark-fin rudder jutting up from its spine and smooth black tires like a child's toy. He had his arm around her waist and was gesturing toward the city. They were both in white: loose clothing, bare legs, spotless white sun shoes. Neither of them seemed aware of the beams of my headlights. He was saying something wise and strong, and she was nodding, and suddenly I was frightened, frightened in an entirely different way. Sanity had ceased to be an issue; I knew, somehow, that the city behind me was Tucson—a dream Tucson thrown up out of the collective yearning of an era. That it was real, entirely real. But the couple in front of me lived in it, and they frightened me.

2. One or both of the two adjacent cities of that name lying on either side of the Arizona-Mexico border.
3. British science-fiction film (1936) conceived by H. G. Wells (1866–1946) about a decades-long world war that begins in 1940 and the utopia that—by the twenty-first century—replaces the civilization that war destroys. *Metropolis*: German silent science-fiction film (1927) about a vast future city of towering high-rises occupied by the wealthy and powered by machines operated by laborers living and toiling belowground.
4. Iconic Manhattan skyscraper heralded as the world's tallest building when completed in 1931.

They were the children of Dialta Downes's '80-that-wasn't; they were Heirs to the Dream. They were white, blond, and they probably had blue eyes. They were American. Dialta had said that the Future had come to America first, but had finally passed it by. But not here, in the heart of the Dream. Here, we'd gone on and on, in a dream logic that knew nothing of pollution, the finite bounds of fossil fuel, or foreign wars it was possible to lose. They were smug, happy, and utterly content with themselves and their world. And in the Dream, it was *their* world.

Behind me, the illuminated city: Searchlights swept the sky for the sheer joy of it. I imagined them thronging the plazas of white marble, orderly and alert, their bright eyes shining with enthusiasm for their floodlit avenues and silver cars.

It had all the sinister fruitiness of Hitler Youth[5] propaganda.

50   I put the car in gear and drove forward slowly, until the bumper was within three feet of them. They still hadn't seen me. I rolled the window down and listened to what the man was saying. His words were bright and hollow as the pitch in some Chamber of Commerce brochure, and I knew that he believed in them absolutely.

"John," I heard the woman say, "we've forgotten to take our food pills." She clicked two bright wafers from a thing on her belt and passed one to him. I backed onto the highway and headed for Los Angeles, wincing and shaking my head.

I phoned Kihn from a gas station. A new one, in bad Spanish Modern. He was back from his expedition and didn't seem to mind the call.

"Yeah, that is a weird one. Did you try to get any pictures? Not that they ever come out, but it adds an interesting *frisson*[6] to your story, not having the pictures turn out. . . ."

But what should I do?

55   "Watch lots of television, particularly game shows and soaps. Go to porn movies. Ever see *Nazi Love Motel*? They've got it on cable, here. Really awful. Just what you need."

What was he talking about?

"Quit yelling and listen to me. I'm letting you in on a trade secret: Really bad media can exorcise your semiotic ghosts. If it keeps the saucer people off my back, it can keep these Art Deco[7] futuroids off yours. Try it. What have you got to lose?"

Then he begged off, pleading an early-morning date with the Elect.

"The who?"

60   "These oldsters from Vegas; the ones with the microwaves."

I considered putting a collect call through to London, getting Cohen at Barris-Watford and telling him his photographer was checked out for a pro-

5. Youth organization of the German Nazi Party, founded in the 1920s; membership became compulsory for those over seventeen in 1939; two years later, the age was lowered to ten. Key to Hitler's plan to create an Aryan master race, it emphasized both physical training and ideological indoctrination.
6. Sudden, brief, shiver-inducing thrill.
7. Popular, self-consciously modern design style of the 1920s and 1930s featuring bold outlines, geometric forms, and the use of cutting-edge materials such as plastic.

tracted season in the Twilight Zone.[8] In the end, I let a machine mix me a really impossible cup of black coffee and climbed back into the Toyota for the haul to Los Angeles.

Los Angeles was a bad idea, and I spent two weeks there. It was prime Downes country; too much of the Dream there, and too many fragments of the Dream waiting to snare me. I nearly wrecked the car on a stretch of overpass near Disneyland, when the road fanned out like an origami trick and left me swerving through a dozen minilanes of whizzing chrome teardrops with shark fins. Even worse, Hollywood was full of people who looked too much like the couple I'd seen in Arizona. I hired an Italian director who was making ends meet doing darkroom work and installing patio decks around swimming pools until his ship came in; he made prints of all the negatives I'd accumulated on the Downes job. I didn't want to look at the stuff myself. It didn't seem to bother Leonardo, though, and when he was finished I checked the prints, riffling through them like a deck of cards, sealed them up, and sent them air freight to London. Then I took a taxi to a theater that was showing *Nazi Love Motel*, and kept my eyes shut all the way.

Cohen's congratulatory wire was forwarded to me in San Francisco a week later. Dialta had loved the pictures. He admired the way I'd "really gotten into it," and looked forward to working with me again. That afternoon I spotted a flying wing over Castro Street,[9] but there was something tenuous about it, as though it were only half there. I rushed into the nearest newsstand and gathered up as much as I could find on the petroleum crisis[1] and the nuclear energy hazard.[2] I'd just decided to buy a plane ticket for New York.

"Hell of a world we live in, huh?" The proprietor was a thin black man with bad teeth and an obvious wig. I nodded, fishing in my jeans for change, anxious to find a park bench where I could submerge myself in hard evidence of the human near-dystopia we live in. "But it could be worse, huh?"

"That's right," I said, "or even worse, it could be perfect."

He watched me as I headed down the street with my little bundle of condensed catastrophe.

1981

QUESTIONS

1. What exactly is Merv Kihn's explanation for what happens to the narrator in Bolinas? How might the rest of the story either validate or complicate his explanation?

8. Literally, an in-between space or one outside ordinary legal or ethical limits; figuratively, a fantastic or illusory world; also the title of a popular American television series (1959–64) featuring unrelated stories usually involving a bizarre, often macabre premise or ending with an unexpected twist.

9. Main thoroughfare of one of the oldest and most famous gay neighborhoods in the United States.

1. Throughout the 1970s, the United States faced a series of "energy" or "oil crises" caused by unprecedentedly high demand, increasing reliance on imported oil, and various actions taken by oil-producing nations motivated, in part, by anger over U.S. actions in the Middle East.

2. A partial meltdown at Pennsylvania's Three Mile Island nuclear plant on March 28, 1979, crystallized the concerns of a growing national antinuclear movement.

2. Why and how might it matter that the story begins in England but takes place mainly in the American West? that the conversation with which the story ends takes place on Castro Street in San Francisco?

3. In addition to making evocative use of setting, what might THE GERNSBACK CONTINUUM have to say *about* setting or about the worlds created in and by fiction (among other things)?

AUTHORS ON THEIR WORK

WILLIAM GIBSON (b. 1948)

From "Maximus Clarke Talks with William Gibson about His 'Speculative Novels of Last Wednesday'" (2010)*

WG [WILLIAM GIBSON]: I forget who it was [. . .] who said something to the effect that people make a terribly big deal about the future, but when we get there, it's just as shabby and small as the present.

MC [INTERVIEWER MAXIMUS CLARKE]: And I think what you did early on that grabbed a lot of people's attention was to refract the future through that lens— to make the future not shiny—to make it just sort of a place. It was the overturning of the utopian "raygun gothic" future, as you satirized it in "The Gernsback Continuum," and its replacement with something that felt more like a real place. I don't know whether you thought of that story as a kind of manifesto for what you wanted to do, but it feels retrospectively like one.

WG: It was, to some extent. [. . .] Actually, how the story came to be written is that I was writing little bits and pieces of non-fiction for fanzines and little amateur science fiction magazines. Someone had given me a book called *The Streamlined Decade*, which was a sort of paperbound coffee table book of Art Moderne design. And I wrote a review of it, comparing it to Hugo Gernsback's universe, and submitted it to one of these little magazines. And they rejected it.

* * * *

When I started writing it as a story, I didn't particularly expect that it would work.

Then as I proceeded with it, it was building momentum, and actually working, in spite of this unlikely pile of socio-artistic analysis that I was building it with. And the bricolage aspect of it really impressed me. I thought, "Hmm, that's the way to do this! I thought I just had to sit here and make stuff up, but actually I can import material, and build things out of it, and somehow the thing takes on a life of its own."

*"Maximus Clarke Talks with William Gibson about His 'Speculative Novels of Last Wednesday.'" Interview by Maximus Clarke. *Maud Newton*, 22 Sept. 2010, maudnewton.com/blog/maximus-clarke-talks-with-william-gibson-about-his-speculative-novels-of-last-wednesday/.

RAY BRADBURY
(1920–2012)

The Veldt[1]

The only writer ever both to receive a National Medal of Arts (2004) and to have a lunar crater (1971) and a Mars rover landing site (2012) named in his honor, Ray Bradbury was born and raised mostly in Waukegan, Illinois, until 1934, when the Great Depression took his family to Los Angeles. Here he began publishing short stories in the "pulp" magazines that had first introduced him (at age eight) to science fiction. Publishing what he referred to as his first "really fine story," "The Lake," in 1944, Bradbury left off selling newspapers to become a full-time writer. He never looked back. Arguably the twentieth century's most widely read science-fiction/fantasy writer and the first to attract a mainstream audience, Bradbury is perhaps most famous for two books. More a collection of interlinked stories than a novel, *The Martian Chronicles* (1950) imagines the colonization of Mars circa 1999–2026, focusing on how the human colonists both interact with the planet's gentle, shape-shifting, telepathic inhabitants and project their own desires and cultural values onto their new home. The novel *Fahrenheit 451* (1953) features what novelist Kingsley Amis hailed as "the most skillfully drawn of all science fiction's conformist hells"—a future in which reading is outlawed and firemen are tasked with burning books. In addition to other novels, including *Something Wicked This Way Comes* (1962) and *Farewell Summer* (2006), Bradbury wrote for both stage and screen, even featuring in his own television series, *The Ray Bradbury Theater*, from 1985 to 1992. First and foremost, however, Bradbury was a short-story writer; *The Stories of Ray Bradbury* (1980) and *Ray Bradbury Stories, Volume 2* (2009) gather some of his best.

"George, I wish you'd look at the nursery."

"What's wrong with it?"

"I don't know."

"Well, then."

"I just want you to look at it, is all, or call a psychologist in to look at it."   5

"What would a psychologist want with a nursery?"

"You know very well what he'd want." His wife paused in the middle of the kitchen and watched the stove busy humming to itself, making supper for four.

"It's just that the nursery is different now than it was."

"All right, let's have a look."

They walked down the hall of their soundproofed, Happylife Home, which   10 had cost them thirty thousand dollars installed, this house which clothed and fed and rocked them to sleep and played and sang and was good to them. Their approach sensitized a switch somewhere and the nursery light flicked on when

---

1. Area of grassy land with scattered trees and shrubs, especially in southern (sub-Saharan) Africa.

they came within ten feet of it. Similarly, behind them, in the halls, lights went on and off as they left them behind, with a soft automaticity.

"Well," said George Hadley.

They stood on the thatched floor of the nursery. It was forty feet across by forty feet long and thirty feet high; it had cost half again as much as the rest of the house. "But nothing's too good for our children," George had said.

The nursery was silent. It was empty as a jungle glade at hot high noon. The walls were blank and two dimensional. Now, as George and Lydia Hadley stood in the center of the room, the walls began to purr and recede into crystalline distance, it seemed, and presently an African veldt appeared, in three dimensions; on all sides, in colors reproduced to the final pebble and bit of straw. The ceiling above them became a deep sky with a hot yellow sun.

George Hadley felt the perspiration start on his brow.

15   "Let's get out of the sun," he said. "This is a little too real. But I don't see anything wrong."

"Wait a moment, you'll see," said his wife.

Now the hidden odorophonics were beginning to blow a wind of odor at the two people in the middle of the baked veldtland. The hot straw smell of lion grass, the cool green smell of the hidden water hole, the great rusty smell of animals, the smell of dust like a red paprika in the hot air. And now the sounds: the thump of distant antelope feet on grassy sod, the papery rustling of vultures. A shadow passed through the sky. The shadow flickered on George Hadley's upturned, sweating face.

"Filthy creatures," he heard his wife say.

"The vultures."

20   "You see, there are the lions, far over, that way. Now they're on their way to the water hole. They've just been eating," said Lydia. "I don't know what."

"Some animal." George Hadley put his hand up to shield off the burning light from his squinted eyes. "A zebra or a baby giraffe, maybe."

"Are you sure?" His wife sounded peculiarly tense.

"No, it's a little late to be sure," he said, amused. "Nothing over there I can see but cleaned bone, and the vultures dropping for what's left."

"Did you hear that scream?" she asked.

25   "No."

"About a minute ago?"

"Sorry, no."

The lions were coming. And again George Hadley was filled with admiration for the mechanical genius who had conceived this room. A miracle of efficiency selling for an absurdly low price. Every home should have one. Oh, occasionally they frightened you with their clinical accuracy, they startled you, gave you a twinge, but most of the time what fun for everyone, not only your own son and daughter, but for yourself when you felt like a quick jaunt to a foreign land, a quick change of scenery. Well, here it was!

And here were the lions now, fifteen feet away, so real, so feverishly and startlingly real that you could feel the prickling fur on your hand, and your mouth was stuffed with the dusty upholstery smell of their heated pelts, and the yellow of them was in your eyes like the yellow of an exquisite French tapestry, the yellows of lions and summer grass, and the sound of the matted lion lungs exhaling on the silent noontide, and the smell of meat from the panting, dripping mouths.

The lions stood looking at George and Lydia Hadley with terrible green-yellow eyes.

"Watch out!" screamed Lydia.

The lions came running at them.

Lydia bolted and ran. Instinctively, George sprang after her. Outside, in the hall, with the door slammed, he was laughing and she was crying, and they both stood appalled at the other's reaction.

"George!"

"Lydia! Oh, my dear poor sweet Lydia!"

"They almost got us!"

"Walls, Lydia, remember; crystal walls, that's all they are. Oh, they look real, I must admit—Africa in your parlor—but it's all dimensional superreactionary, supersensitive color film and mental tape film behind glass screens. It's all odorophonics and sonics, Lydia. Here's my handkerchief."

"I'm afraid." She came to him and put her body against him and cried steadily. "Did you see? Did you *feel*? It's too real."

"Now, Lydia . . ."

"You've got to tell Wendy and Peter[2] not to read any more on Africa."

"Of course—of course." He patted her.

"Promise?"

"Sure."

"And lock the nursery for a few days until I get my nerves settled."

"You know how difficult Peter is about that. When I punished him a month ago by locking the nursery for even a few hours—the tantrum he threw! And Wendy too. They *live* for the nursery."

"It's got to be locked, that's all there is to it."

"All right." Reluctantly he locked the huge door. "You've been working too hard. You need a rest."

"I don't know—I don't know," she said, blowing her nose, sitting down in a chair that immediately began to rock and comfort her. "Maybe I don't have enough to do. Maybe I have time to think too much. Why don't we shut the whole house off for a few days and take a vacation?"

"You mean you want to fry my eggs for me?"

"Yes." She nodded.

"And darn my socks?"

"Yes." A frantic, watery-eyed nodding.

"And sweep the house?"

"Yes, yes—oh, yes!"

"But I thought that's why we bought this house, so we wouldn't have to do anything?"

"That's just it. I feel like I don't belong here. The house is wife and mother now and nursemaid. Can I compete with an African veldt? Can I give a bath and scrub the children as efficiently or quickly as the automatic scrub bath

<hr>

2. The Hadley children bear the same names as characters featured in the work of English author J. M. Barrie (1860–1937), including his play *Peter Pan, or the Boy Who Wouldn't Grow Up* (1904).

can? I can not. And it isn't just me. It's you. You've been awfully nervous lately."

"I suppose I have been smoking too much."

"You look as if you didn't know what to do with yourself in this house, either. You smoke a little more every morning and drink a little more every afternoon and need a little more sedative every night. You're beginning to feel unnecessary too."

"Am I?" He paused and tried to feel into himself to see what was really there.

60   "Oh, George!" She looked beyond him, at the nursery door. "Those lions can't get out of there, can they?"

He looked at the door and saw it tremble as if something had jumped against it from the other side.

"Of course not," he said.

At dinner they ate alone, for Wendy and Peter were at a special plastic carnival across town and had televised home to say they'd be late, to go ahead eating. So George Hadley, bemused, sat watching the dining-room table produce warm dishes of food from its mechanical interior.

"We forgot the ketchup," he said.

65   "Sorry," said a small voice within the table, and ketchup appeared.

As for the nursery, thought George Hadley, it won't hurt for the children to be locked out of it awhile. Too much of anything isn't good for anyone. And it was clearly indicated that the children had been spending a little too much time on Africa. That sun. He could feel it on his neck, still, like a hot paw. And the lions. And the smell of blood. Remarkable how the nursery caught the telepathic emanations of the children's minds and created life to fill their every desire. The children thought lions, and there were lions. The children thought zebras, and there were zebras. Sun—sun. Giraffes—giraffes. Death and death.

That last. He chewed tastelessly on the meat that the table had cut for him. Death thoughts. They were awfully young, Wendy and Peter, for death thoughts. Or, no, you were never too young, really. Long before you knew what death was you were wishing it on someone else. When you were two years old you were shooting people with cap pistols.

But this—the long, hot African veldt—the awful death in the jaws of a lion. And repeated again and again.

"Where are you going?"

70   He didn't answer Lydia. Preoccupied, he let the lights glow softly on ahead of him, extinguished behind him as he padded to the nursery door. He listened against it. Far away, a lion roared.

He unlocked the door and opened it. Just before he stepped inside, he heard a faraway scream. And then another roar from the lions, which subsided quickly.

He stepped into Africa. How many times in the last year had he opened this door and found Wonderland, Alice, the Mock Turtle, or Aladdin and his Magical Lamp, or Jack Pumpkinhead of Oz, or Dr. Doolittle, or the cow jumping over a very real-appearing moon[3]—all the delightful contraptions of a make-

---

3. Places and characters from famous works of children's literature, including Lewis Carroll's *Alice's Adventures in Wonderland* (1865); the Middle Eastern folktale "Aladdin and the Magic [or Wonderful] Lamp," about a young orphan and the genie of the lamp who grants his wishes; L. Frank Baum's novels, beginning with *The Wonderful Wizard of Oz* (1900); Hugh Lofting's Doctor Dolittle series (1920–52); and the nursery rhyme "Hey Diddle Diddle."

believe world. How often had he seen Pegasus[4] flying in the sky ceiling, or seen fountains of red fireworks, or heard angel voices singing. But now, this yellow hot Africa, this bake oven with murder in the heat. Perhaps Lydia was right. Perhaps they needed a little vacation from the fantasy which was growing a bit too real for ten-year-old children. It was all right to exercise one's mind with gymnastic[5] fantasies, but when the lively child mind settled on *one* pattern . . . ? It seemed that, at a distance, for the past month, he had heard lions roaring, and smelled their strong odor seeping as far away as his study door. But, being busy, he had paid it no attention.

George Hadley stood on the African grassland alone. The lions looked up from their feeding, watching him. The only flaw to the illusion was the open door through which he could see his wife, far down the dark hall, like a framed picture, eating her dinner abstractedly.

"Go away," he said to the lions.

They did not go.   75

He knew the principle of the room exactly. You sent out your thoughts. Whatever you thought would appear.

"Let's have Aladdin and his lamp," he snapped.

The veldtland remained; the lions remained.

"Come on, room! I demand Aladdin!" he said.

Nothing happened. The lions mumbled in their baked pelts.   80

"Aladdin!"

He went back to dinner. "The fool room's out of order," he said. "It won't respond."

"Or—"

"Or what?"

"Or it *can't* respond," said Lydia, "because the children have thought about   85
Africa and lions and killing so many days that the room's in a rut."

"Could be."

"Or Peter's set it to remain that way."

"*Set* it?"

"He may have got into the machinery and fixed something."

"Peter doesn't know machinery."   90

"He's a wise one for ten. That I.Q. of his—"

"Nevertheless—"

"Hello, Mom. Hello, Dad."

The Hadleys turned. Wendy and Peter were coming in the front door, cheeks like peppermint candy, eyes like bright blue agate marbles, a smell of ozone on their jumpers from their trip in the helicopter.

"You're just in time for supper," said both parents.   95

"We're full of strawberry ice cream and hot dogs," said the children, holding hands. "But we'll sit and watch."

"Yes, come tell us about the nursery," said George Hadley.

The brother and sister blinked at him and then at each other. "Nursery?"

"All about Africa and everything," said the father with false joviality.

"I don't understand," said Peter.   100

4. Flying horse of Greek myth.
5. Athletic.

"Your mother and I were just traveling through Africa with rod and reel; Tom Swift[6] and his Electric Lion," said George Hadley.

"There's no Africa in the nursery," said Peter simply.

"Oh, come now, Peter. We know better."

"I don't remember any Africa," said Peter to Wendy. "Do you?"

105 "No."

"Run see and come tell."

She obeyed.

"Wendy, come back here!" said George Hadley, but she was gone. The house lights followed her like a flock of fireflies. Too late, he realized he had forgotten to lock the nursery door after his last inspection.

"Wendy'll look and come tell us," said Peter.

110 "She doesn't have to tell *me*. I've seen it."

"I'm sure you're mistaken, Father."

"I'm not, Peter. Come along now."

But Wendy was back. "It's not Africa," she said breathlessly.

"We'll see about this," said George Hadley, and they all walked down the hall together and opened the nursery door.

115 There was a green, lovely forest, a lovely river, a purple mountain, high voices singing, and Rima,[7] lovely and mysterious, lurking in the trees with colorful flights of butterflies, like animated bouquets, lingering on her long hair. The African veldtland was gone. The lions were gone. Only Rima was here now, singing a song so beautiful that it brought tears to your eyes.

George Hadley looked in at the changed scene. "Go to bed," he said to the children.

They opened their mouths.

"You heard me," he said.

They went off to the air closet, where a wind sucked them like brown leaves up the flue to their slumber rooms.

120 George Hadley walked through the singing glade and picked up something that lay in the corner near where the lions had been. He walked slowly back to his wife.

"What is that?" she asked.

"An old wallet of mine," he said.

He showed it to her. The smell of hot grass was on it and the smell of a lion. There were drops of saliva on it, it had been chewed, and there were blood smears on both sides.

He closed the nursery door and locked it, tight.

125 In the middle of the night he was still awake and he knew his wife was awake. "Do you think Wendy changed it?" she said at last, in the dark room.

"Of course."

"Made it from a veldt into a forest and put Rima there instead of lions?"

---

6. Hero of a series of books launched in 1910 and relating adventures made possible by his ingenious inventions.

7. South American forest-dwelling heroine of W. H. Hudson's *Green Mansions: A Romance of the Tropical Forest* (1904).

"Yes."

"Why?"

"I don't know. But it's staying locked until I find out." 130

"How did your wallet get there?"

"I don't know anything," he said, "except that I'm beginning to be sorry we bought that room for the children. If children are neurotic at all, a room like that—"

"It's supposed to help them work off their neuroses in a healthful way."

"I'm starting to wonder." He stared at the ceiling.

"We've given the children everything they ever wanted. Is this our reward— 135 secrecy, disobedience?"

"Who was it said, 'Children are carpets, they should be stepped on occasionally'? We've never lifted a hand. They're insufferable—let's admit it. They come and go when they like; they treat us as if we were offspring. They're spoiled and we're spoiled."

"They've been acting funny ever since you forbade them to take the rocket to New York a few months ago."

"They're not old enough to do that alone, I explained."

"Nevertheless, I've noticed they've been decidedly cool toward us since."

"I think I'll have David McClean come tomorrow morning to have a look at 140 Africa."

"But it's not Africa now, it's Green Mansions country and Rima."

"I have a feeling it'll be Africa again before then."

A moment later they heard the screams.

Two screams. Two people screaming from downstairs. And then a roar of lions.

"Wendy and Peter aren't in their rooms," said his wife. 145

He lay in his bed with his beating heart. "No," he said. "They've broken into the nursery."

"Those screams—they sound familiar."

"Do they?"

"Yes, awfully."

And although their beds tried very hard, the two adults couldn't be rocked to 150 sleep for another hour. A smell of cats was in the night air.

"Father?" said Peter.

"Yes."

Peter looked at his shoes. He never looked at his father any more, nor at his mother. "You aren't going to lock up the nursery for good, are you?"

"That all depends."

"On what?" snapped Peter. 155

"On you and your sister. If you intersperse this Africa with a little variety— oh, Sweden perhaps, or Denmark or China—"

"I thought we were free to play as we wished."

"You are, within reasonable bounds."

"What's wrong with Africa, Father?"

"Oh, so now you admit you have been conjuring up Africa, do you?" 160

"I wouldn't want the nursery locked up," said Peter coldly. "Ever."

"Matter of fact, we're thinking of turning the whole house off for about a month. Live sort of a carefree one-for-all existence."

"That sounds dreadful! Would I have to tie my own shoes instead of letting the shoe tier do it? And brush my own teeth and comb my hair and give myself a bath?"

"It would be fun for a change, don't you think?"

165   "No, it would be horrid. I didn't like it when you took out the picture painter last month."

"That's because I wanted you to learn to paint all by yourself, son."

"I don't want to do anything but look and listen and smell; what else *is* there to do?"

"All right, go play in Africa."

"Will you shut off the house sometime soon?"

170   "We're considering it."

"I don't think you'd better consider it any more, Father."

"I won't have any threats from my son!"

"Very well." And Peter strolled off to the nursery.

"Am I on time?" said David McClean.

175   "Breakfast?" asked George Hadley.

"Thanks, had some. What's the trouble?"

"David, you're a psychologist."

"I should hope so."

"Well, then, have a look at our nursery. You saw it a year ago when you dropped by; did you notice anything peculiar about it then?"

180   "Can't say I did; the usual violences, a tendency toward a slight paranoia here or there, usual in children because they feel persecuted by parents constantly, but, oh, really nothing."

They walked down the hall. "I locked the nursery up," explained the father, "and the children broke back into it during the night. I let them stay so they could form the patterns for you to see."

There was a terrible screaming from the nursery.

"There it is," said George Hadley. "See what you make of it."

They walked in on the children without rapping.

185   The screams had faded. The lions were feeding.

"Run outside a moment, children," said George Hadley. "No, don't change the mental combination. Leave the walls as they are. Get!"

With the children gone, the two men stood studying the lions clustered at a distance, eating with great relish whatever it was they had caught.

"I wish I knew what it was," said George Hadley. "Sometimes I can almost see. Do you think if I brought high-powered binoculars here and—"

David McClean laughed dryly. "Hardly." He turned to study all four walls. "How long has this been going on?"

190   "A little over a month."

"It certainly doesn't *feel* good."

"I want facts, not feelings."

"My dear George, a psychologist never saw a fact in his life. He only hears about feelings; vague things. This doesn't feel good, I tell you. Trust my hunches and my instincts. I have a nose for something bad. This is very bad. My advice to you is to have the whole damn room torn down and your children brought to me every day during the next year for treatment."

"Is it that bad?"

"I'm afraid so. One of the original uses of these nurseries was so that we could study the patterns left on the walls by the child's mind, study at our leisure, and help the child. In this case, however, the room has become a channel toward—destructive thoughts, instead of a release away from them."

"Didn't you sense this before?"

"I sensed only that you had spoiled your children more than most. And now you're letting them down in some way. What way?"

"I wouldn't let them go to New York."

"What else?"

"I've taken a few machines from the house and threatened them, a month ago, with closing up the nursery unless they did their homework. I did close it for a few days to show I meant business."

"Ah, ha!"

"Does that mean anything?"

"Everything. Where before they had a Santa Claus now they have a Scrooge.[8] Children prefer Santas. You've let this room and this house replace you and your wife in your children's affections. This room is their mother and father, far more important in their lives than their real parents. And now you come along and want to shut it off. No wonder there's hatred here. You can feel it coming out of the sky. Feel that sun. George, you'll have to change your life. Like too many others, you've built it around creature comforts. Why, you'd starve tomorrow if something went wrong in your kitchen. You wouldn't know how to tap an egg. Nevertheless, turn everything off. Start new. It'll take time. But we'll make good children out of bad in a year, wait and see."

"But won't the shock be too much for the children, shutting the room up abruptly, for good?"

"I don't want them going any deeper into this, that's all."

The lions were finished with their red feast.

The lions were standing on the edge of the clearing watching the two men.

"Now *I'm* feeling persecuted," said McClean. "Let's get out of here. I never have cared for these damned rooms. Make me nervous."

"The lions look real, don't they?" said George Hadley. "I don't suppose there's any way—"

"What?"

"—that they could *become* real?"

"Not that I know."

"Some flaw in the machinery, a tampering or something?"

"No."

They went to the door.

"I don't imagine the room will like being turned off," said the father.

"Nothing ever likes to die—even a room."

"I wonder if it hates me for wanting to switch it off?"

---

8. Miserly, hard-hearted protagonist of Charles Dickens's *A Christmas Carol* (1843).

"Paranoia is thick around here today," said David McClean. "You can follow it like a spoor. Hello." He bent and picked up a bloody scarf. "This yours?"

220   "No." George Hadley's face was rigid. "It belongs to Lydia."

They went to the fuse box together and threw the switch that killed the nursery.

The two children were in hysterics. They screamed and pranced and threw things. They yelled and sobbed and swore and jumped at the furniture.

"You can't do that to the nursery, you can't!"

"Now, children."

225   The children flung themselves onto a couch, weeping.

"George," said Lydia Hadley, "turn on the nursery, just for a few moments. You can't be so abrupt."

"No."

"You can't be so cruel."

"Lydia, it's off, and it stays off. And the whole damn house dies as of here and now. The more I see of the mess we've put ourselves in, the more it sickens me. We've been contemplating our mechanical, electronic navels for too long. My God, how we need a breath of honest air!"

230   And he marched about the house turning off the voice clocks, the stoves, the heaters, the shoe shiners, the shoe lacers, the body scrubbers and swabbers and massagers, and every other machine he could put his hand to.

The house was full of dead bodies, it seemed. It felt like a mechanical cemetery. So silent. None of the humming hidden energy of machines waiting to function at the tap of a button.

"Don't let them do it!" wailed Peter at the ceiling, as if he was talking to the house, the nursery. "Don't let Father kill everything." He turned to his father. "Oh, I hate you!"

"Insults won't get you anywhere."

"I wish you were dead!"

235   "We were, for a long while. Now we're going to really start living. Instead of being handled and massaged, we're going to *live*."

Wendy was still crying and Peter joined her again. "Just a moment, just one moment, just another moment of nursery," they wailed.

"Oh, George," said the wife, "it can't hurt."

"All right—all right, if they'll only just shut up. One minute, mind you, and then off forever."

"Daddy, Daddy, Daddy!" sang the children, smiling with wet faces.

240   "And then we're going on a vacation. David McClean is coming back in half an hour to help us move out and get to the airport. I'm going to dress. You turn the nursery on for a minute, Lydia, just a minute, mind you."

And the three of them went babbling off while he let himself be vacuumed upstairs through the air flue and set about dressing himself. A minute later Lydia appeared.

"I'll be glad when we get away," she sighed.

"Did you leave them in the nursery?"

"I wanted to dress too. Oh, that horrid Africa. What can they see in it?"

245   "Well, in five minutes we'll be on our way to Iowa. Lord, how did we ever get in this house? What prompted us to buy a nightmare?"

"Pride, money, foolishness."

"I think we'd better get downstairs before those kids get engrossed with those damned beasts again."

Just then they heard the children calling, "Daddy, Mommy, come quick—quick!"

They went downstairs in the air flue and ran down the hall. The children were nowhere in sight. "Wendy? Peter!"

They ran into the nursery. The veldtland was empty save for the lions wait-   250
ing, looking at them. "Peter, Wendy?"

The door slammed.

"Wendy, Peter!"

George Hadley and his wife whirled and ran back to the door.

"Open the door!" cried George Hadley, trying the knob. "Why, they've locked it from the outside! Peter!" He beat at the door. "Open up!"

He heard Peter's voice outside, against the door.   255

"Don't let them switch off the nursery and the house," he was saying.

Mr. and Mrs. George Hadley beat at the door. "Now, don't be ridiculous, children. It's time to go. Mr. McClean'll be here in a minute and . . ."

And then they heard the sounds.

The lions on three sides of them, in the yellow veldt grass, padding through the dry straw, rumbling and roaring in their throats.

The lions.   260

Mr. Hadley looked at his wife and they turned and looked back at the beasts edging slowly forward, crouching, tails stiff.

Mr. and Mrs. Hadley screamed.

And suddenly they realized why those other screams had sounded familiar.

"Well, here I am," said David McClean in the nursery doorway. "Oh, hello." He stared at the two children seated in the center of the open glade eating a little picnic lunch. Beyond them was the water hole and the yellow veldtland; above was the hot sun. He began to perspire. "Where are your father and mother?"

The children looked up and smiled. "Oh, they'll be here directly."   265

"Good, we must get going." At a distance Mr. McClean saw the lions fighting and clawing and then quieting down to feed in silence under the shady trees.

He squinted at the lions with his hand up to his eyes.

Now the lions were done feeding. They moved to the water hole to drink.

A shadow flickered over Mr. McClean's hot face. Many shadows flickered. The vultures were dropping down the blazing sky.

"A cup of tea?" asked Wendy in the silence.   270

                                                                            1951

QUESTIONS

1. Only George and Lydia Hadley appear in THE VELDT's first part: How are they and their lives characterized? How does each parent view their Happylife Home and especially the nursery? What might account for the differences in their views at this stage?

2. How and why do those views, especially George's, evolve over the course of the story?

3. As the story makes clear, the nursery could have turned into any setting either Peter and Wendy or their creator, Ray Bradbury, chose. How might the choice of an African veldt affect the story's characterization of the children and of their relationship to their parents? How might it affect the story's theme?

AUTHORS ON THEIR WORK

RAY BRADBURY (1920–2012)

From "Tangent Online Presents: An Interview with Ray Bradbury" (1976)*

BRADBURY: You write stories of murder because we want to kill people. It's the reverse of love and this is part of the dichotomy, or paradox, of being human. Unless we can accept the fact that we have love-hate relationships quite often, our friends, our lovers, our mothers and fathers—then we'll never be human. If we try to deny the darkness in our souls then we'll become completely dark. [. . .] The Greek philosophies teach us that we are a combination of dark and light, good and evil, and murderer and savior, hmm? And until we know this completely about ourselves we cannot love well, and we cannot forgive ourselves.

[. . .] Any child, at some time or another, has had thoughts of murdering their mother and father . . . like my story "The Veldt." Every child who reads this, where lions come out of the walls of the room, in order to devour the parents, all the kids go "Whoopee! Hurray! I know that." [. . . W]e've *all* wanted to kill—in that moment of love—the person that we love. It's part of the human mechanism. *Why* the mechanism works the way it does is a mystery to us; we can't expect anything too perfect.

TANGENT: A lot of people feel there is too much violence on TV today. How do you feel about this?

BRADBURY: [. . .] There is a kind of violence at times that is so inordinate that it is *sick*. [. . .] So, we can't even talk about it.

But ordinary violence, which comes in a way of comparing good and evil, helps exorcize those spirits within ourselves which need to be exorcized. [. . . O]ur arts must help us to free the violence that is in our soul. Now, I don't know what all of the rules of the game are, but if our movies and our televisions don't have a certain amount of this we will become a society bound *completely* by laws, so the anarchy that rages within us on occasion will burst out and be ten times worse. So, if we need these steam valves to let some of this out of us occasionally—and we have to look at this very carefully—to find the right proportion for our children, and for ourselves. Somehow we've got to find the right proportion if we want to build a society that allows itself to vent its rages, so that we don't have to go outside the law for it.

*"Tangent Online Presents: An Interview with Ray Bradbury." 1976. Interview by Robert Jacobs, Dave Truesdale, and Bob Wayne. *Tangent*, 9 June 2012, www.tangentonline.com/ interviews-columnsmenu-166/1864-classic-ray-bradbury-interview.

OCTAVIA E. BUTLER

(1947–2006)

Bloodchild

The first science-fiction writer to win a MacArthur "genius grant," Octavia Butler used the money it brought her to buy a house with her mother, the strict Baptist maid who raised Butler after her father's death. An only child forbidden to dance or wear make-up and an undiagnosed dyslexic who reached six feet tall by age fifteen, Butler was, in her words, "a perennial 'out kid.'" In her twenties, she took classes—mainly in literature, creative writing, history, and anthropology—at various Southern California institutions, earning her AA at Pasadena City College while supporting herself with odd jobs. Butler's first break came in 1969, when she took a class with famed science-fiction writer Harlan Ellison (1934–2018). Armed with his encouragement and a loan from her mother, she attended the Clarion Science Fiction Writers' Workshop, a six-week "boot camp" through which she met "another 25 outsiders" and sold her first short story. Butler's later stories netted science fiction's highest honors, including Hugos for "Speech Sounds" and "Bloodchild," which also won Locus and Nebula awards. Her fifteen novels include those in her Patternist, Xenogenesis/Lillith's Brood, and Earthseed series, as well as the best-selling *Kindred* (1979)—the story of a young African American writer who time-travels from modern Los Angeles to a nineteenth-century Maryland plantation. The first African American woman to become a major force in the field of science fiction, Butler is today widely hailed as a mother of Afrofuturism. In 2020, Amazon announced that it is partnering with Academy Award–nominated director Ava DuVernay on a television adaptation of Butler's *Dawn* (1987). In March 2021, NASA named the Mars landing site of its *Perseverance* rover "Octavia E. Butler Landing."

M y last night of childhood began with a visit home. T'Gatoi's sister had given us two sterile eggs. T'Gatoi gave one to my mother, brother, and sisters. She insisted that I eat the other one alone. It didn't matter. There was still enough to leave everyone feeling good. Almost everyone. My mother wouldn't take any. She sat, watching everyone drifting and dreaming without her. Most of the time she watched me.

I lay against T'Gatoi's long, velvet underside, sipping from my egg now and then, wondering why my mother denied herself such a harmless pleasure. Less of her hair would be gray if she indulged now and then. The eggs prolonged life, prolonged vigor. My father, who had never refused one in his life, had lived more than twice as long as he should have. And toward the end of his life, when he should have been slowing down, he had married my mother and fathered four children.

But my mother seemed content to age before she had to. I saw her turn away as several of T'Gatoi's limbs secured me closer. T'Gatoi liked our body heat and took advantage of it whenever she could. When I was little and at home more, my mother used to try to tell me how to behave with T'Gatoi—how to be

respectful and always obedient because T'Gatoi was the Tlic government official in charge of the Preserve, and thus the most important of her kind to deal
directly with Terrans. It was an honor, my mother said, that such a person had
chosen to come into the family. My mother was at her most formal and severe
when she was lying.

I had no idea why she was lying, or even what she was lying about. It *was* an
honor to have T'Gatoi in the family, but it was hardly a novelty. T'Gatoi and my
mother had been friends all my mother's life, and T'Gatoi was not interested in
being honored in the house she considered her second home. She simply came
in, climbed onto one of her special couches, and called me over to keep her
warm. It was impossible to be formal with her while lying against her and hearing her complain as usual that I was too skinny.

5   "You're better," she said this time, probing me with six or seven of her limbs.
"You're gaining weight finally. Thinness is dangerous." The probing changed
subtly, became a series of caresses.

"He's still too thin," my mother said sharply.

T'Gatoi lifted her head and perhaps a meter of her body off the couch as
though she were sitting up. She looked at my mother, and my mother, her face
lined and old looking, turned away.

"Lien, I would like you to have what's left of Gan's egg."

"The eggs are for the children," my mother said.

10   "They are for the family. Please take it."

Unwillingly obedient, my mother took it from me and put it to her mouth.
There were only a few drops left in the now-shrunken, elastic shell, but she
squeezed them out, swallowed them, and after a few moments some of the lines
of tension began to smooth from her face.

"It's good," she whispered. "Sometimes I forget how good it is."

"You should take more," T'Gatoi said. "Why are you in such a hurry to be old?"

My mother said nothing.

15   "I like being able to come here," T'Gatoi said. "This place is a refuge because
of you, yet you won't take care of yourself."

T'Gatoi was hounded on the outside. Her people wanted more of us made
available. Only she and her political faction stood between us and the hordes
who did not understand why there was a Preserve—why any Terran could not
be courted, paid, drafted, in some way made available to them. Or they did
understand, but in their desperation, they did not care. She parceled us out to
the desperate and sold us to the rich and powerful for their political support.
Thus, we were necessities, status symbols, and an independent people. She
oversaw the joining of families, putting an end to the final remnants of the
earlier system of breaking up Terran families to suit impatient Tlic. I had lived
outside with her. I had seen the desperate eagerness in the way some people
looked at me. It was a little frightening to know that only she stood between us
and that desperation that could so easily swallow us. My mother would look at
her sometimes and say to me, "Take care of her." And I would remember that
she too had been outside, had seen.

Now T'Gatoi used four of her limbs to push me away from her onto the floor.
"Go on, Gan," she said. "Sit down there with your sisters and enjoy not being
sober. You had most of the egg. Lien, come warm me."

My mother hesitated for no reason that I could see. One of my earliest memories is of my mother stretched alongside T'Gatoi, talking about things I could not understand, picking me up from the floor and laughing as she sat me on one of T'Gatoi's segments. She ate her share of eggs then. I wondered when she had stopped, and why.

She lay down now against T'Gatoi, and the whole left row of T'Gatoi's limbs closed her, holding her loosely, but securely. I had always found it comfortable to lie that way, but except for my older sister, no one else in the family liked it. They said it made them feel caged.

T'Gatoi meant to cage my mother. Once she had, she moved her tail slightly, 20
then spoke. "Not enough egg, Lien. You should have taken it when it was passed to you. You need it badly now."

T'Gatoi's tail moved once more, its whip motion so swift I wouldn't have seen it if I hadn't been watching for it. Her sting drew only a single drop of blood from my mother's bare leg.

My mother cried out—probably in surprise. Being stung doesn't hurt. Then she sighed and I could see her body relax. She moved languidly into a more comfortable position within the cage of T'Gatoi's limbs. "Why did you do that?" she asked, sounding half asleep.

"I could not watch you sitting and suffering any longer."

My mother managed to move her shoulders in a small shrug. "Tomorrow," she said.

"Yes. Tomorrow you will resume your suffering—if you must. But just now, 25
just for now, lie here and warm me and let me ease your way a little."

"He's still mine, you know," my mother said suddenly.

"Nothing can buy him from me." Sober, she would not have permitted herself to refer to such things.

"Nothing," T'Gatoi agreed, humoring her.

"Did you think I would sell him for eggs? For long life? My son?"

"Not for anything," T'Gatoi said, stroking my mother's shoulders, toying with 30
her long, graying hair.

I would like to have touched my mother, shared that moment with her. She would take my hand if I touched her now. Freed by the egg and the sting, she would smile and perhaps say things long held in. But tomorrow, she would remember all this as a humiliation. I did not want to be part of a remembered humiliation. Best just be still and know she loved me under all the duty and pride and pain.

"Xuan Hoa, take off her shoes," T'Gatoi said. "In a little while I'll sting her again and she can sleep."

My older sister obeyed, swaying drunkenly as she stood up. When she had finished, she sat down beside me and took my hand. We had always been a unit, she and I.

My mother put the back of her head against T'Gatoi's underside and tried from that impossible angle to look up into the broad, round face. "You're going to sting me again?"

"Yes, Lien." 35

"I'll sleep until tomorrow noon."

"Good. You need it. When did you sleep last?"

My mother made a wordless sound of annoyance. "I should have stepped on you when you were small enough," she muttered.

It was an old joke between them. They had grown up together, sort of, though T'Gatoi had not, in my mother's lifetime, been small enough for any Terran to step on. She was nearly three time my mother's present age, yet would still be young when my mother died of age. But T'Gatoi and my mother had met as T'Gatoi was coming into a period of rapid development—a kind of Tlic adolescence. My mother was only a child, but for a while they developed at the same rate and had no better friends than each other.

40   T'Gatoi had even introduced my mother to the man who became my father. My parents, pleased with each other in spite of their different ages, married as T'Gatoi was going into her family's business—politics. She and my mother saw each other less. But sometime before my older sister was born, my mother promised T'Gatoi one of her children. She would have to give one of us to someone, and she preferred T'Gatoi to some stranger.

Years passed. T'Gatoi traveled and increased her influence. The Preserve was hers by the time she came back to my mother to collect what she probably saw as her just reward for her hard work. My older sister took an instant liking to her and wanted to be chosen, but my mother was just coming to term with me and T'Gatoi liked the idea of choosing an infant and watching and taking part in all the phases of development. I'm told I was first caged within T'Gatoi's many limbs only three minutes after my birth. A few days later, I was given my first taste of egg. I tell Terrans that when they ask whether I was ever afraid of her. And I tell it to Tlic when T'Gatoi suggests a young Terran child for them and they, anxious and ignorant, demand an adolescent. Even my brother who had somehow grown up to fear and distrust the Tlic could probably have gone smoothly into one of their families if he had been adopted early enough. Sometimes, I think for his sake he should have been. I looked at him, stretched out on the floor across the room, his eyes open, but glazed as he dreamed his egg dream. No matter what he felt toward the Tlic, he always demanded his share of egg.

"Lien, can you stand up?" T'Gatoi asked suddenly.

"Stand?" my mother said. "I thought I was going to sleep."

"Later. Something sounds wrong outside." The cage was abruptly gone.

45   "What?"

"Up, Lien!"

My mother recognized her tone and got up just in time to avoid being dumped on the floor. T'Gatoi whipped her three meters of body off her couch, toward the door, and out at full speed. She had bones—ribs, a long spine, a skull, four sets of limb bones per segment. But when she moved that way, twisting, hurling herself into controlled falls, landing running, she seemed not only boneless, but aquatic—something swimming through the air as though it were water. I loved watching her move.

I left my sister and started to follow her out the door, though I wasn't very steady on my own feet. It would have been better to sit and dream, better yet to find a girl and share a waking dream with her. Back when the Tlic saw us as not much more than convenient, big, warm-blooded animals, they would pen several of us together, male and female, and feed us only eggs. That way they could be sure of getting another generation of us no matter how we tried to hold out. We were lucky that didn't go on long. A few generations of it and we would have *been* little more than convenient, big animals.

"Hold the door open, Gan," T'Gatoi said. "And tell the family to stay back."

"What is it?" I asked.

"N'Tlic."

I shrank back against the door. "Here? Alone?"

"He was trying to reach a call box, I suppose." She carried the man past me, unconscious, folded like a coat over some of her limbs. He looked young—my brother's age perhaps—and he was thinner than he should have been. What T'Gatoi would have called dangerously thin.

"Gan, go to the call box," she said. She put the man on the floor and began stripping off his clothing.

I did not move.

After a moment, she looked up at me, her sudden stillness a sign of deep impatience.

"Send Qui," I told her. "I'll stay here. Maybe I can help."

She let her limbs begin to move again, lifting the man and pulling his shirt over his head. "You don't want to see this," she said. "It will be hard. I can't help this man the way his Tlic could."

"I know. But send Qui. He won't want to be of any help here. I'm at least willing to try."

She looked at my brother—older, bigger, stronger, certainly more able to help her here. He was sitting up now, braced against the wall, staring at the man on the floor with undisguised fear and revulsion. Even she could see that he would be useless.

"Qui, go!" she said.

He didn't argue. He stood up, swayed briefly, then steadied, frightened sober.

"This man's name is Bram Lomas," she told him, reading from the man's armband. I fingered my own armband in sympathy. "He needs T'Khotgif Teh. Do you hear?"

"Bram Lomas, T'Khotgif Teh," my brother said. "I'm going." He edged around Lomas and ran out the door.

Lomas began to regain consciousness. He only moaned at first and clutched spasmodically at a pair of T'Gatoi's limbs. My younger sister, finally awake from her egg dream, came close to look at him, until my mother pulled her back.

T'Gatoi removed the man's shoes, then his pants, all the while leaving him two of her limbs to grip. Except for the final few, all her limbs were equally dexterous. "I want no argument from you this time, Gan," she said.

I straightened. "What shall I do?"

"Go out and slaughter an animal that is at least half your size."

"Slaughter? But I've never—"

She knocked me across the room. Her tail was an efficient weapon whether she exposed the sting or not.

I got up, feeling stupid for having ignored her warning, and went into the kitchen. Maybe I could kill something with a knife or an ax. My mother raised a few Terran animals for the table and several thousand local ones for their fur. T'Gatoi would probably prefer something local. An achti, perhaps. Some of those were the right size, though they had about three times as many teeth as I did and a real love of using them. My mother, Hoa, and Qui could kill them with knives. I had never killed one at all, had never slaughtered any animal. I had spent most of my time with T'Gatoi while my brother and sisters were learning the family business. T'Gatoi had been right. I should have been the one to go to the call box. At least I could do that.

I went to the corner cabinet where my mother kept her large house and garden tools. At the back of the cabinet there was a pipe that carried off waste water from the kitchen—except that it didn't anymore. My father had rerouted the waste water below before I was born. Now the pipe could be turned so that one half slid around the other and a rifle could be stored inside. This wasn't our only gun, but it was our most easily accessible one. I would have to use it to shoot one of the biggest of the achti. Then T'Gatoi would probably confiscate it. Firearms were illegal in the Preserve. There had been incidents right after the Preserve was established—Terrans shooting Tlic, shooting N'Tlic. This was before the joining of families began, before everyone had a personal stake in keeping the peace. No one had shot a Tlic in my lifetime or my mother's, but the law still stood—for our protection, we were told. There were stories of whole Terran families wiped out in reprisal back during the assassinations.

I went out to the cages and shot the biggest achti I could find. It was a handsome breeding male, and my mother would not be pleased to see me bring it in. But it was the right size, and I was in a hurry.

I put the achti's long, warm body over my shoulder—glad that some of the weight I'd gained was muscle—and took it to the kitchen. There, I put the gun back in its hiding place. If T'Gatoi noticed the achti's wounds and demanded the gun, I would give it to her. Otherwise, let it stay where my father wanted it.

75   I turned to take the achti to her, then hesitated. For several seconds, I stood in front of the closed door wondering why I was suddenly afraid. I knew what was going to happen. I hadn't seen it before but T'Gatoi had shown me diagrams and drawings. She had made sure I knew the truth as soon as I was old enough to understand it.

Yet I did not want to go into that room. I wasted a little time choosing a knife from the carved, wooden box in which my mother kept them. T'Gatoi might want one, I told myself, for the tough, heavily furred hide of the achti.

"Gan!" T'Gatoi called, her voice harsh with urgency.

I swallowed. I had not imagined a single moving of the feet could be so difficult. I realized I was trembling and that shamed me. Shame impelled me through the door.

I put the achti down near T'Gatoi and saw that Lomas was unconscious again. She, Lomas, and I were alone in the room—my mother and sisters probably sent out so they would not have to watch. I envied them.

80   But my mother came back into the room as T'Gatoi seized the achti. Ignoring the knife I offered her, she extended claws from several of her limbs and slit the achti from throat to anus. She looked at me, her yellow eyes intent. "Hold this man's shoulders, Gan."

I stared at Lomas in panic, realizing that I did not want to touch him, let alone hold him. This would not be like shooting an animal. Not as quick, not as merciful, and, I hoped, not as final, but there was nothing I wanted less than to be part of it.

My mother came forward. "Gan, you hold his right side," she said. "I'll hold his left." And if he came to, he would throw her off without realizing he had done it. She was a tiny woman. She often wondered aloud how she had produced, as she said, such "huge" children.

"Never mind," I told her, taking the man's shoulders. "I'll do it." She hovered nearby.

"Don't worry," I said. "I won't shame you. You don't have to stay and watch."

She looked at me uncertainly, then touched my face in a rare caress. Finally, she went back to her bedroom. 85

T'Gatoi lowered her head in relief. "Thank you, Gan," she said with courtesy more Terran than Tlic. "That one . . . she is always finding new ways for me to make her suffer."

Lomas began to groan and make choked sounds. I had hoped he would stay unconscious. T'Gatoi put her face near his so that he focused on her.

"I've stung you as much as I dare for now," she told him. "When this is over, I'll sting you to sleep and you won't hurt anymore."

"Please," the man begged. "Wait . . ."

"There's no more time, Bram. I'll sting you as soon as it's over. When T'Khotgif arrives she'll give you eggs to help you heal. It will be over soon." 90

"T'Khotgif!" the man shouted, straining against my hands.

"Soon, Bram." T'Gatoi glanced at me, then placed a claw against his abdomen slightly to the right of the middle, just below the left rib. There was movement on the right side—tiny, seemingly random pulsations moving his brown flesh, creating a concavity here, a convexity there, over and over until I could see the rhythm of it and knew where the next pulse would be.

Lomas's entire body stiffened under T'Gatoi's claw, though she merely rested it against him as she wound the rear section of her body around his legs. He might break my grip, but he would not break hers. He wept helplessly as she used his pants to tie his hands, then pushed his hands above his head so that I could kneel on the cloth between them and pin them in place. She rolled up his shirt and gave it to him to bite down on.

And she opened him.

His body convulsed with the first cut. He almost tore himself away from me. The sound he made . . . I had never heard such sounds come from anything human. T'Gatoi seemed to pay no attention as she lengthened and deepened the cut, now and then pausing to lick away blood. His blood vessels contracted, reacting to the chemistry of her saliva, and the bleeding slowed. 95

I felt as though I were helping her torture him, helping her consume him. I knew I would vomit soon, didn't know why I hadn't already. I couldn't possibly last until she was finished.

She found the first grub. It was fat and deep red with his blood—both inside and out. It had already eaten its own egg case but apparently had not yet begun to eat its host. At this stage, it would eat any flesh except its mother's. Let alone, it would have gone on excreting the poisons that had both sickened and alerted Lomas. Eventually it would have begun to eat. By the time it ate its way out of Lomas's flesh, Lomas would be dead or dying—and unable to take revenge on the thing that was killing him. There was always a grace period between the time the host sickened and the time the grubs began to eat him.

T'Gatoi picked up the writhing grub carefully and looked at it, somehow ignoring the terrible groans of the man.

Abruptly, the man lost consciousness.

100 "Good," T'Gatoi looked down at him. "I wish you Terrans could do that at will." She felt nothing. And the thing she held . . .

It was limbless and boneless at this stage, perhaps fifteen centimeters long and two thick, blind and slimy with blood. It was like a large worm. T'Gatoi put it into the belly of the achti, and it began at once to burrow. It would stay there and eat as long as there was anything to eat.

Probing through Lomas's flesh, she found two more, one of them smaller and more vigorous. "A male!" she said happily. He would be dead before I would. He would be through his metamorphosis and screwing everything that would hold still before his sisters even had limbs. He was the only one to make a serious effort to bite T'Gatoi as she placed him in the achti.

Paler worms oozed to visibility in Lomas's flesh. I closed my eyes. It was worse than finding something dead, rotting, and filled with tiny animal grubs. And it was far worse than any drawing or diagram.

"Ah, there are more," T'Gatoi said, plucking out two long, thick grubs. "You may have to kill another animal, Gan. Everything lives inside you Terrans."

105 I had been told all my life that this was a good and necessary thing Tlic and Terran did together—a kind of birth. I had believed it until now. I knew birth was painful and bloody, no matter what. But this was something else, something worse. And I wasn't ready to see it. Maybe I never would be. Yet I couldn't not see it. Closing my eyes didn't help.

T'Gatoi found a grub still eating its egg case. The remains of the case were still wired into a blood vessel by their own little tube or hook or whatever. That was the way the grubs were anchored and the way they fed. They took only blood until they were ready to emerge. Then they ate their stretched, elastic egg cases. Then they ate their hosts.

T'Gatoi bit away the egg case, licked away the blood. Did she like the taste? Did childhood habits die hard—or not die at all?

The whole procedure was wrong, alien. I wouldn't have thought anything about her could seem alien to me.

"One more, I think," she said. "Perhaps two. A good family. In a host animal these days, we would be happy to find one or two alive." She glanced at me. "Go outside, Gan, and empty your stomach. Go now while the man is unconscious."

110 I staggered out, barely made it. Beneath the tree just beyond the front door, I vomited until there was nothing left to bring up. Finally, I stood shaking, tears streaming down my face. I did not know why I was crying, but I could not stop. I went further from the house to avoid being seen. Every time I closed my eyes I saw red worms crawling over redder human flesh.

There was a car coming toward the house. Since Terrans were forbidden motorized vehicles except for certain farm equipment, I knew this must be Lomas's Tlic with Qui and perhaps a Terran doctor. I wiped my face on my shirt, struggled for control.

"Gan," Qui called as the car stopped. "What happened?" He crawled out of the low, round, Tlic-convenient car door. Another Terran crawled out the other side and went into the house without speaking to me. The doctor. With his help and a few eggs, Lomas might make it.

"T'Khotgif Teh?" I said.

The Tlic driver surged out of her car, reared up half her length before me. She was paler and smaller than T'Gatoi—probably born from the body of an animal. Tlic from Terran bodies were always larger as well as more numerous.

"Six young," I told her. "Maybe seven, all alive. At least one male." 115

"Lomas?" she said harshly. I liked her for the question and the concern in her voice when she asked it. The last coherent thing he had said was her name.

"He's alive," I said.

She surged away to the house without another word.

"She's been sick," my brother said, watching her go. "When I called, I could hear people telling her she wasn't well enough to go out even for this."

I said nothing. I had extended courtesy to the Tlic. Now I didn't want to talk 120 to anyone. I hoped he would go in—out of curiosity if nothing else.

"Finally found out more than you wanted to know, eh?"

I looked at him.

"Don't give me one of *her* looks," he said. "You're not her. You're just her property."

One of her looks. Had I picked up even an ability to imitate her expressions?

"What'd you do, puke?" He sniffed the air. "So now you know what you're in 125 for."

I walked away from him. He and I had been close when we were kids. He would let me follow him around when I was home, and sometimes T'Gatoi would let me bring him along when she took me into the city. But something had happened when he reached adolescence. I never knew what. He began keeping out of T'Gatoi's way. Then he began running away—until he realized there was no "away." Not in the Preserve. Certainly not outside. After that he concentrated on getting his share of every egg that came into the house and on looking out for me in a way that made me all but hate him—a way that clearly said, as long as I was all right, he was safe from the Tlic.

"How was it, really?" he demanded, following me.

"I killed an achti. The young ate it."

"You didn't run out of the house and puke because they ate an achti."

"I had . . . never seen a person cut open before." That was true, and enough 130 for him to know. I couldn't talk about the other. Not with him.

"Oh," he said. He glanced at me as though he wanted to say more, but he kept quiet.

We walked, not really headed anywhere. Toward the back, toward the cages, toward the fields.

"Did he say anything?" Qui asked. "Lomas, I mean."

Who else would he mean? "He said 'T'Khotgif.'"

Qui shuddered. "If she had done that to me, she'd be the last person I'd call for." 135

"You'd call for her. Her sting would ease your pain without killing the grubs in you."

"You think I'd care if they died?"

No. Of course he wouldn't. Would I?

"Shit!" He drew a deep breath. "I've seen what they do. You think this thing with Lomas was bad? It was nothing."

140 I didn't argue. He didn't know what he was talking about.

"I saw them eat a man," he said.

I turned to face him. "You're lying!"

"*I saw them eat a man.*" He paused. "It was when I was little. I had been to the Hartmund house and I was on my way home. Halfway here, I saw a man and a Tlic and the man was N'Tlic. The ground was hilly. I was able to hide from them and watch. The Tlic wouldn't open the man because she had nothing to feed the grubs. The man couldn't go any further and there were no houses around. He was in so much pain, he told her to kill him. He begged her to kill him. Finally, she did. She cut his throat. One swipe of one claw. I saw the grubs eat their way out, then burrow in again, still eating."

His words made me see Lomas's flesh again, parasitized, crawling. "Why didn't you tell me that?" I whispered.

145 He looked startled as though he'd forgotten I was listening. "I don't know."

"You started to run away not long after that, didn't you?"

"Yeah. Stupid. Running inside the Preserve. Running in a cage."

I shook my head, said what I should have said to him long ago. "She wouldn't take you, Qui. You don't have to worry."

"She would . . . if anything happened to you."

150 "No. She'd take Xuan Hoa. Hoa . . . wants it." She wouldn't if she had stayed to watch Lomas.

"They don't take women," he said with contempt.

"They do sometimes." I glanced at him. "Actually, they prefer women. You should be around them when they talk among themselves. They say women have more body fat to protect the grubs. But they usually take men to leave the women free to bear their own young."

"To provide the next generation of host animals," he said, switching from contempt to bitterness.

"It's more than that!" I countered. Was it?

155 "If it were going to happen to me, I'd want to believe it was more, too."

"It *is* more!" I felt like a kid. Stupid argument.

"Did you think so while T'Gatoi was picking worms out of that guy's guts?"

"It's not supposed to happen that way."

"Sure it is. You weren't supposed to see it, that's all. And his Tlic was supposed to do it. She could sting him unconscious and the operation wouldn't have been as painful. But she'd still open him, pick out the grubs, and if she missed even one, it would poison him and eat him from the inside out."

160 There was actually a time when my mother told me to show respect for Qui because he was my older brother. I walked away, hating him. In his way, he was gloating. He was safe and I wasn't. I could have hit him, but I didn't think I would be able to stand it when he refused to hit back, when he looked at me with contempt and pity.

He wouldn't let me get away. Longer legged, he swung ahead of me and made me feel as though I were following him.

"I'm sorry," he said.

I strode on, sick and furious.

"Look, it probably won't be that bad with you. T'Gatoi likes you. She'll be careful."

I turned back toward the house, almost running from him.   165

"Has she done it to you yet?" he asked, keeping up easily. "I mean, you're about the right age for implantation. Has she—"

I hit him. I didn't know I was going to do it, but I think I meant to kill him. If he hadn't been bigger and stronger, I think I would have.

He tried to hold me off, but in the end, had to defend himself. He only hit me a couple of times. That was plenty. I don't remember going down, but when I came to, he was gone. It was worth the pain to be rid of him.

I got up and walked slowly toward the house. The back was dark. No one was in the kitchen. My mother and sisters were sleeping in their bedrooms—or pretending to.

Once I was in the kitchen, I could hear voices—Tlic and Terran from the   170
next room. I couldn't make out what they were saying—didn't want to make it out.

I sat down at my mother's table, waiting for quiet. The table was smooth and worn, heavy and well crafted. My father had made it for her just before he died. I remembered hanging around underfoot when he built it. He didn't mind. Now I sat leaning on it, missing him. I could have talked to him. He had done it three times in his long life. Three clutches of eggs, three times being opened up and sewed up. How had he done it? How did anyone do it?

I got up, took the rifle from its hiding place, and sat down again with it. It needed cleaning, oiling.

All I did was load it.

"Gan?"

She made a lot of little clicking sounds when she walked on bare floor, each   175
limb clicking in succession as it touched down. Waves of little clicks.

She came to the table, raised the front half of her body above it, and surged onto it. Sometimes she moved so smoothly she seemed to flow like water itself. She coiled herself into a small hill in the middle of the table and looked at me.

"That was bad," she said softly. "You should not have seen it. It need not be that way."

"I know."

"T'Khotgif—Ch'Khotgif now—she will die of her disease. She will not live to raise her children. But her sister will provide for them, and for Bram Lomas." Sterile sister. One fertile female in every lot. One to keep the family going. That sister owed Lomas more than she could ever repay.

"He'll live then?"   180

"Yes."

"I wonder if he would do it again."

"No one would ask him to do that again."

I looked into the yellow eyes, wondering how much I saw and understood there, and how much I only imagined. "No one ever asks us," I said. "You never asked me."

She moved her head slightly. "What's the matter with your face?"   185

"Nothing. Nothing important." Human eyes probably wouldn't have noticed the swelling in the darkness. The only light was from one of the moons, shining through a window across the room.

"Did you use the rifle to shoot the achti?"

"Yes."

"And do you mean to use it to shoot me?"

190   I stared at her, outlined in the moonlight—coiled, graceful body. "What does Terran blood taste like to you?"

She said nothing.

"What are you?" I whispered. "What are we to you?"

She lay still, rested her head on her topmost coil. "You know me as no other does," she said softly. "You must decide."

"That's what happened to my face," I told her.

195   "What?"

"Qui goaded me into deciding to do something. It didn't turn out very well." I moved the gun slightly, brought the barrel up diagonally under my own chin. "At least it was a decision I made."

"As this will be."

"Ask me, Gatoi."

"For my children's lives?"

200   She would say something like that. She knew how to manipulate people, Terran and Tlic. But not this time.

"I don't want to be a host animal," I said. "Not even yours."

It took her a long time to answer. "We use almost no host animals these days," she said. "You know that."

"You use us."

"We do. We wait long years for you and teach you and join our families to yours." She moved restlessly. "You know you aren't animals to us."

205   I stared at her, saying nothing.

"The animals we once used began killing most of our eggs after implantation long before your ancestors arrived," she said softly. "You know these things, Gan. Because your people arrived, we are relearning what it means to be a healthy, thriving people. And your ancestors, fleeing from their home-world, from their own kind who would have killed or enslaved them—they survived because of us. We saw them as people and gave them the Preserve when they still tried to kill us as worms."

At the word "worms," I jumped. I couldn't help it, and she couldn't help noticing it.

"I see," she said quietly. "Would you really rather die than bear my young, Gan?"

I didn't answer.

210   "Shall I go to Xuan Hoa?"

"Yes!" Hoa wanted it. Let her have it. She hadn't had to watch Lomas. She'd be proud. . . . Not terrified.

T'Gatoi flowed off the table onto the floor, startling me almost too much.

"I'll sleep in Hoa's room tonight," she said. "And sometime tonight or in the morning, I'll tell her."

This was going too fast. My sister Hoa had had almost as much to do with raising me as my mother. I was still close to her—not like Qui. She could want T'Gatoi and still love me.

"Wait! Gatoi!"   215

She looked back, then raised nearly half her length off the floor and turned to face me. "These are adult things, Gan. This is my life, my family!"

"But she's . . . my sister."

"I have done what you demanded. I have asked you!"

"But—"

"It will be easier for Hoa. She has always expected to carry other lives inside   220 her."

Human lives. Human young who should someday drink at her breasts, not at her veins.

I shook my head. "Don't do it to her, Gatoi." I was not Qui. It seemed I could become him, though, with no effort at all. I could make Xuan Hoa my shield. Would it be easier to know that red worms were growing in her flesh instead of mine?

"Don't do it to Hoa," I repeated.

She stared at me, utterly still.

I looked away, then back at her. "Do it to me."   225

I lowered the gun from my throat and she leaned forward to take it.

"No," I told her.

"It's the law," she said.

"Leave it for the family. One of them might use it to save my life someday."

She grasped the rifle barrel, but I wouldn't let go. I was pulled into a standing   230 position over her.

"Leave it here!" I repeated. "If we're not your animals, if these are adult things, accept the risk. There is risk, Gatoi, in dealing with a partner."

It was clearly hard for her to let go of the rifle. A shudder went through her and she made a hissing sound of distress. It occurred to me that she was afraid. She was old enough to have seen what guns could do to people. Now her young and this gun would be together in the same house. She did not know about the other guns. In this dispute, they did not matter.

"I will implant the first egg tonight," she said as I put the gun away. "Do you hear, Gan?"

Why else had I been given a whole egg to eat while the rest of the family was left to share one? Why else had my mother kept looking at me as though I were going away from her, going where she could not follow? Did T'Gatoi imagine I hadn't known?

"I hear."   235

"Now!" I let her push me out of the kitchen, then walked ahead of her toward my bedroom. The sudden urgency in her voice sounded real. "You would have done it to Hoa tonight!" I accused.

"I must do it to someone tonight."

I stopped in spite of her urgency and stood in her way. "Don't you care who?"

She flowed around me and into my bedroom. I found her waiting on the couch we shared. There was nothing in Hoa's room that she could have used.

She would have done it to Hoa on the floor. The thought of her doing it to Hoa at all disturbed me in a different way now, and I was suddenly angry.

240   Yet I undressed and lay down beside her. I knew what to do, what to expect. I had been told all my life. I felt the familiar sting, narcotic, mildly pleasant. Then the blind probing of her ovipositor.[1] The puncture was painless, easy. So easy going in. She undulated slowly against me, her muscles forcing the egg from her body into mine. I held on to a pair of her limbs until I remembered Lomas holding her that way. Then I let go, moved inadvertently, and hurt her. She gave a low cry of pain and I expected to be caged at once within her limbs. When I wasn't, I held on to her again, feeling oddly ashamed.

"I'm sorry," I whispered.

She rubbed my shoulders with four of her limbs.

"Do you care?" I asked. "Do you care that it's me?"

She did not answer for some time. Finally, "You were the one making the choices tonight, Gan. I made mine long ago."

245   "Would you have gone to Hoa?"

"Yes. How could I put my children into the care of one who hates them?"

"It wasn't . . . hate."

"I know what it was."

"I was afraid."

250   Silence.

"I still am." I could admit it to her here, now.

"But you came to me . . . to save Hoa."

"Yes." I leaned my forehead against her. She was cool velvet, deceptively soft. "And to keep you for myself," I said. It was so. I didn't understand it, but it was so.

She made a soft hum of contentment. "I couldn't believe I had made such a mistake with you," she said. "I chose you. I believed you had grown to choose me."

255   "I had, but . . ."

"Lomas."

"Yes."

"I had never known a Terran to see a birth and take it well. Qui has seen one, hasn't he?"

"Yes."

260   "Terrans should be protected from seeing."

I didn't like the sound of that—and I doubted that it was possible. "Not protected," I said. "Shown. Shown when we're young kids, and shown more than once. Gatoi, no Terran ever sees a birth that goes right. All we see is N'Tlic—pain and terror and maybe death."

She looked down at me. "It is a private thing. It has always been a private thing."

Her tone kept me from insisting—that and the knowledge that if she changed her mind, I might be the first public example. But I had planted the thought in her mind. Chances were it would grow, and eventually she would experiment.

"You won't see it again," she said. "I don't want you thinking any more about shooting me."

1. Organ through which a female fish or insect deposits eggs.

The small amount of fluid that came into me with her egg relaxed me as 265 completely as a sterile egg would have, so that I could remember the rifle in my hands and my feelings of fear and revulsion, anger and despair. I could remember the feelings without reviving them. I could talk about them.

"I wouldn't have shot you," I said. "Not you." She had been taken from my father's flesh when he was my age.

"You could have," she insisted.

"Not you." She stood between us and her own people, protecting, interweaving.

"Would you have destroyed yourself?"

I moved carefully, uncomfortable. "I could have done that. I nearly did. 270 That's Qui's 'away.' I wonder if he knows."

"What?"

I did not answer.

"You will live now."

"Yes." *Take care of her,* my mother used to say. Yes.

"I'm healthy and young," she said. "I won't leave you as Lomas was left— 275 alone, N'Tlic. I'll take care of you."

1984, 1995

QUESTIONS

1. BLOODCHILD focuses on what Gan calls his "last night of childhood" (par. 1). What does he mean? How and why do his feelings about T'Gatoi evolve over the course of the story? Why might he make the decision he ultimately does?

2. Why does Gan's mother, Lien, refuse to eat eggs? Why does she lie as and when she does? Might she be conflicted? How and why so?

3. How does the story's setting contribute to its characterization of the relationship between Tlic and Terran generally and among the story's major characters specifically, especially the fact that the story unfolds both on a planet occupied by the Tlic long before Terran arrived (par. 206) and on "the Preserve" (par. 3)? What is the effect of when and how the story gives us this and other background information (or **exposition**)?

AUTHORS ON THEIR WORK

OCTAVIA E. BUTLER (1947–2006)
From Afterword [to "Bloodchild"] (1995)*

It amazes me that some people have seen "Bloodchild" as a story of slavery. It isn't. It's a number of other things, though. On one level, it's a love story between two very different beings. On another, it's a coming-of-age story in which a boy must absorb disturbing information and use it to make a decision that will affect the rest of his life.

On a third level, "Bloodchild" is my pregnant man story. I've always wanted to explore what it might be like for a man to be put into that most unlikely of all positions. Could I write a story in which a man chose to become pregnant *not* through some sort of misplaced competitiveness to prove that a man could do anything a woman could do, not because he was forced to, not even out of curiosity? I wanted to see whether I could write a dramatic story of a man becoming pregnant as an act of love—choosing pregnancy in spite of as well as because of surrounding difficulties.

Also, "Bloodchild" was my effort to ease an old fear of mine. I was going to travel to the Peruvian Amazon to do research for my Xenogenesis books (*Dawn, Adulthood Rites,* and *Imago*), and I worried about my possible reactions to some of the insect life of the area. In particular, I worried about the botfly—an insect with, what seemed to me then, horror-movie habits. There was no shortage of botflies in the part of Peru that I intended to visit.

The botfly lays its eggs in wounds left by the bites of other insects. I found the idea of a maggot living and growing under my skin, eating my flesh as it grew, to be so intolerable, so terrifying that I didn't know how I could stand it if it happened to me.

. . .

When I have to deal with something that disturbs me as much as the botfly did, I write about it. [. . .] Writing "Bloodchild" didn't make me like botflies, but for a while, it made them seem more interesting than horrifying.

There's one more thing I tried to do in "Bloodchild." I tried to write a story about paying the rent—a story about an isolated colony of human beings on an inhabited, extrasolar world. At best, they would be a lifetime away from reinforcements. It wouldn't be the British Empire in space, and it wouldn't be *Star Trek.* Sooner or later, the humans would have to make some kind of accommodation with their um . . . their hosts. Chances are this would be an unusual accommodation. Who knows what we humans have that others might be willing to take in trade for a livable space on a world not our own?

*Afterword. *Bloodchild and Other Stories,* Four Walls Eight Windows, 1995, pp. 30–32.

ZADIE SMITH
(b. 1975)

Meet the President!

Sadie Smith grew up in North London, a self-described "working-class kid" who lived in public housing until she was eight and enjoyed a "black and white and mixed" life like that "of millions of people throughout the world." Part of a "big and boisterous" family headed by a Jamaican-born Rastafarian who earned a social-work degree in her thirties and a much older, "short white" World War II veteran who left school at twelve, Smith attended public school, read voraciously, took tap-dancing lessons, changed her name to "Zadie" (at fourteen), and dreamed of someday appearing in Hollywood musicals. Both of her younger brothers eventually did become entertainers. But Smith instead attended Cambridge University, publishing short stories and penning her first novel. A multi-award-winning international best seller about two multicultural families in North London, *White Teeth* (2000) made Smith, at age twenty-two, a critics' darling, a household name, and what some called a "drop-dead cool" "poster girl for the new Britain." Committed to "taking risks," Smith has since produced a remarkably diverse body of work. Though she is best known for her novels—*The Autograph Man* (2002), *On Beauty* (2005), *NW* (2012), and *Swing Time* (2016)—Smith's nonfiction, some of which is collected in *Changing My Mind* (2009) and *Feel Free* (2018), ranges from interviews with Jay-Z to meditations on the work of Franz Kafka. Her equally varied short stories, most of which appear in *Grand Union* (2019), include the BBC National Short Story Award finalist "Miss Adele Amidst the Corsets" (2014), about an aging transgender New Yorker. Mostly a New Yorker herself these days, a married mother of two, and a fellow of the Royal Society of Literature, Smith teaches creative writing at NYU but spends her summers in North London; here, she says, "my life returns to its previous state"—"complication" and "chaos."

"What you got there, then?"

The boy didn't hear the question. He stood at the end of a ruined pier, believing himself quite alone. But now he registered the presence at his back, and turned.

"What you got there?"

A very old person, a woman, stood before him, gripping the narrow shoulder of a girl child. Both of them local, typically stunted, dim: they stared up at him stupidly. The boy turned again to the sea. All week long he had been hoping for a clear day to try out the new technology—not new to the world, but new to the boy—and now at last here was a break in the rain. Gray sky met gray sea. Not ideal, but sufficient. Ideally he would be standing on a cairn in Scotland or some other tropical spot, experiencing backlit clarity. Ideally he would be—

"Is it one of them what you see through?"   5

A hand, lousy with blue veins, reached out for the light encircling the boy's head, as if it were a substantial thing, to be grasped like the handle of a mug.

"Ooh, look at the green, Aggie. That shows you it's on."

The boy was ready to play. He touched the node on his finger to the node at his temple, raising the volume.

"Course, he'd have to be somebody, Aggs, cos they don't give 'em to nobody"— the boy felt the shocking touch of a hand on his own flesh. "Are you somebody, then?"

She had shuffled around until she stood square in front of him, unavoidable. 10 Hair as white as paper. A long, shapeless black dress, made of some kind of cloth, and what appeared to be a pair of actual glasses. Forty-nine years old, type O, a likelihood of ovarian cancer, some ancient debt infraction—nothing more. A blank, more or less. Same went for the girl: never left the country, eighty-five-per-cent chance of macular degeneration,[1] an uncle on the database, long ago located, eliminated. She would be nine in two days. Melinda Durham and Agatha Hanwell. They shared no more DNA than strangers.

---

1. Degenerative eye disease that destroys the central part of the retina, or "macula."

"Can you see us?" The old woman let go of her charge and waved her hands wildly. The tips of her fingers barely reached the top of the boy's head. "Are we in it? What are we?"

The boy, unused to proximity, took a single step forward. Farther he could not go. Beyond was the ocean; above, a mess of weather, clouds closing in on blue wherever blue tried to assert itself. A dozen or so craft darted up and down, diving low like seabirds after a fish, and no bigger than seabirds, skimming the dirty foam, then returning to the heavens, directed by unseen hands. On his first day here the boy had trailed his father on an inspection tour to meet those hands: intent young men at their monitors, over whose shoulders the boy's father leaned, as he sometimes leaned over the boy to insure he ate breakfast.

"What d'you call one of them there?"

The boy tucked his shirt in all round: "AG 12."

15   The old woman snorted as a mark of satisfaction, but did not leave.

He tried looking the females directly in their dull brown eyes. It was what his mother would have done, a kindly woman with a great mass of waist-length flame-colored hair, famed for her patience with locals. But his mother was long dead, he had never known her, he was losing what little light the day afforded. He blinked twice, said, "Hand to hand." Then, having a change of heart: "Weaponry." He looked down at his torso, to which he now attached a quantity of guns.

"You carry on, lad," the old woman said. "We won't get in your way. He can see it all, duck," she told the girl, who paid her no mind. "Got something in his hands—or thinks he does."

She took a packet of tobacco from a deep pocket in the front of her garment and began to roll a cigarette, using the girl as a shield from the wind.

"Them clouds, dark as bulls. Racing, racing. They always win." To illustrate, she tried turning Aggie's eyes to the sky, lifting the child's chin with a finger, but the girl would only gawk stubbornly at the woman's elbow. "They'll dump on us before we even get there. If you didn't have to, I wouldn't go, Aggie, no chance, not in this. It's for you I do it. I've been wet and wet and wet. All my life. And I bet he's looking at blazing suns and people in their what-have-yous and all-togethers! Int yer? Course you are! And who'd blame you?" She laughed so loud the boy heard her. And then the child—who did not laugh, whose pale face, with its triangle chin and enormous, fair-lashed eyes, seemed capable only of astonishment—pulled at his actual leg, forcing him to mute for a moment and listen to her question.

20   "Well, I'm Bill Peek," he replied, and felt very silly, like somebody in an old movie.

"Bill Peek!" the old woman cried. "Oh, but we've had Peeks in Anglia[2] a long time. You'll find a Peek or two or three down in Sutton Hoo.[3] Bill Peek! You from round here, Bill Peek?"

---

2. Originally, the medieval Latin name for England; today, one name for one of its easternmost and thus partly coastal regions.
3. Located in East Anglia and one of England's most famous archaeological sites; the wealth of Anglo-Saxon artifacts discovered here includes an entire seventh-century ship.

His grandparents? Very possibly. Local and English—or his great-grandparents. His hair and eyes and skin and name suggested it. But it was not a topic likely to engage his father, and the boy himself had never felt any need or desire to pursue it. He was simply global, accompanying his father on his inspections, though usually to livelier spots than this. What a sodden dump it was! Just as everyone had warned him it would be. The only people left in England were the ones who couldn't leave.

"From round here, are you? Or maybe a Norfolk[4] one? He looks like a Norfolk one, Aggs, wouldn't you say?"

Bill Peek raised his eyes to the encampment on the hill, pretending to follow with great interest those dozen circling, diving craft, as if he, uniquely, as the child of personnel, had nothing to fear from them. But the woman was occupied with her fag[5] and the girl only sang "Bill Peek, Bill Peek, Bill Peek" to herself, and smiled sadly at her own turned-in feet. They were too local even to understand the implied threat. He jumped off the pier onto the deserted beach. It was low tide—it seemed you could walk to Holland. He focussed upon the thousands of tiny spirals on the sand, like miniature turds stretching out to the horizon.

Felixstowe, England. A Norman[6] village; later, briefly, a resort, made popular   25 by the German royal family; much fishing, once upon a time. A hundred years earlier, almost to the very month, a quaint flood had killed only forty-eight people. Over the years, the place had been serially flooded, mostly abandoned. Now the sad little town had retreated three miles inland and up a hill. Pop.: 850. The boy blinked twice more; he did not care much for history. He narrowed his attention to a single turd. *Arenicola marina.* Sandworms. Lugworms. These were its coiled castings. Castings? But here he found his interest fading once again. He touched his temple and said, "Blood Head 4." Then: "Washington." It was his first time at this level. Another world began to construct itself around Bill Peek, a shining city on a hill.

"Poor little thing," Melinda Durham said. She sat on the pier, legs dangling, and pulled the girl into her lap. "Demented with grief she is. We're going to a laying out. Aggie's sister is laid out today. Her last and only relation. Course, the cold truth is, Aggie's sister weren't much better than trash, and a laying out's a sight too good for her—she'd be better off laid out on this beach here and left for the gulls. But I ain't going for *her.* I do it for Aggie. Aggie knows why. Aggie's been a great help to me what with one thing and another."

While he waited, as incidental music played, the boy idly checked a message from his father: at what time could he be expected back at the encampment? *At what time could he be expected.* This was a pleasing development, being an inquiry rather than an order. He would be fifteen in May, almost a man! A man who could let another man know when he could be expected, and let him know in his own sweet time, when he had the inclination. He performed some rudimentary stretches and bounced up and down on the balls of his feet.

4. County in East Anglia.
5. Cigarette (British slang).
6. Peoples of Normandy, in northern France, who invaded and conquered England in 1066.

"Maud, that was her name. And she was born under the same steeple she'll be buried under. Twelve years old. But so whorish—" Melinda covered Aggie's ears, and the girl leaned into the gesture, having mistaken it for affection. "So whorish she looked like a crone. If you lived round here, Bill Peek, you'd've *known* Maud, if you understand me correctly. You would've known Maud right up to the Biblical and beyond. Terrible. But Aggie's cut from quite different sod, thank goodness!" Aggie was released and patted on the head. "And she's no one left, so here I am, muggins here, taking her to a laying out when I've a million other stones to be lifted off the pile."

The boy placed a number of grenades about his person. In each chapter of the Pathways Global Institute (in Paris, New York, Shanghai, Nairobi, Jerusalem, Tokyo), the boy had enjoyed debating with friends the question of whether it was better to augment around the "facts on the ground," incorporating whatever was at hand ("flagging," it was called, the pleasure being the unpredictability), or to choose spots where there were barely any facts to work around. The boy was of the latter sensibility. He wanted to augment in clean, blank places, where he was free to fully extend, unhindered. He looked down the beach as the oil streaks in the sand were overlaid now with a gleaming pavement, lined on either side by the National Guard, saluting him. It was three miles to the White House. He picked out a large pair of breasts to wear, for reasons of his own, and a long, scaled tail, for purposes of strangulation.

30 "Oh, fuck a duck—you wouldn't do me an awful favor and keep an eye on Aggie just a minute, would you?—I've left my rosary! I can't go to no laying out without it. It's more than my soul's worth. Oh, Aggie, how did you ever let me leave without it? She's a good girl, but she's thoughtless sometimes—her sister were thoughtless, too. Bill Peek, you will keep an eye on her, won't you? I won't be a moment. We're shacked up just on that hill by the old Martello[7] tower. Eight minutes I'll be. No more. Would you do that for me, Bill Peek?"

Bill Peek nodded his head, once rightward, twice leftward. Knives shot out of his wrists and splayed beautifully like the fronds of a fern.

It was perhaps twenty minutes later, as he approached the pile of rubble— pounded by enemy craft—that had once been the Monument, that young Bill Peek felt again a presence at his back and turned and found Aggie Hanwell with her fist in her mouth, tears streaming, jaw working up and down in an agonized fashion. He couldn't hear her over the explosions. Reluctantly, he paused.

"She ain't come back."

"Excuse me?"

35 "She went but she ain't come back!"

"Who?" he asked, but then scrolled back until he found it. "M. Durham?"

The girl gave him that same astonished look.

"My Melly," she said. "She promised to take me but she went and she ain't come back!"

The boy swiftly located M. Durham—as much an expedience as an act of charity—and experienced the novelty of sharing the information with the girl,

---

7. Small, round forts first built throughout southeast England during the early nineteenth century, mainly to defend against a possible French invasion.

in the only way she appeared able to receive it. "She's two miles away," he said, with his own mouth. "Heading north."

Aggie Hanwell sat down on her bum in the wet sand. She rolled something 40 in her hand. The boy looked at it and learned that it was a periwinkle—a snail of the sea! He recoiled, disliking those things which crawled and slithered upon the earth. But this one proved broken, with only a pearlescent nothing inside it.

"So it was all a lie," Aggie said, throwing her head back dramatically to consider the sky. "Plus one of them's got my number. I've done nothing wrong but still Melly's gone and left me and one of them thing's been following me, since the pier—even before that."

"If you've done nothing wrong," Bill Peek said, solemnly parroting his father, "you've nothing to worry about. It's a precise business." He had been raised to despair of the type of people who spread misinformation about the Program. Yet along with his new maturity had come fresh insight into the complexities of his father's world. For didn't those with bad intent on occasion happen to stand beside the good, the innocent, or the underaged? And in those circumstances could precision be entirely guaranteed? "Anyway, they don't track children. Don't you understand anything?"

Hearing this, the girl laughed—a bitter and cynical cackle, at odds with her pale little face—and Bill Peek made the mistake of being, for a moment, rather impressed. But she was only imitating her elders, as he was imitating his.

"Go home," he said.

Instead she set about burrowing her feet into the wet sand. 45

"Everyone's got a good angel and a bad angel," she explained. "And if it's a bad angel that picks you out"—she pointed to a craft swooping low—"there's no escaping it. You're done for."

He listened in wonderment. Of course he'd always known there were people who thought in this way—there was a module you did on them in sixth grade— but he had never met anyone who really harbored what his anthrosoc teacher, Mr. Lin, called "animist beliefs."[8]

The girl sighed, scooped up more handfuls of sand, and added them to the two mounds she had made on top of her feet, patting them down, encasing herself up to the ankles. Meanwhile all around her Bill Peek's scene of fabulous chaos was frozen—a Minotaur[9] sat in the lap of stony Abe Lincoln and a dozen carefully planted I.E.D.s awaited detonation. He was impatient to return.

"Must advance," he said, pointing down the long stretch of beach, but she held up her hands, she wanted pulling up. He pulled. Standing, she clung to him, hugging his knees. He felt her face damp against his leg.

"Oh, it's awful bad luck to miss a laying out! Melly's the one knew where to 50 go. She's got the whole town up here," she said, tapping her temple, making the boy smile. "Memoried. No one knows town like Melly. She'll say, 'This used to be here, but they knocked it down,' or, 'There was a pub here with a mark on the wall where the water rose.' She's memoried every corner. She's my friend."

---

8. "Animism" involves the attribution of life and consciousness to inanimate objects.
9. In Greek myth, the monster—part bull, part human—imprisoned in the labyrinth of King Minos, where he fed on the young men and women sent to him in tribute.

"Some friend!" the boy remarked. He succeeded in unpeeling the girl from his body, and strode on down the beach, firefighting a gang of Russian commandoes as they parachuted into view. Alongside him a scurrying shape ran; sometimes a dog, sometimes a droid, sometimes a huddle of rats. Her voice rose out of it.

"Can I see?"

Bill Peek disembowelled a fawn to his left. "Do you have an Augmentor?"

"No."

55 "Do you have a complementary system?"

"No."

He knew he was being cruel—but she was ruining his concentration. He stopped running and split the visuals, the better to stare her down.

"Any system?"

"No."

60 "Therefore no. No, you can't."

Her nose was pink, a drop of moisture hung from it. She had an innocence that practically begged to be corrupted. Bill Peek could think of more than a few Pathways boys of his acquaintance who wouldn't hesitate to take her under the next boardwalk and put a finger inside her. And the rest. As the son of personnel, however, Bill Peek was held to a different standard.

"Jimmy Kane had one—he was a fella of Maud's, her main fella. He flew in and then he flew out—you never knew when he'd be flying in again. He was a captain in the Army. He had an old one of them . . . but said it still worked. He said it made her nicer to look at when they were doing it. He was from nowhere, too."

"Nowhere?"

"Like you."

65 Not for the first time the boy was struck by the great human mysteries of this world. He was almost fifteen, almost a man, and the great human mysteries of this world were striking him with satisfying regularity, as was correct for his stage of development. (From the Pathways Global Institute prospectus: "As our students reach tenth grade they begin to gain insight into the great human mysteries of this world, and a special sympathy for locals, the poor, ideologues, and all those who have chosen to limit their own human capital in ways that it can be difficult at times for us to comprehend.") From the age of six months, when he was first enrolled in the school, he had hit every mark that Pathways expected of its pupils—walking, talking, divesting, monetizing,[1] programming, augmenting—and so it was all the more shocking to find himself face-to-face with an almost nine-year-old so absolutely blind, so lost, so developmentally debased.

"This"—he indicated Felixstowe, from the beach with its turd castings and broken piers, to the empty-shell buildings and useless flood walls, up to the hill where his father hoped to expect him—"is nowhere. If you can't move, you're no one from nowhere. 'Capital must flow.'" (This last was the motto of his school,

---

1. Like *divesting*, primarily a banking/investment term. To "monetize" something is to turn it into money, as when a debt is purchased so as to increase the supply of ready money. To "divest" is to shed something or to dispossess someone else of it.

though she needn't know that.) "Now, if you're asking me where I was born, the event of my birth occurred in Bangkok,[2] but wherever I was born I would remain a member of the Incipio Security Group, which employs my father—and within which I have the highest clearance." He was surprised by the extent of the pleasure this final, outright lie gave him. It was like telling a story, but in a completely new way—a story that could not be verified or checked, and which only total innocence would accept. Only someone with no access of any kind. Never before had he met someone like this, who could move only in tiny local spirals, a turd on a beach.

Moved, the boy bent down suddenly and touched the girl gently on her face. As he did so he had a hunch that he probably looked like the first prophet of some monotheistic[3] religion, bestowing his blessing on a recent convert, and, upon re-watching the moment and finding this was so, he sent it out, both to Mr. Lin and to his fellow Pathways boys, for peer review. It would surely count toward completion of Module 19, which emphasized empathy for the dispossessed.

"Where is it you want to go, my child?"

She lit up with gratitude, her little hand gripped his, the last of her tears rolling into her mouth and down her neck. "St. Jude's!"[4] she cried. She kept talking as he replayed the moment to himself and added a small note of explanatory context for Mr. Lin, before he refocussed on her stream of prattle: "And I'll say goodbye to her. And I'll kiss her on her face and nose. Whatever they said about her she was my own sister and I loved her and she's going to a better place— I don't care if she's stone cold in that church, I'll hold her!"

"Not a church," the boy corrected. "14 Ware Street, built 1950, originally 70 domestic property, situated on a floodplain, condemned for safety. Site of 'St. Jude's'—local, outlier congregation. Has no official status."

"St. Jude's is where she'll be laid out," she said and squeezed his hand. "And I'll kiss her no matter how cold she is."

The boy shook his head and sighed.

"We're going in the same direction. Just follow me. No speaking." He put his finger to his lips, and she tucked her chin into her neck meekly, seeming to understand. Restarting, he flagged her effectively, transforming little Aggie Hanwell into his sidekick, his familiar,[5] a sleek reddish fox. He was impressed by the perfect visual reconstruction of the original animal, apparently once common in this part of the world. Re-named Mystus, she provided cover for his left flank and mutely admired Bill Peek as he took the traitor Vice-President hostage and dragged him down the Mall[6] with a knife to his neck.

After a spell they came to the end of the beach. Here the sand shaded into pebbles and then a rocky cove, and barnacles held on furiously where so much else had been washed away. Above their heads, the craft were finishing their

2. Capital of Thailand.
3. Having one god.
4. Named for the patron saint of desperate and lost causes.
5. Attendant spirit usually embodied in an animal; in folklore, a cat often serves as a witch's familiar.
6. National park in downtown Washington, D.C., stretching from the Lincoln Memorial to the U.S. Capitol, with the Washington Monument at its center.

Sallies and had clustered like bees, moving as one back to the landing bay at the encampment. Bill Peek and his familiar were also nearing the end of their journey, moments away from kicking in the door to the Oval Office, where—if all went well—they would meet the President and be thanked for their efforts. But at the threshold, unaccountably, Bill Peek's mind began to wander. Despite the many friends around the world watching (there was a certain amount of kudos granted to any boy who successfully met the President in good, if not record, time, on his first run-through), he found himself pausing to stroke Mystus and worry about whether his father would revoke his AG after this trip. It had been a bribe and a sop in the first place—it was unregistered. Bill had wanted to stay on at the Tokyo campus for the whole summer, and then move to Norway, before tsunami season, for a pleasant fall. His father had wanted him by his side, here, in the damp, unlit graylands. An AG 12 was the compromise. But these later models were security risks, easily hacked, and the children of personnel were not meant to carry hackable devices. That's how much my father loves me, Bill Peek thought hopefully, that's how much he wants me around.

75   Previously the boy had believed that the greatest testament to love was the guarantee—which he had had all his life—of total personal security. He could count on one hand the amount of times he'd met a local; radicals were entirely unknown to him; he had never travelled by any mode of transport that held more than four people. But now, almost adult, he had a new thought, saw the matter from a fresh perspective, which he hoped would impress Mr. Lin with its age-appropriate intersectionality.[7] He rested against the Oval Office door and sent his thought to the whole Pathways family: "Daring to risk personal security can be a sign of love, too." Feeling inspired, he split the visual in order to pause and once more appreciate the human mysteries of this world slash how far he'd come.

He found that he was resting on a slimy rock, his fingers tangled in the unclean hair follicles of Agatha Hanwell. She saw him looking at her. She said, "Are we there yet?" The full weight of her innocence emboldened him. They were five minutes from Ware Street. Wasn't that all the time he needed? No matter what lay beyond that door, it would be dispatched by Bill Peek, brutally, beautifully; he would step forward, into his destiny. He would meet the President! He would shake the President's hand.

"Follow me."

She was quick on the rocks, perhaps even a little quicker than he, moving on all fours like an animal. They took a right, a left, and Bill Peek slit many throats. The blood ran down the walls of the Oval Office and stained the Presidential seal and at the open windows a crowd of cheering, anonymous well-wishers pressed in. At which point Mystus strayed from him and rubbed herself along their bodies, and was stroked and petted in turn.

"So many people come to see your Maud. Does the soul good."

80   "How are you, Aggie, love? Bearing up?"

"They took her from the sky. Boom! 'Public depravity.' I mean, I ask you!"

"Come here, Aggs, give us a hug."

"Who's that with her?"

7. Study of how different forces intersect with each other.

"Look, that's the little sis. Saw it all. Poor little thing."

"She's in the back room, child. You go straight through. You've more right than anybody." 85

All Bill Peek knew is that many bodies were lying on the ground and a space was being made for him to approach. He stepped forward like a king. The President saluted him. The two men shook hands. But the light was failing, and then failed again; the celebrations were lost in infuriating darkness. . . . The boy touched his temple, hot with rage: a low-ceilinged parlor came into view, with its filthy window, further shaded by a ragged net curtain, the whole musty hovel lit by candles. He couldn't even extend an arm—there were people everywhere, local, offensive to the nose, to all other senses. He tried to locate Agatha Hanwell, but her precise coördinates were of no use here; she was packed deep into this crowd—he could no more get to her than to the moon. A fat man put a hand on his shoulder and asked, "You in the right place, boy?" A distressing female with few teeth said, "Leave him be." Bill Peek felt himself being pushed forward, deeper into the darkness. A song was being sung, by human voices, and though each individual sang softly, when placed side by side like this, like rows of wheat in the wind, they formed a weird unity, heavy and light at the same time. *"Because I do not hope to turn again . . . Because I do not hope . . ."*[8] In one voice, like a great beast moaning. A single craft carrying the right hardware could take out the lot of them, but they seemed to have no fear of that. Swaying, singing.

Bill Peek touched his sweaty temple and tried to focus on a long message from his father—something about a successful inspection and Mexico in the morning—but he was being pushed by many hands, ever forward, until he reached the back wall where a long box, made of the kind of wood you saw washed up on the beach, sat on a simple table, with candles all around it. The singing grew ever louder. Still, as he passed through their number, it seemed that no man or woman among them sang above a whisper. Then, cutting across it all like a stick through the sand, a child's voice wailed, an acute, high-pitched sound, such as a small animal makes when, out of sheer boredom, you break its leg. Onward they pushed him; he saw it all perfectly clearly in the candlelight— the people in black, weeping, and Aggie on her knees by the table, and inside the driftwood box the lifeless body of a real girl, the first object of its kind that young Bill Peek had ever seen. Her hair was red and set in large, infantile curls, her skin very white, and her eyes wide open and green. A slight smile revealed the gaps in her teeth, and suggested secret knowledge, the kind of smile he had seen before on the successful sons of powerful men with full clearance—the boys who never lose. Yet none of it struck him quite as much as the sensation that there was someone or something else in that grim room, both unseen and present, and coming for him as much as for anybody.

2013

---

8. First lines of T. S. Eliot's long poem *Ash Wednesday* (1930); published after his conversion to Anglicanism, it traces the speaker's struggle to embrace faith in both God and the possibility of human salvation.

QUESTIONS

1. What are the most important characteristics—social, environmental or ecological, and technological—of the future Zadie Smith imagines in MEET THE PRESIDENT!? What might the story imply about how this future came to be?
2. What might be the significance and effect of Smith's choice of geographical setting? of the characters' references to real places in, and real features of, that setting? How are characters characterized, in part, by their relationship to (this) place?
3. How would you describe what happens to Bill Peek over the course of the story? Does he change or learn something new? How and why so, or not?

SUGGESTIONS FOR WRITING

1. Write a response paper or essay reflecting on the ways in which THE VELDT or MEET THE PRESIDENT! engage in extrapolation. What developments or trends of the early 1950s or the 2010s does the story comment on by imagining the specific future it does?
2. Write an essay exploring what THE GERNSBACK CONTINUUM might suggest about the nature and social role of science fiction. Alternatively, draw on the definitions in this album or on other definitions you discover on your own, as well as evidence from the story, to explore just whether and why THE GERNSBACK CONTINUUM should count as science fiction.
3. In the afterword excerpted in this album, Octavia Butler claims that BLOODCHILD is, among other things, "a love story between two very different beings." Write an essay that supports and develops this claim. What might the story ultimately show us about love and/or family? Alternatively, write an essay exploring and developing Butler's claim that her story offers a picture of human-alien relations and, perhaps, of humanity's role in the universe that challenges the picture offered by conventional science fiction, especially the original *Star Trek* series.
4. Write an essay comparing what at least two stories in this album suggest about technology's effects on human relationships.
5. Write an essay comparing the role of place in two stories in this album. What is the effect, for example, of Bradbury's choice to focus exclusively on the Hadley home in THE VELDT and to ignore the world outside its borders? of the numerous, specific, actual places in which the action of THE GERNSBACK CONTINUUM unfolds?

6 | SYMBOLISM AND FIGURATIVE LANGUAGE

A **symbol** is something that represents something else. Sometimes a symbol resembles or closely relates to what it represents, but often the association is arbitrary or subtle. Even so, through common usage, many symbols are instantly understood by almost everyone in a particular group. Although we rarely think of them as such, the letters of the English alphabet are themselves symbols, representing different sounds. We simply learn to recognize them, however, without thinking about whether there is any resemblance between what the symbols look like and what they represent. In other languages, one character may stand for an object or concept, such as the Chinese characters for "fire." Yet some symbols do help us by resembling what they stand for, such as the symbol for a fire alarm.

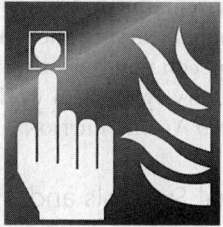

Similarly, abstractions may be represented by symbols that resemble things that are associated with them:

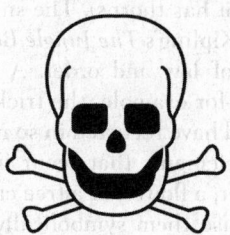

Although the smiley face can simply mean "Smile!" its meanings when used as an emoji range from "I like this" to "Just joking." The skull and crossbones symbol is used on warning labels to indicate that the contents are poisonous, but it has also been associated with death, cemeteries, and pirates.

Other symbols are more arbitrary, having no literal connection with what they represent. Octagons and the color red have little to do with stopping a car, but most Americans understand what a stop sign means. Such symbols, though not based on resemblances, elicit an unconscious and reflexive response from us. The meaning of a symbol is not always so concrete and practical, however. The U.S. flag is an arbitrary symbol, having no direct resemblance to what it represents, but most people recognize its primary significance; the "stars and stripes" undoubtedly stands for the United States. Nevertheless, the flag differs from a traffic sign in that the flag evokes much more varied, complex, even conflicting responses.

LITERARY SYMBOLISM

A symbol usually conveys an abstraction or cluster of abstractions, from the ideal to the imperceptible or the irrational, in a more concrete form. In a literary work, a symbol compares or puts together two things that are in some ways dissimilar. But literary symbolism rarely comes down to a simple equation of one thing to another. Unlike an arbitrary symbol such as a letter or traffic sign, a symbol in literature usually carries richer and more varied meanings, as does a flag or a religious image. And because of its significance, a symbol usually appears or is hinted at numerous times throughout the work. In reading literature, it may be challenging to recognize symbols, and readers may have good reasons to disagree about their interpretation, since literary works often incorporate symbolism for which there is no single "correct" interpretation. Reading a short story is not like a treasure hunt for some shiny symbol that clearly reveals all the hidden meanings; the complexity remains and requires further exploration even when we have recognized a symbol's significance. A literary symbol may be understood as an extended figure of speech that rewards further interpretation. (For one fiction writer's views of how literary symbolism works, see the excerpt from Flannery O'Connor's THE NATURE AND AIM OF FICTION.)

Traditional Symbols and Archetypes

Some symbols have been in use by many people for a long time (in which case they are known as *traditional symbols*); a white dove, for example, is a traditional symbol of peace and love. A rose can be a symbol of godly love, of romantic desire, of female beauty, of mortality (because the flower wilts), or of hidden cruelty (because it has thorns). The snake has traditionally been a symbol of evil, but in Rudyard Kipling's *The Jungle Book* (1894), the python Ka, while frightening, is on the side of law and order. A few symbolic character types, plots, objects, or settings—for example, the trickster, the quest, the garden—have become so pervasive and have recurred in so many cultures that they are considered **archetypes** (literary elements that recur in the literature and myths of multiple cultures). Fire, water, a flower, or a tree can all be considered archetypes because numerous cultures use them symbolically, often within their systems of religion or myth. Literary symbolism frequently borrows from the symbols and archetypes associated with such systems.

Allegory and Myth

A common literary form, especially in works written by and for religious believers, is the **allegory**, which may be regarded as an "extended" symbol or series of symbols that encompasses a whole work. In an allegory, concrete things and abstract concepts may be associated with each other across a narrative that consistently maintains at least two distinct levels of meaning. Because allegories set up series of correspondences, they usually help the reader translate these correspondences through the use of names that readily function as labels, often with obvious moral implications. In *The Pilgrim's Progress* (1678), the most famous prose allegory in English, the central character is named Christian; he is born in the City of Destruction and sets out for the Celestial City, passes through the Slough of Despond and Vanity Fair, meets men named Pliable and Obstinate, and so on. The point of an allegory is not to make us hunt for disguised meanings, so it is no defect if an allegory's intended meaning is clear. Instead, the purpose is to let us enjoy an invented world where everything is especially meaningful and everything corresponds to something else according to a moral or otherwise "correct" plan.

When an entire story is allegorical or symbolic, it is sometimes called a **myth**. *Myth* originally referred to a story of communal origin providing an explanation or religious interpretation of humanity, nature, the universe, or the relations among them. Sometimes we apply the term *myth* to stories associated with religions we do not believe in, and sometimes to literature that seeks to express experiences or truths that transcend any one location, culture, or time.

FIGURES OF SPEECH

Figures of speech, or **figurative language**, are similar to symbols in that they supplement or replace literal meaning, often by creating imaginative connections between our ideas and our senses. Sometimes referred to as *tropes* (literally, "turnings"), figures of speech could be described as *bending* the usual meaning of language and *shaping* our response to a work. Whether or not they have anything to do with spatial forms or "figures," or whether they rely on vision, such tropes contribute to what are called the **images** or **imagery** of a story. Many figures of speech are known by the Latin or Greek names used in classical Greek and Roman **rhetoric**, the art and science of speech and persuasion.

Just as you can enjoy gymnastics or diving competitions without knowing the names of the specific twists and turns, you can enjoy the figurative language in a story without identifying each figure of speech. Yet for the purposes of interpreting and writing about literature, it is important to learn some basic terms and distinctions so that you have access to a shared and economical language for describing your responses and the techniques that trigger them. The box below defines some of the most common figures of speech.

Key Figures of Speech

allegory   an extended association, often sustained in every element (character, plot, setting, etc.) and throughout an entire work, between two levels of meaning, usually literal and abstract. In *Animal Farm* (1945), for example, George Orwell uses an uprising of barnyard animals as an allegory for the Bolshevik revolution in Russia.

allusion   a reference, usually brief, to another text or some person or entity external to the work. Examples may range from a direct quotation of the Bible to the mention of a famous name.

irony   a meaning or outcome contrary to what is expected; in *verbal irony*, a speaker or narrator says one thing and means the reverse. When the intended meaning is harshly critical or mocking, it is called *sarcasm*. If a teenager says, "I just love it when my mom lectures me," she may well be using irony.

metaphor   a representation of one thing as if it were something else, without a verbal signal such as *like* or *as*. When, in SONNY'S BLUES, the narrator remarks that the musician Creole "let out the reins" (par. 237), he does not speak literally. Rather, he suggests the freer, faster way that the fiddler begins to play by implicitly likening it to the way a rider slackens her hold on the reins that constrain her horse's movements.

metonymy   using the name of one thing to refer to another thing associated with it. The common phrase *red tape* is a metonym for excessive paperwork and procedure that slows down an official transaction, based on the fact that such paperwork used to be tied up with red tape.

oxymoron   a combination of contradictory or opposite ideas, qualities, or entities, as in *wise fool* or *jumbo shrimp*.

personification   sometimes called *anthropomorphism*, attributing human qualities to objects or animals. When he observes "the drums talked back," "the horn insisted" (par. 237), the narrator of SONNY'S BLUES personifies these musical instruments.

simile   a representation of one thing as if it were something else, with an explicit verbal signal such as *like* or *as*. In *To Kill a Mockingbird* (1960), Scout describes a teacher who "looked and smelled like a peppermint drop" and bored students "wriggling like a bucket of Catawba worms."

symbol   a person, place, object, or image that represents more than its literal meaning. A symbol is more than a passing comparison (such as a simile); instead, as in allegory, its meaning usually relates to most details and themes of the work. Unlike allegory, a symbol usually associates more than two entities or ideas and may be obscure or ambiguous in its meaning. Literary works may refer to their central symbolic figure in their titles, as in Raymond Carver's CATHEDRAL.

synecdoche   a form of metonymy (or name substitution) in which the part represents the whole (a *sail* refers to a ship, *wheels* to a car).

INTERPRETING SYMBOLISM AND FIGURATIVE LANGUAGE

The context of an entire story or poem or play can guide you in deciding how far to push your own "translation" of a figure of speech or whether a metaphor has the deeper significance of a symbol. It is best to read the entire story and note all of the figures of speech or imagery before you examine one as a symbol. Often, a symbol is a focal point in a story, a single object or situation that draws the attention of one or more characters.

In F. Scott Fitzgerald's *The Great Gatsby* (1925), for example, a faded billboard featuring a pair of bespectacled eyes takes on a central and multilayered significance, though there is no longstanding tradition of symbolic meaning for billboards or spectacles. Although the billboard is a purely realistic detail of setting (one can easily imagine seeing something like it along any highway today), it comes to function as a symbol, too, because of the number of times and specific ways it is discussed by the narrator and characters. When one character, George Wilson, looks up at the looming eyes and remarks, "God sees everything," it becomes pretty clear what the billboard symbolizes to him. Yet when another character immediately reminds Wilson that what he sees is only "an advertisement," we are forced to consider both what Wilson's interpretation might tell us about him and with what alternative or additional meanings the rest of the novel might invest this object. The symbol remains ambiguous and complex.

Effective symbols and figurative language cannot be extracted from the story they serve, but they can leave a lasting image of what the story is about. With guidance and practice, identifying and interpreting literary symbolism and other figurative language will begin to feel almost as familiar to you as reading the letter symbols on a page, though the meanings may be subtle, ambiguous, and far-reaching rather than straightforward.

Responding to Symbolism: Some Guidelines

- Read the story carefully, noting any details that seem to have exceptional significance, such as names, repeated actions or statements, recurring references to objects, peculiar places, allusions, or other figures of speech.
- Using your list of such possibly symbolic details, look back through the story to find the passages that feature these details. Are any of the passages connected to each other in a pattern? Do any of these interconnected details suggest themes?
- Note any symbols or images that you recognize from mythology, religion, or any other literature, art, or popular culture. Look again at the way the story presents such material. What are the signals that the fire is more than a fire, the tree is more than a tree, the ring is more than a ring? If the story invents its own symbol, find any words in the story that show how the characters see something meaningful in it.
- Once you have found a symbol—an aspect of the story that is a figure of speech, trope, image, or connection between literal and nonliteral; is extended beyond a few sentences; is more complicated than an allegory's one-to-one translation; and may be interpreted in multiple ways—review every aspect of the story, on the literal level, that relates to this symbol.
- As you write about the symbol or symbolism in a story, consider your claims about its meaning. Try not to narrow down the possible meanings of either the symbol or the story, but at the same time don't make overly grand claims for their ability to reveal the meaning of life. When in doubt, refer back to the story and its characterization, plot, and setting.
- Remember to cite specific passages that will help your reader understand the symbol's significance. Your reader may suspect that you are reading too much into it or miscasting its meanings, so this evidence is crucial to explaining your interpretation and persuading your reader that it is reasonable.

NATHANIEL HAWTHORNE

(1804–64)

The Birth-Mark

Nathaniel Hawthorne was born in Salem, Massachusetts, a descendant of Puritan immigrants. Educated at Bowdoin College, he was agonizingly slow in winning recognition for his work and supported himself from time to time in government service—working in the customhouses of Boston and Salem and serving as the U.S. consul in Liverpool, England. His early collections of stories, *Twice-Told Tales* (1837) and *Mosses from an Old Manse* (1846), did not sell well, and it was not until the publication of his most famous novel, *The Scarlet Letter* (1850), that his fame spread beyond a discerning few. His other novels include *The House of the Seven Gables* (1851) and *The Blithedale Romance* (1852). Burdened by a deep sense of guilt for his family's role in the notorious Salem witchcraft trials over a century before he was born (one ancestor had been a judge), Hawthorne used fiction as a means of exploring the moral dimensions of sin and the human soul.

I n the latter part of the last century[1] there lived a man of science, an eminent proficient in every branch of natural philosophy,[2] who not long before our story opens had made experience of a spiritual affinity more attractive than any chemical one. He had left his laboratory to the care of an assistant, cleared his fine countenance from the furnace-smoke, washed the stain of acids from his fingers, and persuaded a beautiful woman to become his wife. In those days, when the comparatively recent discovery of electricity and other kindred mysteries of Nature seemed to open paths into the region of miracle, it was not unusual for the love of science to rival the love of woman in its depth and absorbing energy. The higher intellect, the imagination, the spirit, and even the heart might all find their congenial aliment in pursuits which, as some of their ardent votaries believed, would ascend from one step of powerful intelligence to another, until the philosopher should lay his hand on the secret of creative force and perhaps make new worlds for himself. We know not whether Aylmer possessed this degree of faith in man's ultimate control over nature. He had devoted himself, however, too unreservedly to scientific studies ever to be weakened from them by any second passion. His love for his young wife might prove the stronger of the two; but it could only be by intertwining itself with his love of science and uniting the strength of the latter to his own.

Such a union accordingly took place, and was attended with truly remarkable consequences and a deeply impressive moral. One day, very soon after their marriage, Aylmer sat gazing at his wife with a trouble in his countenance that grew stronger until he spoke.

1. That is, the eighteenth century; this story was first published in 1843.
2. The body of knowledge we now call science.

"Georgiana," said he, "has it never occurred to you that the mark upon your cheek might be removed?"

"No, indeed," said she, smiling; but, perceiving the seriousness of his manner, she blushed deeply. "To tell you the truth, it has been so often called a charm, that I was simple enough to imagine it might be so."

"Ah, upon another face perhaps it might," replied her husband; "but never on yours. No, dearest Georgiana, you came so nearly perfect from the hand of Nature, that this slightest possible defect, which we hesitate whether to term a defect or a beauty, shocks me, as being the visible mark of earthly imperfection."

"Shocks you, my husband!" cried Georgiana, deeply hurt; at first reddening with momentary anger, but then bursting into tears. "Then why did you take me from my mother's side? You cannot love what shocks you!"

To explain this conversation, it must be mentioned that in the center of Georgiana's left cheek there was a singular mark, deeply interwoven, as it were, with the texture and substance of her face. In the usual state of her complexion— a healthy though delicate bloom—the mark wore a tint of deeper crimson, which imperfectly defined its shape amid the surrounding rosiness. When she blushed it gradually became more indistinct, and finally vanished amid the triumphant rush of blood that bathed the whole cheek with its brilliant glow. But if any shifting motion caused her to turn pale there was the mark again, a crimson stain upon the snow, in what Aylmer sometimes deemed an almost fearful distinctness. Its shape bore not a little similarity to the human hand, though of the smallest pygmy size. Georgiana's lovers were wont to say that some fairy at her birth-hour had laid her tiny hand upon the infant's cheek, and left this impress there in token of the magic endowments that were to give her such sway over all hearts. Many a desperate swain would have risked life for the privilege of pressing his lips to the mysterious hand. It must not be concealed, however, that the impression wrought by this fairy sign-manual varied exceedingly according to the difference of temperament in the beholders. Some fastidious persons—but they were exclusively of her own sex—affirmed that the bloody hand, as they chose to call it, quite destroyed the effect of Georgiana's beauty and rendered her countenance even hideous. But it would be as reasonable to say that one of those small blue stains which sometimes occur in the purest statuary marble would convert the Eve of Powers[3] to a monster. Masculine observers, if the birth-mark did not heighten their admiration, contented themselves with wishing it away, that the world might possess one living specimen of ideal loveliness without the semblance of a flaw. After his marriage—for he thought little or nothing of the matter before—Aylmer discovered that this was the case with himself.

Had she been less beautiful—if Envy's self could have found aught else to sneer at—he might have felt his affection heightened by the prettiness of this mimic hand, now vaguely portrayed, now lost, now stealing forth again and glimmering to and fro with every pulse of emotion that throbbed within her heart; but, seeing her otherwise so perfect, he found this one defect grow more and more intolerable with every moment of their united lives. It was the fatal

3. Hiram Powers (1805–73), American sculptor and friend of Hawthorne, produced noted marble statues, including *Eve Tempted* and *Eve Disconsolate*.

flaw of humanity which Nature, in one shape or another, stamps ineffaceably on all her productions, either to imply that they are temporary and finite, or that their perfection must be wrought by toil and pain. The crimson hand expressed the ineludible gripe in which mortality clutches the highest and purest of earthly mould, degrading them into kindred with the lowest, and even with the very brutes, like whom their visible frames return to dust. In this manner, selecting it as the symbol of his wife's liability to sin, sorrow, decay, and death, Aylmer's somber imagination was not long in rendering the birth-mark a frightful object, causing him more trouble and horror than ever Georgiana's beauty, whether of soul or sense, had given him delight.

At all the seasons which should have been their happiest he invariably, and without intending it, nay, in spite of a purpose to the contrary, reverted to this one disastrous topic. Trifling as it at first appeared, it so connected itself with innumerable trains of thought and modes of feeling that it became the central point of all. With the morning twilight Aylmer opened his eyes upon his wife's face and recognized the symbol of imperfection; and when they sat together at the evening hearth his eyes wandered stealthily to her cheek, and beheld, flickering with the blaze of the wood-fire, the spectral hand that wrote mortality where he would fain[4] have worshipped. Georgiana soon learned to shudder at his gaze. It needed but a glance with the peculiar expression that his face often wore to change the roses of her cheek into a death-like paleness, amid which the crimson hand was brought strongly out, like a bas-relief of ruby on the whitest marble.

10   Late one night, when the lights were growing dim so as hardly to betray the stain on the poor wife's cheek, she herself, for the first time, voluntarily took up the subject.

"Do you remember, my dear Aylmer," said she, with a feeble attempt at a smile, "have you any recollection, of a dream last night about this odious hand?"

"None! none whatever!" replied Aylmer, starting; but then he added, in a dry, cold tone, affected for the sake of concealing the real depth of his emotion, "I might well dream of it; for, before I fell asleep, it had taken a pretty firm hold of my fancy."

"And you did dream of it?" continued Georgiana, hastily; for she dreaded lest a gush of tears should interrupt what she had to say. "A terrible dream! I wonder that you can forget it. Is it possible to forget this one expression?—'It is in her heart now; we must have it out!' Reflect, my husband; for by all means I would have you recall that dream."

The mind is in a sad state when Sleep, the all-involving, cannot confine her specters within the dim region of her sway, but suffers them to break forth, affrighting this actual life with secrets that perchance belong to a deeper one. Aylmer now remembered his dream. He had fancied himself with his servant Aminadab attempting an operation for the removal of the birth-mark; but the deeper went the knife, the deeper sank the hand, until at length its tiny grasp appeared to have caught hold of Georgiana's heart; whence, however, her husband was inexorably resolved to cut or wrench it away.

4. Eagerly, preferably.

When the dream had shaped itself perfectly in his memory, Aylmer sat in his 15 wife's presence with a guilty feeling. Truth often finds its way to the mind close muffled in robes of sleep, and then speaks with uncompromising directness of matters in regard to which we practice an unconscious self-deception during our waking moments. Until now he had not been aware of the tyrannizing influence acquired by one idea over his mind, and of the lengths which he might find in his heart to go for the sake of giving himself peace.

"Aylmer," resumed Georgiana, solemnly, "I know not what may be the cost to both of us to rid me of this fatal birth-mark. Perhaps its removal may cause cureless deformity; or it may be the stain goes as deep as life itself. Again: do we know that there is a possibility, on any terms, of unclasping the firm gripe of this little hand which was laid upon me before I came into the world?"

"Dearest Georgiana, I have spent much thought upon the subject," hastily interrupted Aylmer. "I am convinced of the perfect practicability of its removal."

"If there be the remotest possibility of it," continued Georgiana, "let the attempt be made, at whatever risk. Danger is nothing to me; for life, while this hateful mark makes me the object of your horror and disgust—life is a burden which I would fling down with joy. Either remove this dreadful hand, or take my wretched life! You have deep science. All the world bears witness of it. You have achieved great wonders. Cannot you remove this little, little mark, which I cover with the tips of two small fingers? Is this beyond your power, for the sake of your own peace, and to save your poor wife from madness?"

"Noblest, dearest, tenderest wife," cried Aylmer, rapturously, "doubt not my power. I have already given this matter the deepest thought—thought which might almost have enlightened me to create a being less perfect than yourself. Georgiana, you have led me deeper than ever into the heart of science. I feel myself fully competent to render this dear cheek as faultless as its fellow; and then, most beloved, what will be my triumph when I shall have corrected what Nature left imperfect in her fairest work! Even Pygmalion,[5] when his sculptured woman assumed life, felt not greater ecstasy than mine will be."

"It is resolved, then," said Georgiana, faintly smiling. "And, Aylmer, spare me 20 not, though you should find the birth-mark take refuge in my heart at last."

Her husband tenderly kissed her cheek—her right cheek—not that which bore the impress of the crimson hand.

The next day Aylmer apprised his wife of a plan that he had formed whereby he might have opportunity for the intense thought and constant watchfulness which the proposed operation would require; while Georgiana, likewise, would enjoy the perfect repose essential to its success. They were to seclude themselves in the extensive apartments occupied by Aylmer as a laboratory, and where, during his toilsome youth, he had made discoveries in the elemental powers of Nature that had roused the admiration of all the learned societies in Europe. Seated calmly in this laboratory, the pale philosopher had investigated the secrets of the highest cloud-region and of the profoundest mines; he had satisfied himself of the causes that kindled and kept alive the fires of the volcano; and had explained the mystery of fountains, and how it is that they gush

---

5. Pygmalion was a legendary artist of Cyprus who fell in love with the statue he made of a beautiful woman; in Ovid's *Metamorphoses* (8 CE), she comes to life.

forth, some so bright and pure, and others with such rich medicinal virtues, from the dark bosom of the earth. Here, too, at an earlier period, he had studied the wonders of the human frame, and attempted to fathom the very process by which Nature assimilates all her precious influences from earth and air, and from the spiritual world, to create and foster man, her masterpiece. The latter pursuit, however, Aylmer had long laid aside in unwilling recognition of the truth—against which all seekers sooner or later stumble—that our great creative Mother, while she amuses us with apparently working in the broadest sunshine, is yet severely careful to keep her own secrets, and, in spite of her pretended openness, shows us nothing but results. She permits us, indeed, to mar, but seldom to mend, and, like a jealous patentee, on no account to make. Now, however, Aylmer resumed these half-forgotten investigations; not, of course, with such hopes or wishes as first suggested them; but because they involved much physiological truth and lay in the path of his proposed scheme for the treatment of Georgiana.

As he led her over the threshold of the laboratory Georgiana was cold and tremulous. Aylmer looked cheerfully into her face, with intent to reassure her, but was so startled with the intense glow of the birth-mark upon the whiteness of her cheek that he could not restrain a strong convulsive shudder. His wife fainted.

"Aminadab! Aminadab!" shouted Aylmer, stamping violently on the floor.

25   Forthwith there issued from an inner apartment a man of low stature, but bulky frame, with shaggy hair hanging about his visage, which was grimed with the vapors of the furnace. This personage had been Aylmer's underworker during his whole scientific career, and was admirably fitted for that office by his great mechanical readiness, and the skill with which, while incapable of comprehending a single principle, he executed all the details of his master's experiments. With his vast strength, his shaggy hair, his smoky aspect, and the indescribable earthiness that incrusted him, he seemed to represent man's physical nature; while Aylmer's slender figure, and pale, intellectual face, were no less apt a type of the spiritual element.

"Throw open the door of the boudoir, Aminadab," said Aylmer, "and burn a pastil."[6]

"Yes, master," answered Aminadab, looking intently at the lifeless form of Georgiana; and then he muttered to himself, "If she were my wife, I'd never part with that birth-mark."

When Georgiana recovered consciousness she found herself breathing an atmosphere of penetrating fragrance, the gentle potency of which had recalled her from her death-like faintness. The scene around her looked like enchantment. Aylmer had converted those smoky, dingy, somber rooms, where he had spent his brightest years in recondite pursuits, into a series of beautiful apartments not unfit to be the secluded abode of a lovely woman. The walls were hung with gorgeous curtains, which imparted the combination of grandeur and grace that no other species of adornment can achieve; and, as they fell from the ceiling to the floor, their rich and ponderous folds, concealing all angles and straight lines, appeared to shut in the scene from infinite space. For aught

---

6. Pastille, a lozenge or tablet of medicinal incense.

Georgiana knew, it might be a pavilion among the clouds. And Aylmer, excluding the sunshine, which would have interfered with his chemical processes, had supplied its place with perfumed lamps, emitting flames of various hue, but all uniting in a soft, impurpled radiance. He now knelt by his wife's side, watching her earnestly, but without alarm; for he was confident in his science, and felt that he could draw a magic circle round her within which no evil might intrude.

"Where am I? Ah, I remember," said Georgiana, faintly; and she placed her hand over her cheek to hide the terrible mark from her husband's eyes.

"Fear not, dearest!" exclaimed he. "Do not shrink from me! Believe me, 30 Georgiana, I even rejoice in this single imperfection, since it will be such a rapture to remove it."

"O, spare me!" sadly replied his wife. "Pray do not look at it again. I never can forget that convulsive shudder."

In order to soothe Georgiana, and, as it were, to release her mind from the burden of actual things, Aylmer now put in practice some of the light and playful secrets which science had taught him among its profounder lore. Airy figures, absolutely bodiless ideas, and forms of unsubstantial beauty came and danced before her, imprinting their momentary footsteps on beams of light. Though she had some indistinct idea of the method of these optical phenomena, still the illusion was almost perfect enough to warrant the belief that her husband possessed say over the spiritual world. Then again, when she felt a wish to look forth from her seclusion, immediately, as if her thoughts were answered, the procession of external existence flitted across a screen. The scenery and the figures of actual life were perfectly represented but with that bewitching yet indescribable difference which always makes a picture, an image, or a shadow so much more attractive than the original. When wearied of this, Aylmer bade her cast her eyes upon a vessel containing a quantity of earth. She did so, with little interest at first; but was soon startled to perceive the germ of a plant shooting upward from the soil. Then came the slender stalk; the leaves gradually unfolded themselves; and amid them was a perfect and lovely flower.

"It is magical!" cried Georgiana. "I dare not touch it."

"Nay, pluck it," answered Aylmer—"pluck it, and inhale its brief perfume while you may. The flower will wither in a few moments and leave nothing save its brown seed vessels; but thence may be perpetuated a race as ephemeral as itself."

But Georgiana had no sooner touched the flower than the whole plant suf- 35 fered a blight, its leaves turning coal-black as if by the agency of fire.

"There was too powerful a stimulus," said Aylmer, thoughtfully.

To make up for this abortive experiment, he proposed to take her portrait by a scientific process of his own invention. It was to be affected by rays of light striking upon a polished plate of metal. Georgiana assented; but, on looking at the result, was affrighted to find the features of the portrait blurred and indefinable; while the minute figure of a hand appeared where the cheek should have been. Aylmer snatched the metallic plate and threw it into a jar of corrosive acid.

Soon, however, he forgot these mortifying failures. In the intervals of study and chemical experiment he came to her flushed and exhausted, but seemed invigorated by her presence, and spoke in glowing language of the resources of his art. He gave a history of the long dynasty of the alchemists, who spent so many ages in quest of the universal solvent by which the golden principle might be elicited from all things vile and base.[7] Aylmer appeared to believe that, by the plainest scientific logic, it was altogether within the limits of possibility to discover this long-sought medium. "But," he added, "a philosopher who should go deep enough to acquire the power would attain too lofty a wisdom to stoop to the exercise of it." Not less singular were his opinions in regard to the elixir vitae.[8] He more than intimated that it was at his option to concoct a liquid that should prolong life for years, perhaps interminably; but that it would produce a discord in Nature which all the world, and chiefly the quaffer of the immortal nostrum, would find cause to curse.

"Aylmer, are you in earnest?" asked Georgiana, looking at him with amazement and fear. "It is terrible to possess such power, or even to dream of possessing it."

40   "O, do not tremble, my love," said her husband. "I would not wrong either you or myself by working such inharmonious effects upon our lives; but I would have you consider how trifling, in comparison, is the skill requisite to remove this little hand."

At the mention of the birth-mark, Georgiana, as usual, shrank as if a red-hot iron had touched her cheek.

Again Aylmer applied himself to his labors. She could hear his voice in the distant furnace-room giving directions to Aminadab, whose harsh, uncouth, misshapen tones were audible in response, more like the grunt or growl of a brute than human speech. After hours of absence, Aylmer reappeared and proposed that she should now examine his cabinet of chemical products and natural treasures of the earth. Among the former he showed her a small vial, in which, he remarked, was contained a gentle yet most powerful fragrance, capable of impregnating all the breezes that blow across a kingdom. They were of inestimable value, the contents of that little vial; and, as he said so, he threw some of the perfume into the air and filled the room with piercing and invigorating delight.

"And what is this?" asked Georgiana, pointing to a small crystal globe containing a gold-colored liquid. "It is so beautiful to the eye that I could imagine it the elixir of life."

"In one sense it is," replied Aylmer; "or rather, the elixir of immortality. It is the most precious poison that ever was concocted in this world. By its aid I could apportion the lifetime of any mortal at whom you might point your finger. The strength of the dose would determine whether he were to linger out years, or drop dead in the midst of a breath. No king on his guarded throne could keep his life if I, in my private station, should deem that the welfare of millions justified me in depriving him of it."

45   "Why do you keep such a terrific drug?" inquired Georgiana, in horror.

"Do not mistrust me, dearest," said her husband, smiling; "its virtuous potency is yet greater than its harmful one. But see! here is a powerful cosmetic. With a

---

7. Before the advent of modern chemistry, alchemists studied the properties of matter in a search for spiritual essences and the secret of transforming base metals into gold.
8. Literally, the drink or potion of life (Latin), imagined to give immortality.

few drops of this in a vase of water, freckles may be washed away as easily as the hands are cleansed. A stronger infusion would take the blood out of the cheek, and leave the rosiest beauty a pale ghost."

"Is it with this lotion that you intend to bathe my cheek?" asked Georgiana, anxiously.

"O no," hastily replied her husband; "this is merely superficial. Your case demands a remedy that shall go deeper."

In his interviews with Georgiana, Aylmer generally made minute inquiries as to her sensations, and whether the confinement of the rooms and the temperature of the atmosphere agreed with her. These questions had such a particular drift that Georgiana began to conjecture that she was already subjected to certain physical influences, either breathed in with the fragrant air or taken with her food. She fancied likewise, but it might be altogether fancy, that there was a stirring up of her system—a strange, indefinite sensation creeping through her veins, and tingling, half painfully, half pleasurably, at her heart. Still, whenever she dared to look into the mirror, there she beheld herself pale as a white rose and with the crimson birth-mark stamped upon her cheek. Not even Aylmer now hated it so much as she.

To dispel the tedium of the hours which her husband found it necessary to 50 devote to the processes of combination and analysis, Georgiana turned over the volumes of his scientific library. In many dark old tomes she met with chapters full of romance and poetry. They were the works of the philosophers of the Middle Ages, such as Albertus Magnus, Cornelius Agrippa, Paracelsus, and the famous friar who created the prophetic Brazen Head.[9] All these antique naturalists stood in advance of their centuries, yet were imbued with some of their credulity, and therefore were believed, and perhaps imagined themselves to have acquired from the investigation of Nature a power above Nature, and from physics a sway over the spiritual world. Hardly less curious and imaginative were the early volumes of the Transactions of the Royal Society,[1] in which the members, knowing little of the limits of natural possibility, were continually recording wonders or proposing methods whereby wonders might be wrought.

But, to Georgiana, the most engrossing volume was a large folio from her husband's own hand, in which he had recorded every experiment of his scientific career, its original aim, the methods adopted for its development, and its final success or failure, with the circumstances to which either event was attributable. The book, in truth, was both the history and emblem of his ardent, ambitious, imaginative, yet practical and laborious life. He handled physical details as if there were nothing beyond them; yet spiritualized them all, and redeemed himself from materialism by his strong and eager aspiration towards the infinite. In his grasp the veriest clod of earth assumed a soul. Georgiana, as she read, reverenced Aylmer and loved him more profoundly than ever, but with a less entire dependence on his judgment than heretofore. Much as he had

9. The Brazen Head, a brass bust of a man, was supposed to be able to answer any question; the "famous friar" is Roger Bacon (c. 1219–c. 92), an English natural philosopher, as scientists were then called. Albertus Magnus (1193?–1280), Agrippa (1486–1535), and Paracelsus (1493–1541) were all European experimenters reputed to have near-magical powers in alchemy or astrology.

1. *The Philosophical Transactions of the Royal Society* is the oldest English-language scientific journal, published since 1665.

accomplished, she could not but observe that his most splendid successes were almost invariably failures, if compared with the ideal at which he aimed. His brightest diamonds were the merest pebbles, and felt to be so by himself, in comparison with the inestimable gems which lay hidden beyond his reach. The volume, rich with achievements that had won renown for its author, was yet as melancholy a record as ever mortal hand had penned. It was the sad confession and continual exemplification of the shortcomings of the composite man, the spirit burdened with clay and working in matter, and of the despair that assails the higher nature at finding itself so miserably thwarted by the earthly part. Perhaps every man of genius, in whatever sphere, might recognize the image of his own experience in Aylmer's journal.

So deeply did these reflections affect Georgiana that she laid her face upon the open volume and burst into tears. In this situation she was found by her husband.

"It is dangerous to read in a sorcerer's books," said he with a smile, though his countenance was uneasy and displeased. "Georgiana, there are pages in that volume which I can scarcely glance over and keep my senses. Take heed lest it prove as detrimental to you."

"It has made me worship you more than ever," said she.

55   "Ah, wait for this one success," rejoined he, "then worship me if you will. I shall deem myself hardly unworthy of it. But come, I have sought you for the luxury of your voice. Sing to me, dearest."

So she poured out the liquid music of her voice to quench the thirst of his spirit. He then took his leave with a boyish exuberance of gayety, assuring her that her seclusion would endure but a little longer, and that the result was already certain. Scarcely had he departed when Georgiana felt irresistibly impelled to follow him. She had forgotten to inform Aylmer of a symptom which for two or three hours past had begun to excite her attention. It was a sensation in the fatal birth-mark, not painful, but which induced a restlessness through-out her system. Hastening after her husband, she intruded for the first time into the laboratory.

The first thing that struck her eye was the furnace, that hot and feverish worker, with the intense glow of its fire, which by the quantities of soot clus-tered above it seemed to have been burning for ages. There was a distilling-apparatus in full operation. Around the room were retorts, tubes, cylinders, crucibles, and other apparatus of chemical research. An electrical machine stood ready for immediate use. The atmosphere felt oppressively close, and was tainted with gaseous odors which had been tormented forth by the processes of science. The severe and homely simplicity of the apartment, with its naked walls and brick pavement, looked strange, accustomed as Georgiana had become to the fantastic elegance of her boudoir. But what chiefly, indeed almost solely, drew her attention, was the aspect of Aylmer himself.

He was pale as death, anxious and absorbed, and hung over the furnace as if it depended upon his utmost watchfulness whether the liquid which it was dis-tilling should be the draught of immortal happiness or misery. How different from the sanguine and joyous mien that he had assumed for Georgiana's encouragement!

"Carefully now, Aminadab; carefully, thou human machine; carefully, thou man of clay," muttered Aylmer, more to himself than his assistant. "Now, if there be a thought too much or too little, it is all over."

"Ho! ho!" mumbled Aminadab. "Look, master! look!" 60

Aylmer raised his eyes hastily, and at first reddened, then grew paler than ever, on beholding Georgiana. He rushed towards her and seized her arm with a gripe that left the print of his fingers upon it.

"Why do you come hither? Have you no trust in your husband?" cried he, impetuously. "Would you throw the blight of that fatal birth-mark over my labors? It is not well done. Go, prying woman! go!"

"Nay, Aylmer," said Georgiana with the firmness of which she possessed no stinted endowment, "it is not you that have a right to complain. You mistrust your wife; you have concealed the anxiety with which you watch the development of this experiment. Think not so unworthily of me, my husband. Tell me all the risk we run, and fear not that I shall shrink; for my share in it is far less than your own."

"No, no, Georgiana!" said Aylmer, impatiently; "it must not be."

"I submit," replied she, calmly. "And, Aylmer, I shall quaff whatever draught 65 you bring me; but it will be on the same principle that would induce me to take a dose of poison if offered by your hand."

"My noble wife," said Aylmer, deeply moved, "I knew not the height and depth of your nature until now. Nothing shall be concealed. Know, then, that this crimson hand, superficial as it seems, has clutched its grasp into your being with a strength of which I had no previous conception. I have already administered agents powerful enough to do aught except to change your entire physical system. Only one thing remains to be tried. If that fail us we are ruined."

"Why did you hesitate to tell me this?" asked she.

"Because, Georgiana," said Aylmer, in a low voice, "there is danger."

"Danger? There is but one danger—that this horrible stigma shall be left upon my cheek!" cried Georgiana. "Remove it, remove it, whatever be the cost, or we shall both go mad!"

"Heaven knows your words are too true," said Aylmer, sadly. "And now, dear- 70 est, return to your boudoir. In a little while all will be tested."

He conducted her back and took leave of her with a solemn tenderness which spoke far more than his words how much was now at stake. After his departure Georgiana became rapt in musings. She considered the character of Aylmer, and did it completer justice than at any previous moment. Her heart exulted, while it trembled, at his honorable love—so pure and lofty that it would accept nothing less than perfection, nor miserably make itself contented with an earthlier nature than he had dreamed of. She felt how much more precious was such a sentiment than that meaner kind which would have borne with the imperfection for her sake, and have been guilty of treason to holy love by degrading its perfect idea to the level of the actual; and with her whole spirit she prayed that, for a single moment, she might satisfy his highest and deepest conception. Longer than one moment she well knew it could not be; for his spirit was ever on the march, ever ascending, and each instant required something that was beyond the scope of the instant before.

The sound of her husband's footsteps aroused her. He bore a crystal goblet containing a liquor colorless as water, but bright enough to be the draught of immortality. Aylmer was pale; but it seemed rather the consequence of a highly wrought state of mind and tension of spirit than of fear or doubt.

"The concoction of the draught has been perfect," said he, in answer to Georgiana's look. "Unless all my science have deceived me, it cannot fail."

"Save on your account, my dearest Aylmer," observed his wife, "I might wish to put off this birth-mark of mortality by relinquishing mortality itself in preference to any other mode. Life is but a sad possession to those who have attained precisely the degree of moral advancement at which I stand. Were I weaker and blinder, it might be happiness. Were I stronger, it might be endured hopefully. But, being what I find myself, methinks I am of all mortals the most fit to die."

75   "You are fit for heaven without tasting death!" replied her husband. "But why do we speak of dying? The draught cannot fail. Behold its effect upon this plant."

On the window-seat there stood a geranium diseased with yellow blotches, which had overspread all its leaves. Aylmer poured a small quantity of the liquid upon the soil in which it grew. In a little time, when the roots of the plant had taken up the moisture, the unsightly blotches began to be extinguished in a living verdure.

"There needed no proof," said Georgiana, quietly. "Give me the goblet. I joyfully stake all upon your word."

"Drink, then, thou lofty creature!" exclaimed Aylmer, with fervid admiration. "There is no taint of imperfection on thy spirit. Thy sensible frame, too, shall soon be all perfect."

She quaffed the liquid and returned the goblet to his hand.

80   "It is grateful," said she, with a placid smile. "Methinks it is like water from a heavenly fountain; for it contains I know not what of unobtrusive fragrance and deliciousness. It allays a feverish thirst that had parched me for many days. Now, dearest, let me sleep. My earthly senses are closing over my spirit like the leaves around the heart of a rose at sunset."

She spoke the last words with a gentle reluctance, as if it required almost more energy than she could command to pronounce the faint and lingering syllables. Scarcely had they loitered through her lips ere she was lost in slumber. Aylmer sat by her side, watching her aspect with the emotions proper to a man, the whole value of whose existence was involved in the process now to be tested. Mingled with this mood, however, was the philosophic investigation characteristic of the man of science. Not the minutest symptom escaped him. A heightened flush of the cheek, a slight irregularity of breath, a quiver of the eyelid, a hardly perceptible tremor through the frame—such were the details which, as the moments passed, he wrote down in his folio volume. Intense thought had set its stamp upon every previous page of that volume; but the thoughts of years were all concentrated upon the last.

While thus employed, he failed not to gaze often at the fatal hand, and not without a shudder. Yet once, by a strange and unaccountable impulse, he pressed it with his lips. His spirit recoiled, however, in the very act; and Georgiana, out of the midst of her deep sleep, moved uneasily and murmured, as if in remonstrance. Again Aylmer resumed his watch. Nor was it without avail.

The crimson hand, which at first had been strongly visible upon the marble paleness of Georgiana's cheek, now grew more faintly outlined. She remained not less pale than ever; but the birth-mark, with every breath that came and went, lost somewhat of its former distinctness. Its presence had been awful; its departure was more awful still. Watch the stain of the rainbow fading out of the sky, and you will know how that mysterious symbol passed away.

"By Heaven! it is wellnigh gone!" said Aylmer to himself, in almost irrepressible ecstasy. "I can scarcely trace it now. Success! success! And now it is like the faintest rose-color. The lightest flush of blood across her cheek would overcome it. But she is so pale!"

He drew aside the window-curtain and suffered the light of natural day to fall into the room and rest upon her cheek. At the same time he heard a gross, hoarse chuckle, which he had long known as his servant Aminadab's expression of delight.

"Ah, clod! ah, earthly mass!" cried Aylmer, laughing in a sort of frenzy, "you have served me well! Matter and spirit—earth and heaven—have both done their part in this! Laugh, thing of the senses! You have earned the right to laugh."

These exclamations broke Georgiana's sleep. She slowly unclosed her eyes and gazed into the mirror which her husband had arranged for that purpose. A faint smile flitted over her lips when she recognized how barely perceptible was now that crimson hand which had once blazed forth with such disastrous brilliancy as to scare away all their happiness. But then her eyes sought Aylmer's face with a trouble and anxiety that he could by no means account for.

"My poor Aylmer!" murmured she.

"Poor? Nay, richest, happiest, most favored!" exclaimed he. "My peerless bride, it is successful! You are perfect!"

"My poor Aylmer," she repeated, with a more than human tenderness, "you have aimed loftily; you have done nobly. Do not repent that, with so high and pure a feeling, you have rejected the best the earth could offer. Aylmer, dearest Aylmer, I am dying!"

Alas! it was too true! The fatal hand had grappled with the mystery of life, and was the bond by which an angelic spirit kept itself in union with a mortal frame. As the last crimson tint of the birth-mark—that sole token of human imperfection—faded from her cheek, the parting breath of the now perfect woman passed into the atmosphere, and her soul, lingering a moment near her husband, took its heavenward flight. Then a hoarse, chuckling laugh was heard again! Thus ever does the gross fatality of earth exult in its invariable triumph over the immortal essence which, in this dim sphere of half-development, demands the completeness of a higher state. Yet, had Aylmer reached a profounder wisdom, he need not thus have flung away the happiness which would have woven his mortal life of the self-same texture with the celestial. The momentary circumstance was too strong for him; he failed to look beyond the shadowy scope of time, and, living once for all in eternity, to find the perfect future in the present.

1843

QUESTIONS

1. What difference would it make if the mark on Georgiana's cheek were shaped like a fish, a heart, or an irregular oval? Why (and when) does the mark appear redder or more visible or faint? If the birthmark is explicitly a "symbol of imperfection" (par. 9), what *kinds* of imperfection does it represent?
2. Aylmer says to his wife, "Even Pygmalion, when his sculptured woman assumed life, felt not greater ecstasy than mine will be" (par. 19). How does this literary allusion to the myth of Pygmalion enhance the meaning of THE BIRTH-MARK? Is this allusion ironic, given what happens to Alymer's project to make his wife perfect?
3. Look closely at the specific settings of the story, from the laboratory to the boudoir. Note the similes, metaphors, and other figures of speech that help characterize these places. How do these different patterns of imagery contribute to the symbolism of the story? to an allegorical reading of the story?

A. S. BYATT

(b. 1936)

The Thing in the Forest

The oldest of four children (and sister of novelist Margaret Drabble), Antonia Susan Byatt was born in Sheffield, England; graduated from Newnham College, Cambridge; and worked toward a PhD in English literature at Bryn Mawr College in Pennsylvania and at the University of Oxford. In the early 1960s Byatt began teaching at the University of London and published her first novel, *The Shadow of the Sun* (1964). By far the most successful of the numerous works that followed is *Possession: A Romance* (1990), the Booker Prize–winning best seller that inspired a 1996 film starring Gwyneth Paltrow. Interweaving the story of the unlikely romance between two Victorian poets reminiscent of Christina Rossetti and Robert Browning, on the one hand, with the tale of the two modern academics who uncover it, on the other, along with poems and tales ostensibly written by its protagonists, *Possession* is simultaneously a fascinating blend of literary genres—from detective and historical fiction to romance, fairy tale, and dramatic monologue—and a reflection *on* literature—how we use it to make sense of and thus "possess" our present and our past, and why it often takes "possession" of us. In this, it resembles other Byatt novels such as *The Children's Book* (2009), the novellas in *Angels and Insects* (1992), and many of her short stories. Made a Dame Commander of the British Empire in 1999, Dame Byatt is also a distinguished literary critic who has written books on novelist Iris Murdoch and on poets William Wordsworth and Samuel Taylor Coleridge, as well as *Portraits in Fiction* (2001), a collection of biographical essays.

There were once two little girls who saw, or believed they saw, a thing in a forest. The two little girls were evacuees, who had been sent away from the city by train with a large number of other children.[1] They all had their names attached to their coats with safety pins, and they carried little bags or satchels, and the regulation gas mask. They wore knitted scarves and bonnets or caps, and many had knitted gloves attached to long tapes that ran along their sleeves, inside their coats, and over their shoulders and out, so that they could leave their ten woollen fingers dangling, like a spare pair of hands, like a scarecrow. They all had bare legs and scuffed shoes and wrinkled socks. Most had wounds on their knees in varying stages of freshness and scabbiness. They were at the age when children fall often and their knees were unprotected. With their suitcases, some of which were almost too big to carry, and their other impedimenta, a doll, a toy car, a comic, they were like a disorderly dwarf regiment, stomping along the platform.

The two little girls had not met before, and made friends on the train. They shared a square of chocolate, and took alternate bites at an apple. Their names were Penny and Primrose. Penny was thin and dark and taller, possibly older, than Primrose, who was plump and blond and curly. Primrose had bitten nails, and a velvet collar on her dressy green coat. Penny had a bloodless transparent paleness, a touch of blue in her fine lips. Neither of them knew where they were going, nor how long the journey might take. They did not even know why they were going, since neither of their mothers had quite known how to explain the danger to them. How do you say to your child, I am sending you away, because enemy bombs may fall out of the sky, but I myself am staying here, in what I believe may be daily danger of burning, being buried alive, gas, and ultimately perhaps a gray army rolling in on tanks over the suburbs? So the mothers (who did not resemble each other at all) behaved alike, and explained nothing—it was easier. Their daughters, they knew, were little girls, who would not be able to understand or imagine.

The girls discussed whether it was a sort of holiday or a sort of punishment, or a bit of both. Both had the idea that these were all perhaps not very good children, possibly being sent away for that reason. They were pleased to be able to define each other as "nice." They would stick together, they agreed.

The train crawled sluggishly farther and farther away from the city and their homes. It was not a clean train—the upholstery of their carriage had the dank smell of unwashed trousers, and the gusts of hot steam rolling backward past their windows were full of specks of flimsy ash, and sharp grit, and occasionally fiery sparks that pricked face and fingers like hot needles if you opened the window. It was very noisy, too, whenever it picked up a little speed. The window-panes were both grimy and misted up. The train stopped frequently, and when it stopped they used their gloves to wipe rounds, through which they peered out at flooded fields, furrowed hillsides, and tiny stations whose names were carefully blacked out, whose platforms were empty of life.

---

1. The story begins during the Blitz—that is, during the period (1940–41) when British cities were frequently bombed by German warplanes. Many children were evacuated from cities to safer locations in the countryside.

5   The children did not know that the namelessness was meant to baffle or delude an invading army. They felt—they did not think it out, but somewhere inside them the idea sprouted—that the erasure was because of them, because they were not meant to know where they were going or, like Hansel and Gretel, to find the way back. They did not speak to each other of this anxiety, but began the kind of conversation children have about things they really dislike, things that upset, or disgust, or frighten them. Semolina pudding with its grainy texture, mushy peas, fat on roast meat. Having your head held roughly back over the basin to have your hair washed, with cold water running down inside your liberty bodice. Gangs in playgrounds. They felt the pressure of all the other alien children in all the other carriages as a potential gang. They shared another square of chocolate, and licked their fingers, and looked out at a great white goose flapping its wings beside an inky pond.

    The sky grew dark gray and in the end the train halted. The children got out, and lined up in a crocodile,[2] and were led to a mud-colored bus. Penny and Primrose managed to get a seat together, although it was over the wheel, and both of them began to feel sick as the bus bumped along snaking country lanes, under whipping branches, with torn strips of thin cloud streaming across a full moon.

    They were billeted in a mansion commandeered from its owner. The children were told they were there temporarily, until families were found to take them. Penny and Primrose held hands, and said to each other that it would be wizard if they could go to the same family, because at least they would have each other. They didn't say anything to the rather tired-looking ladies who were ordering them about, because, with the cunning of little children, they knew that requests were most often counterproductive—adults liked saying no. They imagined possible families into which they might be thrust. They did not discuss what they imagined, as these pictures, like the black station signs, were too frightening, and words might make some horror solid, in some magical way. Penny, who was a reading child, imagined Victorian dark pillars of severity, like Jane Eyre's Mr. Brocklehurst, or David Copperfield's Mr. Murdstone. Primrose imagined—she didn't know why—a fat woman with a white cap and round red arms who smiled nicely but made the children wear sacking aprons and scrub the steps and the stove. "It's like we were orphans," she said to Penny. "But we're not." Penny said, "If we manage to stick together. . . ."

The great house had a double flight of imposing stairs to its front door, and carved griffins and unicorns on its balustrade. There was no lighting, because of the blackout. All the windows were shuttered. The children trudged up the staircase in their crocodile, and were given supper (Irish stew and rice pudding with a dollop of blood-red jam) before going to bed in long makeshift dormitories, where once servants had slept. They had camp beds (military issue) and gray shoddy blankets. Penny and Primrose got beds together but couldn't get a corner. They queued[3] to brush their teeth in a tiny washroom, and both suffered (again without speaking) suffocating anxiety about what would happen if they

---

2. Group of people lined up two by two.
3. Lined up.

wanted to pee in the middle of the night. They also suffered from a fear that in the dark the other children would start laughing and rushing and teasing, and turn themselves into a gang. But that did not happen. Everyone was tired and anxious and orphaned. An uneasy silence, a drift of perturbed sleep, came over them all. The only sounds—from all parts of the great dormitory, it seemed— were suppressed snuffles and sobs, from faces pressed into thin pillows.

When daylight came, things seemed, as they mostly do, brighter and better. The children were given breakfast in a large vaulted room, at trestle tables, porridge made with water, and a dab of the red jam, heavy cups of strong tea. Then they were told they could go out and play until lunchtime. Children in those days—wherever they came from—were not closely watched, were allowed to come and go freely, and those evacuated children were not herded into any kind of holding pen or transit camp. They were told they should be back for lunch at twelve-thirty, by which time those in charge hoped to have sorted out their provisional future lives. It was not known how they would know when it was twelve-thirty, but it was expected that—despite the fact that few of them had wristwatches—they would know how to keep an eye on the time. It was what they were used to.

Penny and Primrose went out together, in their respectable coats and laced shoes, onto the terrace. The terrace appeared to them to be vast. It was covered with a fine layer of damp gravel, stained here and there bright green, or invaded by mosses. Beyond it was a stone balustrade, with a staircase leading down to a lawn. Across the lawn was a sculpted yew hedge. In the middle of the hedge was a wicket gate, and beyond the gate were trees. A forest, the little girls said to themselves.

"Let's go into the forest," said Penny, as though the sentence were required of her.

Primrose hesitated. Most of the other children were running up and down the terrace. Some boys were kicking a ball on the grass.

"O.K.," said Primrose. "We needn't go far."

"No. I've never been in a forest."

"Nor me."

"We ought to look at it, while we've got the opportunity," said Penny.

There was a very small child—one of the smallest—whose name, she told everyone, was Alys. With a "y," she told those who could spell, and those who couldn't, which surely included herself. She was barely out of nappies.[4] She was quite extraordinarily pretty, pink and white, with large pale-blue eyes, and sparse little golden curls all over her head and neck, through which her pink skin could be seen. Nobody seemed to be in charge of her, no elder brother or sister. She had not quite managed to wash the tearstains from her dimpled cheeks.

She had made several attempts to attach herself to Penny and Primrose. They did not want her. They were excited about meeting and liking each other. She said now, "I'm coming, too, into the forest."

"No, you aren't," said Primrose.

"You are too little, you must stay here," said Penny.

"You'll get lost," said Primrose.

4. Diapers.

"You won't get lost. I'll come with you," said the little creature, with an engaging smile, made for loving parents and grandparents.

"We don't want you, you see," said Primrose.

"It's for your own good," said Penny.

25   Alys went on smiling hopefully, the smile becoming more of a mask.

"It will be all right," said Alys.

"Run," said Primrose.

They ran; they ran down the steps and across the lawn, and through the gate, into the forest. They didn't look back. They were long-legged little girls. The trees were silent round them, holding out their branches to the sun.

Primrose touched the warm skin of the nearest saplings, taking off her gloves to feel the cracks and knots. Penny looked into the thick of the forest. There was undergrowth—a mat of brambles and bracken. There were no obvious paths. Dark and light came and went, inviting and mysterious, as the wind pushed clouds across the face of the sun.

30   "We have to be careful not to get lost," she said. "In stories, people make marks on tree trunks, or unroll a thread, or leave a trail of white pebbles—to find their way back."

"We needn't go out of sight of the gate," said Primrose. "We could just explore a little bit."

They set off, very slowly. They went on tiptoe, making their own narrow passages through the undergrowth, which sometimes came as high as their thin shoulders. They were urban, and unaccustomed to silence. Then they began to hear small sounds. The chatter and repeated lilt and alarm of invisible birds, high up, further in. Rustling in dry leaves. Slitherings, dry coughs, sharp cracks. They went on, pointing out to each other creepers draped with glistening berries, crimson, black, and emerald, little crops of toadstools, some scarlet, some ghostly pale, some a dead-flesh purple, some like tiny parasols—and some like pieces of meat protruding from tree trunks. They met blackberries, but didn't pick them, in case in this place they were dangerous or deceptive. They admired from a safe distance the stiff upright fruiting rods of the lords-and-ladies,[5] packed with fat red berries.

Did they hear it first or smell it? Both sound and scent were at first infinitesimal and dispersed. They gave the strange impression of moving in—in waves—from the whole perimeter of the forest. Both increased very slowly in intensity, and both were mixed, a sound and a smell fabricated of many disparate sounds and smells. A crunching, a crackling, a crushing, a heavy thumping, combining with threshing and thrashing, and added to that a gulping, heaving, boiling, bursting, steaming sound, full of bubbles and farts, piffs and explosions, swallowings and wallowings. The smell was worse, and more aggressive, than the sound. It was a liquid smell of putrefaction, the smell of maggoty things at the bottom of untended dustbins, blocked drains, mixed with the smell of bad eggs, and of rotten carpets and ancient polluted bedding. The ordinary forest smells and sounds were extinguished. The two little girls looked at each other, and

5. Wild arum, a flowering perennial common to southern Britain.

took each other's hand. Speechlessly and instinctively, they crouched down behind a fallen tree trunk, and trembled, as the thing came into view.

Its head appeared to form, or first become visible in the distance, between the trees. Its face—which was triangular—appeared like a rubbery or fleshy mask over a shapeless sprouting bulb of a head, like a monstrous turnip. Its color was the color of flayed flesh, pitted with wormholes, and its expression was neither wrath nor greed but pure misery. Its most defined feature was a vast mouth, pulled down and down at the corners, tight with a kind of pain. Its lips were thin, and raised, like welts from whip-strokes. It had blind, opaque white eyes, fringed with fleshy lashes and brows like the feelers of sea anemones. Its face was close to the ground and moved toward the children between its forearms, which were squat, thick, powerful, and akimbo, like a cross between a washer-woman's and a primeval dragon's. The flesh on these forearms was glistening and mottled.

The rest of its very large body appeared to be glued together, like still wet papier-mâché, or the carapace of stones and straws and twigs worn by caddis flies underwater. It had a tubular shape, as a turd has a tubular shape, a provisional amalgam. It was made of rank meat, and decaying vegetation, but it also trailed veils and prostheses of man-made materials, bits of wire netting, foul dishcloths, wire-wool full of pan scrubbings, rusty nuts and bolts. It had feeble stubs and stumps of very slender legs, growing out of it at all angles, wavering and rippling like the suckered feet of a caterpillar or the squirming fringe of a centipede. On and on it came, bending and crushing whatever lay in its path, including bushes, though not substantial trees, which it wound between, awkwardly. The little girls observed, with horrified fascination, that when it met a sharp stone, or a narrow tree trunk, it allowed itself to be sliced through, flowed sluggishly round in two or three smaller worms, convulsed, and reunited. Its progress was apparently very painful, for it moaned and whined among its other burblings and belchings. They thought it could not see, or certainly could not see clearly. It and its stench passed within a few feet of their tree trunk, humping along, leaving behind it a trail of bloody slime and dead foliage.

Its end was flat and blunt, almost transparent, like some earthworms.

When it had gone, Penny and Primrose, kneeling on the moss and dead leaves, put their arms about each other, and hugged each other, shaking with dry sobs. Then they stood up, still silent, and stared together, hand in hand, at the trail of obliteration and destruction, which wound out of the forest and into it again. They went back, hand in hand, without looking behind them, afraid that the wicket gate, the lawn, the stone steps, the balustrade, the terrace, and the great house would be transmogrified, or simply not there. But the boys were still playing football on the lawn, a group of girls were skipping and singing shrilly on the gravel. They let go each other's hand, and went back in.

They did not speak to each other again.

The next day, they were separated and placed with strange families. Their stay in these families—Primrose was in a dairy farm, Penny was in a parsonage—did not in fact last very long, though then the time seemed slow-motion and endless. Later, Primrose remembered the sound of milk spurting in the pail, and Penny remembered the empty corsets of the Vicar's wife, hanging bony on the line. They remembered dandelion clocks, but you can remember

35

those from anywhere, any time. They remembered the thing they had seen in the forest, on the contrary, in the way you remember those very few dreams— almost all nightmares—that have the quality of life itself. (Though what are dreams if not life itself?) They remembered too solid flesh, too precise a stink, a rattle and a soughing that thrilled the nerves and the cartilage of their growing ears. In the memory, as in such a dream, they felt, I cannot get out, this is a real thing in a real place.

40   They returned from evacuation, like many evacuees, so early that they then lived through wartime in the city, bombardment, blitz, unearthly light and roaring, changed landscapes, holes in their world where the newly dead had been. Both lost their fathers. Primrose's father was in the Army, and was killed, very late in the war, on a crowded troop carrier sunk in the Far East. Penny's father, a much older man, was in the Auxiliary Fire Service, and died in a sheet of flame in the East India Docks on the Thames, pumping evaporating water from a puny coil of hose. They found it hard, after the war, to remember these different men. The claspers of memory could not grip the drowned and the burned. Primrose saw an inane grin under a khaki cap, because her mother had a snapshot. Penny thought she remembered her father, already gray-headed, brushing ash off his boots and trouser cuffs as he put on his tin hat to go out. She thought she remembered a quaver of fear in his tired face, and the muscles composing themselves into resolution. It was not much what either of them remembered.

After the war, their fates were still similar and dissimilar. Penny's widowed mother embraced grief, closed her face and her curtains. Primrose's mother married one of the many admirers she had had before the ship went down, gave birth to another five children, and developed varicose veins and a smoker's cough. She dyed her blond hair with peroxide when it faded. Both Primrose and Penny were only children who now, because of the war, lived in amputated or unreal families. Penny was a good student and in due course went to university, where she chose to study developmental psychology. Primrose had little education. She was always being kept off school to look after the others. She, too, dyed her blond curls with peroxide when they turned mousy and faded. She got fat as Penny got thin. Neither of them married. Penny became a child psychologist, working with the abused, the displaced, the disturbed. Primrose did this and that. She was a barmaid. She worked in a shop. She went to help at various church crèches and Salvation Army gatherings, and discovered she had a talent for storytelling. She became Aunty Primrose, with her own repertoire. She was employed to tell tales to kindergartens and entertain at children's parties. She was much in demand at Halloween, and had her own circle of bright-colored plastic chairs in a local shopping mall, where she kept an eye on the children of burdened women, keeping them safe, offering them just a frisson of fear and terror, which made them wriggle with pleasure.

The house in the country aged differently. During this period of time—while the little girls became women—it was handed over to the nation, which turned it into a living museum. Guided tours took place in it, at regulated times. During these tours, the ballroom and intimate drawing rooms were fenced off with crimson twisted ropes on little brass one-eyed pedestals. The bored and the curious peered in at four-poster beds and pink silk fauteuils,[6] at silver-framed photographs of wartime royalty, and crackling crazing[7] Renaissance and Enlightenment portraits. In the room where the evacuees had eaten their rationed meals, the history of the house was displayed, on posters, in glass cases, with helpful notices and opened copies of old diaries and records. There was no mention of the evacuees, whose presence appeared to have been too brief to have left any trace.

The two women met in this room on an autumn day in 1984. They had come with a group, walking in a chattering crocodile behind a guide. They prowled around the room, each alone with herself, in opposite directions, each without acknowledging the other's presence. Their mothers had died that spring, within a week of each other, though this coincidence was unknown to them. It had made both of them think of taking a holiday, and both had chosen that part of the world. Penny was wearing a charcoal trouser suit and a black velvet hat. Primrose wore a floral knit long jacket over a shell-pink cashmere sweater, over a rustling long skirt with an elastic waist, in a mustard-colored tapestry print. Her hips and bosom were bulky. Both of them, at the same moment, leaned over an image in a medieval-looking illustrated book. Primrose thought it was a very old book. Penny assumed it was nineteenth-century mock-medieval. It showed a knight, on foot, in a forest, lifting his sword to slay something. The knight shone on the rounded slope of the page, in the light, which caught the gilding on his helmet and sword belt. It was not possible to see what was being slain. This was because, both in the tangled vegetation of the image and in the way the book was displayed in the case, the enemy, or victim, was in shadows.

Neither of them could read the ancient (or pseudo-ancient) black letter of the text beside the illustration. There was a typed description, under the book. They had to lean forward to read it, and to see what was worming its way into, or out of, the deep spine of the book, and that was how each came to see the other's face, close up, in the glass, which was both transparent and reflective. Their transparent reflected faces lost detail—cracked lipstick, pouches, fine lines of wrinkles—and looked both younger and grayer, less substantial. And that is how they came to recognize each other, as they might not have done, plump face to bony face. They breathed each other's names—Penny, Primrose—and their breath misted the glass, obscuring the knight and his opponent. I could have died, I could have wet my knickers, said Penny and Primrose afterward to each other, and both experienced this still moment as pure, dangerous shock. They read the caption, which was about the Loathly Worm, which, tradition held, had infested the countryside and had been killed more than once by scions of that house—Sir Lionel, Sir Boris, Sir Guillem. The Worm, the typewriter had tapped out, was an English worm, not a European dragon, and, like most such worms, was wingless. In some sightings it was reported as having vestigial legs, hands, or feet. In others it was limbless. It had, in monstrous form, the capacity of common or garden worms to sprout new heads or trunks if it was divided, so that two worms, or more, replaced one. This was why it had been killed so often, yet reappeared. It had been reported travelling with a slithering pack of young ones, but these may have been only revitalized segments.

6. Armchairs.
7. Sealed with varnish that, with age, has cracked in patterns.

The Lambdon Worm, as depicted in
Fairy-Gold: A Book of Old English Fairy Tales (1906)

45   Being English, they thought of tea. There was a tearoom in the great house, in a converted stable at the back. There they stood silently side by side, clutching floral plastic trays spread with briar roses, and purchased scones, superior raspberry jam in tiny jam jars, little plastic tubs of clotted cream. "You couldn't get cream or real jam in the war," said Primrose as they found a corner table. She said wartime rationing had made her permanently greedy, and thin Penny agreed it had—clotted cream was still a treat.

They watched each other warily, offering bland snippets of autobiography in politely hushed voices. Primrose thought Penny looked gaunt, and Penny thought Primrose looked raddled.[8] They established the skein of coincidences— dead fathers, unmarried status, child-caring professions, recently dead mothers. Circling like beaters,[9] they approached the covert thing in the forest. They discussed the great house, politely. Primrose admired the quality of the carpets. Penny said it was nice to see the old pictures back on the wall. Primrose said, Funny really, that there was all that history, but no sign that they, the children, that was, had ever been there. Funny, said Penny, that they should meet each other next to that book, with that picture. "Creepy," said Primrose in a light, light cobweb voice, not looking at Penny. "We saw that thing. When we went in the forest."

"Yes, we did," said Penny. "We saw it."

---

8. Frazzled.
9. Hunters who beat the bushes to drive out game.

"Did you ever wonder," asked Primrose, "if we really saw it?"

"Never for a moment," said Penny. "That is, I don't know what it was, but I've always been quite sure we saw it."

"Does it change—do you remember all of it?"

"It was a horrible thing, and yes, I remember all of it, there isn't a bit of it I can manage to forget. Though I forget all sorts of things," said Penny, in a thin voice, a vanishing voice.

"And have you ever told anyone of it, spoken of it?" asked Primrose more urgently, leaning forward.

"No," said Penny. She had not. She said, "Who would believe it?"

"That's what I thought," said Primrose. "I didn't speak. But it stuck in my mind like a tapeworm in your gut. I think it did me no good."

"It did me no good either," said Penny. "No good at all. I've thought about it," she said to the aging woman opposite, whose face quivered under her dyed goldilocks. "I think, I think there are things that are real—more real than we are—but mostly we don't cross their paths, or they don't cross ours. Maybe at very bad times we get into their world, or notice what they are doing in ours."

Primrose nodded energetically. She looked as though sharing was solace, and Penny, to whom it was not solace, grimaced with pain.

"Sometimes I think that thing finished me off," Penny said to Primrose, a child's voice rising in a woman's gullet, arousing a little girl's scared smile, which wasn't a smile on Primrose's face.

Primrose said, "It did finish her off, that little one, didn't it? She got into its path, didn't she? And when it had gone by—she wasn't anywhere," said Primrose. "That was how it was?"

"Nobody ever asked where she was or looked for her," said Penny.

"I wondered if we'd made her up," said Primrose. "But I didn't, we didn't."

"Her name was Alys."

"With a 'y.'"

There had been a mess, a disgusting mess, they remembered, but no particular sign of anything that might have been, or been part of, or belonged to, a persistent little girl called Alys.

Primrose shrugged voluptuously, let out a gale of a sigh, and rearranged her flesh in her clothes.

"Well, we know we're not mad, anyway," she said. "We've got into a mystery, but we didn't make it up. It wasn't a delusion. So it was good we met, because now we needn't be afraid we're mad, need we—we can get on with things, so to speak?"

They arranged to have dinner together the following evening. They were staying in different bed-and-breakfasts and neither of them thought of exchanging addresses. They agreed on a restaurant in the market square of the local town— Seraphina's Hot Pot—and a time, seven-thirty. They did not even discuss spending the next day together. Primrose went on a local bus tour. Penny took a long solitary walk. The weather was gray, spitting fine rain. Both arrived at their lodgings with headaches, and both made tea with the tea bags and kettle provided in their rooms. They sat on their beds. Penny's had a quilt with blowsy cabbage roses. Primrose's had a black-and-white checked gingham duvet. They turned on their televisions, watched the same game show, listened to the inordinate jolly laughter.

Seven-thirty came and went, and neither woman moved. Both, indistinctly, imagined the other waiting at a table, watching a door open and shut. Neither moved. What could they have said, they asked themselves, but only perfunctorily.

The next day, Penny thought about the wood, put on her walking shoes, and set off obliquely in the opposite direction. Primrose sat over her breakfast, which was English and ample. The wood, the real and imagined wood—both before and after she had entered it with Penny—had always been simultaneously a source of attraction and of discomfort, shading into terror. Without speaking to herself a sentence in her head—"I shall go there"—Primrose decided. And she went straight there, full of warm food, arriving as the morning brightened with the first busload of tourists, and giving them the slip, to take the path they had once taken, across the lawn and through the wicket gate.

The wood was much the same, but denser and more inviting in its new greenness. Primrose's body decided to set off in a rather different direction from the one the little girls had taken. New bracken was uncoiling with snaky force. Yesterday's rain still glittered on limp new hazel leaves and threads of gossamer. Small feathered throats above her whistled and trilled with enchanting territorial aggression and male self-assertion, which were to Primrose simply the chorus. She found a mossy bank, with posies of primroses, which she recognized and took vaguely as a good sign, a personal sign. She was better at flowers than birds, because there had been Flower Fairies in the school bookshelves when she was little, with the flowers painted accurately, accompanied by truly pretty human creatures, all children, clothed in the blues and golds, russets and purples of the flowers and fruits. Here she saw and recognized them, windflower and bryony, self-heal and dead nettle, and had—despite where she was—a lovely lapping sense of invisible, just invisible life swarming in the leaves and along the twigs.

70   She stopped. She did not like the sound of her own toiling breath. She was not very fit. She saw, then, a whisking in the bracken, a twirl of fur, thin and flaming, quivering on a tree trunk. She saw a squirrel, a red squirrel, watching her from a bough. She had to sit down, as she remembered her mother. She sat on a hummock of grass, rather heavily. She remembered them all, Nutkin and Moldywarp, Brock and Sleepy Dormouse, Natty Newt and Ferdy Frog. Her mother hadn't told stories and hadn't opened gates into imaginary worlds. But she had been good with her fingers. Every Christmas during the war, when toys, and indeed materials, were not to be had, Primrose had woken to find in her stocking a new stuffed creature, made from fur fabric, with button eyes and horny claws. There had been an artistry to them. The stuffed squirrel was the essence of squirrel, the fox was watchful, the newt was slithery. They did not wear anthropomorphic jackets or caps, which made it easier to invest them with imaginary natures. She believed in Father Christmas, and the discovery that her mother had made the toys, the vanishing of magic, had been a breathtaking blow. She could not be grateful for the skill and the imagination, so uncharacteristic of her flirtatious mother. The creatures continued to accumulate. A spider, a Bambi. She told herself stories at night about a girlwoman, an enchantress in a fairy wood, loved and protected by an army of wise and gentle animals. She

slept banked in by stuffed creatures, as the house in the blitz was banked in by inadequate sandbags.

Primrose registered the red squirrel as disappointing—stringier and more ratlike than its plump gray city cousins. But she knew it was special, and when it took off from branch to branch, flicking its extended tail like a sail, gripping with its tiny hands, she set out to follow it. It would take her to the center, she thought. It could easily have leaped out of sight, she thought, but it didn't. She pushed through brambles into denser, greener shadows. Juices stained her skirts and skin. She began to tell herself a story about staunch Primrose, not giving up, making her way to "the center." Her childhood stories had all been in the third person. "She was not afraid." "She faced up to the wild beasts. They cowered." She laddered her tights and muddied her shoes and breathed heavier. The squirrel stopped to clean its face. She crushed bluebells and saw the sinister hoods of arum lilies.

She had no idea how far she had come, but she decided that the clearing where she found herself was the center. The squirrel had stopped, and was running up and down a single tree. There was a mossy mound that could have had a thronelike aspect, if you were being imaginative. So she sat on it. "She came to the center and sat on the mossy chair."

Now what?

She had not forgotten what they had seen, the blank miserable face, the powerful claws, the raggle-taggle train of accumulated decay. She had come neither to look for it nor to confront it, but she had come because it was there. She had known all her life that she, Primrose, had really been in a magic forest. She knew that the forest was the source of terror. She had never frightened the littluns she entertained, with tales of lost children in forests. She frightened them with slimy things that came up the plughole, or swarmed out of the U-bend in the lavatory, and were dispatched by bravery and magic. But the woods in her tales bred glamour. They were places where you used words like "spangles" and "sequins" for real dewdrops on real dock leaves. Primrose knew that glamour and the thing they had seen, brilliance and the ashen stink, came from the same place. She made both things safe for the littluns by restricting them to pantomime flats and sweet illustrations. She didn't look at what she knew, better not, but she did know she knew, she recognized confusedly.

Now what?

She sat on the moss, and a voice in her head said, "I want to go home." And she heard herself give a bitter, entirely grownup little laugh, for what was home? What did she know about home?

Where she lived was above a Chinese takeaway. She had a dangerous cupboard-corner she cooked in, a bed, a clothes-rail, an armchair deformed by generations of bottoms. She thought of this place in faded browns and beiges, seen through drifting coils of Chinese cooking steam, scented with stewing pork and a bubbling chicken broth. Home was not real, as all the sturdy twigs and roots in the wood were real. The stuffed animals were piled on the bed and the carpet, their fur rubbed, their pristine stare gone from their scratched eyes. She thought about what one thought was real, sitting there on the moss throne at the center. When Mum had come in, snivelling, to say Dad was dead, Primrose herself had been preoccupied with whether pudding would be tapioca or semolina, whether there would be jam, and, subsequently, how ugly Mum's dripping nose was, how she looked as though she were putting it on.[1] She remembered the semolina and the rather nasty blackberry jam, the taste and the texture, to this day. So was that real, was that home?

She had later invented a picture of a cloudy aquamarine sea under a gold sun, in which a huge fountain of white curling water rose from a foundering ship. It was very beautiful but not real. She could not remember Dad. She could remember the Thing in the Forest, and she could remember Alys. The fact that the mossy tump had lovely colors—crimson and emerald—didn't mean she didn't remember the Thing. She remembered what Penny had said about "things that are more real than we are." She had met one. Here at the center, the spout of water was more real than the semolina, because she was where such things reign. The word she found was "reign." She had understood something, and did not know what she had understood. She wanted badly to go home, and she wanted never to move. The light was lovely in the leaves. The squirrel flirted its tail and suddenly set off again, springing into the branches. The woman lumbered to her feet and licked the bramble scratches on the back of her hands.

Penny walked very steadily, keeping to hedgerows and field-edge paths. She remembered the Thing. She remembered it clearly and daily. But she walked away, noticing and not noticing that her path was deflected by field forms and the lay of the land into a snaking sickle shape. As the day wore on, she settled into her stride and lifted her eyes. When she saw the wood on the horizon, she knew it was the wood, although she was seeing it from an unfamiliar aspect, from where it appeared to be perched on a conical hillock, ridged as though it had been grasped and squeezed by coils of strength. It was almost dusk. She mounted the slope, and went in over a suddenly discovered stile.[2]

80   Once inside, she moved cautiously. She stood stock-still, and snuffed the air for the remembered rottenness: she listened to the sounds of the trees and the creatures. She smelled rottenness, but it was normal rottenness, leaves and stems mulching back into earth. She heard sounds. Not birdsong, for it was too late in the day, but the odd raucous warning croak. She heard her own heartbeat in the thickening brown air.

It was no use looking for familiar tree trunks or tussocks. They had had a lifetime, her lifetime, to alter out of recognition.

She began to think she discerned dark tunnels in the undergrowth, where something might have rolled and slid. Mashed seedlings, broken twigs and fronds, none of it very recent. There were things caught in the thorns, flimsy colorless shreds of damp wool or fur. She peered down the tunnels and noted where the scrapings hung thickest. She forced herself to go into the dark, stooping, occasionally crawling on hands and knees. The silence was heavy. She found threadworms of knitting wool, unravelled dishcloth cotton, clinging newsprint. She found odd sausage-shaped tubes of membrane, containing fragments of hair and bone and other inanimate stuffs. They were like monstrous owl pellets, or the gut-shaped hairballs vomited by cats. Penny went forward,

---

1. Pretending.
2. Set of steps for climbing over a fence or hedge.

putting aside briars and tough stems with careful fingers. It had been here, but how long ago?

Quite suddenly, she came out at a place she remembered. The clearing was larger, the tree trunks were thicker, but the great log behind which they had hidden still lay there. The place was almost the ghost of a camp. The trees round about were hung with pennants and streamers, like the scorched, hacked, threadbare banners in the chapel of the great house, with their brown stains of earth or blood. It had been here, it had never gone away.

Penny moved slowly and dreamily round, looking for things. She found a mock-tortoiseshell hairslide, and a shoe button with a metal shank. She found a bird skeleton, quite fresh, bashed flat. She found ambivalent shards and several teeth, of varying sizes and shapes. She found—spread around, half hidden by roots, stained green but glinting white—a collection of small bones, finger bones, tiny toes, a rib, and finally what might be a brainpan and brow. She thought of putting them in her knapsack, and then thought she could not. She was not an anatomist. The tiny bones might have been badger or fox.

She sat down, with her back against the fallen trunk. She thought, Now I am watching myself as you do in a safe dream, but then, when I saw it, it was one of those dreams where you are inside and cannot get out. Except that it wasn't a dream. 85

It was the encounter with the Thing that had led her to deal professionally in dreams. Something that resembled unreality had lumbered into reality, and she had seen it. She had been the reading child, but after the sight of the Thing she had not been able to inhabit the customary and charming unreality of books. She had become good at studying what could not be seen. She took an interest in the dead, who inhabited real history. She was drawn to the invisible forces that moved in molecules and caused them to coagulate or dissipate. She had become a psychotherapist "to be useful." That was not quite accurate. The corner of the blanket that covered the unthinkable had been turned back enough for her to catch sight of it. She was in its world. It was not by accident that she had come to specialize in severely autistic children, children who twittered, or banged, or stared, who sat damp and absent on Penny's official lap and told her no dreams. The world they knew was a real world. Often Penny thought it was the real world, from which even their desperate parents were at least partly shielded. Somebody had to occupy themselves with the hopeless. Penny felt she could.

All the leaves of the forest began slowly to quaver and then to clatter. Far away, there was the sound of something heavy, and sluggish, stirring. Penny sat very still and expectant. She heard the old blind rumble, she sniffed the old stink. It came from no direction; it was all around; as though the Thing encompassed the wood, or as though it travelled in multiple fragments, as it was described in the old text. It was dark now. What was visible had no distinct color, only shades of ink and elephant.

Now, thought Penny, and just as suddenly as it had begun the turmoil ceased. It was as though the Thing had turned away; she could feel the tremble of the wood recede and become still. Quite rapidly, over the treetops, a huge disk of white gold mounted and hung. Penny remembered her father, standing in the cold light of the full moon, and saying wryly that the bombers would not come tonight, they were safe under a cloudless full moon. He had vanished in an oven of red-yellow roaring, Penny had guessed, or been told, or imagined. Her mother had sent her away before allowing the fireman to speak, who had come with the news. She had been a creep-mouse on stairs and in cubbyholes, trying to over-hear what was being imparted. Her mother didn't, or couldn't, want her com-pany. She caught odd phrases of talk—"nothing really to identify," "absolutely no doubt." He had been a tired, gentle man with ash in his trouser turnups. There had been a funeral. Penny remembered thinking there was nothing, or next to nothing, in the coffin his fellow-firemen shouldered. It went up so lightly. It was so easy to set down on the crematorium slab.

They had been living behind the blackout anyway, but her mother went on living behind drawn curtains long after the war was over.

90   The moon had released the wood, it seemed. Penny stood up and brushed leaf mold off her clothes. She had been ready for it, and it had not come. She felt disappointed. But she accepted her release and found her way back to the fields and her village along liquid trails of moonlight.

The two women took the same train back to the city, but did not encounter each other until they got out. The passengers scurried and shuffled toward the exit, mostly heads down. Both women remembered how they had set out in the wartime dark, with their twig legs and gas masks. Both raised their heads as they neared the barrier, not in hope of being met, for they would not be, but automatically, to calculate where to go and what to do. They saw each other's faces in the cavernous gloom, two pale, recognizable rounds, far enough apart for speech, and even greetings, to be awkward. In the dimness, they were reduced to similarity—dark eyeholes, set mouth. For a moment or two, they stood and simply stared. On that first occasion the station vault had been full of curling steam, and the air gritty with ash. Now the blunt-nosed sleek diesel they had left was blue and gold under a layer of grime. They saw each other through the black imagined veil that grief or pain or despair hangs over the visible world. Each saw the other's face and thought of the unforgettable misery of the face they had seen in the forest. Each thought that the other was the witness, who made the thing certainly real, who prevented her from slipping into the comfort of believing she had imagined it or made it up. So they stared at each other, blankly, without acknowledgment, then picked up their baggage, and turned away into the crowd.

Penny found that the black veil had somehow become part of her vision. She thought constantly about faces, her father's, her mother's, Primrose's face, the hopeful little girl, the woman staring up at her from the glass case, staring at her conspiratorially over the clotted cream. The blond infant Alys, an ingratiat-ing sweet smile. The half-human face of the Thing. She tried to remember that face completely, and suffered over the detail of the dreadful droop of its mouth, the exact inanity of its blind squinnying.[3] Present faces were blank disks, shad-owed moons. Her patients came and went. She was increasingly unable to dis-tinguish one from another. The face of the Thing hung in her brain, jealously soliciting her attention, distracting her from dailiness. She had gone back to its place, and had not seen it. She needed to see it. Why she needed it was because

3. Squinting.

it was more real than she was. She would go and face it. What else was there, she asked herself, and answered herself, nothing.

So she made her way back, sitting alone in the train as the fields streaked past, drowsing through a century-long night under the cabbage quilt in the B. and B. This time, she went in the old way, from the house, through the garden gate; she found the old trail quickly, her sharp eye picked up the trace of its detritus, and soon enough she was back in the clearing, where her cairn of tiny bones by the tree trunk was undisturbed. She gave a little sigh, dropped to her knees, and then sat with her back to the rotting wood and silently called the Thing. Almost immediately, she sensed its perturbation, saw the trouble in the branches, heard the lumbering, smelled its ancient smell. It was a grayish, unremarkable day. She closed her eyes briefly as the noise and movement grew stronger. When it came, she would look it in the face, she would see what it was. She clasped her hands loosely in her lap. Her nerves relaxed. Her blood slowed. She was ready.

Primrose was in the shopping mall, putting out her circle of rainbow-colored plastic chairs. She creaked as she bent over them. It was pouring with rain outside, but the mall was enclosed like a crystal palace in a casing of glass. The floor under the rainbow chairs was gleaming dappled marble. They were in front of a dimpling fountain, with lights shining up through the greenish water, making golden rings round the polished pebbles and wishing coins that lay there. The little children collected round her: their mothers kissed them good-bye, told them to be good and quiet and listen to the nice lady. They had little transparent plastic cups of shining orange juice, and each had a biscuit in silver foil. They were all colors—black skin, brown skin, pink skin, freckled skin, pink jacket, yellow jacket, purple hood, scarlet hood. Some grinned and some whimpered, some wriggled, some were still. Primrose sat on the edge of the fountain. She had decided what to do. She smiled her best, most comfortable smile, and adjusted her golden locks. Listen to me, she told them, and I'll tell you something amazing, a story that's never been told before.

There were once two little girls who saw, or believed they saw, a thing in a   95 forest. . . .

2002, 2004

QUESTIONS

1. Traditional fairy tales often rely on symbolic objects, actions, settings, or characters. How is THE THING IN THE FOREST like a fairy tale in this respect? How is it different? Are there figures of speech in this story that you would argue are not symbolic?
2. Is the "Loathly Worm" (par. 44) supernatural, imaginary, or real? Notice the description of its appearances. Can you identify different *kinds* of literal or physical traits that people see in it? Can you identify three or more concepts, feelings, or historical conditions that it might represent? Is it personified? Does it resemble other monsters in literature, art, or media?
3. Are "Penny" and "Primrose" allegorical names? How do the differences between the characters add to the symbolic meaning of the Thing? How do their different actions in the story help reveal its meanings?

EDWIDGE DANTICAT
(b. 1969)

A Wall of Fire Rising

At age twelve, Edwidge Danticat moved from Port-au-Prince, Haiti, to Brooklyn, New York, where her parents had relocated eight years before. Having grown up speaking only French and Creole, Danticat published her first writing in English at age fourteen, a newspaper article about her immigration to the United States that developed into her first novel, *Breath, Eyes, Memory* (1994). Danticat received a degree in French literature from Barnard College and an MFA from Brown University. *Krik? Krak!* (1995), a collection of short stories, was nominated for the National Book Award. Her second novel, *The Farming of Bones* (1998), is based on the 1937 massacre of Haitians at the border of the Dominican Republic. In 2002, Danticat published *After the Dance: A Walk through Carnival in Jacmel, Haiti*, an account of her travels. Other publications include *The Dew Breaker* (2004), a collection of interlinked stories examining the life of a Haitian torturer; *Brother, I'm Dying* (2007), winner of the National Book Critics Circle Award for Autobiography; the essay collection *Create Dangerously: The Immigrant Artist at Work* (2010); and the novel *Claire of the Sea Light* (2013). Danticat is also the author of young-adult novels, including *Untwine* (2015). Her 2019 short-story collection, *Everything Inside*, garnered her yet another National Book Critics Circle Award.

"Listen to what happened today," Guy said as he barged through the rattling door of his tiny shack.

His wife, Lili, was squatting in the middle of their one-room home, spreading cornmeal mush on banana leaves for their supper.

"Listen to what happened to *me* today!" Guy's seven-year-old son—Little Guy—dashed from a corner and grabbed his father's hand. The boy dropped his composition notebook as he leaped to his father, nearly stepping into the corn mush and herring that his mother had set out in a trio of half gourds on the clay floor.

"Our boy is in a play." Lili quickly robbed Little Guy of the honor of telling his father the news.

5   "A play?" Guy affectionately stroked the boy's hair.

The boy had such tiny corkscrew curls that no amount of brushing could ever make them all look like a single entity. The other boys at the Lycée Jean-Jacques[1] called him "pepper head" because each separate kinky strand was coiled into a tight tiny ball that looked like small peppercorns.

---

1. Haiti is French speaking; Little Guy attends a *lycée* (school) named after Jean-Jacques Dessalines (1758–1806), founder of independent Haiti. A former slave, Dessalines was declared emperor Jacques I in 1804.

"When is this play?" Guy asked both the boy and his wife. "Are we going to have to buy new clothes for this?"

Lili got up from the floor and inclined her face towards her husband's in order to receive her nightly peck on the cheek.

"What role do you have in the play?" Guy asked, slowly rubbing the tip of his nails across the boy's scalp. His fingers made a soft grating noise with each invisible circle drawn around the perimeters of the boy's head. Guy's fingers finally landed inside the boy's ears, forcing the boy to giggle until he almost gave himself the hiccups.

"Tell me, what is your part in the play?" Guy asked again, pulling his fingers away from his son's ear. 10

"I am Boukman," the boy huffed out, as though there was some laughter caught in his throat.

"Show Papy your lines," Lili told the boy as she arranged the three open gourds on a piece of plywood raised like a table on two bricks, in the middle of the room. "My love, Boukman is the hero of the play."

The boy went back to the corner where he had been studying and pulled out a thick book carefully covered in brown paper.

"You're going to spend a lifetime learning those." Guy took the book from the boy's hand and flipped through the pages quickly. He had to strain his eyes to see the words by the light of an old kerosene lamp, which that night—like all others—flickered as though it was burning its very last wick.

"All these words seem so long and heavy," Guy said. "You think you can do this, son?" 15

"He has one very good speech," Lili said. "Page forty, remember, son?"

The boy took back the book from his father. His face was crimped in an of-course-I-remember look as he searched for page forty.

"Bouk-man," Guy struggled with the letters of the slave revolutionary's name as he looked over his son's shoulders. "I see some very hard words here, son."

"He already knows his speech," Lili told her husband.

"Does he now?" asked Guy. 20

"We've been at it all afternoon," Lili said. "Why don't you go on and recite that speech for your father?"

The boy tipped his head towards the rusting tin on the roof as he prepared to recite his lines.

Lili wiped her hands on an old apron tied around her waist and stopped to listen.

"Remember what you are," Lili said, "a great rebel leader. Remember, it is the revolution."

"Do we want him to be all of that?" Guy asked. 25

"He is Boukman," Lili said. "What is the only thing on your mind now, Boukman?"

"Supper," Guy whispered, enviously eyeing the food cooling off in the middle of the room. He and the boy looked at each other and began to snicker.

"Tell us the other thing that is on your mind," Lili said, joining in their laughter.

"Freedom!" shouted the boy, as he quickly slipped into his role.

"Louder!" urged Lili. 30

"Freedom is on my mind!" yelled the boy.

"Why don't you start, son?" said Guy. "If you don't, we'll never get to that other thing that we have on our minds."

The boy closed his eyes and took a deep breath. At first, his lips parted but nothing came out. Lili pushed her head forward as though she were holding her breath. Then like the last burst of lightning out of clearing sky, the boy began.

"A wall of fire is rising and in the ashes, I see the bones of my people. Not only those people whose dark hollow faces I see daily in the fields, but all those souls who have gone ahead to haunt my dreams. At night I relive once more the last caresses from the hand of a loving father, a valiant love, a beloved friend."[2]

35   It was obvious that this was a speech written by a European man, who gave to the slave revolutionary Boukman the kind of European phrasing that might have sent the real Boukman turning in his grave. However, the speech made Lili and Guy stand on the tips of their toes from great pride. As their applause thundered in the small space of their shack that night, they felt as though for a moment they had been given the rare pleasure of hearing the voice of one of the forefathers of Haitian independence in the forced baritone of their only child. The experience left them both with a strange feeling that they could not explain. It left the hair on the back of their necks standing on end. It left them feeling much more love than they ever knew that they could add to their feeling for their son.

"Bravo," Lili cheered, pressing her son into the folds of her apron. "Long live Boukman and long live my boy."

"Long live our supper," Guy said, quickly batting his eyelashes to keep tears from rolling down his face.

The boy kept his eyes on his book as they ate their supper that night. Usually Guy and Lili would not have allowed that, but this was a special occasion. They watched proudly as the boy muttered his lines between swallows of cornmeal.

The boy was still mumbling the same words as the three of them used the last of the rainwater trapped in old gasoline containers and sugarcane pulp from the nearby sugarcane mill to scrub the gourds that they had eaten from.

40   When things were really bad for the family, they boiled clean sugarcane pulp to make what Lili called her special sweet water tea. It was supposed to suppress gas and kill the vermin in the stomach that made poor children hungry. That and a pinch of salt under the tongue could usually quench hunger until Guy found a day's work or Lili could manage to buy spices on credit and then peddle them for a profit at the marketplace.

That night, anyway, things were good. Everyone had eaten enough to put all their hunger vermin to sleep.

The boy was sitting in front of the shack on an old plastic bucket turned upside down, straining his eyes to find the words on the page. Sometimes when there was no kerosene for the lamp, the boy would have to go sit by the side of

2. On the night of August 22, 1791, slaves led by a slave foreman named Boukman (who was secretly a voodoo high priest) built a "wall of fire" that destroyed many plantations in the French colony of Saint-Domingue, marking the beginning of a mass slave revolt that would lead, fourteen years later, to the establishment of independent Haiti.

the road and study under the street lamps with the rest of the neighborhood children. Tonight, at least, they had a bit of their own light.

Guy bent down by a small clump of old mushrooms near the boy's feet, trying to get a better look at the plant. He emptied the last drops of rainwater from a gasoline container on the mushroom, wetting the bulging toes sticking out of his sons' sandals, which were already coming apart around his endlessly growing feet.

Guy tried to pluck some of the mushrooms, which were being pushed into the dust as though they wanted to grow beneath the ground as roots. He took one of the mushrooms in his hand, running his smallest finger over the round bulb. He clipped the stem and buried the top in a thick strand of his wife's hair.

The mushroom looked like a dried insect in Lili's hair.   45

"It sure makes you look special," Guy said, teasing her.

"Thank you so much," Lili said, tapping her husband's arm. "It's nice to know that I deserve these much more than roses."

Taking his wife's hand, Guy said, "Let's go to the sugar mill."

"Can I study my lines there?" the boy asked.

"You know them well enough already," Guy said.   50

"I need many repetitions," the boy said.

Their feet sounded as though they were playing a wet wind instrument as they slipped in and out of the puddles between the shacks in the shantytown. Near the sugar mill was a large television screen in an iron grill cage that the government had installed so that the shantytown dwellers could watch the state-sponsored news at eight o'clock every night. After the news, a gendarme[3] would come and turn off the television set, taking home the key. On most nights, the people stayed at the site long after this gendarme had gone and told stories to one another beneath the big blank screen. They made bonfires with dried sticks, corn husks, and paper, cursing the authorities under their breath.

There was a crowd already gathering for the nightly news event. The sugar mill workers sat in the front row in chairs or on old buckets.

Lili and Guy passed the group, clinging to their son so that in his childhood naïveté he wouldn't accidentally glance at the wrong person and be called an insolent child. They didn't like the ambiance of the nightly news watch. They spared themselves trouble by going instead to the sugar mill, where in the past year they had discovered their own wonder.

Everyone knew that the family who owned the sugar mill were eccentric   55 "Arabs," Haitians of Lebanese or Palestinian descent whose family had been in the country for generations. The Assad family had a son who, it seems, was into all manner of odd things, the most recent of which was a hot-air balloon, which he had brought to Haiti from America and occasionally flew over the shantytown skies.

As they approached the fence surrounding the field where the large wicker basket and deflated balloon rested on the ground, Guy let go of the hands of both his wife and the boy.

---

3. Policeman or guard (French).

Lili walked on slowly with her son. For the last few weeks, she had been feeling as though Guy was lost to her each time he reached this point, twelve feet away from the balloon. As Guy pushed his hand through the barbed wire, she could tell from the look on his face that he was thinking of sitting inside the square basket while the smooth rainbow surface of the balloon itself floated above his head. During the day, when the field was open, Guy would walk up to the basket, staring at it with the same kind of longing that most men display when they admire very pretty girls.

Lili and the boy stood watching from a distance as Guy tried to push his hand deeper, beyond the chain link fence that separated him from the balloon. He reached into his pants pocket and pulled out a small pocketknife, sharpening the edges on the metal surface of the fence. When his wife and child moved closer, he put the knife back in his pocket, letting his fingers slide across his son's tightly coiled curls.

"I wager you I can make this thing fly," Guy said.

60 "Why do you think you can do that?" Lili asked.

"I know it," Guy replied.

He followed her as she circled the sugar mill, leading to their favorite spot under a watch light. Little Guy lagged faithfully behind them. From this distance, the hot-air balloon looked like an odd spaceship.

Lili stretched her body out in the knee-high grass in the field. Guy reached over and tried to touch her between her legs.

"You're not one to worry, Lili," he said. "You're not afraid of the frogs, lizards, or snakes that could be hiding in this grass?"

65 "I am here with my husband," she said. "You are here to protect me if anything happens."

Guy reached into his shirt pocket and pulled out a lighter and a crumpled piece of paper. He lit the paper until it burned to an ashy film. The burning paper floated in the night breeze for a while, landing in fragments on the grass.

"Did you see that, Lili?" Guy asked with a flame in his eyes brighter than the lighter's. "Did you see how the paper floated when it was burned? This is how that balloon flies."

"What did you mean by saying that you could make it fly?" Lili asked.

"You already know all my secrets," Guy said as the boy came charging towards them.

70 "Papa, could you play *Lago* with me?" the boy asked.

Lili lay peacefully on the grass as her son and husband played hide-and-seek. Guy kept hiding and his son kept finding him as each time Guy made it easier for the boy.

"We rest now." Guy was becoming breathless.

The stars were circling the peaks of the mountains, dipping into the cane fields belonging to the sugar mill. As Guy caught his breath, the boy raced around the fence, running as fast as he could to purposely make himself dizzy.

"Listen to what happened today," Guy whispered softly in Lili's ear.

75 "I heard you say that when you walked in the house tonight," Lili said. "With the boy's play, I forgot to ask you."

The boy sneaked up behind them, his face lit up, though his brain was spinning. He wrapped his arms around both their necks.

"We will go back home soon," Lili said.

"Can I recite my lines?" asked the boy.

"We have heard them," Guy said. "Don't tire your lips."

The boy mumbled something under his breath. Guy grabbed his ear and 80 twirled it until it was a tiny ball in his hand. The boy's face contorted with agony as Guy made him kneel in the deep grass in punishment.

Lili looked tortured as she watched the boy squirming in the grass, obviously terrified of the crickets, lizards, and small snakes that might be there.

"Perhaps we should take him home to bed," she said.

"He will never learn," Guy said, "if I say one thing and you say another."

Guy got up and angrily started walking home. Lili walked over, took her son's hand, and raised him from his knees.

"You know you must not mumble," she said. 85

"I was saying my lines," the boy said.

"Next time say them loud," Lili said, "so he knows what is coming out of your mouth."

That night Lili could hear her son muttering his lines as he tucked himself in his corner of the room and drifted off to sleep. The boy still had the book with his monologue in it clasped under his arm as he slept.

Guy stayed outside in front of the shack as Lili undressed for bed. She loosened the ribbon that held the old light blue cotton skirt around her waist and let it drop past her knees. She grabbed half a lemon that she kept in the corner by the folded mat that she and Guy unrolled to sleep on every night. Lili let her blouse drop to the floor as she smoothed the lemon over her ashen legs.

Guy came in just at that moment and saw her bare chest by the light of the 90 smaller castor oil lamp that they used for the later hours of the night. Her skin had coarsened a bit over the years, he thought. Her breasts now drooped from having nursed their son for two years after he was born. It was now easier for him to imagine their son's lips around those breasts than to imagine his anywhere near them.

He turned his face away as she fumbled for her nightgown. He helped her open the mat, tucking the blanket edges underneath.

Fully clothed, Guy dropped onto the mat next to her. He laid his head on her chest, rubbing the spiky edges of his hair against her nipples.

"What was it that happened today?" Lili asked, running her fingers along Guy's hairline, an angular hairline, almost like a triangle, in the middle of his forehead. She nearly didn't marry him because it was said that people with angular hairlines often have very troubled lives.

"I got a few hours' work for tomorrow at the sugar mill," Guy said. "That's what happened today."

"It was such a long time coming," Lili said. 95

It was almost six months since the last time Guy had gotten work there. The jobs at the sugar mill were few and far between. The people who had them never left, or when they did they would pass the job on to another family member who was already waiting on line.

Guy did not seem overjoyed about the one day's work.

"I wish I had paid more attention when you came in with the news," Lili said. "I was just so happy about the boy."

"I was born in the shadow of that sugar mill," Guy said. "Probably the first thing my mother gave me to drink as a baby was some sweet water tea from the pulp of the sugarcane. If anyone deserves to work there, I should."

100 "What will you be doing for your day's work?"

"Would you really like to know?"

"There is never any shame in honest work," she said.

"They want me to scrub the latrines."

"It's honest work," Lili said, trying to console him.

105 "I am still number seventy-eight on the permanent hire list," he said. "I was thinking of putting the boy on the list now, so maybe by the time he becomes a man he can be up for a job."

Lili's body jerked forward, rising straight up in the air. Guy's head dropped with a loud thump onto the mat.

"I don't want him on that list," she said. "For a young boy to be on any list like that might influence his destiny. I don't want him on the list."

"Look at me," Guy said. "If my father had worked there, if he had me on the list, don't you think I would be working?"

"If you have any regard for me," she said, "you will not put him on the list."

110 She groped for her husband's chest in the dark and laid her head on it. She could hear his heart beating loudly as though it were pumping double, triple its normal rate.

"You won't put the boy on any lists, will you?" she implored.

"Please, Lili, no more about the boy. He will not go on the list."

"Thank you."

"Tonight I was looking at that balloon in the yard behind the sugar mill," he said. "I have been watching it real close."

115 "I know."

"I have seen the man who owns it," he said. "I've seen him get in it and put it in the sky and go up there like it was some kind of kite and he was the kite master. I see the men who run after it trying to figure out where it will land. Once I was there and I was one of those men who were running and I actually guessed correctly. I picked a spot in the sugarcane fields. I picked the spot from a distance and it actually landed there."

"Let me say something to you, Guy—"

"Pretend that this is the time of miracles and we believed in them. I watched the owner for a long time, and I think I can fly that balloon. The first time I saw him do it, it looked like a miracle, but the more and more I saw it, the more ordinary it became."

"You're probably intelligent enough to do it," she said.

120 "I am intelligent enough to do it. You're right to say that I can."

"Don't you think about hurting yourself?"

"Think like this. Can't you see yourself up there? Up in the clouds some-where like some kind of bird?"

"If God wanted people to fly, he would have given us wings on our backs."

"You're right, Lili, you're right. But look what he gave us instead. He gave us reasons to want to fly. He gave us the air, the birds, our son."

"I don't understand you," she said. 125

"Our son, your son, you do not want him cleaning latrines."

"He can do other things."

"Me too. I can do other things too."

A loud scream came from the corner where the boy was sleeping. Lili and Guy rushed to him and tried to wake him. The boy was trembling when he opened his eyes.

"What is the matter?" Guy asked. 130

"I cannot remember my lines," the boy said.

Lili tried to string together what she could remember of her son's lines. The words slowly came back to the boy. By the time he fell back to sleep, it was almost dawn.

The light was slowly coming up behind the trees. Lili could hear the whispers of the market women, their hisses and swearing as their sandals dug into the sharp-edged rocks on the road.

She turned her back to her husband as she slipped out of her nightgown, quickly putting on her day clothes.

"Imagine this," Guy said from the mat on the floor. "I have never really seen 135 your entire body in broad daylight."

Lili shut the door behind her, making her way out to the yard. The empty gasoline containers rested easily on her head as she walked a few miles to the public water fountains. It was harder to keep them steady when the containers were full. The water splashed all over her blouse and rippled down her back.

The sky was blue as it was most mornings, a dark indigo-shaded turquoise that would get lighter when the sun was fully risen.

Guy and the boy were standing in the yard waiting for her when she got back.

"You did not get much sleep, my handsome boy," she said, running her wet fingers over the boy's face.

"He'll be late for school if we do not go right now," Guy said. "I want to drop 140 him off before I start work."

"Do we remember our lines this morning?" Lili asked, tucking the boy's shirt down deep into his short pants.

"We just recited them," Guy said. "Even I know them now."

Lili watched them walk down the footpath, her eyes following them until they disappeared.

As soon as they were out of sight, she poured the water she had fetched into a large calabash, letting it stand beside the house.

She went back into the room and slipped into a dry blouse. It was never too 145 early to start looking around, to scrape together that night's meal.

"Listen to what happened again today," Lili said when Guy walked through the door that afternoon.

Guy blotted his face with a dust rag as he prepared to hear the news. After the day he'd had at the factory, he wanted to sit under a tree and have a leisurely smoke, but he did not want to set a bad example for his son by indulging his very small pleasures.

"You tell him, son," Lili urged the boy, who was quietly sitting in a corner, reading.

"I've got more lines," the boy announced, springing up to his feet. "Papy, do you want to hear them?"

150   "They are giving him more things to say in the play," Lili explained, "because he did such a good job memorizing so fast."

"My compliments, son. Do you have your new lines memorized too?" Guy asked.

"Why don't you recite your new lines for your father?" Lili said.

The boy walked to the middle of the room and prepared to recite. He cleared his throat, raising his eyes towards the ceiling.

"There is so much sadness in the faces of my people. I have called on their gods, now I call on our gods. I call on our young. I call on our old. I call on our mighty and the weak. I call on everyone and anyone so that we shall all let out one piercing cry that we may either live freely or we should die."

155   "I see your new lines have as much drama as the old ones," Guy said. He wiped a tear away, walked over to the chair, and took the boy in his arms. He pressed the boy's body against his chest before lowering him to the ground.

"Your new lines are wonderful, son. They're every bit as affecting as the old." He tapped the boy's shoulder and walked out of the house.

"What's the matter with Papy?" the boy asked as the door slammed shut behind Guy.

"His heart hurts," Lili said.

After supper, Lili took her son to the field where she knew her husband would be. While the boy ran around, she found her husband sitting in his favorite spot behind the sugar mill.

160   "Nothing, Lili," he said. "Ask me nothing about this day that I have had."

She sat down on the grass next to him, for once feeling the sharp edges of the grass blades against her ankles.

"You're really good with that boy," he said, drawing circles with his smallest finger on her elbow. "You will make a performer of him. I know you will. You can see the best in that whole situation. It's because you have those stars in your eyes. That's the first thing I noticed about you when I met you. It was your eyes, Lili, so dark and deep. They drew me like danger draws a fool."

He turned over on the grass so that he was staring directly at the moon up in the sky. She could tell that he was also watching the hot-air balloon behind the sugar mill fence out of the corner of his eye.

"Sometimes I know you want to believe in me," he said. "I know you're wishing things for me. You want me to work at the mill. You want me to get a pretty house for us. I know you want these things too, but mostly you want me to feel like a man. That's why you're not one to worry about, Lili. I know you can take things as they come."

165   "I don't like it when you talk this way," she said.

"Listen to this, Lili. I want to tell you a secret. Sometimes, I just want to take that big balloon and ride it up in the air. I'd like to sail off somewhere and keep floating until I got to a really nice place with a nice plot of land where I could be something new. I'd build my own house, keep my own garden. Just *be* something new."

"I want you to stay away from there."

"I know you don't think I should take it. That can't keep me from wanting."

"You could be injured. Do you ever think about that?"

"Don't you ever want to be something new?" 170

"I don't like it," she said.

"Please don't get angry with me," he said, his voice straining almost like the boy's.

"If you were to take that balloon and fly away, would you take me and the boy?"

"First you don't want me to take it and now you want to go?"

"I just want to know that when you dream, me and the boy, we're always in 175
your dreams."

He leaned his head on her shoulders and drifted off to sleep. Her back ached as she sat there with his face pressed against her collar bone. He drooled and the saliva dripped down to her breasts, soaking her frayed polyester bra. She listened to the crickets while watching her son play, muttering his lines to himself as he went in a circle around the field. The moon was glowing above their heads. Winking at them, as Guy liked to say, on its way to brighter shores.

Opening his eyes, Guy asked her, "How do you think a man is judged after he's gone?"

How did he expect her to answer something like that?

"People don't eat riches," she said. "They eat what it can buy."

"What does that mean, Lili? Don't talk to me in parables. Talk to me 180
honestly."

"A man is judged by his deeds," she said. "The boy never goes to bed hungry. For as long as he's been with us, he's always been fed."

Just as if he had heard himself mentioned, the boy came dashing from the other side of the field, crashing in a heap on top of his parents.

"My new lines," he said. "I have forgotten my new lines."

"Is this how you will be the day of this play, son?" Guy asked. "When people give you big responsibilities, you have to try to live up to them."

The boy had relearned his new lines by the time they went to bed. 185

That night, Guy watched his wife very closely as she undressed for bed.

"I would like to be the one to rub that piece of lemon on your knees tonight," he said.

She handed him the half lemon, then raised her skirt above her knees.

Her body began to tremble as he rubbed his fingers over her skin.

"You know that question I asked you before," he said, "how a man is remem- 190
bered after he's gone? I know the answer now. I know because I remember my father, who was a very poor struggling man all his life. I remember him as a man that I would never want to be."

Lili got up with the break of dawn the next day. The light came up quickly above the trees. Lili greeted some of the market women as they walked together to the public water fountain.

On her way back, the sun had already melted a few gray clouds. She found the boy standing alone in the yard with a terrified expression on his face, the old withered mushrooms uprooted at his feet. He ran up to meet her, nearly knocking her off balance.

"What happened?" she asked. "Have you forgotten your lines?"

The boy was breathing so heavily that his lips could not form a single word.

195   "What is it?" Lili asked, almost shaking him with anxiety.

"It's Papa," he said finally, raising a stiff finger in the air.

The boy covered his face as his mother looked up at the sky. A rainbow-colored balloon was floating aimlessly above their heads.

"It's Papa," the boy said. "He is in it."

She wanted to look down at her son and tell him that it wasn't his father, but she immediately recognized the spindly arms, in a bright flowered shirt that she had made, gripping the cables.

200   From the field behind the sugar mill a group of workers were watching the balloon floating in the air. Many were clapping and cheering, calling out Guy's name. A few of the women were waving their head rags at the sky, shouting, "Go! Beautiful, go!"

Lili edged her way to the front of the crowd. Everyone was waiting, watching the balloon drift higher up into the clouds.

"He seems to be right over our heads," said the factory foreman, a short slender mulatto with large buckteeth.

Just then, Lili noticed young Assad, his thick black hair sticking to the beads of sweat on his forehead. His face had the crumpled expression of disrupted sleep.

"He's further away than he seems," said young Assad. "I still don't understand. How did he get up there? You need a whole crew to fly these things."

205   "I don't know," the foreman said. "One of my workers just came in saying there was a man flying above the factory."

"But how the hell did he start it?" Young Assad was perplexed.

"He just did it," the foreman said.

"Look, he's trying to get out!" someone hollered.

A chorus of screams broke out among the workers.

210   The boy was looking up, trying to see if his father was really trying to jump out of the balloon. Guy was climbing over the side of the basket. Lili pressed her son's face into her skirt.

Within seconds, Guy was in the air hurtling down towards the crowd. Lili held her breath as she watched him fall. He crashed not far from where Lili and the boy were standing, his blood immediately soaking the landing spot.

The balloon kept floating free, drifting on its way to brighter shores. Young Assad rushed towards the body. He dropped to his knees and checked the wrist for a pulse, then dropped the arm back to the ground.

"It's over!" The foreman ordered the workers back to work.

Lili tried to keep her son's head pressed against her skirt as she moved closer to the body. The boy yanked himself away and raced to the edge of the field where his father's body was lying on the grass. He reached the body as young Assad still knelt examining the corpse. Lili rushed after him.

215   "He is mine," she said to young Assad. "He is my family. He belongs to me."

Young Assad got up and raised his head to search the sky for his aimless balloon, trying to guess where it would land. He took one last glance at Guy's bloody corpse, then raced to his car and sped away.

The foreman and another worker carried a cot and blanket from the factory.

Little Guy was breathing quickly as he looked at his father's body on the ground. While the foreman draped a sheet over Guy's corpse, his son began to recite the lines from his play.

"A wall of fire is rising and in the ashes, I see the bones of my people. Not only those people whose dark hollow faces I see daily in the fields, but all those souls who have gone ahead to haunt my dreams. At night I relive once more the last caresses from the hand of a loving father, a valiant love, a beloved friend."

"Let me look at him one last time," Lili said, pulling back the sheet.   220

She leaned in very close to get a better look at Guy's face. There was little left of that countenance that she had loved so much. Those lips that curled when he was teasing her. That large flat nose that felt like a feather when rubbed against hers. And those eyes, those night-colored eyes. Though clouded with blood, Guy's eyes were still bulging open. Lili was searching for some kind of sign—a blink, a smile, a wink—something that would remind her of the man that she had married.

"His eyes aren't closed," the foreman said to Lili. "Do you want to close them, or should I?"

The boy continued reciting his lines, his voice rising to a man's grieving roar. He kept his eyes closed, his fists balled at his side as he continued with his newest lines.

"There is so much sadness in the faces of my people. I have called on their gods, now I call on our gods. I call on our young. I call on our old. I call on our mighty and the weak. I call on everyone and anyone so that we shall all let out one piercing cry that we may either live freely or we should die."

"Do you want to close the eyes?" the foreman repeated impatiently.   225

"No, leave them open," Lili said. "My husband, he likes to look at the sky."

1991

QUESTIONS

1. What does the hot-air balloon symbolize to Assad, its owner? to Guy? to the implied author?
2. The title of the story alludes to a speech that Little Guy must memorize for a school play about Haiti's history. The lines of the speech are rich in figurative language, including metaphors: "A wall of fire is rising and in the ashes, I see the bones of my people" (par. 34). How do the title's allusion and other aspects of the story confirm that the speech's image of "a wall of fire" is symbolic?
3. What do you think happens at the end of A WALL OF FIRE RISING? Is Guy's plunge to the earth a deliberate suicide or an accident? What are some symbolic interpretations of both possibilities?

HARUKI MURAKAMI

(b. 1949)

Barn Burning[1]

A devoted runner; a devotee of baseball and music, especially jazz; and, by his own estimate, a "very good" sandwich-maker who doesn't "do socialization much," Haruki Murakami has long enjoyed fame of both an intensity and a reach reserved for few writers: The "cult" of this "oxymoronic thing, a mainstream experimentalist," as a *Wall Street Journal* reviewer marvels, "spreads across the globe." Born in Kyoto and raised in Kobe, Japan, the only child of two teachers, and, in his youth, a voracious reader of everything but the Japanese literature they taught—Murakami, by his own account, came to writing both late and suddenly, in 1978: A twenty-nine-year-old running a successful jazz club with the wife he met in college, he went to a baseball game and had "some kind of epiphany" that he "could write." The novel he subsequently composed in English, translated into Japanese, and submitted for a prestigious first-novel award won that prize. And Murakami never stopped writing. In addition to numerous novels including *Norwegian Wood* (1987), *The Wind-Up Bird Chronicle* (1994–95), and *Kafka on the Shore* (2002), a memoir about running, and *Absolutely on Music: Conversations* (2011), Murakami's expansive and eclectic oeuvre includes *Underground: The Tokyo Gas Attack and the Japanese Psyche* (1997); the short-story collections *The Elephant Vanishes* (1993), *After the Quake* (2000), *Blind Willow, Sleeping Woman* (2006), and *Men without Women* (2014); and Japanese translations of writers such as F. Scott Fitzgerald, Raymond Carver, Tim O'Brien, and Ursula K. Le Guin. Credited with single-handedly "smash[ing]" the "continuum of Japanese writing" on behalf of a postwar generation soaked in an American popular culture they experienced as intoxicatingly liberating, Murakami's fiction manages to be at once instantly recognizable and impossible to categorize, oscillating between a blend of science and detective fiction, postmodernism, magic realism, and fantasy, on the one hand, and, on the other, an almost deadpan realism that endows the seemingly most banal events and characters with strangeness and mystery. Stage and screen adaptations of Murakami's work are numerous and include South Korean director and screenwriter Lee Chang-dong's *Burning* (2018), a film inspired by "Barn Burning."

I met her at a friend's wedding reception here in Tokyo, and we got to know each other. Three years ago. There was nearly a dozen years' age difference between us, she being twenty and I thirty-one. Not that it mattered much. I had a lot else on my mind then, and didn't have time to worry about things like age. And she didn't care about the difference at all. I was married, too, but that didn't bother her either. For her, your age or marital status or income were like your shoe size, how high or low your voice is, the shape of your fingernails—in

1. Translated from the Japanese by Philip Gabriel. Murakami's title echoes that of a well-known 1939 short story by William Faulkner (pp. 146–58).

other words, not the kind of thing you can do anything about. Come to think of it, I guess she's right.

She was studying with that guy—I can't remember his name—the famous mime, and working as an advertising model to make ends meet. But she usually found it too much trouble to go out on the assignments her agent got her, so her income didn't amount to much. What it didn't cover, her boyfriends made up. Of course, I don't know for sure. But things she said seemed to hint at that kind of arrangement.

I'm not saying that she slept with men for money. Maybe there were times when something close to that took place. But that's not the point. Something else was at work in her relations with men. There was a simplicity about her that attracted a certain type of man. He would look at that unabashed simplicity and want to put it together with his own complicated, bottled-up feelings. I can't explain it well, but I think that's what was going on. You could say that she lived on her simplicity.

Naturally, you couldn't expect things to work that way all the time. That would turn the whole structure of the universe upside down. It could only happen under certain conditions, in a certain time and place. The way it did with the Tangerine Peeling. Let me tell you about this Tangerine Peeling. As I mentioned, when I first met her she told me she was studying mime. "Is that so?" I said. Didn't surprise me too much. Young women these days are all studying something or other. But she didn't seem the type who'd be serious about perfecting a skill.

Then she showed me the Tangerine Peeling. As the name says, it involves 5 peeling a tangerine. On her left was a bowl piled high with tangerines; on her right, a bowl for the peels. At least that was the idea—actually there wasn't anything there at all. She'd take an imaginary tangerine in her hand, slowly peel it, put one section in her mouth, and spit out the seeds. When she'd finished one tangerine, she'd wrap up all the seeds in the peel and deposit it in the bowl to her right. She repeated these movements over and over again. When you try to put it in words it doesn't sound like anything special. But if you see it with your own eyes for ten or twenty minutes (we were just chatting at the bar, and, almost without thinking, she kept on performing it) gradually the sense of reality is sucked right out of everything around you. It's a very strange feeling. A long time ago, when Adolf Eichmann[2] was on trial in an Israeli court, someone said that a fitting punishment for him would be locking him in an airtight room and slowly pumping all the air out. I don't know how he actually died. . . . The story just sort of popped into my head.

"You're pretty talented," I told her.

2. German high official (1906–62) who organized the round-up and transportation of Jews to Nazi death camps during World War II. His 1961 trial by the Israeli state, which ended with a death sentence carried out the following year, is the subject of the controversial book *Eichmann in Jerusalem* (1963), in which philosopher Hannah Arendt develops her influential concept of the "banality of evil": the idea that Eichmann's and others' evil deeds resulted from and demonstrate not their peculiarly wicked, depraved, or abnormal character or ideology but rather the way in which ordinary but ambitious individuals fail to imagine or reflect on the human consequences of their actions.

"This? It's easy. Has nothing to do with talent. What you do isn't make your-self believe that there are tangerines there. You forget that the tangerines are *not* there. That's all."

"Sounds like Zen."[3]

I could see we were going to get along.

10   We didn't go out all that often. About once a month, twice at most. I'd call her up and ask her where she'd like to go. We'd have something to eat, have a few drinks in a bar. And talk up a storm. I'd listen to her talk, she'd listen to me. We had hardly anything in common to talk about, but that didn't matter. I guess you'd say we were friends. Naturally, I paid for everything, all the food and drink. A few times she called me up, usually when she'd run out of money and was hungry. On those occasions she ate like you wouldn't believe.

I was completely relaxed when I was with her. I could erase everything from my mind—all the work I didn't want to do, the jumble of senseless ideas people carry around in their heads. She had that effect on me. She didn't talk about anything in particular. Often I would just keep nodding my head, not really picking up the gist of her words. But listening to her made me feel relaxed, as if I were gazing at drifting clouds far off in the distance.

I talked about all sorts of things, too. I told her, as honestly as I could, my thoughts on everything, from personal dilemmas to the state of the world. You name it. Maybe she was doing the same thing I did—just nodding her head as she listened to me, without any of it sinking in. But I didn't care. What I was looking for was a certain *feeling*. A feeling that had nothing to do with sympa-thy—or understanding.

In the spring of the year after we met, her father had died of heart disease, and she inherited a little money from him. At least that's what she told me. She said she wanted to use the money to go to North Africa. I don't know why she picked North Africa, but I went ahead and introduced her to a girl I knew who worked at the Algerian Embassy in Tokyo. So off she went to Algeria. As things turned out, I went to see her off at the airport. She carried just one beat-up old bag with a few changes of clothes stuffed inside. Going through the luggage check, she looked more like she was going *home* to North Africa than taking a trip there.

"Are you going to come back to Japan?" I asked her, jokingly.

15   "Of course I am," she replied.

Three months later she was back, seven pounds lighter and tanned a deep brown. And with a new boyfriend. It seemed the two of them met at a restaurant in Algiers.[4] Since there weren't many Japanese there, they grew close and soon became lovers. As far as I knew, he was the first steady boyfriend she'd ever had.

He was in his late twenties, tall, impeccably dressed, and well-spoken. His face was somewhat expressionless, but he was handsome enough, and came across as a pleasant sort of guy. His hands were large, with long fingers.

I knew that much about him because I went to pick her up at the airport. A telegram had come all of a sudden from Beirut[5] with just the date and flight

3. Japanese school of Buddhism stressing the achievement of enlightenment through meditation.
4. Capital of Algeria, on North Africa's Mediterranean coast.
5. Capital, largest city, and chief port of Lebanon, on the Mediterranean Sea.

number. When the plane arrived (four hours late, because of bad weather—I sat in the airport coffee shop and read through three magazines) the two of them appeared at the gate arm in arm, for all the world like some nice young married couple. She introduced me to him, and we shook hands. He had the firm handshake of a person who'd lived abroad a long time. She said she was dying for a bowl of tempura and rice, so we went to a restaurant, and she had some while he and I had a couple of draught beers.

"I'm in the import-export business," he told me. But he didn't say anything more about it. Maybe he didn't want to talk about his job, or maybe he thought I'd find it boring, I really don't know. I didn't have much interest in hearing about trade, so I didn't ask any questions. Having nothing much to talk about, we talked about how dangerous Beirut had become, and about the water system in Tunis.[6] He seemed to be up on everything from North Africa to the Middle East.

When she'd finished her tempura, she gave a deep yawn and said she was 20 sleepy. She looked like she was going to conk out right on the spot; she had the habit of nodding off at the most unexpected times. He said he'd take her home by cab. I told them the train would be faster for me. I had no idea why I'd gone to all the trouble of coming out to the airport.

"I'm glad I could get to know you," he said, somewhat apologetically.

"Same here," I replied.

I saw him again several times after that. Whenever I ran into her, there he'd be, right beside her. And if I had a date with her he'd drive her to wherever we were supposed to meet. He drove a silver sports car, German. I know next to nothing about cars, so I can't really describe it well, but it looked like it belonged in a black-and-white Fellini[7] film.

"He must be pretty well off, don't you think?" I asked her once.

"Yeah," she answered without much interest. "Guess so."   25

"I wonder if you can make that much in foreign trade."

"Foreign trade?"

"That's what he told me. Said he was in foreign trade."

"Well, I guess he must be. But I don't know. He doesn't seem to be working anywhere. He meets a lot of people and makes a lot of phone calls, but he doesn't seem to be too wrapped up in it."

Just like Gatsby,[8] I thought. A young man who's a riddle: you have no idea 30 what he does, really, but he never seems to be hurting for money.

She called me one Sunday afternoon in October. My wife had left in the morning to visit relatives and I was alone. It was a beautiful, clear Sunday, and I was gazing at the camphor tree in the garden, eating an apple. I must have eaten seven apples that day. This happens from time to time—I get a pathological craving for apples.

"We were just in the neighborhood and wondered if we could drop by to see you," she said.

6. Capital of Tunisia, in North Africa.
7. Federico Fellini (1920–93), internationally acclaimed Italian film director renowned for superimposing dreamlike, hallucinatory imagery on ordinary situations.
8. Jay Gatsby, protagonist of F. Scott Fitzgerald's novel *The Great Gatsby* (1925), a mysterious, charismatic millionaire who raises himself out of poverty by questionable, even criminal means.

"We?" I asked.

"Him and me," she said.

35   "Sure, come on," I said.

"O.K.—we'll be over in half an hour," she said. And hung up.

I lay vacantly on the couch for a while, then got up and showered and shaved. Drying off, I cleaned my ears. I couldn't decide whether I should straighten up the house, and in the end decided not to. There wasn't enough time to do a thorough job of it, and if it can't be done right, I thought, better not bother with it at all. The room was littered with books, magazines, letters, records, pencils, and sweaters, but it didn't look that messy. I'd just finished a job and was feeling lazy. I sat down on the sofa and, gazing at the camphor tree, had myself another apple.

A little after two, I heard a car pull up to the house. When I opened the door, I saw the silver sports car at the curb. She stuck her face out the window and waved. I showed them where to park, out in back.

"Well, here we are!" she said with a smile. She wore a light shirt that showed the outline of her nipples through it, and an olive-green miniskirt.

40   He had on a navy-blue blazer. Somehow he seemed different, probably because of his two-day growth of beard. You'd think the whiskers would make him look scruffy; instead they gave him a certain presence. Getting out of the car, he took off his sunglasses and stuck them in his pocket.

"I'm really sorry to drop in like this all of a sudden on your day off," he said.

"No problem," I said. "It's like every day's a day off for me. And I was just ready for some company."

"We brought a meal," she said, and she hauled a large white paper sack from the rear seat of the car.

"A meal?"

45   "Nothing special. We just thought that since we dropped in on you on a Sunday we'd better bring something to eat," he said.

"Great. All I've had today is apples."

We went inside and laid the food out on the table. Quite a spread: roast-beef sandwiches, salad, smoked salmon, and blueberry ice cream—and plenty of everything. While she arranged it all on plates, I got some white wine out of the refrigerator and uncorked it. It looked like we were having ourselves a little party.

"Let's eat. I'm starved," she said, famished as usual.

We munched our sandwiches, ate our salad, and helped ourselves to the smoked salmon. When we'd polished off the wine, we drank some canned beer from the fridge. One thing you can always count on at my place is a fridge full of beer.

50   His color didn't change at all, no matter how much he drank. I am a pretty good beer drinker myself. She had a couple of cans with us, and in less than an hour the table was lined with empties. She selected a couple of records from the shelf and set them on the player. The first tune was Miles Davis doing "Airegin."[9]

"You don't see too many of these automatic changers these days," he said.

---

9. Jazz standard first recorded in 1954 by the Miles Davis Quintet, led by the trumpeter and composer of the same name (1926–91), arguably the single most revered, if also notoriously prickly, figure in American jazz.

I explained how I was a fan of automatic changers, and how I'd had a tough time coming up with a Garrard[1] in good shape. Nodding from time to time, he listened politely.

We talked about audio equipment for a while, and he fell quiet. Then he said, "I've got some grass, if you'd care for a smoke."

I wasn't sure how to react. I'd just given up smoking cigarettes a month before; it was touch and go whether I could shake the habit for good, and I had no idea what effect smoking marijuana would have on me. But I decided to give it a try. He took out the dark-colored leaves in a foil wrapper from the bottom of the paper sack, rolled the grass into a sheet of cigarette paper, and licked the glued edge. He lit up with his lighter and took a few drags to make sure the joint was going before passing it over to me. The grass was terrific. We sat there silently for a while, each taking a toke and then handing it along. Miles Davis was over, and a collection of Strauss[2] waltzes began to play. Not your usual programming, I thought. But not bad.

After we finished the first joint, she said she was sleepy. She hadn't gotten 55 enough rest the night before, apparently, and the three beers and the grass knocked her out. I showed her upstairs and put her to bed. She asked to borrow a T-shirt. I gave her one, she stripped down to her panties, pulled on the shirt, and lay down on the bed. "Are you cold?" I asked, but she was already snoring away. Shaking my head, I went back downstairs.

In the living room her boyfriend was rolling a second joint. He was something. Given a choice, I'd rather have snuggled up next to her in bed and taken a good nap, but that was out. I smoked the second joint with him, the Strauss waltzes still going. For some reason I remembered a play we'd done back in grade school. I was the owner of a glove shop. A baby fox comes in looking for gloves, but he doesn't have enough money to buy them.

"You can't buy gloves with that," I say. The villain.

"But Mama is so cold. Her paws are all chapped. *Please!*" the baby fox begs.

"Sorry, but it's not enough. Save up your money and come back later. If you do—"

"—sometimes I burn down barns," he said.   60

"Excuse me?" I said. I was drifting off, and I must have heard him wrong.

"Sometimes I burn down barns," he said again.

I looked at him. He was tracing the design on his lighter with the tip of his fingernail. He sucked the marijuana smoke deep into his lungs, held it there for ten seconds, then slowly let it out. The smoke swirled up like ectoplasm from his mouth. He passed me the joint.

"Pretty good stuff," I said.

He nodded. "I brought it back from India. The best they had. You smoke this 65 and all kinds of memories rush out at you. Light, smells, things like that. The quality of your memory"—he paused in a leisurely way, and, as if searching for

1. Device produced by Garrard Engineering and Manufacturing, a British company (founded 1915) once famous for its high-quality turntables and related equipment—in this case a mechanism enabling a turntable to automatically play multiple phonograph records in sequence (rather than one at a time).
2. German composer Richard Strauss (1864–1949).

the right words, lightly snapped his fingers a couple of times—"is like something you've never experienced before. Don't you think so?"

I do, I told him. I was lost in memories of the commotion on the grade-school
stage, of the smell of paint on the cardboard scenery.

"I'd like to hear about the barns," I said.

He gazed at me. His face, as usual, was expressionless.

"You don't mind me telling you about it?" he asked.

70 "Go right ahead," I replied.

"It's very simple, really. You pour gasoline around, throw on a lighted match
and *whoosh!* it's all over. Takes less than fifteen minutes to burn to the ground.
Of course, I'm not talking about large barns. More like sheds, really."

"So . . ." I said, and I stopped. I couldn't figure out how to go on. "So why do
you burn down barns?"

"Is it strange?"

"I'm not sure. You burn barns, and I don't. Obviously there's a difference
between the two. Rather than say which is strange and which isn't, what I'd like
to pin down is *how* they're different. But you're the one who brought up this
barn burning in the first place, right?"

75 "Yes," he said. "Right you are. Oh, by the way—do you have any Ravi Shankar[3]
records?"

"I don't," I told him.

He sat there blankly for a time. His mind seemed all twisted around, like
putty. Or maybe it was *my* mind that was all twisted around.

"I burn roughly one barn every two months," he said. And snapped his fingers again. "That seems about the right pace. For me, that is."

I nodded vaguely. *The right pace?*

80 "So, are these your own barns you burn?" I asked.

He looked at me as if he had no idea what I was talking about. "Why would
I burn down my own barns? What makes you think I own so many barns?"

"So, what you're telling me," I said, "is you burn other people's barns,
correct?"

"That's right," he said. "Of course that's right. Other people's barns. So it's illegal. Just like you and me sitting here smoking grass—definitely against the law."

I was silent, resting my elbows on the arms of the chair.

85 "I burn other people's barns without their permission. Of course, I always
choose one that won't turn into a four-alarm blaze. I don't want to start a fire—
just burn down barns."

I nodded, and snuffed out the stub of the joint. "But if you're caught you'll be
in trouble. It's arson, after all. You blow it and you could wind up in jail."

"I won't get caught," he said casually. "I pour on the gasoline, strike a match,
and take off. Then I have a good time watching it all from a distance with binoculars. I won't get caught. The police aren't going to comb the streets over a
lousy little barn burning down."

---

3. Legendary Indian musician and composer of Hindustani classical music (1920–2012); his world
tours and collaborations with others, particularly the Beatles, in the 1960s did much to popularize
Indian, particularly sitar, music in the West.

He was probably right, I thought. And no one would ever think that a well-dressed young man driving an expensive foreign car would be running around torching barns.

"Does she know about it?" I asked, pointing upstairs.

"She doesn't know a thing. Actually, I've never told another soul. It's not the 90 kind of topic you can bring up with just anybody."

"Then why me?"

He spread the fingers of his left hand straight out and rubbed his cheek. The whiskers made a scratchy, dry sound, like a bug crawling over a taut sheet of paper. "You're a writer, so I thought you must be interested in patterns of human behavior. Writers are supposed to appreciate something for what it is, before they hand down a judgment or whatever. If 'appreciate' isn't the right word, maybe you can say they can accept things for what they are. That's why I told you. Besides, I wanted to talk about it with someone."

I nodded. But in what way was I supposed to accept this as it was? Frankly, I had no idea.

He laughed. "The way I'm explaining it might be a little weird, I guess." He spread both hands in front of him and clapped them together. "The world's full of barns, that are, like, waiting for me to burn them down. A barn all by itself beside the ocean, a barn in the middle of a rice paddy[4] . . . Anyhow, all kinds of barns. Give me fifteen minutes, and I'll burn them clear to the ground. So it looks like there was never any barn there to begin with. No one gets choked up over it. It just . . . disappears. *Whoosh!*"

"But you're the one who judges that they're expendable, right?" 95

"I don't judge anything. The barns are waiting to be burned. I just accept that. I merely accept what's there. It's like the rain. The rain falls. The river swells up. Something gets carried away in the flow. Is the rain making a judgment? It's not like I'm out to commit an immoral act. I have my own code of morality. A sense of morality is important; people can't live without it. I think of it like this: morality is the delicate balance that's involved in parallel existence."

"Parallel existence? What do you mean?"

"In other words, I'm right here, but I'm over *there*, too. I'm in Tokyo, and at the same time I'm in Tunis. I can blame people and forgive them, all at once. There's a *balance* involved, and without it I don't think we'd be able to live. It's like a clasp—if it came undone we'd fall to pieces. But because it's there we can experience this kind of parallel existence."

"And burning down barns is consistent with your code of morality?"

"Not exactly. It's more an act that sustains that morality. But enough of this 100 morality talk. That's not the point I'm getting at. What I'm trying to say is that the world is filled with these barns. You've got your barns, I've got mine. Trust me, I know what I'm talking about. I've been almost everywhere in the world, done everything you could possibly imagine. Even stared death in the face a couple of times. Don't get me wrong, I'm not trying to brag or anything. But why don't we change the subject? I'm usually not this talkative—the grass makes me run off at the mouth."

4. Wet field in which rice is grown.

We sat there, silent and still for a while, waiting, it seemed, for the glow to wear off. I had no clue what I should say next. I felt as if I were looking through a train window watching a weird landscape flash in and out of view. My body was relaxed, yet I couldn't grasp the details of the scenes passing by. But I could grasp, quite distinctly, the presence of my own body. And with it a trace of parallel existence: here's me, over here thinking. And here's another me, *watching* the first me thinking. Time ticked by in polyrhythmic precision.

"Care for another beer?" I asked after a while.

"Thanks. Don't mind if I do."

I brought out four cans from the kitchen, along with some Camembert cheese.[5] We had two beers each and ate the cheese.

105 "When was the last time you burned down a barn?" I asked him.

"Let me see." He lightly gripped his empty beer can and thought for a while. "This summer, the end of August."

"And when are you going to burn down your next one?"

"I don't know. I'm not going by some schedule, circling dates on the calendar and holding off till then. I burn a barn when I get the urge to."

"But when you want to burn one, there isn't always the kind you're looking for just waiting for you, is there?"

110 "Of course not," he said quietly. "So I make sure I've got a good one picked out in advance."

"You lay in a supply, in other words."

"That's right."

"Can I ask you one more thing?"

"Sure."

115 "Have you already decided on your next barn?"

Frown lines formed between his eyes. And he breathed in a rush of air through his nose. "Yes. I've already found it."

I didn't say anything, just sipped at what was left of my beer.

"It's a wonderful barn. It's a long time since I've seen one so well worth burning. Actually, I came over here today to check it out."

"You mean it's around here?"

120 "Very close by," he said.

So ended our discussion of barns.

He woke up his girlfriend at five, and apologized again for having dropped in on me out of the blue. Even though he'd drunk a huge amount of beer, he was cold sober. He drove the car out from behind the house. It had one small nick, near the headlight.

"I'll keep an eye out for those barns," I said in farewell.

"Right," he said. "Anyhow, remember it's right nearby."

125 "What do you mean, 'barns'?" she asked.

"Just something between us men," he replied.

"I see," she said.

And they disappeared.

---

5. Strong-flavored, soft, creamy cheese named after the northern French village in which it was first produced.

I returned to the living room and plopped down on the sofa. The tabletop was covered with all kinds of garbage. I picked up my duffel coat from where it lay on the floor, covered myself with it, and fell sound asleep.

When I woke up, the room was pitch-dark. Seven o'clock.   130

A bluish pall and the pungent smell of the marijuana lay over the room. The darkness was strangely uneven. Still sacked out on the sofa, I tried to conjure up more memories of the school play, but I couldn't get a clear picture in my head. Did the baby fox ever get the gloves?

I got up from the sofa, opened the windows for some fresh air, made coffee in the kitchen, and drank it.

The next day, I went to the bookstore and bought a map of the part of town where I live. One of those black-and-white maps on a scale of one to twenty thousand, showing even the smallest lanes and alleys. Map in hand, I walked the neighborhood, marking with a pencil the location of every barn. Over three days, I explored an area some two and a half miles in each direction. My home was on the outskirts of town, with quite a few farms still around, so there were lots of barns. I counted sixteen.

The barn he planned to burn must be one of those. The way he'd said that it was right nearby made me sure it wasn't beyond the area I'd covered.

Next, I made a careful check of each of the sixteen barns. First, I eliminated the ones too close to people's houses or to those plastic-covered greenhouses farmers use. Next, I crossed off the ones that had farm tools and pesticides inside—that is, ones that looked as though someone was using them every day. I was sure he wouldn't want to burn one of those.

That left five barns. Five barns that could be burned. The kind that could   135 burn down in fifteen minutes, and would burn clear to the ground—and wouldn't be any loss. But I couldn't decide which of the five he'd pick. It was a question of personal preference. I was dying to find out which one it would be.

I spread out the map and erased all but five of the "X"s I'd made. Then I got out my T-square, French curve, and divider,[6] and I mapped out the shortest route that would pass all five barns and take me back home. The route curved along the river and over some hills, so the project took longer than I thought it would. The course ended up being four and one-third miles, no matter how many times I measured it.

At six the next morning I put on my jogging outfit and running shoes and ran the length of the course I'd mapped out. Since I usually do three and a half miles every morning, adding an extra mile didn't bother me too much. The scenery wasn't bad, and though there were two railroad crossings along the way, they didn't really slow me down.

The course circled the athletic grounds of the college near my house, then ran along the river and nearly two miles up a deserted dirt road. The first barn was halfway up the road. Then the course cut through a wood and up a slight slope. Another barn. A little way off, there was a stable for a racetrack. The horses might kick up a little ruckus if they saw a fire, but that's all; they wouldn't get hurt or anything.

6. Measuring compass. *T-square*: T-shaped instrument for drawing or testing right angles. *French curve*: template used for drawing curved lines.

The third and fourth barns looked alike, like two ugly old twins. They were only two hundred or so yards apart. Both of them were dilapidated and filthy. If you were going to burn down one of them, you might as well burn the pair.

140   The last barn stood beside a railroad crossing, at about the three-and-a-half-mile mark. It was clearly abandoned. It faced the road and had a tin Pepsi-Cola sign nailed to it. The building itself—I'm not sure you could even call it a building anymore—had mostly collapsed. It fit his description—a building just waiting for someone to commit it to the flames.

I stopped in front of the last barn, took a few deep breaths, then crossed the railroad tracks and headed home. The run took thirty-one minutes and thirty seconds. I took a shower and had breakfast. Then I lay on the sofa, listening to a record and, when that was finished, started work.

I ran the same course every morning for a month. But none of the barns burned down.

Sometimes the thought hit me that maybe he was trying to get *me* to burn down a barn. As if he'd filled my head with the image of a barn burning and were steadily pumping it up more and more, like putting air in a bicycle tire. There were even times when I thought that, as long as I was waiting for him to do it, I might as well go ahead and strike a match and burn one down. It's just a beat-up old barn, right?

But that's going too far. After all, it's not me who burns barns, it's *him*. No matter how much the image of burning barns might swell up in my head, I'm just not the barn-burning type.

145   Maybe he decided on some other barn somewhere. Or was too busy to find the time to burn one. I didn't hear from her at all.

December came, and with it the end of fall, and the morning air turned piercingly cold. No change in the barns, just white frost covering their roofs. In frozen woods, winter birds noisily flapped their wings. The world moved on as always.

The next time I saw him was that December, a few days before Christmas. Wherever you went, Christmas carols were playing. I was busy walking around town buying presents for all sorts of people. Over near Nogizaki,[7] I spotted his car in the parking lot of a coffee shop. There was no mistaking that silver sports car, with its Shinagawa[8] plates and the small scratch next to the left headlight. The car didn't look as bright and shiny as it used to. The silver seemed faded, but that may have just been my imagination. I have a tendency to rework my memories to suit me. Without thinking, I went inside.

The interior of the shop was dark, with a strong aroma of coffee. People's voices were muted, and baroque music[9] played softly in the background. I spotted him right away. Seated by the window, he was drinking café au lait.[1] The shop was hot enough to fog up your glasses, but he hadn't removed his cashmere coat. Or his muffler.

7. Subway station in Minato City, an expensive, fashionable ward (or district) of Tokyo.
8. Another ward of Tokyo.
9. A style of Western classical music produced c. 1600–1750, characterized by complexity and expressiveness.
1. Literally, "coffee with milk" (French); a combination of roughly equal parts hot milk and coffee.

I was a little flustered, but I just said hello. I didn't tell him I'd seen his car parked out front; I happened to come into the shop and happened to run into him.

"Mind if I sit down?" I asked. 150

"Not at all. Please go ahead," he said.

We chatted for a while. But our conversation went nowhere. We didn't have much to say to each other, and his thoughts seemed to be elsewhere. Even so, he didn't appear to mind my sharing his table. He told me about the harbor in Tunisia. And about the shrimp they catch there. It wasn't that he felt obliged to talk; he just wanted to tell me about the shrimp. But the story ran out halfway through, like a trickle of water being sucked up by sand.

He raised his hand, called a waiter over, and ordered a second cup of café au lait.

"By the way, whatever happened to that barn?" I ventured to ask him.

A trace of a smile played at the corners of his mouth. "Ah—you still remem- 155 ber, I see," he said. He took his handkerchief out of his pocket, wiped his mouth, and put the handkerchief back in his pocket. "I burned it, of course. Burned it right down. Just like I said I would."

"Near my house?"

"Yes. Right nearby."

"When?"

"A while back, ten days after we dropped by your house."

I told him about marking the locations of the barns on a map and running 160 past them once a day. "So I couldn't have missed it," I said.

"You're quite meticulous, aren't you?" he said brightly. "Meticulous and logi-cal. But you must have overlooked it. That happens sometimes. A thing's too close and you miss it."

"Well, I don't get it."

He straightened his tie and glanced at his watch. "It's too close," he said. "But I have to be going. Why don't we have a nice long talk about it next time? You'll have to excuse me, but someone's waiting for me."

There was no reason to keep him any longer. He stood up and put his ciga-rettes and lighter in his pocket.

"Oh, by the way, have you seen her since that day?" he asked. 165

"No, I haven't. Have you?"

"No. I can't get hold of her. She isn't in her apartment, I can't get through by phone, and she hasn't been going to her mime class for a long time."

"I imagine she just took off for somewhere. She's done that a number of times."

He stood there, hands stuck in his pockets, and stared at the tabletop. "With no money, for a month and a half? She's not the kind who can make it on her own, you know."

He snapped his fingers inside his pocket a couple of times. 170

"She doesn't have a cent," he continued. "Or any real friends, either. Her address book is crammed, but those are just names. There's not a single per-son she can depend on. You're the only one she trusted. I'm not saying that to be polite. You were someone special to her. Even made me a bit jealous. And I'm not the kind of person who's ever jealous." He gave a slight sigh and looked at his watch again. "I've really got to be going. Let's get together again sometime."

I nodded. But the right words wouldn't come out. It was always that way. Whenever I was with him the words just wouldn't flow.

I tried calling her a couple of times after that, until the phone company shut off her phone. I was a little worried, so I went to her apartment. Her door was locked. A sheaf of junk mail was stuffed in her mailbox. I couldn't locate the building supervisor, so I couldn't even find out if she still lived there. I tore a page from my appointment book, wrote a note saying, "Get in touch with me," signed my name, and dropped it in her mailbox.

Not a word.

175   The next time I visited her apartment, there was someone else's nameplate on the door. I knocked, but no one answered. Just like the last time, the super was nowhere to be found.

So I gave up. That was almost a year ago. She just disappeared.

I still run past the five barns every morning. No barn in my neighborhood has burned down. And I haven't heard about any barn burning. December's come again, and the winter birds fly overhead. And I keep on getting older.

1992

QUESTIONS

1. Toward the end of BARN BURNING, the narrator suggests that the story's female character "just took off for somewhere" (par. 168). What do you surmise happens to her, and what cues in the story lead you to that conclusion?
2. What, if anything, might barns and barn burning come to stand for or even to symbolize in Murakami's story? What evidence supports your interpretation?
3. BARN BURNING makes frequent use of allusion, even borrowing its title from a William Faulkner story about a young boy faced with the choice of either abetting his sharecropper father's burning of barns or trying to stop it. Which of Murakami's allusions seem most meaningful, and why and how so? When and how might an allusion contribute to characterization? to conflict or theme?

SUGGESTIONS FOR WRITING

1. Choose any story in this chapter, read it thoroughly, and follow the guidelines for responding to symbolism that appear earlier in this chapter. Write an essay in which you explore the various meanings of the story's major symbol and the way these emerge over the course of the story.
2. In THE BIRTH-MARK, Aylmer the scientist is portrayed as "spiritual" and "intellectual," in contrast with his crudely physical laboratory assistant, Aminadab (par. 25). Write an essay in which you argue that the allegory of Aylmer's terrible experiment on his wife refers not only to a man's desire for immortal beauty but also to his desire for control of everything physical, including the laborer.
3. Write an essay in which you compare the way symbolism works in THE BIRTH-MARK and either A WALL OF FIRE RISING or BARN BURNING. For example, what is the effect and significance of both the magical atmosphere of Byatt's story and the way its characters explicitly refer to particular objects as symbols? How might symbolism work differently in Danticat's or Murakami's story because of its realistic, contemporary setting and plot and the fact that its characters don't explicitly refer to anything as a symbol?

4. To what extent are characters aware of the symbolism in a story? Do characters accept the symbolism as objective and real, even if what happens seems magical or impossible? Write an essay focused on characters' different ways of responding to or believing in a symbol or symbolism in one or two stories. For instance, in THE THING IN THE FOREST, Primrose says, "We've got into a mystery, but we didn't make it up" (par. 65). What else in the story confirms that the girls' memories are more than illusion? How do the two women respond differently after they meet again? You might raise similar questions concerning THE BIRTH-MARK and compare the characters' awareness and response to the respective symbols in Byatt's and Hawthorne's stories.

SAMPLE WRITING: COMPARATIVE ESSAY

The essay below compares two stories by exploring the role symbolism plays in each. More specifically, it tackles questions posed in the fourth writing suggestion at the end of chapter 6: To what extent does anything within a story (or stories) become a symbol not only for readers but also for the characters themselves? What, for these characters, does the thing symbolize? What seems alike and different about how various characters perceive or interpret and respond to the same symbol? What is the significance and effect of their various perceptions and responses?

As you read the essay, try to identify the specific strategies and techniques this student writer uses to tackle the single greatest challenge of the comparative essay—creating one coherent argument out of observations about two different literary texts. (For more on comparative essays, see 30.2.1.)

For ease of reference, we have altered the citations in this essay to refer to paragraph numbers. Unless your instructor indicates otherwise, you should follow convention by instead citing page numbers when writing about fiction.

Collins 1

Charles Collins
Dr. Mays
English 298
15 May 2021

Symbolism in "The Birth-Mark" and "The Thing in the Forest"

In "The Birth-Mark" by Nathaniel Hawthorne and A. S. Byatt's "The Thing in the Forest," the symbols of the birthmark and the Thing move the plots of the stories. Characters in both stories are compelled by these objects to act, though in different ways. In "The Birth-Mark," the main character, Aylmer, views his wife's birthmark as a flaw in her beauty, as well as a symbol of human imperfection, and tries to remove it. In "The Thing in the Forest," the protagonists, Penny and Primrose, react to the Thing both as a real thing and as a symbol. The characters' interpretation of these things is what creates conflict, and the stories are both shaped by the symbolic meanings that the characters ascribe to those things.

In "The Birth-Mark," Aylmer, a "natural philosopher," becomes obsessed with a birthmark in the shape of a small hand on his wife's face. The plot of the story concerns his attempt to remove the mark, which results in the death of Georgiana,

Collins 2

his wife. The reader finds out in the very beginning that Aylmer views Georgiana's birthmark as more than a mere birthmark. In fact, it is because he views the mark as symbolic that he becomes obsessed with it. He makes his thoughts clear when he says to his wife, in response to her stating that other people have found her birthmark attractive, "No, dearest Georgiana, you came so nearly perfect from the hand of Nature, that this slightest possible defect, which we hesitate whether to term a defect or a beauty, shocks me, as being the visible mark of earthly imperfection" (par. 5). Aylmer sees his wife as nearly perfect, so when he sees something that does not seem consistent with his idea of beauty, he is disturbed by it and begins to view it as having a greater meaning. The narrator later clarifies this point by saying, "In this manner, selecting it as the symbol of his wife's liability to sin, sorrow, decay, and death, Aylmer's somber imagination was not long in rendering the birth-mark a frightful object, causing him more trouble and horror than ever Georgiana's beauty, whether of soul or sense, had given him delight" (par. 8). Here the story explicitly states that Aylmer sees his wife's birthmark as more than a physical feature; to him, it is a symbol of all of the imperfect things about humans.

Though the narrator suggests that "[w]e know not whether Aylmer possessed this degree of faith in man's ultimate control over nature," such that "the philosopher should lay his hand on the secret of creative force and perhaps make new worlds for himself" (par. 1), Aylmer's actions throughout the story suggest that he does believe this. Once Aylmer sees the birthmark as a "frightful object," he becomes intent upon removing it. The birthmark to him symbolizes human imperfection, and so it is a challenge to him to conquer that imperfection and control the "defect" that Nature placed upon his wife. It is only because he views the birthmark as a symbol that it comes to have this level of control over him and to motivate his actions and thus the plot of the story.

Unfortunately for Aylmer, he does not realize the cost of getting rid of the birthmark. He succeeds in his plan, but by succeeding he ends up killing his wife. What he sees as a symbol of imperfection the reader can see as a symbol of life. In Aylmer's dream the birthmark is tied to Georgiana's heart, and he must remove her heart to remove the birthmark. Georgiana's heart and her birthmark are actually symbolic of the human spark of life that keeps her alive. Perhaps part of this spark involves imperfection, or perhaps it is "a charm," but either way Georgiana cannot live without it. Aminadab seems to understand this and remarks to himself that "[i]f she were my wife, I'd never part with that birthmark" (par. 27).

However, both Aylmer and Georgiana are so horrified by what the birthmark represents that they are willing to take incredible risks to get rid of it. Georgiana even acknowledges that removing the birthmark might kill her, but says, "Danger is nothing to me; for life, while this hateful mark makes me the object of your horror and disgust . . . is a burden which I would fling down with joy" (par. 18). Because Aylmer and Georgiana view the birthmark as a mark of human imperfection, they are willing to try to remove it, so much so that Aylmer fails to see how the birthmark is tied to Georgiana's life and that Georgiana is willing to lose her life to be rid of it. Aylmer misinterprets the birthmark, thinking that it represents imperfection instead of life, and so he ends up losing his perfect wife.

The symbolism in "The Birth-Mark" is fairly straightforward. The characters openly acknowledge the power of the symbol, and the narrator of the story clearly states what meaning Aylmer finds in it. In "The Thing in the Forest" what the Thing represents is not as clear. Penny and Primrose, the story's main characters, do not view the Thing as symbolic, as Aylmer does the birthmark. Neither the narrator nor the characters directly say why the Thing is important to Penny and Primrose or even whether the Thing they see in the forest is the monster, the Loathly Worm, that they later read about in the book at the mansion. Instead of viewing the Thing as a symbol, Penny and Primrose view the Thing as real and physical. Penny says, "I think, I think there are things that are real—more real than we are—but mostly we don't cross their paths, or they don't cross ours" (par. 55). When Primrose returns to the forest she also realizes that the Thing is real, even more real than her everyday life at home. Penny and Primrose comfort each other by acknowledging that the Thing really exists, that they saw it, and that it "finished off" Alys. But despite their assertions that the Thing exists, they do not say what it is. Primrose says to Penny, "We've got into a mystery, but we didn't make it up. It wasn't a delusion" (par. 65). Though they reassure one another that the Thing is real, they recognize that what they saw is more mysterious than the mythical Loathly Worm.

Though they do not define the Thing, it motivates Penny and Primrose to act just as the birthmark causes Aylmer to act. However, each girl responds in a different way. On the one hand, Primrose, who makes her living telling fantastic stories to children, "had never frightened the littluns she entertained, with tales of lost children in forests" (par. 74). Primrose has avoided the Thing by entering a world of fairy tales where she speaks of the forest in unrealistic terms. After going to the forest and realizing "[s]he had understood something, and did not know what she had understood" (par. 78), she is able to continue with her life by finally telling the story of their encounter with the Thing as a fairy tale to children. She makes the Thing unreal and is therefore able to live with it.

Penny, on the other hand, tries to study the Thing because "[s]omething that resembled unreality had lumbered into reality, and she had seen it" (par. 86). After seeing the Thing, she becomes uninterested in fiction, like the stories Primrose told or like the novels she read as a child, and instead becomes a child psychologist who tries to scientifically study children who see things that are "more real." Upon the death of her mother and her visit to the mansion and the forest, Penny feels compelled to confront the Thing, refusing to take it as a symbol. She goes into the forest to seek out the Thing, but it does not come to her. As time passes, she begins to see the darkness of the thing all around her, and so she goes back to the forest once again to confront the Thing, where presumably it "finishes her off," as there is no account of her life after the encounter. When Penny goes to see the Thing for the final time, "she would look it in the face, she would see what it was. She clasped her hands loosely in her lap. Her nerves relaxed. Her blood slowed. She was ready" (par. 93). Penny treats the Thing as real, and so there are real consequences for her. Though the story does not state so explicitly, presumably the Thing kills Penny as it did Alys.

Though the characters in the story do not state what the Thing represents, the story suggests that it is a symbol of suffering and death, among other

Collins 4

things. The women's visits to the Thing correspond with the deaths of their parents. The first time the girls see the Thing is during the bombing of London during World War II, shortly before their fathers die. When they go to the mansion the second time, it is shortly after the deaths of their mothers. When the adult Primrose goes into the forest, instead of seeing the worm, she recognizes that the memory of her mother telling her about her father's death was "real," like the Thing. The Thing also looks and smells like something that has died, like "liquid . . . putrefaction" and "maggoty things at the bottom of untended dustbins" (par. 33), something that is decomposing. Furthermore, the characters believe that the Thing got Alys, that is, that she died. All of this suggests that the Thing is a symbol for death and that the story is about how different people handle death.

While symbolism is present in both "The Birth-Mark" and "The Thing in the Forest," it is handled in different ways. In "The Birth-Mark," on the one hand, Aylmer consistently views the birthmark as a symbol. He is obsessed with the birthmark because of what he thinks it represents. He has little concern for the birthmark as a physical, real thing. Penny and Primrose, on the other hand, are initially worried about the Thing as something real and physical. Penny never views the Thing as a symbol, but instead views it as a real thing, a monster, and presumably at the end of the story she faces it, and it kills her. Primrose, however, understands that the Thing is real, but chooses to make it a part of a fairy tale and thereby deals with it as a type of symbol, even though she does not understand what the Thing is a symbol of. By choosing to tell a story about the Thing, she makes it unreal, and it does not harm her. In both stories, the power given to symbolism or its rejection is what motivates the actions of the characters and determines the consequences they suffer.

Collins 5

Works Cited

Byatt, A. S. "The Thing in the Forest." Mays, pp. 379-93.

Hawthorne, Nathaniel. "The Birth-Mark." Mays, pp. 366-77.

Mays, Kelly J., editor. *The Norton Introduction to Literature.* Shorter 14th ed., W. W. Norton, 2021.

7 | THEME

At some point, a responsive reader of any story or novel will inevitably ask, *Why does it all matter? What does it all mean? What's the point?* When we ask what a text means, we are inquiring, at least in part, about its **theme**—a general idea or insight conveyed by the work in its entirety. Theme is certainly not the only way fiction matters nor the only thing we take away from our experience of reading it. Nor is theme fiction's *point* in the sense of its sole "objective" or "purpose." Yet theme is a fictional work's *point* in the sense of its "essential meaning" (or meanings). And our experience of any work isn't complete unless we grapple with the question of its theme.

On rare occasions, we might not have to grapple hard or look far: A very few texts, such as **fables** and certain fairy tales and folktales, explicitly state their themes. To succeed, however, even these works must ultimately "earn" their themes, bringing a raw statement to life through their characters, plot, setting, symbols, and narration. The following fable, by Aesop, succinctly makes its point through a brief dialogue.

AESOP

The Two Crabs

One fine day two crabs came out from their home to take a stroll on the sand. "Child," said the mother, "you are walking very ungracefully. You should accustom yourself to walking straight forward without twisting from side to side."

"Pray, mother," said the young one, "do but set the example yourself, and I will follow you."

"EXAMPLE IS THE BEST PRECEPT."

*   *   *

In most literary works, all the elements work together to imply an unstated theme that usually requires re-reading to decipher. Even the most careful and responsive readers will likely disagree about just what the theme is or how best to state it. And each statement of a given theme will imply a slightly different view of what matters most and why.

THEME(S): SINGULAR OR PLURAL?

In practice, readers even disagree about the precise meaning of the term *theme* itself. One source of disagreement hinges on the question of whether any single work of fiction can convey more than one theme. On one side of the debate are those who use the word *theme* to refer only to the central or main idea of a work. On the other are those who use the term, as we generally do in this book, to refer to any idea a work conveys. While the former readers tend to talk about *the* theme, the latter instead refer to *a* theme in order to stress that each theme is only one of many. Regardless of whether we call all of the ideas expressed in a work *themes* or instead refer to some of them as *subthemes*, the essential points on which all agree are that a single literary work often expresses multiple ideas and that at least one of those ideas is likely to be more central or overarching and inclusive than others.

THE TWO CRABS demonstrates that even the most simple and straightforward of stories can convey more than one idea. This fable's stated theme, "Example is the best precept," emerges only because the little crab "back talks" to its mother, implicitly suggesting another theme: that children are sometimes wiser than their parents or even that we sometimes learn by questioning, rather than blindly following, authority. The fact that crabs naturally "twist from side to side"—that no crab *can* walk straight—certainly adds **irony** to the fable, but might it also imply yet another theme?

BE SPECIFIC: THEME AS IDEA VERSUS TOPIC OR SUBJECT

Often, you will see the term *theme* used very loosely to refer to a topic or subject captured in a noun phrase—"the wisdom of youth," "loss of innocence," "the dangers of perfectionism"—or even a single noun—"loss," "youth," "grief," or "prejudice." Identifying such topics—especially those specific enough to require a noun phrase rather than a single noun—can be a useful first step on the way to figuring out a particular story's themes and also to grouping stories together for the purpose of comparison.

For now, though, we urge you to consider this merely a first step on the path to interpreting a story. The truth is, we haven't yet said anything very insightful, revealing, or debatable about the meaning of an individual story until we articulate the idea it expresses *about* a topic such as love, prejudice, or grief. To state a theme in this much more restricted and helpful sense, you will need at least one complete sentence. Note, however, that a complete sentence is still not necessarily a statement of theme. For example, an online student essay begins with the less than scintillating sentence, "In Nathaniel Hawthorne's 'The Birth-Mark' the reader finds several themes—guilt, evil, love, and alienation." One reason this sentence is both unexciting and unhelpful is that—despite its specific list of topics—we could in fact substitute for THE BIRTH-MARK almost any other story in this book. (Try it yourself.) Notice how much more interesting things get, however, when we instead articulate the story's particular insight about just one of these very general topics: "Nathaniel Hawthorne's 'The Birth-Mark' shows us that we too often destroy the very thing we love by trying to turn the good into the perfect."

DON'T BE TOO SPECIFIC: THEME AS *GENERAL* IDEA

Though a theme is specific in the sense that it is a complete idea or statement rather than a topic, it is nonetheless a *general* idea rather than one that describes the characters, plot, or settings unique to one story. Theme is a general insight illustrated *through* these elements rather than an insight *about* any of them. Look again at the statement above—"Nathaniel Hawthorne's 'The Birth-Mark' shows us that we too often destroy the very thing we love by trying to turn the good into the perfect." Now compare this statement with one such as this: "In Nathaniel Hawthorne's 'The Birth-Mark,' the scientist Aylmer kills his wife because he can't tolerate imperfection." Though both statements are valid, only the first of them is truly a statement of theme—of what the story shows us about love through Aylmer rather than what the story suggests about Aylmer himself.

THEME VERSUS MORAL

In some cases, a theme may take the form of a **moral**—a rule of conduct or maxim for living. But most themes are instead general observations and insights about how humans actually *do* behave, or about how life, the world, or some particular corner of it actually *is*, rather than moral imperatives about how people *should* behave or how life *should* ideally be. As one contemporary critic puts it, a responsive reader should thus "ask not *What does this story teach?* but *What does this story reveal?*" By the same token, we're usually on safer and more fertile ground if we phrase a theme as a statement rather than as a command. Hawthorne's "The Birth-Mark," for example, certainly demonstrates the dangers of arrogantly seeking a perfection that isn't natural or human. As a result, we might well be tempted to reduce its theme to a moral such as "Accept imperfection," "Avoid arrogance," or "Don't mess with Mother Nature." None of these statements is wholly inappropriate to the story. Yet each of them seems to underestimate the story's complexity and its implicit emphasis on all that humanity gains, as well as loses, in the search for perfection. As a result, a better statement of the story's theme might be "Paradoxically, both our drive for perfection and our inevitable imperfection make us human."

As you decipher and discuss the themes of the stories that follow, keep in mind that to identify a theme is not to "close the case" but rather to begin a more searching investigation of the details that make each story vivid and unique. Theme is an abstraction from the story; the story and its details do not disappear or lose significance once distilled into theme, nor could you reconstruct a story merely from a statement of its theme. Indeed, theme and story are fused, inseparable. Or, as Flannery O'Connor puts it, "You tell a story because a statement [alone] would be inadequate" (see WRITING SHORT STORIES in ch. 8). Often difficult to put into words, themes are nonetheless the essential common ground that helps you care about a story and relate it to your own life—even though it seems to be about lives and experiences very different from your own.

Tips for Identifying Themes

Because theme emerges from a work in its entirety and from all the other elements working together, there is no "one-size-fits-all" method for identifying theme. Here, however, are some things to look for and consider as you read and re-read the work.

TIP	EXAMPLE
1. Pay attention to the title. A title will seldom spell out in full a work's main theme, but some titles do suggest a central topic or topics or a clue to theme. Probe the rest of the story to see what, if any, insights about that topic it ultimately seems to offer.	What might Bharati Mukherjee's "The Management of Grief" suggest about whether and how grief can be "managed"?
2. List any recurring phrases and words, especially those for abstract concepts (e.g., love, honor). Certain concrete terms (especially if noted in the title) may likewise provide clues; objects of value or potency might attract significant attention in the text (an heirloom, a weapon, a tree in a garden). Then probe the story to see how and where else it might implicitly deal with that concept or entity and what, if any, conclusions the story proposes.	Versions of the word "blind" occur six times in the relatively short first paragraph of Raymond Carver's "Cathedral," and the word recurs throughout the story. What different kinds of blindness does the story depict? What truth or insight about blindness might it ultimately offer?
3. Identify any statements that the characters or narrator(s) make about a general concept, issue, or topic such as human nature, the natural world, and so on. Look, too, for statements that potentially have a general meaning or application beyond the story, even if they refer to a specific situation in it. Then consider whether and how the story as a whole corroborates, overturns, or complicates any one such view or statement.	In A. S. Byatt's "The Thing in the Forest," one of the two protagonists observes, "[. . .] I think there are things that are real—more real than we are—but mostly we don't cross their paths, or they don't cross ours. Maybe at very bad times we get into their world, or notice what they are doing in ours" (par. 55). How does the rest of the story both flesh out what these "things" might be and either corroborate or complicate this character's generalization about them?
4. If a character changes over the course of the story, articulate the truth or insight that he or she seems to discover. Then consider whether and how the story as a whole corroborates or complicates that insight.	The end of "The Thing in the Forest" implies that one of its protagonists has come to believe that even the most fantastic stories have an important function in real life. What is that function? Does the story as a whole confirm her conclusions?

TIP	EXAMPLE
5. Identify a conflict depicted in the work and state it in general terms or turn it into a general question, leaving out any reference to specific characters, situations, and so on. Then think about the insight or theme that might be implied by the way the conflict is resolved.	Through Sarty, William Faulkner's "Barn Burning" raises the question of how we should reconcile loyalty to our family with our own individual sense of right and wrong. In the end, the story implies that following our own moral code can sometimes be the more painful, as well as the more noble, option.

GABRIEL GARCÍA MÁRQUEZ
(1927–2014)

A Very Old Man with Enormous Wings: A Tale for Children[1]

Born in Aracataca, Colombia, a remote town near the Caribbean coast, Gabriel García Márquez studied law at the University of Bogotá and then worked as a journalist in Latin America, Europe, and the United States. From 1967 to 1975, he lived in Barcelona, Spain, later dividing his time between Mexico City, Mexico; Paris, France; and Havana, Cuba. His first published book, *Leaf Storm* (1955), set in the fictional small town of Macondo, is based on the myths and legends of his childhood home. His most famous novel, *One Hundred Years of Solitude* (1967), fuses magic, reality, fable, and fantasy to present six generations of one Macondo family, a microcosm of many of the social, political, and economic problems of Latin America. Among his many other works are *The Autumn of the Patriarch* (1975), *Chronicle of a Death Foretold* (1981), *Love in the Time of Cholera* (1985), *Of Love and Other Demons* (1994), and *Living to Tell the Tale* (2002), a three-volume set of memoirs. García Márquez won the Nobel Prize in Literature in 1982.

O n the third day of rain they had killed so many crabs inside the house that Pelayo had to cross his drenched courtyard and throw them into the sea, because the newborn child had a temperature all night and they thought it was due to the stench. The world had been sad since Tuesday. Sea and sky were a single ash-gray thing and the sands of the beach, which on March nights glimmered like powdered light, had become a stew of mud and rotten shellfish. The light was so weak at noon that when Pelayo was coming back to the house after throwing away the crabs, it was hard for him to see what it was that was moving and groaning in the rear of the courtyard. He had to go very close to see that it was an old man, a very old man, lying face down in the mud, who, in

1. Translated from the Spanish by Gregory Rabassa.

spite of his tremendous efforts, couldn't get up, impeded by his enormous wings.

Frightened by that nightmare, Pelayo ran to get Elisenda, his wife, who was putting compresses on the sick child, and he took her to the rear of the court-yard. They both looked at the fallen body with mute stupor. He was dressed like a ragpicker.[2] There were only a few faded hairs left on his bald skull and very few teeth in his mouth, and his pitiful condition of a drenched great-grandfather had taken away any sense of grandeur he might have had. His huge buzzard wings, dirty and half-plucked, were forever entangled in the mud. They looked at him so long and so closely that Pelayo and Elisenda very soon overcame their surprise and in the end found him familiar. Then they dared speak to him, and he answered in an incomprehensible dialect with a strong sailor's voice. That was how they skipped over the inconvenience of the wings and quite intelli-gently concluded that he was a lonely castaway from some foreign ship wrecked by the storm. And yet, they called in a neighbor woman who knew everything about life and death to see him, and all she needed was one look to show them their mistake.

"He's an angel," she told them. "He must have been coming for the child, but the poor fellow is so old that the rain knocked him down."

On the following day everyone knew that a flesh-and-blood angel was held captive in Pelayo's house. Against the judgment of the wise neighbor woman, for whom angels in those times were the fugitive survivors of a celestial con-spiracy, they did not have the heart to club him to death. Pelayo watched over him all afternoon from the kitchen, armed with his bailiff's[3] club, and before going to bed he dragged him out of the mud and locked him up with the hens in the wire chicken coop. In the middle of the night, when the rain stopped, Pelayo and Elisenda were still killing crabs. A short time afterward the child woke up without a fever and with a desire to eat. Then they felt magnanimous and decided to put the angel on a raft with fresh water and provisions for three days and leave him to his fate on the high seas. But when they went out into the courtyard with the first light of dawn, they found the whole neighborhood in front of the chicken coop having fun with the angel, without the slightest rever-ence, tossing him things to eat through the openings in the wire as if he weren't a supernatural creature but a circus animal.

Father Gonzaga arrived before seven o'clock, alarmed at the strange news. 5 By that time onlookers less frivolous than those at dawn had already arrived and they were making all kinds of conjectures concerning the captive's future. The simplest among them thought that he should be named mayor of the world. Others of sterner mind felt that he should be promoted to the rank of five-star general in order to win all wars. Some visionaries hoped that he could be put to stud in order to implant on earth a race of winged wise men who could take charge of the universe. But Father Gonzaga, before becoming a priest, had been a robust woodcutter. Standing by the wire, he reviewed his catechism in an instant and asked them to open the door so that he could take a close look at that pitiful man who looked more like a huge decrepit hen among the fascinated

2. Someone who earns a living by collecting rags and other refuse.
3. Local government official, usually one employed to make arrests and serve warrants.

chickens. He was lying in a corner drying his open wings in the sunlight among the fruit peels and breakfast leftovers that the early risers had thrown him. Alien to the impertinences of the world, he only lifted his antiquarian eyes and murmured something in his dialect when Father Gonzaga went into the chicken coop and said good morning to him in Latin. The parish priest had his first suspicion of an imposter when he saw that he did not understand the language of God or know how to greet His ministers. Then he noticed that seen close up he was much too human: he had an unbearable smell of the outdoors, the back side of his wings was strewn with parasites and his main feathers had been mistreated by terrestrial winds, and nothing about him measured up to the proud dignity of angels. Then he came out of the chicken coop and in a brief sermon warned the curious against the risks of being ingenuous. He reminded them that the devil had the bad habit of making use of carnival tricks in order to confuse the unwary. He argued that if wings were not the essential element in determining the difference between a hawk and an airplane, they were even less so in the recognition of angels. Nevertheless, he promised to write a letter to his bishop so that the latter would write to his primate[4] so that the latter would write to the Supreme Pontiff in order to get the final verdict from the highest courts.

His prudence fell on sterile hearts. The news of the captive angel spread with such rapidity that after a few hours the courtyard had the bustle of a marketplace and they had to call in troops with fixed bayonets to disperse the mob that was about to knock the house down. Elisenda, her spine all twisted from sweeping up so much marketplace trash, then got the idea of fencing in the yard and charging five cents admission to see the angel.

The curious came from far away. A traveling carnival arrived with a flying acrobat who buzzed over the crowd several times, but no one paid any attention to him because his wings were not those of an angel but, rather, those of a sidereal[5] bat. The most unfortunate invalids on earth came in search of health: a poor woman who since childhood had been counting her heartbeats and had run out of numbers; a Portuguese man who couldn't sleep because the noise of the stars disturbed him; a sleepwalker who got up at night to undo the things he had done while awake; and many others with less serious ailments. In the midst of that shipwreck disorder that made the earth tremble, Pelayo and Elisenda were happy with fatigue, for in less than a week they had crammed their rooms with money and the line of pilgrims waiting their turn to enter still reached beyond the horizon.

The angel was the only one who took no part in his own act. He spent his time trying to get comfortable in his borrowed nest, befuddled by the hellish heat of the oil lamps and sacramental candles that had been placed along the wire. At first they tried to make him eat some mothballs, which, according to the wisdom of the wise neighbor woman, were the food prescribed for angels. But he turned them down, just as he turned down the papal lunches[6] that the

---

4. Highest bishop of a given state.
5. Of, or relating to, the stars.
6. Expensive, elaborately prepared meals.

penitents brought him, and they never found out whether it was because he was an angel or because he was an old man that in the end he ate nothing but eggplant mush. His only supernatural virtue seemed to be patience. Especially during the first days, when the hens pecked at him, searching for the stellar parasites that proliferated in his wings, and the cripples pulled out feathers to touch their defective parts with, and even the most merciful threw stones at him, trying to get him to rise so they could see him standing. The only time they succeeded in arousing him was when they burned his side with an iron for branding steers, for he had been motionless for so many hours that they thought he was dead. He awoke with a start, ranting in his hermetic language and with tears in his eyes, and he flapped his wings a couple of times, which brought on a whirlwind of chicken dung and lunar dust and a gale of panic that did not seem to be of this world. Although many thought that his reaction had been one not of rage but of pain, from then on they were careful not to annoy him, because the majority understood that his passivity was not that of a hero taking his ease but that of a cataclysm in repose.

Father Gonzaga held back the crowd's frivolity with formulas of maidservant inspiration while awaiting the arrival of a final judgment on the nature of the captive. But the mail from Rome showed no sense of urgency. They spent their time finding out if the prisoner had a navel, if his dialect had any connection with Aramaic, how many times he could fit on the head of a pin, or whether he wasn't just a Norwegian with wings. Those meager letters might have come and gone until the end of time if a providential event had not put an end to the priest's tribulations.

It so happened that during those days, among so many other carnival attrac- 10 tions, there arrived in town the traveling show of the woman who had been changed into a spider for having disobeyed her parents. The admission to see her was not only less than the admission to see the angel, but people were permitted to ask her all manner of questions about her absurd state and to examine her up and down so that no one would ever doubt the truth of her horror. She was a frightful tarantula the size of a ram and with the head of a sad maiden. What was most heartrending, however, was not her outlandish shape but the sincere affliction with which she recounted the details of her misfortune. While still practically a child she had sneaked out of her parents' house to go to a dance, and while she was coming back through the woods after having danced all night without permission, a fearful thunderclap rent the sky in two and through the crack came the lightning bolt of brimstone that changed her into a spider. Her only nourishment came from the meatballs that charitable souls chose to toss into her mouth. A spectacle like that, full of so much human truth and with such a fearful lesson, was bound to defeat without even trying that of a haughty angel who scarcely deigned to look at mortals. Besides, the few miracles attributed to the angel showed a certain mental disorder, like the blind man who didn't recover his sight but grew three new teeth, or the paralytic who didn't get to walk but almost won the lottery, and the leper whose sores sprouted sunflowers. Those consolation miracles, which were more like mocking fun, had already ruined the angel's reputation when the woman who had been changed into a spider finally crushed him completely. That was how Father

Gonzaga was cured forever of his insomnia and Pelayo's courtyard went back to being as empty as during the time it had rained for three days and crabs walked through the bedrooms.

The owners of the house had no reason to lament. With the money they saved they built a two-story mansion with balconies and gardens and high netting so that crabs wouldn't get in during the winter, and with iron bars on the windows so that angels wouldn't get in. Pelayo also set up a rabbit warren close to town and gave up his job as bailiff for good, and Elisenda bought some satin pumps with high heels and many dresses of iridescent silk, the kind worn on Sunday by the most desirable women in those times. The chicken coop was the only thing that didn't receive any attention. If they washed it down with creolin[7] and burned tears of myrrh inside it every so often, it was not in homage to the angel but to drive away the dungheap stench that still hung everywhere like a ghost and was turning the new house into an old one. At first, when the child learned to walk, they were careful that he not get too close to the chicken coop. But then they began to lose their fears and got used to the smell, and before the child got his second teeth he'd gone inside the chicken coop to play, where the wires were falling apart. The angel was no less standoffish with him than with other mortals, but he tolerated the most ingenious infamies with the patience of a dog who had no illusions. They both came down with chicken pox at the same time. The doctor who took care of the child couldn't resist the temptation to listen to the angel's heart, and he found so much whistling in the heart and so many sounds in his kidneys that it seemed impossible for him to be alive. What surprised him most, however, was the logic of his wings. They seemed so natural on that completely human organism that he couldn't understand why other men didn't have them too.

When the child began school it had been some time since the sun and rain had caused the collapse of the chicken coop. The angel went dragging himself about here and there like a stray dying man. They would drive him out of the bedroom with a broom and a moment later find him in the kitchen. He seemed to be in so many places at the same time that they grew to think that he'd been duplicated, that he was reproducing himself all through the house, and the exasperated and unhinged Elisenda shouted that it was awful living in that hell full of angels. He could scarcely eat and his antiquarian eyes had also become so foggy that he went about bumping into posts. All he had left were the bare cannulae of his last feathers. Pelayo threw a blanket over him and extended him the charity of letting him sleep in the shed, and only then did they notice that he had a temperature at night, and was delirious with the tongue twisters of an old Norwegian. That was one of the few times they became alarmed, for they thought he was going to die and not even the wise neighbor woman had been able to tell them what to do with dead angels.

And yet he not only survived his worst winter, but seemed improved with the first sunny days. He remained motionless for several days in the farthest corner of the courtyard, where no one would see him, and at the beginning of December some large, stiff feathers began to grow on his wings, the feathers of a scarecrow, which looked more like another misfortune of decrepitude. But he must

7. Disinfectant.

have known the reason for those changes, for he was quite careful that no one should notice them, that no one should hear the sea chanteys that he sometimes sang under the stars. One morning Elisenda was cutting some bunches of onions for lunch when a wind that seemed to come from the high seas blew into the kitchen. Then she went to the window and caught the angel in his first attempts at flight. They were so clumsy that his fingernails opened a furrow in the vegetable patch and he was on the point of knocking the shed down with the ungainly flapping that slipped on the light and couldn't get a grip on the air. But he did manage to gain altitude. Elisenda let out a sigh of relief, for herself and for him, when she saw him pass over the last houses, holding himself up in some way with the risky flapping of a senile vulture. She kept watching him even when she was through cutting the onions and she kept on watching until it was no longer possible for her to see him, because then he was no longer an annoyance in her life but an imaginary dot on the horizon of the sea.

1968

QUESTIONS

1. The subtitle of this story is "A Tale for Children." Why and how does this seem like an apt description? an inapt or ironic one?
2. How do the various characters interpret the winged man? How do they arrive at their interpretations? What might their interpretations reveal about them? about people and/or the process of interpretation in general?
3. Why do so many people at first come to see the winged man and later stop doing so? Why is Elisenda so relieved when the man finally flies away? What insights into human behavior might be revealed here? Might any constitute a theme?

YASUNARI KAWABATA
(1899–1972)

The Grasshopper and the Bell Cricket[1]

Born in Osaka, Japan, to a prosperous family, Yasunari Kawabata graduated from Tokyo Imperial University in 1924 and had his first literary success with the semiautobiographical novella *The Izu Dancer* (1926). He cofounded the journal *Contemporary Literature* in support of the Neosensualist movement, which had much in common with the European literary movements of Dadaism, Expressionism, and Cubism. His best-known works include *Snow Country* (1948), *Thousand Cranes* (1952), *The Sound of the Mountain* (1954), *The Lake* (1954), *The Sleeping Beauty* (1961), *The Old Capital* (1962), and the collection *Palm-of-the-Hand Stories* (published in English in 1988). Kawabata was awarded the Nobel Prize in Literature in 1968. After long suffering from poor health, he committed suicide in 1972.

---

1. Translated from the Japanese by Lane Dunlop.

Walking along the tile-roofed wall of the university, I turned aside and approached the upper school. Behind the white board fence of the school playground, from a dusky clump of bushes under the black cherry trees, an insect's voice could be heard. Walking more slowly and listening to that voice, and furthermore reluctant to part with it, I turned right so as not to leave the playground behind. When I turned to the left, the fence gave way to an embankment planted with orange trees. At the corner, I exclaimed with surprise. My eyes gleaming at what they saw up ahead, I hurried forward with short steps.

At the base of the embankment was a bobbing cluster of beautiful varicolored lanterns, such as one might see at a festival in a remote country village. Without going any farther, I knew that it was a group of children on an insect chase among the bushes of the embankment. There were about twenty lanterns. Not only were there crimson, pink, indigo, green, purple, and yellow lanterns, but one lantern glowed with five colors at once. There were even some little red store-bought lanterns. But most of the lanterns were beautiful square ones which the children had made themselves with love and care. The bobbing lanterns, the coming together of children on this lonely slope—surely it was a scene from a fairy tale?

One of the neighborhood children had heard an insect sing on this slope one night. Buying a red lantern, he had come back the next night to find the insect. The night after that, there was another child. This new child could not buy a lantern. Cutting out the back and front of a small carton and papering it, he placed a candle on the bottom and fastened a string to the top. The number of children grew to five, and then to seven. They learned how to color the paper that they stretched over the windows of the cutout cartons, and to draw pictures on it. Then these wise child-artists, cutting out round, three-cornered, and lozenge leaf shapes in the cartons, coloring each little window a different color, with circles and diamonds, red and green, made a single and whole decorative pattern. The child with the red lantern discarded it as a tasteless object that could be bought at a store. The child who had made his own lantern threw it away because the design was too simple. The pattern of light that one had had in hand the night before was unsatisfying the morning after. Each day, with cardboard, paper, brush, scissors, penknife, and glue, the children made new lanterns out of their hearts and minds. Look at my lantern! Be the most unusually beautiful! And each night, they had gone out on their insect hunts. These were the twenty children and their beautiful lanterns that I now saw before me.

Wide-eyed, I loitered near them. Not only did the square lanterns have old-fashioned patterns and flower shapes, but the names of the children who had made them were cut out in squared letters of the syllabary. Different from the painted-over red lanterns, others (made of thick cutout cardboard) had their designs drawn onto the paper windows, so that the candle's light seemed to emanate from the form and color of the design itself. The lanterns brought out the shadows of the bushes like dark light. The children crouched eagerly on the slope wherever they heard an insect's voice.

5   "Does anyone want a grasshopper?" A boy, who had been peering into a bush about thirty feet away from the other children, suddenly straightened up and shouted.

"Yes! Give it to me!" Six or seven children came running up. Crowding behind the boy who had found the grasshopper, they peered into the bush. Brushing away their outstretched hands and spreading out his arms, the boy stood as if guarding the bush where the insect was. Waving the lantern in his right hand, he called again to the other children.

"Does anyone want a grasshopper? A grasshopper!"

"I do! I do!" Four or five more children came running up. It seemed you could not catch a more precious insect than a grasshopper. The boy called out a third time.

"Doesn't anyone want a grasshopper?"

Two or three more children came over.

"Yes. I want it."

It was a girl, who just now had come up behind the boy who'd discovered the insect. Lightly turning his body, the boy gracefully bent forward. Shifting the lantern to his left hand, he reached his right hand into the bush.

"It's a grasshopper."

"Yes. I'd like to have it."

The boy quickly stood up. As if to say "Here!" he thrust out his fist that held the insect at the girl. She, slipping her left wrist under the string of her lantern, enclosed the boy's fist with both hands. The boy quietly opened his fist. The insect was transferred to between the girl's thumb and index finger.

"Oh! It's not a grasshopper. It's a bell cricket." The girl's eyes shone as she looked at the small brown insect.

"It's a bell cricket! It's a bell cricket!" The children echoed in an envious chorus.

"It's a bell cricket. It's a bell cricket."

Glancing with her bright intelligent eyes at the boy who had given her the cricket, the girl opened the little insect cage hanging at her side and released the cricket in it.

"It's a bell cricket."

"Oh, it's a bell cricket," the boy who'd captured it muttered. Holding up the insect cage close to his eyes, he looked inside it. By the light of his beautiful many-colored lantern, also held up at eye level, he glanced at the girl's face.

Oh, I thought. I felt slightly jealous of the boy, and sheepish. How silly of me not to have understood his actions until now! Then I caught my breath in surprise. Look! It was something on the girl's breast which neither the boy who had given her the cricket, nor she who had accepted it, nor the children who were looking at them noticed.

In the faint greenish light that fell on the girl's breast, wasn't the name "Fujio" clearly discernible? The boy's lantern, which he held up alongside the girl's insect cage, inscribed his name, cut out in the green papered aperture, onto her white cotton kimono. The girl's lantern, which dangled loosely from her wrist, did not project its pattern so clearly, but still one could make out, in a trembling patch of red on the boy's waist, the name "Kiyoko." This chance interplay of red and green—if it was chance or play—neither Fujio nor Kiyoko knew about.

Even if they remembered forever that Fujio had given her the cricket and that Kiyoko had accepted it, not even in dreams would Fujio ever know that his name had been written in green on Kiyoko's breast or that Kiyoko's name had been inscribed in red on his waist, nor would Kiyoko ever know that Fujio's name had been inscribed in green on her breast or that her own name had been written in red on Fujio's waist.

25   Fujio! Even when you have become a young man, laugh with pleasure at a girl's delight when, told that it's a grasshopper, she is given a bell cricket; laugh with affection at a girl's chagrin when, told that it's a bell cricket, she is given a grasshopper.

Even if you have the wit to look by yourself in a bush away from the other children, there are not many bell crickets in the world. Probably you will find a girl like a grasshopper whom you think is a bell cricket.

And finally, to your clouded, wounded heart, even a true bell cricket will seem like a grasshopper. Should that day come, when it seems to you that the world is only full of grasshoppers, I will think it a pity that you have no way to remember tonight's play of light, when your name was written in green by your beautiful lantern on a girl's breast.

1924

QUESTIONS

1. Who might the narrator of this story be? What clues are provided in the story?
2. What might the grasshopper and the bell cricket each come to symbolize in the story?
3. Might the final three paragraphs of this story come close to stating its theme(s)? How would you state the theme(s)?

JUNOT DÍAZ
(b. 1968)

Wildwood

Aptly described by one British newspaper as "a truly all-American writer" and by himself as an "African diasporic, migrant, Caribbean, Dominican, Jersey boy," MIT professor and MacArthur "genius grant" winner Junot Díaz lived in the Dominican Republic until age six, when he and the rest of his family joined his father in the United States. While his mother worked on a factory assembly line and his father, a former military policeman, drove a forklift, Díaz and his four siblings navigated life in what he calls a "very black, very Puerto Rican and very poor" New Jersey neighborhood. Díaz supported himself through college, earning a BA in English from Rutgers and a Cornell MFA. A year after graduating, Díaz published *Drown* (1996), a collection of interrelated short stories. A decade later, his novel *The Brief Wondrous Life of Oscar Wao* (2007) won numerous prizes, including both a National Book Critics Circle Award and a Pulitzer. Hailed in a 2015 poll as the greatest novel of the twenty-first century (so far), *Oscar Wao* is a tale of a lovelorn and utterly lovable "ghetto nerd," who dreams of becoming the next J. R. R. Tolkien, and three generations of his Dominican American family. In addition to publishing a second short-story collection, *This Is How You Lose Her* (2012), and the children's book *Islandborn* (2018), Díaz cofounded the pioneering Voices of Our Nations Arts Foundation to nurture the work of writers of color. "Wildwood," published almost simultaneously as both a short story and a chapter of *Oscar Wao*, is something of a departure for Díaz thanks to its female narrator-protagonist. But it is utterly characteristic in its creation of an entirely new fictional language to capture the unique voices, experiences, and outlooks of its funny, complicated, thoroughly all-American cast of characters.

I t's never the changes we want that change everything.

This is how it all starts: with your mother calling you into the bathroom. You will remember what you were doing at that precise moment for the rest of your life: you were reading "Watership Down"[1] and the bucks and their does were making the dash for the raft and you didn't want to stop reading, the book had to go back to your brother tomorrow, but then she called you again, louder, her I'm-not-fucking-around voice, and you mumbled irritably, Sí, señora.

She is standing in front of the medicine-cabinet mirror, naked from the waist up, her bra slung about her hips like a torn sail, the scar on her back as vast and inconsolable as the sea. You want to return to your book, to pretend you didn't hear her, but it is too late. Her eyes meet yours, the same big smoky eyes you

---

1. Richard Adams's classic novel (1972) about the adventures of a community of English rabbits who, inspired by the prophetic vision of one of their youngest and smallest members, flee their doomed warren and create a new home.

will have in the future. Ven acá,[2] she commands. She is frowning at something on one of her breasts.

Your mother's breasts are immensities. One of the wonders of the world. The only ones you've seen that are bigger are in nudie magazines or on really fat ladies. They're forty-two triple Ds and the aureoles are as big as saucers and black as pitch and at their edges are fierce hairs that sometimes she plucks and sometimes she doesn't. These breasts have always embarrassed you and when you walk in public with her you are conscious of them. After her face and her hair, her tetas are what she is most proud of. Your father could never get enough of them, she always brags. But given the fact that he ran off on her after their third year of marriage it seemed in the end that he could.

5   You dread conversations with your mother. These one-sided dressing-downs. You figure that she has called you in to give you another earful about your diet. Your mom's convinced that if you only eat more plátanos you will suddenly acquire her extraordinary train-wrecking secondary sex characteristics. Even at that age you are nothing if not your mother's daughter. You are twelve years old and already as tall as her, a long slender-necked ibis of a girl. You have her straight hair, which makes you look more Hindu than Dominican, and a behind that the boys haven't been able to stop talking about since the fifth grade and whose appeal you do not yet understand. You have her complexion, too, which means you are dark as night. But for all your similarities the tides of inheritance have yet to reach your chest. You have only the slightest hint of breasts: from most angles you're flat as a board and you're thinking she's going to order you to stop wearing bras again because they're suffocating your potential breasts, discouraging them from popping out. You're ready to argue with her to the death, because you're as possessive of your bras as you are of the pads you now buy yourself.

But no, she doesn't say a word about eating more plátanos. Instead, she takes your right hand and guides you. Your mom is rough in all things, but this time she is gentle. You did not think her capable of it.

Do you feel that? she asks in her too familiar raspy voice.

At first all you feel is the density of the tissue and the heat of her, like a bread that never stopped rising. She kneads your fingers into her. You're as close as you've ever been and your breathing is what you hear.

Don't you feel that?

10   She turns toward you. Coño, muchacha,[3] stop looking at me and feel.

So you close your eyes and your fingers are pushing down and you're thinking of Helen Keller[4] and how when you were little you wanted to be her except more nunnish and then suddenly you do feel something. A knot just beneath her skin, tight and secretive as a plot. And at that moment, for reasons you will never quite understand, you are overcome by the feeling, the premonition, that something in your life is about to change. You become light-headed and you can feel a throbbing in your blood, a rhythm, a drum. Bright lights zoom through you

2. Come here (Spanish).
3. Damn, girl (Dominican Spanish).
4. Famously blind and deaf American author, activist, and lecturer (1880–1968).

like photon torpedoes, like comets. You don't know how or why you know this thing, but that you know it cannot be doubted. It is exhilarating. For as long as you've been alive you've had bruja[5] ways; even your mother will not begrudge you that much. Hija de Liborio, she called you after you picked your tía's[6] winning numbers for her and when you guessed correctly how old to the day she'd been when she left home for the U.S. (a fact she'd never told anyone). You assumed Liborio was a relative. That was before Santo Domingo, before you knew about the Great Power of God.

I feel it, you say, too loudly. Lo siento.[7]

And like that, everything changes. Before the winter is out the doctors remove that breast you were kneading and its partner, along with the auxiliary lymph nodes. Because of the operations, your mother will have trouble lifting her arms over her head for the rest of her life. Her hair begins to fall out and one day she pulls it all out herself and puts it in a plastic bag. You change, too. Not right away, but it happens. And it's in that bathroom that it all begins. That you begin.

A punk chick. That's what I became. A Siouxsie and the Banshees-loving[8] punk chick. The Puerto Rican kids on the block couldn't stop laughing when they saw my hair; they called me Blacula. And the morenos,[9] they didn't know what to say; they just called me devil-bitch. Yo, devil-bitch, yo, yo! My tía Rubelka thought it was some kind of mental illness. Hija, she said while frying pastelitos, maybe you need help. But my mother was the worst. It's the last straw, she screamed. The. Last. Straw. But it always was with her. Mornings when I came downstairs she'd be in the kitchen making her coffee in la greca and listening to Radio WADO[1] and when she saw me and my hair she'd get mad all over again, as if during the night she'd forgotten who I was.

My mother was one of the tallest women in Paterson[2] and her anger was just 15 as tall. It pincered you in its long arms, and if you showed any weakness you were finished. Que muchacha tan fea,[3] she said in disgust, splashing the rest of her coffee in the sink. Fea had become my name. It was nothing new, to tell the truth. She'd been saying stuff like that all our lives. My mother would never win any awards, believe me. You could call her an absentee parent: if she wasn't at work she was sleeping and when she wasn't sleeping all she did was scream and hit. As kids, me and Oscar were more scared of our mother than we were of the

---

5. Witch (Spanish).
6. Aunt's (Spanish). *Hija de Liborio*: literally, "child of Liborio" (Spanish), an allusion to Olivorio Liborio Mateo (1876–1922), a peasant farmer turned messianic faith healer regarded by his followers as an incarnation of Christ; remnants of his once-powerful Liborista movement still survive.
7. I feel it (Spanish).
8. English rock band (1976–96) created and fronted by Siouxsie Sioux, hailed by the London *Times* as inventing "a form of post-punk discord [. . .] as influential as it was underrated."
9. Literally, "browns" (Spanish), a term for people with dark skin.
1. Spanish-language news and talk station owned by Univision. *La greca*: Italian-style aluminum stovetop espresso pot (Spanish).
2. New Jersey city in the New York metropolitan area, home to many Hispanic and Middle Eastern immigrants.
3. What an ugly girl (Spanish).

dark or el cuco.[4] She would hit us anywhere, in front of anyone, always free with the chanclas and the correa,[5] but now with her cancer there wasn't much she could do anymore. The last time she tried to whale on me it was because of my hair, but instead of cringing or running I punched her hand. It was a reflex more than anything, but once it happened I knew I couldn't take it back, not ever, and so I just kept my fist clenched, waiting for whatever came next, for her to attack me with her teeth like she had this one lady in the Pathmark.[6] But she just stood there shaking, in her stupid wig and her stupid bata,[7] with two huge foam prostheses in her bra, the smell of burning wig all around us. I almost felt sorry for her. This is how you treat your mother? she cried. And if I could I would have broken the entire length of my life across her face, but instead I screamed back, And this is how you treat your daughter?

Things had been bad between us all year. How could they not have been? She was my Old World Dominican mother who had come alone to the United States and I was her only daughter, the one she had raised up herself with the help of nobody, which meant it was her duty to keep me crushed under her heel. I was fourteen and desperate for my own patch of world that had nothing to do with her. I wanted the life that I used to see when I watched "Big Blue Marble"[8] as a kid, the life that drove me to make pen pals and to borrow atlases from school. The life that existed beyond Paterson, beyond my family, beyond Spanish. And as soon as she became sick I saw my chance and I'm not going to pretend or apologize; I saw my chance and eventually I took it.

If you didn't grow up like I did then you don't know and if you don't know it's probably better you don't judge. You don't know the hold our mothers have on us, even the ones that are never around—*especially* the ones that are never around. What it's like to be the perfect Dominican daughter, which is just a nice way of saying a perfect Dominican slave. You don't know what it's like to grow up with a mother who never said anything that wasn't negative, who was always suspicious, always tearing you down and splitting your dreams straight down the seams. On TV and in books mothers talk to daughters, about life, about themselves, but on Main Street in Paterson mothers say not a word unless it's to hurt you. When my first pen pal, Tomoko, stopped writing me after three letters my mother was the one who said, You think someone's going to lose life writing to you? Of course I cried; I was eight and I had already planned that Tomoko and her family would adopt me. My mother, of course, saw clean into the marrow of those dreams and laughed. I wouldn't write to you, either, she said.

She was that kind of mother: who makes you doubt yourself, who would wipe you out if you let her. But I'm not going to pretend, either. For a long time I let her say what she wanted about me and, what was worse, for a long time I believed her. I was a fea, I was a worthless, I was an idiota. From ages two to thirteen I believed her and because I believed her I was the perfect hija. I was

4. Mythical ghost-monster, a sort of Spanish-language "bogeyman."
5. Belt (Spanish). *Chanclas*: flip-flops (Spanish).
6. Grocery store, part of a chain owned by the Great Atlantic and Pacific Tea Company.
7. Bathrobe (Spanish).
8. American television series for children (1974–83); featuring stories about children around the world, the show sponsored an international pen-pal club.

the one cooking, cleaning, doing the wash, buying groceries, writing letters to the bank to explain why a house payment was going to be late, translating. I had the best grades in my class. I never caused trouble, even when the morenas used to come after me with scissors because of my straight straight hair. I stayed at home and made sure my little brother Oscar was fed and everything ran right while she was at work. I raised him and I raised me. I was the one. You're my hija, she said, that's what you're supposed to be doing. When that thing happened to me when I was eight and I finally told her what our neighbor had done she told me to shut my mouth and stop crying and I did exactly that, I shut my mouth and clenched my legs and my mind and within a year I couldn't have told you what he looked like or even his name. All you do is complain, she said to me, but you have no idea what life really is. Sí, señora.

When she told me that I could go on my sixth-grade sleepaway to Bear Mountain[9] and I bought a backpack with my own paper-route money and wrote Bobby Santos notes because he was promising to break into my cabin and kiss me in front of everyone I believed her and when on the morning of the trip she announced that I wasn't going and I said, But you promised, and she said, Muchacha del diablo,[1] I promised you nothing, I didn't throw my backpack at her or pull out my hair, and when it was Laura Saenz who ended up kissing Bobby Santos, not me, I didn't say anything, either. I just lay in my room with stupid Bear-Bear and sang under my breath, imagining where I would run away to when I grew up. To Japan maybe, where I would track down Tomoko, or to Austria, where my singing would inspire a remake of "The Sound of Music."

All my favorite books from that period were about runaways—"Watership Down," "The Incredible Journey," "My Side of the Mountain"[2]—and when Bon Jovi's "Runaway"[3] came out I imagined it was me they were singing about. No one had any idea. I was the tallest, dorkiest girl in school, the one who dressed up as Wonder Woman[4] every Halloween, the one who never said a word. People saw me in my glasses and my hand-me-down clothes and could not have imagined what I was capable of. And then when I was twelve I got that feeling, the scary witchy one, and before I knew it my mother was sick and the wildness that had been in me all along, that I had tried to tamp down with chores and with homework and with promises that once I reached college I would be able to do whatever I pleased, burst out. I couldn't help it. I tried to keep it down, but it just flooded through all my quiet spaces. It was a message more than a feeling, a message that tolled like a bell: Change, change, change.

It didn't happen overnight. Yes the wildness was in me, yes it kept my heart beating fast all the long day, yes it danced around me while I walked down the street, yes it let me look boys straight in the face when they stared at me, yes it

20

turned my laugh from a cough into a wild fever, but I was still scared. How could I not be? I was my mother's daughter. Her hold on me was stronger than love. And then one day I was walking home with Karen Cepeda, who at that time was my friend. Karen did the goth thing really well; she had spiky Robert Smith[5] hair and wore all black and had the skin color of a ghost. Walking with her in Paterson was like walking with the bearded lady. Everybody would stare and it was the scariest thing and that was, I guess, why I did it.

We were walking down Main and being glared at by everybody and out of nowhere I said, Karen, I want you to cut my hair. As soon as I said it I knew. The feeling in my blood, the rattle, came over me again. Karen raised her eyebrow: What about your mother? You see, it wasn't just me—everybody was scared of Belicia de León.

Fuck her, I said.

Karen looked at me like I was being stupid—I never cursed, but that was something else that was about to change. The next day we locked ourselves in her bathroom while downstairs her father and uncles were bellowing at some soccer game. Well, how do you want it? she asked. I looked at the girl in the mirror for a long time. All I knew was that I didn't want to see her ever again. I put the clippers in Karen's hand, turned them on, and guided her hand until it was all gone.

25   So now you're punk? Karen asked uncertainly.

Yes, I said.

The next day my mother threw the wig at me. You're going to wear this. You're going to wear it every day. And if I see you without it on I'm going to kill you!

I didn't say a word. I held the wig over the burner.

Don't do it, she said as the burner clicked. Don't you dare—

30   It went up in a flash, like gasoline, like a stupid hope, and if I hadn't thrown it in the sink it would have taken my hand. The smell was horrible, like all the chemicals from all the factories in Elizabeth.[6]

That was when she slapped at me, when I struck her hand and she snatched it back, like I was the fire.

Of course everyone thought I was the worst daughter ever. My tía and our neighbors kept saying, Hija, she's your mother, she's dying, but I wouldn't listen. When I hit her hand, a door opened. And I wasn't about to turn my back on it.

But God how we fought! Sick or not, dying or not, my mother wasn't going to go down easy. She wasn't una pendeja.[7] I'd seen her slap grown men, push white police officers onto their asses, curse a whole group of bochincheras.[8] She had raised me and my brother by herself, she had worked three jobs until she could buy this house we lived in, she had survived being abandoned by my father, she

5. Former Siouxsie and the Banshees guitarist (b. 1959) and (since 1976) lead singer-songwriter of the English rock band the Cure.
6. Elizabeth, New Jersey, is home to a major oil refinery consistently ranked as among the nation's worst polluters.
7. Dumbass, fool, pushover, or coward (Spanish).
8. Gossips (Spanish).

had come from Santo Domingo all by herself, and as a young girl she'd been beaten, set on fire, left for dead. (This last part she didn't tell me, my tía Rubelka did, in a whisper, Your mother almost died, she almost died, and when I asked my mother about it at dinner she took my dinner and gave it to my brother.) That was my mother and there was no way she was going to let me go without killing me first. Figurín de mierda, she called me. You think you're someone, but you ain't nada.[9]

She dug hard, looking for my seams, wanting me to tear like always, but I didn't, I wasn't going to. It was that feeling I had that my life was waiting for me on the other side that made me fearless. When she threw away my Smiths and Sisters of Mercy posters—aquí yo no quiero maricones[1]—I bought replacements. When she threatened to rip up my new clothes I started keeping them in my locker and at Karen's house. When she told me that I had to quit my job at the Greek diner I explained to my boss that my mother was starting to lose it because of her chemo, and when she called to say I couldn't work there anymore he just handed me the phone and stared out at his customers in embarrassment. When she changed the locks on me—I had started staying out late, going to the Limelight because even though I was fourteen I looked twenty-five—I would knock on Oscar's window and he would let me in, scared because the next day my mother would run around the house screaming, Who the hell let that hija de la gran puta[2] in the house? Who? Who? And Oscar would be at the breakfast table stammering, I don't know, Mami, I don't.

Her rage filled the house, like flat stale smoke. It got into everything, into our   35 hair and our food, like the fallout they told us about in school that would one day drift down soft as snow. My brother didn't know what to do. He stayed in his room, though sometimes he would lamely try to ask me what was going on. Nothing. You can tell me, Lola, he said, and I could only laugh. You need to lose weight, I told him.

In those final weeks I knew better than to go near my mother. Most of the time she just looked at me with the stink eye, but sometimes without warning she would grab me by my throat and hang on until I pried her fingers off. She didn't bother talking to me unless it was to make death threats: When you grow up you'll meet me in a dark alley when you least expect it and then I'll kill you and nobody will know I did it! Gloating as she said this.

You're crazy, I told her.

You don't call me crazy, she said, and then she sat down panting.

It was bad, but no one expected what came next. So obvious when you think about it.

All my life I'd been swearing that one day I would just disappear.   40

And one day I did.

---

9. Nothing (Spanish). *Figurín de mierda*: literally, perhaps something like "figure made of crap"; figuratively, "a phony," something that only looks refined (Spanish).

1. I don't want to have those fags here (Spanish). *Smiths and Sisters of Mercy*: influential British alternative rock bands of the 1980s, fronted by highly literary singer-songwriter Morrissey (who once described himself as "humasexual") and Andrew Eldritch, respectively.

2. Daughter of a bitch (Spanish).

I ran off, dique,[3] because of a boy.

What can I really tell you about him? He was like all boys: beautiful and callow and, like an insect, he couldn't sit still. Un blanquito[4] with long hairy legs who I met one night at the Limelight.

His name was Aldo.

45   He was nineteen and lived down at the Jersey Shore with his seventy-four-year-old father. In the back of his Oldsmobile on University I pulled my leather skirt up and my fishnet stockings down and the smell of me was everywhere. I didn't let him go all the way, but still. The spring of my sophomore year we wrote and called each other at least once a day. I even drove down with Karen to visit him in Wildwood[5] (she had a license, I didn't). He lived and worked near the boardwalk, one of three guys who operated the bumper cars, the only one without tattoos. You should stay, he told me that night while Karen walked ahead of us on the beach. Where would I live? I asked, and he smiled. With me. Don't lie, I said, but he looked out at the surf. I want you to come, he said seriously.

He asked me three times. I counted, I know.

That summer my brother announced that he was going to dedicate his life to designing role-playing games, and my mother was trying to keep a second job for the first time since her operation. It wasn't working out. She was coming home exhausted, and since I wasn't helping, nothing around the house was getting done. Some weekends my tía Rubelka would help out with the cooking and cleaning and would lecture us both, but she had her own family to look after, so most of the time we were on our own. Come, he said on the phone. And then in August Karen left for Slippery Rock.[6] She had graduated from high school a year early. If I don't see Paterson again it will be too soon, she said before she left. Five days later, school started. I cut class six times in the first two weeks. I just couldn't do school anymore. Something inside wouldn't let me. It didn't help that I was reading "The Fountainhead" and had decided that I was Dominique and Aldo was Roark.[7] And finally what we'd all been waiting for happened. My mother announced at dinner, quietly, I want you both to listen to me: the doctor is running more tests on me.

Oscar looked like he was going to cry. He put his head down. And my reaction? I looked at her and said, Could you please pass the salt?

These days I don't blame her for smacking me across my face, but right then it was all I needed. We jumped on each other and the table fell and the sancocho[8] spilled all over the floor and Oscar just stood in the corner bellowing, Stop it, stop it, stop it!

---

3. Supposedly or so they say (Dominican Spanish).

4. Little white boy (Spanish).

5. Beachfront community on the Jersey shore; the town's population surges from around 5,000 in the off-season to over 200,000 in season.

6. University in Pennsylvania about fifty miles north of Pittsburgh.

7. Influential and controversial best seller (1943) by Ayn Rand; a celebration of individualism, it chronicles young architect Howard Roark's struggles to achieve success without compromising, even with the equally headstrong architect's daughter (Dominique Francon) with whom he falls in love.

8. Thick soup or stew common in South America and the Caribbean.

Hija de tu maldita madre![9] she shrieked. And I said, This time I hope you die 50 from it.

For a couple of days the house was a war zone, and then on Friday she let me out of my room and I was allowed to sit next to her on the sofa and watch novelas with her. She was waiting for her blood work to come back, but you would never have known her life was in the balance. She watched the TV like it was the only thing that mattered, and whenever one of the characters did something underhanded she would start waving her arms: Someone has to stop her! Can't they see what that puta[1] is up to?

I hate you, I said very quietly, but she didn't hear.

Go get me some water, she said. Put an ice cube in it.

That was the last thing I did for her. The next morning I was on the bus bound for the shore. One bag, two hundred dollars in tips, Tío[2] Rudolfo's old knife, and the only picture my mother had of my father, which she had hidden under her bed (she was in the picture, too, but I pretended not to notice). I was so scared. I couldn't stop shaking. The whole ride down I was expecting the sky to split open and my mother to reach down and shake me. But it didn't happen. Nobody but the man across the aisle noticed me. You're really beautiful, he said. Like a girl I once knew.

I didn't write them a note. That's how much I hated them. Her. 55

That night while Aldo and I lay in his sweltering kitty-litter-infested room I told him: I want you to do it to me.

He started unbuttoning my pants. Are you sure?

Definitely, I said grimly.

He had a long thin dick that hurt like hell, but the whole time I just said, Oh yes, Aldo, yes, because that was what I imagined you were supposed to say while you were losing your virginity to some boy you thought you loved.

It was like the stupidest thing I ever did. I was miserable. And so bored. But of 60 course I wouldn't admit it. I had run away, so I was happy! Happy!

Aldo had neglected to mention, all those times he asked me to live with him, that his father hated him like I hated my mother. Aldo, Sr., had been in the Second World War and he'd never forgiven the "Japs" for all the friends he had lost. My dad's so full of shit, Aldo said. He never left Fort Dix.[3] I don't think his father said nine words to me the whole time I lived with them. He was one mean viejito[4] and even had a padlock on the refrigerator. Stay the hell out of it, he told me. We couldn't even get ice cubes out.

Aldo and his dad lived in one of the cheapest little bungalows on New Jersey Avenue, and me and Aldo slept in a room where his father kept the litter box for his two cats, and at night we would move it out into the hallway, but he always woke up before us and put it back in the room: I told you to leave my crap alone! Which is funny when you think about it. But it wasn't funny then. I got a job selling French fries on the boardwalk and between the hot oil and the cat piss I

9. Child of a motherfucker, considered one of the worst possible insults in Dominican Spanish.
1. Whore (Spanish).
2. Uncle (Spanish).
3. U.S. military post just south of Trenton, New Jersey.
4. Old man (Spanish).

couldn't smell anything else. On my days off I would drink with Aldo or I would sit in the sand dressed in all black and try to write in my journal, which I was sure would form the foundation for a utopian society after we blew ourselves into radioactive kibble. Sometimes boys would walk up to me and throw lines at me like, Who fuckin' died? They would sit down next to me in the sand. You a good-looking girl, you should be in a bikini. Why, so you can rape me? Jesus Christ, one of them said, jumping to his feet. What the hell is wrong with you?

To this day I don't know how I lasted. At the beginning of October I was laid off from the French-fry palace; by then most of the boardwalk was closed up and I had nothing to do except hang out at the public library, which was even smaller than my high-school one. Aldo had moved on to working with his dad at his garage, which only made them more pissed off at each other and by extension more pissed off at me. When they got home they would drink Schlitz[5] and complain about the Phillies. I guess I should count myself lucky that they didn't decide to bury the hatchet by gangbanging me. I stayed out as much as I could and waited for the feeling to come back to me, to tell me what I should do next, but I was bone dry, bereft, no visions whatsoever. I started to think that maybe it was like in the books: as soon as I lost my virginity I lost my power. I got really mad at Aldo after that. You're a drunk, I told him. And an idiot. So what, he shot back. Your pussy smells. Then stay out of it! I will!

But of course I was happy! Happy! I kept waiting to run into my family posting flyers of me on the boardwalk—my mom, the tallest blackest chestiest thing in sight, Oscar looking like the Brown Blob, my tía Rubelka, maybe even my tío if they could get him off the heroin long enough—but the closest I came to any of that was some flyers someone had put up for a lost cat. That's white people for you. They lose a cat and it's an all-points bulletin, but we Dominicans lose a daughter and we might not even cancel our appointment at the salon.

65   By November I was so finished. I would sit there with Aldo and his putrid father and the old shows would come on the TV, the ones me and my brother used to watch when we were kids, "Three's Company," "What's Happening!!," "The Jeffersons,"[6] and my disappointment would grind against some organ that was very soft and tender. It was starting to get cold, too, and wind just walked right into the bungalow and got under your blankets or jumped in the shower with you. It was awful. I kept having these stupid visions of my brother trying to cook for himself. Don't ask me why. I was the one who cooked for us. The only thing Oscar knew how to make was grilled cheese. I imagined him thin as a reed, wandering around the kitchen, opening cabinets forlornly. I even started dreaming about my mother, except in my dreams she was young, my age, and it was because of those dreams that I realized something obvious: she had run away, too, and that was why we were all in the United States.

5. Notoriously cheap American beer.
6. Like *Three's Company* (1977–84) and *What's Happening!!* (1976–79), a popular American sitcom (1975–85). Where *What's Happening!!* features three working-class African American teens in Los Angeles, both *The Jeffersons* and *Three's Company* focus on the conflicts and humor arising from particular living arrangements: The former features a newly affluent African American family who move from working-class Queens into a luxurious Manhattan high-rise; in the latter, which has an all-Caucasian cast, two young women keep their apartment only by convincing their landlord that their male roommate is gay.

I put away the photo of her and my father, but the dreams didn't stop. I guess when a person is with you they're only with you when they're with you, but when they're gone, when they're really gone, they're with you forever.

And then at the end of November Aldo, my wonderful boyfriend, decided to be cute. I knew he was getting unhappy with us, but I didn't know exactly how bad it was until one night he had his friends over. His father had gone to Atlantic City[7] and they were all drinking and smoking and telling dumb jokes and suddenly Aldo says, Do you know what Pontiac stands for? Poor Old Nigger Thinks It's A Cadillac. Who was he looking at when he told his punch line? He was looking straight at me.

That night he wanted me but I pushed his hand away. Don't touch me.

Don't get sore, he said, putting my hand on his cock. It wasn't nothing.

And then he laughed. 70

So what did I do a couple days later—a really dumb thing. I called home. The first time no one answered. The second time it was Oscar. The de León residence, how may I direct your call? That was my brother for you. This is why everybody in the world hated his guts.

It's me, dumb-ass.

Lola. He was so quiet and then I realized he was crying. Where *are* you?

You don't want to know. I switched ears, trying to keep my voice casual. How is everybody?

Lola, Mami's going to *kill* you. 75

Dumb-ass, could you keep your voice down. Mami isn't home, is she?

She's working.

What a surprise, I said. Mami working. On the last minute of the last hour of the last day my mother would be at work. She would be at work when the missiles were in the air.

I guess I must have missed him real bad or I just wanted to see somebody who knew anything about me, or the cat piss had damaged my common sense, because I gave him the address of a coffee shop on the boardwalk and told him to bring my clothes and some of my books.

Bring me money, too. 80

He paused. I don't know where Mami keeps it.

You know, Mister. Just bring it.

How much? he asked timidly.

All of it.

That's a lot of money, Lola. 85

Just bring me the money, Oscar.

O.K., O.K. He inhaled deeply. Will you at least tell me if you're O.K. or not?

I'm O.K., I said, and that was the only point in the conversation where I almost cried. I kept quiet until I could speak again and then I asked him how he was going to get down here without our mother finding out.

You know me, he said weakly. I might be a dork, but I'm a resourceful dork.

7. Somewhat rundown New Jersey beach town renowned for its casinos.

90   I should have known not to trust anybody whose favorite books as a child were Encyclopedia Brown.[8] But I wasn't really thinking; I was so looking forward to seeing him.

By then I had this plan. I was going to convince my brother to run away with me. My plan was that we would go to Dublin. I had met a bunch of Irish guys on the boardwalk and they had sold me on their country. I would become a backup singer for U2[9] and both Bono and the drummer would fall in love with me, and Oscar could become the Dominican James Joyce.[1] I really believed it would happen, too. That's how deluded I was by then.

The next day I walked into the coffee shop, looking brand-new, and he was there, with the bag. Oscar, I said, laughing. You're so fat!

I know, he said, ashamed. I was worried about you.

We embraced for like an hour and then he started crying. Lola, I'm sorry.

95   It's O.K., I said, and that's when I looked up and saw my mother and my tía Rubelka and my tío Rudolfo boiling out of the kitchen.

Oscar! I screamed, but it was too late. My mother already had me in her hands. She looked so thin and worn, almost like a hag, but she was holding on to me like I was her last nickel, and underneath her red wig her green eyes were *furious*. I noticed, absently, that she had dressed up for the occasion. That was typical. Muchacha del diablo, she shrieked. I managed to haul her out of the coffee shop and when she pulled back her hand to smack me I broke free. I ran for it. Behind me I could feel her sprawling, hitting the curb hard with a crack, but I wasn't looking back. No—I was running. In elementary school, whenever we had field day I was always the fastest girl in my grade, took home all the ribbons; they said it wasn't fair, because I was so big, but I didn't care. I could even have beaten the boys if I'd wanted to, so there was no way my sick mother, my messed-up tíos, and my fat brother were going to catch me. I was going to run as fast as my long legs could carry me. I was going to run down the boardwalk, past Aldo's miserable house, out of Wildwood, out of New Jersey, and I wasn't going to stop. I was going to *fly*.

Anyway, that's how it *should* have worked out. But I looked back. I couldn't help it. It's not like I didn't know my Bible, all the pillars-of-salt stuff,[2] but when you're someone's daughter that she raised by herself with no help from nobody habits die hard. I just wanted to make sure my mom hadn't broken her arm or smashed open her skull. I mean, really, who the hell wants to kill her own mother by accident? That's the only reason I glanced back. She was sprawled on the ground, her wig had fallen out of reach, her poor bald head out in the day like something private and shameful, and she was bawling like a lost calf, Hija,

8. Fictional series (1963–present) about the adventures of bookish boy detective Leroy ("Encyclopedia") Brown.

9. Wildly successful Irish rock band formed in Dublin in 1976 by frontman Bono, guitarist the Edge, bassist Adam Clayton, and drummer Larry Mullen, Jr.

1. Celebrated Dublin-born author (1882–1941) of books including the short-story collection *Dubliners* (1914), which includes "Araby" (pp. 284–88).

2. In the book of Genesis, Lot and his wife flee the iniquitous Sodom at the behest of angels who warn them not to look back lest they share in that city's well-earned destruction; when Lot's wife ignores the warning, she turns into a pillar of salt.

hija! And there I was wanting to run off into my future. It was right then that I needed that feeling to guide me, but it wasn't anywhere in sight. Only me. In the end I didn't have the ovaries. She was on the ground, bald as a baby, crying, probably a month away from dying, and here I was, her one and only daughter. And there was nothing I could do about it. So I walked back and when I reached down to help her she clamped on to me with both hands. That was when I realized she hadn't been crying at all. She'd been faking! Her smile was like a lion's.

Ya te tengo,[3] she said, jumping triumphantly to her feet. Te tengo.

And that is how I ended up in Santo Domingo.[4] I guess my mother thought it would be harder for me to run away from an island where I knew no one, and in a way she was right. I'm into my sixth month here and these days I'm just trying to be philosophical about the whole thing. I wasn't like that at first, but in the end I had to let it go. It was like the fight between the egg and the rock, my abuela[5] said. No winning.

I'm actually going to school, not that it's going to count when I return to Paterson, but it keeps me busy and out of trouble and around people my own age. You don't need to be around us viejos all day, Abuela says. I have mixed feelings about the school. For one thing, it's improved my Spanish a lot. It's a private school, a Carol Morgan[6] wanna-be filled with people my tío Carlos Moya calls los hijos de mami y papi.[7] And then there's me. If you think it was tough being a goth in Paterson, try being a Dominican york in one of those private schools back in D.R. You will never meet bitchier girls in your whole life. They whisper about me to death. Someone else would have had a nervous breakdown, but after Wildwood I'm not so brittle. I don't let it get to me.

And the irony of all ironies? I'm on our school's track team. I joined because my friend Rosio, the scholarship girl from Los Mina,[8] told me I could win a spot on the team on the length of my legs alone. Those are the pins of a winner, she prophesied. Well, she must have known something I didn't, because I'm now our school's top runner in the four hundred metres and under. That I have talent at this simple thing never ceases to amaze me. Karen would pass out if she could see me running sprints out behind my school while Coach Cortés screams at us, first in Spanish and then in Catalán. Breathe, breathe, *breathe!* I've got like no fat left on me and the musculature of my legs impresses everyone, even me. I can't wear shorts anymore without causing traffic jams, and the other day when my abuela accidentally locked us out of the house she turned to me in frustration and said, Hija, just kick the door open. That pushed a laugh out of both of us.

So much has changed these last months, in my head, my heart. Rosio has me dressing up like a real Dominican girl. She's the one who fixes my hair and

3. Now I've got you (Spanish).
4. Capital (founded 1496) of the Dominican Republic, which, along with the Republic of Haiti, occupies Hispaniola Island.
5. Grandmother (Spanish).
6. Prestigious English-language school in Santo Domingo, founded in 1933 by U.S. missionaries Carol and Barney Morgan.
7. Spoiled kids, something like "Daddy's girls" and "Mommy's boys" (Spanish).
8. Neighborhood in Santo Domingo.

helps me with my makeup, and sometimes when I see myself in mirrors I don't even know who I am anymore. Not that I'm unhappy or anything. Even if I found a hot-air balloon that would whisk me straight to U2's house I'm not sure I would take it. (I'm still not talking to my traitor brother, though.) The truth is I'm even thinking of staying one more year. Abuela doesn't want me ever to leave—I'll miss you, she says so simply it can't be anything but true—and my mom has told me I can stay if I want to but that I would be welcome at home, too. Tía Rubelka tells me she's hanging tough, my mother, that she's back to two jobs. They sent me a picture of the whole family and Abuela framed it and I can't look at it without misting up. My mother's not wearing her fakies in it; she looks so thin I don't even recognize her.

Just know that I would die for you, she told me the last time we talked. And before I could say anything she hung up.

But that's not what I wanted to tell you. It's about that crazy feeling that started this whole mess, the bruja feeling that comes singing out of my bones, that takes hold of me the way blood seizes cotton. The feeling that tells me that everything in my life is about to change. It's come back. Just the other day I woke up from all these dreams and it was there, pulsing inside of me. I imagine this is what it feels like to have a child in you. At first I was scared, because I thought it was telling me to run away again, but every time I looked around our house, every time I saw my abuela the feeling got stronger, so I knew this was something different.

105　　I was dating a boy by then, a sweet morenito[9] by the name of Max Sánchez, who I had met in Los Mina while visiting Rosio. He's short, but his smile and his snappy dressing make up for a lot. Because I'm from Nueba Yol[1] he talks about how rich he's going to become and I try to explain to him that I don't care about that, but he looks at me like I'm crazy. I'm going to get a white Mercedes-Benz, he says. Tú verás.[2] But it's the job he has that I love best, that got me and him started. In Santo Domingo two or three theatres often share the same set of reels for a movie, so when the first theatre finishes with the first reel they put it in Max's hands and he rides his motorcycle like crazy to make it to the second theatre and then he drives back, waits, picks up the second reel, and so on. If he's held up or gets into an accident the first reel will end and there will be no second reel and the people in the audience will throw bottles. So far he's been blessed, he tells me while kissing his San Miguel[3] medal. Because of me, he brags, one movie becomes three. I'm the man who puts together the pictures. Max is not from la clase alta,[4] as my abuela would describe it, and if any of the stuck-up bitches in school saw us they would just about die, but I'm fond of him. He holds open doors, he calls me his morena; when he's feeling brave he touches my arm gently and then pulls back.

9. Literally, moreno (brown) plus -ito (a diminutive suffix) equals "little brown" (Spanish), that is, a little brown-skinned boy.
1. New York City (Dominican slang).
2. You'll see (Spanish).
3. St. Michael (Spanish), leader of God's army and angel of death, who ensures the redeemed soul's safe passage to heaven.
4. The upper class (Spanish).

Anyway I thought maybe the feeling was about Max, and so one day I let him take me to one of the love motels. He was so excited he almost fell off the bed, and the first thing he wanted was to look at my ass. I never knew my big ass could be such a star attraction, but he kissed it, four, five times, gave me goose bumps with his breath, and pronounced it a tesoro. When we were done and he was in the bathroom washing himself I stood in front of the mirror naked and looked at my culo for the first time. A tesoro,[5] I repeated. A treasure.

Well? Rosio asked at school. And I nodded once, quickly, and she grabbed me and laughed and all the girls I hated turned to look, but what could they do? Happiness, when it comes, is stronger than all the jerk girls in Santo Domingo combined.

But I was still confused. Because the feeling, it just kept getting stronger and stronger, wouldn't let me sleep, wouldn't give me any peace. I started losing races, which was something I never did.

You ain't so great, are you, gringa,[6] the girls on the other teams hissed at me, and I could only hang my head. Coach Cortés was so unhappy he just locked himself in his car and wouldn't say anything to any of us.

The whole thing was driving me crazy, and then one night I came home from 110 being out with Max. He had taken me for a walk along the Malecón[7]—he never had money for anything else—and we had watched the bats zigzagging over the palms and an old ship head into the distance. While I stretched my hamstrings, he talked quietly about moving to the U.S. My abuela was waiting for me at the living-room table. Even though she still wears black to mourn the husband she lost when she was young she's one of the most handsome women I've ever known. We have the same jagged lightning-bolt part, and when I saw her at the airport, the first time in ten years, I didn't want to admit it but I knew that things were going to be O.K. between us. She stood like she was her own best thing[8] and when she saw me she said, Hija, I have waited for you since the day you left. And then she hugged me and kissed me and said, I'm your abuela, but you can call me La Inca.[9]

Standing over her that night, her part like a crack in her hair, I felt a surge of tenderness. I put my arms around her and that was when I noticed that she was looking at photos. Old photos, the kind I'd never seen in my house. Photos of my mother when she was young, before she had her breasts. She was even skinnier than me! I picked the smallest photo up. Mami was standing in front of a bakery. Even with an apron on she looked potent, like someone who was going to be someone.

She was very guapa, I said casually.

5. Treasure (Spanish). *Culo:* ass (Spanish).
6. English-speaking foreigner (Spanish).
7. Santo Domingo's world-famous oceanfront promenade.
8. Perhaps an allusion to Toni Morrison's novel *Beloved* (1987), in which a man works to convince his lover, a mother grieving for her children, that she, not they, is her "own best thing." In interviews, Díaz has referred to his "relationship with" Morrison's work as "the most sustained love of mine, the one that's carried me through all these years."
9. The Incan (Spanish), a noble, member, or follower of the Indian peoples who established, in what is now Peru, pre-Columbian America's largest empire (c. thirteenth century through 1572).

Abuela snorted. Guapa soy yo. Your mother was a diosa. But so cabeza dura. When she was your age we never got along. She was cabeza dura and I was . . . exigente.[1] You and her are more alike than you think.

I know she ran away. From you. From Santo Domingo.

115   La Inca stared at me, incredulous. Your mother didn't run away. We had to *send* her away. To keep her from being murdered. To keep us all from being murdered. She didn't listen and she fell in love with the wrong man. She didn't listen. Jesu Cristo, hija—

She was about to say something more and then she stopped.

And that's when it hit with the force of a hurricane. The *feeling*. My abuela was sitting there, forlorn, trying to cobble together the right words, and I could not move or breathe. I felt like I always did in the last seconds of a race, when I was sure that I was going to explode. She was about to say something and I was waiting for whatever she was going to give me. I was waiting to begin.

2007

QUESTIONS

1. WILDWOOD begins with Lola's observation that "[i]t's never the changes we want that change everything." How and why exactly does Lola change over the course of the story?
2. WILDWOOD ends with Lola's remark, "I was waiting to begin." Why do you think the story ends with reference to a beginning, or how does this line shape the way you understand the nature and significance of the changes Lola has undergone up to this point?
3. How do Díaz's specific ways of intermixing Spanish and English, as well as his frequent allusions (literary, musical, televisual, and biblical), help to flesh out the story's central conflicts and/or theme(s)?

SUGGESTIONS FOR WRITING

1. Choose any story in this chapter and write an essay exploring how character, point of view, setting, symbolism, or any recurring word or phrase contributes to the development of theme. Be sure to state that theme in a sentence.
2. Sometimes the theme in a work of literature can be expressed as a strong, clear statement: "A always follows from B," or "An X can never be a Y." More often, though, especially in modern literature, authors offer subtler, often ambiguous themes that deliberately undermine our faith in simple absolutes: "A doesn't necessarily always follow B," or "There are times when an X can be a Y." Write an essay in which you argue that one of the stories in this chapter has an "always" or "never" kind of theme, and contrast it to the more indeterminate theme of another story. Alternatively, use your essay to explain why we might be both tempted and wrong to see one of these stories as having an "always" or "never" theme. What is the overly simplistic version of the theme, and what is the more complex one?
3. Write an essay exploring how theme is developed through the juxtaposition of realistic detail and fantastic elements in A VERY OLD MAN WITH ENORMOUS WINGS, especially (but not exclusively) in the description of the winged man himself.
4. Though the main theme of WILDWOOD may well be a universal one (an insight that applies to all or most people), its major characters are all contemporary working-class

1. Demanding. *Guapa soy yo*: I am pretty or attractive. *Diosa*: goddess. *Cabeza dura*: hardheaded (all Spanish).

Dominican Americans. Write an essay exploring how the story characterizes their life and how this characterization shapes the story's theme, perhaps giving the story a culturally and historically specific, as well as universal, resonance and relevance.

5. Write your own fable, perhaps reworking or modernizing one by Aesop. Be sure both to state the theme and to make sure it is demonstrated in the fable itself.

Cross-Cultural Encounters

AN ALBUM

Few of us in today's increasingly wired world either inhabit or trace our roots to a single culture. Rather, most of us live across cultures and identify with multiple "tribes," habitually performing rituals both ancient and modern—whether we recognize them as such or not. Whether or not we choose to watch Netflix, see Hollywood movies, eat at McDonald's, or post to *Facebook*, few of us can avoid being heavily influenced by these phenomena or participating in the shared culture they help constitute. Yet each of us has a slightly different relationship to that common culture, depending in part upon where we, our parents, and even our grandparents grew up; on what languages we speak or read; on what faiths we follow.

Increased mobility, globalization, and the Internet have done as much to enhance awareness of cultural diversity as they have to erode it. They also ensure that all of us have to navigate cultural differences—to communicate and collaborate with people whose experiences, habits, worldviews, and values differ dramatically from our own. Such cross-cultural encounters—whether they occur between people or within a single person—can be exhilarating and enlightening, as well as difficult and painful. Paradoxically, it is often only by encountering a foreign culture that we come to appreciate what is specific, special, even foreign and funny about our own, or even to recognize it as our own. As a character in Nobel Prize–winning author Wole Soyinka's 1975 play *Death and the King's Horseman* remarks, he didn't understand what he "took" from his Nigerian homeland until he left for another country: "But I found out over there. I am grateful [. . .] for that. And I will never give it up."

Like many authors studied in English literature classes today, Soyinka hails neither from England nor from America, but from a former British colony, Nigeria—a reminder that English is today a world language and a world literature, thanks in part to imperialism and the far from equitable cross-cultural encounters it entailed, as well as the rich hybrid cultures, literatures, and languages it created. One of the most exciting literary developments of the past half century has been the emergence of so-called *postcolonial literature*—that is, works written either by those raised in former colonies (like Soyinka or Salman Rushdie) or by their children and grandchildren, people (like Jhumpa Lahiri) who may never have even visited their "cultural homelands." Not surprisingly, postcolonial literature often investigates the varied ways in which cultures intersect and clash today, as well as the ways in which today's world has been shaped by the cultural confrontations of yesterday.

By exploring such issues, postcolonial literature may help us to navigate our own distinctly modern world. But it also builds on a tradition stretching back to literature's very beginnings. What else, after all, are Homer's *Odyssey*, Shakespeare's *The Tempest*, and even, perhaps, the Christian Bible about, if not cross-cultural encounters? Conversely, how many contemporary movies can you think of that are essentially what Hollywood calls "fish out of water" stories about cultural difference? (Have you ever seen *E.T.* or *Borat*?)

Such stories can be comic as well as tragic and everything in between, just as the conclusions they reach vary widely. The stories in this album vividly demonstrate that range of tone and theme. In many of them, characters find themselves in the position of translator, forced to interpret one language or culture to another, and in the process learning much about those cultures and themselves. Just what do each of these characters learn, and what might their stories reveal about the way culture and environment shape us—both linking us to, and dividing us from, others? What might the stories suggest about when and why cross-cultural communication or translation fails? How do the stories define the costs and benefits of literally and figuratively learning a new language, journeying outside our familiar world, even seeing ourselves and our own culture as others do? When and how might cultural belonging and identity become a matter of choice? And when they do, why do people seem to make the choices they do? Which stories envision the clash or choice of cultures as one between "ancient" and "modern" traditions? How do they envision the strengths and weaknesses of each?

BHARATI MUKHERJEE

(1940–2017)

The Management of Grief

Bharati Mukherjee grew up in Calcutta (now Kolkata), India, in what she called an "extraordinarily close-knit" and wealthy Hindu family of which her highly educated chemist father was "the benevolent patriarch." Moving with her family among Calcutta, London, and Switzerland, Mukherjee attended mainly English-language private schools, both Protestant and Catholic. Armed with a University of Calcutta BA and an MA in English and Ancient Indian Culture from the University of Baroda, in western India, she moved to the United States in 1961, earning both an MFA in creative writing and a PhD in English and comparative literature at the University of Iowa. There, too, she met and married Canadian Clark Blaise, abandoning her plan to return to India and let her father choose her spouse. Teaching at various Canadian and U.S. universities, the couple cowrote two works of nonfiction—*Days and Nights in Calcutta* (1977), which chronicles a 1972 visit to India, and *The Sorrow and the Terror* (1987), a carefully researched account of a 1985 Air India terrorist bombing that killed 329 and also inspired "The Management of Grief." Though Mukherjee had previously published novels, beginning with *The Tiger's Daughter* (1971), and one short-story collection (*Darkness* [1985]), *Days and Nights* remained her most highly acclaimed book until *The Middleman and Other Stories* won the National Book Critics Circle Award in 1988. Here and in novels such as *Jasmine* (1989), *The Holder of the World* (1993), *The Tree Bride* (2004), and *Miss New India* (2011), Mukherjee explores what she called the "extreme transformations" wrought by immigration—on individuals, families, and the texture of both American and Indian life and identity.

A woman I don't know is boiling tea the Indian way in my kitchen. There are a lot of women I don't know in my kitchen, whispering, and moving tactfully. They open doors, rummage through the pantry, and try not to ask me where things are kept. They remind me of when my sons were small, on Mother's Day or when Vikram and I were tired, and they would make big, sloppy omelets. I would lie in bed pretending I didn't hear them.

Dr. Sharma, the treasurer of the Indo-Canada Society, pulls me into the hallway. He wants to know if I am worried about money. His wife, who has just come up from the basement with a tray of empty cups and glasses, scolds him. "Don't bother Mrs. Bhave with mundane details." She looks so monstrously pregnant her baby must be days overdue. I tell her she shouldn't be carrying heavy things. "Shaila," she says, smiling, "this is the fifth." Then she grabs a teenager by his shirttails. He slips his Walkman[1] off his head. He has to be one of her four children, they have the same domed and dented foreheads. "What's the official word now?" she demands. The boy slips the headphones back on. "They're acting evasive, Ma. They're saying it could be an accident or a terrorist bomb."

All morning, the boys have been muttering, Sikh Bomb, Sikh[2] Bomb. The men, not using the word, bow their heads in agreement. Mrs. Sharma touches her forehead at such a word. At least they've stopped talking about space debris and Russian lasers.

Two radios are going in the dining room. They are tuned to different stations. Someone must have brought the radios down from my boys' bedrooms. I haven't gone into their rooms since Kusum came running across the front lawn in her bathrobe. She looked so funny, I was laughing when I opened the door.

The big TV in the den is being whizzed through American networks and   5
cable channels.

"Damn!" some man swears bitterly. "How can these preachers carry on like nothing's happened?" I want to tell him we're not that important. You look at the audience, and at the preacher in his blue robe with his beautiful white hair, the potted palm trees under a blue sky, and you know they care about nothing.

The phone rings and rings. Dr. Sharma's taken charge. "We're with her," he keeps saying. "Yes, yes, the doctor has given calming pills. Yes, yes, pills are having necessary effect." I wonder if pills alone explain this calm. Not peace, just a deadening quiet. I was always controlled, but never repressed. Sound can reach me, but my body is tensed, ready to scream. I hear their voices all around me. I hear my boys and Vikram cry, "Mommy, Shaila!" and their screams insulate me, like headphones.

The woman boiling water tells her story again and again. "I got the news first. My cousin called from Halifax before six A.M., can you imagine? He'd gotten up for prayers and his son was studying for medical exams and he heard on a rock channel that something had happened to a plane. They said first it had disappeared from the radar, like a giant eraser just reached out. His father called me, so I said to him, what do you mean, 'something bad'? You mean a hijacking?

---

1. Handheld audiocassette or CD player.
2. Sikhs are adherents of Sikhism, a religion founded c. 1500; they constitute a substantial minority of India's population.

And he said, *behn*,[3] there is no confirmation of anything yet, but check with your neighbors because a lot of them must be on that plane. So I called poor Kusum straightaway. I knew Kusum's husband and daughter were booked to go yesterday."

Kusum lives across the street from me. She and Satish had moved in less than a month ago. They said they needed a bigger place. All these people, the Sharmas and friends from the Indo-Canada Society, had been there for the housewarming. Satish and Kusum made homemade tandoori on their big gas grill and even the white neighbors piled their plates high with that luridly red, charred, juicy chicken. Their younger daughter had danced, and even our boys had broken away from the Stanley Cup telecast to put in a reluctant appearance. Everyone took pictures for their albums and for the community newspapers—another of our families had made it big in Toronto—and now I wonder how many of those happy faces are gone. "Why does God give us so much if all along He intends to take it away?" Kusum asks me.

10   I nod. We sit on carpeted stairs, holding hands like children. "I never once told him that I loved him," I say. I was too much the well brought up woman. I was so well brought up I never felt comfortable calling my husband by his first name.

"It's all right," Kusum says. "He knew. My husband knew. They felt it. Modern young girls have to say it because what they feel is fake."

Kusum's daughter, Pam, runs in with an overnight case. Pam's in her McDonald's uniform. "Mummy! You have to get dressed!" Panic makes her cranky. "A reporter's on his way here."

"Why?"

"You want to talk to him in your bathrobe?" She starts to brush her mother's long hair. She's the daughter who's always in trouble. She dates Canadian boys and hangs out in the mall, shopping for tight sweaters. The younger one, the goody-goody one according to Pam, the one with a voice so sweet that when she sang *bhajans*[4] for Ethiopian relief even a frugal man like my husband wrote out a hundred dollar check, *she* was on that plane. *She* was going to spend July and August with grandparents because Pam wouldn't go. Pam said she'd rather waitress at McDonald's. "If it's a choice between Bombay and Wonderland,[5] I'm picking Wonderland," she'd said.

15   "Leave me alone," Kusum yells. "You know what I want to do? If I didn't have to look after you now, I'd hang myself."

Pam's young face goes blotchy with pain. "Thanks," she says, "don't let me stop you."

"Hush," pregnant Mrs. Sharma scolds Pam. "Leave your mother alone. Mr. Sharma will tackle the reporters and fill out the forms. He'll say what has to be said."

Pam stands her ground. "You think I don't know what Mummy's thinking? *Why her?* that's what. That's sick! Mummy wishes my little sister were alive and I were dead."

Kusum's hand in mine is trembly hot. We continue to sit on the stairs.

3. Sister (Hindi).
4. Hymns (Hindi).
5. Toronto amusement park.

She calls before she arrives, wondering if there's anything I need. Her name is 20
Judith Templeton and she's an appointee of the provincial government. "Multi-
culturalism?" I ask, and she says, "partially," but that her mandate is bigger. "I've
been told you knew many of the people on the flight," she says. "Perhaps if you'd
agree to help us reach the others . . . ?"

She gives me time at least to put on tea water and pick up the mess in the
front room. I have a few *samosas*[6] from Kusum's housewarming that I could fry
up, but then I think, why prolong this visit?

Judith Templeton is much younger than she sounded. She wears a blue suit
with a white blouse and a polka dot tie. Her blond hair is cut short, her only
jewelry is pearl drop earrings. Her briefcase is new and expensive looking, a
gleaming cordovan leather. She sits with it across her lap. When she looks out
the front windows onto the street, her contact lenses seem to float in front of
her light blue eyes.

"What sort of help do you want from me?" I ask. She has refused the tea, out
of politeness, but I insist, along with some slightly stale biscuits.[7]

"I have no experience," she admits. "That is, I have an MSW[8] and I've worked
in liaison with accident victims, but I mean I have no experience with a tragedy
of this scale—"

"Who could?" I ask. 25

"—and with the complications of culture, language, and customs. Someone
mentioned that Mrs. Bhave is a pillar—because you've taken it more calmly."

At this, perhaps, I frown, for she reaches forward, almost to take my hand. "I
hope you understand my meaning, Mrs. Bhave. There are hundreds of people
in Metro[9] directly affected, like you, and some of them speak no English. There
are some widows who've never handled money or gone on a bus, and there are
old parents who still haven't eaten or gone outside their bedrooms. Some houses
and apartments have been looted. Some wives are still hysterical. Some husbands are in shock and profound depression. We want to help, but our hands
are tied in so many ways. We have to distribute money to some people, and
there are legal documents—these things can be done. We have interpreters,
but we don't always have the human touch, or maybe the right human touch.
We don't want to make mistakes, Mrs. Bhave, and that's why we'd like to ask
you to help us."

"More mistakes, you mean," I say.

"Police matters are not in my hands," she answers.

"Nothing I can do will make any difference," I say. "We must all grieve in our 30
own way."

"But you are coping very well. All the people said, Mrs. Bhave is the strongest
person of all. Perhaps if the others could see you, talk with you, it would help
them."

"By the standards of the people you call hysterical, I am behaving very oddly
and very badly, Miss Templeton." I want to say to her, *I wish I could scream,*

6. Fried turnovers filled with finely chopped meat or vegetables.
7. Cookies.
8. Master's degree in social work.
9. That is, the municipality of metropolitan Toronto.

starve, walk into Lake Ontario, jump from a bridge. "They would not see me as a model. I do not see myself as a model."

I am a freak. No one who has ever known me would think of me reacting this way. This terrible calm will not go away.

She asks me if she may call again, after I get back from a long trip that we all must make. "Of course," I say. "Feel free to call, anytime."

35 Four days later, I find Kusum squatting on a rock overlooking a bay in Ireland. It isn't a big rock, but it juts sharply out over water. This is as close as we'll ever get to them. June breezes balloon out her sari and unpin her knee-length hair. She has the bewildered look of a sea creature whom the tides have stranded.

It's been one hundred hours since Kusum came stumbling and screaming across my lawn. Waiting around the hospital, we've heard many stories. The police, the diplomats, they tell us things thinking that we're strong, that knowledge is helpful to the grieving, and maybe it is. Some, I know, prefer ignorance, or their own versions. The plane broke into two, they say. Unconsciousness was instantaneous. No one suffered. My boys must have just finished their breakfasts. They loved eating on planes, they loved the smallness of plates, knives, and forks. Last year they saved the airline salt and pepper shakers. Half an hour more and they would have made it to Heathrow.[1]

Kusum says that we can't escape our fate. She says that all those people—our husbands, my boys, her girl with the nightingale voice, all those Hindus, Christians, Sikhs, Muslims, Parsis, and atheists on that plane—were fated to die together off this beautiful bay. She learned this from a swami[2] in Toronto.

I have my Valium.

Six of us "relatives"—two widows and four widowers—choose to spend the day today by the waters instead of sitting in a hospital room and scanning photographs of the dead. That's what they call us now: relatives. I've looked through twenty-seven photos in two days. They're very kind to us, the Irish are very understanding. Sometimes understanding means freeing a tourist bus for this trip to the bay, so we can pretend to spy our loved ones through the glassiness of waves or in sunspeckled cloud shapes.

40 I could die here, too, and be content.

"What is that, out there?" She's standing and flapping her hands and for a moment I see a head shape bobbing in the waves. She's standing in the water, I, on the boulder. The tide is low, and a round, black, head-sized rock has just risen from the waves. She returns, her sari end dripping and ruined and her face is a twisted remnant of hope, the way mine was a hundred hours ago, still laughing but inwardly knowing that nothing but the ultimate tragedy could bring two women together at six o'clock on a Sunday morning. I watch her face sag into blankness.

"That water felt warm, Shaila," she says at length.

"You can't," I say. "We have to wait for our turn to come."

I haven't eaten in four days, haven't brushed my teeth.

1. Major London airport.
2. Hindu religious teacher.

"I know," she says. "I tell myself I have no right to grieve. They are in a better 45 place than we are. My swami says I should be thrilled for them. My swami says depression is a sign of our selfishness."

Maybe I'm selfish. Selfishly I break away from Kusum and run, sandals slapping against stones, to the water's edge. What if my boys aren't lying pinned under the debris? What if they aren't stuck a mile below that innocent blue chop? What if, given the strong currents. . . .

Now I've ruined my sari, one of my best. Kusum has joined me, knee-deep in water that feels to me like a swimming pool. I could settle in the water, and my husband would take my hand and the boys would slap water in my face just to see me scream.

"Do you remember what good swimmers my boys were, Kusum?"

"I saw the medals," she says.

One of the widowers, Dr. Ranganathan from Montreal, walks out to us, 50 carrying his shoes in one hand. He's an electrical engineer. Someone at the hotel mentioned his work is famous around the world, something about the place where physics and electricity come together. He has lost a huge family, something indescribable. "With some luck," Dr. Ranganathan suggests to me, "a good swimmer could make it safely to some island. It is quite possible that there may be many, many microscopic islets scattered around."

"You're not just saying that?" I tell Dr. Ranganathan about Vinod, my elder son. Last year he took diving as well.

"It's a parent's duty to hope," he says. "It is foolish to rule out possibilities that have not been tested. I myself have not surrendered hope."

Kusum is sobbing once again. "Dear lady," he says, laying his free hand on her arm, and she calms down.

"Vinod is how old?" he asks me. He's very careful, as we all are. *Is*, not was.

"Fourteen. Yesterday he was fourteen. His father and uncle were going to 55 take him down to the Taj and give him a big birthday party. I couldn't go with them because I couldn't get two weeks off from my stupid job in June." I process bills for a travel agent. June is a big travel month.

Dr. Ranganathan whips the pockets of his suit jacket inside out. Squashed roses, in darkening shades of pink, float on the water. He tore the roses off creepers in somebody's garden. He didn't ask anyone if he could pluck the roses, but now there's been an article about it in the local papers. When you see an Indian person, it says, please give him or her flowers.

"A strong youth of fourteen," he says, "can very likely pull to safety a younger one."

My sons, though four years apart, were very close. Vinod wouldn't let Mithun drown. *Electrical engineering*, I think, foolishly perhaps: this man knows important secrets of the universe, things closed to me. Relief spins me lightheaded. No wonder my boys' photographs haven't turned up in the gallery of photos of the recovered dead. "Such pretty roses," I say.

"My wife loved pink roses. Every Friday I had to bring a bunch home. I used to say, why? After twenty-odd years of marriage you're still needing proof positive of my love?" He has identified his wife and three of his children. Then others from Montreal, the lucky ones, intact families with no survivors. He chuckles as he wades back to shore. Then he swings around to ask me a question.

"Mrs. Bhave, you are wanting to throw in some roses for your loved ones? I have two big ones left."

60   But I have other things to float: Vinod's pocket calculator; a half-painted model B-52 for my Mithun. They'd want them on their island. And for my husband? For him I let fall into the calm, glassy waters a poem I wrote in the hospital yesterday. Finally he'll know my feelings for him.

"Don't tumble, the rocks are slippery," Dr. Ranganathan cautions. He holds out a hand for me to grab.

Then it's time to get back on the bus, time to rush back to our waiting posts on hospital benches.

Kusum is one of the lucky ones. The lucky ones flew here, identified in multiplicate their loved ones, then will fly to India with the bodies for proper ceremonies. Satish is one of the few males who surfaced. The photos of faces we saw on the walls in an office at Heathrow and here in the hospital are mostly of women. Women have more body fat, a nun said to me matter-of-factly. They float better. Today I was stopped by a young sailor on the street. He had loaded bodies, he'd gone into the water when—he checks my face for signs of strength—when the sharks were first spotted. I don't blush, and he breaks down. "It's all right," I say. "Thank you." I had heard about the sharks from Dr. Ranganathan. In his orderly mind, science brings understanding, it holds no terror. It is the shark's duty. For every deer there is a hunter, for every fish a fisherman.

The Irish are not shy; they rush to me and give me hugs and some are crying. I cannot imagine reactions like that on the streets of Toronto. Just strangers, and I am touched. Some carry flowers with them and give them to any Indian they see.

65   After lunch, a policeman I have gotten to know quite well catches hold of me. He says he thinks he has a match for Vinod. I explain what a good swimmer Vinod is.

"You want me with you when you look at photos?" Dr. Ranganathan walks ahead of me into the picture gallery. In these matters, he is a scientist, and I am grateful. It is a new perspective. "They have performed miracles," he says. "We are indebted to them."

The first day or two the policemen showed us relatives only one picture at a time; now they're in a hurry, they're eager to lay out the possibles, and even the probables.

The face on the photo is of a boy much like Vinod; the same intelligent eyes, the same thick brows dipping into a V. But this boy's features, even his cheeks, are puffier, wider, mushier.

"No." My gaze is pulled by other pictures. There are five other boys who look like Vinod.

70   The nun assigned to console me rubs the first picture with a fingertip. "When they've been in the water for a while, love, they look a little heavier." The bones under the skin are broken, they said on the first day—try to adjust your memories. It's important.

"It's not him. I'm his mother. I'd know."

"I know this one!" Dr. Ranganathan cries out suddenly from the back of the gallery. "And this one!" I think he senses that I don't want to find my boys. "They are the Kutty brothers. They were also from Montreal." I don't mean to be crying. On the contrary, I am ecstatic. My suitcase in the hotel is packed heavy with dry clothes for my boys.

The policeman starts to cry. "I am so sorry, I am so sorry, ma'am. I really thought we had a match."

With the nun ahead of us and the policeman behind, we, the unlucky ones without our children's bodies, file out of the makeshift gallery.

From Ireland most of us go on to India. Kusum and I take the same direct flight 75 to Bombay, so I can help her clear customs quickly. But we have to argue with a man in uniform. He has large boils on his face. The boils swell and glow with sweat as we argue with him. He wants Kusum to wait in line and he refuses to take authority because his boss is on a tea break. But Kusum won't let her coffins out of sight, and I shan't desert her though I know that my parents, elderly and diabetic, must be waiting in a stuffy car in a scorching lot.

"You bastard!" I scream at the man with the popping boils. Other passengers press closer. "You think we're smuggling contraband in those coffins!"

Once upon a time we were well brought up women; we were dutiful wives who kept our heads veiled, our voices shy and sweet.

In India, I become, once again, an only child of rich, ailing parents. Old friends of the family come to pay their respects. Some are Sikh, and inwardly, involuntarily, I cringe. My parents are progressive people; they do not blame communities for a few individuals.

In Canada it is a different story now.

"Stay longer," my mother pleads. "Canada is a cold place. Why would you 80 want to be all by yourself?" I stay.

Three months pass. Then another.

"Vikram wouldn't have wanted you to give up things!" they protest. They call my husband by the name he was born with. In Toronto he'd changed to Vik so the men he worked with at his office would find his name as easy as Rod or Chris. "You know, the dead aren't cut off from us!"

My grandmother, the spoiled daughter of a rich *zamindar*,[3] shaved her head with rusty razor blades when she was widowed at sixteen. My grandfather died of childhood diabetes when he was nineteen, and she saw herself as the harbinger of bad luck. My mother grew up without parents, raised indifferently by an uncle, while her true mother slept in a hut behind the main estate house and took her food with the servants. She grew up a rationalist. My parents abhor mindless mortification.

The zamindar's daughter kept stubborn faith in Vedic[4] rituals; my parents rebelled. I am trapped between two modes of knowledge. At thirty-six, I am too old to start over and too young to give up. Like my husband's spirit, I flutter between worlds.

3. Landowner (Hindi).
4. Of or relating to the Vedas, Hinduism's most ancient and authoritative texts.

85 Courting aphasia,[5] we travel. We travel with our phalanx of servants and poor relatives. To hill stations and to beach resorts. We play contract bridge in dusty gymkhana clubs. We ride stubby ponies up crumbly mountain trails. At tea dances, we let ourselves be twirled twice round the ballroom. We hit the holy spots we hadn't made time for before. In Varanasi, Kalighat, Rishikesh, Hardwar, astrologers and palmists seek me out and for a fee offer me cosmic consolations.

Already the widowers among us are being shown new bride candidates. They cannot resist the call of custom, the authority of their parents and older brothers. They must marry; it is the duty of a man to look after a wife. The new wives will be young widows with children, destitute but of good family. They will make loving wives, but the men will shun them. I've had calls from the men over crackling Indian telephone lines. "Save me," they say, these substantial, educated, successful men of forty. "My parents are arranging a marriage for me." In a month they will have buried one family and returned to Canada with a new bride and partial family.

I am comparatively lucky. No one here thinks of arranging a husband for an unlucky widow.

Then, on the third day of the sixth month into this odyssey, in an abandoned temple in a tiny Himalayan village, as I make my offering of flowers and sweetmeats to the god of a tribe of animists, my husband descends to me. He is squatting next to a scrawny *sadhu*[6] in moth-eaten robes. Vikram wears the vanilla suit he wore the last time I hugged him. The *sadhu* tosses petals on a butter-fed flame, reciting Sanskrit mantras and sweeps his face of flies. My husband takes my hands in his.

You're beautiful, he starts. Then, *What are you doing here?*

90 *Shall I stay?* I ask. He only smiles, but already the image is fading. *You must finish alone what we started together.* No seaweed wreathes his mouth. He speaks too fast just as he used to when we were an envied family in our pink split-level. He is gone.

In the windowless altar room, smoky with joss sticks and clarified butter lamps, a sweaty hand gropes for my blouse. I do not shriek. The *sadhu* arranges his robe. The lamps hiss and sputter out.

When we come out of the temple, my mother says, "Did you feel something weird in there?"

My mother has no patience with ghosts, prophetic dreams, holy men, and cults.

"No," I lie. "Nothing."

95 But she knows that she's lost me. She knows that in days I shall be leaving.

Kusum's put her house up for sale. She wants to live in an ashram[7] in Hardwar. Moving to Hardwar was her swami's idea. Her swami runs two ashrams, the one in Hardwar and another here in Toronto.

"Don't run away," I tell her.

5. Loss of the ability to articulate ideas or comprehend language.
6. Hindu holy man.
7. Residence of a Hindu religious community and its particular leader or guru.

"I'm not running away," she says. "I'm pursuing inner peace. You think you or that Ranganathan fellow are better off?"

Pam's left for California. She wants to do some modelling, she says. She says when she comes into her share of the insurance money she'll open a yoga-cum-aerobics studio in Hollywood. She sends me postcards so naughty I daren't leave them on the coffee table. Her mother has withdrawn from her and the world.

The rest of us don't lose touch, that's the point. Talk is all we have, says   100
Dr. Ranganathan, who has also resisted his relatives and returned to Montreal and to his job, alone. He says, whom better to talk with than other relatives? We've been melted down and recast as a new tribe.

He calls me twice a week from Montreal. Every Wednesday night and every Saturday afternoon. He is changing jobs, going to Ottawa. But Ottawa is over a hundred miles away, and he is forced to drive two hundred and twenty miles a day. He can't bring himself to sell his house. The house is a temple, he says; the king-sized bed in the master bedroom is a shrine. He sleeps on a folding cot. A devotee.

There are still some hysterical relatives. Judith Templeton's list of those needing help and those who've "accepted" is in nearly perfect balance. Acceptance means you speak of your family in the past tense and you make active plans for moving ahead with your life. There are courses at Seneca and Ryerson[8] we could be taking. Her gleaming leather briefcase is full of college catalogues and lists of cultural societies that need our help. She has done impressive work, I tell her.

"In the textbooks on grief management," she replies—I am her confidante, I realize, one of the few whose grief has not sprung bizarre obsessions—"there are stages to pass through: rejection, depression, acceptance, reconstruction." She has compiled a chart and finds that six months after the tragedy, none of us still reject reality, but only a handful are reconstructing. "Depressed Acceptance" is the plateau we've reached. Remarriage is a major step in reconstruction (though she's a little surprised, even shocked, over *how* quickly some of the men have taken on new families). Selling one's house and changing jobs and cities is healthy.

How do I tell Judith Templeton that my family surrounds me, and that like creatures in epics, they've changed shapes? She sees me as calm and accepting but worries that I have no job, no career. My closest friends are worse off than I. I cannot tell her my days, even my nights, are thrilling.

She asks me to help with families she can't reach at all. An elderly couple in   105
Agincourt whose sons were killed just weeks after they had brought their parents over from a village in Punjab. From their names, I know they are Sikh. Judith Templeton and a translator have visited them twice with offers of money for air fare to Ireland, with bank forms, power-of-attorney forms, but they have refused to sign, or to leave their tiny apartment. Their sons' money is frozen in the bank. Their sons' investment apartments have been trashed by tenants, the furnishings sold off. The parents fear that anything they sign or any money they

8. Seneca College of Applied Arts and Technology, in Willowdale; Ryerson Polytechnical Institute, Toronto.

receive will end the company's or the country's obligations to them. They fear they are selling their sons for two airline tickets to a place they've never seen.

The high-rise apartment is a tower of Indians and West Indians, with a sprinkling of Orientals. The nearest bus stop kiosk is lined with women in saris. Boys practice cricket in the parking lot. Inside the building, even I wince a bit from the ferocity of onion fumes, the distinctive and immediate Indianness of frying *ghee*,[9] but Judith Templeton maintains a steady flow of information. These poor old people are in imminent danger of losing their place and all their services.

I say to her, "They are Sikh. They will not open up to a Hindu woman." And what I want to add is, as much as I try not to, I stiffen now at the sight of beards and turbans. I remember a time when we all trusted each other in this new country, it was only the new country we worried about.

The two rooms are dark and stuffy. The lights are off, and an oil lamp sputters on the coffee table. The bent old lady has let us in, and her husband is wrapping a white turban over his oiled, hip-length hair. She immediately goes to the kitchen, and I hear the most familiar sound of an Indian home, tap water hitting and filling a teapot.

They have not paid their utility bills, out of fear and the inability to write a check. The telephone is gone; electricity and gas and water are soon to follow. They have told Judith their sons will provide. They are good boys, and they have always earned and looked after their parents.

110   We converse a bit in Hindi. They do not ask about the crash and I wonder if I should bring it up. If they think I am here merely as a translator, then they may feel insulted. There are thousands of Punjabi-speakers, Sikhs, in Toronto to do a better job. And so I say to the old lady, "I too have lost my sons, and my husband, in the crash."

Her eyes immediately fill with tears. The man mutters a few words which sound like a blessing. "God provides and God takes away," he says.

I want to say, but only men destroy and give back nothing. "My boys and my husband are not coming back," I say. "We have to understand that."

Now the old woman responds. "But who is to say? Man alone does not decide these things." To this her husband adds his agreement.

Judith asks about the bank papers, the release forms. With a stroke of the pen, they will have a provincial trustee to pay their bills, invest their money, send them a monthly pension.

115   "Do you know this woman?" I ask them.

The man raises his hand from the table, turns it over and seems to regard each finger separately before he answers. "This young lady is always coming here, we make tea for her and she leaves papers for us to sign." His eyes scan a pile of papers in the corner of the room. "Soon we will be out of tea, then will she go away?"

The old lady adds, "I have asked my neighbors and no one else gets *angrezi*[1] visitors. What have we done?"

9. Clarified butter.
1. English, Anglo (Hindi).

"It's her job," I try to explain. "The government is worried. Soon you will have no place to stay, no lights, no gas, no water."

"Government will get its money. Tell her not to worry, we are honorable people."

I try to explain the government wishes to give money, not take. He raises his 120 hand. "Let them take," he says. "We are accustomed to that. That is no problem."

"We are strong people," says the wife. "Tell her that."

"Who needs all this machinery?" demands the husband. "It is unhealthy, the bright lights, the cold air on a hot day, the cold food, the four gas rings. God will provide, not government."

"When our boys return," the mother says. Her husband sucks his teeth. "Enough talk," he says.

Judith breaks in. "Have you convinced them?" The snaps on her cordovan briefcase go off like firecrackers in that quiet apartment. She lays the sheaf of legal papers on the coffee table. "If they can't write their names, an X will do— I've told them that."

Now the old lady has shuffled to the kitchen and soon emerges with a pot of 125 tea and two cups. "I think my bladder will go first on a job like this," Judith says to me, smiling. "If only there was some way of reaching them. Please thank her for the tea. Tell her she's very kind."

I nod in Judith's direction and tell them in Hindi, "She thanks you for the tea. She thinks you are being very hospitable but she doesn't have the slightest idea what it means."

I want to say, humor her. I want to say, my boys and my husband are with me too, more than ever. I look in the old man's eyes and I can read his stubborn, peasant's message: *I have protected this woman as best I can. She is the only person I have left. Give to me or take from me what you will, but I will not sign for it. I will not pretend that I accept.*

In the car, Judith says, "You see what I'm up against? I'm sure they're lovely people, but their stubbornness and ignorance are driving me crazy. They think signing a paper is signing their sons' death warrants, don't they?"

I am looking out the window. I want to say, *In our culture, it is a parent's duty to hope.*

"Now Shaila, this next woman is a real mess. She cries day and night, and 130 she refuses all medical help. We may have to—"

"—Let me out at the subway," I say.

"I beg your pardon?" I can feel those blue eyes staring at me.

It would not be like her to disobey. She merely disapproves, and slows at a corner to let me out. Her voice is plaintive. "Is there anything I said? Anything I did?"

I could answer her suddenly in a dozen ways, but I choose not to. "Shaila? Let's talk about it," I hear, then slam the door.

A wife and mother begins her new life in a new country, and that life is cut 135 short. Yet her husband tells her: Complete what we have started. We, who stayed out of politics and came halfway around the world to avoid religious and political feuding have been the first in the New World to die from it. I no longer know what we started, nor how to complete it. I write letters to the editors of local papers and to members of Parliament. Now at least they admit it was a bomb. One MP[2] answers back, with sympathy, but with a challenge. You want to make a difference? Work on a campaign. Work on mine. Politicize the Indian voter.

My husband's old lawyer helps me set up a trust. Vikram was a saver and a careful investor. He had saved the boys' boarding school and college fees. I sell the pink house at four times what we paid for it and take a small apartment downtown. I am looking for a charity to support.

We are deep in the Toronto winter, gray skies, icy pavements. I stay indoors, watching television. I have tried to assess my situation, how best to live my life, to complete what we began so many years ago. Kusum has written me from Hardwar that her life is now serene. She has seen Satish and has heard her daughter sing again. Kusum was on a pilgrimage, passing through a village when she heard a young girl's voice, singing one of her daughter's favorite *bhajans*. She followed the music through the squalor of a Himalayan village, to a hut where a young girl, an exact replica of her daughter, was fanning coals under the kitchen fire. When she appeared, the girl cried out, "Ma!" and ran away. What did I think of that?

I think I can only envy her.

Pam didn't make it to California, but writes me from Vancouver. She works in a department store, giving make-up hints to Indian and Oriental girls. Dr. Ranganathan has given up his commute, given up his house and job, and accepted an academic position in Texas where no one knows his story and he has vowed not to tell it. He calls me now once a week.

140   I wait, I listen, and I pray, but Vikram has not returned to me. The voices and the shapes and the nights filled with visions ended abruptly several weeks ago.

I take it as a sign.

One rare, beautiful, sunny day last week, returning from a small errand on Yonge Street, I was walking through the park from the subway to my apartment. I live equidistant from the Ontario Houses of Parliament and the University of Toronto. The day was not cold, but something in the bare trees caught my attention. I looked up from the gravel, into the branches and the clear blue sky beyond. I thought I heard the rustling of larger forms, and I waited a moment for voices. Nothing.

"What?" I asked.

Then as I stood in the path looking north to Queen's Park and west to the university, I heard the voices of my family one last time. *Your time has come,* they said. *Go, be brave.*

145   I do not know where this voyage I have begun will end. I do not know which direction I will take. I dropped the package on a park bench and started walking.

1988

---

2. Member of Parliament.

QUESTIONS

1. How would you characterize Shaila Bhave's central conflict? In what ways might it resemble that of any grieving wife and mother? of any victim of terrorism? How is it created or exacerbated by her particular cultural location and situation?
2. Why does Shaila choose to return to Canada? What exactly does she seem to be choosing at the story's end? How do her choices compare to those of other characters in the story? What is the thematic significance of those choices?
3. How does Shaila's work with Judith affect her and the story's themes?

AUTHORS ON THEIR WORK

BHARATI MUKHERJEE (1940–2017)

From "Author Interviews: Bharati Mukherjee Runs the West Coast Offense" (2002)*

MUKHERJEE: My husband, Clark Blaise, and I wrote a nonfiction book [*The Sorrow and the Terror* (1987)] about the terrorist bombing of an Air India jet that took off from Toronto on its way to Bombay with 329 people on board, ninety percent of whom were Canadians of Indian origin. The bad guys were Canadians, but Sikh, militant [. . .] in politics. It was the bloodiest terrorist incident until WTC [World Trade Center].

[. . .] The book was a nonfiction bestseller in Canada. We were under death threat for two years. When I sat down to write *The Middleman and Other Stories* [1988] as a collection of stories about diaspora, "The Management of Grief" came out in one sitting. It was a very sad story to write.

I would have been on that plane if I hadn't left Canada for the U.S. five years before—that's the plane we used to take to India, the first one after school closing. I lost a friend on that flight.

DAVE: Having created two products from one body of research, [. . .] how do you account for the[ir] life spans being so different?

MUKHERJEE: [. . .] Yes, they've long forgotten the nonfiction book, [. . .] but the story lives on.

The persuasive power of fiction was heartening. [. . .] The story of individual families or individual victims lived on and spoke to people in ways that the statement of facts didn't.

*"Author Interviews: Bharati Mukherjee Runs the West Coast Offense." Interview by Dave Welch. *PowellsBooks Blog*, 4 Apr. 2002, www.powells.com/post/interviews/bharati-mukherjee-runs-the-west-coast-offense.

JHUMPA LAHIRI
(b. 1967)

Interpreter of Maladies

Born in London and raised in Rhode Island, Jhumpa Lahiri is the daughter of Bengali parents; much of her fiction addresses the difficulty of reconciling an Indian heritage with life in the United States. Lahiri earned a BA from Barnard College and several degrees from Boston University: an MA in English, an MFA in creative writing, an MA in comparative studies in literature and the arts, and a PhD in Renaissance studies. She has published many stories in well-known periodicals such as the *New Yorker* and won the 2000 Pulitzer Prize for her first collection, *Interpreter of Maladies* (1999), a best seller that has been translated into at least twenty-nine languages. Her second, award-winning collection, *Unaccustomed Earth* (2008), debuted at the top of the *New York Times* best-seller list. Lahiri debuted as a novelist with *The Namesake* (2003), made into a film in 2006; *The Lowland* (2013) was short-listed for both the Man Booker Prize and the National Book Award. Now living in Rome, she published her first Italian-language novel, *Dove mi trovo*, in 2018 and later translated it into English as *Whereabouts* (2021).

At the tea stall Mr. and Mrs. Das bickered about who should take Tina to the toilet. Eventually Mrs. Das relented when Mr. Das pointed out that he had given the girl her bath the night before. In the rearview mirror Mr. Kapasi watched as Mrs. Das emerged slowly from his bulky white Ambassador, dragging her shaved, largely bare legs across the back seat. She did not hold the little girl's hand as they walked to the rest room.

They were on their way to see the Sun Temple at Konarak.[1] It was a dry, bright Saturday, the mid-July heat tempered by a steady ocean breeze, ideal weather for sightseeing. Ordinarily Mr. Kapasi would not have stopped so soon along the way, but less than five minutes after he'd picked up the family that morning in front of Hotel Sandy Villa, the little girl had complained. The first thing Mr. Kapasi had noticed when he saw Mr. and Mrs. Das, standing with their children under the portico of the hotel, was that they were very young, perhaps not even thirty. In addition to Tina they had two boys, Ronny and Bobby, who appeared very close in age and had teeth covered in a network of flashing silver wires. The family looked Indian but dressed as foreigners did, the children in stiff, brightly colored clothing and caps with translucent visors. Mr. Kapasi was accustomed to foreign tourists; he was assigned to them regularly because he could speak English. Yesterday he had driven an elderly couple

---

1. In paragraphs 91–98, the story provides an accurate history and description of the Sun Temple at Konark (or Konarak), still a pilgrimage as well as tourist site near the east coast in India's Orissa region. According to legend, the temple was built because Samba, son of Lord Krishna, was cured of leprosy by Surya, the sun god.

from Scotland, both with spotted faces and fluffy white hair so thin it exposed their sunburnt scalps. In comparison, the tanned, youthful faces of Mr. and Mrs. Das were all the more striking. When he'd introduced himself, Mr. Kapasi had pressed his palms together in greeting, but Mr. Das squeezed hands like an American so that Mr. Kapasi felt it in his elbow. Mrs. Das, for her part, had flexed one side of her mouth, smiling dutifully at Mr. Kapasi, without displaying any interest in him.

As they waited at the tea stall, Ronny, who looked like the older of the two boys, clambered suddenly out of the back seat, intrigued by a goat tied to a stake in the ground.

"Don't touch it," Mr. Das said. He glanced up from his paperback tour book, which said "INDIA" in yellow letters and looked as if it had been published abroad. His voice, somehow tentative and a little shrill, sounded as though it had not yet settled into maturity.

"I want to give it a piece of gum," the boy called back as he trotted ahead.   5

Mr. Das stepped out of the car and stretched his legs by squatting briefly to the ground. A clean-shaven man, he looked exactly like a magnified version of Ronny. He had a sapphire blue visor, and was dressed in shorts, sneakers, and a T-shirt. The camera slung around his neck, with an impressive telephoto lens and numerous buttons and markings, was the only complicated thing he wore. He frowned, watching as Ronny rushed toward the goat, but appeared to have no intention of intervening. "Bobby, make sure that your brother doesn't do any-thing stupid."

"I don't feel like it," Bobby said, not moving. He was sitting in the front seat beside Mr. Kapasi, studying a picture of the elephant god taped to the glove compartment.

"No need to worry," Mr. Kapasi said. "They are quite tame." Mr. Kapasi was forty-six years old, with receding hair that had gone completely silver, but his butterscotch complexion and his unlined brow, which he treated in spare moments to dabs of lotus-oil balm, made it easy to imagine what he must have looked like at an earlier age. He wore gray trousers and a matching jacket-style shirt, tapered at the waist, with short sleeves and a large pointed collar, made of a thin but durable synthetic material. He had specified both the cut and the fabric to his tailor—it was his preferred uniform for giving tours because it did not get crushed during his long hours behind the wheel. Through the wind-shield he watched as Ronny circled around the goat, touched it quickly on its side, then trotted back to the car.

"You left India as a child?" Mr. Kapasi asked when Mr. Das had settled once again into the passenger seat.

"Oh, Mina and I were both born in America," Mr. Das announced with an   10 air of sudden confidence. "Born and raised. Our parents live here now, in Assan-sol.[2] They retired. We visit them every couple years." He turned to watch as the little girl ran toward the car, the wide purple bows of her sundress flopping on her narrow brown shoulders. She was holding to her chest a doll with yellow

2. Or Asonsol, a city in northeastern India, not far from Kolkata and about three hundred miles from Puri, the coastal city in Orissa that the Das family is visiting. Puri is both a tourist resort and a Hindu holy city, said to be dominated by the forces of both the gods and humanity.

hair that looked as if it had been chopped, as a punitive measure, with a pair of dull scissors. "This is Tina's first trip to India, isn't it, Tina?"

"I don't have to go to the bathroom anymore," Tina announced.

"Where's Mina?" Mr. Das asked.

Mr. Kapasi found it strange that Mr. Das should refer to his wife by her first name when speaking to the little girl. Tina pointed to where Mrs. Das was purchasing something from one of the shirtless men who worked at the tea stall. Mr. Kapasi heard one of the shirtless men sing a phrase from a popular Hindi love song as Mrs. Das walked back to the car, but she did not appear to understand the words of the song, for she did not express irritation, or embarrassment, or react in any other way to the man's declarations.

He observed her. She wore a red-and-white-checkered skirt that stopped above her knees, slip-on shoes with a square wooden heel, and a close-fitting blouse styled like a man's undershirt. The blouse was decorated at chest-level with a calico appliqué in the shape of a strawberry. She was a short woman, with small hands like paws, her frosty pink fingernails painted to match her lips, and was slightly plump in her figure. Her hair, shorn only a little longer than her husband's, was parted far to one side. She was wearing large dark brown sunglasses with a pinkish tint to them, and carried a big straw bag, almost as big as her torso, shaped like a bowl, with a water bottle poking out of it. She walked slowly, carrying some puffed rice tossed with peanuts and chili peppers in a large packet made from newspapers. Mr. Kapasi turned to Mr. Das.

15   "Where in America do you live?"

"New Brunswick, New Jersey."

"Next to New York?"

"Exactly. I teach middle school there."

"What subject?"

20   "Science. In fact, every year I take my students on a trip to the Museum of Natural History in New York City. In a way we have a lot in common, you could say, you and I. How long have you been a tour guide, Mr. Kapasi?"

"Five years."

Mrs. Das reached the car. "How long's the trip?" she asked, shutting the door.

"About two and a half hours," Mr. Kapasi replied.

At this Mrs. Das gave an impatient sigh, as if she had been traveling her whole life without pause. She fanned herself with a folded Bombay film magazine written in English.

25   "I thought that the Sun Temple is only eighteen miles north of Puri," Mr. Das said, tapping on the tour book.

"The roads to Konarak are poor. Actually it is a distance of fifty-two miles," Mr. Kapasi explained.

Mr. Das nodded, readjusting the camera strap where it had begun to chafe the back of his neck.

Before starting the ignition, Mr. Kapasi reached back to make sure the cranklike locks on the inside of each of the back doors were secured. As soon as the car began to move the little girl began to play with the lock on her side, clicking it with some effort forward and backward, but Mrs. Das said nothing to stop her. She sat a bit slouched at one end of the back seat, not offering her puffed rice to anyone. Ronny and Tina sat on either side of her, both snapping bright green gum.

"Look," Bobby said as the car began to gather speed. He pointed with his finger to the tall trees that lined the road. "Look."

"Monkeys!" Ronny shrieked. "Wow!"   30

They were seated in groups along the branches, with shining black faces, silver bodies, horizontal eyebrows, and crested heads. Their long gray tails dangled like a series of ropes among the leaves. A few scratched themselves with black leathery hands, or swung their feet, staring as the car passed.

"We call them the hanuman," Mr. Kapasi said. "They are quite common in the area."

As soon as he spoke, one of the monkeys leaped into the middle of the road, causing Mr. Kapasi to brake suddenly. Another bounced onto the hood of the car, then sprang away. Mr. Kapasi beeped his horn. The children began to get excited, sucking in their breath and covering their faces partly with their hands. They had never seen monkeys outside of a zoo, Mr. Das explained. He asked Mr. Kapasi to stop the car so that he could take a picture.

While Mr. Das adjusted his telephoto lens, Mrs. Das reached into her straw bag and pulled out a bottle of colorless nail polish, which she proceeded to stroke on the tip of her index finger.

The little girl stuck out a hand. "Mine too. Mommy, do mine too."   35

"Leave me alone," Mrs. Das said, blowing on her nail and turning her body slightly. "You're making me mess up."

The little girl occupied herself by buttoning and unbuttoning a pinafore on the doll's plastic body.

"All set," Mr. Das said, replacing the lens cap.

The car rattled considerably as it raced along the dusty road, causing them all to pop up from their seats every now and then, but Mrs. Das continued to polish her nails. Mr. Kapasi eased up on the accelerator, hoping to produce a smoother ride. When he reached for the gearshift the boy in front accommodated him by swinging his hairless knees out of the way. Mr. Kapasi noted that this boy was slightly paler than the other children. "Daddy, why is the driver sitting on the wrong side in this car, too?" the boy asked.

"They all do that here, dummy," Ronny said.   40

"Don't call your brother a dummy," Mr. Das said. He turned to Mr. Kapasi. "In America, you know . . . it confuses them."

"Oh yes, I am well aware," Mr. Kapasi said. As delicately as he could, he shifted gears again, accelerating as they approached a hill in the road. "I see it on *Dallas*, the steering wheels are on the left-hand side."

"What's *Dallas*?" Tina asked, banging her now naked doll on the seat behind Mr. Kapasi.

"It went off the air," Mr. Das explained. "It's a television show."[3]

They were all like siblings, Mr. Kapasi thought as they passed a row of date   45
trees. Mr. and Mrs. Das behaved like an older brother and sister, not parents. It seemed that they were in charge of the children only for the day; it was hard to

---

3. Internationally popular American television show (1978–91) featuring the rich, dysfunctional Ewing family of Dallas.

believe they were regularly responsible for anything other than themselves. Mr. Das tapped on his lens cap, and his tour book, dragging his thumbnail occasionally across the pages so that they made a scraping sound. Mrs. Das continued to polish her nails. She had still not removed her sunglasses. Every now and then Tina renewed her plea that she wanted her nails done, too, and so at one point Mrs. Das flicked a drop of polish on the little girl's finger before depositing the bottle back inside her straw bag.

"Isn't this an air-conditioned car?" she asked, still blowing on her hand. The window on Tina's side was broken and could not be rolled down.

"Quit complaining," Mr. Das said. "It isn't so hot."

"I told you to get a car with air-conditioning," Mrs. Das continued. "Why do you do this, Raj, just to save a few stupid rupees. What are you saving us, fifty cents?"

Their accents sounded just like the ones Mr. Kapasi heard on American television programs, though not like the ones on *Dallas.*

50   "Doesn't it get tiresome, Mr. Kapasi, showing people the same thing every day?" Mr. Das asked, rolling down his own window all the way. "Hey, do you mind stopping the car. I just want to get a shot of this guy."

Mr. Kapasi pulled over to the side of the road as Mr. Das took a picture of a barefoot man, his head wrapped in a dirty turban, seated on top of a cart of grain sacks pulled by a pair of bullocks. Both the man and the bullocks were emaciated. In the back seat Mrs. Das gazed out another window, at the sky, where nearly transparent clouds passed quickly in front of one another.

"I look forward to it, actually," Mr. Kapasi said as they continued on their way. "The Sun Temple is one of my favorite places. In that way it is a reward for me. I give tours on Fridays and Saturdays only. I have another job during the week."

"Oh? Where?" Mr. Das asked.

"I work in a doctor's office."

55   "You're a doctor?"

"I am not a doctor. I work with one. As an interpreter."

"What does a doctor need an interpreter for?"

"He has a number of Gujarati patients. My father was Gujarati, but many people do not speak Gujarati in this area,[4] including the doctor. And so the doctor asked me to work in his office, interpreting what the patients say."

"Interesting. I've never heard of anything like that," Mr. Das said.

60   Mr. Kapasi shrugged. "It is a job like any other."

"But so romantic," Mrs. Das said dreamily, breaking her extended silence. She lifted her pinkish brown sunglasses and arranged them on top of her head like a tiara. For the first time, her eyes met Mr. Kapasi's in the rearview mirror: pale, a bit small, their gaze fixed but drowsy.

Mr. Das craned to look at her. "What's so romantic about it?"

"I don't know. Something." She shrugged, knitting her brows together for an instant. "Would you like a piece of gum, Mr. Kapasi?" she asked brightly. She

---

4. Gujarat is a northwestern region of India, on the Arabian Sea. Mr. Kapasi speaks several of India's disparate regional languages—those of Bengal and Orissa, near where he lives, and Gujarati, from the opposite coast—along with the more widespread Hindi and English.

reached into her straw bag and handed him a small square wrapped in green-and-white-striped paper. As soon as Mr. Kapasi put the gum in his mouth a thick sweet liquid burst onto his tongue.

"Tell us more about your job, Mr. Kapasi," Mrs. Das said.

"What would you like to know, madame?" 65

"I don't know," she shrugged, munching on some puffed rice and licking the mustard oil from the corners of her mouth. "Tell us a typical situation." She settled back in her seat, her head tilted in a patch of sun, and closed her eyes. "I want to picture what happens."

"Very well. The other day a man came in with a pain in his throat."

"Did he smoke cigarettes?"

"No. It was very curious. He complained that he felt as if there were long pieces of straw stuck in his throat. When I told the doctor he was able to prescribe the proper medication."

"That's so neat." 70

"Yes," Mr. Kapasi agreed after some hesitation.

"So these patients are totally dependent on you," Mrs. Das said. She spoke slowly, as if she were thinking aloud. "In a way, more dependent on you than the doctor."

"How do you mean? How could it be?"

"Well, for example, you could tell the doctor that the pain felt like a burning, not straw. The patient would never know what you had told the doctor, and the doctor wouldn't know that you had told the wrong thing. It's a big responsibility."

"Yes, a big responsibility you have there, Mr. Kapasi," Mr. Das agreed. 75

Mr. Kapasi had never thought of his job in such complimentary terms. To him it was a thankless occupation. He found nothing noble in interpreting people's maladies, assiduously translating the symptoms of so many swollen bones, countless cramps of bellies and bowels, spots on people's palms that changed color, shape, or size. The doctor, nearly half his age, had an affinity for bell-bottom trousers and made humorless jokes about the Congress party.[5] Together they worked in a stale little infirmary where Mr. Kapasi's smartly tailored clothes clung to him in the heat, in spite of the blackened blades of a ceiling fan churning over their heads.

The job was a sign of his failings. In his youth he'd been a devoted scholar of foreign languages, the owner of an impressive collection of dictionaries. He had dreamed of being an interpreter for diplomats and dignitaries, resolving conflicts between people and nations, settling disputes of which he alone could understand both sides. He was a self-educated man. In a series of notebooks, in the evenings before his parents settled his marriage, he had listed the common etymologies of words, and at one point in his life he was confident that he could converse, if given the opportunity, in English, French, Russian, Portuguese, and Italian, not to mention Hindi, Bengali, Orissi, and Gujarati. Now only a handful

5. The Indian National Congress party, founded in 1885, led the movement for independence from Britain (gained in 1947) through the successive leadership of Mohandas Gandhi (1869–1948) and Jawaharlal Nehru (1889–1964). The party divided and subdivided, but a faction once led by Indira Gandhi (1917–84) dominated through the 1980s and much of the 1990s, despite being constantly accused of corruption and the use of violent tactics.

of European phrases remained in his memory, scattered words for things like saucers and chairs. English was the only non-Indian language he spoke fluently anymore. Mr. Kapasi knew it was not a remarkable talent. Sometimes he feared that his children knew better English than he did, just from watching television. Still, it came in handy for the tours.

He had taken the job as an interpreter after his first son, at the age of seven, contracted typhoid—that was how he had first made the acquaintance of the doctor. At the time Mr. Kapasi had been teaching English in a grammar school, and he bartered his skills as an interpreter to pay the increasingly exorbitant medical bills. In the end the boy had died one evening in his mother's arms, his limbs burning with fever, but then there was the funeral to pay for, and the other children who were born soon enough, and the newer, bigger house, and the good schools and tutors, and the fine shoes and the television, and the countless other ways he tried to console his wife and to keep her from crying in her sleep, and so when the doctor offered to pay him twice as much as he earned at the grammar school, he accepted. Mr. Kapasi knew that his wife had little regard for his career as an interpreter. He knew it reminded her of the son she'd lost, and that she resented the other lives he helped, in his own small way, to save. If ever she referred to his position, she used the phrase "doctor's assistant," as if the process of interpretation were equal to taking someone's temperature, or changing a bedpan. She never asked him about the patients who came to the doctor's office, or said that his job was a big responsibility.

For this reason it flattered Mr. Kapasi that Mrs. Das was so intrigued by his job. Unlike his wife, she had reminded him of its intellectual challenges. She had also used the word "romantic." She did not behave in a romantic way toward her husband, and yet she had used the word to describe him. He wondered if Mr. and Mrs. Das were a bad match, just as he and his wife were. Perhaps they, too, had little in common apart from three children and a decade of their lives. The signs he recognized from his own marriage were there—the bickering, the indifference, the protracted silences. Her sudden interest in him, an interest she did not express in either her husband or her children, was mildly intoxicating. When Mr. Kapasi thought once again about how she had said "romantic," the feeling of intoxication grew.

80   He began to check his reflection in the rearview mirror as he drove, feeling grateful that he had chosen the gray suit that morning and not the brown one, which tended to sag a little in the knees. From time to time he glanced through the mirror at Mrs. Das. In addition to glancing at her face he glanced at the strawberry between her breasts, and the golden brown hollow in her throat. He decided to tell Mrs. Das about another patient, and another: the young woman who had complained of a sensation of raindrops in her spine, the gentleman whose birthmark had begun to sprout hairs. Mrs. Das listened attentively, stroking her hair with a small plastic brush that resembled an oval bed of nails, asking more questions, for yet another example. The children were quiet, intent on spotting more monkeys in the trees, and Mr. Das was absorbed by his tour book, so it seemed like a private conversation between Mr. Kapasi and Mrs. Das. In this manner the next half hour passed, and when they stopped for lunch at a roadside restaurant that sold fritters and omelette sandwiches, usually something Mr. Kapasi looked forward to on his tours so that he could sit in peace

and enjoy some hot tea, he was disappointed. As the Das family settled together under a magenta umbrella fringed with white and orange tassels, and placed their orders with one of the waiters who marched about in tricornered caps, Mr. Kapasi reluctantly headed toward a neighboring table.

"Mr. Kapasi, wait. There's room here," Mrs. Das called out. She gathered Tina onto her lap, insisting that he accompany them. And so, together, they had bottled mango juice and sandwiches and plates of onions and potatoes deep-fried in graham-flour batter. After finishing two omelette sandwiches Mr. Das took more pictures of the group as they ate.

"How much longer?" he asked Mr. Kapasi as he paused to load a new roll of film in the camera.

"About half an hour more."

By now the children had gotten up from the table to look at more monkeys perched in a nearby tree, so there was a considerable space between Mrs. Das and Mr. Kapasi. Mr. Das placed the camera to his face and squeezed one eye shut, his tongue exposed at one corner of his mouth. "This looks funny. Mina, you need to lean in closer to Mr. Kapasi."

She did. He could smell a scent on her skin, like a mixture of whiskey and 85 rosewater. He worried suddenly that she could smell his perspiration, which he knew had collected beneath the synthetic material of his shirt. He polished off his mango juice in one gulp and smoothed his silver hair with his hands. A bit of the juice dripped onto his chin. He wondered if Mrs. Das had noticed.

She had not. "What's your address, Mr. Kapasi?" she inquired, fishing for something inside her straw bag.

"You would like my address?"

"So we can send you copies," she said. "Of the pictures." She handed him a scrap of paper which she had hastily ripped from a page of her film magazine. The blank portion was limited, for the narrow strip was crowded by lines of text and a tiny picture of a hero and heroine embracing under a eucalyptus tree.

The paper curled as Mr. Kapasi wrote his address in clear, careful letters. She would write to him, asking about his days interpreting at the doctor's office, and he would respond eloquently, choosing only the most entertaining anec-dotes, ones that would make her laugh out loud as she read them in her house in New Jersey. In time she would reveal the disappointment of her marriage, and he his. In this way their friendship would grow, and flourish. He would pos-sess a picture of the two of them, eating fried onions under a magenta umbrella, which he would keep, he decided, safely tucked between the pages of his Rus-sian grammar. As his mind raced, Mr. Kapasi experienced a mild and pleasant shock. It was similar to a feeling he used to experience long ago when, after months of translating with the aid of a dictionary, he would finally read a pas-sage from a French novel, or an Italian sonnet, and understand the words, one after another, unencumbered by his own efforts. In those moments Mr. Kapasi used to believe that all was right with the world, that all struggles were rewarded, that all of life's mistakes made sense in the end. The promise that he would hear from Mrs. Das now filled him with the same belief.

When he finished writing his address Mr. Kapasi handed her the paper, but 90 as soon as he did so he worried that he had either misspelled his name, or acci-dentally reversed the numbers of his postal code. He dreaded the possibility of a lost letter, the photograph never reaching him, hovering somewhere in Orissa, close but ultimately unattainable. He thought of asking for the slip of paper again, just to make sure he had written his address accurately, but Mrs. Das had already dropped it into the jumble of her bag.

They reached Konarak at two-thirty. The temple, made of sandstone, was a massive pyramid-like structure in the shape of a chariot. It was dedicated to the great master of life, the sun, which struck three sides of the edifice as it made its journey each day across the sky. Twenty-four giant wheels were carved on the north and south sides of the plinth. The whole thing was drawn by a team of seven horses, speeding as if through the heavens. As they approached, Mr. Kapasi explained that the temple had been built between A.D. 1243 and 1255, with the efforts of twelve hundred artisans, by the great ruler of the Ganga dynasty, King Narasimhadeva the First, to commemorate his victory against the Muslim army.

"It says the temple occupies about a hundred and seventy acres of land," Mr. Das said, reading from his book.

"It's like a desert," Ronny said, his eyes wandering across the sand that stretched on all sides beyond the temple.

"The Chandrabhaga River once flowed one mile north of here. It is dry now," Mr. Kapasi said, turning off the engine.

95   They got out and walked toward the temple, posing first for pictures by the pair of lions that flanked the steps. Mr. Kapasi led them next to one of the wheels of the chariot, higher than any human being, nine feet in diameter.

"'The wheels are supposed to symbolize the wheel of life,'" Mr. Das read. "'They depict the cycle of creation, preservation, and achievement of realization.' Cool." He turned the page of his book. "'Each wheel is divided into eight thick and thin spokes, dividing the day into eight equal parts. The rims are carved with designs of birds and animals, whereas the medallions in the spokes are carved with women in luxurious poses, largely erotic in nature.'"

What he referred to were the countless friezes of entwined naked bodies, making love in various positions, women clinging to the necks of men, their knees wrapped eternally around their lovers' thighs. In addition to these were assorted scenes from daily life, of hunting and trading, of deer being killed with bows and arrows and marching warriors holding swords in their hands.

It was no longer possible to enter the temple, for it had filled with rubble years ago, but they admired the exterior, as did all the tourists Mr. Kapasi brought there, slowly strolling along each of its sides. Mr. Das trailed behind, taking pictures. The children ran ahead, pointing to figures of naked people, intrigued in particular by the Nagamithunas, the half-human, half-serpentine couples who were said, Mr. Kapasi told them, to live in the deepest waters of the sea. Mr. Kapasi was pleased that they liked the temple, pleased especially that it appealed to Mrs. Das. She stopped every three or four paces, staring silently at the carved lovers, and the processions of elephants, and the topless female musicians beating on two-sided drums.

Though Mr. Kapasi had been to the temple countless times, it occurred to him, as he, too, gazed at the topless women, that he had never seen his own wife fully naked. Even when they had made love she kept the panels of her blouse hooked together, the string of her petticoat knotted around her waist. He had never admired the backs of his wife's legs the way he now admired those of Mrs. Das, walking as if for his benefit alone. He had, of course, seen plenty of bare limbs before, belonging to the American and European ladies who took his tours. But Mrs. Das was different. Unlike the other women, who had an interest only in the temple, and kept their noses buried in a guidebook, or their eyes behind the lens of a camera, Mrs. Das had taken an interest in him.

Mr. Kapasi was anxious to be alone with her, to continue their private conversation, yet he felt nervous to walk at her side. She was lost behind her sunglasses, ignoring her husband's requests that she pose for another picture, walking past her children as if they were strangers. Worried that he might disturb her, Mr. Kapasi walked ahead, to admire, as he always did, the three life-sized bronze avatars of Surya, the sun god, each emerging from its own niche on the temple facade to greet the sun at dawn, noon, and evening. They wore elaborate headdresses, their languid, elongated eyes closed, their bare chests draped with carved chains and amulets. Hibiscus petals, offerings from previous visitors, were strewn at their gray-green feet. The last statue, on the northern wall of the temple, was Mr. Kapasi's favorite. This Surya had a tired expression, weary after a hard day of work, sitting astride a horse with folded legs. Even his horse's eyes were drowsy. Around his body were smaller sculptures of women in pairs, their hips thrust to one side.

"Who's that?" Mrs. Das asked. He was startled to see that she was standing beside him.

"He is the Astachala-Surya," Mr. Kapasi said. "The setting sun."

"So in a couple of hours the sun will set right here?" She slipped a foot out of one of her square-heeled shoes, rubbed her toes on the back of her other leg.

"That is correct."

She raised her sunglasses for a moment, then put them back on again. "Neat."

Mr. Kapasi was not certain exactly what the word suggested, but he had a feeling it was a favorable response. He hoped that Mrs. Das had understood Surya's beauty, his power. Perhaps they would discuss it further in their letters. He would explain things to her, things about India, and she would explain things to him about America. In its own way this correspondence would fulfill his dream, of serving as an interpreter between nations. He looked at her straw bag, delighted that his address lay nestled among its contents. When he pictured her so many thousands of miles away he plummeted, so much so that he had an overwhelming urge to wrap his arms around her, to freeze with her, even for an instant, in an embrace witnessed by his favorite Surya. But Mrs. Das had already started walking.

"When do you return to America?" he asked, trying to sound placid.

"In ten days."

He calculated: A week to settle in, a week to develop the pictures, a few days to compose her letter, two weeks to get to India by air. According to his schedule, allowing room for delays, he would hear from Mrs. Das in approximately six weeks' time.

The family was silent as Mr. Kapasi drove them back, a little past four-thirty, to Hotel Sandy Villa. The children had bought miniature granite versions of the chariot's wheels at a souvenir stand, and they turned them round in their hands. Mr. Das continued to read his book. Mrs. Das untangled Tina's hair with her brush and divided it into two little ponytails.

Mr. Kapasi was beginning to dread the thought of dropping them off. He was not prepared to begin his six-week wait to hear from Mrs. Das. As he stole glances at her in the rearview mirror, wrapping elastic bands around Tina's hair, he wondered how he might make the tour last a little longer. Ordinarily he sped back to Puri using a shortcut, eager to return home, scrub his feet and hands with sandalwood soap, and enjoy the evening newspaper and a cup of tea that his wife would serve him in silence. The thought of that silence, something to which he'd long been resigned, now oppressed him. It was then that he suggested visiting the hills at Udayagiri and Khandagiri, where a number of monastic dwellings were hewn out of the ground, facing one another across a defile. It was some miles away, but well worth seeing, Mr. Kapasi told them.

"Oh yeah, there's something mentioned about it in this book," Mr. Das said. "Built by a Jain king or something."[6]

"Shall we go then?" Mr. Kapasi asked. He paused at a turn in the road. "It's to the left."

Mr. Das turned to look at Mrs. Das. Both of them shrugged.

115   "Left, left," the children chanted.

Mr. Kapasi turned the wheel, almost delirious with relief. He did not know what he would do or say to Mrs. Das once they arrived at the hills. Perhaps he would tell her what a pleasing smile she had. Perhaps he would compliment her strawberry shirt, which he found irresistibly becoming. Perhaps, when Mr. Das was busy taking a picture, he would take her hand.

He did not have to worry. When they got to the hills, divided by a steep path thick with trees, Mrs. Das refused to get out of the car. All along the path, dozens of monkeys were seated on stones, as well as on the branches of the trees. Their hind legs were stretched out in front and raised to shoulder level, their arms resting on their knees.

"My legs are tired," she said, sinking low in her seat. "I'll stay here."

"Why did you have to wear those stupid shoes?" Mr. Das said. "You won't be in the pictures."

120   "Pretend I'm there."

"But we could use one of these pictures for our Christmas card this year. We didn't get one of all five of us at the Sun Temple. Mr. Kapasi could take it."

"I'm not coming. Anyway, those monkeys give me the creeps."

"But they're harmless," Mr. Das said. He turned to Mr. Kapasi. "Aren't they?"

"They are more hungry than dangerous," Mr. Kapasi said. "Do not provoke them with food, and they will not bother you."

125   Mr. Das headed up the defile with the children, the boys at his side, the little girl on his shoulders. Mr. Kapasi watched as they crossed paths with a Japanese man and woman, the only other tourists there, who paused for a final photograph, then stepped into a nearby car and drove away. As the car disappeared

6. This site is not a major tourist attraction; "giri" means mountain. Jainism, one of India's several major religions, is a nontheistic sect that emerged from Hinduism around 580 BCE, at about the same time as Buddhism.

out of view some of the monkeys called out, emitting soft whooping sounds, and then walked on their flat black hands and feet up the path. At one point a group of them formed a little ring around Mr. Das and the children. Tina screamed in delight. Ronny ran in circles around his father. Bobby bent down and picked up a fat stick on the ground. When he extended it, one of the monkeys approached him and snatched it, then briefly beat the ground.

"I'll join them," Mr. Kapasi said, unlocking the door on his side. "There is much to explain about the caves."

"No. Stay a minute," Mrs. Das said. She got out of the back seat and slipped in beside Mr. Kapasi. "Raj has his dumb book anyway." Together, through the windshield, Mrs. Das and Mr. Kapasi watched as Bobby and the monkey passed the stick back and forth between them.

"A brave little boy," Mr. Kapasi commented.

"It's not so surprising," Mrs. Das said.

"No?"

"He's not his." 130

"I beg your pardon?"

"Raj's. He's not Raj's son."

Mr. Kapasi felt a prickle on his skin. He reached into his shirt pocket for the small tin of lotus-oil balm he carried with him at all times, and applied it to three spots on his forehead. He knew that Mrs. Das was watching him, but he did not turn to face her. Instead he watched as the figures of Mr. Das and the children grew smaller, climbing up the steep path, pausing every now and then for a picture, surrounded by a growing number of monkeys.

"Are you surprised?" The way she put it made him choose his words with 135 care.

"It's not the type of thing one assumes," Mr. Kapasi replied slowly. He put the tin of lotus-oil balm back in his pocket.

"No, of course not. And no one knows, of course. No one at all. I've kept it a secret for eight whole years." She looked at Mr. Kapasi, tilting her chin as if to gain a fresh perspective. "But now I've told you."

Mr. Kapasi nodded. He felt suddenly parched, and his forehead was warm and slightly numb from the balm. He considered asking Mrs. Das for a sip of water, then decided against it.

"We met when we were very young," she said. She reached into her straw bag in search of something, then pulled out a packet of puffed rice. "Want some?"

"No, thank you." 140

She put a fistful in her mouth, sank into the seat a little, and looked away from Mr. Kapasi, out the window on her side of the car. "We married when we were still in college. We were in high school when he proposed. We went to the same college, of course. Back then we couldn't stand the thought of being separated, not for a day, not for a minute. Our parents were best friends who lived in the same town. My entire life I saw him every weekend, either at our house or theirs. We were sent upstairs to play together while our parents joked about our marriage. Imagine! They never caught us at anything, though in a way I think it was all more or less a setup. The things we did those Friday and Saturday nights, while our parents sat downstairs drinking tea . . . I could tell you stories, Mr. Kapasi."

As a result of spending all her time in college with Raj, she continued, she did not make many close friends. There was no one to confide in about him at the end of a difficult day, or to share a passing thought or a worry. Her parents now lived on the other side of the world, but she had never been very close to them, anyway. After marrying so young she was overwhelmed by it all, having a child so quickly, and nursing, and warming up bottles of milk and testing their temperature against her wrist while Raj was at work, dressed in sweaters and corduroy pants, teaching his students about rocks and dinosaurs. Raj never looked cross or harried, or plump as she had become after the first baby.

Always tired, she declined invitations from her one or two college girlfriends, to have lunch or shop in Manhattan. Eventually the friends stopped calling her, so that she was left at home all day with the baby, surrounded by toys that made her trip when she walked or wince when she sat, always cross and tired. Only occasionally did they go out after Ronny was born, and even more rarely did they entertain. Raj didn't mind; he looked forward to coming home from teaching and watching television and bouncing Ronny on his knee. She had been outraged when Raj told her that a Punjabi friend,[7] someone whom she had once met but did not remember, would be staying with them for a week for some job interviews in the New Brunswick area.

Bobby was conceived in the afternoon, on a sofa littered with rubber teething toys, after the friend learned that a London pharmaceutical company had hired him, while Ronny cried to be freed from his playpen. She made no protest when the friend touched the small of her back as she was about to make a pot of coffee, then pulled her against his crisp navy suit. He made love to her swiftly, in silence, with an expertise she had never known, without the meaningful expressions and smiles Raj always insisted on afterward. The next day Raj drove the friend to JFK.[8] He was married now, to a Punjabi girl, and they lived in London still, and every year they exchanged Christmas cards with Raj and Mina, each couple tucking photos of their families into the envelopes. He did not know that he was Bobby's father. He never would.

145   "I beg your pardon, Mrs. Das, but why have you told me this information?" Mr. Kapasi asked when she had finally finished speaking, and had turned to face him once again.

"For God's sake, stop calling me Mrs. Das. I'm twenty-eight. You probably have children my age."

"Not quite." It disturbed Mr. Kapasi to learn that she thought of him as a parent. The feeling he had had toward her, that had made him check his reflection in the rearview mirror as they drove, evaporated a little.

"I told you because of your talents." She put the packet of puffed rice back into her bag without folding over the top.

"I don't understand," Mr. Kapasi said.

150   "Don't you see? For eight years I haven't been able to express this to anybody, not to friends, certainly not to Raj. He doesn't even suspect it. He thinks I'm still in love with him. Well, don't you have anything to say?"

"About what?"

7. Person from the Punjab, a northern region of India, near Pakistan.
8. John F. Kennedy International Airport, in New York City.

"About what I've just told you. About my secret, and about how terrible it makes me feel. I feel terrible looking at my children, and at Raj, always terrible. I have terrible urges, Mr. Kapasi, to throw things away. One day I had the urge to throw everything I own out of the window, the television, the children, everything. Don't you think it's unhealthy?"

He was silent.

"Mr. Kapasi, don't you have anything to say? I thought that was your job."

"My job is to give tours, Mrs. Das." 155

"Not that. Your other job. As an interpreter."

"But we do not face a language barrier. What need is there for an interpreter?"

"That's not what I mean. I would never have told you otherwise. Don't you realize what it means for me to tell you?"

"What does it mean?"

"It means that I'm tired of feeling so terrible all the time. Eight years, 160 Mr. Kapasi, I've been in pain eight years. I was hoping you could help me feel better, say the right thing. Suggest some kind of remedy."

He looked at her, in her red plaid skirt and strawberry T-shirt, a woman not yet thirty, who loved neither her husband nor her children, who had already fallen out of love with life. Her confession depressed him, depressed him all the more when he thought of Mr. Das at the top of the path, Tina clinging to his shoulders, taking pictures of ancient monastic cells cut into the hills to show his students in America, unsuspecting and unaware that one of his sons was not his own. Mr. Kapasi felt insulted that Mrs. Das should ask him to interpret her common, trivial little secret. She did not resemble the patients in the doctor's office, those who came glassy-eyed and desperate, unable to sleep or breathe or urinate with ease, unable, above all, to give words to their pains. Still, Mr. Kapasi believed it was his duty to assist Mrs. Das. Perhaps he ought to tell her to confess the truth to Mr. Das. He would explain that honesty was the best policy. Honesty, surely, would help her feel better, as she'd put it. Perhaps he would offer to preside over the discussion, as a mediator. He decided to begin with the most obvious question, to get to the heart of the matter, and so he asked, "Is it really pain you feel, Mrs. Das, or is it guilt?"

She turned to him and glared, mustard oil thick on her frosty pink lips. She opened her mouth to say something, but as she glared at Mr. Kapasi some certain knowledge seemed to pass before her eyes, and she stopped. It crushed him; he knew at that moment that he was not even important enough to be properly insulted. She opened the car door and began walking up the path, wobbling a little on her square wooden heels, reaching into her straw bag to eat handfuls of puffed rice. It fell through her fingers, leaving a zigzagging trail, causing a monkey to leap down from a tree and devour the little white grains. In search of more, the monkey began to follow Mrs. Das. Others joined him, so that she was soon being followed by about half a dozen of them, their velvety tails dragging behind.

Mr. Kapasi stepped out of the car. He wanted to holler, to alert her in some way, but he worried that if she knew they were behind her, she would grow nervous. Perhaps she would lose her balance. Perhaps they would pull at her bag or her hair. He began to jog up the path, taking a fallen branch in his hand to scare away the monkeys. Mrs. Das continued walking, oblivious, trailing grains of puffed rice. Near the top of the incline, before a group of cells fronted by a row of squat stone pillars, Mr. Das was kneeling on the ground, focusing the lens of his camera. The children stood under the arcade, now hiding, now emerging from view.

"Wait for me," Mrs. Das called out. "I'm coming."

165   Tina jumped up and down. "Here comes Mommy!"

"Great," Mr. Das said without looking up. "Just in time. We'll get Mr. Kapasi to take a picture of the five of us."

Mr. Kapasi quickened his pace, waving his branch so that the monkeys scampered away, distracted, in another direction.

"Where's Bobby?" Mrs. Das asked when she stopped.

Mr. Das looked up from the camera. "I don't know. Ronny, where's Bobby?"

170   Ronny shrugged. "I thought he was right here."

"Where is he?" Mrs. Das repeated sharply. "What's wrong with all of you?"

They began calling his name, wandering up and down the path a bit. Because they were calling, they did not initially hear the boy's screams. When they found him, a little farther down the path under a tree, he was surrounded by a group of monkeys, over a dozen of them, pulling at his T-shirt with their long black fingers. The puffed rice Mrs. Das had spilled was scattered at his feet, raked over by the monkeys' hands. The boy was silent, his body frozen, swift tears running down his startled face. His bare legs were dusty and red with welts from where one of the monkeys struck him repeatedly with the stick he had given to it earlier.

"Daddy, the monkey's hurting Bobby," Tina said.

Mr. Das wiped his palms on the front of his shorts. In his nervousness he accidentally pressed the shutter on his camera; the whirring noise of the advancing film excited the monkeys, and the one with the stick began to beat Bobby more intently. "What are we supposed to do? What if they start attacking?"

175   "Mr. Kapasi," Mrs. Das shrieked, noticing him standing to one side. "Do something, for God's sake, do something!"

Mr. Kapasi took his branch and shooed them away, hissing at the ones that remained, stomping his feet to scare them. The animals retreated slowly, with a measured gait, obedient but unintimidated. Mr. Kapasi gathered Bobby in his arms and brought him back to where his parents and siblings were standing. As he carried him he was tempted to whisper a secret into the boy's ear. But Bobby was stunned, and shivering with fright, his legs bleeding slightly where the stick had broken the skin. When Mr. Kapasi delivered him to his parents, Mr. Das brushed some dirt off the boy's T-shirt and put the visor on him the right way. Mrs. Das reached into her straw bag to find a bandage which she taped over the cut on his knee. Ronny offered his brother a fresh piece of gum. "He's fine. Just a little scared, right, Bobby?" Mr. Das said, patting the top of his head.

"God, let's get out of here," Mrs. Das said. She folded her arms across the strawberry on her chest. "This place gives me the creeps."

"Yeah. Back to the hotel, definitely," Mr. Das agreed.

"Poor Bobby," Mrs. Das said. "Come here a second. Let Mommy fix your hair." Again she reached into her straw bag, this time for her hairbrush, and began to run it around the edges of the translucent visor. When she whipped out the hairbrush, the slip of paper with Mr. Kapasi's address on it fluttered away in the wind. No one but Mr. Kapasi noticed. He watched as it rose, carried higher and higher by the breeze, into the trees where the monkeys now sat, solemnly observing the scene below. Mr. Kapasi observed it too, knowing that this was the picture of the Das family he would preserve forever in his mind.

1998, 1999

QUESTIONS

1. How does it matter—to Mr. Kapasi and this story—that the Das family both are and aren't "foreign" (par. 2)?
2. How might his encounter with the Das family alter Mr. Kapasi's sense of what it means to be Indian? Why is it important that this encounter has as its background a visit to ancient Indian religious shrines?
3. What is the thematic significance of the secret that Mrs. Das reveals to Mr. Kapasi? What is its relationship to the rest of the story and to aspects of human behavior that transcend culture and upbringing?

AUTHORS ON THEIR WORK

JHUMPA LAHIRI (b. 1967)

From "Interviews: Jhumpa Lahiri" (2008)*

[INTERVIEWER:] One thing that fascinates me about your previous stories is the way you view the marriages of people in your parents' generation. [. . .] Was that a fascination for you growing up: *What is going on with my folks?* And do you think it was especially interesting to you because you were growing up in [London, in] a culture different from the one in which they grew up [in India]?

[LAHIRI:] I don't know why, but the older I get the more interested I get in my parents' marriage. [. . .] I do think it's a question that has preoccupied me in all the books I've written. My parents had an arranged marriage, as did so many other people when I was growing up. My father came and had a life in the United States one way and my mother had a different one, and I was very aware of those things. I continue to wonder about it, and I will continue to write about it.

From "Interview with Jhumpa Lahiri" (2003)**

[INTERVIEWER: Your 2003 novel] *The Namesake* deals with Indian immigrants in the United States as well as their children. What, in your opinion, distinguishes the experiences of the former from the latter?

[LAHIRI:] In a sense, very little. The question of identity is always a difficult one, but especially so for those who are culturally displaced, as immigrants are, or those who grow up in two worlds simultaneously, as is the case for their children. The older I get, the more I am aware that I have somehow inherited a sense of exile from my parents, even though in many ways I am so much more American than they are. In fact, it is still very hard to think of myself as an American. (This is of course complicated by the fact that I was born in London.) I think that for immigrants, the challenges of exile, the loneliness, the constant sense of alienation, the knowledge of and longing for a lost world, are more explicit and distressing than for their children. On the other hand, the problem for the children of immigrants—those with strong ties to their country of origin—is that they feel neither one thing nor the other. This has been my experience, in any case. For example, I never know how to answer the question "Where are you from?" If I say I'm from Rhode Island, people are seldom satisfied. They want to know more, based on things such as my name, my appearance, etc. Alternatively, if I say I'm from India, a place where I was not born and have never lived, this is also inaccurate. It bothers me less now. But it bothered me growing up, the feeling that there was no single place to which I fully belonged.

*"Interviews: Jhumpa Lahiri." Interview by Isaac Chotiner. *The Atlantic*, Apr. 2008, www.theatlantic.com/magazine/archive/2008/04/jhumpa-lahiri/306725/.
**"A Conversation with Jhumpa Lahiri." Houghton Mifflin Harcourt, 2004. www.houghtonmifflinbooks.com/booksellers/press_release/lahiri/. Press release.

SANDRA CISNEROS
(b. 1954)

Mericans

In her 1990 essay "Only Daughter," Sandra Cisneros declares, "I am the only daughter in a Mexican family of six sons," "the only daughter of a Mexican father and a Mexican-American mother," "the only daughter of a working-class family of nine," "only *a* daughter"— "All of these had everything to do with who I am today." Arguably the most widely recognized, widely read Chicana writer, Cisneros grew up moving between two places: Chicago, Illinois, where her family eventually purchased a home in a mainly Puerto Rican neighborhood on the northside; and Mexico City, Mexico, where her father was raised and her paternal grandparents still lived. After graduating from Loyola University in 1976, Cisneros earned an MFA at the University of Iowa's famed Writers' Workshop (1978). Convinced by her own discomfort in that program that her distinctly Latina experience and perspective constituted her true "writing power," Cisneros published her first book, the poetry collection *Bad Boys*, in 1980, while teaching at Chicago's Latino Youth High School. She exploded onto the literary scene four years later with *The House on Mango Street*, simultaneously a coming-of-age novel, short-story collection, and series of prose poems tracing the transformation of Esperanza, the novel's Cisneros-esque protagonist, from uncertain, lonely adolescent to ambitious, self-aware writer. Among the more prominent of Cisneros's later works are volumes of poetry including *Loose Woman* (1994); the award-winning *Caramelo* (2002), a novel interweaving the story of Chicago teenager Celaya Reyes with that of the Mexican woman who would become her "Awful Grandmother"; the memoir-in-essays *A House of My Own: Stories from My Life* (2015); and *Vintage Cisneros* (2004), which gathers a selection of her earlier work. Her multi-award-winning short-story collection *Woman Hollering Creek and Other Stories* (1991) depicts (mostly female) Mexican American characters living across the U.S.-Mexico borderlands, or *la frontera*. Having herself for many years lived and taught creative writing in San Antonio, Texas, Cisneros today makes her home in Guanajuato, Mexico. Her innumerable honors include a MacArthur Fellowship (1995), the National Medal of the Arts (2015), and the PEN/Nabokov Award for Achievement in International Literature (2019).

W e're waiting for the awful grandmother who is inside dropping pesos into *la ofrenda* box before the altar to La Divina Providencia.[1] Lighting votive candles and genuflecting. Blessing herself and kissing her thumb. Running a crystal rosary between her fingers. Mumbling, mumbling, mumbling.

There are so many prayers and promises and thanks-be-to-God to be given in the name of the husband and the sons and the only daughter who never attend mass. It doesn't matter. Like La Virgen de Guadalupe,[2] the awful grandmother intercedes on their behalf. For the grandfather who hasn't believed in anything since the first PRI[3] elections. For my father, El Periquín,[4] so skinny he needs his sleep. For Auntie Light-skin, who only a few hours before was breakfasting on brain and goat tacos after dancing all night in the pink zone.[5] For Uncle Fat-face, the blackest of the black sheep—*Always remember your Uncle Fat-face in your prayers.* And Uncle Baby—*You go for me, Mamá—God listens to you.*

The awful grandmother has been gone a long time. She disappeared behind the heavy leather outer curtain and the dusty velvet inner. We must stay near the church entrance. We must not wander over to the balloon and punch-ball vendors. We cannot spend our allowance on fried cookies or Familia Burrón[6] comic books or those clear cone-shaped suckers that make everything look like a rainbow when you look through them. We cannot run off and have our picture taken on the wooden ponies. We must not climb the steps up the hill behind the church and chase each other through the cemetery. We have promised to stay right where the awful grandmother left us until she returns.

There are those walking to church on their knees. Some with fat rags tied around their legs and others with pillows, one to kneel on, and one to flop ahead. There are women with black shawls crossing and uncrossing themselves. There are armies of penitents carrying banners and flowered arches while musicians play tinny trumpets and tinny drums.

La Virgen de Guadalupe is waiting inside behind a plate of thick glass. There's also a gold crucifix bent crooked as a mesquite tree when someone once threw a bomb. La Virgen de Guadalupe on the main altar because she's a big miracle, the crooked crucifix on a side altar because that's a little miracle. 5

But we're outside in the sun. My big brother Junior hunkered against the wall with his eyes shut. My little brother Keeks running around in circles.

Maybe and most probably my little brother is imagining he's a flying feather dancer, like the ones we saw swinging high up from a pole on the Virgin's birthday. I want to be a flying feather dancer too, but when he circles past me he shouts, "I'm a B-Fifty-two[7] bomber, you're a German," and shoots me with an

1. Divine Providence. *La ofrenda*: the offering (Spanish).
2. Catholic title of Virgin Mary in her appearance before St. Juan Diego in a 1531 vision, near what is now Mexico City, Mexico; this figure holds an important place in Mexican religion, sometimes serving as a symbol of the nation itself.
3. Acronym for Partido Revolucionario Institucional, or Institutional Revolutionary Party (Spanish); political party that governed Mexico from 1929 to 2000.
4. The Parakeet (Spanish).
5. A.k.a. Zona Rosa, Mexico City neighborhood famous for its bohemian character, cafés, and nightlife.
6. Burrón family (Spanish), central characters in a popular Mexican comic series (1948–2009).
7. U.S. long-range heavy bomber; Keeks's reference to shooting Germans from a B-52 is anachronistic, as the plane was introduced into military service only after World War II (1939–45), remaining so until the early 2000s. *Flying feather dancer*: the Voladores, or fliers, of Papantla, who, in a cultural tradition of the Totonac people of Veracruz, Mexico, launch themselves headfirst (in groups of four or

invisible machine gun. I'd rather play flying feather dancers, but if I tell my brother this, he might not play with me at all.

"*Girl*. We can't play with a *girl*." *Girl*. It's my brothers' favorite insult now instead of "sissy." "You *girl*," they yell at each other. "You throw that ball like a *girl*."

I've already made up my mind to be a German when Keeks swoops past again, this time yelling, "I'm Flash Gordon. You're Ming the Merciless and the Mud People."[8] I don't mind being Ming the Merciless, but I don't like being the Mud People. Something wants to come out of the corners of my eyes, but I don't let it. Crying is what *girls* do.

10   I leave Keeks running around in circles—"I'm the Lone Ranger, you're Tonto."[9] I leave Junior squatting on his ankles and go look for the awful grandmother.

Why do churches smell like the inside of an ear? Like incense and the dark and candles in blue glass? And why does holy water smell of tears? The awful grandmother makes me kneel and fold my hands. The ceiling high and everyone's prayers bumping up there like balloons.

If I stare at the eyes of the saints long enough, they move and wink at me, which makes me a sort of saint too. When I get tired of winking saints, I count the awful grandmother's mustache hairs while she prays for Uncle Old, sick from the worm, and Auntie Cuca, suffering from a life of troubles that left half her face crooked and the other half sad.

There must be a long, long list of relatives who haven't gone to church. The awful grandmother knits the names of the dead and the living into one long prayer fringed with the grandchildren born in that barbaric country with its barbarian ways.

I put my weight on one knee, then the other, and when they both grow fat as a mattress of pins, I slap them each awake. *Micaela, you may wait outside with Alfredito and Enrique.* The awful grandmother says it all in Spanish, which I understand when I'm paying attention. "What?" I say, though it's neither proper nor polite. "What?" which the awful grandmother hears as "*¿Güat?*" But she only gives me a look and shoves me toward the door.

15   After all that dust and dark, the light from the plaza makes me squinch my eyes like if I just came out of the movies. My brother Keeks is drawing squiggly lines on the concrete with a wedge of glass and the heel of his shoe. My brother Junior squatting against the entrance, talking to a lady and man.

They're not from here. Ladies don't come to church dressed in pants. And everybody knows men aren't supposed to wear shorts.

"*¿Quieres chicle?*"[1] the lady asks in a Spanish too big for her mouth.

"*Gracias.*" The lady gives him a whole handful of gum for free, little cellophane cubes of Chiclets, cinnamon and aqua and the white ones that don't taste like anything but are good for pretend buck teeth.

---

five) from a tall pole to which they are connected by ropes; their colorful costumes and headpieces were originally made of feathers.

8. Or Clay People, tribe depicted as inhabiting Mars's caves and underground tunnels in the popular Flash Gordon series; originating as a comic in the 1930s, it later spawned multiple film, as well as live-action and animated television, series. *Ming the Merciless*: villain of the same series; emperor of the imaginary planet Mongo.

9. Since 1933, Native American sidekick of the Lone Ranger, masked hero of the famous Western radio—and, later, television and film—series.

1. Do you want gum? (Spanish).

"Por favor,"[2] says the lady. *"¿Un foto?"*[3] pointing to her camera.

"*Sí.*" 20

She's so busy taking Junior's picture, she doesn't notice me and Keeks.

"Hey, Michele, Keeks. You guys want gum?"

"But you speak English!"

"Yeah," my brother says, "we're Mericans."

We're Mericans, we're Mericans, and inside the awful grandmother prays. 25

1991

QUESTIONS

1. How are the grandmother, the grandchildren, and the relation between them characterized in the story? What role, if any, do cultural differences and perceptions play in that relationship? In these terms, how might details of setting become significant? allusions? narration, including when and how the narrator uses first-person plural ("we") and/versus first-person singular ("I")?

2. What is the attitude of the tourists toward the children and vice versa? Why might the tourists be surprised that the children speak English, and what is the significance of that surprise?

3. Why might "Mericans" be an especially appropriate title for this story?

AUTHORS ON THEIR WORK

SANDRA CISNEROS (b. 1954)

From "Interviewing Sandra Cisneros: Living on the Frontera" (1996)*

What I think is so wonderful about being born on any borderline, be it the border between France and Spain, or the border of México and Tejas is that if you live on the border you can see the opposite country in a way the opposite country cannot see itself, and I think for those of us who are living in those borderlines it's just an incredible time in history because we are presenting mirrors to each country, to ourselves, and to all the citizens of the world, that have never been held up before. So, we have a particular ear, and a particular vision. I can hear things and see things that most citizens cannot see themselves unless you happen to be on the border. That for me is, I suppose, part of my job as a translator, to hold up that mirror, that tape recorder, and to let each side see themselves in the way the others see them, in a way that they do not see themselves, and by seeing themselves in that light I think there's communication, and I hope compassion for the misunderstandings that have grown up. I like the work that I'm doing in the story "Mericans." It's so important for Mexicans to understand how Americans view them; it's an incredible commentary for U.S. readers to see how they view Mexicans as opposed to how they view Mexican-Americans [. . .].

*"Interviewing Sandra Cisneros: Living on the Frontera." Interview by Pilar Godayol Nogué. *Lectora: revista de dones i textualitat*, no. 2, 1996, pp. 61–68.

2. Please (Spanish).
3. A photo? (Spanish).

DAVID SEDARIS
(b. 1956)

Jesus Shaves

Dubbed by some "the funniest writer alive," David Sedaris uses his own life and the absurdities of the everyday as fodder for stories that often blur the line between fiction and nonfiction. Juxtaposing the highbrow with the lowbrow, they treat everything from his fleeting interests in crystal meth and bee-sized suits of armor to his brother's basement barbecue-sauce business. Sedaris was raised in the suburbs of Raleigh, North Carolina, after his Greek American family moved there from New York. Openly gay, Sedaris points to his inability to play jazz guitar as the source of his father's disappointment—"Fortunately there were six of us," so "it was easy to get lost in the crowd." After graduating from the School of the Art Institute of Chicago, he worked a series of now-well-documented menial jobs in New York City and Chicago before radio host Ira Glass discovered him at a Chicago nightclub, reading from his diary. "Santa-land Diaries," which recounts his adventures as a department-store elf, was later featured on National Public Radio, making Sedaris an overnight sensation. Author of multiple *New York Times* best sellers, including *Me Talk Pretty One Day* (2000), *When You Are Engulfed in Flames* (2008), and *Calypso* (2018), as well as *Squirrel Seeks Chipmunk* (2010), "a collection of fables without morals," Sedaris has also collaborated with his sister, actress-comedian Amy Sedaris, on a number of plays, including *Incident at Cobbler's Knob* (1997) and *The Book of Liz* (2002). As renowned for his voice and comic timing as for his writing, Sedaris draws sellout crowds on his worldwide reading tours and has an app called *David's Diary*.

"And what does one do on the fourteenth of July? Does one celebrate Bastille Day?"

It was my second month of French class, and the teacher was leading us in an exercise designed to promote the use of *one*, our latest personal pronoun.

"Might one sing on Bastille Day?" she asked. "Might one dance in the street? Somebody give me an answer."

Printed in our textbooks was a list of major holidays alongside a scattered arrangement of photos depicting French people in the act of celebration. The object was to match the holiday with the corresponding picture. It was simple enough but seemed an exercise better suited to the use of the word *they*. I didn't know about the rest of the class, but when Bastille Day eventually rolled around, I planned to stay home and clean my oven.

5   Normally, when working from the book, it was my habit to tune out my fellow students and scout ahead, concentrating on the question I'd calculated might fall to me, but this afternoon, we were veering from the usual format. Questions were answered on a volunteer basis, and I was able to sit back, confident that the same few students would do the talking. Today's discussion was dominated by an Italian nanny, two chatty Poles, and a pouty, plump Moroccan

woman who had grown up speaking French and had enrolled in the class to improve her spelling.[1] She'd covered these lessons back in the third grade and took every opportunity to demonstrate her superiority. A question would be asked and she'd give the answer, behaving as though this were a game show and, if quick enough, she might go home with a tropical vacation or a side-by-side refrigerator-freezer. By the end of her first day, she'd raised her hand so many times, her shoulder had given out. Now she just leaned back in her seat and shouted the answers, her bronzed arms folded across her chest like some great grammar genie.

We finished discussing Bastille Day, and the teacher moved on to Easter, which was represented in our textbook by a black-and-white photograph of a chocolate bell lying upon a bed of palm fronds.

"And what does one do on Easter? Would anyone like to tell us?"

The Italian nanny was attempting to answer the question when the Moroccan student interrupted, shouting, "Excuse me, but what's an Easter?"

Despite her having grown up in a Muslim country, it seemed she might have heard it mentioned once or twice, but no. "I mean it," she said. "I have no idea what you people are talking about."

The teacher then called upon the rest of us to explain.   10

The Poles led the charge to the best of their ability. "It is," said one, "a party for the little boy of God who call his self Jesus and . . . oh, shit."

She faltered, and her fellow countryman came to her aid.

"He call his self Jesus, and then he be die one day on two . . . morsels of . . . lumber."

The rest of the class jumped in, offering bits of information that would have given the pope an aneurysm.

"He die one day, and then he go above of my head to live with your father."   15

"He weared the long hair, and after he died, the first day he come back here for to say hello to the peoples."

"He nice, the Jesus."

"He make the good things, and on the Easter we be sad because somebody makes him dead today."

Part of the problem had to do with grammar. Simple nouns such as *cross* and *resurrection* were beyond our grasp, let alone such complicated reflexive phrases as "To give of yourself your only begotten son." Faced with the challenge of explaining the cornerstone of Christianity, we did what any self-respecting group of people might do. We talked about food instead.

"Easter is a party for to eat of the lamb," the Italian nanny explained. "One,   20 too, may eat of the chocolate."

"And who brings the chocolate?" the teacher asked.

I knew the word, and so I raised my hand, saying, "The Rabbit of Easter. He bring of the chocolate."

My classmates reacted as though I'd attributed the delivery to the Antichrist. They were mortified.

1. France controlled most of Morocco between 1912 and 1956; as a result, though Arabic is now the latter country's official language, French is still widely taught and serves as the primary language of business and government.

"A rabbit?" The teacher, assuming I'd used the wrong word, positioned her index fingers on top of her head, wiggling them as though they were ears. "You mean one of these? A rabbit rabbit?"

25 "Well, sure," I said. "He come in the night when one sleep on a bed. With a hand he have the basket and foods."

The teacher sadly shook her head, as if this explained everything that was wrong with my country. "No, no," she said. "Here in France the chocolate is brought by the big bell that flies in from Rome."[2]

I called for a time-out. "But how do the bell know where you live?"

"Well," she said, "how does a rabbit?"

It was a decent point, but at least a rabbit has eyes. That's a start. Rabbits move from place to place, while most bells can only go back and forth—and they can't even do that on their own power. On top of that, the Easter Bunny has character; he's someone you'd like to meet and shake hands with. A bell has all the personality of a cast-iron skillet. It's like saying that come Christmas, a magic dustpan flies in from the North Pole, led by eight flying cinder blocks. Who wants to stay up all night so they can see a bell? And why fly one in from Rome when they've got more bells than they know what to do with right here in Paris? That's the most implausible aspect of the whole story, as there's no way the bells of France would allow a foreign worker to fly in and take their jobs. That Roman bell would be lucky to get work cleaning up after a French bell's dog—and even then he'd need papers. It just didn't add up.

30 Nothing we said was of any help to the Moroccan student. A dead man with long hair supposedly living with her father, a leg of lamb served with palm fronds and chocolate. Confused and disgusted, she shrugged her massive shoulders and turned her attention back to the comic book she kept hidden beneath her binder. I wondered then if, without the language barrier, my classmates and I could have done a better job making sense of Christianity, an idea that sounds pretty far-fetched to begin with.

In communicating any religious belief, the operative word is *faith*, a concept illustrated by our very presence in that classroom. Why bother struggling with the grammar lessons of a six-year-old if each of us didn't believe that, against all reason, we might eventually improve? If I could hope to one day carry on a fluent conversation, it was a relatively short leap to believing that a rabbit might visit my home in the middle of the night, leaving behind a handful of chocolate kisses and a carton of menthol cigarettes. So why stop there? If I could believe in myself, why not give other improbabilities the benefit of the doubt? I accepted the idea that an omniscient God had cast me in his own image and that he watched over me and guided me from one place to the next. The virgin birth, the resurrection, and the countless miracles—my heart expanded to encompass all the wonders and possibilities of the universe.

A bell, though, that's fucked up.

2000

---

2. In remembrance of Jesus's death, bells across France are customarily silenced from the Thursday before Good Friday until Easter morning; children are encouraged to believe that the bells fly to Rome to visit the pope, returning with gifts.

QUESTIONS

1. How might it matter thematically that the class exercise focuses on use of the pronoun *one*?

2. At one point, the narrator claims that grammar is "[p]art of the problem" (par. 19). How does grammar contribute to the humor of JESUS SHAVES? to its theme?

3. What "lesson" does the narrator seem to draw from this class exercise? In these terms, what might be significant, as well as funny, about the story's last sentence?

SUGGESTIONS FOR WRITING

1. Write a response paper comparing your reactions to JESUS SHAVES, on the one hand, and to either THE MANAGEMENT OF GRIEF, INTERPRETER OF MALADIES, or MERICANS, on the other. How does your personal relationship to the various cultural traditions depicted in the two stories, especially those of each protagonist, affect your response?

2. In THE MANAGEMENT OF GRIEF, Shaila describes herself as "trapped between two modes of knowledge" (par. 84). Write an essay exploring whether and how this claim holds true both for Shaila and for a character in any other story in this album. What "two [or more] modes of knowledge" inform the characters' thinking and behavior, and how so? In what ways is each character "trapped" and in what ways liberated or even empowered by that situation?

3. Write an essay exploring how THE MANAGEMENT OF GRIEF and INTERPRETER OF MALADIES characterize what the former story calls "the New World" versus the Old (par. 135). According to these stories, what is distinctive about the life and people of North America and about the values or worldview of those who live there? What seems to be most and least attractive about them? How do the two stories ultimately differ (or not) in their attitudes toward North America and North Americans?

4. Compare how any two stories in this album treat the issue of linguistic and cultural interpretation and translation. What does each story imply about when, how, and why such translation works or fails, and about what those who act as interpreters or translators might learn from doing so? How does narration contribute to each story's articulation of its theme?

5. Write an essay exploring how any other story, poem, or play in this anthology depicts a cross-cultural encounter and what its major conclusion about that (or its theme) seems to be, perhaps comparing this work to one of the stories in this album.

Exploring Contexts

8 | THE AUTHOR'S WORK AS CONTEXT: FLANNERY O'CONNOR

As soon as we read more than one work by an author, we begin to recognize similar qualities in the works, as if we are getting to know a personality. Each story, poem, or play is part of the author's entire body of work, or **oeuvre**. Though the voice and vision may vary from work to work, there will be continuities. The concerns and assumptions that permeate an author's oeuvre do more than relate the individual works to one another; they also serve as the author's trademark. We read each new work by the same author with certain expectations about setting, characterization, style, tone, and other elements.

Unless a work of literature is anonymous or ancient, it is relatively easy to find out about the person who wrote it. In this book we provide short biographies of writers, and numerous print and online sources can add detail and complexity to your first impressions of an author. Curiosity about a writer may lead you not only to biographies but also to other things the author produced, including essays, lectures, letters, diaries, interviews, and memoirs—anything that promises insight into the experience, the worldview, and the process that helped produce the work.

In this chapter we will look closely at the work of the American fiction writer Flannery O'Connor (1925–64), focusing on three stories: the title stories of both her first collection, *A Good Man Is Hard to Find* (1955), and her last, *Everything That Rises Must Converge* (published posthumously in 1965), as well as "Good Country People," which appeared in the first collection. O'Connor's career was short, hampered by her struggles with lupus, but her accomplishments were considerable: Raised in Milledgeville, Georgia, she died there at thirty-nine, having published some thirty-one stories and two novels, as well as numerous essays and reviews.

O'Connor's settings are most often in the American South, rural or urban, and her characters most often Southerners, White or Black. Consequently, her subject is often what she called "the race business." O'Connor has a keen eye for realistic detail and for the truth that lies beneath the surface of language and self-image. Her means of uncovering this truth is often violence that shocks the reader and, usually, her characters. O'Connor was a deeply religious and serious writer, a Roman Catholic in a milieu in which most were Protestant Evangelicals. But her stories are replete with irony and wit and are often downright funny. Indeed, as you will see, she is not above mixing comedy and horror or using comic pratfalls to achieve serious (even tragic) ends. It is not difficult to recognize a story by Flannery O'Connor.

In the rest of this chapter, we first offer general guidance on biographical approaches to authors and their works. Then we discuss more fully some terms and concepts that you have encountered in earlier chapters, but that are especially useful in reading and responding to multiple works by the same author: the distinctions

Flannery O'Connor at home at Andalusia Farm, near Milledgeville, Georgia, 1962

among types of narration as well as matters of tone, style, and imagery. To round out the picture of Flannery O'Connor and to provide material you might use for a critical essay, the chapter concludes with passages from O'Connor's essays and letters, a biographical timeline, and samples of biographical criticism of her work.

BIOGRAPHICAL APPROACHES TO LITERATURE

An author's works always relate in some way to his or her life, though they rarely, if ever, offer a direct account of actual experience. A biographical approach to interpretation not only brings us closer to the person behind the work but also gives us a stronger sense of the work's origins. Even a few biographical facts about the author can help guide our expectations about the work and place its **themes** in perspective.

Before you write about any work, it is always a good idea to find out when and where an author lived and wrote, just as you would notice the **setting** (the time and place) within the work. Any essay on a work of literature may include carefully cited information or evidence about the author's life, career, and views. For example, it may be useful to know that A HUNGER ARTIST author Franz Kafka (1883–1924) was a well-educated Jewish civil servant who wrote in German while living in Prague and Vienna. His fiction, then, should not be read as if it were written yesterday in a suburb of Los Angeles. And it *may* be read, in part, as a response to the mixture of assimilation and exile that many Eastern European Jews experienced at the turn of the twentieth century.

Be aware, however, that the biographical approach has some limitations and drawbacks. In a short essay on one or more works by a single author, it is usually better to focus on the works themselves. But even if you are writing a longer paper, you should always be careful not to misread a fictional work as factual autobiography or to treat features of the work as direct results of some biographical cause. Such cause-and-effect biographical critiques ignore other explanations and interpretations. Any literary work that spoke exclusively about or to one individual's personal experience (rather than being informed by it) would likely not be worth reading. Finally, when you read essays, reviews, and criticism in which writers reflect on their own work, it is tempting to take such comments as the final word about the work. But anyone who has ever tried to write knows that the result can have unintended effects on other people. Literary writing opens itself up to multiple interpretations, and any evidence of a writer's conscious intentions shouldn't close down the interpretive process.

It is possible to avoid these pitfalls and take a moderate approach to biographical criticism, however. After all, the text didn't pop into existence in a vacuum; a real human being in a specific historical time and place did write it. Knowing more about the context in which a work was produced—including the circumstances and vision of the author who created it—can lead you to deeper understanding and appreciation.

IMPLIED AUTHOR OR NARRATOR

Chapter 2 introduces key concepts about narrators that will help you in reading Flannery O'Connor's stories. A GOOD MAN IS HARD TO FIND, GOOD COUNTRY PEOPLE, and EVERYTHING THAT RISES MUST CONVERGE, like the rest of O'Connor's stories, are narrated in the third person. Yet the narrators of these stories are not all the same.

Each narrator adopts a slightly different position toward the focal character. Immediately this difference reminds us that Flannery O'Connor, who wrote all of the stories, is *not* the fictional teller or narrator of them. Did the real Flannery O'Connor share the voice and perspective of any of her narrators? What did the real O'Connor hope to teach her readers? We have only a few of her statements to go on; the actual author is inaccessible to us. These gaps in what a reader can access or know have inspired the concept of the *implied author*. This concept helps us to avoid reading a story as the writer's direct personal communication, allows for a variety of stories by one writer, and reminds us not only that the narrator of a story is *not* the author of it but also that we aren't talking about the flesh-and-blood person who wrote other works as well. When writing your critical essays, be sure to identify the narrator (as a character or not) and to distinguish the narrator from the author.

STYLE AND TONE

Exploring multiple works by the same author immediately gives you a broader view of the way that author writes. Each author has certain tendencies of **style**, which includes **figures of speech** and **imagery**. A writer's style also includes **diction** or word choice—whether *formal* or *informal* (think *implement* versus *tool*, or *coiffure* versus *hairdo*), whether ornate, standard, colloquial, dialect, or slang. The diction of many of the stories in this book is somewhat informal, particularly those narrated in the first person. An author may highlight the regional or dialect differences of a narrator's language, just as Flannery O'Connor filters the everyday Southern speech patterns of her characters through an articulate, perceptive narrator with correct diction.

In O'Connor's fiction, such distinctions between the narrator's diction and syntax and that of the characters contribute to **tone**, or the attitude of the implied author and the narrator toward the characters and events, an element somewhat analogous to tone of voice. When what is being said and how it is said (tone) are in harmony, it is difficult to separate one from the other; when there seems to be a discrepancy, we have a number of terms to describe the difference. If the language seems exaggerated, we call it **overstatement**, or *hyperbole*. Sometimes it will be the narrator, sometimes a character, who uses language so intensive or exaggerated that we must read it at a discount, as it were, and judge the speaker's accuracy or honesty in the process. The opposite of overstatement is **understatement**, or **litotes**.

O'Connor's work is also characterized by **irony**. When a word or expression carries not only its literal meaning but a different meaning for the speaker as well, we have an example of *verbal irony*. For example, the phrase "good country people" accumulates ironies when Hulga, a character who has groaned at the idea, uses it herself. As you read O'Connor's stories, look out also for nonverbal forms of irony. The most common form is *situational irony*, which occurs when a character holds a position or has an expectation that is reversed or fulfilled in an unexpected way. A form of situational irony known as *dramatic irony* occurs when a gap opens between what a character believes or expects and what the reader or audience knows. This gap may be revealed when a character says something that has unintended alternative meanings to a better-informed listener or that later becomes true in an unintended way. Dramatic irony also may be sustained throughout an entire work by an unreliable first-person narrator, who perceives or tries to "spin" his or her circumstances in a distorted way. All three types of irony occur throughout O'Connor's stories. Rather than demeaning her characters, O'Connor's ironic treatment testifies to her keen observation of the limits of all human awareness and of the way people tend to rationalize and misconstrue their situations and their own characters.

The distinctive Southern voices of the dialogue in an O'Connor story and the vivid setting and imagery are hallmarks of this author's style. But even more, we know an O'Connor story by the dryly humorous distance her narrators maintain from all characters, the often violent harm characters do to one another, the belated revelation that destroys a character's pride in knowing more than others—the commandment, in a sense, to awaken before we meet eternal damnation.

THREE STORIES BY FLANNERY O'CONNOR

A Good Man Is Hard to Find

The grandmother didn't want to go to Florida. She wanted to visit some of her connections in east Tennessee and she was seizing at every chance to change Bailey's mind. Bailey was the son she lived with, her only boy. He was sitting on the edge of his chair at the table, bent over the orange sports section of the *Journal*. "Now look here, Bailey," she said, "see here, read this," and she stood with one hand on her thin hip and the other rattling the newspaper at his bald head. "Here this fellow that calls himself The Misfit is aloose from the Federal Pen and headed toward Florida and you read here what it says he did to these people. Just you read it. I wouldn't take my children in any direction with a criminal like that aloose in it. I couldn't answer to my conscience if I did."

Bailey didn't look up from his reading so she wheeled around then and faced the children's mother, a young woman in slacks, whose face was as broad and innocent as a cabbage and was tied around with a green head-kerchief that had two points on the top like a rabbit's ears. She was sitting on the sofa, feeding the baby his apricots out of a jar. "The children have been to Florida before," the old lady said. "You all ought to take them somewhere else for a change so they would see different parts of the world and be broad. They never have been to east Tennessee."

The children's mother didn't seem to hear her but the eight-year-old boy, John Wesley, a stocky child with glasses, said, "If you don't want to go to Florida, why dontcha stay at home?" He and the little girl, June Star, were reading the funny papers on the floor.

"She wouldn't stay at home to be queen for a day," June Star said without raising her yellow head.

5   "Yes and what would you do if this fellow, The Misfit, caught you?" the grandmother asked.

"I'd smack his face," John Wesley said.

"She wouldn't stay at home for a million bucks," June Star said. "Afraid she'd miss something. She has to go everywhere we go."

"All right, Miss," the grandmother said. "Just remember that the next time you want me to curl your hair."

June Star said her hair was naturally curly.

10   The next morning the grandmother was the first one in the car, ready to go. She had her big black valise that looked like the head of a hippopotamus in one corner, and underneath it she was hiding a basket with Pitty Sing,[1] the cat, in it. She didn't intend for the cat to be left alone in the house for three days because he would miss her too much and she was afraid he might brush against one of the gas burners and accidentally asphyxiate himself. Her son, Bailey, didn't like to arrive at a motel with a cat.

---

1. Named after Pitti-Sing, one of the "three little maids from school" in W. S. Gilbert and Arthur Sullivan's operetta *The Mikado* (1885).

She sat in the middle of the back seat with John Wesley and June Star on either side of her. Bailey and the children's mother and the baby sat in front and they left Atlanta at eight forty-five with the mileage on the car at 55890. The grandmother wrote this down because she thought it would be interesting to say how many miles they had been when they got back. It took them twenty minutes to reach the outskirts of the city.

The old lady settled herself comfortably, removing her white cotton gloves and putting them up with her purse on the shelf in front of the back window. The children's mother still had on slacks and still had her head tied up in a green kerchief, but the grandmother had on a navy blue straw sailor hat with a bunch of white violets on the brim and a navy blue dress with a small white dot in the print. Her collars and cuffs were white organdy trimmed with lace and at her neckline she had pinned a purple spray of cloth violets containing a sachet. In case of an accident, anyone seeing her dead on the highway would know at once that she was a lady.

She said she thought it was going to be a good day for driving, neither too hot nor too cold, and she cautioned Bailey that the speed limit was fifty-five miles an hour and that the patrolmen hid themselves behind billboards and small clumps of trees and sped out after you before you had a chance to slow down. She pointed out interesting details of the scenery: Stone Mountain; the blue granite that in some places came up to both sides of the highway; the brilliant red clay banks slightly streaked with purple; and the various crops that made rows of green lace-work on the ground. The trees were full of silver-white sunlight and the meanest of them sparkled. The children were reading comic magazines and their mother had gone back to sleep.

"Let's go through Georgia fast so we won't have to look at it much," John Wesley said.

"If I were a little boy," said the grandmother, "I wouldn't talk about my native 15 state that way. Tennessee has the mountains and Georgia has the hills."

"Tennessee is just a hillbilly dumping ground," John Wesley said, "and Georgia is a lousy state too."

"You said it," June Star said.

"In my time," said the grandmother, folding her thin veined fingers, "children were more respectful of their native states and their parents and everything else. People did right then. Oh look at the cute little pickaninny!" she said and pointed to a Negro child standing in the door of a shack. "Wouldn't that make a picture, now?" she asked and they all turned and looked at the little Negro out of the back window. He waved.

"He didn't have any britches on," June Star said.

"He probably didn't have any," the grandmother explained. "Little niggers in 20 the country don't have things like we do. If I could paint, I'd paint that picture," she said.

The children exchanged comic books.

The grandmother offered to hold the baby and the children's mother passed him over the front seat to her. She set him on her knee and bounced him and told him about the things they were passing. She rolled her eyes and screwed up her mouth and stuck her leathery thin face into his smooth bland one. Occasionally he gave her a faraway smile. They passed a large cotton field with five or six graves fenced in the middle of it, like a small island. "Look at the graveyard!" the grandmother said, pointing it out. "That was the old family burying ground. That belonged to the plantation."

"Where's the plantation?" John Wesley asked.

"Gone with the Wind,"[2] said the grandmother. "Ha. Ha."

25   When the children finished all the comic books they had brought, they opened the lunch and ate it. The grandmother ate a peanut butter sandwich and an olive and would not let the children throw the box and the paper napkins out the window. When there was nothing else to do they played a game by choosing a cloud and making the other two guess what shape it suggested. John Wesley took one the shape of a cow and June Star guessed a cow and John Wesley said, no, an automobile, and June Star said he didn't play fair, and they began to slap each other over the grandmother.

The grandmother said she would tell them a story if they would keep quiet. When she told a story, she rolled her eyes and waved her head and was very dramatic. She said once when she was a maiden lady she had been courted by a Mr. Edgar Atkins Teagarden from Jasper, Georgia. She said he was a very good-looking man and a gentleman and that he brought her a watermelon every Saturday afternoon with his initials cut in it, E. A. T. Well, one Saturday, she said, Mr. Teagarden brought the watermelon and there was nobody at home and he left it on the front porch and returned in his buggy to Jasper, but she never got the watermelon, she said, because a nigger boy ate it when he saw the initials, E. A. T.! This story tickled John Wesley's funny bone and he giggled and giggled but June Star didn't think it was any good. She said she wouldn't marry a man that just brought her a watermelon on Saturday. The grandmother said she would have done well to marry Mr. Teagarden because he was a gentleman and had bought Coca-Cola stock when it first came out and that he had died only a few years ago, a very wealthy man.

They stopped at The Tower for barbecued sandwiches. The Tower was a part stucco and part wood filling station and dance hall set in a clearing outside of Timothy. A fat man named Red Sammy Butts ran it and there were signs stuck here and there on the building and for miles up and down the highway saying, TRY RED SAMMY'S FAMOUS BARBECUE. NONE LIKE FAMOUS RED SAMMY'S! RED SAM! THE FAT BOY WITH THE HAPPY LAUGH! A VETERAN! RED SAMMY'S YOUR MAN!

Red Sammy was lying on the bare ground outside The Tower with his head under a truck while a gray monkey about a foot high, chained to a small chinaberry tree, chattered nearby. The monkey sprang back into the tree and got on the highest limb as soon as he saw the children jump out of the car and run toward him.

Inside, The Tower was a long dark room with a counter at one end and tables at the other and dancing space in the middle. They all sat down at a board table next to the nickelodeon[3] and Red Sam's wife, a tall burnt-brown woman with hair and eyes lighter than her skin, came and took their order. The children's

---

2. Title of an immensely popular novel, published in 1936, by Margaret Mitchell (1900–49); the novel depicts a large, prosperous Georgia plantation, Tara, that is destroyed by Northern troops in the American Civil War.

3. Jukebox.

mother put a dime in the machine and played "The Tennessee Waltz," and the grandmother said that tune always made her want to dance. She asked Bailey if he would like to dance but he only glared at her. He didn't have a naturally sunny disposition like she did and trips made him nervous. The grandmother's brown eyes were very bright. She swayed her head from side to side and pretended she was dancing in her chair. June Star said play something she could tap to so the children's mother put in another dime and played a fast number and June Star stepped out onto the dance floor and did her tap routine.

"Ain't she cute?" Red Sam's wife said, leaning over the counter. "Would you 30 like to come be my little girl?"

"No I certainly wouldn't," June Star said. "I wouldn't live in a broken-down place like this for a million bucks!" and she ran back to the table.

"Ain't she cute?" the woman repeated, stretching her mouth politely.

"Aren't you ashamed?" hissed the grandmother.

Red Sam came in and told his wife to quit lounging on the counter and hurry up with these people's order. His khaki trousers reached just to his hip bones and his stomach hung over them like a sack of meal swaying under his shirt. He came over and sat down at a table nearby and let out a combination sigh and yodel. "You can't win," he said. "You can't win," and he wiped his sweating red face off with a gray handkerchief. "These days you don't know who to trust," he said. "Ain't that the truth?"

"People are certainly not nice like they used to be," said the grandmother. 35

"Two fellers come in here last week," Red Sammy said, "driving a Chrysler. It was a old beat-up car but it was a good one and these boys looked all right to me. Said they worked at the mill and you know I let them fellers charge the gas they bought? Now why did I do that?"

"Because you're a good man!" the grandmother said at once.

"Yes'm, I suppose so," Red Sam said as if he were struck with this answer.

His wife brought the orders, carrying the five plates all at once without a tray, two in each hand and one balanced on her arm. "It isn't a soul in this green world of God's that you can trust," she said. "And I don't count nobody out of that, not nobody," she repeated, looking at Red Sammy.

"Did you read about that criminal, The Misfit, that's escaped?" asked the 40 grandmother.

"I wouldn't be a bit surprised if he didn't attact this place right here," said the woman. "If he hears about it being here, I wouldn't be none surprised to see him. If he hears it's two cent in the cash register, I wouldn't be a tall surprised if he . . ."

"That'll do," Red Sam said. "Go bring these people their Co'-Colas," and the woman went off to get the rest of the order.

"A good man is hard to find," Red Sammy said. "Everything is getting terrible. I remember the day you could go off and leave your screen door unlatched. Not no more."

He and the grandmother discussed better times. The old lady said that in her opinion Europe was entirely to blame for the way things were now. She said the way Europe acted you would think we were made of money and Red Sam said it was no use talking about it, she was exactly right. The children ran outside into the white sunlight and looked at the monkey in the lacy chinaberry tree.

He was busy catching fleas on himself and biting each one carefully between his teeth as if it were a delicacy.

45   They drove off again into the hot afternoon. The grandmother took cat naps and woke up every few minutes with her own snoring. Outside of Toombsboro she woke up and recalled an old plantation that she had visited in this neighborhood once when she was a young lady. She said the house had six white columns across the front and that there was an avenue of oaks leading up to it and two little wooden trellis arbors on either side in front where you sat down with your suitor after a stroll in the garden. She recalled exactly which road to turn off to get to it. She knew that Bailey would not be willing to lose any time looking at an old house, but the more she talked about it, the more she wanted to see it once again and find out if the little twin arbors were still standing. "There was a secret panel in this house," she said craftily, not telling the truth but wishing that she were, "and the story went that all the family silver was hidden in it when Sherman came through but it was never found . . ."

"Hey!" John Wesley said. "Let's go see it! We'll find it! We'll poke all the woodwork and find it! Who lives there? Where do you turn off at? Hey Pop, can't we turn off there?"

"We never have seen a house with a secret panel!" June Star shrieked. "Let's go to the house with the secret panel! Hey Pop, can't we go see the house with the secret panel!"

"It's not far from here, I know," the grandmother said. "It wouldn't take over twenty minutes."

Bailey was looking straight ahead. His jaw was as rigid as a horseshoe. "No," he said.

50   The children began to yell and scream that they wanted to see the house with the secret panel. John Wesley kicked the back of the front seat and June Star hung over her mother's shoulder and whined desperately into her ear that they never had any fun even on their vacation, that they could never do what THEY wanted to do. The baby began to scream and John Wesley kicked the back of the seat so hard that his father could feel the blows in his kidney.

"All right!" he shouted and drew the car to a stop at the side of the road. "Will you all shut up? Will you all just shut up for one second? If you don't shut up, we won't go anywhere."

"It would be very educational for them," the grandmother murmured.

"All right," Bailey said, "but get this: this is the only time we're going to stop for anything like this. This is the one and only time."

"The dirt road that you have to turn down is about a mile back," the grandmother directed. "I marked it when we passed."

55   "A dirt road," Bailey groaned.

After they had turned around and were headed toward the dirt road, the grandmother recalled other points about the house, the beautiful glass over the front doorway and the candle-lamp in the hall. John Wesley said that the secret panel was probably in the fireplace.

"You can't go inside this house," Bailey said. "You don't know who lives there."

"While you all talk to the people in front, I'll run around behind and get in a window," John Wesley suggested.

"We'll all stay in the car," his mother said.

They turned onto the dirt road and the car raced roughly along in a swirl of 60
pink dust. The grandmother recalled the times when there were no paved roads
and thirty miles was a day's journey. The dirt road was hilly and there were sudden washes in it and sharp curves on dangerous embankments. All at once they
would be on a hill, looking down over the blue tops of trees for miles around,
then the next minute, they would be in a red depression with the dust-coated
trees looking down on them.

"This place had better turn up in a minute," Bailey said, "or I'm going to turn
around."

The road looked as if no one had traveled on it in months.

"It's not much farther," the grandmother said and just as she said it, a horrible
thought came to her. The thought was so embarrassing that she turned red in
the face and her eyes dilated and her feet jumped up, upsetting her valise in the
corner. The instant the valise moved, the newspaper top she had over the basket
under it rose with a snarl and Pitty Sing, the cat, sprang onto Bailey's shoulder.

The children were thrown to the floor and their mother, clutching the baby,
out the door onto the ground; the old lady was thrown into the front seat. The
car turned over once and landed right-side-up in a gulch off the side of the road.
Bailey remained in the driver's seat with the cat—gray-striped with a broad
white face and an orange nose—clinging to his neck like a caterpillar.

As soon as the children saw they could move their arms and legs, they scram- 65
bled out of the car, shouting, "We've had an ACCIDENT!" The grandmother
was curled up under the dashboard, hoping she was injured so that Bailey's
wrath would not come down on her all at once. The horrible thought she had
had before the accident was that the house she had remembered so vividly was
not in Georgia but in Tennessee.

Bailey removed the cat from his neck with both hands and flung it out the
window against the side of a pine tree. Then he got out of the car and started
looking for the children's mother. She was sitting against the side of the red gutted ditch, holding the screaming baby, but she only had a cut down her face and
a broken shoulder. "We've had an ACCIDENT!" the children screamed in a
frenzy of delight.

"But nobody's killed," June Star said with disappointment as the grandmother
limped out of the car, her hat still pinned to her head but the broken front brim
standing up at a jaunty angle and the violet spray hanging off the side. They all
sat down in the ditch, except the children, to recover from the shock. They were
all shaking.

"Maybe a car will come along," said the children's mother hoarsely.

"I believe I have injured an organ," said the grandmother, pressing her side,
but no one answered her. Bailey's teeth were clattering. He had on a yellow
sport shirt with bright blue parrots designed in it and his face was as yellow as
the shirt. The grandmother decided that she would not mention that the house
was in Tennessee.

The road was about ten feet above and they could see only the tops of the 70
trees on the other side of it. Behind the ditch they were sitting in there were
more woods, tall and dark and deep. In a few minutes they saw a car some distance away on top of a hill, coming slowly as if the occupants were watching
them. The grandmother stood up and waved both arms dramatically to attract

their attention. The car continued to come on slowly, disappeared around a bend and appeared again, moving even slower, on top of the hill they had gone over. It was a big black battered hearselike automobile. There were three men in it.

It came to a stop just over them and for some minutes, the driver looked down with a steady expressionless gaze to where they were sitting, and didn't speak. Then he turned his head and muttered something to the other two and they got out. One was a fat boy in black trousers and a red sweat shirt with a silver stallion embossed on the front of it. He moved around on the right side of them and stood staring, his mouth partly open in a kind of loose grin. The other had on khaki pants and a blue striped coat and a gray hat pulled down very low, hiding most of his face. He came around slowly on the left side. Neither spoke.

The driver got out of the car and stood by the side of it, looking down at them. He was an older man than the other two. His hair was just beginning to gray and he wore silver-rimmed spectacles that gave him a scholarly look. He had a long creased face and didn't have on any shirt or undershirt. He had on blue jeans that were too tight for him and was holding a black hat and a gun. The two boys also had guns.

"We've had an ACCIDENT!" the children screamed.

The grandmother had the peculiar feeling that the bespectacled man was someone she knew. His face was as familiar to her as if she had known him all her life but she could not recall who he was. He moved away from the car and began to come down the embankment, placing his feet carefully so that he wouldn't slip. He had on tan and white shoes and no socks, and his ankles were red and thin. "Good afternoon," he said. "I see you all had you a little spill."

75   "We turned over twice!" said the grandmother.

"Oncet," he corrected. "We seen it happen. Try their car and see will it run, Hiram," he said quietly to the boy with the gray hat.

"What you got that gun for?" John Wesley asked. "Whatcha gonna do with that gun?"

"Lady," the man said to the children's mother, "would you mind calling them children to sit down by you? Children make me nervous. I want all you all to sit down right together there where you're at."

"What are you telling US what to do for?" June Star asked.

80   Behind them the line of woods gaped like a dark open mouth. "Come here," said their mother.

"Look here now," Bailey began suddenly, "we're in a predicament! We're in . . ."

The grandmother shrieked. She scrambled to her feet and stood staring. "You're The Misfit!" she said. "I recognized you at once!"

"Yes'm," the man said, smiling slightly as if he were pleased in spite of himself to be known, "but it would have been better for all of you, lady, if you hadn't of reckernized me."

Bailey turned his head sharply and said something to his mother that shocked even the children. The old lady began to cry and The Misfit reddened.

85   "Lady," he said, "don't you get upset. Sometimes a man says things he don't mean. I don't reckon he meant to talk to you thataway."

"You wouldn't shoot a lady, would you?" the grandmother said and removed a clean handkerchief from her cuff and began to slap at her eyes with it.

The Misfit pointed the toe of his shoe into the ground and made a little hole and then covered it up again. "I would hate to have to," he said.

"Listen," the grandmother almost screamed, "I know you're a good man. You don't look a bit like you have common blood. I know you must come from nice people!"

"Yes mam," he said, "finest people in the world." When he smiled he showed a row of strong white teeth. "God never made a finer woman than my mother and my daddy's heart was pure gold," he said. The boy with the red sweat shirt had come around behind them and was standing with his gun at his hip. The Misfit squatted down on the ground. "Watch them children, Bobby Lee," he said. "You know they make me nervous." He looked at the six of them huddled together in front of him and he seemed to be embarrassed as if he couldn't think of anything to say. "Ain't a cloud in the sky," he remarked, looking up at it. "Don't see no sun but don't see no cloud neither."

"Yes, it's a beautiful day," said the grandmother. "Listen," she said, "you 90 shouldn't call yourself The Misfit because I know you're a good man at heart. I can just look at you and tell."

"Hush!" Bailey yelled. "Hush! Everybody shut up and let me handle this!" He was squatting in the position of a runner about to sprint forward but he didn't move.

"I pre-chate that, lady," The Misfit said and drew a little circle in the ground with the butt of his gun.

"It'll take a half a hour to fix this here car," Hiram called, looking over the raised hood of it.

"Well, first you and Bobby Lee get him and that little boy to step over yonder with you," The Misfit said, pointing to Bailey and John Wesley. "The boys want to ast you something," he said to Bailey. "Would you mind stepping back in them woods there with them?"

"Listen," Bailey began, "we're in a terrible predicament! Nobody realizes 95 what this is," and his voice cracked. His eyes were as blue and intense as the parrots in his shirt and he remained perfectly still.

The grandmother reached up to adjust her hat brim as if she were going to the woods with him but it came off in her hand. She stood staring at it and after a second she let it fall on the ground. Hiram pulled Bailey up by the arm as if he were assisting an old man. John Wesley caught hold of his father's hand and Bobby Lee followed. They went off toward the woods and just as they reached the dark edge, Bailey turned and supporting himself against a gray naked pine trunk, he shouted, "I'll be back in a minute, Mamma, wait on me!"

"Come back this instant!" his mother shrilled but they all disappeared into the woods.

"Bailey Boy!" the grandmother called in a tragic voice but she found she was looking at The Misfit squatting on the ground in front of her. "I just know you're a good man," she said desperately. "You're not a bit common!"

"Nome,[4] I ain't a good man," The Misfit said after a second as if he had considered her statement carefully, "but I ain't the worst in the world neither. My

---

4. Contraction of "No, ma'am."

daddy said I was a different breed of dog from my brothers and sisters. 'You know,' Daddy said, 'it's some that can live their whole life out without asking about it and it's others has to know why it is, and this boy is one of the latters. He's going to be into everything!'" He put on his black hat and looked up suddenly and then away deep into the woods as if he were embarrassed again. "I'm sorry I don't have on a shirt before you ladies," he said, hunching his shoulders slightly. "We buried our clothes that we had on when we escaped and we're just making do until we can get better. We borrowed these from some folks we met," he explained.

100 "That's perfectly all right," the grandmother said. "Maybe Bailey has an extra shirt in his suitcase."

"I'll look and see terrectly," The Misfit said.

"Where are they taking him?" the children's mother screamed.

"Daddy was a card himself," The Misfit said. "You couldn't put anything over on him. He never got in trouble with the Authorities though. Just had the knack of handling them."

"You could be honest too if you'd only try," said the grandmother. "Think how wonderful it would be to settle down and live a comfortable life and not have to think about somebody chasing you all the time."

105 The Misfit kept scratching in the ground with the butt of his gun as if he were thinking about it. "Yes'm, somebody is always after you," he murmured.

The grandmother noticed how thin his shoulder blades were just behind his hat because she was standing up looking down on him. "Do you ever pray?" she asked.

He shook his head. All she saw was the black hat wiggle between his shoulder blades. "Nome," he said.

There was a pistol shot from the woods, followed closely by another. Then silence. The old lady's head jerked around. She could hear the wind move through the tree tops like a long satisfied insuck of breath. "Bailey Boy!" she called.

"I was a gospel singer for a while," The Misfit said. "I been most everything. Been in the arm service, both land and sea, at home and abroad, been twict married, been an undertaker, been with the railroads, plowed Mother Earth, been in a tornado, seen a man burnt alive oncet," and looked up at the children's mother and the little girl who were sitting close together, their faces white and their eyes glassy; "I even seen a woman flogged," he said.

110 "Pray, pray," the grandmother began, "pray, pray. . . ."

"I never was a bad boy that I remember of," The Misfit said in an almost dreamy voice, "but somewheres along the line I done something wrong and got sent to the penitentiary. I was buried alive," and he looked up and held her attention to him by a steady stare.

"That's when you should have started to pray," she said. "What did you do to get sent to the penitentiary that first time?"

"Turn to the right, it was a wall," The Misfit said, looking up again at the cloudless sky. "Turn to the left, it was a wall. Look up it was a ceiling, look down it was a floor. I forgot what I done, lady. I set there and set there, trying to remember what it was I done and I ain't recalled it to this day. Oncet in a while, I would think it was coming to me, but it never come."

"Maybe they put you in by mistake," the old lady said vaguely.

"Nome," he said. "It wasn't no mistake. They had the papers on me."   115

"You must have stolen something," she said.

The Misfit sneered slightly. "Nobody had nothing I wanted," he said. "It was a head-doctor at the penitentiary said what I had done was kill my daddy but I known that for a lie. My daddy died in nineteen ought nineteen of the epidemic flu and I never had a thing to do with it. He was buried in the Mount Hopewell Baptist churchyard and you can go there and see for yourself."

"If you would pray," the old lady said, "Jesus would help you."

"That's right," The Misfit said.

"Well then, why don't you pray?" she asked trembling with delight suddenly.   120

"I don't want no hep," he said. "I'm doing all right by myself."

Bobby Lee and Hiram came ambling back from the woods. Bobby Lee was dragging a yellow shirt with bright blue parrots in it.

"Thow me that shirt, Bobby Lee," The Misfit said. The shirt came flying at him and landed on his shoulder and he put it on. The grandmother couldn't name what the shirt reminded her of. "No, lady," The Misfit said while he was buttoning it up, "I found out the crime don't matter. You can do one thing or you can do another, kill a man or take a tire off his car, because sooner or later you're going to forget what it was you done and just be punished for it."

The children's mother had begun to make heaving noises as if she couldn't get her breath. "Lady," he asked, "would you and that little girl like to step off yonder with Bobby Lee and Hiram and join your husband?"

"Yes, thank you," the mother said faintly. Her left arm dangled helplessly and   125
she was holding the baby, who had gone to sleep, in the other. "Hep that lady up, Hiram," The Misfit said as she struggled to climb out of the ditch, "and Bobby Lee, you hold onto that little girl's hand."

"I don't want to hold hands with him," June Star said. "He reminds me of a pig."

The fat boy blushed and laughed and caught her by the arm and pulled her off into the woods after Hiram and her mother.

Alone with The Misfit, the grandmother found that she had lost her voice. There was not a cloud in the sky nor any sun. There was nothing around her but woods. She wanted to tell him that he must pray. She opened and closed her mouth several times before anything came out. Finally she found herself saying, "Jesus, Jesus," meaning, Jesus will help you, but the way she was saying it, it sounded as if she might be cursing.

"Yes'm," The Misfit said as if he agreed. "Jesus thown everything off balance. It was the same case with Him as with me except He hadn't committed any crime and they could prove I had committed one because they had the papers on me. Of course," he said, "they never shown me my papers. That's why I sign myself now. I said long ago, you get you a signature and sign everything you do and keep a copy of it. Then you'll know what you done and you can hold up the crime to the punishment and see do they match and in the end you'll have something to prove you ain't been treated right. I call myself The Misfit," he said, "because I can't make what all I done wrong fit what all I gone through in punishment."

There was a piercing scream from the woods, followed closely by a pistol   130
report. "Does it seem right to you, lady, that one is punished a heap and another ain't punished at all?"

"Jesus!" the old lady cried. "You've got good blood! I know you wouldn't shoot a lady! I know you come from nice people! Pray! Jesus, you ought not to shoot a lady. I'll give you all the money I've got!"

"Lady," The Misfit said, looking beyond her far into the woods, "there never was a body that give the undertaker a tip."

There were two more pistol reports and the grandmother raised her head like a parched old turkey hen crying for water and called, "Bailey Boy, Bailey Boy!" as if her heart would break.

"Jesus was the only One that ever raised the dead," The Misfit continued, "and He shouldn't have done it. He thown everything off balance. If He did what He said, then it's nothing for you to do but thow away everything and follow Him, and if He didn't, then it's nothing for you to do but enjoy the few minutes you got left the best way you can—by killing somebody or burning down his house or doing some other meanness to him. No pleasure but meanness," he said and his voice had become almost a snarl.

135   "Maybe He didn't raise the dead," the old lady mumbled, not knowing what she was saying and feeling so dizzy that she sank down in the ditch with her legs twisted under her.

"I wasn't there so I can't say He didn't," The Misfit said. "I wisht I had of been there," he said, hitting the ground with his fist. "It ain't right I wasn't there because if I had of been there I would of known. Listen lady," he said in a high voice, "if I had of been there I would of known and I wouldn't be like I am now." His voice seemed about to crack and the grandmother's head cleared for an instant. She saw the man's face twisted close to her own as if he were going to cry and she murmured, "Why you're one of my babies. You're one of my own children!" She reached out and touched him on the shoulder. The Misfit sprang back as if a snake had bitten him and shot her three times through the chest. Then he put his gun down on the ground and took off his glasses and began to clean them.

Hiram and Bobby Lee returned from the woods and stood over the ditch, looking down at the grandmother who half sat and half lay in a puddle of blood with her legs crossed under her like a child's and her face smiling up at the cloudless sky.

Without his glasses, The Misfit's eyes were red-rimmed and pale and defenseless-looking. "Take her off and thow her where you thown the others," he said, picking up the cat that was rubbing itself against his leg.

"She was a talker, wasn't she?" Bobby Lee said, sliding down the ditch with a yodel.

140   "She would of been a good woman," The Misfit said, "if it had been somebody there to shoot her every minute of her life."

"Some fun!" Bobby Lee said.

"Shut up, Bobby Lee," The Misfit said. "It's no real pleasure in life."

1953

Good Country People

B esides the neutral expression that she wore when she was alone, Mrs. Freeman had two others, forward and reverse, that she used for all her human dealings. Her forward expression was steady and driving like the advance of a heavy truck. Her eyes never swerved to left or right but turned as the story turned as if they followed a yellow line down the center of it. She seldom used the other expression because it was not often necessary for her to retract a statement, but when she did, her face came to a complete stop, there was an almost imperceptible movement of her black eyes, during which they seemed to be receding, and then the observer would see that Mrs. Freeman, though she might stand there as real as several grain sacks thrown on top of each other, was no longer there in spirit. As for getting anything across to her when this was the case, Mrs. Hopewell had given it up. She might talk her head off. Mrs. Freeman could never be brought to admit herself wrong on any point. She would stand there and if she could be brought to say anything, it was something like, "Well, I wouldn't of said it was and I wouldn't of said it wasn't," or letting her gaze range over the top kitchen shelf where there was an assortment of dusty bottles, she might remark, "I see you ain't ate many of them figs you put up last summer."

They carried on their most important business in the kitchen at breakfast. Every morning Mrs. Hopewell got up at seven o'clock and lit her gas heater and Joy's. Joy was her daughter, a large blonde girl who had an artificial leg. Mrs. Hopewell thought of her as a child though she was thirty-two years old and highly educated. Joy would get up while her mother was eating and lumber into the bathroom and slam the door, and before long, Mrs. Freeman would arrive at the back door. Joy would hear her mother call, "Come on in," and then they would talk for a while in low voices that were indistinguishable in the bathroom. By the time Joy came in, they had usually finished the weather report and were on one or the other of Mrs. Freeman's daughters, Glynese or Carramae, Joy called them Glycerin and Caramel. Glynese, a redhead, was eighteen and had many admirers; Carramae, a blonde, was only fifteen but already married and pregnant. She could not keep anything on her stomach. Every morning Mrs. Freeman told Mrs. Hopewell how many times she had vomited since the last report.

Mrs. Hopewell liked to tell people that Glynese and Carramae were two of the finest girls she knew and that Mrs. Freeman was a *lady* and that she was never ashamed to take her anywhere or introduce her to anybody they might meet. Then she would tell how she had happened to hire the Freemans in the first place and how they were a godsend to her and how she had had them four years. The reason for her keeping them so long was that they were not trash. They were good country people. She had telephoned the man whose name they had given as a reference and he had told her that Mr. Freeman was a good farmer but that his wife was the nosiest woman ever to walk the earth. "She's got to be into everything," the man said. "If she don't get there before the dust settles, you can bet she's dead, that's all. She'll want to know all your business. I can stand him real good," he had said, "but me nor my wife neither could have stood that woman one more minute on this place." That had put Mrs. Hopewell off for a few days.

She had hired them in the end because there were no other applicants but she had made up her mind beforehand exactly how she would handle the woman. Since she was the type who had to be into everything, then, Mrs. Hopewell had decided, she would not only let her be into everything, she would *see to it* that she was into everything—she would give her the responsibility of everything, she would put her in charge. Mrs. Hopewell had no bad qualities of her own but she was able to use other people's in such a constructive way that she never felt the lack. She had hired the Freemans and she had kept them four years.

5   Nothing is perfect. This was one of Mrs. Hopewell's favorite sayings. Another was: that is life! And still another, the most important, was: well, other people have their opinions too. She would make these statements, usually at the table, in a tone of gentle insistence as if no one held them but her, and the large hulking Joy, whose constant outrage had obliterated every expression from her face, would stare just a little to the side of her, her eyes icy blue, with the look of someone who has achieved blindness by an act of will and means to keep it.

When Mrs. Hopewell said to Mrs. Freeman that life was like that, Mrs. Freeman would say, "I always said so myself." Nothing had been arrived at by anyone that had not first been arrived at by her. She was quicker than Mr. Freeman. When Mrs. Hopewell said to her after they had been on the place a while, "You know, you're the wheel behind the wheel," and winked, Mrs. Freeman had said, "I know it. I've always been quick. It's some that are quicker than others."

"Everybody is different," Mrs. Hopewell said.

"Yes, most people is," Mrs. Freeman said.

"It takes all kinds to make the world."

10   "I always said it did myself."

The girl was used to this kind of dialogue for breakfast and more of it for dinner; sometimes they had it for supper too. When they had no guest they ate in the kitchen because that was easier. Mrs. Freeman always managed to arrive at some point during the meal and to watch them finish it. She would stand in the doorway if it were summer but in the winter she would stand with one elbow on top of the refrigerator and look down on them, or she would stand by the gas heater, lifting the back of her skirt slightly. Occasionally she would stand against the wall and roll her head from side to side. At no time was she in any hurry to leave. All this was very trying on Mrs. Hopewell but she was a woman of great patience. She realized that nothing is perfect and that in the Freemans she had good country people and that if, in this day and age, you get good country people, you had better hang onto them.

She had had plenty of experience with trash. Before the Freemans she had averaged one tenant family a year. The wives of these farmers were not the kind you would want to be around you for very long. Mrs. Hopewell, who had divorced her husband long ago, needed someone to walk over the fields with her; and when Joy had to be impressed for these services, her remarks were usually so ugly and her face so glum that Mrs. Hopewell would say, "If you can't come pleasantly, I don't want you at all," to which the girl, standing square and rigid-shouldered with her neck thrust slightly forward, would reply, "If you want me, here I am—LIKE I AM."

Mrs. Hopewell excused this attitude because of the leg (which had been shot off in a hunting accident when Joy was ten). It was hard for Mrs. Hopewell to realize that her child was thirty-two now and that for more than twenty years she had had only one leg. She thought of her still as a child because it tore her heart to think instead of the poor stout girl in her thirties who had never danced a step or had any *normal* good times. Her name was really Joy but as soon as she was twenty-one and away from home, she had had it legally changed. Mrs. Hopewell was certain that she had thought and thought until she had hit upon the ugliest name in any language. Then she had gone and had the beautiful name, Joy, changed without telling her mother until after she had done it. Her legal name was Hulga.

When Mrs. Hopewell thought the name, Hulga, she thought of the broad blank hull of a battleship. She would not use it. She continued to call her Joy to which the girl responded but in a purely mechanical way.

Hulga had learned to tolerate Mrs. Freeman who saved her from taking walks with her mother. Even Glynese and Carramae were useful when they occupied attention that might otherwise have been directed at her. At first she had thought she could not stand Mrs. Freeman for she had found that it was not possible to be rude to her. Mrs. Freeman would take on strange resentments and for days together she would be sullen but the source of her displeasure was always obscure; a direct attack, a positive leer, blatant ugliness to her face— these never touched her. And without warning one day, she began calling her Hulga.

She did not call her that in front of Mrs. Hopewell who would have been incensed but when she and the girl happened to be out of the house together, she would say something and add the name Hulga to the end of it, and the big spectacled Joy-Hulga would scowl and redden as if her privacy had been intruded upon. She considered the name her personal affair. She had arrived at it first purely on the basis of its ugly sound and then the full genius of its fitness had struck her. She had a vision of the name working like the ugly sweating Vulcan who stayed in the furnace and to whom, presumably, the goddess had to come when called. She saw it as the name of her highest creative act. One of her major triumphs was that her mother had not been able to turn her dust into Joy, but the greater one was that she had been able to turn it herself into Hulga. However, Mrs. Freeman's relish for using the name only irritated her. It was as if Mrs. Freeman's beady steel-pointed eyes had penetrated far enough behind her face to reach some secret fact. Something about her seemed to fascinate Mrs. Freeman and then one day Hulga realized that it was the artificial leg. Mrs. Freeman had a special fondness for the details of secret infections, hidden deformities, assaults upon children. Of diseases, she preferred the lingering or incurable. Hulga had heard Mrs. Hopewell give her the details of the hunting accident, how the leg had been literally blasted off, how she had never lost consciousness. Mrs. Freeman could listen to it any time as if it had happened an hour ago.

When Hulga stumped into the kitchen in the morning (she could walk without making the awful noise but she made it—Mrs. Hopewell was certain— because it was ugly-sounding), she glanced at them and did not speak. Mrs. Hopewell would be in her red kimono with her hair tied around her head in rags. She would be sitting at the table, finishing her breakfast and

Mrs. Freeman would be hanging by her elbow outward from the refrigerator, looking down at the table. Hulga always put her eggs on the stove to boil and then stood over them with her arms folded, and Mrs. Hopewell would look at her—a kind of indirect gaze divided between her and Mrs. Freeman—and would think that if she would only keep herself up a little, she wouldn't be so bad looking. There was nothing wrong with her face that a pleasant expression wouldn't help. Mrs. Hopewell said that people who looked on the bright side of things would be beautiful even if they were not.

Whenever she looked at Joy this way, she could not help but feel that it would have been better if the child had not taken the Ph.D. It had certainly not brought her out any and now that she had it, there was no more excuse for her to go to school again. Mrs. Hopewell thought it was nice for girls to go to school to have a good time but Joy had "gone through." Anyhow, she would not have been strong enough to go again. The doctors had told Mrs. Hopewell that with the best of care, Joy might see forty-five. She had a weak heart. Joy had made it plain that if it had not been for this condition, she would be far from these red hills[1] and good country people. She would be in a university lecturing to people who knew what she was talking about. And Mrs. Hopewell could very well picture her there, looking like a scarecrow and lecturing to more of the same. Here she went about all day in a six-year-old skirt and a yellow sweat shirt with a faded cowboy on a horse embossed on it. She thought this was funny; Mrs. Hopewell thought it was idiotic and showed simply that she was still a child. She was brilliant but she didn't have a grain of sense. It seemed to Mrs. Hopewell that every year she grew less like other people and more like herself—bloated, rude, and squint-eyed. And she said such strange things! To her own mother she had said—without warning, without excuse, standing up in the middle of a meal with her face purple and her mouth half full—"Woman! do you ever look inside? Do you ever look inside and see what you are *not*? God!" she had cried sinking down again and staring at her plate, "Malebranche[2] was right: we are not our own light. We are not our own light!" Mrs. Hopewell had no idea to this day what brought that on. She had only made the remark, hoping Joy would take it in, that a smile never hurt anyone.

The girl had taken the Ph.D. in philosophy and this left Mrs. Hopewell at a complete loss. You could say, "My daughter is a nurse," or "My daughter is a schoolteacher," or even, "My daughter is a chemical engineer." You could not say, "My daughter is a philosopher." That was something that had ended with the Greeks and Romans. All day Joy sat on her neck in a deep chair, reading. Sometimes she went for walks but she didn't like dogs or cats or birds or flowers or nature or nice young men. She looked at nice young men as if she could smell their stupidity.

20   One day Mrs. Hopewell had picked up one of the books the girl had just put down and opening it at random, she read, "Science, on the other hand, has to

1. Like many of O'Connor's stories, this one is set in rural Georgia, in a hilly landscape of red soil similar to the surroundings of O'Connor's mother's farm, Andalusia, near Milledgeville, Georgia.
2. Nicolas Malebranche (1638–1715), renowned philosopher and author of *The Search after Truth*, expressing his skepticism about the human capacity to know one's own mind or the world except through God. Here, Hulga rephrases Malebranche's quotation from St. Augustine to the effect that we are not our own "light."

assert its soberness and seriousness afresh and declare that it is concerned solely with what-is. Nothing—how can it be for science anything but a horror and a phantasm? If science is right, then one thing stands firm: science wishes to know nothing of nothing. Such is after all the strictly scientific approach to Nothing. We know it by wishing to know nothing of Nothing."[3] These words had been underlined with a blue pencil and they worked on Mrs. Hopewell like some evil incantation in gibberish. She shut the book quickly and went out of the room as if she were having a chill.

This morning when the girl came in, Mrs. Freeman was on Carramae. "She thrown up four times after supper," she said, "and was up twict in the night after three o'clock. Yesterday she didn't do nothing but ramble in the bureau drawer. All she did. Stand up there and see what she could run up on."

"She's got to eat," Mrs. Hopewell muttered, sipping her coffee, while she watched Joy's back at the stove. She was wondering what the child had said to the Bible salesman. She could not imagine what kind of a conversation she could possibly have had with him.

He was a tall gaunt hatless youth who had called yesterday to sell them a Bible. He had appeared at the door, carrying a large black suitcase that weighted him so heavily on one side that he had to brace himself against the door facing. He seemed on the point of collapse but he said in a cheerful voice, "Good morning, Mrs. Cedars!" and set the suitcase down on the mat. He was not a bad-looking young man though he had on a bright blue suit and yellow socks that were not pulled up far enough. He had prominent face bones and a streak of sticky-looking brown hair falling across his forehead.

"I'm Mrs. Hopewell," she said.

"Oh!" he said, pretending to look puzzled but with his eyes sparkling, "I saw 25 it said 'The Cedars' on the mailbox so I thought you was Mrs. Cedars!" and he burst out in a pleasant laugh. He picked up the satchel and under cover of a pant, he fell forward into her hall. It was rather as if the suitcase had moved first, jerking him after it. "Mrs. Hopewell!" he said and grabbed her hand. "I hope you are well!" and he laughed again and then all at once his face sobered completely. He paused and gave her a straight earnest look and said, "Lady, I've come to speak of serious things."

"Well, come in," she muttered, none too pleased because her dinner was almost ready. He came into the parlor and sat down on the edge of a straight chair and put the suitcase between his feet and glanced around the room as if he were sizing her up by it. Her silver gleamed on the two sideboards; she decided he had never been in a room as elegant as this.

"Mrs. Hopewell," he began, using her name in a way that sounded almost intimate, "I know you believe in Chrustian service."

"Well yes," she murmured.

"I know," he said and paused, looking very wise with his head cocked on one side, "that you're a good woman. Friends have told me."

Mrs. Hopewell never liked to be taken for a fool. "What are you selling?" she 30 asked.

3. Passage from German philosopher Martin Heidegger's (1889–1976) inaugural lecture (1929) at the University of Freiburg, "What Is Metaphysics?"

"Bibles," the young man said and his eye raced around the room before he added, "I see you have no family Bible in your parlor, I see that is the one lack you got!"

Mrs. Hopewell could not say, "My daughter is an atheist and won't let me keep the Bible in the parlor." She said, stiffening slightly, "I keep my Bible by my bedside." This was not the truth. It was in the attic somewhere.

"Lady," he said, "the word of God ought to be in the parlor."

"Well, I think that's a matter of taste," she began. "I think. . . ."

35   "Lady," he said, "for a Christian, the word of God ought to be in every room in the house besides in his heart. I know you're a Christian because I can see it in every line of your face."

She stood up and said, "Well, young man, I don't want to buy a Bible and I smell my dinner burning."

He didn't get up. He began to twist his hands and looking down at them, he said softly, "Well lady, I'll tell you the truth—not many people want to buy one nowadays and besides, I know I'm real simple. I don't know how to say a thing but to say it. I'm just a country boy." He glanced up into her unfriendly face. "People like you don't like to fool with country people like me!"

"Why!" she cried, "good country people are the salt of the earth! Besides, we all have different ways of doing, it takes all kinds to make the world go 'round. That's life!"

"You said a mouthful," he said.

40   "Why, I think there aren't enough good country people in the world!" she said, stirred. "I think that's what's wrong with it!"

His face had brightened. "I didn't inraduce myself," he said. "I'm Manley Pointer from out in the country around Willohobie, not even from a place, just from near a place."

"You wait a minute," she said. "I have to see about my dinner." She went out to the kitchen and found Joy standing near the door where she had been listening.

"Get rid of the salt of the earth," she said, "and let's eat."

Mrs. Hopewell gave her a pained look and turned the heat down under the vegetables. "I can't be rude to anybody," she murmured and went back into the parlor.

45   He had opened the suitcase and was sitting with a Bible on each knee.

"You might as well put those up," she told him. "I don't want one."

"I appreciate your honesty," he said. "You don't see any more real honest people unless you go way out in the country."

"I know," she said, "real genuine folks!" Through the crack in the door she heard a groan.

"I guess a lot of boys come telling you they're working their way through college," he said, "but I'm not going to tell you that. Somehow," he said, "I don't want to go to college. I want to devote my life to Christian service. See," he said, lowering his voice, "I got this heart condition. I may not live long. When you know it's something wrong with you and you may not live long, well then, lady . . ." He paused, with his mouth open, and stared at her.

50   He and Joy had the same condition! She knew that her eyes were filling with tears but she collected herself quickly and murmured, "Won't you stay for dinner? We'd love to have you!" and was sorry the instant she heard herself say it.

"Yes mam," he said in an abashed voice, "I would sher love to do that!"

Joy had given him one look on being introduced to him and then throughout the meal had not glanced at him again. He had addressed several remarks to her, which she had pretended not to hear. Mrs. Hopewell could not understand deliberate rudeness, although she lived with it, and she felt she had always to overflow with hospitality to make up for Joy's lack of courtesy. She urged him to talk about himself and he did. He said he was the seventh child of twelve and that his father had been crushed under a tree when he himself was eight year old. He had been crushed very badly, in fact, almost cut in two and was practically not recognizable. His mother had got along the best she could by hard working and she had always seen that her children went to Sunday School and that they read the Bible every evening. He was now nineteen year old and he had been selling Bibles for four months. In that time he had sold seventy-seven Bibles and had the promise of two more sales. He wanted to become a missionary because he thought that was the way you could do most for people. "He who losest his life shall find it," he said simply and he was so sincere, so genuine and earnest that Mrs. Hopewell would not for the world have smiled. He prevented his peas from sliding onto the table by blocking them with a piece of bread which he later cleaned his plate with. She could see Joy observing sidewise how he handled his knife and fork and she saw too that every few minutes, the boy would dart a keen appraising glance at the girl as if he were trying to attract her attention.

After dinner Joy cleared the dishes off the table and disappeared and Mrs. Hopewell was left to talk with him. He told her again about his childhood and his father's accident and about various things that had happened to him. Every five minutes or so she would stifle a yawn. He sat for two hours until finally she told him she must go because she had an appointment in town. He packed his Bibles and thanked her and prepared to leave, but in the doorway he stopped and wrung her hand and said that not on any of his trips had he met a lady as nice as her and he asked if he could come again. She had said she would always be happy to see him.

Joy had been standing in the road, apparently looking at something in the distance, when he came down the steps toward her, bent to the side with his heavy valise. He stopped where she was standing and confronted her directly. Mrs. Hopewell could not hear what he said but she trembled to think what Joy would say to him. She could see that after a minute Joy said something and that then the boy began to speak again, making an excited gesture with his free hand. After a minute Joy said something else at which the boy began to speak once more. Then to her amazement, Mrs. Hopewell saw the two of them walk off together, toward the gate. Joy had walked all the way to the gate with him and Mrs. Hopewell could not imagine what they had said to each other, and she had not yet dared to ask.

Mrs. Freeman was insisting upon her attention. She had moved from the refrigerator to the heater so that Mrs. Hopewell had to turn and face her in order to seem to be listening. "Glynese gone out with Harvey Hill again last night," she said. "She had this sty."

"Hill," Mrs. Hopewell said absently, "is that the one who works in the garage?"

55

"Nome,[4] he's the one that goes to chiropracter school," Mrs. Freeman said. "She had this sty. Been had it two days. So she says when he brought her in the other night he says, 'Lemme get rid of that sty for you,' and she says, 'How?' and he says, 'You just lay yourself down acrost the seat of that car and I'll show you.' So she done it and he popped her neck. Kept on a-popping it several times until she made him quit. This morning," Mrs. Freeman said, "she ain't got no sty. She ain't got no traces of a sty."

"I never heard of that before," Mrs. Hopewell said.

"He ast her to marry him before the Ordinary,"[5] Mrs. Freeman went on, "and she told him she wasn't going to be married in no *office*."

60 "Well, Glynese is a fine girl," Mrs. Hopewell said. "Glynese and Carramae are both fine girls."

"Carramae said when her and Lyman was married Lyman said it sure felt sacred to him. She said he said he wouldn't take five hundred dollars for being married by a preacher."

"How much would he take?" the girl asked from the stove.

"He said he wouldn't take five hundred dollars," Mrs. Freeman repeated.

"Well we all have work to do," Mrs. Hopewell said.

65 "Lyman said it just felt more sacred to him," Mrs. Freeman said. "The doctor wants Carramae to eat prunes. Says instead of medicine. Says them cramps is coming from pressure. You know where I think it is?"

"She'll be better in a few weeks," Mrs. Hopewell said.

"In the tube,"[6] Mrs. Freeman said. "Else she wouldn't be as sick as she is."

Hulga had cracked her two eggs into a saucer and was bringing them to the table along with a cup of coffee that she had filled too full. She sat down carefully and began to eat, meaning to keep Mrs. Freeman there by questions if for any reason she showed an inclination to leave. She could perceive her mother's eye on her. The first round-about question would be about the Bible salesman and she did not wish to bring it on. "How did he pop her neck?" she asked.

Mrs. Freeman went into a description of how he had popped her neck. She said he owned a '55 Mercury but that Glynese said she would rather marry a man with only a '36 Plymouth who would be married by a preacher. The girl asked what if he had a '32 Plymouth and Mrs. Freeman said what Glynese had said was a '36 Plymouth.

70 Mrs. Hopewell said there were not many girls with Glynese's common sense. She said what she admired in those girls was their common sense. She said that reminded her that they had had a nice visitor yesterday, a young man selling Bibles. "Lord," she said, "he bored me to death but he was so sincere and genuine I couldn't be rude to him. He was just good country people, you know," she said, "—just the salt of the earth."

"I seen him walk up," Mrs. Freeman said, "and then later—I seen him walk off," and Hulga could feel the slight shift in her voice, the slight insinuation, that he had not walked off alone, had he? Her face remained expressionless but the color rose into her neck and she seemed to swallow it down with the next

---

4. Contraction of "No, ma'am."

5. That is, a legal official, in the local county courthouse.

6. That is, an ectopic or tubal pregnancy outside the uterus, a life-threatening condition for both mother and fetus.

spoonful of egg. Mrs. Freeman was looking at her as if they had a secret together.

"Well, it takes all kinds of people to make the world go 'round," Mrs. Hopewell said. "It's very good we aren't all alike."

"Some people are more alike than others," Mrs. Freeman said.

Hulga got up and stumped, with about twice the noise that was necessary, into her room and locked the door. She was to meet the Bible salesman at ten o'clock at the gate. She had thought about it half the night. She had started thinking of it as a great joke and then she had begun to see profound implications in it. She had lain in bed imagining dialogues for them that were insane on the surface but that reached below to depths that no Bible salesman would be aware of. Their conversation yesterday had been of this kind.

He had stopped in front of her and had simply stood there. His face was bony 75 and sweaty and bright, with a little pointed nose in the center of it, and his look was different from what it had been at the dinner table. He was gazing at her with open curiosity, with fascination, like a child watching a new fantastic animal at the zoo, and he was breathing as if he had run a great distance to reach her. His gaze seemed somehow familiar but she could not think where she had been regarded with it before. For almost a minute he didn't say anything. Then on what seemed an insuck of breath, he whispered, "You ever ate a chicken that was two days old?"

The girl looked at him stonily. He might have just put this question up for consideration at the meeting of a philosophical association. "Yes," she presently replied as if she had considered it from all angles.

"It must have been mighty small!" he said triumphantly and shook all over with little nervous giggles, getting very red in the face, and subsiding finally into his gaze of complete admiration, while the girl's expression remained exactly the same.

"How old are you?" he asked softly.

She waited some time before she answered. Then in a flat voice she said, "Seventeen."

His smiles came in succession like waves breaking on the surface of a little lake. 80 "I see you got a wooden leg," he said. "I think you're brave. I think you're real sweet."

The girl stood blank and solid and silent.

"Walk to the gate with me," he said. "You're a brave sweet little thing and I liked you the minute I seen you walk in the door."

Hulga began to move forward.

"What's your name?" he asked, smiling down on the top of her head.

"Hulga," she said.   85

"Hulga," he murmured, "Hulga. Hulga. I never heard of anybody name Hulga before. You're shy, aren't you, Hulga?" he asked.

She nodded, watching his large red hand on the handle of the giant valise.

"I like girls that wear glasses," he said. "I think a lot. I'm not like these people that a serious thought don't ever enter their heads. It's because I may die."

"I may die too," she said suddenly and looked up at him. His eyes were very small and brown, glittering feverishly.

"Listen," he said, "don't you think some people was meant to meet on account 90 of what all they got in common and all? Like they both think serious thoughts and all?" He shifted the valise to his other hand so that the hand nearest her was free. He caught hold of her elbow and shook it a little. "I don't work on Saturday," he said. "I like to walk in the woods and see what Mother Nature is wearing. O'er the hills and far away. Pic-nics and things. Couldn't we go on a pic-nic tomorrow? Say yes, Hulga," he said and gave her a dying look as if he felt his insides about to drop out of him. He had even seemed to sway slightly toward her.

During the night she had imagined that she seduced him. She imagined that the two of them walked on the place until they came to the storage barn beyond the two back fields and there, she imagined, that things came to such a pass that she very easily seduced him and that then, of course, she had to reckon with his remorse. True genius can get an idea across even to an inferior mind. She imagined that she took his remorse in hand and changed it into a deeper understanding of life. She took all his shame away and turned it into something useful.

She set off for the gate at exactly ten o'clock, escaping without drawing Mrs. Hopewell's attention. She didn't take anything to eat, forgetting that food is usually taken on a picnic. She wore a pair of slacks and a dirty white shirt, and as an afterthought, she had put some Vapex[7] on the collar of it since she did not own any perfume. When she reached the gate no one was there.

She looked up and down the empty highway and had the furious feeling that she had been tricked, that he had only meant to make her walk to the gate after the idea of him. Then suddenly he stood up, very tall, from behind a bush on the opposite embankment. Smiling, he lifted his hat which was new and wide-brimmed. He had not worn it yesterday and she wondered if he had bought it for the occasion. It was toast-colored with a red and white band around it and was slightly too large for him. He stepped from behind the bush still carrying the black valise. He had on the same suit and the same yellow socks sucked down in his shoes from walking. He crossed the highway and said, "I knew you'd come!"

The girl wondered acidly how he had known this. She pointed to the valise and asked, "Why did you bring your Bibles?"

95 He took her elbow, smiling down on her as if he could not stop. "You can never tell when you'll need the word of God, Hulga," he said. She had a moment in which she doubted that this was actually happening and then they began to climb the embankment. They went down into the pasture toward the woods. The boy walked lightly by her side, bouncing on his toes. The valise did not seem to be heavy today; he even swung it. They crossed half the pasture without saying anything and then, putting his hand easily on the small of her back, he asked softly, "Where does your wooden leg join on?"

She turned an ugly red and glared at him and for an instant the boy looked abashed. "I didn't mean you no harm," he said. "I only meant you're so brave and all. I guess God takes care of you."

"No," she said, looking forward and walking fast, "I don't even believe in God."

At this he stopped and whistled. "No!" he exclaimed as if he were too astonished to say anything else.

7. Brand of nasal decongestant.

She walked on and in a second he was bouncing at her side, fanning with his hat. "That's very unusual for a girl," he remarked, watching her out of the corner of his eye. When they reached the edge of the wood, he put his hand on her back again and drew her against him without a word and kissed her heavily.

The kiss, which had more pressure than feeling behind it, produced that 100 extra surge of adrenaline in the girl that enables one to carry a packed trunk out of a burning house, but in her, the power went at once to the brain. Even before he released her, her mind, clear and detached and ironic anyway, was regarding him from a great distance, with amusement but with pity. She had never been kissed before and she was pleased to discover that it was an unexceptional experience and all a matter of the mind's control. Some people might enjoy drain water if they were told it was vodka. When the boy, looking expectant but uncertain, pushed her gently away, she turned and walked on, saying nothing as if such business, for her, were common enough.

He came along panting at her side, trying to help her when he saw a root that she might trip over. He caught and held back the long swaying blades of thorn vine until she had passed beyond them. She led the way and he came breathing heavily behind her. Then they came out on a sunlit hillside, sloping softly into another one a little smaller. Beyond, they could see the rusted top of the old barn where the extra hay was stored.

The hill was sprinkled with small pink weeds. "Then you ain't saved?" he asked suddenly, stopping.

The girl smiled. It was the first time she had smiled at him at all. "In my economy," she said, "I'm saved and you are damned but I told you I didn't believe in God."

Nothing seemed to destroy the boy's look of admiration. He gazed at her now as if the fantastic animal at the zoo had put its paw through the bars and given him a loving poke. She thought he looked as if he wanted to kiss her again and she walked on before he had the chance.

"Ain't there somewheres we can sit down sometime?" he murmured, his 105 voice softening toward the end of the sentence.

"In that barn," she said.

They made for it rapidly as if it might slide away like a train. It was a large two-story barn, cool and dark inside. The boy pointed up the ladder that led into the loft and said, "It's too bad we can't go up there."

"Why can't we?" she asked.

"Yer leg," he said reverently.

The girl gave him a contemptuous look and putting both hands on the ladder, 110 she climbed it while he stood below, apparently awestruck. She pulled herself expertly through the opening and then looked down at him and said, "Well, come on if you're coming," and he began to climb the ladder, awkwardly bringing the suitcase with him.

"We won't need the Bible," she observed.

"You never can tell," he said, panting. After he had got into the loft, he was a few seconds catching his breath. She had sat down in a pile of straw. A wide sheath of sunlight, filled with dust particles, slanted over her. She lay back against a bale, her face turned away, looking out the front opening of the barn where hay was thrown from a wagon into the loft. The two pink-speckled hillsides lay back against a dark ridge of woods. The sky was cloudless and cold blue. The boy dropped down by her side and put one arm under her and the other over her and began methodically kissing her face, making little noises like a fish. He did not remove his hat but it was pushed far enough back not to interfere. When her glasses got in his way, he took them off of her and slipped them into his pocket.

The girl at first did not return any of the kisses but presently she began to and after she had put several on his cheek, she reached his lips and remained there, kissing him again and again as if she were trying to draw all the breath out of him. His breath was clear and sweet like a child's and the kisses were sticky like a child's. He mumbled about loving her and about knowing when he first seen her that he loved her, but the mumbling was like the sleepy fretting of a child being put to sleep by his mother. Her mind, throughout this, never stopped or lost itself for a second to her feelings. "You ain't said you loved me none," he whispered finally, pulling back from her. "You got to say that."

She looked away from him off into the hollow sky and then down at a black ridge and then down farther into what appeared to be two green swelling lakes. She didn't realize he had taken her glasses but this landscape could not seem exceptional to her for she seldom paid any close attention to her surroundings.

115   "You got to say it," he repeated. "You got to say you love me."

She was always careful how she committed herself. "In a sense," she began, "if you use the word loosely, you might say that. But it's not a word I use. I don't have illusions. I'm one of those people who see *through* to nothing."

The boy was frowning. "You got to say it. I said it and you got to say it," he said.

The girl looked at him almost tenderly. "You poor baby," she murmured. "It's just as well you don't understand," and she pulled him by the neck, face-down, against her. "We are all damned," she said, "but some of us have taken off our blindfolds and see that there's nothing to see. It's a kind of salvation."

The boy's astonished eyes looked blankly through the ends of her hair. "Okay," he almost whined, "but do you love me or don'tcher?"

120   "Yes," she said and added, "in a sense. But I must tell you something. There mustn't be anything dishonest between us." She lifted his head and looked him in the eye. "I am thirty years old," she said. "I have a number of degrees."

The boy's look was irritated but dogged. "I don't care," he said. "I don't care a thing about what all you done. I just want to know if you love me or don'tcher?" and he caught her to him and wildly planted her face with kisses until she said, "Yes, yes."

"Okay then," he said, letting her go. "Prove it."

She smiled, looking dreamily out on the shifty landscape. She had seduced him without even making up her mind to try. "How?" she asked, feeling that he should be delayed a little.

He leaned over and put his lips to her ear. "Show me where your wooden leg joins on," he whispered.

125   The girl uttered a sharp little cry and her face instantly drained of color. The obscenity of the suggestion was not what shocked her. As a child she had sometimes been subject to feelings of shame but education had removed the last traces of that as a good surgeon scrapes for cancer; she would no more have felt it over what he was asking than she would have believed in his Bible. But she

was as sensitive about the artificial leg as a peacock about his tail. No one ever touched it but her. She took care of it as someone else would his soul, in private and almost with her own eyes turned away. "No," she said.

"I known it," he muttered, sitting up. "You're just playing me for a sucker."

"Oh no no!" she cried. "It joins on at the knee. Only at the knee. Why do you want to see it?"

The boy gave her a long penetrating look. "Because," he said, "it's what makes you different. You ain't like anybody else."

She sat staring at him. There was nothing about her face or her round freezing-blue eyes to indicate that this had moved her; but she felt as if her heart had stopped and left her mind to pump her blood. She decided that for the first time in her life she was face to face with real innocence. This boy, with an instinct that came from beyond wisdom, had touched the truth about her. When after a minute, she said in a hoarse high voice, "All right," it was like surrendering to him completely. It was like losing her own life and finding it again, miraculously, in his.

Very gently he began to roll the slack leg up. The artificial limb, in a white   130
sock and brown flat shoe, was bound in a heavy material like canvas and ended in an ugly jointure where it was attached to the stump. The boy's face and his voice were entirely reverent as he uncovered it and said, "Now show me how to take it off and on."

She took it off for him and put it back on again and then he took it off himself, handling it as tenderly as if it were a real one. "See!" he said with a delighted child's face. "Now I can do it myself!"

"Put it back on," she said. She was thinking that she would run away with him and that every night he would take the leg off and every morning put it back on again. "Put it back on," she said.

"Not yet," he murmured, setting it on its foot out of her reach. "Leave it off for a while. You got me instead."

She gave a little cry of alarm but he pushed her down and began to kiss her again. Without the leg she felt entirely dependent on him. Her brain seemed to have stopped thinking altogether and to be about some other function that it was not very good at. Different expressions raced back and forth over her face. Every now and then the boy, his eyes like two steel spikes, would glance behind him where the leg stood. Finally she pushed him off and said, "Put it back on me now."

"Wait," he said. He leaned the other way and pulled the valise toward him   135
and opened it. It had a pale blue spotted lining and there were only two Bibles in it. He took one of these out and opened the cover of it. It was hollow and contained a pocket flask of whiskey, a pack of cards, and a small blue box with printing on it. He laid these out in front of her one at a time in an evenly-spaced row, like one presenting offerings at the shrine of a goddess. He put the blue box in her hand. THIS PRODUCT TO BE USED ONLY FOR THE PREVENTION OF DISEASE, she read, and dropped it. The boy was unscrewing the top of the flask. He stopped and pointed, with a smile, to the deck of cards. It was not an ordinary deck but one with an obscene picture on the back of each card. "Take a swig," he said, offering her the bottle first. He held it in front of her, but like one mesmerized, she did not move.

Her voice when she spoke had an almost pleading sound. "Aren't you," she murmured, "aren't you just good country people?"

The boy cocked his head. He looked as if he were just beginning to understand that she might be trying to insult him. "Yeah," he said, curling his lip slightly, "but it ain't held me back none. I'm as good as you any day in the week."

"Give me my leg," she said.

He pushed it farther away with his foot. "Come on now, let's begin to have us a good time," he said coaxingly. "We ain't got to know one another good yet."

140 "Give me my leg!" she screamed and tried to lunge for it but he pushed her down easily.

"What's the matter with you all of a sudden?" he asked, frowning as he screwed the top on the flask and put it quickly back inside the Bible. "You just a while ago said you didn't believe in nothing. I thought you was some girl!"

Her face was almost purple. "You're a Christian!" she hissed. "You're a fine Christian! You're just like them all—say one thing and do another. You're a perfect Christian, you're . . ."

The boy's mouth was set angrily. "I hope you don't think," he said in a lofty indignant tone, "that I believe in that crap! I may sell Bibles but I know which end is up and I wasn't born yesterday and I know where I'm going!"

"Give me my leg!" she screeched. He jumped up so quickly that she barely saw him sweep the cards and the blue box into the Bible and throw the Bible into the valise. She saw him grab the leg and then she saw it for an instant slanted forlornly across the inside of the suitcase with a Bible at either side of its opposite ends. He slammed the lid shut and snatched up the valise and swung it down the hole and then stepped through himself.

145 When all of him had passed but his head, he turned and regarded her with a look that no longer had any admiration in it. "I've gotten a lot of interesting things," he said. "One time I got a woman's glass eye this way. And you needn't to think you'll catch me because Pointer ain't really my name. I use a different name at every house I call at and don't stay nowhere long. And I'll tell you another thing, Hulga," he said, using the name as if he didn't think much of it, "you ain't so smart. I been believing in nothing ever since I was born!" and then the toast-colored hat disappeared down the hole and the girl was left, sitting on the straw in the dusty sunlight. When she turned her churning face toward the opening, she saw his blue figure struggling successfully over the green speckled lake.

Mrs. Hopewell and Mrs. Freeman, who were in the back pasture, digging up onions, saw him emerge a little later from the woods and head across the meadow toward the highway. "Why, that looks like that nice dull young man that tried to sell me a Bible yesterday," Mrs. Hopewell said, squinting. "He must have been selling them to the Negroes back in there. He was so simple," she said, "but I guess the world would be better off if we were all that simple."

Mrs. Freeman's gaze drove forward and just touched him before he disappeared under the hill. Then she returned her attention to the evil-smelling onion shoot she was lifting from the ground. "Some can't be that simple," she said. "I know I never could."

1955

Everything That Rises Must Converge

Her doctor had told Julian's mother that she must lose twenty pounds on account of her blood pressure, so on Wednesday nights Julian had to take her downtown on the bus for a reducing class at the Y. The reducing class was designed for working girls over fifty, who weighed from 165 to 200 pounds. His mother was one of the slimmer ones, but she said ladies did not tell their age or weight. She would not ride the buses by herself at night since they had been integrated, and because the reducing class was one of her few pleasures, necessary for her health, and *free*, she said Julian could at least put himself out to take her, considering all she did for him. Julian did not like to consider all she did for him, but every Wednesday night he braced himself and took her.

She was almost ready to go, standing before the hall mirror, putting on her hat, while he, his hands behind him, appeared pinned to the door frame, waiting like Saint Sebastian for the arrows to begin piercing him.[1] The hat was new and had cost her seven dollars and a half. She kept saying, "Maybe I shouldn't have paid that for it. No, I shouldn't have. I'll take it off and return it tomorrow. I shouldn't have bought it."

Julian raised his eyes to heaven. "Yes, you should have bought it," he said. "Put it on and let's go." It was a hideous hat. A purple velvet flap came down on one side of it and stood up on the other; the rest of it was green and looked like a cushion with the stuffing out. He decided it was less comical than jaunty and pathetic. Everything that gave her pleasure was small and depressed him.

She lifted the hat one more time and set it down slowly on top of her head. Two wings of gray hair protruded on either side of her florid face, but her eyes, sky-blue, were as innocent and untouched by experience as they must have been when she was ten. Were it not that she was a widow who had struggled fiercely to feed and clothe and put him through school and who was supporting him still, "until he got on his feet," she might have been a little girl that he had to take to town.

"It's all right, it's all right," he said. "Let's go." He opened the door himself and started down the walk to get her going. The sky was a dying violet and the houses stood out darkly against it, bulbous liver-colored monstrosities of a uniform ugliness though no two were alike. Since this had been a fashionable neighborhood forty years ago, his mother persisted in thinking they did well to have an apartment in it. Each house had a narrow collar of dirt around it in which sat, usually, a grubby child. Julian walked with his hands in his pockets, his head down and thrust forward and his eyes glazed with the determination to make himself completely numb during the time he would be sacrificed to her pleasure.

The door closed and he turned to find the dumpy figure, surmounted by the atrocious hat, coming toward him. "Well," she said, "you only live once and paying a little more for it, I at least won't meet myself coming and going."

---

1. Discovered to be a Christian, Sebastian, a Roman commander in Milan, was tied to a tree, shot with arrows, and left for dead. (He recovered, but when he reasserted his faith he was clubbed to death.)

"Some day I'll start making money," Julian said gloomily—he knew he never would—"and you can have one of those jokes whenever you take the fit." But first they would move. He visualized a place where the nearest neighbors would be three miles away on either side.

"I think you're doing fine," she said, drawing on her gloves. "You've only been out of school a year. Rome wasn't built in a day."

She was one of the few members of the Y reducing class who arrived in hat and gloves and who had a son who had been to college. "It takes time," she said, "and the world is in such a mess. This hat looked better on me than any of the others, though when she brought it out I said, 'Take that thing back. I wouldn't have it on my head,' and she said, 'Now wait till you see it on,' and when she put it on me, I said, 'We-ull,' and she said, 'If you ask me, that hat does something for you and you do something for the hat, and besides,' she said, 'with that hat, you won't meet yourself coming and going.'"

10   Julian thought he could have stood his lot better if she had been selfish, if she had been an old hag who drank and screamed at him. He walked along, saturated in depression, as if in the midst of his martyrdom he had lost his faith. Catching sight of his long, hopeless, irritated face, she stopped suddenly with a grief-stricken look, and pulled back on his arm. "Wait on me," she said. "I'm going back to the house and take this thing off and tomorrow I'm going to return it. I was out of my head. I can pay the gas bill with that seven-fifty."

He caught her arm in a vicious grip. "You are not going to take it back," he said. "I like it."

"Well," she said, "I don't think I ought . . ."

"Shut up and enjoy it," he muttered, more depressed than ever.

"With the world in the mess it's in," she said, "it's a wonder we can enjoy anything. I tell you, the bottom rail is on the top."

15   Julian sighed.

"Of course," she said, "if you know who you are, you can go anywhere." She said this every time he took her to the reducing class. "Most of them in it are not our kind of people," she said, "but I can be gracious to anybody. I know who I am."

"They don't give a damn for your graciousness," Julian said savagely. "Knowing who you are is good for one generation only. You haven't the foggiest idea where you stand now or who you are."

She stopped and allowed her eyes to flash at him. "I most certainly do know who I am," she said, "and if you don't know who you are, I'm ashamed of you."

"Oh hell," Julian said.

20   "Your great-grandfather was a former governor of this state," she said. "Your grandfather was a prosperous landowner. Your grandmother was a Godhigh."

"Will you look around you," he said tensely, "and see where you are now?" and he swept his arm jerkily out to indicate the neighborhood, which the growing darkness at least made less dingy.

"You remain what you are," she said. "Your great-grandfather had a plantation and two hundred slaves."

"There are no more slaves," he said irritably.

"They were better off when they were," she said. He groaned to see that she was off on that topic. She rolled onto it every few days like a train on an open track. He knew every stop, every junction, every swamp along the way, and knew the exact point at which her conclusion would roll majestically into the station: "It's ridiculous. It's simply not realistic. They should rise, yes, but on their own side of the fence."

"Let's skip it," Julian said.   25

"The ones I feel sorry for," she said, "are the ones that are half white. They're tragic."

"Will you skip it?"

"Suppose we were half white. We would certainly have mixed feelings."

"I have mixed feelings now," he groaned.

"Well let's talk about something pleasant," she said. "I remember going to   30
Grandpa's when I was a little girl. Then the house had double stairways that went up to what was really the second floor—all the cooking was done on the first. I used to like to stay down in the kitchen on account of the way the walls smelled. I would sit with my nose pressed against the plaster and take deep breaths. Actually the place belonged to the Godhighs but your grandfather Chestny paid the mortgage and saved it for them. They were in reduced circumstances," she said, "but reduced or not, they never forgot who they were."

"Doubtless that decayed mansion reminded them," Julian muttered. He never spoke of it without contempt or thought of it without longing. He had seen it once when he was a child before it had been sold. The double stairways had rotted and been torn down. Negroes were living in it. But it remained in his mind as his mother had known it. It appeared in his dreams regularly. He would stand on the wide porch, listening to the rustle of oak leaves, then wander through the high-ceilinged hall into the parlor that opened onto it and gaze at the worn rugs and faded draperies. It occurred to him that it was he, not she, who could have appreciated it. He preferred its threadbare elegance to anything he could name and it was because of it that all the neighborhoods they had lived in had been a torment to him—whereas she had hardly known the difference. She called her insensitivity "being adjustable."

"And I remember the old darky who was my nurse, Caroline. There was no better person in the world. I've always had a great respect for my colored friends," she said. "I'd do anything in the world for them and they'd . . ."

"Will you for God's sake get off that subject?" Julian said. When he got on a bus by himself, he made it a point to sit down beside a Negro, in reparation as it were for his mother's sins.

"You're mighty touchy tonight," she said. "Do you feel all right?"

"Yes I feel all right," he said. "Now lay off."   35

She pursed her lips. "Well, you certainly are in a vile humor," she observed. "I just won't speak to you at all."

They had reached the bus stop. There was no bus in sight and Julian, his hands still jammed in his pockets and his head thrust forward, scowled down the empty street. The frustration of having to wait on the bus as well as ride on it began to creep up his neck like a hot hand. The presence of his mother was borne in upon him as she gave a pained sigh. He looked at her bleakly. She was holding herself very erect under the preposterous hat, wearing it like a banner of her imaginary dignity. There was in him an evil urge to break her spirit. He suddenly unloosened his tie and pulled it off and put it in his pocket.

She stiffened. "Why must you look like *that* when you take me to town?" she said. "Why must you deliberately embarrass me?"

"If you'll never learn where you are," he said, "you can at least learn where I am."

40   "You look like a—thug," she said.

"Then I must be one," he murmured.

"I'll just go home," she said. "I will not bother you. If you can't do a little thing like that for me . . ."

Rolling his eyes upward, he put his tie back on. "Restored to my class," he muttered. He thrust his face toward her and hissed, "True culture is in the mind, the *mind*," he said, and tapped his head, "the mind."

"It's in the heart," she said, "and in how you do things and how you do things is because of who you *are*."

45   "Nobody in the damn bus cares who you are."

"I care who I am," she said icily.

The lighted bus appeared on top of the next hill and as it approached, they moved out into the street to meet it. He put his hand under her elbow and hoisted her up on the creaking step. She entered with a little smile, as if she were going into a drawing room where everyone had been waiting for her. While he put in the tokens, she sat down on one of the broad front seats for three which faced the aisle. A thin woman with protruding teeth and long yellow hair was sitting on the end of it. His mother moved up beside her and left room for Julian beside herself. He sat down and looked at the floor across the aisle where a pair of thin feet in red and white canvas sandals were planted.

His mother immediately began a general conversation meant to attract anyone who felt like talking. "Can it get any hotter?" she said and removed from her purse a folding fan, black with a Japanese scene on it, which she began to flutter before her.

"I reckon it might could," the woman with the protruding teeth said, "but I know for a fact my apartment couldn't get no hotter."

50   "It must get the afternoon sun," his mother said. She sat forward and looked up and down the bus. It was half filled. Everybody was white. "I see we have the bus to ourselves," she said. Julian cringed.

"For a change," said the woman across the aisle, the owner of the red and white canvas sandals. "I come on one the other day and they were thick as fleas—up front and all through."

"The world is in a mess everywhere," his mother said. "I don't know how we've let it get in this fix."

"What gets my goat is all those boys from good families stealing automobile tires," the woman with the protruding teeth said. "I told my boy, I said you may not be rich but you been raised right and if I ever catch you in any such mess, they can send you on to the reformatory. Be exactly where you belong."

"Training tells," his mother said. "Is your boy in high school?"

55   "Ninth grade," the woman said.

"My son just finished college last year. He wants to write but he's selling typewriters until he gets started," his mother said.

The woman leaned forward and peered at Julian. He threw her such a malevolent look that she subsided against the seat. On the floor across the aisle there was an abandoned newspaper. He got up and got it and opened it out in front of him. His mother discreetly continued the conversation in a lower tone but the woman across the aisle said in a loud voice, "Well that's nice. Selling typewriters is close to writing. He can go right from one to the other."

"I tell him," his mother said, "that Rome wasn't built in a day."

Behind the newspaper Julian was withdrawing into the inner compartment of his mind where he spent most of his time. This was a kind of mental bubble in which he established himself when he could not bear to be a part of what was going on around him. From it he could see out and judge but in it he was safe from any kind of penetration from without. It was the only place where he felt free of the general idiocy of his fellows. His mother had never entered it but from it he could see her with absolute clarity.

The old lady was clever enough and he thought that if she had started from any of the right premises, more might have been expected of her. She lived according to the laws of her own fantasy world, outside of which he had never seen her set foot. The law of it was to sacrifice herself for him after she had first created the necessity to do so by making a mess of things. If he had permitted her sacrifices, it was only because her lack of foresight had made them necessary. All of her life had been a struggle to act like a Chestny without the Chestny goods, and to give him everything she thought a Chestny ought to have; but since, said she, it was fun to struggle, why complain? And when you had won, as she had won, what fun to look back on the hard times! He could not forgive her that she had enjoyed the struggle and that she thought *she* had won.

What she meant when she said she had won was that she had brought him up successfully and had sent him to college and that he had turned out so well—good looking (her teeth had gone unfilled so that his could be straightened), intelligent (he realized he was too intelligent to be a success), and with a future ahead of him (there was of course no future ahead of him). She excused his gloominess on the grounds that he was still growing up and his radical ideas on his lack of practical experience. She said he didn't yet know a thing about "life," that he hadn't even entered the real world—when already he was as disenchanted with it as a man of fifty.

The further irony of all this was that in spite of her, he had turned out so well. In spite of going to only a third-rate college, he had, on his own initiative, come out with a first-rate education; in spite of growing up dominated by a small mind, he had ended up with a large one; in spite of all her foolish views, he was free of prejudice and unafraid to face facts. Most miraculous of all, instead of being blinded by love for her as she was for him, he had cut himself emotionally free of her and could see her with complete objectivity. He was not dominated by his mother.

The bus stopped with a sudden jerk and shook him from his meditation. A woman from the back lurched forward with little steps and barely escaped falling in his newspaper as she righted herself. She got off and a large Negro got on. Julian kept his paper lowered to watch. It gave him a certain satisfaction to see injustice in daily operation. It confirmed his view that with a few exceptions there was no one worth knowing within a radius of three hundred miles. The Negro was well dressed and carried a briefcase. He looked around and then sat down on the other end of the seat where the woman with the red and white canvas sandals was sitting. He immediately unfolded a newspaper and obscured himself behind it. Julian's mother's elbow at once prodded insistently into his ribs. "Now you see why I won't ride on these buses by myself," she whispered.

The woman with the red and white canvas sandals had risen at the same time the Negro sat down and had gone further back in the bus and taken the seat of the woman who had got off. His mother leaned forward and cast her an approving look.

65   Julian rose, crossed the aisle, and sat down in the place of the woman with the canvas sandals. From this position, he looked serenely across at his mother. Her face had turned an angry red. He stared at her, making his eyes the eyes of a stranger. He felt his tension suddenly lift as if he had openly declared war on her.

He would have liked to get in conversation with the Negro and to talk with him about art or politics or any subject that would be above the comprehension of those around them, but the man remained entrenched behind his paper. He was either ignoring the change of seating or had never noticed it. There was no way for Julian to convey his sympathy.

His mother kept her eyes fixed reproachfully on his face. The woman with the protruding teeth was looking at him avidly as if he were a type of monster new to her.

"Do you have a light?" he asked the Negro.

Without looking away from his paper, the man reached in his pocket and handed him a packet of matches.

70   "Thanks," Julian said. For a moment he held the matches foolishly. A NO SMOKING sign looked down upon him from over the door. This alone would not have deterred him; he had no cigarettes. He had quit smoking some months before because he could not afford it. "Sorry," he muttered and handed back the matches. The Negro lowered the paper and gave him an annoyed look. He took the matches and raised the paper again.

His mother continued to gaze at him but she did not take advantage of his momentary discomfort. Her eyes retained their battered look. Her face seemed to be unnaturally red, as if her blood pressure had risen. Julian allowed no glimmer of sympathy to show on his face. Having got the advantage, he wanted desperately to keep it and carry it through. He would have liked to teach her a lesson that would last her a while, but there seemed no way to continue the point. The Negro refused to come out from behind his paper.

Julian folded his arms and looked stolidly before him, facing her but as if he did not see her, as if he had ceased to recognize her existence. He visualized a scene in which, the bus having reached their stop, he would remain in his seat and when she said, "Aren't you going to get off?" he would look at her as a stranger who had rashly addressed him. The corner they got off on was usually deserted, but it was well lighted and it would not hurt her to walk by herself the four blocks to the Y. He decided to wait until the time came and then decide whether or not he would let her get off by herself. He would have to be at the Y at ten to bring her back, but he could leave her wondering if he was going to show up. There was no reason for her to think she could always depend on him.

He retired again into the high-ceilinged room sparsely settled with large pieces of antique furniture. His soul expanded momentarily but then he became aware of his mother across from him and the vision shriveled. He studied her coldly. Her feet in little pumps dangled like a child's and did not quite reach the floor. She was training on him an exaggerated look of reproach. He felt completely detached from her. At that moment he could with pleasure have slapped her as he would have slapped a particularly obnoxious child in his charge.

He began to imagine various unlikely ways by which he could teach her a lesson. He might make friends with some distinguished Negro professor or lawyer and bring him home to spend the evening. He would be entirely justified but her blood pressure would rise to 300. He could not push her to the extent of making her have a stroke, and moreover, he had never been successful at making any Negro friends. He had tried to strike up an acquaintance on the bus with some of the better types, with ones that looked like professors or ministers or lawyers. One morning he had sat down next to a distinguished-looking dark brown man who had answered his questions with a sonorous solemnity but who had turned out to be an undertaker. Another day he had sat down beside a cigar-smoking Negro with a diamond ring on his finger, but after a few stilted pleasantries, the Negro had rung the buzzer and risen, slipping two lottery tickets into Julian's hand as he climbed over him to leave.

He imagined his mother lying desperately ill and his being able to secure only a Negro doctor for her. He toyed with that idea for a few minutes and then dropped it for a momentary vision of himself participating as a sympathizer in a sit-in demonstration. This was possible but he did not linger with it. Instead, he approached the ultimate horror. He brought home a beautiful suspiciously Negroid woman. Prepare yourself, he said. There is nothing you can do about it. This is the woman I've chosen. She's intelligent, dignified, even good, and she's suffered and she hasn't thought it *fun*. Now persecute us, go ahead and persecute us. Drive her out of here, but remember, you're driving me too. His eyes were narrowed and through the indignation he had generated, he saw his mother across the aisle, purple-faced, shrunken to the dwarf-like proportions of her moral nature, sitting like a mummy beneath the ridiculous banner of her hat.

He was tilted out of his fantasy again as the bus stopped. The door opened with a sucking hiss and out of the dark a large, gaily dressed, sullen-looking colored woman got on with a little boy. The child, who might have been four, had on a short plaid suit and a Tyrolean hat with a blue feather in it. Julian hoped that he would sit down beside him and that the woman would push in beside his mother. He could think of no better arrangement.

As she waited for her tokens, the woman was surveying the seating possibilities—he hoped with the idea of sitting where she was least wanted. There was something familiar-looking about her but Julian could not place what it was. She was a giant of a woman. Her face was set not only to meet opposition but to seek it out. The downward tilt of her large lower lip was like a warning sign: DON'T TAMPER WITH ME. Her bulging figure was encased in a green crepe dress and her feet overflowed in red shoes. She had on a hideous hat. A purple velvet flap came down on one side of it and stood up on the other; the rest of it was green and looked like a cushion with the stuffing out. She carried a mammoth red pocketbook that bulged throughout as if it were stuffed with rocks.

To Julian's disappointment, the little boy climbed up on the empty seat beside his mother. His mother lumped all children, black and white, into the

75

common category, "cute," and she thought little Negroes were on the whole cuter than little white children. She smiled at the little boy as he climbed on the seat.

Meanwhile the woman was bearing down upon the empty seat beside Julian. To his annoyance, she squeezed herself into it. He saw his mother's face change as the woman settled herself next to him and he realized with satisfaction that this was more objectionable to her than it was to him. Her face seemed almost gray and there was a look of dull recognition in her eyes, as if suddenly she had sickened at some awful confrontation. Julian saw that it was because she and the woman had, in a sense, swapped sons. Though his mother would not realize the symbolic significance of this, she would feel it. His amusement showed plainly on his face.

80   The woman next to him muttered something unintelligible to herself. He was conscious of a kind of bristling next to him, a muted growling like that of an angry cat. He could not see anything but the red pocketbook upright on the bulging green thighs. He visualized the woman as she had stood waiting for her tokens—the ponderous figure, rising from the red shoes upward over the solid hips, the mammoth bosom, the haughty face, to the green and purple hat.

His eyes widened.

The vision of the two hats, identical, broke upon him with the radiance of a brilliant sunrise. His face was suddenly lit with joy. He could not believe that Fate had thrust upon his mother such a lesson. He gave a loud chuckle so that she would look at him and see that he saw. She turned her eyes on him slowly. The blue in them seemed to have turned a bruised purple. For a moment he had an uncomfortable sense of her innocence, but it lasted only a second before principle rescued him. Justice entitled him to laugh. His grin hardened until it said to her as plainly as if he were saying aloud: Your punishment exactly fits your pettiness. This should teach you a permanent lesson.

Her eyes shifted to the woman. She seemed unable to bear looking at him and to find the woman preferable. He became conscious again of the bristling presence at his side. The woman was rumbling like a volcano about to become active. His mother's mouth began to twitch slightly at one corner. With a sinking heart, he saw incipient signs of recovery on her face and realized that this was going to strike her suddenly as funny and was going to be no lesson at all. She kept her eyes on the woman and an amused smile came over her face as if the woman were a monkey that had stolen her hat. The little Negro was looking up at her with large fascinated eyes. He had been trying to attract her attention for some time.

"Carver!" the woman said suddenly. "Come heah!"

85   When he saw that the spotlight was on him at last, Carver drew his feet up and turned himself toward Julian's mother and giggled.

"Carver!" the woman said. "You heah me? Come heah!"

Carver slid down from the seat but remained squatting with his back against the base of it, his head turned slyly around toward Julian's mother, who was smiling at him. The woman reached a hand across the aisle and snatched him to her. He righted himself and hung backwards on her knees, grinning at Julian's mother. "Isn't he cute?" Julian's mother said to the woman with the protruding teeth.

"I reckon he is," the woman said without conviction.

The Negress yanked him upright but he eased out of her grip and shot across the aisle and scrambled, giggling wildly, onto the seat beside his love.

"I think he likes me," Julian's mother said, and smiled at the woman. It was 90 the smile she used when she was being particularly gracious to an inferior. Julian saw everything was lost. The lesson had rolled off her like rain on a roof.

The woman stood up and yanked the little boy off the seat as if she were snatching him from contagion. Julian could feel the rage in her at having no weapon like his mother's smile. She gave the child a sharp slap across his leg. He howled once and then thrust his head into her stomach and kicked his feet against her shins. "Behave," she said vehemently.

The bus stopped and the Negro who had been reading the newspaper got off. The woman moved over and set the little boy down with a thump between herself and Julian. She held him firmly by the knee. In a moment he put his hands in front of his face and peeped at Julian's mother through his fingers.

"I see yoooooooo!" she said and put her hand in front of her face and peeped at him.

The woman slapped his hand down. "Quit yo' foolishness," she said, "before I knock the living Jesus out of you!"

Julian was thankful that the next stop was theirs. He reached up and pulled 95 the cord. The woman reached up and pulled it at the same time. Oh my God, he thought. He had the terrible intuition that when they got off the bus together, his mother would open her purse and give the little boy a nickel. The gesture would be as natural to her as breathing. The bus stopped and the woman got up and lunged to the front, dragging the child, who wished to stay on, after her. Julian and his mother got up and followed. As they neared the door, Julian tried to relieve her of her pocketbook.

"No," she murmured, "I want to give the little boy a nickel."

"No!" Julian hissed. "No!"

She smiled down at the child and opened her bag. The bus door opened and the woman picked him up by the arm and descended with him, hanging at her hip. Once in the street she set him down and shook him.

Julian's mother had to close her purse while she got down the bus step but as soon as her feet were on the ground, she opened it again and began to rummage inside. "I can't find but a penny," she whispered, "but it looks like a new one."

"Don't do it!" Julian said fiercely between his teeth. There was a streetlight 100 on the corner and she hurried to get under it so that she could better see into her pocketbook. The woman was heading off rapidly down the street with the child still hanging backward on her hand.

"Oh little boy!" Julian's mother called and took a few quick steps and caught up with them just beyond the lamppost. "Here's a bright new penny for you," and she held out the coin, which shone bronze in the dim light.

The huge woman turned and for a moment stood, her shoulders lifted and her face frozen with frustrated rage, and stared at Julian's mother. Then all at once she seemed to explode like a piece of machinery that had been given one ounce of pressure too much. Julian saw the black fist swing out with the red pocketbook. He shut his eyes and cringed as he heard the woman shout, "He don't take nobody's pennies!" When he opened his eyes, the woman was disappearing down the street with the little boy staring wide-eyed over her shoulder. Julian's mother was sitting on the sidewalk.

"I told you not to do that," Julian said angrily. "I told you not to do that!"

He stood over her for a minute, gritting his teeth. Her legs were stretched out in front of her and her hat was on her lap. He squatted down and looked her in the face. It was totally expressionless. "You got exactly what you deserved," he said. "Now get up."

105   He picked up her pocketbook and put what had fallen out back in it. He picked the hat up off her lap. The penny caught his eye on the sidewalk and he picked that up and let it drop before her eyes into the purse. Then he stood up and leaned over and held his hands out to pull her up. She remained immobile. He sighed. Rising above them on either side were black apartment buildings, marked with irregular rectangles of light. At the end of the block a man came out of a door and walked off in the opposite direction. "All right," he said, "suppose somebody happens by and wants to know why you're sitting on the sidewalk?"

She took the hand and, breathing hard, pulled heavily up on it and then stood for a moment, swaying slightly as if the spots of light in the darkness were circling around her. Her eyes, shadowed and confused, finally settled on his face. He did not try to conceal his irritation. "I hope this teaches you a lesson," he said. She leaned forward and her eyes raked his face. She seemed trying to determine his identity. Then, as if she found nothing familiar about him, she started off with a headlong movement in the wrong direction.

"Aren't you going on to the Y?" he asked.

"Home," she muttered.

"Well, are we walking?"

110   For answer she kept going. Julian followed along, his hands behind him. He saw no reason to let the lesson she had had go without backing it up with an explanation of its meaning. She might as well be made to understand what had happened to her. "Don't think that was just an uppity Negro woman," he said. "That was the whole colored race which will no longer take your condescending pennies. That was your black double. She can wear the same hat as you, and to be sure," he added gratuitously (because he thought it was funny), "it looked better on her than it did on you. What all this means," he said, "is that the old world is gone. The old manners are obsolete and your graciousness is not worth a damn." He thought bitterly of the house that had been lost for him. "You aren't who you think you are," he said.

She continued to plow ahead, paying no attention to him. Her hair had come undone on one side. She dropped her pocketbook and took no notice. He stooped and picked it up and handed it to her but she did not take it.

"You needn't act as if the world had come to an end," he said, "because it hasn't. From now on you've got to live in a new world and face a few realities for a change. Buck up," he said, "it won't kill you."

She was breathing fast.

"Let's wait on the bus," he said.

115   "Home," she said thickly.

"I hate to see you behave like this," he said. "Just like a child. I should be able to expect more of you." He decided to stop where he was and make her stop and wait for a bus. "I'm not going any farther," he said stopping. "We're going on the bus."

She continued to go on as if she had not heard him. He took a few steps and caught her arm and stopped her. He looked into her face and caught his breath. He was looking into a face he had never seen before. "Tell Grandpa to come get me," she said.

He stared, stricken.

"Tell Caroline to come get me," she said.

Stunned, he let her go and she lurched forward again, walking as if one   120 leg were shorter than the other. A tide of darkness seemed to be sweeping her from him. "Mother!" he cried. "Darling, sweetheart, wait!" Crumpling, she fell to the pavement. He dashed forward and fell at her side, crying, "Mamma, Mamma!" He turned her over. Her face was fiercely distorted. One eye, large and staring, moved slightly to the left as if it had become unmoored. The other remained fixed on him, raked his face again, found nothing and closed.

"Wait here, wait here!" he cried and jumped up and began to run for help toward a cluster of lights he saw in the distance ahead of him. "Help, help!" he shouted, but his voice was thin, scarcely a thread of sound. The lights drifted farther away the faster he ran and his feet moved numbly as if they carried him nowhere. The tide of darkness seemed to sweep him back to her, postponing from moment to moment his entry into the world of guilt and sorrow.

1961

Passages from Flannery O'Connor's Essays and Letters

ESSAYS[1]

From The Fiction Writer and His Country (1957)[2]

[W]hen I look at stories I have written I find that they are, for the most part, about people who are poor, who are afflicted in both mind and body, who have little—or at best a distorted—sense of spiritual purpose, and whose actions do not apparently give the reader a great assurance of the joy of life.

Yet how is this? For I am no disbeliever in spiritual purpose and no vague believer. I see from the standpoint of Christian orthodoxy. This means that for me the meaning of life is centered in our Redemption by Christ and what I see in the world I see in its relation to that. [. . .]

Some may blame preoccupation with the grotesque on the fact that here we have a Southern writer and that this is just the type of imagination that Southern life fosters. [. . . .] I find it hard to believe that what is observable behavior in one

---

1. All but the first of these selections are composites, edited from O'Connor manuscripts by Sally and Robert Fitzgerald and published (along with the first) in *Mystery and Manners: Occasional Prose.* Farrar, Straus & Giroux, 1969.
2. Originally published in *The Living Novel: A Symposium,* edited by Granville Hicks, Macmillan, 1957, pp. 157–64.

section can be entirely without parallel in another. At least, of late, Southern writers have had the opportunity of pointing out that none of us invented Elvis Presley and that that youth is himself probably less an occasion for concern than his popularity, which is not restricted to the Southern part of the country.

* * *

When you can assume that your audience holds the same beliefs you do, you can relax a little and use more normal means of talking to it; when you have to assume that it does not, then you have to make your vision apparent by shock— to the hard of hearing you shout, and for the almost-blind you draw large and startling figures.

From The Nature and Aim of Fiction (posthumously published in 1969)

The beginning of human knowledge is through the senses, and the fiction writer begins where human perception begins. He appeals through the senses, and you cannot appeal to the senses with abstractions.

Now the word *symbol* scares a good many people off, just as the word *art* does. They seem to feel that a symbol is some mysterious thing put in arbitrarily by the writer to frighten the common reader [. . .]. They seem to think that it is a way of saying something that you aren't actually saying, and so [. . .] they approach it as if it were a problem in algebra. Find *x*. And when they do find or think they find this abstraction, *x*, then they go off with an elaborate sense of satisfaction and the notion that they have "understood" the story. [. . .]

I think for the fiction writer himself, symbols are something he uses simply as a matter of course. You might say that these are details that, while having their essential place in the literal level of the story, operate in depth as well as on the surface, increasing the story in every direction.

From Writing Short Stories (posthumously published in 1969)

Nothing essential to the main experience can be left out of a short story. All the action has to be satisfactorily accounted for in terms of motivation, and there has to be a beginning, a middle, and an end, though not necessarily in that order.

* * *

People talk about the theme of a story as if the theme were like the string that a sack of chicken feed is tied with. They think that if you can pick out the theme, the way you pick the right thread in the chicken-feed sack, you can rip the story open and feed the chickens. But this is not the way meaning works in fiction.

When you can state the theme of a story, when you can separate it from the story itself, then you can be sure the story is not a very good one. The meaning of

Flannery O'Connor, 1952

a story has to be embodied in it, has to be made concrete in it. A story is a way to say something that can't be said any other way, and it takes every word in the story to say what the meaning is. You tell a story because a statement would be inadequate.

.   .   .   .

An idiom characterizes a society, and when you ignore the idiom, you are very likely ignoring the whole social fabric that could make a meaningful character. You can't cut characters off from their society and say much about them as individuals. You can't say anything meaningful about the mystery of a personality unless you put that personality in a believable and significant social context.

From On Her Own Work (posthumously published in 1969)

I often ask myself what makes a story work, and what makes it hold up as a story, and I have decided that it is probably some action, some gesture of a character that is unlike any other in the story, one which indicates where the real heart of the story lies. This would have to be an action or a gesture which was both totally right and totally unexpected; it would have to be one that was both in character and beyond character; it would have to suggest both the world and eternity. The action or gesture I'm talking about would have to be on the anagogical level, that is, the level which has to do with the Divine life and our participation in it. It would be a gesture that transcended any neat allegory that might have been intended or any pat moral categories a reader could make. It would be a gesture which somehow made contact with mystery.

.   .   .   .

[I]n my own stories I have found that violence is strangely capable of returning my characters to reality and preparing them to accept their moment of grace.

.   .   .   .

We hear many complaints about the prevalence of violence in modern fiction, and it is always assumed that this violence is a bad thing and meant to be an end in itself. With the serious writer, violence is never an end in itself. It is the extreme situation that best reveals what we are essentially [. . .].

From "Novelist and Believer" (written 1963; posthumously published in 1969)

Great fiction [. . .] is not simply an imitation of feeling. The good novelist not only finds a symbol for feeling, he finds a symbol and a way of lodging it which tells the intelligent reader whether this feeling is adequate or inadequate, whether it is moral or immoral, whether it is good or evil. And his theology, even in its most remote reaches, will have a direct bearing on this.

∗   ∗   ∗

The artist penetrates the concrete world in order to find at its depths the image of its source, the image of ultimate reality. This in no way hinders his perception of evil but rather sharpens it, for only when the natural world is seen as good does evil become intelligible as a destructive force and a necessary result of our freedom.

LETTERS[1]

To Louise and Tom Gossett,[2] 10 April 1961

I have just read a review of my book [*The Violent Bear It Away*], long and damming [sic], which says it don't give us hope and courage and that all novels should give us hope and courage. I think if the novel is to give us virtue the selection of hope and courage is rather arbitrary—why not charity, peace, patience, joy, benignity, long-suffering and fear of the Lord? Or faith? The fact of the matter is that the modern mind opposes courage to faith. It also demands that the novel provide us with gifts that only religion can give. I don't think the novel can offend against the truth, but I think its truths are more particular than general. But this is a large subject and I ain't no aesthetician.

To Roslyn Barnes,[3] 17 June 1961

Can you tell me if the statement: "everything that rises must converge" is a true proposition in physics? I can easily see its moral, historical and evolutionary significance, but I want to know if it is also a correct physical statement.

To John Hawkes,[4] 28 November 1961

You haven't convinced me that I write with the Devil's will or belong in the romantic tradition and I'm prepared to argue some more with you on this if I

1. None of the letters below is reproduced in full; each is an excerpt.
2. The Drs. Gossett were literary scholars; Thomas (1916–2005), a professor of English, was suspended from his position at Wesleyan College, in Macon, Georgia, for supporting racial integration. His best-known book is *Race: The History of an Idea in America* (1963, 1997).
3. Roslyn Barnes began a long correspondence and friendship with O'Connor while a student at O'Connor's alma mater, Georgia State College for Women (now Georgia College & State University) in Milledgeville.
4. American novelist and short-story writer (1925–98).

can remember where we left off at. I think the reason we can't agree on this is because there is a difference in our two devils. My Devil has a name, a history and a definite plan. His name is Lucifer, he's a fallen angel, his sin is pride, and his aim is the destruction of the Divine plan. Now I judge that your Devil is co-equal to God, not his creature: that pride is his virtue not his sin; and that his aim is not to destroy the Divine plan because there isn't any Divine plan to destroy. My Devil is objective and yours is subjective. You say one becomes "evil" when one leaves the herd. I say that depends entirely on what the herd is doing.

To "A," 9 December 1961

Some friends of mine in Texas wrote me that a friend of theirs went into a bookstore looking for a paperback copy of *A Good Man*. The clerk said, "We don't have that one but we have another by that author, called *The Bear That Ran Away With It*."[5] I foresee the trouble I am going to have with "Everything That Rises Must Converge"—"Every Rabbit That Rises Is a Sage."

To "A," 1 September 1963

The topical is poison. I got away with it in "Everything That Rises" but only because I say a plague on everybody's house as far as the race business goes.

CHRONOLOGY

1925	Born Mary Flannery O'Connor on March 25 to Roman Catholic parents of Irish descent in Savannah, Georgia, where she will attend Catholic schools.
1938	Moves with her parents briefly to Atlanta (where her father takes a new job), then, with her mother, to her mother's hometown of Milledgeville, where she attends Peabody High School.
1940	Increasingly ill with lupus (a debilitating autoimmune disease), O'Connor's father retires, joining his wife and daughter in Milledgeville.
1941	Father dies of lupus.
1942	Enrolls in three-year accelerated program at Georgia State College for Women, in Milledgeville (now Georgia College & State University).
1945	Earns BA and enrolls in the graduate journalism program at the University of Iowa but soon transfers to the Iowa Writers' Workshop, which has recently granted the country's first MFA degrees.
1946	Publishes her first short story, "The Geranium," in *Accent* magazine.
1947	Earns her MFA; wins Rinehart-Iowa Fiction Award.
1948	Accepted into the prestigious Yaddo artists' colony in Saratoga Springs, New York, where she moves in June.

5. The actual title of O'Connor's 1960 novel is *The Violent Bear It Away*.

1949   Moves briefly to a New York apartment, then to the Connecticut home of Sally and Robert Fitzgerald (a poet and eminent translator of classical literature).

1950   Diagnosed with lupus, receives intensive (and debilitating) steroid treatments.

1951   When her illness worsens, moves back in with her mother at Andalusia, the family farm near Milledgeville where she writes for three hours daily and raises chickens and peacocks.

1952   Publishes her first novel, *Wise Blood*; receives *Kenyon Review* fellowship.

1955   Publishes her first short-story collection, *A Good Man Is Hard to Find and Other Stories*.

1957   Receives an American Academy of Arts and Letters grant, her first O. Henry Award (for "Greenleaf"), and an Alumnae Achievement Award from her alma mater.

1958   Makes her only trip abroad, visiting, with her mother, London, Paris, Rome (where she has a private audience with Pope Pius XII), and Lourdes.

1959   Receives a Ford Foundation grant for literary accomplishment.

1960   Publishes second novel, *The Violent Bear It Away*.

1963   Receives second O. Henry Award for "Everything That Rises Must Converge" and an honorary doctorate from Smith College, in Massachusetts. Undergoes surgery for a fibroid tumor, reportedly hiding her manuscript-in-progress under her hospital pillow for fear she won't be allowed to continue working on it.

1964   Rehospitalized twice due to a postoperative kidney infection and reactivated lupus, falls into a coma before dying, of kidney failure, on August 3, age thirty-nine.

1965   Second short-story collection, *Everything That Rises Must Converge*, posthumously published. "Revelation" wins O. Henry Award.

1969   Sally and Robert Fitzgerald publish *Mystery and Manners: Occasional Prose*.

1971   *The Complete Stories of Flannery O'Connor* is published, winning the National Book Award for Fiction (1972).

1995   O'Connor's mother dies in Milledgeville, age ninety-nine.

CRITICAL EXCERPTS

MARY GORDON

From Flannery's Kiss (2004)[1]

I have been asked to speak at an academic conference devoted to Flannery O'Connor. It is taking place in her home town, Milledgeville, Georgia. I arrive

1. Mary Gordon, "Flannery's Kiss." *Michigan Quarterly Review*, no. 43, summer 2004, pp. 328–49. Unless otherwise indicated, all footnotes have been added by the editor.

in the middle of a session. One of the speakers is a young Jesuit. He talks about some letters of Flannery O'Connor's that were not included in Sally Fitzgerald's collection.[2] They were written in 1955, to a young Danish man who was a book salesman for her publisher, Harcourt Brace. The Jesuit reads the letters. They are girlish. If there are not triple exclamation points, there should be. She tells the Dane how much she enjoys his company. "If you were here we could talk for about a million years," she says. The Jesuit tracks the Dane down in Denmark. He is now an old man, but he remembers the encounter with Flannery vividly. He tells the Jesuit that he enjoyed Flannery's companionship very much and that one day when he'd taken her for a drive in the country, it occurs to him that she is a woman, and that she would like him to kiss her. When he does kiss her, the experience horrifies him. He says that Flannery did not know how to kiss. Whereas when he had kissed other women they had offered him soft lips, Flannery presented him with teeth. He remembered that she was chronically ill and he felt like he was kissing a skull. Worried that she was in love with him, he returned quite soon to Denmark. Six months later, he wrote her that he was engaged to be married. Flannery sat down upon receiving the letter and within a matter of days completed her story, "Good Country People," which is about a Bible salesman who is a fetishist of prosthetic devices and who steals a girl's wooden leg when she thinks she is seducing him. Flannery sends the story to the Dane and tells him not to think it's about him, even though the fetishist, whose name is Manley Pointer, is a Bible salesman and the Dane is a book salesman.

In a letter to a friend, Flannery says that the character she most identifies with is the girl whose wooden leg is stolen.

* * *

Flannery O'Connor represents two images of the artist, both of which suggest that the way I have lived my life means I cannot be a real artist.[3] The Catholic and the Romantic, both insisting on the inferiority of human connectedness, the superiority of artistic isolation. Among the least acceptable of human connections for the artist: the connection to one's children. When Faulkner's daughter complained that he didn't pay attention to her, he replied, "Whoever heard of Shakespeare's daughter?" Even Virginia Woolf only spoke of Shakespeare's sister.[4] Until very recently, no important woman writer has had children. I am the mother of a daughter and a son.

For a variety of reasons then, Flannery has for many years caused me to feel unworthy. She has for many years caused me to feel ashamed. And in revenge, the words come to me unbidden, "No one would say I don't know how to kiss."

* * *

2. All citations from Flannery O'Connor's letters are from *Flannery O'Connor: The Habit of Being: Letters Selected and with an Introduction by Sally Fitzgerald* (NY: Farrar, Straus, Giroux, 1979) [Gordon's note].

3. Gordon (b. 1949) is a novelist and memoirist, as well as a literary critic.

4. In her famous 1929 lecture/essay *A Room of One's Own*, Woolf imagines what might have happened had Shakespeare had a sister who yearned to be a writer.

Miraculously, Flannery got herself out of Milledgeville, a town that was once the state capital of Georgia, a town noted for its prison and its mental hospital, a town of fewer than ten thousand people not any of whom, perhaps, really understood her, to the Writers' Workshop at the University of Iowa. Having graduated from Iowa, she went to the writers' colony Yaddo, in Saratoga Springs, briefly to New York, and then to live with Sally and Robert Fitzgerald in their house in Connecticut. But then she became ill; she was diagnosed with lupus, the disease that had killed her father. She resigned herself to the life of an invalid. She resigned herself to being taken care of by her mother.

Andalusia, which is pronounced AnduLOOZia, not AndaluTHEEa, is a dairy farm on a gently sloping tract of land. The line of trees which finds its way into so many of O'Connor's stories is visible from the front porch, screened in, with many rockers, looking as if they belonged more properly on the front porch of a small hotel. Just inside the front door, your eye falls on a velvet rope, cordoning something off. It is Flannery's bedroom. I ask the curator if I can go behind the velvet ropes and he says no.

I have rarely seen a more uncomfortable room. Her bed is single, dark wooden, monastic. The desk is near the bed, so she could get to it easily in the days when walking was difficult for her. The bedspread and the drapes are a heavy ungiving blue. There is a black and white picture of the Sacred Heart, books in bookcases, some knickknacks on the mantle which I cannot see from the doorway across which the velvet rope stretches. Propped against the wall are Flannery's crutches, cruel-looking steel devices with semicircles where her arms might rest. The most famous picture of Flannery O'Connor catches her standing on the porch, leaning on her crutches. One of her peacocks stands beside her, a little to her left, on a lower porch step.

* * *

If Flannery had not been ill, would she have traveled? Met new people, had experiences that would have changed the quality of her work? She says in one of her letters: "I have never been anywhere but sick. In a sense sickness is a place, more instructive than a long trip to Europe, and it's always a place where there's no company, where nobody can follow. . . . The surface hereabouts has always been very flat. I come from a family where the only emotion respectable to show is irritation. In some this tendency produces hives, in others literature, in me both."

If she had traveled, if she had met new people, if she had been able to give and receive more affection (which she gives and receives in her letters, written from the house that she never leaves), would her work have changed?

Do we want that work changed?

* * *

She would deny that her stories are loveless. She would say that the love of God scalds, it does not comfort. Let us take her on her own terms. In her stories there is very little comfort. But there is also very little kindness from the author to her characters. And after reading her for a while, I become impatient at the partialness of her vision. At what is left out. Love. I can see the mocking spelling she might use for the word love. She might spell it *looove*. Or *lurv*.

O'Connor does not allow her characters to feel the pain of loss. They are denied the experience of grieving. I have often wondered if people are more comfortable with violence than with grief: violence is sharp, clear, bounded; grief can be eternal; it percolates and permutates. Its path is gradual and slow. It's the kind of thing that, as an artist, O'Connor can't do. [. . .] She is interested in the climactic moment, not in the consequences of the climax. She is interested in redemption, but not in forgiveness. Consider the vast tonal difference in the two words: *redemption* and *forgiveness*. [. . .] In Catholic sacramentology, sins can only be forgiven in the sacrament if the sinner asks forgiveness. As we all go on sinning, we must constantly be forgiven. Indeed re-forgiven. Redemption took place once in history; forgiveness must be relived.

In trying to understand my feelings about Flannery O'Connor, the best I can say is that I often do not like Flannery O'Connor, but I can't get over loving her. The woman and the work. I go back and back to her. The reason for that is something she would despise. I am drawn not only to Flannery O'Connor the writer, but to Flannery O'Connor the woman. The woman who lived the life I refused and was grateful not to have to live. But who lived it with purity and gallantry. With singleness of heart. With bravery and good humor. She is the good Catholic I can never be. And yet she made me feel there was a place for me, or for the likes of me.

ANN E. REUMAN

From Revolting Fictions: Flannery O'Connor's Letter to Her Mother (1993)[1]

In her letters, O'Connor sketches the portrait of Regina Cline O'Connor, who, though slight in build, possessed a commanding presence. Proud of her patrician family and immensely self-assured, Regina was more Cline than O'Connor, conscious of lineage, propriety, and appearance. [. . .] With proud reverence for the past, she hosted at the Cline House visitors who made the annual garden club pilgrimage to notable, historic homes in the community. When walking through the town center, she would be recognized for her social prominence before her daughter would be remembered for her nationally acclaimed literature. And, as manager of her house and affairs, she expected unquestioning observance of her rules, with gratitude for her generosity. [. . .] Attentive to appearances, Mrs. O'Connor checked extensions of herself—her house, her

1. Ann E. Reuman, "Revolting Fictions: Flannery O'Connor's Letter to Her Mother." *Papers on Language and Literature*, vol. 29, no. 2, 1993, pp. 197–214. The essay's bibliography has been edited.

daughter—as she checked herself. She displayed the Cline family portraits in her parlor, proud of their visible claim to an honorable heritage; [. . .] she tried to show her daughter to advantage, spotlighting her public awards and curtaining her less glamorous habits. Writing to the Fitzgeralds about her recent receipt of the Kenyon Fellowship awarded on the basis of her work on *Wise Blood* (her first novel, dedicated to her mother), O'Connor comments, "My mamma [sic] is getting a big bang out of notifying all the kin who didn't like the book that the Rockerfeller [sic] Foundation, etc. etc.—this very casual like on the back of Christmas cards. Money talks, she says, and the name Rockerfeller don't hurt a bit" (*Habit* 49). And in a later note regarding a television play of one of her stories, she remarks, "My mother has been collecting congratulations . . . all week like eggs in a basket" (207).

Yet, while she praised what was already publicly acclaimed, O'Connor's mother worked just as hard to repress the socially unacceptable in her daughter's writing and behavior, urging O'Connor not to publish near the reading populace of Millidgeville [sic] a story which she found objectionable from the local standpoint; clearly expressing her disapproval of Flannery's tendency to "make a spectacle" of herself by wearing adolescent clothes into her thirties; and tersely reminding her daughter that her language was a reflection on herself. As O'Connor reports in one of her letters in a seemingly offhand way, her mother once said, "You talk just like a nigger and someday you are going to be away from home and do it and people are going to wonder WHERE YOU CAME FROM" (148; O'Connor's emphasis).

Clearly, under the surface of controlled and witty letters in which Mrs. O'Connor appears to be as Sally Fitzgerald sees her, "relished and admired, joked with and about, altogether clearly loved" (Fitzgerald x) by her daughter, O'Connor hints at a darker and more complicated portrait. [. . .] Punctuating her letters with refrains of "You can't get ahead of mother" and "My parent is back at large," O'Connor hints at a domineering, invasive, and aloof mother whose presence "never contribute[d] to [O'Connor's] articulateness" ([*Habit*] 195).

O'Connor's recurrent bouts with lupus [. . .] redirected her course, first sending her back to Millidgeville for medical tests and ultimately returning her to her mother's home. [. . .] O'Connor found little escape from her mother's presence while living under the same roof. Bottled up by Southern codes of silence and Catholic respect for elders, and aggravated by dependence on her mother without hope of change in her status, O'Connor's adolescent resentment carried into adulthood, building in intensity and exploding into her fiction.

Clearly there is a change in tone, characterization, and focus in O'Connor's stories written after 1951 when she was forced to live with her mother and move to Andalusia. In her earlier works, O'Connor deals primarily with Georgia folks, often displaced by a move to the city, usually struggling against personal fears to assert themselves or gain affection. [. . .] In each of these stories, though the character has a fearful glimpse of his or her vulnerability and impotence, the action is minimal, the tone is subdued, and the focus is primarily on an individual protagonist. The shift from passive and personal experience to explosive interaction, from humility and withdrawal to angry and violent revelation, from timid attempts to win love to fierce refusal of it, marks an abrupt redirection in O'Connor's writing after her return home, as if to dramatize her mother's crippling influence on her life.

· · ·

Like the literal-minded mother in [O'Connor's short story] "The Enduring Chill" who wishes her son would go out and do work—real work, not writing— and who urges him to write something good like *Gone With the Wind*, Mrs. O'Connor, an inveterate subscriber to *Reader's Digest*, does not seem to appreciate her daughter's brand of writing. O'Connor's confession to a fellow writer tells much:

> The other day [my mother] asked me why I didn't try to write something that people liked instead of the kind of thing I do write. Do you think, she said, that you are really using the talent God gave you when you don't write something that a lot, a LOT, of people like? This always leaves me shaking and speechless, raises my blood pressure 140 degrees, etc. All I can ever say is, if you have to ask, you'll never know. (*Habit* 326)

[. . .] O'Connor may have written her stories for her mother, hiding the "letter to her parent" in her text, eager to have her mother find her private revelation yet protecting her from public embarrassment. As O'Connor suggested in several letters, her mother was her primary and most trying reader, preferring O'Connor's painting (which she felt she could understand) to her writing, and constantly falling asleep on her books.

Where relative passivity and emotional suicide fail to register with her mother, O'Connor lodges her discontent in more violent, boldly stroked stories, filled with troops of Flannerys and Reginas in a wild assortment of shapes, sizes, ages, and sexes, but always quite recognizable versions of the original pair. In "The Comforts of Home" and "Everything That Rises Must Converge," effeminate sons bristle against overpowering mothers.

· · ·

[I]n "Everything That Rises Must Converge," Julian Chestny, a thirty-year-old unappreciated writer, strikes out indirectly at his mother's ignorance, bigotry, and oppressive expectation of gratitude. In the portrait of the mother, O'Connor once again draws from material in her own life. [. . .]

[. . .] Unable either to communicate with his mother or break the tie that binds him, Julian—much like O'Connor in her fiction—retreats into his fantasy world. [. . .] Stating in one of her letters her annoyance with her mother's repeated "assault" on her bedroom, which she periodically would invade and clean, installing revolting curtains and changing her rug—an experience which O'Connor tellingly claimed made her feel "like she was being sawed in two without ether" (*Habit* 158–59)—O'Connor suggests that her "fiction," expressive of herself and unviolated by her mother's penchant for "tidiness," is the only "room" which she can preserve intact.

. . .

The recurrence in O'Connor's later fiction of these intolerable parents and murderous children struggling for articulation and dominance suggests an intense and urgent need expressible only in violent action—and in fiction. In one letter, O'Connor herself remarks, "Most of the violences carried to their logical conclusions in the stories manage to be warded off in fact here [at the dairy farm]—*though most of them exist in potentiality*" (198; emphasis added). [. . .]

That O'Connor saw herself in her fiction is clear. As she wrote to one correspondent, "My heroine already is, and is Hulga . . . a projection of myself into this kind of tragic comic action" (106).

WORKS CITED

Fitzgerald, Sally. Introduction. In O'Connor, *The Habit of Being.*
O'Connor, Flannery. *The Habit of Being: Letters.* Ed. Sally Fitzgerald. New York: Farrar, Straus & Giroux, 1979.

EILEEN POLLACK

From Flannery O'Connor and the New Criticism: A Response to Mark McGurl (2007)[1]

To writers who teach to earn their living, Flannery O'Connor has long represented the benefits that accrue to writers who refuse to teach (or, in O'Connor's case, are prevented from doing so by illness). Her continued exposure to irritating Southern matrons and Jesus-haunted backwoods preachers kept her fiction gritty and eccentric in ways that might have been impossible if she had remained in the academy.

However, as Mark McGurl so ably demonstrates, studying for two years at Iowa was enough to influence O'Connor's fiction for the rest of her life. Although legend would have it that she arrived in Iowa City fully formed as a writer,[2] then sat quietly in the back of her workshops except for the "occasional amused and shy smile at something absurd" (as Robert Giroux tells us in his introduction to the collected stories) (viii), McGurl wisely points out that the New Critical

1. Eileen Pollack, "Flannery O'Connor and the New Criticism." *American Literary History,* no. 19, 2007, pp. 546–56. Pollack's essay responded to another essay in the same journal issue: Mark McGurl's "Understanding Iowa: Flannery O'Connor, B.A., M.F.A." Unless otherwise indicated, all footnotes have been added by the editor.
2. O'Connor graduated with an MFA degree from the prestigious Iowa Writers' Workshop at the University of Iowa in 1947.

approach O'Connor absorbed from studying with Robert Penn Warren and reading the textbook/anthology he authored with Cleanth Brooks is evident in everything she ever published.[3]

· · ·

For O'Connor, the advice that she write what she know took the form of setting her stories in rural Georgia and centering each story on the thematic question of what it might take to get a sinner to recognize the central mysteries of Christianity. Her problem as an artist was how to write about such a theme for an audience composed largely of nonbelievers. Preaching or moralizing about her characters' sins would have been not only inartistic but ineffective. The advice that she show rather than tell was particularly well suited to her thematic concerns as a Christian because it would allow her to bring alive for her readers the spiritual struggles of characters unlike themselves, creating on the page the power of unfamiliar sacraments such as baptism and/or the operation of grace in the material world.[4]

In addition, she believed that the divine (the thematic, the expository, that which must be told) is immanent in the concrete details of the material world (that which can be shown). Just as the spirit is made flesh in the Word, just as God assumed the body of a man and suffered as humans suffered, so too the grand themes of Christianity can be embodied in the physical particulars of a flawed character's very human struggles against the devil. The fiction writer, O'Connor tells us in "The Teaching of Literature," "is concerned with mystery that is lived. He's concerned with ultimate mystery as we find it embodied in the concrete world of sense experience" (*Mystery* 125).

In the same way, O'Connor's obsessive use of the effaced third-person narrator was a choice that came not from her time at Iowa or a mindless adherence to some stricture laid down by Brooks and Warren but rather from the demands imposed by the Southern setting of her work, her thematic concerns as a believing Christian, and her friendship with the novelist Caroline Gordon.[5] [. . .] It is clear from O'Connor's letters that she sent nearly everything she ever wrote to Gordon for editing and that Gordon scolded her every time she lapsed from strict adherence to this limited third-person point of view.[6]

[. . .] O'Connor could not use first-person narrators because those narrators would have spoken in a thick rural Southern dialect that few readers would have understood or had the patience to decipher, just as Engel[7] could not understand O'Connor's speech when she showed up in his office to try to worm her way into his workshop. [. . .] O'Connor chose to rely on narrators who spoke

---

3. Novelist Robert Penn Warren (1905–89) and critic Cleanth Brooks (1906–94) collaborated on an influential series of essays and textbooks that helped lay the foundations for what came to be known as the New Criticism, which urged the importance of "close reading" and rejected the use of biography and secondary sources in literary studies.

4. See O'Connor, *Mystery*, 162 [Pollack's note].

5. American novelist Caroline Ferguson Gordon (1895–1981); like O'Connor, she was best known for her short stories and her Roman Catholicism.

6. See O'Connor, *Habit*, 69, 95, 157, 260, 295 [Pollack's note].

7. American writer Paul Engel (1908–91), O'Connor's teacher at the Iowa Writers' Workshop.

standard English, allowing her characters to speak dialect only in limited and easily digestible doses in dialogue.

. . .

[. . .] O'Connor endowed her narrators with perfect diction in accordance with Gordon's dictum that allowing the narrator to slip into dialect lowers the tone of a story and saps it of the tension that might otherwise have accrued from the subtle conflict between the cultures represented by the two ways of speaking.

. . .

We have seen, then, that O'Connor chose to show rather than tell and used limited third-person narrators because this style and this technique suited her particular needs as a Southerner and a Christian rather than because she was slavishly adhering to some New Critical creed she picked up at Iowa.

. . .

As she wrote in a letter to Betty Hester ("A") in September 1955, "I understand that something of oneself gets through and often something that one is not conscious of. Also to have sympathy for any character, you have to put a good deal of yourself into him." [. . . The artist must] make sure that those elements of the author's personality "that don't bear on the subject at hand are excluded. Everything has to be subordinated to a whole which is not you" (*Habit* 105).

WORKS CITED

O'Connor, Flannery. *The Complete Stories*. New York: Farrar, Straus, Giroux, 1973.
———. *The Habit of Being: Letters of Flannery O'Connor*. Ed. Sally Fitzgerald. New York: Farrar, Straus, Giroux, 1979.
———. *Mystery and Manners*. Ed. Sally Fitzgerald and Robert Fitzgerald. New York: Farrar, Straus, Giroux, 1970.

SUGGESTIONS FOR WRITING

1. Flannery O'Connor wrote that "[t]he beginning of human knowledge is through the senses, and the fiction writer begins where human perception begins." Citing examples from the O'Connor stories and the nonfiction passages in this chapter, write an essay exploring O'Connor's use of imagery, including figurative language (metaphor, simile, symbol) and references to vision or other senses. Are the senses trustworthy? How does the physical world portrayed through this imagery affect other elements of the story or stories (characterization, plot, theme, etc.)?

2. Flannery O'Connor wrote both that "in my own stories I have found that violence is strangely capable of returning my characters to reality and preparing them to accept their moment of grace" and that violence "is the extreme situation that best reveals what we are essentially." Write an essay analyzing the three stories by O'Connor in this chapter in light of these statements about violence. What "moments of grace" do you see? Can you assess what O'Connor considers the essence of humanity ("what we are")?

3. Like all writers, O'Connor is fascinated with certain character types—in these stories, for example, middle-aged or elderly White women who are also mothers and (in two stories) their better-educated, even self-consciously "intellectual" children. Drawing on evidence from at least two stories in this album, write an essay analyzing one of these character types. What qualities and attitudes do characters of this type share? What about them helps to create conflict? How, if at all, are they changed by their experience? What, ultimately, might O'Connor show us through these characters?

4. Write an essay interpreting some aspect of one of Flannery O'Connor's stories in light of information about her life. Be sure to cite O'Connor's own words from her letters and essays excerpted in this chapter, from the critical essays, or from other sources. What does the biographical context help explain? What qualities or aspects of the story does your biographical approach *not* account for?

5. Choose two of the stories in this chapter and write an essay comparing the way they are narrated (see the excerpt from Pollack's essay above). Pay close attention to passages in which the narrator relates the voice, vision, thoughts, or perspective of a focal character. How does the treatment of each character contribute to tone, irony, or other effects of the story?

6. After making your own list of what all three stories in this chapter have in common, write a short story in the Flannery O'Connor manner. Are you able to make it a little humorous without being too absurd? violent or shocking without being too cruel? unsettling but not disgusting? Is your story at all autobiographical?

7. Choose any story in this book (perhaps your favorite) and read at least one other story by the same writer. Write an essay comparing the stories, focusing on a specific element or aspect of them. Judging by these stories, what seems most distinctive about this author's work or worldview?

Louise Erdrich

AN ALBUM

Is there anyone but Louise? I don't think there is.
—ANN PATCHETT

She is, above all, an American original [. . .].
—ROBERT NEWLEN (LIBRARY OF CONGRESS)

When readers today consider Flannery O'Connor's work, it often appears to us a perfectly rounded, concentrated whole thanks not only to the passage of time and to all that has already been said and written about that work but also to the very brevity of O'Connor's life and career. Complex and influential as O'Connor's fiction is, there is a very limited amount—all produced in just nineteen of her short thirty-nine years. In these terms, as in others, the case of Louise Erdrich couldn't be more different—that of a best-selling, acclaimed, even beloved contemporary writer whose career, now in its fourth decade, is already nearly as long as O'Connor's entire life was. Often mentioned as a strong contender to be the first Native American author to win the Nobel Prize in Literature, Erdrich has already received more than one prestigious lifetime achievement award. Yet neither her achievement nor her evolution as a writer nor her **oeuvre** nor even the stories of her fictional characters are anything like complete. For example, published in 2017, *Future Home of the Living God* may be Erdrich's fifteenth single-authored novel for adults, but it's also her first foray into future fiction and a major contribution to the emergent subgenre of *cli-fi*, or *climate fiction*. And Erdrich's large, growing body of work also embraces fiction for children; varied nonfiction, both essays and books; three poetry collections; and numerous short stories, only some of which are collected in *The Red Convertible: Selected and New Stories, 1978–2008*.

Erdrich's fiction is in every way as diverse as its characters and settings, which range from the nineteenth century through the twenty-first and beyond, and from Germany to New Hampshire to the Caribbean. Yet the work for which Erdrich is best known concentrates, just as O'Connor's does, on the places and peoples the author knows best. For Erdrich—who is of German, French, and Ojibwe, or Chippewa, descent and an enrolled member of the Turtle Mountain Band of Chippewa Indians—that means both Native and European American characters in the American Northwest, especially Minnesota and the Dakotas. By her own account, Erdrich thus writes about "where I'm from" in multiple ways and senses: "I'm writing out of the mixture of cultures. Knowing both sides of my family really infused my life with a sense that I lived in many times and in many places as many people. It was never just me. I was always filled with the stories [. . .]."

Though Erdrich is primarily known as a novelist, many see the story as her true forté, just as it is O'Connor's. Stories and storytelling are a central concern, as well as feature, of Erdrich's fiction, partly because stories and storytelling are so very important to the peoples whose mingled cultures and histories her fiction honors and explores. Like *Love Medicine* (1984) and *The Plague of Doves* (2008), many of her novels began life as short stories. Many can be and are read as collections of interlinked stories, offering us a diverse cast of related narrators' and focal characters' perspectives on the same events. As a result, events rarely come to us in chronological order, and truth never appears uncomplicated or singular. Such effects are greatly amplified by the fact that many of Erdrich's novels themselves interlink, with later novels as often as not moving backward, rather than forward, in time, functioning more as prequels than sequels. (A character who debuts in one novel as an eminent Catholic priest, for example, is revealed, in another, to have once been a nun.)

All these features of Erdrich's work have earned her frequent comparisons to William Faulkner, that other American master known for creating a fictional place all his own, peopled with the most tangled of family trees. Yet the persistent presence of the marvelous, even magical and miraculous, in Erdrich's fictional universe ensures that she is just as often compared to Latin American magical realist Gabriel García Márquez. In awarding her its coveted Prize for American Fiction, the U.S. Library of Congress hailed Erdrich for, among other things, "connecting a dreamworld of Ojibwe legend to stark realities of the modern-day." Today often describing herself as both deeply spiritual and committed to no single religion, Erdrich equally credits her Roman Catholic upbringing for the mystical, marvelous aspect of her fiction and worldview.

Erdrich's fiction, like O'Connor's, often deals with dark, even violent, subject matter—accidental shootings, domestic abuse, lynching, rape, alcoholism, and racism, to name a few. Yet in a manner simultaneously like and very different from O'Connor's, Erdrich, too, always combines great seriousness with great humor. (As she told one interviewer, "writing humor into a book" may be "the hardest thing," but it is also, for her, "essential.") Partly as a result, Erdrich's fiction ultimately tends to be hopeful rather than mournful, emphasizing the resilience of cultures, communities, families, and individuals in the face of hardship and loss, both collective and personal. In her early essay "Where I Ought to Be: A Writer's Sense of Place" (1985), Erdrich describes the "task" of Native writers like herself as striving, "[i]n the light of enormous loss," to "tell the stories of contemporary survivors while protecting and celebrating the cores of cultures left in the wake of" their near-annihilation. As one might predict of an oeuvre that includes a Justice trilogy, Erdrich's insists on our need to confront the wrongs of the past and their very real effects on our present, even as it foregrounds empathy, understanding, and forgiveness. ("Justice," as she says in one interview, "is the foundation of a trusting society. It's the foundation of going forward and making a life.")

All of these and many other characteristic features and concerns of Erdrich's fiction may be found in the three stories we include in this anthology: LOVE MEDICINE (1984) and THE YEARS OF MY BIRTH (2011) appear in this album, along with a timeline of Erdrich's life and career; THE PLAGUE OF DOVES (2004), together with a brief Erdrich biography, can be found in "Telling Stories: An Album." Though written in different decades, these three stories are chosen to highlight the continuities in Erdrich's oeuvre more than its remarkable breadth.

At the heart of that body of work arguably lies, first and foremost, the human heart itself—love, whether romantic or familial, fierce or gentle, fading as suddenly and mysteriously as it strikes or enduring over and even beyond a lifetime. As the protagonist of her novel *The Painted Drum* (2005) avows, "Nobody can protect you from" heartbreak, even from being broken, nor will "living alone," "for solitude will also break you with its yearning. You have to love. You have to feel. It is the reason you are here on earth. You are here to risk your heart. You are here to be swallowed up." Second—and as central to Erdrich's fiction as it has been in her own life—is family, which Erdrich represents as enormously vital, complex, and fluid precisely because it is also something humans must and do create, for ourselves and each other, rather than simply inherit ready-made.

As you read and discuss Erdrich's stories, test for yourself the claims we have made here about the patterns in her fiction. But work, too, to identify other similarities, as well as differences, among these three examples of the author's work. What seems to you most interesting and distinctive about the form and style of these stories? about their narrators and narration? about their characters and settings? about their plots and the conflicts at their center? about their themes? What, for you, might make Erdrich and all of her characters authentic "American originals"?

Love Medicine

I never really done much with my life, I suppose. I never had a television. Grandma Kashpaw had one inside her apartment at the Senior Citizens, so I used to go there and watch my favorite shows. For a while she used to call me the biggest waste on the reservation and hark back to how she saved me from my own mother, who wanted to tie me in a potato sack and throw me in a slough. Sure, I was grateful to Grandma Kashpaw for saving me like that, for raising me, but gratitude gets old. After a while, stale. I had to stop thanking her. One day I told her I had paid her back in full by staying at her beck and call. I'd do anything for Grandma. She knew that. Besides, I took care of Grandpa like nobody else could, on account of what a handful he'd gotten to be.

But that was nothing. I know the tricks of mind and body inside out without ever having trained for it, because I got the touch. It's a thing you got to be born with. I got secrets in my hands that nobody ever knew to ask. Take Grandma Kashpaw with her tired veins all knotted up in her legs like clumps of blue snails. I take my fingers and I snap them on the knots. The medicine flows out of me. The touch. I run my fingers up the maps of those rivers of veins or I knock very gentle above their hearts or I make a circling motion on their stomachs, and it helps them. They feel much better. Some women pay me five dollars.

I couldn't do the touch for Grandpa, though. He was a hard nut. You know, some people fall right through the hole in their lives. It's invisible, but they come to it after time, never knowing where. There is this woman here, Lulu Lamartine, who always had a thing for Grandpa. She loved him since she was a girl and always said he was a genius. Now she says that his mind got so full it exploded.

How can I doubt that? I know the feeling when your mental power builds up too far. I always used to say that's why the Indians got drunk. Even statistically we're the smartest people on the earth. Anyhow with Grandpa I couldn't hardly believe it, because all my youth he stood out as a hero to me. When he started getting toward second childhood he went through different moods. He would stand in the woods and cry at the top of his shirt. It scared me, scared everyone, Grandma worst of all.

5   Yet he was so smart—do you believe it?—that he *knew* he was getting foolish.

He said so. He told me that December I failed school and come back on the train to Hoopdance. I didn't have nowhere else to go. He picked me up there and he said it straight out: "I'm getting into my second childhood." And then he said something else I still remember: "I been chosen for it. I couldn't say no." So I figure that a man so smart all his life—tribal chairman and the star of movies and even pictured in the statehouse and on cans of snuff—would know what he's doing by saying yes. I think he was called to second childhood like anybody else gets a call for the priesthood or the army or whatever. So I really did not listen too hard when the doctor said this was some kind of disease old people got eating too much sugar. You just can't tell me that a man who went to Washington and gave them bureaucrats what for could lose his mind from eating too much Milky Way. No, he put second childhood on himself.

Behind those songs he sings out in the middle of Mass, and back of those stories that everybody knows by heart, Grandpa is thinking hard about life. I know the feeling. Sometimes I'll throw up a smokescreen to think behind. I'll hitch up to Winnipeg and play the Space Invaders[1] for six hours, but all the time there and back I will be thinking some fairly deep thoughts that surprise even me, and I'm used to it. As for him, if it was just the thoughts there wouldn't be no problem. Smokescreen is what irritates the social structure, see, and Grandpa has done things that just distract people to the point they want to throw him in the cookie jar where they keep the mentally insane. He's far from that, I know for sure, but even Grandma had trouble keeping her patience once he started sneaking off to Lamartine's place. He's not supposed to have his candy, and Lulu feeds it to him. That's *one* of the reasons why he goes.

Grandma tried to get me to put the touch on Grandpa soon after he began stepping out. I didn't want to, but before Grandma started telling me again what a bad state my bare behind was in when she first took me home, I thought I should at least pretend.

I put my hands on either side of Grandpa's head. You wouldn't look at him and say he was crazy. He's a fine figure of a man, as Lamartine would say, with all his hair and half his teeth, a beak like a hawk, and cheeks like the blades of a hatchet. They put his picture on all the tourist guides to North Dakota and even copied his face for artistic paintings. I guess you could call him a monument all of himself. He started grinning when I put my hands on his templates,[2] and I knew right then he knew how come I touched him. I knew the smokescreen was going to fall.

10   And I was right: just for a moment it fell.

"Let's pitch whoopee," he said across my shoulder to Grandma.

They don't use that expression much around here anymore, but for damn sure it must have meant something. It got her goat right quick.

---

1. Popular 1980s video arcade game.
2. Blunder for "temples," one of many malapropisms in the story.

She threw my hands off his head herself and stood in front of him, over-matching him pound for pound, and taller too, for she had a growth spurt in middle age while he had shrunk, so now the length and breadth of her surpassed him. She glared and spoke her piece into his face about how he was off at all hours tomcatting and chasing Lamartine again and making a damn old fool of himself.

"And you got no more whoopee to pitch anymore anyhow!" she yelled at last, surprising me so my jaw just dropped, for us kids all had pretended for so long that those rustling sounds we heard from their side of the room at night never happened. She sure had pretended it, up till now, anyway. I saw that tears were in her eyes. And that's when I saw how much grief and love she felt for him. And it gave me a real shock to the system. You see I thought love got easier over the years so it didn't hurt so bad when it hurt, or feel so good when it felt good. I thought it smoothed out and old people hardly noticed it. I thought it curled up and died, I guess. Now I saw it rear up like a whip and lash.

She loved him. She was jealous. She mourned him like the dead.   15

And he just smiled into the air, trapped in the seams of his mind.

So I didn't know what to do. I was in a laundry then. They was like parents to me, the way they had took me home and reared me. I could see her point for wanting to get him back the way he was so at least she could argue with him, sleep with him, not be shamed out by Lamartine. She'd always love him. That hit me like a ton of bricks. For one whole day I felt this odd feeling that cramped my hands. When you have the touch, that's where longing gets you. I never loved like that. It made me feel all inspired to see them fight, and I wanted to go out and find a woman who I would love until one of us died or went crazy. But I'm not like that really. From time to time I heal a person all up good inside, however when it comes to the long shot I doubt that I got staying power.

And you need that, staying power, going out to love somebody. I knew this quality was not going to jump on me with no effort. So I turned my thoughts back to Grandma and Grandpa. I felt her side of it with my hands and my tangled guts, and I felt his side of it within the stretch of my mentality. He had gone out to lunch one day and never came back. He was fishing in the middle of Matchimanito. And there was big thoughts on his line, and he kept throwing them back for even bigger ones that would explain to him, say, the meaning of how we got here and why we have to leave so soon. All in all, I could not see myself treating Grandpa with the touch, bringing him back, when the real part of him had chose to be off thinking somewhere. It was only the rest of him that stayed around causing trouble, after all, and we could handle most of it without any problem.

Besides, it was hard to argue with his reasons for doing some things. Take Holy Mass. I used to go there just every so often, when I got frustrated mostly, because even though I know the Higher Power dwells everyplace, there's something very calming about the cool greenish inside of our mission. Or so I thought, anyway. Grandpa was the one who stripped off my delusions in this matter, for it was he who busted right through what Father calls the sacred serenity of the place.

We filed in that time. Me and Grandpa. We sat down in our pews. Then the   20
rosary got started up pre-Mass and that's when Grandpa filled up his chest and opened his mouth and belted out them words.

HAIL MARIE FULL OF GRACE.

He had a powerful set of lungs.

And he kept on like that. He did not let up. He hollered and he yelled them prayers, and I guess people was used to him by now, because they only muttered theirs and did not quit and gawk like I did. I was getting red-faced, I admit. I give him the elbow once or twice, but that wasn't nothing to him. He kept on. He shrieked to heaven and he pleaded like a movie actor and he pounded his chest like Tarzan in the Lord I Am Not Worthies.[3] I thought he might hurt himself. Then after a while I guess I got used to it, and that's when I wondered: how come?

So afterwards I out and asked him. "How come? How come you yelled?"

"God don't hear me otherwise," said Grandpa Kashpaw.

I sweat. I broke right into a little cold sweat at my hairline because I knew this was perfectly right and for years not one damn other person had noticed it. God's been going deaf. Since the Old Testament, God's been deafening up on us. I read, see. Besides the dictionary, which I'm constantly in use of, I had this Bible once. I read it. I found there was discrepancies between then and now. It struck me. Here God used to raineth bread from clouds, smite the Phillipines,[4] sling fire down on red-light districts where people got stabbed. He even appeared in person every once in a while. God used to pay attention, is what I'm saying.

Now there's your God in the Old Testament and there is Chippewa Gods as well. Indian Gods, good and bad, like tricky Nanabozho or the water monster, Missepeshu,[5] who lives over in Matchimanito. That water monster was the last God I ever heard to appear. It had a weakness for young girls and grabbed one of the Pillagers off her rowboat. She got to shore all right, but only after this monster had its way with her. She's an old lady now. Old Lady Pillager. She still doesn't like to see her family fish that lake.

Our Gods aren't perfect, is what I'm saying, but at least they come around. They'll do a favor if you ask them right. You don't have to yell. But you do have to know, like I said, how to ask in the right way. That makes problems, because to ask proper was an art that was lost to the Chippewas once the Catholics gained ground. Even now, I have to wonder if Higher Power turned it back, if we got to yell, or if we just don't speak its language.

I looked around me. How else could I explain what all I had seen in my short life—King smashing his fist in things, Gordie drinking himself down to the Bismarck hospitals, or Aunt June left by a white man to wander off in the snow. How else to explain the times my touch don't work, and farther back, to the old-time Indians who was swept away in the outright germ warfare and dirty-dog killing of the whites. In those times, us Indians was so much kindlier than now. We took them in.

---

3. "Lord, I am not worthy that you should enter under my roof, but only say the word and my soul shall be healed"—words spoken by Roman Catholic congregants before taking Communion, an echo of those spoken to Jesus by a Roman centurion in begging that his sick servant might be healed (Matt. 8). *Tarzan*: oft-revisited fictional character who debuted in Edgar Rice Burroughs's novel *Tarzan of the Apes* (1912); an orphan of English noble blood raised in the jungle by great apes.

4. Blunder for "Philistines."

5. Literally, "the great Lynx"; powerful lake-dwelling being resembling a big cat, but with horns, palmed paws, and scales in Anishinaabe, especially Ojibwe, tradition. *Nanabozho*: trickster figure.

Oh yes, I'm bitter as an old cutworm[6] just thinking of how they done to us and doing still.

So Grandpa Kashpaw just opened my eyes a little there. Was there any sense relying on a God whose ears was stopped? Just like the government? I says then, right off, maybe we got nothing but ourselves. And that's not much, just personally speaking. I know I don't got the cold hard potatoes it takes to understand everything. Still, there's things I'd like to do. For instance, I'd like to help some people like my Grandpa and Grandma Kashpaw get back some happiness within the tail ends of their lives.

I told you once before I couldn't see my way clear to putting the direct touch on Grandpa's mind, and I kept my moral there, but something soon happened to make me think a little bit of mental adjustment wouldn't do him and the rest of us no harm.

It was after we saw him one afternoon in the sunshine courtyard of the Senior Citizens with Lulu Lamartine. Grandpa used to like to dig there. He had his little dandelion fork out, and he was prying up them dandelions right and left while Lamartine watched him.

"He's scratching up the dirt, all right," said Grandma, watching Lamartine 35 watch Grandpa out the window.

Now Lamartine was about half the considerable size of Grandma, but you would never think of sizes anyway. They were different in an even more noticeable way. It was the difference between a house fixed up with paint and picky fence, and a house left to weather away into the soft earth, is what I'm saying. Lamartine was jacked up, latticed, shuttered, and vinyl sided, while Grandma sagged and bulged on her slipped foundations and let her hair go the silver gray of rain-dried lumber. Right now, she eyed the Lamartine's pert flowery dress with such a look it despaired me. I knew what this could lead to with Grandma. Alternating tongue storms and rock-hard silences was hard on a man, even one who didn't notice, like Grandpa. So I went fetching him.

But he was gone when I popped through the little screen door that led out on the courtyard. There was nobody out there either, to point which way they went. Just the dandelion fork quibbling upright in the ground. That gave me an idea. I snookered over to the Lamartine's door and I listened in first, then knocked. But nobody. So I went walking through the lounges and around the card tables. Still nobody. Finally it was my touch that led me to the laundry room. I cracked the door. I went in. There they were. And he was really loving her up good, boy, and she was going hell for leather. Sheets was flapping on the lines above, and washcloths, pillowcases, shirts was also flying through the air, for they was trying to clear out a place for themselves in a high-heaped but shallow laundry cart. The washers and dryers was all on, chock-full of quarters, shaking and moaning. I couldn't hear what Grandpa and the Lamartine was billing and cooing, and they couldn't hear me.

I didn't know what to do, so I went inside and shut the door.

The Lamartine wore a big curly light-brown wig. Looked like one of them squeaky little white-people dogs. Poodles they call them. Anyway, that wig is what saved us from the worse. For I could hardly shout and tell them I was in

6. Nocturnal moth caterpillar that feeds on young stems.

there, no more could I try and grab him. I was trapped where I was. There was nothing I could really do but hold the door shut. I was scared of somebody else upsetting in and really getting an eyeful. Turned out though, in the heat of the clinch, as I was trying to avert my eyes you see, the Lamartine's curly wig jumped off her head. And if you ever been in the midst of something and had a big change like that occur in the someone, you can't help know how it devastates your basic urges. Not only that, but her wig was almost with a life of its own. Grandpa's eyes were bugging at the change already, and swear to God if the thing didn't rear up and pop him in the face like it was going to start something. He scrambled up, Grandpa did, and the Lamartine jumped up after him all addled looking. They just stared at each other, huffing and puffing, with quizzical expression. The surprise seemed to drive all sense completely out of Grandpa's mind.

40 "The letter was what started the fire," he said. "I never would have done it."

"What letter?" said the Lamartine. She was stiff-necked now, and elegant, even bald, like some alien queen. I gave her back the wig. The Lamartine replaced it on her head, and whenever I saw her after that, I couldn't help thinking of her bald, with special powers, as if from another planet.

"That was a close call," I said to Grandpa after she had left.

But I think he had already forgot the incident. He just stood there all quiet and thoughtful. You really wouldn't think he was crazy. He looked like he was just about to say something important, explaining himself. He said something, all right, but it didn't have nothing to do with anything that made sense.

He wondered where the heck he put his dandelion fork. That's when I decided about the mental adjustment.

45 Now what was mostly our problem was not so much that he was not all there, but that what was there of him often hankered after Lamartine. If we could put a stop to that, I thought, we might be getting someplace. But here, see, my touch was of no use. For what could I snap my fingers at to make him faithful to Grandma? Like the quality of staying power, this faithfulness was invisible. I know it's something that you got to acquire, but I never known where from. Maybe there's no rhyme or reason to it, like my getting the touch, and then again maybe it's a kind of magic.

It was Grandma Kashpaw who thought of it in the end. She knows things. Although she will not admit she has a scrap of Indian blood in her, there's no doubt in my mind she's got some Chippewa. How else would you explain the way she'll be sitting there, in front of her TV story, rocking in her armchair and suddenly she turns on me, her brown eyes hard as lake-bed flint.

"Lipsha Morrissey," she'll say, "you went out last night and got drunk."

How did she know that? I'll hardly remember it myself. Then she'll say she just had a feeling or ache in the scar of her hand or a creak in her shoulder. She is constantly being told things by little aggravations in her joints or by her household appliances. One time she told Gordie never to ride with a crazy Lamartine boy. She had seen something in the polished-up tin of her bread toaster. So he didn't. Sure enough, the time came we heard how Lyman and Henry went out of control in their car, ending up in the river. Lyman swam to the top, but Henry never made it.

Thanks to Grandma's toaster, Gordie was probably spared.

Someplace in the blood Grandma Kashpaw knows things. She also remem- 50
bers things, I found. She keeps things filed away. She's got a memory like them
video games that don't forget your score. One reason she remembers so many
details about the trouble I gave her in early life is so she can flash back her total
when she needs to.

Like now. Take the love medicine. I don't know where she remembered that
from. It came tumbling from her mind like an asteroid off the corner of the
screen.[7]

Of course she starts out by mentioning the time I had this accident in church
and did she leave me there with wet overhalls? No she didn't. And ain't I glad?
Yes I am. Now what you want now, Grandma?

But when she mentions them love medicines, I feel my back prickle at the
danger. These love medicines is something of an old Chippewa specialty. No
other tribe has got them down so well. But love medicines is not for the layman
to handle. You don't just go out and get one without paying for it. Before you get
one, even, you should go through one hell of a lot of mental condensation. You
got to think it over. Choose the right one. You could really mess up your life
grinding up the wrong little thing.

So anyhow, I said to Grandma I'd give this love medicine some thought. I
knew the best thing was to go ask a specialist like Old Lady Pillager, who lives
up in a tangle of bush and never shows herself. But the truth is I was afraid of
her, like everyone else. She was known for putting the twisted mouth on people,
seizing up their hearts. Old Lady Pillager was serious business, and I have
always thought it best to steer clear of that whenever I could. That's why I took
the powers in my own hands. That's why I did what I could.

I put my whole mentality to it, nothing held back. After a while I started to 55
remember things I'd heard gossiped over.

I heard of this person once who carried a charm of seeds that looked like
baby pearls. They was attracted to a metal knife, which made them powerful.
But I didn't know where them seeds grew. Another love charm I heard about I
couldn't go along with, because how was I suppose to catch frogs in the act,
which it required. Them little creatures is slippery and fast. And then the pow-
erfullest of all, the most extreme, involved nail clips and such. I wasn't anywhere near asking Grandma to provide me all the little body bits that this last
love recipe called for. I went walking around for days just trying to think up
something that would work.

Well I got it. If it hadn't been the early fall of the year, I never would have got
it. But I was sitting underneath a tree one day down near the school just watching people's feet go by when something tells me, look up! Look up! So I look up,
and I see two honkers, Canada geese, the kind with little masks on their faces,
a bird what mates for life. I see them flying right over my head naturally preparing to land in some slough on the reservation, which they certainly won't get off
of alive.

It hits me, anyway. Them geese, they mate for life. And I think to myself, just
what if I went out and got a pair? And just what if I fed some part—say the

7. Allusion to *Asteroids*, another popular 1980s video arcade game.

goose heart—of the female to Grandma and Grandpa ate the other heart? Wouldn't that work? Maybe it's all invisible, and then maybe again it's magic. Love is a stony road. We know that for sure. If it's true that the higher feelings of devotion get lodged in the heart like people say, then we'd be home free. If not, eating goose heart couldn't harm nobody anyway. I thought it was worth my effort, and Grandma Kashpaw thought so, too. She had always known a good idea when she heard one. She borrowed me Grandpa's gun.

So I went out to this particular slough, maybe the exact same slough I never got thrown in by my mother, thanks to Grandma Kashpaw, and I hunched down in a good comfortable pile of rushes. I got my gun loaded up. I ate a few of these soft baloney sandwiches Grandma made me for lunch. And then I waited. The cattails blown back and forth above my head. Them stringy blue herons was spearing up their prey. The thing I know how to do best in this world, the thing I been training for all my life, is to wait. Sitting there and sitting there was no hardship on me. I got to thinking about some funny things that happened. There was this one time that Lulu Lamartine's little blue tweety bird, a para-clete, I guess you'd call it, flown up inside her dress and got lost within there. I recalled her running out into the hallway trying to yell something, shaking. She was doing a right good jig there, cutting the rug for sure, and the thing is it *never* flown out. To this day people speculate where it went. They fear she might per-haps of crushed it in her corsets. It sure hasn't ever yet been seen alive. I thought of funny things for a while, but then I used them up, and strange things that happened started weaseling their way into my mind.

60   I got to thinking quite naturally of the Lamartine's cousin named Wrist-watch. I never knew what his real name was. They called him Wristwatch because he got his father's broken wristwatch as a young boy when his father passed on. Never in his whole life did Wristwatch take his father's watch off. He didn't care if it worked, although after a while he got sensitive when people asked what time it was, teasing him. He often put it to his ear like he was listen-ing to the tick. But it was broken for good and forever, people said so, at least that's what they thought.

Well I saw Wristwatch smoking in his pickup one afternoon and by nine that evening he was dead.

He died sitting at the Lamartine's table, too. As she told it, Wristwatch had just eaten himself a good-size dinner and she said would he take seconds on the hot dish when he fell over to the floor. They turnt him over. He was gone. But here's the strange thing: when the Senior Citizen's orderly took the pulse he noticed that the wristwatch Wristwatch wore was now working. The moment he died the wristwatch started keeping perfect time. They buried him with the watch still ticking on his arm.

I got to thinking. What if some gravediggers dug up Wristwatch's casket in two hundred years and that watch was still going? I thought what question they would ask and it was this: Whose hand wound it?

I started shaking like a piece of grass at just the thought.

65   Not to get off the subject or nothing. I was still hunkered in the slough. It was passing late into the afternoon and still no honkers had touched down. Now I don't need to tell you that the waiting did not get to me, it was the chill. The rushes was very soft, but damp. I was getting cold and debating to leave,

when they landed. Two geese swimming here and there as big as life, looking deep into each other's little pinhole eyes. Just the ones I was looking for. So I lifted Grandpa's gun to my shoulder and I aimed perfectly, and *blam! Blam!* I delivered two accurate shots. But the thing is, them shots missed. I couldn't hardly believe it. Whether it was that the stock had warped or the barrel got bent someways, I don't quite know, but anyway them geese flown off into the dim sky, and Lipsha Morrissey was left there in the rushes with evening fallen and his two cold hands empty. He had before him just the prospect of another day of bone-cracking chill in them rushes, and the thought of it got him depressed.

Now it isn't my style, in no way, to get depressed.

So I said to myself, Lipsha Morrissey, you're a happy S.O.B. who could be covered up with weeds by now down at the bottom of this slough, but instead you're alive to tell the tale. You might have problems in life, but you still got the touch. You got the power, Lipsha Morrissey. Can't argue that. So put your mind to it and figure out how not to be depressed.

I took my advice. I put my mind to it. But I never saw at the time how my thoughts led me astray toward a tragic outcome none could have known. I ignored all the danger, all the limits, for I was tired of sitting in the slough and my feet were numb. My face was aching. I was chilled, so I played with fire. I told myself love medicine was simple. I told myself the old superstitions was just that—strange beliefs. I told myself to take the ten dollars Mary MacDonald had paid me for putting the touch on her arthritis joint, and the other five I hadn't spent yet from winning bingo last Thursday. I told myself to go down to the Red Owl store.

And here is what I did that made the medicine backfire. I took an evil short-cut. I looked at birds that was dead and froze.

All right. So now I guess you will say, "Slap a malpractice suit on Lipsha Morrissey." 70

I heard of those suits. I used to think it was a color clothing quack doctors had to wear so you could tell them from the good ones. Now I know better that it's law.

As I walked back from the Red Owl with the rock-hard, heavy turkeys, I argued to myself about malpractice. I thought of faith. I thought to myself that faith could be called belief against the odds and whether or not there's any proof. How does that sound? I thought how we might have to yell to be heard by Higher Power, but that's not saying it's not *there*. And that is faith for you. It's belief even when the goods don't deliver. Higher Power makes promises we all know they can't back up, but anybody ever go and slap an old malpractice suit on God? Or the U.S. government? No they don't. Faith might be stupid, but it gets us through. So what I'm heading at is this. I finally convinced myself that the real actual power to the love medicine was not the goose heart itself but the faith in the cure.

I didn't believe it, I knew it was wrong, but by then I had waded so far into my lie I was stuck there. And then I went one step further.

The next day, I cleaned the hearts away from the paper packages of gizzards inside the turkeys. Then I wrapped them hearts with a clean hankie and brung them both to get blessed up at the mission. I wanted to get official blessings from the priest, but when Father answered the door to the rectory, wiping his hands on a little towel, I could tell he was a busy man.

75 "Booshoo,[8] Father," I said. "I got a slight request to make of you this afternoon."

"What is it?" he said.

"Would you bless this package?" I held out the hankie with the hearts tied inside it.

He looked at the package, questioning it.

"It's turkey hearts," I honestly had to reply.

80 A look of annoyance crossed his face.

"Why don't you bring this matter over to Sister Martin," he said. "I have duties."

And so, although the blessing wouldn't be as powerful, I went over to the Sisters with the package.

I rung the bell, and they brought Sister Martin to the door. I had her as a music teacher, but I was always so shy then. I never talked out loud. Now, I had grown taller than Sister Martin. Looking down, I saw that she was not feeling up to snuff. Brown circles hung under her eyes.

"What's the matter?" she said, not noticing who I was.

85 "Remember me, Sister?"

She squinted up at me.

"Oh yes," she said after a moment. "I'm sorry, you're the youngest of the Kashpaws. Gordie's brother."

Her face warmed up.

"Lipsha," I said, "that's my name."

90 "Well, Lipsha," she said, smiling broad at me now, "what can I do for you?"

They always said she was the kindest-hearted of the Sisters up the hill, and she was. She brought me back into their own kitchen and made me take a big yellow wedge of cake and a glass of milk.

"Now tell me," she said, nodding at my package. "What have you got wrapped up so carefully in those handkerchiefs?"

Like before, I answered honestly.

"Ah," said Sister Martin. "Turkey hearts." She waited.

95 "I hoped you could bless them."

She waited some more, smiling with her eyes. Kindhearted though she was, I began to sweat. A person could not pull the wool down over Sister Martin. I stumbled through my mind for an explanation, quick, that wouldn't scare her off.

"They're a present," I said, "for Saint Kateri's[9] statue."

"She's not a saint yet."

"I know," I stuttered on. "In the hopes they will crown her."

100 "Lipsha," she said, "I never heard of such a thing."

So I told her. "Well the truth is," I said, "it's a kind of medicine."

"For what?"

---

8. Or *boozhoo*: "hello," "greetings" (Ojibwe or Chippewa).

9. Kateri Tekakwitha (1656–80), "Lily of the Mohawk," born in what is now upstate New York to a Mohawk father and a devoutly Christian Algonquin mother. Following the deaths of her parents, Kateri moved to a Jesuit mission near Montreal, Canada, to spend the rest of her short life in prayer and chastity. Credited with miracles after her death, she was beatified in 1980 and canonized in 1991.

"Love."

"Oh Lipsha," she said after a moment, "you don't need any medicine. I'm sure any girl would like you exactly the way you are."

I just sat there. I felt miserable, caught in my pack of lies.   105

"Tell you what," she said, seeing how bad I felt, "my blessing won't make any difference anyway. But there is something you can do."

I looked up at her, hopeless.

"Just be yourself."

I looked down at my plate. I knew I wasn't much to brag about right then, and I shortly became even less. For as I walked out the door I stuck my fingers in the cup of holy water that was sacred from their touches. I put my fingers in and blessed the hearts, quick, with my own hand.

I went back to Grandma and sat down in her little kitchen at the Senior Citi- 110
zens. I unwrapped them hearts on the table, and her hard agate eyes went soft. She said she wasn't even going to cook those hearts up but eat them raw so their power would go down strong as possible.

I couldn't hardly watch when she munched hers. Now that's true love. I was worried about how she would get Grandpa to eat his, but she told me she'd think of something and don't worry. So I did not. I was supposed to hide off in her bedroom while she put dinner on a plate for Grandpa and fixed up the heart so he'd eat it. I caught a glint of the plate she was making for him. She put that heart smack on a piece of lettuce like in a restaurant and then attached to it a little heap of boiled peas.

He sat down. I was listening in the next room.

She said, "Why don't you have some mash potato?" So he had some mash potato. Then she gave him a little piece of boiled meat. He ate that. Then she said, "Why you didn't never touch your salad yet. See that heart? I'm feeding you it because the doctor said your blood needs building up."

I couldn't help it, at that point I peeked through a crack in the door.

I saw Grandpa picking at that heart on his plate with a certain look. He   115
didn't look appetized at all, is what I'm saying. I doubted our plan was going to work. Grandma was getting worried, too. She told him one more time, loudly, that he had to eat that heart.

"Swallow it down," she said. "You'll hardly notice it."

He just looked at her straight on. The way he looked at her made me think I was going to see the smokescreen drop a second time, and sure enough it happened.

"What you want me to eat this for so bad?" he asked her uncannily.

Now Grandma knew the jig was up. She knew that he knew she was work-ing medicine. He put his fork down. He rolled the heart around his saucer plate.

"I don't want to eat this," he said to Grandma. "It don't look good."   120

"Why it's fresh grade-A," she told him. "One hundred percent."

He didn't ask percent what, but his eyes took on an even more warier look.

"Just go on and try it," she said, taking the salt shaker up in her hand. She was getting annoyed. "Not tasty enough? You want me to salt it for you?" She waved the shaker over his plate.

"All right, skinny white girl!" She had got Grandpa mad. Oopsy-daisy, he popped the heart into his mouth. I was about to yawn loudly and come out of the bedroom. I was about ready for this crash of wills to be over, when I saw he was still up to his old tricks. First he rolled it into one side of his cheek. "Mmmmm," he said. Then he rolled it into the other side of his cheek. "Mmm-mmmm," again. Then he stuck his tongue out with the heart on it and put it back, and there was no time to react. He had pulled Grandma's leg once too far. Her goat was got. She was so mad she hopped up quick as a wink and slugged him between the shoulderblades to make him swallow.

125   Only thing is, he choked.

He choked real bad. A person can choke to death. You ever sit down at a restaurant table and up above you there is a list of instructions what to do if something slides down the wrong pipe? It sure makes you chew slow, that's for damn sure. When Grandpa fell off his chair better believe me that little graphic illustrated poster fled into my mind. I jumped out the bedroom. I done everything within my power that I could do to unlodge what was choking him. I squeezed underneath his rib cage. I socked him in the back. I was desperate. But here's the factor of decision: he wasn't choking on the heart alone. There was more to it than that. It was other things that choked him as well. It didn't seem like he wanted to struggle or fight. Death came and tapped his chest, so he went just like that. I'm sorry all through my body at what I done to him with that heart, and there's those who will say Lipsha Morrissey is just excusing himself off the hook by giving song and dance about how Grandpa gave up.

Maybe I can't admit what I did. My touch had gone worthless, that is true. But here is what I seen while he lay in my arms.

You hear a person's life will flash before their eyes when they're in danger. It was him in danger, not me, but it was *his* life come over me. I saw him dying, and it was like someone pulled the shade down in a room. His eyes clouded over and squeezed shut, but just before that I looked in. He was still fishing in the middle of Matchimanito. Big thoughts was on his line and he had half a case of beer in the boat. He waved at me, grinned, and then the bobber went under.

Grandma had gone out of the room crying for help. I bunched my force up in my hands and I held him. I was so wound up I couldn't even breathe. All the moments he had spent with me, all the times he had hoisted me on his shoulders or pointed into the leaves was concentrated in that moment. Time was flashing back and forth like a pinball machine. Lights blinked and balls hopped and rubber bands chirped, until suddenly I realized the last ball had gone down the drain and there was nothing. I felt his force leaving him, flowing out of Grandpa never to return. I felt his mind weakening. The bobber going under in the lake. And I felt the touch retreat back into the darkness inside my body, from where it came.

130   One time, long ago, both of us were fishing together. We caught a big old snapper what started towing us around like it was a motor. "This here fishline is pretty damn good," Grandpa said. "Let's keep this turtle on and see where he takes us." So we rode along behind that turtle, watching as from time to time it surfaced. The thing was just about the size of a washtub. It took us all around the lake twice, and as it was traveling, Grandpa said something as a joke. "Lipsha,"

he said, "we are glad your mother didn't want you because we was always looking for a boy like you who would tow us around the lake."

"I ain't no snapper. Snappers is so stupid they stay alive when their head's
chopped off," I said.

"That ain't stupidity," said Grandpa. "Their brain's just in their heart, like
yours is."

When I looked up, I knew the fuse had blown between my heart and my
mind and that a terrible understanding was to be given.

Grandma got back into the room and I saw her stumble. And then she went
down too. It was like a house you can't hardly believe has stood so long, through
years of record weather, suddenly goes down in the worst yet. It makes sense, is
what I'm saying, but you still can't hardly believe it. You think a person you
know has got through death and illness and being broke and living on commodity rice[1] will get through anything. Then they fold and you see how fragile were
the stones that underpinned them. You see how instantly the ground can shift
you thought was solid. You see the stop signs and the yellow dividing markers of
roads you traveled and all the instructions you had played according to vanish.
You see how all the everyday things you counted on was just a dream you had
been having by which you run your whole life. She had been over me, like a
sheer overhang of rock dividing Lipsha Morrissey from outer space. And now
she went underneath. It was as though the banks gave way on the shores of
Matchimanito, and where Grandpa's passing was just the bobber swallowed
under by his biggest thought, her fall was the house and the rock under it sliding after, sending half the lake splashing up to the clouds.

Where there was nothing.

135

You play them games never knowing what you see. When I fell into the
dream alongside of both of them I saw that the dominions I had defended
myself from anciently was but delusions of the screen. Blips of light. And I was
scot-free now, whistling through space.

I don't know how I come back. I don't know from where. They was slapping my
face when I arrived back at Senior Citizens and they was oxygenating her. I saw
her chest move, almost unwilling. She sighed the way she would when somebody bothered her in the middle of a row of beads she was counting. I think it
irritated her to no end that they brought her back. I knew from the way she
looked after they took the mask off, she was not going to forgive them disturbing her restful peace. Nor was she forgiving Lipsha Morrissey. She had been
stepping out onto the road of death, she told the children later at the funeral. I
asked was there any stop signs or dividing markers on that road, but she clamped
her lips in a vise the way she always done when she was mad.

Which didn't bother me. I knew when things had cleared out she wouldn't
have no choice. I was not going to speculate where the blame was put for
Grandpa's death. We was in it together. She had slugged him between the
shoulders. My touch had failed him, never to return.

1. That is, rice distributed as part of the U.S. government's Food Distribution Program on Indian
Reservations (FDPIR); FDPIR foods are often called "commodity foods" because they come from
government purchases of surplus agricultural commodities.

All the blood children and the took-ins, like me, came home from Minneapolis and Chicago, where they had relocated years ago. They stayed with friends on the reservation or with Aurelia or slept on Grandma's floor. They were struck down with grief and bereavement to be sure, every one of them. At the funeral I sat down in the back of the church with Albertine. She had gotten all skinny and ragged haired from cramming all her years of study into two or three. She had decided that to be a nurse was not enough for her so she was going to be a doctor. But the way she was straining her mind didn't look too hopeful. Her eyes were bloodshot from driving and crying. She took my hand. From the back we watched all the children and the mourners as they hunched over their prayers, their hands stuffed full of Kleenex. It was someplace in that long sad service that my vision shifted. I began to see things different, more clear. The family kneeling down turned to rocks in a field. It struck me how strong and reliable grief was, and death. Until the end of time, death would be our rock.

140   So I had perspective on it all, for death gives you that. All the Kashpaw children had done various things to me in their lives—shared their folks with me, loaned me cash, beat me up in secret—and I decided, because of death, then and there I'd call it quits. If I ever saw King[2] again, I'd shake his hand. Forgiving somebody else made the whole thing easier to bear.

Everybody saw Grandpa off into the next world. And then the Kashpaws had to get back to their jobs, which was numerous and impressive. I had a few beers with them and I went back to Grandma, who had sort of got lost in the shuffle of everybody being sad about Grandpa and glad to see one another.

Zelda had sat beside her the whole time and was sitting with her now. I wanted to talk to Grandma, say how sorry I was, that it wasn't her fault, but only mine. I would have, but Zelda gave me one of her looks of strict warning as if to say, "I'll take care of Grandma. Don't horn in on the women."

If only Zelda knew, I thought, the sad realities would change her. But of course I couldn't tell the dark truth.

It was evening, late. Grandma's light was on underneath a crack in the door. About a week had passed since we buried Grandpa. I knocked first but there wasn't no answer, so I went right in. The door was unlocked. She was there but she didn't notice me at first. Her hands were tied up in her rosary, and her gaze was fully absorbed in the easy chair opposite her, the one that had always been Grandpa's favorite. I stood there, staring with her, at the little green nubs in the cloth and plastic armrest covers and the sad little hair-tonic stain he had made on the white doily where he laid his head. For the life of me I couldn't figure what she was staring at. Thin space. Then she turned.

145   "He ain't gone yet," she said.

Remember that chill I luckily didn't get from waiting in the slough? I got it now. I felt it start from the very center of me, where fear hides, waiting to attack. It spiraled outward so that in minutes my fingers and teeth were shaking and clattering. I knew she told the truth. She seen Grandpa. Whether or not he

---

2. King Howard Kashpaw, another (biological) grandchild of Marie (Grandma) and Nector (Grandpa) Kashpaw; a ne'er-do-well who, in childhood, often torments Lipsha.

had been there is not the point. She had *seen* him, and that meant anybody else could see him, too. Not only that but, as is usually the case with these here ghosts, he had a certain uneasy reason to come back. And of course Grandma Kashpaw had scanned it out.

I sat down. We sat together on the couch watching his chair out of the corner of our eyes. She had found him sitting in his chair when she walked in the door.

"It's the love medicine, my Lipsha," she said. "It was stronger than we thought. He came back even after death to claim me to his side."

I was afraid. "We shouldn't have tampered with it," I said. She agreed. For a while we sat still. I don't know what she thought, but my head felt screwed on backward. I couldn't accurately consider the situation, so I told Grandma to go to bed. I would sleep on the couch keeping my eye on Grandpa's chair. Maybe he would come back and maybe he wouldn't. I guess I feared the one as much as the other, but I got to thinking, see, as I lay there in darkness, that perhaps even through my terrible mistakes some good might come. If Grandpa did come back, I thought he'd return in his right mind. I could talk with him. I could tell him it was all my fault for playing with power I did not understand. Maybe he'd forgive me and rest in peace. I hoped this. I calmed myself and waited for him all night.

He fooled me though. He knew what I was waiting for, and it wasn't what he 150 was looking to hear. Come dawn I heard a blood-splitting cry from the bedroom and I rushed in there. Grandma turnt the lights on. She was sitting on the edge of the bed and her face looked harsh, pinched-up, gray.

"He was here," she said. "He came and laid down next to me in bed. And he touched me."

Her heart broke down. She cried. His touch was so cold. She laid back in bed after a while, as it was morning, and I went to the couch. As I lay there, falling asleep, I suddenly felt Grandpa's presence and the barrier between us like a swollen river. I felt how I had wronged him. How awful was the place where I had sent him. Behind the wall of death, he'd watched the living eat and cry and get drunk. He was lonesome, but I understood he meant no harm.

"Go back," I said to the dark, afraid and yet full of pity. "You got to be with your own kind now," I said. I felt him retreating, like a sigh, growing less. I felt his spirit as it shrunk back through the walls, the blinds, the brick courtyard of Senior Citizens. "Look up Aunt June," I whispered as he left.

I slept late the next morning, a good hard sleep allowing the sun to rise and warm the earth. It was past noon when I awoke. There is nothing, to my mind, like a long sleep to make those hard decisions that you neglect under stress of wakefulness. Soon as I woke up that morning, I saw exactly what I'd say to Grandma. I had gotten humble in the past week, not just losing the touch but getting jolted into the understanding that would prey on me from here on out. Your life feels different on you, once you greet death and understand your heart's position. You wear your life like a garment from the mission bundle sale ever after—lightly because you realize you never paid nothing for it, cherishing because you know you won't ever come by such a bargain again. Also you have the feeling someone wore it before you and someone will after. I can't explain that, not yet, but I'm putting my mind to it.

155   "Grandma," I said, "I got to be honest about the love medicine."

She listened. I knew from then on she would be listening to me the way I had listened to her before. I told her about the turkey hearts and how I had them blessed. I told her what I used as love medicine was purely a fake, and then I said to her what my understanding brought me.

"Love medicine ain't what brings him back to you, Grandma. No, it's something else. He loved you over time and distance, but he went off so quick he never got the chance to tell you how he loves you, how he doesn't blame you, how he understands. It's true feeling, not no magic. No supermarket heart could have brung him back."

She looked at me. She was seeing the years and days I had no way of knowing, and she didn't believe me. I could tell this. Yet a look came on her face. It was like the look of mothers drinking sweetness from their children's eyes. It was tenderness.

"Lipsha," she said, "you was always my favorite."

160   She took the beads off the bedpost, where she kept them to say at night, and she told me to put out my hand. When I did this, she shut the beads inside of my fist and held them there a long minute, tight, so my hand hurt. I almost cried when she did this. I don't really know why. Tears shot up behind my eyelids, and yet it was nothing. I didn't understand, except her hand was so strong, squeezing mine.

The earth was full of life and there were dandelions growing out the window, thick as thieves, already seeded, fat as big yellow plungers. She let my hand go. I got up. "I'll go out and dig a few dandelions," I told her.

Outside, the sun was hot and heavy as a hand on my back. I felt it flow down my arms, out my fingers, arrowing through the ends of the fork into the earth. With every root I prized up there was return, as if I was kin to its secret lesson. The touch got stronger as I worked through the grassy afternoon. Uncurling from me like a seed out of the blackness where I was lost, the touch spread. The spiked leaves full of bitter mother's milk. A buried root. A nuisance people dig up and throw in the sun to wither. A globe of frail seeds that's indestructible.

1984

QUESTIONS

1. How are Lipsha, his world, and his worldview characterized, in part, by how he narrates his story, including his diction, imagery, allusions, and seeming digressions?
2. What do you see as Lipsha's conflicts in the story? What might he learn over the course of it?
3. At least twice in LOVE MEDICINE, Lipsha refers explicitly to the U.S. government and implicitly to its treatment of American Indians. In terms of the story as a whole, what might be the meaning and significance of such references?

The Years of My Birth

The nurse had wrapped my brother in a blue flannel blanket and was just about to hand him to his mother when she whispered, "Oh, God, there's another one," and out I slid, half dead. I then proceeded to die in earnest, going from slightly pink to a dull gray-blue, at which point the nurse tried to scoop me into a bed warmed by lights. She was stopped by the doctor, who pointed out my head and legs. Stepping between me and the mother, the doctor addressed her.

"Mrs. Lasher, I have something important to say. Your other child has a congenital deformity and may die. Shall we use extraordinary means to salvage it?"

She looked at the doctor with utter incomprehension at first, then cried, "No!"

While the doctor's back was turned, the nurse cleared my mouth with her finger, shook me upside down, and swaddled me tightly in another blanket, pink. I took a blazing breath.

"Nurse," the doctor said.   5

"Too late," she answered.

I was left in the nursery with a bottle strapped to my face while the county tried to decide what to do with me. I was too young to be admitted to any state-run institution, and Mr. and Mrs. George Lasher refused to have me in their house, which was at the edge of a nearby town, where Mr. Lasher owned and ran a farm-implements dealership.

The night janitor at the hospital, a woman from the reservation named Betty Wishkob, asked the head maternity nurse for permission to hold me on her break. While cradling me, with her back to the observation window, Betty also nursed me—she was still nursing her youngest child at home. As she fed me, she molded and rounded my skull with her powerful hand. Nobody in the hospital knew that she was feeding me at night, or that she was doctoring me and had made up her mind to keep me. This was five decades ago. When Betty asked if she could take me home, there was relief and not a lot of paperwork involved, at least in the beginning. So I was saved, and grew up with the Wishkobs. I lived on the reservation and eventually was educated as my Chippewa siblings were—first at a school run by the Catholic mission and later at one run by the government.

Around the age of two, I was taken away for the first time and placed alone in a room. I remember the smell of disinfectant and what I would now call despair. Into this disinfected despair, there came a presence, someone or something, who grieved with me and held my hand. That presence would come to me again at other moments in my life. Its return is partly what this story is about.

The second time that an officious welfare officer decided to find a more suit-   10 able home for me, I was four. As Betty argued with her in the dust of our yard, the matted hackles on the dog's back rose. I stood beside Betty and held her skirt—green cotton. I pressed the fine weave between my fingers and hid my face in its scent of heated cloth. Then I was in the back seat of a car that sped soundlessly in some infinite direction. I slept. I woke alone in another white room. My bed was narrow, and the sheets were tucked tightly down, so that I had to struggle to get out. I sat on the edge of the bed for what seemed like a long time, waiting.

When you are little, you do not always know when you are screaming or crying—your feelings and the sound that comes out of you are all one thing. I remember that I opened my mouth, that is all, and that I did not shut it until I was back with Betty.

Every morning until I was about eleven, Betty and her husband, Albert, tried to straighten me by stretching out my legs. They woke me before the other children and brought me into the kitchen. I drank a glass of thin, blue milk by the woodstove. Then Betty sat in a kitchen chair and put me in her lap. Albert sat across from us in another chair.

"Put your feet out, Tuffy," he said.

I put my feet in Albert's hands, and he pulled me one way while Betty pulled the other. Slowly, as I grew, my legs untwisted, though one was always a little shorter than the other. I was the youngest of their four children—it was Sheryl whom Betty had been nursing when she cared for me in the hospital. Their older son, Cedric, gave me the name Tuffy because he knew that once I went to school I would get a nickname anyway. He didn't want it to be one that mocked my rolling walk or my head. My head—so misshapen when I was born that the doctor had diagnosed a birth defect—was still a bit flat on one side, where I had been crushed in the womb by my twin. But it had been shaped enough by Betty's squeezing and kneading that by the time I was old enough to look in a mirror I thought I was pretty.

15   Neither Betty nor Albert ever told me I was wrong; it was Sheryl who gave me the news.

"Tuffy, you are so ugly you're cute," she said.

I looked in the mirror the next chance I got and realized that she was telling the truth.

The house we lived in had a smell that permeates it still—old wood, onions, fried coot,[1] the salty outdoors scent of children. Betty was always trying to keep us clean, and Albert was always getting us dirty. He took us into the woods and showed us how to spot a rabbit run and set a snare. We yanked gophers from their holes with loops of string and picked pail after pail of berries. We rode a mean little bucking pony, fished perch from a nearby lake, dug potatoes every year to make money for school clothes. Betty's job at the hospital had not lasted. Albert sold firewood, corn, squash. We never went hungry. Not long ago, I read a memoir by a man named Peter Razor,[2] who was abandoned like me, only he ended up in an institution. He wrote of the one time that he remembered being held, and said that it remained one of the strangest and happiest moments of his life. I don't remember being held as something special. Which tells me that I

---

1. Small, dark, duck-like bird that lives near rivers and lakes.
2. Enrolled member of the Fond du Lac Band of Ojibwe (b. c. 1929); in *While the Locust Slept: A Memoir* (2001) he recounts his childhood experience in a state-run Minnesota orphanage and his indenture to an abusive farming family.

must have been held so often that the sensation became a part of me, inseparable from my memory of the world.

I know that I was loved, because it was a complicated matter for Betty and Albert to claim me from the welfare system, though I had aided their efforts with my endless scream. A full adoption involved hiring a lawyer, which they didn't have the money to do. I was afflicted with nightmares of being chased down and captured, and many nights I scrambled into the warm cleft of mattress between them, then held my breath and lay perfectly still until they had rolled over and gone back to sleep. When I knew that I was safe, I opened my eyes and looked into the darkness, which was never entirely black but alive with shifting green panels and tiny zigzags of fractured light. Then I'd feel myself sliding down into a safe, warm sleep, their slow and even breathing like a gentle rope, keeping me from slipping too far.

All of which is not to say that they were perfect. Albert drank from time to   20
time and passed out on the floor. Betty's temper was explosive. She never hit, but she yelled and raved. She could say awful things. Once, Sheryl was twirling around in the house. There was a shelf set snugly in the corner of the living room, and on that shelf there was a cut-glass vase that was very precious to Betty. When we brought her wildflower bouquets, she'd put them in that vase. I'd seen her washing the vase with soap and polishing it with an old pillowcase. Sheryl's arm knocked the vase off the shelf, and it struck the floor with a bright sound and shattered into splinters.

Betty was working at the stove. She spun around, threw her hands out, and stared.

"Damn you, Sheryl," she said. "That was the only beautiful thing I ever had."

"Tuffy broke it!" Sheryl said, and bolted out the door.

I stood mute and too frozen to speak. Betty began to cry, harshly, wiping her face with her forearm. I moved to sweep up the pieces for her, but she said to leave them, in such a heartsick voice that I went to find Sheryl, who was hiding in her usual place on the far side of the henhouse. When I asked her why she'd blamed me, she gave me a glaring, hateful look and said, "Because you're white."

Children can be brutal when it comes to gaining the attention and favor of   25
their parents. I didn't hold anything Sheryl did or said against her, and we became close later on. I am very glad for that, as I have never married, and I needed to confide in someone when, six months ago, I was contacted by my birth mother.

Until Betty and Albert died, I lived in an addition tacked onto the tiny house where all of us grew up. They died one right after the other, in the space of a few months, as the long-married sometimes do. By then, the other children had either moved off reservation or built new houses closer to town. I stayed on. Even now that Betty and Albert were gone and I had the whole house, I spent most of my time in my room. One difference was that I let the dog, a descendant of the one that had growled at the welfare lady, live inside with me. Betty had believed in outside dogs, but I petted and pampered this one. I'd had a fireplace installed, with a glass front and fans that threw the heat into a cozy circle in front of it, and there I'd sit every evening, with the dog at my feet, reading or crocheting while I listened to music.

Then one night the telephone rang.

I answered it with a simple hello. There was a pause. A woman asked if this was Linda Wishkob speaking.

"It is," I said, and then I experienced a skip of apprehension.

30　　"This is Nancy Lasher." The voice was tight and nervous. "I am your mother."

I took a breath, let it out. I said nothing but simply set the phone back in the cradle. Later, that moment struck me as funny. It was a kind of replay of my birth. I'd done it over. But this time I had instinctively rejected my mother, left her in the cradle just as she'd left me.

I work in the reservation post office. I am a government employee. At any time, I could have found out my birth parents' address. I could have called them up or, had I been another sort of person, got drunk and stood in their yard and railed at them. But not only did I not care—I actively did not want to know where they lived. Why would I? Everything I did know about them was painful, and I have always tried to avoid pain—which is perhaps why I've never married or had children.

That night, after I'd hung up the phone, I made a cup of tea and busied myself with crossword puzzles. One stumped me. The clue was "double-goer," twelve spaces, and it took me the longest time and a dictionary to come up with the word "doppelganger."[3]

Growing up in the midst of a large family, I had never registered the visitations from my presence, at those rare moments when I was alone, as something strange. The first time I was aware of it was when I was taken from Betty and put in a white room. After that, I occasionally had the sensation that there was someone walking beside me or sitting behind me, always just beyond my peripheral vision. One of the reasons I let the dog live inside was that it kept away this presence, which over the years had grown to seem anxious, needy, helpless in some way I could not define. I had never before thought of the presence in relation to my twin, who'd grown up not an hour's drive away from me, but that night the combination of the phone call out of the blue and the twelve-letter word in my puzzle set my thoughts flowing.

35　　Betty had told me all she knew of the circumstances of my birth. She was never one to keep things from people for their own good. She always let you have the truth square. But as I'd never thought to ask her about my brother she hadn't talked about him. Nor had any of my siblings—mainly because I don't think they really cared. Perhaps they didn't even associate me with the Lashers. I searched my memory and could not pull out much, except that my twin had been a boy, born first. I had no idea what the Lashers had named him. Of course, we were fraternal twins and supposedly no more alike than any other brother and sister. So I was free, that night, to actually hate and resent him. I'd heard my birth mother's voice for the first time. He'd heard it all his life.

She had called herself, simply, my mother. Not my birth mother—that careful, distancing term—but my mother. It could have been plain arrogance, but then there had also been distress in her tone. My brain had taped the eight words she'd said. All that night and the next morning, too, they played on a

---

3. Literally, "double-goer" (German); double; alter ego; ghostly counterpart.

loop. By the end of the second day, however, the intonation grew fainter, and I was relieved that on the third day it stopped.

On the fourth day, she called again.

She began by apologizing: "I am sorry to bother you." She went on to say that she had always wanted to meet me but had been afraid to find out where I was. She said that George, my father, was dead and she lived alone and that my twin brother was a postal worker in Bismarck.[4] It was then that I couldn't help myself. I had to ask his name.

"Linden," she told me. "It's an old family name."

"Was mine an old family name as well?" I asked.   40

"No," she said, "but it matched your brother's name."

She told me that George had written my name down on the birth certificate, but that they had never seen me. She told me that he had died of a heart attack, and she had nearly moved down to Bismarck to be near Linden, but she couldn't sell her home. She said that she hadn't known I lived so close by or she would have called me long before. Her light, conversational chatter must have caused a dreamlike amnesia to come over me, because when she asked if we could meet, if she could take me out to dinner at Vert's Supper Club, the only place in the area that served full dinners with drinks, I said yes and agreed on a day.

When I finally hung up the phone, I stared for a long time at the little log fire in my fireplace. I'd laid the fire before the call and had been looking forward to popping some corn. Whenever I did, I threw kernels high in the air for the dog to catch. Now I was gripped by something new—a dreadful array of feelings. Which should I choose to succumb to first? I couldn't decide. The dog came and put his head in my lap, and we sat there until I realized that one of the reactions I could have was numbness. Relieved, feeling nothing, I let the dog out, let him in, and went to bed.

She was shorter than me. And so ordinary. I was sure that I must have seen her in the street, or at the grocery, or in the bank, perhaps. It would have been hard not to have crossed paths with her at some point around here. But I would not have suspected her of being my mother. I could detect nothing familiar or like myself about her.

We did not shake hands or hug. We sat across from each other in a leather- 45
ette booth.

"You aren't . . ."

"Retarded? Lame?"

She composed herself. "You got your coloring from your father," she said. "George had dark hair."

Nancy Lasher had red-rimmed blue eyes behind bifocals, a sharp nose, a tiny, lipless bow of a mouth. Her hair was typical for a woman of seventy-seven—tightly permanented, gray-white. At one time, she had been a handsome woman, I thought, with strong features. Now she wore stained dentures, big earrings made of cultured pearls, a pale-blue pants suit. Walking in, I'd noticed her square-toed lace-up therapy shoes. There wasn't anything about her that called to me. She was just any little old lady you wouldn't want to approach.

4. Capital of North Dakota.

People on the reservation didn't go near women who looked like her—I can't say why. A mutual instinct for avoidance, perhaps.

50   "Would you like to order?" she asked, touching the menu. "Have anything you like—it's all on me."

"No, thank you, we will split the check," I answered.

I'd thought about this in advance and concluded that, if she wanted to assuage her guilt in some way, taking me out to dinner was far too cheap. So we ordered and ate and drank our glasses of sour white wine. As we did so, she talked. She asked me about myself. She drew me out, as they might say in a novel. She made sounds of interest and surprise and sympathy. She said that she admired me. We got through the dinner of walleye and pilaf.[5] Tears came into her eyes over a bowl of chocolate ice cream.

"I wish I'd known you were going to be so normal. I wish I hadn't ever given you up," she said.

I was alarmed at the effect that these words had on me, and quickly asked, "How's Linden?"

55   Her tears dried up and her face became sharp and direct.

"He's very sick," she said. "He's got kidney failure and is on dialysis. He's waiting for a kidney. I'd give him one of mine, but I'm a bad match and my kidney is old. George is dead. You are your brother's only hope."

I put my napkin to my lips and felt myself floating up off my chair. Someone floated with me, just barely with me, and I could feel his anxious breathing there. Now would be the time to call Sheryl, I thought. I should have called her before. She won't believe this. It seemed best to me, too, not to believe what I had just heard and felt. I had a twenty-dollar bill with me, and I put that money on the table and walked out the door. I got to my car, but before I could get in I had to run to the scarp of grass and weed that surrounded the parking lot. I was heaving and crying when I felt Nancy Lasher's hand stroking my back. It was the first time my birth mother had ever touched me, and although I quieted beneath her hand, I could detect a stupid triumph in her murmuring voice. She'd known where I lived all along, of course. I pushed her away, repelled by hatred, like an animal sprung from a trap.

"What should I do?" I asked Sheryl.

"I'm calling Cedric." He lived in Bismarck. "Listen here, Tuffy. I'll get Cedric to go to the hospital and pull the plug on this Linden, and you can forget this crap."

60   That was Sheryl—who else could have made me laugh under the circumstances?

It was the morning after the dinner, and I was still in bed. I'd called in sick for the first time in years.

"You're not seriously even considering it," Sheryl said. Then, when I didn't answer, "Are you?"

"I don't know."

"Then I really am calling Cedric up. Those people ditched you. They turned their backs on you. They would have left you in the street to die. You're *my*

---

5. Dish made with seasoned rice. *Walleye*: perch-like freshwater fish.

sister. I don't want you to share your kidneys. Hey, what if I need one of your kidneys someday? Did you ever think of that? Save your damn kidney for me!"

"O.K.," I said.   65

"I love you," she said, and I said it back.

"Tuffy, don't you do it," she warned, but her voice was suddenly small, vulnerable.

After she hung up, I called the numbers on the card my mother had given me and made appointments for the tests.

While I was down in Bismarck, I stayed with Cedric and his wife, whose name is Cheryl with a "C." She's a quiet person, but she put out little towels for me that she had appliquéd with the shapes of wild animals. And tiny motel soaps she'd swiped. She made my bed. She tried to show me that she approved of what I was doing, although the others in my family did not. She is very Christian. But this was not a do-unto-others sort of thing for me. I've already said that I don't seek pain, and I would not have contemplated going through with it unless I found the alternative unbearable.

All my life, knowing without knowing it, I had waited for this to happen. My   70
twin had been the one beside me, just out of sight. He did not know that he had been there, I was sure. He did not know that when I was stolen from Betty and alone in the whiteness he had held my hand, sat with me, and grieved. And now that I'd met his mother I understood something more. In a small town people knew everything; they knew what she had done by abandoning me. She'd have had to turn her fury with herself, her shame, on someone else—the child she'd chosen. She'd have blamed Linden. I had felt the contempt and the triumph in her touch. I was grateful now for the way things had turned out. Before we were born, my twin had had the compassion to crush me, to improve me by deforming me: I was the one who was spared.

"I'll tell you what," the doctor, a woman, who gave me the results of the tests and conducted the interview said. "You are a match, but I know your story. And I think it only fair that you know that Linden Lasher's kidney failure is his own fault. He has issues. He tried to commit suicide with a massive dose of acetaminophen, aspirin, and alcohol. That's why he is on dialysis. I think you should take that into account when making your decision."

Later that day, I sat with Linden, who said, "You don't have to do this. You don't have to be a Jesus."

"I know what you did," I said. "I'm not religious."

"Interesting," Linden said. He stared at me. "We sure don't look alike."

I realized that this was not a compliment, because he was nice-looking. He'd   75
got the best of his mother's features. But there was something else, too—his eyes shifted around the room. He kept biting his lip, whistling, rolling his blanket between his fingers.

"Are you a mail carrier?" he asked.

"I work behind the counter, mostly."

"I've got a good route," he said, yawning. "A regular route—I could do it in my sleep. Every Christmas, my people leave me cards, money, cookies, that sort of thing."

"Did you ever think," I said, "that there was someone walking your route just beside you or just behind you? Someone there when you closed your eyes, gone when you opened them?"

80   "No," he said. "Are you crazy?"

"That was me," I said.

I picked up his hand, and he let it go limp. We sat there together, silent. After a while, he pulled his hand out of mine and massaged it as though my grip had hurt.

"I don't like you," he said. "This was my mother's idea. I don't want your kidney. I don't want a piece of you inside me. I'd rather get on a list. Frankly, you're kind of a disgusting woman. I mean, I'm sorry, but you've probably heard this before."

"No," I said. "Nobody's ever told me that."

85   "You probably have a dog," he said. "Dogs love whoever feeds them. I doubt you could get a husband, or whatever, unless you put a bag over your head. And even then it would have to come off at night."

"Are you saying this to drive me away?" My throat clamped down on my voice. I swallowed, drew a deep breath to stop the shakes that had started in my body. "You want to die. You don't want to be saved, right? I'm not saving you for any reason. You won't owe me anything."

"Owe you?"

He seemed genuinely surprised. His teeth were so straight that I was sure he'd had orthodontic work done when he was young. He started laughing now, showing all those beautiful teeth. He shook his head, wagged his finger at me, laughing so hard he seemed overcome. When I bent down awkwardly to pick up my purse, he was infected by such a bout of hilarity that he nearly choked. I tried to get away from him, to get to the door, but instead I backed up against the wall and was stuck there in that white, white room.

2011

QUESTIONS

1. What do you think Tuffy will decide about whether to donate her kidney to Linden? What evidence from the story supports your hypothesis? What might Erdrich gain by leaving this question unanswered?

2. Near the beginning of the story, after telling the reader about the recurring "presence" she first experienced at age two, Tuffy remarks, "Its return is partly what this story is about" (par. 9). What does the story seem to suggest about what this presence is, why it appears to Tuffy as and when it does, why it matters to her, and what it does for her? If the story is only "partly" about that presence, what else is it about?

3. How are Tuffy's adoptive and birth families characterized? How and why do her impressions and feelings, particularly toward her birth family, evolve over the course of the story?

Chronology

1954   Born Karen Louise Erdrich on June 7 in Little Falls, Minnesota, the eldest of the seven children of Rita Joanne Gourneau (member of the Turtle Mountain Band of Chippewa Indians and daughter of former tribal chair Pat Gourneau) and Ralph Louis Erdrich (son of German immigrants who ran a butcher shop). She will, like her French-Ojibwe mother and grandfather, be raised Roman Catholic in Wahpeton, North Dakota, a small town on the Minnesota border where both her parents teach at the Bureau of Indian Affairs boarding school.

1972	Enters Dartmouth College, the year it first admits women and launches a Native American Studies program chaired by anthropologist Michael Dorris, with whom Erdrich takes classes. (Her "crazy jobs" during and after college include beet-hoeing, cucumber-picking, life-guarding, waitressing, and working as a signal flagperson for a construction crew.)
1976–77	Earns her BA in English; serves as visiting poet/teacher in the North Dakota Poets in the Schools Program.
1978	Enters MA writing program at Johns Hopkins University.
1979	Earns MA; edits *The Circle*, the Boston Indian Council newspaper; returns to Dartmouth for a reading and re-meets Dorris.
1981	Publishes a writing textbook for children (*Imagination*); returns to Dartmouth as writer-in-residence; marries Dorris and begins co-parenting his three adopted Sioux children, Abel, Sava, and Madeline. The couple also begin a close artistic collaboration, producing romance fiction under the pseudonym "Milou North."
1982	Wins Nelson Algren Literary Award for "The World's Greatest Fisherman," a story later incorporated into *Love Medicine*.
1983	Wins Pushcart Prize for the poem "Indian Boarding School: The Runaways." "Scales," another story later worked into *Love Medicine*, is chosen for *The Best American Short Stories 1983*.
1984	Publishes *Jacklight* (poetry collection) and *Love Medicine*; gives birth to the first of four biological daughters, Persia Andromeda. (The first novel in the so-called North Dakota or Argus cycle, *Love Medicine* wins multiple prizes including the National Book Critics Circle Award for Fiction.)
1985	Publishes *The Beet Queen* (second novel in the Argus series), a finalist for the National Book Critics Circle Award for Fiction; is awarded a Guggenheim Fellowship; gives birth to daughter Pallas Antigone.
1987	Wins O. Henry Award for "Fleur" (short story).
1988	Publishes *Tracks* (third novel in the Argus series). "Snares" chosen for *The Best American Short Stories 1988*.
1989	Publishes *Baptism of Desire* (poetry collection). Dorris publishes *The Broken Cord: A Family's Ongoing Struggle with Fetal Alcohol Syndrome*, with an introduction by Erdrich. Based on the life of their son Abel, it wins the National Book Critics Circle Award for Nonfiction and is later adapted into a television movie (1992).
1990	Named one of *People* magazine's "50 Most Beautiful People."
1991	Publishes *The Crown of Columbus* (novel coauthored with Dorris); Abel Dorris dies of injuries suffered in a hit-and-run accident.
1993	Moves with Dorris from New Hampshire to Minneapolis; publishes expanded edition of *Love Medicine*.

1994   Publishes *The Bingo Palace* (fourth novel in the Argus series).

1995   Publishes *The Blue Jay's Dance: A Birth Year* (memoir).

1996   Publishes *Tales of Burning Love* (novel) and *Grandmother's Pigeon* (her first children's book); separates from Dorris.

1997   Dorris commits suicide.

1998   Publishes *The Antelope Wife* (novel), which wins the World Fantasy Award.

1999   Publishes *The Birchbark House,* a finalist for the National Book Award for Young People's Literature and the first book in her illustrated Birchbark children's series.

2000   Receives Lifetime Achievement Award from the Native Writers' Circle of the Americas; gives birth to daughter Azure.

2001   Publishes *The Last Report on the Miracles at Little No Horse*, a finalist for the National Book Award for Fiction; opens Birchbark Books & Native Arts.

2003   Publishes *Original Fire: New and Selected Poems* and *The Master Butchers Singing Club* (novel).

2008   Publishes *The Plague of Doves*; the first novel in the Justice trilogy, it is short-listed for the Pulitzer Prize in Fiction.

2009   Publishes her only short-story collection, *The Red Convertible: Selected and New Stories 1978–2008.*

2010   Publishes *Shadow Tag* (novel).

2012   Publishes *The Round House*; the second novel in the Justice trilogy and winner of the National Book Award for Fiction, it includes the short story "The Years of My Birth."

2014   Wins PEN/Saul Bellow Award for Achievement in American Fiction and the Richard C. Holbrooke Award from the Dayton Literary Peace Prize Foundation.

2015   Wins U.S. Library of Congress Prize for American Fiction.

2016   Publishes *LaRose*, the third novel in the Justice trilogy, winner of the National Book Critics Circle Award for Fiction.

2017   Publishes *Future Home of the Living God*, her first novel set in the future.

2020   Publishes *The Night Watchman* (novel), winner of the Pulitzer Prize in Fiction.

SUGGESTIONS FOR WRITING

1. Both Love Medicine and The Years of My Birth feature narrator-protagonists who are adoptees, or what Lipsha, the former story's narrator, calls "took-ins" rather than "blood children" (par. 139). Write an essay exploring the patterns you see in Erdrich's portrayal of such characters and their families. What, through them, might she suggest or show us about the nature and importance of family in general

or of a specific type of family relationship such as that between siblings, grandparents and grandchildren, or parents and children?

2. Though Erdrich deploys all sorts of narrators and types of narration in her fiction, first-person narrators are especially common. By analyzing at least two Erdrich stories, write an essay exploring the significance and effect of Erdrich's use of first-person narrators and/or the ways in which she characterizes her protagonists—either by the form and style, as well as content, of their narratives, or by *how* they tell their stories and *what* stories they tell. Also or instead, consider the effects of the narrators' different genders and/or ages.

3. Toward the end of LOVE MEDICINE, Lipsha tells his grandmother that it was not "love medicine" that brought her husband's ghost back to her but love itself, not "magic" but "true feeling" (par. 157). Much earlier, he admits to being shocked to discover, through his grandparents, that love doesn't get "easier over the years" (par. 14). Write an essay analyzing how love, particularly "true" love, is depicted in at least two Erdrich stories. What might the narrator-protagonists of these stories themselves learn or discover about romantic love, and why and how so?

4. At one point in LOVE MEDICINE, Lipsha defines faith as "belief against the odds and whether or not there's any proof," avowing that though "[f]aith might be stupid, [. . .] it gets us through" (par. 72). Though Lipsha here refers to religious faith, especially faith in "Higher Power," one might see both this Erdrich story and others as dealing with other kinds of faith as well. Write an essay about faith in at least two Erdrich stories: How might these stories deal with the issue of faith generally or religious faith specifically? What kinds of faith do they consider? How, if at all, might they uphold and/or complicate the claims about faith that Lipsha makes in the quoted passage?

CULTURAL AND HISTORICAL CONTEXTS:

9 | WOMEN IN TURN-OF-THE-CENTURY AMERICA

Over the past two hundred years, the meaning of the word *culture* has broadened considerably, from "cultivation" (as in *agriculture*) to "the arts or familiarity with the arts" (*high culture, a cultured person*) to "a whole way of life" (*American culture, African American culture*). The fact that we still use the one word for both "the arts" and "a whole way of life" implies a close, even fundamental relationship between the two. The double implications of "culture" suggest that works of art both reflect and help shape the way we live.

On the one hand, art in a particular time and place takes the form it does because of the larger cultural context—what the nineteenth-century writer William Hazlitt called "the spirit of the age." In other words, authors, like the rest of us, live in particular times and places, and authorial visions, however unique, are inevitably shaped by cultural and historical context.

On the other hand, literature can shape history, too. Testifying to the powerful effect that writers can exercise, one member of the generation born just after World War I noted that Ernest Hemingway's "impact upon us was tremendous"; "We could follow him, ape his manner"; "we began unconsciously to [. . .] impose on everything we did and felt the particular emotions [his fiction] aroused in us." Authors sometimes choose to write precisely because they want to affect the way their contemporaries think, feel, and behave. Our understanding of a particular text or of an author's entire body of work is often enhanced if we learn more about that context.

But what happens to either the personal or the universal aspects of a literary work as we focus on its relationship to its cultural and historical context? At its best, the process is one of addition rather than subtraction. Reading a text in light of its context simply gives us a different but complementary perspective to that gained by reading the text on its own terms. Indeed, what makes the study of literature both exciting and enriching is its multilayered, multidimensional quality: the way that Flannery O'Connor's EVERYTHING THAT RISES MUST CONVERGE, for example, simultaneously embodies its author's personal vision of the association between violence and enlightenment, explores the universal problem of generational conflict, and evaluates the dramatic cultural transformations particular to the American South during the 1950s. The point, then, of reading with an eye toward cultural and historical context is not to foreclose other ways of reading but rather to enrich our experience of the text and, through it, our sense of what is both constant and variable about human experience across ages and cultures.

WOMEN AT THE TURN OF THE CENTURY:
AN OVERVIEW

The period between about 1890 and 1920, often referred to as "the turn of the twentieth century" and the Progressive Era, saw transformations in many aspects of society in the United States. The nation's rapid industrialization and urbanization, in changing the way people worked and lived, also inspired a number of economic, political, and social reforms. The Progressive Era brought attempts to regulate corporations and improve working conditions through the creation of new government agencies and the passage of labor laws. In the social sphere, reformers sought advances in education, sanitation, and health care. Many of these efforts, perhaps most notably the women's suffrage and temperance movements, were spearheaded by middle-class women, trying to improve their own circumstances and those of women of all socioeconomic classes and races.

Works of literature written by American women during this period provide valuable insights into the predicaments of married middle-class White women in Progressive-Era America. This chapter examines three classics in the context of women's roles at the turn of the century: Charlotte Perkins Gilman's THE YELLOW WALLPAPER (1892), Kate Chopin's THE STORY OF AN HOUR (1894), and Susan Glaspell's A JURY OF HER PEERS (1917, based on her 1916 play TRIFLES). Without directly commenting on historic developments, these realistic stories about married women in domestic settings reflect changing outlooks. The chapter includes a selective chronology of relevant biographical and historical events and a sample of contemporary documents on relevant topics. The list of sources and the writing suggestions at the end of the chapter point out several possible avenues for interpreting and writing about these stories. But first, we introduce some of the issues women faced at the time: work inside and outside the home; marriage law, domestic violence, and divorce; and the medical treatment of women—all matters that came under scrutiny thanks to Charlotte Perkins Gilman and other women leaders of the time.

In the Progressive Era, it was still the norm for a married White woman to serve as full-time manager of the home and any servants in it: By 1920, only 6.5 percent of married White women in the United States held paying jobs. In contrast, married African American women, who in the post–Civil War South had long been forced to work for minimal pay in the fields or as laundresses or cooks in White households, continued to seek paid work after migrating to Northern cities. Among single women of all races, half worked as paid employees at this time.

Work in the home, for wives or servants, could be very hard. For decades after the Civil War, women of all classes and races produced most of their households' clothing and food, quilts and curtains, and were kept busy tending wood or coal fires, making candles, or tending oil or gas lamps. Water had to be pumped, carried, and heated over fires, and laundry took more than a day's hard labor. It was rare, even among poorer families, for a house to be run without at least part-time hired help.

Toward the end of the nineteenth century, a series of inventions reduced domestic chores, and so domestic service declined. After the 1850s, sewing machines gradually became affordable not only for manufacturers but also for individuals, and the invention of the Mason jar in 1857 enabled families to preserve their homegrown fruits and vegetables for the winter. In 1931, the National

Susan Glaspell at typewriter (Berg Collection, New York Public Library)

Association of Real Estate Boards looked back at changes in the home: A newspaper article, "Home Necessities Once Were Luxury," quotes the association's finding that since the 1870s, "The electric light and the development of the array of electrical appliances did the work of the modern housewife," while bathtubs, once rare, newsworthy luxuries, were now installed in many homes (*New York Times,* 18 Jan. 1931).

Some Innovations in Travel and Communication

- **Train**—first available for passengers in the 1820s, but not widely used in the United States until the 1890s.
- **Automobile**—mass-produced by 1908, though horse-drawn carts and carriages remained in use in many areas through the 1930s.
- **Telegraph**—first developed in the 1830s; transatlantic in 1866; improved in the 1870s; wireless by the 1890s.
- **Telephone**—Alexander Graham Bell's first patent was granted in 1876; hand-crank telephones reached Iowa farms by 1900, with households sharing "party" lines.
- **Typewriter**—available in less expensive models for more businesses from the 1870s onward; women began to work as "typewriters."

A new convenience or labor-saving device, from the automobile to electricity to the telephone, could free a housewife from hours of work and allow her to pursue another occupation, to stay in touch with friends, to develop artistic talents, or to experience the world. The changes spread slowly, however, and were more common in urban areas and well-to-do homes than on farms or in working-class tenements. Social expectations for upper-class women kept many of them idle and dependent on servants.

Middle-class women's usefulness as household producers declined before opportunities for education and meaningful careers opened up. Medicine and law became organized, standardized professions at the turn of the century, for example, but both of these highly paid fields excluded women (and many men). At the same time, medical treatments and legal procedures that responded to any of the dysfunctions of married life tended to directly and indirectly increase men's domination of women. The "rest cure," psychoanalysis, and other medical practices developed by professional men became common ways to treat women suffering from the illnesses and depression that may have resulted in part from their feelings of purposelessness and inactivity. A woman might find her desire to pursue a career diagnosed as an illness; her acts of self-determination or resistance might be prohibited, punished, or judged insane.

Well into the twentieth century, divorce was expensive and difficult and usually resulted in a clouded reputation for the woman (as it did for the divorced Charlotte Stetson before she married George Houghton Gilman). Not until 1900 were some women able to sue successfully for divorce on the grounds of the husband's "mental cruelty"; previously, they would have needed to prove that he was violent or had committed adultery.

WOMEN WRITERS IN A CHANGING WORLD

In the United States and Europe, women's roles were slowly changing, however, thanks to the efforts of reform groups. Both Gilman and Glaspell participated in such efforts, on behalf of women and others, through their work with Heterodoxy, a New York group that advocated women's civil rights and suffrage. Gilman, in testimony before Congress on January 28, 1896, argued that extending the vote to women would "improve the [human] race by improving the women." "You can not have as good a citizen, as good a class of people, where half the people are no part of the Government," she argued, "[a]nd to debar any part of the race from its development is to carry along with society a dead weight, a part of the organism which is not living organic matter, which is a thing to be carried instead of to help. To give suffrage to this half of the race will develop it as it never has been developed before."[1] Gilman and Glaspell both lived to see U.S. women gain the vote in 1920.

Especially after 1870, women began to gain access to higher education and to demand entrance to careers other than teaching, writing, or the arts. By the beginning of the twentieth century, some women pursued careers in nursing, social work, libraries, fashion, and business, though most were employed in lower-paid positions, as clerical or support staff rather than as managers. Writing had long been a way to earn a living for some educated women, but the spread of newspapers and mass-market magazines from the 1890s onward provided openings for a new kind of worker, the woman journalist.

Chopin, Gilman, and Glaspell, needing to earn a living, embraced such opportunities. Susan Glaspell began her journalism career after college, as a reporter in

---

1. Charlotte Perkins Gilman, testimony before Congress of the National American Woman Suffrage Association Committee on the Judiciary in Washington, D.C., 28 Jan. 1896. Originally published in *In This Our World*, Small, Maynard, 1893, pp. 95–100.

The Woman in Business
—*how big is her Future?*

What first projected women into business?

The Typewriter.

Who built the first practical typewriter and employed the first typist to run it?

Remington!

Since 1874 Remington has introduced more than 2,000,000 women to paying positions and the means to a bigger life. Each year this number is increased by about 75,000.

Thanks to Remington, who threw open the doors of opportunity, women have advanced to high achievement in the business world.

Today:—

A woman who started as a typist is the private secretary and real advisor to one of America's greatest financiers.

Another is advertising manager of America's greatest premium business.

A salary of about $9000 a year is paid to a woman concerned with the promotion of a highly esteemed proprietary remedy. She started as a typist.

Another woman who not so long ago was written of as the "highest salaried woman in America" thanks the typewriter for her start.

And these few instances but typify many others.

How to Start

How big is the future of the woman today who contemplates business as a career?

Business tells us that it cannot find enough of the kind of women it wants. Business fairly clamors for girls of high intelligence and good education. Executives say that an efficient private secretary is invaluable.

REMINGTON

Remington typewriter advertisement, 1919

Iowa, and covered a scandalous murder case similar to the one in her story "A Jury of Her Peers." These writers' careers and writings, including the works featured here, reflect both the expanding prospects and continuing limitations on women's lives in this transitional period.

KATE CHOPIN
(1850–1904)

The Story of an Hour

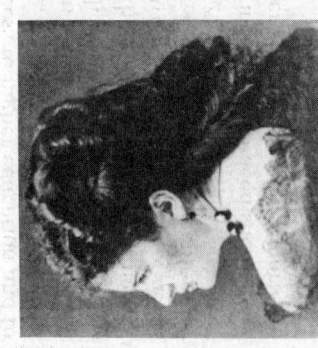

Katherine O'Flaherty was born in St. Louis, Missouri, to a high-ranking Creole-Irish family. Her father died when she was four, and Kate was raised by her mother, grandmother, and great-grandmother. Well-read at a young age, she received her formal education at the St. Louis Academy of the Sacred Heart. In 1870, she married Oscar Chopin, a Louisiana businessman, and lived with him in Natchitoches Parish and New Orleans, where she became a close observer of

Creole and Cajun life. Following her husband's sudden death in 1884, she returned to St. Louis, where she raised her six children and began her literary career. In slightly more than a decade she produced a substantial body of work, including the story collections *Bayou Folk* (1894) and *A Night in Acadie* (1897). Her classic novella *The Awakening* (1899) was greeted with a storm of criticism for its frank treatment of female sexuality.

K nowing that Mrs. Mallard was afflicted with a heart trouble, great care was taken to break to her as gently as possible the news of her husband's death.

It was her sister Josephine who told her, in broken sentences; veiled hints that revealed in half concealing. Her husband's friend Richards was there, too, near her. It was he who had been in the newspaper office when intelligence of the railroad disaster was received, with Brently Mallard's name leading the list of "killed." He had only taken the time to assure himself of its truth by a second telegram, and had hastened to forestall any less careful, less tender friend in bearing the sad message.

She did not hear the story as many women have heard the same, with a paralyzed inability to accept its significance. She wept at once, with sudden, wild abandonment, in her sister's arms. When the storm of grief had spent itself she went away to her room alone. She would have no one follow her.

There stood, facing the open window, a comfortable, roomy armchair. Into this she sank, pressed down by a physical exhaustion that haunted her body and seemed to reach into her soul.

She could see in the open square before her house the tops of trees that were all aquiver with the new spring life. The delicious breath of rain was in the air. In the street below a peddler was crying his wares. The notes of a distant song which some one was singing reached her faintly, and countless sparrows were twittering in the eaves. 5

There were patches of blue sky showing here and there through the clouds that had met and piled one above the other in the west facing her window.

She sat with her head thrown back upon the cushion of the chair, quite motionless, except when a sob came up into her throat and shook her, as a child who has cried itself to sleep continues to sob in its dreams.

She was young, with a fair, calm face, whose lines bespoke repression and even a certain strength. But now there was a dull stare in her eyes, whose gaze was fixed away off yonder on one of those patches of blue sky. It was not a glance of reflection, but rather indicated a suspension of intelligent thought.

There was something coming to her and she was waiting for it, fearfully. What was it? She did not know; it was too subtle and elusive to name. But she felt it, creeping out of the sky, reaching toward her through the sounds, the scents, the color that filled the air.

Now her bosom rose and fell tumultuously. She was beginning to recognize 10 this thing that was approaching to possess her, and she was striving to beat it back with her will—as powerless as her two white slender hands would have been.

When she abandoned herself a little whispered word escaped her slightly parted lips. She said it over and over under her breath: "free, free, free!" The vacant stare and the look of terror that had followed it went from her eyes. They stayed keen and bright. Her pulses beat fast, and the coursing blood warmed and relaxed every inch of her body.

She did not stop to ask if it were or were not a monstrous joy that held her. A clear and exalted perception enabled her to dismiss the suggestion as trivial.

She knew that she would weep again when she saw the kind, tender hands folded in death; the face that had never looked save with love upon her, fixed and gray and dead. But she saw beyond that bitter moment a long procession of years to come that would belong to her absolutely. And she opened and spread her arms out to them in welcome.

There would be no one to live for her during those coming years; she would live for herself. There would be no powerful will bending hers in that blind persistence with which men and women believe they have a right to impose a private will upon a fellow-creature. A kind intention or a cruel intention made the act seem no less a crime as she looked upon it in that brief moment of illumination.

15   And yet she had loved him—sometimes. Often she had not. What did it matter! What could love, the unsolved mystery, count for in face of this possession of self-assertion which she suddenly recognized as the strongest impulse of her being!

"Free! Body and soul free!" she kept whispering.

Josephine was kneeling before the closed door with her lips to the keyhole, imploring for admission. "Louise, open the door! I beg; open the door—you will make yourself ill. What are you doing, Louise? For heaven's sake open the door."

"Go away. I am not making myself ill." No; she was drinking in a very elixir of life through that open window.

Her fancy was running riot along those days ahead of her. Spring days, and summer days, and all sorts of days that would be her own. She breathed a quick prayer that life might be long. It was only yesterday she had thought with a shudder that life might be long.

20   She arose at length and opened the door to her sister's importunities. There was a feverish triumph in her eyes, and she carried herself unwittingly like a goddess of Victory. She clasped her sister's waist, and together they descended the stairs. Richards stood waiting for them at the bottom.

Some one was opening the front door with a latchkey. It was Brently Mallard who entered, a little travel-stained, composedly carrying his grip-sack and umbrella. He had been far from the scene of accident, and did not even know there had been one. He stood amazed at Josephine's piercing cry; at Richards' quick motion to screen him from the view of his wife.

But Richards was too late.

When the doctors came they said she had died of heart disease—of joy that kills.

1894

CHARLOTTE PERKINS GILMAN
(1860–1935)

The Yellow Wallpaper

Charlotte Anna Perkins was born in Hartford, Connecticut. After a painful, lonely childhood and several years of supporting herself as a governess, art teacher, and designer of greeting cards, Perkins married the artist Charles Stetson. Following her several extended periods of depression, Charles Stetson put his wife in the care of a doctor who, in her own words, "sent me home with the solemn advice to 'live as domestic a life as [. . .] possible,' to 'have but two hours' intellectual life a day,' and 'never to touch pen, brush, or pencil again' as long as I lived." Three months of this regimen brought her "near the borderline of utter mortal ruin" and inspired her masterpiece, "The Yellow Wallpaper." In 1900, she married George Houghton Gilman, having divorced Stetson in 1892. Her nonfiction works, springing from the early women's movement, include *Women and Economics* (1898) and *The Man-Made World* (1911). She also wrote several utopian novels, including *Moving the Mountain* (1911) and *Herland* (1915).

I t is very seldom that mere ordinary people like John and myself secure ancestral halls for the summer.

A colonial mansion, a hereditary estate, I would say a haunted house, and reach the height of romantic felicity—but that would be asking too much of fate!

Still I will proudly declare that there is something queer about it.

Else, why should it be let so cheaply? And why have stood so long untenanted?

John laughs at me, of course, but one expects that in marriage.   5

John is practical in the extreme. He has no patience with faith, an intense horror of superstition, and he scoffs openly at any talk of things not to be felt and seen and put down in figures.

John is a physician, and *perhaps*—(I would not say it to a living soul, of course, but this is dead paper and a great relief to my mind—) *perhaps* that is one reason I do not get well faster.

You see he does not believe I am sick!

And what can one do?

If a physician of high standing, and one's own husband, assures friends and   10
relatives that there is really nothing the matter with one but temporary nervous depression—a slight hysterical tendency—what is one to do?

My brother is also a physician, and also of high standing, and he says the same thing.

So I take phosphates or phosphites—whichever it is, and tonics, and journeys, and air, and exercise, and am absolutely forbidden to "work" until I am well again.

Personally, I disagree with their ideas.

Personally, I believe that congenial work, with excitement and change, would do me good.

15   But what is one to do?

I did write for a while in spite of them; but it *does* exhaust me a good deal—having to be so sly about it, or else meet with heavy opposition.

I sometimes fancy that in my condition if I had less opposition and more society and stimulus—but John says the very worst thing I can do is to think about my condition, and I confess it always makes me feel bad.

So I will let it alone and talk about the house.

The most beautiful place! It is quite alone, standing well back from the road, quite three miles from the village. It makes me think of English places that you read about, for there are hedges and walls and gates that lock, and lots of separate little houses for the gardeners and people.

20   There is a *delicious* garden! I never saw such a garden—large and shady, full of box-bordered paths, and lined with long grape-covered arbors with seats under them.

There were greenhouses, too, but they are all broken now.

There was some legal trouble, I believe, something about the heirs and co-heirs; anyhow, the place has been empty for years.

That spoils my ghostliness, I am afraid, but I don't care—there is something strange about the house—I can feel it.

I even said so to John one moonlight evening, but he said what I felt was a *draught*, and shut the window.

25   I get unreasonably angry with John sometimes. I'm sure I never used to be so sensitive. I think it is due to this nervous condition.

But John says if I feel so, I shall neglect proper self-control; so I take pains to control myself—before him, at least, and that makes me very tired.

I don't like our room a bit. I wanted one downstairs that opened on the piazza and had roses all over the window, and such pretty old-fashioned chintz hangings! but John would not hear of it.

He said there was only one window and not room for two beds, and no near room for him if he took another.

He is very careful and loving, and hardly lets me stir without special direction.

30   I have a schedule prescription for each hour in the day; he takes all care from me, and so I feel basely ungrateful not to value it more.

He said we came here solely on my account, that I was to have perfect rest and all the air I could get. "Your exercise depends on your strength, my dear," said he, "and your food somewhat on your appetite; but air you can absorb all the time." So we took the nursery at the top of the house.

It is a big, airy room, the whole floor nearly, with windows that look all ways, and air and sunshine galore. It was nursery first and then playroom and gymnasium, I should judge; for the windows are barred for little children, and there are rings and things in the walls.

The paint and paper look as if a boys' school had used it. It is stripped off—the paper—in great patches all around the head of my bed, about as far as I can reach, and in a great place on the other side of the room low down. I never saw a worse paper in my life.

One of those sprawling flamboyant patterns committing every artistic sin.

It is dull enough to confuse the eye in following, pronounced enough to constantly irritate and provoke study, and when you follow the lame uncertain curves for a little distance they suddenly commit suicide—plunge off at outrageous angles, destroy themselves in unheard of contradictions.

The color is repellant, almost revolting; a smouldering unclean yellow, strangely faded by the slow-turning sunlight.

It is a dull yet lurid orange in some places, a sickly sulphur tint in others.

No wonder the children hated it! I should hate it myself if I had to live in this room long.

There comes John, and I must put this away,—he hates to have me write a word.

We have been here two weeks, and I haven't felt like writing before, since that first day.

I am sitting by the window now, up in this atrocious nursery, and there is nothing to hinder my writing as much as I please, save lack of strength.

John is away all day, and even some nights when his cases are serious.

I am glad my case is not serious!

But these nervous troubles are dreadfully depressing.

John does not know how much I really suffer. He knows there is no *reason* to suffer, and that satisfies him.

Of course it is only nervousness. It does weigh on me so not to do my duty in any way!

I mean to be such a help to John, such a real rest and comfort, and here I am a comparative burden already!

Nobody would believe what an effort it is to do what little I am able,—to dress and entertain, and order things.

It is fortunate Mary is so good with the baby. Such a dear baby!

And yet I *cannot* be with him, it makes me so nervous.

I suppose John never was nervous in his life. He laughs at me so about this wallpaper!

At first he meant to repaper the room, but afterwards he said that I was letting it get the better of me, and that nothing was worse for a nervous patient than to give way to such fancies.

He said that after the wallpaper was changed it would be the heavy bedstead, and then the barred windows, and then that gate at the head of the stairs, and so on.

"You know the place is doing you good," he said, "and really, dear, I don't care to renovate the house just for a three months' rental."

"Then do let us go downstairs," I said, "there are such pretty rooms there."

Then he took me in his arms and called me a blessed little goose, and said he would go down cellar, if I wished, and have it whitewashed into the bargain.

But he is right enough about the beds and windows and things.

It is an airy and comfortable room as any one need wish, and, of course, I would not be so silly as to make him uncomfortable just for a whim.

I'm really getting quite fond of the big room, all but that horrid paper.

Out of one window I can see the garden, those mysterious deep-shaded arbors, the riotous old-fashioned flowers, and bushes and gnarly trees.

Out of another I get a lovely view of the bay and a little private wharf belonging to the estate. There is a beautiful shaded lane that runs down there from the house. I always fancy I see people walking in these numerous paths and arbors, but John has cautioned me not to give way to fancy in the least. He says that with my imaginative power and habit of story-making, a nervous weakness like mine is sure to lead to all manner of excited fancies, and that I ought to use my will and good sense to check the tendency. So I try.

I think sometimes that if I were only well enough to write a little it would relieve the press of ideas and rest me.

But I find I get pretty tired when I try.

It is so discouraging not to have any advice and companionship about my work. When I get really well, John says we will ask Cousin Henry and Julia down for a long visit; but he says he would as soon put fireworks in my pillow-case as to let me have those stimulating people about now.

65   I wish I could get well faster.

But I must not think about that. This paper looks to me as if it *knew* what a vicious influence it had!

There is a recurrent spot where the pattern lolls like a broken neck and two bulbous eyes stare at you upside down.

I get positively angry with the impertinence of it and the everlastingness. Up and down and sideways they crawl, and those absurd, unblinking eyes are everywhere. There is one place where two breadths didn't match, and the eyes go all up and down the line, one a little higher than the other.

I never saw so much expression in an inanimate thing before, and we all know how much expression they have! I used to lie awake as a child and get more entertainment and terror out of blank walls and plain furniture than most children could find in a toy-store.

70   I remember what a kindly wink the knobs of our big, old bureau used to have, and there was one chair that always seemed like a strong friend.

I used to feel that if any of the other things looked too fierce I could always hop into that chair and be safe.

The furniture in this room is no worse than inharmonious, however, for we had to bring it all from downstairs. I suppose when this was used as a playroom they had to take the nursery things out, and no wonder! I never saw such ravages as the children have made here.

The wallpaper, as I said before, is torn off in spots, and it sticketh closer than a brother—they must have had perseverance as well as hatred.

Then the floor is scratched and gouged and splintered, the plaster itself is dug out here and there, and this great heavy bed which is all we found in the room, looks as if it had been through the wars.

75   But I don't mind it a bit—only the paper.

There comes John's sister. Such a dear girl as she is, and so careful of me! I must not let her find me writing.

She is a perfect and enthusiastic housekeeper, and hopes for no better profession. I verily believe she thinks it is the writing which made me sick!

But I can write when she is out, and see her a long way off from these windows.

There is one that commands the road, a lovely shaded winding road, and one that just looks off over the country. A lovely country, too, full of great elms and velvet meadows.

This wallpaper has a kind of sub-pattern in a different shade, a particularly 80
irritating one, for you can only see it in certain lights, and not clearly then.

But in the places where it isn't faded and where the sun is just so—I can see
a strange, provoking, formless sort of figure, that seems to skulk about behind
that silly and conspicuous front design.

There's sister on the stairs!

Well, the Fourth of July is over! The people are all gone and I am tired out. John
thought it might do me good to see a little company, so we just had mother and
Nellie and the children down for a week.

Of course I didn't do a thing. Jennie sees to everything now.

But it tired me all the same. 85

John says if I don't pick up faster he shall send me to Weir Mitchell[1] in
the fall.

But I don't want to go there at all. I had a friend who was in his hands once,
and she says he is just like John and my brother, only more so!

Besides, it is such an undertaking to go so far.

I don't feel as if it was worth while to turn my hand over for anything, and I'm
getting dreadfully fretful and querulous.

I cry at nothing, and cry most of the time. 90

Of course I don't when John is here, or anybody else, but when I am alone.

And I am alone a good deal just now. John is kept in town very often by serious cases, and Jennie is good and lets me alone when I want her to.

So I walk a little in the garden or down that lovely lane, sit on the porch
under the roses, and lie down up here a good deal.

I'm getting really fond of the room in spite of the wallpaper. Perhaps *because*
of the wallpaper.

It dwells in my mind so! 95

I lie here on this great immovable bed—it is nailed down, I believe—and
follow that pattern about by the hour. It is as good as gymnastics, I assure you.
I start, we'll say, at the bottom, down in the corner over there where it has not
been touched, and I determine for the thousandth time that I *will* follow that
pointless pattern to some sort of conclusion.

I know a little of the principle of design, and I know this thing was not
arranged on any laws of radiation, or alternation, or repetition, or symmetry, or
anything else that I ever heard of.

It is repeated, of course, by the breadths, but not otherwise.

Looked at in one way each breadth stands alone, the bloated curves and
flourishes—a kind of "debased Romanesque" with *delirium tremens*—go waddling up and down in isolated columns of fatuity.

But, on the other hand, they connect diagonally, and the sprawling outlines 100
run off in great slanting waves of optic horror, like a lot of wallowing seaweeds
in full chase.

The whole thing goes horizontally, too, at least it seems so, and I exhaust
myself in trying to distinguish the order of its going in that direction.

1. Silas Weir Mitchell (1829–1914), American physician, novelist, and specialist in nerve disorders,
popularized the rest cure.

They have used a horizontal breadth for a frieze, and that adds wonderfully to the confusion.

There is one end of the room where it is almost intact, and there, when the crosslights fade and the low sun shines directly upon it, I can almost fancy radiation after all,—the interminable grotesque seem to form around a common center and rush off in headlong plunges of equal distraction.

It makes me tired to follow it. I will take a nap I guess.

105   I don't know why I should write this.

I don't want to.

I don't feel able.

And I know John would think it absurd. But I *must* say what I feel and think in some way—it is such a relief!

But the effort is getting to be greater than the relief.

110   Half the time now I am awfully lazy, and lie down ever so much.

John says I mustn't lose my strength, and has me take cod liver oil and lots of tonics and things, to say nothing of ale and wine and rare meat.

Dear John! He loves me very dearly, and hates to have me sick. I tried to have a real earnest reasonable talk with him the other day, and tell him how I wish he would let me go and make a visit to Cousin Henry and Julia.

But he said I wasn't able to go, nor able to stand it after I got there; and I did not make out a very good case for myself, for I was crying before I had finished.

It is getting to be a great effort for me to think straight. Just this nervous weakness I suppose.

115   And dear John gathered me up in his arms, and just carried me upstairs and laid me on the bed, and sat by me and read to me till it tired my head.

He said I was his darling and his comfort and all he had, and that I must take care of myself for his sake, and keep well.

He says no one but myself can help me out of it, that I must use my will and self-control and not let any silly fancies run away with me.

There's one comfort, the baby is well and happy, and does not have to occupy this nursery with the horrid wallpaper.

If we had not used it, that blessed child would have! What a fortunate escape! Why, I wouldn't have a child of mine, an impressionable little thing, live in such a room for worlds.

120   I never thought of it before, but it is lucky that John kept me here after all, I can stand it so much easier than a baby, you see.

Of course I never mention it to them any more—I am too wise,—but I keep watch of it all the same.

There are things in that paper that nobody knows but me, or ever will.

Behind that outside pattern the dim shapes get clearer every day.

It is always the same shape, only very numerous.

125   And it is like a woman stooping down and creeping about behind that pattern. I don't like it a bit. I wonder—I begin to think—I wish John would take me away from here!

It is so hard to talk with John about my case, because he is so wise, and because he loves me so.

But I tried it last night.

It was moonlight. The moon shines in all around just as the sun does.

I hate to see it sometimes, it creeps so slowly, and always comes in by one window or another.

John was asleep and I hated to waken him, so I kept still and watched the 130 moonlight on that undulating wallpaper till I felt creepy.

The faint figure behind seemed to shake the pattern, just as if she wanted to get out.

I got up softly and went to feel and see if the paper *did* move, and when I came back John was awake.

"What is it, little girl?" he said. "Don't go walking about like that—you'll get cold."

I thought it was a good time to talk, so I told him that I really was not gaining here, and that I wished he would take me away.

"Why, darling!" said he, "our lease will be up in three weeks, and I can't see 135 how to leave before.

"The repairs are not done at home, and I cannot possibly leave town just now. Of course if you were in any danger, I could and would, but you really are better, dear, whether you can see it or not. I am a doctor, dear, and I know. You are gaining flesh and color, your appetite is better, I feel really much easier about you."

"I don't weigh a bit more," said I, "nor as much; and my appetite may be better in the evening when you are here, but it is worse in the morning when you are away!"

"Bless her little heart!" said he with a big hug, "she shall be as sick as she pleases! But now let's improve the shining hours by going to sleep, and talk about it in the morning!"

"And you won't go away?" I asked gloomily.

"Why, how can I, dear? It is only three weeks more and then we will take a 140 nice little trip of a few days while Jennie is getting the house ready. Really dear you are better!"

"Better in body perhaps—" I began, and stopped short, for he sat up straight and looked at me with such a stern, reproachful look that I could not say another word.

"My darling," said he, "I beg of you, for my sake and for our child's sake, as well as for your own, that you will never for one instant let that idea enter your mind! There is nothing so dangerous, so fascinating, to a temperament like yours. It is a false and foolish fancy. Can you not trust me as a physician when I tell you so?"

So of course I said no more on that score, and we went to sleep before long. He thought I was asleep first, but I wasn't, and lay there for hours trying to decide whether that front pattern and the back pattern really did move together or separately.

On a pattern like this, by daylight, there is a lack of sequence, a defiance of law, that is a constant irritant to a normal mind.

The color is hideous enough, and unreliable enough, and infuriating enough, 145 but the pattern is torturing.

You think you have mastered it, but just as you get well underway in following, it turns a back-somersault and there you are. It slaps you in the face, knocks you down, and tramples upon you. It is like a bad dream.

The outside pattern is a florid arabesque, reminding one of a fungus. If you can imagine a toadstool in joints, an interminable string of toadstools, budding and sprouting in endless convolutions—why, that is something like it.

That is, sometimes!

There is one marked peculiarity about this paper, a thing nobody seems to notice but myself, and that is that it changes as the light changes.

150   When the sun shoots in through the east window—I always watch for that first long, straight ray—it changes so quickly that I never can quite believe it.

That is why I watch it always.

By moonlight—the moon shines in all night when there is a moon—I wouldn't know it was the same paper.

At night in any kind of light, in twilight, candlelight, lamplight, and worst of all by moonlight, it becomes bars! The outside pattern I mean, and the woman behind it is as plain as can be.

I didn't realize for a long time what the thing was that showed behind, that dim sub-pattern, but now I am quite sure it is a woman.

155   By daylight she is subdued, quiet. I fancy it is the pattern that keeps her so still. It is so puzzling. It keeps me quiet by the hour.

I lie down ever so much now. John says it is good for me, and to sleep all I can.

Indeed he started the habit by making me lie down for an hour after each meal.

It is a very bad habit I am convinced, for you see I don't sleep.

And that cultivates deceit, for I don't tell them I'm awake—O no!

160   The fact is I am getting a little afraid of John.

He seems very queer sometimes, and even Jennie has an inexplicable look.

It strikes me occasionally, just as a scientific hypothesis,—that perhaps it is the paper!

I have watched John when he did not know I was looking, and come into the room suddenly on the most innocent excuses, and I've caught him several times *looking at the paper*! And Jennie too. I caught Jennie with her hand on it once.

She didn't know I was in the room, and when I asked her in a quiet, a very quiet voice, with the most restrained manner possible, what she was doing with the paper—she turned around as if she had been caught stealing, and looked quite angry—asked me why I should frighten her so!

165   Then she said that the paper stained everything it touched, that she had found yellow smooches on all my clothes and John's, and she wished we would be more careful!

Did not that sound innocent? But I know she was studying that pattern, and I am determined that nobody shall find it out but myself!

Life is very much more exciting now than it used to be. You see I have something more to expect, to look forward to, to watch. I really do eat better, and am more quiet than I was.

John is so pleased to see me improve! He laughed a little the other day, and said I seemed to be flourishing in spite of my wallpaper.

I turned it off with a laugh. I had no intention of telling him it was *because* of the wallpaper—he would make fun of me. He might even want to take me away.

I don't want to leave now until I have found it out. There is a week more, and I think that will be enough.

I'm feeling ever so much better! I don't sleep much at night, for it is so interesting to watch developments; but I sleep a good deal in the daytime.

In the daytime it is tiresome and perplexing.

There are always new shoots on the fungus, and new shades of yellow all over it. I cannot keep count of them, though I have tried conscientiously.

It is the strangest yellow, that wallpaper! It makes me think of all the yellow things I ever saw—not beautiful ones like buttercups, but old foul, bad yellow things.

But there is something else about that paper—the smell! I noticed it the moment we came into the room, but with so much air and sun it was not bad. Now we have had a week of fog and rain, and whether the windows are open or not, the smell is here.

It creeps all over the house.

I find it hovering in the dining-room, skulking in the parlor, hiding in the hall, lying in wait for me on the stairs.

It gets into my hair.

Even when I go to ride, if I turn my head suddenly and surprise it—there is that smell!

Such a peculiar odor, too! I have spent hours in trying to analyze it, to find what it smelled like.

It is not bad—at first, and very gentle, but quite the subtlest, most enduring odor I ever met.

In this damp weather it is awful, I wake up in the night and find it hanging over me.

It used to disturb me at first. I thought seriously of burning the house—to reach the smell.

But now I am used to it. The only thing I can think of that it is like is the *color* of the paper! A yellow smell.

There is a very funny mark on this wall, low down, near the mopboard. A streak that runs round the room. It goes behind every piece of furniture, except the bed, a long, straight, even *smooch*, as if it had been rubbed over and over.

I wonder how it was done and who did it, and what they did it for. Round and round and round—round and round and round—it makes me dizzy!

I really have discovered something at last.

Through watching so much at night, when it changes so, I have finally found out.

The front pattern *does* move—and no wonder! The woman behind shakes it!

Sometimes I think there are a great many women behind, and sometimes only one, and she crawls around fast, and her crawling shakes it all over.

Then in the very bright spots she keeps still, and in the very shady spots she just takes hold of the bars and shakes them hard.

And she is all the time trying to climb through. But nobody could climb through that pattern—it strangles so; I think that is why it has so many heads.

They get through, and then the pattern strangles them off and turns them upside down, and makes their eyes white!

If those heads were covered or taken off it would not be half so bad.

195   I think that woman gets out in the daytime!

And I'll tell you why—privately—I've seen her!

I can see her out of every one of my windows!

It is the same woman, I know, for she is always creeping, and most women do not creep by daylight.

I see her in that long shaded lane, creeping up and down. I see her in those dark grape arbors, creeping all around the garden.

200   I see her on that long road under the trees, creeping along, and when a carriage comes she hides under the blackberry vines.

I don't blame her a bit. It must be very humiliating to be caught creeping by daylight!

I always lock the door when I creep by daylight. I can't do it at night, for I know John would suspect something at once.

And John is so queer now, that I don't want to irritate him. I wish he would take another room! Besides, I don't want anybody to get that woman out at night but myself.

I often wonder if I could see her out of all the windows at once.

205   But, turn as fast as I can, I can only see out of one at one time.

And though I always see her, she *may* be able to creep faster than I can turn!

I have watched her sometimes away off in the open country, creeping as fast as a cloud shadow in a high wind.

If only that top pattern could be gotten off from the under one! I mean to try it, little by little.

I have found out another funny thing, but I shan't tell it this time! It does not do to trust people too much.

210   There are only two more days to get this paper off, and I believe John is beginning to notice. I don't like the look in his eyes.

And I heard him ask Jennie a lot of professional questions about me. She had a very good report to give.

She said I slept a good deal in the daytime.

John knows I don't sleep very well at night, for all I'm so quiet!

He asked me all sorts of questions, too, and pretended to be very loving and kind.

215   As if I couldn't see through him!

Still, I don't wonder he acts so, sleeping under this paper for three months.

It only interests me, but I feel sure John and Jennie are secretly affected by it.

Hurrah! This is the last day, but it is enough. John is to stay in town over night, and won't be out until this evening.

Jennie wanted to sleep with me—the sly thing! but I told her I should undoubtedly rest better for a night all alone.

That was clever, for really I wasn't alone a bit! As soon as it was moonlight 220
and that poor thing began to crawl and shake the pattern, I got up and ran to
help her.

I pulled and she shook, I shook and she pulled, and before morning we had
peeled off yards of that paper.

A strip about as high as my head and half around the room.

And then when the sun came and that awful pattern began to laugh at me, I
declared I would finish it to-day!

We go away to-morrow, and they are moving all my furniture down again to
leave things as they were before.

Jennie looked at the wall in amazement, but I told her merrily that I did it out 225
of pure spite at the vicious thing.

She laughed and said she wouldn't mind doing it herself, but I must not get
tired.

How she betrayed herself that time!

But I am here, and no person touches this paper but me,—not *alive!*

She tried to get me out of the room—it was too patent! But I said it was so
quiet and empty and clean now that I believed I would lie down again and
sleep all I could; and not to wake me even for dinner—I would call when I
woke.

So now she is gone, and the servants are gone, and the things are gone, and 230
there is nothing left but that great bedstead nailed down, with the canvas mattress we found on it.

We shall sleep downstairs to-night, and take the boat home to-morrow.

I quite enjoy the room, now it is bare again.

How those children did tear about here!

This bedstead is fairly gnawed!

But I must get to work. 235

I have locked the door and thrown the key down into the front path.

I don't want to go out, and I don't want to have anybody come in, till John
comes.

I want to astonish him.

I've got a rope up here that even Jennie did not find. If that woman does get
out, and tries to get away, I can tie her!

But I forgot I could not reach far without anything to stand on! 240

This bed will *not* move!

I tried to lift and push it until I was lame, and then I got so angry I bit off a
little piece at one corner—but it hurt my teeth.

Then I peeled off all the paper I could reach standing on the floor. It sticks
horribly and the pattern just enjoys it! All those strangled heads and bulbous
eyes and waddling fungus growths just shriek with derision!

I am getting angry enough to do something desperate. To jump out of the
window would be admirable exercise, but the bars are too strong even to try.

Besides I wouldn't do it. Of course not. I know well enough that a step like 245
that is improper and might be misconstrued.

I don't like to *look* out of the windows even—there are so many of those
creeping women, and they creep so fast.

I wonder if they all come out of that wallpaper as I did?

But I am securely fastened now by my well-hidden rope—you don't get *me* out in the road there!

I suppose I shall have to get back behind the pattern when it comes night, and that is hard!

250 It is so pleasant to be out in this great room and creep around as I please!

I don't want to go outside. I won't, even if Jennie asks me to.

For outside you have to creep on the ground, and everything is green instead of yellow.

But here I can creep smoothly on the floor, and my shoulder just fits in that long smooch around the wall, so I cannot lose my way.

Why there's John at the door!

255 It is no use, young man, you can't open it!

How he does call and pound!

Now he's crying for an axe.

It would be a shame to break down that beautiful door!

"John dear!" said I in the gentlest voice, "the key is down by the front steps, under a plantain leaf!"

260 That silenced him for a few moments.

Then he said—very quietly indeed, "Open the door, my darling!"

"I can't," said I. "The key is down by the front door under a plantain leaf!"

And then I said it again, several times, very gently and slowly, and said it so often that he had to go and see, and he got it of course, and came in. He stopped short by the door.

"What is the matter?" he cried. "For God's sake, what are you doing!"

265 I kept on creeping just the same, but I looked at him over my shoulder.

"I've got out at last," said I, "in spite of you and Jane. And I've pulled off most of the paper, so you can't put me back!"

Now why should that man have fainted? But he did, and right across my path by the wall, so that I had to creep over him every time!

1892

SUSAN GLASPELL

(1876–1948)

A Jury of Her Peers

Though today remembered almost exclusively for her masterful one-act play *Trifles* (1916), Susan Glaspell wrote over a dozen plays, fifty short stories, nine novels, and a memoir, in addition to playing a key role in the development of twentieth-century American theater. Born in Davenport, Iowa, she graduated from Drake University in 1899 and spent two years at the *Des Moines Daily News*, where she covered the trial of a fifty-seven-year-old woman accused of murdering her sleeping husband with an axe. When Glaspell's short stories began appearing in magazines, she returned to Davenport. There, she became involved with George Cram Cook, a former English professor, socialist, and married father of two. The two wed in 1913 and moved

east, eventually settling in New York's Greenwich Village and in Cape Cod, Massachusetts, where they founded the Provincetown Players, an extraordinary collective at the
Provincetown Playhouse of freethinking, Left-leaning actors, directors, and playwrights
that included Edna St. Vincent Millay and a then-unknown Eugene O'Neill. Between
1916 and 1922 this pioneering group reportedly staged more plays by women than any
other contemporary theater; among them were eleven by Glaspell, ranging from realistic dramas such as *Trifles* and satirical comedies like *Woman's Honor* (1918) to her
expressionistic *The Verge* (1921). Widowed in 1924, Glaspell ended a brief second marriage in 1931, the same year that her last play, *Alison's House*, won the Pulitzer Prize.
Having published her first novel in 1909 and multiple best sellers in the 1920s and
1930s, Glaspell spent the last years of her life writing fiction in Provincetown.

When Martha Hale opened the storm door and got a cut of the north
wind, she ran back for her big woolen scarf. As she hurriedly wound
that round her head her eye made a scandalized sweep of her kitchen. It was
no ordinary thing that called her away—it was probably farther from ordinary
than anything that had ever happened in Dickson County. But what her eye
took in was that her kitchen was in no shape for leaving: her bread all ready for
mixing, half the flour sifted and half unsifted.

She hated to see things half done; but she had been at that when the team
from town stopped to get Mr. Hale, and then the sheriff came running in to say
his wife wished Mrs. Hale would come too—adding, with a grin, that he
guessed she was getting scary and wanted another woman along. So she had
dropped everything right where it was.

"Martha!" now came her husband's impatient voice. "Don't keep folks waiting
out here in the cold."

She again opened the storm door, and this time joined the three men and the
one woman waiting for her in the big two-seated buggy.

After she had the robes tucked around her she took another look at the   5
woman who sat beside her on the back seat. She had met Mrs. Peters the year
before at the county fair, and the thing she remembered about her was that she
didn't seem like a sheriff's wife. She was small and thin and didn't have a strong
voice. Mrs. Gorman, sheriff's wife before Gorman went out and Peters came in,
had a voice that somehow seemed to be backing up the law with every word.
But if Mrs. Peters didn't look like a sheriff's wife, Peters made it up in looking
like a sheriff. He was to a dot the kind of man who could get himself elected
sheriff—a heavy man with a big voice, who was particularly genial with the law-
abiding, as if to make it plain that he knew the difference between criminals
and noncriminals. And right there it came into Mrs. Hale's mind, with a stab,
that this man who was so pleasant and lively with all of them was going to the
Wrights' now as a sheriff.

"The country's not very pleasant this time of year," Mrs. Peters at last ventured, as if she felt they ought to be talking as well as the men.

Mrs. Hale scarcely finished her reply, for they had gone up a little hill and
could see the Wright place now, and seeing it did not make her feel like talking.
It looked very lonesome this cold March morning. It had always been a

lonesome-looking place. It was down in a hollow, and the poplar trees around it were lonesome-looking trees. The men were looking at it and talking about what had happened. The county attorney was bending to one side of the buggy, and kept looking steadily at the place as they drew up to it.

"I'm glad you came with me," Mrs. Peters said nervously, as the two women were about to follow the men in through the kitchen door.

Even after she had her foot on the doorstep, her hand on the knob, Martha Hale had a moment of feeling she could not cross that threshold. And the reason it seemed she couldn't cross it now was simply because she hadn't crossed it before. Time and time again it had been in her mind. "I ought to go over and see Minnie Foster"—she still thought of her as Minnie Foster, though for twenty years she had been Mrs. Wright. And then there was always something to do and Minnie Foster would go from her mind. But *now* she could come.

10   The men went over to the stove. The women stood close together by the door. Young Henderson, the county attorney, turned around and said, "Come up to the fire, ladies."

Mrs. Peters took a step forward, then stopped. "I'm not—cold," she said.

And so the two women stood by the door, at first not even so much as looking around the kitchen.

The men talked for a minute about what a good thing it was the sheriff had sent his deputy out that morning to make a fire for them, and then Sheriff Peters stepped back from the stove, unbuttoned his outer coat, and leaned his hands on the kitchen table in a way that seemed to mark the beginning of official business. "Now, Mr. Hale," he said in a sort of semi-official voice, "before we move things about, you tell Mr. Henderson just what it was you saw when you came here yesterday morning."

The county attorney was looking around the kitchen.

15   "By the way," he said, "has anything been moved?" He turned to the sheriff. "Are things just as you left them yesterday?"

Peters looked from cupboard to sink; from that to a small worn rocker a little to one side of the kitchen table.

"It's just the same."

"Somebody should have been left here yesterday," said the county attorney.

"Oh—yesterday," returned the sheriff, with a little gesture as of yesterday having been more than he could bear to think of. "When I had to send Frank to Morris Center for that man who went crazy—let me tell you, I had my hands full *yesterday*. I knew you could get back from Omaha by today, George, and as long as I went over everything here myself—"

20   "Well, Mr. Hale," said the county attorney, in a way of letting what was past and gone go, "tell just what happened when you came here yesterday morning."

Mrs. Hale, still leaning against the door, had that sinking feeling of the mother whose child is about to speak a piece. Lewis often wandered along and got things mixed up in a story. She hoped he would tell this straight and plain, and not say unnecessary things that would just make things harder for Minnie Foster. He didn't begin at once, and she noticed that he looked queer—as if standing in that kitchen and having to tell what he had seen there yesterday morning made him almost sick.

"Yes, Mr. Hale?" the county attorney reminded.

"Harry and I had started to town with a load of potatoes," Mrs. Hale's husband began.

Harry was Mrs. Hale's oldest boy. He wasn't with them now, for the very good reason that those potatoes never got to town yesterday and he was taking them this morning, so he hadn't been home when the sheriff stopped to say he wanted Mr. Hale to come over to the Wright place and tell the county attorney his story there, where he could point it all out. With all Mrs. Hale's other emotions came the fear that maybe Harry wasn't dressed warm enough—they hadn't any of them realized how that north wind did bite.

"We come along this road," Hale was going on, with a motion of his hand to the road over which they had just come, "and as we got in sight of the house I says to Harry, 'I'm goin' to see if I can't get John Wright to take a telephone.' You see," he explained to Henderson, "unless I can get somebody to go in with me they won't come out this branch road except for a price I can't pay. I'd spoke to Wright about it once before; but he put me off, saying folks talked too much anyway, and all he asked was peace and quiet—guess you know about how much he talked himself. But I thought maybe if I went to the house and talked about it before his wife, and said all the womenfolks liked the telephones, and that in this lonesome stretch of road it would be a good thing—well, I said to Harry that that was what I was going to say—though I said at the same time that I didn't know as what his wife wanted made much difference to John—" 25

Now, there he was!—saying things he didn't need to say. Mrs. Hale tried to catch her husband's eye, but fortunately the county attorney interrupted with:

"Let's talk about that a little later, Mr. Hale. I do want to talk about that, but I'm anxious now to get along to just what happened when you got here."

When he began this time, it was very deliberately and carefully:

"I didn't see or hear anything. I knocked at the door. And still it was all quiet inside. I knew they must be up—it was past eight o'clock. So I knocked again, louder, and I thought I heard somebody say 'Come in.' I wasn't sure—I'm not sure yet. But I opened the door—this door," jerking a hand toward the door by which the two women stood, "and there, in that rocker"—pointing to it—"sat Mrs. Wright."

Everyone in the kitchen looked at the rocker. It came into Mrs. Hale's mind that the rocker didn't look in the least like Minnie Foster—the Minnie Foster of twenty years before. It was a dingy red, with wooden rungs up the back, and the middle rung was gone, and the chair sagged to one side. 30

"How did she—look?" the county attorney was inquiring.

"Well," said Hale, "she looked—queer."

"How do you mean—queer?"

As he asked it he took out a notebook and pencil. Mrs. Hale did not like the sight of that pencil. She kept her eye fixed on her husband, as if to keep him from saying unnecessary things that would go into that notebook and make trouble.

Hale did speak guardedly, as if the pencil had affected him too. 35

"Well, as if she didn't know what she was going to do next. And kind of—done up."

"How did she seem to feel about your coming?"

"Why, I don't think she minded—one way or other. She didn't pay much attention. I said, 'Ho' do, Mrs. Wright? It's cold, ain't it!' And she said, 'Is it?'— and went on pleatin' at her apron.

"Well, I was surprised. She didn't ask me to come up to the stove, or to sit down, but just set there, not even lookin' at me. And so I said: 'I want to see John.'

40 "And then she—laughed. I guess you would call it a laugh.

"I thought of Harry and the team outside, so I said, a little sharp, 'Can I see John?' 'No,' says she—kind of dull like. 'Ain't he home?' says I. Then she looked at me. 'Yes,' says she, 'he's home.' 'Then why can't I see him?' I asked her, out of patience with her now. 'Cause he's dead,' says she, just as quiet and dull—and fell to pleatin' her apron. 'Dead?' says I, like you do when you can't take in what you've heard.

"She just nodded her head, not getting a bit excited, but rockin' back and forth.

"'Why—where is he?' says I, not knowing *what* to say.

"She just pointed upstairs—like this"—pointing to the room above.

45 "I got up, with the idea of going up there myself. By this time I—didn't know what to do. I walked from there to here; then I says: 'Why, what did he die of?'

"'He died of a rope around his neck,' says she; and just went on pleatin' at her apron."

Hale stopped speaking, and stood staring at the rocker, as if he were still seeing the woman who had sat there the morning before. Nobody spoke; it was as if everyone were seeing the woman who had sat there the morning before.

"And what did you do then?" the county attorney at last broke the silence.

"I went out and called Harry. I thought I might—need help. I got Harry in, and we went upstairs." His voice fell almost to a whisper. "There he was—lying over the—"

50 "I think I'd rather have you go into that upstairs," the county attorney interrupted, "where you can point it all out. Just go on now with the rest of the story."

"Well, my first thought was to get that rope off. It looked—"

He stopped, his face twitching.

"But Harry, he went up to him, and he said, 'No, he's dead all right, and we'd better not touch anything.' So we went downstairs.

"She was still sitting the same way. 'Has anybody been notified?' I asked. 'No,' says she, unconcerned.

55 "'Who did this, Mrs. Wright?' said Harry. He said it business-like, and she stopped pleatin' at her apron. 'I don't know,' she says. 'You don't *know*?' says Harry. 'Weren't you sleepin' in the bed with him?' 'Yes,' says she, 'but I was on the inside.' 'Somebody slipped a rope round his neck and strangled him, and you didn't wake up?' says Harry. 'I didn't wake up,' she said after him.

"We may have looked as if we didn't see how that could be, for after a minute she said, 'I sleep sound.'

"Harry was going to ask her more questions, but I said maybe that weren't our business; maybe we ought to let her tell her story first to the coroner or the sheriff. So Harry went fast as he could over to High Road—the Rivers' place, where there's a telephone."

"And what did she do when she knew you had gone for the coroner?" The attorney got his pencil in his hand all ready for writing.

"She moved from that chair to this one over here"—Hale pointed to a small chair in the corner—"and just sat there with her hands held together and looking down. I got a feeling that I ought to make some conversation, so I said I had come in to see if John wanted to put in a telephone; and at that she started to laugh, and then she stopped and looked at me—scared."

At the sound of a moving pencil the man who was telling the story looked up. 60

"I dunno—maybe it wasn't scared," he hastened; "I wouldn't like to say it was. Soon Harry got back, and then Dr. Lloyd came, and you, Mr. Peters, and so I guess that's all I know that you don't."

He said that last with relief, and moved a little, as if relaxing. Everyone moved a little. The county attorney walked toward the stair door.

"I guess we'll go upstairs first—then out to the barn and around there."

He paused and looked around the kitchen.

"You're convinced there was nothing important here?" he asked the sheriff. 65 "Nothing that would—point to any motive?"

The sheriff too looked all around, as if to reconvince himself.

"Nothing here but kitchen things," he said, with a little laugh for the insignificance of kitchen things.

The county attorney was looking at the cupboard—a peculiar, ungainly structure, half closet and half cupboard, the upper part of it being built in the wall, and the lower part just the old-fashioned kitchen cupboard. As if its queerness attracted him, he got a chair and opened the upper part and looked in. After a moment he drew his hand away sticky.

"Here's a nice mess," he said resentfully.

The two women had drawn nearer, and now the sheriff's wife spoke. 70

"Oh—her fruit," she said, looking to Mrs. Hale for sympathetic understanding. She turned back to the county attorney and explained: "She worried about that when it turned so cold last night. She said the fire would go out and her jars might burst."

Mrs. Peters' husband broke into a laugh.

"Well, can you beat the women! Held for murder, and worrying about her preserves!"

The young attorney set his lips.

"I guess before we're through with her she may have something more serious 75 than preserves to worry about."

"Oh, well," said Mrs. Hale's husband, with good-natured superiority, "women are used to worrying over trifles."

The two women moved a little closer together. Neither of them spoke. The county attorney seemed suddenly to remember his manners—and think of his future.

"And yet," said he, with the gallantry of a young politician, "for all their worries, what would we do without the ladies?"

The women did not speak, did not unbend. He went to the sink and began washing his hands. He turned to wipe them on the roller towel—whirled it for a cleaner place.

"Dirty towels! Not much of a housekeeper, would you say, ladies?" 80

He kicked his foot against some dirty pans under the sink.

"There's a great deal of work to be done on a farm," said Mrs. Hale stiffly.

"To be sure. And yet"—with a little bow to her—"I know there are some Dickson County farmhouses that do not have such roller towels." He gave it a pull to expose its full length again.

"Those towels get dirty awful quick. Men's hands aren't always as clean as they might be."

85   "Ah, loyal to your sex, I see," he laughed. He stopped and gave her a keen look. "But you and Mrs. Wright were neighbors. I suppose you were friends, too."

Martha Hale shook her head.

"I've seen little enough of her of late years. I've not been in this house—it's more than a year."

"And why was that? You didn't like her?"

"I liked her well enough," she replied with spirit. "Farmers' wives have their hands full, Mr. Henderson. And then"—She looked around the kitchen.

90   "Yes?" he encouraged.

"It never seemed a very cheerful place," said she, more to herself than to him.

"No," he agreed; "I don't think anyone would call it cheerful. I shouldn't say she had the homemaking instinct."

"Well, I don't know as Wright had, either," she muttered.

"You mean they didn't get on very well?" he was quick to ask.

95   "No; I don't mean anything," she answered, with decision. As she turned a little away from him, she added: "But I don't think a place would be any the cheerfuler for John Wright's bein' in it."

"I'd like to talk to you about that a little later, Mrs. Hale," he said. "I'm anxious to get the lay of things upstairs now."

He moved toward the stair door, followed by the two men.

"I suppose anything Mrs. Peters does'll be all right?" the sheriff inquired. "She was to take in some clothes for her, you know—and a few little things. We left in such a hurry yesterday."

The county attorney looked at the two women whom they were leaving alone there among the kitchen things.

100   "Yes—Mrs. Peters," he said, his glance resting on the woman who was not Mrs. Peters, the big farmer woman who stood behind the sheriff's wife. "Of course Mrs. Peters is one of us," he said, in a manner of entrusting responsibility. "And keep your eye out, Mrs. Peters, for anything that might be of use. No telling; you women might come upon a clue to the motive—and that's the thing we need."

Mr. Hale rubbed his face after the fashion of a showman getting ready for a pleasantry.

"But would the women know a clue if they did come upon it?" he said; and, having delivered himself of this, he followed the others through the stair door.

The women stood motionless and silent, listening to the footsteps, first upon the stairs, then in the room above them.

Then, as if releasing herself from something strange, Mrs. Hale began to arrange the dirty pans under the sink, which the county attorney's disdainful push of the foot had deranged.

105   "I'd hate to have men comin' into my kitchen," she said testily—"snoopin' round and criticizin'."

"Of course it's no more than their duty," said the sheriff's wife, in her manner of timid acquiescence.

"Duty's all right," replied Mrs. Hale bluffly; "but I guess that deputy sheriff that come out to make the fire might have got a little of this on." She gave the roller towel a pull. "Wish I'd thought of that sooner! Seems mean to talk about her for not having things slicked up, when she had to come away in such a hurry."

She looked around the kitchen. Certainly it was not "slicked up." Her eye was held by a bucket of sugar on a low shelf. The cover was off the wooden bucket, and beside it was a paper bag—half full.

Mrs. Hale moved toward it.

"She was putting this in there," she said to herself—slowly.   110

She thought of the flour in her kitchen at home—half sifted, half not sifted. She had been interrupted and had left things half done. What had interrupted Minnie Foster? Why had that work been left half done? She made a move as if to finish it,—unfinished things always bothered her,—and then she glanced around and saw that Mrs. Peters was watching her—and she didn't want Mrs. Peters to get that feeling she had got of work begun and then—for some reason—not finished.

"It's a shame about her fruit," she said, and walked toward the cupboard that the county attorney had opened, and got on the chair, murmuring: "I wonder if it's all gone."

It was a sorry enough looking sight, but "Here's one that's all right," she said at last. She held it toward the light. "This is cherries, too." She looked again. "I declare I believe that's the only one."

With a sigh, she got down from the chair, went to the sink, and wiped off the bottle.

"She'll feel awful bad, after all her hard work in the hot weather. I remember   115
the afternoon I put up my cherries last summer."

She set the bottle on the table, and, with another sigh, started to sit down in the rocker. But she did not sit down. Something kept her from sitting down in that chair. She straightened—stepped back, and, half turned away, stood looking at it, seeing the woman who sat there "pleatin' at her apron."

The thin voice of the sheriff's wife broke in upon her: "I must be getting those things from the front room closet." She opened the door into the other room, started in, stepped back. "You coming with me, Mrs. Hale?" she asked nervously. "You—you could help me get them."

They were soon back—the stark coldness of that shut-up room was not a thing to linger in.

"My!" said Mrs. Peters, dropping the things on the table and hurrying to the stove.

Mrs. Hale stood examining the clothes the woman who was being detained   120
in town had said she wanted.

"Wright was close!" she exclaimed, holding up a shabby black skirt that bore the marks of much making over. "I think maybe that's why she kept so much to herself. I s'pose she felt she couldn't do her part; and then, you don't enjoy things when you feel shabby. She used to wear pretty clothes and be lively— when she was Minnie Foster, one of the town girls, singing in the choir. But that—oh, that was twenty years ago."

With a carefulness in which there was something tender, she folded the shabby clothes and piled them at one corner of the table. She looked at Mrs. Peters, and there was something in the other woman's look that irritated her.

"She don't care," she said to herself. "Much difference it makes to her whether Minnie Foster had pretty clothes when she was a girl."

Then she looked again, and she wasn't so sure; in fact, she hadn't at any time been perfectly sure about Mrs. Peters. She had that shrinking manner, and yet her eyes looked as if they could see a long way into things.

125　"This all you was to take in?" asked Mrs. Hale.

"No," said the sheriff's wife; "she said she wanted an apron. Funny thing to want," she ventured in her nervous little way, "for there's not much to get you dirty in jail, goodness knows. But I suppose just to make her feel more natural. If you're used to wearing an apron—. She said they were in the bottom drawer of this cupboard. Yes—here they are. And then her little shawl that always hung on the stair door."

She took the small gray shawl from behind the door leading upstairs, and stood a minute looking at it.

Suddenly Mrs. Hale took a quick step toward the other woman.

"Mrs. Peters!"

130　"Yes, Mrs. Hale?"

"Do you think she—did it?"

A frightened look blurred the other things in Mrs. Peters' eyes.

"Oh, I don't know," she said, in a voice that seemed to shrink away from the subject.

"Well, I don't think she did," affirmed Mrs. Hale stoutly. "Asking for an apron, and her little shawl. Worryin' about her fruit."

135　"Mr. Peters says—" Footsteps were heard in the room above; she stopped, looked up, then went on in a lowered voice: "Mr. Peters says—it looks bad for her. Mr. Henderson is awful sarcastic in a speech, and he's going to make fun of her saying she didn't—wake up."

For a moment Mrs. Hale had no answer. Then, "Well, I guess John Wright didn't wake up—when they was slippin' that rope under his neck," she muttered.

"No, it's *strange*," breathed Mrs. Peters. "They think it was such a—funny way to kill a man."

She began to laugh; at sound of the laugh, abruptly stopped.

"That's just what Mr. Hale said," said Mrs. Hale, in a resolutely natural voice. "There was a gun in the house. He says that's what he can't understand."

140　"Mr. Henderson said, coming out, that what was needed for the case was a motive. Something to show anger—or sudden feeling."

"Well, I don't see any signs of anger around here," said Mrs. Hale. "I don't—"

She stopped. It was as if her mind tripped on something. Her eye was caught by a dish towel in the middle of the kitchen table. Slowly she moved toward the table. One half of it was wiped clean, the other half messy. Her eyes made a slow, almost unwilling turn to the bucket of sugar and the half empty bag beside it. Things begun—and not finished.

After a moment she stepped back, and said, in that manner of releasing herself:

"Wonder how they're finding things upstairs? I hope she had it a little more red-up[1] up there. You know,"—she paused, and feeling gathered,—"it seems kind of *sneaking*; locking her up in town and coming out here to get her own house to turn against her!"

"But, Mrs. Hale," said the sheriff's wife, "the law is the law." 145

"I s'pose 'tis," answered Mrs. Hale shortly.

She turned to the stove, saying something about that fire not being much to brag of. She worked with it a minute, and when she straightened up she said aggressively:

"The law is the law—and a bad stove is a bad stove. How'd you like to cook on this?"—pointing with the poker to the broken lining. She opened the oven door and started to express her opinion of the oven; but she was swept into her own thoughts, thinking of what it would mean, year after year, to have that stove to wrestle with. The thought of Minnie Foster trying to bake in that oven—and the thought of her never going over to see Minnie Foster—.

She was startled by hearing Mrs. Peters say: "A person gets discouraged—and loses heart."

The sheriff's wife had looked from the stove to the sink—to the pail of water 150 which had been carried in from outside. The two women stood there silent, above them the footsteps of the men who were looking for evidence against the woman who had worked in that kitchen. That look of seeing into things, of seeing through a thing to something else, was in the eyes of the sheriff's wife now. When Mrs. Hale next spoke to her, it was gently:

"Better loosen up your things, Mrs. Peters. We'll not feel them when we go out."

Mrs. Peters went to the back of the room to hang up the fur tippet she was wearing. A moment later she exclaimed, "Why, she was piecing a quilt," and held up a large sewing basket piled high with quilt pieces.

Mrs. Hale spread some of the blocks on the table.

"It's log-cabin pattern," she said, putting several of them together. "Pretty, isn't it?"

They were so engaged with the quilt that they did not hear the footsteps on 155 the stairs. Just as the stair door opened Mrs. Hale was saying:

"Do you suppose she was going to quilt it or just knot it?"

The sheriff threw up his hands.

"They wonder whether she was going to quilt it or just knot it!"

There was a laugh for the ways of women, a warming of hands over the stove, and then the county attorney said briskly:

"Well, let's go right out to the barn and get that cleared up." 160

"I don't see as there's anything so strange," Mrs. Hale said resentfully, after the outside door had closed on the three men—"our taking up our time with little things while we're waiting for them to get the evidence. I don't see as it's anything to laugh about."

"Of course they've got awful important things on their minds," said the sheriff's wife apologetically.

1. Tidy.

They returned to an inspection of the blocks for the quilt. Mrs. Hale was looking at the fine, even sewing, and preoccupied with thoughts of the woman who
had done that sewing, when she heard the sheriff's wife say, in a queer tone:

"Why, look at this one."

165   She turned to take the block held out to her.

"The sewing," said Mrs. Peters, in a troubled way. "All the rest of them have
been so nice and even—but—this one. Why, it looks as if she didn't know what
she was about!"

Their eyes met—something flashed to life, passed between them; then, as if
with an effort, they seemed to pull away from each other. A moment Mrs. Hale
sat there, her hands folded over that sewing which was so unlike all the rest of
the sewing. Then she had pulled a knot and drawn the threads.

"Oh, what are you doing, Mrs. Hale?" asked the sheriff's wife, startled.

"Just pulling out a stitch or two that's not sewed very good," said Mrs. Hale
mildly.

170   "I don't think we ought to touch things," Mrs. Peters said, a little helplessly.

"I'd just finish up this end," answered Mrs. Hale, still in that mild, matter-of-
fact fashion.

She threaded a needle and started to replace bad sewing with good. For a
little while she sewed in silence. Then, in that thin, timid voice, she heard:

"Mrs. Hale!"

"Yes, Mrs. Peters?"

175   "What do you suppose she was so—nervous about?"

"Oh, *I* don't know," said Mrs. Hale, as if dismissing a thing not important
enough to spend much time on. "I don't know as she was—nervous. I sew awful
queer sometimes when I'm just tired."

She cut a thread, and out of the corner of her eye looked up at Mrs. Peters.
The small, lean face of the sheriff's wife seemed to have tightened up. Her eyes
had that look of peering into something. But the next moment she moved, and
said in her thin, indecisive way:

"Well, I must get those clothes wrapped. They may be through sooner than
we think. I wonder where I could find a piece of paper—and string."

"In that cupboard, maybe," suggested Mrs. Hale, after a glance around.

180   One piece of the crazy sewing remained unripped. Mrs. Peters' back turned,
Martha Hale now scrutinized that piece, compared it with the dainty, accurate
sewing of the other blocks. The difference was startling. Holding this block made
her feel queer, as if the distracted thoughts of the woman who had perhaps turned
to it to try and quiet herself were communicating themselves to her.

Mrs. Peters' voice roused her.

"Here's a birdcage," she said. "Did she have a bird, Mrs. Hale?"

"Why, I don't know whether she did or not." She turned to look at the cage
Mrs. Peters was holding up. "I've not been here in so long." She sighed. "There
was a man round last year selling canaries cheap—but I don't know as she took
one. Maybe she did. She used to sing real pretty herself."

Mrs. Peters looked around the kitchen.

185   "Seems kind of funny to think of a bird here." She half laughed—an attempt
to put up a barrier. "But she must have had one—or why would she have a cage?
I wonder what happened to it."

"I suppose maybe the cat got it," suggested Mrs. Hale, resuming her sewing.

"No; she didn't have a cat. She's got that feeling some people have about cats—being afraid of them. When they brought her to our house yesterday, my cat got in the room, and she was real upset and asked me to take it out."

"My sister Bessie was like that," laughed Mrs. Hale.

The sheriff's wife did not reply. The silence made Mrs. Hale turn round. Mrs. Peters was examining the birdcage.

"Look at this door," she said slowly. "It's broke. One hinge has been pulled apart." 190

Mrs. Hale came nearer.

"Looks as if someone must have been—rough with it."

Again their eyes met—startled, questioning, apprehensive. For a moment neither spoke nor stirred. Then Mrs. Hale, turning away, said brusquely:

"If they're going to find any evidence, I wish they'd be about it. I don't like this place."

"But I'm awful glad you came with me, Mrs. Hale." Mrs. Peters put the bird- 195 cage on the table and sat down. "It would be lonesome for me—sitting here alone."

"Yes, it would, wouldn't it?" agreed Mrs. Hale, a certain determined natural- ness in her voice. She picked up the sewing, but now it dropped in her lap, and she murmured in a different voice: "But I tell you what I *do* wish, Mrs. Peters. I wish I had come over sometimes when she was here. I wish—I had."

"But of course you were awful busy, Mrs. Hale. Your house—and your children."

"I could've come," retorted Mrs. Hale shortly. "I stayed away because it weren't cheerful—and that's why I ought to have come. I"—she looked around— "I've never liked this place. Maybe because it's down in a hollow and you don't see the road. I don't know what it is, but it's a lonesome place, and always was. I wish I had come over to see Minnie Foster sometimes. I can see now—" She did not put it into words.

"Well, you mustn't reproach yourself," counseled Mrs. Peters. "Somehow, we just don't see how it is with other folks till—something comes up."

"Not having children makes less work," mused Mrs. Hale, after a silence, 200 "but it makes a quiet house—and Wright out to work all day—and no company when he did come in. Did you know John Wright, Mrs. Peters?"

"Not to know him. I've seen him in town. They say he was a good man."

"Yes—good," conceded John Wright's neighbor grimly. "He didn't drink, and kept his word as well as most, I guess, and paid his debts. But he was a hard man, Mrs. Peters. Just to pass the time of day with him—." She stopped, shiv- ered a little. "Like a raw wind that gets to the bone." Her eye fell upon the cage on the table before her, and she added, almost bitterly: "I should think she would've wanted a bird!"

Suddenly she leaned forward, looking intently at the cage. "But what do you s'pose went wrong with it?"

"I don't know," returned Mrs. Peters; "unless it got sick and died."

But after she said it she reached over and swung the broken door. Both 205 women watched it as if somehow held by it.

"You didn't know—her?" Mrs. Hale asked, a gentler note in her voice.

"Not till they brought her yesterday," said the sheriff's wife.

"She—come to think of it, she was kind of like a bird herself. Real sweet and pretty, but kind of timid and—fluttery. How—she—did—change."

That held her for a long time. Finally, as if struck with a happy thought and relieved to get back to everyday things, she exclaimed:

210 "Tell you what, Mrs. Peters, why don't you take the quilt in with you? It might take up her mind."

"Why, I think that's a real nice idea, Mrs. Hale," agreed the sheriff's wife, as if she too were glad to come into the atmosphere of a simple kindness. "There couldn't possibly be any objection to that, could there? Now, just what will I take? I wonder if her patches are in here—and her things."

They turned to the sewing basket.

"Here's some red," said Mrs. Hale, bringing out a roll of cloth. Underneath that was a box. "Here, maybe her scissors are in here—and her things." She held it up. "What a pretty box! I'll warrant that was something she had a long time ago—when she was a girl."

She held it in her hand a moment; then, with a little sigh, opened it.

215 Instantly her hand went to her nose.

"Why—!"

Mrs. Peters drew nearer—then turned away.

"There's something wrapped up in this piece of silk," faltered Mrs. Hale.

"This isn't her scissors," said Mrs. Peters in a shrinking voice.

220 Her hand not steady, Mrs. Hale raised the piece of silk. "Oh, Mrs. Peters!" she cried. "It's—"

Mrs. Peters bent closer.

"It's the bird," she whispered.

"But, Mrs. Peters!" cried Mrs. Hale. "*Look* at it! Its neck—look at its neck! It's all—other side *to.*"

She held the box away from her.

225 The sheriff's wife again bent closer.

"Somebody wrung its neck," said she, in a voice that was slow and deep.

And then again the eyes of the two women met—this time clung together in a look of dawning comprehension, of growing horror. Mrs. Peters looked from the dead bird to the broken door of the cage. Again their eyes met. And just then there was a sound at the outside door.

Mrs. Hale slipped the box under the quilt pieces in the basket, and sank into the chair before it. Mrs. Peters stood holding to the table. The county attorney and the sheriff came in from outside.

"Well, ladies," said the county attorney, as one turning from serious things to little pleasantries, "have you decided whether she was going to quilt it or knot it?"

230 "We think," began the sheriff's wife in a flurried voice, "that she was going to—knot it."

He was too preoccupied to notice the change that came in her voice on that last.

"Well, that's very interesting, I'm sure," he said tolerantly. He caught sight of the birdcage. "Has the bird flown?"

"We think the cat got it," said Mrs. Hale in a voice curiously even.

He was walking up and down, as if thinking something out.

235 "Is there a cat?" he asked absently.

Mrs. Hale shot a look up at the sheriff's wife.

"Well, not *now*," said Mrs. Peters. "They're superstitious, you know; they leave." She sank into her chair.

The county attorney did not heed her. "No sign at all of anyone having come in from the outside," he said to Peters, in the manner of continuing an interrupted conversation. "Their own rope. Now let's go upstairs again and go over it, piece by piece. It would have to have been someone who knew just the—"

The stair door closed behind them and their voices were lost.   240

The two women sat motionless, not looking at each other, but as if peering into something and at the same time holding back. When they spoke now it was as if they were afraid of what they were saying, but as if they could not help saying it.

"She liked the bird," said Martha Hale, low and slowly. "She was going to bury it in that pretty box."

"When I was a girl," said Mrs. Peters, under her breath, "my kitten—there was a boy took a hatchet, and before my eyes—before I could get there—" She covered her face an instant. "If they hadn't held me back I would have"—she caught herself, looked upstairs where footsteps were heard, and finished weakly—"hurt him."

Then they sat without speaking or moving.

"I wonder how it would seem," Mrs. Hale at last began, as if feeling her way 245 over strange ground—"never to have had any children around?" Her eyes made a slow sweep of the kitchen, as if seeing what that kitchen had meant through all the years. "No, Wright wouldn't like the bird," she said after that—"a thing that sang. She used to sing. He killed that too." Her voice tightened.

Mrs. Peters moved uneasily.

"Of course we don't know who killed the bird."

"I knew John Wright," was Mrs. Hale's answer.

"It was an awful thing was done in this house that night, Mrs. Hale," said the sheriff's wife. "Killing a man while he slept—slipping a thing round his neck that choked the life out of him."

Mrs. Hale's hand went out to the birdcage.   250

"His neck. Choked the life out of him."

"We don't *know* who killed him," whispered Mrs. Peters wildly. "We don't *know.*"

Mrs. Hale had not moved. "If there had been years and years of—nothing, then a bird to sing to you, it would be awful—still—after the bird was still."

It was as if something within her not herself had spoken, and it found in Mrs. Peters something she did not know as herself.

"I know what stillness is," she said, in a queer, monotonous voice. "When we 255 homesteaded in Dakota, and my first baby died—after he was two years old— and me with no other then—"

Mrs. Hale stirred.

"How soon do you suppose they'll be through looking for evidence?"

"I know what stillness is," repeated Mrs. Peters, in just that same way. Then she too pulled back. "The law has got to punish crime, Mrs. Hale," she said in her tight little way.

"I wish you'd seen Minnie Foster," was the answer, "when she wore a white dress with blue ribbons, and stood up there in the choir and sang."

260   The picture of that girl, the fact that she had lived neighbor to that girl for twenty years, and had let her die for lack of life, was suddenly more than she could bear.

"Oh, I *wish* I'd come over here once in a while!" she cried. "That was a crime! That was a crime! Who's going to punish that?"

"We mustn't take on," said Mrs. Peters, with a frightened look toward the stairs.

"I might 'a' *known* she needed help! I tell you, it's *queer*, Mrs. Peters. We live close together, and we live far apart. We all go through the same things—it's all just a different kind of the same thing! If it weren't—why do you and I *understand*? Why do we *know*—what we know this minute?"

She dashed her hand across her eyes. Then, seeing the jar of fruit on the table, she reached for it and choked out:

265   "If I was you I wouldn't *tell* her her fruit was gone! Tell her it *ain't*. Tell her it's all right—all of it. Here—take this in to prove it to her! She—she may never know whether it was broke or not."

She turned away.

Mrs. Peters reached out for the bottle of fruit as if she were glad to take it— as if touching a familiar thing, having something to do, could keep her from something else. She got up, looked about for something to wrap the fruit in, took a petticoat from the pile of clothes she had brought from the front room, and nervously started winding that round the bottle.

"My!" she began, in a high, false voice, "it's a good thing the men couldn't hear us! Getting all stirred up over a little thing like a—dead canary." She hurried over that. "As if that could have anything to do with—with—My, wouldn't they *laugh*?"

Footsteps were heard on the stairs.

270   "Maybe they would," muttered Mrs. Hale—"maybe they wouldn't."

"No, Peters," said the county attorney incisively; "it's all perfectly clear, except the reason for doing it. But you know juries when it comes to women. If there was some definite thing—something to show. Something to make a story about. A thing that would connect up with this clumsy way of doing it."

In a covert way Mrs. Hale looked at Mrs. Peters. Mrs. Peters was looking at her. Quickly they looked away from each other. The outer door opened and Mr. Hale came in.

"I've got the team round now," he said. "Pretty cold out there."

"I'm going to stay here awhile by myself," the county attorney suddenly announced. "You can send Frank out for me, can't you?" he asked the sheriff. "I want to go over everything. I'm not satisfied we can't do better."

275   Again, for one brief moment, the two women's eyes found one another.

The sheriff came up to the table.

"Did you want to see what Mrs. Peters was going to take in?"

The county attorney picked up the apron. He laughed.

"Oh, I guess they're not very dangerous things the ladies have picked out."

280   Mrs. Hale's hand was on the sewing basket in which the box was concealed. She felt that she ought to take her hand off the basket. She did not seem able to. He picked up one of the quilt blocks which she had piled on to cover the box. Her eyes felt like fire. She had a feeling that if he took up the basket she would snatch it from him.

But he did not take it up. With another little laugh, he turned away, saying:

"No; Mrs. Peters doesn't need supervising. For that matter, a sheriff's wife is married to the law. Ever think of it that way, Mrs. Peters?"

Mrs. Peters was standing beside the table. Mrs. Hale shot a look up at her; but she could not see her face. Mrs. Peters had turned away. When she spoke, her voice was muffled.

"Not—just that way," she said.

"Married to the law!" chuckled Mrs. Peters' husband. He moved toward the door into the front room, and said to the county attorney: 285

"I just want you to come in here a minute, George. We ought to take a look at these windows."

"Oh—windows," said the county attorney scoffingly.

"We'll be right out, Mr. Hale," said the sheriff to the farmer, who was still waiting by the door.

Hale went to look after the horses. The sheriff followed the county attorney into the other room. Again—for one moment—the two women were alone in that kitchen.

Martha Hale sprang up, her hands tight together, looking at that other woman, with whom it rested. At first she could not see her eyes, for the sheriff's 290 wife had not turned back, since she turned away at that suggestion of being married to the law. But now Mrs. Hale made her turn back. Her eyes made her turn back. Slowly, unwillingly, Mrs. Peters turned her head until her eyes met the eyes of the other woman. There was a moment when they held each other in a steady, burning look in which there was no evasion nor flinching. Then Martha Hale's eyes pointed the way to the basket in which was hidden the thing that would make certain the conviction of the other woman—that woman who was not there and yet who had been there with them all through the hour.

For a moment Mrs. Peters did not move. And then she did it. With a rush forward, she threw back the quilt pieces, got the box, tried to put it in her hand-bag. It was too big. Desperately she opened it, started to take the bird out. But there she broke—she could not touch the bird. She stood helpless, foolish.

There was the sound of a knob turning in the inner door. Martha Hale snatched the box from the sheriff's wife, and got it in the pocket of her big coat just as the sheriff and the county attorney came back into the kitchen.

"Well, Henry," said the county attorney facetiously, "at least we found out that she was not going to quilt it. She was going to—what is it you call it, ladies?"

Mrs. Hale's hand was against the pocket of her coat.

"We call it—knot it, Mr. Henderson." 295

1917

Chronology

1861–65	American Civil War
1866	American Equal Rights Association founded.
1870	Kate O'Flaherty marries Oscar Chopin of Louisiana.
1874	Women's Christian Temperance Union founded.
1876	Susan Glaspell born in Davenport, Iowa.
1884	Widowed, Kate Chopin moves with her children to St. Louis, publishing her first short story in 1889.
	Charlotte Perkins marries fellow artist Walter Stetson.
1888	Charlotte Perkins Stetson separates from her husband and moves with her daughter and mother to California.
1890	Wyoming becomes the first state to grant women the vote; National American Woman Suffrage Association formed.
1892	Charlotte Perkins Stetson publishes "The Yellow Wallpaper" in *New England Magazine*.
1894	Kate Chopin publishes "The Story of an Hour" in *Vogue*.
1898	Charlotte Perkins publishes *Women and Economics* and divorces Stetson.
1899	Chopin publishes *The Awakening*.
1900	Charlotte Perkins marries Charles Houghton Gilman.
	Planned collection of Kate Chopin's stories, *A Vocation and a Voice*, to include "The Story of an Hour"; publisher may have backed off because of controversy over *The Awakening*.
	Susan Glaspell reports on the Hossack murder for the *Des Moines Daily News*: twenty-six stories by April 11, 1901.
	By now, every state has passed legislation granting married women some control over their property and earnings.
1903	Height of suffragette agitation in Britain (1903–14). Gilman addresses International Congress of Women in Berlin, Germany.
1904	Kate Chopin dies.
1909	Gilman begins producing her own magazine, *The Forerunner*.
1910	Glaspell cofounds Heterodoxy, a group of feminist socialists in New York, including Charlotte Perkins Gilman; it lasts through 1920.
1913	Susan Glaspell marries George Cram Cook.
1914–18	World War I
1915	Glaspell and Cook form the Provincetown Players in a theater in an abandoned wharf in Provincetown, Massachusetts.
1916	Glaspell's play *Trifles* first performed at Wharf Theatre.
1917	Russian Revolution. Glaspell's "A Jury of Her Peers" published in *Everyweek*.
1920	Nineteenth Amendment to Constitution grants women the vote.

1929	Stock market crash
1931	Glaspell's full-length play *Alison's House* wins the Pulitzer Prize.
1935	Charlotte Perkins Gilman, with incurable breast cancer, commits suicide.
1939–45	World War II
1948	Susan Glaspell dies in Provincetown, Massachusetts.

CONTEXTUAL EXCERPTS

CHARLOTTE PERKINS GILMAN
From Similar Cases (1893)[1]

> There was once a Neolithic Man,
> An enterprising wight,
> Who made his chopping implements
> Unusually bright.
> 5 Unusually clever he,
> Unusually brave,
> And he drew delightful Mammoths
> On the borders of his cave.
> To his Neolithic neighbors,
> 10 Who were startled and surprised,
> Said he, "My friends, in course of time,
> We shall be civilized!
> We are going to live in cities!
> We are going to fight in wars!
> 15 We are going to eat three times a day
> Without the natural cause!
> We are going to turn life upside down
> About a thing called gold!
> We are going to want the earth, and take
> 20 As much as we can hold!
> We are going to wear great piles of stuff
> Outside our proper skins!
> We are going to have diseases!
> And Accomplishments!! And Sins!!!"
> 25 Then they all rose up in fury
> Against their boastful friend,

1. Charlotte Perkins Stetson, "Similar Cases." *In This Our World*, Small, Maynard, 1893, pp. 95–100. Like many at the turn of the century, Charlotte Perkins Stetson, later Gilman, applied Darwin's theory of evolution to society. She advocated *eugenics*—literally "good breeding" or racial improvement—through restricting the reproduction of those considered to be mentally or physically deficient. She believed that traditional domestic relations were retarding human progress. This eugenicist poem spread throughout the newspaper press in 1893 and made "Mrs. Stetson" famous. In the first stanzas, an advanced "Eohippus" (evolutionary ancestor of the horse) predicts that he will evolve into a horse, only to be laughed to scorn by other primitive creatures; later an ape foretells that he will be a man, encountering similar mockery from his inferior contemporaries. The poem's concluding stanzas appear here.

> For prehistoric patience
> Cometh quickly to an end.
> Said one, "This is chimerical!
30 Utopian! Absurd!"
> Said another, "What a stupid life!
> Too dull, upon my word!"
> Cried all, "Before such things can come,
> You idiotic child,
35 You must alter Human Nature!"
> And they all sat back and smiled.
> Thought they, "An answer to that last
> It will be hard to find!"
> It was a clinching argument
40 To the Neolithic Mind!

CHARLOTTE PERKINS GILMAN

From Women and Economics: A Study of the Economic Relation between Men and Women as a Factor in Social Evolution (1898)[1]

In the human species the condition [of women's economic dependence on men] is permanent and general, though there are exceptions, and though the present century is witnessing the beginnings of a great change in this respect. [. . .]

To many this view will not seem clear at first; and the case of working peasant women or females of savage tribes, and the general household industry of women, will be instanced against it. Some careful and honest discrimination is needed to make plain to ourselves the essential facts of the relation, even in these cases. The horse, in his free natural condition, is economically independent. He gets his living by his own exertions, irrespective of any other creature. The horse, in his present condition of slavery, is economically dependent. He gets his living at the hands of his master; and his exertions, though strenuous, bear no direct relation to his living. In fact, the horses who are the best fed and cared for and the horses who are the hardest worked are quite different animals. The horse works, it is true; but what he gets to eat depends on the power and will of his master. His living comes through another. He is economically dependent. So with the hard-worked savage or peasant women. Their labor is the property of another: they work under another will; and what they receive depends not on their labor, but on the power and will of another. They are economically dependent. This is true of the human female both individually and collectively.

---

1. Charlotte Perkins Stetson, *Women and Economics: A Study of the Economic Relation between Men and Women as a Factor in Social Evolution.* Small, Maynard, 1898, pp. 6–7.

BARBARA BOYD

From Heart and Home Talks: Politics and Milk (1911)[1]

Politics are no longer outside the home. They are very apt to be inside the baby, as Charlotte Perkins Gilman cleverly remarks. And being inside the baby, they certainly become a matter of woman's concerns.

The sphere of politics has changed within the last 50 years. And the sphere of woman's work has changed. Consequently, they are overlapping each other. [. . .]

Politics, in their workings out, have entered the home. Women, in their new fields of labor, have entered domains affected by politics. As a result, women, both in the home and out of it, must take into consideration politics as a factor in their lives.

[. . .] The condition of the milk supplied to all large cities comes under the thumb of politics. Whether it is up to certain healthful requirements or not depends almost altogether upon the laws upon the subject, and upon the inspectors. And both these depend upon politics.

But not only the milk that enters the home and goes inside the baby, but many other things affecting the health of the family depend today upon politics. And so the woman in the home is affected by politics. [. . .] Thus, politics today are her concern, if things that vitally affect the home and family are her concern.

In the field of labor, politics enter with equal importance into her life. The conditions under which she works, the hours of labor, wages even, can all be affected by the ballot box. And she needs to have a voice in saying what all these shall be, if justice is to be done her.

So no longer can women say that politics have nothing to do with her.

MRS. ARTHUR LYTTELTON

From Women and Their Work (1901)[1]

[A]t present the supply [of servants] is unequal to the demand. This is due to several causes. First, to the fact that many occupations are now open to women which were formerly closed, and that therefore a girl has a choice [. . .]. Then there is the large increase in the number of families who keep servants, for while the larger households have in many cases diminished their establishments, many people who formerly kept no servant now keep one, and those who kept one keep two or more, and consequently the mistresses of the middle class now do less work in the household than was formerly the case. Lastly, there is the fact that in spite of the great rise in the wages of domestic servants, service is looked down upon by the girls of the poorer classes. [. . . T]he "business

1. Barbara Boyd, "Heart and Home Talks: Politics and Milk." *The Washington Post*, 11 Sept. 1911.
1. Mrs. Arthur Lyttelton [Kathleen Clive], *Women and Their Work*. Methuen, 1901, pp. 59–61. Lyttelton's reference to cooperative kitchens would have been recognized as an idea promoted by Charlotte Perkins Gilman in both her magazine, *Forerunner*, and her internationally influential book *Women and Economics* (1898).

young lady" and the factory girl consider themselves as higher in the social scale than the parlour-maid or the cook. [. . .]

[. . .] Some [. . .] think that by a system of co-operative kitchens and other labour-saving appliances, we may almost succeed in doing without servants altogether. But probably the best remedy of all would be to raise the whole profession of domestic service [. . .]. [W]e must begin at the top, and convince women of the upper and middle classes that it is their part to learn to manage households [. . .]. The discomfort and misery and ill-health caused by badly-managed households is incalculable, while, on the other hand, a woman who can manage a household properly [. . .] is fitted for every sort of work outside the home. The administrative gifts, when properly trained, are just those which prove most useful in many kinds of philanthropic and social work.

RHETA CHILDE DORR
From What Eight Million Women Want (1910)[1]

Men, ardently, eternally, interested in Woman—one woman at a time—are almost never even faintly interested in women. Strangely, deliberately ignorant of women, they argue that their ignorance is justified by an innate unknowableness of the sex.

I am persuaded that the time is at hand when this sentimental, half contemptuous attitude of half the population towards the other half will have to be abandoned. [. . .]

The Census of 1900 reported nearly six million women in the United States engaged in wage earning outside their homes. Between 1890 and 1900 the number of women in industry increased faster than the number of men in industry. [. . .] Nine million women who have forsaken the traditions of the hearth and are competing with men in the world of paid labor, means that women are rapidly passing from the domestic control of their fathers and their husbands. Surely this is the most important economic fact in the world to-day.

Within the past twenty years no less than nine hundred and fifty-four thousand divorces have been granted in the United States. Two thirds of these divorces were granted to aggrieved wives. In spite [. . .] of tradition and [. . .] social ostracism, [. . .] more than six hundred thousand women, in the short space of twenty years, repudiated the burden of uncongenial marriage. Without any doubt this is the most important social fact we have had to face since the slavery question was settled.

[. . .] In half a dozen countries women are already completely enfranchised. In England the opposition is seeking terms of surrender. In the United States the stoutest enemy of the movement acknowledges that woman suffrage is ultimately inevitable. [. . .] Does any one question that this is the most important political fact the modern world has ever faced?

---

1. Rheta Childe Dorr, *What Eight Million Women Want*. Small, Maynard, 1910, pp. 2–4. A journalist from Nebraska, Dorr was a follower of Gilman; she praises Gilman's *Women and Economics* (1898) in this book.

THE NEW YORK TIMES

From Mrs. Delong Acquitted. She Killed Her Husband, But the Jury Has Set Her Free (1 Dec. 1892)[1]

In October, 1891, Mrs. Delong found her husband with a woman of low character. She remonstrated and a quarrel ensued, which led up to the shooting of her husband. The plea put in by the defense was insanity and self-defense. The evidence was at times quite contradictory, but the story of wrongs and abuse which the defendant had suffered at the hands of her husband [. . .] evidently satisfied the jury that Mrs. Delong acted in self-defense.

. . .

The scene in the courtroom when the verdict was announced was one of great excitement. The prisoner at the bar was sobbing, but when the verdict was given the room was filled with cheers and hurrahs, the clapping of hands, and the stamping of feet. The defendant raised her hands and implored God's blessing upon the jury.

THE WASHINGTON POST

From The Chances of Divorce (28 Nov. 1909)

If you are married or about to be married, the Government's latest statistics showing the probability of divorce may be of interest. During the twenty-year period from 1887 to 1906 the records of all registered marriages in the United States totaled 12,832,044 and the Courts granted freedom to 820,264 unhappy couples.

From this it is plain to be seen that your chances of divorce are about one in fifteen, so the odds are fairly long that if you are already married or later do marry, death, and not the Divorce Court, will sever your bonds.

Wives who seek freedom will be interested to know that 66.6 per cent of all decrees have been granted to wives, and that alimony has been also allowed in two cases out of every twenty-two.

Divorce is most frequent in the fourth and fifth years of married life. Actors and showmen are the most frequently divorced classes. Commercial travelers come next on the list of guilty. Agricultural laborers are the prize winners for matrimonial constancy. Clergymen are next desirable.

About one third of those divorced remarry, and divorcees enjoy an advantage over widows in this respect, due, as the unfeeling Government ungallantly remarks, to the fact that those who get rid of their husbands by law are usually younger than those who leave his removal to Providence.

1. On December 2, 1900, in Indianola, Iowa, someone killed farmer John Hossack with an axe as he was sleeping in bed beside his wife. Susan Glaspell's reporting and public opinion were largely against Mrs. Hossack, and the first trial ended in a guilty verdict; a retrial ended without a verdict. (Sixteen years after the Hossack murder, Glaspell adapted the case into a play and story, written from a more sympathetic perspective.) At the turn of the twentieth century, public opinion about such cases frequently sided with the wife of an abusive husband, as this newspaper account of an earlier murder trial suggests.

CHARLOTTE PERKINS GILMAN

From Why I Wrote The Yellow Wallpaper (1913)[1]

For many years I suffered from a severe and continuous nervous breakdown tending to melancholia—and beyond. During about the third year of this trouble I went, in devout faith and some faint stir of hope, to a noted specialist in nervous diseases, the best known in the country. This wise man put me to bed and applied the rest cure, to which a still good physique responded so promptly that he concluded that there was nothing much the matter with me, and sent me home with solemn advice to "live as domestic a life as possible," to "have but two hours' intelligent life a day," and "never to touch pen, brush or pencil again as long as I lived."

THE WASHINGTON POST

The Rest Cure (4 Aug. 1902)

Silas Weir Mitchell, 1829–1914

What makes people tired is not overwork, but overconcentration, overniceness in clinging to one settled rule till the nerves rebel.

What is most needed for recreation is relaxation. In carrying burdens, either mental or physical, there is nothing like "changing hands" often.

Recreation need not always consist of social diversion—of going to the theater or the show. One must vary his routine, if nothing more than to change his position while at work.

Routine kills more Americans than anything else. It brings about depression, despondency, and nervous breakdowns.

These general principles and their application constitute what the doctors call "the rest cure." There's nothing like keeping out of the ruts.

THE WASHINGTON POST

From Egotism of the Rest Cure (10 Sept. 1905)

Many a smart dame spends August at a rest cure, but the woman who would enjoy such a holiday is to be pitied, for the essential point about a rest cure is the egotism of the patient's attitude to herself and those about her. It is signifi-

---

1. Published in Gilman's magazine *The Forerunner*, vol. 4, no. 10, Oct. 1913, p. 271. Gilman suffered postpartum depression after the birth of her daughter. In 1886, she sought treatment by S. Weir Mitchell. Though Gilman repeatedly affirmed that the horrors she described in "The Yellow Wallpaper" (pp. 585–96) had persuaded Weir Mitchell to abandon the "rest cure" treatment, and biographers have tended to repeat this assertion, there is no evidence it was true.

cant that this type of holiday is one very rarely advised in the case of a man or in the case of a real worker.

SUGGESTIONS FOR FURTHER READING

Ben-Zvi, Linda. "'Murder, She Wrote': The Genesis of Susan Glaspell's *Trifles*." *Susan Glaspell: Essays on Her Theater and Fiction*, edited by Linda Ben-Zvi, U of Michigan P, 1995, pp. 19–48.

Bose, Christine E. *Women in 1900*. Temple UP, 2001.

Edelstein, Sari. "Charlotte Perkins Gilman and the Yellow Newspaper." *Legacy*, vol. 24, no. 1, 2007, pp. 72–92.

Griswold, Robert L. "Law, Sex, Cruelty, and Divorce in Victorian America, 1840–1900." Hawes and Nybakken, pp. 145–72.

Hard, William. *The Women of To-Morrow*. Baker, 1911.

Hawes, Joseph M., and Elizabeth I. Nybakken, editors. *Family and Society in American History*. U of Illinois P, 2001.

Hedges, Elaine. "Small Things Reconsidered: 'A Jury of Her Peers.'" *Susan Glaspell: Essays on Her Theater and Fiction*, edited by Linda Ben-Zvi, U of Michigan P, 1995, pp. 49–69.

Karpinski, Joanne B., editor. *Critical Essays on Charlotte Perkins Gilman*. G. K. Hall, 1992.

Kleinberg, S. J. *Women in the United States, 1830–1945*. Macmillan, 1999.

Koloski, Bernard. *Kate Chopin: A Study of the Short Fiction*. Twayne, 1996.

Leach, William R. *True Love and Perfect Union: The Feminist Reform of Sex and Society*. Basic Books, 1980.

Llewellyn, K. N. "Behind the Law of Divorce: I." *Columbia Law Review*, vol. 32, no. 8, Dec. 1932, pp. 1281–1308.

Roosevelt, Eleanor [Mrs. Franklin D.]. *It's Up to the Women*. Frederick A. Stokes, 1933.

Smith-Rosenberg, Carroll. *Disorderly Conduct: Visions of Gender in Victorian America*. Alfred A. Knopf, 1985.

SUGGESTIONS FOR WRITING

1. In THE STORY OF AN HOUR Louise Mallard receives the false report—relayed in two telegrams to a newspaper office and then through her sister—of her husband's death in a railroad accident. Other than these particulars of transportation and communication, the story's simple setting and action might belong to an earlier period. Looking closely at details of the story, write an essay that examines its relation to the historical context of 1894, when it was published. In what respects does the story reflect changes or continuities in family life? Could the same events have happened without the modern means of travel and communication? What role do time or history play in this short incident?

2. The narrator of THE YELLOW WALLPAPER declares, "congenial work [. . .] would do me good. But what is one to do?" (par. 14–15). Notice places in the story where the patient's views or wishes are contradicted, or where she is able to do something to change how she is treated. Write an essay bringing a historical perspective to this story's representation of women's work or ability to act, or "do." The essay might include reference to S. Weir Mitchell's rest cure or other treatments of women's illness in 1880–1920.

3. In A JURY OF HER PEERS, Mrs. Peters is "married to the law" (in the form of her husband the sheriff, par. 282), whereas Mrs. Hale is married to the farmer who first discovers the murder. In what ways, including dress, speech and manners, action, and attitude, are the two visiting women alike or different? In what ways do they identify with or distance themselves from the absent wife, Mrs. Wright? How do the men and women take sides separately or together? Is the idea that the murder was provoked a sign of the story's realistic portrayal of marriage around 1900? Write an essay focusing on turn-of-the-century marriage, the law, and alliances as well as differences between men and women ("peers") in this story.

4. THE STORY OF AN HOUR, A JURY OF HER PEERS, and THE YELLOW WALLPAPER all take place inside a house, and almost entirely within one room of that house. Entering through a door or gazing out a window may play a significant part in the action. Write an essay in which you focus on domestic space and women's confinement in this period of U.S. history, comparing at least two of these stories.

5. At the end of each of these stories, a husband or wife has collapsed or is dead— a marriage has ended. Write an essay in which you analyze one or more of these three stories as an indirect commentary on turn-of-the-century views of marriage and divorce.

6. Examine the details of the women's housekeeping in A JURY OF HER PEERS and TRIFLES, the play by Susan Glaspell, both in the physical setting of the farm kitchen and in the characters' conversations or thoughts. Write an essay on women's work at the turn of the twentieth century as reflected in Glaspell's story and play.

7. Charlotte Perkins Gilman and Barbara Boyd acknowledged that many women were opposed to the idea of changing traditional feminine roles and did not want the vote. Examine sources on the history of the women's movement in the United States—for instance, by consulting the National Women's History Project website or printed sources. Write an essay on the ways that women such as the sisters in THE STORY OF AN HOUR or THE YELLOW WALLPAPER or the more timid Mrs. Peters in A JURY OF HER PEERS might resist or slow down what Chopin, Gilman, or Glaspell considered to be progress for women. Choose one or two stories and focus on a specific issue such as the idea that women are naturally domestic and subordinate to husbands.

8. For a biographical and historical approach to one of these stories, consult the biography of Chopin, Gilman, or Glaspell in this volume and the entry on this author in the online or print Dictionary of National Biography, the online Gale Literature, Literature Online, or other reliable resources available on the Web or in your library. Compare at least three versions of the author's biography to confirm some of the general facts. Write an essay that interprets the story by this author (THE STORY OF AN HOUR, THE YELLOW WALLPAPER, or A JURY OF HER PEERS) in relation both to her life and career and to women's changing roles and conditions as outlined in this chapter.

10 | CRITICAL CONTEXTS: TIM O'BRIEN'S "THE THINGS THEY CARRIED"

We have already seen that, although stories may be read as if they stand alone, they are enriched by being situated in authorial, literary, or cultural and historical contexts. Once a work has earned a place in the **canon** of literature, it has already become surrounded by a critical context as well—a conversation among readers that works very much like the conversations about a work that you have in (and beyond) the classroom but that takes place on the page rather than in person and extends over decades, even centuries, rather than hours or days. To write critically about a work of literature is to engage not only the text but also other readers who have written about it. In a critical context essay, the literary text typically functions as your primary source, published criticism as your secondary sources.

Reading criticism about a work should not rob you of, or substitute for, your individual response to the work any more than discussing it with your friends or classmates does. Rather, in addition to being informative in various ways, reading criticism can help you to clarify and enrich your response and to move from response to argument. After all, we sometimes discover that we have something particular to say or that what we have to say is worth saying only when we learn that someone else has already said something very different—something that we either disagree with or that seems to us to miss "the real point" or at least a point we think shouldn't be missed.

Sometimes entering a critical conversation can seem a daunting prospect, at least at first. What, you might think, can I, a mere student, possibly add? What is left for *anyone* to say about a story about which so much has been said already? The truth, however, is that *all* critics—even the most informed and experienced—must confront a version of the same questions every time they sit down to write. As important, they—like you—must implicitly answer those questions *in* their writing. When a work has engaged a number of critics, that is, subsequent commentators need to not only acknowledge the previous readings but also, by contradicting or modifying their conclusions, articulate a **motive** for writing—and, more important, for reading—yet another essay on the work. Trying to identify, as you read the work of other and especially more experienced literary critics, the specific moves, techniques, and strategies that they use to describe and insert themselves into a conversation—to acknowledge and respond to the work of others—can give you concrete examples of how to do the same thing.

The conversation about a work of literature is, in other words, a true conversation, even, at times, a debate. And wherever there is debate there is motive and opportunity—to reconsider both "sides," to take one side or the other, to offer an alternative point of view or one that somehow reconciles seemingly opposed stances, or to simply change the subject. To identify such opportunities, however, you first have to get a handle on how an array of individual arguments fit together as part of *one* conversation. Like any conversation or debate, including the sorts in which you participate every day, a conversation about a literary text tends to circle around a few key issues and questions and, almost inevitably, to ignore or at least slight others. In reading criticism, one of your first tasks is thus to figure out

- what those specific issues and questions are;
- where each of the individual critics stands on them, or what the various "sides" are;
- where, when, and why you find yourself agreeing with their various stances and arguments; and—finally—
- what aspects of the text or what ways of looking at it *aren't* brought up at all or at least aren't thoroughly addressed in the conversation that you think should be.

To give you practice at doing just that, this chapter includes both a short story—Vietnam veteran Tim O'Brien's THE THINGS THEY CARRIED—and excerpts from three scholarly essays about it. We've made your job a bit easier by choosing a story at once universally admired and highly controversial, in part because of its subject matter: a war mainly fought not by volunteers but by draftees, the first war the United States ever lost, and one so fiercely, widely, and publicly contested that many feared it might tear the country apart. Focusing on the fortunes and misfortunes of a company of soldiers fighting—as O'Brien himself did—in the jungles of Vietnam in the late 1960s, the story originally debuted in *Esquire* magazine in 1986, eleven years after the Fall of Saigon ended the war the story depicts and only four years before the start of the Gulf War (1990–91), the first of the series of American military engagements that has unfortunately helped to give O'Brien's work—and the controversies over it—new relevance. Included in *The Best American Short Stories 1987*, "The Things They Carried" became something of an instant classic after its republication in O'Brien's 1990 collection of the same name. So interlinked, in fact, are the twenty-two stories that make up *The Things They Carried*—beginning with the title story and ending with THE LIVES OF THE DEAD—that some commentators refer to the book not as a short-story collection, sequence, or cycle at all but rather as a novel. Whether they categorize "The Things They Carried" as a short story (as we do) or as a novel chapter, however, critics seldom, if ever, analyze it in isolation. Instead, they tend to consider how it works and means in the context of the book of which it is a part, of its critical context, and, often, of O'Brien's **oeuvre** or authorial canon as a whole, of other literature about Vietnam, and/or of the story's historical and cultural contexts (not only the late 1960s, in which it is set, but also the late 1980s, when it was written and first published).

We've made your job somewhat easier, too, by handpicking just three essays about the story that directly address—and often vehemently disagree with—one another. Though we have omitted those portions of each essay that deal with stories not included in this anthology, the essays are otherwise reproduced entire. This might add to your reading load, but it also ensures that you can read and really *use* these essays not only as contributions to the critical conversation about O'Brien's story but also as models of how to engage effectively in a critical conversation about any text or how, that is, to craft compelling arguments about a text by considering its critical context.

Reading critical essays in this light (as models), what you most want to pay attention to is less their various arguments than the formal or rhetorical strategies and techniques writers deploy to insert themselves into the ongoing conversation and to convince you of the worthiness of their contribution to it. The goal is to identify "moves" that you can try out in your own writing. When and how and for what specific purposes, for example, do these writers allude to, paraphrase, summarize, or quote from the arguments of other writers (their own secondary sources)? What specific techniques do they use to signal to you, the reader, when they are referring to or even reproducing the ideas of a source as opposed to their own ideas? What does each writer suggest about why his or her argument is both different from others' and important to the conversation? What, in other words, are their motives? How exactly do these writers work to convince you that they are being fair and balanced in their approach both to the primary source (the literary text) and to their secondary sources (others' arguments about it)?

Just as considering other readers' views of any work of fiction can help you to discover and refine your own, so identifying the specific techniques other writers use to draw on the work of other critics both to make their cases and to convince readers the case is worth making will help you discover new ways to do that, too.

TIM O'BRIEN
The Things They Carried
(See O'Brien biography on p. 56.)

First Lieutenant Jimmy Cross carried letters from a girl named Martha, a junior at Mount Sebastian College in New Jersey. They were not love letters, but Lieutenant Cross was hoping, so he kept them folded in plastic at the bottom of his rucksack. In the late afternoon, after a day's march, he would dig his foxhole, wash his hands under a canteen, unwrap the letters, hold them with the tips of his fingers, and spend the last hour of light pretending. He would imagine romantic camping trips into the White Mountains in New Hampshire. He would sometimes taste the envelope flaps, knowing her tongue had been there. More than anything, he wanted Martha to love him as he loved her, but the letters were mostly chatty, elusive on the matter of love. She was a virgin, he was almost sure. She was an English major at Mount Sebastian, and she wrote beautifully about her professors and roommates and midterm exams, about her respect for Chaucer and her great affection for Virginia Woolf.[1] She often quoted lines of poetry; she never mentioned the war, except to say, Jimmy, take care of yourself. The letters weighed 4 ounces. They were signed Love, Martha, but Lieutenant Cross understood that Love was only a way of signing and did not mean what he sometimes pretended it meant. At dusk, he would carefully return the letters to his rucksack. Slowly, a bit distracted, he would get up and move among his men, checking the perimeter, then at full dark he would return to his hole and watch the night and wonder if Martha was a virgin.

---

1. British novelist (1882–1941) and author of *A Room of One's Own* (1929), which explores the difficulties that have inhibited women writers. *Chaucer:* *Canterbury Tales* author Geoffrey Chaucer (c. 1343–1400), often hailed as the first English poet and the greatest before Shakespeare.

Tim O'Brien in Vietnam, c. 1969–70

The things they carried were largely determined by necessity. Among the necessities or near-necessities were P-38 can openers, pocket knives, heat tabs,[2] wristwatches, dog tags, mosquito repellent, chewing gum, candy, cigarettes, salt tablets, packets of Kool-Aid, lighters, matches, sewing kits, Military Payment Certificates, C rations,[3] and two or three canteens of water. Together, these items weighed between 12 and 18 pounds, depending upon a man's habits or rate of metabolism. Henry Dobbins, who was a big man, carried extra rations; he was especially fond of canned peaches in heavy syrup over pound cake. Dave Jensen, who practiced field hygiene, carried a toothbrush, dental floss, and several hotel-sized bars of soap he'd stolen on R&R[4] in Sydney, Australia. Ted Lavender, who was scared, carried tranquilizers until he was shot in the head outside the village of Than Khe in mid-April. By necessity, and because it was SOP,[5] they all carried steel helmets that weighed 5 pounds including the liner and camouflage cover. They carried the standard fatigue jackets and trousers. Very few carried underwear. On their feet they carried jungle boots—2.1 pounds—and Dave Jensen carried three pairs of socks and a can of Dr. Scholl's foot powder as a precaution against trench foot.[6]

2. Flammable tablets used to heat rations. *P-38 can openers*: small can openers developed in 1942 and issued as part of the field rations of U.S. forces between World War II and the 1980s.
3. Combat rations, canned meals for use in the field, c. 1940–58. *Military Payment Certificates*: form of currency used to pay U.S. military in some foreign countries from the end of World War II until the late 1970s.
4. Rest and recuperation or relaxation, leave (military acronym/slang).
5. Standard operating procedure (military acronym/slang).
6. Serious medical condition caused by prolonged exposure to damp, cold, unsanitary conditions; so named because of its prevalence among soldiers serving in the trenches of World War I.

Until he was shot, Ted Lavender carried 6 or 7 ounces of premium dope, which for him was a necessity. Mitchell Sanders, the RTO,[7] carried condoms. Norman Bowker carried a diary. Rat Kiley carried comic books. Kiowa, a devout Baptist, carried an illustrated New Testament that had been presented to him by his father, who taught Sunday school in Oklahoma City, Oklahoma. As a hedge against bad times, however, Kiowa also carried his grandmother's distrust of the white man, his grandfather's old hunting hatchet. Necessity dictated. Because the land was mined and booby-trapped, it was SOP for each man to carry a steel-centered, nylon-covered flak jacket, which weighed 6.7 pounds, but which on hot days seemed much heavier. Because you could die so quickly, each man carried at least one large compress bandage, usually in the helmet band for easy access. Because the nights were cold, and because the monsoons were wet, each carried a green plastic poncho that could be used as a raincoat or groundsheet or make-shift tent. With its quilted liner, the poncho weighed almost 2 pounds, but it was worth every ounce. In April, for instance, when Ted Lavender was shot, they used his poncho to wrap him up, then to carry him across the paddy,[8] then to lift him into the chopper that took him away.

They were called legs or grunts.

To carry something was to hump it, as when Lieutenant Jimmy Cross humped his love for Martha up the hills and through the swamps. In its intransitive form,[9] to hump meant to walk, or to march, but it implied burdens far beyond the intransitive.

Almost everyone humped photographs. In his wallet, Lieutenant Cross carried two photographs of Martha. The first was a Kodacolor[1] snapshot signed Love, though he knew better. She stood against a brick wall. Her eyes were gray and neutral, her lips slightly open as she stared straight-on at the camera. At night, sometimes, Lieutenant Cross wondered who had taken the picture, because he knew she had boyfriends, because he loved her so much, and because he could see the shadow of the picture-taker spreading out against the brick wall. The second photograph had been clipped from the 1968 Mount Sebastian yearbook. It was an action shot—women's volleyball—and Martha was bent horizontal to the floor, reaching, the palms of her hands in sharp focus, the tongue taut, the expression frank and competitive. There was no visible sweat. She wore white gym shorts. Her legs, he thought, were almost certainly the legs of a virgin, dry and without hair, the left knee cocked and carrying her entire weight, which was just over 117 pounds. Lieutenant Cross remembered touching that left knee. A dark theater, he remembered, and the movie was *Bonnie and Clyde*,[2] and Martha wore a tweed skirt, and during the final scene, when he touched her knee, she turned and looked at him in a sad, sober way that made him pull his hand back, but he would always remember

5

7. Radio telephone operator (military acronym/slang).
8. Usually swampy field where rice is grown.
9. That is, when used without a direct object.
1. First color film made by the Eastman Kodak Company, c. 1942–63.
2. Oscar-winning film (1967) in which Warren Beatty and Faye Dunaway portray Depression-era out-laws Clyde Barrow (1909–34) and Bonnie Parker (1910–34); in its graphic final scene, shot partly in slow motion, the couple dies in a hail of machine-gun fire.

the feel of the tweed skirt and the knee beneath it and the sound of the gunfire that killed Bonnie and Clyde, how embarrassing it was, how slow and oppressive. He remembered kissing her good night at the dorm door. Right then, he thought, he should've done something brave. He should've carried her up the stairs to her room and tied her to the bed and touched that left knee all night long. He should've risked it. Whenever he looked at the photographs, he thought of new things he should've done.

What they carried was partly a function of rank, partly of field specialty.

As a first lieutenant and platoon leader, Jimmy Cross carried a compass, maps, code books, binoculars, and a .45-caliber pistol that weighed 2.9 pounds fully loaded. He carried a strobe light and the responsibility for the lives of his men.

As an RTO, Mitchell Sanders carried the PRC-25 radio, a killer, 26 pounds with its battery.

As a medic, Rat Kiley carried a canvas satchel filled with morphine and plasma and malaria tablets and surgical tape and comic books and all the things a medic must carry, including M&M's for especially bad wounds,[3] for a total weight of nearly 18 pounds.

10   As a big man, therefore a machine gunner, Henry Dobbins carried the M-60, which weighed 23 pounds unloaded, but which was almost always loaded. In addition, Dobbins carried between 10 and 15 pounds of ammunition draped in belts across his chest and shoulders.

As PFCs or Spec 4s,[4] most of them were common grunts and carried the standard M-16 gas-operated assault rifle. The weapon weighed 7.5 pounds unloaded, 8.2 pounds with its full 20-round magazine. Depending on numerous factors, such as topography and psychology, the riflemen carried anywhere from 12 to 20 magazines, usually in cloth bandoliers, adding on another 8.4 pounds at minimum, 14 pounds at maximum. When it was available, they also carried M-16 maintenance gear—rods and steel brushes and swabs and tubes of LSA oil[5]—all of which weighed about a pound. Among the grunts, some carried the M-79 grenade launcher, 5.9 pounds unloaded, a reasonably light weapon except for the ammunition, which was heavy. A single round weighed 10 ounces. The typical load was 25 rounds. But Ted Lavender, who was scared, carried 34 rounds when he was shot and killed outside Than Khe, and he went down under an exceptional burden, more than 20 pounds of ammunition, plus the flak jacket and helmet and rations and water and toilet paper and tranquilizers and all the rest, plus the unweighed fear. He was dead weight. There was no twitching or flopping. Kiowa, who saw it happen, said it was like watching a rock fall, or a big sandbag or something—just boom, then down—not like the movies where the dead guy rolls around and does fancy spins and goes ass over

---

3. Medics in Vietnam administered M&M candies as a placebo to those so severely wounded that they wouldn't benefit from treatment.

4. Those holding the rank of Specialist Fourth Class, the rank immediately above Private First Class. PFC: Private First Class (military acronym/slang), rank between private (PVT) and lance-corporal (LCP).

5. Military acronym/slang for either "lubricant, small arms" or "lubricant, semifluid, automatic [weapons]."

U.S. soldiers on "Search and Destroy" patrol in Vietnam, 1966

teakettle—not like that, Kiowa said, the poor bastard just flat-fuck fell. Boom. Down. Nothing else. It was a bright morning in mid-April. Lieutenant Cross felt the pain. He blamed himself. They stripped off Lavender's canteens and ammo, all the heavy things, and Rat Kiley said the obvious, the guy's dead, and Mitchell Sanders used his radio to report one U.S. KIA[6] and to request a chopper. Then they wrapped Lavender in his poncho. They carried him out to a dry paddy, established security, and sat smoking the dead man's dope until the chopper came. Lieutenant Cross kept to himself. He pictured Martha's smooth young face, thinking he loved her more than anything, more than his men, and now Ted Lavender was dead because he loved her so much and could not stop thinking about her. When the dustoff[7] arrived, they carried Lavender aboard. Afterward they burned Than Khe. They marched until dusk, then dug their holes, and that night Kiowa kept explaining how you had to be there, how fast it was, how the poor guy just dropped like so much concrete. Boom-down, he said. Like cement.

In addition to the three standard weapons—the M-60, M-16 and M-79—they carried whatever presented itself, or whatever seemed appropriate as a means of killing or staying alive. They carried catch-as-catch-can. At various times, in various situations, they carried M-14s and CAR-15s and Swedish Ks and grease

6. Killed in action (military acronym/slang).
7. Medical evacuation helicopter, perhaps an acronym for Dedicated Unhesitating Service To Our Fighting Forces.

guns and captured AK-47s and Chi-Coms and RPGs[8] and Simonov carbines and black market Uzis and .38-caliber Smith & Wesson handguns and 66 mm LAWs and shotguns and silencers and blackjacks[9] and bayonets and C-4 plastic explosives. Lee Strunk carried a slingshot, a weapon of last resort, he called it. Mitchell Sanders carried brass knuckles. Kiowa carried his grandfather's feathered hatchet. Every third or fourth man carried a Claymore antipersonnel mine[1]—3.5 pounds with its firing device. They all carried fragmentation grenades[2]—14 ounces each. They all carried at least one M-18 colored smoke grenade—24 ounces. Some carried CS or tear gas grenades. Some carried white phosphorus grenades. They carried all they could bear, and then some, including a silent awe for the terrible power of the things they carried.

In the first week of April, before Lavender died, Lieutenant Jimmy Cross received a good-luck charm from Martha. It was a simple pebble, an ounce at most. Smooth to the touch, it was a milky white color with flecks of orange and violet, oval-shaped, like a miniature egg. In the accompanying letter, Martha wrote that she had found the pebble on the Jersey shoreline, precisely where the land touched water at high tide, where things came together but also separated. It was this separate-but-together quality, she wrote, that had inspired her to pick up the pebble and to carry it in her breast pocket for several days, where it seemed weightless, and then to send it through the mail, by air, as a token of her truest feelings for him. Lieutenant Cross found this romantic. But he wondered what her truest feelings were, exactly, and what she meant by separate-but-together. He wondered how the tides and waves had come into play on that afternoon along the Jersey shoreline when Martha saw the pebble and bent down to rescue it from geology. He imagined bare feet. Martha was a poet, with the poet's sensibilities, and her feet would be brown and bare, the toenails unpainted, the eyes chilly and somber like the ocean in March, and though it was painful, he wondered who had been with her that afternoon. He imagined a pair of shadows moving along the strip of sand where things came together but also separated. It was phantom jealousy, he knew, but he couldn't help himself. He loved her so much. On the march, through the hot days of early April, he carried the pebble in his mouth, turning it with his tongue, tasting sea salt and moisture. His mind wandered. He had difficulty keeping his attention on the war. On occasion he would yell at his men to spread out the column, to keep their eyes open, but then he would slip away into daydreams, just pretending, walking barefoot along the Jersey shore, with Martha, carrying nothing. He would feel himself rising. Sun and waves and gentle winds, all love and lightness.

What they carried varied by mission.

15   When a mission took them to the mountains, they carried mosquito netting, machetes, canvas tarps, and extra bug juice.

8. Rocket-propelled grenades (military acronym/slang).

9. Leather-covered, often lead-filled clubs with flexible handles. *LAWs:* light antitank or antiarmor weapons (military acronym/slang).

1. Remote-control mine that fires steel balls.

2. The most common type of grenade; they fire small projectiles or "fragments."

If a mission seemed especially hazardous, or if it involved a place they knew to be bad, they carried everything they could. In certain heavily mined AOs, where the land was dense with Toe Poppers and Bouncing Betties,[3] they took turns humping a 28-pound mine detector. With its headphones and big sensing plate, the equipment was a stress on the lower back and shoulders, awkward to handle, often useless because of the shrapnel in the earth, but they carried it anyway, partly for safety, partly for the illusion of safety.

On ambush, or other night missions, they carried peculiar little odds and ends. Kiowa always took along his New Testament and a pair of moccasins for silence. Dave Jensen carried night-sight vitamins high in carotene. Lee Strunk carried his slingshot; ammo, he claimed, would never be a problem. Rat Kiley carried brandy and M&M's candy. Until he was shot, Ted Lavender carried the starlight scope,[4] which weighed 6.3 pounds with its aluminum carrying case. Henry Dobbins carried his girlfriend's pantyhose wrapped around his neck as a comforter. They all carried ghosts. When dark came, they would move out single file across the meadows and paddies to their ambush coordinates, where they would quietly set up the Claymores and lie down and spend the night waiting.

Other missions were more complicated and required special equipment. In mid-April, it was their mission to search out and destroy the elaborate tunnel complexes[5] in the Than Khe area south of Chu Lai. To blow the tunnels, they carried one-pound blocks of pentrite high explosives, four blocks to a man, 68 pounds in all. They carried wiring, detonators, and battery-powered clackers.[6] Dave Jensen carried earplugs. Most often, before blowing the tunnels, they were ordered by higher command to search them, which was considered bad news, but by and large they just shrugged and carried out orders. Because he was a big man, Henry Dobbins was excused from tunnel duty. The others would draw numbers. Before Lavender died there were 17 men in the platoon, and whoever drew the number 17 would strip off his gear and crawl in headfirst with a flashlight and Lieutenant Cross's .45-caliber pistol. The rest of them would fan out as security. They would sit down or kneel, not facing the hole, listening to the ground beneath them, imagining cobwebs and ghosts, whatever was down there—the tunnel walls squeezing in—how the flashlight seemed impossibly heavy in the hand and how it was tunnel vision in the very strictest sense, compression in all ways, even time, and how you had to wiggle in—ass and elbows—a swallowed-up feeling—and how you found yourself worrying about odd things: Will your flashlight go dead? Do rats carry rabies? If you screamed, how far would the sound carry? Would your buddies hear it? Would they have the courage to drag you out? In some respects, though not many, the waiting was worse than the tunnel itself. Imagination was a killer.

On April 16, when Lee Strunk drew the number 17, he laughed and muttered something and went down quickly. The morning was hot and very still. Not good, Kiowa said. He looked at the tunnel opening, then out across a dry

3. Like *Toe Poppers*, slang for a type of land mine. *AOs*: areas of operation (military acronym/slang).
4. Night-vision device.
5. During the war, a vast system of tunnels was constructed throughout South Vietnam as a stronghold and base for attacks; some contained living areas, storage depots, even hospitals.
6. Handheld firing device for Claymore mines.

paddy toward the village of Than Khe. Nothing moved. No clouds or birds or people. As they waited, the men smoked and drank Kool-Aid, not talking much, feeling sympathy for Lee Strunk but also feeling the luck of the draw. You win some, you lose some, said Mitchell Sanders, and sometimes you settle for a rain check. It was a tired line and no one laughed.

20   Henry Dobbins ate a tropical chocolate bar.[7] Ted Lavender popped a tranquilizer and went off to pee.

After five minutes, Lieutenant Jimmy Cross moved to the tunnel, leaned down, and examined the darkness. Trouble, he thought—a cave-in maybe. And then suddenly, without willing it, he was thinking about Martha. The stresses and fractures, the quick collapse, the two of them buried alive under all that weight. Dense, crushing love. Kneeling, watching the hole, he tried to concentrate on Lee Strunk and the war, all the dangers, but his love was too much for him, he felt paralyzed, he wanted to sleep inside her lungs and breathe her blood and be smothered. He wanted her to be a virgin and not a virgin, all at once. He wanted to know her. Intimate secrets: Why poetry? Why so sad? Why that grayness in her eyes? Why so alone? Not lonely, just alone—riding her bike across campus or sitting off by herself in the cafeteria—even dancing, she danced alone—and it was the aloneness that filled him with love. He remembered telling her that one evening. How she nodded and looked away. And how, later, when he kissed her, she received the kiss without returning it, her eyes wide open, not afraid, not a virgin's eyes, just flat and uninvolved.

Lieutenant Cross gazed at the tunnel. But he was not there. He was buried with Martha under the white sand at the Jersey shore. They were pressed together, and the pebble in his mouth was her tongue. He was smiling. Vaguely, he was aware of how quiet the day was, the sullen paddies, yet he could not bring himself to worry about matters of security. He was beyond that. He was just a kid at war, in love. He was twenty-four years old. He couldn't help it.

A few moments later Lee Strunk crawled out of the tunnel. He came up grinning, filthy but alive. Lieutenant Cross nodded and closed his eyes while the others clapped Strunk on the back and made jokes about rising from the dead.

Worms, Rat Kiley said. Right out of the grave. Fuckin' zombie.

25   The men laughed. They all felt great relief.

Spook[8] city, said Mitchell Sanders.

Lee Strunk made a funny ghost sound, a kind of moaning, yet very happy, and right then, when Strunk made that high happy moaning sound, when he went *Ahhooooo*, right then Ted Lavender was shot in the head on his way back from peeing. He lay with his mouth open. The teeth were broken. There was a swollen black bruise under his left eye. The cheekbone was gone. Oh shit, Rat Kiley said, the guy's dead. The guy's dead, he kept saying, which seemed profound—the guy's dead. I mean really.

7. Candy bar originally developed for the military in World War II, designed to withstand extreme heat.
8. Ghost, but also used, since the 1940s, as a racial slur, especially with reference to African Americans.

The things they carried were determined to some extent by superstition. Lieutenant Cross carried his good-luck pebble. Dave Jensen carried a rabbit's foot. Norman Bowker, otherwise a very gentle person, carried a thumb that had been presented to him as a gift by Mitchell Sanders. The thumb was dark brown, rubbery to the touch, and weighed 3 ounces at most. It had been cut from a VC[9] corpse, a boy of fifteen or sixteen. They'd found him at the bottom of an irrigation ditch, badly burned, flies in his mouth and eyes. The boy wore black shorts and sandals. At the time of his death he had been carrying a pouch of rice, a rifle, and three magazines of ammunition.

You want my opinion, Mitchell Sanders said, there's a definite moral here.

He put his hand on the dead boy's wrist. He was quiet for a time, as if counting a pulse, then he patted the stomach, almost affectionately, and used Kiowa's hunting hatchet to remove the thumb.   30

Henry Dobbins asked what the moral was.

Moral?

You know. *Moral.*

Sanders wrapped the thumb in toilet paper and handed it across to Norman Bowker. There was no blood. Smiling, he kicked the boy's head, watched the flies scatter, and said, Its like with that old TV show—Paladin.[1] Have gun, will travel.

Henry Dobbins thought about it.   35

Yeah, well, he finally said. I don't see no moral.

There it *is*, man.

Fuck off.

They carried USO stationery and pencils and pens. They carried Sterno, safety pins, trip flares, signal flares, spools of wire, razor blades, chewing tobacco, liberated joss sticks and statuettes of the smiling Buddha, candles, grease pencils, *The Stars and Stripes*, fingernail clippers, Psy Ops[2] leaflets, bush hats, bolos, and much more. Twice a week, when the resupply choppers came in, they carried hot chow in green mermite cans[3] and large canvas bags filled with iced beer and soda pop. They carried plastic water containers, each with a 2-gallon capacity. Mitchell Sanders carried a set of starched tiger fatigues[4] for special occasions. Henry Dobbins carried Black Flag insecticide. Dave Jensen carried empty sandbags that could be filled at night for added protection. Lee Strunk

9. Viet Cong (military acronym/slang), short for *Viet Nam Cong San*, meaning "Vietnamese Communists," the guerrilla force that fought, with the support of the North Vietnamese Army, against both South Vietnam and the United States during the Vietnam War.

1. Gunfighter-protagonist of *Have Gun—Will Travel*, a popular television Western, 1957–63.

2. Short for psychological operations, military operations designed to affect the mental state of opposing forces. USO: United Service Organizations (acronym), nonprofit organization (founded 1941) providing programs, services, and entertainment to U.S. military personnel and their families. *Sterno*: canned flammable jelly used as a portable heat source, usually for cooking. *Trip flares*: devices used to secure an area and detect infiltrators; each consists of a trip wire that sends up a flare when disturbed or "tripped." *Joss*: incense. *Grease pencils*: pencils made of colored grease, usually used for writing on glossy surfaces. *The Stars and Stripes*: newspaper produced by the U.S. Department of Defense since World War II.

3. Insulated aluminum canisters used to transport hot or cold meals to troops in the field.

4. Camouflage uniform designed for jungle combat.

carried tanning lotion. Some things they carried in common. Taking turns, they carried the big PRC-77 scrambler radio, which weighed 30 pounds with its battery. They shared the weight of memory. They took up what others could no longer bear. Often, they carried each other, the wounded or weak. They carried infections. They carried chess sets, basketballs, Vietnamese-English dictionaries, insignia of rank, Bronze Stars and Purple Hearts, plastic cards imprinted with the Code of Conduct. They carried diseases, among them malaria and dysentery. They carried lice and ringworm and leeches and paddy algae and various rots and molds. They carried the land itself—Vietnam, the place, the soil—a powdery orange-red dust that covered their boots and fatigues and faces. They carried the sky. The whole atmosphere, they carried it, the humidity, the monsoons, the stink of fungus and decay, all of it, they carried gravity. They moved like mules. By daylight they took sniper fire, at night they were mortared, but it was not battle, it was just the endless march, village to village, without purpose, nothing won or lost. They marched for the sake of the march. They plodded along slowly, dumbly, leaning forward against the heat, unthinking, all blood and bone, simple grunts, soldiering with their legs, toiling up the hills and down into the paddies and across the rivers and up again and down, just humping, one step and then the next and then another, but no volition, no will, because it was automatic, it was anatomy, and the war was entirely a matter of posture and carriage, the hump was everything, a kind of inertia, a kind of emptiness, a dullness of desire and intellect and conscience and hope and human sensibility. Their principles were in their feet. Their calculations were biological. They had no sense of strategy or mission. They searched the villages without knowing what to look for, not caring, kicking over jars of rice, frisking children and old men, blowing tunnels, sometimes setting fires and sometimes not, then forming up and moving on to the next village, then other villages, where it would always be the same. They carried their own lives. The pressures were enormous. In the heat of early afternoon, they would remove their helmets and flak jackets, walking bare, which was dangerous but which helped ease the strain. They would often discard things along the route of march. Purely for comfort, they would throw away rations, blow their Claymores and grenades, no matter, because by nightfall the resupply choppers would arrive with more of the same, then a day or two later still more, fresh watermelons and crates of ammunition and sunglasses and woolen sweaters—the resources were stunning—sparklers for the Fourth of July, colored eggs for Easter—it was the great American war chest—the fruits of science, the smokestacks, the canneries, the arsenals at Hartford, the Minnesota forests, the machine shops, the vast fields of corn and wheat—they carried like freight trains; they carried it on their backs and shoulders—and for all the ambiguities of Vietnam, all the mysteries and unknowns, there was at least the single abiding certainty that they would never be at a loss for things to carry.

40 After the chopper took Lavender away, Lieutenant Jimmy Cross led his men into the village of Than Khe. They burned everything. They shot chickens and dogs, they trashed the village well, they called in artillery and watched the wreckage, then they marched for several hours through the hot afternoon, and

then at dusk, while Kiowa explained how Lavender died, Lieutenant Cross found himself trembling.

He tried not to cry. With his entrenching tool, which weighed 5 pounds, he began digging a hole in the earth.

He felt shame. He hated himself. He had loved Martha more than his men, and as a consequence Lavender was now dead, and this was something he would have to carry like a stone in his stomach for the rest of the war.

All he could do was dig. He used his entrenching tool like an ax, slashing, feeling both love and hate, and then later, when it was full dark, he sat at the bottom of his foxhole and wept. It went on for a long while. In part, he was grieving for Ted Lavender, but mostly it was for Martha, and for himself, because she belonged to another world, which was not quite real, and because she was a junior at Mount Sebastian College in New Jersey, a poet and a virgin and uninvolved, and because he realized she did not love him and never would.

Like cement, Kiowa whispered in the dark. I swear to God—boom, down. Not a word.

I've heard this, said Norman Bowker.

A pisser, you know? Still zipping himself up. Zapped while zipping.

All right, fine. That's enough.

Yeah, but you had to see it, the guy just—

I *heard*, man. Cement. So why not shut the fuck *up?*

Kiowa shook his head sadly and glanced over at the hole where Lieutenant Jimmy Cross sat watching the night. The air was thick and wet. A warm dense fog had settled over the paddies and there was the stillness that precedes rain.

After a time Kiowa sighed.

One thing for sure, he said. The lieutenant's in some deep hurt. I mean that crying jag—the way he was carrying on—it wasn't fake or anything, it was real heavy-duty hurt. The man cares.

Sure, Norman Bowker said.

Say what you want, the man does care.

We all got problems.

Not Lavender.

No, I guess not, Bowker said. Do me a favor, though.

Shut up?

That's a smart Indian. Shut up.

Shrugging, Kiowa pulled off his boots. He wanted to say more, just to lighten up his sleep, but instead he opened his New Testament and arranged it beneath his head as a pillow. The fog made things seem hollow and unattached. He tried not to think about Ted Lavender, but then he was thinking how fast it was, no drama, down and dead, and how it was hard to feel anything except surprise. It seemed unchristian. He wished he could find some great sadness, or even anger, but the emotion wasn't there and he couldn't make it happen. Mostly he felt pleased to be alive. He liked the smell of the New Testament under his cheek, the leather and ink and paper and glue, whatever the chemicals were. He liked hearing the sounds of night. Even his fatigue, it felt fine, the stiff muscles and the prickly awareness of his own body, a floating feeling. He enjoyed not being dead. Lying there, Kiowa admired Lieutenant Jimmy Cross's capacity for grief. He wanted to share the man's pain, he wanted to care as Jimmy Cross cared. And yet when he closed his eyes, all he could think was Boom-down, and all he could feel was the pleasure of having his boots off and the fog curling in around him and the damp soil and the Bible smells and the plush comfort of night.

After a moment Norman Bowker sat up in the dark.

What the hell, he said. You want to talk, *talk*. Tell it to me.

Forget it.

No, man, go on. One thing I hate, it's a silent Indian.

65　For the most part they carried themselves with poise, a kind of dignity. Now and then, however, there were times of panic, when they squealed or wanted to squeal but couldn't, when they twitched and made moaning sounds and covered their heads and said Dear Jesus and flopped around on the earth and fired their weapons blindly and cringed and sobbed and begged for the noise to stop and went wild and made stupid promises to themselves and to God and to their mothers and fathers, hoping not to die. In different ways, it happened to all of them. Afterward, when the firing ended, they would blink and peek up. They would touch their bodies, feeling shame, then quickly hiding it. They would force themselves to stand. As if in slow motion, frame by frame, the world would take on the old logic—absolute silence, then the wind, then sunlight, then voices. It was the burden of being alive. Awkwardly, the men would reassemble themselves, first in private, then in groups, becoming soldiers again. They would repair the leaks in their eyes. They would check for casualties, call in dustoffs, light cigarettes, try to smile, clear their throats and spit and begin cleaning their weapons. After a time someone would shake his head and say, No lie, I almost shit my pants, and someone else would laugh, which meant it was bad, yes, but the guy had obviously not shit his pants, it wasn't that bad, and in any case nobody would ever do such a thing and then go ahead and talk about it. They would squint into the dense, oppressive sunlight. For a few moments, perhaps, they would fall silent, lighting a joint and tracking its passage from man to man, inhaling, holding in the humiliation. Scary stuff, one of them might say. But then someone else would grin or flick his eyebrows and say, Roger-dodger, almost cut me a new asshole, *almost*.

There were numerous such poses. Some carried themselves with a sort of wistful resignation, others with pride or stiff soldierly discipline or good humor or macho zeal. They were afraid of dying but they were even more afraid to show it.

They found jokes to tell.

They used a hard vocabulary to contain the terrible softness. *Greased* they'd say. *Offed, lit up, zapped while zipping.* It wasn't cruelty, just stage presence. They were actors. When someone died, it wasn't quite dying, because in a curious way it seemed scripted, and because they had their lines mostly memorized, irony mixed with tragedy, and because they called it by other names, as if to encyst and destroy the reality of death itself. They kicked corpses. They cut off thumbs. They talked grunt lingo. They told stories about Ted Lavender's supply of tranquilizers, how the poor guy didn't feel a thing, how incredibly tranquil he was.

There's a moral here, said Mitchell Sanders.

They were waiting for Lavender's chopper, smoking the dead man's dope. 70

The moral's pretty obvious, Sanders said, and winked. Stay away from drugs. No joke, they'll ruin your day every time.

Cute, said Henry Dobbins.

Mind blower, get it? Talk about wiggy. Nothing left, just blood and brains.

They made themselves laugh.

There it is, they'd say. Over and over—there it is, my friend, there it is—as if 75 the repetition itself were an act of poise, a balance between crazy and almost crazy, knowing without going, there it is, which meant be cool, let it ride, because Oh yeah, man, you can't change what can't be changed, there it is, there it absolutely and positively and fucking well *is*.

They were tough.

They carried all the emotional baggage of men who might die. Grief, terror, love, longing—these were intangibles, but the intangibles had their own mass and specific gravity, they had tangible weight. They carried shameful memories. They carried the common secret of cowardice barely restrained, the instinct to run or freeze or hide, and in many respects this was the heaviest burden of all, for it could never be put down, it required perfect balance and perfect posture. They carried their reputations. They carried the soldier's greatest fear, which was the fear of blushing. Men killed, and died, because they were embarrassed not to. It was what had brought them to the war in the first place, nothing positive, no dreams of glory or honor, just to avoid the blush of dishonor. They died so as not to die of embarrassment. They crawled into tunnels and walked point and advanced under fire. Each morning, despite the unknowns, they made their legs move. They endured. They kept humping. They did not submit to the obvious alternative, which was simply to close the eyes and fall. So easy, really. Go limp and tumble to the ground and let the muscles unwind and not speak and not budge until your buddies picked you up and lifted you into the chopper that would roar and dip its nose and carry you off to the world. A mere matter of falling, yet no one ever fell. It was not courage, exactly; the object was not valor. Rather, they were too frightened to be cowards.

By and large they carried these things inside, maintaining the masks of composure. They sneered at sick call. They spoke bitterly about guys who had found release by shooting off their own toes or fingers. Pussies, they'd say. Candyasses. It was fierce, mocking talk, with only a trace of envy or awe, but even so the image played itself out behind their eyes.

They imagined the muzzle against flesh. So easy: squeeze the trigger and blow away a toe. They imagined it. They imagined the quick, sweet pain, then the evacuation to Japan, then a hospital with warm beds and cute geisha nurses.

And they dreamed of freedom birds. 80

At night, on guard, staring into the dark, they were carried away by jumbo jets. They felt the rush of takeoff. Gone! they yelled. And then velocity—wings and engines—a smiling stewardess—but it was more than a plane, it was a real bird, a big sleek silver bird with feathers and talons and high screeching. They were flying. The weights fell off; there was nothing to bear. They laughed and held on tight, feeling the cold slap of wind and altitude, soaring, thinking *It's over, I'm gone!*—they were naked, they were light and free—it was all lightness, bright and fast and buoyant, light as light, a helium buzz in the brain, a giddy bubbling in the lungs as they were taken up over the clouds and the war, beyond duty, beyond gravity and mortification and global entanglements—*Sin loi!,*[5] they yelled. *I'm sorry, motherfuckers, but I'm out of it, I'm goofed, I'm on a space cruise, I'm gone!*—and it was a restful, unencumbered sensation, just riding the light waves, sailing that big silver freedom bird over the mountains and oceans, over America, over the farms and great sleeping cities and cemeteries and highways and the golden arches of McDonald's, it was flight, a kind of fleeing, a kind of falling, falling higher and higher, spinning off the edge of the earth and beyond the sun and through the vast, silent vacuum where there were no burdens and where everything weighed exactly nothing—*Gone!* they screamed. *I'm sorry but I'm gone!*—and so at night, not quite dreaming, they gave themselves over to lightness, they were carried, they were purely borne.

On the morning after Ted Lavender died, First Lieutenant Jimmy Cross crouched at the bottom of his foxhole and burned Martha's letters. Then he burned the two photographs. There was a steady rain falling, which made it difficult, but he used heat tabs and Sterno to build a small fire, screening it with his body, holding the photographs over the tight blue flame with the tips of his fingers.

He realized it was only a gesture. Stupid, he thought. Sentimental, too, but mostly just stupid.

Lavender was dead. You couldn't burn the blame.

85   Besides, the letters were in his head. And even now, without photographs, Lieutenant Cross could see Martha playing volleyball in her white gym shorts and yellow T-shirt. He could see her moving in the rain.

When the fire died out, Lieutenant Cross pulled his poncho over his shoulders and ate breakfast from a can.

There was no great mystery, he decided.

In those burned letters Martha had never mentioned the war, except to say, Jimmy, take care of yourself. She wasn't involved. She signed the letters Love, but it wasn't love, and all the fine lines and technicalities did not matter. Virginity was no longer an issue. He hated her. Yes, he did. He hated her. Love, too, but it was a hard, hating kind of love.

The morning came up wet and blurry. Everything seemed part of everything else, the fog and Martha and the deepening rain.

90   He was a soldier, after all.

Half smiling, Lieutenant Jimmy Cross took out his maps. He shook his head hard, as if to clear it, then bent forward and began planning the day's march. In ten minutes, or maybe twenty, he would rouse the men and they would pack up and head west, where the maps showed the country to be green and inviting. They would do what they had always done. The rain might add some weight, but otherwise it would be one more day layered upon all the other days.

He was realistic about it. There was that new hardness in his stomach. He loved her but he hated her.

5. Sorry or Excuse me (Vietnamese).

No more fantasies, he told himself.

Henceforth, when he thought about Martha, it would be only to think that she belonged elsewhere. He would shut down the daydreams. This was not Mount Sebastian, it was another world, where there were no pretty poems or midterm exams, a place where men died because of carelessness and gross stupidity. Kiowa was right. Boom-down, and you were dead, never partly dead.

Briefly, in the rain, Lieutenant Cross saw Martha's gray eyes gazing back   95
at him.

He understood.

It was very sad, he thought. The things men carried inside. The things men did or felt they had to do.

He almost nodded at her, but didn't.

Instead he went back to his maps. He was now determined to perform his duties firmly and without negligence. It wouldn't help Lavender, he knew that, but from this point on he would comport himself as an officer. He would dispose of his good-luck pebble. Swallow it, maybe, or use Lee Strunk's slingshot, or just drop it along the trail. On the march he would impose strict field discipline. He would be careful to send out flank security, to prevent straggling or bunching up, to keep his troops moving at the proper pace and at the proper interval. He would insist on clean weapons. He would confiscate the remainder of Lavender's dope. Later in the day, perhaps, he would call the men together and speak to them plainly. He would accept the blame for what had happened to Ted Lavender. He would be a man about it. He would look them in the eyes, keeping his chin level, and he would issue the new SOPs in a calm, impersonal tone of voice, a lieutenant's voice, leaving no room for argument or discussion. Commencing immediately, he'd tell them, they would no longer abandon equipment along the route of march. They would police up their acts. They would get their shit together, and keep it together, and maintain it neatly and in good working order.

He would not tolerate laxity. He would show strength, distancing himself.   100

Among the men there would be grumbling, of course, and maybe worse, because their days would seem longer and their loads heavier, but Lieutenant Jimmy Cross reminded himself that his obligation was not to be loved but to lead. He would dispense with love; it was not now a factor. And if anyone quarreled or complained, he would simply tighten his lips and arrange his shoulders in the correct command posture. He might give a curt little nod. Or he might not. He might just shrug and say, Carry on, then they would saddle up and form into a column and move out toward the villages west of Than Khe.

1986, 1990

CRITICAL EXCERPTS

Steven Kaplan

From The Undying Uncertainty of the Narrator in Tim O'Brien's *The Things They Carried* (1993)[1]

Before the United States became militarily involved in defending the sovereignty of South Vietnam, it had to, as one historian recently put it, "invent" (Baritz 142–43) the country and the political issues at stake there. The Vietnam War was in many ways a wild and terrible work of fiction written by some dangerous and frightening storytellers. First the United States decided what constituted good and evil, right and wrong, civilized and uncivilized, freedom and oppression for Vietnam, according to American standards; then it traveled the long physical distance to Vietnam and attempted to make its own notions about these things clear to the Vietnamese people—ultimately by brute, technological force. For the U.S. military and government; the Vietnam that they had in effect invented became fact. For the soldiers that the government then sent there, however, the facts that their government had created about who was the enemy, what were the issues, and how the war was to be won were quickly overshadowed by a world of uncertainty. Ultimately, trying to stay alive long enough to return home in one piece was the only thing that made any sense to them. As David Halberstam puts it in his novel, *One Very Hot Day*, the only fact of which an American soldier in Vietnam could be certain was that "yes was no longer yes, no was no longer no, maybe was more certainly maybe" (127). Almost all of the literature on the war, both fictional and nonfictional, makes clear that the only certain thing during the Vietnam War was that nothing was certain. Philip Beidler has pointed out in an impressive study of the literature of that war that "most of the time in Vietnam, there were some things that seemed just too terrible and strange to be true and others that were just too terrible and true to be strange" (4).

The main question that Beidler's study raises is how, in light of the overwhelming ambiguity that characterized the Vietnam experience, could any sense or meaning be derived from what happened and, above all, how could this meaning, if it were found, be conveyed to those who had not experienced the war? The answer Beidler's book offers, as Beidler himself recently said at a conference on writing about the war, is that "words are all we have. In the hands of true artists . . . they may yet preserve us against the darkness" (Lomperis 87). Similarly, for the novelist Tim O'Brien, the language of fiction is the most accurate means for conveying, as Beidler so incisively puts it, "what happened (in Vietnam) . . . what might have happened, what could have happened, what should have happened, and maybe also what can be kept from happening or what can be made to happen" (87). If the experience of Vietnam and its accompanying sense of chaos and confusion can be shown at all, then for Tim O'Brien

1. Steven Kaplan, "The Undying Uncertainty of the Narrator in Tim O'Brien's *The Things They Carried*." *Critique*, vol. 35, no. 1, fall 1993, pp. 43–52. *Taylor & Francis Online*, https://doi.org/10.1080/00 111619.1993.9936466. All footnotes are Kaplan's. Some notes and works-cited entries are omitted.

it will not be in the fictions created by politicians but in the stories told by writers of fiction.

One of Tim O'Brien's most important statements about the inherent problems of understanding and writing about the Vietnam experience appears in a chapter of his novel, *Going After Cacciato*, appropriately titled "The Things They Didn't Know." The novel's protagonist, Paul Berlin, briefly interrupts his fantasy about chasing the deserter Cacciato, who is en route from Vietnam to Paris, to come to terms with the fact that although he is physically in Vietnam and fighting a war, his understanding of where he is and what he is doing there is light-years away. At the center of the chapter is a long catalogue of the things that Berlin and his comrades did not know about Vietnam, and the chapter closes with the statement that what "they" *knew* above all else were the "uncertainties never articulated in war stories" (319). In that chapter Tim O'Brien shows that recognizing and exploring the uncertainties about the war is perhaps the closest one can come to finding anything certain at all. Paul Berlin, in his fantasy about escaping the war and chasing Cacciato to Paris, is in fact attempting to confront and, as far as possible, understand the uncertainties of the Vietnam War through the prism of his imagination. [. . .]

In his most recent work of fiction,[2] *The Things They Carried*, Tim O'Brien takes the act of trying to reveal and understand the uncertainties about the war one step further, by looking at it through the imagination. He completely destroys the fine line dividing fact from fiction and tries to show, even more so than in *Cacciato*, that fiction (or the imagined world) can often be truer, especially in the case of Vietnam, than fact. In the first chapter, an almost documentary account of the items referred to in the book's title, O'Brien introduces the reader to some of the things, both imaginary and concrete, emotional and physical, that the average foot soldier had to carry through the jungles of Vietnam. All of the "things" are depicted in a style that is almost scientific in its precision. We are told how much each subject weighs, either psychologically or physically, and, in the case of artillery, we are even told how many ounces each round weighed [. . .].

Even the most insignificant details seem worth mentioning. One main character is not just from Oklahoma City but from "Oklahoma City, Oklahoma" (5), as if mentioning the state somehow makes the location more factual, more certain. More striking than this obsession with even the minutest detail, however, is the academic tone that at times makes the narrative sound like a government report. We find such transitional phrases as "for instance" (5) and "in addition" (7), and whole paragraphs are dominated by sentences that begin with "because" (5). These strengthen our impression that the narrator is striving, above all else, to convince us of the reality, of the concrete certainty, of the things they carried.

In the midst of this factuality and certainty, however, are signals that all the information in this opening chapter will not amount to much: that the certain-

2. The reviewers of this book are split on whether to call it a novel or a collection of short stories. In a recent interview, I asked Tim O'Brien what he felt was the most adequate designation. He said that *The Things They Carried* is neither a collection of stories nor a novel: he preferred to call it a work of fiction.

ties are merely there to conceal uncertainties and that the words following the frequent "becauses" do not provide an explanation of anything. We are told in the opening page that the most important thing that First Lieutenant Jimmy Cross carried were some letters from a girl he loved. The narrator [. . .] tells us that the girl did not love Cross, but that he constantly indulged in "hoping" and "pretending" (3) in an effort to turn her love into fact. We are also told "she was a virgin," but this is immediately qualified by the statement that "he was almost sure" of this (3). On the next page, Cross becomes increasingly uncertain as he sits at "night and wonder(s) if Martha was a virgin" (4). Shortly after this, Cross wonders who had taken the pictures he now holds in his hands "because he knew she had boyfriends" (5), but we are never told how he "knew" this. At the end of the chapter, after one of Cross's men has died because Cross was too busy thinking of Martha, Cross sits at the bottom of his foxhole crying, not so much for the member of his platoon who has been killed "but mostly it was for Martha, and for himself, because she belonged to another world, and because she was . . . a poet and a virgin and uninvolved" (17).

This pattern of stating facts and then quickly calling them into question that is typical of Jimmy Cross's thoughts in these opening pages characterizes how the narrator portrays events throughout this book: the facts about an event are given; they then are quickly qualified or called into question; from this uncertainty emerges a new set of facts about the same subject that are again called into question—on and on, without end.

By giving the reader facts and then calling those facts into question, by telling stories and then saying that those stories happened (147), and then that they did not happen (203), and then that they might have happened (204), O'Brien puts more emphasis in *The Things They Carried* on the question that he first posed in *Going After Cacciato*: how can a work of fiction become paradoxically more real than the events upon which it is based, and how can the confusing experiences of the average soldier in Vietnam be conveyed in such a way that they will acquire at least a momentary sense of certainty.

When we conceptualize life, we attempt to step outside ourselves and look at who we are. We constantly make new attempts to conceptualize our lives and uncover our true identities because looking at who we might be is as close as we can come to discovering who we actually are. Similarly, representing events in fiction is an attempt to understand them by detaching them from the "real world" and placing them in a world that is being staged. In *The Things They Carried*, Tim O'Brien desperately struggles to make his readers believe that what they are reading is true because he wants them to step outside their everyday reality and participate in the events that he is portraying: he wants us to believe in his stories to the point where we are virtually in the stories so that we might gain a more thorough understanding of, or feeling for, what is being portrayed in them. Representation as O'Brien practices it in this book is not a mimetic act but a "game," as [Wolfgang] Iser calls it in [. . .] "The Play of the Text," a process of acting things out:

> Now since the latter (the text) is fictional, it automatically invokes a convention-governed contract between author and reader indicating that the textual world is to be viewed not as reality but as if it *were* reality. And so whatever is repeated in the text is not meant to denote the world, but merely a world enacted. This may well repeat an identifiable reality, but it contains one all-important difference: what happens within it is relieved of the consequences inherent in the real world referred to. Hence in disclosing itself, fictionality signalizes that everything is only to be taken *as if* it were what it seems to be, to be taken—in other words—as play. (251)

In *The Things They Carried*, representation includes staging what might have happened in Vietnam while simultaneously questioning the accuracy and credibility of the narrative act itself. The reader is thus made fully aware of being made a participant in a game, in a "performative act," and thereby also is asked to become immediately involved in the incredibly frustrating act of trying to make sense of events that resist understanding. The reader is permitted to experience at first hand the uncertainty that characterized being in Vietnam.

. . . .

The narrative strategy that O'Brien uses in this book to portray the uncertainty of what happened in Vietnam is not restricted to depicting war, and O'Brien does not limit it to the war alone. He concludes his book with a chapter titled "The Lives of the Dead" in which he moves from his experiences in Vietnam back to when he was nine years old. On the surface, the book's last chapter is about O'Brien's first date, his first love, a girl named Linda who died of a brain tumor a few months after he had taken her to see the movie, *The Man Who Never Was*. What this chapter is really about, however, as its title suggests, is how the dead (which also include people who may never have actually existed) can be given life in a work of fiction. In a story, O'Brien tells us, "memory and imagination and language combine to make spirits in the head. There is the illusion of aliveness" (260). Like the man who never was in the film of that title, the people that never were except in memories and the imagination can become real or alive, if only for a moment, through the act of storytelling.

According to O'Brien, when you tell a story, really tell it, "you objectify your own experience. You separate it from yourself" (178). By doing this you are able to externalize "a swirl of memories that might otherwise have ended in paralysis or worse" (179). However, the storyteller does not just escape from the events and people in a story by placing them on paper; as we have seen, the act of telling a given story is an ongoing and never-ending process. By constantly involving and then re-involving the reader in the task of determining what "actually" happened in a given situation, in a story, and by forcing the reader to experience the impossibility of ever knowing with any certainty what actually happened, O'Brien liberates himself from the lonesome responsibility of remembering and trying to understand events. He also creates a community of individuals immersed in the act of experiencing the uncertainty or indeterminacy of all events, regardless of whether they occurred in Vietnam, in a small town in Minnesota (253–273), or somewhere in the reader's own life.

O'Brien thus saves himself, as he puts it in the last sentence of his book, from the fate of his character Norman Bowker who, in a chapter called "Speaking of Courage," kills himself because he cannot find some lasting meaning in the horrible things he experienced in Vietnam. O'Brien saves himself by demonstrating in this book that the most important thing is to be able to recognize and accept that events have no fixed or final meaning and that the only meaning that events can have is one that emerges momentarily and then shifts and changes each time that the events come alive as they are remembered or portrayed.

The character Norman Bowker hangs himself in the locker room of the local YMCA after playing basketball with some friends (181), partially because he has a story locked up inside of himself that he feels he cannot tell because no one would want to hear it. [. . .]

O'Brien, after his war, took on the task "of grabbing people by the shirt and explaining exactly what had happened to me" (179). He explains in *The Things They Carried* that it is impossible to know "exactly what had happened." He wants us to know all of the things he/they/we did not know about Vietnam and will probably never know. He wants us to feel the sense of uncertainty that his character/narrator Tim O'Brien experiences twenty years after the war when he returns to the place where his friend Kiowa sank into a "field of shit" and tries to find "something meaningful and right" (212) to say but ultimately can only say, "well . . . there it is" (212). Each time we, the readers of *The Things They Carried*, return to Vietnam through O'Brien's labyrinth of stories, we become more and more aware that this statement is the closest we probably ever will come to knowing the "real truth," the undying uncertainty of the Vietnam War.

WORKS CITED

Baritz, Loren. *Backfire: A History of How American Culture Led Us into Vietnam and Made Us Fight the Way We Did*. New York: Morrow, 1985.

Beidler, Philip. *American Literature and the Experience of Vietnam*. Athens: U of Georgia P, 1982.

Halberstam, David. *One Very Hot Day*. New York: Houghton, 1967.

Iser, Wolfgang. *Prospecting: From Reader Response to Literary Anthropology*. Baltimore: Johns Hopkins UP, 1989.

Lomperis, Timothy. *"Reading the Wind": The Literature of the Vietnam War: An Interpretative Critique*. Durham: Duke UP, 1989.

O'Brien, Tim. *Going After Cacciato*. New York: Dell, 1978.

———. *The Things They Carried*. Boston: Houghton, 1990.

LORRIE N. SMITH

From "The Things Men Do": The Gendered Subtext in Tim O'Brien's *Esquire* Stories (1994)[1]

Tim O'Brien's 1990 book of interlocked stories, *The Things They Carried*, garnered one rave review after another, reinforcing O'Brien's already established position as one of the most important veteran writers of the Vietnam War. The Penguin paperback edition serves up six pages of superlative blurbs like "consummate artistry," "classic," "the best American writer of his generation," "unique," and "master work." A brilliant metafictionist,[2] O'Brien captures the moral and ontological uncertainty experienced by men at war, along with enough visceral realism to "make the stomach believe," as his fictional narrator, Tim O'Brien, puts it. [. . .] Yet, O'Brien—and his reviewers—seem curiously unselfconscious about this book's obsession with and ambivalence about representations of masculinity and femininity, particularly in the five stories originally published during the 1980s in *Esquire*. If this observation is accurate, and if, as one reviewer (Harris) claims, O'Brien's book "exposes the nature of all war stories," then we might postulate that "all war stories" are constituted by what Eve Kosofsky Sedgwick calls, in another context, a "drama of gender difference" (6). The book diverts attention from this central play by constructing an elaborate and captivating metafictional surface, but the drama is finally exposed by the sheer exaggeration and aggressiveness of its gendered roles and gendering gestures. "The things" his male characters "carried" to war, it turns out, include plenty of patriarchal baggage. O'Brien purports to tell "true" war stories, but stops short of fully interrogating their ideological underpinnings—either in terms of the binary construction of gender that permeates representations of war in our culture, or in terms of the Vietnam War itself as a political event implicated in racist, ethnocentric assumptions. Hence, the text offers no challenge to a discourse of war in which apparently innocent American men are tragically wounded and women are objectified, excluded, and silenced. My intent in bringing this subtext to light is not to devalue O'Brien's technical skill or emotional depth, but to account for my own discomfort as a female reader and to position *The Things They Carried* within a larger cultural project to rewrite the Vietnam War from a masculinist and strictly American perspective.

As much about the act of writing as about war itself, O'Brien's book celebrates the reconstructive power of the imagination, which gives shape, substance, and significance to slippery emotion and memory. We might even say that imagination itself—as embodied in the act of storytelling—plays the hero in this book, countering our national propensity for amnesia and offering the hope of personal redemption. O'Brien has often spoken of the imagination as a

1. Lorrie N. Smith, "'The Things Men Do': The Gendered Subtext in Tim O'Brien's *Esquire* Stories." *Critique*, vol. 36, no. 1, fall 1994, pp. 16–40. *Taylor & Francis Online*, https://doi.org/10.1080/00111619. 1994.9935239. Unless otherwise indicated, all footnotes have been added by the editor. Some of Smith's works-cited entries are omitted.
2. That is, a writer of *metafiction*, fiction that draws attention to its status as fiction in order to explore the nature of fiction and the role of authors and readers.

morally weighted force shaping the narratives and myths we live by. In Timothy Lomperis's *Reading the Wind*, for instance, O'Brien comments, "It's a real thing and I think influences in a major way the kind of real-life decisions we made to go to the war or not to go to the war. Either way, we imagine our futures and then try to step into our own imaginations . . . the purpose of fiction is to explore moral quandaries" (48, 52). In a more recent interview, he claims "exercising the imagination is the main way of finding truth" (Naparsteck 10). Taking his cue from O'Brien, critic Philip Beidler asserts that form, theme, and moral imperative merge in *The Things They Carried*: "It is at once a summation of Tim O'Brien's re-writing of the old dialectic of facts and fictions and a literally exponential prediction of new contexts of vision and insight, of new worlds to remember, imagine, believe" (32–33).

[. . .] By the end of the book, storytelling even carries the power of salvation and transubstantiation: "As a writer now, I want to save Linda's life . . . in a story I can steal her soul. I can revive, at least briefly, that which is absolute and unchanging. In a story, miracles can happen" (265). Writing, like life, entails choice; unlike life, it also offers endless possibility. Hence, O'Brien's stories often offer multiple versions of "reality," complicating the ambiguously entwined experience, memory, and retelling of Vietnam [. . .]. The book insistently asserts that "story-truth is truer sometimes than happening truth" (203) and admits that some stories, are simply "beyond telling" (79), can only be apprehended by those who experienced the event. Storytelling is finally a ritual both private and shared, a yearning toward wholeness, coherence, and meaning even while admitting their elusiveness.[3]

But who is invited to share this ritual? Despite its valorization of storytelling, *The Things They Carried* repeatedly underscores the incommunicability of war. This paradox has been identified by Kali Tal, who defines writing by Vietnam veterans as a literature of trauma, with analogues to writing by survivors of the Holocaust, slavery, incest, rape, and torture. For Tal, "Trauma literature demonstrates the unbridgeable gap between writer and reader and thus defines itself by the impossibility of its task—the communication of the traumatic experience" ("Speaking" 218). Tal challenges critics to account for the "inherent contradiction within literature by Vietnam veterans" by recognizing that "the symbols generated by liminality are readable only to those familiar with the alphabet of trauma" (239). I agree in general with this claim but would qualify it with Susan Jeffords's argument that revisionist cultural and literary productions over the past decade have restored the once-stigmatized Vietnam veteran to a position of power and status. Indeed, thanks largely to Oliver Stone, Sylvester

---

3. Like Toni Morrison's *Beloved*, *The Things They Carried* is fueled by the problem of how to tell stories about unspeakable trauma and how to make peace with the ghosts of the dead. This comparison sheds light on how texts and narrative strategies are gendered. Morrison's narrative of "re-memory" circles around the central story in a complex interplay of voices and sub-stories; its impulse is generous, inclusive, and collective, aimed at regeneration for a whole community as well as Sethe and her traumatized family. For a fuller treatment of this idea in Morrison, see Linda Krumholz. O'Brien's stories, as I hope to show, deal with trauma and the threat to the masculine subject by excluding women, both as readers and as characters. Though storytelling often reinforces camaraderie and redeems the solitary narrator, it does not include a whole community traumatized by the Vietnam War, nor does it attempt, as Morrison's story does, to recover a collective repressed history [Smith's note].

Stallone,[4] and Ron Kovic, veteran writers have increasingly had access to a discourse that is all *too* readable and familiar in our culture. The "alphabet of trauma," that is, has been encoded as a narrative of wounded American manhood that depends, for its meaning—whether tragic, ironic, or redemptive—on the positioning of women and Vietnamese as others.[5]

In an earlier essay, Tal found connections between the aims of feminist criticism and literature of Vietnam combat veterans who choose "to renounce their inherited white male power" ("Feminist Criticism" 199). Such texts, not surprisingly, are rare; more often, veterans' narratives fight bitterly to regain and sustain the power that the war temporarily disrupted. Hence, a consideration of how gender constructs affect the Vietnam veteran's rewriting of trauma opens a deeper gap than Tal identifies, in terms of both textual representation and the position and response of the reader. O'Brien often depicts war as inaccessible to nonveterans, creating a storytelling loop between characters within stories that excludes the uninitiated reader and privileges the authority of the soldiers' experience. But it is important to note that the moments of deepest trauma in the book occur when the masculine subject is threatened with dissolution or displacement. All readers are to some extent subjugated by O'Brien's shifty narrator: however, the female reader, in particular, is rendered marginal and mute, faced with the choice throughout the book of either staying outside the story or reading against herself from a masculine point of view. O'Brien repeatedly inscribes the outsider as female, hence reinforcing masculine bonds that lessen the survivor/outsider distinction for male readers. Male characters are granted many moments of mutual understanding, whereas women pointedly won't, don't, or can't understand war stories. In short, O'Brien writes women out of the war and the female reader out of the storytelling circle.

For all its polyphonic, postmodernist blurring of fact and fiction, *The Things They Carried* preserves a very traditional gender dichotomy, insistently representing abject femininity to reinforce dominant masculinity and to preserve the writing of war stories as a masculine privilege. Specifically, O'Brien uses female figures to mediate the process in homosocial[6] bonding, a narrative strategy Sedgwick plots as a triangulation:

> In the presence of a woman who can't be seen as pitiable or contemptible, men are able to exchange power and to confirm each other's value even in the context of the remaining inequalities in their power. The sexually pitiable or contemptible female figure is a solvent that not only facilitates the relative democratization that grows up with capitalism and cash exchange, but goes a long way—for the men whom she leaves bonded together—toward palliating its gaps and failures. (160)

4. Star (b. 1946) of (mainly action) films including *First Blood* (1982), the first of three movies about troubled Vietnam veteran John Rambo. *Oliver Stone*: Vietnam veteran (b. 1946) and director of films including *Born on the Fourth of July* (1989), based on the best-selling autobiography of paralyzed Vietnam veteran turned antiwar activist Ron Kovic (b. 1946).

5. For elaborations on the ways Vietnam War literature has worked to rehabilitate male veterans and masculinity, see Susan Jeffords, Jacqueline Lawson, and Lorrie Smith. Lynne Hanley explores female alternatives to "belligerent" narratives [Smith's note].

6. Involving social relationships among people of the same sex.

If we transfer Sedgwick's paradigm from the realm of class struggle to the current cultural contest over the meaning, communicability, and "gaps and failures" of the Vietnam War, we can understand how O'Brien's representations of "contemptible" femininity strengthen male bonds and deflect the contemporaneous assaults of an emasculating lost war, the women's movement, and feminist theory. We might even place the female reader at one corner of the triangle, her exclusion facilitating the bond between male writer and reader. Anxiety over the general incommunicabilty of trauma is thus greatly eased by the shared language of patriarchy.

Starring the now conventional trope of a democratic platoon of characters, this collection of stories suppresses any signifiers of age, race, class, or ideology to accentuate the common bond of masculinity. O'Brien closes male ranks in this book, celebrating camaraderie and preempting complicity or identification on the part of the female reader. Lavishing sensitive attention to the depth and complexity of men's emotions and rescuing their humanity in the face of a dehumanizing war, O'Brien represents women not as characters with agency and sensibility of their own, but as projections of a narrator trying to resolve the trauma of the war. Although he seems at points to engage and question conventional gender constructions, in the end he does so only to quell threats to masculinity and to re-assert patriarchal order. For all its internal resistance to narrative closure, the book's framing narrative is a hermeneutic circle: men at war act like men at war, and only men can write about it and understand it. [. . .]

Critics like Beidler who ignore gender can thus read *The Things They Carried* as a high achievement in the cultural project he sees writers of the Vietnam generation undertaking: to "reconstitute [American cultural mythology] as a medium both of historical self-reconsideration and, in the same moment, of historical self-renewal and even self-invention" (5). Such a grand(iose) humanistic accomplishment can only be achieved if we overlook how dominant conceptions of culture, self, and history erase or subjugate the female subject. Once we admit this asymmetry and oppression, totalizing myths of "universal truth" like those Beidler reads in O'Brien and other writers of the Vietnam generation become impossible. A feminist reading of fiction by Vietnam veterans reveals quite a different cultural and discursive project: what I have elsewhere labeled "backlash" and what Susan Jeffords calls "the remasculinization of America." Jeffords details how the proliferation of texts and films about the Vietnam War, especially during the 1980s, has contributed to "the large-scale renegotiation and regeneration of the interests, values, and projects of patriarchy now taking place in U.S. social relations." More specifically, "the representational features of the Vietnam War are structurally written through relations of gender, relations designed primarily to reinforce the interests of masculinity and patriarchy" (xi). Because Tim O'Brien is indisputably canonized as a major "Vietnam author in his generation" and *The Things They Carried* is widely acclaimed, it merits close examination in the context of this larger cultural work of consolidating the masculine subject, cementing male bonds, and preempting or silencing feminist dissent.

II

The core of *The Things They Carried* consists of five long stories originally published in *Esquire* during the late 1980s—the period in which Susan Faludi documents an "undeclared war on American women" and Jeffords locates the rehabilitation of temporarily outcast male Vietnam veterans. (Women veterans, of course, have never been visible enough to be cast out.)

III

[. . .] It seems more than coincidental that the [O'Brien] stories that most deeply probe and most emphatically reassert masculinity should appear in this glossy, upscale men's magazine famous, as Faludi puts it, for its "screeds against women." The intended audience for this magazine (subtitled "Man at His Best") is unabashedly male, and though O'Brien's stories rarely show men at their best, they do speak to a self-conscious and perhaps threatened masculinity. (Anyone familiar with Vietnam studies will also associate *Esquire* with a controversial and often-quoted article by William Broyles entitled "Why Men Love War.") As with *Playboy*, the female reader opening these pages ventures into alien and dangerous territory. Ultimately, reading war, like experiencing, remembering, and writing it, is constructed as a masculine rite.

The narrative structure of these stories is very similar: alternating radically disjunctive passages of past and present, fiction and commentary, war and memory. The force that presumes to reconcile these dualities and overcome the confounding incommunicability of war is the writer's imagination, articulated from a masculine point of view. In both the opening and closing stories of the volume, imagination is linked to an idealized, unattainable woman—Martha, a girlfriend at home, and Linda, a childhood sweetheart who died at nine. The first story plays one of the many variations on the imagination-reality motif and picks up where O'Brien's earlier novel, *Going After Cacciato*, left off, with Paul Berlin imagining himself pleading for peace at the Paris Peace Talks but admitting: "Even in imagination we must be true to our obligations, for, even in imagination, obligation cannot be outrun. Imagination, like reality, has its limits" (378). "The Things They Carried" goes further to limit the imagination, asserting that in battle, "Imagination was a killer." What this means, on one level, is that the nerve-wracking tension in the field could lead soldiers to imagine the worst or make a fatal mistake. But the story also establishes an inexorable equation: imagination = women = distraction = danger = death. The story's dramatic resolution turns on recovering masculine power by suppressing femininity in both female and male characters. Survival itself depends on excluding women from the masculine bond. In this first story, the renunciation of femininity is a sad but necessary cost of war, admitted only after real emotional struggle. It establishes a pattern, however, for the rest of the book.

"The Things They Carried" introduces the cast of Alpha Company and establishes their identity as a cohesive group, each manfully carrying his own weight but also sharing the burden of war. The story features Lieutenant Jimmy Cross, the platoon's 24-year-old C. O., who fell into the war via ROTC. He is presented as a man of integrity, honesty, and deep compassion for his men, a cautious, somewhat stiff and unseasoned commander with no inherent lust for death and destruction. The story is fundamentally an initiation narrative whose tension lies in Jimmy Cross's need to deal with guilt and harden himself to battle realities, which are here distinctly differentiated from the realm of imagination. Jimmy Cross's story alternates with lyrical passages cataloguing all the "things" men at war carry, including "all the emotional baggage of men who might die." These passages, echoing O'Brien's earlier constraints of "obligation," insistently repeat the idea that "the things they carried were largely determined by necessity. [. . .]" (4, 5).

Lieutenant Jimmy Cross's survival and his coming of age as an effective soldier depend on letting go of all that is not necessary and immediate—here equated completely with the feminine, the romantic, the imaginary. Becoming a warrior entails a pattern of desire, guilt, and renunciation in relation to a woman. The story opens by describing in detail Jimmy Cross's most precious cargo:

> First Lieutenant Jimmy Cross carried letters from a girl named Martha, a junior at Mount Sebastian College in New Jersey. They were not love letters, but Lieutenant Cross was hoping, so he kept them folded in plastic at the bottom of his rucksack. In the late afternoon, after a day's march, he would dig his foxhole, wash his hands under a canteen, unwrap the letters, hold them with the tips of his fingers, and spend the last hour of light pretending. He would imagine romantic camping trips. [. . .] More than anything, he wanted Martha to love him as he loved her, but the letters were mostly chatty, elusive on the matter of love. She was a virgin, he was almost sure. (4)

Martha's writing—and, implicitly, her reading of his war experience—are sexualized through association: her inability to respond to his love and his longing suggest the blank page of virginity in patriarchal discourse. Though Jimmy Cross tries to realize a connection with Martha through this sacramental/sexual ritual, she is represented as aloof and untouchable, a poet with "grey, neutral" eyes inhabiting "another world, which was not quite real." Martha's words are never presented directly, but are paraphrased by the narrator, who reminds us twice that she never mentions the war in her letters. Like other women in the book, she represents all those back home who will never understand the warrior's trauma. In addition to the letters, Jimmy Cross carries two pictures of Martha and a good-luck charm—a stone Martha sent from the Jersey Shore [. . .]. As the story progresses, Martha—rather these metonymic objects signifying Martha—becomes a distraction from the immediate work of war and caring for his men. His mind wanders, usually into the realm of sexual fantasy: "Slowly, a bit distracted, he would get up and move among his men, checking the perimeter, then at full dark he would return to his hole and watch the night and wonder if Martha was a virgin" (4). Memory and desire intertwine in a fantasy that fuses courage and virility and, by extension, fighting and writing upon her blank virgin page. In one of the book's several retrospective "should haves," Jimmy Cross remembers a date with Martha and thinks "he should've done something brave. He should've carried her up the stairs to her room and tied her to the bed and touched that left knee all night long. He should've risked it. Whenever he looked at the photographs, he thought of new things he should've done" (6). We are meant to see the move from chivalry to sado-masochistic erotica as natural and understandable, because "He was just a kid at war, in love," after all. That Jimmy Cross's sexual "bravery" might have been earned through violation and coercion is not considered in the story. The focus is on the male's empowering fantasy.

Jimmy Cross's distraction climaxes with the sniper shooting of Ted Lavender "on his way back from peeing." Just before this incident, the company had waited tensely for Lee Strunk to emerge from clearing out a Vietcong tunnel. The language of sexual desire and union, coming just before Lee Strunk's "rising from the dead" and Lavender's death, links Jimmy's imagination of Martha—his merging with the feminine—with annihilation of the self. As he gazes suggestively down into the dark tunnel, he leaves the war and succumbs to a fantasy of perfect union between masculine and feminine, death and desire:

> And then suddenly, without willing it, he was thinking about Martha. The stresses and fractures, the quick collapse, the two of them buried alive under all that weight. Dense, crushing love. Kneeling, watching the hole, he tried to concentrate on Lee Strunk and the war, all the dangers, but his love was too much for him, he felt paralyzed, he wanted to sleep inside her lungs and breathe her blood and be smothered. He wanted his to be a virgin and not a virgin, all at once. He wanted to know her. (12)

Such unraveling of gender duality, however, is dangerous, such paradoxes unsustainable. At the moment of Jimmy's imagined dissolution, Ted Lavender is shot. As if to punish himself for daydreaming and forgetting "about matters of security"—but more deeply for abandoning his men in the desire to know the feminine—Jimmy Cross goes to the extreme of rejecting desire for Martha altogether. He reacts to the trauma of Lavender's death in two significant ways. The first is one of the book's parallel scenes of My Lai–like[7] retribution, here bluntly told but not shown: "Lieutenant Jimmy Cross led his men into the village of Than Khe. They burned everything" (16). The second is guilt, entangled with anger that his love for Martha is unrequited. He reverts to a familiar binary choice—either Martha or his men: "He felt shame. He hated himself. He had loved Martha more than his men, and as a consequence Lavender was now dead, and this was something he would have to carry, like a stone in his stomach for the rest of the war" (16)—his good luck charm transformed to the weight of guilt. That night he cries "for Ted Lavender" but also for the realization, or perhaps rationalization, that "Martha did not love him and never would." Jimmy Cross regains a "mask of composure" necessary to survive war's horror, burns Martha's letters and photographs in a purgative ritual reversing the opening blessing, and wills himself to renounce Martha and all she signifies: "He hated her. Yes, he did. He hated her. Love, too, but it was a hard, hating kind of love" (23). With this rejection and a newly hardened, terse idiom, Jimmy Cross completes his transformation: "He was a soldier, after all. . . . He was realistic about it. . . . He would be a man about it. . . . No more fantasies. . . . from this point

7. In the infamous My Lai Massacre, a company of U.S. soldiers, several of whose members had been maimed or killed in previous weeks, marched into the village of My Lai on March 16, 1968, and, without provocation, killed over three hundred apparently unarmed civilians.

on he would comport himself as an officer. . . . he would dispense with love; it was not now a factor" (23–24). His survival as a soldier and a leader depends upon absolute separation from the feminine world and rejection of his own femininity: "Henceforth, when he thought about Martha, it would be only to think that she belonged elsewhere. He would shut down the day-dreams. This was not Mount Sebastian, it was another world, where there were no pretty poems or midterm exams, a place where men died because of carelessness and gross stupidity" (24).

How are we meant to read this rejection? O'Brien is not blaming Martha for male suffering, for of course, the story isn't *about* Martha at all, though she introduces the book's protypical figure of the woman incapable of understanding war. Rather, he uses her to define "necessary" codes of male behavior in war and to establish Jimmy's "proper" bond with his men. We are given no rationale for why Jimmy perceives his choice in such absolute terms, nor are we invited to critique Jimmy for this rigidity, though we do pity him and recognize his naivete. Jimmy Cross's rejection of the feminine is portrayed as one of the burdensome but self-evident "necessities" of war, and O'Brien grants Jimmy this recognition: "It was very sad, he thought. The things men carried inside. The things men did or felt they had to do." Most sad and ironic of all, Jimmy ends up suffering alone because of his status as an officer: "He would show strength, distancing himself." Jimmy Cross's allegorical initials even encourage us to read his youthful renunciation in Christian terms.

At the very end, however, masculine bonds prevail and compensate for Jimmy's losses. O'Brien places the men of Alpha Company in a larger cultural landscape of men without women by alluding to cowboy movies and Huckleberry Finn: "He might just shrug and say, Carry on, then they would saddle up and form into a column and move out toward to villages west of Than Khe." The narrative voice here is very carefully distinguished from the characters, and it is hard to know how to take the conditional "might" and the self-conscious diction: as parody? as straight allusion? as Jimmy Cross's self-deluding macho fantasy? One possibility is that O'Brien means to expose and critique the social construction of masculinity, suggesting that soldiers' behavior in Vietnam is conditioned by years of John Wayne movies, as indeed numerous veterans' memoirs attest is true. Likewise, the story unmasks the soldiers' macho "stage presence," "pose," and "hard vocabulary": "Men killed, and died, because they were embarrassed not to"; they do what they "felt they had to do." But these constructions are inevitably converted into behavior that seems natural and inevitable—"necessary"—within the ur-story underlying all war stories: the tragic destruction of male innocence. O'Brien's depth as a writer allows him to reveal the socialized nature of soldiering and to show compassion for the vulnerable men behind the pose. But he stops short of undoing and revising these constructions. In the end, men *are* how they act, just as they *are* their stories and culture *is* its myths. The story rescues the humanity of men at war and consigns femininity to the margins, thus assuring the seamless continuity and endless repetition of masculine war stories.

VI

In the story that closes the book, "The Lives of the Dead," O'Brien makes a turn toward wholeness, closure, and regeneration. Here, for once, the feminine occupies a position in the same precious realm of the imagination as the masculine, although alternating sections again keep the war stories, the childhood stories, and the present-day metafictional commentary separate. The imagination, which was so dangerously distracting in "The Things They Carried," is now a force that keeps the dead alive and integrates the self by mixing memory and desire, "bringing body and soul back together," unifying through the shaping force of language and narrative form, "a little kid, twenty-three-year-old infantry sergeant, a middle-aged writer knowing guilt and sorrow" (265). The narrator alternates in this story two primal experiences of death: his view of a Vietcong corpse on his fourth day in Vietnam, and his experience of love and loss at age nine. The story resurrects Linda, his fourth grade sweetheart, who died of a brain tumor. In retrospect, he imagines their first love as "pure knowing," imbued with the knowledge that "beyond language . . . we were sharing something huge and permanent" (259). At this point in the book, the concept of merging wholly with another through "pure knowing" has accumulated the weight of fear (Jimmy Cross and Martha) and danger [. . .], both of which are also associated with transgressing normal gender codes and dissolving the socially constructed self. Here, the impulse seems to be to idealize youthful passion, distinguishing it from more frightening forms of grown-up "knowing." The narrator remembers that, in fact, his urge to tell stories has always been connected with resuscitating the dead. Grieving after Linda's death, he dreams of Linda coming back to comfort him: "Timmy, stop crying. It doesn't *matter.*" In the months following, he begins to make up elaborate stories to bring Linda alive and call her into his dreams. He writes the stories down and in their vividness they become real. He gives Linda a voice (which of course is only his own dream voice, the feminine within himself) and imagines her expressing herself with a literary metaphor, once more reinforcing the connection between gender and writing/storytelling, with the female figured as absence: "'Well, right now,' she said, 'I'm *not* dead. But when I am, it's like . . . I don't know, I guess it's like being inside a book that nobody's reading.'" The strategy stuck with him, for "In Vietnam, too, we had ways of making the dead seem not quite so dead." The most important way, the book makes clear, is to both read and write the dead by telling stories woven "in the spell of memory and imagination."

"The Lives of the Dead" reverses the book's opening story, "The Things They Carried," for here the imagination, linked with the memory of a girl, is not a dangerous force but is redemptive and regenerative. The story also moves beyond the antagonistic polarity of gender that marks the other *Esquire* stories. Linda is forever innocent and forever young, an idealized Laura or Beatrice or Annabel Lee[8] who comes when bidden as muse for the narrator's cathartic

---

8. Young, dead, but beloved heroine of the last (1849) poem by Edgar Allan Poe (1809–49), who famously declares in "The Philosophy of Composition" (1846), "the death [. . .] of a beautiful woman is, unquestionably, the most poetical topic in the world." *Laura*: beautiful but married woman, whether real or fictional, at the sight of whom the Italian Renaissance poet Petrarch (1304–74) supposedly gave up his priestly vocation; she became the muse who inspired his influential sonnets.

stories. Although it sounds ungenerous to critique such a moving and lovely story, one must wonder whether the book's only positive and unthreatening representation of femininity is possible because she is forever pre-pubescent, safely encased in memory, dream, death, and narrative. Unlike Martha [. . .], she never grows up to be a castrating "cooze" or savage monster. She never touches the war, thus never intrudes upon his homosocial bonds; rather, the narrator uses her, as male writers have always used female muses, to find his voice and arrive at his own understanding of his traumas. In the context of all the other war stories in the book, Linda still functions as part of a triangle; she is the mediator that facilitates the narrator's reconciliation with his own past in Vietnam and his recovery of a whole self. It is tempting to read that self as universally human, but the force of the whole preceding book cautions us that it is a masculine self wounded in war and recovered in war stories. Woman can only play dead or absent muse to the central masculine subject.

The Things They Carried contributes significantly to the canon of Vietnam War fiction. It is a remarkable treatment of the epistemology of writing and the psychology of soldiering. It dismantles many stereotypes that have dominated Hollywood treatments of the Vietnam War and distorted our understanding: the basket-case veteran (the book's narrator is reasonably well-adjusted), the macho war lover (characters such as Azar are presented as extreme aberrations), the callous officer (Jimmy Cross is fallible and sympathetic), the soldier as victim of government machinations, the peace movement, or apathetic civilians. The book probes the vulnerability of soldiers betrayed by cultural myths and registers how deeply war in our culture is a gendered activity. But O'Brien inscribes no critique of his characters' misogyny or the artificial binary opposition of masculinity and femininity, no redefinition of power, no fissure in the patriarchal discourse of war. However ambiguous and horrible Vietnam may be, and however many new combinations of memory, fact, and imagination O'Brien composes, war is still presented as an inevitable, natural phenomenon deeply meaningful to the male psyche and hostile to femininity. More pernicious, these stories seem to warn women readers away from any empathetic grasp of "the things men do." [. . .] Tim O'Brien's imaginative flights are heady, but his exclusion of women as readers and as characters finally reveals a failure of the imagination and muddy, clay feet.

WORKS CITED

Beidler, Philip D. *Re-Writing America: Vietnam Authors in Their Generation*. Athens: U of Georgia P, 1991.

Broyles, William. "Why Men Love War." *Esquire* (Nov 84): 55–65.

Faludi, Susan. *Backlash: The Undeclared War on American Women*. New York: Crown, 1991.

Hanley, Lynne. *Writing War: Fiction, Gender and Memory*. Amherst: U of Massachusetts P, 1991.

Harris, Robert R. "Too Embarrassed Not to Kill." Review of *The Things They Carried*. *New York Times Book Review* 11 Mar 1990.

Beatrice—whom the poet Dante (1265–1321) met in childhood and who died at age twenty-four, just three years after marrying another man—performs a similar role in his life and work.

Jeffords, Susan. *The Remasculinization of America: Gender and the Vietnam War.* Bloomington: Indiana UP, 1991.

Krumholz, Linda. "The Ghosts of Slavery: Historical Recovery in Toni Morrison's *Beloved.*" *African American Review* 26:3 (Fall 92): 395–408.

Lawson, Jacqueline. "'She a Pretty Woman . . . for a Gook': The Misogyny of the Vietnam War." In Philip K. Jason, ed. *Fourteen Landing Zones: Approaches to Vietnam War Literature.* Iowa City: U of Iowa P, 1990.

Lomperis, Timothy. *"Reading the Wind": The Literature of the Vietnam War.* Durham: Duke UP, 1987.

Naparsteck, Martin. "An Interview with Tim O'Brien." *Contemporary Literature* 32:1 (Spring 91): 1–11.

O'Brien, Tim. *Going After Cacciato.* New York: Dell, 1978.

———. *The Things They Carried.* New York: Penguin, 1990.

Sedgwick, Eve Kosofsky. *Between Men: English Literature and Male Homosocial Desire.* New York: Columbia UP, 1985.

Smith, Lorrie. "Back against the Wall: Anti-Feminist Backlash in Vietnam War Literature." *Vietnam Generation* 1:3–4 (Summer–Fall, 1989): 115–126. Special issue on "Gender and the War: Men, Women and Vietnam."

Tal, Kali. "Feminist Criticism and the Literature of the Vietnam Combat Veteran." *Vietnam Generation* 1:3–4 (Summer–Fall, 1989): 190–202.

———. "Speaking the Language of Pain: Vietnam War Literature in the Context of a Literature of Trauma." In Philip K. Jason, ed. *Fourteen Landing Zones: Approaches to Vietnam War Literature.* Iowa City: U of Iowa P, 1991.

SUSAN FARRELL

From Tim O'Brien and Gender: A Defense of *The Things They Carried*[1]

Alongside the popularity and critical acclaim awarded the outpouring of recent U.S. accounts of the Vietnam War sit some more quietly voiced criticisms of this body of literature. Perhaps the most compelling of these critiques has emerged from recent feminist scholars who argue that much Vietnam War literature replicates traditional western notions of gender and thus reinforces patriarchal institutions and beliefs. Two key works published in 1989 set the stage for much of the feminist criticism of Vietnam War literature that was to follow. Susan Jeffords' *The Remasculinization of America: Gender and the Vietnam War* (1989) explores popular film and narrative representations of the war. Jeffords argues for reading the war as a "construction of gendered interests," despite the fact that war might initially seem to be the domain of men and not relevant to gender analysis (81). A special issue of the journal *Vietnam Generation* devoted to the topic of gender and the war also appeared in 1989. In her introduction to this special issue, editor Jacqueline Lawson responds to a much-read *Esquire* article by ex-Marine William Broyles, Jr., "Why Men Love War." While Broyles claims that "war is the enduring condition of man, period," Lawson writes that

1. Susan Farrell, "Tim O'Brien and Gender: A Defense of *The Things They Carried.*" *CEA Critic*, vol. 66, no. 1, fall 2003, pp. 1–21. Farrell's list of works cited has been abbreviated.

she hopes this issue of the journal will dispel such a "canard—that war is the exclusive province of men, a closed and gendered activity inscribed by myth, informed by ritual, and enacted solely through the power relations of patriarchy" (6). To this end, she has explored some of the brutal rape and torture scenes of Vietnamese women that occur regularly in the literature.

[. . .] Critic Lorrie Smith has added to the debate, pointing out that "most popular treatments of the war—for all their claims to 'tell it like it was'—reveal more about the cultural and political climate of the 1980's than about the war itself" ("Back" 115). Smith connects a 1980s backlash against the feminist movement to the misogyny she reads in Vietnam War literature, a misogyny which she describes as "very visible," as seemingly "natural and expected." In popular representations, Smith argues, the "Vietnam War is being reconstructed as a site where white American manhood—figuratively as well as literally wounded during the war and assaulted by the women's movement for twenty years—can reassert its dominance in the social hierarchy" ("Back" 115).

The work of Tim O'Brien, while highly praised, has not been exempt from the criticism of feminist scholars. Lorrie Smith argues that the short fiction that eventually came together to make up *The Things They Carried* silences women and re-enforces traditional masculine views of war and gender. Smith writes that O'Brien's "text offers no challenge to a discourse of war in which apparently innocent American men are tragically wounded and women are objectified, excluded, and silenced" ("Things" 17). While Smith points out that her intent "is not to devalue O'Brien's technical skill or emotional depth," she does want to "account for [her] own discomfort as a female reader and to position *The Things They Carried* within a larger cultural project to rewrite the Vietnam War from a masculinist and strictly American perspective" (17). She argues that, even though O'Brien's narrator says that only those who were there can fully understand the events which occurred, he still permits a bond to form between male readers and the characters on the basis that women are completely unable to understand "the things men do." Male readers become less marked as outsiders than women as the stories progress since "the shared language of patriarchy" eases the general incommunicability of the war trauma for men (19).

Smith supports her argument with a close reading of both the longer stories that first appeared in *Esquire* magazine and the shorter vignettes that O'Brien added when he collected the material as a book. She argues that the opening, title story of the collection "establishes a pattern . . . for the rest of the book" in that it teaches readers that survival in war depends on "suppressing femininity" (24). Readers learn, as does Lieutenant Jimmy Cross, that the renunciation of the feminine, is "a sad but necessary cost of war" (24). Martha in the opening story, along with [the book's other female characters,] all represent another world: those back home who will never understand the war. Even more, this inability to understand is at least partly willful: they do not understand because they do not listen. [. . .]

While I find Smith's article thoughtful and intriguing, and while I agree with much feminist criticism of Vietnam War literature, this essay proposes that the work of Tim O'Brien, particularly *The Things They Carried*, stands apart from the genre as a whole. O'Brien is much more self-consciously aware of gender issues and critical of traditional gender dichotomies than are the bulk of U.S.

writers about the Vietnam War. Though it is often tempting to forget it, readers must always bear in mind the distinction between O'Brien-the-narrator and O'Brien-the-author. This difference is crucial to understanding the book's central questions: What is truth and how can truth best be communicated? How can we truly understand the experiences of another human being? I would suggest that O'Brien posits two very different responses to these questions and that his responses are directly related to some of the concerns about gender raised by feminist critics. The male characters in the book do indeed subscribe to patriarchal and condescending attitudes about gender; they believe that knowledge is attained experientially and thus they exclude women from understanding the war experience. Yet, always running counter to this view is its corrective: that trauma is communicable, that understanding may be attained though the imaginative acts of storytelling and reading, and that the male characters do not necessarily understand war and gender as well as they think they do.

I. "The Things They Carried" [. . .]

The book's opening story, "The Things They Carried," offers two competing narratives: the ultra-realistic, precise details of what the men carry (down to brand names and weights of objects listed in ounces) versus the more personal, more traumatic story of the death of Ted Lavender. Such a form underscores one of the novel's main concerns, the relation between fact and fiction. [. . .] The concrete specificity of the lists in the opening story [. . .] set[s] readers up to expect a hard-nosed, factual account of the war. Thus, we might mistakenly read Jimmy Cross's story as fact as well—an omniscient, third-person account of the reality of war experience. Such a reading would be a mistake, though. We must remember that the story of Ted Lavender's death is filtered through the subjective experience of Lieutenant Jimmy Cross. It is a narrative that increasingly interrupts and subsumes the more objective story of the items the men carry with them in the field. Yet, it is *not* a story about men at war having to renounce the feminine. Rather, it is about the inevitable guilt associated with war deaths and what soldiers do with that guilt.

While Jimmy Cross certainly views Martha as inhabiting another world, separate from the war, and thus as representing home, purity, an innocence he no longer retains, I'd argue that readers are not supposed to make the same easy gender classifications that Cross does. This point is driven home by Cross's reaction to Lavender's death. Cross is not only a romantic who fantasizes a love affair that's not really there with Martha, he greatly exaggerates his responsibility for Lavender's death. The very randomness of Lavender's death—he is "zapped while zipping," shot after separating from the men briefly to urinate—belies Jimmy Cross's responsibility for the death. Cross blames himself for the death because, as the narrator tells us in a later story, "In the Field," "When a man died, there had to be blame" (177). The soldiers wish to find a reason for the deaths they witness in order to make them less frightening, less random and meaningless. Blame can provide the illusion that war deaths such as those of Lavender and Kiowa are preventable, if only someone behaves differently, more responsibly, in the future. So, Cross determines that his love for Martha, his fantasies about her, are the cause of Lavender's death and that, to prevent such deaths in the future, he will strictly follow standard operating procedures and "dispense with love," focusing instead on duty. Ironically, Lavender dies after the platoon has just finished searching Viet Cong tunnels, a tactic that *was* standard operating procedure, but an extremely dangerous undertaking. While Lee Strunk emerges intact from such a risky assignment, Ted Lavender dies a few moments later completely unexpectedly, while conducting the ordinary business of living.

Again, readers are supposed to see the irrationality of both Cross's burden of guilt as well as his resolve to be a better officer. In fact, it is his very refusal to question orders, to deviate from standard operating procedure, that leads him to camp in the "shitfield" later in the book and inadvertently brings about the death of Kiowa, another accident, and one which many different characters claim blame for. Readers, then, are not supposed to see Cross's burning of Martha's picture and renunciation of the imagination as "sad but necessary" consequences of war, but rather as the attempts of a romantic and guilt-ridden young man to gain control over a situation in which he actually has very little power (Smith, "Things" 24). Because the burning of Martha's picture is linked to the burning of the Vietnamese village, readers see even more fully how mistaken and irrational Cross is in his reaction to Lavender's death.

V. "The Lives of the Dead"

"The Lives of the Dead" is as much a love story as it is a war story. The book, in fact, could be said to be framed by two love stories—the opening story which tells of Jimmy Cross's love for Martha and the final story which tells of the narrator's love as a nine-year-old for Linda, the little girl who dies of a brain tumor. [. . .] In "The Lives of the Dead," O'Brien deliberately juxtaposes traumatic war deaths with the traumatic death of Linda in order to undermine the old cliché of Vietnam War fiction: "if you weren't there, you can't possibly understand." "The Lives of the Dead" argues for the power of fiction, of imaginative creation. In stories, the dead *can* come to life; experiences *can* be communicated imaginatively.

The powerful status of fiction is perhaps nowhere so well illustrated as in the plot of the movie that nine-year-old Timmy attends on his date with Linda: *The Man Who Never Was*. In the film, the Allies plant false documents on the body of a dead British soldier to mislead the Germans about the site of the upcoming landings in Europe. "The Germans find the documents," O'Brien writes, and "the deception wins the war" (232). The dead soldier's fictional identity is more influential than his actual, biographical identity, which we never discover. In many ways, narrator O'Brien in the book is "the man who never was." He is a created persona whose stories teach us about the difficulty of getting to the truth of individual identity. The narrator looks at a photograph of himself from 1956, realizing that, "in the important ways" he has not changed at all: "the essence remains the same . . . the human life is all one thing, like a blade tracing loops on ice" (236). What shapes a person, then, is difficult to unravel. An individual seems to be the product of biological predisposition as well as a jumble of experiences: wartime experience as well as larger life experience. In any case, human essence and selfhood remain mysterious.

Because O'Brien works so diligently to connect war experience to human experience in general, I do not read his work as excluding or silencing women. One of O'Brien's most moving pieces is a personal essay he published in the *New York Times Magazine* in 1994, called "The Vietnam in Me." In this essay, O'Brien tells two stories simultaneously—the tale of his return to Vietnam over twenty years after having been a soldier there and the story of the disintegration of a serious love relationship. Nearly suicidal over the break-up, O'Brien has difficulty sleeping and writes that he is on "war time, which is the time we're all on at one point or another: when fathers die, when husbands ask for divorce, when women you love are fast asleep beside men you wish were you" (55). Just as in "The Lives of the Dead" O'Brien links the physical corpse of the old Vietnamese man to those of Ted Lavender, Curt Lemon, and Kiowa, and finally to Linda's, O'Brien links wartime experience and life experience in this article. "If there's a lesson in this," he writes, "which there is not, it's very simple. You don't have to be in Nam to be in Nam" (55). While much Vietnam War literature expresses the "incommunicability" of war trauma, which is eased for men because of a shared patriarchal language, O'Brien's work expresses the exact opposite: that through imaginative acts of storytelling and reading, the atrocity of war can begin to be understood and thus can begin to heal.

WORKS CITED

Broyles, Jr., William. "Why Men Love War." *Esquire* (November 1984): 55–65.

Jeffords, Susan. *The Remasculinization of America: Gender and the Vietnam War.* Bloomington: Indiana UP, 1989.

Lawson, Jacqueline. Introduction. *Vietnam Generation Special Issue. Gender and the War: Men, Women, and Vietnam* 1.3–4 (Summer–Fall 1989): 6–11.

O'Brien, Tim. *The Things They Carried.* New York: Houghton Mifflin, 1990.

———. "The Vietnam in Me." *New York Times Magazine* 2 October 1994: 48–57.

Smith, Lorrie N. "Back against the Wall: Anti-Feminist Backlash in Vietnam War Literature." *Vietnam Generation Special Issue. Gender and the War: Men, Women, and Vietnam* 1.3–4 (Summer–Fall 1989): 115–126.

———. "'The Things Men Do': The Gendered Subtext in Tim O'Brien's *Esquire* Stories." *Critique: Studies in Contemporary Fiction* 36.1 (Fall 1994): 16–40.

SUGGESTIONS FOR WRITING

1. Though THE THINGS THEY CARRIED may be more obviously a "war story" than any other in this anthology, several others also deal with war or its aftereffects on combatants or civilians. These include William Faulkner's BARN BURNING, Amy Tan's A PAIR OF TICKETS, Jamil Jan Kochai's PLAYING METAL GEAR SOLID V: THE PHANTOM PAIN, and A. S. Byatt's THE THING IN THE FOREST. Additionally, this anthology contains both a play featuring an Iraq War veteran (WATER BY THE SPOONFUL) and an array of war-related poems including THE CALL, THE DEATH OF THE BALL TURRET GUNNER, DISABLED, DULCE ET DECORUM EST, PILGRIMAGE, and Vietnam veteran Yusef Komunyakaa's TU DO STREET and FACING IT. Write an essay comparing the treatment of war in at least two of these works. What's similar and what's unique about what each work shows us about war and its effects?

2. THE THINGS THEY CARRIED is written in the third person, oscillating between sections that (like the title) refer to the entire platoon, as if seen from a distance, and sections that instead home in on a single focal character or consciousness. Usually, that consciousness is Jimmy Cross's. But not always. Write an essay exploring how point of view and/or other aspects of narration shape the story's effects and meaning. Why and how might it matter, for example, that in one section we "overhear" a conversation—between Bowker and Kiowa—that Jimmy isn't privy to, and even spend one paragraph inside Kiowa's consciousness?

3. Like almost every literary critic who writes about *The Things They Carried*, those whose work appears in this chapter all seem to agree that the stories in this collection are **metafictional**—that is, they in various ways draw attention to the fact that they *are* stories and thus also become *about* stories and about the relationship between fiction and reality, stories and truth. THE THINGS THEY CARRIED, however, may well be the least metafictional story in the sequence. Write a response paper or essay in which you analyze what, if anything, seems metafictional in and about the story and why and how exactly that might matter. Do the story's metafictional aspects make it seem less or more "true" or emotionally engaging, and in what ways?

4. One topic of debate among scholars who write about THE THINGS THEY CARRIED is the extent to which it does and/or doesn't reproduce traditional and potentially damaging notions of masculinity and femininity. Drawing upon both THE THINGS THEY CARRIED and the critical excerpts in this chapter, write an essay laying out your own case. Do you agree with one or another of the critics, or might both sides have missed something? Why and how so?

5. At one point in her essay, Lorrie N. Smith suggests, in passing, that THE THINGS THEY CARRIED is "fundamentally an initiation narrative" not unlike those featured in this anthology's "Initiation Stories" album. Write an essay exploring how O'Brien's story works in these terms, perhaps by comparing this story to at least one other. Who is initiated? into what? In making your case, be sure to consider the different arguments the critical excerpts in this chapter make, especially about how the story as a whole encourages us to understand and feel about Jimmy Cross's thoughts and actions at the story's end.

6. *The Things They Carried* opens with the story of the same name, and it ends with THE LIVES OF THE DEAD. Write an essay interrelating or comparing the two stories, perhaps by considering some or all of the following questions: How and why exactly might THE THINGS THEY CARRIED work and mean differently when read alongside THE LIVES OF THE DEAD or vice versa? Why and how might THE THINGS THEY CARRIED work well as a sort of introduction to a fictional meditation on Vietnam and THE LIVES OF THE DEAD as a conclusion to that meditation? In these or any terms, what might be the significance and effect of the two stories' very different styles of narration? of the way they each (differently) move back and forth in time and between different episodes or narrative modes?

7. In this chapter you have seen how a single work of literature can generate a broad range of critical responses. Taken together, these texts represent a kind of ongoing conversation between a "primary text" and "secondary texts" and among the "secondary texts." Using secondary texts available to you at a library and on the Internet, write an essay in which you join in the critical "conversation" about any of the stories you have read in another chapter or album in this book.

Reading More Fiction

JAMES BALDWIN
(1924–87)

Sonny's Blues

For much of his life, James Baldwin was a—perhaps even *the*—leading literary spokesman for civil rights and racial equality. Raised with his eight younger siblings in Depression-era Harlem—often, as he once put it, with a child in one hand and a book in the other—he would spend much of his adult life in France. Here, when he first arrived in late 1948, Baldwin would experience poverty so extreme that he had to sell his clothes and typewriter. But only here, he said, could he get "over—and a lot beyond [. . .] all the terms in which Americans identified me—in my own mind." He first attracted critical attention with two extraordinary novels, *Go Tell It on the Mountain* (1953), which draws on his past as a teenage preacher in the Fireside Pentecostal Church, and *Giovanni's Room* (1956), which deals with the anguish of being Black and homosexual in a largely White and heterosexual society. In addition to his novels and the short-story collection *Going to Meet the Man* (1965), Baldwin also had a long flirtation with the theater; his play *Blues for Mister Charlie* (1964) is based partly on the real-life murder of Emmett Till (1955). But Baldwin is perhaps best remembered today for the essays collected in books such as *Notes of a Native Son* (1955) and the best-selling *The Fire Next Time* (1963). Here especially, as Nobel Laureate Toni Morrison avowed, her beloved friend Jimmy "made American English honest," "reshap[ing] it until it was truly modern," "representative, humane"; "un-gat[ing] it for black people so that in your wake we could enter it, occupy it, restructure it in order to accommodate [. . .] our intricate, difficult, demanding beauty, our tragic, insistent knowledge, our lived reality."

I read about it in the paper, in the subway, on my way to work. I read it, and I couldn't believe it, and I read it again. Then perhaps I just stared at it, at the newsprint spelling out his name, spelling out the story. I stared at it in the swinging lights of the subway car, and in the faces and bodies of the people, and in my own face, trapped in the darkness which roared outside.

It was not to be believed and I kept telling myself that, as I walked from the subway station to the high school. And at the same time I couldn't doubt it. I was scared, scared for Sonny. He became real to me again. A great block of ice got settled in my belly and kept melting there slowly all day long, while I taught my classes algebra. It was a special kind of ice. It kept melting, sending trickles of ice water all up and down my veins, but it never got less. Sometimes it hardened and seemed to expand until I felt my guts were going to come spilling out or that I was going to choke or scream. This would always be at a moment when I was remembering some specific thing Sonny had once said or done.

When he was about as old as the boys in my classes his face had been bright and open, there was a lot of copper in it; and he'd had wonderfully direct brown eyes, and great gentleness and privacy. I wondered what he looked like now. He had been picked up, the evening before, in a raid on an apartment downtown, for peddling and using heroin.

I couldn't believe it: but what I mean by that is that I couldn't find any room for it anywhere inside me. I had kept it outside me for a long time. I hadn't wanted to know. I had had suspicions, but I didn't name them, I kept putting them away. I told myself that Sonny was wild, but he wasn't crazy. And he'd always been a good boy, he hadn't ever turned hard or evil or disrespectful, the way kids can, so quick, so quick, especially in Harlem. I didn't want to believe that I'd ever see my brother going down, coming to nothing, all that light in his face gone out, in the condition I'd already seen so many others. Yet it had happened and here I was, talking about algebra to a lot of boys who might, every one of them for all I knew, be popping off needles every time they went to the head.[1] Maybe it did more for them than algebra could.

5   I was sure that the first time Sonny had ever had horse,[2] he couldn't have been much older than these boys were now. These boys, now, were living as we'd been living then, they were growing up with a rush and their heads bumped abruptly against the low ceiling of their actual possibilities. They were filled with rage. All they really knew were two darknesses, the darkness of their lives, which was now closing in on them, and the darkness of the movies, which had blinded them to that other darkness, and in which they now, vindictively, dreamed, at once more together than they were at any other time, and more alone.

When the last bell rang, the last class ended, I let out my breath. It seemed I'd been holding it for all that time. My clothes were wet—I may have looked as though I'd been sitting in a steam bath, all dressed up, all afternoon. I sat alone in the classroom a long time. I listened to the boys outside, downstairs, shouting and cursing and laughing. Their laughter struck me for perhaps the first time. It was not the joyous laughter which—God knows why—one associates with children. It was mocking and insular, its intent was to denigrate. It was disenchanted, and in this, also, lay the authority of their curses. Perhaps I was listening to them because I was thinking about my brother and in them I heard my brother. And myself.

One boy was whistling a tune, at once very complicated and very simple, it seemed to be pouring out of him as though he were a bird, and it sounded very cool and moving through all that harsh, bright air, only just holding its own through all those other sounds.

1. Lavatory.
2. Heroin.

I stood up and walked over to the window and looked down into the courtyard. It was the beginning of the spring and the sap was rising in the boys. A
teacher passed through them every now and again, quickly, as though he or she
couldn't wait to get out of that courtyard, to get those boys out of their sight and
off their minds. I started collecting my stuff. I thought I'd better get home and
talk to Isabel.

The courtyard was almost deserted by the time I got downstairs. I saw this
boy standing in the shadow of a doorway, looking just like Sonny. I almost called
his name. Then I saw that it wasn't Sonny, but somebody we used to know, a
boy from around our block. He'd been Sonny's friend. He'd never been mine,
having been too young for me, and, anyway, I'd never liked him. And now, even
though he was a grown-up man, he still hung around that block, still spent
hours on the street corners, was always high and raggy. I used to run into him
from time to time and he'd often work around to asking me for a quarter or fifty
cents. He always had some real good excuse, too, and I always gave it to him. I
don't know why.

But now, abruptly, I hated him. I couldn't stand the way he looked at me, 10
partly like a dog, partly like a cunning child. I wanted to ask him what the hell
he was doing in the school courtyard.

He sort of shuffled over to me, and he said, "I see you got the papers. So you
already know about it."

"You mean about Sonny? Yes, I already know about it. How come they didn't
get you?"

He grinned. It made him repulsive and it also brought to mind what he'd
looked like as a kid. "I wasn't there. I stay away from them people."

"Good for you." I offered him a cigarette and I watched him through the
smoke. "You come all the way down here just to tell me about Sonny?"

"That's right." He was sort of shaking his head and his eyes looked strange, as 15
though they were about to cross. The bright sun deadened his damp dark brown
skin and it made his eyes look yellow and showed up the dirt in his kinked hair.
He smelled funky. I moved a little away from him and I said, "Well, thanks. But
I already know about it and I got to get home."

"I'll walk you a little ways," he said. We started walking. There were a couple
of kids still loitering in the courtyard and one of them said goodnight to me and
looked strangely at the boy beside me.

"What're you going to do?" he asked me. "I mean, about Sonny?"

"Look. I haven't seen Sonny for over a year, I'm not sure I'm going to do anything. Anyway, what the hell *can* I do?"

"That's right," he said quickly, "ain't nothing you can do. Can't much help old
Sonny no more, I guess."

It was what I was thinking and so it seemed to me he had no right to say it. 20

"I'm surprised at Sonny, though," he went on—he had a funny way of talking,
he looked straight ahead as though he were talking to himself—"I thought
Sonny was a smart boy, I thought he was too smart to get hung."

"I guess he thought so too," I said sharply, "and that's how he got hung. And
how about you? You're pretty goddamn smart, I bet."

Then he looked directly at me, just for a minute. "I ain't smart," he said. "If I
was smart, I'd have reached for a pistol a long time ago."

"Look. Don't tell *me* your sad story, if it was up to me, I'd give you one." Then I felt guilty—guilty, probably, for never having supposed that the poor bastard *had* a story of his own, much less a sad one, and I asked, quickly, "What's going to happen to him now?"

25 He didn't answer this. He was off by himself some place.

"Funny thing," he said, and from his tone we might have been discussing the quickest way to get to Brooklyn, "when I saw the papers this morning, the first thing I asked myself was if I had anything to do with it. I felt sort of responsible."

I began to listen more carefully. The subway station was on the corner, just before us, and I stopped. He stopped, too. We were in front of a bar and he ducked slightly, peering in, but whoever he was looking for didn't seem to be there. The juke box was blasting away with something black and bouncy and I half watched the barmaid as she danced her way from the juke box to her place behind the bar. And I watched her face as she laughingly responded to something someone said to her, still keeping time to the music. When she smiled one saw the little girl, one sensed the doomed, still-struggling woman beneath the battered face of the semi-whore.

"I never *give* Sonny nothing," the boy said finally, "but a long time ago I come to school high and Sonny asked me how it felt." He paused, I couldn't bear to watch him, I watched the barmaid, and I listened to the music which seemed to be causing the pavement to shake. "I told him it felt great." The music stopped, the barmaid paused and watched the juke box until the music began again. "It did."

All this was carrying me some place I didn't want to go. I certainly didn't want to know how it felt. It filled everything, the people, the houses, the music, the dark, quicksilver barmaid, with menace; and this menace was their reality.

30 "What's going to happen to him now?" I asked again.

"They'll send him away some place and they'll try to cure him." He shook his head. "Maybe he'll even think he's kicked the habit. Then they'll let him loose"—he gestured, throwing his cigarette into the gutter. "That's all."

"What do you mean, that's *all*?"

But I knew what he meant.

"I *mean*, that's *all*." He turned his head and looked at me, pulling down the corners of his mouth. "Don't you know what I mean?" he asked, softly.

35 "How the hell *would* I know what you mean?" I almost whispered it, I don't know why.

"That's right," he said to the air, "how would *he* know what I mean?" He turned toward me again, patient and calm, and yet I somehow felt him shaking, shaking as though he were going to fall apart. I felt that ice in my guts again, the dread I'd felt all afternoon; and again I watched the barmaid, moving about the bar, washing glasses, and singing. "Listen. They'll let him out and then it'll just start all over again. That's what I mean."

"You mean—they'll let him out. And then he'll just start working his way back in again. You mean he'll never kick the habit. Is that what you mean?"

"That's right," he said, cheerfully. "*You* see what I mean."

"Tell me," I said at last, "why does he want to die? He must want to die, he's killing himself, why does he want to die?"

He looked at me in surprise. He licked his lips. "He don't want to die. He   40
wants to live. Don't nobody want to die, ever."

Then I wanted to ask him—too many things. He could not have answered, or
if he had, I could not have borne the answers. I started walking. "Well, I guess
it's none of my business."

"It's going to be rough on old Sonny," he said. We reached the subway station.
"This is your station?" he asked. I nodded. I took one step down. "Damn!" he
said, suddenly. I looked up at him. He grinned again. "Damn it if I didn't leave
all my money home. You ain't got a dollar on you, have you? Just for a couple of
days, is all."

All at once something inside gave and threatened to come pouring out of me. I
didn't hate him any more. I felt that in another moment I'd start crying like a child.

"Sure," I said. "Don't sweat." I looked in my wallet and didn't have a dollar, I
only had a five. "Here," I said. "That hold you?"

He didn't look at it—he didn't want to look at it. A terrible, closed look came   45
over his face, as though he were keeping the number on the bill a secret from
him and me. "Thanks," he said, and now he was dying to see me go. "Don't
worry about Sonny. Maybe I'll write him or something."

"Sure," I said. "You do that. So long."

"Be seeing you," he said. I went on down the steps.

And I didn't write Sonny or send him anything for a long time. When I finally
did, it was just after my little girl died, and he wrote me back a letter which
made me feel like a bastard.

Here's what he said:

Dear brother,   50

   You don't know how much I needed to hear from you. I wanted to write
you many a time but I dug how much I must have hurt you and so I didn't
write. But now I feel like a man who's been trying to climb up out of some
deep, real deep and funky hole and just saw the sun up there, outside. I got to
get outside.

   I can't tell you much about how I got here. I mean I don't know how to tell
you. I guess I was afraid of something or I was trying to escape from something and you know I have never been very strong in the head (smile). I'm glad
Mama and Daddy are dead and can't see what's happened to their son and I
swear if I'd known what I was doing I would never have hurt you so, you and
a lot of other fine people who were nice to me and who believed in me.

   I don't want you to think it had anything to do with me being a musician.
It's more than that. Or maybe less than that. I can't get anything straight in
my head down here and I try not to think about what's going to happen to me
when I get outside again. Sometime I think I'm going to flip and *never* get
outside and sometime I think I'll come straight back. I tell you one thing,
though, I'd rather blow my brains out than go through this again. But that's
what they all say, so they tell me. If I tell you when I'm coming to New York
and if you could meet me, I sure would appreciate it. Give my love to Isabel
and the kids and I was sure sorry to hear about little Gracie. I wish I could be
like Mama and say the Lord's will be done, but I don't know it seems to me
that trouble is the one thing that never does get stopped and I don't know what

good it does to blame it on the Lord. But maybe it does some good if you believe it.

Your brother,
Sonny

Then I kept in constant touch with him and I sent him whatever I could and I went to meet him when he came back to New York. When I saw him many things I thought I had forgotten came flooding back to me. This was because I had begun, finally, to wonder about Sonny, about the life that Sonny lived inside. This life, whatever it was, had made him older and thinner and it had deepened the distant stillness in which he had always moved. He looked very unlike my baby brother. Yet, when he smiled, when we shook hands, the baby brother I'd never known looked out from the depths of his private life, like an animal waiting to be coaxed into the light.

"How you been keeping?" he asked me.

55 "All right. And you?"

"Just fine." He was smiling all over his face. "It's good to see you again."

"It's good to see you."

The seven years' difference in our ages lay between us like a chasm: I wondered if these years would ever operate between us as a bridge. I was remembering, and it made it hard to catch my breath, that I had been there when he was born; and I had heard the first words he had ever spoken. When he started to walk, he walked from our mother straight to me. I caught him just before he fell when he took the first steps he ever took in this world.

"How's Isabel?"

60 "Just fine. She's dying to see you."

"And the boys?"

"They're fine, too. They're anxious to see their uncle."

"Oh, come on. You know they don't remember me."

"Are you kidding? Of course they remember you."

65 He grinned again. We got into a taxi. We had a lot to say to each other, far too much to know how to begin.

As the taxi began to move, I asked, "You still want to go to India?"

He laughed. "You still remember that. Hell, no. This place is Indian enough for me."

"It used to belong to them," I said.

And he laughed again. "They damn sure knew what they were doing when they got rid of it."

70 Years ago, when he was around fourteen, he'd been all hipped on the idea of going to India. He read books about people sitting on rocks, naked, in all kinds of weather, but mostly bad, naturally, and walking barefoot through hot coals and arriving at wisdom. I used to say that it sounded to me as though they were getting away from wisdom as fast as they could. I think he sort of looked down on me for that.

"Do you mind," he asked, "if we have the driver drive alongside the park? On the west side—I haven't seen the city in so long."

"Of course not," I said. I was afraid that I might sound as though I were humoring him, but I hoped he wouldn't take it that way.

So we drove along, between the green of the park and the stony, lifeless elegance of hotels and apartment buildings, toward the vivid, killing streets of our childhood. These streets hadn't changed, though housing projects jutted up out of them now like rocks in the middle of a boiling sea. Most of the houses in which we had grown up had vanished, as had the stores from which we had stolen, the basements in which we had first tried sex, the rooftops from which we had hurled tin cans and bricks. But houses exactly like the houses of our past yet dominated the landscape, boys exactly like the boys we once had been found themselves smothering in these houses, came down into the streets for light and air and found themselves encircled by disaster. Some escaped the trap, most didn't. Those who got out always left something of themselves behind, as some animals amputate a leg and leave it in the trap. It might be said, perhaps, that I had escaped, after all, I was a school teacher; or that Sonny had, he hadn't lived in Harlem for years. Yet, as the cab moved uptown through streets which seemed, with a rush, to darken with dark people, and as I covertly studied Sonny's face, it came to me that what we both were seeking through our separate cab windows was that part of ourselves which had been left behind. It's always at the hour of trouble and confrontation that the missing member aches.

We hit 110th Street and started rolling up Lenox Avenue. And I'd known this avenue all my life, but it seemed to me again, as it had seemed on the day I'd first heard about Sonny's trouble, filled with a hidden menace which was its very breath of life.

"We almost there," said Sonny.   75

"Almost." We were both too nervous to say anything more.

We live in a housing project. It hasn't been up long. A few days after it was up it seemed uninhabitably new, now, of course, it's already rundown. It looks like a parody of the good, clean, faceless life—God knows the people who live in it do their best to make it a parody. The beat-looking grass lying around isn't enough to make their lives green, the hedges will never hold out the streets, and they know it. The big windows fool no one, they aren't big enough to make space out of no space. They don't bother with the windows, they watch the TV screen instead. The playground is most popular with the children who don't play at jacks, or skip rope, or roller skate, or swing, and they can be found in it after dark. We moved in partly because it's not too far from where I teach, and partly for the kids; but it's really just like the houses in which Sonny and I grew up. The same things happen, they'll have the same things to remember. The moment Sonny and I started into the house I had the feeling that I was simply bringing him back into the danger he had almost died trying to escape.

Sonny has never been talkative. So I don't know why I was sure he'd be dying to talk to me when supper was over the first night. Everything went fine, the oldest boy remembered him, and the youngest boy liked him, and Sonny had remembered to bring something for each of them; and Isabel, who is really much nicer than I am, more open and giving, had gone to a lot of trouble about dinner and was genuinely glad to see him. And she's always been able to tease Sonny in a way that I haven't. It was nice to see her face so vivid again and to hear her laugh and watch her make Sonny laugh. She wasn't, or, anyway, she didn't seem to be, at all uneasy or embarrassed. She chatted as though there were no subject which had to be avoided and she got Sonny past his first, faint stiffness. And thank God she was there, for I was filled with that icy dread again. Everything I did seemed awkward to me, and everything I said sounded freighted with hidden meaning. I was trying to remember everything I'd heard about dope addiction and I couldn't help watching Sonny for signs. I wasn't doing it out of malice. I was trying to find out something about my brother. I was dying to hear him tell me he was safe.

"Safe!" my father grunted, whenever Mama suggested trying to move to a neighborhood which might be safer for children. "Safe, hell! Ain't no place safe for kids, nor nobody."

80   He always went on like this, but he wasn't, ever, really as bad as he sounded, not even on weekends, when he got drunk. As a matter of fact, he was always on the lookout for "something a little better," but he died before he found it. He died suddenly, during a drunken weekend in the middle of the war, when Sonny was fifteen. He and Sonny hadn't ever got on too well. And this was partly because Sonny was the apple of his father's eye. It was because he loved Sonny so much and was frightened for him, that he was always fighting with him. It doesn't do any good to fight with Sonny. Sonny just moves back, inside himself, where he can't be reached. But the principal reason that they never hit it off is that they were so much alike. Daddy was big and rough and loud-talking, just the opposite of Sonny, but they both had—that same privacy.

Mama tried to tell me something about this, just after Daddy died. I was home on leave from the army.

This was the last time I ever saw my mother alive. Just the same, this picture gets all mixed up in my mind with pictures I had of her when she was younger. The way I always see her is the way she used to be on a Sunday afternoon, say, when the old folks were talking after the big Sunday dinner. I always see her wearing pale blue. She'd be sitting on the sofa. And my father would be sitting in the easy chair, not far from her. And the living room would be full of church folks and relatives. There they sit, in chairs all around the living room, and the night is creeping up outside, but nobody knows it yet. You can see the darkness growing against the windowpanes and you hear the street noises every now and again, or maybe the jangling beat of a tambourine from one of the churches close by, but it's real quiet in the room. For a moment nobody's talking, but every face looks darkening, like the sky outside. And my mother rocks a little from the waist, and my father's eyes are closed. Everyone is looking at something a child can't see. For a minute they've forgotten the children. Maybe a kid is lying on the rug, half asleep. Maybe somebody's got a kid in his lap and is absent-mindedly stroking the kid's head. Maybe there's a kid, quiet and big-eyed, curled up in a big chair in the corner. The silence, the darkness coming, and the darkness in the faces frighten the child obscurely. He hopes that the hand which strokes his forehead will never stop—will never die. He hopes that there will never come a time when the old folks won't be sitting around the living room, talking about where they've come from, and what they've seen, and what's happened to them and their kinfolk.

But something deep and watchful in the child knows that this is bound to end, is already ending. In a moment someone will get up and turn on the light. Then the old folks will remember the children and they won't talk any more that day. And when light fills the room, the child is filled with darkness. He knows that every time this happens he's moved just a little closer to that darkness outside. The darkness outside is what the old folks have been talking about. It's what they've come from. It's what they endure. The child knows that they won't talk any more because if he knows too much about what's happened to *them,* he'll know too much too soon, about what's going to happen to *him.*

The last time I talked to my mother, I remember I was restless. I wanted to get out and see Isabel. We weren't married then and we had a lot to straighten out between us.

There Mama sat, in black, by the window. She was humming an old church song, *Lord, you brought me from a long ways off.* Sonny was out somewhere. Mama kept watching the streets. 85

"I don't know," she said, "if I'll ever see you again, after you go off from here. But I hope you'll remember the things I tried to teach you."

"Don't talk like that," I said, and smiled. "You'll be here a long time yet."

She smiled, too, but she said nothing. She was quiet for a long time. And I said, "Mama, don't you worry about nothing. I'll be writing all the time, and you be getting the checks. . . ."

"I want to talk to you about your brother," she said, suddenly. "If anything happens to me he ain't going to have nobody to look out for him."

"Mama," I said, "ain't nothing going to happen to you *or* Sonny. Sonny's all 90 right. He's a good boy and he's got good sense."

"It ain't a question of his being a good boy," Mama said, "nor of his having good sense. It ain't only the bad ones, nor yet the dumb ones that gets sucked under." She stopped, looking at me. "Your Daddy once had a brother," she said, and she smiled in a way that made me feel she was in pain. "You didn't never know that, did you?"

"No," I said, "I never knew that," and I watched her face.

"Oh, yes," she said, "your Daddy had a brother." She looked out of the window again. "I know you never saw your Daddy cry. But *I* did—many a time, through all these years."

I asked her, "What happened to his brother? How come nobody's ever talked about him?"

This was the first time I ever saw my mother look old. 95

"His brother got killed," she said, "when he was just a little younger than you are now. I knew him. He was a fine boy. He was maybe a little full of the devil, but he didn't mean nobody no harm."

Then she stopped and the room was silent, exactly as it had sometimes been on those Sunday afternoons. Mama kept looking out into the streets.

"He used to have a job in the mill," she said, "and, like all young folks, he just liked to perform on Saturday nights. Saturday nights, him and your father would drift around to different places, go to dances and things like that, or just sit around with people they knew, and your father's brother would sing, he had a fine voice, and play along with himself on his guitar. Well, this particular Saturday night, him and your father was coming home from some place, and they were both a little drunk and there was a moon that night, it was bright like day. Your father's brother was feeling kind of good, and he was whistling to himself, and he had his guitar slung over his shoulder. They was coming down a hill and beneath them was a road that turned off from the highway. Well, your father's brother, being always kind of frisky, decided to run down this hill, and he did, with that guitar banging and clanging behind him, and he ran across the road, and he was making water behind a tree. And your father was sort of amused at him and he was still coming down the hill, kind of slow. Then he heard a car motor and that same minute his brother stepped from behind the tree, into the road, in the moonlight. And he started to cross the road. And your father started to run down the hill, he says he don't know why. This car was full of white men. They was all drunk, and when they seen your father's brother they let out a great whoop and holler and they aimed the car straight at him. They was having fun, they just wanted to scare him, the way they do sometimes, you know. But they was drunk. And I guess the boy, being drunk, too, and scared, kind of lost his head. By the time he jumped it was too late. Your father says he heard his brother scream when the car rolled over him, and he heard the wood of that guitar when it give, and he heard them strings go flying, and he heard them white men shouting, and the car kept on a-going and it ain't stopped till this day. And, time your father got down the hill, his brother weren't nothing but blood and pulp."

Tears were gleaming on my mother's face. There wasn't anything I could say.

100 "He never mentioned it," she said, "because I never let him mention it before you children. Your Daddy was like a crazy man that night and for many a night thereafter. He says he never in his life seen anything as dark as that road after the lights of that car had gone away. Weren't nothing, weren't nobody on that road, just your Daddy and his brother and that busted guitar. Oh, yes. Your Daddy never did really get right again. Till the day he died he weren't sure but that every white man he saw was the man that killed his brother."

She stopped and took out her handkerchief and dried her eyes and looked at me.

"I ain't telling you all this," she said, "to make you scared or bitter or to make you hate nobody. I'm telling you this because you got a brother. And the world ain't changed."

I guess I didn't want to believe this. I guess she saw this in my face. She turned away from me, toward the window again, searching those streets.

"But I praise my Redeemer," she said at last, "that He called your Daddy home before me. I ain't saying it to throw no flowers at myself, but, I declare, it keeps me from feeling too cast down to know I helped your father get safely through this world. Your father always acted like he was the roughest, strongest man on earth. And everybody took him to be like that. But if he hadn't had me there—to see his tears!"

105 She was crying again. Still, I couldn't move. I said, "Lord, Lord, Mama, I didn't know it was like that."

"Oh, honey," she said, "there's a lot that you don't know. But you are going to find out." She stood up from the window and came over to me. "You got to hold on to your brother," she said, "and don't let him fall, no matter what it looks like is happening to him and no matter how evil you gets with him. You going to be evil with him many a time. But don't you forget what I told you, you hear?"

"I won't forget," I said. "Don't you worry, I won't forget. I won't let nothing happen to Sonny."

My mother smiled as though she was amused at something she saw in my face. Then, "You may not be able to stop nothing from happening. But you got to let him know you's *there*."

Two days later I was married, and then I was gone. And I had a lot of things on my mind and I pretty well forgot my promise to Mama until I got shipped home on a special furlough for her funeral.

And, after the funeral, with just Sonny and me alone in the empty kitchen, I tried to find out something about him. 110

"What do you want to do?" I asked him.

"I'm going to be a musician," he said.

For he had graduated, in the time I had been away, from dancing to the juke box to finding out who was playing what, and what they were doing with it, and he had bought himself a set of drums.

"You mean, you want to be a drummer?" I somehow had the feeling that being a drummer might be all right for other people but not for my brother Sonny.

"I don't think," he said, looking at me very gravely, "that I'll ever be a good 115 drummer. But I think I can play a piano."

I frowned. I'd never played the role of the oldest brother quite so seriously before, had scarcely ever, in fact, *asked* Sonny a damn thing. I sensed myself in the presence of something I didn't really know how to handle, didn't understand. So I made my frown a little deeper as I asked: "What kind of musician do you want to be?"

He grinned. "How many kinds do you think there are?"

"Be *serious*," I said.

He laughed, throwing his head back, and then looked at me. "I *am* serious."

"Well, then, for Christ's sake, stop kidding around and answer a serious 120 question. I mean, do you want to be a concert pianist, you want to play classical music and all that, or—or what?" Long before I finished he was laughing again. "For Christ's *sake*, Sonny!"

He sobered, but with difficulty. "I'm sorry. But you sound so—*scared!*" and he was off again.

"Well, you may think it's funny now, baby, but it's not going to be so funny when you have to make your living at it, let me tell you *that*." I was furious because I knew he was laughing at me and I didn't know why.

"No," he said, very sober now, and afraid, perhaps, that he'd hurt me, "I don't want to be a classical pianist. That isn't what interests me. I mean"—he paused, looking hard at me, as though his eyes would help me to understand, and then gestured helplessly, as though perhaps his hand would help—"I mean, I'll have a lot of studying to do, and I'll have to study *everything*, but, I mean, I want to play *with*—jazz musicians." He stopped. "I want to play jazz," he said.

Well, the word had never before sounded as heavy, as real, as it sounded that afternoon in Sonny's mouth. I just looked at him and I was probably frowning a real frown by this time. I simply couldn't see why on earth he'd want to spend his time hanging around nightclubs, clowning around on bandstands, while people pushed each other around a dance floor. It seemed—beneath him, somehow. I had never thought about it before, had never been forced to, but I suppose I had always put jazz musicians in a class with what Daddy called "good-time people."

"Are you *serious*?" 125

"Hell, *yes*, I'm serious."

He looked more helpless than ever, and annoyed, and deeply hurt.

I suggested, helpfully: "You mean—like Louis Armstrong?"[3]

His face closed as though I'd struck him. "No. I'm not talking about none of that old-time, down-home crap."

130   "Well, look, Sonny, I'm sorry, don't get mad. I just don't altogether get it, that's all. Name somebody—you know, a jazz musician you admire."

"Bird."

"Who?"

"Bird! Charlie Parker![4] Don't they teach you nothing in the goddamn army?"

I lit a cigarette. I was surprised and then a little amused to discover that I was trembling. "I've been out of touch," I said. "You'll have to be patient with me. Now. Who's this Parker character?"

135   "He's just one of the greatest jazz musicians alive," said Sonny, sullenly, his hands in his pockets, his back to me. "Maybe *the* greatest," he added, bitterly, "that's probably why *you* never heard of him."

"All right," I said, "I'm ignorant. I'm sorry. I'll go out and buy all the cat's records right away, all right?"

"It don't," said Sonny, with dignity, "make any difference to me. I don't care what you listen to. Don't do me no favors."

I was beginning to realize that I'd never seen him so upset before. With another part of my mind I was thinking that this would probably turn out to be one of those things kids go through and that I shouldn't make it seem important by pushing it too hard. Still, I didn't think it would do any harm to ask: "Doesn't all this take a lot of time? Can you make a living at it?"

He turned back to me and half leaned, half sat, on the kitchen table. "Everything takes time," he said, "and—well, yes, sure, I can make a living at it. But what I don't seem to be able to make you understand is that it's the only thing I want to do."

140   "Well, Sonny," I said gently, "you know people can't always do exactly what they *want* to do—"

"*No*, I don't know that," said Sonny, surprising me. "I think people *ought* to do what they want to do, what else are they alive for?"

"You getting to be a big boy," I said desperately, "it's time you started thinking about your future."

"I'm thinking about my future," said Sonny, grimly. "I think about it all the time."

I gave up. I decided, if he didn't change his mind, that we could always talk about it later. "In the meantime," I said, "you got to finish school." We had already decided that he'd have to move in with Isabel and her folks. I knew this wasn't the ideal arrangement because Isabel's folks are inclined to be dicty[5] and they hadn't especially wanted Isabel to marry me. But I didn't know what else to do. "And we have to get you fixed up at Isabel's."

3. New Orleans–born trumpeter and singer (1901–71); by the 1950s, his music would have seemed old-fashioned to jazz aficionados.
4. Charlie ("Bird") Parker (1920–55), brilliant saxophonist, jazz innovator, and narcotics addict; working in New York in the mid-1940s, he developed, with Dizzy Gillespie and others, the style of jazz called "bebop."
5. Snobbish, bossy.

There was a long silence. He moved from the kitchen table to the window. 145
"That's a terrible idea. You know it yourself."

"Do you have a *better* idea?"

He just walked up and down the kitchen for a minute. He was as tall as I was. He had started to shave. I suddenly had the feeling that I didn't know him at all.

He stopped at the kitchen table and picked up my cigarettes. Looking at me with a kind of mocking, amused defiance, he put one between his lips. "You mind?"

"You smoking already?"

He lit the cigarette and nodded, watching me through the smoke. "I just 150
wanted to see if I'd have the courage to smoke in front of you." He grinned and blew a great cloud of smoke to the ceiling. "It was easy." He looked at my face. "Come on, now. I bet you was smoking at my age, tell the truth."

I didn't say anything but the truth was on my face, and he laughed. But now there was something very strained in his laugh. "Sure. And I bet that ain't all you was doing."

He was frightening me a little. "Cut the crap," I said. "We already decided that you was going to go and live at Isabel's. Now what's got into you all of a sudden?"

"*You* decided it," he pointed out. "*I* didn't decide nothing." He stopped in front of me, leaning against the stove, arms loosely folded. "Look, brother. I don't want to stay in Harlem no more, I really don't." He was very earnest. He looked at me, then over toward the kitchen window. There was something in his eyes I'd never seen before, some thoughtfulness, some worry all his own. He rubbed the muscle of one arm. "It's time I was getting out of here."

"Where do you want to *go*, Sonny?"

"I want to join the army. Or the navy, I don't care. If I say I'm old enough, 155
they'll believe me."

Then I got mad. It was because I was so scared. "You must be crazy. You god-damn fool, what the hell do you want to go and join the *army* for?"

"I just told you. To get out of Harlem."

"Sonny, you haven't even finished *school.* And if you really want to be a musician, how do you expect to study if you're in the *army?*"

He looked at me, trapped, and in anguish. "There's ways. I might be able to work out some kind of deal. Anyway, I'll have the G.I. Bill when I come out."

"*If* you come out." We stared at each other. "Sonny, please. Be reasonable. I 160
know the setup is far from perfect. But we got to do the best we can."

"I ain't learning nothing in school," he said. "Even when I go." He turned away from me and opened the window and threw his cigarette out into the narrow alley. I watched his back. "At least, I ain't learning nothing you'd want me to learn." He slammed the window so hard I thought the glass would fly out, and turned back to me. "And I'm sick of the stink of these garbage cans!"

"Sonny," I said, "I know how you feel. But if you don't finish school now, you're going to be sorry later that you didn't." I grabbed him by the shoulders. "And you only got another year. It ain't so bad. And I'll come back and I swear I'll help you do *whatever* you want to do. Just try to put up with it till I come back. Will you please do that? For me?"

He didn't answer and he wouldn't look at me.

"Sonny. You hear me?"

165   He pulled away. "I hear you. But you never hear anything *I* say."

I didn't know what to say to that. He looked out of the window and then back at me. "OK," he said, and sighed. "I'll try."

Then I said, trying to cheer him up a little, "They got a piano at Isabel's. You can practice on it."

And as a matter of fact, it did cheer him up for a minute. "That's right," he said to himself. "I forgot that." His face relaxed a little. But the worry, the thoughtfulness, played on it still, the way shadows play on a face which is staring into the fire.

But I thought I'd never hear the end of that piano. At first, Isabel would write me, saying how nice it was that Sonny was so serious about his music and how, as soon as he came in from school, or wherever he had been when he was supposed to be at school, he went straight to that piano and stayed there until suppertime. And, after supper, he went back to that piano and stayed there until everybody went to bed. He was at the piano all day Saturday and all day Sunday. Then he bought a record player and started playing records. He'd play one record over and over again, all day long sometimes, and he'd improvise along with it on the piano. Or he'd play one section of the record, one chord, one change, one progression, then he'd do it on the piano. Then back to the record. Then back to the piano.

170   Well, I really don't know how they stood it. Isabel finally confessed that it wasn't like living with a person at all, it was like living with sound. And the sound didn't make any sense to her, didn't make any sense to any of them— naturally. They began, in a way, to be afflicted by this presence that was living in their home. It was as though Sonny were some sort of god, or monster. He moved in an atmosphere which wasn't like theirs at all. They fed him and he ate, he washed himself, he walked in and out of their door; he certainly wasn't nasty or unpleasant or rude, Sonny isn't any of those things; but it was as though he were all wrapped up in some cloud, some fire, some vision all his own; and there wasn't any way to reach him.

At the same time, he wasn't really a man yet, he was still a child, and they had to watch out for him in all kinds of ways. They certainly couldn't throw him out. Neither did they dare to make a great scene about that piano because even they dimly sensed, as I sensed, from so many thousands of miles away, that Sonny was at that piano playing for his life.

But he hadn't been going to school. One day a letter came from the school board and Isabel's mother got it—there had, apparently, been other letters but Sonny had torn them up. This day, when Sonny came in, Isabel's mother showed him the letter and asked where he'd been spending his time. And she finally got it out of him that he'd been down in Greenwich Village, with musicians and other characters, in a white girl's apartment. And this scared her and she started to scream at him and what came up, once she began—though she denies it to this day—was what sacrifices they were making to give Sonny a decent home and how little he appreciated it.

Sonny didn't play the piano that day. By evening, Isabel's mother had calmed down but then there was the old man to deal with, and Isabel herself. Isabel says she did her best to be calm but she broke down and started crying. She says she just watched Sonny's face. She could tell, by watching him, what was happening with him. And what was happening was that they penetrated his cloud, they had reached him. Even if their fingers had been a thousand times more gentle than human fingers ever are, he could hardly help feeling that they had stripped him naked and were spitting on that nakedness. For he also had to see that his presence, that music, which was life or death to him, had been torture for them and that they had endured it, not at all for his sake, but only for mine. And Sonny couldn't take that. He can take it a little better today than he could then but he's still not very good at it and, frankly, I don't know anybody who is.

The silence of the next few days must have been louder than the sound of all the music ever played since time began. One morning, before she went to work, Isabel was in his room for something and she suddenly realized that all of his records were gone. And she knew for certain that he was gone. And he was. He went as far as the navy would carry him. He finally sent me a postcard from some place in Greece and that was the first I knew that Sonny was still alive. I didn't see him any more until we were both back in New York and the war had long been over.

He was a man by then, of course, but I wasn't willing to see it. He came by $\qquad$ 175 the house from time to time, but we fought almost every time we met. I didn't like the way he carried himself, loose and dreamlike all the time, and I didn't like his friends, and his music seemed to be merely an excuse for the life he led. It sounded just that weird and disordered.

Then we had a fight, a pretty awful fight, and I didn't see him for months. By and by I looked him up, where he was living, in a furnished room in the Village, and I tried to make it up. But there were lots of other people in the room and Sonny just lay on his bed, and he wouldn't come downstairs with me, and he treated these other people as though they were his family and I weren't. So I got mad and then he got mad, and then I told him that he might just as well be dead as live the way he was living. Then he stood up and he told me not to worry about him any more in life, that he *was* dead as far as I was concerned. Then he pushed me to the door and the other people looked on as though nothing were happening, and he slammed the door behind me. I stood in the hallway, staring at the door. I heard somebody laugh in the room and then the tears came to my eyes. I started down the steps, whistling to keep from crying, I kept whistling to myself, *You going to need me, baby, one of these cold, rainy days.*

I read about Sonny's trouble in the spring. Little Grace died in the fall. She was a beautiful little girl. But she only lived a little over two years. She died of polio and she suffered. She had a slight fever for a couple of days, but it didn't seem like anything and we just kept her in bed. And we would certainly have called the doctor, but the fever dropped, she seemed to be all right. So we thought it had just been a cold. Then, one day, she was up, playing, Isabel was in the kitchen fixing lunch for the two boys when they'd come in from school, and she heard Grace fall down in the living room. When you have a lot of children you don't always start running when one of them falls, unless they start screaming or something. And, this time, Gracie was quiet. Yet, Isabel says that when she heard that *thump* and then that silence, something happened to her to make her afraid. And she ran to the living room and there was little Grace on the floor, all twisted up, and the reason she hadn't screamed was that she couldn't get her breath. And when she did scream, it was the worst sound, Isabel says, that she'd ever heard in all her life, and she still hears it sometimes in her dreams. Isabel will sometimes wake me up with a low, moaning, strangling sound and I have to be quick to awaken her and hold her to me and where Isabel is weeping against me seems a mortal wound.

I think I may have written Sonny the very day that little Grace was buried. I was sitting in the living room in the dark, by myself, and I suddenly thought of Sonny. My trouble made his real.

One Saturday afternoon, when Sonny had been living with us, or anyway, been in our house, for nearly two weeks, I found myself wandering aimlessly about the living room, drinking from a can of beer, and trying to work up courage to search Sonny's room. He was out, he was usually out whenever I was home, and Isabel had taken the children to see their grandparents. Suddenly I was standing still in front of the living room window, watching Seventh Avenue. The idea of searching Sonny's room made me still. I scarcely dared to admit to myself what I'd be searching for. I didn't know what I'd do if I found it. Or if I didn't.

180   On the sidewalk across from me, near the entrance to a barbecue joint, some people were holding an old-fashioned revival meeting. The barbecue cook, wearing a dirty white apron, his conked[6] hair reddish and metallic in the pale sun, and a cigarette between his lips, stood in the doorway, watching them. Kids and older people paused in their errands and stood there, along with some older men and a couple of very tough-looking women who watched everything that happened on the avenue, as though they owned it, or were maybe owned by it. Well, they were watching this, too. The revival was being carried on by three sisters in black, and a brother. All they had were their voices and their Bibles and a tambourine. The brother was testifying[7] and while he testified two of the sisters stood together, seeming to say, amen, and the third sister walked around with the tambourine outstretched and a couple of people dropped coins into it. Then the brother's testimony ended and the sister who had been taking up the collection dumped the coins into her palm and transferred them to the pocket of her long black robe. Then she raised both hands, striking the tambourine against the air, and then against one hand, and she started to sing. And the two other sisters and the brother joined in.

It was strange, suddenly, to watch, though I had been seeing these meetings all my life. So, of course, had everybody else down there. Yet, they paused and watched and listened and I stood still at the window. *"'Tis the old ship of Zion,"* they sang, and the sister with the tambourine kept a steady, jangling beat, *"it has rescued many a thousand!"* Not a soul under the sound of their voices was hearing this song for the first time, not one of them had been rescued. Nor had they seen much in the way of rescue work being done around them. Neither did they especially believe in the holiness of the three sisters and the brother, they

6. Processed: straightened and greased.
7. Publicly professing belief.

knew too much about them, knew where they lived, and how. The woman with the tambourine, whose voice dominated the air, whose face was bright with joy, was divided by very little from the woman who stood watching her, a cigarette between her heavy, chapped lips, her hair a cuckoo's nest, her face scarred and swollen from many beatings, and her black eyes glittering like coal. Perhaps they both knew this, which was why, when, as rarely, they addressed each other, they addressed each other as Sister. As the singing filled the air the watching, listening faces underwent a change, the eyes focusing on something within; the music seemed to soothe a poison out of them; and time seemed, nearly, to fall away from the sullen, belligerent, battered faces, as though they were fleeing back to their first condition, while dreaming of their last. The barbecue cook half shook his head and smiled, and dropped his cigarette and disappeared into his joint. A man fumbled in his pockets for change and stood holding it in his hand impatiently, as though he had just remembered a pressing appointment further up the avenue. He looked furious. Then I saw Sonny, standing on the edge of the crowd. He was carrying a wide, flat notebook with a green cover, and it made him look, from where I was standing, almost like a schoolboy. The coppery sun brought out the copper in his skin, he was very faintly smiling, standing very still. Then the singing stopped, the tambourine turned into a collection plate again. The furious man dropped in his coins and vanished, so did a couple of the women, and Sonny dropped some change in the plate, looking directly at the woman with a little smile. He started across the avenue, toward the house. He has a slow, loping walk, something like the way Harlem hipsters walk, only he's imposed on this his own half-beat. I had never really noticed it before.

I stayed at the window, both relieved and apprehensive. As Sonny disappeared from my sight, they began singing again. And they were still singing when his key turned in the lock.

"Hey," he said.

"Hey, yourself. You want some beer?"

"No. Well, maybe." But he came up to the window and stood beside me, 185 looking out. "What a warm voice," he said.

They were singing *If I could only hear my mother pray again!*

"Yes," I said, "and she can sure beat that tambourine."

"But what a terrible song," he said, and laughed. He dropped his notebook on the sofa and disappeared into the kitchen. "Where's Isabel and the kids?"

"I think they went to see their grandparents. You hungry?"

"No." He came back into the living room with his can of beer. "You want to 190 come some place with me tonight?"

I sensed, I don't know how, that I couldn't possibly say no. "Sure. Where?"

He sat down on the sofa and picked up his notebook and started leafing through it. "I'm going to sit in with some fellows in a joint in the Village."

"You mean, you're going to play, tonight?"

"That's right." He took a swallow of his beer and moved back to the window. He gave me a sidelong look. "If you can stand it."

"I'll try," I said. 195

He smiled to himself and we both watched as the meeting across the way broke up. The three sisters and the brother, heads bowed, were singing *God be with you till we meet again*. The faces around them were very quiet. Then the song ended. The small crowd dispersed. We watched the three women and the lone man walk slowly up the avenue.

"When she was singing before," said Sonny, abruptly, "her voice reminded me for a minute of what heroin feels like sometimes—when it's in your veins. It makes you feel sort of warm and cool at the same time. And distant. And—and sure." He sipped his beer, very deliberately not looking at me. I watched his face. "It makes you feel—in control. Sometimes you've got to have that feeling."

"Do you?" I sat down slowly in the easy chair.

"Sometimes." He went to the sofa and picked up his notebook again. "Some people do."

200 "In order," I asked, "to play?" And my voice was very ugly, full of contempt and anger.

"Well"—he looked at me with great, troubled eyes, as though, in fact, he hoped his eyes would tell me things he could never otherwise say—"they *think* so. And *if* they think so—!"

"And what do *you* think?" I asked.

He sat on the sofa and put his can of beer on the floor. "I don't know," he said, and I couldn't be sure if he were answering my question or pursuing his thoughts. His face didn't tell me. "It's not so much to *play*. It's to *stand* it, to be able to make it at all. On any level." He frowned and smiled: "In order to keep from shaking to pieces."

"But these friends of yours," I said, "they seem to shake themselves to pieces pretty goddamn fast."

205 "Maybe." He played with the notebook. And something told me that I should curb my tongue, that Sonny was doing his best to talk, that I should listen. "But of course you only know the ones that've gone to pieces. Some don't—or at least they haven't *yet* and that's just about all *any* of us can say." He paused. "And then there are some who just live, really, in hell, and they know it and they see what's happening and they go right on. I don't know." He sighed, dropped the notebook, folded his arms. "Some guys, you can tell from the way they play, they on something *all* the time. And you can see that, well, it makes something real for them. But of course," he picked up his beer from the floor and sipped it and put the can down again, "they *want* to, too, you've got to see that. Even some of them that say they don't—*some*, not all."

"And what about you?" I asked—I couldn't help it. "What about you? Do *you* want to?"

He stood up and walked to the window and I remained silent for a long time. Then he sighed. "Me," he said. Then: "While I was downstairs before, on my way here, listening to that woman sing, it struck me all of a sudden how much suffering she must have had to go through—to sing like that. It's *repulsive* to think you have to suffer that much."

I said: "But there's no way not to suffer—is there, Sonny?"

"I believe not," he said and smiled, "but that's never stopped anyone from trying." He looked at me. "Has it?" I realized, with this mocking look, that there stood between us, forever, beyond the power of time or forgiveness, the fact that I had held silence—so long!—when he had needed human speech to help him.

He turned back to the window. "No, there's no way not to suffer. But you try all kinds of ways to keep from drowning in it, to keep on top of it, and to make it seem—well, like *you*. Like you did something, all right, and now you're suffering for it. You know?" I said nothing. "Well you know," he said, impatiently, "why *do* people suffer? Maybe it's better to do something to give it a reason, *any* reason."

"But we just agreed," I said, "that there's no way not to suffer. Isn't it better, then, just to—take it?" 210

"But nobody just takes it," Sonny cried, "that's what I'm telling you! *Everybody* tries not to. You're just hung up on the *way* some people try—it's not *your* way!"

The hair on my face began to itch, my face felt wet. "That's not true," I said, "that's not true. I don't give a damn what other people do, I don't even care how they suffer. I just care how *you* suffer." And he looked at me. "Please believe me," I said, "I don't want to see you—die—trying not to suffer."

"I won't," he said flatly, "die trying not to suffer. At least, not any faster than anybody else."

"But there's no need," I said, trying to laugh, "is there? in killing yourself."

I wanted to say more, but I couldn't. I wanted to talk about will power and 215 how life could be—well, beautiful. I wanted to say that it was all within; but was it? or, rather, wasn't that exactly the trouble? And I wanted to promise that I would never fail him again. But it would all have sounded—empty words and lies.

So I made the promise to myself and prayed that I would keep it.

"It's terrible sometimes, inside," he said, "that's what's the trouble. You walk these streets, black and funky and cold, and there's not really a living ass to talk to, and there's nothing shaking, and there's no way of getting it out—that storm inside. You can't talk it and you can't make love with it, and when you finally try to get with it and play it, you realize *nobody's* listening. So *you've* got to listen. You got to find a way to listen."

And then he walked away from the window and sat on the sofa again, as though all the wind had suddenly been knocked out of him. "Sometimes you'll do *anything* to play, even cut your mother's throat." He laughed and looked at me. "Or your brother's." Then he sobered. "Or your own." Then: "Don't worry. I'm all right now and I think I'll *be* all right. But I can't forget—where I've been. I don't mean just the physical place I've been, I mean where I've *been*. And *what* I've been."

"What have you been, Sonny?" I asked.

He smiled—but sat sideways on the sofa, his elbow resting on the back, his 220 fingers playing with his mouth and chin, not looking at me. "I've been something I didn't recognize, didn't know I could be. Didn't know anybody could be." He stopped, looking inward, looking helplessly young, looking old. "I'm not talking about it now because I feel *guilty* or anything like that—maybe it would be better if I did, I don't know. Anyway, I can't really talk about it. Not to you, not to anybody," and now he turned and faced me. "Sometimes, you know, and it was actually when I was most *out* of the world, I felt that I was in it, that I was *with* it, really, and I could play or I didn't really have to *play*, it just came out of me, it was there. And I don't know how I played, thinking about it now, but I know I did awful things, those times, sometimes, to people. Or it wasn't that I *did* anything to them—it was that they weren't real." He picked up the beer can; it was empty; he rolled it between his palms: "And other times—well, I needed a fix, I needed to find a place to lean, I needed to clear a space to *listen*—and I couldn't find it, and I—went crazy, I did terrible things to *me*, I was terrible *for* me." He began pressing the beer can between his hands, I watched the metal begin to give. It glittered, as he played with it like a knife, and I was afraid he would cut himself, but I said nothing. "Oh well. I can never tell you. I was all by myself at the bottom of something, stinking and sweating and crying and shaking, and I smelled it, you know? *my* stink, and I thought I'd die if I couldn't get away from it and yet, all the same, I knew that everything I was doing was just locking me in with it. And I didn't know," he paused, still flattening the beer can, "I didn't know, I still *don't* know, something kept telling me that maybe it was good to smell your own stink, but I didn't think that *that* was what I'd been trying to do—and—who can stand it?" and he abruptly dropped the ruined beer can, looking at me with a small, still smile, and then rose, walking to the window as though it were the lodestone rock. I watched his face, he watched the avenue. "I couldn't tell you when Mama died—but the reason I wanted to leave Harlem so bad was to get away from drugs. And then, when I ran away, that's what I was running from—really. When I came back, nothing had changed, *I* hadn't changed, I was just—older." And he stopped, drumming with his fingers on the windowpane. The sun had vanished, soon darkness would fall. I watched his face. "It can come again," he said, almost as though speaking to himself. Then he turned to me. "It can come again," he repeated. "I just want you to know that."

"All right," I said, at last. "So it can come again. All right."

He smiled, but the smile was sorrowful. "I had to try to tell you," he said.

"Yes," I said. "I understand that."

"You're my brother," he said, looking straight at me, and not smiling at all.

225   "Yes," I repeated, "yes. I understand that."

He turned back to the window, looking out. "All that hatred down there," he said, "all that hatred and misery and love. It's a wonder it doesn't blow the avenue apart."

We went to the only nightclub on a short, dark street, downtown. We squeezed through the narrow, chattering, jampacked bar to the entrance of the big room, where the bandstand was. And we stood there for a moment, for the lights were very dim in this room and we couldn't see. Then, "Hello, boy," said the voice and an enormous black man, much older than Sonny or myself, erupted out of all that atmospheric lighting and put an arm around Sonny's shoulder. "I been sitting right here," he said, "waiting for you."

He had a big voice, too, and heads in the darkness turned toward us.

Sonny grinned and pulled a little away, and said, "Creole, this is my brother. I told you about him."

230   Creole shook my hand. "I'm glad to meet you, son," he said, and it was clear that he was glad to meet me *there*, for Sonny's sake. And he smiled, "You got a real musician in *your* family," and he took his arm from Sonny's shoulder and slapped him, lightly, affectionately, with the back of his hand.

"Well. Now I've heard it all," said a voice behind us. This was another musician, and a friend of Sonny's, a coal-black, cheerful-looking man, built close to the ground. He immediately began confiding to me, at the top of his lungs, the most terrible things about Sonny, his teeth gleaming like a lighthouse and his laugh coming up out of him like the beginning of an earthquake. And it turned out that everyone at the bar knew Sonny, or almost everyone; some were musicians, working there, or nearby, or not working, some were simply hangers-on, and some were there to hear Sonny play. I was introduced to all of them and they were all very polite to me. Yet, it was clear that, for them, I was only Sonny's brother. Here, I was in Sonny's world. Or, rather: his kingdom. Here, it was not even a question that his veins bore royal blood.

They were going to play soon and Creole installed me, by myself, at a table in a dark corner. Then I watched them, Creole, and the little black man, and Sonny, and the others, while they horsed around, standing just below the bandstand. The light from the bandstand spilled just a little short of them and, watching them laughing and gesturing and moving about, I had the feeling that they, nevertheless, were being most careful not to step into that circle of light too suddenly; that if they moved into the light too suddenly, without thinking, they would perish in flame. Then, while I watched, one of them, the small black man, moved into the light and crossed the bandstand and started fooling around with his drums. Then—being funny and being, also, extremely ceremonious—Creole took Sonny by the arm and led him to the piano. A woman's voice called Sonny's name and a few hands started clapping. And Sonny, also being funny and being ceremonious, and so touched, I think, that he could have cried, but neither hiding it nor showing it, riding it like a man, grinned, and put both hands to his heart and bowed from the waist.

Creole then went to the bass fiddle and a lean, very bright-skinned brown man jumped up on the bandstand and picked up his horn. So there they were, and the atmosphere on the bandstand and in the room began to change and tighten. Someone stepped up to the microphone and announced them. Then there were all kinds of murmurs. Some people at the bar shushed others. The waitress ran around, frantically getting in the last orders, guys and chicks got closer to each other, and the lights on the bandstand, on the quartet, turned to a kind of indigo. Then they all looked different there. Creole looked about him for the last time, as though he were making certain that all his chickens were in the coop, and then he—jumped and struck the fiddle. And there they were.

All I know about music is that not many people ever really hear it. And even then, on the rare occasions when something opens within, and the music enters, what we mainly hear, or hear corroborated, are personal, private, vanishing evocations. But the man who creates the music is hearing something else, is dealing with the roar rising from the void and imposing order on it as it hits the air. What is evoked in him, then, is of another order, more terrible because it has no words, and triumphant, too, for that same reason. And his triumph, when he triumphs, is ours. I just watched Sonny's face. His face was troubled, he was working hard, but he wasn't with it. And I had the feeling that, in a way, everyone on the bandstand was waiting for him, both waiting for him and pushing him along. But as I began to watch Creole, I realized that it was Creole who held them all back. He had them on a short rein. Up there, keeping the beat with his whole body, wailing on the fiddle, with his eyes half closed, he was listening to everything, but he was listening to Sonny. He was having a dialogue with Sonny. He wanted Sonny to leave the shoreline and strike out for the deep water. He was Sonny's witness that deep water and drowning were not the same thing—he had been there, and he knew. And he wanted Sonny to know. He was waiting for Sonny to do the things on the keys which would let Creole know that Sonny was in the water.

235   And, while Creole listened, Sonny moved, deep within, exactly like someone in torment. I had never before thought of how awful the relationship must be between the musician and his instrument. He has to fill it, this instrument, with the breath of life, his own. He has to make it do what he wants it to do. And a piano is just a piano. It's made out of so much wood and wires and little hammers and big ones, and ivory. While there's only so much you can do with it, the only way to find this out is to try; to try and make it do everything.

And Sonny hadn't been near a piano for over a year. And he wasn't on much better terms with his life, not the life that stretched before him now. He and the piano stammered, started one way, got scared, stopped; started another way, panicked, marked time, started again; then seemed to have found a direction, panicked again, got stuck. And the face I saw on Sonny I'd never seen before. Everything had been burned out of it, and, at the same time, things usually hidden were being burned in, by the fire and fury of the battle which was occurring in him up there.

Yet, watching Creole's face as they neared the end of the first set, I had the feeling that something had happened, something I hadn't heard. Then they finished, there was scattered applause, and then, without an instant's warning, Creole started into something else, it was almost sardonic, it was *Am I Blue*.[8] And, as though he commanded, Sonny began to play. Something began to happen. And Creole let out the reins. The dry, low, black man said something awful on the drums, Creole answered, and the drums talked back. Then the horn insisted, sweet and high, slightly detached perhaps, and Creole listened, commenting now and then, dry, and driving, beautiful and calm and old. Then they all came together again, and Sonny was part of the family again. I could tell this from his face. He seemed to have found, right there beneath his fingers, a damn brand-new piano. It seemed that he couldn't get over it. Then, for a while, just being happy with Sonny, they seemed to be agreeing with him that brand-new pianos certainly were a gas.

Then Creole stepped forward to remind them that what they were playing was the blues. He hit something in all of them, he hit something in me, myself, and the music tightened and deepened, apprehension began to beat the air. Creole began to tell us what the blues were all about. They were not about anything very new. He and his boys up there were keeping it new, at the risk of ruin, destruction, madness, and death, in order to find new ways to make us listen. For, while the tale of how we suffer, and how we are delighted, and how we may triumph is never new, it always must be heard. There isn't any other tale to tell, it's the only light we've got in all this darkness.

And this tale, according to that face, that body, those strong hands on those strings, has another aspect in every country, and a new depth in every genera-

8. Jazz standard brilliantly recorded by Billie Holiday (1915–59).

tion. Listen, Creole seemed to be saying, listen. Now these are Sonny's blues. He made the little black man on the drums know it, and the bright, brown man on the horn. Creole wasn't trying any longer to get Sonny in the water. He was wishing him Godspeed. Then he stepped back, very slowly, filling the air with the immense suggestion that Sonny speak for himself.

Then they all gathered around Sonny and Sonny played. Every now and 240 again one of them seemed to say, amen. Sonny's fingers filled the air with life, his life. But that life contained so many others. And Sonny went all the way back, he really began with the spare, flat statement of the opening phrase of the song. Then he began to make it his. It was very beautiful because it wasn't hurried and it was no longer a lament. I seemed to hear with what burning he had made it his, and what burning we had yet to make it ours, how we could cease lamenting. Freedom lurked around us and I understood, at last, that he could help us to be free if we would listen, that he would never be free until we did. Yet, there was no battle in his face now, I heard what he had gone through, and would continue to go through until he came to rest in earth. He had made it his: that long line, of which we knew only Mama and Daddy. And he was giving it back, as everything must be given back, so that, passing through death, it can live forever. I saw my mother's face again, and felt, for the first time, how the stones of the road she had walked on must have bruised her feet. I saw the moonlit road where my father's brother died. And it brought something else back to me, and carried me past it, I saw my little girl again and felt Isabel's tears again, and I felt my own tears begin to rise. And I was yet aware that this was only a moment, that the world waited outside, as hungry as a tiger, and that trouble stretched above us, longer than the sky.

Then it was over. Creole and Sonny let out their breath, both soaking wet, and grinning. There was a lot of applause and some of it was real. In the dark, the girl came by and I asked her to take drinks to the bandstand. There was a long pause, while they talked up there in the indigo light and after awhile I saw the girl put a Scotch and milk on top of the piano for Sonny. He didn't seem to notice it, but just before they started playing again, he sipped from it and looked toward me, and nodded. Then he put it back on top of the piano. For me, then, as they began to play again, it glowed and shook above my brother's head like the very cup of trembling.[9]

1957

9. See Isaiah 51.17, 22–23: "Awake, awake, stand up, O Jerusalem, which hast drunk at the hand of the Lord the cup of his fury; thou hast drunken the dregs of the cup of trembling, and wrung them out. [. . .] Behold, I have taken out of thine hand the cup of trembling, even the dregs of the cup of my fury; thou shalt no more drink it again: But I will put it into the hand of them that afflict thee [. . .]."

RAYMOND CARVER

(1938–88)

Cathedral

Born in the logging town of Clatskanie, Oregon, to a working-class family, Raymond Carver married at nineteen and had two children by the time he was twenty-one. Despite these early responsibilities and a lifelong struggle with alcoholism, Carver published his first story in 1961 and graduated from Humboldt State College in 1963. He published his first book, *Near Klamath*, a collection of poems, in 1968 and thereafter supported himself with visiting lectureships at the University of California at Berkeley, Syracuse University, and the Iowa Writers' Workshop, among other institutions. Described by the *New York Times* as "surely the most influential writer of American short stories in the second half of the twentieth century"; credited by others with "reviving what was once thought of as a dying literary form"; and compared to such literary luminaries as Ernest Hemingway, Stephen Crane, and Anton Chekhov, Carver often portrays characters whom one reviewer describes as living, much as Carver long did, "on the edge: of poverty, alcoholic self-destruction, loneliness." The author himself labeled them the sort of "good people," "doing the best they could," who "filled" America. Dubbed a "minimalist" due to his spare style and low-key plots, Carver himself suffered an early death, of lung cancer, at age fifty. His major short-story collections include *Will You Please Be Quiet, Please?* (1976), *What We Talk about When We Talk about Love* (1981), and the posthumously published *Call If You Need Me* (2001).

This blind man, an old friend of my wife's, he was on his way to spend the night. His wife had died. So he was visiting the dead wife's relatives in Connecticut. He called my wife from his in-laws'. Arrangements were made. He would come by train, a five-hour trip, and my wife would meet him at the station. She hadn't seen him since she worked for him one summer in Seattle ten years ago. But she and the blind man had kept in touch. They made tapes and mailed them back and forth. I wasn't enthusiastic about his visit. He was no one I knew. And his being blind bothered me. My idea of blindness came from the movies. In the movies, the blind moved slowly and never laughed. Sometimes they were led by seeing-eye dogs. A blind man in my house was not something I looked forward to.

That summer in Seattle she had needed a job. She didn't have any money. The man she was going to marry at the end of the summer was in officers' training school. He didn't have any money, either. But she was in love with the guy, and he was in love with her, etc. She'd seen something in the paper: HELP WANTED—*Reading to Blind Man*, and a telephone number. She phoned and went over, was hired on the spot. She'd worked with this blind man all summer. She read stuff to him, case studies, reports, that sort of thing. She helped him organize his little office in the county social-service department. They'd become good friends, my wife and the blind man. How do I know these things? She told me. And she told me something else. On her last day in the office, the blind man asked if he could touch her face. She agreed to this. She told me he touched his fingers to every part of her face, her nose—even her neck! She never forgot it. She even tried to write a poem about it. She was always trying to write a poem. She wrote a poem or two every year, usually after something really important had happened to her.

When we first started going out together, she showed me the poem. In the poem, she recalled his fingers and the way they had moved around over her face. In the poem, she talked about what she had felt at the time, about what went through her mind when the blind man touched her nose and lips. I can remember I didn't think much of the poem. Of course, I didn't tell her that. Maybe I just don't understand poetry. I admit it's not the first thing I reach for when I pick up something to read.

Anyway, this man who'd first enjoyed her favors, the officer-to-be, he'd been her childhood sweetheart. So okay. I'm saying that at the end of the summer she let the blind man run his hands over her face, said goodbye to him, married her childhood etc., who was now a commissioned officer, and she moved away from Seattle. But they'd kept in touch, she and the blind man. She made the first contact after a year or so. She called him up one night from an Air Force base in Alabama. She wanted to talk. They talked. He asked her to send him a tape and tell him about her life. She did this. She sent the tape. On the tape, she told the blind man about her husband and about their life together in the military. She told the blind man she loved her husband but she didn't like it where they lived and she didn't like it that he was a part of the military-industrial thing. She told the blind man she'd written a poem and he was in it. She told him that she was writing a poem about what it was like to be an Air Force officer's wife. The poem wasn't finished yet. She was still writing it. The blind man made a tape. He sent her the tape. She made a tape. This went on for years. My wife's officer was posted to one base and then another. She sent tapes from Moody AFB, McGuire, McConnell, and finally Travis, near Sacramento, where one night she got to feeling lonely and cut off from people she kept losing in that moving-around life. She got to feeling she couldn't go it another step. She went in and swallowed all the pills and capsules in the medicine chest and washed them down with a bottle of gin. Then she got into a hot bath and passed out.

But instead of dying, she got sick. She threw up. Her officer—why should he 5 have a name? he was the childhood sweetheart, and what more does he want?—came home from somewhere, found her, and called the ambulance. In time, she put it all on a tape and sent the tape to the blind man. Over the years, she put all kinds of stuff on tapes and sent the tapes off lickety-split. Next to writing a poem every year, I think it was her chief means of recreation. On one tape, she told the blind man she'd decided to live away from her officer for a time. On another tape, she told him about her divorce. She and I began going out, and of course she told her blind man about it. She told him everything, or so it seemed to me. Once she asked me if I'd like to hear the latest tape from the blind man. This was a year ago. I was on the tape, she said. So I said okay, I'd listen to it. I got us drinks and we settled down in the living room. We made ready to listen. First she inserted the tape into the player and adjusted a couple of dials. Then she pushed a lever. The tape squeaked and someone began to talk in this loud voice. She lowered the volume. After a few minutes of harmless chitchat, I heard my own name in the mouth of this stranger, this blind man I didn't even know! And then this: "From all you've said about him, I can only conclude—" But we were interrupted, a knock at the door, something, and we didn't ever get back to the tape. Maybe it was just as well. I'd heard all I wanted to.

Now this same blind man was coming to sleep in my house.

"Maybe I could take him bowling," I said to my wife. She was at the draining board doing scalloped potatoes. She put down the knife she was using and turned around.

"If you love me," she said, "you can do this for me. If you don't love me, okay. But if you had a friend, any friend, and the friend came to visit, I'd make him feel comfortable." She wiped her hands with the dish towel.

"I don't have any blind friends," I said.

10   "You don't have *any* friends," she said. "Period. Besides," she said, "goddamn it, his wife's just died! Don't you understand that? The man's lost his wife!"

I didn't answer. She'd told me a little about the blind man's wife. Her name was Beulah. Beulah! That's a name for a colored woman.

"Was his wife a Negro?" I asked.

"Are you crazy?" my wife said. "Have you just flipped or something?" She picked up a potato. I saw it hit the floor, then roll under the stove. "What's wrong with you?" she said. "Are you drunk?"

"I'm just asking," I said.

15   Right then my wife filled me in with more detail than I cared to know. I made a drink and sat at the kitchen table to listen. Pieces of the story began to fall into place.

Beulah had gone to work for the blind man the summer after my wife had stopped working for him. Pretty soon Beulah and the blind man had themselves a church wedding. It was a little wedding—who'd want to go to such a wedding in the first place?—just the two of them, plus the minister and the minister's wife. But it was a church wedding just the same. It was what Beulah had wanted, he'd said. But even then Beulah must have been carrying the cancer in her glands. After they had been inseparable for eight years—my wife's word, *inseparable*—Beulah's health went into a rapid decline. She died in a Seattle hospital room, the blind man sitting beside the bed and holding on to her hand. They'd married, lived and worked together, slept together—had sex, sure—and then the blind man had to bury her. All this without his having ever seen what the goddamned woman looked like. It was beyond my understanding. Hearing this, I felt sorry for the blind man for a little bit. And then I found myself think-ing what a pitiful life this woman must have led. Imagine a woman who could never see herself as she was seen in the eyes of her loved one. A woman who could go on day after day and never receive the smallest compliment from her beloved. A woman whose husband could never read the expression on her face, be it misery or something better. Someone who could wear makeup or not— what difference to him? She could, if she wanted, wear green eye-shadow around one eye, a straight pin in her nostril, yellow slacks and purple shoes, no matter. And then to slip off into death, the blind man's hand on her hand, his blind eyes streaming tears—I'm imagining now—her last thought maybe this: that he never even knew what she looked like, and she on an express to the grave. Robert was left with a small insurance policy and half of a twenty-peso Mexican coin. The other half of the coin went into the box with her. Pathetic.

So when the time rolled around, my wife went to the depot to pick him up. With nothing to do but wait—sure, I blamed him for that—I was having a drink and watching the TV when I heard the car pull into the drive. I got up from the sofa with my drink and went to the window to have a look.

I saw my wife laughing as she parked the car. I saw her get out of the car and shut the door. She was still wearing a smile. Just amazing. She went around to the other side of the car to where the blind man was already starting to get out. This blind man, feature this, he was wearing a full beard! A beard on a blind man! Too much, I say. The blind man reached into the back seat and dragged out a suitcase. My wife took his arm, shut the car door, and, talking all the way, moved him down the drive and then up the steps to the front porch. I turned off the TV. I finished my drink, rinsed the glass, dried my hands. Then I went to the door.

My wife said, "I want you to meet Robert. Robert, this is my husband. I've told you all about him." She was beaming. She had this blind man by his coat sleeve.

The blind man let go of his suitcase and up came his hand.   20

I took it. He squeezed hard, held my hand, and then he let it go.

"I feel like we've already met," he boomed.

"Likewise," I said. I didn't know what else to say. Then I said, "Welcome. I've heard a lot about you." We began to move then, a little group, from the porch into the living room, my wife guiding him by the arm. The blind man was carrying his suitcase in his other hand. My wife said things like, "To your left here, Robert. That's right. Now watch it, there's a chair. That's it. Sit down right here. This is the sofa. We just bought this sofa two weeks ago."

I started to say something about the old sofa. I'd liked that old sofa. But I didn't say anything. Then I wanted to say something else, small-talk, about the scenic ride along the Hudson. How going *to* New York, you should sit on the right-hand side of the train, and coming *from* New York, the left-hand side.

"Did you have a good train ride?" I said. "Which side of the train did you sit   25
on, by the way?"

"What a question, which side!" my wife said. "What's it matter which side?" she said.

"I just asked," I said.

"Right side," the blind man said. "I hadn't been on a train in nearly forty years. Not since I was a kid. With my folks. That's been a long time. I'd nearly forgotten the sensation. I have winter in my beard now," he said. "So I've been told, anyway. Do I look distinguished, my dear?" the blind man said to my wife.

"You look distinguished, Robert," she said. "Robert," she said. "Robert, it's just so good to see you."

My wife finally took her eyes off the blind man and looked at me. I had the   30
feeling she didn't like what she saw. I shrugged.

I've never met, or personally known, anyone who was blind. This blind man was late forties, a heavy-set, balding man with stooped shoulders, as if he carried a great weight there. He wore brown slacks, brown shoes, a light-brown shirt, a tie, a sports coat. Spiffy. He also had this full beard. But he didn't use a cane and he didn't wear dark glasses. I'd always thought dark glasses were a must for the blind. Fact was, I wished he had a pair. At first glance, his eyes looked like anyone else's eyes. But if you looked close, there was something different about them. Too much white in the iris, for one thing, and the pupils seemed to move around in the sockets without his knowing it or being able to stop it. Creepy. As I stared at his face, I saw the left pupil turn in toward his nose while the other made an effort to keep in one place. But it was only an effort, for that eye was on the roam without his knowing it or wanting it to be.

I said, "Let me get you a drink. What's your pleasure? We have a little of everything. It's one of our pastimes."

"Bub, I'm a Scotch man myself," he said fast enough in this big voice.

"Right," I said. Bub! "Sure you are. I knew it."

35   He let his fingers touch his suitcase, which was sitting alongside the sofa. He was taking his bearings. I didn't blame him for that.

"I'll move that up to your room," my wife said.

"No, that's fine," the blind man said loudly. "It can go up when I go up."

"A little water with the Scotch?" I said.

"Very little," he said.

40   "I knew it," I said.

He said, "Just a tad. The Irish actor, Barry Fitzgerald? I'm like that fellow. When I drink water, Fitzgerald said, I drink water. When I drink whiskey, I drink whiskey." My wife laughed. The blind man brought his hand up under his beard. He lifted his beard slowly and let it drop.

I did the drinks, three big glasses of Scotch with a splash of water in each. Then we made ourselves comfortable and talked about Robert's travels. First the long flight from the West Coast to Connecticut, we covered that. Then from Connecticut up here by train. We had another drink concerning that leg of the trip.

I remembered having read somewhere that the blind didn't smoke because, as speculation had it, they couldn't see the smoke they exhaled. I thought I knew that much and that much only about blind people. But this blind man smoked his cigarette down to the nubbin and then lit another one. This blind man filled his ashtray and my wife emptied it.

When we sat down at the table for dinner, we had another drink. My wife heaped Robert's plate with cube steak, scalloped potatoes, green beans. I buttered him up two slices of bread. I said, "Here's bread and butter for you." I swallowed some of my drink. "Now let us pray," I said, and the blind man lowered his head. My wife looked at me, her mouth agape. "Pray the phone won't ring and the food doesn't get cold," I said.

45   We dug in. We ate everything there was to eat on the table. We ate like there was no tomorrow. We didn't talk. We ate. We scarfed. We grazed that table. We were into serious eating. The blind man had right away located his foods, he knew just where everything was on his plate. I watched with admiration as he used his knife and fork on the meat. He'd cut two pieces of meat, fork the meat into his mouth, and then go all out for the scalloped potatoes, the beans next, and then he'd tear off a hunk of buttered bread and eat that. He'd follow this up with a big drink of milk. It didn't seem to bother him to use his fingers once in a while, either.

We finished everything, including half a strawberry pie. For a few moments, we sat as if stunned. Sweat beaded on our faces. Finally, we got up from the table and left the dirty plates. We didn't look back. We took ourselves into the living room and sank into our places again. Robert and my wife sat on the sofa. I took the big chair. We had us two or three more drinks while they talked about the major things that had come to pass for them in the past ten years. For the most part, I just listened. Now and then I joined in. I didn't want him to think I'd left the room, and I didn't want her to think I was feeling left out. They talked of things that had happened to them—to them!—these past ten years. I waited in vain to hear my name on my wife's sweet lips: "And then my dear husband came into my life"—something like that. But I heard nothing of the sort. More talk of Robert. Robert had done a little of everything, it seemed, a regular blind jack-of-all-trades. But most recently he and his wife had had an Amway distributorship, from which, I gathered, they'd earned their living, such as it was. The blind man was also a ham radio operator. He talked in his loud voice about conversations he'd had with fellow operators in Guam, in the Philippines, in Alaska, and even in Tahiti. He said he'd have a lot of friends there if he ever wanted to go visit those places. From time to time, he'd turn his blind face toward me, put his hand under his beard, ask me something. How long had I been in my present position? (Three years.) Did I like my work? (I didn't.) Was I going to stay with it? (What were the options?) Finally, when I thought he was beginning to run down, I got up and turned on the TV.

My wife looked at me with irritation. She was heading toward a boil. Then she looked at the blind man and said, "Robert, do you have a TV?"

The blind man said, "My dear, I have two TVs. I have a color set and a black-and-white thing, an old relic. It's funny, but if I turn the TV on, and I'm always turning it on, I turn on the color set. It's funny, don't you think?"

I didn't know what to say to that. I had absolutely nothing to say to that. No opinion. So I watched the news program and tried to listen to what the announcer was saying.

"This is a color TV," the blind man said. "Don't ask me how, but I can tell." 50

"We traded up a while ago," I said.

The blind man had another taste of his drink. He lifted his beard, sniffed it, and let it fall. He leaned forward on the sofa. He positioned his ashtray on the coffee table, then put the lighter to his cigarette. He leaned back on the sofa and crossed his legs at the ankles.

My wife covered her mouth, and then she yawned. She stretched. She said, "I think I'll go upstairs and put on my robe. I think I'll change into something else. Robert, you make yourself comfortable," she said.

"I'm comfortable," the blind man said.

"I want you to feel comfortable in this house," she said. 55

"I am comfortable," the blind man said.

After she'd left the room, he and I listened to the weather report and then to the sports roundup. By that time, she'd been gone so long I didn't know if she was going to come back. I thought she might have gone to bed. I wished she'd come back downstairs. I didn't want to be left alone with a blind man. I asked him if he wanted another drink, and he said sure. Then I asked if he wanted to smoke some dope with me. I said I'd just rolled a number. I hadn't, but I planned to do so in about two shakes.

"I'll try some with you," he said.

"Damn right," I said. "That's the stuff."

60   I got our drinks and sat down on the sofa with him. Then I rolled us two fat numbers. I lit one and passed it. I brought it to his fingers. He took it and inhaled.

"Hold it as long as you can," I said. I could tell he didn't know the first thing.

My wife came back downstairs wearing her pink robe and her pink slippers.

"What do I smell?" she said.

"We thought we'd have us some cannabis," I said.

65   My wife gave me a savage look. Then she looked at the blind man and said, "Robert, I didn't know you smoked."

He said, "I do now, my dear. There's a first time for everything. But I don't feel anything yet."

"This stuff is pretty mellow," I said. "This stuff is mild. It's dope you can reason with," I said. "It doesn't mess you up."

"Not much it doesn't, bub," he said, and laughed.

My wife sat on the sofa between the blind man and me. I passed her the number. She took it and toked and then passed it back to me. "Which way is this going?" she said. Then she said, "I shouldn't be smoking this. I can hardly keep my eyes open as it is. That dinner did me in. I shouldn't have eaten so much."

70   "It was the strawberry pie," the blind man said. "That's what did it," he said, and he laughed his big laugh. Then he shook his head.

"There's more strawberry pie," I said.

"Do you want some more, Robert?" my wife said.

"Maybe in a little while," he said.

We gave our attention to the TV. My wife yawned again. She said, "Your bed is made up when you feel like going to bed, Robert. I know you must have had a long day. When you're ready to go to bed, say so." She pulled his arm. "Robert?"

75   He came to and said, "I've had a real nice time. This beats tapes, doesn't it?"

I said, "Coming at you," and I put the number between his fingers. He inhaled, held the smoke, and then let it go. It was like he'd been doing it since he was nine years old.

"Thanks, bub," he said. "But I think this is all for me. I think I'm beginning to feel it," he said. He held the burning roach out for my wife.

"Same here," she said. "Ditto. Me, too." She took the roach and passed it to me. "I may just sit here for a while between you two guys with my eyes closed. But don't let me bother you, okay? Either one of you. If it bothers you, say so. Otherwise, I may just sit here with my eyes closed until you're ready to go to bed," she said. "Your bed's made up, Robert, when you're ready. It's right next to our room at the top of the stairs. We'll show you up when you're ready. You wake me up now, you guys, if I fall asleep." She said that and then she closed her eyes and went to sleep.

The news program ended. I got up and changed the channel. I sat back down on the sofa. I wished my wife hadn't pooped out. Her head lay across the back of the sofa, her mouth open. She'd turned so that her robe had slipped away from her legs, exposing a juicy thigh. I reached to draw her robe back over her, and it was then that I glanced at the blind man. What the hell! I flipped the robe open again.

"You say when you want some strawberry pie," I said. 80

"I will," he said.

I said, "Are you tired? Do you want me to take you up to your bed? Are you ready to hit the hay?"

"Not yet," he said. "No, I'll stay up with you, bub. If that's all right. I'll stay up until you're ready to turn in. We haven't had a chance to talk. Know what I mean? I feel like me and her monopolized the evening." He lifted his beard and he let it fall. He picked up his cigarettes and his lighter.

"That's all right," I said. Then I said, "I'm glad for the company."

And I guess I was. Every night I smoked dope and stayed up as long as I 85 could before I fell asleep. My wife and I hardly ever went to bed at the same time. When I did go to sleep, I had these dreams. Sometimes I'd wake up from one of them, my heart going crazy.

Something about the church and the Middle Ages was on the TV. Not your run-of-the-mill TV fare. I wanted to watch something else. I turned to the other channels. But there was nothing on them, either. So I turned back to the first channel and apologized.

"Bub, it's all right," the blind man said. "It's fine with me. Whatever you want to watch is okay. I'm always learning something. Learning never ends. It won't hurt me to learn something tonight. I got ears," he said.

We didn't say anything for a time. He was leaning forward with his head turned at me, his right ear aimed in the direction of the set. Very disconcerting. Now and then his eyelids drooped and then they snapped open again. Now and then he put his fingers into his beard and tugged, like he was thinking about something he was hearing on the television.

On the screen, a group of men wearing cowls was being set upon and tormented by men dressed in skeleton costumes and men dressed as devils. The men dressed as devils wore devil masks, horns, and long tails. This pageant was part of a procession. The Englishman who was narrating the thing said it took place in Spain once a year. I tried to explain to the blind man what was happening.

"Skeletons," he said. "I know about skeletons," he said, and he nodded. 90

The TV showed this one cathedral. Then there was a long, slow look at another one. Finally, the picture switched to the famous one in Paris, with its flying buttresses and its spires reaching up to the clouds. The camera pulled away to show the whole of the cathedral rising above the skyline.

There were times when the Englishman who was telling the thing would shut up, would simply let the camera move around over the cathedrals. Or else the camera would tour the countryside, men in fields walking behind oxen. I waited as long as I could. Then I felt I had to say something. I said, "They're showing the outside of this cathedral now. Gargoyles. Little statues carved to look like monsters. Now I guess they're in Italy. Yeah, they're in Italy. There's paintings on the walls of this one church."

"Are those fresco paintings, bub?" he asked, and he sipped from his drink.

I reached for my glass. But it was empty. I tried to remember what I could remember. "You're asking me are those frescoes?" I said. "That's a good question. I don't know."

95   The camera moved to a cathedral outside Lisbon. The differences in the Portuguese cathedral compared with the French and Italian were not that great. But they were there. Mostly the interior stuff. Then something occurred to me, and I said, "Something has occurred to me. Do you have any idea what a cathedral is? What they look like, that is? Do you follow me? If somebody says cathedral to you, do you have any notion what they're talking about? Do you know the difference between that and a Baptist church, say?"

He let the smoke dribble from his mouth. "I know they took hundreds of workers fifty or a hundred years to build," he said. "I just heard the man say that, of course. I know generations of the same families worked on a cathedral. I heard him say that, too. The men who began their life's work on them, they never lived to see the completion of their work. In that wise, bub, they're no different from the rest of us, right?" He laughed. Then his eyelids drooped again. His head nodded. He seemed to be snoozing. Maybe he was imagining himself in Portugal. The TV was showing another cathedral now. This one was in Germany. The Englishman's voice droned on. "Cathedrals," the blind man said. He sat up and rolled his head back and forth. "If you want the truth, bub, that's about all I know. What I just said. What I heard him say. But maybe you could describe one to me? I wish you'd do it. I'd like that. If you want to know, I really don't have a good idea."

I stared hard at the shot of the cathedral on the TV. How could I even begin to describe it? But say my life depended on it. Say my life was being threatened by an insane guy who said I had to do it or else.

I stared some more at the cathedral before the picture flipped off into the countryside. There was no use. I turned to the blind man and said, "To begin with, they're very tall." I was looking around the room for clues. "They reach way up. Up and up. Toward the sky. They're so big, some of them, they have to have these supports. To help hold them up, so to speak. These supports are called buttresses. They remind me of viaducts, for some reason. But maybe you don't know viaducts, either? Sometimes the cathedrals have devils and such carved into the front. Sometimes lords and ladies. Don't ask me why this is," I said.

He was nodding. The whole upper part of his body seemed to be moving back and forth.

100   "I'm not doing so good, am I?" I said.

He stopped nodding and leaned forward on the edge of the sofa. As he listened to me, he was running his fingers through his beard. I wasn't getting through to him, I could see that. But he waited for me to go on just the same. He nodded, like he was trying to encourage me. I tried to think what else to say. "They're really big," I said. "They're massive. They're built of stone. Marble, too, sometimes. In those olden days, when they built cathedrals, men wanted to be close to God. In those olden days, God was an important part of everyone's life. You could tell this from their cathedral-building. I'm sorry," I said, "but it looks like that's the best I can do for you. I'm just no good at it."

"That's all right, bub," the blind man said. "Hey, listen. I hope you don't mind my asking you. Can I ask you something? Let me ask you a simple question, yes or no. I'm just curious and there's no offense. You're my host. But let me ask if you are in any way religious? You don't mind my asking?"

I shook my head. He couldn't see that, though. A wink is the same as a nod to a blind man. "I guess I don't believe in it. In anything. Sometimes it's hard. You know what I'm saying?"

"Sure, I do," he said.

"Right," I said. 105

The Englishman was still holding forth. My wife sighed in her sleep. She drew a long breath and went on with her sleeping.

"You'll have to forgive me," I said. "But I can't tell you what a cathedral looks like. It just isn't in me to do it. I can't do any more than I've done."

The blind man sat very still, his head down, as he listened to me.

I said, "The truth is, cathedrals don't mean anything special to me. Nothing. Cathedrals. They're something to look at on late-night TV. That's all they are."

It was then that the blind man cleared his throat. He brought something up. 110 He took a handkerchief from his back pocket. Then he said, "I get it, bub. It's okay. It happens. Don't worry about it," he said. "Hey, listen to me. Will you do me a favor? I got an idea. Why don't you find us some heavy paper? And a pen. We'll do something. We'll draw one together. Get us a pen and some heavy paper. Go on, bub, get the stuff," he said.

So I went upstairs. My legs felt like they didn't have any strength in them. They felt like they did after I'd done some running. In my wife's room, I looked around. I found some ballpoints in a little basket on her table. And then I tried to think where to look for the kind of paper he was talking about.

Downstairs, in the kitchen, I found a shopping bag with onion skins in the bottom of the bag. I emptied the bag and shook it. I brought it into the living room and sat down with it near his legs. I moved some things, smoothed the wrinkles from the bag, spread it out on the coffee table.

The blind man got down from the sofa and sat next to me on the carpet.

He ran his fingers over the paper. He went up and down the sides of the paper. The edges, even the edges. He fingered the corners.

"All right," he said. "All right, let's do her." 115

He found my hand, the hand with the pen. He closed his hand over my hand. "Go ahead, bub, draw," he said. "Draw. You'll see. I'll follow along with you. It'll be okay. Just begin now like I'm telling you. You'll see. Draw," the blind man said.

So I began. First I drew a box that looked like a house. It could have been the house I lived in. Then I put a roof on it. At either end of the roof, I drew spires. Crazy.

"Swell," he said. "Terrific. You're doing fine," he said. "Never thought anything like this could happen in your lifetime, did you, bub? Well, it's a strange life, we all know that. Go on now. Keep it up."

I put in windows with arches. I drew flying buttresses. I hung great doors. I couldn't stop. The TV station went off the air. I put down the pen and closed and opened my fingers. The blind man felt around over the paper. He moved the tips of his fingers over the paper, all over what I had drawn, and he nodded.

"Doing fine," the blind man said. 120

I took up the pen again, and he found my hand. I kept at it. I'm no artist. But I kept drawing just the same.

My wife opened up her eyes and gazed at us. She sat up on the sofa, her robe hanging open. She said, "What are you doing? Tell me, I want to know."

I didn't answer her.

The blind man said, "We're drawing a cathedral. Me and him are working on it. Press hard," he said to me. "That's right. That's good," he said. "Sure. You got it, bub. I can tell. You didn't think you could. But you can, can't you? You're cooking with gas now. You know what I'm saying? We're going to really have us something here in a minute. How's the old arm?" he said. "Put some people in there now. What's a cathedral without people?"

125   My wife said, "What's going on? Robert, what are you doing? What's going on?"

"It's all right," he said to her. "Close your eyes now," the blind man said to me.

I did it. I closed them just like he said.

"Are they closed?" he said. "Don't fudge."

"They're closed," I said.

130   "Keep them that way," he said. He said, "Don't stop now. Draw."

So we kept on with it. His fingers rode my fingers as my hand went over the paper. It was like nothing else in my life up to now.

Then he said, "I think that's it. I think you got it," he said. "Take a look. What do you think?"

But I had my eyes closed. I thought I'd keep them that way for a little longer. I thought it was something I ought to do.

"Well?" he said. "Are you looking?"

135   My eyes were still closed. I was in my house. I knew that. But I didn't feel like I was inside anything.

"It's really something," I said.

1981, 1983

WILLIAM FAULKNER

A Rose for Emily
(See Faulkner biography on p. 146.)

I

When Miss Emily Grierson died, our whole town went to her funeral: the men through a sort of respectful affection for a fallen monument, the women mostly out of curiosity to see the inside of her house, which no one save an old manservant—a combined gardener and cook—had seen in at least ten years.

It was a big, squarish frame house that had once been white, decorated with cupolas and spires and scrolled balconies in the heavily lightsome style of the seventies,[1] set on what had once been our most select street. But garages and cotton gins had encroached and obliterated even the august names of that neighborhood; only Miss Emily's house was left, lifting its stubborn and

---

1. The 1870s, the decade following the Civil War between the "Union and Confederate soldiers" mentioned at the end of the paragraph.

coquettish decay above the cotton wagons and the gasoline pumps—an eyesore among eyesores. And now Miss Emily had gone to join the representatives of those august names where they lay in the cedar-bemused cemetery among the ranked and anonymous graves of Union and Confederate soldiers who fell at the battle of Jefferson.

Alive, Miss Emily had been a tradition, a duty, and a care; a sort of hereditary obligation upon the town, dating from that day in 1894 when Colonel Sartoris, the mayor—he who fathered the edict that no Negro woman should appear on the streets without an apron—remitted her taxes, the dispensation dating from the death of her father on into perpetuity. Not that Miss Emily would have accepted charity. Colonel Sartoris invented an involved tale to the effect that Miss Emily's father had loaned money to the town, which the town, as a matter of business, preferred this way of repaying. Only a man of Colonel Sartoris' generation and thought could have invented it, and only a woman could have believed it.

When the next generation, with its more modern ideas, became mayors and aldermen, this arrangement created some little dissatisfaction. On the first of the year they mailed her a tax notice. February came, and there was no reply. They wrote her a formal letter, asking her to call at the sheriff's office at her convenience. A week later the mayor wrote her himself, offering to call or to send his car for her, and received in reply a note on paper of an archaic shape, in a thin, flowing calligraphy in faded ink, to the effect that she no longer went out at all. The tax notice was also enclosed, without comment.

They called a special meeting of the Board of Aldermen. A deputation waited 5 upon her, knocked at the door through which no visitor had passed since she ceased giving china-painting lessons eight or ten years earlier. They were admitted by the old Negro into a dim hall from which a stairway mounted into still more shadow. It smelled of dust and disuse—a close, dank smell. The Negro led them into the parlor. It was furnished in heavy, leather-covered furniture. When the Negro opened the blinds of one window, a faint dust rose sluggishly about their thighs, spinning with slow motes in the single sun-ray. On a tarnished gilt easel before the fireplace stood a crayon portrait of Miss Emily's father.

They rose when she entered—a small, fat woman in black, with a thin gold chain descending to her waist and vanishing into her belt, leaning on an ebony cane with a tarnished gold head. Her skeleton was small and spare; perhaps that was why what would have been merely plumpness in another was obesity in her. She looked bloated, like a body long submerged in motionless water, and of that pallid hue. Her eyes, lost in the fatty ridges of her face, looked like two small pieces of coal pressed into a lump of dough as they moved from one face to another while the visitors stated their errand.

She did not ask them to sit. She just stood in the door and listened quietly until the spokesman came to a stumbling halt. Then they could hear the invisible watch ticking at the end of the gold chain.

Her voice was dry and cold. "I have no taxes in Jefferson. Colonel Sartoris explained it to me. Perhaps one of you can gain access to the city records and satisfy yourselves."

"But we have. We are the city authorities, Miss Emily. Didn't you get a notice from the sheriff, signed by him?"

10   "I received a paper, yes," Miss Emily said. "Perhaps he considers himself the sheriff. . . . I have no taxes in Jefferson."

"But there is nothing on the books to show that, you see. We must go by the—"

"See Colonel Sartoris. I have no taxes in Jefferson."

"But, Miss Emily—"

"See Colonel Sartoris." (Colonel Sartoris had been dead almost ten years.) "I have no taxes in Jefferson. Tobe!" The Negro appeared. "Show these gentlemen out."

II

15 So she vanquished them, horse and foot, just as she had vanquished their fathers thirty years before about the smell. That was two years after her father's death and a short time after her sweetheart—the one we believed would marry her—had deserted her. After her father's death she went out very little; after her sweetheart went away, people hardly saw her at all. A few of the ladies had the temerity to call, but were not received, and the only sign of life about the place was the Negro man—a young man then—going in and out with a market basket.

"Just as if a man—any man—could keep a kitchen properly," the ladies said; so they were not surprised when the smell developed. It was another link between the gross, teeming world and the high and mighty Griersons.

A neighbor, a woman, complained to the mayor, Judge Stevens, eighty years old.

"But what will you have me do about it, madam?" he said.

"Why, send her word to stop it," the woman said. "Isn't there a law?"

20   "I'm sure that won't be necessary," Judge Stevens said. "It's probably just a snake or a rat that nigger of hers killed in the yard. I'll speak to him about it."

The next day he received two more complaints, one from a man who came in diffident deprecation. "We really must do something about it, Judge. I'd be the last one in the world to bother Miss Emily, but we've got to do something." That night the Board of Aldermen met—three gray-beards and one younger man, a member of the rising generation.

"It's simple enough," he said. "Send her word to have her place cleaned up. Give her a certain time to do it in, and if she don't . . ."

"Dammit, sir," Judge Stevens said, "will you accuse a lady to her face of smelling bad?"

So the next night, after midnight, four men crossed Miss Emily's lawn and slunk about the house like burglars, sniffing along the base of the brickwork and at the cellar openings while one of them performed a regular sowing motion with his hand out of a sack slung from his shoulder. They broke open the cellar door and sprinkled lime there, and in all the outbuildings. As they recrossed the lawn, a window that had been dark was lighted and Miss Emily sat in it, the light behind her, and her upright torso motionless as that of an idol. They crept quietly across the lawn and into the shadow of the locusts that lined the street. After a week or two the smell went away.

That was when people had begun to feel really sorry for her. People in our town, remembering how old lady Wyatt, her great-aunt, had gone completely crazy at last, believed that the Griersons held themselves a little too high for what they really were. None of the young men were quite good enough for Miss Emily and such. We had long thought of them as a tableau; Miss Emily a slender figure in white in the background, her father a spraddled silhouette in the foreground, his back to her and clutching a horsewhip, the two of them framed by the back-flung front door. So when she got to be thirty and was still single, we were not pleased exactly, but vindicated; even with insanity in the family she wouldn't have turned down all of her chances if they had really materialized.

When her father died, it got about that the house was all that was left to her; and in a way, people were glad. At last they could pity Miss Emily. Being left alone, and a pauper, she had become humanized. Now she too would know the old thrill and the old despair of a penny more or less.

The day after his death all the ladies prepared to call at the house and offer condolence and aid, as is our custom. Miss Emily met them at the door, dressed as usual and with no trace of grief on her face. She told them that her father was not dead. She did that for three days, with the ministers calling on her, and the doctors, trying to persuade her to let them dispose of the body. Just as they were about to resort to law and force, she broke down, and they buried her father quickly.

We did not say she was crazy then. We believed she had to do that. We remembered all the young men her father had driven away, and we knew that with nothing left, she would have to cling to that which had robbed her, as people will.

III

She was sick for a long time. When we saw her again, her hair was cut short, making her look like a girl, with a vague resemblance to those angels in colored church windows—sort of tragic and serene.

The town had just let the contracts for paving the sidewalks, and in the summer after her father's death they began to work. The construction company came with niggers and mules and machinery, and a foreman named Homer Barron, a Yankee—a big, dark, ready man, with a big voice and eyes lighter than his face. The little boys would follow in groups to hear him cuss the niggers, and the niggers singing in time to the rise and fall of picks. Pretty soon he knew everybody in town. Whenever you heard a lot of laughing anywhere about the square, Homer Barron would be in the center of the group. Presently we began to see him and Miss Emily on Sunday afternoons driving in the yellow-wheeled buggy and the matched team of bays from the livery stable.

At first we were glad that Miss Emily would have an interest, because the ladies all said, "Of course a Grierson would not think seriously of a Northerner, a day laborer." But there were still others, older people, who said that even grief could not cause a real lady to forget noblesse oblige—without calling it noblesse oblige.[2] They just said, "Poor Emily. Her kinsfolk should come to her." She had

2. Obligation, coming with noble or upper-class birth, to behave with honor and generosity toward those less privileged.

some kin in Alabama; but years ago her father had fallen out with them over the estate of old lady Wyatt, the crazy woman, and there was no communication between the two families. They had not even been represented at the funeral.

And as soon as the old people said, "Poor Emily," the whispering began. "Do you suppose it's really so?" they said to one another. "Of course it is. What else could . . ." This behind their hands; rustling of craned silk and satin behind jalousies[3] closed upon the sun of Sunday afternoon as the thin, swift clop-clop-clop of the matched team passed: "Poor Emily."

She carried her head high enough—even when we believed that she was fallen. It was as if she demanded more than ever the recognition of her dignity as the last Grierson; as if it had wanted that touch of earthiness to reaffirm her imperviousness. Like when she bought the rat poison, the arsenic. That was over a year after they had begun to say "Poor Emily," and while the two female cousins were visiting her.

"I want some poison," she said to the druggist. She was over thirty then, still a slight woman, though thinner than usual, with cold, haughty black eyes in a face the flesh of which was strained across the temples and about the eyesockets as you imagine a lighthouse-keeper's face ought to look. "I want some poison," she said.

35   "Yes, Miss Emily. What kind? For rats and such? I'd recom—"

"I want the best you have. I don't care what kind."

The druggist named several. "They'll kill anything up to an elephant. But what you want is—"

"Arsenic," Miss Emily said. "Is that a good one?"

"Is . . . arsenic? Yes ma'am. But what you want—"

40   "I want arsenic."

The druggist looked down at her. She looked back at him, erect, her face like a strained flag. "Why, of course," the druggist said. "If that's what you want. But the law requires you to tell what you are going to use it for."

Miss Emily just stared at him, her head tilted back in order to look him eye for eye, until he looked away and went and got the arsenic and wrapped it up. The Negro delivery boy brought her the package; the druggist didn't come back. When she opened the package at home there was written on the box, under the skull and bones: "For rats."

IV

So the next day we all said, "She will kill herself"; and we said it would be the best thing. When she had first begun to be seen with Homer Barron, we had said, "She will marry him." Then we said, "She will persuade him yet," because Homer himself had remarked—he liked men, and it was known that he drank with the younger men in the Elk's Club—that he was not a marrying man. Later we said, "Poor Emily," behind the jalousies as they passed on Sunday afternoon in the glittering buggy, Miss Emily with her head high and Homer Barron with his hat cocked and a cigar in his teeth, reins and whip in a yellow glove.

3. Window blinds made of adjustable horizontal slats.

Then some of the ladies began to say that it was a disgrace to the town and a bad example to the young people. The men did not want to interfere, but at last the ladies forced the Baptist minister—Miss Emily's people were Episcopal—to call upon her. He would never divulge what happened during that interview, but he refused to go back again. The next Sunday they again drove about the streets, and the following day the minister's wife wrote to Miss Emily's relations in Alabama.

So she had blood-kin under her roof again and we sat back to watch developments. At first nothing happened. Then we were sure that they were to be married. We learned that Miss Emily had been to the jeweler's and ordered a man's toilet set in silver, with the letters H. B. on each piece. Two days later we learned that she had bought a complete outfit of men's clothing, including a nightshirt, and we said, "They are married." We were really glad. We were glad because the two female cousins were even more Grierson than Miss Emily had ever been.

So we were not surprised when Homer Barron—the streets had been finished some time since—was gone. We were a little disappointed that there was not a public blowing-off, but we believed that he had gone on to prepare for Miss Emily's coming, or to give her a chance to get rid of the cousins. (By that time it was a cabal, and we were all Miss Emily's allies to help circumvent the cousins.) Sure enough, after another week they departed. And, as we had expected all along, within three days Homer Barron was back in town. A neighbor saw the Negro man admit him at the kitchen door at dusk one evening.

And that was the last we saw of Homer Barron. And of Miss Emily for some time. The Negro man went in and out with the market basket, but the front door remained closed. Now and then we would see her at a window for a moment, as the men did that night when they sprinkled the lime, but for almost six months she did not appear on the streets. Then we knew that this was to be expected too; as if that quality of her father which had thwarted her woman's life so many times had been too virulent and too furious to die.

When we next saw Miss Emily, she had grown fat and her hair was turning gray. During the next few years it grew grayer and grayer until it attained an even pepper-and-salt iron-gray, when it ceased turning. Up to the day of her death at seventy-four it was still that vigorous iron-gray, like the hair of an active man.

From that time on her front door remained closed, save for a period of six or seven years, when she was about forty, during which she gave lessons in china-painting. She fitted up a studio in one of the downstairs rooms, where the daughters and grand-daughters of Colonel Sartoris' contemporaries were sent to her with the same regularity and in the same spirit that they were sent on Sundays with a twenty-five cent piece for the collection plate. Meanwhile her taxes had been remitted.

Then the newer generation became the backbone and the spirit of the town, and the painting pupils grew up and fell away and did not send their children to her with boxes of color and tedious brushes and pictures cut from the ladies' magazines. The front door closed upon the last one and remained closed for good. When the town got free postal delivery Miss Emily alone refused to let them fasten the metal numbers above her door and attach a mailbox to it. She would not listen to them.

Daily, monthly, yearly we watched the Negro grow grayer and more stooped, going in and out with the market basket. Each December we sent her a tax notice, which would be returned by the post office a week later, unclaimed. Now and then we would see her in one of the downstairs windows—she had evidently shut up the top floor of the house—like the carven torso of an idol in a niche, looking or not looking at us, we could never tell which. Thus she passed from generation to generation—dear, inescapable, impervious, tranquil, and perverse.

And so she died. Fell ill in the house filled with dust and shadows, with only a doddering Negro man to wait on her. We did not even know she was sick; we had long since given up trying to get any information from the Negro. He talked to no one, probably not even to her, for his voice had grown harsh and rusty, as if from disuse.

She died in one of the downstairs rooms, in a heavy walnut bed with a curtain, her gray head propped on a pillow yellow and moldy with age and lack of sunlight.

V

The Negro met the first of the ladies at the front door and let them in, with their hushed, sibilant voices and their quick, curious glances, and then he disappeared. He walked right through the house and out the back and was not seen again.

55   The two female cousins came at once. They held the funeral on the second day, with the town coming to look at Miss Emily beneath a mass of bought flowers, with the crayon face of her father musing profoundly above the bier and the ladies sibilant and macabre; and the very old men—some in their brushed Confederate uniforms—on the porch and the lawn, talking of Miss Emily as if she had been a contemporary of theirs, believing that they had danced with her and courted her perhaps, confusing time with its mathematical progression, as the old do, to whom all the past is not a diminishing road, but, instead, a huge meadow which no winter ever quite touches, divided from them now by the narrow bottleneck of the most recent decade of years.

Already we knew that there was one room in that region above stairs which no one had seen in forty years, and which would have to be forced. They waited until Miss Emily was decently in the ground before they opened it.

The violence of breaking down the door seemed to fill this room with pervading dust. A thin, acrid pall as of the tomb seemed to lie everywhere upon this room decked and furnished as for a bridal: upon the valance curtains of faded rose color, upon the rose-shaded lights, upon the dressing table, upon the delicate array of crystal and the man's toilet things backed with tarnished silver, silver so tarnished that the monogram was obscured. Among them lay a collar and tie, as if they had just been removed, which, lifted, left upon the surface a pale crescent in the dust. Upon a chair hung the suit, carefully folded; beneath it the two mute shoes and the discarded socks.

The man himself lay in the bed.

For a long while we just stood there, looking down at the profound and fleshless grin. The body had apparently once lain in the attitude of an embrace, but now the long sleep that outlasts love, that conquers even the grimace of love, had cuckolded him. What was left of him, rotted beneath what was left of the nightshirt, had become inextricable from the bed in which he lay; and upon him and upon the pillow beside him lay that even coating of the patient and biding dust.

Then we noticed that in the second pillow was the indentation of a head. One of us lifted something from it, and leaning forward, that faint and invisible dust dry and acrid in the nostrils, we saw a long strand of iron-gray hair.

60

1930

ERNEST HEMINGWAY
(1899–1961)

Hills Like White Elephants

Among the most distinctively American of writers, even if he rarely wrote about America, Ernest Hemingway grew up in an upscale Chicago suburb, but spent his summers on Lake Walloon in northern Michigan. Here, his physician father nurtured his love of hunting and fishing. Hemingway graduated from high school just two months after the United States entered World War I. Forbidden to enlist by his parents and uninterested in college, he worked as a reporter for the *Kansas City Star* before volunteering as a Red Cross ambulance driver. Badly wounded on the Italian front, he returned to the States and to journalism. Then, in 1921, he moved to Paris, France, entering the famed expatriate circle that included Ezra Pound, Gertrude Stein, and F. Scott Fitzgerald. Two volumes of stories, *In Our Time* (1925) and *Men without Women* (1927), and two major novels, *The Sun Also Rises* (1926) and *A Farewell to Arms* (1929), established Hemingway's international reputation as both a masterful literary craftsman and a chief spokesman for the "Lost Generation," while later, less critically acclaimed books on topics such as bullfighting (*Death in the Afternoon* [1932]) and big-game hunting (*Green Hills of Africa* [1935]) helped confirm his status as an almost mythic figure, patron saint of what the *New York Times* called a "cult" of daring and danger. Hemingway supported the Loyalists in the Spanish Civil War, the subject of his novel *For Whom the Bell Tolls* (1940); served as a war correspondent during World War II; and survived two plane crashes and four marriages. Severely depressed and suffering an array of physical ailments, he took his own life shortly before his sixty-second birthday, only a few years after earning both a Pulitzer—for *The Old Man and the Sea* (1952)—and the Nobel Prize in Literature (1954).

The hills across the valley of the Ebro[1] were long and white. On this side there was no shade and no trees and the station was between two lines of rails in the sun. Close against the side of the station there was the warm shadow of the building and a curtain, made of strings of bamboo beads, hung

1. River in northern Spain.

across the open door into the bar, to keep out flies. The American and the girl with him sat at a table in the shade, outside the building. It was very hot and the express from Barcelona would come in forty minutes. It stopped at this junction for two minutes and went on to Madrid.

"What should we drink?" the girl asked. She had taken off her hat and put it on the table.

"It's pretty hot," the man said.

"Let's drink beer."

5   "Dos cervezas," the man said into the curtain.

"Big ones?" a woman asked from the doorway.

"Yes. Two big ones."

The woman brought two glasses of beer and two felt pads. She put the felt pads and the beer glasses on the table and looked at the man and the girl. The girl was looking off at the line of hills. They were white in the sun and the country was brown and dry.

"They look like white elephants," she said.

10   "I've never seen one," the man drank his beer.

"No, you wouldn't have."

"I might have," the man said. "Just because you say I wouldn't have doesn't prove anything."

The girl looked at the bead curtain. "They've painted something on it," she said. "What does it say?"

"Anis del Toro. It's a drink."

15   "Could we try it?"

The man called "Listen" through the curtain. The woman came out from the bar.

"Four reales."[2]

"We want two Anis del Toro."

"With water?"

20   "Do you want it with water?"

"I don't know," the girl said. "Is it good with water?"

"It's all right."

"You want them with water?" asked the woman.

"Yes, with water."

25   "It tastes like licorice," the girl said and put the glass down.

"That's the way with everything."

"Yes," said the girl. "Everything tastes of licorice. Especially all the things you've waited so long for, like absinthe."

"Oh, cut it out."

"You started it," the girl said. "I was being amused. I was having a fine time."

30   "Well, let's try and have a fine time."

"All right. I was trying. I said the mountains looked like white elephants. Wasn't that bright?"

"That was bright."

"I wanted to try this new drink. That's all we do, isn't it—look at things and try new drinks?"

2. Spanish coins.

"I guess so."

The girl looked across at the hills.   35

"They're lovely hills," she said. "They don't really look like white elephants. I just meant the coloring of their skin through the trees."

"Should we have another drink?"

"All right."

The warm wind blew the bead curtain against the table.

"The beer's nice and cool," the man said.   40

"It's lovely," the girl said.

"It's really an awfully simple operation, Jig," the man said. "It's not really an operation at all."

The girl looked at the ground the table legs rested on.

"I know you wouldn't mind it, Jig. It's really not anything. It's just to let the air in."

The girl did not say anything.   45

"I'll go with you and I'll stay with you all the time. They just let the air in and then it's all perfectly natural."

"Then what will we do afterward?"

"We'll be fine afterward. Just like we were before."

"What makes you think so?"

"That's the only thing that bothers us. It's the only thing that's made us 50 unhappy."

The girl looked at the bead curtain, put her hand out and took hold of two of the strings of beads.

"And you think then we'll be all right and be happy."

"I know we will. You don't have to be afraid. I've known lots of people that have done it."

"So have I," said the girl. "And afterward they were all so happy."

"Well," the man said, "if you don't want to you don't have to. I wouldn't have 55 you do it if you didn't want to. But I know it's perfectly simple."

"And you really want to?"

"I think it's the best thing to do. But I don't want you to do it if you don't really want to."

"And if I do it you'll be happy and things will be like they were and you'll love me?"

"I love you now. You know I love you."

"I know. But if I do it, then it will be nice again if I say things are like white 60 elephants, and you'll like it?"

"I'll love it. I love it now but I just can't think about it. You know how I get when I worry."

"If I do it you won't ever worry?"

"I won't worry about that because it's perfectly simple."

"Then I'll do it. Because I don't care about me."

"What do you mean?"   65

"I don't care about me."

"Well, I care about you."

"Oh, yes. But I don't care about me. And I'll do it and then everything will be fine."

"I don't want you to do it if you feel that way."

70   The girl stood up and walked to the end of the station. Across, on the other side, were fields of grain and trees along the banks of the Ebro. Far away, beyond the river, were mountains. The shadow of a cloud moved across the field of grain and she saw the river through the trees.

"And we could have all this," she said. "And we could have everything and every day we make it more impossible."

"What did you say?"

"I said we could have everything."

"We can have everything."

75   "No, we can't."

"We can have the whole world."

"No, we can't."

"We can go everywhere."

"No, we can't. It isn't ours anymore."

80   "It's ours."

"No, it isn't. And once they take it away, you never get it back."

"But they haven't taken it away."

"We'll wait and see."

"Come on back in the shade," he said. "You mustn't feel that way."

85   "I don't feel any way," the girl said. "I just know things."

"I don't want you to do anything that you don't want to do—"

"Nor that isn't good for me," she said. "I know. Could we have another beer?"

"All right. But you've got to realize—"

"I realize," the girl said. "Can't we maybe stop talking?"

90   They sat down at the table and the girl looked across at the hills on the dry side of the valley and the man looked at her and at the table.

"You've got to realize," he said, "that I don't want you to do it if you don't want to. I'm perfectly willing to go through with it if it means anything to you."

"Doesn't it mean anything to you? We could get along."

"Of course it does. But I don't want anybody but you. I don't want any one else. And I know it's perfectly simple."

"Yes, you know it's perfectly simple."

95   "It's all right for you to say that, but I do know it."

"Would you do something for me now?"

"I'd do anything for you."

"Would you please please please please please please please stop talking?"

He did not say anything but looked at the bags against the wall of the station. There were labels on them from all the hotels where they had spent nights.

100   "But I don't want you to," he said, "I don't care anything about it."

"I'll scream," the girl said.

The woman came out through the curtains with two glasses of beer and put them down on the damp felt pads. "The train comes in five minutes," she said.

"What did she say?" asked the girl.

"That the train is coming in five minutes."

105   The girl smiled brightly at the woman, to thank her.

"I'd better take the bags over to the other side of the station," the man said. She smiled at him.

"All right. Then come back and we'll finish the beer."

He picked up the two heavy bags and carried them around the station to the other tracks. He looked up the tracks but could not see the train. Coming back, he walked through the barroom, where people waiting for the train were drinking. He drank an Anis at the bar and looked at the people. They were all waiting reasonably for the train. He went out through the bead curtain. She was sitting at the table and smiled at him.

"Do you feel better?" he asked.

"I feel fine," she said. "There's nothing wrong with me. I feel fine."

110

1927

FRANZ KAFKA

(1883–1924)

A Hunger Artist[1]

Born into a middle-class Jewish family in Prague, Franz Kafka earned a doctorate in law from the German University in that city and held an inconspicuous position in the civil service for many years. Emotionally and physically ill for the last seven or eight years of his short life, he died of tuberculosis in Vienna, never having married (though he was twice engaged to the same woman and lived with an actress in Berlin for some time before he died) and not having published his three major novels, *The Trial* (1925), *The Castle* (1926), and *Amerika* (1927). Indeed, Kafka ordered his friend Max Brod to destroy these and other works he had left in manuscript. Fortunately, Brod did not, and not long after Kafka's death, his sometimes-dreamlike, sometimes-nightmarish work became known and admired all over the world. His stories in English translation are collected in *The Great Wall of China* (1933), *The Penal Colony* (1948), and *The Complete Stories* (1971).

During these last decades the interest in professional fasting has markedly diminished. It used to pay very well to stage such great performances under one's own management, but today that is quite impossible. We live in a different world now. At one time the whole town took a lively interest in the hunger artist; from day to day of his fast the excitement mounted; everybody wanted to see him at least once a day; there were people who bought season tickets for the last few days and sat from morning till night in front of his small barred cage; even in the nighttime there were visiting hours, when the whole effect was heightened by torch flares; on fine days the cage was set out in the open air, and then it was the children's special treat to see the hunger artist; for their elders he was often just a joke that happened to be in fashion, but the children stood open-mouthed, holding each other's hands for greater security, marveling at him as he sat there pallid in black tights, with his ribs sticking out

1. Translated from the German by Edwin and Willa Muir.

so prominently, not even on a seat but down among straw on the ground, sometimes giving a courteous nod, answering questions with a constrained smile, or perhaps stretching an arm through the bars so that one might feel how thin it was, and then again withdrawing deep into himself, paying no attention to anyone or anything, not even to the all-important striking of the clock that was the only piece of furniture in his cage, but merely staring into vacancy with half-shut eyes, now and then taking a sip from a tiny glass of water to moisten his lips.

Besides casual onlookers there were also relays of permanent watchers selected by the public, usually butchers, strangely enough, and it was their task to watch the hunger artist day and night, three of them at a time, in case he should have some secret recourse to nourishment. This was nothing but a formality, instituted to reassure the masses, for the initiates knew well enough that during his fast the artist would never in any circumstances, not even under forcible compulsion, swallow the smallest morsel of food: the honor of his profession forbade it. Not every watcher, of course, was capable of understanding this, there were often groups of night watchers who were very lax in carrying out their duties and deliberately huddled together in a retired corner to play cards with great absorption, obviously intending to give the hunger artist the chance of a little refreshment, which they supposed he could draw from some private hoard. Nothing annoyed the artist more than such watchers; they made him miserable; they made his fast seem unendurable; sometimes he mastered his feebleness sufficiently to sing during their watch for as long as he could keep going, to show them how unjust their suspicions were. But that was of little use; they only wondered at his cleverness in being able to fill his mouth even while singing. Much more to his taste were the watchers who sat close up to the bars, who were not content with the dim night lighting of the hall but focused him in the full glare of the electric pocket torch[2] given them by the impresario. The harsh light did not trouble him at all, in any case he could never sleep properly, and he could always drowse a little, whatever the light, at any hour, even when the hall was thronged with noisy onlookers. He was quite happy at the prospect of spending a sleepless night with such watchers; he was ready to exchange jokes with them, to tell them stories out of his nomadic life, anything at all to keep them awake and demonstrate to them again that he had no eatables in his cage and that he was fasting as not one of them could fast. But his happiest moment was when the morning came and an enormous breakfast was brought them, at his expense, on which they flung themselves with the keen appetite of healthy men after a weary night of wakefulness. Of course there were people who argued that this breakfast was an unfair attempt to bribe the watchers, but that was going rather too far, and when they were invited to take on a night's vigil without a breakfast, merely for the sake of the cause, they made themselves scarce, although they stuck stubbornly to their suspicions.

Such suspicions, anyhow, were a necessary accompaniment to the profession of fasting. No one could possibly watch the hunger artist continuously, day and night, and so no one could produce first-hand evidence that the fast had really been rigorous and continuous; only the artist himself could know that, he was

2. Flashlight.

therefore bound to be the sole completely satisfied spectator of his own fast. Yet for other reasons he was never satisfied; it was not perhaps mere fasting that had brought him to such skeleton thinness that many people had regretfully to keep away from his exhibitions, because the sight of him was too much for them, perhaps it was dissatisfaction with himself that had worn him down. For he alone knew, what no other initiate knew, how easy it was to fast. It was the easiest thing in the world. He made no secret of this, yet people did not believe him, at the best they set him down as modest; most of them, however, thought he was out for publicity or else was some kind of cheat who found it easy to fast because he had discovered a way of making it easy, and then had the impudence to admit the fact, more or less. He had to put up with all that, and in the course of time had got used to it, but his inner dissatisfaction always rankled, and never yet, after any term of fasting—this must be granted to his credit—had he left the cage of his own free will. The longest period of fasting was fixed by his impresario at forty days,[3] beyond that term he was not allowed to go, not even in great cities, and there was good reason for it, too. Experience had proved that for about forty days the interest of the public could be stimulated by a steadily increasing pressure of advertisement, but after that the town began to lose interest, sympathetic support began notably to fall off; there were of course local variations as between one town and another or one country and another, but as a general rule forty days marked the limit. So on the fortieth day the flower-bedecked cage was opened, enthusiastic spectators filled the hall, a military band played, two doctors entered the cage to measure the results of the fast, which were announced through a megaphone, and finally two young ladies appeared, blissful at having been selected for the honor, to help the hunger artist down the few steps leading to a small table on which was spread a carefully chosen invalid repast. And at this very moment the artist always turned stubborn. True, he would entrust his bony arms to the outstretched helping hands of the ladies bending over him, but stand up he would not. Why stop fasting at this particular moment, after forty days of it? He had held out for a long time, an illimitably long time; why stop now, when he was in his best fasting form, or rather, not yet quite in his best fasting form? Why should he be cheated of the fame he would get for fasting longer, for being not only the record hunger artist of all time, which presumably he was already, but for beating his own record by a performance beyond human imagination, since he felt that there were no limits to his capacity for fasting? His public pretended to admire him so much, why should it have so little patience with him; if he could endure fasting longer, why shouldn't the public endure it? Besides, he was tired, he was comfortable sitting in the straw, and now he was supposed to lift himself to his full height and go down to a meal the very thought of which gave him a nausea that only the presence of the ladies kept him from betraying, and even that with an effort. And he looked up into the eyes of the ladies who were apparently so friendly and in reality so cruel, and shook his head, which felt too heavy on its strengthless neck. But then there happened yet again what always happened. The impresario came forward, without a word—for the band made speech impossible—lifted

3. Common biblical length of time; in the New Testament, Jesus fasts for forty days in the desert and has visions of both God and the devil.

his arms in the air above the artist, as if inviting Heaven to look down upon its creature here in the straw, this suffering martyr, which indeed he was, although in quite another sense; grasped him round the emaciated waist, with exaggerated caution, so that the frail condition he was in might be appreciated; and committed him to the care of the blenching ladies, not without secretly giving him a shaking so that his legs and body tottered and swayed. The artist now submitted completely; his head lolled on his breast as if it had landed there by chance; his body was hollowed out; his legs in a spasm of self-preservation clung close to each other at the knees, yet scraped on the ground as if it were not really solid ground, as if they were only trying to find solid ground; and the whole weight of his body, a feather-weight after all, relapsed onto one of the ladies, who, looking round for help and panting a little—this post of honor was not at all what she had expected it to be—first stretched her neck as far as she could to keep her face at least free from contact with the artist, when finding this impossible, and her more fortunate companion not coming to her aid but merely holding extended on her own trembling hand the little bunch of knuckle-bones that was the artist's, to the great delight of the spectators burst into tears and had to be replaced by an attendant who had long been stationed in readiness. Then came the food, a little of which the impresario managed to get between the artist's lips, while he sat in a kind of half-fainting trance, to the accompaniment of cheerful patter designed to distract the public's attention from the artist's condition; after that, a toast was drunk to the public, supposedly prompted by a whisper from the artist in the impresario's ear; the band confirmed it with a mighty flourish, the spectators melted away, and no one had any cause to be dissatisfied with the proceedings, no one except the hunger artist himself, he only, as always.

So he lived for many years, with small regular intervals of recuperation, in visible glory, honored by the world, yet in spite of that troubled in spirit, and all the more troubled because no one would take his trouble seriously. What comfort could he possibly need? What more could he possibly wish for? And if some good-natured person, feeling sorry for him, tried to console him by pointing out that his melancholy was probably caused by fasting, it could happen, especially when he had been fasting for some time, that he reacted with an outburst of fury and to the general alarm began to shake the bars of his cage like a wild animal. Yet the impresario had a way of punishing these outbreaks which he rather enjoyed putting into operation. He would apologize publicly for the artist's behavior, which was only to be excused, he admitted, because of the irritability caused by fasting, a condition hardly to be understood by well-fed people; then by natural transition he went on to mention the artist's equally incomprehensible boast that he could fast for much longer than he was doing; he praised the high ambition, the good will, the great self-denial undoubtedly implicit in such a statement; and then quite simply countered it by bringing out photographs, which were also on sale to the public, showing the artist on the fortieth day of a fast lying in bed almost dead from exhaustion. This perversion of the truth, familiar to the artist though it was, always unnerved him afresh and proved too much for him. What was a consequence of the premature ending of his fast was here presented as the cause of it! To fight against this lack of understanding, against a whole world of non-understanding, was impossible. Time and again in good faith he stood by the bars listening to the impresario, but as soon as the photographs appeared he always let go and sank with a groan back on to his straw, and the reassured public could once more come close and gaze at him.

A few years later when the witnesses of such scenes called them to mind, they often failed to understand themselves at all. For meanwhile the aforementioned change in public interest had set in; it seemed to happen almost overnight; there may have been profound causes for it, but who was going to bother about that; at any rate the pampered hunger artist suddenly found himself deserted one fine day by the amusement seekers, who went streaming past him to other more favored attractions. For the last time the impresario hurried him over half Europe to discover whether the old interest might still survive here and there; all in vain; everywhere, as if by secret agreement, a positive revulsion from professional fasting was in evidence. Of course it could not really have sprung up so suddenly as all that, and many premonitory symptoms which had not been sufficiently remarked or suppressed during the rush and glitter of success now came retrospectively to mind, but it was now too late to take any countermeasures. Fasting would surely come into fashion again at some future date, yet that was no comfort for those living in the present. What, then, was the hunger artist to do? He had been applauded by thousands in his time and could hardly come down to showing himself in a street booth at village fairs, and as for adopting another profession, he was not only too old for that but too fanatically devoted to fasting. So he took leave of the impresario, his partner in an unparalleled career, and hired himself to a large circus; in order to spare his own feelings he avoided reading the conditions of his contract.

A large circus with its enormous traffic in replacing and recruiting men, animals and apparatus can always find a use for people at any time, even for a hunger artist, provided of course that he does not ask too much, and in this particular case anyhow it was not only the artist who was taken on but his famous and long-known name as well, indeed considering the peculiar nature of his performance, which was not impaired by advancing age, it could not be objected that here was an artist past his prime, no longer at the height of his professional skill, seeking a refuge in some quiet corner of a circus; on the contrary, the hunger artist averred that he could fast as well as ever, which was entirely credible, he even alleged that if he were allowed to fast as he liked, and this was at once promised him without more ado, he could astound the world by establishing a record never yet achieved, a statement which certainly provoked a smile among the other professionals, since it left out of account the change in public opinion, which the hunger artist in his zeal conveniently forgot.

He had not, however, actually lost his sense of the real situation and took it as a matter of course that he and his cage should be stationed, not in the middle of the ring as a main attraction, but outside, near the animal cages, on a site that was after all easily accessible. Large and gaily painted placards made a frame for the cage and announced what was to be seen inside it. When the public came thronging out in the intervals to see the animals, they could hardly avoid passing the hunger artist's cage and stopping there for a moment, perhaps they might even have stayed longer had not those pressing behind them in the narrow gangway, who did not understand why they should be held up on their way toward the excitements of the menagerie, made it impossible for anyone to stand gazing quietly for any length of time. And that was the reason why the hunger artist, who had of course been looking forward to these visiting hours as the main achievement of his life, began instead to shrink from them. At first he could hardly wait for the intervals; it was exhilarating to watch the crowds come streaming his way, until only too soon—not even the most obstinate self-deception, clung to almost consciously, could hold out against the fact—the conviction was borne in upon him that these people, most of them, to judge from their actions, again and again, without exception, were all on their way to the menagerie. And the first sight of them from the distance remained the best. For when they reached his cage he was at once deafened by the storm of shouting and abuse that arose from the two contending factions, which renewed themselves continuously, of those who wanted to stop and stare at him—he soon began to dislike them more than the others—not out of real interest but only out of obstinate self-assertiveness, and those who wanted to go straight on to the animals. When the first great rush was past, the stragglers came along, and these, whom nothing could have prevented from stopping to look at him as long as they had breath, raced past with long strides, hardly even glancing at him, in their haste to get to the menagerie in time. And all too rarely did it happen that he had a stroke of luck, when some father of a family fetched up before him with his children, pointed a finger at the hunger artist and explained at length what the phenomenon meant, telling stories of earlier years when he himself had watched similar but much more thrilling performances, and the children, still rather uncomprehending, since neither inside nor outside school had they been sufficiently prepared for this lesson—what did they care about fasting?—yet showed by the brightness of their intent eyes that new and better times might be coming. Perhaps, said the hunger artist to himself many a time, things would be a little better if his cage were set not quite so near the menagerie. That made it too easy for people to make their choice, to say nothing of what he suffered from the stench of the menagerie, the animals' restlessness by night, the carrying past of raw lumps of flesh for the beasts of prey, the roaring at feeding times, which depressed him continually. But he did not dare to lodge a complaint with the management; after all, he had the animals to thank for the troops of people who passed his cage, among whom there might always be one here and there to take an interest in him, and who could tell where they might seclude him if he called attention to his existence and thereby to the fact that, strictly speaking, he was only an impediment on the way to the menagerie.

A small impediment, to be sure, one that grew steadily less. People grew familiar with the strange idea that they could be expected, in times like these, to take an interest in a hunger artist, and with this familiarity the verdict went out against him. He might fast as much as he could, and he did so; but nothing could save him now, people passed him by. Just try to explain to anyone the art of fasting! Anyone who has no feeling for it cannot be made to understand it. The fine placards grew dirty and illegible, they were torn down; the little notice board telling the number of fast days achieved, which at first was changed carefully every day, had long stayed at the same figure, for after the first few weeks even this small task seemed pointless to the staff; and so the artist simply fasted on and on, as he had once dreamed of doing, and it was no trouble to him, just as he had always foretold, but no one counted the days, no one, not even the artist himself, knew what records he was already breaking, and his heart grew heavy. And when once in a time some leisurely passer-by stopped, made merry over the old figure on the board and spoke of swindling, that was in its way the stupidest lie ever invented by indifference and inborn malice, since it was not the hunger artist who was cheating; he was working honestly, but the world was cheating him of his reward.

Many more days went by, however, and that too came to an end. An overseer's eye fell on the cage one day and he asked the attendants why this perfectly good cage should be left standing there unused with dirty straw inside it; nobody knew, until one man, helped out by the notice board, remembered about the hunger artist. They poked into the straw with sticks and found him in it. "Are you still fasting?" asked the overseer. "When on earth do you mean to stop?" "Forgive me, everybody," whispered the hunger artist; only the overseer, who had his ear to the bars, understood him. "Of course," said the overseer, and tapped his forehead with a finger to let the attendants know what state the man was in, "we forgive you." "I always wanted you to admire my fasting," said the hunger artist. "We do admire it," said the overseer, affably. "But you shouldn't admire it," said the hunger artist. "Well, then we don't admire it," said the overseer, "but why shouldn't we admire it?" "Because I have to fast, I can't help it," said the hunger artist. "What a fellow you are," said the overseer, "and why can't you help it?" "Because," said the hunger artist, lifting his head a little and speaking, with his lips pursed, as if for a kiss, right into the overseer's ear, so that no syllable might be lost, "because I couldn't find the food I liked. If I had found it, believe me, I should have made no fuss and stuffed myself like you or anyone else." These were his last words, but in his dimming eyes remained the firm though no longer proud persuasion that he was still continuing to fast.

"Well, clear this out now!" said the overseer, and they buried the hunger artist, straw and all. Into the cage they put a young panther. Even the most insensitive felt it refreshing to see this wild creature leaping around the cage that had so long been dreary. The panther was all right. The food he liked was brought him without hesitation by the attendants; he seemed not even to miss his freedom; his noble body, furnished almost to the bursting point with all that it needed, seemed to carry freedom around with it too; somewhere in his jaws it seemed to lurk; and the joy of life streamed with such ardent passion from his throat that for the onlookers it was not easy to stand the shock of it. But they braced themselves, crowded round the cage, and did not want ever to move away.

1922, 1924

JAMAICA KINCAID
(b. 1949)

Girl

Raised in poverty by her homemaker mother and carpenter stepfather on the small Caribbean island of Antigua, Elaine Potter Richardson was sent to the United States to earn her own living at age seventeen, much like the protagonists of her first novels, *Annie John* (1985) and *Lucy* (1990). Working as an au pair and receptionist, she earned her high-school equivalency degree and studied photography at the New School for Social Research in New York and, briefly, Franconia College in New Hampshire. Returning to New York, she took the name of a character in a George Bernard Shaw play, at least in part out of resentment toward her mother, with whom she had once been very close. After a short stint as a freelance journalist, Kincaid worked as a regular contributor to the *New Yorker* from 1976 until 1995, in 1979 marrying its editor's son, composer Allen Shawn, with whom she would eventually move to Bennington, Vermont, and raise two children. "Girl," her first published story, appeared in the *New Yorker* in 1978 and was later republished in her first collection, *At the Bottom of the River* (1983). Subsequent novels include *The Autobiography of My Mother* (1996), paradoxically the least autobiographical of her books; *Mr. Potter* (2002), a fictionalized account of her efforts to understand the biological father she never knew; and *See Now Then* (2013). Kincaid's equally impressive nonfiction includes *My Brother* (1997), a memoir inspired by her youngest brother's death from AIDS; *A Small Place* (1988), an essay exploring the profound economic and psychological impact of Antigua's dependence on tourism; and *Among Flowers: A Walk in the Himalayas* (2005). Divorced in 2002, Kincaid is currently Professor of African and African American Studies in Residence at Harvard.

Wash the white clothes on Monday and put them on the stone heap; wash the color clothes on Tuesday and put them on the clothesline to dry; don't walk barehead in the hot sun; cook pumpkin fritters in very hot sweet oil; soak your little cloths right after you take them off; when buying cotton to make yourself a nice blouse, be sure that it doesn't have gum on it, because that way it won't hold up well after a wash; soak salt fish overnight before you cook it; is it true that you sing benna[1] in Sunday school?; always eat your food in such a way that it won't turn someone else's stomach; on Sundays try to walk like a lady and not like the slut you are so bent on becoming; don't sing benna in Sunday school; you mustn't speak to wharf-rat boys, not even to give directions; don't eat fruits on the street—flies will follow you; *but I don't sing benna on Sundays at all and never in Sunday school*; this is how to sew on a button; this is how to make a buttonhole for the button you have just sewed on; this is how to hem a dress when you see the hem coming down and so to prevent

---

1. Caribbean folk-music style.

yourself from looking like the slut I know you are so bent on becoming; this is how you iron your father's khaki shirt so that it doesn't have a crease; this is how you iron your father's khaki pants so that they don't have a crease; this is how you grow okra—far from the house, because okra tree harbors red ants; when you are growing dasheen, make sure it gets plenty of water or else it makes your throat itch when you are eating it; this is how you sweep a corner; this is how you sweep a whole house; this is how you sweep a yard; this is how you smile to someone you don't like too much; this is how you smile to someone you don't like at all; this is how you smile to someone you like completely; this is how you set a table for tea; this is how you set a table for dinner; this is how you set a table for dinner with an important guest; this is how you set a table for lunch; this is how you set a table for breakfast; this is how to behave in the presence of men who don't know you very well, and this way they won't recognize immediately the slut I have warned you against becoming; be sure to wash every day, even if it is with your own spit; don't squat down to play marbles—you are not a boy, you know; don't pick people's flowers—you might catch something; don't throw stones at blackbirds, because it might not be a blackbird at all; this is how to make a bread pudding; this is how to make doukona;[2] this is how to make pepper pot; this is how to make a good medicine for a cold; this is how to make a good medicine to throw away a child before it even becomes a child; this is how to catch a fish; this is how to throw back a fish you don't like, and that way something bad won't fall on you; this is how to bully a man; this is how a man bullies you; this is how to love a man, and if this doesn't work there are other ways, and if they don't work don't feel too bad about giving up; this is how to spit up in the air if you feel like it, and this is how to move quick so that it doesn't fall on you; this is how to make ends meet; always squeeze bread to make sure it's fresh; *but what if the baker won't let me feel the bread?*; you mean to say that after all you are really going to be the kind of woman who the baker won't let near the bread?

1978, 1983

BOBBIE ANN MASON

(b. 1940)

Shiloh

Bobbie Ann Mason grew up on her parents' dairy farm in western Kentucky, the region where many of her stories are set. She received a BA from the University of Kentucky, an MA from the State University of New York at Binghamton, and a PhD in English from the University of Connecticut. In addition to writing a dissertation on the work of Vladimir Nabokov, later published as a book (1974), and *The Girl Sleuth: A Feminist Guide* (1975), Mason began to publish the short stories eventually collected in the highly acclaimed *Shiloh and Other Stories* (1982), winner of the PEN Hemingway Award. That book, combined with her first

---

2. Spicy pudding, often made from plantain and wrapped in a plantain or banana leaf.

novel, *In Country* (1985; filmed 1989), inspired one reviewer to dub her writing "Shopping Mall Realism." Mason has continued to write novels, including *Feather Crowns* (1993), *An Atomic Romance* (2005), *The Girl in the Blue Beret* (2011), and *Dear Ann* (2020), as well as nonfiction ranging from a biography of Elvis Presley (2002) to *Clear Springs: A Memoir* (1999), a nominee for the Pulitzer Prize. She is best known and most highly praised, however, for short-story collections like *Zigzagging down a Wild Trail* (2001) and *Nancy Culpepper* (2006). Novelist Ann Tyler describes Mason as "a full-fledged master of the short story," while fiction writer Lorrie Moore suggests that her "strongest form may be neither the novel nor the story, but the story *collection*."

L eroy Moffitt's wife, Norma Jean, is working on her pectorals. She lifts three-pound dumbbells to warm up, then progresses to a twenty-pound barbell. Standing with her legs apart, she reminds Leroy of Wonder Woman.

"I'd give anything if I could just get these muscles to where they're real hard," says Norma Jean. "Feel this arm. It's not as hard as the other one."

"That's cause you're right-handed," says Leroy, dodging as she swings the barbell in an arc.

"Do you think so?"

5   "Sure."

Leroy is a truck driver. He injured his leg in a highway accident four months ago, and his physical therapy, which involves weights and a pulley, prompted Norma Jean to try building herself up. Now she is attending a body-building class. Leroy has been collecting temporary disability since his tractor-trailer jack-knifed in Missouri, badly twisting his left leg in its socket. He has a steel pin in his hip. He will probably not be able to drive his rig again. It sits in the backyard, like a gigantic bird that has flown home to roost. Leroy has been home in Kentucky for three months, and his leg is almost healed, but the accident frightened him and he does not want to drive any more long hauls. He is not sure what to do next. In the meantime, he makes things from craft kits. He started by building a miniature log cabin from notched Popsicle sticks. He varnished it and placed it on the TV set, where it remains. It reminds him of a rustic Nativity scene. Then he tried string art (sailing ships on black velvet), a macramé owl kit, a snap-together B-17 Flying Fortress,[1] and a lamp made out of a model truck, with a light fixture screwed in the top of the cab. At first the kits were diversions, something to kill time, but now he is thinking about building a full-scale log house from a kit. It would be considerably cheaper than building a regular house, and besides, Leroy has grown to appreciate how things are put together. He has begun to realize that in all the years he was on the road he never took time to examine anything. He was always flying past scenery.

"They won't let you build a log cabin in any of the new subdivisions," Norma Jean tells him.

"They will if I tell them it's for you," he says, teasing her. Ever since they were married, he has promised Norma Jean he would build her a new home one day.

---

1. American World War II bomber.

They have always rented, and the house they live in is small and nondescript. It does not even feel like a home, Leroy realizes now.

Norma Jean works at the Rexall drugstore, and she has acquired an amazing amount of information about cosmetics. When she explains to Leroy the three stages of complexion care, involving creams, toners, and moisturizers, he thinks happily of other petroleum products—axle grease, diesel fuel. This is a connection between him and Norma Jean. Since he has been home, he has felt unusually tender about his wife and guilty over his long absences. But he can't tell what she feels about him. Norma Jean has never complained about his traveling; she has never made hurt remarks, like calling his truck a "widow-maker." He is reasonably certain she has been faithful to him, but he wishes she would celebrate his permanent homecoming more happily. Norma Jean is often startled to find Leroy at home, and he thinks she seems a little disappointed about it. Perhaps he reminds her too much of the early days of their marriage, before he went on the road. They had a child who died as an infant, years ago. They never speak about their memories of Randy, which have almost faded, but now that Leroy is home all the time, they sometimes feel awkward around each other, and Leroy wonders if one of them should mention the child. He has the feeling that they are waking up out of a dream together—that they must create a new marriage, start afresh. They are lucky they are still married. Leroy has read that for most people losing a child destroys the marriage—or else he heard this on *Donahue*.[2] He can't always remember where he learns things anymore.

At Christmas, Leroy bought an electric organ for Norma Jean. She used to   10
play the piano when she was in high school. "It don't leave you," she told him once. "It's like riding a bicycle."

The new instrument had so many keys and buttons that she was bewildered by it at first. She touched the keys tentatively, pushed some buttons, then pecked out "Chopsticks." It came out in an amplified fox-trot rhythm, with marimba sounds.

"It's an orchestra!" she cried.

The organ had a pecan-look finish and eighteen preset chords, with optional flute, violin, trumpet, clarinet, and banjo accompaniments. Norma Jean mastered the organ almost immediately. At first she played Christmas songs. Then she bought *The Sixties Songbook* and learned every tune in it, adding variations to each with the rows of brightly colored buttons.

"I didn't like these old songs back then," she said. "But I have this crazy feeling I missed something."

"You didn't miss a thing," said Leroy.   15

Leroy likes to lie on the couch and smoke a joint and listen to Norma Jean play "Can't Take My Eyes Off You" and "I'll Be Back."[3] He is back again. After fifteen years on the road, he is finally settling down with the woman he loves. She is still pretty. Her skin is flawless. Her frosted curls resemble pencil trimmings.

---

2. Long-running American talk show (1970–96) hosted by journalist Phil Donahue.
3. Hit songs of the 1960s.

Now that Leroy has come home to stay, he notices how much the town has changed. Subdivisions are spreading across western Kentucky like an oil slick. The sign at the edge of town says "Pop: 11,500"—only seven hundred more than it said twenty years before. Leroy can't figure out who is living in all the new houses. The farmers who used to gather around the courthouse square on Saturday afternoons to play checkers and spit tobacco juice have gone. It has been years since Leroy has thought about the farmers, and they have disappeared without his noticing.

Leroy meets a kid named Stevie Hamilton in the parking lot at the new shopping center. While they pretend to be strangers meeting over a stalled car, Stevie tosses an ounce of marijuana under the front seat of Leroy's car. Stevie is wearing orange jogging shoes and a T-shirt that says CHATTAHOOCHEE SUPER-RAT. His father is a prominent doctor who lives in one of the expensive subdivisions in a new white-columned brick house that looks like a funeral parlor. In the phone book under his name there is a separate number, with the listing "Teenagers."

"Where do you get this stuff?" asks Leroy. "From your pappy?"

20   "That's for me to know and you to find out," Stevie says. He is slit-eyed and skinny.

"What else you got?"

"What you interested in?"

"Nothing special. Just wondered."

Leroy used to take speed on the road. Now he has to go slowly. He needs to be mellow. He leans back against the car and says, "I'm aiming to build me a log house, soon as I get time. My wife, though, I don't think she likes the idea."

25   "Well, let me know when you want me again," Stevie says. He has a cigarette in his cupped palm, as though sheltering it from the wind. He takes a long drag, then stomps it on the asphalt and slouches away.

Stevie's father was two years ahead of Leroy in high school. Leroy is thirty-four. He married Norma Jean when they were both eighteen, and their child Randy was born a few months later, but he died at the age of four months and three days. He would be about Stevie's age now. Norma Jean and Leroy were at the drive-in, watching a double feature (*Dr. Strangelove* and *Lover Come Back*),[4] and the baby was sleeping in the back seat. When the first movie ended, the baby was dead. It was the sudden infant death syndrome. Leroy remembers handing Randy to a nurse at the emergency room, as though he were offering her a large doll as a present. A dead baby feels like a sack of flour. "It just happens sometimes," said the doctor, in what Leroy always recalls as a nonchalant tone. Leroy can hardly remember the child anymore, but he still sees vividly a scene from *Dr. Strangelove* in which the President of the United States was talking in a folksy voice on the hot line to the Soviet premier about the bomber accidentally headed toward Russia. He was in the War Room, and the world map was lit up. Leroy remembers Norma Jean catatonically beside him in the hospital and himself thinking: Who is this strange girl? He had forgotten who

---

4. A 1963 satire on nuclear war and a 1961 Rock Hudson–Doris Day romantic comedy satirizing the advertising business, respectively.

she was. Now scientists are saying that crib death is caused by a virus. Nobody knows anything, Leroy thinks. The answers are always changing.

When Leroy gets home from the shopping center, Norma Jean's mother, Mabel Beasley, is there. Until this year, Leroy has not realized how much time she spends with Norma Jean. When she visits, she inspects the closets and then the plants, informing Norma Jean when a plant is droopy or yellow. Mabel calls the plants "flowers," although there are never any blooms. She always notices if Norma Jean's laundry is piling up. Mabel is a short, overweight woman whose tight, brown-dyed curls look more like a wig than the actual wig she sometimes wears. Today she has brought Norma Jean an off-white dust ruffle she made for the bed; Mabel works in a custom-upholstery shop.

"This is the tenth one I made this year," Mabel says. "I got started and couldn't stop."

"It's real pretty," says Norma Jean.

"Now we can hide things under the bed," says Leroy, who gets along with his   30
mother-in-law primarily by joking with her. Mabel has never really forgiven him for disgracing her by getting Norma Jean pregnant. When the baby died, she said that fate was mocking her.

"What's that thing?" Mabel says to Leroy in a loud voice, pointing to a tangle of yarn on a piece of canvas.

Leroy holds it up for Mabel to see. "It's my needlepoint," he explains. "This is a *Star Trek* pillow cover."

"That's what a woman would do," says Mabel. "Great day in the morning!"

"All the big football players on TV do it," he says.

"Why, Leroy, you're always trying to fool me. I don't believe you for one min-   35
ute. You don't know what to do with yourself—that's the whole trouble. Sewing!"

"I'm aiming to build us a log house," says Leroy. "Soon as my plans come."

"Like *heck* you are," says Norma Jean. She takes Leroy's needlepoint and shoves it into a drawer. "You have to find a job first. Nobody can afford to build now anyway."

Mabel straightens her girdle and says, "I still think before you get tied down y'all ought to take a little run to Shiloh."

"One of these days, Mama," Norma Jean says impatiently.

Mabel is talking about Shiloh, Tennessee. For the past few years, she has   40
been urging Leroy and Norma Jean to visit the Civil War battleground there.[5]
Mabel went there on her honeymoon—the only real trip she ever took. Her husband died of a perforated ulcer when Norma Jean was ten, but Mabel, who was accepted into the United Daughters of the Confederacy in 1975, is still preoccupied with going back to Shiloh.

"I've been to kingdom come and back in that truck out yonder," Leroy says to Mabel, "but we never yet set foot in that battleground. Ain't that something? How did I miss it?"

5. Where, in April 1862, more than twenty-three thousand troops of the North and South, one-quarter of those who fought there, died. This was the first real indication of how bitter and bloody the war was to be. When Union reinforcements arrived, General Ulysses S. Grant drove the Confederate forces, who had gained an initial victory by a surprise attack, back to their base in Corinth, Mississippi.

"It's not even that far," Mabel says.

After Mabel leaves, Norma Jean reads to Leroy from a list she has made. "Thing you could do," she announces. "You could get a job as a guard at Union Carbide, where they'd let you set on a stool. You could get on at the lumberyard. You could do a little carpenter work, if you want to build so bad. You could—"

"I can't do something where I'd have to stand up all day."

45 "You ought to try standing up all day behind a cosmetics counter. It's amazing that I have strong feet, coming from two parents that never had strong feet at all." At the moment Norma Jean is holding on to the kitchen counter, raising her knees one at a time as she talks. She is wearing two-pound ankle weights.

"Don't worry," says Leroy. "I'll do something."

"You could truck calves to slaughter for somebody. You wouldn't have to drive any big old truck for that."

"I'm going to build you this house," says Leroy. "I want to make you a real home."

"I don't want to live in any log cabin."

50 "It's not a cabin. It's a house."

"I don't care. It looks like a cabin."

"You and me together could lift those logs. It's just like lifting weights."

Norma Jean doesn't answer. Under her breath, she is counting. Now she is marching through the kitchen. She is doing goose steps.

Before his accident, when Leroy came home he used to stay in the house with Norma Jean, watching TV in bed and playing cards. She would cook fried chicken, picnic ham, chocolate pie—all his favorites. Now he is home alone much of the time. In the mornings, Norma Jean disappears, leaving a cooling place in the bed. She eats a cereal called Body Buddies, and she leaves the bowl on the table, with soggy tan balls floating in a milk puddle. He sees things about Norma Jean that he never realized before. When she chops onions, she stares off into a corner, as if she can't bear to look. She puts on her house slippers almost precisely at nine o'clock every evening and nudges her jogging shoes under the couch. She saves bread heels for the birds. Leroy watches the birds at the feeder. He notices the peculiar way goldfinches fly past the window. They close their wings, then fall, then spread their wings to catch and lift themselves. He wonders if they close their eyes when they fall. Norma Jean closes her eyes when they are in bed. She wants the lights turned out. Even then, he is sure she closes her eyes.

55 He goes for long drives around town. He tends to drive a car rather carelessly. Power steering and an automatic shift make a car feel so small and inconsequential that his body is hardly involved in the driving process. His injured leg stretches out comfortably. Once or twice he has almost hit something, but even the prospect of an accident seems minor in a car. He cruises the new subdivisions, feeling like a criminal rehearsing for a robbery. Norma Jean is probably right about a log house being inappropriate here in the new subdivisions. All the houses look grand and complicated. They depress him.

One day when Leroy comes home from a drive he finds Norma Jean in tears. She is in the kitchen making a potato and mushroom-soup casserole, with grated-cheese topping. She is crying because her mother caught her smoking.

"I didn't hear her coming. I was standing here puffing away pretty as you please," Norma Jean says, wiping her eyes.

"I knew it would happen sooner or later," says Leroy, putting his arm around her.

"She don't know the meaning of the word 'knock,'" says Norma Jean. "It's a wonder she hadn't caught me years ago."

"Think of it this way," Leroy says. "What if she caught me with a joint?" 60

"You better not let her!" Norma Jean shrieks. "I'm warning you, Leroy Moffitt!"

"I'm just kidding. Here, play me a tune. That'll help you relax."

Norma Jean puts the casserole in the oven and sets the timer. Then she plays a ragtime tune, with horns and banjo, as Leroy lights up a joint and lies on the couch, laughing to himself about Mabel's catching him at it. He thinks of Stevie Hamilton—a doctor's son pushing grass. Everything is funny. The whole town seems crazy and small. He is reminded of Virgil Mathis, a boastful policeman Leroy used to shoot pool with. Virgil recently led a drug bust in a back room at a bowling alley, where he seized ten thousand dollars' worth of marijuana. The newspaper had a picture of him holding up the bags of grass and grinning widely. Right now, Leroy can imagine Virgil breaking down the door and arresting him with a lungful of smoke. Virgil would probably have been alerted to the scene because of all the racket Norma Jean is making. Now she sounds like a hard-rock band. Norma Jean is terrific. When she switches to a Latin-rhythm version of "Sunshine Superman," Leroy hums along. Norma Jean's foot goes up and down, up and down.

"Well, what do you think?" Leroy says, when Norma Jean pauses to search through her music.

"What do I think about what?" 65

His mind has gone blank. Then he says, "I'll sell my rig and build us a house." That wasn't what he wanted to say. He wanted to know what she thought— what she *really* thought—about them.

"Don't start in on that again," says Norma Jean. She begins playing "Who'll Be the Next in Line?"

Leroy used to tell hitchhikers his whole life story—about his travels, his hometown, the baby. He would end with a question: "Well, what do you think?" It was just a rhetorical question. In time, he had the feeling that he'd been telling the same story over and over to the same hitchhikers. He quit talking to hitchhikers when he realized how his voice sounded—whining and self-pitying, like some teenage-tragedy song. Now Leroy has the sudden impulse to tell Norma Jean about himself, as if he had just met her. They have known each other so long they have forgotten a lot about each other. They could become reacquainted. But when the oven timer goes off and she runs to the kitchen, he forgets why he wants to do this.

The next day, Mabel drops by. It is Saturday and Norma Jean is cleaning. Leroy is studying the plans of his log house, which have finally come in the mail. He has them spread out on the table—big sheets of stiff blue paper, with diagrams and numbers printed in white. While Norma Jean runs the vacuum, Mabel drinks coffee. She sets her coffee cup on a blueprint.

70 "I'm just waiting for time to pass," she says to Leroy, drumming her fingers on the table.

As soon as Norma Jean switches off the vacuum, Mabel says in a loud voice, "Did you hear about the datsun dog that killed the baby?"

Norma Jean says, "The word is 'dachshund.'"

"They put the dog on trial. It chewed the baby's legs off. The mother was in the next room all the time." She raises her voice. "They thought it was neglect."

Norma Jean is holding her ears. Leroy manages to open the refrigerator and get some Diet Pepsi to offer Mabel. Mabel still has some coffee and she waves away the Pepsi.

75 "Datsuns are like that," Mabel says. "They're jealous dogs. They'll tear a place to pieces if you don't keep an eye on them."

"You better watch out what you're saying, Mabel," says Leroy.

"Well, facts is facts."

Leroy looks out the window at his rig. It is like a huge piece of furniture gathering dust in the backyard. Pretty soon it will be an antique. He hears the vacuum cleaner. Norma Jean seems to be cleaning the living room rug again.

Later, she says to Leroy, "She just said that about the baby because she caught me smoking. She's trying to pay me back."

80 "What are you talking about?" Leroy says, nervously shuffling blueprints.

"You know good and well," Norma Jean says. She is sitting in a kitchen chair with her feet up and her arms wrapped around her knees. She looks small and helpless. She says, "The very idea, her bringing up a subject like that! Saying it was neglect."

"She didn't mean that," Leroy says.

"She might not have *thought* she meant it. She always says things like that. You don't know how she goes on."

"But she didn't really mean it. She was just talking."

85 Leroy opens a king-sized bottle of beer and pours it into two glasses, dividing it carefully. He hands a glass to Norma Jean and she takes it from him mechanically. For a long time, they sit by the kitchen window watching the birds at the feeder.

Something is happening. Norma Jean is going to night school. She has graduated from her six-week body-building course and now she is taking an adult-education course in composition at Paducah Community College. She spends her evenings outlining paragraphs.

"First you have a topic sentence," she explains to Leroy. "Then you divide it up. Your secondary topic has to be connected to your primary topic."

To Leroy, this sounds intimidating. "I never was any good in English," he says.

"It makes a lot of sense."

90 "What are you doing this for, anyhow?"

She shrugs. "It's something to do." She stands up and lifts her dumbbells a few times.

"Driving a rig, nobody cared about my English."

"I'm not criticizing your English."

Norma Jean used to say, "If I lose ten minutes' sleep, I just drag all day." Now she stays up late, writing compositions. She got a B on her first paper—a how-to theme on soup-based casseroles. Recently Norma Jean has been cooking unusual foods—tacos, lasagna, Bombay chicken. She doesn't play the organ anymore, though her second paper was called "Why Music Is Important to Me." She sits at the kitchen table, concentrating on her outlines, while Leroy plays with his log house plans, practicing with a set of Lincoln Logs. The thought of getting a truckload of notched, numbered logs scares him, and he wants to be prepared. As he and Norma Jean work together at the kitchen table, Leroy has the hopeful thought that they are sharing something, but he knows he is a fool to think this. Norma Jean is miles away. He knows he is going to lose her. Like Mabel, he is just waiting for time to pass.

One day, Mabel is there before Norma Jean gets home from work, and Leroy 95 finds himself confiding in her. Mabel, he realizes, must know Norma Jean better than he does.

"I don't know what's got into that girl," Mabel says. "She used to go to bed with the chickens. Now you say she's up all hours. Plus her a-smoking. I like to died."

"I want to make her this beautiful home," Leroy says, indicating the Lincoln Logs. "I don't think she even wants it. Maybe she was happier with me gone."

"She don't know what to make of you, coming home like this."

"Is that it?"

Mabel takes the roof off his Lincoln Log cabin. "You couldn't get *me* in a log 100 cabin," she says. "I was raised in one. It's no picnic, let me tell you."

"They're different now," says Leroy.

"I tell you what," Mabel says, smiling oddly at Leroy.

"What?"

"Take her on down to Shiloh. Y'all need to get out together, stir a little. Her brain's all balled up over them books."

Leroy can see traces of Norma Jean's features in her mother's face. Mabel's 105 face has the texture of crinkled cotton, but suddenly she looks pretty. It occurs to Leroy that Mabel has been hinting all along that she wants them to take her with them to Shiloh.

"Let's all go to Shiloh," he says. "You and me and her. Come Sunday."

Mabel throws up her hands in protest. "Oh, no, not me. Young folks want to be by theirselves."

When Norma Jean comes in with groceries, Leroy says excitedly, "Your mama here's been dying to go to Shiloh for thirty-five years. It's about time we went, don't you think?"

"I'm not going to butt in on anybody's second honeymoon," Mabel says.

"Who's going on a honeymoon, for Christ's sake?" Norma Jean says loudly. 110

"I never raised no daughter of mine to talk that-a-way," Mabel says.

"You ain't seen nothing yet," says Norma Jean. She starts putting away boxes and cans, slamming cabinet doors.

"There's a log cabin at Shiloh." Mabel says, "It was there during the battle. There's bullet holes in it."

"When are you going to *shut up* about Shiloh, Mama?" asks Norma Jean.

"I always thought Shiloh was the prettiest place, so full of history," Mabel 115 goes on. "I just hoped y'all could see it once before I die, so you could tell me about it." Later, she whispers to Leroy, "You do what I said. A little change is what she needs."

"Your name means 'the king,'" Norma Jean says to Leroy that evening. He is trying to get her to go to Shiloh, and she is reading a book about another century.

"Well, I reckon I ought to be right proud."

"I guess so."

"Am I still king around here?"

120   Norma Jean flexes her biceps and feels them for hardness. "I'm not fooling around with anybody, if that's what you mean," she says.

"Would you tell me if you were?"

"I don't know."

"What does *your* name mean?"

"It was Marilyn Monroe's real name."

125   "No kidding!"

"Norma comes from the Normans. They were invaders," she says. She closes her book and looks hard at Leroy. "I'll go to Shiloh with you if you'll stop staring at me."

On Sunday, Norma Jean packs a picnic and they go to Shiloh. To Leroy's relief, Mabel says she does not want to come with them. Norma Jean drives, and Leroy, sitting beside her, feels like some boring hitchhiker she has picked up. He tries some conversation, but she answers him in monosyllables. At Shiloh, she drives aimlessly through the park, past bluffs and trails and steep ravines. Shiloh is an immense place, and Leroy cannot see it as a battleground. It is not what he expected. He thought it would look like a golf course. Monuments are everywhere, showing through the thick clusters of trees. Norma Jean passes the log cabin Mabel mentioned. It is surrounded by tourists looking for bullet holes.

"That's not the kind of log house I've got in mind," says Leroy apologetically.

"I know *that*."

130   "This is a pretty place. Your mama was right."

"It's O.K.," says Norma Jean. "Well, we've seen it. I hope she's satisfied."

They burst out laughing together.

At the park museum, a movie on Shiloh is shown every half hour, but they decide that they don't want to see it. They buy a souvenir Confederate flag for Mabel, and then they find a picnic spot near the cemetery. Norma Jean has brought a picnic cooler, with pimiento sandwiches, soft drinks, and Yodels. Leroy eats a sandwich and then smokes a joint, hiding it behind the picnic cooler. Norma Jean has quit smoking altogether. She is picking cake crumbs from the cellophane wrapper, like a fussy bird.

Leroy says, "So the boys in gray ended up in Corinth. The Union soldiers zapped 'em finally. April 7, 1862."

135   They both know that he doesn't know any history. He is just talking about some of the historical plaques they have read. He feels awkward, like a boy on a date with an older girl. They are still just making conversation.

"Corinth is where Mama eloped to," says Norma Jean.

They sit in silence and stare at the cemetery for the Union dead and, beyond, at a tall cluster of trees. Campers are parked nearby, bumper to bumper, and small children in bright clothing are cavorting and squealing. Norma Jean wads up the cake wrapper and squeezes it tightly in her hand. Without looking at Leroy, she says, "I want to leave you."

Leroy takes a bottle of Coke out of the cooler and flips off the cap. He holds the bottle poised near his mouth but cannot remember to take a drink. Finally he says, "No, you don't."

"Yes, I do."

"I won't let you." 140

"You can't stop me."

"Don't do me that way."

Leroy knows Norma Jean will have her own way. "Didn't I promise to be home from now on?" he says.

"In some ways, a woman prefers a man who wanders," says Norma Jean. "That sounds crazy, I know."

"You're not crazy." 145

Leroy remembers to drink from his Coke. Then he says, "Yes, you *are* crazy. You and me could start all over again. Right back at the beginning."

"We *have* started all over again," says Norma Jean. "And this is how it turned out."

"What did I do wrong?"

"Nothing."

"Is this one of those women's lib things?" Leroy asks. 150

"Don't be funny."

The cemetery, a green slope dotted with white markers, looks like a subdivision site. Leroy is trying to comprehend that his marriage is breaking up, but for some reason he is wondering about white slabs in a graveyard.

"Everything was fine till Mama caught me smoking," says Norma Jean, standing up. "That set something off."

"What are you talking about?"

"She won't leave me alone—*you* won't leave me alone." Norma Jean seems to 155 be crying, but she is looking away from him. "I feel eighteen again. I can't face that all over again." She starts walking away. "No, it *wasn't* fine. I don't know what I'm saying. Forget it."

Leroy takes a lungful of smoke and closes his eyes as Norma Jean's words sink in. He tries to focus on the fact that thirty-five hundred soldiers died on the grounds around him. He can only think of that war as a board game with plastic soldiers. Leroy almost smiles, as he compares the Confederates' daring attack on the Union camps and Virgil Mathis's raid on the bowling alley. General Grant, drunk and furious, shoved the Southerners back to Corinth, where Mabel and Jet Beasley were married years later, when Mabel was still thin and good-looking. The next day, Mabel and Jet visited the battleground, and then Norma Jean was born, and then she married Leroy and they had a baby, which they lost, and now Leroy and Norma Jean are here at the same battleground. Leroy knows he is leaving out a lot. He is leaving out the insides of history. History was always just names and dates to him. It occurs to him that building a house out of logs is similarly empty—too simple. And the real inner workings of a marriage, like most of history, have escaped him. Now he sees that building a log house is the dumbest idea he could have had. It was clumsy of him to think Norma Jean would want a log house. It was a crazy idea. He'll have to think of something else, quickly. He will wad the blueprints into tight balls and fling them into the lake. Then he'll get moving again. He opens his eyes. Norma Jean has moved away and is walking through the cemetery, following a serpentine brick path.

Leroy gets up to follow his wife, but his good leg is asleep and his bad leg still hurts him. Norma Jean is far away, walking rapidly toward the bluff by the river, and he tries to hobble toward her. Some children run past him, screaming noisily. Norma Jean has reached the bluff, and she is looking out over the Tennessee River. Now she turns toward Leroy and waves her arms. Is she beckoning to him? She seems to be doing an exercise for her chest muscles. The sky is unusually pale—the color of the dust ruffle Mabel made for their bed.

1980, 1982

GUY DE MAUPASSANT
(1850–93)
The Jewelry[1]

Born Henri René Albert in Normandy, France, Guy de Maupassant was expelled at sixteen from a Rouen seminary and finished his education at a public high school. After serving in the Franco-Prussian War, he worked as a government clerk in Paris for ten years. A protégé of novelist Gustave Flaubert, Maupassant published during the 1880s some three hundred stories, half a dozen novels, and plays. The short stories, which appeared regularly in popular periodicals, sampled military and peasant life, the decadent world of politics and journalism, prostitution, the supernatural, and the hypocrisies of solid citizens; with Anton Chekhov, Maupassant may be said to have created the modern short story. His life ended somewhat like one of his own stories: He died of syphilis in an asylum. His novels include *A Life* (1883), *Handsome Friend* (1885), and *Pierre et Jean* (1888).

H aving met the girl one evening, at the house of the office-superintendent, M. Lantin became enveloped in love as in a net.

She was the daughter of a country-tutor, who had been dead for several years. Afterward she had come to Paris with her mother, who made regular visits to several bourgeois families of the neighborhood, in hopes of being able to get her daughter married. They were poor and respectable, quiet and gentle. The young girl seemed to be the very ideal of that pure good woman to whom every young man dreams of entrusting his future. Her modest beauty had a charm of angelic shyness; and the slight smile that always dwelt about her lips seemed a reflection of her heart.

Everybody sang her praises; all who knew her kept saying: "The man who gets her will be lucky. No one could find a nicer girl than that."

---

1. Translated from the French by Lafcadio Hearn.

M. Lantin, who was then chief clerk in the office of the Minister of the Interior, with a salary of 3,500 francs a year,[2] demanded her hand, and married her.

He was unutterably happy with her. She ruled his home with an economy so 5 adroit that they really seemed to live in luxury. It would be impossible to conceive of any attentions, tendernesses, playful caresses which she did not lavish upon her husband; and such was the charm of her person that, six years after he married her, he loved her even more than he did the first day.

There were only two points upon which he ever found fault with her—her love of the theater, and her passion for false jewelry.

Her lady-friends (she was acquainted with the wives of several small office holders) were always bringing her tickets for the theaters; whenever there was a performance that made a sensation, she always had her *loge* secured, even for first performances; and she would drag her husband with her to all these entertainments, which used to tire him horribly after his day's work. So at last he begged her to go to the theater with some lady-acquaintances who would consent to see her home afterward. She refused for quite a while—thinking it would not look very well to go out thus unaccompanied by her husband. But finally she yielded, just to please him; and he felt infinitely grateful to her therefore.

Now this passion for the theater at last evoked in her the desire of dress. It was true that her toilette remained simple, always in good taste, but modest; and her sweet grace, her irresistible grace, ever smiling and shy, seemed to take fresh charm from the simplicity of her robes. But she got into the habit of suspending in her pretty ears two big cut pebbles, fashioned in imitation of diamonds; and she wore necklaces of false pearls, bracelets of false gold, and haircombs studded with paste-imitations of precious stones.

Her husband, who felt shocked by this love of tinsel and show, would often say—"My dear, when one has not the means to afford real jewelry, one should appear adorned with one's natural beauty and grace only—and these gifts are the rarest of jewels."

But she would smile sweetly and answer: "What does it matter? I like those 10 things—that is my little whim. I know you are right; but one can't make oneself over again. I've always loved jewelry so much!"

And then she would roll the pearls of the necklaces between her fingers, and make the facets of the cut crystals flash in the light, repeating: "Now look at them—see how well the work is done. You would swear it was real jewelry."

He would then smile in his turn, and declare to her: "You have the tastes of a regular Gypsy."

Sometimes, in the evening, when they were having a chat by the fire, she would rise and fetch the morocco box in which she kept her "stock" (as M. Lantin called it)—would put it on the tea-table, and begin to examine the false jewelry with passionate delight, as if she experienced some secret and mysterious sensations of pleasure in their contemplation; and she would insist on putting one of the necklaces round her husband's neck, and laugh till she couldn't laugh any more, crying out: "Oh! how funny you look!" Then she would rush into his arms, and kiss him furiously.

2. Midlevel functionary's wage, perhaps about $40,000 to $50,000 today.

One winter's night, after she had been to the Opera, she came home chilled through, and trembling. Next day she had a bad cough. Eight days after that, she died of pneumonia.

15 Lantin was very nearly following her into the tomb. His despair was so frightful that in one single month his hair turned white. He wept from morning till night, feeling his heart torn by inexpressible suffering—ever haunted by the memory of her, by the smile, by the voice, by all the charm of the dead woman.

Time did not assuage his grief. Often during office hours his fellow-clerks went off to a corner to chat about this or that topic of the day—his cheeks might have been seen to swell up all of a sudden, his nose wrinkle, his eyes fill with water—he would pull a frightful face, and begin to sob.

He had kept his dead companion's room just in the order she had left it, and he used to lock himself up in it every evening to think about her—all the furniture, and even all her dresses, remained in the same place they had been on the last day of her life.

But life became hard for him. His salary, which, in his wife's hands, had amply sufficed for all household needs, now proved scarcely sufficient to supply his own few wants. And he asked himself in astonishment how she had managed always to furnish him with excellent wines and with delicate eating which he could not now afford at all with his scanty means.

He got a little into debt, like men obliged to live by their wits. At last one morning that he happened to find himself without a cent in his pocket, and a whole week to wait before he could draw his monthly salary, he thought of selling something; and almost immediately it occurred to him to sell his wife's "stock"—for he had always borne a secret grudge against the flash-jewelry that used to annoy him so much in former days. The mere sight of it, day after day, somewhat spoiled the sad pleasure of thinking of his darling.

20 He tried a long time to make a choice among the heap of trinkets she had left behind her—for up to the very last day of her life she had kept obstinately buying them, bringing home some new thing almost every night—and finally he resolved to take the big pearl necklace which she used to like the best of all, and which he thought ought certainly to be worth six or eight francs, as it was really very nicely mounted for an imitation necklace.

He put it in his pocket, and walked toward the office, following the boulevards, and looking for some jewelry-store on the way, where he could enter with confidence.

Finally he saw a place and went in; feeling a little ashamed of thus exposing his misery, and of trying to sell such a trifling object.

"Sir," he said to the jeweler, "please tell me what this is worth."

The jeweler took the necklace, examined it, weighed it, took up a magnifying glass, called his clerk, talked to him in whispers, put down the necklace on the counter, and drew back a little bit to judge of its effect at a distance.

25 M. Lantin, feeling very much embarrassed by all these ceremonies, opened his mouth and began to declare—"Oh! I know it can't be worth much".... when the jeweler interrupted him saying:

"Well, sir, that is worth between twelve and fifteen thousand francs; but I cannot buy it unless you can let me know exactly how you came by it."

The widower's eyes opened enormously, and he stood gaping—unable to understand. Then after a while he stammered out: "You said? . . . Are you sure?" The jeweler, misconstruing the cause of this astonishment, replied in a dry tone—"Go elsewhere if you like, and see if you can get any more for it. The very most I would give for it is fifteen thousand. Come back and see me again, if you can't do better."

M. Lantin, feeling perfectly idiotic, took his necklace and departed; obeying a confused desire to find himself alone and to get a chance to think.

But the moment he found himself in the street again, he began to laugh, and he muttered to himself: "The fool!—oh! what a fool; If I had only taken him at his word. Well, well!—a jeweler who can't tell paste from real jewelry!"

And he entered another jewelry-store, at the corner of the Rue de la Paix. 30 The moment the jeweler set eyes on the necklace, he examined—"Hello! I know that necklace well—it was sold here!"

M. Lantin, very nervous, asked:

"What's it worth?"

"Sir, I sold it for twenty-five thousand francs. I am willing to buy it back again for eighteen thousand—if you can prove to me satisfactorily, according to legal presciptions, how you came into possession of it."—This time, M. Lantin was simply paralyzed with astonishment. He said: "Well . . . but please look at it again, sir. I always thought until now that it was . . . was false."

The jeweler said:

"Will you give me your name, sir?" 35

"Certainly. My name is Lantin; I am employed at the office of the Minister of the Interior. I live at No. 16, Rue des Martyrs."

The merchant opened the register, looked, and said: "Yes; this necklace was sent to the address of Madame Lantin, 16 Rue des Martyrs, on July 20th, 1876."

And the two men looked into each other's eyes—the clerk wild with surprise; the jeweler suspecting he had a thief before him.

The jeweler resumed:

"Will you be kind enough to leave this article here for twenty-four hours 40 only—I'll give you a receipt."

M. Lantin stuttered: "Yes—ah! certainly." And he went out folding up the receipt, which he put in his pocket.

Then he crossed the street, went the wrong way, found out his mistake, returned by way of the Tuileries, crossed the Seine, found out he had taken the wrong road again, and went back to the Champs-Élysées without being able to get one clear idea into his head. He tried to reason, to understand. His wife could never have bought so valuable an object as that. Certainly not. But then, it must have been a present! . . . A present from whom? What for?

He stopped and stood stock-still in the middle of the avenue.

A horrible suspicion swept across his mind. . . . She? . . . But then all those other pieces of jewelry must have been presents also! . . . Then it seemed to him that the ground was heaving under his feet; that a tree, right in front of him, was falling toward him; he thrust out his arms instinctively, and fell senseless.

He recovered his consciousness again in a drug-store to which some bystand- 45 ers had carried him. He had them lead him home, and he locked himself into his room.

Until nightfall he cried without stopping, biting his handkerchief to keep himself from screaming out. Then, completely worn out with grief and fatigue, he went to bed, and slept a leaden sleep.

A ray of sunshine awakened him, and he rose and dressed himself slowly to go to the office. It was hard to have to work after such a shock. Then he reflected that he might be able to excuse himself to the superintendent, and he wrote to him. Then he remembered he would have to go back to the jeweler's; and shame made his face purple. He remained thinking a long time. Still he could not leave the necklace there; he put on his coat and went out.

It was a fine day; the sky extended all blue over the city, and seemed to make it smile. Strollers were walking aimlessly about, with their hands in their pockets.

Lantin thought as he watched them passing: "How lucky the men are who have fortunes! With money a man can even shake off grief—you can go where you please—travel—amuse yourself! Oh! if I were only rich!"

50   He suddenly discovered he was hungry—not having eaten anything since the evening before. But his pockets were empty; and he remembered the necklace. Eighteen thousand francs! Eighteen thousand francs!—that was a sum—that was!

He made his way to the Rue de la Paix and began to walk backward and forward on the sidewalk in front of the store. Eighteen thousand francs! Twenty times he started to go in; but shame always kept him back.

Still he was hungry—very hungry—and had not a cent. He made one brusque resolve, and crossed the street almost at a run, so as not to let himself have time to think over the matter; and he rushed into the jeweler's.

As soon as he saw him, the merchant hurried forward, and offered him a chair with smiling politeness. Even the clerks came forward to stare at Lantin, with gaiety in their eyes and smiles about their lips.

The jeweler said: "Sir, I made inquiries; and if you are still so disposed, I am ready to pay you down the price I offered you."

55   The clerk stammered: "Why, yes—sir, certainly."

The jeweler took from a drawer eighteen big bills,[3] counted them, and held them out to Lantin, who signed a little receipt, and thrust the money feverishly into his pocket.

Then, as he was on the point of leaving, he turned to the ever-smiling merchant, and said, lowering his eyes: "I have some—I have some other jewelry, which came to me in the same—from the same inheritance. Would you purchase them also from me?"

The merchant bowed, and answered: "Why, certainly, sir—certainly. . . ." One of the clerks rushed out to laugh at his ease; another kept blowing his nose as hard as he could.

Lantin, impassive, flushed and serious, said: "I will bring them to you."

60   And he hired a cab to get the jewelry.

When he returned to the store, an hour later, he had not yet breakfasted. They examined the jewelry—piece by piece—putting a value on each. Nearly all had been purchased from that very house.

---

3. French paper money varied in size; the larger the bill, the larger the denomination.

Lantin, now, disputed estimates made, got angry, insisted on seeing the books, and talked louder and louder the higher the estimates grew.

The big diamond earrings were worth 20,000 francs; the bracelets, 35,000; the brooches, rings and medallions, 16,000; a set of emeralds and sapphires, 14,000; solitaire, suspended to a gold neckchain, 40,000; the total value being estimated at 196,000 francs.

The merchant observed with mischievous good nature: "The person who owned these must have put all her savings into jewelry."

Lantin answered with gravity: "Perhaps that is as good a way of saving money 65 as any other." And he went off, after having agreed with the merchant that an expert should make a counter-estimate for him the next day.

When he found himself in the street again, he looked at the Column Vendôme[4] with the desire to climb it, as if it were a May pole. He felt jolly enough to play leapfrog over the Emperor's head—up there in the blue sky.

He breakfasted at Voisin's[5] restaurant, and ordered wine at 20 francs a bottle.

Then he hired a cab and drove out to the Bois.[6] He looked at the carriages passing with a sort of contempt, and a wild desire to yell out to the passers-by: "I am rich, too—I am! I have 200,000 francs!"

The recollection of the office suddenly came back to him. He drove there, walked right into the superintendent's private room, and said: "Sir, I come to give you my resignation. I have just come into a fortune of *three* hundred thousand francs." Then he shook hands all round with his fellow-clerks; and told them all about his plans for a new career. Then he went to dinner at the Café Anglais.

Finding himself seated at the same table with a man who seemed to him 70 quite genteel, he could not resist the itching desire to tell him, with a certain air of coquetry, that he had just inherited a fortune of *four* hundred thousand francs.

For the first time in his life he went to the theater without feeling bored by the performance; and he passed the night in revelry and debauch.

Six months after he married again. His second wife was the most upright of spouses, but had a terrible temper. She made his life very miserable.

1883

AMY TAN

(b. 1952)

A Pair of Tickets

Amy Tan was born in Oakland, California, just two and a half years after her parents immigrated from China. She received her MA in linguistics from San Jose State University and has worked on programs for disabled children and as a freelance writer. In 1987, at age thirty-five, she visited China for the first

---

4. Famous column with a statue of the emperor Napoleon at the top.
5. Like the Café Anglais below, a well-known and high-priced restaurant.
6. Large Parisian park where the rich took their outings.

time—"As soon as my feet touched China, I became Chinese"—and returned to write her first book, *The Joy Luck Club* (1989), a novel composed of stories told by four Chinese immigrant women and their American-born daughters. Tan has written more bestselling novels—including *The Kitchen God's Wife* (1991), *The Hundred Secret Senses* (1995), *The Bonesetter's Daughter* (2001), *Saving Fish from Drowning* (2005), and *The Valley of Amazement* (2013)—and has coauthored two children's books. Her nonfiction includes *The Opposite of Fate: A Book of Musings* (2003), which explores lucky accidents, choice, and memory, and *Where the Past Begins: A Writer's Memoir* (2017). Tan is also a backup singer for the Rock Bottom Remainders, a rock band made up of fellow writers, including Stephen King and Dave Barry; they make appearances at benefits that support literacy programs for children.

The minute our train leaves the Hong Kong border and enters Shenzhen, China, I feel different. I can feel the skin on my forehead tingling, my blood rushing through a new course, my bones aching with a familiar old pain. And I think, My mother was right. I am becoming Chinese.

"Cannot be helped," my mother said when I was fifteen and had vigorously denied that I had any Chinese whatsoever below my skin. I was a sophomore at Galileo High in San Francisco, and all my Caucasian friends agreed: I was about as Chinese as they were. But my mother had studied at a famous nursing school in Shanghai, and she said she knew all about genetics. So there was no doubt in her mind, whether I agreed or not: Once you are born Chinese, you cannot help but feel and think Chinese.

"Someday you will see," said my mother. "It's in your blood, waiting to be let go."

And when she said this, I saw myself transforming like a werewolf, a mutant tag of DNA suddenly triggered, replicating itself insidiously into a *syndrome*, a cluster of telltale Chinese behaviors, all those things my mother did to embarrass me—haggling with store owners, pecking her mouth with a toothpick in public, being color-blind to the fact that lemon yellow and pale pink are not good combinations for winter clothes.

5   But today I realize I've never really known what it means to be Chinese. I am thirty-six years old. My mother is dead and I am on a train, carrying with me her dreams of coming home. I am going to China.

We are going to Guangzhou, my seventy-two-year-old father, Canning Woo, and I, where we will visit his aunt, whom he has not seen since he was ten years old. And I don't know whether it's the prospect of seeing his aunt or if it's because he's back in China, but now he looks like he's a young boy, so innocent and happy I want to button his sweater and pat his head. We are sitting across from each other, separated by a little table with two cold cups of tea. For the first time I can ever remember, my father has tears in his eyes, and all he is seeing out the train window is a sectioned field of yellow, green, and brown, a narrow canal flanking the tracks, low rising hills, and three people in blue jackets riding an ox-driven cart on this early October morning. And I can't help myself. I also have misty eyes, as if I had seen this a long, long time ago, and had almost forgotten.

In less than three hours, we will be in Guangzhou, which my guidebook tells me is how one properly refers to Canton these days. It seems all the cities I have heard of, except Shanghai, have changed their spellings. I think they are saying China has changed in other ways as well. Chungking is Chongqing. And Kwei-lin is Guilin. I have looked these names up, because after we see my father's aunt in Guangzhou, we will catch a plane to Shanghai, where I will meet my two half-sisters for the first time.

They are my mother's twin daughters from her first marriage, little babies she was forced to abandon on a road as she was fleeing Kweilin for Chungking in 1944. That was all my mother had told me about these daughters, so they had remained babies in my mind, all these years, sitting on the side of a road, listening to bombs whistling in the distance while sucking their patient red thumbs.

And it was only this year that someone found them and wrote with this joyful news. A letter came from Shanghai, addressed to my mother. When I first heard about this, that they were alive, I imagined my identical sisters transforming from little babies into six-year-old girls. In my mind, they were seated next to each other at a table, taking turns with the fountain pen. One would write a neat row of characters: *Dearest Mama. We are alive.* She would brush back her wispy bangs and hand the other sister the pen, and she would write: *Come get us. Please hurry.*

Of course they could not know that my mother had died three months 10 before, suddenly, when a blood vessel in her brain burst. One minute she was talking to my father, complaining about the tenants upstairs, scheming how to evict them under the pretense that relatives from China were moving in. The next minute she was holding her head, her eyes squeezed shut, groping for the sofa, and then crumpling softly to the floor with fluttering hands.

So my father had been the first one to open the letter, a long letter it turned out. And they did call her Mama. They said they always revered her as their true mother. They kept a framed picture of her. They told her about their life, from the time my mother last saw them on the road leaving Kweilin to when they were finally found.

And the letter had broken my father's heart so much—these daughters calling my mother from another life he never knew—that he gave the letter to my mother's old friend Auntie Lindo and asked her to write back and tell my sisters, in the gentlest way possible, that my mother was dead.

But instead Auntie Lindo took the letter to the Joy Luck Club and discussed with Auntie Ying and Auntie An-mei what should be done, because they had known for many years about my mother's search for her twin daughters, her endless hope. Auntie Lindo and the others cried over this double tragedy, of losing my mother three months before, and now again. And so they couldn't help but think of some miracle, some possible way of reviving her from the dead, so my mother could fulfill her dream.

So this is what they wrote to my sisters in Shanghai: "Dearest Daughters, I too have never forgotten you in my memory or in my heart. I never gave up hope that we would see each other again in a joyous reunion. I am only sorry it has been too long. I want to tell you everything about my life since I last saw you. I want to tell you this when our family comes to see you in China. . . ." They signed it with my mother's name.

15   It wasn't until all this had been done that they first told me about my sisters, the letter they received, the one they wrote back.

"They'll think she's coming, then," I murmured. And I had imagined my sisters now being ten or eleven, jumping up and down, holding hands, their pigtails bouncing, excited that their mother—*their* mother—was coming, whereas my mother was dead.

"How can you say she is not coming in a letter?" said Auntie Lindo. "She is their mother. She is your mother. You must be the one to tell them. All these years, they have been dreaming of her." And I thought she was right.

But then I started dreaming, too, of my mother and my sisters and how it would be if I arrived in Shanghai. All these years, while they waited to be found, I had lived with my mother and then had lost her. I imagined seeing my sisters at the airport. They would be standing on their tiptoes, looking anxiously, scanning from one dark head to another as we got off the plane. And I would recognize them instantly, their faces with the identical worried look.

Jyejye, Jyejye. Sister, Sister. We are here," I saw myself saying in my poor version of Chinese.

20   "Where is Mama?" they would say, and look around, still smiling, two flushed and eager faces. "Is she hiding?" And this would have been like my mother, to stand behind just a bit, to tease a little and make people's patience pull a little on their hearts. I would shake my head and tell my sisters she was not hiding.

"Oh, that must be Mama, no?" one of my sisters would whisper excitedly, pointing to another small woman completely engulfed in a tower of presents. And that, too, would have been like my mother, to bring mountains of gifts, food, and toys for children—all bought on sale—shunning thanks, saying the gifts were nothing, and later turning the labels over to show my sisters, "Calvin Klein, 100% wool."

I imagined myself starting to say, "Sisters, I am sorry, I have come alone . . ." and before I could tell them—they could see it in my face—they were wailing, pulling their hair, their lips twisted in pain, as they ran away from me. And then I saw myself getting back on the plane and coming home.

After I had dreamed this scene many times—watching their despair turn from horror into anger—I begged Auntie Lindo to write another letter. And at first she refused.

"How can I say she is dead? I cannot write this," said Auntie Lindo with a stubborn look.

25   "But it's cruel to have them believe she's coming on the plane," I said. "When they see it's just me, they'll hate me."

"Hate you? Cannot be." She was scowling. "You are their own sister, their only family."

"You don't understand," I protested.

"What I don't understand?" she said.

And I whispered, "They'll think I'm responsible, that she died because I didn't appreciate her."

30   And Auntie Lindo looked satisfied and sad at the same time, as if this were true and I had finally realized it. She sat down for an hour, and when she stood up she handed me a two-page letter. She had tears in her eyes. I realized that

the very thing I had feared, she had done. So even if she had written the news of my mother's death in English, I wouldn't have had the heart to read it.

"Thank you," I whispered.

The landscape has become gray, filled with low flat cement buildings, old factories, and then tracks and more tracks filled with trains like ours passing by in the opposite direction. I see platforms crowded with people wearing drab Western clothes, with spots of bright colors: little children wearing pink and yellow, red and peach. And there are soldiers in olive green and red, and old ladies in gray tops and pants that stop mid-calf. We are in Guangzhou.

Before the train even comes to a stop, people are bringing down their belongings from above their seats. For a moment there is a dangerous shower of heavy suitcases laden with gifts to relatives, half-broken boxes wrapped in miles of string to keep the contents from spilling out, plastic bags filled with yarn and vegetables and packages of dried mushrooms, and camera cases. And then we are caught in a stream of people rushing, shoving, pushing us along, until we find ourselves in one of a dozen lines waiting to go through customs. I feel as if I were getting on a number 30 Stockton bus in San Francisco. I am in China, I remind myself. And somehow the crowds don't bother me. It feels right. I start pushing too.

I take out the declaration forms and my passport. "Woo," it says at the top, and below that, "June May," who was born in "California, U.S.A.," in 1951. I wonder if the customs people will question whether I'm the same person as in the passport photo. In this picture, my chin-length hair is swept back and artfully styled. I am wearing false eyelashes, eye shadow, and lip liner. My cheeks are hollowed out by bronze blusher. But I had not expected the heat in October. And now my hair hangs limp with the humidity. I wear no makeup; in Hong Kong my mascara had melted into dark circles and everything else had felt like layers of grease. So today my face is plain, unadorned except for a thin mist of shiny sweat on my forehead and nose.

Even without makeup, I could never pass for true Chinese. I stand five-foot- 35 six, and my head pokes above the crowd so that I am eye level only with other tourists. My mother once told me my height came from my grandfather, who was a northerner, and may have even had some Mongol blood. "This is what your grandmother once told me," explained my mother. "But now it is too late to ask her. They are all dead, your grandparents, your uncles, and their wives and children, all killed in the war, when a bomb fell on our house. So many generations in one instant."

She had said this so matter-of-factly that I thought she had long since gotten over any grief she had. And then I wondered how she knew they were all dead.

"Maybe they left the house before the bomb fell," I suggested.

"No," said my mother. "Our whole family is gone. It is just you and I."

"But how do you know? Some of them could have escaped."

"Cannot be," said my mother, this time almost angrily. And then her frown 40 was washed over by a puzzled blank look, and she began to talk as if she were trying to remember where she had misplaced something. "I went back to that house. I kept looking up to where the house used to be. And it wasn't a house, just the sky. And below, underneath my feet, were four stories of burnt bricks and wood, all the life of our house. Then off to the side I saw things blown into the yard, nothing valuable. There was a bed someone used to sleep in, really just a metal frame twisted up at one corner. And a book, I don't know what kind, because every page had turned black. And I saw a teacup which was unbroken but filled with ashes. And then I found my doll, with her hands and legs broken, her hair burned off. . . . When I was a little girl, I had cried for that doll, seeing it all alone in the store window, and my mother had bought it for me. It was an American doll with yellow hair. It could turn its legs and arms. The eyes moved up and down. And when I married and left my family home, I gave the doll to my youngest niece, because she was like me. She cried if that doll was not with her always. Do you see? If she was in the house with that doll, her parents were there, and so everybody was there, waiting together, because that's how our family was."

The woman in the customs booth stares at my documents, then glances at me briefly, and with two quick movements stamps everything and sternly nods me along. And soon my father and I find ourselves in a large area filled with thousands of people and suitcases. I feel lost and my father looks helpless.

"Excuse me," I say to a man who looks like an American. "Can you tell me where I can get a taxi?" He mumbles something that sounds Swedish or Dutch.

"Syau Yen! Syau Yen!" I hear a piercing voice shout from behind me. An old woman in a yellow knit beret is holding up a pink plastic bag filled with wrapped trinkets. I guess she is trying to sell us something. But my father is staring down at this tiny sparrow of a woman, squinting into her eyes. And then his eyes widen, his face opens up and he smiles like a pleased little boy.

"Aiyi! Aiyi!"—Auntie Auntie!—he says softly.

45   "Syau Yen!" coos my great-aunt. I think it's funny she has just called my father "Little Wild Goose." It must be his baby milk name, the name used to discourage ghosts from stealing children.

They clasp each other's hands—they do not hug—and hold on like this, taking turns saying, "Look at you! You are so old. Look how old you've become!" They are both crying openly, laughing at the same time, and I bite my lip, trying not to cry. I'm afraid to feel their joy. Because I am thinking how different our arrival in Shanghai will be tomorrow, how awkward it will feel.

Now Aiyi beams and points to a Polaroid picture of my father. My father had wisely sent pictures when he wrote and said we were coming. See how smart she was, she seems to intone as she compares the picture to my father. In the letter, my father had said we would call her from the hotel once we arrived, so this is a surprise, that they've come to meet us. I wonder if my sisters will be at the airport.

It is only then that I remember the camera. I had meant to take a picture of my father and his aunt the moment they met. It's not too late.

"Here, stand together over here," I say, holding up the Polaroid. The camera flashes and I hand them the snapshot. Aiyi and my father still stand close together, each of them holding a corner of the picture, watching as their images begin to form. They are almost reverentially quiet. Aiyi is only five years older than my father, which makes her around seventy-seven. But she looks ancient, shrunken, a mummified relic. Her thin hair is pure white, her teeth are brown with decay. So much for stories of Chinese women looking young forever, I think to myself.

Now Aiyi is crooning to me: *"Jandale."* So big already. She looks up at me, at my full height, and then peers into her pink plastic bag—her gifts to us, I have figured out—as if she is wondering what she will give to me, now that I am so old and big. And then she grabs my elbow with her sharp pincerlike grasp and turns me around. A man and a woman in their fifties are shaking hands with my father, everybody smiling and saying, "Ah! Ah!" They are Aiyi's oldest son and his wife, and standing next to them are four other people, around my age, and a little girl who's around ten. The introductions go by so fast, all I know is that one of them is Aiyi's grandson, with his wife, and the other is her granddaughter, with her husband. And the little girl is Lili, Aiyi's great-granddaughter.

Aiyi and my father speak the Mandarin dialect from their childhood, but the rest of the family speaks only the Cantonese of their village. I understand only Mandarin but can't speak it that well. So Aiyi and my father gossip unrestrained in Mandarin, exchanging news about people from their old village. And they stop only occasionally to talk to the rest of us, sometimes in Cantonese, sometimes in English.

"Oh, it is as I suspected," says my father, turning to me. "He died last summer." And I already understood this. I just don't know who this person, Li Gong, is. I feel as if I were in the United Nations and the translators had run amok.

"Hello," I say to the little girl. "My name is Jing-mei." But the little girl squirms to look away, causing her parents to laugh with embarrassment. I try to think of Cantonese words I can say to her, stuff I learned from friends in Chinatown, but all I can think of are swear words, terms for bodily functions, and short phrases like "tastes good," "tastes like garbage," and "she's really ugly." And then I have another plan: I hold up the Polaroid camera, beckoning Lili with my finger. She immediately jumps forward, places one hand on her hip in the manner of a fashion model, juts out her chest, and flashes me a toothy smile. As soon as I take the picture she is standing next to me, jumping and giggling every few seconds as she watches herself appear on the greenish film.

By the time we hail taxis for the ride to the hotel, Lili is holding tight onto my hand, pulling me along.

In the taxi, Aiyi talks nonstop, so I have no chance to ask her about the different sights we are passing by.

"You wrote and said you would come only for one day," says Aiyi to my father in an agitated tone. "One day! How can you see your family in one day! Toishan is many hours' drive from Guangzhou. And this idea to call us when you arrive. This is nonsense. We have no telephone."

My heart races a little. I wonder if Auntie Lindo told my sisters we would call from the hotel in Shanghai?

Aiyi continues to scold my father. "I was so beside myself, ask my son, almost turned heaven and earth upside down trying to think of a way! So we decided the best was for us to take the bus from Toishan and come into Guangzhou—meet you right from the start."

And now I am holding my breath as the taxi driver dodges between trucks and buses, honking his horn constantly. We seem to be on some sort of long

freeway overpass, like a bridge above the city. I can see row after row of apartments, each floor cluttered with laundry hanging out to dry on the balcony. We
pass a public bus, with people jammed in so tight their faces are nearly wedged
against the window. Then I see the skyline of what must be downtown Guangzhou. From a distance, it looks like a major American city, with highrises and
construction going on everywhere. As we slow down in the more congested part
of the city, I see scores of little shops, dark inside, lined with counters and
shelves. And then there is a building, its front laced with scaffolding made of
bamboo poles held together with plastic strips. Men and women are standing
on narrow platforms, scraping the sides, working without safety straps or helmets. Oh, would OSHA[1] have a field day here, I think.

60   Aiyi's shrill voice rises up again: "So it is a shame you can't see our village,
our house. My sons have been quite successful, selling our vegetables in the
free market. We had enough these last few years to build a big house, three
stories, all of new brick, big enough for our whole family and then some. And
every year, the money is even better. You Americans aren't the only ones who
know how to get rich!"

The taxi stops and I assume we've arrived, but then I peer out at what looks
like a grander version of the Hyatt Regency. "This is communist China?" I wonder out loud. And then I shake my head toward my father. "This must be the
wrong hotel." I quickly pull out our itinerary, travel tickets, and reservations. I
had explicitly instructed my travel agent to choose something inexpensive, in
the thirty-to-forty-dollar range. I'm sure of this. And there it says on our itinerary: Garden Hotel, Huanshi Dong Lu. Well, our travel agent had better be prepared to eat the extra, that's all I have to say.

The hotel is magnificent. A bellboy complete with uniform and sharp-
creased cap jumps forward and begins to carry our bags into the lobby. Inside,
the hotel looks like an orgy of shopping arcades and restaurants all encased in
granite and glass. And rather than be impressed, I am worried about the
expense, as well as the appearance it must give Aiyi, that we rich Americans
cannot be without our luxuries even for one night.

But when I step up to the reservation desk, ready to haggle over this booking
mistake, it is confirmed. Our rooms are prepaid, thirty-four dollars each. I feel
sheepish, and Aiyi and the others seem delighted by our temporary surroundings. Lili is looking wide-eyed at an arcade filled with video games.

Our whole family crowds into one elevator, and the bellboy waves, saying he
will meet us on the eighteenth floor. As soon as the elevator door shuts, everybody becomes very quiet, and when the door finally opens again, everybody
talks at once in what sounds like relieved voices. I have the feeling Aiyi and the
others have never been on such a long elevator ride.

65   Our rooms are next to each other and are identical. The rugs, drapes, bed-
spreads are all in shades of taupe. There's a color television with remote-control
panels built into the lamp table between the two twin beds. The bathroom has
marble walls and floors. I find a built-in wet bar with a small refrigerator stocked
with Heineken beer, Coke Classic, and Seven-Up, mini-bottles of Johnnie

---

1. The Occupational Safety and Health Administration (acronym), a division of the U.S. Department
of Labor.

Walker Red, Bacardi rum, and Smirnoff vodka, and packets of M & M's, honey-roasted cashews, and Cadbury chocolate bars. And again I say out loud, "This is communist China?"

My father comes into my room. "They decided we should just stay here and visit," he says, shrugging his shoulders. "They say, Less trouble that way. More time to talk."

"What about dinner?" I ask. I have been envisioning my first real Chinese feast for many days already, a big banquet with one of those soups steaming out of a carved winter melon, chicken wrapped in clay, Peking duck, the works.

My father walks over and picks up a room service book next to a *Travel & Leisure* magazine. He flips through the pages quickly and then points to the menu. "This is what they want," says my father.

So it's decided. We are going to dine tonight in our rooms, with our family, sharing hamburgers, french fries, and apple pie à la mode.

Aiyi and her family are browsing the shops while we clean up. After a hot ride 70
on the train, I'm eager for a shower and cooler clothes.

The hotel has provided little packets of shampoo which, upon opening, I discover is the consistency and color of hoisin sauce.[2] This is more like it, I think. This is China. And I rub some in my damp hair.

Standing in the shower, I realize this is the first time I've been by myself in what seems like days. But instead of feeling relieved, I feel forlorn. I think about what my mother said, about activating my genes and becoming Chinese. And I wonder what she meant.

Right after my mother died, I asked myself a lot of things, things that couldn't be answered, to force myself to grieve more. It seemed as if I wanted to sustain my grief, to assure myself that I had cared deeply enough.

But now I ask the questions mostly because I want to know the answers. What was that pork stuff she used to make that had the texture of sawdust? What were the names of the uncles who died in Shanghai? What had she dreamt all these years about her other daughters? All the times when she got mad at me, was she really thinking about them? Did she wish I were they? Did she regret that I wasn't?

At one o'clock in the morning, I awake to tapping sounds on the window. I must 75
have dozed off and now I feel my body uncramping itself. I'm sitting on the floor, leaning against one of the twin beds. Lili is lying next to me. The others are asleep, too, sprawled out on the beds and floor. Aiyi is seated at a little table, looking very sleepy. And my father is staring out the window, tapping his fingers on the glass. The last time I listened my father was telling Aiyi about his life since he last saw her. How he had gone to Yenching University, later got a post with a newspaper in Chungking, met my mother there, a young widow. How they later fled together to Shanghai to try to find my mother's family house, but there was nothing there. And then they traveled eventually to Canton and then to Hong Kong, then Haiphong and finally to San Francisco. . . .

---

2. Sweet brownish-red sauce made from soybeans, sugar, water, spices, garlic, and chili.

"Suyuan didn't tell me she was trying all these years to find her daughters," he is now saying in a quiet voice. "Naturally, I did not discuss her daughters with her. I thought she was ashamed she had left them behind."

"Where did she leave them?" asks Aiyi. "How were they found?"

I am wide awake now. Although I have heard parts of this story from my mother's friends.

"It happened when the Japanese took over Kweilin," says my father.

80 "Japanese in Kweilin?" says Aiyi. "That was never the case. Couldn't be. The Japanese never came to Kweilin."

"Yes, that is what the newspapers reported. I know this because I was working for the news bureau at the time. The Kuomintang[3] often told us what we could say and could not say. But we knew the Japanese had come into Kwangsi Province. We had sources who told us how they had captured the Wuchang-Canton railway. How they were coming overland, making very fast progress, marching toward the provincial capital."

Aiyi looks astonished. "If people did not know this, how could Suyuan know the Japanese were coming?"

"An officer of the Kuomintang secretly warned her," explains my father. "Suyuan's husband also was an officer and everybody knew that officers and their families would be the first to be killed. So she gathered a few possessions and, in the middle of the night, she picked up her daughters and fled on foot. The babies were not even one year old."

"How could she give up those babies!" sighs Aiyi. "Twin girls. We have never had such luck in our family." And then she yawns again.

85 "What were they named?" she asks. I listen carefully. I had been planning on using just the familiar "Sister" to address them both. But now I want to know how to pronounce their names.

"They have their father's surname, Wang," says my father. "And their given names are Chwun Yu and Chwun Hwa."

"What do the names mean?" I ask.

"Ah." My father draws imaginary characters on the window. "One means 'Spring Rain,' the other 'Spring Flower,'" he explains in English, "because they born in the spring, and of course rain come before flower, same order these girls are born. Your mother like a poet, don't you think?"

I nod my head. I see Aiyi nod her head forward, too. But it falls forward and stays there. She is breathing deeply, noisily. She is asleep.

90 "And what does Ma's name mean?" I whisper.

"'Suyuan,'" he says, writing more invisible characters on the glass. "The way she write it in Chinese, it mean 'Long-Cherished Wish.' Quite a fancy name, not so ordinary like flower name. See this first character, it mean something like 'Forever Never Forgotten.' But there is another way to write 'Suyuan.' Sound exactly the same, but the meaning is opposite." His finger creates the brushstrokes of another character. "The first part look the same: 'Never Forgotten.'

3. National People's Party, led by Generalissimo Chiang Kai-shek (1887–1975), which fought successfully against the Japanese occupation before being defeated militarily in 1949 by the Chinese Communist Party, led by Mao Zedong (1893–1976).

But the last part add to first part make the whole word mean 'Long-Held Grudge.' Your mother get angry with me, I tell her her name should be Grudge."

My father is looking at me, moist-eyed. "See, I pretty clever, too, hah?"

I nod, wishing I could find some way to comfort him. "And what about my name," I ask, "what does 'Jing-mei' mean?"

"Your name also special," he says. I wonder if any name in Chinese is not something special. "'Jing' like excellent *jing*. Not just good, it's something pure, essential, the best quality. *Jing* is good leftover stuff when you take impurities out of something like gold, or rice, or salt. So what is left—just pure essence. And 'Mei,' this is common *mei*, as in *meimei*, 'younger sister.'"

I think about this. My mother's long-cherished wish. Me, the younger sister 95 who was supposed to be the essence of the others. I feed myself with the old grief, wondering how disappointed my mother must have been. Tiny Aiyi stirs suddenly, her head rolls and then falls back, her mouth opens as if to answer my question. She grunts in her sleep, tucking her body more closely into the chair.

"So why did she abandon those babies on the road?" I need to know, because now I feel abandoned too.

"Long time I wondered this myself," says my father. "But then I read that letter from her daughters in Shanghai now, and I talk to Auntie Lindo, all the others. And then I knew. No shame in what she done. None."

"What happened?"

"Your mother running away—" begins my father.

"No, tell me in Chinese," I interrupt. "Really, I can understand." 100

He begins to talk, still standing at the window, looking into the night.

After fleeing Kweilin, your mother walked for several days trying to find a main road. Her thought was to catch a ride on a truck or wagon, to catch enough rides until she reached Chungking, where her husband was stationed.

She had sewn money and jewelry into the lining of her dress, enough, she thought, to barter rides all the way. If I am lucky, she thought, I will not have to trade the heavy gold bracelet and jade ring. These were things from her mother, your grandmother.

By the third day, she had traded nothing. The roads were filled with people, everybody running and begging for rides from passing trucks. The trucks rushed by, afraid to stop. So your mother found no rides, only the start of dysentery pains in her stomach.

Her shoulders ached from the two babies swinging from scarf slings. Blisters 105 grew on the palms from holding two leather suitcases. And then the blisters burst and began to bleed. After a while, she left the suitcases behind, keeping only the food and a few clothes. And later she also dropped the bags of wheat flour and rice and kept walking like this for many miles, singing songs to her little girls, until she was delirious with pain and fever.

Finally, there was not one more step left in her body. She didn't have the strength to carry those babies any farther. She slumped to the ground. She knew she would die of her sickness, or perhaps from thirst, from starvation, or from the Japanese, who she was sure were marching right behind her.

She took the babies out of the slings and sat them on the side of the road, then lay down next to them. You babies are so good, she said, so quiet. They smiled back, reaching their chubby hands for her, wanting to be picked up again. And then she knew she could not bear to watch her babies die with her.

She saw a family with three young children in a cart going by. "Take my babies, I beg you," she cried to them. But they stared back with empty eyes and never stopped.

She saw another person pass and called out again. This time a man turned around, and he had such a terrible expression—your mother said it looked like death itself—she shivered and looked away.

110   When the road grew quiet, she tore open the lining of her dress, and stuffed jewelry under the shirt of one baby and money under the other. She reached into her pocket and drew out the photos of her family, the picture of her father and mother, the picture of herself and her husband on their wedding day. And she wrote on the back of each the names of the babies and this same message: "Please care for these babies with the money and valuables provided. When it is safe to come, if you bring them to Shanghai, 9 Weichang Lu, the Li family will be glad to give you a generous reward. Li Suyuan and Wang Fuchi."

And then she touched each baby's cheek and told her not to cry. She would go down the road to find them some food and would be back. And without looking back, she walked down the road, stumbling and crying, thinking only of this one last hope, that her daughters would be found by a kindhearted person who would care for them. She would not allow herself to imagine anything else.

She did not remember how far she walked, which direction she went, when she fainted, or how she was found. When she awoke, she was in the back of a bouncing truck with several other sick people, all moaning. And she began to scream, thinking she was now on a journey to Buddhist hell. But the face of an American missionary lady bent over her and smiled, talking to her in a soothing language she did not understand. And yet she could somehow understand. She had been saved for no good reason, and it was now too late to go back and save her babies.

When she arrived in Chungking, she learned her husband had died two weeks before. She told me later she laughed when the officers told her this news, she was so delirious with madness and disease. To come so far, to lose so much and to find nothing.

I met her in a hospital. She was lying on a cot, hardly able to move, her dysentery had drained her so thin. I had come in for my foot, my missing toe, which was cut off by a piece of falling rubble. She was talking to herself, mumbling.

115   "Look at these clothes," she said, and I saw she had on a rather unusual dress for wartime. It was silk satin, quite dirty, but there was no doubt it was a beautiful dress.

"Look at this face," she said, and I saw her dusty face and hollow cheeks, her eyes shining black. "Do you see my foolish hope?"

"I thought I had lost everything, except these two things," she murmured. "And I wondered which I would lose next. Clothes or hope? Hope or clothes?"

"But now, see here, look what is happening," she said, laughing, as if all her prayers had been answered. And she was pulling hair out of her head as easily as one lifts new wheat from wet soil.

It was an old peasant woman who found them. "How could I resist?" the peasant woman later told your sisters when they were older. They were still sitting obediently near where your mother had left them, looking like little fairy queens waiting for their sedan to arrive.

The woman, Mei Ching, and her husband, Mei Han, lived in a stone cave. 120 There were thousands of hidden caves like that in and around Kweilin so secret that the people remained hidden even after the war ended. The Meis would come out of their cave every few days and forage for food supplies left on the road, and sometimes they would see something that they both agreed was a tragedy to leave behind. So one day they took back to their cave a delicately painted set of rice bowls, another day a little footstool with a velvet cushion and two new wedding blankets. And once, it was your sisters.

They were pious people, Muslims, who believed the twin babies were a sign of double luck, and they were sure of this when, later in the evening, they discovered how valuable the babies were. She and her husband had never seen rings and bracelets like those. And while they admired the pictures, knowing the babies came from a good family, neither of them could read or write. It was not until many months later that Mei Ching found someone who could read the writing on the back. By then, she loved these baby girls like her own.

In 1952 Mei Han, the husband, died. The twins were already eight years old, and Mei Ching now decided it was time to find your sisters' true family.

She showed the girls the picture of their mother and told them they had been born into a great family and she would take them back to see their true mother and grandparents. Mei Ching told them about the reward, but she swore she would refuse it. She loved these girls so much, she only wanted them to have what they were entitled to—a better life, a fine house, educated ways. Maybe the family would let her stay on as the girls' amah.[4] Yes, she was certain they would insist.

Of course, when she found the place at 9 Weichang Lu, in the old French Concession, it was something completely different. It was the site of a factory building, recently constructed, and none of the workers knew what had become of the family whose house had burned down on that spot.

Mei Ching could not have known, of course, that your mother and I, her new 125 husband, had already returned to that same place in 1945 in hopes of finding both her family and her daughters.

Your mother and I stayed in China until 1947. We went to many different cities—back to Kweilin, to Changsha, as far south as Kunming. She was always looking out of one corner of her eye for twin babies, then little girls. Later we went to Hong Kong, and when we finally left in 1949 for the United States, I think she was even looking for them on the boat. But when we arrived, she no longer talked about them. I thought, At last, they have died in her heart.

When letters could be openly exchanged between China and the United States, she wrote immediately to old friends in Shanghai and Kweilin. I did not know she did this. Auntie Lindo told me. But of course, by then, all the street names had changed. Some people had died, others had moved away. So it took many years to find a contact. And when she did find an old schoolmate's address and wrote asking her to look for her daughters, her friend wrote back and said this was impossible, like looking for a needle on the bottom of the ocean. How

4. Maidservant or nurse.

did she know her daughters were in Shanghai and not somewhere else in China? The friend, of course, did not ask, How do you know your daughters are still alive?

So her schoolmate did not look. Finding babies lost during the war was a matter of foolish imagination, and she had no time for that.

But every year, your mother wrote to different people. And this last year, I think she got a big idea in her head, to go to China and find them herself. I remember she told me, "Canning, we should go, before it is too late, before we are too old." And I told her we were already too old, it was already too late.

130   I just thought she wanted to be a tourist! I didn't know she wanted to go and look for her daughters. So when I said it was too late, that must have put a terrible thought in her head that her daughters might be dead. And I think this possibility grew bigger and bigger in her head, until it killed her.

Maybe it was your mother's dead spirit who guided her Shanghai schoolmate to find her daughters. Because after your mother died, the schoolmate saw your sisters, by chance, while shopping for shoes at the Number One Department Store on Nanjing Dong Road. She said it was like a dream, seeing these two women who looked so much alike, moving down the stairs together. There was something about their facial expressions that reminded the schoolmate of your mother.

She quickly walked over to them and called their names, which of course, they did not recognize at first, because Mei Ching had changed their names. But your mother's friend was so sure, she persisted. "Are you not Wang Chwun Yu and Wang Chwun Hwa?" she asked them. And then these double-image women became very excited, because they remembered the names written on the back of an old photo, a photo of a young man and woman they still honored, as their much-loved first parents, who had died and become spirit ghosts still roaming the earth looking for them.

At the airport, I am exhausted. I could not sleep last night. Aiyi had followed me into my room at three in the morning, and she instantly fell asleep on one of the twin beds, snoring with the might of a lumberjack. I lay awake thinking about my mother's story, realizing how much I have never known about her, grieving that my sisters and I had both lost her.

And now at the airport, after shaking hands with everybody, waving good-bye, I think about all the different ways we leave people in this world. Cheerily waving good-bye to some at airports, knowing we'll never see each other again. Leaving others on the side of the road, hoping that we will. Finding my mother in my father's story and saying good-bye before I have a chance to know her better.

135   Aiyi smiles at me as we wait for our gate to be called. She is so old. I put one arm around her and one arm around Lili. They are the same size, it seems. And then it's time. As we wave good-bye one more time and enter the waiting area, I get the sense I am going from one funeral to another. In my hand I'm clutching a pair of tickets to Shanghai. In two hours we'll be there.

The plane takes off. I close my eyes. How can I describe to them in my broken Chinese about our mother's life? Where should I begin?

"Wake up, we're here," says my father. And I awake with my heart pounding in my throat. I look out the window and we're already on the runway. It's gray outside.

And now I'm walking down the steps of the plane, onto the tarmac and toward the building. If only, I think, if only my mother had lived long enough to be the one walking toward them. I am so nervous I cannot even feel my feet. I am just moving somehow.

Somebody shouts, "She's arrived!" And then I see her. Her short hair. Her small body. And that same look on her face. She has the back of her hand pressed hard against her mouth. She is crying as though she had gone through a terrible ordeal and were happy it is over.

And I know it's not my mother, yet it is the same look she had when I was five 140 and had disappeared all afternoon, for such a long time, that she was convinced I was dead. And when I miraculously appeared, sleepy-eyed, crawling from underneath my bed, she wept and laughed, biting the back of her hand to make sure it was true.

And now I see her again, two of her, waving, and in one hand there is a photo, the Polaroid I sent them. As soon as I get beyond the gate, we run toward each other, all three of us embracing, all hesitations and expectations forgotten.

"Mama, Mama," we all murmur, as if she is among us.

My sisters look at me, proudly. *"Meimei jandale,"* says one sister proudly to the other. "Little Sister has grown up." I look at their faces again and I see no trace of my mother in them. Yet they still look familiar. And now I also see what part of me is Chinese. It is so obvious. It is my family. It is in our blood. After all these years, it can finally be let go.

My sisters and I stand, arms around each other, laughing and wiping the tears from each other's eyes. The flash of the Polaroid goes off and my father hands me the snapshot. My sisters and I watch quietly together, eager to see what develops.

The gray-green surface changes to the bright colors of our three images, 145 sharpening and deepening all at once. And although we don't speak, I know we all see it: Together we look like our mother. Her same eyes, her same mouth, open in surprise to see, at last, her long-cherished wish.

1989

EUDORA WELTY
(1909–2001)

Why I Live at the P.O.

Known as the "First Lady of Southern Literature," Eudora Welty grew up in Jackson, Mississippi, attended Mississippi State College for Women, and earned a BA from the University of Wisconsin. Among the countless awards she received were two Guggenheim Fellowships, six O. Henry Awards, a Pulitzer Prize, the French Legion of Honor, the National Medal for Literature, and the Presidential Medal of Freedom. Although she wrote five novels, including *The Robber Bridegroom* (1942), *Ponder Heart* (1954), and *The Optimist's Daughter* (1972), Welty is best known for her short stories, many of which appear in *The Collected Stories of Eudora Welty* (1980). Among her nonfiction works are *One Writer's Beginnings* (1984), *A Writer's Eye: Collected Book Reviews* (1994), and five collections of her photographs, including *One Place, One Time* (1971) and *Photographs* (1989). In 1998 the Library of America published a two-volume edition of her selected works, making her the first living author to appear in the series.

I was getting along fine with Mama, Papa-Daddy, and Uncle Rondo until my sister Stella-Rondo just separated from her husband and came back home again. Mr. Whitaker! Of course I went with Mr. Whitaker first, when he first appeared here in China Grove, taking "Pose Yourself" photos, and Stella-Rondo broke us up. Told him I was one-sided. Bigger on one side than the other, which is a deliberate, calculated falsehood: I'm the same. Stella-Rondo is exactly twelve months to the day younger than I am and for that reason she's spoiled.

She's always had anything in the world she wanted and then she'd throw it away. Papa-Daddy give her this gorgeous Add-a-Pearl necklace when she was eight years old and she threw it away playing baseball when she was nine, with only two pearls.

So as soon as she got married and moved away from home the first thing she did was separate! From Mr. Whitaker! This photographer with the popeyes she said she trusted. Came home from one of those towns up in Illinois and to our complete surprise brought this child of two.

Mama said she like to make her drop dead for a second. "Here you had this marvelous blonde child and never so much as wrote your mother a word about it," says Mama. "I'm thoroughly ashamed of you." But of course she wasn't.

5   Stella-Rondo just calmly takes off this *hat*, I wish you could see it. She says, "Why, Mama, Shirley-T.'s adopted, I can prove it."

"How?" says Mama, but all I says was, "H'm!" There I was over the hot stove, trying to stretch two chickens over five people and a completely unexpected child into the bargain without one moment's notice.

"What do you mean—'H'm'?" says Stella-Rondo, and Mama says, "I heard that, Sister."

I said that oh, I didn't mean a thing, only that whoever Shirley-T. was, she was the spit-image of Papa-Daddy if he'd cut off his beard, which of course he'd never do in the world. Papa-Daddy's Mama's papa and sulks.

Stella-Rondo got furious! She said, "Sister, I don't need to tell you you got a lot of nerve and always did have and I'll thank you to make no future reference to my adopted child whatsoever."

10   "Very well," I said. "Very well, very well. Of course I noticed at once she looks like Mr. Whitaker's side too. That frown. She looks like a cross between Mr. Whitaker and Papa-Daddy."

"Well, all I can say is she isn't."

"She looks exactly like Shirley Temple to me," says Mama, but Shirley-T. just ran away from her.

So the first thing Stella-Rondo did at the table was turn Papa-Daddy against me.

"Papa-Daddy," she says. He was trying to cut up his meat. "Papa-Daddy!" I was taken completely by surprise. Papa-Daddy is about a million years old and's got this long-long beard. "Papa-Daddy, Sister says she fails to understand why you don't cut off your beard."

So Papa-Daddy l-a-y-s down his knife and fork! He's real rich. Mama says he is, he says he isn't. So he says, "Have I heard correctly? You don't understand why I don't cut off my beard?" 15

"Why," I says, "Papa-Daddy, of course I understand, I did not say any such a thing, the idea!"

He says, "Hussy!"

I says, "Papa-Daddy, you know I wouldn't any more want you to cut off your beard than the man in the moon. It was the farthest thing from my mind! Stella-Rondo sat there and made that up while she was eating breast of chicken."

But he says, "So the postmistress fails to understand why I don't cut off my beard. Which job I got you through my influence with the government. 'Bird's nest'—is that what you call it?"

Not that it isn't the next to smallest P.O. in the entire state of Mississippi. 20

I says, "Oh, Papa-Daddy," I says, "I didn't say any such a thing, I never dreamed it was a bird's nest, I have always been grateful though this is the next to smallest P.O. in the state of Mississippi, and I do not enjoy being referred to as a hussy by my own grandfather."

But Stella-Rondo says, "Yes, you did say it too. Anybody in the world could of heard you, that had ears."

"Stop right there," says Mama, looking at *me*.

So I pulled my napkin straight back through the napkin ring and left the table.

As soon as I was out of the room Mama says, "Call her back, or she'll starve to death," but Papa-Daddy says, "This is the beard I started growing on the Coast when I was fifteen years old." He would of gone on till nightfall if Shirley-T. hadn't lost the Milky Way she ate in Cairo. 25

So Papa-Daddy says, "I am going out and lie in the hammock, and you can all sit here and remember my words: I'll never cut off my beard as long as I live, even one inch, and I don't appreciate it in you at all." Passed right by me in the hall and went straight out and got in the hammock.

It would be a holiday. It wasn't five minutes before Uncle Rondo suddenly appeared in the hall in one of Stella-Rondo's flesh-colored kimonos, all cut on the bias, like something Mr. Whitaker probably thought was gorgeous.

"Uncle Rondo!" I says. "I didn't know who that was! Where are you going?"

"Sister," he says, "get out of my way, I'm poisoned."

"If you're poisoned stay away from Papa-Daddy," I says. "Keep out of the hammock. Papa-Daddy will certainly beat you on the head if you come within forty miles of him. He thinks I deliberately said he ought to cut off his beard after he got me the P.O., and I've told him and told him and told him, and he acts like he just don't hear me. Papa-Daddy must of gone stone deaf." 30

"He picked a fine day to do it then," says Uncle Rondo, and before you could say "Jack Robinson" flew out in the yard.

What he'd really done, he'd drunk another bottle of that prescription. He does it every single Fourth of July as sure as shooting, and it's horribly expensive. Then he falls over in the hammock and snores. So he insisted on zigzagging right on out to the hammock, looking like a half-wit.

Papa-Daddy woke with this horrible yell and right there without moving an inch he tried to turn Uncle Rondo against me. I heard every word he said. Oh, he told Uncle Rondo I didn't learn to read till I was eight years old and he didn't see how in the world I ever got the mail put up at the P.O., much less read it all, and he said if Uncle Rondo could only fathom the lengths he had gone to get me that job! And he said on the other hand he thought Stella-Rondo had a brilliant mind and deserved credit for getting out of town. All the time he was just lying there swinging as pretty as you please and looping out his beard, and poor Uncle Rondo was *pleading* with him to slow down the hammock, it was making him as dizzy as a witch to watch it. But that's what Papa-Daddy likes about a hammock. So Uncle Rondo was too dizzy to get turned against me for the time being. He's Mama's only brother and is a good case of a one-track mind. Ask anybody. A certified pharmacist.

Just then I heard Stella-Rondo raising the upstairs window. While she was married she got this peculiar idea that it's cooler with the windows shut and locked. So she has to raise the window before she can make a soul hear her outdoors.

35   So she raises the window and says, "*Oh!*" You would have thought she was mortally wounded.

Uncle Rondo and Papa-Daddy didn't even look up, but kept right on with what they were doing. I had to laugh.

I flew up the stairs and threw the door open! I says, "What in the wide world's the matter, Stella-Rondo? You mortally wounded?"

"No," she says, "I am not mortally wounded but I wish you would do me the favor of looking out that window there and telling me what you see."

So I shade my eyes and look out the window.

40   "I see the front yard," I says.

"Don't you see any human beings?"

"I see Uncle Rondo trying to run Papa-Daddy out of the hammock," I says. "Nothing more. Naturally, it's so suffocating-hot in the house, with all the windows shut and locked, everybody who cares to stay in their right mind will have to go out and get in the hammock before the Fourth of July is over."

"Don't you notice anything different about Uncle Rondo?" asks Stella-Rondo.

"Why, no, except he's got on some terrible-looking flesh-colored contraption I wouldn't be found dead in, is all I can see," I says.

45   "Never mind, you won't be found dead in it, because it happens to be part of my trousseau, and Mr. Whitaker took several dozen photographs of me in it," says Stella-Rondo. "What on earth could Uncle Rondo *mean* by wearing part of my trousseau out in the broad open daylight without saying so much as 'Kiss my foot,' *knowing* I only got home this morning after my separation and hung my negligee up on the bathroom door, just as nervous as I could be?"

"I'm sure I don't know, and what do you expect me to do about it?" I says. "Jump out the window?"

"No, I expect nothing of the kind. I simply declare that Uncle Rondo looks like a fool in it, that's all," she says. "It makes me sick to my stomach."

"Well, he looks as good as he can," I says. "As good as anybody in reason could." I stood up for Uncle Rondo, please remember. And I said to Stella-Rondo, "I think I would do well not to criticize so freely if I were you and came home with a two-year-old child I had never said a word about, and no explanation whatever about my separation."

"I asked you the instant I entered this house not to refer one more time to my adopted child, and you gave me your word of honor you would not," was all Stella-Rondo would say, and started pulling out every one of her eyebrows with some cheap Kress tweezers.

So I merely slammed the door behind me and went down and made some green-tomato pickle. Somebody had to do it. Of course Mama had turned both the Negroes loose; she always said no earthly power could hold one anyway on the Fourth of July, so she wouldn't even try. It turned out that Jaypan fell in the lake and came within a very narrow limit of drowning.

So Mama trots in. Lifts up the lid and says, "H'm! Not very good for your Uncle Rondo in his precarious condition, I must say. Or poor little adopted Shirley-T. Shame on you!"

That made me tired. I says, "Well, Stella-Rondo had better thank her lucky stars it was her instead of me came trotting in with that very peculiar-looking child. Now if it had been me that trotted in from Illinois and brought a peculiar-looking child of two, I shudder to think of the reception I'd of got, much less controlled the diet of an entire family."

"But you must remember, Sister, that you were never married to Mr. Whitaker in the first place and didn't go up to Illinois to live," says Mama, shaking a spoon in my face. "If you had I would of been just as overjoyed to see you and your little adopted girl as I was to see Stella-Rondo, when you wound up with your separation and came on back home."

"You would not," I says.

"Don't contradict me, I would," says Mama.

But I said she couldn't convince me though she talked till she was blue in the face. Then I said, "Besides, you know as well as I do that that child is not adopted."

"She most certainly is adopted," says Mama, stiff as a poker.

I says, "Why, Mama, Stella-Rondo had her just as sure as anything in this world, and just too stuck up to admit it."

"Why, Sister," said Mama. "Here I thought we were going to have a pleasant Fourth of July, and you start right out not believing a word your own baby sister tells you!"

"Just like Cousin Annie Flo. Went to her grave denying the facts of life," I reminded Mama.

"I told you if you ever mentioned Annie Flo's name I'd slap your face," says Mama, and slaps my face.

"All right, you wait and see," I says.

"I," says Mama, "I prefer to take my children's word for anything when it's humanly possible." You ought to see Mama, she weighs two hundred pounds and has real tiny feet.

Just then something perfectly horrible occurred to me.

65   "Mama," I says, "can that child talk?" I simply had to whisper! "Mama, I won-der if that child can be—you know—in any way? Do you realize?" I says, "that she hasn't spoke one single, solitary word to a human being up to this minute? This is the way she looks," I says, and I looked like this.

Well, Mama and I just stood there and stared at each other. It was horrible!

"I remember well that Joe Whitaker frequently drank like a fish," says Mama. "I believed to my soul he drank *chemicals*." And without another word she marches to the foot of the stairs and calls Stella-Rondo.

"Stella-Rondo? O-o-o-o-o! Stella-Rondo!"

"What?" says Stella-Rondo from upstairs. Not even the grace to get up off the bed.

70   "Can that child of yours talk?" asks Mama.

Stella-Rondo says, "Can she what?"

"Talk! Talk!" says Mama. "Burdyburdyburdyburdy!"

So Stella-Rondo yells back, "Who says she can't talk?"

"Sister says so," says Mama.

75   "You didn't have to tell me, I know whose word of honor don't mean a thing in this house," says Stella-Rondo.

And in a minute the loudest Yankee voice I ever heard in my life yells out, "OE'm Pop-OE the Sailor-r-r-r Ma-a-an!" and then somebody jumps up and down in the upstairs hall. In another second the house would of fallen down.

"Not only talks, she can tap-dance!" calls Stella-Rondo. "Which is more than some people I won't name can do."

"Why, the little precious darling thing!" Mama says, so surprised. "Just as smart as she can be!" Starts talking baby talk right there. Then she turns on me. "Sister, you ought to be thoroughly ashamed! Run upstairs this instant and apol-ogize to Stella-Rondo and Shirley-T."

"Apologize for what?" I says. "I merely wondered if the child was normal, that's all. Now that she's proved she is, why, I have nothing further to say."

80   But Mama just turned on her heel and flew out, furious. She ran right upstairs and hugged the baby. She believed it was adopted. Stella-Rondo hadn't done a thing but turn her against me from upstairs while I stood there helpless over the hot stove. So that made Mama, Papa-Daddy, and the baby all on Stella-Rondo's side.

Next, Uncle Rondo.

I must say that Uncle Rondo has been marvelous to me at various times in the past and I was completely unprepared to be made to jump out of my skin, the way it turned out. Once Stella-Rondo did something perfectly horrible to him—broke a chain letter from Flanders Field—and he took the radio back he had given her and gave it to me. Stella-Rondo was furious! For six months we all had to call her Stella instead of Stella-Rondo, or she wouldn't answer. I always thought Uncle Rondo had all the brains of the entire family. Another time he sent me to Mammoth Cave with all expenses paid.

But this would be the day he was drinking that prescription, the Fourth of July.

So at supper Stella-Rondo speaks up and says she thinks Uncle Rondo ought to try to eat a little something. So finally Uncle Rondo said he would try a little cold biscuits and ketchup, but that was all. So *she* brought it to him.

"Do you think it wise to disport with ketchup in Stella-Rondo's flesh-colored 85 kimono?" I says. Trying to be considerate! If Stella-Rondo couldn't watch out for her trousseau, somebody had to.

"Any objections?" asks Uncle Rondo, just about to pour out all of the ketchup.

"Don't mind what she says, Uncle Rondo," says Stella-Rondo. "Sister has been devoting this solid afternoon to sneering out my bedroom window at the way you look."

"What's that?" says Uncle Rondo. Uncle Rondo has got the most terrible temper in the world. Anything is liable to make him tear the house down if it comes at the wrong time.

So Stella-Rondo says, "Sister says, 'Uncle Rondo certainly does look like a fool in that pink kimono!'"

Do you remember who it was really said that? 90

Uncle Rondo spills out all the ketchup and jumps out of his chair and tears off the kimono and throws it down on the dirty floor and puts his foot on it. It had to be sent all the way to Jackson to the cleaners and re-pleated.

"So that's your opinion of your Uncle Rondo, is it?" he says. "I look like a fool, do I? Well, that's the last straw. A whole day in this house with nothing to do, and then to hear you come out with a remark like that behind my back!"

"I didn't say any such of a thing, Uncle Rondo," I says, "and I'm not saying who did, either. Why, I think you look all right. Just try to take care of yourself and not talk and eat at the same time," I says. "I think you better go lie down."

"Lie down my foot," says Uncle Rondo. I ought to of known by that he was fixing to do something perfectly horrible.

So he didn't do anything that night in the precarious state he was in—just 95 played Casino with Mama and Stella-Rondo and Shirley-T. and gave Shirley-T. a nickel with a head on both sides. It tickled her nearly to death, and she called him "Papa." But at 6:30 A.M. the next morning, he threw a whole five-cent package of some unsold one-inch firecrackers from the store as hard as he could into my bedroom and they every one went off. Not one bad one in the string. Anybody else, there'd be one that wouldn't go off.

Well, I'm just terribly susceptible to noise of any kind, the doctor has always told me I was the most sensitive person he had ever seen in his whole life, and I was simply prostrated. I couldn't eat! People tell me they heard it as far as the cemetery, and old Aunt Jep Patterson, that had been holding her own so good, thought it was Judgment Day and she was going to meet her whole family. It's usually so quiet here.

And I'll tell you it didn't take me any longer than a minute to make up my mind what to do. There I was with the whole entire house on Stella-Rondo's side and turned against me. If I have anything at all I have pride.

So I just decided I'd go straight down to the P.O. There's plenty of room there in the back, I says to myself.

Well! I made no bones about letting the family catch on to what I was up to. I didn't try to conceal it.

100   The first thing they knew, I marched in where they were all playing Old
Maid and pulled the electric oscillating fan out by the plug, and everything got
real hot. Next I snatched the pillow I'd done the needlepoint on right off the
davenport from behind Papa-Daddy. He went "Ugh!" I beat Stella-Rondo up the
stairs and finally found my charm bracelet in her bureau drawer under a picture
of Nelson Eddy.[1]

   "So that's the way the land lies," says Uncle Rondo. There he was, piecing on
the ham. "Well, Sister, I'll be glad to donate my army cot if you got any place to
set it up, providing you'll leave right this minute and let me get some peace."
Uncle Rondo was in France.

   "Thank you kindly for the cot and 'peace' is hardly the word I would select if
I had to resort to firecrackers at 6:30 A.M. in a young girl's bedroom," I says to
him. "And as to where I intend to go, you seem to forget my position as postmistress of China Grove, Mississippi," I says. "I've always got the P.O."

   Well, that made them all sit up and take notice.

   I went out front and started digging up some four-o'clocks to plant around
the P.O.

105   "Ah-ah-ah!" says Mama, raising the window. "Those happen to be my four-
o'clocks. Everything planted in that star is mine. I've never known you to make
anything grow in your life."

   "Very well," I says. "But I take the fern. Even you, Mama, can't stand there
and deny that I'm the one watered that fern. And I happen to know where I can
send in a box top and get a packet of one thousand mixed seeds, no two the
same kind, free."

   "Oh, where?" Mama wants to know.

   But I says, "Too late. You 'tend to your house, and I'll 'tend to mine. You hear
things like that all the time if you know how to listen to the radio. Perfectly
marvelous offers. Get anything you want free."

   So I hope to tell you I marched in and got that radio, and they could of all bit
a nail in two, especially Stella-Rondo, that it used to belong to, and she well
knew she couldn't get it back, I'd sue for it like a shot. And I very politely took
the sewing-machine motor I helped pay the most on to give Mama for Christmas back in 1929, and a good big calendar, with the first-aid remedies on it. The
thermometer and the Hawaiian ukulele certainly were rightfully mine, and I
stood on the step-ladder and got all my watermelon-rind preserves and every
fruit and vegetable I'd put up, every jar. Then I began to pull the tacks out of the
bluebird wall vases on the archway to the dining room.

110   "Who told you you could have those, Miss Priss?" says Mama, fanning as
hard as she could.

   "I bought 'em and I'll keep track of 'em," I says. "I'll tack 'em up one on each
side of the post-office window, and you can see 'em when you come to ask me
for your mail, if you're so dead to see 'em."

---

1. Opera singer (1901–67) who enjoyed phenomenal popularity in the 1930s and 1940s when he
costarred in numerous film musicals with Jeanette MacDonald. The two were known as "America's
Singing Sweethearts."

"Not I! I'll never darken the door to that post office again if I live to be a hundred," Mama says. "Ungrateful child! After all the money we spent on you at the Normal."[2]

"Me either," says Stella-Rondo. "You can just let my mail lie there and *rot*, for all I care. I'll never come and relieve you of a single, solitary piece."

"I should worry," I says. "And who you think's going to sit down and write you all those big fat letters and postcards, by the way? Mr. Whitaker? Just because he was the only man ever dropped down in China Grove and you got him— unfairly—is he going to sit down and write you a lengthy correspondence after you come home giving no rhyme nor reason whatsoever for your separation and no explanation for the presence of that child? I may not have your brilliant mind, but I fail to see it."

So Mama says, "Sister, I've told you a thousand times that Stella-Rondo sim- 115
ply got homesick, and this child is far too big to be hers," and she says, "Now, why don't you just sit down and play Casino?"

Then Shirley-T. sticks out her tongue at me in this perfectly horrible way. She has no more manners than the man in the moon. I told her she was going to cross her eyes like that some day and they'd stick.

"It's too late to stop me now," I says. "You should have tried that yesterday. I'm going to the P.O. and the only way you can possibly see me is to visit me there."

So Papa-Daddy says, "You'll never catch me setting foot in that post office, even if I should take a notion into my head to write a letter some place." He says, "I won't have you reachin' out of that little old window with a pair of shears and cuttin' off any beard of mine. I'm too smart for you!"

"We all are," says Stella-Rondo.

But I said, "If you're so smart, where's Mr. Whitaker?"   120

So then Uncle Rondo says, "I'll thank you from now on to stop reading all the orders I get on postcards and telling everybody in China Grove what you think is the matter with them," but I says, "I draw my own conclusions and will continue in the future to draw them." I says, "If people want to write their innermost secrets on penny postcards, there's nothing in the wide world you can do about it, Uncle Rondo."

"And if you think we'll ever *write* another postcard you're sadly mistaken," says Mama.

"Cutting off your nose to spite your face then," I says. "But if you're all determined to have no more to do with the U.S. mail, think of this: What will Stella-Rondo do now, if she wants to tell Mr. Whitaker to come after her?"

"Wah!" says Stella-Rondo. I knew she'd cry. She had a conniption fit right there in the kitchen.

"It will be interesting to see how long she holds out," I says. "And now—I am   125
leaving."

"Good-bye," says Uncle Rondo.

"Oh, I declare," says Mama, "to think that a family of mine should quarrel on the Fourth of July, or the day after, over Stella-Rondo leaving old Mr. Whitaker and having the sweetest little adopted child! It looks like we'd all be glad!"

"Wah!" says Stella-Rondo, and has a fresh conniption fit.

---

2. That is, normal school (teachers' college).

"He left *her*—you mark my words," I says. "That's Mr. Whitaker. I know Mr. Whitaker. After all, I knew him first. I said from the beginning he'd up and leave her. I foretold every single thing that's happened."

130   "Where did he go?" asks Mama.

"Probably to the North Pole, if he knows what's good for him," I says.

But Stella-Rondo just bawled and wouldn't say another word. She flew to her room and slammed the door.

"Now look what you've gone and done, Sister," says Mama. "You go apologize."

"I haven't the time, I'm leaving," I says.

135   "Well, what are you waiting around for?" asks Uncle Rondo.

So I just picked up the kitchen clock and marched off, without saying, "Kiss my foot," or anything, and never did tell Stella-Rondo good-bye.

There was a girl going along on a little wagon right in front.

"Nigger girl," I says, "come help me haul these things down the hill, I'm going to live in the post office."

Took her nine trips in her express wagon. Uncle Rondo came out on the porch and threw her a nickel.

140   And that's the last I've laid eyes on any of my family or my family laid eyes on me for five solid days and nights. Stella-Rondo may be telling the most horrible tales in the world about Mr. Whitaker, but I haven't heard them. As I tell everybody, I draw my own conclusions.

But oh, I like it here. It's ideal, as I've been saying. You see, I've got everything cater-cornered, the way I like it. Hear the radio? All the war news. Radio, sewing machine, book ends, ironing board and that great big piano lamp—peace, that's what I like. Butter-bean vines planted all along the front where the strings are.

Of course, there's not much mail. My family are naturally the main people in China Grove, and if they prefer to vanish from the face of the earth, for all the mail they get or the mail they write, why, I'm not going to open my mouth. Some of the folks here in town are taking up for me and some turned against me. I know which is which. There are always people who will quit buying stamps just to get on the right side of Papa-Daddy.

But here I am, and here I'll stay. I want the world to know I'm happy.

And if Stella-Rondo should come to me this minute, on bended knees, and *attempt* to explain the incidents of her life with Mr. Whitaker, I'd simply put my fingers in both my ears and refuse to listen.

1941

PART TWO Poetry

Danez Smith

11 | POETRY: READING, RESPONDING, WRITING

Ways of reading poetry and reasons for doing so differ almost as widely as poems themselves, and in ways we can perhaps best appreciate by considering poetry's functions in other times and places. Though you might be aware, for example, that medieval noblemen paid courtly bards to commemorate their achievements and thereby help them to maintain their prestige and power, you might be surprised to learn that since 2007 millions of people across the Middle East have tuned in to watch *Prince of Poets*, a reality show in which poets rather than pop singers compete for audience votes. Closer to home, you may or may not remember that in 2019 the sonnet below took center stage in heated debates over U.S. immigration policies, precisely because the same poem had—over a century earlier—helped both to fund installation of what has since become the nation's single-most iconic monument and to re-shape that monument's very meanings.

EMMA LAZARUS
The New Colossus

Not like the brazen giant of Greek
    fame,[1]
With conquering limbs astride
    from land to land;
Here at our sea-washed, sunset
    gates shall stand
A mighty woman with a torch,
    whose flame
5 Is the imprisoned lightning, and
    her name
Mother of Exiles. From her beacon-hand
Glows world-wide welcome; her mild eyes command
The air-bridged harbor that twin cities[2] frame.
"Keep, ancient lands, your storied pomp!" cries she
10 With silent lips. "Give me your tired, your poor,
Your huddled masses yearning to breathe free,

---

1. The Colossus of Rhodes, one of the seven wonders of the ancient world, a hundred-foot statue of Helios, the sun god. *New Colossus*: the Statue of Liberty, in New York Harbor; Lazarus's poem was originally written to help raise funds to erect a pedestal for the statue; a plaque bearing her poem was added in 1903.
2. Manhattan and Brooklyn.

> The wretched refuse of your teeming shore.
> Send these, the homeless, tempest-tost to me,
> I lift my lamp beside the golden door!"

1883

Such phenomena might come as a surprise to us simply because today, at least in the West, we often don't think of poetry as having great popular appeal or political potency. Millions of us may be moved by the way hip-hop artists wield poetic techniques to "celebrate and sing" themselves, much as poet Walt Whitman did. Yet poetry itself seems to many of us a thing apart, something to suffer, to cherish, or to be simply baffled and intimidated by because it seems so arcane, so different and difficult, so essentially irrelevant to the rest of our lives. Though one rarely hears anyone say of all fiction "I hate it" or "I love it" or "I just don't get it," if you're like most people, you've probably said, thought, or heard someone else say at least one of these things about poetry.

Such attitudes seem to be changing, however. According to one National Endowment for the Arts (NEA) study, the percentage of U.S. adults reading poetry grew an astounding 76 percent between 2012 and 2017, with the most dramatic increase reported by young people: Among those aged eighteen to twenty-four, poetry reading *doubled* in those five years. Whether that's due to social media or our desire to escape it, to the success of spoken-word and slam poetry, to our increased political activism and consciousness (wokeness?), to the greater diversity and inclusivity of poetry itself, or to some combination of all these, poetry in general and political poetry in particular are, to quote the headlines, "*hot* again."

This chapter and the ones that follow welcome poetry lovers. But they neither require you to be one nor aim to convert you. They do, we hope, demonstrate a few key points:

- Poetry isn't all one thing: *Poems differ as much as the people who write and read them, or as much as music or movies do.* They can be by turns goofy, sad, or angry; they can tell a story, demand social justice, or simply describe the look of a certain time of day. Deciding that you "love," "hate," "get," or "don't get" all poetry based on your experience of one poem or of one kind of poetry is a little like deciding you hate sports because watching golf on TV bores you.
- *A good poem is not a secret message one needs a special decoder ring or an advanced degree to decipher.* Any thoughtful person who's willing to try can make sense of it, though some poems certainly do invite us to rethink our idea of what "making sense" might mean. (As poet Lucille Clifton puts it, some poems aim "to afflict the comfortable," not just "to comfort the afflicted.") Poetry has spoken to millions of ordinary people across the centuries and around the world, so at least some poems can speak to us, too, if we give both them and ourselves a chance. By the same token, even the most devoted, experienced poetry lovers among us can become better, more responsive, more thoughtful readers only by reading more and different kinds of poetry and by exploring, as the following chapters do, the various elements and techniques with which poetry is made.
- People around the world have often turned to poetry to express their feelings and longings precisely because *poetry is, in certain vital ways, distinct from other forms of writing.* Each genre plays by its own rules and has its own history and traditions, so reading poetry effectively, like succeeding in a video game, does involve learning and playing by certain rules.

- Any one poem may open itself to multiple responses and interpretations, just as a game may allow you many ways of advancing to the next level. But in both cases there are limits. Neither is a free-for-all in which "anything goes." (In both cases, too, some difficulty can be essential to the fun.) *A poem wouldn't mean anything if it could mean everything.*
- *Yet the questions we ask of a poem and the techniques we use to understand it are simply variations of the same ones we use in reading fiction or drama.* Indeed, some poems narrate action just as a short story does; others work much like **scenes** from plays.
- Finally, *poems aren't nearly as fragile as we take them to be when we worry about "over-reading" or "analyzing them to death."* You can't kill a poem. But a poem does experience a sort of living death if it's not read, re-read, and pondered over. Poems need you. They can bear the weight of your careful attention, and they deserve it: The best of them are, after all, the result of someone else's. William Wordsworth may have done much to shape our contemporary ideas about poetry when he famously described it as "the spontaneous overflow of powerful feelings," but his own poems were, like most great poems, the result of weeks, even years, of writing and revision.

DEFINING POETRY

But what, after all, is poetry? Trying to define poetry is a bit like trying to catch a snowflake; you can do it, but at the very same moment, the snowflake begins to melt and disappear. With poems, as with fiction, one can always come up with particular examples that don't do what the definition insists they must, as well as numerous writers and readers who will disagree. Yet to claim that poetry eludes all definition is merely to reinforce the idea that it is simply too mysterious for ordinary mortals. Without being all-sufficient or entirely satisfying, a dictionary definition can at least give us a starting point. Here are two such definitions of poetry:

1. Writing that formulates a *concentrated* imaginative awareness of experience in language chosen and *arranged* to create a specific *emotional response* through meaning, sound, and **rhythm**. (*Merriam-Webster*)
2. Composition in verse or some comparable *patterned arrangement* of language in which the expression of *feelings* and ideas is given *intensity* by the use of distinctive style and *rhythm* [. . .]. Traditionally associated with explicit formal departure from the *patterns* of ordinary speech or prose, e.g., in the use of elevated diction, figurative language, and syntactical reordering. (*The Oxford English Dictionary*)

Different as they are, both of these definitions stress four elements (which we've italicized above): 1) the "patterned arrangement of language" to 2) generate "rhythm" and thereby both 3) express and evoke specific "emotion[s]" or "feelings" in 4) a "concentrated" way, or with "intensity."

But what does all that really mean? To test drive this definition, let's look at an example. And let's pick a tough one: Head, Heart, taken from *The Collected Stories of Lydia Davis*, is usually classified as a work of fiction, and it certainly does have the elements of one, including **characters** and some **action** arranged into a **plot** related to us by a **narrator**. Yet one reviewer of Davis's *Collected Stories* tellingly describes this one as "a poem of a story." What specific features of the following story might make it work like a poem? Which, if any, of the features essential to poetry might it lack?

LYDIA DAVIS
Head, Heart

Heart weeps.
Head tries to help heart.
Head tells heart how it is, again:
You will lose the ones you love. They will all go. But even the earth will
   go, someday.
5 Heart feels better, then.
But the words of head do not remain long in the ears of heart.
Heart is so new to this.
I want them back, says heart.
Head is all heart has.
10 Help, head. Help heart.

2007

If difficulty were essential to poetry, "Head, Heart" would not seem to qualify. It's hard to imagine less formal, even more elementary, **diction** or **syntax**. And the whole seems relatively easy to paraphrase (often a helpful thing to do when first encountering a poem): When we're sad about losing someone we love, we reason with ourselves that loss is inevitable because everything earthly, even the earth itself, can't last forever. Such rational explanations give us comfort, but that comfort is itself temporary; we still miss those we've lost and have to keep calling on our heads to help our hearts cope.

We do have emotion here, then, as well as a **conflict** between emotion and reason—and even when they lack plots, most poems do explore conflicts, just as stories and plays do. But do we have a poem? Does it matter that "Head, Heart" depends entirely on two **figures of speech**—**metonymy**, the use of the name of one thing for another closely associated thing (here, "head" for "reason," and "heart" for "emotion"), as well as **personification**, the representation of an object or an abstraction (here, "head" and "heart") as a person (capable of weeping and talking, for example)? Though fiction and drama both use figurative language, we often describe such language as "poetic," even when it occurs in a story or play, because poems do tend to depend much more on it (as we discuss further in ch. 16).

Does it matter that "Head, Heart" is short—just seventy-one words? Though poems come in every size, many poems are short or at least shorter than the typical work of fiction. Brevity is one way that *some* poems achieve the "concentration" and "intensity" the dictionaries take to be essential. Such concentration invites, even requires, ours. As former U.S. Poet Laureate Tracy K. Smith puts it, "Poetry invites [readers] to take their time, to move slowly, to process things gradually, which is an impluse counter to the breakneck pace at which so much else occurs." The very brevity of a poem can teach us simply to slow down for a moment and pay attention—not only to the details within the poem, but also, through them, to whatever in the world or in ourselves the poem attends to. Sometimes that's all a poem does—simply invites us to pay attention to something we wouldn't notice otherwise.

Regardless of their overall length, moreover, most poems concentrate our attention and modulate our pace by doling out words a few at a time, arranging them
not just into sentences (as in prose) but into discrete **lines**. One result is much more
blank space and thus more silences and pauses than in prose. For this reason alone,
"Head, Heart" looks and works somewhat like a poem. And the deliberateness
with which it does so is signaled by the fact that one of its sentences is divided so
as to span multiple lines. (Line 3 ends with a colon, not a period.) By arranging
words into lines and, often, into **stanzas**, the poet, not a typesetter or printer, determines where words fall on the page. And that perhaps is the most important aspect
of that arrangement of language into verse that has differentiated poetry from prose
since poetry became a written, as well as spoken, art (an issue discussed further in
ch. 20). All printings of a poem in verse, if accurate, reproduce exactly the same
breaks and space the words precisely the same way on the page.

AUTHORS ON THEIR WORK

BILLY COLLINS (b. 1941)

From "A Brisk Walk: An Interview with Billy Collins" (2006)*

I'm a line-maker. I think that's what makes poets different from prose-
writers. [. . .] We think not just in sentences the way prose writers do but
also in lines. [. . .] When I'm constructing a poem, I'm trying to write one good
line after another. [. . .] I'm not thinking of just writing a paragraph and then
chopping it up. I'm very conscious of the fact that every line should have a
cadence to it. It should contribute to the progress of the poem. And that the
ending of the line is a way of turning the reader's attention back into the
interior of the poem.

*"A Brisk Walk: An Interview with Billy Collins." Interview by Joel Whitney. *Guernica*, 14
June 2006, www.guernicamag.com/interviews/a_brisk_walk/.

One result is that line endings and beginnings inevitably get more of our attention, bear more oomph and meaning. Notice how many of the lines of "Head,
Heart" begin with *head* and *heart* and how these words repeat in a pattern (*Heart,
Head, Head, Heart, Heart, Head*—and then *Help*), as if the line beginnings themselves enact the same interplay between "head" and "heart" that the sentences
describe. Conversely, certain end words reverberate: *Again*, for example, suggests
the repetitive familiarity of this conflict, one that paradoxically seems all the more
difficult or poignant because it's both repetitive (each person goes through this
again and again) and common (all of us go through this); *then* alerts us to the tempo-
rariness of the comfort head offers heart, preparing us for the *But* in the next line.
   Again and *then* also reverberate in us and with each other because they **rhyme**,
just as *head*, *heart*, and *help* **alliterate**. These words share a special aural, as well
as spatial and visual, relationship to one another. Though prose writers certainly
make their appeal to us in part through sound, poetry remains, as it has been for
thousands of years, a more insistently aural form—one that through aural patterning addresses itself to what Davis here humorously, but not wrongly, calls "the ears

of heart" (line 6). As poet Mary Oliver puts it, "To make a poem, we must make sounds. Not random sounds, but chosen sounds."

But are there qualities essential to poetry that "Head, Heart" lacks? Is it, for example, sufficiently aural in its appeal? Does it have genuine rhythm? Perhaps so, perhaps not. As you work your way through the rest of the chapters in this section and read more poems, we encourage you to keep thinking critically about our definitions in order to hone your own sense of just what poetry is, how it works, and what it does.

THE PROSE POEM

As you think through such questions, you might want to consider that strange creature called the **prose poem,** a poem that uses all the strategies and tactics of poetry save that one essential to verse: the line break. First recognized and cultivated as a genre in the late nineteenth century, at the same time and by some of the same poets who pioneered **free verse** or *vers libre* (to use the French term), prose poetry, as poet and literary critic David Lehman observes, "does away with the line as the unit of composition," "[j]ust as free verse did away with meter and rhyme." As a result, he suggests, we might think of prose poetry as "poetry that disguises its true nature," a hybrid form "us[ing] the means of prose toward the ends of poetry." Alternatively, we might envision the prose poem, as poet Campbell McGrath does, as occupying "the twilight zone between poetry and prose," requiring "some sort of music, a rhythmic intensity or flow," "a different movement and different kind of closure" than the fiction it otherwise sometimes resembles.

How might Lehman's or McGrath's descriptions apply to either of the following very different examples? How, in turn, might these examples help you to refine your sense of just what strategies, tactics, movements, and "ends" constitute poetry?

CAMPBELL McGRATH
Section XI: My Library *from* Sleepwork

Assembled with such care over the decades, with its shelves of well-thumbed *Collected Poems,* its ponderous chronicles, tea-stained chapbooks, and paperbacks asterisked with mildew, after all these years my library slips its anchor and sails ever more certainly into the past. Soon even the methods and substance of its origin—paper and ink, the printing press—will resemble fragments of ash and animal bone in an ancient digging, yet I feel no particular sense of regret that I will not live to see our futuristic tropes put to the final test, whatever dire exigency that might consist of. All I have ever wanted is to write a poem as ineradicable as the sun, singular as a wolf in its kingdom of moonlit ice. But who has time, anymore, for idle tasks? Why should anyone bother to adjudicate the petty crimes of language, border disputes between synonyms, lexical transgressions opaque as tax legislation? Pea vines are climbing the neighbor's trellis, the kids are looking for a surfboard behind the garage, wind rustles the branches which respond with shrugs and apologetic bows. In the shelter of their anthologies, the poems talk softly in the darkness, huddled together for warmth, waiting.

2019

ADA LIMÓN
Sacred Objects

I'm driving down to Tennessee, but before I get there, I stop at the
Kentucky state line to fuel up and pee. The dog's in the car and the weather's
fine. As I pump the gas a man in his black Ford F150 yells out his window
about my body. I actually can't remember what it was. Nice tits. Nice ass.
Something common that I've been hearing my whole life. Except sometimes it's not *Nice ass*, it's *Big ass* or something a bit more cruel. I pretend
not to hear him. I pretend my sunglasses hide my whole body and I'm made
invisible. Right then, a man with black hair, who could be an uncle of
mine, pulls by in his truck and nods. He's towing a trailer that's painted
gray with white letters. The letters read: *Sacred Objects*. I imagine a trailer
full of Las Virgens de Guadalupe[3] all wobbly from their travels, concrete, or
marble, or wood. All of these female statues hidden together in this secret
shadowed place on their way to find a place where they'll be safe, even
worshipped, or at the very least allowed to live in the light.

2017

POETIC SUBGENRES AND KINDS

All poems share some common elements, use some of the same techniques, and
thus require us to ask some of the same questions. Later in this chapter, we'll outline steps you can follow and questions you can pose as you read, respond to, and
write about any poem. But as the prose poem suggests, different sorts of poems
also work by slightly different rules and thus invite somewhat different responses
and questions.

Poems may be classified into subgenres based on various characteristics, including their length, appearance, and formal features (patterns of rhyme and rhythm,
for example); their subject; or even the type of **situation** and **setting** (time and
place) they depict. (A **sonnet**, for example, traditionally has fourteen lines. Defined
broadly, an **elegy** is a poem about death.) A single poem might well represent multiple subgenres or at least might contain elements of more than one. (One could
write an elegy that is also a sonnet, for instance.)

Since Aristotle's time, however, readers and writers have also often divided
poems into three broad categories or subgenres—**narrative, dramatic,** or **lyric**—
based upon their mode of presentation. Put simply, poems that have a plot are
either narrative poems (if they feature a narrator) or dramatic poems (if they don't),
and many poems that lack a plot are lyrics. The rest of this section describes each
of these subgenres in more detail, starting with the one that most resembles fiction
and ending with the dramatic monologue, a sort of hybrid that combines features
of both dramatic and lyric poetry.

As the dramatic monologue demonstrates, the borders between narrative, dramatic, and lyric poetry are fuzzy, contestable, and shifting. Some poems will cross
those borders; others will resist these categories altogether. And the very definition
of lyric poetry has not only changed over time, but also remains contested today.

---

3. Catholic title of Virgin Mary in her appearance before St. Juan Diego in a 1531 vision, near what
is now Mexico City.

The ultimate goal isn't to definitively pigeonhole every poem but rather to develop a language through which to recognize, describe, and explore different poetic modes. Knowing which mode dominates in a particular poem can help ensure that we privilege the right questions as we read and write about it. Learning the **conventions** of particular subgenres and kinds allows us to better adjust to individual poems, to compare them to each other, and to appreciate how each creatively uses, reworks, or even defies or questions generic conventions.

Narrative Poetry

Like a work of prose fiction, a narrative poem tells a story; in other words, it has a plot related by a narrator, though its plot might be based on actual rather than made-up events. Comprising the same elements discussed in the Fiction section of this book, a narrative poem encourages us to ask the same questions—about character, plot, narration, and so on—that we do when reading a short story or novel. (See "Questions about the Elements of Fiction" in ch. 1.)

In centuries past, narrative poetry was a—even *the*—dominant subgenre of poetry. As a result, there are many different kinds of narrative poems, including book-length **epics** like Homer's *Iliad*; chivalric **romances**; grisly murder **ballads**, often rooted in actual events; and a range of harder-to-classify works of varying lengths such as the relatively short example below.

EAVAN BOLAND
Quarantine

In the worst hour of the worst season
   of the worst year of a whole people
a man set out from the workhouse with his wife.
He was walking—they were both walking—north.

5 She was sick with famine fever and could not keep up.
   He lifted her and put her on his back.
He walked like that west and west and north.
Until at nightfall under freezing stars they arrived.

In the morning they were both found dead.
10   Of cold. Of hunger. Of the toxins of a whole history.
But her feet were held against his breastbone.
The last heat of his flesh was his last gift to her.

Let no love poem ever come to this threshold.
   There is no place here for the inexact
15 praise of the easy graces and sensuality of the body.
There is only time for this merciless inventory:

Their death together in the winter of 1847.[4]
   Also what they suffered. How they lived.
And what there is between a man and woman.
20 And in which darkness it can best be proved.

                                      2001

---

4. The worst year of the Irish Famine, or Great Hunger (1845–49), which killed an estimated one million people and led to the emigration of another million.

• How are the man and woman's journey and death characterized in the poem's first three stanzas? What might the poem's last two stanzas encourage us to see as meaningful about these events?

AUTHORS ON THEIR WORK

EAVAN BOLAND (1944–2020)

From "Interview with Irish Poet Eavan Boland" (2008)*

INTERVIEWER: What do we get out of poems that deal with individual lives that we don't get from history books or the evening news?

BOLAND: [. . .] History is the official version of events, and in some ways like the old poetic elegy has this undertone that it has to be about something important. You know, the poem isn't tied to that. The poem is set up by its music and its meaning to try to commend something *to be* important. But it doesn't have to begin with the sense that it must be important.

INTERVIEWER: So does the writing of a poem about something make it important?

BOLAND: I think if a poem works, it definitely holds together something, and it protects something from the erosions of space and time. And in some barely conscious way the fact that it's been protected makes you think this thing is like a photograph; it's like a snapshot; it was kept when all the other things were let go.

⋅ ⋅ ⋅ ⋅ ⋅

I think what really came to be the starting point [for "Quarantine"] was [. . .] my sense that the love poem is another form of official history. It records glamor and desire and the beauty of a moment, but these steadfastnesses don't get recorded. And I felt that was really wrong [. . .].

*"Interview with Irish Poet Eavan Boland." Interview by Elizabeth Austen. KUOW Public Radio, 3 Mar. 2008, beta.prx.org/stories/24834.

Dramatic Poetry

For centuries, plays were written in verse; as a result, drama itself was understood not as a genre in its own right (as we think of it today) but rather as a subgenre of poetry. *Dramatic poetry* thus meant and still can mean actual plays in verse (or *verse drama*). But any poem that consists wholly of **dialogue** among characters, unmediated by a narrator, counts as a dramatic poem. And we might even apply that label to poems like the following, in which narration is kept to the barest minimum. Indeed, this narrator's only words are "said she," and since every other word in the poem is spoken by one female character to another, the poem essentially reads like a scene from a play. Notice, though, that the poem also depends on techniques of formal organization and patterning unique to verse: In each of the poem's six stanzas, for example, one woman speaks the first lines, while her companion gets the last line (or two).

THOMAS HARDY
The Ruined Maid

"O 'Melia,[5] my dear, this does everything crown!
Who could have supposed I should meet you in Town?
And whence such fair garments, such prosperi-ty?"—
"O didn't you know I'd been ruined?" said she.

5 —"You left us in tatters, without shoes or socks,
Tired of digging potatoes, and spudding up docks;[6]
And now you've gay bracelets and bright feathers three!"—
"Yes: that's how we dress when we're ruined," said she.

—"At home in the barton[7] you said 'thee' and 'thou,'
10 And 'thik oon,' and 'theäs oon,' and 't'other'; but now
Your talking quite fits 'ee for high compa-ny!"—
"Some polish is gained with one's ruin," said she.

—"Your hands were like paws then, your face blue and bleak
But now I'm bewitched by your delicate cheek,
15 And your little gloves fit as on any la-dy!"—
"We never do work when we're ruined," said she.

—"You used to call home-life a hag-ridden dream,
And you'd sigh, and you'd sock;[8] but at present you seem
To know not of megrims[9] or melancho-ly!"—
20 "True. One's pretty lively when ruined," said she.

—"I wish I had feathers, a fine sweeping gown,
And a delicate face, and could strut about Town!"—
"My dear—a raw country girl, such as you be,
Cannot quite expect that. You ain't ruined," said she.

1866   1901

When we read and write about dramatic poems, we can usefully bring to bear the same questions we do in reading drama. (See "Questions to Ask When Reading a Play" in ch. 24.) But when it comes to short poems like THE RUINED MAID, questions about sets, staging, and even plot will usually be much less relevant than those related to character and conflict, as well as setting, tone, language, symbol, and theme. In Hardy's poem, for example, how are each of the two speakers characterized by *how* they speak, as well as *what* they say? How is our view of them, and especially of 'Melia, "the ruined maid," affected by the formal pattern mentioned earlier, which ensures (among other things) that she gets the last line? How might this pattern, along with rhythm and rhyme, also add **irony** to the poem?

5. Short for Amelia.
6. Spading up weeds.
7. Farmyard.
8. Sigh (English dialect).
9. Migraine headaches.

Lyric Poetry

For good historical reasons, lyric poems probably best fulfill your expectations of what poetry should be like. Yet lyric poetry has been and still is defined in myriad ways. The word *lyric* derives from the ancient Greeks, for whom it designated a short poem chanted or sung by a single singer to the accompaniment of a stringed instrument called a lyre (hence, the word *lyric* and the fact that we today also use the word *lyrics* to denote the words of any song). Scholars believe that the earliest "lyrics" in the Greek sense were likely associated with religious occasions and feelings, especially those related to celebration, praise, and mourning. Ever since, the lyric has been associated with brevity, musicality, a single speaker, and the expression of intense feeling. Not surprisingly, at least a few specific kinds of lyric, including the **ode** and the elegy, originated in the ancient world.

Over the centuries, the lyric's boundaries have expanded and become fuzzier. Few lyrics are intended to be sung at all, much less to a lyre. But everyone agrees that relatively short poems that focus primarily on the feelings, impressions, and thoughts—that is, on the subjective, inward experience—of a single first-person speaker are lyrics. (By this definition, both prose poems appearing earlier in this chapter are thus lyrics.)

Below are two examples very different from each other in subject matter and tone. Yet with these, as with all lyrics, our initial questions in both reading and writing will likely focus on each speaker's situation and inward experience of it. What is each speaker experiencing, feeling, and thinking, and how exactly does the poem make that state of mood and mind at once vivid and relevant to us?

WILLIAM WORDSWORTH
I wandered lonely as a cloud[1]

I wandered lonely as a cloud
That floats on high o'er vales and hills,
When all at once I saw a crowd,
A host, of golden daffodils;
5 Beside the lake, beneath the trees,
Fluttering and dancing in the breeze.

Continuous as the stars that shine
And twinkle on the milky way,
They stretched in never-ending line
10 Along the margin of a bay:
Ten thousand saw I at a glance,
Tossing their heads in sprightly dance.

The waves beside them danced; but they
Out-did the sparkling waves in glee:
15 A poet could not but be gay,
In such a jocund company:

1. When any poem lacks a title, it is conventional to substitute the poem's first line, maintaining original capitalization (or lack thereof).

I gazed—and gazed—but little thought
What wealth the show to me had brought:

For oft, when on my couch I lie
20 In vacant or in pensive mood,
They flash upon that inward eye
Which is the bliss of solitude;
And then my heart with pleasure fills,
And dances with the daffodils.

1807

- According to the speaker, what is "the bliss of solitude" (line 22)? Why and how does "solitude" become less "lonely" for him (1)?
- What about the relationship between human beings and nature might be implied by the speaker's description of his particular experience?

ELISA GONZALEZ
In Quarantine, I Reflect on the Death of Ophelia[2]

I wake early and angry, I eat oatmeal with thyme honey,
I call my sister, I call my mother, I call my other sisters, my brothers,
I worry about my feverish lover, I worry about my siblings, jobless now.
I send an ill-advised e-mail, I don't send an ill-advised tweet.

5 I'm alone so I'm lonely. That's what my sister says.

Time to stay indoors, the doctor says, all the doctors say,
but the open window betrays that not everyone's voice dies to solitude.
Shut up, shut up! the window slams.
Time to embrace the virtues of boredom, the price of happiness again, after.

10 The window shows men digging a place for survivors of the future, the
      rich ones.
It will be a condo tower, glass walls for better envy.
They've built the frames, I see, around the holes where doors will
      someday go.
Capitalism! So full of holes and hope.

If I try to remember what it was like, childhood, a period of kudzu[3]
15 growth that *felt* like stasis in the white-glazed room where days upon days
      my father shut me—
if I try, I see the ceiling, that water stain trailing down
like brown Pre-Raphaelite curls,[4] hair of a drowning girl among reeds,
which later I recognized in a painting of a pale drowning Ophelia.

2. Love interest of the eponymous protagonist of Shakespeare's play *Hamlet* (c. 1599–1601); she falls into a fit of madness and drowns.
3. Fast-growing Asian climbing vine common in the southeastern United States.
4. The Pre-Raphaelites were a group of nineteenth-century British painters whose work often features beautiful but melancholic women with long, thick hair; John Everett Millais's painting of a drowned Ophelia (1851–52) is a famous example, partly thanks to the myth that Millais's model died of the cold she caught from the chilly bathwater in which she posed.

I love alone, I tell my sister. She says, You just want to.

20 I agree I want the past.
For a magnolia to bloom on a crowded street, all safe in beauty, for I
still love the world, though it drowns
and dies like that girl, avoidably.

A professor once asked, pleased we wouldn't know,
25 Who is really responsible for the death of Ophelia?
The answer, he said, ought to feel like we have arrived together
at a skyscraper's peak, where the inhuman
view reveals in windows and in streets
the small, sick or potentially sick bodies—each one a new array of
questions.

30 The only possible epiphany is that the ending of a thought is never such.

Together. I liked the word in the professor's mouth.
But if I am alone, and if I am lonely, and if I am not alone in loneliness,
and if the everyone
together suffers, and if this everyone suffers and dies by the unguided
motion of matter, and if
also by the motion of craven, murderous men, and if also by the motion of
money, and if of course
35 you were always going to die, Ophelia, and if even so your death remains
unforgivable,
then what are the questions I should ask? All I have is sleeplessness and
rage,
and that's no answer, it's not even a thought, though it might not end till
my body does,

John Everett Millais, *Ophelia*, 1851–52

perhaps not even then, as I can imagine it going on past my ending,
   and really—
what more suitable ghost could I leave behind? Since I do love the world.

2020

• What does this lyric's speaker communicate about her own particular situation and feelings and about COVID-19 in general by means of **allusion** both to Shakespeare's Ophelia and to John Everett Millais's famous painting of that "drown[ed] girl among reeds" (line 17)?

What makes these lyrics different from narrative and dramatic poems? Though both of the examples above include action ("wander[ing]," "wak[ing]," "eat[ing]," and so on), that action doesn't quite add up to a plot; what we have might be better described as a situation, scene, or incident. Similarly, though the poems vividly describe external things such as "golden daffodils" and a "white-glazed room," greater emphasis ultimately falls on how the "I" experiences and feels about them—the internal experience or state of mind and mood that those outward things inspire or reflect. Both poems thus encourage us to focus almost exclusively on the complex emotional experience and thoughts of a particular speaker in a specific situation, but ones that we can, if the poem is effective, ultimately understand as having a much wider, sometimes even universal, resonance and relevance.

Most lyrics require us to infer a general theme from a specific experience, but some offer more explicit reflection, commentary, even argument. As you read the following example, notice what happens in line 5 (exactly halfway through the poem), as the speaker turns from personal statements to more impersonal, argumentative ones. How does personal reflection relate to, even enable, argument here?

Frontispiece to Phillis Wheatley's *Poems on Various Subjects, Religious and Moral*, 1773

PHILLIS WHEATLEY
On Being Brought from Africa to America

'Twas mercy brought me from my
    Pagan land,
Taught my benighted soul to
    understand
That there's a God, that there's a
    Saviour too:
Once I redemption neither sought
    nor knew.
5 Some view our sable race with
    scornful eye,
"Their colour is a diabolic die."
Remember, Christians, Negroes,
    black as Cain,[5]
May be refin'd, and join th' angelic
    train.

1773

5. One of Adam's sons, who killed his brother Abel. (See Gen. 4.)

- What do the poem's first four lines imply about how the speaker feels about "being brought from Africa to America" and about what motivates these feelings?
- What two "view[s]" (line 5) of Africans are contrasted in the last four lines? According to the entire poem, which is the right view, and why and how so?

Descriptive or Observational Lyrics

As Wheatley's poem demonstrates, lyrics come in many varieties. Quite a few are more exclusively descriptive or observational than the examples above, insofar as they describe something or someone to us without bringing much attention to the speaker's state of mind or feelings. As we've noted, after all, some poems simply give us the opportunity to look more closely and carefully at something in the world around us. Nineteenth-century poet Percy Bysshe Shelley suggested, in fact, that all poetry's major purpose is just that—helping us see in a new way. Poetry, he said, "strips the veil of familiarity from the world, and lays bare [its] naked and sleeping beauty" and "wonder." Over a century later, American poet James Dickey expressed a similar idea somewhat differently when he defined a poet as "someone who notices and is enormously taken by things that somebody else would walk by."

Obviously, any descriptive poem inevitably reflects its speaker's point of view. Yet lyrics of this type invite us to focus more on what they describe than on the subjective, internal experience or feelings of the speaker doing the describing. As a result, our focus in reading and writing will probably be how the poem characterizes, and encourages us to see, think, and feel about, whatever it describes—whether a moment, a person, an object, or a phenomenon. What is described in each of the poems that follow? What figures of speech are used, and with what implications and effects?

EMILY DICKINSON
The Sky is low—the Clouds are mean

The Sky is low—the Clouds are mean.
A Travelling Flake of Snow
Across a Barn or through a Rut
Debates if it will go—
5 A Narrow Wind complains all Day
How some one treated him
Nature, like Us, is sometimes caught
Without her Diadem—

1866

- Whom does the speaker seem to mean by "Us," and what might this poem imply about the similarity between "Nature" and "Us" (line 7)?

BILLY COLLINS
Divorce

Once, two spoons in bed,
now tined forks

across a granite table
and the knives they have hired.

2008

- This poem consists almost entirely of **metaphor** (implied comparison). What
  is compared to what here? How would you describe the poem's **tone**? (Is it
  funny, sad, bitter, or some combination of these?) Why and how so?

The Dramatic Monologue

Finally, we come to the **dramatic monologue**, a subgenre of poem that—by residing somewhere in between lyric and dramatic poetry—can teach us more about
both. Robert Browning, the nineteenth-century British poet often credited with
inventing this kind of poem, tellingly labeled his own works "dramatic lyrics,"
describing them as "dramatic in principle," "lyric in expression." On the one hand,
the dramatic monologue is "lyric in expression" or like a lyric poem because it
features a single speaker who speaks in the first person. On the other hand, it is
"dramatic in principle" or resembles a scene from a play for at least two reasons.
First, the poem's primary focus is characterization, an obviously fictional or historical speaker's often unintentional revelation of his or her personality, outlook, and
values. Such poems tend to offer us a window into an entire, complex psychology
and even life history rather than simply one experience or feeling of a speaker we
otherwise discover little about (as in lyrics). Often, too, dramatic monologues
invite us to see their speakers and situations somewhat differently than the speakers themselves do, much as does fiction narrated by *unreliable narrators*. Second,
the speaker of a dramatic monologue conventionally addresses one or more silent
auditors whose identity we can only infer from the speaker's words *to* them. Often,
speaker and auditor are caught in a very specific and "dramatic" moment or situation, one which we also have to tease out from the clues the speaker gives us and
which frequently involves some sort of persuasion on the speaker's part. The questions we pose in reading and writing about such poems thus often center on character and characterization and on the comparison of our perception of the speaker
and his or her situation with the speaker's own self-representation.

Today this subgenre remains as popular with songwriters as with poets. Bruce
Springsteen's albums *Nebraska* (1982) and *The Rising* (2002), for instance, consist
mainly of dramatic monologues. Below, you will find the lyrics to one of these, followed by a poem that takes the form of an imaginary letter, thus putting an interesting twist on the conventions regarding "speakers" and "auditors."

BRUCE SPRINGSTEEN
Nebraska

I saw her standin' on her front lawn
    just twirlin' her baton
Me and her went for a ride, sir, and ten
    innocent people died

5 From the town of Lincoln, Nebraska,
    with a sawed-off .410 on my lap
Through the badlands of Wyoming I
    killed everything in my path

I can't say that I'm sorry for the things
10 that we done
At least for a little while, sir, me and
    her we had us some fun

The jury brought in a guilty verdict and
    the judge he sentenced me to death
15 Midnight in a prison storeroom with
    leather straps across my chest

Sheriff, when the man pulls that
    switch, sir, and snaps my poor head back
You make sure my pretty baby is sittin'
20 right there on my lap

They declared me unfit to live, said into
    that great void my soul'd be hurled
They wanted to know why I did what I did
    Well, sir, I guess there's just a meanness in this world[6]

                      1982

• What different motives and explanations for the speaker's actions might
NEBRASKA provide by means of what he says, how he speaks, and how his
speech is rendered on the page? Might the song as a whole offer explanations
that the speaker doesn't offer, at least consciously or directly?

ROBERT HAYDEN
A Letter from Phillis Wheatley

(London, 1773)

Dear Obour[7]
    Our crossing was without
event. I could not help, at times,

---

6. Allusion to words spoken by a murderer in Flannery O'Connor's "A Good Man Is Hard to Find"
(par. 134; p. 508).
7. Obour Tanner, a Rhode Island slave and Wheatley's intimate friend and frequent correspondent.

reflecting on that first—my Destined—
5   voyage long ago (I yet
have some remembrance of its Horrors)[8]
and marvelling at God's Ways.
        Last evening, her Ladyship[9] presented me
to her illustrious Friends.
10   I scarce could tell them anything
of Africa, though much of Boston
and my hope of Heaven. I read
my latest Elegies to them.
"O Sable Muse!" the Countess cried,
15   embracing me, when I had done.
I held back tears, as is my wont,
and there were tears in Dear
Nathaniel's eyes.
        At supper—I dined apart
20   like captive Royalty—
the Countess and her Guests promised
signatures affirming me
True Poetess, albeit once a slave.[1]
Indeed, they were most kind, and spoke,
25   moreover, of presenting me
at Court (I thought of Pocahontas)[2]—
an Honor, to be sure, but one,
I should, no doubt, as Patriot decline.
        My health is much improved;
30   I feel I may, if God so Wills,
entirely recover here.
Idyllic England! Alas, there is
no Eden without its Serpent. Beneath
chiming Complaisance I hear him hiss;
35   I see his flickering tongue
when foppish would-be Wits
murmur of the Yankee Pedlar
and his Cannibal Mockingbird.
        Sister, forgive th'intrusion of
40   my Sombreness—Nocturnal Mood
I would not share with any save

8. Born in Africa c. 1753–54, Phillis Wheatley was taken at around age eight on the slave ship *Phillis* to America, where she was purchased by Boston merchant John Wheatley. In 1773, he sent her to London with his son, Nathaniel, a visit partly motivated by concerns about her health.
9. Selina Hastings, Countess of Huntingdon (1707–91), helped arrange publication of Wheatley's first book of poems, which appeared in London just months after the poet's return to the United States.
1. Wheatley's *Poems on Various Subjects, Religious and Moral* (1773) was prefaced by a letter, signed by seventeen eminent Bostonians, attesting to the poems' authenticity, which had been questioned because of her race.
2. Daughter of an Algonquian Indian chief (c. 1595–1617), Pocahontas famously befriended Virginia's first English colonists, led by Captain John Smith; she died while visiting England, where she had been presented at the court of King James I.

your trusted Self. Let me disperse,
in closing, such unseemly Gloom
by mention of an Incident
45 you may, as I, consider Droll:
Today, a little Chimney Sweep,
his face and hands with soot quite Black,
staring hard at me, politely asked:
"Does you, M'lady, sweep chimneys too?"
50 I was amused, but Dear Nathaniel
(ever Solicitous) was not.
    I pray the Blessings of Our Lord
    and Saviour Jesus Christ
    will Abundantly be yours.
55   Phillis

                                              1977

- What internal and external conflicts seem to be revealed here? What conflict does the speaker herself seem aware of? Why might Hayden have chosen both this particular moment in Wheatley's life and this particular addressee (Obour Tanner)?
- How does Hayden's portrayal of both Wheatley's feelings and others' views of her compare to Wheatley's own characterization of these in On Being Brought from Africa to America?

RESPONDING TO POETRY

Not all poems are as readily accessible as those in this chapter, and even those that are take on additional meanings if we approach them systematically, bringing to bear specific reading habits and skills and some knowledge of poetic genres, conventions, and traditions. Experience will give you a sense of what to expect, but knowing what to expect isn't everything. As a reader of poetry, you should always be open—to new experiences, new feelings, new ideas, new forms of expression. Every poem is a potential new experience, and you will often discover something new with every re-reading.

Steps to Follow, Questions to Ask, and Sample Reading Notes

No one can give you a method that will offer you total experience of all poems. But because individual poems share characteristics with other poems, taking certain steps can prompt you both to ask the right questions and to devise compelling answers. If you are relatively new to poetry, encounter a poem that seems especially difficult, or plan to write about a poem, you may need to tackle the following steps one at a time, pausing to write even as you read and respond. With further experience, you will often find that you can skip some steps or run through them quickly and almost automatically, though your experience and understanding of any poem will be enriched if you slow down and take your time.

  Try the first step on your own, then we will both detail and demonstrate the others.

1. **Listen to a poem first.** When you encounter a new poem, read through it once without thinking too much about what it means. Try to simply listen to the poem, even if you read silently, much as you might a song on the radio. Better yet, read it aloud. Doing so will help you hear the poem's sound qualities, get a clearer impression of its **tone**, and start making sense of its **syntax**, the way words combine into sentences.

APHRA BEHN
On Her Loving Two Equally

I

How strongly does my passion flow,
Divided equally twixt[3] two?
Damon had ne'er subdued my heart,
Had not Alexis took his part;
5   Nor could Alexis powerful prove,
Without my Damon's aid, to gain my love.

II

When my Alexis present is,
Then I for Damon sigh and mourn;
But when Alexis I do miss,
10   Damon gains nothing but my scorn.
But if it chance they both are by,
For both alike I languish, sigh, and die.

III

Cure then, thou mighty wingèd god,[4]
This restless fever in my blood;
15   One golden-pointed dart take back:
But which, O Cupid, wilt thou take?
If Damon's, all my hopes are crossed;
Or that of my Alexis, I am lost.

1684

Now that you've read Behn's poem, read through the remaining steps and see how one reader used them as a guide for responding. Later, return to these steps as you read and respond to other poems.

2. **Articulate your expectations, starting with the title.** Poets often try to surprise readers, but you can appreciate such surprises only if you first define your expectations. As you read a poem, take note of what you expect and where, when, and how the poem does and doesn't fulfill your expectations.

---

3. Between.
4. Cupid, who, according to myth, shot darts of lead and of gold at the hearts of lovers, corresponding to false love and true love, respectively.

The title of Aphra Behn's "On Her Loving Two Equally" makes me think the poem will be about a woman. But can someone really "love two equally"? Maybe this is the question the poem will ask. If so, I expect its answer to be no, because I don't think this is possible. If so, maybe the title is a sort of pun—"On Her Loving *Too* Equally."

3. **Read the syntax literally.** What the sentences literally say is only a starting point, but it is vital. You cannot begin to explore what a poem *means* unless you first know what it *says*. Though poets arrange words into lines and stanzas, they usually write in complete sentences, just as writers in other genres do. At the same time and partly in order to create the sort of aural and visual patterns discussed earlier in this chapter, poets make much more frequent use of **inversion** (a change in normal word order or syntax). To ensure you don't misread, first "translate" the poem rather than fixing on certain words and free-associating or leaping to conclusions. To translate accurately, especially with poems written before the twentieth century, you may need to break this step down into the following smaller steps:

   a. *Identify sentences.* For now, ignore the line breaks and look for sentences or independent clauses (word groups that can function as complete sentences). These will typically be preceded and followed by a period (.), a semicolon (;), a colon (:), or a dash (—).

   The eighteen lines of Behn's poem can be broken down into nine sentences.
   1. How strongly does my passion flow, Divided equally twixt two?
   2. Damon had ne'er subdued my heart, Had not Alexis took his part;
   3. Nor could Alexis powerful prove, Without my Damon's aid, to gain my love.
   4. When my Alexis present is, Then I for Damon sigh and mourn;
   5. But when Alexis I do miss, Damon gains nothing but my scorn.
   6. But if it chance they both are by, For both alike I languish, sigh, and die.
   7. Cure then, thou mighty wingèd god, This restless fever in my blood;
   8. One golden-pointed dart take back: But which, O Cupid, wilt thou take?
   9. If Damon's, all my hopes are crossed; Or that of my Alexis, I am lost.

   b. *Reorder sentences.* Identify the main elements—subject(s), verb(s), object(s)—of each sentence or independent clause, and if necessary rearrange them in normative word order. (In English, this order tends to be subject-verb-object except in the case of a question; in either case, dependent clauses come at the beginning or end of the main clause and next to whatever element they modify.)

   c. *Replace each pronoun with the antecedent noun it replaces;* if the antecedent is ambiguous, indicate all the possibilities.

   In the following sentences, the reordered words appear in italics, nouns substituted for pronouns appear in parentheses:

1. How strongly does my passion flow, Divided equally twixt two?
2. Damon had ne'er subdued my heart, Had not Alexis took (Alexis's or Damon's) part;
3. Nor could Alexis *prove* powerful *to gain my love* Without my Damon's aid.
4. When my Alexis *is* present, Then I *sigh and mourn* for Damon;
5. But when *I do miss* Alexis, Damon gains nothing but my scorn.
6. But if it chance *both* (Damon and Alexis) are by, *I languish, sigh, and die* For both (Damon and Alexis) alike.
7. *thou mighty wingèd god,* Cure then This restless fever in my blood;
8. *take back* One golden-pointed dart: But which *wilt thou take,* O Cupid?
9. If Damon's, all my hopes are crossed; Or that (dart) of my Alexis, I am lost.

d. *Translate sentences into modern prose.* Use a dictionary to define unfamiliar or ambiguous words or words that seem to be used in an unfamiliar or unexpected way. Add any implied words necessary to link the parts of a sentence to each other and one sentence logically to the next. At this stage, don't move to outright paraphrase; instead, stick closely to the original.

Below, added words appear in brackets, substituted definitions in parentheses:

1. How strongly does my passion flow [when it is] divided equally between two [people]?
2. Damon would never have (*conquered* or *tamed*) my heart if Alexis had not taken (Damon's or Alexis's) (*portion*) [of my heart].
3. Nor could Alexis [have] prove[n] powerful [enough] to gain my love without my Damon's aid.
4. When my Alexis is present, then I sigh and mourn for Damon;
5. But when I miss Alexis, Damon doesn't gain anything (*except*) my scorn.
6. But if it (*so happens*) that both (Damon and Alexis) are [near]by [me], I languish, sigh, and die for both (Damon and Alexis) alike.
7. [Cupid], (*you*) mighty god (*with wings*), cure then this restless fever in my blood;
8. Take back one [of your two] darts [with] pointed gold [tips]: But which [of these darts] will you take, O Cupid?
9. If [on the one hand, you take away] Damon's [dart], all my hopes are (*opposed, invalidated, spoiled*); Or [if, on the other hand, you take away] Alexis's [arrow], I am (*desperate, ruined, destroyed; no longer claimed or possessed by anyone; helpless or unable to find my way*).

e. *Note any ambiguities in the original language that you might have ignored in your translation.* For example, look for modifiers that might modify more than one thing; verbs that might have multiple subjects or objects; words that have multiple relevant meanings.

In the second sentence, "his" could refer either to Damon or to Alexis since both names appear in the first part of this sentence; in other words, this could say either "Alexis took Damon's part" or "Alexis took his own part." But what about the word *part*? I translated this as *portion*, and I assumed it referred back to "heart," partly because the two words come at the ends of lines 3 ("heart") and 4 ("part") and also rhyme. But two other definitions of *part* might make sense here: "the role of a character in a play" or "one's . . . allotted task (as in an action)," and "one of the opposing sides in a conflict or dispute," which in this case could be the "conflict" over the speaker's love. On the one hand, then, I could translate this as "Alexis took his own portion of my heart"; "Alexis played his own role in my life or in this three-way courtship drama"; or "Alexis defended his own side in the battle for my love." On the other hand, I could translate it as "Alexis took Damon's part of my heart"; "Alexis played Damon's role"; or even "Alexis defended Damon's side in the battle for my love."

4. **Consult reference works.** In addition to using a dictionary to define unfamiliar or ambiguous words, look up anything else to which the poem refers that you either don't understand or that you suspect might be ambiguous: a place, a person, a myth, a quotation, an idea, etc.

According to *Britannica.com*, Cupid was the "ancient Roman god of love" and "often appeared as a winged infant carrying a bow and a quiver of arrows whose wounds inspired love or passion in his every victim." It makes sense, then, that the speaker of this poem would think that she might stop loving one of these men if Cupid took back the arrow that made her love him. But the poem wasn't written in ancient Rome (it's dated 1684), so is the speaker just kidding or being deliberately "poetic" when she calls on Cupid? And what about the names "Damon" and "Alexis"? Were those common in the seventeenth century? Maybe so, if a poet could be named Aphra Behn.

5. **Figure out who, where, when, and what happens.** Once you have gotten a sense of the literal meaning of each sentence, ask the following very general factual questions about the whole poem. Remember that not all of the questions will suit every poem. (Which questions apply will depend in part on whether the poem is narrative, dramatic, or lyric.) At this point, stick to the facts. What do you know for sure?

Who?
• Who is, or who are, the poem's **speaker(s)**?
• Who is, or who are, the **auditor(s)**, if any?
• Who are the other **characters**, if any, that appear in the poem?

The title suggests that the speaker is a woman who loves two people. In the poem, she identifies these as two men—Damon and Alexis. The speaker doesn't seem to address anyone in particular (certainly not the two men she talks about) except in the third stanza, when she addresses Cupid—first through the **epithet** "mighty wingèd god" (line 13) and then by name (16). (Because Cupid isn't present, this is an **apostrophe**.)

Where? When?
• Where is the speaker?
• Where and when do any actions described in the poem take place? That is, what is the poem's **setting**?

No place or time is specified in Behn's poem. The poem is dated 1684, and the antiquated diction ("twixt," line 2; "wilt," 16) seems appropriate to that time. But nothing in the poem makes the situation or feelings it describes specific to a time or place. The speaker doesn't say things like "Last Thursday, when Damon and I were hanging out in the garden . . . ," for example. She seems to describe situations that keep happening repeatedly rather than specific incidents.

What?

- What is the **situation** described in the poem?
- What, if anything, literally happens over the course of it, or what **action**, if any, does it describe?
- Or, if the poem doesn't have a **plot**, then how would you describe its internal structure? Even when a poem seems less interested in telling a story than in simply capturing a feeling or describing something or someone, you can still usually read in it some kind of progression or development or even an argument. When and how does the subject matter or focus or address shift over the course of the poem?

The basic situation is that the speaker loves two men equally. In the second stanza she describes recurring situations—being with one of the men and not the other or being with both of them at once—and the feelings that result. Then, in the third stanza, she imagines what would happen if she stopped loving one of them. The topic or subject essentially remains the same throughout, but there are two subtle shifts. First is the shift from addressing anyone in stanzas one and two to addressing Cupid in stanza three. Second, there are shifts in verb tense and time: the first stanza floats among various tenses ("does," line 1; "took," 4), the second sticks to the present tense ("is," "sigh," "mourn," etc.), and the third shifts to future ("wilt," 16). As a result, I would say that the poem has two parts: in one, the speaker characterizes her situation in the present and recent past; in the other she explores a possible alternative future (that she ends up not liking any better).

6. **Formulate tentative answers to the questions, *Why does it matter? What does it all mean?***

- Why should the poem matter to anyone other than the poet, or what might the poem show and say to readers?
- What problems, issues, questions, or **conflicts** does the poem explore that might be relevant to people other than the speaker(s) or the poet—to humanity in general, to the poet's contemporaries, to people of a certain type or in a certain situation, and so forth?
- How is each problem or conflict developed and resolved over the course of the poem, or how is each question answered? What conclusions does the poem seem to reach about these, or what are its **themes**?

The title and first two lines pose a question: how strong is our love if we love two people instead of one? We tend to assume that anything that is "divided" is less strong than something unified. The use of the word *flow* in the first line reinforces that assumption because it implicitly compares love to something that flows: a river, for example, "flows," and when a river divides into two streams, each stream is smaller and its flow less strong than the river's. So the way the speaker articulates the question implies an answer: love, like a river, isn't strong and sure when divided.

But the rest of the poem undermines that answer. In the first stanza, the speaker points out that each lover and his love has "aided" and added to the "power" of the other: neither man would have "gain[ed her] love" if the other hadn't. The second stanza gives a more concrete sense of why: since we tend to yearn for what we don't have at the moment, being with one of these men makes her miss the other one. But if both men are present, she feels the same about both and perhaps even feels *more* complete and satisfied.

As if realizing she can't solve the problem herself, she turns in the third stanza to Cupid and asks him to help by taking away her love for either Damon or Alexis. As soon as she asks for this, though, she indicates the result would be unhappiness. In the end, the poem seems to say (or its theme is) that love *doesn't* flow or work like a river because love can actually be stronger when we love more than one person, as if it's multiplied instead of lessened by division.

Clearly, this is the opposite of what I expected, which was that the poem would ask whether it was possible to love two people and conclude it wasn't. The conflict is also different than I expected—though there's an external conflict between the two men (maybe), the focus is on the speaker's internal conflict, but that conflict isn't over which guy to choose but about how this is actually working (*I love both of them equally; each love reinforces the other*) versus how she thinks things *should* work (*I'm not supposed to love two equally*).

7. **Consider how the poem's form contributes to its effect and meaning.**

   - How is the poem organized on the page, into lines and/or stanzas, for example? (What are the lines and stanzas like in terms of length, shape, and so on? Are they all alike, or do they vary? Are lines **enjambed** or **end-stopped**?)
   - What are the poem's other formal features? (Is there **rhyme** or another form of aural patterning such as **alliteration**? What is the poem's base **meter**, and are there interesting variations? If not, how else might you describe the poem's rhythm?)
   - How do the poem's overall form and its various formal features contribute to its meaning and effect? In other words, what gets lost when you translate the poem into modern prose?

The stanza organization underscores shifts in the speaker's approach to her situation. But organization reinforces meaning in other ways as well. On the one hand, the division into three stanzas and the choice to number them, plus the fact that each stanza has three sentences, mirror the three-way struggle or love triangle described in the poem. On the other hand, because the poem has eighteen *lines* and nine *sentences*, every sentence is "divided equally twixt two" *lines*. Sound and especially rhyme reinforce this pattern, since the two lines that make up one sentence usually rhyme with each other (to form a couplet). The only lines that aren't couplets are those that begin the second stanza, where we instead have alternating rhyme—*is* (line 7) rhymes with *miss* (9), *mourn* (8) rhymes with *scorn* (10). But these lines describe how the speaker "miss[es]" one man when the other is "by," a sensation she arguably reproduces in readers by ensuring that we twice "miss" the rhyme that the rest of the poem leads us to expect.

8. **Investigate and consider the ways the poem both uses and departs from poetic conventions, especially those related to form and subgenre.**

- Does the poem use a traditional verse form (such as **blank verse**) or a traditional stanza form (such as **ballad stanza**)? Is it a specific subgenre or kind of poem—a **sonnet**, an **ode**, a **ballad**, for example? If so, how does that affect its meaning?

Over time, stanza and verse forms have been used in certain ways and to certain ends, and particular subgenres have observed certain conventions. As a result, they generate particular expectations for readers familiar with such traditions, and poems gain additional meaning by both fulfilling and defying those expectations. For example, **anapestic** meter (two unstressed syllables followed by a stressed one, as in *Tennessee*) is usually used for comic poems, so when poets use it in a serious poem they are probably making a point.

9. **Argue.** Discussion with others—both out loud and in writing—usually results in clarification and keeps you from being too dependent on personal biases and preoccupations, which sometimes mislead even the best readers. Discussing a poem with someone else (especially someone who thinks very differently) or sharing what you've written about the poem can expand your perspective and enrich your experience.

WRITING ABOUT POETRY

If you follow the steps outlined above and keep notes on your personal responses to the poems you read, you will have already begun writing informally. You have also generated ideas and material you can use in more formal writing. To demonstrate how, we conclude this chapter with two examples of such writing. Both grow out of the notes earlier in this chapter. Yet each is quite different in form and content. The first example is a relatively informal response paper that investigates the allusions in Aphra Behn's On Her Loving Two Equally, following up on the discoveries and questions generated by consulting reference works (as in step 4 above). The second example is an essay on the poem that defends and develops as a thesis one answer to the questions *Why does it matter? What does it all mean?* (as in step 6 above) by drawing on discoveries made in earlier and later steps.

As these examples illustrate, there are many different ways to write about poems, just as there are many different things to say about any one. But all such writing begins with a clear sense of the poem itself and your responses to it. Effective writing also depends on a willingness to listen carefully to the poem and to ask genuine questions about how it works, what it says and means, and how it both fulfills and challenges your expectations about life and about poetry.

From bardic chronicles to imaginary letters, brief introspective lyrics to action-packed epics, poetry comes in many sizes, shapes, and varieties; serves myriad purposes for many diverse audiences; and offers pleasures and rewards both like and unlike those we get from fiction, drama, music, or any other art form. In part, though, that's because poetry is something of a trickster and a trespasser, crossing in and out of those other generic domains and trying on their clothes, even as it inhabits and wears very special ones all its own. Poetry speaks to head, as well as heart; ears, as well as eyes. If you keep yours open, it just might speak to you in ways you never expected.

SAMPLE WRITING: RESPONSE PAPER

The following response paper investigates the allusions in Aphra Behn's ON HER LOVING TWO EQUALLY by drawing upon information from reference works. Few response papers involve research, but we have included one that does in order to demonstrate both how you can use information from credible secondary sources to test and deepen your personal response to a poem and how you can develop reading notes like those in chapter 11 into a thoughtful informal response paper.

Names in "On Her Loving Two Equally"

Aphra Behn's "On Her Loving Two Equally" is dated 1684, but refers to an ancient pagan god. That seems weird and made me curious about what he was doing in the poem. According to the *Encyclopedia Britannica Online*, Cupid was the "ancient Roman god of love," "often appeared as a winged infant carrying a bow and a quiver of arrows whose wounds inspired love or passion in his every victim," and "was sometimes portrayed wearing armour like that of Mars, the God of war, perhaps to suggest ironic parallels between warfare and romance" ("Cupid"). It makes sense, then, that the speaker of this poem would think that she might stop loving one of these guys if Cupid took back the arrow that made her love him. And the reference to Cupid also reinforces the association in the poem "between warfare" or at least conflict "and romance." (The speaker is internally conflicted, and there is also an external conflict between the two male lovers.)

I'm still not sure whether the speaker is kidding or being deliberately "poetic" by talking to an ancient Roman god. But either way, this reinforces the idea I had when I was reading, that the poem isn't very specific about time or place. The poem makes the speaker's situation seem like something that has happened or could happen any time, anywhere.

But what about the names Damon and Alexis? Were these real names in seventeenth-century England, which is apparently where Behn was from? According to the Oxford *Dictionary of First Names*, Damon is "a classical Greek name" that was

> made famous in antiquity by the story of Damon and Pythias. In the early 4th century BC Pythias was condemned to death by Dionysius, ruler of Syracuse. His friend Damon offered to stand surety for him, and took his place in the condemned cell while Pythias put his affairs in order. When Pythias duly returned to be executed rather than absconding and leaving his friend to his fate, Dionysius was so impressed by the

trust and friendship of the two young men that he pardoned both of them. ("Damon")

This doesn't tell me for sure whether there were really men named Damon in seventeenth-century England, but it's now clear that using the name "Damon" is another way of alluding to "antiquity" and maybe making this situation and poem seem "antique." But the story of Damon and Pythias seems even more relevant. When I was translating this poem, I noticed that it could imply that Damon and Alexis were actually helping each other, not just fighting over the speaker (especially because "his," in line 4, could refer to either man). Does the fact that the most famous Damon was willing to sit in prison and even be executed to help his best friend give me more evidence that I'm right? On the other hand, does it matter that the name comes from a word meaning " 'to tame, subdue' (often a euphemism for 'kill')" ("Damon")?

I couldn't find anything nearly this interesting about "Alexis," except that it is a Latin form of a Greek name that originally came from a word that means "to defend" ("Alexis").

To sum up, I think two things are important: (1) by referring to Cupid and naming her boyfriends Damon and Alexis, Behn makes her poem and her speaker's situation seem "antique," even for the seventeenth century, and implies her situation could happen any time anywhere; and (2) the fact that the men's names mean "to tame, subdue," even "kill," and "to defend" makes the conflict in the poem more intense, but the fact that the world's most famous Damon sacrificed himself for his friend might add fuel to the idea that these rivals are also friends who are helping each other. Maybe there's even more "loving two equally" going on here than I thought at first? If the speaker loves each of these guys more because she loves the other one, is that true of them, too? This poem is crazy!

Works Cited

"Alexis." Hanks et al.

Behn, Aphra. "On Her Loving Two Equally." *The Norton Introduction to Literature*, edited by Kelly J. Mays, shorter 14th ed., W. W. Norton, 2021, p. 771.

"Cupid." *Encyclopaedia Britannica Online*, www.britannica.com/topic/Cupid.

"Damon." Hanks et al.

Hanks, Patrick, et al., editors. *A Dictionary of First Names*. 2nd ed., Oxford UP, 2006. *Oxford Reference Online*, https://doi:10.1093/acref/9780198610601.001.0001.

SAMPLE WRITING: ESSAY

The following sample essay develops the observations about Aphra Behn's ON HER LOVING TWO EQUALLY in chapter 11, demonstrating how you can turn notes about a poem into a coherent, well-structured essay. As this essay also shows, however, you will often discover new ways of looking at a poem (or any literary text) in the very process of writing about it.

  The writer begins by considering why she is drawn to the poem, even though it does not express her ideal of love. She then uses her personal response to the poem as a starting point for analyzing it in greater depth. (For guidelines on correctly quoting and citing poetry, see "Writing about Literature," ch. 33.)

Multiplying by Dividing in Aphra Behn's "On Her Loving Two Equally"

  My favorite poem in "Reading, Responding, Writing" is Aphra Behn's "On Her Loving Two Equally"—not because it expresses my ideal of love, but because it challenges conventional ideals. The main ideal or assumption explored in the poem is that true love is exclusive and monogamous, as the very titles of poems like "How do *I* [singular] love *thee* [singular]?" or "To *My* Dear and Loving [and One and Only] Husband" insist (emphasis added). The mere title of Behn's poem upsets that idea by insisting that at least one woman is capable of "Loving Two Equally." In fact, one thing that is immediately interesting about Behn's poem is that, though it poses and explores a question, its question is not "Can a woman love two equally?" The title and the poem take it for granted that she can. Instead, the poem asks whether equally loving two people lessens the power or quality of love—or, as the speaker puts it in the first two lines, "How strongly does my passion flow, / Divided equally twixt two?" Every aspect of this poem suggests that when it comes to love, as opposed to math, division leads to multiplication.

  This answer grabs attention because it is so counterintuitive and unconventional. Forget love for just a minute: It's common sense that anything that is divided is smaller and weaker than something unified. In math, for example, division is the opposite of multiplication; if we divide one number by another, we get a number smaller than the first number, if not the second. Although Behn's use of the word *flow* to frame her question compares love to a river instead of a number, the implication is the same: When a river divides into two streams, each of them is smaller than the river, and its flow less strong; as a result, each stream is more easily dammed up or diverted than the undivided river. So the way the speaker initially poses her question seems to support the conventional view: love is stronger when it "flows" toward one person, weaker when divided between two.

As conventional and comforting as that implied answer is, however, it's one the poem immediately rejects. In the remaining lines of the first stanza, the speaker insists that each of her two lovers and the love she feels for him has *not* lessened the strength of her feelings for the other, but the reverse. Each lover and each love has "aid[ed]" (line 6) the other, making him and it more "powerful" (5). Indeed, she says, neither man would have "subdued [her] heart" (3) or "gain[ed her] love" (6) at all if the other hadn't done so as well.

In the second stanza, the speaker gives us a somewhat more concrete sense of why this might be the case. On the one hand, being with either one of these men ("When my Alexis present is," 7) actually makes her both "scorn" him (10) and "miss" (9) the man who's not there ("I for Damon sigh and mourn," 8). This isn't really a paradox; we often yearn more for the person or thing we don't have (the grass is always greener on the *other* side of the fence), and we often lose our appreciation for nearby, familiar things and people. What is far away and inaccessible is often dearer to us because its absence either makes us aware of what it means to us or allows us to forget its flaws and idealize it.

Perhaps because all of this makes the speaker feel that she can't possibly solve the problem by herself, the speaker turns in the third stanza to Cupid—the deity who is supposed to control these things by shooting a "golden-pointed dart" (15) into the heart of each lover. She asks him to solve her dilemma for her by "tak[ing] back" her love for either Damon or Alexis (15). As with her question in the first stanza, however, this plea is revoked as soon as it's formulated, for if she loses Damon, "all [her] hopes are crossed"; if she loses Alexis, she is "lost" (17-18).

Here and throughout the poem, the speaker's main preoccupation seems to be what *she* feels and what this situation is like for *her*—"*my* passion" (1), "*my* heart" (3), "*my* Damon's aid, . . . *my* love" (6), "*my* Alexis" (7), "*I* . . . sigh and mourn" (8), "*I* do miss" (9), "*my* scorn" (10), "*I* languish, sigh, and die" (12), "This restless fever in *my* blood" (14), "*my* hopes" (17), "*my* Alexis" and "*I* am lost" (18). Yet the poem implies that the payoff here is not hers alone and that her feelings are not purely selfish. Both times the word *gain* appears in the poem, for example, her lovers' gains and feelings are the focus—the fact that Alexis is able "to gain [her] love" thanks to "Damon's aid" (6) and that "Damon gains nothing but my scorn" when she is missing Alexis (10). Moreover, ambiguous wording in the first stanza suggests that the men here may be actively, intentionally helping to create this situation and even acting in contradictory, selfish and unselfish, ways. When the speaker says that "Damon had ne'er subdued my heart / Had not Alexis took his part" (3-4), *his* could refer to Alexis or Damon and *part* could mean "a portion" (of her "heart," presumably), "a role" (in her life or in this courtship drama), or a "side in a dispute or conflict" (over her love). Thus, she could be saying that Alexis (unselfishly) defended Damon's suit; (selfishly) fought against Damon or took a share or role that properly belonged to Damon; and/or (neutrally) took his (Alexis's) own share or role or defended his (Alexis's) own cause. Perhaps all of this *has* been the case at various times; people do behave in contradictory ways when they are in love, especially when they perceive that they have a rival. It's also true that men and women alike often more highly prize something or someone that someone else prizes, too. So perhaps each lover's "passion" for her also "flow[s]" more strongly than it would otherwise precisely because he has a rival.

In the end, the poem thus seems to say that love *doesn't* flow or work like a river because love isn't a tangible or quantifiable thing. As a result, love is also different from the sort of battle implied by the martial language of the first stanza in which someone wins only if someone else loses. The poem attributes this to the perversity of the human heart—especially our tendency to yearn for what we can't have and what we think other people want, too.

Through its form, the poem demonstrates that division can increase instead of lessen meaning, as well as love. On the one hand, just as the poem's content stresses the power of the love among *three people*, so the poem's form also stresses "threeness" as well as "twoness." It is after all divided into *three* distinctly numbered stanzas, and each stanza consists of *three* sentences. On the other hand, every *sentence* is "divided equally twixt two" *lines*, just as the speaker's "passion" is divided equally between two men. Formally, then, the poem mirrors the kinds of division it describes. Sound and especially rhyme reinforce this pattern since the two lines that make up one sentence usually rhyme with each other to form a couplet. The only lines that don't conform to this pattern come at the beginning of the second stanza where we instead have alternating rhyme—*is* (7) rhymes with *miss* (9), *mourn* (8) rhymes with *scorn* (10). But here, again, form reinforces content since these lines describe how the speaker "miss[es]" one man when the other is "by," a sensation that she arguably reproduces in us as we read by ensuring we twice "miss" the rhyme that the rest of the poem leads us to expect.

Because of the way it challenges our expectations and our conventional ideas about romantic love, the poem might well make us uncomfortable, perhaps all the more so because the speaker and poet here are female. For though we tend to think all true lovers should be loyal and monogamous, this has been expected even more of women than of men. What the poem says about love might make more sense and seem less strange and even objection-able, however, if we think of other, nonromantic kinds of love: after all, do we really think that our mother and father love us less if their love is "divided equally twixt" ourselves and our siblings, or do we love each of our parents less because there are two of *them*? If we think of these familial kinds of love, it becomes much easier to accept Behn's suggestion that love multiplies when we spread it around.

Work Cited

Behn, Aphra. "On Her Loving Two Equally." *The Norton Introduction to Literature,* edited by Kelly J. Mays, shorter 14th ed., W. W. Norton, 2021, p. 771.

who
soar
then
luscious
delirious
live
has
drunk
these
need
ful
not
to
delicate
your
sleep
there
let
honey
sausage
death
this
language
above
moon
my
said
smooth
ship
egg
on
blow
all
stare
am
juice
the
skin
symphony
day
bed
ing
as
sing
after
want
white

The Art of
(Reading) Poetry
AN ALBUM

oets obviously have a keen, even vested, interest in offering their own answers to the questions of what poetry is and why and how it should be written and read. Not surprisingly, many poets have found poetry itself the best medium through which to tackle those questions. Such poems, as well as prose works devoted to the same topic, constitute a genre of sorts— the "Ars Poetica," a Latin phrase meaning "Art of Poetry" that many writers also use in the titles of individual works of this kind. In so doing, these writers deliberately insert themselves into a conversation that began many centuries ago, by alluding directly to a treatise on poetry with just that name by the Roman poet Horace (65–8 BCE).

You won't find any quotations from Horace in this album. But it does gather a range of more recent "Ars Poetica" poems and invite you to compare their visions of the art of poetry, both to each other and with your own ideas and experience. As you read the poems, consider the relationship between the vision of poetry that the poems articulate (by virtue of *what* they say) and enact (by virtue of *how* they say it)— that is, the relationship between content and form, theory and practice. Does each poem manage to be or to do the things it suggests poetry must? Does the poem invite the sort of readerly response it envisions as ideal? How so or not? Which poems found elsewhere in this book do you think each of the poets in this album might like or admire the most? the least? Why and how so?

HOWARD NEMEROV
Because You Asked about the Line between Prose and Poetry

Sparrows were feeding in a freezing drizzle
That while you watched turned to pieces of snow
Riding a gradient invisible
From silver aslant to random, white, and slow.

5 There came a moment that you couldn't tell.
And then they clearly flew instead of fell.

1980

- What "couldn't" you "tell" (line 5)? Who or what is "they" (6)?
- What answers, in the end, might this poem describing birds and snow offer to the question implied in its title: What defines the difference or "Line between Prose and Poetry"?

ARCHIBALD MacLEISH
Ars Poetica[1]

A poem should be palpable and mute
As a globed fruit,

Dumb
As old medallions to the thumb,

5 Silent as the sleeve-worn stone
Of casement ledges where the moss has grown—

A poem should be wordless
As the flight of birds.

A poem should be motionless in time
10 As the moon climbs,

Leaving, as the moon releases
Twig by twig the night-entangled trees,

Leaving, as the moon behind the winter leaves,
Memory by memory the mind—

15 A poem should be motionless in time
As the moon climbs.

A poem should be equal to:
Not true.

For all the history of grief
20 An empty doorway and a maple leaf.

For love
The leaning grasses and two lights above the sea—

A poem should not mean
But be.

1926

• How can a poem "be wordless" (line 7)? "not mean / But be" (23–24)? How
  does or doesn't this poem manage both?

ELIZABETH ALEXANDER
Ars Poetica #100: I Believe

Poetry, I tell my students,
is idiosyncratic. Poetry

is where we are ourselves
(though Sterling Brown[2] said

---

1. "Art of Poetry" (Latin), title of a poetical treatise by the Roman poet Horace (65–8 BCE). (See album introduction.)
2. African American poet (1901–89) and literary critic.

5 "Every 'I' is a dramatic 'I' "),
  digging in the clam flats

  for the shell that snaps,
  emptying the proverbial pocketbook.

  Poetry is what you find
10 in the dirt in the corner,

  overhear on the bus, God
  in the details, the only way

  to get from here to there.
  Poetry (and now my voice is rising)

15 is not all love, love, love,
  and I'm sorry the dog died.

  Poetry (here I hear myself loudest)
  is the human voice,

  and are we not of interest to each other?

2005

• What competing ideas about poetry are articulated in this poem, and what
  is the speaker's view of each? Why might the poem end with a question?

MARIANNE MOORE
Poetry

I, too, dislike it: there are things that are important beyond all this
    fiddle.
    Reading it, however, with a perfect contempt for it, one discovers in
    it after all, a place for the genuine.
        Hands that can grasp, eyes
5   that can dilate, hair that can rise
            if it must, these things are important not because a

high-sounding interpretation can be put upon them but because they are
    useful. When they become so derivative as to become unintelligible,
    the same thing may be said for all of us, that we
10 do not admire what
    we cannot understand: the bat
        holding on upside down or in quest of something to

eat, elephants pushing, a wild horse taking a roll, a tireless wolf under
    a tree, the immovable critic twitching his skin like a horse that feels a
        flea, the base-
15 ball fan, the statistician—
        nor is it valid
            to discriminate against "business documents and

school-books";[3] all these phenomena are important. One must make a
  distinction
    however: when dragged into prominence by half poets, the result is not
      poetry,

20   nor till the poets among us can be
        "literalists of
        the imagination"[4]—above
          insolence and triviality and can present

  for inspection, "imaginary gardens with real toads in them," shall we have
25   it. In the meantime, if you demand on the one hand,
      the raw material of poetry in
        all its rawness and
        that which is on the other hand
          genuine, you are interested in poetry.

1919

• Does your interpretation of the meaning and tone of this poem's first line
  change as you read the rest of the poem? When and how so? By the poem's
  end, what might you conclude about what the speaker "dislike[s]" or feels "a
  perfect contempt for" (lines 1–2)?

JULIA ALVAREZ
"Poetry Makes Nothing Happen"?

—W. H. AUDEN[5]

Listening to a poem on the radio,
Mike Holmquist stayed awake on his drive home
from Laramie[6] on Interstate 80,
tapping his hand to the beat of some lines
5 by Longfellow;[7] while overcome by grief
one lonesome night when the bathroom cabinet
still held her husband's meds, May Quinn reached out
for a book by Yeats instead and fell asleep
cradling "When You Are Old," not the poet's best,
10 but still . . . poetry made nothing happen,

---

3. *Diary of Tolstoy* (Dutton), p. 84. "Where the boundary between prose and poetry lies, I shall never
be able to understand. The question is raised in manuals of style, yet the answer to it lies beyond me.
Poetry is verse: Prose is not verse. Or else poetry is everything with the exception of business
documents and school books" [Moore's note].
4. Yeats, *Ideas of Good and Evil* (A. H. Bullen, 1903), p. 182. "The limitation of [William Blake's] view was
from the very intensity of his vision; he was a too literal realist of imagination, as others are of nature; and
because he believed that the figures seen by the mind's eye, when exalted by inspiration, were 'eternal
existences,' symbols of divine essences, he hated every grace of style that might obscure their lineaments"
[Moore's note]. The phrase "imaginary [. . .] in them," in the next stanza, has no known source.
5. See "In Memory of W. B. Yeats" (line 36; p. 1076).
6. In Wyoming.
7. American poet Henry Wadsworth Longfellow (1807–82).

which was good, given what May had in mind.
Writing a paper on a Bishop[8] poem,
Jenny Klein missed her ride but arrived home
to the cancer news in a better frame of mind.
15 While troops dropped down into Afghanistan
in the living room, Naomi Stella clapped
to the nursery rhyme her father had turned on,
All the king's horses and all the king's men . . .
If only poetry had made nothing happen!
20 If only the president had listened to Auden!

Faith Chaney, Lulú Pérez, Sunghee Chen—
there's a list as long as an epic poem
of folks who'll swear a poem has never done
a thing for them . . . except . . . perhaps adjust
25 the sunset view one cloudy afternoon,
which made them see themselves or see the world
in a different light—degrees of change so small
only a poem registers them at all.
That's why they can be trusted, why poems might
30 still save us from what happens in the world.

2003

• How does this poem answer the question in its title: What, if anything, does
poetry "make happen" or keep from happening? What is the effect of the
poem's specificity about names and situations? of the way each stanza differently plays on the word "happens?"

BILLY COLLINS

Introduction to Poetry

I ask them to take a poem
and hold it up to the light
like a color slide

or press an ear against its hive.

5 I say drop a mouse into a poem
and watch him probe his way out,

or walk inside the poem's room
and feel the walls for a light switch.

I want them to water-ski
10 across the surface of a poem
waving at the author's name on the shore.

But all they want to do
is tie the poem to a chair with rope
and torture a confession out of it.

8. Elizabeth Bishop (1911–79).

15   They begin beating it with a hose
   to find out what it really means.

1988

• Who is "them" (line 1), and what is the effect of the speaker's choice to refer to "them" and "they" (12) in this way? What different approaches to reading poetry come into conflict here? Why and how?

OCTAVIO PAZ
Proem[9]

At times poetry is the vertigo of bodies and the vertigo of joy and the vertigo of death;

   the walk with eyes closed along the edge of the cliff, and the verbena in submarine gardens;

   the laughter that sets fire to rules and the holy commandments;

   the descent of parachuting words onto the sands of the page;[1]

5   the despair that boards a paper boat and crosses,

   for forty nights and forty days, the night-sorrow sea and the day-sorrow desert;[2]

   the idolatry of the self and the desecration of the self and the dissipation of the self;

   the beheading of epithets, the burial of mirrors;

   the recollection of pronouns freshly cut in the garden of Epicurus, and the garden of Netzahualcoyotl;[3]

10   the flute solo on the terrace of memory and the dance of flames in the cave of thought;[4]

   the migrations of millions of verbs, wings and claws, seeds and hands;

   the nouns, bony and full of roots, planted on the waves of language;

   the love unseen and the love unheard and the love unsaid: the love in love.

Syllables seeds.

1987

---

9. Translated from the Spanish by Eliot Weinberger. *Proem*: preface or preamble, but also suggesting a combination of *prose* and *poem*.

1. Allusion to *Altazor, or A Voyage in a Parachute* (1931), a book-length poem by avant-garde Chilean poet Vicente Huidobro (1893–1948).

2. See Matthew 4.1–11, in which Jesus is tempted by the devil during a forty-day fast in the Judean desert.

3. Central Mexican state or its namesake, the renowned philosopher, warrior, and poet-king who turned the pre-Columbian city-state of Texcoco into "the Athens of the Western World." *Epicurus*: Greek philosopher (341–270 BCE) who championed simple pleasure, friendship, and retirement, as symbolized by the private garden outside of Athens where members of his school gathered.

4. The Allegory of the Cave, in Plato's *Republic* (c. 375 BCE), describes people chained in a cave, able to see not the actual people or things behind them but only the shadows of those forms cast onto the wall by firelight.

Understanding the Text

12 | SPEAKER: WHOSE VOICE DO WE HEAR?

Poems are personal. The thoughts and feelings they express belong to a specific person, and however general or universal their sentiments seem to be, poems come to us as the expression of an individual human voice. That voice is often a voice of the poet, but not always. Poets sometimes create characters just as writers of fiction or drama do. And the **speaker** of a poem may express ideas or feelings very different from the poet's own and in a distinct voice.

Usually there is much more to a poem than the characterization of the speaker, but often it is necessary first to identify the speaker and determine his or her character before we can appreciate what else goes on in the poem. And sometimes, in looking for the speaker of the poem, we discover the gist of the entire poem.

NARRATIVE POEMS AND THEIR SPEAKERS

In the following narrative poem, the poet relies mainly on one speaker with a highly distinctive voice. This speaker acts as a **narrator**. Generally speaking in the third-person plural, on behalf of a group, however, the speaker sometimes quotes the remarks of individual members of the group (lines 1–2, 16–20), who are thus also speakers in the poem, even if they are never individually identified. As you read the poem, notice how your impressions of Hard Rock and of the group are shaped by both the narrator's words and those of the speakers he quotes.

ETHERIDGE KNIGHT

Hard Rock Returns to Prison from the Hospital for the Criminal Insane

Hard Rock was "known not to take no shit
From nobody," and he had the scars to prove it:
Split purple lips, lumped ears, welts above
His yellow eyes, and one long scar that cut
5 Across his temple and plowed through a thick
Canopy of kinky hair.

The WORD was that Hard Rock wasn't a mean nigger
Anymore, that the doctors had bored a hole in his head,
Cut out part of his brain, and shot electricity
10 Through the rest. When they brought Hard Rock back,
Handcuffed and chained, he was turned loose,
Like a freshly gelded stallion, to try his new status.

- "Creationism," the avant-garde literary school founded by the poet to whom Paz alludes in line 4, held that every poet should create a highly personal, imaginary world rather than simply describe the actual or natural world. To what extent and how might you see Paz's poem as either embracing or complicating that view of poetry? What, in these terms, might you make of the poem's organic language and metaphors?

SUGGESTIONS FOR WRITING

1. Both Billy Collins's INTRODUCTION TO POETRY and Elizabeth Alexander's ARS POETICA #100: I BELIEVE can be interpreted as exploring, from a teacher's perspective, what happens among teachers, students, and poems in a classroom. Write a response paper in which you reflect on how either of those poems characterizes that situation and how that depiction compares to your own classroom experience.

2. Consider your responses to all the poems in this album. Which one most accurately expresses your view of what poetry is, what it does, and how we should read it? Why and how so? What does your choice say about you? Write an essay in which you reflect on how at least two of these poems express, reinforce, refine, or perhaps challenge your views of poetry.

3. Pick any poem in this album and write an essay that both explains what qualities it attributes to good poetry and then demonstrates whether, why, and how any other poem in the anthology has those qualities. Be sure to use concrete evidence from both poems to make your case.

BIN TRAVELER FORM

Cut By Mateuska Urllea   **Qty** 19   **Date** 06/28/24

Scanned By Susana Rodziguez   **Qty** ____   **Date** 06/29/24

Regines = (2.86)
(8)

Scanned Batch IDs   9025496Z   9025540Z

Notes/Exceptions

_____

_____

_____

_____

_____

_____

And we all waited and watched, like indians at a corral,
To see if the WORD was true.

15 As we waited we wrapped ourselves in the cloak
Of his exploits: "Man, the last time, it took eight
Screws to put him in the Hole."[1] "Yeah, remember when he
Smacked the captain with his dinner tray?" "He set
The record for time in the Hole—67 straight days!"
20 "Ol Hard Rock! man, that's one crazy nigger."
And then the jewel of a myth that Hard Rock had once bit
A screw on the thumb and poisoned him with syphilitic spit.

The testing came, to see if Hard Rock was really tame.
A hillbilly called him a black son of a bitch
25 And didn't lose his teeth, a screw who knew Hard Rock
From before shook him down and barked in his face.
And Hard Rock did *nothing*. Just grinned and looked silly,
His eyes empty like knot holes in a fence.

And even after we discovered that it took Hard Rock
30 Exactly 3 minutes to tell you his first name,
We told ourselves that he had just wised up,
Was being cool; but we could not fool ourselves for long,
And we turned away, our eyes on the ground. Crushed.
He had been our Destroyer, the doer of things
35 We dreamed of doing but could not bring ourselves to do,
The fears of years, like a biting whip,
Had cut grooves too deeply across our backs.

1968

   As we might expect, we learn a good deal in this poem about its title character:
The first stanza lets us know that he is a Black prison inmate and vividly describes
his hair and his various "scars" (line 2) as evidence of his fierce, indomitable character, his refusal ever to back down or let anyone treat him badly. In the third
stanza we hear about some of his more famous past "exploits" (16). But by the time
we get to the third stanza we've been warned that *this* Hard Rock might already be
a thing of the past. And the fourth stanza and the first part of the fifth and final
one confirm that fear, presenting a man radically transformed and reduced by the
lobotomy and electroshock therapy described in stanza two. The poem thus
becomes, in part, the tragic tale of Hard Rock's fast, hard fall. And it would be
worthwhile to think further about just what other aspects of the poem help to
make that fall seem so fast, so hard, so poignant.

   One might be the fact that Hard Rock is literally never allowed to speak for himself in the poem. Everything we learn about him comes to us from the narrator
and the other speakers whom that narrator quotes—all Hard Rock's fellow inmates.
And it is this group, this "we," and its perceptions of Hard Rock even more than
the man himself that arguably emerge as HARD ROCK RETURNS's major focus. The
poem begins, after all, with what "was 'known'"—and, as the quotation marks
here stress, *said*—about Hard Rock by these men (1). It ends with a stanza devoted

---

1. Solitary confinement. *Screws*: guards.

almost exclusively to their collective reaction to his transformation. How else might the poem work to train our focus on its speakers? How, ultimately, does it characterize them, through how they speak and what they say? What exactly does Hard Rock and Hard Rock's fall mean to these men, and why?

Not all narrative poems are as much *about* their speakers as "Hard Rock Returns" is. Eavan Boland's QUARANTINE, for instance, features as its main speaker a third-person omniscient narrator, one who isn't a character in the story she tells and about whom we learn nothing specific. "Quarantine" thereby keeps our attention riveted on the characters and the action themselves. Yet this poem's effect ultimately depends on this very fact and thus, like all narrative poems, on *its* particular narrator and mode of narration, on all its speaker's words. To fully experience and better understand such poems, we can always draw upon the very same concepts and questions about narrators and characters that we draw upon when reading fiction (see chs. 3 and 4).

SPEAKERS IN THE DRAMATIC MONOLOGUE

Like all **dramatic monologues**, the following poem has no narrator. Rather, it consists entirely of the words a single fictional speaker speaks to a fictional **auditor** in a specific time, place, and dramatic situation, much as would a character in a play. As you read the poem, pay attention to the details that alert you to the time, place, and situation and that help to characterize the speaker, the auditor, and their relationship.

A. E. STALLINGS
Hades[2] Welcomes His Bride

Come now, child, adjust your eyes, for sight
Is here a lesser sense. Here you must learn
Directions through your fingertips and feet
And map them in your mind. I think some shapes
5   Will gradually appear. The pale things twisting
Overhead are mostly roots, although some worms
Arrive here clinging to their dead. Turn here.
Ah.   And in this hall will sit our thrones,
And here you shall be queen, my dear, the queen
10 Of all men ever to be born. No smile?
Well, some solemnity befits a queen.
These thrones I have commissioned to be made
Are unlike any you imagined; they glow
Of deep-black diamonds and lead, subtler
15 And in better taste than gold, as will suit
Your timid beauty and pale throat. Come now,
Down these winding stairs, the air more still
And dry and easier to breathe. Here is a room

2. Greek god of the underworld (also called Hades) and of death; he married Persephone after abducting her from her mother, Demeter, goddess of corn, grain, and the earth's harvest.

For your diversions. Here I've set a loom
20 And silk unraveled from the finest shrouds
And dyed the richest, rarest shades of black.
Such pictures you shall weave! Such tapestries!
For you I chose those three thin shadows[3] there,
And they shall be your friends and loyal maids,
25 And do not fear from them such gossiping
As servants usually are wont. They have
Not mouth nor eyes and cannot thus speak ill
Of you. Come, come. This is the greatest room;
I had it specially made after great thought
30 So you would feel at home. I had the ceiling
Painted to recall some evening sky—
But without the garish stars and lurid moon.
What?   That stark shape crouching in the corner?
Sweet, that is to be our bed. Our bed.
35 Ah!   Your hand is trembling! I fear
There is, as yet, too much pulse in it.

1993

So, what do you think of the speaker, his bride-auditor, and their bower of wormy wedded bliss? Stallings's title alerts us that the former is Hades. If we know our Greek mythology (or simply read the handy footnote), we go into the poem knowing, too, that his bride is also his kidnap victim, Persephone (whose name, interestingly enough, never appears here). Yet Hades Welcomes His Bride puts a unique new spin on this old, familiar story by presenting it from the perspective of Hades—or, in Stallings's words, from "the bad guy's point of view"—so as to also make him seem anything but the straightforwardly ghoulish devil or brutish villain we might expect. Hades, after all, speaks formally, respectfully, even tenderly to his bride and "queen" from the beginning (line 9), inviting her into a new home to which he recognizes she must "adjust" (1) and offering advice about how to do so (1–5). As he leads her through its rooms and points out its various features, it becomes clear (long before he explicitly says so, in lines 29–30) that he has taken pains to create an environment as tasteful, grand, and hospitable, even homey, as he knows how. He is also sensitive to his bride's reactions, noticing that she isn't smiling (10); that she seems startled by what turns out to be the bed she will share with him; that after he twice utters the words "our bed. Our bed," she "is trembling" (34–35). The fact that he repeats those words also implies that he's eagerly anticipating his wedding night. As the details accumulate, the horrors of this home and of the life and marriage to which this bride is doomed become as palpably apparent to readers as they are to her. Yet Hades's character remains ambiguous: Is he being knowingly malevolent, grandiose, even abusive by arranging and presenting things as he does and by rationalizing his bride's reactions? Is he enjoying scaring the pants off his bride, as it were? Or might he instead be, as one reviewer contends, "engag[ing] in the same self-deception as" any ordinary "mortal lover" might, so genuinely bent on his bride sharing his delight and so inured to his own literally hellish milieu that he can't or won't see the truth?

3. Especially in the sense of "phantoms"; also suggesting *shades*, another word both for "ghost" and for Hades.

Your answers and your interpretation of the speaker here, as in all dramatic monologues, depend entirely on the speaker's own words—on *what* he says and *when* and *how* he says it. The details accumulate into a fairly full, if—in this case—delightfully ambiguous, wonderfully creepy portrait, even though we do not have either a narrator's description or another speaker to give us perspective (as in Knight's "Hard Rock Returns"). As in other dramatic monologues, we do get some hint of another perspective via the reactions of the auditor, but we can only deduce what those reactions might be from what the speaker himself says.

THE LYRIC AND ITS SPEAKER

With narrative poems and dramatic monologues, we are usually in no danger of mistaking the speaker for the poet. Lyrics may present more of a challenge. When there is a pointed discrepancy between the speaker of a **lyric** and what we know of the poet—when the speaker is a woman, for example, and the poet is a man—we know we have a fictional speaker to contend with and that the point (or at least *one* point) of the poem is to observe the characterization carefully.

Sometimes even in lyrics poets "borrow" a character from history and ask readers to factor in historical facts and contexts. At other times, poets instead do as Gwendolyn Brooks does in the following poem: By adopting the voice and perspective of an invented but nonetheless representative speaker, they personalize—by both imagining and helping us to imagine, from the inside—the experience and feelings of many real people.

GWENDOLYN BROOKS

the mother

Abortions will not let you forget.
You remember the children you got that you did not get,
The damp small pulps with a little or with no hair,
The singers and workers that never handled the air.
5 You will never neglect or beat
Them, or silence or buy with a sweet.
You will never wind up the sucking-thumb
Or scuttle off ghosts that come.
You will never leave them, controlling your luscious sigh,
10 Return for a snack of them, with gobbling mother-eye.

I have heard in the voices of the wind the voices of my dim killed
    children.
I have contracted. I have eased
My dim dears at the breasts they could never suck.
I have said, Sweets, if I sinned, if I seized
15 Your luck
And your lives from your unfinished reach,
If I stole your births and your names,
Your straight baby tears and your games,
Your stilted or lovely loves, your tumults, your marriages, aches, and your
    deaths,

20 If I poisoned the beginnings of your breaths,
Believe that even in my deliberateness I was not deliberate.
Though why should I whine,
Whine that the crime was other than mine?—
Since anyhow you are dead.
25 Or rather, or instead,
You were never made.
But that too, I am afraid,
Is faulty: oh, what shall I say, how is the truth to be said?
You were born, you had body, you died.
30 It is just that you never giggled or planned or cried.

Believe me, I loved you all.
Believe me, I knew you, though faintly, and I loved, I loved you
All.

1945

Even when poets present themselves as if they were speaking directly to us in their own voices, their poems present only a partial portrait, something considerably less than the full personality and character of the poet. Though there is not an obviously created character—someone with distinct characteristics that are different from those of the poet—strategies of characterization are used to present the person speaking in one way and not another. As a result, you should still differentiate between the speaker and the poet.

Although the poet who wrote the following poem is probably writing about a personal, actual experience, he is also making a character of himself—that is, characterizing himself in a certain way, emphasizing some parts of himself and not others. We call this character a **persona**.

WILLIAM WORDSWORTH
She dwelt among the untrodden ways

She dwelt among the untrodden ways
   Beside the springs of Dove,[4]
A Maid whom there were none to praise,
   And very few to love.

5 A Violet by a mossy stone
   Half-hidden from the eye!
—Fair as a star, when only one
   Is shining in the sky.

She lived unknown, and few could know
10   When Lucy ceased to be;
But she is in her Grave, and, oh,
   The difference to me!

1800, 1815

---

4. Small stream in the Lake District in northern England, near where Wordsworth lived.

Did Lucy actually live? Was she a friend of the poet? We don't know; the poem doesn't tell us, and even biographers of Wordsworth are unsure. What we do know is that Wordsworth was able to represent grief very powerfully. Whether the speaker is the historical Wordsworth or not, that speaker is a major focus of the poem, and it is his feelings that the poem isolates and expresses. We need to recognize some characteristics of the speaker and be sensitive to his feelings for the poem to work.

* * *

The poems we have looked at in this chapter—and those that follow—all suggest the value of beginning the reading of any poem with three simple questions: Who is speaking? What do we know about the speaker? What kind of person is the speaker? Putting together the evidence that the poem presents in answer to such questions can often take us a long way into the poem. For some poems, such questions won't help a great deal because the speaking voice is too indistinct or the character too scantily presented. But starting with such questions will often lead you toward the central experience the poem offers.

POEMS FOR FURTHER STUDY

WALT WHITMAN
I celebrate myself, and sing myself

> I celebrate myself, and sing myself,
> And what I assume you shall assume,
> For every atom belonging to me as good belongs to you.
>
> I loafe and invite my soul,
> 5 I lean and loafe at my ease observing a spear of summer grass.
>
> My tongue, every atom of my blood, form'd from this soil, this air,
> Born here of parents born here from parents the same, and their parents
>   the same,
> I, now thirty-seven years old in perfect health begin,
> Hoping to cease not till death.
>
> 10 Creeds and schools in abeyance,
> Retiring back a while suffced at what they are, but never forgotten,
> I harbor for good or bad, I permit to speak at every hazard,
> Nature without check with original energy.

                                                        1855, 1881

• What might be characteristically American about the speaker of this poem?

PHILIP SCHULTZ
Googling Ourselves

> These strangers with my name,
> busy being kidnapped, embezzled,
> honored and dying at a frightening rate.

The cross-dressing exterminator convicted of rape
5 in Kensington, Ohio, sentenced
to 72 years without bail, the policeman killed
stopping a burglary in Thermopolis, WY—could they
have imagined a Florida painter with their name
communicating with extraterrestrials through sculptures
10 made out of railroad tracks, or being written about
in a poem by another member of our redundant family
for a reason none of us can explain?

Sometimes I fear I'm imaginary, don't really exist.
Catch myself wondering why I only seem to like myself
15 when, say, I'm wearing a teacher's face—
because I see myself only through others' eyes?
In that case, who am I really? Alone at night,
watching a ballgame, I'm always surprised when
I speak to myself in the third person, wondering why
20 this man cares so much about something he plays no part in.
It's easier to wonder why Nietzsche[5] sought
his soul's sympathy, a truth he knew he'd despise,
probably feared he wouldn't survive. To imagine him up late,
seeking his ever-evolving, unidentifiable self,
25 a past more inhabitable and less unforgiving,
anxious to know why someone with his name would say,
"Poets lie too much . . . who among us has not adulterated his wine?"

Late at night the Web is a dangerous swamp
of voyeuristic self-scrutiny and addictive impersonation,
30 the ego testifying for and against itself, seeking evidence
of triumph and complicity, sanction without malice,
pretext or God. Who is this man obsessively looking up
all his persona narrators, feeling like a hodgepodge,
trapped somewhere between Heaven and earth,
35 spitting against the wind? Is it because he knows
he's getting closer to the end, will soon vanish
and become nothing? Is this why he's studying
everyone who answers to his name, because
one may have invented time or sympathy or God
40 and will love him, even momentarily, for who he is?

2017

- Over the course of this poem, we learn that its speaker is a poet (line 11), a teacher (15), and a "man" (20) "closer to the end" of his life than to its beginning (36). How do and don't these facts matter to the questions the poem raises about why we might Google ourselves and what the strange or estranging effects of doing so might be? What might the poem ask or say about identity, the self, "who [someone] is" (40), even the lyric "I"?

5. Influential German philosopher Friedrich Nietzsche (1844–1900); the last line of this stanza comes from *Thus Spoke Zarathustra* (1883–85), a meditation on core Nietzschean concepts such as "the eternal recurrence of the same" and "the death of God."

E. E. CUMMINGS
"next to of course god america i

"next to of course god america i
love you land of the pilgrims' and so forth oh
say can you see by the dawn's early my
country 'tis of centuries come and go
5 and are no more what of it we should worry
in every language even deafanddumb
thy sons acclaim your glorious name by gorry
by jingo by gee by gosh by gum
why talk of beauty what could be more beaut-
10 iful than these heroic happy dead
who rushed like lions to the roaring slaughter
they did not stop to think they died instead
then shall the voice of liberty be mute?"

He spoke.   And drank rapidly a glass of water

1926

- Except for the last line, this poem works much like a dramatic monologue.
  What can you discern about the situation in which the quoted words are
  spoken? about the speaker and his or her audience? about the poem's attitude
  toward the speaker?

LUCILLE CLIFTON
cream of wheat

sometimes at night
we stroll the market aisles
ben and jemima and me   they
walk in front   remembering this and that
5 i lag behind
trying to remove my chefs cap
wondering about what ever pictured me
then left me personless
Rastus
10 i read in an old paper
i was called rastus
but no mother ever
gave that to her son   toward dawn
we return to our shelves
15 our boxes   ben and jemima and me
we pose and smile   i simmer   what
is my name

1 · 9 · 2 · 3

Cream of Wheat advertisement
featuring Rastus

2008

- At what point and how did you begin to figure out just who the speaker of
  this poem is? What is the effect of the shifts between plural and singular,
  "we" and "I"?

LORNA DEE CERVANTES
Beneath the Shadow of the Freeway

1

Across the street—the freeway,
blind worm, wrapping the valley up
from Los Altos to Sal Si Puedes.[6]
I watched it from my porch
5   unwinding. Every day at dusk
as Grandma watered geraniums
the shadow of the freeway lengthened.

2

We were a woman family:
Grandma, our innocent Queen;
10   Mama, the Swift Knight, Fearless Warrior.
Mama wanted to be Princess instead.
I know that. Even now she dreams of taffeta
and foot-high tiaras.

Myself: I could never decide.
15   So I turned to books, those staunch, upright men.
I became Scribe: Translator of Foreign Mail,
interpreting letters from the government, notices
of dissolved marriages and Welfare stipulations.
I paid the bills, did light man-work, fixed faucets,
20   insured everything
against all leaks.

3

Before rain I notice seagulls.
They walk in flocks,
cautious across lawns: splayed toes,
25   indecisive beaks. Grandma says
seagulls mean storm.

In California in the summer,
mockingbirds sing all night.
Grandma says they are singing for their nesting wives.
30   "They don't leave their families
borrachando."[7]

She likes the ways of birds,
respects how they show themselves
for toast and a whistle.

---

6. Literally, "Escape If You Can" (Spanish), unofficial name of an old barrio in east San Jose, California, about thirty miles south of Los Altos, a wealthy, mostly White enclave whose name means "The Heights."
7. To get drunk (Spanish).

35   She believes in myths and birds.
     She trusts only what she builds
     with her own hands.

4

     She built her house,
     cocky, disheveled carpentry,
40   after living twenty-five years
     with a man who tried to kill her.

     Grandma, from the hills of Santa Barbara,
     I would open my eyes to see her stir mush
     in the morning, her hair in loose braids,
45   tucked close around her head
     with a yellow scarf.

     Mama said, "It's her own fault,
     getting screwed by a man for that long.
     Sure as shit wasn't hard."
50   soft she was soft

5

     in the night I would hear it
     glass bottles shattering the street
     words cracked into shrill screams
     inside my throat a cold fear
55   as it entered the house in hard
     unsteady steps stopping at my door
     my name bathrobe slippers
     outside a 3 A.M. mist heavy
     as a breath full of whiskey
60   stop it go home come inside
     mama if he comes here again
     I'll call the police

     inside
     a gray kitten a touchstone
65   purring beneath the quilts
     grandma stitched
     from his suits
     the patchwork singing
     of mockingbirds

6

70   "You're too soft always were.
     You'll get nothing but shit.
     Baby, don't count on nobody."

     —a mother's wisdom.
     Soft. I haven't changed,
75   maybe grown more silent, cynical
     on the outside.

"O Mama, with what's inside of me
I could wash that all away. I could."

"But Mama, if you're good to them
80　they'll be good to you back."

Back. The freeway is across the street.
It's summer now. Every night I sleep with a gentle man
to the hymn of mockingbirds,

and in time, I plant geraniums.
85　I tie up my hair into loose braids,
and trust only what I have built
with my own hands.

1981

- In addition to the main, first-person ("I") speaker, this poem features two other characters who also speak, her mother and grandmother. How are the mother and grandmother and their outlooks characterized, in part through their speech? By the end, how are the adult speaker's life and outlook characterized, especially in relation to those of her mother and grandmother?

SUGGESTIONS FOR WRITING

1　In June 2020, Quaker Oats both responded to ongoing debates and sparked new ones by announcing that, because its "origins are based on a racial stereotype," the "Aunt Jemima" brand of syrup and pancake mix would, after 130 years, get a new image and a new name (The Pearl Milling Company). Find at least two articles or editorials published in response to this announcement. Drawing on both the articles and Lucille Clifton's CREAM OF WHEAT, write an essay exploring how the poem might be seen to contribute to this debate. Does it implicitly offer support to one side or the other? How so, or how not? What sort of insight might a poem be able to offer that an article, editorial, or essay cannot? In these terms, how might both Clifton's choice of speaker and her characterization of him matter?

2. Gwendolyn Brooks's THE MOTHER, like Patricia Smith's SAGAS OF THE ACCIDENTAL SAINTS, Reginald Dwayne Betts's PARKING LOT, TOO, and Anna Laetitia Barbauld's THE MOUSE'S PETITION, is a lyric tackling a complex and controversial topic by making an invented but representative character its first-person speaker. Write an essay analyzing at least one of these poems, exploring the effects and effectiveness of this technique. If you choose to write about multiple poems, be sure to consider any important differences in the particular ways each handles or presents its invented lyric speaker. How might each poet's technique be especially appropriate to the specific issues or situations the poem explores?

3. Write an essay in which you compare the speakers in any two poems in this chapter. What kinds of self-image do they have? In each poem, what is the implied distance between the speaker and the poet?

4. Choose any of the poems in this or the previous chapter and write an essay about the way a poet can create irony and humor through the use of a speaker who either is or is not clearly distinct from the poet himself or herself.

5. Write a poem, short story, or personal essay in which the speaker or narrator is a character mentioned by a speaker in any of the poems in this chapter—for example, a pre-op Hard Rock, Ben and Jemima in CREAM OF WHEAT, or Persephone in Stallings's HADES WELCOMES HIS BRIDE. How might the same situation, as well as the main speaker of these poems, look and sound different when viewed from another speaker's point of view and described in another speaker's voice?

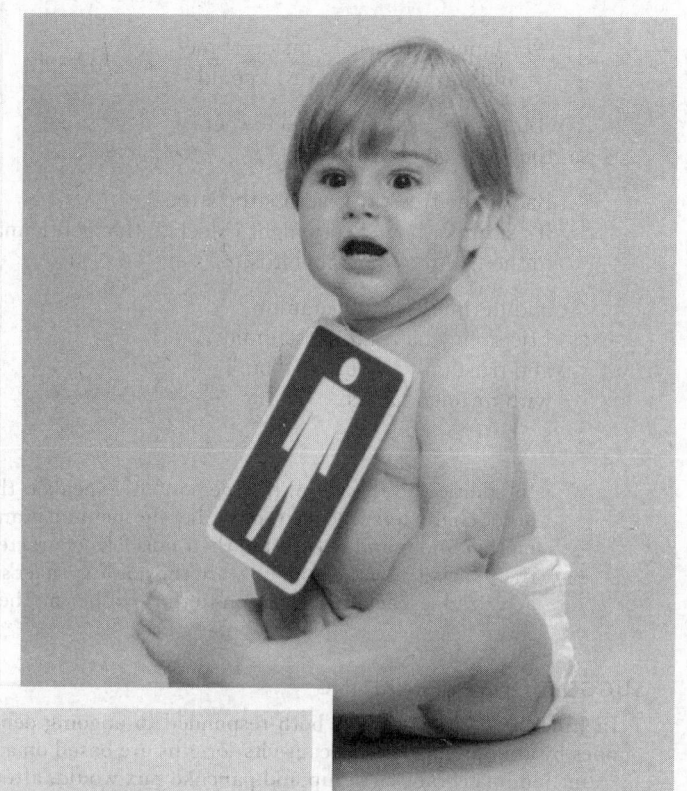

Exploring Gender

AN ALBUM

As far as I'm concerned, being any gender is a drag.
—PATTI SMITH

I
n poetry, as in life, the meaning of what is said to us depends in great part on who says it. In both contexts, too, our sense of who a **speaker** (or any person) is has much to do with gender, even when we aren't aware of it. Is this person a *he* or a *she*? Those little pronouns make all the difference, which is one reason why many people today opt to refuse the binary these pronouns imply by adopting the gender-neutral *they*.

As an experiment, look back at one or two of the poems in the last chapter. At what point, and for what reason, did you first decide that a poem's speaker was male or female? Did you ever change your mind? Does any speaker's gender seem more ambiguous now, on a second reading of the poem, than it did on the first reading? What difference does the speaker's gender make to your response? How might your response relate to the ways the poem does or doesn't conform to your expectations of men and women? What is the effect of the correspondence (or lack thereof) between the **author**'s gender and the speaker's?

Despite all we have said about the danger of confusing the author of a poem with its speaker(s), in practice we usually draw on our knowledge of an author's gender in determining a speaker's gender, particularly when the latter is ambiguous. Consider William Wordsworth's poem SHE DWELT AMONG THE UNTRODDEN WAYS. The title tells us that the poem describes a "she," whom we later learn is "A Maid"—that is, an unmarried woman, probably young and virginal, named Lucy (lines 3, 10). But what about the speaker? On the one hand, we know that Lucy's death and burial make all "[t]he difference" to this person (12), and the poem also gives us plenty of reasons to suspect that the speaker is among the "very few" who "love[d]" Lucy (4), finding her flowerlike and "[f]air" (5, 7). On the other hand, you might be surprised to discover that nothing in the poem offers definitive proof of the speaker's gender. Yet based on these few cues—on the fact that the poem is written by *William* Wordsworth, on our assumptions about men, women, and the way they tend to feel and talk about each other, and on the ways a **lyric** is likely to portray a lost beloved—we almost inevitably assume as we read that the speaker is a man.

In the absence of definitive textual cues about a speaker's gender, such assumptions are common and conventional. But it is nonetheless important (and just plain interesting) to notice that when we assign gender to the speaker of some poems, we *are* making an assumption—one that greatly affects our reading and response. Notice, too, that in assigning gender we not only tend to assume that there are only two options but also often draw on assumptions about sexuality as well, often taking for granted a heterosexual norm. When it comes to gender we need to pay attention to all the details that a poem gives us, as well as to those it withholds.

We also need to be ready for surprises and to look for evidence that might over-turn, or at least complicate, our assumptions. For example, Shakespeare's sonnets famously include some addressed to a young man, others addressed to a woman, and still others that are ambiguous, especially when read independently of the rest of the sonnets in the **sequence**. In some cases, the erotic charge of the poems, com-bined with our own tendency to believe that love poems must be addressed from a man to a woman or vice versa, might well lead us to make inappropriate, even hetero-sexist inferences about the gender of the speaker or the lover.

To help you think more about these issues, this album gathers poems whose speakers vary widely. In one way or another, however, all of these poems invite us to explore our ideas and feelings about gender and, to a lesser extent, sexuality. What does it mean to be a man or a woman? What has it meant in other times and places? Might gender be more complex than the phrases *man* or *woman* and *he* or *she* suggest? When, where, and how do we acquire our ideas about gender-appropriate roles, qualities, behavior, and appearance? Are some or all of these "ideas" not learned at all, but rather innate or instinctual? When and why might having a gender be a burden? a pleasure? How does gender shape our experi-ence? our sense of ourselves and others? our interactions with, and our emotional responses to, poems and people?

RICHARD LOVELACE
Song: To Lucasta, Going to the Wars

Tell me not, sweet, I am unkind,
    That from the nunnery
Of thy chaste breast and quiet mind
    To war and arms I fly.

5 True: a new mistress now I chase,
    The first foe in the field;
And with a stronger faith embrace
    A sword, a horse, a shield.

Yet this inconstancy is such
10   As you too shall adore;
I could not love thee, dear, so much,
    Loved I not honor more.

1649

• What might this poem imply about men's and women's attitudes toward love and war?

LADY MARY CHUDLEIGH
To the Ladies

Wife and servant are the same,
But only differ in the name:
For when that fatal knot is tied,

Which nothing, nothing can divide,
5 When she the word *Obey* has said,
And man by law supreme has made,
Then all that's kind is laid aside,
And nothing left but state[1] and pride.
Fierce as an eastern prince he grows,
10 And all his innate rigor shows:
Then but to look, to laugh, or speak,
Will the nuptial contract break.
Like mutes, she signs alone must make,
And never any freedom take,
15 But still be governed by a nod,
And fear her husband as her god:
Him still must serve, him still obey,
And nothing act, and nothing say,
But what her haughty lord thinks fit,
20 Who, with the power, has all the wit.
Then shun, oh! shun that wretched state,
And all the fawning flatterers hate.
Value yourselves, and men despise:
You must be proud, if you'll be wise.

1703

• What might the speaker mean when she says a husband "with the power, has all the wit" (line 20)? How might that statement multiply the meanings of the poem's last line?

WILFRED OWEN
Disabled

He sat in a wheeled chair, waiting for dark,
And shivered in his ghastly suit of grey,
Legless, sewn short at elbow. Through the park
Voices of boys rang saddening like a hymn,
5 Voices of play and pleasure after day,
Till gathering sleep had mothered them from him.

About this time Town used to swing so gay
When glow-lamps budded in the light blue trees,
And girls glanced lovelier as the air grew dim,—
10 In the old times, before he threw away his knees.
Now he will never feel again how slim
Girls' waists are, or how warm their subtle hands;
All of them touch him like some queer disease.

There was an artist silly for his face,
15 For it was younger than his youth, last year.

1. Social position.

Now, he is old; his back will never brace;
He's lost his color very far from here,
Poured it down shell-holes till the veins ran dry,
And half his lifetime lapsed in the hot race,
20 And leap of purple spurted from his thigh.

One time he liked a blood-smear down his leg,
After the matches,[2] carried shoulder-high.
It was after football, when he'd drunk a peg,[3]
He thought he'd better join.—He wonders why.
25 Someone had said he'd look a god in kilts,
That's why; and may be, too, to please his Meg;
Aye, that was it, to please the giddy jilts
He asked to join. He didn't have to beg;
Smiling they wrote his lie; aged nineteen years.

30 Germans he scarcely thought of; all their guilt,
And Austria's, did not move him. And no fears
Of Fear came yet. He thought of jeweled hilts
For daggers in plaid socks; of smart salutes;
And care of arms; and leave; and pay arrears;
35 *Esprit de corps*; and hints for young recruits.
And soon, he was drafted out with drums and cheers.

Some cheered him home, but not as crowds cheer Goal.
Only a solemn man who brought him fruits
Thanked him; and then inquired about his soul.

40 Now, he will spend a few sick years in Institutes,
And do what things the rules consider wise,
And take whatever pity they may dole.
Tonight he noticed how the women's eyes
Passed from him to the strong men that were whole.
45 How cold and late it is! Why don't they come
And put him into bed? Why don't they come?

1917

- How might you respond differently to this poem if the soldier himself were
  the speaker? if the poem described the events of his life in the order in which
  they happened? if the poem lacked its last two lines?

ALICE DUNBAR-NELSON
I Sit and Sew

I sit and sew—a useless task it seems,
My hands grown tired, my head weighed down with dreams—
The panoply of war, the martial tread of men,

2. Soccer games.
3. A drink, usually brandy and soda.

Grim faced, stern eyed, gazing beyond the ken
5   Of lesser souls, whose eyes have not seen Death,
Nor learned to hold their lives but as a breath—
But—I must sit and sew.

I sit and sew—my heart aches with desire—
That pageant terrible, that fiercely pouring fire
10   On wasted fields, and writhing grotesque things
Once men. My soul in pity flings
Appealing cries, yearning only to go
There in that holocaust of hell, those fields of woe—
But—I must sit and sew

15   The little useless seam, the idle patch;
Why dream I here beneath my homely thatch,
When there they lie in sodden mud and rain,
Pitifully calling me, the quick[4] ones and the slain?
You need me, Christ. It is no roseate dream
20   That beckons me—this pretty futile seam
It stifles me—God, *must* I sit and sew?

1918

• How might repetition help to bring home to the reader the speaker's situation and feelings?

ELIZABETH BISHOP
Exchanging Hats

Unfunny uncles who insist
in trying on a lady's hat,
—oh, even if the joke falls flat,
we share your slight transvestite twist

5   in spite of our embarrassment.
Costume and custom are complex.
The headgear of the other sex
inspires us to experiment.

Anandrous[5] aunts, who, at the beach
10   with paper plates upon your laps,
keep putting on the yachtsmen's caps
with exhibitionistic screech,

the visors hanging o'er the ear
so that the golden anchors drag,
15   —the tides of fashion never lag.
Such caps may not be worn next year.

4. Mainly in the sense of living; alive.
5. Literally, "husbandless."

Or you who don the paper plate
itself, and put some grapes upon it,
or sport the Indian's feather bonnet,
20   —perversities may aggravate

the natural madness of the hatter.
And if the opera hats collapse
and crowns grow drafty, then, perhaps,
he thinks what might a miter matter?

25   Unfunny uncle, you who wore a
hat too big, or one too many,
tell us, can't you, are there any
stars inside your black fedora?

Aunt exemplary and slim,
30   with avernal[6] eyes, we wonder
what slow changes they see under
their vast, shady, turned-down brim.

                                           1956

• The speaker in this poem uses the first-person plural ("we," line 4; "our," 5;
  "us," 8). Who might "we" be? How might your response to the poem change
  if the speaker instead used the first-person singular ("I") or the third-person
  plural ("they")?

DAVID WAGONER
My Father's Garden

On his way to the open hearth where white-hot steel
Boiled against furnace walls in wait for his lance
To pierce the fireclay and set loose demons
And dragons in molten tons, blazing
5   Down to the huge satanic caldrons,
Each day he would pass the scrapyard, his kind of garden.

In rusty rockeries of stoves and brake drums,
In grottoes of sewing machines and refrigerators,
He would pick flowers for us: small gears and cogwheels
10   With teeth like petals, with holes for anthers,
Long stalks of lead to be poured into toy soldiers,
Ball bearings as big as grapes to knock them down.

He was called a melter. He tried to keep his brain
From melting in those tyger-mouthed mills
15   Where the same steel reappeared over and over
To be reborn in the fire as something better

6. Infernal.

Or worse: cannons or cars, needles or girders,
Flagpoles, swords, or plowshares.

But it melted. His classical learning ran
20 Down and away from him, not burning bright.[7]
His fingers culled a few cold scraps of Latin
And Greek, *magna sine laude*,[8] for crosswords
And brought home lumps of tin and sewer grills
As if they were his ripe prize vegetables.

1980, 1987

• What facts do we learn here about the speaker's father and his life? What are
the speaker's feelings about both?

JUDITH ORTIZ COFER
The Changeling

As a young girl
vying for my father's attention,
I invented a game that made him look up
from his reading and shake his head
5 as if both baffled and amused.

In my brother's closet, I'd change
into his dungarees—the rough material
molding me into boy shape; hide
my long hair under an army helmet
10 he'd been given by Father, and emerge
transformed into the legendary Ché[9]
of grown-up talk.

Strutting around the room,
I'd tell of life in the mountains,
15 of carnage and rivers of blood,
and of manly feasts with rum and music
to celebrate victories *para la libertad*.[1]
He would listen with a smile
to my tales of battles and brotherhood
20 until Mother called us to dinner.

She was not amused
by my transformations, sternly forbidding me
from sitting down with them as a man.
She'd order me back to the dark cubicle
25 that smelled of adventure, to shed

7. Like "tyger-mouthed" (line 14), an allusion to William Blake's poem "The Tyger" (1794; p. 1187).
8. Without great distinction (Latin); a reversal of the usual *magna cum laude*.
9. Ernesto "Che" Guevara (1928–67), Argentinian-born Cuban revolutionary leader.
1. For freedom (Spanish).

my costume, to braid my hair furiously
with blind hands, and to return invisible,
as myself,
to the real world of her kitchen.

1993

• Why do you think the speaker's father is amused by her "transformations"
(line 22), and why does her mother forbid them? What does this poem imply
about all three characters?

MARIE HOWE
Practicing

I want to write a love poem for the girls I kissed in seventh grade,
a song for what we did on the floor in the basement

of somebody's parents' house, a hymn for what we didn't say but thought:
That feels good or *I like that*, when we learned how to open each other's
    mouths

5 how to move our tongues to make somebody moan. We called it
    practicing, and
one was the boy, and we paired off—maybe six or eight girls—and turned out
the lights and kissed and kissed until we were stoned on kisses, and
    lifted our
nightgowns or let the straps drop, and, Now you be the boy:

concrete floor, sleeping bag or couch, playroom, game room, train room,
    laundry.
10 Linda's basement was like a boat with booths and portholes

instead of windows. Gloria's father had a bar downstairs with stools that
    spun,
plush carpeting. We kissed each other's throats.

We sucked each other's breasts, and we left marks, and never spoke of it
    upstairs
outdoors, in daylight, not once. We did it, and it was

15 practicing, and slept, sprawled so our legs still locked or crossed, a hand
    still lost
in someone's hair . . . and we grew up and hardly mentioned who

the first kiss really was—a girl like us, still sticky with the moisturizer we'd
shared in the bathroom. I want to write a song

for that thick silence in the dark, and the first pure thrill of unreluctant desire,
20 just before we made ourselves stop.

1998

• What does the speaker of this poem imply about why her memories of "practicing" matter to her now that she is an adult? What does she imply about
how being a girl compares to being a woman?

AUTHORS ON THEIR WORK

MARIE HOWE (b. 1950)

From "Marie Howe" (1997)*

M[ARIE] H[OWE]: [. . .] I was interested in what it means to be a woman, what it means to be a man. [. . .]

In this culture, our mothers don't tell us about their first sexual experience, they don't tell us about their marriage, their lives, their sexual life in marriage, they don't tell us anything. My mother told us nothing. [. . .] So, I've been really aware lately, at 46 years old, that I still need my sisters and my friends to teach me and help me figure out how to be a "girl."

[INTERVIEWER]: So much of our time as girls and women is spent trying to figure out what is allowed, by men and by other women as well. What is not talked about and what is talked about. How we can have an authentic sexuality.

MH: In learning how to be a girl in this culture, we are learning how to be objects. [. . .]

So in the poems, I was trying to find places in my young life where I was actually the subject, and I found it was in practicing how to kiss, which I did with other girls. I got to be a boy-girl and a girl-girl—I got to kiss the girl and kiss the boy. I loved that.

From "The Complexity of the Human Heart: A Conversation with Marie Howe" (2004)**

[INTERVIEWER]: I was interested in your saying you don't want to write personal poems anymore. Is one of the dangers having people confuse your poetry with your life? Once I heard someone say to Sharon Olds, "Tell me, how old are your son and daughter now?" And she said, "I have no son or daughter. Those are fictitious children."

MH: I understand what she means. For example, with that poem "Practicing," [. . .] the New Yorker legal department called up and said, "Are those girls identifiable?" I said, well, Linda's basement was like a boat and Gloria's father did have a bar downstairs with plush carpeting, but I didn't kiss those girls. So, yes, they're identifiable, because the poem has great, great details from my childhood, but that to me is the answer to the question of whether it is autobiographical. It's all constructed. I didn't kiss those two girls. They were my best friends when I was a kid. I kissed other girls, but how could you give up those gorgeous details with those basements, and it poured into the poems. [. . .] But what comes together in a poem isn't true [. . .].

[. . .] I'm making something, like [the artist] Joseph Cornell makes his boxes and everyone looks into them, but it's the box you look into; it's not the man or the woman. It's alchemy of language and memory and imagination and time and music and sounds that gets made, and that's different from "Here is what happened to

me when I was ten." That poem is a good example. Linda's boat basement and
Gloria's plush carpeting were there, but they weren't *there* there.

*"Marie Howe." Interview by Victoria Redel. *BOMB: A Quarterly Arts and Culture Magazine*,
fall 1997, bombmagazine.org/article/2105/marie-howe.
**"The Complexity of the Human Heart: A Conversation with Marie Howe." Interview by
David Elliott. *AGNI Online*, 2004, agnionline.bu.edu/interview/the-complexity-of-the
-human-heart-a-conversation-with-marie-howe

BOB HICOK

O my pa-pa

Our fathers have formed a poetry workshop.
They sit in a circle of disappointment over our fastballs
and wives. We thought they didn't read our stuff,
whole anthologies of poems that begin, My father never,
5   or those that end, and he was silent as a carp,
or those with middles which, if you think
of the right side as a sketch, look like a paunch
of beer and worry, but secretly, with flashlights
in the woods, they've read every word and noticed
10 that our nine happy poems have balloons and sex
and giraffes inside, but not one dad waving hello
from the top of a hill at dusk. Theirs
is the revenge school of poetry, with titles like
"My Yellow Sheet Lad" and "Given Your Mother's Taste
15 for Vodka, I'm Pretty Sure You're Not Mine."
They're not trying to make the poems better
so much as sharper or louder, more like a fishhook
or electrocution, as a group
they overcome their individual senilities,
20 their complete distaste for language, how cloying
it is, how like tears it can be, and remember
every mention of their long hours at the office
or how tired they were when they came home,
when they were dragged through the door
25 by their shadows. I don't know why it's so hard
to write a simple and kind poem to my father, who worked,
not like a dog, dogs sleep most of the day in a ball
of wanting to chase something, but like a man, a man
with seven kids and a house to feed, whose absence
30 was his presence, his present, the Cheerios,
the PF Flyers, who taught me things about trees,
that they're the most intricate version of standing up,
who built a grandfather clock with me so I would know
that time is a constructed thing, a passing, ticking fancy.
35 A bomb. A bomb that'll go off soon for him, for me,
and I notice in our fathers' poems a reciprocal dwelling
on absence, that they wonder why we disappeared

as soon as we got our licenses, why we wanted
the rocket cars, as if running away from them
40 to kiss girls who looked like mirrors of our mothers
wasn't fast enough, and it turns out they did
start to say something, to form the words hey
or stay, but we'd turned into a door full of sun,
into the burning leave, and were gone
45 before it came to them that it was all right
to shout, that they should have knocked us down
with a hand on our shoulders, that they too are mystified
by the distance men need in their love.

2007

- What does the speaker seem to discover about fathers, sons, and men by imagining the poems "Our fathers" might write (line 1)? What does the poem imply
about the relationship between poetry, "language" (20), and gender?

TERRANCE HAYES
Mr. T—[2]

A man made of scrap muscle & the steam
engine's imagination, white feathers
flapping in each lobe for the skull's migration,
should the need arise. Sometimes drugged
5 & duffled (by white men) in a cockpit
bound for the next adventure. And liable
to crush a fool's face like newsprint; headlines
of Hollywood blood and wincing. Half Step 'N Fetchit,[3]
half John Henry. What were we, the skinny B-boys,[4]
10 to learn from him? How to hulk through Chicago
in a hedgerow afro, an ox-grunt kicking dust
behind the teeth; those eighteen glammering
gold chains around the throat of pity,
that fat hollow medallion like the sun on a leash—

2002

- How does the poem characterize Mr. T and the speaker's feelings about
him? Why might it matter that the speaker uses the first-person plural
("we") versus the singular ("I")?

2. Stage name of bodyguard-turned-actor Lawrence Tureaud (b. 1952), star of the 1980s action-
adventure series *The A-Team* and the film *Rocky III* (1982). His boast "I pity the fool" became a
popular catchphrase.
3. Born Lincoln Theodore Perry (1902–85), "Stepin Fetchit" is widely regarded as the first African
American movie star; he became famous and controversial in the 1930s by repeatedly playing the
same stereotypically simpleminded character.
4. Hip-hop dancers or "breakers." *John Henry*: American folk hero portrayed as an enormously strong
railroad worker who dies from exhaustion after winning a contest against a steam-powered drill.

Mr. T (a.k.a. Lawrence Tureaud, top left), Stepin Fetchit (a.k.a. Lincoln Perry, bottom left), and John Henry (right)

STACEY WAITE
The Kind of Man I Am at the DMV

"Mommy, that man is a girl," says the little boy
pointing his finger, like a narrow spotlight,
targeting the center of my back, his kid-hand
learning to assert what he sees, his kid-hand
5 learning the failure of gender's tidy little
story about itself. I try not to look at him

because, yes that man is a girl. I, man, am a girl.
I am the kind of man who is a girl and because
the kind of man I am is patient with children
10 I try not to hear the meanness in his voice,
his boy voice that sounds like a girl voice
because his boy voice is young and pitched high
like the tent in his pants will be years later
because he will grow to be the kind of man
15 who is a man, or so his mother thinks.

His mother snatches his finger from the air,
of course he's not, she says, pulling him
back to his seat, *what number does it say we are?*
she says to her boy, bringing his attention
20 to numbers, to counting and its solid sense.

But he has earrings, the boy complains
now sounding desperate like he's been
the boy who cries wolf, like he's been
the hub of disbelief before, but this time
25 he knows he is oh so right. The kind
of man I am is a girl, the kind of man
I am is push-ups on the basement
floor, is chest bound tight against himself,
is thick gripping hands to the wheel
30 when the kind of man I am drives away
from the boy who will become a boy
except for now while he's still a girl voice,
a girl face, a hairless arm, a powerless hand.
That boy is a girl that man who is a girl
35 thinks to himself, as he pulls out of the lot,
his girl eyes shining in the Midwest sun.

2013

- According to the poem, what is wrong with "gender's tidy little / story about itself," or what is its "failure" (lines 5–6)? How does the speaker characterize and seem to feel about the little boy? his mother? Why and how so?

SAEED JONES
Boy in a Stolen Evening Gown

In this field of thistle, I am the improbable
lady. How I wear the word: sequined weight
snagging my saunter into overgrown grass, blonde
split-end blades. I waltz in an acre of bad wigs.

5 Sir who is no one, sir who is yet to come, I need you
to undo this zipped back, trace the chiffon
body I've borrowed. See how I switch my hips

for you, dry grass cracking under my pretend
high heels? Call me and I'm at your side,
10 one wildflower behind my ear. Ask me
and I'll slip out of this softness, the dress

a black cloud at my feet. I could be the boy
wearing nothing, a negligee of gnats.

2014

- According to the poem, what does it feel like to be a "boy," or *this* boy, "in a stolen evening gown," "an improbable lady" (lines 1, 2)? In what specific ways is the experience exciting and pleasurable, or not? In these terms, what role is played by the imaginary male addressee ("sir") introduced in the second stanza (5)?
- Why and how might it matter that this thirteen-line poem, though not quite a conventional sonnet, in some ways resembles one?

SUGGESTIONS FOR WRITING

1. Identify the poem in this album that moves you the most, whether to anger, frustration, sadness, delight, or any other emotion. Write an essay exploring why and how the poem evokes the emotions it does, focusing especially on the way your emotional response relates, on the one hand, to the poem's representation of gender and, on the other hand, either to your own experience of being a certain gender (or not) or to your own ideas about gender. Alternatively, choose any poem in the album that you find especially good or interesting, and write an essay exploring what it shows about gender and how it does so.

2. Some of the poems in this album explore the relationship between adults and children from the grown-up child's perspective (David Wagoner's MY FATHER'S GARDEN, Judith Ortiz Cofer's THE CHANGELING, Elizabeth Bishop's EXCHANGING HATS, Bob Hicok's O MY PA-PA). Write an essay comparing the way at least two of these poems portray either these relationships or the role of parents in teaching their children what it means to be a certain gender. What feelings do the poems express about these relationships or roles?

3. Richard Lovelace's SONG: TO LUCASTA, GOING TO THE WARS, Wilfred Owen's DISABLED, Alice Dunbar-Nelson's I SIT AND SEW, and Judith Ortiz Cofer's THE CHANGELING all deal with war and men's and women's relationship to it. Write an essay in which you compare at least two of these poems and their implications about the role of war in defining masculinity and femininity.

4. Elizabeth Bishop's EXCHANGING HATS, Judith Ortiz Cofer's THE CHANGELING, Marie Howe's PRACTICING, and Saeed Jones's BOY IN A STOLEN EVENING GOWN all describe games, experiments, or experiences that involve trying on different roles, sometimes by trying on different clothes. Write an essay in which you compare at least two of these poems and the experiences they describe. What does each experience and each poem illustrate about social roles and rules? about the difference between "play" and "real life" or between childhood and adulthood? If you focus on PRACTICING, feel free to draw on the excerpts from the Howe interviews, as well as the poem.

5. Choose any poem from another chapter or album in this book, and write an essay exploring how the poem's meaning and emotional impact are affected by the fact that its speaker either is or is not clearly identified as male or female.

13 | SITUATION AND SETTING: WHAT HAPPENS? WHERE? WHEN?

Questions about the **speaker** in a poem (*Who?* questions) lead to questions about *What?* and *Why?* as well as *Where?* and *When?* First you identify the imagined **situation** in the poem: To whom is the speaker speaking? Is there an **auditor** in the poem? Is anyone else present or referred to in the poem? What is happening? Why is this event or communication occurring, and why is it significant? As soon as you zoom in on answers to such questions about persons and actions, you also encounter questions about place and time. (Where and when does the action or communication take place?) In other words, situation entails **setting**.

The place involved in a poem is its *spatial setting*, and the time is its *temporal setting*. The temporal setting may be a specific date or an era, a season of the year or a time of day. Temporal and spatial settings often influence our expectations, although a poet may surprise us by making something very different of what we had thought was familiar. We tend, for example, to think of spring as a time of discovery and growth, and poems set in spring are likely to make use of that association. Similarly, morning usually suggests discovery—beginnings, vitality, the world fresh and new.

Not all poems have an identifiable situation or setting, just as not all poems have a speaker who is easily distinguishable from the author. **Lyrics** that simply present a series of thoughts and feelings directly, in a reflective way, may not present anything resembling a scene with action, dialogue, or description. But many poems depend crucially on a sense of place, a sense of time, and scenes that resemble those in plays or films. And questions about these matters will often lead you to define not only the "facts" but also the feelings central to the design a poem has on its readers.

To understand the dialogue in Thomas Hardy's THE RUINED MAID, for example, we need to recognize that the two women are meeting after an extended period of separation (the situation) and that they meet in a town rather than the rural area in which they grew up together (the setting). We infer (from the opening lines) that the meeting is accidental and that no one else is present for the conversation. The poem depends on their situation: After leading separate lives for a while, they have some catching up to do. We don't know what specific town they are in or what year, season, or time of day it is—and those details are not important to the poem's effect.

More specific settings matter in other poems. Etheridge Knight's HARD ROCK RETURNS TO PRISON FROM THE HOSPITAL FOR THE CRIMINAL INSANE depends entirely on its prison setting, as does A. E. Stallings's HADES WELCOMES HIS BRIDE on all the vividly rendered objects that make up its version of the underworld. Here, the contrast between the actuality of the setting and the alternately matter-of-fact and glowing terms in which the speaker presents it generates **irony**, adds to the overall creepiness, and helps define the ambiguities of the speaker's character.

Situation and setting may be treated in various ways in a poem, ranging from silence to the barest hints of description to full photographic detail. Often it is relatively easy to identify the situation at the beginning of a poem, but the implications of setting, and what happens as the poem unfolds, may be subtler. Poets often rely on readers to fill in the gaps, drawing on their knowledge of circumstances and familiar experiences in the present or in the past. The poem may specify only a few aspects of a *kind* of setting, such as a motel room in the afternoon.

SITUATION

The following poem portrays a situation that should be—at least in some of its aspects—familiar to you. How would you summarize that situation?

RITA DOVE
Daystar

> She wanted a little room for thinking:
> but she saw diapers steaming on the line,
> a doll slumped behind the door.
> So she lugged a chair behind the garage
> 5   to sit out the children's naps.
>
> Sometimes there were things to watch—
> the pinched armor of a vanished cricket,
> a floating maple leaf. Other days
> she stared until she was assured
> 10   when she closed her eyes
> she'd see only her own vivid blood.
>
> She had an hour, at best, before Liza appeared
> pouting from the top of the stairs.
> And just *what* was mother doing
> 15   out back with the field mice? Why,
> building a palace. Later
> that night when Thomas rolled over and
> lurched into her, she would open her eyes
> and think of the place that was hers
> 20   for an hour—where
> she was nothing,
> pure nothing, in the middle of the day.

1986

   The mother in Dove's DAYSTAR, overwhelmed by the demands of young children, needs a room of her own. All she can manage, however, is a brief hour of respite. The situation is virtually the whole story here. Nothing really happens except that daily events (washing diapers, picking up toys, explaining the world to children, having sex) that surround her brief private hour and make it precious. Being "nothing" (lines 21 and 22) takes on great value in these circumstances.

   Not every poem presents, as Dove's does, familiar and real or realistic situations (any more than all fiction does). Yet even poems that present imaginary or fantastic situations must make them somehow real-seeming and relevant to us. The two poems below are good examples. Both contemplate imaginary situations but of very differ-ent kinds. The first works by simply twisting a familiar situation: The poem describes the speaker's experience as a student in a college course, only the course is in Humani*ty*, not Humani*ties*. The second poem is more abstract and speculative: Like the genre of fiction and film to which its title refers (science fiction), it imagines a possible future. As you read the poems, think about what each suggests about real-world situations ("what is") by the way it depicts its wholly imaginary ("what if") one.

DENISE DUHAMEL
Humanity 101

I was on my way to becoming a philanthropist,
or the president, or at least someone who gave a shit,
but I was a nontraditional student
with a lot of catching up to do. I enrolled in Humanity 101
5   (not to be confused with the Humanities,
a whole separate department). When I flunked
the final exam, my professor suggested
I take Remedial Humanity where I'd learn the basics
that I'd missed so far. I may have been a nontraditional student,
10 but I was a traditional person, she said, the way a professor
can say intimate things sometimes, as though
your face and soul are aglow in one of those
magnified (10x) makeup mirrors.

So I took Remedial Humanity, which sounds like an easy A,
15 but, believe me, it was actually quite challenging.
There were analogy questions, such as:
Paris Hilton[1] is to a rich U.S. suburban kid
as a U.S. middle-class kid is to:
1.) a U.S. poverty-stricken kid,
20 2.) a U.S. kid with nothing in the fridge,
or
3.) a Third World kid with no fridge at all.
We were required to write essays about the cause of war—
Was it a phenomenon? Was it our lower animal selves?
25 Was it economics? Was it psychological/sexual/religious
(good vs. evil and all that stuff)? For homework
we had to bend down to talk to a homeless person
slouched against a building. We didn't necessarily have to
give them money or food, but we had to say something like
30 *How are you?* or *What is your favorite color?*
We took field trips to nursing homes, prisons,
day-care centers. We stood near bedsides
or sat on the floor to color with strange little people
who cried and were afraid of us at first.
35 I almost dropped out. I went to see the professor

(handwritten margin note: Tone: humor / self-awareness / introspection)

---

1. Socialite and media personality (b. 1981), great-granddaughter of Hilton Hotels founder Conrad Hilton.

during his office hours because I wanted to change my major.
He asked, "Is that because your heart is being smashed?"
He thought I should stick it out, that I could make it,
if I just escaped for an hour a day blasting music
40 into my earbuds or slumping in front of the TV.
I said, "But that's just it. Now I see humanity everywhere,
even on sitcoms, even in pop songs,
even in beer commercials." He closed his door
and showed me the scars under his shirt
45 where he had been stabbed. He said I had to assume
everyone had such a wound, whether I could see it or not.

He assured me that it really did get easier in time,
and that it was hard to make music when you were still
learning how to play the scales. He made me see
50 my potential. He convinced me of my own humanity,
that one day I might even be able to get a PhD. But first
I had to, for extra credit, write a treatise on detachment.

2015

• What does the speaker learn from her Humanity class? Why, according to
  the poem, might we all need one? What aspects of the situation imagined
  here seem especially funny or ironic? How does the poem use specific
  aspects of familiar situations?

TRACY K. SMITH
Sci-Fi

There will be no edges, but curves.
Clean lines pointing only forward.

History, with its hard spine & dog-eared
Corners, will be replaced with nuance,

5 Just like the dinosaurs gave way
To mounds and mounds of ice.

Women will still be women, but
The distinction will be empty. Sex,

Having outlived every threat, will gratify
10 Only the mind, which is where it will exist.

For kicks, we'll dance for ourselves
Before mirrors studded with golden bulbs.

The oldest among us will recognize that glow—
But the word *sun* will have been re-assigned

15 To a Standard Uranium-Neutralizing device
Found in households and nursing homes.

And yes, we'll live to be much older, thanks
To popular consensus. Weightless, unhinged,

Eons from even our own moon, we'll drift
20 In the haze of space, which will be, once
And for all, scrutable and safe.

2011

• Does the poem present the future it imagines as positive? negative? both? How might this poem's version of the future compare to those convention- ally offered up in science fiction and film? Might the poem comment on such conventional representations?

SETTING

Frequently a poem's setting draws on common notions of a particular time or place. Setting a poem in a garden, for example, or writing about apples almost inevitably reminds readers of the Garden of Eden because it is an important and widely recog- nized part of the Western heritage. Even people who don't read at all or who lack Judeo- Christian religious commitments are likely to know about Eden, and poets writing in Western cultures can count on that knowledge. A reference to something outside the poem that carries a history of meaning and strong emotional associations is called an **allusion**. For example, gardens may carry suggestions of innocence and order, or temp- tation and the Fall, or both, depending on how the poem handles the allusion.

Specific, well-known places may similarly be associated with particular ideas, val- ues, ways of life, or natural phenomena. The titles of many poems refer, like the fol- lowing one, directly to specific places or times. As you read the poem, pay attention to when and where it takes place and to the details of setting, as well as situation.

MATTHEW ARNOLD
Dover Beach[2]

The sea is calm tonight.
The tide is full, the moon lies fair
Upon the straits; on the French coast the light
Gleams and is gone; the cliffs of England stand,
5 Glimmering and vast, out in the tranquil bay.
Come to the window, sweet is the night-air!
Only, from the long line of spray
Where the sea meets the moon-blanched land,
Listen! you hear the grating roar
10 Of pebbles which the waves draw back, and fling,
At their return, up the high strand,
Begin, and cease, and then again begin,
With tremulous cadence slow, and bring
The eternal note of sadness in.

15 Sophocles long ago
Heard it on the Aegean, and it brought
Into his mind the turbid ebb and flow

2. At the narrowest point on the English Channel. The light on the French coast (lines 3–4) would be about twenty miles away.

Of human misery,[3] we
Find also in the sound a thought,
20   Hearing it by this distant northern sea.

The Sea of Faith
Was once, too, at the full, and round earth's shore
Lay like the folds of a bright girdle furled.
But now I only hear
25   Its melancholy, long, withdrawing roar,
Retreating, to the breath
Of the night-wind, down the vast edges drear
And naked shingles[4] of the world.

Ah, love, let us be true
30   To one another! for the world, which seems
To lie before us like a land of dreams,
So various, so beautiful, so new,
Hath really neither joy, nor love, nor light,
Nor certitude, nor peace, nor help for pain;
35   And we are here as on a darkling plain
Swept with confused alarms of struggle and flight,
Where ignorant armies clash by night.

c. 1851   1867

The situation and setting of DOVER BEACH are concrete and specific. It is night by
the seashore, and the speaker is gazing at the view from a room with someone he
invites to "Come to the window" (line 6) and "Listen" (9); later he says to this person, "Ah, love, let us be true / To one another!" (29–30). Most readers have assumed
that the speaker and his companion are about to travel from Dover across the sea to
France and that the situation is a honeymoon, or at least that the couple is young
and married; after all, the "world [. . .] seems / To lie before us [. . .] / so new" (30–
32). Although this poem is not a prayer, it is a kind of plea for hope despite the
modern loss of faith. The tide is now full, but the poet hears a destructive repetition
of rising and falling waves (the pebbles will be worn down eventually), and he dwells
on the "withdrawing" side of this pattern. For centuries, Christian belief, "The Sea
of Faith" (21), was at high tide, but now the speaker can only "hear" it "[r]etreating"
(24, 26). On the one hand, then, the specifics of setting—the fact that it is night,
that the speaker looks out on a stony beach lined with cliffs, and so on—seem to
evoke the sense of danger, isolation, and uncertainty the speaker feels as a result of
the loss of faith. On the other hand, how might details of setting introduce hope
into the poem, especially when we combine them with our knowledge of how tides
ebb and flow and how the dark of night gives way to the light of day?

ONE POEM, MULTIPLE SITUATIONS AND SETTINGS

Though many poems depict one situation and setting, a single poem will sometimes
juxtapose multiple "scenes." In such cases, we need both to determine the situ-

---

3. In Sophocles's *Antigone* (lines 637–46; p. 1668), the chorus compares the fate of the house of
Oedipus to the waves of the sea.
4. Pebble-strewn beaches.

ation and setting particular to each scene and to consider how the poem interrelates its various scenes to create a singular effect and meaning.

The following poem describes several scenes. Some seem to have actually occurred at particular places and times (when the main speaker was "[i]n sixth grade," for example [line 1]). Others seem hypothetical, abstract, or generic—events that might or often do happen almost anywhere to almost anybody (like "choos[ing] / persimmons," 6–7). Still others seem indeterminate as to time and/or place (Did "Donna undres[s]" only once [18]? When?). How many different scenes of each type can you discern? What connects them to each other? For example, how might at least some of these scenes demonstrate or discuss various kinds of "precision" (5, 82)? How so, and what kinds?

LI-YOUNG LEE
Persimmons

In sixth grade Mrs. Walker
slapped the back of my head
and made me stand in the corner
for not knowing the difference
5 between *persimmon* and *precision*.
How to choose
persimmons. This is precision.
Ripe ones are soft and brown-spotted.
Sniff the bottoms. The sweet one
10 will be fragrant. How to eat:
put the knife away, lay down newspaper.
Peel the skin tenderly, not to tear the meat.
Chew the skin, suck it,
and swallow. Now, eat
15 the meat of the fruit,
so sweet,
all of it, to the heart.

Donna undresses, her stomach is white.
In the yard, dewy and shivering
20 with crickets, we lie naked,
face-up, face-down.
I teach her Chinese.
Crickets: *chiu chiu.* Dew: I've forgotten.
Naked: I've forgotten.
25 *Ni, wo:*   you and me.
I part her legs,
remember to tell her
she is beautiful as the moon.

Other words
30 that got me into trouble were
fight and *fright*, *wren* and *yarn*.
Fight was what I did when I was frightened,
fright was what I felt when I was fighting.

Wrens are small, plain birds,
35 yarn is what one knits with.
Wrens are soft as yarn.
My mother made birds out of yarn.
I loved to watch her tie the stuff;
a bird, a rabbit, a wee man.

40 Mrs. Walker brought a persimmon to class
and cut it up
so everyone could taste
a *Chinese apple*. Knowing
it wasn't ripe or sweet, I didn't eat
45 but watched the other faces.

My mother said every persimmon has a sun
inside, something golden, glowing,
warm as my face.

Once, in the cellar, I found two wrapped in newspaper,
50 forgotten and not yet ripe.
I took them and set both on my bedroom windowsill,
where each morning a cardinal
sang, *The sun, the sun.*
Finally understanding
55 he was going blind,
my father sat up all one night
waiting for a song, a ghost.
I gave him the persimmons,
swelled, heavy as sadness,
60 and sweet as love.

This year, in the muddy lighting
of my parents' cellar, I rummage, looking
for something I lost.
My father sits on the tired, wooden stairs,
65 black cane between his knees,
hand over hand, gripping the handle.

He's so happy that I've come home.
I ask how his eyes are, a stupid question.
All gone, he answers.

70 Under some blankets, I find a box.
Inside the box I find three scrolls.
I sit beside him and untie
three paintings by my father:
Hibiscus leaf and a white flower.
75 Two cats preening.
Two persimmons, so full they want to drop from the cloth.

He raises both hands to touch the cloth,
asks, *Which is this?*

This is persimmons, Father.

80   *Oh, the feel of the wolftail on the silk,*
   the strength, the tense
   precision in the wrist.
   I painted them hundreds of times
   eyes closed. These I painted blind.
85   *Some things never leave a person:*
   scent of the hair of one you love,
   the texture of persimmons,
   in your palm, the ripe weight.

1986

ONE SITUATION AND SETTING, MULTIPLE POEMS

Careful attention to situation and setting can be helpful not only in understanding how any one poem works and means but also in appreciating the differences among poems. We can usefully compare *any* two or more poems that focus on a similar situation or setting. But some poems deliberately invite such comparison by revisiting precisely the same situation and setting depicted in other, earlier poems.

   The following two poems, by Christopher Marlowe and Sir Walter Raleigh, respectively, provide a famous example of this sort of response. Like all **pastoral** poems, these are both set in a rural landscape and concerned with the simple life of country folk, usually (as here) shepherds, who live an outdoor life and tend to basic human needs. Yet Marlowe's is the more conventional of the two insofar as it presents that landscape and that life in stylized, idealized terms—as a simple, timeless world of beauty, music, and love that implicitly operates as a kind of counter to, and interlude from, the more urbane, adult, complicated, time-bound "real world." Raleigh's poem is only one of many replies to Marlowe's, which itself indirectly alludes and responds to countless, even earlier works in the pastoral tradition.

CHRISTOPHER MARLOWE
The Passionate Shepherd to His Love

   Come live with me and be my love,
   And we will all the pleasures prove[5]
   That valleys, groves, hills, and fields,
   Woods, or steepy mountain yields.

5   And we will sit upon the rocks,
   Seeing the shepherds feed their flocks,
   By shallow rivers to whose falls
   Melodious birds sing madrigals.

   And I will make thee beds of roses
10   And a thousand fragrant posies,
   A cap of flowers, and a kirtle[6]
   Embroidered all with leaves of myrtle;

5. Experience.
6. Gown.

A gown made of the finest wool
Which from our pretty lambs we pull;
15 Fair linèd slippers for the cold,
With buckles of the purest gold;

A belt of straw and ivy buds,
With coral clasps and amber studs:
And if these pleasures may thee move,
20 Come live with me, and be my love.

The shepherd swains[7] shall dance and sing
For thy delight each May morning:
If these delights thy mind may move,
Then live with me and be my love.

1599, 1600

• What, according to the speaker, are the specific virtues of the ideal world (or setting) and the life to which he invites his "love" (line 1)? How, by implication, might the poem characterize the (real) world he invites her to leave behind?

SIR WALTER RALEIGH
The Nymph's Reply to the Shepherd

If all the world and love were young,
And truth in every shepherd's tongue,
These pretty pleasures might me move
To live with thee and be thy love.

5 Time drives the flocks from field to fold,
When rivers rage, and rocks grow cold,
And Philomel[8] becometh dumb;
The rest complain of cares to come.

The flowers do fade, and wanton fields
10 To wayward winter reckoning yields:
A honey tongue, a heart of gall,
Is fancy's spring, but sorrow's fall.

Thy gowns, thy shoes, thy beds of roses,
Thy cap, thy kirtle, and thy posies
15 Soon break, soon wither, soon forgotten;
In folly ripe, in reason rotten.

Thy belt of straw and ivy buds,
Thy coral clasps and amber studs,
All these in me no means can move
20 To come to thee and be thy love.

7. Youths.
8. The nightingale.

But could youth last, and love still breed,
Had joys no date,[9] nor age no need,
Then these delights my mind might move
To live with thee and be thy love.

1600

- Raleigh's poem works by presenting the same situation and setting Marlowe's does from a different speaker's perspective and having that speaker, in turn, present a sort of "if/then" scenario (*If all this were true, then I would say yes*): For what specific reasons is this nymph *not* going to accept her shepherd's offer? What's the effect of the poem's "if/then" structure?

THE OCCASIONAL POEM

Some subgenres or kinds of poetry are defined mostly, even wholly, by the way they handle situation or setting or by the specific sorts of situation and/or setting they depict, and these will be the major focus of the rest of this chapter. In fact, we've already discussed one: the pastoral poem, which by definition portrays an idyllic rural setting with certain conventional features.

Rather than depicting a particular kind of setting, an **occasional poem** is a poem written about or for a specific real, especially public and ceremonial, occasion. In the past, writing—and often publicly reading—poems in honor of royal birthdays and other state occasions or commemorating military victories and other major national events was considered an obligation of those serving as Poet Laureate. Since 1961, U.S. presidents have sometimes invited poets to recite at their inaugurations poems written for the occasion. (John F. Kennedy was the first to do so, with Robert Frost; Joe Biden was, to date, the last.) But not all poets have needed an invitation to write occasional poems, nor are all occasional poems celebratory: Though written while he was Poet Laureate, Alfred Tennyson's THE CHARGE OF THE LIGHT BRIGADE commemorates an infamously disastrous battle. Occasional poems can even consider much more ordinary, even personal "occasions." Yet the occasional poem and its history are a healthy reminder that, while we often today think of *all* poems as addressing an individual reader and expressing exclusively personal feelings, a good deal of poetry written over the centuries has had a more public, civic focus and purpose, speaking about and to an entire community and its history. Written for, and read at, the 57th U.S. presidential inauguration, Barack Obama's second, in 2013, the following, quite modern poem is a good example.

RICHARD BLANCO
One Today

One sun rose on us today, kindled over our shores,
peeking over the Smokies, greeting the faces
of the Great Lakes, spreading a simple truth
across the Great Plains, then charging across the Rockies.
5 One light, waking up rooftops, under each one, a story
told by our silent gestures moving behind windows.

9. End.

My face, your face, millions of faces in morning's mirrors,
each one yawning to life, crescendoing into our day:
pencil-yellow school buses, the rhythm of traffic lights,
10 fruit stands: apples, limes, and oranges arrayed like rainbows
begging our praise. Silver trucks heavy with oil or paper—
bricks or milk, teeming over highways alongside us,
on our way to clean tables, read ledgers, or save lives—
to teach geometry, or ring-up groceries as my mother did
15 for twenty years, so I could write this poem.

All of us as vital as the one light we move through,
the same light on blackboards with lessons for the day:
equations to solve, history to question, or atoms imagined,
the "I have a dream"[1] we keep dreaming,
20 or the impossible vocabulary of sorrow that won't explain
the empty desks of twenty children marked absent
today, and forever.[2] Many prayers, but one light
breathing color into stained glass windows,
life into the faces of bronze statues, warmth
25 onto the steps of our museums and park benches
as mothers watch children slide into the day.

One ground. Our ground, rooting us to every stalk
of corn, every head of wheat sown by sweat
and hands, hands gleaning coal or planting windmills
30 in deserts and hilltops that keep us warm, hands
digging trenches, routing pipes and cables, hands
as worn as my father's cutting sugarcane
so my brother and I could have books and shoes.

The dust of farms and deserts, cities and plains
35 mingled by one wind—our breath. Breathe. Hear it
through the day's gorgeous din of honking cabs,
buses launching down avenues, the symphony
of footsteps, guitars, and screeching subways,
the unexpected song bird on your clothes line.

40 Hear: squeaky playground swings, trains whistling,
or whispers across café tables, Hear: the doors we open
for each other all day, saying: hello / shalom,
buon giorno / howdy / namaste / or buenos días[3]
in the language my mother taught me—in every language

1. Title of the famous speech delivered by Martin Luther King, Jr., during the August 1963 March on Washington; one of its most quoted sentences reads, "I have a dream that my four little children will one day live in a nation where they will not be judged by the color of their skin but by the content of their character."
2. On December 14, 2012, Adam Lanza shot and killed twenty-six people, including twenty children ages six and seven, at Sandy Hook Elementary School in Newtown, Connecticut.
3. The words following *hello* are similar greetings in different languages including Hebrew (*shalom*), Italian (*buon giorno*), Hindi (*namaste*), and Spanish (*buenos días*).

45 spoken into one wind carrying our lives
    without prejudice, as these words break from my lips.

    One sky: since the Appalachians and Sierras claimed
    their majesty, and the Mississippi and Colorado worked
    their way to the sea. Thank the work of our hands:
50 weaving steel into bridges, finishing one more report
    for the boss on time, stitching another wound
    or uniform, the first brush stroke on a portrait,
    or the last floor on the Freedom Tower[4]
    jutting into a sky that yields to our resilience.

55 One sky, toward which we sometimes lift our eyes
    tired from work: some days guessing at the weather
    of our lives, some days giving thanks for a love
    that loves you back, sometimes praising a mother
    who knew how to give, or forgiving a father
60 who couldn't give what you wanted.

    We head home: through the gloss of rain or weight
    of snow, or the plum blush of dusk, but always—home,
    always under one sky, our sky. And always one moon
    like a silent drum tapping on every rooftop
65 and every window, of one country—all of us—
    facing the stars
    hope—a new constellation
    waiting for us to map it,
    waiting for us to name it—together

                                                        2013

- As Blanco remarked to an interviewer, the inaugural "occasion demanded"
  a poem that was not exclusively or primarily "autobiographical." Yet his
  poem does include autobiographical details. What are those, and how do
  they contribute to the poem?
- Why might "One Today" be a good title for this poem? What are the various, different ways the poem might encourage you to interpret that phrase?

THE CARPE DIEM POEM

The following two poems from the 1600s represent similar situations: In each, a
male speaker addresses a female auditor whom he desires. The poems belong to the
tradition of **carpe diem** (Latin for "seize the day") because the speaker is urging his
auditor, his lover, to enjoy pleasures now, before they die. The woman is resisting
because of her concern for chastity or social rules. The action of these poems is
implied in the shifts in what the speaker is saying. What does the woman do in THE
FLEA? Can you imagine the woman's response in TO HIS COY MISTRESS?

4. Main building of the World Trade Center, as rebuilt after the terrorist attacks of September 11,
2001.

JOHN DONNE
The Flea

Mark but this flea, and mark in this,[5]
How little that which thou deny'st me is;
It sucked me first, and now sucks thee,
And in this flea our two bloods mingled be;
5 Thou know'st that this cannot be said
A sin, nor shame, nor loss of maidenhead.
      Yet this enjoys before it woo,
      And pampered[6] swells with one blood made of two,
      And this, alas, is more than we would do.[7]

10 Oh stay,[8] three lives in one flea spare,
Where we almost, yea more than, married are.
This flea is you and I, and this
Our marriage bed, and marriage temple is;
Though parents grudge, and you, we're met
15 And cloistered in these living walls of jet.
      Though use[9] make you apt to kill me,
      Let not to that, self-murder added be,
      And sacrilege, three sins in killing three.

Cruel and sudden, hast thou since
20 Purpled thy nail in blood of innocence?
Wherein could this flea guilty be,
Except in that drop which it sucked from thee?
Yet thou triumph'st, and say'st that thou
Find'st not thyself, nor me, the weaker now;
25   'Tis true; then learn how false fears be;
      Just so much honor, when thou yield'st to me,
      Will waste, as this flea's death took life from thee.

1633

• What lines help you imagine what the speaker is doing as he speaks? what
  the auditor does or says?

---

5. Medieval preachers and rhetoricians asked their hearers to "mark" (look at) an object that
illustrated a moral or philosophical lesson they wished to emphasize.
6. Fed luxuriously.
7. According to seventeenth-century medical theory, conception involved the literal mingling of the
lovers' blood.
8. Desist.
9. Habit.

ANDREW MARVELL
To His Coy Mistress

    Had we but world enough, and time,
This coyness,[1] lady, were no crime.
We would sit down, and think which way
To walk, and pass our long love's day.
5 Thou by the Indian Ganges' side
Shouldst rubies[2] find: I by the tide
Of Humber would complain.[3] I would
Love you ten years before the Flood,
And you should if you please refuse
10 Till the conversion of the Jews.[4]
My vegetable love[5] should grow
Vaster than empires, and more slow;
An hundred years should go to praise
Thine eyes, and on thy forehead gaze;
15 Two hundred to adore each breast,
But thirty thousand to the rest.
An age at least to every part,
And the last age should show your heart.
For, lady, you deserve this state;[6]
20 Nor would I love at lower rate.
    But at my back I always hear
Time's wingèd chariot hurrying near;
And yonder all before us lie
Deserts of vast eternity.
25 Thy beauty shall no more be found,
Nor, in thy marble vault, shall sound
My echoing song; then worms shall try
That long preserved virginity,
And your quaint honor turn to dust,
30 And into ashes all my lust:
The grave's a fine and private place,
But none, I think, do there embrace.
    Now therefore, while the youthful hue
Sits on thy skin like morning dew,[7]
35 And while thy willing soul transpires[8]

1. Hesitancy, modesty (not necessarily suggesting calculation).
2. Talismans believed to preserve virginity.
3. Write love complaints, conventional songs lamenting the cruelty of love. *Humber*: a river and estuary in Marvell's hometown of Hull, England.
4. Which, according to popular Christian belief, will occur just before the end of the world.
5. Which is capable only of passive growth, not of consciousness. The "vegetable soul" is lower than the other two divisions of the soul, "animal" and "rational."
6. Dignity.
7. The text reads "glew." "Lew" (warmth) has also been suggested as an emendation.
8. Breathes forth.

At every pore with instant fires,
Now let us sport us while we may,
And now, like am'rous birds of prey,
Rather at once our time devour
40   Than languish in his slow-chapped[9] pow'r.
Let us roll all our strength and all
Our sweetness up into one ball,
And tear our pleasures with rough strife
Thorough[1] the iron gates of life.
45   Thus, though we cannot make our sun
Stand still,[2] yet we will make him run.[3]

1681

• How does each stanza develop the speaker's argument? Is it persuasive?

THE AUBADE

An **aubade**, broadly defined, is any poem set in and focusing on morning. (*Aubade*
comes from the French term for "dawn".) Although morning suggests fresh beginnings and hope, an aubade often expresses sadness because the new day means
that two lovers must part—time has moved on. Indeed, *aubade*, narrowly defined,
indicates a poem that deals with this specific situation—two lovers waking up to
a dawn that spells an end to a night of joyous union. (The aubade thus shares with
the **carpe diem** poem and even the sonnet, with which it is also historically linked,
an interest in the relationship between love, sex, time, and mortality.)

Below you will find two aubades ripe for study and comparison: The first is among
the best-known and most influential examples in the English-language tradition. As
such, it helped to establish the conventions with which the second example plays by
featuring an elderly speaker whose lover isn't an actual woman but "Life" itself. We
can, in other words, fully appreciate this LATE AUBADE, its peculiar situation, its
humor and poignancy, only if we know something about how earlier aubades work.

JOHN DONNE
The Sun Rising

Busy old fool, unruly sun,
    Why dost thou thus,
Through windows, and through curtains, call on us?
Must to thy motions lovers' seasons run?
5   Saucy pedantic wretch, go chide
        Late schoolboys, and sour prentices,[4]
    Go tell court-huntsmen that the king will ride,

9. Slow-jawed. Chronos (Time), ruler of the world in early Greek myth, devoured all of his children
except Zeus, who was hidden. Later, Zeus seized power (see line 46 and note).
1. Through.
2. To lengthen his night of love with Alcmene, Zeus made the sun stand still.
3. Each sex act was believed to shorten life by one day.
4. Apprentices.

Call country ants[5] to harvest offices;
Love, all alike, no season knows, nor clime,
10 Nor hours, days, months, which are the rags of time.
Thy beams, so reverend and strong
why shouldst thou think?
I could eclipse and cloud them with a wink,
But that I would not lose her sight so long:
15   If her eyes have not blinded thine,
Look, and tomorrow late, tell me
Whether both the Indias[6] of spice and mine
Be where thou left'st them, or lie here with me.
Ask for those kings whom thou saw'st yesterday,
20 And thou shalt hear, all here in one bed lay.

She is all states, and all princes I,
Nothing else is.
Princes do but play us; compared to this,
All honor's mimic,[7] all wealth alchemy.
25   Thou, sun, art half as happy as we,
In that the world's contracted thus;
Thine age asks[8] ease, and since thy duties be
To warm the world, that's done in warming us.
Shine here to us, and thou art every where;
30 This bed thy center[9] is, these walls thy sphere.

1633

• What cues in the poem alert you to the specific situation and setting?
What is the speaker feeling? How does he communicate his feelings about
his lover by addressing the sun rather than the lover? What is the speaker
arguing in each stanza? How does one argument build on, or relate to, the
last?

JAMES RICHARDSON
Late Aubade

after Hardy[1]

So what do you think, Life, it seemed pretty good to me,
though quiet, I guess, and unspectacular.
It's been so long, I don't know any more how these things go.
I don't know what it means that we've had this time together.

5 I get that the coffee, the sunlight on glassware, the Sunday paper
and our studious lightness, not hearing the phone, are iconic
of living regretless in the Now. A Cool that's beyond me:

5. Farmworkers.
6. The East and West Indies, commercial sources of spices and gold.
7. Mimicry.
8. Requires.
9. Of orbit.
1. Poet and novelist Thomas Hardy (1840–1928).

I'm having some trouble acting suitably poised and ironic.

It's sensible to be calm, not to make too much of a little thing
10   and just see what happens, as I think you are saying
with your amused look, sipping and letting me monologue,
and young as you are, Life, you would know: you have done it all.

If I get up a little reluctantly, tapping my wallet, keys, tickets,
I'm giving you time to say *Stay, it's a dream*
15   *that you're old—no one notices—years never happened—*
but I see you have already given me all that you can.

Those clear eyes are ancient; you've done this with billions of others,
but you are my first life, Life. I feel helplessly young.
I'm a kid checking mail, a kid on his cell with his questions:
20   are we in love, Life, are we exclusive, are we forever?

                                                                        2014

• In what various ways and senses is this a "late" aubade? Is "late aubade" an
oxymoron? How might that relate to the speaker's characterization of himself
and of Life? How do they each manage to be both young and old at the same
time? How might the poem literalize the notion of being "in love" with life?

POEMS FOR FURTHER STUDY

Consider the *Who? What? Why? Where?* and *When?* questions as you read the
following poems.

TERRANCE HAYES
Carp Poem

After I have parked below the spray paint caked in the granite
grooves of the Frederick Douglass[2] Middle School sign,

where men-size children loiter like shadows draped in outsize
denim, jerseys, braids, and boots that mean I am no longer young;

5   after I have made my way to the New Orleans Parish Jail down the
         block,
where the black prison guard wearing the same weariness

my prison guard father wears buzzes me in. I follow his pistol and shield
along each corridor trying not to look at the black men

boxed and bunked around me until I reach the tiny classroom
10   where two dozen black boys are dressed in jumpsuits orange as the carp

I saw in a pond in Japan once, so many fat, snaggletoothed fish
ganged in and lurching for food that a lightweight tourist could have
         crossed

the water on their backs so long as he had tiny rice balls or bread
to drop into the mouths below his footsteps, which I'm thinking

2. Prominent African American abolitionist, politician, and former slave (c. 1818–95).

15 is how Jesus must have walked on the lake that day, the crackers and
        crumbs
  falling from the folds of his robe, and how maybe it was the one fish

  so hungry it leaped up his sleeve that he later miraculously changed
  into a narrow loaf of bread, something that could stick to a believer's
        ribs,

  and don't get me wrong, I'm a believer too, in the power of food at least,
20 having seen a footbridge of carp packed gill to gill, packed tighter

  than a room of boy prisoners waiting to talk poetry with a young black
        poet,
  packed so close they'd have eaten each other had there been nothing
        else to eat.

                                                                        2010

• What is this poem's central setting and situation? How do details of setting
  help to define the situation and its significance? What two other situations
  and settings appear in the poem? How does the poem relate these three
  scenes?

NATASHA TRETHEWEY
Pilgrimage

Vicksburg, Mississippi[3]

Here, the Mississippi carved
        its mud-dark path, a graveyard

for skeletons of sunken riverboats.
        Here, the river changed its course,

5 turning away from the city
        as one turns, forgetting, from the past—

the abandoned bluffs, land sloping up
        above the river's bend—where now

the Yazoo fills the Mississippi's empty bed.
10   Here, the dead stand up in stone, white

marble, on Confederate Avenue. I stand
        on ground once hollowed by a web of caves;

they must have seemed like catacombs,
        in 1863, to the woman sitting in her parlor,

15 candlelit, underground. I can see her
        listening to shells explode, writing herself

3. On July 4, 1863, the city surrendered to Union forces under Ulysses S. Grant after a forty-day
siege; coming just a day after the Confederate defeat at Gettysburg, Vicksburg's surrender is regarded
as a major turning point in the Civil War.

into history, asking *what is to become*
      of all the living things in this place?

This whole city is a grave. Every spring—
20   *Pilgrimage*—the living come to mingle

with the dead, brush against their cold shoulders
      in the long hallways, listen all night

to their silence and indifference, relive
      their dying on the green battlefield.

25 At the museum, we marvel at their clothes—
      preserved under glass—so much smaller

than our own, as if those who wore them
      were only children. We sleep in their beds,

the old mansions hunkered on the bluffs, draped
30   in flowers—funereal—a blur

of petals against the river's gray.
      The brochure in my room calls this

living history. The brass plate on the door reads
      Prissy's[4] *Room.* A window frames

35 the river's crawl toward the Gulf. In my dream,
      the ghost of history lies down beside me,

rolls over, pins me beneath a heavy arm.

                                          2006

• What different historical times and situations meet in a single place in this
poem? Why and how so?

MAHMOUD DARWISH
Identity Card[5]

Write down:
I am Arab
my I.D. number, 50,000
my children, eight
5 and the ninth due next summer
—Does that anger you?

Write down:
Arab.
I work with my struggling friends in a quarry

---

4. Scarlett O'Hara's maid (a slave) in Margaret Mitchell's novel *Gone with the Wind* (1936).
5. Translated from the Arabic by John Mikhail Asfour. Israeli law requires all citizens sixteen and over
to carry a government-issued identity card at all times, to be presented on demand to police, military,
or government officials. Until 2005, the cards indicated the bearer's ethnicity (Arab, Jew, etc.).

Palestinians showing ID to soldier at an Israeli checkpoint, 2016

10 and my children are eight.
   I chip a loaf of bread for them,
   clothes and notebooks
   from the rocks.
   I will not beg for a handout at your door
15 nor humble myself
   on your threshold
   —Does that anger you?

   Write down:
   Arab,
20 a name with no friendly diminutive.
   A patient man, in a country
   brimming with anger.
   My roots have gripped this soil
   since time began,
25 before the opening of ages
   before the cypress and the olive,
   before the grasses flourished.
   My father came from a line of plowmen,
   and my grandfather was a peasant
30 who taught me about the sun's glory
   before teaching me to read.
   My home is a watchman's shack
   made of reeds and sticks
   —Does my condition anger you?

35 There is no gentle name,
write down:
Arab.
The color of my hair, jet black—
eyes, brown—
40 trademarks,
a headband over a *keffiyeh*[6]
and a hand whose touch grates
rough as a rock.
My address is a weaponless village
45 with nameless streets.
All its men are in the field and quarry
—Does that anger you?

Write down, then
at the top of Page One:
50 I do not hate
and do not steal
but starve me, and I will eat
my assailant's flesh.
Beware of my hunger
55 and of my anger.

1964

- Based on the speaker's words and the poem's title, to whom and in what situation and setting do you imagine him speaking?

YEHUDA AMICHAI
On Yom Kippur in 1967 . . .[7]

On Yom Kippur in 1967, the Year of Forgetting,[8] I put on
my dark holiday clothes and walked to the Old City of Jerusalem.
For a long time I stood in front of an Arab's hole-in-the-wall shop,
not far from the Damascus Gate,[9] a shop with
5 buttons and zippers and spools of thread
in every color and snaps and buckles.
A rare light and many colors, like an open Ark.

6. Traditional male headdress consisting of a square of cloth secured by a cord.
7. From the sequence "Jerusalem, 1967." Translated from the Hebrew by Stephen Mitchell. *Yom Kippur*: the Day of Atonement, culmination of the High Holy Days, during which Jews seek forgiveness for wrongs committed against God and other people; usually falls in September or October.
8. In the so-called Six Day War of June 1967, Israel waged a successful campaign against Syria, Jordan, and Egypt, capturing the mainly Arab-occupied West Bank, along with the Sinai and Golan Heights. According to the translator, "the date 1967 (=5728) is expressed in Hebrew letters that also form the word for 'forget.'"
9. One of the main entrances to the Old City of Jerusalem, so called because it leads to a highway once stretching all the way to Syria's capital, Damascus.

Shops in the Muslim Quarter, Old City, Jerusalem

I told him in my heart that my father too
had a shop like this, with thread and buttons.
10   I explained to him in my heart about all the decades
and the causes and the events, why I am now here
and my father's shop was burned there and he is buried here.[1]

When I finished, it was time for the Closing of the Gates prayer.
He too lowered the shutters and locked the gate
15   and I returned, with all the worshipers, home.

1968

• Why and how is it important that the poem is set on Yom Kippur? that it
ends with the word "home"?

HAI-DANG PHAN
Osprey

Swelling out of the ocean like a bad feeling,
heard before seen slouching toward Miramar[2]
over Venice Beach, it's the Bell Boeing V-22,

1. Amichai's father was a prosperous German merchant who moved his family to what was then
Palestine in 1936, three years after Adolf Hitler became Germany's chancellor, three years before the
start of World War II, and twelve years before the state of Israel was founded.
2. Marine Corps Air Station Miramar in San Diego, California; see also the last lines of W. B. Yeats's
"The Second Coming" (p. 1073): "And what rough beast, its hour come round at last, / Slouches
towards Bethehem to be born?"

not sleek but versatile, able to launch
5 from Al Asad, fly to Mudaysis,[3] perform pickup,
then return, all within the golden hour,
fast enough to outrun a difficult past,
the budgetary hurdles and crashes in R. & D.,
the $72-million price tag, flyaway,[4]
10 its many modes, and we think moods;
you remember its namesake in another state,

fled from some outer dark, gliding above
the diamond, from left field to center,
where it made its home up in the stadium lights,
15 a crown of wooden swords for its nest,
hovering in the swampy air like forethought
as the crack of a bat sent a tiny moon
into orbit, a wave rippling through
the crowd, the lights on their tall stems
20 powered on, day powered down,
and you had no team, you did not know
whom to root for, home or away.

2018

- Phan's poem juxtaposes two occasions or scenes, as well as two kinds of osprey (one a military aircraft, the other a fish-eating hawk). How does the poem connect the two scenes, situations, and settings? How, through them, might the poem encourage us to understand the multiple meanings of the speaker's concluding remark, "you did not know / whom to root for, home or away"?

SUGGESTIONS FOR WRITING

1. Matthew Arnold's DOVER BEACH and Natasha Trethewey's PILGRIMAGE are meditations on history and human destiny derived from the poets' close observation of particular places and times. Write an essay in which you examine one poem's descriptive language and the way it creates a suitable setting for the speaker's philosophical musings.

2. Write an essay either comparing the two carpe diem poems in this chapter or comparing one of these poems to John Donne's THE SUN RISING. If you choose the former option, concentrate on how each poem differently handles the same basic situation: How does each speaker go about convincing his auditor to "seize the day"? If you choose the latter option, explore how Donne's aubade might work as a sort of sequel to the carpe diem poem: In what ways are the two poems alike, and what difference do their different situations make?

3. Like Li-Young Lee's PERSIMMONS, both Terrance Hayes's CARP POEM and Hai-Dang Phan's OSPREY describe and interrelate at least two different scenes, involving different situations and settings. Choose one of these poems and write an essay exploring how its various scenes are interrelated to form one meaningful whole. What

3. Like Al Asad, a military air base in Iraq, used at various times by U.S., as well as Iraqi, forces.
4. Of or relating to an aircraft ready to fly, as in "the plane's flyaway price." R. & D.: Research and Development (acronym).

does each scene contribute to the overall meaning and effect of the poem, and how so? Alternatively, write an essay comparing the different ways in which any two of these poems interrelate multiple scenes, situations, and settings to each other, and with what effects.

4. Write an essay analyzing how Richard Blanco's ONE TODAY characterizes contemporary America. In these terms, what role is played by the autobiographical details incorporated into the poem? the allusions both to particular settings such as "the Smokies" (line 2) and generic ones such as "rooftops" (5), as well as past events such as the Sandy Hook shooting? Alternatively, compare Blanco's characterization to that offered in Walt Whitman's I HEAR AMERICA SINGING.

5. Wildly different as they and their handling of setting are, Etheridge Knight's HARD ROCK RETURNS TO PRISON FROM THE HOSPITAL FOR THE CRIMINAL INSANE and Terrance Hayes's CARP POEM are both set in a prison. Write an essay comparing the two poems' characterizations of prison life and the role that descriptions of setting—both time and place—play in each poem. Or compare any other two poems in this book that depict similar settings and/or situations.

6. Choose any poem in this anthology in which you think setting is especially key to the poem's effect and meaning or in which you think the meaningfulness of setting depends on the associations of particular times and/or places. Write an essay explaining why and how so.

7. Write your own occasional poem about a recent event that you believe others in your community should see as having major significance. What community are you writing about and to? What exactly makes this event so meaningful? Alternatively, write a response—in verse or prose—to any poem in this chapter: Like Walter Raleigh's THE NYMPH'S REPLY TO THE SHEPHERD, your response should depict the same situation and setting as the original poem does, but viewed from another speaker's point of view and in his or her distinctive voice. How, for example, might the shepherd respond to the nymph's reply?

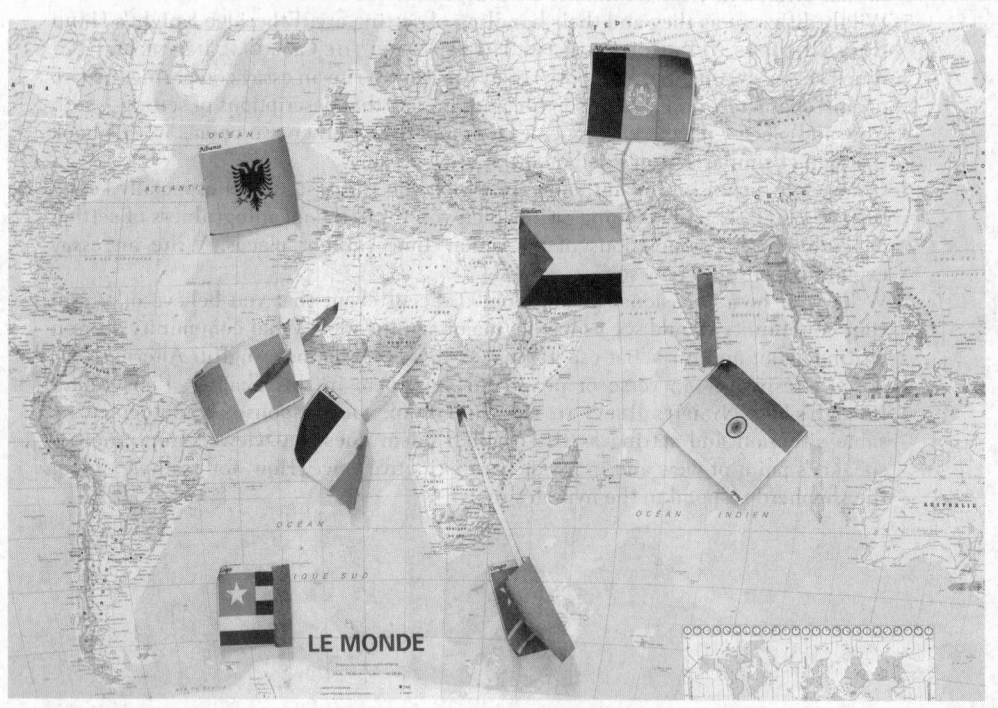
LE MONDE

Homelands
AN ALBUM

O ne of the most ancient literary **motifs** is the quest or journey away from home. Sacred literature, including the Bible, tells of exile and a long period of suffering before arrival at or return to a homeland. **Epics** and **romances** may concern the hero's wanderings or adventures to reach or to defend a realm closely associated with his birth, inheritance, or fate. Since the 1500s, global exploration, colonialism, slavery, mass migration, and economic transformation have meant that many of the world's populations have experienced dislocation and deracination (loss of roots). Those who find themselves displaced try to remember where they came from; they may seek to honor their heritage or yearn for a sense of belonging.

The poems in this album were written at different times in different places and cultural contexts. Each speaker suggests some kind of double vision on the past and present, on a more modern or recent location and a former, perhaps ancestral home. What is the role of dislocation or altered identity in these poems? How do these poems represent the speaker's divided loyalties or distance from home? How do they indicate the passage of time, whether in history, over generations, or within one person's life?

MAYA ANGELOU
Africa

    Thus she had lain
    sugar cane sweet
    deserts her hair
    golden her feet
5   mountains her breasts
    two Niles her tears.
    Thus she has lain
    Black through the years.

    Over the white seas
10 rime white and cold
    brigands ungentled
    icicle bold
    took her young daughters
    sold her strong sons
15 churched her with Jesus
    bled her with guns.
    Thus she has lain.

    Now she is rising
    remember her pain

20 remember the losses
her screams loud and vain
remember her riches
her history slain
now she is striding
25 although she had lain.

1975

• What is the effect of the way the phrases describing Africa's action—"had
lain" (line 1), "is rising" (18), and so forth—repeat with variations throughout the poem?

AUTHORS ON THEIR WORK

MAYA ANGELOU (1928–2014)

From "Maya Angelou, The Art of Fiction No. 119" (1990)*

I never agreed, even as a young person, with the Thomas Wolfe
title You Can't Go Home Again. Instinctively I didn't. But the
truth is, you can never leave home. You take it with you; it's
under your fingernails; it's in the hair follicles; it's in the way
you smile; it's in the ride of your hips, in the passage of your
breasts; it's all there, no matter where you go. You can take on the affectations
and the postures of other places and even learn to speak their ways. But the truth
is, home is between your teeth. Everybody's always looking for it: Jews go to
Israel; black Americans and Africans in the Diaspora go to Africa; Europeans,
Anglo-Saxons go to England and Ireland; people of Germanic background go to
Germany. It's a very queer quest. We can kid ourselves; we can tell ourselves, Oh
yes, honey, I live in Tel Aviv, actually. . . . The truth is a stubborn fact.

*"Maya Angelou, The Art of Fiction No. 119." Interview by George Plimpton. The Paris
Review, no. 116, fall 1990, www.theparisreview.org/interviews/2279/the-art-of-fiction-no-119
-maya-angelou.

DEREK WALCOTT
A Far Cry from Africa

A wind is ruffling the tawny pelt
Of Africa. Kikuyu,[1] quick as flies,
Batten upon the bloodstreams of the veldt.[2]
Corpses are scattered through a paradise.

---

1. East African tribe whose members, as Mau Mau fighters, conducted an eight-year insurrection
against British colonists in Kenya.
2. Open plains, neither cultivated nor thickly forested (Afrikaans).

5 Only the worm, colonel of carrion, cries:
"Waste no compassion on these separate dead!"
Statistics justify and scholars seize
The salients of colonial policy.
What is that to the white child hacked in bed?
10 To savages, expendable as Jews?

Threshed out by beaters,[3] the long rushes break
In a white dust of ibises whose cries
Have wheeled since civilization's dawn
From the parched river or beast-teeming plain.
15 The violence of beast on beast is read
As natural law, but upright man
Seeks his divinity by inflicting pain.
Delirious as these worried beasts, his wars
Dance to the tightened carcass of a drum,
20 While he calls courage still that native dread
Of the white peace contracted by the dead.

Again brutish necessity wipes its hands
Upon the napkin of a dirty cause, again
A waste of our compassion, as with Spain,[4]
25 The gorilla wrestles with the superman.
I who am poisoned with the blood of both,
Where shall I turn, divided to the vein?
I who have cursed
The drunken officer of British rule, how choose
30 Between this Africa and the English tongue I love?
Betray them both, or give back what they give?
How can I face such slaughter and be cool?
How can I turn from Africa and live?

1962

> • How does the speaker express his divided loyalties in the questions that
> conclude the poem? What various meanings might the poem's title accrue
> by the end?

---

3. In big-game hunting, natives are hired to beat the brush, driving birds—such as ibises—and other animals into the open.
4. Spanish Civil War (1936–39), in which Republican loyalists supported politically by liberals in the West and militarily by Soviet Communists fought Nationalist rebels aided by Nazi Germany and Fascist Italy.

AUTHORS ON THEIR WORK

DEREK WALCOTT (1930–2017)

From "An Interview with Derek Walcott" (1979)*

[QUESTION:] Do you want to talk about the Caribbean writer's special relationship to Africa?

[ANSWER: . . .] I have been British; I have been a citizen of the Caribbean federation; now I'm supposed to be either a Trinidadian or a St. Lucian but with a British passport. I find that I am able to make a living in America (and I owe America a great deal for its recognition and the fact that I can work here); and there is the same danger, the same seduction in saying I really am African and should be in Africa, or that my whole experience is African. This can be simply another longing, even a slave longing, for another master. There is no West Indian who is black, or even one who is not black, who is not aware of the existence of Africa in all of us. [. . .] The fact is that every West Indian has been severed from a continent, whether he be Indian, Chinese, Portuguese, or black. To have the population induced into a mass nostalgia to be somewhere else seemed to me about as ennobling as wishing that the whole population was in Brooklyn, or Brickston. [. . .] It would be equally abhorrent to me to say "I wish we were English again" as to say "I wish we were African again." The reality is that one has to build in the West Indies. But that is not to say one doesn't know who one is: our music, our speech—all the things that are organic in the way we live—are African.

I [. . .] felt that it was a privilege to grow up as an English colonial child [in the West Indies] because politically and culturally the British heritage was supposed to be mine. It was no problem for me to feel that since I was writing in English, I was in tune with the growth of the language. I was the contemporary of anyone writing in English anywhere in the world. What is more important, however— and I'm still working on this—was to find a voice that was not inflected by influences. One didn't develop an English accent in speech; one kept as close as possible to an inflection that was West Indian. The aim was that a West Indian or an Englishman could read a single poem, each with his own accent, without either one feeling that it was written in dialect.

*"An Interview with Derek Walcott." Interview by Edward Hirsch. *Contemporary Literature*, vol. 20, no. 3, summer 1979, pp. 279–92.

CLAUDE McKAY

The Tropics in New York

Bananas ripe and green, and ginger-root,
　　Cocoa in pods and alligator pears,
And tangerines and mangoes and grape fruit,
　　Fit for the highest prize at parish fairs,

5　Set in the window, bringing memories
　　Of fruit-trees laden by low-singing rills,
And dewy dawns, and mystical blue skies
　　In benediction over nun-like hills.

My eyes grew dim, and I could no more gaze;
10　A wave of longing through my body swept,
And, hungry for the old, familiar ways,
　　I turned aside and bowed my head and wept.

1920

JUDITH ORTIZ COFER

The Latin Deli: An Ars Poetica[5]

Presiding over a formica counter,
plastic Mother and Child magnetized
to the top of an ancient register,
the heady mix of smells from the open bins
5　of dried codfish, the green plantains
hanging in stalks like votive offerings,
she is the Patroness of Exiles,
a woman of no-age who was never pretty,
who spends her days selling canned memories
10　while listening to the Puerto Ricans complain
that it would be cheaper to fly to San Juan
than to buy a pound of Bustelo coffee here,
and to Cubans perfecting their speech
of a "glorious return" to Havana—where no one
15　has been allowed to die and nothing to change until then;
to Mexicans who pass through, talking lyrically
of dólares to be made in El Norte[6]—
　　　　　　　　　　　all wanting the comfort
of spoken Spanish, to gaze upon the family portrait
20　of her plain wide face, her ample bosom
resting on her plump arms, her look of maternal interest
as they speak to her and each other
of their dreams and their disillusions—

---

5. "Art of Poetry" (Latin), after the title of a treatise by the Roman poet Horace (65–8 BCE).
6. The North (referring to the United States). *Dólares*: dollars (Spanish).

how she smiles understanding,
25   when they walk down the narrow aisles of her store
reading the labels of packages aloud, as if
they were the names of lost lovers: *Suspiros,*[7]
Merengues, the stale candy of everyone's childhood.
                              She spends her days
30   slicing *jamón y queso*[8] and wrapping it in wax paper
tied with string: plain ham and cheese
that would cost less at the A&P,[9] but it would not satisfy
the hunger of the fragile old man lost in the folds
of his winter coat, who brings her lists of items
35   that he reads to her like poetry, or the others,
whose needs she must divine, conjuring up products
from places that now exist only in their hearts—
closed ports she must trade with.

                                              1993

- What keeps people shopping at the Latin Deli (versus a chain store)? How is
  this poem an "ars poetica," or what might it say about "the art of poetry" as
  practiced by a Puerto Rican American poet like Cofer?

MARTÍN ESPADA
Coca-Cola and Coco Frío[1]

On his first visit to Puerto Rico,
island of family folklore,
the fat boy wandered
from table to table
5   with his mouth open.
At every table, some great-aunt
would steer him with cool spotted hands
to a glass of Coca-Cola.
One even sang to him, in all the English
10   she could remember, a Coca-Cola jingle
from the forties. He drank obediently, though
he was bored with this potion, familiar
from soda fountains in Brooklyn.

Then, at a roadside stand off the beach, the fat boy
15   opened his mouth to coco frío, a coconut
chilled, then scalped by a machete
so that a straw could inhale the clear milk.
The boy tilted the green shell overhead

7. Literally "sighs" (Spanish); like *Merengues* (line 28), a type of candy.
8. Ham and cheese (Spanish).
9. Great Atlantic and Pacific Tea Company, a major U.S. grocery store chain founded in 1859.
1. Literally, "cold coconut" (Spanish).

and drooled coconut milk down his chin;
20 suddenly, Puerto Rico was not Coca-Cola
or Brooklyn, and neither was he.

For years afterward, the boy marveled at an island
where the people drank Coca-Cola
and sang jingles from World War II
25 in a language they did not speak,
while so many coconuts in the trees
sagged heavy with milk, swollen
and unsuckled.

1993

• What might the poem encourage us to see as ironic or paradoxical either
about the boy's experiences in Puerto Rico or about his relatives' behavior?

CATHY SONG

Heaven

He thinks when we die we'll go to China.
Think of it—a Chinese heaven
where, except for his blond hair,
the part that belongs to his father,
5 everyone will look like him.
China, that blue flower on the map,
bluer than the sea
his hand must span like a bridge
to reach it.
10 An octave away.

I've never seen it.
It's as if I can't sing that far.
But look—
on the map, this black dot.
15 Here is where we live,
on the pancake plains
just east of the Rockies,
on the other side of the clouds.
A mile above the sea,
20 the air is so thin, you can starve on it.
No bamboo trees
but the alpine equivalent,
reedy aspen with light, fluttering leaves.
Did a boy in Guangzhou² dream of this
25 as his last stop?
I've heard the trains at night
whistling past our yards,

2. Usually called Canton, a seaport city in southeastern China.

what we've come to own,
the broken fences, the whiny dog, the rattletrap cars.
30　It's still the wild west,
mean and grubby,
the shootouts and fistfights in the back alley.
With my son the dreamer
and my daughter, who is too young to walk,
35　I've sat in this spot
and wondered why here?
Why in this short life,
this town, this creek they call a river?

He had never planned to stay,
40　the boy who helped to build
the railroads for a dollar a day.
He had always meant to go back.
When did he finally know
that each mile of track led him further away,
45　that he would die in his sleep,
dispossessed,
having seen Gold Mountain,
the icy wind tunneling through it,
these landlocked, makeshift ghost towns?

50　It must be in the blood,
this notion of returning.
It skipped two generations, lay fallow,
the garden an unmarked grave.
On a spring sweater day
55　it's as if we remember him.
I call to the children.
We can see the mountains
shimmering blue above the air.
If you look really hard
60　says my son the dreamer,
leaning out from the laundry's rigging,
the work shirts fluttering like sails,
you can see all the way to heaven.

1988

• Who is "He" in this poem's first line? What family history is recounted in
the poem? How does the poem make use of contrast?

AGHA SHAHID ALI
Postcard from Kashmir

Kashmir shrinks into my mailbox,
my home a neat four by six inches.

I always loved neatness. Now I hold
the half-inch Himalayas in my hand.

5   This is home. And this the closest
     I'll ever be to home. When I return,
     the colors won't be so brilliant,
     the Jhelum's[3] waters so clean,
     so ultramarine. My love
10   so overexposed.

     And my memory will be a little
     out of focus, in it
     a giant negative, black
     and white, still undeveloped.

     (for Pavan Sahgal)

1987

- What words characterize the speaker's dreams of home in this poem? What
  words reveal a more realistic attitude?

ADRIENNE SU
Escape from the Old Country

     I never had to make one,
     no sickening weeks by ocean,

     no waiting for the aerogrammes[4]
     that gradually ceased to come.

5   Spent the babysitting money
     on novels, shoes, and movies,

     yet the neighborhood stayed empty.
     It had nothing to do with a journey

     not undertaken, nor with dialect,
10   nor with a land that waited

     to be rediscovered, then rejected.
     As acid rain collected

     above the suburban hills, I tried
     to imagine being nothing, tried

15   to be able to claim, "I have
     no culture," and be believed.

     Yet the land occupies the person
     even as the semblance of freedom

     invites a kind of recklessness.
20   Tradition, unobserved, unasked,

     hangs on tight; ancestors roam
     into reverie, interfering at the most

3. The river Jhelum runs through Kashmir and Pakistan.
4. Airmail letters, especially those on specially designed stationery.

awkward moments, first flirtations,
in doorways and dressing rooms—

25 But of course. Here in America,
no one escapes. In the end, each traveler

returns to the town where, everyone
knew, she hadn't even been born.

2006

- To what does "one" refer, in line 1? In the context of the rest of the poem, what are the various possible meanings of the sentence "Here in America, / no one escapes" (lines 25–26)?

SUGGESTIONS FOR WRITING

1. Write a response paper or essay exploring how Africa or any other homeland and the speaker's relationship to it are characterized in at least one or two poems in this album.

2. Multiple poems in this album explore the way we tend to idealize the place we or our forebears have left. Write an essay comparing what at least two poems suggest about how and why we do so. Which, if any, poems seem to see such idealization as a problem? Why and how so?

3. In The Tropics in New York, the speaker's "memories" of his (Caribbean) home are stirred by the site of fruits in a shop window (line 5); Coca-Cola and Coca Frío turns on the contrast between the familiar drink a boy's relatives offer him when he visits Puerto Rico and the one he there discovers on his own; and certain coffee, candies, ham, and cheese are, in part, what the customers of The Latin Deli seek there, despite the expense involved. Write an essay analyzing what at least two of these poems suggest about why and how food and drink might loom so large in our memories and/or experiences of our personal or familial homelands. How might any of the experiences described here resemble or give you new insight into any of your own experiences?

4. Look closely at the three stanzas of A Far Cry from Africa by Derek Walcott. Be sure to note any changes—rhyme patterns or **meter**, subject matter or attitude— across the three stanzas. Where does the speaker clarify who he is and where his loyalties lie? Why is the last part of the poem a series of questions? Write an essay in which you interpret the form and theme of the poem as itself a kind of "far cry from Africa," in every sense: far from that homeland, part of a non-African tradition, "crying" for connection.

5. In the interview excerpted earlier in this chapter, Maya Angelou claims that "the truth is, you can never *leave* home. You take it with you." Write an essay in which you use Angelou's arguments to analyze Adrienne Su's Escape from the Old Country. According to Angelou, how and why exactly do we always take our ancestral "home" with us? Does the speaker or **implied author** of Su's poem seem to agree with Angelou? How and why so, or not?

6. Imagine receiving in your mailbox a postcard from the place where you or your parents were born. (Alternatively, imagine receiving digital pictures or messages in other formats.) Write a poem or a short prose description in which you express a response similar to the speaker's in Agha Shahid Ali's Postcard from Kashmir: How would the place be changed if you could visit, and how would it differ from the way you or your family think about it now?

14 | THEME AND TONE

Poetry is full of surprises. Poems express anger or outrage just as effectively as love or sadness or hilarity, and good poems can be written about going to a rock concert or mowing the lawn, as well as about making love or smelling flowers. Even poems on predictable subjects can surprise us with unpredicted attitudes or sudden twists. Knowing that a poem is about some particular subject or topic—love, for example, or death—may give us a general idea of what to expect, but it never tells us exactly what we will find in a particular poem. Labeling a poem a "love poem" or a "death poem" is a convenient way to speak of its topic. But poems that may be loosely called "love poems" or "death poems" may have little else in common, may express utterly different attitudes or ideas, and may concentrate on very different aspects of the subject. Letting a poem speak to us means more than merely figuring out its topic; it means listening to *how* the poem says what it says. *What* a poem says about its topic is its **theme**. *How* a poem makes that statement involves its **tone**—the poem's attitude or feelings toward its topic. No two poems on the same subject affect us in exactly the same way; their themes and tones vary, and even similar themes may be expressed in various ways, creating different tones and effects.

TONE

Tone, a term borrowed from acoustics and music, refers to the qualities of the language a speaker uses in social situations or in a poem, and it also refers to a speaker's intended effect. Tone is closely related to style and **diction**; it is an effect of the speaker's expressions, *as if* showing a real person's feelings, manner, and attitude or relationship to a listener and to the particular subject or situation. Thus, the speaker may use angry or mocking words, may address the listener intimately or distantly, may sincerely confess or coolly observe, may paint a grand picture or narrate a **legend**.

The following poem is brief but complex, particularly in tone. As you read the poem, work first to identify its **speaker**, **situation**, and **setting**. Then try both to capture its tone in a single word or two and to figure out which features of the poem most help to create that tone. Last but not least, be sure to note when, how, and why the poem's tone might shift or change.

LORNA DEE CERVANTES
Freeway 280

Las casitas[1] near the gray cannery,
nestled amid wild abrazos[2] of climbing roses
and man-high red geraniums
are gone now. The freeway conceals it
5 all beneath a raised scar.

But under the fake windsounds of the open lanes,
in the abandoned lots below, new grasses sprout,
wild mustard remembers, old gardens
come back stronger than they were,
10 trees have been left standing in their yards.
Albaricoqueros, cerezos, nogales . . .[3]
Viejitas[4] come here with paper bags to gather greens.
Espinaca, verdolagas, yerbabuena . . .[5]

I scramble over the wire fence
15 that would have kept me out.
Once, I wanted out, wanted the rigid lanes
to take me to a place without sun,
without the smell of tomatoes burning
on swing shift in the greasy summer air.
20 Maybe it's here
en los campos extraños de esta ciudad[6]
where I'll find it, that part of me
mown under
like a corpse
25 or a loose seed.

1981

The situation and setting of FREEWAY 280 unfolds slowly but surely: The speaker has returned to a place she once lived, a neighborhood now "conceal[ed]" by the freeway built overhead (line 4). As we might expect, given that scenario, the poem's tone is initially somber: The first stanza mostly describes all that is "gone now" (4), the sense of wounding and loss emphasized by the **metaphor** likening the freeway to a "scar" (5). Yet the word *But*, which begins the second stanza, signals a shift in tone, as well as focus, as what initially seem to be "abandoned lots" (7) reveal themselves to be full of life: Old women harvest the produce of "gardens" not merely surviving but thriving, "com[ing] back stronger than they were" (9) to produce a bounty whose variety and beauty are made vividly apparent by the lists (in Spanish) that make up lines 11 and 13. If the poem to this point juxtaposes images

1. The little houses (Spanish).
2. Hugs (Spanish).
3. Apricot trees, cherry trees, walnut trees (Spanish).
4. Old women (Spanish); the suffix *-itas* is a diminutive connoting affection.
5. Spinach, purslane, mint (Spanish).
6. In the strange fields of this city (Spanish).

of loss and life, a somber, mournful tone with a bright, even celebratory, one, the poem's last two stanzas arguably maintain and expand upon, by also personalizing, those dualities. It is only in the third stanza, after all, that the speaker first refers to herself, letting us know that she once lived in this place even as she foregrounds the irony of her past and present relationship to it: She is now fighting to get into a place that she once wanted only to escape by means of the freeway itself; she now sees her old neighborhood as also representing a "part of" her (22). If, like the neighborhood and its gardens, that part of herself, her identity, has been buried, or "mown under," it, too, can be envisioned as "a loose seed" ripe for cultivation rather than a dead "corpse" to be mourned (23–25). Though we might thus describe the poem's ultimate tone as hopeful, we can appreciate—and, as importantly, effectively *show* someone else—that it is so only by attending to the many tones the poem, over its course, shifts among and sometimes balances simultaneously.

And what is true of this poem is true of many. Certainly, we want to capture, for ourselves and others, a poem's single dominant or ultimate tone. But we can often do that best by allowing for two possibilities: one, that this tone is complex, even contradictory; and two, that this tone might be, to speak figuratively, a place at which a poem arrives rather than the place it starts or inhabits consistently. Like people, tone can be multifaceted; tone can evolve.

THEME

Our response to the tone(s) of a poem, however it surprises or jars or stirs us, guides us to understand its theme (or themes): what the poem expresses about its topic. A theme is not simply a work's subject or topic; it is a statement *about* that topic. Although we can usually agree on a poem's topic without much difficulty, it is harder to determine how to state a poem's theme. A single theme may be expressed in several different ways, and a single poem may also have more than one theme. Sometimes the poet explicitly states a poem's theme, and such a statement may clarify why the author chose a particular mode of presentation and how the poem fits into the author's own patterns of thinking and growing. However, the author's words may give a misleading view of how most people read the poem, just as a person's self-assessment may not be all we need in order to understand his or her character. Further study of the poem is necessary to understand how it fulfills—or fails to fulfill—the author's intentions. Despite the difficulty of identifying and expressing themes, doing so is an important step in understanding and writing about poetry.

Topic versus Tone and Theme: A Comparative Exercise

Reading two or more poems with similar topics side by side may suggest how each is distinctive in what it has to say and how it does so—its theme and tone. The following two poems are about animals, although both of them place their final emphasis on human beings: The animal in each case is only the means to the end of exploring human nature. The poems share the assumption that animal behavior may appear to reflect human habits and conduct and that it may reveal much about us; in each case the character central to the poem is revealed to be surprisingly unlike the way she thinks of herself. But the poems differ in their tones, in the specific relationship between the woman and the animals, and in their themes.

How would you describe the tone of the following poem? its topic and theme?

MAXINE KUMIN
Woodchucks

Gassing the woodchucks didn't turn out right.
The knockout bomb from the Feed and Grain Exchange
was featured as merciful, quick at the bone
and the case we had against them was airtight,
5 both exits shoehorned shut with puddingstone,[7]
but they had a sub-sub-basement out of range.

Next morning they turned up again, no worse
for the cyanide than we for our cigarettes
and state-store Scotch, all of us up to scratch.
10 They brought down the marigolds as a matter of course
and then took over the vegetable patch
nipping the broccoli shoots, beheading the carrots.

The food from our mouths, I said, righteously thrilling
to the feel of the .22, the bullets' neat noses.
15 I, a lapsed pacifist fallen from grace
puffed with Darwinian pieties for killing,
now drew a bead on the littlest woodchuck's face.
He died down in the everbearing roses.

Ten minutes later I dropped the mother. She
20 flipflopped in the air and fell, her needle teeth
still hooked in a leaf of early Swiss chard.
Another baby next. O one-two-three
the murderer inside me rose up hard,
the hawkeye killer came on stage forthwith.

25 There's one chuck left. Old wily fellow, he keeps
me cocked and ready day after day after day.
All night I hunt his humped-up form. I dream
I sight along the barrel in my sleep.
If only they'd all consented to die unseen
30 gassed underground the quiet Nazi way.

1972

As you read WOODCHUCKS aloud, how does your tone of voice change from beginning to end? What tone do you use to read the ending? How does the hunter feel about her increasing attraction to violence? Why does the poem begin by call-ing the gassing of the woodchucks "merciful" (line 3) and end by describing it as

---

7. Mixture of cement, pebbles, and gravel.

"the quiet Nazi way" (30)? What names does the hunter call herself? How does the name-calling affect your feelings about her? Exactly when does the hunter begin to *enjoy* the feel of the gun and the idea of killing? How does the poet make that clear? What, ultimately, might the poem as a whole say or show us about ourselves—especially, perhaps, our relation to animals? to violence?

ADRIENNE RICH
Aunt Jennifer's Tigers

Aunt Jennifer's tigers prance across a screen,
Bright topaz denizens of a world of green.
They do not fear the men beneath the tree;
They pace in sleek chivalric certainty.

5 Aunt Jennifer's fingers fluttering through her wool
Find even the ivory needle hard to pull.
The massive weight of Uncle's wedding band
Sits heavily upon Aunt Jennifer's hand.

When Aunt is dead, her terrified hands will lie
10 Still ringed with ordeals she was mastered by.
The tigers in the panel that she made
Will go on prancing, proud and unafraid.

1951

In this poem, why are tigers a particularly appropriate animal? What words describing the tigers seem especially significant? Why are Aunt Jennifer's hands described as "terrified" (line 9)? What clues does the poem give about why Aunt Jennifer is so afraid? How does the poem make you feel about Aunt Jennifer's life and death? How would you describe the tone of the poem? Why does the poem begin and end with the tigers? Might the poem's theme be a universal one (about all or most people)? Or is the theme more specific (about, say, women versus men or about married people)?

AUTHORS ON THEIR WORK

ADRIENNE RICH (1929–2012)

From "When We Dead Awaken: Writing as Re-Vision" (1971)*

In writing this poem, composed and apparently cool as it is, I thought I was creating a portrait of an imaginary woman. But this woman suffers from the opposition of her imagination, worked out in tapestry, and her lifestyle, "ringed with ordeals she was mastered by." It was important to me that Aunt Jennifer was a person as distinct from myself as possible—distanced by the formalism of the poem, by its objective, observant tone—even by putting the woman in a different generation.

*"When We Dead Awaken: Writing as Re-Vision." Forum of the Commission on the Status of Women in the Profession. MLA Annual Convention, Dec. 1971, Chicago.

THEME AND CONFLICT

Since a theme is an idea implied by all of the elements of the poem working together, identifying theme—as opposed to topic and tone—can sometimes be a tough and tricky business. In reading and writing about poetry, then, it often helps to focus first—and most—on conflict. Though we usually think of conflict as an aspect of **plot,** even perfectly plotless poems are almost always organized around and devoted to exploring conflicts and tensions. To begin to identify these, look for contrasts and think about the conflict they imply.

Take, for example, Aunt Jennifer's Tigers. Though it might be hard to say at first just what the theme of Rich's poem might be, it's hard to miss the contrast at its center. Where the tigers Aunt Jennifer embroiders "prance" and "pace" freely, "proud and unafraid," through a world as colorful and as lasting as they are (lines 1, 4, 12), Aunt Jennifer and her world seem just the opposite: Nothing but her fingers and hands move in the poem, and even they are "terrified" and tentative, "fluttering through her wool," "weight[ed]" down by a heavy "wedding band" in life and stilled permanently by death (9, 5, 7). We have, then, not just a contrast but a multifaceted conflict—between imaginary and real worlds, between individual vision and social obligation. What the poem concludes about this conflict is its theme, but starting with questions about conflict often provides not only an easier way into the poem but also a much richer, more textured experience and understanding of it. And very good essays can be written about a poem or poems' conflicts.

The following poem is all about this issue—the role of conflict in poetry. As you read the poem, try to identify the contrasts it sets up, the underlying conflict those contrasts point to, and the theme that ultimately emerges. Then test your own interpretation of the poem against the author's comments about how the poem came to be and what, for her, it's all about.

ADRIENNE SU
On Writing

A love poem risks becoming a ruin,
public, irretrievable, a form of tattooing,

while loss, being permanent,
can sustain a thousand documents.

5   Loss predominates in history,
smorgasbord of death, betrayal, heresy,

crime, contagion, deployment, divorce.
A writer could remain aboard

the ship of grief and thrive, never
10 approaching the shores of rapture.

What can be said about elation
that the elated, seeking consolation

from their joy, will go to books for?
It's wiser and quicker to look for

15 a poem in the dentist's chair
than in the luxury suite where

eternal love, declared, turns out
to be eternal. Who cares about

a stranger's bliss? Thus the juncture
20 where I'm stalled, unaccustomed

to integrity, despite your presence,
our tranquility, and every confidence.

2012

AUTHORS ON THEIR WORK

ADRIENNE SU (b. 1967)

From *The Best American Poetry 2013* (2013)*

When I started assembling my newest manuscript, *The House Unburned*, I found it to be suffering from structural gaps and an excess of grief and regret. [. . .]

To round it out, I needed to come up with some poems of happiness, or at least the absence of unhappiness. This presented a problem, since, as I'm always telling students, successful poems are born of uncertainty, interior conflict, the modes of struggle that lack clear solutions. I went back and forth between two selves: the editor, whose vision for the collection required some happier poems, and the poet, who raged against the affront of an assignment so lacking in ambiguity. How, argued the poet, can happiness, gratification, or success be complex enough to give life to a poem?

Eventually, the answer came with a shift in setting. If the poem could be about writing, conflict would be inherent in the question. So I gave myself permission to write about writing. Now that I had a conflict, the road to the poem appeared.

The Best American Poetry 2013. Edited by Denise Duhamel, Scribner Poetry, 2013, p. 198. The Best American Poetry series, edited by David Lehman.

POEMS FOR FURTHER STUDY

ANNA LAETITIA BARBAULD
The Mouse's Petition[8]

Found in the trap where he had been confined all night by Dr. Priestley, for the
sake of making experiments with different kinds of air

"Parcere subjectis, et debellare superbos."
—Virgil

Oh hear a pensive prisoner's prayer,
For liberty that sighs;
And never let thine heart be shut
Against the wretch's cries.

5 For here forlorn and sad I sit,
Within the wiry gate;
And tremble at th' approaching morn,
Which brings impending fate.

If e'er thy breast with freedom glow'd,
10 And spurn'd a tyrant's chain,
Let not thy strong oppressive force
A free-born mouse detain.

Oh do not stain with guiltless blood
Thy hospitable hearth;
15 Nor triumph that thy wiles betray'd
A prize so little worth.

The scatter'd gleanings of a feast
My frugal meals supply;
But if thine unrelenting heart
20 That slender boon deny,

The cheerful light, the vital air,
Are blessings widely given;
Let nature's commoners enjoy
The common gifts of heaven.

25 The well-taught philosophic mind
To all compassion gives;
Casts round the world an equal eye,
And feels for all that lives.

---

8. Addressed to the clergyman, political theorist, and scientist Joseph Priestley (1733–1804), a radical
who embraced the French Revolution and the rights of man. The imagined speaker (the petitioning
mouse) is destined to participate in just the sort of experiment that led Priestley, a few years later, to
the discovery of "phlogiston"—what we now call oxygen. Tradition has it that when Barbauld showed
him the lines, Priestley set the mouse free. The Latin epigraph is from the *Aeneid* 6.853, "To spare
the humbled, and to tame in war the proud."

If mind, as ancient sages taught,[9]
30 A never dying flame,
Still shifts through matter's varying forms,
In every form the same,

Beware, lest in the worm you crush
A brother's soul you find;
35 And tremble lest thy luckless hand
Dislodge a kindred mind.

Or, if this transient gleam of day
Be *all* of life we share,
Let pity plead within thy breast
40 That little *all* to spare.

So may thy hospitable board
With health and peace be crown'd;
And every charm of heartfelt ease
Beneath thy roof be found.

45 So, when destruction lurks unseen,
Which men, like mice, may share,
May some kind angel clear thy path,
And break the hidden snare.

1773

• What implicit and explicit arguments does the mouse make to bolster his "petition" to be released? How might these add up to a theme? In all these terms, what is the effect of Barbauld's choice to make the mouse the poem's speaker?

ROBERT BURNS

To a Mouse

*On Turning Her up in Her Nest with the Plough,
November, 1785*

Wee, sleeket,° cowran, tim'rous beastie,   *sleek*
O, what a panic's in thy breastie!
Thou need na start awa sae hasty,
            Wi' bickering brattle!°   *With headlong scamper*
5   I wad be laith° to rin an' chase thee   *loath*
            Wi' murd'ring pattle!°   *plowstaff*

I'm truly sorry Man's dominion
Has broken Nature's social union,
An' justifies that ill opinion,
10   Which makes thee startle,
At me, thy poor, earth-born companion,
            An' fellow mortal!

9. Lines 29–36 play on the idea of transmigration of souls, a doctrine Priestley had earlier embraced.

I doubt na, whyles,° but thou may thieve;   *sometimes*
What then? poor beastie, thou maun° live!   *must*
15 A daimen-icker in a thrave[1]
   'S a sma' request:
I'll get a blessin wi' the lave,°   *remainder*
   An' never miss't!

Thy wee-bit housie, too, in ruin!
20 It's silly wa's° the win's are strewin!   *frail walls*
An' naething, now, to big° a new ane,   *build*
   O' foggage° green!   *Of coarse grass*
An' bleak December's winds ensuin,
   Baith snell° an' keen!   *Both bitter*

25 Thou saw the fields laid bare an' waste,
An' weary Winter comin fast,
An' cozie here, beneath the blast,
   Thou thought to dwell,
Till crash! the cruel coulter° past   *cutter blade*
30   Out thro' thy cell.

That wee-bit heap o' leaves an' stibble°   *stubble*
Has cost thee monie a weary nibble!
Now thou's turn'd out, for a' thy trouble,
   But° house or hald,[2]   *Without*
35 To thole° the Winter's sleety dribble,   *endure*
   An' cranreuch could!°   *hoarfrost cold*

But Mousie, thou art no thy-lane,°   *not alone*
In proving foresight may be vain:
The best laid schemes o' Mice an' Men
40   Gang aft agley,°   *Go oft awry*
An' lea'e us nought but grief an' pain,
   For promis'd joy!

Still, thou art blest, compar'd wi' me!
The present only toucheth thee:
45 But Och! I backward cast my e'e,
   On prospects drear!
An' forward tho' I canna see,
   I guess an' fear!

             1786

• Why and how does the speaker of this poem, a poor Scottish plowman, identify with the mouse, or what cues might there be that he is projecting his own
experiences and fears onto the mouse, as well as responding to the mouse's
situation? How does that affect the poem's tone? shape its theme(s)?

1. An occasional ear in twenty-four sheaves.
2. Hold, holding (i.e., land).

FRANK O'HARA
Poem

Lana Turner[3] has collapsed!
I was trotting along and suddenly
it started raining and snowing
and you said it was hailing
5   but hailing hits you on the head
hard so it was really snowing and
raining and I was in such a hurry
to meet you but the traffic
was acting exactly like the sky
10   and suddenly I see a headline
LANA TURNER HAS COLLAPSED!
there is no snow in Hollywood
there is no rain in California
I have been to lots of parties
15   and acted perfectly disgraceful
but I never actually collapsed
oh Lana Turner we love you get up

1962

Lana Turner testifying at the John Stompanato inquest, April 1958

3. American actress (1921–95); in 1958, Turner's lover, John Stompanato, Jr., was stabbed to death by her daughter, who was determined to have acted in self-defense.

- What or whom exactly does this poem seem to make fun of? Does the poem also convey more serious sentiments?
- What current celebrity seems to you the best potential substitute for Lana Turner? What about both this celebrity's public persona and the poem itself make your choice seem especially appropriate?

MAYA ANGELOU
Still I Rise

You may write me down in history
With your bitter, twisted lies,
You may trod me in the very dirt
But still, like dust, I'll rise.

5 Does my sassiness upset you?
Why are you beset with gloom?
'Cause I walk like I've got oil wells
Pumping in my living room.

Just like moons and like suns,
10 With the certainty of tides,
Just like hopes springing high,
Still I'll rise.

Did you want to see me broken?
Bowed head and lowered eyes?
15 Shoulders falling down like teardrops,
Weakened by my soulful cries.

Does my haughtiness offend you?
Don't you take it awful hard
'Cause I laugh like I've got gold mines
20 Diggin' in my own back yard.

You may shoot me with your words,
You may cut me with your eyes,
You may kill me with your hatefulness,
But still, like air, I'll rise.

25 Does my sexiness upset you?
Does it come as a surprise
That I dance like I've got diamonds
At the meeting of my thighs?

Out of the huts of history's shame
30 I rise
Up from a past that's rooted in pain
I rise
I'm a black ocean, leaping and wide,
Welling and swelling I bear in the tide.

35 Leaving behind nights of terror and fear
I rise

Into a daybreak that's wondrously clear
I rise
Bringing the gifts that my ancestors gave,
40 I am the dream and the hope of the slave.
I rise
I rise
I rise.

1978

- Who seems to be the "you" addressed in the poem? How would you describe the poem's tone, and which features of the poem seem most key to determining the tone? What's the effect, for example, of the use of questions? Does the tone remain consistent or change over the course of the poem?

SUGGESTIONS FOR WRITING

1. Choose any two poems in this chapter that express positive and negative feelings about their topics. How do the tones of the poems combine or contrast the feelings? Is there a shift in tone in each poem? If so, where? How is the shift revealed through language? Write an essay in which you compare the way each poet accomplishes this shifting of tone.
2. Write an essay in which you consider the use of language to create tone in any two or more poems on the same subject. How do the tones suit the themes of these poems?
3. Write an essay on Maxine Kumin's WOODCHUCKS in which you show that the speaker's conflict between sympathy and murderous instinct is reflected in the mixed tone and varied vocabulary. Focus on formal and informal **diction**, noting phrases from law or religion—"the case we had against them"; "fallen from grace" (4, 15)—or from everyday speech—"up to scratch," "food from our mouths" (9, 13). How does the diction, or word choice, of the poem affect its tone?
4. The first humane societies for the protection of animals were founded, in England, in the late eighteenth century, around the same time that THE MOUSE'S PETITION and TO A MOUSE were written, and these societies are sometimes seen as the beginning of the modern animal-rights movement. Write an essay exploring whether and how one might see either or both of these poems and/or Maxine Kumin's WOODCHUCKS as animal-rights poems or as poems that defend the rights of animals or the value of animal life. According to these poems, what sort of rights do or should animals have, and why so, or what makes animal life potentially as valuable as human life? Alternatively, write an essay demonstrating that these poems, which might seem to be about the treatment of animals or the relative value of animal and/versus human life, are actually just as much or more about the treatment of certain sorts of human beings and the relative value of different human lives. Regardless of which topic you choose, be sure to articulate what you see as each poem's theme.
5. Write your own version (in verse or prose) of any poem in this chapter, working to present the situation it depicts from a different angle and in a different tone. For example, what might the mouse addressed in TO A MOUSE have to say about his situation and the plowman's words to him? How might his view and tone differ from that of Burns's speaker? What theme might emerge if the situation were viewed this way? Or, to take another example, what if the speaker in FREEWAY 280 were more disgusted than attracted by the current state of her old neighborhood, seeing its condition as proof that she was right to take to the "rigid lanes" of the highway and leave her old life and self behind (line 16)? Again, what conflict might drive your poem, and what theme might it ultimately suggest?

SAMPLE WRITING: RESPONSE PAPER

The response paper below reads like a draft of what could be a quite effective essay on the theme of Anna Laetitia Barauld's THE MOUSE'S PETITION. If its writer, Zoeie Neal, were your classmate, what would you suggest to her are the draft's major strengths? What three things would you suggest she most needs to do in order to turn this response into a compelling essay? How might she better introduce, support, and develop her argument about the poem and its theme?

Neal 1

Zoeie Neal
Dr. Kelly Mays
ENG 298
23 September 2021

Response to "The Mouse's Petition"

The smallest mouse is hardly of any significance to the scheme of man and nature. It is small, and we are men. What do men owe a mouse, of all creatures? Anna Barbauld creates a strong case for the mouse, using its own voice. Interestingly, her case could be applied to any people or animals subject to oppression.

The poem's first stanza speaks of "liberty." The notion that was catching steam in Barbauld's day was that all men were born with it. When the mouse states, "Oh hear a pensive prisoner's prayer / For liberty that sighs" (lines 1-2), the mouse begs for his liberty. He is trapped in a cage and wishes to be free, as men do. If men are born free, then so is he. Later the mouse builds on this when he says, "Let nature's commoners enjoy / The common gifts of heaven" (23-24). He implies things like "light" and "air" (21), like liberty, are bestowed on all living creatures, even "commoners," not just the rich and mighty. The person that denies any creature heaven's "common gifts" goes against "heaven."

The poem expands on religion about halfway through. Even with the widespread acceptance of heaven and hell and of God, some people believe in reincarnation. These beliefs are not mutually exclusive either. First, the mouse appeals to belief in reincarnation when he says, "Beware, lest in the worm you crush / A brother's soul you find" (33-34). The mouse says that a worm, a creature even more lowly than him, might have the reincarnated soul of someone

Neal 2

you loved that died. He implores the scientist that has him caged to think of whose soul he might crush if he crushes the mouse. Then he turns around and also appeals to people who don't believe in reincarnation, when he says,

> Or, if this transient gleam of day
> Be *all* of life we share,
> Let pity plead within thy breast
> That little *all* to spare. (37-40)

In this stanza, the reasoning is that if we in fact do not reincarnate, then we must spare what life we can because one life is so short.

Perhaps the biggest argument for releasing the mouse is the empathy that man possesses. Humans can empathize with members of their own species and with other animals, to feel as they do. "The well-taught philosophic mind," the mouse says, "Casts round the world an equal eye, / And feels for all that lives" (25-28). Notice that it's a "philosophic mind" that does this, not a scientific mind. For one studied in philosophy has at least thought about how one should live; the only logical conclusion is to circle back to the idea that we are all equal and empathize with our equals. All lives are equal in value, and we should not see it any other way; to do so would be inhuman. Barbauld really drives home this point in her last stanza: "May some kind angel clear thy path, / And break the hidden snare" (47-48). Like the mouse, we may be trapped. We would wish some kind stranger to help and deliver us from evil. This empathy that we feel is natural, and we should wield it as if we were protecting ourselves.

This poem, on the surface, is a defense of this poor unlucky mouse. However, it delves deeper than this; its theme is that we should feel empathy not only for the mouse but also for our fellow humans.

Neal 3

Work Cited

Barbauld, Anna Laetitia. "The Mouse's Petition." *The Norton Introduction to Literature*, edited by Kelly J. Mays, shorter 14th ed., W. W. Norton, 2021, pp. 862-63.

Family

AN ALBUM

Families are the groundwork of society, and most people's earliest memories involve family members. Families may be nuclear or extended, biological or adoptive, emotionally demonstrative or distant. Families may pass down traditions that younger generations may choose to abandon, embrace, or simply tolerate. Adults who have left home may dwell on memories, good or bad, of their mothers, fathers, brothers, or sisters. Each renewed contact with family can spark conflicting thoughts and feelings. Hope, disappointment, or grief for one's child can find expression as a concentrated moment in a poem. A spouse or a child can remind the speaker of the passage of time and mortality.

Because the family is such a basic unit of social interaction, many poems explore family relations. The following poems are all, in different ways, about family. What do these poems have in common? How do they differ? Which best capture your feelings and ideas about family relationships? Can you find two poems that express the same **theme**—in other words, can you accurately state their themes in the same way? How do any two poems compare in **tone**? Which poems have surprising shifts in tone? Do any poems express surprising or disturbing attitudes toward loved ones?

SIMON J. ORTIZ
My Father's Song

Wanting to say things,
I miss my father tonight.
His voice, the slight catch,
the depth from his thin chest,
5 the tremble of emotion
in something he has just said
to his son, his song:

We planted corn one Spring at Acu[1]—
we planted several times
10 but this one particular time
I remember the soft damp sand
in my hand.

My father had stopped at one point
to show me an overturned furrow;
15 the plowshare had unearthed
the burrow nest of a mouse
in the soft moist sand.

---

1. Alternative name for Acoma village and/or pueblo, about sixty miles west of Albuquerque, New Mexico. Sometimes translated as "the place that always was," Acu is the oldest continuously inhabited community in the United States.

Very gently, he scooped tiny pink animals
into the palm of his hand
20 and told me to touch them.
We took them to the edge
of the field and put them in the shade
of a sand moist clod.

I remember the very softness
25 of cool and warm sand and tiny alive mice
and my father saying things.

1976

• What are the "things" that the speaker wants to say (line 1)? Are they the
same "things" he remembers his father saying (26)? Does the poem itself say
these things?

ROBERT HAYDEN
Those Winter Sundays

Sundays too my father got up early
and put his clothes on in the blueblack cold,
then with cracked hands that ached
from labor in the weekday weather made
5 banked fires blaze. No one ever thanked him.

I'd wake and hear the cold splintering, breaking.
When the rooms were warm, he'd call,
and slowly I would rise and dress,
fearing the chronic angers of that house,

10 Speaking indifferently to him,
who had driven out the cold
and polished my good shoes as well.
What did I know, what did I know
of love's austere and lonely offices?

1966

• Why might the poem begin with the words "Sundays too" (rather than, say,
"On Sundays")? What are the "austere and lonely offices" to which the poem's
final line refers?

ELLEN BRYANT VOIGT
My Mother

my mother my mother my mother she
could do anything so she did everything the world
was an unplowed field a dress to be hemmed a scraped knee it needed
a casserole it needed another alto in the choir her motto was apply
    yourself

5　the secret of life was spreading your gifts why hide your light
　　under a bushel[2] you might

　　forget it there in the dark times the lonely times
　　the sun gone down on her resolve she slept a little first
　　so she'd be fresh she put on a little lipstick drawing on her smile
10　she pulled that hair up off her face she pulled her stockings on she
　　　　stepped
　　into her pumps she took up her matching purse already
　　packed with everything they all would learn
　　they would be nice they would

　　apologize they would be grateful whenever
15　they had forgotten what to pack she never did
　　she had a spare she kissed your cheek she wiped the mark
　　away with her own spit she marched you out again unless you were
　　that awful sort of stubborn broody[3] child who more and more
　　I was who once had been so sweet so mild staying put
20　where she put me what happened

　　must have been the bushel I was hiding in
　　the sun gone down on her resolve she slept a little first
　　so she'd be fresh she pulled her stockings on she'd packed
　　the words for my every lack she had a little lipstick on her teeth the
　　　　mark
25　on my cheek would not rub off she gave the fluids from her mouth
　　to it she gave the tissues in her ample purse to it I never did
　　apologize I let my sister succor those in need and suffer
　　the little children[4] my mother

　　knew we are self-canceling she gave herself
30　a lifetime C an average grade from then on out she kept
　　the lights on day and night a garden needs the light the sun
　　could not be counted on she slept a little day and night she didn't need
　　her stockings or her purse she watered she weeded she fertilized she
　　　　stood
　　in front the tallest stalk keeping the deer the birds all
35　the world's idle shameless thieves away

2011

- How might this poem's form, especially its lack of punctuation and capitalization, contribute to tone? to its characterization of the speaker's
  mother?

2. See the Sermon on the Mount (Matt. 5.15–16): "Neither do men light a candle, and put it under a
bushel, but on a candlestick; and it giveth light unto all that are in the house. / Let your light so shine
before men, that they may see your good works, and glorify your Father which is in heaven."
3. Thoughtful and unhappy, given to brooding or worrying.
4. See Matthew 19.14: "But Jesus said, Suffer little children, and forbid them not, to come unto me:
for of such is the kingdom of heaven."

MARTÍN ESPADA
Of the Threads That Connect the Stars

Did you ever see stars? asked my father with a cackle. He was not
speaking of the heavens, but the white flash in his head when a fist burst
between his eyes. In Brooklyn, this would cause men and boys to slap
the table with glee; this might be the only heavenly light we'd ever see.

5   I never saw stars. The sky in Brooklyn was a tide of smoke rolling over us
from the factory across the avenue, the mattresses burning in the junkyard,
the ruins where squatters would sleep, the riots of 1966[5] that kept me
locked in my room like a suspect. My father talked truce on the streets.

My son can see the stars through the tall barrel of a telescope.
10 He names the galaxies with the numbers and letters of astronomy.
I cannot see what he sees in the telescope, no matter how many eyes
   I shut.
I understand a smoking mattress better than the language of galaxies.

My father saw stars. My son sees stars. The earth rolls beneath
our feet. We lurch ahead, and one day we have walked this far.

2013

• How does the poem differentiate and connect three generations of one family
by describing the stars that each did or didn't, do or don't, see?

EMILY GROSHOLZ
Eden

In lurid cartoon colors, the big baby
Dinosaur steps backwards under the shadow
Of an approaching tyrannosaurus rex.
"His mommy going to fix it," you remark,
5 Serenely anxious, hoping for the best.

After the big explosion, after the lights
Go down inside the house and up the street,
We rush outdoors to find a squirrel stopped
In straws of half-gnawed cable. I explain,
10 Trying to fit the facts, "The squirrel is dead."

No, you explain it otherwise to me.
"He's sleeping. And his mommy going to come."
Later, when the squirrel has been removed,
"His mommy fix him," you insist, insisting
15 On the right to know what you believe.

---

5. In July 1966, violent conflict repeatedly erupted between Black and Puerto Rican residents of
Brooklyn's troubled Bedford-Stuyvesant neighborhood.

The world is truly full of fabulous
Great and curious small inhabitants,
And you're the freshly minted, unashamed
Adam in this garden. You preside,
20 Appreciate, and judge our proper names.

Like God, I brought you here.
Like God, I seem to be omnipotent,
Mostly helpful, sometimes angry as hell.
I fix whatever minor faults arise
25 With bandaids, batteries, masking tape, and pills.

But I am powerless, as you must know,
To chase the serpent sliding in the grass,
Or the tall angel with the flaming sword
Who scares you when he rises suddenly
30 Behind the gates of sunset.

1992

• How does Grosholz use language to elevate the poem's subject matter from
  the trivial and childish to the biblical and profound?

PHILIP LARKIN
This Be the Verse

They fuck you up, your mum and dad.
    They may not mean to, but they do.
They fill you with the faults they had
    And add some extra, just for you.

5 But they were fucked up in their turn
    By fools in old-style hats and coats,
Who half the time were soppy-stern
    And half at one another's throats.

Man hands on misery to man.
10   It deepens like a coastal shelf.[6]
Get out as early as you can,
    And don't have any kids yourself.

1971

• This poem opens with one of the most (in)famous lines in all of English-
  language poetry. What tone does that line establish, and how so? How does
  the rest of the poem either maintain or complicate that tone? How might
  the poem's sound qualities—especially its **rhyme** and/or **meter**—contribute
  to tone? Is the poem's first line an adequate statement of its theme?

6. Part of a continent that lies under the ocean and typically ends in a steep slope down to the ocean
floor.

AUTHORS ON THEIR WORK

PHILIP LARKIN (1922–85)

From "An Interview with John Haffenden" (1981)*

Was it your intention, in using bad language in one or two poems, to provide a shock tactic?

Yes. I mean, these words are part of the palette. You use them when you want to shock. I don't think I've ever shocked for the sake of shocking. "They fuck you up" is funny because it's ambiguous. Parents bring about your conception and also bugger you up once you are born. Professional parents in particular don't like that poem.

*"An Interview with John Haffenden." *Further Requirements: Interviews, Broadcasts, Statements and Book Reviews,* edited by Anthony Thwaite, Faber and Faber, 2001, pp. 47–62. Originally published in *Viewpoints: Poets in Conversation with John Haffenden,* 1981.

JIMMY SANTIAGO BACA
Green Chile

I prefer red chile over my eggs
and potatoes for breakfast.
Red chile *ristras*[7] decorate my door,
dry on my roof, and hang from eaves.
5　They lend open-air vegetable stands
historical grandeur, and gently swing
with an air of festive welcome.
I can hear them talking in the wind,
haggard, yellowing, crisp, rasping
10　tongues of old men, licking the breeze.

　　But grandmother loves green chile.
When I visit her,
she holds the green chile pepper
in her wrinkled hands.
15　Ah, voluptuous, masculine,
an air of authority and youth simmers
from its swan-neck stem, tapering to a flowery
collar, fermenting resinous spice.
A well-dressed gentleman at the door
20　my grandmother takes sensuously in her hand,
rubbing its firm glossed sides,
caressing the oily rubbery serpent,

---

7. Braided strings of dried peppers.

with mouth-watering fulfillment,
fondling its curves with gentle fingers.
25 Its bearing magnificent and taut
as flanks of a tiger in mid-leap,
she thrusts her blade into
as cuts it open, with lust
on her hot mouth, sweating over the stove,
30 bandanna round her forehead,
mysterious passion on her face
and she serves me green chile con carne
between soft warm leaves of corn tortillas,
with beans and rice—her sacrifice
35 to her little prince.
I slurp from my plate
with last bit of tortilla, my mouth burns
and I hiss and drink a tall glass of cold water.

All over New Mexico, sunburned men and women
40 drive rickety trucks stuffed with gunny-sacks
of green chile, from Belen, Veguita, Willard, Estancia,
San Antonio y[8] Socorro, from fields
to roadside stands, you see them roasting green chile
in screen-sided homemade barrels, and for a dollar a bag,
45 we relive this old, beautiful ritual again and again.

1989

- What different qualities do the red and green chiles have? Which words in
the poem help personify the chiles? How fully do these words reflect the differences between the speaker and the grandmother?

PAUL MARTÍNEZ POMPA
The Abuelita[9] Poem

I. Skin & Corn

Her brown skin glistens as the sun
pours through the kitchen window
like gold *leche*.[1] After grinding
the <u>*nixtamal*</u>,[2] a word so beautifully ethnic
5 it must not only be italicized but underlined
to let you, the reader, know you've encountered
something beautifully ethnic, she kneads
with the hands of centuries-old ancestor
spirits who magically yet realistically possess her
10 until the *masa* is smooth as a *lowrider's*

8. And (Spanish).
9. Grandmother (Spanish).
1. Milk (Spanish).
2. Treated corn to make *masa* (line 10), the dough used in tortillas.

chrome bumper. And I know she must do this
with care because it says so on a website
that explains how to make homemade corn *tortillas*.
So much labor for this peasant bread
15 this edible art birthed from *Abuelita's*
brown skin, which is still glistening
in the sun.

II. Apology

Before she died I called my abuelita
grandma. I cannot remember
20 if she made corn tortillas from scratch
but, O, how she'd flip the factory fresh
El Milagros[3] (Quality Since 1950)
on the burner, bathe them in butter
& salt for her grandchildren.
25 How she'd knead the buttons
on the telephone, order me food
from Pizza Hut. I assure you,
gentle reader, this was done
with the spirit of Mesoamérica[4]
30 ablaze in her fingertips.

2009

• How does this poem play on the expectations potentially created by its title?
  What does the poem ultimately seem to suggest about those expectations?

ANDREW HUDGINS
Begotten

I've never, as some children do,
looked at my folks and thought, I *must*
have come from someone else—
rich parents who'd misplaced me, but
5 who would, as in a myth or novel,
return and claim me. Hell, no. I saw
my face in cousins' faces, heard
my voice in their high drawls. And Sundays,
after the dinner plates were cleared,
10 I lingered, elbow propped on red
oilcloth, and studied great-uncles, aunts,
and cousins new to me. They squirmed.
I stared till I discerned the features
they'd gotten from the family larder:
15 eyes, nose, lips, hair? I stared until,

---

3. An actual brand, but meaning "miracles" (Spanish).
4. Literally, "Middle America" (Spanish), a region extending roughly from central Mexico to Nicaragua.

uncomfortable, they'd snap, "Hey, boy—
what are you looking at? At me?"
"No, sir," I'd lie. "No, ma'am." I'd count ten
and then continue staring at them.
20 I never had to ask, What am I?
I stared at my blood-kin, and thought,
So *this*, dear God, is what I am.

1994

- What can you infer from the language in this poem about the speaker's attitude toward his life and his family? What does the poem's title evoke?

SUGGESTIONS FOR WRITING

1. Compare the portrayal of the parent-child relationship in any two poems in this
   album, focusing especially on the poems' tones and themes.
2. What words in Robert Hayden's THOSE WINTER SUNDAYS suggest the son's feelings
   toward his father and his home? What words indicate that his attitudes have changed
   since the time depicted in the poem? Write an essay in which you compare the
   speaker's feelings, as a youth and then later as a man, about his father and his home.
3. Write an essay comparing the way grandmothers and their relationship to food and
   family are portrayed in Jimmy Santiago Baca's GREEN CHILE and Paul Martínez
   Pompa's THE ABUELITA POEM. How might Martínez Pompa's poem respond to and
   comment on Baca's?
4. Pick the poem in this album that you like most and the one you like least. Write an
   informal response paper or essay comparing your reactions to the two poems and
   exploring why and how the poems provoke those disparate reactions. What role do
   the poem's tones and themes play here? What role is played by your own experiences
   of, and feelings and ideas about, family?

15 | LANGUAGE: WORD CHOICE AND ORDER

Fiction and drama depend on language just as poetry does, but in a poem almost everything comes down to the particular meanings and implications, as well as sound, shape, and location of individual words. When we read stories and plays, we generally focus our attention on character and plot, and although words determine how we imagine those characters and how we respond to what happens to them, we are not as likely to pause over any one word as we may need to when reading a poem, even one with characters and a plot. Because poems are often short and because even long poems are usually broken up into relatively short lines, much depends on every word in them. Sometimes, as though they were distilled prose, poems contain only the essential words. They say just barely enough to communicate in the most basic way, using elemental signs—each of which is chosen for exactly the right shade of meaning or feeling or both. But elemental does not necessarily mean simple, and these signs may be very rich in their meanings and complex in their effects. The poet's word choice—the **diction** of a poem—determines not only meaning but also just about every effect the poem produces.

PRECISION AND AMBIGUITY

Let's look first at poems that create some of their effects by examining—or playing with—a single word. Here, multiple meanings or the shiftiness, ambiguity, and uncertainty of a word are at issue. The following short poem, for example, depends almost entirely on the ways we use the word "play."

SARAH CLEGHORN
The golf links lie so near the mill

The golf links lie so near the mill
That almost every day
The laboring children can look out
And see the men at play.

1915

While traveling in the American South, Cleghorn had seen, right next to a golf course, a textile mill that employed quite young children. Her poem doesn't *say* that we expect men to work and children to play; it just assumes our expectation and builds an effect of **situational irony**—an incongruity between what we expect and what actually occurs—out of the observation. The poem saves almost all of its devastating effect for the final word, after the situation has been carefully described and the irony set up.

In the following poem, a word used repeatedly acquires multiple meanings and refuses to be limited to a single one. Here, the importance of a word involves its ambiguity (that is, its having more than one possible meaning) rather than its precision or exactness. How many different meanings of the words *leave(s)* and *leaving* can you distinguish in the poem? How might the poem capitalize on the ambiguity of other words?

LI-YOUNG LEE
Leaving

Each day, less leaves
in the tree outside my window.
More leave, and every day
more sky. More of the far,
5   and every night more stars.

Day after shortening day, more
day in my panes, more missing
in the branches, fewer places
for the birds to hide, their abandoned nests exposed.
10 And night after increasing night,
the disappearances multiply.

The leaves leap from fire
to colder fire,
from belonging to darker belonging,
15 from membership to ownership.

Their growing absence
leaves no lack, nothing wanting,
and their gone outnumbers their going
through the door they leave ajar.

2018

DENOTATION AND CONNOTATION

Although the unambiguous or "dictionary" meaning of words—that is, their **denotation**—is important, words are more than hard blocks of meaning on whose sense everyone agrees. They also carry emotional force and shades of suggestion. The words we use indicate not only what we mean but also how we feel about it and want to encourage others to feel. A person who holds office is, quite literally (and unemotionally), an *officeholder*—the word denotes what he or she does in a relatively neutral way. But if we want to imply that a particular officeholder is wise, trustworthy, and deserving of political support, we may call that person a *public servant*, a *political leader*, or an *elected official*, whereas if we want to promote distrust or contempt of the same officeholder we might say *politician* or *bureaucrat* or *political hack*. These terms have clear **connotations**—suggestions of emotional coloration that imply our attitude and invite a similar one from our hearers. In poems, as in life, what words connote can be just as important as what they denote.

The following **epitaph**, for example, which describes one person's mixed feelings about another, depends heavily on the connotations of fairly common words.

WALTER DE LA MARE
Slim Cunning Hands

Slim cunning hands at rest, and cozening eyes—
Under this stone one loved too wildly lies;
How false she was, no granite could declare;
    Nor all earth's flowers, how fair.

1950

What the speaker in SLIM CUNNING HANDS remembers about the dead woman—her hands, her eyes—tells part of the story; her physical presence was clearly important to him. The poem's other nouns—*stone, granite, flowers*—all remind us of her death and its finality. All these words denote objects central to the rituals that memorialize a departed life. Granite and stone connote finality as well, while flowers connote fragility and suggest the brevity of life (which is why they have become the symbolic language of funerals). The way the speaker talks about the woman expresses, in just a few words, the complexity of his love for her. She was loved, he says, too "wildly"—by him perhaps, and apparently by others. The excitement she offered is suggested by the word, as is the lack of control. The words *cunning* and *cozening* imply her falsity; they suggest her calculation, cleverness, and untrustworthiness, as well as her skill, persuasiveness, and ability to please. Moreover, coming at the end of the second line, the word *lies* has more than one meaning. The body "lies" under the stone, but falsity has by now become too prominent to ignore as a second meaning. And the word *fair*, a simple yet very inclusive word, suggests how totally attractive the speaker finds her: Her beauty can no more be expressed by flowers than her fickleness can be expressed by something as permanent as words in stone. But the word *fair*, in the emphatic position as the final word, also implies two other meanings that seem to resonate, ironically, with what we have already learned about her from the speaker: "impartial" and "just." "Impartial" she may be in her preferences (as the word *false* suggests), but to the speaker she is hardly "just," and the final defining word speaks both to her appearance and (ironically) to her character. Simple words here tell us perhaps all we need to know of a long story—or at least the speaker's version of it.

Words like *fair* and *cozening* are clearly loaded. They imply more emotionally than they mean literally. They have strong, clear connotations; they tell us what to think, what evaluation to make; and they suggest the basis for the evaluation. Sometimes word choice in poems is less dramatic and less obviously significant. But it is always important. Often simple appropriateness makes the words in a poem work, and words that do not call special attention to themselves can nonetheless be the most effective. Precision of denotation may be just as impressive and productive of specific effects as the resonance or ambiguous suggestiveness of connotation. Often poems achieve their power by a combination of verbal effects, setting off elaborate **figures of speech** or other complicated strategies with simple words chosen to indicate exact actions, moments, or states of mind.

Words are the starting point for all poetry, of course, and almost every word is likely to be significant, either denotatively or connotatively or both. Poets who know their craft pick each word with care to express exactly what needs to be expressed and to suggest every emotional shade that the poem is calculated to evoke in us.

Word Choice: An Example and an Exercise

Before you read the following poem, notice the three words in the title. What do they lead you to expect? What questions do they raise? Jot down your thoughts on a piece of paper. Then, as you read the poem, take note of key words and try to be conscious of the emotional effects and impressions they create.

THEODORE ROETHKE
My Papa's Waltz

The whiskey on your breath
Could make a small boy dizzy;
But I hung on like death:
Such waltzing was not easy.

5 We romped until the pans
Slid from the kitchen shelf;
My mother's countenance
Could not unfrown itself.

The hand that held my wrist
10 Was battered on one knuckle;
At every step you missed
My right ear scraped a buckle.

You beat time on my head
With a palm caked hard by dirt,
15 Then waltzed me off to bed
Still clinging to your shirt.

1948

Exactly how does the situation in MY PAPA'S WALTZ and the poem itself fulfill or defy the expectations created by the title? How does the poem answer your questions? How does it characterize the waltz and the speaker's feelings about it? Which words are most suggestive in these terms? What clues are there in the word choice that an adult is remembering a childhood experience? How scared was the boy at the time? How does the grown adult now evaluate the emotions he felt when he was a boy?

WORD ORDER AND PLACEMENT

Individual words qualify and amplify one another—suggestions clarify other suggestions, and meanings grow upon meanings—and thus how words are put together and where individual words are located matters. Notice, for example, that in "Slim Cunning Hands" the final emphasis is on how *fair* in appearance the woman was; the speaker's last word describes the quality he can't forget despite her lack of a different kind of fairness and his distrust of her. Even though it doesn't justify everything else, her beauty mitigates all the disappointment and hurt. Putting the word *fair* at the end of the line and of the poem gives it special emphasis and meaning.

That one word, *fair*, does not stand all by itself, however, any more than any other word in a poem does. Every word exists within larger units of meaning— sentences, patterns of comparison and contrast, the whole poem—and where the word is and how it is used are important. The final word or words may be especially emphatic (as in "Slim Cunning Hands"), and words that are repeated take on a special intensity, as *leave* does in LEAVING. Certain words may stand out because they are unusual or used in an unusual way (like *unfrown* or *waltzing* in "My Papa's Waltz" [lines 8, 4]) or because they are given an artificial prominence—through unusual sentence structure, for example, or because the title calls special attention to them. In verse, as opposed to prose, moreover, the number and placement of words in a line and the spacing of the words and lines stays the same in every printed version. Where words come—in a line, in a stanza—and how they are spatially and visually related to other words also helps to determine their force and meaning.

The subtlety and force of word choice are sometimes strongly affected by **syntax**—the way the sentences are put together. When you find unusual syntax or spacing, you can be pretty sure that something there merits special attention. Notice the odd sentence constructions in the second and third stanzas of "My Papa's Waltz"—the way the speaker talks about the abrasion of buckle on ear in line 12, for example. He does not say that the buckle scraped his ear, as we would expect, but rather "My right ear scraped a buckle." Reversing the expected word order makes a big difference in the effect created; the speaker avoids placing blame and refuses to specify any unpleasant effect. Had he said that the buckle scraped his ear, we would have to worry about the fragile ear. The syntax channels our feeling and helps control what we think of the "waltz."

In the most curious part of the poem, the second stanza, the silent mother appears, and the syntax on both sides of the semicolon is peculiar. In lines 5–6, the connection between the romping and the pans falling is stated oddly: "We romped *until* the pans / Slid from the kitchen shelf" (emphasis added). The speaker does not say that they knocked down the pans or imply awkwardness, but he does suggest energetic activity and duration. He implies intensity, almost intention—as though the romping would not be complete until the pans fell. And the clause about the mother—odd but effective—makes her position clear. A silent bystander in this male ritual, she doesn't seem frightened or angry. She seems to be holding a frown, or to have it molded on her face, as though it were part of her own ritual and perhaps a facet of her stern character as well. The syntax implies that she *has to* maintain the frown, and the falling of the pans almost seems to be for her benefit. She disapproves, but she remains their audience.

Sometimes poems create, as well, a powerful sense of the way minds and emotions work by varying normal syntactical order in special ways. Listen for and watch, for example, what happens a few lines into the following poem. What does it suggest about what is happening inside the speaker?

SHARON OLDS
Sex without Love

> How do they do it, the ones who make love
> without love? Beautiful as dancers,
> gliding over each other like ice-skaters
> over the ice, fingers hooked
> 5 inside each other's bodies, faces
> red as steak, wine, wet as the
> children at birth whose mothers are going to
> give them away. How do they come to the
> come to the   come to the   God   come to the
> 10 still waters, and not love
> the one who came there with them, light
> rising slowly as steam off their joined
> skin? These are the true religious,
> the purists, the pros, the ones who will not
> 15 accept a false Messiah, love the
> priest instead of the God. They do not
> mistake the lover for their own pleasure,
> they are like great runners: they know they are alone
> with the road surface, the cold, the wind,
> 20 the fit of their shoes, their over-all cardio-
> vascular health—just factors, like the partner
> in the bed, and not the truth, which is the
> single body alone in the universe
> against its own best time.

1984

The poem starts calmly enough, with a simple rhetorical question implying that the speaker just cannot understand sex without love. Lines 2–4 carefully compare such sexual activity with two other artful activities, and the speaker—although plainly disapproving—seems coolly in control of the analysis and evaluation. But by the end of the fourth line, something begins to seem odd: "[H]ooked" seems too ugly and extreme a way to characterize the lovers' fingers, however much the speaker may disapprove, and by line 6 the syntax seems to break down. How does "wine" fit the syntax of the line? Is it parallel with "steak," another example of redness? Or is it somehow related to the last part of the sentence, parallel with "faces"? Neither of these possibilities quite works. At best, the punctuation is inadequate; at worst, the speaker's mind is working too fast for the language it generates, scrambling its images. We can't yet be sure what is going on, but by the ninth line the lack of control is manifest with the compulsive repeating (three times) of "come to the" and the interjected "God."

Such verbal behavior—here concretized by the way the poem orders its words and spaces them on the page—invites us to reevaluate the speaker's moralizing relative to her emotional involvement with the issues and with her representation of sexuality itself. The speaker's own values, as well as those who have sex without love, become a subject for evaluation.

AUTHORS ON THEIR WORK

SHARON OLDS (b. 1942)

From "Sharon Olds" (1996)*

I don't think that sex has been written about a lot in poetry. And I want to be able to write about any subject. There [. . .] are subjects that are probably a lot harder to write about than others. I think that love is almost the hardest thing to write about. Not a general state of being in love, but a particular love for a particular person. Just one's taste for that one. And if you look at all the love poetry in our tradition, there isn't much that helps us know why that one. I'm just interested in human stuff like hate, love, sexual love, and sex. I don't see why not. It just seems to me if writers can assemble, in language, something that bears any relation to experience—especially important experience, experience we care about, moving and powerful experience—then it is worth trying.

*"Sharon Olds." Interview by Dwight Garner. *Salon*, 1 July 1996, www.salon.com/1996/07/01 /interview_19/.

Words, the basic materials of poetry, come in many varieties and can be used in many different ways and in myriad—sometimes surprising—combinations. They are seldom simple or transparent, even when we know their meanings and recognize their syntactical combinations as ordinary and conventional. Carefully examining them, individually and collectively, is a crucial part of reading poems, and being able to ask good questions about the words that poems use and the way they use them is one of the most basic, rewarding, and useful skills a reader of poetry can develop.

POEMS FOR FURTHER STUDY

WILLIAM BLAKE
London

I wander through each chartered[1] street,
Near where the chartered Thames does flow,
And mark in every face I meet
Marks of weakness, marks of woe.

1. "Given liberty," but also, ironically, "licensed," "controlled," "preempted as private property."

5   In every cry of every man,
    In every Infant's cry of fear,
    In every voice, in every ban,[2]
    The mind-forged manacles I hear.

    How the Chimney-sweeper's cry
10 Every black'ning Church appalls;
    And the hapless Soldier's sigh
    Runs in blood down Palace walls.

    But most through midnight streets I hear
    How the youthful Harlot's curse
15 Blasts the new-born Infant's tear,
    And blights with plagues the Marriage hearse.

                                                    1794

• Does the tone of this poem seem sad, angry, or both? Why and how so?
  How might the repeated word "chartered" (lines 1, 2) suggest a theme?

ROBERT FROST
"Out, Out—"

    The buzz saw snarled and rattled in the yard
    And made dust and dropped stove-length sticks of wood,
    Sweet-scented stuff when the breeze drew across it.
    And from there those that lifted eyes could count
5   Five mountain ranges one behind the other
    Under the sunset far into Vermont.
    And the saw snarled and rattled, snarled and rattled,
    As it ran light, or had to bear a load.
    And nothing happened: day was all but done.
10 Call it a day, I wish they might have said
    To please the boy by giving him the half hour
    That a boy counts so much when saved from work.
    His sister stood beside them in her apron
    To tell them "Supper." At the word, the saw,
15 As if to prove saws knew what supper meant,
    Leaped out at the boy's hand, or seemed to leap—
    He must have given the hand. However it was,
    Neither refused the meeting. But the hand!
    The boy's first outcry was a rueful laugh,
20 As he swung toward them holding up the hand
    Half in appeal, but half as if to keep
    The life from spilling. Then the boy saw all—
    Since he was old enough to know, big boy

2. Prohibition, curse, or public condemnation, but also suggesting *banns*, official proclamation of an intended marriage.

Doing a man's work though a child at heart—
25 He saw all spoiled. "Don't let him cut my hand off—
The doctor, when he comes. Don't let him, sister!"
So. But the hand was gone already.
The doctor put him in the dark of ether.
He lay and puffed his lips out with his breath.
30 And then—the watcher at his pulse took fright.
No one believed. They listened at his heart.
Little—less—nothing!—and that ended it.
No more to build on there. And they, since they
Were not the one dead, turned to their affairs.

1916

• Which particular words and arrangements of syntax here seem to you
especially effective? Which seem, at least at first, especially odd? Why and
how so? What might Frost achieve through the odd or unexpected diction
or syntax?

GERARD MANLEY HOPKINS
Pied Beauty[3]

Glory be to God for dappled things—
    For skies of couple-color as a brinded[4] cow;
        For rose-moles all in stipple[5] upon trout that swim;
Fresh-firecoal chestnut-falls;[6] finches' wings;
5   Landscape plotted and pieced—fold, fallow, and plow;
        And all trades, their gear and tackle and trim.
All things counter, original, spare, strange;
    Whatever is fickle, freckled (who knows how?)
        With swift, slow; sweet, sour; adazzle, dim;
10 He fathers-forth whose beauty is past change;
        Praise him.

1887

• How many ways of expressing mixed color can you find in this poem? How
does Hopkins expand the meaning of "pied beauty"?

3. Particolored beauty: having patches or sections of more than one color.
4. Streaked or spotted.
5. Rose-colored dots or flecks.
6. Fallen chestnuts as red as burning coals.

WILLIAM CARLOS WILLIAMS
The Red Wheelbarrow

so much depends
upon

a red wheel
barrow

5 glazed with rain
water

beside the white
chickens.

1923

- How does setting the words "barrow," "water," and "chickens" on lines of their own help to substantiate the poem's first line?

This Is Just to Say

I have eaten
the plums
that were in
the icebox

5 and which
you were probably
saving
for breakfast

Forgive me
10 they were delicious
so sweet
and so cold

1934

- What is meant by "This" in the poem's title? What is the apparent occasion for this poem?

AUTHORS ON THEIR WORK

WILLIAM CARLOS WILLIAMS (1883–1963)

From reading and commentary at Princeton University (1952)*

I've [. . .] gotten some fame, but I should probably say notoriety, from a very brief little poem called "The Red Wheelbarrow." [. . .] I had a letter from a lady in Boston [. . .] that said, "I love it. It's perfectly wonderful. But what does it *mean*?" [audience laughs] In the first place, I say modestly it's a perfect poem [laughs] [. . .]. It means just the same as the opening lines of [John Keats's] *Endymion*, "A thing of beauty is a joy forever." And so much depends upon it. But instead of saying "A thing of beauty," I say, "a red wheel / barrow // glazed with rain / water // beside the white / chickens." Isn't that beautiful?

• • •

From Interview with John W. Gerber (1950)**

WILLIAMS: It actually took place just as it [. . .] says here [in "This Is Just to Say"]. And my wife being out, I left a note for her just that way, and she replied very beautifully. Unfortunately, I lost it. [. . .] I think what she wrote was quite as good as this, a little more complex, but quite as good. Perhaps the virtue of this is its simplicity.

INTERVIEWER: Now, what I want to ask you about that [is], What makes that a poem?

WILLIAMS: In the first place, it's metrically absolutely regular. [. . . reads poem] So, dogmatically speaking, it has to be a poem because it goes that way, don't you see?

INTERVIEWER: Well, this goes against so many preconceived ideas of the poem, though, because it's the kind of thing that almost anybody might say.

WILLIAMS: Yes, because no one believes that poetry can exist in its own light. That's one of our immediate fallacies. [. . .] Imagine reading a poem in the American dialects, how impossible! That's the first hazard, that's the first hurdle. We have to get over that. [. . .] It can't be that we poor colonials, as we have been ever since the Revolution, we poor people who are not living in the centers of Europe can have anything happen in our lives important enough to be put down in words and given a form. But everything in our lives, if it's sufficiently authentic to our lives and touches us deeply enough, with a certain amount of feeling, is capable of being organized into a form which can be a poem. [. . .] Your wife, [. . .] the woman who's there with whom you are supposed to be in love and sometimes are [. . .] had these things saved for supper, and here you come along and raid it. Why, it's practically rape of the icebox, and there you are. So I think that's material for a poem. [laughs] That's a definite poem—without even writing it. But then if you can give it conventional metrical form, why [. . .] you're just simply superb, that's all. [laughs] You've done a great deed.

*Reading and commentary at Princeton University. 19 Mar. 1952. *PennSound*, writing.upenn .edu/pennsound/x/Williams-WC.php.

**Interview with John W. Gerber, Rutherford, NJ. June 1950. *PennSound*, writing.upenn .edu/pennsound/x/Williams-WC.php.

KAY RYAN
Blandeur

If it please God,
let less happen.
Even out Earth's
rondure, flatten

5   Eiger,[7] blanden
the Grand Canyon.
Make valleys
slightly higher,
widen fissures
10 to arable land,
remand your
terrible glaciers
and silence
their calving,
15 halving or doubling
all geographical features
toward the mean.
Unlean against our hearts.
Withdraw your grandeur
20 from these parts.

2000

• How does the poem define the made-up words (or neologisms) *blandeur* and
blanden (line 5)? How does it play on the word *grandeur* and its connotations?

MARTHA COLLINS
The Irish were not, the Germans[8]

The Irish were not, the Germans
were not, the Jews Italians Slavs and others
were not, or were not exactly or not quite
at various times in American history.

5   Before us the Greeks themselves
were not (though the weaker enemy
Persians[9] were), the next-up Romans
themselves were not either.

And later the Europeans were not
10 until Linnaeus[1] named by color,
red white yellow and black.

Even the English settlers were only
vaguely at first to contrast with natives,
but then with Africans, more and more

7. Mountain in the Swiss Alps.
8. From *White Papers*, a book-length sequence of numbered poems. A white paper is a detailed,
authoritative report issued by a government or business.
9. Allusion to the Greco-Persian Wars (c. 492–449 BCE), in which Greek city-states eventually
triumphed over the initially far more powerful Persian Empire.
1. Swedish scientist (1707–78) who developed an elaborate system for classifying all living beings into
genus, species, and so on; the system divided human beings into four species—*Americanus, Asiaticus,
Africanus,* and *Europaeus*—based, in part, on skin tone.

15 of them slaves to be irreversibly,
    totally different from, they were.

    Then others were not, then were,
    or were not, but gradually became,
    leaving only, for a time, black
20 and yellow to be not.

    Then there were other words
    for those who were still or newly
    (see *immigrant, Arab*) somehow not
    the same and therefore not.

25 Thus history leaves us nothing
    but not: like children playing at being
    something, we made, we keep
    making our whiteness up.

                                        2011

> • What is the effect of Collins's choice not to refer to the color white or to
> Whiteness until the poem's very last line? of her frequent use of the word
> *not*? of her sometimes odd syntax?

RICHARD BLANCO
My Father in English

First half of his life lived in Spanish: the long syntax
of *las montañas*[2] that lined his village, the rhyme
of *sol* with his soul—a Cuban *alma*[3]—that swayed
with *las palmas*,[4] the sharp rhythm of his *machete*
5 cutting through *caña*, the syllables of his *canarios*[5]
that sung into *la brisa*[6] of the island home he left
to spell out the second half of his life in English—
the vernacular of New York City sleet, neon, glass—
and the brick factory where he learned to polish
10 steel twelve hours a day. Enough to save enough
to buy a used Spanish–English dictionary he kept
bedside like a bible—studied fifteen new words
after his prayers each night, then practiced them
on us the next day: *Buenos días, indeed, my family.*
15 *Indeed más*[7] *coffee. Have a good day today, indeed—*
and again in the evening: *Gracias to my bella wife,*
indeed, for dinner. Hicistes tu[8] *homework, indeed?*

2. The mountains (Spanish).
3. Soul (Spanish). *Sol*: sun (Spanish).
4. The palms (Spanish).
5. Canaries (Spanish). *Caña*: (sugar) cane (Spanish).
6. The breeze (Spanish).
7. More (Spanish).
8. Did you (Spanish).

La vida is indeed *difícil.*[9] Indeed did indeed become
his favorite word, which, like the rest of his new life,
20 he never quite grasped: overused and misused often
to my embarrassment. Yet the word I most learned
to love and know him through: *indeed,* the exile who
tried to master the language he chose to master him,
indeed, the husband who refused to say *I love you*
25 in English to my mother, the man who died without
true translation. *Indeed,* meaning: in fact/*en efecto,*
meaning: in reality/*de hecho,*[1] meaning to say now
what I always meant to tell him in both languages:
thank you/*gracias* for surrendering the past tense
30 of your life so that I might conjugate myself here
in the present of this country, in truth/*así es,*[2] *indeed.*

2019

- In what ways and senses, and for what reasons, does *indeed* become such
  an important word here, one that accurately captures the speaker's father?

SUGGESTIONS FOR WRITING

1. Choose one poem in this book in which a single word seems to be especially crucial.
   Write an essay in which you work out carefully why and how that's the case.
2. Choose one poem in this book in which syntax (the order of words in sentences) or the
   placement of words on the page seems especially key to the poem's overall effect and
   meaning. Write an essay explaining how and why considering word order, in either or
   both of these senses, might change or deepen a reader's understanding of the poem.
3. Language is a topic of (as well as a tool used in) many poems in this anthology, including Richard Blanco's MY FATHER IN ENGLISH. Write an essay exploring what any of
   these poems has to say about poetry or language and how word choice, order, and
   placement help the poem express or illustrate it.
4. Look up the words *charter* and *ban*, as well as *banns*, in a good online dictionary. Then
   write an essay explaining how they contribute to the tone and theme of Blake's LONDON.
   How do all of the varied, even contradictory, meanings of these words matter?

9. Life is indeed hard (Spanish).
1. In fact (Spanish).
2. Quite so (Spanish).

16 | VISUAL IMAGERY AND FIGURES OF SPEECH

The language of poetry is often visual and pictorial. Rather than depending primarily on abstract ideas and elaborate reasoning, poems depend more on concrete and specific words that create images in our minds. Poems thus help us see things afresh or feel them suggestively through our other physical senses, such as hearing or touch. Sound is, as we will see, a vital aspect of poetry. But most poems use the sense of sight to help us form, in our minds, visual impressions, images that communicate more directly than concepts. We "see" yellow leaves on a branch or a father and son waltzing precariously, so that our response begins from a vivid visual impression of exactly what is happening. Some people think that those media and arts that challenge the imagination of a hearer or reader—radio drama, for example, or poetry—allow us to respond more fully than those (such as television or theater) that actually show things, appealing to our physical senses. Certainly these media leave more to our imagination, to our mind's eye.

Poems are sometimes quite abstract—they can even be *about* abstractions like grandeur or history. But usually they are quite concrete in what they ask us to see. One reason is that they often begin in a poet's mind with a picture or an image: of a person, a place, an event, or any other object of observation. That image may be based on something the poet has actually seen, but it may also be totally imaginary and only based on the "real world" in the sense that it draws on the poet's sense of what the world is or might be like. Even when a poet begins with an idea that draws on visual experience, however, the reader still has to *imagine* (through the poem's words) whatever the poem describes. The poet must rely on words to help the reader flesh out that mental image. In a sense, then, the reader becomes a visual artist, but the poet directs the visualization by evoking specific responses through words. *How* that happens can involve quite complicated verbal strategies—or even *visual* ones that draw on the possibilities of print (see ch. 20).

Seeing in the mind's eye—the re-creation of visual experience—requires different skills from poets and readers. Poets use all the linguistic strategies they can think of to re-create for us something they have already "seen." Poets depend on our having had a rich variety of visual experiences and try to draw on those experiences by using common, evocative words and then refining the process through more elaborate verbal devices. We as readers inhabit the process the other way around, trying to draw on our previous knowledge so that we can "see" by following verbal clues.

The languages of description are quite varied. The visual qualities of poetry result partly from the two aspects of poetic language described in chapter 15: on the one hand, the precision of individual words, and, on the other hand, precision's opposite—the reach, richness, and ambiguity of suggestion that words sometimes accrue. Visualization can also derive from sophisticated rhetorical and literary devices (**figures of speech**, for example, as we will see later in this chapter). But often description begins simply with naming—providing the word (noun, verb, adjective, or adverb) that will trigger images familiar from a reader's own experience. A reader can readily imagine a *dog* or *cat* or *house* or *flower* when each word is named, but not all readers will envision the same kind of dog or flower until the word is qualified in some way. So the poet may specify that the dog is a greyhound or poodle, or that the flower is a daffodil or a lilac; or the poet may indicate colors, sizes, specific movements, or particular identifying features. Such description can involve either narrowing by category (*daffodil* versus *flower*) or expanding through detail ("golden daffodils; / Beside the lake, beneath the trees"). And often comparisons are either explicitly or implicitly involved. Notice how this works in the three poems below, which move from the least to the most elaborate in their descriptive techniques. As you read each, look for instances of *narrowing by category*, *expanding by detail*, and implicit or explicit *comparing*, and consider how these help to create a vivid, cohesive visual picture.

DAVID BOTTOMS
Hubert Blankenship

Needing credit, he edges through the heavy door, head down,
and quietly closes the screen behind him.

This is Blankenship, father of five, owner of a plow horse and a cow.

Out of habit he leans against the counter by the stove.
5 He pats the pockets of his overalls

for the grocery list penciled on a torn paper bag,
then rolls into a strip of newsprint

the last of his Prince Albert.[1]
He hardly takes his eyes off his boot, sliced on one side

10 to accommodate his bunion, and hands
the list to my grandfather. Bull of the Woods,[2] three tins

of sardines, Spam, peanut butter, two loaves of bread (Colonial),[3]
then back to the musty feed room

where he ignores the hand truck leaning against the wall

15 and hefts onto his shoulder a hundred-pound bag of horse feed.
He rises to full height, snorting

but hardly burdened,
and parades, head high, to the bed of his pickup.

2015

---

1. Brand of tobacco, introduced by R. J. Reynolds in 1907, named after the British prince who served as King Edward VII, 1901–10.
2. Brand of chewing tobacco introduced c. 1883.
3. Brand originally introduced by the Colonial Baking Company (c. 1928–58).

CLAUDE McKAY
The Harlem Dancer

Applauding youths laughed with young prostitutes
And watched her perfect, half-clothed body sway;
Her voice was like the sound of blended flutes
Blown by black players upon a picnic day.
5 She sang and danced on gracefully and calm,
The light gauze hanging loose about her form;
To me she seemed a proudly-swaying palm
Grown lovelier for passing through a storm.
Upon her swarthy neck black shiny curls
10 Luxuriant fell; and tossing coins in praise,
The wine-flushed, bold-eyed boys, and even the girls,
Devoured her shape with eager, passionate gaze;
But looking at her falsely-smiling face,
I knew her self was not in that strange place.

1922

ADA LIMÓN
Dandelion Insomnia

The big-ass bees are back, tipsy, sun drunk
and heavy with thick knitted leg warmers
of pollen. I was up all night again so today's
yellow hours seem strange and hallucinogenic.
5 The neighborhood is lousy with mowers, crazy
dogs, and people mending what winter ruined.
What I can't get over is something simple, easy:
How could a dandelion seed head seemingly
grow overnight? A neighbor mows the lawn
10 and bam, the next morning, there's a hundred
dandelion seed heads straight as arrows
and proud as cats high above any green blade
of manicured grass. It must bug some folks,
a flower so tricky it can reproduce asexually,
15 making perfect identical selves, bam, another me,
bam, another me. I can't help it—I root
for that persecuted rosette so hyper in its
own making it seems to devour the land.
Even its name, translated from the French
20 *dent de lion,* means lion's tooth. It's vicious,
made for a time that requires tenacity, a way
of remaking the toughest self while everyone
else is asleep.

2018

More than just a matter of naming, using precise words, and providing basic information, description involves qualification and comparison. Sometimes, the poet needs to tell us what *not* to picture, dissociating what the poem describes from other possible images we may have in mind. Different features in the language of description add up to something that describes a whole—a picture or scene—as well as a series of individualized objects.

SIMILE AND ANALOGY

As we've seen, the vividness of the picture writers create in our minds often depends on comparisons. Such comparisons are often made through figures of speech. What we are trying to imagine is pictured or characterized in terms of something else familiar to us, and we are asked to think of one thing as if it were something else. Many such comparisons, in which something is pictured or figured forth in terms of something already familiar to us, are taken for granted in daily life. Things we can't see or that aren't familiar to us are imaged as things we already know; for example, God is said to be like a father; Italy is said to be shaped like a boot; life is compared to a forest, a journey, or a sea.

Sometimes, comparisons are made explicitly, as when, in THE HARLEM DANCER, the dancer's "voice" is said to be "like the sound of blended flutes / Blown by black players upon a picnic day" (lines 3–4). Such *explicit* comparisons are called similes, and usually (as here) the comparison involves the words *like* or *as*. Usually similes are made passingly; they make a quick comparison and usually do not elaborate. Similes sometimes develop into more elaborate comparisons, however, and occasionally, as in the poem below, even govern a poem (in which case they are called analogies).

TODD BOSS
My Love for You Is So Embarrassingly

grand . . . would you mind terribly, my groundling,[4]
    if I compared it to the *Hindenburg*[5] (I mean,
  before it burned)—that vulnerable, elephantine

dream of transport, a fabric *Titanic*[6] on an ocean
5 of air? There: with binoculars, dear, you can
  just make me out, in a gondola window, wildly

    flapping both arms as the ship's shadow
    moves like a vagrant country across the
  country where you live in relative safety. I pull

10 that oblong shadow along behind me wherever
    I go. It is so big, and goes so slowly, it alters
    ground temperatures noticeably, makes

4. Literally, someone on the ground; figuratively, a person of unsophisticated taste, like a spectator who stood in the pit of an Elizabethan theater.
5. German airship destroyed by fire during a failed docking attempt over New Jersey, May 6, 1937.
6. British passenger liner sunk on April 15, 1912, after colliding with an iceberg on its maiden voyage.

> housewives part kitchen curtains, wrings
> whimpers from German shepherds. Aren't I
> 15   ridiculous? Isn't it anachronistic, this
>
> dirigible devotion, this Zeppelin affection, a moon
> that touches, with a kiss of wheels, the ground
> you take for granted beneath your heels?—

2011

METAPHOR

When a comparison is implicit, describing something as if it were something else, it is called a **metaphor**. In the poem that follows, the poet helps us visualize old age and approaching death through metaphors comparing these with familiar things— the coming of winter, the approach of sunset, and the dying embers of a fire.

WILLIAM SHAKESPEARE

That time of year thou mayst in me behold

That time of year thou mayst in me behold
When yellow leaves, or none, or few, do hang
Upon those boughs which shake against the cold,
Bare ruined choirs, where late the sweet birds sang.
5   In me thou see'st the twilight of such day
As after sunset fadeth in the west;
Which by and by[7] black night doth take away,
Death's second self,[8] that seals up all in rest.
In me thou see'st the glowing of such fire,
10 That on the ashes of his youth doth lie,
As the deathbed whereon it must expire,
Consumed with that which it was nourished by.
This thou perceiv'st, which makes thy love more strong,
To love that well which thou must leave ere long.

1609

The first four lines of THAT TIME OF YEAR evoke images of the late autumn, but notice that the poet does not have the speaker say directly that his physical condition and age make him resemble autumn. He draws the comparison without stating it as a comparison: You can see my own state, he says, in the coming of winter, when almost all the leaves have fallen from the trees. The speaker portrays himself *indirectly* by talking about the passing of the year. Again, then, one thing is pictured *as if* it were something else. "That time of year" goes on to another metaphor in lines 5–8 and still another in lines 9–12, and each metaphor contributes to our understanding of the speaker's sense of his old age and approaching death. More important, however, is the way the metaphors give us feelings, an

7. Shortly.
8. Sleep.

emotional sense of the speaker's age and of his own attitude toward aging. Through the metaphors we come to understand, appreciate, and to some extent share the increasing sense of urgency that the poem expresses. Our emotional sense of the poem depends largely on the way each metaphor is developed and by the way each metaphor leads, with its own kind of internal logic, to another, even as later metaphors build on earlier ones. Look back at the poem. What does each metaphor contribute? How does each build on the last?

"That time of year" represents an unusually intricate use of images to organize a poem and focus its emotional impact. Not all poems depend on such a full and varied use of metaphor. Sometimes rather than accumulating metaphors, a poet presents a single metaphor that extends over a section of a poem (in which case it is called an *extended metaphor*) or even over the whole poem (in which case it is called a *controlling metaphor*). The following poem depends from the beginning—even from its title—on a single controlling metaphor. What is the metaphor? How is it developed over the course of the poem? What does the poem thereby convey about what the experience of mothering looks and feels like, especially to a new mother?

LIZ BERRY
The Republic of Motherhood

> I crossed the border into the Republic of Motherhood
> and found it a queendom, a wild queendom.
> I handed over my clothes and took its uniform,
> its dressing gown and undergarments, a cardigan
> 5 soft as a creature, smelling of birth and milk,
> and I lay down in Motherhood's bed, the bed I had made
> but could not sleep in, for I was called at once to work
> in the factory of Motherhood. The owl shift,
> the graveyard shift. Feedingcleaninglovingfeeding.
> 10 I walked home, heartsore, through pale streets,
> the coins of Motherhood singing in my pockets.
> Then I soaked my spindled bones
> in the chill municipal baths of Motherhood,
> watching strands of my hair float from my fingers.
> 15 Each day I pushed my pram through freeze and blossom
> down the wide boulevards of Motherhood
> where poplars bent their branches to stroke my brow.
> I stood with my sisters in the queues of Motherhood—
> the weighing clinic, the supermarket—waiting
> 20 for Motherhood's bureaucracies to open their doors.
> As required, I stood beneath the flag of Motherhood
> and opened my mouth although I did not know the anthem.
> When darkness fell I pushed my pram home again,
> and by lamplight wrote urgent letters of complaint
> 25 to the Department of Motherhood but received no response.
> I grew sick and was healed in the hospitals of Motherhood
> with their long-closed isolation wards

and narrow beds watched over by a fat moon.
The doctors were slender and efficient
30 and when I was well they gave me my pram again
so I could stare at the daffodils in the parks of Motherhood
while winds pierced my breasts like silver arrows.
In snowfall, I haunted Motherhood's cemeteries,
the sweet fallen beneath my feet—
35 Our Lady of the Birth Trauma, Our Lady of Psychosis.
I wanted to speak to them, tell them I understood,
but the words came out scrambled, so I knelt instead
and prayed in the chapel of Motherhood, prayed
for that whole wild fucking queendom,
40 its sorrow, its unbearable skinless beauty,
and all the souls that were in it. I prayed and prayed
until my voice was a nightcry
and sunlight pixelated my face like a kaleidoscope.

2017

AUTHORS ON THEIR WORK

LIZ BERRY (b. 1980)

From "In Conversation: Liz Berry & Mona Arshi" (2019)*

I was definitely afraid of "The Republic of Motherhood"! When it was accepted by *Granta* [magazine], I rang my friend, another poet and mum, in tears as I wasn't sure if it was the right thing to do to publish it. I was afraid that everyone would tell me I was a terrible mother or that one day my sons might grow up and read the poem and think I didn't love them. Yet in my heart I knew that it was a poem that I'd had to write.

I had such a hard time when my first son was born. [. . .] I longed for poems to meet me in my sorrow and help me know how to live in that new world, how to survive it. Yet there were hardly any poems about that, so I felt that these feelings, this new world of mine, must be trivial or embarrassing [. . .] or something to be ashamed of. Awful! So when I was ready to write again I wanted to make the poems I'd needed to read. It seemed no good hiding behind masks or monologues as that felt like a way of disowning it and pushing it away, pretending it wasn't my feeling because I was ashamed of it. I didn't want to feel ashamed any more. I wanted to write those poems barely and openly, as I might speak to a friend or another new mother, and let them know that they were not alone and that there was nothing to be ashamed of, that in sharing these poems we might share the heartache and also the joy, find solace.

*"In Conversation: Liz Berry & Mona Arshi." *Granta*, 13 May 2019, granta.com/liz-berry-and -mona-arshi-in-conversation/.

PERSONIFICATION

Another figure of speech, **personification**, involves treating an abstraction, such as death or justice or beauty, as if it were a person. When Shakespeare's "That time of year" talks about the coming of night and of sleep, for example, sleep is personified as the "second self" of death (that is, as a kind of "double" for death [line 8]). If personification in this poem is a brief gesture, it proves much more obvious and central in the following poem, though in this case, too, it is death that the poet personifies. How so, and with what implications and effects?

EMILY DICKINSON
Because I could not stop for Death—

Because I could not stop for Death—
He kindly stopped for me—
The Carriage held but just Ourselves—
And Immortality.

5   We slowly drove—He knew no haste
And I had put away
My labor and my leisure too,
For His Civility—

We passed the School, where Children strove
10   At Recess—in the Ring—
We passed the Fields of Gazing Grain—
We passed the Setting Sun—

Or rather—He passed Us—
The Dews drew quivering and chill—
15   For only Gossamer,[9] my Gown—
My Tippet—only Tulle[1]—

We paused before a House that seemed
A Swelling of the Ground—
The Roof was scarcely visible—
20   The Cornice—in the Ground—

Since then—'tis Centuries—and yet
Feels shorter than the Day
I first surmised the Horses' Heads
Were toward Eternity—

                                                          c. 1863

---

9. Soft, sheer fabric.
1. Fine net fabric. *Tippet:* shawl.

METONYMY AND SYNECDOCHE

Simile, analogy, metaphor, and personification all insist on the similarity between two ostensibly unlike things, things we might normally never think of putting together—a dancer and a palm tree swaying in the wind, dying and being driven away in a carriage. **Metonymy** instead relies on the fact that we already associate one thing with another, since it entails referring to a thing by instead naming something else associated with it. Though this sounds complicated, it's not: When you say, "The White House issued a press release," "Harry and Sally are walking down the aisle this summer," or "The suits disapproved," you aren't speaking literally. Instead you're using *White House* as a metonym for the people who work in that building (the U.S. president and his administration); *walking down the aisle* as a metonym for getting married; and *suits* to mean people in authority. The most common type of metonymy—so common that it is treated as a figure of speech in its own right—is **synecdoche**, which involves referring to a thing by naming only a part of it, as when we either say that someone has "a lot of mouths to feed" or demand "all hands on deck."

What metonyms can you identify in the following sonnet? What other figures of speech? What does the poet gain from each?

WILLIAM WORDSWORTH
London, 1802

Milton![2] thou should'st be living at this hour:
England hath need of thee: she is a fen
Of stagnant waters: altar, sword and pen,
Fireside, the heroic wealth of hall and bower,
5 Have forfeited their ancient English dower[3]
Of inward happiness. We are selfish men;
Oh! raise us up, return to us again;
And give us manners, virtue, freedom, power.
Thy soul was like a Star and dwelt apart:
10 Thou hadst a voice whose sound was like the sea;
Pure as the naked heavens, majestic, free,
So didst thou travel on life's common way,
In chearful godliness; and yet thy heart
The lowliest duties on itself did lay.

1807

2. Poet John Milton (1608–74), who also wrote pamphlets championing various freedoms, including those of speech and of the press, and backed the anti-royalist cause in the English Civil War.
3. Gift, endowment.

Figurative Language:
A Comparative Exercise

Indulging in metaphors, personification, and other figures of speech is not the exclusive pastime of poets but something we all do, every day, usually without thinking about it: We "fall head over heels in love" and hope the stock market doesn't "take a dive." Our chairs have "arms" and "legs." We say that the body "houses" the soul. A physician might tell a woman (as one physician did tell a poet whose work appears below) that it's unlikely her "womb could viably house a fetus." Then we look at the house across the street and see a human face staring back at us—with windows for eyes, a door mouth, and so on. One thing poetry can do is to reawaken us to the figures of speech buried in everyday language—to make us see again the visual images they *should* but often no longer do conjure up—and to consider, even feel, their implications.

The two poems below do just that. And both do so by taking as their ostensible subject houses—or rather "house" in general. Yet the two poems are in some ways polar opposites, especially in their use of, and attitude toward, figures of speech. In the first, Tracy K. Smith's ASH, "house" functions as part of a controlling metaphor, something to which the poem is implicitly comparing another thing that's never named. Identifying that other thing is key to fully experiencing and understanding this riddle-like poem. And doing so will require paying close attention to the specific features, qualities, and actions the poem attributes to "house," in part through yet more figures of speech. The second poem, Emma Bolden's HOUSE IS AN ENIGMA, instead seems to take aim at our very tendency to speak—and even think and *see*—"house" figuratively. What, according to this poem, might be the negative effects of doing so? How does the poem use figures of speech to point out the potential problems with figures of speech—at least or especially those involving "house"?

TRACY K. SMITH
Ash

Strange house we must keep and fill.

House that eats and pleads and kills.

House on legs. House on fire. House infested

With desire. Haunted house. Lonely house.

5 House of trick and suck and shrug.

Give-it-to-me house. *I-need-you-baby* house.

House whose rooms are pooled with blood.

House with hands. House of guilt. House

That other houses built. House of lies

10 And pride and bone. House afraid to be alone.

House like an engine that churns and stalls.

House with skin and hair for walls.

House the seasons singe and douse.

House that believes it is not a house.

2015

EMMA BOLDEN
House Is an Enigma

House is not a metaphor. House has nothing
to do with beak or wing.[4] House is not two

hands held angled towards each other. House is
not its roof or the pine straw on its roof. At night,

5   its windows and doors look nothing like a face.
Its stairs are not vertebrae. Its walls may be

white. They are not pale skin. House does not
appreciate your pun on its panes as pains.

House does not appreciate because house
10   does not have feelings. House has no aesthetic

program. House does what it does, which is
not doing. House does not sit on its foundations.

House exists in its foundations, and when the wind
pushes itself to full gale, house is never the one crying.

2014

AUTHORS ON THEIR WORK

TRACY K. SMITH (b. 1972)

From "Love Is a Language / Few Practice, but All, or Near All Speak" (2018)*

This ["Ash"] is a poem—it's sort of strange. It's a metaphor-based poem. It feels, even as I read it, that the metaphor's slippery. I wrote it thinking about one thing. And then, hearing people talk about it and ask about it, it's come to mean some-

---

4. The phrase *beak and wing* features in many poems, including Christopher Smart's (1722–71) "A Song to David," where it functions as a synecdoche for birds: "every beak and wing / Which cheer the winter, hail the spring" (lines 133–34).

thing else for me. [. . .] I wrote that poem thinking about the body, thinking about what it means to be alive in this human form and how strange it is that it's temporary, that we are not just the body, but something else. That's the way I've read it the first many times that I read it, or, at least, what I heard myself saying. But there's a lot of ambiguity in the poem, and so people have questions about it. Someone has told me it feels like a poem that, more than just being in the body, is about being a woman and that sense of vulnerability and also sheltering something. Then, because a lot of these poems in this book are thinking about nationhood and American history, I was really excited to hear it described as a poem that is about the country as a house, and taking us back even to Abraham Lincoln in the sense of "a house divided against itself." I love that active readers can give you a good enough argument to re-hear and see what you've made yourself.

*"Love Is a Language / Few Practice, but All, or Near All Speak." *On Being with Krista Tippett*, 1 Nov. 2018, onbeing.org/programs/tracy-k-smith-love-is-a-language-few-practice-but -all-or-near-all-speak-nov2018/.

ALLUSION

Like many poems, Todd Boss's MY LOVE FOR YOU IS SO EMBARRASSINGLY depends on multiple figures of speech: By comparing his love to the *Hindenburg* and, in turn, the *Hindenburg* (line 2) to the *Titanic* (4), the speaker makes use not only of analogy and metaphor but also of **allusion**, a brief reference to a fictitious or actual person, place, or thing and, usually, to the stories or **myth** surrounding it. Like metaphor and simile, allusion allows poets to economically suggest a wealth of sometimes complex images, feelings, and ideas by relying on widely shared literary and cultural knowledge. In this particular case, knowing something about both what happened to the *Hindenburg* and the *Titanic* and what "dream[s]" of human ingenuity and power were destroyed along with them gives us a more specific, vivid picture of how something might be simultaneously "vulnerable" and "elephantine," exhilarating and terrifying, transcendent and potentially disastrous (4, 3).

Sometimes "getting" an allusion or even recognizing one requires us to learn something new. Many of the footnotes in this book aim to help you with that. But whenever you come across a name or other reference in a poem that you don't understand or a phrase that seems oddly familiar, it's well worth your while to consult a reference book or to Google up a reliable source. Allusions are one of the ways poems engage with the larger world, participating in a vast conversation they invite and even expect you, too, to be a part of.

The poem below relies on an array of allusions. As you read it, try not only to spot all the allusions but also to tease out what specifically each contributes to the poem.

AMIT MAJMUDAR
Dothead

Well yes, I said, my mother wears a dot.
I know they said "third eye" in class, but it's not
an *eye* eye, not like that. It's not some freak
third eye that opens on your forehead like

5   on some Chernobyl baby.[5] What it means
    is, what it's *showing* is, there's this unseen
    eye, on the inside. And she's marking it.
    It's how the X that says where treasure's at
    is not the treasure, but as good as treasure.—
10 All right. What I said wasn't half so measured.
    In fact, I didn't say a thing. Their laughter
    had made my mouth go dry. Lunch was after
    World History; that week was India—myths,
    caste system, suttee,[6] all the Greatest Hits.
15 The white kids I was sitting with were friends,
    at least as I defined a friend back then.
    So wait, said Nick, does *your* mom wear a dot?
    I nodded, and I caught a smirk on Todd—
    She wear it to the shower? And to bed?—
20 while Jesse sucked his chocolate milk and Brad
    was getting ready for another stab.
    I said, Hand me that ketchup packet there.
    And Nick said, What? I snatched it, twitched the tear,
    and squeezed a dollop on my thumb and worked
25 circles till the red planet entered the house of war
    and on my forehead for the world to see
    my third eye burned those schoolboys in their seats,
    their flesh in little puddles underneath,
    pale pools where Nataraja[7] cooled his feet.

                                                    2011

• • •

All figurative language involves an attempt to clarify something *and* to prompt readers to feel a certain way about it. Once you start looking for them, you will find figures of speech in poem after poem; they are among the most common devices through which poets share their visions with us, helping us to see our world and our language anew.

POEMS FOR FURTHER STUDY

WILLIAM SHAKESPEARE
Shall I compare thee to a summer's day?

Shall I compare thee to a summer's day?
Thou art more lovely and more temperate.
Rough winds do shake the darling buds of May,

---

5. That is, a baby born with birth defects as a result of the explosion that occurred in April 1986 at the Chernobyl Nuclear Power Plant in Ukraine.
6. Custom of a Hindu widow voluntarily being cremated on her husband's funeral pyre.
7. The Lord of Dancers, an avatar of the Hindu god Shiva, whose ecstatic twirling expresses the cyclic energy of the universe.

And summer's lease hath all too short a date.
5 Sometime too hot the eye of heaven shines,
And often is his gold complexion dimmed;
And every fair from fair sometime declines,
By chance or nature's changing course untrimmed.
But thy eternal summer shall not fade,
10 Nor lose possession of that fair thou ow'st,
Nor shall Death brag thou wand'rest in his shade,
When in eternal lines to time thou grow'st.
   So long as men can breathe or eyes can see,
   So long lives this,[8] and this gives life to thee.

1609

• What sort of promise does the speaker make with this poem? Why can he boast that "thy eternal summer shall not fade" (line 9)?

ANONYMOUS
The Twenty-Third Psalm[9]

The Lord is my shepherd; I shall not want.
He maketh me to lie down in green pastures: he leadeth me beside
   the still waters.
He restoreth my soul: he leadeth me in the paths of righteousness
   for his name's sake.
Yea, though I walk through the valley of the shadow of death,
   I will fear no evil: for thou art with me;
   thy rod and thy staff they comfort me.
5 Thou preparest a table before me in the presence of mine enemies:
   thou anointest my head with oil; my cup runneth over.
Surely goodness and mercy shall follow me all the days of my life:
   and I will dwell in the house of the Lord for ever.

• What is the controlling metaphor in this poem? At what point in the psalm does the controlling metaphor shift?

JOHN DONNE
Batter my heart, three-personed God[1]

Batter my heart, three-personed God; for You
As yet but knock, breathe, shine, and seek to mend;
That I may rise and stand, o'erthrow me, and bend
Your force, to break, blow, burn, and make me new.

---

8. This poem.
9. Traditionally attributed to King David. This English translation is from the King James Version of the Bible (1611).
1. From the sequence known as "Holy Sonnets."

5 I, like an usurped town, to another due,
  Labor to admit You, but Oh, to no end!
  Reason, Your viceroy[2] in me, me should defend,
  But is captived, and proves weak or untrue.
  Yet dearly I love You, and would be loved fain,[3]
10 But am betrothed unto Your enemy:
  Divorce me, untie or break that knot again,
  Take me to You, imprison me, for I,
  Except You enthrall me, never shall be free,
  Nor ever chaste, except You ravish me.

1633

- In the poem's controlling metaphor, who is the speaker? Who, or what, is
  God? To whom is the speaker "betrothed" (line 10)?

Gunner climbing into ball turret, c. 1942

RANDALL JARRELL
The Death of the Ball Turret Gunner[4]

From my mother's sleep I fell into the State,
And I hunched in its belly till my wet fur froze.
Six miles from earth, loosed from its dream of life,

2. One who rules as the representative of someone of higher rank.
3. Gladly.
4. A ball turret was a Plexiglas sphere set into the belly of a B-17 or B-24 [airplane] and inhabited by two .50 caliber machine-guns and one man, a short small man. When this gunner tracked with his machine-guns a fighter attacking his bomber from below, he revolved with the turret; hunched

I woke to black flak and the nightmare fighters.
5   When I died they washed me out of the turret with a hose.

1945

- What is meant by "I fell into the State (line 1)"? What do the words "sleep," "dream," and "nightmare" (1, 3, 4) suggest about the situation?

NATALIE DIAZ

When the Beloved Asks, "What Would You Do If You Woke Up and I Was a Shark?"

My lover doesn't realize that I've contemplated this scenario,
fingered it like the smooth inner iridescence of a nautilus shell
in the shadow-long waters of many 2 a.m.s—drunk on the brine

of shoulder blades, those pale horns of shore I am wrecked upon,
5   my mind treading the wine-dark waves of luxuria's[5] tempests—
as a matter of preparedness, and because I do not sleep for fear

of such things or even other things—I've read that the ocean
is a large pot of Apocalypse soup soon to boil over with our sins—
but a thing is a thing, especially if it's a 420-million-year-old beast,

10   especially if you have wronged so many as I. Beauty, it is simple,
more simple than a beloved can imagine: I wouldn't fight, not kick,
flail, not carry on like one driven mad by the black neoprene wetsuit

of death, not like sad-mouthed, despair-eyed albacore or blubbery
pinnipeds, wouldn't rage the city's flickering streets of ampullae
15   of Lorenzini,[6] nor slug my ferocious, streamlined lover's titanium

white nose, that bull's-eye of cartilage, no, I wouldn't prolong it.
Instead, I'd place my head onto that dark altar of jaws, prostrated
pilgrim at Melville's[7] glittering gates, climb into that mysterious

window starred with teeth—the one lit room in the charnel house.
20   I, at once mariner, at once pirate, would navigate my want by those
throbbing constellations. I'd wear those jaws like a toothy cilice,[8]

slip into the glitzy red gown of penance, and it would be no different
from what I do each day—voyaging the salt-sharp sea of your body,
sometimes mooring the ports or sighting the sextant, then mending

---

upside-down in his little sphere, he looked like the foetus in the womb. The fighters which attacked him were armed with cannon firing explosive shells. The hose was a steam hose [Jarrell's note].
5. Luxuriance; excess; lust (Latin).
6. Series of sensory organs just beneath the skin of cartilaginous fish such as sharks and rays that, by detecting electrical fields, aid in the detection of prey. *Pinnipeds*: carnivorous aquatic mammals such as seals or walruses.
7. Reference to Herman Melville's *Moby-Dick* (1851), about a sea captain's obsessive quest to kill the giant white whale that consumed half his leg.
8. Spiked garter or other device worn by religious penitents and ascetics as a means of mortifying the flesh or doing penance.

25 the purple sails and hoisting the masts before being bound to them.
Be-loved, *is* loved, what you cannot know is I am overboard for this
metamorphosis, ready to be raptured to that mouth, reduced to a swell
of wet clothes, as you roll back your eyes and drag me into the fathoms.

2012

- What is the poem's controlling metaphor? What feelings about her lover
and herself does the speaker communicate through the specific ways she
develops and elaborates on that metaphor? Why a shark?

SUGGESTIONS FOR WRITING

1. Choose any poem in this chapter and explore the meaning and effect of its meta-
phor(s). Does the poem make use of an extended or controlling metaphor or of multiple metaphors? If the latter, how do the metaphors relate to and build on each other?
2. Choose any poem in this book that uses personification and write an essay exploring
how this figure of speech contributes both to the emotional effect of the poem and its
theme(s). (In addition to the Emily Dickinson poem in this chapter, other good options
include Jimmy Santiago Baca's GREEN CHILE, John Keats's TO AUTUMN, and John
Donne's DEATH, BE NOT PROUD.)
3. This chapter contains two quite different love poems, Todd Boss's MY LOVE FOR YOU
IS SO EMBARRASSINGLY and Natalie Diaz's WHEN THE BELOVED ASKS, "WHAT WOULD
YOU DO IF YOU WOKE UP AND I WAS A SHARK?" Which of these two poems most
appeals to you, or which best captures either how you have felt or would like to feel
about a lover or how you would like a lover to feel about you? Write a response paper
in which you explain why and how the poem you've chosen appeals to you, being sure
to say something about how the poem uses imagery or figures of speech to communicate feeling.
4. Research the design of World War II bombers like the B-17 and the B-24. Examine
a picture of the gunner in the ball turret of such an airplane, and note carefully his
body position. Write an essay in which you explain how Randall Jarrell's THE DEATH
OF THE BALL TURRET GUNNER uses visual details to create its fetal and birth metaphors.
5. Choose any poem in this book that relies on at least one allusion to something or
someone initially unfamiliar to you. After researching whatever the poem alludes
to, write an informal response paper or essay exploring how the poem works and
means differently to an informed reader.
6. Look online for the lyrics to some of your favorite songs and identify the figures of
speech used in each. Write an essay explaining which of these figures seem the most
creative and effective, and why.

17 | SYMBOL

Properly used, the term *symbol* suggests one of the most basic things about poems—their ability to get beyond what words signify and to make larger claims about meanings in the verbal world. All words go beyond themselves. They are not simply a collection of sounds: They signify something beyond their sounds, often things or actions or ideas. Words describe not only a verbal universe but also a world in which actions occur, acts have implications, and events have meaning. Sometimes words signify something beyond themselves, say, *rock* or *tree* or *cloud*, and symbolize something as well, such as solidity or life or dreams. Words can—when their implications are agreed on by tradition, convention, or habit—stand for things beyond their most immediate meanings or significations and become symbols, and even simple words that have accumulated no special power from previous use may be given special significance in special circumstances—in poetry as in life itself.

A **symbol** is, put simply, something that stands for something else. The everyday world is full of examples; a flag, a logo, a trademark, or a skull and crossbones all suggest things beyond themselves, and everyone likely understands what their display indicates, whether or not each viewer shares a commitment to what is thus represented. In common usage a prison symbolizes confinement, constriction, and loss of freedom, and in specialized traditional usage a cross may symbolize oppression, cruelty, suffering, death, resurrection, triumph, or an intersection of some kind (as in *crossroads* and *crosscurrents*). The specific symbolic significance depends on the context; for example, a reader might determine significance by looking at contiguous details in a poem and by examining the poem's attitude toward a particular tradition or body of beliefs. A star means one thing to a Jewish poet and something else to a Christian poet, still something else to a sailor or an actor. In a very literal sense, words themselves are all symbols (they stand for objects, actions, or qualities, not just for letters or sounds), but symbols in poetry are those words and phrases that have a range of reference beyond their literal signification or **denotation**.

THE INVENTED SYMBOL

Poems sometimes create a symbol out of a thing, action, or event that has no previously agreed-upon symbolic significance. Such a symbol is sometimes called an *invented symbol*. The following poem, for example, gives an action symbolic significance.

JAMES DICKEY
The Leap

The only thing I have of Jane MacNaughton
Is one instant of a dancing-class dance.
She was the fastest runner in the seventh grade,
My scrapbook says, even when boys were beginning
5   To be as big as the girls,
But I do not have her running in my mind,
Though Frances Lane is there, Agnes Fraser,
Fat Betty Lou Black in the boys-against-girls
Relays we ran at recess: she must have run

10   Like the other girls, with her skirts tucked up
So they would be like bloomers,
But I cannot tell; that part of her is gone.
What I do have is when she came,
With the hem of her skirt where it should be
15   For a young lady, into the annual dance
Of the dancing class we all hated, and with a light
Grave leap, jumped up and touched the end
Of one of the paper-ring decorations

To see if she could reach it. She could,
20   And reached me now as well, hanging in my mind
From a brown chain of brittle paper, thin
And muscular, wide-mouthed, eager to prove
Whatever it proves when you leap
In a new dress, a new womanhood, among the boys
25   Whom you easily left in the dust
Of the passionless playground. If I said I saw
In the paper where Jane MacNaughton Hill,

Mother of four, leapt to her death from a window
Of a downtown hotel, and that her body crushed-in
30   The top of a parked taxi, and that I held
Without trembling a picture of her lying cradled
In that papery steel as though lying in the grass,
One shoe idly off, arms folded across her breast,
I would not believe myself. I would say
35   The convenient thing, that it was a bad dream
Of maturity, to see that eternal process

Most obsessively wrong with the world
Come out of her light, earth-spurning feet
Grown heavy: would say that in the dusty heels
40   Of the playground some boy who did not depend
On speed of foot, caught and betrayed her.
Jane, stay where you are in my first mind:
It was odd in that school, at that dance.

I and the other slow-footed yokels sat in corners
45 Cutting rings out of drawing paper

Before you leapt in your new dress
And touched the end of something I began,
Above the couples struggling on the floor,
New men and women clutching at each other
50 And prancing foolishly as bears: hold on
To that ring I made for you, Jane—
My feet are nailed to the ground
By dust I swallowed thirty years ago—
While I examine my hands.

1967

Memory is crucial to THE LEAP. The fact that Jane MacNaughton's graceful leap in dancing class has stuck in the speaker's mind all these years means that this leap was important to him, meant something to him, stood for something in his mind. For the speaker, the leap is an "instant" and the "only thing" he has of Jane (lines 2, 1). He remembers its grace and ease, and he struggles at several points to articulate its meaning (16–26, 44–50), but even without articulation or explanation it remains in his head as a visual memory, a symbol of something beyond himself, something he cannot do, something he wanted to be. What that leap stood for, or symbolized, was boldness, confidence, accomplishment, maturity, Jane's ability to go beyond her fellow students in dancing class—the transcending of childhood by someone entering adulthood. Her feet now seem "earth-spurning" (38) in that original leap, and they separate her from everyone else. Jane MacNaughton was beyond the speaker's abilities and any attempt he could make to articulate his hopes, but she was not beyond his dreams. And even before he could say so, she symbolized a dream.

The leap to her death seems cruelly wrong and ironic after the grace of her earlier leap. In memory she is suspended in air, as if there were no gravity, no coming back to earth, as if life could exist as dream. And so the photograph, re-created in precise detail, is a cruel dashing of the speaker's dream—a detailed record of the ending of a leap, a denial of the suspension in which his memory had held her. His dream is grounded; her mortality is insistent. But the speaker still wants to hang on to that symbolic moment (42), which he confronts in a more mature context but will never altogether replace or surrender.

The leap is ultimately symbolic in the *poem*, too, not just in the speaker's mind. In the poem (and for us as readers) its symbolism is double: The first leap symbolizes aspiration, and the second symbolizes the frustration and grounding of high hopes; the two are complementary, one impossible to imagine without the other. The poem is horrifying in some ways, a dramatic reminder that human beings don't ultimately transcend their mortality, their limits, no matter how heroic or unencumbered by gravity they may once have seemed. But the poem is not altogether sad and despairing, partly because it still affirms the validity of the original leap and partly because it creates and elaborates another symbol: the paper chain.

The chain connects Jane to the speaker both literally and figuratively. It is, in part, *his* paper chain that she had leaped to touch in dancing class (18–19), and he thinks of her first leap as "touch[ing] the end of something I began" (47). He and the other earthbound, "slow-footed yokels" (44) made the chain, and it connects them to her original leap, just as a photograph glimpsed in the newspaper connects the speaker to her second leap. And so the paper chain becomes the poem's symbol of linkage, connecting lower accomplishment to higher possibility, the artisan to the artist, material substance to the act of imagination. At the end the speaker examines the hands that made the chain because those hands certify his connection to her and to the imaginative leap she had made for him. The chain thus symbolizes not only the lower capabilities of those who cannot leap like the budding Jane could, but also (later) the connection with her leap as both transcendence and mortality.

Like the leap, the chain is elevated to special meaning, given symbolic significance, only by the poet's treatment of it. A leap and a chain have no necessary significance in themselves—at least no significance that we have all agreed upon—but the poet here makes them significant, symbolic.

THE TRADITIONAL SYMBOL

Some objects and acts have a built-in significance because of past usage in literature, or tradition, or the stories a culture develops to explain itself and its beliefs. Such things have acquired an agreed-upon significance, an accepted value in our minds. They already stand for something before the poet cites them; they are *traditional symbols*. Poets assume that their readers will recognize the traditional meanings of these symbols. Birds, for example, traditionally symbolize flight, freedom from confinement, detachment from earthbound limits, the ability to soar beyond rationality and transcend mortal limits. Traditionally, birds have also been linked with the soul and with imagination, especially poetic imagination, and poets often identify with them as pure and ideal singers of songs.

One traditional symbol, the rose, may be a simple and fairly plentiful flower in its season, but it has so long stood for particular qualities that merely to name it creates predictable expectations. Its beauty, delicacy, fragrance, shortness of life, and depth of color have made it a symbol of the transitoriness of beauty, and countless poets have relied on its accepted symbolism—sometimes to compliment a friend, sometimes to make a point about the nature of symbolism. The following poem draws, in quite a traditional way, on the traditional meanings.

EDMUND WALLER
Song

Go, lovely rose!
Tell her that wastes her time and me
That now she knows,
When I resemble[1] her to thee,
5   How sweet and fair she seems to be.

Tell her that's young,
And shuns to have her graces spied,
That hadst thou sprung
In deserts, where no men abide,
10   Thou must have uncommended died.

1. Compare.

Small is the worth
Of beauty from the light retired;
   Bid her come forth,
Suffer herself to be desired,
15   And not blush so to be admired.

   Then die! that she
The common fate of all things rare
   May read in thee;
How small a part of time they share
20   That are so wondrous sweet and fair!

                                                                1645

The speaker in Song sends the rose to his love in order to have it speak its traditional meanings of beauty and transitoriness. He counts on accepted symbolism to make his point and hurry her into accepting his advances. The poet does not elaborate or argue these things because he does not need to; he relies on the familiarity of the tradition (though, of course, readers unfamiliar with the tradition will not respond in the same way—that is one reason it is difficult to fully appreciate texts from another linguistic or cultural tradition).

Poets may use traditional symbols to invoke predictable responses—in effect using shortcuts to meaning by repeating acts of signification sanctioned by time and cultural habit. But often poets examine the tradition even as they employ it, and sometimes they revise or reverse traditional, expected meanings. Symbols do not necessarily stay the same over time, and poets often turn even the most traditional symbols to their own original uses. Knowing the traditions of poetry—reading a lot of poems and observing how they tend to use certain words, metaphors, and symbols—can be very useful in reading new poems, but traditions evolve, and individual poems do highly individual things. Knowing the past never means being able to interpret new texts with certainty. Symbolism makes things happen, but individual poets and texts determine what will happen and how. How does the following poem both draw and comment on the traditional symbolism of roses?

DOROTHY PARKER
One Perfect Rose

A single flow'r he sent me, since we met.
   All tenderly his messenger he chose;
Deep-hearted, pure, with scented dew still wet—
   One perfect rose.

5 I knew the language of the floweret;
   "My fragile leaves," it said, "his heart enclose."
Love long has taken for his amulet
   One perfect rose.

Why is it no one ever sent me yet
10   One perfect limousine, do you suppose?
Ah no, it's always just my luck to get
   One perfect rose.

                                                                1937

THE SYMBOLIC POEM

Sometimes symbols—traditional or not—become so insistent in the world of a poem that the larger referential world is left almost totally behind. In such cases the symbol is everything, and the poem does not just *use* symbols but becomes a symbolic poem, usually a highly individualized one dependent on a system introduced by the individual poet. Here is one such poem.

WILLIAM BLAKE
The Sick Rose[2]

O rose, thou art sick.
The invisible worm
That flies in the night
In the howling storm

5 Has found out thy bed
Of crimson joy,
And his dark secret love
Does thy life destroy.

1794

William Blake's poem does not seem to be about or refer to a real rose. Rather the poem is about what the rose represents—not in this case something altogether understandable through the traditional meanings of *rose*.

We usually associate the rose with beauty and love, often with sex; and here several key terms have sexual connotations: "worm," "bed," and "crimson joy" (lines 2, 5, 6). The violation of the rose by the worm is the poem's main concern; the violation seems to have involved secrecy, deceit, and "dark" motives (7), and the result is sickness rather than the joy of love. The poem is sad; it involves a sense of hurt and tragedy, nearly of despair. The poem cries out against the misuse of the rose, against its desecration, implying that instead of a healthy joy in sensuality and sexuality, there has been in this case destruction and hurt, perhaps because of misunderstanding, repression, and lack of sensitivity.

But to say so much about this poem we have to extrapolate from other poems by Blake, and we have to introduce information from outside the poem. Fully symbolic poems often require that we thus go beyond the formal procedures of close reading that we have discussed so far. As presented in this poem, the rose is not part of the normal world that we ordinarily see, and it is symbolic in a special sense. The poet does not simply take an object from our everyday world and give it special significance, making it a symbol in the same way that James Dickey does with the leap. In Blake's poem the rose instead seems to belong to its own world, a world made entirely inside the poem or the poet's head. The rose is not referential, or not primarily so. The whole poem is symbolic; it lives in its own world. But what is the rose here a symbol of? In general terms, we can say from what the poem tells us; but we may not be as confident as we can be in the more nearly recognizable world of "The

2. In Renaissance emblem books, the scarab beetle, worm, and rose are closely associated: The beetle feeds on dung, and the smell of the rose is fatal to it.

Leap" or ONE PERFECT ROSE. In THE SICK ROSE, it seems inappropriate to ask the standard questions: What rose? Where? Which worm? What are the particulars here? In the world of this poem worms can fly and may be invisible. We are altogether in a world of meanings that have been formulated according to a special system of knowledge and code of belief. We will feel comfortable and confident in that world only if we read many poems written by the poet (in this case, William Blake) within the same symbolic system.

Negotiation of meanings in symbolic poems can be very difficult indeed. Reading symbolic poems is an advanced skill that depends on knowledge of context, especially the lives and work of authors and the special literary and cultural traditions they draw from. But usually the symbols you will find in poems *are* referential of meanings we all share, and you can readily discover these meanings by carefully studying the poems themselves.

POEMS FOR FURTHER STUDY

JOHN KEATS
Ode to a Nightingale

I

My heart aches, and a drowsy numbness pains
   My sense, as though of hemlock I had drunk,
Or emptied some dull opiate to the drains
   One minute past, and Lethe-wards[3] had sunk:
5 'Tis not through envy of thy happy lot,
   But being too happy in thine happiness,
      That thou, light-wingèd Dryad[4] of the trees,
         In some melodious plot
   Of beechen green, and shadows numberless,
10   Singest of summer in full-throated ease.

II

O, for a draught of vintage! that hath been
   Cooled a long age in the deep-delvèd earth,
Tasting of Flora[5] and the country green,
   Dance, and Provençal song,[6] and sunburnt mirth!
15 O for a beaker full of the warm South,
   Full of the true, the blushful Hippocrene,[7]
      With beaded bubbles winking at the brim,
         And purple-stainèd mouth;
   That I might drink, and leave the world unseen,
20   And with thee fade away into the forest dim:

3. Toward the river of forgetfulness (Lethe) in Hades, the underworld of classical myth.
4. Wood nymph.
5. Roman goddess of flowers.
6. The medieval troubadours of Provence were famous for their love songs.
7. Fountain of the Muses on Mount Helicon, whose waters bring poetic inspiration.

III

Fade far away, dissolve, and quite forget
    What thou among the leaves hast never known,
The weariness, the fever, and the fret
    Here, where men sit and hear each other groan;
25 Where palsy shakes a few, sad, last gray hairs,
    Where youth grows pale, and specter-thin, and dies;
        Where but to think is to be full of sorrow
           And leaden-eyed despairs,
    Where Beauty cannot keep her lustrous eyes,
30   Or new Love pine at them beyond tomorrow.

IV

Away! away! for I will fly to thee,
    Not charioted by Bacchus and his pards,[8]
But on the viewless[9] wings of Poesy,
    Though the dull brain perplexes and retards:
35 Already with thee! tender is the night,
    And haply the Queen-Moon is on her throne,
        Clustered around by all her starry Fays;[1]
           But here there is no light,
    Save what from heaven is with the breezes blown
40   Through verdurous glooms and winding mossy ways.

V

I cannot see what flowers are at my feet,
    Nor what soft incense hangs upon the boughs,
But, in embalmèd[2] darkness, guess each sweet
    Wherewith the seasonable month endows
45 The grass, the thicket, and the fruit-tree wild;
    White hawthorn, and the pastoral eglantine;[3]
        Fast fading violets covered up in leaves;
           And mid-May's eldest child,
    The coming musk-rose, full of dewy wine,
50   The murmurous haunt of flies on summer eves.

VI

Darkling[4] I listen; and, for many a time
    I have been half in love with easeful Death,
Called him soft names in many a musèd rhyme,
    To take into the air my quiet breath;
55 Now more than ever seems it rich to die,
    To cease upon the midnight with no pain,
        While thou art pouring forth thy soul abroad
           In such an ecstasy!

---

8. The Roman god of wine was sometimes portrayed in a chariot drawn by leopards.
9. Invisible.
1. Fairies.
2. Fragrant, aromatic.
3. Sweetbriar or honeysuckle.
4. In the dark.

Still wouldst thou sing, and I have ears in vain—
60   To thy high requiem become a sod.

VII

Thou wast not born for death, immortal Bird!
No hungry generations tread thee down;
The voice I hear this passing night was heard
In ancient days by emperor and clown:
65 Perhaps the selfsame song that found a path
Through the sad heart of Ruth,[5] when, sick for home,
She stood in tears amid the alien corn;
The same that ofttimes hath
Charmed magic casements, opening on the foam
70   Of perilous seas, in faery lands forlorn.

VIII

Forlorn! the very word is like a bell
To toll me back from thee to my sole self!
Adieu! the fancy cannot cheat so well
As she is famed to do, deceiving elf.
75 Adieu! adieu! thy plaintive anthem fades
Past the near meadows, over the still stream,
Up the hillside; and now 'tis buried deep
In the next valley-glades:
Was it a vision, or a waking dream?
80   Fled is that music:—Do I wake or sleep?

May 1819   1819

• Since birds obviously die, just as humans do, what might the speaker mean
  when he declares, "Thou wast not born for death, immortal Bird!" (line 61)?
  That is, how, according to the poem, is the bird "immortal" in a way the
  speaker isn't? How might this help you begin to understand what the bird
  comes to symbolize in the poem?

ROBERT FROST
The Road Not Taken

Two roads diverged in a yellow wood,
And sorry I could not travel both
And be one traveler, long I stood
And looked down one as far as I could
5 To where it bent in the undergrowth;

Then took the other, as just as fair,
And having perhaps the better claim,
Because it was grassy and wanted wear;
Though as for that the passing there
10 Had worn them really about the same,

5. Virtuous Moabite widow who, according to the Old Testament book of Ruth, left her own country to
accompany her mother-in-law, Naomi, back to Naomi's native land. She supported herself as a gleaner.

And both that morning equally lay
In leaves no step had trodden black.
Oh, I kept the first for another day!
Yet knowing how way leads on to way,
15 I doubted if I should ever come back.

I shall be telling this with a sigh
Somewhere ages and ages hence:
Two roads diverged in a wood, and I—
I took the one less traveled by,
20 And that has made all the difference.

1916

• What sort of choices might the fork in the road represent? In these terms,
what seems most important about the description of the roads? Why and
how might it matter that the poem's famous last lines (about the great "difference" [line 20] it made to take the road "less traveled by" [19]) are framed
as something the speaker imagines saying "with a sigh" at some point in the
distant future (16)?

PAUL LAURENCE DUNBAR

Sympathy

I know what the caged bird feels, alas!
    When the sun is bright on the upland slopes;
When the wind stirs soft through the springing grass,
And the river flows like a stream of glass;
5   When the first bird sings and the first bud opens,
And the faint perfume from its chalice steals—
I know what the caged bird feels!

I know why the caged bird beats his wing
    Till its blood is red on the cruel bars;
10 For he must fly back to his perch and cling
When he fain[6] would be on the bough a-swing;
    And a pain still throbs in the old, old scars
And they pulse again with a keener sting—
I know why he beats his wing!

15 I know why the caged bird sings, ah me,
    When his wing is bruised and his bosom sore,—
When he beats his bars and he would be free;
It is not a carol of joy or glee,
    But a prayer that he sends from his heart's deep core,
20 But a plea, that upward to Heaven he flings—
I know why the caged bird sings!

1893

6. Gladly.

• How might your interpretation of this poem's symbolism change depending
  on whether or not you consider the date of its publication and/or the fact
  that its author was African American?

HOWARD NEMEROV
The Vacuum

The house is so quiet now
The vacuum cleaner sulks in the corner closet,
Its bag limp as a stopped lung, its mouth
Grinning into the floor, maybe at my
5   Slovenly life, my dog-dead youth.

I've lived this way long enough,
But when my old woman died her soul
Went into that vacuum cleaner, and I can't bear
To see the bag swell like a belly, eating the dust
10 And the woolen mice, and begin to howl

Because there is old filth everywhere
She used to crawl, in the corner and under the stair.
I know now how life is cheap as dirt,
And still the hungry, angry heart
15 Hangs on and howls, biting at air.

1955

• What does the vacuum come to symbolize? How might the poem play on
  the various meanings of the word "vacuum"?

ADRIENNE RICH
Diving into the Wreck

First having read the book of myths,
and loaded the camera,
and checked the edge of the knife-blade,
I put on
5   the body-armor of black rubber
the absurd flippers
the grave and awkward mask.
I am having to do this
not like Cousteau[7] with his
10 assiduous team
aboard the sun-flooded schooner
but here alone.

There is a ladder.
The ladder is always there

---

7. Jacques-Yves Cousteau (1910–97), French writer and underwater explorer.

15 hanging innocently
    close to the side of the schooner.
    We know what it is for,
    we who have used it.
    Otherwise
20 it's a piece of maritime floss
    some sundry equipment.

    I go down.
    Rung after rung and still
    the oxygen immerses me
25 the blue light
    the clear atoms
    of our human air.
    I go down.
    My flippers cripple me,
30 I crawl like an insect down the ladder
    and there is no one
    to tell me when the ocean
    will begin.

    First the air is blue and then
35 it is bluer and then green and then
    black I am blacking out and yet
    my mask is powerful
    it pumps my blood with power
    the sea is another story
40 the sea is not a question of power
    I have to learn alone
    to turn my body without force
    in the deep element.

    And now: it is easy to forget
45 what I came for
    among so many who have always
    lived here
    swaying their crenellated fans
    between the reefs
50 and besides
    you breathe differently down here.

    I came to explore the wreck.
    The words are purposes.
    The words are maps.
55 I came to see the damage that was done
    and the treasures that prevail.
    I stroke the beam of my lamp
    slowly along the flank
    of something more permanent
60 than fish or weed

    the thing I came for:
    the wreck and not the story of the wreck

the thing itself and not the myth
the drowned face always staring
65 toward the sun
the evidence of damage
worn by salt and sway into this threadbare beauty
the ribs of the disaster
curving their assertion
70 among the tentative haunters.

This is the place.
And I am here, the mermaid whose dark hair
streams black, the merman in his armored body
We circle silently
75 about the wreck
we dive into the hold.
I am she: I am he

whose drowned face sleeps with open eyes
whose breasts still bear the stress
80 whose silver, copper, vermeil cargo lies
obscurely inside barrels
half-wedged and left to rot
we are the half-destroyed instruments
that once held to a course
85 the water-eaten log
the fouled compass

We are, I am, you are
by cowardice or courage
the one who find our way
90 back to this scene
carrying a knife, a camera
a book of myths
in which
our names do not appear.

1972   1973

- What word or phrase first signals that DIVING INTO THE WRECK is to be
  understood symbolically, not literally? What are some possible symbolic
  interpretations of the wreck and the dive?

ADA LIMÓN
The Leash

After the birthing of bombs of forks and fear,
the frantic automatic weapons unleashed,
the spray of bullets into a crowd holding hands,
that brute sky opening in a slate-metal maw
5 that swallows only the unsayable in each of us, what's
left? Even the hidden nowhere river is poisoned

orange and acidic by a coal mine. How can
you not fear humanity, want to lick the creek
bottom dry, to suck the deadly water up into
10 your own lungs, like venom? Reader, I want to
say: *Don't die.* Even when silvery fish after fish
comes back belly up, and the country plummets
into a crepitating crater of hatred, isn't there still
something singing? The truth is: I don't know.
15 But sometimes I swear I hear it, the wound closing
like a rusted-over garage door, and I can still move
my living limbs into the world without too much
pain, can still marvel at how the dog runs straight
toward the pickup trucks breaknecking down
20 the road, because she thinks she loves them,
because she's sure, without a doubt, that the loud
roaring things will love her back, her soft small self
alive with desire to share her goddamn enthusiasm,
until I yank the leash back to save her because
25 I want her to survive forever. *Don't die,* I say,
and we decide to walk for a bit longer, starlings
high and fevered above us, winter coming to lay
her cold corpse down upon this little plot of earth.
Perhaps we are always hurtling our bodies toward
30 the thing that will obliterate us, begging for love
from the speeding passage of time, and so maybe,
like the dog obedient at my heels, we can walk together
peacefully, at least until the next truck comes.

2018

- How might the leash or the dog's actions come to function as symbols, and
  for what?

SUGGESTIONS FOR WRITING

1. Consider the poems about roses in this chapter, and write a paragraph about each poem
   showing how it establishes specific symbolism for the rose. What generalizations can
   you draw about the rose's traditional meanings in poetry? If you can, find other poems
   about roses outside of this anthology to determine if your generalizations still apply.
2. Is there a "correct" interpretation of Adrienne Rich's DIVING INTO THE WRECK? If one
   interpretation seems to fit all the particulars of the poem, does that mean it's better
   than other possible interpretations? Write an essay in which you explore the poem's
   symbolism and argue for or against the idea that there is a single best way to understand its symbolism. Can ambiguity serve a poet's purpose, or does it ultimately under-
   cut a poem's meaning and significance?
3. Choose any poem in this book in which an object or action seems to function as a
   symbol. Write an essay exploring that symbol's various possible meanings.

18 | THE SOUNDS OF POETRY

Much of what happens in a poem happens in your mind's eye, but some of it happens in your "mind's ear" and in your voice. Poems are full of meaningful sounds and silences as well as words and sentences. Besides choosing words for their meanings, poets choose words because they have certain sounds, and poems use sound effects to create a mood or establish a tone, just as films do.

Historically, poetry began as an oral phenomenon. Early bards in many cultures chanted or recited their verses, often accompanied by a musical instrument of some kind, and poetry remains a vocal art, dependent on the human voice. Often poems that seem very difficult when looked at silently come alive when read aloud, turned into sound. The music and rhythms become clearer, and saying the words or hearing them spoken is very good practice for learning to hear in your mind's ear when you read silently.

RHYME

Rhyme—repetition or correspondence of the terminal sounds of words—is perhaps the single most familiar sound device poets use, though of course not all poems use it. Early English poetry, in fact, used **alliteration**, instead of rhyming words at the end of the poetic lines, to balance the first and second half of each line, and much, if not most, modern poetry is written in **free verse**—that is, without rhyme or regular **meter**. From the later Middle Ages until the twentieth century, however, the music of rhyme was central to both the sound and the formal conception of most poems in the Western world. Because poetry was originally an oral art (many poems were only later written down, if at all), various kinds of memory devices (sometimes called *mnemonic devices*) were built into poems to help reciters remember them. Rhyme was one such device, and most people still find it easier to memorize poetry that rhymes. The simple pleasure of hearing familiar sounds repeated at regular intervals may help account for the traditional popularity of rhyme. Rhyme also gives poetry a special aural quality. According to the established taste in eras before our own, there was a decorum or proper behavior in poetry as in other things: A poem, it was thought, should not in any way be mistaken for prose, which was considered artistically inferior to poetry and primarily utilitarian.

Some English poets (especially in the Renaissance) did experiment—often very successfully—with unrhymed verse, but the cultural pressure for rhyme was almost constant. Why? Custom, combined with the sense of proper decorum, accounted in part for the assumption that rhyme was necessary to poetry, but so, too, did a sense that poetry was an imitation of larger relationships in the universe. It seemed natural to use rhyme to represent or re-create a sense of pattern, harmony, correspondence, symmetry, and order. The sounds of poetry were thus, poets reasoned, reminders of cosmic harmony, of the music of the spheres that animated all creation. In a modern world increasingly perceived as fragmented and chaotic, there may be less of a tendency to assume or assert a sense of harmony and symmetry. It would be too simple to say that rhyme in a poem necessarily means that the poet has a firm sense of cosmic order or that an unrhymed poem testifies to chaos. But the cultural assumptions of different times have influenced the expectations and practices of both poets and readers.

Rhyme also provides a kind of discipline for the poet, a way of harnessing poetic talents and keeping a rein on the imagination. Robert Frost declared writing free verse pointless, like playing tennis without a net. Frost speaks for many traditional (or so-called *formalist* or *neo-formalist*) poets in suggesting that writing good poetry requires discipline and great care with formal elements such as rhyme or rhythm. Other poets have chosen to play by new rules or to invent their own, preferring the sparer tones that unrhymed poetry provides. Such poets of course still care about the sounds of their poetry, but they may replace rhyme with other aural devices or mix regular rhyme and meter with more flexible lines, paying tribute to tradition as well as the unexpectedness of experience.

End Rhyme and Rhyme Scheme

When we think of rhyme in poetry, we likely think first of the most common type—*end rhyme*, which occurs when the last words in two or more lines of a poem rhyme with each other. When we speak of a poem's *rhyme scheme*, we refer to its particular pattern of end rhymes. To indicate rhyme scheme, we conventionally assign a different letter of the alphabet to each rhyme sound, reusing the same letter every time the same terminal sound repeats in later lines. Here, for example, are the first two stanzas of Thomas Hardy's THE RUINED MAID, which have a rhyme scheme of *aabb, ccbb* thanks to the way each stanza ends with the very same (long *e*) sound:

> "O 'Melia, my dear, this does everything crown!   *a*
> Who could have supposed I should meet you in Town?   *a*
> And whence such fair garments, such prosperi-ty?"—   *b*
> "O didn't you know I'd been ruined?" said she.   *b*
>
> —"You left us in tatters, without shoes or socks,   *c*
> Tired of digging potatoes, and spudding up docks;   *c*
> And now you've gay bracelets and bright feathers three!"—   *b*
> "Yes: that's how we dress when we're ruined," said she.   *b*

Since any two adjacent lines that rhyme form a **couplet**, we could also or instead describe "The Ruined Maid" as a poem comprised entirely of rhyming couplets.

Internal, Slant, and Eye Rhyme

Though end rhyme alone determines a poem's rhyme scheme, it isn't the only kind: *Internal rhyme* occurs when a word within (and thus *internal to*) a line rhymes with another word in the same or adjacent lines, as in the following lines from Samuel Taylor Coleridge's "The Rime of the Ancient Mariner" (internal rhyming words appear in italics):

> In mist or *cloud*, on mast or *shroud*,
> It perched for vespers nine;
> Whiles all the *night*, through fog-smoke *white*,
> Glimmered the *white* moonshine.

Whether end or internal, rhymes differ, too, in type. Technically, rhyme (or what is sometimes called *perfect, true,* or *full rhyme*) requires that words share consonants and vowel sounds, as do "cloud" and "shroud," "night" and "white." When words share one but not the other, we have a version of what's variously called *off, half, near,* or *slant rhyme*—that is, a rhyme slightly "off" or only approximate. (The words *all* and *bowl,* for example, share consonant sounds, but their vowel sounds differ, and the opposite is true of *dark* and *heart*.) Another device more common in poetry written since the later nineteenth century, and (like internal rhyme) ubiquitous in hip-hop lyrics, slant rhyme can produce a variety of effects, all deriving from the poem's failure to provide the sounds our ears expect, whether our brains know it or not. Much the same in reverse is true of *eye rhyme*: As much a visual as an aural device, it occurs, as its name suggests, when words *look* like they should rhyme, but don't, as with *bear* and *ear, Yeats* and *Keats.*

OTHER SOUND DEVICES

Sometimes the sounds in poems just provide special effects, rather like a musical score behind a film, setting the mood and getting us into an appropriate frame of mind. But often sound and meaning go hand in hand, and the poet finds words whose sounds echo the action or make a point by stressing the relationship among words and the things they signify.

A single word that captures or approximates the sound of what it describes, such as *splash* or *squish* or *murmur,* is an *onomatopoeic* word, and the device itself is **onomatopoeia**.

But poets can also turn sound into sense by choosing and ordering words so as to create distinctive, meaningful aural patterns. Rhyme is one such device, but four other important ones are

- **alliteration**—the repetition of usually initial consonant sounds through a sequence of words, as in "The *b*ig-ass *b*ees are *b*ack" (from Ada Limón's DANDELION INSOMNIA) or "The *W*icked *W*itch of the *W*est";
- **consonance**—the repetition of consonant sounds, especially at the end of words or syllables, without the correspondence of vowel sounds necessary to create rhyme, as in "Abstruser musings" (from Coleridge's FROST AT MIDNIGHT) or "That was a stroke of luck";
- **assonance**—the repetition of vowel sounds in a sequence of words with different endings, as in "*E*ons from *e*ven our own moon, w*e*'ll drift" (from Tracy K. Smith's SCI-FI); and
- **anaphora**—the repetition of the same word or series of words at or near the beginning of successive sentences or clauses, as in "*The words are* purposes. *The words are* maps" (from Adrienne Rich's DIVING INTO THE WRECK). Like the other sound devices here, this one is a favorite of speechwriters as well as poets, as demonstrated by Pat Buchanan's address to the 1992 Republican National Convention: "That's change, all right. But that's *not the kind of change* America needs. It's *not the kind of change* America

wants. And it's *not the kind of change* we can abide in a nation we still call 'God's country.'"

Used effectively, such devices are powerful tools, generating meaning, as well as creating mood or simply providing emphasis. A case in point is the following excerpt from the world's most famous *mock epic*, which describes a scene that may seem at once foreign and familiar to you: A young woman (or "nymph," line 125) sits at a mirrored dressing table (or "toilet," 123), littered with cosmetics and other accoutrements, and, with the help of her lady's maid, prepares herself for the day ahead—fixing her hair, applying makeup, and so on. Given the way these activities are characterized as a distinctly twisted religious ritual (in lines 123–30), what is the effect and significance of alliteration, particularly in line 140 (which here appears in bold)?

ALEXANDER POPE
From The Rape of the Lock

123   And now, unveil'd, the toilet stands displayed,
      Each silver vase in mystic order laid.
125 First, rob'd in white, the nymph intent adores
      With head uncover'd, the cosmetic pow'rs.
      A heav'nly image in the glass appears,
      To that she bends, to that her eyes she rears;
      Th' inferior priestess,[1] at her altar's side,
130 Trembling, begins the sacred rites of pride.
      Unnumber'd treasures ope at once, and here
      The various off'rings of the world appear;
      From each she nicely culls with curious[2] toil,
      And decks the goddess with the glitt'ring spoil.
135 This casket India's glowing gems unlocks,
      And all Arabia breathes from yonder box.
      The tortoise here and elephant unite,
      Transform'd to combs, the speckled and the white.[3]
      Here files of pins extend their shining rows,
140 **Puffs, powders, patches, bibles, billet-doux.**[4]
      Now awful[5] beauty puts on all its arms;
      The fair each moment rises in her charms,
      Repairs her smiles, awakens ev'ry grace,
      And calls forth all the wonders of her face

1712, 1714

1. That is, the lady's maid.
2. Strange, unusual.
3. The hair combs, in other words, are made from tortoiseshell (which is "speckled") and ivory from an elephant's tusk (which is "white").
4. Love letter (French). *Patches*: tiny pieces of silk or plaster worn to hide a blemish or heighten one's beauty.
5. Awe-inspiring.

SOUND POEMS

The following poems place especially heavy emphasis on sound and aural patterning.
As you read them, try to identify which sound devices they use and with what effects.

HELEN CHASIN
The Word *Plum*

The word *plum* is delicious

pout and push, luxury of
self-love, and savoring murmur

full in the mouth and falling
5   like fruit

taut skin
pierced, bitten, provoked into
juice, and tart flesh

question
10   and reply, lip and tongue
of pleasure.

1968

ALEXANDER POPE
Sound and Sense[6]

337   But most by numbers[7] judge a poet's song,
       And smooth or rough, with them, is right or wrong;
       In the bright muse though thousand charms conspire,[8]
340   Her voice is all these tuneful fools admire,
       Who haunt Parnassus[9] but to please their ear,
       Not mend their minds; as some to church repair,
       Not for the doctrine, but the music there.
       These, equal syllables[1] alone require,
345   Though oft the ear the open vowels tire,
       While expletives[2] their feeble aid do join,
       And ten low words oft creep in one dull line,
       While they ring round the same unvaried chimes,
       With sure returns of still expected rhymes.

6. From *An Essay on Criticism*, Pope's poem on the art of poetry and the problems of literary criticism.
The passage excerpted here follows a discussion of several common weaknesses of critics—failure to
regard an author's intention, for example, or overemphasis on clever metaphors and ornate style.
7. Meter, rhythm, sound.
8. Unite.
9. Mountain in Greece, traditionally associated with the Muses and considered the seat of poetry and
music.
1. Regular accents.
2. Filler words, such as "do."

350 Where'er you find "the cooling western breeze,"
    In the next line, it "whispers through the trees";
    If crystal streams "with pleasing murmurs creep,"
    The reader's threatened (not in vain) with "sleep."
    Then, at the last and only couplet fraught
355 With some unmeaning thing they call a thought,
    A needless Alexandrine[3] ends the song,
    That, like a wounded snake, drags its slow length along.
    Leave such to tune their own dull rhymes, and know
    What's roundly smooth, or languishingly slow;
360 And praise the easy vigor of a line,
    Where Denham's strength and Waller's[4] sweetness join.
    True ease in writing comes from art, not chance,
    As those move easiest who have learned to dance.
    'Tis not enough no harshness gives offense,
365 The sound must seem an echo to the sense:
    Soft is the strain when Zephyr[5] gently blows,
    And the smooth stream in smoother numbers flows;
    But when loud surges lash the sounding shore,
    The hoarse, rough verse should like the torrent roar.
370 When Ajax[6] strives, some rock's vast weight to throw,
    The line too labors, and the words move slow;
    Not so, when swift Camilla[7] scours the plain,
    Flies o'er th' unbending corn, and skims along the main.
    Hear how Timotheus'[8] varied lays surprise,
375 And bid alternate passions fall and rise!
    While, at each change, the son of Libyan Jove[9]
    Now burns with glory, and then melts with love;
    Now his fierce eyes with sparkling fury glow,
    Now sighs steal out, and tears begin to flow:
380 Persians and Greeks like turns of nature[1] found,
    And the world's victor stood subdued by sound!
    The pow'r of music all our hearts allow,
    And what Timotheus was, is DRYDEN now.

                                                    1711

Helen Chasin's poem THE WORD *PLUM* savors the sounds of the word as well as
the taste and feel of the fruit itself. It is almost as if the poem is tasting the sounds
and rolling them slowly on the tongue. The alliterative second and third lines even

3. Line of six metrical feet, sometimes used in pentameter poems to vary the pace mechanically. Line
357 is an alexandrine.
4. Sir John Denham and Edmund Waller, seventeenth-century poets credited with perfecting the
heroic couplet.
5. The west wind.
6. Greek hero of the Trojan War, noted for his strength.
7. A woman warrior in Virgil's *Aeneid*.
8. Court musician of Alexander the Great, celebrated in a famous poem by John Dryden (see line 383)
for the power of his music over Alexander's emotions.
9. In Greek tradition, the chief god of any people was often given the name Zeus (Jove), and the chief
god of Libya (the Greek name for all of Africa) was called Zeus Ammon. Alexander visited his oracle
and was proclaimed son of the god.
1. Similar alternations of emotion.

replicate the *p*, *l*, *uh*, and *m* sounds of the word while imitating the squishy sounds of eating the fruit. Words like "delicious" and "luxury" sound juicy, and other words, such as "murmur," imitate sounds of satisfaction and pleasure. Even the process of eating is in part re-created aurally. The tight, clipped sounds of "taut skin / pierced" (lines 6–7) suggest the way teeth sharply break the skin and slice quickly into the soft flesh of a plum, and the words describing the tartness ("provoked," "question," 7, 9) force the lips to pucker and the tongue and palate to meet and hold, as if the mouth were savoring a tart fruit. The poet is having fun here refashioning the sensual appeal of a plum, teasing the sounds and meanings out of available words. The words must mean something appropriate and describe something accurately first of all, of course, but when they also imitate the sounds and feel of the process they describe, they do double duty.

Written in a very different era and style, Pope's SOUND AND SENSE uses a number of echoic or onomatopoeic words. In some lines pleasant and unpleasant consonant sounds underline a particular point or emphasize a mood. When the poet talks about a particular weakness in poetry, he illustrates it at the same time—by using open vowels (line 345), expletives (346), monosyllabic words (347), predictable rhymes (350–53), or long, slow lines (357). He similarly illustrates the good qualities of poetry as well (360, for example). But the main effects of the passage come from an interaction of several ingenious strategies at once. In lines 339 and 340, for example, Pope produces complex sound effects in addition to the harmony of a rhyming couplet ("conspire," "admire"). Assonance echoes in the *oo* vowel sounds in "muse," "tuneful," and "fools"; alliteration repeats consonants in "*r*ight or *wr*ong" and "tune*ful fool*s." Ironically, the *muse*-ical voice here is a bit out of tune to those who have good poetic taste: Pope intends the *r* and *f* sounds to feel both cute and awkward, as a comment on people who only want easy listening and miss poetry's other "charms," including its meaning (compared to the "doctrine" that is the real purpose of a church service, in line 343).

With a similar technique of demonstrating principles of poetic style and taste, the pace of lines 347, 357, and 359 is controlled by clashing consonant sounds as well as long vowels. Line 347 seems much longer than it is because almost every one-syllable word ends in a consonant that refuses to blend with the beginning of the next word, making the words hard to say without distinct, awkward pauses between them. In lines 357 and 359, long vowels such as those in "wounded," "snake," "slow," "along," "roundly," and "smooth" slow down the pace, and awkward, hard-to-pronounce consonants are again juxtaposed. The commas also provide nearly full stops in the middle of these lines to slow us down still more. Similarly, the harsh lashing of the shore in lines 368–69 is accomplished partly by onomatopoeia and partly by the dominance of rough consonants in line 369. (In Pope's time, the English *r* was still trilled gruffly so that it could be made to sound extremely *rrr*ough and har*rr*sh.) Almost every line in this passage demonstrates how to make sound echo sense.

POETIC METER

We can thank the ancient Greeks for systematizing an understanding of meter and providing a vocabulary (including the words *rhythm* and *meter*) that enables us to discuss the art of poetry. *Meter* comes from a Greek word meaning "measure": What we measure in the English language are the patterns of stressed (or accented) syllables that occur naturally when we speak, and, just as when we measure length, the unit we use in measuring poetry is the **foot**. Most traditional poetry in English uses the accentual-syllabic form of meter—meaning that its rhythmic pattern is based on both a set number of syllables per line and a regular pattern of accents in each line. Not all poems have a regular metrical pattern, and not all metered poems follow only one pattern throughout. But like everyday speech, the language of poetry always has *some* accents (as in this italic emphasis on "some"), and poets arrange that rhythm for effect. Thus in nonmetrical as well as metrical poetry, a reader should "listen" for patterns of stress.

The Basic Metrical Feet of Poetry in English

iamb: an unstressed or unaccented syllable followed by a stressed or accented one ("she wént," "belíeve"). This meter is called *iambic*.

trochee: a stressed syllable followed by an unstressed one ("méter," "Hómer"). This meter is called *trochaic*.

anapest: two unstressed syllables followed by a stressed one ("comprehénd," "after yóu"). This meter is called *anapestic*.

dactyl: a stressed syllable followed by two unstressed ones ("róundabout," "dínnertime"). This meter is called *dactylic*.

rising or falling: the above feet either begin or end with the stressed syllable, as if they lose or gain momentum or "height." Hence iambic and anapestic are called rising meters, and trochaic and dactylic are called falling meters.

Other Kinds of Feet

spondee: two stressed syllables. Spondaic feet vary or interrupt the prevailing rhythm, emphasizing a syllable that we would expect to be unstressed ("Lást cáll," "Dón't gó").

pyrrhic: two unstressed syllables. Pyrrhic feet similarly interrupt the expected rising or falling beats, placing an unstressed syllable where we expect an emphasis ("ŭntŏ," "ĭs ă").

Spondees and pyrrhic feet depend on prevailing meter and usually appear singly or only a few times in a row. It is difficult to imagine (or to write or speak) a line or sentence that either has no unstressed syllables—a constant strong beat (spondaic)—or lacks stressed syllables—a rippling monotone (pyrrhic).

Because the concept of meter derives from poetic traditions in Greek and Latin that counted syllables rather than accents, other possible combinations of syllables acquired names, for instance, *amphibrach* (unstressed, stressed, unstressed—noted by Coleridge in his demonstration of meter, METRICAL FEET, below). But since most meter in poetry in English depends on accents rather than the number of syllables, the terms above cover most of the variations that you will encounter.

Counting Feet, or Meter

A line of poetry is subdivided into feet in order to "measure" its meter. The terms are easy enough to understand if you recall geometry or other numeric terminology. Remember that this is a count of the number *not* of syllables but of stresses; thus, for example, monometer could have two or three syllables per line.

monometer:	one foot
dimeter:	two feet
trimeter:	three feet
tetrameter:	four feet
pentameter:	five feet
hexameter:	six feet
heptameter:	seven feet
octameter:	eight feet

Counting the number of feet—that is, the number of accents, stresses, or strong beats per line—helps you identify the *kind* of feet in the line. Thus the terms are combined: *Iambic pentameter* has five iambs per line; *trochaic tetrameter* has four trochees per line, and so on.

Scansion

Scansion is the technique of listening to and marking stressed and unstressed syllables, counting the syllables and feet. Often, you will need to scan several lines before you can be sure of the "controlling" metrical pattern or "base meter" of a poem.

In the following poem, Samuel Taylor Coleridge playfully names and illustrates many types of meter. By marking syllables himself as stressed or unstressed, he also illustrates how scansion works.

SAMUEL TAYLOR COLERIDGE
Metrical Feet

Lesson for a Boy[2]

Trōchĕe trīps frŏm lōng tŏ shōrt;[3]
From long to long in solemn sort
Slōw Spōndēe stālks; strŏng fŏot! yet ill able
Ēvĕr tŏ cōme ŭp wĭth Dāctўl trĭsўllăblĕ.
5 Ĭāmbĭcs mārch frŏm shōrt tŏ lōng—
With ă leāp ănd ă bōund thĕ swĭft Ānăpĕsts thrōng;
One syllable long, with one short at each side,
Ămphībrăchўs hāstes wĭth ă stātelў stride—
Fīrst ănd lāst bēĭng lōng, mĭddlĕ shōrt, Ămphĭmācer
10 Strīkes hĭs thūndērĭng hōofs līke ă prōud hĭgh-brĕd Rācer.
If Derwent be innocent, steady, and wise,
And delight in the things of earth, water, and skies;
Tender warmth at his heart, with these meters to show it,
With sound sense in his brains, may make Derwent a poet—
15 May crown him with fame, and must win him the love
Of his father on earth and his Father above.
　　　　　My dear, dear child!

2. Written originally for Coleridge's son Hartley, the poem was later adapted for his younger son, Derwent.
3. Long and short marks over syllables are Coleridge's.

Could you stand upon Skiddaw,[4] you would not from its whole ridge
See a man who so loves you as your fond s. t. coleridge.

                                                                    1806

Hearing a poem properly involves practice—listening to others read poetry and especially listening to yourself as you read poems aloud. Your dictionary will show you the stresses for every word of more than one syllable, and the governing stress of individual words will largely control the patterns in a line: If you read a line for its sense (almost as if it were prose), you will usually see the line's basic pattern. But single-syllable words can be a challenge because they may or may not be stressed, depending on their syntactic function and the full meaning of the sentence. Normally, important functional words, such as one-syllable nouns and verbs, are stressed (as in normal conversation or in prose), while conjunctions (such as *and* or *but*), prepositions (such as *on* or *with*), and articles (such as *an* or *the*) are unstressed.

Here are the first two lines of Alexander Pope's "Sound and Sense," marked to show the stressed syllables:

But móst | by núm- | bers júdge | a pó- | et's sóng,
And smóoth | or róugh, | with thém, | is ríght | or wróng.

These lines, like so many in English literature, provide an example of *iambic pentameter*—that is, each line consists of five iambic feet. Notice that there is nothing forced or artificial in the sound of these lines; the words flow easily. In fact, linguists contend that English is naturally iambic, and even the most ordinary, "unpoetic" utterances often fall into this pattern: "Please tell me if you've heard this one before." "They said she had a certain way with words." "The baseball game was televised at nine."

Here are a few more examples of various meters.

iambic pentameter: "In sé- | quent tóil | all fór- | wards dó | conténd" (William Shakespeare, LIKE AS THE WAVES . . .)
trochaic octameter: "Ónce u- | pón a | mídnight | dréary, | whíle I | póndered, | wéak and | wéary" (Edgar Allan Poe, THE RAVEN)
anapestic tetrameter: "There are mán- | y who sáy | that a dóg | has his dáy" (Dylan Thomas)

Although scanning lines of poetry by reading them aloud, marking syllables as unstressed or stressed, and adding up feet may seem like a counting game that has little to do with poetry's meaning, it is an important way to understand the sound effects of a poem. Like different styles of music, different meters tend to express different moods or to suit different themes. When you know the basic meter of a poem, you are more alert to subtle variations in the pattern. Poets avoid the predictable or the lulling by using certain "change-ups" in the dominant meter or line length, such as substitution of a different foot (e.g., a trochee or spondee instead of an iamb); **caesura**, a short pause within a line often signaled by punctuation; or **enjambment**, extending the end of the grammatical sentence beyond the end of the poetic line.

Notice that the following example is perfectly regular dactylic hexameter until the final foot, a trochee. Also notice that Longfellow has placed a caesura within a long line.

---

4. Mountain in the lake country of northern England (where Coleridge lived in his early years), near the town of Derwent.

"Thís is the | fórest pri- | méval. The | múrmuring | pínes and the | hémlocks" (Henry Wadsworth Longfellow, *Evangeline*)

Substitution of one metrical foot for another—to accommodate idioms and conversational habits or to create a special effect—is quite common, especially in the first foot of a line. Shakespeare often begins an iambic line with a trochee:

Líke as | the wáves | make towárds | the péb- | bled shóre

Or consider this line from John Milton's *Paradise Lost*, a poem written mainly in iambic pentameter:

Rócks, cáves, | lákes, féns, | bógs, déns, | and Shádes | of Déath

Here Milton substitutes three spondees for the first three iambs in a pentameter line. John Dryden's "To the Memory of Mr. Oldham" arguably begins with two spondees, a pyrrhic, and an iamb before settling into a regular iambic pentameter:

Fárewéll, | tóo lít | tle, and | tóo láte | ly knówn

As Dryden's poem shows, meter does leave room for discussion; some readers might read the line above as iambic throughout, and others might read the last three feet as iambic: The natural emphasis on the first word after the caesura, "and," could make the predictable word "too" unstressed. The way you actually read a line, once you have "heard" the basic rhythm, is influenced by two factors: normal pronunciation and prose sense (on the one hand) and the predominant pattern of the poem (on the other). Since these two forces are constantly in tension and are sometimes contradictory, you can almost never fully predict the actual reading of a line, and good reading aloud (like every other art) depends less on formula than on subtlety and flexibility. And, again, very good readers sometimes disagree about whether or not to stress certain syllables. We have noted the use of substitution, and many poems since around 1900 have taken liberties with meter and rhyme. Some poets (such as Marianne Moore) have favored counting syllables rather than accents. Even more widespread is free verse, which does without any governing pattern of stresses or line lengths.

Scansion: An Exercise

Each of the following poems is written in a different meter. Using the terms defined in "Poetic Meter" (on pp. 931–33), as well as in Coleridge's poem "Metrical Feet," pair the following poems with their corresponding meters (e.g., iambic pentameter). (The answers are on p. 937.)

1. ANONYMOUS
There was a young girl from St. Paul

There was a young girl from St. Paul,
Wore a newspaper-dress to a ball.
  The dress caught on fire

And burned her entire
5 Front page, sporting section and all.

(Note that this poem is a **limerick** and uses a meter common to this
subgenre.)

2. ALFRED, LORD TENNYSON
From The Charge of the Light Brigade[5]

1.

Half a league, half a league,
    Half a league onward,
All in the valley of Death
    Rode the six hundred.
5 "Forward, the Light Brigade!
"Charge for the guns!" he said:
Into the valley of Death
    Rode the six hundred.

2.

"Forward, the Light Brigade!"
10 Was there a man dismay'd?
Not tho' the soldier knew
    Someone had blunder'd:
Theirs not to make reply,
Theirs not to reason why,
15 Theirs but to do and die:
Into the valley of Death
    Rode the six hundred.

1854

3. JANE TAYLOR
The Star

'Twinkle, twinkle, little star,
How I wonder what you are!
Up above the world so high,
Like a diamond in the sky.

5 When the blazing sun is gone,
When he nothing shines upon,

---

5. On October 25, 1854—during the Crimean War—miscommunication among commanders led a
British cavalry troop to charge directly into a Russian artillery assault, leading to heavy casualties
and an ignominious defeat.

Then you show your little light,
Twinkle, twinkle, all the night.

Then the trav'ller in the dark,
10 Thanks you for your tiny spark;
He could not see which way to go,
If you did not twinkle so.

In the dark blue sky you keep,
And often through my curtains peep,
15 For you never shut your eye
Till the sun is in the sky.

As your bright and tiny spark
Lights the trav'ller in the dark,
Though I know not what you are,
20 Twinkle, twinkle, little star.

1806

4. PHILLIS WHEATLEY
An Hymn to the Evening

Soon as the sun forsook the eastern main
The peals of thunder shook the heav'nly plain;
Majestic grandeur! From zephyrs wing,
Exhales the incense of the blooming spring.
5 Soft purl the streams, the birds renew their notes,
And through the air their mingled music floats
Through all the heav'ns what beauteous dyes are spread,
But the west glories in the deepest red;
So may our breasts with ev'ry virtue glow,
10   The living temples of our God below!

Filled with the praise of him who gives the light,
And draws the sable curtains of the night,
Let placid slumbers sooth each weary mind,
At morn to wake more heav'nly, more refin'd,
15 So shall the labours of the day begin
More pure, more guarded from the snares of sin.

Night's leaden sceptre seals my drowsy eyes,
Then cease, my song, till fair *Aurora*[6] rise.

1773

ANSWERS TO SCANSION EXERCISE: 1. anapestic trimeter (lines 1, 2, and 5) and dimeter
(3–4), 2. dactylic dimeter, 3. trocaic tetrameter, 4. iambic pentameter

6. Goddess of dawn.

Sound and Sense: A Comparative Exercise

To get a vivid sense of the difference sound can make to the tone and meaning of a poem—and just how you can *use* what you've learned about meter, rhyme, and other sound devices—try comparing the two following poems, both inspired by World War I (1914–18). The first is the most famous of several poems originally published in the British newspaper the *Daily Mail* by Jessie Pope (1868–1941), an English journalist famous, before the war, as a writer of light verse. The second poem is the work of Wilfred Owen (1893–1918), an aspiring English poet who voluntarily enlisted in 1915 (the same year Pope's poem appeared) and, from January 1917, served as an officer on the French front. Begun some nine months later, during Owen's hospitalization for shell shock, and originally entitled "To Jessie Pope," his poem is in some ways as much about traditional poetic representations of war as it is about war itself.

As you read the two poems, pay careful attention to how each uses all of the various sound devices discussed in this chapter, particularly meter and rhyme. How precisely do such sound effects contribute to the poems' very different tones and themes and their very different views of war?

JESSIE POPE
The Call

Who's for the trench—
    Are you, my laddie?
Who'll follow French[7]—
    Will you, my laddie?
5 Who's fretting to begin,
Who's going out to win?
And who wants to save his skin—
    Do you, my laddie?

Who's for the khaki suit—
10   Are you, my laddie?
Who longs to charge and shoot—
    Do you, my laddie?
Who's keen on getting fit,
Who means to show his grit,
15 And who'd rather wait a bit—
    Would you, my laddie?

Who'll earn the Empire's[8] thanks—
    Will you, my laddie?

7. Field-Marshall John French (1852–1925), commander in chief of the British Expeditionary Force for the first two years of World War I (1914–16).
8. At the start of World War I, the British Empire was the largest in human history, covering over eleven million square miles of the earth's surface; the desire to maintain or expand empire was one major cause of the war.

Who'll swell the victor's ranks—
20   Will you, my laddie?
When that procession comes,
Banners and rolling drums—
Who'll stand and bite his thumbs—
        Will you, my laddie?

1915

WILFRED OWEN

Dulce et Decorum Est[9]

Bent double, like old beggars under sacks,
Knock-kneed, coughing like hags, we cursed through sludge,
Till on the haunting flares we turned our backs
And towards our distant rest began to trudge.
5   Men marched asleep. Many had lost their boots
But limped on, blood-shod. All went lame; all blind;
Drunk with fatigue; deaf even to the hoots
Of disappointed shells that dropped behind.

Gas! Gas! Quick, boys!—An ecstasy of fumbling,
10 Fitting the clumsy helmets just in time;
But someone still was yelling out and stumbling
And floundering like a man in fire or lime.—
Dim, through the misty panes and thick green light
As under a green sea, I saw him drowning.

15 In all my dreams, before my helpless sight,
He plunges at me, guttering, choking, drowning.

If in some smothering dreams you too could pace
Behind the wagon that we flung him in,
And watch the white eyes writhing in his face,
20 His hanging face, like a devil's sick of sin;
If you could hear, at every jolt, the blood
Come gargling from the froth-corrupted lungs,
Obscene as cancer, bitter as the cud
Of vile, incurable sores on innocent tongues,—
25 My friend, you would not tell with such high zest
To children ardent for some desperate glory,
The old Lie: Dulce et decorum est
Pro patria mori.

1917

9. Part of a phrase from Horace (Roman poet and satirist, 65–8 BCE), quoted in full in the last lines
of Owen's poem: "It is sweet and proper to die for one's country" (Latin).

POEMS FOR FURTHER STUDY

WILLIAM SHAKESPEARE

Like as the waves make towards the pebbled shore

Like as the waves make towards the pebbled shore,
So do our minutes hasten to their end,
Each changing place with that which goes before,
In sequent toil all forwards do contend.[1]
5 Nativity, once in the main[2] of light,
Crawls to maturity, wherewith being crowned,
Crooked[3] eclipses 'gainst his glory fight,
And Time that gave doth now his gift confound.[4]
Time doth transfix[5] the flourish set on youth
10 And delves the parallels[6] in beauty's brow,
Feeds on the rarities of nature's truth,
And nothing stands but for his scythe to mow.
And yet to times in hope[7] my verse shall stand,
Praising thy worth, despite his cruel hand.

1609

• Which lines in this poem vary the basic iambic meter? What is the effect of
  these variations?

GERARD MANLEY HOPKINS
The Windhover[8]

To Christ our Lord

I caught this morning morning's minion,[9] king-
    dom of daylight's dauphin,[1] dapple-dawn-drawn Falcon, in his riding
    Of the rolling level underneath him steady air, and striding
High there, how he rung upon the rein of a wimpling[2] wing
5 In his ecstasy! then off, off forth on swing,
    As a skate's heel sweeps smooth on a bow-bend: the hurl and gliding
    Rebuffed the big wind. My heart in hiding
Stirred for a bird,—the achieve of, the mastery of the thing!

1. Struggle. *Sequent:* successive.
2. High seas. *Nativity:* newborn life.
3. Perverse.
4. Bring to nothing.
5. Pierce.
6. Lines, wrinkles.
7. The future.
8. Small hawk, the kestrel, which habitually hovers in the air, headed into the wind.
9. Favorite, beloved.
1. Heir to regal splendor.
2. Rippling.

Brute beauty and valor and act, oh, air, pride, plume, here
10   Buckle![3] AND the fire that breaks from thee then, a billion
Times told lovelier, more dangerous, O my chevalier![4]

No wonder of it: shéer plód makes plow down sillion[5]
Shine, and blue-bleak embers, ah my dear,
Fall, gall themselves, and gash gold-vermilion.

1877   1918

• What aural devices does Hopkins use here? How do they help him both to
characterize the bird and its flight and to express (even reproduce in us) the
speaker's feeling about them?

AMIT MAJMUDAR
Ode to a Drone

Hellraiser, razor-feathered
riser, windhover over
Peshawar,[6]

power's
5   joystick-blithe
thousand-mile scythe,

proxy executioner's
proxy axe
pinged by a proxy server,

10   winged victory,
pilot cipher
unburdened by aught

but fuel and bombs,
fool of God, savage
15   idiot savant[7]

sucking your benumbed
trigger-finger
gamer's thumb.

2013

• How do sound effects contribute to tone and characterization in this poem?
How might the poem echo Hopkins's THE WINDHOVER in its sound, as well
as content? What is the effect of these echoes, or what point might Majmudar make through them?

---

3. Several meanings may apply: to join closely, to prepare for battle, to grapple with, to collapse.
4. Horseman, knight.
5. Narrow strip of land between furrows in an open field divided for separate cultivation.
6. City in Pakistan. *Windhover*: see above, n. 8.
7. Someone highly knowledgeable or skilled in one area but seriously deficient in all others or even
mentally disabled.

WALT WHITMAN
A Noiseless Patient Spider

A noiseless patient spider,
I marked where on a little promontory it stood isolated,
Marked how to explore the vacant vast surrounding,
It launched forth filament, filament, filament, out of itself,
5 Ever unreeling them, ever tirelessly speeding them.

And you O my soul where you stand,
Surrounded, detached, in measureless oceans of space,
Ceaselessly musing, venturing, throwing, seeking the spheres to
    connect them,
Till the bridge you will need be formed, till the ductile anchor hold,
10 Till the gossamer thread you fling catch somewhere, O my soul.

1881

• Like all poems in free verse, Whitman's lacks regular meter and rhyme. By
  what other means does he here create meaningful sound effects?

RITA DOVE
Pedestrian Crossing, Charlottesville

A gaggle of girls giggle over the bricks
leading off Court Square. We brake

dutifully, and wait, but there's at least
twenty of these knob-kneed creatures,

5 blond and curly, still at an age that thinks
impudence is cute. Look how they dart

and dither, changing flanks as they lurch
along—golden gobbets of infuriating foolishness

or pure joy, depending on one's disposition.
10 At the moment mine's sour—this is taking

far too long; don't they have minders?
Just behind my shoulder in the city park

the Southern general still stands, stonewalling[8] us all.
When I was their age I judged Goldilocks

15 nothing more than a pint-size criminal
who flounced into others' lives, then

assumed their clemency. Unfair,
I know, my aggression—to lump them

---

8. Pun on Stonewall Jackson (1824–63), Confederate general in the American Civil War.

> into a gaggle (silly geese!) when all
> 20 they're guilty of is being young. So far.

2020

- Which sound devices are used most in the poem, and with what effect, especially in terms of tone and characterization?

SUGGESTIONS FOR WRITING

1. Read Pope's SOUND AND SENSE carefully twice—once silently and once aloud—and then mark the stressed and unstressed syllables. Single out all the lines that have major variations from the basic iambic pentameter pattern. Pick out six lines with variations that seem to you worthy of comment, and write a paragraph on each in which you show how the variation contributes to the specific effects achieved in that line and the corresponding point Pope conveys about poetic style.

2. Try your hand at writing limericks in imitation of THERE WAS A YOUNG GIRL FROM ST. PAUL; study the rhythmic patterns and line lengths carefully, and imitate them exactly in your poem. Begin your limerick with "There once was a _____ from _____" (using a place for which you think you can find a comic rhyme).

3. Write an essay exploring how Wilfred Owen uses meter (including substitutions) and rhyme, as well as other sound devices, in DULCE ET DECORUM EST both to capture the experience of war and its effects and to respond critically to traditional war poetry, perhaps by comparing this poem to Jessie Pope's THE CALL. If you choose to draw on Pope's poem, however, you might also want to consider how the poem works and means differently when titled DULCE ET DECORUM EST rather than (as it originally was) "To Jessie Pope."

4. Pope's SOUND AND SENSE contains this advice for poets: "But when loud surges lash the sounding shore, / The hoarse, rough verse should like the torrent roar" (lines 368–69). In other words, he counsels that the sound of the poet's description should match the sense of what the poem is describing. Write an essay in which you examine the sound and sense in Shakespeare's LIKE AS THE WAVES MAKE TOWARDS THE PEBBLED SHORE or any other poem in this chapter. How does the poem achieve a harmony of meaning and sound?

5. Drawing on the questions posed earlier about ODE TO A DRONE, write an essay analyzing the effect and significance of the way it echoes and alludes to THE WINDHOVER. Do you see any validity in one reviewer's claim that the "juxtaposition of Hopkins's religious ecstasy and the dispassion of a 'joystick-blithe [gamer]' assassinating unsuspecting victims" is "irritating," even potentially "offensive"?

6. Write an essay in which you discuss any poem in this book in which sound seems a more important element than anything else, even the meaning of words. What is the point of writing and reading this kind of poetry? Can it achieve its effects through silent reading, or must it be experienced aloud?

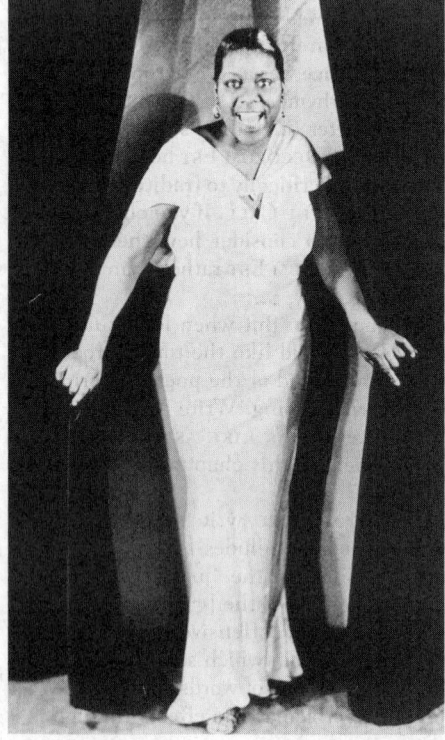

Words and Music

AN ALBUM

People often associate poetry with music, for good reason. The word *lyric* derives from the ancient Greeks' practice of reciting certain poems to the accompaniment of a harplike instrument, the lyre. Throughout history, poems have often been set to music, and today we call the words of any song *lyrics*. Many poems, especially during the Renaissance, were simply called "Song" (or "Chanson" or "Lied" or similar terms in other languages), and some were constructed in hybrid musical-poetic forms such as the madrigal, the dirge, and the hymn. Another, even older and more common such form is the **ballad**: a type of narrative poem originally intended for singing and characterized by features such as stock imagery, a refrain, and simple **diction**, **meter** and **rhyme scheme**. (So common is one such pattern of rhyme and meter that it is called **ballad stanza**, even when used in other types of poems.)

The most fundamental link between poetry and music involves their almost equal dependence on the principles of rhythm. Both art forms have a basis in mathematics: A regular beat or syncopated sound pattern shapes their phrasing and formal movement. Performers of both arts must keep count and consider quantities as well as qualities of sounds. Just as good musicians learn to listen and count so easily that it seems "natural," so poets develop an ear for rhythm that makes their sound choices seem effortless. Readers, too, can develop such an ear.

Both poetry and music use representational or imitative strategies to create the illusion of sounds—bells, waves, motorcycles, for example—but words operate referentially in a way that sounds normally do not, and their syntax is of a different kind from that in musical composition. The referential fact of language almost always alters the "pure" effects of sound.

But what of the relation between poetry and song lyrics as opposed to music itself? Are song lyrics poetry? This remains a complex, open, sometimes hotly debated question, and one brought to the fore in recent years by events including Yale University Press's publication of *The Anthology of Rap* (2010), edited by Adam Bradley and Andrew DuBois, with a foreword by literary scholar Henry Louis Gates, Jr., and an afterword by rappers Chuck D and Common; and the granting, in 2016, of the Nobel Prize in Literature to singer-songwriter Bob Dylan. Suffice it to say that some poets, even or especially those whose work most engages with—even resembles—rap or other musical styles and forms, think it nonetheless important to insist on the difference between their art and that of songwriters. As these poets point out, poetry must make music exclusively with words: A good poem has roughly the same rhythm and sound regardless of who reads it because it relies on normal patterns of stress or "beats," for example. But the same typically isn't true of song lyrics, which instead rely on musical accompaniment and are often sung so as to accommodate the rhythms *it* supplies. For this reason, even highly effective song lyrics don't always work as well on the page, especially if we haven't already heard the song they are really only one half of.

In the end, the real question isn't which form is superior but rather how these two equally vital art forms resemble and differ from each other. If, in debating the issue, poets occasionally seem to overstate the claims of their art and *their* right to Nobel Prizes, that's primarily because—let's face it—modern Western society doesn't tend to accord them anything approaching the public recognition and material rewards lavished on singer-songwriters and rappers.

This album invites you to think for yourself—and discuss with others—the complex relationships between poetry, music, and song. The poems in the album were all written for, in conjunction with, or to imitate or comment on music. They include one traditional and one more contemporary ballad, as well as song lyrics. (For another example of the latter, see Bruce Springsteen's NEBRASKA.) But we also invite you to consider as well as song lyrics by your favorite artists. Are the words as effective without the music? Do they make good poems? Can you, in the lyrics you know well, separate the actual musical implications from those of the words alone?

THOMAS CAMPION
When to her lute Corinna sings

When to her lute Corinna sings,
Her voice revives the leaden[1] strings,
And doth in highest notes appear
As any challenged[2] echo clear;
5   But when she doth of mourning speak,
Ev'n with her sighs the strings do break.

And as her lute doth live or die,
Led by her passion, so must I:
For when of pleasure she doth sing,
10   My thoughts enjoy a sudden spring;
But if she doth of sorrow speak,
Ev'n from my heart the strings do break.

1601

• How does Campion mimic an "echo" in this poem? What is the effect of this echoing?

ANONYMOUS
Sir Patrick Spens

The king sits in Dumferling toune,[3]
    Drinking the blude-reid[4] wine:
"O whar will I get guid sailor,
    To sail this ship of mine?"

1. Heavy.
2. Aroused.
3. Town.
4. Bloodred.

5 Up and spake an eldern knicht,
    Sat at the king's richt knee:
"Sir Patrick Spens is the best sailor
    That sails upon the sea."

The king has written a braid[5] letter
10   And signed it wi' his hand,
And sent it to Sir Patrick Spens,
    Was walking on the sand.

The first line that Sir Patrick read,
    A loud lauch[6] lauched he;
15 The next line that Sir Patrick read,
    The tear blinded his ee.[7]

"O wha is this has done this deed,
    This il deed done to me,
To send me out this time o' the year,
20   To sail upon the sea?

"Make haste, make haste, my merry men all,
    Our guid ship sails the morn."
"O say na sae,[8] my master dear,
    For I fear a deadly storm.

25 "Late, late yestre'en I saw the new moon
    Wi' the auld moon in her arm,
And I fear, I fear, my dear mastér,
    That we will come to harm."

O our Scots nobles were richt laith[9]
30   To weet their cork-heeled shoon,[1]
But lang owre a[2] the play were played
    Their hats they swam aboon.[3]

O lang, lang, may their ladies sit,
    Wi' their fans into their hand,
35 Or ere they see Sir Patrick Spens
    Come sailing to the land.

O lang, lang, may the ladies stand
    Wi' their gold kems[4] in their hair,
Waiting for their ain[5] dear lords,
40   For they'll see them na mair.

---

5. Broad: explicit.
6. Laugh.
7. Eye.
8. Not so.
9. Right loath: very reluctant.
1. To wet their cork-heeled shoes. Because cork was expensive, such shoes were a mark of wealth and status.
2. Before all.
3. Above.
4. Combs.
5. Own.

Half o'er, half o'er to Aberdour
   It's fifty fadom deep,
And there lies guid Sir Patrick Spens
   Wi' the Scots lords at his feet.

c. 13th century

- Often ballads' plots either involve extraordinary, even violent, events experienced by ordinary folk or center on a conflict between people of different social ranks. Is that true of Sir Patrick Spens? What might the ballad suggest about "nobles" (line 29) through its form, and especially its "music," as well as its content?

DUDLEY RANDALL
Ballad of Birmingham

(On the bombing of a church in Birmingham, Alabama, 1963)[6]

"Mother dear, may I go downtown
Instead of out to play,
And march the streets of Birmingham
In a Freedom March today?"

5 "No, baby, no, you may not go,
For the dogs are fierce and wild,
And clubs and hoses, guns and jails
Aren't good for a little child."

"But, mother, I won't be alone.
10 Other children will go with me,
And march the streets of Birmingham
To make our country free."

"No, baby, no, you may not go,
For I fear those guns will fire.
15 But you may go to church instead
And sing in the children's choir."

She has combed and brushed her night-dark hair,
And bathed rose petal sweet,
And drawn white gloves on her small brown hands,
20 And white shoes on her feet.

The mother smiled to know her child
Was in the sacred place,
But that smile was the last smile
To come upon her face.

25 For when she heard the explosion,
Her eyes grew wet and wild.

6. Just before Sunday services on September 15, 1963, a bomb exploded in Birmingham, Alabama's Sixteenth Street Baptist Church, killing four girls, aged eleven to fourteen, and injuring at least twenty-one other members of the predominantly African American congregation.

She raced through the streets of Birmingham
Calling for her child.

She clawed through bits of glass and brick,
30 Then lifted out a shoe.
"Oh, here's the shoe my baby wore,
But, baby, where are you?"

1969

• Compare this poem to other ballads in this volume and elsewhere. Why is
the form appropriate and effective for commemorating this violent event?

AUGUSTUS MONTAGUE TOPLADY
A Prayer, Living and Dying

I

ROCK of ages, cleft for me,
Let me hide myself in Thee!
Let the Water and the Blood,
From thy riven Side which flow'd,
5 Be of sin the double cure;
Cleanse me from its guilt and pow'r.

II

Not the labors of my hands
Can fulfill thy Law's demands:
Could my zeal no respite know,
10 Could my tears for ever flow,
All for sin could not atone;
Thou must save, and Thou alone.

III

Nothing in my hand I bring;
Simply to thy Cross I cling;
15 Naked, come to Thee for dress;
Helpless, look to Thee for grace;
Foul, I to the Fountain fly:
Wash me, SAVIOR, or I die!

IV

While I draw this fleeting breath—
20 When my eye-strings break in death—
When I soar to worlds unknown—
See Thee on thy judgment-throne—
ROCK of ages, cleft for me,
Let me hide myself in Thee!

1776

• What aspects of this poem might make it suitable for communal singing by
untrained singers?

ROBERT HAYDEN

Homage to the Empress of the Blues[7]

Because there was a man somewhere in a candystripe silk shirt,
gracile and dangerous as a jaguar and because a woman moaned
for him in sixty-watt gloom and mourned him Faithless Love
Twotiming Love Oh Love Oh Careless Aggravating Love,

5   She came out on the stage in yards of pearls, emerging like
a favorite scenic view, flashed her golden smile and sang.

Because grey laths began somewhere to show from underneath
torn hurdygurdy[8] lithographs of dollfaced heaven;
and because there were those who feared alarming fists of snow
10 on the door and those who feared the riot-squad of statistics,

She came out on the stage in ostrich feathers, beaded satin,
and shone that smile on us and sang.

1962

- How do the two short stanzas beginning with "She came out" complete the
thoughts of the longer stanzas that start with "Because"?

BOB DYLAN

The Times They Are A-Changin'

Come gather 'round people
Wherever you roam
And admit that the waters
Around you have grown
5 And accept it that soon
You'll be drenched to the bone
If your time to you is worth savin'
Then you better start swimmin' or you'll sink like a stone
For the times they are a-changin'

10 Come writers and critics
Who prophesize with your pen
And keep your eyes wide
The chance won't come again
And don't speak too soon
15 For the wheel's still in spin
And there's no tellin' who that it's namin'
For the loser now will be later to win
For the times they are a-changin'

---

7. Bessie Smith (1894?–1937), legendary blues singer whose theatrical style grew out of the Black
American vaudeville tradition.
8. Disreputable kind of dance hall.

Come senators, congressmen
20 Please heed the call
Don't stand in the doorway
Don't block up the hall
For he that gets hurt
Will be he who has stalled
25 There's a battle outside and it is ragin'
It'll soon shake your windows and rattle your walls
For the times they are a-changin'

Come mothers and fathers
Throughout the land
30 And don't criticize
What you can't understand
Your sons and your daughters
Are beyond your command
Your old road is rapidly agin'
35 Please get out of the new one if you can't lend your hand
For the times they are a-changin'

The line it is drawn
The curse it is cast
The slow one now
40 Will later be fast
As the present now
Will later be past
The order is rapidly fadin'
And the first one now will later be last
45 For the times they are a-changin'

1963, 1964

• How does familiarity with THE TIMES THEY ARE A-CHANGIN' as a song affect
your sense of it as a poem? How do the lyrics work as poetry? Are there any
ways or moments that they don't?

MOS DEF
Hip Hop

You say one for the treble, two for the time
Come on, y'all, let's rock this!
You say one for the treble, two for the time
Come on!

5 *Speech is my hammer, bang the world into shape, now let it fall . . . (Hungh!!)*

My restlessness is my nemesis, it's hard
To really chill and sit still, committed to page
I write a rhyme, sometimes won't finish for days
Scrutinize my literature from the large to the miniature
10 I mathematically add-minister, subtract the wack
Selector, wheel it back, I'm feelin that

(Ha ha ha) From the core to the perimeter, Black
You know the motto: stay fluid even in staccato (Mos Def)
Full blooded, full throttle, breathe deep inside the drum hollow
15 . . . There's the hum
Young man, where you from? Brooklyn, number one
Native Son,[9] speaking in the native tongue
I got my eyes on tomorrow (there it is), while you still tryna
Find where it is, I'm on the ave' where it lives and dies
20 Violently, silently . . . Shine
So vibrantly that eyes squint to catch a glimpse
Embrace the bass with my dark ink fingertips
Used to speak the King's English, but caught a rash on my lips
See, now my chat just like this
25 Long range from the baseline (swish). Move like an apparition
Go to the ground with ammunition (chi-chi-POW)
Move from the gate, voice cued on your tape
Putting food on your plate, many crews can relate
Who choosing your fate, yo
30 We went from picking cotton, to chain-gang line chopping
To be-bopping, to hip-hopping
Blues people got the blue-chip stock option
Invisible Man,[1] got the whole world watching
(Where ya at?) I'm high, low, east, west, all over your map
35 I'm getting big props with this thing called hip hop
Where you can either get paid or get shot, when your product in stock
The fair-weather friends flock, when your chart position drop
Then the phone calls . . .
Chill for a minute, let's see who else hot
40 Snatch your shelf spot. Don't gas yourself, ock
The industry just a better-built cell block
A long way from the shell tops
And the bells that L rocked (rock, rock, rock, rock . . .)[2]

Hip hop is prosecution evidence
45 A out of court settlement, ad space for liquor
Sick without benefits (hungh!), luxury tenements
Choking the skyline, it's low life getting tree-top high
It is a backwater remedy
Bitter intent to memory, a class C felony[3]
50 Facing the death penalty (hungh!), stimulant and sedative
Original repetitive, violently competitive
A school unaccredited (there it is)
The break beats you get broken with on time and inappropriate
Hip hop went from selling crack to smoking it

9. Title of a 1940 novel by Richard Wright (1908–60) about Bigger Thomas, an impoverished
twenty-year-old living on Chicago's South Side.
1. Title of Ralph Ellison's 1952 novel, narrated by an unnamed African American protagonist.
2. Allusion to LL Cool J's 1985 hit "Rock the Bells."
3. States categorize felonies as A, B, C, etc. based on their seriousness, and penalties are apportioned
accordingly.

55 Medicine for loneliness, remind me of Thelonious and Dizzy[4]
    Propers to b-boys[5] getting busy
    The wartime snapshot, the working man's jackpot
    A two dollar snack box sold beneath the crack spot
    Olympic sponsor of the black Glock[6]
60 Gold medalist in the back shot from the sovereign state
    Of the have-nots where farmers have trouble with cash crops
    It's all-city like Phase 2, hip hop will simply amaze you
    Praise you, pay you
    Do whatever you say do, but Black, it can't save you

                                                            1999

    • What does this song suggest about the character, origin, and significance of
      hip-hop?

SUGGESTIONS FOR WRITING

1. Is there a meaningful difference between poetry and song lyrics? between poetry and
   rap? Is hip-hop a form of literature? Write an essay in which you explore the definitions of "poetry" and "lyrics." Be sure to cite examples to illustrate your ideas.
2. Find on the Internet the lyrics of a song (of any genre) that in your opinion uses
   words well, and download or print out one or more versions. First, notice any variations between the text(s) you find and the words you hear when listening to the
   song. Using a correct version of the lyrics (as you determine it), scan the lines for
   meter and rhyme. Are any words or syllables used to keep the beat without adding
   to the meaning (like the word "do" in Pope's SOUND AND SENSE)? Are any rhymes
   dependent on vowel sounds rather than consonants (that is, do they not quite rhyme
   in print)? How does the refrain (if any) vary from the rest of the lyrics, and how does
   it relate to the title or theme of the song? Which lines or verses are most important
   to the "story" or the feeling relayed by the song? How would you describe the speaker's diction and tone, and how does it compare with the vocal style of the singer?
   Write a descriptive response paper on these words as a poem without music, and as
   lyrics within the song. Are they as successful in print as they are when performed
   with music?
3. Drawing on Mos Def's HIP HOP and the lyrics to at least two other songs, write an
   essay exploring the rhythm and sound devices peculiar to hip-hop or rap. How especially do its rhythmic patterns compare to those of metered poetry?

---

4. Dizzy Gillespie (1917–93), American jazz musician, as was Thelonious Monk (1917–82).
5. Hip-hop dancers or "breakers."
6. Pistol, especially semiautomatic.

19 | INTERNAL STRUCTURE

"Proper words in proper places": That is how one great writer of English prose, Jonathan Swift, described good writing. A good poet finds appropriate words, and already we have looked at some implications for readers of the verbal choices a poet makes. But the poet must also decide where to put those words—how to arrange them for maximum semantic, as well as visual and aural, effect—because individual words, figures of speech, symbols, and sounds exist not only within phrases and sentences and rhythmic patterns, but also within the larger whole of the poem. How should the words be arranged and the poem organized? What comes first and what last? What principle or idea of organization will inform the poem? How do the parts combine into a whole? And what is the effect of that arrangement? Considering these questions from the poet's point of view (What is my plan? Where shall I begin? Where do I want to go?) can help us notice the effects of structural choices.

DIVIDING POEMS INTO "PARTS"

It's useful to think of most poems—whether narrative, dramatic, or **lyric**—as informally divisible into parts, distinguished from each other by shifts in subject matter or topic, in **tone**, in address, in tense, or in mode (from narration to reflection or description, for example), and so on. As you read a new poem, look out for such shifts, however subtle, to determine how many parts you think the poem has and how each part relates to, and builds on, the one before. The following lyric, for example, seems to have two parts. How does each part relate to the other? What differentiates and connects them?

PAT MORA
Sonrisas[1]

I live in a doorway
between two rooms, I hear
quiet clicks, cups of black
coffee, *click, click* like facts
5   budgets, tenure, curriculum,
from careful women in crisp beige
suits, quick beige smiles
that seldom sneak into their eyes.

1. Smiles (Spanish).

I peek
10 in the other room señoras
in faded dresses stir sweet
milk coffee, laughter whirls
with steam from fresh *tamales*
  sh, sh, mucho ruido,[2]
15 they scold one another,
press their lips, trap smiles
in their dark, Mexican eyes.

1986

This poem's two parts closely resemble each other in that each describes the women who inhabit one of the "two rooms" the speaker "live[s]" "between." Both descriptions include sights ("crisp beige / suits," "faded dresses"), sounds ("quiet clicks," "laughter"), and even the suggestion of tastes ("black / coffee," "sweet / milk coffee"). Yet the relation between the two parts and the two rooms is clearly one of contrast ("crisp [. . .] / suits" *versus* "faded dresses," "quiet clicks" *versus* "laughter," etc.). Here different languages, habits, sights, sounds, and values characterize the worlds symbolized by the two rooms, and the poem is organized around the contrast between them. The meaning of the poem (the difference between the two worlds and the experience of living between them) is very nearly the same as the structure.

To fully understand that meaning and the poem, we would need to tease out all those contrasts and their implications. We would also need to consider the significance of the author's choice not only to make the two parts roughly equal in length, but also to order them as she does. How would the poem and our sense of the speaker's feelings about the two rooms be different if we simply rearranged its **stanzas**, as follows?

I live in a doorway
between two rooms, I hear señoras
in faded dresses stir sweet
milk coffee, laughter whirls
with steam from fresh *tamales*
sh, sh, mucho ruido,
they scold one another,
press their lips, trap smiles
in their dark, Mexican eyes.

I peek
in the other room, I hear
quiet clicks, cups of black
coffee, *click, click* like facts
budgets, tenure, curriculum,
from careful women in crisp beige
suits, quick beige smiles
that seldom sneak into their eyes.

2. A lot of noise (Spanish).

INTERNAL VERSUS EXTERNAL OR FORMAL "PARTS"

In Sonrisas, the internal division created by the speaker's shift in focus (from one room and world to another) corresponds to the poem's formal or "external" division into two stanzas and two sentences. Internal and external or formal divisions need not always coincide with each other, however. Major shifts in a poem sometimes occur in the middle of a stanza, a line, even a sentence. Take the following poem. Only one sentence and one stanza long, it has no formal divisions at all. Yet it, too, arguably divides into two parts. As you read the poem, consider whether you agree and, if so, where you think the shift occurs.

GALWAY KINNELL
Blackberry Eating

I love to go out in late September
among the fat, overripe, icy, black blackberries
to eat blackberries for breakfast,
the stalks very prickly, a penalty
5   they earn for knowing the black art
of blackberry-making; and as I stand among them
lifting the stalks to my mouth, the ripest berries
fall almost unbidden to my tongue,
as words sometimes do, certain peculiar words
10   like *strengths* or *squinched*,
many-lettered, one-syllabled lumps,
which I squeeze, squinch open, and splurge well
in the silent, startled, icy, black language
of blackberry-eating in late September.

1980

The poem's first eight lines relate the speaker's experience of just what the title leads us to expect—blackberry eating. But notice what happens in line 9: The speaker's focus shifts from the topic of blackberries to the topic of words, with the word "as" signaling that we're entering the second phase of an **analogy** (or extended **simile**) comparing the experience we've just read about (eating blackberries) to the one we now begin to read about (forming words), with both berries and words "fall[ing] almost unbidden to [the] tongue" (line 8). Here, then, the relation between the poem's two parts and the two objects and experiences they describe is one of likeness rather than contrast (as in "Sonrisas"). Fittingly enough for a poem about connection and comparison, as well as vaguely round "lumps" of things (11), the poem's final line ends with the same words as its first ("in late September"). In a sense, then, the poem might be described as having a circular, as well as two-part (or "bipartite"), structure.

LYRICS AS INTERNAL DRAMAS

Obviously, not all poems consist of only two parts, as do those above. The following poem, for example, arguably divides into three parts. Just as important, in this poem the relationship between the parts seems to be one of development, tracing a change of outlook or attitude *within* the speaker.

SEAMUS HEANEY
Punishment[3]

I can feel the tug
of the halter at the nape
of her neck, the wind
on her naked front.

5 It blows her nipples
to amber beads,
it shakes the frail rigging
of her ribs.

I can see her drowned
10 body in the bog,
the weighing stone,
the floating rods and boughs.

Under which at first
she was a barked sapling
15 that is dug up
oak-bone, brain-firkin:

her shaved head
like a stubble of black corn,
her blindfold a soiled bandage,
20 her noose a ring

to store
the memories of love.
Little adulteress,
before they punished you

25 you were flaxen-haired,
undernourished, and your
tar-black face was beautiful.
My poor scapegoat,

I almost love you
30 but would have cast, I know,
the stones of silence.
I am the artful voyeur

of your brain's exposed
and darkened combs,
35 your muscles' webbing
and all your numbered bones:

---

3. According to the Roman historian Tacitus (c. 56–120 CE), Germanic peoples punished adulterous women by first shaving their heads and then banishing or killing them. In 1951, in Windeby, Germany, the naked body of a young girl from the first century CE was pulled from the bog where she had been murdered. In modern Ireland, "betraying sisters" (line 38) were sometimes punished by the Irish Republican Army (IRA) for associating with British soldiers.

> I who have stood dumb
> when your betraying sisters,
> cauled[4] in tar,
> 40 wept by the railings,
>
> who would connive
> in civilized outrage
> yet understand the exact
> and tribal, intimate revenge.

1975

In PUNISHMENT, the first shift seems to come in line 23 (again, in the middle of a stanza rather than at its beginning): Up to this point, the speaker has described the long-dead girl in the third person (e.g., "*her* neck," "*her* nipples," lines 3, 5; emphasis added). And despite his twice-repeated emphasis on his own perceptions and responses ("I can feel," "I can see," 1, 9; emphasis added), the girl herself gets most of the attention. Starting in line 23, however, the speaker begins to speak to the girl directly, addressing her in the second person ("you") and through **epithets** ("Little adulteress," "poor scapegoat," 23, 28). Verb tense shifts, too ("were," 25), as the speaker begins to imagine the girl's life "before they punished" her (24). In at least two ways, then, the speaker seems to be coming closer to the girl, now seeing and addressing her as a human being with a history rather than as a thing to be looked at and talked *about*. At the same time, the speaker focuses more on himself as well, expressing his emotions ("I almost love you," 29) and reflecting somewhat critically on the way he looked at the girl's body—and allowed us to—earlier in the poem ("I am the artful voyeur," 32).

Subject matter and tense shift again, however, in line 37: The poem's final two stanzas consider the speaker's behavior toward the "betraying sisters" (38) in an indeterminate past ("I [. . .] have," 37), as if here he describes not one experience, but rather a composite of many. Aside from the "your," in line 38, the girl herself seems to have disappeared from the poem (so much so that even that "your" now seems potentially ambiguous: Might it now also refer to someone else?). Though in this poem, unlike BLACKBERRY EATING, we don't have the word *as* to signal an analogy, it seems clear that Heaney's speaker has, over the course of the poem, come to see a similarity between his attitude toward the long-dead girl and the "betraying sisters," the behavior of those responsible for these women's punishments, and even between writing a poem about such women and punishing them. How and why so?

Though "Punishment" is by no means a dramatic poem in the literal sense, it does—like some other lyrics—relate an internal drama of sorts, tracing the process through which its speaker comes to see or accept, as well as share with us, some truth about or insight into the world or himself that he didn't see or accept previously, somewhat as a fictional character might in a dramatic or narrative poem or in a short story. In reading and writing about such poems, a good topic to explore might be what insight the speaker comes to over the course of the poem, and when and why so.

---

4. Wrapped or enclosed as if in a caul (the inner fetal membrane of higher vertebrates that sometimes covers the head at birth).

Analyzing Internal Structure: An Exercise

Like "Punishment," both of the following poems trace a development in their speakers' perceptions of themselves or the world around them, even if the realizations to which the speakers come and the processes by which they get there differ. As you read each poem, think about where and why the shifts come both in the poem and in the speaker's outlook. In which poem does the change within the speaker seem to happen *during* the poem itself (as in "Punishment"), and which poem might instead depict the change as one that happened at some earlier, unspecified point in time?

SAMUEL TAYLOR COLERIDGE
Frost at Midnight

The frost performs its secret ministry,
Unhelped by any wind. The owlet's cry
Came loud—and hark, again! loud as before.
The inmates of my cottage, all at rest,
5 Have left me to that solitude, which suits
Abstruser musings: save that at my side
My cradled infant slumbers peacefully.
'Tis calm indeed! so calm, that it disturbs
And vexes meditation with its strange
10 And extreme silentness. Sea, hill, and wood,
This populous village! Sea, and hill, and wood,
With all the numberless goings on of life,
Inaudible as dreams! the thin blue flame
Lies on my low burnt fire, and quivers not;
15 Only that film,[5] which fluttered on the grate,
Still flutters there, the sole unquiet thing.
Methinks, its motion in this hush of nature
Gives it dim sympathies with me who live,
Making it a companionable form,
20 Whose puny flaps and freaks the idling Spirit
By its own moods interprets, every where
Echo or mirror seeking of itself,
And makes a toy of Thought.

                   But O! how oft,
25 How oft, at school, with most believing mind,
Presageful, have I gazed upon the bars,
To watch that fluttering stranger! and as oft
With unclosed lids, already had I dreamt

5. In all parts of the kingdom these films are called *strangers* and supposed to portend the arrival of some absent friend [Coleridge's note]. The "film" is a piece of soot fluttering on the bar of the grate.

Of my sweet birth-place, and the old church-tower,
30 Whose bells, the poor man's only music, rang
From morn to evening, all the hot Fair-day,
So sweetly, that they stirred and haunted me
With a wild pleasure, falling on mine ear
Most like articulate sounds of things to come!
35 So gazed I, till the soothing things I dreamt
Lulled me to sleep, and sleep prolonged my dreams!
And so I brooded all the following morn,
Awed by the stern preceptor's face, mine eye
Fixed with mock study on my swimming book:
40 Save if the door half opened, and I snatched
A hasty glance, and still my heart leaped up,
For still I hoped to see the stranger's face,
Townsman, or aunt, or sister more beloved,
My play-mate when we both were clothed alike![6]

45   Dear Babe, that sleepest cradled by my side,
Whose gentle breathings, heard in this deep calm,
Fill up the interspersed vacancies
And momentary pauses of the thought!
My babe so beautiful! it thrills my heart
50 With tender gladness, thus to look at thee,
And think that thou shalt learn far other lore
And in far other scenes! For I was reared
In the great city, pent 'mid cloisters dim,
And saw nought lovely but the sky and stars.
55 But thou, my babe! shalt wander like a breeze
By lakes and sandy shores, beneath the crags
Of ancient mountain, and beneath the clouds,
Which image in their bulk both lakes and shores
And mountain crags: so shalt thou see and hear
60 The lovely shapes and sounds intelligible
Of that eternal language, which thy God
Utters, who from eternity doth teach
Himself in all, and all things in himself.
Great universal Teacher! he shall mould
65 Thy spirit, and by giving make it ask.

    Therefore all seasons shall be sweet to thee,
Whether the summer clothe the general earth
With greenness, or the redbreast sit and sing
Betwixt the tufts of snow on the bare branch
70 Of mossy apple-tree, while the nigh thatch
Smokes in the sun-thaw; whether the eave-drops fall
Heard only in the trances of the blast,

---

6. Late eighteenth-century custom called for all infants to wear dresses, regardless of gender.

Or if the secret ministry of frost
Shall hang them up in silent icicles,
75 Quietly shining to the quiet Moon.

1798

- Coleridge described some of his poems, including FROST AT MID-
  NIGHT, as having a circular structure. How and why might this poem
  seem circular, or in what way does its end resemble its beginning? In
  what way are the two different? How might the resemblance and difference help us recognize the change in the speaker's outlook?

SHARON OLDS
The Victims

When Mother divorced you, we were glad. She took it and
took it, in silence, all those years and then
kicked you out, suddenly, and her
kids loved it. Then you were fired, and we
5 grinned inside, the way people grinned when
Nixon's helicopter lifted off the South
Lawn for the last time.[7] We were tickled
to think of your office taken away,
your secretaries taken away,
10 your lunches with three double bourbons,
your pencils, your reams of paper. Would they take your
suits back, too, those dark
carcasses hung in your closet, and the black
noses of your shoes with their large pores?
15 She had taught us to take it, to hate you and take it
until we pricked with her for your
annihilation, Father. Now I
pass the bums in doorways, the white
slugs of their bodies gleaming through slits in their
20 suits of compressed silt, the stained
flippers of their hands, the underwater
fire of their eyes, ships gone down with the
lanterns lit, and I wonder who took it and
took it from them in silence until they had
25 given it all away and had nothing
left but this.

1984

- How are the speaker's shifting attitudes toward her father (and the
  poem's parts) both related and differentiated by repetition of the
  word "took"?

7. When Richard Nixon resigned the U.S. presidency on August 8, 1974, his exit from the White
House (by helicopter from the lawn) was televised live.

MAKING ARGUMENTS ABOUT STRUCTURE

Dividing a poem into parts and analyzing its internal structure as we have here isn't an exact science: Different readers might well come to slightly different conclusions about the nature, timing, and significance of key shifts and thus about how many parts a poem might be said to have, how one part relates to another, and what sort of whole those parts create. It seems quite possible, for example, to argue that THE VICTIMS has either two parts or three, depending on what you make of lines 15–17 (up to the word "Now"), or that FROST AT MIDNIGHT has three, four, even five parts. In these cases, as in many others, there is no single correct answer. Indeed, ample room for disagreement is in a way precisely the point: Formulating your own ideas about where important shifts come in a poem and why they're important, identifying good evidence to support your conclusions, and considering alternative ways of understanding the poem's structure may take you far down the path to developing your own argument about how the poem as a whole works and means.

POEMS WITHOUT "PARTS"

As we've seen, too, dividing a poem into parts is simply a useful way to *begin* to explore and analyze its structure rather than the entire point or end of such analysis. And this is all the more obviously true with those poems that contain no major shifts and thus no distinct "parts" at all. Such poems nonetheless have a meaningful structure; their authors, too, must figure out how to organize their material so as to create something like a beginning, middle, and end. And here, too, such structural choices determine how the poem moves and means. The following poem is a case in point: One sentence and one stanza long, with no major shifts, how does it nonetheless manage both to cohere and to develop? What picture of America results both from its particular details and from the way they are organized?

WALT WHITMAN
I Hear America Singing

I hear America singing, the varied carols I hear,
Those of mechanics, each one singing his as it should be blithe and
    strong,
The carpenter singing his as he measures his plank or beam,
The mason singing his as he makes ready for work, or leaves off work,
5 The boatman singing what belongs to him in his boat, the deckhand
    singing on the steamboat deck,
The shoemaker singing as he sits on his bench, the hatter singing as he
    stands,
The wood-cutter's song, the ploughboy's on his way in the morning, or
    at noon intermission or at sundown,
The delicious singing of the mother, or of the young wife at work, or of
    the girl sewing or washing,

Each singing what belongs to him or her and to none else,
10 The day what belongs to the day—at night the party of young fellows,
        robust, friendly,
    Singing with open mouths their strong melodious songs.

1860, 1881

By limiting himself to a single sentence and a single stanza, which nonetheless refers to a multitude of people and "songs," Whitman produces a poem that structurally embodies the Latin motto on the U.S. seal—*e pluribus unum*, "Out of many, one." The "many ones" with whom the poem begins are all ordinary men who work with their hands: From "mechanics" (line 2) to a "boatman" (5) and "ploughboy" (7), they work on land and shore, in city and country. Though line 8 doesn't constitute a major shift, it does subtly broaden the poem's picture of America: Women enter the poem; and though they, too, are depicted "at work," the fact that they are identified specifically as a "mother," "young wife," and "girl" introduces, too, the idea both of generations and of family, two important social groups that intervene between many individuals, on the one hand, and an entire nation, on the other. Finally, at the poem's end, we move from "day" to "night" and from labor to leisure, in a way that makes clear that these oppositions and time itself have also been structuring principles all along: Line 4, after all, describes the mason as singing "as he makes ready for [. . .] or leaves off work," line 7 the ploughboy and wood-cutter each making "his way in the morning, or at noon intermission or at sundown." By its close, then, the poem has shown us a full day of life in Whitman's version of America and in the lives of those whose various, unique "carols" (1) combine to create a single American song.

POEMS FOR FURTHER STUDY

As you read each of the following poems, consider the following questions: Does the poem seem to divide into internal "parts"? If so, where and why? What are the major shifts? How does each part build on the last? How do the parts combine into a meaningful whole? If the poem doesn't seem divisible into parts, what are its organizing principles? How does the poem build and develop, and what overall picture or even **theme** results?

WILLIAM SHAKESPEARE
Th' expense of spirit in a waste of shame

Th' expense of spirit in a waste[8] of shame
Is lust in action; and, till action, lust
Is perjured, murderous, bloody, full of blame,
Savage, extreme, rude, cruel, not to trust;
5 Enjoyed no sooner but despisèd straight:
Past reason hunted; and no sooner had,
Past reason hated, as a swallowed bait,
On purpose laid to make the taker mad:

---

8. Using up; also, desert. *Expense*: expending.

Mad in pursuit, and in possession so;
10 Had, having, and in quest to have, extreme;
A bliss in proof,[9] and proved, a very woe;
Before, a joy proposed; behind, a dream.
All this the world well knows; yet none knows well
To shun the heaven that leads men to this hell.

1609

• Paraphrase this poem. What emotional stages accompany the carrying out of a violent or lustful act? Is Shakespeare an insightful psychologist? What is his major insight about how lust works?

PERCY BYSSHE SHELLEY
Ode to the West Wind

I

O wild West Wind, thou breath of Autumn's being,
Thou, from whose unseen presence the leaves dead
Are driven, like ghosts from an enchanter fleeing,

Yellow, and black, and pale, and hectic red,
5 Pestilence-stricken multitudes: O thou,
Who chariotest to their dark wintry bed

The wingèd seeds, where they lie cold and low,
Each like a corpse within its grave, until
Thine azure sister of the Spring shall blow

10 Her clarion[1] o'er the dreaming earth, and fill
(Driving sweet buds like flocks to feed in air)
With living hues and odors plain and hill:

Wild Spirit, which art moving everywhere;
Destroyer and preserver; hear, oh, hear!

II

15 Thou on whose stream, mid the steep sky's commotion,
Loose clouds like earth's decaying leaves are shed,
Shook from the tangled boughs of Heaven and Ocean,

Angels[2] of rain and lightning: there are spread
On the blue surface of thine aëry surge,
20 Like the bright hair uplifted from the head

Of some fierce Maenad,[3] even from the dim verge
Of the horizon to the zenith's height,
The locks of the approaching storm. Thou dirge

---

9. In the act.
1. Trumpet call.
2. Messengers.
3. Frenzied female votary of Dionysus, the Greek god of vegetation and fertility who was supposed to die in the fall and rise again each spring.

Of the dying year, to which this closing night
25 Will be the dome of a vast sepulcher,
Vaulted with all thy congregated might

Of vapors, from whose solid atmosphere
Black rain, and fire, and hail will burst: oh, hear!

III

Thou who didst waken from his summer dreams
30 The blue Mediterranean, where he lay,
Lulled by the coil of his crystàlline streams,

Beside a pumice isle in Baiae's bay,[4]
And saw in sleep old palaces and towers
Quivering within the wave's intenser day,

35 All overgrown with azure moss and flowers
So sweet, the sense faints picturing them! Thou
For whose path the Atlantic's level powers

Cleave themselves into chasms, while far below
The sea-blooms and the oozy woods which wear
40 The sapless foliage of the ocean, know

Thy voice, and suddenly grow gray with fear,
And tremble and despoil themselves:[5] oh, hear!

IV

If I were a dead leaf thou mightest bear;
If I were a swift cloud to fly with thee;
45 A wave to pant beneath thy power, and share

The impulse of thy strength, only less free
Than thou, O uncontrollable! If even
I were as in my boyhood, and could be

The comrade of thy wanderings over Heaven,
50 As then, when to outstrip thy skyey speed
Scarce seemed a vision; I would ne'er have striven

As thus with thee in prayer in my sore need.
Oh, lift me as a wave, a leaf, a cloud!
I fall upon the thorns of life! I bleed!

55 A heavy weight of hours has chained and bowed
One too like thee: tameless, and swift, and proud.

V

Make me thy lyre, even as the forest is:
What if my leaves are falling like its own!
The tumult of thy mighty harmonies

4. Where Roman emperors had erected villas, west of Naples.
5. The vegetation at the bottom of the sea [. . .] sympathizes with that of the land in the change of
seasons [Shelley's note].

60   Will take from both a deep, autumnal tone,
      Sweet though in sadness. Be thou, Spirit fierce,
      My spirit! Be thou me, impetuous one!

      Drive my dead thoughts over the universe
      Like withered leaves to quicken a new birth!
65   And, by the incantation of this verse,

      Scatter, as from an unextinguished hearth
      Ashes and sparks, my words among mankind!
      Be through my lips to unawakened earth

      The trumpet of a prophecy! O Wind,
70   If Winter comes, can Spring be far behind?

1819   1820

   • What attributes of the West Wind does the speaker want his poetry to
     embody? In what ways is this poem like the wind it describes? What is the
     effect of its structure?

PHILIP LARKIN
Church Going

      Once I am sure there's nothing going on
      I step inside, letting the door thud shut.
      Another church: matting, seats, and stone,
      And little books; sprawlings of flowers, cut
5   For Sunday, brownish now; some brass and stuff
      Up at the holy end; the small neat organ;
      And a tense, musty, unignorable silence,
      Brewed God knows how long. Hatless, I take off
      My cycle-clips in awkward reverence,

10   Move forward, run my hand around the font.
      From where I stand, the roof looks almost new—
      Cleaned, or restored? Someone would know: I don't.
      Mounting the lectern, I peruse a few
      Hectoring large-scale verses, and pronounce
15   "Here endeth" much more loudly than I'd meant.
      The echoes snigger briefly. Back at the door
      I sign the book, donate an Irish sixpence,
      Reflect the place was not worth stopping for.

      Yet stop I did: in fact I often do,
20   And always end much at a loss like this,
      Wondering what to look for; wondering, too,
      When churches fall completely out of use
      What we shall turn them into, if we shall keep
      A few cathedrals chronically on show,
25   Their parchment, plate and pyx in locked cases,
      And let the rest rent-free to rain and sheep.
      Shall we avoid them as unlucky places?

Or, after dark, will dubious women come
To make their children touch a particular stone;
30 Pick simples[6] for a cancer; or on some
Advised night see walking a dead one?
Power of some sort or other will go on
In games, in riddles, seemingly at random;
But superstition, like belief, must die,
35 And what remains when disbelief has gone?
Grass, weedy pavement, brambles, buttress, sky,

A shape less recognizable each week,
A purpose more obscure. I wonder who
Will be the last, the very last, to seek
40 This place for what it was; one of the crew
That tap and jot and know what rood-lofts[7] were?
Some ruin-bibber,[8] randy for antique,
Or Christmas-addict, counting on a whiff
Of gown-and-bands and organ-pipes and myrrh?
45 Or will he be my representative,

Bored, uninformed, knowing the ghostly silt
Dispersed, yet tending to this cross of ground
Through suburb scrub because it held unspilt
So long and equably what since is found
50 Only in separation—marriage, and birth,
And death, and thoughts of these—for whom was built
This special shell? For, though I've no idea
What this accoutered frowsty barn is worth,
It pleases me to stand in silence here;

55 A serious house on serious earth it is,
In whose blent[9] air all our compulsions meet,
Are recognized, and robed as destinies.
And that much never can be obsolete,
Since someone will forever be surprising
60 A hunger in himself to be more serious,
And gravitating with it to this ground,
Which, he once heard, was proper to grow wise in,
If only that so many dead lie round.

1955

> • Describe the parts of this poem. How do the first two stanzas differ from the
> rest of the poem? Where and how does the poem shift from the personal to
> the general?

6. Medicinal herbs.
7. Galleries atop the screens (on which crosses ["roods"] are mounted) that divide the naves or main
bodies of churches from the choirs or chancels.
8. Literally, ruin-drinker: someone extremely attracted to antiquarian objects.
9. Blended.

AUTHORS ON THEIR WORK

PHILIP LARKIN (1922–85)

From "A Conversation with Ian Hamilton" (1964)*

It ["Church Going"] is of course an entirely secular poem. I was a bit irritated by an American who insisted to me it was a religious poem. It isn't religious at all. Religion surely means that the affairs of this world are under divine surveillance, and so on, and I go to some pains to point out that I don't bother about that kind of thing. [. . .]

[. . . T]he poem is about going to church, not religion—I tried to suggest this by the title—and the union of the important stages of human life—birth, marriage and death—that going to church represents; and my own feeling that when they are dispersed into the registry office and the crematorium chapel life will become thinner in consequence.

· · ·

From "An Interview with John Haffenden" (1981)**

It ["Church Going"] came from the first time I saw a ruined church in Northern Ireland, and I'd never seen a ruined church before—discarded. It shocked me. Now of course it's commonplace: churches are not so much ruined as turned into bingo-halls, warehouses for refrigerators or split-level houses for architects.

It's not clear in the poem that you began with a ruined church.
No, it wasn't in the poem, but when you go into a church there's a feeling of something . . . well . . . over, derelict.

Some critics have discerned in it a yearning for a latter-day Christian or religious sanction. Is that so?
I suppose so. I'm not someone who's lost faith: I never had it. I was baptized [. . .] but not confirmed. Aren't religions shaped in terms of what people want? No one could help hoping Christianity was true, or at least the happy ending—rising from the dead and our sins forgiven. One longs for these miracles, and so in a sense one longs for religion. But "Church Going" isn't that kind of poem: it's a humanist poem, a celebration of the dignity of . . . well, you know what it says.

---

*"A Conversation with Ian Hamilton." *Further Requirements: Interviews, Broadcasts, Statements and Book Reviews*, edited by Anthony Thwaite, Faber and Faber, 2001, pp. 19–26. Originally published in *London Magazine*, Nov. 1946.
**"An Interview with John Haffenden." *Further Requirements*, pp. 47–62. Originally published in *Viewpoints: Poets in Conversation with John Haffenden*, 1981.

KEVIN YOUNG
Greening

It never ends, the bruise
        of being—messy,
untimely, the breath

of newborns uneven, half
5   pant, as they find
their rhythm, inexact

as vengeance. Son,
        while you sleep
we watch you like a kettle

10 learning to whistle.
        Awake, older,
you fumble now

in the most graceful
        way—grateful
15 to have seen you, on your own

steam, simply eating, slow,
        chewing—this bloom
of being. Almost beautiful

how you flounder, mouth full, bite
20   the edges of this world
that doesn't want

a thing but to keep turning
        with, or without you—
with. With. Child, hold fast

25 I say, to this greening thing
     as it erodes
and spins.

2011, 2014

- When, how, and why might the speaker's outlook or attitude shift over the course of the poem?

SUGGESTIONS FOR WRITING

1. What words and patterns are repeated in the different stanzas of Shelley's ODE TO THE WEST WIND? What differences are there from stanza to stanza? What "progress" does the poem make? Write an essay in which you discuss the ways that meaning and structure are intertwined in Shelley's poem.

2. Write an essay that explores the use of contrast in Pat Mora's SONRISAS. How is each of the two rooms in the poem characterized by way of contrast with the other? What do they individually and jointly symbolize? What does the poem show through this

contrast? Alternatively, write an essay about BLACKBERRY EATING, focusing on the comparison it makes.

3. Pick out any poem you have read in this book that seems particularly effective in the way it is put together. Write an essay in which you consider how the poem is organized—that is, what structural principles it employs. What do the choices of speaker, situation, and setting have to do with the poem's structure? What other artistic decisions contribute to its structure?

SAMPLE WRITING: ESSAY IN PROGRESS

The following piece of writing by student Lindsay Gibson was originally just one section of a longer essay on multiple poems by Philip Larkin. Though the beginning and middle of the piece work fine out of that context, you'll notice that we haven't supplied either the title or the real conclusion that the piece needs to have in order to become a complete, effective essay. What should the piece be titled? How might it be brought to a more satisfying conclusion?

You will notice, too, that the essay focuses only partly and somewhat unevenly on issues related to internal structure. How might the essay make more of the poem's structure? More generally, what are the essay's weakest and strongest moments and aspects? How might its argument be improved or expanded? Answering such questions for yourself or discussing them with your classmates can be a useful way to better understand the qualities of a good argument, a good title, and a good conclusion.

Lindsay Gibson
Dr. Nick Lolordo
Modern British Poetry
27 April 2021

Philip Larkin's "Church Going"

Philip Larkin is one of the semester's most fascinating poets. His use of colloquial language, regular meter, and rhyme sets him slightly apart from other poets of his day, many of whom write in varying forms of verse, use nearly indecipherable language, and rarely, if ever, make use of rhyme at all. Many of his poems are fraught with existential crises, the nature of which only someone living in the postmodern world could understand; consequently, his poems contain a lot of meaning for the contemporary reader.

Larkin's most fascinating poem, "Church Going," embodies many of his best attributes as a poet: it uses everyday, standard English and is therefore easy to read and understand, yet its stanzas contain a real search for meaning that its simple language might not immediately invite the reader to ponder. The poem also addresses one of Larkin's main preoccupations: religion, and specifically the role of religion in a postmodern world. Even with all of this, the most engaging aspect of the poem is the duality reflected in its structure: at first and on the one hand, the speaker makes quiet fun of religion; later and on the other hand, he reveals to us his own search for meaning and the answers that he realizes religion may or may not be able to give him.

The first two stanzas of "Church Going" contain a narrative of a seemingly secular man entering a church he has passed along his way. The speaker observes the layout of the building, the various accoutrements common to a church, and views it all with a mild sense of sarcasm or awkward reverence. His language almost insists on his self-proclaimed ignorance: "Someone would know; I don't" (line 12). And he foreshadows the rest of the poem when appraising the roof of the church as one would an antique: "Cleaned, or restored?" (12). At the end of the second stanza, the speaker reflects that "the place was not worth stopping for" (18). Yet stop he did, and that tells us volumes about what the rest of the poem is about.

In the third stanza, the poem's tone and the speaker's attitude shift as the speaker begins to ponder big questions about religion in today's world: Does it have any meaning left? Should it? The speaker reveals to us that he often stops at churches like these, searching for meaning, yet "Wondering what to look for" (21), not even knowing what the questions are that he wants answered. His use of words like "parchment, plate and pyx" (25) reveals to us that he is not as ignorant about religious liturgy as he would have us believe— which, in turn, is further evidence of the dual nature of the poem: the speaker wants us to believe he doesn't know or care about anything to do with religion, yet he has been on his quest for meaning long enough to know the names of things he claims he does not. The last line of the third stanza poses another compelling question, this time about the future: after churches fall out of use, "Shall we avoid them as unlucky places?" (27). The question of whether, when faith is finally dead, people will still cling to superstitions such as luck and supernatural powers of whatever nature is a fascinating one.

The speaker goes on to explore this question in the next few stanzas by imagining some specific ways in which superstition might persist after religion is gone: women might take their children to "touch a particular stone" (29) or pick herbs around the church to use for medicinal purposes. But in all these imagined examples, no one actually goes to the church to worship anymore. In stanza 4, the speaker presents various tableaus of people using the church for more and more mundane uses, such as a student of architecture, someone else who only likes to see the ruins of old buildings simply because they're old, and finally, and somewhat paradoxically, a "Christmas-addict" (43) who (presumably) wants to see the last religious remnants of his beloved, commoditized, and commercial-ized holiday. The last person who might visit the church in this post-religion world might even be a doppelganger of the speaker himself, who, though claiming to be "Bored" and "uninformed" (46), visits the church because "it held unspilt / So long and equably what since is found / Only in separation—marriage, and birth, / And death, and thoughts of these" (48-51). Once again the speaker insists that he is ignorant and careless of religion, but goes on to betray the fact that even if he does not believe in the religion itself, he is fascinated by the idea that it held "unspilt" what people now only find in marriages, births, and deaths: meaning. It is at this point that the reader can truly appreciate the point and purpose of this whole poem: meaning, and the search for it. It seems poignant that the speaker realizes there is more *meaning* in the church itself than any other place, whether actual belief in religion is there or not.

The last stanza seems to be an attempt on the speaker's part to reconcile the opposing forces of the poem—the speaker's insistence that he cares nothing for religion and that religion is meaningless anyway versus his existential need to find some kind of meaning that will justify his existence and maybe even the beliefs of others. The speaker finally respects what the church does for people, including himself: one's "compulsions meet, / Are recognized, and robed as destinies" (56-57). When one wonders if compulsions are merely that, one can go to church and be told that he or she is part of a larger whole—one's destiny. And if compulsions can be transformed into destinies, at least in the mind of the wonderer, then there will always be value in such a service: "that much never can be obsolete" (58), according to the speaker of the poem.

The last stanzas of the poem are devoted to a man who gravitates to the church because he "once heard [it] was proper to grow wise in, / If only that so many dead lie round" (62-63). Once again, the speaker shows us that even when belief in the religion associated with the church is completely gone, a sense of reverence, if only for the dead, will remain. The belief may be gone, but the sense of a community among people searching for, and perhaps finding, meaning will remain, and people will always be drawn to that, no matter what their belief system (or lack thereof).

The poem itself has another overarching concern that merits discussion: death. There are many images of or mentions of death throughout the poem: There are "flowers, cut / For Sunday, brownish now" (4-5), the words "Here endeth" (15) echoing through the small church, the possibility of someone seeing a "walking [. . .] dead one" (31), the assertion that "superstition, like belief, must die" (34), talk of the "ghostly silt / Dispersed" (46-47), thoughts of "marriage, and birth, / And death" (50-51). And finally, the last image in the poem is the abandoned church's graveyard in which "so many dead lie round" (63). Through-out the poem there is death: death of people, death of ideas, death of faith. Death's pervasiveness is one more way the poem struggles with its dual nature: the poem narrates a serious search for meaning, yet the very definition of death is that there *is* no meaning. Death is the end, there is nothing more. Any search for meaning is rendered meaningless anyway upon one's death. The speaker implies that there is even an end to the search for meaning itself. The speaker asks in line 35, perhaps the most powerful line of the whole poem, "And what remains when disbelief has gone?" What is left over when even "disbelief" has died? Is it the beginning of another cycle in the search for meaning, or has even the "faith" that there is nothing out there died as well?

The poem "Church Going" is a very layered, intensive look at all the things that matter to us as human beings: meaning, death, hope, hopelessness, and the way all of these things blend together in the perpetual existential crisis that is man's very existence.

Work Cited

Larkin, Philip. "Church Going." *The Norton Introduction to Literature*, edited by Kelly J. Mays, shorter 14th ed., W. W. Norton, 2021, pp. 966-67.

20 | EXTERNAL FORM

Previous chapters have discussed many of the *internal* features of a poem that make it unique: the **tone** and characteristics of its **speaker**; its **situation** and **setting** and its **themes**; its **diction**, **imagery**, and sounds. This chapter ventures into the *external* form of a poem, including its arrangement on the page and into both visual and verbal units. These formal aspects are external in being recognizable; like the fashion and fabric of clothing that expresses the personality of an individual, the external form is an appropriate garb or guise for the unique internal action and meaning of the poem. When reading a poem, you might immediately notice its stanza breaks. Or you might quickly recognize that the poem takes a traditional form such as the sonnet, or that it simply looks odd. These formal features guide readers as well as poets. They help readers feel and appreciate repetitions and connections, changes and gaps, in the language as well as the meaning of the poem.

STANZAS

Most poems of more than a few lines are divided into **stanzas**—groups of lines divided from other groups by white space on the page. Putting some space between groupings of lines has the effect of sectioning a poem, giving its physical appearance a series of divisions that sometimes correspond to turns of thought, changes of scene or image, or other shifts in structure or direction of the kind examined in the last chapter. In Donne's THE FLEA, for example, the stanza divisions mark distinct stages in the action: Between the first and second stanzas, the speaker stops his companion from killing the flea; between the second and third stanzas, the companion follows through on her intention and kills the flea. Any formal division of a poem into stanzas is important to consider; what appear to be gaps or silences may be structural markers.

Historically, stanzas have most often been organized by patterns of **rhyme,** and often of **meter,** too; thus stanza divisions have traditionally been a visual indicator of patterns in sound. In most traditional stanza forms, the pattern of rhyme is repeated in stanza after stanza throughout the poem, until voice and ear become familiar with the pattern and come to expect it. The repetition of pattern allows us to hear deviations from the pattern as well, just as we do in music.

TRADITIONAL STANZA FORMS

As the poems in this anthology demonstrate, stanzas can take myriad forms. Over time, however, certain stanza forms have become traditional, or "fixed." In using such stanza forms, poets thus often implicitly or explicitly allude and even respond to previous poets and poems that have used the same form. Like musicians, they also generate new effects, meanings, and music through meaningful variations on traditional forms.

Terza Rima

In the following poem, the first and third lines in each stanza rhyme, and the middle line then rhymes with the first and third lines of the next stanza.

ROBERT FROST
Acquainted with the Night

I have been one acquainted with the night.
I have walked out in rain—and back in rain.
I have outwalked the furthest city light.

I have looked down the saddest city lane.
5   I have passed by the watchman on his beat
And dropped my eyes, unwilling to explain.

I have stood still and stopped the sound of feet
When far away an interrupted cry
Came over houses from another street,

10   But not to call me back or say good-by;
And further still at an unearthly height,
One luminary clock against the sky

Proclaimed the time was neither wrong nor right.
I have been one acquainted with the night.

1928

In this stanza form, known as **terza rima**, the stanzas are linked to each other by a common sound: one rhyme sound from each stanza is picked up in the next stanza, and so on to the end of the poem (though sometimes poems in this form have sections that use varied rhyme schemes). Most traditional stanza forms involve a metrical pattern as well as a rhyme scheme. Terza rima, like most English fixed stanza and verse forms, involves **iambic** meter (unstressed and stressed syllables alternating regularly), and each line has five beats (**pentameter**).

Because terza rima requires many rhymes, and thus many different rhyme words, it is not very common in English, a language less rich in rhyme possibilities than Italian or French because it derives from so many different language families.

Spenserian Stanza

Named for Edmund Spenser, who used it to great effect in his long poem *The Faerie Queene*, the **Spenserian stanza** is even more rhyme rich than terza rima, using only three rhyme sounds in nine rhymed lines, as in this stanza from John Keats's "The Eve of St. Agnes":

Her falt'ring hand upon the balustrade,	*a*
Old Angela was feeling for the stair,	*b*
When Madeline, St. Agnes' charmèd maid,	*a*
Rose, like a missioned spirit, unaware:	*b*
With silver taper's light, and pious care,	*b*
She turned, and down the agèd gossip led	*c*
To a safe level matting. Now prepare,	*b*
Young Porphyro, for gazing on that bed;	*c*
She comes, she comes again, like ring dove frayed and fled	*c*

Notice that while the first eight lines of a Spenserian stanza are in iambic pentameter, the ninth has one extra foot, making it iambic **hexameter**.

Ballad Stanza

The much more common **ballad stanza** has only one set of rhymes in four lines; lines 1 and 3 in each stanza do not rhyme at all. And while those lines are in iambic **tetrameter** (4 beats/feet), lines 2 and 4 are rhymed iambic **trimeter** (3 beats/feet). As its name suggests, this stanza form is often used in **ballads** including SIR PATRICK SPENS, which begins with the following stanza:

The king sits in Dumferling toune,	*a*
Drinking the blude-reid wine:	*b*
"O whar will I get guid sailor,	*c*
To sail this ship of mine?"	*b*

TRADITIONAL VERSE FORMS

Stanza forms are not themselves subgenres of poetry, but rather a form that can be used for various kinds of poems. The same is true of other traditional verse forms—set patterns of rhythm and rhyme that govern whole poems or parts of them rather than individual stanzas. Three verse forms especially useful to know are the rhyming **couplet**, blank verse, and free verse.

Any pair of consecutive lines that share *end rhymes* is called a *rhyming couplet*. Andrew Marvell's TO HIS COY MISTRESS, for example, consists entirely of iambic tetrameter couplets, beginning with these two:

Had we but world enough, and time,	*a*
This coyness, lady, were no crime.	*a*
We would sit down, and think which way	*b*
To walk, and pass our long love's day.	*b*

A *heroic couplet* requires iambic pentameter, as in Phillis Wheatley's ON BEING BROUGHT FROM AFRICA TO AMERICA:

'Twas mercy brought me from my Pagan land,	*a*
Taught my benighted soul to understand	*a*
That there's a God, that there's a Saviour, too:	*b*
Once I redemption neither sought nor knew.	*b*

Near the other end of the spectrum from the heroic couplet sits **blank verse**, which consists of lines with regular meter, usually iambic pentameter, but no discernible rhyme scheme, as in these lines, which Adam speaks to Eve in John Milton's *Paradise Lost*:

> Well hast thou motioned, well thy thoughts employed,
> How we might best fulfil the work which here
> God hath assigned us; nor of me shalt pass
> Unpraised: for nothing lovelier can be found
> In woman, than to study household good,
> And good works in her husband to promote.

Though here used by Milton to describe lofty events of cosmic significance, blank verse was among the least formal and most natural of traditional verse forms until the explosion of **free verse** in the twentieth century. Now perhaps the most common of verse forms, free verse is "free" because it lacks both regular meter and rhyme. The wildly different lengths of the following lines from Lorna Dee Cervantes's Beneath the Shadow of the Freeway make its use of free verse especially obvious:

> inside
> a gray kitten a touchstone
> purring beneath the quilts
> grandma stitched

FIXED FORMS OR FORM-BASED SUBGENRES

Again, all these stanza and verse forms can be used in many different kinds of poems. But some kinds or subgenres of poetry are defined wholly by their use of particular formal patterns. Perhaps the most famous of these are the **sonnet** and the **haiku**, to which we devote the first two albums that follow this chapter. Others include the **limerick** (see, for example, There was a young girl from St. Paul), the **villanelle** (Do Not Go Gentle into That Good Night, below), the **palindrome** (Myth, below), and the **abecedarian** and **sestina** (see below). Though relatively rare for much of the twentieth century, such traditional fixed forms have in recent years become increasingly popular once again, even as new ones like the **golden shovel** continue to be invented.

You can probably deduce the principles involved in each of these fixed forms by looking carefully at an example; if you have trouble, consult the definitions in the glossary.

TRADITIONAL FORMS: POEMS FOR FURTHER STUDY

DYLAN THOMAS
Do Not Go Gentle into That Good Night[1]

> Do not go gentle into that good night,
> Old age should burn and rave at close of day;
> Rage, rage against the dying of the light.

---

1. Written during the final illness of the poet's father.

Though wise men at their end know dark is right,
5 Because their words had forked no lightning they
Do not go gentle into that good night.

Good men, the last wave by, crying how bright
Their frail deeds might have danced in a green bay,
Rage, rage against the dying of the light.

10 Wild men who caught and sang the sun in flight,
And learn, too late, they grieved it on its way,
Do not go gentle into that good night.

Grave men, near death, who see with blinding sight
Blind eyes could blaze like meteors and be gay,
15 Rage, rage against the dying of the light.

And you, my father, there on the sad height,
Curse, bless, me now with your fierce tears, I pray.
Do not go gentle into that good night.
Rage, rage against the dying of the light.

                                                                    1951, 1952

• What do the "wise," "good," "wild," and "grave" men have in common with
  the speaker's father? Why do you think Thomas chose such a strict form,
  the villanelle, for such an emotionally charged subject?

NATASHA TRETHEWEY
Myth

I was asleep while you were dying.
It's as if you slipped through some rift, a hollow
I make between my slumber and my waking,

the Erebus[2] I keep you in, still trying
5 not to let go. You'll be dead again tomorrow,
but in dreams you live. So I try taking

you back into morning. Sleep-heavy, turning,
my eyes open, I find you do not follow.
Again and again, this constant forsaking.

10 Again and again, this constant forsaking:
my eyes open, I find you do not follow.
You back into morning, sleep-heavy, turning.

But in dreams you live. So I try taking,
not to let go. You'll be dead again tomorrow.
15 The Erebus I keep you in—still, trying—

---

2. In Greek mythology, the dark region of the underworld through which the dead pass en route to
Hades.

I make between my slumber and my waking.
It's as if you slipped through some rift, a hollow.
I was asleep while you were dying.

2007

• How does Trethewey's use of a palindromic structure contribute to the
poem's evocation of grief? Why do you think the poem is called "Myth"?

ELIZABETH BISHOP
Sestina

September rain falls on the house.
In the failing light, the old grandmother
sits in the kitchen with the child
beside the Little Marvel Stove,
5 reading the jokes from the almanac,
laughing and talking to hide her tears.

She thinks that her equinoctial tears
and the rain that beats on the roof of the house
were both foretold by the almanac,
10 but only known to a grandmother.
The iron kettle sings on the stove.
She cuts some bread and says to the child,

It's time for tea now; but the child
is watching the teakettle's small hard tears
15 dance like mad on the hot black stove,
the way the rain must dance on the house.
Tidying up, the old grandmother
hangs up the clever almanac

on its string. Birdlike, the almanac
20 hovers half open above the child,
hovers above the old grandmother
and her teacup full of dark brown tears.
She shivers and says she thinks the house
feels chilly, and puts more wood in the stove.

25 *It was to be*, says the Marvel Stove.
I know what I know, says the almanac.
With crayons the child draws a rigid house
and a winding pathway. Then the child
puts in a man with buttons like tears
30 and shows it proudly to the grandmother.

But secretly, while the grandmother
busies herself about the stove,
the little moons fall down like tears
from between the pages of the almanac

35 into the flower bed the child
has carefully placed in the front of the house.

Time to plant tears, says the almanac.
The grandmother sings to the marvellous stove
and the child draws another inscrutable house.

1965

• Try to derive from SESTINA the "rules" that govern the sestina form. Why do
you think Bishop chose this form for her poem?

A. E. STALLINGS
Sestina: Like

With a nod to Jonah Winter[3]

Now we're all "friends," there is no love but Like,
A semi-demi goddess, something like
A reality-TV star look-alike,
Named Simile or Me Two. So we like
5   In order to be liked. It isn't like
There's Love or Hate now. Even plain "dislike"

Is frowned on: there's no button for it. Like
Is something you can quantify: each "like"
You gather's almost something money-like,
10   Token of virtual support. "Please like
This page to stamp out hunger." And you'd *like*
To end hunger and climate change alike,

But it's unlikely Like does diddly. Like
Just twiddles its unopposing thumbs-ups, like-
15   Wise props up scarecrow silences. *"I'm like,
So OVER him,"* I overhear. "But, like,
He doesn't get it. Like, you know? He's like
It's all OK. Like I don't even LIKE

Him anymore. Whatever. I'm all like . . ."
20   Take "like" out of our chat, we'd all alike
Flounder, agape, gesticulating like
A foreign film sans subtitles, fall like
Dumb phones to mooted desuetude. Unlike
With other crutches, um, when we use "like,"

25   We're not just buying time on credit: Like
Displaces other words; crowds, cuckoo-like,

---

3. Poet and children's book author (b. 1962); every line of his breakup poem "Sestina: Bob" (1999)
ends with the word *bob*.

Endangered hatchlings from the nest.[4] (Click "like"
If you're against extinction!) Like is like
Invasive zebra mussels, or it's like
30   Those nutria-things, or kudzu,[5] or belike

Redundant fast food franchises, each like
(More like) the next. Those poets who dislike
Inversions, archaisms, who just like
Plain English as she's spoke—why isn't "like"
35   Their (literally) every other word? I'd like
Us just to admit that's what real speech is like.

But as you like, my friend. Yes, we're alike,
How we pronounce, say, lichen, and dislike
Cancer and war. So like this page. Click *Like*.

2013

• How does Stallings here bend sestina conventions to make her point about
"real speech" (line 36) and poetry?

NATALIE DIAZ

Abecedarian Requiring Further Examination of Anglikan Seraphym[6] Subjugation of a Wild Indian Rezervation

Angels don't come to the reservation.
Bats, maybe, or owls, boxy mottled things.
Coyotes, too. They all mean the same thing—
death. And death
5   eats angels, I guess, because I haven't seen an angel
fly through this valley ever.
Gabriel?[7] Never heard of him. Know a guy named Gabe though—
he came through here one powwow[8] and stayed, typical
Indian. Sure he had wings,
10   jailbird that he was. He flies around in stolen cars. Wherever he stops,
kids grow like gourds from women's bellies.
Like I said, no Indian I've ever heard of has ever been or seen an angel.
Maybe in a Christmas pageant or something—

4. Some cuckoo species lay their eggs in other birds' nests.
5. Invasive plant of Asian origin, especially ubiquitous in the southern United States. *Nutria*: invasive species of large, semiaquatic rodent, originally from South America.
6. Antiquated spelling of *seraphim* (literally, "burning ones," in Hebrew); highly ranked celestial beings in Jewish, Islamic, and Christian traditions.
7. Divine messenger in Jewish, Christian, and Islamic traditions. In the Bible, he appears to Mary to announce that she will bear Jesus and is also said to be the angelic trumpeter who will announce the arrival of the Last Judgment and Christ's second coming.
8. American Indian ceremony or social gathering.

Nazarene[9] church holds one every December,
15 organized by Pastor John's wife. It's no wonder
Pastor John's son is the angel—everyone knows angels are white.
Quit bothering with angels, I say. They're no good for Indians.
Remember what happened last time
some white god came floating across the ocean?
20 Truth is, there may be angels, but if there are angels
up there, living on clouds or sitting on thrones across the sea wearing
velvet robes and golden rings, drinking whiskey from silver cups,
we're better off if they stay rich and fat and ugly and
'xactly where they are—in their own distant heavens.
25 You better hope you never see angels on the rez. If you do, they'll be marching you off to
Zion[1] or Oklahoma, or some other hell they've mapped out for us.

2012

• This poem arguably treats serious issues in a humorous, ironic way. What techniques does Diaz use to balance seriousness and humor? How does the abecedarian form add to that effect?

EVIE SHOCKLEY

acrobatic

acrophiliac[2] i'm not, so don't try putting me on the balance
beam. the rings,[3] too, are a bad idea—it doesn't help having
chalk on my hands. it seems that when you think of me, you think
daredevil, some simone biles,[4] but that's just ignorant. as
5 everybody else knows, i'm a close-to-the-mat
freestyler, just bouncing along to the music from *rocky*.[5] you couldn't
get me as far off the ground as the uneven bars.
heights make my skin break out and my eyes
implode. since as far back as i can remember, i've avoided
10 jungle gyms—if god meant us to climb, he'd have given all
kindergarteners tails. you'll never catch me on a ski
lift, a ski slope, or a ski. there are just too
many ways to die, when you start fucking with altitude.
next, you'll be asking me to high dive. listen: i need my

9. Evangelical Christian denomination deriving from nineteenth-century Methodism.
1. Hill of Jerusalem on which the city of David was built; the city of Jerusalem or the Jewish promised land, in Jewish tradition; in Christian theology, the heavenly city or kingdom of heaven.
2. Lover of heights; someone aroused by heights or high altitudes.
3. Gymnastic apparatus consisting of two small circles suspended by straps from the ceiling.
4. Belizean American athlete (b. 1997) who holds more World/Olympic medals than anyone else in the history of U.S. gymnastics.
5. Movie (1976) telling the unlikely rags-to-riches story of fictional Italian American boxer Rocky Balboa; its theme song, "Gonna Fly Now," ranks on the American Film Institute's top one hundred list.

15 oxygen. if i was any taller, i'd get dizzy
    parting my hair. surely you know that mountains are—without
    question—the greatest mistake mother nature made. give me
        one good
    reason to ride a roller coaster. i don't even like mood
    swings. you can keep the carnival—the flying
20 trapeze is an absolute no-go, even with a safety net
    underneath. i start dragging my heels at the suggestion of the pole
    vault—i'd never let go. i'll watch the fabulous janelle monae[6]
    walk the tightrope all day, but that's not my dance. i'm as
    xenial[7] as anyone, but my out-of-towners don't get tours of towers. my
25 yoga routine revolves around downward facing dog.[8] really, not even
    zeus[9] in his swan suit could sweep me off my feet.

                                                                        2017

• How might the abecedarian form of this poem both underscore and complicate its speaker's apparent inaptitude for "acrobatics"?

THE WAY A POEM LOOKS

Like stanza breaks, other arrangements of print and space help guide the voice
and the mind to a clearer sense of sound, meaning, and feeling. But poems are
written to be seen as well as heard, and their appearance on the page is crucial to
their effect. E. E. Cummings's poem L(A, for example, tries to visualize typograph-
ically what the poet asks you to see in your mind's eye.

E. E. CUMMINGS
l(a

l(a

le

af

fa

ll

s)

one

l

iness

                                                                        1958

6. African American singer, songwriter, rapper, and actress (b. 1985).
7. Of or related to hospitality or relations between guests and hosts.
8. Resting inversion yoga pose in which the body forms a V, with hands and feet pushing into the floor
and hips pushing upward.
9. Supreme deity of the ancient Greeks; according to myth, he disguised himself as a swan in order to
rape Leda, a mortal princess.

The unusual spacing of words in the following poem, with some run together and others widely separated, provides a guide to reading, regulating both speed and sense, so that the poem can capture aloud the wonder of a spring day.

E. E. CUMMINGS
in Just-[1]

in Just-
spring   when the world is mud-
luscious the little
lame balloonman

5   whistles   far   and wee

and eddieandbill come
running from marbles and
piracies and it's
spring

10   when the world is puddle-wonderful

the queer
old balloonman whistles
far   and   wee
and bettyandisbel come dancing

15   from hop-scotch and jump-rope and

it's
spring
and
    the
20   goat-footed

balloonMan[2] whistles
far
and
wee

1923

CONCRETE POETRY

Occasionally, poems are composed in a specific shape so that they resemble physical objects. The idea that poems can be related to the visual arts is an old one. Theodoric in ancient Greece is credited with inventing *technopaegnia*—that is,

1. First poem in the series *Chansons innocentes* (French for "Songs of Innocence").
2. Pan, whose Greek name means "everything," is traditionally represented with a syrinx (or the pipes of Pan). The upper half of his body is human, the lower half goat; as the father of Silenus he is associated with the spring rites of the god Dionysus.

the construction of poems with visual appeal. Once, the shaping of words to resemble an object was thought to have mystical power, but more recent attempts at **concrete poetry,** or shaped verse, simply attempt to supplement (or replace) verbal meanings with devices from painting and sculpture. Here are two examples.

GEORGE HERBERT
Easter Wings

Lord, who createdst man in wealth and store,[3]
Though foolishly he lost the same,
Decaying more and more
Till he became
Most poor:
With thee
O let me rise
As larks,[4] harmoniously,
And sing this day thy victories:
Then shall the fall further the flight in me.

My tender age in sorrow did begin;
And still with sicknesses and shame
Thou didst so punish sin,
That I became
Most thin.
With thee
Let me combine,
And feel this day thy victory;
For, if I imp[5] my wing on thine,
Affliction shall advance the flight in me.

1633

- How do this poem's decreasing and increasing line lengths correspond to the meaning of the words? Why do you think Herbert has chosen to present the poem sideways?

3. In plenty.
4. Which herald the morning.
5. Engraft: in falconry, to engraft feathers in a damaged wing, so as to restore the powers of flight.

JUSTIN PHILLIP REED
Portrait with Stiff Upper Lip

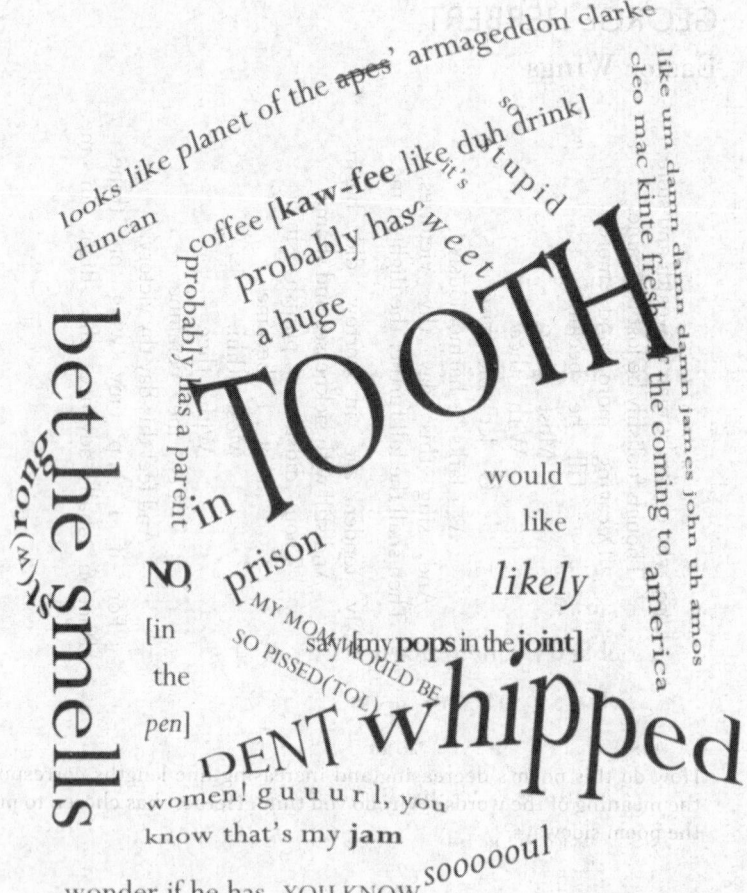

2018

• In what different ways and senses do the words here form a "portrait"? Who
  are the poem's speakers? Why might the person portrayed have or need a
  "stiff upper lip"?

SUGGESTIONS FOR WRITING

1. Trace the variations in imagery of light and darkness in Thomas's Do Not Go Gentle into That Good Night. How do we know that light represents life and darkness death (rather than, say, sight and blindness)? How does the poet use the strict formal requirements of the villanelle to emphasize this interplay of light and darkness? Write an essay in which you discuss the interaction of form and content in Do Not Go Gentle into That Good Night.

2. Which of the poems either mentioned or reproduced in this chapter do you think makes the most effective use of any traditional stanza or verse form? Why and how so? Write a response paper in which you explore your response to the poem and how it is shaped by the poet's choice of a traditional form.

3. Write an essay analyzing what A. E. Stallings's Sestina: Like suggests about social media and its effects on our language and on our sensibilities, paying special attention to the poem's play on the word "like" and with the sestina form.

4. Every poem has a particular form, whether or not it adheres to a traditional stanza or verse form or to conventional ideas about line, rhythm, or spacing. Examine closely the form of any poem in this book, including its arrangement on the page and division into lines and stanzas. How does the poet use form to shape sound, emotion, and meaning? Write an essay examining the relationship between the poem's theme and its external form.

5. Try your hand at writing an abecedarian. What sort of situations or topics might suit this form, and vice versa? Are such poems inevitably at least partly humorous? Why and how so, or not?

From *Black, Grey and White: A Book of Visual Sonnets* (2011), by David Miller

The Sonnet

AN ALBUM

The **sonnet**, one of the most persistent and familiar fixed forms, originated in medieval Italy and France. It dominated English poetry in the late sixteenth and early seventeenth centuries and then was revived several times from the late eighteenth century onward. Except for some experiments with length, the sonnet has always been fourteen lines long, and it usually is written in **iambic pentameter**. It is often printed as a single stanza, although it actually has formal divisions defined by its various rhyme schemes. For more than four centuries, the sonnet has been surprisingly resilient, and it continues to attract a variety of poets. As a verse form, the sonnet is contained, compact, demanding; whatever it does, it must do concisely. It is best suited to intensity of feeling and concentration of figurative language and expression.

Conventional sonnets are structured according to one of two principles of division. The *English*, or *Shakespearean*, *sonnet* is divided into three units of four lines each (**quatrains**) and a final unit of two lines (couplet), and sometimes the line spacing reflects this division. Ordinarily its rhyme scheme reflects the structure: The scheme of *abab cdcd efef gg* is the classic one, but many variations from that pattern still reflect the basic 4-4-4-2 division. In the *Italian*, or *Petrarchan*, *sonnet* (the Italian poet Francesco Petrarch was an early master of this form), the fundamental break is between the first eight lines (called an **octave**) and the last six (called a **sestet**). Its "typical" rhyme scheme is *abbaabba cdecde*, although it, too, produces many variations that still reflect the basic division into two parts, an octave and a sestet.

The two kinds of sonnet structures are useful for different sorts of argument. The 4-4-4-2 structure works very well for a poem that makes a three-step argument (with either a quick summary or a dramatic turn at the end) or for setting up brief, cumulative images. Shakespeare's THAT TIME OF YEAR THOU MAYST IN ME BEHOLD, for example, uses the 4-4-4-2 structure to mark the progressive steps toward death and the parting of lovers by using three distinct metaphors and then summarizing. In the two-part structure of the Italian sonnet, the octave often states a proposition or generalization, and the sestet provides a particular example, consequence, or application of it; alternatively, the second part may turn away from the first to present a new position or response. The final lines may, for example, reverse the first eight and achieve a paradox or irony in the poem, or the poem may nearly balance two comparable arguments or images. Basically, the 8-6 structure lends itself to poems with two points to make, or to those that make one point and then illustrate or complicate it.

During the Renaissance, poets regularly employed the sonnet for love poems; many modern sonnets continue to be about love or private life, and many poets continue to use a personal, apparently open and sincere **tone** in their sonnets. Time, (human) mortality, and (art's) immortality are also conventional topics, reinforced by the form itself: Sonnets are, after all, necessarily brief (just as, they sometimes remind us, all things humans are), yet simultaneously fixed, static, even rigid in somewhat the way monuments are. Today, centuries after the sonnet's introduction, the very fact that the form has endured so long and has been so highly revered can't help but reinforce its association with both immortality and artistic tradition.

But poets often find the sonnet form useful for a variety of other subjects and tones. Sonnets may be about politics, philosophy, motherhood, social media. And their tones vary widely, too, from anger and remorse to tender awe or snark. Sometimes poets take the kind of comfort in the careful limits of the form that William Wordsworth describes in NUNS FRET NOT AT THEIR CONVENT'S NARROW ROOM, finding in its two basic variations, the English sonnet and the Italian sonnet, a wealth of ways to organize their materials into coherent structures. Sometimes a neat and precise structure is instead altered as particular needs or effects may demand. And the two basic structures, Shakespearean and Petrarchan, certainly do not define all the structural possibilities within a fourteen-line poem.

Which of the following sonnets follow the Italian model? the English? In each case, how do form, structure, and content work together? How does each poet adapt the traditional form to his or her particular purpose? Aside from particular patterns of rhyme and meter, what other conventions of the sonnet can you identify? How do individual poems use, rework, even comment on those conventions? (To see how one student answered some of these questions by comparing sonnets by two different writers, read Melissa Makolin's essay OUT-SONNETING SHAKESPEARE . . . .)

FRANCESCO PETRARCH
Upon the breeze she spread her golden hair[1]

Upon the breeze she spread her golden hair
that in a thousand gentle knots was turned,
and the sweet light beyond all measure burned
in eyes where now that radiance is rare;

5   and in her face there seemed to come an air
of pity, true or false, that I discerned:
I had love's tinder in my breast unburned,
was it a wonder if it kindled there?

She moved not like a mortal, but as though
10   she bore an angel's form, her words had then
a sound that simple human voices lack;

a heavenly spirit, a living sun
was what I saw; now, if it is not so,
the wound's not healed because the bow grows slack.

c. 1334–38

• What might this sonnet imply about the relationship between the speaker and the woman described? What do both structure and form contribute to that characterization?

---

1. Translated from the Italian by Anthony Mortimer.

HENRY CONSTABLE
My lady's presence makes the roses red

My lady's presence makes the roses red,
Because to see her lips they blush for shame.
The lily's leaves, for envy, pale became,
And her white hands in them this envy bred.
5 The marigold the leaves abroad doth spread,
Because the sun's and her power is the same.
The violet of purple colour came,
Dyed in the blood she made my heart to shed.
In brief: all flowers from her their virtue take;
10 From her sweet breath their sweet smells do proceed;
The living heat which her eyebeams doth make
Warmeth the ground and quickeneth the seed.
The rain, wherewith she watereth the flowers,
Falls from mine eyes, which she dissolves in showers.

1594

• Which type of sonnet is this? How do external form and internal structure
here work together?

WILLIAM SHAKESPEARE
My mistress' eyes are nothing like the sun

My mistress' eyes are nothing like the sun;
Coral is far more red than her lips' red;
If snow be white, why then her breasts are dun,[2]
If hairs be wires, black wires grow on her head.
5 I have seen roses damasked[3] red and white,
But no such roses see I in her cheeks;
And in some perfumes is there more delight
Than in the breath that from my mistress reeks.
I love to hear her speak, yet well I know
10 That music hath a far more pleasing sound;
I grant I never saw a goddess go;[4]
My mistress, when she walks, treads on the ground.
And yet, by heaven, I think my love as rare
As any she belied with false compare.

1609

• How might this poem respond to sonnets like Constable's My lady's presence . . . and Petrarch's Upon the breeze . . . ?

2. Mouse-colored.
3. Variegated.
4. Walk.

Not marble, nor the gilded monuments

Not marble, nor the gilded monuments
Of princes, shall outlive this powerful rhyme;
But you shall shine more bright in these contènts
Than unswept stone, besmeared with sluttish time.
5 When wasteful war shall statues overturn,
And broils[5] root out the work of masonry,
Nor Mars his[6] sword nor war's quick fire shall burn
The living record of your memory.
'Gainst death and all-oblivious enmity
10 Shall you pace forth; your praise shall still find room
Even in the eyes of all posterity
That wear this world out to the ending doom.[7]
So, till the judgment that yourself arise,
You live in this, and dwell in lovers' eyes.

1609

• How does each quatrain build on the last?

Let me not to the marriage of true minds

Let me not to the marriage of true minds
Admit impediments.[8] Love is not love
Which alters when it alteration finds,
Or bends with the remover to remove:
5 Oh, no! it is an ever-fixèd mark,
That looks on tempests and is never shaken;
It is the star to every wandering bark,
Whose worth's unknown, although his height be taken.[9]
Love's not Time's fool, though rosy lips and cheeks
10 Within his bending sickle's compass come;
Love alters not with his brief hours and weeks,
But bears it out even to the edge of doom.
If this be error and upon me proved,
I never writ, nor no man ever loved.

1609

• What might the speaker mean when he says that love doesn't "ben[d] with the remover to remove" (line 4)? How might the rest of the poem explain and develop this statement?

5. Roots of plants.
6. Mars his: Mars's. Nor: neither.
7. Judgment Day.
8. The Church of England's marriage service contains this address to the witnesses: "If any of you know cause or just impediments why these persons should not be joined together [. . .]."
9. That is, measuring the altitude of stars (for purposes of navigation) is not a way to measure value.

JOHN MILTON
When I consider how my light is spent

When I consider how my light is spent,
    Ere half my days, in this dark world and wide,
    And that one talent which is death to hide[1]
    Lodged with me useless, though my soul more bent
5 To serve therewith my Maker, and present
    My true account, lest he returning chide;
    "Doth God exact day-labor, light denied?"
    I fondly ask; but Patience to prevent[2]
That murmur, soon replies, "God doth not need
10   Either man's work or his own gifts; who best
    Bear his mild yoke, they serve him best. His state
Is kingly. Thousands at his bidding speed
    And post o'er land and ocean without rest:
    They also serve who only stand and wait."

                           c. 1652

• How might the timing of the poem's shift to Patience (in the middle of line 8) be meaningful? Paraphrase the speaker's question and Patience's reply.

SOR JUANA INÉS DE LA CRUZ
O rose divine, in gentle cultivation[3]

In which she morally censures a rose, and thereby all that resemble it

O rose divine, in gentle cultivation
you are, with all your fragrant subtlety,
tuition, purple-hued, to loveliness,
snow-white instruction to the beautiful;

5 intimation of a human structure,
example of gentility in vain,
in whose one being nature has united
the joyful cradle and the mournful grave;

how haughty in your pomp, presumptuous one,
10 how proud when you disdain the threat of death,
then, in a swoon and shriveling, you give
a withered vision of a failing self;

1. In the parable of the talents (Matt. 25), the servants who earn interest on their master's money (his talents) while he is away are called "good and faithful"; the one who simply hides the money and then returns it is condemned and sent away.
2. Forestall. *Fondly*: foolishly.
3. Translated from the Spanish by Edith Grossman.

and so, with your wise death and foolish life,
in living you deceive, dying you teach!

1692

• What conventions of the sonnet can you identify here? In what respects
does this poem depart from the tradition of the sonnet?

WILLIAM WORDSWORTH
Nuns fret not at their convent's narrow room

Nuns fret not at their convent's narrow room;
And hermits are contented with their cells;
And students with their pensive citadels;
Maids at the wheel, the weaver at his loom,
5   Sit blithe and happy; bees that soar for bloom,
High as the highest Peak of Furness-fells,[4]
Will murmur by the hour in foxglove bells:
In truth the prison, unto which we doom
Ourselves, no prison is: and hence for me,
10 In sundry moods, 'twas pastime to be bound
Within the sonnet's scanty plot of ground;
Pleased if some souls (for such there needs must be)
Who have felt the weight of too much liberty,
Should find brief solace there, as I have found.

1807

• What does this poem imply about the sonnet's appeal?

The world is too much with us

The world is too much with us; late and soon,
Getting and spending, we lay waste our powers:
Little we see in Nature that is ours;
We have given our hearts away, a sordid boon![5]
5   This Sea that bares her bosom to the moon;
The winds that will be howling at all hours,
And are up-gathered now like sleeping flowers;
For this, for every thing, we are out of tune;
It moves us not.—Great God! I'd rather be
10 A Pagan suckled in a creed outworn;
So might I, standing on this pleasant lea,
Have glimpses that would make me less forlorn;

---

4. Mountains in England's Lake District, where Wordsworth lived.
5. Gift. It is the act of giving the heart away that is "sordid."

Have sight of Proteus rising from the sea;
Or hear old Triton[6] blow his wreathèd horn.

1807

• How does the poem characterize the "Pagan" worldview (line 10) as opposed
to "ou[r]" modern one? What does it mean to "see in Nature" nothing or
"Little [. . .] that is ours" (3)?

ELIZABETH BARRETT BROWNING
How do I love thee? Let me count the ways

How do I love thee? Let me count the ways.
I love thee to the depth and breadth and height
My soul can reach, when feeling out of sight
For the ends of Being and ideal Grace.
5 I love thee to the level of every day's
Most quiet need, by sun and candlelight.
I love thee freely, as men strive for Right;
I love thee purely, as they turn from Praise;
I love thee with the passion put to use
10 In my old griefs, and with my childhood's faith.
I love thee with a love I seemed to lose
With my lost saints—I love thee with the breath,
Smiles, tears of all my life!—and, if God choose,
I shall but love thee better after death.

1850

• How many "ways" of loving does the speaker "count" in the poem (line 1)?
How do these ways relate to and build on each other?

CHRISTINA ROSSETTI
In an Artist's Studio

One face looks out from all his canvases,
    One selfsame figure sits or walks or leans;
    We found her hidden just behind those screens,
That mirror gave back all her loveliness.
5 A queen in opal or in ruby dress,
    A nameless girl in freshest summer-greens,
    A saint, an angel—every canvas means
The same one meaning, neither more nor less.
He feeds upon her face by day and night,
10   And she with true kind eyes looks back on him
Fair as the moon and joyful as the light:
    Not wan with waiting, not with sorrow dim;

6. Sea deity, usually represented as blowing on a conch shell. *Proteus*: an old man of the sea who (in
the *Odyssey*) can assume a variety of shapes.

Not as she is, but was when hope shone bright;
   Not as she is, but as she fills his dream.

1856

• What might this poem suggest about the relationship between painter and subject? How might the poem's form encourage us to compare painting to poetry?

EDNA ST. VINCENT MILLAY

What lips my lips have kissed, and where, and why

What lips my lips have kissed, and where, and why,
I have forgotten, and what arms have lain
Under my head till morning; but the rain
Is full of ghosts tonight, that tap and sigh
5 Upon the glass and listen for reply,
And in my heart there stirs a quiet pain
For unremembered lads that not again
Will turn to me at midnight with a cry.
Thus in the winter stands the lonely tree,
10 Nor knows what birds have vanished one by one,
Yet knows its boughs more silent than before:
I cannot say what loves have come and gone;
I only know that summer sang in me
A little while, that in me sings no more.

1923

• What are the poem's principal parts? Why does the Italian/Petrarchan model suit this sonnet?

Women have loved before as I love now

Women have loved before as I love now;
At least, in lively chronicles of the past—
Of Irish waters by a Cornish prow
Or Trojan waters by a Spartan mast
5 Much to their cost invaded—here and there,
Hunting the amorous line, skimming the rest,
I find some woman bearing as I bear
Love like a burning city in the breast.
I think however that of all alive
10 I only in such utter, ancient way
Do suffer love; in me alone survive
The unregenerate passions of a day
When treacherous queens, with death upon the tread,
Heedless and wilful, took their knights to bed.

1931

• What does this poem imply about the difference between ancient and modern ways of loving?

I, being born a woman and distressed

I, being born a woman and distressed
By all the needs and notions of my kind,
Am urged by your propinquity to find
Your person fair, and feel a certain zest
5 To bear your body's weight upon my breast:
So subtly is the fume of life designed,
To clarify the pulse and cloud the mind,
And leave me once again undone, possessed.
Think not for this, however, the poor treason
10 Of my stout blood against my staggering brain,
I shall remember you with love, or season
My scorn with pity,—let me make it plain:
I find this frenzy insufficient reason
For conversation when we meet again.

                                                                            1923

• What feelings are expressed here? What does the poem imply about the
source or cause of these feelings?

I will put Chaos into fourteen lines

I will put Chaos[7] into fourteen lines
And keep him there; and let him thence escape
If he be lucky; let him twist, and ape
Flood, fire, and demon—his adroit designs
5 Will strain to nothing in the strict confines
Of this sweet Order, where, in pious rape,
I hold his essence and amorphous shape,
Till he with Order mingles and combines.
Past are the hours, the years, of our duress,
10 His arrogance, our awful servitude:
I have him. He is nothing more nor less
Than something simple not yet understood;
I shall not even force him to confess;
Or answer. I will only make him good.

                                                                            1923

• What might this sonnet suggest about the value or appeal of the sonnet
form?

7. In Greek mythology, the formless void preceding creation. But Millay's Chaos recalls another
mythological figure, Proteus. A sea god endowed with both a knowledge of all things (past, present, and
future) and the ability to assume any form in order to elude humans, he would divulge his knowledge
only to a captor able to hold him fast through all his mutations—hence the English term *protean*.

GWENDOLYN BROOKS
First Fight. Then Fiddle.

First fight. Then fiddle. Ply the slipping string
With feathery sorcery; muzzle the note
With hurting love; the music that they wrote
Bewitch, bewilder. Qualify to sing
5   Threadwise. Devise no salt, no hempen thing
For the dear instrument to bear. Devote
The bow to silks and honey. Be remote
A while from malice and from murdering.
But first to arms, to armor. Carry hate
10   In front of you and harmony behind.
Be deaf to music and to beauty blind.
Win war. Rise bloody, maybe not too late
For having first to civilize a space
Wherein to play your violin with grace.

1949

• After advising "First fight. Then fiddle," the speaker discusses first music,
then conflict. Why do you think the poet has arranged her material this way?
Why a sonnet?

GWEN HARWOOD
In the Park

She sits in the park. Her clothes are out of date.
Two children whine and bicker, tug her skirt.
A third draws aimless patterns in the dirt.
Someone she loved once passes by—too late

5   to feign indifference to that casual nod.
"How nice," et cetera. "Time holds great surprises."
From his neat head unquestionably rises
a small balloon . . . "but for the grace of God . . ."

They stand a while in flickering light, rehearsing
10   the children's names and birthdays. "It's so sweet
to hear their chatter, watch them grow and thrive,"
she says to his departing smile. Then, nursing
the youngest child, sits staring at her feet.
To the Wind she says, "They have eaten me alive."

1963

• What is the implication of the "small balloon" (line 8) that rises from the
head of the man who passes by?

JUNE JORDAN

Something Like a Sonnet for Phillis Miracle Wheatley[8]

Girl from the realm of birds florid and fleet
flying full feather in far or near weather
Who fell to a dollar lust coffled[9] like meat
Captured by avarice and hate spit together
5   Trembling asthmatic alone on the slave block
built by a savagery travelling by carriage
viewed like a species of flaw in the livestock
A child without safety of mother or marriage

Chosen by whimsy but born to surprise
10   They taught you to read but you learned how to write
Begging the universe into your eyes:
They dressed you in light but you dreamed with the night.
From Africa singing of justice and grace,
Your early verse sweetens the fame of our Race.

1989

- Phillis Wheatley usually wrote in heroic couplets—rhyming couplets of iambic pentameter. What is the effect of Jordan's use of dactylic meter, unusual for a sonnet?

BILLY COLLINS

Sonnet

All we need is fourteen lines, well, thirteen now,
and after this one just a dozen
to launch a little ship on love's storm-tossed seas,
then only ten more left like rows of beans.
5   How easily it goes unless you get Elizabethan
and insist the iambic bongos must be played
and rhymes positioned at the ends of lines,
one for every station of the cross.
But hang on here while we make the turn
10   into the final six where all will be resolved,
where longing and heartache will find an end,
where Laura will tell Petrarch[1] to put down his pen,

8. African-born poet (1753–84) brought to the United States and enslaved at the age of seven or eight.
9. Chained together in a line.
1. Italian poet Francesco Petrarch (1304–74), regarded as a father of the sonnet form. Many of his love poems were inspired by Laura, who may have been the wife of a local nobleman.

take off those crazy medieval tights,
blow out the lights, and come at last to bed.

1999

• In what respects is Collins's poem a traditional sonnet? In what respects is
it not? What might it suggest about the relationship between love and
poetry, especially as conventionally portrayed in sonnets?

HARRYETTE MULLEN
Dim Lady[2]

My honeybunch's peepers are nothing like neon. Today's
special at Red Lobster is redder than her kisser. If Liquid Paper
is white, her racks are institutional beige. If her mop were
Slinkys, dishwater Slinkys would grow on her noggin. I have
5 seen tablecloths in Shakey's Pizza Parlors, red and white, but
no such picnic colors do I see in her mug. And in some minty-
fresh mouthwashes there is more sweetness than in the garlic
breeze my main squeeze wheezes. I love to hear her rap, yet
I'm aware that Muzak has a hipper beat. I don't know any
10 Marilyn Monroes. My ball and chain is plain from head to toe.
And yet, by gosh, my scrumptious Twinkie has as much sex
appeal for me as any lanky model or platinum movie idol
who's hyped beyond belief.

2002

• How might Mullen's poem essentially "do unto" Shakespeare's MY MIS-
TRESS' EYES ARE NOTHING LIKE THE SUN much as Shakespeare's poem does
to earlier, especially Petrarchan, sonnets? What is the effect of Mullen's
diction? her use of brand names? Is DIM LADY a sonnet?

SUGGESTIONS FOR WRITING

1. Consider carefully the structure of, and sequencing in, Brooks's FIRST FIGHT. THEN
   FIDDLE. How do various uses of sound in the poem (**rhyme**, **onomatopoeia**, and
   alliteration, for example) reinforce its themes and tones? Write an essay in which
   you explore the relationship between sound and sense in the poem.
2. Some of the sonnets in this book, including those by Shakespeare, adhere closely to
   the classic English model; others, such as Milton's WHEN I CONSIDER HOW MY LIGHT
   IS SPENT, follow the Italian model; and some, including those by Billy Collins and
   June Jordan, bear only slight resemblance to either of the traditional sonnet models.
   Take any four sonnets in this book as the basis for an essay in which you compare
   the various ways poets have used the sonnet form to achieve their unique artistic
   purposes.
3. Several poems in this album are not only sonnets but also commentaries on the sonnet or on certain conventions associated with it such as Petrarchan "conceits"

---

2. Shakespeare's sonnets frequently address or refer to the so-called Dark Lady.

(Shakespeare's MY MISTRESS' EYES . . .) or the relation between (male) speaker and (female) subject or love object. Write an essay comparing at least two of these poems. What does each ultimately suggest about the sonnet through both its form and its content?

4. Choose two sonnets from this album that offer what you see as either very similar or very different, even opposed, visions of love. Write an essay comparing the two, being sure to consider how each poet uses the sonnet form.

Yoshitoshi, *Since the Crescent Moon*, circa 1885–92

A woodblock print featuring haiku master Matsuo Bashō speaking to two farmers. The haiku on the print reads:

Since the crescent moon
I have been waiting
for tonight

Haiku

AN ALBUM

The **haiku**, an import into the English poetic tradition, has a long history in Japanese poetry. Originally, the haiku (then called *hokku*) was a short section of a longer poem (called a *renga* or *haikai*) composed by several poets who wrote segments in response to one another. Traditionally, the Japanese haiku was an unrhymed poem consisting of seventeen sounds (or, rather, characters representing seventeen sounds) and distributed over three lines in a 5-7-5 pattern—that is, five distinctive sounds in the first line, seven in the second, and five in the third. "Sounds" in the Japanese language are not exactly the same as "syllables" in English, but when English writers began to compose haiku about a century ago, they ordinarily translated the sound requirement into syllables.

Haiku aim for compression; they leave a lot unsaid. Typically, haiku describe a natural object and imply a state of mind. They usually have a "seasonal" requirement, so that each poem associates itself with one season of the year in a revolving pattern of change. This seasonal association may be suggested quite subtly and indirectly through, for example, an allusion to a seasonal flower. Haiku more generally involve descriptions of nature, reflecting the Buddhist sense of nature as orderly and benign but also contingent and transient.

When adapted into other languages and cultures, haiku cannot rely on the same spiritual assumptions or worldview, but these poems usually retain a sense of the human and natural as being mutually reflective and interdependent. Haiku often combine observation and imagination, blurring the Western distinction between seeing something literally and having some "vision" of its end or meaning.

Some of the traditional Japanese masters of haiku from the seventeenth to the early twentieth century—Bashō and Buson, for example—are represented (in English translations) in this album. So, too, are some of the many later poets and translators who have tried their hand at haiku, without always strictly observing the seventeen-syllable and three-line requirements. Some (as you'll see) create long poems made up of haiku. As haiku has become an international form, its conventions have, like those of other fixed forms, proven both demanding and adaptable to the particular needs of different cultural contexts, different languages, and different poets.

TRADITIONAL JAPANESE HAIKU

CHIYOJO
Whether astringent[1]

Whether astringent
I do not know. This is my first
Persimmon picking.

---

1. Translated from the Japanese by Daniel C. Buchanan. Chiyojo (1703–75) is probably the most famous Japanese woman haiku poet. Tradition has it that she wrote this poem at the time of (and about) her engagement.

BASHŌ

A village without bells—[2]

A village without bells—
    how do they live?
       spring dusk.

This road—

    This road—
no one goes down it,
    autumn evening.

BUSON

Coolness—[3]

Coolness—
    the sound of the bell
      as it leaves the bell.

Listening to the moon

    Listening to the moon,
gazing at the croaking of frogs
    in a field of ripe rice.

ONE HAIKU, FOUR TRANSLATIONS

Perhaps the single most famous haiku is by Bashō. Here are four different English translations of that poem. (The source of these poems, Hiroaki Sato's *One Hundred Frogs: From Matsuo Bashō to Allen Ginsberg*, contains many more examples.)

LAFCADIO HEARN

Old pond—

Old pond—frogs jumped in—sound of water.

1898

CLARA A. WALSH

An old-time pond

An old-time pond, from off whose shadowed depth
Is heard the splash where some lithe frog leaps in.

1910

2. This poem and the next translated from the Japanese by Robert Hass. Matsuo Bashō (1644–94) is usually considered the first great master of haiku.
3. This poem and the next translated from the Japanese by Robert Hass. Yosa Buson (1716–83) was a renowned painter, as well as a haiku master.

EARL MINER

The still old pond

The still old pond
and as a frog leaps in it
   the sound of a splash.

1979

ALLEN GINSBERG

The old pond

The old pond—a frog jumps in, kerplunk!

1979

MODERN HAIKU

EZRA POUND

In a Station of the Metro[4]

The apparition of these faces in the crowd;
Petals on a wet, black bough.

1913

ALLEN GINSBERG

Looking over my shoulder

Looking over my shoulder
my behind was covered
with cherry blossoms.

1955

RICHARD WRIGHT

In the falling snow

In the falling snow
A laughing boy holds out his palms
Until they are white.

1960

4. Paris subway.

ETHERIDGE KNIGHT

Eastern guard tower

Eastern guard tower
glints in sunset; convicts rest
like lizards on rocks.

The falling snow flakes

The falling snow flakes
Cannot blunt the hard aches nor
Match the steel stillness.

Making jazz swing in

Making jazz swing in
Seventeen syllables AIN'T
No square poet's job.

1960

AUTHORS ON THEIR WORK

ETHERIDGE KNIGHT (1931–91)

From "A MELUS Interview: Etheridge Knight" (1985)*

Gwendolyn Brooks. Yeah, she's the first one turned me on to *haiku*. She used to come visit me when I was in prison. And this is in the Sixties, remember, this is long before they had poets-in-the-prison programs and poets in schools. [. . .] She brought me some books and Japanese *haiku*. Years later I asked her how come and she said, "It was because you were too wordy in your poems." And I like *haiku*. I try to use it, I try to follow the general form. I try to bring my own American consciousness to it. You know. [. . .] I like them because you gotta deal with the noun and the verb. You ain't got too much time to fool around with some abstractions, you know, a lot of adverbs and adjectives and stuff. But I like them.

*"A MELUS Interview: Etheridge Knight." Interview by Steven C. Tracy. *MELUS*, vol. 12, no. 2, summer 1985, pp. 7–23. *JSTOR*, www.jstor.org/stable/467427.

OCTAVIO PAZ
Basho An[5]

The whole world fits in-
to seventeen syllables,
and you in this hut.

Straw thatch and tree trunks:
5   they come in through the crannies:
Buddhas and insects.

Made out of thin air,
between the pines and the rocks
the poem sprouts up.

10   An interweaving
of vowels and the consonants:
the house of the world.

Centuries of bones,
mountains: sorrow turned to stone:
15   here they are weightless.

What I am saying
barely fills up the three lines:
hut of syllables.

1987

SONIA SANCHEZ
From 9 Haiku (for Freedom's Sisters)[6]

5.

(Fannie Lou Hamer)[7]

feet deep
in cotton you shifted
the country's eyes

---

5. In about 1670 Matsuo Basho traveled on foot through the mountains and valleys surrounding Kyoto, composing poems. He stayed for a short while in a tiny hut next to the Kompukuji temple. In memory of the poet they have named the hut Basho-An. In 1760 another poet and painter, Yosa Buson, visited the same places and discovered the ruins of Basho's cabin. He moved nearby and, with the help of three disciples, rebuilt the hut. Buson died in 1783. His tomb was erected there, as were the tombs of other of his poet-disciples. In 1984 my wife and I visited Basho-An, a place as solitary now as it was 300 years ago [Paz's note]. Translated from the Spanish by Mark Weinberger.
6. Each haiku in this sequence is dedicated to a specific African American woman.
7. *Fannie Lou Hamer* was the vice-chair of the Mississippi Freedom Democratic Party, a voting-rights activist, and a civil rights leader [Sanchez's note]. A Mississippi Delta sharecropper's daughter, Hamer (1917–77) grew up picking cotton alongside her nineteen siblings; in 1968, she became the first African American delegate to a national party convention since Reconstruction and Mississippi's first-ever female delegate.

7.

(Rosa Parks)[8]

baptizer of
morning light walking us away
from reserved spaces

2010

SUE STANDING
Diamond Haiku

Major or minor,
says Baseball Diamond Sutra,[9]
what does it matter?

The boys of summer
5   know that nirvana[1] is just
one inning away.

Deep in the outfield,
a glove reaches toward sky—
fireflies blink on.

10 Over the bleachers,
a blank scoreboard announces
no wins, no losses.

2011

TWAIKU

With its 280-character limit (previously 140), *Twitter* has given haiku a new lease
on life, inspiring thousands of people around the world to try their hand at crafting what some now dub "twaiku." You can find countless examples—on topics
ranging from cats and zombies to NASCAR—online and via *Facebook* pages like
"The Twitter Haiku Movement." But the "movement" (if such it is) first grabbed
headlines in early 2010, when Sun Microsystems' CEO Jonathan Schwartz chose
to tweet (or "twaiku") his resignation:

Financial crisis
Stalled too many customers
CEO no more.

8. *Rosa Parks* was an African American civil rights activist whom the U.S. Congress called the
"Mother of the Modern-Day Civil Rights Movement" [Sanchez's note]. Parks (1913–2005) helped to
spark the famous Montgomery Bus Boycott when she refused in 1955 to give up her bus seat to a
White passenger.
9. The *Diamond Sutra* is one of Buddhism's most ancient and sacred texts, but in her 1993 article
"The Baseball Diamond Sutra," Helen Tworkov suggests that some modern enthusiasts credit
baseball's putative "inventor," Union general Abner Doubleday (1819–93), with infusing the game
with many veiled Buddhist references, including the baseball "diamond."
1. In Buddhism, state of bliss and peace reached through the effort to extinguish desire and
transcend individual consciousness.

SUGGESTIONS FOR WRITING 1009

SUGGESTIONS FOR WRITING

1. What is gained, and what is lost, when an artistic tradition like Japanese haiku is imported, through translation, imitation, and inspiration, into another language and culture? Using the poems in this album and your own research, write an essay in which you analyze the way that haiku has established itself as part of English-language literary culture. What might be distinctive about English-language or specifically American haiku? Or how exactly have writers in this tradition adapted the form to suit and reflect a distinctively modern, Western perspective and experience?

2. As this album begins to demonstrate, haiku has proven especially attractive to twentieth- and twenty-first-century African American poets. Gwendolyn Brooks, for example, introduced the form to Etheridge Knight, and Sonia Sanchez in a sense walks in their footsteps. Using the poems in this album and your own research, write an essay in which you explore how one or two of these poets, or others, have made their own distinctive use of the form.

3. Write an essay exploring the seasonal imagery in at least three of the more traditional haiku in this album. How does each refer to a season, however indirectly? What does each manage to suggest about the particular character or feeling of that season, and how so?

The Golden Shovel

AN ALBUM

T he sonnet and haiku are centuries old. But contemporary poets continue to invent new fixed forms, even as they re-invent old ones. Take, for example, the **golden shovel**—an accessible, flexible form that its champions predict might ultimately become for our own, twenty-first, century what the sonnet was to earlier ones. In a golden shovel, the last words of each line, read sequentially, reproduce at least one line of another poem (or song lyric). Credit for pioneering the form goes to the ever-inventive Terrance Hayes. His 2010 poem THE GOLDEN SHOVEL takes its inspiration and title from another poem that Hayes's end-words reproduce not once but twice: Gwendolyn Brooks's WE REAL COOL, set in a pool hall called the Golden Shovel. Credit for popularizing the form, however, goes to poets Peter Kahn (also a high-school teacher), Ravi Shankar, and Patricia Smith, editors of *The Golden Shovel Anthology: New Poems Honoring Gwendolyn Brooks*. Originally published in 2017, the centenary of Brooks's birth, this volume "both introduc[ing] a new form and celebrat[ing her] legacy" proved so popular that a second edition appeared just two years later, now including poems not only by an impressive array of contemporary poets, both established and emerging, but also by students (like you) whose work was selected through an international competition.

Like the anthology that helped introduce it to the world, the golden shovel has already proven a uniquely accessible and inspiring, "beguiling and mind-expanding," "substantial and dynamic contribution to" English-language literature, to quote admiring reviewers. But what makes this new form so appealing to poetry novices and experts alike? We hope that this album, which includes a selection of Gwendolyn Brooks poems alongside a handful of the innumerable golden shovels those poems have inspired, will encourage you to ask and answer this question for yourself.

But here are a few possibilities to get you started. As Shankar notes, the golden shovel is "one of the few [poetic] forms that work both horizontally and vertically," operating a bit like a "verbal sudoku." Like a sudoku, the golden shovel, moreover, doesn't require poets to start from scratch, with a blank slate or a dauntingly blank page. Rather, this form offers a head-start, a starting place, an inspiration—in this case, the line (or more) of another poem a writer selects to provide the end-words of each line of his or her new poem. If, as we suggest throughout this book, all writing comes out of engaged reading, if literature itself is a never-ending conversation inviting all comers, then the golden shovel foregrounds and capitalizes on that. In Shankar's words, "an inherently collaborative effort, a dialogue, a response," the golden shovel offers the poet a chance not only to pay homage to specific work, words, and wordsmiths that inspire her but also to "sample," while reinterpreting, that work. As such, it's a form very much in the spirit of a cultural moment like our own that "values collage and sampling, cross-fertilizing, riffing, and remixing." That the golden shovel was originally invented by a poet as conversant with hip hop as with the traditional poetic canon seems anything but accidental. As music critic Jason Draper insists, after all, sampling has given hip hop "the power to bring old music to new ears, helping music to evolve while paying respect to the artists that came before."

As we hope this album will help you appreciate, the golden shovel does poetry's music the same service. Which golden shovels in this album seem to revisit, from a new angle, situations, settings, or topics explored in the Brooks poem they sample? Which of these golden shovels instead help us to see in an entirely new way the poetic line(s) they borrow? Either way, how does each golden shovel mean and work differently when you not only read it "horizontally," line by line, but also read its end words "vertically"? Individually and collectively, what might these Brooks-inspired golden shovels help you to see or appreciate about her poetry that you might not have otherwise?

GWENDOLYN BROOKS
We Real Cool

The Pool Players.
Seven at the Golden Shovel.

We real cool. We
Left school. We

5 Lurk late. We
Strike straight. We

Sing sin. We
Thin gin. We

Jazz June. We
10 Die soon.

1950

- Who are "we" in this poem? Do you think that the speaker and the poet share the same idea of what is "cool"?

GWENDOLYN BROOKS (1917–2000)

From "An Interview with Gwendolyn Brooks" (1970)*

Q[UESTION:] Are your characters literally true to your experience or do you set out to change experience?

A[NSWER:] Some of them are, are invented, some of them are very real people.

Q[UESTION:] How about the seven pool players in the poem "We Real Cool"?

A[NSWER:] They have no pretensions to any glamor. They are supposedly dropouts, or at least they're in the poolroom when they should possibly be in school, since they're probably young enough, or at least those I saw were when I looked in a poolroom [. . .]. First of all, let me tell you how that's supposed to be said, because there's a reason why I set it out as I did. These are people who are essentially saying, "Kilroy is here. We are." But they're a little uncertain of the strength of their identity. [. . .]

The "We"—you're supposed to stop after the "We" and think about their validity, and of course there's no way for you to tell whether it should be said softly or not, I suppose, but I say it rather softly because I want to represent their basic uncertainty, which they don't bother to question every day, of course.

Q[UESTION:] Are you saying that the form of this poem, then, was determined by the colloquial rhythm you were trying to catch?

A[NSWER:] No, determined by my feeling about these boys, these young men.

*"An Interview with Gwendolyn Brooks." Interview by George Stavros. *Contemporary Literature*, vol. 11, no. 1, winter 1970, pp. 1–20. *JSTOR*, www.jstor.org/stable/1207502.

TERRANCE HAYES
The Golden Shovel

After Gwendolyn Brooks

I. 1981

When I am so small Da's sock covers my arm, we
cruise at twilight until we find the place the real

men lean, bloodshot and translucent with cool.
His smile is a gold-plated incantation as we

5 drift by women on bar stools, with nothing left
in them but approachlessness. This is a school

I do not know yet. But the cue sticks mean we
are rubbed by light, smooth as wood, the lurk

of smoke thinned to song. We won't be out late.
10 Standing in the middle of the street last night we

watched the moonlit lawns and a neighbor strike
his son in the face. A shadow knocked straight

Da promised to leave me everything: the shovel we
used to bury the dog, the words he loved to sing

15 his rusted pistol, his squeaky Bible, his sin.
The boy's sneakers were light on the road. We

watched him run to us looking wounded and thin.
He'd been caught lying or drinking his father's gin.

He'd been defending his ma, trying to be a man. We
20 stood in the road, and my father talked about jazz,

how sometimes a tune is born of outrage. By June
the boy would be locked upstate. That night we

got down on our knees in my room. If I should die
before I wake. Da said to me, it will be too soon.

II. 1991

25 Into the tented city we go, weakened by the fire's ethereal

afterglow. Born lost and cooler than heartache. What we

know is what we know. The left
30 hand severed and school-

ed by cleverness. A plate of we-
ekdays cooking. The hour lurk-

ing in the afterglow. A late-
night chant. Into the city we

35 go. Close your eyes and strike
a blow. Light can be straight-

ened by its shadow. What we
break is what we hold. A sing-

ular blue note. An outcry sin-
40 ged exiting the throat. We

push until we thin, thin-
king we won't creep back again.

While God licks his kin, we
sing until our blood is jazz,

45 we swing from June to June.
We sweat to keep from we-

eping. Groomed on a die-
t of hunger, we end too soon.

2010

- The first part of Hayes's poem seems to share the pool-hall setting of Brooks's WE REAL COOL, as well as its focus on (Black) men and masculinity. What vision of all three—pool hall, (Black) men, and (Black) masculinity—does Hayes's poem offer?
- The second part of THE GOLDEN SHOVEL seems more enigmatic, both taking more liberties with the words it incorporates from WE REAL COOL (as with "thin- / king," lines 41–42) and more closely resembling Brooks's poem in terms of style. What do you make of this second part of THE GOLDEN SHOVEL and how it relates to the first part?

GWENDOLYN BROOKS

a song in the front yard

I've stayed in the front yard all my life.
I want a peek at the back
Where it's rough and untended and hungry weed grows.
A girl gets sick of a rose.

5   I want to go in the back yard now
And maybe down the alley,
To where the charity children play.
I want a good time today.

They do some wonderful things.
10 They have some wonderful fun.
My mother sneers, but I say it's fine
How they don't have to go in at quarter to nine.
My mother, she tells me that Johnnie Mae
Will grow up to be a bad woman.
15 That George'll be taken to Jail soon or late
(On account of last winter he sold our back gate).

But I say it's fine. Honest, I do.
And I'd like to be a bad woman, too,
And wear the brave stockings of night-black lace
20 And strut down the streets with paint on my face.

1945

• Who is this poem's speaker, and what is her situation? What do "the front
yard" and "the back" (lines 1, 2) come to stand for or symbolize in the poem?

EVIE SHOCKLEY

song in the back yard

—a golden shovel for rihanna[1]

the more you see   the less you see me   tattoos and
thighs crowd your eyes   i'm young but i've seen scenes i'd
pay well to unwitness   plays as old as power   an ancient script   you like
my hair   my ass   my tits   if you had to
5   sell my voice   how would you package it   would it be
pretty in pink   with dancehall in my spit and a
childhood of training in denial   mi make it *good girl gone bad*
gone red   seen red   seen blue black scream-swollen song scene   woman
down   i didn't do it   *this was done to me*   and *my love is too*

1. Stage name of internationally famous Barbadian singer-songwriter and fashion icon Robyn
Rihanna Fenty (b. 1988); her third album, *Good Girl Gone Bad* (2007), referenced in line 7, earned
her the first of many Grammy awards, for the chart-topping single "Umbrella" (line 27).

10   *complicated to have thrown back in my face*[2]   and
            it's got nothing to do with the clothes i wear
        he was my friend   he was my father   i was my mother   the
    ancient script again   now casting a new generation   you got to be brave
      when every minute of your day is a press / release   my stockings
15   my sheerest armor   my filly signal   just one sign of
    the fearless core you do not want to mess wit   my strength is night-black
           is island-rock   is hard but alive as coral reef   the lace

      the caribbean sea makes   no surprise *i'm so hard* eh   *chains and*
          whips excite me[3]   i love leather   i will strut
20   the red carpet in any city in the world   in necklines down
           to there   shorts rising up to here   but i'm the
    barbadian mirage   the weed-hungry boys in the back alleys and busy streets
        of the world   dem cah look but never touch   i'm dizzy with
 power   but rubber-muscled from the weight of the role i model   mi paint
25   mi politics pon mi lips for de young girls to read   slip on
   courage like stilettos   and in return   fair-weather fans bring roses to my
   door   real love brings an *umbrella*   shelter for my only human face
                                 2017

- How is Rihanna characterized in the poem, and how—through her—might this "song" offer a different perspective on issues raised in Brooks's A SONG IN THE FRONT YARD?

GWENDOLYN BROOKS
Riot

A riot is the language of the unheard.

—*Martin Luther King*[4]

John Cabot,[5] out of Wilma, once a Wycliffe,
all whitebluerose below his golden hair,
wrapped richly in right linen and right wool,
almost forgot his Jaguar and Lake Bluff;[6]
5 almost forgot Grandtully (which is The

2. Quotation from African American poet-playwright Ntozake Shange's Obie Award-winning play *For Colored Girls Who Have Considered Suicide / When the Rainbow Is Enuf* (1975), which explores, in a series of verse monologues, the pain and promise of "bein alive & bein a woman & bein colored."
3. Lyric from Rihanna's single "S&M," from *Loud* (2010). *I'm so hard*: refrain of Rihanna's single "Hard," from *Rated R* (2009).
4. In a 1966 *60 Minutes* interview, King (1929–68) responded to questions about the "increasingly vocal minority who disagree totally" with his campaign of nonviolence by contending that though this "group represents a numerical minority," "we've got to see that a riot is the language of the unheard. And, what is it that America has failed to hear? It has failed to hear that the economic plight of the Negro poor has worsened over the last few years."
5. A prominent American family since the early eighteenth century, the Cabots made their original fortune through trade, especially of rum, slaves, and opium.
6. Wealthy village in the Chicago metropolitan area, on the shore of Lake Michigan; in 2010, its population was 92 percent White, 0.58 percent African American.

Best Thing That Ever Happened To Scotch); almost
forgot the sculpture at the Richard Gray
and Distelheim; the kidney pie at Maxim's,[7]
the Grenadine de Boeuf at Maison Henri.

10 Because the Negroes were coming down the street.

Because the Poor were sweaty and unpretty
(not like Two Dainty Negroes in Winnetka)[8]
and they were coming toward him in rough ranks.
In seas. In windsweep. They were black and loud.
15 And not detainable. And not discreet.

Gross. Gross. *"Que tu es grossier!"*[9] John Cabot
itched instantly beneath the nourished white
that told his story of glory to the World.
"Don't let It touch me! the blackness! Lord!" he whispered
20 to any handy angel in the sky.

But, in a thrilling announcement, on It drove
and breathed on him: and touched him. In that breath
the fume of pig foot, chitterling[1] and cheap chili,
malign, mocked John. And, in terrific touch, old
25 averted doubt jerked forward decently,
cried "Cabot! John! You are a desperate man,
and the desperate die expensively today."

John Cabot went down in the smoke and fire
and broken glass and blood, and he cried "Lord!
30 Forgive these nigguhs that know not what they do."

1969

• How does the poem characterize John Cabot and his response to the riot?
  What types of **irony** might be at work in the poem?

LIZ LOCHHEAD
Beyond It

The bad weather is trying to get in
so veils of rain become blatterings,[2] seas
over-arch, they pound and rake our shores. In
they come—far, far beyond the high-tide mark with windsweep
5 and drag, splintering all they suck back in. They
make a nothing of all things that once were

7. Like "Maison Henri" (line 9), pricy, exclusive Chicago restaurant (founded 1963). *Distelheim*: like
"the Richard Gray" (founded 1963, line 7), a private Chicago art gallery.
8. Prosperous Chicago suburb.
9. How crude you are! (French).
1. Small intestines of animals, usually fried or boiled.
2. In Scots, "blatter" means a rainstorm, a heavy fall, or "a volley of clattering words, or sound of
rapid motion."

our all-in-all, stood proud. The skies go black
with thick murk, this impenetrable cloud, and
more-than-weather stirs one boiling broth of chaos, irresistible
   and loud.

2017

• How might Lochhead re-interpret by recontextualizing the line she takes
from RIOT?

GWENDOLYN BROOKS
Behind the Scenes

When I see a President, a Vice President, a Secretary of
State on sparkling tile,
beside noble columns of white,
I think to myself: "Somebody got there early,
5 and swept, and scrubbed; somebody dusted."

Before the President came,
somebody buffed his shoes.
The not too-stiffened white of his shirt
was not achieved by his own agility.

10 At the invisible controls: some little
weak-kneed, stricken, or powerful woman or man.

c. 1993 2003

• What different conceptions of importance and "powe[r]" (line 11) might be
contrasted in this poem?

JULIA ALVAREZ
Behind the Scenes

After you, Ms. Brooks
from behind the scenes

You don't fool me pretending that you're gone, I
see you in the white margins even if you think
you're now invisible, even if you look like print to
everybody else. I'm in this line of work myself,
5 so I know how you've toiled to become the nobody somebody
reading doesn't see, as if the not-too stiffened stanzas got
ironed out, the sparkling rhymes buffed & put there
by themselves, and not because Nobody got there early

and was gone before the ink dried on her thumb. Early
10 on, I learned from reading your poems that there
are no shortcuts writing them, that each time I've got
to give up being the *VIP* Somebody,

get down on my weak knees, discard *myself,*
become the work we love. So here's to
15 you at the invisible controls, not gone as some think
but powerfully alive in poems swept clean of *I.*

2017

• How does Alvarez here characterize Brooks's work as an author, or what does she suggest she learned from that work about being a poet?

SUGGESTIONS FOR WRITING

1. Which of the golden shovels in this album do you find most compelling, either on its own terms or in terms of its relation to the Brooks poem it samples? Write a response paper in which you explore your own choice and response: What makes the poem you picked especially compelling to you in either of the terms suggested above?

2. Write an essay in which you draw on both BEHIND THE SCENES and at least two other Brooks poems to develop the thesis that this poem can give us a key to Brooks's poetry. How, that is, might her poems demonstrate an interest in looking "behind the scenes," particularly at those who often remain "invisible," yet "powerful" (Brooks, BEHIND THE SCENES, lines 10, 11).

3. Write an essay comparing any of the Brooks poems in this album to the golden shovel it inspired. How specifically does the golden shovel offer a new perspective either on the sort of issues, characters, settings, or situations explored in Brooks's poem or on the line the golden shovel takes from Brooks?

4. Choose at least one line from any poem in this anthology or, if your instructor allows, from a song whose lyrics you find especially effective. Then write your own golden shovel, using the words of your chosen line as your end words. When you finish (or even as you work), write a paragraph or two reflecting on what, if anything, is especially challenging about this writing exercise and what it might show you—about poetry; about working within a fixed form; about the way golden shovels work; and/or about the line, poem, or lyrics that you began with.

Exploring Contexts

The more knowledge you have—both general knowledge and knowledge of poetic and literary traditions—the better a reader of poetry (and everything else) you are likely to be. Poems often draw on a fund of human knowledge about all sorts of things, asking us to bring to bear facts and beliefs we have acquired from earlier reading or from our everyday experiences. In the previous chapters, we have looked at how practice, specific skills, and a knowledge of basic literary terms make interpretation easier and better. This contextual section focuses more on other types of information that will help you read richly and fully: information about authors and their work, about events that influenced authors or inspired their writing, and about the ways other readers and critics have interpreted the work. Poets always write in a specific time and place, under unique circumstances, and with some awareness of the world around them, whether or not they explicitly refer to contemporary matters. Poems not only *refer* to people, places, and events—things that exist in time—but also *reflect* given moments and even try to shape those moments; they are the products of both the potentialities and the limitations of the times in which they are created. Many poems—like many works of drama and fiction—have something to say not only about seemingly universal situations and concerns but also about those specific to particular times and cultures.

What we need to bring to our reading varies from poem to poem. For example, to understand Wilfred Owen's DULCE ET DECORUM EST we need to know that poison gas was used in World War I; the green tint through which the speaker sees the world in lines 13–14 comes from the green glass in the goggles of the gas mask he has just put on. But some broader issues matter as well, such as the climate of opinion that surrounded the war and the way war had been represented in earlier literary works. No doubt you will read a poem more intelligently—and with more feeling—the more you know about its cultural, historical, and literary contexts. But at the same time, your sense of these subjects will grow as a result of reading the poems themselves sensitively and thoughtfully and relating them to your own time, too. Reading poetry can be a way to gain knowledge as well as an aesthetic experience. Although we don't generally turn to poetry for information as such, poems often give us more than we expect, insofar as we are aware of real-world contexts. As important, they can give us insights into times and cultures other than our own that history books cannot or typically do not.

To get at appropriate factual, cultural, and historical information, we need to ask three kinds of questions of ourselves. The first is obvious: Do I understand all (or most) of the references in the poem? When events, places, or people unfamiliar to you come up, you will need to find out what, where, or whom they are. The second question is more difficult: How do I know, in a poem that does *not* refer specifically to events, people, or ideas that I do not recognize, that I need to know more? That is, when a poem has no specific references to look up, no people or events to identify, how do I know that it has a specific context? Usually, good poets will not puzzle you more than necessary, so you can safely assume that anything that is not self-explanatory merits close attention and possibly some digging in the library and/or careful Googling. References that are not in themselves clear provide a strong clue that you need more information. When something doesn't click, when the information given seems insufficient, you need to trust your puzzlement and try to find the missing facts that will help you to make sense of the poem. But how? Often the date of the poem helps; sometimes the title gives a clue or a point of departure; sometimes you can uncover, by reading about the author, some of the things he or she was interested in or concerned about. There is no single all-purpose way to discover what to look for, but that kind of research—looking for clues, adding up the evidence—can be interesting in itself and very rewarding when it is successful. The third question for every factual reference is *Why?* Why does the poem refer to this particular person instead of some other? What function does the reference serve?

21 | THE AUTHOR'S WORK AS CONTEXT: ADRIENNE RICH

Even though all poets share the medium of language and usually have some common notions about their craft, they put the unique resources of their individual personalities, experiences, and outlooks into every poem they create. A poet may rely on tradition extensively and use devices that others have developed without surrendering his or her individuality, just as any individual shares certain characteristics with others—political affiliations, religious beliefs, tastes in clothes and music—without compromising his or her integrity and uniqueness. Sometimes a person's uniqueness is hard to define. But it is always there, and we recognize and depend on it in our relationships with other people. And so with poets: Most don't make a conscious effort to put an individual stamp on their work; they don't have to. The stamp is there in the very subjects, words, images, and forms they choose. Every individual's unique consciousness marks what it records and imagines.

Experienced readers can often identify a poem as the distinctive work of an individual poet even though they may never have seen that poem before, much as experienced listeners can identify a new piece of music as the work of a particular composer, singer, or group after hearing only a few phrases. This ability depends on a lot of reading or a lot of listening to music, and any reasonably sensitive reader can learn, over time, to do it with remarkable accuracy. Yet this ability is not an end in itself; rather, it is a by-product of learning to appreciate the distinctive qualities of a poet's work. Once you've read several poems by the same poet, you will usually see some features that the poems all share. Many people have favorite poets, just as they have favorite rock groups or rap artists. In both cases, we are attracted to the artist's work because, consciously or not, we recognize and appreciate that artist's distinctive style and outlook.

The work of any writer will display a characteristic way of thinking. It will have certain identifiable *tendencies*. But this does not mean that every poem by a particular author will be predictable and contain all of the same features. Poets test their talents and their views—as well as their readers—by experimenting with various subjects and points of view, formal structures and devices. Like all of us, poets also grow and change over time. As readers, then, we want to strive to recognize differences, as well as similarities, among individual poems and to appreciate the ways an author's work does and doesn't change over the years.

Of what practical use is it to learn to recognize and understand the distinctive voice and mind of a particular poet? Just as you learn from watching other people, seeing how they react and respond to various situations and events, so you can learn from watching poets at work—seeing how they learn and develop, how they change their minds or test alternative points of view, how they discover the reach and limits of their imaginations and talents, how they find their distinctive voices and come to terms with their own identities. Each poem exists separately and individually, but the whole body of a poet's work also records the workings and the evolution of a distinctive artistic consciousness as it confronts a world that is itself perpetually changing.

In addition, the more you know about a poet and the more of his or her poems you read, the better a reader you will likely be of any individual poem by the poet. When you grow accustomed to a writer's habits and manners and means of expression, you learn what to expect. Coming to a new poem by a familiar poet, you know what to look for and have clear expectations. At the same time, you are better prepared to appreciate the surprises each poem holds in store.

THE POETRY OF ADRIENNE RICH

You will find both continuity and change, similarities and differences, in the work of any good poet, and this chapter introduces you to a great one. Adrienne Rich (1929–2012) was an especially active, prolific poet whom many readers and critics regard as the best of her generation. A careful reader of her work will find similarities of interest and strategy from her earliest poems—published shortly after World War II, in 1951—to her twenty-first-century ones. A distinctive mind and orientation are at work.

But over the years Rich's work changed quite a lot, too, as she modified her views on a number of issues. Such changes were the result both of her personal experiences and of those shared experiences that helped define her era. Many of the changes in Rich's ideas and attitudes, for example, reflect changing concerns among American intellectuals (especially women) in the second half of the twentieth century, and her poems represent both changed social conditions and sharply altered social, political, and philosophical attitudes. But her poems also reflect altered personal circumstances. Rich married in her early twenties and had three children by the time she was thirty; many of her early poems are about heterosexual love, and some of them are quite explicitly about sex. Later, she was involved in a long-term lesbian relationship and wrote, again quite explicitly, about sex between women, as well as enormously influential essays including "Compulsory Heterosexuality and Lesbian Existence" (1980). In Rich's poems, then, we may not only trace the contours of an evolving personal life and outlook but also—and even more important for the study of poetry generally—see how changes *within* the poet and in her social and cultural context alter the subjects, themes, and form of her poetry.

Just as information about an author's life and times can help us in this enterprise, so, too, can the essays, letters, and interviews in which authors reflect on the character and aims of their poetry and on the topics the poetry explores. In the case of Rich, we have a bounty of such material from a poet who was also a remarkably prolific, articulate, and influential prose writer. Gathered at the end of this chapter are excerpts from these writings, including both essays that express Rich's outlook at a particular moment and retrospective pieces in which she reflects on the development of her work over time.

It is fitting that the titles of two of Adrienne Rich's books—*A Change of World* (1951) and *The Will to Change* (1971)—prominently feature the word *change*. For change is both a consistent concern of her poetry and a hallmark of her poetic career. Published when their author was just twenty-one, poems such as AT A BACH CONCERT, STORM WARNINGS, and AUNT JENNIFER'S TIGERS seem, at first glance, preternaturally mature. With their tightly controlled structure, their regular rhythm (and, often, rhyme), and their coolly observant tone, these early poems both embody and celebrate the "discipline" that "masters feelings" and the "proud restraining purity" by which art lends order to life ("At a Bach Concert," lines 4, 5, 11). (Versions of the word *master*, in fact, appear in all three poems.) Explaining why he chose *A Change of World* for the prestigious Yale Younger Poets Series, poet W. H. Auden singled out just such qualities and attitudes, praising Rich for a "craftsmanship" based on that "capacity for detachment from the self and its emotions without which no art is possible." If "poems are analogous to persons," Auden continued, then these poems are "neatly and modestly dressed, speak quietly but do not mumble, respect their elders but are not cowed by them, and do not tell fibs."

Adrienne Rich, 1951

Less than a decade later, however, Rich began to see the very "neatness" and "detachment" of her own early poems as itself a kind of "fib." As she put it in 1964, the early poems, "even the ones I liked best and in which I felt I'd said most, were queerly limited" because "in many cases I [. . .] suppressed, omitted, falsified even, certain disturbing elements to gain the perfection of order." From this point forward, Rich's work attempted to do the opposite—to, in Matthew Arnold's words, "see life steadily and see it whole," in all its disturbing, disorderly imperfection. Indeed, one of the major themes of the later poems is both the necessity and the difficulty of breaking through the web of "myth" and illusion in order to get to "the thing itself" (DIVING INTO THE WRECK, line 63).

In its attempt to do just that, Rich's poetry itself became less neat and orderly, less quiet, modest, and respectful. Beginning with the collection *Snapshots of a Daughter-in-Law* (1963), the poems speak in many radically different voices and tones and take many different forms. Rich's evolution as a poet was not a matter of pursuing any kind of single-minded mastery over her materials. "I find that I can no longer go to write a poem with a neat handful of materials and express those materials according to a prior plan," Rich explained in 1964; "the poem itself engenders new sensations, new awareness in me as it progresses." What results are "poems that *are* experiences" rather than "poems *about* experiences."

In becoming more informal, exploratory, and emotional, Rich's poems also

Adrienne Rich, 1966

became more personal and autobiographical, more willing to enter and lay bare what "Storm Warnings" calls the "troubled regions" of the poet's own life, heart, and mind (28). In fact, Rich suggested that her artistic growth was, in part, a matter of closing the gap between "the woman in the poem and the woman writing the poem." And in "Roofwalker," a 1961 poem that articulated her new poetic ideal, Rich compares herself both to a roofer standing atop a half-built house and to "a naked man fleeing / across" those very roofs. Like both, she now dared to be "exposed, larger than life, / and due to break my neck."

At the same time, Rich's work also became steadily more social, political, and historical. HISTORY is, in fact, the title of one poem in this chapter and the subject of many others. As early as 1956, Rich also began to insist on the historicity of her own poems by dating each one. "It seems to me now that this was an oblique political statement," Rich insists in the 1984 essay "Blood, Bread, and Poetry": "It was a declaration that placed poetry in a historical continuity, not above or outside history." "For Rich," as one critic argues, "a deepening subjectivity does not mean withdrawal, as it did for [Emily] Dickinson, but, on the contrary, a more searching engagement with people and with social forces."

In Rich's life, as in her work, the movement into the self fueled the movement outward—into the world and back into the past—and vice versa. On the one hand, it was in part her personal feelings and experiences—the fact that she felt "unfit, disempowered, adrift" as a housewife and mother in the mid-1950s—that sent her to the work of "political" writers such as Mary Wollstonecraft, Simone de Beauvoir, and James Baldwin, and, later, into the antiwar, civil rights, and women's movements. On the other hand, it was these writers and movements that eventually encouraged her to see her "private turmoil"—indeed, her consciousness itself—as the product of historically specific social and political forces. As she explains in "Blood, Bread, and Poetry,"

> my personal world view [. . .] was [. . .] created by political conditions. I was not a man;
> I was white in a white-supremacist society; I was [. . .] educated from the perspective
> of a particular class; my father was an "assimilated" Jew in an anti-Semitic world, my
> mother a white southern Protestant; there were particular historical currents on
> which my consciousness would come together, piece by piece. [. . .] My personal world
> view, which like so many young people I carried as a conviction of my own uniqueness,
> was not original with me, but was, rather, my untutored and half-conscious rendering
> of the facts of blood and bread, the social and political forces of my time and place.

Rich's mature poetry often scrutinizes the "social and political forces" that shape our lives and our relationships with one another and with the planet we inhabit. In this way, "the personal is political" for and in Rich—and so, too, is the literary. Yet her poetry works as poetry largely because in it the converse is always equally true. Her "poems compel us," as critic Albert Gelpi suggests, "precisely because [. . .] the politics [are] not abstracted and depersonalized but tested on the nerve-ends."

Despite—or even because of—all the changes, Rich's work also demonstrates a real and rare sort of consistency. From the very beginning of her career in the 1950s to her death in 2012, Rich conceived poems with a powerful sense of functional structure and cast them in **lyric** modes that sensitively reflect their moods and tones. She engaged readers viscerally and intellectually through vivid images. And certain images and objects—knives and coffee pots, ruins and rubble, maps and monsters, wintry weather— recur in multiple poems, binding the poems together even as they help us track a process of evolution and change that, Rich reminds us, isn't simple or straightforward. "If you think you can grasp me, think again," she warns us in the poem "Delta"; "my story flows in more than one direction."

Adrienne Rich, 2006

POEMS BY ADRIENNE RICH

At a Bach Concert

Coming by evening through the wintry city
We said that art is out of love with life.
Here we approach a love that is not pity.

This antique discipline, tenderly severe,
5 Renews belief in love yet masters feeling,
Asking of us a grace in what we bear.

Form is the ultimate gift that love can offer—
The vital union of necessity
With all that we desire, all that we suffer.

10 A too-compassionate art is half an art.
Only such proud restraining purity
Restores the else-betrayed, too-human heart.

                                                      1951

Storm Warnings

The glass has been falling all the afternoon,
And knowing better than the instrument
What winds are walking overhead, what zone
Of gray unrest is moving across the land,
5 I leave the book upon a pillowed chair
And walk from window to closed window, watching
Boughs strain against the sky

And think again, as often when the air
Moves inward toward a silent core of waiting,
10 How with a single purpose time has traveled
By secret currents of the undiscerned
Into this polar realm. Weather abroad
And weather in the heart alike come on
Regardless of prediction.

15 Between foreseeing and averting change
Lies all the mastery of elements
Which clocks and weatherglasses cannot alter.
Time in the hand is not control of time,
Nor shattered fragments of an instrument
20 A proof against the wind; the wind will rise,
We can only close the shutters.

I draw the curtains as the sky goes black
And set a match to candles sheathed in glass
Against the keyhole draught, the insistent whine
25 Of weather through the unsealed aperture.

This is our sole defense against the season;
These are the things that we have learned to do
Who live in troubled regions.

1951

Snapshots of a Daughter-in-Law

1

You, once a belle in Shreveport,
with henna-colored hair, skin like a peachbud,
still have your dresses copied from that time,
and play a Chopin prelude
5   called by Cortot:[1] *"Delicious recollections
float like perfume through the memory."*

Your mind now, mouldering like wedding-cake,
heavy with useless experience, rich
with suspicion, rumor, fantasy,
10   crumbling to pieces under the knife-edge
of mere fact. In the prime of your life.
Nervy, glowering, your daughter
wipes the teaspoons, grows another way.

2

Banging the coffee-pot into the sink
15   she hears the angels chiding, and looks out
past the raked gardens to the sloppy sky.
Only a week since They said: *Have no patience.*

The next time it was: *Be insatiable.*
Then: *Save yourself; others you cannot save.*[2]
20   Sometimes she's let the tapstream scald her arm,
a match burn to her thumbnail,

or held her hand above the kettle's snout
right in the woolly steam. They are probably angels,
since nothing hurts her anymore, except
25   each morning's grit blowing into her eyes.

3

A thinking woman sleeps with monsters.
The beak that grips her, she becomes. And Nature,
that sprung-lidded, still commodious
steamer-trunk of *tempora* and *mores*[3]
30   gets stuffed with it all: the mildewed orange-flowers,

1. Alfred Cortot (1877–1962), Franco-Swiss pianist and conductor.
2. According to Matthew 27.42, the chief priests, scribes, and elders mocked the crucified Jesus by
saying, "He saved others; himself he cannot save."
3. Times and customs (Latin).

the female pills, the terrible breasts
of Boadicea[4] beneath flat foxes' heads and orchids.

Two handsome women, gripped in argument,
each proud, acute, subtle, I hear scream
35   across the cut glass and majolica
like Furies[5] cornered from their prey:
The argument *ad feminam*,[6] all the old knives
that have rusted in my back, I drive in yours,
ma semblable, ma soeur![7]

4

40   Knowing themselves too well in one another:
their gifts no pure fruition, but a thorn,
the prick filed sharp against a hint of scorn . . .
Reading while waiting
for the iron to heat,
45   writing, *My Life had stood—a Loaded Gun—*[8]
in that Amherst pantry while the jellies boil and scum,
or, more often,
iron-eyed and beaked and purposed as a bird,
dusting everything on the whatnot every day of life.

5

50   *Dulce ridens, dulce loquens*,[9]
she shaves her legs until they gleam
like petrified mammoth-tusk.

6

When to her lute Corinna sings[1]
neither words nor music are her own;
55   only the long hair dipping
over her cheek, only the song
of silk against her knees
and these
adjusted in reflections of an eye.

---

4. Queen of the ancient Britons. When her husband died, the Romans seized the territory he ruled and scourged Boadicea; she then led a heroic but ultimately unsuccessful revolt. *Female pills*: medicines for gynecological ailments.
5. In Roman mythology, the three sisters were the avenging spirits of retributive justice.
6. To the woman (Latin). The *argumentum ad hominem* (literally, "argument to the man") is (in classical rhetoric) an argument aimed at a person's individual prejudices or special interests.
7. My mirror-image or double, my sister (French). Charles Baudelaire (1821–67), in the prefatory poem to *Les Fleurs du Mal* (1857), addresses (and attacks) his "hypocrite reader" as "mon semblable, mon frère" (my double, my brother).
8. "My Life had stood—a Loaded Gun—" [Poem No. 754], Emily Dickinson, *Complete Poems*, ed. T. H. Johnson, 1960, p. 369 [Rich's note]. See the Emily Dickinson album that follows this chapter.
9. Sweet laughter, sweet chatter (Latin). The phrase (slightly modified here) concludes Horace's *Ode* 1.22, describing the appeal of a mistress.
1. Opening line of a lyric by Thomas Campion (1567–1620; p. 946).

60 Poised, trembling and unsatisfied, before
an unlocked door, that cage of cages,
tell us, you bird, you tragical machine—
is this *fertilisante douleur*?[2] Pinned down
by love, for you the only natural action,
65 are you edged more keen
to prise the secrets of the vault? has Nature shown
her household books to you, daughter-in-law,
that her sons never saw?

7

"To have in this uncertain world some stay
70 *which cannot be undermined, is*
of the utmost consequence."[3]
                              Thus wrote
a woman, partly brave and partly good,
who fought with what she partly understood.
75 Few men about her would or could do more,
hence she was labeled harpy, shrew and whore.

8

"You all die at fifteen," said Diderot,[4]
and turn part legend, part convention.
Still, eyes inaccurately dream
80 behind closed windows blankening with steam.
Deliciously, all that we might have been,
all that we were—fire, tears,
wit, taste, martyred ambition—
stirs like the memory of refused adultery
85 the drained and flagging bosom of our middle years.

9

Not that it is done well, but
that it is done at all?[5] Yes, think
of the odds! or shrug them off forever.
This luxury of the precocious child,
90 Time's precious chronic invalid,—
would we, darlings, resign it if we could?
Our blight has been our sinecure:

2. Enriching pain (French).

3. ". . . is of the utmost consequence," from Mary Wollstonecraft, *Thoughts on the Education of Daughters*, London, 1787 [Rich's note]. Wollstonecraft (1759–97) also wrote *A Vindication of the Rights of Woman* (1792).

4. "Vous mourez toutes a quinze ans," from the *Lettres à Sophie Volland*, quoted by Simone de Beauvoir in *Le Deuxième Sexe*, vol. II, pp. 123–4 [Rich's note]. Editor of the *Encyclopédie* (the central document of the French Enlightenment), Denis Diderot (1713–84) became disillusioned with the traditional education of women and undertook an experimental education for his own daughter. French philosopher Simone de Beauvoir's (1908–86) landmark book, *The Second Sex* (1949), explores what she calls the "myths" and supposed "facts" that have historically made women "secondary" to men.

5. Samuel Johnson's (1709–84) comment on women preachers: "Sir, a woman's preaching is like a dog's walking on his hinder legs. It is not done well, but you are surprised to find it done at all."

mere talent was enough for us—
glitter in fragments and rough drafts.

95 Sigh no more, ladies.[6]
                    Time is male
and in his cups drinks to the fair.
Bemused by gallantry, we hear
our mediocrities over-praised,
100 indolence read as abnegation,
slattern thought styled intuition,
every lapse forgiven, our crime
only to cast too bold a shadow
or smash the mould straight off.

105 For that, solitary confinement,
tear gas, attrition shelling.
Few applicants for that honor.

        10
                    Well,
she's long about her coming, who must be
110 more merciless to herself than history.[7]
Her mind full to the wind, I see her plunge
breasted and glancing through the currents,
taking the light upon her
at least as beautiful as any boy
115 or helicopter,
                    poised, still coming,
her fine blades making the air wince

but her cargo
no promise then:
120 delivered
palpable
ours.

                                        1958–60

6. Opening words of a song in Shakespeare's *Much Ado about Nothing* (Act 2, Scene 3); sung by a minor male character, it explains that "Men were deceivers ever" and urges women to "sigh not so, but let them go, / And be you blithe and bonny."

7. Cf. *Le Deuxième See*, vol. II, p. 574: ". . . elle arrive du fond des ages, de Thèbes, de Minos, de Chichen Itza; et elle est aussi le totem planté au coeur de la brousse africaine; c'est un helicoptère et c'est un oiseau; et voilà la plus grande merveille: sous ses cheveux peints le bruissement des feuillages devient une pensée et des paroles s'échappent de ses seins" [Rich's note]. "[S]he comes from the remotest ages, from Thebes, Minos, Chichén Itzá; and she is also the totem planted in the heart of the African jungle; she is a helicopter and she is a bird; and here is the greatest wonder: beneath her painted hair, the rustling of leaves becomes a thought and words escape from her breasts" (Simone de Beauvoir's *The Second Sex*, translated by Constance Borde and Sheila Malovany, Alfred A. Knopf, 2009, p. 764).

AUTHORS ON THEIR WORK

ADRIENNE RICH (1929–2012)

From "When We Dead Awaken" (1979)*

Over two years I wrote a 10-part poem called "Snapshots of a Daughter-in-Law," in a longer, looser mode than I'd ever trusted myself with before. It was an extraordinary relief to write that poem. It strikes me now as too literary, too dependent on allusion; I hadn't found the courage yet to do without authorities, or even to use the pronoun "I"—the woman in the poem is always "she." One section of it, #2, concerns a woman who thinks she is going mad; she is haunted by voices telling her to resist and rebel, voices which she can hear but not obey.

*"When We Dead Awaken: Writing as Re-Vision." *On Lies, Secrets, and Silence: Selected Prose: 1966–1978.* W. W. Norton, 1979, pp. 33–49.

Planetarium

(*Thinking of Caroline Herschel, 1750–1848, astronomer, sister of William;*[8] *and others*)

A woman in the shape of a monster
a monster in the shape of a woman
the skies are full of them

a woman   "in the snow
5   among the Clocks and instruments
or measuring the ground with poles"

in her 98 years to discover
8 comets
she whom the moon ruled
10   like us
levitating into the night sky
riding the polished lenses
Galaxies of women, there
doing penance for impetuousness
15   ribs chilled
in those spaces   of the mind

An eye,
        "virile, precise and absolutely certain"

8. In 1781, William Herschel (1738–1822) became the first astronomer since antiquity to discover a planet, Uranus, earning appointment as court astronomer to King George III, election to the world-famous Royal Society, and a knighthood.

from the mad webs of Uranisborg[9]
20   encountering the NOVA
every impulse of light exploding
from the core
as life flies out of us

Tycho whispering at last
25   "Let me not seem to have lived in vain"[1]

What we see, we see
and seeing is changing

the light that shrivels a mountain
and leaves a man alive

30   Heartbeat of the pulsar
heart sweating through my body

The radio impulse
pouring in from Taurus
I am bombarded yet   I stand

35   I have been standing all my life in the
direct path of a battery of signals
the most accurately transmitted most
untranslatable language in the universe
I am a galactic cloud so deep   so invo-
40   luted that a light wave could take 15
years to travel through me   And has
taken   I am an instrument in the shape
of a woman trying to translate pulsations
into images   for the relief of the body
45   and the reconstruction of the mind.

1968

For the Record

The clouds and the stars didn't wage this war
the brooks gave no information
if the mountain spewed stones of fire into the river
it was not taking sides
5   the raindrop faintly swaying under the leaf
had no political opinions

and if here or there a house
filled with backed-up raw sewage

---

9. Actually Uraniborg, the elaborate palace-laboratory-observatory of Danish astronomer Tycho Brahe
(1546–1601), whose cosmology tried to fuse the Ptolemaic and Copernican systems. Brahe discovered and described (in *De nova stella*, 1574) a new star in what had previously been considered a
fixed-star system. The quotation is from Brahe.
1. Reportedly Brahe's dying words, spoken to fellow astronomer and mathematician Johannes Kepler
(1571–1630).

or poisoned those who lived there
10 with slow fumes, over years
the houses were not at war
nor did the tinned-up buildings

intend to refuse shelter
to homeless old women and roaming children
15 they had no policy to keep them roaming
or dying, no, the cities were not the problem
the bridges were non-partisan
the freeways burned, but not with hatred

Even the miles of barbed-wire
20 stretched around crouching temporary huts
designed to keep the unwanted
at a safe distance, out of sight
even the boards that had to absorb
year upon year, so many human sounds

25 so many depths of vomit, tears
slow-soaking blood
had not offered themselves for this
The trees didn't volunteer to be cut into boards
nor the thorns for tearing flesh
30 Look around at all of it

and ask whose signature
is stamped on the orders, traced
in the corner of the building plans
Ask where the illiterate, big-bellied
35 women were, the drunks and crazies,
the ones you fear most of all: ask where you were.

1983

My mouth hovers across your breasts[2]

My mouth hovers across your breasts
in the short grey winter afternoon
in this bed   we are delicate
and tough   so hot with joy we amaze ourselves
5 tough   and delicate   we play rings
around each other   our daytime candle burns
with its peculiar light   and if the snow
begins to fall outside   filling the branches
and if the night falls   without announcement
10 these are the pleasures of winter
sudden, wild and delicate   your fingers
exact   my tongue exact at the same moment

2. Poem 3 in Rich's sequence "Tracking Poems."

stopping to laugh at a joke
my love   hot on your scent   on the cusp of winter

1986

History[3]

Should I simplify my life for you?
Don't ask how I began to love men.
Don't ask how I began to love women.
Remember the forties songs, the slowdance numbers
5   the small sex-filled gas-rationed Chevrolet?
Remember walking in the snow and who was gay?
Cigarette smoke of the movies, silver-and-gray
profiles, dreaming the dreams of he-and-she
breathing the dissolution of the wisping silver plume?
10 Dreaming that dream we leaned applying lipstick
by the gravestone's mirror when we found ourselves
playing in the cemetery. In Current Events she said
the war in Europe is over, the Allies
and she wore no lipstick have won the war[4]
15 and we raced screaming out of Sixth Period.

Dreaming that dream
we had to maze our ways through a wood
where lips were knives breasts razors and I hid
in the cage of my mind scribbling
20 *this map stops where it all begins*
into a red-and-black notebook.
Remember after the war when peace came down
as plenty for some and they said we were saved
in an eternal present and we knew the world could end?
25 —Remember after the war when peace rained down
on the winds from Hiroshima Nagasaki Utah Nevada?[5]
and the socialist queer Christian teacher jumps from the hotel
      window?[6]
and L.G. saying *I want to sleep with you but not for sex*
and the red-and-black enamelled coffee-pot dripped slow through the
      dark grounds
30 —appetite terror power tenderness
the long kiss in the stairwell the switch thrown
on two Jewish Communists[7] married to each other

3. Poem 4 in Rich's sequence "Inscriptions."
4. World War II (1939–45), fought between the Allies or Allied powers (including France, Great
Britain, the United States, and the Soviet Union) and the Axis powers (Germany, Japan, Italy).
5. Sites of atomic bomb explosions, the first two in Japan near the end of World War II, the last two at
test sites in the American West.
6. Allusion to the critic Francis Otto Matthiessen (1902–50), who taught at Harvard while Rich was
an undergraduate there.
7. Julius and Ethel Rosenberg, executed as spies by the United States in 1953.

the definitive crunch of glass at the end of the wedding?[8]
(When shall we learn, what should be clear as day,
35 *We cannot choose what we are free to love?)*[9]

1995

Transparencies

That the meek word like the righteous word can bully
that an Israeli soldier interviewed years
after the first Intifada[1] could mourn on camera
what under orders he did, saw done, did not refuse
5 that another leaving Beit Jala[2] could scrawl
on a wall: *We are truely sorry for the mess we made*
is merely routine   word that would cancel deed
That human equals innocent and guilty
That we grasp for innocence whether or no
10 is elementary   That words can translate into broken bones
That the power to hurl words is a weapon
That the body can be a weapon
any child on playground knows   That asked your favorite word
in a game
15 you always named a thing, a quality, *freedom* or *river*
(never a pronoun never *God* or *War*)
is taken for granted   That word and body
are all we have to lay on the line
That words are windowpanes in a ransacked hut, smeared
20 by time's dirty rains, we might argue
likewise that words are clear as glass till the sun strikes it blinding

But that in a dark windowpane you have seen your face
That when you wipe your glasses the text grows clearer
That the sound of crunching glass comes at the height of the
25   wedding[3]
That I can look through glass
into my neighbor's house
but not my neighbor's life
That glass is sometimes broken to save lives
30 That a word can be crushed like a goblet underfoot
is only what it seems, part question, part answer: how
you live it

2002   2004

8. At Jewish weddings the groom breaks a glass to commemorate the loss of Jerusalem and the Temple.
9. Opening lines of W. H. Auden's poem "Canzone" (1942).
1. Rebellion (Arabic); specifically, armed uprising of Palestinians against Israeli occupation of the
West Bank and Gaza Strip. The first began in 1987.
2. Town in the West Bank of Palestine inhabited mainly by Arab Christians.
3. See n. 8 above.

Tonight No Poetry Will Serve

Saw you walking barefoot
taking a long look
at the new moon's eyelid

later spread
5   sleep-fallen, naked in your dark hair
asleep but not oblivious
of the unslept unsleeping
elsewhere

Tonight I think
10   no poetry
will serve

Syntax of rendition:[4]

verb pilots the plane
adverb modifies action

15   verb force-feeds noun
submerges the subject
noun is choking
verb   disgraced   goes on doing

now diagram the sentence

2007   2011

PASSAGES FROM RICH'S ESSAYS

From When We Dead Awaken: Writing as Re-Vision (1972, 1979)[5]

Most, if not all, human lives are full of fantasy—passive daydreaming which
need not be acted on. But to write poetry or fiction, or even to think well, is not to
fantasize, or to put fantasies on paper. For a poem to coalesce, for a character or
an action to take shape, there has to be an imaginative transformation of reality
which is in no way passive. And a certain freedom of the mind is needed—
freedom to press on, to enter the currents of your thought like a glider pilot,
knowing that your motion can be sustained, that the buoyancy of your attention
will not be suddenly snatched away. Moreover, if the imagination is to transcend
and transform experience it has to question, to challenge, to conceive of alternatives, perhaps to the very life you are living at that moment. You have to be free to
play around with the notion that day might be night, love might be hate; nothing

---

4. Perhaps an allusion to the practice of "extraordinary rendition"—transporting suspected terrorists
to other countries, including those that condone torture.
5. "When We Dead Awaken: Writing as Re-Vision." *On Lies, Secrets, and Silence: Selected Prose: 1966–1978*,
W. W. Norton, 1979, pp. 33–49. Originally published in slightly different form in *College English*, 1972.

can be too sacred for the imagination to turn into its opposite or to call experimentally by another name. For writing is re-naming. Now, to be maternally with small children all day in the old way, to be with a man in the old way of marriage, requires a holding-back, a putting-aside of that imaginative activity, and demands instead a kind of conservatism. I want to make it clear that I am *not* saying that in order to write well, or think well, it is necessary to become unavailable to others, or to become a devouring ego. This has been the myth of the masculine artist and thinker; and I do not accept it. But to be a female human being trying to fulfill traditional female functions in a traditional way *is* in direct conflict with the subversive function of the imagination. The word traditional is important here. There must be ways, and we will be finding out more and more about them, in which the energy of creation and the energy of relation can be united. But in those earlier years I always felt the conflict as a failure of love in myself. I had thought I was choosing a full life: the life available to most men, in which sexuality, work, and parenthood could coexist. But I felt, at twenty-nine, guilt toward the people closest to me, and guilty toward my own being.

I wanted, then, more than anything, the one thing of which there was never enough: time to think, time to write. The fifties and early sixties were years of rapid revelations: the sit-ins and marches in the South, the Bay of Pigs, the early antiwar movement,[6] raised large questions—questions for which the masculine world of the academy around me seemed to have expert and fluent answers. But I needed to think for myself—about pacifism and dissent and violence, about poetry and society, and about my own relationship to all these things. For about ten years I was reading in fierce snatches, scribbling in notebooks, writing poetry in fragments; I was looking desperately for clues, because if there were no clues then I thought I might be insane. I wrote in a notebook about this time:

> Paralyzed by the sense that there exists a mesh of relationships—e.g., between my anger at the children, my sensual life, pacifism, sex (I mean sex in its broadest significance, not merely sexual desire)—an interconnectedness which, if I could see it, make it valid, would give me back myself, make it possible to function lucidly and passionately. Yet I grope in and out among these dark webs.

I think I began at this point to feel that politics was not something "out there" but something "in here" and of the essence of my condition.

In the late fifties I was able to write, for the first time, directly about experiencing myself as a woman. The poem[7] was jotted in fragments during children's naps, brief hours in a library, or at 3 A.M. after rising with a wakeful child. I despaired of doing any continuous work at this time. Yet I began to feel that my fragments and scraps had a common consciousness and a common theme, one which I would have been very unwilling to put on paper at an earlier time because I had been taught that poetry should be "universal," which meant, of course, nonfemale. Until then I had tried very much *not* to identify myself as a female poet.

6. That is, the movement opposing the Vietnam War (c. 1955–75). *Bay of Pigs:* On April 17, 1961, 1,400 Cuban exiles, backed by the CIA, launched a botched invasion of Communist Cuba at the Bay of Pigs, on the island's south coast.
7. "Snapshots of a Daughter-in-Law" (p. 1027).

From A Communal Poetry (1993)[8]

One day in New York in the late 1980s, I had lunch with a poet I'd known for more than twenty years. Many of his poems were—are—embedded in my life. We had read together at the antiwar events of the Vietnam years.[9] Then, for a long time, we hardly met. As a friend, he had seemed to me withheld, defended in a certain way I defined as masculine and with which I was becoming in general impatient; yet often, in their painful beauty, his poems told another story. On this day, he was as I had remembered him: distant, stiff, shy perhaps. The conversation stumbled along as we talked about our experiences with teaching poetry, which seemed a safe ground. I made some remark about how long it was since last we'd talked. Suddenly, his whole manner changed: *You disappeared! You simply disappeared.* I realized he meant not so much from his life as from a landscape of poetry to which he thought we both belonged and were in some sense loyal.

If anything, those intervening years had made me feel more apparent, more visible—to myself and to others—as a poet. The powerful magnet of the women's liberation movement—and the women's poetry movement it released—had drawn me to coffeehouses where women were reading new kinds of poems; to emerging "journals of liberation" that published women's poems, often in a context of political articles and the beginnings of feminist criticism; to bookstores selling chapbooks and pamphlets from the new women's presses; to a woman poet's workshops with women in prison; to meetings with other women poets in Chinese restaurants, coffee shops, apartments, where we talked not only of poetry, but of the conditions that make it possible or impossible. It had never occurred to me that I was disappearing—rather, that I was, along with other women poets, beginning to appear. In fact, we were taking part in an immense shift in human consciousness.

My old friend had, I believe, not much awareness of any of this. It was, for him, so off-to-the-edge, so out-of-the-way; perhaps so dangerous, it seemed I had sunk, or dived, into a black hole. Only later, in a less constrained and happier meeting, were we able to speak of the different ways we had perceived that time.

He thought there had been a known, defined poetic landscape and that as poetic contemporaries we simply shared it. But whatever poetic "generation" I belonged to, in the 1950s I was a mother, under thirty, raising three small children. Notwithstanding the prize and the fellowship to Europe that my first book of poems had won me,[1] there was little or no "appearance" I then felt able to claim as a poet, against that other profound and as yet unworded reality.

---

8. "A Communal Poetry." *What Is Found There: Notebooks on Poetry and Politics*, W. W. Norton, 1993, pp. 164–80.
9. Circa 1955–75.
1. Rich won the Yale Younger Poets Prize in 1951 and traveled on a Guggenheim Fellowship 1952–53.

From **Why I Refused the National Medal for the Arts (2001)**[2]

July 3, 1997

Jane Alexander, Chair
The National Endowment for the Arts
1100 Pennsylvania Avenue
Washington, D.C. 20506

Dear Jane Alexander,

I just spoke with a young man from your office, who informed me that I had been chosen to be one of twelve recipients of the National Medal for the Arts at a ceremony at the White House in the fall. I told him at once that I could not accept such an award from President Clinton or this White House because the very meaning of art, as I understand it, is incompatible with the cynical politics of this administration. I want to clarify to you what I meant by my refusal.

Anyone familiar with my work from the early sixties on knows that I believe in art's social presence—as breaker of official silences, as voice for those whose voices are disregarded, and as a human birthright. In my lifetime I have seen the space for the arts opened by movements for social justice, the power of art to break despair. Over the past two decades I have witnessed the increasingly brutal impact of racial and economic injustice in our country.

There is no simple formula for the relationship of art to justice. But I do know that art—in my own case the art of poetry—means nothing if it simply decorates the dinner table of power that holds it hostage. The radical disparities of wealth and power in America are widening at a devastating rate. A president cannot meaningfully honor certain token artists while the people at large are so dishonored.

I know you have been engaged in a serious and disheartening struggle to save government funding for the arts, against those whose fear and suspicion of art is nakedly repressive. In the end, I don't think we can separate art from overall human dignity and hope. My concern for my country is inextricable from my concerns as an artist. I could not participate in a ritual that would feel so hypocritical to me.

Sincerely,
Adrienne Rich

cc: President Clinton

The invitation from the White House came by telephone on July 3. After several years' erosion of arts funding and hostile propaganda from the religious right

2. "Why I Refused the National Medal for the Arts." *Arts of the Possible: Essays and Conversations,* W. W. Norton, 2001, pp. 98–105.

After the text of my letter to Jane Alexander, then chair of the National Endowment for the Arts, had been fragmentarily quoted in various news stories, Steve Wasserman, editor of the *Los Angeles Times Book Review,* asked me for an article expanding on my reasons. Herewith the letter and the article [Rich's note].

and the Republican Congress, the House vote to end the National Endowment for the Arts was looming. That vote would break as news on July 10; my refusal of the National Medal for the Arts would run as a sidebar story in the *New York Times* and the *San Francisco Chronicle*.

In fact, I was unaware of the timing. My refusal came directly out of my work as a poet and essayist and citizen drawn to the interfold of personal and public experience. I had recently been thinking and writing about the shrinking of the social compact, of whatever it was this country had ever meant when it called itself a democracy: the shredding of the vision of *government of the people, by the people, for the people.*

"We the people—still an excellent phrase," said the playwright Lorraine Hansberry in 1962, well aware who had been excluded, yet believing the phrase might someday come to embrace us all. And I had for years been feeling both personal and public grief, fear, hunger, and the need to render this, my time, in the language of my art.

Whatever was "newsworthy" about my refusal was not about a single individual—not myself, not President Clinton. Nor was it about a single political party. Both major parties have displayed a crude affinity for the interests of corporate power, while deserting the majority of the people, especially the most vulnerable. Like so many others, I've watched the dismantling of our public education, the steep rise in our incarceration rates, the demonization of our young black men, the accusations against our teen-age mothers, the selling of health care—public and private—to the highest bidders, the export of subsistence-level jobs in the United States to even lower-wage countries, the use of below-minimum-wage prison labor to break strikes and raise profits, the scapegoating of immigrants, the denial of dignity and minimal security to working and poor people. At the same time, we've witnessed the acquisition of publishing houses, once risk-taking conduits of creativity, by conglomerates driven single-mindedly to fast profits, the acquisition of major communications and media by those same interests, the sacrifice of the arts and public libraries in stripped-down school and civic budgets, and, most recently, the evisceration of the National Endowment for the Arts. Piece by piece the democratic process has been losing ground to the accumulation of private wealth.

There is no political leadership in the White House or the Congress that has spoken to and for the people who, in a very real sense, have felt abandoned by their government.

⋆   ⋆   ⋆

And what about art? Mistrusted, adored, pietized, condemned, dismissed as entertainment, commodified, auctioned at Sotheby's, purchased by investment-seeking celebrities, it dies into the "art object" of a thousand museum basements. It's also reborn hourly in prisons, women's shelters, small-town garages, community-college workshops, halfway houses, wherever someone picks up a pencil, a wood-burning tool, a copy of *The Tempest*,[3] a tag-sale camera, a whittling knife, a stick of charcoal, a pawnshop horn, a video of *Citizen Kane*,[4] what-

---

3. Late Shakespeare play about the exiled Duke of Milan, a magician; widely regarded as the playwright's dramatic exploration of his own art.
4. Celebrated 1941 film about an unscrupulous publishing tycoon very loosely based on U.S. newspaper magnate William Randolph Hearst (1863–1951).

ever lets you know again that this deeply instinctual yet self-conscious expressive language, this regenerative process, could help you save your life. "If there were no poetry on any day in the world," the poet Muriel Rukeyser wrote, "poetry would be invented that day. For there would be an intolerable hunger."

Art can never be totally legislated by any system, even those that reward obedience and send dissident artists to hard labor and death; nor can it, in our specifically compromised system, be really free. It may push up through cracked macadam, by the merest means, but it needs breathing space, cultivation, protection to fulfill itself. Just as people do. New artists, young or old, need education in their art, the tools of their craft, chances to study examples from the past and meet practitioners in the present, get the criticism and encouragement of mentors, learn that they are not alone. As the social compact withers, fewer and fewer people will be told *Yes, you can do this; this also belongs to you.* Like government, art needs the participation of the many in order not to become the property of a powerful and narrowly self-interested few.

Art is our human birthright, our most powerful means of access to our own and another's experience and imaginative life. In continually rediscovering and recovering the humanity of human beings, art is crucial to the democratic vision. A government tending further and further away from the search for democracy will see less and less "use" in encouraging artists, will see art as obscenity or hoax.

     ·   ·   ·

Federal funding for the arts, like the philanthropy of private arts patrons, can be given and taken away. In the long run art needs to grow organically out of a social compost nourishing to everyone, a literate citizenry, a free, universal, public education complex with art as an integral element, a society honoring both human individuality and the search for a decent, sustainable common life. In such conditions, art would still be a voice of hunger, desire, discontent, passion, reminding us that the democratic project is never-ending.

For that to happen, what else would have to change?

From **Poetry and the Forgotten Future** (2006)[5]

2

What I'd like to do here is touch on some aspects of poetry as it's created and received in [a] violently politicized and brutally divided world [. . .].

I'll flash back to 1821: Shelley's[6] claim, in "The Defence of Poetry," that "poets are the unacknowledged legislators of the world." Piously overquoted, mostly out

5. "Poetry and the Forgotten Future." Plenary lecture. Conference on Poetry and Politics, 13 July 2006, University of Stirling, Scotland. Here taken from *A Human Eye: Essays on Art in Society, 1997–2008*, W. W. Norton, 2009, pp. 126–46. Originally published as *Poetry and Commitment*, W. W. Norton, 2007.
6. Percy Bysshe Shelley, British poet (1792–1822).

of context, it's taken to suggest that simply by virtue of composing verse, poets exert some exemplary moral power—in a vague, unthreatening way. In fact, in his earlier political essay "A Philosophic View of Reform," Shelley had written that "Poets *and philosophers* [italics mine] are the unacknowledged" etc. The philosophers he was talking about were revolutionary-minded: Thomas Paine, William Godwin, Voltaire, Mary Wollstonecraft.[7]

And Shelley was, no mistake, out to change the legislation of his time. For him there was no contradiction among poetry, political philosophy, and active confrontation with illegitimate authority [. . .].

Shelley, in fact, saw powerful institutions, not original sin or "human nature," as the source of human misery. For him, art bore an integral relationship to the "struggle between Revolution and Oppression." His West Wind was the "trumpet of a prophecy," driving "dead thoughts . . . like withered leaves, to quicken a new birth."[8]

He did *not* say, "Poets are the unacknowledged interior decorators of the world."

3

Pursuing this theme of the committed poet and the action of poetry in the world: two interviews, both from 1970.

A high official of the Greek military junta asks the poet Yannis Ritsos, then under house arrest: "You are a poet. Why do you get mixed up in politics?"

Ritsos answers, "A poet is the first citizen of his country and for this very reason it is the duty of the poet to be concerned about the politics of his country."

⋅   ⋅   ⋅   ⋅

Second interview. The South African poet Dennis Brutus, when asked about poetry and political activity: "I believe that the poet—as a poet—has no obligation to be committed, but the man—as a man—has an obligation to be committed. What I'm saying is that I think everybody ought to be committed and the poet is just one of the many 'everybodies.'"

Dennis Brutus wrote, acted on, was imprisoned then exiled for his opposition to the South African apartheid[9] regime [. . .].

What's at stake here is the recognition of poetry as what James Scully calls "social practice." He distinguishes between "protest poetry" and "dissident poetry": Protest poetry is "conceptually shallow," "reactive," predictable in its means, too often a hand-wringing from the sidelines.

---

7. British author (1759–97) whose works include *A Vindication of the Rights of Men* (1790) and *A Vindication of the Rights of Woman* (1792); Wollstonecraft's daughter (by William Godwin) married Percy Bysshe Shelley. *Voltaire*: French Enlightenment philosopher (1694–78). *William Godwin*: Radical British philosopher (1756–1836) whose works include *An Enquiry Concerning Political Justice* (1793), also husband and first biographer of Mary Wollstonecraft. *Thomas Paine*: British-born author (1737–1809) of both *Common Sense* (1776) and *Rights of Man* (1791).
8. See Shelley's "Ode to the West Wind" (p. 964).
9. Literally, "apartness" (Afrikaans); system of legalized racial segregation practiced in South Africa from 1948 until 1991.

Dissident poetry, however [he writes] does not respect boundaries between private and public, self and other. In breaking boundaries, it breaks silences, speaking for, or at best, with, the silenced; opening poetry up, putting it into the middle of life. . . . It is a poetry that talks back, that would act as part of the world, not simply as a mirror of it.

4

I'm both a poet and one of the "everybodies" of my country. I live, in poetry and daily experience, with manipulated fear, ignorance, cultural confusion, and social antagonism huddling together on the fault line of an empire. In my life-time I've seen the breakdown of rights and citizenship where ordinary "every-bodies," poets or not, have left politics to a political class bent on shoveling the elemental resources, the public commons of the entire world, into private con-trol. Where democracy has been left to the raiding of "acknowledged" legisla-tors, the highest bidders. In short, to a criminal element.

Ordinary, comfortable Americans have looked aside when our fraternally-twinned parties—Democrat and Republican—have backed dictatorships against popular movements abroad; as their covert agencies, through torture and assassi-nation, through supplied weapons and military training, have propped up repres-sive parties and regimes in the name of anticommunism and our "national interests." Why did we think fascistic methods, the subversion of civil and human rights, would be contained somewhere else? Because as a nation, we've clung to a self-righteous false innocence, eyes shut to our own scenario, our body politic's internal bleeding.

But internal bleeding is no sudden symptom. That uncannily prescient African American writer James Baldwin asked his country, a quarter century ago: "If you don't know my father, how can you know the people in the streets of Tehran?"[1]

This year, a report from the Bureau of Justice Statistics finds that 1 out of every 136 residents of the United States is behind bars: many in jails, uncon-victed. That the percentage of black men in prison or jail is almost 12 to 1 over white male prisoners. That the states with the highest rates of incarceration and execution are those with the poorest populations.

We often hear that—by contrast with, say, Nigeria or Egypt, China or the for-mer Soviet Union—the West doesn't imprison dissident writers. But when a nation's criminal justice system imprisons so many—often on tawdry evidence and botched due process—to be tortured in maximum security units or on death row, overwhelmingly because of color and class, it is in effect—and intention—silencing potential and actual writers, intellectuals, artists, journalists: a whole intelligentsia. The internationally known case of Mumia Abu-Jamal[2] is emblem-atic but hardly unique. The methods of Abu Ghraib and Guantánamo[3] have long been practiced in the prisons and policing of the United States.

What has all this to do with poetry? [. . .]

1. Capital of Iran.
2. African American activist and radio journalist (b. 1954) sentenced to death in 1982 (later reduced to life without parole) for the murder of a Philadelphia police officer; many believe he was wrongfully convicted.
3. Prisons in Iraq and Cuba, respectively. Established by the United States in 2002, the Guantánamo Bay Detention Camp houses prisoners of war, mainly from Afghanistan. Between 2004 and 2006, several U.S. soldiers were convicted of torturing inmates of Abu Ghraib while that facility was jointly controlled by U.S. and Iraqi forces (2003–6).

[. . . L]et's never discount it—within every official, statistical, designated nation, there breathes another nation: of unappointed, unappeased, unacknowledged clusters of people who daily, with fierce imagination and tenacity, confront cruelties, exclusions, and indignities, signaling through those carriers—which are often literal cages—in poetry, music, street theater, murals, videos, Web sites—and through many forms of direct activism.

5

I hope never to idealize poetry—it has suffered enough from that. Poetry is not a healing lotion, an emotional massage, a kind of linguistic aromatherapy. Neither is it a blueprint, nor an instruction manual, nor a billboard [. . .].

Walt Whitman never separated his poetry from his vision of American democracy—a vision severely tested in a Civil War fought over the economics of slavery. Late in life he called "poetic lore [. . .] a conversation overheard in the dusk, from speakers far or hid, of which we get only a few broken murmurs"—the obscurity, we might think now, of democracy itself.

But also of those "dark times" in and about which Bertolt Brecht[4] assured us there would be songs.

Poetry has been charged with "aestheticizing," thus being complicit in, the violent realities of power, of practices like collective punishment, torture, rape, and genocide. This accusation was famously invoked in Adorno's[5] "after the Holocaust lyric poetry is impossible"—which Adorno later retracted and which a succession of Jewish poets have in their practice rejected [. . .].

If to "aestheticize" is to glide across brutality and cruelty, treat them merely as dramatic occasions for the artist rather than structures of power to be revealed and dismantled—much hangs on the words "merely" and "rather than." Opportunism isn't the same as committed attention. But we can also define the "aesthetic" not as a privileged and sequestered rendering of human suffering, but as news of an awareness, a resistance, that totalizing systems want to quell: art reaching into us for what's still passionate, still unintimidated, still unquenched.

Poetry has been written off on other counts: (1) it's not a mass-market "product": it doesn't get sold on airport newsstands or in supermarket aisles; (2) the actual consumption figures for poetry can't be quantified at the checkout counter; (3) it's too "difficult" for the average mind; (4) it's too elite, but the wealthy don't bid for it at Sotheby's. It is, in short, redundant. This might be called the free-market critique of poetry.

There's actually an odd correlation between these ideas: poetry is either inadequate, even immoral, in the face of human suffering, or it's unprofitable, hence useless. Either way, poets are advised to hang our heads or fold our tents. Yet in

4. In "Motto," the German poet and playwright (1898–1956) asks, "In dark times, will there also be singing?" And he answers, "Yes, there will be singing. About the dark times."
5. German philosopher Theodor Adorno (1903–69).

fact, throughout the world, transfusions of poetic language can and do quite literally keep bodies and souls together—and more.

. . .

7

Poetry has the capacity—in its own ways and by its own means—to remind us of something we are forbidden to see. A forgotten future: a still-uncreated site whose moral architecture is founded not on ownership and dispossession, the subjection of women, torture and bribes, outcast and tribe, but on the continuous redefining of freedom—that word now held under house arrest by the rhetoric of the "free" market. This ongoing future, written off over and over, is still within view. All over the world its paths are being rediscovered and reinvented: through collective action, through many kinds of art. Its elementary condition is the recovery and redistribution of the world's resources that have been extracted from the many by the few.

. . .

Finally: there is always that in poetry which will not be grasped, which cannot be described, which survives our ardent attention, our critical theories, our classrooms, our late-night arguments. There is always (I am quoting the poet/translator Américo Ferrari) "an unspeakable where, perhaps, the nucleus of the living relation between the poem and the world resides."

The living relation between the poem and the world: difficult knowledge, operating theater where the poet, committed, goes on working.

BIBLIOGRAPHY[6]

Brutus, Dennis. *Poetry and Protest: A Dennis Brutus Reader.* Ed. Lee Sustar and Aisha Karim. Chicago: Haymarket, 2006.

Franklin, H. Bruce. "The American Prison and the Normalization of Torture." historiansagainstwar.org/resources/torture/brucefranklin.html

Holmes, Richard. *Shelley: The Pursuit.* New ed. New York: New York Review of Books, 2003.

Ritsos, Yannis. *Yannis Ritsos, Selected Poems 1938–1988.* Ed. and trans. Kimon Friar and Kostas Myrsiades. Brockport, NY: BOA, 1989.

Scully, James. *Line Break: Poetry as Social Practice.* Foreword by Adrienne Rich. Willimantic, CT: Curbstone, 2005.

Vallejo, César. *Trilce.* Trans. Clayton Eshleman. Intro. by Américo Ferrari. New York: Marsilio, 1992.

White, Elizabeth. "1 in 136 U.S. Residents Behind Bars: U.S. Prisons, Jails Grew by 1,000 Inmates a Week from '04 to '05." Associated Press (22 May 2006).

Whitman, Walt. *Walt Whitman: Complete Poetry and Collected Prose.* Ed. Justin Kaplan. New York: Library of America, 1982.

6. Rich's bibliography has been abbreviated.

A POEM FOR ADRIENNE RICH

JOY HARJO
By the Way

For Adrienne Rich

I've given it time, as if time were mine to give.
There was a dam, larger than Hoover[7] or the President or the patent
For the metal creature that sucks up all the dust.
Words had to stop and ask permission before crossing over.
5 Oh, sometimes they were wild with the urgency of sweet
And leaped—
Mostly the rest were kept in the net
Of swallowed or forbidden language.

I want to go back and rewrite all the letters.
10 I lied frequently.
No. I was not O.K.
And neither was James Baldwin,[8] though his essays
Were perfect spinning platters of comprehension of the fight
To assert humanness in a black-and-white world.

15 That's how blues emerged, by the way—
Our spirits needed a way to dance through the heavy mess.
The music, a sack that carries the bones of those left alongside
The trail of tears[9] when we were forced
To leave everything we knew by the way—

20 I constructed an individual life in the so-called *civilized* world.
We all did—far from the trees and plants
Who had born us and fed us.
All I wanted was the music, I would tell you now—
Within it, what we cannot carry.
25 I talk about *then* from a hotel room just miles
From your home in the East
Before you fled on your personal path of tears
To the West, that worn-out American Dream
Dogging your steps.

30 You lived on a pedestal for me then, the driven diver[1] who climbed

---

7. Straddling the border of Nevada and Arizona, Hoover Dam was the world's largest when it opened in 1935.
8. African American novelist, civil rights activist, and social critic whose influential essays are collected in books including *The Fire Next Time* (1963) and *Notes of a Native Son* (1955).
9. Forced relocation, in the 1830s, of the Cherokee, Muscogee, and other Native peoples from the Southeastern United States to "Indian Territory" in what is now Oklahoma—some five thousand miles west.
1. See Rich's "Diving into the Wreck" (p. 921).

Back up from the abyss, Venus on a seashell[2] with a dagger
In her hands,
I had to look, and followed your tracks in the poems
Cut by suffering.
35 Aren't they all?
We're in the apocalyptic age of addiction and forgetting.
It's worse now.

But that dam, I had to tell you. I broke it open stone by stone.
It took a saxophone, flowers, and your words
40 Had something to do with it
I can't say exactly how.
The trajectory wasn't clean, even though it was sure.
Does that make sense?
Maybe it does only in the precincts of dreams and poetry,
45 Not in a country lit twenty-four hours a day to keep dreams stuck
Turning in a wheel
In the houses of money.

I read about transcendence, how the light
Came in through the window of a nearby traveller
50 And every cell of creation opened its mouth
To drink grace.

That's what I never told you.

2016

Chronology

1929   Born in Baltimore, Maryland, May 16. Begins writing poetry as a child with the encouragement of her father, Dr. Arnold Rich.

1951   AB, Radcliffe College. *A Change of World* chosen by poet W. H. Auden for publication in the Yale Younger Poets series.

1952–53   Wins Guggenheim Fellowship; travels in Europe and England; marries Harvard economist Alfred H. Conrad.

1955   Birth of David Conrad. Publishes *The Diamond Cutters and Other Poems*.

1957   Birth of Paul Conrad.

1959   Birth of Jacob Conrad.

1960   Wins National Institute of Arts and Letters Award for poetry.

1961–62   Wins Guggenheim Fellowship; resides with family in the Netherlands.

1962–63   Wins Amy Lowell Travelling Fellowship.

1963   Publishes *Snapshots of a Daughter-in-Law*; wins *Poetry* magazine's Bess Hokin Prize.

---

2. Sandro Botticello's painting *The Birth of Venus* (c. 1485) depicts the Roman goddess of love standing nude on a giant scallop shell.

1966   Publishes *Necessities of Life*; moves to New York City and becomes increasingly active in protests against the war in Vietnam.

1966–68   Becomes lecturer at Swarthmore College.

1967–69   Becomes adjunct professor of writing in the Graduate School of the Arts, Columbia University.

1968   Begins teaching in the SEEK and Open Admissions Programs at City College of New York.

1969   Publishes *Leaflets*.

1970   Alfred Conrad dies.

1971   Publishes *The Will to Change*; becomes increasingly active in the women's movement.

1972–73   Becomes Fannie Hurst Visiting Professor of Creative Literature at Brandeis University.

1973   Publishes *Diving into the Wreck*.

1974   Wins National Book Award for *Diving into the Wreck*. Rich rejects the award as an individual, but accepts it, in a statement written with fellow nominees Audre Lorde and Alice Walker, in the name of all women. Becomes Professor of English, City College of New York.

1975   Publishes *Poems: Selected and New*.

1976   Becomes Professor of English at Douglass College; publishes *Of Woman Born: Motherhood as Experience and Institution* and *Twenty-one Love Poems*.

1978   Publishes *The Dream of a Common Language: Poems 1974–1977*.

1979   Publishes *On Lies, Secrets, and Silence: Selected Prose 1966–1978*; moves to Montague, Massachusetts; edits, with Michelle Cliff, the lesbian-feminist journal *Sinister Wisdom*.

1981   Publishes *A Wild Patience Has Taken Me This Far: Poems 1978–1981*.

1984   Publishes *The Fact of a Doorframe: Poems Selected and New 1950–1984*; moves to Santa Cruz, California, and becomes professor of English, San Jose State University.

1986   Publishes *Blood, Bread, and Poetry: Selected Prose 1979–1985*; becomes professor of English, Stanford University.

1989   Publishes *Time's Power: Poems 1985–1988*.

1991   Publishes *An Atlas of the Difficult World: Poems 1988–1991*.

1992   Wins *Los Angeles Times* Book Prize for *An Atlas of the Difficult World*, the Lenore Marshall/*Nation* Prize for Poetry, and the Nicholas Roerich Museum Poet's Prize; is co-winner of the Frost Silver Medal for distinguished lifetime achievement.

1993   Publishes *What Is Found There: Notebooks on Poetry and Politics*.

1994   Awarded MacArthur Fellowship.

1995   Publishes *Dark Fields of the Republic: Poems 1991–1995*.

1996   Awarded the Academy of American Poets (AAP) Dorothea Tanning Prize.

1997   Refuses the National Medal for the Arts on political grounds and wins the
              AAP's Wallace Stevens Award.

1999   Elected a chancellor of the AAP; receives Lannan Foundation's Lifetime
              Achievement Award; publishes *Midnight Salvage: Poems 1995–1998*.

2001   Publishes *Fox: Poems 1998–2000* and *Arts of the Possible: Essays and
              Conversations*.

2002   Publishes *The Fact of a Doorframe: Poems Selected and New 1950–2000*.

2004   Publishes *The School among the Ruins: Poems 2000–2004*, winner of the
              National Book Critics Circle Award.

2006   Awarded the National Book Foundation's Medal for Distinguished Contri-
              bution to American Letters.

2007   Publishes *Telephone Ringing in the Labyrinth: Poems 2004–2006* and (with
              Mark Doty) *Poetry and Commitment*.

2009   Publishes *A Human Eye: Essays on Art in Society, 1997–2008*.

2010   Publishes *Tonight No Poetry Will Serve: Poems 2007–2010*.

2012   Dies at age eighty-two, of complications from rheumatoid arthritis.

SUGGESTIONS FOR WRITING

1. In her 1951 poem AT A BACH CONCERT, Adrienne Rich describes "Form" as "the ultimate gift that love can offer" (line 7). What, exactly, is the case for the "discipline"
of formal art argued by this poem (4)? How does Rich's later work both embody and
reject formalism? Considering as evidence the selections of Rich's poetry and prose
in this and previous chapters, write an essay in which you discuss how Rich's
thoughts about formality and form evolved throughout her career.
2. Carefully considering plot, characterization, and structure, write an essay in which
you detail the ways DIVING INTO THE WRECK is and is not typical of Rich's work.
3. In poems such as SNAPSHOTS OF A DAUGHTER-IN-LAW and PLANETARIUM, Rich considers the creative accomplishments of women throughout history. What role do
these women play in Rich's poetry, separately and together? How is that role both
constrained and unconstrained by their gender? Write an essay in which you examine the way Rich portrays creative women. Are they role models in her work, or
something else?
4. Rich once said of her college days in the late 1940s,

> I had no political ideas of my own, only the era's vague and hallucinatory anti-
> Communism and the encroaching privatism of the 1950s. Drenched in invisible
> assumptions of my class and race, unable to fathom the pervasive ideology of gender,
> I felt "politics" as distant, vaguely sinister, the province of powerful older men or of
> people I saw as fanatics. It was in poetry that I sought a grasp on the world and on
> interior events, "ideas of order," even power.

Using the poems by Rich included in this anthology, write an essay that charts the
development of the poet's political consciousness.
5. In the prose excerpts in this chapter, Rich describes and defends the political passions that, she says, animate her life as an artist. How fully do Rich's poems embody

her political beliefs, particularly her commitment to feminism? Write an essay in which you explore Rich's poetry in light of her feminist politics.

6. Choose two or more poems in this book by one author (other than Rich), and write an essay in which you draw on those poems to demonstrate either the distinctive, characteristic qualities and features of that author's work or the way your understanding of one poem by the author is altered or enhanced when you read it in conjunction with the other poem or poems.

SAMPLE WRITING:
COMPARATIVE ESSAY

The student essay below was written in response to the following assignment (a more elaborate version of the last writing suggestion in ch. 21):

> Your second essay for the course should be 6–9 pages long and should analyze two or more poems included in *The Norton Introduction to Literature*. The poems must be by the same author.
>
> You are *strongly* encouraged to pay attention to how the poems' meaning and effect are shaped by some aspect or aspects of their form. Those aspects might include specific formal features such as rhyme, meter, alliteration, or assonance, and/or external form or subgenre—the fact that a poem is a Shakespearean or Petrarchan sonnet, a haiku, or a dramatic monologue, for example. (In terms of the latter, you might consider how the poem's effect and meaning are shaped by the fact that it takes a particular form.)

In her essay, student writer Melissa Makolin draws on three sonnets by William Shakespeare to argue for the distinctiveness and radicalism of the views expressed in two sonnets by another author, Edna St. Vincent Millay. In a sense, then, Makolin's essay focuses simultaneously on external form (ch. 20) and the author's work (ch. 21), even as it explores gender ("Exploring Gender: An Album") and engages in a kind of feminist criticism (see "Critical Approaches"). That's a lot to tackle in a relatively short essay, and you will no doubt find things both to admire and to criticize about Makolin's argument. At what points do you find yourself agreeing with her interpretation? disagreeing? wanting more evidence or more analysis of the evidence provided? more contextual information—about literary tradition, the author, or historical and cultural context? Where and how might the essay's logic seem faulty or its claims contradictory? In the end, what might you take away from this sample essay about how to craft an effective, persuasive argument about an author's work?

Melissa Makolin
Dr. Mays
English 298
15 April 2021

Out-Sonneting Shakespeare: An Examination of
Edna St. Vincent Millay's Use of the Sonnet Form

Edna St. Vincent Millay is known not only for her poetry, but also for the feminist ideals she represents therein. She was an extremely talented poet who turned the sonnet form on its head, using the traditionally restrictive form previously used almost exclusively by male poets to express feminist ideas that were radical for her time. Sonnets, especially as written by Shakespeare and Petrarch, are often about the physical beauty of an idealized but also objectified woman, and they implicitly emphasize the man's dominance over her. Millay uses the sonnet form to assert a much different view of femininity, sexuality, and biological dominance. She uses a form known for its poetic limitations to reject social limitations. She uses a form previously used to objectify women to portray them as sexual beings with power and control over their own bodies and lives. The paradox of Millay's poetry is that she uses a poetically binding, male-dominated form to show that she will not be bound either by literary tradition or societal mores regarding inter-gender relations.

The idea of a woman seeking physical pleasure in defiance of societal constraints is one that was revolutionary when "Women have loved before as I love now" and "I, being born a woman and distressed" were published, in 1931 and 1923 respectively. They are poems about a woman's lust leading her to select a sexual partner based on her physical needs rather than on the desire for love. This is a concept that Shakespeare would have found very contentious for three reasons. First, Shakespeare did not agree with acting on lust of any kind; in fact, this is the topic of his sonnet "Th' expense of spirit in a waste of shame." It is a fourteen-line treatise on the evils that result from acting on lustful urges in which Shakespeare declares,

> Th' expense of spirit in a waste of shame
> Is lust in action; and, till action, lust
> Is perjured, murderous, bloody, full of blame,
> Savage, extreme, rude, cruel, not to trust. (lines 1-4)

Lust, sexual or otherwise, is a pathway to a hell both religious and secular. Seventeenth-century society dramatically constricted the liberties of women in particular and didn't encourage sexual freedom for either gender.

Second, the majority of Shakespeare's sonnets simultaneously idealize and trivialize the two things they celebrate: women and love. In poems such as "My mistress' eyes are nothing like the sun," he treats women either as objects of an ordered, almost courtly love or as objects of mild ridicule. In this poem's first twelve lines, he mocks his mistress by describing her halitosis (7-8), referring to her breasts as "dun" (3) and her hair as "black wires" (4), references to all the contemporary conventions of beauty to which she does not conform. He not only tells her what the ideal of feminine beauty is, but also makes light of the various ways in which she does not live up to it. He justifies these hurtful insults by reassuring the poor woman that she is "as rare / As any she belied with false compare" (13-14). He mocks her appearance by telling her that she is special and beautiful in her own way only because he loves her. Insulting someone, breaking down her self-esteem, and convincing her that she could be loved by no one else are tactics used in abusive relationships to subjugate one's partner. This is not love, and the role of women in the traditional Shakespeare sonnet is far from empowered.

Third and finally, in addition to idealizing while simultaneously trivializing women, Shakespeare's sonnets also demean the concept of love. To Shakespeare, a woman is worthy of love either because she is an ideal of physical beauty or because he is noble enough to love her despite her flaws (as in "My mistress' eyes are nothing like the sun"). He takes this warped concept one step further, though, by creating an ideal of love that is egotistical and unhealthy for both parties. In "Shall I compare thee to a summer's day?," he spends the first twelve lines describing the ways in which this particular woman fulfills the contemporary ideals of beauty. It is clear that he ardently reveres her physical appearance, and the poem ends with the kind of declaration of personal devotion consistent with love. The turn, however, exhibits a malignant narcissism when it reassures the beloved that "So long as men can breathe or eyes can see, / So long lives this, and this gives life to thee" (13-14). The object of the speaker's affection is just that, an object that only exists as an appendage to him. Shakespeare makes it clear that it is only because of his poetic greatness that their love will persist through the ages. He uses the poetic form to relegate women to the position of objects.

The sonnets of Edna St. Vincent Millay use Shakespearean and Petrarchan forms to offer quite a different view of the role of women. She sees herself as a liberated woman, and she is not afraid to defy social conventions by taking lovers and discarding them when necessary. In writing sonnets about actively satisfying her lust, she also defies literary conventions, completely changing the male-female power dynamic of past sonnets by male writers. In "Women have loved before as I love now," Millay discusses how women throughout history have felt the same lust that she feels, but unlike other more timid and traditional women, she is willing to join the ranks of the brave women of antiquity and to satisfy her passions despite the potential cost. This poem celebrates the women who choose to act against the standards set for them. Describing them as "treacherous queens, with death upon the tread, / Heedless and wilful, [who] took their knights to bed" makes them sound heroic, and it shifts control in the sexual relationship from the man to the woman (13-14). In Millay's version, the women sexually dominate the men and temporarily free themselves from the constraints of an oppressive society. Further, by alluding to the famous females of the "lively chronicles of the past" (2), she shows not only that this behavior is natural and heroic, but also that it is historically valid. The specific women she alludes to when referring to "Irish waters by a Cornish prow" (3) and "Trojan waters by a Spartan mast" (4) are respectively Iseult, the adulteress of the classic work of medieval passion *The*

Romance of Tristan and Iseult, and Helen of Troy (or any of the other libidinous women) of the Homeric epics.

The fact that Millay uses the sonnet form to illustrate sexual liberation is significant for several reasons. First, it shows that she understands the restrictions placed upon her, both as a poet and as a woman. Second, using the sonnet shows that she can hold her own against the great male poets and write within the boundaries that they have erected; the subject matter of her poetry shows that she chooses not to. Lastly, it is significant because, in using the sonnet form for her own feminist purposes, she directly confronts Shakespeare's one-dimensional portrayal of women by proposing her own view of ideal femininity.

The second of Edna St. Vincent Millay's sonnets that defies the ideals set forth by Shakespeare is "I, being born a woman and distressed." It is a poem about impermanent lust, not eternal love. The speaker tells her lover that her feelings are purely physical ("a certain zest / To bear your body's weight upon my breast," 4-5) and simply arise out of human biology ("the needs and notions of my kind," 2) and close quarters ("propinquity," 3). Emotional and physical needs are two things which need not be dependent on each other, and temporary desire does not have to lead to anything lasting. Consummation of a relationship was never discussed in the time of Shakespeare as a tenet of courtly love because women were supposed to be angelic ideals rather than real people with carnal desires. Millay's speaker defies these unrealistic and unattainable ideals of eternal adoration by warning her lover not to "Think" that "I shall remember you with love" (9, 11), illustrating that desire is impermanent. In fact, it is just a temporary "frenzy" and "insufficient reason" even to have a "conversation when we meet again" (13-14). Lust in Millay's world is fleeting, whereas the love of Shakespeare's world is final and complete once the man conquers all and the woman takes her place on his arm. Millay's poem might seem cynical, but it represents a more realistic view of female and male interactions; life and love are transitory and to be enjoyed in the moment because sexual urges can be sated, are biologically determined, and essential to survival, while emotional ones are (relatively) inconsequential and satisfied in other ways.

Millay draws on Shakespeare as a kind of foil by using the form so associated with his name as a vehicle for her very different views on the same topics. Millay brings sexual relationships to a far more terrestrial level with her assertions that women have primal urges that must be satisfied and that submission to ascribed gender roles is not necessary in order to obtain this satisfaction. She presents a radically modern view of relationships. She lambastes the Shakespearean paradigm of the idealized woman, a traditionally beautiful possession of the egotistical man. By using the Shakespearean sonnet form to propose her own revamped, modern vision of woman, a self-aware person who fearlessly relishes the idea of her own emotional and sexual independence, Millay redefines both "woman" and "love."

Makolin 4

Works Cited

Mays, Kelly J., editor. *The Norton Introduction to Literature*. Shorter 14th ed.,
    W. W. Norton, 2021.

Millay, Edna St. Vincent. "I, being born a woman and distressed." Mays,
    p. 997.

————. "Women have loved before as I love now." Mays, pp. 996.

Shakespeare, William. "Th' expense of spirit in a waste of shame." Mays, pp. 963-64.

————. "My mistress' eyes are nothing like the sun." Mays, p. 991.

————. "Shall I compare thee to a summer's day?" Mays, pp. 906-07.

Emily Dickinson

AN ALBUM

The bee himself did not evade the schoolboy more than she evaded me; and even at this day I still stand somewhat bewildered, like the boy.
—THOMAS WENTWORTH HIGGINSON

The woman many regard as among America's most original poets was born in her family's home in Amherst, Massachusetts, on December 10, 1830. She would die in the same home at the age of fifty-five, having anonymously published only ten of the almost eighteen hundred poems her sister discovered after her death. Because she never married and rarely, if ever, ventured outside her home in the last twenty years of her life, biographers and critics often contrast the narrowness of Emily Dickinson's life with the tremendous breadth of her posthumous reputation and influence, and the brevity and emotional intensity of her poetry with its sheer formal, emotional, and intellectual audacity and range.

Yet Dickinson's life was not quite as uneventful or narrow as it might outwardly appear. She received a fairly extensive education for a woman of her era, studying classics, science, and other subjects at both Amherst Academy, which she attended for seven years, and the Mount Holyoke Female Seminary (later, Mount Holyoke College), which she attended for one year. She also read widely and deeply throughout her life. Moreover, she had a great deal of indirect knowledge of public and literary affairs, including the abolitionist, feminist, and Transcendentalist movements, as well as the various theological controversies of her day. Her father was a prominent lawyer, college administrator, and politician; Dickinson herself maintained an avid correspondence with some ninety people and included among her friends the clergyman Charles Wadsworth, journalists Samuel Bowles and Thomas Higginson, and novelist Helen Hunt Jackson. Dickinson's friendships also ensured her a select, but astute, audience for her letters and the poems she often included in them.

Dickinson nonetheless did cultivate her privacy and independence, bequeathing us a body of poetry that is in some ways as deliberately elusive, enigmatic, and eccentric as the woman herself apparently was, even to those who knew her best. As a result, hers is also a poetry that holds especially rich rewards for readers willing both to read individual poems multiple times and to read multiple poems with an eye on the light each sheds on the others.

As you read the Dickinson poems gathered in this album and in other chapters, try to identify the various formal features and strategies that seem to you most characteristic of Dickinson's poetry, including its **diction**, syntax, punctuation, **meter**, and **rhyme**. Pay attention, too, to the varying **tone** of the poems and the **persona** Dickinson creates in and through them. To what extent and how and why do the speakers of these varied **lyrics** seem like versions of the same person? what sort of person? What patterns do you notice in the objects depicted and in the topics or questions explored in these poems? What sorts of feelings are communicated,

Dickinson family home in Amherst, Massachusetts

and what might the poems have to say about feeling, as well as thought and imagination? Why might (or might not) Dickinson's poems seem "torn up by the roots, with rain and dew and earth still clinging to them," as Higginson once declared? Or how might the poems help you understand what Dickinson meant when she wrote, "Tell all the truth but tell it slant— Success in Circuit lies"?

As you work to answer these questions for yourself, you may—like countless readers before you—find yourself as intrigued by the poet behind the work as by the work itself, and rightly so. Yet critic Molly McQuade's cautionary words are worth remembering: "Because [Dickinson] lived in seclusion by choice, and because her poetry also steadfastly reflects the author's coveting of privacy, to read the life in the poetry is perilous, if not impossible. Likewise, to search the life for the origins of her poetry would be treacherous."

Another factor that may make both a biographical approach to Dickinson's poetry and claims about how it changed over time unusually difficult is the fact that we cannot precisely date her poems. Instead, we have to rely on the approximate dates scholars assign based on a study of the letters and the hand-sewn books that hold the only surviving copies. In a way, then, the case of Emily Dickinson is a bit like that of William Shakespeare—one in which all that we *don't* know about the author makes the work all the more intriguing.

POEMS BY EMILY DICKINSON

Wild Nights—Wild Nights!

Wild Nights—Wild Nights!
Were I with thee

Wild Nights should be
Our luxury!

5   Futile—the Winds—
To a Heart in port—
Done with the Compass—
Done with the Chart!

Rowing in Eden—
10 Ah, the Sea!
Might I but moor—Tonight—
In Thee!

1861

- Whom might the speaker be addressing? What might it mean to be "Done
with the Chart" (line 8)?

"Hope" is the thing with feathers—

"Hope" is the thing with feathers—
That perches in the soul—
And sings the tune without the words—
And never stops—at all—

5   And sweetest—in the Gale—is heard—
And sore must be the storm—
That could abash the little Bird
That kept so many warm—

I've heard it in the chillest land—
10 And on the strangest Sea—
Yet—never—in Extremity,
It asked a crumb—of me.

1862

- What might be both expected and unexpected or surprising about the
poem's controlling metaphor and the way it develops? How might the
imagery in this poem compare to that in other Dickinson poems? Or
how might the *use* of imagery (rather than the images themselves)
compare?

After great pain, a formal feeling comes—

After great pain, a formal feeling comes—
The Nerves sit ceremonious, like Tombs—
The stiff Heart questions was it He, that bore,
And Yesterday, or Centuries before?

5   The Feet, mechanical, go round—
A Wooden way
Of Ground, or Air, or Ought—
Regardless grown,
A Quartz contentment, like a stone—

10 This is the Hour of Lead—
   Remembered, if outlived,
   As Freezing Persons recollect the Snow—
   First—Chill—then Stupor—then the letting go—

c. 1862

• What different metaphors and similes are used here, and what does each
  contribute to the poem's portrayal of how we feel "After great pain"?

I heard a Fly buzz—when I died—

   I heard a Fly buzz—when I died—
   The Stillness in the Room
   Was like the Stillness in the Air—
   Between the Heaves of Storm—

5 The Eyes around—had wrung them dry—
   And Breaths were gathering firm
   For that last Onset—when the King
   Be witnessed—in the Room—

   I willed my Keepsakes—Signed away
10 What portion of me be
   Assignable—and then it was
   There interposed a Fly—

   With Blue—uncertain—stumbling Buzz—
   Between the light—and me—
15 And then the Windows failed—and then
   I could not see to see—

1863

• How would you describe this poem's internal structure? That is, how would
  you divide it into parts, and characterize the relationship between them or
  the way one part differs from the other? Why a fly?

My Life had stood—a Loaded Gun—

   My Life had stood—a Loaded Gun—
   In Corners—till a Day
   The Owner passed—identified—
   And carried Me away—

5 And now We roam in Sovereign Woods—
   And now We hunt the Doe—
   And every time I speak for Him—
   The Mountains straight reply—

   And do I smile, such cordial light
10 Upon the Valley glow—
   It is as a Vesuvian face
   Had let its pleasure through—

And when at Night—Our good Day done—
I guard My Master's Head—
15 'Tis better than the Eider-Duck's
Deep Pillow—to have shared—

To foe of His—I'm deadly foe—
None stir the second time—
On whom I lay a Yellow Eye—
20 Or an emphatic Thumb—

Though I than He—may longer live
He longer must—than I—
For I have but the power to kill,
Without—the power to die—

c. 1863

- How does Dickinson set up and then defy expectations through the poem's
  controlling metaphor? How do the poem's quirks (e.g., the jerky rhythm, the
  strange syntax, the slant rhymes) contribute to its overall effect?

I stepped from Plank to Plank

I stepped from Plank to Plank
A slow and cautious way
The Stars about my Head I felt
About my Feet the Sea.

5 I knew not but the next
Would be my final inch—
This gave me that precarious Gait
Some call Experience.

1865

- For what does "stepp[ing] from Plank to Plank" become a metaphor in the
  poem? Is this experience a positive or a negative one?

Tell all the truth but tell it slant—

Tell all the truth but tell it slant—
Success in Circuit lies
Too bright for our infirm Delight
The Truth's superb surprise
5 As Lightning to the Children eased
With explanation kind
The Truth must dazzle gradually
Or every man be blind—

1872

- What meanings of the word "Circuit" (line 2) seem especially appropriate
  and relevant here? Why and how so?

POEMS ABOUT EMILY DICKINSON

WENDY COPE
Emily Dickinson

Higgledy-piggledy
Emily Dickinson
Liked to use dashes
Instead of full stops.

5 Nowadays, faced with such
Idiosyncrasy,
Critics and editors
Send for the cops.

1986

• What does the use of dactyls (each metrical foot consisting of a stressed syllable followed by two unstressed syllables) contribute to this poem? How do this meter and the poem's other formal features underscore its depiction of both Dickinson's poetry and the attitudes of modern "Critics and editors" (line 7)?

BILLY COLLINS
Taking Off Emily Dickinson's Clothes

First, her tippet[1] made of tulle,
easily lifted off her shoulders and laid
on the back of a wooden chair.

And her bonnet,
5 the bow undone with a light forward pull.

Then the long white dress, a more
complicated matter with mother-of-pearl
buttons down the back,
so tiny and numerous that it takes forever
10 before my hands can part the fabric,
like a swimmer's dividing water,
and slip inside.

You will want to know
that she was standing
15 by an open window in an upstairs bedroom,
motionless, a little wide-eyed,
looking out at the orchard below,
the white dress puddled at her feet
on the wide-board, hardwood floor.

___
1. Shoulder cape with hanging ends.

20 The complexity of women's undergarments
   in nineteenth-century America
   is not to be waved off,
   and I proceeded like a polar explorer
   through clips, clasps, and moorings,
25 catches, straps, and whalebone stays,
   sailing toward the iceberg of her nakedness.

   Later, I wrote in a notebook
   it was like riding a swan into the night,
   but, of course, I cannot tell you everything—
30 the way she closed her eyes to the orchard,
   how her hair tumbled free of its pins,
   how there were sudden dashes
   whenever we spoke.

   What I can tell you is
35 it was terribly quiet in Amherst
   that Sabbath afternoon,
   nothing but a carriage passing the house,
   a fly buzzing in a windowpane.

   So I could plainly hear her inhale
40 when I undid the very top
   hook-and-eye fastener of her corset

   and I could hear her sigh when finally it was unloosed,
   the way some readers sigh when they realize
   that Hope has feathers,
45 that Reason is a plank,
   that Life is a loaded gun
   that looks right at you with a yellow eye.

                                                        1998

• How does this poem use figures of speech to characterize the act of disrob-
  ing Dickinson? For what does that act, in turn, become a metaphor? How
  does the poem use allusions to specific Dickinson poems?

Chronology

1830   Born on December 10 in Amherst, Massachusetts, second of the three chil-
        dren of Emily Norcross Dickinson and Edward Dickinson, son of the founder
        of Amherst College and himself both a treasurer of the college and a lawyer.

1841   After attending two local primary schools, enters Amherst Academy; one of her
        teachers will later describe her "as a very bright, but rather delicate and frail-
        looking girl; an excellent scholar; of exemplary deportment, faithful in all school
        duties; but somewhat shy and nervous." "Her compositions," he added, "were
        strikingly original."

1842–43 Dickinson's father serves two terms as a state senator, later joining the Gov-
        ernor's Executive Council (1846–47).

1844	After the death of a cousin, spends a month with her aunt in Boston.
1847	Leaves Amherst Academy for one year at Mount Holyoke Female Seminary (later Mount Holyoke College).
1852	Publishes the first of seven poems to appear anonymously in the local *Springfield Daily Republican*, a newspaper with liberal, abolitionist leanings.
1853–55	Dickinson's father serves in the U.S. Congress; in spring 1855, Dickinson goes to Washington, D.C., with her father and sister, visiting a cousin in Philadelphia on the way home. Also in 1855, her elder brother, Austin, declares himself "saved," and Emily becomes the only member of her immediate family not to undergo a similar religious conversion experience.
1856	Austin Dickinson marries Susan Huntington Gilbert, who will become one of Emily Dickinson's most intimate friends and the recipient of many letters and approximately ninety poems—by far the most of any correspondent.
1858	Meets *Springfield Daily Republican* editor Samuel Bowles (1826–78), who becomes a frequent visitor.
1862	Initiates a lifelong correspondence with *Atlantic Monthly* literary editor, abolitionist, and feminist Thomas Wentworth Higginson (1823–1911); though she will send many of her poems to Higginson, he advises against publication.
1864–65	Eye trouble sends Dickinson on two extended stays in Cambridgeport, where she is treated by a Boston ophthalmologist. After her return, Dickinson will seldom leave the family home, though she will receive visits from intimates including Higginson, Bowles, and the Reverend Charles Wadsworth.
1874	Dickinson's father dies.
1875	Dickinson's always-frail mother suffers a major stroke; Dickinson becomes her bedridden mother's primary caretaker.
1877	After the death of his wife, Judge Otis P. Lord, an old friend, engages Dickinson in what one journalist calls "an astonishingly candid, erotic correspondence," though Dickinson apparently refuses a marriage proposal.
1886	Dies at home on May 15, age fifty-five. In an obituary, sister-in-law Susan Dickinson observes, "Very few in the village, except among older inhabitants, knew Miss Emily personally, although the facts of her seclusion and her intellectual brilliancy were familiar Amherst traditions." After Dickinson's death, her sister discovers almost eighteen hundred poems and three volumes of letters.
1890	Austin Dickinson's mistress, Mabel Loomis Todd (1856–1932), and Thomas Higginson coedit and publish a posthumous collection of selected poems by Emily Dickinson.
1891	Responding to "a constant and earnest demand by readers for further information in regard to her," Higginson publishes excerpts from selected Dickinson letters.

SUGGESTIONS FOR WRITING

1. One immediately apparent feature of Dickinson's poetry is her rather odd use of punctuation, especially her frequent use of the dash. Write an essay that explains how punctuation contributes to the effect and meaning of at least two Dickinson poems.

2. Write an essay exploring the various kinds of "circuits" or "circuitousness" at work in at least two Dickinson poems and the way such "circuits" contribute to the poems' success.

3. Write an essay explaining the way Dickinson's poetry is characterized in one poem about Dickinson included in this album; be sure to draw on at least one of Dickinson's poems to assess whether, why, and how that characterization seems apt.

W. B. Yeats

AN ALBUM

Mad Ireland hurt you into poetry.
—W. H. AUDEN

I f it is difficult to make claims about either biographical elements in Emily Dickinson's poems or her poetry's development over time, the opposite holds true of the work of W. B. Yeats. Whereas Dickinson left us guessing about her inner life, the timing and revision of her poems, and her ideas about the nature and goals of her craft, Yeats left us a trove of memoirs, essays, and manuscripts on which to draw. As such, his poetry may well move and speak to us more as we discover more about the author's personal experience and beliefs; about the order in which the poems were written (and often rewritten); and about the historical events that helped shape the author and his work. Whereas Dickinson published few poems in her lifetime and soared to fame only after her death, Yeats was a prolific and celebrated, if controversial, public figure who received the Nobel Prize for Literature some twenty-five years before his death.

William Butler Yeats was born in Dublin in 1865. Though he spent much of his youth in London and is today regarded as one of the greatest **lyric** poets in the English language, he is best known as the preeminent Irish poet of the twentieth century. Well versed in Irish history, folklore, and politics, Yeats attended art school for a time before devoting himself to writing poetry that was, early in his career, self-consciously dreamy and ethereal. (A great admirer of poets Percy Shelley [1792–1822] and William Blake [1782–1827], Yeats once labeled himself "the last Romantic.") Yeats's poems became tighter, more concrete, direct, and passionate with his involvement (mainly through theater) with the Irish nationalist cause, his desperate love for the actress and activist Maud Gonne (1866–1953), his exposure to the work of the German philosopher Friedrich Nietzsche (1844–1900), and his friendship with the American poet Ezra Pound (1885–1972). Yeats served as a senator in the newly independent Irish government before withdrawing from active public life to Thoor Ballylee, a crumbling, ancient tower fashioned into a home by Yeats and Georgie Hyde-Lees (1892–1968), the young Englishwoman he ultimately married.

Yeats and his work were profoundly shaped by shifts in the character and fortunes of Irish nationalism—both the political movement to liberate Ireland from British control and its cultural cousin, the Celtic Revival, which sought to rejuvenate a distinctively Irish literature and culture. Deeply involved in both movements in a way that his younger countryman, James Joyce (1882–1941), never was, Yeats nonetheless—at various times and in various ways—found himself in profound conflict with their aims, their methods, and their vision of both art and Ireland. Though he was particularly averse to the idea of art as propaganda, his early poetry and plays draw heavily on the oral folk traditions and rhythms to which he was first introduced during childhood visits to County Sligo and which he began to research more seriously after his introduction to Irish nationalists. Though such folk sources would become less important to his later work, Yeats strove throughout his life to preserve and reinvigorate Irish culture.

Yeats was also deeply influenced by events and movements that stretched well beyond his native country, including World War I (1914–18), the spiritualist movement, and the birth of psychology. As Yeats himself recognized, his deep immersion in the occult, as well as his lifelong search for a satisfactory belief system to replace the Protestant Christianity of his forebears, was a reaction to the materialistic, rationalistic spirit of his age (or what he called "the despotism of fact" that for him culminated in the First World War) and one common among the artists and intellectuals of his day. Ultimately, Yeats came to believe fervently in what his contemporary Carl Jung (1875–1961) labeled the "collective unconscious"—a sort of universal memory shared by all human beings—and in the idea that the poet, like the priest, the prophet, and the magician, taps into the collective unconscious and moves his audience through symbols. The comparison between priest and poet is key, for Yeats also believed that the arts, including poetry, should perform a quasi-religious function. He claimed in his essay "The Autumn of the Body" (1898) that "The arts are [. . .] about to take upon their shoulders the burdens that have fallen from the shoulders of priests, and to lead us back upon our journey by filling our thoughts with the essence of things, and not with things." Elsewhere, he declared that he "made a new religion, almost an infallible church of poetic tradition."

Such beliefs shape not only the complex symbolism of Yeats's verse but also its external form. Yeats eschewed the **free verse** popular with his contemporaries at least in part because, as he explains in "The Symbolism of Poetry" (1900),

> The purpose of rhythm [. . .] is to prolong the moment [. . .] when we are both asleep and awake, [. . .] by hushing us with an alluring monotony, which holds us waking by variety, to keep us in that state of perhaps real trance, in which the mind liberated from the pressure of the will is unfolded in symbols [. . .]. In the making and in the understanding of a work of art, and the more easily if it is full of patterns and symbols and music, we are lured to the threshold of sleep, and it may be far beyond it, without knowing that we have ever set our feet upon the steps of horn or of ivory.

To achieve those incantatory rhythms, Yeats experimented with various meters and verse forms, ranging from **ballad stanza** to **ottava rima**.

The chronology at the end of this album and the footnotes that accompany the poems will provide you with more information about Yeats, and you can find much more online and in the library. Even without that information, however, you will learn much about Yeats, his art, his beliefs, and the way all three changed over time by carefully reading the poems in this album one by one, paying attention to all that you observe, and discussing them with other readers. As you do so, consider the following questions:

- What patterns can you detect in the poems' external form, as well as internal structure?
- Where do symbols occur and recur, and what role do they play?
- What vision of art and the artist is conveyed by both the content and the form of these poems?
- Do you agree with those scholars who see dramatic shifts of both form and content from early poems such as THE LAKE ISLE OF INNISFREE (1890) to midcareer poems such as EASTER 1916 (1916) to late poems such as LEDA AND THE SWAN (1923) and SAILING TO BYZANTIUM (1927)?

- If you do detect three distinct phases and kinds of poems here, then do you think THE SECOND COMING (1919) fits more with the poems of Yeats's second or middle phase, or more with those of his third or late phase? Why and how so?
- If you see all the poems as more alike than different, what are the features that make them both alike and distinctive?

POEMS BY W. B. YEATS

The Lake Isle of Innisfree[1]

I will arise and go now, and go to Innisfree,
And a small cabin build there, of clay and wattles made,
Nine bean-rows will I have there, a hive for the honey-bee,
And live alone in the bee-loud glade.

5 And I shall have some peace there, for peace comes dropping slow,
Dropping from the veils of the morning to where the cricket sings;
There midnight's all a glimmer, and noon a purple glow,
And evening full of the linnet's wings.

I will arise and go now, for always night and day
10 I hear lake water lapping with low sounds by the shore;
While I stand on the roadway, or on the pavements grey,
I hear it in the deep heart's core.

1890

- Why does the speaker vow to go to Innisfree, and how does the life he imagines living there compare to the one he now lives? In what ways might his imagined future seem like a return to the past?

AUTHORS ON THEIR WORK

W. B. YEATS (1865–1939)

From *The Trembling of the Veil* (1922)*

Sometimes I told myself very adventurous love-stories with myself for hero, and at other times I planned out a life of lonely austerity, and at other times mixed the ideals and planned a life of lonely austerity mitigated by periodical lapses. I had still the ambition, formed in Sligo in my teens, of living in imitation of Thoreau[2] on Innisfree, a little island in Lough Gill, and when walking through Fleet Street very homesick I heard a little tinkle of water and saw a fountain in a shop-window which balanced a little ball upon its jet, and began to remember lake water. From the sudden remembrance came my poem *Innisfree*, my first lyric with anything in its rhythm of my own music. I had begun to loosen rhythm as an escape from rhetoric and from that emotion of

1. Island in Lough Gill, County Sligo, Ireland.
2. Henry David Thoreau (1817–62) spent two years living in an isolated cabin near Walden Pond, in Massachusetts, experiences described in *Walden; or, Life in the Woods* (1854).

the crowd that rhetoric brings, but I only understood vaguely and occasionally that I must for my special purpose use nothing but the common syntax. A couple of years later I would not have written that first line with its conventional archaism—"Arise and go"—nor the inversion in the last stanza. Passing another day by the new Law Courts [. . .] I grew suddenly oppressed by the great weight of stone, and thought, "There are miles and miles of stone and brick all round me," and presently added, "If John the Baptist or his like were to come again and had his mind set upon it, he could make all these people go out into some wilderness leaving their buildings empty," and that thought, which does not seem very valuable now, so enlightened the day that it is still vivid in the memory [. . .].

*The Autobiography of William Butler Yeats. Macmillan, 1953. In this excerpt from his autobiography, Yeats describes the period in the 1880s when he was in his twenties and living in London with his family.

Easter 1916[3]

    I have met them at close of day
    Coming with vivid faces
    From counter or desk among gray
    Eighteenth-century houses.
5   I have passed with a nod of the head
    Or polite meaningless words,
    Or have lingered awhile and said
    Polite meaningless words,
    And thought before I had done
10 Of a mocking tale or a gibe
    To please a companion
    Around the fire at the club,
    Being certain that they and I
    But lived where motley is worn:
15 All changed, changed utterly:
    A terrible beauty is born.

    That woman's[4] days were spent
    In ignorant good-will,
    Her nights in argument
20 Until her voice grew shrill.
    What voice more sweet than hers
    When, young and beautiful,
    She rode to harriers?

3. On Easter Monday, 1916, nationalist leaders proclaimed an Irish Republic. After a week of street fighting, the British government put down the Easter Rebellion and executed a number of prominent nationalists, including the four mentioned in lines 75–76, all of whom Yeats knew personally.
4. Countess Constance Georgina Markievicz (1868–1927), a beautiful and well-born young woman from County Sligo who became a vigorous nationalist. She was initially condemned to death, but her sentence was later commuted to life imprisonment, and she was granted amnesty in 1917.

This man[5] had kept a school
25   And rode our wingèd horse,[6]
This other[7] his helper and friend
Was coming into his force;
He might have won fame in the end,
So sensitive his nature seemed,
30   So daring and sweet his thought.
This other man[8] I had dreamed
A drunken, vainglorious lout.
He had done most bitter wrong
To some who are near my heart,
35   Yet I number him in the song;
He, too, has resigned his part
In the casual comedy;
He, too, has been changed in his turn,
Transformed utterly:
40   A terrible beauty is born.

Hearts with one purpose alone
Through summer and winter seem
Enchanted to a stone
To trouble the living stream.
45   The horse that comes from the road,
The rider, the birds that range
From cloud to tumbling cloud,
Minute by minute they change;
A shadow of cloud on the stream
50   Changes minute by minute;
A horse-hoof slides on the brim,
And a horse plashes within it;
The long-legged moor-hens dive,
And hens to moor-cocks call;
55   Minute by minute they live:
The stone's in the midst of all.

Too long a sacrifice
Can make a stone of the heart.
O when may it suffice?
60   That is Heaven's part, our part
To murmur name upon name,
As a mother names her child
When sleep at last has come
On limbs that had run wild.

5. Patrick Pearse (1879–1916), who led the assault on the Dublin Post Office, from which the proclamation of a republic was issued. A schoolmaster by profession, he had championed the restoration of the Gaelic language in Ireland and was an active political writer and poet.
6. The mythological Pegasus, a traditional symbol of poetic inspiration.
7. Thomas MacDonagh (1878–1916), also a writer and teacher.
8. Major John MacBride (1868–1916), who had married Yeats's beloved Maud Gonne in 1903 but separated from her two years later.

65   What is it but nightfall?
      No, no, not night but death;
      Was it needless death after all?
      For England may keep faith[9]
      For all that is done and said.
70   We know their dream; enough
      To know they dreamed and are dead;
      And what if excess of love
      Bewildered them till they died?
      I write it out in a verse—
75   MacDonagh and MacBride
      And Connolly[1] and Pearse
      Now and in time to be,
      Wherever green is worn,
      Are changed, changed utterly;
80   A terrible beauty is born.

                                                                1916

- The phrase "A terrible beauty is born" becomes a kind of refrain in this
  poem. What does the poem suggest about why the events of Easter 1916
  and the kind of political passion and commitment that went into it were
  simultaneously "terrible" and "beautiful"? What do the stone and the stream
  seem to symbolize?

The Second Coming[2]

Turning and turning in the widening gyre[3]
The falcon cannot hear the falconer;
Things fall apart; the center cannot hold;
Mere anarchy is loosed upon the world,
5   The blood-dimmed tide is loosed, and everywhere
The ceremony of innocence is drowned;
The best lack all conviction, while the worst
Are full of passionate intensity.

Surely some revelation is at hand;
10   Surely the Second Coming is at hand.
The Second Coming! Hardly are those words out
When a vast image out of *Spiritus Mundi*[4]
Troubles my sight: somewhere in sands of the desert
A shape with lion body and the head of a man,

9. Before the uprising, the English had promised eventual home rule to Ireland.
1. James Connolly (1868–1916), leader of the Easter uprising.
2. The Second Coming of Christ, according to Matthew 24.29–44, will follow a time of "tribulation."
In *A Vision* (1937), Yeats describes his view of history as dependent on cycles of about two thousand
years: The birth of Christ had ended the cycle of Greco-Roman civilization, and now the Christian
cycle seemed near an end, to be followed by an antithetical cycle, ominous in its portents.
3. Literally, the widening spiral of a falcon's flight. "Gyre" is Yeats's term for a cycle of history, which
he diagrammed as a series of interpenetrating cones.
4. Or *Anima Mundi* (Latin), the spirit or soul of the world. Yeats considered this universal consciousness or memory a fund from which poets drew their images and symbols.

15 A gaze blank and pitiless as the sun,
   Is moving its slow thighs, while all about it
   Reel shadows of the indignant desert birds.[5]
   The darkness drops again; but now I know
   That twenty centuries of stony sleep
20 Were vexed to nightmare by a rocking cradle,
   And what rough beast, its hour come round at last,
   Slouches towards Bethlehem to be born?

January 1919   1920, 1921

> • What vision of the contemporary world is implied by the metaphors in the
> poem's first half? What vision of its future is suggested in the poem's sec-
> ond half?

Leda and the Swan[6]

A sudden blow: the great wings beating still
Above the staggering girl, her thighs caressed
By the dark webs, her nape caught in his bill,
He holds her helpless breast upon his breast.

5 How can those terrified vague fingers push
The feathered glory from her loosening thighs?
And how can body, laid in that white rush,
But feel the strange heart beating where it lies?

A shudder in the loins engenders there
10 The broken wall, the burning roof and tower
And Agamemnon dead.
                              Being so caught up,
So mastered by the brute blood of the air,
Did she put on his knowledge with his power
15 Before the indifferent beak could let her drop?

                                                            1923

> • If THE SECOND COMING predicts the end of one historical cycle and its gov-
> erning (Christian) myth, LEDA AND THE SWAN imagines the beginning of the
> preceding cycle. How does the poem characterize that beginning? Might we
> again have here (as in EASTER 1916) a kind of "terrible beauty"? How would
> you paraphrase the question the speaker poses at the poem's end? Why
> might questions loom so large in this poem?

---

5. Yeats later wrote of the "brazen winged beast [. . .] described in my poem *The Second Coming*" as
"associated with laughing, ecstatic destruction."
6. According to Greek myth, Zeus took the form of a swan to rape Leda, who became the mother of
Helen of Troy, Castor, and Clytemnestra, Agamemnon's wife and murderer. Helen's abduction from
her husband, Menelaus, brother of Agamemnon, began the Trojan War (line 10). Yeats described the
visit of Zeus to Leda as an annunciation like that to Mary (see Luke 1.26–38); "I imagine the
annunciation that founded Greece as made to Leda" (*A Vision*).

Sailing to Byzantium[7]

I

That[8] is no country for old men. The young
In one another's arms, birds in the trees
—Those dying generations—at their song,
The salmon-falls, the mackerel-crowded seas,
5 Fish, flesh, or fowl, commend all summer long
Whatever is begotten, born, and dies.
Caught in that sensual music all neglect
Monuments of unaging intellect.

II

An aged man is but a paltry thing,
10 A tattered coat upon a stick, unless
Soul clap its hands and sing, and louder sing
For every tatter in its mortal dress,
Nor is there singing school but studying
Monuments of its own magnificence;
15 And therefore I have sailed the seas and come
To the holy city of Byzantium.

III

O sages standing in God's holy fire
As in the gold mosaic of a wall,
Come from the holy fire, perne in a gyre,[9]
20 And be the singing-masters of my soul.
Consume my heart away; sick with desire
And fastened to a dying animal
It knows not what it is; and gather me
Into the artifice of eternity.

IV

25 Once out of nature I shall never take
My bodily form from any natural thing,
But such a form as Grecian goldsmiths make
Of hammered gold and gold enameling
To keep a drowsy Emperor awake;[1]
30 Or set upon a golden bough[2] to sing

---

7. Ancient name of Istanbul, Turkey, the capital and holy city of Eastern Christendom from the late fourth century until 1453. It was famous for its stylized and formal mosaics; its symbolic, nonnaturalistic art; and its highly developed intellectual life. Yeats repeatedly uses it to symbolize a world of artifice and timelessness, free from the decay and death of the natural, sensual world.
8. Ireland, as an instance of the natural, temporal world.
9. That is, whirl in a coiling motion, so that his soul may merge with its motion as the timeless world invades the cycles of history and nature. "Perne" is Yeats's coinage (from the noun *pirn*): to spin around in the kind of spiral pattern that thread makes as it comes off a bobbin or spool.
1. I have read somewhere that in the Emperor's palace at Byzantium was a tree made of gold and silver, and artificial birds that sang [Yeats's note].
2. In book 6 of the *Aeneid*, the sibyl tells Aeneas that he must pluck the golden bough from a nearby tree in order to descend to Hades, the underworld. Each time Aeneas plucks the branch, an identical one takes its place.

To lords and ladies of Byzantium
Of what is past, or passing, or to come.

1927

• Like THE LAKE ISLE OF INNISFREE, this poem focuses on an imaginary journey and on a contrast between then and there versus here and now, yet this
poem deals more directly with the subject of art and especially of poetry
or song: what it might be like, where it might come from, what it might do for
us. How does this poem both pose and answer those questions?

A POEM ABOUT W. B. YEATS

W. H. AUDEN
In Memory of W. B. Yeats

(d. January, 1939)

I

He disappeared in the dead of winter:
The brooks were frozen, the airports almost deserted,
And snow disfigured the public statues;
The mercury sank in the mouth of the dying day.
5   What instruments we have agree
The day of his death was a dark cold day.

Far from his illness
The wolves ran on through the evergreen forests,
The peasant river was untempted by the fashionable quays;
10   By mourning tongues
The death of the poet was kept from his poems.

But for him it was his last afternoon as himself,
An afternoon of nurses and rumors;
The provinces of his body revolted,
15   The squares of his mind were empty,
Silence invaded the suburbs,
The current of his feeling failed; he became his admirers.

Now he is scattered among a hundred cities
And wholly given over to unfamiliar affections,
20   To find his happiness in another kind of wood
And be punished under a foreign code of conscience.
The words of a dead man
Are modified in the guts of the living.

But in the importance and noise of tomorrow
25   When the brokers are roaring like beasts on the floor of the Bourse,[3]
And the poor have the sufferings to which they are fairly accustomed,
And each in the cell of himself is almost convinced of his freedom,
A few thousand will think of this day
As one thinks of a day when one did something slightly unusual.

3. Paris stock exchange.

30 What instruments we have agree
    The day of his death was a dark cold day.

                    II

    You were silly like us; your gift survived it all:
    The parish of rich women, physical decay,
    Yourself. Mad Ireland hurt you into poetry.
35 Now Ireland has her madness and her weather still,
    For poetry makes nothing happen: it survives
    In the valley of its making where executives
    Would never want to tamper, flows on south
    From ranches of isolation and the busy griefs,
40 Raw towns that we believe and die in; it survives,
    A way of happening, a mouth.

                    III

    Earth, receive an honored guest:
    William Yeats is laid to rest.
    Let the Irish vessel lie
45 Emptied of its poetry.

    In the nightmare of the dark
    All the dogs of Europe bark,
    And the living nations wait,
    Each sequestered in its hate;

50 Intellectual disgrace
    Stares from every human face,
    And the seas of pity lie
    Locked and frozen in each eye.

    Follow, poet, follow right
55 To the bottom of the night,
    With your unconstraining voice
    Still persuade us to rejoice;

    With the farming of a verse
    Make a vineyard of the curse,
60 Sing of human unsuccess
    In a rapture of distress;

    In the deserts of the heart
    Let the healing fountain start,
    In the prison of his days
65 Teach the free man how to praise.

                                                    1939

• Does Auden's **elegy** as a whole affirm that "poetry makes nothing happen"
  (line 36)? Why does the death of Yeats seem to inspire the speaker to reflect
  on this possibility?

AUTHORS ON THEIR WORK

W. H. AUDEN (1907–73)

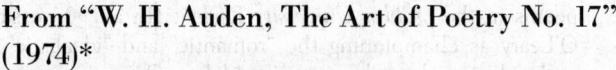

From "W. H. Auden, The Art of Poetry No. 17" (1974)*

INTERVIEWER: How about writers as leaders? Yeats, for instance, held office.

AUDEN: And he was terrible! Writers seldom make good leaders. They're self-employed, for one thing, and they have very little contact with their customers. It's very easy for a writer to be unrealistic. I have not lost my interest in politics, but I have come to realize that, in cases of social or political injustice, only two things are effective: political action and straight journalistic reportage of the facts. The arts can do nothing. The social and political history of Europe would be what it has been if Dante, Shakespeare, Michelangelo, Mozart, et al., had never lived. A poet, *qua* poet, has only one political duty, namely, in his own writing to set an example of the correct use of his mother tongue which is always being corrupted. When words lose their meaning, physical force takes over. By all means, let a poet, if he wants to, write what is now called an "engagé" ["engaged"] poem, so long as he realizes that it is mainly himself who will benefit from it. It will enhance his literary reputation among those who feel the same as he does.

INTERVIEWER: Would you care to comment on Yeats?

AUDEN: I find it very difficult to be fair to Yeats because he had a bad influence on me. He tempted me into a rhetoric which was, for me, oversimplified. Needless to say, the fault was mine, not his. He was, of course, a very great poet.

*"W. H. Auden, The Art of Poetry No. 17." Interview by Michael Newman. *The Paris Review*, no. 57, spring 1974, www.theparisreview.org/interviews/3970/the-art-of-poetry-no-17-w-h-auden.

Chronology

1865   Born on June 13 in Dublin, Ireland, the eldest child of merchant's daughter Susan Pollexfen Yeats and well-known, but often financially strapped, lawyer-turned-painter John Butler Yeats.

1867   To further his career as an artist, John Yeats moves his family to London.

1872   With his mother and siblings, spends two years at his maternal grandparents' home in Sligo, on Ireland's rural west coast.

1874   Returns to London with his family and attends the Godolphin School.

1880   Financial difficulties force John Yeats to move his family back to Dublin, where his eldest son attends a local high school.

1884　Enters Dublin's Metropolitan School of Art, where he will study until 1886. With fellow writer and art student George Russell (known as "AE"), Yeats begins his research into spiritualism and the occult.

1885　Meets Irish nationalist John O'Leary and, with O'Leary's help, publishes his first poems in the *Dublin University Review*. (In a 1907 essay, Yeats will describe O'Leary as championing the "romantic" and "idealistic" "conception of Irish nationality [. . .] in whose service I labour.")

1887　Returns to London with his family and edits *Poems and Ballads of Young Ireland*.

1888　Joins the spiritualist Theosophical Society and edits *Fairy and Folk Tales of the Irish Peasantry*.

1889　Publishes his first volume of poetry, *The Wanderings of Oisin and Other Poems*, and meets and falls in love with the actress and Irish revolutionary Maud Gonne.

1891　Gonne rejects the first of at least three marriage proposals from Yeats.

1892　With others founds the London-based Irish Literary Society; publishes *The Countess Cathleen and Various Legends and Lyrics*, a collection of plays and poems.

1893　Publishes an edition of William Blake's poems and a prose work, *The Celtic Twilight*.

1895　Publishes *Poems*, which includes revised versions of works in his first two collections and which is sometimes said to mark the end of his early period.

1896　Meets fellow writer and Celtic Revivalist Lady Augusta Gregory and begins to spend holidays at her estate, Coole Park, in rural County Galway, Ireland.

1899　With Lady Gregory founds the Irish Literary Theatre, later called the Abbey Theatre, in Dublin, which produces his *Countess Cathleen*.

1902　Maud Gonne stars in Yeats's *Cathleen ni Houlihan*.

1903　Gonne marries war veteran John MacBride, from whom she will separate in 1905.

1904　Yeats's middle period arguably begins with the publication of the collection *In the Seven Woods*. He begins a six-year stint as manager of the Abbey Theatre, coming into conflict both with conservative Catholics offended by the supposed immorality and impiety of Abbey productions and with Irish nationalists convinced that Abbey plays should promote a wholly positive view of Ireland and the Irish.

1907　An Abbey performance of J. M. Synge's *The Playboy of the Western World* sparks riots over its supposedly negative portrayal of the Irish.

1913　Spends the first of three winters with the young American poet Ezra Pound.

1914　World War I begins (in August). Yeats publishes *Responsibilities*, his first pointedly Modernist, as well as avowedly public and political, poetry collection.

1916　In London, debuts *At the Hawk's Well*, the first of his plays influenced by Japanese Noh drama (rather than Irish history and legend), and publishes *Reveries of Childhood and Youth*, the first volume of his autobiography. In April, Irish nationalists stage the Easter Uprising in Dublin. Proclaiming Ireland an independent republic, the seven hundred volunteers are defeated by British troops after a week of bloody fighting; their leaders, including John MacBride, are executed for treason in May. Yeats proposes to Maud Gonne for the last time.

1917　The Russian Revolution begins, and T. S. Eliot publishes his first poetry collection, which includes *The Love Song of J. Alfred Prufrock* and which, Yeats later claimed, announced the birth of a new, self-consciously "modern" poetry that he "disliked" and yet admired for its "satiric intensity." Yeats marries Georgie Hyde-Lees; while still on their honeymoon, Georgie begins the spirit-inspired automatic writing that will be the basis for *A Vision* (1925).

1918   World War I ends. Yeats and his wife move to Thoor (literally, "Castle") Ballylee, an ancient Norman tower near Lady Gregory's estate; the tower and its winding staircase will become a central symbol in his later poetry.

1919   In January, Russian revolutionaries kill four grand dukes, bringing to seventeen the number of members of the former Russian emperor's family to die in the revolution. Yeats writes "The Second Coming" and publishes *The Wild Swans at Coole*, the last collection of his so-called middle period. His first child, a daughter, is born in Dublin. Ireland enters a period of civil unrest.

1921   A truce brings temporary peace to Ireland. Yeats's second child, a son, is born, and Yeats publishes the poetry collection *Michael Robartes and the Dancer*.

1922   Irish Civil War begins. Yeats's father dies. Yeats publishes *The Trembling of the Veil*, the second volume of his autobiography, and begins a six-year stint as a senator in the first Irish government.

1923   Wins the Nobel Prize in Literature.

1925   Publishes *A Vision*, a work of nonfiction outlining his system of symbols and cyclical vision of history.

1928   Publishes *The Tower* and resigns from the Irish Senate.

1933   Publishes *The Winding Stair and Other Poems*.

1939   Dies in France on January 28, age seventy-six. World War II begins.

1948   Yeats's remains are returned to Ireland and buried in County Sligo under a stone bearing the epitaph he composed: "Cast a cold eye / On Life, on Death. / Horseman, pass by!"

SUGGESTIONS FOR WRITING

1. Write an essay in which you compare THE LAKE ISLE OF INNISFREE and SAILING TO BYZANTIUM in order to show how Yeats's poetry both did and didn't change over the course of his career. How might the first of these poems seem like the work of a young man and poet, and the latter like that of a mature or even elderly one?

2. Write an essay that explains the significance of any one recurring image or symbol, or set of related images or symbols, in at least two Yeats poems. Alternatively, use your essay to explore why terror and beauty seem to go together in Yeats's poems.

3. Drawing on at least three poems, write an essay explaining whether and how Yeats's poetry seems distinctly "Irish." How, for example, might the troubled history of his native country or his own troubled relationship to Irish nationalism, as well as the middle-class Irish public, be explored in the poems, including the later ones that outwardly seem resolutely non-Irish in content and form?

4. Write an essay comparing the way W. H. Auden's poem about Yeats portrays the nature, source, and function of poetry to the way Yeats's poems, such as SAILING TO BYZANTIUM, do. Alternatively, compare the way each poet handles the contrast between physical, mortal life and "decay" (Auden, line 33), on the one hand, and the life lived in the imagination and poetry, on the other. Do the two poets seem to agree about the immortality and importance of poetry?

Pat Mora

AN ALBUM

A ward-winning contemporary writer Pat Mora was born in 1942 in El Paso, Texas, a city on the Mexican border to which all four of her Spanish-speaking grandparents migrated during the Mexican Revolution (c. 1910–20). After earning a BA and MA from the University of Texas, El Paso, Mora taught both high-school and college English but did not devote herself seriously to writing until after her 1981 divorce, when, as she once joked to an interviewer, "I saw the age of forty coming for me." In the years since, she has seen her three children into adulthood; remarried; and left Texas for Cincinnati, Ohio, and Santa Fe, New Mexico (her two current homes). She has also flourished as a writer, publishing collections of poetry including *Borders* (1986), *Agua Santa/Holy Water* (1995), *Aunt Carmen's Book of Practical Saints* (1997), *Adobe Odes* (2007), and *Encantado: Desert Monologues* (2018); a book of essays, *Nepantla: Essays from the Land in the Middle* (1993); a family memoir; and over twenty-five books for children and young adults, including poetry, picture books, biographies, and retellings of Mayan folktales.

Avowing that she "take[s] pride in being a Hispanic writer," Mora sees her work for both children and adults as bound up with the effort to promote literacy, a wider knowledge and appreciation of Hispanic culture and heritage, and cross-cultural understanding. In *Nepantla*, she likens the work of the poet to that of the *curandera*, or traditional healer, sounding not unlike poet W. B. Yeats when she argues that

> [t]he Chicana writer seeks to heal cultural wounds of historical neglect by providing opportunities to remember the past, to share and ease bitterness, to describe what has been viewed as unworthy of description, to cure by incantations and rhythms, by listening with her entire being and responding. She then gathers the tales and myths, weaves them together, and, if lucky, casts spells.

Though she makes frequent use of Spanish terms and phrases in her work, Mora writes primarily in English because she is, in her own words, "bilingual, though English-dominant," living on the figurative border between languages and cultures or in what she calls "the land in the middle." Much of her work explores that land. Yet in interviews, Mora roundly rejects the idea that the experience of living "in the middle" is entirely negative. Rather, she insists that, while "there are situations where, yes, it's plenty difficult" or where she is uncertain about where she belongs or who she is, there is also a flip side: "it's double pleasure in a way," offering "the advantage of moving back and forth." As Mora also suggests, people from all backgrounds "experience borders of many kinds throughout life." And by exploring some of these divides—between men and women, for example, or among different generations—Mora's work stresses the ubiquity of the border experience, as well as the pleasures and conflicts it entails.

Literal, physical borders in particular and space and place in general also intrigue Mora—all the more, she suggests, since a 1989 move from the Southwest to the Midwest heightened her awareness of both the distinctiveness of her native landscape and her own relationship to it. Whenever she flew west, she explained to one interviewer,

> I would look out at this tremendous space and think how totally I felt at home there. Many of my Midwestern friends would confide to me that they found the desert sometimes even terrifying. I remember one of the brightest women I know who is an academic in Cincinnati said to me that the first time she came to the Southwest she was afraid she would fall off because she was so used to the protection of trees [. . .]. Our early geography shapes us in complex ways.

Geography, landscape, and the immigrant experience are only some of the many things you will find to explore in Mora's poems, including those gathered in this album and in other chapters. What might her poems individually and collectively suggest about what both is and isn't unique about the Mexican American experience? about the positive and negative aspects of living "in the land of the middle"? about what unites and divides Mexican Americans of different classes, generations, and genders? about family? about the power and the limits of language? In what ways might Mora's poems perform the *curandera*-like work she ascribes to the poet in *Nepantla*?

POEMS BY PAT MORA

Elena

My Spanish isn't enough.
I remember how I'd smile
listening to my little ones,
understanding every word they'd say,
5   their jokes, their songs, their plots.
     Vamos a pedirle dulces a mamá. Vamos.[1]
But that was in Mexico.
Now my children go to American high schools.
They speak English. At night they sit around
10   the kitchen table, laugh with one another.
I stand by the stove and feel dumb, alone.
I bought a book to learn English.
My husband frowned, drank more beer.
My oldest said, "*Mamá*, he doesn't want you
15   to be smarter than he is." I'm forty,
embarrassed at mispronouncing words,
embarrassed at the laughter of my children,
the grocer, the mailman. Sometimes I take
my English book and lock myself in the bathroom,
20   say the thick words softly,
for if I stop trying, I will be deaf
when my children need my help.

1985

- What does the speaker mean by the first line—"My Spanish isn't enough"? What other words in the poem address the inadequacy of language?

---

1. Let's go ask mama for sweets. Let's go (Spanish).

Gentle Communion

Even the long-dead are willing to move.
Without a word, she came with me from the desert.
Mornings she wanders through my rooms
making beds, folding socks.

5 Since she can't hear me anymore,
Mamande[2] ignores the questions I never knew
to ask, about her younger days, her red
hair, the time she fell and broke her nose
in the snow. I will never know.

10 When I try to make her laugh,
to disprove her sad album face, she leaves
the room, resists me as she resisted
grinning for cameras, make-up, English.

While I write, she sits and prays,
15 feet apart, legs never crossed,
the blue housecoat buttoned high
as her hair dries white, girlish
around her head and shoulders.

She closes her eyes, bows her head,
20 and like a child presses her hands together,
her patient flesh steeple, the skin
worn, like the pages of her prayer book.

Sometimes I sit in her wide-armed
chair as I once sat in her lap.
25 Alone, we played a quiet I Spy.
She peeled grapes I still taste.

She removes the thin skin, places
the luminous coolness on my tongue.
I know not to bite or chew. I wait
30 for the thick melt,
our private green honey.

1991

• How does this poem draw on the various meanings of the word *communion*? Why might it be significant that the grandmother comes "Without a
word" (line 2)?

Mothers and Daughters

The arm-in-arm-mother-daughter-stroll
in villages and shopping malls
evenings and weekends

2. Child's conflation of *mama grande* (Spanish for "grandmother").

the w a l k - t a l k slow,
5   arm-in-arm
                around the world.

Sometimes they feed one another
memories sweet as hot bread
and lemon tea. Sometimes it's mother-stories
the young one can't remember:

10   "When you were new, I'd nest you
in one arm, while I cooked,
whisper, what am I to do with you?"

Sometimes it's tug
-of-war that started in the womb
15   the fight for space
the sharp jab deep inside
as the weight shifts,
arm-in-arm
                around the world

always the bodytalk thick,
20   always the recipes
hints for feeding
more with less.

                                                        1991

• How does the poem's form, especially its visual appearance and rhythm,
  contribute to its characterization of the mother-daughter relationship?

La Migra

                I

Let's play La Migra[3]
I'll be the Border Patrol.
You be the Mexican maid.
I get the badge and sunglasses.
5   You can hide and run,
but you can't get away
because I have a jeep
I can take you wherever
I want, but don't ask
10   questions because
I don't speak Spanish.
I can touch you wherever
I want but don't complain
too much because I've got
15   boots and kick—if I have to,
and I have handcuffs.

3. Mexican slang for U.S. border patrol agents (an abbreviation of the word *immigration*).

Oh, and a gun.
Get ready, get set, run.

                 II
Let's play *La Migra*
20   You be the Border Patrol.
     I'll be the Mexican woman.
     Your jeep has a flat,
     and you have been spotted
     by the sun.
25   All you have is heavy: hat,
     glasses, badge, shoes, gun.
     I know this desert,
     where to rest,
     where to drink.
30   Oh, I am not alone.
     You hear us singing
     and laughing with the wind,
     Agua dulce brota aquí,
     aquí, aquí,[4] but since you
35   can't speak Spanish,
     you do not understand.
     Get ready.

                                                     1993

• Who seems to be the speaker of this poem, or are there more than one? What
is the game of "hide and run" the speaker proposes (line 5)? Who will win?

Ode to Adobe

          Your blue mouth,
     door of a thousand river-rolled stories,
              opens.
     Walls whisper,
5   voices of earth and straw.
          Clay flower,
     each of your rooms welcomes
              like a wish,
     tastes a different color—
10   mango, papaya, persimmon, quince.
     In your nichos, Santa Rita and San Judas,[5]
              patron saints of the impossible,

4. Sweet water springs here, here, here (Spanish).
5. One of Jesus's twelve apostles, St. Jude Thaddeus is the patron saint of desperate causes because
his New Testament letter stresses that the faithful should persevere in the face of difficult circumstances. *Santa Rita*: Patroness of impossible causes, Italian-born St. Rita (1381–1457) was mistreated
for twenty years by the husband her parents forced her to marry and entered a convent after both he
and her two sons died. *Nichos*: small shelves carved into a wall.

shake their heads,
    gossip
15 about an aunt's pastel
    lust, while they pretend to pray.

    Mud song,
growing to your interior music,
    dream cave,
20 honey-hive shaped by a choir
    of muddy hands,
ballad of eloquent bricks,
    kitchen of unending banquets,
beans simmering for centuries,
25   sun-baked loaf, you rise
        from the desert into a luminaria.[6]

Traditional adobe dwelling found in the southwestern United States and
northern Mexico

    Serenata de barro,
cantadora de la tierra,[7]
    our hands stroke you, wrinkled
30   and delicious,
smell the layered legacy
    that shelters us in the arms
    of candle and piñon smoke.

    Your melodies, washed and ironed
35   by generations of mothers,

---

6. Traditional Mexican Christmas lantern made by setting a candle inside a paper bag weighted with
sand.
7. Serenader of mud, singer of the popular songs of the earth, land, or soil (Spanish).

drift out,

lure departed spirits home again
to dream in the crackle
of kiva fireplaces
40 warmed by sips of humor
and old desires, the taste
of guacamole, the silk
of skin.

In your candlelit mirror,
45 eternal vanity:
a spirit powders her bony nose.

2006

• To what is adobe compared in the poem? How do these comparisons work together to characterize both the adobe and the life lived within it?

Chronology

1942 Born on January 19 in El Paso, Texas, to Raul Antonio Mora, an optician, and his wife, Estela; both are bilingual, second-generation El Pasoans of Mexican descent.

1963 Marries William H. Burnside, Jr., with whom she will have a son and two daughters; earns her BA from Texas Western College (now the University of Texas, El Paso, or UTEP); and begins a three-year stint teaching in the El Paso Independent School District.

1967 Earns her MA from UTEP.

1971 Begins working as a part-time English and communications instructor at El Paso Community College.

1979 Begins working as a part-time English instructor at UTEP.

1981 After her first marriage ends in divorce, devotes more time to writing, while also working as assistant to UTEP's Vice President of Academic Affairs.

1984 Marries Vernon Lee Scarborough, an archaeologist teaching at UTEP, and publishes her first poetry collection, *Chants*, winner of the Harvey L. Johnson and Southwest Book awards.

1986 Wins her second Southwest Book Award for her second poetry collection, *Borders*.

1988 Becomes director of UTEP's natural history museum and assistant to the university president.

1989 Leaves UTEP to take up full-time writing, lecturing, and promoting literacy; moves to the Cincinnati/northern Kentucky area when her husband joins the University of Cincinnati anthropology department. (The couple will make a second home in Santa Fe, New Mexico.)

1991 Publishes *Communion*, a collection of poems chronicling her travels to Cuba, India, and Pakistan.

1992 Publishes *A Birthday Basket for Tia*, the first of many children's books.

1993   Publishes *Nepantla: Essays from the Land in the Middle*.

1994   Wins a National Endowment for the Arts fellowship to complete her poetry collection *Agua Santa / Holy Water* (1995).

1997   Publishes *House of Houses*, a family memoir, and the poetry collection *Aunt Carmen's Book of Practical Saints*, and spearheads creation of a national day of celebration of children's bilingual literacy (El día de los niños, El día de los libros/ Children's Day, Book Day).

2001   Publishes *My Own True Name: New and Selected Poems for Young Adults*.

2006   Publishes *Adobe Odes*.

2010   Publishes both her second poetry collection for young adults (*Dizzy In Your Eyes: Poems about Love*) and *Zing! Seven Creativity Practices for Educators and Students* (simultaneously a guide for educators and students and "an epistolary memoir of her journey as a writer").

2012   Wins the Association of Writers & Writing Programs (AWP) Con Tinta Achievement Award for Literary Activism.

2017   Wins the Texas Institute of Letters Lon Tinkle Award for Lifetime Achievement.

2018   Publishes *Encantado: Desert Monologues*.

SUGGESTIONS FOR WRITING

1. Food, cooking, and related imagery figure in many of Mora's poems. Write an essay exploring the significance of such references. What might the poems suggest about the roles food, cooking, and eating play in our lives?

2. Drawing on at least three of Mora's poems, write an essay that explores her vision of the role of language. When, how, and why does language both unite and divide people? When, why, and how might nonverbal forms of communication prove superior?

3. As the introduction to this album suggests, Pat Mora takes pride in being a Latina writer and identifies one of her goals as chronicling the experience and feelings of contemporary Latinos and Latinas. Write an essay in which you compare at least two of Mora's poems, exploring what they together imply about what it is like to be Latina/o and how that experience differs across generations, classes, and/or genders.

4. The poems reprinted here were originally included in various collections, each of which has a distinct focus and flavor. GENTLE COMMUNION, for example, appears in Mora's third volume, *Communion* (1991), which some critics see as the culmination of the earliest phase of her career and as the reflection of both a widening of the world depicted in her work (through poems inspired by her travels to other countries) and a greater concentration on the situation of women and on the relationships both among women and between women and men. Pick the Mora poem you like most, identify the collection in which it originally appeared, and read some other poems included in that collection. Then write an essay that either compares your chosen poem to others in the collection or that explains how your interpretation of the original poem changes when you read it in conjunction with the other poems.

22 | CULTURAL AND HISTORICAL CONTEXTS: THE HARLEM RENAISSANCE

Poetry may be read in private moments or experienced in a great variety of communal settings—in classrooms or theaters, for example, or at poetry slams or public readings. It is nonetheless almost always *written* in solitude by a single author. Collaborative composition is rare in poetry, even rarer than in other arts. Still, there is a sense in which many poems represent collaborative acts. Traditions, group identities, shared experiences, desires, and communal needs may come together in a particular moment and location to produce poetry that has a distinctive stamp of time, place, and vision. One such phenomenon was the Harlem Renaissance, a period of ten or fifteen years early in the twentieth century when an extraordinarily talented group of people came together in uptown Manhattan to celebrate and embody the awakening of a new African American consciousness. It was an unprecedented moment in American poetry and in American culture at large, and it produced some of the twentieth century's most compelling and original poems, as well as significant works of art in a variety of other genres and media.

The Harlem Renaissance was not exactly a movement in the sense of having a formal structure; no one originated it or called it to order, and it was not consciously planned or organized by any person or group. There was no founder, no architect, no leader, and it is hard to say why or how—or even exactly when—it began or ended. It happened, as the needs and desires of Black intellectuals and artists became manifest and began to coalesce in a particular time and place, and it ended—or rather scattered its energy—when conditions in the world at large dictated that other priorities, especially economic ones, began to trump those that had brought it together. But it was not, of course, independent of history or without cause. It was a product of many circumstances, most of them involving the long-term aftereffects of slavery and the increasingly articulated desire of African Americans to produce a distinctive Black American culture within the larger national culture. The Harlem Renaissance represented powerful assertions: that America had to include the voices of Black Americans in order to find its own full definition and, equally, that artistic creativity—including literary creativity—was essential to Black Americans' realization and assertion of their full humanity. To live in Harlem and to be Black and creative was not an altogether happy experience, and the poetry that exploded out of that time and place is a poetry of anger, resentment, conflict, and torn loyalties. It is also a poetry of energy, sensitivity, humanity, and high ideals.

What was the Harlem Renaissance? It was first of all a migration or, rather, part of a migration: Around the end of World War I, Black Americans relocated in large numbers from the South to the North and from rural areas to cities. New York was only one of many destinations; Chicago, Philadelphia, Detroit, Washington, Cleveland, Buffalo, and other urban centers all received huge

The Cotton Club, circa 1930

numbers of Black migrants. But New York was the largest and most vibrant seat of culture in America, beginning to rival European capitals as a site where active artistic communities produced and consumed culture of all kinds—high, low, and in between. More than 100,000 Blacks migrated to Harlem during the 1920s, taking over and transforming a Manhattan neighborhood north of Central Park and turning it into a distinctive, creative, independent center of art and performance that drew the rest of New York City to it. For most of the 1920s—called "the Roaring '20s" because of the era's daring, rebellious attitudes and booming economic growth—Harlem was a magnet for avant-garde Whites in New York. They flocked to speakeasies, nightclubs, and theaters. They were fascinated by the kinds of music, dance, and performance art they could find there—productions quite different from those on Broadway or in other parts of the city, though White venues increasingly tried to capture, in their own productions, something of the life and energy that patrons sought in Harlem. White readers and many White artists showed enormous—sometimes mawkish or even ghoulish—curiosity about Black life in America. Before the Harlem Renaissance had ended,

A dancer entertains a crowd at Small's Paradise Club, 1929. As at many of Harlem's best-known nightclubs, the entertainers and staff at Small's were primarily African American, the clientele mainly White.

many novels and a large number of Broadway productions—Marc Connelly's *Green Pastures* (1930), Eugene O'Neill's *The Emperor Jones* (1920), and *All God's Chillun Got Wings* (1924), for example—tried to represent the Black experience for White audiences. Black artists and writers (and their readers) were not always happy with the way White writers either portrayed Black experience and Black concerns or "adapted" (some would say "appropriated") work originally created by African Americans, but the widespread curiosity provided a wider audience for Black literature and arts than ever before.

The height of the Harlem Renaissance was the 1920s. Some historians, pointing to the political ferment caused by U.S. entry into World War I in 1917, date its beginnings in the mid to late teens, and some regard it as lasting until the outbreak of World War II in the late 1930s. But the decade of the 1920s saw most of the productivity and creative energy that we associate with the flourishing of Harlem. And it was in the early 1920s when most of the leading writers in the group actually moved to New York. Many historians regard the stock-market crash of 1929 and the depression that followed as signs of the end. Certainly the mood of the whole nation changed rapidly then, and by the early 1930s most of the leading figures of the Renaissance had moved away from New York, sometimes forming smaller communities elsewhere. Harlem itself began a slow economic decline.

Between the wars, though, Harlem's productivity and impact were dramatic. Before 1917, there had been few publishing outlets hospitable to young Black writers; only Paul Laurence Dunbar among African American poets was widely read or known, and he had died in 1906. But rising political and social concerns during and immediately after World War I produced several new periodicals: *The Messenger*, founded in 1917 by A. Philip Randolph and Chandler Owen, claimed to be "The only Radical Negro Magazine in America," and in 1923 the Urban League started its own magazine, *Opportunity*. Both of these new journals saw themselves as activist alternatives to the NAACP's official journal, *Crisis*, edited by W. E. B. Du Bois. Other magazines came and went. *Fire!!* managed only a single issue, but brought verbal and visual art spectacularly together. Meanwhile—and perhaps just as important in a different way—mainstream magazines and publishers began to feature younger Black writers, who soon developed a broad readership.

Claude McKay, circa 1930

Some historians date the Harlem Renaissance from the composition of Claude McKay's fiery sonnet IF WE MUST DIE, written in the summer of 1919. McKay later denied that the poem referred specifically to Blacks and Whites, but the many anti-Black riots that broke out in several American cities that summer—sometimes called "the Red Summer"—certainly shaped the poem. Another milestone was the publication in 1922 of James Weldon Johnson's *Book of American Negro Poetry*, which, in the words of the editors of *The Norton Anthology of African American Literature*, "emphasized the youthful promise of the new writers and established some of the terms of the

Countee Cullen, circa 1935

emerging movement." But it was Alain Locke's landmark anthology *The New Negro* that, in 1925, effectively announced the significance of the Harlem Renaissance. Locke, a sociology professor at Howard University and the first African American Rhodes Scholar, gathered all kinds of material—poems, fiction, essays, visual art—by authors old and young, Black and White—into a working definition of the "new Negro."

The major figures of the Harlem Renaissance were, however, highly individual. And though they shared many ideals and aspirations, they never confined themselves to a creed or hardened into a "school." Langston Hughes, with a wonderful **lyric** voice and an eye for telling details, pursued the relationship of poetry to Black music and experimented with a variety of forms and rhythms. Countee Cullen was instead deeply committed to conventional poetic forms and felt most at home poetically when he was working in traditional fixed forms. Claude McKay, born in Jamaica, lived briefly in New York but mostly in Greenwich Village rather than Harlem, and spent much of his career abroad (in Russia, France, and North Africa). He always followed his own star in poetry, too; his work is sometimes violent and incendiary, but equally strong is his sense of nostalgia and natural spiritualism and his affinity for traditional fixed forms. (He is a master of the **sonnet**.) Despite setting a militant tone in a founding poem of the Harlem Renaissance, "If We Must Die," he wrote only two poems that were directly about Harlem experiences and themes. Likewise, novelists like Zora Neale Hurston, Jean Toomer, Jesse Fauset, and

Vendor selling books and pamphlets from a cart on 125th Street in Harlem, June 1943

Nella Larsen pursued individual styles and themes in their fiction. What held the group together was a dedication both to producing first-rate writing and to raising the aspirations of American Blacks of all backgrounds and abilities.

The question of who was to benefit from the ambitious art of the Harlem Renaissance was hotly debated. Was it ordinary people, who could stretch the horizons of their reading and their own ambitions? African Americans generally? Or was it primarily intellectuals and artists who might raise expectations for Black thought and art? W. E. B. Du Bois, who was a lightning rod for many members of the militant and radical new generation, had famously championed the "talented tenth," a select group whose natural gifts authoritatively raised them above others. And opinions split over whether the beneficiaries of the Harlem Renaissance were to be ordinary readers and viewers or the creative geniuses themselves, in the service of a higher aesthetic quite distinct from social progress. It's fair to say that writers remained divided, alternately championing the triumph of art and hoping for a larger cultural impact that would benefit readers (especially Black readers) more generally.

The role of Whites in the Harlem Renaissance is also a matter of debate. The most controversial, though undeniably influential figure was Carl Van Vechten, whose parties legendarily brought young Black writers into the company of famous and powerful White celebrities, many of whom proved helpful to Black writers' careers. Van Vechten was a gifted photographer whose portraits of many rising figures chronicle the Harlem years brilliantly, and he undeniably fostered many useful connections that resulted in publication and fame. (He took the photos of Countee Cullen, Arna Bontemps, Claude McKay, and Zora Neale Hurston reproduced in this chapter.) But some felt Van Vechten's motives were self-serving, and his well-meaning novel about Harlem life, *Nigger Heaven* (1926), was widely disparaged, though critics equally suspected "realistic" accounts of everyday life by Black writers. (See, for example, the Du Bois review of a Claude McKay novel later in this chapter.) There is no doubt that figures like Van Vechten fostered interaction between prominent Whites and rising figures in the Black artistic community, but not everyone regarded the results as helpful to the Black cause overall. Some historians view White participation in the Harlem Renaissance as exploitative, others as sincere but bumbling; still others view such Black-White collaboration as an early demonstration of racial unity.

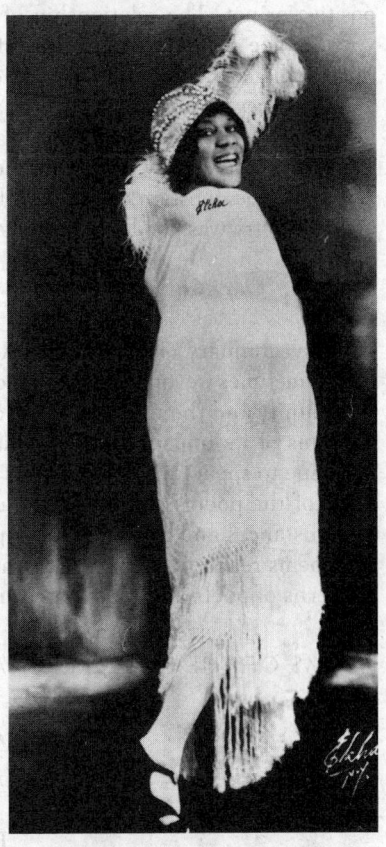

Known as the "Empress of the Blues," Bessie Smith was one of the most popular entertainers in America during the 1920s.

Another set of questions involves elitism—whether the renaissance had truly salutary effects on the larger Black community. Du Bois insisted on the obligation of "the talented tenth" to use their artistic and intellectual gifts to improve the lot of others. Critics of Du Bois find his position divisive and patronizing toward the majority of the Black community; defenders see the idea as a strategy for achieving community improvement by cultivating potential leaders. At the heart of this controversy is disagreement about how leadership works to promote both improved social conditions and audience engagement. (Similar arguments rage today over the stardom of Black athletes and entertainers.)

Two other, related controversies concern the influence of the church on Black culture and the relationship of the ambitious new "high art" of poetry, novels, and painting to popular-culture phenomena such as jazz, blues, and dance. There is little doubt that religion was a powerful force in the Black community, but observers continue to debate, as the artists themselves then did, whether it fostered and furthered artistic expression or served as a restraining and discouraging force. Often readers can see in poetry about even the most secular subjects traces of religious ideas and traditions; you will have to decide for yourself whether the effects are positive or not. The relationship of radical art to popular culture was even more vexed. Some central figures in the Harlem Renaissance regarded their own aims as "above" the "attractions" and "spectacles" that drew large numbers of Whites to Harlem, and they regarded the performance arts as, at best, distractions from, or dilutions of, the main flow of radical artistic expression. And while nearly everyone agrees that the quality of various theatrical arts in the many venues of Harlem was very high, the question of whether, beyond jazz and blues, the influence of popular arts on poetry was good or bad remains open.

No easy summary of the Harlem Renaissance will do. Its ambitions—often radical, sometimes revolutionary—made enormous waves in both the Black urban community and the world of art. However one measures the Harlem Renaissance in terms of its impact on later writers, Black and White, the poems themselves continue to speak to readers across divides of time and culture. You will find that some of the poems can hardly be understood without knowledge of the specific circumstances and conditions that produced them; you will also find that many of the poems reach insistently for connections both to the past and to the enduring concerns of poets and readers in far-flung times and places.

POEMS OF THE HARLEM RENAISSANCE

Arna Bontemps, 1939

ARNA BONTEMPS
A Black Man Talks of Reaping

I have sown beside all waters in my day.
I planted deep, within my heart the fear
That wind or fowl would take the grain away.
I planted safe against this stark, lean year.

5   I scattered seed enough to plant the land
In rows from Canada to Mexico
But for my reaping only what the hand
Can hold at once is all that I can show.

Yet what I sowed and what the orchard yields
10 My brother's sons are gathering stalk and root,
Small wonder then my children glean in fields
They have not sown, and feed on bitter fruit.

1926

COUNTEE CULLEN
Yet Do I Marvel

I doubt not God is good, well-meaning, kind,
And did He stoop to quibble could tell why
The little buried mole continues blind,
Why flesh that mirrors Him must some day die,
5   Make plain the reason tortured Tantalus[1]
Is baited by the fickle fruit, declare
If merely brute caprice dooms Sisyphus[2]
To struggle up a never-ending stair.
Inscrutable His ways are, and immune
10 To catechism by a mind too strewn
With petty cares to slightly understand
What awful brain compels His awful hand.
Yet do I marvel at this curious thing:
To make a poet black, and bid him sing!

1925

Incident

Once riding in old Baltimore,
    Heart-filled, head-filled with glee,
I saw a Baltimorean
    Keep looking straight at me.

5   Now I was eight and very small,
    And he was no whit bigger,
And so I smiled, but he poked out
    His tongue, and called me, "Nigger."

I saw the whole of Baltimore
10   From May until December;
Of all the things that happened there
    That's all that I remember.

1925

1. Figure in Greek myth condemned to stand up to his neck in water he couldn't drink and to look
upon fruit he couldn't reach to eat.
2. King of Corinth who, in Greek myth, was condemned eternally to roll a huge stone uphill.

Saturday's Child[3]

Some are teethed on a silver spoon,
　　With the stars strung for a rattle;
I cut my teeth as the black raccoon—
　　For implements of battle.

5　Some are swaddled in silk and down,
　　And heralded by a star;[4]
They swathed my limbs in a sackcloth gown
　　On a night that was black as tar.

For some, godfather and goddame
10　　The opulent fairies be;
Dame Poverty gave me my name,
　　And Pain godfathered me.

For I was born on Saturday—
　　"Bad time for planting a seed,"
15　Was all my father had to say,
　　And, "One mouth more to feed."

Death cut the strings that gave me life,
　　And handed me to Sorrow,
The only kind of middle wife
20　　My folks could beg or borrow.

　　　　　　　　　　　　　　　　　　　1925

ANGELINA GRIMKÉ
The Black Finger

Angelina Grimké, circa 1905

I have just seen a beautiful thing
　　Slim and still,
Against a gold, gold sky,
　　A straight cypress,
5　　Sensitive
　　Exquisite,
A black finger
Pointing upwards.
Why, beautiful, still finger are you black?
10　And why are you pointing upwards?

　　　　　　　　　　　　　　　　　　　1925

---

3. According to a popular nursery rhyme, "Saturday's child works hard for his living."
4. According to Matthew 2.7–10, Jesus's birth was accompanied by the appearance of a new star.

Tenebris[5]

There is a tree, by day,
That, at night,
Has a shadow,
A hand huge and black,
5   With fingers long and black.
    All through the dark,
Against the white man's house,
    In the little wind,
The black hand plucks and plucks
10   At the bricks.
The bricks are the color of blood and very small.
    Is it a black hand,
    Or is it a shadow?

1927

LANGSTON HUGHES
The Weary Blues

Droning a drowsy syncopated tune,
Rocking back and forth to a mellow
    croon,
    I heard a Negro play.
Down on Lenox Avenue[6] the other
    night
5   By the pale dull pallor of an old gas
    light
    He did a lazy sway. . . .
    He did a lazy sway. . . .
To the tune o' those Weary Blues.
With his ebony hands on each ivory
    key
10 He made that poor piano moan with
    melody.
    O Blues!
Swaying to and fro on his rickety stool
He played that sad raggy tune like a musical fool.
    Sweet Blues!
15 Coming from a black man's soul.
    O Blues!
In a deep song voice with a melancholy tone
I heard that Negro sing, that old piano moan—
    "Ain't got nobody in all this world,
20   Ain't got nobody but ma self.

Langston Hughes, circa 1926

5. In darkness (Latin).
6. Major Harlem thoroughfare, a.k.a. Malcolm X Boulevard since 1987.

I's gwine to quit ma frownin'
And put ma troubles on the shelf."

Thump, thump, thump, went his foot on the floor.
He played a few chords then he sang some more—
25   "I got the Weary Blues
And I can't be satisfied.
Got the Weary Blues
And can't be satisfied—
I ain't happy no mo'
30   And I wish that I had died."
And far into the night he crooned that tune.
The stars went out and so did the moon.
The singer stopped playing and went to bed
While the Weary Blues echoed through his head.
35 He slept like a rock or a man that's dead.

1923   1925

The Negro Speaks of Rivers

I've known rivers:
I've known rivers ancient as the world and older than the flow of
        human blood in human veins.

My soul has grown deep like the rivers.

I bathed in the Euphrates when dawns were young.
5   I built my hut near the Congo and it lulled me to sleep.
I looked upon the Nile and raised the pyramids above it.
I heard the singing of the Mississippi when Abe Lincoln went down to
        New Orleans, and I've seen its muddy bosom turn all golden in
        the sunset.

Pen-and-ink illustration by the artist Aaron Douglas made to accompany Hughes's
"The Negro Speaks of Rivers"

I've known rivers:
Ancient, dusky rivers.

10 My soul has grown deep like the rivers.

1926

I, Too

I, too, sing America.

I am the darker brother.
They send me to eat in the kitchen
When company comes,
5 But I laugh,
And eat well,
And grow strong.

Tomorrow,
I'll sit at the table.
10 When company comes
Nobody'll dare
Say to me,
"Eat in the kitchen,"
Then.

15 Besides,
They'll see how beautiful I am
And be ashamed—

I, too, am America.

1932

Harlem

What happens to a dream deferred?

Does it dry up
Like a raisin in the sun?
Or fester like a sore—
5 And then run?
Does it stink like rotten meat?
Or crust and sugar over—
Like a syrupy sweet?
Maybe it just sags
10 Like a heavy load.

Or does it explode?

1951

HELENE JOHNSON
Sonnet to a Negro in Harlem

You are disdainful and magnificent—
Your perfect body and your pompous gait,
Your dark eyes flashing solemnly with hate,
Small wonder that you are incompetent
5 To imitate those whom you so despise—
Your shoulders towering high above the throng,
Your head thrown back in rich, barbaric song,
Palm trees and mangoes stretched before your eyes.
Let others toil and sweat for labor's sake
10 And wring from grasping hands their meed[7] of gold.
Why urge ahead your supercilious feet?
Scorn will efface each footprint that you make.
I love your laughter arrogant and bold.
You are too splendid for this city street.

1927

CLAUDE McKAY
Harlem Shadows

I hear the halting footsteps of a lass
    In Negro Harlem when the night lets fall
Its veil. I see the shapes of girls who pass
    To bend and barter at desire's call.
5 Ah, little dark girls who in slippered feet
    Go prowling through the night from street to street!

Through the long night until the silver break
    Of day the little gray feet know no rest;
Through the lone night until the last snow-flake
10   Has dropped from heaven upon the earth's white breast,
The dusky, half-clad girls of tired feet
Are trudging, thinly shod, from street to street.

Ah, stern harsh world, that in the wretched way
    Of poverty, dishonor and disgrace,
15 Has pushed the timid little feet of clay,
    The sacred brown feet of my fallen race!
Ah, heart of me, the weary, weary feet
In Harlem wandering from street to street.

1918

7. Reward.

If We Must Die

If we must die, let it not be like hogs
Hunted and penned in an inglorious spot,
While round us bark the mad and hungry dogs,
Making their mock at our accursed lot.
5   If we must die, O let us nobly die,
So that our precious blood may not be shed
In vain; then even the monsters we defy
Shall be constrained to honor us though dead!
O kinsmen! we must meet the common foe!
10 Though far outnumbered let us show us brave,
And for their thousand blows deal one deathblow!
What though before us lies the open grave?
Like men we'll face the murderous, cowardly pack,
Pressed to the wall, dying, but fighting back!

1919

America

Although she feeds me bread of bitterness,
And sinks into my throat her tiger's tooth,
Stealing my breath of life, I will confess
I love this cultured hell that tests my youth!
5   Her vigor flows like tides into my blood,
Giving me strength erect against her hate.
Her bigness sweeps my being like a flood.
Yet as a rebel fronts a king in state,
I stand within her walls with not a shred
10 Of terror, malice nor even a word of jeer.
Darkly I gaze into the days ahead
To see her might and granite wonders there,
Beneath the touch of Time's unerring hand,
Like ancient treasures buried in the sand.

1921

The White House

Your door is shut against my tightened face,
And I am sharp as steel with discontent;
But I possess the courage and the grace
To bear my anger proudly and unbent.
5   The pavement slabs burn loose beneath my feet,
And passion rends my vitals as I pass,
A chafing savage, down the decent street,
Where boldly shines your shuttered door of glass.
Oh, I must search for wisdom every hour,
10 Deep in my wrathful bosom sore and raw,

And find in it the superhuman power
To hold me to the letter of your law!
Oh, I must keep my heart inviolate
Against the poison of your deadly hate.

1937

CONTEXTUAL EXCERPTS

JAMES WELDON JOHNSON

From the preface to The Book of American Negro Poetry (1921)[1]

James Weldon Johnson, circa 1920

This preface has gone far beyond what I had in mind when I started. It was my intention to gather together the best verses I could find by Negro poets and present them with a bare word of introduction. It was not my plan to make this collection inclusive nor to make the book in any sense a book of criticism. I planned to present only verses by contemporary writers; but, perhaps, because this is the first collection of its kind, I realized the absence of a starting-point and was led to provide one and to fill in with historical data what I felt to be a gap.

It may be surprising to many to see how little of the poetry being written by Negro poets today is being written in Negro dialect. The newer Negro poets show a tendency to discard dialect; much of the subject-matter which went into the making of traditional dialect poetry, 'possums, watermelons, etc., they have discarded altogether, at least, as poetic material. This tendency will, no doubt, be regretted by the majority of white readers; and, indeed, it would be a distinct loss if the American Negro poets threw away this quaint and musical folk speech as a medium of expression. And yet, after all, these poets are working through a problem not realized by the reader, and, perhaps, by many of these poets themselves not realized consciously. They are trying to break away from, not Negro dialect itself, but the limitations on Negro dialect imposed by the fixing effects of long convention.

The Negro in the United States has achieved or been placed in a certain artistic niche. When he is thought of artistically, it is as a happy-go-lucky, singing, shuffling, banjo-picking being or as a more or less pathetic figure. The picture of him is in a log cabin amid fields of cotton or along the levees. Negro dialect is naturally and by long association the exact instrument for

1. James Weldon Johnson, preface. *The Book of American Negro Poetry*, edited by Johnson, Harcourt, Brace, 1922, pp. vii–xlviii.

voicing this phase of Negro life; and by that very exactness it is an instrument with but two full stops, humor and pathos. So even when he confines himself to purely racial themes, the Aframerican poet realizes that there are phases of Negro life in the United States which cannot be treated in the dialect either adequately or artistically. Take, for example, the phases rising out of life in Harlem, that most wonderful Negro city in the world. I do not deny that a Negro in a log cabin is more picturesque than a Negro in a Harlem flat, but the Negro in the Harlem flat is here, and he is but part of a group growing everywhere in the country, a group whose ideals are becoming increasingly more vital than those of the traditionally artistic group, even if its members are less picturesque.

What the colored poet in the United States needs to do is something like what Synge[2] did for the Irish; he needs to find a form that will express the racial spirit by symbols from within rather than by symbols from without, such as the mere mutilation of English spelling and pronunciation. He needs a form that is freer and larger than dialect, but which will still hold the racial flavor; a form expressing the imagery, the idioms, the peculiar turns of thought, and the distinctive humor and pathos, too, of the Negro, but which will also be capable of voicing the deepest and highest emotions and aspirations, and allow of the widest range of subjects and the widest scope of treatment.

Negro dialect is at present a medium that is not capable of giving expression to the varied conditions of Negro life in America, and much less is it capable of giving the fullest interpretation of Negro character and psychology. This is no indictment against the dialect as dialect, but against the mold of convention in which Negro dialect in the United States has been set. In time these conventions may become lost, and the colored poet in the United States may sit down to write in dialect without feeling that his first line will put the general reader in a frame of mind which demands that the poem be humorous or pathetic. In the meantime, there is no reason why these poets should not continue to do the beautiful things that can be done, and done best, in the dialect.

In stating the need for Aframerican poets in the United States to work out a new and distinctive form of expression I do not wish to be understood to hold any theory that they should limit themselves to Negro poetry, to racial themes; the sooner they are able to write *American* poetry spontaneously, the better. Nevertheless, I believe that the richest contribution the Negro poet can make to the American literature of the future will be the fusion into it of his own individual artistic gifts.

ALAIN LOCKE

From The New Negro (1925)[1]

The tide of Negro migration, northward and city-ward, is not to be fully explained as a blind flood started by the demands of war industry coupled with the shutting off of foreign migration, or by the pressure of poor crops coupled with increased

---

2. John Millington Synge (1871–1909), Irish dramatist whose works celebrate Irish traditions.
1. Alain Locke, *The New Negro: Voices of the Harlem Renaissance*, edited by Locke. 1925. Touchstone, 1997, pp. 3–16.

social terrorism in certain sections of the South and Southwest. Neither labor demand, the bollweevil,[2] nor the Ku Klux Klan is a basic factor, however contributory any or all of them may have been. The wash and rush of this human tide on the beach line of the northern city centers is to be explained primarily in terms of a new vision of opportunity, of social and economic freedom, of a spirit to seize, even in the face of an extortionate and heavy toll, a chance for the improvement of conditions. With each successive wave of it, the movement of the Negro becomes more and more a mass movement toward the larger and the more democratic chance—in the Negro's case a deliberate flight not only from countryside to city, but from medieval America to modern.

Take Harlem as an instance of this. Here in Manhattan is not merely the largest Negro community in the world, but the first concentration in history of so many diverse elements of Negro life. It has attracted the African, the West Indian, the Negro American; has brought together the Negro of the North and the Negro of the South; the man from the city and the man from the town and village; the peasant, the student, the business man, the professional man, artist, poet, musician, adventurer and worker, preacher and criminal, exploiter and social outcast. Each group has come with its own separate motives and for its own special ends, but their greatest experience has been the finding of one another. Proscription and prejudice have thrown these dissimilar elements into a common area of contact and interaction. Within this area, race sympathy and unity have determined a further fusing of sentiment and experience. So what began in terms of segregation becomes more and more, as its elements mix and react, the laboratory of a great race-welding. Hitherto, it must be admitted that American Negroes have been a race more in name than in fact, or to be exact, more in sentiment than in experience. The chief bond between them has been that of a common condition rather than a common consciousness; a problem in common rather than a life in common. In Harlem, Negro life is seizing upon its first chances for group expression and self-determination. It is—or promises at least to be—a race capital. That is why our comparison is taken with those nascent centers of folk-expression and self-determination which are playing a creative part in the world today. Without pretense to their political significance, Harlem has the same role to play for the New Negro as Dublin has had for the New Ireland or Prague for the New Czechoslovakia.

Harlem, I grant you, isn't typical—but it is significant, it is prophetic. No sane observer, however sympathetic to the new trend, would contend that the great masses are articulate as yet, but they stir, they move, they are more than physically restless. The challenge of the new intellectuals among them is clear enough—the "race radicals" and realists who have broken with the old epoch of philanthropic guidance, sentimental appeal and protest. But are we after all only reading into the stirrings of a sleeping giant the dreams of an agitator? The answer is in the migrating peasant. It is the "man farthest down" who is most active in getting up. One of the most characteristic symptoms of this is the professional man, himself migrating to recapture his constituency after a vain effort to maintain in some Southern corner what for years back seemed an established living and clientele. The clergyman following his errant flock, the

2. Beetle notorious for destroying cotton crops.

physician or lawyer trailing his clients, supply the true clues. In a real sense it is the rank and file who are leading, and the leaders who are following. A transformed and transforming psychology permeates the masses.

When the racial leaders of twenty years ago spoke of developing race-pride and stimulating race-consciousness, and of the desirability of race solidarity, they could not in any accurate degree have anticipated the abrupt feeling that has surged up and now pervades the awakened centers. [. . .] It is a social disservice to blunt the fact that the Negro of the Northern centers has reached a stage where tutelage, even of the most interested and well-intentioned sort, must give place to new relationships, where positive self-direction must be reckoned with in ever increasing measure. The American mind must reckon with a fundamentally changed Negro.

The Negro too, for his part, has idols of the tribe to smash. If on the one hand the white man has erred in making the Negro appear to be that which would excuse or extenuate his treatment of him, the Negro, in turn, has too often unnecessarily excused himself because of the way he has been treated. The intelligent Negro of today is resolved not to make discrimination an extenuation for his shortcomings in performance, individual or collective; he is trying to hold himself at par, neither inflated by sentimental allowances nor depreciated by current social discounts. For this he must know himself and be known for precisely what he is, and for that reason he welcomes the new scientific rather than the old sentimental interest. Sentimental interest in the Negro has ebbed. We used to lament this as the falling off of our friends; now we rejoice and pray to be delivered both from self-pity and condescension. The mind of each racial group has had a bitter weaning, apathy or hatred on one side matching disillusionment or resentment on the other; but they face each other today with the possibility at least of entirely new mutual attitudes. [. . .]

The fiction is that the life of the races is separate, and increasingly so. The fact is that they have touched too closely at the unfavorable and too lightly at the favorable levels.

While inter-racial councils have sprung up in the South, drawing on forward elements of both races, in the Northern cities manual laborers may brush elbows in their everyday work, but the community and business leaders have experienced no such interplay or far too little of it. These segments must achieve contact or the race situation in America becomes desperate. Fortunately this is happening. There is a growing realization that in social effort the cooperative basis must supplant long-distance philanthropy, and that the only safeguard for mass relations in the future must be provided in the carefully maintained contacts of the enlightened minorities of both race groups. In the intellectual realm a renewed and keen curiosity is replacing the recent apathy; the Negro is being carefully studied, not just talked about and discussed. In art and letters, instead of being wholly caricatured, he is being seriously portrayed and painted.

To all of this the New Negro is keenly responsive as an augury of a new democracy in American culture. He is contributing his share to the new social understanding. But the desire to be understood would never in itself have been sufficient to have opened so completely the protectively closed portals of the thinking Negro's mind. There is still too much possibility of being snubbed or patronized for that. It was rather the necessity for fuller, truer self-expression, the realization of the unwisdom of allowing social discrimination to segregate him mentally, and a counter-attitude to cramp and fetter his own living—and so the "spite-wall" that the intellectuals built over the "color-line" has happily been taken down. Much of this reopening of intellectual contacts has centered in New York and has been richly fruitful not merely in the enlarging of personal experience, but in the definite enrichment of American art and letters and in the clarifying of our common vision of the social tasks ahead.

The particular significance in the re-establishment of contact between the more advanced and representative classes is that it promises to offset some of the unfavorable reactions of the past, or at least to re-surface race contacts somewhat for the future. Subtly the conditions that are molding a New Negro are molding a new American attitude.

However, this new phase of things is delicate; it will call for less charity but more justice; less help, but infinitely closer understanding. This is indeed a critical stage of race relationships because of the likelihood, if the new temper is not understood, of engendering sharp group antagonism and a second crop of more calculated prejudice. In some quarters, it has already done so. Having weaned the Negro, public opinion cannot continue to paternalize. The Negro today is inevitably moving forward under the control largely of his own objectives. What are these objectives? Those of his outer life are happily already well and finally formulated, for they are none other than the ideals of American institutions and democracy. Those of his inner life are yet in process of formation, for the new psychology at present is more of a consensus of feeling than of opinion, of attitude rather than of program. Still some points seem to have crystallized.

Up to the present one may adequately describe the Negro's "inner objectives" as an attempt to repair a damaged group psychology and reshape a warped social perspective. Their realization has required a new mentality for the American Negro. And as it matures we begin to see its effects; at first, negative, iconoclastic, and then positive and constructive. In this new group psychology we note the lapse of sentimental appeal, then the development of a more positive self-respect and self-reliance; the repudiation of social dependence, and then the gradual recovery from hyper-sensitiveness and "touchy" nerves, the repudiation of the double standard of judgment with its special philanthropic allowances and then the sturdier desire for objective and scientific appraisal; and finally the rise from social disillusionment to race pride, from the sense of social debt to the responsibilities of social contribution, and offsetting the necessary working and commonsense acceptance of restricted conditions, the belief in ultimate esteem and recognition.

The Negro mind reaches out as yet to nothing but American wants, American ideas. But this forced attempt to build his Americanism on race values is a unique social experiment, and its ultimate success is impossible except through the fullest sharing of American culture and institutions. There should be no delusion about this. American nerves in sections unstrung with race hysteria are often fed the opiate that the trend of Negro advance is wholly separatist, and that the effect of its operation will be to encyst the Negro as a benign foreign body in the body politic. This cannot be—even if it were desirable. The racialism of the Negro is no limitation or reservation with respect to American life; it is only a constructive effort to build the obstructions in the stream of his progress into an efficient dam of social energy and power. Democracy itself is obstructed and stagnated to the extent that any of its channels are closed. Indeed they cannot be selectively closed. So the choice is not between one way for the Negro and another way for the rest, but between American institutions frustrated on the one hand and American ideals progressively fulfilled and realized on the other.

More and more, however, an intelligent realization of the great discrepancy between the American social creed and the American social practice forces upon the Negro the taking of the moral advantage that is his. Only the steadying and sobering effect of a truly characteristic gentleness of spirit prevents the rapid rise of a definite cynicism and counter-hate and a defiant superiority feeling. Human as this reaction would be, the majority still deprecate its advent, and would gladly see it forestalled by the speedy amelioration of its causes. We wish our race pride to be a healthier, more positive achievement than a feeling based upon a realization of the shortcomings of others. But all paths toward the attainment of a sound social attitude have been difficult; only a relatively few enlightened minds have been able as the phrase puts it "to rise above" prejudice. The ordinary man has had until recently only a hard choice between the alternatives of supine and humiliating submission and stimulating but hurtful counter-prejudice. Fortunately from some inner, desperate resourcefulness has recently sprung up the simple expedient of fighting prejudice by mental passive resistance, in other words by trying to ignore it. For the few, this manna may perhaps be effective, but the masses cannot thrive upon it.

Fortunately there are constructive channels opening out into which the balked social feelings of the American Negro can flow freely.

Without them there would be much more pressure and danger than there is. These compensating interests are racial but in a new and enlarged way. One is the consciousness of acting as the advance-guard of the African peoples in their contact with Twentieth Century civilization; the other, the sense of a mission of rehabilitating the race in world esteem from that loss of prestige for which the fate and conditions of slavery have so largely been responsible. Harlem, as we shall see, is the center of both these movements; she is the home of the Negro's "Zionism."[3] The pulse of the Negro world has begun to beat in Harlem. A Negro newspaper carrying news material in English, French, and Spanish, gathered from all quarters of America, the West Indies, and Africa has maintained itself in Harlem for over five years. Two important magazines,[4] both edited from New York, maintain their news and circulation consistently on a

3. International movement aimed at securing a homeland for the Jewish people. The modern state of Israel was not founded until 1948.
4. Probably *Opportunity* and *The Crisis*.

cosmopolitan scale. Under American auspices and backing, three pan-African congresses have been held abroad for the discussion of common interests, colonial questions, and the future cooperative development of Africa. In terms of the race question as a world problem, the Negro mind has leapt, so to speak, upon the parapets of prejudice and extended its cramped horizons. In so doing it has linked up with the growing group consciousness of the dark-peoples and is gradually learning their common interests. As one of our writers has recently put it: "It is imperative that we understand the white world in its relations to the non-white world." As with the Jew, persecution is making the Negro international.

As a world phenomenon this wider race consciousness is a different thing from the much asserted rising tide of color. Its inevitable causes are not of our making. The consequences are not necessarily damaging to the best interests of civilization. Whether it actually brings into being new Armadas of conflict or argosies[5] of cultural exchange and enlightenment can only be decided by the attitude of the dominant races in an era of critical change. With the American Negro, his new internationalism is primarily an effort to recapture contact with the scattered peoples of African derivation. Garveyism[6] may be a transient, if spectacular, phenomenon, but the possible role of the American Negro in the future development of Africa is one of the most constructive and universally helpful missions that any modern people can lay claim to.

RUDOLPH FISHER

From The Caucasian Storms Harlem (1927)[1]

I

It might not have been such a jolt had my five years' absence from Harlem been spent otherwise. But the study of medicine includes no courses in cabareting; and, anyway, the Negro cabarets in Washington, where I studied, are all uncompromisingly black. Accordingly I was entirely unprepared for what I found when I returned to Harlem recently.

I remembered one place especially where my own crowd used to hold forth; and, hoping to find some old-timers there still, I sought it out one midnight. The old, familiar plunkety-plunk welcomed me from below as I entered. I descended the same old narrow stairs, came into the same smoke-misty basement, and found myself a chair at one of the ancient white-porcelain, mirror-smooth tables. I drew a deep breath and looked about, seeking familiar faces. "What a lot of 'fays!"[2] I thought, as I noticed the number of white guests. Presently I grew puzzled and began to stare, then I gaped—and gasped. I found myself wondering if this was the right place—if, indeed, this was Harlem at all. I suddenly became

---

5. Merchant ships. *Armadas*: fleets of warships.
6. The Back to Africa movement of Marcus Garvey (1887–1940).
1. Rudolph Fisher, "The Caucasian Storms Harlem." *The American Mercury*, vol. 11, Aug. 1927, pp. 393–98.
2. Short for "ofays," a derogatory term for Whites.

aware that, except for the waiters and members of the orchestra, I was the only Negro in the place.

After a while I left it and wandered about in a daze from night-club to night-club. I tried the Nest, Small's, Connie's Inn, the Capitol, Happy's, the Cotton Club. There was no mistake; my discovery was real and was repeatedly confirmed. No wonder my old crowd was not to be found in any of them. The best of Harlem's black cabarets have changed their names and turned white.

Such a discovery renders a moment's recollection irresistible. As irresistible as were the cabarets themselves to me seven or eight years ago. Just out of college in a town where cabarets were something only read about. A year of graduate work ahead. A Summer of rest at hand. Cabarets. Cabarets night after night, and one after another. There was no cover-charge then, and a fifteen-cent bottle of Whistle lasted an hour. It was just after the war[3]—the heroes were home—cabarets were the thing.

How the Lybia prospered in those happy days! It was the gathering place of the swellest Harlem set: if you didn't go to the Lybia, why, my dear, you just didn't belong. The people you saw at church in the morning you met at the Lybia at night. What romance in those war-tinged days and nights! Officers from Camp Upton,[4] with pretty maids from Brooklyn! Gay lieutenants, handsome captains—all whirling the lively onestep. Poor non-coms[5] completely ignored; what sensible girl wanted a corporal or even a sergeant? That white, old-fashioned house, standing alone in 138th street, near the corner of Seventh Avenue—doomed to be torn down a few months thence—how it shook with the dancing and laughter of the dark merry crowds!

But the first place really popular with my friends was a Chinese restaurant in 136th Street, which had been known as Hayne's Café and then became the Oriental. It occupied an entire house of three stories, and had carpeted floors and a quiet, superior air. There was excellent food and incredibly good tea and two unusual entertainers: a Cuban girl, who could so vary popular airs that they sounded like real music, and a slender little "brown" with a voice of silver and a way of singing a song that made you forget your food. One could dance in the Oriental if one liked, but one danced to a piano only, and wound one's way between linen-clad tables over velvety, noiseless floors.

Here we gathered: Fritz Pollard, All-American halfback,[6] selling Negro stock to prosperous Negro physicians; Henry Creamer and Turner Layton, who had written "After You've Gone" and a dozen more songs, and were going to write "Strut, Miss Lizzie;" Paul Robeson,[7] All-American end, on the point of tackling law, quite unaware that the stage would intervene; Preacher Harry Bragg, Harvard Jimmie MacLendon and a half a dozen others. Here at a little table, just inside the door, Bert Williams[8] had supper every night, and afterward some-

---

3. World War I.
4. Military facility near Manhattan.
5. Noncommissioned officers.
6. In 1916 at Brown University. He was the first Black professional football player (Akron Indians, 1919).
7. Star football player at Rutgers before entering Columbia University Law School in 1919 (1898–1976); he would later gain international renown as a singer and civil rights spokesman.
8. Popular Black comedian and actor (c. 1874–1922).

times joined us upstairs and sang songs with us and lampooned the Actors' Equity Association, which had barred him because of his color. Never did white guests come to the Oriental except as guests of Negroes. But the manager soon was stricken with a psychosis of some sort, became a black Jew, grew himself a bushy, square-cut beard, donned a skull-cap and abandoned the Oriental. And so we were robbed of our favorite resort, and thereafter became mere rounders.

II

Such places, those real Negro cabarets that we met in the course of our rounds! There was Edmonds' in Fifth Avenue at 130th Street. It was a sure-enough honky-tonk, occupying the cellar of a saloon. It was the social center of what was then, and still is, Negro Harlem's kitchen. Here a tall brown-skin girl, unmistakably the one guaranteed in the song to make a preacher lay his Bible down, used to sing and dance her own peculiar numbers, vesting them with her own originality. She was known simply as Ethel,[9] and was a genuine drawing-card. She knew her importance, too. Other girls wore themselves ragged trying to rise above the inattentive din of conversation, and soon, literally, yelled themselves hoarse; eventually they lost whatever music there was in their voices and acquired that familiar throaty roughness which is so frequent among blues singers, and which, though admired as characteristically African, is as a matter of fact nothing but a form of chronic laryngitis. Other girls did these things, but not Ethel. She took it easy. She would stride with great leisure and self-assurance to the center of the floor, stand there with a half-contemptuous nonchalance, and wait. All would become silent at once. Then she'd begin her song, genuine blues, which, for all their humorous lines, emanated tragedy and heartbreak:

> Woke up this mawnin'
> The day was dawnin'
> And I was sad and blue, so blue, Lord—
> Didn' have nobody
> To tell my troubles to—

It was Ethel who first made popular the song, "Tryin' to Teach My Good Man Right from Wrong," in the slow, meditative measures in which she complained:

> I'm gettin' sick and tired of my railroad man
> I'm gettin' sick and tired of my railroad man—
> Can't get him when I want him—
> I get him when I can.

It wasn't long before this song-bird escaped her dingy cage. Her name is a vaudeville attraction now, and she uses it all—Ethel Waters. Is there anyone who hasn't heard her sing "Shake That Thing!"?

.   .   .

There were the Lybia, then, and Hayne's, Connor's, the Oriental, Edmonds' and the Garden of Joy, each distinctive, standing for a type, some living up to

---

9. Ethel Waters (1896–1977).

their names, others living down to them, but all predominantly black. Regularly I made the rounds among these places and saw only incidental white people. I have seen them occasionally in numbers, but such parties were out on a lark. They weren't in their natural habitat and they often weren't any too comfortable.

But what of Barron's, you say? Certainly they were at home there. Yes, I know about Barron's. I have been turned away from Barron's because I was too dark to be welcome. I have been a member of a group that was told, "No more room," when we could see plenty of room. Negroes were never actually wanted in Barron's save to work. Dark skins were always discouraged or barred. In short, the fact about Barron's was this: it simply wasn't a Negro cabaret; it was a cabaret run by Negroes for whites. It wasn't even on the lists of those who lived in Harlem— they'd no more think of going there than of going to the Winter Garden Roof.[1] But these other places were Negro through and through. Negroes supported them, not merely in now-and-then parties, but steadily, night after night.

IV

Some think it's just a fad. White people have always more or less sought Negro entertainment as diversion. The old shows of the early nineteen hundreds, Williams and Walker[2] and Cole and Johnson, are brought to mind as examples. The howling success—literally that—of J. Leubrie Hill[3] around 1913 is another; on the road his "Darktown Follies" played in numerous white theatres. In Harlem it played at the black Lafayette and, behold, the Lafayette temporarily became white. And so now, it is held, we are observing merely one aspect of a meteoric phenomenon, which simply presents itself differently in different circumstances: Roland Hayes and Paul Robeson, Jean Toomer and Walter White, Charles Gilpin and Florence Mills[4]—"Green Thursday," "Porgy," "In Abraham's Bosom"[5]— Negro spirituals—the startling new African groups proposed for the Metropolitan Museum of Art. Negro stock is going up, and everybody's buying.

V

[. . .] It may be a season's whim, then, this sudden, contagious interest in everything Negro. If so, when I go into a familiar cabaret, or the place where a familiar cabaret used to be, and find it transformed and relatively colorless, I may be observing just one form that the season's whim has taken.

But suppose it is a fad—to say that explains nothing. How came the fad? What occasions the focusing of attention on this particular thing—rounds up and gathers these seasonal whims, and centers them about the Negro? Cabarets are

1. Prominent Manhattan nightclub.
2. Bert Williams and George Nash Walker formed an immensely popular vaudeville team in 1895.
3. Songwriter (1869–1916).
4. Performer (1895–1927). Hayes (1887–1976), singer. Toomer (1894–1967), author of *Cane*. White (1893–1955), writer and civil rights leader. Gilpin (1878–1930), actor.
5. 1926 play by White writer Paul Green. *Porgy*: a novel by Du Bose Heyward (1925).

peculiar, mind you. They're not like theatres and concert halls. You don't just go to a cabaret and sit back and wait to be entertained. You get out on the floor and join the pow-wow and help entertain yourself. Granted that white people have long enjoyed the Negro entertainment as a diversion, is it not something different, something more, when they bodily throw themselves into Negro entertainment in cabarets? "Now Negroes go to their own cabarets to see how white people act."

And what do we see? Why, we see them actually playing Negro games. I watch them in that epidemic Negroism, the Charleston. I look on and envy them. They camel and fish-tail and turkey, they geche and black-bottom and scronch, they skate and buzzard and mess-around[6]—and they do them all better than I! This interest in the Negro is an active and participating interest. It is almost as if a traveler from the North stood watching an African tribe-dance, then suddenly found himself swept wildly into it, caught in its tidal rhythm.

Willingly would I be an outsider in this if I could know that I read it aright— that out of this change in the old familiar ways some finer thing may come. Is this interest akin to that of the Virginians on the veranda of a plantation's big-house—sitting genuinely spellbound as they hear the lugubrious strains floating up from the Negro quarters? Is it akin to that of the African explorer, Stanley,[7] leaving a village far behind, but halting in spite of himself to catch the boom of its distant drum? Is it significant of basic human responses, the effect of which, once admitted, will extend far beyond cabarets? Maybe these Nordics at last have tuned in on our wave-length. Maybe they are at last learning to speak our language.

W. E. B. DU BOIS

From Two Novels (1928)[1]

Claude McKay's *Home to Harlem* [. . .] for the most part nauseates me, and after the dirtier parts of its filth I feel distinctly like taking a bath. This does not mean that the book is wholly bad. McKay is too great a poet to make any complete failure in writing. There are bits of *Home to Harlem* beautiful and fascinating: the continued changes upon the theme of the beauty of colored skins; the portrayal of the fascination of their new yearnings for each other which Negroes are developing. The chief character, Jake, has something appealing, and the glimpses of the Haitian, Ray, have all the materials of a great piece of fiction.

But it looks as though, despite this, McKay has set out to cater for that prurient demand on the part of white folk for a portrayal in Negroes of that utter licentiousness which conventional civilization holds white folk back from enjoying—if enjoyment it can be called. That which a certain decadent section of the white American world, centered particularly in New York, longs for with fierce

6. Various popular dances.
7. Sir Henry Morgan Stanley (1841–1904), English explorer of Africa.
1. W. E. B. Du Bois, "Two Novels." *The Crisis*, vol. 35, no. 6, June 1928, pp. 202+. The excerpt omits Du Bois's comments on Nella Larsen's novel *Quicksand*.

and unrestrained passions, it wants to see written out in black and white, and saddled on black Harlem. This demand, as voiced by a number of New York publishers, McKay has certainly satisfied, and added much for good measure. He has used every art and emphasis to paint drunkenness, fighting, lascivious sexual promiscuity, and utter absence of restraint in as bold and as bright colors as he can.

[. . .] As a picture of Harlem life or of Negro life anywhere, it is, of course, nonsense. Untrue, not so much on account of its facts, but on account of its emphasis and glaring colors. I am sorry that the author of *Harlem Shadows* stooped to this. I sincerely hope that he will some day rise above it and give us in fiction the strong, well-knit as well as beautiful theme, that it seems to me he might do.

Cover of the first edition of Claude McKay's *Home to Harlem* (1928)

ZORA NEALE HURSTON

How It Feels to Be Colored Me (1928)[1]

I am colored but I offer nothing in the way of extenuating circumstances except the fact that I am the only Negro in the United States whose grandfather on the mother's side was *not* an Indian chief.

I remember the very day that I became colored. Up to my thirteenth year I lived in the little Negro town of Eatonville, Florida. It is exclusively a colored town. The only white people I knew passed through the town going to or coming from Orlando. The native whites rode dusty horses, the Northern tourists chugged down the sandy village road in automobiles. The town knew the Southerners and never stopped cane chewing when they passed. But the Northerners were something else again. They were peered at cautiously from behind curtains by the timid. The more venturesome would come out on the porch to watch them go past and got just as much pleasure out of the tourists as the tourists got out of the village.

The front porch might seem a daring place for the rest of the town, but it was a gallery seat for me. My favorite place was atop the gate-post. Proscenium box[2] for a born first-nighter. Not only did I enjoy the show, but I didn't mind the actors knowing that I liked it. I usually spoke to them in passing. I'd wave at them and when they returned my salute, I would say something like

1. Zora Neale Hurston, "How It Feels to Be Colored Me." *The World Tomorrow*, vol. 11, May 1928, pp. 215–16.
2. The box seats in a theater on either side of and nearest to the stage.

this: "Howdy-do-well-I-thank-you-where-you-goin'?" Usually automobile or the horse paused at this, and after a queer exchange of compliments, I would probably "go a piece of the way" with them, as we say in farthest Florida. If one of my family happened to come to the front in time to see me, of course negotiations would be rudely broken off. But even so, it is clear that I was the first "welcome-to-our-state" Floridian, and I hope the Miami Chamber of Commerce will please take notice.

During this period, white people differed from colored to me only in that they rode through town and never lived there. They liked to hear me "speak pieces" and sing and wanted to see me dance the parse-me-la, and gave me generously of their small silver for doing these things, which seemed strange to me for I wanted to do them so much that I needed bribing to stop. Only they didn't know it. The colored people gave no dimes. They deplored any joyful tendencies in me, but I was their Zora nevertheless. I belonged to them, to the nearby hotels, to the county—everybody's Zora.

Zora Neale Hurston, 1935

But changes came in the family when I was thirteen, and I was sent to school in Jacksonville. I left Eatonville, the town of the oleanders, as Zora. When I disembarked from the river-boat at Jacksonville, she was no more. It seemed that I had suffered a sea change. I was not Zora of Orange County any more, I was now a little colored girl. I found it out in certain ways. In my heart as well as in the mirror, I became a fast[3] brown—warranted not to rub nor run.

But I am not tragically colored. There is no great sorrow dammed up in my soul, nor lurking behind my eyes. I do not mind at all. I do not belong to the sobbing school of Negrohood who hold that nature somehow has given them a lowdown dirty deal and whose feelings are all hurt about it. Even in the helter-skelter skirmish that is my life, I have seen that the world is to the strong regardless of a little pigmentation more or less. No, I do not weep at the world—I am too busy sharpening my oyster knife.[4]

Someone is always at my elbow reminding me that I am the grand-daughter of slaves. It fails to register depression with me. Slavery is sixty years in the past. The operation was successful and the patient is doing well, thank you. The terrible struggle that made me an American out of a potential slave said "On the line!" The Reconstruction said "Get set!"; and the generation before said "Go!" I am off to a flying start and I must not halt in the stretch to look behind and weep. Slavery is the price I paid for civilization, and the choice was not with me.

3. That is, colorfast.
4. Allusion to Shakespeare's *The Merry Wives of Windsor*: "Why, then the world's mine oyster, / Which I with sword will open" (2.2.4–5).

It is a bully adventure and worth all that I have paid through my ancestors for it. No one on earth ever had a greater chance for glory. The world to be won and nothing to be lost. It is thrilling to think—to know that for any act of mine, I shall get twice as much praise or twice as much blame. It is quite exciting to hold the center of the national stage, with the spectators not knowing whether to laugh or to weep.

The position of my white neighbor is much more difficult. No brown specter pulls up a chair beside me when I sit down to eat. No dark ghost thrusts its leg against mine in bed. The game of keeping what one has is never so exciting as the game of getting.

I do not always feel colored. Even now I often achieve the unconscious Zora of Eatonville before the Hegira.[5] I feel most colored when I am thrown against a sharp white background.

For instance at Barnard.[6] "Beside the waters of the Hudson" I feel my race. Among the thousand white persons, I am a dark rock surged upon, and over-swept, but through it all, I remain myself. When covered by the waters, I am; and the ebb but reveals me again.

Sometimes it is the other way around. A white person is set down in our midst, but the contrast is just as sharp for me. For instance, when I sit in the drafty basement that is The New World Cabaret with a white person, my color comes. We enter chatting about any little nothing that we have in common and are seated by the jazz waiters. In the abrupt way that jazz orchestras have, this one plunges into a number. It loses no time in circumlocutions, but gets right down to business. It constricts the thorax and splits the heart with its tempo and narcotic harmonies. This orchestra grows rambunctious, rears on its hind legs and attacks the tonal veil with primitive fury, rending it, clawing it until it breaks through to the jungle beyond. I follow those heathen—follow them exultingly. I dance wildly inside myself; I yell within, I whoop; I shake my assegai[7] above my head, I hurl it true to the mark *yeeeeooww!* I am in the jungle and living in the jungle way. My face is painted red and yellow and my body is painted blue. My pulse is throbbing like a war drum. I want to slaughter something—give pain, give death to what, I do not know. But the piece ends. The men of the orchestra wipe their lips and rest their fingers. I creep back slowly to the veneer we call civilization with the last tone and find the white friend sitting motionless in his seat, smoking calmly.

"Good music they have here," he remarks, drumming the table with his fingertips.

Music. The great blobs of purple and red emotion have not touched him. He has only heard what I felt. He is far away and I see him but dimly across the ocean and the continent that have fallen between us. He is so pale with his whiteness then and I am *so* colored.

At certain times I have no race, I am *me*. When I set my hat at a certain angle and saunter down Seventh Avenue, Harlem City, feeling as snooty as the lions

---

5. In Islam, Muhammad's emigration from Mecca to Medina in 622 CE; here, the journey to Jacksonville.
6. Barnard College in Manhattan, then a private women's school, now part of Columbia University.
7. Spear.

in front of the Forty-Second Street Library,[8] for instance. So far as my feelings are concerned, Peggy Hopkins Joyce on the Boule Mich[9] with her gorgeous raiment, stately carriage, knees knocking together in a most aristocratic manner, has nothing on me. The cosmic Zora emerges. I belong to no race nor time. I am the eternal feminine with its string of beads.

I have no separate feeling about being an American citizen and colored. I am merely a fragment of the Great Soul that surges within the boundaries. My country, right or wrong.

Sometimes, I feel discriminated against, but it does not make me angry. It merely astonishes me. How *can* any deny themselves the pleasure of my company? It's beyond me.

But in the main, I feel like a brown bag of miscellany propped against a wall. Against a wall in company with other bags, white, red and yellow. Pour out the contents, and there is discovered a jumble of small things priceless and worthless. A first-water diamond,[1] an empty spool, bits of broken glass, lengths of string, a key to a door long since crumbled away, a rusty knife-blade, old shoes saved for a road that never was and never will be, a nail bent under the weight of things too heavy for any nail, a dried flower or two still a little fragrant. In your hand is the brown bag. On the ground before you is the jumble it held—so much like the jumble in the bags, could they be emptied, that all might be dumped in a single heap and the bags refilled without altering the content of any greatly. A bit of colored glass more or less would not matter. Perhaps that is how the Great Stuffer of Bags filled them in the first place—who knows?

LANGSTON HUGHES

From The Big Sea (1940)[1]

Harlem Literati

The summer of 1926, I lived in a rooming house on 137th Street, where Wallace Thurman and Harcourt Tynes[2] also lived. Thurman was then managing editor of the *Messenger*, a Negro magazine that had a curious career. It began by being very radical, racial, and socialistic, just after the war. I believe it received a grant from the Garland Fund[3] in its early days. Then it later became a kind of Negro society magazine and a plugger for Negro business, with photographs of prominent colored ladies and their nice homes in it. A. Philip Randolph, now President of the Brotherhood of Sleeping Car Porters, Chandler Owen, and

---

8. Headquarters of the New York Public Library.
9. Elegant boulevard St. Michel in Paris.
1. That is, a diamond of the highest quality.
1. Langston Hughes, *The Big Sea*. 1940. Hill and Wang, 1993, pp. 233–41.
2. Thurman (1902–34) and Tynes were friends. *House on 137th Street*: The rooming house appears in Thurman's novel *Infants of the Spring* (1932) as "Niggerati Manor."
3. The American Fund for Public Service, established in 1920 by Charles Garland.

George S. Schuyler were connected with it. Schuyler's editorials, à la Mencken,[4] were the most interesting things in the magazine, verbal brickbats that said sometimes one thing, sometimes another, but always vigorously. I asked Thurman what kind of magazine the *Messenger* was, and he said it reflected the policy of whoever paid off best at the time.

Anyway, the *Messenger* bought my first short stories. They paid me ten dollars a story. Wallace Thurman wrote me that they were very bad stories, but better than any others they could find, so he published them.

Thurman had recently come from California to New York. He was a strangely brilliant black boy, who had read everything, and whose critical mind could find something wrong with everything he read. I have no critical mind, so I usually either like a book or don't. But I am not capable of liking a book and then finding a million things wrong with it, too—as Thurman was capable of doing.

Thurman had read so many books because he could read eleven lines at a time. He would get from the library a great pile of volumes that would have taken me a year to read. But he would go through them in less than a week, and be able to discuss each one at great length with anybody. That was why, I suppose, he was later given a job as a reader at Macaulay's—the only Negro reader, so far as I know, to be employed by any of the larger publishing firms.

. . .

Wallace Thurman wanted to be a great writer, but none of his own work ever made him happy. *The Blacker the Berry*,[5] his first book, was an important novel on a subject little dwelt upon in Negro fiction—the plight of the very dark Negro woman, who encounters in some communities a double wall of color prejudice within and without the race. His play, *Harlem*, considerably distorted for box office purposes, was, nevertheless, a compelling study—and the only one in the theater—of the impact of Harlem on a Negro family fresh from the South. And his *Infants of the Spring*, a superb and bitter study of the bohemian fringe of Harlem's literary and artistic life, is a compelling book.

But none of these things pleased Wallace Thurman. He wanted to be a *very* great writer, like Gorki or Thomas Mann,[6] and he felt that he was merely a journalistic writer. His critical mind, comparing his pages to the thousands of other pages he had read, by Proust, Melville, Tolstoy, Galsworthy, Dostoyevski, Henry James, Sainte-Beuve, Taine, Anatole France,[7] found his own

4. Henry Louis Mencken (1880–1956), prominent Baltimore essayist, critic, and editor who was a friend of Schuyler's. Randolph (1889–1979) and Owen (1889–1967), editors at the *Messenger*, who hired Schuyler as a writer in 1923. Schuyler (1895–1977), conservative Black writer.
5. Published in 1929.
6. German novelist (1875–1955). Maxim Gorki was the pen name of Russian writer Aleksey Maksimovich Pyeshkov (1868–1936).
7. Pen name of French novelist and essayist Jacques Anatole François Thibault (1844–1924). Marcel Proust (1871–1922), French novelist. Herman Melville (1819–91), U.S. writer. Leo Tolstoy (1828–1910), Russian novelist and social critic. John Galsworthy (1867–1933), English novelist. Fyodor Dostoyevski (1821–81), Russian novelist. Henry James (1843–1916), U.S. novelist and critic. Charles Augustin Sainte-Beuve (1804–69), French critic and poet. Hippolyte Adolphe Taine (1828–93), French critic and historian.

pages vastly wanting. So he contented himself by writing a great deal for money, laughing bitterly at his fabulously concocted "true stories," creating two bad motion pictures[8] of the "Adults Only" type for Hollywood, drinking more and more gin, and then threatening to jump out of windows at people's parties and kill himself.

During the summer of 1926, Wallace Thurman, Zora Neale Hurston, Aaron Douglas, John P. Davis, Bruce Nugent, Gwendolyn Bennett,[9] and I decided to publish "a Negro quarterly of the arts" to be called *Fire*—the idea being that it would burn up a lot of the old, dead conventional Negro-white ideas of the past, *épater le bourgeois*[1] into a realization of the existence of the younger Negro writers and artists, and provide us with an outlet for publication not available in the limited pages of the small Negro magazines then existing, the *Crisis, Opportunity,* and the *Messenger*—the first two being house organs of inter-racial organizations, and the latter being God knows what.

Sweltering summer evenings we met to plan *Fire*. Each of the seven of us agreed to give fifty dollars to finance the first issue. Thurman was to edit it, John P. Davis to handle the business end, and Bruce Nugent to take charge of distribution. The rest of us were to serve as an editorial board to collect material, contribute our own work, and act in any useful way that we could.

* * *

I don't know how Thurman persuaded the printer to let us have all the copies to distribute, but he did. I think Alain Locke, among others, signed notes guaranteeing payments. But since Thurman was the only one of the seven of us with a regular job, for the next three or four years his checks were constantly being attached and his income seized to pay for *Fire*. And whenever I sold a poem, mine went there, too—to *Fire*.

None of the older Negro intellectuals would have anything to do with *Fire*. Dr. DuBois[2] in the *Crisis* roasted it. The Negro press called it all sorts of bad names, largely because of a green and purple story by Bruce Nugent, in the Oscar Wilde[3] tradition, which we had included. Rean Graves, the critic for the *Baltimore Afro-American*, began his review by saying: "I have just tossed the first issue of *Fire* into the fire." Commenting upon various of our contributors, he said: "Aaron Douglas who, in spite of himself and the meaningless grotesqueness of his creations, has gained a reputation as an artist, is permitted to spoil three perfectly good pages and a cover with his pen and ink hudge pudge. Countee Cullen has written a beautiful poem in his 'From a Dark Tower,' but tries his best to obscure the thought in superfluous sentences. Langston Hughes displays his usual ability to say nothing in many words."

8. *Tomorrow's Children* (1934) and *High School Girl* (1935).
9. Poet (1902–81). Hurston (1891–1960), novelist and folklorist. Douglas (1898–1979), artist. Davis (1905–73), lawyer and prominent leftist. Nugent (1906–87), illustrator and writer.
1. Shock the middle class (French).
2. W. E. B. Du Bois (1868–1963), African American writer, editor of *Crisis*, and cofounder of the NAACP.
3. Irish poet, novelist, and playwright (1854–1900), a proponent of the Art for Art's Sake movement. *Green and purple story*: the first installment of a novel called *Smoke, Lilies and Jade* (1926).

So *Fire* had plenty of cold water thrown on it by the colored critics. The white critics (except for an excellent editorial in the *Bookman* for November, 1926) scarcely noticed it at all. We had no way of getting it distributed to bookstands or news stands. Bruce Nugent took it around New York on foot and some of the Greenwich Village bookshops put it on display, and sold it for us. But then Bruce, who had no job, would collect the money and, on account of salary, eat it up before he got back to Harlem.

Finally, irony of ironies, several hundred copies of *Fire* were stored in the basement of an apartment where an actual fire occurred and the bulk of the whole issue was burned up. Even after that Thurman had to go on paying the printer.

Now *Fire* is a collector's item, and very difficult to get, being mostly ashes.

That taught me a lesson about little magazines. But since white folks had them, we Negroes thought we could have one, too. But we didn't have the money.

[. . .] About the future of Negro literature Thurman was very pessimistic. He thought the Negro vogue had made us all too conscious of ourselves, had flattered and spoiled us, and had provided too many easy opportunities for some of us to drink gin and more gin, on which he thought we would always be drunk. With his bitter sense of humor, he called the Harlem literati, the "niggerati."

Of this "niggerati," Zora Neale Hurston was certainly the most amusing. Only to reach a wider audience, need she ever write books—because she is a perfect book of entertainment in herself. In her youth she was always getting scholarships and things from wealthy white people, some of whom simply paid her just to sit around and represent the Negro race for them, she did it in such a racy fashion. She was full of side-splitting anecdotes, humorous tales, and tragicomic stories, remembered out of her life in the South as a daughter of a travelling minister of God. She could make you laugh one minute and cry the next. To many of her white friends, no doubt, she was a perfect "darkie," in the nice meaning they give the term—that is a naïve, childlike, sweet, humorous, and highly colored Negro.

But Miss Hurston was clever, too—a student who didn't let college give her a broad *a* and who had great scorn for all pretensions, academic or otherwise. That is why she was such a fine folk-lore collector,[4] able to go among the people and never act as if she had been to school at all. Almost nobody else could stop the average Harlemite on Lenox Avenue and measure his head with a strange-looking, anthropological device and not get bawled out for the attempt, except Zora, who used to stop anyone whose head looked interesting, and measure it.

Harlem was like a great magnet for the Negro intellectual, pulling him from everywhere. Or perhaps the magnet was New York—but once in New York, he had to live in Harlem, for rooms were hardly to be found elsewhere unless one could pass for white or Mexican or Eurasian and perhaps live in the Village[5]— which always seemed to me a very arty locale, in spite of the many real artists and writers who lived there. Only a few of the New Negroes lived in the Village, Harlem being their real stamping ground.

4. Hurston published two such collections, *Mules and Men* (1935) and *Tell My Horse* (1938).
5. Greenwich Village, Manhattan district long known as a haunt of writers and radicals.

SUGGESTIONS FOR WRITING

1. Many poets of the Harlem Renaissance made extensive use of the sonnet form; this chapter contains such examples as Helene Johnson's SONNET TO A NEGRO IN HARLEM and Claude McKay's IF WE MUST DIE, and you will find other McKay sonnets elsewhere in this book. Write an essay in which you compare some of the sonnets written during the Harlem Renaissance. How do different approaches to the sonnet form signal different thematic concerns? What might attract these writers to the sonnet or make it an especially effective form in this context and for their purposes in particular poems?

2. In 1921, James Weldon Johnson wrote of "the need for Aframerican poets in the United States to work out a new and distinctive form of expression." Judging from the selections in this chapter, do you think that poets such as Langston Hughes and Claude McKay met the need articulated by Johnson? Write an essay in which you examine both traditionalism and innovation in the poetry of the Harlem Renaissance. How distinct are the works of Black and White poets during this period?

3. In *The New Negro*, Alain Locke declares, "In Harlem, Negro life is seizing upon its first chances for group expression and self-determination." Do poems such as Arna Bontemps's A BLACK MAN TALKS OF REAPING, Angelina Grimké's THE BLACK FINGER, and Langston Hughes's I, TOO achieve a common social consciousness—Locke's "group expression"? What political effect do you think these poets hoped to achieve through their work? Write an essay in which you analyze the political ideas in the poetry of the Harlem Renaissance.

4. Some poems of the Harlem Renaissance—Langston Hughes's THE WEARY BLUES and Claude McKay's THE HARLEM DANCER, for example—are explicitly about music; others, such as Countee Cullen's SATURDAY's CHILD, with its ballad form, and Angelina Grimké's improvisational TENEBRIS, take a distinctly musical approach. Write an essay about the interplay of words and music in the poetry of this period.

5. In his review of Claude McKay's *Home to Harlem*, W. E. B. Du Bois laments that McKay "stooped" to betraying the Black cause by portraying "drunkenness, fighting, lascivious sexual promiscuity, and utter absence of restraint" in his novel's Black characters. Do writers have a particular duty to portray positive role models? Do writers from ethnic groups engaged in social struggle have an obligation to participate in that struggle? Citing evidence from the selections in this chapter, write an essay in which you weigh the demands of artistic duty against the demands of artistic freedom.

6. What does it mean for a group of artists to be considered a "school"—that is, a group whose work appears to share common themes, styles, and goals? Write an essay in which you discuss whether or not the writers of the Harlem Renaissance spoke with a unified voice. How might a grouping like "the Harlem Renaissance" help our understanding of this period and the art it produced, and how might such a grouping or label obscure the individual achievements of the artists?

7. Identify any two poets in this anthology whose work interests you and who lived and wrote in roughly the same time and place. (The biographies at the end of the Poetry section might be a helpful place to start.) Then do a bit of research. Did your two poets have similar backgrounds? Are they considered part of the same or competing "movements" or "schools"? Drawing on your research, write an essay in which you compare at least one poem by each poet and explore how the poems were each shaped by historical and cultural context. Alternatively, choose two poets in this anthology who wrote poems on similar topics or of the same type or genre (odes or sonnets, for example) but who lived and wrote in very different times and/or places. Then write a research essay exploring how historical and/or cultural context might shape the different ways in which each writer approaches the same topic or genre.

SAMPLE WRITING: RESEARCH ESSAY

As chapters 9, 22, and 27 suggest, essays about cultural and historical context must do more than simply report the facts about the context in or about which a poem (or any other literary text) is written. Rather, these essays must draw on such facts to illuminate the text, to show us something about how the text works and means that we might not otherwise see. Many such essays thus originate with the same broad, interpretive question: How does a particular text not only *reflect* but also *respond to* and *comment on* a specific historical moment and situation? To be effective, however, each essay must narrow this question, homing in on some particular difficulty or question endemic to the moment or situation and the literary text.

The following essay is a case in point. Reading Langston Hughes's poem I, Too in the context of the Harlem Renaissance, the essay focuses specifically on how the poem envisions the plight and possibilities of the Black poet in 1920s and 1930s America, demonstrating the distinctiveness of Hughes's vision by comparing it to that of other Harlem Renaissance writers.

To do so, the essay's writer, Irene Morstan, draws upon primary and secondary sources she discovered online, as well as material included in chapter 22. What purpose does each source serve in the essay, or how exactly does Morstan use each source to make her argument? How effectively does she use her sources? integrate and balance textual and contextual analysis? To what aspects of the poem might she pay more attention?

Irene Morstan
Dr. Mays
English 298
15 April 2021

"They'll See How Beautiful I Am": "I, Too" and the Harlem Renaissance

Langston Hughes begins his 1926 essay "The Negro Artist and the Racial Mountain" with a statement made to him by another Black poet: "I want to be a poet—not a Negro poet." Hughes takes this to mean that the poet wishes he were a white poet, and pities the poet for this. He believes that the Black poet

---

should accept his Blackness. The goal for Black poets should not be to sound like white poets but to celebrate and embrace their Black identity.

Hughes was a central figure in a movement called the Harlem Renaissance, which was "a period of ten or fifteen years in the early twentieth century when an extraordinarily talented group of people came together . . . to celebrate and embody the awakening of a new African American consciousness" (Mays, "Cultural" 1065). *The Norton Introduction to Literature* states, "The Harlem Renaissance represented powerful assertions: that America had to include the voices of Black Americans in order to find its own full definition and, equally, that artistic creativity . . . was essential to Black Americans' realization and assertion of their full humanity" (Mays, "Cultural" 1089). Hughes speaks to both of those assertions in his poem "I, Too." He insists upon the place of the Black poet, and person, at the American "table" and upon the power of the Black poet to "sing."

The opening of "I, Too" is a declaration of the Black man as a poet, despite being historically excluded from such a title. In the first line of the poem "I, too, sing America," Hughes indicates that the speaker is a poet. Hughes related poetry to music, suggesting that he thinks music making and writing poetry are related. Not only is the speaker a poet, but he is a Black poet. By the second line of the poem the race of the speaker is clear; he refers to himself as the "darker brother." The "too" in the first line implies that the speaker has been set apart from another group of people, that he has been excluded from "sing[ing] America." However, the speaker is responding to this exclusion with an affirmative statement that he is both a Black poet and part of the American family, despite being set aside by white people.

Refusing to be set aside was an important part of the Harlem Renaissance. James Weldon Johnson, in his preface to *The Book of American Negro Poetry*, says Black poets moved away from writing in dialect to keep white people from thinking of them as "a happy-go-lucky, singing, shuffling, banjo-picking being or as a more or less pathetic figure" (1102). Black poets in the Harlem Renaissance did not want to be stereotyped by whites; they did not want to be Jim from Mark Twain's *Adventures of Huckleberry Finn*. Such stereotypes made Black people easy to overlook because they were represented as caricatures of people. These figures did not accurately represent the Black person as a complex human being capable of artistic achievement. Not all Harlem Renaissance poets responded to this in the same way. The author of "Literature of the Harlem Renaissance" states, "Countee Cullen insisted that the Black poet is a part of the universal community of all poets, while Langston Hughes asserted his unique racial qualities" (260). While Hughes, in "The Negro Artist and the Racial Mountain," says that he does not believe that Black people should give up any of the things associated with Black identity, including writing in dialect, he does explore the dismissal of the Black poet by the white audience through "I, Too."

This theme of Black exclusion surfaces in the second stanza where the speaker talks about how "They send me to eat in the kitchen / When company comes" (lines 3-4). Here "they" refers to white people who dismiss the Black poet from the "table" (9). These lines suggest that the white people are perhaps ashamed of "the darker brother" and do not want him to be present in front of the other white guests, the "company." Maybe they don't even see him as a brother, just a servant. This reflects the place of the Black artist in the 1920s and 1930s. While the Black artist might occasionally be present, he was meant to be a source of entertainment for white people, not an equal. Rudolph Fisher discusses the white interest in Harlem in *The Caucasian Storms Harlem*, where he notes, "White people have always more or less sought Negro entertainment as diversion" (1111). Despite being suspicious of white peoples' impulses to go to Harlem nightclubs, Fisher hopes that this white interest in Black artistry will be the beginning of "finer thing[s]" and that "they are at last learning to speak our language" (1112).

The speaker of "I, Too" also sees that finer things are on the horizon. Even though he has been sent to the kitchen, a place reminiscent of the institution of slavery where Black slaves worked to feed their white masters, the speaker of the poem says, "I laugh, / And eat well, / And grow strong" (lines 5-7). This dismissal has not crushed his spirit, and "Tomorrow, / I'll sit at the table" (8-9). Hughes's speaker anticipates the time when the Black poet will no longer be cast aside. Because of his strength and his spirit he is undeniable. In the future,

> Nobody'll dare
> Say to me,
> "Eat in the kitchen" (11-13)

And the Black spirit was undeniable during the Harlem Renaissance. The number of notable Black authors and artists gathered in one place was incredible. During the 1920s and 1930s writers like Claude McKay, Countee Cullen, Zora Neale Hurston, Jean Toomer, Angelina Grimké, as well as Langston Hughes, were all in Harlem. This was one of the first times that Black people from all over America were in one place together, as "more than 100,000 Blacks migrated to Harlem during the 1920s" (Mays, "Cultural" 1090). Alain Locke, author of *The New Negro*, saw this as a turning point in Black history and in the history of America, even arguing that it created a real Black "race." In 1925, he wrote,

> Hitherto, it must be admitted that American Negroes have been a race
> more in name than in fact, or to be exact, more in sentiment than in
> experience. The chief bond between them has been that of a common
> condition rather than a common consciousness; a problem in common
> rather than a life in common. In Harlem, Negro life is seizing upon its
> first chances for group expression and self-determination. (1104)

The Harlem Renaissance was a movement where Black writers, even though they may have had some differences, joined together to create Black art according to their own rules, not the rules of white people. Black artists had "grow[n] strong," and it is this strength that the speaker of "I, Too" sees as causing change between Blacks and whites.

However, as hopeful as the speaker is, he acknowledges that this has not yet happened. By placing "then" on its own line and at the end of the sentence (line 14), Hughes highlights that these actions are yet to come. The "then" in the poem sounds wistful, as if the speaker gets very excited about the prospect of being acknowledged and respected, only to remember the difficulties that lie between the current state of affairs and the one dreamt of for the future. Racial inequality was still prevalent at the time of the Harlem Renaissance, and the situation did not improve for some time. During the 1920s and 1930s segregation was still normal. (Langston Hughes said that an African American who moved to New York "had to live in Harlem, for rooms were hardly to be found elsewhere unless one could pass for white or Mexican or Eurasian" [*The Big Sea* 1119], and Fisher says that Blacks like him were surprisingly even excluded from some Harlem clubs [1111].) On the other hand, the isolation of the "then" on its own line also could be read as being firmly insistent that a positive change will come. This echoes the goal of the writers of the Harlem Renaissance, "to [raise] the aspirations of American Blacks of all backgrounds and abilities" (Mays, "Cultural" 1092). In this reading, "then" is both a statement of faith about the future and a call to action about now.

These two readings reflect two different Black views of Harlem Renaissance literature. Some people were cynical and did not believe that change had come or would. Langston Hughes recounts that "[a]bout the future of Negro literature [Wallace] Thurman was very pessimistic. He thought the Negro vogue had made us all too conscious of ourselves, had flattered and spoiled us, and had provided too many easy opportunities for some of us to drink gin and more gin, on which he thought we would always be drunk" (*The Big Sea* 1119). In contrast to this dark view of the Harlem Renaissance is novelist Zora Neale Hurston's view of the position of Black people in 1920s America. In "How It Feels to Be Colored Me," she states, "I am not tragically colored. There is no great sorrow dammed up in my soul nor lurking behind my eyes. . . . I do not belong to the sobbing school of Negrohood who hold that nature somehow has given them a lowdown dirty deal. . . . I do not weep at the world—I am too busy sharpening my oyster knife" (1114). Here Hurston is expressing that she is not brought down by the slavery of the past, but is making herself ready to make the world hers. Her view is the positive one found in Hughes's poem.

Just as the writers of the Harlem Renaissance wanted their creative abilities to be appreciated, so they also wanted Black people and culture to be appreciated and embraced by the American public. The speaker of "I, Too" makes this apparent at the end of the poem when he says,

> Besides,
> They'll see how beautiful I am
> And be ashamed—
>
> I, too, am America. (lines 15-18)

The speaker is asserting that being Black is being beautiful and that people who have discriminated against Blacks will be ashamed of their behavior when they really see what Black people are like. Not only are Black people beautiful, they are part of America as well. The speaker of the poem makes this clear when he says that he *is* America. This "darker brother" is just as much a part of America as a white person (2), so he should not be excluded, either physically or literarily. Hughes, like many other writers of the Harlem Renaissance, is insisting that all Americans recognize the place of Black people, both culturally and creatively, in the American identity.

Hughes speaks not only to white people in "I, Too" but also to other writers during the Harlem Renaissance. As is illustrated in the opening anecdote, Hughes was insistent about honoring Blackness and common Black life. He thought that all aspects of Black life were worth celebrating, and "[u]nlike other notable black poets of the period" including Claude McKay and Countee Cullen "Hughes refused to differentiate between his personal experience and the common experience of Black America. He wanted to tell the stories of his people in ways that reflected their actual culture, including both their suffering and their love of music, laughter, and language itself" ("Langston Hughes"). Hughes's references to race and beauty throughout "I, Too" show that he was committed to representing Black life in a positive way.

Langston Hughes and the writers of the Harlem Renaissance are an important part of American history and have had a lasting impact on American literature. The quality of their works and power of their message shaped American culture. Through creative pieces like "I, Too," Hughes shows audiences how Black literature and Black people were valuable parts of the American identity.

Works Cited

Fisher, Rudolph. "From *The Caucasian Storms Harlem*." Mays, *Norton*, pp. 1108-12.

Hughes, Langston. "From *The Big Sea*." Mays, *Norton*, pp. 1116-19.

———. "I, Too." Mays, *Norton*, p. 1099.

———. "The Negro Artist and the Racial Mountain." 1926. *Poetry Foundation*, 13 Oct. 2009, www.poetryfoundation.org/resources/learning/essays/detail /69395.

Hurston, Zora Neale. "How It Feels to Be Colored Me." Mays, *Norton*, pp. 1113-16.

Johnson, James Weldon. "From the preface to *The Book of American Negro Poetry*." Mays, *Norton*, pp. 1102-03.

"Langston Hughes." *Poets.org*, Academy of American Poets, www.poets.org /poetsorg/poet/langston-hughes.

"Literature of the Harlem Renaissance." *Twentieth-Century Literary Criticism*, edited by Thomas J. Schoenberg and Lawrence J. Trudeau, vol. 218, Gale, 2009, pp. 260-376.

Locke, Alain. "From *The New Negro*." Mays, *Norton*, pp. 1103-08.

Mays, Kelly J. "Cultural and Historical Contexts: The Harlem Renaissance." Mays, *Norton*, pp. 1089-94.

———, editor. *The Norton Introduction to Literature*. Shorter 14th ed., W. W. Norton, 2021.

#BlackLivesMatter

AN ALBUM

We must create work that refuses to leave this world the same. . . .

—DANEZ SMITH, "WE MUST BE THE NEW GUARDS:
OPEN LETTER TO WHITE POETS" (2014)

According to multiple pollsters, between fifteen and twenty-six million Americans took to the streets in the late spring and summer of 2020—an estimated 500,000 on June 6 alone. As many as half of them reported never having before participated in a demonstration. Yet now, in the midst of a global pandemic, they masked and marched. They marched by the thousands in New York and Chicago, Atlanta and Portland. They stood, by the hundreds or the handful, in the town squares and along the roadsides of communities of all shapes, sizes, and political leanings—in Holland, Arkansas (pop. 552), where Chad Jones, a White farmer, staged a protest of one, to "help change hearts and minds" and to prove to his kids that anyone, everyone can make a difference; in Chambersburg, Pennsylvania (pop. 17,862), where the county's Republican district attorney wrote an open letter of support; in Fort Dodge, Iowa (pop. 25,000), where Jayden Johnson, a Black nineteen-year-old, took to *SnapChat*, inviting friends to join her downtown, only to end up leading over one hundred African American, Latino, and White teenagers and young adults in the first public protest in the town's memory. All told, every U.S. state and some 40 percent of U.S. counties played host to such events. According to one well-regarded, widely cited study, 93 percent of those events were entirely peaceful.

But violence inspired them. Horrified by the violent deaths, at the hands of acting and former police officers, of George Floyd, in Minneapolis, Minnesota; of emergency medical technician Breonna Taylor, in Louisville, Kentucky; of jogger Ahmaud Arbery, in Brunswick, Georgia, those millions gathered under the banner of Black Lives Matter (BLM). Initially a hashtag, later an organization created by Black activists Patrisse Cullors, Opal Tometi, and Alicia Garza following the 2013 acquittal of George Zimmerman for the shooting death of unarmed Black teenager Trayvon Marvin, and first gaining national attention a year later, in the wake of the fatal police shooting of Michael Brown, in Ferguson, Missouri, BLM became, as of July 2020, not only the single largest but also the single most diverse movement in U.S. history—exponentially more so, by every measure, than the civil rights movement of the 1960s. As political scientist Alvin Tillery notes, BLM, as of 2020, became a very "broad umbrella for social justice campaigns" coalescing not around any one organization or any one platform or policy solution but rather around two basic ideas with which polls suggest a majority of Americans agreed: that racial and ethnic discrimination is a major problem and that the U.S. criminal justice system needs reform so as to ensure—to paraphrase poet Danez Smith—"with liberty & justice" truly does hold "for all."[1]

---

1. To take just two examples, a June 2020 Associated Press-NORC Center for Public Affairs Research poll found that only 5 percent of Americans believed that the U.S. criminal justice system required no

If, in important ways, BLM thus became, as of 2020, both a broadly and a peculiarly American movement, "Black Lives Matter" nonetheless also became a rallying cry for protesters around the globe—from Brussels, Belgium, and Bristol, England, to Seoul, Korea, and Sydney, Australia. Even in civil war–torn Idlib, Syria, a lone wall standing in a sea of rubble sprouted a mural honoring George Floyd. ("When we draw on the walls of destroyed buildings," the mural's two young creators affirmed, "we are telling the world that [. . .] there was injustice here, just like there's injustice in America.")

Perhaps any movement that so galvanizes a nation, even a world, deserves attention—not despite but because of the controversy it generates. But BLM merits consideration in this particular context for a different reason—the way both the movement and the events and concerns inspiring it have galvanized poets and poetry readers, utterly transforming the landscape of contemporary American poetry and doing much to give that poetry the new rawness, urgency, and immediacy at least partly responsible for the recent upsurge of interest in it, especially among young readers. In its own way, BLM may thus ultimately prove as important a phenomenon in the history of poetry as the Harlem Renaissance.

In fact, if we ask the question posed in a 2018 *New York Times* editorial, "Who First Showed Us That Black Lives Matter?," one answer would be the writers of the Harlem Renaissance. Yet in at least one important sense the two movements are exact opposites: Where the Harlem Renaissance was an artistic movement with a social justice component, BLM is a social justice movement that has nonetheless both nurtured and been nurtured by art. Though that art takes many forms, the "newly invigorated conversations about systemic racism" inspired by BLM are ones in which poets and poetry have assumed uniquely "active and visible roles," to quote the editors of the important recent anthology *Revisiting the Elegy in the Black Lives Matter Era* (2020).

This album invites you to enter that conversation and to consider poetry's unique contribution to it. By gathering a small selection of poems, as well as two essays by poets, published between 2015 and July 2020, this album invites you, too, to consider poetry in relation not to a different, distant historical and cultural context but rather to our very own.

If you compare these recent poems to those of the Harlem Renaissance, what important continuities and differences might you see? What might these two sets of poems, considered together, demonstrate about both the continuities and the differences between the state of America and of American race relations in the earlier twentieth century and/versus the early twenty-first? Or, to misquote Zora Neale Hurston, what might the poems individually and collectively convey about "What It Feels Like to Be Black Me" or "Black Us" today as opposed to "What It Felt to Be Colored Me" in the 1920s and 1930s?

Considered on their own terms and in their own context, in what various ways do the poems in this album work to affirm and insist that Black lives do, indeed, matter? What, conversely, do they urge us to see, feel, and understand about why that affirmation is so urgently needed—or, that is, about why and how Black lives are too often devalued? How might the poems represent racism and its effects as systemic—involving not merely individual prejudice but also, even primarily, the

---

change, with 69 percent instead advocating either "major changes" or "a complete overhaul"; according to a July 2020 Monmouth University poll, 67 percent of Americans saw racial and ethnic discrimination in the U.S. as a big problem, just 7 percent as no problem at all.

policies and practices of established institutions? What might poetry be able to illuminate about the experience and effects of systemic racism that other forms of expression cannot? And what, ultimately, might these poems demonstrate about the peculiar power of poetry itself as a vehicle of protest?

Like poems ranging from Langston Hughes's I, Too to Wilfred Owen's DULCE ET DECORUM EST and Adrienne Rich's TONIGHT NO POETRY WILL SERVE, all those gathered in this album might be classified as "protest poetry"—a very old, very loosely defined genre that Edward Hirsch's *A Poet's Glossary* characterizes as "[p]oetry of dissent, of social criticism," "timely, oppositional, reactive, urgent," "born from outrage and linked to social action."

Many of these poems are also elegies that nonetheless, as *Revisiting the Elegy*'s editors and contributors demonstrate, rework the conventions of that genre in important ways. Like conventional elegies such as W. H. Auden's IN MEMORY OF W. B. YEATS, that is, multiple poems in this album work both to memorialize the dead and to express the intense grief provoked by their loss, "carv[ing] out a *public* space for black grief" and "countering [. . .] media representations that either ignore black pain or individualize it," often by also transforming "victims [. . .] into criminals who somehow deserved their fate." Yet where conventional elegies also ultimately work to provide readers comfort and solace, poems like Danez Smith's NOT AN ELEGY FOR MIKE BROWN actively "resis[t] the turn toward consolation," "encourag[ing]" readers "to become more than passive bystanders," unsettling us "in order to provoke [us] into action." Urging us to recognize, just as the essay by poet Claudia Rankine excerpted here also does, that both the fact and the threat of death, hence mourning, are and long have been endemic to "Black Life" in the United States, they warn us, too, that—without concerted action—that will not change.

DANEZ SMITH
not an elegy for Mike Brown[2]

> I am sick of writing this poem
> but bring the boy. his new name
>
> his same old body. ordinary, black
> dead thing. bring him & we will mourn
> 5 until we forget what we are mourning
>
> & isn't that what being black is about?
> not the joy of it, but the feeling
>
> you get when you are looking
> at your child, turn your head,
> 10 then, poof, no more child.
>
> that feeling. that's black.
>
>   //
>
> think: once, a white girl

---

2. Unarmed Black eighteen-year-old whose death at the hands of a White Ferguson, Missouri, police officer on August 9, 2014, touched off the months of sometimes violent protests that first brought national attention to the Black Lives Matter movement.

was kidnapped & that's the Trojan war.[3]

later, up the block, Troy got shot
15   & that was Tuesday. are we not worthy

of a city of ash? of 1,000 ships
launched because we are missed?

always, something deserves to be burned.
it's never the right thing.

20   I demand a war to bring the dead boy back
no matter what his name is this time.

I at least demand a song.   a head.
a song will do for now.

//

look at what the lord has made.
25   above Missouri, sweet smoke.

2015

- In what different ways and senses is Danez Smith's poems "not an elegy"? "not an elegy for Mike Brown" specifically?
- How does the poem characterize "being black" (line 6)? In these terms, what role is played by the juxtaposition of the two Troys? of the fire that razed ancient Troy and the fires lit in Ferguson, Missouri, in the wake of Brown's death?

ROSS GAY
A Small Needful Fact

Is that Eric Garner[4] worked
for some time for the Parks and Rec.
Horticultural Department, which means,
perhaps, that with his very large hands,
5   perhaps, in all likelihood,
he put gently into the earth
some plants which, most likely,
some of them, in all likelihood,
continue to grow, continue
10   to do what such plants do, like house

---

3. In classical mythology, the war between Greece and Troy, which ends with the latter's fiery destruction, is sparked either by the "kidnap[ping]" by Paris of King Menelaus's beautiful wife Helen or her choice to flee to Troy with Paris; Christopher Marlowe's *Doctor Faustus* thus famously refers to Helen's as "the face that launch'd a thousand ships."
4. Unarmed Black forty-three-year-old who suffered a fatal asthma attack on July 17, 2014, after being put into a chokehold and pinned to the ground by a White police officer, in Staten Island, New York; the medical examiner ruled Garner's death a homicide.

and feed small and necessary creatures,
like being pleasant to touch and smell,
like converting sunlight
into food, like making it easier
15 for us to breathe.

2015

- Why, according to Ross Gay's poem, is the "fact" that Eric Garner "worked /
  [. . .] for the Parks and Rec. / Horticultural Department" (lines 1–3) a "small,"
  yet "needful" one? What significance does the poem give to that fact?
- What is the significance and effect of the poem's repetitions, especially of
  the end words/phrases "likelihood" (5, 8) and "most likely" (7)?

PATRICIA SMITH
Sagas of the Accidental Saint

For the mothers of the lost

I don't expect you'll recognize my voice.
I don't believe this saga I've suppressed
will ever sound familiar. I am just

a stooped and accidental saint, no choice
5   except to strain the limits of my throat.
I am the mama weep beneath the fold,

that paragraph you skip, the wink of gold
inside a rotted mouth, that shredding note
of grief. Excuse what's inexcusable

10 in me—the shifting wildfire-tinted weave,
my ankles blue with fluid, how I grieve
in gospel you can't clutch—a fusible

display of doubled negatives I spew
whenever someone says my child is gone
15 and then goes on to pile the blame upon

my child for being gone. Or maybe you
believe the wretched mess is rightly traced
right back to *me*, whose body housed the crime—

my daughter out of dollars, out of time,
20 my son just seeking ways to be erased.
So many ways they stride into the line

of gunfire, tease the trigger, crave the shot,
just living through their days as if they're not
about to die. He totes a paper bag of wine,

25 or tussles, laughing, with his kid or rolls
a joint or asks his boo to braid his hair
while lazing on the stoop, or dares to glare

when someone shoves. She fights against the holds
around her throat or somehow looks the same
30   as someone else or sits inside her car

or someone else's car, or leaves ajar
a door she should have closed. He plays a game
of hoops to clear his head, or doesn't raise

his hands, or raises them, or doesn't stop
35   or does, or, when commanded, fails to drop
his wallet, keys or phone. He sets ablaze

a heap of trash, somebody's car or store,
while shouting slogans meant to make you care
that he's alive. She's killed if she's not there

40   although she said she'd be, or there before
she should have been, or on her way to work,
or coming home not walking like she should,

not walking down the street she normally would.
He walks too close behind, you have to jerk
45   your purse out of the way, you palm the mace,

he passes, spitting lyric vile and blue,
not giving damns that he's offending you.
All you can remember is his race.

You ask him to succumb, he dares decline,
50   the situation quickly falls apart.
A weapon's raised to line up with his heart

because he feels entitled to his spine.
She fumbles in her pocket for some change
or jumps the A train turnstile on a dare.

55   She mumbles like her mind is not all there,
or titters in a way you think is strange.
He wrecks his Chevy, waves for help, he calls

the 9 the 1, the 1. He's *waiting* wrong,
the folks around him said he didn't belong.
60   He coughs or sneezes, looks away, he brawls

with brothers, sisters, father, wife. He waves
a Walmart toy, or he can't find his place
in line, he laughs too loud, he can't retrace

his steps, he droops his pants, he misbehaves.
65   She turns her back or whirls around or could
be packin', could be wanted, could be strong

enough to snap your neck. She moves all wrong.
He wanders into someone else's hood
in colors that he struggles to explain.

70 He prances, strides, he's plotting an escape,
he stops and spins on you, he's here to rape
your daughter. Or he scoffs when you complain

about his smell, he crafts a sign, he parks
behind your Chevy, thrusts his massive fist
75 into or through the air, he wakes up pissed

but right on time, then smokes a blunt or arcs
his brow when someone asks *You good?* He waits
his turn or takes a break, he takes a leak,

he frightens everyone with his physique,
80 the situation's bound to escalate.
So many ways they're asking not to be.

She's wearing out her welcome, being black
when no one's asked her to, you've seen her lack
of grace, the space she occupies, her glee

85 when chicken, weed or welfare checks roll in.
He goes to class, he graduates, he takes
the seat right next to you, his shoulder makes

you quake inside. You simply don't know when
he'll blow. She shops beneath the winking eye
90 of video, but then pays with a card

that *can't* be hers. His chest and arms are scarred
with scrape and blood tattoos—so why untie
the noose shaped like his neck? His clothes are blue

or red, he wants your job, he's scoped your wife,
95 he craves your home, your cash, your perfect life,
that textbook in his hand's not fooling you.

She hawks and spits, she begs for change, she blows
a harp, she blows through blow, she blows her chance,
a victim, yet again, of circumstance.

100 He's fighting back, but everybody knows
that he's too coarse, too dumb, too street, too black,
too dense, too doomed, too thick, too much of those,

too vicious pose, too quick to come to blows,
too likely he could spark your heart attack.
105 He flares his nostrils, hides his hands, he flees

without explaining why. She lifts, she steals,
she swipes, she grabs, she snatches, cuts a deal.
He stumbles, trips, he trips a wire, he sees

too much, she needs too much, he feels too much,
110 her skin's too mud, his skin's too light, he fights
too dirty, fights for breath, the savage nights

are huge with him, the voodoo in his touch—
he shoots himself while handcuffed to a pole,
or hangs himself while hanging from a tree,

115 or wrings his neck although his hands aren't free.
He always seems to fail at self-control.
He's monster, ogre, he's the looming threat,

insisting he didn't do that thing he did,
denying that she'd hidden what she hid,
120 confusing you by getting so upset.

He claims he's innocent, he files a case,
he lives too large, too long, he must believe
that he is white or free. He's so naive—

with every step he takes, he falls from grace.
125 He steps inside or out, or through or down,
she bellows, jumps or hisses, struts or spins,

he stalks a street, steps off a curb. His sins
should be enough to drive him out of town,
where he'd be out of sight and out of mind

130 and out of bounds but thankfully not out
of range. And if you think he's all about
the kill, the drops, the guns and gangster grind,

you know for sure as soon as you see me—
his mama, grieving ugly, wailing 'bout
135 *my chile, my chile,* and plucking Jesus out

of every bag. You just can't see why he
deserves such stupid love—my wailing thrusts,
each *Lord have mercy on my baby's soul,*

my sad theatrics as my child goes cold.
140 And then the hungry cameras readjust
my howls—until it's not my child who's dead,

but something feral, edged in leak, a threat
to shrubbery and Sundays. While he's wet
and seeping into street, they frame his head

145 and mine inside a single shot and ask
my nappy hair and bulging eyes just what
I think. I keen, implode on cue. They cut

the camera back to frame the blooded mask
and splay. You don't remember what I say,
150 or hear his name, but you are borderline

obsessed with my collapse, my crumpled whine
and holy-ghosted flail, the matinee
of mama. You are entertained until

you aren't. And then I'm just an open maw,
155 a blur and tongue. You shouldn't waste your awe
on my unleashed display of overkill.

Ignore the blackish bruiser, dripping bile,
the spittle-spewing me, still bellowing
my Lord my Lord why would you let this thing

160 disrupt your day? I disappear. And while
I'm relegated to an anecdote
on way to nothing, all you can recall

is sputtered gospel woe and caterwaul,
that corpse the tightened wire around my throat.

165 *that's my son collapsed there my son*
crumpled there my son lying there
my son positioned there my daughter
repositioned there my daughter as
exhibit A there my daughter dumped
170 *over there my son hidden away there*
my son blue there my son dangling
there my son caged there my daughter
on the gurney there on the slab there
in the drawer there my daughter splayed
175 *there my son locked down there my*
son hanging there my son bleeding
out there my son growing frigid there
my daughter deposited there my son
inside the chalk there my daughter
180 *being bagged there my son on the slab*
there my son crushed there my son
rearranged there my son crumpled
in the door there my daughter's neck
shrinking in the noose there my son's
185 *left eye over there my son as exhibit B*
there my son behind the wheel there
my son under the wheels there my son
slumped over the wheel there my son
my daughter blooded and not moving
190 *in the doorway on the stoop down*
the block in front of her kids just inside
the barbershop facedown in the street
outside the bodega inside the bodega
in the black alley behind the bodega
195 *on the videotape a block from home*
leaving home hanging out at home
in the schoolyard on the blacktop
in his bed in her kitchen in my arms
in my arms in my arms that's my son
200 *shot to look thug that's my daughter*

> shot to look more animal shot as kill
> shot as prey shot as conquest shot as
> solution shot as lesson shot as warning
> shot as comeback shot as payback shot
> 205 for sport shot for history that's my son
> not being alive any more there that's my
> child coming to rest one layer below
> the surface of the
>
> rest
>
> 210 of my life
>
>   there

                                               2017

- Who is the speaker of Patricia Smith's poem, and at what point and based on what cues do you begin to identify the speaker? In what ways and senses is the speaker an "accidental saint"? What is the effect and significance of Smith's choice of speaker?
- What does Smith's poem suggest about how both "the mothers of the lost" to whom she dedicates the poem, as well as "the lost" themselves, tend to be viewed by "you"?

DANEZ SMITH
dear white america

i've left Earth in search of darker planets, a solar system revolving too near a black hole. i've left in search of a new God. i do not trust the God you have given us. my grandmother's hallelujah is only outdone by the fear she nurses every time the blood-fat summer swallows another child who used to sing in the choir. take your God back. though his songs are beautiful, his miracles are inconsistent. i want the fate of Lazarus for Renisha, want Chucky, Bo, Meech, Trayvon, Sean & Jonylah[5] risen three days after their entombing, their ghost re-gifted flesh & blood, their flesh & blood re-gifted their children. i've left Earth, i am equal parts sick of your *go back to Africa & i just don't see race.* neither did the poplar tree. we did not build your boats (though we did leave a trail of kin to guide us home). we did not build your prisons (though we did & we fill them too). we did not ask to be part of your America (though are we not America? her

---

5. Jonylah Watkins, six-month-old fatally shot in Chicago on March 11, 2013. Here, both victim and shooter were Black, and no police were involved, unlike the cases of Renisha McBride, unarmed Black nineteen-year-old fatally shot in Dearborn Heights, Michigan, by a White homeowner (November 2, 2013); Clifford "Chucky" Howell, Black thirteen-year-old fatally shot by a White police officer in nearby Detroit (September 13, 1969); Burrell ("Bo") Ramsey-White, Black twenty-six-year-old fatally shot by a Boston policeman (August 21, 2012); Wardel ("Meech") Davis, who died of an acute asthma attack during a struggle with Buffalo, New York, police officers (February 7, 2017); Trayvon Martin, fatally shot by volunteer neighborhood watchman George Zimmerman in Sandford, Florida (February 26, 2012); and Sean Bell, fatally shot by police officers in New York City (November 25, 2006). *Lazarus:* man restored to life by Jesus, four days after his death (John 11.1–44).

joints brittle & dragging a ripped gown through Oakland?). i can't stand your ground.[6] i'm sick of calling your recklessness the law. each night, i count my brothers. & in the morning, when some do not survive to be counted, i count the holes they leave. i reach for black folks & touch only air. your master magic trick, America. now he's breath-ing, now he don't. abra-cadaver. white bread voodoo. sorcery you claim not to practice, hand my cousin a pistol to do your work. i tried, white people. i tried to love you, but you spent my brother's funeral making plans for brunch, talking too loud next to his bones. you took one look at the river, plump with the body of boy after girl after sweet boi & ask *why does it always have to be about race?* because you made it that way! be-cause you put an asterisk on my sister's gorgeous face! call her pretty (for a black girl)! because black girls go missing without so much as a whisper of where?! because there are no amber alerts[7] for amber-skinned girls! because Jordan boomed. because Emmett[8] whistled. because Huey P. spoke. because Martin[9] preached. because black boys can al-ways be too loud to live. because it's taken my papa's & my grandma's time, my father's time, my mother's time, my aunt's time, my uncle's time, my brother's & my sister's time . . . how much time do you want for your progress? i've left Earth to find a place where my kin can be safe, where black people ain't but people the same color as the good, wet earth, until that means something, until then i bid you well, i bid you war, i bid you our lives to gamble with no more. i've left Earth & i am touching everything you beg your telescopes to show you. i'm giving the stars their right names. & this life, this new story & history you cannot steal or sell or cast overboard or hang or beat or drown or own or redline[1] or shackle or silence or cheat or choke or cover up or jail or shoot or jail or shoot or jail or shoot or ruin

this, if only this one, is ours.

2015, 2017

- If one thing DEAR WHITE AMERICA expresses is the outrage characteristic of protest poetry, then what exactly is the speaker outraged about?
- What other feelings are conveyed in the poem? Why, for example, is the speaker "sick" and "tired"? How might the poem also express love, and for what and whom?

---

6. Play on the phrase "stand your ground," a term for laws, like those invoked in the Trayvon Martin case, allowing people to use deadly force in any situation in which they reasonably believe it necessary to defend against imminent threat. (The alternative are laws entailing a "duty to retreat"—that is, sanctioning use of force only when there is no possibility of avoiding or retreating from a threat.)
7. Emergency response system that disseminates information about a missing person, usually a child, so named after Amber Hagerman, a White nine-year-old Texas girl abducted and murdered in 1996.
8. Emmett Till (1941–55), Black fourteen-year-old lynched in Mississippi after purportedly whistling at White storeowner Carolyn Bryant.
9. Civil rights leader Martin Luther King, Jr., (1929–68) was fatally shot by James Earl Ray hours after delivering his "I've Been to the Mountaintop" address at a Memphis, Tennessee, church. *Huey P.*: Black activist and Black Panther Party cofounder Huey P. Newton (1942–89) was fatally shot by Tyrone Robinson in West Oakland, California.
1. The systematic denial of various services such as loans to specific groups of people or to people living in designated areas, so named because in 1935 the U.S. Federal Home Loan Bank Board mandated the creation of maps ranking geographic areas in terms of their desirability to mortgage lenders and other investors; areas considered most risky were outlined in red.

EVIE SHOCKLEY

of speech

they spoke with blue they
blued they gave us
the blues their presence was
bluing they blue us over
5 aside they spoke with metal with
their barricades they
barricaded they barred they
used bars to divide
the sidewalk they used
10 bars to divide us
from other people they barred
us in a few bars of the blues

the barricades were
bare the barricades were
15 blue they spoke with
badge they spoke with badger they
spoke with loudspeakers
that spoke louder
than the speakers at our rally we
20 rallied we spoke together we
spoke louder than the loudspeakers
we spoke over
the blues we spoke of the blues

they spoke with laws they
25 spoke of laws they spoke
of enforcement they
spoke of force they meant
force they meant us to be in
force in their force they
30 are force they are in forces their
forces spoke with loudspeakers
their forces blue us away
with the force of their speech they
drowned us in their blue speech

35 they spoke of arrest they
did not arrest our
attention we spoke of freedom
we spoke of speech we spoke
of browns and blacks they
40 spoke with numbers we
spoke with numbers we spoke
of numbers we numbered
their crimes we have

their number their blues
45 number their days are
numbered our days are numbered

they spoke with blue with
barricade with badge
with authority but not with
50 impunity their bullets speak
with impunity they
speak with handcuffs their
speech is handcuffed their speech
is not free their unfreedom
55 of speech is blue their blacks
speak blue their browns speak
blue their whites speak blue

we   have the freedom of speech
we used the freedom   of speech to speak
60 of freedom loudly we   spoke freedom
loudly and in   that place and
in that speaking we lived and did not die
we spoke and   did not die we
spoke freedom and   nothing happened
65 except   this poem this freedom we
spoke with freedom and   our speech
of freedom spoke   louder than
blues than badges our   speech of
freedom spoke over their   loudspeakers
70 our freedom spoke   over their barricades
and onto this page   ¡yes!   one freedom

led to another

—millions march rally, columbus circle,
nyc, july 17, 2015, one year after
the murder of eric garner[2]

2017

- In this poem about, as well as of, protest, "we" are clearly the protesters. Who are "they," and how does the poem figure the conflict between the two and their "speech"?
- How might this poem celebrate the power of speech not only through what it says but also through how it does so? What specific forms of wordplay are at work in the poem? What is their individual and collective significance and effect?

2. Unarmed Black forty-three-year-old who suffered a fatal asthma attack on July 17, 2014, after being put into a chokehold and pinned to the ground by a White police officer, in Staten Island, New York; the medical examiner ruled Garner's death a homicide.

Jonathan Bachman's award-winning photograph *Unrest in Baton Rouge* (July 9, 2016) features Ieshia Evans, a twenty-seven-year-old Pennsylvania nurse who traveled to Baton Rouge, Louisiana, to protest the fatal police shooting of Alton Sterling.

TRACY K. SMITH
Unrest in Baton Rouge

after the photo by Jonathan Bachman

Our bodies run with ink dark blood.
Blood pools in the pavement's seams.

Is it strange to say love is a language
Few practice, but all, or near all speak?

5 Even the men in black armor, the ones
Jangling handcuffs and keys, what else

Are they so buffered against, if not love's blade
Sizing up the heart's familiar meat?

We watch and grieve. We sleep, stir, eat.
10 Love: the heart sliced open, gutted, clean.

Love: naked almost in the everlasting street,
Skirt lifted by a different kind of breeze.

2018

• How might this poem, read alongside the photo that inspired it, explain and develop the idea—broached as a question or possibility here—that love might be "a language / Few practice, but all, or near all speak" (lines 3–4)?

KEVIN YOUNG
Not Guilty [A Frieze for Sandra Bland]³

Because the night has no
   number, because
the thunder doesn't

     mean rain
5 Because maybe
     Because we must

say your names
   & the list grows
longer & more

10   endless
I am writing this:
     you are no gun

nor holster, no
     finger aimed, thumb
15 a hammer cocked

     back, all the way—
I refuse
     to bury you, to inter

your name in earth
20   or to burn you back
to bone, to what

     we all know, the soft
song of your skull
     as an infant, the place

25 God or your mother
     or same thing
left untouched

     by hands—
that halo grown whole
30   till they said you weren't—

said that Death
     could be your breath—
could be a body

     or less—& you
35 grew more black
     & blue.

3. From the three-poem sequence "Triptych for Trayvon Martin." (On Martin, see this album's
introduction and Chronology.) *Sandra Bland*: Black twenty-eight-year-old found hanged in her jail
cell in Walter County, Texas, on July 13, 2015, three days after being pulled over for a traffic violation
and arrested on suspicion of felony assault on a public servant. A Texas grand jury later decided
against indictments in her death, while indicting the arresting officer for misdemeanor perjury.

I refuse
    to watch. I refuse.
Not guilty. Not

40   *guilty.* I know you
will stay & rise
    like the sea—

the tide
    all salt & shifting.
45 Don't ever leave.

                                         2018

   • Why, according to the speaker, is he "writing this" (line 11)?
   • What does the speaker "refuse" to do, and why and how so (lines 17, 37)?

REGINALD DWAYNE BETTS
When I Think of Tamir Rice[4] While Driving

in the backseat my sons laugh & tussle,
far from Tamir's age, adorned with his
complexion & cadence & already warned

about toy pistols, though my rhetoric
5 ain't about fear, but dislike—about
how guns have haunted me since I first gripped

a pistol; I think of Tamir, twice-blink
& confront my weeping's inadequacy, how
some loss invents the geometry that baffles.

10 The Second Amendment[5]—cold, cruel,
a constitutional violence, a ruthless
thing worrying me still; should be it predicts

the heft in my hand, arm sag, burdened by
what I bear: My bare arms collaged
15 with wings as if hope alone can bring

back a buried child. A child, a toy gun,
a blue shield's rapid rapid rabid shit. This
is how misery sounds: my boys

playing in the backseat juxtaposed against
20 a twelve-year-old's murder playing
in my head. My tongue cleaves to the roof

---

4. Black twelve-year-old fatally shot by Cleveland, Ohio, police while in possession of a toy gun (November 22, 2014).
5. Variously interpreted, hence controversial, amendment to the U.S. Constitution guaranteeing "the right of the people to keep and bear Arms" on the grounds that a "well regulated Militia" is "necessary to the security of a free State."

of my mouth, my right hand has forgotten.
This is the brick & mortar of the America
that murdered Tamir & may stalk the laughter

25 in my backseat. I am a father driving
his Black sons to school & the death
of a Black boy rides shotgun & this

could be a funeral procession. The death
a silent thing in the air, unmentioned—
30 because mentioning death invites taboo:

if you touch my sons the blood washed
away from the concrete must, at some
point, belong to you, & not just to you, to

the artifice of justice that is draped like a blue
35 g-d around your shoulders, the badge that
justifies the echo of the fired pistol; taboo:

the thing that stays freedom is a murderer's body
mangled & disrupted by my constitutional
rights come to burden, because the killer's mind

40 refused the narrative of a brown child, his dignity,
his right to breathe, his actual fucking existence,
with all the crystalline brilliance I saw when

my boys first reached for me. This world best
invite more than the story of the children bleeding
45 on crisp fall days. Tamir's death must be more

than warning about recklessness & abandoned
justice & white terror's ghost—& this is
why I hate it all, the protests & their counters,

the Civil Rights attorneys that stalk the bodies
50 of the murdered, this dance of ours that reduces
humanity to the dichotomy of the veil. We are

not permitted to articulate the reasons we might
yearn to see a man die. A mind may abandon
sanity. What if all I had stomach for was blood?

55 But history is no sieve & sanity is no elixir
& I am bound to be haunted by the strength
that lets Tamir's father, mother, kinfolk resist

the temptation to turn everything they see
into a grave & make home the series of cells
60 that so many brothers already call their tomb.

2019

• How does Betts's poem interrelate the situation of the speaker ("a father driving / his Black sons to school," lines 25–26) and that of Tamir Rice's parents?

Parking Lot, Too

A confession began when I walked out of that parking lot.
A confession began when I walked Black out of that parking lot.
A confession began when I, without combing my hair, dressed
For a day that would find me walking out of that parking lot.
5 There is so much to be said of a Black man with unkempt hair:
He meets the description of the suspect; suspect is running.
I ran away from things far less frightening than the police.
A confession began when I robed myself in black. A confession
Began when I walked out of that parking lot wearing a black
10 Hoodie. Things get exponentially worse when a hoodie is pulled
Over my unkempt air. A confession began when I walked out
Of that parking lot Black. A confession began when I walked
Out of that parking lot a Negro. A confession begins when
That nigga walked into the parking lot. A confession begins
15 When that nigga & the pistol he carries like a dick walked
Into that parking lot. A confession begins when everything you
See him doing is seen as sex. A confession begins when
That nigga walked into a parking lot & drove away with everything
Belonging to that white man. A confession begins when
20 My mother laid up with a man the complexion of that nigga's
Daddy. A confession begins when my mother births a child
In a city close enough to make me & that nigga almost related.
A confession begins when the police perceive us as one. We must
Be one. He could not have walked in & driven out & I walked
25 In & walked out on the same night & whatever gaps in the story
& slight differences in the features of our faces was just
More evidence that niggers will lie. A confession begins even if
I didn't have the fucking car. A confession begins, my confession
Began, with a woman stitching stars and stripes into a flag.

2019

- What does Parking Lot, Too suggest about how and why a Black man might be considered guilty, even confess, to a crime he didn't commit? How do the speaker's assertions about that develop over the course of the poem?
- In these terms, what is the significance and effect of the poem's use of **anaphora**?

CLAUDIA RANKINE
Weather

On a scrap of paper in the archive is written
I have forgotten my umbrella. Turns out
in a pandemic everyone, not just the philosopher,[6]

6. Friedrich Nietzsche (1844–1900). *I have forgotten . . .*: The enigmatic sentence, appearing in a manuscript discovered after the German philosopher's death, has long fascinated scholars, testifying for some to the impossibility of ever arriving at one definitive interpretation of any statement, for

is without. We scramble in the drought of information
5 held back by inside traders.[7] Drop by drop. Face
covering? No, yes. Social distancing? Six feet
under for underlying conditions. Black.
Just us and the blues kneeling on a neck
with the full weight of a man in blue.
10 Eight minutes and forty-six seconds.[8]
In extremis, *I can't breathe* gives way
to asphyxiation, to giving up this world,
and then *mama*, called to, a call
to protest, fire, glass, say their names, say
15 their names, *white silence equals violence,*
the violence of again, a militarized police
force teargassing, bullets ricochet, and civil
unrest taking it, burning it down. Whatever
contracts keep us social compel us now
20 to disorder the disorder. Peace. We're out
to repair the future. There's an umbrella
by the door, not for yesterday but for the weather
that's here. I say weather but I mean
a form of governing that deals out death
25 and names it living. I say weather but I mean
a November[9] that won't be held off. This time
nothing, no one forgotten. We are here for the storm
that's storming because what's taken matters.

June 15, 2020

- How does WEATHER interrelate the COVID-19 pandemic and its handling
  to the death of George Floyd?
- Though WEATHER twice repeats an important motto of Black Lives Matter,
  "say their names, say / their names" (lines 14–15), what might the poem
  gain by *not* mentioning any names, including Floyd's?

From The Condition of Black Life Is One of Mourning

A friend recently told me that when she gave birth to her son, before naming
him, before even nursing him, her first thought was, I have to get him out of this

---

others to the idea that history and memory, like an umbrella, are alternately closed and forgotten, opened
and remembered, when they serve us. In interviews, Claudia Rankine also refers to "the umbrella of
safety" afforded to some but not others in the United States.
7. Those who trade in public company stock about which they have relevant information not available
publicly, often a serious crime.
8. The length of time, according to video evidence, that Minneapolis police officer Derek Chauvin
kept his knee on the neck of George Floyd, while Floyd lay prone on the ground repeating the phrase
"I can't breathe" (line 11) and crying out for his dead mother (line 13) before dying of heart failure.
9. U.S. general elections for federal public officials are held the first Tuesday after November 1. Those
held on November 3, 2020, included enough competitive races to potentially shift the Senate majority
from Republican to Democrat (which did not happen until a special election for the Senate seats in
Georgia in January 2021), as well as the presidential contest resulting in the defeat of Republican
incumbent Donald Trump (b. 1946) by former vice president and Delaware senator Joe Biden
(Democrat, b. 1942).

country. We both laughed. Perhaps our black humor had to do with understanding that getting out was neither an option nor the real desire. This is it, our life. Here we work, hold citizenship, pensions, health insurance, family, friends and on and on. She couldn't, she didn't leave. Years after his birth, whenever her son steps out of their home, her status as the mother of a living human being remains as precarious as ever. Added to the natural fears of every parent facing the randomness of life is this other knowledge of the ways in which institutional racism works in our country. Ours was the laughter of vulnerability, fear, recognition and an absurd stuckness.

I asked another friend what it's like being the mother of a black son. "The condition of black life is one of mourning," she said bluntly. For her, mourning lived in real time inside her and her son's reality: At any moment she might lose her reason for living. Though the white liberal imagination likes to feel temporarily bad about black suffering, there really is no mode of empathy that can replicate the daily strain of knowing that as a black person you can be killed for simply being black: no hands in your pockets, no playing music, no sudden movements, no driving your car, no walking at night, no walking in the day, no turning onto this street, no entering this building, no standing your ground, no standing here, no standing there, no talking back, no playing with toy guns,[1] no living while black.

Eleven days after I was born, on Sept. 15, 1963, four black girls were killed in the bombing of the 16th Street Baptist Church in Birmingham, Ala.[2] Now, 52 years later, six black women and three black men have been shot to death while at a Bible-study meeting at the historic Emanuel African Methodist Episcopal Church in Charleston, S.C. They were killed by a homegrown terrorist, self-identified as a white supremacist, who might also be a "disturbed young man" (as various news outlets have described him).[3] It has been reported that a black woman and her 5-year-old granddaughter survived the shooting by playing dead. They are two of the three survivors of the attack. The white family of the suspect says that for them this is a difficult time. This is indisputable. But for African-American families, this living in a state of mourning and fear remains commonplace.

. . .

We live in a country where Americans assimilate corpses in their daily comings and goings. Dead blacks are a part of normal life here. Dying in ship hulls, tossed into the Atlantic, hanging from trees, beaten, shot in churches, gunned down by the police or warehoused in prisons: Historically, there is no quotidian without the enslaved, chained or dead black body to gaze upon or to hear about or to position a self against. When blacks become overwhelmed by our culture's

1. On November 22, 2014, Black twelve-year-old Tamir Rice was fatally shot by police in Cleveland, Ohio, while in possession of a toy gun. *Standing your ground:* See p. 1136, n. 6.

2. For a poetic response to this event, see Dudley Randall's "Ballad of Birmingham" (p. 948).

3. Dylann Roof (b. 1994); the mass shooting occurred on June 17, 2015 (see Chronology). *Disturbed young man:* Republican South Carolina Senator Lindsay Graham, for example, explaining that his niece attended school with Roof, described the twenty-four-year-old shooter as a "strange, disturbed young man."

disorder and protest (ultimately to our own detriment, because protest gives the police justification to militarize, as they did in Ferguson[4]), the wrongheaded question that is asked is, What kind of savages are we? Rather than, What kind of country do we live in?

In 1955, when Emmett Till's[5] mutilated and bloated body was recovered from the Tallahatchie River and placed for burial in a nailed-shut pine box, his mother, Mamie Till Mobley, demanded his body be transported from Mississippi, where Till had been visiting relatives, to his home in Chicago. Once the Chicago funeral home received the body, she made a decision that would create a new pathway for how to think about a lynched body. She requested an open coffin and allowed photographs to be taken and published of her dead son's disfigured body.

Mobley's refusal to keep private grief private allowed a body that meant nothing to the criminal-justice system to stand as evidence. By placing both herself and her son's corpse in positions of refusal relative to the etiquette of grief, she "disidentified" with the tradition of the lynched figure left out in public view as a warning to the black community, thereby using the lynching tradition against itself. The spectacle of the black body, in her hands, publicized the injustice mapped onto her son's corpse. "Let the people see what I see," she said, adding, "I believe that the whole United States is mourning with me."

Mamie Till-Mobley mourns at the funeral of her lynched son, Emmett Till, 1955.

4. Ferguson, Missouri, where heavily armed police clashed with protesters in the months following the fatal police shooting of eighteen-year-old Michael Brown on August 9, 2014.
5. Black fourteen-year-old (1941–55) lynched in Mississippi after an encounter with White storeowner Carolyn Bryant.

It's very unlikely that her belief in a national mourning was fully realized, but her desire to make mourning enter our day-to-day world was a new kind of logic. In refusing to look away from the flesh of our domestic murders, by insisting we look with her upon the dead, she reframed mourning as a method of acknowledgment that helped energize the civil rights movement in the 1950s and '60s.

[. . . I]n Ferguson, [. . .] the police, in their refusal to move Michael Brown's body, perhaps unknowingly continued where Till's mother left off.

After Brown was shot six times, twice in the head, his body was left face-down in the street by the police officers. Whatever their reasoning, by not moving Brown's corpse for four hours after his shooting, the police made mourning his death part of what it meant to take in the details of his story. No one could consider the facts of Michael Brown's interaction with the Ferguson police officer Darren Wilson without also thinking of the bullet-riddled body bleeding on the asphalt. It would be a mistake to presume that everyone who saw the image mourned Brown, but once exposed to it, a person had to decide whether his dead black body mattered enough to be mourned. [. . .]

Black Lives Matter, the movement founded by the activists Alicia Garza, Patrisse Cullors and Opal Tometi, began with the premise that the incommensurable experiences of systemic racism creates an unequal playing field. The American imagination has never been able to fully recover from its white-supremacist beginnings. Consequently, our laws and attitudes have been straining against the devaluation of the black body. Despite good intentions, the associations of blackness with inarticulate, bestial criminality persist beneath the appearance of white civility. This assumption both frames and determines our individual interactions and experiences as citizens.

The American tendency to normalize situations by centralizing whiteness was consciously or unconsciously demonstrated again when certain whites, like the president of Smith College,[6] sought to alter the language of "Black Lives Matter" to "All Lives Matter." What on its surface was intended to be interpreted as a humanist move—"aren't we all just people here?"—didn't take into account a system inured to black corpses in our public spaces. When the judge in the Charleston bond hearing for Dylann Storm Roof called for support of Roof's family, it was also a subtle shift away from valuing the black body in our time of deep despair.

Anti-black racism is in the culture. It's in our laws, in our advertisements, in our friendships, in our segregated cities, in our schools, in our Congress, in our scientific experiments, in our language, on the Internet, in our bodies no matter our race, in our communities and, perhaps most devastatingly, in our justice system. The unarmed, slain black bodies in public spaces turn grief into our everyday feeling that something is wrong everywhere and all the time, even if locally things appear normal. Having coffee, walking the dog, reading the paper, taking the elevator to the office, dropping the kids off at school: All of this good

---

6. Kathleen McCartney (b. 1956), who later apologized for using "All Lives Matter" as the subject line of a December 5, 2014, email responding to the police-involved deaths of both Michael Brown and Eric Garner (an unarmed Black forty-three-year-old whose death, on July 17, 2014, in Staten Island, New York, was later ruled a homicide).

life is surrounded by the ambient feeling that at any given moment, a black person is being killed in the street or in his home by the armed hatred of a fellow American.

The Black Lives Matter movement can be read as an attempt to keep mourning an open dynamic in our culture because black lives exist in a state of precariousness. Mourning then bears both the vulnerability inherent in black lives and the instability regarding a future for those lives. Unlike earlier black-power movements that tried to fight or segregate for self-preservation, Black Lives Matter aligns with the dead, continues the mourning and refuses the forgetting in front of all of us. If the Rev. Martin Luther King Jr.'s civil rights movement made demands that altered the course of American lives and backed up those demands with the willingness to give up your life in service of your civil rights, with Black Lives Matter, a more internalized change is being asked for: recognition.

The truth, as I see it, is that if black men and women, black boys and girls, mattered, if we were seen as living, we would not be dying simply because whites don't like us. Our deaths inside a system of racism existed before we were born. The legacy of black bodies as property and subsequently three-fifths human[7] continues to pollute the white imagination. To inhabit our citizenry fully, we have to not only understand this, but also grasp it. In the words of playwright Lorraine Hansberry, "The problem is we have to find some way with these dialogues to show and to encourage the white liberal to stop being a liberal and become an American radical." And, as my friend the critic and poet Fred Moten has written: "I believe in the world and want to be in it. I want to be in it all the way to the end of it because I believe in another world and I want to be in that." This other world, that world, would presumably be one where black living matters. But we can't get there without fully recognizing what is here.

Dylann Storm Roof's unmediated hatred of black people; Black Lives Matter; citizens' videotaping the killings of blacks; the Ferguson Police Department leaving Brown's body in the street—all these actions support Mamie Till Mobley's belief that we need to see or hear the truth. We need the truth of how the bodies died to interrupt the course of normal life. But if keeping the dead at the forefront of our consciousness is crucial for our body politic, what of the families of the dead? How must it feel to a family member for the deceased to be more important as evidence than as an individual to be buried and laid to rest?

Michael Brown's mother, Lesley McSpadden, was kept away from her son's body because it was evidence. She was denied the rights of a mother, a sad fact reminiscent of pre-Civil War times, when as a slave she would have had no legal claim to her offspring. McSpadden learned of her new identity as a mother of a dead son from bystanders [. . .].

McSpadden, unlike Mamie Till Mobley, seemed to have little desire to expose her son's corpse to the media. Her son was not an orphan body for everyone to look upon. She wanted him covered and removed from sight. He belonged to her, her baby. After Brown's corpse was finally taken away, two weeks passed

---

7. Superseded by the fourteenth amendment in 1868, Article 1, Section 2, Clause 3 of the U.S. Constitution calls for state population counts to include all "free persons, including those bound to Service for a Term of Years," as well as "three-fifths of all other Persons," with slaves being the "other Persons" drafters of the clause had foremost in mind.

before his family was able to see him. This loss of control and authority might explain why after Brown's death, McSpadden was supposedly in the precarious position of accosting vendors selling T-shirts that demanded justice for Michael Brown that used her son's name. Not only were the procedures around her son's corpse out of her hands; his name had been commoditized and assimilated into our modes of capitalism.

Regardless of the wishes of these mothers—mothers of men like Brown, John Crawford III or Eric Garner, and also mothers of women and girls like Rekia Boyd and Aiyana Stanley-Jones,[8] each of whom was killed by the police— their children's deaths will remain within the public discourse. For those who believe the same behavior that got them killed if exhibited by a white man or boy would not have ended his life, the subsequent failure to indict or convict the police officers involved in these various cases requires that public mourning continue and remain present indefinitely. [. . .]

The Charleston murders alerted us to the reality that a system so steeped in anti-black racism means that on any given day it can be open season on any black person—old or young, man, woman or child. There exists no equivalent reality for white Americans. The Confederate battle flag continues to fly at South Carolina's statehouse[9] as a reminder of a history marked by lynched black bodies. We can distance ourselves from this fact until the next horrific killing, but we won't be able to outrun it. History's authority over us is not broken by maintaining a silence about its continued effects.

A sustained state of national mourning for black lives is called for in order to point to the undeniability of their devaluation. The hope is that recognition will break a momentum that laws haven't altered. [. . .] One friend said, "I am so afraid, every day." Her son's childhood feels impossible, because he will have to be—has to be—so much more careful. Our mourning, this mourning, is in time with our lives. There is no life outside of our reality here. Is this something that can be seen and known by parents of white children? This is the question that nags me. National mourning, as advocated by Black Lives Matter, is a mode of intervention and interruption that might itself be assimilated into the category of public annoyance. This is altogether possible; but also possible is the recognition that it's a lack of feeling for another that is our problem. Grief, then, for these deceased others might align some of us, for the first time, with the living.

June 22, 2015

8. Black seven-year-old fatally shot by a police officer in Detroit, Michigan, during a raid on her home (May 16, 2010). *John Crawford III*: Black twenty-two-year-old fatally shot by police in a Beavercreek, Ohio, Walmart while holding an unloaded BB gun (August 5, 2014). *Rekia Boyd*: unarmed Black twenty-two-year-old fatally shot by an off-duty Chicago police detective (March 21, 2012).
9. State legislators ended this practice on July 10, 2015, permanently moving the flag to the Confederate Relic Room & Military Museum.

TRACY K. SMITH

Dear Black America: A Letter

Dear Black America—

We are many things, aren't we? We are hair. God yes, we are hair. And song. And memory. We are a language so deep it has no need for words. And we are words that feint, dart and wheel like birds. Like James Brown, we feel good.[1] Like Fannie Lou Hamer,[2] we are sick and tired. We are fearsome. We are fire. Like God, we are that we are.

I've always felt great freedom in the countless territories making up the realm of Blackness. So many routes to wholeness. So many versions of joy. In Blackness I am local. In Blackness I am also distant kin. Indigenous and immigrant at once. Host and welcome guest.

But in the country of America—the physical and psychic territory in which the physical and psychic domain of Black America is situated—we are made to huddle together. By force. By the feelings of rage, threat, exhaustion, disappointment and longsuffering that extend toward us from this nation that loathes, fears, regrets and cannot yet fully bear to accept the fact of us.

And I hear my uncles saying, "Tell me something I don't know," with laughter in their throats. And it is that laughter—our laughter—that I cleave to.

We revel in the depth and the flair and the belief and the secrecy of Blackness. We are lucky to be who we are, and we know it. And I hear my aunts saying, "Amen," and their deep intaking of breath, followed by steep exhalation.

Black, we revel in the resourcefulness and the resilience and the poise and the knowhow and the grace and the anger and the prayers to all manner of being that have kept us alive. Alive despite attempt after concerted attempt to annihilate us.

I see you in all your forms, Black America, and I feel inside me a welling up of pride, reverence and fierce protection. These threats we live subject to— these ceaseless, baseless, unending and uneradicated threats to our black bodies, spirits and minds—do you know what I think they are? They are the grotesque and perverse ends to which a nation founded in shame has gone in order to avoid atoning for its crimes. They are defensive acts, based on the belief that, if we were allowed to dwell in our full power, what we would bestow upon this nation would be vengeance.

But we know better, don't we? Look what we do with our voices. Look what we build with our hands. Look what we hold together with just our arms.

Once a friend told me, "I think we came to this earth to save it."

---

1. Chorus and alternate title of "I Got You," iconic hit song of the legendary South Carolina–born singer (1933–2006).
2. Mississippi-born Black sharecropper's daughter (1917–77) and influential civil rights activist who famously declared, on behalf of all Blacks in the Jim Crow South, that she was "sick and tired of being sick and tired."

Once, I wrote in a notebook, "Maybe we are operating at a heightened spiritual frequency."

Why else do we call it Soul?

Black America, I feel myself cradled by this thing we share. When I call it race, I'm told that race is false. When I call it a movement, I'm reminded that we have moved through countless other movements before now. When I call it culture, I feel the seams of the word splitting at the great moving heft it attempts to contain.

We are here in America now as we have been in America always. When we are struck down and held back. When our bodies are corrupted by the violence of others. When we love. When, as now, we are trapped inside of finitude and flesh. During all of this and then some, Black America, we are agents of the eternal.

July 2, 2020

Chronology

This necessarily selective chronology refers only to events alluded to in this album's introduction and literary selections and that occurred between 2010 and early 2021.

2010   May 16, Detroit, Michigan: White police officer Joseph Weekley fatally shoots unarmed Black seven-year-old **Aiyana Stanley-Jones** while executing a search warrant on her family's home.

2011   October 4, Michigan: Grand jury indicts Officer Weekley for involuntary manslaughter in the death of Aiyana Stanley-Jones.

2012   February 26, Sandford, Florida: Twenty-eight-year-old volunteer neighborhood watch coordinator George Zimmerman, who identifies as mixed race, fatally shoots unarmed seventeen-year-old Black high school student **Trayvon Martin.**

March 21, Chicago, Illinois: White off-duty police detective Dante Servin fatally shoots unarmed Black twenty-two-year-old **Rekia Boyd.**

August 21, Boston, Massachusetts: White plainclothes police officer Mathew Pieroway fatally shoots armed Black 26-year-old **Burrell ("Bo") Ramsey-White.**

2013   March 11, Chicago: Black thirty-three-year-old Koman Willis fatally shoots Black six-month-old **Jonylah Watkins** during a dispute with her father over a stolen PlayStation system. City Council approves $4.5 million settlement with Rekia Boyd's family.

May 27, Chicago: Koman Willis is charged with first-degree murder in Jonylah Watkins's death.

June 18, Detroit: Officer Weekley's trial for manslaughter in the death of Aiyana Stanley-Jones ends in jury deadlock. (The second trial, in October 2014, will end with the judge's dismissal of the manslaughter charge and another deadlocked jury.)

July 13, Florida: George Zimmerman found not guilty of second-degree murder in the shooting of Trayvon Martin. In response, activist Alicia Garza posts to Facebook "a love letter to black people" ending with the words "Black people. I love you. I love us. Our lives matter." Shortly thereafter, friend and fellow activist Patrisse Cullors creates the hashtag #BlackLivesMatter.

November 2, Dearborn Heights, Michigan: White homeowner Theodore Wafer fatally shoots unarmed Black nineteen-year-old **Renisha McBride.**

November 13, Chicago: Detective Servin is charged with involuntary manslaughter in the death of Rekia Boyd.

December 17, Massachusetts: Suffolk County District Attorney releases report clearing Officer Pieroway of wrongdoing in the shooting death of Bo Ramsey-White.

2014 July 17, Staten Island, New York: Unarmed Black forty-three-year-old **Eric Garner** dies after being put into a chokehold and pinned to the ground by twenty-nine-year-old White police officer Daniel Pantaleo.

August 1, New York: Medical Examiner's Office rules Eric Garner's death a homicide.

August 5, Beavercreek, Ohio: Twenty-two-year-old White police officer Sean Williams shoots Black twenty-two-year-old **John Crawford III** while he is holding an unloaded BB gun inside a Walmart.

August 7, Michigan: Theodore Wafer is convicted of second-degree murder in the death of Renisha McBride.

August 9, Ferguson, Missouri: Twenty-eight-year-old White police officer Darren Wilson fatally shoots unarmed Black eighteen-year-old **Michael ("Mike") Brown, Jr.**

September 24, Ohio: Grand jury declines to indict Officer Williams for the death of John Crawford.

November 22, Cleveland, Ohio: Twenty-six-year-old White police officer Timothy Loehmann fatally shoots Black twelve-year-old **Tamir Rice** while he is in possession of a toy gun.

November 24, Missouri: Grand jury decides against any indictment in the case of Michael Brown.

December 3, New York: Grand jury decides against any indictment in the case of Eric Garner.

December 28, Ohio: Grand jury decides against any indictment in the case of Tamir Rice.

2015 April 19, Baltimore, Maryland: Black twenty-five-year-old **Freddie Gray, Jr.,** dies of injuries to his spinal cord sustained in the wake of his arrest, seven days earlier, for possessing a knife.

April 20, Chicago: Judge Dennis J. Porter clears Detective Servin of all charges in the death of Rekia Boyd.

May 1, Baltimore: After the medical examiner rules Freddie Gray's death a homicide, six Baltimore police officers (three White, three Black) are charged with crimes including second-degree depraved-heart murder.

June 17, Charleston, South Carolina: Twenty-one-year-old White supremacist Dylann Roof (b. 1994) opens fire in the Emanuel African Methodist Episcopal Church, killing nine Black parishioners. (According to his online manifesto, he was "truly awakened" by coverage of the Trayvon Martin shooting.)

July 13, Waller County, Texas: Black twenty-eight-year-old **Sandra Bland** is found hanged in her jail cell, three days after being pulled over for a traffic violation, by thirty-year-old White state trooper Brian Encinia, and arrested on suspicion of felony assault on a public servant.

December 23, Texas: Grand jury decides against indictments in the death of Sandra Bland.

2016   January 6, Texas: Grand jury indicts Officer Encinia for misdemeanor perjury related to the arrest of Sandra Bland.

May 23, Maryland: Circuit Judge Barry Williams declares Officer Edward M. Nero not guilty on all charges related to the homicide of Freddie Gray.

June 23, Maryland: Judge Williams declares Officer Caesar R. Goodson, Jr., not guilty on all charges related to the homicide of Freddie Gray.

July 5, Baton Rouge, Louisiana: White police officer Blane Salamoni fatally shoots armed Black thirty-seven-year-old **Alton Sterling.**

July 18, Maryland: Judge Williams declares Baltimore police lieutenant Brian W. Rice not guilty on all charges related to the homicide of Freddie Gray.

July 27, Maryland: After his first trial ends in a jury deadlock, Officer William G. Porter, as well as Officer Garrett E. Miller and Sergeant Alicia D. White, has all charges dropped in the homicide of Freddie Gray.

December 15, South Carolina: Dylann Roof is convicted on thirty-three federal charges, including nine counts of using a firearm to commit murder and twenty-four civil rights violations. (At the jury's recommendation, he is sentenced to death by lethal injection, January 2017.)

2017   February 7, Buffalo, New York: Black twenty-year-old **Wardel ("Meech") Davis** dies of an acute asthma attack during a struggle with police officers Todd C. McAlister and Nicholas J. Parisi.

May 2, Louisiana: U.S. Department of Justice concludes its investigation of the Alton Sterling case, announcing it will not bring charges against the officers involved.

September 12, Maryland: After a two-year investigation, the U.S. Department of Justice announces that it will not bring federal charges against officers involved in Freddie Gray's homicide.

December 13, New York: State Attorney General releases report clearing police officers of any wrongdoing in the death of Meech Davis but "uncover[ing] policies in real need of reform by the Buffalo Police Department and the Erie County Medical Examiner."

2018   March, Louisiana: After State Attorney General concludes its investigation of the shooting death of Alton Sterling, announcing no charges against the officer, Officer Salamoni is fired for violating use of force policies.

2020   February 23, Glynn County, Georgia: Sixty-four-year-old White former police officer Gregory McMichael; his thirty-four-year-old son, Travis; and friend William ("Roddie") Bryan chase and fatally shoot unarmed Black twenty-five-year-old jogger **Ahmaud Arbery.**

March 13, Louisville, Kentucky: Police officers executing a "no-knock" search warrant fatally shoot twenty-six-year-old Black emergency room technician **Breonna Taylor.**

May 7, Georgia: All three suspects in the killing of Ahmaud Arbery are charged with murder and aggravated assault.

May 25, Minneapolis, Minnesota: Unarmed Black forty-six-year-old **George Perry Floyd, Jr.**, dies after forty-four-year-old White police officer Derek Chauvin kneels on his neck while he is lying handcuffed on the ground.

May 29, Minneapolis: Officer Chauvin is arrested for third-degree murder and second-degree manslaughter.

June 24, Georgia: Grand jury indicts all three suspects in the killing of Ahmaud Arbery.

September 23, Kentucky: Grand jury indicts one police officer involved in the Breonna Taylor shooting for wanton endangerment.

2021   March 12, Minneapolis: City officials agree to pay $27 million to settle civil lawsuit filed by the family of George Floyd.

March 31, Georgia: Inspired by the killing of Ahmaud Arbery, state legislature approves bill gutting Civil War–era law allowing citizens to arrest others they suspect of committing a crime.

April 20, Minneapolis: Jury finds former police officer Derek Chauvin guilty on all three charges in the George Floyd case (second-degree unintentional murder, third-degree murder, and second-degree manslaughter).

June 25, Minneapolis: Derek Chauvin is sentenced to twenty-two-and-a-half years in prison.

SELECT BIBLIOGRAPHY

Choosing the poems and essays for this album was extraordinarily difficult. Below we list just a few of the many others we considered, along with important collections either not represented at all here or represented by only one or two selections.

Alexander, Elizabeth. "The Trayvon Generation." *The New Yorker*, 22 June 2020, www .newyorker.com/magazine/2020/06/22/the-trayvon-generation.

Alleyne, Lauren K. "Martin Luther King Jr. Mourns Trayvon Martin." *The Atlantic*, 26 Feb. 2018, www.theatlantic.com/magazine/archive/2018/02/trayvon-martin-martin -luther-king-jr/552596/.

Ashgar, Fatimah. "for mike brown." *PEN America*, 15 July 2015, pen.org/for-mike-brown/.

Bennett, Joshua. "Mike Brown Is a Type of Christ." *The American Poetry Review*, vol. 46, no. 2, aprweb.org/poems/mike-brown-is-a-type-of-christ.

Betts, Reginald Dwayne. *Felon: Poems*. W. W. Norton, 2019.

Brown, Jericho. "Bullet Points." *Poetry Foundation*, www.poetryfoundation.org/poems /152728/bullet-points. Originally published in *The Tradition*, Copper Canyon Press, 2019.

Clark, Tiana. "The Ayes Have It." *I Can't Talk about the Trees without the Blood*, U of Pittsburgh P, 2018, pp. 35–37.

Diaz, Natalie. "American Arithmetic." *Literary Hub*, 5 Oct. 2018, lithub.com/american -arithmetic/. Originally published in *Tales of Two Americas: Stories of Inequality in a Divided Nation*, edited by John Feeman, Penguin, 2017.

Dove, Rita. "Trayvon, Redux." *The Root*, 16 July 2013, www.theroot.com/trayvon-redux -by-rita-dove-1790897314.

Hayes, Terrance. "George Floyd." *The New Yorker*, 22 June 2020, p. 68.

———. *American Sonnets for My Past and Future Assassin*. Penguin, 2018.

Herrera, Juan Felipe. "@ the Crossroads—A Sudden American Poem." *Poem-a-Day*, Academy of American Poets, 10 July 2016.

Jackson, Major. "Ferguson." *Boston Review*, 2 Mar. 2016, bostonreview.net/poetry /major-jackson-ferguson.

Medina, Tony, editor. *Resisting Arrest: Poems to Stretch the Sky*. Jacar Press, 2016.

Rankine, Claudia. *Citizen: An American Lyric*. Graywolf Press, 2014.

———. "The Condition of Black Life Is One of Mourning." *New York Times*, 22 June 2015, www.nytimes.com/2015/06/22/magazine/the-condition-of-black-life-is-one -of-mourning.html.

———. *Just Us: An American Conversation*. Graywolf Press, 2020.

Senior, Olive. "B for Breathe: A Poem for George Floyd." *CBC Books*, 10 June 2020, www.cbc.ca/books/transmission/the-death-of-george-floyd-inspired-this-powerful -poem-by-olive-senior-1.5603544.

Shockley, Evie. *semiautomatic*. Wesleyan UP, 2017.

Smith, Danez. *Don't Call Us Dead*. Graywolf Press, 2017.

———. "We Must Be the New Guards: Open Letter to White Poets." *Squandermania and Other Foibles*, 25 Nov. 2014, donshore.blogspot.com/2014/11/open-letter-to -white-poets-from-danez.html.

Smith, Patricia. *Incendiary Art: Poems*. Northwestern UP, 2017.

Smith, Tracy K. *Wade in the Water: Poems*. Graywolf Press, 2017.

Young, Kevin. *Brown: Poems*. Alfred A. Knopf, 2018.

SUGGESTIONS FOR WRITING

1. Write an essay in which you explore what Patricia Smith's SAGAS OF THE ACCIDEN-TAL SAINTS and/or Reginald Dwayne Betts's WHEN I THINK OF TAMIR RICE WHILE DRIVING suggest about the peculiar challenges faced by Black parents, perhaps by drawing, too, on Danez Smith's NOT AN ELEGY FOR MIKE BROWN and/or Claudia Rankine's essay THE CONDITION OF BLACK LIFE IS ONE OF MOURNING.

2. Write an essay exploring what NOT AN ELEGY FOR MIKE BROWN and at least one other poem in this album suggest about conventional attitudes to the "black / dead" (lines

3–4). How specifically does each poem work to challenge and to change those attitudes?

3. In THE CONDITION OF BLACK LIFE IS ONE OF MOURNING, Claudia Rankine argues that "the associations of blackness with inarticulate, bestial criminality persist," "fram[ing] and determin[ing] our individual interactions and experiences" (par. 10). Write an essay in which you analyze how at least two poems in this album might demonstrate and develop Rankine's claim.

4. Black Lives Matter has become a global rallying cry and movement. Yet Danez Smith's DEAR WHITE AMERICA explicitly addresses an American audience about what it—like at least some other poems in this album, as well as many Harlem Renaissance poems—arguably frames as a peculiarly American situation and history. Write an essay in which you explore this issue, either focusing exclusively on poems and, perhaps, essays in this album or comparing at least one poem from this album to at least one from the Harlem Renaissance.

As the previous Exploring Contexts chapters have suggested, poems draw on all kinds of earlier texts, experiences, and events. But they also produce new contexts of discussion and interpretation, ongoing conversations about the poems themselves. Different readers of poems see different things in them, so naturally a variety of interpretations develop around any poem that is read repeatedly by various readers over many years. Many of those interpretations are published in specialized journals and books (the selections that follow are all reprinted from published sources), and a kind of dialogue develops among readers, producing a body of commentary about the poem. Professional interpreters of texts are called *literary critics*, and the textual analysis they provide is called **literary criticism**— not because their work is necessarily negative or corrective, but because they ask hard, analytical, "critical" questions and interpret texts through a wide variety of literary, historical, biographical, psychological, aesthetic, moral, political, or social lenses.

Your own interpretive work may seem to you more private and far removed from such professional writing about poems. But once you engage in class discussion or talk informally about a poem, you are practicing literary criticism—offering comments, analyzing, judging, putting the poem into some kind of perspective that makes it more intelligible. You are, in effect, joining the ongoing conversation about the poem. And when you *write* about the poem, you implicitly or explicitly engage the opinions of others—your teacher, fellow students, or published critics. You may not have the experience or specific expertise of professional critics, but you can respond to their work and use it in your own.

There are many ways to engage literary criticism and put it to work for you. The most common is to draw on published work for specific information about the poem: glossings of particular terms; explanations of references or situations you don't recognize; accounts of how, when, and under what circumstances the poem was written. Such material, as well as the interpretive claims of critics, can also serve as a springboard for your own interpretation, as you build on what someone else has argued or, if you disagree, use that argument as a point of departure.

When you use the work of others, you must give full credit, carefully indicating the sources of all direct quotations and all borrowed ideas. You must always tell your reader exactly how to find the material you quote, paraphrase, or summarize. Usually, you do this through careful notes and a list of citations (that is, a bibliography) at the end of your paper. (See ch. 33 for help with citation and documentation.)

It is usually best to do your own extensive analysis of a poem *before* consulting other critics. Your own reading experience gives you a legitimate perspective. You always want to take in new information and to challenge both your first impressions and your considered analyses—but don't be too quick simply to adopt somebody else's ideas. The best way to test the views of others is to compare them critically to your own conclusions, which you might then want to supplement, refine, extend, or even scrap altogether. You can sharpen your skills by testing your views against those of people with extensive interpretive experience and specialist expertise. As you will discover, even the experts disagree. One measure of a poem's greatness is its ability to stimulate disagreement and a broad range of interpretation.

Judged by that standard, the poem featured in this chapter is among the very greatest of the twentieth century. First published posthumously in 1965 and famously declared "monstrous" by distinguished Jewish American critic Irving Howe, Sylvia Plath's DADDY has generated countless interpretations and unusually heated debate among a wide array of readers. As the rash of newspaper, magazine, and Web articles that appeared in 2013, the fiftieth anniversary of Plath's suicide, suggest, moreover, it is a debate still very much ongoing. This chapter invites you to enter that debate: Beginning with the poem itself (which is where we hope you, too, will begin), it features excerpts from several especially influential commentaries published over the last fifty years (including Howe's), as well as an exercise and "Suggestions for Writing" designed to help you develop your own informed response to both the poem and its critical context.

SYLVIA PLATH
Daddy

You do not do, you do not do
Any more, black shoe
In which I have lived like a foot
For thirty years, poor and white,
5 Barely daring to breathe or Achoo.

Daddy, I have had to kill you.
You died before I had time—
Marble-heavy, a bag full of God,
Ghastly statue with one gray toe[1]
10 Big as a Frisco seal

And a head in the freakish Atlantic
Where it pours bean green over blue
In the waters off beautiful Nauset.[2]
I used to pray to recover you.
15 Ach, du.[3]

In the German tongue, in the Polish town[4]
Scraped flat by the roller
Of wars, wars, wars.
But the name of the town is common.
20 My Polack friend

1. Otto Plath, Sylvia's father, lost a toe to gangrene resulting from diabetes.
2. Inlet on Cape Cod, Massachusetts.
3. Oh, you (German).
4. Otto Plath, an ethnic German, was born in Grabow, Poland.

Says there are a dozen or two.
So I never could tell where you
Put your foot, your root,
I never could talk to you.
25 The tongue stuck in my jaw.

It stuck in a barb wire snare.
Ich,[5] ich, ich, ich,
I could hardly speak.
I thought every German was you.
30 And the language obscene

An engine, an engine
Chuffing me off like a Jew.
A Jew to Dachau, Auschwitz, Belsen.[6]
I began to talk like a Jew.
35 I think I may well be a Jew.

The snows of the Tyrol, the clear beer of Vienna[7]
Are not very pure or true.
With my gypsy-ancestress and my weird luck
And my Taroc[8] pack and my Taroc pack
40 I may be a bit of a Jew.

I have always been scared of *you*,
With your Luftwaffe,[9] your gobbledygoo.
And your neat moustache
And your Aryan[1] eye, bright blue.
45 Panzer[2]-man, panzer-man, O You—

Not God but a swastika
So black no sky could squeak through.
Every woman adores a Fascist,
The boot in the face, the brute
50 Brute heart of a brute like you.

You stand at the blackboard, daddy,
In the picture I have of you,
A cleft in your chin instead of your foot
But no less a devil for that, no not
55 Any less the black man who

Bit my pretty red heart in two.
I was ten when they buried you.
At twenty I tried to die

5. German for "I."
6. Sites of World War II Nazi death camps.
7. The snow in the Tyrol (an Alpine region in Austria and northern Italy) is, legendarily, as pure as the beer is clear in Vienna.
8. Tarot, playing cards used mainly for fortune-telling.
9. German air force.
1. People of Germanic lineage, often blond-haired and blue-eyed.
2. Literally "panther" (German), the Nazi tank corps's term for an armored vehicle.

Sylvia Plath, 1961

And get back, back, back to you.
60 I thought even the bones would do

But they pulled me out of the sack,
And they stuck me together with glue.[3]
And then I knew what to do.
I made a model of you,
65 A man in black with a Meinkampf[4] look

And a love of the rack and the screw.
And I said I do, I do.
So daddy, I'm finally through.
The black telephone's off at the root,
70 The voices just can't worm through.

If I've killed one man, I've killed two—
The vampire who said he was you
And drank my blood for a year,
Seven years, if you want to know.
75 Daddy, you can lie back now.

There's a stake in your fat black heart
And the villagers never liked you.
They are dancing and stamping on you.
They always *knew* it was you.
80 Daddy, daddy, you bastard, I'm through.

1962   1965

3. Perhaps an allusion to Plath's recovery from her first suicide attempt in 1953.
4. Title of Adolf Hitler's autobiography and manifesto (1925–27); German for "my struggle."

Preparing a Response to Critical Contexts:
An Exercise

Before you read the criticism on Sylvia Plath's "Daddy" reprinted in this chapter, carefully read the poem itself several times. Ask all the analytical questions you have found useful in other cases: Who is speaking? to whom? when? under what conditions? What is the full situation? What kind of language does the poem use? How does the poem use **metaphor**? **allusion**? historical reference? What strategies of rhythm and sound does the poem use? What is the poem's **tone**? When was the poem written, and how does it reflect its time? What do you know about the person who wrote it? In what ways is this poem like others you have read by this poet or by this poet's contemporaries?

Once you have a preliminary "reading" of your own and have noted answers to these questions, look at the selections that follow. In order to come up with ideas for an essay incorporating the selections, you might follow these basic steps:

- Read each critical piece carefully and keep close track of all the things with which you agree and (even more important) disagree.
- Look specifically for information and facts that are new to you; examine the information carefully.
- Look for points of disagreement among the critics, make a list of the most important issues raised, and look for the parts of the poem over which disagreements occur.
- Once you have prepared your notes and absorbed some of the criticism, how do you participate in the debate about Sylvia Plath's poem? Here are some possible topics for an essay that draws on published criticism:
  - *Your essay could show that others have overlooked or misinterpreted something significant.* Do critics ignore something in or about the poem that should be explored? Do they make some observation or claim in passing that seems worthy of further consideration?
  - *Your essay could be an overview of critical trends in the study of this poem, making clear which interpretations you find helpful, and where your own interpretation differs from others.* Sort the critics into two or three groups according to their interpretation of "Daddy." Which critics place the most emphasis on Plath's psychology, personal experience, and self-expression? Which critics stress her development as a poet with a specific style? Which critics highlight her social criticism, either of anti-Semitism and the Holocaust or of sexism and women's oppression, or both? (See "Critical Approaches" for help identifying and describing the approaches of these critics or groups of critics.)
- In one or two sentences, write a **thesis** statement expressing your views on various critical approaches, such as the following:

° Criticism of Sylvia Plath's "Daddy" has gone too far with a biographical approach, whereas myth criticism would facilitate a better understanding of the poem.

° The life of Sylvia Plath provides a key to a reading of her poem "Daddy." As suggested by critics (including George Steiner, A. Alvarez, and Steven Gould Axelrod) and biographical sources, the poem expresses violent emotional aspects of her life, including her unresolved attachment to her father, Otto Plath; her power struggle with her husband, Ted Hughes; and her suicide attempt.

° Feminist readings of Sylvia Plath's "Daddy" have taken different approaches: Some focus on biographical evidence of Plath's experience as a woman, whereas others, such as Margaret Homans's "A Feminine Tradition," consider a "literal" identification of the woman poet with the female speaker of the poem to be a reinforcement of the idea that women can never escape their personal, physical lives. This essay balances these feminist approaches to "Daddy," examining it as a semi-autobiographical dramatic monologue: The speaker responds to some experiences Plath had as a daughter and wife, but the poem is not wholly autobiographical.

See also the writing suggestions at the end of this chapter.

CRITICAL EXCERPTS

GEORGE STEINER

From Dying Is an Art (1967)[1]

Sylvia Plath's last poems have already passed into legend as both representative of our present tone of emotional life and unique in their implacable, harsh brilliance [. . .].

The spell does not lie wholly in the poems themselves. The suicide of Sylvia Plath at the age of thirty-one in 1963, and the personality of this young woman who had come from Massachusetts to study and live in England (where she married Ted Hughes, himself a gifted poet), are vital parts of it. To those who knew her and to the greatly enlarged circle who were electrified by her last poems and sudden death, she had come to signify the specific honesties and risks of the poet's condition. Her personal style, and the price in private harrowing she so obviously paid to achieve the intensity and candor of her principal poems, have taken on their own dramatic authority.

All this makes it difficult to judge the poems. I mean that the vehemence and intimacy of the verse is such as to constitute a very powerful rhetoric of

---

1. George Steiner, "Dying Is an Art." 1965. *Language and Silence: Essays on Language, Literature, and the Inhuman*, Atheneum, 1974, pp. 295–302. All footnotes have been added by the editor.

sincerity. The poems play on our nerves with their own proud nakedness, making claims so immediate and sharply urged that the reader flinches, embarrassed by the routine discretions and evasions of his own sensibility. Yet if these poems are to take life among us, if they are to be more than exhibits in the history of modern psychological stress, they must be read with all the intelligence and scruple we can muster. They are too honest, they have cost too much, to be yielded to myth.

It requires no biographical impertinence to realize that Sylvia Plath's life was harried by bouts of physical pain, that she sometimes looked on the accumulated exactions of her own nerve and body as "a trash / To annihilate each decade."[2] She was haunted by the piecemeal, strung-together mechanics of the flesh. [. . .] The hospital ward was her exemplary ground:

> My patent leather overnight case like a black pillbox,
> My husband and child smiling out of the family photo;
> Their smiles catch onto my skin, little smiling hooks.[3]

This brokenness, so sharply feminine and contemporary, is, I think, her principal realization [. . .]. This new frankness of women about the specific hurts and tangles of their nervous-physiological makeup is as vital to the poetry of Sylvia Plath as it is to the tracts of Simone de Beauvoir[4] or to the novels of Edna O'Brien and Brigid Brophy.[5] Women speak out as never before [. . .].

* * *

Where Emily Dickinson could—indeed was obliged to—shut the door on the riot and humiliations of the flesh, thus achieving her particular dry lightness, Sylvia Plath "fully assumed her own condition." This alone would assure her of a place in modern literature. But she took one step further, assuming a burden that was not naturally or necessarily hers.

Born in Boston in 1932 of German and Austrian parents, Sylvia Plath had no personal, immediate contact with the world of the concentration camps. I may be mistaken, but so far as I know there was nothing Jewish in her background. But her last, greatest poems culminate in an act of identification, of total communion with those tortured and massacred. [Here Steiner quotes lines 31–40 of "Daddy."]

Sylvia Plath is only one of a number of young contemporary poets, novelists, and playwrights, themselves in no way implicated in the actual holocaust, who

2. Steiner here quotes Plath's "Lady Lazarus" (lines 23–24; p. 1205).
3. Plath, "Tulips" (1962), lines 19–21.
4. French philosopher (1908–86) best known as author of *The Second Sex* (1949), a foundational text of modern feminism.
5. Irish novelist, essayist, and dramatist (1929–95) and vocal champion of women's and animal rights. *Edna O'Brien*: Irish novelist (b. 1930).

have done most to counter the general inclination to forget the death camps. Perhaps it is only those who had no part in the events who *can* focus on them rationally and imaginatively; to those who experienced the thing, it has lost the hard edges of possibility, it has stepped outside the real.

Committing the whole of her poetic and formal authority to the metaphor, to the mask of language, Sylvia Plath *became* a woman being transported to Auschwitz on the death trains. The notorious shards of massacre seemed to enter into her own being:

> A cake of soap,
> A wedding ring,
> A gold filling.[6]

In "Daddy" she wrote one of the very few poems I know of in any language to come near the last horror. It achieves the classic act of generalization, translating a private, obviously intolerable hurt into a code of plain statement, of instantaneously public images which concern us all. It is the "Guernica"[7] of modern poetry. And it is both histrionic and, in some ways, "arty," as is Picasso's outcry.

Pablo Picasso, *Guernica* (1937)

Are these final poems entirely legitimate? In what sense does anyone, himself uninvolved and long after the event, commit a subtle larceny when he invokes the echoes and trappings of Auschwitz and appropriates an enormity of ready emotion to his own private design? Was there latent in Sylvia Plath's sensibility, as in that of many of us who remember only by fiat of imagination, a fearful envy, a dim resentment at not having been there, of having missed the rendezvous with hell? In "Lady Lazarus" and "Daddy" the realization seems to me so complete, the sheer rawness and control so great, that only irresistible need could have brought it off. These poems take tremendous risks, extending Sylvia Plath's essentially austere manner to the very limit. They are a bitter triumph, proof of the capacity of poetry to give to reality the greater permanence of the imagined. She could not return from them.

6. Plath, "Lady Lazarus" (lines 76–78; p. 1205).
7. Pablo Picasso's famous painting (1937) depicting the brutalities of war.

A. ALVAREZ

From Sylvia Plath (1968)[1]

The reasons for Sylvia Plath's images are always there, though sometimes you have to work hard to find them. She is, in short, always in intelligent control of her feelings. Her work bears out her theories:

> I think my poems come immediately out of the sensuous and emotional experiences I have, but I must say I cannot sympathise with these cries from the heart that are informed by nothing except a needle or a knife or whatever it is. I believe that one should be able to control and manipulate experiences, even the most terrifying—like madness, being tortured, this kind of experience— and one should be able to manipulate these experiences with an informed and intelligent mind. I think that personal experience shouldn't be a kind of shut box and mirror-looking narcissistic experience. I believe it should be generally relevant, to such things as Hiroshima and Dachau, and so on.

It seems to me that it was only by her determination both to face her most inward and terrifying experiences and to use her intelligence in doing so—so as not to be overwhelmed by them—that she managed to write these extraordinary last poems, which are at once deeply autobiographical and yet detached, generally relevant.

[. . .] She assumes the suffering of all the modern victims. Above all, she becomes an imaginary Jew. I think this is a vitally important element in her work. For two reasons. First, because anyone whose subject is suffering has a ready-made modern example of hell on earth in the concentration camps. And what matters in them is not so much the physical torture—since sadism is general and perennial—but the way modern, as it were industrial, techniques can be used to destroy utterly the human identity. [. . .] This anonymity of pain, which makes all dignity impossible, was Sylvia Plath's subject. Second, she seemed convinced, in these last poems, that the root of her suffering was the death of her father, whom she loved, who abandoned her, and who dragged her after him into death. And in her fantasies her father was pure German, pure Aryan, pure anti-semite.

It all comes together in the most powerful of her last poems, "Daddy," about which she wrote the following bleak note:

> The poem is spoken by a girl with an Electra complex. Her father died while she thought he was God. Her case is complicated by the fact that her father was also a Nazi and her mother very possibly part Jewish. In the daughter the two strains marry and paralyse each other—she has to act out the awful little allegory once over before she is free of it.[2]

---

1. A. Alvarez, "Sylvia Plath." *Beyond All This Fiddle: Essays, 1955–1967*, Penguin, 1968, pp. 56–57.
2. From the introductory notes to "New Poems," a reading prepared for the BBC Third Programme but never broadcast [Alvarez's note]. *Electra complex* is the psychoanalytic term for a girl's sense of competition with her mother for her father's affection, coined by Carl Jung (1875–1961) and alluding to the eponymous heroine of Sophocles's tragedy *Electra*. In the play, Electra and her brother conspire to kill their mother to avenge their father's murder.

[. . .] What comes through most powerfully, I think, is the terrible *unforgiving-ness* of her verse, the continual sense not so much of violence—although there is a good deal of that—as of violent resentment that this should have been done to *her*. What she does in the poem is, with a weird detachment, to turn the violence against herself so as to show that she can equal her oppressors with her self-inflicted oppression. And this is the strategy of the concentration camps. When suffering is there whatever you do, by inflicting it upon yourself you achieve your identity, you set yourself free.

Yet the tone of the poem, like its psychological mechanisms, is not single or simple, and she uses a great deal of skill to keep it complex. Basically, her trick is to tell this horror story in a verse form as insistently jaunty and ritualistic as a nursery rhyme. And this helps her to maintain towards all the protagonists—her father, her husband and herself—a note of hard and sardonic anger, as though she were almost amused that her own suffering should be so extreme, so grotesque. [. . .] When she first read me the poem a few days after she wrote it, she called it a piece of "light verse." It obviously isn't, yet equally obviously it also isn't the racking personal confession that a mere description or précis of it might make it sound.

Yet neither is it unchangingly vindictive or angry. The whole poem works on one single, returning note and rhyme, echoing from start to finish:

> You do not do, you do not do . . .
> . . . I used to pray to recover you.
> Ach, du . . .

There is a kind of cooing tenderness in this which complicates the other, more savage note of resentment. It brings in an element of pity, less for herself and her own suffering than for the person who made her suffer. Despite everything, "Daddy" is a love poem.

IRVING HOWE

From The Plath Celebration: A Partial Dissent (1973)[1]

Sylvia Plath's most famous poem, adored by many sons and daughters, is "Daddy." It is a poem with an affecting theme, the feelings of the speaker as she regathers the pain of her father's premature death and her persuasion that he has betrayed her by dying:

> I was ten when they buried you.
> At twenty I tried to die
> And get back, back, back to you.

In the poem Sylvia Plath identifies the father (we recall his German birth) with the Nazis ("Panzer-man, panzer-man, O You") and flares out with assaults for which nothing in the poem (nor, so far as we know, in Sylvia Plath's own life) offers any warrant: "A cleft in your chin instead of your foot / But no less a devil

---

1. Irving Howe, "The Plath Celebration: A Partial Dissent." 1973. *The Critical Point of Literature and Culture*, Horizon Press, 1977, pp. 231–33. All footnotes have been added by the editor.

for that. . . ." Nor does anything in the poem offer warrant, other than the free-flowing hysteria of the speaker, for the assault of such lines as, "There's a stake in your fat black heart / And the villagers never liked you." [. . .]

What we have here is a revenge fantasy, feeding upon filial love-hatred, and thereby mostly of clinical interest. But seemingly aware that the merely clinical can't provide the materials for a satisfying poem, Sylvia Plath tries to enlarge upon the personal plight, give meaning to the personal outcry, by fancying the girl as victim of a Nazi father: "An engine, an engine / Chuffing me off like a Jew. . . ."

The more sophisticated admirers of this poem may say that I fail to see it as a dramatic presentation, a monologue spoken by a disturbed girl not necessarily to be identified with Sylvia Plath, despite the similarities of detail between the events of the poem and the events of her life. I cannot accept this view. The personal-confessional element, strident and undisciplined, is simply too obtrusive to suppose the poem no more than a dramatic picture of a certain style of disturbance. If, however, we did accept such a reading of "Daddy," we would fatally narrow its claims to emotional or moral significance, for we would be confining it to a mere vivid imagining of a pathological state. That, surely, is not how its admirers really take the poem.

It is clearly not how the critic George Steiner takes the poem when he calls it "the 'Guernica' of modern poetry."[2] But then, in an astonishing turn, he asks: "In what sense does anyone, himself uninvolved and long after the event, commit a subtle larceny when he invokes the echoes and trappings of Auschwitz and appropriates an enormity of ready emotion to his own private design?" The question is devastating to his early comparison with "Guernica." Picasso's painting objectifies the horrors of Guernica, through the distancing of art; no one can suppose that he shares or participates in them. Plath's poem aggrandizes on the "enormity of ready emotion" invoked by references to the concentration camps, in behalf of an ill-controlled if occasionally brilliant outburst. There is something monstrous, utterly disproportionate, when tangled emotions about one's father are deliberately compared with the historical fate of the European Jews; something sad, if the comparison is made spontaneously. "Daddy" persuades once again, through the force of negative example, of how accurate T. S. Eliot was in saying, "The more perfect the artist, the more completely separate in him will be the man who suffers and the mind which creates."[3]

---

2. See above, p. 1165 and footnote 7. Picasso's painting was inspired by the German and Italian air assault on Guernica, a village in northern Spain, on April 26, 1937, during the Spanish Civil War.
3. In "Tradition and the Individual Talent" (1919).

JUDITH KROLL

From Rituals of Exorcism: "Daddy" (1976)[1]

Poems explicitly about the protagonist's father, read in order of composition, show that the attitude toward him evolves from nostalgic mournfulness, regret, and guilt, to resentment and a bitter resolve to break his hold on her. [. . .]

The recital of the myth in "Daddy" ends in a ritual intended to cancel the earlier "sacred marriage" which has suffocated her:

> You do not do, you do not do
> Any more, black shoe
> In which I have lived like a foot
> For thirty years, poor and white,
> Barely daring to breathe or Achoo.[2]

In this image of passive and victimized domesticity, the speaker implicitly compares her past self to the "old woman who lived in a shoe" who "didn't know what to do"; now, however, she makes it clear that she does know what to do.

As a preamble to the exorcism, [. . .] Daddy must be cast in this new light, transformed from god to devil, if he is to be successfully expelled, but there must also be some real basis for it. To be effectively exposed, he must first appear as godly. But the speaker soon shows that she now attributes his godliness in part to his authoritarianism and personal inaccessibility—qualities which became intensified through his death, and which later became transferred to "a model of you"—her husband. [. . .] Loving a man literally or metaphorically dead [. . .] becomes a kind of persecution or punishment; and so, by the end of the incantation, Daddy deserves to be cast out. The "black telephone . . . off at the root," conveys the finality of the intended exorcism.

The "venomousness," ambiguous from the beginning, is not the whole story. "Daddy" is not primarily a poem of "father-hatred" or abuse as Robert Lowell, Elizabeth Hardwick, and others have contended. The need for exorcising her father's ghost lies, after all, in the extremity of her attachment to him. Alvarez very justly remarks that [. . .] "'Daddy' is a love poem."[3] [. . .] The love is not merely conveyed by the rhythm and sound of the poem, it is a necessary part of the poem's meaning, a part of the logic of its act.

The exorcism serves another purpose because through it she attempts to reject the pattern of being abandoned and made to suffer by a god, a man who is "chock-full of power": she creates "a model of you"—an image of her father—and marries this proxy. Then she kills both father and husband at once, magically

---

1. Judith Kroll, "Rituals of Exorcism: 'Daddy.'" *Chapters in a Mythology: The Poetry of Sylvia Plath*, Harper and Row, 1976, pp. 122–26. Unless otherwise indicated, all notes are Kroll's.

2. When Plath introduced "Daddy" as being about "a girl with an Electra complex" (with, in effect, the female version of an Oedipus complex), she gave a clue to what may be a play on words in the poem. "Oedipus" means "swell-foot," and therefore the speaker's identification of herself as a "foot" may be a private way of saying "I am Oedipus" and incorporating into the poem an allusion to the Electra complex.

3. Alvarez, "Sylvia Plath" [see p. 1166].

using each as the other's representative.[4] Each death entails that of the other: the stake in her father's heart also kills the "vampire who said he was you"; and the killing of her marriage (for which she now claims to take responsibility, as she does for having allowed her marriage to perpetuate, by proxy, her relationship to her father) finally permits Daddy to "lie back." The marriage to and killing of her father by proxy are acts of what Frazer[5] calls "sympathetic magic," in which "things act on each other at a distance through a secret sympathy." [. . .]

Plath was familiar with and used such ideas. [. . .] The notion that "as the image suffers, so does the man"—affecting the real subject through a proxy— nicely describes marriage to a model of Daddy, and explains why "If I've killed one man, I've killed two." The earlier attempt of the speaker in "Daddy" to recover her father also involved sympathetic magic; she had tried to rejoin him by dying and becoming like him:

> At twenty I tried to die
> And get back, back, back to you.

She finally exorcises her father as if he were a scapegoat invested with the evils of her spoiled history. Frazer's discussion of rituals in which the dying god is also a scapegoat is germane here. He conjectures that two originally separate rituals merged. [. . . T]he father in "Daddy" may well be described as such a divine scapegoat figure.

MARY LYNN BROE

From Protean Poetic: The Poetry of Sylvia Plath (1980)[1]

Among the other poems that display the performing self, "Daddy" and "Lady Lazarus" are two of the most often quoted, but most frequently misunderstood, poems in the Plath canon. The speaker in "Daddy" performs a mock poetic exorcism of an event that has already happened—the death of her father, who she feels withdrew his love from her by dying prematurely: "Daddy, I have had to kill you. / You died before I had time—."

The speaker attempts to exorcise not just the memory of her father but her own *Mein Kampf* model of him as well as her inherited behavioral traits that lead her graveward under the Freudian banner of death instinct or Thanatos's[2] libido. But her ritual reenactment simply does not take. The event comically backfires as pure self-parody: the metaphorical murder of the father dwindles into Hollywood spectacle, while the poet is lost in the clutter of the collective unconscious.[3]

---

4. The biographical basis for this identification is evident in *Letters Home*. [. . .]

5. Sir James George Frazer (1854–1941), Scottish anthropologist whose book *The Golden Bough* analyzes early religious and magical practices [editor's note].

1. Mary Lynn Broe, *Protean Poetic: The Poetry of Sylvia Plath*. U of Missouri P, 1980. The following excerpt appears on pages 172–75. Unless otherwise indicated, all footnotes have been added by the editor.

2. In Greek mythology, Thanatos is a personification of death.

3. According to psychologist Carl Jung (1875–1961), a reservoir of memories and images shared by all, but inaccessible to the conscious mind.

Early in the poem, the ritual gets off on the wrong foot both literally and figuratively. A sudden rhythmic break midway through the first stanza interrupts the insistent and mesmeric chant of the poet's own freedom:

> You do not do, you do not do
> Any more, black shoe
> In which I have lived like a foot
> For thirty years, poor and white,
> Barely daring to breathe or Achoo.

The break suggests, on the one hand, that the nursery-rhyme world of contained terror is here abandoned; on the other, that the poet-exorcist's mesmeric control is superficial, founded in a shaky faith and an unsure heart—the worst possible state for the strong, disciplined exorcist.

At first she kills her father succinctly with her own words, demythologizing him to a ludicrous piece of statuary that is hardly a Poseidon or the Colossus of Rhodes.[4] [. . .]

Then as she tries to patch together the narrative of him, his tribal myth (the "common" town, the "German tongue," the war-scraped culture), she begins to lose her own powers of description to a senseless Germanic prattle ("The tongue stuck in my jaw. / It stuck in a barb wire snare. / Ich, ich, ich, ich"). The individual man is absorbed by his inhuman archetype, the "panzer man," "an engine / Chuffing me off like a Jew." Losing the exorcist's power that binds the spirit and then casts out the demon, she is the classic helpless victim of the swastika man. As she calls up her own picture of him as a devil, he refuses to adopt this stereotype. Instead he jumbles his trademark:

> A cleft in your chin instead of your foot
> But no less a devil for that, no not
> Any less the black man who
>
> Bit my pretty red heart in two.

The overt Nazi-Jew allegory throughout the poem suggests that, by a simple inversion of power, father and daughter grow more alike. But when she tries to imitate his action of dying, making all the appropriate grand gestures, she once again fails: "but they pulled me out of the sack, / And they stuck me together with glue." She retreats to a safe world of icons and replicas, but even the doll image she constructs turns out to be "the vampire who said he was you." At last, she abandons her father to the collective unconscious where it is *he* who is finally recognized ("they always *knew* it was you"). *She* is lost, impersonally absorbed by his irate persecutors, bereft of both her power and her conjuror's discipline, and possessed by the incensed villagers. The exorcist's ritual, one of purifying, cleansing, commanding silence and then ordering the evil spirit's departure, has dwindled to a comic picture from the heart of darkness. Mad villagers stamp on the devil-vampire creation. [. . .]

[. . .] It would seem that the real victim is the poet-performer who, despite her straining toward identification with the public events of holocaust and

---

4. One of the seven wonders of the ancient world, a gigantic statue of the Greek sun god, Helios. *Poseidon:* the chief sea god in the Greek pantheon.

destruction of World War II, becomes more murderously persecuting than the "panzer-man" who smothered her, and who abandoned her with a paradoxical love, guilt, and fear. [. . .]

The failure of the exorcism and the emotional ambivalence are echoed in the curious rhythm. The incantatory safety of the nursery-rhyme thump (seemingly one of controlled, familiar terrors) also suggests some sinister brooding by its repetition. The poem opens with a suspiciously emphatic protest, a kind of psychological whistling-in-the-dark. As it proceeds, "Daddy"'s continuous life-rhythms— the assonance, consonance, and especially the sustained *oo* sounds—triumph over either the personal or the cultural-historical imagery. The sheer sense of organic life in the interwoven sounds carries the verse forward in boisterous spirit and communicates an underlying feeling of comedy that is also echoed in the repeated failure of the speaker to perform her exorcism.

Ultimately, "Daddy" is like an emotional, psychological, and historical autopsy, a final report. There is no real progress. The poet is in the same place in the beginning as in the end. [. . .] Although it seems that the speaker has moved from identification with the persecuted to identity as persecutor, Jew to vampire-killer, powerless to powerful, she has simply enacted a performance that allows her to live with what is unchangeable. She has used her art to stave off suffocation, and performs her self-contempt with a degree of bravado.[5]

MARGARET HOMANS
From A Feminine Tradition (1982)[1]

The current belief in a literal "I" present in poetry is responsible for the popular superstition that Sylvia Plath's death was the purposeful completion of her poetry's project, the assumption being that if the speaker is precisely the same as the biographical Plath, the poetry's self-destructive violence is directed toward Plath herself, not toward an imagined speaker. This reading of Plath is unfair to the woman and, by calling it merely unmediated self-expression, obscures her poetry's real power. In poem after poem depicting or wishing for physical violence, the imagery of violence is part of a symmetrical figurative system, and death is figured as a way of achieving rebirth or some other transcendence.[2] Plath's project may not thus be very different from that of [Emily] Dickinson, who speaks quite often from beyond the grave, reimagining and repossessing death as her own in order to dispel the terrors of literal death. However, within that figurative system the poet embraces a self-destructive program that must soon have been poetically terminal, even if it did not bring about the actual death.

5. What remains the most thorough and enlightening account of the poem is A. R. Jones, "On 'Daddy,'" *The Art of Sylvia Plath*, [ed. Newman,] pp. 230–36 [Broe's note].

1. Margaret Homans, "A Feminine Tradition." *Women Writers and Poetic Identity: Dorothy Words- worth, Emily Brontë, and Emily Dickinson*, Princeton UP, 1982, pp. 218–21.

2. I am indebted here, for their persuasively positive readings of Plath, to Judith Kroll, *Chapters in a Mythology: The Poetry of Sylvia Plath* (New York: Harper & Row, 1976), and to Stacy Pies, "Coming Clear of the Shadow: The Poetry of Sylvia Plath," unpublished essay (Yale University, 1979) [Homans's note].

Several of Plath's late poems come to terms with a father figure (who may include the poetic fathers she acknowledges in *The Colossus*), whose crime, no different from that identified by nineteenth-century women, is of attempting to transform the feminine self into objects.

"Daddy" uses Nazi imagery to make the same accusation about objectification brought against men as oppressors in "Lady Lazarus" and makes the corollary accusation against the father (and the husband modelled after him) that objectification has silenced her: "I never could talk to you. / . . . I could hardly speak." In this context defiance and retribution take the form of her speaking, but again this counterattack is counterproductive. Punning on the expression "being through" to mean both establishing a telephone connection and being finished, she at once makes and conclusively severs communication:

> So daddy, I'm finally through.
> The black telephone's off at the root,
> The voices just can't worm through.

The poem concludes, "Daddy, daddy, you bastard, I'm through." Suppressing the power of the one who silenced her, she simultaneously returns herself to the silence that the poem came into being to protest.

PAMELA J. ANNAS

From A Disturbance in Mirrors: The Poetry of Sylvia Plath (1988)[1]

The particular sexual metaphor in "Daddy" is sado-masochism, which stands for the authority structure of a partriarchal and war-making society. [. . .] "Daddy" is an analysis of the structure of the society in which the individual is enmeshed. Intertwined with the image of sadist and masochist in "Daddy" is a parallel image of vampire and victim. In "Daddy," father, husband, and a larger patriarchal and competitive authority structure, which the speaker of the poem sees as having been responsible for the various imperialisms of the twentieth century, all melt together and become demonic, finally a gigantic vampire figure. In the modulation from one image to another to form an accumulated image that is characteristic of many of Plath's late poems, the male figure at the center of "Daddy" takes four major forms: the statue, the Gestapo officer, the professor, and the vampire. The poem begins, however, with an image of a black shoe, an image which, like the black shoe in "The Munich Mannequins" and like the black suit in "The Applicant," can be seen to stand for corporate man. The second stanza of the poem refers back to the title poem of *The Colossus*, where the speaker's father, representative of a gigantic male other, so dominated

1. Pamela J. Annas, *A Disturbance in Mirrors: The Poetry of Sylvia Plath*. Greenwood Press, 1988. Contributions in Women's Studies 89. The following excerpt appears on pages 139–43. All notes are Annas's.

her world that her horizon was bounded by his scattered pieces. [. . .] Here the image of her father, grown larger than the earlier Colossus of Rhodes, stretches across and subsumes the whole of the United States, from the Pacific to the Atlantic ocean.

The next seven stanzas of "Daddy" construct the image of the Gestapo officer, using her family background—her parents were both of German origin—to mediate between her personal sense of suffocation and the social history of the Nazi invasions. The black shoe of the first stanza in which she says she has been wedged like a foot "barely daring to breathe" becomes in stanza ten, at the end of the Nazi section, a larger social image of suffocation: "Not God but a swastika / So black no sky could squeak through." The Gestapo figure recurs briefly three stanzas later as the speaker of the poem transfers the image from father to husband and incidentally suggests that the victim has some control in a brutalized association—at least to the extent she chooses to be there.[2] "I made a model of you, . . . And I said I do, I do." The Gestapo figure becomes "Herr Professor" in stanza eleven, an actual image of Plath's father, and also an image of what has for centuries been seen as the prototypical and even ideal relationship between a man and a woman.[3] The professor, who is a man, talks and is active; the woman, who is a student, listens and is passive. [. . .] But Plath places this image between the images of Nazi/Jew and vampire/victim so that it becomes the center of a series. Indeed, the image of daddy as teacher turns almost immediately into a devil/demon/vampire. [. . .]

The last two stanzas of "Daddy" are like the conclusion of "Lady Lazarus" in their assertion that the speaker of the poem is breaking out of the cycle and that, in order to do so, she must turn on and kill Herr God, Herr Lucifer in the one poem, and Daddy in his final metamorphosis as vampire in the other poem [. . .].

The cycle of victim/vampire is, left alone, a closed and repetitious cycle, like the repeated suicides of "Lady Lazarus." According to the legends and the Hollywood film versions of these legends we all grew up on, once consumed by a vampire, one dies and is reborn a vampire and preys upon others, who in their turn die and become vampires. The vampire imagery in Sylvia Plath's poetry intersects on one level with her World War II imagery and its exploitation and victimization and on another level intersects with her images of a bureaucratic, fragmented, and dead—in the sense of numbed and unaware—society. The connections are sometimes confused, but certainly World War II is often imaged in her poetry as a kind of grisly, vampiric feast. [. . .]

The whole of "Daddy" is an exorcism to banish the demon, put a stake through the vampire's heart, and thus break the cycle of vampire → victim. It is

2. See Wilhelm Reich's *The Mass Psychology of Fascism* (New York: Simon and Schuster, 1969), particularly his chapter on "The Authoritarian Personality," for an analysis of how an oppressed class can contribute to its own oppression. Judith Lewis Herman, in *Father-Daughter Incest* (Cambridge, Mass.: Harvard University Press, 1981), discusses the history of the suppression of incest beginning with Freud and continuing into contemporary psychological literature, the attribution of reports of incest to hysterical female oedipal fantasizing or, when the fact of incest is impossible to deny, assigning blame to the victim: what Herman calls the Seductive Daughter and/or the Collusive Mother (Chapter 1, "A Common Occurrence"). Writing in the early 1960s and familiar with some of these attitudes, [. . .] Plath assigns some culpability to the victim.
3. This photograph of Otto Plath is reproduced on page 17 of *Letters Home*.

crucial to the poem that the exorcism is accomplished through communal action by the "villagers." The rhythm of the poem is powerfully and deliberately primitive: a child's chant, a formal curse. The hard sounds, short lines, and repeated rhymes of "do," "you," "Jew," and "through" give a hard pounding quality to the poem that is close to the sound of a heart beat. [. . .]

Purity, which is what exorcism aims at, is for Plath an ambiguous concept. On the one hand it means integrity of self, wholeness rather than fragmentation, an unspoiled state of being, rest, perfection, aesthetic beauty, and loss of self through transformation into some reborn other. On the other hand, it also means absence, isolation, blindness, a kind of autism which shuts out the world, stasis and death, and a loss of self through dispersal into some other. In "Lady Lazarus" and "Fever 103°" the emphasis is on exorcising the poet's previous selves, though within a social context that makes that unlikely. "Daddy," however, is a purification of the world; in "Daddy" it is the various avatars of the other—the male figure who represents the patriarchal society she lives in—that are being exorcised. [. . .] The more the speaker of the poems defines her situation as desperate, the more violent and vengeful becomes the agent of purification and transformation.

STEVEN GOULD AXELROD

From Sylvia Plath: The Wound and the Cure of Words (1990)[1]

Although this poem too ["Daddy"] has traditionally been read as "personal" (Aird 78) or "confessional" (M. L. Rosenthal 82), Margaret Homans has more recently suggested that it concerns a woman's dislocated relations to speech (*Women Writers* 220–21). Plath herself introduced it on the BBC as the opposite of confession, as a constructed fiction: "Here is a poem spoken by a girl with an Electra complex. [. . .]" (*CP* 293).[2] [. . .] However we interpret Plath's preface, we must agree that "Daddy" is dramatic and allegorical, since its details depart freely from the facts of her biography. In this poem she [. . .] figures her unresolved conflicts with paternal authority as a textual issue. Significantly, her father was a published writer, and his successor, her husband, was also a writer. Her preface asserts that the poem concerns a young woman's paralyzing self-division, which she can defeat only through allegorical representation. Recalling that paralysis was one of Plath's main tropes for literary incapacity, we begin to see that the poem evokes the female poet's anxiety of authorship and specifically Plath's strategy of delivering herself from that anxiety by making it the topic of her discourse. Viewed from this perspective, "Daddy" enacts the woman poet's struggle with "daddy-poetry." It represents her effort to reject the "buried male muse" from her invention process and the "jealous gods" from her audience (*J* 223; *CP* 179).[3]

1. Steven Gould Axelrod, *Sylvia Plath: The Wound and the Cure of Words*. Johns Hopkins UP, 1990. The excerpts below appear on pages 51–70. All footnotes have been added by the editor, and Axelrod's bibliography has been abbreviated.
2. For the full quotation, see the Alvarez excerpt above. *CP* is Axelrod's abbreviation for Plath's *Collected Poems*.
3. *J* is Axelrod's abbreviation for Plath's *Journals*.

Plath wrote "Daddy" several months after Hughes left her, on the day she learned that he had agreed to a divorce (October 12, 1962). George Brown and Tirril Harris have shown that early loss makes one especially vulnerable to subsequent loss (Bowlby 250–59), and Plath seems to have defended against depression by almost literally throwing herself into her poetry. She followed "Daddy" with a host of poems that she considered her greatest achievement to date: "Medusa," "The Jailer," "Lady Lazarus," "Ariel," the bee sequence, and others. The letters she wrote to her mother and brother on the day of "Daddy," and then again four days later, brim with a sense of artistic self-discovery: "Writing like mad. . . . Terrific stuff, as if domesticity had choked me" (*LH* 466).[4] Composing at the "still blue, almost eternal hour before the baby's cry, before the glassy music of the milkman, setting his bottles" (quoted in Alvarez, *Savage God* 21), she experienced an "enormous" surge in creative energy (*LH* 467). [. . . S]he wrote "Daddy" to demonstrate the existence of her voice, which had been silent or subservient for so long. She wrote it to prove her "genius" (*LH* 468).

Plath projected her struggle for textual identity onto the figure of a partly Jewish young woman who learns to express her anger at the patriarch and at his language of male mastery, which is as foreign to her as German, as "obscene" as murder (st. 6),[5] and as meaningless as "gobbledygoo" (st. 9). [. . .] At a basic level, "Daddy" concerns its own violent, transgressive birth as a text, its origin in a culture that regards it as illegitimate—a judgment the speaker hurls back on the patriarch himself when she labels *him* a bastard (st. 16). Plath's unaccommodating worldview, which was validated by much in her childhood and adult experience, led her to understand literary tradition not as an expanding universe of beneficial influence [. . .] but as a closed universe in which every addition required a corresponding subtraction [. . .]. If Plath's speaker was to be born as a poet, a patriarch must die.

As in "The Colossus," the father here appears as a force or an object rather than as a person. Initially he takes the form of an immense "black shoe," capable of stamping on his victim (st. 1). Immediately thereafter he becomes a marble "statue" (st. 2) [. . .]. He then transforms into Nazi Germany (st. 6–7, 9–10), the archetypal totalitarian state. [. . .] Eventually the father declines in stature from God (st. 2) to a devil (st. 11) to a dying vampire (st. 15). Perhaps he shrinks under the force of his victim's denunciation, which de-creates him as a power as it creates him as a figure. But whatever his size, he never assumes human dimensions, aspirations, and relations—except when posing as a teacher in a photograph (st. 11). Like the colossus, he remains figurative and symbolic, not individual.

[. . . Unlike the father figure in "The Colossus,"] "Daddy" remains silent, apart from the gobbledygoo attributed to him once (st. 9). He uses his mouth primarily for biting and for drinking blood. The poem emphasizes his feet and, implicitly, his phallus. He is a "black shoe" (st. 1), a statue with "one gray toe" (st. 2), a "boot" (st. 10). [. . . The speaker] is herself silenced by his shoe: "I never could talk to you" (st. 5). Daddy is [. . .] a male censor. His boot in the face of "every woman" is presumably lodged in her mouth (st. 10). He stands for all the ele-

---

4. *LH* is Axelrod's abbreviation for Plath's *Letters Home*.
5. When referring to "Daddy," Axelrod cites stanza (st.) rather than line numbers.

ments in the literary situation and in the female ephebe's[6] internalization of it, that prevent her from producing any words at all, even copied or subservient ones. Appropriately, Daddy can be killed only by being stamped on: he lives and dies by force, not language. If "The Colossus" tells a tale of the patriarch's speech, [. . .] "Daddy" tells a tale of the daughter's effort to speak.

Thus we are led to another important difference between the two poems. The "I" of "The Colossus" acquires her identity only through serving her "father," whereas the "I" of "Daddy" actuates her gift only through opposition to him. The later poem precisely inscribes the plot of Plath's dream novel of 1958: "a girl's search for the dead father—for an outside authority which must be developed, instead, from the inside" (*J* 258). As the child of a Nazi, the girl could "hardly speak" (st. 6), but as a Jew she begins "to talk" and to acquire an identity (st. 7). In Plath's allegory, the outsider Jew corresponds to "the rebel, the artist, the odd" (*JP* 55),[7] and particularly to the woman artist. Otto Rank's *Beyond Psychology*, which had a lasting influence on her, explicitly compares women to Jews, since "woman . . . has suffered from the very beginning a fate similar to that of the Jew, namely, suppression, slavery, confinement, and subsequent persecution" (287–88). Rank, whose discourse I would consider tainted by anti-Semitism, argues that Jews speak a language [. . .] that differs essentially from the language of the majority cultures in which they find themselves (191, 281–84). He analogously [. . .] argues that woman speaks in a language different from man's, and that as a result of man's denial of woman's world, "woman's 'native tongue' has hitherto been unknown or at least unheard" (248). [. . . H]is idea of linguistic difference based on gender and his analogy between Jewish and female speech seem to have embedded themselves in the substructure of "Daddy" (and in many of Plath's other texts as well). For Plath, as later for Adrienne Rich, the Holocaust and the patriarchy's silencing of women were linked outcomes of the masculinist interpretation of the world. Political insurrection and female self-assertion also interlaced symbolically. In "Daddy," Plath's speaker finds her voice and motive by identifying herself as antithetical to her Fascist father. [. . .] Previously devoted to the patriarch—both in "The Colossus" and in memories evoked in "Daddy" of trying to "get back" to him (st. 12)—she now seeks only to escape from him and to see him destroyed.

Plath has unleashed the anger, normal in mourning as well as in revolt, that she suppressed in the earlier poem. But she has done so at a cost. Let us consider her childlike speaking voice. The language of "Daddy," beginning with its title, is often regressive. The "I" articulates herself by moving backwards in time, using the language of nursery rhymes and fairy tales (the little old woman who lived in a shoe, the black man of the forest). Such language accords with a child's conception of the world, not an adult's. Plath's assault on the language of "daddy-poetry" has turned inward, on the language of her own poem, which teeters precariously on the edge of a preverbal abyss—represented by the eerie, keening "oo" sound with which a majority of the verses end. And then let us consider the play on "through" at the poem's conclusion. Although that last line allows for multiple readings, one interpretation is that the "I" has unconsciously carried out her father's

6. Youth, especially a young man, in training; apprentice.
7. *JP* is Axelrod's abbreviation for Plath's *Johnny Panic and the Bible of Dreams.*

wish: her discourse, by transforming itself into cathartic oversimplifications, has undone itself.

Yet the poem does contain its verbal violence by means more productive than silence. In a letter to her brother, Plath referred to "Daddy" as "gruesome" (*LH* 472), while on almost the same day she described it to A. Alvarez as a piece of "light verse" (Alvarez, *Beyond* 56). She later read it on the BBC in a highly ironic tone of voice. The poem's unique spell derives from its rhetorical complexity: its variegated and perhaps bizarre fusion of the horrendous and the comic. As [Margaret] Uroff has remarked, it both shares and remains detached from the fixation of its protagonist (159). [. . .] Plath's speaker uses potentially self-mocking melodramatic terms to describe both her opponent ("so black no sky could squeak through" [st. 10]) and herself ("poor and white" [st. 1]). While this aboriginal speaker quite literally expresses black-and-white thinking, her civilized double possesses a sensibility sophisticated enough to subject such thinking to irony. Thus the poem expresses feelings that it simultaneously parodies—it may be parodying the very idea of feeling. The tension between erudition and simplicity in the speaker's voice appears in her pairings that juxtapose adult with childlike diction: "breathe or Achoo," "your Luftewaffe, your gobbledygoo" (st. 1, 9). She can expound on such adult topics as Taroc packs, Viennese beer, and Tyrolean snowfall; can specify death camps by name; and can employ an adult vocabulary of "recover," "ancestress," "Aryan," "*Meinkampf,*" "obscene," and "bastard." Yet she also has recourse to a more primitive lexicon that includes "chuffing," "your black heart," and "my pretty red heart." She proves herself capable of careful intellectual discriminations ("so I never could tell" [st. 5]), conventionalized description ("beautiful Nauset" [st. 3]), and moral analogy ("if I've killed one man, I've killed two" [st. 15]), while also exhibiting regressive fantasies (vampires), repetitions ("wars, wars, wars" [st. 4]), and inarticulateness ("panzer-man, panzer-man, O You—" [st. 9]). She oscillates between calm reflection ("You stand at the blackboard, daddy, / In the picture I have of you" [st. 11]) and mad incoherence ("Ich, ich, ich, ich" [st. 6]). Her sophisticated language puts her wild language in an ironic perspective, removing the discourse from the control of the archaic self who understands experience only in extreme terms.

The ironies in "Daddy" proliferate in unexpected ways, however. When the speaker proclaims categorically that "every woman adores a Fascist" (st. 10), she is subjecting her victimization to irony by suggesting that sufferers choose, or at least accommodate themselves to, their suffering. But she is also subjecting her authority to irony, since her claim about "every woman" is transparently false. It simply parodies patriarchal commonplaces, such as those advanced by Helene Deutsch concerning "feminine masochism" (192–99, 245–85). [. . .] Plath's mother wished that Plath would write about "decent, courageous people" (*LH* 477), and she herself heard an inner voice demanding that she be a perfect "paragon" in her language and feeling (*J* 176). But in the speaker of "Daddy," she inscribed the opposite of such a paragon: a divided self whose veneer of civilization is breached and infected by unhealthy instincts.

Plath's irony cuts both ways. At the same time that the speaker's sophisticated voice undercuts her childish voice, reducing its melodrama to comedy, the childish or maddened voice undercuts the pretensions of the sophisticated voice, revealing the extremity of suffering masked by its ironies. While demonstrating the inadequacy of thinking and feeling in opposites, the poem implies that such a mode can locate truths denied more complex cognitive and affective systems. The very moderation of the normal adult intelligence, its tolerance of ambiguity, its defenses against the primal energies of the id, results in falsification. Reflecting Schiller's[8] idea that the creative artist experiences a "momentary and passing madness" (quoted by Freud in a passage of *The Interpretation of Dreams* [193] that Plath underscored), "Daddy" gives voice to that madness. Yet the poem's sophisticated awareness, its comic vision, probably wins out in the end, since the poem concludes by curtailing the power of its extreme discourse [. . .]. Furthermore, Plath distanced herself from the poem's aboriginal voice by introducing her text as "a poem spoken by a girl with an Electra complex"—that is, as a study of the *girl's* pathology rather than her father's—and as an allegory that will "free" her from that pathology. She also distanced herself by reading the poem in a tone that emphasized its irony. And finally, she distanced herself by laying the poem's wild voice permanently to rest after October. The aboriginal vision was indeed purged. "Daddy" represents not Dickinson's madness that is divinest sense,[9] but rather an entry into a style of discourse and a mastery of it. [. . .]

Plath's poetic revolt in "Daddy" liberated her pent-up creativity, but the momentary success sustained her little more than self-sacrifice had done. "Daddy" became another stage in her development, an unrepeatable experiment, a vocal opening that closed itself at once. The poem is not an elegy for the power of "daddy-poetry" but for the powers of speech Plath discovered in composing it.

When we consider "Daddy" generically, a further range of implications presents itself. Although we could profitably consider the poem as the dramatic monologue Plath called it in her BBC broadcast, let us regard it instead as the kind of poem most readers have taken it to be: a domestic poem. [. . .] I shall define the domestic poem as one that represents and comments on a protagonist's relationship to one or more family members, usually a parent, child, or spouse. To focus our discussion even further, I shall emphasize poetry that specifically concerns a father.

In the 1950s the "domestic poem" proper appeared on the scene, with its own conventions and expectations, and with its own complex cultural and literary reasons for being. Perhaps [. . .] its precise timing depended on a reaction against modernism's aesthetic of impersonality.[1] Theodore Roethke wrote several early poems that initiated the genre: "My Papa's Waltz" (1948), "The Lost Son" (1948), and "Where Knock Is Open Wide" (1951). [Robert] Lowell's "Life Studies" sequence (1959) was, and is, the genre's most prominent landmark. [. . .] In all these poems, the parent-child relationship serves as a locus for psychological investigation. In many of them it also serves as a means of representing the acquisition of poetic identity and of exploring the bounds of textuality itself. [. . .] The

8. German poet-philosopher Friedrich Schiller (1759–1805).
9. One Emily Dickinson poem begins, "Much Madness is divinest Sense— / To a discerning Eye— / Much Sense—the starkest Madness."
1. In "Tradition and the Individual Talent" (1919), Modernist poet T. S. Eliot articulates an "impersonal theory of poetry," arguing, "the more perfect the artist, the more completely separate in him will be the man who suffers and the mind which creates."

"domestic poem" became a system of signs in which each individual text's adherence to the system and deviations within the system produced its particular literary meaning.

During Plath's trying time of 1958–59 [. . .] she struggled [. . .] to "break into a new line of poetry" (*J* 321). As always, her method was to "read others and think hard" (*J* 302). The two male poets she read most intently, the two who most instructed her, were Roethke and Lowell.

In 1959 [when she attended Lowell's Boston University poetry courses] Plath did not consciously attempt to write in the domestic poem genre, perhaps because she was not yet ready to assume her majority. [. . .] But by fall 1962, when she had already lost so much, she was ready to chance tackling poetic tradition, and specifically her chief male instructors, Roethke and Lowell. In "Daddy" she achieved her victory in two ways. First, as we have seen, she symbolically assaults a father figure who is identified with male control of language. All her anxiety of influence comes to the fore in the poem: her sense of belatedness, her awareness of constraint, her fears of inadequacy, her furious need to overcome her dependency, her guilt at her own aggressivity. Since the precursors "do not do / Any more" (st. 1), she wishes to escape their paralyzing influence and to empty the "bag full of God" that has kept her tongue stuck in her jaw for so long (st. 2, 5). The father whose power she attacks is not simply Roethke or Lowell, or even Hughes or Otto Plath, but a literary character who includes reference to all of them as categories of masculine authority. [. . .]

In addition to killing the father in its fictional plot, the poem seeks to discredit the forefathers through its status as poetic act. Taking a genre established by Roethke and Lowell, "Daddy" fundamentally alters it through antithesis and parody. Like all strong poems, it transforms its genre and therefore the way we perceive the precursive examples [. . .]. Her poem attempts to conclude the genre, to represent the final possible stroke, or at the very least to inaugurate some new and important genre, of which the whole domestic genre was but a foreshadowing.

"Daddy" swerves sharply from its precursors, curtailing their power. It turns the psychological depth of Roethke's poem and the ironically detached surface of Lowell's poem into a fury of denunciation, an extravagance of emotion, an exaggeration of acts and effects, perhaps revealing the subtexts of both precursors. [. . .] It unmasks Roethke's implicitly oppressive father figure as a monster and Lowell's sophisticated comedy as slapstick. It transforms the domestic genre alternately into a horror show, encapsulating every political, cultural, and familial atrocity of the age, and a theater of cruelty, evoking nervous laughter. "Daddy" takes the genre as far as it can go—and then further.

WORKS CITED

PRIMARY TEXTS

Plath, Sylvia. *Collected Poems.* Ed. Ted Hughes. New York: Harper & Row, 1981.
———. *Johnny Panic and the Bible of Dreams: Short Stories, Prose, and Diary Excerpts.* New York: Harper & Row, 1979.
———. *Journals of Sylvia Plath.* Ed. Frances McCullough and Ted Hughes. New York: Dial, 1982.
———. *Letters Home: Correspondence: 1950–1963.* Ed. Aurelia Schober Plath. New York: Harper & Row, 1975.

SECONDARY TEXTS

Aird, Eileen. *Sylvia Plath: Her Life and Work.* New York: Harper & Row, 1973.
Alvarez, A. *Beyond All This Fiddle.* London: Allen Lane-Penguin, 1968.
———. *The Savage God: A Study of Suicide.* 1971. New York: Bantam, 1973.
Bowlby, John. *Attachment and Loss.* Vol. 3. *Loss: Sadness and Depression.* London: Hogarth, 1980.
Deutsch, Helene. *The Psychology of Women,* Vol. 1. *Girlhood.* 1944. New York: Bantam, 1973.
Freud, Sigmund. *The Interpretation of Dreams.* 1900. Trans. A. A. Brill. *Basic Writings.* New York: Random House/Modern Library, 1938. 181–549.
Homans, Margaret. *Women Writers and Poetic Identity: Dorothy Wordsworth, Emily Brontë, and Emily Dickinson.* Princeton: Princeton UP, 1980.
Rank, Otto. *Beyond Psychology.* 1941. New York: Dover, 1958.
Rosenthal, M. L. *The New Poets: American and British Poetry since World War II.* London: Oxford UP, 1967.
Uroff, Margaret Dickie. *Sylvia Plath and Ted Hughes.* Urbana: U of Illinois P, 1979.

LISA NARBESHUBER

From The Poetics of Torture: The Spectacle of Sylvia Plath's Poetry (2004)[1]

Plath's poetry reacts against the absence, especially for women, of a public space, indeed a language for debate, wherein one might make visible and deconstruct the given order of things. In the following, I argue that Plath deliberately blurs the borders between the public and the private in two of the most celebrated, controversial, and critiqued of her poems: "Daddy" and "Lady Lazarus." Transforming the conventional female body of the 1950s into a kind of transgressive dialect, Plath makes her personae speak in and to a public realm dominated by male desires. [. . . I]n order to bring their private selves into the public realm, the speakers in "Daddy" and "Lady Lazarus" become public performers and rebellious exaggerators [. . .]. They [. . .] may have trouble communicating (as we will see most obviously in "Daddy"), but this serves to reveal their public

1. Lisa Narbeshuber, "The Poetics of Torture: The Spectacle of Sylvia Plath's Poetry." *Canadian Review of American Studies,* vol. 34, no. 2, 2004, pp. 185–203. All footnotes are Narbeshuber's; her bibliography has been abbreviated.

voicelessness. Plath's speakers should not be read as pathological case studies; rather it is the culture, written on their bodies, which is expressed as pathological. Likewise, their acts of rebellion almost necessarily contain an unacceptable, self-destructive side. In various ways, Plath brashly pairs the private with the public, to the point where the personal all but dissolves into a ludicrous public performance or event, with the body as displayed object.

This desire in Plath's poetry to trace the connection between the private and the public has not been explored in any depth in Plath criticism.[2] Instead, most criticism reads "Daddy" and "Lady Lazarus" around the psychology of Plath's life, if not exclusively as biography, then as the feminist struggles of a victorious woman over a man or men. For example, critics regard the irrepressible "Lady Lazarus" as "a triumph of vitality" (Broe 175); [. . .] a wonderful, "searingly self-confident" (Van Dyne 55) exhibition of the speaker's "true identity as a triumphant resurrecting goddess, the fully liberated, fiery true self . . ." (Kroll 118–9) [. . .]. Plath's poetry [. . .] does not so much demonstrate the crushing of the authentic or "real" self by the patriarchal, as show the role of (social) fantasy in the construction of the subject. More than an attack on the male (or in particular her husband or father), her poetry confronts the mentality of the status quo that accepts the ideology of the individual and notions of the natural, or even the personal, self. She unveils and critiques the private, the hidden, and the normalized by parodying various public discourses of power (gendered male), while portraying her personae as objects of those discourses and, thereby, both the agents and the spectacles of punishment.

* * *

By radically redefining herself in terms of historically grounded, collective worlds, Plath (whether justified or not) successfully displaces the solitary, private individual. When identifying herself with the concentration camp Jew, she compares herself to a community, just as she identifies her father and husband, who play the tormenting Nazis, as part of an historical political organization. In all of this, Plath suggests that her own contemporary experience—everyday conceptions of femininity, individualism, and the privacy of the family—conforms to collective patterns. She fights the disappearance of the public, its retreat to the privacy of the home, and "seriality" in general.[3] One cannot see the whole from these little pockets of private perception. Stressing, then, the collective

2. Plath criticism still contains her within the private framework of the individual: looking at her as a confessional poet, reading her poetry as biography or psychological case study. Recent criticism has explored the exceptional fascination readers have with her life. Elisabeth Bronfen, for one, believes that Plath's "life and her poetry are so inextricably implicated that we can do nothing but read her poetry within the biographical appraisal that has reworked her life for us" (7). Some critics (including Bronfen) despair over this reductive approach to reading Plath's poetry. Bruce Bawer concludes that "the real interest lies not in Plath's art but in her life" (19). See Jacqueline Rose, Al Strangeways, and Linda Wagner-Martin for a few book-length discussions on the subject.

3. "Seriality," a term Sartre develops in *Critique of Dialectical Reason*, describes a mode of social interaction in which members of a group cannot see their profound connection to one another. Sartre gives the example of a grouping of people waiting for a bus at a bus stop: "[W]e are concerned here with a plurality of isolations: these people do not care about or speak to each other and, in general, they do not look at one another; they exist side by side alongside a bus stop" (256). The individual "constitutes himself in the gathering as an objective element of a series" (266).

engineering of so-called "private experience," Plath charts a metaphorical map, linking invisible worlds to the cultural processes that inform them.

"Daddy," notoriously, re-stages secret family conflicts between parents and children, husbands and wives. It lifts a veil covering shameful social relations. And just as significantly, Plath "talks back." The opening lines [1–5] vividly picture a claustrophobic domestic space [. . .]. This (cultural) space allows for little movement or even speech—she can't "breathe or Achoo." For Plath, the domestic realm stands out in the open, but unnoticed, hidden, or—as the poem suggests—*underfoot*. Plath wants to dismantle the interiority of the "shoe"-house, revealing its contents. As the progression of "Daddy" underscores, her new theatre is external, a decidedly worldly place, full of worldly struggles and a worldly language: "Atlantic" (11), "Polish town[s]" (16), "wars" (18), "Dachau, Auschwitz, Belsen" (33), "[t]he snows of the Tyrol, the clear beer of Vienna" (36), "swastika[s]" (46), "Fascist[s]" (48), and so forth.

In "Daddy," private "family matters" link up with large historical struggles, social organizations, and linguistic systems. Moving from the private, "shoe"-world to the just as stifling political world, consciousness can grasp the machinery that produces and oppresses it. The German language acts like a repressive mechanical power, bearing down on the collective body:

> And the language obscene
>
> An engine, an engine
> Chuffing me off like a Jew.
> A Jew to Dachau, Auschwitz, Belsen.
> I began to talk like a Jew.
> I think I may well be a Jew. (30–5)

In general, Plath suggests the power of language ("an engine") to subject the self. But more specifically, she implies that certain styles of discourse violate body and soul more than others. She emphasizes the word "obscene" by placing it at the end of the stanza. To her, German is "the language obscene," but the word "obscene," falling where it does, also introduces her own words: as if to suggest her situation *and* her metaphors are indecent. Through such audacious, dramatic comparisons, Plath pictures human relationships as violent and grotesque *spectacles*, giving individual, private relationships public currency. At the same time, by having to *force* the domestic into the public arena, she highlights how these relationships normally remain serialized and closed off from social life.

Within this world of conflict, Plath, as I suggested earlier, "talks back," fantasizing possible alternatives to the pact of silence common among families. She occupies the position of speechlessness, but she struggles to respond:

> I never could talk to you.
> The tongue stuck in my jaw.
>
> It stuck in a barb wire snare.
> Ich, ich, ich, ich,
> I could hardly speak. (24–8)

Even though she may stutter—a shameful defect?—the persona does not hide her deficiency but gives voice to her fear and anger. Her fixed "ich" may also be seen to mirror the stuttering repetition of the oppressor's language ("An engine, an engine"), which "chuffs" out the same sound over and over again, revealing itself as a homogenizing, mechanical force. She responds in kind, with her similarly aggressive "obscene" language: She speaks crudely, and in a most unladylike way, of her "Polack friend" (20) and says to her father, "Daddy, daddy, you bastard" (80). By speaking not only "the language obscene" but also the actual German language ("Ich, ich, ich, ich"), the persona demonstrates that, even as she attempts to escape her oppressor's (male) language, it makes heavy claims on her. It may even suggest her complicity.[4] Her underlying desire to be desired by her father ("[e]very woman adores a fascist" [48]) has caused her, at times, to play along with the terms of his game, living within the rigid configurations of his language. "Daddy" embodies tremendous socio-psychological tension: for Plath utilizes a language of mastery[5] (clarity, directness, multiple worldly allusions) that she simultaneously subverts with her startling array of marginal voices (with nursery rhymes, baby talk, speech defects, "hysteria"). [. . .] Plath dramatizes both her imprisonment in the oppressor's script—doing the important work of laying out dominant discursive codes—*and* the important points of resistance, on the margins.

Within these boundaries, her persona fantasizes herself as powerful, overpowering her tormentors, as when she imagines killing them ("If I've killed one man, I've killed two—" [71]), even driving a stake into her father's heart. Significantly, in the final act, she desires a collective judgment of this drama:

> And the villagers never liked you.
> They are dancing and stamping on you.
> They always *knew* it was you. (77–9)

She does not want to be alone in her condemnation of the Other. For Plath, this collective problem deserves a collective response, and she aims to give it one.

It should be noted, especially in the case of Plath, whose biography attracts so much attention, how she moves from the literary universe to the "real world." Jacqueline Rose tells how an "old friend wrote Plath's mother on publication of the poem in the review of *Ariel* in *Time* in 1966 to insist that Plath's father had been nothing like the image in the poem" (229). As this quotation demonstrates, Plath's poems, intentionally or not, perform a sort of "talk back" or "back talk," a rudely public, counter-discourse that rejects the family code of silence. By making feelings and ideas public, Plath risks a great deal. She risks banishment by her family and by a public anxious to preserve the status quo of middle-class family life.

In "Daddy," Plath reframes the private in terms of a public discourse, framing personal, family conflicts within larger cultural processes (language, homogenization, technology, politics). Making abstract processes concrete, she gives human faces to collective activities, forcing them into a dramatic, conflictual dialogue. In

---

4. Various critics have made similar observations. Janice Markey, for one, writes, "Plath makes it clear in this poem that the exploitation of women in a patriarchal society is in part due to women's compliance in the sado-masochism involved" (16). In *The Psychic Life of Power*, Judith Butler offers a psychological justification for the woman's willingness and desire to be oppressed, arguing that we all discover sexual pleasure within the power structures that dominate us.

5. According to Alice Suskin Ostriker, "[c]ontrol, impersonality, and dispassionateness are supposedly normative, masculine virtues" (88–9) and what characterizes "the oppressor's language" (168), along with Plath's poetic style here.

much of her late poetry, Plath repeatedly imagines a fragile self (very often *feminized*), subject to inhuman, and specifically modern, processes of rationalization (i.e., where the self is "paved over" by logic, statistics, uniformity, etc., processes that are most often viewed, by her, as patriarchal). [. . . F]or Plath, rationalized worlds eliminate any form of public stage. [. . .] Against this absence of public forum, Plath [. . .] exposes and challenges the deep rift between non-public and public types of discourse, between individual and collective experiences and responses.

[Plath's] personae expose both the contemporary social organization and themselves as constructed, rather than simply given or natural. Their identities, therefore, have the potential to be countered and reconfigured. The shape and meaning of *human being* is open for debate and change. [. . .] Both "Lady Lazarus" and "Daddy" work out where power can be located, as well as pointing out how this society has become a "serial" one, within which the self cannot gain a view of the whole. Plath stands outside, views, and addresses the very community she silently, passively inhabited. The poems confront the community by staging dramas of punishment. These spectacles of torture, although educational, are simultaneously self-destructive, as the speakers in both poems desire their own deaths. And yet, through these self-flagellating, suicidal personae, we may see diverse aspects of constructed female identity.

WORKS CITED

Bawer, Bruce. "Sylvia Plath and the Poetry of Confession." *New Criterion* 9.6 (1991): 18–27.

Broe, Mary Lynn. *Protean Poetic: The Poetry of Sylvia Plath*. Columbia: U of Missouri P, 1980.

Bronfen, Elisabeth. *Sylvia Plath*. Writers and Their Work Ser. Plymouth, UK: Northcote, 1998.

Butler, Judith. *The Psychic Life of Power: Theories in Subjection*. Stanford: Stanford UP, 1997.

Kroll, Judith. *Chapters in a Mythology: The Poetry of Sylvia Plath*. New York: Harper, 1976.

Markey, Janice. *A Journey into the Red Eye: The Poetry of Sylvia Plath: A Critique*. London: Women's, 1993.

Ostriker, Alicia Suskin. *Stealing the Language: The Emergence of Women's Poetry in America*. Boston: Beacon, 1986.

Plath, Sylvia. *Collected Poems*. London: Faber, 1981.

Rose, Jacqueline. *The Haunting of Sylvia Plath*. Cambridge: Harvard UP, 1992.

Sartre, Jean-Paul. *Theory of Practical Ensembles*. Vol. 1 of *Critique of Dialectical Reason*. 1960. Trans. Alan Sheridan-Smith. Ed. Jonathan Rée. London: NLB, 1976.

Strangeways, Al. *Sylvia Plath: The Shaping of Shadows*. Madison: Fairleigh Dickinson UP, 1998.

Van Dyne, Susan R. *Revising Life: Sylvia Plath's Ariel Poems*. Chapel Hill: U of North Carolina P, 1993.

Wagner-Martin, Linda. *Sylvia Plath: A Literary Life*. Literary Life Ser. London: Macmillan, 1999.

SUGGESTIONS FOR WRITING

1. In his essay DYING IS AN ART, George Steiner argues that Plath's poems "are too honest, they have cost too much, to be yielded to myth" (1164). Do you think that DADDY is an "honest" poem? Write an essay exploring what "honesty" means in modern poetry and whether or not DADDY is an "honest" poem. Draw on DADDY and the critical essays found in this chapter, citing them when appropriate.

2. Several of the critics in this chapter make competing claims about the meaning and significance of the form of DADDY, particularly its nursery-rhyme-like qualities. Using those claims as a springboard, write an essay in which you make your own argument about the relationship between form and content in DADDY.

3. In THE PLATH CELEBRATION: A PARTIAL DISSENT, Irving Howe argues, "There is something monstrous, utterly disproportionate, when tangled emotions about one's father are deliberately compared with the historical fate of the European Jews" (1168). Is Plath's personal, artistic use of a great historical tragedy truly "monstrous," as Howe says, or is it acceptable and effective, as other critics here contend? Write an essay in which you discuss the appropriateness and effects of Plath's references to the Holocaust, being sure to relate your interpretation to those of the critics in this chapter.

4. Mary Lynn Broe, Judith Kroll, Margaret Homans, Pamela Annas, and Steven Gould Axelrod all claim that DADDY portrays the speaker's attempt to successfully "exorcise" one demon or another, though they disagree both about what or who that demon is and about whether and how that exorcism (not the poem) succeeds. Using their arguments as a starting point, write an essay in which you offer your own interpretation of the process of exorcism enacted in the poem.

5. In SYLVIA PLATH, A. Alvarez quotes Plath's own interpretation of DADDY as a poem "spoken by a girl with an Electra complex" (1166). (Other articles also mention this statement.) Research the term *Electra complex*, which originated with Carl Jung. Is it useful to interpret DADDY through the lens of the Electra complex? Citing critics included in this chapter, write an essay in which you discuss Plath's Freudian explanation of DADDY.

6. In SYLVIA PLATH: THE WOUND AND THE CURE OF WORDS, Steven Gould Axelrod argues that DADDY is a response to "the domestic poem" created in the late 1940s and 1950s by American male poets, especially poems such as Theodore Roethke's MY PAPA'S WALTZ that depict fathers and sons. Write an essay comparing Plath's and Roethke's poems, drawing on, and in one way or another responding to, Axelrod's arguments. Do you agree, for example, with his claim that where one poem represents the father figure as merely "implicitly oppressive," the other "unmasks" him as a "monster" (1180)? Alternatively, might Axelrod be right that reading DADDY changes forever the way we read MY PAPA'S WALTZ? How and why so, or not?

7. Is DADDY a feminist poem? Citing the essays by Margaret Homans and other critics in this chapter, write an essay in which you explore the validity of a feminist interpretation.

Reading More Poetry

WILLIAM BLAKE
The Lamb

    Little Lamb, who made thee?
    Dost thou know who made thee?
Gave thee life, and bid thee feed
By the stream and o'er the mead;
5 Gave thee clothing of delight,
Softest clothing woolly bright;
Gave thee such a tender voice,
Making all the vales rejoice?
    Little Lamb, who made thee?
10   Dost thou know who made thee?

    Little Lamb, I'll tell thee!
    Little Lamb, I'll tell thee:
He is calléd by thy name,
For he calls himself a Lamb,
15 He is meek and he is mild;
He became a little child.
I a child and thou a lamb,
We are calléd by his name.
    Little Lamb, God bless thee!
20   Little Lamb, God bless thee!

1789

The Tyger

Tyger! Tyger! burning bright
In the forests of the night,
What immortal hand or eye
Could frame thy fearful symmetry?

5 In what distant deeps or skies
Burnt the fire of thine eyes?
On what wings dare he aspire?
What the hand dare seize the fire?

And what shoulder, & what art,
10 Could twist the sinews of thy heart?
And when thy heart began to beat,
What dread hand? & what dread feet?

What the hammer? what the chain?
In what furnace was thy brain?
15   What the anvil? what dread grasp
Dare its deadly terrors clasp?

When the stars threw down their spears
And water'd heaven with their tears,
Did he smile his work to see?
20   Did he who made the Lamb make thee?

Tyger! Tyger! burning bright
In the forests of the night,
What immortal hand or eye
Dare frame thy fearful symmetry?

1794

ROBERT BROWNING
My Last Duchess

Ferrara[1]

That's my last Duchess painted on the wall,
Looking as if she were alive. I call
That piece a wonder, now: Frà Pandolf's[2] hands
Worked busily a day, and there she stands.
5   Will't please you sit and look at her? I said
"Frà Pandolf" by design, for never read
Strangers like you that pictured countenance,
The depth and passion of its earnest glance,
But to myself they turned (since none puts by
10   The curtain I have drawn for you, but I)
And seemed as they would ask me, if they durst,
How such a glance came there; so, not the first
Are you to turn and ask thus. Sir, 'twas not
Her husband's presence only, called that spot
15   Of joy into the Duchess' cheek: perhaps
Frà Pandolf chanced to say "Her mantle laps
Over my lady's wrist too much," or "Paint
Must never hope to reproduce the faint
Half-flush that dies along her throat": such stuff
20   Was courtesy, she thought, and cause enough
For calling up that spot of joy. She had
A heart—how shall I say?—too soon made glad,

1. Alfonso II, Duke of Ferrara in Italy in the mid-sixteenth century, is the presumed speaker of this **dramatic monologue**, which is loosely based on historical events. When the duke's first wife—whom he had married when she was fourteen—died at seventeen under suspicious circumstances, he negotiated through an agent (this poem's **auditor**) for marriage to the niece of the count of Tyrol in Austria.
2. Frà Pandolf is, like Claus (line 56), fictitious.

Too easily impressed; she liked whate'er
She looked on, and her looks went everywhere.
25 Sir, 'twas all one! My favor at her breast,
The dropping of the daylight in the West,
The bough of cherries some officious fool
Broke in the orchard for her, the white mule
She rode with round the terrace—all and each
30 Would draw from her alike the approving speech,
Or blush, at least. She thanked men,—good! but thanked
Somehow—I know not how—as if she ranked
My gift of a nine-hundred-years-old name
With anybody's gift. Who'd stoop to blame
35 This sort of trifling? Even had you skill
In speech—which I have not—to make your will
Quite clear to such an one, and say, "Just this
Or that in you disgusts me; here you miss,
Or there exceed the mark"—and if she let
40 Herself be lessoned so, nor plainly set
Her wits to yours, forsooth, and made excuse,
—E'en then would be some stooping; and I choose
Never to stoop. Oh sir, she smiled, no doubt,
Whene'er I passed her; but who passed without
45 Much the same smile? This grew; I gave commands;
Then all smiles stopped together. There she stands
As if alive. Will't please you rise? We'll meet
The company below, then. I repeat,
The Count your master's known munificence
50 Is ample warrant that no just pretense
Of mine for dowry will be disallowed;
Though his fair daughter's self, as I avowed
At starting, is my object. Nay, we'll go
Together down, sir. Notice Neptune, though,
55 Taming a sea-horse, thought a rarity,
Which Claus of Innsbruck cast in bronze for me!

1842

SAMUEL TAYLOR COLERIDGE
Kubla Khan

Or, a Vision in a Dream[3]

In Xanadu did Kubla Khan
A stately pleasure-dome decree:
Where Alph, the sacred river, ran
Through caverns measureless to man

---

3. Coleridge claimed that he wrote this fragment immediately after waking from an opium dream and that after he was interrupted by a visitor he was unable to finish the poem.

5   Down to a sunless sea.
       So twice five miles of fertile ground
       With walls and towers were girdled round:
       And here were gardens bright with sinuous rills
       Where blossomed many an incense-bearing tree;
10   And here were forests ancient as the hills,
       Enfolding sunny spots of greenery.
       But oh! that deep romantic chasm which slanted
       Down the green hill athwart a cedarn cover![4]
       A savage place! as holy and enchanted
15   As e'er beneath a waning moon was haunted
       By woman wailing for her demon-lover![5]
       And from this chasm, with ceaseless turmoil seething,
       As if this earth in fast thick pants were breathing,
       A mighty fountain momently[6] was forced,
20   Amid whose swift half-intermitted burst
       Huge fragments vaulted like rebounding hail,
       Or chaffy grain beneath the thresher's flail:
       And 'mid these dancing rocks at once and ever
       It flung up momently the sacred river.
25   Five miles meandering with a mazy motion
       Through wood and dale the sacred river ran,
       Then reached the caverns measureless to man,
       And sank in tumult to a lifeless ocean:
       And 'mid this tumult Kubla heard from far
30   Ancestral voices prophesying war!

          The shadow of the dome of pleasure
          Floated midway on the waves;
          Where was heard the mingled measure
          From the fountain and the caves.
35   It was a miracle of rare device,
       A sunny pleasure-dome with caves of ice!

          A damsel with a dulcimer
          In a vision once I saw:
          It was an Abyssinian maid,
40   And on her dulcimer she played,
          Singing of Mount Abora.
          Could I revive within me
          Her symphony and song,
          To such a deep delight 'twould win me,
45   That with music loud and long,
       I would build that dome in air,
       That sunny dome! those caves of ice!

---

4. That is, from side to side beneath a cover of cedar trees.
5. In a famous and often-imitated German ballad, the lady Lenore is carried off on horseback by the
specter of her lover and married to him at his grave.
6. Suddenly.

And all who heard should see them there,
And all should cry, Beware! Beware!
50 His flashing eyes, his floating hair!
Weave a circle round him thrice,
And close your eyes with holy dread,
For he on honey-dew hath fed,
And drunk the milk of Paradise.

1797–98   1816

JOHN DONNE
Death, be not proud

Death, be not proud, though some have callèd thee
Mighty and dreadful, for thou art not so;
For those whom thou think'st thou dost overthrow
Die not, poor Death, nor yet canst thou kill me.
5 From rest and sleep, which but thy pictures[7] be,
Much pleasure; then from thee much more must flow,
And soonest[8] our best men with thee do go,
Rest of their bones, and soul's delivery.[9]
Thou art slave to Fate, Chance, kings, and desperate men,
10 And dost with Poison, War, and Sickness dwell;
And poppy or charms can make us sleep as well,
And better than thy stroke; why swell'st[1] thou then?
One short sleep past, we wake eternally
And death shall be no more; Death, thou shalt die.

1633

The Good-Morrow

I wonder, by my troth, what thou and I
Did, till we loved? Were we not weaned till then
But sucked on country pleasures, childishly?
Or snorted in the seven sleepers' den?[2]
5 'Twas so; but[3] this, all pleasures fancies be.
If ever any beauty I did see,
Which I desired, and got,[4] 'twas but a dream of thee.

And now good morrow to our waking souls,
Which watch not one another out of fear;

---

7. Likenesses.
8. Most willingly.
9. Deliverance.
1. Puff with pride.
2. According to legend, seven Christian youths escaped Roman persecution by sleeping in a cave for
187 years. *Snorted*: snored.
3. Except for.
4. Sexually possessed.

10 For love all love of other sights controls,
    And makes one little room an everywhere.
    Let sea-discoverers to new worlds have gone,
    Let maps to other,[5] worlds on worlds have shown:
    Let us possess one world; each hath one, and is one.

15 My face in thine eye, thine in mine appears,[6]
    And true plain hearts do in the faces rest;
    Where can we find two better hemispheres,
    Without sharp North, without declining West?
    Whatever dies was not mixed equally;[7]
20 If our two loves be one, or thou and I
    Love so alike that none do slacken, none can die.

                                                        1633

A Valediction: Forbidding Mourning

    As virtuous men pass mildly away,
        And whisper to their souls to go,
    Whilst some of their sad friends do say,
        "The breath goes now," and some say, "No,"

5   So let us melt, and make no noise,
        No tear-floods, nor sigh-tempests move;
    'Twere profanation of our joys
        To tell the laity our love.

    Moving of the earth[8] brings harms and fears,
10   Men reckon what it did and meant;
    But trepidation of the spheres,[9]
        Though greater far, is innocent.

    Dull sublunary[1] lovers' love
        (Whose soul is sense) cannot admit
15 Absence, because it doth remove
        Those things which elemented[2] it.

    But we, by a love so much refined
        That our selves know not what it is,
    Inter-assured of the mind,
20   Care less, eyes, lips, and hands to miss.

---

5. Other people.
6. That is, each is reflected in the other's eyes.
7. Perfectly mixed elements, according to scholastic philosophy, were stable and immortal.
8. Earthquakes.
9. Renaissance theory that the celestial spheres trembled and thus caused unexpected variations in their orbits. Such movements are "innocent" because earthlings do not observe or fret about them.
1. Below the moon—that is, changeable. According to the traditional cosmology that Donne invokes here, the moon is the dividing line between the immutable celestial world and the mutable earthly one.
2. Comprised, made up its elements.

Our two souls therefore, which are one,
    Though I must go, endure not yet
A breach, but an expansion,
    Like gold to airy thinness beat.

25 If they be two, they are two so
    As stiff twin compasses are two:
Thy soul, the fixed foot, makes no show
    To move, but doth, if the other do;

And though it in the center sit,
30   Yet when the other far doth roam,
It leans, and hearkens after it,
    And grows erect, as that comes home.

Such wilt thou be to me, who must,
    Like the other foot, obliquely run;
35 Thy firmness makes my circle[3] just,
    And makes me end where I begun.

1633

PAUL LAURENCE DUNBAR
We Wear the Mask

We wear the mask that grins and lies,
It hides our cheeks and shades our eyes,—
This debt we pay to human guile;
With torn and bleeding hearts we smile,
5 And mouth with myriad subtleties.

Why should the world be over-wise,
In counting all our tears and sighs?
Nay, let them only see us, while
    We wear the mask.

10 We smile, but, O great Christ, our cries
To thee from tortured souls arise.
We sing, but oh the clay is vile
Beneath our feet, and long the mile;
But let the world dream otherwise,
15   We wear the mask!

1895

---

3. Traditional symbol of perfection.

ROBERT FROST
Fire and Ice

Some say the world will end in fire,
Some say in ice.
From what I've tasted of desire
I hold with those who favor fire.
5   But if it had to perish twice,
I think I know enough of hate
To say that for destruction ice
Is also great
And would suffice.

1920

Stopping by Woods on a Snowy Evening

Whose woods these are I think I know.
His house is in the village though;
He will not see me stopping here
To watch his woods fill up with snow.

5   My little horse must think it queer
To stop without a farmhouse near
Between the woods and frozen lake
The darkest evening of the year.

He gives his harness bells a shake
10 To ask if there is some mistake.
The only other sound's the sweep
Of easy wind and downy flake.

The woods are lovely, dark, and deep,
But I have promises to keep,
15 And miles to go before I sleep,
And miles to go before I sleep.

1923

JOY HARJO
The Woman Hanging from the Thirteenth Floor Window

She is the woman hanging from the 13th floor
window. Her hands are pressed white against the
concrete moulding of the tenement building. She
hangs from the 13th floor window in east Chicago,
5   with a swirl of birds over her head. They could
be a halo, or a storm of glass waiting to crush her.

She thinks she will be set free.

The woman hanging from the 13th floor window
on the east side of Chicago is not alone.
10   She is a woman of children, of the baby, Carlos
and of Margaret, and of Jimmy who is the oldest.
She is her mother's daughter and her father's son.
She is several pieces between the two husbands
she has had. She is all the women of the apartment
15   building who stand watching her, watching themselves.

When she was young she ate wild rice on scraped down
plates in warm wood rooms. It was in the farther
north and she was the baby then. They rocked her.

She sees Lake Michigan lapping at the shores of
20   herself. It is a dizzy hole of water and the rich
live in tall glass houses at the edge of it. In some
places Lake Michigan speaks softly, here, it just sputters
and butts itself against the asphalt. She sees
other buildings just like hers. She sees other
25   women hanging from many-floored windows
counting their lives in the palms of their hands
and in the palms of their children's hands.

She is the woman hanging from the 13th floor window
on the Indian side of town. Her belly is soft from
30   her children's births, her worn Levi's swing down below
her waist, and then her feet, and then her heart.
She is dangling.

The woman hanging from the 13th floor hears voices.
They come to her in the night when the lights have gone
35   dim. Sometimes they are little cats mewing and scratching
at the door; sometimes they are her grandmother's voice,
and sometimes they are gigantic men of light whispering
to her to get up, to get up, to get up. That's when she wants
to have another child to hold onto in the night, to be able
40   to fall back into dreams.

And the woman hanging from the 13th floor window
hears other voices. Some of them scream out from below
for her to jump, they would push her over. Others cry softly
from the sidewalks, pull their children up like flowers and gather
45   them into their arms. They would help her, like themselves.
But she is the woman hanging from the 13th floor window,
and she knows she is hanging by her own fingers, her
own skin, her own thread of indecision.

She thinks of Carlos, of Margaret, of Jimmy.
50   She thinks of her father, and of her mother
She thinks of all the women she has been, of all
the men. She thinks of the color of her skin, and

of Chicago streets, and of waterfalls and pines.
She thinks of moonlight nights, and of cool spring storms.
55   Her mind chatters like neon and northside bars.
She thinks of the 4 A.M. lonelinesses that have folded
her up like death, discordant, without logical and
beautiful conclusion. Her teeth break off at the edges.
She would speak.

60   The woman hangs from the 13th floor crying for
the lost beauty of her own life. She sees the
sun falling west over the gray plane of Chicago.
She thinks she remembers listening to her own life
break loose, as she falls from the 13th floor
65   window on the east side of Chicago, or as she
climbs back up to claim herself again.

                                                            1983

SEAMUS HEANEY
Digging

Between my finger and my thumb
The squat pen rests; snug as a gun.

Under my window, a clean rasping sound
When the spade sinks into gravelly ground:
5   My father, digging. I look down

Till his straining rump among the flowerbeds
Bends low, comes up twenty years away
Stooping in rhythm through potato drills⁴
Where he was digging.

10   The coarse boot nestled on the lug, the shaft
Against the inside knee was levered firmly.
He rooted out tall tops, buried the bright edge deep
To scatter new potatoes that we picked
Loving their cool hardness in our hands.

15   By God, the old man could handle a spade.
Just like his old man.

My grandfather cut more turf⁵ in a day
Than any other man on Toner's bog.
Once I carried him milk in a bottle
20   Corked sloppily with paper. He straightened up
To drink it, then fell to right away
Nicking and slicing neatly, heaving sods

---

4. Small furrows in which seeds are sown.
5. Peat cut into slabs and dried to be used as fuel in stoves and furnaces.

Over his shoulder, going down and down
For the good turf. Digging.

25 The cold smell of potato mould, the squelch and slap
Of soggy peat, the curt cuts of an edge
Through living roots awaken in my head.
But I've no spade to follow men like them.

Between my finger and my thumb
30 The squat pen rests.
I'll dig with it.

1966

GERARD MANLEY HOPKINS
God's Grandeur

The world is charged with the grandeur of God.
    It will flame out, like shining from shook foil;[6]
    It gathers to a greatness, like the ooze of oil
Crushed. Why do men then now not reck his rod?[7]
5 Generations have trod, have trod, have trod;
    And all is seared with trade; bleared, smeared with toil;
    And wears man's smudge and shares man's smell: the soil
Is bare now, nor can foot feel, being shod.

And for all this, nature is never spent;
10   There lives the dearest freshness deep down things;
And though the last lights off the black West went
    Oh, morning, at the brown brink eastward, springs—
Because the Holy Ghost over the bent
    World broods with warm breast and with ah! bright wings.

c. 1877

Spring and Fall

to a young child

Márgarét áre you gríeving[8]
Over Goldengrove unleaving?
Leáves, like the things of man, you
With your fresh thoughts care for, can you?

---

6. "I mean foil in its sense of leaf or tinsel [. . .]. Shaken goldfoil gives off broad glares like sheet lightning and also, and this is true of nothing else, owing to its zig-zag dints and creasings and network of small many cornered facets, a sort of fork lightning too" (*Letters of Gerard Manley Hopkins to Robert Bridges*, edited by C. C. Abbott, 1955, p. 169).
7. Heed his authority.
8. Hopkins's own accent markings.

5   Áh! ás the heart grows older
    It will-come to such sights colder
    By and by, nor spare a sigh
    Though worlds of wanwood leafmeal⁹ lie;
    And yet you wíll weep and know why.
10 Now no matter, child, the name:
    Sórrow's spríngs áre the same.
    Nor mouth had, no nor mind, expressed
    What heart heard of, ghost¹ guessed:
    It ís the blight man was born for,
15 It is Margaret you mourn for.

                                          1880

JOHN KEATS
Ode on a Grecian Urn

I

Thou still unravished bride of quietness,
    Thou foster-child of silence and slow time,
Sylvan historian, who canst thus express
    A flowery tale more sweetly than our rhyme:
5   What leaf-fringed legend haunts about thy shape
        Of deities or mortals, or of both,
            In Tempe or the dales of Arcady?²
    What men or gods are these? What maidens loath?
        What mad pursuit? What struggle to escape?
10   What pipes and timbrels? What wild ecstasy?

II

Heard melodies are sweet, but those unheard
    Are sweeter; therefore, ye soft pipes, play on;
Not to the sensual³ ear, but, more endeared,
    Pipe to the spirit ditties of no tone:
15 Fair youth, beneath the trees, thou canst not leave
        Thy song, nor ever can those trees be bare;
            Bold Lover, never, never canst thou kiss,
    Though winning near the goal—yet, do not grieve;
        She cannot fade, though thou hast not thy bliss,
20   For ever wilt thou love, and she be fair!

---

9. Broken up, leaf by leaf (analogous to "piecemeal"). *Wanwood*: pale, gloomy woods.
1. Soul.
2. Arcadia. Tempe is a beautiful valley near Mount Olympus in Greece, and the valleys ("dales") of Arcadia are a picturesque section of the Peloponnesus; both came to be associated with the pastoral ideal.
3. Of the senses, as distinguished from the "ear" of the spirit or imagination.

III

Ah, happy, happy boughs! that cannot shed
    Your leaves, nor ever bid the Spring adieu;
And, happy melodist, unwearièd,
    For ever piping songs for ever new;
25 More happy love! more happy, happy love!
    For ever warm and still to be enjoyed,
        For ever panting, and for ever young;
All breathing human passion far above,
    That leaves a heart high-sorrowful and cloyed,
30   A burning forehead, and a parching tongue.

Greek vase featuring Hercules driving
a bull to sacrifice, c. 525–520 BCE

IV

Who are these coming to the sacrifice?
    To what green altar, O mysterious priest,
Lead'st thou that heifer lowing at the skies,
    And all her silken flanks with garlands dressed?
35 What little town by river or sea shore,
    Or mountain-built with peaceful citadel,
        Is emptied of its folk, this pious morn?
And, little town, thy streets for evermore
    Will silent be; and not a soul to tell
40   Why thou art desolate, can e'er return.

V

O Attic shape! Fair attitude! with brede[4]
   Of marble men and maidens overwrought,[5]
With forest branches and the trodden weed;
   Thou, silent form, dost tease us out of thought
45 As doth eternity: Cold Pastoral!
     When old age shall this generation waste,
       Thou shalt remain, in midst of other woe
Than ours, a friend to man, to whom thou say'st,
     Beauty is truth, truth beauty[6]—that is all
50   Ye know on earth, and all ye need to know.

May 1819   1820

To Autumn

I

Season of mists and mellow fruitfulness,
   Close bosom-friend of the maturing sun;
Conspiring with him how to load and bless
   With fruit the vines that round the thatch-eves run;
5 To bend with apples the mossed cottage-trees,
   And fill all fruit with ripeness to the core;
     To swell the gourd, and plump the hazel shells
With a sweet kernel; to set budding more,
   And still more, later flowers for the bees,
10   Until they think warm days will never cease,
     For Summer has o'er-brimmed their clammy cells.

II

Who hath not seen thee oft amid thy store?
   Sometimes whoever seeks abroad may find
Thee sitting careless on a granary floor,
15   Thy hair soft-lifted by the winnowing wind,[7]
Or on a half-reaped furrow sound asleep,
   Drowsed with the fume of poppies, while thy hook[8]
     Spares the next swath and all its twinèd flowers:
And sometimes like a gleaner thou dost keep
20   Steady thy laden head across a brook;
   Or by a cider-press, with patient look,
     Thou watchest the last oozings hours by hours.

---

4. Woven pattern. *Attic:* Attica was the district of ancient Greece surrounding Athens.
5. Ornamented all over.
6. In some printings of the poem, "Beauty is truth, truth beauty" is in quotation marks, and in some texts it is not, leading to critical disagreements about whether the last line and a half are also inscribed on the urn or spoken by the poem's speaker.
7. Which sifts the grain from the chaff.
8. Scythe or sickle.

III

Where are the songs of Spring? Ay, where are they?
    Think not of them, thou hast thy music too—
25 While barrèd clouds bloom the soft-dying day,
    And touch the stubble-plains with rosy hue;
Then in a wailful choir the small gnats mourn
    Among the river sallows,[9] borne aloft
        Or sinking as the light wind lives or dies;
30 And full-grown lambs loud bleat from hilly bourn;[1]
    Hedge-crickets sing; and now with treble soft
    The red-breast whistles from a garden-croft;[2]
        And gathering swallows twitter in the skies.

September 19, 1819   1820

YUSEF KOMUNYAKAA

Facing It

My black face fades,
hiding inside the black granite.
I said I wouldn't,
dammit: No tears.
5 I'm stone. I'm flesh.
My clouded reflection eyes me
like a bird of prey, the profile of night
slanted against morning. I turn
this way—I'm inside
10 the Vietnam Veterans Memorial[3]
again, depending on the light
to make a difference.
I go down the 58,022 names,
half-expecting to find
15 my own in letters like smoke.
I touch the name Andrew Johnson;[4]
I see the booby trap's white flash.
Names shimmer on a woman's blouse
but when she walks away
20 the names stay on the wall.
Brushstrokes flash, a red bird's

9. Shallows.
1. Domain.
2. Enclosed garden near a house.
3. Designed by Maya Ying Lin, this Washington, D.C., memorial features two black, highly reflective
stone walls, each almost 247 feet long, etched with the names of servicemen declared either missing
or killed in action during the Vietnam War.
4. Soldier from Komunyakaa's hometown, Bogalusa, Louisiana. He shared the name of the U.S.
president who, after succeeding the recently assassinated Abraham Lincoln in 1865, both vetoed bills
designed to stop Southern states from depriving freed slaves of their civil liberties and opposed
passage of the Fourteenth Amendment (1868) granting citizenship to African Americans.

Veteran at the Vietnam Veterans Memorial, Washington, D.C., 2016

wings cutting across my stare.
The sky. A plane in the sky.
A white vet's image floats
25 closer to me, then his eyes
look through mine. I'm a window.
He's lost his right arm
inside the stone. In the black mirror
a woman's trying to erase names:
30 No, she's brushing a boy's hair.

1988

AUTHORS ON THEIR WORK

YUSEF KOMUNYAKAA (b. 1947)

From "Facing It" (2000)*

Now, as I think back to 1984, when I wrote "Facing It," with the humidity hanging over New Orleans [. . .] in early summer, I remember that it seemed several lifetimes from those fiery years in Vietnam. [. . .] I had meditated on the Vietnam Veterans Memorial as if the century's blues songs had been solidified into something monumental and concrete. Our wailing, our ranting, our singing of spirituals and kaddish and rock anthems, it was all captured and refined into a shaped destiny that attempted to portray personal and public feelings about war and human loss. It became a shrine overnight: a blackness that plays with light—a reflected motion in the stone that balances a dance between grass and sky. Whoever faces the granite becomes a part of it. The reflections move into and through each other. A dance between the dead and the living. Even in its heft and weight, emotionally and physically, it still seems to defy immediate description, constantly incorporating into its shape all the new reflections and shapes brought to it: one of the poignant shrines of the twentieth century.

*"Facing It." Blue Notes: Essays, Interviews, and Commentaries, edited by Radiclani Clytus, U of Michigan P, 2000, pp. 54–55.

Tu Do Street[5]

Searching for love, a woman,
someone to help ease down the cocked hammer
of my nerves & senses. The music
divides the evening into black
5 & white—soul, country & western,
acid rock, & Frank Sinatra.
I close my eyes & can see
men drawing lines in the dust,
daring each other to step across.
10 America pushes through the membrane
of mist & smoke, & I'm a small boy
again in Bogalusa[6] skirting tough talk
coming out of bars with White Only
signs & Hank Snow.[7] But tonight,
15 here in Saigon, just for the hell of it,
I walk into a place with Hank Williams[8]
calling from the jukebox. The bar girls
fade behind a smokescreen, fluttering
like tropical birds in a cage, not
20 speaking with their eyes & usual
painted smiles. I get the silent
treatment. We have played Judas
for each other out in the boonies
but only enemy machinegun fire
25 can bring us together again.

5. Literally, "Liberty Street" (Vietnamese), famous thoroughfare in the French quarter of Saigon, Vietnam; so named only during the war between North and South Vietnam (1955–75).
6. Industrial city in southeastern Louisiana.
7. Renowned Canadian-born country singer (1914–99).
8. Famously troubled country music singer-songwriter (1923–53) whose many hits include "I'm So Lonesome I Could Cry."

When I order a beer, the mama-san[9]
behind the counter acts as if she
can't understand, while her
eyes caress a white face;
30 down the street the black GIs
hold to their turf also.
An off-limits sign pulls me
deeper into alleys; I look
for a softness behind these voices
35 wounded by their beauty & war.
Back in the bush at Dak To
& Khe Sahn, we fought
the brothers of these women
we now run to hold in our arms.
40 There's more than a nation divided
inside us, as black & white
soldiers touch the same lovers
minutes apart, tasting
each other's breath,
45 without knowing these rooms
run into each other like tunnels
leading to the underworld.

1988

LINDA PASTAN
To a Daughter Leaving Home

When I taught you
at eight to ride
a bicycle, loping along
beside you
5 as you wobbled away
on two round wheels,
my own mouth rounding
in surprise when you pulled
ahead down the curved
10 path of the park,
I kept waiting
for the thud
of your crash as I
sprinted to catch up,
15 while you grew
smaller, more breakable
with distance,

---

9. In East Asia, a woman in authority; in Japanese, *san* is an honorific suffix, a title (not unlike "Mrs.")
added to names and proper nouns to indicate respect.

pumping, pumping
for your life, screaming
20   with laughter,
the hair flapping
behind you like a
handkerchief waving
goodbye.

1988

MARGE PIERCY
Barbie Doll

This girlchild was born as usual
and presented dolls that did pee-pee
and miniature GE stoves and irons
and wee lipsticks the color of cherry candy.
5   Then in the magic of puberty, a classmate said:
You have a great big nose and fat legs.

She was healthy, tested intelligent,
possessed strong arms and back,
abundant sexual drive and manual dexterity.
10   She went to and fro apologizing.
Everyone saw a fat nose on thick legs.

She was advised to play coy,
exhorted to come on hearty,
exercise, diet, smile and wheedle.
15   Her good nature wore out
like a fan belt.
So she cut off her nose and her legs
and offered them up.

In the casket displayed on satin she lay
20   with the undertaker's cosmetics painted on,
a turned-up putty nose,
dressed in a pink and white nightie.
Doesn't she look pretty? everyone said.
Consummation at last.
25   To every woman a happy ending.

1973

SYLVIA PLATH
Lady Lazarus

I have done it again.
One year in every ten
I manage it—

A sort of walking miracle, my skin
5   Bright as a Nazi lampshade,
My right foot

A paperweight,
My face a featureless, fine
Jew linen.[1]

10 Peel off the napkin
O my enemy.
Do I terrify?—

The nose, the eye pits, the full set of teeth?
The sour breath
15 Will vanish in a day.

Soon, soon the flesh
The grave cave ate will be
At home on me

And I a smiling woman.
20 I am only thirty.
And like the cat I have nine times to die.

This is Number Three.
What a trash
To annihilate each decade.

25 What a million filaments.
The peanut-crunching crowd
Shoves in to see

Them unwrap me hand and foot—
The big strip tease.
30 Gentlemen, ladies

These are my hands
My knees.
I may be skin and bone,

Nevertheless, I am the same, identical woman.
35 The first time it happened I was ten.
It was an accident.

The second time I meant
To last it out and not come back at all.
I rocked shut

40 As a seashell.
They had to call and call
And pick the worms off me like sticky pearls.

---

1. During World War II, prisoners in some Nazi camps were gassed to death and their body parts then turned into objects such as lampshades and paperweights.

Dying
Is an art, like everything else.
45 I do it exceptionally well.

I do it so it feels like hell.
I do it so it feels real.
I guess you could say I've a call.

It's easy enough to do it in a cell.
50 It's easy enough to do it and stay put.
It's the theatrical

Comeback in broad day
To the same place, the same face, the same brute
Amused shout:

55 "A miracle!"
That knocks me out.
There is a charge

For the eyeing of my scars, there is a charge
For the hearing of my heart—
60 It really goes.

And there is a charge, a very large charge
For a word or a touch
Or a bit of blood

Or a piece of my hair or my clothes.
65 So, so Herr Doktor.
So, Herr Enemy.

I am your opus,
I am your valuable,
The pure gold baby

70 That melts to a shriek.
I turn and burn.
Do not think I underestimate your great concern

Ash, ash—
You poke and stir.
75 Flesh, bone, there is nothing there—

A cake of soap,
A wedding ring,
A gold filling.

Herr God, Herr Lucifer
80 Beware
Beware.

Out of the ash
I rise with my red hair
And I eat men like air.

1965

Morning Song

Love set you going like a fat gold watch.
The midwife slapped your footsoles, and your bald cry
Took its place among the elements.

Our voices echo, magnifying your arrival. New statue.
5   In a drafty museum, your nakedness
Shadows our safety. We stand round blankly as walls.

I'm no more your mother
Than the cloud that distils a mirror to reflect its own slow
Effacement at the wind's hand.

10 All night your moth-breath
Flickers among the flat pink roses. I wake to listen:
A far sea moves in my ear.

One cry, and I stumble from bed, cow-heavy and floral
In my Victorian nightgown.
15 Your mouth opens clean as a cat's. The window square

Whitens and swallows its dull stars. And now you try
Your handful of notes;
The clear vowels rise like balloons.

1961

EDGAR ALLAN POE
The Raven

Once upon a midnight dreary, while I pondered, weak and weary,
Over many a quaint and curious volume of forgotten lore,
While I nodded, nearly napping, suddenly there came a tapping,
As of some one gently rapping, rapping at my chamber door.
5   "'Tis some visitor," I muttered, "tapping at my chamber door—
Only this, and nothing more."

Ah, distinctly I remember it was in the bleak December,
And each separate dying ember wrought its ghost upon the floor.
Eagerly I wished the morrow;—vainly I had sought to borrow
10 From my books surcease of sorrow—sorrow for the lost Lenore—
For the rare and radiant maiden whom the angels name Lenore—
Nameless here for evermore.

And the silken sad uncertain rustling of each purple curtain
Thrilled me—filled me with fantastic terrors never felt before;
15 So that now, to still the beating of my heart, I stood repeating
"'Tis some visitor entreating entrance at my chamber door;—
Some late visitor entreating entrance at my chamber door;
This it is, and nothing more."

Presently my soul grew stronger; hesitating then no longer,
20 "Sir," said I, "or Madam, truly your forgiveness I implore;
But the fact is I was napping, and so gently you came rapping,
And so faintly you came tapping, tapping at my chamber door,
That I scarce was sure I heard you"—here I opened wide the door;—
Darkness there, and nothing more.

25 Deep into that darkness peering, long I stood there wondering, fearing,
Doubting, dreaming dreams no mortal ever dared to dream before;
But the silence was unbroken, and the darkness gave no token,
And the only word there spoken was the whispered word, "Lenore!"
This I whispered, and an echo murmured back the word, "Lenore!"—
30 Merely this, and nothing more.

Back into the chamber turning, all my soul within me burning,
Soon I heard again a tapping somewhat louder than before.
"Surely," said I, "surely that is something at my window lattice;
Let me see, then, what thereat is, and this mystery explore—
35 Let my heart be still a moment and this mystery explore;—
'Tis the wind and nothing more!"

Open here I flung the shutter, when, with many a flirt and flutter,
In there stepped a stately raven of the saintly days of yore;
Not the least obeisance made he; not an instant stopped or stayed he;
40 But, with mien of lord or lady, perched above my chamber door—
Perched upon a bust of Pallas² just above my chamber door—
Perched, and sat, and nothing more.

Then this ebony bird beguiling my sad fancy into smiling,
By the grave and stern decorum of the countenance it wore,
45 "Though thy crest be shorn and shaven, thou," I said, "art sure no craven,
Ghastly grim and ancient raven wandering from the Nightly shore—
Tell me what thy lordly name is on the Night's Plutonian³ shore!"
Quoth the raven, "Nevermore."

Much I marvelled this ungainly fowl to hear discourse so plainly,
50 Though its answer little meaning—little relevancy bore,
For we cannot help agreeing that no living human being
Ever yet was blessed with seeing bird above his chamber door—
Bird or beast upon the sculptured bust above his chamber door,
With such name as "Nevermore."

55 But the raven, sitting lonely on the placid bust, spoke only
That one word, as if his soul in that one word he did outpour.
Nothing farther then he uttered—not a feather then he fluttered—
Till I scarcely more than muttered "Other friends have flown before—
On the morrow *he* will leave me, as my hopes have flown before."
60 Then the bird said "Nevermore."

Startled at the stillness broken by reply so aptly spoken,
"Doubtless," said I, "what it utters is its only stock and store

2. Athena, Greek goddess of wisdom.
3. Dark; Pluto was the ancient Greek god of the underworld.

Caught from some unhappy master whom unmerciful Disaster
Followed fast and followed faster till his songs one burden bore—
65 Till the dirges of his Hope that melancholy burden bore
                    Of 'Never—nevermore.'"

But the raven still beguiling all my sad soul into smiling,
Straight I wheeled a cushioned seat in front of bird and bust and door;
Then, upon the velvet sinking, I betook myself to linking
70 Fancy unto fancy, thinking what this ominous bird of yore—
What this grim, ungainly, ghastly, gaunt, and ominous bird of yore
                    Meant in croaking "Nevermore."

This I sat engaged in guessing, but no syllable expressing
To the fowl whose fiery eyes now burned into my bosom's core;
75 This and more I sat divining, with my head at ease reclining
On the cushion's velvet lining that the lamplight gloated o'er,
But whose velvet violet lining with the lamplight gloating o'er,
                    She shall press, ah, nevermore!

Then, methought, the air grew denser, perfumed from an unseen censer
80 Swung by angels whose faint foot-falls tinkled on the tufted floor.
"Wretch," I cried, "thy God hath lent thee—by these angels he hath sent
        thee
Respite—respite and nepenthe[4] from thy memories of Lenore!
Quaff, oh quaff this kind nepenthe and forget this lost Lenore!"
                    Quoth the raven, "Nevermore."

85 "Prophet!" said I, "thing of evil!—prophet still, if bird or devil!—
Whether Tempter sent, or whether tempest tossed thee here ashore,
Desolate, yet all undaunted, on this desert land enchanted—
On this home by Horror haunted—tell me truly, I implore—
Is there—*is* there balm in Gilead?[5]—tell me—tell me, I implore!"
90   Quoth the raven, "Nevermore."

"Prophet!" said I, "thing of evil—prophet still, if bird or devil!
By that Heaven that bends above us—by that God we both adore—
Tell this soul with sorrow laden if, within the distant Aidenn,[6]
It shall clasp a sainted maiden whom the angels name Lenore—
95 Clasp a rare and radiant maiden whom the angels name Lenore."
                    Quoth the raven, "Nevermore."

"Be that word our sign of parting, bird or fiend!" I shrieked upstarting—
"Get thee back into the tempest and the Night's Plutonian shore!
Leave no black plume as a token of that lie thy soul hath spoken!
100 Leave my loneliness unbroken!—quit the bust above my door!
Take thy beak from out my heart, and take thy form from off my door!"
                    Quoth the raven, "Nevermore."

And the raven, never flitting, still is sitting, still is sitting
On the pallid bust of Pallas just above my chamber door;

4. Drug reputed by the Greeks to cause forgetfulness or sorrow (pronounced "ne-PEN-thee").
5. See Jeremiah 8.22.
6. Eden.

105   And his eyes have all the seeming of a demon's that is dreaming,
      And the lamp-light o'er him streaming throws his shadow on the floor;
      And my soul from out that shadow that lies floating on the floor
                              Shall be lifted—nevermore!

                                                                        1844

CHRISTINA ROSSETTI
Goblin Market

Morning and evening
Maids heard the goblins cry:
"Come buy our orchard fruits,
Come buy, come buy:
5   Apples and quinces,
Lemons and oranges,
Plump unpecked cherries,
Melons and raspberries,
Bloom-down-cheeked peaches,
10   Swart[7]-headed mulberries,
Wild free-born cranberries,
Crab-apples, dewberries,
Pine-apples, blackberries,
Apricots, strawberries;—
15   All ripe together
In summer weather,—
Morns that pass by,
Fair eves that fly;
Come buy, come buy:
20   Our grapes fresh from the vine,
Pomegranates full and fine,
Dates and sharp bullaces,
Rare pears and greengages,
Damsons[8] and bilberries,
25   Taste them and try:
Currants and gooseberries,
Bright-fire-like barberries,
Figs to fill your mouth,
Citrons from the South,
30   Sweet to tongue and sound to eye;
Come buy, come buy."

Evening by evening
Among the brookside rushes,
Laura bowed her head to hear,
35   Lizzie veiled her blushes:

---

7. Dark.
8. Plums; "bullaces" (line 22) and "greengages" (23) are other varieties of the same fruit.

Crouching close together
In the cooling weather,
With clasping arms and cautioning lips,
With tingling cheeks and finger tips.
40 "Lie close," Laura said,
Pricking up her golden head:
"We must not look at goblin men,
We must not buy their fruits:
Who knows upon what soil they fed
45 Their hungry thirsty roots?"
"Come buy," call the goblins
Hobbling down the glen.
"Oh," cried Lizzie, "Laura, Laura,
You should not peep at goblin men."
50 Lizzie covered up her eyes,
Covered close lest they should look;
Laura reared her glossy head,
And whispered like the restless brook:
"Look, Lizzie, look, Lizzie,
55 Down the glen tramp little men.
One hauls a basket,
One bears a plate,
One lugs a golden dish
Of many pounds weight.
60 How fair the vine must grow
Whose grapes are so luscious;
How warm the wind must blow
Thro' those fruit bushes."
"No," said Lizzie: "No, no, no;
65 Their offers should not charm us,
Their evil gifts would harm us."
She thrust a dimpled finger
In each ear, shut eyes and ran:
Curious Laura chose to linger
70 Wondering at each merchant man.
One had a cat's face,
One whisked a tail,
One tramped at a rat's pace,
One crawled like a snail,
75 One like a wombat prowled obtuse and furry,
One like a ratel[9] tumbled hurry skurry.
She heard a voice like voice of doves
Cooing all together:
They sounded kind and full of loves
80 In the pleasant weather.

Laura stretched her gleaming neck
Like a rush-imbedded swan,

---

9. Badger-like mammal native to Asia and Africa (pronounced "RAY-tl").

Like a lily from the beck,[1]
Like a moonlit poplar branch,
85 Like a vessel at the launch
When its last restraint is gone.

Backwards up the mossy glen
Turned and trooped the goblin men,
With their shrill repeated cry,
90 "Come buy, come buy."
When they reached where Laura was
They stood stock still upon the moss,
Leering at each other,
Brother with queer brother;
95 Signalling each other,
Brother with sly brother.
One set his basket down,
One reared[2] his plate;
One began to weave a crown
100 Of tendrils, leaves and rough nuts brown
(Men sell not such in any town);
One heaved the golden weight
Of dish and fruit to offer her:
"Come buy, come buy," was still their cry.

105 Laura stared but did not stir,
Longed but had no money:
The whisk-tailed merchant bade her taste
In tones as smooth as honey,
The cat-faced purr'd,
110 The rat-paced spoke a word
Of welcome, and the snail-paced even was heard;
One parrot-voiced and jolly
Cried "Pretty Goblin" still[3] for "Pretty Polly;"—
One whistled like a bird.

115 But sweet-tooth Laura spoke in haste:
"Good folk, I have no coin;
To take were to purloin:
I have no copper in my purse,
I have no silver either,
120 And all my gold is on the furze[4]
That shakes in windy weather
Above the rusty heather."
"You have much gold upon your head,"
They answered all together:
125 "Buy from us with a golden curl."

1. Stream.
2. Raised.
3. Always.
4. Spiny shrub with yellow flowers.

She clipped a precious golden lock,
She dropped a tear more rare than pearl,
Then sucked their fruit globes fair or red:
Sweeter than honey from the rock,[5]
130 Stronger than man-rejoicing wine,
Clearer than water flowed that juice;
She never tasted such before,
How should it cloy with length of use?
She sucked and sucked and sucked the more
135 Fruits which that unknown orchard bore;
She sucked until her lips were sore;
Then flung the emptied rinds away
But gathered up one kernel-stone,
And knew not was it night or day
140 As she turned home alone.

Lizzie met her at the gate
Full of wise upbraidings:
"Dear, you should not stay so late,
Twilight is not good for maidens;
145 Should not loiter in the glen
In the haunts of goblin men.
Do you not remember Jeanie,
How she met them in the moonlight,
Took their gifts both choice and many,
150 Ate their fruits and wore their flowers
Plucked from bowers
Where summer ripens at all hours?
But ever in the noonlight
She pined and pined away;
155 Sought them by night and day,
Found them no more but dwindled and grew grey;
Then fell with the first snow,
While to this day no grass will grow
Where she lies low:
160 I planted daisies there a year ago
That never blow.[6]
You should not loiter so."
"Nay, hush," said Laura:
"Nay, hush, my sister:
165 I ate and ate my fill,
Yet my mouth waters still;
Tomorrow night I will
Buy more:" and kissed her:
"Have done with sorrow;
170 I'll bring you plums tomorrow

---

5. See Psalms 81.16: "He should have fed them also with the finest of the wheat: and with honey out of the rock should I have satisfied thee."
6. Bloom.

Fresh on their mother twigs,
Cherries worth getting;
You cannot think what figs
My teeth have met in,
175 What melons icy-cold
Piled on a dish of gold
Too huge for me to hold,
What peaches with a velvet nap,
Pellucid[7] grapes without one seed:
180 Odorous indeed must be the mead
Whereon they grow, and pure the wave they drink
With lilies at the brink,
And sugar-sweet their sap."

Golden head by golden head,
185 Like two pigeons in one nest
Folded in each other's wings,
They lay down in their curtained bed:
Like two blossoms on one stem,
Like two flakes of new-fall'n snow,
190 Like two wands of ivory
Tipped with gold for awful[8] kings.
Moon and stars gazed in at them,
Wind sang to them lullaby,
Lumbering owls forbore to fly,
195 Not a bat flapped to and fro
Round their rest:
Cheek to cheek and breast to breast
Locked together in one nest.

Early in the morning
200 When the first cock crowed his warning,
Neat like bees, as sweet and busy,
Laura rose with Lizzie:
Fetched in honey, milked the cows,
Aired and set to rights the house,
205 Kneaded cakes of whitest wheat,
Cakes for dainty mouths to eat,
Next churned butter, whipped up cream,
Fed their poultry, sat and sewed;
Talked as modest maidens should:
210 Lizzie with an open heart,
Laura in an absent dream,
One content, one sick in part;
One warbling for the mere bright day's delight,
One longing for the night.
215 At length slow evening came:
They went with pitchers to the reedy brook;

7. Translucent.
8. Awe-inspiring.

GOBLIN MARKET
and other poems
by Christina Rossetti

"Golden head by golden head"

London and Cambridge
Macmillan and Co. 1862

Frontispiece featuring artwork by Christina Rossetti's brother,
painter-poet Dante Gabriel Rossetti

Lizzie most placid in her look,
Laura most like a leaping flame.
They drew the gurgling water from its deep;
220 Lizzie plucked purple and rich golden flags,[9]
Then turning homewards said: "The sunset flushes
Those furthest loftiest crags;
Come, Laura, not another maiden lags,
No wilful squirrel wags,
225 The beasts and birds are fast asleep."
But Laura loitered still among the rushes
And said the bank was steep.

And said the hour was early still,
The dew not fall'n, the wind not chill:
230 Listening ever, but not catching

9. Irises.

The customary cry,
"Come buy, come buy,"
With its iterated jingle
Of sugar-baited words:
235 Not for all her watching
Once discerning even one goblin
Racing, whisking, tumbling, hobbling;
Let alone the herds
That used to tramp along the glen,
240 In groups or single,
Of brisk fruit-merchant men.
Till Lizzie urged, "O Laura, come;
I hear the fruit-call but I dare not look:
You should not loiter longer at this brook:
245 Come with me home.
The stars rise, the moon bends her arc,
Each glowworm winks her spark,
Let us get home before the night grows dark:
For clouds may gather
250 Tho' this is summer weather,
Put out the lights and drench us thro';
Then if we lost our way what should we do?"

Laura turned cold as stone
To find her sister heard that cry alone,
255 That goblin cry,
"Come buy our fruits, come buy."
Must she then buy no more such dainty fruit?
Must she no more such succous[1] pasture find,
Gone deaf and blind?
260 Her tree of life drooped from the root:
She said not one word in her heart's sore ache;
But peering thro' the dimness, nought discerning,
Trudged home, her pitcher dripping all the way;
So crept to bed, and lay
265 Silent till Lizzie slept;
Then sat up in a passionate yearning,
And gnashed her teeth for baulked desire, and wept
As if her heart would break.

Day after day, night after night,
270 Laura kept watch in vain
In sullen silence of exceeding pain.
She never caught again the goblin cry:
"Come buy, come buy;"—
She never spied the goblin men
275 Hawking their fruits along the glen:
But when the noon waxed bright
Her hair grew thin and gray;

1. Juicy.

She dwindled, as the fair full moon doth turn
To swift decay and burn
280   Her fire away.

One day remembering her kernel-stone
She set it by a wall that faced the south;
Dewed it with tears, hoped for a root,
Watched for a waxing shoot,
285   But there came none;
It never saw the sun,
It never felt the trickling moisture run:
While with sunk eyes and faded mouth
She dreamed of melons, as a traveler sees
290   False waves in desert drouth
With shade of leaf-crowned trees,
And burns the thirstier in the sandful breeze.

She no more swept the house,
Tended the fowls or cows,
295   Fetched honey, kneaded cakes of wheat,
Brought water from the brook:
But sat down listless in the chimney-nook
And would not eat.

Tender Lizzie could not bear
300   To watch her sister's cankerous² care
Yet not to share.
She night and morning
Caught the goblins' cry:
"Come buy our orchard fruits,
305   Come buy, come buy:"—
Beside the brook, along the glen,
She heard the tramp of goblin men,
The voice and stir
Poor Laura could not hear;
310   Longed to buy fruit to comfort her,
But feared to pay too dear.
She thought of Jeanie in her grave,
Who should have been a bride;
But who for joys brides hope to have
315   Fell sick and died
In her gay prime,
In earliest Winter time,
With the first glazing rime,
With the first snow-fall of crisp Winter time.

320   Till Laura dwindling
Seemed knocking at Death's door:
Then Lizzie weighed³ no more

2. Corroding.
3. Evaluated, considered.

Better and worse;
But put a silver penny in her purse,
325 Kissed Laura, crossed the heath with clumps of furze
At twilight, halted by the brook:
And for the first time in her life
Began to listen and look.

Laughed every goblin
330 When they spied her peeping:
Came towards her hobbling,
Flying, running, leaping,
Puffing and blowing,
Chuckling, clapping, crowing,
335 Clucking and gobbling,
Mopping and mowing,[4]
Full of airs and graces,
Pulling wry faces,
Demure grimaces,
340 Cat-like and rat-like,
Ratel- and wombat-like,
Snail-paced in a hurry,
Parrot-voiced and whistler,
Helter skelter, hurry skurry,
345 Chattering like magpies,
Fluttering like pigeons,
Gliding like fishes,—
Hugged her and kissed her,
Squeezed and caressed her:
350 Stretched up their dishes,
Panniers,[5] and plates:
"Look at our apples
Russet and dun,
Bob at our cherries,
355 Bite at our peaches,
Citrons and dates,
Grapes for the asking,
Pears red with basking
Out in the sun,
360 Plums on their twigs;
Pluck them and suck them,
Pomegranates, figs."—

"Good folk," said Lizzie,
Mindful of Jeanie:
365 "Give me much and many:"—
Held out her apron,
Tossed them her penny.
"Nay, take a seat with us,

4. Making faces.
5. Baskets for carrying provisions.

Honour and eat with us,"
370 They answered grinning:
"Our feast is but beginning.
Night yet is early,
Warm and dew-pearly,
Wakeful and starry:
375 Such fruits as these
No man can carry;
Half their bloom would fly,
Half their dew would dry,
Half their flavour would pass by.
380 Sit down and feast with us,
Be welcome guest with us,
Cheer you and rest with us."—
"Thank you," said Lizzie: "But one waits
At home alone for me:
385 So without further parleying,
If you will not sell me any
Of your fruits tho' much and many,
Give me back my silver penny
I tossed you for a fee."—
390 They began to scratch their pates,
No longer wagging, purring,
But visibly demurring,
Grunting and snarling.
One called her proud,
395 Cross-grained, uncivil;
Their tones waxed loud,
Their looks were evil.
Lashing their tails
They trod and hustled her,
400 Elbowed and jostled her,
Clawed with their nails,
Barking, mewing, hissing, mocking,
Tore her gown and soiled her stocking,
Twitched her hair out by the roots,
405 Stamped upon her tender feet,
Held her hands and squeezed their fruits
Against her mouth to make her eat.
White and golden Lizzie stood,
Like a lily in a flood,—
410 Like a rock of blue-veined stone
Lashed by tides obstreperously,—
Like a beacon left alone
In a hoary roaring sea,
Sending up a golden fire,—
415 Like a fruit-crowned orange-tree
White with blossoms honey-sweet
Sore beset by wasp and bee,—
Like a royal virgin town

Topped with gilded dome and spire
420 Close beleaguered by a fleet
Mad to tug her standard down.

One may lead a horse to water,
Twenty cannot make him drink.
Tho' the goblins cuffed and caught her,
425 Coaxed and fought her,
Bullied and besought her,
Scratched her, pinched her black as ink,
Kicked and knocked her,
Mauled and mocked her,
430 Lizzie uttered not a word;
Would not open lip from lip
Lest they should cram a mouthful in:
But laughed in heart to feel the drip
Of juice that syrupped all her face,
435 And lodged in dimples of her chin,
And streaked her neck which quaked like curd.
At last the evil people
Worn out by her resistance
Flung back her penny, kicked their fruit
440 Along whichever road they took,
Not leaving root or stone or shoot;
Some writhed into the ground,
Some dived into the brook
With ring and ripple,
445 Some scudded on the gale without a sound,
Some vanished in the distance.
In a smart, ache, tingle,
Lizzie went her way;
Knew not was it night or day;
450 Sprang up the bank, tore thro' the furze,
Threaded copse and dingle,[6]
And heard her penny jingle
Bouncing in her purse,
Its bounce was music to her ear.
455 She ran and ran
As if she feared some goblin man
Dogged her with gibe or curse
Or something worse:
But not one goblin skurried after,
460 Nor was she pricked by fear;
The kind heart made her windy-paced
That urged her home quite out of breath with haste
And inward laughter.

She cried "Laura," up the garden,
465 "Did you miss me?

6. Deep wooded valley or dell. *Copse*: small cluster of trees.

Come and kiss me.
Never mind my bruises,
Hug me, kiss me, suck my juices
Squeezed from goblin fruits for you,
470 Goblin pulp and goblin dew.
Eat me, drink me, love me;[7]
Laura, make much of me:
For your sake I have braved the glen
And had to do with goblin merchant men."

475 Laura started from her chair,
Flung her arms up in the air,
Clutched her hair:
"Lizzie, Lizzie, have you tasted
For my sake the fruit forbidden?
480 Must your light like mine be hidden,
Your young life like mine be wasted,
Undone in mine undoing
And ruined in my ruin,
Thirsty, cankered, goblin-ridden?"—
485 She clung about her sister,
Kissed and kissed and kissed her:
Tears once again
Refreshed her shrunken eyes,
Dropping like rain
490 After long sultry drouth;
Shaking with aguish[8] fear, and pain,
She kissed and kissed her with a hungry mouth.

Her lips began to scorch,
That juice was wormwood[9] to her tongue,
495 She loathed the feast:
Writhing as one possessed she leaped and sung,
Rent all her robe, and wrung
Her hands in lamentable haste,
And beat her breast.
500 Her locks streamed like the torch
Borne by a racer at full speed,
Or like the mane of horses in their flight,
Or like an eagle when she stems the light
Straight toward the sun,
505 Or like a caged thing freed,
Or like a flying flag when armies run.

Swift fire spread thro' her veins, knocked at her heart,
Met the fire smouldering there
And overbore its lesser flame;

7. Echo of Jesus's words at the Last Supper: See Mark 14.22–24 and Luke 22.19–20.
8. Feverish.
9. Bitter-tasting woody shrub sometimes used in medicine, as well as in vermouth and absinthe.

510 She gorged on bitterness without a name:
Ah! fool, to choose such part
Of soul-consuming care!
Sense failed in the mortal strife:
Like the watch-tower of a town
515 Which an earthquake shatters down,
Like a lightning-stricken mast,
Like a wind-uprooted tree
Spun about,
Like a foam-topped waterspout
520 Cast down headlong in the sea,
She fell at last;
Pleasure past and anguish past,
Is it death or is it life?

Life out of death.
525 That night long Lizzie watched by her,
Counted her pulse's flagging stir,
Felt for her breath,
Held water to her lips, and cooled her face
With tears and fanning leaves:
530 But when the first birds chirped about their eaves,
And early reapers plodded to the place
Of golden sheaves,
And dew-wet grass
Bowed in the morning winds so brisk to pass,
535 And new buds with new day
Opened of cup-like lilies on the stream,
Laura awoke as from a dream,
Laughed in the innocent old way,
Hugged Lizzie but not[1] twice or thrice;
540 Her gleaming locks showed not one thread of grey,
Her breath was sweet as May
And light danced in her eyes.

Days, weeks, months, years
Afterwards, when both were wives
545 With children of their own;
Their mother-hearts beset with fears,
Their lives bound up in tender lives;
Laura would call the little ones
And tell them of her early prime,
550 Those pleasant days long gone
Of not-returning time:
Would talk about the haunted glen,
The wicked, quaint[2] fruit-merchant men,
Their fruits like honey to the throat
555 But poison in the blood;

1. Not only.
2. Strange.

(Men sell not such in any town:)
Would tell them how her sister stood
In deadly peril to do her good,

And win the fiery antidote:
560 Then joining hands to little hands
Would bid them cling together,
"For there is no friend like a sister
In calm or stormy weather;
To cheer one on the tedious way,
565 To fetch one if one goes astray,
To lift one if one totters down,
To strengthen whilst one stands."

1862

WALLACE STEVENS
Anecdote of the Jar

I placed a jar in Tennessee,
And round it was, upon a hill.
It made the slovenly wilderness
Surround that hill.

5 The wilderness rose up to it,
And sprawled around, no longer wild.
The jar was round upon the ground
And tall and of a port in air.

It took dominion everywhere.
10 The jar was gray and bare.
It did not give of bird or bush,
Like nothing else in Tennessee.

1923

ALFRED, LORD TENNYSON
Ulysses[3]

It little profits that an idle king,
By this still hearth, among these barren crags,
Matched with an agèd wife,[4] mete and dole
Unequal laws unto a savage race,
5 That hoard, and sleep, and feed, and know not me.

---

3. After the Trojan War ended, Ulysses (or Odysseus), king of Ithaca and one of the war's Greek heroes, returned to his island home (line 34). Homer's account of the situation appears in Book 11 of *The Odyssey*, but Dante's account of Ulysses in canto 26 of the *Inferno* is the more immediate background of Tennyson's poem.
4. Penelope.

I cannot rest from travel; I will drink
Life to the lees.[5] All times I have enjoyed
Greatly, have suffered greatly, both with those
That loved me, and alone; on shore, and when
10 Through scudding drifts the rainy Hyades[6]
Vexed the dim sea. I am become a name;
For always roaming with a hungry heart
Much have I seen and known—cities of men
And manners, climates, councils, governments,
15 Myself not least, but honored of them all—
And drunk delight of battle with my peers,
Far on the ringing plains of windy Troy.
I am a part of all that I have met;
Yet all experience is an arch wherethrough
20 Gleams that untraveled world, whose margin fades
For ever and for ever when I move.
How dull it is to pause, to make an end,
To rust unburnished, not to shine in use!
As though to breathe were life. Life piled on life
25 Were all too little, and of one to me
Little remains; but every hour is saved
From that eternal silence, something more,
A bringer of new things; and vile it were
For some three suns to store and hoard myself,
30 And this gray spirit yearning in desire
To follow knowledge like a sinking star,
Beyond the utmost bound of human thought.

This is my son, mine own Telemachus,
To whom I leave the scepter and the isle—
35 Well-loved of me, discerning to fulfill
This labor, by slow prudence to make mild
A rugged people, and through soft degrees
Subdue them to the useful and the good.
Most blameless is he, centered in the sphere
40 Of common duties, decent not to fail
In offices of tenderness, and pay
Meet adoration to my household gods,
When I am gone. He works his work, I mine.

There lies the port; the vessel puffs her sail:
45 There gloom the dark, broad seas. My mariners,
Souls that have toiled, and wrought, and thought with me—
That ever with a frolic welcome took
The thunder and the sunshine, and opposed
Free hearts, free foreheads—you and I are old;
50 Old age hath yet his honor and his toil.
Death closes all; but something ere the end,

---

5. That is, all the way down to the bottom of the cup.
6. Group of stars believed to predict the rain when they rose at the same time as the sun.

Some work of noble note, may yet be done,
Not unbecoming men that strove with Gods.
The lights begin to twinkle from the rocks;
55 The long day wanes; the slow moon climbs; the deep
Moans round with many voices. Come, my friends,
'Tis not too late to seek a newer world.
Push off, and sitting well in order smite
The sounding furrows; for my purpose holds
60 To sail beyond the sunset, and the baths
Of all the western stars, until I die.
It may be that the gulfs will wash us down;[7]
It may be we shall touch the Happy Isles,[8]
And see the great Achilles, whom we knew.
65 Though much is taken, much abides; and though
We are not now that strength which in old days
Moved earth and heaven, that which we are, we are:
One equal temper of heroic hearts,
Made weak by time and fate, but strong in will
70 To strive, to seek, to find, and not to yield.

1833

WALT WHITMAN
Facing West from California's Shores

Facing west from California's shores,
Inquiring, tireless, seeking what is yet unfound,
I, a child, very old, over waves, towards the house of maternity,[9] the
    land of migrations, look afar,
Look off the shores of my Western sea, the circle almost circled;
5 For starting westward from Hindustan, from the vales of Kashmere,
From Asia, from the north, from the God, the sage, and the hero,
From the south, from the flowery peninsulas and the spice islands,
Long having wander'd since, round the earth having wander'd,
Now I face home again, very pleas'd and joyous,
10 (But where is what I started for so long ago?
And why is it yet unfound?)

1860, 1881

---

7. Beyond the Gulf of Gibraltar was supposed to lie a chasm that led to Hades, the underworld.
8. Elysium, the Islands of the Blessed, where heroes like Achilles (line 64) go after death.
9. Asia, as the supposed birthplace of the human race.

RICHARD WILBUR
Love Calls Us to the Things of This World

The eyes open to a cry of pulleys,
And spirited from sleep, the astounded soul
Hangs for a moment bodiless and simple
As false dawn.
5   Outside the open window
The morning air is all awash with angels.

Some are in bed-sheets, some are in blouses,
Some are in smocks: but truly there they are.
Now they are rising together in calm swells
10 Of halcyon[1] feeling, filling whatever they wear
With the deep joy of their impersonal breathing;

Now they are flying in place, conveying
The terrible speed of their omnipresence, moving
And staying like white water; and now of a sudden
15 They swoon down into so rapt a quiet
That nobody seems to be there.
                              The soul shrinks

From all that it is about to remember,
From the punctual rape of every blessed day,
20 And cries,
              "Oh, let there be nothing on earth but laundry,
Nothing but rosy hands in the rising steam
And clear dances done in the sight of heaven."

Yet, as the sun acknowledges
25 With a warm look the world's hunks and colors,
The soul descends once more in bitter love
To accept the waking body, saying now
In a changed voice as the man yawns and rises,
      "Bring them down from their ruddy gallows;
30 Let there be clean linen for the backs of thieves;
Let lovers go fresh and sweet to be undone,
And the heaviest nuns walk in a pure floating
Of dark habits,
              keeping their difficult balance."

1956

---

1. Serene.

Biographical Sketches: Poets

Sketches are included for all poets represented by two or more poems.

JULIA ALVAREZ (b. 1950)

Thanks especially to her bestselling, award-winning *How the García Girls Lost Their Accents* (1991), Julia Alvarez is today best known for her novels, as well as books of fiction for young readers (including the Tía Lola series) and nonfiction for adults (including *Once Upon a Quinceañera: Coming of Age in the USA* [2007]). Yet Alvarez—whom President Barack Obama awarded the National Medal of Arts in 2014—began her career with poetry, a form she has never abandoned and which often looms large in her fictional characters' lives. Born in New York, Alvarez, along with her three sisters, was raised in her Dominican parents' homeland until age ten, when (in 1960) their involvement in the underground movement to oust dictator Rafael Trujillo forced the family to flee. Resettled in New York City, Alvarez initially struggled with her new environment and new language. Yet this very "radical uprooting from my culture, my native language, my country" also became, she explains, "the reason I began writing." Ultimately, she says, "English, not the United States, was where I landed and sunk deep roots," embracing "[l]anguage [a]s the only homeland." The joys and challenges of the immigrant experience and of lives lived across cultures and languages feature prominently in the poetry collected in her *Homecoming* (1984), *The Other Side / El Otro Lado* (1995), and *The Woman I Kept to Myself* (2004). A graduate of Middlebury College (BA, 1971) and Syracuse University (MA, 1975), Alvarez served many years on the faculty of her undergraduate alma mater, where she today holds the title of Writer in Residence Emerita.

MAYA ANGELOU (1928–2014)

Alongside the brother who nicknamed her "Maya," St. Louis–born Marguerite Ann Johnson was raised mainly by her grandmother, in Jim Crow–era Arkansas, and by her mother, in San Francisco. Raped at age eight, she refused to speak for five years, nurturing her love of language through the work of writers ranging from Shakespeare and Dickens to the Harlem Renaissance poets. Bearing her only son just weeks after graduating from high school, Johnson worked as short-order cook, car paint stripper, streetcar conductor, and sex worker before launching her career as dancer-singer-actress "Maya Angelou." Though she would perform professionally all her life, in the 1960s Angelou also branched out, joining the Harlem Writers Guild, working as a civil rights activist, and living briefly in Egypt and West Africa before penning (at James Baldwin's urging) *I Know Why the Caged Bird Sings* (1970), the first and most acclaimed of her six memoirs. In 1971 Angelou made her poetic debut, with *Just Give Me a Cool Drink of Water 'fore I Diiie*. Angelou was also an essayist; the creator of children's books, cookbooks, and her own line of Hallmark greeting cards; a playwright, screenwriter, and composer; a film director; a teacher; and a public speaker renowned for her regal demeanor and deep, sonorous voice. Angelou's greatest fame came well after age sixty, thanks partly to two famous fans—Oprah Winfrey, who frequently celebrated her "mentor-mother-sister-friend," and Bill Clinton, who, in 1993, invited Angelou to become only the second poet in U.S. history to recite her work at a presidential inauguration. Granted the Presidential Medal of Freedom, her nation's highest civilian honor, some eighteen years later, Angelou once described all her writing as forwarding the same "thesis" her remarkable life arguably did: "We may encounter many defeats, but we must not be defeated."

BASHŌ (1644–94)

Born Matsuo Munefusa, the second son of a low-ranking provincial samurai, the haiku poet who came to be known as Bashō at first put aside his literary interests and entered into service with the local ruling military house. In 1666, following the feudal lord's death, Bashō left for Edo (now Tokyo), the military capital of the shogun's new government, to pursue a career as a professional poet. He supported himself as a teacher and editor of other people's poetry but ultimately developed a following and a sizable group of students. A seasoned traveler, Bashō maintained an austere existence on the road and at home, casting himself in travel narratives such as *The Narrow Road to the Interior* (1694) as a pilgrim devoted to nature and Zen.

REGINALD DWAYNE BETTS (b. 1980)

"Poets tell various kinds of down-and-out stories about being rescued by their vocations," notes *The New Yorker*'s Dan Chiasson, but that of lawyer-poet, memoirist, and teacher Reginald Dwayne Betts has to be "among the most amazing." Born in Maryland, Betts was a sixteen-year-old high school honors student when he and a friend carjacked a man at gunpoint outside a mall. Charged as an adult, Betts confessed and spent over eight years in prison where, at some point during his fourteen months in solitary confinement, someone slipped a copy of Dudley Randall's edited collection *The Black Poets* under his door. Inspired especially by the work of Robert Hayden, Sonia Sanchez, and Lucille Clifton, Betts determined to be a poet, earned his high school degree, and—after his release—worked at a bookstore while attending community college, ultimately finishing his BA at the University of Maryland and earning his MFA at Warren Wilson College (2010). After also publishing two award-winning books, *A Question of Freedom: A Memoir of Learning, Survival, and Coming of Age in Prison* (2009) and the poetry collection *Shahid Reads His Own Palm* (2010), Betts was appointed by President Barack Obama to the Coordinating Council on Juvenile Justice and Delinquency Prevention in 2012 and served as national spokesperson for the Campaign for Youth Justice. On the way to a Yale law degree (2016) and admission to the Connecticut bar (2017), Betts won yet another major award for his second volume of poetry, *Bastards of the Reagan Era* (2015), while also spending his summers working for the American Civil Liberties Union (ACLU) and the D.C. Public Defender office. Today a doctoral candidate in law at Yale and a married father of two, Betts published his third award-winning collection, *Felon*, in 2019. A searingly moving, inventive, often lyric meditation on the experience and effects of incarceration, it fully realizes Betts's ambition to be not a lawyer *and* a poet but "a lawyer-poet," "encouraging conversations that help to change and shift people's lives."

ELIZABETH BISHOP (1911–79)

Born in Worcester, Massachusetts, Elizabeth Bishop endured the death of her father before she was a year old and the institutionalization of her mother four years later. Bishop was raised first by her maternal grandmother in Nova Scotia, then by her paternal grandparents back in Worcester. At Vassar College she met the poet Marianne Moore, who encouraged her to give up plans for medical school and pursue a career in poetry. Bishop traveled through Canada, Europe, and South America, finally settling in Rio de Janeiro, Brazil, where she lived for nearly twenty years. Her four volumes of poetry are *North and South* (1946); *A Cold Spring* (1955), which won the Pulitzer Prize; *Questions of Travel* (1965); and *Geography III* (1976), which won the National Book Critics Circle Award.

WILLIAM BLAKE (1757–1828)

The son of a London haberdasher and his wife, William Blake studied drawing at ten and at fourteen began a seven-year apprenticeship to an engraver. After a first book of poems, *Poetical Sketches* (1783), he began experimenting with what he called "illuminated printing"—the words and pictures of each page were engraved in relief on copper, which was used to print sheets that were then partly colored by hand—a laborious and time-consuming process that resulted in books of singular beauty, no two of which are exactly alike. His great *Songs of Innocence and of Experience* (1794) was produced in this manner, as were his increasingly mythic and prophetic books, including *The Marriage of Heaven and Hell*

(1793), *The Four Zoas* (1803), *Milton* (1804), and *Jerusalem* (1809). Blake devoted his later life to pictorial art, illustrating *Chaucer's Canterbury Tales*, the Book of Job, and Dante's *Divine Comedy*, on which he was hard at work when he died.

RICHARD BLANCO (b. 1968)

Only the sixth poet ever invited to read at a U.S. presidential inauguration, as well as the only openly gay person, immigrant, Latino, or civil engineer so honored (thus far), Richard Blanco often jokes that he was "made in Cuba, born in Spain, and assembled in America." Blanco's mother was seven months pregnant when the family first fled Cuba for Spain, then—five months later—immigrated to the United States. Like many Cuban exiles, they would eventually settle in Miami, Florida, where three generations shared one house and Richard helped out at the family bodega while struggling, in his own words, "to understand his place in America" and "grappl[e] with his burgeoning artistic and sexual identities." Since earning civil engineering and MFA degrees from Florida International University (in 1991 and 1997, respectively), Blanco has pursued both callings at various times, while also doing a good deal of teaching and public speaking. Today, he serves as the Academy of American Poets's Education Ambassador and lives in Maine with his long-time partner, a molecular cell biologist and CEO. In addition to chapbooks featuring other occasional poems (including one commemorating the 2015 reopening of the U.S. Embassy in Havana, Cuba), Blanco's oeuvre includes poetry collections ranging from the award winners *Directions to the Beach of the Dead* (2005) and *Looking for the Gulf Motel* (2012) to *How to Love a Country* (2019), as well as two well-received memoirs—*For All of Us, One Today: An Inaugural Poet's Journey* (2013) and *The Prince of los Cocuyos* (2014), winner of a Lambda Literary Award.

GWENDOLYN BROOKS (1917–2000)

Gwendolyn Brooks was born in Topeka, Kansas, and raised in Chicago, Illinois, where she began writing poetry at the age of seven, and where she graduated from Wilson Junior College in 1936. Shortly after beginning her formal study of modern poetry at the Southside Community Art Center,

Brooks produced her first book of poems, *A Street in Bronzeville* (1945). With her second volume, *Annie Allen* (1949), she became the first African American to win the Pulitzer Prize. Though her early work focused on what Langston Hughes called the "ordinary aspects of black life," during the mid-1960s she devoted her poetry to raising African American consciousness and to social activism. In 1968, she was named the Poet Laureate of Illinois; in 1985, she became the first Black woman ever to serve as poetry consultant to the Library of Congress.

LORNA DEE CERVANTES (b. 1954)

Among the most important Chicana writers of the twentieth century, Lorna Dee Cervantes credits poetry with "sav[ing] my life, on a literal level as well as on a figurative level." A Californian of Mexican, Chumash, and Tarascan ancestry, Cervantes was born in San Francisco but grew up poor in San Jose, where she and her brother were raised by their mother and much-beloved grandmother after the divorce of their parents. Though Cervantes's mother, a house cleaner, discouraged her daughter from speaking Spanish and from reading, she was herself an avid reader, especially of poetry. Cervantes became one, too, tracing the start of her career as poet and activist in the women's and Chicana/o movements to her discovery, at age fifteen, of Latin American poet Pablo Neruda and just-emerging African American women poets including Maya Angelou. Their work first convinced Cervantes that poetry was neither a dead art nor one reserved "for the aristocratic classes." The most influential literary results of that realization were *Mango* (founded 1976), one of the earliest literary magazines to feature Chicana/o writers' work, and her own American Book Award–winning poetry collection *Emplumada* (1981). Rocked by her mother's 1982 murder, Cervantes earned a BA at San Jose State University and studied for a PhD at the University of California, Santa Cruz, before resuming a career ultimately including four more poetry collections, teaching stints at various universities, and abundant awards and accolades. Decades later, Cervantes's most famous works nonetheless remain those in her groundbreaking first book—poems written, says Cervantes, "to give back that gift that had saved me," especially to "some little Chicana [. . .] scanning the shelves, like I used to do," looking "for women's names or Spanish surnames," something to "relate to": "This is what I can give to my *Raza* [people]."

JUDITH ORTIZ COFER (1952–2016)

Born in Hormigueros, Puerto Rico, Judith Ortiz Cofer just two years later moved with her family, first to New Jersey and later to Georgia, experiences that would inspire much of her later fiction and poetry. "How can you inject passion and purpose into your work if it has no roots?" she asked, avowing that her own roots included a long line of women storytellers who "infected" her at a very early age with the desire to tell stories both on and off the page. After earning an MA at Florida Atlantic University (1977), Cofer returned to Georgia, teaching at the University of Georgia for over 26 years. Among her numerous publications are *The Line of the Sun* (1989), a novel in which a young girl relates the history of her ne'er-do-well uncle's emigration from Puerto Rico; the poetry collection *A Love Story Beginning in Spanish* (2005); *The Latin Deli: Prose and Poetry* (1993); and the memoir *In the Cruel Country: Notes for an Elegy* (2015).

SAMUEL TAYLOR COLERIDGE (1772–1834)

Born in the small town of Ottery St. Mary in rural Devonshire, England, Samuel Taylor Coleridge is among the greatest and most original of the nineteenth-century Romantic poets. He wrote three of the most haunting and powerful poems in English—"The Rime of the Ancient Mariner" (1798), *Christabel* (1816), and "Kubla Khan" (1816)—as well as immensely influential literary criticism and a treatise on biology. In 1795, in the midst of a failed experiment to establish a "Pantisocracy" (his form of ideal community), he met William Wordsworth, and in 1798 they jointly published their enormously influential *Lyrical Ballads*. Coleridge's physical ailments, addiction to opium, and profound sense of despair made his life difficult and tumultuous and certainly affected his work. Still, he remains a central figure in English literature.

BILLY COLLINS (b. 1941)

Once described as "the most popular poet in America," Billy Collins enjoys the sort of celebrity status usually reserved for Hollywood actors like his friend Bill Murray, reportedly signing six-figure contracts for books in progress. As U.S. Poet Laureate (2001–3), Collins both refused to publish and hence profit from his poem "The Names," written in honor of the victims of the 9/11 attacks, and initiated philanthropic projects like *Poetry 180*, aimed at exciting high schoolers' interest in poetry. Born in New York City, Collins credits his mother with awakening his love of poetry and teaching him the importance of "reading poetry as poetry," "as a set of sounds set to rhythm"— lessons reinforced by his studies at the College of Holy Cross and the University of California–Riverside. Though Collins began publishing his work in the 1980s, it wasn't until 1991 that his book *Questions about Angels* thrust him into the spotlight. Since that time, he has published numerous collections, including *The Art of Drowning* (1995), *Taking Off Emily Dickinson's Clothes* (2000), *Ballistics* (2008), and *Whale Day and Other Poems* (2020). By his own account "unashamedly" "suburban," "domestic," and "middle class," Collins's deceptively simple poetry uses the material of the everyday to, as one reader put it, "help us feel the mystery of being alive."

COUNTEE CULLEN (1903–46)

During his own lifetime, Countee Cullen was the most celebrated and honored poet of the Harlem Renaissance, and he claimed New York City as his birthplace. In fact, he may have been born in Louisville, Kentucky, and the circumstances of his childhood adoption by the Reverend Frederick Cullen remain obscure. It is certain, though, that the poet received a good education at New York's DeWitt Clinton High School and then New York University. After receiving his MA at Harvard, Cullen returned to New York in 1926 and soon established himself as the leading figure in the Harlem literary world, winning numerous awards for his poetry and editing the influential monthly column "The Dark Tower" for *Opportunity: Journal of Negro Life*. A playwright, novelist, translator, and anthologist, Cullen is best remembered as a poet; his work is collected in *My Soul's High Song: The Collected Writings of Countee Cullen, Voice of the Harlem Renaissance* (1991).

E. E. CUMMINGS (1894–1962)

Born in Cambridge, Massachusetts, the son of a Congregationalist minister, Edward Estlin Cummings attended Harvard University, where he wrote poetry in the Pre-Raphaelite and Metaphysical traditions. He joined the ambulance corps in France the day after the United States entered World War I but was imprisoned by the French due to his outspoken opposition to the war; he transmuted the experience into his first literary success, the novel *The Enormous Room* (1922). After the war, Cummings established himself as a poet and artist in New York City's Greenwich Village, made frequent trips to France and New Hampshire, and showed little interest in wealth or his growing celebrity. His variety of Modernism is distinguished by its playfulness, its formal experimentation, its lyrical directness, and its celebration of the individual.

NATALIE DIAZ (b. 1978)

In 2016, an interviewer asked acclaimed novelist Louise Erdrich what "new Native American authors" she most wanted to see "reach a wider audience." By far the youngest person on Erdrich's list and the only former professional basketball player was poet and future MacArthur "genius grant" recipient Natalie Diaz. An enrolled member of the Gila River Indian Community, Diaz describes herself as both "an indigenous woman, a queer woman, a Latinx woman" and someone acutely aware of how "identity tends to be used as a thing to pin us down and hold us still." Raised in the Fort Mojave Indian Village in Needles, California, daughter of a Mojave mother and Latino father, the trilingual Diaz attended Old Dominion University on a basketball scholarship. A point guard, she reached the NCAA Final Four as a freshman and, after graduation, played professionally in Europe and Asia before returning to her alma mater to earn her MFA (2006). Proving her as agile and inventive on the page as on the court, while also reflecting her interest in "the way we deserve love, our capacities for love, and all of the innovative ways we've managed to find to express that love to one another," Diaz's dazzling debut collection—*When My Brother Was an Aztec* (2012)—moves from poems about modern reservation life, as experienced through characters ranging from a grandmother who lost her legs to diabetes to "The last Mojave Indian Barbie"; to vivid, viscerally poignant poems about a brother's methamphetamine addiction and its complex effects on the family; to poems of erotic love. Having served as founder-director of the Fort Mojave Language Recovery Program and become both the first Native American winner of the Pulitzer Prize for Poetry, for her second collection, *Postcolonial Love Poem* (2020), and the youngest person ever elected to the Academy of American Poets Board of Chancellors, Diaz is today Maxine and Jonathan Marshall Chair in Modern and Con-

temporary Poetry at Arizona State University, where she also serves as founder-director of the Center for Imagination in the Borderlands.

EMILY DICKINSON (1830–86)

From childhood on, Emily Dickinson led a sequestered and obscure life. Yet her verse has traveled far beyond the cultured yet relatively circumscribed environment in which she lived: her room, her father's house, her family, a few close friends, and the small town of Amherst, Massachusetts. Indeed, along with Walt Whitman, her far more public contemporary, she all but invented American poetry. Born in Amherst, the daughter of a respected lawyer whom she revered ("His heart was pure and terrible," she once wrote), Dickinson studied for less than a year at the Mount Holyoke Female Seminary, returning permanently to her family home. She became more and more reclusive, dressing only in white, seeing no visitors, yet working ceaselessly at her poems—nearly eighteen hundred in all, only a few of which were published during her lifetime. After her death, her sister Lavinia discovered the rest in a trunk, neatly bound into packets with blue ribbons—among the most important bodies of work in all of American literature.

JOHN DONNE (1572–1631)

The first and greatest of the English writers who came to be known as the Metaphysical poets, John Donne wrote in a revolutionary style that combined highly intellectual conceits with complex, compressed phrasing. Born into an old Roman Catholic family at a time when Catholics were subject to constant harassment and barred from many forms of employment, Donne quietly abandoned his religion and pursued a promising legal career until a politically disastrous marriage ruined his worldly aspirations. He struggled for years to support a large family; impoverished and despairing, he even wrote a treatise (*Biathanatos*) on the lawfulness of suicide. King James (who had ambitions for him as a preacher) eventually pressured Donne to take Anglican orders in 1615, and Donne became one of the great sermonizers of his day, rising to the position of dean of St. Paul's Cathedral in 1621. Donne's private devotions (*Meditations*) were published in 1624, and he continued to write poetry until a few years before his death.

RITA DOVE (b. 1952)

A native of Akron, Ohio; daughter of one of the tire industry's first Black chemists; and today holder of no fewer than twenty-eight honorary doctorates (among countless other awards), poet Rita Dove graduated *summa cum laude* from Miami University in Ohio (1973) and earned her MFA in creative writing from the famed University of Iowa Writers' Workshop (1977). In 1987, Dove became only the second African American poet (after Gwendolyn Brooks) to win the Pulitzer Prize, for her verse novel *Thomas and Beulah*. Six years later, in 1993, she became—at age 40—the youngest poet and first African American ever named Poet Laureate of the United States. As important, Dove was arguably the first U.S. laureate to make advocacy for the literary arts a major obligation of the post. In this and so many ways—including her editorship of the *Penguin Anthology of Twentieth-Century American Poetry* (2011)—Dove has had an enormous influence on contemporary American letters. Her many books of poetry include National Book Critics Circle Award finalist *On the Bus with Rosa Parks* (1999) and *Collected Poems: 1974–2004* (2016), winner of the NAACP Image and Library of Virginia awards and finalist for the National Book Award. Today Commonwealth Professor of English at the University of Virginia and a married mother of one, Dove has also published numerous essays and poetry columns, as well as a short-story collection (*Fifth Sunday*, 1985), a novel (*Through the Ivory Gate*, 1992), and a play (*The Darker Face of the Earth*, 1994). Honored with the National Medal of the Arts in 2011, Dove achieved yet another of her remarkable firsts by becoming the first poet ever to receive both this award and the National Humanities Medal (1996).

PAUL LAURENCE DUNBAR (1872–1906)

The son of former slaves, Paul Laurence Dunbar was born in Dayton, Ohio. He attended a White high school, where he showed an early talent for writing and was elected class president. Unable to afford further education, he then worked as an elevator operator, writing poems and newspaper articles in his spare time. Dunbar took out a loan to subsidize the printing of his first book, *Oak and Ivy* (1893), but with the publi-cation of *Majors and Minors* (1895) and *Lyrics of Lowly Life* (1896), his growing reputation enabled him to support himself by writing and lecturing. Though acclaimed during his lifetime for his lyrical use of rural Black dialect in volumes such as *Candle-Lightin' Time* (1902), Dunbar was later criticized for adopting "White" literary conventions and for supposedly pandering to racist images of slaves and ex-slaves. He wrote novels and short stories in addition to poetry and dealt frankly with racial injustice in works such as *The Sport of the Gods* (1903) and *The Fourth of July and Race Outrages* (1903).

MARTÍN ESPADA (b. 1957)

At the age of thirteen, New Yorker Martín Espada moved with his family to a Long Island neighborhood where they were the only Puerto Ricans, an experience he describes as "more traumatic than anything that ever happened to me on the so-called mean streets" of the racially diverse Brooklyn neighborhood he previously called home. By working everywhere from a bar and a ballpark to a primate lab and a transient hotel, Espada put himself through college, graduating from the University of Wisconsin–Madison with a BA in history. After earning a law degree at Northeastern University, in Boston, he went to work as a lawyer, specializing first in bilingual education, later in housing law. From age twenty, however, Espada was also writing poetry, inspired initially by a family friend's gift of both an anthology of Latin American revolutionary poetry and the prediction that "Tri tambien seras poeta" ("You will also become a poet"). Featuring barrio photos taken by his father, a community activist, Espada's first collection, *The Immigrant Iceboy's Bolero*, appeared in 1982. But it was his third, prize-winning book, *Rebellion Is the Circle of a Lover's Hand* (1990), that led the *New York Times* to predict he would be "the Latino poet of his generation." In the years since, Espada has done much to justify that title, securing a professorship at the University of Massachusetts–Amherst (in 1993) and publishing poetry collections ranging from *City of Coughing and Dead Radiators* (1993) to *The Republic of Poetry* (2006, a finalist for the Pulitzer) and *Floaters* (2021), books of essays including *Zapata's Disciple* (1998), anthologies of Latina/o and Chicana/o poetry, and translations. What drives all that work, says Espada, is the same commitment he had as a lawyer: "to speak on behalf of" all those who lack not the ability but the "opportunity" to "speak for themselves."

ROBERT FROST (1874–1963)

Though his poetry identifies Robert Frost with rural New England, he was born and lived to the age of eleven in San Francisco, California. Moving to New England after his father's death, Frost studied classics in high school, entered and dropped out of both Dartmouth and Harvard, and spent difficult years as an unrecognized poet before his first book, *A Boy's Will* (1913), was accepted and published in England. Frost's character was full of contradiction—he held "that we get forward as much by hating as by loving"—yet by the end of his long life he was one of the most honored poets of his time, as well as the most widely read. In 1961, two years before his death, he was invited to read a poem at John F. Kennedy's presidential inauguration ceremony. Frost's poems—masterfully crafted, sometimes deceptively simple—are collected in *The Poetry of Robert Frost* (1969).

ALLEN GINSBERG (1926–97)

After a childhood in Paterson, New Jersey, overshadowed by his mother's mental illness, Allen Ginsberg enrolled at Columbia University, intent upon following his father's advice by becoming a labor lawyer. At the center of a circle that included Lucien Carr, Jack Kerouac, William S. Burroughs, and Neal Cassady, Ginsberg became interested in experimental poetry and alternative lifestyles. He graduated in 1948 and then joined the literary scene in San Francisco, California. In 1956, he published *Howl and Other Poems*, with an introduction by his mentor William Carlos Williams. The title poem, which condemns bourgeois culture and celebrates the emerging counterculture, became a manifesto for the Beat movement and catapulted Ginsberg to fame. Deeply involved in radical politics and Eastern spiritualism, Ginsberg went on to write such prose works as *Declaration of Independence for Dr. Timothy Leary* (1971) in addition to many volumes of poetry.

ANGELINA GRIMKÉ (1880–1958)

Born in Boston, Massachusetts, Angelina Grimké was the descendent of Black slaves, White slaveholders, free Blacks, and prominent White abolitionists, including her namesake, Angelina Weld Grimké. As a child, Angelina was abandoned by her White mother, whose middle-class family disapproved of her marriage to Archibald Grimké, a biracial lawyer and author who eventually became vice president of the NAACP. Grimké graduated from the Boston Normal School of Gymnastics in 1902 and then moved with her father to Washington, D.C., where she worked as a teacher and began to write poetry, essays, short stories, and plays. By the 1920s, she was publishing her work in the leading journals and anthologies of the Harlem Renaissance—*The Crisis, Opportunity*, Alain Locke's *The New Negro* (1925), Countee Cullen's *Caroling Dusk* (1927), and Robert Kerlin's *Negro Poets and Their Poems* (1928). Much of her finest writing can be found in *Selected Works of Angelina Weld Grimké* (1991).

JOY HARJO (b. 1951)

Tulsa, Oklahoma-born author and musician Joy Harjo (née Foster) traces her affinity for art to the women in her immediate family and to the long line of Native American leaders and orators from whom she descends. A cook and waitress with an eighth-grade education, Harjo's mother loved the poetry of William Blake, penned songs, and performed with a country swing band. Though Harjo's father—a mechanic and sheet-metal worker who battled alcoholism—abandoned the family when she and her three siblings were very young, his mother and sister were painters whose art adorned her childhood home. Intent on following in their footsteps and escaping an abusive stepfather, Harjo attended the Institute of American Indian Arts in Santa Fe, New Mexico, the boarding school where a "suicidal" teenager was, she says, first "given permission to be an Indian artist," "given permission to be human." She graduated in 1968, the same year she gave birth to her first child. Two years later, she became "Joy Harjo," adopting her paternal grandmother and favorite aunt's surname and enrolling as a member of the Muskogee Nation. A single mother of two by age 21, Harjo worked odd jobs while pursuing her education. Inspired by mentors including Simon Ortiz, she abandoned painting for poetry, publishing her first collection in 1975 and earning a BA in English at the University of New Mexico (1976) and an MFA in Creative Writing at the University of Iowa (1978). In the decades since, Harjo has emerged as among the best-known Native American voices of her generation. Her work—including numerous books of poetry, a memoir, a children's book, and four albums—has won her honors including a Native Writers Circle of the Americas' Lifetime Achievement Award, William Carlos Williams and Wallace Stevens poetry prizes, and a Native American Music Award for Best Female Artist of the Year. In 2019, she became the first Native American ever to serve as U.S. Poet Laureate.

ROBERT HAYDEN (1913–80)

Born in a Detroit, Michigan, ghetto, Asa Sheffey became "Robert Hayden" at eighteen months, when he was unofficially adopted by the neighbors who would raise him and whom he would remember in poems such as "Those Winter Sundays." Inspired by the Harlem Renaissance writers he discovered as a teenager, Hayden published his first poem in 1931. Severely nearsighted, he attended Detroit City College (1932–36), thanks only to state rehabilitation grants, and worked for the Federal Writers Project (1936–39), before studying with W. H. Auden at the University of Michigan (MA, 1944). Becoming "a poet who teaches [. . .] so that he can write a poem or two now and then," Hayden held professorships at historically Black Fisk University (1946–69) and at the University of Michigan (1969–80). International acclaim came late: In 1966, Langston Hughes and seven other judges unanimously awarded Hayden the Grand Prize for Poetry at the First World Festival of Negro Arts in Senegal, Africa, and in 1976 he became the first African American appointed to the post now known as U.S. Poet Laureate. Like his masterpiece "Middle Passage" (1962), much of Hayden's poetry aims, he said, to "correct the distortions of Afro-American history." Yet he insisted that he was not a "black artist" but an American one. Today he is widely and rightly regarded as among the very best of both.

TERRANCE HAYES (b. 1971)

Born in Columbia, South Carolina, Terrance Hayes attended Coker College on a basketball scholarship, shifting his attention to poetry only in his senior year and going on to earn an MFA from the University of Pittsburgh (1997). His first book of poetry, *Muscular Music* (1999), explores popular culture's impact on African American identity and notions of masculinity. It was followed by *Hip Logic* (2002), a National Poetry Series winner; *Wind in a Box* (2006), listed by *Publishers Weekly* as one of the top 100 books of 2006; and, more recently, *How to Be Drawn* (2015) and *American Sonnets*

for *My Past and Future Assassin* (2018). Characterized as "an elegant and adventurous writer" whose work deftly combines humor and sincerity, Hayes has garnered numerous honors and awards, including a National Book Award for his fourth collection, *Lighthead* (2010), multiple Best American Poetry selections, a Pushcart Prize, and a MacArthur Fellowship. Though he is continually drawn to questions of identity, masculinity, race, culture, and community, he "aspire[s] to a poetic style that resists style"; and indeed, his collections contain poetic forms ranging from pecha kucha, a format for Japanese business presentations, to terza rima, while adopting the voices of poets from Harryette Mullen to Dr. Seuss. Today a professor of English at New York University, Hayes is also author of the award-winning *To Float in the Space Between: Drawings and Essays in Conversation with Etheridge Knight* (2018).

SEAMUS HEANEY (1939–2013)

Considered "the most important Irish poet since Yeats," 1995 Nobel Prize winner Seamus Heaney grew up with his eight siblings on Mossbawm Farm in rural County Derry, Northern Ireland. At twelve, however, scholarships took Heaney first to St. Columb's College and then Queen's University, Belfast, where he studied Irish, Latin, and Old English. Here, too, he discovered the poetry of authors such as Ted Hughes, Patrick Kavanagh, and Robert Frost, which, he said, first taught him to "trust" in the value of that "local" childhood experience that he once "considered archaic and irrelevant to 'the modern world.'" Rural life and labor, as well as the relationship between past and present, the "archaic" and the "modern," loom large from his earliest collection, *Death of a Naturalist* (1966), to later ones such as *District and Circle* (2006). Most famous, perhaps, is *North* (1975), especially its sequence of poems inspired by both the ancient, yet somehow ageless, corpses discovered in Irish and Scandinavian bogs, and by the increasingly violent conflict between Protestants and Catholics in Northern Ireland. Having earned virtually all of the highest honors that a contemporary poet could, Heaney also won acclaim both as a versatile and creative translator, most famously of *Beowulf* (2000) and *Antigone* (*The Burial at Thebes*, 2004), and as an essayist; his *Finders Keepers: Selected Prose, 1971–2001* (2002) won the Truman Capote Award for Literary Criticism, the largest annual prize of its kind. After teaching at Harvard from 1985 until 2006, Heaney lived in Dublin until his death.

GERARD MANLEY HOPKINS (1844–89)

The eldest of the eight children of a marine-insurance adjuster and his wife, Gerard Manley Hopkins attended Oxford University, where his ambition was to become a painter—until, at the age of twenty-two, he converted to Roman Catholicism and burned all his early poetry as too worldly. Not until after his seminary training and ordination as a Jesuit priest, in 1877, did he resume writing poetry, though he made few attempts to publish his verse, which many of his contemporaries found nearly incomprehensible. Near the end of his life, Hopkins was appointed professor of Greek at University College, Dublin, where—out of place, deeply depressed, and all but unknown—he died of typhoid. His poetry, collected and published by his friends, has been championed by modern poets, who admire its controlled tension, strong rhythm, and sheer exuberance.

LANGSTON HUGHES (1902–67)

Born in Joplin, Missouri, Langston Hughes was raised mainly by his maternal grandmother, though he lived intermittently with each of his parents. He studied at Columbia University but left to travel and work at a variety of jobs. Having already published poems in periodicals, anthologies, and his own first collection, *The Weary Blues* (1926), he graduated from Lincoln University; published a successful novel, *Not without Laughter* (1930); and became a major writer of the Harlem Renaissance. During the 1930s, he became involved in radical politics and traveled the world as a correspondent and columnist; during the 1950s, though, the FBI classified him as a security risk and limited his ability to travel. In addition to poems and novels, he wrote essays, plays, screenplays, and an autobiography; he also edited anthologies of literature and folklore.

JOHN KEATS (1795–1821)

Because John Keats was the son of a London livery stable owner and his wife, reviewers would later disparage him as a working-class "Cockney poet." At fifteen he was apprenticed to a surgeon, and at twenty-one he became a licensed pharmacist—in the same year that his first two published poems, including the sonnet "On First Looking into Chapman's Homer," appeared in *The Examiner*, a journal edited by radical critic-poet Leigh Hunt. Hunt introduced Keats to such literary figures as the poet Percy Bysshe Shelley and helped him publish his *Poems by John Keats* (1817). When his second book, the long poem *Endymion* (1818), was fiercely attacked by critics, Keats, suffering from a steadily worsening case of tuberculosis, knew that he would not live to realize his poetic promise. In July 1820, he published *Lamia, Isabella, The Eve of St. Agnes, and Other Poems*, which contained the poignant "To Autumn" and three other great odes: "Ode on a Grecian Urn," "Ode on Melancholy," and "Ode to a Nightingale"; early the next year, he died in Rome. In the years after Keats's death, his letters became almost as famous as his poetry.

ETHERIDGE KNIGHT (1931–91)

A native of Corinth, Mississippi, Etheridge Knight spent much of his adolescence carousing in pool halls, bars, and juke joints, developing a skillful oratorical style in an environment that prized verbal agility. During this time, he also became addicted to narcotics. He served in the U.S. Army from 1947 to 1951; in 1960 he was sentenced to eight years for robbery. At the Indiana State Prison in Michigan City, he began to write poetry and in 1968 published his first collection, *Poems from Prison*. After his release, Knight joined the Black Arts movement, taught at a number of universities, and published works including *Black Voices from Prison* (1970), *Belly Song and Other Poems* (1973), and *Born of a Woman* (1980).

YUSEF KOMUNYAKAA (b. 1947)

The first African American man to win a Pulitzer Prize for Poetry, Yusef Komunyakaa once described his life and work as a "process" of "healing" from "two places." The first place was Bogalusa, Louisiana—the segregated rural mill town where James Willie Brown, Jr., grew up, learning "the importance of music and metaphor" from the Bible and the family radio, "the value of tools" and "precision" from a carpenter father unable to read or write. The second place was Vietnam, where twenty-one-year-old Komunyakaa—who eventually adopted the surname his great-grandparents gave up when they emigrated from Trinidad—earned a Bronze Star for meritorious wartime service. While pursuing a BA (University of Colorado, 1975), an MA (Colorado State, 1979), and an MFA (University of California–Irvine, 1980), Komunyakaa began to turn the first of these places into poetry, initially gaining recognition with the jazz- and blues-inflected collection *Copacetic* (1984). National acclaim came with *Dien Cai Dau* (1988), the book in which, twenty years after the fact, the poet finally, in his own words, stopped "writing around the war." In the years since, Komunyakaa's numerous collections have garnered him some of poetry's highest honors, including a Pulitzer (for *Neon Vernacular: New & Selected Poems 1977–1989* [1994]), the Ruth Lilly Poetry Prize (2001), and the Wallace Stevens Award (2011). Today Global Distinguished Professor of English at New York University, Komunyakaa is also the editor of multiple poetry anthologies; cotranslator (with Martha Collins) of Vietnamese poet Nguyen Quan Thieu's *The Insomnia of Fire* (1995); author of two non-fiction collections; and, with Chad Gracia, author of *Gilgamesh: A Verse Play* (2006).

PHILIP LARKIN (1922–85)

Postwar England's most widely known and popular poet, so-called "laureate of the common man" Philip Larkin endured what he later described as a boring childhood the second, belated, rather shy—because also nearsighted and stuttering—child of Coventry's city treasurer. Exempted from service in World War II because of his eyesight, Larkin graduated from Oxford in 1943 and became a librarian, mainly at Hull, where he headed the university library for thirty years (1955–85). Larkin credited his rediscovery of Thomas Hardy's poetry with "cur[ing]" him of the Yeatsian "Celtic fever" of his first collection, *The North Ship* (1945), and helping him to develop the mature style debuted in his second, *The Less Deceived* (1955). This critically acclaimed book made Larkin the undisputed leading light of "the Movement," a group of young poets who rejected the enigmatic, allusive, and—in their eyes—elitist Modernism of T. S. Eliot and Ezra Pound in favor of a more straightforward and robust, if also skeptical and ironic, style. Notoriously publicity averse, Larkin declined the position of Poet Laureate of the United Kingdom just a year before his death. In his lifetime, he published only two other volumes of verse, *The Whitsun Weddings* (1964) and *High Windows* (1974); two novels, *Jill* (1946) and *A Girl in Winter* (1947); *All What Jazz* (1970), a collection of jazz reviews originally written for the *Daily Telegraph*; and the best-selling *Required Writing: Miscellaneous Pieces 1955–1982* (1983).

LI-YOUNG LEE (b. 1957)

Often categorized as an Asian American writer, Academy of American Poets Fellow Li-Young Lee is perhaps better understood as the "global poet" he himself aspires to be, one whose work is deeply influenced by the classical Chinese poetry and the King James Bible in which his father steeped him, as well as his experiences in both Asia and America; as refugee and exile; and as son, brother, husband, and father (of two sons, now grown). Raised in a small Pennsylvania town, Lee was born in Jakarta, Indonesia, where his parents, both from prominent Chinese families, fled after the establishment in 1949 of the People's Republic of China by Mao Zedong, to whom Lee's father had been personal physician. After helping to found Gamaliel University and, partly as a result, suffering political imprisonment and torture, Lee's father was forced once again to flee with his family when Lee was just two, wandering from Indonesia to Singapore, Japan, Malaysia, Hong Kong, and, finally, in 1964, the United States, where Lee Kuo Yuan (Richard) was ordained a Presbyterian minister and Lee, by his own account, "started writing poems as soon as I started learning the English language" (his third). After earning a biochemistry degree at the University of Pittsburgh (1979) and marrying his wife, Donna, Lee turned seriously to writing, studying at the University of Arizona (1979–80) and the State University of New York at Brockport (1980–81) on the way to publishing the first of his award-winning poetry collections, *Rose* (1986). A much-admired memoir sometimes described as an extended prose poem, Lee's *The Winged Seed* (1995) won the Before Columbus Foundation's American Book Award, and *Breaking the Alabaster Jar: Conversations with Li-Young Lee* (2006) collects interviews conducted at various stages of his career. As Lee avows in one, "life is worth living" only "if [. . .] there is such a thing as meaning," and "Poetry is the only way I know to make meaning."

ADA LIMÓN (b. 1976)

A native of Sonoma, California, poet Ada Limón describes herself as the child of a "grandfather who crossed a border and went from living in a chicken coop to becoming one of the first Mexican Americans to graduate from San Diego State," of a father and stepfather "who taught [her] tenacity and storytelling," and of an artist-mother "who showed [her] how to create"—and whose paintings today grace the cover of her books. A theater major at the University of Washington (BA, 1998), Limón earned her MFA at New York University (2001), where she studied with poets including Sharon Olds, Philip Levine, and Marie Howe. Published four years later, her first collection, *Lucky Wreck* (2006), won the Autumn House Poetry Prize, while two more recent ones earned even more impressive honors and accolades: A *New York Times* notable book, *Bright Dead Things* (2015) was a finalist for both the National Book and National Book Critics Circle awards for poetry, while *The Carrying* (2018) not only nabbed the latter award but also made the best book lists of publications ranging from *Publishers Weekly* and the *Chicago Review of Books* to the *Washington Post* and *BuzzFeed*. Though Limón today teaches in the Queens University of Charlotte Low Residency MFA Program, as well as the online and summer programs for the Provincetown Fine Arts Work Center, her main "day job" has long been writing of a different sort. After twelve years in New York, working for magazines including *Martha Stewart Living*, *GQ*, and *Travel + Leisure*, Limón today splits her time between Sonoma and Lexington, Kentucky, where she works as a freelance writer.

AMIT MAJMUDAR (b. 1979)

A diagnostic nuclear radiologist, Ohio's first-ever Poet Laureate, and the son of Indian immigrants (both doctors), Amit Majmudar grew up mainly in and around Cleveland, Ohio, "bec[oming]," he says, "a citizen of the library," most "at ease" amid "a crowd of books." With a BS from the University of Akron and an MD from Northeast Ohio Medical University, Majmudar is, as a writer, entirely self-taught. (As he puts it, "My [only] teachers have been dead poets, mostly, and no one dead poet in particular.") Majmudar's poetry collections include *0°, 0°* (2009), a finalist for the Poetry Society of America's Norma Farber First Book Award; *Heaven and Earth* (2011), selected by A. E. Stallings for a Donald Justice prize; *Dothead* (2016), a book tackling, as one reviewer aptly observes, every topic from "Adam and Eve's sex life" and "the art of the semi-colon" to "T.S.A. security lines" and the 2012 Sandy Hook school shooting; and *What He Did in Solitary* (2020). Majmudar has also won praise for his fiction, especially the novels *Partitions* (2011), about four characters caught up in the 1947 partition of India and Pakistan, and *The Abundance* (2013), about an Indian American family coping with the terminal illness of their wife/mother/grandmother. A married father of three, Majmudar sees his two vocations as united by the search for patterns: As a radiologist, he explains in an NPR interview, "what I do is I recognize the patterns of disease" as revealed in "X-rays, CT scans, PET scans"; then, "when I go home and write [. . .], I'm basically creating patterns in language," working with its "mathematical, musical aspect" to "quicke[n] it into poetry."

CLAUDE McKAY (1889–1948)

Festus Claudius McKay was born and raised in Sunny Ville, Clarendon Parish, Jamaica, the youngest of eleven children. He worked as a wheelwright and cabinetmaker, then briefly as a police constable, before writing and publishing two books of poetry in Jamaican dialect. In 1912, he emigrated to the United States, where he attended Booker T. Washington's Tuskegee Institute in Alabama and studied agricultural science at Kansas State College before moving to New York City. McKay supported himself through various jobs while becoming a prominent literary and political figure. The oldest Harlem Renaissance writer, McKay was also the first to publish, with the poetry collection *Harlem Shadows* (1922). His other works include the novels *Home to Harlem* (1928) and *Banana Bottom* (1933) and his autobiography, *A Long Way from Home* (1937).

EDNA ST. VINCENT MILLAY (1892–1950)

Born in Rockland, Maine, Edna St. Vincent Millay published her first poem at twenty, her first poetry collection at twenty-five. After graduating from Vassar College, she moved to New York City's Greenwich

Village, where she both gained a reputation as a brilliant poet and became notorious for her bohemian lifestyle and her association with prominent artists, writers, and radicals. In 1923, she won the Pulitzer Prize for her collection *The Ballad of the Harp-Weaver*; in 1925, growing weary of fame, she and her husband moved to Austerlitz, New York, where she lived for the rest of her life. Although her work fell out of favor with mid-twentieth-century Modernists, who rejected her formalism as old-fashioned, her poetry—witty, acerbic, and superbly crafted—has found many new admirers today.

PAT MORA (b. 1942)

Born to Mexican American parents in El Paso, Texas, Pat Mora earned a BA and an MA from the University of Texas at El Paso. She has been a consultant on U.S.-Mexico youth exchanges; a museum director and administrator at her alma mater; and a teacher of English at all levels. Her poetry—collected in *Chants* (1985), *Borders* (1986), *Communion* (1991), *Agua Santa/Holy Water* (1995), *Aunt Carmen's Book of Practical Saints* (1997), *Adobe Odes* (2006), and *Encantado: Desert Monologues* (2018)—reflects and addresses her Chicana and southwestern background. Mora's other publications include *Nepantla: Essays from the Land in the Middle* (1993); a family memoir, *House of Houses* (1997); and many works for children and young adults.

HOWARD NEMEROV (1920–91)

Howard Nemerov grew up in New York City, part of a wealthy, cultured Jewish family of Russian descent that included his parents (owners of a department store) and two younger sisters, famed photographer Diane Arbus and sculptor Renée Sparkia. Graduating from Harvard in the middle of World War II, Nemerov served first in the Royal Canadian Air Force, later in the U.S. Air Force (1942–45). The first of his many poetry collections, *The Image and the Law*, appeared in 1947; his first novel, *The Melodramatists*, was published a year later. Nemerov taught at various U.S. colleges and universities, spending the last two-plus decades of his life at Washington University in St. Louis, Missouri, which in 1999 named a dormitory in his honor. A married father of three sons, Nemerov also served as poetry consultant to the Library of Congress (1963–64) and as U.S. Poet Laureate (1988–90); his *Collected Poems* (1977) netted a National Book Award and both the Pulitzer and Bollingen prizes; ten years later he received the National Medal of Arts. Dubbed by some a "formalist," prized by many for his wit, Nemerov defies easy classification: Novelist Joyce Carol Oates styled him "romantic, realist, comedian, satirist, relentless and indefatigable brooder upon the most ancient mysteries." In his own self-reflective 1966 essay "Attentiveness and Obedience," Nemerov cites T. S. Eliot and John Donne as major influences, from whom he learned "irony, difficulty, erudition." Yet "I now," he goes on to insist, "regard simplicity and the appearance of ease in the measure as primary values."

SHARON OLDS (b. 1942)

Born in San Francisco, California; raised in nearby Berkeley by fiercely religious, yet troubled parents; and educated at Stanford (BA, 1964) and Columbia (PhD, 1972) universities (where she wrote a dissertation on Ralph Waldo Emerson), poet Sharon Olds was thirty-seven when she published her first book of poetry, *Satan Says*, in 1981. Since then, she has come to rank as one of America's most important living poets, garnering National Book Critics Circle Awards for her 1984 collection *The Dead and the Living* and for *Strike Spark: Selected Poems* (2002). In 2013, she became the first woman to win the T. S. Eliot Prize for Poetry, for *Stag's Leap*, a collection that also earned a Pulitzer. Like the work of two writers to whom Olds is often compared, Walt Whitman and Sylvia Plath, however, hers has consistently provoked controversy, thanks mainly to its unflinching attention to, and distinctly female perspective on, the pleasures and pains of both the human body and the family, as well as emotional and physical violence. *The Dead and the Living* is divided between "Poems for the Living," about the poet's experience as daughter and mother, and "Poems for the Dead," about the victims of international conflicts; *The Father* (1992) chronicles her father's death (from cancer), *One Secret Thing* (2008), her mother's. *Stag's Leap* (2013) deals with the disintegration of her thirty-two-year marriage. As famous for her reticence off the page as for her candor on it, Olds teaches creative writing at New York University. Her most recent collections include *Odes* (2016) and *Arias* (2019).

WILFRED OWEN (1893–1918)

Born in Shropshire, England, Wilfred Owen left school in 1911, having failed to win a scholarship to London University. He served as assistant to a vicar in Oxfordshire until 1913, when he left to teach English at a Berlitz school in Bordeaux. In 1915, Owen returned to England to enlist in the army and was sent to the front lines in France. Suffering from shell shock two years later, he was evacuated to Craiglockhart War Hospital, where he met the poets Siegfried Sassoon and Robert Graves. Five of Owen's poems were published in 1918, the year he returned to combat; he was killed in battle one week before the signing of the armistice. His poems, which portray the horror of trench warfare and satirize the unthinking patriotism of those who cheered the war from their armchairs, are collected in the two-volume *Complete Poems and Fragments* (1983).

OCTAVIO PAZ (1914–98)

Winner of the 1990 Nobel Prize in Literature, Octavio Paz was among the twentieth century's most prolific, influential, and truly international of poets and public intellectuals. Born near Mexico City, Mexico, in 1914, he was the scion of a prominent family: The grandfather from whose vast library Paz drew his early education was a well-known liberal intellectual and novelist, Paz's father a lawyer who had served as assistant to Emiliano Zapata, leader in the Mexican Revolution (c. 1910–20). Having published his first poem at seventeen and his first poetry collection, *Wild Moon*, when he was only nineteen, Paz headed to Europe four years later, in 1937, attending the Second International Congress of Anti-Fascist Writers at the urging of famed Chilean poet Pablo Neruda. In 1945, Paz began his two-decade career as a diplomat. Six years as Mexico's ambassador to India (1962–68) spawned a lifelong immersion in Eastern literature and thought reflected in both Paz's poetry and

books such as *The Monkey Grammarian* (1974). Here, as in so much of his work, Paz—as one critic aptly notes—"deliberately wr[ites] at the edges of genres," creating highly experimental blends of narrative, essay, and poetry. Resigning his ambassadorship in 1968 over his government's violent repression of student protesters, he later became a controversial figure in leftist circles. Mexican President Ernesto Zedillo nonetheless expressed the feelings of many when he described Paz's 1998 death as "an irreplaceable loss for contemporary thought and culture—not just for Latin America but for the entire world." Paz's vast oeuvre includes at least twenty volumes of poetry, some of which is gathered in *Collected Poems, 1957–1987* (1987); translations of poets working in languages ranging from English to Japanese; and numerous books of nonfiction.

HAI-DANG PHAN (b. 1980)

Born in Vietnam, Hai-Dang Phan grew up in Wisconsin, where his family arrived in 1982 after ten harrowing days at sea followed by months in refugee camps in Malaysia and the Philippines. Phan earned his MFA in creative writing from the University of Florida and a PhD in literary studies from the University of Wisconsin–Madison. A 2017 National Endowment for the Arts Fellow and winner of both the *New England Review* Emerging Writers Award (2016) and *Poetry* magazine's Frederick Bock Prize (2016), Phan is currently an associate professor of English at Grinnell College, where he teaches ethnic American literature, the craft of poetry, and introduction to literary analysis. His first collection, *Reenactments*, appeared in 2019; his translation of *Paper Bells*, a volume of new and selected poems by Vietnamese writer Phan Nhiên Hạo, in 2020. Asked about the title of his collection, Phan describes "reenactment" as "carr[ying] with it the very human impulse to do things over, to see what you missed, to say what you mean, to get things right, to do better." "That seems to me an essential thing that poetry gives us as writers and readers," he explains, "the ability to recreate and reexperience the most vivid moments of our lives, to notice the ordinary things we missed because they were ordinary, and also to imaginatively inhabit other lives and other times."

SYLVIA PLATH (1932–63)

Sylvia Plath was born in Boston, Massachusetts; her father, a Polish immigrant, died when she was eight. After graduating from Smith College, Plath attended Cambridge University on a Fulbright scholarship, and there met and married English poet Ted Hughes, with whom she had two children. As she documented in her novel *The Bell Jar* (1963), in 1953—between her junior and senior years of college—Plath became seriously depressed, attempted suicide, and was hospitalized. In 1963, the breakup of her marriage led to another suicide attempt, this time successful. Plath has attained cult status as much for her poems as for her "martyrdom" to art and life. In addition to her first volume of poetry, *The Colossus* (1960), Plath's work has been collected in *Ariel* (1966), *Crossing the Water* (1971), and *Winter Trees* (1972). Her selected letters were published in 1975; her expurgated journals in 1983; and her unabridged journals in 2000.

ALEXANDER POPE (1688–1744)

Son of a wealthy merchant, London-born Alexander Pope managed to become the greatest poet of his age, one of the most accomplished versifiers and satirists in English literary history, and the first British writer to make his living entirely by his pen despite—or, rather, thanks to—two obvious handicaps. One, tuberculosis of the spine, contracted in infancy, ensured that Pope was, in the words of his contemporaries, only "about four feet six high; very humpbacked," plagued with "the headache four days in a week, and [. . .] sick [. . .] the other three." Two, as a Roman Catholic, Pope was legally debarred from voting or holding public office, inheriting or purchasing land, living within ten miles of London, or attending any of England's so-called public schools or universities. Largely self-taught and unable to rely on patronage, the pugnacious, politically conservative Pope launched his career with poems celebrating natural beauty and love (*Pastorals* [1709] and *Windsor Forest* [1713]) but leapt to fame with two book-length poems in a very different spirit—the didactic *An Essay on Criticism* (1711) and the brilliant mock epic *The Rape of the Lock* (1712, 1714). Made wealthy by his translations of Homer's *Iliad*

(1720) and *Odyssey* (1726), Pope retired to a five-acre villa in Twickenham, outside London. By the time of his death at age fifty-six, he had produced an unrivaled body of work that includes at least two other masterpieces, *The Dunciad* (1728) and *An Essay on Man* (1734).

CLAUDIA RANKINE (b. 1963)

Jamaica-born Claudia Rankine immigrated at age seven to New York City, where her father worked as an orderly, her mother as a nurse's aide. While earning a BA at Williams College (1986), Rankine was first inspired to take writing classes by the work of Adrienne Rich and James Baldwin, who "together," in her own words, "began to give me language to speak." Since earning her MFA at Columbia University (1994), Rankine has emerged as among the most influential writers and thinkers of her generation, a "fearless poet," in the words of Mark Doty, "extend[ing] American poetry in invigorating new directions" by "investigating many kinds of boundaries: the unsettled territory between poetry and prose, between the word and the visual image, between what it's like to be a subject and the ways we're defined from outside by skin color, economics, and global corporate culture." A playwright who has also collaborated on numerous multimedia and performance pieces; editor of collections including *American Poets in the Twenty-First Century: The New Poetics* (2007); founder-curator of the Racial Imaginary Institute; MacArthur Fellow; former chancellor of the Academy of American Poets; and today Frederick Iseman Professor of Poetry at Yale University, Rankine is best known for books bending and blending genre—verse, prose poem, essay, and image. The most important is *Citizen: An American Lyric* (2014). Among the most influential books of the early twenty-first century, this best-selling, multi-award-winning "anatomy of American racism in the new millennium" (to quote *Bookforum*) was the first book ever named as a finalist for National Book Critics Circle Awards in both poetry and criticism. Reviewers describe her much-anticipated follow-up, *Just Us: An American Conversation* (2020), as another "utterly original and desperately needed" work of "disarming intimacy and searing honesty," which "should move, challenge, and transform every reader who encounters it."

ADRIENNE RICH (1929–2012)

One of the foremost poets and public intellectuals of her time, Adrienne Rich was born in Baltimore, Maryland, daughter of a former concert pianist and of a renowned Johns Hopkins University pathologist. Rich's career as a poet began in 1951, when the Radcliffe College senior's first volume, *A Change of World* (1951), was selected by W. H. Auden for the prestigious Yale Younger Poets Award. Two years later, Rich married Harvard economist Alfred Conrad, with whom she had three children. As the 1950s gave way to the 1960s and 1970s, Rich's life and work changed profoundly. Beginning with her 1963 collection, *Snapshots of a Daughter-in-Law,* her poetry became ever less tightly controlled and formal, as it became ever more politically and personally charged, reflecting her deep engagement with the feminist, antiwar, and civil rights movements. After her estranged husband's suicide (1970) and publication of the National Book Award–winning *Diving into the Wreck* (1974), Rich began a lifelong partnership with Jamaica-born novelist and editor Michelle Cliff and published her two most influential prose works, *Of Woman Born: Motherhood as Experience and Institution* (1976) and *On Lies, Secrets, and Silence* (1979), which includes her landmark essay "Compulsory Heterosexuality and Lesbian Existence." In the decades that followed, Rich never rested on her countless laurels, fiercely pursuing both her craft and her work for social justice. Her thirtieth and last volume of verse, *Tonight No Poetry Will Serve,* came out in 2010, just two years before her death, at age eighty-two, from the rheumatoid arthritis she had battled for decades. In its obituary, the *New York Times* hailed Rich as "a poet of towering reputation," whose work is "distinguished by an unswerving progressive vision and a dazzling, empathetic ferocity."

CHRISTINA ROSSETTI (1830–94)

Ranking with Emily Dickinson and Elizabeth Barrett Browning as among the nineteenth century's most important women poets, Christina Rossetti spent her outwardly uneventful life in London, part of a uniquely talented family. Her father, an Italian political exile, was a poet, Dante scholar, and Italian professor, her mother an Anglo-Italian former governess. Rossetti's older sister and youngest brother ultimately became distinguished literature and art critics, and her eldest brother, Dante Gabriel, an influential painter-poet. According to her brother, Christina composed her first poem before she was old enough to write and was, as a girl, so "vivacious, and open to pleasurable impressions" that everyone expected her to "develop into a woman [. . .] fond of society and diversions, and taking a part in them of more than average brilliancy." Yet "[w]hat came to pass was [. . .] quite the contrary." In the 1840s, the illness and virtual blindness of the teenaged Rossetti's father rendered her family's financial situation precarious; her own health broke down, and she became much more devout. For the rest of her life, Rossetti battled illness and sin in equal measure. Seeking to adhere strictly to her Protestant faith, she refused to marry any of her various suitors, eschewed once-loved "diversions" such as opera, and undertook volunteer work, including ten years at the St. Mary Magdalene Penitentiary, a charitable institution dedicated to the reform of so-called fallen or ruined women. All the while, however, Rossetti kept writing and publishing, producing a remarkable body of poetry including lyrics, devotional verse, narrative fables, and ballads. Her first and best-known book, *Goblin Market and Other Poems,* appeared in 1862.

WILLIAM SHAKESPEARE (1554–1616)

Considering the great fame of his work, surprisingly little is known of William Shakespeare's life. Between 1585 and 1592, he left his birthplace of Stratford-upon-Avon for London to begin a career as playwright and actor. No dates of his professional career are recorded, however, nor can the order in which he composed his plays and poems be determined with absolute certainty. By 1594, he had established himself as a poet with two long works—*Venus and Adonis* and *The Rape of Lucrece*—and his more than 150 sonnets are supreme expressions of the form. His reputation, though, rests on the works he wrote for the theater. Shakespeare produced perhaps thirty-five plays in twenty-five years, proving himself a master of every dramatic genre: tragedy (in works such as *Macbeth, Hamlet, King Lear,* and *Othello*); historical drama (for example, *Richard III* and *Henry IV*); comedy (*Twelfth Night, As You Like It,* and many more); and romance (including *The Tempest* and *Cymbeline*).

EVIE SHOCKLEY (b. 1965)

Born and raised in Nashville, Tennessee, poet-critic Evie Shockley is the daughter of a jazz musician who also taught kindergarten. After earning a BA at Northwestern University (1988) and a JD at the University of Michigan (1991), she clerked for a U.S. Court of Appeals judge and practiced law in Chicago only to find herself, as she told one interviewer, "more and more miserable." Fearing that an MFA in creative writing was "too risky for someone who still had law school loans to pay off," she instead opted to study literature at Duke, graduating with a PhD in English, Women's Studies, and African and African American Studies in 2002. Even before that, however, Shockley published *The Gorgon Goddess* (2001), the first of an ensemble of poetry collections now also including *a half-red sea* (2006), *the new black* (2011), and *semiautomatic* (2017). A finalist for the Pulitzer Prize and the second of Shockley's books to win a Hurston/Wright Legacy Award, *semioautomatic* is aptly styled by the Pulitzer committee as "a brilliant leap of faith [. . .] part rap, part rant, part slam, part performance art, that leaves the reader unsettled, challenged—and bettered." Simultaneously "playful and dead serious," in the words of one reviewer, Shockley's poetry is notable, too, for its formal experimentation, the importance of which she teases out in *Renegade Poetics: Black Aesthetics and Formal Innovation in African American Poetry* (2011). A former Cave Canem fellow and winner of both the Holmes National Poetry Prize (2012) and the Stephen Henderson Award for Outstanding Achievement in Poetry (2015), Shockley is today a professor of English at Rutgers University, where she teaches contemporary, especially African American and African diaspora, literatures; critical race studies; and creative writing.

DANEZ SMITH (b. 1988?)

Like the Dark Noise Collective Danez Smith cofounded, the work of this Black, Queer, nonbinary Minnesotan "explodes archaic notions of page vs. stage" as "arenas of verse." A two-time Individual World Poetry Slam finalist, Smith earned a BA at the University of Wisconsin–Madison (2012) as part of the inaugural cohort of the pioneering First Wave spoken word and hip-hop arts program. Also a graduate of the University of Michigan MFA program (2017), Smith is only one of two creative writers to make *Forbes* magazine's 2019 "30 under 30: Media" list, becoming, to quote *American Poets*, "one of a generation's most noticed poets" by proving "at once a stunning performer and a tersely effective arranger of words on the page." Those "stunning performance[s]" include a 2014 reading of Smith's poem "dear white america" that went viral via *YouTube* and a 2016 *Late Show with Stephen Colbert* appearance with Macklemore in a dramatic interpretation of the rapper's "White Privilege II." Just as stunning are Smith's three published collections: the latest, *Homie* (2020); the first, *[insert] boy* (2014), winner of the Lambda Literary Award for Gay Poetry, the Kate Tufts Discovery Award, and *Ploughshares'* John C. Zacharis First Book Award; and the most acclaimed, *Don't Call Us Dead* (2017). A National Book Award finalist and winner of the Forward Prize for Best Collection (an honor Smith is the youngest author ever to receive), its long opening sequence of quasi-sonnets, imagining a "summer, somewhere" where murdered Black boys find "everything is sanctuary / & nothing is gun," earned the Poetry Society of America/T. S. Eliot Foundation's inaugural Four Quartets Prize. Cohost of the Poetry Foundation's podcast *VS*, Smith's ideal is a poetry "that is alive" not only "in the air," "when you read it aloud," "but also on the page," and whose goal is "inspiring a next generation" by "distill[ing] something" of a "humanity" at once "ugly and gorgeous."

TRACY K. SMITH (b. 1972)

Pulitzer Prize–winning poet Tracy K. Smith credits her "love of language" and "sense of [. . .] hearing voices and imagining the lives inside" them to her parents—a mother who was also a teacher with a great "gift for storytelling and mimicry" and an optical-engineer father who "was always reading and pushing us to read." Though raised with her four older siblings mainly in California, Smith has spent much of her life in the Northeast: Born in Massachusetts, she returned there to attend Harvard (BA, 1994), studying with Seamus Heaney, while also—like fellow poets Natasha Trethewey and Kevin Young—participating in the Boston-based writers' group/reading series known as the Dark Room Collective. Grieving her mother's death from cancer,

Smith nonetheless moved on to Columbia University, earning her MFA in 1997. Today a mother of three and director of Princeton University's Lewis Center for the Arts, Smith won rave reviews and multiple awards for her first two collections—*The Body's Question* (2003), which she describes as "grappling with the idea of the body as a site for experience, memory, and loss," "discovery and joy," and *Duende* (2007)—and for her 2015 memoir (*Ordinary Light*). But what earned her a Pulitzer and secured her reputation as one of America's most innovative and exciting young poets was *Life on Mars* (2011), a collection shaped equally by grief over her father's death, his work on the Hubble Space Telescope, and her interest in exploring (with nods to David Bowie and *2001: A Space Odyssey*) "space" and humans' enduring fascination with—and fantasies about—space "as a kind of metaphor through which to consider some of the facts and problems of life here on Earth." Smith served as U.S. Poet Laureate from 2017 to 2019 and hosts the radio show/podcast *The Slowdown*.

A. E. STALLINGS (b. 1968)

Alicia Elsbeth Stallings's biography—which could be titled *All the Way from Athens to Athens*—is an unusual one for a contemporary American poet. Admittedly, this daughter of a librarian and a Georgia Tech professor grew up in a bookish home, publishing her first poem—in *Seventeen* magazine—at age sixteen. But at the University of Georgia (in Athens, Georgia) and, later, Oxford University (in England), where she earned her MA, Stallings chose to study not English but ancient Greek and Latin language and literature, inspired, as she explains, both by a love of mythology rooted in a fascination with fairy tales and by her awareness that "the English poets whom [she] admired" most—including T. S. Eliot and A. E. Housman—"had studied the Classics and not English, which wasn't even a discipline then." Stallings has lived abroad—in Athens, Greece—since her 1999 marriage. Published the same year, her Richard Wilbur Award–winning first collection, *Archaic Smile*, assured her reputation as among America's foremost contemporary "New Formalists," a label simultaneously affirmed and greatly complicated by her later collections, *Hapax* (2006), *Olives* (2012), and *Like* (2018); by essays such as "Crooked Roads without Improvement: Some Thoughts on Formal Verse" (2000); and by her Poetry Foundation–sponsored blog *Harriet*

(2007–8). Also a prizewinning translator of poets ranging from Lucretius (99–55 BCE) and Plutarch (46–120 CE) to Angelos Sikelianos (1884–1951), Stallings has garnered numerous highly coveted honors, ranging from a Nemerov Sonnet Award (2004) to a MacArthur Foundation "genius grant" (2011), and currently serves as poetry program director of the Athens Centre. Despite all that, she is, by her own report, usually known in Greece simply as "Aliki Psaropoulou, wife of Yannis, mother of Jason and Atalanta," thus enjoying an oddly "freeing" sort of "invisibility."

ADRIENNE SU (b. 1967)

Adrienne Su grew up in Atlanta, Georgia, unaware, she says, of the ironies involved in being "viewed as Chinese," while "I knew no Chinese and thrived on the study of Latin." A graduate of Harvard and the University of Virginia, where she studied with poets Rita Dove, Gregory Orr, and Charles Wright, Su, by her own account, "started writing as soon as I could form a sentence on paper" and "started sending out work" while still in high school. Having worked as a freelance editor and writer, Su is today an associate professor of English and poet in residence at Pennsylvania's Dickinson College; a wife and mother; and the author of poetry collections including *Middle Kingdom* (1997), *Sanctuary* (2006), *Having None of It* (2009), *Living Quarters* (2015), and *Peach State* (2020). Crediting her high school Latin teacher and the ancient Roman poet Virgil with first teaching her the art of meter, and her early involvement in poetry slams with bolstering her commitment to writing "poems that on some levels can be read by anyone," Su also, in her words, "prefer[s] the daily to the exotic as subject matter," seeing writing as best when "it's woven into everyday life, as a ritual that fits somewhere between making pancakes for my kids and preparing a class for college students."

ALFRED, LORD TENNYSON (1809–92)

The most popular and important of the Victorian poets, Alfred, Lord Tennyson demonstrated his talents at an early age; he published his first volume in 1827. Encouraged to devote his life to poetry by a group of undergraduates at Cambridge University known as the "Apostles," Tennyson was particularly close to Arthur Hallam, whose sudden death in 1833 inspired the long elegy *In Memoriam* (1850). With that poem Tennyson achieved lasting fame and recognition; he was appointed Poet Laureate the year of its publication, succeeding William Wordsworth. Despite the great popularity of his "journalistic" poems—"The Charge of the Light Brigade" (1854) is perhaps the best known—Tennyson's great theme was the past, both personal (*In the Valley of Cauteretz*, 1864) and national (*Idylls of the King*, 1869). Tennyson was made a baron in 1884; when he died, eight years later, he was buried in Poets' Corner in London's Westminster Abbey.

NATASHA TRETHEWEY (b. 1966)

Daughter of a social worker and a Canadian poet who met at a Kentucky college, but who had to marry in Ohio because of laws banning interracial unions, Natasha Trethewey was born in her mother's hometown of Gulfport, Mississippi. After her parents' divorce, she lived with her mother in Atlanta, Georgia, summering on the Gulf Coast with both her father and her mother's family. In 1985, Trethewey was just beginning her studies at the University of Georgia when her stepfather murdered her mother. Turning to poetry to deal with her grief, Trethewey earned her BA in 1989; an MA from Virginia's Hollins College, where her father was a professor (1991); and an MFA from the University of Massachusetts at Amherst (1995). After a short stint teaching at Auburn University, Trethewey moved to Emory University and, in 2007, became only the fourth African American poet ever to win the Pulitzer Prize, for *Native Guard*. Her third collection, it explores the problem of individual and collective historical amnesia through elegies to her mother and a sonnet sequence written from the perspective of a Black Civil War soldier. The years 2007–8, however, also brought Trethewey loss and hardship when her brother was imprisoned on drug-related charges and her beloved grandmother died. Interweaving poetry, essays, and letters, her memoir *Beyond Katrina: A Meditation on the Mississippi Gulf Coast* (2010) reflects on both the region and her family's efforts to remember and rebuild; *Memorial Drive: A Daughter's Memoir* (2020) explores her mother's death and its aftermath. Trethewey's most recent collections include *Thrall* (2012) and *Monument: Poems New and Selected* (2018). Having served as U.S. Poet Laureate from 2012 to 2014, Trethewey is today Board of Trustees Professor of English at Northwestern University.

PHILLIS WHEATLEY (c. 1753–84)

The second American woman and first African American to publish a book of poems, Phillis Wheatley lived most of her life in slavery, her first name that of the ship in which she was trafficked from West Africa to the New World at around age seven. Deemed too "slender" and "frail," according to a retrospective (1834) account, for the hard labor demanded of slaves in the West Indies/Caribbean or Southern colonies, the asthmatic Wheatley was instead transported to Boston and sold "for a trifle" to merchant John Wheatley and his wife, Susanna, whom she served as a domestic. Convinced of her precocity, the Wheatleys (including children Nathaniel and Mary) taught Phillis to read and write and encouraged her study of the Bible, as well as classical and British literature (especially John Milton and Alexander Pope). Having published her first poem at thirteen, Wheatley gained international attention three years later with her elegy for British evangelist George Whitefield. Unable to interest an American publisher in her poems, the Wheatleys contacted Whitefield's patron, a wealthy countess and abolitionist. Thanks to her, Wheatley and Nathaniel in 1771 visited England, where her *Poems on Various Subjects, Religious and Moral* was published two years later. Legally freed shortly before her mistress's death in 1774, she remained with the family until 1778, when—in the wake of John's and Mary's death and the married Nathaniel's move to England—Wheatley married. Though Wheatley continued to publish poems for the rest of her life, she and her husband, like many free Blacks, struggled to make ends meet. She and her only surviving child died while her husband was jailed for debt. The first American edition of *Poems on Various Subjects*, a second collection Wheatley had tried unsuccessfully to publish by subscription in 1779, appeared two years later.

WALT WHITMAN (1819–92)

Walt Whitman was born on a farm in West Hills, Long Island, to a British father and a Dutch mother. After working as a journalist throughout New York for many years, he taught for a time and founded his own newspaper, *The Long Islander*, in 1838; he then left journalism to work on *Leaves of Grass*, originally intended as a poetic treatise on American democratic idealism. Published privately in multiple editions from 1855 to 1874, the book of poems at first failed to reach a mass audience. In 1881, Boston's Osgood and Company published another edition of *Leaves of Grass*, which sold well until the district attorney called it "obscene literature" and stipulated that Whitman remove certain poems and phrases. He refused, and it was many years before his works were again published, this time in Philadelphia. By the time Whitman died, his work was revered, as it still is today, for its greatness of spirit and its exuberant American voice. Along with Emily Dickinson, Whitman is widely credited with pioneering a distinctly American poetry.

WILLIAM CARLOS WILLIAMS (1883–1963)

Born in Rutherford, New Jersey, William Carlos Williams attended school in Switzerland and New York and studied medicine at the University of Pennsylvania and the University of Leipzig in Germany. He spent most of his life in Rutherford, practicing medicine and gradually establishing himself as one of America's great poets. Early in his writing career he left the European-inspired Imagist movement to develop a more uniquely American poetic style comprised of vital, local language, and "no ideas but in things." His shorter poems have been published in numerous collections, including the Pulitzer Prize–winning *Brueghel, and Other Poems* (1963); his five-volume philosophical poem, *Paterson*, was published in 1963. Among his other works are plays such as *A Dream of Love* (1948) and *Many Loves* (1950); a trilogy of novels— *White Mules* (1937), *In the Money* (1940), and *The Build-Up* (1952); his *Autobiography* (1951); his *Selected Essays* (1954); and his *Selected Letters* (1957).

WILLIAM WORDSWORTH (1770–1850)

Regarded by many as the greatest of the Romantic poets, William Wordsworth was born in Cockermouth in the English Lake District, a beautiful, mountainous region that his poetry helped make a popular tourist destination even in his own lifetime. He studied at Cambridge University and then spent a year in France, hoping to witness the French Revolution firsthand; as the revolution's "glorious renovation" dissolved into anarchy and then tyranny, Wordsworth was forced to return to England. Remarkably, he managed to establish "a saving intercourse with my true self" and to write some of his finest poetry, including the early version of his autobiographical masterpiece, *The Prelude*, which first appeared in 1805 and then again, much altered, in 1850. In 1798, Wordsworth and his friend Samuel Taylor Coleridge published *Lyrical Ballads*, which contained many of their greatest poems and is widely considered the founding document of English Romanticism. Revered by the reading public, Wordsworth served as Poet Laureate from 1843 until his death in 1850.

WILLIAM BUTLER YEATS (1865–1939)

William Butler Yeats was born in Dublin, Ireland, and, though he spent most of his youth in London, became the preeminent Irish poet of the twentieth century. Immersed in Irish history, folklore, and politics, as well as spiritualism and the occult, he attended art school for a time but left to devote himself to poetry that was, early in his career, self-consciously dreamy and ethereal. Yeats's poems became tighter and more passionate with his reading of philosophers such as Nietzsche, his involvement (mainly through theater) with the Irish nationalist cause, and his desperate love for the actress and nationalist Maud Gonne. He was briefly a senator in the newly independent Irish government before withdrawing from active public life to Thoor Ballylee, a crumbling Norman tower that Yeats and his wife fashioned into a home. There he developed an elaborate mythology (published as *A Vision* in 1925) and wrote poems that explored fundamental questions of history and identity. He was awarded the Nobel Prize for Literature in 1923.

KEVIN YOUNG (b. 1970)

Poet Kevin Young was born in Lincoln, Nebraska, and grew up mainly in the Midwest, before heading east to Harvard University. There, he took courses with Seamus Heaney, participated in the influential Dark Room Collective, and wrote many of the poems that would make up his first, award-winning collection (*Most Way Home*, 1995) on the way to earning a BA in English and American literature (1992). Shuttling between coasts, Young spent two years at Stanford University, in Northern California, before completing his MFA at Brown University, in Rhode Island. Young also has deep Southern roots. Both his mother—among the first Black women to earn a PhD (in chemistry) from the University of Nebraska—and his father—an ophthalmologist who was also an avid hunter and cook—grew up in rural Louisiana, where much of Young's extended family still lives. His diverse collections of verse include *Black Maria* (2005), about fictional private eye A. K. A. Jones; *Ardency* (2011), about the real-life Africans who managed to wrest control of the slave ship *Amistad* in 1839; *Book of Hours* (2014), which includes poems both grappling with his father's 2004 death, in a hunting accident, and inspired by the birth of Young's first son some two years later; *Blue Laws: Selected and Uncollected Poems 1995–2015* (2016); and *Brown: Poems* (2018). Currently director of the Smithsonian's National Museum of African American History and Culture and *New Yorker* poetry editor, Young is also the editor of multiple anthologies and author of *Bunk: The Rise of Hoaxes, Humbug, Plagiarists, Phonies, Post-Facts, and Fake News* (2017).

PART THREE Drama

Quiara Alegría Hudes

24 | DRAMA: READING, RESPONDING, WRITING

Many cultures have had oral literatures: histories, **romances**, poems to be recited or sung. Our own era has its share of oral art forms, of course, and many of us enjoy audiobooks. But most contemporary fiction writers and poets write with an expectation that their work will be read and enjoyed privately, silently, from the printed page.

In contrast, **drama** is written primarily to be performed—by actors, on a stage, for an audience. Playwrights or dramatists (the two terms are used interchangeably) work with an understanding that the words on the page are just the first step—a map of sorts—toward the ultimate goal: a collaborative, publicly performed work of art. They create plays fully aware of the possibilities that go beyond printed words and extend to physical actions, stage devices, and other theatrical techniques for creating effects and modifying audience responses. Although the script of a play may be the most essential piece in the puzzle that makes up the final work of art, the play text is not the final, complete work.

To attend a play—that is, to be part of an audience—represents a very different kind of experience from the usually solitary act of reading. On the stage, real human beings, standing for imaginary characters, deliver lines and perform actions for you to see and hear. In turn, the actors adapt in subtle ways to the reactions of the people who attend the performance and whose responses are no longer wholly private but have become, in part, communal.

When you attend the performance of a play, then, you become a collaborator in the creation of a unique work of art: not the play *text* but instead a specific *interpretation* of that text. No two performances of a play can ever be identical, just as no two interpretations of a play can be exactly the same.

READING DRAMA

In many respects, of course, reading drama is similar to reading fiction. In both cases we anticipate what will happen next; we imagine the characters, settings, and actions; we respond to the symbolic suggestiveness of images; and we identify themes. But because most plays are written to be performed, reading plays is also somewhat different from reading fiction or poetry. In fiction, for example, there is a mediator or **narrator**, someone standing between us and the events. In contrast, drama rarely has such an interpreter or mediator to tell us what is happening or to shape our responses. Play texts instead rely on **stage directions** (the italicized descriptions of the set, characters, and actions), while **exposition** (the explanation of the past and current situation) emerges only here and there through **dialogue**.

For this reason, reading drama may place a greater demand on the imagination than reading fiction does: The reader must be his or her own narrator and interpreter. Such exercise for the imagination can prove rewarding, however, for it has much in common with the imaginative work that a director, actors, and other artists involved in a staged production do. In re-creating a play as we read it, we are essentially imagining the play as if it were being performed by live actors in real time. We "cast" the characters, we design the set with its furniture and props, and we choreograph or "block" the physical action, according to the cues in the text.

In reading drama even more than in reading fiction, we construct our ideas of character and personality from what characters say. In some plays, especially those with an experimental bent, certain lines of dialogue can be mystifying; other characters, as well as the audience or readers, can be left wondering what a speech means. On the one hand, such puzzling lines can become clearer in performance when we see and hear actors deliver them. On the other hand, plays that call for several characters to speak at once or to talk at cross purposes can be much easier to understand when read than they are in performance. In interpreting dialogue, you will naturally draw on your own experiences of comparable situations or similar personalities, as well as your familiarity with other plays or stories.

Questions to Ask When Reading a Play

In reading drama as in reading fiction, you can begin to understand a text by asking some basic questions about the elements of drama.

- **Expectations:** What do you expect
  - from the title? from the first sentence, paragraph, or speech?
  - after the first events or interactions of characters?
  - as the **conflict** is resolved?
- **Characterization:** Who are the characters? Is there a list of characters printed after the title of the play? What do you notice about their names or any identification of their roles, character types, or relationships?
  - Who is/are the **protagonist**(s)?
  - Who is/are the **antagonist**(s)?
  - Who are the other characters?
  - What does each character know at any moment in the **action**? What does each character expect at any point? What does the audience know or expect that is different from what the characters know or expect?
- **Plot:** What happens in the play?
  - Do the characters or situations change during the play?
  - What are the differences between the beginning, middle, and end of the play?
  - Is it divided into acts? Would there be an intermission in a performance?
  - Can you summarize the plot? Is it a recognizable kind or genre such as **tragedy, comedy, farce**, or mystery?
- **Setting:** What is the setting of the play?
  - *When* does the action occur? Do the stage directions specify a year or era, a day of the week, a season, a time of day?
  - Are there any time changes during the play? Are the **scenes** in chronological order, or are there any scenes that are supposed to take place earlier or simultaneously? Does the passage of time in the lives of the

characters correspond with the passage of time onstage? Or do we understand that time has passed and events have occurred between scenes?
- ○ *Where* does the action take place? Is it in the United States or another country, or in a specific town or region? Do the stage directions describe the scene that an audience would see onstage, and does this remain the same or change during the play? How many scene changes are there?
- **Style:** What do you notice about how the play is written?
  - ○ What is the style of the dialogue? Are the sentences and speeches short or long? Is the vocabulary simple or complex? Do characters ever speak at the same time, or do they always take turns? Does the play instruct actors to be silent for periods of time?
  - ○ Which characters speak most often? How might their speech patterns differ?
  - ○ Are there any **images** or figures of speech?
  - ○ What is the **tone** or mood? Does the play make the reader or audience feel sad, amused, worried, curious?
- **Theme:** What does the play mean? Can you express its theme or themes?
  - ○ Answers to these big questions may be found in many instances by returning to your answers to the questions above. The play's meaning or theme depends on all its features.

THINKING THEATRICALLY

As you read a play, you should not only make mental or written notes but also raise some of the questions an actor might ask in preparing a role or a director might ask before choosing a cast: How should this line be spoken? What kind of person is this character, and what are his or her motives in each scene? What does the play suggest about what made the character this way—family, environment, experience? Which characters are present or absent (onstage or off) in which scenes, and how do the characters onstage or off influence one another? Would you, as "director" of an imaginary performance, tell the actors to move in certain directions, together or apart; to express certain emotions and intentions; to speak in quiet, angry, sarcastic, or agonized tones?

Besides trying to understand the characters, you should consider ways that the play could be produced, designed, and staged. How might a set designer create a kitchen, street corner, garden, woods, or other space for the actors to move in, and how many set changes are there in the play? What would the audience see through any windows or doors in an imaginary building? How would lighting give an impression of the time of day or season? Would sound effects or music be necessary (such as a gunshot or telephone)? What sort of costumes are specified in the stage directions, and how would costumes help express character types and their relationships, as well as the historical time period? What essential props must be provided for the actors to use, and what other props are optional?

As you read Susan Glaspell's TRIFLES, keep these questions in mind, and list any others that occur to you. Try to create a mental image of the settings and of each character, and think about different ways the lines might be delivered and about their effect on an audience.

FICTION

*Chimamanda Ngozi Adichie
Aesop
*Isabel Allende
Margaret Atwood
James Baldwin
Toni Cade Bambara
Jorge Luis Borges
Ray Bradbury
Linda Brewer
Octavia E. Butler
A. S. Byatt
Italo Calvino
Raymond Carver
Anton Chekov
Kate Chopin

*Sandra Cisneros
Judith Ortiz Cofer
Edwidge Danticat
Junot Díaz
Ralph Ellison
Louise Erdrich
William Faulkner
Jules Feiffer
Gabriel García Márquez
William Gibson
Charlotte Perkins Gilman
Susan Glaspell
Jacob and Wilhelm Grimm
Nathaniel Hawthorne
Ernest Hemingway

Adam Johnson
James Joyce
Franz Kafka
Yasunari Kawabata
Jamaica Kincaid
*Jamil Jan Kochai
Jhumpa Lahiri
*Yiyun Li
Bobbie Ann Mason
Guy de Maupassant
Toni Morrison
Bharati Mukherjee
Alice Munro
*Haruki Murakami
Viet Thanh Nguyen

Alissa Nutting
Joyce Carol Oates
Tim O'Brien
Flannery O'Connor
Edgar Allan Poe
Annie Proulx
Karen Russell
George Saunders
David Sedaris
*Zadie Smith
Amy Tan
David Foster Wallace
Eudora Welty
Virginia Woolf

POETRY

Elizabeth Alexander
Agha Shahid Ali
Julia Alvarez
Yehuda Amichai
Maya Angelou
Matthew Arnold
W. H. Auden
Jimmy Santiago Baca
*Anna Laetitia Barbauld
Bashō
Aphra Behn
*Liz Berry
*Reginald Dwayne Betts
Elizabeth Bishop
William Blake
*Richard Blanco
*Eavan Boland
Emma Bolden
Arna Bontemps
Todd Boss
David Bottoms
Gwendolyn Brooks
Elizabeth Barrett Browning
Robert Browning

*Robert Burns
Buson
Thomas Campion
*Lorna Dee Cervantes
Helen Chasin
Chiyojo
Lady Mary Chudleigh
Sarah Cleghorn
Lucille Clifton
Judith Ortiz Cofer
Samuel Taylor Coleridge
Billy Collins
Martha Collins
Henry Constable
Wendy Cope
Countee Cullen
E. E. Cummings
Mahmoud Darwish
Lydia Davis
Walter de la Mare
*Natalie Diaz
James Dickey
Emily Dickinson
John Donne

Rita Dove
Denise Duhamel
Paul Laurence Dunbar
*Alice Dunbar-Nelson
Bob Dylan
Martín Espada
Robert Frost
*Ross Gay
Allen Ginsberg
*Elisa Gonzalez
Angelina Grimké
Emily Grosholz
Thomas Hardy
Joy Harjo
Gwen Harwood
Robert Hayden
Terrance Hayes
Seamus Heaney
Lafcadio Hearn
George Herbert
Bob Hicok
Gerard Manley Hopkins
Marie Howe
Andrew Hudgins

Langston Hughes
Randall Jarrell
Helene Johnson
*Saeed Jones
Ben Jonson
June Jordan
*Sor Juana Inés de la Cruz
John Keats
Galway Kinnell
Etheridge Knight
Yusef Komunyakaa
Maxine Kumin
Philip Larkin
*Emma Lazarus
Li-Young Lee
*Ada Limón
*Liz Lochhead
Richard Lovelace
Archibald MacLeish
Amit Majmudar
Christopher Marlowe
Paul Martinez Pompa
Andrew Marvell
*Campbell McGrath

SUSAN GLASPELL

(1876–1948)

Trifles

Though today remembered almost exclusively for her masterful *Trifles* (1916), Susan Glaspell wrote over a dozen plays, fifty short stories, nine novels, and a memoir, in addition to playing a key role in the development of twentieth-century American theater. Born in Davenport, Iowa, she graduated from Drake University in 1899 and spent two years at the *Des Moines Daily News*, where she covered the trial of a fifty-seven-year-old woman accused of murdering her sleeping husband with an axe. When Glaspell's short stories began appearing in magazines, she returned to Davenport. There, she became involved with George Cram Cook, a former English professor and married father of two. The two wed in 1913 and moved east, eventually settling in New York's Greenwich Village and Cape Cod, Massachusetts, where they founded the Provincetown Players, an extraordinary collective of freethinking, Left-leaning actors, directors, and playwrights that included Edna St. Vincent Millay and Eugene O'Neill. Between 1916 and 1922 at the Provincetown Playhouse, this pioneering group reportedly staged more plays by women than any other contemporary theater. Among them were eleven by Glaspell, ranging from realistic dramas such as *Trifles* and satirical comedies like *Woman's Honor* (1918) to her expressionistic *The Verge* (1921). Widowed in 1924, Glaspell ended a brief second marriage in 1931, the same year that her last play, *Alison's House*, won the Pulitzer Prize for Drama. Having published her first novel in 1909 and multiple best sellers in the 1920s and 1930s, Glaspell spent the last years of her life writing fiction in Provincetown.

CHARACTERS

SHERIFF	MRS. PETERS, *Sheriff's wife*
COUNTY ATTORNEY	MRS. HALE
HALE	

SCENE: *The kitchen in the now abandoned farmhouse of* JOHN WRIGHT, *a gloomy kitchen, and left without having been put in order—unwashed pans under the sink, a loaf of bread outside the bread-box, a dish-towel on the table—other signs of incompleted work. At the rear the outer door opens and the* SHERIFF *comes in followed by the* COUNTY ATTORNEY *and* HALE. *The* SHERIFF *and* HALE *are men in middle life, the* COUNTY ATTORNEY *is a young man; all are much bundled up and go at once to the stove. They are followed by the two women—the* SHERIFF's *wife first; she is a slight wiry woman, a thin nervous face.* MRS. HALE *is larger and would ordinarily be called more comfortable looking, but she is disturbed now and looks fearfully about as she enters. The women have come in slowly, and stand close together near the door.*

Marjorie Vonnegut, Elinor Cox, John King, Arthur Hohl, and T. W. Gibson
in a 1916 production of *Trifles*

COUNTY ATTORNEY: [*Rubbing his hands.*] This feels good. Come up to the fire, ladies.

MRS. PETERS: [*After taking a step forward.*] I'm not—cold.

SHERIFF: [*Unbuttoning his overcoat and stepping away from the stove as if to mark the beginning of official business.*] Now, Mr. Hale, before we move things about, you explain to Mr. Henderson just what you saw when you came here yesterday morning.

COUNTY ATTORNEY: By the way, has anything been moved? Are things just as you left them yesterday?

SHERIFF: [*Looking about.*] It's just the same. When it dropped below zero last night I thought I'd better send Frank out this morning to make a fire for us— no use getting pneumonia with a big case on, but I told him not to touch anything except the stove—and you know Frank.

COUNTY ATTORNEY: Somebody should have been left here yesterday.

SHERIFF: Oh—yesterday. When I had to send Frank to Morris Center for that man who went crazy—I want you to know I had my hands full yesterday. I knew you could get back from Omaha by today and as long as I went over everything here myself—

COUNTY ATTORNEY: Well, Mr. Hale, tell just what happened when you came here yesterday morning.

HALE: Harry and I had started to town with a load of potatoes. We came along the road from my place and as I got here I said, "I'm going to see if I can't get

John Wright to go in with me on a party telephone."[1] I spoke to Wright about it once before and he put me off, saying folks talked too much anyway, and all he asked was peace and quiet—I guess you know about how much he talked himself; but I thought maybe if I went to the house and talked about it before his wife, though I said to Harry that I didn't know as what his wife wanted made much difference to John—

COUNTY ATTORNEY: Let's talk about that later, Mr. Hale. I do want to talk about that, but tell now just what happened when you got to the house.

HALE: I didn't hear or see anything; I knocked at the door, and still it was all quiet inside. I knew they must be up, it was past eight o'clock. So I knocked again, and I thought I heard somebody say, "Come in." I wasn't sure, I'm not sure yet, but I opened the door—this door [Indicating the door by which the two women are still standing.] and there in that rocker—[Pointing to it.] sat Mrs. Wright.

[They all look at the rocker.]

COUNTY ATTORNEY: What—was she doing?

HALE: She was rockin' back and forth. She had her apron in her hand and was kind of—pleating it.

COUNTY ATTORNEY: And how did she—look?

HALE: Well, she looked queer.

COUNTY ATTORNEY: How do you mean—queer?

HALE: Well, as if she didn't know what she was going to do next. And kind of done up.

COUNTY ATTORNEY: How did she seem to feel about your coming?

HALE: Why, I don't think she minded—one way or other. She didn't pay much attention. I said, "How do, Mrs. Wright, it's cold, ain't it?" And she said, "Is it?"—and went on kind of pleating at her apron. Well, I was surprised; she didn't ask me to come up to the stove, or to set down, but just sat there, not even looking at me, so I said, "I want to see John." And then she— laughed. I guess you would call it a laugh. I thought of Harry and the team outside, so I said a little sharp: "Can't I see John?" "No," she says, kind o' dull like. "Ain't he home?" says I. "Yes," says she, "he's home." "Then why can't I see him?" I asked her, out of patience. "'Cause he's dead," says she. "Dead?" says I. She just nodded her head, not getting a bit excited, but rockin' back and forth. "Why—where is he?" says I, not knowing what to say. She just pointed upstairs—like that. [Himself pointing to the room above.] I got up, with the idea of going up there. I walked from there to here—then I says, "Why, what did he die of?" "He died of a rope round his neck," says she, and just went on pleatin' at her apron. Well, I went out and called Harry. I thought I might—need help. We went upstairs and there he was lyin'—

COUNTY ATTORNEY: I think I'd rather have you go into that upstairs, where you can point it all out. Just go on now with the rest of the story.

1. That is, a party line in which a number of households each have extensions, a common arrangement in the early twentieth century, especially in rural areas.

HALE: Well, my first thought was to get that rope off. It looked . . . [*Stops, his face twitches.*] . . . but Harry, he went up to him, and he said, "No, he's dead all right, and we'd better not touch anything." So we went back downstairs. She was still sitting that same way. "Has anybody been notified?" I asked. "No," says she, unconcerned. "Who did this, Mrs. Wright?" said Harry. He said it business-like—and she stopped pleatin' of her apron. "I don't know," she says. "You don't *know*?" says Harry. "No," says she. "Weren't you sleepin' in the bed with him?" says Harry. "Yes," says she, "but I was on the inside." "Somebody slipped a rope round his neck and strangled him and you didn't wake up?" says Harry. "I didn't wake up," she said after him. We must 'a looked as if we didn't see how that could be, for after a minute she said, "I sleep sound." Harry was going to ask her more questions but I said maybe we ought to let her tell her story first to the coroner, or the sheriff, so Harry went fast as he could to Rivers' place, where there's a telephone.

COUNTY ATTORNEY: And what did Mrs. Wright do when she knew that you had gone for the coroner?

HALE: She moved from that chair to this one over here [*Pointing to a small chair in the corner.*] and just sat there with her hands held together and looking down. I got a feeling that I ought to make some conversation, so I said I had come in to see if John wanted to put in a telephone, and at that she started to laugh, and then she stopped and looked at me—scared. [*The* COUNTY ATTOR-NEY, *who has had his notebook out, makes a note.*] I dunno, maybe it wasn't scared. I wouldn't like to say it was. Soon Harry got back, and then Dr. Lloyd came, and you, Mr. Peters, and so I guess that's all I know that you don't.

COUNTY ATTORNEY: [*Looking around.*] I guess we'll go upstairs first—and then out to the barn and around there. [*To the* SHERIFF.] You're convinced that there was nothing important here—nothing that would point to any motive?

SHERIFF: Nothing here but kitchen things.

[*The* COUNTY ATTORNEY, *after again looking around the kitchen, opens the door of a cupboard closet. He gets up on a chair and looks on a shelf. Pulls his hand away, sticky.*]

COUNTY ATTORNEY: Here's a nice mess.

[*The women draw nearer.*]

MRS. PETERS: [*To the other woman.*] Oh, her fruit; it did freeze. [*To the* LAWYER.] She worried about that when it turned so cold. She said the fire'd go out and her jars would break.

SHERIFF: Well, can you beat the women! Held for murder and worryin' about her preserves.

COUNTY ATTORNEY: I guess before we're through she may have something more serious than preserves to worry about.

HALE: Well, women are used to worrying over trifles.

[*The two women move a little closer together.*]

COUNTY ATTORNEY: [*With the gallantry of a young politician.*] And yet, for all their worries, what would we do without the ladies? [*The women do not unbend. He goes to the sink, takes a dipperful of water from the pail and pouring* it into a basin, washes his hands. Starts to wipe them on the roller towel, turns it for a cleaner place.] Dirty towels! [Kicks his foot against the pans under the sink.] Not much of a housekeeper, would you say, ladies?

MRS. HALE: [Stiffly.] There's a great deal of work to be done on a farm.

COUNTY ATTORNEY: To be sure. And yet [With a little bow to her.] I know there are some Dickson county farmhouses which do not have such roller towels. [He gives it a pull to expose its length again.]

MRS. HALE: Those towels get dirty awful quick. Men's hands aren't always as clean as they might be.

COUNTY ATTORNEY: Ah, loyal to your sex, I see. But you and Mrs. Wright were neighbors. I suppose you were friends, too.

MRS. HALE: [Shaking her head.] I've not seen much of her of late years. I've not been in this house—it's more than a year.

COUNTY ATTORNEY: And why was that? You didn't like her?

MRS. HALE: I liked her all well enough. Farmers' wives have their hands full, Mr. Henderson. And then—

COUNTY ATTORNEY: Yes—?

MRS. HALE: [Looking about.] It never seemed a very cheerful place.

COUNTY ATTORNEY: No—it's not cheerful. I shouldn't say she had the home-making instinct.

MRS. HALE: Well, I don't know as Wright had, either.

COUNTY ATTORNEY: You mean that they didn't get on very well?

MRS. HALE: No, I don't mean anything. But I don't think a place'd be any cheer-fuller for John Wright's being in it.

COUNTY ATTORNEY: I'd like to talk more of that a little later. I want to get the lay of things upstairs now. [He goes to the left, where three steps lead to a stair door.]

SHERIFF: I suppose anything Mrs. Peters does'll be all right. She was to take in some clothes for her, you know, and a few little things. We left in such a hurry yesterday.

COUNTY ATTORNEY: Yes, but I would like to see what you take, Mrs. Peters, and keep an eye out for anything that might be of use to us.

MRS. PETERS: Yes, Mr. Henderson. [The women listen to the men's steps on the stairs, then look about the kitchen.]

MRS. HALE: I'd hate to have men coming into my kitchen, snooping around and criticizing. [She arranges the pans under the sink which the LAWYER had shoved out of place.]

MRS. PETERS: Of course it's no more than their duty.

MRS. HALE: Duty's all right, but I guess that deputy sheriff that came out to make the fire might have got a little of this on. [Gives the roller towel a pull.] Wish I'd thought of that sooner. Seems mean to talk about her for not having things slicked up when she had to come away in such a hurry.

MRS. PETERS: [Who has gone to a small table in the left rear corner of the room, and lifted one end of a towel that covers a pan.] She had bread set. [Stands still.]

MRS. HALE: [Eyes fixed on a loaf of bread beside the bread box, which is on a low shelf at the other side of the room. Moves slowly toward it.] She was going to put this in there. [Picks up loaf, then abruptly drops it. In a manner of return-ing to familiar things.] It's a shame about her fruit. I wonder if it's all gone.

[*Gets up on the chair and looks.*] I think there's some here that's all right, Mrs. Peters. Yes—here; [*Holding it toward the window.*] this is cherries, too. [*Looking again.*] I declare I believe that's the only one. [*Gets down, bottle in her hand. Goes to the sink and wipes it off on the outside.*] She'll feel awful bad after all her hard work in the hot weather. I remember the afternoon I put up my cherries last summer. [*She puts the bottle on the big kitchen table, center of the room. With a sigh, is about to sit down in the rocking-chair. Before she is seated realizes what chair it is; with a slow look at it, steps back. The chair, which she has touched, rocks back and forth.*] *Symbolic – she still there*

MRS. PETERS: Well, I must get those things from the front room closet. [*She goes to the door at the right, but after looking into the other room, steps back.*] You coming with me, Mrs. Hale? You could help me carry them. [*They go in the other room; reappear,* MRS. PETERS *carrying a dress and skirt,* MRS. HALE *following with a pair of shoes.*] My, it's cold in there. [*She puts the clothes on the big table, and hurries to the stove.*]

MRS. HALE: [*Examining the skirt.*] Wright was close. I think maybe that's why she kept so much to herself. She didn't even belong to the Ladies Aid. I suppose she felt she couldn't do her part, and then you don't enjoy things when you feel shabby. She used to wear pretty clothes and be lively, when she was Minnie Foster, one of the town girls singing in the choir. But that—oh, that was thirty years ago. This all you was to take in? *domestic job*

MRS. PETERS: She said she wanted an apron. Funny thing to want, for there isn't much to get you dirty in jail, goodness knows. But I suppose just to make her feel more natural. She said they was in the top drawer in this cupboard. Yes, here. And then her little shawl that always hung behind the door. [*Opens stair door and looks.*] Yes, here it is. [*Quickly shuts door leading upstairs.*]

MRS. HALE: [*Abruptly moving toward her.*] Mrs. Peters?

MRS. PETERS: Yes, Mrs. Hale?

MRS. HALE: Do you think she did it?

MRS. PETERS: [*In a frightened voice.*] Oh, I don't know.

MRS. HALE: Well, I don't think she did. Asking for an apron and her little shawl. Worrying about her fruit.

MRS. PETERS: [*Starts to speak, glances up, where footsteps are heard in the room above. In a low voice.*] Mr. Peters says it looks bad for her. Mr. Henderson is awful sarcastic in a speech and he'll make fun of her sayin' she didn't wake up.

MRS. HALE: Well, I guess John Wright didn't wake when they was slipping that rope under his neck.

MRS. PETERS: No, it's strange. It must have been done awful crafty and still. They say it was such a—funny way to kill a man, rigging it all up like that.

MRS. HALE: That's just what Mr. Hale said. There was a gun in the house. He says that's what he can't understand.

MRS. PETERS: Mr. Henderson said coming out that what was needed for the case was a motive; something to show anger, or—sudden feeling.

MRS. HALE: [*Who is standing by the table.*] Well, I don't see any signs of anger around here. [*She puts her hand on the dish towel which lies on the table, stands looking down at table, one half of which is clean, the other half messy.*] It's wiped to here. [*Makes a move as if to finish work, then turns and looks at loaf of bread outside the bread box. Drops towel. In that voice of coming back to*

No longer exist

familiar things.] Wonder how they are finding things upstairs. I hope she had it a little more red-up[2] up there. You know, it seems kind of *sneaking*. Locking her up in town and then coming out here and trying to get her own house to turn against her!

MRS. PETERS: But Mrs. Hale, the law is the law.

MRS. HALE: I s'pose 'tis. [*Unbuttoning her coat.*] Better loosen up your things, Mrs. Peters. You won't feel them when you go out.

[MRS. PETERS *takes off her fur tippet, goes to hang it on hook at back of room, stands looking at the under part of the small corner table.*]

MRS. PETERS: She was piecing a quilt. [*She brings the large sewing basket and they look at the bright pieces.*]

MRS. HALE: It's log cabin pattern. Pretty, isn't it? I wonder if she was goin' to quilt it or just knot it?

[*Footsteps have been heard coming down the stairs. The* SHERIFF *enters followed by* HALE *and the* COUNTY ATTORNEY.]

SHERIFF: They wonder if she was going to quilt it or just knot it!

[*The men laugh, the women look abashed.*]

COUNTY ATTORNEY: [*Rubbing his hands over the stove.*] Frank's fire didn't do much up there, did it? Well, let's go out to the barn and get that cleared up.

[*The men go outside.*]

MRS. HALE: [*Resentfully.*] I don't know as there's anything so strange, our takin' up our time with little things while we're waiting for them to get the evidence. [*She sits down at the big table smoothing out a block with decision.*] I don't see as it's anything to laugh about.

MRS. PETERS: [*Apologetically.*] Of course they've got awful important things on their minds. [*Pulls up a chair and joins* MRS. HALE *at the table.*]

MRS. HALE: [*Examining another block.*] Mrs. Peters, look at this one. Here, this is the one she was working on, and look at the sewing! All the rest of it has been so nice and even. And look at this! It's all over the place! Why, it looks as if she didn't know what she was about! [*After she has said this they look at each other, then start to glance back at the door. After an instant* MRS. HALE *has pulled at a knot and ripped the sewing.*]

MRS. PETERS: Oh, what are you doing, Mrs. Hale?

MRS. HALE: [*Mildly.*] Just pulling out a stitch or two that's not sewed very good. [*Threading the needle.*] Bad sewing always made me fidgety.

MRS. PETERS: [*Nervously.*] I don't think we ought to touch things.

MRS. HALE: I'll just finish up this end. [*Suddenly stopping and leaning forward.*] Mrs. Peters?

MRS. PETERS: Yes, Mrs. Hale?

MRS. HALE: What do you suppose she was so nervous about?

MRS. PETERS: Oh—I don't know. I don't know as she was nervous. I sometimes sew awful queer when I'm just tired. [MRS. HALE *starts to say something, looks*

2. Tidied up.

at MRS. PETERS, *then goes on sewing.*] Well, I must get these things wrapped up. They may be through sooner than we think. [*Putting apron and other things together.*] I wonder where I can find a piece of paper, and string.

MRS. HALE: In that cupboard, maybe.

MRS. PETERS: [*Looking in cupboard.*] Why, here's a bird-cage. [*Holds it up.*] Did she have a bird, Mrs. Hale?

MRS. HALE: Why, I don't know whether she did or not—I've not been here for so long. There was a man around last year selling canaries cheap, but I don't know as she took one; maybe she did. She used to sing real pretty herself.

MRS. PETERS: [*Glancing around.*] Seems funny to think of a bird here. But she must have had one, or why would she have a cage? I wonder what happened to it.

MRS. HALE: I s'pose maybe the cat got it.

MRS. PETERS: No, she didn't have a cat. She's got that feeling some people have about cats—being afraid of them. My cat got in her room and she was real upset and asked me to take it out.

MRS. HALE: My sister Bessie was like that. Queer, ain't it?

MRS. PETERS: [*Examining the cage.*] Why, look at this door. It's broke. One hinge is pulled apart.

MRS. HALE: [*Looking too.*] Looks as if someone must have been rough with it.

MRS. PETERS: Why, yes. [*She brings the cage forward and puts it on the table.*]

MRS. HALE: I wish if they're going to find any evidence they'd be about it. I don't like this place.

MRS. PETERS: But I'm awful glad you came with me, Mrs. Hale. It would be lonesome for me sitting here alone.

MRS. HALE: It would, wouldn't it? [*Dropping her sewing.*] But I tell you what I do wish, Mrs. Peters. I wish I had come over sometimes when *she* was here. I—[*Looking around the room.*]—wish I had.

MRS. PETERS: But of course you were awful busy, Mrs. Hale—your house and your children.

MRS. HALE: I could've come. I stayed away because it weren't cheerful—and that's why I ought to have come. I—I've never liked this place. Maybe because it's down in a hollow and you don't see the road. I dunno what it is, but it's a lonesome place and always was. I wish I had come over to see Minnie Foster sometimes. I can see now—[*Shakes her head.*]

MRS. PETERS: Well, you mustn't reproach yourself, Mrs. Hale. Somehow we just don't see how it is with other folks until—something comes up.

MRS. HALE: Not having children makes less work—but it makes a quiet house, and Wright out to work all day, and no company when he did come in. Did you know John Wright, Mrs. Peters?

MRS. PETERS: Not to know him; I've seen him in town. They say he was a good man.

MRS. HALE: Yes—good; he didn't drink, and kept his word as well as most, I guess, and paid his debts. But he was a hard man, Mrs. Peters. Just to pass the time of day with him—[*Shivers.*] Like a raw wind that gets to the bone. [*Pauses, her eye falling on the cage.*] I should think she would 'a wanted a bird. But what do you suppose went with it?

MRS. PETERS: I don't know, unless it got sick and died. [*She reaches over and swings the broken door, swings it again, both women watch it.*]

MRS. HALE: You weren't raised round here, were you? [MRS. PETERS *shakes her head.*] You didn't know—her?

MRS. PETERS: Not till they brought her yesterday.

MRS. HALE: She—come to think of it, she was kind of like a bird herself—real sweet and pretty, but kind of timid and—fluttery. How—she—did—change. [*Silence; then as if struck by a happy thought and relieved to get back to everyday things.*] Tell you what, Mrs. Peters, why don't you take the quilt in with you? It might take up her mind.

MRS. PETERS: Why, I think that's a real nice idea, Mrs. Hale. There couldn't possibly be any objection to it, could there? Now, just what would I take? I wonder if her patches are in here—and her things. [*They look in the sewing basket.*]

MRS. HALE: Here's some red. I expect this has got sewing things in it. [*Brings out a fancy box.*] What a pretty box. Looks like something somebody would give you. Maybe her scissors are in here. [*Opens box. Suddenly puts her hand to her nose.*] Why—[MRS. PETERS *bends nearer, then turns her face away.*] There's something wrapped up in this piece of silk.

MRS. PETERS: Why, this isn't her scissors.

MRS. HALE: [*Lifting the silk.*] Oh, Mrs. Peters—it's—

[MRS. PETERS *bends closer.*]

MRS. PETERS: It's the bird.

MRS. HALE: [*Jumping up.*] But, Mrs. Peters—look at it! Its neck! Look at its neck! It's all—other side *to.*

MRS. PETERS: Somebody—wrung—its—neck.

[*Their eyes meet. A look of growing comprehension, of horror. Steps are heard outside.* MRS. HALE *slips box under quilt pieces, and sinks into her chair. Enter* SHERIFF *and* COUNTY ATTORNEY. MRS. PETERS *rises.*]

COUNTY ATTORNEY: [*As one turning from serious things to little pleasantries.*] Well ladies, have you decided whether she was going to quilt it or knot it?

MRS. PETERS: We think she was going to—knot it.

COUNTY ATTORNEY: Well, that's interesting, I'm sure. [*Seeing the bird-cage.*] Has the bird flown?

MRS. HALE: [*Putting more quilt pieces over the box.*] We think the—cat got it.

COUNTY ATTORNEY: [*Preoccupied.*] Is there a cat?

[MRS. HALE *glances in a quick covert way at* MRS. PETERS.]

MRS. PETERS: Well, not *now.* They're superstitious, you know. They leave.

COUNTY ATTORNEY: [*To* SHERIFF PETERS, *continuing an interrupted conversation.*] No sign at all of anyone having come from the outside. Their own rope. Now let's go up again and go over it piece by piece. [*They start upstairs.*] It would have to have been someone who knew just the—

[MRS. PETERS *sits down. The two women sit there not looking at one another, but as if peering into something and at the same time holding back. When they talk now it is in the manner of feeling their way over strange ground, as if afraid of what they are saying, but as if they cannot help saying it.*]

MRS. HALE: She liked the bird. She was going to bury it in that pretty box.

MRS. PETERS: [*In a whisper.*] When I was a girl—my kitten—there was a boy took a hatchet, and before my eyes—and before I could get there—[*Covers her face an instant.*] If they hadn't held me back I would have—[*Catches herself, looks upstairs where steps are heard, falters weakly.*]—hurt him.

MRS. HALE: [*With a slow look around her.*] I wonder how it would seem never to have had any children around. [*Pause.*] No, Wright wouldn't like the bird—a thing that sang. She used to sing. He killed that, too.

MRS. PETERS: [*Moving uneasily.*] We don't know who killed the bird.

MRS. HALE: I knew John Wright.

MRS. PETERS: It was an awful thing was done in this house that night, Mrs. Hale. Killing a man while he slept, slipping a rope around his neck that choked the life out of him.

MRS. HALE: His neck. Choked the life out of him. [*Her hand goes out and rests on the bird-cage.*]

MRS. PETERS: [*With rising voice.*] We don't know who killed him. We don't know.

MRS. HALE: [*Her own feeling not interrupted.*] If there's been years and years of nothing, then a bird to sing to you, it would be awful—still, after the bird was still.

MRS. PETERS: [*Something within her speaking.*] I know what stillness is. When we homesteaded in Dakota, and my first baby died—after he was two years old, and me with no other then—

MRS. HALE: [*Moving.*] How soon do you suppose they'll be through, looking for the evidence?

MRS. PETERS: I know what stillness is. [*Pulling herself back.*] The law has got to punish crime, Mrs. Hale.

MRS. HALE: [*Not as if answering that.*] I wish you'd seen Minnie Foster when she wore a white dress with blue ribbons and stood up there in the choir and sang. [*A look around the room.*] Oh, I *wish* I'd come over here once in a while! That was a crime! That was a crime! Who's going to punish that?

MRS. PETERS: [*Looking upstairs.*] We mustn't—take on.

MRS. HALE: I might have known she needed help! I know how things can be—for women. I tell you, it's queer, Mrs. Peters. We live close together and we live far apart. We all go through the same things—it's all just a different kind of the same thing. [*Brushes her eyes, noticing the bottle of fruit, reaches out for it.*] If I was you, I wouldn't tell her her fruit was gone. Tell her it *ain't*. Tell her it's all right. Take this in to prove it to her. She—she may never know whether it was broke or not.

MRS. PETERS: [*Takes the bottle, looks about for something to wrap it in; takes petticoat from the clothes brought from the other room, very nervously begins winding this around the bottle. In a false voice.*] My, it's a good thing the men couldn't hear us. Wouldn't they just laugh! Getting all stirred up over a little thing like a—dead canary. As if that could have anything to do with—with—wouldn't they *laugh*!

[*The men are heard coming down stairs.*]

MRS. HALE: [*Under her breath.*] Maybe they would—maybe they wouldn't.

COUNTY ATTORNEY: No, Peters, it's all perfectly clear except a reason for doing it. But you know juries when it comes to women. If there was some definite thing. Something to show—something to make a story about—a thing that would connect up with this strange way of doing it—

[*The women's eyes meet for an instant. Enter* HALE *from outer door.*]

HALE: Well, I've got the team around. Pretty cold out there.

COUNTY ATTORNEY: I'm going to stay here a while by myself. [*To the* SHERIFF.] You can send Frank out for me, can't you? I want to go over everything. I'm not satisfied that we can't do better.

SHERIFF: Do you want to see what Mrs. Peters is going to take in?

[*The* LAWYER *goes to the table, picks up the apron, laughs.*]

COUNTY ATTORNEY: Oh, I guess they're not very dangerous things the ladies have picked out. [*Moves a few things about, disturbing the quilt pieces which cover the box. Steps back.*] No, Mrs. Peters doesn't need supervising. For that matter, a sheriff's wife is married to the law. Ever think of it that way, Mrs. Peters?

MRS. PETERS: Not—just that way.

SHERIFF: [*Chuckling.*] Married to the law. [*Moves toward the other room.*] I just want you to come in here a minute, George. We ought to take a look at these windows.

COUNTY ATTORNEY: [*Scoffingly.*] Oh, windows!

SHERIFF: We'll be right out, Mr. Hale.

[HALE *goes outside. The* SHERIFF *follows the* COUNTY ATTORNEY *into the other room. Then* MRS. HALE *rises, hands tight together, looking intensely at* MRS. PETERS, *whose eyes make a slow turn, finally meeting* MRS. HALE'S. *A moment* MRS. HALE *holds her, then her own eyes point the way to where the box is concealed. Suddenly* MRS. PETERS *throws back quilt pieces and tries to put the box in the bag she is wearing. It is too big. She opens box, starts to take bird out, cannot touch it, goes to pieces, stands there helpless. Sound of a knob turning in the other room.* MRS. HALE *snatches the box and puts it in the pocket of her big coat. Enter* COUNTY ATTORNEY *and* SHERIFF.]

COUNTY ATTORNEY: [*Facetiously.*] Well, Henry, at least we found out that she was not going to quilt it. She was going to—what is it you call it, ladies?

MRS. HALE: [*Her hand against her pocket.*] We call it—knot it, Mr. Henderson.

CURTAIN

1916

QUESTIONS

1. If we were watching a production of TRIFLES and had no cast list, how would we gradually piece together the fact that Mrs. Peters is the sheriff's wife? What are the earliest lines of dialogue that allow an audience to infer this fact?
2. What lines in the play characterize Mrs. Hale's reaction to the men's behavior and attitudes? What lines characterize Mrs. Peters's reaction to the men early in the play, and what lines show her feelings changing later in the play? What might account for the two women's initial differences and their evolving solidarity with Mrs. Wright?
3. What are the "trifles" that the men ignore and the two women notice? Why do the men dismiss them, and why do the women see these things as significant clues? What is the thematic importance of these "trifles"?
4. How would you stage the key moment of the play, Mrs. Hale's discovery of the bird in the sewing basket? What facial expression would she have? What body language? Where would you place Mrs. Peters, and what would she be doing? How would you use lighting to heighten the effectiveness of the scene?
5. If a twenty-first-century playwright were to write an updated version of TRIFLES, what details of plot, character, and setting would be different from those in Glaspell's play? What would be the same? What are some possible "trifles" that might serve the same dramatic functions as those in Glaspell's play?

RESPONDING TO DRAMA

When reading a play in order to write about it, you will need to keep a record of how you respond and what you observe as the action unfolds. Recording your thoughts as you read will help you clarify your expectations and attend to the way the play elicits and manages them. Below you will find examples of two ways of responding to a play. The first shows how you might jot down your initial impressions and questions in the margins as you read. The second shows how one reader used the questions on pages 1251–52 to take more comprehensive, methodical notes on the same play. Each of these methods of note-taking has certain advantages, and you may well find that a combination of the two works best.

SAMPLE WRITING: ANNOTATION OF *TRIFLES*

Though the passage chosen for annotation here is the play's opening, any passage in a play—including stage directions, as well as dialogue—will reward close analysis.

A "trifle" is something unimportant and also a kind of dessert. So is the play going to be about unimportant things? Is it a comedy?

Trifles

CHARACTERS

Only character *not* identified either by job or relationship to somebody else. (Why not "Mr. Hale"?)

SHERIFF	MRS. PETERS, *Sheriff's wife*
COUNTY ATTORNEY	MRS. HALE
HALE	

SCENE: *The kitchen in the now abandoned farmhouse of* JOHN WRIGHT, *a gloomy kitchen, and left without having been put in order—*

Why "now abandoned"? Who's John

Wright? "Gloomy" doesn't sound like a comedy.

Is this a crime scene? Why refer to "work" (not "eating" or something)?

Women described more than men. They look different, but even the "comfortable looking" one (funny expression) isn't comfortable. They stick together.

Why hesitate?

Now attorney gets a name. Sounds like they are in court.

Second mention of things being moved: they're worried about evidence.

So this *is* "a big case." Is John Wright the criminal or victim?

Everyone knows everyone else. It's very cold, a harsh environment outside this kitchen. And it takes work to make it warm (lighting a fire).

It's a small town (in Nebraska?), but a lot of bad stuff is happening! Sheriff is defensive with attorney—source of conflict?

Again, everybody knows about everybody else.

unwashed pans under the sink, a loaf of bread outside the bread-box, a dish-towel on the table—other signs of incompleted work. At the rear the outer door opens and the SHERIFF *comes in followed by the* COUNTY ATTOR-NEY *and* HALE. *The* SHERIFF *and* HALE *are men in middle life, the* COUNTY ATTORNEY *is a young man; all are much bundled up and go at once to the stove. They are followed by the two women—the* SHERIFF'S *wife first; she is a slight wiry woman, a thin nervous face.* MRS. HALE *is larger and would ordinarily be called more comfortable looking, but she is disturbed now and looks fearfully about as she enters. The women have come in slowly, and stand close together near the door.*

COUNTY ATTORNEY: [*Rubbing his hands.*] This feels good. Come up to the fire, ladies.

MRS. PETERS: [*After taking a step forward.*] I'm not—cold.

SHERIFF: [*Unbuttoning his overcoat and stepping away from the stove as if to mark the beginning of official business.*] Now, Mr. Hale, before we move things about, you explain to Mr. Henderson just what you saw when you came here yesterday morning.

COUNTY ATTORNEY: By the way, has anything been moved? Are things just as you left them yesterday?

SHERIFF: [*Looking about.*] It's just the same. When it dropped below zero last night I thought I'd better send Frank out this morning to make a fire for us—no use getting pneumonia with a big case on, but I told him not to touch anything except the stove—and you know Frank.

COUNTY ATTORNEY: Somebody should have been left here yesterday.

SHERIFF: Oh—yesterday. When I had to send Frank to Morris Center for that man who went crazy—I want you to know I had my hands full yesterday. I knew you could get back from Omaha by today and as long as I went over everything here myself—

COUNTY ATTORNEY: Well, Mr. Hale, tell just what happened when you came here yesterday morning.

HALE: Harry and I had started to town with a load of potatoes. We came along the road from my place and as I got here I said, "I'm going to see if I can't get John Wright to go in with me on a party telephone." I spoke to Wright about it once before and he put me

Hale assumes most husbands would act differently around their wives, care about what they want—but maybe not Wright.

off, saying folks talked too much anyway, and all he asked was peace and quiet—I guess you know about how much he talked himself; but I thought maybe if I went to the house and talked about it before his wife, though I said to Harry that I didn't know as what his wife wanted made much difference to John—

Attorney is worried about being "official," sticking to "business," and thinks "that" (Wright's personality or feelings?) doesn't count.

COUNTY ATTORNEY: Let's talk about that later, Mr. Hale. I do want to talk about that, but tell now just what happened when you got to the house.

Everyone gets up early—because of all the work they have to do?

HALE: I didn't hear or see anything; I knocked at the door, and still it was all quiet inside. I knew they must be up, it was past eight o'clock. So I knocked again, and I thought I heard somebody say, "Come in." I wasn't sure, I'm not sure yet, but I opened the door—this door [*Indicat-*

Ordinary things now seem creepy. Why are the women still standing by the door? Are they afraid? not part of "official business"? witnesses? Why are they here?

ing the door by which the two women are still standing.] and there in that rocker—[*Pointing to it.*] sat Mrs. Wright.

She's not listed as a character either. What happened?

SAMPLE WRITING: READING NOTES

Below are examples of the questions an experienced reader might ask when reading TRIFLES for the first time, as well as responses to those questions. (See pp. 1251–52.) Any of these notes might inspire ideas for essay topics. This is just a selection of the many details that could be observed about this lasting play, in which details certainly matter.

Expectations

Does the title suggest anything? "Trifles" sounds like a comedy (a trifle is something trivial), but it might be ironic. But why does Hale say that "women are used to worrying over trifles"? I expect to find out that the title is significant in some way, even that the theme is somehow connected to "trifles."

Characterization

Who are the characters? What are they like? Three men and two women in the cast of characters. What kind of situation would bring together a sheriff, a county attorney, a farmer, and two wives? No actors are needed to play either Mr. Wright or Mrs. Wright. Some men who help Mr. Hale (Harry) and Mr. Peters (deputy Frank) are mentioned as coming and going but are never onstage.

The "county attorney" acts like a detective; he seems businesslike and thinks he's smarter than farmers and women. The stage directions specify that he speaks "[w]ith the gallantry of a young politician," but his flattery toward the women doesn't work. We find out his name is Mr. Henderson.

According to the stage directions, Mrs. Peters, the sheriff's wife, is "a slight wiry woman, a thin nervous face"; Mrs. Hale, the farmer's wife, is "larger and would ordinarily be called more comfortable looking." The casting of the two women would be important for contrast; a wider range of physical types would be suitable for the men. Everyone is cold, but only the men take comfort by the fire in the kitchen; the women are upset.

Is there a protagonist, an antagonist, or other types? There isn't a hero or heroine of this play, and I wouldn't call anyone the villain unless it's the dead man or his murderer. Who the real villain is seems like an important question.

Are the characters' names significant? There's nothing especially meaningful or unusual about the names, although "Hale" means healthy (as in "hale and hearty"), and "Wright" sounds like "right," though obviously something's wrong in this house. Interesting how "Mrs. Wright" becomes "Minnie Foster" to the women. Think about when. And about why it matters.

Plot

What happens? The big event has already happened; this is the scene of the crime. The men are looking for clues and leave the women in the kitchen, where they discover possible causes or motives for the crime. The women decide not to tell the men about either the evidence they find or their interpretation of it.

Are there scene changes? The whole scene is a fairly short uninterrupted period in one part of a farmhouse. Characters go offstage to other rooms or outdoors to the barn.

How is exposition handled? The county attorney asks Hale to "tell just what happened"; Hale explains what happened before the play started, describing how Mrs. Wright behaved. It comes as a shock to learn that Mrs. Wright told Hale he couldn't see John Wright "'Cause [he was] dead." Shouldn't she have run to tell someone about the murder or have told Hale as soon as he arrived? When Hale reports that Mrs. Wright said her husband "died of a rope round his neck," it sounds suspicious. Could she have slept so soundly that she didn't realize someone had strangled her husband?

What events mark the rising action? When the men go upstairs and Mrs. Hale says, "I'd hate to have men coming into my kitchen, snooping around and criticizing," the women have a chance to notice more in the kitchen. Mrs. Hale recalls her relationship to Mrs. Wright, and the women discuss whether the wife really murdered her husband.

The men return to the kitchen on their way out to the barn just after the women discover the quilt pieces with the bad stitching. The next dialogue between the women is more open and brings out Mrs. Hale's regret for not having visited and supported Mrs. Wright in her unhappy marriage. They notice the empty birdcage.

What is the climax? Mrs. Hale finds the dead bird in the pretty box, and the two women understand what it means just before the men return to the kitchen briefly. From then on the women utter small lies to the men. Mrs. Peters for the first time shares personal memories that suggest she can imagine Mrs. Wright's motives.

What is the resolution? As everyone prepares to leave, Mrs. Peters pretends the bird is insignificant, joining Mrs. Hale in protecting Mrs. Wright and playing along with the men's assumption that there's nothing to notice in the kitchen. The women collaborate in hiding the bird.

What kind of play or plot is it? Like some detective stories, the play doesn't ask "whodunnit?" but why the murder was committed. Its mode of representation is a familiar type—domestic realism—in which the places, people, things, and even events are more or less ordinary. (Unfortunately, domestic violence is common.)

Setting
When does the action occur? The play appears to be contemporary with 1916 (a stove heater, party-line telephones, a horse-drawn wagon). It is a winter morning, and the scene takes perhaps an hour.

Where does the action occur? It is obviously Nebraska farm country, where farms are very far apart.

What is the atmosphere? The freezing weather reflects the feeling of the play and gives the characters a motive for gathering in the kitchen. John Wright is described as a chilly wind. The frozen house has ruined Mrs. Wright's preserves. The mess in the kitchen, especially the sticky spill of red fruit in the cupboard, seems related to the unhappiness and horror of the marriage and the crime. Also just shows how hard their lives are maybe.

Are there scene changes? Instead of several scenes over a longer time, showing the deteriorating marriage, the crisis over the bird, the murder itself, Mrs. Wright's sleepless night, and Mr. Hale's visit, the story unfolds in a single scene, in one room, on the second morning after the murder, between the entrance and exit of Mrs. Hale and Mrs. Peters. It is essential that the play focus on "kitchen things" and what the women visitors notice and think.

Style, Tone, Imagery
What is the style of the dialogue? The dialogue seems similar to everyday speech. There are some differences in speaking style that show the Hales are more rustic than the Peters and the county attorney. Hale has a relaxed way of

telling a story: "then I says," etc. Mrs. Hale: "Those towels get dirty awful quick" and "If I was you, I wouldn't tell her her fruit was gone. Tell her it *ain't*."

How do nonverbal gestures and actions convey meaning? Many specific actions indicated in the stage directions are crucial to the play: everyone looking at the rocking chair, pointing to the room upstairs, looking at the loaf of bread that should have been put back in the bread box, etc.

Do any of the props seem to have symbolic meaning? Some objects in the play are so important they seem symbolic, though the play tries not to be too heavily poetic. All kinds of "trifles" are clues. For instance, the women get Mrs. Wright's clothes to bring to her in jail. "MRS. HALE: [*Examining the skirt.*] Wright was close," meaning stingy. Mrs. Hale's words convey a quick impression: the skirt looks "shabby" because John Wright didn't give his wife any money for clothes (he was "good" but stingy and cold).

There would be some colorful props onstage—the jar of cherries, the red cloth and other quilt material, the pretty box—all of them signs of what has gone wrong. The room itself is "gloomy" and has some dirty and messy things in plain sight; other things in the cupboards are eventually revealed. These props would add to the uncomfortable feeling of the play.

The closest thing to a symbol is the caged songbird. Even the men notice the broken door and missing bird. Mrs. Hale underlines the comparison to Mrs. Wright twice: "she was kind of like a bird," and later, "No, Wright wouldn't like the bird—a thing that sang. She used to sing. He killed that, too."

Theme
What is the theme of the play? The title calls attention to what the play is about. Glaspell didn't call it *The Caged Songbird* or *Murder in the Midwest* or something heavy-handed. The main action is a search for a motive to confirm what everyone believes, that Minnie Wright must have strangled her husband while he was sleeping. But the underlying theme of the play seems to be about men's and women's different perspectives. How can women's everyday things be important? Why would anyone charged with murder worry about preserves? Even the women hope that Mrs. Wright's worry about having her apron and shawl in jail means she didn't commit the crime. The kitchen things—the trifles in her own house—"turn against her," but the women are able to hide evidence because the men consider it insignificant.

WRITING ABOUT DRAMA

Writing an essay about drama, like writing about fiction or poetry, can sharpen your responses and focus your reading; at the same time, it can illuminate aspects of the work that other readers may have missed. When you write about drama, in a very real sense you perform the role that directors and actors take on in a stage performance: You offer your "reading" of the text, interpreting it in order to guide other readers' responses. But you also shape and refine your own response by attempting to express it clearly.

Using the notes you have taken while reading a play, try to locate the specific lines and actions that have contributed to your expectations or your discoveries. Are these at the beginning, the middle, or the end of the play? Who gives most of the hints or misleading information? If there is one character who is especially unseeing, especially devious, or especially insightful, you might decide to write an essay describing the function of that character in the play. A good way to undertake such a study of a character in drama (as in fiction) is to imagine the work without that character. Mrs. Hale in *Trifles* is certainly the cleverest "detective," so why do we need Mrs. Peters as well? One obvious answer is that plays need dialogue, and we would find it artificial if Mrs. Hale talked mainly to herself. But a more interesting answer is that in a play the audience learns by witnessing characters with different temperaments and worldviews responding to the same situation. As these remarks suggest, you can also develop essays that compare characters.

In addition to character studies, essays on drama can focus on the kinds of observations made above: expectations and plot structure; the presence and absence of characters or actions onstage; the different degrees of awareness of characters and audience at various points in the action; titles, stage directions, and other stylistic details, including **metaphors** or other imagery; and, of course, themes. As you write, you will probably discover that you can imagine directing or acting in a performance of the play, and you'll realize that interpreting a play is a crucial step in bringing it to life.

SUGGESTIONS FOR WRITING

1. The action in Glaspell's play unfolds continuously and without interruption, in a single, relatively small room (the kitchen of a farmhouse), with the two female characters never leaving the stage. Write a response paper or essay discussing how these three factors affect your responses to the play, to the crime being investigated, and to the various characters.

2. How do your sympathies for Mrs. Peters change over the course of TRIFLES? What might Mrs. Peters be said to represent in the clash of attitudes at the heart of the play? Write an essay in which you examine both Mrs. Peters's evolving character as it is revealed in TRIFLES and her significance to the play's theme.

3. How would you characterize Susan Glaspell's feminism as revealed in TRIFLES— does it seem radical or moderate? How does it compare to feminist political and social ideas of our own time? (Consult three or more educational or library websites for biographical background on Glaspell; there are several sites offering teaching materials on TRIFLES as well. If time allows, you might also pursue sources that provide an overview of women's movements in the United States in the twentieth and twenty-first centuries.) Write an essay in which you explore the political leanings apparent in TRIFLES, both in the context of Glaspell's play (published in 1916) and in the broader historical context of the struggle for women's rights over the past century.

4. Write an essay in which you propose a production of TRIFLES, complete with details of how you would handle the casting, costumes, set design, lighting, and direction of the actors. What would be your overall controlling vision for the production? Would you attempt to reproduce faithfully the look and feel of the play as it might have been in 1916, or would you introduce innovations, even "update" the play? How would you justify your choices in terms of dramatic effectiveness?

5. Write an essay in which you draw on both TRIFLES and A JURY of HER PEERS to consider the similarities and differences between an effective story and an effective play. Does the play work better than the story or vice versa? Why and how so? Why the different titles?

SAMPLE WRITING: RESPONSE PAPER

Response papers are a great way to begin moving from informal notes to a more formal essay. Though many response-paper assignments invite you to respond to any aspect or element of a literary text that grabs your attention, the following example was written in response to a more targeted assignment, one that asked students to "explore something specific about the way TRIFLES handles plot. For example, what are the major internal and/or external conflicts? Or what would you argue is the play's turning point, and why?" Student writer Jessica Zezulka explored the last question. Marginal comments below are the instructor's. But what do you think of this writer's answer? How might she strengthen and develop the argument she begins to make here about the play's turning point? What alternative answers or arguments occur to you?

Zezulka 1

Jessica Zezulka
Professor Mays
English 298
10 September 2021

Trifles Plot Response Paper

While the men dillydally over the facts, the so-called "evidence," the women in *Trifles* discover the missing piece: a motive for murder. The moment Mrs. Hale and Mrs. Peters find the dead canary in the hidden box is the turning point in the play. Up until that instant, their conversation seems trivial, to both a reader and the men involved. Upon discussing the little trifles, the quilt and the sewing, these two women have inadvertently stumbled across what the men are so desperate to find. This turning point changes the way the play is read, as well as the way you view the wife of the dead man.

Mrs. Wright, accused of murdering her husband, appears almost crazy for just up and killing her spouse. The reader is as confused as the men at first, wondering why on earth would she do it? When you realize, along with the two women, that her motive was his brutal killing of the canary, you suddenly become privy to a secret that the men seemingly never learn. The play uses dramatic irony, where the reader knows the truth but the characters in the play are oblivious.

Marginal comments (instructor's):

Might it be possible to read their conversation as less trivial (even up to this point) than the male characters do?

Again, though, don't we have relevant evidence before that about the possible state (and effects) of this marriage, which might be just as relevant to motive? If so, what *really* makes this moment stand out?

Interesting! Irony certainly is key to the play, but not all the characters are equally "oblivious," right?

Zezulka 2

Susan Glaspell timed this moment perfectly, giving the reader time to be both confused and then suddenly enlightened.

This turning point breeds sympathy for the accused murderess. Mrs. Wright is no longer just a good wife gone bad. You as the reader follow the emotions of the two women in the empty house and can feel their almost immediate comprehension and understanding of both the situation and the woman involved. The wife becomes someone we can relate to, almost having a just cause for murdering her husband. As I said, Glaspell builds the tension to that point perfectly; the reader is all for the law being upheld until you know what led up to the murder. If you asked me, I'd say he deserved it. The women's discussion of *trifles* led to the heart of the matter, a turning point that all but justifies John Wright's death.

So might the play also turn on the conflict—or at least the contrast—between two possible ways of defining "innocence" or even two kinds of "law"?

Zezulka 3

Work Cited

Glaspell, Susan. *Trifles. The Norton Introduction to Literature*, edited by Kelly J. Mays, shorter 14th ed., W. W. Norton, 2021, pp. 1253-63.

SAMPLE WRITING: ESSAY

The following student essay demonstrates how you might develop an early response to a play into a more formal and thorough argument about it. In her essay on Susan Glaspell's TRIFLES, Stephanie Ortega explores the relationship among the female characters in order to offer her own answers to more than one of the questions posed in the previous chapter's "Suggestions for Writing": How does Mrs. Peters's character evolve over the course of *Trifles*? How is that evolution significant to the play's theme, or how might it help to define the play's particular version of feminism?

As always, we encourage you to read the sample with a critical eye, identifying what works and what doesn't so as to discover specific ways to improve your own writing and reading. At what moments in the essay do you find yourself strongly agreeing? discovering something new about or in Glaspell's play? At what moments might you instead find yourself disagreeing or feeling either confused or simply dissatisfied, wanting more? What exactly makes each of these moments especially satisfying, interesting, persuasive, enlightening—or the reverse? If Stephanie Ortega were your classmate, what three specific things would you suggest she do in order to improve the essay in revision? Alternatively, what three qualities or strategies of this essay might you want to emulate in your own work?

Stephanie Ortega
Professor Mays
English 298
23 September 2021

A Journey of Sisterhood

Trifles begins at the start of a murder investigation. Mrs. Wright has allegedly murdered her harsh husband, John Wright; and the sheriff and his wife, Mrs. Peters; the county attorney; and the neighbors, Mr. and Mrs. Hale, all come to the Wright house to investigate. Throughout the entire play the women are always onstage, whereas the men enter and exit, so the women are the play's focus. But Glaspell's *Trifles* is a feminist play not only because of that, but also because of how it shows two or even three very different women coming together in sisterhood.

Mrs. Peters and Mrs. Hale are first introduced as they stand together by the door of the house where the murder took place, yet though the women stand together, their behavior and views initially seem wide apart. Whereas Mrs. Hale stands up for her counterparts, Mrs. Peters and Mrs. Wright, from the beginning, Mrs. Peters at first tends to stick up more for the men. When the county attorney makes a remark about Mrs. Wright not having been much of a homemaker and having a dirty home, we see that Mrs. Hale doesn't like men poking in Mrs. Wright's business and having input in the doings of a house. Putting herself in Mrs. Wright's shoes, Mrs. Hale says, "I'd hate to have men coming into *my* kitchen, snooping around and criticizing" (1257; emphasis added). But Mrs. Peters states that since it is an investigation, "it's no more than th[e men's] duty" to poke around (1257). Later, when Mrs. Hale actually interferes with the investigation by trying to tidy up the place and resew the badly stitched quilt they discover, Mrs. Peters steps in, "*[n]ervously*" saying, "I don't think we ought to touch things" (1259). Mrs. Peters's only view is that of her husband; she knows and seems to care very little about Mrs. Wright or her life before marriage, as Minnie Foster. As far as Mrs. Peters is concerned, "the law is the law" (1259), and she is "married to" it, as the county attorney will say at the end of the play (1263); therefore she must abide by it.

Mrs. Hale's identification with Minnie Foster only intensifies as the play progresses. She remembers Minnie Foster as a carefree woman full of energy and life, bright and cheery like a canary, implying that marriage to John Wright "change[d]" all that (1261). Mrs. Hale starts feeling guilty for not visiting Mrs. Wright, telling Mrs. Peters multiple times that she "wish[es she] had come over sometimes when *she* was here," and eventually even suggesting that not coming to see Mrs. Wright was "a crime" (1260, 1262).

In part because of the way Mrs. Hale talks about her, Minnie Foster's figurative presence becomes ever stronger, bringing Mrs. Hale and Mrs. Peters together as they put themselves into her place, speculating about her feelings and responses to the conditions of her life. When the women come upon a box containing a bird that had its neck wrung, Mrs. Hale associates Mr. Wright's presumed killing of the songbird with his destruction of part of Mrs. Wright, speculating about her feelings: "No, Wright wouldn't like the bird—a thing that sang. She used to sing. He killed that, too" (1260). Thus, Mr. Wright's killing of the bird is a symbolic killing of Minnie Foster's spirit. At this point, the women come to understand that Mrs. Wright was indeed the one who killed her husband because when the women realize that Mr. Wright wrung the bird's neck, the women finally know the reason for Mrs. Wright's "funny way" of killing him (1258). (It's now that "*Their eyes meet*" with "*[a] look of growing comprehension, of horror*" [1261].)

More important, here is where we really start to see a change in Mrs. Peters. For the first time she, too, interferes with the investigators, even though she doesn't actually destroy evidence or lie, when she responds to a question about the cat by simply saying that there is not one "*now*" (1261). She expresses sympathy for Minnie Foster and identifies with her, based on her own memories of the way she felt both when her kitten was killed with a hatchet and, much later, when her first baby died, leaving her and her husband alone in the "stillness" of their isolated house (1262). Mrs. Peters also states that had she gotten hold of the boy who killed her kitten long ago she would have gotten revenge just as Mrs. Peters and Mrs. Hale now speculate that Minnie Foster Wright did. The women each sympathize with Minnie Foster and the distant person she has become, Mrs. Wright.

By sympathizing with Mrs. Wright and paying attention to the "little things" the men don't consider solid "evidence" (1259), the women have single-handedly sorted out a plausible sequence of events and, more importantly, a reason why Mrs. Wright killed her husband the way she did. Yet rather than reveal what they've learned, they slowly, in the silence of mutual sympathy, work together to cover Mrs. Wright's tracks and to protect her. Mrs. Peters is defying the actual law and starting to protect the law of women and sisterhood instead. Mrs. Hale, Mrs. Peters, and Mrs. Wright become one unit, opposing their intuitive feminine selves to the logical and analytical men.

Although Mrs. Wright never once appears onstage, her presence is what brings all three women closer. They are able to attain information that the men simply overlook. And it is this which brings the women forth in the union of sisterhood at the end of the play as they realize that "We [women] all go through the same things—it's all just a different kind of the same thing" (1262).

Work Cited

Glaspell, Susan. *Trifles. The Norton Introduction to Literature*, edited by Kelly J. Mays, shorter 14th ed., W. W. Norton, 2021, pp. 1253–63.

Understanding the Text

25 | ELEMENTS OF DRAMA

Most of us read more fiction than drama and are likely to encounter drama by watching filmed versions of it. Nonetheless, the skills you have developed in reading stories and poems come in handy when you read plays. And just as with fiction and poetry, you will understand and appreciate drama more fully by becoming familiar with the various elements and conventions of the **genre**.

CHARACTER

Character is possibly the most familiar and accessible of the elements; both fiction and drama feature one or more imaginary persons who take part in the action. The word *character* refers not only to a person represented in an imagined plot, whether narrated or acted out, but also to the unique qualities that make up a personality. From one point of view, "character" as a part in a plot and "character" as a kind of personality are both predictions: This sort of person is likely to see things from a certain angle and behave in certain ways. Notice that the idea of character includes both the individual differences among people and the classification of similar people into types. Whereas much realistic fiction emphasizes unique individuals rather than general character types, drama often compresses and simplifies personalities—a play has only about two hours at the most (sometimes much less) in which to show situations, appearances, and behaviors, without description or background other than **exposition** provided in the dialogue. The advantage of portraying character in broader strokes is that it heightens the contrasts between character types, adding to the drama: Differences provoke stronger reactions.

Plays are especially concerned with character because of the concrete manner in which they portray people on the stage. With a few exceptions (such as experiments in multimedia performance), the only words in the performance of a play are spoken by actors, and usually these actors are *in character*—that is, speaking as though they really are the people they play in the drama. (Rarely, plays have a **narrator** who observes and comments on the action from the sidelines, and in some plays a character may address the audience directly, but even when the actors apparently step outside of the imaginary frame, they are still part of the play and are still playing characters.) In fiction, the narrator's description and commentary can guide a reader's judgment about characters. Reading a play, you will have no such guide because drama relies almost exclusively on *indirect characterization* (see ch. 4). Apart from some clues about characters in the **stage directions**, you will need to imagine the appearance, manners, and movement of someone speaking the lines assigned to any one character. You can do this even as you read through a play for the first time, discovering the characters' attitudes and motivations as the scenes unfold. This ability to predict character and then to revise expectations as situations change is based not only on our experiences of people in real life but also on our familiarity with recurring types of characters or roles.

Consider the patterns of characters in many stories that are narrated or acted out, whether in novels, comic books, television series, Hollywood films, or video games. In many of these forms, there is a leading role, a main character: the **protagonist**. The titles of plays such as ANTIGONE or THE TRAGEDY OF OTHELLO, THE MOOR OF VENICE imply that the play will be about a central character, the chief object of the playwright's and the reader's or audience's concern. Understanding the character of the protagonist—often in contrast with an **antagonist**, the opponent of the main character—becomes the consuming interest of such a play. Especially in more traditional or popular genres, the protagonist may be called a **hero** or **heroine**, and the antagonist may be called the **villain**. Most great drama, however, avoids depicting pure good and pure evil in a fight to the death. Most characters possess both negative and redeeming qualities.

As in other genres that represent people in action, in drama there are *minor characters* or supporting roles. At least since ancient Rome, romantic comedies have been structured around a leading man and woman, along with a comparable pair (often the "buddies" of the leads) whose problems may be less serious, whose characters may be less complex, or who in other ways support or complicate rather than dominate the action. Sometimes a minor character serves as a **foil**, a character designed to bring out the qualities of another character by means of contrast. The main point to remember is that all the characters in a drama are interdependent and help characterize one another. Through dialogue and behavior, each brings out what is characteristic in the others.

Indeed, in some plays for stage and screen, the line between major and minor characters may be thin to the point of nonexistence. Instead of foregrounding one or even two protagonists, such dramas instead give roughly equal time and attention to an entire ensemble of characters. Different as they otherwise are, the movie *Avengers: Endgame* (2019) and Lynn Nottage's Pulitzer Prize–winning play SWEAT (2015) are both examples of what is sometimes called *ensemble drama*. In Nottage's play, which features two generations of Pennsylvania factory workers, one might say that all the characters collectively act as protagonist, a once-unified community that erupts into conflict due primarily to external forces, which here become the true antagonist(s).

All plays, like all movies, must respect certain limitations: the time an audience can be expected to sit and watch, the attention and sympathy an audience is likely to give to various characters, the amount of exposition that can be shown rather than spoken aloud. Because of these constraints, playwrights, screenwriters, casting directors, and actors must rely on shortcuts to convey character. Everyone involved, including the audience, consciously or unconsciously relies on stereotypes of various social roles to flesh out the dramatic action. Even a play that seeks to undermine stereotypes must still invoke them. In the United States today, casting—or typecasting—usually relies on an actor's social identity, from gender and race to occupation, region, and age. However, plays that rely too much on stereotypes, positive or negative, may leave everyone disappointed (or offended); a role that defies stereotypes can be more interesting to perform and to watch. Alternatively, a character can be so exceptional and unfamiliar that audiences will fail to recognize any connection to people they might meet, and their responses will fall flat. All dramatic roles, then, must have some connection to types of personality, and good roles modify such types just enough to make the character interesting. Playwrights often overturn or modify expectations of character in order to surprise an audience. So, too, do the actors who play those parts.

Every performance of a given character, like every production of a play, is an interpretation. Not just "adaptations"—Greek or Elizabethan plays set in modern times and performed in modern dress, for example—but even productions that seek to adhere faithfully to the written play are interpretations of what is vital or essential in it. John Malkovich, in the 1984 production of Arthur Miller's *Death of a Salesman*, did not portray Biff Loman as the outgoing, successful, hail-fellow-well-met jock the play text might lead us to expect. Instead Malkovich saw Biff as only pretending to be a jock. Big-time athletes, he insisted, don't glad-hand people; they wait for people to come to them. The actor did not change the **author**'s words, but by intonation, body language, and "stage business" (wordless gestures and actions) he suggested his own view of the character. In other words, he broke with the expectations associated with the character's type. As you read and develop your own interpretation of a play, try imagining various interpretations of its characters in order to reveal different possible meanings in the drama.

Questions about Character

- Who is the protagonist? Why and how so? Which other characters, if any, are main or major characters? Which are minor characters? Alternatively, might this play be better understood as an ensemble drama?
- Whether the play features a single protagonist or an ensemble that functions as one, what are the protagonist's most distinctive traits? What is most distinctive about the protagonist's outlook and values? What motivates the protagonist? What is it about the protagonist that creates internal and/or external conflict? Which lines or stage directions reveal most about the protagonist?
- What are the roles of other characters? Which, if any, functions as an antagonist? Which, if any, serves as a foil? Does any character function as a narrator or **chorus**, providing background information and commentary? Why and how so?
- To what extent are any of the characters in the play "types"? How might this affect an audience's experience of the play? In what ways might a director or actor choose to go against the expected types, and how would this complicate the play's overall effect and meaning?
- Which of the characters, or which aspects of the characters, does the play encourage us to sympathize with or to admire? to view negatively? Why and how so? Are there characters who might be more or less sympathetic, depending on how the role is cast and interpreted?
- If you were directing a production of this play, whom among your friends and acquaintances would you cast in each role, and why? If you were directing a movie version, what professional actors would you cast?

PLOT AND STRUCTURE

An important part of any storyteller's task, whether in narrative or dramatic genres, is the invention, selection, and arrangement of some **action**. Even carefully structured action cannot properly be called a full-scale **plot** without some unifying sense of purpose. That is, what happens should seem to happen for meaningful reasons. This does not mean, of course, that characters or the audience must be satisfied in their hopes or expectations, or that effective plays need to wrap up every loose end. It does mean that a reader or theatergoer should feel that the playwright has completed *this* play—that nothing essential is missing—though the play's outcome or overall effect may be difficult to sum up.

Conflict is the engine that drives plot, and the presentation of conflict shapes the dramatic structure of a play. A conflict whose outcome is never in doubt may have other kinds of interest, but it is not truly dramatic. In a dramatic conflict, each of the opposing forces must at some point seem likely to triumph or worthy of such triumph—whether conflict is *external* (one character versus another, or one group of characters versus another group, each of whom may represent a different worldview) or *internal* (within a single character torn between competing views, duties, needs, or desires), or even one idea or ideology versus another one. In *Antigone*, for example, our interest in the struggle between Antigone and Creon depends on their being evenly matched. Creon possesses the throne, but Antigone's position as both a member of the ruling family and the fiancée of Creon's presumptive heir helps to offset her opponent's strength.

The typical plot in drama, as in fiction, involves five stages: exposition, rising action, climax, falling action, and conclusion. **Exposition**, the first phase of plot, provides essential background information about the characters and situation as they exist at the beginning of a play and perhaps also about the events that got the characters to this point—as when, early in TRIFLES, Mr. Hale describes what happened before the play opens. The second phase, **rising action**, begins when an **inciting incident** leads to conflict—as when, in *Trifles*, the men leave the women alone with what the latter soon discover to be crucial evidence. The moment when the conflict reaches its greatest pitch of intensity and its outcome is decided is the plot's third phase, its **climax** or **turning point**—in *Trifles*, perhaps the discovery of the dead bird and the act of covering up the evidence. The fourth stage, **falling action**, brings a release of emotional tension and moves the characters toward the **resolution** of their conflict and the plot itself toward its fifth and final stage, the **conclusion**. In *Trifles*, the men's return to the kitchen because, they believe, no evidence has been found can be called the falling action. The women's apparent decision to remain mute about what they have discovered can be called the resolution. The play concludes as the characters leave the Wrights' house.

Unlike *Trifles*, some lengthy plays feature more than one plot. In such cases, the plot to which less time and attention is devoted is called the **subplot**.

Many older plays in the Western tradition, such as Shakespeare's, have five acts, each act roughly corresponding to—and thus emphasizing—a particular phase of plot. Acts are often further subdivided into scenes, each of which usually takes place in a somewhat different time and place and features a somewhat different combination of characters. Ancient Greek plays such as OEDIPUS THE KING are structured differently, such that individual scenes or *episodes* are separated by choral songs—that is, odes spoken or sung by the group of characters known as the chorus. Modern plays tend to have fewer acts and scenes than those of earlier eras, and plays such as *Trifles*—in which the action unfolds continuously and, usually, in a single time and place—have become so common that they have their own name: the *one-act play*.

Whatever their length, plays need not, of course, depict events in chronological order. Though much of the action in Nottage's *Sweat* takes place in 2000, for example, these scenes effectively function as **flashbacks** thanks to an opening scene, as well as some later ones, set in 2008. The play's very first scene, moreover, transitions seamlessly from one man's meeting with his parole officer to the same officer's meeting with another client, without clearly indicating in what order the two meetings might have actually occurred. With drama, as with fiction, then, it's helpful to remember that authors have choices about the sequencing, as well as pacing, of action. Analyzing plot thus means considering the significance not only of what happens but also of when and how that "what" is presented to us.

In the performance of a play longer than one act, it has become customary to have at least one intermission, in part for the practical reason that the audience may need restrooms or refreshments. Breaks may be signaled by turning down stage lights, turning up the house lights, and lowering the curtain (if there is one).

On rare occasions, very long plays (such as Tony Kushner's *Angels in America* [1993–94]) are performed over more than one evening, with the obvious challenge of finding an audience willing and able to afford tickets and time for more than one performance; those who read such play "cycles" or **sequences** at their own pace at home have a certain advantage.

The key point is that the form of a play and the breaks between scenes or acts affect our experience and interpretation of the play. Breaks can create suspense, as when a curtain comes down after an unexplained gunshot; they can provide relief from tension or an emotional crisis; they can sharpen and shape our sense of the relation among scenes and characters.

Questions about Plot

- Read the first scene or the first few pages and then stop. What potential for conflict do you see here? What do you expect to happen in the rest of the play?
- How is the play divided into acts, scenes, or episodes, if at all? What is the effect of this structure? Does the division of the play correspond at all to the five stages of plot development—exposition, rising action, climax, resolution, conclusion?
- Does the play show a relatively clear progression through the traditional stages of plot development, or does it seem to defy such conventions? If so, how, and what might the playwright achieve through these departures from tradition?
- What is the inciting incident or destabilizing event? How and why does this event destabilize the initial situation? How would you describe the conflict that develops? To what extent is it external, internal, or both?
- What is the climax, or turning point? Why and how so? How is the conflict resolved? How and why might this resolution fulfill or defy your expectations?
- Does the play ever present events out of chronological order or make that order seem uncertain? How might this make the action mean differently to you than it otherwise would?

STAGES, SETS, AND SETTING

Most of us have been to a theater at one time or another, and we know what a conventional modern stage (the **proscenium stage**) looks like: a room with the wall missing between us and it (the so-called *fourth wall*). So when we read a modern play—that is, one written during the past three or four hundred years—and

Theater in the ancient Greek city of Hierapolis (in modern-day Turkey)

imagine it taking place before us, we think of it as happening on this kind of stage. Though there are also other modern types of stages—the **thrust stage**, where the audience sits around three sides of the major acting area, and the **arena stage**, where the audience sits all the way around the acting area and players make their entrances and their exits through the auditorium—most plays today are performed on a proscenium stage. Most of the plays in this book can be readily imagined as taking place on such a stage.

Ancient Greek and Elizabethan plays, including those of Shakespeare, were originally staged quite differently from most modern plays, however, and although they may be played today on a proscenium stage, we might be confused as we read if we are unaware of the layout of the theaters for which they were first written. In the Greek theater, the audience sat on a raised semicircle of seats (**amphitheater**) halfway around a circular area (**orchestra**) used primarily for dancing by the chorus. At the back of the orchestra was the **skene**, or stage house, representing the palace or temple before which the action took place. (See the photo above.) Shakespeare's stage, in contrast, basically involved a rectangular area built inside one end of a large enclosure like a circular walled-in yard; the audience stood on the ground or sat in stacked balconies around three sides of the principal acting area (rather like a thrust stage). There were additional acting areas on either side of this stage, as well as a recessed area at its back (which could represent Queen Gertrude's chamber in *Hamlet*, for example) and an upper acting area (which could serve as Juliet's balcony in *Romeo and Juliet*). A trapdoor in the stage floor was used for occasional effects; the ghost of Hamlet's father probably entered and exited this way. Until three centuries ago—and certainly in Shakespeare's time—plays for large paying audiences were performed outdoors in daylight because of the difficulty and expense of lighting. If you are curious about Shakespeare's stage, you can visit a reconstruction of his Globe Theatre in Southwark, London, England, either in person or online at www.shakespearesglobe.com. (See also the photo on the next page.) Every

Opening performance at the new Globe Theatre, London, 1997

summer, plays by Shakespeare are performed there for large international audiences willing to sit on hard benches around the arena or to stand as "groundlings" (a lucky few of whom can lean on the stage near the feet of the actors). The walls in the background of the stage are beautifully carved and painted, but there is no painted scenery, minimal furniture, few costume changes, no lighting, and no curtain around the stage (a cloth hanging usually covers the recessed area at the back of the stage). Three or four musicians may play period instruments on the balcony.

As the design of the Globe suggests, the conventions of dramatic writing and stage production have changed considerably over the centuries. Certainly this is true of the way playwrights convey a sense of place—one of the two key ingredients that make up a play's **setting**. Usually the audience is asked to imagine that the featured section of the auditorium is actually a particular place somewhere else. The audience of course knows it is a stage, more or less bare or elaborately disguised, but they accept it as a kitchen, a public square, a wooded park, a bar, or a room in a castle or a hut. *Oedipus the King* takes place entirely before the palace at Thebes. Following the general convention of ancient Greek drama, the play's setting never changes. When the action demands the presence of Teiresias, for example, the scene does not shift to him; instead, escorts bring him to the front of the palace. Similarly, important events that take place elsewhere are described by witnesses who arrive on the scene.

In Shakespeare's theater the conventions of place are quite different: The acting arena does not represent a single specific place but assumes a temporary identity according to the characters who inhabit it, their costumes, and their speeches. At the opening of *Hamlet* we know we are at a sentry station because a man dressed as a soldier challenges two others. By line 15, we know that we are in Denmark because the actors profess to be "liegemen to the Dane." At the end of the scene the actors leave the stage and in a sense take the sentry station with them. Shortly thereafter, a group of people dressed in court costumes and a man and a woman wearing crowns appear. As a theater audience, we must surmise from the costumes and dialogue that the acting area has now become a royal court; when we read the play, the stage directions give us a cue that the place has changed.

In a modern play, there are likely to be several changes of scene, sometimes marked by the lowering of the curtain or the darkening of the stage while different sets and props are arranged. **Sets** (the design, decoration, and scenery) and **props** (articles or objects used onstage) vary greatly in modern productions of plays written in any period. Sometimes space is merely suggested—a circle of sand at one end of the stage, a blank wall behind—to emphasize universal themes or to stimulate the audience's imagination. Often, a set instead uses realistic aids to the imagination. The set of *Trifles*, for example, must include at least a sink, a cupboard, a stove, a small table, a large kitchen table, and a rocking chair, as well as certain props: a birdcage, quilting pieces, and an ornamental box.

Time is the second key ingredient of setting, and conventions for representing time have also altered across the centuries. Three or four centuries ago, European dramatists and critics admired the conventions of classical Greek drama, which, they believed, dictated that the action of a play should represent a very short time—sometimes as short as the actual performance time (two or three hours), and certainly no longer than a single day. This unity of time, one of the three so-called **classical unities**, impels a dramatist to select the moment when a stable situation should change and to fill in the necessary prior details by exposition. (These same critics maintained that a play should be unified in place and action as well; the kind of leaping from Venice to Cyprus, or from court to forest, that happens in Shakespeare's plays, as well as subplots, were off-limits according to such standards. In *Trifles*, which observes the three classical unities, all the action before the investigators' visit to the farmhouse is summarized by characters during their brief visit, and the kitchen is the only part of the house seen by the audience.)

When there are gaps and shifts in time, they are often indicated between scenes with the help of scenery, sound effects, stage directions, or notes in the program. An actor must assist in conveying the idea of time if his or her character appears at different ages. Various conventions of classical or Elizabethan drama have also worked effectively to communicate to the audience the idea of the passage of time, from the choral odes in *Oedipus the King* to the breaks between scenes in Shakespeare plays.

Action within a play thus can take place in a wide range of locations and over many years rather than in the one place and the twenty-four-hour period demanded by critics who believed in the classical unities. And we can learn much about how a particular play works and what it means by paying attention to the way it handles setting and sets.

Questions about Setting and Staging

- Does all the action occur in one time and place, or in more than one? If the latter, what are those times and places? How much time tends to pass between scenes or episodes?
- How important do the general time, place, and social milieu seem to be, and in what ways are they important? What about the plot and characters would remain the same if a director chose to set the play in a different time and place? What wouldn't?

- What patterns do you notice regarding where and when things happen? Which characters are associated with each setting? How do different characters relate to the same setting? When, how, and why do scenes change from one setting to another? Are there significant deviations?
- Do the stage directions describe particular settings and props in detail? If so, what seems significant about the details? How might they establish mood, reveal character, and affect individual characters and their interactions with one another? Is there anything in the stage directions that seems to be intended more for readers than for a director staging a production?
- Does the date of the play tell you anything about the way it was originally intended to be staged? Does the representation of time and place in the play implicitly call for a certain type of stage?
- If you were staging the play today, what kind of stage, sets, and props might you use, and why? How might your choices affect how the play works on audiences and what it means to them?

TONE, LANGUAGE, AND SYMBOL

In plays, as in other literary genres, **tone** is difficult to specify or explain. Perhaps tone is especially important in drama because it is, in performance, a spoken form, and vocal tone always affects the meaning of spoken words to some extent, in any culture or language. The actor—and any reader who wishes to imagine a play as spoken aloud—must infer from the written language just how to read a line, what tone of voice to use. The choice of tone must be a negotiation between the words of the playwright and the interpretation and skill of the actor or reader. At times stage directions will specify the tone of a line of dialogue, though even that must be only a hint, since there are many ways of speaking "intensely" or "angrily." Find a line in one of the plays printed here that has a stage direction telling the actor how to deliver it, and with one or two other people take turns saying it that way. If nothing else, such an experiment may help you appreciate the talent of good actors who can put on a certain tone of voice and make it seem natural and convincing. But it will also show you the many options for interpreting tone.

Dramatic irony, in which a character's perception is contradicted by what the audience knows, and even *situational irony*, in which a character's (and the audience's) expectations about what will happen are contradicted by what actually does happen, are relatively easy to detect. But *verbal irony*, in which a statement implies a meaning quite different from its obvious, literal meaning, can be fairly subtle and easy to miss. In the absence of clear stage directions, verbal irony—like other aspects of tone—can also be a matter of interpretation. That is, directors and actors, as well as readers and audiences, will often have to decide which lines in a play should be interpreted ironically. All three types of irony are nonetheless crucial to drama. As the very term *dramatic irony* suggests, drama—even more than fiction—depends for its effects on gaps between what the various characters and the audience know. And situational irony—the gap between expectations and outcomes and even between what characters seem to deserve and what they get— is an especially key component of **tragedy**.

Never hesitate to apply to drama the skills you have developed in interpreting poetry; after all, most early plays were written in some form of verse. Aspects of poetry often emerge in modern plays; for example, **monologues** or extended speeches by one character, while they rarely rhyme or have regular **meter**, may allow greater eloquence than is usual in everyday speech and may include revealing imagery and **figures of speech**. A character in Lorraine Hansberry's A RAISIN IN THE SUN, for example, uses **personification**, as well as **alliteration**, to great effect when she remarks (in act 3) that "death done come in this here house. [. . .] Done come walking in my house."

Simple actions or objects, too, often have metaphorical significance or turn into **symbols**. Effective plays often use props in this way, as *Trifles* does with the bird and its cage. And some plays, like some poems, may even be organized around *controlling* **metaphors**. As you read, pay close attention to metaphors or images, whether in language or in more concrete form.

Allusions, references to other works of literature or art or to something else external to the play, can enrich the text in similar ways. Though New Orleans, where Tennessee Williams's A STREETCAR NAMED DESIRE takes place, actually does contain a street called Elysian Fields, the play gets a good deal of symbolic mileage out of using this as a setting thanks to the allusion to Greek mythology (in which the Elysian Fields were the final resting place of heroic and virtuous souls). Awareness of all the stylistic choices in a play can help you reach a clearer, more comprehensive interpretation of it.

Questions about Tone, Language, and Symbol

- Which lines in the play strike you as most ambiguous when it comes to the tone in which they should be spoken? Why and how so? What is the effect of that ambiguity, or how might an actor's or reader's decision about tone here affect the play as a whole?
- How would you describe the overall tone of the entire play? Do any moments or entire scenes or acts in the play seem interestingly different in terms of their tone?
- How do the play's characters differ from one another in terms of their tone? Does any character's tone change over the course of the play?
- Are any details—such as names; actions or statements; references to objects, props, or other details of setting; or allusions, metaphors, or other figures of speech—repeated throughout the play? Do any of these repeated details seem to have special significance? If so, what might that significance be?
- What types of irony, if any, are at work in the play? What is the effect of the irony?

THEME

Theme—a statement a work seems to make about a given issue or subject—is by its very nature the most comprehensive of the elements, embracing the impact of the entire work. Indeed, theme is not part of the work but is abstracted from it by the reader or audience. Since we, as interpreters, infer the theme and put it in our own words, we understandably often disagree about it. (And great plays arguably have multiple themes.) To arrive at your own statement of a theme, you need to consider all the elements of a play together: character, structure, setting (including time and place), tone, and other aspects of the style or the potential staging that create the entire effect.

Tips for Identifying Theme

Because theme emerges from a work in its entirety and from all the other elements working together, there's no one-size-fits-all method for discovering theme. Here, however, are some things to look for and consider as you read and re-read a play.

- Pay attention to the title. A title will seldom indicate a play's theme directly, but some titles do suggest a central topic or a key question. Probe the rest of the play to see what insights, if any, about that topic or answers to that question it ultimately seems to offer.
- Identify any statements that the characters make about a general concept, issue, or topic such as human nature, the natural world, and so on, particularly in monologues or in debates between major characters. Look, too, for statements that potentially have a general meaning or application beyond the play, even if they refer to a specific situation. Then consider whether and how the play as a whole corroborates, overturns, or complicates any one such view or statement.
- If a character changes over the course of the play, try to articulate the truth or insight that the character seems to discover. Then consider whether and how the play as a whole corroborates or complicates that insight.
- Identify a conflict depicted in the play and state it in general terms or turn it into a general question, leaving out any reference to specific characters, setting, and so on. Then think about the insight or theme that might be implied by the way the conflict is resolved.

* * * *

Above all, try to understand a play on its own terms and to separate interpretation from evaluation. You may dislike symbolic or unrealistic drama until you get more used to it; if a play is not supposed to represent what real people would do in everyday life, then it should not be criticized for failing to do so. Alternatively, you may find realistic plays about ordinary adults in middle America in the mid-twentieth century to be lacking in excitement or appeal. Yet if you read carefully, you may discover vigorous, moving portrayals of people trapped in situations all too familiar to them, if alien to you. Tastes may vary as widely as tones of speech, but if you are familiar with the elements of drama and the ways dramatic **conventions** vary over time and across cultures, you can become a good judge of theatrical literature, and you will notice more and more of the fine effects it can achieve. Nothing replaces the exhilaration and immediacy of a live theater performance, but reading and re-reading plays can yield a rich and rewarding appreciation of the dramatic art. A great play is one that works on the page as well as on the stage.

AUGUST WILSON
(1945–2005)
Fences

August Wilson died of liver cancer when he was only sixty. One of the most important dramatists in American theater history, he had come a long way, the hard way. Frederick August Kittel, Jr., (who would later take his mother's maiden name) was the son of a White, German-born baker and his wife, a Black cleaning woman who singlehandedly raised their six children in Pittsburgh's down-at-heel Hill District. In 1957, when Wilson was twelve, his mother remarried. Her new husband was an African American sewer-department worker who, as Wilson learned only after his stepfather's death, had been both a high-school football star unable to secure a college scholarship and an ex-convict. After a series of bad experiences, Wilson left school at fifteen. Armed with a tenth-grade education, he worked a number of menial jobs, read his way through the public library, and served briefly in the army. In 1968, he returned to the Hill, cofounding the Black Horizon Theater and debuting his first play. Fourteen years later, Wilson struck artistic gold with a play recently turned into a Netflix film starring Viola Davis—*Ma Rainey's Black Bottom* (1982), his first Broadway play and the second in what would become a ten-play cycle. Set mostly in the Hill and chronicling African American life in every decade of the twentieth century, the series earned Wilson two Pulitzers (for *Fences*, 1987, and *The Piano Lesson*, 1990); a Tony (for *Fences*); a Grammy (for the original *Ma Rainey's* cast album); an Emmy (for his adaptation of *Piano Lesson*); and eight Drama Critics' Circle awards. A noteworthy creator of ensemble drama, Wilson often described *Fences* as his least representative, most conventional play, thanks to the way it revolves around a single "big character." Yet this, his best-known work, is also arguably among his most personal, set in the period of his youth and aimed, he said, at "uncover[ing] the nobility and the dignity" of the adults he grew up around—"that generation, which shielded its children from all of the indignities they went through."

For Lloyd Richards,[1]
who adds to whatever he touches

CHARACTERS

TROY MAXSON
JIM BONO, *Troy's friend*
ROSE, *Troy's wife*
LYONS, *Troy's oldest son by a previous marriage*

GABRIEL, *Troy's brother*
CORY, *Troy and Rose's son*
RAYNELL, *Troy's daughter*

1. Influential Canadian American director-actor (1919–2006) whom August Wilson called his "guide, mentor, and provocateur." The first Black director of a Broadway play (Lorraine Hansberry's *A Raisin in the Sun*, 1959, p. 1555), artistic director of the Eugene O'Neill Theater Center and the Yale Repertory Theatre, and dean of the Yale School of Drama, Richards oversaw the first productions of all of Wilson's plays, beginning with *Ma Rainey's Black Bottom* (1982).

Denzel Washington as Troy and Viola Davis as Rose in the 2016 film adaptation of *Fences*

SETTING: *The setting is the yard which fronts the only entrance to the Maxson household, an ancient two-story brick house set back off a small alley in a big-city neighborhood. The entrance to the house is gained by two or three steps leading to a wooden porch badly in need of paint.*

A relatively recent addition to the house and running its full width, the porch lacks congruence. It is a sturdy porch with a flat roof. One or two chairs of dubious value sit at one end where the kitchen window opens onto the porch. An old-fashioned icebox stands silent guard at the opposite end.

The yard is a small dirt yard, partially fenced (except during the last scene), with a wooden sawhorse, a pile of lumber, and other fence-building equipment off to the side. Opposite is a tree from which hangs a ball made of rags. A baseball bat leans against the tree. Two oil drums serve as garbage receptacles and sit near the house at right to complete the setting.

THE PLAY: *Near the turn of the century, the destitute of Europe sprang on the city with tenacious claws and an honest and solid dream. The city devoured them. They swelled its belly until it burst into a thousand furnaces and sewing machines, a thousand butcher shops and bakers' ovens, a thousand churches and hospitals and funeral parlors and moneylenders. The city grew. It nourished itself and offered each man a partnership limited only by his talent, his guile and his willingness and capacity for hard work. For the immigrants of Europe, a dream dared and won true.*

The descendants of African slaves were offered no such welcome or participation. They came from places called the Carolinas and the Virginias, Georgia, Alabama, Mississippi and Tennessee. They came strong, eager, searching. The city rejected them and they fled and settled along the riverbanks and under bridges in shallow, ramshackle houses made of sticks and tar paper. They collected rags and wood. They sold the use of their muscles and their bodies. They cleaned houses and washed clothes, they shined shoes, and in quiet desperation and vengeful pride, they stole, and lived in pursuit of their own dream. That they could breathe free, finally, and stand to meet life with the force of dignity and whatever eloquence the heart could call upon.

By 1957, the hard-won victories of the European immigrants had solidified the industrial might of America. War had been confronted and won with new energies that used loyalty and patriotism as its fuel. Life was rich, full and flourishing. The Milwaukee Braves won the World Series, and the hot winds of change that would make the sixties a turbulent, racing, dangerous and provocative decade had not yet begun to blow full.

When the sins of our fathers visit us
We do not have to play host.
We can banish them with forgiveness
As God, in His Largeness and Laws.

—AUGUST WILSON

ACT ONE

Scene 1

It is 1957. Troy and Bono enter the yard, engaged in conversation. Troy is fifty-three years old, a large man with thick, heavy hands; it is this largeness that he strives to fill out and make an accommodation with. Together with his blackness, his largeness informs his sensibilities and the choices he has made in his life.

Of the two men, Bono is obviously the follower. His commitment to their friendship of thirty-odd years is rooted in his admiration of Troy's honesty, capacity for hard work, and his strength, which Bono seeks to emulate.

It is Friday night, payday, and the one night of the week the two men engage in a ritual of talk and drink. Troy is usually the most talkative and at times he can be crude and almost vulgar, though he is capable of rising to profound heights of expression. The men carry lunch buckets and wear or carry burlap aprons and are dressed in clothes suitable to their jobs as garbage collectors.

BONO: Troy, you ought to stop that lying!

TROY: I ain't lying! The nigger had a watermelon this big. (*Indicates with his hands*) Talking about . . . "What watermelon, Mr. Rand?" I like to fell out! "What watermelon, Mr. Rand?" . . . And it sitting there big as life.

BONO: What did Mr. Rand say?

TROY: Ain't said nothing. Figure if the nigger too dumb to know he carrying a watermelon, he wasn't gonna get much sense out of him. Trying to hide that great big old watermelon under his coat. Afraid to let the white man see him carry it home.

BONO: I'm like you . . . I ain't got no time for them kind of people.

TROY: Now what he look like getting mad 'cause he see the man from the union talking to Mr. Rand?

BONO: He come talking to me about . . . "Maxson gonna get us fired." I told him to get away from me with that. He walked away from me calling you a troublemaker. What Mr. Rand say?

TROY: Ain't said nothing. He told me to go down the commissioner's office next Friday. They called me down there to see them.

BONO: Well, as long as you got your complaint filed, they can't fire you. That's what one of them white fellows tell me.

TROY: I ain't worried about them firing me. They gonna fire me 'cause I asked a question? That's all I did. I went to Mr. Rand and asked him, "Why? Why you got the white mens driving and the colored lifting?" Told him, "What's the matter, don't I count? You think only white fellows got sense enough to drive a truck. That ain't no paper job! Hell, anybody can drive a truck. How come you got all whites driving and the colored lifting?" He told me, "Take it to the union." Well, hell, that's what I done! Now they wanna come up with this pack of lies.

BONO: I told Brownie if the man come and ask him any questions . . . just tell the truth! It ain't nothing but something they done trumped up on you 'cause you filed a complaint on them.

TROY: Brownie don't understand nothing. All I want them to do is change the job description. Give everybody a chance to drive the truck. Brownie can't see that. He ain't got that much sense.

BONO: How you figure he be making out with that gal be up at Taylors' all the time . . . that Alberta gal?

TROY: Same as you and me. Getting as much as we is. Which is to say nothing.

BONO: It is, huh? I figure you doing a little better than me . . . and I ain't saying what I'm doing.

TROY: Aw, nigger, look here . . . I know you. If you had got anywhere near that gal, twenty minutes later you be looking to tell somebody. And the first one you gonna tell . . . that you gonna want to brag to . . . is gonna be me.

BONO: I ain't saying that. I see where you be eyeing her.

TROY: I eye all the women. I don't miss nothing. Don't never let nobody tell you Troy Maxson don't eye the women.

BONO: You been doing more than eyeing her. You done bought her a drink or two.

TROY: Hell yeah, I bought her a drink! What that mean? I bought you one, too. What that mean 'cause I buy her a drink? I'm just being polite.

BONO: It's all right to buy her one drink. That's what you call being polite. But when you wanna be buying two or three . . . that's what you call eyeing her.

TROY: Look here, as long as you known me . . . you ever known me to chase after women?

BONO: Hell yeah! Long as I done known you. You forgetting I knew you when.

TROY: Naw, I'm talking about since I been married to Rose?

BONO: Oh, not since you been married to Rose. Now, that's the truth, there. I can say that.

TROY: All right then! Case closed.

BONO: I see you be walking up around Alberta's house. You supposed to be at Taylors' and you be walking up around there.

TROY: What you watching where I'm walking for? I ain't watching after you.

BONO: I seen you walking around there more than once.

TROY: Hell, you liable to see me walking anywhere! That don't mean nothing 'cause you see me walking around there.

BONO: Where she come from anyway? She just kinda showed up one day.

TROY: Tallahassee. You can look at her and tell she one of them Florida gals. They got some big healthy women down there. Grow them right up out the ground. Got a little bit of Indian in her. Most of them niggers down in Florida got some Indian in them.

BONO: I don't know about that Indian part. But she damn sure big and healthy. Woman wear some big stockings. Got them great big old legs and hips as wide as the Mississippi River.

TROY: Legs don't mean nothing. You don't do nothing but push them out of the way. But them hips cushion the ride!

BONO: Troy, you ain't got no sense.

TROY: It's the truth! Like you riding on Goodyears!

> (*Rose enters from the house. She is ten years younger than Troy. Her devotion to him stems from her recognition of the possibilities of her life without him: a succession of abusive men and their babies, a life of partying and running the streets, the church, or aloneness with its attendant pain and frustration. She recognizes Troy's spirit as a fine and illuminating one and she either ignores or forgives his faults, only some of which she recognizes. Though she doesn't drink, her presence is an integral part of the Friday night rituals. She alternates between the porch and the kitchen, where supper preparations are under way.*)

ROSE: What you all out here getting into?

TROY: What you worried about what we getting into for? This is men talk, woman.

ROSE: What I care what you talking about? Bono, you gonna stay for supper?

BONO: No, I thank you, Rose. But Lucille say she cooking up a pot of pigfeet.

TROY: Pigfeet! Hell, I'm going home with you! Might even stay the night if you got some pigfeet. You got something in there to top them pigfeet, Rose?

ROSE: I'm cooking up some chicken. I got some chicken and collard greens.

TROY: Well, go on back in the house and let me and Bono finish what we was talking about. This is men talk. I got some talk for you later. You know what kind of talk I mean. You go on and powder it up.

ROSE: Troy Maxson, don't you start that now!

TROY (*Puts his arm around her*): Aw, woman . . . come here. Look here, Bono . . . when I met this woman . . . I got out that place, say, "Hitch up my pony, saddle up my mare . . . there's a woman out there for me somewhere. I looked here. Looked there. Saw Rose and latched on to her." I latched on to her and told her—I'm gonna tell you the truth—I told her, "Baby, I don't wanna marry, I just wanna be your man." Rose told me . . . tell him what you told me, Rose.

ROSE: I told him if he wasn't the marrying kind, then move out the way so the marrying kind could find me.

TROY: That's what she told me. "Nigger, you in my way. You blocking the view! Move out the way so I can find me a husband." I thought it over two or three days. Come back—

ROSE: Ain't no two or three days nothing. You was back the same night.

TROY: Come back, told her . . . "Okay, baby . . . but I'm gonna buy me a banty rooster and put him out there in the backyard . . . and when he see a stranger come, he'll flap his wings and crow . . ." Look here, Bono, I could watch the front door by myself . . . it was that back door I was worried about.

ROSE: Troy, you ought not talk like that. Troy ain't doing nothing but telling a lie.

TROY: Only thing is . . . when we first got married . . . forget the rooster . . . we ain't had no yard!

BONO: I hear you tell it. Me and Lucille was staying down there on Logan Street. Had two rooms with the outhouse in the back. I ain't mind the outhouse none. But when that goddamn wind blow through there in the winter . . . that's what I'm talking about! To this day I wonder why in the hell I ever stayed down there for six long years. But see, I didn't know I could do no better. I thought only white folks had inside toilets and things.

ROSE: There's a lot of people don't know they can do no better than they doing now. That's just something you got to learn. A lot of folks still shop at Bella's.

TROY: Ain't nothing wrong with shopping at Bella's. She got fresh food.

ROSE: I ain't said nothing about if she got fresh food. I'm talking about what she charge. She charge ten cents more than the A&P.[2]

TROY: The A&P ain't never done nothing for me. I spends my money where I'm treated right. I go down to Bella, say, "I need a loaf of bread, I'll pay you Friday." She give it to me. What sense that make when I got money to go and spend it somewhere else and ignore the person who done right by me? That ain't in the Bible.

ROSE: We ain't talking about what's in the Bible. What sense it make to shop there when she overcharge?

TROY: You shop where you want to. I'll do my shopping where the people been good to me.

ROSE: Well, I don't think it's right for her to overcharge. That's all I was saying.

BONO: Look here . . . . I got to get on. Lucille be raising all kind of hell.

TROY: Where you going, nigger? We ain't finished this pint. Come here, finish this pint.

BONO: Well, hell, I am . . . if you ever turn the bottle loose.

TROY (*Hands him the bottle*): The only thing I say about the A&P is I'm glad Cory got that job down there. Help him take care of his school clothes and things. Gabe done moved out and things getting tight around here. He got that job . . . He can start to look out for himself.

ROSE: Cory done went and got recruited by a college football team.

TROY: I told that boy about that football stuff. The white man ain't gonna let him get nowhere with that football. I told him when he first come to me with it. Now you come telling me he done went and got more tied up in it. He ought

2. By the 1930s, the Great Atlantic and Pacific Tea Company, so named in 1859, was the leading supermarket chain in the United States.

to go and get recruited in how to fix cars or something where he can make a living.

ROSE: He ain't talking about making no living playing football. It's just something the boys in school do. They gonna send a recruiter by to talk to you. He'll tell you he ain't talking about making no living playing football. It's a honor to be recruited.

TROY: It ain't gonna get him nowhere. Bono'll tell you that.

BONO: If he be like you in the sports . . . he's gonna be all right. Ain't but two men ever played baseball as good as you. That's Babe Ruth and Josh Gibson.[3] Them's the only two men ever hit more home runs than you.

TROY: What it ever get me? Ain't got a pot to piss in or a window to throw it out of.

ROSE: Times have changed since you was playing baseball, Troy. That was before the war.[4] Times have changed a lot since then.

TROY: How in hell they done changed?

ROSE: They got lots of colored boys playing ball now. Baseball and football.

BONO: You right about that, Rose. Times have changed, Troy. You just come along too early.

TROY: There ought not never have been no time called too early! Now you take that fellow . . . what's that fellow they had playing right field for the Yankees back then? You know who I'm talking about, Bono. Used to play right field for the Yankees.

ROSE: Selkirk?[5]

TROY: Selkirk! That's it! Man batting .269, understand? .269. What kind of sense that make? I was hitting .432 with thirty-seven home runs! Man batting .269 and playing right field for the Yankees! I saw Josh Gibson's daughter yesterday. She walking around with raggedy shoes on her feet. Now I bet you Selkirk's daughter ain't walking around with raggedy shoes on her feet! I bet you that!

ROSE: They got a lot of colored baseball players now. Jackie Robinson[6] was the first. Folks had to wait for Jackie Robinson.

TROY: I done seen a hundred niggers play baseball better than Jackie Robinson. Hell, I know some teams Jackie Robinson couldn't even make! What you talking about Jackie Robinson. Jackie Robinson wasn't nobody. I'm talking about if you could play ball then they ought to have let you play. Don't care what color you were. Come telling me I come along too early. If you could play . . . then they ought to have let you play.

(*Troy takes a long drink from the bottle.*)

ROSE: You gonna drink yourself to death. You don't need to be drinking like that.

---

3. Georgia-born catcher (1911–47) often called "the Black Babe Ruth." Hailed by the Baseball Hall of Fame as "the greatest power hitter in black baseball," he died three months before integration of the major leagues. *Babe Ruth*: legendary outfielder, pitcher, and power hitter (1895–1948) for the Boston Red Sox and New York Yankees.

4. World War II (1939–45).

5. George Selkirk (1908–87), Canadian-born player who succeeded Babe Ruth as the New York Yankees right fielder.

6. Brooklyn Dodgers first baseman (1919–72); in 1947, he became the first Black player in the major leagues and, in 1949, the first Black winner of the National League MVP Award.

TROY: Death ain't nothing. I done seen him. Done wrassled with him. You can't tell me nothing about death. Death ain't nothing but a fastball on the outside corner. And you know what I'll do to that! Lookee here, Bono . . . am I lying? You get one of them fastballs, about waist high, over the outside corner of the plate where you can get the meat of the bat on it . . . and good God! You can kiss it good-bye. Now, am I lying?

BONO: Naw, you telling the truth there. I seen you do it.

TROY: If I'm lying . . . that 450 feet worth of lying! (*Pause*) That's all death is to me. A fastball on the outside corner.

ROSE: I don't know why you want to get on talking about death.

TROY: Ain't nothing wrong with talking about death. That's part of life. Everybody gonna die. You gonna die, I'm gonna die. Bono's gonna die. Hell, we all gonna die.

ROSE: But you ain't got to talk about it. I don't like to talk about it.

TROY: You the one brought it up. Me and Bono was talking about baseball . . . you tell me I'm gonna drink myself to death. Ain't that right, Bono? You know I don't drink this but one night out of the week. That's Friday night. I'm gonna drink just enough to where I can handle it. Then I cuts it loose. I leave it alone. So don't you worry about me drinking myself to death. 'Cause I ain't worried about Death. I done seen him. I done wrestled with him.

Look here, Bono . . . I looked up one day and Death was marching straight at me. Like Soldiers on Parade! The Army of Death was marching straight at me. The middle of July, 1941. It got real cold just like it be winter. It seem like Death himself reached out and touched me on the shoulder. He touch me just like I touch you. I got cold as ice and Death standing there grinning at me.

ROSE: Troy, why don't you hush that talk.

TROY: I say . . . What you want, Mr. Death? You be wanting me? You done brought your army to be getting me? I looked him dead in the eye. I wasn't fearing nothing. I was ready to tangle. Just like I'm ready to tangle now. The Bible say be ever vigilant. That's why I don't get but so drunk. I got to keep watch.

ROSE: Troy was right down there in Mercy Hospital. You remember he had pneumonia? Laying there with a fever talking plumb out of his head.

TROY: Death standing there staring at me . . . carrying that sickle in his hand. Finally he say, "You want bound over for another year?" See, just like that . . . "You want bound over for another year?" I told him, "Bound over hell! Let's settle this now!"

It seem like he kinda fell back when I said that, and all the cold went out of me. I reached down and grabbed that sickle and threw it just as far as I could throw it . . . and me and him commenced to wrestling.

We wrestled for three days and three nights. I can't say where I found the strength from. Every time it seemed like he was gonna get the best of me, I'd reach way down deep inside myself and find the strength to do him one better.

ROSE: Every time Troy tell that story he find different ways to tell it. Different things to make up about it.

TROY: I ain't making up nothing. I'm telling you the facts of what happened. I wrestled with Death for three days and three nights and I'm standing here to tell you about it. (*Pause*) All right. At the end of the third night we done weakened each other to where we can't hardly move. Death stood up, throwed on his robe . . . had him a white robe with a hood on it. He throwed on that robe and went off to look for his sickle. Say, "I'll be back." Just like that. "I'll be back." I told him say, "Yeah, but . . . you gonna have to find me!" I wasn't no fool. I wasn't going looking for him. Death ain't nothing to play with. And I know he's gonna get me. I know I got to join his army . . . his camp followers. But as long as I keep my strength and see him coming . . . as long as I keep up my vigilance . . . he's gonna have to fight to get me. I ain't going easy.

BONO: Well, look here, since you got to keep up your vigilance . . . let me have the bottle.

TROY: Aw hell, I shouldn't have told you that part. I should have left out that part.

ROSE: Troy be talking that stuff and half the time don't even know what he be talking about.

TROY: Bono know me better than that.

BONO: That's right. I know you. I know you got some Uncle Remus[7] in your blood. You got more stories than the devil got sinners.

TROY: Aw hell, I done seen him too! Done talked with the devil.

ROSE: Troy, don't nobody want to be hearing all that stuff.

> (*Lyons enters the yard from the street. Thirty-four years old, Troy's son from a previous marriage, he sports a neatly trimmed goatee, sport coat and white shirt, tieless and buttoned at the collar. Though he fancies himself a musician, he is more caught up in the rituals and "idea" of being a musician than in the actual practice of the music. He has come to borrow money from Troy and, while he knows he will be successful, he is uncertain as to what extent his lifestyle will be held up to scrutiny and ridicule.*)

LYONS: Hey, Pop.

TROY: What you come "Hey, Popping" me for?

LYONS: How you doing, Rose? (*Kisses her*) Mr. Bono. How you doing?

BONO: Hey, Lyons . . . how you been?

TROY: He must have been doing all right. I ain't seen him around here last week.

ROSE: Troy, leave your boy alone. He come by to see you and you wanna start all that nonsense.

TROY: I ain't bothering Lyons. (*Offers him the bottle*) Here, get you a drink. We got an understanding. I know why he come by to see me and he know I know.

LYONS: Come on, Pop . . . I just stopped by to say hi . . . see how you was doing.

TROY: You ain't stopped by yesterday.

ROSE: You gonna stay for supper, Lyons? I got some chicken cooking in the oven.

LYONS: No, Rose . . . thanks. I was just in the neighborhood and thought I'd stop by for a minute.

TROY: You was in the neighborhood all right, nigger. You telling the truth there. You was in the neighborhood 'cause it's my payday.

LYONS: Well, hell, since you mentioned it . . . let me have ten dollars.

---

7. African American narrator of the folktales, adapted from African American originals, published by White Georgia journalist Joel Chandler Harris beginning in 1879, and featuring Br'er Rabbit.

TROY: I'll be damned! I'll die and go to hell and play blackjack with the devil before I give you ten dollars.

BONO: That's what I want to know about . . . that devil you done seen.

LYONS: What . . . Pop done seen the devil? You too much, Pops.

TROY: Yeah, I done seen him. Talked to him too!

ROSE: You ain't seen no devil. I done told you that man ain't had nothing to do with the devil. Anything you can't understand, you want to call it the devil.

TROY: Look here, Bono . . . I went down to see Hertzberger about some furniture. Got three rooms for two-ninety-eight. That what it say on the radio. "Three rooms . . . two-ninety-eight." Even made up a little song about it. Go down there . . . man tell me I can't get no credit. I'm working every day and can't get no credit. What to do? I got an empty house with some raggedy furniture in it. Cory ain't got no bed. He's sleeping on a pile of rags on the floor. Working every day and can't get no credit. Come back here—Rose'll tell you—madder than hell. Sit down . . . try to figure what I'm gonna do. Come a knock on the door. Ain't been living here but three days. Who know I'm here? Open the door . . . devil standing there bigger than life. White fellow . . . got on good clothes and everything. Standing there with a clipboard in his hand. I ain't had to say nothing. First words come out of his mouth was . . . "I understand you need some furniture and can't get no credit." I liked to fell over. He say, "I'll give you all the credit you want, but you got to pay the interest on it." I told him, "Give me three rooms' worth and charge whatever you want." Next day a truck pulled up here and two men unloaded them three rooms. Man what drove the truck give me a book. Say send ten dollars, first of every month to the address in the book and everything will be all right. Say if I miss a payment the devil was coming back and it'll be hell to pay. That was fifteen years ago. To this day . . . the first of the month I send my ten dollars, Rose'll tell you.

ROSE: Troy lying.

TROY: I ain't never seen that man since. Now you tell me who else that could have been but the devil? I ain't sold my soul or nothing like that, you understand. Naw, I wouldn't have truck with the devil about nothing like that. I got my furniture and pays my ten dollars the first of the month just like clockwork.

BONO: How long you say you been paying this ten dollars a month?

TROY: Fifteen years!

BONO: Hell, ain't you finished paying for it yet? How much the man done charged you.

TROY: Aw hell, I done paid for it. I done paid for it ten times over! The fact is I'm scared to stop paying it.

ROSE: Troy lying. We got that furniture from Mr. Glickman, He ain't paying no ten dollars a month to nobody.

TROY: Aw hell, woman. Bono know I ain't that big a fool.

LYONS: I was just getting ready to say . . . I know where there's a bridge for sale.

TROY: Look here, I'll tell you this . . . it don't matter to me if he was the devil. It don't matter if the devil give credit. Somebody has got to give it.

ROSE: It ought to matter. You going around talking about having truck with the devil . . . God's the one you gonna have to answer to. He's the one gonna be at the Judgment.

LYONS: Yeah, well, look here, Pop . . . let me have that ten dollars. I'll give it back to you. Bonnie got a job working at the hospital.

TROY: What I tell you, Bono? The only time I see this nigger is when he wants something. That's the only time I see him.

LYONS: Come on, Pop, Mr. Bono don't want to hear all that. Let me have the ten dollars. I told you Bonnie working.

TROY: What that mean to me? "Bonnie working." I don't care if she working. Go ask her for the ten dollars if she working. Talking about "Bonnie working." Why ain't you working?

LYONS: Aw, Pop, you know I can't find no decent job. Where am I gonna get a job at? You know I can't get no job.

TROY: I told you I know some people down there. I can get you on the rubbish if you want to work. I told you that the last time you came by here asking me for something.

LYONS: Naw, Pop . . . thanks. That ain't for me. I don't wanna be carrying nobody's rubbish. I don't wanna be punching nobody's time clock.

TROY: What's the matter, you too good to carry people's rubbish? Where you think that ten dollars you talking about come from? I'm just supposed to haul people's rubbish and give my money to you 'cause you too lazy to work. You too lazy to work and wanna know why you ain't got what I got.

ROSE: What hospital Bonnie working at? Mercy?

LYONS: She's down at Passavant working in the laundry.

TROY: I ain't got nothing as it is. I give you that ten dollars and I got to eat beans the rest of the week. Naw . . . you ain't getting no ten dollars here.

LYONS: You ain't got to be eating no beans. I don't know why you wanna say that.

TROY: I ain't got no extra money. Gabe done moved over to Miss Pearl's paying her the rent and things done got tight around here. I can't afford to be giving you every payday.

LYONS: I ain't asked you to give me nothing. I asked you to loan me ten dollars. I know you got ten dollars.

TROY: Yeah, I got it. You know why I got it? 'Cause I don't throw my money away out there in the streets. You living the fast life . . . wanna be a musician . . . running around in them clubs and things . . . then, you learn to take care of yourself. You ain't gonna find me going and asking nobody for nothing. I done spent too many years without.

LYONS: You and me is two different people, Pop.

TROY: I done learned my mistake and learned to do what's right by it. You still trying to get something for nothing. Life don't owe you nothing. You owe it to yourself. Ask Bono. He'll tell you I'm right.

LYONS: You got your way of dealing with the world . . . I got mine. The only thing that matters to me is the music.

TROY: Yeah, I can see that! It don't matter how you gonna eat . . . where your next dollar is coming from. You telling the truth there.

LYONS: I know I got to eat. But I got to live too. I need something that gonna help me to get out of the bed in the morning. Make me feel like I belong in the world. I don't bother nobody. I just stay with my music 'cause that's the only way I can find to live in the world. Otherwise there ain't no telling what

I might do. Now I don't come criticizing you and how you live. I just come by to ask you for ten dollars. I don't wanna hear all that about how I live.

TROY: Boy, your mama did a hell of a job raising you.

LYONS: You can't change me, Pop. I'm thirty-four years old. If you wanted to change me, you should have been there when I was growing up. I come by to see you . . . ask for ten dollars and you want to talk about how I was raised. You don't know nothing about how I was raised.

ROSE: Let the boy have ten dollars, Troy.

TROY (*To Lyons*): What the hell you looking at me for? I ain't got no ten dollars. You know what I do with my money. (*To Rose*) Give him ten dollars if you want him to have it.

ROSE: I will. Just as soon as you turn it loose.

TROY (*Handing Rose the money*): There it is. Seventy-six dollars and forty-two cents. You see this, Bono? Now, I ain't gonna get but six of that back.

ROSE: You ought to stop telling that lie. Here, Lyons. (*Hands him the money*)

LYONS: Thanks, Rose. Look . . . I got to run . . . I'll see you later.

TROY: Wait a minute. You gonna say, "Thanks, Rose," and ain't gonna look to see where she got that ten dollars from? See how they do me, Bono?

LYONS: I know she got it from you, Pop. Thanks. I'll give it back to you.

TROY: There he go telling another lie. Time I see that ten dollars . . . he'll be owing me thirty more.

LYONS: See you, Mr. Bono.

BONO: Take care, Lyons!

LYONS: Thanks, Pop. I'll see you again.

(*Lyons exits the yard.*)

TROY: I don't know why he don't go and get him a decent job and take care of that woman he got.

BONO: He'll be all right, Troy. The boy is still young.

TROY: The *boy* is thirty-four years old.

ROSE: Let's not get off into all that.

BONO: Look here . . . I got to be going. I got to be getting on. Lucille gonna be waiting.

TROY (*Puts his arm around Rose*): See this woman, Bono? I love this woman. I love this woman so much it hurts. I love her so much . . . I done run out of ways of loving her. So I got to go back to basics. Don't you come by my house Monday morning talking about time to go to work . . .'cause I'm still gonna be stroking!

ROSE: Troy! Stop it now!

BONO: I ain't paying him no mind, Rose. That ain't nothing but gin-talk. Go on, Troy. I'll see you Monday.

TROY: Don't you come by my house, nigger! I done told you what I'm gonna be doing.

(*The lights fade to black.*)

Scene 2

The lights come up on Rose hanging up clothes. She hums and sings softly to herself. It is the following morning.

ROSE (*Singing*):
> Jesus, be a fence all around me every day
> Jesus, I want you to protect me as I travel on my way.
> Jesus, be a fence all around me every day.

(*Troy enters from the house.*)

> Jesus, I want you to protect me
> As I travel on my way.

(*To Troy*) 'Morning. You ready for breakfast? I can fix it soon as I finish hanging up these clothes?

TROY: I got the coffee on. That'll be all right. I'll just drink some of that this morning.

ROSE: That 651 hit yesterday. That's the second time this month. Miss Pearl hit for a dollar . . . seem like those that need the least always get lucky. Poor folks can't get nothing.

TROY: Them numbers don't know nobody. I don't know why you fool with them. You and Lyons both.

ROSE: It's something to do.

TROY: You ain't doing nothing but throwing your money away.

ROSE: Troy, you know I don't play foolishly. I just play a nickel here and a nickel there.

TROY: That's two nickels you done thrown away.

ROSE: Now I hit sometimes . . . that makes up for it. It always comes in handy when I do hit. I don't hear you complaining then.

TROY: I ain't complaining now. I just say it's foolish. Trying to guess out of six hundred ways which way the number gonna come. If I had all the money niggers, these Negroes, throw away on numbers for one week—just one week—I'd be a rich man.

ROSE: Well, you wishing and calling it foolish ain't gonna stop folks from playing numbers. That's one thing for sure. Besides . . . some good things come from playing numbers. Look where Pope done bought him that restaurant off of numbers.

TROY: I can't stand niggers like that. Man ain't had two dimes to rub together. He walking around with his shoes all run over bumming money for cigarettes. All right. Got lucky there and hit the numbers . . .

ROSE: Troy, I know all about it.

TROY: Had good sense, I'll say that for him. He ain't throwed his money away. I seen niggers hit the numbers and go through two thousand dollars in four days. Man bought him that restaurant down there . . . fixed it up real nice . . . and then didn't want nobody to come in it! A Negro go in there and can't get no kind of service. I seen a white fellow come in there and order a bowl of stew. Pope picked all the meat out the pot for him. Man ain't had nothing but a bowl of meat! Negro come behind him and ain't got nothing but the potatoes and carrots. Talking about what numbers do for people, you picked a wrong example. Ain't done nothing but make a worser fool out of him than he was before.

ROSE: Troy, you ought to stop worrying about what happened at work yesterday.

TROY: I ain't worried. Just told me to be down there at the commissioner's office on Friday. Everybody think they gonna fire me. I ain't worried about them firing me. You ain't got to worry about that. (*Pause*) Where's Cory? Cory in the house? (*Calls*) Cory?

ROSE: He gone out.

TROY: Out, huh? He gone out 'cause he know I want him to help me with this fence. I know how he is. That boy scared of work.

(*Gabriel enters. He comes halfway down the alley and, hearing Troy's voice, stops.*)

He ain't done a lick of work in his life.

ROSE: He had to go to football practice. Coach wanted them to get in a little extra practice before the season start.

TROY: I got his practice . . . running out of here before he get his chores done.

ROSE: Troy, what is wrong with you this morning? Don't nothing set right with you. Go on back in there and go to bed . . . get up on the other side.

TROY: Why something got to be wrong with me? I ain't said nothing wrong with me.

ROSE: You got something to say about everything. First it's the numbers . . . then it's the way the man runs his restaurant . . . then you done got on Cory. What's it gonna be next? Take a look up there and see if the weather suits you . . . or is it gonna be how you gonna put up the fence with the clothes hanging in the yard.

TROY: You hit the nail on the head then.

ROSE: I know you like I know the back of my hand. Go on in there and get you some coffee . . . see if that straighten you up. 'Cause you ain't right this morning.

(*Troy starts into the house and sees Gabriel. Gabriel starts singing. Troy's brother, he is seven years younger than Troy. Injured in World War II, he has a metal plate in his head. He carries an old trumpet tied around his waist and believes with every fiber of his being that he is the archangel Gabriel.[8] He carries a chipped basket with an assortment of discarded fruits and vegetables he has picked up in the strip district[9] and which he attempts to sell.*)

GABRIEL (*Singing*):
Yes, ma'am, I got plums
You ask me how I sell them
Oh ten cents apiece
Three for a quarter

8. Divine messenger in Jewish, Christian, and Islamic traditions. In the Bible, he appears to Daniel (to explain his visions), to Zacharias (to prophesy John the Baptist's birth), and to Mary (to announce that she will bear Jesus). He is also said to be the angelic trumpeter who will announce the arrival of the Last Judgment and Christ's second coming.
9. Market district located on a narrow strip of land northeast of downtown Pittsburgh.

>   Come and buy now
>   'Cause I'm here today
>   And tomorrow I'll be gone.

(*Rose enters.*)

Hey, Rose!

ROSE: How you doing, Gabe?

GABRIEL: There's Troy . . . Hey, Troy!

TROY: Hey, Gabe.

(*Troy exits into the kitchen.*)

ROSE (*To Gabriel*): What you got there?

GABRIEL: You know what I got, Rose. I got fruits and vegetables.

ROSE (*Looking in the basket*): Where's all these plums you talking about?

GABRIEL: I ain't got no plums today, Rose. I was just singing that. Have some tomorrow. Put me in a big order for plums. Have enough plums tomorrow for Saint Peter[1] and everybody.

(*Troy reenters from the kitchen and crosses to the steps.*)

(*To Rose*) Troy's mad at me.

TROY: I ain't mad at you. What I got to be mad at you about? You ain't done nothing to me.

GABRIEL: I just moved over to Miss Pearl's to keep out from in your way. I ain't mean no harm by it.

TROY: Who said anything about that? I ain't said anything about that.

GABRIEL: You ain't mad at me, is you?

TROY: Naw . . . I ain't mad at you, Gabe. If I was mad at you I'd tell you about it.

GABRIEL: Got me two rooms. In the basement. Got my own door too. Wanna see my key? (*Holds up a key*) That's my own key! Ain't nobody else got a key like that. That's my key! My two rooms!

TROY: Well, that's good, Gabe. You got your own key . . . that's good.

ROSE: You hungry, Gabe? I was just fixing to cook Troy his breakfast.

GABRIEL: I'll take some biscuits. You got some biscuits? Did you know when I was in Heaven . . . every morning me and Saint Peter would sit down by the Gate and eat some big fat biscuits? Oh, yeah! We had us a good time. We'd sit there and eat us them biscuits and then Saint Peter would go off to sleep and tell me to wake him up when it's time to open the Gates for the Judgment.

ROSE: Well, come on . . . I'll make up a batch of biscuits.

(*Rose exits into the house.*)

GABRIEL: Troy . . . Saint Peter got your name in the book. I seen it. It say . . . Troy Maxson. I say . . . I know him! He got the same name like what I got. That's my brother!

TROY: How many times you gonna tell me that, Gabe?

---

1. Apostle traditionally represented as guardian of heaven's gates because, in Matthew 16.19, Jesus tells him, "I will give unto thee the keys of the kingdom of heaven."

GABRIEL: Ain't got my name in the book. Don't have to have my name. I done died and went to Heaven. He got your name though. One morning Saint Peter was looking at his book . . . marking it up for the Judgment . . . and he let me see your name. Got it in there under M. Got Rose's name . . . I ain't seen it like I seen yours . . . but I know it's in there. He got a great big book. Got everybody's name what was ever been born. That's what he told me. But I seen your name. Seen it with my own eyes.

TROY: Go on in the house there. Rose going to fix you something to eat.

GABRIEL: Oh, I ain't hungry. I done had breakfast with Aunt Jemima. She come by and cooked me up a whole mess of flapjacks. Remember how we used to eat them flapjacks?

TROY: Go on in the house and get you something to eat now.

GABRIEL: I got to go sell my plums. I done sold some tomatoes. Got me two quarters. Wanna see? (*Shows Troy his quarters*) I'm gonna save them and buy me a new horn so Saint Peter can hear me when it's time to open the Gates. (*Stops suddenly. Listens*) Hear that? That's the hellhounds. I got to chase them out of here. Go on get out of here! Get out! (*Exits singing:*)

> Better get ready for the Judgment
> Better get ready for the Judgment
> My Lord is coming down.

> (*Rose enters from the house.*)

TROY: He gone off somewhere.

GABRIEL (*Offstage*):
> Better get ready for the Judgment
> Better get ready for the Judgment morning
> Better get ready for the Judgment
> My God is coming down.

ROSE: He ain't eating right. Miss Pearl say she can't get him to eat nothing.

TROY: What you want me to do about it, Rose? I done did everything I can for the man. I can't make him get well. Man got half his head blown away . . . what you expect?

ROSE: Seem like something ought to be done to help him.

TROY: Man don't bother nobody. He just mixed up from that metal plate he got in his head. Ain't no sense for him to go back into the hospital.

ROSE: Least he be eating right. They can help him take care of himself.

TROY: Don't nobody wanna be locked up, Rose. What you wanna lock him up for? Man go over there and fight the war . . . messin' around with them Japs, get half his head blown off . . . and they give him a lousy three thousand dollars. And I had to swoop down on that.

ROSE: Is you fixing to go into that again?

TROY: That's the only way I got a roof over my head . . .'cause of that metal plate.

ROSE: Ain't no sense you blaming yourself for nothing. Gabe wasn't in no condition to manage that money. You done what was right by him. Can't nobody say you ain't done what was right by him. Look how long you took care of him . . . till he wanted to have his own place and moved over there with Miss Pearl.

TROY: That ain't what I'm saying, woman! I'm just stating the facts. If my brother didn't have that metal plate in his head . . . I wouldn't have a pot to piss in or a window to throw it out of. And I'm fifty-three years old. Now see if you can understand that!

(*He gets up from the porch and starts to exit the yard.*)

ROSE: Where you going off to? You been running out of here every Saturday for weeks. I thought you was gonna work on this fence?

TROY: I'm gonna walk down to Taylors'. Listen to the ball game. I'll be back in a bit. I'll work on it when I get back.

(*He exits the yard. The lights fade to black.*)

Scene 3

The lights come up on the yard. It is four hours later. Rose is taking down the clothes from the line. Cory enters carrying his football equipment.

ROSE: Your daddy like to had a fit with you running out of here this morning without doing your chores.

CORY: I told you I had to go to practice.

ROSE: He say you were supposed to help him with this fence.

CORY: He been saying that the last four or five Saturdays, and then he don't never do nothing, but go down to Taylors'. Did you tell him about the recruiter?

ROSE: Yeah, I told him.

CORY: What he say?

ROSE: He ain't said nothing too much. You get in there and get started on your chores before he gets back. Go on and scrub down them steps before he gets back here hollering and carrying on.

CORY: I'm hungry. What you got to eat, Mama?

ROSE: Go on and get started on your chores. I got some meat loaf in there. Go on and make you a sandwich . . . and don't leave no mess in there.

(*Cory exits into the house. Rose continues to take down the clothes. Troy enters the yard and sneaks up and grabs her from behind.*)

Troy! Go on, now. You liked to scared me to death. What was the score of the game? Lucille had me on the phone and I couldn't keep up with it.

TROY: What I care about the game? Come here, woman. (*Tries to kiss her*)

ROSE: I thought you went down Taylors' to listen to the game. Go on, Troy! You supposed to be putting up this fence.

TROY (*Attempting to kiss her again*): I'll put it up when I finish with what is at hand.

ROSE: Go on, Troy. I ain't studying you.

TROY (*Chasing after her*): I'm studying you . . . fixing to do my homework!

ROSE: Troy, you better leave me alone.

TROY: Where's Cory? That boy brought his butt home yet?

ROSE: He's in the house doing his chores.

TROY (*Calling*): Cory! Get your butt out here, boy!

(*Rose exits into the house with the laundry. Troy goes over to the pile of wood, picks up a board, and starts sawing. Cory enters from the house.*)

You just now coming in here from leaving this morning?

CORY: Yeah, I had to go to football practice.

TROY: Yeah, what?

CORY: Yessir.

TROY: I ain't but two seconds off you noway. The garbage sitting in there overflowing . . . you ain't done none of your chores . . . and you come in here talking about, "Yeah."

CORY: I was just getting ready to do my chores now, Pop . . .

TROY: Your first chore is to help me with this fence on Saturday. Everything else come after that. Now get that saw and cut them boards.

(*Cory takes the saw and begins cutting the boards. Troy continues working. There is a long pause.*)

CORY: Hey, Pop . . . why don't you buy a TV?

TROY: What I want with a TV? What I want one of them for?

CORY: Everybody got one. Earl, Ba Bra . . . Jesse!

TROY: I ain't asked you who had one. I say what I want with one?

CORY: So you can watch it. They got lots of things on TV. Baseball games and everything. We could watch the World Series.

TROY: Yeah . . . and how much this TV cost?

CORY: I don't know. They got them on sale for around two hundred dollars.

TROY: Two hundred dollars, huh?

CORY: That ain't that much, Pop.

TROY: Naw, it's just two hundred dollars. See that roof you got over your head at night? Let me tell you something about that roof. It's been over ten years since that roof was last tarred. See now . . . the snow come this winter and sit up there on that roof like it is . . . and it's gonna seep inside. It's just gonna be a little bit . . . ain't gonna hardly notice it. Then the next thing you know, it's gonna be leaking all over the house. Then the wood rot from all that water and you gonna need a whole new roof. Now, how much you think it cost to get that roof tarred?

CORY: I don't know.

TROY: Two hundred and sixty-four dollars . . . cash money. While you thinking about a TV, I got to be thinking about the roof . . . and whatever else go wrong around here. Now if you had two hundred dollars, what would you do . . . fix the roof or buy a TV?

CORY: I'd buy a TV. Then when the roof started to leak . . . when it needed fixing . . . I'd fix it.

TROY: Where are you gonna get the money from? You done spent it for a TV. You gonna sit up and watch the water run all over your brand-new TV.

CORY: Aw, Pop. You got money. I know you do.

TROY: Where I got it at, huh?

CORY: You got it in the bank.

TROY: You wanna see my bankbook? You wanna see that seventy-three dollars and twenty-two cents I got sitting up in there.

CORY: You ain't got to pay for it all at one time. You can put a down payment on it and carry it home with you.

TROY: Not me. I ain't gonna owe nobody nothing if I can help it. Miss a payment and they come and snatch it right out house. Then what you got? Now, soon as I get two hundred dollars clear, then I'll buy a TV. Right now, as soon as I get two hundred and sixty-four dollars, I'm gonna have this roof tarred.

CORY: Aw . . . Pop!

TROY: You go on and get you two hundred dollars and buy one if ya want it. I got better things to do with my money.

CORY: I can't get no two hundred dollars. I ain't never seen two hundred dollars.

TROY: I'll tell you what . . . you get you a hundred dollars and I'll put the other hundred with it.

CORY: All right, I'm gonna show you.

TROY: You gonna show me how you can cut them boards right now.

(*Cory begins to cut the boards. There is a long pause.*)

CORY: The Pirates won today. That makes five in a row.

TROY: I ain't thinking about the Pirates. Got an all-white team. Got that boy . . . that Puerto Rican boy . . . Clemente.[2] Don't even half-play him. That boy could be something if they give him a chance. Play him one day and sit him on the bench the next.

CORY: He gets a lot of chances to play.

TROY: I'm talking about playing regular. Playing every day so you can get your timing. That's what I'm talking about.

CORY: They got some white guys on the team that don't play every day. You can't play everybody at the same time.

TROY: If they got a white fellow sitting on the bench . . . you can bet your last dollar he can't play! The colored guy got to be twice as good before he get on the team. That's why I don't want you to get all tied up in them sports. Man on the team and what it get him? They got colored on the team and don't use them. Same as not having them. All them teams the same.

CORY: The Braves got Hank Aaron and Wes Covington.[3] Hank Aaron hit two home runs today. That makes forty-three.

TROY: Hank Aaron ain't nobody. That's what you supposed to do. That's how you supposed to play the game. Ain't nothing to it. It's just a matter of timing . . . getting the right follow-through. Hell, I can hit forty-three home runs right now!

CORY: Not off no major-league pitching, you couldn't.

TROY: We had better pitching in the Negro leagues. I hit seven home runs off of Satchel Paige.[4] You can't get no better than that!

2. Roberto Clemente (1934–72), Pittsburgh Pirates right fielder (1955–72), four-time National League batting champion, and winner of twelve Gold Gloves.

3. African American fielder (1932–2011) who played for the Milwaukee Braves from 1956 to 1961. *Hank Aaron*: legendary African American batsman (1934–2021) who played twenty-one seasons with the Milwaukee, later Atlanta, Braves (1954–74) and, in 1974–75, broke Babe Ruth's records for most home runs and runs batted in (RBIs).

4. Pitcher (1906–82). Arguably the Negro Leagues' most famous player (1926–47), he pitched in the newly integrated major leagues from age forty-two to sixty (1948–66).

CORY: Sandy Koufax.[5] He's leading the league in strikeouts.

TROY: I ain't thinking of no Sandy Koufax.

CORY: You got Warren Spahn and Lew Burdette.[6] I bet you couldn't hit no home runs off of Warren Spahn.

TROY: I'm through with it now. You go on and cut them boards. (*Pause*) Your mama tell me you done got recruited by a college football team? Is that right?

CORY: Yeah. Coach Zellman say the recruiter gonna be coming by to talk to you. Get you to sign the permission papers.

TROY: I thought you supposed to be working down there at the A&P. Ain't you supposed to be working down there after school?

CORY: Mr. Stawicki say he gonna hold my job for me until after the football season. Say starting next week I can work weekends.

TROY: I thought we had an understanding about this football stuff? You suppose to keep up with your chores and hold that job down at the A&P. Ain't been around here all day on a Saturday. Ain't none of your chores done . . . and now you telling me you done quit your job.

CORY: I'm gonna be working weekends.

TROY: You damn right you are! And ain't no need for nobody coming around here to talk to me about signing nothing.

CORY: Hey, Pop . . . you can't do that. He's coming all the way from North Carolina.

TROY: I don't care where he coming from. The white man ain't gonna let you get nowhere with that football noway. You go on and get your book-learning so you can work yourself up in that A&P or learn how to fix cars or build houses or something, get you a trade. That way you have something can't nobody take away from you. You go on and learn how to put your hands to some good use. Besides hauling people's garbage.

CORY: I get good grades, Pop. That's why the recruiter wants to talk with you. You got to keep up your grades to get recruited. This way I'll be going to college. I'll get a chance . . .

TROY: First you gonna get your butt down there to the A&P and get your job back.

CORY: Mr. Stawicki done already hired somebody else 'cause I told him I was playing football.

TROY: You a bigger fool than I thought . . . to let somebody take away your job so you can play some football. Where you gonna get your money to take out your girlfriend and whatnot? What kind of foolishness is that to let somebody take away your job?

CORY: I'm still gonna be working weekends.

TROY: Naw . . . naw. You getting your butt out of here and finding you another job.

CORY: Come on, Pop! I got to practice. I can't work after school and play football too. The team needs me. That's what Coach Zellman say . . .

---

5. Brooklyn, later Los Angeles, Dodgers pitcher (b. 1935), the first player ever to win three Cy Young awards, and the youngest ever elected to Baseball's Hall of Fame.

6. Like 1957 Cy Young Award winner Warren Spahn (1921–2003), a pitcher for the Boston, later Milwaukee, Braves (1926–2007). Burdette was MVP of the 1957 World Series, the only World Series the Milwaukee Braves ever won and the first, since 1948, won by any non–New York team.

TROY: I don't care what nobody else say. I'm the boss . . . you understand? I'm the boss around here. I do the only saying what counts.

CORY: Come on, Pop!

TROY: I asked you . . . did you understand?

CORY: Yeah . . .

TROY: What!?!

CORY: Yessir.

TROY: You go on down there to that A&P and see if you can get your job back. If you can't do both . . . then you quit the football team. You've got to take the crookeds with the straights.

CORY: Yessir. (*Pause*) Can I ask you a question?

TROY: What the hell you wanna ask me? Mr. Stawicki the one you got the questions for.

CORY: How come you ain't never liked me?

TROY: Liked you? Who the hell say I got to like you? What law is there say I got to like you? Wanna stand up in my face and ask a damn fool-ass question like that. Talking about liking somebody. Come here, boy, when I talk to you.

(*Cory comes over to where Troy is working. He stands slouched over and Troy shoves him on his shoulder.*)

Straighten up, goddamn it! I asked you a question . . . what law is there say I got to like you?

CORY: None.

TROY: Well, all right then! Don't you eat every day? (*Pause*) Answer me when I talk to you! Don't you eat every day?

CORY: Yeah.

TROY: Nigger, as long as you in my house, you put that sir on the end of it when you talk to me!

CORY: Yes . . . sir.

TROY: You eat every day.

CORY: Yessir!

TROY: Got a roof over your head.

CORY: Yessir!

TROY: Got clothes on your back.

CORY: Yessir.

TROY: Why you think that is?

CORY: 'Cause of you.

TROY: Aw, hell, I know it's 'cause of me . . . but why do you think that is?

CORY (*Hesitant*): 'Cause you like me.

TROY: Like you? I go out of here every morning . . . bust my butt . . . putting up with them crackers every day . . .'cause I like you? You about the biggest fool I ever saw. (*Pause*) It's my job. It's my responsibility! You understand that? A man got to take care of his family. You live in my house . . . sleep you behind on my bedclothes . . . fill you belly up with my food . . .'cause you my son. You my flesh and blood. Not 'cause I like you! 'Cause it's my duty to take care of you. I owe a responsibility to you!

Let's get this straight right here . . . before it go along any further . . . I ain't got to like you. Mr. Rand don't give me my money come payday 'cause he likes me. He gives me 'cause he owe me. I done give you everything I had to give. I gave you your life! Me and your mama worked that out between us. And liking your black ass wasn't part of the bargain. Don't you try and go through life worrying about if somebody like you or not. You best be making sure they doing right by you. You understand what I'm saying, boy?

CORY: Yessir.

TROY: Then get the hell out of my face, and get on down to that A&P.

(*Rose has been standing behind the screen door for much of the scene. She enters as Cory exits.*)

ROSE: Why don't you let the boy go ahead and play football, Troy? Ain't no harm in that. He's just trying to be like you with the sports.

TROY: I don't want him to be like me! I want him to move as far away from my life as he can get. You the only decent thing that ever happened to me. I wish him that. But I don't wish him a thing else from my life. I decided seventeen years ago that boy wasn't getting involved in no sports. Not after what they did to me in the sports.

ROSE: Troy, why don't you admit you was too old to play in the major leagues? For once . . . why don't you admit that?

TROY: What do you mean too old? Don't come telling me I was too old. I just wasn't the right color. Hell, I'm fifty-three years old and can do better than Selkirk's .269 right now!

ROSE: How's was you gonna play ball when you were over forty? Sometimes I can't get no sense out of you.

TROY: I got good sense, woman. I got sense enough not to let my boy get hurt over playing no sports. You been mothering that boy too much. Worried about if people like him.

ROSE: Everything that boy do . . . he do for you. He wants you to say, "Good job, son." That's all.

TROY: Rose, I ain't got time for that. He's alive. He's healthy. He's got to make his own way. I made mine. Ain't nobody gonna hold his hand when he get out there in that world.

ROSE: Times have changed from when you was young, Troy. People change. The world's changing around you and you can't even see it.

TROY (*Slow, methodical*): Woman . . . I do the best I can do. I come in here every Friday. I carry a sack of potatoes and a bucket of lard. You all line up at the door with your hands out. I give you the lint from my pockets. I give you my sweat and my blood. I ain't got no tears. I done spent them. We go upstairs in that room at night . . . and I fall down on you and try to blast a hole into forever. I get up Monday morning . . . find my lunch on the table. I go out. Make my way. Find my strength to carry me through to the next Friday. (*Pause*) That's all I got, Rose. That's all I got to give. I can't give nothing else.

(*Troy exits into the house. The lights fade to black.*)

Scene 4

It is Friday. Two weeks later. Cory starts out of the house with his football equipment. The phone rings.

CORY (*Calling*): I got it! (*Answers the phone, stands in the screen door talking*) Hello? Hey, Jesse. Naw . . . I was just getting ready to leave now.

ROSE (*Calling*): Cory!

CORY: I told you, man, them spikes is all tore up. You can use them if you want, but they ain't no good. Earl got some spikes.

ROSE (*Calling*): Cory!

CORY (*Calling to Rose*): Mam? I'm talking to Jesse. (*Into phone*) When she say that? (*Pause*) Aw, you lying, man. I'm gonna tell her you said that.

ROSE (*Calling*): Cory, don't you go nowhere!

CORY: I got to go to the game, Ma! (*Into the phone*) Yeah, hey, look, I'll talk to you later. Yeah, I'll meet you over Earl's house. Later. Bye, Ma.

(*Cory exits the house and starts out the yard.*)

ROSE: Cory, where you going off to? You got that stuff all pulled out and thrown all over your room.

CORY (*In the yard*): I was looking for my spikes. Jesse wanted to borrow my spikes.

ROSE: Get up there and get that cleaned up before your daddy get back in here.

CORY: I got to go to the game! I'll clean it up *when I get back.*

(*He exits.*)

ROSE: That's all he need to do is see that room all messed up.

(*Rose exits into the house. Troy and Bono enter the yard with a bottle. Troy is dressed in clothes other than his work clothes.*)

BONO: He told him the same thing he told you. Take it to the union.

TROY: Brownie ain't got that much sense. Man wasn't thinking about nothing. He wait until I confront them on it . . . then he wanna come crying seniority. (*Calls*) Hey, Rose!

BONO: I wish I could have seen Mr. Rand's face when he told you.

TROY: He couldn't get it out of his mouth! Liked to bit his tongue! When they called me down there to the commissioner's office . . . he thought they was gonna fire me. Like everybody else.

BONO: I didn't think they was gonna fire you. I thought they was gonna put you on the warning paper.

TROY: Hey, Rose! (*To Bono*) Yeah, Mr. Rand like to bit his tongue.

(*Troy breaks the seal on the bottle, takes a drink, and hands it to Bono.*)

BONO: I see you run right down to Taylors' and told that Alberta gal.

TROY (*Calling*): Hey, Rose! (*To Bono*) I told everybody. Hey, Rose! I went down there to cash my check.

ROSE (*Entering from the house*): Hush all that hollering, man! I know you out here. What they say down there at the commissioner's office?

TROY: You supposed to come when I call you, woman. Bono'll tell you that. (*To Bono*) Don't Lucille come when you call her?

ROSE: Man, hush your mouth. I ain't no dog . . . talk about "come when you call me."

TROY (*Puts his arm around Rose*): You hear this, Bono? I had me an old dog used to get uppity like that. You say, "C'mere, Blue!" . . . and he just lay there and look at you. End up getting a stick and chasing him away trying to make him come.

ROSE: I ain't studying you and your dog. I remember you used to sing that old song.

TROY (*Singing*):
Hear it ring! Hear it ring!
I had a dog his name was Blue.

ROSE: Don't nobody wanna hear you sing that old song.

TROY (*Singing*):
You know Blue was mighty true.

ROSE: Used to have Cory running around here singing that song.

BONO: Hell, I remember that song myself.

TROY (*Singing*):
You know Blue was a good old dog.
Blue treed a possum in a hollow log.

That was my daddy's song. My daddy made up that song.

ROSE: I don't care who made it up. Don't nobody wanna hear you sing it.

TROY (*Makes a song like calling a dog*): Come here, woman.

ROSE: You come in here carrying on, I reckon they ain't fired you. What they say down there at the commissioner's office?

TROY: Look here, Rose . . . Mr. Rand called me into his office today when I got back from talking to them people down there . . . it come from up top . . . he called me in and told me they was making me a driver.

ROSE: Troy, you kidding!

TROY: No I ain't. Ask Bono.

ROSE: Well, that's great, Troy. Now you don't have to hassle them people no more.

(*Lyons enters from the street.*)

TROY: Aw hell, I wasn't looking to see you today. I thought you was in jail. Got it all over the front page of the *Courier* about them raiding Seefus' place . . . where you be hanging out with all them thugs.

LYONS: Hey, Pop . . . that ain't got nothing to do with me. I don't go down there gambling. I go down there to sit in with the band. I ain't got nothing to do with the gambling part. They got some good music down there.

TROY: They got some rogues . . . is what they got.

LYONS: How you been, Mr. Bono? Hi, Rose.

BONO: I see where you playing down at the Crawford Grill tonight.

ROSE: How come you ain't brought Bonnie like I told you. You should have brought Bonnie with you, she ain't been over in a month of Sundays.

LYONS: I was just in the neighborhood . . . thought I'd stop by.

TROY: Here he come . . .

BONO: Your daddy got a promotion on the rubbish. He's gonna be the first colored driver. Ain't got to do nothing but sit up there and read the paper like them white fellows.

LYONS: Hey, Pop . . . if you knew how to read you'd be all right.

BONO: Naw . . . naw . . . you mean if the nigger knew how to *drive* he'd be all right. Been fighting with them people about driving and ain't even got a license. Mr. Rand know you ain't got no driver's license?

TROY: Driving ain't nothing. All you do is point the truck where you want it to go. Driving ain't nothing.

BONO: Do Mr. Rand know you ain't got no driver's license? That's what I'm talking about. I ain't asked if driving was easy. I asked if Mr. Rand know you ain't got no driver's license.

TROY: He ain't got to know. The man ain't got to know my business. Time he find out, I have two or three driver's licenses.

LYONS (*Going into his pocket*): Say, look here, Pop . . .

TROY: I knew it was coming. Didn't I tell you, Bono? I know what kind of "look here, Pop" that was. The nigger fixing to ask me for some money. It's Friday night. It's my payday. All them rogues down there on the avenue . . . the ones that ain't in jail . . . and Lyons is hopping in his shoes to get down there with them.

LYONS: See, Pop . . . if you'd give somebody else a chance to talk sometime, you'd see that I was fixing to pay you back your ten dollars like I told you. Here . . . I told you I'd pay you when Bonnie got paid.

TROY: Naw . . . you go ahead and keep that ten dollars. Put it in the bank. The next time you feel like you wanna come by here and ask me for something . . . you go on down there and get that.

LYONS: Here's your ten dollars, Pop. I told you I don't want you to give me nothing. I just wanted to borrow ten dollars.

TROY: Naw . . . you go on and keep that for the next time you want to ask me.

LYONS: Come on, Pop . . . here go your ten dollars.

ROSE: Why don't you go on and let the boy pay you back, Troy?

LYONS: Here you go, Rose. If you don't take it I'm gonna have to hear about it for the next six months. (*Hands her the money*)

ROSE: You can hand yours over here too, Troy.

TROY: You see this, Bono. You see how they do me.

BONO: Yeah, Lucille do me the same way.

(*Gabriel is heard singing offstage. He enters.*)

GABRIEL: Better get ready for the Judgment! Better get ready for . . . Hey! . . . Hey! There's Troy's boy!

LYONS: How you doing, Uncle Gabe?

GABRIEL: Lyons . . . The King of the Jungle! Rose . . . hey, Rose. Got a flower for you. (*Takes a rose from his pocket*) Picked it myself. That's the same rose like you is!

ROSE: That's right nice of you, Gabe.

LYONS: What you been doing, Uncle Gabe?

GABRIEL: Oh, I been chasing hellhounds and waiting on the time to tell Saint Peter to open the Gates.

LYONS: You been chasing hellhounds, huh? Well . . . you doing the right thing, Uncle Gabe. Somebody got to chase them.

GABRIEL: Oh, yeah . . . I know it. The devil's strong. The devil ain't no pushover. Hellhounds snipping at everybody's heels. But I got my trumpet waiting on the Judgment time.

LYONS: Waiting on the Battle of Armageddon,[7] huh?

GABRIEL: Ain't gonna be too much of a battle when God get to waving that Judgment sword. But the people's gonna have a hell of a time trying to get into Heaven if them Gates ain't open.

LYONS (*Putting his arm around Gabriel*): You hear this, Pop. Uncle Gabe, you all right!

GABRIEL (*Laughing with Lyons*): Lyons! King of the Jungle.

ROSE: You gonna stay for supper, Gabe. Want me to fix you a plate?

GABRIEL: I'll just take a sandwich, Rose. Don't want no plate. Just wanna eat with my hands. I'll take a sandwich.

ROSE: How about you, Lyons? You staying? Got some short ribs cooking.

LYONS: Naw, I won't eat nothing till after we finished playing. (*Pause*) You ought to come down and listen to me play, Pop.

TROY: I don't like that Chinese music. All that noise.

ROSE: Go on in the house and wash up, Gabe . . . I'll fix you a sandwich.

GABRIEL (*As he exits, to Lyons*): Troy's mad at me.

LYONS: What you mad at Uncle Gabe for, Pop.

ROSE: He thinks Troy's mad at him 'cause he moved over to Miss Pearl's.

TROY: I ain't mad at the man. He can live where he want to live at.

LYONS: What he move over there for? Miss Pearl don't like nobody.

ROSE: She don't mind him none. She treats him real nice. She just don't allow all that singing.

TROY: She don't mind that rent he be paying . . . that's what she don't mind.

ROSE: Troy, I ain't going through that with you no more. He's over there 'cause he want to have his own place. He can come and go as he please.

TROY: Hell, he could come and go as he please here. I wasn't stopping him. I ain't put no rules on him.

ROSE: It ain't the same thing, Troy. And you know it.

(*Gabriel comes to the screen door.*)

Now, that's the last I wanna hear about that. I don't wanna hear nothing else about Gabe and Miss Pearl. And next week . . .

GABRIEL: I'm ready for my sandwich, Rose.

ROSE: And next week . . . when that recruiter come from that school . . . I want you to sign that paper and go on and let Cory play football. Then that'll be the last I have to hear about that.

TROY (*To Rose as she exits into the house*): I ain't thinking about Cory nothing.

LYONS: What . . . Cory got recruited? What school he going to?

TROY: That boy walking around here smelling his piss . . . thinking he's grown. Thinking he's gonna do what he want, irrespective of what I say. Look here, Bono . . . I left the commissioner's office and went down to the A&P . . . that

---

7. In Christian tradition, the final, history-ending battle between the armies of good and evil.

boy ain't working down there. He lying to me. Telling me he got his job back . . . telling me he working weekends . . . telling me he working after school . . . Mr. Stawicki tell me he ain't working down there at all!

LYONS: Cory just growing up. He's just busting at the seams trying to fill out your shoes.

TROY: I don't care what he's doing. When he get to the point where he wanna disobey me . . . then it's time for him to move on. Bono'll tell you that I bet he ain't never disobeyed his daddy without paying the consequences.

BONO: I ain't never had a chance. My daddy came on through . . . but I ain't never knew him to see him . . . or what he had on his mind or where he went. Just moving on through. Searching out the New Land. That's what the old folks used to call it. See a fellow moving around from place to place . . . woman to woman . . . called it Searching out the New Land. I can't say if he ever found it. I come along, didn't want no kids. Didn't know if I was gonna be in one place long enough to fix on them right as their daddy. I figured I was going searching too. As it turned out I been hooked up with Lucille near about as long as your daddy been with Rose. Going on sixteen years.

TROY: Sometimes I wish I hadn't known my daddy. He ain't cared nothing about no kids. A kid to him wasn't nothing. All he wanted was for you to learn how to walk so he could start you to working. When it come time for eating . . . he ate first. If there was anything left over, that's what you got. Man would sit down and eat two chickens and give you the wing.

LYONS: You ought to stop that, Pop. Everybody feed their kids. No matter how hard times is . . . everybody care about their kids. Make sure they have something to eat.

TROY: The only thing my daddy cared about was getting them bales of cotton in to Mr. Lubin. That's the only thing that mattered to him. Sometimes I used to wonder why he was living. Wonder why the devil hadn't come and got him. "Get them bales of cotton in to Mr. Lubin" and find out he owe him money . . . .

LYONS: He should have just went on and left when he saw he couldn't get nowhere. That's what I would have done.

TROY: How he gonna leave with eleven kids? And where he gonna go? He ain't knew how to do nothing but farm. No, he was trapped and I think he knew it. But I'll say this for him . . . he felt a responsibility toward us. Maybe he ain't treated us the way I felt he should have . . . but without that responsibility he could have walked off and left us . . . made his own way.

BONO: A lot of them did. Back in those days what you talking about . . . . they walk out their front door and just take on down one road or another and keep on walking.

LYONS: There you go! That's what I'm talking about.

BONO: Just keep on walking till you come to something else. Ain't you never heard of nobody having the walking blues? Well, that's what you call it when you just take off like that.

TROY: My daddy ain't had them walking blues! What you talking about? He stayed right there with his family. But he was just as evil as he could be. My mama couldn't stand him. Couldn't stand that evilness. She run off when I was about eight. She sneaked off one night after he had gone to sleep. Told me she was coming back for me. I ain't never seen her no more. All his women run off and left him. He wasn't good for nobody.

When my turn come to head out, I was fourteen and got to sniffing around Joe Canewell's daughter. Had us an old mule we called Greyboy. My daddy sent me out to do some plowing and I tied up Greyboy and went to fooling around with Joe Canewell's daughter. We done found us a nice spot, got real cozy with each other. She about thirteen and we done figured we was grown anyway . . . so we down there enjoying ourselves . . . ain't thinking about nothing. We didn't know Greyboy had got loose and wandered back to the house and my daddy was looking for me. We down there by the creek enjoying ourselves when my daddy come up on us. Surprised us. He had them leather straps off the mule and commenced to whupping me like there was no tomorrow. I jumped up, mad and embarrassed. I was scared of my daddy. When he commenced to whupping on me . . . quite naturally I run to get out of the way. (*Pause*) Now I thought he was mad 'cause I ain't done my work. But I see where he was chasing me off so he could have the gal for himself. When I see what the matter of it was, I lost all fear of my daddy. Right there is where I become a man . . . at fourteen years of age. (*Pause*) Now it was my turn to run him off. I picked up them same reins that he had used on me. I picked up them reins and commenced to whupping on him. The gal jumped up and run off . . . and when my daddy turned to face me, I could see why the devil had never come to get him . . .'cause he was the devil himself. I don't know what happened. When I woke up, I was laying right there by the creek, and Blue . . . this old dog we had . . . was licking my face. I thought I was blind. I couldn't see nothing. Both my eyes were swollen shut. I laid there and cried. I didn't know what I was gonna do. The only thing I knew was the time had come for me to leave my daddy's house. And right there the world suddenly got big. And it was a long time before I could cut it down to where I could handle it.

Part of that cutting down was when I got to the place where I could feel him kicking in my blood and knew that the only thing that separated us was the matter of a few years.

(*Gabriel enters from the house with a sandwich.*)

LYONS: What you got there, Uncle Gabe?

GABRIEL: Got me a ham sandwich. Rose gave me a ham sandwich.

TROY: I don't know what happened to him. I done lost touch with everybody except Gabriel. But I hope he's dead. I hope he found some peace.

LYONS: That's a heavy story, Pop. I didn't know you left home when you was fourteen.

TROY: And didn't know nothing. The only part of the world I knew was the forty-two acres of Mr. Lubin's land. That's all I knew about life.

LYONS: Fourteen's kinda young to be out on your own. (*Phone rings*) I don't even think I was ready to be out on my own at fourteen. I don't know what I would have done.

TROY: I got up from the creek and walked on down to Mobile.[8] I was through with farming. Figured I could do better in the city. So I walked the two hundred miles to Mobile.

---

8. City in southwest Alabama, on the Gulf Coast near the Florida state line.

LYONS: Wait a minute . . . you ain't walked no two hundred miles, Pop. Ain't nobody gonna walk no two hundred miles. You talking about some walking there.

BONO: That's the only way you got anywhere back in them days.

LYONS: Shhh. Damn if I wouldn't have hitched a ride with somebody!

TROY: Who you gonna hitch it with? They ain't had no cars and things like they got now. We talking about 1918.

ROSE (*Entering*): What you all out here getting into?

TROY (*To Rose*): I'm telling Lyons how good he got it. He don't know nothing about this I'm talking.

ROSE: Lyons, that was Bonnie on the phone. She say you supposed to pick her up.

LYONS: Yeah, okay, Rose.

TROY: I walked on down to Mobile and hitched up with some of them fellows that was heading this way. Got up here and found out . . . not only couldn't you get a job . . . you couldn't find no place to live. I thought I was in freedom. Shhh. Colored folks living down there on the riverbanks in whatever kind of shelter they could find for themselves. Right down there under the Brady Street Bridge. Living in shacks made of sticks and tarpaper. Messed around there and went from bad to worse. Started stealing. First it was food. Then I figured, hell, if I steal money I can buy me some food. Buy me some shoes too! One thing led to another. Met your mama. I was young and anxious to be a man. Met your mama and had you. What I do that for? Now I got to worry about feeding you and her. Got to steal three times as much. Went out one day looking for somebody to rob . . . that's what I was, a robber. I'll tell you the truth. I'm ashamed of it today. But it's the truth. Went to rob this fellow . . . pulled out my knife . . . and he pulled out a gun. Shot me in the chest. It felt just like somebody had taken a hot branding iron and laid it on me. When he shot me I jumped at him with my knife. They told me I killed him and they put me in the penitentiary and locked me up for fifteen years. That's where I met Bono. That's where I learned how to play baseball. Got out that place and your mama had taken you and went on to make life without me. Fifteen years was a long time for her to wait. But that fifteen years cured me of that robbing stuff. Rose'll tell you. She asked me when I met her if I had gotten all that foolishness out of my system. And I told her, "Baby, it's you and baseball all what count with me." You hear me, Bono? I meant it too. She say, "Which one comes first?" I told her, "Baby, ain't no doubt it's baseball . . . but you stick and get old with me and we'll both outlive this baseball." Am I right, Rose? And it's true.

ROSE: Man, hush your mouth. You ain't said no such thing. Talking about, "Baby, you know you'll always be number one with me." That's what you was talking.

TROY: You hear that, Bono. That's why I love her.

BONO: Rose'll keep you straight. You get off the track, she'll straighten you up.

ROSE: Lyons, you better get on up and get Bonnie. She waiting on you.

LYONS (*Gets up to go*): Hey, Pop, why don't you come on down to the Grill and hear me play?

TROY: I ain't going down there. I'm too old to be sitting around in them clubs.

BONO: You got to be good to play down at the Grill.

LYONS: Come on, Pop . . .

TROY: I got to get up in the morning.

LYONS: You ain't got to stay long.

TROY: Naw, I'm gonna get my supper and go on to bed.

LYONS: Well, I got to go. I'll see you again.

TROY: Don't you come around my house on my payday.

ROSE: Pick up the phone and let somebody know you coming. And bring Bonnie with you. You know I'm always glad to see her.

LYONS: Yeah, I'll do that, Rose. You take care now. See you, Pop. See you, Mr. Bono. See you, Uncle Gabe.

GABRIEL: Lyons! King of the Jungle!

(*Lyons exits.*)

TROY: Is supper ready, woman? Me and you got some business to take care of. I'm gonna tear it up too.

ROSE: Troy, I done told you now!

TROY (*Puts his arm around Bono*): Aw hell, woman . . . this is Bono. Bono like family. I done known this nigger since . . . how long I done know you?

BONO: It's been a long time.

TROY: I done known this nigger since Skippy was a pup. Me and him done been through some times.

BONO: You sure right about that.

TROY: Hell, I done know him longer than I known you. And we still standing shoulder to shoulder. Hey, look here, Bono . . . a man can't ask for no more than that. (*Drinks to him*) I love you, nigger.

BONO: Hell, I love you too . . . but I got to get home see my woman. You got yours in hand. I got to go get mine.

(*Bono starts to exit as Cory enters the yard, dressed in his football uniform. He gives Troy a hard, uncompromising look.*)

CORY: What you do that for, Pop? (*Throws his helmet down in the direction of Troy*)

ROSE: What's the matter? Cory . . . what's the matter?

CORY: Papa done went up to the school and told Coach Zellman I can't play football no more. Wouldn't even let me play the game. Told him to tell the recruiter not to come.

ROSE: Troy . . .

TROY: What you Troying me for. Yeah, I did it. And the boy know why I did it.

CORY: Why you wanna do that to me? That was the one chance I had.

ROSE: Ain't nothing wrong with Cory playing football, Troy.

TROY: The boy lied to me. I told the nigger if he wanna play football . . . to keep up his chores and hold down that job at the A&P. That was the conditions. Stopped down there to see Mr. Stawicki . . .

CORY: I can't work after school during the football season, Pop! I tried to tell you that Mr. Stawicki's holding my job for me. You don't never want to listen to nobody. And then you wanna go and do this to me!

TROY: I ain't done nothing to you. You done it to yourself.

CORY: Just 'cause you didn't have a chance! You just scared I'm gonna be better than you, that's all.

TROY: Come here.

ROSE: Troy . . .

(*Cory reluctantly crosses over to Troy.*)

TROY: All right! See. You done made a mistake.

CORY: I didn't even do nothing!

TROY: I'm gonna tell you what your mistake was. See . . . you swung at the ball and didn't hit it. That's strike one. See, you in the batter's box now. You swung and you missed. That's strike one. Don't you strike out!

(*The lights go down on the scene.*)

ACT TWO

Scene 1

The following morning. Cory is at the tree hitting the ball with the bat. He tries to mimic Troy, but his swing is awkward, less sure. Rose enters from the house.

ROSE: Cory, I want you to help me with this cupboard.

CORY: I ain't quitting the team. I don't care what Poppa say.

ROSE: I'll talk to him when he gets back. He had to go see about your Uncle Gabe. The police done arrested him. Say he was disturbing the peace. He'll be back directly. Come on in here and help me clean out the top of this cupboard.

(*Cory exits into the house. Rose sees Troy and Bono coming down the alley.*)

Troy . . . what they say down there?

TROY: Ain't said nothing. I give them fifty dollars and they let him go. I'll talk to you about it. Where's Cory?

ROSE: He's in there helping me clean out these cupboards.

TROY: Tell him to get his butt out here.

(*Troy and Bono go over to the pile of wood. Bono picks up the saw and begins sawing.*)

(*To Bono*) All they want is the money. That makes six or seven times I done went down there and got him. See me coming they stick out their *hands*.

BONO: Yeah, I know what you mean. That's all they care about . . . that money. They don't care about what's right. (*Pause*) Nigger, why you got to go and get some hard wood? You ain't doing nothing but building a little old fence. Get you some soft pine wood. That's all you need.

TROY: I know what I'm doing. This is outside wood. You put pine wood inside the house. Pine wood is inside wood. This here is outside wood. Now you tell me where the fence is gonna be?

BONO: You don't need this wood. You can put it up with pine wood and it'll stand as long as you gonna be here looking at it.

TROY: How you know how long I'm gonna be here, nigger? Hell, I might just live forever. Live longer than old man Horsely.

BONO: That's what Magee used to say.

TROY: Magee's a damn fool. Now you tell me who you ever heard of gonna pull their own teeth with a pair of rusty pliers.

BONO: The old folks . . . my granddaddy used to pull his teeth with pliers. They ain't had no dentists for the colored folks back then.

TROY: Get clean pliers! You understand? Clean pliers! Sterilize them! Besides we ain't living back then. All Magee had to do was walk over to Doc Goldblum's.

BONO: I see where you and that Tallahassee gal . . . that Alberta . . . I see where you all done got tight.

TROY: What you mean "got tight"?

BONO: I see where you be laughing and joking with her all the time.

TROY: I laughs and jokes with all of them, Bono. You know me.

BONO: That ain't the kind of laughing and joking I'm talking about.

(Cory enters from the house.)

CORY: How you doing, Mr. Bono?

TROY: Cory? Get that saw from Bono and cut some wood. He talking about the wood's too hard to cut. Stand back there, Jim, and let that young boy show you how it's done.

BONO: He's sure welcome to it.

(Cory takes the saw and begins to cut the wood.)

Whew-e-e! Look at that. Big old strong boy. Look like Joe Louis.[9] Hell, must be getting old the way I'm watching that boy whip through that wood.

CORY: I don't see why Mama want a fence around the yard noways.

TROY: Damn if I know either. What the hell she keeping out with it? She ain't got nothing nobody want.

BONO: Some people build fences to keep people out . . . and other people build fences to keep people in. Rose wants to hold on to you all. She loves you.

TROY: Hell, nigger, I don't need nobody to tell me my wife loves me, Cory . . . go on in the house and see if you can find that other saw.

CORY: Where's it at?

TROY: I said find it! Look for it till you find it!

(Cory exits into the house.)

What's that supposed to mean? Wanna keep us in?

BONO: Troy . . . I done known you seem like damn near my whole life. You and Rose both. I done know both of you all for a long time. I remember when you met Rose. When you was hitting them baseball out the park. A lot of them old gals was after you then. You had the pick of the litter. When you picked Rose, I was happy for you. That was the first time I knew you had any sense. I said . . . My man Troy knows what he's doing . . . I'm gonna follow this nigger . . . he might take me somewhere. I been following you too. I done learned a whole heap of things about life watching you. I done learned how to tell where the shit lies. How to tell it from the alfalfa. You done learned me a lot of things. You showed me how to not make the same mistakes . . . to

9. Alabama-born boxer (1914–81) known as the "Brown Bomber," world heavyweight champion 1937–49.

take life as it comes along and keep putting one foot in front of the other. (*Pause*) Rose a good woman, Troy.

TROY: Hell, nigger, I know she a good woman. I been married to her for eighteen years. What you got on your mind, Bono?

BONO: I just say she a good woman. Just like I say anything. I ain't got to have nothing on my mind.

TROY: You just gonna say she a good woman and leave it hanging out there like that? Why you telling me she a good woman?

BONO: She loves you, Troy. Rose loves you.

TROY: You saying I don't measure up. That's what you trying to say. I don't measure up 'cause I'm seeing this other gal. I know what you trying to say.

BONO: I know what Rose means to you, Troy. I'm just trying to say I don't want to see you mess up.

TROY: Yeah, I appreciate that, Bono. If you was messing around on Lucille I'd be telling you the same thing.

BONO: Well, that's all I got to say. I just say that because I love you both.

TROY: Hell, you know me . . . I wasn't out there looking for nothing. You can't find a better woman than Rose. I know that. But seems like this woman just stuck on to me where I can't shake her loose. I done wrestled with it, tried to throw her off me . . . but she just stuck on tighter. Now she's stuck on for good.

BONO: You's in control . . . that's what you tell me all the time. You responsible for what you do.

TROY: I ain't ducking the responsibility of it. As long as it sets right in my heart . . . then I'm okay. 'Cause that's all I listen to. It'll tell me right from wrong every time. And I ain't talking about doing Rose no bad turn. I love Rose. She done carried me a long ways and I love and respect her for that.

BONO: I know you do. That's why I don't want to see you hurt her. But what you gonna do when she find out? What you got then? If you try and juggle both of them . . . sooner or later you gonna drop one of them. That's common sense.

TROY: Yeah, I hear what you saying, Bono. I been trying to figure a way to work it out.

BONO: Work it out right, Troy. I don't want to be getting all up between you and Rose's business . . . but work it so it come out right.

TROY: Aw hell, I get all up between you and Lucille's business. When you gonna get that woman that refrigerator she been wanting? Don't tell me you ain't got no money now. I know who your banker is. Mellon don't need that money bad as Lucille want that refrigerator. I'll tell you that.

BONO: Tell you what I'll do . . . when you finish building this fence for Rose . . . I'll buy Lucille that refrigerator.

TROY: You done stuck your foot in your mouth now!

(*Troy grabs up a board and begins to saw. Bono starts to walk out the yard.*)

Hey, nigger . . . where you going?

BONO: I'm going home. I know you don't expect me to help you now. I'm protecting my money. I wanna see you put up that fence by yourself. That's what I want to see. You'll be here another six months without me.

TROY: Nigger, you ain't right.

BONO: When it comes to my money . . . I'm as right as fireworks on the Fourth of July.

TROY: All right, we gonna see now. You better get out your bankbook.

(*Bono exits, and Troy continues to work. Rose enters from the house.*)

ROSE: What they say down there? What's happening with Gabe?

TROY: I went down there and got him out. Cost me fifty dollars. Say he was disturbing the peace. Judge set up a hearing for him in three weeks. Say to show cause why he shouldn't be recommitted.

ROSE: What was he doing that cause them to arrest him?

TROY: Some kids was teasing him and he run them off home. Say he was howling and carrying on. Some folks seen him and called the police. That's all it was.

ROSE: Well, what's you say? What'd you tell the judge?

TROY: Told him I'd look after him. It didn't make no sense to recommit the man. He stuck out his big greasy palm and told me to give him fifty dollars and take him on home.

ROSE: Where's he at now? Where'd he go off to?

TROY: He's gone on about his business. He don't need nobody to hold his hand.

ROSE: Well, I don't know. Seem like that would be the best place for him if they did put him into the hospital. I know what you're gonna say. But that's what I think would be best.

TROY: The man done had his life ruined fighting for what? And they wanna take and lock him up. Let him be free. He don't bother nobody.

ROSE: Well, everybody got their own way of looking at it I guess. Come on and get your lunch. I got a bowl of lima beans and some cornbread in the oven. Come on get something to eat. Ain't no sense you fretting over Gabe. (*Turns to go in the house*)

TROY: Rose . . . got something to tell you.

ROSE: Well, come on . . . wait till I get this food on the table.

TROY: Rose!

(*She stops and turns around.*)

I don't know how to say this. (*Pause*) I can't explain it none. It just sort of grows on you till it gets out of hand. It starts out like a little bush . . . and the next thing you know it's a whole forest.

ROSE: Troy . . . what is you talking about?

TROY: I'm talking, woman, let me talk. I'm trying to find a way to tell you . . . I'm gonna be a daddy. I'm gonna be somebody's daddy.

ROSE: Troy . . . you're not telling me this? You're gonna be . . . what?

TROY: Rose . . . now . . . see . . .

ROSE: You telling me you gonna be somebody's daddy? You telling your *wife* this?

(*Gabriel enters from the street. He carries a rose in his hand.*)

GABRIEL: Hey, Troy! Hey, Rose!

ROSE: I have to wait eighteen years to hear something like this.

GABRIEL: Hey, Rose . . . I got a flower for you. (*Hands it to her*) That's a rose. Same rose like you is.

ROSE: Thanks, Gabe.

GABRIEL: Troy, you ain't mad at me is you? Them bad mens come and put me away. You ain't mad at me is you?

TROY: Naw, Gabe, I ain't mad at you.

ROSE: Eighteen years and you wanna come with this.

GABRIEL (*Takes a quarter out of his pocket*): See what I got? Got a brand-new quarter.

TROY: Rose . . . it's just . . .

ROSE: Ain't nothing you can say, Troy. Ain't no way of explaining that.

GABRIEL: Fellow that give me this quarter had a whole mess of them. I'm gonna keep this quarter till it stop shining.

ROSE: Gabe, go on in the house there. I got some watermelon in the frigidaire. Go on and get you a piece.

GABRIEL: Say, Rose . . . you know I was chasing hellhounds and them bad mens come and get me and take me away. Troy helped me. He come down there and told them they better let me go before he beat them up. Yeah, he did!

ROSE: You go on and get you a piece of watermelon, Gabe. Them bad mens is gone now.

GABRIEL: Okay, Rose . . . gonna get me some watermelon. The kind with the stripes on it.

(*Gabriel exits into the house.*)

ROSE: Why, Troy? Why? After all these years to come dragging this in to me now. It don't make no sense at your age. I could have expected this ten or fifteen years ago, but not now.

TROY: Age ain't got nothing to do with it, Rose.

ROSE: I done tried to be everything a wife should be. Everything a wife could be. Been married eighteen years and I got to live to see the day you tell me you been seeing another woman and done fathered a child by her. And you know I ain't never wanted no half nothing in my family. My whole family is half. Everybody got different fathers and mothers . . . my two sisters and my brother. Can't hardly tell who's who. Can't never sit down and talk about Papa and Mama. It's your papa and your mama and my papa and my mama . . .

TROY: Rose . . . stop it now.

ROSE: I ain't never wanted that for none of my children. And now you wanna drag your behind in here and tell me something like this.

TROY: You ought to know. It's time for you to know.

ROSE: Well, I don't want to know, goddamn it!

TROY: I can't just make it go away. It's done now. I can't wish the circumstance of the thing away.

ROSE: And you don't want to either. Maybe you want to wish me and my boy away. Maybe that's what you want? Well, you can't wish us away. I've got eighteen years of my life invested in you. You ought to have stayed upstairs in my bed where you belong.

TROY: Rose . . . now listen to me . . . we can get a handle on this thing. We can talk this out . . . come to an understanding.

ROSE: All of a sudden it's "we." Where was "we" at when you was down there rolling around with some godforsaken woman? "We" should have come to an understanding before you started making a damn fool of yourself. You're a day late and a dollar short when it comes to an understanding with me.

TROY: It's just . . . She gives me a different idea . . . a different understanding about myself. I can step out of this house and get away from the pressures and problems . . . be a different man. I ain't got to wonder how I'm gonna pay the bills or get the roof fixed. I can just be a part of myself that I ain't never been.

ROSE: What I want to know . . . is do you plan to continue seeing her. That's all you can say to me.

TROY: I can sit up in her house and laugh. Do you understand what I'm saying. I can laugh out loud . . . and it feels good. It reaches all the way down to the bottom of my shoes. (*Pause*) Rose, I can't give that up.

ROSE: Maybe you ought to go on and stay down there with her . . . if she a better woman than me.

TROY: It ain't about nobody being a better woman or nothing. Rose, you ain't to blame. A man couldn't ask for no woman to be a better wife than you've been. I'm responsible for it. I done locked myself into a pattern trying to take care of you all that I forgot about myself.

ROSE: What the hell was I there for? That was my job, not somebody else's.

TROY: Rose, I done tried all my life to live decent . . . to live a clean . . . hard . . . useful life. I tried to be a good husband to you. In every way I knew how. Maybe I come into the world backwards, I don't know. But . . . you born with two strikes on you before you come to the plate. You got to guard it closely . . . always looking for the curveball on the inside corner. You can't afford to let none get past you. You can't afford a call strike. If you going down . . . you going down swinging. Everything lined up against you. What you gonna do. I fooled them, Rose. I bunted. When I found you and Cory and a halfway decent job . . . I was safe. Couldn't nothing touch me. I wasn't gonna strike out no more. I wasn't going back to the penitentiary, I wasn't gonna lay in the streets with a bottle of wine. I was safe. I had me a family. A job. I wasn't gonna get that last strike. I was on first looking for one of them boys to knock me in. To get me home.

ROSE: You should have stayed in my bed, Troy.

TROY: Then when I saw that girl . . . she firmed up my backbone. And I got to thinking that if I tried . . . I just might be able to steal second. Do you understand, after eighteen years I wanted to steal second.

ROSE: You should have held me tight. You should have grabbed me and held on.

TROY: I stood on first base for eighteen years and I thought . . . well, goddamn it . . . go on for it!

ROSE: We're not talking about baseball! We're talking about you going off to lay in bed with another woman . . . and then bring it home to me. That's what we're talking about. We ain't talking about no baseball.

TROY: Rose, you're not listening to me. I'm trying the best I can to explain it to you. It's not easy for me to admit that I been standing in the same place for eighteen years.

ROSE: I been standing with you! I been right here with you, Troy. I got a life too. I gave eighteen years of my life to stand in the same spot with you. Don't you think I ever wanted other things? Don't you think I had dreams and hopes?

What about my life? What about me? Don't you think it ever crossed my mind to want to know other men? That I wanted to lay up somewhere and forget about my responsibilities? That I wanted someone to make me laugh so I could feel good? You not the only one who's got wants and needs. But I held on to you, Troy. I took all my feelings, my wants and needs, my dreams . . . and I buried them inside you. I planted a seed and watched and prayed over it. I planted myself inside you and waited to bloom. And it didn't take me no eighteen years to find out the soil was hard and rocky and it wasn't never gonna bloom.

But I held on to you, Troy. I held you tighter. You was my husband. I owed you everything I had. Every part of me I could find to give you. And upstairs in that room . . . with the darkness falling in on me . . . I gave everything I had to try and erase the doubt that you wasn't the finest man in the world. And wherever you was going . . . I wanted to be there with you. 'Cause you was my husband. 'Cause that's the only way I was gonna survive as your wife. You always talking about what you give . . . and what you don't have to give. But you take too. You take . . . and don't even know nobody's giving!

(*Rose turns to exit into the house; Troy grabs her arm.*)

TROY: You say I take and don't give!
ROSE: Troy! You're hurting me.
TROY: You say I take and don't give.
ROSE: Troy . . . you're hurting my arm! Let go!
TROY: I done give you everything I got. Don't you tell that lie on me.
ROSE: Troy!
TROY: Don't you tell that lie on me!

(*Cory enters from the house.*)

CORY: Mama!
ROSE: Troy, you're hurting me.
TROY: Don't you tell me about no taking and giving.

(*Cory comes up behind Troy and grabs him. Troy, surprised, is thrown off balance just as Cory throws a glancing blow that catches him on the chest and knocks him down. Troy is stunned, as is Cory.*)

ROSE: Troy. Troy. No!

(*Troy gets to his feet and starts at Cory.*)

Troy . . . no. Please! Troy!

(*Rose pulls on Troy to hold him back. Troy stops himself.*)

TROY (*To Cory*): All right. That's strike two. You stay away from around me, boy. Don't you strike out. You living with a full count. Don't you strike out.

(*Troy exits out the yard as the lights go down on the scene.*)

Scene 2

It is six months later, early afternoon. Troy enters from the house and starts to exit the yard. Rose enters from the house.

ROSE: Troy, I want to talk to you.

TROY: All of a sudden, after all this time, you want to talk to me, huh? You ain't wanted to talk to me for months. You ain't wanted to talk to me last night. You ain't wanted no part of me then. What you wanna talk to me about now?

ROSE: Tomorrow's Friday.

TROY: I know what day tomorrow is. You think I don't know tomorrow's Friday? My whole life I ain't done nothing but look to see Friday coming and you got to tell me it's Friday.

ROSE: I want to know if you're coming home.

TROY: I always come home, Rose. You know that. There ain't never been a night I ain't come home.

ROSE: That ain't what I mean . . . and you know it. I want to know if you're coming straight home after work.

TROY: I figured I'd cash my check . . . hang out at Taylors' with the boys . . . maybe play a game of checkers . . .

ROSE: Troy, I can't live like this. I won't live like this. You livin' on borrowed time with me. It's been going on six months now you ain't been coming home.

TROY: I be here every night. Every night of the year. That's three hundred sixty-five days.

ROSE: I want you to come home tomorrow after work.

TROY: Rose . . . I don't mess up my pay. You know that now. I take my pay and I give it to you. I don't have no money but what you give me back. I just want to have a little time to myself . . . a little time to enjoy life.

ROSE: What about me? When's my time to enjoy life?

TROY: I don't know what to tell you, Rose. I'm doing the best I can.

ROSE: You ain't come home from work but time enough to change your clothes and run out . . . and you wanna call that the best you can do?

TROY: I'm going over to the hospital to see Alberta. She went into the hospital this afternoon. Look like she might have the baby early. I won't be gone long.

ROSE: Well, you ought to know. They went over to Miss Pearl's and got Gabe today. She said you told them to go ahead and lock him up.

TROY: I ain't said no such thing. Whoever told you that is telling a lie. Pearl ain't doing nothing but telling a big fat lie.

ROSE: She ain't had to tell me. I read it on the papers.

TROY: I ain't told them nothing of the kind.

ROSE: I saw it right there on the papers.

TROY: What it say, huh?

ROSE: It said you told them to take him.

TROY: Then they screwed that up, just the way they screw up everything. I ain't worried about what they got on the paper.

ROSE: Say the government send part of his check to the hospital and the other part to you.

TROY: I ain't got nothing to do with that if that's the way it works. I ain't made up the rules about how it work.

ROSE: You did Gabe just like you did Cory. You wouldn't sign the paper for Cory . . . but you signed for Gabe. You signed that paper.

(*The phone is heard ringing inside the house.*)

TROY: I told you I ain't signed nothing, woman! The only thing I signed was the release form. Hell, I can't read, I don't know what they had on that paper! I ain't signed nothing about sending Gabe away.

ROSE: I said send him to the hospital . . . you said let him be free . . . now you done went down there and signed him to the hospital for half his money. You went back on yourself, Troy. You gonna have to answer for that.

TROY: See now . . . you been over there talking to Miss Pearl. She done got mad 'cause she ain't getting Gabe's rent money. That's all it is. She's liable to say anything.

ROSE: Troy, I seen where you signed the paper.

TROY: You ain't seen nothing I signed. What she doing got papers on my brother anyway? Miss Pearl telling a big fat lie. And I'm gonna tell her about it too! You ain't seen nothing I signed. Say . . . you ain't seen nothing I signed.

(*Rose exits into the house to answer the phone. She returns.*)

ROSE: Troy . . . that was the hospital. Alberta had the baby.

TROY: What she have? What is it?

ROSE: It's a girl.

TROY: I better get on down to the hospital to see her.

ROSE: Troy . . .

TROY: Rose . . . I got to go see her now. That's only right . . . what's the matter . . . the baby's all right, ain't it?

ROSE: Alberta died having the baby.

TROY: Died . . . you say she's dead? Alberta's dead?

ROSE: They said they done all they could. They couldn't do nothing for her.

TROY: The baby? How's the baby?

ROSE: They say it's healthy. I wonder who's gonna bury her.

TROY: She had family, Rose. She wasn't living in the world by herself.

ROSE: I know she wasn't living in the world by herself.

TROY: Next thing you gonna want to know if she had any insurance.

ROSE: Troy, you ain't got to talk like that.

TROY: That's the first thing that jumped out your mouth. "Who's gonna bury her?" Like I'm fixing to take on that task for myself.

ROSE: I am your wife. Don't push me away.

TROY: I ain't pushing nobody away. Just give me some space. That's all. Just give me some room to breathe.

(*Rose exits into the house. Troy walks about the yard.*)

(*With a quiet rage that threatens to consume him*) All right . . . Mr. Death. See now . . . I'm gonna tell you what I'm gonna do. I'm gonna take and build me a fence around this yard. See? I'm gonna build me a fence around what belongs to me. And then I want you to stay on the other side. See? You stay over there until you're ready for me. Then you come on. Bring your army. Bring your sickle. Bring your wrestling clothes. I ain't gonna fall down on my vigilance this time. You ain't gonna sneak up on me no more. When you ready for me . . . when the top of your list say "Troy Maxson" . . . that's when you come around here. You come up and knock on the front door. Ain't nobody else got nothing to do with this. This is between you and me. Man to man. You stay on the other side of that fence until you ready for me. Then you come up and knock on the front door. Anytime you want. I'll be ready for you.

(*The lights fade to black.*)

Scene 3

The lights come up on the porch. It is late evening three days later. Rose sits listening to the ball game, waiting for Troy. The final out of the game is made and Rose switches off the radio. Troy enters the yard carrying an infant wrapped in blankets. He stands back from the house and calls.

Rose enters and stands on the porch. There is a long, awkward silence, the weight of which grows heavier with each passing second.

TROY: Rose . . . I'm standing here with my daughter in my arms. She ain't but a wee bitty little old thing. She don't know nothing about grownups' business. She innocent . . . and she ain't got no mama.

ROSE: What you telling me for, Troy?

(*She turns and exits into the house.*)

TROY: Well . . . I guess we'll just sit out here on the porch.

(*He sits down on the porch. There is an awkward indelicateness about the way he handles the baby. His largeness engulfs and seems to swallow her. He speaks loud enough for Rose to hear:*)

A man's got to do what's right for him. I ain't sorry for nothing I done. It felt right in my heart. (*To the baby*) What you smiling at? Your daddy's a big man. Got these great big old hands. But sometimes he's scared. And right now your daddy's scared 'cause we sitting out here and ain't got no home. Oh, I been homeless before. I ain't had no little baby with me. But I been homeless. You just be out on the road by your lonesome and you see one of them trains coming and you just kinda go like this . . . (*Singing, as a lullaby:*)

Please, Mr. Engineer, let a man ride the line
Please, Mr. Engineer, let a man ride the line
I ain't got no ticket please let me ride the blinds.[1]

(*Rose enters from the house. Troy hearing her steps behind him, stands and faces her.*)

She's my daughter, Rose. My own flesh and blood. I can't deny her no more than I can deny them boys. (*Pause*) You and them boys is my family. You and

---

1. That is, hitch a free ride on the platform outside a rail car with no door at one end (hence, "blind").

them and this child is all I got in the world. So I guess what I'm saying is . . .
I'd appreciate it if you'd help me take care of her.
ROSE: Okay, Troy . . . you're right. I'll take care of your baby for you . . .'cause . . .
like you say . . . she's innocent . . . and you can't visit the sins of the father
upon the child. A motherless child has got a hard time. (*Takes the baby from
him*) From right now . . . this child got a mother. But you a womanless man.

(*Rose turns and exits into the house with the baby. The lights fade to black.*)

Scene 4

*It is two months later. Lyons enters from the street. He knocks on the door
and calls.*

LYONS: Hey, Rose! (*Pause*) Rose!
ROSE (*From inside the house*): Stop that yelling. You gonna wake up Raynell. I
just got her to sleep.
LYONS: I just stopped by to pay Papa this twenty dollars I owe him. Where's
Papa at?
ROSE: He should be here in a minute. I'm getting ready to go down to the church.
Sit down and wait on him.
LYONS: I got to go pick up Bonnie over her mother's house.
ROSE: Well, sit it down there on the table. He'll get it.
LYONS: (*Enters the house and sets the money on the table*): Tell Papa I said thanks.
I'll see you again.
ROSE: All right, Lyons. We'll see you.

(*Lyons starts to exit as Cory enters.*)

CORY: Hey, Lyons.
LYONS: What's happening, Cory. Say man, I'm sorry I missed your graduation.
You know I had a gig and couldn't get away. Otherwise, I would have been
there, man. So what you doing?
CORY: I'm trying to find a job.
LYONS: Yeah, I know how that go, man. It's rough out here. Jobs are scarce.
CORY: Yeah, I know.
LYONS: Look here, I got to run. Talk to Papa . . . he know some people. He'll be
able to help get you a job. Talk to him . . . see what he say.
CORY: Yeah . . . all right, Lyons.
LYONS: You take care. I'll talk to you soon. We'll find some time to talk.

(*Lyons exits the yard. Cory wanders over to the tree, picks up the bat and
assumes a batting stance. He studies an imaginary pitcher and swings. Dissatisfied with the result, he tries again. Troy enters. They eye each other for a
beat. Cory puts the bat down and exits the yard. Troy starts into the house as
Rose exits with Raynell. She is carrying a cake.*)

TROY: I'm coming in and everybody's going out.
ROSE: I'm taking this cake down to the church for the bake sale. Lyons was by
to see you. He stopped by to pay you your twenty dollars. It's laying in there
on the table.

TROY (*Going into his pocket*): Well . . . here go this money.

ROSE: Put it in there on the table, Troy. I'll get it.

TROY: What time you coming back?

ROSE: Ain't no use in you studying me. It don't matter what time I come back.

TROY: I just asked you a question, woman. What's the matter . . . can't I ask you a question?

ROSE: Troy, I don't want to go into it. Your dinner's in there on the stove. All you got to do is heat it up. And don't you be eating the rest of them cakes in there. I'm coming back for them. We having a bake sale at the church tomorrow.

(*Rose exits the yard. Troy sits down on the steps, takes a pint bottle from his pocket, opens it and drinks. He begins to sing:*)

TROY:

> Hear it ring! Hear it ring!
> Had an old dog his name was Blue
> You know Blue was mighty true
> You know Blue was a good old dog
> Blue treed a possum in a hollow log
> You know from that he was a good old dog.

(*Bono enters the yard.*)

BONO: Hey, Troy.

TROY: Hey, what's happening, Bono?

BONO: I just thought I'd stop by to see you.

TROY: What you stop by and see me for? You ain't stopped by in a month of Sundays. Hell, I must owe you money or something.

BONO: Since you got your promotion I can't keep up with you. Used to see you every day. Now I don't even know what route you working.

TROY: They keep switching me around. Got me out in Greentree now . . . hauling white folks' garbage.

BONO: Greentree, huh? You lucky, at least you ain't got to be lifting them barrels. Damn if they ain't getting heavier. I'm gonna put in my two years and call it quits.

TROY: I'm thinking about retiring myself.

BONO: You got it easy. You can *drive* for another five years.

TROY: It ain't the same, Bono. It ain't like working the back of the truck. Ain't got nobody to talk to . . . feel like you working by yourself. Naw, I'm thinking about retiring. How's Lucille?

BONO: She all right. Her arthritis get to acting up on her sometime. Saw Rose on my way in. She going down to the church, huh?

TROY: Yeah, she took up going down there. All them preachers looking for somebody to fatten their pockets. (*Pause*) Got some gin here.

BONO: Naw, thanks. I just stopped by to say hello.

TROY: Hell, nigger . . . you can take a drink. I ain't never known you to say no to a drink. You ain't got to work tomorrow.

BONO: I just stopped by. I'm fixing to go over to Skinner's. We got us a domino game going over his house every Friday.

TROY: Nigger, you can't play no dominoes. I used to whup you four games out of five.

BONO: Well, that learned me. I'm getting better.

TROY: Yeah? Well, that's all right.

BONO: Look here . . . I got to be getting on. Stop by sometime, huh?

TROY: Yeah, I'll do that, Bono. Lucille told Rose you bought her a new refrigerator.

BONO: Yeah, Rose told Lucille you had finally built your fence . . . so I figured we'd call it even.

TROY: I knew you would.

BONO: Yeah . . . okay. I'll be talking to you.

TROY: Yeah, take care, Bono. Good to see you. I'm gonna stop over.

BONO: Yeah. Okay, Troy.

(*Bono exits. Troy drinks from the bottle.*)

TROY:

Old Blue died and I dug his grave
Let him down with a golden chain
Every night when I hear old Blue bark
I know Blue treed a possum in Noah's Ark.
Hear it ring! Hear it ring!

(*Cory enters the yard. Cory and Troy eye each other for a beat. Cory walks over to Troy, who sits in the middle of the steps.*)

CORY: I got to get by.

TROY: Say what? What's you say?

CORY: You in my way. I got to get by.

TROY: You got to get by where? This is my house. Bought and paid for. In full. Took me fifteen years. And if you wanna go in my house and I'm sitting on the steps . . . you say excuse me. Like your mama taught you.

CORY: Come on, Pop . . . I got to get by.

(*Cory starts to maneuver his way past Troy. Troy grabs his leg and shoves him back.*)

TROY: You just gonna walk over top of me?

CORY: I live here too!

TROY (*Advancing on him*): You just gonna walk over top of me in my own house?

CORY: I ain't scared of you.

TROY: I ain't asked if you was scared of me. I asked you if you was fixing to walk over top of me in my own house? That's the question. You ain't gonna say excuse me? You just gonna walk over top of me?

CORY: If you wanna put it like that.

TROY: How else am I gonna put it?

CORY: I was walking by you to go into the house 'cause you sitting on the steps drunk, singing to yourself. You can put it like that.

TROY: Without saying excuse me??? (*Cory doesn't respond*) I asked you a question. Without saying excuse me???

CORY: I ain't got to say excuse me to you. You don't count around here no more.

TROY: Oh, I see . . . I don't count around here no more. You ain't got to say excuse me to your daddy. All of a sudden you done got so grown that your daddy don't count around here no more . . . Around here in his own house and yard that he done paid for with the sweat of his brow. You done got so grown to where you gonna take over. You gonna take over my house. Is that right? You gonna wear my pants. You gonna go in there and stretch out on my bed. You ain't got to say excuse me 'cause I don't count around here no more. Is that right?

CORY: That's right. You always talking this dumb stuff. Now, why don't you just get out my way.

TROY: I guess you got someplace to sleep and something to put in your belly. You got that, huh? You got that? That's what you need. You got that, huh?

CORY: You don't know what I got. You ain't got to worry about what I got.

TROY: You right! You one hundred percent right! I done spent the last seventeen years worrying about what you got. Now it's your turn, see? I'll tell you what to do. You grown . . . we done established that. You a man. Now, let's see you act like one. Turn your behind around and walk out this yard. And when you get out there in the alley . . . you can forget about this house. See? 'Cause this is my house. You go on and be a man and get your own house. You can forget about this. 'Cause this is mine. You go on and get yours 'cause I'm through with doing for you.

CORY: You talking about what you did for me . . . what'd you ever give me?

TROY: Them feet and bones! That pumping heart, nigger! I give you more than anybody else is ever gonna give you.

CORY: You ain't never gave me nothing! You ain't never done nothing but hold me back. Afraid I was gonna be better than you. All you ever did was try and make me scared of you. I used to tremble every time you called my name. Every time I heard your footsteps in the house. Wondering all the time . . . what's Papa gonna say if I do this? . . . What's he gonna say if I do that? . . . What's Papa gonna say if I turn on the radio? And Mama, too . . . she tries . . . but she's scared of you.

TROY: You leave your mama out of this. She ain't got nothing to do with this.

CORY: I don't know how she stand you . . . after what you did to her.

TROY: I told you to leave your mama out of this! (*Advances on Cory*)

CORY: What you gonna do . . . give me a whupping? You can't whup me no more. You're too old. You just an old man.

TROY (*Shoves him on his shoulder*): Nigger! That's what you are! You just another nigger on the street to me!

CORY: You crazy! You know that?

TROY: Go on now! You got the devil in you. Get on away from me!

CORY: You just a crazy old man . . . talking about I got the devil in me.

TROY: Yeah, I'm crazy! If you don't get on the other side of that yard . . . I'm gonna show you how crazy I am! Go on . . . get the hell out of my yard.

CORY: It ain't your yard. You took Uncle Gabe's money he got from the Army to buy this house and then you put him out.

TROY (*Advances on Cory*): Get your black ass out of my yard!

(*Troy's advance backs Cory up against the tree. Cory grabs the bat.*)

CORY: I ain't going nowhere! Come on . . . put me out! I ain't scared of you.

TROY: That's my bat!

CORY: Come on!

TROY: Put my bat down!

CORY: Come on, put me out.

(*Cory swings at Troy, who backs across the yard.*)

What's the matter? You so bad . . . put me out!

(*Troy advances on Cory, who backs up.*)

Come on! Come on!

TROY: You're gonna have to use it! You wanna draw that bat back on me . . . you're gonna have to use it.

CORY: Come on! . . . Come on!

(*Cory swings the bat at Troy a second time. He misses. Troy continues to advance on him.*)

TROY: You're gonna have to kill me! You wanna draw that bat back on me. You're gonna have to kill me.

(*Cory, backed up against the tree, can go no farther. Troy taunts him. He sticks out his head and offers him a target.*)

Come on! Come on!

(*Cory is unable to swing the bat. Troy grabs it.*)

Then I'll show you.

(*Cory and Troy struggle over the bat. The struggle is fierce and fully engaged. Troy ultimately is the stronger, and takes the bat from Cory and stands over him ready to swing. He stops himself.*)

Go on and get away from around my house.

(*Cory, stung by his defeat, picks himself up, walks slowly out of the yard and up the alley.*)

CORY: Tell Mama I'll be back for my things. (*Exits*)

TROY: They'll be on the other side of that fence.

I can't taste nothing. Hallelujah! I can't taste nothing no more. (*Assumes a batting posture and begins to taunt Death, the fastball in the outside corner*) Come on! It's between you and me now! Come on! Anytime you want! Come on! I be ready for you . . . but I ain't gonna be easy.

(*The lights go down on the scene.*)

Scene 5

The time is 1965. The lights come up in the yard. It is the morning of Troy's funeral. A funeral plaque with a light hangs beside the door. There is a small garden plot off to the side. There is noise and activity in the house as Rose, Gabriel,

Lyons and Bono have gathered. The door opens and Raynell, seven years old, enters dressed in a flannel nightgown. She crosses to the garden and pokes around with a stick. Rose calls from the house.

ROSE: Raynell!
RAYNELL: Mam?
ROSE: What you doing out there?
RAYNELL: Nothing.

(*Rose comes to the screen door.*)

ROSE: Girl, get in here and get dressed. What you doing?
RAYNELL: Seeing if my garden growed.
ROSE: I told you it ain't gonna grow overnight. You got to wait.
RAYNELL: It don't look like it never gonna grow. Dag!
ROSE: I told you a watched pot never boils. Get in here and get dressed.
RAYNELL: This ain't even no pot, Mama.
ROSE: You just have to give it a chance. It'll grow. Now you come on and do what I told you. We got to be getting ready. This ain't no morning to be playing around. You hear me?
RAYNELL: Yes, Mam.

(*Rose exits into the house. Raynell continues to poke at her garden with a stick. Cory enters. He is dressed in a Marine corporal's uniform, and carries a duffel bag. His posture is that of a military man, and his speech has a clipped sternness.*)

CORY (*To Raynell*): Hi. (*Pause*) I bet your name is Raynell.
RAYNELL: Uh-huh.
CORY: Is your mama home?

(*Raynell runs up on the porch and calls through the screen door:*)

RAYNELL: Mama . . . there's some man out here. Mama?

(*Rose comes to the screen door.*)

ROSE: Cory? Lord have mercy! Look here, you all!

(*Rose and Cory embrace in a tearful reunion as Bono and Lyons enter from the house dressed in funeral clothes.*)

BONO: Aw, looka here . . .
ROSE: Done got all grown up!
CORY: Don't cry, Mama. What you crying about?
ROSE: I'm just so glad you made it.
CORY: Hey, Lyons. How you doing, Mr. Bono?

(*Lyons goes to embrace Cory.*)

LYONS: Look at you, man. Look at you. Don't he look good, Rose. Got them corporal stripes.
ROSE: What took you so long.
CORY: You know how the Marines are, Mama. They got to get all their paperwork straight before they let you do anything.

ROSE: Well, I'm sure glad you made it. They let Lyons come. Your Uncle Gabe's still in the hospital. They don't know if they gonna let him out or not. I just talked to them a little while ago.

LYONS: A corporal in the United States Marines.

BONO: Your daddy knew you had it in you. He used to tell me all the time.

LYONS: Don't he look good, Mr. Bono?

BONO: Yeah, he remind me of Troy when I first met him. (*Pause*) Say, Rose, Lucille's down at the church with the choir. I'm gonna go down and get the pallbearers lined up. I'll be back to get you all.

ROSE: Thanks, Jim.

CORY: See you, Mr. Bono.

(*Bono exits.*)

LYONS (*With his arm around Raynell*): Cory . . . look at Raynell. Ain't she precious? She gonna break a whole lot of hearts.

ROSE: Raynell, come and say hello to your brother. This is your brother, Cory. You remember Cory.

RAYNELL: No, Mam.

CORY: She don't remember me, Mama.

ROSE: Well, we talk about you. She heard us talk about you. (*To Raynell*) This is your brother Cory. Come on and say hello.

RAYNELL: Hi.

CORY: Hi. So you're Raynell. Mama told me a lot about you.

ROSE: You all come on into the house and let me fix you some breakfast. Keep up your strength.

CORY: I ain't hungry, Mama.

LYONS: You can fix me something, Rose. I'll be in there in a minute.

ROSE: Cory, you sure you don't want nothing. I know they ain't feeding you right.

CORY: No, Mama . . . thanks. I don't feel like eating. I'll get something later.

ROSE: Raynell . . . get on upstairs and get that dress on like I told you.

(*Rose and Raynell exit into the house.*)

LYONS: So . . . I hear you thinking about getting married.

CORY: Yeah, I done found the right one, Lyons. It's about time.

LYONS: Me and Bonnie been split up about four years now. About the time Papa retired. I guess she just got tired of all them changes I was putting her through. (*Pause*) I always knew you was gonna make something out yourself. Your head was always in the right direction. So . . . you gonna stay in . . . make it a career . . . put in your twenty years?

CORY: I don't know. I got six already, I think that's enough.

LYONS: Stick with Uncle Sam and retire early. Ain't nothing out here. I guess Rose told you what happened with me. They got me down the workhouse. I thought I was being slick cashing other people's checks.

CORY: How much time you doing?

LYONS: They give me three years. I got that beat now. I ain't got but nine more months. It ain't so bad. You learn to deal with it like anything else. You got to take the crookeds with the straights. That's what Papa used to say. He used to say that when he struck out. I seen him strike out three times in a row . . .

and the next time up he hit the ball over the grandstand. Right out there in Homestead Field.[2] He wasn't satisfied hitting in the seats . . . he wanted to hit it over everything! After the game he had two hundred people standing around waiting to shake his hand. You got to take the crookeds with the straights. Yeah, Papa was something else.

CORY: You still playing?

LYONS: Cory . . . you know I'm gonna do that. There's some fellows down there we got us a band . . . we gonna try and stay together when we get out . . . but yeah, I'm still playing. It still helps me to get out of bed in the morning. As long as it do that I'm gonna be right there playing and trying to make some sense out of it.

ROSE (Calling): Lyons, I got these eggs in the pan.

LYONS: Let me go on and get these eggs, man. Get ready to go bury Papa. (Pause) How you doing? You doing all right?

(Cory nods. Lyons touches him on the shoulder and they share a moment of silent grief. Lyons exits into the house. Cory wanders about the yard. Raynell enters.)

RAYNELL: Hi.

CORY: Hi.

RAYNELL: Did you used to sleep in my room?

CORY: Yeah . . . that used to be my room.

RAYNELL: That's what Papa call it. "Cory's room." It got your football in the closet.

(Rose comes to the screen door.)

ROSE: Raynell, get in there and get them good shoes on.

RAYNELL: Mama, can't I wear these? Them other one hurt my feet.

ROSE: Well, they just gonna have to hurt your feet for a while. You ain't said they hurt your feet when you went down to the store and got them.

RAYNELL: They didn't hurt then. My feet done got bigger.

ROSE: Don't you give me no backtalk now. You get in there and get them shoes on.

(Raynell exits into the house.)

Ain't too much changed. He still got that piece of rag tied to that tree. He was out here swinging that bat. I was just ready to go back in the house. He swung that bat and then he just fell over. Seem like he swung it and stood there with this grin on his face . . . and then he just fell over. They carried him on down to the hospital, but I knew there wasn't no need . . . Why don't you come on in the house?

CORY: Mama . . . I got something to tell you. I don't know how to tell you this . . . but I've got to tell you . . . I'm not going to Papa's funeral.

ROSE: Boy, hush your mouth. That's your daddy you talking about. I don't want hear that kind of talk this morning. I done raised you to come to this? You standing there all healthy and grown talking about you ain't going to your daddy's funeral?

CORY: Mama . . . listen . . .

ROSE: I don't want to hear it, Cory. You just get that thought out of your head.

2. Among the most renowned teams in the Negro League, the Homestead Grays originated in Homestead, Pennsylvania, just south of Pittsburgh, but moved to Pittsburgh's Forbes Field in the late 1930s.

CORY: I can't drag Papa with me everywhere I go. I've got to say no to him. One time in my life I've got to say no.

ROSE: Don't nobody have to listen to nothing like that. I know you and your daddy ain't seen eye to eye, but I ain't got to listen to that kind of talk this morning. Whatever was between you and your daddy . . . the time has come to put it aside. Just take it and set it over there on the shelf and forget about it. Disrespecting your daddy ain't gonna make you a man, Cory. You got to find a way to come to that on your own. Not going to your daddy's funeral ain't gonna make you a man.

CORY: The whole time I was growing up . . . living in his house . . . Papa was like a shadow that followed you everywhere. It weighed on you and sunk into your flesh. It would wrap around you and lay there until you couldn't tell which one was you anymore. That shadow digging in your flesh. Trying to crawl in. Trying to live through you. Everywhere I looked, Troy Maxson was staring back at me . . . hiding under the bed . . . in the closet. I'm just saying I've got to find a way to get rid of that shadow, Mama.

ROSE: You just like him. You got him in you good.

CORY: Don't you tell me that, Mama.

ROSE: You Troy Maxson all over again.

CORY: I don't want to be Troy Maxson. I want to be me.

ROSE: You can't be nobody but who you are, Cory. That shadow wasn't nothing but you growing into yourself. You either got to grow into it or cut it down to fit you. But that's all you got to make life with. That's all you got to measure yourself against that world out there. Your daddy wanted you to be everything he wasn't . . . and at the same time he tried to make you into everything he was. I don't know if he was right or wrong . . . but I do know he meant to do more good than he meant to do harm. He wasn't always right. Sometimes when he touched he bruised. And sometimes when he took me in his arms he cut.

When I first met your daddy I thought, "Here is a man I can lay down with and make a baby." That's the first thing I thought when I seen him. I was thirty years old and had done seen my share of men. But when he walked up to me and said, "I can dance a waltz that'll make you dizzy," I thought, "Rose Lee, here is a man that you can open yourself up to and be filled to bursting. Here is a man that can fill all them empty spaces you been tipping around the edges of." One of them empty spaces was being somebody's mother.

I married your daddy and settle down to cooking his supper and keeping clean sheets on the bed. When your daddy walked through the house he was so big he filled it up. That was my first mistake. Not to make him leave some room for me. For my part in the matter. But at that time I wanted that. I wanted a house that I could sing in. And that's what your daddy gave me. I didn't know to keep up his strength I had to give up little pieces of mine. I did that. I took on his life as mine and mixed up the pieces so that you couldn't hardly tell which was which anymore. It was my choice. It was my life and I didn't have to live it like that. But that's what life offered me in the way of being a woman and I took it. I grabbed hold of it with both hands.

By the time Raynell came into the house, me and your daddy had done lost touch with one another. I didn't want to make my blessing off of nobody's misfortune . . . but I took on to Raynell like she was all them babies I had wanted and never had. (*The phone rings*) Like I'd been blessed to relive a part of my life. And if the Lord see fit to keep up my strength . . . I'm gonna do her just like your daddy did you . . . I'm gonna give her the best of what's in me.

RAYNELL (*Entering, still with her old shoes*): Mama . . . Reverend Tolliver on the phone.

(*Rose exits into the house.*)

Hi.

CORY: Hi.

RAYNELL: You in the Army or the Marines?

CORY: Marines.

RAYNELL: Papa said it was the Army. Did you know Blue?

CORY: Blue? Who's Blue?

RAYNELL: Papa's dog what he sing about all the time.

CORY (*Singing*):
> Hear it ring! Hear it ring!
> I had a dog his name was Blue
> You know Blue was mighty true
> You know Blue was a good old dog
> Blue treed a possum in a hollow log
> You know from that he was a good old dog.
> Hear it ring! Hear it ring!

(*Raynell joins in singing.*)

CORY AND RAYNELL:
> Blue treed a possum out on a limb
> Blue looked at me and I looked at him
> Grabbed that possum and put him in a sack
> Blue stayed there till I came back
> Old Blue's feets was big and round
> Never allowed a possum to touch the ground.
>
> Old Blue died and I dug his grave
> I dug his grave with a silver spade
> Let him down with a golden chain
> And every night I call his name
> Go on Blue, you good dog you
> Go on Blue, you good dog you

RAYNELL:
> Blue laid down and died like a man
> Blue laid down and died . . .

CORY AND RAYNELL:
> Blue laid down and died like a man
> Now he's treeing possums in the Promised Land
> I'm gonna tell you this to let you know

Blue's gone where the good dogs go
When I hear Old Blue bark
When I hear Old Blue bark
Blue treed a possum in Noah's Ark
Blue treed a possum in Noah's Ark.

(*Rose comes to the screen door.*)

ROSE: Cory, we gonna be ready to go in a minute.
CORY (*To Raynell*): You go on in the house and change them shoes like Mama told you so we can go to Papa's funeral.
RAYNELL: Okay, I'll be back.

(*Raynell exits into the house. Cory gets up and crosses over to the tree. Rose stands at the screen door watching him. Gabriel enters from the alley.*)

GABRIEL (*Calling*): Hey, Rose!
ROSE: Gabe?
GABRIEL: I'm here, Rose. Hey, Rose, I'm here!

(*Rose enters from the house.*)

ROSE: Lord . . . Look here, Lyons!
LYONS (*Enters from the house*): See, I told you, Rose . . . I told you they'd let him come.
CORY: How you doing, Uncle Gabe?
LYONS: How you doing, Uncle Gabe?
GABRIEL: Hey, Rose. It's time. It's time to tell Saint Peter to open the Gates. Troy, you ready? You ready, Troy. I'm gonna tell Saint Peter to open the Gates. You get ready now.

(*Gabriel, with great fanfare, braces himself to blow. The trumpet is without a mouthpiece. He puts the end of it into his mouth and blows with great force, like a man who has been waiting some twenty-odd years for this single moment. No sound comes out of the trumpet. He braces himself and blows again with the same result. A third time he blows. There is a weight of impossible description that falls away and leaves him bare and exposed to a frightful realization. It is a trauma that a sane and normal mind would be unable to withstand. He begins to dance. A slow, strange dance, eerie and life-giving. A dance of atavistic[3] signature and ritual. Lyons attempts to embrace him. Gabriel pushes Lyons away. Gabriel begins to howl in what is an attempt at song, or perhaps a song turning back into itself in an attempt at speech. He finishes his dance and the Gates of Heaven stand open as wide as God's closet.*)

That's the way that go!

(*Blackout.*)

1987

---

3. Characterized by a reversion to an ancient or ancestral form.

QUESTIONS

1. In interviews, August Wilson describes FENCES as revolving so completely around its central character that it might "almost" be called "*The Life of Troy Maxson* or just *Troy Maxson*." To what extent does and doesn't that seem true?
2. Wilson also describes the play as "examin[ing] Troy's life layer by layer" to "find out why he made the choices he made" (see "Authors on Their Work" below). How do you think the play ultimately answers that question? What does it seem to present as the key to Troy's character or as the thing he values most?
3. According to the play, how have circumstances helped to make Troy the man he is? How might he and his life have been different had he turned fifty-three in either 1947 or 1967? had he been White?
4. Does Troy's character develop over the course of the play or only the way others see him? Why and how so?
5. What is the effect and significance of the fact that the play ends after Troy's death? How would the play work differently and carry a different meaning if its final scene were omitted? if Troy died onstage?
6. What might the fence come to stand for or symbolize in the play? Why might *Fences*, plural, be a more apt title than *The Fence*?
7. How are father-son relationships depicted in the play? How does Troy's relationship with his father compare to and shape his relationship with his sons? Why do you think the play includes Lyons, as well as Cory?
8. How might Rose or your impression of her evolve over the course of the play? Why does she adopt Raynell, and what effect does this choice seem to have? Why might she begin to attend church?
9. What is the significance and effect of Wilson's choice to set the play in the Maxson's front yard? to punctuate the play with scenes that take place on Friday nights? not to show us Troy at work, Cory playing football, and so on?

AUTHORS ON THEIR WORK

AUGUST WILSON (1945–2005)

From "Hurdling *Fences*" (1989)*

I wanted to explore our commonalities of culture. What you have in *Fences* is a very specific situation, a black family which the forces of racism have molded and shaped, but you also have a husband-wife, father-son. White America looks at black America in this glancing manner. They pass right by the Troy Maxsons of the world and never stop to look at them. They talk about niggers as lazy and shiftless. Well, here's a man with responsibilities as prime to his life. I wanted to examine Troy's life layer by layer and find out why he made the choices he made.

• • •

From "Men, Women, and Culture: A Conversation with August Wilson" (1993)**

[INTERVIEWER]: What makes Troy heroic? He's an ex-con, ex-baseball player, now a garbage collector; he exploits his brother and cheats on his wife—what is redeeming about him as an African American man?

WILSON: I think that, for me, this may be nothing more than his willingness to wrestle with his life, his willingness to engage no matter what the circumstances of his life. He hasn't given up despite the twists and turns it's given him. I find that both noble and heroic.

*"Hurdling *Fences*." Interview by Dennis Watlington. *Vanity Fair*, no. 52, Apr. 1989, pp. 102–13.

**"Men, Women, and Culture: A Conversation with August Wilson." Interview by Nathan L. Grant. *American Drama*, vol. 5, no. 2, spring 1996, pp. 100–122.

SUGGESTIONS FOR WRITING

1. Why is Troy Maxson so insistent that his son quit the football team? What about your own cultural and historical context might make his attitude seem surprising (or not)? Write a response paper or essay exploring these questions.
2. Write an essay exploring Gabriel's role in the play. What is significant about his injuries and their cause, for example? about his fixation with Judgment Day? about his actions in the play's final scene? What might his final, "*frightful realization*" (1338) be, and why, according to Wilson's stage directions, might "*the Gates of Heaven stand open as wide as God's closet*" only after that realization and the "*atavistic*" dance that follows it?
3. Write an essay exploring Wilson's characterization of Rose. What might the play suggest, through her, about the options available to, or conflicts faced by, women in general or African American women in particular in the 1950s? To what extent might Wilson's play reproduce or challenge our preconceptions about such women? Alternatively, consider how FENCES might reproduce or challenge stereotypical views of Black men.
4. Research theories of tragedy and the tragic hero. Drawing on both these and evidence from Wilson's play, explain whether and how FENCES might be considered a tragedy or Troy Maxson a tragic hero.
5. Write an epilogue to FENCES, a scene depicting Rose, Lyons, Cory, or Raynell in 1975. What do you imagine has happened to this character, and why and how so? If Cory had a child, for example, what would his relationship with that child be like? What might he say to his child about his father, his mother, and his own childhood?

QUIARA ALEGRÍA HUDES
(b. 1977)

Water by the Spoonful

Though she now lives in New York City with her lawyer husband and two children, Quiara Alegría Hudes hails from Philadelphia, Pennsylvania, the city that still serves as inspiration and setting for much of her work. The daughter of a Jewish carpenter and a Puerto Rican mother and stepfather, Hudes spent her childhood exploring the city's ethnically and economically diverse neighborhoods, especially the predominantly African American West Philly area she called home and the North Philly barrios where many of her maternal relatives still live. Hudes had her first play produced by Philadelphia Young Playwrights when she was only ten. Yet when she became the first in her family to attend college, at Yale, she majored in music. After graduation, Hudes returned home, launching a successful career as a musician-composer before heading to Brown University. Here she earned an MFA (2003) and completed two plays—the award-winning *Yemaya's Belly* (2005), about a young Cuban boy who dreams of immigrating to the United States, and *The Adventures of Barrio Grrl!*, which she later turned into a children's musical. Hudes received the first of three Pulitzer nominations for her work on another musical, the Tony Award–winning *In the Heights* (2007), featuring music and lyrics by *Hamilton* creator Lin-Manuel Miranda. Though *In the Heights* was successfully adapted into a film (2021), Hudes's real acclaim as a dramatist rests on a trilogy inspired by, and developed partly in collaboration with, her "story-centric family," especially Elliot Ruiz, a cousin wounded in the Iraq War (2003–11). *Water by the Spoonful* (2011), which won a Pulitzer, is the second play in the sequence that also includes *Elliot, A Soldier's Fugue* (2006) and *The Happiest Song Plays Last* (2013). Together, says Hudes, these plays tell a distinctly "American story" about issues and people we too often "don't talk about," in part by exploiting and exploring diverse, often distinctly twenty-first-century ways of both talking and storytelling.

CHARACTERS

ELLIOT ORTIZ, an Iraq vet with a slight limp, works at Subway sandwich shop, scores an occasional job as a model or actor, Yazmin's cousin, Odessa's birth son, Puerto Rican, twenty-four.

YAZMIN ORTIZ, in her first year as an adjunct professor of music, Odessa's niece and Elliot's cousin, Puerto Rican, twenty-nine.

HAIKUMOM, aka Odessa Ortiz, founder of www.recover-together.com, works odd janitorial jobs, lives one notch above squalor, Puerto Rican, thirty-nine.

FOUNTAINHEAD, aka John, a computer programmer and entrepreneur, lives on Philadelphia's Main Line,[1] white, forty-one.

CHUTES&LADDERS, lives in San Diego, has worked a low-level job at the IRS since the Reagan years,[2] his real name is Clayton "Buddy" Wilkie, African American, fifty-six.

ORANGUTAN, a recent community college graduate, her real name is Madeleine Mays and before that Yoshiko Sakai, Japanese by birth, thirty-one.

A GHOST, also plays Professor Aman, an Arabic professor at Swarthmore;[3] also plays a Policeman in Japan.

SETTING: 2009. *Six years after Elliot left for Iraq. Philadelphia, San Diego, Japan and Puerto Rico.*

The stage has two worlds. The "real world" is populated with chairs. The chairs are from many locations—living rooms, an office, a seminar room, a church, a diner, internet cafés, etc. They all have the worn-in feel of life. A duct-taped La-Z-Boy. Salvaged trash chairs. A busted-up metal folding chair from a rec center.

1. Series of affluent towns in Philadelphia's western suburbs, along the old Main Line of the Pennsylvania Railroad.
2. 1981–89, during the presidency of Ronald Reagan (1911–2004). *IRS*: Internal Revenue Service (acronym).
3. Highly ranked private liberal arts college (founded 1864) located eleven miles southwest of Philadelphia.

An Aero chair. An Eames chair.[4] *A chair/desk from a college classroom. Diner chairs. A chair from an internet café in Japan. Living room chairs. Library chairs. A church pew. Facing in all different directions.*

The "online world" is an empty space. A space that connects the chairs.

MUSIC: *Jazz. John Coltrane.*[5] *The sublime stuff* (A Love Supreme). *And the noise* (Ascension).

NOTE: *Unless specifically noted, when characters are online, don't have actors typing on a keyboard. Treat it like regular conversation rather than the act of writing or typing. They can be doing things people do in the comfort of their home, like eating potato chips, walking around in jammies, cooking, doing dishes, clipping nails, etc.*

Scene One

Swarthmore College. Elliot and Yaz eat breakfast. Elliot wears a Subway sandwich shop polo shirt.

ELLIOT: This guy ain't coming. How do you know him?

YAZ: We're on a committee together.

ELLIOT: My shift starts in fifteen.

YAZ: All right, we'll go.

ELLIOT: Five more minutes. Tonight on the way home, we gotta stop by Whole Foods.

YAZ: Sure, I need toothpaste.

ELLIOT: You gotta help me with my mom, Yaz.

YAZ: You said she had a good morning.

ELLIOT: She cooked breakfast.

YAZ: Progress.

ELLIOT: No. The docs said she can't be eating all that junk, it'll mess with her chemo, so she crawls out of bed for the first time in days and cooks eggs for breakfast. In two inches of pork-chop fat. I'm like, Mom, recycle glass and plastic, not grease. She thinks putting the egg on top of a paper towel after you cook it makes it healthy. I told her, Mom, you gotta cook egg whites. In Pam spray. But it has to be her way. Like, "That's how we ate them in Puerto Rico and we turned out fine." You gotta talk to her. I'm trying to teach her about quinoa. Broccoli rabe. Healthy shit. So I get home the other day, she had made quinoa with bacon. She was like, "It's healthy!"

YAZ: That's Ginny. The more stubborn she's being, the better she's feeling.

ELLIOT: I gave those eggs to the dogs when she went to the bathroom.

YAZ (*Pulls some papers from her purse*): You wanna be my witness?

ELLIOT: To what?

(*Yaz signs the papers.*)

---

4. High-end chair designed in 1956 by renowned husband-and-wife team Charles (1907–78) and Ray Eames (1912–88).

5. American jazz saxophonist and composer (1926–67), pioneer of "free jazz."

Liza Colón-Zayas, Sue Jean Kim, and Frankie R. Faison in the Second Stage Theater
production of *Water by the Spoonful*, 2012

YAZ: My now-legal failure. I'm divorced.

ELLIOT: Yaz. I don't want to hear that.

YAZ: You've been saying that for months and I've been keeping my mouth closed.
I just need a John Hancock.

ELLIOT: What happened to "trial separation"?

YAZ: There was a verdict. William fell out of love with me.

ELLIOT: I've never seen you two argue.

YAZ: We did, we just had smiles on our faces.

ELLIOT: That's bullshit. You don't divorce someone before you even have a fight
with them. I'm calling him.

YAZ: Go ahead.

ELLIOT: He was just texting me about going to the Phillies game on Sunday.

YAZ: So, go. He didn't fall out of love with the family, just me.

ELLIOT: I'm going to ask him who he's been screwing behind your back.

YAZ: No one, Elliot.

ELLIOT: You were tappin' some extra on the side?

YAZ: He woke up one day and I was the same as any other person passing by on
the street, and life is short, and you can only live in mediocrity so long.

ELLIOT: You two are the dog and the owner that look like each other. Ya'll are
the *Cosby Show*.[6] Conundrum, Yaz and William make a funny, end-of episode. You show all us cousins, maybe we can't ever do it ourselves, but it *is*
possible.

6. Television sitcom (1984–92) about a close-knit upper-middle-class African American family starring comedian Bill Cosby (b. 1937).

YAZ: Did I ever say, "It's possible"?

ELLIOT: By example.

YAZ: Did I ever say those words?

(*Professor Aman enters.*)

AMAN: Yazmin, forgive me. You must be . . .

ELLIOT: Elliot Ortiz. Nice to meet you, I appreciate it.

AMAN: Professor Aman. (*They shake*) We'll have to make this short and sweet, my lecture begins . . . began . . . well, talk fast.

ELLIOT: Yaz, give us a second?

YAZ: I'll be in the car. (*Exits*)

ELLIOT: I'm late, too, so . . .

AMAN: You need something translated.

ELLIOT: Just a phrase. Thanks, man.

AMAN: Eh, your sister's cute.

ELLIOT: Cousin. I wrote it phonetically. You grow up speaking Arabic?

AMAN: English. What's your native tongue?

ELLIOT: Spanglish. (*Hands Aman a piece of paper*)

AMAN: Mom-ken men fad-luck ted-dini ga-waz saf-far-i. Mom-ken men-fadluck ted-dini gawaz saffari. Am I saying that right?

ELLIOT (*Spooked*): Spot on.

AMAN: You must have some familiarity with Arabic to remember it so clearly.

ELLIOT: Maybe I heard it on TV or something.

AMAN: An odd phrase.

ELLIOT: It's like a song I can't get out of my head.

AMAN: Yazmin didn't tell me what this is for.

ELLIOT: It's not for anything.

AMAN: Do you mind me asking, what's around your neck?

ELLIOT: Something my girl gave me.

AMAN: Can I see? (*Elliot pulls dog tags from under his shirt*) Romantic gift. You were in the army.

ELLIOT: Marines.

AMAN: Iraq?

ELLIOT: For a minute.

AMAN: Were you reluctant to tell me that?

ELLIOT: No.

AMAN: Still in the service?

ELLIOT: Honorable discharge. Leg injury.

AMAN: When?

ELLIOT: A few years ago.

AMAN: This is a long time to have a phrase stuck in your head.

ELLIOT: What is this, man?

AMAN: You tell me.

ELLIOT: It's just a phrase. If you don't want to translate, just say so.

AMAN: A college buddy is making a film about Marines in Iraq. Gritty, documentary-style. He's looking for some veterans to interview. Get an authentic point of view. Maybe I could pass your number on to him.

ELLIOT: Nope. No interviews for this guy.

AMAN: You're asking me for a favor. (*Pause*) Yazmin told me you're an actor. Every actor needs a break, right?

ELLIOT: I did enough Q&As about the service. People manipulate you with the questions.

AMAN: It's not just to interview. He needs a right-hand man, an expert to help him. How do Marines hold a gun? How do they kick in civilian doors, this sort of thing. How do they say "Ooh-rah" in a patriotic manner?

ELLIOT: Are you his headhunter or something?

AMAN: I'm helping with the translations, I have a small stake and I want the movie to be accurate. And you seem not unintelligent. For a maker of sandwiches. (*Hands him a business card*) He's in L.A. In case you want a career change. I give you a cup of sugar, you give me a cup of sugar.

ELLIOT: If I have a minute, I'll dial the digits. (*Takes the business card*) So what's it mean?

AMAN: Momken men-fadluck ted-dini gawaz saffari. Rough translation, "Can I please have my passport back?"

Scene Two

Odessa's living room and kitchen. She makes coffee. She goes over to her computer, clicks a button. On a screen we see:

HAIKUMOM, SITEADMIN
STATUS: ONLINE

HAIKUMOM: Rise and shine, kiddos, the rooster's a-crowin', it's a beautiful day to be sober. (*No response*) Your Thursday morning haiku:[7]

> if you get restless
> buy a hydrangea or rose
> water it, wait, bloom

(*Odessa continues making coffee. A computer dings and on another screen we see:*)

ORANGUTAN
STATUS: ONLINE

ORANGUTAN: Ninety-one days. Smiley face.

HAIKUMOM (*Relieved*): Orangutan! Jesus, I thought my primate friend had disappeared back to the jungle.

ORANGUTAN: Disappeared? Yes. Jungle? Happily, no.

HAIKUMOM: I'm trying to put a high-five emoticon, but my computer is being a capital B. So, high-five!

---

7. Originally Japanese poetic form that, in its English-language incarnations, traditionally consists of seventeen syllables divided into three lines of five, seven, and five syllables, respectively.

(They high-five in the air. Another computer screen lights up:)

CHUTES&LADDERS
STATUS: ONLINE

CHUTES&LADDERS: Orangutan? I was about to send a search party after your rear end. Kid, *log on.* No news is bad news.

ORANGUTAN: Chutes&Ladders, giving me a hard time as usual. I'd expect nothing less.

CHUTES&LADDERS: Your last post says: "Day One. Packing bags, gotta run," and then you don't log on for three months?

ORANGUTAN: I was going to Japan, I had to figure out what shoes to bring.

HAIKUMOM: The country?

CHUTES&LADDERS: What happened to Maine?

ORANGUTAN: And I quote, "Get a hobby, find a new job, an exciting city, go teach English in a foreign country." Did you guys think I wouldn't take your seasoned advice? I was batting 0 for ten, and for the first time, guys, I feel fucking free.

HAIKUMOM *(Nonjudgmental)*: Censored.

ORANGUTAN: I wake up and I think, What's the world got up its sleeve today? And I look forward to the answer. So, thank you.

CHUTES&LADDERS: We told you so.

ORANGUTAN *(Playful)*: Shut up.

HAIKUMOM: You're welcome.

ORANGUTAN: I gave my parents the URL. My username, my password. They logged on and read every post I've ever put on here and for once they said they understood. They had completely cut me off, but after reading this site they bought me the plane ticket. One way. I teach English in the mornings. I have a class of children, a class of teens, and a class of adults, most of whom are older than me. I am free in the afternoons. I have a paycheck which I use for legal things like ice cream, noodles and socks. I walk around feeling like maybe I *am* normal. Maybe, just possibly, I'm not that different. Or maybe it's just homeland delusions.

CHUTES&LADDERS AND HAIKUMOM: Homeland?

HAIKUMOM: You're Japanese?

ORANGUTAN: I *was*, for the first eight days of my life. Yoshiko Sakai. Then on day nine I was adopted and moved to Cape Lewiston, Maine, where I became Ma—M.M., and where in all my days I have witnessed *one* other Asian. In the Superfresh. Deli counter.

CHUTES&LADDERS: Japan . . . Wow, that little white rock sure doesn't discriminate.

HAIKUMOM: Amen.

ORANGUTAN: Mango Internet Café. I'm sitting in an orange plastic chair, a little view of the Hokkaido waterfront.

HAIKUMOM: Japan has a waterfront?

CHUTES&LADDERS: It's an island.

HAIKUMOM: Really? Are there beaches? Can you go swimming?

ORANGUTAN: The ocean reminds me of Maine. Cold water, very quiet, fisherman, boats, the breeze. I wouldn't try swimming. I'm just a looker. I was never one to actually have an experience.

CHUTES&LADDERS: Ah, the ocean . . . There's only one thing on this planet I'm more scared of than that big blue lady.

HAIKUMOM: Let me guess: landing on a sliding board square?[8]

CHUTES&LADDERS: Lol, truer words have never been spoken. You know I was born just a few miles from the Pacific. In the fresh salt air. Back in "those days" I'm at Coronado Beach[9] with a few "friends" doing my "thing" and I get sucked up under this wave. I gasp, I breathe in and my lungs fill with water. I'm like, this is it, I'm going to meet my maker. I had never felt so heavy, not even during my two OD's.[1] I was sinking to the bottom and my head hit the sand like a lead ball. My body just felt like an anvil. The next thing I know there's fingers digging in my ankles. This lifeguard pulls me out, I'm throwing up salt water. I say to him, "Hey blondie, you don't know me from Adam but you are my witness: today's the day I start to *live*." And this lifeguard, I mean he was young with these muscles, this kid looks at me like, "Who is this big black dude who can't even doggy paddle?" When I stand up and brush the sand off me, people *applaud*. An old lady touches my cheek and says, "I thought you were done for." I get back to San Diego that night, make one phone call, the next day I'm in my first meeting, sitting in a folding chair, saying the serenity prayer.[2]

ORANGUTAN: I hate to inflate your already swollen ego, but that was a lucid, touching story. By the way, did you get the lifeguard's name? He sounds hot.

HAIKUMOM: Hey Chutes&Ladders, it's never too late to learn. Most YMCAs offer adult swimming classes.

CHUTES&LADDERS: I'll do the world a favor and stay out of a speedo.

ORANGUTAN: Sober air toast. To lifeguards.

CHUTES&LADDERS AND HAIKUMOM: To lifeguards.

ORANGUTAN, CHUTES&LADDERS AND HAIKUMOM: Clink.

HAIKUMOM: Chutes&Ladders, I'm buying you a pair of water wings.

Scene Three

John Coltrane's A Love Supreme *plays. A Subway sandwich shop on Philadelphia's Main Line. Elliot sits behind the counter. The phone rings. He gets up, hobbles to it—he walks with a limp.*

ELLIOT: Subway Main Line. Lar! Laaar, what's it doing for you today? Staying in the shade? I got you, how many you need? Listen, the delivery guy's out and

---

8. In Milton Bradley's board game Chutes & Ladders (based on the ancient Indian game Snakes and Ladders), some squares are connected by pictures of sliding boards, or "chutes." Players landing on the square picturing the top of the chute "slide" directly down to the square picturing the bottom of the chute.

9. On Coronado Island, just off the coast of San Diego, California.

1. Overdoses (acronym).

2. Authored by American theologian Reinhold Niebuhr (1892–1971) and adopted by Alcoholics Anonymous and other twelve-step addiction-recovery programs, it reads, "God, grant me the serenity to accept the things I cannot change, / The courage to change the things I can, / And the wisdom to know the difference."

my little sports injury is giving me hell so can you pick up? Cool, sorry for the inconvenience. Let me grab a pen. A'ight, pick a hoagie, any hoagie!

(*Elliot begins writing the order.*

Lights rise to a seminar room at Swarthmore College. We find Yaz mid-class. She hits a button on a stereo and the Coltrane stops playing.)

YAZ: Coltrane's *A Love Supreme*, 1964. Dissonance is still a gateway to resolution. A B-diminished chord is still resolving to? C-major. A tritone is still resolving up to? The major sixth. Diminished chords, tritones, still didn't have the right to be their own independent thought. In 1965 something changed. The ugliness bore no promise of a happy ending. The ugliness became an end in itself. Coltrane democratized the notes. He said, they're all equal. Freedom. It was called Free Jazz but freedom is a hard thing to express musically without spinning into noise. This is from *Ascension*, 1965.

(*She plays* Ascension. *It sounds uglier than the first sample. In the Subway, a figure comes into view. It is the Ghost.*)

GHOST: Momken men-fadluck ted-dini gawaz saffari?

(*Elliot tries to ignore the Ghost, reading off the order.*)

ELLIOT: That's three teriyaki onion with chicken. First with hots and onions. Second with everything. Third with extra bacon. Two spicy Italian with American cheese on whole grain. One BMT on flatbread. Good so far?

GHOST: Momken men-fadluck ted-dini gawaz saffari?

ELLIOT: Five chocolate chip cookies, one oatmeal raisin. Three Baked Lay's, three Doritos. Two Sprite Zeros, one Barq's, one Coke, two orange sodas. How'd I do?

GHOST: Momken men-fadluck ted-dini gawaz saffari?

ELLIOT: All right, that'll be ready in fifteen minutes. One sec for your total.

(*Elliot gets a text message. He reads it; his entire demeanor shifts.*)

Lar, I just got a text. There's a family emergency, I can't do this order right now.

(*Elliot hangs up. He exits, limping away.*)

YAZ: Oh come on, don't make that face. I know it feels academic. You're going to leave here and become R&B hit makers and Sondheim[3] clones and never think about this noise again. But this is Coltrane, people, this is not Schoenberg![4] This is jazz, stuff people listen to *voluntarily*. Shopping period is still on—go sit in one session of "Germans and Noise" down the hall and you'll come running back begging for this muzak.

(*Yaz turns off the music.*)

---

3. Stephen Sondheim (b. 1930), multi-award-winning American composer-lyricist best known for hit Broadway musicals including *West Side Story* (1957), for which he wrote the lyrics only; *Sweeney Todd* (1979); and *Into the Woods* (1986).

4. Arnold Schoenberg (1874–1951), influential avant-garde Austrian classical pianist, composer, and music theorist.

In fact, change the syllabus. No listening report next week. Instead, I want you to pinpoint the first time you really noticed dissonance. The composer, the piece, the measures. Two pages analyzing the notes and two pages describing the experience personally. This is your creation myth.[5] Before you leave this school you better figure out that story and cling to it for dear life or you'll be a stockbroker within a year.

I was thirteen, I worked in a corrugated box factory all summer, I saved up enough to find my first music teacher—up to that point I was self-taught, playing to the radio. I walked into Don Rappaport's room at Settlement Music School.[6] He was old, he had jowls, he was sitting at the piano and he said, "What do you do?" I said, "I'm a composer, sir." Presumptuous, right? I sat down and played Mr. Rappaport a Yazmin original. He said, "It's pretty, everything goes together. It's like an outfit where your socks are blue and your pants, shirt, hat are all blue." Then he said, "Play an F-sharp major in your left hand." Then he said, "Play a C-major in your right hand." "Now play them together." He asked me, "Does it go together?" I told him, "No, sir." He said, "Now go home and write." My first music lesson was seven minutes long. I had never really heard dissonance before.

(*Yaz's phone vibrates. She sees the caller with concern.*)

Let's take five.

(*As students file out, Yaz makes a phone call. Lights up on Elliot outside the Subway.*)

(*"What's the bad news?"*) You called three times.

ELLIOT: She's still alive.

YAZ: Okay.

ELLIOT: Jefferson Hospital. They admitted her three hours ago. Pop had the courtesy to text me.

YAZ: Are you still at work?

ELLIOT: Just smashed the bathroom mirror all over the floor. Boss sent me out to the parking lot.

YAZ: Wait there. I'm on my way.

ELLIOT: "Your mom is on breathing machine." Who texts that? Who texts that and then doesn't pick up the phone?

YAZ: I'll be there within twenty.

ELLIOT: Why did I come to work today?

YAZ: She had a good morning. You wanted your thing translated.

ELLIOT: She cooked and I wouldn't eat a bite off the fork. There's a Subway hoagies around the corner and I had to work half an hour away.

YAZ: You didn't want your buddies to see you working a normal job.

ELLIOT: Not normal job. Shit job. I'm a butler. A porter of sandwiches.

5. Narrative recounting a particular culture or religion's understanding of how something (usually the world itself) came to be.
6. Philadelphia institution originally founded (1908) to provide free music instruction to newly arrived immigrants but today offering music, dance, and visual arts classes to children and adults across the city "without regard to age, background, ability or economic circumstances." Hudes is an alumna.

YAZ: Ginny's been to Hades and back, stronger each time.

ELLIOT: What is Hades?

YAZ: In Greek mythology, the river through the underworld—

ELLIOT: My mom's on a machine and you're dropping vocab words?!

(*A ding.*)

YAZ: Text message, don't hang up. (*She looks at her phone. A moment, then*) You still there?

ELLIOT: It was my dad wasn't it? Yaz, spit it out.

YAZ: It was your dad.

ELLIOT: And? Yaz, I'm about to start walking down Lancaster Avenue for thirty miles till I get back to Philly and I don't care if I snap every wire out my leg and back—I need to get out of here. I need to see Mom, I need to talk to her!

YAZ: He said, "Waiting for Elliot till we turn off the machine."

Scene Four

The chat room. A screen lights up:

[NO IMAGE]
FOUNTAINHEAD[7]
STATUS: ONLINE

FOUNTAINHEAD: I've uh, wow, hello there everyone. Delete, delete. Good afternoon. Evening. Delete.

(*Deep breath.*)

Things I am taking:

—My life into my own hands.

—My gorgeous, deserving wife out for our seventh anniversary.

Me: mildly athletic, but work twice as hard. Won state for javelin two years straight. Ran a half marathon last fall. Animated arguer. Two medals for undergrad debate. MBA from Wharton.[8] Beautiful wife, two sons. Built a programming company from the ground up, featured in the *New York Times'* Circuits section, sold it at its peak, bought a yellow Porsche, got a day job to keep myself honest. Salary was 300K, company was run by morons, got laid off, handsome severance, which left me swimming in cash and free time.

Me and crack: long story short, I was at a conference with our CFO and two programmers and a not-unattractive lady in HR.[9] They snorted, invited me to join. A few weeks later that little rock waltzed right into my hand. I've been using off and on since. One eight ball every Saturday, strict rations, portion control. Though the last three or four weeks, it's less like getting high

---

7. Title of a best-selling 1943 novel by Ayn Rand (1905–82), a famous evocation of her individualist philosophy.

8. Famed business school (founded 1881) of the University of Pennsylvania, in Philadelphia. *MBA*: master of business administration (acronym).

9. Human resources (acronym). *CFO*: chief financial officer (acronym).

and more like trying to build a time machine. Anything to get back the romance of that virgin smoke.

Last weekend I let myself buy more than my predetermined allotment—I buy in small quantity, because as with my food, I eat what's on my plate. Anyway, I ran over a curb, damaged the underside of my Porsche. Now it's in the shop and I'm driving a rental Mustang. So, not rock bottom but a rental Ford is as close to rock bottom as I'd like to get. Fast forward to tonight. I'm watching my wife's eyelids fall and telling myself, "You are on punishment, Poppa. Daddy's on time out. Do not get out of bed, do not tiptoe down those stairs, do not go down to that basement, do not sit beside that foosball table, do not smoke, and please do not crawl on the carpet looking for one last hit in the fibers."

(*Pause.*)

In kindergarten my son tested into G and T. Gifted and talented. You meet with the school, they tailor the program to the kid. Math, reading, art, whatever the parent chooses. I said, "Teach my son how to learn. How to use a library. How to find original source material, read a map, track down the experts so he becomes an expert." Which gets me to—

You: the experts. It's the first day of school and I'm knocking at your classroom door. I got my No. 2 pencils, I'll sit in the front row, pay attention, and do my homework. No lesson is too basic. Teach me every technique. Any tip so that Saturday doesn't become every day. Any actions that keep you in the driver seat. Healthy habits and rational thoughts to blot out that voice in the back of my head.

Today, I quit. My wife cannot know, she'd get suspicious if I were at meetings all the time. There can be no medical records, so therapy is out. At least it's not heroin, I'm not facing a physical war. It's a psychological battle and I'm armed with two weapons: willpower and the experts.

I'm taking my wife out tomorrow for our seventh anniversary and little does she know that when we clink glasses, I'll be toasting to Day One.

(*Odessa is emotional. Chutes&Ladders and Orangutan seem awestruck.*)

ORANGUTAN (*Clapping*): That was brave.
CHUTES&LADDERS: What. The.
HAIKUMOM: Careful.
CHUTES&LADDERS: Fuck.
HAIKUMOM: Censored.
ORANGUTAN: I'm making popcorn. Oh, this is gonna be fun!
CHUTES&LADDERS: Fountainhead, speaking of experts, I've been meaning to become an asshole. Can you teach me how?
HAIKUMOM: Censored!
ORANGUTAN: "Tips"? This isn't a cooking website. And what is a half marathon?
CHUTES&LADDERS: Maybe it's something like a half crack addict. Or a half husband.
ORANGUTAN: Was that an addiction coming out or an online dating profile? "Married Male Dope Fiend. Smokin' hot."

CHUTES&LADDERS: Fountainhead, you sound like the kind of guy who's read *The 7 Habits of Highly Effective People*[1] cover to cover. Was one of those habits crack? Give the essays a rest and type three words. "I'm. A. Crackhead."

ORANGUTAN: You know, adderall is like totes[2] cool. Us crackheads, we're like yucky and stuff. We're like so nineties. Go try the adderall edge!

HAIKUMOM: Hey.

ORANGUTAN: The guy's a hoax. Twenty bucks says he's pranking. Let's start a new thread.

HAIKUMOM: Hi, Fountainhead, welcome. As the site administrator, I want to honestly congratulate you for accomplishing what so many addicts only hope for: one clean day. Any time you feel like using, log on here instead. It's worked for me. When it comes to junkies, I dug lower than the dungeon. Once upon a time I had a beautiful family, too. Now all I have is six years clean. Don't lose what I lost, what Chutes&Ladders lost.

CHUTES&LADDERS: Excuse me.

HAIKUMOM: Orangutan, I just checked and Fountainhead has no aliases and has never logged onto this site before under a different pseudonym, which are the usual markers of a scam.

ORANGUTAN: I'm just saying. Who toasts to their first day of sobriety?

CHUTES&LADDERS: I hope it's seltzer in that there champagne glass.

ORANGUTAN: Ginger ale, shirley temple.

CHUTES&LADDERS: "A toast, honey. I had that seven-year itch so I became a crackhead."

CHUTES&LADDERS AND ORANGUTAN: Clink.

HAIKUMOM: Hey; kiddos. Your smiley administrator doesn't want to start purging messages. For rules of the forums click on this link. No personal attacks.

ORANGUTAN: We don't come to this site for a pat on the back.

HAIKUMOM: I'm just saying. R-e-s-p-e-c-t.

CHUTES&LADDERS: I will always give *crack* the respect it deserves. Some purebred poodle comes pissing on my tree trunk? Damn straight I'll chase his ass out my forest.

HAIKUMOM: This here is my forest. You two think you were all humble pie when you started out? Check your original posts.

ORANGUTAN: Oh, I know mine. "I-am-scared-I-will-kill-myself-talk-me-off-the-ledge."

HAIKUMOM: So unless someone gets that desperate they don't deserve our noble company? "Suffer like me, or you ain't legit"?

ORANGUTAN: Haikumom's growing claws.

HAIKUMOM: Just don't act entitled because you got so low. (*To Fountainhead*) Sorry. Fountainhead, forgive us. We get very passionate because—

CHUTES&LADDERS: Fountainhead, your Porsche has a massive engine. You got bulging marathon muscles. I'm sure your penis is as big as that javelin you used to throw.

1. Popular business self-help book (1989) by Stephen R. Covey (1932–2012) stressing the principles of independence and self-mastery, interdependence, and continuous improvement.
2. Totally (slang). *Adderall*: stimulant used to treat narcolepsy and attention deficit hyperactivity disorder (ADHD).

HAIKUMOM: Censored.

CHUTES&LADDERS: But none of those things come close to the size of your ego. If you can put that aside, you may, *may* stand a chance. Otherwise, you're fucked, my friend.

HAIKUMOM: Message purged.

ORANGUTAN: OH MY GOD, WE'RE DYING HERE, DO WE HAVE TO BE SO POLITE ABOUT IT?

HAIKUMOM: Censored.

ORANGUTAN: Oh my G-zero-D. Democracy or dictatorship?

CHUTES&LADDERS: Hey Fountainhead, why the silence?

> (*Fountainhead logs off.*)

HAIKUMOM: Nice work, guys. Congratulations.

CHUTES&LADDERS: You don't suppose he's . . . crawling on the carpet looking for one last rock??

ORANGUTAN: Lordy lord lord, I'm about to go over his house and start looking for one myself!

HAIKUMOM: That's why you're in Japan, little monkey. For now, I'm closing this thread. Fountainhead, if you want to reopen it, email me directly.

Scene Five

A flower shop in Center City[3] *Philadelphia. Yaz looks over some brochures. Elliot enters, his limp looking worse.*

YAZ: I was starting to get worried. How you holding?

ELLIOT: Joe's Gym, perfect remedy.

YAZ: You went boxing? Really?

ELLIOT: I had to blow off steam. Women don't get it.

YAZ: Don't be a pig. You've had four leg surgeries, no more boxing.

ELLIOT: Did Odessa call?

YAZ: You know how she is. Shutting herself out from the world.

ELLIOT: We need help this week.

YAZ: And I got your back.

ELLIOT: I'm just saying, pick up the phone and ask, "Do you need anything, Elliot?"

YAZ: I did speak to your dad. Everyone's gathering at the house. People start arriving from PR[4] in a few hours. The next door neighbor brought over two trays of pigs feet.

ELLIOT: I just threw up in my mouth.

YAZ: Apparently a fight broke out over who gets your mom's pocketbooks.

ELLIOT: Those pleather things from the ten-dollar store?

YAZ: Thank you, it's not like she had Gucci purses!

ELLIOT: People just need to manufacture drama.

---

3. Downtown district, the city's business and transportation hub.
4. Puerto Rico (acronym).

YAZ: He said they were tearing through Ginny's closets like it was a shopping spree. "I want this necklace!" "I want the photo album!" "Yo, those chancletas[5] are mine!" I'm like, damn, let the woman be buried first.

ELLIOT: Yo, let's spend the day here.

YAZ (*Handing him some papers*): Brochures. I was being indecisive so the florist went to work on a wedding bouquet. I ruled out seven, you make the final call. Celebration of Life, Blooming Garden, Eternity Wreath.

ELLIOT: All of those have carnations. I don't want a carnation within a block of the church.

YAZ: You told me to eliminate seven. I eliminated seven. Close your eyes and point.

ELLIOT: Am I a particularly demanding person?

YAZ: Yes. What's so wrong with a carnation?

ELLIOT: You know what a carnation says to the world? That they were out of roses at the 7-Eleven. It should look something like Mom's garden.

YAZ (*In agreement*): Graveside Remembrances? That looks something like it . . . I'm renominating Graveside Remembrances. Putting it back on the table.

ELLIOT: You couldn't find anything tropical? Yaz, you could find a needle in a damn haystack and you couldn't find a bird of paradise or something?

YAZ: He just shoved some brochures in my hand.

ELLIOT (*Stares her down*): You have an awful poker face.

YAZ: Now, look here.

ELLIOT: You did find something.

YAZ: No. Not exactly.

ELLIOT: How much does it cost? Yaz, this is my mom we're talking about.

YAZ: Five hundred more. Just for the casket piece.

ELLIOT: You can't lie for shit, you never could.

YAZ: Orchid Paradise.

(*Yaz hands him another brochure. They look at it together.*)

ELLIOT: Aw damn. Damn. That looks like her garden.

YAZ: Spitting image.

ELLIOT (*Pointing*): I think she grew those.

YAZ: Right next to the tomatoes.

ELLIOT: But hers were yellow. Fuck.

YAZ: It's very odd to order flowers when someone dies. Because the flowers are just gonna die, too. "Would you like some death with your death?"

ELLIOT (*A confession*): I didn't water them.

YAZ (*Getting it*): What, are you supposed to be a gardener all of a sudden?

ELLIOT: It doesn't rain for a month and do I grab the hose and water Mom's garden one time?

YAZ: You were feeding her. Giving her meds. Bathing her. I could've come over and watered a leaf. A single petal.

ELLIOT: The last four days, she'd wake me up in the middle of the night. "Did you water the flowers?" "Yeah, Mom, just like you told me to yesterday." "Carry me out back, I want to see." "Mom, you're too heavy, I can't carry you down those steps one more time today."

5. Sandals or flip-flops (Spanish slang).

YAZ: Little white lies.

ELLIOT: Can you do the sermon?

YAZ: This is becoming a second career.

ELLIOT: Because you're the only one who doesn't cry.

YAZ: Unlike Julia.

ELLIOT (*Imitating*): "¡Ay dios mio![6] ¡Ay! ¡Ay!"

YAZ: I hate public speaking.

ELLIOT: You're a teacher.

YAZ: It's different when it's ideas. Talking about ideas isn't saying something, it's making syllables with your mouth.

ELLIOT: You love ideas. All you ever wanted to do was have ideas.

YAZ: It was an elaborate bait and switch. The ideas don't fill the void, they just help you articulate it.

ELLIOT: You've spoken at city hall. On the radio.

YAZ: You're the face of Main Line Chevrolet. (*Pause*) Can I do it in English?

ELLIOT: You could do it in Russian for all I care. I'll just be in the front row acting like my cheek is itchy so no one sees me crying.

YAZ: The elders want a good Spanish sermon.

ELLIOT: Mami Ginny was it. You're the elder now.

YAZ: I'm twenty-nine.

ELLIOT: But you don't look a day over fifty.

YAZ: You gotta do me a favor in return. I know this is your tragedy but . . . Call William. Ask him not to come to the funeral.

ELLIOT: Oh shit.

YAZ: He saw the obit in the *Daily News*.

ELLIOT: They were close. Mami Ginny loved that blond hair. She was the madrina[7] of your wedding.

YAZ: William relinquished mourning privileges. You fall out of love with me, you lose certain rights. He calls talking about, "I want the condo." Fuck that. Fuck that. Coming from you it won't seem bitter. Wants the fucking condo all for hisself. That I decorated, that I painted. "Oh, and where's the funeral, by the way?" You know, he's been to four funerals in the Ortiz clan and I could feel it, there was a part of him, under it all, that was disgusted. The open casket. The prayers.

ELLIOT: It is disgusting.

YAZ: Sitting in the pew knowing what freaks we are.

ELLIOT: He's good people.

YAZ: I was probably at his side doing the same thing, thinking I'm removed, that I'm somehow different.

ELLIOT: Hey, hey, done.

YAZ: One more condition. I go to Puerto Rico with you. We scatter her ashes together.

ELLIOT: Mami Ginny couldn't be buried in Philly. She had to have her ashes thrown at a waterfall in El Yunque,[8] just to be the most Puerto Rican motherfucker around.

6. Oh Lord or Oh my God (Spanish).

7. Matron of honor (Spanish).

8. Tropical rain forest in Puerto Rico, part of the U.S. National Forest System.

YAZ: I saw your Colgate ad.

ELLIOT: Dang, cousin Yaz watches Spanish TV?

YAZ: Shut up.

ELLIOT: I walked into the casting office, flashed my pearly whites, showed them my military ID and I charmed them.

YAZ: Do it.

ELLIOT: Give me a dollar.

YAZ: For that big cheeseburger smile?

> (*She gives him a dollar.*)

ELLIOT (*Smiling*): "Sonrisa,[9] baby!"

> (*Yaz cracks up laughing, which devolves into tears.*)

How we gonna pay for Orchid Paradise?

YAZ: They should have a frequent-flower card. They punch a hole. Buy nine funeral bouquets, get the tenth free. We'd be living in a house full of lilies. Look at that guy. Arranging his daisies like little treasures. What do you think it's like to be him? To be normal?

ELLIOT: Normal? A hundred bucks says that dude has a closet full of animal porno at home.

YAZ: I bet in his family, funerals are rare occasions. I bet he's never seen a cousin get arrested. Let alone one under the age of eighteen. I bet he never saw his eight-year-old cousin sipping rum through a twisty straw or . . . I just remembered this time cousin Maria was babysitting me . . .

ELLIOT: Fat Maria or Buck Tooth Maria?

YAZ: Pig.

ELLIOT: Ah, Fat Maria.

YAZ: I was dyeing her hair. I had never dyed hair before so I asked her to read me the next step and she handed me the box and said, "You read it." And I said, "My rubber gloves are covered in toxic goop, I can't really hold that right now." And so she held it in front of my eyes and said, "You gonna have to read it because I sure as hell can't."

ELLIOT: I been knowed that.

YAZ: I said, "But you graduated from high school." She said, "They just pass you, I just stood in the back." I was in fourth grade. *I* could read! (*Pause*) I have a degree written in Latin that I don't even understand. I paid seventeen thousand dollars for my piano.

ELLIOT: Oh shit.

YAZ: I have a mortgage on my piano. Drive two miles north? William told me every time I went to North Philly, I'd come back different. His family has Quaker Oats for DNA. They play Pictionary on New Year's. I'd sit there wishing I could scoop the blood out my veins like you scoop the seeds out a pumpkin and he'd be like, "Whatchu thinking about, honey?" And I'd be like, "Nothing. Let's play some Pictionary."

ELLIOT: Yo, being the scholarship case at an all-white prep school really fucked with your head, didn't it?

9. Smile (Spanish).

YAZ: I should've gone to Edison.

ELLIOT: Public school in el barrio.[1] You wouldn't have survived there for a day.

YAZ: Half our cousins didn't survive there.

ELLIOT: True. But you would've pissed your pants. At least their pants was dry when they went down.

YAZ: You're sick.

ELLIOT: And the ladies love me.

YAZ: I thought abuela[2] dying, that would be the end of us. But Ginny grabbed the torch. Christmas, Easter. Now what? Our family may be fucked-up but we had somewhere to go. A kitchen that connected us. Plastic-covered sofas where we could park our communal asses.

ELLIOT: Pop's selling the house. And the plastic-covered sofas. He's moving back to the Bronx, be with his sisters.

YAZ: You going with him? (Elliot shrugs) Wow. I mean, once that living room is gone, I may never step foot in North Philly again.

ELLIOT: Washed up at age twenty-four. Disabled vet. Motherless chil'. Working at Subway. Soon-to-be homeless.

YAZ: My couch is your couch.

ELLIOT: Until William takes your couch.

YAZ: My cardboard box is your cardboard box.

ELLIOT: I could go out to L.A. and be a movie star.

YAZ: You need a manager? Shoot I'm coming witchu. Forget Philly.

ELLIOT: Change of scene, baby. Dream team.

YAZ: Probably we should order some flowers first, though. Don'tcha think? (Elliot nods. To the florist) Sir?

Scene Six

> *The chat room. Orangutan is online, seems upset.*

ORANGUTAN: 2:38 A.M. Tuesday. The witching hour.

> (*Chutes&Ladders logs on.*)

CHUTES&LADDERS: 1:38 P.M. Monday. The lunch hour.

ORANGUTAN: I'm in a gay bar slash internet café in the city of Sapporo. Deafening dance music.

CHUTES&LADDERS: Sure you should be in a bar, little monkey?

ORANGUTAN (*Disappointed*): I flew halfway around the world and guess what? It was still me who got off the plane. (*Taking comfort*) Sapporo is always open. The world turns upside down at night.

CHUTES&LADDERS: You're in a city named after a beer sitting in a bar. Go home.

ORANGUTAN: Everything in this country makes sense but me. The noodles in soup make sense. The woodpecker outside my window every evening? Completely logical. The girls getting out of school in their miniskirts and shy smiles? Perfectly natural. I'm floating. I'm a cloud. My existence is one sustained out-of-body experience. It doesn't matter if I change my shoes, there's

---

1. Spanish-speaking district or neighborhood.
2. Grandmother (Spanish).

not a pair I've ever been able to fill. I'm a baby in a basket on an endless river. Wherever I go I don't make sense there.

CHUTES&LADDERS: Hey, little monkey. How many days you got?

ORANGUTAN: I think day ninety-six is when the demons really come out to play.

CHUTES&LADDERS: Ninety-six? Girl, hang your hat on that.

ORANGUTAN: I really really really want to smoke crack.

CHUTES&LADDERS: Yeah, well *don't*.

ORANGUTAN: Distract me from myself. What do you really really really want, Chutes&Ladders?

CHUTES&LADDERS: I wouldn't say no to a new car—my Tercel is one sorry sight.

ORANGUTAN: What else?

CHUTES&LADDERS: Tuesday's crossword. On Monday I'm done by the time I sit at my desk. I wish every day could be a Tuesday.

ORANGUTAN: What about your son? Don't you really really really want to call him?

CHUTES&LADDERS: By all accounts, having me be a stranger these ten years has given him the best decade of his life.

ORANGUTAN: I've known you for how long?

CHUTES&LADDERS: Three Christmas Eves. When you logged on you were a stone-cold user. We sang Christmas carols online all night. Now you've got ninety days.

ORANGUTAN: Can I ask you a personal question? What's your day job?

CHUTES&LADDERS: IRS. GS4 paper pusher.

ORANGUTAN: Got any vacation days?

CHUTES&LADDERS: A solid collection. I haven't taken a vacation in ten years.

ORANGUTAN: Do you have money?

CHUTES&LADDERS: Enough to eat steak on Friday nights. Enough to buy pay-per-view boxing.

ORANGUTAN: Yeah, I bet that's all the pay-per-view you buy. (*Pause*) Enough money to fly to Japan?

(*Pause.*)

CHUTES&LADDERS: You should know I'm fifty years old on a good day. I eat three and a half doughnuts for breakfast and save the remaining half for brunch. I have small hands, six toes on my left foot. And my face resembles a corgi.

ORANGUTAN: If I was looking for a hot screw I wouldn't be logging on to this site.

CHUTES&LADDERS: Damn, was it something I said?

ORANGUTAN (*With honest admiration*): I've been on this planet for thirty-one years and you're the only person I've ever met who's more sarcastic than I am yet still believes in God.

CHUTES&LADDERS (*Taking the compliment*): Says the agnostic.

ORANGUTAN: The atheist. Who is very envious of believers. My brain is my biggest enemy—always arguing my soul into a corner. (*Pause*) I like you. Come to Japan. We can go get an ice cream. I can show you the countryside.

CHUTES&LADDERS: I don't have a passport. If my Tercel can't drive there, I generally don't go.

ORANGUTAN: Come save me in Japan. Be my knight in shining armor.

CHUTES&LADDERS: I'll admit, I'm a dashing concept. If you saw my flesh and blood, you'd be disappointed.

ORANGUTAN: I see my flesh and blood every day and I've learned to live with the disappointment.

CHUTES&LADDERS: I'm the squarest of the square. I live in a square house on a square block watching a square box eating square-cut fries.

ORANGUTAN: I get it. You were the kid who colored inside the lines.

CHUTES&LADDERS: No, I was the kid who ate the crayons. *Was.* I went clean and all personality left my life. Flew right out the window. I had to take life on life's terms. Messy, disappointing, bad shit happens to good people, coffee stains on my necktie, boring life.

ORANGUTAN: Maybe we could hang out and have a relationship that has very little to do with crack or addiction or history. We could watch DVDs and microwave popcorn and take walks on the waterfront while we gossip about celebrities. It could be the land of the living.

CHUTES&LADDERS: Stay in the box. Keep things in their place. It's a simple, effective recipe for ten clean years.

ORANGUTAN: Forget simple. I want a goddamn challenge.

CHUTES&LADDERS: You're in recovery and work in a foreign country. That's a challenge.

ORANGUTAN: No. No it's fucking not. Not if I just stay anonymous and alone. Like every day of my shit life so far. A friend, the kind that is nice to you and you are nice to in return. *That* would push the comfort zone. The invitation is open. Come tear my shyness open.

CHUTES&LADDERS: All right, now you're being weird. Can we change the subject?

(*Haikumom appears. She's reading the newspaper.*)

HAIKUMOM: Orangutan, cover your ears.

ORANGUTAN: Big Brother, always watching.

HAIKUMOM: Cover your ears, kiddo.

ORANGUTAN: That doesn't really work online.

HAIKUMOM: Okay, Chutes and Ladders, can we g-chat? One on one?

ORANGUTAN: Come on! No talking behind backs.

HAIKUMOM: Fine. Chutes&Ladders, you listening?

CHUTES&LADDERS: Lord have mercy spit it out.

HAIKUMOM: Orangutan may be immature . . .

ORANGUTAN: Hey.

HAIKUMOM: She may be annoying at times . . .

ORANGUTAN: What the f?

HAIKUMOM: She may be overbearing and self-obsessed and a little bit of a concern troll and she can type faster than she can think which often leads to diarrhea of the keyboard—

CHUTES&LADDERS: Your point?

HAIKUMOM: But she's telling you, "Be my friend." When's the last time someone opened your closet door, saw all them skeletons, and said, "Wassup?! Can I join the party?"

CHUTES&LADDERS: All right, my wrist is officially slapped. Thank you, oh nagging wives.

HAIKUMOM: Internal Revenue Service, 300 North Los Angeles Street 90012? Is that you?

CHUTES&LADDERS: Need my name, too? It's Wilkie. I'll leave it at that.

HAIKUMOM: I'm sending you a care package. Orangutan, you can uncover your ears now. I love you.

ORANGUTAN: Middle finger.

(*Fountainhead's log-on appears.*)

FOUNTAINHEAD: Hey all, thanks for the warm two-by-four to my head.

HAIKUMOM: All right, look who's back.

FOUNTAINHEAD: Knives sharpened? Last night we ran out of butter while my wife was cooking and she sent me to the store and it took every bit of strength I could summon not to make a "wrong turn" to that parking lot I know so well. I got the butter and on the car ride home, I couldn't help it, I drove by the lot, and there was my dealer in the shadows. My brain went on attack. "Use one more time just to prove you won't need another hit tomorrow." I managed to keep on driving and bring the butter home. Major victory. And my wife pulls it out of the plastic bag and says, "This is unsalted. I said salted." Then she feels guilty so she says never mind, never mind, she'll just add a little extra salt to the pie crust but I insist. "No, no, no, my wife deserves the right kind of butter and she's gonna get it!" I mean, I bark it, I'm already halfway out the door, my heart was racing all the way to the parking lot and raced even harder when I sat in the car and smoked. So, Michael Jordan[3] is benched with a broken foot. But he'll come back in the finals.

HAIKUMOM: Thanks for the update, Fountainhead. You may not believe this, but we were missing you and worried about you. Don't beat yourself up about the slip. You had three days clean. This time you'll make it to day four.

FOUNTAINHEAD: Be ambitious. Why not reach for a whopping five?

ORANGUTAN: Maybe you'll make it to day thirty if you tell your wife.

FOUNTAINHEAD: I told you, I have my reasons, I cannot do that. My wife has some emotional issues.

ORANGUTAN (*Sarcastic*): No!

FOUNTAINHEAD: Listen? Please? Are you capable of that? She's in therapy twice a week. Depression, manic. I don't want to be the reason she goes down a tailspin. I actually have her best interest in mind.

CHUTES&LADDERS: Yawn.

FOUNTAINHEAD: Ah, Chutes&Ladders. I could feel you circling like a vulture. Weigh in, by all means.

CHUTES&LADDERS: And I repeat. Yawn.

FOUNTAINHEAD: Chutes&Ladders, why do I get the feeling you'd be the first in line for tickets to watch me smoke again? That you'd be in the bleachers cheering if I relapse?

CHUTES&LADDERS: How can you relapse when you don't even think you're addicted?

FOUNTAINHEAD: If you read my original post clearly, I wrote that it's a psychological addiction, not like heroin.

CHUTES&LADDERS: Well see then, you're not a junkie after all.

---

3. Former Chicago Bull (b. 1963) hailed by the NBA as "the greatest basketball player of all time."

FOUNTAINHEAD: What is this, first-grade recess?

CHUTES&LADDERS: No, this is a site for crackheads trying not to be crackheads anymore. If you're not a crackhead, leave, we don't want you, you are irrelevant, get off my lawn, go.

HAIKUMOM: Chutes&Ladders, please.

CHUTES&LADDERS: I got this.

ORANGUTAN: He's still logged on.

CHUTES&LADDERS: Hey Fountainhead, why did you come to this website?

FOUNTAINHEAD: Because I thoroughly enjoy getting shit on.

HAIKUMOM: Censored.

CHUTES&LADDERS: Why do you want to be here?

FOUNTAINHEAD: Want? The two times I've logged on here I've *wanted* to vomit.

CHUTES&LADDERS: Well? Did you receive some sort of invitation? Did one of us ask you here?

FOUNTAINHEAD: Look, I'm the first to say it. I have a problem.

CHUTES&LADDERS: Adam had problems. Eve had problems. Why are *you here?*

FOUNTAINHEAD: To get information.

CHUTES&LADDERS: Go to Wikipedia. Why are you *here?*

FOUNTAINHEAD: Because I smoke crack.

CHUTES&LADDERS: Go to a dealer. Why are you here?

FOUNTAINHEAD: Because I plan to stop smoking crack.

CHUTES&LADDERS: Fine, when your son has a tummy-ache in the middle of the night and walks in on you tweaking and geeking just tell him, "Don't worry, Junior, Daddy's sucking on a glass dick—"

HAIKUMOM (*Overlaps*): Hey!

CHUTES&LADDERS: "—but Daddy makes 300K and this is all a part of Daddy's Plan!"

FOUNTAINHEAD: I'M A FUCKING CRACKHEAD.

HAIKUMOM (*Apologetic*): Censored.

FOUNTAINHEAD: Fuck you, Chutes&Ladders.

HAIKUMOM: Bleep.

FOUNTAINHEAD: Fuck you . . . Don't talk about my sons. Don't fucking talk about my boys.

HAIKUMOM: Bleep again.

FOUNTAINHEAD: Are you happy, Chutes&Ladders?

CHUTES&LADDERS: Absolutely not, my friend. I'm a crackhead, too, and I wouldn't wish it on my worst enemy.

FOUNTAINHEAD: And I *made* 300K, I'm currently unemployed. An unemployed crackhead. At least I still have all my teeth. (*They laugh*) Better than I can say for my dealer.

CHUTES&LADDERS (*Being a friend*): Ex-dealer, man.

FOUNTAINHEAD: Ex-dealer. Thank you.

HAIKUMOM: Fountainhead, welcome to the dinner party. Granted, it's a party we never wanted to be invited to, but pull up a chair and pass the salt. Some people here may pour it in your wounds. Just like you, we've all crawled on the floor with a flashlight. We've thrown out the brillo and bought some more. But guess what? You had three days. For three days straight, you didn't try to kill yourself on an hourly basis. Please. Talk to your wife about your addiction. You need every supporting resource. You are in for the fight of your life. You mentioned Wharton. I live in Philly. If you're still in the area and you have an emergency or even a craving, email me directly. Any time of night. Don't take it lightly when I say a sober day for you is a sober day for me. I know you can do this but I know you can't do it alone. So stop being a highly functioning isolator and start being a highly dysfunctional *person*. The only way out it is through it.

ORANGUTAN (*Nostalgic*): Slogans . . .

HAIKUMOM: Ya'll know I know 'em all.

CHUTES&LADDERS: They saved my life.

ORANGUTAN: Your personal favorite. Go.

HAIKUMOM: "Nothing changes if nothing changes."

(*Elliot appears at the boxing gym, punching a bag. The Ghost watches him.*)

GHOST: Momken men-fadluck ted-dini gawaz saffari?

ORANGUTAN: "It came to pass, it didn't come to stay."

FOUNTAINHEAD: "I obsessively pursue feeling good, no matter how bad it makes me feel."

CHUTES&LADDERS: Okay, now!

ORANGUTAN: Nice!

HAIKUMOM: Rookie don't play!

GHOST: Momken men-fadluck ted-dini gawaz saffari?

ORANGUTAN: "One hit is too many, one thousand never enough."

HAIKUMOM: "Have an at-ti-tude of gra-ti-tude."

CHUTES&LADDERS: "If you are eating a shit sandwich, chances are you ordered it."

ORANGUTAN: Ding ding ding. We have a winner!

HAIKUMOM: Censored. But good one.

GHOST: Momken men-fadluck ted-dini gawaz saffari?

HAIKUMOM (*Turning a page in the paper*): Oh shit!

ORANGUTAN: CENSORED!!!!!! YES!!!!!! Whooooooo!

HAIKUMOM: You got me.

ORANGUTAN (*Victorious*): You know how long I've been waiting to do that?!

HAIKUMOM: My sister Ginny's in the *Daily News*! A nice big picture!

GHOST: Momken men-fadluck ted-dini gawaz saffari?

HAIKUMOM: "Eugenia P. Ortiz, A Force For Good In Philadelphia!" Okay, now!

(*Elliot punches harder. His leg is starting to bother him.*)

ELLIOT: Your leg feels great. Your leg feels like a million bucks. No pain. No pain.

HAIKUMOM: "In lieu of flowers contributions may be made to . . ."

(*Haikumom drops the newspaper.*
The Ghost blows on Elliot, knocking him to the floor.)

GHOST: Momken men-fadluck ted-dini gawaz saffari?

(*Intermission.*)

Scene Seven

> *A diner. Odessa and John, aka Fountainhead, sit in a booth.*

ODESSA: To lapsed Catholics. (*They clink coffee mugs*) And you thought we had nothing in common.

JOHN: When did you become interested in Buddhism?

ODESSA: My older brother used to terrorize me during mass. He would point to a statue, tell me about the evil spirit hiding behind it. Fangs, claws. I thought Saint Lazarus[4] was gonna come to life and suck my eyes out. Buddhism? Not scary. If there's spirits, they're hiding inside you.

JOHN: Aren't those the scariest kind?

ODESSA: So, how many days do you have? It should be two now.

JOHN: I put my sons' picture on my cell phone so if I get the urge, I can just look at them instead.

ODESSA: How many days?

JOHN (*Small talk*): I love Puerto Rico. On my honeymoon we stayed at that hotel in Old San Juan, the old convent. (*Odessa shrugs*) And that Spanish fort at the top of the city? El Morro?

ODESSA: I've always been meaning to make it there.

JOHN: There are these keyholes where the cannons used to fit, and the view of the waves through them, you can practically see the Spanish armada approaching.

ODESSA: I mean, one of these days I've gotta make it to PR.

JOHN: Oh. I just figured . . .

ODESSA: The Jersey Shore. Atlantic City. The Philadelphia airport. Oh, I've been places.

JOHN: On an actual plane?

ODESSA: I only fly first-class, and I'm still saving for that ticket.

> (*Odessa's cell phone rings.*)

JOHN: You're a popular lady.

ODESSA (*Into her phone, her demeanor completely changing*): What? I told you, the diner on Spring Garden and Third. I'm busy, come in an hour. One hour. Now stop calling me and asking fucking directions. (*She hangs up*)

JOHN: Says the one who censors.

ODESSA: My sister died.

JOHN: Right. You sure you're okay?

ODESSA: She's dead, ain't nothing left to do. People act like the world is going to fall apart.

JOHN: You write very Zen[5] messages. And yet.

ODESSA: My family knows every button to push.

JOHN: My condolences. (*Pause*) You don't strike me as a computer nerd. I used to employ an entire floor of them.

ODESSA: You should've seen me at first, pecking with two fingers. Now I'm like an octopus with ten little tentacles. In my neck of the woods staying clean is like

---

4. In the Gospel of John, Jesus restores Lazarus to life four days after his death.
5. Japanese school of Buddhism stressing the achievement of enlightenment through meditation, often using brief, enigmatic, often paradoxical statements (koans) to transcend rational thought.

trying to tap-dance on a minefield. The website fills the hours. So how are we gonna fill yours, huh? When was the last time you picked up a javelin?

JOHN: Senior year of high school.

ODESSA (*Hands him a sheet of paper*): There's a sober softball league. Fairmount Park, games on Sundays. Sober bowling on Thursdays.

JOHN: I lied in my first post. I've been smoking crack for two years. I've tried quitting hundreds of times. Day two? Please, I'm in the seven-hundredth day of hell.

ODESSA: You got it out of your system. Most people lie at one time or another on the site. The good news is, two years in, there's still time. (*Hands him another sheet of paper*) Talbott Recovery Center in Atlanta. It's designed for professionals with addictions. Paradise Recovery in Hawaii. They actually check your income before admitting you. Just for the wealthy. This place in Jersey, it's right over the bridge, they have an outpatient program for professionals like you.

JOHN: I'm tenacious. I'm driven. I love my parents.

ODESSA: Pitchforks against tanks.

JOHN: I relish in paying my taxes.

ODESSA: And you could be dead tomorrow. (*Pause*) Is your dealer male or female?

JOHN: I had a few. Flushed their numbers down the toilet like you suggested.

ODESSA: Your original connection. The one who got you hooked.

JOHN: Female.

ODESSA: Did you have sex with her?

JOHN: You don't beat around the bush do you?

ODESSA: I'll take that as a yes. (*No answer*) Do you prefer sex when you're high to sex when you're sober?

JOHN: I've never really analyzed it.

ODESSA: It can be a dangerous cocktail. Some men get off on smoking and fucking.

JOHN: All men get off on fucking.

ODESSA: Are you scared your wife will find out you're addicted to crack? Or are you scared she'll find out what came of your wedding vows?

JOHN: I should go.

ODESSA: We just ordered.

JOHN: I promised my son. There's a science fair tomorrow. Something about dioramas and crazy glue.

ODESSA: Don't talk about them. Get sober for them.

JOHN: Fuck you.

ODESSA: Leave me three bucks for your coffee cuz I ain't got it.

(*He stands, pulls out three dollars. She throws the money back at him.*)

You picked up the phone and called me.

JOHN (*He sits down again*): I don't know how to do this. I've never done this before.

ODESSA: I have and it usually doesn't end up so good. One in twenty, maybe, hang around. Most people just don't write one day and then thirty days and then you're wondering . . . And sometimes you get the answer. Cuz their wife looks on their computer and sees the website and logs on and writes, "I found him face down in the snow."

JOHN: How many day ones did you have?

ODESSA: Seven years' worth.

JOHN: Do you still crave?

ODESSA: On the good days, only every hour. Would you rather be honest with your wife, or would you rather end up like me? (*Pause*) That wasn't rhetorical.

JOHN: You're not exactly what I wanted to be when I grew up.

ODESSA: Truth. Now we're talking.

(*Elliot and Yaz enter.*)

YAZ: There she is.

(*Elliot and Yaz sit down in the booth.*)

ELLIOT: You were supposed to meet us at the flower place.

YAZ: The deposit was due at nine.

ODESSA: My alarm clock didn't go off.

ELLIOT: Were you up on that chat room all night?

ODESSA (*Ignoring him, to a waiter, off*): Can I get a refill, please?

ELLIOT: Where's the money?

ODESSA: I told you I don't have any money.

ELLIOT: And you think I do? I been paying for Mami Ginny's meds for six months straight—

ODESSA: Well get it from Yaz's mom.

YAZ: My mom put in for the headstone. She got an expensive one.

ODESSA: Headstone? She's getting cremated.

YAZ: She still needs a proper Catholic piece of granite. Right beside abuela, right beside your dad and sister and brother.

ELLIOT: And daughter.

YAZ: Everyone agreed.

ODESSA: No one asked my opinion.

ELLIOT: Everyone who showed up to the family meeting.

ODESSA: I wasn't invited.

YAZ: I texted you twice.

ODESSA: I was out of minutes.

ELLIOT: We just spoke on the phone.

ODESSA: Whatchu want me to do, Elliot, if I say I ain't got no fucking money, I ain't got no money.

JOHN: Hi, I'm John, nice to meet you.

YAZ: Yazmin.

ELLIOT: You one of Mom's rehab buddies?

JOHN: We know each other from work.

ELLIOT: You scrub toilets?

ODESSA (*To John*): I'm a practitioner of the custodial arts.

ELLIOT: Is she your sponsor?

JOHN (*To Odessa*): I thought this was going to be a private meeting.

ELLIOT: I'm her son.

JOHN (*To Odessa*): You must have been young.

ELLIOT: But I was raised by my Aunt Ginny and that particular aunt just died. (*To Odessa*) So now, you got three hours to find some money to pay for one basket of flowers in the funeral of the woman who changed my pampers.

YAZ: We're all supposed to be helping out.

ODESSA: You both know I run out of minutes all the time. No one could be bothered to drive by and tell me face to face?

ELLIOT: Because you always bothered to drive by and say hello to Mami Ginny when you knew she was sick? Because you bothered to hit me up one time this week and say, "Elliot, I'm sorry your mom died."

ODESSA: You still got one mom alive.

ELLIOT: Really? You want to go there?

YAZ: The flower place needs the money today.

ODESSA: She was my sister and you are my son, too.

YAZ: Guys. Two hundred dollars by end of business day.

ODESSA: That's my rent.

ELLIOT: Then fifty.

ODESSA: I just spent fifty getting my phone back on.

ELLIOT: Ten dollars. For the woman who raised your son! Do we hear ten dollars? Going once!

ODESSA: I spent my last ten at the post office.

ELLIOT: Going twice!

(*John goes into his wallet.*)

JOHN: Here's fifty.

(*They all look at him like he's crazy. He pulls out some more money.*)

Two hundred?

(*Elliot pushes the money back to John with one pointer finger, as if the bills might be contaminated.*)

ELLIOT: No offense, I don't take money from users.

JOHN: I'm not . . . I think that was my cue.

ODESSA: Sit down. My son was just going.

ELLIOT: Did World's Best Mom here tell you about her daughter?

ODESSA: I'm about to throw this coffee in your fucking face.

YAZ: Come on, Elliot, I'll pay for the flowers.

(*Elliot doesn't get up.*)

ELLIOT: I looked at that chat room once. The woman I saw there? She's literally not the same person I know. (*To John*) Did she tell you how she became such a saint?

JOHN: We all have skeletons.

ELLIOT: Yeah well she's an archaeological dig. Did she tell you about her daughter?

ODESSA (*Suddenly resigned*): Go ahead, I ain't got no secrets.

YAZ (*Getting up*): Excuse me.

ELLIOT: Sit here and listen, Yaz. You were born with a silver spoon and you need to know how it was for me.

YAZ: I said I'd pay for the goddamn flowers so LET'S GO. NOW!

ELLIOT: My sister and I had the stomach flu, right? For a whole day we couldn't keep nothing down.

ODESSA: Three days . . . You were vomiting three days straight.

ELLIOT: Medicine, juice, anything we ate, it would come right back up. (*To John*) Your co-worker here took us to Children's Hospital.

ODESSA: Jefferson.

ELLIOT: It was wall-to-wall packed. Every kid in Philly had this bug. ERs were turning kids away. They gave us a flier about stomach flu and sent us home. Bright blue paper. Little cartoon diagrams. It said give your kids a spoonful of water every five minutes.

ODESSA: A teaspoon.

ELLIOT: A small enough amount that they can keep it down. Five minutes. Spoon. Five minutes. Spoon. I remember thinking, Wow, this is it. Family time. Quality time. Just the three of us. Because it was gentle, the way you said, "Open up." I opened my mouth, you put that little spoon of water into my mouth. That little bit of relief. And then I watched you do the same thing with my little sister. And I remember being like, "Wow, I love you, Mom. My moms is all right." Five minutes. Spoon. Five minutes. Spoon. But you couldn't stick to something simple like that. You couldn't sit still like that. You had to have your thing. That's where I stop remembering.

ODESSA: I left.

ELLIOT: A Department of Human Services report. That's my memory. Six hours later a neighbor kicks in the door. Me and my sister are lying in a pile of laundry. My shorts was all messed up. And what I really don't remember is my sister. Quote: "Female infant, approximately two years, pamper and tear ducts dry, likely cause of death, dehydration." Cuz when you dehydrate you can't form a single tear.

JOHN (*To Elliot*): I'm very sorry . . . (*He puts some money on the table*) For the coffee. (*Exits*)

ELLIOT: That's some friend you got there.

(*Pause.*)

YAZ: Mary Lou. We can at least say her name out loud. Mary Lou. Mary Lou. (*To Odessa*) One time you came to babysit me, you brought Elliot and Mary Lou— she was still in pampers—and Mary Lou had this soda from 7-Eleven. She didn't want to give me a sip. You yelled at her so bad, you totally cursed her out and I said, "You're not supposed to yell at people like that!" And you said, "No, Yaz, let her cry. She's gotta learn that ya'll are cousins, ya'll are flesh and blood, and we share everything. You hear me, Yaz? In this family we share *everything*." You walked out of the room, came back from the kitchen with four straws in your hand, sat us down on the floor in a circle, pointed to me and said, "You first." I sipped. "Elliot's turn." He sipped. "Mary Lou's turn." She sipped. Then you sipped. You made us do like that, taking turns, going around the circle, till the cup was empty.

(*Odessa hands Elliot a key.*)

ODESSA: The pawn shop closes at five. Go into my house. Take my computer. Pawn it. However much you get, put towards a few flowers, okay?

(*Odessa exits.*)

Scene Eight

Split scene: Odessa's living room and the chat room.
Chutes&Ladders holds a phone.

ORANGUTAN: Did you hit the call button yet?

CHUTES&LADDERS: I'm working on it.

ORANGUTAN: Where are you? Are you at home?

CHUTES&LADDERS: *Jeopardy!*'s on mute.

ORANGUTAN: Dude, turn off the tube. This is serious. Did you even dial?

CHUTES&LADDERS: Yeah, yeah. (*He does*) All right, it's ringing. What am I going to say?

ORANGUTAN: "Hi, Son, it's Dad."

CHUTES&LADDERS: Wendell. That's his name. (*Hangs up*) No answer.

ORANGUTAN: As in, you hung up?

CHUTES&LADDERS: Yes. I hung up.

ORANGUTAN: Dude, way too quick!

CHUTES&LADDERS: What do you have, a stopwatch? Do you know the average time before someone answers a telephone?

ORANGUTAN: 3.2 rings.

CHUTES&LADDERS: According to . . .

ORANGUTAN: I don't reveal my sources.

CHUTES&LADDERS: Look, my son's a grown man with a good life.

ORANGUTAN: Quit moping and dial Wendell's number.

CHUTES&LADDERS: This Japan thing is cramping my style. Different networks, different time zones. No concurrent *Jeopardy!* watching.

ORANGUTAN: Deflection: nostalgia.

CHUTES&LADDERS: Humor me.

ORANGUTAN (*Humoring him*): How's my little Trebeky[6] doing?

CHUTES&LADDERS: He's had work done. Man looks younger than he did twenty years ago.

ORANGUTAN: Needle or knife?

CHUTES&LADDERS: Needle. His eyes are still in the right place.

ORANGUTAN: Well, it's working. Meow. Purrrrr. Any good categories?

CHUTES&LADDERS: Before and After.

ORANGUTAN: I love Before and After! But I'll go with . . . Quit Stalling for two hundred. (*She hums the* Jeopardy! *theme*)

CHUTES&LADDERS: It's ringing.

ORANGUTAN: My stopwatch is running.

CHUTES&LADDERS: Still ringing.

ORANGUTAN: You're going to be great.

CHUTES&LADDERS: It rang again.

ORANGUTAN: You're a brave soul.

(*We hear a man's voice at the other end of the line say, "Hello?" Chutes&Ladders hangs up.*)

CHUTES&LADDERS: He must not be around.

6. Alex Trebek (1940–2020), longtime host of the television game show *Jeopardy!*

ORANGUTAN: Leave a voice mail.

CHUTES&LADDERS: Maybe next time.

> (*Chutes&Ladders logs off.*)

ORANGUTAN: Hey! Don't log off, come on. Chutes&Ladders. Whatever happened to tough love? Log back on, we'll do a crossword. You can't fly before "Final Jeopardy!" Sigh. Anyone else online? Haikumom? I'm still waiting for that daily poem . . . Bueller? Bueller?

> (*In Odessa's living room, Elliot and Yaz enter.*)

YAZ: Wow, look at that computer. Stone age.

ELLIOT: Fred Flinstone shit.

YAZ: Positively Dr. Who.[7]

ELLIOT: Dr. Who?

YAZ: That computer is actually worse than what they give the adjuncts[8] at Swarthmore.

ELLIOT: What does "adjunct" even mean?

YAZ: Exactly. It's the nicest thing she owns.

ELLIOT: Let's not act like this is some heroic sacrifice. Like this makes her the world's martyr.

YAZ: We're not going to get more than fifteen bucks for it.

ELLIOT: Symbols matter, Yaz. This isn't about the money. This is shaking hands. This is tipping your hat. This is holding the door open. This is the bare minimum, the least effort possible to earn the label "person." (*Looks at the screen*) What do you think her password is? (*Types*) "Odessa." Nope. "Odessaortiz." Nope.

YAZ: It's probably Elliot.

> (*He types. Haikumom's log-on appears.*)

ELLIOT: The irony.

YAZ: I think legally that might be like breaking and entering.

ELLIOT (*Typing*): Hello? Oh shit it posted.

ORANGUTAN: Haikumom! Hit me with those seventeen syllables, baby!

YAZ: Haikumom? What the hell is that?

ELLIOT: Her username. She has the whole world thinking she's some Chinese prophet.

YAZ: Haiku are Japanese.

ELLIOT: "Haiku are Japanese." (*Typing*) Hello, Orangutan. How are you?

ORANGUTAN (*Formal*): I am fine. How are you?

ELLIOT (*Typing*): So, I guess you like monkeys, huh?

ORANGUTAN: An orangutan is a primate.

YAZ: Elliot.

ELLIOT: Chill.

---

7. British science-fiction television program (1963–present), a cult classic known for its cheesy props and special effects.

8. College instructors hired on a temporary, usually part-time basis as opposed to permanent, tenure-track faculty.

ORANGUTAN: And this primate has ninety-eight days. That deserves a poem, don't you think?

ELLIOT (*Typing*): I don't have a poem, but I have a question. What does crack feel like?

ORANGUTAN: What?

YAZ: Elliot, cut it out.

ELLIOT (*Typing*): Sometimes I'm amazed I don't know firsthand.

ORANGUTAN: Who is this?

ELLIOT (*Typing*): How does it make your brain feel?

ORANGUTAN: Like it's flooded with dopamine.[9] Listen, cyber-stalker, if you came here for shits and giggles, we are a sadly unfunny bunch.

ELLIOT (*Typing*): Are you just a smoker or do you inject it right into your eyeballs?

ORANGUTAN: Who the fuck is this?

ELLIOT (*Typing*): Haikumom.

ORANGUTAN: Bullshit, you didn't censor me. Quit screwing around, hacker, who are you?

YAZ: You think Ginny would want you acting this way?

ELLIOT: I think Mami Ginny would want Mami Odessa to pay for a single flower on her fucking casket.

YAZ (*Types*): This is not Haikumom. It's her son.

ORANGUTAN: Well, if you're looking for the friends and family thread, you have to go to the home page and create a new log-on. This particular forum is for people actually in recovery. Wait, her son the actor? From the Crest ad?

ELLIOT (*Typing*): Colgate.

ORANGUTAN: "Sonrisa baby!" I saw that on YouTube! Your teeth are insanely white. Ever worked in Hollywood?

ELLIOT (*Typing*): Psh. I just had this guy begging me to do a feature film. Gritty, documentary-style, about Marines in Iraq. I just don't want to do anything cheesy.

ORANGUTAN: So you're the war hero . . .

ELLIOT (*Typing*): Haikumom brags.

ORANGUTAN: How's your recovery going? (*No answer*) This is the crack forum, but there's a really good pain-meds forum on this site, too. Link here.

YAZ: What is she talking about?

ORANGUTAN: There's a few war vets on that forum, just like you. You'd be in good company.

YAZ: Pain meds? Elliot? (*He doesn't respond. Yaz types*) What are you talking about?

ORANGUTAN: Haikumom told us about your history.

YAZ (*Typing*): What history?

ORANGUTAN: Sorry. Maybe she told us in confidence.

ELLIOT: Confidence? They call this shit "world wide" for a reason.

YAZ (*Typing*): I can search all the threads right now.

ORANGUTAN: That you had a bunch of leg surgeries in Iraq. That if a soldier said they hurt, the docs practically threw pills at them. That you OD'd three

---

9. A primary neurotransmitter (a chemical used to send signals between nerve cells), affecting motor function, emotions, learning, and behavior, associated especially with pleasure.

times and were in the hospital for it. She was real messed up about it. I guess she had hoped the fruit would fall a little farther from the tree.

YAZ (*To Elliot*): Is this true?

ELLIOT: I wasn't a soldier. I was a Marine. Soldiers is the army.

YAZ: Oh my god.

ELLIOT (*Takes the keyboard, types*): What I am: sober. What I am not and never will be: a pathetic junkie like you.

(*He unplugs the computer. He throws the keyboard on the ground. He starts unplugging cables violently.*)

YAZ: Hold on. Just stop it, Elliot! Stop it!

ELLIOT: The one time I ever reached out to her for anything and she made me a story on a website.

YAZ: Why wouldn't you ask me for help? Why would you deal with that alone?

ELLIOT: The opposite of alone. I seen barracks that looked like dope houses. It was four months in my life, it's over. We've chopped up a lot of shit together, Yaz, but we ain't gonna chop this up. This shit stays in the vault. You got me?

YAZ: No!

ELLIOT: Yaz. (*He looks her straight in the eye*) Please. Please.

YAZ: I want to grab the sky and smash it into pieces. Are you clean?

ELLIOT: The only thing I got left from those days is the nightmares. That's when he came, and some days I swear he ain't never gonna leave.

YAZ: Who?

(*Elliot tries to walk away from the conversation, but the Ghost is there, blocking his path.*)

Who?!

ELLIOT (*Almost like a child*): Please, Yaz. Please end this conversation. Don't make me beg, Yaz.

YAZ: The pawn shop closes in fifteen minutes. I'll get the monitor, you grab the computer.

Scene Nine

Chutes&Ladders is at work, on his desk phone. A bundled pile of mail is on his desk. He takes off the rubber band, browses. Junk, mostly.

CHUTES&LADDERS (*Into the work phone*): That's right. Three Ws. Dot. Not the word, the punctuation mark. I-R-S. Not "F" like flamingo; "S" like Sam. Dot. Yup, another one. Gov. Grover orange victor.

(*Orangutan appears, online.*)

ORANGUTAN: I'm doing it. I'm almost there. *And* I can chat! Japan is so advanced. Internet cafes are like parking meters here.

CHUTES&LADDERS: Where are you and what are you doing?

ORANGUTAN: Sapporo train station. Just did some research. Get this: in the early eighties, they straightened all the rivers in Hokkaido.

CHUTES&LADDERS: Why?

ORANGUTAN: To create jobs the government straightened the rivers! Huge bodies of water, manual laborers, scientists, engineers, bulldozers, and the rivers became straight! How nuts is that?

CHUTES&LADDERS: People can't leave good enough alone. Why are humans so damn restless?

ORANGUTAN: It's not restlessness. It's ego. Massive, bizarre ego.

CHUTES&LADDERS: Can't let a river be a river. (*Into the phone*) The forms link is on the left.

ORANGUTAN: Now it's the aughts, people keep being born, jobs still need creating, but there's no curves left to straighten, so, drum roll, the government is beginning a new program to put all the original turns back in the rivers!

CHUTES&LADDERS: Well good luck to them, but no amount of engineering can put a wrinkle back in Nicole Kidman's[1] forehead.

ORANGUTAN: Ever heard of Kushiro?

CHUTES&LADDERS: Is that your new boyfriend's name?

ORANGUTAN: Ha. Ha ha ha. It's home of the hundred-mile-long Kushiro River, which is the pilot project, the first river they're trying to recurve.

CHUTES&LADDERS: Kushiro River. Got it. Burned in the brain. One day I'll win a Trivial Pursuit's[2] wedge with that. (*Into the phone*) You, too, ma'am. (*He hangs up*)

ORANGUTAN: My train to Kushiro leaves in twenty minutes. My heart is pounding.

CHUTES&LADDERS: I don't follow.

ORANGUTAN: Kushiro is the town where I was born. I'm going. I'm doing it.

CHUTES&LADDERS: Hold on, now you're throwing curveballs.

ORANGUTAN: In my hand is a sheet of paper. On the paper is the address of the house where my birth parents once lived. I'm going to knock on their door.

(*Chutes&Ladder's desk phone rings.*)

CHUTES&LADDERS (*Into the phone*): Help desk, please hold. (*To Orangutan*) How long have you had that address for?

ORANGUTAN: It's been burning a hole in my pocket for two days. I hounded my mom before I left Maine. She finally wrote down the name of the adoption agency. The first clue, the first evidence of who I was I ever had. I made a vow to myself, if I could stay sober for three months, I would track my parents down. So a few days ago class ended early, I went to the agency, showed my passport, and thirty minutes later I had an address on a piece of paper. Ask me anything about Kushiro. All I've done the last two days is research it. I'm an expert. Population, 190,000. There's a tech school, there's an airport.

CHUTES&LADDERS: Why are you telling me this? To get my blessing?

ORANGUTAN: I tell you about the things I do.

CHUTES&LADDERS: You don't want my opinion, you want my approval.

ORANGUTAN: Hand it over.

---

1. Australian actress (b. 1967) whose adventures in plastic surgery have been the stuff of tabloid rumor since at least 2008.

2. Board game in which players win wedge-shaped game pieces by correctly answering trivia questions.

CHUTES&LADDERS: No.

ORANGUTAN: Don't get monosyllabic.

CHUTES&LADDERS: Take that piece of paper and use it as kindling for a warm winter fire.

ORANGUTAN: Jeez, what did they slip into your Wheaties this morning?

CHUTES&LADDERS: Do a ritual burning and never look back. You have three months. Do you know the worth in gold of three months? Don't give yourself a reason to go back to the shadows.

ORANGUTAN: I'm in recovery. I have no illusions about catharsis. I realize what will most likely happen is nothing. Maybe something tiny. A microscopic butterfly flapping her microscopic wings.

CHUTES&LADDERS: Live in the past, follow your ass.

ORANGUTAN: Don't you have the slightest ambition?

CHUTES&LADDERS: Yes, and I achieve it every day: Don't use and don't hurt anyone. Two things I used to do on a daily basis. I don't do them anymore. Done. Dream realized. No more dreaming.

(*His phone rings again.*)

(*Into the phone*) Continue holding, please.

ORANGUTAN: When was the last time you went out on a limb?

CHUTES&LADDERS: Three odd weeks ago.

ORANGUTAN: Did you try hazelnut instead of french roast? Did you listen to *Soul Mornings* instead of NPR?[3]

CHUTES&LADDERS: There's a new secretary down the hall, she's got a nice smile. I decided to go say hello. We had a little back and forth. I said, let's have lunch, she said maybe but meant no, I turned away, looked down and my tie was floating in my coffee cup.

ORANGUTAN: I waited three months to tell you this, every step of the way, the train ride, what the river looks like. What their front door looks like. (*Pause*) I'm quitting this site. I hate this site. I fucking hate this site.

CHUTES&LADDERS: You're already losing it and you haven't even gotten on the train.

ORANGUTAN: Three days ago I suggested you and I meet face to face and you blew a fucking gasket.

CHUTES&LADDERS: That's what this is about?

ORANGUTAN: Don't flatter yourself. This is about me wanting relationships. With humans, not ones and zeroes. So we were once junkies. It's superficial. It's not real friendship.

CHUTES&LADDERS: I beg to differ.

ORANGUTAN: Prove me wrong.

CHUTES&LADDERS: Search down that address and a hundred bucks says your heart comes back a shattered light bulb.

ORANGUTAN: You mean, gasp, I'll actually FEEL something?

CHUTES&LADDERS: What are you going to do if the address is wrong? What if the building's been bulldozed? What if some new tenant lives there? What if the woman who gave you birth then gave you away answers the door?

3. National Public Radio (acronym).

ORANGUTAN: I DON'T KNOW! A concept you clearly avoid at all costs. Learn how to live, that's all I'm goddamn trying to do!

(*His phone rings. He picks up the receiver and hangs it up.*)

CHUTES&LADDERS: I have three grandsons. You know how I know that? Because I rang my son's doorbell one day. Step 9,[4] make amends. And his wife answered, and I don't blame her for hating me. But I saw three little boys in that living room and one of those boys said, "Daddy, who's that man at the door?" And my son said to *my grandson*, "I don't know. He must be lost." My son came outside, closed the door behind him, exchanged a few cordial words and then asked me to go.

ORANGUTAN: So I shouldn't even try.

CHUTES&LADDERS: I had five years sober until that day.

ORANGUTAN: You really believe in your heart of hearts I should not even try. (*Pause*) Coward.

(*His phone rings. He unplugs the phone line.*)

CHUTES&LADDERS: You think it's easy being your friend?

ORANGUTAN: Sissy. You walk the goddamn earth scared of your own shadow, getting smaller and smaller, until you disappear.

CHUTES&LADDERS: You tease me. You insult me. It's like breathing to you.

ORANGUTAN: You fucking idiot. Why do little girls tease little boys on the playground at recess? Why the fuck were cooties invented? You fucking imbecile!

CHUTES&LADDERS: You disappeared for three months. I couldn't sleep for three months!

ORANGUTAN: I wanted to impress you. I wanted to log on and show you I could be better. And I was an idiot because you're just looking for cowards like you. I'm logging off. This is it. It's over.

CHUTES&LADDERS: Orangutan.

ORANGUTAN: Into the abyss I climb, looking for a flesh-and-blood hand to grasp onto.

CHUTES&LADDERS: Little monkey, stop it.

ORANGUTAN: I'm in the station. My train is in five minutes, you gave me all the motivational speech I need, I'm going to the platform, I'm getting on the train, I'm going to see the house where I was born.

(*She logs off. Chutes&Ladders grabs his phone and hurls it into his wastebasket. He throws his calculator, his mail pile, his pen cup to the ground. Left on his desk is one padded envelope.*)

CHUTES&LADDERS: "To Chutes&Ladders Wilkie." "From Haikumom Ortiz."

(*He rips it open, pulls out a deflated orange water wing, puts it over his hand.*)

---

4. In the twelve-step addiction-recovery program first pioneered by Alcoholics Anonymous. In their original form, steps 8 and 9 read, "Made a list of all persons we had harmed and became willing to make amends to them all" and "Made direct amends to such people wherever possible, except when to do so would injure them or others."

Scene Ten

Split scene. Lights rise on a church. Elliot and Yaz stand at the lectern.

YAZ: It is time to honor a woman.[5]
ELLIOT: A woman who built her community with a hammer and nails.
YAZ: A woman who knew her nation's history. Its African roots. European roots. Indigenous roots. A woman who refused to be enslaved but lived to serve.
ELLIOT: A carpenter, a nurse, a comedian, a cook.
YAZ: Eugenia Ortiz.
ELLIOT: Mami Ginny.

(*Lights rise on Odessa's house. She sits on her floor. She scoops a spoonful of water from a mug, pours it onto the floor in a slow ribbon.*)

YAZ: She grew vegetables in her garden lot and left the gate open so anyone could walk in and pick dinner off the vine.
ELLIOT: She drank beer and told dirty jokes and even the never-crack-a-smile church ladies would be rolling laughing.
YAZ: She told me every time I visited, "Yaz, you're going to Juilliard."[6]
ELLIOT: Every morning when I left for school, "Elliot, nobody can make you invisible but you."

(*Lights rise on the Sapporo train station. Orangutan is on the platform.*)

LOUDSPEAKER (*An announcement in Japanese*): 3:00 express to Kushiro now boarding on track one. Please have tickets out and ready for inspection.
YAZ: Zero.
ELLIOT: Birth children.
YAZ: One.
ELLIOT: Adopted son.

(*Odessa pours another spoonful of water on the floor. Again, it creates a slow ribbon.*)

YAZ: Three.
ELLIOT: Years in the army nurse corps.
YAZ: Three.
ELLIOT: Arrests for civil disobedience. I was in Iraq and she was demonstrating for peace.
YAZ: Forty-seven.
ELLIOT: Wheelchair ramps she installed in homes with disabled children or elderly.

(*Odessa pours another spoonful of water on the floor. A small pool is forming.*)

---

5. This eulogy is inspired by and owes much debt to Roger Zepernick's eulogy for Eugenia Burgos [Hudes's note]. Zepernick is an ordained Lutheran minister and onetime director of Centro Pedro Claver, a North Philadelphia social services organization. Eugenia "Ginny" Perez Burgos—Hudes's maternal aunt and a North Philadelphia neighborhood activist and city administrator—died of bone cancer in 2009 at age fifty-nine; obituaries credit her with raising two sons, Shawn Ortiz and Elliot Ruiz.
6. Elite performing arts conservatory (founded 1905) housed in New York City's Lincoln Center for the Performing Arts.

YAZ: Twelve.

ELLIOT: Abandoned lots she turned into city-recognized public gardens.

(*Another spoonful.*)

YAZ: Twenty-two.

ELLIOT: Godchildren recognized by this church.

(*Another spoonful.*)

YAZ: One hundred and thirty.

ELLIOT: Abandoned homes she refurbished and sold to young families.

LOUDSPEAKER (*Another announcement in Japanese*): Final boarding call, 3:00 express to Kushiro, track one.

(*Orangutan is still on the platform. She seems frozen, like she cannot move.*)

YAZ: All while having a fresh pot of rice and beans on the stove every night. For any hungry stranger. And the pilgrims stopped. And they planted roots, because she was here. We are the living, breathing proof.

ELLIOT: I am the . . . Excuse me.

(*He exits.*)

YAZ: Elliot is the standing, walking testimony to a life. She. Was. Here.

(*Odessa turns the cup upside down. It is empty.*)

Scene Eleven

Chutes&Ladders at his desk. In front of him: an inflated orange water wing.

CHUTES&LADDERS (*On the phone*): Yeah, it's a 1995 Tercel. Midnight blue. It's got a few miles. A hundred and twenty thousand. But like I said, I'll give it to you for three hundred below Kelley Blue Book. Yup, automatic. Just got new brake pads. Cassette deck, mint condition. I'll even throw in a few tapes. Tina Turner and Lionel Richie.[7] Oh, hold on, call-waiting.

(*He presses mute. Sings to himself:*)

> A tisket, a tasket.
> A green and yellow basket.
> I bought a basket for my mommy.
> On the way I dropped it.
> Was it red? No no no no!
> Was it brown? No no no no![8]

(*Back into the phone*) Sorry about that. I got someone else interested. No, it's all right, I have them on hold. You need to see this thing tonight if you're serious.

---

7. American pop singer-songwriter (b. 1949) popular in the 1980s. *Tina Turner:* singer-actress (b. 1939) widely known as "the Queen of Rock 'n' Roll"; first rocketing to fame in the 1960s (alongside husband Ike), she enjoyed a new wave of international success thanks to her comeback album, *Private Dancer* (1984).

8. Slightly mangled version of "A-Tisket, A-Tasket," a song first recorded in 1938 by jazz legend Ella Fitzgerald (1917–96), based on a traditional nursery rhyme.

I put this listing up thirty minutes ago, my phone is ringing off the hook. 6:30? Hey I didn't mention. Little lady has racing stripes.

Scene Twelve

Split scene. Lights rise on the Sapporo train station, same as before. Orangutan has laid down on the platform and fallen asleep, her backpack like a pillow.

Lights rise on Odessa's house, that night. Her phone rings. We hear loud knocking.

ELLIOT (*Offstage*): Mami Odessa! Open the door!

(*More ringing.*)

(*Offstage*) Yo, Mom!

YAZ (*Offstage*): She's not there.

ELLIOT (*Offstage*): Can't you hear her phone ringing? Move out the way.

YAZ (*Offstage*): Be careful, your leg!

(*A few kicks and the door bursts open. Yaz and Elliot enter, switch on the lights. Odessa is in a heap, motionless, on the floor. Yaz runs and holds Odessa in her arms.*)

Oh shit. Odessa! Odessa! Wake up.

(*Yaz slaps Odessa's face a few times.*)

Her pulse is racing.

(*Yaz opens her cell phone, dials.*
Elliot finds a spoon on the floor.)

ELLIOT: Oh no. Oh no you fucking didn't! MOM!!! Get up!

YAZ (*Into the phone*): Hi, I need an ambulance. I have someone unconscious here. I think it's an overdose, crack cocaine. Yes, she has a pulse. 33 Ontario Street. No, no seizures, she's just a lump. Well what should we do while we wait? Okay. Yes. (*She hangs up*) They're on their way. Elevate her feet.

ELLIOT: Help me get her to the sofa. One, two, three.

(*Elliot lifts her with Yaz's help. They struggle under her weight. In fact they lift the air. Odessa stands up, lucid, and watches the action: Elliot and Yaz struggling under her invisible weight.*)

YAZ: Watch her head.

ELLIOT: Aw, fuck, my leg.

YAZ: Careful.

(*They set "Odessa" on the sofa, while Odessa watches, unseen, calm.*)

ODESSA: I must be in the terminal. Between flights. The layover.

YAZ: Oh god, not two in one day, please.

ELLIOT: She's been through this shit a million times. She's a survivor! WAKE UP! Call your mom. She'll get here before the ambulance.

(*Yaz dials.*)

ODESSA: I've been to the airport, one time. My dad flew here from Puerto Rico. First time I met him. We stood by the baggage claim, his flight was late, we waited forever. There was one single, lone suitcase, spinning around a carousel.

YAZ (*To Elliot*): Voice mail. (*Into the phone*) Mom? Call me back immediately, it's an emergency.

ELLIOT: Give me that. (*Grabs the phone*) Titi, Odessa fucking OD'd and she's dying on her living room floor and I can't take this anymore! COME GET US before I walk off and leave her on the sofa! (*He hangs up*)

YAZ: If you need to, go. No guilt. I got this.

ELLIOT: She's my *mom*. Can I be angry? Can you let me be angry?

YAZ: Why is this family plagued? (*Elliot moves to go*) Where are you going?

ELLIOT: To find something fragile.

> (*He exits. We hear something shatter.*)

ODESSA: Everyone had cleared away from the carousel. Everyone had their bags. But this one was unclaimed. It could still be there for all I know. Spiraling. Spinning. Looking for an owner. Abandoned.

> (*In the Sapporo station, a Policeman enters with a bright, beaming flashlight and points it at Orangutan.*
>
>   *In Odessa's house, a radiant white light suddenly pours in from above. Odessa looks up, is overwhelmed. It is beautiful. Yaz sees it.*)

YAZ: Dear god, do you see that?

> (*Elliot enters. Watching Yaz, he looks up.*)

ELLIOT (*Not seeing it*): What?

YAZ (*To Odessa*): It's okay, Odessa, go, go, we love you, I love you Titi,[9] you are good, you *are* good. Oh my god, she's beautiful.

ELLIOT: What are you talking about?

YAZ: It's okay, it's okay. We love you Odessa.

POLICEMAN (*In Japanese*): Miss, miss, are you okay?

ORANGUTAN (*Waking*): English, please.

POLICEMAN: No sleeping on the floor.

ORANGUTAN (*Getting up slowly*): Sorry.

POLICEMAN: Are you sick?

ORANGUTAN: No.

POLICEMAN: Are you intoxicated?

ORANGUTAN: No. I'm very sorry. I just got tired. I'll go. I'm going.

POLICEMAN: Please, can I give you a hand?

ORANGUTAN: No. I got it.

> (*Orangutan exits. The Policeman turns off his flashlight, exits.*
>
>   *The sound of an ambulance siren. Suddenly the white light disappears. Odessa crawls onto the couch and slips into Yaz's arms, where she's been all along.*)

YAZ: Holy shit . . .

---

9. Auntie (Spanish).

ELLIOT: What's happening, Yaz? What the fuck was that?

YAZ: You've got to forgive her, Elliot. You have to.

Scene Thirteen

The chat room.

CHUTES&LADDERS: Oh nagging wives? Orangutan? Hello? Earth to Orangutan. Come on, three days straight I been worrying about you. I have time-sensitive information. Ground control to Major Orangutan.[1]

ORANGUTAN: Ta-da.

CHUTES&LADDERS: Where you been?

ORANGUTAN: Here. There. Morrissey and Nine Inch Nails[2] on loop.

CHUTES&LADDERS: Is that what the kids like these days?

ORANGUTAN (*Rolls eyes*): That was me rolling my eyes.

CHUTES&LADDERS: Guess what I did.

ORANGUTAN (*Shrugs*): That was me shrugging.

CHUTES&LADDERS: Guess.

ORANGUTAN: Guess what I didn't do?

CHUTES&LADDERS: Meet your birth parents?

ORANGUTAN: Board the train.

CHUTES&LADDERS: Sorry.

ORANGUTAN: Don't apologize. You had my number.

CHUTES&LADDERS: Guess what I did.

ORANGUTAN: Told me so. Had my shit pegged.

CHUTES&LADDERS: I sold my Tercel. My plane lands in Narita Airport a week from this Wednesday.

ORANGUTAN: What?

CHUTES&LADDERS: American Airlines Flight 3312. Arriving 10:01 A.M.

ORANGUTAN: You're a dumbass. Tokyo? Do you have any idea how far that is from Hokkaido? And how much a ticket on the train costs? Oy, and how the hell am I going to get out of teaching that day? Oh, you dollface, you ducky!

CHUTES&LADDERS: I'll be wearing a jean jacket and a Padres cap. That's how you'll know me.

ORANGUTAN: Oh Chutes&Ladders. You old bag of bones, you! You old so-and-so, you mensch,[3] you human being! Why the hell didn't you tell me?

CHUTES&LADDERS: I'm just hoping I have the guts to get on the plane.

ORANGUTAN: Of course you're getting on that damn plane! For me you did this?

(*Fountainhead logs on.*)

FOUNTAINHEAD: Hey everyone. I managed to find one computer here at the hospital that works. Odessa asked me to post a message on her behalf. She landed on: "Go." Hit reset on the timer. Back to day one.

1. David Bowie's 1969 song "Space Oddity" includes the lines "Ground Control to Major Tom: your circuit's dead, there's something wrong."

2. American industrial rock band (founded 1988). *Morrissey*: English singer-songwriter (b. 1959), vocalist of the influential rock band the Smiths (1982–87).

3. Person of great integrity; a really good, stand-up guy (Yiddish).

ORANGUTAN: Who's Odessa?

FOUNTAINHEAD: Sorry. Haikumom.

ORANGUTAN: What? Do you log on here just to mock us?

CHUTES&LADDERS: Hold on, is she okay?

FOUNTAINHEAD: Cardiac arrest. They said she was one hair from a coma. She hadn't used in six years and her system went nuts.

CHUTES&LADDERS: So she's alive?

FOUNTAINHEAD: And just barely ticking. Tubes in and out of her nose. She's responsive, she mumbled a few words.

ORANGUTAN: You can't be serious.

CHUTES&LADDERS: Why are you there? Were you using with her?

FOUNTAINHEAD: No.

CHUTES&LADDERS: Did you sell her the stuff?

FOUNTAINHEAD: No, Jesus, of course not. She gave them my number, I'm her emergency contact. Why, I have no idea, we're practically strangers. Getting her to the hospital, seeing her like that . . . I don't mean this as an insult, but she looked not human. Bones with skin covering. Mummy-like.

ORANGUTAN: Fuck. You.

FOUNTAINHEAD: I'm being descriptive. I'm being honest. The thought of my boys walking in on me like that. My wife finding me . . .

ORANGUTAN: That woman is the reason I'm. Oh god, you get complacent for one second! One second! You get comfortable for one minute! Fountainhead, go to the stats page. You'll see. There's thousands of members on this site. People she has saved, people she may yet save some day. I am one of them. You are one of them.

CHUTES&LADDERS: Fountainhead, does she have family there? Has anyone come through her room?

FOUNTAINHEAD: Apparently a son and a niece but they had to catch a flight to San Juan.[4]

CHUTES&LADDERS: No parents? No other children? A friend? A neighbor?

FOUNTAINHEAD: None showed up.

CHUTES&LADDERS: Fountainhead. You have a family, I absolutely understand that, and I mean zero disrespect when I say, when I beg of you this: your job on this earth has just changed. It is not to stay clean. It's not to be a husband or a father or a CEO. It's to stay by that woman's side. Make sure she gets home safe. Bathe her. Feed her. Get her checked into a rehab, inpatient. Do not leave her side for a second. Can you do this?

FOUNTAINHEAD: I have one day clean. I'm not meant to be a saint.

CHUTES&LADDERS: Tell me now, swear on your mother's name, otherwise I'm on the first flight to Philadelphia.

FOUNTAINHEAD: I don't know.

CHUTES&LADDERS: Look man, do you believe in God?

FOUNTAINHEAD: Sure, along with unicorns and the boogeyman.

CHUTES&LADDERS: How about miracles?

FOUNTAINHEAD: When the Phils are winning.

CHUTES&LADDERS: How about actions? I bet you believe in those.

---

4. Capital of Puerto Rico.

FOUNTAINHEAD: Yeah.

CHUTES&LADDERS: Your lifeboat has just arrived. Get on board or get out of the way.

FOUNTAINHEAD: I'll take care of Odessa. You have my word. My solemn word. (*Pause*) She did manage to say one thing: Someone has to take over site admin. She doesn't want the chat room full of curse words.

(*Yaz appears. A screen lights up:*)

FREEDOM&NOISE
STATUS: ONLINE

FREEDOM&NOISE: I'm good with computers. I'll throw my hat in the ring.

CHUTES&LADDERS: Freedom&Noise, are you new here?

FREEDOM&NOISE: Yes. Very.

(*Fountainhead's phone rings.*)

FOUNTAINHEAD: Freedom&Noise, email me offline. Link attached. I gotta go.

CHUTES&LADDERS: You gave us your word. Don't be a stranger.

(*Fountainhead logs off. Into the phone:*)

FOUNTAINHEAD: Hi, honey, sorry I haven't called sooner. Something came up. Listen, I'm not coming home tonight, just order in. I have a friend who got sick, she's having an emergency. No, it's not a romantic friend. I will tell you about it. When I get home. When I—Honey? Honey . . .

(*The call is over. He writes a text message.*)

Honey, under my bookmarks, click on "Fantasy Football" link. My username is "Fountainhead." My password is "Porsche71." Log on and read. Send.

Scene Fourteen

Puerto Rico. A hotel room. Yaz is online.

FREEDOM&NOISE: Hello, I am Freedom&Noise, your interim site manager, currently logging on from the Rainforest B&B in Puerto Rico. I am not a user, I've smoked pot twice, both times when I was thirteen, and am therefore unqualified for this position. There was a young woman I once knew. Let's call her "O." My crazy aunt, a fun babysitter, the baddest hide-and-seek player north of Girard Avenue. We played dress-up, built booby traps and forts, and when I was eight, she disappeared. No explanation, no acknowledgment she had ever existed, the grown-ups in the family had taken a vow of silence, and O. had been erased. My freshman year at college, I returned home for Thanksgiving, and thanks to a snow delay I walked into the middle of turkey dinner itself, and there was O., a plate full of food, chowing down. I hadn't seen her in ten years. After dinner she told me to congratulate her, it was her anniversary. I said, "Did you get married?" She pulled a necklace out from under her shirt and said, "You know what these gold letters mean? The

'N' is for narcotics, the 'A' is for anonymous and today is my two-year anniversary of being clean." (*Pause*) A few days ago I met a new woman: Haikumom. A woman who created a living, breathing ecosystem, and since I've never sown a single seed, let alone planted a garden, the least I can do is censor you, fix glitches—and one other thing . . . Formulating first line. Did Haikumom really do these on the fly? Five-seven-five, right? (*Counting the syllables on her fingers*) Box full of ashes . . .

(*Elliot enters from the bathroom, freshly showered, pulling on a shirt*)

ELLIOT: Whatchu looking at, Willis?[5]

YAZ: Sh. I'm counting syllables.

(*Elliot looks over Yaz's shoulder at the computer.*)

ELLIOT: Hold up. Don't read that shit, Yaz.

YAZ: You know how Odessa got into haiku in the first place?

ELLIOT: For real, close the computer.

YAZ: I went through this Japanese minimalist phase freshman year. Rock Gardens, Zen Buddhism, the works. I gave her a haiku collection for Christmas.

ELLIOT: Yeah, and you gave me a midget tree that died by New Year's.

YAZ: Bonsai. You didn't water it.

ELLIOT (*Closing Yaz's laptop*): For the two days I'm away from Philly, let me be away from Philly?

YAZ: You know where I was gonna be by thirty? Two kids. Equal-housework marriage. Tenure, no question. Waaaay tenured, like by the age of twenty-four. Carnegie Hall debuts: Yazmin Ortiz's "Oratorio for Electric Guitar and Children's Choir." I wrote a list on a piece of paper and dug a hole in Fairmount Park and put it in the ground and said, "When I turn thirty, I'll dig it up and cross it all off." And I promise you I'll never have the courage to go to that spot with a shovel and face my list full of crumbs, decoys and bandaids.

ELLIOT: Married with kids, what an awful goal.

YAZ: Odessa's done things.

ELLIOT: Well, when you throw her a parade, don't expect me to come.

YAZ: You've done things.

ELLIOT: I wouldn't come to my own parade, either.

YAZ: Ginny did things. What have I done?

ELLIOT: Second-grade Language Arts. You glued my book report.

YAZ: I couldn't stop your leg from getting chewed up.

ELLIOT: Fairmount little league basketball. You kept score, you brought our equipment.

YAZ: I didn't hold your hand when you were in the desert popping pills trying to make yourself disappear. I didn't keep Odessa away from that needle. I didn't water a single plant in Ginny's garden. We're in PR and I'm gonna dig a new hole and I'm not putting a wish or a list in there, I'm putting a scream in there. And I'm gonna sow it like the ugliest foulest and most necessary seed in the world and it's going to bloom! This time it's going to fucking bloom!

5. Play on "Whatchu talkin' about, Willis?," catchphrase of an African American character (played by diminutive actor Gary Coleman [1968–2010]) on the popular 1980s sitcom *Diff'rent Strokes*.

ELLIOT: My eyes just did this weird thing. For a second, it was Mom standing in front of me.

YAZ: Odessa?

ELLIOT: Ginny.

YAZ: Elliot, your birth mother saved your life by giving you away. Tell me I'm wrong.

(*Elliot doesn't respond. Yaz begins gathering her stuff hastily.*)

Now we got some ashes to throw. El Yunque closes in an hour and a half.

ELLIOT: Maybe we should do this tomorrow.

YAZ: I gotta make a call. I'll be in the lobby!

(*She exits.*)

ELLIOT: Yaz?

(*The Ghost appears. He's probably been there the whole time.*)

Yaz!

GHOST: Momken men-fadluck ted-dini gawaz saffari?

(*The Ghost reaches out his hand to touch Elliot.*)

Momken men-fadluck ted-dini gawaz saffari?

(*The second they make contact, Elliot spins on his heels and grabs the Ghost. The Ghost defends himself, pulling away. They start pushing, grabbing, fighting. The Ghost is looking for something—is it Elliot's wallet?*)

Momken men-fadluck ted-dini gawaz saffari?

(*The Ghost finds Elliot's wallet and tears through it, hurling its contents onto the floor. Elliot attacks again, but this time the Ghost reaches out his hand and touches Elliot's face. Elliot freezes, unable to move, as the Ghost's hands glide across his features, considering each one with authority, taking inventory.*)

Momken men-fadluck ted-dini gawaz saffari?

(*The Ghost is gone. Elliot catches his breath, shaken. He reaches into his pocket and pulls out a bottle of pills. He puts one pill in his hand. Then he empties the entire bottle of pills into his hand. He stares at the pills, wanting to throw them away.*)

Scene Fifteen

Split scene. Odessa's bathroom. The bathtub is filled with water. John enters, carrying a very weak Odessa. Odessa is wearing shorts and a bra, a modest outfit for bathing. John lowers her gently into the bathtub.

JOHN: Does that feel okay?

(*Odessa barely nods.*)

It's not too hot or cold?

(*Odessa shakes her head.*)

I don't know how to do this. These are things women do. Take care of sick people. Make the wounds go away.

(*He takes a sponge and starts to bathe her.*)

Is this okay?

(*He lifts her arms and washes her armpits. Embarrassed at first, but quickly gets the swing of it.*)

We check you in at 4:30 so we have plenty of time to clean you up and get you in good clothes, okay? You'll go in there looking like a decent woman.

(*Odessa whispers something inaudible.*)

What was that?

(*She gestures for him to lean in. She whispers into his ear.*)

One more time.

(*She whispers a little louder.*)

Did someone take swimming lessons?

(*She whispers again.*)

Did someone put on water wings?

(*She nods. He continues to bathe her, gently, in silence as:*
   Lights rise on Tokyo. Narita Airport. Orangutan sits on the floor by the luggage carousel. At her feet is a sign that says Chutes&Ladders. She throws the sign like a frisbee across the floor and gets up to leave. Chutes&Ladders enters, rolling a suitcase behind him. He waves to Orangutan.)

CHUTES&LADDERS: Orangutan?

ORANGUTAN: What the holy hell?

CHUTES&LADDERS: Sorry. Sorry. I tried calling but my cell doesn't work here. I told you I'm no good at this fancy kind of living.

ORANGUTAN: You were supposed to land yesterday, you were too scared to get on the plane. You rebook, you were supposed to land today, forty-five minutes ago. Everyone got their luggage already. The last person pulled the last suitcase from the carousel half an hour ago. I thought, Wow, this one sure knows how to play a joke on the ladies. I thought you had left me at the fucking altar.

CHUTES&LADDERS: I got sick on the flight. Totally embarrassing. I had a panic attack as the plane landed and I started tossing into the doggy bag right next to this nice old lady. I've been sitting on the bathroom floor emptying my stomach. Then I had to find a toothbrush and toothpaste and mouthwash because I didn't want to greet you with bad breath and all.

(*She looks skeptical. She sniffs his mouth quickly.*)

ORANGUTAN: Minty. (*Pause*) Oh, you dummy, you big old dummy. COME HERE, you San Diego Padre.

(*They hug. A warm and brief greeting.*)

What's your name?

CHUTES&LADDERS: Clay. Clayton "Buddy" Wilkie.

ORANGUTAN: I'm Madeleine Mays.

CHUTES&LADDERS: It's weird, huh?

ORANGUTAN: Totally weird. The land of the living.

(*They hug. They melt into each other's arms. A hug of basic survival and necessary friendship. Then, they exit, rolling Chutes&Ladders's suitcase off as lights rise in:*
   Puerto Rico. A rock outcropping looking out over a waterfall. Elliot is there, looking down at the water.)

ELLIOT (*Looking down*): Oh shit! Yaz, you gotta see this! Yaz? Fucking Johnny Appleseed of El Yunque.

(*Yaz enters holding a soil-covered flower bulb. She compares the root against a field book.*)

YAZ: I found my spiral ginger! This is going right next to the aloe by the kitchen door, baby!

ELLIOT: Yo, this science experiment ain't getting past security.

YAZ: Experiment my ass. I'm planting these in Ginny's garden.

ELLIOT: Customs gonna sniff that shit from a mile away.

YAZ (*Putting the bulb in a ziploc baggie full of dirt and bulbs*): China rose . . . Sea grape . . . Some kind of fern . . .

ELLIOT: When they cuff those wrists, I don't know you.

YAZ: I'll hide them in my tampon box.

ELLIOT: That don't work. My first trip to PR, Mami Ginny smuggled a coqui[6] back with her kotex and got arrested. Front page of the *Daily News*.

YAZ: Good shit. (*A dirty little secret*) You know what Grandma did?

ELLIOT: Do I want to?

YAZ: She used to smuggle stuff back, too. She'd tuck it below her boobs. She had storage space under there!

ELLIOT: Yeah after she was sixty and had nursed seven kids. Yo you think if I jumped off this rock right now and dove into that water, I'd survive?

YAZ: Just watch out for the huge boulders and the footbridge.

ELLIOT: It's tempting. That spray. (*His phone beeps*) Reception in the rainforest.

YAZ: Kind of ruins the romance.

ELLIOT (*Reads a text message*): Damn, that was fast.

YAZ: What?

ELLIOT: Pop sold the house. Did he even put out a listing?

YAZ: Not that I know of.

ELLIOT: That's like a VW bus going from zero to sixty in three seconds. Don't make no sense.

YAZ: Must have been an inside job.

ELLIOT: I guess so.

---

6. Singing tree frog native to Puerto Rico.

YAZ: A way way inside job . . .

ELLIOT: Yaz . . .

YAZ (*Conspiratorially*): Yeeeees?

ELLIOT: What did you do?

YAZ (*Very conspiratorially*): Nothing . . .

ELLIOT: Holy shit!

YAZ: Put my Steinway[7] on craigslist. Got four responses before you made it down to the lobby. My eighty-eight keys are worth more than Ginny's whole house. Sadly. I'll buy an upright.

ELLIOT: You are one crazy motherfucking adjunct! Yo, I don't know if el barrio is ready for you. I don't know if they can handle you!

YAZ: Oh, they gonna handle me.

ELLIOT: Wait wait wait. You need a title.

YAZ: Yaz will do just fine.

ELLIOT: Hells no. Command respect. I step on those corners, I'm Big El. (*Pause*) "Professor."

YAZ: "Professor."

ELLIOT: You like that, huh?

YAZ: It'll be the Cousins House. We'll renovate the kitchen. You redo the plumbing, I'll hook up a little tile backsplash.

ELLIOT: I watched Bob Vila[8] with Pop, but I ain't no handyman.

YAZ: Just wait, Mr. Home Depot. You're gonna be like, "Fuacata,[9] fuacata, fuacata," with your power drill and nail gun and vise grips.

ELLIOT: Something like that.

YAZ: Well? Get to it. Toss 'em.

ELLIOT: Me? Why the hell do you think I let you come along?

(*He hands Yaz the box.*)

YAZ: Well then say something. Pray.

ELLIOT: I'm all out of prayers.

YAZ: Me, too. Make a toast.

ELLIOT: To LAX. I'm not flying back with you.

YAZ: What do you mean?

ELLIOT: I called from the hotel and changed my flight. One-way ticket. Watch out, Hollywood. (*Pause*) You know how you had to shake me awake last night?

YAZ (*Demeanor shifting*): You were literally sobbing in your sleep.

ELLIOT: This dream was different than usual. I'm fixing a Subway hoagie, I feel eyes on the back of my neck, I turn around and expect to see him, the first guy I shot down in Iraq. But instead it's Mami Ginny. Standing next to the bread oven, smiling. You know how her eyes smile?

YAZ: Best smile in the world.

ELLIOT: Looking at me, her son. Coming to say good-bye.

YAZ: That's beautiful.

---

7. Piano made by the legendary German American firm Steinway & Sons (founded 1853).
8. Host (b. 1946) of a series of home-improvement shows, beginning with *This Old House* (1979–89).
9. Onomatopoeic interjection akin to "Wham!" or "Bam!" (Cuban Spanish).

ELLIOT: She puts on her glasses to see my face even better. She squints and something changes. The moment I come into focus, her eyes widen. Her jaw drops, she starts trembling. Then she starts to cry. Something she's seeing scares her. Then she starts to scream. Loud, like, "Ahhh! Ahhh!" She won't stop looking at me, but she's terrified, horrified by what she sees. And I don't know if my lip is bleeding or there's a gash on my forehead or she's looking through my eyes and seeing straight into my fucking soul.

YAZ: Jesus.

ELLIOT: I wanted Mami Odessa to relapse, Yaz. I wanted her to pick up that needle. I knew precisely what to do, what buttons to push, I engineered that shit, I might as well have pushed the thing into her vein. Because I thought, Why would God take the good one? Yo, take the bad mom instead! I was like, Why wouldn't you take the bad fucking mom? If I stay in Philly, I'm gonna turn into it. I'm gonna become one of them. I'm already halfway there. You've got armor, you've got ideas, but I don't.

YAZ: Go. Go and don't you ever, ever look back.

(*She takes his hand.*)

But if you do, there will be a plastic-covered sofa waiting for you.

(*Below them, in Philadelphia, John is done bathing Odessa. He lifts her and holds her like an angel above the bathtub. She is dripping wet and seems almost radiant, and yet deeply, deeply sick.*)

I'm the elder now. I stay home. I hold down the fort.

ELLIOT: I'm walking.

YAZ: On three?

YAZ AND ELLIOT: One.

Two.

Three.

(*They toss the ashes. Blackout.*)

2011

QUESTIONS

1. WATER BY THE SPOONFUL features many entirely fictional characters, situations, and events, including the online community created by "Haikumom" and the death of Elliot's infant sister. Yet as the biographical headnote and textual footnotes suggest, the play was also inspired in part by real people and events: Hudes's cousin Elliot Ruiz was raised by their aunt Ginny, who died of cancer; he was wounded in the U.S. war with Iraq; Odessa is based in part on a cousin who is a former drug addict; and so on. How, if at all, might this knowledge affect your response to the play and its characters?

2. How do the characters of Elliot and Yaz each develop over the course of the play? What role in that development is played by their experiences in both real and online worlds?

3. As readers or spectators of Hudes's play, we first get to know Odessa via her online interactions, and throughout the play we see much more of these than does Elliott or Yaz. How does that affect how we view and feel about Odessa, Elliott, and their individual and mutual conflicts? Why might Hudes have chosen to structure the play in this way?

4. How would you articulate the play's main theme? Might it have to do with notions of family? with the ways we help and hurt others? with the process of trauma and recovery? something else entirely?

5. How might Yaz's discussion of musical dissonance provide a language for articulating the play's themes or describing its structure?

6. Especially in terms of conflict or theme, what role is played by Fountainhead, Chutes&Ladders, and Orangutan? How, if at all, might it matter that Fountainhead is the play's only White or upper-middle-class character? that Chutes&Ladders and Orangutan end up meeting in the real world?

SUGGESTIONS FOR WRITING

1. Though WATER BY THE SPOONFUL begins by alternating scenes set entirely in the real world with scenes set wholly in the virtual world, later scenes tend to be more complicated. Scene 10, for example, is a "split scene" that shifts among Ginny's funeral, Odessa's house, and a train station in Sapporo, Japan. Choose one of these "split scenes" and write an informal response paper about it. How do the various elements of the scene work together and perhaps comment on each other? How might the scene be staged so as to emphasize those connections without confusing the audience?

2. Write an essay exploring what WATER BY THE SPOONFUL seems to suggest about the power and limits of online selves and communities. What might the virtual world allow us to be and do that the real world doesn't, and vice versa?

3. Write an essay exploring the water imagery in Hudes's play. By its end, what various meanings might the phrase "water by the spoonful" accrue?

4. WATER BY THE SPOONFUL features a cast of characters who at first seem very different from one another in terms of their personalities, their backgrounds, their situations in life, and their conflicts. Yet over the course of the play we and they arguably discover just how similar they are. Choose any two characters from the play, perhaps those that initially seem the most different or far removed from each other. Then write an essay comparing the characters and their development over the course of the play. What similarities emerge as the play progresses? To what extent and how do the characters themselves come to appreciate these similarities? What might the play ultimately say or show us through these characters?

5. Charles Isherwood, writing in *The New York Times*, describes WATER BY THE SPOON-FUL's theme as involving "the myriad ways in which human lives can intersect, and the potentially great rewards—or irreparable damage—that can result from the unlikely spark of those connections." Others instead describe the play as exploring

the difficulty and importance of forgiving both ourselves and others; the idea "that no one is above reproach—or beyond redemption"; "the true meaning of family" (theatreworks.org); or the "life-affirming message" that "[p]eople instinctively take care of each other" and that "hitting bottom is the start of the trip back up" (Richard Zoglin, in *Time*). Write an essay defending and developing one of these claims.

Exploring Contexts

26 | THE AUTHOR'S WORK AS CONTEXT: WILLIAM SHAKESPEARE

When we read, we inevitably compare. We compare the writer's style to the styles of other writers; we compare characters within a story or play to one another and to people we know; we compare our life experiences to the many imaginary experiences that unfold before us as we read. Our interpretations of literature are fueled by comparison.

Reading several works by a single author is among the most rewarding and enlightening types of comparison we can employ as active readers of literature. Such comparisons serve a variety of purposes: They help us develop a sense of the overall shape of the writer's work (that is, the writer's **oeuvre**, or **canon**); they reveal the kinds of characters, plots, and dramatic situations the author tends to create; they offer a glimpse into the author's particular way of looking at the world. At the same time, such comparisons can enrich our understanding of any one work by drawing our attention to features we might not have thought much about otherwise, including those unique to it.

THE LIFE OF SHAKESPEARE: A BIOGRAPHICAL MYSTERY

This chapter offers you the opportunity to compare two plays by one of history's most vital and versatile playwrights: William Shakespeare. Shakespeare is a particularly enticing subject for this kind of comparative study in part because we know so little about him. While we can enhance our reading of many writers' work by studying the letters, essays, diaries, and other documents in which they comment directly on their lives and writing, Shakespeare left behind none of these. The only records that exist are a handful of official ones such as marriage licenses, property deeds, and wills.

William Shakespeare

These tell a brief story. Shakespeare's origins were humble: His grandfather, Richard, rented the land he farmed, near Stratford-upon-Avon, a market town in the English midlands. Richard's son, John, married the daughter of one of Richard's former landlords and moved to town. There he became a tradesman prosperous and respected enough to buy quite a bit of property and to hold several important civic offices, including that of bailiff, or mayor. The family's star was on the rise by the time William (the third of eight

Shakespeare's birthplace in Stratford-upon-Avon

children) was born, sometime in April 1564. Though neither of Shakespeare's parents had formal schooling and his mother was likely unable to read or write, his father's involvement in city government brought with it the privilege of enrolling William in the local free grammar school. Here Shakespeare learned how to read and write, not only in English but also in Latin and perhaps Greek. His schoolmasters also probably required him to read such standard classical works as Ovid's *Metamorphoses* and the plays of Plautus and Terence (which greatly influenced the plays he would later write). In 1582, at the age of eighteen, Shakespeare married twenty-six-year-old Anne Hatha-way, the daughter of a local farmer. The couple's first child (a daughter) was baptized six months later and followed in 1585 by a set of twins.

From the time of the twins' birth until 1592, Shakespeare's life becomes—for us—a blank: All we know is that by the latter date he was a successful actor and playwright spending most of his time in London. We know this, in part, because Shakespeare was prominent enough to be called an "upstart crow" in a book pub-lished by a rival playwright in 1592; apparently, this London-born, university-educated author felt a bit threatened by the undereducated provincial. Though, in 1594, the "upstart crow" achieved a measure of renown as a poet by publishing two lengthy narrative poems (*Venus and Adonis* and *The Rape of Lucrece*), his career from this time until his death centered mainly on his work with the Lord Chamberlain's (later King's) Men—one of the two most prominent acting compa-nies of his day. Shakespeare's work with the company was multifaceted: An actor with the troupe and its chief dramatist, he was also a shareholder who helped manage the troupe's affairs (including the building of the Globe Theatre, on the South Bank of the River Thames, in 1599). Being a shareholder ensured that he prospered along with the company, especially after they secured the patronage of the king in 1603. As a result, Shakespeare enjoyed a level of economic prosperity and a kind of status that wouldn't have been possible to a mere actor, playwright, or poet. Though Shakespeare's father had by this point fallen into debt, the Crown nonetheless granted him (and thus his playwright son) the title of "gentleman" in the late 1590s. And at his death in 1616, Shakespeare left his family substantial property in both London and Stratford, where the family had continued to live and where he likely spent most of his last few years.

Such facts remind us that Shakespeare was, after all, a real and in some ways rather ordinary person—who ultimately convinced audiences and rivals alike that he was more than an "upstart crow," but who did not, to quote one biographer, "in his own day inspire the mysterious veneration that afterwards came to surround him." These mundane facts tell us almost nothing, however, about the man's or the artist's inner life—his personal opinions, his motives, his loves, his dislikes, his politics, his "philosophy." These we can only infer by reading and comparing his poems and plays. Luckily, Shakespeare left us a lot of these, including 154 sonnets (some of which appear in this book) and at least thirty-eight plays. Scholars believe Shakespeare cowrote many more plays, and others may yet be discovered and authenticated.

EXPLORING SHAKESPEARE'S WORK:
A MIDSUMMER NIGHT'S DREAM AND *OTHELLO*

Given that his plays include comedies, tragedies, English histories, and **romances**, variety is a distinctive feature of Shakespeare's work as a playwright. It is fitting, then, that the two plays included in this chapter—A MIDSUMMER NIGHT'S DREAM and THE TRAGEDY OF OTHELLO, THE MOOR OF VENICE—seem, at first glance, so different. *A Midsummer Night's Dream*, written in about 1595, is generally considered among the last of Shakespeare's "apprentice" plays—the work of a young writer just beginning to find his own voice and dramatic style, but still quite dependent on classical models. Written c. 1601–3, *Othello* is instead regarded as one of the greatest works of a seasoned writer. Differences proliferate: *Dream*, a **comedy**, culminates in marriage (several marriages, in fact); *Othello*, a **tragedy**, concludes with multiple gruesome deaths. *Dream* is among Shakespeare's shortest plays; *Othello*, among his longest. Featuring the smallest cast of any Shakespearean tragedy, *Othello* presents us with only four highly individualized characters, including Iago—that most unforgettable of villains who dominates the play, speaking over 30 percent of its lines (two hundred more than the **protagonist** himself). *Dream*, in contrast, flits among many characters, the play's humor depending in part on our having as hard a time as the characters themselves do remembering who is who and who loves whom. Finally, where *Othello* entirely lacks **subplots**, *Midsummer Night's Dream* features at least four parallel yet contrasting plots, each featuring a pair of lovers whose happiness is, or has been, threatened by their own failures to understand each other or by others' opposition to their relationship. Here, as in other Shakespeare plays, the subplots can be divided into **underplots**, which are romantic or parodic versions of the main plot, and **overplots**, which foreground the play's political dimensions. In *A Midsummer Night's Dream*, Bottom becomes the protagonist of the underplot, Theseus and Hippolyta (and, perhaps, Titania and Oberon) protagonists of the overplot(s).

But while *A Midsummer Night's Dream* and *Othello* have important and revealing differences, they have equally significant similarities, and by attending to these similarities we may come to understand and appreciate Shakespeare's particular way of looking at the world. To begin with, we may approach such similarities (within these or any plays) by concentrating on the elements, looking for patterns in character, setting, structure, tone, and theme, remembering that these elements ultimately combine to shape our experience of any one play.

Different as their **settings** might be, for example, both *A Midsummer Night's Dream* and *Othello*—like most Shakespearean tragedies and comedies—unfold in foreign climes and at least somewhat foreign times: ancient Athens, in one case; late sixteenth-century Venice and Cyprus, in the other. As important, each play juxtaposes two settings, one of which it characterizes as more civilized, courtly, and cultured than the other. *A Midsummer Night's Dream* opens and closes in Athens proper, in the court of Theseus, and in daylight. But the bulk of its action takes place in the contrasting, simultaneously more natural and more dreamlike and magical, "green world" of a moonlit wood. Likewise, *Othello* begins in Venice, a city-state regarded as "the crown jewel" of Renaissance Italy, a major seaport and commercial center renowned for its prowess in the arts; its relatively cosmopolitan, even multicultural population; and its political intrigue. Yet in act 3 the play transports its characters and audience to a very different place: an island off the Turkish coast legendary as the birthplace of Aphrodite (a.k.a. Venus), goddess of love, on the one hand; and, on the other hand, as a rough-and-ready military outpost on the very margin of the Christian West (versus the Islamic East). (Cyprus, as represented in the play, might thus remind modern readers of the frontier fort as imagined in many an American Western.)

In thinking about **character**, notice that many major characters in *A Midsummer Night's Dream* and *Othello* occupy or aspire to high position. These characters' choices and behavior deeply affect the communities that they lead and/or defend. In fact, Shakespeare's plays often remind us of the general effects and communal significance of such characters' actions, taking for granted the idea that "on [a leader's] choice depends / The safety and health of th[e] whole state" (*Hamlet*) and tracing the effects of the particular choices made by kings, princes, dukes, and generals.

Shakespeare and his contemporaries often compared the relationship between a king and his subjects to that between a father and his children or between a husband and his wife. For example, an early Shakespeare comedy, *The Taming of the Shrew*, concludes with a speech in which the tamed shrew declares, "Thy husband is thy lord, thy life, thy keeper, / Thy head, thy sovereign." Building on this idea, she argues both that a woman's duty to her husband is the same "as the subject owes the prince" and that a woman who refuses to obey her husband is exactly like "a foul contending rebel / And graceless traitor." We might see similar analogies at work in *A Midsummer Night's Dream* and

Alessandro de' Medici, Duke of Florence (1510–37), nicknamed "Il Moro" (Spanish for "the Moor")

Judi Dench as Titania and Ian Richardson as Oberon in the 1968 film adaptation of *A Midsummer Night's Dream*

Judi Dench as Titania and Oliver Chris as Bottom in *A Midsummer Night's Dream* at the Rose Theatre, Kingston-upon-Thames, 2010

Othello, both of which begin with a father attempting to dictate whom his daughter will marry.

We pay attention to these high-ranking characters' effects on their environments in part because Shakespeare's plays also include characters who occupy positions much lower on the social ladder. In addition to Titania, Oberon, Theseus, and Hippolyta (rulers of the divine and human realms), *A Midsummer Night's Dream* introduces us to the Athenian craftsmen (or "mechanicals") led by the fittingly named Bottom. And while *Othello* focuses predominantly on Venice's military leaders and their wives, its cast also includes a prostitute and a clown. As a result, the two plays demonstrate Shakespeare's tendency to people his plays with a socially diverse cast of characters and to thereby create a socially inclusive dramatic world.

Indeed, *Othello* is virtually unique among Shakespearean tragedies in featuring a protagonist and an **antagonist** who are themselves neither nobly born nor former, current, or prospective heads of state. Renowned and respected general though he is, Othello leads Venice's armies rather than Venice itself, while Iago aspires only to be Othello's lieutenant. Identified as a Moor (often as "*the* Moor")—a term in Shakespeare's day denoting Muslims and/or (North) Africans—Othello has, moreover, earned rather than inherited his position. That he is both a foreigner to Venice and of a different race than the play's other characters arguably makes his position more tenuous and does much to shape his character, the play's **plot**, and thus his fate. For modern audiences and theatrical producers, questions about just what role such factors play thus tend to loom large, as do questions about whether and how Shakespeare's play ultimately upholds, as well as critiques, racial stereotypes.

Paul Robeson as Othello and Uta Hagen
as Desdemona in the 1943 Broadway
production of *Othello*

Chiwetel Ejiofor as Othello and Ewan
McGregor as Iago in *Othello* at the
Donmar Warehouse, London, 2007

As inclusive as Shakespeare's dramatic world is, after all, it is far from *demo-cratic* (as the speech from *The Taming of the Shrew* suggests). As you read more plays by Shakespeare, you will probably become more attuned to the different ways in which they depict "high" and "low" characters, for example. *A Midsummer Night's Dream* is typical in the way it associates socially low characters with **low or physical comedy** (as opposed to **high** or **verbal** comedy). Bottom wears an ass's head for much of the play. Yet Bottom is also typical of Shakespeare's socially humble characters in possessing a kind of wisdom his social betters lack.

Despite the tendency to insist on certain social distinctions, then, Shakespearean drama draws our attention to fundamental human experiences that cut across social, cultural, even racial lines. *Othello* and *A Midsummer Night's Dream* remind us that neither a fairy queen nor a great general is any more immune to love's magic or foolishness than the lowliest of mortals. The joys of love, the destructive force of jealousy and self-doubt—these experiences link us and remind us of our common humanity.

Reading *Othello* and *A Midsummer Night's Dream* side by side may also help us appreciate the tonal complexity of Shakespeare's plays—their incorporation of both comic and tragic, light-hearted and somber, elements. While *A Midsummer Night's Dream* plunges us into a nighttime world dominated by the intertwining forces of magic, love, and humor, it also continually reminds us of the dangerous aspects of the night, of the struggles that human beings endure in their pursuit of love and happiness, of the brevity and fragility of human joy and life, even of what Hamlet calls the "thousand natural shocks / That flesh is heir to." The specter of violence and death hovers in the background of *A Midsummer Night's Dream* as surely as it occupies the foreground of *Othello*, which, like other Shakespearean tragedies, includes comic scenes.

As you read *Othello* and *A Midsummer Night's Dream*, you will discover many more parallels of theme, character, setting, and structure whose significance you will want to ponder and investigate. But you should consider, too, another and perhaps more elusive element: language. Shakespeare is justly celebrated for his use of language, and we pay homage to it, unwittingly or not, every time we use any one of the many idiomatic expressions that originated in his plays. (If, for example, you conclude that Shakespeare is "Greek to me," you have proved otherwise by quoting from his play *Julius Caesar*.) In Shakespearean drama, language is never an end in itself but instead establishes character and tone, structures the play, shapes our emotional response to it, and enunciates theme.

The musical and visual qualities of Shakespeare's language are integral to its meaning. Though written mainly in verse, Shakespeare's plays include prose passages; and though most of the poetry is **blank verse** (unrhymed **iambic pentameter**), Shakespeare also uses **rhyme** and rhythmic variation to great effect. As you read the plays, then, you will want to pay attention to the texture and **rhythm** of the language—to the effect of *sound* on *sense*. You will also want to attend to the way Shakespeare uses language to appeal to your eye, as well as your ear. Visual **imagery**, like sound, consistently serves both structural and thematic ends, linking various moments and ideas, actions and themes. In *A Midsummer Night's Dream*, for example, characters frequently refer to their eyes. Such references begin in the very first scene: When Hermia wishes that her father "looked but with my eyes," Theseus responds that "your eyes must with his judgment look" (lines 56–57). These lines prepare us for a drama in which eyes will play a major part, in which love and vision tend to go hand in hand, in which both love and vision often conflict with "judgment." The character's talk of eyes thus connects directly to the plot; through both, the play asks us to think about the tremendous power of vision and the dangers of relying too heavily on it. So, too, perhaps, might a tragedy hinging, as *Othello* does, on what its protagonist dubs "ocular proof" (3.3.357).

.   .   .   .

Reading multiple plays by a single playwright will help you better recognize stylistic as well as structural and thematic patterns: Each additional play you read will bring you closer to an understanding and appreciation of its creator's unique way of looking at the world and of the way his or her views and technique changed over time. You will gain a sense of the author's development as a dramatist even as, ideally, you develop your own skills as a reader of drama.

WILLIAM SHAKESPEARE
A Midsummer Night's Dream[1]

[THE PERSONS OF THE PLAY

THESEUS, Duke of Athens
HIPPOLYTA, Queen of the Amazons,
   betrothed to Theseus
EGEUS, father to Hermia
HERMIA, daughter to Egeus, in love
   with Lysander
LYSANDER, in love with Hermia

OBERON, King of the Fairies
TITANIA, Queen of the Fairies
ROBIN Goodfellow, a puck°   *an imp or a mischievous sprite*
PEASEBLOSSOM
COBWEB
MOTH   } fairies in Titania's service
MUSTARDSEED
Other FAIRIES

DEMETRIUS, in love with Hermia
HELENA, in love with Demetrius
PHILOSTRATE, Master of the Revels at the
   court of Theseus
Lords and Attendants on Theseus and
   Hippolyta

Peter QUINCE, a carpenter, Prologue in
   the Interlude
Nick BOTTOM, a weaver, Pyramus in
   the Interlude
Francis FLUTE, a bellows-mender,
   Thisbe in the Interlude

Tom SNOUT, a tinker, Wall in the Interlude
SNUG, a joiner, Lion in the Interlude
Robin STARVELING, a tailor, Moonshine in
   the Interlude]

ACT I

Scene 1

Theseus's palace in Athens. Enter THESEUS, HIPPOLYTA,
[and PHILOSTRATE,*] with others.*

THESEUS: Now, fair Hippolyta, our nuptial hour
   Draws on apace. Four happy days bring in
   Another moon; but, oh, methinks, how slow
   This old moon wanes! She lingers° my desires   *delays fulfillment of*
   Like to a stepdame° or a dowager   *stepmother* 5
   Long withering out a young man's revenue.[2]
HIPPOLYTA: Four days will quickly steep° themselves in night;   *plunge*
   Four nights will quickly dream away the time;
   And then the moon—like to a silver bow
   Now bent in heaven—shall behold the night   10
   Of our solemnities.

---

1. Text, glosses, and notes are based on those in *The Norton Shakespeare*, 3rd ed., edited by Stephen
Greenblatt.
2. A widow using up the inheritance that will go to her husband's (young) heir on her death.

THESEUS: Go, Philostrate,
Stir up the Athenian youth to merriments,
Awake the pert and nimble spirit of mirth,
Turn melancholy forth to funerals;
15   The pale companion is not for our pomp.

[*Exit* PHILOSTRATE.]

Hippolyta, I wooed thee with my sword
And won thy love doing thee injuries;[3]
But I will wed thee in another key,
With pomp, with triumph,° and with reveling.   *public festivity*

Enter EGEUS *and his daughter* HERMIA, *and* LYSANDER
and DEMETRIUS.

20 EGEUS: Happy be Theseus, our renownèd duke!
THESEUS: Thanks, good Egeus. What's the news with thee?
EGEUS: Full of vexation come I, with complaint
Against my child, my daughter Hermia.
—Stand forth, Demetrius.—My noble lord,
25   This man hath my consent to marry her.
—Stand forth, Lysander.—And, my gracious duke,
This man hath bewitched the bosom of my child.
—Thou, thou, Lysander, thou hast given her rhymes,
And interchanged love tokens with my child.
30   Thou hast by moonlight at her window sung
With feigning[4] voice verses of feigning love,
And stolen the impression of her fantasy[5]
With bracelets of thy hair, rings, gauds,° conceits,°   *trinkets / clever gifts*
Knacks,° trifles, nosegays,° sweetmeats—messengers *Knickknacks / bouquets*
35   Of strong prevailment° in unhardened youth.   *persuasiveness*
With cunning hast thou filched my daughter's heart,
Turned her obedience, which is due to me,
To stubborn harshness.—And, my gracious duke,
Be it so° she will not here before your grace   *If*
40   Consent to marry with Demetrius,
I beg the ancient privilege of Athens:
As she is mine, I may dispose of her,
Which shall be either to this gentleman
Or to her death, according to our law
45   Immediately° provided in that case.   *Expressly*
THESEUS: What say you, Hermia? Be advised, fair maid:
To you your father should be as a god,
One that composed° your beauties, yea, and one   *fashioned*
To whom you are but as a form in wax

---

3. Theseus captured Hippolyta in his military conquest of the Amazons.
4. Pun: deceitful; desiring ("faining"); soft (in music).
5. By craftily impressing your image on her imagination, like a seal in wax, (you have) stolen her love.

By him imprinted,[6] and within his power   50
To leave° the figure or disfigure° it.   *maintain / destroy*
Demetrius is a worthy gentleman.
HERMIA: So is Lysander.
THESEUS: In himself he is,
But in this kind,° wanting your father's voice,[7]   *respect*
The other must be held the worthier.   55
HERMIA: I would my father looked but with my eyes.
THESEUS: Rather your eyes must with his judgment look.
HERMIA: I do entreat your grace to pardon me.
I know not by what power I am made bold,
Nor how it may concern° my modesty   *befit* 60
In such a presence here to plead my thoughts,
But I beseech your grace that I may know
The worst that may befall me in this case
If I refuse to wed Demetrius.
THESEUS: Either to die the death° or to abjure   *be executed* 65
For ever the society of men.
Therefore, fair Hermia, question your desires,
Know° of your youth, examine well your blood,°   *Inquire / passions*
Whether, if you yield not to your father's choice,
You can endure the livery° of a nun,[8]   *habit* 70
For aye° to be in shady cloister mewed,°   *ever / caged*
To live a barren sister all your life,
Chanting faint hymns to the cold fruitless moon.[9]
Thrice blessèd they that master so their blood
To undergo such maiden pilgrimage;°   *life as a virgin* 75
But earthlier happy is the rose distilled[1]
Than that which, withering on the virgin thorn,
Grows, lives, and dies in single blessedness.°   *in celibacy*
HERMIA: So will I grow, so live, so die, my lord,
Ere I will yield my virgin patent[2] up   80
Unto his lordship whose unwishèd yoke
My soul consents not to give sovereignty.
THESEUS: Take time to pause, and by the next new moon—
The sealing day betwixt my love and me
For everlasting bond of fellowship—   85
Upon that day either prepare to die
For disobedience to your father's will,
Or else to wed Demetrius, as he would,
Or on Diana's altar to protest°   *vow*

6. You are merely a wax impression of his seal.
7. Lacking your father's consent or vote.
8. Christian orders of nuns were established in the Middle Ages, but Elizabethans used the term as well for women devoted to a religious life in classical antiquity.
9. Emblem of Diana, goddess of chastity.
1. Preserved in a perfume (figuratively, preserved in her children). *Earthlier happy:* happier on earth.
2. My right to remain a virgin.

90   For aye° austerity and single life.   *ever*

DEMETRIUS: Relent, sweet Hermia, and, Lysander, yield

      Thy crazèd title° to my certain right.   *flawed claim*

LYSANDER: You have her father's love, Demetrius;

      Let me have Hermia's. Do you marry him.

95 EGEUS: Scornful Lysander! True, he hath my love,

      And what is mine my love shall render him;

      And she is mine, and all my right of her

      I do estate° unto Demetrius.   *settle; bestow*

LYSANDER [*to* THESEUS]: I am, my lord, as well derived° as he,   *descended*

100   As well possessed,° my love is more than his,   *endowed with wealth*

      My fortunes every way as fairly ranked,

      If not with vantage,° as Demetrius'.   *superiority*

      And, which is more than all these boasts can be,

      I am beloved of beauteous Hermia.

105   Why should not I then prosecute° my right?   *pursue*

      Demetrius, I'll avouch it to his head,°   *face*

      Made love to° Nedar's daughter, Helena,   *Wooed*

      And won her soul, and she, sweet lady, dotes,

      Devoutly dotes, dotes in idolatry

110   Upon this spotted and inconstant° man.   *fickle*

THESEUS: I must confess that I have heard so much

      And with Demetrius thought to have spoke thereof,

      But, being overfull of self-affairs,°   *my own concerns*

      My mind did lose it.—But, Demetrius, come,

115   —And come, Egeus; you shall go with me.

      I have some private schooling° for you both.   *advice*

      —For you, fair Hermia, look you arm° yourself   *prepare*

      To fit your fancies° to your father's will,   *desires*

      Or else the law of Athens yields you up,

120   Which by no means we may extenuate,°   *mitigate*

      To death or to a vow of single life.

      —Come, my Hippolyta. What cheer, my love?

      —Demetrius and Egeus, go along.

      I must employ you in some business

125   Against° our nuptial and confer with you   *In preparation for*

      Of something nearly that³ concerns yourselves.

EGEUS: With duty and desire we follow you.

                *Exeunt*⁴ [*all but* LYSANDER *and* HERMIA].

LYSANDER: How now, my love, why is your cheek so pale?

      How chance the roses there do fade so fast?

130 HERMIA: Belike° for want of rain, which I could well   *Probably*

      Beteem° them from the tempest of my eyes.   *Afford; grant*

LYSANDER: Ay me! For aught that I could ever read,

      Could ever hear by tale or history,

---

3. That closely.

4. Exit the stage (Latin for "they go out").

The course of true love never did run smooth,
But either it was different in blood°—   *hereditary rank*   135
HERMIA: Oh, cross!° Too high to be enthralled to low.   *vexation*
LYSANDER: Or else misgraffèd° in respect of years—   *badly matched*
HERMIA: Oh, spite! Too old to be engaged to young.
LYSANDER: Or else it stood° upon the choice of friends°—   *rested / kin*
HERMIA: Oh, hell! To choose love by another's eyes.   140
LYSANDER: Or if there were a sympathy° in choice,   *an agreement*
War, death, or sickness did lay siege to it,
Making it momentany° as a sound,   *momentary*
Swift as a shadow, short as any dream,
Brief as the lightning in the collied° night   *coal-black*   145
That in a spleen° unfolds° both heaven and earth   *swift impulse / reveals*
And ere a man hath power to say "Behold!"
The jaws of darkness do devour it up.
So quick bright things come to confusion.
HERMIA: If then true lovers have been ever° crossed,   *always*   150
It stands as an edict in destiny.
Then let us teach our trial patience⁵
Because it is a customary cross,
As due to love as thoughts and dreams and sighs,
Wishes and tears, poor fancy's° followers.   *love's*   155
LYSANDER: A good persuasion.° Therefore hear me, Hermia: *argument; principle*
I have a widow aunt, a dowager
Of great revenue, and she hath no child.
From Athens is her house remote seven leagues,
And she respects° me as her only son.   *regards*   160
There, gentle Hermia, may I marry thee,
And to that place the sharp Athenian law
Cannot pursue us. If thou lovest me then
Steal forth thy father's house tomorrow night,
And in the wood, a league without° the town,   *outside*   165
Where I did meet thee once with Helena
To do observance to a morn of May,°   *To celebrate May Day*
There will I stay for thee.
HERMIA: My good Lysander,
I swear to thee by Cupid's strongest bow,
By his best arrow with the golden head,⁶   170
By the simplicity° of Venus' doves,⁷   *innocence*
By that which knitteth souls and prospers loves,
And by that fire which burned the Carthage Queen
When the false Trojan under sail was seen,⁸
By all the vows that ever men have broke,   175
In number more than ever women spoke,

---

5. Let us teach ourselves to be patient in this trial.
6. Cupid's sharp golden arrow was said to create love; his blunt lead arrow caused dislike.
7. Said to draw Venus's chariot.
8. Dido, Queen of Carthage, burned herself on a funeral pyre when her lover, Aeneas, sailed away.

In that same place thou hast appointed me
Tomorrow truly will I meet with thee.
LYSANDER: Keep promise, love. Look, here comes Helena.

    Enter HELENA.

180 HERMIA: God speed, fair[9] Helena! Whither away?
HELENA: Call you me fair? That "fair" again unsay.
    Demetrius loves your fair; oh, happy fair!°   *fortunate beauty*
    Your eyes are lodestars,° and your tongue's sweet air°   *guiding stars / melody*
    More tunable° than lark to shepherd's ear   *tuneful*
185   When wheat is green, when hawthorn buds appear.
    Sickness is catching; oh, were favor° so,   *looks; charms*
    Your words I catch, fair Hermia, ere I go;
    My ear should catch your voice, my eye your eye,
    My tongue should catch your tongue's sweet melody.
190   Were the world mine, Demetrius being bated,°   *excepted*
    The rest I'd give to be to you translated.
    Oh, teach me how you look, and with what art
    You sway the motion of Demetrius' heart.
HERMIA: I frown upon him, yet he loves me still.
195 HELENA: Oh, that your frowns would teach my smiles such skill!
HERMIA: I give him curses, yet he gives me love.
HELENA: Oh, that my prayers could such affection move!
HERMIA: The more I hate, the more he follows me.
HELENA: The more I love, the more he hateth me.
200 HERMIA: His folly, Helena, is no fault of mine.
HELENA: None but your beauty; would that fault were mine!
HERMIA: Take comfort: he no more shall see my face.
    Lysander and myself will fly this place.
    Before the time I did Lysander see
205   Seemed Athens as a paradise to me.
    Oh, then, what graces in my love do dwell
    That he hath turned a heaven unto a hell?
LYSANDER: Helen, to you our minds we will unfold:
    Tomorrow night, when Phoebe° doth behold   *Diana (the moon)*
210   Her silver visage in the watery glass,
    Decking with liquid pearl the bladed grass,
    A time that lovers' flights doth still° conceal,   *always*
    Through Athens' gates have we devised to steal.
HERMIA: And in the wood where often you and I
215   Upon faint° primrose beds were wont° to lie,   *pale / accustomed*
    Emptying our bosoms of their counsel sweet,
    There my Lysander and myself shall meet,
    And thence from Athens turn away our eyes
    To seek new friends and stranger companies.°   *the company of strangers*

---

9. The dialogue plays on the meanings "blonde," "beautiful," "beauty." Helena is presumably fair-haired and Hermia (called a "raven" at 2.2.114) a brunette.

Farewell, sweet playfellow; pray thou for us,   220
And good luck grant thee thy Demetrius.
—Keep word, Lysander; we must starve our sight
From lovers' food till morrow deep midnight.   *Exit.*
LYSANDER: I will, my Hermia.—Helena, adieu.
As you on him, Demetrius dote on you.   *Exit.*   225
HELENA: How happy some o'er other some¹ can be!
Through Athens I am thought as fair as she.
But what of that? Demetrius thinks not so.
He will not know what all but he do know.
And as he errs, doting on Hermia's eyes,   230
So I, admiring of his qualities.
Things base and vile, holding no quantity,°   *shape; proportion*
Love can transpose to form and dignity.
Love looks not with the eyes but with the mind,²
And therefore is winged Cupid painted blind.   235
Nor hath love's mind of any judgment taste,°   *any trace of judgment*
Wings and no eyes figure° unheedy haste.   *symbolize*
And therefore is love said to be a child
Because in choice he is so oft beguiled.
As waggish° boys in game° themselves forswear,   *playful / sport; play* 240
So the boy Love is perjured everywhere.
For ere Demetrius looked on Hermia's eyne,°   *eyes*
He hailed down oaths that he was only mine.
And when this hail some heat from Hermia felt,
So he dissolved,° and showers of oaths did melt.   *broke faith; melted* 245
I will go tell him of fair Hermia's flight:
Then to the wood will he tomorrow night
Pursue her; and for this intelligence°   *information*
If I have thanks, it is a dear³ expense.
But herein mean I to enrich my pain,   250
To have his sight thither and back again.   *Exit.*

Scene 2

Somewhere in the city of Athens. Enter QUINCE *the car-
penter, and* SNUG *the joiner, and* BOTTOM *the weaver, and*
FLUTE *the bellows-mender, and* SNOUT *the tinker, and*
STARVELING *the tailor.*⁴

---

1. In comparison with others.
2. Love is promoted not by the evidence of the senses, but by the fancies of the mind.
3. Costly (because of the betrayal of secrecy and because it leads Demetrius to Hermia); or welcome
(because the potential return is Demetrius's love regained).
4. The artisans' names recall their occupations. Quince's name is probably derived from "quoins,"
wooden wedges used by carpenters who made buildings such as houses and theaters. The name "Snug"
evokes well-finished wooden furniture made by joiners. A bottom was the piece of wood on which
thread was wound; Bottom's name also connotes "ass" and "lowest point." As Flute's name suggests,
domestic bellows whistle through holes when needing repair. Snout's name may refer to the spouts of
the kettles he repairs or to his nose. Tailors, as Starveling's name recalls, were proverbially thin.

QUINCE: Is all our company here?

BOTTOM: You were best to call them generally,[5] man by
man, according to the scrip.°   script; list

QUINCE: Here is the scroll of every man's name which is thought
5   fit through all Athens to play in our interlude° before the   brief play
Duke and the Duchess on his wedding day at night.

BOTTOM: First, good Peter Quince, say what the play treats on;
then read the names of the actors; and so grow° to a point.°   draw / conclusion

QUINCE: Marry,° our play is *The Most Lamentable Comedy*   By the virgin Mary
10   *and Most Cruel Death of Pyramus and Thisbe.*[6]

BOTTOM: A very good piece of work, I assure you, and a
merry. Now, good Peter Quince, call forth your actors by
the scroll. Masters, spread yourselves.

QUINCE: Answer as I call you.—Nick Bottom, the weaver?

15   BOTTOM: Ready. Name what part I am for, and proceed.

QUINCE: You, Nick Bottom, are set down for Pyramus.

BOTTOM: What is Pyramus? A lover or a tyrant?

QUINCE: A lover that kills himself, most gallant, for love.

BOTTOM: That will ask some tears in the true performing of
20   it. If I do it, let the audience look to their eyes. I will move
storms. I will condole° in some measure. To the rest.—Yet   lament; arouse pity
my chief humor° is for a tyrant. I could play Ercles[7] rarely,°   inclination / excellently
or a part to tear a cat° in, to make all split.°   to rant / go to pieces

          The raging rocks
25   And shivering shocks°   shattering blows
          Shall break the locks
          Of prison gates,
          And Phibbus' car[8]
          Shall shine from far
30   And make and mar
          The foolish Fates.

This was lofty. Now name the rest of the players. This is
Ercles' vein, a tyrant's vein. A lover is more condoling.

QUINCE: Francis Flute, the bellows-mender?

35   FLUTE: Here, Peter Quince.

QUINCE: Flute, you must take Thisbe on you.

FLUTE: What is Thisbe, a wandering knight?°   knight-errant

QUINCE: It is the lady that Pyramus must love.

FLUTE: Nay, faith, let not me play a woman:[9] I have a beard
40   coming.

---

5. Bottom's error for "individually" (he frequently misuses words in this manner).

6. Parodying titles such as that of Thomas Preston's *Cambyses: A Lamentable Tragedy Mixed Full of
Pleasant Mirth* . . . (c. 1570).

7. Hercules (a stock ranting role in early plays).

8. The chariot of Phoebus Apollo, the sun god (the odd spelling may represent Bottom's pronunciation).

9. On the Elizabethan stage, women's parts were played by boys and young men.

QUINCE: That's all one.° You shall play it in a mask,[1] and you *irrelevent*
   may speak as small° as you will. *high-pitched; shrill*
BOTTOM: An° I may hide my face, let me play Thisbe too. I'll *If*
   speak in a monstrous little voice, "Thisne, Thisne!"[2]—"Ah,
   Pyramus, my lover dear, thy Thisbe dear and lady dear." 45
QUINCE: No, no, you must play Pyramus; and Flute, you Thisbe.
BOTTOM: Well, proceed.
QUINCE: Robin Starveling, the tailor?
STARVELING: Here, Peter Quince.
QUINCE: Robin Starveling, you must play Thisbe's mother. 50
   —Tom Snout, the tinker?
SNOUT: Here, Peter Quince.
QUINCE: You, Pyramus' father; myself, Thisbe's father; Snug the
   joiner, you, the lion's part; and I hope here is a play fitted.° *(well) cast*
SNUG: Have you the lion's part written? Pray you, if it be, 55
   give it me, for I am slow of study.
QUINCE: You may do it extempore, for it is nothing but roaring.
BOTTOM: Let me play the lion too. I will roar that I will do any
   man's heart good to hear me. I will roar that I will make
   the Duke say, "Let him roar again! Let him roar again!" 60
QUINCE: An you should do it too terribly, you would fright
   the Duchess and the ladies that they would shriek, and
   that were enough to hang us all.
ALL: That would hang us, every mother's son.
BOTTOM: I grant you, friends, if you should fright the ladies 65
   out of their wits, they would have no more discretion but
   to hang us. But I will aggravate° my voice so that I will *(for "moderate")*
   roar you as gently as any sucking dove.[3] I will roar you an
   'twere° any nightingale *as though it were*
QUINCE: You can play no part but Pyramus; for Pyramus is a 70
   sweet-faced man, a proper° man as one shall see in a *handsome*
   summer's day, a most lovely, gentlemanlike man. Therefore you must needs play Pyramus.
BOTTOM: Well, I will undertake it. What beard were I best
   to play it in? 75
QUINCE: Why, what you will.
BOTTOM: I will discharge° it in either your straw-color beard, *perform*
   your orange-tawny[4] beard, your purple-in-grain° beard, or *very deep red*
   your French-crown-color° beard, your perfect yellow. *gold coin-colored*
QUINCE: Some of your French crowns have no hair at all,[5] 80
   and then you will play bare-faced.°—But, masters, here *beardless; undisguised*

1. Elizabethan ladies regularly wore masks to remain anonymous and to protect their complexions.
2. Probably intended as a pet name for Thisbe; or it may mean "in this manner" ("thissen").
3. Bottom confuses "sitting dove" and "sucking lamb."
4. Dark yellow, a recognized name for the dye. (Bottom the weaver shows his professional knowledge.)
5. Referring to the baldness caused by venereal disease (called "the French disease").

are your parts,[6] and I am to entreat you, request you, and
desire you to con° them by tomorrow night, and meet me   *memorize*
in the palace wood, a mile without the town, by moon-
85   light. There will we rehearse; for if we meet in the city, we
shall be dogged with company, and our devices° known.   *plans*
In the meantime, I will draw a bill° of properties such as   *list*
our play wants. I pray you, fail me not.
        BOTTOM: We will meet, and there we may rehearse most
90   obscenely and courageously. Take pains; be perfect.[7] Adieu.
        QUINCE: At the Duke's oak we meet.
        BOTTOM: Enough! Hold, or cut bowstrings.[8]   *Exeunt.*

ACT II

Scene 1

A wood near Athens. Enter a FAIRY *at one door and* ROBIN
Goodfellow[, *a puck,*][9] *at another.*

        ROBIN: How now, spirit, whither wander you?
        FAIRY: Over hill, over dale,
                Thorough° bush, thorough briar,   *Through*
                Over park, over pale,°   *enclosure; fence*
5   Thorough flood, thorough fire,
                I do wander everywhere
                Swifter than the moon's sphere;[1]
                And I serve the Fairy Queen
                To dew her orbs[2] upon the green.
10   The cowslips tall her pensioners° be;   *royal bodyguards*
                In their gold coats spots you see.
                Those be rubies, fairy favors,°   *gifts*
                In those freckles live their savors.°   *scent*
                I must go seek some dewdrops here
15   And hang a pearl in every cowslip's ear.
                Farewell, thou lob° of spirits, I'll be gone.   *country bumpkin*
                Our queen and all her elves come here anon.
        ROBIN: The King doth keep his revels here tonight.
                Take heed the Queen come not within his sight,
20   For Oberon is passing fell and wrath[3]

6. Literally; an Elizabethan actor was generally given only his own lines and cues.
7. Be letter perfect in learning your parts. *Obscenely*: comic blunder, possibly for "out of sight" ("from
the scene" or "from being seen").
8. (From military archery): Be present at the rehearsal, or else quit the troupe (?).
9. Imp or mischievous sprite; in Elizabethan folklore, Robin Goodfellow was a puck who would do
housework if well treated.
1. Each planet, including the moon, was thought to be fixed in a transparent hollow globe revolving
around the earth.
2. To sprinkle her fairy rings (circles of dark grass).
3. Exceedingly fierce and angry.

Because that she as her attendant hath
A lovely boy stolen from an Indian king—
She never had so sweet a changeling[4]—
And jealous Oberon would have the child
Knight of his train, to trace° the forests wild.   range 25
But she perforce° withholds the lovèd boy,   forcibly
Crowns him with flowers, and makes him all her joy.
And now they never meet in grove or green,
By fountain° clear or spangled starlight sheen,°   spring / shining starlight
But they do square,° that all their elves for fear   quarrel 30
Creep into acorn cups and hide them there.
FAIRY: Either I mistake your shape and making° quite,   form
Or else you are that shrewd° and knavish sprite   mischievous
Called Robin Goodfellow. Are not you he
That frights the maidens of the villagery,°   villages 35
Skim milk, and sometimes labor in the quern,°   hand mill
And bootless° make the breathless housewife churn,   in vain
And sometime° make the drink to bear no barm,°   at times / froth on ale
Mislead night-wanderers, laughing at their harm?
Those that "hobgoblin" call you, and "sweet puck,"   40
You do their work, and they shall have good luck.
Are not you he?
ROBIN: Thou speakest aright;
I am that merry wanderer of the night.
I jest to Oberon and make him smile
When I a fat and bean-fed horse beguile,°   trick 45
Neighing in likeness of a filly foal.
And sometime lurk I in a gossip's° bowl   an old woman's
In very likeness of a roasted crab,[5]
And when she drinks, against her lips I bob,
And on her withered dewlap° pour the ale.   loose skin on the neck 50
The wisest aunt° telling the saddest° tale   old woman / most serious
Sometime for three-foot stool mistaketh me.
Then slip I from her bum, down topples she,
And "tailor" cries,[6] and falls into a cough;
And then the whole choir° hold their hips and laugh,   company 55
And waxen° in their mirth, and neeze,° and swear   increase / sneeze
A merrier hour was never wasted there.
But room, fairy: here comes Oberon.
FAIRY: And here my mistress. Would that he were gone.

*Enter [OBERON,] the King of Fairies, at one door, with
his train, and [TITANIA,] the Queen, at another, with
hers.*

4. Usually a child left by fairies in exchange for one stolen, but here the stolen child.
5. Crab apple ("lamb's wool," a winter drink, was made with roasted apples and warm ale).
6. Possibly the old woman cries this because she ends up cross-legged on the floor, as tailors sat to do
their work, or because she falls on her "tail."

60 OBERON: Ill met by moonlight, proud Titania.
    TITANIA: What, jealous Oberon?—Fairy, skip hence.
        I have forsworn his bed and company.
    OBERON: Tarry, rash wanton!° Am not I thy lord?   *impetuous creature*
    TITANIA: Then I must be thy lady; but I know
65   When thou hast stolen away from fairyland
        And in the shape of Corin[7] sat all day
        Playing on pipes of corn and versing love[8]
        To amorous Phillida. Why art thou here
        Come from the farthest step° of India   *limit*
70   But that, forsooth, the bouncing° Amazon,   *vigorous*
        Your buskined° mistress and your warrior love,   *boot-wearing*
        To Theseus must be wedded, and you come
        To give their bed joy and prosperity?
    OBERON: How canst thou thus, for shame, Titania,
75   Glance at my credit° with Hippolyta,   *Question my good name*
        Knowing I know thy love to Theseus?
        Didst not thou lead him through the glimmering night
        From Perigenia, whom he ravishèd,
        And make him with fair Aegles[9] break his faith,
80   With Ariadne, and Antiopa?[1]
    TITANIA: These are the forgeries of jealousy;
        And never since the middle summer's spring°   *beginning of midsummer*
        Met we on hill, in dale, forest, or mead,
        By pavèd° fountain or by rushy[2] brook,   *pebbled*
85   Or in° the beachèd margin° of the sea   *on / shore*
        To dance our ringlets° to the whistling wind,   *circle dances*
        But with thy brawls thou hast disturbed our sport.
        Therefore the winds, piping to us in vain,
        As in revenge have sucked up from the sea
90   Contagious fogs which, falling in the land,
        Hath every pelting° river made so proud   *paltry*
        That they have overborne their continents.°   *banks*
        The ox hath therefore stretched his yoke in vain,
        The plowman lost his sweat, and the green corn°   *grain*
95   Hath rotted ere his youth attained a beard.
        The fold stands empty in the drownèd field,
        And crows are fatted with the murrain° flock;   *dead of disease*

7. "Corin" and "Phillida" (line 68) are typical names for a shepherd and shepherdess in pastoral poetry.
8. Making or reciting love poetry. *Pipes of corn*: musical instruments made of oat stalks.
9. In Plutarch's *Lives*, Theseus previously had mistresses named Perigouna and Aegles. "Perigenia" (line 78) may be Shakespeare's alteration.
1. Taken from Plutarch; some writers used "Antiopa" as an alternative name for the Amazonian queen whom Theseus married, although here it seems to refer to a different woman. Ariadne helped Theseus to kill the Minotaur and escape from his labyrinth on Crete; she fled with Theseus, but he deserted her on Naxos.
2. Fringed with reeds.

The nine-men's morris[3] is filled up with mud,
And the quaint mazes in the wanton green[4]
For lack of tread are undistinguishable. 100
The human mortals want° their winter cheer;[5]   *lack*
No night is now with hymn or carol blessed.
Therefore[6] the moon, the governess of floods,
Pale in her anger, washes° all the air,   *moistens; wets*
That rheumatic[7] diseases do abound. 105
And thorough this distemperature° we see   *bad weather; disturbance*
The seasons alter; hoary-headed frosts
Fall in the fresh lap of the crimson rose,
And on old Hiems'° chin and icy crown   *winter's*
An odorous chaplet° of sweet summer buds   *wreath* 110
Is, as in mockery, set. The spring, the summer,
The childing° autumn, angry winter, change   *fruitful*
Their wonted liveries,[8] and the mazèd° world   *bewildered*
By their increase° now knows not which is which.   *crop yield*
And this same progeny of evils comes 115
From our debate,° from our dissension;   *quarrel*
We are their parents and original.°   *origin*
OBERON: Do you amend it then; it lies in you.
Why should Titania cross her Oberon?
I do but beg a little changeling boy 120
To be my henchman.°   *page of honor*
TITANIA: Set your heart at rest.[9]
The fairyland buys not the child of me.
His mother was a votress[1] of my order,
And in the spicèd Indian air by night
Full often hath she gossiped by my side 125
And sat with me on Neptune's yellow sands,
Marking the embarkèd traders° on the flood,°   *merchant ships / tide*
When we have laughed to see the sails conceive
And grow big-bellied with the wanton° wind,   *playful; amorous*
Which she, with pretty and with swimming[2] gait 130
Following°—her womb then rich with my young squire—   *Copying*
Would imitate, and sail upon the land
To fetch me trifles and return again,
As from a voyage, rich with merchandise.

3. The playing area for this outdoor game (traditionally, a board game played with nine pebbles or pegs) was cut in turf.
4. Luxuriant grass. *Quaint mazes:* intricate arrangements of paths (kept visible by frequent use).
5. Winter cheer would include the hymns and carols of the Yuletide.
6. As in lines 88 and 93 above, referring to the consequences of their quarrel.
7. Characterized by rheum: colds, coughs, and the like.
8. Customary clothing.
9. Proverbial expression for "Abandon that idea."
1. Woman who has taken a vow to serve (often, religious).
2. As though gliding through the waves.

135   But she, being mortal, of that boy did die,
      And for her sake do I rear up her boy,
      And for her sake I will not part with him.
OBERON: How long within this wood intend you stay?
TITANIA: Perchance till after Theseus' wedding day.
140   If you will patiently dance in our round
      And see our moonlight revels, go with us.
      If not, shun me, and I will spare° your haunts.   *avoid*
OBERON: Give me that boy, and I will go with thee.
TITANIA: Not for thy fairy kingdom.—Fairies, away!
145   We shall chide° downright if I longer stay.   *quarrel*

                    Exeunt [TITANIA *and her train*].

OBERON: Well, go thy way. Thou shalt not from° this grove   *go from*
      Till I torment thee for this injury.
      —My gentle puck, come hither. Thou rememberest
      Since° once I sat upon a promontory   *When*
150   And heard a mermaid on a dolphin's back
      Uttering such dulcet° and harmonious breath°   *sweet / voice; song*
      That the rude° sea grew civil at her song   *rough*
      And certain stars shot madly from their spheres°   *orbits*
      To hear the sea-maid's music?
ROBIN: I remember.
155 OBERON: That very time I saw—but thou couldst not—
      Flying between the cold moon and the earth,
      Cupid, all armed. A certain aim he took
      At a fair vestal thronèd by the west,[3]
      And loosed his love-shaft° smartly from his bow   *golden arrow*
160   As° it should pierce a hundred thousand hearts.   *As though*
      But I might° see young Cupid's fiery shaft   *could*
      Quenched in the chaste beams of the watery moon;
      And the imperial votress passèd on
      In maiden meditation, fancy-free.°   *free of love thoughts*
165   Yet marked I where the bolt° of Cupid fell.   *arrow*
      It fell upon a little western flower,
      Before milk-white, now purple with love's wound,
      And maidens call it "love-in-idleness."[4]
      Fetch me that flower. The herb I showed thee once:
170   The juice of it on sleeping eyelids laid
      Will make or° man or woman madly dote   *either*
      Upon the next live creature that it sees.
      Fetch me this herb, and be thou here again

---

3. To the west of India; in England. *Vestal*: virgin (a compliment to Queen Elizabeth, the Virgin Queen, and possibly an allusion to a specific entertainment in her honor, such as the water pageant at Elvetham in 1591).
4. Pansy. (Classical legend describes how the mulberry turned purple with Pyramus's blood and the hyacinth with Hyacinthus's, but it does not mention the pansy.)

Ere the leviathan[5] can swim a league.

ROBIN: I'll put a girdle° round about the earth   *circle*   175
    In forty minutes.

OBERON: Having once this juice,
    I'll watch Titania when she is asleep
    And drop the liquor° of it in her eyes.   *juice*
    The next thing then she waking looks upon—
    Be it on lion, bear, or wolf, or bull,   180
    On meddling monkey or on busy ape—
    She shall pursue it with the soul of love.
    And ere I take this charm from off her sight—
    As I can take it with another herb—
    I'll make her render up her page to me.   185
    But who comes here? I am invisible,
    And I will overhear their conference.

Enter DEMETRIUS, HELENA *following him.*

DEMETRIUS: I love thee not, therefore pursue me not.
    Where is Lysander and fair Hermia?
    The one I'll stay, the other stayeth me.[6]   190
    Thou told'st me they were stolen unto this wood,
    And here am I, and wood° within this wood   *insane*
    Because I cannot meet my Hermia.
    Hence, get thee gone, and follow me no more.

HELENA: You draw me, you hard-hearted adamant,[7]   195
    But yet you draw not iron, for my heart
    Is true as steel.[8] Leave you° your power to draw,   *Relinquish*
    And I shall have no power to follow you.

DEMETRIUS: Do I entice you? Do I speak you fair?[9]
    Or rather do I not in plainest truth   200
    Tell you I do not nor I cannot love you?

HELENA: And even for that do I love you the more.
    I am your spaniel, and, Demetrius,
    The more you beat me I will fawn on you.
    Use me but as your spaniel: spurn me, strike me,   205
    Neglect me, lose me—only give me leave,
    Unworthy as I am, to follow you.
    What worser place can I beg in your love—
    And yet a place of high respect with me—
    Than to be usèd as you use your dog?   210

DEMETRIUS: Tempt not too much the hatred of my spirit,
    For I am sick when I do look on thee.

5. Biblical sea monster, identified with the whale.
6. The one (Lysander) I'll bring to a halt, the other (Hermia) stops me in my tracks.
7. Very hard stone supposed to have magnetic properties. *Draw me:* that is, with the magnetic power of attraction.
8. Hermia contrasts the base metal iron with steel, which holds its temper.
9. Do I speak kindly to you?

HELENA: And I am sick when I look not on you.

DEMETRIUS: You do impeach° your modesty too much   *call into question*
215   To leave the city and commit yourself
     Into the hands of one that loves you not,
     To trust the opportunity of night
     And the ill counsel of a desert° place   *deserted*
     With the rich worth of your virginity.

220 HELENA: Your virtue is my privilege.° For that°   *protection / Because*
     It is not night when I do see your face.
     Therefore I think I am not in the night,
     Nor doth this wood lack worlds of company,
     For you in my respect° are all the world.   *as far as I am concerned*
225   Then how can it be said I am alone
     When all the world is here to look on me?

DEMETRIUS: I'll run from thee and hide me in the brakes,°   *thickets*
     And leave thee to the mercy of wild beasts.

HELENA: The wildest hath not such a heart as you.
230   Run when you will. The story shall be changed:
     Apollo flies, and Daphne holds the chase;[1]
     The dove pursues the griffin;[2] the mild hind°   *doe*
     Makes speed to catch the tiger: bootless° speed   *useless*
     When cowardice pursues and valor flies.

235 DEMETRIUS: I will not stay thy questions.[3] Let me go!
     Or if thou follow me, do not believe
     But I shall do thee mischief in the wood.   *[Exit.]*[4]

HELENA: Ay, in the temple, in the town, the field,
     You do me mischief. Fie, Demetrius,
240   Your wrongs do set a scandal on my sex.[5]
     We cannot fight for love as men may do;
     We should be wooed and were not made to woo.
     I'll follow thee and make a heaven of hell
     To die upon the hand I love so well.   *[Exit.]*

245 OBERON: Fare thee well, nymph. Ere he do leave this grove
     Thou shalt fly him, and he shall seek thy love.

     *Enter [*ROBIN *Goodfellow, the] puck.*

     Hast thou the flower there? Welcome, wanderer.

ROBIN: Ay, there it is.

OBERON: I pray thee give it me.
     I know a bank where the wild thyme blows,

---

1. Reversal of the traditional myth in which the nymph Daphne, flying from Apollo, was transformed into a laurel tree to escape him.
2. Fabulous monster with a lion's body and an eagle's head and wings.
3. I will not wait here any longer to hear you talk.
4. Some versions of the play provide no exit for Demetrius in this scene; however, when exactly he leaves has important implications for the tone of Helena's speech.
5. Your injustices to me cause me to behave in a way that disgraces my sex (by wooing him rather than being wooed).

Where oxlips[6] and the nodding violet grows,   250
Quite over-canopied with luscious woodbine,°   *honeysuckle*
With sweet musk-roses,[7] and with eglantine.°   *sweetbrier (a type of rose)*
There sleeps Titania sometime of the night,
Lulled in these flowers with dances and delight;
And there the snake throws° her enameled skin,   *throws off; casts away* 255
Weed° wide enough to wrap a fairy in.   *Garment*
And with the juice of this I'll streak° her eyes,   *anoint*
And make her full of hateful fantasies.
Take thou some of it, and seek through this grove.
A sweet Athenian lady is in love   260
With a disdainful youth. Anoint his eyes,
But do it when the next thing he espies
May be the lady. Thou shalt know the man
By the Athenian garments he hath on.
Effect it with some care, that he may prove   265
More fond° on her than she upon her love.   *doting*
And look thou meet me ere the first cock crow.[8]

ROBIN: Fear not, my lord; your servant shall do so. *Exeunt.*

Scene 2

The wood. Enter TITANIA, *Queen of Fairies, with her train.*

TITANIA: Come, now a roundel° and a fairy song;   *circle dance*
    Then, for the third part of a minute,[9] hence,
    Some to kill cankers° in the musk-rose buds,   *caterpillars*
    Some war with reremice° for their leathern wings   *bats*
    To make my small elves coats, and some keep back   5
    The clamorous owl that nightly hoots and wonders
    At our quaint° spirits. Sing me now asleep;   *dainty*
    Then to your offices, and let me rest.

    [*She lies down.*] FAIRIES *sing* [*and dance*].

FIRST FAIRY: You spotted snakes with double° tongue,   *forked*
    Thorny hedgehogs, be not seen;   10
    Newts and blindworms,[1] do no wrong,
    Come not near our Fairy Queen.
CHORUS: Philomel,[2] with melody
    Sing in our sweet lullaby;
    Lulla, lulla, lullaby, lulla, lulla, lullaby.   15
    Never harm,

---

6. Hybrid between primrose and cowslip.
7. Large rambling white roses.
8. Some spirits were thought unable to bear daylight.
9. The fairies are quick enough to do their tasks in twenty seconds.
1. Newts (water lizards) and blindworms were thought to be poisonous, as were spiders (line 20).
2. The nightingale (in classical mythology, a woman who, having been raped by her sister's husband, was transformed into a bird).

   Nor spell, nor charm
   Come our lovely lady nigh.
   So good night, with lullaby.
20 FIRST FAIRY: Weaving spiders, come not here;
    Hence, you long-legged spinners, hence!
    Beetles black, approach not near;
    Worm nor snail, do no offense.
CHORUS: Philomel, with melody, etc.

  [TITANIA *sleeps.*]

25 SECOND FAIRY: Hence, away! Now all is well.
   One aloof° stand sentinel.   *at a distance*

   [*Exeunt* FAIRIES, *leaving one sentinel.*]

Enter OBERON. [*He squeezes the juice on* TITANIA'S *eyes.*]

OBERON: What thou seest when thou dost wake,
   Do it for thy true love take;
   Love and languish for his sake.
30   Be it ounce° or cat or bear,   *lynx*
   Pard,° or boar with bristled hair,   *Leopard*
   In thy eye that shall appear
   When thou wak'st, it is thy dear.
   Wake when some vile thing is near.   [*Exit.*]

Enter LYSANDER *and* HERMIA.

35 LYSANDER: Fair love, you faint with wandering in the wood,
   And to speak truth, I have forgot our way.
   We'll rest us, Hermia, if you think it good,
   And tarry for the comfort of the day.
HERMIA: Be it so, Lysander. Find you out a bed,
40   For I upon this bank will rest my head.
LYSANDER: One turf shall serve as pillow for us both;
   One heart, one bed, two bosoms, and one troth.°   *pledged faith*
HERMIA: Nay, good Lysander: for my sake, my dear,
   Lie further off yet; do not lie so near.
45 LYSANDER: Oh, take the sense,° sweet, of my innocence!   *true meaning*
   Love takes the meaning in love's conference.[3]
   I mean that my heart unto yours is knit,
   So that but one heart we can make of it.
   Two bosoms interchainèd with an oath;
50   So, then, two bosoms and a single troth.
   Then by your side no bed-room me deny,
   For lying so, Hermia, I do not lie.[4]
HERMIA: Lysander riddles very prettily.
   Now much beshrew° my manners and my pride   *curse*

3. Love should enable lovers truly to understand each other.
4. Deceive; punning on "lie down."

If Hermia meant to say Lysander lied.   55
But, gentle friend, for love and courtesy
Lie further off in human° modesty.   *courteous*
Such separation as may well be said
Becomes a virtuous bachelor and a maid,
So far be distant. And good night, sweet friend;   60
Thy love ne'er alter till thy sweet life end.
LYSANDER: Amen, amen, to that fair prayer say I,
And then end life when I end loyalty.
Here is my bed. Sleep give thee all his rest.
HERMIA: With half that wish the wisher's eyes be pressed.[5]   65

[*They sleep separately.*]

Enter [ROBIN *Goodfellow, the*] *puck.*

ROBIN: Through the forest have I gone,
But Athenian found I none
On whose eyes I might approve°   *test*
This flower's force in stirring love.
Night and silence. Who is here?   70
Weeds of Athens he doth wear.
This is he my master said
Despisèd the Athenian maid;
And here the maiden, sleeping sound
On the dank and dirty ground.   75
Pretty soul, she durst not lie
Near this lack-love, this kill-courtesy.
Churl,° upon thy eyes I throw   *Rude fellow*
All the power this charm doth owe.°   *own*

[*He squeezes the juice on* LYSANDER'S *eyes.*]

When thou wak'st, let love forbid   80
Sleep his seat on thy eyelid.[6]
So awake when I am gone,
For I must now to Oberon.   *Exit.*

Enter DEMETRIUS *and* HELENA, *running.*

HELENA: Stay, though thou kill me, sweet Demetrius.
DEMETRIUS: I charge thee: hence, and do not haunt me thus.   85
HELENA: Oh, wilt thou darkling° leave me? Do not so.   *in darkness*
DEMETRIUS: Stay, on thy peril;[7] I alone will go.   [*Exit.*]
HELENA: Oh, I am out of breath in this fond° chase.   *foolish*
The more my prayer, the lesser is my grace.°   *reward*
Happy is Hermia, wheresoe'er she lies,   90
For she hath blessèd and attractive° eyes.   *magnetic*

5. May sleep's rest be shared between us. *Pressed:* closed in sleep.
6. Prevent you from sleeping.
7. Stay here, or risk peril (if you follow me).

How came her eyes so bright? Not with salt tears;
If so, my eyes are oftener washed than hers.
No, no; I am as ugly as a bear,
95　For beasts that meet me run away for fear.
Therefore no marvel though Demetrius
Do, as° a monster, fly my presence thus.　　　　　　　　　*as if I were*
What wicked and dissembling glass of mine
Made me compare° with Hermia's sphery eyne?°　　　*compete / starry eyes*
100　But who is here? Lysander, on the ground?
Dead or asleep? I see no blood, no wound.
Lysander, if you live, good sir, awake.

LYSANDER: [*awaking*]　And run through fire I will for thy
　　sweet sake.
Transparent[8] Helena, nature shows art°　　　　　　*skill; magic power*
105　That through thy bosom makes me see thy heart.
Where is Demetrius? Oh, how fit a word
Is that vile name to perish on my sword!

HELENA: Do not say so, Lysander; say not so.
What though he love your Hermia? Lord, what though?
110　Yet Hermia still loves you; then be content.

LYSANDER: Content with Hermia? No, I do repent
The tedious minutes I with her have spent.
Not Hermia but Helena I love.
Who will not change a raven for a dove?
115　The will of man is by his reason swayed,[9]
And reason says you are the worthier maid.
Things growing are not ripe until their season,
So I, being young, till now ripe not to reason.
And, touching now the point of human skill,[1]
120　Reason becomes the marshal[2] to my will
And leads me to your eyes, where I o'erlook°　　　　*look over; read*
Love's stories written in love's richest book.

HELENA: Wherefore was I to this keen° mockery born?　　*sharp*
When at your hands did I deserve this scorn?
125　Is't not enough, is't not enough, young man,
That I did never—no, nor never can—
Deserve a sweet look from Demetrius' eye,
But you must flout my insufficiency?[3]
Good troth,° you do me wrong—good sooth,° you do—　　*Truly / indeed*
130　In such disdainful manner me to woo.
But fare you well. Perforce I must confess
I thought you lord of more true gentleness.°　　　　　*courtesy; breeding*

8. Radiant; capable of being seen through.
9. Renaissance psychology considered the will (that is, the passions) to be in constant conflict with, and ideally subject to, the faculty of reason.
1. Reaching (only) now the highest point of human judgment.
2. Officer who led guests to their appointed places.
3. Mock my shortcomings by pretending they are wonderful qualities.

Oh, that a lady of one man refused
Should of° another therefore be abused!   *Exit.*   *by*
LYSANDER: She sees not Hermia.—Hermia, sleep thou there,   135
And never mayst thou come Lysander near;
For as a surfeit of the sweetest things
The deepest loathing to the stomach brings,
Or as the heresies that men do leave
Are hated most of those they did deceive,[4]   140
So thou, my surfeit and my heresy,
Of all be hated, but the most of me!
And, all my powers, address° your love and might   *direct; apply*
To honor Helen and to be her knight.   *Exit.*
HERMIA: [*awaking*]   Help me, Lysander, help me! Do thy best   145
To pluck this crawling serpent from my breast!
Ay me, for pity! What a dream was here!
Lysander, look how I do quake with fear.
Methought a serpent ate my heart away,
And you sat smiling at his cruel prey.°   *act of preying*   150
Lysander? What, removed? Lysander! Lord!
What, out of hearing, gone? No sound, no word?
Alack, where are you? Speak an if° you hear,   *an if = if*
Speak, of° all loves! I swoon almost with fear.   *for the sake of*
No? Then I well perceive you are not nigh.   155
Either death or you I'll find immediately.

Exit. [TITANIA *remains lying asleep.*]

ACT III

Scene 1

The wood. Enter the clowns° [, BOTTOM, QUINCE, SNOUT,   *rustics*
STARVELING, FLUTE, *and* SNUG].

BOTTOM: Are we all met?
QUINCE: Pat,° pat; and here's a marvelous convenient place   *On the dot*
    for our rehearsal. This green plot shall be our stage, this
    hawthorn brake° our tiring-house,° and we will do it in   *thicket / dressing room*
    action as we will do it before the Duke.   5
BOTTOM: Peter Quince?
QUINCE: What sayest thou, bully° Bottom?   *good fellow; jolly*
BOTTOM: There are things in this comedy of Pyramus and
    Thisbe that will never please. First, Pyramus must draw
    a sword to kill himself, which the ladies cannot abide.   10
    How answer you that?
SNOUT: By'r lakin,[5] a parlous° fear.   *perilous*

---

4. As men most hate the false opinions they once held.
5. By our ladykin (Virgin Mary): a mild oath.

STARVELING: I believe we must leave the killing out, when
    all is done.[6]

15 BOTTOM: Not a whit. I have a device to make all well. Write
    me a prologue, and let the prologue seem to say we will
    do no harm with our swords, and that Pyramus is not
    killed indeed. And for the more better assurance, tell
    them that I, Pyramus, am not Pyramus but Bottom the
20   weaver. This will put them out of fear.

QUINCE: Well, we will have such a prologue, and it shall be
    written in eight and six.[7]

BOTTOM: No, make it two more: let it be written in eight and
    eight.

25 SNOUT: Will not the ladies be afeard of the lion?

STARVELING: I fear it, I promise you.

BOTTOM: Masters, you ought to consider with yourself, to
    bring in—God shield us!—a lion among ladies is a most
    dreadful thing.[8] For there is not a more fearful° wildfowl   *frightening*
30   than your lion living. And we ought to look to't.

SNOUT: Therefore another prologue must tell he is not a lion.

BOTTOM: Nay, you must name his name, and half his face
    must be seen through the lion's neck, and he himself must
    speak through, saying thus or to the same defect:° "Ladies,"   *(for "effect")*
35   or "Fair Ladies, I would wish you," or "I would request
    you," or "I would entreat you not to fear, not to tremble.
    My life for yours.[9] If you think I come hither as a lion, it
    were pity of° my life. No, I am no such thing. I am a man   *a threat to*
    as other men are"—and there indeed let him name his
40   name, and tell them plainly he is Snug the joiner.

QUINCE: Well, it shall be so. But there is two hard things:
    that is, to bring the moonlight into a chamber—for you
    know Pyramus and Thisbe meet by moonlight.

SNOUT:[1] Doth the moon shine that night we play our play?

45 BOTTOM: A calendar, a calendar! Look in the almanac; find
    out moonshine, find out moonshine!

QUINCE: Yes, it doth shine that night.

BOTTOM: Why, then may you leave a casement of the great
    chamber window where we play open, and the moon may
50   shine in at the casement.

QUINCE: Ay, or else one must come in with a bush of thorns
    and a lantern and say he comes to disfigure,[2] or to present,°   *represent*

---

6. When all is said and done.
7. Alternate lines of eight and six syllables (a common ballad measure).
8. In 1594, at a feast in honor of the christening of King James's son, a tame lion that was supposed
to draw a chariot was replaced by a Black African man in order to avoid frightening the audience.
9. I pledge my life to defend yours.
1. Or Snug.
2. Blunder for "figure," represent. *Bush of thorns*: bundle of thornbush kindling (like the lantern, a
traditional accessory of the man in the moon).

the person of Moonshine. Then there is another thing: we must have a wall in the great chamber; for Pyramus and Thisbe, says the story, did talk through the chink of a wall.   55

SNOUT: You can never bring in a wall. What say you, Bottom?

BOTTOM: Some man or other must present Wall; and let him have some plaster, or some loam, or some roughcast³ about him to signify "wall"; or let him hold his fingers thus, and through that cranny shall Pyramus and Thisbe whisper.   60

QUINCE: If that may be, then all is well. Come, sit down, every mother's son, and rehearse your parts. Pyramus, you begin. When you have spoken your speech, enter into that brake, and so everyone according to his cue.   65

    Enter ROBIN[*, invisible*].

ROBIN [*aside*]:   What hempen homespuns⁴ have we swaggering here
    So near the cradle of the Fairy Queen?
    What, a play toward?° I'll be an auditor—   *in preparation*
    An actor too perhaps, if I see cause.

QUINCE: Speak, Pyramus.—Thisbe, stand forth.   70

BOTTOM [*as Pyramus*]: "Thisbe, the flowers of odious° savors   (*for* "*odorous*")
    sweet—"

QUINCE: Odors—"odorous"!

BOTTOM [*as Pyramus*]: "—Odors savors sweet.
    So hath thy breath, my dearest Thisbe dear.
    But hark, a voice! Stay thou but here a while,   75
    And by and by I will to thee appear."   *Exit.*

QUINCE: A stranger Pyramus than e'er played here.   [*Exit.*]

FLUTE: Must I speak now?

QUINCE: Ay, marry, must you. For you must understand he goes but to see a noise that he heard and is to come again.   80

FLUTE [*as Thisbe*]: "Most radiant Pyramus, most lily-white of hue,
    Of color like the red rose on triumphant briar,
    Most brisky juvenal° and eke° most lovely Jew,⁵   *lively youth (juvenile) / also*
    As true as truest horse that yet would never tire,
    I'll meet thee, Pyramus, at Ninny's tomb—"   85

QUINCE: "Ninus'⁶ tomb," man! Why, you must not speak that yet; that you answer to Pyramus. You speak all your part at once, cues and all.—Pyramus, enter! Your cue is past; it is "never tire."

---

3. Mixture of lime and gravel used to plaster exterior walls.
4. Peasants, or country bumpkins, dressed in coarse homespun fabric made from hemp.
5. Not often considered "lovely" by Elizabethan Christians; usually, a term of abuse (here, echoing the first syllable of "juvenal").
6. Mythical founder of Nineveh, whose wife, Semiramis, was believed to have founded Babylon, the setting for the story of Pyramus and Thisbe. Flute's mistake, "Ninny," means "fool."

90 FLUTE: Oh,
     [*as Thisbe*]: "As true as truest horse that yet would never
       tire."

     [*Enter* ROBIN, *invisible, and* BOTTOM *with the ass
       head on.*]

BOTTOM [*as Pyramus*]:   "If I were fair,° Thisbe, I were° only   handsome / would be
     thine."
QUINCE: Oh, monstrous! Oh, strange! We are haunted! Pray,
     masters! Fly, masters! Help!

                    [*Exeunt* QUINCE, SNOUT, STARVELING,
                                FLUTE, *and* SNUG.]

95 ROBIN: I'll follow you, I'll lead you about a round,°   in circles
     Through bog, through bush, through brake, through
        briar.
     Sometime a horse I'll be, sometime a hound,
     A hog, a headless bear, sometime a fire,°   will-o'-the-wisp
     And neigh and bark and grunt and roar and burn,
100   Like horse, hound, hog, bear, fire, at every turn.   *Exit.*
BOTTOM: Why do they run away? This is a knavery of them
     to make me afeard.

     Enter SNOUT.

SNOUT: O Bottom, thou art changed! What do I see on thee?
BOTTOM: What do you see? You see an ass head of your
105   own,[7] do you?   [*Exit* SNOUT.]

     Enter QUINCE.

QUINCE: Bless thee, Bottom, bless thee! Thou art translated.°   transformed

                                               Exit.

BOTTOM: I see their knavery. This is to make an ass of me,
     to fright me, if they could. But I will not stir from this
     place, do what they can. I will walk up and down here,
110   and I will sing, that they shall hear I am not afraid.
     [*Sings.*]   The ouzel cock,° so black of hue,   male blackbird
                  With orange-tawny bill,
                  The throstle° with his note so true,   song thrush
                  The wren with little quill°—   feathers
115 TITANIA [*awaking*]:   What angel wakes me from my flowery bed?
BOTTOM [*sings*]:   The finch, the sparrow, and the lark,
                  The plainsong[8] cuckoo gray,
                  Whose note full many a man doth mark
                  And dares not answer "Nay"[9]—

---

7. You see a figment of your own asinine imagination.
8. Melody sung without adornment (that is, the cuckoo's call).
9. Deny. (The cuckoo's call was associated with cuckoldry.)

for indeed, who would set his wit to° so foolish a bird?   *pay heed to*   120
Who would give a bird the lie,[1] though he cry "cuckoo"
never so?°   *ever so much*

TITANIA: I pray thee, gentle mortal, sing again.
    Mine ear is much enamored of thy note;
    So is mine eye enthrallèd to thy shape,   125
    And thy fair virtue's force[2] perforce doth move me
    On the first view to say, to swear, I love thee.

BOTTOM: Methinks, mistress, you should have little reason
    for that. And yet, to say the truth, reason and love keep
    little company together nowadays—the more the pity   130
    that some honest neighbors will not make them friends.
    Nay, I can gleek° upon occasion.   *make jokes*

TITANIA: Thou art as wise as thou art beautiful.

BOTTOM: Not so neither; but if I had wit enough to get out of
    this wood, I have enough to serve mine own turn.°   *purpose*   135

TITANIA: Out of this wood do not desire to go.
    Thou shalt remain here, whether thou wilt or no.
    I am a spirit of no common rate°—   *rank*
    The summer still° doth tend upon my state[3]—   *always*
    And I do love thee. Therefore go with me.   140
    I'll give thee fairies to attend on thee,
    And they shall fetch thee jewels from the deep
    And sing while thou on pressèd flowers dost sleep.
    And I will purge thy mortal grossness° so   *fleshly being*
    That thou shalt like an airy spirit go.   145
    Peaseblossom, Cobweb, Moth, and Mustardseed!

Enter four FAIRIES[: PEASEBLOSSOM, COBWEB, MOTH,[4]
and MUSTARDSEED].

PEASEBLOSSOM: Ready.
COBWEB: And I.
MOTH: And I.
MUSTARDSEED: And I.
ALL: Where shall we go?

TITANIA: Be kind and courteous to this gentleman.
    Hop in his walks and gambol in his eyes;
    Feed him with apricots and dewberries,   150
    With purple grapes, green figs, and mulberries;
    The honey bags steal from the humble-bees,°   *bumblebees*
    And for night-tapers crop their waxen thighs,
    And light them at the fiery glowworms' eyes
    To have° my love to bed and to arise;   *lead*   155
    And pluck the wings from painted butterflies

1. Who would call a bird a liar?
2. The power of your good or beauteous qualities.
3. Serves me, as part of my royal retinue.
4. Or "mote": speck.

To fan the moonbeams from his sleeping eyes.
Nod to him, elves, and do him courtesies.

PEASEBLOSSOM: Hail, mortal!

160 COBWEB: Hail!

MOTH: Hail!

MUSTARDSEED: Hail!

BOTTOM: I cry your worships mercy,[5] heartily.—I beseech
your worship's name.

165 COBWEB: Cobweb.

BOTTOM: I shall desire you of more acquaintance, good
Master Cobweb. If I cut my finger, I shall make bold with
you.[6]—Your name, honest gentleman?

PEASEBLOSSOM: Peaseblossom.

170 BOTTOM: I pray you commend me to Mistress Squash, your
mother, and to Master Peascod,[7] your father. Good Master
Peaseblossom, I shall desire you of more acquaintance
too.—Your name, I beseech you, sir?

MUSTARDSEED: Mustardseed.

175 BOTTOM: Good Master Mustardseed, I know your patience
well. That same cowardly, giant-like ox-beef[8] hath devoured
many a gentleman of your house. I promise you, your
kindred hath made my eyes water ere now. I desire you of
more acquaintance, good Master Mustardseed.

180 TITANIA [to the FAIRIES]:   Come, wait upon him. Lead him to
my bower.
The moon methinks looks with a watery eye,
And when she weeps, weeps every little flower,[9]
Lamenting some enforcèd° chastity.   violated; involuntary
Tie up my lover's tongue;[1] bring him silently.   [Exeunt.]

Scene 2

The wood. Enter [OBERON,] *King of Fairies.*

OBERON: I wonder if Titania be awaked;
Then what it was that next came in her eye,
Which she must dote on in extremity.

Enter ROBIN *Goodfellow.*

Here comes my messenger. How now, mad spirit?
5   What night-rule° now about this haunted grove?   night revels; sports

ROBIN: My mistress with a monster is in love.

---

5. I beg pardon of your honors.
6. Cobwebs were used to stop bleeding.
7. Ripe pea pod (called "your father" because it suggests "codpiece"). *Squash*: unripe pea pod.
8. Because beef is often eaten with mustard, or because oxen munch on mustard plants. *Your patience*: what you have suffered with fortitude.
9. Dew was thought to originate on the moon.
1. Bottom is perhaps making involuntary asinine noises.

Near to her close° and consecrated bower, *private*
While she was in her dull° and sleeping hour, *drowsy*
A crew of patches,° rude mechanicals° *fools / rough workmen*
That work for bread upon Athenian stalls,° *market stands* 10
Were met together to rehearse a play
Intended for great Theseus' nuptial day.
The shallowest thick-skin of that barren sort,° *witless lot*
Who Pyramus presented° in their sport, *acted*
Forsook his scene° and entered in a brake. *stage* 15
When I did him at this advantage take,
An ass's nole° I fixèd on his head. *head*
Anon his Thisbe must be answerèd,
And forth my mimic° comes. When they him spy— *burlesque actor*
As wild geese that the creeping fowler° eye, *bird hunter* 20
Or russet-pated choughs, many in sort,[2]
Rising and cawing at the gun's report,
Sever° themselves and madly sweep the sky— *Scatter*
So at his sight away his fellows fly,
And at our stamp[3] here o'er and o'er one falls. 25
He° "Murder!" cries and help from Athens calls. *One (workman)*
Their sense thus weak, lost with their fears thus strong,
Made senseless things begin to do them wrong.
For briars and thorns at their apparel snatch,
Some sleeves, some hats: from yielders all things catch.[4] 30
I led them on in this distracted fear
And left sweet Pyramus translated there,
When in that moment, so it came to pass,
Titania waked and straightway loved an ass.
OBERON: This falls out better than I could devise. 35
But hast thou yet latched° the Athenian's eyes *anointed*
With the love juice, as I did bid thee do?
ROBIN: I took him sleeping—that is finished, too—
And the Athenian woman by his side,
That° when he waked, of force° she must be eyed. *So that / necessity* 40

Enter DEMETRIUS *and* HERMIA.

OBERON: Stand close. This is the same Athenian.
ROBIN: This is the woman, but not this the man.

[OBERON *and* ROBIN *stand apart.*]

DEMETRIUS: Oh, why rebuke you him that loves you so?
Lay breath so bitter on your bitter foe.
HERMIA: Now I but chide, but I should use thee worse, 45
For thou, I fear, hast given me cause to curse.

---

2. Together, in a flock. *Russet-pated choughs*: gray-headed jackdaws.
3. Editors have wondered how a fairy's presumably tiny foot could cause the human to fall.
4. Everything robs the timid.

If thou hast slain Lysander in his sleep,
Being o'er shoes° in blood, plunge in the deep,   *Having waded so far*
And kill me too.

50   The sun was not so true unto the day
As he to me. Would he have stolen away
From sleeping Hermia? I'll believe as soon
This whole° earth may be bored, and that the moon   *solid*
May through the center creep and so displease

55   Her brother's noontide with the Antipodes.[5]
It cannot be but thou hast murdered him.
So should a murderer look: so dead,° so grim.   *deathly pale*

DEMETRIUS: So should the murdered look, and so should I,
Pierced through the heart with your stern cruelty.

60   Yet you, the murderer, look as bright, as clear,
As yonder Venus in her glimmering sphere.°   *orbit*

HERMIA: What's this to my Lysander? Where is he?
Ah, good Demetrius, wilt thou give him me?

DEMETRIUS: I had rather give his carcass to my hounds.

65   HERMIA: Out, dog! Out, cur! Thou driv'st me past the bounds
Of maiden's patience. Hast thou slain him, then?
Henceforth be never numbered among men.
Oh, once tell true; tell true, even for my sake:
Durst thou have looked upon him being awake,

70   And hast thou killed him sleeping? Oh, brave touch!°   *noble stroke*
Could not a worm,° an adder do so much?   *serpent*
An adder did it; for with doubler[6] tongue
Than thine, thou serpent, never adder stung.

DEMETRIUS: You spend your passion on a misprised mood.°   *in misconceived anger*

75   I am not guilty of Lysander's blood,
Nor is he dead, for aught that I can tell.

HERMIA: I pray thee, tell me then that he is well.

DEMETRIUS: And if I could, what should I get therefore?°   *for that*

HERMIA: A privilege, never to see me more;

80   And from thy hated presence part I so.
See me no more, whether he be dead or no.   *Exit.*

DEMETRIUS: There is no following her in this fierce vein.
Here therefore for a while I will remain.
So sorrow's heaviness[7] doth heavier grow

85   For debt that bankrupt sleep doth sorrow owe,[8]
Which now in some slight measure it will pay,
If for his tender here I make some stay.[9]

5. That the moon could creep through a hole bored through the earth's center and emerge on the other side, the Antipodes, displeasing the inhabitants by displacing the noontime sun with the darkness of night. (Apollo, the sun god, was the brother of Diana, the moon goddess.)
6. More forked (of the adder); more duplicitous (of Demetrius).
7. Sadness (punning on "heavy": drowsy).
8. Because sorrow worsens without sleep.
9. I will rest here awhile, giving sleep capital ("tender") to pay off some of its debt to sorrow.

[He] lies down [and sleeps].

OBERON *[to* ROBIN*]:*   What hast thou done? Thou hast
    mistaken quite
  And laid the love juice on some true love's sight.
  Of thy misprision° must perforce ensue   *mistake* 90
  Some true love turned, and not a false turned true.
ROBIN: Then fate o'errules, that, one man holding troth,°   *faith*
  A million fail, confounding oath on oath.[1]
OBERON: About the wood go swifter than the wind,
  And Helena of Athens look° thou find.   *be sure* 95
  All fancy-sick° she is and pale of cheer°   *lovesick / face*
  With sighs of love that costs the fresh blood dear.[2]
  By some illusion see thou bring her here;
  I'll charm his eyes against° she do appear.   *in readiness for when*
ROBIN: I go, I go; look how I go,   100
  Swifter than arrow from the Tartar's bow.[3]   *[Exit.]*
OBERON *[squeezing the juice on* DEMETRIUS*'s eyes]:*   Flower of
    this purple dye,
  Hit with Cupid's archery,
  Sink in apple° of his eye.   *pupil*
  When his love he doth espy,   105
  Let her shine as gloriously
  As the Venus of the sky.
  When thou wak'st, if she be by,
  Beg of her for remedy.

*Enter [*ROBIN *Goodfellow, the] puck.*

ROBIN: Captain of our fairy band,   110
  Helena is here at hand,
  And the youth mistook by me,
  Pleading for a lover's fee.°   *reward*
  Shall we their fond° pageant see?   *foolish*
  Lord, what fools these mortals be!   115
OBERON: Stand aside. The noise they make
  Will cause Demetrius to awake.
ROBIN: Then will two at once woo one;
  That must needs be sport alone.°   *in itself*
  And those things do best please me   120
  That befall preposterously.°   *ass backward*

[They stand apart.]
Enter LYSANDER *and* HELENA.

LYSANDER: Why should you think that I should woo in scorn?

---

1. Among the millions of faithless men, the one true man's oath has been subverted by fate.
2. Sighs were thought to cause a loss of blood.
3. Tartars, a dark-skinned, supposedly savage people in Asia Minor, were famed for their skills in
archery.

Scorn and derision never come in tears.
Look when I vow, I weep, and vows so born,
125   In their nativity all truth appears.[4]
How can these things in me seem scorn to you,
Bearing the badge of faith[5] to prove them true?

HELENA: You do advance° your cunning more and more.   *increase; display*
When truth kills truth[6]—oh, devilish-holy fray!
130   These vows are Hermia's. Will you give her o'er?
Weigh oath with oath, and you will nothing weigh.[7]
Your vows to her and me put in two scales
Will even weigh, and both as light as tales.°   *lies; fiction*

LYSANDER: I had no judgment when to her I swore.
135 HELENA: Nor none, in my mind, now you give her o'er.
LYSANDER: Demetrius loves her, and he loves not you.
DEMETRIUS [*awaking*]:   O Helen, goddess, nymph, perfect,
        divine!
To what, my love, shall I compare thine eyne?
Crystal is muddy. Oh, how ripe in show°   *appearance*
140   Thy lips, those kissing cherries, tempting grow!
That pure congealèd white, high Taurus'[8] snow,
Fanned with the eastern wind, turns to a crow[9]
When thou hold'st up thy hand. Oh, let me kiss
This princess of pure white, this seal° of bliss!   *pledge*

145 HELENA: Oh, spite! Oh, hell! I see you all are bent
To set against me for your merriment.
If you were civil and knew courtesy,
You would not do me thus much injury.
Can you not hate me, as I know you do,
150   But you must join in souls to mock me too?
If you were men, as men you are in show,
You would not use a gentle° lady so,   *well-born; mild*
To vow and swear and superpraise my parts,°   *overpraise my qualities*
When I am sure you hate me with your hearts.
155   You both are rivals and love Hermia,
And now both rivals to mock Helena.
A trim° exploit, a manly enterprise,   *fine*
To conjure tears up in a poor maid's eyes
With your derision. None of noble sort°   *rank; nature*
160   Would so offend a virgin and extort°   *torture*
A poor soul's patience, all to make you sport.

LYSANDER: You are unkind, Demetrius; be not so.

4. The fact that I am weeping authenticates my vow's sincerity.
5. Insignia, such as that worn on a servant's livery (here, his tears).
6. When one vow nullifies another.
7. You will find that neither oath has any substance; you, Lysander, will be found to have no substance.
8. Range of high mountains in Asia Minor.
9. Appears black by contrast.

For you love Hermia; this you know I know.
And here, with all good will, with all my heart,
In Hermia's love I yield you up my part;   165
And yours of Helena to me bequeath,
Whom I do love and will do till my death.

HELENA: Never did mockers waste more idle breath.

DEMETRIUS: Lysander, keep thy Hermia. I will none.[1]
    If e'er I loved her, all that love is gone.   170
    My heart to her but as guest-wise° sojourned,   *as a guest*
    And now to Helen is it home returned,
    There to remain.

LYSANDER: Helen, it is not so.

DEMETRIUS: Disparage not the faith thou dost not know,
    Lest to thy peril thou aby it dear.°   *pay for it dearly* 175
    Look where thy love comes; yonder is thy dear.

Enter HERMIA.

HERMIA: Dark night, that from the eye his° function takes,   *its*
    The ear more quick of apprehension makes.
    Wherein it doth impair the seeing sense,
    It pays the hearing double recompense.   180
    Thou art not by mine eye, Lysander, found;
    Mine ear, I thank it, brought me to thy sound.
    But why unkindly didst thou leave me so?

LYSANDER: Why should he stay whom love doth press to go?

HERMIA: What love could press Lysander from my side?   185

LYSANDER: Lysander's love, that would not let him bide:
    Fair Helena, who more engilds the night
    Than all yon fiery oes and eyes of light.[2]
    [*to* HERMIA] Why seek'st thou me? Could not this
        make thee know
    The hate I bare thee made me leave thee so?   190

HERMIA: You speak not as you think; it cannot be.

HELENA: Lo, she is one of this confederacy.
    Now I perceive they have conjoined all three
    To fashion this false sport in spite of° me.   *to spite*
    Injurious Hermia, most ungrateful maid,   195
    Have you conspired, have you with these contrived
    To bait[3] me with this foul derision?
    Is all the counsel° that we two have shared,   *intimacy*
    The sisters' vows, the hours that we have spent
    When we have chid the hasty-footed time   200
    For parting us—oh, is all forgot,
    All schooldays' friendship, childhood innocence?

1. I will have nothing to do with her.
2. Stars (punning on the vowels and on lovers' exclamatory "oh"s and "ay"s). An "o" was a spangle.
3. To torment (as Elizabethans set dogs to bait a bear).

We, Hermia, like two artificial° gods   *artfully skilled*
Have with our needles created both one flower,
205 Both on one sampler, sitting on one cushion,
Both warbling of one song, both in one key,
As if our hands, our sides, voices, and minds
Had been incorporate.° So we grew together   *of one body*
Like to a double cherry, seeming parted,
210 But yet an union in partition,
Two lovely berries molded on one stem;
So with two seeming bodies but one heart,
Two of the first,[4] like coats in heraldry,
Due but to one and crownèd with one crest.
215 And will you rent our ancient love asunder,
To join with men in scorning your poor friend?
It is not friendly, 'tis not maidenly.
Our sex as well as I may chide you for it,
Though I alone do feel the injury.
220 HERMIA: I am amazèd at your words.
I scorn you not; it seems that you scorn me.
HELENA: Have you not set Lysander, as in scorn,
To follow me and praise my eyes and face?
And made your other love, Demetrius—
225 Who even but now° did spurn me with his foot—   *just now*
To call me goddess, nymph, divine, and rare,
Precious, celestial? Wherefore speaks he this
To her he hates? And wherefore doth Lysander
Deny your love—so rich within his soul—
230 And tender° me, forsooth, affection,   *offer*
But by your setting on, by your consent?
What though I be not so in grace° as you,   *favor*
So hung upon with love, so fortunate,
But miserable most, to love unloved?
235 This you should pity rather than despise.
HERMIA: I understand not what you mean by this.
HELENA: I do. Persever, counterfeit sad° looks,   *serious*
Make mouths upon° me when I turn my back,   *Make faces at*
Wink each at other, hold the sweet jest up.°   *keep up the joke*
240 This sport well carried shall be chronicled.
If you have any pity, grace, or manners,
You would not make me such an argument.°   *a subject of merriment*
But fare ye well. 'Tis partly my own fault,
Which death or absence soon shall remedy.
245 LYSANDER: Stay, gentle Helena, hear my excuse,
My love, my life, my soul, fair Helena!
HELENA: Oh, excellent!

---

4. A technical phrase in heraldry, referring to the first quartering in a coat of arms, which may be repeated. The friends, then, have two bodies but a single, overarching identity.

HERMIA [*to* LYSANDER]:   Sweet, do not scorn her so.

DEMETRIUS: If she cannot entreat, I can compel.[5]

LYSANDER: Thou canst compel no more than she entreat.
    Thy threats have no more strength than her weak   250
      prayers.
    —Helen, I love thee, by my life, I do!
    I swear by that which I will lose for thee
    To prove him false that says I love thee not.

DEMETRIUS [*to* HELENA]:   I say I love thee more than he can do.

LYSANDER: If thou say so, withdraw,[6] and prove it too.   255

DEMETRIUS: Quick, come!

HERMIA: Lysander, whereto tends all this?

LYSANDER: Away, you Ethiope![7]

[*He tries to break away from* HERMIA.]

DEMETRIUS [*to* HERMIA]:   No, no, he'll
    Seem to break loose.[8] [*to* LYSANDER] Take on as° you   *Pretend*
      would follow,
    But yet come not. You are a tame man, go!

LYSANDER [*to* HERMIA]:   Hang off,° thou cat, thou burr! Vile   *Let go* 260
    thing, let loose,
    Or I will shake thee from me like a serpent.

HERMIA: Why are you grown so rude? What change is this,
      Sweet love?

LYSANDER: Thy love? Out, tawny Tartar, out!
    Out, loathèd medicine![9] O hated potion, hence!

HERMIA: Do you not jest?

HELENA: Yes, sooth,° and so do you.   *truly* 265

LYSANDER: Demetrius, I will keep my word with thee.

DEMETRIUS: I would I had your bond, for I perceive
    A weak bond[1] holds you. I'll not trust your word.

LYSANDER: What? Should I hurt her, strike her, kill her dead?
    Although I hate her, I'll not harm her so.   270

HERMIA: What? Can you do me greater harm than hate?
    Hate me? Wherefore? Oh, me, what news,° my love?   *what has happened*
    Am not I Hermia? Are not you Lysander?
    I am as fair now as I was erewhile.°   *a while ago*
    Since night you loved me, yet since night you left me.   275
    Why then, you left me—oh, the gods forbid—
    In earnest, shall I say?

---

5. If Hermia cannot entreat you to stop, I can make you do it.

6. Come with me ("step outside").

7. Allusion to Hermia's dark hair and complexion. Elizabethans generally regarded light complexions as more beautiful than dark and often stigmatized dark-skinned peoples (such as Ethiopians or Tartars) as ugly.

8. Lysander will only pretend to break free from Hermia.

9. Any drug (including poison).

1. Hermia's weak grasp (with a pun on "bond": signed oath, the meaning in the previous line).

LYSANDER: Ay, by my life,
          And never did desire to see thee more.
          Therefore be out of hope, of question, of doubt;
280   Be certain, nothing truer. 'Tis no jest
          That I do hate thee and love Helena.
HERMIA [*to* HELENA]:   Oh, me, you juggler,° you canker-blossom,[2]   *trickster*
          You thief of love! What, have you come by night
          And stolen my love's heart from him?
HELENA: Fine, i'faith.
285   Have you no modesty, no maiden shame,
          No touch of bashfulness? What, will you tear
          Impatient answers from my gentle tongue?
          Fie, fie, you counterfeit, you puppet,[3] you!
HERMIA: "Puppet"? Why so?—Ay, that way goes the game.
290   Now I perceive that she hath made compare
          Between our statures; she hath urged her height,
          And with her personage, her tall personage,
          Her height, forsooth, she hath prevailed with him.
          —And are you grown so high in his esteem
295   Because I am so dwarfish and so low?
          How low am I, thou painted maypole?[4] Speak!
          How low am I? I am not yet so low
          But that my nails can reach unto thine eyes.
HELENA: I pray you, though you mock me, gentlemen,
300   Let her not hurt me. I was never curst;°   *quarrelsome*
          I have no gift at all in shrewishness.
          I am a right° maid for my cowardice.   *proper*
          Let her not strike me. You perhaps may think
          Because she is something° lower than myself   *somewhat*
          That I can match her.
305 HERMIA: "Lower"? Hark, again!
HELENA: Good Hermia, do not be so bitter with me.
          I evermore did love you, Hermia,
          Did ever keep your counsels, never wronged you,
          Save that, in love unto Demetrius,
310   I told him of your stealth° unto this wood.   *stealing away*
          He followed you; for love I followed him.
          But he hath chid me hence and threatened me
          To strike me, spurn me, nay, to kill me too.
          And now, so° you will let me quiet go,   *if only*
315   To Athens will I bear my folly back
          And follow you no further. Let me go.
          You see how simple and how fond° I am.   *foolish*
HERMIA: Why, get you gone. Who is't that hinders you?

---

2. Worm that devours blossoms (of love).
3. Fraudulent imitation; but Hermia interprets "puppet" as a reference to her height.
4. Proverbial epithet for someone tall and skinny. *Painted:* insulting allusion to the use of cosmetics.

HELENA: A foolish heart that I leave here behind.
HERMIA: What, with Lysander?
HELENA: With Demetrius.   320
LYSANDER: Be not afraid; she shall not harm thee, Helena.
DEMETRIUS: No, sir, she shall not, though you take her part.
HELENA: Oh, when she is angry she is keen° and shrewd.°   *sharp / shrewish*
    She was a vixen when she went to school,
    And though she be but little, she is fierce.   325
HERMIA: "Little" again? Nothing but "low" and "little"?
    Why will you suffer her to flout me thus?
    Let me come to her.
LYSANDER: Get you gone, you dwarf,
    You minimus of hind'ring knot-grass⁵ made,
    You bead, you acorn.
DEMETRIUS: You are too officious   330
    In her behalf that scorns your services.
    Let her alone: speak not of Helena;
    Take not her part. For if thou dost intend
    Never so little° show of love to her,   *Even the smallest*
    Thou shalt aby° it.   *pay for; buy*
LYSANDER: Now she holds me not;   335
    Now follow, if thou dar'st, to try whose right,
    Of thine or mine, is most in Helena.
DEMETRIUS: Follow? Nay, I'll go with thee, cheek by jowl.⁶

                    [*Exeunt* LYSANDER *and* DEMETRIUS.]

HERMIA: You, mistress, all this coil° is long° of you.   *turmoil / because*
    Nay, go not back.
HELENA: I will not trust you, I,   340
    Nor longer stay in your curst company.
    Your hands than mine are quicker for a fray;°   *fight*
    My legs are longer, though, to run away.   [*Exit.*]
HERMIA: I am amazed and know not what to say.   [*Exit.*]

                    [OBERON *and* ROBIN *come forward.*]

OBERON: This is thy negligence. Still° thou mistak'st   *Always* 345
    Or else committ'st thy knaveries willfully.
ROBIN: Believe me, king of shadows,° I mistook.   *fairy spirits*
    Did not you tell me I should know the man
    By the Athenian garments he had on?
    And so far° blameless proves my enterprise   *to this extent* 350
    That I have 'nointed an Athenian's eyes;
    And so far am I glad it so did sort,°   *turn out*
    As° this their jangling° I esteem a sport.   *Since / bickering*

5. Creeping binding weed (its sap was thought to stunt human growth). *Minimus*: diminutive thing
(Latin).
6. Proverbial saying for "side by side."

OBERON: Thou seest these lovers seek a place to fight.
355   Hie° therefore, Robin, overcast the night;   *Hurry*
      The starry welkin° cover thou anon   *sky*
      With drooping fog as black as Acheron,[7]
      And lead these testy rivals so astray
      As° one come not within another's way.   *So that*
360   Like to Lysander sometime frame thy tongue,
      Then stir Demetrius up with bitter wrong;°   *insults*
      And sometime rail thou like Demetrius,
      And from each other look thou lead them thus
      Till o'er their brows death-counterfeiting sleep
365   With leaden legs and batty° wings doth creep.   *batlike*
      Then crush this herb into Lysander's eye,
      Whose liquor hath this virtuous° property: *potent*
      To take from thence all error with his might
      And make his eyeballs roll with wonted° sight. *normal*
370   When they next wake, all this derision
      Shall seem a dream and fruitless° vision,   *inconsequential*
      And back to Athens shall the lovers wend°   *go*
      With league° whose date° till death shall never end. *covenant / duration*
      Whiles I in this affair do thee employ,
375   I'll to my queen and beg her Indian boy;
      And then I will her charmèd° eye release   *enchanted*
      From monster's view, and all things shall be peace.
ROBIN: My fairy lord, this must be done with haste,
      For night's swift dragons[8] cut the clouds full fast,
380   And yonder shines Aurora's harbinger,[9]
      At whose approach ghosts wandering here and there
      Troop home to churchyards; damnèd spirits all,
      That in crossways and floods[1] have burial,
      Already to their wormy beds are gone,
385   For fear lest day should look their shames upon:
      They willfully themselves exile from light
      And must for aye° consort with black-browed night. *ever*
OBERON: But we are spirits of another sort.
      I with the morning's love[2] have oft made sport,
390   And like a forester[3] the groves may tread
      Even till the eastern gate, all fiery red,

---

7. River of hell or Hades, in Greek mythology.
8. Imagined as drawing the chariots of the goddess of night.
9. Herald of the goddess of dawn; the morning star.
1. In which the drowned were "buried," without Christian sacrament. *Crossways*: crossroads (where suicides were buried, also without Christian sacrament). Robin is differentiating here between two types of spirits: those who wandered from their churchyard graves and those who have no proper resting place. These two types, both ghosts of former humans, are differentiated in turn from the fairy spirits by Oberon in the ensuing lines.
2. The love of Aurora, goddess of dawn (or Cephalus, a brave hunter, Aurora's lover).
3. Keeper of a royal forest or private park.

Opening on Neptune° with fair blessèd beams   (the sea)
Turns into yellow gold his salt° green streams.   salty
But notwithstanding, haste, make no delay;
We may effect this business yet ere day.   [Exit.]   395
ROBIN: Up and down, up and down,
I will lead them up and down.
I am feared in field and town.
Goblin,° lead them up and down.   (Robin himself)
Here comes one.   400

Enter LYSANDER.

LYSANDER: Where art thou, proud Demetrius? Speak
    thou now.
ROBIN:[4] Here, villain, drawn° and ready. Where art thou?   with sword drawn
LYSANDER: I will be with thee straight.°   immediately
ROBIN: Follow me then
    To plainer° ground.   [*Exit* LYSANDER.][5]   clearer

Enter DEMETRIUS.

DEMETRIUS: Lysander, speak again.
Thou runaway, thou coward, art thou fled?   405
Speak! In some bush? Where dost thou hide thy head?
ROBIN: Thou coward, art thou bragging to the stars,
Telling the bushes that thou look'st for wars,
And wilt not come? Come, recreant;° come, thou child.   coward; wretch
I'll whip thee with a rod. He is defiled   410
That draws a sword on thee.[6]
DEMETRIUS: Yea, art thou there?
ROBIN: Follow my voice; we'll try° no manhood here.   test

                                Exeunt.

[*Enter* LYSANDER.]

LYSANDER: He goes before me and still dares me on.
When I come where he calls, then he is gone.
The villain is much lighter-heeled than I.   415
I followed fast, but faster he did fly,
That° fallen am I in dark uneven way,   With the result that
And here will rest me.

[*He lies down.*]

                        Come, thou gentle day.
For if but once thou show me thy gray light,
I'll find Demetrius and revenge this spite.   420

[*He sleeps.*]

4. In what follows, Robin presumably mimics the voices of Demetrius and Lysander.
5. He might instead wander about the stage.
6. That is, it would be a disgrace to treat you as an honorable opponent.

[*Enter*] ROBIN *and* DEMETRIUS.

ROBIN: Ho, ho, ho! Coward, why com'st thou not?
DEMETRIUS: Abide° me, if thou dar'st; for well I wot°   *Wait for / know*
    Thou runn'st before me, shifting every place,
    And dar'st not stand nor look me in the face.
    Where art thou now?
425 ROBIN: Come hither; I am here.
DEMETRIUS: Nay, then, thou mock'st me. Thou shalt buy°   *pay for*
    this dear°   *dearly*
    If ever I thy face by daylight see.
    Now, go thy way. Faintness constraineth me
    To measure out my length on this cold bed.

[*He lies down.*]

430   By day's approach look to be visited.

[*He sleeps.*]
Enter HELENA.

HELENA: O weary night, O long and tedious night,
    Abate° thy hours; shine comforts from the east,   *Shorten*
    That I may back to Athens by daylight
    From these that my poor company detest;
435   And sleep, that sometimes shuts up sorrow's eye,
    Steal me a while from mine own company.

[*She lies down and*] *sleep*[*s*].

ROBIN: Yet but three? Come one more;
    Two of both kinds makes up four.

[*Enter* HERMIA.]

    Here she comes, curst° and sad.   *angry*
440   Cupid is a knavish lad
    Thus to make poor females mad.
HERMIA: Never so weary, never so in woe,
    Bedabbled with the dew and torn with briars,
    I can no further crawl, no further go;
445   My legs can keep no pace with my desires.
    Here will I rest me till the break of day.

[*She lies down.*]

    Heavens shield Lysander, if they mean a fray.

[*She sleeps.*]

ROBIN: On the ground,
    Sleep sound.
450   I'll apply

To your eye,
Gentle lover, remedy.

[*He squeezes the juice on* LYSANDER'S *eyes.*]

When thou wak'st,
Thou tak'st
True delight   455
In the sight
Of thy former lady's eye;
And the country proverb known,
That every man should take his own,
In your waking shall be shown.   460
Jack shall have Jill,
Naught shall go ill,
The man shall have his mare again, and all shall
be well.

[*Exit. The lovers remain onstage, asleep.*]

ACT IV

Scene 1

The wood. Enter [TITANIA,] *Queen of Fairies, and* [BOT-
TOM, *the*] *clown* [*with the ass head*], *and* FAIRIES[, PEASE-
BLOSSOM, COBWEB, MOTH, *and* MUSTARDSEED], *and*
[OBERON,] *the King, behind them.*

TITANIA [*to* BOTTOM]: Come, sit thee down upon this flowery
  bed
     While I thy amiable° cheeks do coy,°   lovable / caress
     And stick musk-roses in thy sleek smooth head,
     And kiss thy fair large ears, my gentle joy.
BOTTOM: Where's Peaseblossom?   5
PEASEBLOSSOM: Ready.
BOTTOM: Scratch my head, Peaseblossom.—Where's Monsieur
  Cobweb?
COBWEB: Ready.
BOTTOM: Monsieur Cobweb, good monsieur, get you your   10
  weapons in your hand and kill me a red-hipped humble-
  bee on the top of a thistle; and, good monsieur, bring me
  the honey-bag. Do not fret yourself too much in the action,
  monsieur; and, good monsieur, have a care the honey- bag
  break not. I would be loath to have you overflown with° a   *submerged by* 15
  honey-bag, signor.   [*Exit* COBWEB.]
    —Where's Monsieur Mustardseed?
MUSTARDSEED: Ready.

BOTTOM: Give me your neaf,° Monsieur Mustardseed. Pray   *fist*
20   you leave your courtesy,[7] good monsieur.

MUSTARDSEED: What's your will?

BOTTOM: Nothing, good monsieur, but to help Cavaliery[8] Cob-
     web to scratch. I must to the barber's, monsieur, for
     methinks I am marvelous hairy about the face. And I am
25   such a tender ass, if my hair do but tickle me, I must scratch.

TITANIA: What, wilt thou hear some music, my sweet love?

BOTTOM: I have a reasonable good ear in music. Let's have
     the tongs and the bones.[9]

TITANIA: Or say, sweet love, what thou desir'st to eat.

30 BOTTOM: Truly, a peck of provender.° I could munch your   *fodder*
     good dry oats. Methinks I have a great desire to a bottle°   *bundle*
     of hay. Good hay, sweet hay, hath no fellow.°   *equal*

TITANIA: I have a venturous fairy that shall seek
     The squirrel's hoard and fetch thee off new nuts.

35 BOTTOM: I had rather have a handful or two of dried peas.
     But, I pray you, let none of your people stir me; I have
     an exposition of° sleep come upon me.   *(for "disposition to")*

TITANIA: Sleep thou, and I will wind thee in my arms.
     —Fairies, be gone, and be always° away.   *in every direction*

                     [*Exeunt* FAIRIES.]

40   So° doth the woodbine[1] the sweet honeysuckle   *Thus*
     Gently entwist; the female ivy so
     Enrings the barky fingers of the elm.
     —Oh, how I love thee, how I dote on thee!

[*They sleep.*]
Enter ROBIN *Goodfellow.*

OBERON [*coming forward*]:   Welcome, good Robin. Seest
     thou this sweet sight?
45   Her dotage now I do begin to pity.
     For, meeting her of late behind the wood
     Seeking sweet favors° for this hateful fool,   *love tokens*
     I did upbraid her and fall out with her.
     For she his hairy temples then had rounded
50   With coronet of fresh and fragrant flowers,
     And that same dew which sometime° on the buds   *formerly*
     Was wont° to swell like round and orient[2] pearls   *accustomed*
     Stood now within the pretty flowerets' eyes
     Like tears that did their own disgrace bewail.
55   When I had at my pleasure taunted her,

---

7. Stop bowing, or do not stand bareheaded.
8. Blunder for "Cavalier," perhaps influenced by the Italian term *cavaliere.*
9. Triangle and clappers (rustic musical instruments).
1. Here, "woodbine" cannot mean "honeysuckle," as it did at 2.1.251, and thus must refer to a different plant.
2. Lustrous (the best pearls were from the Far East).

And she in mild terms begged my patience,
I then did ask of her her changeling child,
Which straight she gave me, and her fairy sent
To bear him to my bower in fairyland.
And now I have the boy, I will undo   60
This hateful imperfection of her eyes.
And, gentle puck, take this transformèd scalp
From off the head of this Athenian swain,
That he, awaking when the other° do,   *others*
May all to Athens back again repair   65
And think no more of this night's accidents
But as the fierce vexation of a dream.
But first I will release the Fairy Queen.

[*He squeezes the juice on* TITANIA'S *eyes.*]

Be as thou wast wont to be;
See as thou wast wont to see.   70
Dian's bud o'er Cupid's flower[3]
Hath such force and blessèd power.
Now, my Titania, wake you, my sweet queen.
TITANIA [*awaking*]:   My Oberon, what visions have I seen!
Methought I was enamored of an ass.   75
OBERON: There lies your love.
TITANIA: How came these things to pass?
Oh, how mine eyes do loathe his visage now!
OBERON: Silence a while.—Robin, take off this head.
—Titania, music call, and strike more dead
Than common sleep of all these five[4] the sense.   80
TITANIA: Music, ho—music such as charmeth sleep!

[*Music plays.*]

ROBIN [*to* BOTTOM, *removing the ass head*]:   Now when
thou wak'st with thine own fool's eyes peep.
OBERON: Sound, music! Come, my queen, take hands with me,
And rock the ground whereon these sleepers be.

[*They dance.*]

Now thou and I are new in amity   85
And will tomorrow midnight solemnly
Dance in Duke Theseus' house triumphantly
And bless it to all fair prosperity.
There shall the pairs of faithful lovers be
Wedded, with Theseus, all in jollity.   90
ROBIN: Fairy King, attend and mark:

---

3. "Dian's bud," the herb of 2.1.184 and 3.2.366, is perhaps *Agnus castus*, or chaste tree: said to preserve chastity and hence the antidote to "Cupid's flower," or the "love-in-idleness" of 2.1.168.
4. The lovers and Bottom.

I do hear the morning lark.

OBERON: Then, my queen, in silence sad
    Trip we after night's shade.
95   We the globe can compass° soon,   *orbit*
    Swifter than the wandering moon.

TITANIA: Come, my lord, and in our flight
    Tell me how it came this night
    That I sleeping here was found
100   With these mortals on the ground.

Exeunt [OBERON, TITANIA, *and* ROBIN].

Wind horn. Enter THESEUS [*with* HIPPOLYTA, EGEUS,]
and all his train.

THESEUS: Go, one of you, find out the forester,
    For now our observation[5] is performed.
    And since we have the vanguard° of the day,   *earliest part*
    My love shall hear the music of my hounds.
105   Uncouple[6] in the western valley; let them go.
    Dispatch, I say, and find the forester.
                          [*Exit an Attendant.*]
    —We will, fair Queen, up to the mountain's top
    And mark the musical confusion
    Of hounds and echo in conjunction.
110 HIPPOLYTA: I was with Hercules and Cadmus[7] once
    When in a wood of Crete they bayed° the bear   *hunted*
    With hounds of Sparta.[8] Never did I hear
    Such gallant chiding;° for besides the groves,   *barking*
    The skies, the fountains, every region near
115   Seemed all one mutual cry. I never heard
    So musical a discord, such sweet thunder.

THESEUS: My hounds are bred out of the Spartan kind,
    So flewed,[9] so sanded;° and their heads are hung   *sandy-colored*
    With ears that sweep away the morning dew;
120   Crook-kneed, and dewlapped[1] like Thessalian bulls;
    Slow in pursuit, but matched in mouth like bells,
    Each under each. A cry more tunable[2]
    Was never holla'd to nor cheered with horn
    In Crete, in Sparta, nor in Thessaly.

5. "Observance to a morn of May," as at 1.1.167.
6. Release (the dogs, leashed in pairs).
7. Mythical founder of Thebes. (No source for the anecdote is known.)
8. Famous in antiquity as hunting dogs.
9. Flews were large hanging, fleshy chaps.
1. With hanging folds of skin under the neck (compare 2.1.50).
2. A pack of hounds more well tuned. *Matched in mouth* . . . : harmoniously matched in the pitch of
their barking, like a set of bells.

Judge when you hear. But soft,° what nymphs are   *stop; look* 125
    these?
EGEUS: My lord, this is my daughter here asleep,
    And this Lysander, this Demetrius is,
    This Helena, old Nedar's Helena.
    I wonder of their being here together.
THESEUS: No doubt they rose up early to observe   130
    The rite of May and, hearing our intent,
    Came here in grace of our solemnity.°   *ceremony*
    But speak, Egeus: is not this the day
    That Hermia should give answer of her choice?
EGEUS: It is, my lord.   135
THESEUS: Go bid the huntsmen wake them with their horns.
                         [*Exit an Attendant.*]
    Shout within; wind horns; [the lovers] all start up.

    Good morrow, friends. Saint Valentine is past.
    Begin these woodbirds but to couple now?[3]
LYSANDER: Pardon, my lord.

    [*The lovers kneel.*]

THESEUS: I pray you all, stand up.

    [*The lovers stand.*]
  [*to* DEMETRIUS *and* LYSANDER] I know you two are rival   140
    enemies.
    How comes this gentle concord in the world,
    That hatred is so far from jealousy°   *suspicion*
    To sleep by hate and fear no enmity?
LYSANDER: My lord, I shall reply amazèdly,°   *confusedly*
    Half sleep, half waking. But as yet, I swear,   145
    I cannot truly say how I came here.
    But as I think—for truly would I speak,
    And now I do bethink me, so it is—
    I came with Hermia hither. Our intent
    Was to be gone from Athens where we might   150
    Without° the peril of the Athenian law—   *Outside*
EGEUS [*to* THESEUS]:   Enough, enough, my lord; you have
    enough.
    I beg the law, the law upon his head!
    —They would have stolen away, they would, Demetrius,
    Thereby to have defeated° you and me,   *defrauded* 155
    You of your wife and me of my consent,
    Of my consent that she should be your wife.
DEMETRIUS [*to* THESEUS]:   My lord, fair Helen told me of
    their stealth,
    Of this their purpose hither to this wood,

3. Birds were said to choose their mates on Valentine's Day.

160 And I in fury hither followed them,
   Fair Helena in fancy° following me.   *love*
   But, my good lord, I wot not by what power—
   But by some power it is—my love to Hermia,
   Melted as the snow, seems to me now
165 As the remembrance of an idle gaud°   *a worthless trinket*
   Which in my childhood I did dote upon;
   And all the faith, the virtue of my heart,
   The object and the pleasure of mine eye,
   Is only Helena. To her, my lord,
170 Was I betrothed ere I saw Hermia,
   But like a sickness[4] did I loathe this food;
   But, as in health come to my natural taste,
   Now I do wish it, love it, long for it,
   And will for evermore be true to it.
175 THESEUS: Fair lovers, you are fortunately met.
   Of this discourse we more will hear anon.
   —Egeus, I will overbear your will;
   For in the temple, by and by, with us
   These couples shall eternally be knit.
180 And, for° the morning now is something° worn,   *since / somewhat*
   Our purposed hunting shall be set aside.
   Away with us to Athens. Three and three,
   We'll hold a feast in great solemnity.
   —Come, Hippolyta.

                    [*Exit* THESEUS *with* HIPPOLYTA,
                         EGEUS, *and his train.*]

185 DEMETRIUS: These things seem small and undistinguishable,
   Like far-off mountains turnèd into clouds.
   HERMIA: Methinks I see these things with parted eye,°   *(double vision)*
   When everything seems double.
   HELENA: So methinks;
   And I have found Demetrius like a jewel,
   Mine own and not mine own.
190 DEMETRIUS: Are you sure
   That we are awake? It seems to me
   That yet we sleep, we dream. Do not you think
   The Duke was here and bid us follow him?
   HERMIA: Yea, and my father.
   HELENA: And Hippolyta.
195 LYSANDER: And he did bid us follow to the temple.
   DEMETRIUS: Why, then, we are awake. Let's follow him,
   And by the way let's recount our dreams.

                         [*Exeunt lovers.*]

---

4. Only as a person does when ill or nauseated.

BOTTOM [*awaking*]: When my cue comes, call me, and I
will answer. My next is "Most fair Pyramus." Heigh-ho,° *(a call; perhaps a yawn)*
Peter Quince? Flute the bellows-mender? Snout the tin- 200
ker? Starveling? God's my life!° Stolen hence and left me *Good Lord*
asleep! I have had a most rare vision. I have had a dream
past the wit of man to say what dream it was. Man is but
an ass if he go about° to expound this dream. Methought *try*
I was—there is no man can tell what. Methought I 205
was—and methought I had—but man is but patched a
fool[5] if he will offer° to say what methought I had. The *venture*
eye of man hath not heard, the ear of man hath not seen,
man's hand is not able to taste, his tongue to conceive,
nor his heart to report[6] what my dream was. I will get 210
Peter Quince to write a ballad of this dream. It shall be
called "Bottom's Dream," because it hath no bottom;[7] and
I will sing it in the latter end of a play, before the Duke.
Peradventure,° to make it the more gracious, I shall sing *Perhaps*
it at her° death.   [*Exit.*] *(Thisbe's?)* 215

Scene 2

Athens. Enter QUINCE, FLUTE[, SNOUT, *and* STARVELING].

QUINCE: Have you sent to Bottom's house? Is he come
home yet?
STARVELING: He cannot be heard of. Out of doubt° he is *Doubtless*
transported.[8]
FLUTE: If he come not, then the play is marred. It goes not 5
forward, doth it?
QUINCE: It is not possible. You have not a man in all Athens
able to discharge° Pyramus but he. *perform*
FLUTE: No, he hath simply the best wit° of any handicraft *intellect*
man in Athens. 10
QUINCE: Yea, and the best person° too; and he is a very par- *looks*
amour for a sweet voice.
FLUTE: You must say "paragon." A paramour is—God bless
us—a thing of naught.° *something wicked*

  Enter SNUG *the joiner.*

SNUG: Masters, the Duke is coming from the temple, and 15
there is two or three lords and ladies more married. If our
sport° had gone forward, we had all been made men.[9] *entertainment*

---

5. Patchwork or motley costumes were worn by jesters.
6. Burlesque of scripture: "The eye hath not seen, and the ear hath not heard, neither have entered
into the heart of man" those things that God has prepared (1 Cor. 2.9–10, Bishops' Bible).
7. Because it is unfathomable, or has no substance (foundation).
8. Carried away (by the fairies); transformed.
9. Our fortunes would have been made.

FLUTE: Oh, sweet bully Bottom! Thus hath he lost sixpence
a day[1] during his life; he could not have 'scaped sixpence
20   a day. An° the Duke had not given him sixpence a day for   *If*
playing Pyramus, I'll be hanged. He would have deserved
it. Sixpence a day in Pyramus, or nothing.

      Enter BOTTOM.

BOTTOM: Where are these lads? Where are these hearts?°   *mates*
QUINCE: Bottom! Oh, most courageous[2] day! Oh, most happy
25   hour!
BOTTOM: Masters, I am to discourse wonders; but ask me
not what; for if I tell you, I am not true Athenian. I will
tell you everything right as it fell out.
QUINCE: Let us hear, sweet Bottom.
30 BOTTOM: Not a word of° me. All that I will tell you is that   *out of*
the Duke hath dined. Get your apparel together, good
strings° to your beards, new ribbons to your pumps. Meet   *(to attach the beards)*
presently° at the palace; every man look o'er his part. For   *immediately*
the short and the long is, our play is preferred.° In any   *recommended*
35   case, let Thisbe have clean linen; and let not him that
plays the lion pare his nails, for they shall hang out for
the lion's claws. And, most dear actors, eat no onions nor
garlic, for we are to utter sweet breath; and I do not doubt
but to hear them say it is a sweet comedy. No more
40   words. Away! Go, away!   [*Exeunt.*]

ACT V

Scene 1

Athens. Theseus's palace. Enter THESEUS, HIPPOLYTA,
PHILOSTRATE[, *Lords, and Attendants*].

HIPPOLYTA: 'Tis strange, my Theseus, that° these lovers   *that which*
speak of.
THESEUS: More strange than true. I never may believe
These antique[3] fables, nor these fairy toys.°   *trifles*
Lovers and madmen have such seething brains,
5   Such shaping fantasies,° that apprehend° more   *imaginations / conceive*
Than cool reason ever comprehends.
The lunatic, the lover, and the poet
Are of imagination all compact.°   *composed*
One sees more devils than vast hell can hold;
10   That is the madman. The lover, all as frantic,
Sees Helen's beauty in a brow of Egypt.[4]

1. As a royal pension, considerably more than the average daily wage of an Elizabethan workman.
2. Blunder for "brave," meaning "splendid."
3. Ancient; strange, grotesque (as in "antic").
4. In a gypsy's face. *Helen*: Helen of Troy.

The poet's eye, in a fine frenzy rolling,
Doth glance from heaven to earth, from earth to
   heaven.
And as imagination bodies forth
The forms of things unknown, the poet's pen   15
Turns them to shapes and gives to airy nothing
A local habitation and a name.
Such tricks hath strong imagination
That if it would but apprehend some joy,
It comprehends some bringer° of that joy;   *source* 20
Or in the night, imagining some fear,°   *object to be feared*
How easy is a bush supposed a bear!

HIPPOLYTA: But all the story of the night told over,
  And all their minds transfigured so together,
  More witnesseth than fancy's images[5]   25
  And grows to something of great constancy;°   *consistency*
  But, howsoever,° strange and admirable.°   *in any case / wondrous*

Enter [the] lovers, LYSANDER, DEMETRIUS, HERMIA,
and HELENA.

THESEUS: Here come the lovers, full of joy and mirth.
  Joy, gentle friends, joy and fresh days of love
  Accompany your hearts.
LYSANDER: More than to us   30
  Wait in your royal walks, your board, your bed.[6]
THESEUS: Come now, what masques, what dances shall we
    have
  To wear away this long age of three hours
  Between our after-supper and bedtime?
  Where is our usual manager of mirth?   35
  What revels are in hand? Is there no play
  To ease the anguish of a torturing hour?
  Call Philostrate.
PHILOSTRATE: Here, mighty Theseus.
THESEUS: Say, what abridgement[7] have you for this evening,
  What masque, what music? How shall we beguile   40
  The lazy time if not with some delight?
PHILOSTRATE [*giving* THESEUS *a paper*]:   There is a brief°   *short list*
    how many sports are ripe.
  Make choice of which your highness will see first.
THESEUS [*reads*]: "The battle with the Centaurs,[8] to be sung
  By an Athenian eunuch to the harp."   45
  We'll none of that. That have I told my love

---

5. Testifies to something more than mere figments of the imagination.
6. May even more joy and love attend your daily lives.
7. Pastime, something to make the evening seem shorter.
8. Probably the battle that occurred when the Centaurs tried to carry off the bride of Theseus's
friend Pirithous.

In glory of my kinsman Hercules.[9]
[*Reads.*] "The riot of the tipsy Bacchanals
Tearing the Thracian singer in their rage."[1]
50   That is an old device,° and it was played   show
When I from Thebes came last a conqueror.
[*Reads.*] "*The thrice-three muses mourning for the
        death
Of learning, late deceased in beggary.*"[2]
That is some satire, keen and critical,
55   Not sorting with° a nuptial ceremony.   befitting
[*Reads.*] "A tedious brief scene of young Pyramus
And his love Thisbe; very tragical mirth."
Merry and tragical? Tedious and brief?
That is hot ice and wondrous strange snow!
60   How shall we find the concord of this discord?
PHILOSTRATE: A play there is, my lord, some ten words long,
Which is as brief as I have known a play,
But by ten words, my lord, it is too long,
Which makes it tedious. For in all the play
65   There is not one word apt, one player fitted.°   appropriately cast
And tragical, my noble lord, it is,
For Pyramus therein doth kill himself,
Which, when I saw rehearsed, I must confess,
Made mine eyes water; but more merry tears
70   The passion of loud laughter never shed.
THESEUS: What are they that do play it?
PHILOSTRATE: Hard-handed men that work in Athens here,
Which never labored in their minds till now,
And now have toiled° their unbreathed° memories   taxed / unexercised
75   With this same play against° your nuptial.   in preparation for
THESEUS: And we will hear it.
PHILOSTRATE: No, my noble lord,
It is not for you. I have heard it over,
And it is nothing, nothing in the world;
Unless you can find sport in their intents,
80   Extremely stretched° and conned° with cruel pain,   strained / memorized
To do you service.
THESEUS: I will hear that play.
For never anything can be amiss
When simpleness and duty tender it.
Go, bring them in; and take your places, ladies.

[*Exit* PHILOSTRATE.]

---

9. According to Plutarch, Hercules and Theseus were cousins.
1. The murder of the poet Orpheus by drunken women, devotees of Dionysus.
2. Possibly a topical reference: Robert Greene, Christopher Marlowe, and Thomas Kyd, university
wits who began writing for the stage in the 1580s, all died in desperate circumstances in 1592–94.
But satiric laments on the poverty of scholars and poets were commonplace.

HIPPOLYTA: I love not to see wretchedness o'ercharged,[3]   85
    And duty in his service° perishing.   *its attempt to serve*
THESEUS: Why, gentle sweet, you shall see no such thing.
HIPPOLYTA: He says they can do nothing in° this kind.   *of*
THESEUS: The kinder we, to give them thanks for nothing.
    Our sport shall be to take what they mistake.   90
    And what poor duty cannot do, noble respect°   *consideration*
    Takes it in might, not merit.[4]
    Where I have come, great clerks° have purposèd   *scholars*
    To greet me with premeditated welcomes,
    Where I have seen them shiver and look pale,   95
    Make periods in the midst of sentences,
    Throttle their practiced accent[5] in their fears,
    And in conclusion dumbly have broke off,
    Not paying me a welcome. Trust me, sweet,
    Out of this silence yet I picked a welcome;   100
    And in the modesty of fearful° duty   *frightened*
    I read as much as from the rattling tongue
    Of saucy and audacious eloquence.
    Love, therefore, and tongue-tied simplicity
    In least speak most, to my capacity.°   *in my judgment* 105

    [*Enter* PHILOSTRATE.]

PHILOSTRATE: So please your grace, the Prologue is addressed.[6]
THESEUS: Let him approach.

    Enter [quince as] the Prologue.

QUINCE [*as Prologue*]:   If we offend, it is with our good will.
    That you should think, we come not to offend
    But with good will. To show our simple skill,   110
    That is the true beginning of our end.
    Consider, then, we come but in despite.
    We do not come as minding° to content you,   *intending*
    Our true intent is. All for your delight
    We are not here. That you should here repent you   115
    The actors are at hand; and by their show
    You shall know all that you are like to know.[7]
THESEUS: This fellow doth not stand upon points.[8]
LYSANDER: He hath rid his prologue like a rough° colt: he   *an unbroken*
    knows not the stop.[9] A good moral, my lord: it is not   120
    enough to speak, but to speak true.

---

3. Overburdened. *Wretchedness*: incompetence or weakness; poor people.
4. With respect to the giver's capacity, not the merit of the performance.
5. Rehearsed eloquence; usual manner of speaking.
6. The speaker of the Prologue is ready.
7. The humor of Quince's speech rests in its mispunctuation; repunctuated, it becomes a typical courteous address.
8. Bother about niceties; heed punctuation marks.
9. How to rein the colt to a stop; punctuation mark.

HIPPOLYTA: Indeed he hath played on this prologue like a
    child on a recorder: a sound, but not in government.°   *control*
THESEUS: His speech was like a tangled chain: nothing°   *not at all*
125   impaired, but all disordered. Who is next?

     Enter [BOTTOM *as*] *Pyramus, and* [FLUTE *as*] *Thisbe,*
     and [SNOUT *as*] *Wall, and* [STARVELING *as*] *Moonshine,*
     and [SNUG *as*] *Lion.*

QUINCE [*as Prologue*]:   Gentles, perchance you wonder at
       this show,
    But wonder on till truth make all things plain.
    This man is Pyramus, if you would know;
    This beauteous lady Thisbe is, certain.
130   This man with lime and roughcast doth present
    Wall, that vile wall which did these lovers sunder;
    And through Wall's chink, poor souls, they are content
    To whisper—at the which let no man wonder.
    This man with lantern, dog, and bush of thorn
135   Presenteth Moonshine. For, if you will know,
    By moonshine did these lovers think no scorn°   *(it) no disgrace*
    To meet at Ninus' tomb, there, there to woo.
    This grisly beast, which "Lion" hight° by name,   *is called*
    The trusty Thisbe, coming first by night,
140   Did scare away, or rather did affright;
    And as she fled, her mantle she did fall,°   *drop*
    Which Lion vile with bloody mouth did stain.
    Anon comes Pyramus, sweet youth and tall,°   *handsome*
    And finds his trusty Thisbe's mantle slain;
145   Whereat with blade, with bloody, blameful blade,
    He bravely broached° his boiling bloody breast;   *stabbed*
    And Thisbe, tarrying in mulberry shade,
    His dagger drew and died. For all the rest
    Let Lion, Moonshine, Wall, and lovers twain
150   At large° discourse, while here they do remain.   *length*

     Exeunt [QUINCE *as Prologue,* SNUG *as*] *Lion,*
     [FLUTE *as*] *Thisbe, and* [STARVELING *as*] *Moonshine.*

THESEUS: I wonder if the lion be to speak.
DEMETRIUS: No wonder, my lord; one lion may when many
    asses do.
SNOUT [*as Wall*]:   In this same interlude° it doth befall   *play*
155   That I, one Snout by name, present a wall;
    And such a wall as I would have you think
    That had in it a crannied hole or chink
    Through which the lovers, Pyramus and Thisbe,
    Did whisper often very secretly.
160   This loam, this roughcast, and this stone doth show
    That I am that same wall; the truth is so.

And this the cranny is, right and sinister,[1]
Through which the fearful lovers are to whisper.

THESEUS: Would you desire lime and hair to speak better?

DEMETRIUS: It is the wittiest partition[2] that ever I heard   165
discourse, my lord.

THESEUS: Pyramus draws near the wall: silence!

BOTTOM [*as Pyramus*]:   O grim-looked° night, O night with   *grim-looking*
  hue so black,
  O night, which ever art when day is not,
  O night, O night, alack, alack, alack,   170
  I fear my Thisbe's promise is forgot.
  And thou, O wall, O sweet, O lovely wall,
  That stand'st between her father's ground and mine,
  Thou wall, O wall, O sweet and lovely wall,
  Show me thy chink, to blink through with mine eyne.   175

 [SNOUT, *as Wall, shows his chink.*]

  Thanks, courteous wall; Jove shield thee well for this.
  But what see I? No Thisbe do I see.
  O wicked wall, through whom I see no bliss,
  Cursed be thy stones[3] for thus deceiving me!

THESEUS: The wall, methinks, being sensible,° should curse   *capable of feeling* 180
again.°   *back*

BOTTOM [*to* THESEUS]:   No, in truth, sir, he should not.
"Deceiving me" is Thisbe's cue. She is to enter now, and
I am to spy her through the wall. You shall see it will fall
pat° as I told you. Yonder she comes.   *precisely* 185

 Enter [FLUTE *as*] *Thisbe.*

FLUTE [*as Thisbe*]:   O wall, full often hast thou heard my
  moans
  For parting my fair Pyramus and me.
  My cherry lips have often kissed thy stones,
  Thy stones with lime and hair knit up in thee.

BOTTOM [*as Pyramus*]:   I see a voice; now will I to the chink   190
  To spy an° I can hear my Thisbe's face.   *if*
  Thisbe?

FLUTE [*as Thisbe*]:   My love! Thou art my love, I think.

BOTTOM [*as Pyramus*]:   Think what thou wilt, I am thy lover's
  grace,°   *gracious lover*
And like Limander[4] am I trusty still.

---

1. Left; running horizontally. Or on the one side (Pyramus's) and the other (Thisbe's).
2. Wall; formal term for part of an oration.
3. Punning, unintentionally, on "testicles."
4. Blunder for "Leander," who (in Greek myth) drowned while swimming across the Hellespont to meet
his lover, Hero.

195 FLUTE [*as Thisbe*]:   And I like Helen,[5] till the fates me kill.

BOTTOM [*as Pyramus*]:   Not Shafalus to Procrus[6] was so true.

FLUTE [*as Thisbe*]:   As Shafalus to Procrus, I to you.

BOTTOM [*as Pyramus*]:   Oh, kiss me through the hole of this
vile wall.

FLUTE [*as Thisbe*]:   I kiss the wall's hole, not your lips at all.

200 BOTTOM [*as Pyramus*]:   Wilt thou at Ninny's tomb meet me
straightway?

FLUTE [*as Thisbe*]:   Tide° life, tide death, I come without delay.   Betide; come

[*Exeunt* BOTTOM *and* FLUTE.]

SNOUT [*as Wall*]:   Thus have I, Wall, my part dischargèd so;
And, being done, thus Wall away doth go.   [*Exit.*]

THESEUS: Now is the mural° down between the two neighbors.   wall

205 DEMETRIUS: No remedy, my lord, when walls are so willful
to° hear without warning.[7]   as to

HIPPOLYTA: This is the silliest stuff that ever I heard.

THESEUS: The best in this kind are but shadows,[8] and the
worst are no worse if imagination amend them.

210 HIPPOLYTA: It must be your imagination, then, and not theirs.

THESEUS: If we imagine no worse of them than they of
themselves, they may pass for excellent men. Here come
two noble beasts in, a man and a lion.

Enter [SNUG *as*] *Lion and* [STARVELING *as*] *Moonshine*
[*with a lantern, thornbush, and dog*].

SNUG [*as Lion*]:   You ladies, you whose gentle hearts do fear
215   The smallest monstrous mouse that creeps on floor,
May now, perchance, both quake and tremble here
When lion rough in wildest rage doth roar.
Then know that I as Snug the joiner am
A lion fell,[9] nor else no lion's dam.
220   For if I should as lion come in strife
Into this place, 'twere pity on my life.

THESEUS: A very gentle beast, and of a good conscience.

DEMETRIUS: The very best at a beast, my lord, that e'er I saw.

LYSANDER: This lion is a very fox[1] for his valor.

225 THESEUS: True; and a goose[2] for his discretion.

DEMETRIUS: Not so, my lord. For his valor cannot carry his
discretion, and the fox carries the goose.

---

5. Helen of Troy was notoriously untrustworthy; a blunder for "Hero."
6. Blunder for "Cephalus" and "Procris." Procris was in fact seduced by her husband in disguise as
another man; he later accidentally killed her.
7. Informing the parents. *Hear*: proverbially, "walls have ears."
8. Mere likenesses without substance. *Kind*: profession (that is, actors).
9. Fierce; or skin (punning on the costume to which Snug reassuringly calls attention).
1. Symbolic of low cunning, rather than courage.
2. Symbolic of foolishness.

THESEUS: His discretion, I am sure, cannot carry his valor;
   for the goose carries not the fox. It is well. Leave it to his
   discretion, and let us listen to the moon.   230
STARVELING [as Moonshine]: This lantern doth the hornèd°   crescent
   moon present.
DEMETRIUS: He should have worn the horns on his head.[3]
THESEUS: He is no crescent,[4] and his horns are invisible
   within the circumference.
STARVELING [as Moonshine]: This lantern doth the hornèd   235
   moon present;
Myself the man i'th' moon do seem to be.
THESEUS: This is the greatest error of all the rest: the man
   should be put into the lantern; how is it else the man i'th'
   moon?
DEMETRIUS: He dares not come there for° the candle. For   for fear of 240
   you see it is already in snuff.[5]
HIPPOLYTA: I am aweary of this moon; would he would change!
THESEUS: It appears by his small light of discretion that he is
   in the wane; but yet in courtesy, in all reason, we must
   stay the time.   245
LYSANDER: Proceed, Moon.
STARVELING: All that I have to say is to tell you that the lantern is the moon, I the man i'th' moon, this thornbush
   my thornbush, and this dog my dog.
DEMETRIUS: Why, all these should be in the lantern, for all   250
   these are in the moon. But silence; here comes Thisbe.

   Enter [FLUTE *as*] *Thisbe.*

FLUTE [as Thisbe]: This is old Ninny's tomb. Where is my love?
SNUG [as Lion]: Oh!

   [*Lion roars.*]
   [*Thisbe runs off, dropping her mantle.*]

DEMETRIUS: Well roared, Lion!
THESEUS: Well run, Thisbe!   255
HIPPOLYTA: Well shone, Moon! Truly, the moon shines with
   a good grace.

   [*Lion worries*° *Thisbe's mantle.*]   gnaws on

THESEUS: Well moused,[6] Lion!

   Enter [BOTTOM *as*] *Pyramus.*

DEMETRIUS: And then came Pyramus.   [*Exit* SNUG *as Lion.*]

---

3. The symbol of a cuckold.
4. Waxing moon. Perhaps a joke about Starveling's thinness.
5. In need of snuffing; angry.
6. The mantle is like a mouse in the mouth of a cat.

260 LYSANDER: And so the lion vanished.

BOTTOM [*as Pyramus*]:   Sweet moon, I thank thee for thy
　　　sunny beams;
　　　I thank thee, moon, for shining now so bright.
　　　For by thy gracious, golden, glittering gleams
　　　I trust to take of truest Thisbe sight.
265　　　But stay, oh, spite!
　　　But mark, poor knight,
　　　What dreadful dole° is here?　　　　　　　　　　　　　　*grief*
　　　Eyes, do you see?
　　　How can it be?
270　　　O dainty duck! O dear!
　　　Thy mantle good,
　　　What, stained with blood?
　　　Approach, ye Furies fell!
　　　O Fates,[7] come, come,
275　　　Cut thread and thrum,[8]
　　　Quail,° crush, conclude, and quell!°　　　*Overpower / kill*

THESEUS: This passion, and[9] the death of a dear friend,
　　　would go near to make a man look sad.

HIPPOLYTA: Beshrew my heart, but I pity the man.

280 BOTTOM [*as Pyramus*]:   Oh, wherefore, Nature, didst thou
　　　lions frame,
　　　Since lion vile hath here deflowered[1] my dear?
　　　Which is—no, no, which was—the fairest dame
　　　That lived, that loved, that liked, that looked with cheer.
　　　Come, tears, confound!
285　　　Out, sword, and wound
　　　The pap° of Pyramus,　　　　　　　　　　　　　*breast*
　　　Ay, that left pap,
　　　Where heart doth hop.

　　　[*He stabs himself.*]

　　　Thus die I, thus, thus, thus.
290　　　Now am I dead;
　　　Now am I fled.
　　　My soul is in the sky.
　　　Tongue, lose thy light;
　　　Moon, take thy flight.　　　[*Exit* STARVELING *as Moonshine.*]
295　　　Now die, die, die, die, die.

　　　[*Pyramus dies.*]

7. The three Fates in Greek mythology spun and cut the thread of a person's life.
8. Technical term from Bottom's occupation: the tufted end of a weaver's warp, or set of yarns placed lengthwise in a loom when the woven fabric is cut.
9. Only if combined with. *Passion*: suffering; extravagant speech.
1. Ruined (but commonly suggesting "deprived of her virginity"); his error for "devoured."

DEMETRIUS: No die, but an ace for him; for he is but one.[2]

LYSANDER: Less than an ace, man; for he is dead, he is nothing.

THESEUS: With the help of a surgeon he might yet recover,
and yet prove an ass.

HIPPOLYTA: How chance Moonshine is gone before Thisbe   300
comes back and finds her lover?

THESEUS: She will find him by starlight.

[*Enter* FLUTE *as Thisbe.*]

Here she comes, and her passion° ends the play.   *passionate speech*

HIPPOLYTA: Methinks she should not use a long one for such a
Pyramus; I hope she will be brief.   305

DEMETRIUS: A mote° will turn the balance which Pyramus,   *speck*
which[3] Thisbe, is the better: he for a man, God warrant
us; she for a woman, God bless us.

LYSANDER: She hath spied him already with those sweet eyes.

DEMETRIUS: And thus she means, *videlicet*:[4]   310

FLUTE [*as Thisbe*]:   Asleep, my love?
        What, dead, my dove?
        O Pyramus, arise!
        Speak, speak! Quite dumb?
        Dead, dead? A tomb   315
        Must cover thy sweet eyes.
        These lily lips,
        This cherry nose,
        These yellow cowslip cheeks
        Are gone, are gone.   320
        Lovers, make moan.
        His eyes were green as leeks.
        O sisters three,°   *(the Fates)*
        Come, come to me
        With hands as pale as milk;   325
        Lay them in gore,
        Since you have shore°   *shorn*
        With shears his thread of silk.
        Tongue, not a word!
        Come, trusty sword,   330
        Come, blade, my breast imbrue.°   *stain with blood*

[*She stabs herself.*]

        And farewell, friends,
        Thus Thisbe ends.

---

2. Pun on "die" as one of a pair of dice. *One*: the ace, or lowest throw.
3. Whether . . . or.
4. As follows (Latin). *Means*: moans; lodges a formal legal complaint.

Adieu, adieu, adieu.

[*Thisbe dies.*]

335 THESEUS: Moonshine and Lion are left to bury the dead.

DEMETRIUS: Ay, and Wall too.

BOTTOM [*starting up*]:   No, I assure you, the wall is down
     that parted their fathers. [FLUTE *rises.*] Will it please you
     to see the epilogue or to hear a Bergomask dance[5] between
340   two of our company?

THESEUS: No epilogue, I pray you; for your play needs no excuse.
     Never excuse; for when the players are all dead, there need
     none to be blamed. Marry, if he that writ it had played
     Pyramus and hanged himself in Thisbe's garter, it would
345   have been a fine tragedy; and so it is, truly, and very notably
     discharged. But come, your Bergomask; let your epilogue
     alone.   [BOTTOM *and* FLUTE[6] *dance; then exeunt.*]

	The iron tongue of midnight hath told° twelve.	*counted; tolled*
	Lovers, to bed; 'tis almost fairy time.	
350	I fear we shall outsleep the coming morn	
	As much as we this night have overwatched.°	*stayed awake too late*
	This palpable-gross° play hath well beguiled	*palpably crude*
	The heavy° gait of night. Sweet friends, to bed.	*drowsy; slow*
	A fortnight hold we this solemnity	
355	In nightly revels and new jollity. *Exeunt.*	

Enter [ROBIN *Goodfellow, the*] puck[*, with a broom*].

	ROBIN: Now the hungry lion roars,	
	And the wolf behowls the moon,	
	Whilst the heavy° plowman snores,	*weary*
	All with weary task fordone.°	*"done in"; exhausted*
360	Now the wasted brands° do glow,	*burned-out logs*
	Whilst the screech-owl, screeching loud,	
	Puts the wretch that lies in woe	
	In remembrance of a shroud.	
	Now it is the time of night	
365	That the graves, all gaping wide,	
	Every one° lets forth his sprite°	*(grave) / ghost*
	In the churchway paths to glide;	
	And we fairies that do run	
	By the triple Hecate's[7] team	
370	From the presence of the sun,	
	Following darkness like a dream,	

---

5. Dance named after Bergamo, in Italy (commonly ridiculed for its rusticity).

6. The only "two of our company" onstage at the end of the interlude. The role of Bottom may have been first performed by the actor Will Kemp, who was famous for his dancing.

7. Hecate was goddess of the moon and night, and she had three realms: heaven (as Cynthia), earth (as Diana), and hell (as Proserpine).

Now are frolic.° Not a mouse   *merry*
Shall disturb this hallowed house.
I am sent with broom[8] before
To sweep the dust behind° the door.   *from behind* 375

Enter [OBERON and TITANIA,] King and Queen of
Fairies, with all their train.

OBERON: Through the house give glimmering light
    By the dead and drowsy fire;
    Every elf and fairy sprite
    Hop as light as bird from briar;
    And this ditty after me   380
    Sing, and dance it trippingly.
TITANIA: First rehearse your song by rote,
    To each word a warbling note.
    Hand in hand with fairy grace
    Will we sing and bless this place.   385

[The FAIRIES dance to a song.]

OBERON: Now until the break of day
    Through this house each fairy stray.
    To the best bride-bed will we,[9]
    Which by us shall blessèd be;
    And the issue there create°   *created; conceived* 390
    Ever shall be fortunate.
    So shall all the couples three
    Ever true in loving be.
    And the blots of nature's hand
    Shall not in their issue stand;   395
    Never mole, harelip, nor scar,
    Nor mark prodigious,° such as are   *ominous birthmark*
    Despisèd in nativity,
    Shall upon their children be.
    With this field-dew consecrate[1]   400
    Every fairy take his gait,°   *way*
    And each several° chamber bless   *separate*
    Through this palace with sweet peace;
    And the owner of it blessed
    Ever shall in safety rest.   405
    Trip away, make no stay;
    Meet me all by break of day.   *Exeunt [all but ROBIN].*
ROBIN [*to the audience*]:   If we shadows have offended,
    Think but this, and all is mended,

8. One of his traditional emblems; he helped good housekeepers and punished lazy ones.
9. Oberon and Titania will bless the bed of Theseus and Hippolyta.
1. Consecrated, blessed. Playfully alludes to the traditional Catholic custom of blessing the marriage
bed with holy water.

410   That you have but slumbered here
        While these visions did appear.
        And this weak and idle theme,
        No more yielding but° a dream,   *than*
        Gentles, do not reprehend;
415   If you pardon, we will mend.
        And as I am an honest puck,
        If we have unearnèd luck
        Now to 'scape the serpent's tongue,[2]
        We will make amends ere long;
420   Else the puck a liar call.
        So, good night unto you all.
        Give me your hands,° if we be friends,   *applause*
        And Robin shall restore amends.   [*Exit.*]

ROBIN
GOOD-FELLOVV,
HIS MAD PRANKES AND
MERRY IESTS.

Full of honeſt Mirth, and is a fit Medicine
for Melancholy.

Printed at *London* by *Thomas Cotes*, and are to be ſold by
Francis Grove, at his ſhop on Snow-hill, neere the
Sarazens-head. 1639.

---

2. Hissing from the audience.

The Tragedy of Othello, the Moor of Venice[1]

THE PERSONS OF THE PLAY

OTHELLO, the Moor
BRABANZIO, father to Desdemona
DESDEMONA, wife to Othello
IAGO, a villain
EMILIA, wife to Iago
RODERIGO, a gulled gentleman
DUKE of Venice
MONTANO, Governor of Cyprus
Michael CASSIO, an honorable
    lieutenant
BIANCA, a courtesan
LODOVICO
GRAZIANO } two noble Venetians

FIRST SENATOR
SECOND SENATOR
OFFICERS
SAILOR
MESSENGERS
GENTLEMEN of Cyprus
HERALD
MUSICIANS
CLOWN
Servants, Attendants

ACT I

Scene 1

A street in Venice. Enter RODERIGO *and* IAGO.[2]

RODERIGO: Never tell me![3] I take it much unkindly
    That thou, Iago, who hast had my purse
    As if the strings were thine, shouldst know of this.
IAGO: But you'll not hear me. If ever I did dream
    Of such a matter, abhor me.
RODERIGO: Thou told'st me   5
    Thou didst hold him in thy hate.
IAGO: Despise me
    If I do not. Three great ones of the city,
    In personal suit to make me his lieutenant,
    Off-capped° to him—and, by the faith of man,   *Took off their caps*
    I know my price: I am worth no worse a place—   10
    But he, as loving his own pride and purposes,
    Evades them with a bombast circumstance[4]
    Horribly stuffed with epithets of war;°   *military jargon*
    Nonsuits° my mediators. For, "Certes,"° says he,   *Denies / Certainly*

---

1. Text, glosses, and notes are based on those in *The Norton Shakespeare*, 3rd ed., edited by Stephen Greenblatt.
2. Iago's name may be related to Santiago Matamoros, St. James the Moor Slayer, the patron saint of Spain. The potential irony lies in having a character with a foreign-sounding name express hatred for foreigners on behalf of Venice.
3. Expression of annoyance and/or disbelief.
4. With an inflated circumlocution. *Bombast*: cotton padding in clothes.

15	"I have already chose my officer."	
	And what was he?	
	Forsooth, a great arithmetician:[5]	
	One Michael Cassio, a Florentine,°	*(hence, a foreigner)*
	A fellow almost damned in a fair wife,[6]	
20	That° never set a squadron in the field,	*Who*
	Nor the division° of a battle° knows	*ordering / battalion*
	More than a spinster°—unless the bookish theoric,°	*housewife / learning*
	Wherein the tongùed consuls can propose[7]	
	As masterly as he! Mere prattle without practice	
25	Is all his soldiership. But he, sir, had th'election	
	And I—of whom his° eyes had seen the proof	*(Othello's)*
	At Rhodes, at Cyprus, and on others' grounds,	
	Christened and heathen—must be be-leed° and	*without wind*
	calmed°	*becalmed*
	By debitor and creditor. This counter-caster,[8]	
30	He, in good time,° must his lieutenant be	*in timely fashion (ironic)*
	And I, bless the mark,° his moorship's ensign.[9]	*God help us*
	RODERIGO: By heaven, I rather would have been his hangman!	
	IAGO: Why, there's no remedy. 'Tis the curse of service:	
	Preferment goes by letter and affection[1]	
35	And not by old gradation,° where each second	*traditional seniority*
	Stood heir to th' first. Now, sir, be judge yourself	
	Whether I in any just term am affined°	*am bound in any just way*
	To love the Moor.[2]	
	RODERIGO: I would not follow him, then.	
	IAGO: O sir, content you!°	*be content*
40	I follow him to serve my turn upon him.°	*serve my own interests*
	We cannot all be masters, nor all masters	
	Cannot be truly followed. You shall mark	
	Many a duteous and knee-crooking° knave	*(servilely) knee-bending*
	That, doting on his own obsequious bondage,	
45	Wears out his time,° much like his master's ass,	*Spends his years serving*
	For naught but provender,° and when he's old—	*animal feed*
	cashiered.°	*fired*
	Whip me° such honest knaves! Others there are	*I'd have whipped*
	Who, trimmed° in forms and visages of duty,	*outwardly decorated*
	Keep yet their hearts attending on themselves	

5. Implying that Cassio's knowledge of war is purely theoretical.
6. Obscure. Cassio has not yet met Bianca and is unmarried, although in Shakespeare's source he is. Perhaps Shakespeare's error, a reference to Cassio as a ladies' man, or an oblique, debatable anticipation of the main plot.
7. In which the talkative political leaders (of ancient Rome, but referring to modern Italy) can debate.
8. Like "debitor and creditor," pejorative terms for an accountant (Cassio).
9. As "ensign," Iago is something like a standard-bearer or third-in-command, ranking below "lieutenant" Cassio, the second-in-command. *His moorship*: the first indication of whom Iago is complaining about.
1. Promotion comes through connections and favoritism.
2. Elastic term referring to any or all Muslims, heretics, North Africans, or, by way of general association with Blackness, sub-Saharan Africans.

And, throwing but shows of service on their lords,   50
Do well thrive by them° and, when they have lined   *("shows," "lords")*
   their° coats,   *their own*
Do themselves homage. These fellows have some soul
And such a one do I profess myself. For, sir,
It is as sure as you are Roderigo,
Were I the Moor, I would not be Iago:[3]   55
In following him, I follow but myself.
Heaven is my judge: not I for° love and duty,   *I am not driven by*
But seeming so for my peculiar° end.   *personal*
For when my outward action doth demonstrate
The native act and figure[4] of my heart   60
In complement extern,° 'tis not long after   *outward appearance*
But I will wear my heart upon my sleeve
For draws° to peck at. I am not what I am.[5]   *crowlike birds*
RODERIGO: What a full fortune does the thicklips owe°   *own*
   If he can carry't° thus?   *succeed*
IAGO: Call up her° father: *(Desdemona's)* 65
Rouse him,[6] make after° him, poison his delight,   *hound*
Proclaim° him in the streets, incense her kinsmen,   *Criminally accuse*
And, though he in a fertile climate dwell,
Plague him with flies. Though that his joy be joy,[7]
Yet throw such chances of vexation on't   70
As it may lose some color.[8]
RODERIGO: Here is her father's house. I'll call aloud.
IAGO: Do, with like timorous accent° and dire yell   *the same frightening tone*
As when, by night and negligence, the fire
Is spied in populous cities.   75
RODERIGO: What ho, Brabanzio! Signor Brabanzio, ho!
IAGO: Awake! What ho, Brabanzio! Thieves! Thieves!
Look to your house, your daughter, and your bags!
Thieves! Thieves!

    [Enter] BRABANZIO *above.*

BRABANZIO: What is the reason of this terrible summons?   80
   What is the matter there?
RODERIGO: Signor, is all your family within?

---

3. If I could have Othello's status, I would not want my own position. Or: if I were a person of Othello's (nobler) character—but occupied my current rank—I would not behave so self-servingly. The line perhaps also suggests both a deeper self-loathing and identification with Othello.

4. The internal operation (or motivation) and shape (or nature).

5. Probably: I am not in essence what I seem in appearance, or the opposite, though it comes to the same thing: I am not in appearance what I am in essence. Either way, the language reverses God's "I am what I am" (Exodus 3.14), while perhaps indicating Iago's divided self.

6. Like *him, his, he* (lines 66–69), can refer either to Brabanzio, Desdemona's father, or to Othello, seemingly moving from the former to the latter as the passage proceeds.

7. Though his joy is real.

8. Basis, plausibility, rationale, sign of good health; but perhaps more literally anticipating "old black ram" (line 86).

IAGO: Are your doors locked?

BRABANZIO: Why? Wherefore ask you this?

IAGO: Sir, you're robbed. For shame, put on your gown.

85   Your heart is burst; you have lost half your soul:
        Even now, now, very now, an old black ram[9]
        Is tupping° your white ewe. Arise! Arise!   copulating with
        Awake the snorting° citizens with the bell,   snoring
        Or else the devil will make a grandsire of you.
        Arise, I say!

90 BRABANZIO: What, have you lost your wits?

RODERIGO: Most reverend signor, do you know my voice?

BRABANZIO: Not I. What are you?

RODERIGO: My name is Roderigo.

BRABANZIO: The worser welcome.
        I have charged thee not to haunt about my doors:

95   In honest plainness thou hast heard me say
        My daughter is not for thee, and now in madness,
        Being full of supper and distempering draughts,°   inebriating beverages
        Upon malicious knavery dost thou come
        To start° my quiet?   upset

RODERIGO: Sir! Sir! Sir!

BRABANZIO: But thou must needs be sure:

100   My spirits and my place° have in their power   rank
        To make this bitter to thee.

RODERIGO: Patience, good sir.

BRABANZIO: What, tell'st thou me of robbing?
        This is Venice: my house is not a grange.°   country house

RODERIGO: Most grave Brabanzio,

105   In simple and pure soul I come to you—

IAGO: Sir, you are one of those that will not serve God if the
        devil bid you! Because we come to do you service and you
        think we are ruffians, you'll have your daughter covered with
        a Barbary horse;[1] you'll have your nephews° neigh to you;   grandsons

110   you'll have coursers for cousins and jennets for germans.[2]

BRABANZIO: What profane wretch art thou?

IAGO: I am one, sir, that comes to tell you your daughter and
        the Moor are making the beast with two backs.°   copulating

BRABANZIO: Thou art a villain!

IAGO: You are a senator.[3]

115 BRABANZIO: —This thou shalt answer:° I know thee, Roderigo.   answer for

RODERIGO: Sir, I will answer anything. But, I beseech you,
        If't be your pleasure and most wise consent
        —As partly I find it is—that your fair daughter

---

9. Connoting animalistic, monstrous, diabolical (horned) sexuality.

1. Horse from northwest coastal Africa; an Arab; suggesting Berbers or barbarians. *Covered*: (sexually).

2. You'll have strong horses ("coursers") for kinsmen ("cousins") and small Spanish horses ("jennets") for close relatives ("germans").

3. Ironically respectful. *Villain*: criminal; peasant.

At this odd even° and dull° watch o'th' night   *(near midnight) / sleepy*

Transported with no worse nor better guard   120

But with a knave of common° hire, a gondolier,   *public*

To the gross clasps of a lascivious Moor—

If this be known to you and your allowance,°   *allowed by you*

We then have done you bold and saucy° wrongs.   *impudent*

But if you know not this, my manners tell me   125

We have your wrong rebuke. Do not believe

That, from° the sense of all civility,   *in opposition to*

I thus would play and trifle with your reverence.

Your daughter—if you have not given her leave,°   *permission*

I say again—hath made a gross° revolt,   *foul; brazen* 130

Tying her duty, beauty, wit, and fortunes

In an extravagant° and wheeling° stranger   *vagrant / restless*

Of here and everywhere. Straight° satisfy yourself: *Immediately*

If she be in her chamber or your house,

Let loose on me the justice of the state   135

For thus deluding you.

BRABANZIO [*to Servants within*]:   Strike on the tinder,° ho!   *A light*

Give me a taper!° Call up all my people!   *candle*

[*aside*] This accident° is not unlike my dream;   *event*

Belief of it oppresses me already.

—Light, I say! Light!   *Exit* [*above*].

IAGO [*to* RODERIGO]:   Farewell, for I must leave you.   140

It seems not meet° nor wholesome to my place   *proper*

To be produced°—as, if I stay, I shall—   *presented as witness*

Against the Moor. For I do know the state,°   *(Venice)*

However this may gall him with some check,°   *reprimand*

Cannot with safety cast° him: for he's embarked°   *dismiss / committed* 145

With such loud reason° to the Cyprus wars,   *vociferous, just support*

Which even now stand in act° that, for° their souls,   *are taking place / to save*

Another of his fathom° they have none   *caliber*

To lead their business. In which regard,

Though I do hate him as I do hell pains,   150

Yet, for necessity of present life,°   *livelihood*

I must show out a flag and sign of love,

Which is indeed but sign. That you shall surely find him,

Lead to the Sagittary[4] the raisèd search,°   *awakened searchers*

And there will I be with him. So, farewell.   *Exit.*   155

         Enter BRABANZIO *with Servants and torches.*

BRABANZIO: It is too true an evil: gone she is,

And what's to come of my despisèd time°   *lifetime*

Is naught but bitterness. Now, Roderigo,

Where didst thou see her?—O unhappy girl!

---

4. Perhaps indicating an inn named for the astrological sign Sagittarius, where Othello and Desdemona are staying. It may also suggest Othello himself, since Sagittarius is depicted as a centaur (a mythological being part man, part horse), and Iago has already likened Othello to a "Barbary horse."

160   —With the Moor, say'st thou?—Who would be a father?
    —How didst thou know 'twas she?—Oh, she deceives me
    Past thought!—What said she to you? [*to Servants*] Get
       more tapers!
    Raise all my kindred!—Are they married, think you?
RODERIGO: Truly, I think they are.
BRABANZIO: O heaven!
165   How got she out? Oh, treason of the blood!
    Fathers, from hence trust not your daughters' minds
    By what you see them act. Is there not charms°   *magic*
    By which the property° of youth and maidhood°   *nature / virginity*
    May be abused? Have you not read, Roderigo,
    Of some such thing?
170 RODERIGO: Yes, sir, I have indeed.
BRABANZIO [*to Servants*]:   Call up my brother!—Oh, would
      you had had her!
    [*to Servants*] Some one way, some another.—Do you know
    Where we may apprehend her and the Moor?
RODERIGO: I think I can discover him, if you please
175   To get good guard and go along with me.
BRABANZIO: Pray you, lead on. At every house I'll call:
    I may command° at most.° [*to Servants*] Get   *demand help / (of the houses)*
      weapons, ho!
    And raise some special officers of might.
    —On, good Roderigo: I will deserve° your pains.   *Exeunt.*[5]   *reward*

Scene 2

Another street in Venice, before Othello's lodging. Enter
OTHELLO, IAGO, [*and*] *Attendants with torches.*

IAGO: Though in the trade of war I have slain men,
    Yet do I hold it very stuff° o'th' conscience   *essence*
    To do no contrived° murder. I lack iniquity   *premeditated*
    Sometime to do me service: nine or ten times
5   I had thought t'have yerked° him here under the ribs.   *struck with a dagger*
OTHELLO: 'Tis better as it is.
IAGO: Nay, but he prated
    And spoke such scurvy and provoking terms
    Against your honor
    That, with the little godliness I have,
10   I did full hard forbear him.[6] But I pray you, sir,
    Are you fast° married? Be assured of this: *legitimately*
    That the magnifico° is much beloved,   *(Brabanzio)*
    And hath in his effect a voice potential°   *powerful*

---

5. Exit the stage (Latin for "they go out").
6. I barely restrained myself from attacking him.

As double as the Duke's.[7] He will divorce you,
Or put upon you what restraint or grievance   15
The law, with all his might to enforce it on,
Will give him cable.°   *rope; scope*

OTHELLO: Let him do his spite:
My services which I have done the signory°   *Venetian government*
Shall out-tongue his complaints. 'Tis yet to know°—   *It has never been shown*
Which, when I know that boasting is an honor,   20
I shall promulgate—I fetch my life and being
From men of royal siege,° and my demerits°   *rank / deserts*
May speak unbonneted° to as proud a fortune   *with(out?) deference*
As this that I have reached. For know, Iago,
But that° I love the gentle Desdemona,   *But for the fact that* 25
I would not my unhousèd° free condition   *unconfined*
Put into circumscription and confine°   *confinement*
For the sea's worth—

        Enter CASSIO [*and* OFFICERS] *with torches.*

                        But look, what lights come yond?°   *yonder*

IAGO: Those are the raisèd father and his friends.
    You were best go in.

OTHELLO: Not I: I must be found.   30
    My parts,° my title, and my perfect soul°   *qualities / clear conscience*
    Shall manifest me rightly. Is it they?

IAGO: By Janus,[8] I think no.

OTHELLO: The servants of the Duke's? And my lieutenant?
    —The goodness of the night upon you, friends.   35
    What is the news?

CASSIO: The Duke does greet you, general,
    And he requires your haste-post-haste appearance
    Even on the instant.

OTHELLO: What is the matter, think you?

CASSIO: Something from Cyprus, as I may divine.
    It is a business of some heat:° the galleys   *urgency* 40
    Have sent a dozen sequent° messengers   *successive*
    This very night at one another's heels,
    And many of the consuls, raised and met,
    Are at the Duke's already. You have been hotly called for:
    When, being not at your lodging to be found,   45
    The Senate hath sent about three several quests
    To search you out.

OTHELLO: 'Tis well I am found by you.
    I will but spend a word here in the house,
    And go with you.   [*Exit.*]

CASSIO: Ensign, what makes he here?

7. Like the Duke's, Brabanzio's influence is twice as great as that of any other senator.
8. Two-faced Roman god.

50 IAGO: Faith, he tonight hath boarded a land carrack:°   *large merchant ship*
    If it prove lawful prize,[9] he's made for ever.
CASSIO: I do not understand.
IAGO: He's married.
CASSIO: To who?
IAGO: Marry,° to—   *By Mary (wordplay)*

    [*Enter* OTHELLO.]

    [*to* OTHELLO]   Come, captain, will you go?
OTHELLO: Have with you.°   *Let's go*

    Enter BRABANZIO, RODERIGO, *with* OFFICERS *and torches.*

CASSIO: Here comes another troop to seek for you.
55 IAGO: It is Brabanzio.—General, be advised:
    He comes to° bad intent.   *with*
OTHELLO [*to* BRABANZIO *and* RODERIGO]:   Holla, stand there!
RODERIGO: Signor, it is the Moor.
BRABANZIO: Down with him, thief!
IAGO [*drawing*]:   You, Roderigo! Come, sir, I am for you.
OTHELLO: Keep up° your bright swords, for the dew will rust   *Put away*
    them.
60   [*to* BRABANZIO] Good signor, you shall more command
        with years°   *your age*
    Than with your weapons.
BRABANZIO: O thou foul° thief! Where hast thou stowed my   *(ethically); (in color)*
    daughter?
    Damned as thou art, thou hast enchanted her:
    For I'll refer me to all things of sense,[1]
65   If she in chains of magic were not bound,
    Whether a maid, so tender, fair, and happy,
    So opposite° to marriage that she shunned   *opposed*
    The wealthy curlèd darling° of our nation,   *darlings*
    Would ever have, t'incur a general mock,°   *ridicule*
70   Run from her guardage to the sooty bosom
    Of such a thing as thou—to fear, not to delight.
    Judge me the world if 'tis not gross in sense[2]
    That thou hast practiced on her with foul charms,
    Abused her delicate youth with drugs or minerals
75   That waken motion.[3] I'll have't disputed on:°   *argued; looked into*
    'Tis probable, and palpable to thinking.
    I therefore apprehend and do attach° thee   *arrest*
    For an abuser of the world, a practicer
    Of arts inhibited and out of warrant.°   *prohibited and illegal*

---

9. That is, prize of war, enemy property seized in battle, especially at sea. Since officers were allotted shares of prizes lawfully seized, their fortune would be "made." (Iago speaks metaphorically, as the prize is Desdemona.)
1. For I'll refer the matter to all rational beings.
2. Let the world judge me if it is not patently obvious.
3. Mental agitation.

     [*to* OFFICERS] Lay hold upon him. If he do resist,   80
     Subdue him at his peril.
OTHELLO: Hold your hands,
     Both you of my inclining° and the rest!   *following*
     Were it my cue to fight, I should have known it
     Without a prompter. [*to* BRABANZIO] Whither will° you   *desire*
        that I go
     To answer this your charge?
BRABANZIO: To prison, till fit time   85
     Of law and course of direct session°   *court session*
     Call thee to answer.
OTHELLO: What if I do obey?
     How may the Duke be therewith satisfied,
     Whose messengers are here about my side°   *beside me*
     Upon some present business of the state   90
     To bring me to him?
OFFICER: 'Tis true, most worthy signor:
     The Duke's in council, and your noble self,
     I am sure, is sent for.
BRABANZIO: How? The Duke in council?
     In° this time of the night? Bring him away!°   *At / along*
     Mine's not an idle cause. The Duke himself,   95
     Or any of my brothers of the state,
     Cannot but feel this wrong as 'twere their own:
     For if such actions may have passage free,
     Bondslaves and pagans[4] shall our statesmen be.   *Exeunt.*

Scene 3

     A Venetian council room. Enter DUKE, [FIRST *and*
     SECOND] SENATORS, *and* OFFICERS.

DUKE: There's no composition in this news
     That gives them credit.[5]
FIRST SENATOR: Indeed, they are disproportioned:°   *inconsistent*
     My letters say a hundred and seven galleys—
DUKE: And mine a hundred forty—
SECOND SENATOR: And mine two hundred.
     But though they jump not on a just account°—   *don't exactly agree* 5
     As in these cases where the aim reports,
     'Tis oft with difference[6]—yet do they all confirm
     A Turkish fleet, and bearing up to Cyprus.
DUKE: Nay, it is possible enough to judgment:°   *if one judges rationally*
     I do not so secure me in the error   10
     But the main article I do approve

---

4. Implicitly accusing Othello of being both slave and non-Christian, though he is neither.
5. The reports lack the consistency that would make them believable.
6. Where the reports are estimates, there are often discrepancies among them.

In fearful sense.[7]

SAILOR (*within*):   What ho! What ho! What ho!

Enter SAILOR.

OFFICER: A messenger from the galleys.

DUKE: —Now, what's the business?

SAILOR: The Turkish preparation° makes for Rhodes: *battle-ready fleet*
15   So was I bid report here to the state
        By Signor Angelo.[8]

DUKE [*to* SENATORS]:   How say you by this change?

FIRST SENATOR: This cannot be
        By no assay° of reason: 'tis a pageant   *any test*
        To keep us in false gaze.° When we consider   *To misdirect us*
20   Th'importancy of Cyprus to the Turk,
        And let ourselves again but understand
        That as it more concerns the Turk than Rhodes,
        So may he with more facile question bear it,[9]
        For that it stands not in such warlike brace,
25   But altogether lacks th'abilities
        That Rhodes is dressed in. If we make thought of this,
        We must not think the Turk is so unskillful
        To leave that latest° which concerns him first,   *for last*
        Neglecting an attempt of ease and gain
30   To wake and wage° a danger profitless.   *risk*

DUKE: Nay, in all confidence, he's not for° Rhodes.   *aiming for*

OFFICER: Here is more news.

Enter a MESSENGER.

MESSENGER: The Ottomites,° reverend and gracious,°   *Turks / (the Senators)*
        Steering with due course toward the isle of Rhodes,
35   Have there injointed them with an after° fleet.   *joined with another*

FIRST SENATOR: Ay, so I thought. How many, as you guess?

MESSENGER: Of thirty sail. And now they do restem°   *retrace*
        Their backward course, bearing with frank appearance
        Their purposes toward Cyprus. Signor Montano,
40   Your trusty and most valiant servitor,
        With his free duty recommends you thus,[1]
        And prays you to believe him.

DUKE: 'Tis certain, then, for Cyprus.
        Marcus Luccicos,[2] is not he in town?

45 FIRST SENATOR: He's now in Florence.

---

7. I am not so reassured by the discrepancies as to dismiss the main concern—the approach of the Turkish fleet.

8. Not mentioned elsewhere in the play, Angelus Sorianus was a Venetian sea captain who received the Venetian ambassador bearing from Constantinople the Turkish ultimatum to surrender Cyprus shortly before its capture by the Turks in 1571.

9. So also can the Turkish fleet more easily win it.

1. With his freely given loyalty reports to you thus.

2. Not mentioned elsewhere in the play.

DUKE: Write from us to him, post-post-haste.—Dispatch!

[*Exeunt* MESSENGER *and* SAILOR.]

FIRST SENATOR: Here comes Brabanzio and the valiant Moor.

Enter BRABANZIO, OTHELLO, CASSIO, IAGO, RODERIGO,
and OFFICERS.

DUKE: Valiant Othello, we must straight° employ you   *immediately*
     Against the general enemy° Ottoman.   *(of all Christendom)*
     [*to* BRABANZIO] I did not see you. Welcome, gentle° signor;   *noble*   50
     We lacked your counsel and your help tonight.
BRABANZIO: So did I yours. Good your grace, pardon me:
     Neither my place° nor aught° I heard of business   *official duty / anything*
     Hath raised me from my bed; nor doth the general care
     Take hold on me, for my particular grief   55
     Is of so floodgate° and o'er-bearing nature   *such a drenching*
     That it engluts° and swallows other sorrows,   *drinks up*
     And it is still itself.°   *(unaffected)*
DUKE: Why, what's the matter?
BRABANZIO: My daughter! Oh, my daughter!
FIRST *and* SECOND SENATORS: Dead?
BRABANZIO: Ay—to me.
     She is abused,° stol'n from me, and corrupted   *deluded*   60
     By spells and medicines bought of mountebanks:°   *quacks*
     For nature so preposterously° to err,   *monstrously*
     Being not deficient, blind, or lame of sense,
     Sans° witchcraft could not.   *Without*
DUKE: Whoe'er he be that in this foul proceeding   65
     Hath thus beguiled your daughter of herself
     And you of her, the bloody book of law
     You shall yourself read in the bitter letter
     After your own sense, yea, though our proper son
     Stood in your action.[3]
BRABANZIO: Humbly I thank your grace.   70
     Here is the man: this Moor, whom now it seems
     Your special mandate for the state affairs
     Hath hither brought.
FIRST *and* SECOND SENATORS: We are very sorry for't.
DUKE [*to* OTHELLO]:   What in your own part can you say to this?
BRABANZIO: Nothing, but this is so.   75
OTHELLO: Most potent, grave, and reverend signors,
     My very noble and approved° good masters: *proven; experienced*
     That I have ta'en away this old man's daughter,
     It is most true; true I have married her.
     The very head and front° of my offending   *height and breadth*   80
     Hath this extent, no more. Rude° am I in my speech,   *Unpolished*
     And little blessed with the soft phrase of peace

---

3. You yourself shall interpret the law as you see fit even if you are accusing my own son.

For, since these arms of mine had seven years' pith°   strength
Till now some nine moons wasted,° they have   nine months ago
          used°   performed
85   Their dearest° action in the tented° field,   most valued / military
       And little of this great world can I speak
       More than pertains to feats of broils° and battle;   combats
       And, therefore, little shall I grace my cause
       In speaking for myself. Yet, by your gracious patience,
90   I will a round° unvarnished tale deliver   plain
       Of my whole course of love: what° drugs, what charms,   with what
       What conjuration, and what mighty magic—
       For such proceeding I am charged withal°—   with
       I won his daughter.
BRABANZIO: A maiden never bold,
95   Of spirit so still and quiet that her motion
       Blushed at herself;[4] and she, in spite of nature,
       Of years, of country, credit,° everything,   reputation
       To fall in love with what she feared to look on?
       It is a judgment maimed and most imperfect
100   That will confess perfection so could err
       Against all rules of nature, and must° be driven   (we therefore) must
       To find out practices of cunning hell
       Why this should be. I therefore vouch again
       That with some mixtures powerful o'er the blood,°   passions
105   Or with some dram conjured° to this effect,   enchanted dose
       He wrought upon her.
DUKE: To vouch this is no proof
       Without more wider and more overt test
       Than these thin habits and poor likelihoods
       Of modern seeming do prefer against him.[5]
110 FIRST SENATOR: But, Othello, speak.
       Did you by indirect and forcèd courses°   means
       Subdue and poison this young maid's affections?
       Or came it by request and such fair question°   conversation
       As soul to soul affordeth?
OTHELLO: I do beseech you,
115   Send for the lady to the Sagittary,°   (see 1.1.154 and note)
       And let her speak of me before her father.
       If you do find me foul in her report,
       The trust, the office I do hold of you,
       Not only take away, but let your sentence
120   Even fall upon my life.
DUKE [to OFFICERS]:   Fetch Desdemona hither.
OTHELLO: Ensign, conduct them: you best know the place.

                    [*Exeunt* IAGO *and* OFFICERS.]

4. She blushed at her slightest display of emotion.
5. Without fuller and more direct testimony than mere appearances and conjecture based on current, shallow popular beliefs tell against him.

—And till she come, as truly as to heaven
I do confess the vices of my blood,°   *sins of passion*
So justly to your grave ears I'll present   125
How I did thrive in this fair lady's love
And she in mine.
DUKE: Say it, Othello.
OTHELLO: Her father loved me, oft invited me,
    Still° questioned me the story of my life   *Constantly*
    From year to year: the battles, sieges, fortune,   130
    That I have passed.
    I ran it through, even from my boyish days
    To th' very moment that he bade me tell it,
    Wherein I spoke of most disastrous chances;°   *occurrences*
    Of moving accidents° by flood and field;   *events*   135
    Of hairbreadth scapes i'th' imminent deadly breach;[6]
    Of being taken by the insolent foe
    And sold to slavery; of my redemption thence,
    And portance° in my traveler's history;   *conduct*
    Wherein of antres° vast and deserts idle,   *caves*   140
    Rough quarries, rocks, hills whose head touch heaven,
    It was my hint° to speak—such was my process°—   *occasion / story*
    And of the cannibals that each other eat—
    The *Anthropophagi*[7]—and men whose heads
    Grew beneath their shoulders. These things to hear   145
    Would Desdemona seriously incline;°   *eagerly lean (listen)*
    But still the house affairs would draw her hence,
    Which ever as° she could with haste dispatch,   *Whenever*
    She'd come again, and with a greedy ear
    Devour up my discourse. Which I, observing,   150
    Took once a pliant° hour, and found good means   *convenient*
    To draw from her a prayer of earnest heart
    That I would all my pilgrimage dilate°   *relate*
    Whereof by parcels she had something heard
    But not instinctively.° I did consent,   *with conscious purpose*   155
    And often did beguile her of her tears
    When I did speak of some distressful stroke
    That my youth suffered. My story being done,
    She gave me for my pains a world of kisses.
    She swore, "In faith, 'twas strange, 'twas passing° strange.   *exceptionally*   160
    'Twas pitiful, 'twas wondrous pitiful."
    She wished she had not heard it, yet she wished
    That heaven had made her such a man.[8] She thanked me

---

6. In the deadly gaps in a fortification.
7. Man-eaters. The term comes from the ancient Roman writer Pliny the Elder. Shakespeare was also indebted to the travel literature of the Middle Ages (*Mandeville's Travels*) and the Renaissance (Hakluyt's *Principal Navigations*, among others), as well as to John Pory's English description of Leo Africanus's life in his translation of Leo's *Geographical History*.
8. Made such a man for her; made her into such a man.

And bade me, if I had a friend that loved her,
165   I should but teach him how to tell my story,
And that would woo her. Upon this hint,° I spake.   *opportunity; suggestion*
She loved me for the dangers I had passed,
And I loved her that she did pity them.
This only is the witchcraft I have used.

Enter DESDEMONA, IAGO, [*and*] *Attendants.*

170   Here comes the lady. Let her witness it.
DUKE: I think this tale would win my daughter too.
        —Good Brabanzio, take up this mangled matter at
            the best:°   *as well as you can*
        Men do their broken weapons rather use
        Than their bare hands.
BRABANZIO: I pray you hear her speak.
175   If she confess that she was half the wooer,
        Destruction° on my head if my bad blame   *May destruction fall*
        Light on the man. [*to* DESDEMONA] Come hither,
            gentle mistress:
        Do you perceive in all this noble company
        Where most you owe obedience?
DESDEMONA: My noble father,
180   I do perceive here a divided duty.
        To you I am bound for life and education;
        My life and education both do learn° me   *teach*
        How to respect you. You are the lord of duty;
        I am, hitherto, your daughter. But here's my husband,
185   And so much duty as my mother showed
        To you, preferring you before her father,
        So much I challenge° that I may profess   *assert*
        Due to the Moor my lord.
BRABANZIO: God be with you. I have done.
190   [*to* DUKE] Please it, your grace, on to the state affairs.
        I had rather to adopt a child than get° it.   *beget*
        [*to* OTHELLO] Come hither, Moor.
        I here do give thee that with all my heart
        Which, but° thou hast already, with all my heart   *except that*
195   I would keep from thee. [*to* DESDEMONA] For your
            sake, jewel,
        I am glad at soul I have no other child,
        For thy escape would teach me tyranny,
        To hang clogs[9] on them. [*to* DUKE] I have done, my lord.
DUKE: Let me speak like yourself, and lay a sentence°   *draw a moral*
200   Which as a grece° or step may help these lovers.   *flight of stairs*
        "When remedies are past, the griefs are ended

---

9. Blocks of wood tied to criminals' legs to keep them from escaping.

By seeing the worst, which late on hopes depended.[1]
To mourn a mischief that is past and gone
Is the next way to draw new mischief on.
What cannot be preserved, when Fortune takes,   205
Patience her injury a mockery makes.[2]
The robbed that smiles steals something from the thief;
He robs himself that spends a bootless° grief."   *pointless*
BRABANZIO: So let the Turk of Cyprus us beguile:
We lose it not so long as we can smile.   210
He bears the sentence° well that nothing bears   *saying; judgment*
But the free comfort which from thence he hears;
But he bears both the sentence and the sorrow
That, to pay grief, must of poor patience borrow.
These sentences, to sugar or to gall,°   *both sweet and bitter* 215
Being strong on both sides, are equivocal.°   *equally apt*
But words are words: I never yet did hear
That the bruised heart was piercèd[3] through the ears.
I humbly beseech you, proceed to th'affairs of state.
DUKE: The Turk with a most mighty preparation makes for   220
Cyprus. Othello, the fortitude° of the place is best known   *military layout*
to you, and, though we have there a substitute of most
allowed sufficiency,° yet opinion, a more sovereign mistress   *known ability*
of effects, throws a more safer voice on you.[4] You must
therefore be content to slubber° the gloss of your new for-   *soil* 225
tunes with this more stubborn° and boisterous expedition.   *rough*
OTHELLO: The tyrant custom, most grave senators,
Hath made the flinty and steel coach° of war   *captain's quarters*
My thrice-driven° bed of down. I do agnize°   *sifted / acknowledge*
A natural and prompt alacrity   230
I find in hardness,° and do undertake   *hardship*
This present war against the Ottomites.
Most humbly, therefore, bending to your state,°   *authority*
I crave fit disposition for my wife,
Due reference of place and exhibition[5]   235
With such accommodation and besort°   *suitable attendance*
As levels with° her breeding.   *fits*
DUKE: Why, at her father's.
BRABANZIO: I will not have it so.
OTHELLO: Nor I.
DESDEMONA: Nor would I there reside
To put my father in impatient thoughts   240
By being in his eye.—Most gracious Duke,

1. By seeing those things come to pass that caused grief in anticipation, "griefs are ended." The Duke
paints the moral in rhyming couplets, to which Brabanzio replies in kind.
2. Patience laughs at what cannot be helped (and thus reduces the "injury").
3. Surgically lanced (and presumably cured).
4. Public opinion, which determines what gets done, finds greater security with you.
5. Proper accommodation and maintenance.

To my unfolding° lend your prosperous° ear,	*proposal / receptive*
And let me find a charter° in your voice	*an authorization*
T'assist my simpleness.	

DUKE :   What would you, Desdemona?

245 DESDEMONA: That I love the Moor to live with him
My downright violence and storm of fortunes[6]
May trumpet to the world. My heart's subdued
Even to the very quality of my lord.[7]
I saw Othello's visage in his mind,[8]

250	And to his honors and his valiant parts°	*qualities*

Did I my soul and fortunes consecrate—
So that, dear lords, if I be left behind
A moth of peace, and he go to the war,

The rites° for why I love him are bereft me,	*(of love or war); rights*
255 And I a heavy interim shall support°	*have to bear*

By his dear absence. Let me go with him.

OTHELLO: Let her have your voice.°	*agreement*

Vouch with me, heaven, I therefore beg it not
To please the palate of my appetite,
260 Nor to comply with heat the young affects
In my defunct and proper satisfaction,[9]

But to be free° and bounteous to her mind.	*liberal*

And heaven defend your good souls that you think
I will your serious and great business scant

265 When she is with me. No, when light-winged toys°	*diversions*
Of feathered Cupid seal° with wanton dullness	*blind*

My speculative and officed instrument[1]

That° my disports° corrupt and taint my business,	*So that / sexual pleasures*
Let housewives make a skillet of my helm,°	*helmet*
270 And all indign° and base adversities	*undignified*

Make head against my estimation.[2]
DUKE: Be it as you shall privately determine,
Either for her stay or going. Th'affair cries haste,
And speed must answer it.

FIRST SENATOR: You must away° tonight.	*leave*

275 OTHELLO: With all my heart.
DUKE: At nine i'th' morning here we'll meet again.
Othello, leave some officer behind,
And he shall our commission bring to you,

And such things else of quality and respect°	*weight and importance*
As doth import° you.	*concern*

6. My strong feelings and assault on the constraints I was fated to endure.
7. I love him for what he is (military, adventurous).
8. I saw Othello as he sees himself; or: Othello's face expresses his character; or, perhaps: I looked past his outward appearance (age, skin color) to his inner essence.
9. Nor to fulfill with passion youthful desires in the performed (though possibly suggesting defectiveness: "defunct") and fitting satisfaction (of marital relations).
1. My duty-bound faculties of sense.
2. Raise an army against my good reputation.

OTHELLO: So please your grace, my ensign: 280
    A man he is of honesty and trust.
    To his conveyance I assign my wife
    With what else needful your good grace shall think
    To be sent after me.
DUKE: Let it be so.
    —Good night to everyone. [*to* BRABANZIO] And, noble signor,   285
    If virtue no delighted° beauty lack,   *delightful*
    Your son-in-law is far more fair than black.°   *(ethically); (racially)*
FIRST SENATOR: Adieu, brave Moor; use Desdemona well.
BRABANZIO: Look to her,° Moor, if thou hast eyes to see: *Watch her carefully*
    She has deceived her father, and may thee.   290
OTHELLO: My life upon her faith.

      Exeunt [*all except* OTHELLO, DESDEMONA, IAGO,
            and RODERIGO].

           Honest Iago,
    My Desdemona must I leave to thee.
    I prithee let thy wife attend on her,
    And bring them after in the best advantage.[3]
    —Come, Desdemona, I have but an hour   295
    Of love, of wordly matter, and direction°   *directives*
    To spend with thee. We must obey the time.

        Exeunt [OTHELLO *and* DESDEMONA].

RODERIGO: Iago?
IAGO: What say'st thou, noble heart?
RODERIGO: What will I do, think'st thou?
IAGO: Why, go to bed and sleep.
RODERIGO: I will incontinently° drown myself!   *immediately*   300
IAGO: If thou dost, I shall never love thee after. Why, thou
    silly gentleman!
RODERIGO: It is silliness to live when to live is torment; and then
    have we a prescription° to die when death is our physician.   *right; doctor's order*
IAGO: Oh, villainous!° I have looked upon the world for four times   *absurd; immoral(?)* 305
    seven years and, since I could distinguish betwixt a benefit
    and an injury, I never found man that knew how to love him-
    self. Ere I would say I would drown myself for the love of a
    guinea hen,[4] I would change my humanity with a baboon.
RODERIGO: What should I do? I confess it is my shame to be   310
    so fond, but it is not in my virtue° to amend it.   *nature*
IAGO: Virtue? A fig!° 'Tis in ourselves that we are thus, or thus.   *(obscenity)*
    Our bodies are our gardens, to the which our wills are gar-
    deners, so that if we will plant nettles or sow lettuce, set hys-
    sop° and weed up thyme, supply it with one gender° of herbs   *mint herb / type* 315
    or distract it with many, either to have it sterile with idleness°   *noncultivation*

---

3. And bring them along at the most favorable moment.
4. Prostitute; perhaps a disparaging reference to Guinea in West Africa, picked up by "baboon."

or manured with industry, why the power and corrigible
authority° of this lies in our wills. If the brain of our lives had   *ability to improve*
not one scale of reason to poise° another of sensuality, the   *counterweigh*
320   blood and baseness of our natures would conduct us to most
preposterous conclusions.° But we have reason to cool our   *outcomes*
raging motions,° our carnal stings, or unbitted° lusts——   *impulses / unrestrained*
whereof I take this that you call "love" to be a sect or scion.°   *offshoot*

RODERIGO: It cannot be.

325   IAGO: It is merely a lust of the blood and a permission of the
will. Come, be a man! Drown thyself? Drown cats and
blind puppies! I have professed me° thy friend, and I con-   *myself*
fess me knit to thy deserving with cables of perdurable°   *durable*
toughness. I could never better stead° thee than now. Put   *help*
330   money in thy purse! Follow thou the wars; defeat thy
favor with an usurped beard.[5] I say, put money in thy
purse! It cannot be long that Desdemona should continue her love to the Moor—put money in thy purse!—
nor he his to her. It was a violent commencement° in her,   *an abruptly begun affair*
335   and thou shalt see an answerable sequestration[6]—put but
money in thy purse! These Moors are changeable in their
wills—fill thy purse with money! The food that to him
now is as luscious as locusts[7] shall be to him shortly as
bitter as *coloquintida*.[8] She must change for youth:° when   *a youth*
340   she is sated with his body, she will find the errors of her
choice. Therefore put money in thy purse! If thou wilt
needs° damn thyself, do it a more delicate way than   *If you must*
drowning. Make all the money thou canst. If sancti-
mony° and a frail vow betwixt an erring barbarian[9] and   *holy rite*
345   super-subtle° Venetian be not too hard for my wits and   *deceptive*
all the tribe of hell, thou shalt enjoy her. Therefore, make
money. A pox of drowning thyself! It is clean out of the
way!° Seek thou rather to be hanged in compassing° thy   *unacceptable / obtaining*
joy than to be drowned and go without her.

350   RODERIGO: Wilt thou be fast° to my hopes if I depend on the   *duty bound*
issue?°   *outcome*

IAGO: Thou art° sure of me. Go, make money. I have told   *can be*
thee often and I re-tell thee again and again: I hate the
Moor. My cause is hearted,° thine hath no less reason: *heartfelt*
355   let us be conjunctive° in our revenge against him. If thou   *joined*
canst cuckold him, thou dost thyself a pleasure, me a
sport. There are many events in the womb of Time which
will be delivered. Traverse,° go, provide thy money: we   *Go (to arms)*
will have more of this tomorrow. Adieu.

360   RODERIGO: Where shall we meet i'th' morning?

5. Disguise yourself to look more like a soldier with a fake beard.
6. A correspondingly abrupt separation.
7. A sweet, exotic fruit, perhaps carob or honeysuckle.
8. Colocynth, a purgative—one of Iago's many references to the digestive tract.
9. Wandering (also mistaken) foreigner (savage; native of Barbary in North Africa).

IAGO: At my lodging.

RODERIGO: I'll be with thee betimes.°   *early*

IAGO: Go to. Farewell. Do you hear, Roderigo?

RODERIGO: I'll sell all my land!   *Exit.*

IAGO: Thus do I ever make my fool my purse:

For I mine own gained knowledge should profane   365

If I would time expend with such snipe°   *fools*

But° for my sport and profit. I hate the Moor,   *Except*

And it is thought abroad° that twixt my sheets   *rumored*

He's done my office.° I know not if't be true,   *(sexual)*

But I, for mere suspicion in that kind,°   *regard*   370

Will do° as if for surety.° He holds° me well;   *act / it were true / likes*

The better shall my purpose work on him.

Cassio's a proper° man—let me see now: *handsome*

To get his place° and to plume up° my will   *position / gratify*

In double knavery? How? How? Let's see.   375

After some time, to abuse Othello's ears

That he is too familiar with his wife.[1]

He hath a person and a smooth dispose°   *manner*

To be° suspected, framed to make women false.   *That are to be*

The Moor is of a free° and open nature   *liberal*   380

That thinks men honest that but seem to be so,

And will as tenderly° be led by th' nose   *easily*

As asses are.

I have't! It is engendered. Hell and night

Must bring this monstrous birth to the world's light.   [*Exit.*]   385

ACT II

Scene 1

A seaport in Cyprus; outdoors near the harbor. Enter
MONTANO, *and* [FIRST *and* SECOND] GENTLEMEN.

MONTANO: What from the cape can you discern at sea?

FIRST GENTLEMAN: Nothing at all. It is a high-wrought flood:°   *very rough sea*

I cannot twixt the heaven and the main°   *sea*

Descry° a sail.   *Discern*

MONTANO: Methinks the wind hath spoke aloud at land;   5

A fuller blast ne'er shook our battlements.

If it hath ruffianed° so upon the sea,   *raged*

What ribs of oak, when mountains melt on them,

Can hold the mortise?[2] What shall we hear of this?

SECOND GENTLEMAN: A segregation° of the Turkish fleet: *separation*   10

For do but stand upon the foaming shore,

1. "He" is Cassio (as in line 371), but "his" refers to Othello—a potential confusion of pronouns.
2. What ship (with "ribs of oak") can hold its joints ("mortise") together when "mountains" of water pour on it?

The chidden billow³ seems to pelt the clouds,
The wind-shaked surge° with high and monstrous main°   *fountain / open sea*
Seems to cast water on the burning Bear

15   And quench the guards of th'ever-fixèd pole.⁴
I never did like molestation view°   *such a tumult see*
On the enchafèd° flood.   *heated; tumultuous*
MONTANO: If that the Turkish fleet
Be not ensheltered and embayed, they are drowned.
It is impossible to bear it out.

      Enter [THIRD] GENTLEMAN.

20   THIRD GENTLEMAN: News, lads! Our wars are done.
The desperate tempest hath so banged the Turks
That their designment° halts. A noble ship of Venice   *plan*
Hath seen a grievous wreck and sufferance
On most part of their fleet.
MONTANO: How? Is this true?

25   THIRD GENTLEMAN: The ship is here put in,
A Veronese.⁵ Michael Cassio,
Lieutenant to the warlike Moor, Othello,
Is come on shore; the Moor himself at sea,
And is in full commission here for Cyprus.

30   MONTANO I am glad on't; 'tis a worthy governor.
THIRD GENTLEMAN: But this same Cassio, though he speak
of comfort
Touching° the Turkish loss, yet he looks sadly°   *About / somberly*
And prays the Moor be safe, for they were parted
With foul and violent tempest.
MONTANO: Pray heavens he be!

35   For I have served him, and the man commands
Like a full° soldier. Let's to the sea-side, ho,   *true*
As well to see the vessel that's come in
As to throw out our eyes for brave Othello,
Even till we make the main and th'aerial blue
An indistinct regard.⁶

40   THIRD GENTLEMAN: Come, let's do so,
For every minute is expectancy
Of more arrivancy.°   *arrivals*

      Enter CASSIO.

CASSIO: Thanks, you, the valiant of the warlike isle°   *(Cyprus)*
That so approve the Moor! Oh, let the heavens

45   Give him defense against the elements,
For I have lost him on a dangerous sea.

---

3. The rising ocean, rebuked ("chidden") by the wind or repulsed by the land.
4. Probably two stars in the constellation Ursa Minor ("the burning Bear") that point in a line to the polestar.
5. Meaning unclear: originally from Verona, though now used by the Venetians; a cutter.
6. Until we can't distinguish sea from sky.

MONTANA: Is he well shipped?

CASSIO: His bark is stoutly timbered, and his pilot
　　Of very expert and approved allowance:°　　　　　　　　　*proven ability*
　　Therefore my hopes, not surfeited to death,°　　　　　　*not excessive*　50
　　Stand in bold cure.°　　　　　　　　　　　*Are likely to be rewarded*

VOICES (*within*):　　　　　　A sail! A sail! A sail!

CASSIO: What noise?

SECOND GENTLEMAN: The town is empty: on the brow° o'th' sea　　*cliff at the edge*
　　Stand ranks of people and they cry, "A sail!"

CASSIO: My hopes do shape him for° the governor.　　　　　*make it out to be*　55

　　　　[*A shot is heard.*]

SECOND GENTLEMAN: They do discharge their shot of courtesy.
　　Our friends, at least.

CASSIO [*to* SECOND GENTLEMAN]: I pray you, sir, go forth,
　　And give us truth who 'tis that is arrived.

SECOND GENTLEMAN: I shall.　　　　　　　　　　*Exit.*

MONTANO: But, good lieutenant, is your general wived?　　　　　60

CASSIO: Most fortunately! He hath achieved° a maid　　　　　*won*
　　That paragons° description and wild fame,[7]　　　　　*stands above*
　　One that excels the quirks of blazoning° pens　　　　*praise-giving*
　　And in th'essential vesture of creation
　　Does tire the engineer.[8]

　　　　Enter [SECOND] GENTLEMAN.

　　　　　　　　—How now? Who has put in?　　　　　65

SECOND GENTLEMAN: 'Tis one Iago, ensign to the general.

CASSIO: He's had most favorable and happy speed.
　　Tempests themselves, high seas, and howling winds,
　　The guttered° rocks and congregated° sands—　　　*jagged / accumulated*
　　Traitors ensteeped° to enclog the guiltless keel—　　*underwater*　70
　　As having sense of beauty do omit°　　　　　　　*forgo*
　　Their mortal° natures, letting go safely by　　　　*deadly*
　　The divine Desdemona.

MONTANO:　　　　　　　What is she?

CASSIO: She that I spake of: our great captain's captain,
　　Left in the conduct° of the bold Iago,　　　　　*care*　75
　　Whose footing here anticipates our thoughts
　　A sennight's speed.[9] Great Jove,[1] Othello guard,°　　*guard Othello*
　　And swell his sail with thine own powerful breath,
　　That he may bless this bay with his tall ship,
　　Make love's quick pants in Desdemona's arms,　　　　　80
　　Give renewed fire to our extincted spirits—

　　　　Enter DESDEMONA, IAGO, RODERIGO, *and* EMILIA.

7. Unrestrained rumors.
8. Whose natural beauty exhausts the poet's capacity to invent praise.
9. Whose arrival predates our expectations by a week.
1. A.k.a. Jupiter, supreme god in the religion and mythology of ancient Rome.

                                          Oh, behold!
     The riches of the ship is come on shore.
     You men of Cyprus, let her have your knees.

          [*He kneels.*]

     Hail to thee, lady, and the grace of heaven
85   Before, behind thee, and on every hand
     Enwheel thee round.°   *Encircle you*
DESDEMONA: I thank you, valiant Cassio.

          [CASSIO *rises.*]

     What tidings can you tell of my lord?
CASSIO: He is not yet arrived, nor know I aught
     But that he's well and will be shortly here.
90 DESDEMONA: Oh, but I fear! How lost you company?
CASSIO: The great contention of sea and skies
     Parted our fellowship—
VOICES (*within*):   A sail! A sail!
CASSIO: But hark, a sail!

          [*A shot is heard.*]

SECOND GENTLEMAN: They give this greeting to the citadel;
     This likewise is a friend.
CASSIO [*to* SECOND GENTLEMAN]:   See for the news.

          [*Exit* SECOND GENTLEMAN.]

95   —Good ensign, you are welcome. [*He kisses* EMILIA.]
     Welcome, mistress.
     —Let it not gall your patience, good Iago,
     That I extend my manners: 'tis my breeding
     That gives me this bold show of courtesy.
IAGO: Sir, would she give you so° much of her lips   *as*
100 As of her tongue° she oft bestows on me,   (*scolding*); (*kissing*)
     You would have enough.
DESDEMONA: Alas, she has no speech![2]
IAGO: In faith, too much:
     I find it still when I have leave to sleep.
     Marry, before your ladyship I grant
105 She puts her tongue a little in her heart,[3]
     And chides with thinking.
EMILIA: You have little cause to say so.
IAGO: Come on! Come on! You are pictures out of door,
     Bells in your parlors, wildcats in your kitchens,
110 Saints in your injuries, devils being offended,

---

2. Perhaps: Alas, the accused scolding chatterbox is not even rising to her own defense (both a
defense of Emilia and a prod for her to speak).
3. She keeps her (critical) thoughts to herself.

Players in your housewifery, and housewives in
 your beds.[4]
DESDEMONA: Oh, fie upon thee, slanderer!
IAGO: Nay, it is true, or else I am a Turk:
 You rise to play, and go to bed to work.
EMILIA: You shall not write my praise.
IAGO: No, let me not.   115
DESDEMONA: What wouldst write of me, if thou shouldst
 praise me?
IAGO: O gentle lady, do not put me to't,
 For I am nothing if not critical.
DESDEMONA: Come on: assay.° There's one gone to the harbor? *try*
IAGO: Ay, madam.   120
DESDEMONA: I am not merry, but I do beguile°   *disguise*
 The thing I am° by seeming otherwise.   *(worried for Othello)*
 Come, how wouldst thou praise me?
IAGO: I am about it,
 But, indeed, my invention comes from my pate
 As birdlime[5] does from frieze:° it plucks out brains *coarse wool cloth* 125
  and all.
 But my muse labors° and thus she is delivered: *(in childbirth)*
 "If she be fair and wise, fairness and wit,
 The one's for use, the other useth it."[6]
DESDEMONA: Well praised. How if she be black[7] and witty?
IAGO: "If she be black and thereto have a wit,   130
 She'll find a white[8] that shall her blackness fit."° *(sexual)*
DESDEMONA: Worse and worse!
EMILIA: How if fair and foolish?
IAGO: "She never yet was foolish that was fair,
 For even her folly° helped her to an heir." *foolishness; lechery*
DESDEMONA: These are old fond° paradoxes to make fools *foolish* 135
 laugh i'th' alehouse. What miserable praise hast thou for
 her that's foul° and foolish?   *ugly*
IAGO: "There's none so foul and foolish thereunto° *to boot*
 But does foul° pranks which fair and wise ones do." *lascivious*
DESDEMONA: Oh, heavy ignorance: thou praisest the worst 140
 best! But what praise couldst thou bestow on a deserving
 woman indeed? One that in the authority° of her merit *on the strength*
 did justly put on the vouch° of very malice itself? *compel the approval*
IAGO: "She that was ever fair and never proud,

---

4. Iago shifts from Emilia to women generally in this speech. *Pictures:* models of silent propriety.
Bells: noisy. *Kitchens:* perhaps domestic affairs generally, rather than a specific room. *Saints:* martyrs.
Players in your housewifery: deceptive in managing household expenses. *Housewives:* wanton (perhaps
businesslike, or sparing of sexual favors).
5. Sticky substance used to trap small birds.
6. Intelligence makes use of beauty.
7. Dark-haired; dark-complexioned.
8. Fair-skinned person ("wight" means "person").

145 Had tongue at will and yet was never loud,
  Never lacked gold and yet went never gay,°   *lavishly clothed*
  Fled from her wish and yet said, 'Now I may';[9]
  She that being angered, her revenge being nigh,
  Bade her wrong stay° and her displeasure fly;   *sense of injury end*
150 She that in wisdom never was so frail
  To change the cod's head for the salmon's tail;[1]
  She that could think and never disclose her mind,
  See suitors following and not look behind;
  She was a wight,° if ever such wights were"— *(play on "white," line 131)*
155 DESDEMONA: To do what?
 IAGO: "To suckle fools and chronicle small beer."[2]
 DESDEMONA: Oh, most lame and impotent conclusion! —Do
  not learn of° him, Emilia, though he be thy husband. —How *from*
  say you, Cassio? Is he not a most profane and liberal° *outspoken*
160 counselor?
 CASSIO: He speaks home,° madam: you may relish him *forcefully*
  More in° the soldier than in the scholar. *as*
 IAGO [*aside*]: He takes her by the palm. Ay, well said:° whis- *well done*
  per! With as little a web as this will I ensnare as great a
165 fly as Cassio. Ay, smile upon her, do! I will give° thee in *shackle*
  thine own courtship.° [*to* CASSIO] You say true; 'tis so *courtliness*
  indeed. [*aside*] If such tricks as these strip you out of your
  lieutenantry, it had been better you had not kissed your
  three fingers[3] so oft, which now, again, you are most apt to
170 play the sir° in. Very good: well kissed and excellent curtsy! *gentleman*
  [*to* CASSIO] 'Tis so indeed. [*aside*] Yet again your fingers to
  your lips? Would they were clyster-pipes° for your sake. *enema tubes*

    [*Trumpets within.*]

   —The Moor! I know his trumpet.
 CASSIO: 'Tis truly so.
 DESDEMONA: Let's meet him and receive him.

    Enter OTHELLO *and Attendants.*

 CASSIO: Lo, where he comes!
 OTHELLO: O my fair warrior!
175 DESDEMONA: My dear Othello!
 OTHELLO: It gives me wonder great as my content
  To see you here before me. O my soul's joy!
  If after every tempest come such calms,
  May the winds blow till they have wakened death,

---

9. Voluntarily withstood temptation even when given the choice.
1. To make an unworthy exchange. Probably also suggesting sexual infidelity; "cod" means "penis,"
and "tail" equals "vulva."
2. To breast-feed babies and keep track of trivial domestic goods. That is, such perfect virtue suits
only a dull, complacent, decidedly ungenteel housewife.
3. Kissing one's own hand was a common courtly gesture from a gentleman to a lady.

And let the laboring bark° climb hills of seas   *small ship* 180
Olympus-high,⁴ and duck again as low
As hell's° from heaven. If it were now to die,   *hell is*
'Twere now to be most happy—for I fear
My soul hath her content° so absolute   *contentment*
That not another comfort like to this   185
Succeeds° in unknown fate.°   *Will follow / future*

DESDEMONA: The heavens forbid
But that our loves and comforts should increase
Even as our days do grow.

OTHELLO: Amen to that, sweet powers!
I cannot speak enough of this content;
It° stops me here.° It is too much of joy.   *(Emotion) / now; in my heart* 190

    [*They kiss.*]

And this, and this, the greatest discords be
That e'er our hearts shall make.

IAGO [*aside*]:   Oh, you are well tuned now,
But I'll set down the pegs that make this music,⁵
As honest as I am.

OTHELLO: Come, let us to the castle.
—News, friends! Our wars are done. The Turks are   195
    drowned.
How does° my old acquaintance of this isle?   *fares*
[*to* DESDEMONA] Honey, you shall be well desired° in Cyprus: *welcomed*
I have found great love amongst them. O my sweet,
I prattle out of fashion, and I dote
In mine own comforts.—I prithee, good Iago,   200
Go to the bay and disembark my coffers.
Bring thou the master° to the citadel: *captain*
He is a good one, and his worthiness
Does challenge° much respect.—Come, Desdemona.   *deserve*
—Once more, well met at Cyprus.   205

    Exeunt [all but IAGO *and* RODERIGO].

IAGO: Do thou meet me presently at the harbor. Come thither.
If thou beest valiant—as they say base° men being in love   *lowly born*
have then a nobility in their natures more than is native to
them—list° me. The lieutenant tonight watches on the   *listen to*
court of guard.⁶ First, I must tell thee this: Desdemona is   210
directly in love with him.

RODERIGO: With him? Why, 'tis not possible!

IAGO [*putting a finger to his lips*]:   Lay thy finger thus, and let
thy soul be instructed. Mark me with what violence she

4. Mount Olympus, home of the Greek gods and hence too high for mortals.
5. I'll untune (by loosening) the "pegs" that hold the strings of a musical instrument taut.
6. Cassio is in charge of the watch at the guardhouse.

215 first loved the Moor but° for bragging and telling her fantas-   *merely*
     tical lies. To love him still for prating? Let not thy discreet
     heart think it. Her eye must be fed, and what delight shall
     she have to look on the devil? When the blood is made dull
     with the act of sport, there should° be a game° to inflame   *needs to / (sexual)*
220 it and to give satiety a fresh appetite: loveliness in favor,°   *looks; appearance*
     sympathy in years, manners, and beauties—all which the
     Moor is defective in. Now, for want of these required con-
     veniences,° her delicate tenderness will find itself abused,[7]   *agreements; advantages*
     begin to heave the gorge,° disrelish, and abhor the Moor: *feel nausea*
225 very nature° will instruct her in it, and compel her to some   *nature itself*
     second choice. Now, sir, this granted—as it is a most preg-
     nant° and unforced position—who stands so eminent in   *obvious; (sexual)*
     the degree of[8] this fortune as Cassio does? A knave very
     voluble,° no further conscionable° than in putting on the   *facile / no more ethical*
230 mere form of civil and humane seeming° for the better   *courteous appearance*
     compass° of his salt° and most hidden loose affection.   *achievement / lewd*
     Why, none! Why, none! A slipper° and subtle knave, a   *slippery*
     finder of occasion that has an eye can stamp and counter-
     feit advantages, though true advantage[9] never present itself.
235 A devilish knave! Besides, the knave is handsome, young,
     and hath all those requisites in him that folly° and green   *wantonness*
     minds look after.° A pestilent° complete knave, and the   *seek / damnably*
     woman hath found him already.
     RODERIGO: I cannot believe that in her: she's full of most
240 blessed condition.
     IAGO: Blessed fig's end!° The wine she drinks is made of   *(obscene)*
     grapes. If she had been blessed, she would never have
     loved the Moor. Blessed pudding!° Didst thou not see her   *sausage*
     paddle° with the palm of his hand? Didst not mark that?   *fiddle*
245 RODERIGO: Yes, that I did; but that was but courtesy.
     IAGO: Lechery, by this hand. An index and obscure° pro-   *encoded*
     logue to the history° of lust and foul thoughts.[1] They   *story*
     met so near with their lips that their breaths embraced
     together. Villainous thoughts, Roderigo! When these
250 mutabilities so marshal the way, hard at hand comes the
     master and main exercise:[2] th'incorporate° conclusion.   *fleshly; physical*
     Pish! But, sir, be you ruled by me. I have brought you
     from Venice. Watch you tonight for the command; I'll
     lay't upon you.[3] Cassio knows you not. I'll not be far from
255 you. Do you find some occasion to anger Cassio, either by

7. Mistreated; deceived.
8. As next in line for.
9. Who can (like a counterfeiter) mint his own opportunities.
1. The analogy is to a dirty book. *Index*: table of contents.
2. When these intimacies have cleared the way, the main event follows close behind. Here, the analogy is to an official procession.
3. Stand watch tonight. I'll see that you receive orders.

speaking too loud, or tainting° his discipline, or from   *insulting*
what other course you please, which the time shall more
favorably minister.°   *provide*

RODERIGO: Well?

IAGO: Sir, he's rash and very sudden in choler,° and happily°   *anger / to our benefit* 260
may strike at you. Provoke him that he may, for even out of
that will I cause these of Cyprus to mutiny, whose qualification shall come into no true taste again[4] but by the dis-
planting of Cassio. So shall you have a shorter journey to
your desires by the means I shall then have to prefer° them,   *promote* 265
and the impediment most profitably removed, without the
which there were no expectation of our prosperity.

RODERIGO: I will do this, if you can bring it to any opportunity.

IAGO: I warrant thee. Meet me by and by at the citadel. I
must fetch his necessaries° ashore. Farewell.   *Othello's possessions* 270

RODERIGO: Adieu.   *Exit.*

IAGO: That Cassio loves her, I do well believe't;
    That she loves him, 'tis apt and of great credit.°   *likely and believable*
    The Moor, howbeit that I endure him not,
    Is of a constant, loving, noble nature,   275
    And I dare think he'll prove to Desdemona
    A most dear° husband. Now I do love her, too,   *affectionate; costly*
    Not out of absolute lust—though, peradventure,°   *perhaps*
    I stand accountant° for as great a sin—   *accountable*
    But partly led to diet° my revenge,   *feed* 280
    For that° I do suspect the lusty Moor   *Because*
    Hath leaped into my seat,° the thought whereof   *slept with my wife*
    Doth like a poisonous mineral gnaw my inwards,°   *innards*
    And nothing can, or shall, content my soul
    Till I am evened with him, wife for wife.   285
    Or, failing so, yet that I put the Moor,
    At least, into a jealousy so strong
    That judgment cannot cure. Which thing to do,
    If this poor trash of Venice, whom I trace
    For his quick hunting, stand the putting-on,[5]   290
    I'll have our Michael Cassio on the hip;°   *at my mercy*
    Abuse° him to the Moor in the right garb°—   *Slander / manner*
    For I fear Cassio with my night-cape,° too—   *wife (sexual)*
    Make the Moor thank me, love me, and reward me
    For making him egregiously an ass   295
    And practicing upon° his peace and quiet   *undermining*
    Even to madness. 'Tis here,° but yet confused: *My plan is here*
    Knavery's plain face is never seen till used.   *Exit.*

---

4. Who will not be adequately appeased.
5. If Roderigo, whom I follow (?), train (?), puts weights on to slow him down (?), is successfully set
on the hunt when incited.

Scene 2

A street in Cyprus. Enter Othello's HERALD *with a proclamation.*

HERALD [*reads*]: "It is Othello's pleasure, our noble and
valiant general, that upon certain tidings now arrived,
importing the mere perdition° of the Turkish fleet, every   *entire loss*
man put himself into triumph: some to dance, some to
5   make bonfires, each man to what sport and revels his
addition° leads him. For, besides these beneficial news, it   *rank*
is the celebration of his° nuptial." So much was his plea-   *(Othello's)*
sure should be proclaimed. All offices° are open, and there   *storehouses*
is full liberty of feasting from this present hour of five till
10   the bell have told eleven. Bless the isle of Cyprus and our
noble general Othello!   *Exit.*

Scene 3

The citadel at Cyprus. Enter OTHELLO, DESDEMONA,
CASSIO, *and Attendants.*

OTHELLO: Good Michael, look you to the guard tonight.
Let's teach ourselves that honorable stop°   *self-restraint*
Not to out-sport° discretion.   *pass the limits of*
CASSIO: Iago hath direction what to do,
5   But notwithstanding with my personal eye
Will I look to't.
OTHELLO: Iago is most honest.
Michael, good night: tomorrow with your earliest
Let me have speech with you.—Come, my dear love.
The purchase made, the fruits are to ensue:
10   That profit's yet to come tween me and you.[6]
—Good night.   *Exeunt* [OTHELLO *and* DESDEMONA].

Enter IAGO.

CASSIO: Welcome, Iago. We must to the watch.
IAGO: Not this hour, lieutenant: 'tis not yet ten o'th' clock.
Our general cast° us thus early for the love of his Desde-   *dismissed*
15   mona, who let us not therefore blame: he hath not yet
made wanton the night with her, and she is sport for Jove.
CASSIO: She's a most exquisite lady.
IAGO: And, I'll warrant her, full of game.°   *spirit; (sexual)*
CASSIO: Indeed, she's a most fresh and delicate creature.
20 IAGO: What an eye she has! Methinks it sounds a parley° to   *(military) call*
provocation.
CASSIO: An inviting eye, and yet methinks right modest.

6. We haven't yet consummated our marriage.

IAGO: And when she speaks, is it not an alarum° to love?   *a call (to arms)*

CASSIO: She is indeed perfection.

IAGO: Well, happiness to their sheets. Come, lieutenant, I   25
have a stoup° of wine, and here without° are a brace of°   *bottle / outside / two*
Cyprus gallants that would fain have a measure° to the   *would like to drink*
health of black Othello.

CASSIO: Not tonight, good Iago. I have very poor and
unhappy brains for drinking: I could well wish courtesy   30
would invent some other custom° of entertainment.   *customary form*

IAGO: Oh, they are our friends! But one cup: I'll drink for you.

CASSIO: I have drunk but one cup tonight—and that was
craftily qualified,° too—and behold what innovation° it   *well diluted / disorder*
makes here. I am infortunate in the infirmity, and dare   35
not task my weakness with any more.

IAGO: What, man? 'Tis a night of revels. The gallants desire it.

CASSIO: Where are they?

IAGO: Here, at the door. I pray you call them in.

CASSIO: I'll do't, but it dislikes me.°   *Exit.*   *I don't like doing it*   40

IAGO: If I can fasten but one cup upon him
With that which he hath drunk tonight already,
He'll be as full of quarrel and offense°   *ready to take offense*
As my young mistress' dog. Now, my sick fool Roderigo,
Whom love hath turned almost the wrong side out,   45
To Desdemona hath tonight caroused
Potations pottle-deep, and he's to watch.[7]
Three else° of Cyprus—noble swelling° spirits   *other men / proud*
That hold their honors in a wary distance,[8]
The very elements° of this warlike isle—   *character(istic)s*   50
Have I tonight flustered with flowing cups,
And they watch, too. Now 'mongst this flock of
       drunkards
And I put to° our Cassio in some action°   *to put / fight*
That may offend the isle.

           Enter CASSIO, MONTANO, *and* [*three*] GENTLEMEN
           [*with wine*].

                    But here they come.
If consequence do but approve my dream,[9]   55
My boat sails freely both with wind and stream.°   *current*

CASSIO: Fore heaven, they have given me a rouse° already!   *full draft*

MONTANO: Good faith, a little one: not past a pint, as I am a
soldier!

IAGO: —Some wine, ho!   60
   [*sings*]   And let me the cannikin° clink, clink,   *drinking vessel*

---

7. Consumed drink to the bottom of the tankard, and he's set to watch Cassio.
8. Who are touchy about their honor.
9. If events turn out as I hope.

And let me the cannikin clink.
A soldier's a man, oh, man's life's but a span,
Why, then, let a soldier drink!

65   Some wine, boys!
CASSIO: Fore heaven, an excellent song!
IAGO: I learned it in England, where indeed they are most
potent in potting.[1] Your Dane, your German, and your swag°-   hanging
bellied Hollander—drink, ho!—are nothing to your English.
70 CASSIO: Is your Englishman so exquisite in his drinking?
IAGO: Why, he drinks you with facility° your Dane dead   easily drinks
drunk; he sweats not to overthrow your Almain;° he gives   German
your Hollander a vomit ere the next pottle° can be filled.   tankard
CASSIO: To the health of our general!
75 MONTANO: I am for it, lieutenant, and I'll do you justice.°   match your drinking
IAGO: O sweet England!
[sings]   King Stephen was and a worthy peer,
His breeches cost him but a crown;
He held them sixpence all too dear,
80   With that he called the tailor "loon."°   lout
He was a wight of high renown
And thou art but of low degree:
'Tis pride that pulls the country down,
And take thy old cloak about thee.[2]
85   —Some wine, ho!
CASSIO: Why, this is a more exquisite song than the other!
IAGO: Will you hear't again?
CASSIO: No, for I hold him to be unworthy of his place that
does those things. Well, heaven's above all, and there be
90   souls must be saved, and there be souls must not be saved.[3]
IAGO: It's true, good lieutenant.
CASSIO: For mine own part, no offense to the general nor
any man of quality,° I hope to be saved.   rank
IAGO: And so do I, too, lieutenant.
95 CASSIO: Ay, but by your leave, not before me! The lieutenant
is to be saved before the ensign. Let's have no more of
this. Let's to our affairs. Forgive us our sins.—Gentlemen,
let's look to our business. Do not think, gentlemen, I am
drunk: this is my ensign, this is my right hand, and this is
100   my left. I am not drunk now: I can stand well enough and
I speak well enough.

---

1. Most adept at drinking (self-referential joke).
2. From the early ballad often called "The Old Cloak," in which a farmer who wants to trade his old
clothes for a courtier's expensive attire is convinced by his wife to be satisfied with his lot in life; the
wife is the speaker of the lines Iago sings.
3. Referring to the idea of predestination, the belief held by Calvinist Protestants that some souls are
destined from the outset to be saved and others damned.

GENTLEMEN: Excellent well.

CASSIO: Why, very well, then: you must not think, then, that
I am drunk.   *Exit.*

MONTANO: To th' platform, masters. Come, let's set the watch.   105

[*Exeunt* GENTLEMEN.]

IAGO: You see this fellow that is gone before?
    He's a soldier fit to stand by Caesar[4]
    And give direction; and do but see his vice:
    'Tis to his virtue a just equinox,°   *of equal size*
    The one as long as th'other. 'Tis pity of him.°   *It's a shame*   110
    I fear the trust Othello puts him in
    On some odd time of his infirmity
    Will shake this island.

MONTANO: But is he often thus?

IAGO: 'Tis evermore his prologue to his sleep:
    He'll watch the horologe a double set[5]   115
    If drink rock not his cradle.

MONTANO: It were well
    The general were put in mind° of it.   *told*
    Perhaps he sees it not, or his good nature
    Prizes the virtue that appears in Cassio
    And looks not on his evils. Is not this true?—   120

Enter RODERIGO.

IAGO [*aside*]:   How now, Roderigo?
    I pray you, after the lieutenant: go!   [*Exit* RODERIGO.]

MONTANO: —And 'tis great pity that the noble Moor
    Should hazard such a place as his own second
    With one of an engraft° infirmity.   *ingrained*   125
    It were an honest action to say so
    To the Moor.

IAGO: Not I, for this fair island!
    I do love Cassio well, and would do much
    To cure him of this evil. But hark, what noise?

Enter CASSIO *pursuing* RODERIGO.

CASSIO: You rogue! You rascal!

MONTANO: What's the matter, lieutenant?   130

CASSIO: A knave teach me my duty?
    I'll beat the knave into a twiggen bottle.[6]

RODERIGO: Beat me?

CASSIO: Dost thou prate, rogue?

MONTANO: Nay, good lieutenant!

4. Ancient Roman general-turned-emperor Julius Caesar (100–44 BCE).
5. He'll stay up twice around the clock.
6. Wicker-cased. Hence, smash to pieces or, perhaps, produce wicker-like lashes on Roderigo's back.

I pray you, sir, hold your hand.

CASSIO: Let me go, sir,

    Or I'll knock you o'er the mazard.°   *head*

135 MONTANO: Come, come! You're drunk.

CASSIO: Drunk?

    [*They fight.*]

IAGO [*aside to* RODERIGO]:   Away, I say! Go out and cry a mutiny.

                          [*Exit* RODERIGO.]

    —Nay, good lieutenant. Alas, gentlemen!

    —Help, ho!—Lieutenant! Sir!—Montano!

140   —Help, masters!—Here's a goodly watch indeed.

    [*A bell rings.*]

    Who's that which rings the bell? *Diablo!*° Ho!   *Devil!*

    The town will rise.—Fie, fie, lieutenant,

    You'll be ashamed for ever.

          Enter OTHELLO *and Attendants.*

OTHELLO: What is the matter here?

MONTANO: I bleed still. I am hurt to th' death. He dies!

145 OTHELLO: Hold, for your lives!

IAGO: Hold, ho! Lieutenant! Sir! Montano! Gentlemen!

    Have you forgot all place of sense and duty?

    Hold! The general speaks to you. Hold, for shame!

OTHELLO: Why, how now? Ho! From whence ariseth this?

150   Are we turned Turks, and to ourselves do that

    Which heaven hath forbid the Ottomites?°   (*by raising a storm*)

    For Christian shame, put by this barbarous brawl.

    He that stirs next to carve for his own rage°   *draw a sword in anger*

    Holds his soul light: he dies upon his motion.

155   [*to Attendants*] Silence that dreadful bell: it frights the isle

    From her propriety.   [*Exit Attendant.*]

              —What is the matter, masters?

    —Honest Iago, that looks dead with grieving,

    Speak. Who began this? On thy love I charge thee.

IAGO: I do not know. Friends all but now; even now

160   In quarter° and in terms like bride and groom   *Under control*

    Devesting them° for bed; and then but now,   *Getting undressed*

    As if some planet° had unwitted men,   *astrological influence*

    Swords out, and tilting one at other's breasts

    In opposition bloody. I cannot speak

165   Any beginning to this peevish odds,°   *capricious quarrel*

    And would° in action glorious I had lost   *wish that*

    Those legs that brought me to a part of it.

OTHELLO: How comes it, Michael, you are thus forgot?°   *you thus forgot yourself*

CASSIO: I pray you, pardon me: I cannot speak.

OTHELLO: Worthy Montano, you were wont to be° civil: *you used to be*   170
    The gravity and stillness of your youth
    The world hath noted, and your name is great
    In mouths of wisest censure.° What's the matter°   *judgment / Why is it*
    That you unlace your reputation thus,
    And spend° your rich opinion° for the name   *exchange / good reputation*   175
    Of a night-brawler? Give me answer to it!

MONTANO: Worthy Othello, I am hurt to danger.
    Your officer, Iago, can inform you
    While I spare speech, which something now
      offends me,°   *somewhat now pains me*
    Of all that I do know. Nor know I aught°   *anything*   180
    By me that's said or done amiss this night,
    Unless self-charity° be sometimes a vice,   *care of oneself*
    And to defend ourselves it be a sin
    When violence assails us.

OTHELLO: Now, by heaven,
    My blood begins my safer guides to rule   185
    And passion, having my best judgment collied,[7]
    Assays to lead the way! If I once stir
    Or do but lift this arm, the best of you
    Shall sink in my rebuke. Give me to know
    How this foul rout began, who set it on,   190
    And he that is approved in° this offense,   *shown culpable of*
    Though he had twinned with me, both at a birth,
    Shall lose me. What, in a town of war
    Yet° wild, the peoples' hearts brimful of fear,   *Still*
    To manage° private and domestic quarrel   *carry on*   195
    In night, and on the court and guard of safety?[8]
    'Tis monstrous! Iago, who began't?

MONTANO [*to* IAGO]:   If partially affined or league in office,[9]
    Thou dost deliver more or less than truth,
    Thou art no soldier.

IAGO: Touch me not so near.   200
    I had rather have this tongue cut from my mouth
    Than it should do offense to Michael Cassio.
    Yet, I persuade myself, to speak the truth
    Shall nothing wrong him. This it is, general:
    Montano and myself being in speech,   205
    There comes a fellow crying out for help
    And Cassio following him with determined sword
    To execute upon° him. Sir, this gentleman   *attack*

       [*indicating* MONTANO]

---

7. Obscured by anger (choler); darkened racially.
8. At night, and at the place where safety and security are at stake (on the night watch).
9. If biased (in favor of Cassio) by your ties to him or (by) your holding office together.

Steps in to Cassio and entreats his pause.
210　Myself the crying fellow did pursue
Lest by his clamor, as it so fell out,
The town might fall in fright. He, swift of foot,
Outran my purpose, and I returned then rather
For that° I heard the clink and fall of swords 　　　　　　　*Because*
215　And Cassio high in oath, which till tonight
I ne'er might say before. When I came back—
For this was brief—I found them close together
At blow and thrust, even as again they were
When you yourself did part them.
220　More of this matter cannot I report.
But men are men: the best sometimes forget.
Though Cassio did some little wrong to him,° 　　　　　　　*(Roderigo)*
As men in rage strike those that wish them best,
Yet surely Cassio, I believe, received
225　From him that fled some strange indignity
Which patience could not pass.° 　　　　　　　　　　　　*let pass*
OTHELLO: 　　　　　　　　　　I know, Iago,
Thy honesty and love doth mince° this matter, 　　　　　　*minimize*
Making it light to Cassio.—Cassio, I love thee,
But never more be officer of mine.

Enter DESDEMONA [*and Attendants*].

230　Look if my gentle love be not raised up—
[*to* CASSIO] I'll make thee an example.
DESDEMONA: What is the matter, dear?
OTHELLO: 　　　　　　　　　　　All's well, sweeting.
Come away to bed. [*to* MONTANO] Sir, for your hurts
Myself will be your surgeon. [*to Attendants*] Lead him off.
235　—Iago, look with care about the town,
And silence those whom this vile brawl distracted.
—Come, Desdemona. 'Tis the soldier's life
To have their balmy slumbers waked with strife.

Exeunt [all but IAGO *and* CASSIO].

IAGO: What, are you hurt, lieutenant?
240　CASSIO: Ay, past all surgery.
IAGO: Marry, heaven forbid!
CASSIO: Reputation, reputation, reputation! Oh, I have lost
　　my reputation! I have lost the immortal part of myself,
　　and what remains is bestial. My reputation, Iago, my
245　reputation!
IAGO: As I am an honest man, I had thought you had received
　　some bodily wound; there is more sense in that than in
　　reputation. Reputation is an idle and most false impos-
　　ition,° oft got without merit and lost without deserving. 　*artificial notion*
250　You have lost no reputation at all, unless you repute your-
　　self such a loser. What, man, there are more ways to

recover the general again! You are but now cast in his
mood;° a punishment more in policy[1] than in malice, even   *dismissed in anger*
so as one would beat his offenseless dog to affright an
imperious lion. Sue to° him again, and he's yours.   *Petition* 255

CASSIO: I will rather sue to be despised than to deceive so
good a commander with so slight, so drunken, and so
indiscreet an officer. Drunk? And speak parrot?° And   *rant on*
squabble, swagger, swear? And discourse fustian° with   *nonsense*
one's own shadow? O thou invisible spirit of wine, if thou   260
hast no name to be known by, let us call thee "devil."

IAGO: What was he that you followed with your sword?
What had he done to you?

CASSIO: I know not.

IAGO: Is't possible?   265

CASSIO: I remember a mass of things, but nothing distinctly;
a quarrel, but nothing wherefore.° Oh, that men should   *but not its cause*
put an enemy in their mouths to steal away their brains!
That we should with joy, pleasance,° revel, and applause   *delight; recreation*
transform ourselves into beasts!   270

IAGO: Why, but you are now well enough. How came you
thus recovered?

CASSIO: It hath pleased the devil drunkenness to give place
to the devil wrath: one unperfectness° shows me another   *fault*
to make me frankly despise myself.   275

IAGO: Come, you are too severe a moraler.° As the time, the   *moralizer*
place, and the condition of this country stands, I could
heartily wish this had not befallen; but since it is as it is,
mend it, for your own good.

CASSIO: I will ask him for my place again; he shall tell me I   280
am a drunkard. Had I as many mouths as Hydra,[2] such an
answer would stop them all. To be now a sensible man, by
and by a fool, and presently a beast! Oh, strange! Every
inordinate cup is unblessed, and the ingredient is a devil.

IAGO: Come, come: good wine is a good familiar creature, if   285
it be well used. Exclaim no more against it. And, good
lieutenant, I think you think I love you?

CASSIO: I have well approved° it, sir.—I, drunk?   *tested*

IAGO: You, or any man living, may be drunk at a° time, man. I   *some*
tell you what you shall do. Our general's wife is now the   290
general—I may say so, in this respect, for that he hath
devoted and given up himself to the contemplation, mark,
and devotement of° her parts° and graces. Confess your-   *devotion to / qualities*
self freely to her; importune her help to put you in your
place° again. She is of so free, so kind, so apt, so blessed a   *office* 295
disposition, she holds it a vice in her goodness not to do

1. More as a matter of policy (of public example).
2. Mythical serpent with many heads who grew two more when one was cut off.

more than she is requested.[3] This broken joint° between   *(of a bone)*
you and her husband entreat her to splinter° and, my for-   *heal with a splint*
tunes against any lay° worth naming, this crack of your   *wager*
300   love shall grow stronger than it was before.
CASSIO: You advise me well.
IAGO: I protest,° in the sincerity of love and honest kindness.   *insist*
CASSIO: I think it freely, and betimes° in the morning I will   *early*
beseech the virtuous Desdemona to undertake° for me. I   *stand up*
305   am desperate of my fortunes if they check° me!   *stop*
IAGO: You are in the right. Good night, lieutenant. I must to
    the watch.
CASSIO: Good night, honest Iago.   *Exit* CASSIO.
IAGO: And what's he, then, that says I play the villain
310   When this advice is free I give, and honest,
     Probal° to thinking, and indeed the course   *Wise*
     To win the Moor again? For 'tis most easy
     Th'inclining° Desdemona to subdue   *The well-disposed*
     In any honest suit: she's framed as fruitful°   *generous*
315   As the free elements.° And then for her   *unconstrained nature*
     To win the Moor—were° to renounce his baptism,   *even if it were*
     All seals and symbols of redeemed sin—
     His soul is so enfettered to her love
     That she may make, unmake, do what she list,°   *wishes; wills*
320   Even as her appetite[4] shall play the god
     With his weak function.° How am I then a villain   *(intellectual?); (sexual)*
     To counsel Cassio to this parallel° course   *suitable*
     Directly to his good? Divinity° of hell: *Theology*
     When devils will the blackest sins put on,
325   They do suggest at first with heavenly shows,
     As I do now. For whiles this honest fool
     Plies Desdemona to repair his fortune,
     And she for him pleads strongly to the Moor,
     I'll pour this pestilence into his° ear: *(Othello's)*
330   That she repeals him for° her body's lust   *appeals for him (Cassio) due to*
     And, by how much she strives to do him good,
     She shall undo her credit with the Moor.
     So will I turn her virtue into pitch[5]
     And out of her own goodness make the net
335   That shall enmesh them all—

        Enter RODERIGO.

3. In these lines, Iago may covertly defame Desdemona, unbeknownst to Cassio, through double entendre; line 291: "general" (generally accessible sexually); line 293: "parts"; line 294: "put you in your place" (penetration in intercourse); line 295: "free" (generous, erotically open), "kind" (good-humored about agreeing to make love), "apt" (inclined to help, to engage in amorous behavior). Similar undertones mark his ensuing soliloquy, lines 309–35.
4. Desdemona's wishes or desire for Othello; perhaps, his appetite for her.
5. Black, sticky substance used as a snare. The more the thing caught in it tries to escape, the more stuck it becomes.

—How now, Roderigo?

RODERIGO: I do follow here in the chase, not like a hound
    that hunts but one that fills up the cry.° My money is   *a pack follower*
    almost spent; I have been tonight exceedingly well cud-
    geled; and I think the issue will be I shall have so much°   *only this*
    experience for my pains. And so, with no money at all   340
    and a little more wit, return again to Venice.
IAGO: How poor are they that have not patience!
    What wound did ever heal but by degrees?
    Thou know'st we work by wit and not by witchcraft,
    And wit depends on dilatory° time.   *drawn-out* 345
    Does't not go well? Cassio hath beaten thee,
    And thou by that small hurt hath cashiered° Cassio.   *dismissed*
    Though other things grow fair against the sun,
    Yet fruits that blossom first will first be ripe.[6]
    Content thyself awhile. In troth, 'tis morning!   350
    Pleasure and action make the hours seem short.
    Retire thee; go where thou art billeted.
    Away, I say! Thou shalt know more hereafter.
    Nay, get thee gone!   *Exit* RODERIGO.
            Two things are to be done:
    My wife must move° for Cassio to her mistress—   *plead* 355
    I'll set her on;
    Myself a while to draw the Moor apart
    And bring him jump° when he may Cassio find   *exactly*
    Soliciting his wife. Ay, that's the way.
    Dull not device by coldness and delay.[7]   *Exit.*   360

ACT III

Scene 1

Outside Othello and Desdemona's room. Enter CASSIO
[with] MUSICIANS.

CASSIO: Masters, play here—I will content° your pains—   *reward*
    Something that's brief, and bid "Good morrow, general."

    [MUSICIANS *play.*]
    [*Enter* CLOWN.]

CLOWN: Why, masters, have your instruments been in
    Naples, that they speak i'th' nose thus?[8]
MUSICIAN: How, sir? How?   5

6. Although others prosper only when fully in the sun, your plan will be successful even earlier in the
day (metaphorically) because started first and allowed to develop slowly.
7. Don't let sluggishness and slowness to act weaken the plot.
8. That they sound so nasal; perhaps a reference to venereal disease, often associated with Naples, or
a phallic or anal joke.

CLOWN: Are these, I pray you, wind instruments?[9]

MUSICIAN: Ay, marry are they, sir.

CLOWN: Oh, thereby hangs a tail!

MUSICIAN: Whereby hangs a tale, sir?

10 CLOWN: Marry, sir, by many a wind instrument that I know.
But, masters, here's money for you, and the general so
likes your music that he desires you, for love's sake,[1] to
make no more noise with it.

MUSICIAN: Well, sir, we will not!

15 CLOWN: If you have any music that may not° be heard, to't   *cannot*
again. But, as they say, to hear music the general does
not greatly care.

MUSICIAN: We have none such, sir.

CLOWN: Then put up your pipes in your bag, for I'll away.

20   Go, vanish into air. Away!   *Exeunt* MUSICIANS.

CASSIO: Dost thou hear, mine honest friend?

CLOWN: No, I hear not your honest friend: I hear you.

CASSIO: Prithee, keep up thy quillets.° There's a poor piece   *pack up your puns*
of gold for thee. If the gentlewoman that attends the gen-

25   eral be stirring, tell her there's one Cassio entreats her a
little favor of speech. Wilt thou do this?

CLOWN: She is stirring, sir. If she will stir hither, I shall
seem° to notify unto her.   *Exit* CLOWN.   *arrange*

      Enter IAGO.

CASSIO: In happy time,° Iago.   *I'm glad to see you*

IAGO: You have not been a-bed, then?

30 CASSIO: Why, no: the day had broke before we parted.
I have made bold, Iago, to send in to your wife:
My suit to her is that she will to virtuous
Desdemona procure me some access.

IAGO: I'll send her to you presently,°   *immediately*

35   And I'll devise a mean° to draw the Moor   *means; way*
Out of the way, that your converse and business
May be more free.

CASSIO: I humbly thank you for't.   *Exit* [IAGO].
                I never knew
A Florentine° more kind and honest.   *Even a fellow Florentine*

      Enter EMILIA.

40 EMILIA: Good morrow, good lieutenant. I am sorry
For your displeasure,° but all will sure be well: *troubles*
The general and his wife are talking of it,

---

9. The exchange that follows depends on the connections between wind instruments, flatulence, and "tale/tail."

1. Out of affection for him; so that his lovemaking won't be disturbed.

And she speaks for you stoutly. The Moor replies
That he you hurt is of great fame in Cyprus
And great affinity,° and that, in wholesome wisdom,   *well connected* 45
He might° not but refuse you. But he protests he   *could*
   loves you,
And needs no other suitor but his likings°   *affection for you*
To bring you in again.

CASSIO: Yet, I beseech you,
If you think fit, or that it may be done,
Give me advantage of some brief discourse   50
With Desdemon alone.

EMILIA: Pray you, come in.
I will bestow you where you shall have time
To speak your bosom° freely.   *heart*

CASSIO: I am much bound to you.

[Exeunt.]

Scene 2

The citadel. Enter OTHELLO, IAGO, *and* GENTLEMEN.

OTHELLO: These letters give, Iago, to the pilot,
And by him do my duties° to the Senate.°   *send my respects / (in Venice)*
That done, I will be walking on the works.°   *fortifications*
Repair there to me.

IAGO: Well, my good lord, I'll do't.

OTHELLO: —This fortification, gentlemen, shall we see't?   5

GENTLEMEN: We'll wait upon your lordship.   *Exeunt.*

Scene 3

The citadel's garden. Enter DESDEMONA, CASSIO,
and EMILIA.

DESDEMONA: Be thou assured, good Cassio, I will do
All my abilities° in thy behalf.   *I am able*

EMILIA: Good madam, do. I warrant it grieves my husband
As if the cause were his.

DESDEMONA: Oh, that's an honest fellow.—Do not doubt,   5
   Cassio,
But I will have my lord and you again
As friendly as you were.

CASSIO: Bounteous madam,
Whatever shall become of Michael Cassio,
He's never anything but your true servant.

DESDEMONA: I know't. I thank you. You do love my lord;   10
You have known him long and, be you well assured,

He shall in strangeness stand no farther off
Than in a politic distance.[2]

CASSIO: Ay, but, lady,
That policy may either last so long,

15   Or feed upon such nice and waterish diet,
Or breed itself so out of circumstances[3]
That, I being absent, and my place supplied,°   *filled*
My general will forget my love and service.

DESDEMONA: Do not doubt° that. Before Emilia here   *fear*

20   I give thee warrant° of thy place. Assure thee: *assurance*
If I do vow a friendship, I'll perform it
To the last article. My lord shall never rest:
I'll watch him tame, and talk him out of patience;[4]
His bed shall seem a school, his board a shrift;°   *confessional*

25   I'll intermingle everything he does
With Cassio's suit. Therefore be merry, Cassio,
For thy solicitor° shall rather die   *advocate*
Than give thy cause away.°   *up*

Enter OTHELLO *and* IAGO.

EMILIA: Madam, here comes my lord.
CASSIO: Madam, I'll take my leave.
DESDEMONA: Why, stay and hear me speak.

30 CASSIO: Madam, not now: I am very ill at ease,
Unfit for mine own purposes.
DESDEMONA: Well, do your discretion.°   *Exit* CASSIO.   *as you think best*
IAGO: Ha! I like not that.
OTHELLO: What dost thou say?
IAGO: Nothing, my lord, or if—I know not what.

35 OTHELLO: Was not that Cassio parted from my wife?
IAGO: Cassio, my lord? No, sure. I cannot think it
That he would steal away so guilty-like,
Seeing your coming.
OTHELLO: I do believe 'twas he.
DESDEMONA: How now, my lord?

40   I have been talking with a suitor here,
A man that languishes in your displeasure.
OTHELLO: Who is't you mean?
DESDEMONA: Why, your lieutenant, Cassio. Good my lord,
If I have any grace or power to move you,

45   His present reconciliation take:°   *Accept him now*
For if he be not one that truly loves you,
That errs in ignorance and not in cunning,°   *not knowingly*

---

2. He will distance himself from you only as much as good diplomacy requires.
3. Or persist based on such unimportant and poor justifications (perhaps: such pampered and juicy fare), or continue by chance.
4. I'll keep him awake until he obeys me, and talk to him beyond his endurance.

I have no judgment in° an honest face.   *cannot discern*
I prithee call him back.
OTHELLO: Went he hence now?
DESDEMONA: I'sooth,° so humbled   *Truly* 50
    That he hath left part of his grief with me
    To suffer with him. Good love, call him back.
OTHELLO: Not now, sweet Desdemon. Some other time.
DESDEMONA: But shall't be shortly?
OTHELLO: The sooner, sweet, for you.
DESDEMONA: Shall't be tonight at supper?
OTHELLO: No, not tonight.   55
DESDEMONA: Tomorrow dinner,° then?   *midday meal*
OTHELLO: I shall not dine at home:
    I meet the captains at the citadel.
DESDEMONA: Why, then, tomorrow night? On Tuesday morn?
    On Tuesday noon, or night? On Wednesday morn?
    I prithee,° name the time, but let it not   *pray (or ask) you* 60
    Exceed three days. In faith, he's penitent,
    And yet his trespass, in our common reason°—   *normal judgment*
    Save that, they say, the wars must make example
    Out of her° best—is not almost a fault   *(war's)*
    T'incur a private check.⁵ When shall he come?   65
    Tell me, Othello. I wonder in my soul
    What you would ask me that I should deny,
    Or stand so mammering° on? What, Michael Cassio   *hesitating*
    That came a-wooing with you, and so many a time
    When I have spoke of you dispraisingly   70
    Hath ta'en your part? To have so much to do
    To bring him in?° Trust me, I could do much.⁶   *into favor*
OTHELLO: Prithee, no more. Let him come when he will:
    I will deny thee nothing.
DESDEMONA: Why, this is not a boon.
    'Tis as° I should entreat you wear your gloves,   *as if* 75
    Or feed on nourishing dishes, or keep you warm,
    Or sue to you to do a peculiar profit°   *particular benefit*
    To your own person. Nay, when I have a suit
    Wherein I mean to touch your love indeed,
    It shall be full of poise° and difficult weight,   *balanced judgment* 80
    And fearful to be granted.⁷
OTHELLO: I will deny thee nothing.
    Whereon, I do beseech thee, grant me this:
    To leave me but a little to myself.
DESDEMONA: Shall I deny you? No. Farewell, my lord.   85

5. Is barely worth even private criticism.
6. Do much to make you regret your reluctance (?).
7. Desdemona argues that her request is trivial, that only a far more serious "suit" (line 78) would be
a real test of his devotion.

OTHELLO: Farewell, my Desdemona. I'll come to thee straight.°   *immediately*
DESDEMONA: Emilia, come. [*to* OTHELLO] Be as your fancies
    teach° you: *as your whims lead*
    Whate'er you be, I am obedient.

                Exeunt [DESDEMONA *and* EMILIA].

OTHELLO: Excellent wretch!° Perdition catch my soul   *(affectionate)*
90   But I do love thee; and when I love thee not,
    Chaos is come again.
IAGO: My noble lord?
OTHELLO: What dost thou say, Iago?
IAGO: Did Michael Cassio,
    When you wooed my lady, know of your love?
OTHELLO: He did, from first to last. Why dost thou ask?
95 IAGO: But for a satisfaction of my thought,
    No further harm.
OTHELLO: Why of thy thought, Iago?
IAGO: I did not think he had been acquainted with her.
OTHELLO: Oh, yes, and went between us very oft.
IAGO: Indeed?
100 OTHELLO: Indeed? Ay, indeed! Discern'st thou aught in that?
    Is he not honest?
IAGO: Honest, my lord?
OTHELLO: Honest? Ay, honest.
IAGO: My lord, for aught I know.
OTHELLO: What dost thou think?
IAGO: Think, my lord?
105 OTHELLO: "Think, my lord?" Alas, thou echo'st me
    As if there were some monster in thy thought
    Too hideous to be shown. Thou dost mean something.
    I heard thee say even now thou "lik'st not that"
    When Cassio left my wife. What didst not like?
110   And when I told thee he was of my counsel,°   *in my confidence*
    Of my whole course of wooing, thou cried'st "Indeed?"
    And didst contract and purse thy brow together
    As if thou then hadst shut up in thy brain
    Some horrible conceit.° If thou dost love me,   *conception*
115   Show me thy thought.
IAGO: My lord, you know I love you.
OTHELLO: I think thou dost.
    And, for° I know thou'rt full of love and honesty   *since*
    And weigh'st thy words before thou giv'st them breath,
    Therefore these stops° of thine fright me the more: *disruptive pauses*
120   For such things in a false, disloyal knave
    Are tricks of custom,° but in a man that's just   *habit*
    They're close dilations[8] working from the heart

8. Involuntary hesitations (expansions, censures) of interior, close-kept secrets.

That passion cannot rule.°   *control*

IAGO: For Michael Cassio,
 I dare be sworn, I think that he is honest.

OTHELLO I think so too.

IAGO: Men should be what they seem,   125
 Or those that be not, would they might seem none.[9]

OTHELLO: Certain, men should be what they seem.

IAGO: Why, then, I think Cassio's an honest man.

OTHELLO: Nay, yet there's more in this.
 I prithee, speak to me as to thy thinkings   130
 As thou dost ruminate, and give thy worst of thoughts
 The worst of words.

IAGO: Good my lord, pardon me.
 Though I am bound to every act of duty,
 I am not bound to that: all slaves are free.°   *(to hide their thoughts)*
 Utter my thoughts? Why, say they are vile and false—   135
 As where's that palace whereinto foul things
 Sometimes intrude not?—who has that breast so pure?—
 Wherein uncleanly apprehensions
 Keep leets and law-days, and in sessions sit
 With meditations lawful?[1]   140

OTHELLO: Thou dost conspire against thy friend,° Iago,   *(Othello)*
 If thou but think'st him wronged and mak'st his ear
 A stranger to thy thoughts.

IAGO: I do beseech you,
 Though I perchance am vicious° in my guess—   *culpably mistaken*
 As, I confess, it is my nature's plague   145
 To spy into abuses and of my jealousy°   *suspicion; envy*
 Shape faults that are not—that your wisdom
 From one that so imperfectly conceits°   *imagines*
 Would take no notice, nor build yourself a trouble
 Out of his scattering° and unsure observance.   *incoherent* 150
 It were not° for your quiet, nor your good,   *It would not be good*
 Nor for my manhood, honesty, and wisdom
 To let you know my thoughts.

OTHELLO: What dost thou mean?

IAGO: Good name in man and woman, dear my lord,
 Is the immediate jewel of their souls.   155
 Who steals my purse, steals trash: 'tis something,
  nothing;
 'Twas mine, 'tis his, and has been slave to thousands.
 But he that filches from me my good name
 Robs me of that which not enriches him
 And makes me poor indeed.

9. If only those who are not what they seem didn't seem to be what they are not.
1. (Even in pure breasts) illegitimate thoughts meet in court ("leets") from time to time (on "law-days")
and debate (in court "session") with legitimate ones.

160   OTHELLO: I'll know thy thoughts.
      IAGO: You cannot, if my heart were in your hand,
            Nor shall not, whilst 'tis in my custody.
      OTHELLO: Ha!
      IAGO: Oh, beware, my lord, of jealousy!
            It is the green-eyed monster which doth mock
165   The meat it feeds on.[2] That cuckold lives in bliss
            Who, certain of his fate, loves not his wronger;[3]
            But, oh, what damnèd minutes tells he o'er°   does he note pass by
            Who dotes, yet doubts; suspects, yet soundly loves.
      OTHELLO: Oh, misery!
170   IAGO: Poor and content is rich, and rich enough;
            But riches fineless° is as poor as winter   boundless
            To him that ever fears he shall be poor.
            Good heaven, the souls of all my tribe defend
            From jealousy!
      OTHELLO: Why? Why is this?
175   Think'st thou I'd make a life of jealousy,
            To follow still the changes of the moon°   Always madly to waver
            With fresh suspicions? No, to be once in doubt
            Is to be resolved.° Exchange me for a goat   to be finally settled
            When I shall turn the business of my soul
180   To such exufflicate and blowed° surmises,   inflated and blown-up
            Matching thy inference.° 'Tis not to make me jealous   implication
            To say my wife is fair, feeds well, loves company,
            Is free of speech, sings, plays, and dances:
            Where virtue is, these are more virtuous.
185   Nor from mine own weak merits will I draw
            The smallest fear or doubt of her revolt,°   or worry of her betrayal
            For she had eyes and chose me. No, Iago,
            I'll see before I doubt; when I doubt, prove;
            And, on the proof, there is no more but this:
190   Away at once with love or jealousy.
      IAGO: I am glad of this, for now I shall have reason
            To show the love and duty that I bear you
            With franker spirit. Therefore, as I am bound,
            Receive it from me, I speak not yet of proof:
195   Look to your wife; observe her well with Cassio.
            Wear your eyes thus: not jealous, nor secure.
            I would not have your free and noble nature
            Out of self-bounty be abused.[4] Look to't.
            I know our country° disposition well: (obscene wordplay)
200   In Venice they do let heaven see the pranks
            They dare not show their husbands; their best conscience

2. That tortures, as it consumes, the body and soul of the jealous person.
3. Who, knowing it is his fate to be cuckolded, doesn't love his wife.
4. Be deceived on account of your own goodness.

Is not to leave't undone but kept unknown.
OTHELLO: Dost thou say so?
IAGO: She did deceive her father, marrying you;
    And when she seemed to shake and fear your looks,   205
    She loved them most.
OTHELLO: And so she did.
IAGO: Why, go to,° then!   *that's it*
    She that so young could give out such a seeming
    To seal her father's eyes up, close as oak[5]—
    He thought 'twas witchcraft. But I am much to blame.
    I humbly do beseech you of your pardon   210
    For too much loving you.
OTHELLO: I am bound to thee for ever.
IAGO: I see this hath a little dashed your spirits.
OTHELLO: Not a jot, not a jot.
IAGO: Trust me, I fear it has.
    I hope you will consider what is spoke   215
    Comes from your love. But I do see you're moved.
    I am to pray you not to strain my speech
    To grosser issues,° nor to larger reach   *greater conclusions*
    Than to suspicion.
OTHELLO: I will not.
IAGO: Should you do so, my lord,   220
    My speech should fall into such vile success
    Which my thoughts aimed not at. Cassio's my worthy
       friend.
    My lord, I see you're moved.
OTHELLO: No, not much moved.
    I do not think but Desdemona's honest.
IAGO: Long live she so, and long live you to think so.   225
OTHELLO: And yet, how nature erring from itself—
IAGO: Ay, there's the point! As, to be bold with you,
    Not to affect° many proposed matches   *desire*
    Of her own clime, complexion,° and degree,°   *nature, skin color / rank*
    Whereto we see in all things nature tends.   230
    Faugh!° One may smell in such a will most rank,   *(expressing disgust)*
    Foul disproportions,° thoughts unnatural.   *abnormalities*
    But pardon me, I do not in position°   *argument*
    Distinctly speak of her, though I may fear
    Her will, recoiling to° her better judgment,   *resuming* 235
    May fall to match you with her country forms,[6]
    And happily° repent.   *perhaps*
OTHELLO: Farewell, farewell.
    If more thou dost perceive, let me know more.

---

5. Perhaps: to cover (the homonym "seel" means "to blind") her father's eyes as tightly as oak (a fine-grained wood).
6. May happen to compare you with Venetian (with obscene pun on "country") standards.

Set on thy wife to observe. Leave me, Iago.

240 IAGO: My lord, I take my leave.

OTHELLO: Why did I marry? This honest creature doubtless
Sees and knows more, much more, than he unfolds.

IAGO: My lord, I would I might entreat your honor
To scan this thing no farther: leave it to time.

245 Although 'tis fit that Cassio have his place—
For, sure, he fills it up with great ability—
Yet if you please to hold him off awhile,
You shall by that perceive him and his means.°   *(of regaining his job)*
Note if your lady strain his entertainment°   *urge his reception*

250 With any strong or vehement importunity:
Much will be seen in that. In the meantime,
Let me be thought too busy° in my fears—   *meddlesome*
As worthy cause I have to fear I am—
And hold her free,° I do beseech your honor.   *believe her innocent*

OTHELLO: Fear not my government.°   *self-conduct*

255 IAGO: I once more take my leave.

Exit.

OTHELLO: This fellow's of exceeding honesty,
And knows all quantities with a learned spirit
Of human dealings.[7] If I do prove her haggard,°   *wild (falconry)*
Though that her jesses were my dear heartstrings,

260 I'd whistle her off, and let her down the wind
To prey at fortune.[8] Haply, for° I am black   *Perhaps, because*
And have not those soft parts of° conversation°   *easy / manner; intercourse*
That chamberers° have, or for I am declined   *gallants; valets*
Into the vale of years—yet that's not much—

265 She's gone, I am abused,° and my relief   *deceived*
Must be to loathe her. O curse of marriage,
That we can call these delicate creatures ours
And not their appetites! I had rather be a toad
And live upon the vapor of a dungeon

270 Than keep a corner in the thing I love
For others' uses. Yet 'tis the plague to great ones:
Prerogatived° are they less than the base.°   *Privileged / lowborn*
'Tis destiny unshunnable, like death:
Even then, this forked plague is fated to us
When we do quicken.[9]

Enter DESDEMONA *and* EMILIA.

---

7. Amounts of a commodity in civil commercial transactions (literal); characteristics of human behavior (metaphorical).

8. Even if what tied her ("jesses" were leg straps put on a hawk) were my own heartstrings, I'd set her loose downwind forever to hunt on her own.

9. The "plague" of horns (imagined to grow from the forehead of a cuckold) is our fate as soon as we live.

                              Look where she comes!   275
          If she be false, heaven mocked itself.
          I'll not believe't.
DESDEMONA: How now, my dear Othello?
          Your dinner, and the generous° islanders   noble
          By you invited, do attend° your presence.   wait for
OTHELLO: I am to blame.
DESDEMONA: Why do you speak so faintly?   280
          Are you not well?
OTHELLO: I have a pain upon my forehead here.°   (from cuckold's horns)
DESDEMONA: Why, that's with watching;° 'twill away again.   from lack of sleep
          Let me but bind it hard, within this hour
          It will be well.
OTHELLO: Your napkin° is too little.   handkerchief 285
          Let it alone.

          [They drop the handkerchief.]

                    Come, I'll go in with you.
DESDEMONA: I am very sorry that you are not well.

                    Exeunt [OTHELLO and DESDEMONA].

EMILIA: I am glad I have found this napkin:

          [She picks up the handkerchief.]

          This was her first remembrance from the Moor.
          My wayward husband hath a hundred times   290
          Wooed me to steal it, but she so loves the token—
          For he conjured her[1] she should ever keep it—
          That she reserves it evermore about her
          To kiss and talk to. I'll have the work ta'en out,°   embroidery copied
          And giv't Iago. What he will do with it   295
          Heaven knows, not I.
          I nothing, but to please his fantasy.[2]

                    Enter IAGO.

IAGO: How now? What do you here alone?
EMILIA: Do not you chide: I have a thing for you.
IAGO: You have a thing for me? It is a common thing[3]—   300
EMILIA: Ha!
IAGO: —To have a foolish wife.
EMILIA: Oh, is that all? What will you give me now
          For that same handkerchief?
IAGO: What handkerchief?
EMILIA: What handkerchief?   305

1. Made her swear; perhaps also an unwitting backward glance at Brabanzio's charge in 1.3 that
Othello employed witchcraft to win Desdemona.
2. I do (know; intend) nothing, but to please his fancy (whim).
3. It is a vagina ("thing") available to all.

Why, that the Moor first gave to Desdemona;
That which so often you did bid me steal.

IAGO: Hast° stolen it from her?   *Have you*

EMILIA: No, but she let it drop by negligence,

310   And to th'advantage° I, being here, took't up.   *taking the opportunity*
Look, here 'tis.

IAGO: A good wench. Give it me.

EMILIA: What will you do with't, that you have been so earnest
To have me filch it?

IAGO: Why, what is that to you?

EMILIA: If it be not for some purpose of import,°   *importance*

315   Give't me again. Poor lady, she'll run mad
When she shall lack it.

IAGO: Be not acknown on't.°   *Conceal your role in it*
I have use for it. Go, leave me.   *Exit EMILIA.*
I will in Cassio's lodging lose° this napkin,   *misplace; let loose*
And let him find it. Trifles light as air

320   Are to the jealous confirmations strong
As proofs of holy writ. This may do something.
The Moor already changes with my poison:
Dangerous conceits° are in their natures poisons   *ideas*
Which, at the first, are scarce found to distaste

325   But, with a little,° act upon the blood,   *(time)*
Burn like the mines of sulfur.[4]

     Enter OTHELLO.

                          I did say so!
Look where he comes! Not poppy, nor mandragora,[5]
Nor all the drowsy syrups of the world
Shall ever medicine thee to that sweet sleep
Which thou owed'st° yesterday.   *owned; enjoyed*

330 OTHELLO: Ha! Ha! False to me?

IAGO: Why, how now, general? No more of that.

OTHELLO: Avaunt!° Be gone! Thou hast set me on the rack.[6]   *Leave me!*
I swear 'tis better to be much abused°   *mistreated; deceived*
Than but to know't a little.

IAGO: How now, my lord?

335 OTHELLO: What sense had I in her stolen hours of lust?
I saw't not, thought it not, it harmed not me;
I slept the next night well, fed well, was free and merry;
I found not Cassio's kisses on her lips.
He that is robbed, not wanting° what is stolen,   *missing*

340   Let him not know't, and he's not robbed at all.

---

4. Ancient Roman writer Pliny the Elder describes two islands of sulfur between mainland Italy and
Sicily that were rumored to be always on fire.
5. Sleep-inducing substance made from the mandrake root.
6. Torture device on which victims were stretched, dislocating their joints.

IAGO: I am sorry to hear this.
OTHELLO: I had been happy if the general camp,
    Pioneers° and all, had tasted her sweet body,   *Manual laborers*
    So° I had nothing known. Oh, now forever   *If only*
    Farewell the tranquil mind; farewell content;   345
    Farewell the plumèd troops and the big wars
    That makes ambition virtue! Oh, farewell,
    Farewell the neighing steed and the shrill trump,°   *trumpet*
    The spirit-stirring drum, th'ear-piercing fife,
    The royal banner, and all quality,°   *merit* 350
    Pride,° pomp, and circumstance° of glorious war.   *Magnificence / ceremony*
    And O you mortal engines,° whose rude throats   *deadly cannons*
    Th'immortal Jove's dread clamors° counterfeit,   *thunderclaps*
    Farewell. Othello's occupation's gone.
IAGO: Is't possible, my lord?   355
OTHELLO: Villain, be sure thou prove my love a whore;
    Be sure of it! Give me the ocular proof
    Or, by the worth of mine eternal soul,
    Thou hadst been better have been born a dog
    Than answer my waked wrath.
IAGO: Is't come to this?   360
OTHELLO: Make me to see't, or at the least so prove it
    That the probation° bear no hinge nor loop   *proof*
    To hang a doubt on, or woe upon thy life!
IAGO: My noble lord—
OTHELLO: If thou dost slander her and torture me,   365
    Never pray more; abandon all remorse;
    On horror's head horrors accumulate;
    Do deeds to make heaven weep, all earth amazed;
    For nothing canst thou to damnation add
    Greater than that.
IAGO: O grace! O heaven forgive me!   370
    Are you a man? Have you a soul, or sense?
    God b'wi'you; take mine office.[7] O wretched fool°   *(to himself)*
    That lov'st to make thine honesty a vice!°   *fault*
    O monstrous world! Take note, take note, O world:
    To be direct and honest is not safe.   375
    I thank you for this profit° and, from hence,   *profitable lesson*
    I'll love no friend, sith° love breeds such offense.   *since*
OTHELLO: Nay, stay: thou shouldst be honest.
IAGO: I should be wise, for honesty's a fool,
    And loses that° it works for.   *what*
OTHELLO: By the world,   380
    I think my wife be honest, and think she is not;
    I think that thou art just, and think thou art not.
    I'll have some proof. My name, that was as fresh

7. Good-bye, I resign my official position (ensign).

As Dian's[8] visage, is now begrimed and black
385 As mine own face. If there be cords or knives,
Poison or fire, or suffocating streams,[9]
I'll not endure it. Would I were satisfied!
IAGO: I see you are eaten up with passion;
I do repent me that I put it to you.
You would be satisfied?
390 OTHELLO: Would? Nay, and I will!
IAGO: And may. But how? How satisfied, my lord?
Would you the supervision grossly gape on?[1]
Behold her topped?°   *sexually mounted*
OTHELLO: Death and damnation! Oh!
IAGO: It were a tedious° difficulty, I think,   *disagreeable*
395 To bring them to that prospect.° Damn them, then,   *viewable position*
If ever mortal eyes do see them bolster°   *use a pillow*
More° than their own. What, then? How, then?   *Other*
What shall I say? Where's satisfaction?
It is impossible you should see this,
400 Were they as prime° as goats, as hot as monkeys,   *lustful*
As salt as wolves in pride,[2] and fools as gross
As ignorance made drunk. But yet, I say,
If imputation and strong circumstances[3]—
Which lead directly to the door of truth—
405 Will give you satisfaction, you might have't.
OTHELLO: Give me a living° reason she's disloyal.   *legitimate*
IAGO: I do not like the office.
But, sith I am entered in this cause so far—
Pricked to't° by foolish honesty and love—   *Prodded on*
410 I will go on. I lay with Cassio lately
And, being troubled with a raging tooth,
I could not sleep. There are a kind of men
So loose of soul that in their sleeps will mutter
Their affairs: one of this kind is Cassio.
415 In sleep I heard him say, "Sweet Desdemona,
Let us be wary. Let us hide our loves."
And then, sir, would he grip and wring my hand,
Cry, "O sweet creature!" then kiss me hard
As if he plucked up kisses by the roots
420 That grew upon my lips; laid his leg o'er my thigh,
And sighed, and kissed, and then cried, "Cursèd fate,
That gave thee to the Moor!"
OTHELLO: Oh, monstrous! Monstrous!

---

8. Diana, goddess of chastity and of the (pale) moon, in classical mythology.
9. Methods of suicide or murder.
1. Would you look ("gape") at the sight ("vision") from above ("super")? Would you, the person in the observer's position ("the supervision"), look ("gape") on?
2. As lecherous as wolves in heat.
3. If attribution of fault and strong circumstantial evidence.

IAGO: Nay, this was but his dream.
OTHELLO: But this denoted a foregone conclusion.°   *an earlier event*
  'Tis a shrewd doubt,° though it be but a dream.   *reasonable fear* 425
IAGO: And this may help to thicken other proofs
  That do demonstrate thinly.
OTHELLO: I'll tear her all to pieces!
IAGO: Nay, yet be wise; yet° we see nothing done.   *as of yet*
  She may be honest yet.° Tell me but this: *still*
  Have you not sometimes seen a handkerchief   430
  Spotted with strawberries in your wife's hand?
OTHELLO: I gave her such a one. 'Twas my first gift.
IAGO: I know not that, but such a handkerchief—
  I am sure it was your wife's—did I today
  See Cassio wipe his beard with.
OTHELLO: If it be that—   435
IAGO: If it be that, or any, it was hers.
  It speaks against her with the other proofs.
OTHELLO: Oh, that the slave° had forty thousand lives!   *(Cassio)*
  One is too poor, too weak for my revenge.
  Now do I see 'tis true. Look here, Iago: 440
  All my fond love thus do I blow to heaven. 'Tis gone.

  [OTHELLO *kneels.*]

  Arise, black vengeance, from the hollow hell;
  Yield up, O love, thy crown and hearted throne°   *rule of the heart*
  To tyrannous hate. Swell, bosom, with thy fraught,°   *burden*
  For 'tis of aspics'° tongues.   *poisonous snakes'*
IAGO: Yet be content.   445
OTHELLO: Oh, blood! Blood! Blood!
IAGO: Patience, I say: your mind may change.
OTHELLO: Never, Iago! Like to the Pontic Sea,°   *Black Sea*
  Whose icy current and compulsive course
  Ne'er keeps retiring ebb, but keeps due on
  To the Propontic and the Hellespont,[4]   450
  Even so my bloody thoughts, with violent pace,
  Shall ne'er look back, ne'er ebb to humble love
  Till that a capable° and wide revenge   *capacious*
  Swallow them up. Now, by yond marble heaven,
  In the due reverence of a sacred vow   455
  I here engage my words.
IAGO: Do not rise yet.

  [IAGO *kneels.*[5]]

4. The Pontic, or Black, Sea was said by Pliny to flow in only one direction—into the Propontic, the
body of water bounded by the straits of Bosphorus and the Dardanelles (Hellespont), the latter strait
leading to the Aegean.
5. Parody of the marriage ceremony.

Witness, you ever-burning lights above,
You elements that clip° us round about,   *embrace (sexual?)*
Witness that here Iago doth give up
460 The execution° of his wit, hands, heart,   *command*
To wronged Othello's service. Let him command,
And to obey shall be in me remorse,°   *pity (for Othello)*
What bloody business ever.
OTHELLO: I greet thy love
 Not with vain thanks but with acceptance bounteous,
465 And will upon the instant put thee to't.°   *immediately test it*
Within these three days let me hear thee say
That Cassio's not alive.
IAGO: My friend is dead.
'Tis done at your request. But let her live.
OTHELLO: Damn her, lewd minx!° Oh, damn her! Damn her!   *wanton*
470 Come, go with me apart. I will withdraw
To furnish me with some swift means of death
For the fair devil. Now art thou my lieutenant.
IAGO: I am your own forever.   *Exeunt.*

Scene 4

Before the citadel. Enter DESDEMONA, EMILIA, *and*
CLOWN.

DESDEMONA: Do you know, sirrah,[6] where lieutenant Cassio
 lies?
CLOWN: I dare not say he lies anywhere.
DESDEMONA: Why, man?
5 CLOWN: He's a soldier, and for me to say a soldier lies, 'tis
 stabbing.
DESDEMONA: Go to! Where lodges he?
CLOWN: To tell you where he lodges is to tell you where I lie.
DESDEMONA: Can anything be made of this?
10 CLOWN: I know not where he lodges, and for me to devise a
 lodging and say, "He lies here," or "He lies there," were to
 lie in mine own throat.°   *lie outrageously*
DESDEMONA: Can you inquire him out, and be edified by report?
CLOWN: I will catechize the world for him: that is, make
15 questions and by them answer.°   *find the answer*
DESDEMONA: Seek him. Bid him come hither. Tell him I have
 moved° my lord on his behalf, and hope all will be well. *petitioned*
CLOWN: To do this is within the compass° of man's wit and, *scope*
 therefore, I will attempt the doing it. *Exit* CLOWN.
20 DESDEMONA: Where should° I lose the handkerchief, Emilia? *did*
EMILIA: I know not, madam.

6. A form of address to an inferior.

DESDEMONA: Believe me, I had rather have lost my purse
　　　　Full of *crusados*.[7] And but° my noble Moor　　　　　　　　*Were it not the case that*
　　　　Is true of mind and made of no such baseness
　　　　As jealous creatures are, it were enough　　　　　　　　　　　　　　　　　25
　　　　To put him to ill thinking.
EMILIA:　　　　　　　　　　　　Is he not jealous?
DESDEMONA: Who, he? I think the sun where he was born
　　　　Drew all such humors from him.[8]

　　　　Enter OTHELLO.

EMILIA:　　　　　　　　　　　Look where he comes.
DESDEMONA: I will not leave him now till Cassio be
　　　　Called to him.—How is't with you, my lord?　　　　　　　　　　　30
OTHELLO: Well, my good lady, [*aside*] Oh, hardness to dissemble!
　　　　—How do you, Desdemona?
DESDEMONA:　　　　　　　　　Well, my good lord.
OTHELLO: Give me your hand. This hand is moist,° my lady.　　　*(sign of carnal desire)*
DESDEMONA: It hath felt no age, nor known no sorrow.
OTHELLO: This argues fruitfulness and liberal heart.[9]　　　　　　　　　35
　　　　Hot, hot, and moist: this hand of yours requires
　　　　A sequester from liberty, fasting, and prayer,
　　　　Much castigation, exercise devout,
　　　　For here's a young and sweating devil here
　　　　That commonly rebels. 'Tis a good hand,　　　　　　　　　　　　40
　　　　A frank° one.　　　　　　　　　　　　　　　　　　　　　　*(sexually) open*
DESDEMONA:　　　　You may indeed say so,
　　　　For 'twas that hand that gave away my heart.
OTHELLO: A liberal hand. The hearts of old gave hands,
　　　　But our new heraldry is hands, not hearts.[1]
DESDEMONA: I cannot speak of this. Come now, your　　　　　　　　45
　　　　promise.
OTHELLO: What promise, chuck?°　　　　　　　　　　　*woodchuck (affectionate)*
DESDEMONA: I have sent to bid Cassio come speak with you.
OTHELLO: I have a salt and sorry rheum° offends me.　　　　*badly watering eyes*
　　　　Lend me thy handkerchief.
DESDEMONA:　　　　　　　　Here, my lord.
OTHELLO: That which I gave you.
DESDEMONA:　　　　　　　　I have it not about me.　　　　　　　　50
OTHELLO: Not?
DESDEMONA: No, indeed, my lord.
OTHELLO:　　　　　　　That's a fault. That handkerchief

---

7. Gold coins.
8. The four humors were bodily fluids, the mix of which was believed by classical and Renaissance thinkers to determine one's temperament. Desdemona here repeats a standard position—that the climate of Africa, in its effect on the bodily humors, prevented its inhabitants from easily succumbing to jealousy (but made their jealousy especially fierce once aroused).
9. This demonstrates fertility (perhaps, by implication, lust) and a generous (loose) heart.
1. These days the joining of hands doesn't signify ("herald") the joining of hearts.

Did an Egyptian to my mother give:
She was a charmer,° and could almost read   *sorceress*
55   The thoughts of people. She told her, while she kept it,
'Twould make her amiable,° and subdue my father   *desirable*
Entirely to her love; but if she lost it,
Or made a gift of it, my father's eye
Should hold her loathed, and his spirits should hunt
60   After new fancies. She, dying, gave it me,
And bid me, when my fate would have me wived,
To give it her.° I did so, and take heed on't;   *to my wife*
Make it a darling like° your precious eye;   *as dear to you as*
To lose't or give't away were such perdition°   *loss; damnation*
As nothing else could match.
65 DESDEMONA: Is't possible?
OTHELLO: 'Tis true. There's magic in the web° of it.   *weave*
A sibyl,° that had numbered in the world   *female prophet*
The sun to course two hundred compasses,[2]
In her prophetic fury sewed the work;
70   The worms were hallowed that did breed the silk;
And it was dyed in mummy,[3] which the skillful
Conserved of° maidens' hearts.   *Preserved out of*
DESDEMONA: Indeed? Is't true?
OTHELLO: Most veritable. Therefore look to't well.
DESDEMONA: Then would to heaven that I had never seen't!
75 OTHELLO: Ha! Wherefore?
DESDEMONA: Why do you speak so startingly° and rash?   *impetuously*
OTHELLO: Is't lost? Is't gone? Speak, is't out o'th' way?
DESDEMONA: Bless us!
OTHELLO: Say you?
80 DESDEMONA: It is not lost—but what an if° it were?   *an if = if*
OTHELLO: How?
DESDEMONA: I say it is not lost.
OTHELLO: Fetch't. Let me see't.
DESDEMONA: Why, so I can, but I will not now:
This is a trick to put° me from my suit.   *deflect*
85   Pray you, let Cassio be received again.
OTHELLO: Fetch me the handkerchief! [*aside*] My mind misgives.
DESDEMONA: Come, come. You'll never meet a more sufficient° man.   *complete*
OTHELLO: The handkerchief!
DESDEMONA: A man that all his time
Hath founded his good fortunes on your love,
Shared dangers with you—
90 OTHELLO: The handkerchief!

---

2. Who was two hundred years old.
3. Fluid drained from mummified bodies, supposedly magical.

DESDEMONA: In sooth, you are to blame.
OTHELLO: Away!

Exit OTHELLO.

EMILIA: Is not this man jealous?
DESDEMONA: I ne'er saw this before.
    Sure, there's some wonder in this handkerchief;
    I am most unhappy in the loss of it.
EMILIA: 'Tis not a year or two shows us a man:[4]   95
    They are all but° stomachs, and we all but food;   *nothing but*
    They eat us hungrily, and when they are full
    They belch us.

        Enter IAGO *and* CASSIO.

                        Look you, Cassio and my husband.
IAGO [*to* CASSIO]: There is no other way; 'tis she must do't.
    [*He indicates* DESDEMONA.] And, lo, the happiness![5]   100
        Go and importune her.
DESDEMONA: How now, good Cassio? What's the news with you?
CASSIO: Madam, my former suit. I do beseech you
    That by your virtuous means I may again
    Exist, and be a member of his love
    Whom I, with all the office of my heart,   105
    Entirely honor. I would not be delayed.
    If my offense be of such mortal° kind   *deadly*
    That nor° my service past, nor present sorrows,   *neither*
    Nor purposed° merit in futurity,°   *intended / the future*
    Can ransom me into his love again,   110
    But to know so° must be my benefit.   *Even to know this*
    So° shall I clothe me in a forced content,   *If so*
    And shut myself up in° some other course   *limit myself to*
    To° Fortune's alms.   *To win*
DESDEMONA: Alas, thrice-gentle Cassio,
    My advocation is not now in tune.[6]   115
    My lord is not my lord, nor should I know him
    Were he in favor° as in humor altered.   *appearance*
    So help me every spirit sanctified,
    As I have spoken for you all my best,
    And stood within the blank of° his displeasure   *in the aim of* 120
    For my free speech. You must awhile be patient:
    What I can do, I will, and more I will
    Than for myself I dare. Let that suffice you.
IAGO: Is my lord angry?

---

4. Probably: It doesn't take long to see what men are made of.
5. What a happy coincidence (seeing Desdemona).
6. My advocacy isn't working properly.

EMILIA: He went hence but now,
125   And certainly in strange unquietness.
IAGO: Can he be angry? I have seen the cannon
          When it hath blown his ranks into the air
          And, like the devil, from his very arm
          Puffed his own brother[7]—and is he angry?
130   Something of moment, then. I will go meet him.
          There's matter in't indeed, if he be angry.
DESDEMONA: I prithee, do so.   *Exit* [IAGO].
                              Something, sure, of state,°   *state business*
          Either from Venice or some unhatched practice°   *unfinished plot*
          Made demonstrable° here in Cyprus to him,   *Revealed*
135   Hath puddled° his clear spirit; and in such cases   *fouled; dirtied*
          Men's natures wrangle with inferior things,
          Though great ones are their object. 'Tis even so:
          For let our finger ache, and it endues°   *induces*
          Our other healthful members even to a sense
140   Of pain. Nay, we must think men are not gods,
          Nor of them look for such observancy°   *careful attention*
          As fits the bridal.° Beshrew me° much, Emilia,   *wedding / (mild curse)*
          I was—unhandsome° warrior as I am—   *unskilled*
          Arraigning his unkindness with my soul,
145   But now I find I had suborned the witness,
          And he's indicted falsely.[8]
EMILIA: Pray heaven it be
          State matters, as you think, and no conception
          Nor no jealous toy° concerning you.   *whim*
DESDEMONA: Alas the day! I never gave him cause.
150 EMILIA: But jealous souls will not be answered so.
          They are not ever jealous for the cause,
          But jealous for° they're jealous: it is a monster   *because*
          Begot upon itself, born on itself.
DESDEMONA: Heaven keep the monster from Othello's mind!
155 EMILIA: Lady, amen.
DESDEMONA: I will go seek him.—Cassio, walk here about.
          If I do find him fit, I'll move your suit,
          And seek to effect it to my uttermost.
CASSIO: I humbly thank your ladyship.

                    Exeunt [DESDEMONA *and* EMILIA].
          Enter BIANCA.[9]

BIANCA: Save you,° friend Cassio.   *God save you*
160 CASSIO: What make° you from home?   *brings*

---

7. Blew up his own brother (and Othello wasn't angry even then).
8. Made the witness lie and so accused Othello falsely.
9. "Bianca" means "white" in Italian—perhaps part of the play's ironic reversal of conventional color imagery, given that Bianca is a "customer" (courtesan, 4.1.115).

How is't with you, my most fair Bianca?
Indeed, sweet love, I was coming to your house.
BIANCA: And I was going to your lodging, Cassio.
What, keep a week away? Seven days and nights,
Eight score eight hours—and lovers' absent hours   165
More tedious than the dial eight score times!¹
Oh, weary reck'ning!°   *calculating*
CASSIO: Pardon me, Bianca.
I have this while with leaden thoughts been pressed,
But I shall in a more continuate° time   *opportune*
Strike off° this score of absence. Sweet Bianca,   *Make up* 170

[*He gives her the handkerchief.*]

Take me this work out.°   *Copy this embroidery*
BIANCA: O Cassio, whence came this?
This is some token from a newer friend.
To the felt absence now I feel a cause.
Is't come to this? Well, well!
CASSIO: Go to,° woman!   *Stop it*
Throw your vile guesses in the devil's teeth   175
From whence you have° them. You are jealous now   *got*
That this is from some mistress some remembrance.
No, in good troth, Bianca.
BIANCA: Why, whose is it?
CASSIO: I know not, neither. I found it in my chamber.
I like the work° well: ere it be demanded,°   *embroidery / sought out* 180
As like° enough it will, I would have it copied.   *likely*
Take it, and do't, and leave me for this time.
BIANCA: Leave you? Wherefore?
CASSIO: I do attend here on the general,
And think it no addition,° nor my wish,   *(to my cause)* 185
To have him see me womaned.°   *with a woman*
BIANCA: Why, I pray you?
CASSIO: Not that I love you not.
BIANCA: But that you do not love me.
I pray you, bring me on the way a little,
And say if I shall see you soon at night.
CASSIO: 'Tis but a little way that I can bring you,   190
For I attend here; but I'll see you soon.
BIANCA: 'Tis very good. I must be circumstanced.²

Exeunt all.

1. Each hour lovers are parted is eight score (160) times more tedious than normal clock time.
2. Content with what circumstances offer.

ACT IV

Scene 1

Before the citadel. Enter OTHELLO *and* IAGO.

IAGO: Will you think so?
OTHELLO: Think so, Iago?
IAGO: What,
    To kiss in private?
OTHELLO: An unauthorized kiss!
IAGO: Or to be naked with her friend in bed
    An hour or more, not meaning any harm?
5 OTHELLO: Naked in bed, Iago, and not mean harm?
    It is hypocrisy against the devil.³
    They that mean virtuously, and yet do so,
    The devil their virtue tempts, and they tempt heaven.⁴
IAGO: If they do nothing, 'tis a venial slip;°   *an excusable sin*
    But if I give my wife a handkerchief—
10 OTHELLO: What then?
IAGO: Why, then 'tis hers, my lord, and, being hers,
    She may, I think, bestow't on any man.
OTHELLO: She is protectress of her honor, too.
    May she give that?
15 IAGO: Her honor is an essence that's not seen:
    They° have it very oft that have it not.   *They are reputed to*
    But for the handkerchief—
OTHELLO: By heaven, I would most gladly have forgot it!
    Thou said'st—oh, it comes o'er my memory
20   As doth the raven o'er the infectious house,⁵
    Boding to all—he had my handkerchief.
IAGO: Ay, what of that?
OTHELLO: That's not so good now.
IAGO: What if I had said I had seen him do you wrong?
    Or heard him say—as knaves be such abroad,⁶
25   Who, having by their own importunate suit,
    Or voluntary dotage of some mistress,
    Convinced or supplied° them, cannot choose   *Seduced or satisfied*
    But they must blab—
OTHELLO: Hath he said anything?
IAGO: He hath, my lord, but be you well assured,
    No more than he'll unswear.

---

3. By showing every sign of committing adultery but then stopping just in time, they deliberately mislead the devil, who wrongly takes their apparent intention to sin at face value (just as an ordinary hypocrite deceives by professing virtue).
4. Those who mean well ("virtuously") but act in this lascivious fashion ("so") make it easy for the devil successfully to tempt them, and they violate the biblical prohibition against tempting God.
5. The raven was thought to be an ill omen and a carrier of plague. *Infectious*: plague-infested.
6. As such knaves do exist in the world.

OTHELLO: What hath he said? 30

IAGO: Why, that he did—I know not what he did.

OTHELLO: What? What?

IAGO: Lie.

OTHELLO: With her?

IAGO: With her, on her, what you will.

OTHELLO: Lie with her? Lie on her? We say "lie on her"°   *lie about her; (sexual)*
when they belie° her. Lie with her? That's fulsome!°   *slander / nauseating*
Handkerchief! Confessions! Handkerchief! To confess 35
and be hanged for his labor. First to be hanged and then
to confess. I tremble at it. Nature would not invest herself
in such shadowing passion without some instruction.[7] It is
not words that shakes me thus—pish! Noses, ears, and
lips! Is't possible? Confess? Handkerchief? Oh, devil! 40

     [He] falls in a trance.

IAGO: Work on,
My medicine works! Thus credulous fools are caught,
And many worthy and chaste dames, even thus
All guiltless, meet reproach.—What ho, my lord?
My lord, I say! Othello!

     Enter CASSIO.

                       —How now, Cassio? 45

CASSIO: What's the matter?

IAGO: My lord is fallen into an epilepsy.
This is his second fit; he had one yesterday.

CASSIO: Rub him about the temples.

IAGO: The lethargy° must have his° quiet course: *trance / its* 50
If not, he foams at mouth and, by and by,
Breaks out to savage madness. Look, he stirs.
Do you withdraw yourself a little while.
He will recover straight.° When he is gone,   *immediately*
I would on great occasion° speak with you.   *[Exit* CASSIO.]   *important matters* 55
—How is it, general? Have you not hurt your head?[8]

OTHELLO: Dost thou mock me?

IAGO: I mock you not, by heaven.
Would you would bear your fortune like a man.

OTHELLO: A hornèd man's a monster and a beast.

IAGO: There's many a beast, then, in a populous city, 60
And many a civil° monster.   *city-dwelling*

OTHELLO: Did he confess it?

IAGO: Good sir, be a man.
Think every bearded fellow that's but yoked

7. It isn't natural that I would feel such foreboding ("shadowing") emotion (jealousy) unless there were some cause for it.
8. Othello takes this as suggesting that he has grown cuckold's horns.

May draw with you?[9] There's millions now alive
65   That nightly lie in those unproper beds
Which they dare swear peculiar.[1] Your case is better.
Oh, 'tis the spite of hell, the fiend's arch-mock,°   *devil's greatest jest*
To lip° a wanton in a secure° couch   *kiss / an unsuspected*
And to suppose her chaste. No, let me know
70   And, knowing what I am,° I know what she shall be.   *(a cuckold)*
OTHELLO: Oh, thou art wise, 'tis certain.
IAGO: Stand you awhile apart.
Confine yourself but in a patient list.°   *boundary; bearing; desire*
Whilst you were here, o'erwhelmed with your grief—
A passion most resulting° such a man—   *recoiling upon (?)*
75   Cassio came hither. I shifted him away,
And laid° good 'scuses upon your ecstasy,°   *gave / for your fit*
Bade him anon° return and here speak with me,   *soon*
The which he promised. Do but encave° yourself,   *Only hide*
And mark the fleers,° the jibes, and notable scorns   *sneers*
80   That dwell in every region of his face:
For I will make him tell the tale anew,
Where, how, how oft, how long ago, and when
He hath and is again to cope° your wife.   *copulate with*
I say but mark his gesture. Marry,° patience!   *(mild oath)*
85   Or I shall say you're all-in-all in spleen,°   *completely impulsive*
And nothing of a man.
OTHELLO: Dost thou hear, Iago?
I will be found most cunning in my patience,
But—dost thou hear?—most bloody.
IAGO: That's not amiss.
But yet keep time° in all. Will you withdraw?   *maintain control*

        [OTHELLO *withdraws*.]

90   Now will I question Cassio of° Bianca,   *about*
A housewife that by selling her desires[2]
Buys herself bread and cloth. It° is a creature   *(Bianca)*
That dotes on Cassio, as 'tis the strumpet's plague
To beguile many and be beguiled by one.
95   He, when he hears of her, cannot restrain
From the excess of laughter.

        Enter CASSIO.

                              Here he comes.
As he shall smile, Othello shall go mad,

---

9. Every married man ("yoked," like an ox, to his wife and hence to cuckoldry) labors ("draws") under the same fate.
1. Who lie in beds that don't belong entirely to them but that they would swear are exclusively their own.
2. Desired body. *Housewife*: hussy = prostitute.

And his unbookish jealousy[3] must construe
Poor Cassio's smiles, gestures, and light behaviors
Quite in the wrong. [*to* CASSIO] How do you, lieutenant? 100
CASSIO: The worser that you give me the addition° *title*
Whose want even° kills me. *lack just*
IAGO: Ply Desdemona well, and you are sure on't.
Now, if this suit lay in Bianca's dower° *dowry*
How quickly should you speed?
CASSIO: Alas, poor caitiff!° *wretch* 105
OTHELLO [*apart*]: Look how he laughs already.
IAGO: I never knew woman love man so.
CASSIO: Alas, poor rogue. I think indeed she loves me.
OTHELLO [*apart*]: Now he denies it faintly, and laughs it out.
IAGO: Do you hear, Cassio?—
OTHELLO [*apart*]: Now he importunes him 110
To tell it o'er. Go to: well said, well said.
IAGO: —She gives it out that you shall marry her.
Do you intend it?
CASSIO: Ha, ha, ha!
OTHELLO [*apart*]: Do ye triumph, Roman?[4] Do you triumph?
CASSIO: I marry! What, a customer!° Prithee bear some char- *courtesan* 115
ity to my wit.° Do not think it so unwholesome. Ha, ha, ha! *sense*
OTHELLO [*apart*]: So, so, so, so. They laugh that wins.
IAGO: Why, the cry goes that you marry her.
CASSIO: Prithee say true.
IAGO: I am a very villain else.° *if it's not true (ironic)*
OTHELLO [*apart*]: Have you scored me?[5] Well. 120
CASSIO: This is the monkey's own giving out.° She is per- *Bianca's own story*
suaded I will marry her out of her own love and flattery,
not out of my promise.
OTHELLO [*apart*]: Iago beckons me. Now he begins the story.

[OTHELLO *moves closer.*]

CASSIO: She was here even now; she haunts me in every place. 125
I was the other day talking on the sea-bank with certain
Venetians, and thither comes the bauble° and falls me *toy (Bianca)*
thus about my neck.
OTHELLO [*apart*]: Crying, "O dear Cassio!", as it were: his
gesture imports° it. *indicates* 130
CASSIO: So hangs, and lolls, and weeps upon me; so shakes
and pulls me. Ha, ha, ha!

---

3. Naive; ignorant of the high level of suspiciousness appropriate to an educated Venetian man—given
Othello's refusal to be jealous of Desdemona merely because she "loves company, / Is free of
speech, . . . and dances" (3.3.182–83); not conforming to the bookish notion of the unjealous African.
4. Perhaps Othello draws on associations either with Rome's imperial successes (and subsequent
collapse) or with the Roman practice of holding celebratory processions ("triumphs").
5. Wounded me; sexually conquered at my expense.

OTHELLO [*apart*]:   Now he tells how she plucked him to my
chamber. Oh, I see that nose of yours, but not that dog I
135   shall throw it to.[6]

CASSIO: Well, I must leave her company.

Enter BIANCA.

IAGO: Before me, look where she comes!

CASSIO: 'Tis such another fitchew.[7] Marry, a perfumed one!
[*to* BIANCA] What do you mean by this haunting of me?

140   BIANCA: Let the devil and his dam° haunt you! What did you   *mother*
mean by that same handkerchief you gave me even now? I
was a fine fool to take it. I must take out° the work? A likely   *copy*
piece of work,° that you should find it in your chamber and   *An implausible story*
know not who left it there. This is some minx's token—and
145   I must take out the work? There, give it° your hobby-horse!°   *it to / loose woman*
Wheresoever you had it, I'll take out no work on't.

CASSIO: How now, my sweet Bianca? How now? How now?

OTHELLO [*apart*]:   By heaven, that should° be my handkerchief!   *must*

BIANCA: If you'll come to supper tonight, you may: if you will
150   not, come when you are next prepared for.[8]   Exit.

IAGO: After her! After her!

CASSIO: I must: she'll rail in the streets else.

IAGO: Will you sup there?

CASSIO: Yes, I intend so.

155   IAGO: Well, I may chance to see you, for I would very fain°   *be very well pleased to*
speak with you.

CASSIO: Prithee, come. Will you?

IAGO: Go to. Say no more.   [*Exit* CASSIO.]

OTHELLO: How shall I murder him, Iago?

160   IAGO: Did you perceive how he laughed at his vice?

OTHELLO: O Iago!

IAGO: And did you see the handkerchief?

OTHELLO: Was that mine?

IAGO: Yours, by this hand. And to see how he prizes the fool-
165   ish woman, your wife: she gave it him, and he hath given
it his whore.

OTHELLO: I would have him nine years a-killing.[9] A fine
woman! A fair woman! A sweet woman!

IAGO: Nay, you must forget that.

170   OTHELLO: Ay, let her rot and perish, and be damned tonight,
for she shall not live. No, my heart is turned to stone: I
strike it, and it hurts my hand. Oh, the world hath not a

6. I'm envisioning my revenge, but the time is not yet quite right. Cutting off the enemy's nose was
understood as a form of retribution.
7. Polecat, associated with prostitutes because of its bad smell and presumed lecherousness.
8. Come next time I prepare for you (never).
9. I would (like to) spend nine years killing him.

sweeter creature: she might lie by an emperor's side, and
command him tasks.

IAGO: Nay, that's not your way.°   *(the way to think)* 175

OTHELLO: Hang her! I do but say what she is: so delicate with
her needle; an admirable musician—oh, she will sing the
savageness out of a bear!—of so high and plenteous wit
and invention°—   *imagination*

IAGO: She's the worse for all this.   180

OTHELLO: Oh, a thousand, a thousand times! And, then, of
so gentle° a condition!   *highly born*

IAGO: Ay, too gentle.°   *generous (sexually)*

OTHELLO: Nay, that's certain.
But yet the pity of it, Iago. O Iago, the pity of it, Iago!   185

IAGO: If you are so fond° over her iniquity, give her patent°   *foolish / license*
to offend; for if it touch not you, it comes near nobody.

OTHELLO: I will chop her into messes!° Cuckold me!   *pieces of food*

IAGO: Oh, 'tis foul in her.

OTHELLO: With mine officer!   190

IAGO: That's fouler.

OTHELLO: Get me some poison, Iago, this night. I'll not expos-
tulate with her, lest her body and beauty unprovide my
mind° again. This night, Iago.   *weaken my resolve*

IAGO: Do it not with poison. Strangle her in her bed, even   195
the bed she hath contaminated.

OTHELLO: Good, good. The justice of it pleases. Very good.

IAGO: And for Cassio, let me be his undertaker.° You shall   *murderer*
hear more by midnight.

OTHELLO: Excellent good.

[*A trumpet sounds.*]

What trumpet is that same?   200

IAGO: I warrant, something from Venice.

Enter LODOVICO, DESDEMONA, *and Attendants.*

'Tis Lodovico: this comes from the Duke.
See, your wife's with him.

LODOVICO: Save you, worthy general.

OTHELLO: With all my heart,° sir.   *Thank you*

LODOVICO: The Duke and the senators of Venice greet you.   205

[*He gives* OTHELLO *a letter.*]

OTHELLO: I kiss the instrument° of their pleasures.°   *bearer / commands*

DESDEMONA: And what's the news, good cousin Lodovico?

IAGO: I am very glad to see you, signor.
Welcome to Cyprus.

LODOVICO: I thank you. How does Lieutenant Cassio?   210

IAGO: Lives, sir.

DESDEMONA: Cousin, there's fallen between him and my lord

An unkind° breach, but you shall make all well.   *unnatural; painful*

OTHELLO: Are you sure of that?

215 DESDEMONA: My lord?

OTHELLO [*reads*]:   "This fail you not to do, as you will—"

LODOVICO [*to* DESDEMONA]:   He did not call: he's busy in°   *with*
  the paper.
  Is there division twixt my lord and Cassio?

DESDEMONA: A most unhappy one. I would do much

220   T'atone° them, for the love I bear to Cassio.   *To reconcile*

OTHELLO: Fire and brimstone!

DESDEMONA: My lord?

OTHELLO: Are you wise?

DESDEMONA [*to* LODOVICO]: What, is he angry?

LODOVICO: Maybe the letter moved him,
  For, as I think, they do command him home,
  Deputing Cassio in his government.°   *official position; place*

DESDEMONA: Trust me, I am glad on't.

OTHELLO: Indeed?

225 DESDEMONA: My lord?

OTHELLO: I am glad to see you mad.[1]

DESDEMONA: Why, sweet Othello?

OTHELLO: Devil!

      [*He strikes her.*]

DESDEMONA: I have not deserved this!

LODOVICO: My lord! This would not be believed in Venice,

230   Though I should swear I saw't. 'Tis very much.°   *serious*
  Make her amends: she weeps.

OTHELLO: O devil! Devil!
  If that the earth could teem with° woman's tears,   *become pregnant by*
  Each drop she falls would prove a crocodile.[2]
  —Out of my sight!

DESDEMONA: I will not stay to offend you.

      [*She starts to leave.*]

235 LODOVICO: Truly obedient, lady.
  —I do beseech your lordship, call her back.

OTHELLO: Mistress.

DESDEMONA: My lord?

OTHELLO [*to* LODOVICO]:   What would you° with her, sir?   *do you wish*

LODOVICO: Who? I, my lord?

OTHELLO: Ay, you did wish that I would make her turn.°   *return*

240   Sir, she can turn and turn,° and yet go on   *(sexually)*

---

1. Perhaps Othello is pleased that she's rejoicing in Cassio's promotion and hence revealing their adulterous affair, which she would be "mad" to do in public and in front of him.

2. Each drop would cause the earth to conceive a crocodile (crocodiles proverbially wept false tears for their victims).

And turn again. And she can weep, sir, weep!
And she's obedient, as you say, obedient,
Very obedient. [*to* DESDEMONA] Proceed you in your
　　tears.
[*to* LODOVICO] Concerning this, sir—[*to* DESDEMONA]
　　Oh, well-painted passion!
—I am commanded home. [*to* DESDEMONA] Get you   245
　　away.
I'll send for you anon.—Sir, I obey the mandate
And will return to Venice. [*to* DESDEMONA] Hence!
　　Avaunt!°　　　　　　　　　　　　　　　　　　　　*Begone*

[*Exit* DESDEMONA.]

[*to* LODOVICO] Cassio shall have my place, and, sir,
　　tonight
I do entreat that we may sup together.
You are welcome, sir, to Cyprus.—Goats and monkeys!³   250

　　　　　　　　　　　　　　　　　　　　　　　　Exit.

LODOVICO: Is this the noble Moor whom our full Senate
　　Call all-in-all sufficient? Is this the nature
　　Whom passion could not shake? Whose solid virtue
　　The shot of accident nor dart of chance
　　Could neither graze nor pierce?
IAGO:　　　　　　　　　　　　　　　He is much changed.   255
LODOVICO: Are his wits safe? Is he not light of brain?
IAGO: He's that he is: I may not breathe my censure.
　　What he might be—if what he might, he is not—
　　I would to heaven he were.⁴
LODOVICO:　　　　　　　　　　What, strike his wife?
IAGO: Faith, that was not so well. Yet would° I knew   *I wish that* 260
　　That stroke would prove the worst.
LODOVICO:　　　　　　　　　　　　Is it his use?°   *custom*
　　Or did the letters work upon his blood,°   *passions*
　　And new create his fault?
IAGO:　　　　　　　　　　　　Alas, alas!
　　It is not honesty in me to speak
　　What I have seen and known. You shall observe him,   265
　　And his own courses° will denote him so   *actions*
　　That I may save my speech. Do but go after,
　　And mark how he continues.
LODOVICO: I am sorry that I am deceived in him.　　*Exeunt.*

3. Symbols of lust (borrowing Iago's language, 3.3.400).
4. He is what he is (as Iago says of himself, "I am not what I am," 1.1.63). I won't express my judgment on whether he is sane. What he might be (sane)—if, though he might be (sane), he is not—I
wish he were (sane). That is: If he is not sane, I wish he were. Alternatively: If he is sane, I wish he
were insane (because only that would excuse his bad behavior).

Scene 2

> *The citadel. Enter* OTHELLO *and* EMILIA.

OTHELLO: You have seen nothing, then?

EMILIA: Nor ever heard, nor ever did suspect.

OTHELLO: Yes? You have seen Cassio and she together?

EMILIA: But then I saw no harm; and then I heard

5   Each syllable that breath made up between them.

OTHELLO: What, did they never whisper?

EMILIA: Never, my lord.

OTHELLO: Nor send you out o'th' way?

EMILIA: Never.

OTHELLO: To fetch her fan, her gloves, her mask, nor nothing?

EMILIA: Never, my lord.

10 OTHELLO: That's strange.

EMILIA: I durst, my lord, to wager she is honest:

     Lay down my soul at stake.[5] If you think other,°   *otherwise*

     Remove your thought: it doth abuse your bosom.

     If any wretch have put this in your head,

15   Let heaven requit° it with the serpent's curse,[6]   *requite*

     For if she be not honest, chaste, and true,

     There's no man happy: the purest of their wives

     Is foul as slander.

OTHELLO: Bid her come hither. Go.   *Exit* EMILIA.

     She says enough. Yet she's a simple bawd

20   That cannot say as much.[7] This° is a subtle whore,   *(Desdemona)*

     A closet, lock, and key° of villainous secrets;   *A hider*

     And yet she'll kneel and pray—I have seen her do't.

> *Enter* DESDEMONA *and* EMILIA.

DESDEMONA: My lord, what is your will?

OTHELLO: Pray you, chuck, come hither.

DESDEMONA: What is your pleasure?

OTHELLO: Let me see your eyes.

     Look in my face.

25 DESDEMONA: What horrible fancy's this?

OTHELLO [*to* EMILIA]: Some of your function,[8] mistress.

     Leave procreants° alone, and shut the door.   *copulators*

     Cough or cry "hem!" if anybody come.

     Your mystery, your mystery° may dispatch![9]   *Exit* EMILIA.   *profession*

30 DESDEMONA [*kneeling*]:   Upon my knee, what doth your
       speech import?

     I understand a fury in your words.

---

5. Stake my soul (on it).

6. In Genesis, the curse that God laid on the serpent who deceived Eve.

7. Yet it would be a simpleminded go-between who can't say as much as she did.

8. Fulfill your bawd's function by guarding the door.

9. May send you to your destination.

OTHELLO: Why, what art thou?

DESDEMONA: Your wife, my lord: your true and loyal wife.

OTHELLO: Come, swear it! Damn thyself, lest, being°   *appearing*
    Like one of heaven, the devils themselves   35
    Should fear to seize thee. Therefore be double damned:
    Swear thou art honest.

DESDEMONA: Heaven doth truly know it.

OTHELLO: Heaven truly knows that thou art false as hell.

DESDEMONA: To whom, my lord? With whom? How am I false?

OTHELLO: Ah, Desdemon! Away! Away! Away!   40

DESDEMONA: Alas the heavy day, why do you weep?
    Am I the motive° of these tears, my lord?   *cause*
    If haply° you my father do suspect   *perhaps*
    An instrument of this your calling back,°   *(to Venice)*
    Lay not your blame on me. If you have lost him,   45
    I have lost him too.

OTHELLO: Had it pleased heaven
    To try me with affliction; had they° rained   *the heavens*
    All kind of sores and shames on my bare head;
    Steeped me in poverty to the very lips;
    Given to captivity me and my utmost hopes,   50
    I should have found in some place of my soul
    A drop of patience. But, alas, to make me
    The fixèd figure for the time of scorn
    To point his slow and moving finger at![1]
    Yet could I bear that too, well, very well.   55
    But there, where I have garnered° up my heart,   *stored*
    Where either I must live, or bear no life,
    The fountain[2] from the which my current runs,
    Or else dries up—to be discarded thence,
    Or keep it as a cistern for foul toads   60
    To knot and gender° in! Turn thy complexion there,   *To couple and engender*
    Patience, thou young and rose-lipped cherubin:
    I here look grim as hell.[3]

DESDEMONA: I hope my noble lord esteems me honest.

OTHELLO: Oh, ay. As summer flies are in the shambles,°   *slaughter-house* 65
    That quicken even with blowing.[4] O thou weed,
    Who art so lovely fair and smell'st so sweet
    That the sense aches at thee! Would thou hadst never
        been born!

---

1. The designated object of scorn for this scornful time to point (as on a clock face) its slowly moving hand at.

2. Spring. The language here imagines Desdemona as the source of Othello's emotional vitality.

3. Look there (or change your look for the worse) at the thought of that, Patience, and you "cherubin": I (or: Ay) here look infernally forbidding.

4. Who come to life (or bring their offspring to life and hence make the meat foul) as soon as the eggs are deposited. The point seems to be the speed of breeding, inferred from Desdemona's supposed infidelity.

DESDEMONA: Alas, what ignorant° sin have I committed?   *unwitting*

70 OTHELLO: Was this fair paper, this most goodly book,
      Made to write "whore" upon? "What committed?"
      "Committed?" O thou public commoner!°   *prostitute*
      I should make very forges of my cheeks
      That would to cinders burn up modesty,
75   Did I but speak thy deeds. "What committed?"
      Heaven stops the nose at it, and the moon winks;°   *closes its eyes*
      The bawdy° wind, that kisses all it meets,   *promiscuous*
      Is hushed within the hollow mine of earth,°   *cave of the winds*
      And will not hear't. "What committed?"

80 DESDEMONA: By heaven, you do me wrong!
    OTHELLO: Are not you a strumpet?
    DESDEMONA: No, as I am a Christian!
      If to preserve this vessel for my lord
      From any other foul, unlawful touch
      Be not to be a strumpet, I am none.
    OTHELLO: What, not a whore?
85 DESDEMONA: No, as I shall be saved!
    OTHELLO: Is't possible?
    DESDEMONA: O heaven, forgive us!
    OTHELLO: I cry you mercy,° then;   *I beg your pardon*
      I took you for that cunning whore of Venice
      That married with Othello. [*He calls* EMILIA.] You,
        mistress,

            Enter EMILIA.

90   That have the office opposite to Saint Peter,
      And keeps the gate of hell. You, you! Ay, you!
      We have done our course.° There's money for your pains.   *business*

            [*He gives* EMILIA *money.*]

      I pray you, turn the key, and keep our counsel.   *Exit.*
    EMILIA: Alas, what does this gentleman conceive?°   *believe*
95   —How do you, madam? How do you, my good lady?
    DESDEMONA: Faith, half asleep.
    EMILIA: Good madam, what's the matter with my lord?
    DESDEMONA: With who?
    EMILIA: Why, with my lord, madam.
    DESDEMONA: Who is thy lord?
    EMILIA: He that is yours, sweet lady.
100 DESDEMONA: I have none. Do not talk to me, Emilia.
      I cannot weep, nor answers have I none
      But what should go by water.° Prithee tonight   *appear in tears*
      Lay on my bed my wedding sheets. Remember,
      And call thy husband hither.
    EMILIA: Here's a change indeed.   *Exit.*
105 DESDEMONA: 'Tis meet° I should be used so, very meet.   *fitting*

How have I been behaved, that he might stick
The small'st opinion on my least misuse?⁵

Enter IAGO *and* EMILIA.

IAGO: What is your pleasure, madam?
 How is't with you?
DESDEMONA: I cannot tell. Those that do teach young babes   110
 Do it with gentle means and easy tasks;
 He might have chid me so, for, in good faith,
 I am a child to chiding.°   *new to being reproached*
IAGO: What is the matter, lady?
EMILIA: Alas, Iago, my lord hath so bewhored her,°   *called her whore*
 Thrown such despite° and heavy terms upon her,   *spite* 115
 That true hearts cannot bear it.
DESDEMONA: Am I that name, Iago?
IAGO: What name, fair lady?
DESDEMONA: Such as she said my lord did say I was.
EMILIA: He called her "whore." A beggar in his drink
 Could not have laid such terms upon his callet.°   *whore* 120
IAGO: Why did he so?
DESDEMONA: I do not know; I am sure I am none such.
IAGO: Do not weep, do not weep. Alas the day!
EMILIA: Hath she forsook so many noble matches,°   *marriages*
 Her father, and her country, and her friends,   125
 To be called "whore"? Would it not make one weep?
DESDEMONA: It is my wretched fortune.
IAGO: Beshrew° him for't.   *Curse*
 How comes this trick° upon him?   *behavior*
DESDEMONA: Nay, heaven doth know.
EMILIA: I will be hanged if some eternal villain,
 Some busy° and insinuating rogue,   *meddling* 130
 Some cogging,° cozening° slave, to get some office   *deceiving / cheating*
 Have not devised this slander—I will be hanged else.
IAGO: Fie, there is no such man: it is impossible.
DESDEMONA: If any such there be, heaven pardon him.
EMILIA: A halter° pardon him, and hell gnaw his bones!   *hangman's noose* 135
 Why should he° call her "whore"? Who keeps her   *(Othello)*
  company?
 What place, what time, what form, what likelihood?
 The Moor's abused by some most villainous knave,
 Some base, notorious knave, some scurvy fellow.
 O heavens, that° such companions thou'dst unfold,°   *would that / reveal* 140
 And put in every honest hand a whip
 To lash the rascals naked through the world,
 Even from the East to th' West!
IAGO [*aside to* EMILIA]:   Speak within door.°   *more softly*

5. Which would cause him to suspect even slightly my smallest fault.

EMILIA [*aside to* IAGO]: Oh, fie upon them! Some such
    squire° he was   *fellow*
145   That turned your wit the seamy-side without,°   *wrong side out*
    And made you to suspect me with the Moor.
IAGO [*aside to* EMILIA]:   You are a fool. Go to!
DESDEMONA: Alas, Iago,
    What shall I do to win my lord again?
    Good friend, go to him—for, by this light of heaven,
150   I know not how I lost him. Here I kneel:
    If e'er my will did trespass 'gainst his love,
    Either in discourse of thought or actual deed;
    Or that mine eyes, mine ears, or any sense
    Delighted them, or any other form;[6]
155   Or that I do not yet° and ever did   *still*
    And ever will—though he do shake me off
    To beggarly divorcement—love him dearly,
    Comfort forswear me.° Unkindness may do much,   *Deny me (divine) solace*
    And his unkindness may defeat my life
160   But never taint my love. I cannot say "whore":
    It doth abhor me[7] now I speak the word—
    To do the act that might the addition° earn,   *label*
    Not the world's mass of vanity° could make me.   *all worldly splendor*
IAGO: I pray you, be content: 'tis but his humor.°   *mood*
165   The business of the state does him offense.
DESDEMONA: If 'twere no other—
IAGO: It is but so, I warrant.

        [*Trumpets sound.*]

    Hark how these instruments summon to supper:
    The messengers of Venice stay the meat.°   *are waiting to eat*
    Go in, and weep not: all things shall be well.

              Exeunt DESDEMONA *and* EMILIA.
      Enter RODERIGO.

170   How now, Roderigo?
RODERIGO: I do not find that thou deal'st justly with me.
IAGO: What in the contrary?
RODERIGO: Every day thou dafts me with some device,[8] Iago,
    and rather, as it seems to me now, keep'st from me all conve-
175   niency° than suppliest me with the least advantage of hope.   *opportunity*
    I will indeed no longer endure it, nor am I yet persuaded to
    put up° in peace what already I have foolishly suffered.   *endure*
IAGO: Will you hear me, Roderigo?

---

6. Took pleasure in anyone but him.
7. Fill me with abhorrence; make me abhorrent, with a pun on "ab-whore."
8. You make a fool of me with some trick.

RODERIGO: I have heard too much, and your words and per-
formances are no kin together.   180

IAGO: You charge me most unjustly.

RODERIGO: With naught but truth. I have wasted myself out of
my means: the jewels you have had from me to deliver Des-
demona would half have corrupted a votarist.° You have   *nun*
told me she hath received them, and returned me expecta-   185
tions and comforts of sudden respect and acquaintance,
but I find none.

IAGO: Well, go to.° Very well.   *(expresses remonstrance)*

RODERIGO: "Very well"? "Go to"? I cannot go to,° man, nor 'tis   *succeed sexually*
not very well! Nay, I think it is scurvy,° and begin to find   *shabby*   190
myself fopped° in it.   *made a fool*

IAGO: Very well.

RODERIGO: I tell you, 'tis not very well! I will make myself
known to Desdemona: if she will return me my jewels, I
will give over° my suit, and repent my unlawful solicita-   *up* 195
tion. If not, assure yourself I will seek satisfaction of you.

IAGO: You have said° now.   *finished*

RODERIGO: Ay, and said nothing but what I protest intend-
ment of doing.°   *intend to do*

IAGO: Why, now I see there's mettle in thee, and even from   200
this instant do build on° thee a better opinion than ever   *of*
before. Give me thy hand, Roderigo. Thou hast taken
against me a most just exception, but yet, I protest, I have
dealt most directly in thy affair.

RODERIGO: It hath not appeared.   205

IAGO: I grant indeed it hath not appeared, and your suspicion is not without wit and judgment. But, Roderigo, if
thou hast that in thee indeed which I have greater reason
to believe now than ever—I mean purpose, courage, and
valor—this night show it. If thou, the next night follow-   210
ing, enjoy not Desdemona, take me from this world with
treachery, and devise engines for° my life.   *plots against*

RODERIGO: Well, what is it? Is it within reason and compass?°   *possibility*

IAGO: Sir, there is especial commission come from Venice to
depute Cassio in Othello's place.   215

RODERIGO: Is that true? Why, then Othello and Desdemona
return again to Venice.

IAGO: Oh, no. He goes into Mauretania[9] and taketh away
with him the fair Desdemona, unless his abode be lin-
gered here by some accident, wherein none can be so   220
determinate° as the removing of Cassio.   *effectual*

RODERIGO: How do you mean, removing him?

IAGO: Why, by making him uncapable of Othello's place:
knocking out his brains!

9. Country in the western Sahara.

225 RODERIGO: And that you would have me to do?

IAGO: Ay, if you dare do yourself a profit and a right. He sups tonight with a harlotry,° and thither will I go to him. He knows not yet of his honorable fortune.° If you will watch his going thence, which I will fashion° to fall out between

230 twelve and one, you may take him at your pleasure. I will be near to second your attempt, and he shall fall between us. Come: stand not amazed at it, but go along with me; I will show you such a necessity in his death that you shall think yourself bound to put it on him. It is now high

235 supper-time, and the night grows to waste: about it!

RODERIGO: I will hear further reason for this.

IAGO: And you shall be satisfied.   *Exeunt.*

prostitute

promotion

arrange

Scene 3

Scene continues. Enter OTHELLO, LODOVICO, DESDE-
MONA, EMILIA, *and Attendants.*

LODOVICO: I do beseech you, sir, trouble yourself no further.

OTHELLO: Oh, pardon me. 'Twill do me good to walk.

LODOVICO: —Madam, good night. I humbly thank your ladyship.

DESDEMONA: Your honor is most welcome.

5 OTHELLO: Will you walk, sir?—O Desdemona—

DESDEMONA: My lord?

OTHELLO: Get you to bed on th'instant: I will be returned forthwith. Dismiss your attendant there. Look't be done.

DESDEMONA: I will, my lord.

Exeunt [OTHELLO, LODOVICO, *and Attendants*].

10 EMILIA: How goes it now? He looks gentler than he did.

DESDEMONA: He says he will return incontinent,°
    And hath commanded me to go to bed,
    And bid me to dismiss you.

EMILIA: Dismiss me?

DESDEMONA: It was his bidding: therefore, good Emilia,

15   Give me my nightly wearing,° and adieu.
    We must not now displease him.

EMILIA: I would you had never seen him!

DESDEMONA: So would not I: my love doth so approve him
    That even his stubbornness, his checks, his frowns

20   —Prithee, unpin me—have grace and favor.

EMILIA: I have laid those sheets you bade me on the bed.

DESDEMONA: All's one.°—Good Father, how foolish are our
    minds!
    —If I do die before, prithee shroud me
    In one of these same sheets.

EMILIA: Come, come: you talk!

immediately

night clothes

It doesn't matter

DESDEMONA: My mother had a maid called Barbary:[1]   25
    She was in love, and he she loved proved mad
    And did forsake her. She had a song of "willow":
    An old thing 'twas, but it expressed her fortune,
    And she died singing it. That song tonight
    Will not go from my mind. I have much to do   30
    But to[2] go hang my head all at one side
    And sing it like poor Barbary. Prithee dispatch.
EMILIA: Shall I go fetch your nightgown?
DESDEMONA: No, unpin me here.
    This Lodovico is a proper man.
EMILIA: A very handsome man.
DESDEMONA: He speaks well.   35
EMILIA: I know a lady in Venice would have walked barefoot
    to Palestine for a touch of his nether lip.
DESDEMONA [sings]: The poor soul sat singing by a sycamore
                tree:
                Sing all a green willow.[3]
                Her hand on her bosom, her head on her knee: 40
                Sing willow, willow, willow.
                The fresh streams ran by her and murmured
                    her moans:
                Sing willow, willow, willow.
                Her salt tears fell from her and softened
                    the stones:
                Sing willow, willow, willow—
    [to EMILIA]   Lay by these—   45
    [sings]   Willow, willow—
    [to EMILIA]   Prithee, hie thee:° he'll come anon.   *hurry*
    [sings]   "Sing all a green willow" must be my garland:
                Let nobody blame him, his scorn I approve—[4]
    Nay, that's not next.—Hark, who is't that knocks?
EMILIA: It's the wind.   50
DESDEMONA [sings]: I called my love "false love" but what
                said he then?
                Sing willow, willow, willow.
                "If I court more women, you'll couch with
                    more men."
    [to EMILIA] So, get thee gone: good night. Mine eyes
        do itch.
    Doth that bode weeping?
EMILIA: 'Tis neither here nor there.   55

---

1. Iago compares Othello to a "Barbary horse" (1.1.109).
2. I can barely bring myself not to.
3. Conventional symbol of disappointed love. Desdemona here sings part of a popular ballad usually titled "The Willow Song."
4. Here, Desdemona adds a line not in the original ballad.

DESDEMONA: I have heard it said so. Oh, these men, these men!
    Dost thou in conscience think—tell me, Emilia—
    That there be women do abuse their husbands
    In such gross kind?°   *fashion*
EMILIA: There be some such, no question.
60 DESDEMONA: Wouldst thou do such a deed for all the world?
EMILIA: Why, would not you?
DESDEMONA: No, by this heavenly light.
EMILIA: Nor I neither by this heavenly light:
    I might do't as well i'the dark.
DESDEMONA: Wouldst thou do such a deed for all the world?
65 EMILIA: The world's a huge thing; it is a great price
    For a small vice.
DESDEMONA: In troth, I think thou wouldst not.
EMILIA: In troth, I think I should, and undo't when I had
    done. Marry, I would not do such a thing for a joint ring,[5]
    nor for measures of lawn,° nor for gowns, petticoats, nor   *linen*
70   caps, nor any petty exhibition.° But for all the whole   *gift*
    world? Why, who would not make her husband a cuckold
    to make him a monarch? I should venture° purgatory for't.   *risk, wager*
DESDEMONA: Beshrew me if I would do such a wrong
    For the whole world!
75 EMILIA: Why, the wrong is but a wrong i'the world and, hav-
    ing the world for your labor, 'tis a wrong in your own
    world, and you might quickly make it right!
DESDEMONA: I do not think there is any such woman.
EMILIA: Yes, a dozen! And as many to th' vantage as would
80   store the world they played for.[6]
    But I do think it is their husbands' faults
    If wives do fall. Say that they slack their duties,°   *marital duties*
    And pour our treasures into foreign laps;[7]
    Or else break out in peevish jealousies,
85   Throwing restraint upon us; or say they strike us,
    Or scant our former having in despite:[8]
    Why, we have galls,° and, though we have some grace,   *tempers*
    Yet have we some revenge. Let husbands know
    Their wives have sense like them: they see and smell,
90   And have their palates both for sweet and sour,
    As husbands have. What is it that they do
    When they change° us for others? Is it sport?   *exchange*
    I think it is. And doth affection° breed it?   *lust*
    I think it doth. Is't frailty that thus errs?
95   It is so, too. And have not we affections,
    Desires for sport, and frailty, as men have?

5. A cheap ring in separable halves.
6. And as many more as it would take to populate the world they gained by doing it.
7. And give the semen that belongs to us to other women.
8. Or reduce our allowances out of spite.

Then let them use us well. Else let them know
The ills we do, their ills instruct us so.
DESDEMONA: Good night, good night. Heaven me such uses°   *habits*
    send
Not to pick bad from bad, but by bad, mend.⁹   *Exeunt.*   100

ACT V

Scene 1

A street in Cyprus. Enter IAGO *and* RODERIGO.

IAGO: Here, stand behind this balk:° straight° will he come.   *timber beam / right away*
    Wear thy good rapier bare, and put it home.°   *drive it into him*
    Quick, quick! Fear nothing; I'll be at thy elbow.
    It makes us or it mars us. Think on that,
    And fix most firm thy resolution.   5
RODERIGO: Be near at hand; I may miscarry in't.
IAGO: Here, at thy hand. Be bold, and take thy stand.
RODERIGO [*aside*]:   I have no great devotion to the deed;
    And yet he hath given me satisfying reasons.
    'Tis but a man gone.—Forth my sword: he dies!   10

    [*He draws.*]
    [IAGO *withdraws.*]

IAGO [*aside*]:   I have rubbed this young quat° almost to the   *pimple*
    sense,°   *to the quick*
    And he grows angry. Now, whether he kill Cassio,
    Or Cassio him, or each do kill the other,
    Every way makes my gain. Live Roderigo,°   *If Roderigo lives*
    He calls me to a restitution large   15
    Of gold and jewels that I bobbed from him°   *defrauded him of*
    As gifts to Desdemona—
    It must not be. If Cassio do remain,
    He hath a daily beauty in his life
    That makes me ugly; and, besides, the Moor   20
    May unfold° me to him: there stand I in much peril.   *reveal*
    No, he must die. But so:° I heard him coming.   *so be it*

    [*He draws.*]
    Enter CASSIO.

RODERIGO: I know his gait, 'tis he.—Villain, thou diest!

    [*He thrusts at Cassio.*]

CASSIO: That thrust had been mine enemy indeed,
    But that my coat is better° than thou know'st.   *thicker; more armored*   25

9. Not to take bad behavior as an example, but to know what to avoid.

I will make proof of° thine.   *test*

[*He stabs* RODERIGO.]

RODERIGO: Oh, I am slain!

[IAGO *stabs* CASSIO.]

CASSIO: I am maimed forever! Help, ho! Murder! Murder!

[*Exit* IAGO.]

         Enter OTHELLO [*apart*].

OTHELLO: The voice of Cassio. Iago keeps his word!
RODERIGO: Oh, villain that I am!
OTHELLO: It is even so.
30 CASSIO: Oh, help, ho! Light! A surgeon!
OTHELLO: 'Tis he. O brave Iago, honest and just,
         That hast such noble sense of thy friend's wrong;
         Thou teachest me.—Minion,° your dear lies dead,   *Hussy*
         And your unblest fate hies.° Strumpet, I come: *damnation hurries on*
35   For of° my heart those charms, thine eyes, are   *out of*
         blotted;
         Thy bed, lust-stained, shall with lust's blood be
         spotted.

                        Exit OTHELLO.

         Enter LODOVICO *and* GRAZIANO [*apart*].

CASSIO: What, ho? No watch? No passage?° Murder! Murder!   *passersby*
GRAZIANO [*to* LODOVICO]:   'Tis some mischance. The voice
         is very direful.
CASSIO: Oh, help!
40 LODOVICO [*to* GRAZIANO]:   Hark!
RODERIGO: O wretched villain!
LODOVICO [*to* GRAZIANO]:   Two or three groan! 'Tis heavy° night;   *dark*
         These may be counterfeits. Let's think't unsafe
         To come into° the cry without more help.   *go near*
45 RODERIGO: Nobody come? Then shall I bleed to death!

         Enter IAGO [*with a light*].

LODOVICO [*to* GRAZIANO]:   Hark!
GRAZIANO [*to* LODOVICO]:   Here's one comes in his shirt,
         with light and weapons.
IAGO: Who's there? Whose noise is this that cries on murder?
LODOVICO: We do not know.
IAGO: Do not you hear a cry?
CASSIO: Here! Here! For heaven sake, help me!
50 IAGO [*to* CASSIO]:   What's the matter?
GRAZIANO [*to* LODOVICO]:   This is Othello's ensign, as I take it.
LODOVICO [*to* GRAZIANO]:   The same indeed: a very valiant fellow.
IAGO [*to* CASSIO]: What are you here, that cry so grievously?
CASSIO: Iago? Oh, I am spoiled, undone by villains!

Give me some help.

IAGO: O me, lieutenant!   55
What villains have done this?

CASSIO: I think that one of them is hereabout
And cannot make° away.   *get*

IAGO: O treacherous villains!
[*to* LODOVICO *and* GRAZIANO] What are you there?
Come in and give some help.

RODERIGO: Oh, help me there!

CASSIO: That's one of them!   60

IAGO [*to* RODERIGO]:   O murd'rous slave! O villain!

[*He stabs* RODERIGO.]

RODERIGO: O damned Iago! O inhuman dog!

IAGO: Kill men i'th' dark? Where be these bloody thieves?
How silent is this town! Ho! Murder! Murder!
[*to* LODOVICO *and* GRAZIANO] What may you be? Are   65
you of good or evil?

LODOVICO: As you shall prove us, praise us.

IAGO: Signor Lodovico?

LODOVICO: He, sir.

IAGO: I cry you mercy: here's Cassio hurt by villains.

GRAZIANO: Cassio?

IAGO [*to* CASSIO]:   How is't, brother?

CASSIO: My leg is cut in two.   70

IAGO: Marry, heaven forbid.
—Light, gentlemen! I'll bind it with my shirt.

Enter BIANCA.

BIANCA: What is the matter, ho? Who is't that cried?

IAGO: Who is't that cried?

BIANCA: O my dear Cassio!
My sweet Cassio! O Cassio! Cassio! Cassio!   75

IAGO: O notable strumpet.—Cassio, may you suspect
Who they should be that have thus mangled you?

CASSIO: No.

GRAZIANO: I am sorry to find you thus; I have been to seek you.

IAGO [*to* LODOVICO *and* GRAZIANO]:   Lend me a garter. So.
[*He binds Cassio's leg.*]   Oh, for a chair°   *litter* 80
To bear him easily hence.

BIANCA: Alas, he faints! O Cassio! Cassio! Cassio!

IAGO: Gentlemen all, I do suspect this trash°   (*Bianca*)
To be a party in this injury.
—Patience awhile, good Cassio. [*to* LODOVICO *and*   85
GRAZIANO] Come, come,
Lend me a light. [*He goes to* RODERIGO.] Know we this
face or no?
Alas, my friend and my dear countryman,
Roderigo! No? Yes, sure. Yes, 'tis Roderigo!

GRAZIANO: What, of Venice?

IAGO: Even he, sir. Did you know him?

90 GRAZIANO: Know him? Ay.

IAGO: Signor Graziano? I cry your gentle pardon;
      These bloody accidents must excuse my manners
      That so neglected you.

GRAZIANO: I am glad to see you.

IAGO: —How do you, Cassio?—Oh, a chair! A chair!

95 GRAZIANO: Roderigo?

IAGO: He, he. 'Tis he.

     [*Enter Attendants with a chair.*]

                         Oh, that's well said:° the chair.   *carried out*
      Some good man bear him carefully from hence.
      I'll fetch the general's surgeon. [*to* BIANCA] For you,
          mistress,
      Save you your labor.—He that lies slain here, Cassio,
100   Was my dear friend. What malice was between you?

CASSIO: None in the world, nor do I know the man.

IAGO: What, look you pale? [*to Attendants*] Oh, bear him o'th'
      air.[1] [*Exeunt Attendants with* CASSIO *and* RODERIGO.]
      [*to* LODOVICO *and* GRAZIANO] Stay you, good gentlemen.
      [*to* BIANCA] Look you pale, mistress?
      [*to* LODOVICO *and* GRAZIANO] Do you perceive the
      gastness° of her eye?   *terror*

105   [*to* BIANCA] Nay, if you stare we shall hear more anon.
      [*to* LODOVICO *and* GRAZIANO] Behold her well. I pray
          you, look upon her:
      Do you see, gentlemen? Nay, guiltiness will speak,
      Though tongues were out of use.

     [*Enter* EMILIA.]

EMILIA: Alas, what is the matter?
      What is the matter, husband?

110 IAGO: Cassio hath here been set on in the dark
      By Roderigo and fellows that are scaped:
      He's almost slain, and Roderigo quite dead.

EMILIA: Alas, good gentleman! Alas, good Cassio!

IAGO: This is the fruits of whoring. Prithee, Emilia,

115   Go know of Cassio where he supped tonight.
      [*to* BIANCA] What, do you shake at that?

BIANCA: He supped at my house, but I therefore shake not.

IAGO: Oh, did he so? I charge you go with me.

EMILIA: Oh, fie upon thee, strumpet!

120 BIANCA: I am no strumpet, but of life as honest

---

1. Out of the open air (thought to be bad for wounds).

As you that thus abuse me.

EMILIA: As I? Fie upon thee!

IAGO: Kind gentlemen, let's go see poor Cassio dressed.°   *bandaged*

[*to* BIANCA]   Come, mistress, you must tell's another tale.

—Emilia, run you to the citadel

And tell my lord and lady what hath happed.   125

[*to* LODOVICO *and* GRAZIANO] Will you go on afore?

[*aside*] This is the night

That either makes me or fordoes° me quite.   *Exeunt.*   *undoes*

Scene 2

Desdemona and Othello's bedroom. Enter OTHELLO [*with
a light,*] *and* DESDEMONA *in her bed.*

OTHELLO: It is the cause,[2] it is the cause, my soul.

Let me not name it to you, you chaste stars:

It is the cause. Yet I'll not shed her blood,

Nor scar that whiter skin of hers than snow

And smooth as monumental alabaster;°   *stone used in tombs* 5

Yet she must die, else she'll betray more men.

Put out the light, and then put out the light.[3]

If I quench thee, thou flaming minister,°   *light that serves me*

I can again thy former light restore,

Should I repent me—but once put out thy light,   10

Thou cunning'st pattern of excelling nature,[4]

I know not where is that Promethean heat[5]

That can thy light relume.° When I have plucked thy   *relight*
    rose,

I cannot give it vital growth again:

It needs must wither. I'll smell thee on the tree.   15

[*He kisses her.*]

Oh, balmy breath, that dost almost persuade

Justice to break her sword! One more, one more.

Be thus when thou art dead, and I will kill thee

And love thee after. One more, and that's the last.

[*He kisses her.*]

So sweet was ne'er so fatal. I must weep,   20

But they are cruel tears. This sorrow's heavenly:

---

2. What matters is Desdemona's infidelity; the "cause" of justice, which Othello sees himself defending, as in the subsequent lines.

3. This and the following lines compare the light of Othello's lamp or torch to Desdemona's "light" of life.

4. You most cleverly wrought example of nature's work.

5. Life-giving fire. In Greek mythology, Prometheus stole fire from heaven to give it to humankind; in a different tradition, he is credited with animating humankind from clay.

It strikes where it doth love.[6] She wakes!

DESDEMONA: Who's there? Othello?

OTHELLO: Ay, Desdemona.

DESDEMONA: Will you come to bed, my lord?

OTHELLO: Have you prayed tonight, Desdemon?

25 DESDEMONA: Ay, my lord.

OTHELLO: If you bethink yourself of any crime
    Unreconciled as yet to heaven and grace,
    Solicit° for it straight.°   *Ask forgiveness / straightaway*

DESDEMONA: Alack, my lord,
    What may you mean by that?

30 OTHELLO: Well, do it, and be brief. I will walk by.
    I would not kill thy unpreparèd spirit;
    No, heavens forfend, I would not kill thy soul.

DESDEMONA: Talk you of killing?

OTHELLO: Ay, I do.

DESDEMONA: Then heaven have mercy on me!

OTHELLO: Amen, with all my heart.

35 DESDEMONA: If you say,° I hope you will not kill me.   *Since you say "amen"*

OTHELLO: Hum!

DESDEMONA: And yet I fear you, for you're fatal then
    When your eyes roll so. Why I should fear I know not,
    Since guiltiness I know not, but yet I feel I fear.

OTHELLO: Think on thy sins.

40 DESDEMONA: They are loves I bear to you.

OTHELLO: Ay, and for that thou diest.

DESDEMONA: That death's unnatural that kills for loving.
    Alas, why gnaw you so your nether lip?
    Some bloody passion shakes your very frame.

45   These are portents, but yet I hope, I hope,
    They do not point on me.

OTHELLO: Peace, and be still.

DESDEMONA: I will so. What's the matter?

OTHELLO: That handkerchief,
    Which I so loved and gave thee, thou gav'st to Cassio.

DESDEMONA: No, by my life and soul! Send for the man,
50 And ask him.

OTHELLO: Sweet soul, take heed, take heed of perjury.
    Thou art on thy death-bed.

DESDEMONA: I? But not yet to die?

OTHELLO: Presently.°   *Immediately*
    Therefore confess thee freely of thy sin,
55   For to deny each article with oath
    Cannot remove nor choke the strong conception
    That I do groan withal:[7] thou art to die.

6. See Hebrews 12.6: "For whom the Lord loveth, he chasteneth."
7. Cannot stop the strong conviction I have in your guilt (or the firm plan to kill you), which makes me groan so. The metaphor is from childbirth.

DESDEMONA: O heaven, have mercy on me!
OTHELLO: I say amen.
DESDEMONA: And have you mercy, too. I never did
    Offend you in my life, never loved Cassio   60
    But with such general warranty of heaven
    As I might love. I never gave him token.
OTHELLO: By heaven, I saw my handkerchief in's hand!
    O perjured woman, thou dost stone° my heart,   *harden*
    And makest me call what I intend to do   65
    A murder, which I thought a sacrifice.
    I saw the handkerchief.
DESDEMONA: He found it, then.
    I never gave it him. Send for him hither:
    Let him confess a truth.
OTHELLO: He hath confessed.
DESDEMONA: What, my lord?
OTHELLO: That he hath used thee.
DESDEMONA: How, unlawfully?   70
OTHELLO: Ay.
DESDEMONA: He will not say so.
OTHELLO: No, his mouth is stopped.
    Honest Iago hath ta'en order for't.
DESDEMONA: Oh, my fear interprets. What, is he dead?
OTHELLO: Had all his hairs been lives, my great revenge
    Had stomach for them all.   75
DESDEMONA: Alas, he is betrayed, and I undone.
OTHELLO: Out, strumpet! Weep'st thou for him to my face?
DESDEMONA: Oh, banish me, my lord, but kill me not.
OTHELLO: Down, strumpet!

> [*He attacks her.*]

DESDEMONA [*struggling*]:   Kill me tomorrow; let me live tonight!   80
OTHELLO: Nay, if you strive—
DESDEMONA: But half an hour!
OTHELLO: Being done, there is no pause.[8]
DESDEMONA: But while I say one prayer!
OTHELLO: It is too late.
    [*He*] *smothers her.*
EMILIA: (*at the door*):   My lord! My lord! What ho, my lord!
    My lord!
OTHELLO: What noise is this?—Not dead? Not yet quite dead?   85
    I, that am cruel, am yet merciful:
    I would not have thee linger in thy pain.
    So. So.

> [*He smothers* DESDEMONA *again.*]

EMILIA (*within*):   What ho, my lord! My lord!

8. Now that I've started, there's no stopping.

OTHELLO: Who's there?

EMILIA [*within*]:   O good my lord, I would speak a word with you.

90 OTHELLO: Yes.—'Tis Emilia.—By and by!—She's dead.

'Tis like° she comes to speak of Cassio's death: *likely*

The noise was high.°—Ha, no more moving?   *commotion was loud*

Still as the grave. Shall she come in? Were't good?

I think she stirs again! No. What's best to do?

95 If she come in, she'll sure speak to my wife.

My wife! My wife! What wife? I have no wife.

Oh, insupportable! Oh, heavy hour!

Methinks it should be now a huge eclipse

Of sun and moon, and that th'affrighted globe

Did yawn at alteration.[9]

100 EMILIA [*within*]:   I do beseech you

That I may speak with you, O good my lord!

OTHELLO: I had forgot thee.—Oh, come in, Emilia.

—Soft!°—By and by.—Let me the curtains draw.   *Quiet*

—Where art thou? What's the matter with thee now?

Enter EMILIA.

105 EMILIA: O my good lord, yonder's foul murders done.

OTHELLO: What? Now?

EMILIA: But° now, my lord.   *Just*

OTHELLO: It is the very error° of the moon: *deviation*

She comes more nearer earth than she was wont,

And makes men mad.

110 EMILIA: Cassio, my lord, hath killed

A young Venetian called Roderigo.

OTHELLO: Roderigo killed? And Cassio killed?

EMILIA: No, Cassio is not killed.

OTHELLO [*aside*]:   Not Cassio killed? Then murder's out of
      tune,

And sweet revenge grows harsh.

115 DESDEMONA: Oh, falsely, falsely murdered!

EMILIA: Alas, what cry is that?

OTHELLO: That? What?

EMILIA: Out and alas, that was my lady's voice!

[*She opens the bed curtains.*]

Help! Help, ho! Help!—O lady, speak again!

Sweet Desdemona! O sweet mistress, speak!

DESDEMONA: A guiltless death I die.

120 EMILIA: Oh, who hath done this deed?

DESDEMONA: Nobody. I myself. Farewell.

Commend me to my kind lord. Oh, farewell!

[*She dies.*]

9. Should gape at the change. Earthquakes were associated with eclipses.

OTHELLO: Why, how should she be murdered?

EMILIA: Alas, who knows?

OTHELLO: You hear her say herself it was not I.

EMILIA: She said so. I must needs report the truth.   125

OTHELLO: She's like a liar gone to burning hell:
          'Twas I that killed her.

EMILIA: Oh, the more angel she, and you the blacker devil.

OTHELLO: She turned to folly,° and she was a whore.   *wantonness*

EMILIA: Thou dost belie her, and thou art a devil.   130

OTHELLO: She was false as water.

EMILIA: Thou art rash as fire to say
          That she was false. Oh, she was heavenly true!

OTHELLO: Cassio did top her—ask thy husband else.°   *if you doubt it*
          Oh, I were damned beneath all depth in hell
          But that I did proceed upon just grounds   135
          To this extremity. Thy husband knew it all.

EMILIA: My husband?

OTHELLO: Thy husband.

EMILIA: That she was false to wedlock?

OTHELLO: Ay, with Cassio. Had she been true,
          If heaven would make me such another world
          Of one entire and perfect chrysolite,°   *topaz* 140
          I'd not have sold her for it.

EMILIA: My husband?

OTHELLO: Ay, 'twas he that told me on her first.
          An honest man he is, and hates the slime
          That sticks on filthy deeds—

EMILIA: My husband?

OTHELLO: What needs this iterance,° woman? I say, thy   *repetition* 145
          husband.

EMILIA: O mistress! Villainy hath made mocks with° love.   *at*
          —My husband say she was false?

OTHELLO: He, woman.
          I say, thy husband. Dost understand the word?
          My friend, thy husband, honest, honest Iago.

EMILIA: If he say so, may his pernicious soul   150
          Rot half a grain a day: he lies to th' heart.
          She was too fond of her most filthy bargain.

OTHELLO: Ha!

EMILIA: Do thy worst!
          This deed of thine is no more worthy heaven   155
          Than thou wast worthy her.

OTHELLO: Peace, you were best.[1]

EMILIA: Thou hast not half that power to do me harm
          As I have to be hurt. O gull!° O dolt,   *fool*
          As ignorant as dirt. Thou hast done a deed—

---

1. It would be best for you (to remain silent).

160 I care not for thy sword: I'll make thee known,
 Though I lost twenty lives.—Help! Help, ho! Help!
 The Moor hath killed my mistress. Murder! Murder!

   Enter MONTANO, GRAZIANO, *and* IAGO.

MONTANO: What is the matter? How now, general?
EMILIA: Oh, are you come, Iago? You have done well
165 That men must lay their murders on your neck.
GRAZIANO: What is the matter?
EMILIA [*to* IAGO]: Disprove this villain, if thou beest a man.
 He says thou told'st him that his wife was false.
 I know thou didst not: thou'rt not such a villain.
170 Speak, for my heart is full.
IAGO: I told him what I thought, and told no more
 Than what he found himself was apt and true.
EMILIA: But did you ever tell him she was false?
IAGO: I did.
175 EMILIA: You told a lie, an odious, damned lie!
 Upon my soul, a lie, a wicked lie!
 She false with Cassio? Did you say with Cassio?
IAGO: With Cassio, mistress. Go to, charm° your tongue.   *silence*
EMILIA: I will not charm my tongue: I am bound to speak:
180 My mistress here lies murdered in her bed.
MONTANO *and* GRAZIANO: O heavens forfend!
EMILIA: And your reports have set the murder on.
OTHELLO: Nay, stare not, masters: it is true indeed.
GRAZIANO: 'Tis a strange truth.
MONTANO: Oh, monstrous act!
185 EMILIA: Villainy! Villainy! Villainy!
 I think upon't; I think I smell't. Oh, villainy!
 I thought so, then. I'll kill myself for grief.
 Oh, villainy! Villainy!
IAGO: What, are you mad?
 I charge you, get you home.
190 EMILIA: Good gentlemen, let me have leave to speak.
 'Tis proper I obey him, but not now.
 —Perchance, Iago, I will ne'er go home.
OTHELLO: Oh! Oh! Oh!

   [OTHELLO *falls on the bed.*]

EMILIA: Nay, lay thee down and roar,
 For thou hast killed the sweetest innocent
 That e'er did lift up eye.°   *(to heaven)*
195 OTHELLO: Oh, she was foul!
 [*to* GRAZIANO] I scarce did know you, uncle. There
  lies your niece,
 Whose breath, indeed, these hands have newly
  stopped.
 I know this act shows° horrible and grim.   *appears*

GRAZIANO: Poor Desdemon. I am glad thy father's dead:
    Thy match was mortal to him, and pure grief   200
    Shore his old thread in twain.[2] Did he live now,
    This sight would make him do a desperate turn,°   *act*
    Yea, curse his better angel from his side,
    And fall to reprobance.[3]
OTHELLO: 'Tis pitiful, but yet Iago knows   205
    That she with Cassio hath the act of shame
    A thousand times committed. Cassio confessed it,
    And she did gratify his amorous works
    With that recognizance° and pledge of love   *token*
    Which I first gave her. I saw it in his hand: 210
    It was a handkerchief, an antique token
    My father gave my mother.[4]
EMILIA: O heaven! O heavenly powers!
IAGO: Come, hold your peace!
EMILIA: 'Twill out, 'twill out. I, peace?
    No, I will speak as liberal as the north.[5]
    Let heaven, and men, and devils, let them all,   215
    All, all cry shame against me, yet I'll speak.
IAGO: Be wise, and get you home.

    [He draws.]

EMILIA: I will not.
GRAZIANO: Fie! Your sword upon a woman?
EMILIA: O thou dull Moor, that handkerchief thou speak'st of
    I found by fortune,° and did give my husband: *happenstance* 220
    For often, with a solemn earnestness—
    More than indeed belonged to such a trifle—
    He begged of me to steal't.
IAGO: Villainous whore!
EMILIA: She give it Cassio? No, alas, I found it,
    And I did give't my husband.
IAGO: Filth! Thou liest.   225
EMILIA: By heaven, I do not. I do not, gentlemen.
    [to OTHELLO*]* O murd'rous coxcomb!° What should   *fool*
       such a fool
    Do with so good a wife?
OTHELLO: Are there no stones° in heaven   *thunderbolts*
    But what serves for the thunder? *[to* IAGO*]* Precious° villain!   *Absolute*

    *[*OTHELLO *runs at* IAGO; MONTANO *disarms him.*
    IAGO *stabs* EMILIA.*]*

2. Cut the thread of his life.
3. Reprobation, rejection by God—here for suicide, the unforgivably sinful act of despair, leading to
eternal damnation.
4. Earlier, however, Othello says that his mother got the handkerchief not from his father but from
"an Egyptian . . . charmer" (3.4.53–54).
5. As freely as the north wind.

230 GRAZIANO: The woman falls! Sure, he hath killed his wife.

                                       [*Exit* IAGO.]

EMILIA: Ay! Ay! Oh, lay me by my mistress' side.

    [GRAZIANO *puts her on the bed.*]

GRAZIANO: He's gone, but his wife's killed.

MONTANO: 'Tis a notorious villain. [*to* GRAZIANO] Take you
    this weapon,
    Which I have recovered from the Moor.

235 Come, guard the door without; let him not pass,
    But kill him rather. I'll after that same villain,
    For 'tis a damned slave.   *Exeunt* [MONTANO *and* GRAZIANO].

OTHELLO: I am not valiant, neither,
    But every puny whipster° gets my sword.   *insignificant person*
    But why should honor outlive honesty?°   *integrity*
    Let it go all.

240 EMILIA [*to* DESDEMONA]: What did thy song bode, lady?
    Hark, canst thou hear me? I will play the swan
    And die in music. [*She sings.*] "Willow, willow, willow."
    —Moor, she was chaste. She loved thee, cruel Moor.
    So come my soul to bliss as I speak true;

245 So, speaking as I think, alas, I die.

    [*She dies.*]

OTHELLO: I have another weapon in this chamber:
    It was a sword of Spain, the ice-brook's temper.°   *tempered in icy water*
    Oh, here it is.—Uncle, I must come forth.

GRAZIANO [*within*]: If thou attempt it, it will cost thee dear:

250 Thou hast no weapon, and perforce must suffer.

OTHELLO: Look in upon me, then, and speak with me
    Or, naked° as I am, I will assault thee.   *unarmed*

    [*Enter* GRAZIANO.]

GRAZIANO: What is the matter?

OTHELLO: Behold, I have a weapon:
    A better never did itself sustain

255 Upon a soldier's thigh. I have seen the day
    That, with this little arm and this good sword,
    I have made my way through more impediments
    Than twenty times your stop.° But, oh, vain boast!   *power to stop*
    Who can control his fate? 'Tis not so now.

260 Be not afraid, though you do see me weaponed:
    Here is my journey's end; here is my butt°   *goal*
    And very sea-mark° of my utmost sail.°   *beacon / voyage's limit*
    Do you go back dismayed? 'Tis a lost° fear: *an unnecessary*
    Man but a rush° against Othello's breast,   *Aim even a reed*

265 And he retires. Where should Othello go?

[*to* DESDEMONA] Now, how dost thou look now?
   O ill-starred wench,
Pale as thy smock. When we shall meet at count,°   **Judgment Day**
This look of thine will hurl my soul from heaven,
And fiends will snatch at it. Cold, cold, my girl?
Even like thy chastity. O cursèd, cursèd slave!   270
Whip me, ye devils,
From the possession of this heavenly sight;
Blow me about in winds, roast me in sulfur,
Wash me in steep-down gulfs of liquid fire.
O Desdemon! Dead, Desdemon, dead! Oh! Oh!   275

   Enter LODOVICO, CASSIO [*in a chair*], MONTANO, *and*
   IAGO [*as a prisoner*], *with* OFFICERS.

LODOVICO: Where is this rash and most unfortunate man?
OTHELLO: That's he that was Othello: here I am.
LODOVICO: Where is that viper? [*to* OFFICERS] Bring the
   villain forth.
OTHELLO: I look down towards his feet,[6] but that's a fable.
   [*to* IAGO] If that thou beest a devil, I cannot kill thee.   280

   [*He stabs* IAGO.]

LODOVICO [*to* OFFICERS]:   Wrench his sword from him!
IAGO: I bleed, sir, but not killed.
OTHELLO: I am not sorry, neither: I'd have thee live,
   For, in my sense,° 'tis happiness to die.   *state of feeling*
LODOVICO: O thou, Othello, that was once so good,
   Fallen in the practice° of a cursèd slave,   *plot* 285
   What shall be said to thee?
OTHELLO: Why, anything.
   An honorable murderer, if you will,
   For naught I did in hate, but all in honor.
LODOVICO: This wretch hath part confessed his villainy.
   Did you and he consent in Cassio's death?   290
OTHELLO: Ay.
CASSIO: Dear general, I never gave you cause!
OTHELLO: I do believe it, and I ask your pardon.
   Will you, I pray, demand that demi-devil
   Why he hath thus ensnared my soul and body?   295
IAGO: Demand me nothing. What you know, you know.
   From this time forth I never will speak word.
LODOVICO: What, not to pray?
GRAZIANO: Torments° will ope your lips.   *Tortures*
OTHELLO: Well, thou dost best.[7]
LODOVICO: Sir,   300

---

6. I look for the devil's cloven feet.
7. Addressed to Lodovico and Graziano or, ironically, to Iago.

You shall understand what hath befallen,
Which, as I think, you know not. Here is a letter
Found in the pocket of the slain Roderigo,
And here another: the one of them imports
305 The death of Cassio, to be undertook
By Roderigo.
OTHELLO: O villain!
CASSIO: Most heathenish and most gross!°   *monstrous*
LODOVICO: Now, here's another discontented paper°   *paper listing complaints*
Found in his pocket, too, and this it seems
Roderigo meant t' have sent this damnèd villain
310 But that, belike,° Iago in the interim   *most likely*
Came in and satisfied him.
OTHELLO: O thou pernicious caitiff!°   *wretch*
—How came you, Cassio, by that handkerchief
That was my wife's?
CASSIO: I found it in my chamber,
And he himself confessed it but even now
315 That there he dropped it for a special purpose
Which wrought to his desire.
OTHELLO: O fool! Fool! Fool!
CASSIO: There is, besides, in Roderigo's letter
How he upbraids Iago that he made him
Brave° me upon the watch, whereon it came   *Defy*
320 That I was cast;° and even but now he spake,   *dismissed*
After long seeming dead: Iago hurt him;
Iago set him on.
LODOVICO [*to* OTHELLO]:   You must forsake this room and
go with us:
Your power and your command is taken off,°   *away*
325 And Cassio rules in Cyprus. For this slave,
If there be any cunning cruelty
That can torment him much and hold him° long,   *(alive)*
It shall be his.—You shall close° prisoner rest   *tightly confined*
Till that the nature of your fault be known
330 To the Venetian state. [*to* OFFICERS] Come, bring away.
OTHELLO: Soft you,° a word or two before you go.   *Wait*
I have done the state some service, and they know't—
No more of that. I pray you, in your letters,
When you shall these unlucky deeds relate,
335 Speak of me as I am; nothing extenuate,
Nor set down aught in malice. Then must you speak
Of one that loved not wisely, but too well;
Of one not easily jealous but, being wrought,
Perplexed in the extreme; of one whose hand,
340 Like the base Judean,[8] threw a pearl away

---

8. Native of Judea, kingdom in ancient Palestine; member of the biblical "tribe" (line 341) of Judah; Jew.

Richer than all his tribe; of one whose subdued° eyes,　　　　*(by grief)*
Albeit unusèd to the melting mood,
Drop tears as fast as the Arabian trees
Their medicinable gum.° Set you down this,　　　　　　　*myrrh*
And say, besides, that in Aleppo[9] once,　　　　　　　　　345
Where a malignant and a turbaned Turk
Beat a Venetian and traduced° the state,　　　　　　　　*defamed*
I took by th' throat the circumcisèd dog
And smote him thus.

　　　　[*He stabs himself.*]

LODOVICO:　　　　　　　Oh, bloody period!°　　　　*conclusion; sentence*
GRAZIANO: All that is spoke is marred.　　　　　　　　　350
OTHELLO [*to* DESDEMONA]:　　I kissed thee ere I killed thee.
　　No way but this:
　　Killing myself, to die upon a kiss.

　　　　[*He*] *dies*[.]

CASSIO: This did I fear—but thought he had no weapon—
　　For he was great of heart.
LODOVICO [*to* IAGO]:　　　　　O Spartan dog,[1]
　　More fell° than anguish, hunger, or the sea,　　　　*cruel* 355
　　Look on the tragic loading of this bed:
　　This is thy work. The object poisons sight.
　　Let it be hid.—Graziano, keep° the house,　　　　　*guard*
　　And seize upon the fortunes of the Moor,
　　For they succeed on° you. [*to* CASSIO] To you, Lord　*pass down to* 360
　　　　Governor,
　　Remains the censure° of this hellish villain:　　　　*sentence*
　　The time, the place, the torture—oh, enforce it.
　　Myself will straight aboard, and to the state
　　This heavy act with heavy heart relate.　　　　*Exeunt.*

SUGGESTIONS FOR WRITING

1. In A MIDSUMMER NIGHT'S DREAM's best-known speech, Theseus asserts, "The lunatic, the lover, and the poet / Are of imagination all compact" (5.1.7–8). Citing evidence from the play, write an essay analyzing Shakespeare's characterization of
love—not only in the play's action but also in the words of the love-obsessed characters. Is Shakespearean love merely a kind of madness, or does it contain hints of a
guiding wisdom beyond the awareness of lovers themselves?
2. Early in A MIDSUMMER NIGHT'S DREAM, Helena remarks, "Love looks not with the
eyes but with the mind" (1.1.234). The play is filled with references to eyes and
vision; indeed, the plot hinges on the differences between what characters see
and what they think they see. Using specific examples, write an essay exploring

9. Ottoman city in what later became Syria through which Venice traded with the East.
1. The ancient Greek city-state of Sparta was renowned for the martial prowess, even savagery, of its
armies.

the significance of eyes, sight, and seeing in this play. What does the play suggest about the power and the limitations of human vision?

3. In A MIDSUMMER NIGHT'S DREAM, characters perform a play. What are the functions and effects of this device? What might the play within a play suggest about the value of drama—including the value of plays like Shakespeare's own? What different attitudes toward drama are displayed by various characters in A MIDSUMMER NIGHT'S DREAM? Write an essay exploring the function and significance of the play within a play. What attitudes toward drama does Shakespeare encourage us to adopt?

4. Write an essay considering the oft-debated issue of Iago's motives and methods (or a specific aspect thereof) in OTHELLO. Obviously, Iago resents Othello promoting Cassio, and it's important to consider precisely why or in what terms Iago considers Cassio's promotion unfair, even inappropriate. But does this resentment alone seem a sufficient explanation for Iago's actions? What alternative explanations might the play offer? Might Iago be motivated by prejudices about Moors and/or women? Or might he, as some critics argue, simply play upon others' prejudices rather than acting out his own? Alternatively, might you agree with Samuel Taylor Coleridge that Iago ultimately represents "motiveless Malignity"?

5. In his influential discussion of tragedy (in the *Poetics*), Aristotle presents *hamartia* as the cause of the protagonist's downfall. For years, even centuries, *hamartia* has been interpreted to mean something like "tragic flaw"—some specific, negative character trait or propensity such as hubris. More recently, however, some critics have contended that this is a misreading of both Aristotle and tragedy itself, arguing that *hamartia* means not a moral failing but a mistake, often based on the sort of ignorance or misjudgment to which all human beings are prone. Write an essay exploring which of these two understandings of *hamartia* might best explain Othello and OTHELLO.

6. Write an essay exploring the characterization of the socially lowly characters in A MIDSUMMER NIGHT'S DREAM and OTHELLO and their thematic significance. What might be noteworthy about when such characters appear in each play? about how they speak, as well as what they say and do? Might some or all of these characters display a wisdom lacking in their social betters? If so, what is it, and is it the same or similar in the two plays?

7. Write an essay comparing the way relationships between fathers and daughters or husbands and wives are portrayed in OTHELLO and A MIDSUMMER NIGHT'S DREAM. What might the plays suggest about how and why such relationships tend to go wrong? about how fathers/husbands should treat daughters/wives and vice versa? Alternatively, write an essay exploring relationships among women in the two plays: What brings women together as friends and/or allies? When, why, and on what terms, that is, might female characters in these plays identify with and defend each other? What drives them apart or leads them to turn on, or compete with, each other?

27

CULTURAL AND HISTORICAL CONTEXTS: LORRAINE HANSBERRY'S *A RAISIN IN THE SUN*

Three different levels of time operate in most literary texts, including plays. First, a text represents a particular **time**—the temporal **setting**—in which the action takes place. We can call this *plot time*. Second, the text reflects the time when the author was writing, and, inevitably, the conditions and assumptions of that time inform the text's conception and style; this feature of textual time we may call *authorial time*. Third, readers read in a particular *reader time*, when conditions and assumptions may differ from those that obtain in either the text's or the author's present. (If we encounter a play on the stage, we might instead call this *performance time*.)

In some cases, plot, authorial, and reader time all differ. Wole Soyinka's *Death and the King's Horseman*, for example, is set in the early 1940s in the British colony of Nigeria. Yet it was written in the early 1970s, after Soyinka's country gained its independence. Thus, when we—as twenty-first-century readers—read the play, three distinct historical and cultural contexts are operating at once. Values in these three times will not be identical. How we interpret the actions and thoughts of the characters in part depends not only on our own assumptions about what they should or might do, but also on what we know about the conditions that shaped people's lives in quite different historical and cultural milieus. Keeping these three contexts in mind as we read—and consciously making comparisons when we perceive conflicting values—is a vital part of our response and interpretation.

This can be equally true of plays that represent the times in which they were written. When Lorraine Hansberry's A RAISIN IN THE SUN debuted in 1959, its audience watched scenes that might well have been unfolding at virtually the same moment just down the street. The stage directions, in fact, indicate that the action in the play occurs "in Chicago's Southside, sometime between World War II and the present." In this case, almost no difference exists between plot time and authorial time. Indeed, the play asked its original audiences to believe that they were confronting life exactly as it was happening and being invited to consider issues of immediate consequence. And the play also drew, at least to some extent, on that audience's knowledge of current events, concerns, and issues—knowledge that we, living in a quite different reader time, may have to work to master.

Of course, this does not mean that *A Raisin in the Sun* or any great play can't speak to us unless we "study up" on the worlds about and in which it was written. "Inevitably, [. . .] every work belongs to a given moment," as Soyinka reminds us. But, he adds, "it transcends this" moment, too. Hansberry's play remains relevant because it shows us complex, deeply human characters confronting questions that we face today, too—about family, cultural and personal identity, gender, race and ethnicity, ambition, human dignity and honor, historical change, and generational conflict. Much of what happens in the play could and does still happen in our world, and in much the same way.

But not everything. Consider the abortion that Ruth Younger contemplates near the end of *A Raisin in the Sun*'s first act. In 1959, abortion was illegal in the United States. Women who sought abortions had either to leave the country, usually traveling to Mexico or Puerto Rico (a relatively expensive option), or to seek out shady, back-alley practitioners like the one Ruth consults in the play. Such abortionists typically had little medical expertise and often operated in highly unsanitary conditions. Disease and mortality rates were high, and some of the horror that the Younger family expresses at the thought of abortion can be attributed to reasonable fears about its physical consequences. But their horror also results from the moral and social stigma surrounding abortion. However individuals today might feel about the ethics of abortion, the law prohibited it in 1959, and public opinion weighed heavily against the practice. To appreciate Ruth's situation, understand other characters' responses, and imagine the original audience's reactions, it helps to know about the prevailing legal climate, as well as the various social attitudes and concerns of the day, especially within a respectable, proud, and aspiring Black family like the Youngers.

Some plays offer us a good deal of information about setting that is relevant to the interpretation of specific episodes. But sometimes we have to supply facts that the text doesn't give us. People may share some characteristics across ages and cultures, but behavior and motivation are often conditioned by historically and culturally specific circumstances. Often we have to adjust our expectations because the world of the play or that of its author differs greatly from our own. Identifying the play's setting—in time and place—and considering carefully the historical and cultural context in which the play was written can be crucial to understanding what happens and why.

The rest of this chapter seeks to introduce you to the contexts that inspired and shaped *A Raisin in the Sun* and to some of the historically specific conditions, concerns, and conflicts the play explores.

THE HISTORICAL SIGNIFICANCE OF *A RAISIN IN THE SUN*

The debut of *A Raisin in the Sun* was a significant historical and cultural event in its own right. The first play by an African American woman ever produced on Broadway, it earned its creator, Lorraine Hansberry (1930–65), the New York Drama Critics' Circle Award as the year's best play just two months after it opened. Hansberry thus became—at twenty-nine—the youngest American playwright, the first Black writer, and only the fifth woman ever to receive this prestigious award. Yet when Hansberry's friend and fellow writer James Baldwin hailed her play as a major "historical achievement," he had something else in mind—the unprecedented way that *A Raisin in the Sun* brought African Americans into the theater and onto the stage. "I had never in my life seen so many black people in the theater," Baldwin recalled. "And the reason was that never before, in the entire history of the American theater, had so much of the truth of black people's lives been seen on the stage. Black people [had] ignored the theater because the theater had always ignored them." To Baldwin and others, *A Raisin in the Sun* was an "historical achievement" precisely because of its **realism** and contemporaneity, its truthful depiction of the sorts of lives lived by many ordinary African Americans in the late 1950s. In a sense, the play made history by accurately reflecting a historical and cultural reality previously ignored by dramatists.

THE GREAT MIGRATION

One factor that undoubtedly made the Younger family seem so realistic was the fact that their situation closely resembled that of the 6.5 million African Americans who moved from the rural South to the urban North between 1910 and 1970 as part of the Great Migration. Though these migrants settled in every northern city, the majority eventually made their homes in New York City and Chicago. By 1960, Chica-

Lorraine Hansberry, 1959

go's Black population had grown to 813,000—25 percent of the city's inhabitants.

Like Lena Younger and her husband, those migrant millions flew north on the wings of hope—hope for better jobs at higher wages and for greater safety and freedom than they enjoyed in the Jim Crow–era South. (By 1914, every southern state had passed "Jim Crow" laws mandating racially segregated railroad cars, waiting rooms, bathrooms, restaurants, theaters, recreation areas, and even hospitals.) Not coincidentally, migration increased when northern industries were expanding and when conditions in the South were particularly oppressive or violent. In the 1920s, when the Younger family would have arrived in Chicago, a government-sponsored report on race relations in that city pointed out that over 85 percent of the 2,881 lynchings that occurred in the United States between 1885 and 1918 occurred in southern states and "that numbers of migrants from towns where lynchings had occurred registered for jobs in Chicago very shortly after lynchings." The same report also concluded that Blacks were drawn to the city for more than economic reasons. When recent immigrants interviewed for the report were asked, "What do you like about the North?" their responses were remarkably similar:

1. Freedom in voting and conditions of colored people here.
2. Freedom and chance to make a living; privileges.
3. Freedom and opportunity to acquire something.

10. Freedom of speech and action. Can live without fear. No Jim Crow.

Songs and poems of the 1920s, as well as the African American press, fueled such hopes and imbued them with religious significance. The Great Migration was cast as the "Flight out of Egypt"; migrants were encouraged to see themselves as "Bound for the Promised Land," "Going into Canaan."

Segregated drinking fountain, Oklahoma City, 1939

LIFE IN THE "BLACK METROPOLIS"

In reality, the vast majority of Blacks who migrated north found themselves not in Canaan, but in the all-Black, inner-city enclaves—the so-called Smoketowns, Bronzevilles, and Black Belts—that had begun to develop in all of the North's major cities before the First World War. In Chicago, that meant the South Side, a strip of land extending south along State Street from the Loop (the city's central business district) and bounded by Lake Michigan (to the east), Chicago's famous stockyards (to the west), and White neighborhoods (to the south). By the 1940s, the South Side had become what it remains to this day—"the largest contiguous settlement of African-Americans" (in the words of journalist Nicholas Lemann).

On the one hand, this "Black Metropolis" might well have looked to newcomers very like the African American Promised Land, a thriving city within a city in which "a Black person could be somebody." By the 1940s, the South Side boasted bustling shopping districts; a spacious public park and lakeside beach; nationally known institutions including the Regal Theater, the Savoy Ballroom, and the Hotel Grand; and countless movie houses and nightclubs featuring blues masters like Muddy Waters (1915–83), himself a migrant from the Mississippi Delta. It was also, as Lemann notes,

> home to the heavyweight boxing champion of the world (and the most famous black man in America), Joe Louis; the only black member of Congress, William Dawson; the most prominent black newspaper, the *Defender*; the largest black congregation, J. H. Jackson's Olivet Baptist Church; the greatest black singer, Mahalia Jackson; and a host of lesser-known prosperous people [. . .].

Regal Theater, Chicago, 1953

Undoubtedly, the presence of so many African American luminaries, as well as the sheer existence of such a large Black community, fueled the pride and aspirations of ordinary people like the Youngers. (Tellingly, the nation's first African American first lady, Michelle Obama [b. 1964], would grow up on the South Side, where her future husband also launched his career and where the Barack Obama Presidential Center will ultimately be located.)

On the other hand, however, "prosperous people" were few and far between in the South Side at midcentury. And what lay between them were the thousands who, like the Youngers, occupied lower rungs of the social ladder. For even if northern cities offered African Americans greater safety, freedom, and opportunity than they enjoyed in the South, they were nonetheless paid much lower wages than their White counterparts, barred entirely from many good jobs, fired first in bad economic times, and hired last in good ones. In 1950 (nine years before *A Raisin in the Sun*'s debut), the African American unemployment rate in Chicago was roughly three times that of White workers. Of those Chicagoans who were employed, 70 percent of Black men (versus 36 percent of White men) and 75 percent of Black women (versus 33 percent of White women) held unskilled jobs. Twenty-two percent of Black men and almost 36 percent of Black women worked, as do the Youngers, in the lowest (domestic) "service" sector—as cooks, maids, janitors, and chauffeurs; only 14 percent of White men and 11 percent of White women did so.

HOUSING AND RESIDENTIAL SEGREGATION

If the Youngers' jobs make them representative, so, too, does the fact that they live in a small, "tired," roach-infested apartment. In the 1940s, population density on the South Side averaged about 90,000 people per square mile (as compared with 20,000 in White neighborhoods). Landlords often charged South Side residents much higher rents than were charged elsewhere, while doing little to maintain the apartments hastily carved out of existing buildings. In their 1960 study *Housing a Metropolis*, sociologists Beverly Duncan and Philip M. Hauser estimated that Chicago's non-White renters were more than twice as likely as Whites to live in substandard housing. For home buyers in the South Side, the situation was even worse. Duncan and Hauser estimated that, in the late 1940s, those buyers paid 28 to 51 percent more than they would have in White neighborhoods. And they often got less for their money: In 1960, non-White homeowners were, according to the same source, six times as likely as their White counterparts to live in substandard homes.

Though Chicago's Black Belt expanded southward and westward throughout the Great Migration, this expansion meant movement into formerly White residential areas—an extraordinarily difficult, slow, often violent process. This was so, as sociologists St. Clair Drake and Horace R. Cayton explain in their classic *Black Metropolis* (1945), "primarily because of white people's attitudes toward having Negroes as neighbors. Because some white Chicagoans do not wish colored neighbors, formal and informal social controls are used to isolate the latter within congested all-Negro neighborhoods." The major "formal" means of maintaining residential segregation were restrictive covenants preventing property from being sold or rented to Blacks. By 1930, about 75 percent of the city's residential property was bound by such agreements, while all agents who belonged to the real estate trade association were bound by a code of ethics that forbade moving Blacks into White areas. The U.S. Supreme Court declared such covenants legally unenforceable, though not themselves illegal, in 1948. But both before and after that time—in Chicago, as elsewhere—violence was the chief "informal" means adopted by Whites when restrictive covenants and codes failed to maintain residential segregation. According to Drake and Cayton, almost five hundred attacks on Black residents and/or their residences were reported in Chicago between 1945 and 1950, most involving arson. In 1956 and 1957 alone, 164 such racial "incidents" occurred.

It is here that Hansberry's personal experience intersects with the historical and cultural context about and in which she wrote, though her family was much more comfortably middle-class than the fictional family she created. In 1938, when Hansberry was eight, her father, Carl—a prosperous real estate broker and founder of one of Chicago's first Black-owned banks—decided to test the legality of restrictive covenants by purchasing a house in an all-White neighborhood. When the local neighborhood association secured an injunction prohibiting him from occupying the property, Carl Hansberry, backed by the National Association for the Advancement of Colored People (NAACP), took the case all the way to the U.S. Supreme Court. Though he won the case (on a technicality) in 1940, his victory was a limited and costly one. As Lorraine Hansberry later recalled,

> That fight [. . .] required that our family occupy the disputed property in a hellishly hostile "white neighborhood" in which, literally, howling mobs surrounded our house. One of their missiles almost took [my] life. [. . .] My memories [. . .] include being spat at, cursed, and pummeled in the daily trek to and from school. And I also

Crowded conditions in a Chicago tenement, 1941

remember my desperate and courageous mother, patrolling our house all night with a loaded German luger, doggedly guarding her four children, while my father fought [. . .] in the Washington court.

[. . .] The cost, in emotional turmoil, time, and money [. . .] led to my father's early death as a permanently embittered exile in a foreign country when he saw that after such sacrificial efforts the Negroes of Chicago were as ghetto-locked as ever [. . .].

(The disillusioned Carl Hansberry was arranging to move his family to Mexico when he died in 1946.) Among other things, Hansberry's account of her experience might give readers of her play a deeper appreciation of its complex denouement and of the fact that its plot is propelled by a much-loved, hardworking father's death.

THE CIVIL RIGHTS MOVEMENT

Hansberry's experiences remind us, too, that the African American civil rights struggle was multifaceted and began well before the 1960s. Yet it was entering an entirely new phase in 1959. Just five years earlier, in 1954, the famous *Brown v. Board of Education* Supreme Court decision declared "separate but equal" education policies unconstitutional, initiating the long fight to integrate U.S. schools. One year later, in 1955, the Montgomery Bus Boycott began in Alabama, eventually forcing full integration of public transportation and launching Rev. Martin Luther King, Jr., (1929–68) on his career as one of the nation's most famous and influential civil rights leaders. The modern civil rights movement had begun—one in which "gradualism" gave way to "direct action," and court battles to marches, sit-ins, and other forms of civil disobedience.

One factor propelling change was World War II (1939–45). James Baldwin was only one of many Americans to see that war as marking "a turning point in the Negro's relation to" his country because, as Baldwin wrote in his best-selling book *The Fire Next Time* (1963),

> a certain hope died, a certain respect for white Americans faded. One began to pity them, or to hate them. You must put yourself in the skin of a man who is wearing the uniform of his country, is a candidate for death in its defense, and who is called a

Martin Luther King, Jr., after being hit on the head by a rock at a housing discrimination protest in Chicago, 1966

"nigger" by his comrades-in-arms and his officers; who is almost always given the hardest, ugliest, most menial work to do; [. . .]; who does not dance at the U.S.O. the night white soldiers dance there [. . .]; and who watches German prisoners of war being treated by Americans with more human dignity than he has ever received at their hands. And who, at the same time, as a human being, is far freer in a strange land than he has ever been at home [. . .]. You must consider what happens to this citizen, after all he has endured, when he returns home: search, in his shoes, for a job, for a place to live; ride, in his skin, on segregated buses; see, with his eyes, the signs saying "White" and "Colored" [. . .]; look into the eyes of his wife; look into the eyes of his son; listen, with his ears, to political speeches, North and South; imagine yourself being told to "wait."

Though the modern civil rights movement involved people of every age, it was in some ways, as Howard Zinn would argue in 1964, the first major social movement in U.S. history "led by youngsters." A political scientist and activist, Zinn was speaking specifically of the college students who, in 1960, began conducting sit-ins throughout the South and eventually formed the Student Nonviolent Coordinating Committee (SNCC). But Martin Luther King, Jr., was himself only twenty-six when he was chosen to lead the Montgomery boycott. In a sense, then, the modern civil rights movement was born out of the kinds of generational shifts explored in *A Raisin in the Sun*. Hansberry, for example, described her father as "typical of a generation of Negroes who believed that the 'American way' could successfully be made to work to democratize the United States." But, she said, it was "Negroes my own age and younger" who were beginning to question the "American way" and to advocate a more aggressively confrontational stance, "say[ing] that we must now lie down in the streets, tie up traffic, do whatever we can—take to the hills with guns if necessary—and fight back."

Determined to act on their frustration in ways that their parents wouldn't or couldn't, thousands of young people—many the city-born children of the Great Migration—turned to activism in the 1950s and 1960s. Yet, through Walter's drinking and the crime at the heart of her play, Hansberry also subtly reminds us that there were other ways that frustration found expression. The very same impulses and emotions that inspired SNCC members to head south led many of their peers in a very different direction.

AFRICAN AMERICANS AND AFRICA

In *A Raisin in the Sun*, the differences between and within generations take a variety of shapes, but one such distinction whose meaning may be especially dependent on a knowledge of historical and cultural context involves the character Joseph Asagai. A Nigerian attending college in Chicago, Joseph plans to return home in order to help liberate his country from British

Poster printed and distributed by SNCC
in the late 1960s

colonial rule. Through him, Hansberry thus highlights parallels between the situation of Blacks in the United States and in Africa, drawing on her audience's knowledge of contemporary events on that continent even as she suggests just how little real knowledge of Africa most Americans possess.

Historically speaking, Hansberry's (and Beneatha's) keen interest in both traditional African culture and events in contemporary Africa is no accident. As Earl Thorpe noted in 1959 (in an article excerpted below), various African American intellectuals and activists had worked to spread knowledge about Africa and to improve the situation of colonized Africans since at least the 1920s. But African American interest in Africa was becoming much more widespread and taking on a variety of unprecedented forms at midcentury. Between the late 1950s and early 1970s more African Americans than ever before would, like Beneatha, seek to learn about, and embrace, their African cultural heritage, sometimes adopting African names, giving up hair straighteners in order to grow Afros, or wearing clothes modeled on African styles. Meanwhile, Black activists drew inspiration from modern Africans' struggles to liberate their countries from colonial rule.

Between 1880 and 1912 all of Africa except Liberia and Ethiopia had come under the control of European powers. But in the 1950s, "the winds of change" suddenly began to blow hard across Africa, beginning in the north, where first Libya achieved independence (1951), then Morocco, Sudan, and Tunisia (1956). In 1957 the process moved southward into sub-Saharan or so-called Black Africa when Britain's Gold Coast colony became independent Ghana. Thereafter, almost every year saw the birth of at least one new, self-governing African nation. No wonder, then, that Africa was often in the news and on American minds in the 1950s and 1960s.

Developments in Africa stirred interest and pride among Black Americans for yet another reason. African independence was, in many cases, the result of hard-fought popular campaigns spearheaded by extraordinarily talented, charismatic men very like Joseph Asagai, men educated partially in the West and quite familiar with its culture and ways, yet eager to liberate their people and to embrace and revitalize ancient African folkways. The first and most famous such leader to emerge on the world stage was Jomo Kenyatta (1893?–1978), whose career led him from an obscure village to the presidency of independent Kenya by way of the London School of Economics; a masterful book on the culture of his own people, the Kikuyu (*Facing Mount Kenya* [1938]); and a seven-year imprisonment for sedition against the British colonial state. At least in African American eyes, such leaders might very well seem like modern versions of the great warriors of African history and myth.

THE "AMERICANNESS" OF *A RAISIN IN THE SUN*

As *A Raisin in the Sun* reminds us, however, the differences between African Americans and Africans are just as significant as their historical and cultural ties. And for all its characters' interest in Africa, Hansberry's play is a distinctly American one in both content and style. Hansberry herself was well aware of the way it complemented and contrasted with canonical American masterpieces such as Arthur Miller's *Death of a Salesman* (1949). As she pointed out, "Walter Younger is an American more than he is anything else," and there is "a simple line of descent between" her Walter and Miller's salesman, Willy Loman—"the last great hero in American drama to also *accept* the values of his [American] culture."

Hansberry's play offers you the perfect opportunity to think further about how historical and cultural contexts shape literary texts and how those texts speak both to their historical moment and to ours. To help you make the most of that opportunity, the rest of this chapter contains the text of the play, some of Hansberry's comments on it, a timeline, and contextual materials. Most of those materials focus on three interrelated, but distinct, topics. The first section documents the various challenges that confronted African Americans in Chicago and other northern cities throughout the Great Migration and especially in the late 1950s and early 1960s, focusing particularly on residential segregation as viewed from the perspective of both African Americans (in the excerpts from novelist Richard Wright's semiautobiographical TWELVE MILLION BLACK VOICES and a *New York Times* article by Gertrude Samuels) and their White counterparts (in Robert Gruenberg's article on the effort to integrate one Chicago housing project). The second section, which includes excerpts from Dr. King's famous LETTER FROM BIRMINGHAM JAIL, turns to the aims and aspirations of African Americans in the late 1950s and early 1960s, particularly the way they tended to be cast as distinctly American and/or middle class. The third section considers African Americans' changing attitudes toward Africa and Africans. All of these contextual materials aim to bring more vividly to life the world out of which *A Raisin in the Sun* sprang and the historically and culturally specific conditions and concerns it explores. The chapter ends with an excerpt that we hope will inspire you to think and talk, too, about the play's relevance to our twenty-first-century world. That excerpt comes from CLYBOURNE PARK, a 2010 Pulitzer Prize–winning play that, by revisiting and updating settings, situations, and characters from Hansberry's play, artfully invites us to ponder how America both has and hasn't changed since 1959.

LORRAINE HANSBERRY
A Raisin in the Sun

What happens to a dream deferred?

Does it dry up
Like a raisin in the sun?
Or fester like a sore—
And then run?
Does it stink like rotten meat?
Or crust and sugar over—
Like a syrupy sweet?
Maybe it just sags
Like a heavy load.

Or does it explode?

—LANGSTON HUGHES[1]

---

1. Hughes's poem, published in 1951, is titled "Harlem" (p. 1099).

Ruby Dee as Ruth, Sidney Poitier as Walter, and Diana Sands as Beneatha in
the original 1959 Broadway production of *A Raisin in the Sun*

CAST OF CHARACTERS

RUTH YOUNGER
TRAVIS YOUNGER
WALTER LEE YOUNGER (BROTHER)
BENEATHA YOUNGER
LENA YOUNGER (MAMA)

JOSEPH ASAGAI
GEORGE MURCHISON
KARL LINDNER
BOBO
MOVING MEN

*The action of the play is set in Chicago's Southside, sometime between World
War II and the present.*

ACT I

Scene One

*The Younger living room would be a comfortable and well-ordered room if it were
not for a number of indestructible contradictions to this state of being. Its furnishings*

are typical and undistinguished and their primary feature now is that they have clearly had to accommodate the living of too many people for too many years—and they are tired. Still, we can see that at some time, a time probably no longer remembered by the family (except perhaps for MAMA), the furnishings of this room were actually selected with care and love and even hope—and brought to this apartment and arranged with taste and pride.

That was a long time ago. Now the once loved pattern of the couch upholstery has to fight to show itself from under acres of crocheted doilies and couch covers which have themselves finally come to be more important than the upholstery. And here a table or a chair has been moved to disguise the worn places in the carpet; but the carpet has fought back by showing its weariness, with depressing uniformity, elsewhere on its surface.

Weariness has, in fact, won in this room. Everything has been polished, washed, sat on, used, scrubbed too often. All pretenses but living itself have long since vanished from the very atmosphere of this room.

Moreover, a section of this room, for it is not really a room unto itself, though the landlord's lease would make it seem so, slopes backward to provide a small kitchen area, where the family prepares the meals that are eaten in the living room proper, which must also serve as dining room. The single window that has been provided for these "two" rooms is located in this kitchen area. The sole natural light the family may enjoy in the course of a day is only that which fights its way through this little window.

At left, a door leads to a bedroom which is shared by MAMA and her daughter, BENEATHA. At right, opposite, is a second room (which in the beginning of the life of this apartment was probably a breakfast room) which serves as a bedroom for WALTER and his wife, RUTH.

Time: Sometime between World War II and the present.

Place: Chicago's Southside.

At Rise: It is morning dark in the living room. TRAVIS is asleep on the make-down bed at center. An alarm clock sounds from within the bedroom at right, and presently RUTH enters from that room and closes the door behind her. She crosses sleepily toward the window. As she passes her sleeping son she reaches down and shakes him a little. At the window she raises the shade and a dusky Southside morning light comes in feebly. She fills a pot with water and puts it on to boil. She calls to the boy, between yawns, in a slightly muffled voice.

RUTH is about thirty. We can see that she was a pretty girl, even exceptionally so, but now it is apparent that life has been little that she expected, and disappointment has already begun to hang in her face. In a few years, before thirty-five even, she will be known among her people as a "settled woman."

She crosses to her son and gives him a good, final, rousing shake.

RUTH: Come on now, boy, it's seven thirty! [Her son sits up at last, in a stupor of sleepiness.] I say hurry up, Travis! You ain't the only person in the world got to use a bathroom! [The child, a sturdy, handsome little boy of ten or eleven, drags himself out of the bed and almost blindly takes his towels and "today's clothes" from drawers and a closet and goes out to the bathroom, which is in an outside hall and which is shared by another family or families on the same floor. RUTH crosses to the bedroom door at right and opens it and calls in to her *husband.*] Walter Lee! . . . It's after seven thirty! Lemme see you do some waking up in there now! [*She waits.*] You better get up from there, man! It's after seven thirty I tell you. [*She waits again.*] All right, you just go ahead and lay there and next thing you know Travis be finished and Mr. Johnson'll be in there and you'll be fussing and cussing round here like a mad man! And be late too! [*She waits, at the end of patience.*] Walter Lee—it's time for you to get up!

[*She waits another second and then starts to go into the bedroom, but is apparently satisfied that her husband has begun to get up. She stops, pulls the door to, and returns to the kitchen area. She wipes her face with a moist cloth and runs her fingers through her sleep-disheveled hair in a vain effort and ties an apron around her housecoat. The bedroom door at right opens and her husband stands in the doorway in his pajamas, which are rumpled and mismated. He is a lean, intense young man in his middle thirties, inclined to quick nervous movements and erratic speech habits—and always in his voice there is a quality of indictment.*]

WALTER: Is he out yet?

RUTH: What you mean *out*? He ain't hardly got in there good yet.

WALTER: [*Wandering in, still more oriented to sleep than to a new day.*] Well, what was you doing all that yelling for if I can't even get in there yet? [*Stopping and thinking.*] Check coming today?

RUTH: They *said* Saturday and this is just Friday and I hopes to God you ain't going to get up here first thing this morning and start talking to me 'bout no money—'cause I 'bout don't want to hear it.

WALTER: Something the matter with you this morning?

RUTH: No—I'm just sleepy as the devil. What kind of eggs you want?

WALTER: Not scrambled. [RUTH *starts to scramble eggs.*] Paper come? [RUTH *points impatiently to the rolled up* Tribune *on the table, and he gets it and spreads it out and vaguely reads the front page.*] Set off another bomb yesterday.

RUTH: [*Maximum indifference.*] Did they?

WALTER: [*Looking up.*] What's the matter with you?

RUTH: Ain't nothing the matter with me. And don't keep asking me that this morning.

WALTER: Ain't nobody bothering you. [*Reading the news of the day absently again.*] Say Colonel McCormick[2] is sick.

RUTH: [*Affecting tea-party interest.*] Is he now? Poor thing.

WALTER: [*Sighing and looking at his watch.*] Oh, me. [*He waits.*] Now what is that boy doing in that bathroom all this time? He just going to have to start getting up earlier. I can't be late to work on account of him fooling around in there.

RUTH: [*Turning on him.*] Oh, no he ain't going to be getting up no earlier no such thing! It ain't his fault that he can't get to bed no earlier nights 'cause he got a bunch of crazy good-for-nothing clowns sitting up running their mouths in what is supposed to be his bedroom after ten o'clock at night . . .

---

2. Robert Rutherford McCormick (1880–1955), owner-publisher of the *Chicago Tribune*.

WALTER: That's what you mad about, ain't it? The things I want to talk about with my friends just couldn't be important in your mind, could they?

[He rises and finds a cigarette in her handbag on the table and crosses to the little window and looks out, smoking and deeply enjoying this first one.]

RUTH: [Almost matter of factly, a complaint too automatic to deserve emphasis.] Why you always got to smoke before you eat in the morning?

WALTER: [At the window.] Just look at 'em down there . . . Running and racing to work . . . [He turns and faces his wife and watches her a moment at the stove, and then, suddenly.] You look young this morning, baby.

RUTH: [Indifferently.] Yeah?

WALTER: Just for a second—stirring them eggs. It's gone now—just for a second it was—you looked real young again. [Then, drily.] It's gone now—you look like yourself again.

RUTH: Man, if you don't shut up and leave me alone.

WALTER: [Looking out to the street again.] First thing a man ought to learn in life is not to make love to no colored woman first thing in the morning. You all some evil people at eight o'clock in the morning.

[TRAVIS appears in the hall doorway, almost fully dressed and quite wide awake now, his towels and pajamas across his shoulders. He opens the door and signals for his father to make the bathroom in a hurry.]

TRAVIS: [Watching the bathroom.] Daddy, come on!

[WALTER gets his bathroom utensils and flies out to the bathroom.]

RUTH: Sit down and have your breakfast, Travis.

TRAVIS: Mama, this is Friday. [Gleefully.] Check coming tomorrow, huh?

RUTH: You get your mind off money and eat your breakfast.

TRAVIS: [Eating.] This is the morning we supposed to bring the fifty cents to school.

RUTH: Well, I ain't got no fifty cents this morning.

TRAVIS: Teacher say we have to.

RUTH: I don't care what teacher say. I ain't got it. Eat your breakfast, Travis.

TRAVIS: I am eating.

RUTH: Hush up now and just eat!

[The boy gives her an exasperated look for her lack of understanding, and eats grudgingly.]

TRAVIS: You think Grandmama would have it?

RUTH: No! And I want you to stop asking your grandmother for money, you hear me?

TRAVIS: [Outraged.] Gaaaleee! I don't ask her, she just gimme it sometimes!

RUTH: Travis Willard Younger—I got too much on me this morning to be—

TRAVIS: Maybe Daddy—

RUTH: Travis!

[The boy hushes abruptly. They are both quiet and tense for several seconds.]

TRAVIS: [*Presently.*] Could I maybe go carry some groceries in front of the supermarket for a little while after school then?

RUTH: Just hush, I said. [TRAVIS *jabs his spoon into his cereal bowl viciously, and rests his head in anger upon his fists.*] If you through eating, you can get over there and make up your bed.

[*The boy obeys stiffly and crosses the room, almost mechanically, to the bed and more or less carefully folds the covering. He carries the bedding into his mother's room and returns with his books and cap.*]

TRAVIS: [*Sulking and standing apart from her unnaturally.*] I'm gone.

RUTH: [*Looking up from the stove to inspect him automatically.*] Come here. [*He crosses to her and she studies his head.*] If you don't take this comb and fix this here head, you better! [TRAVIS *puts down his books with a great sigh of oppression, and crosses to the mirror. His mother mutters under her breath about his "slubbornness."*] 'Bout to march out of here with that head looking just like chickens slept in it! I just don't know where you get your slubborn ways . . . And get your jacket, too. Looks chilly out this morning.

TRAVIS: [*With conspicuously brushed hair and jacket.*] I'm gone.

RUTH: Get carfare and milk money—[*Waving one finger.*]—and not a single penny for no caps, you hear me?

TRAVIS: [*With sullen politeness.*] Yes'm.

[*He turns in outrage to leave. His mother watches after him as in his frustration he approaches the door almost comically. When she speaks to him, her voice has become a very gentle tease.*]

RUTH: [*Mocking; as she thinks he would say it.*] Oh, Mama makes me so mad sometimes, I don't know what to do! [*She waits and continues to his back as he stands stock-still in front of the door.*] I wouldn't kiss that woman good-bye for nothing in this world this morning! [*The boy finally turns around and rolls his eyes at her, knowing the mood has changed and he is vindicated; he does not, however, move toward her yet.*] Not for nothing in this world! [*She finally laughs aloud at him and holds out her arms to him and we see that it is a way between them, very old and practiced. He crosses to her and allows her to embrace him warmly but keeps his face fixed with masculine rigidity. She holds him back from her presently and looks at him and runs her fingers over the features of his face. With utter gentleness—*] Now—whose little old angry man are you?

TRAVIS: [*The masculinity and gruffness start to fade at last.*] Aw gaalee—Mama . . .

RUTH: [*Mimicking.*] Aw—gaaaaalleeeee, Mama! [*She pushes him, with rough playfulness and finality, toward the door.*] Get on out of here or you going to be late.

TRAVIS: [*In the face of love, new aggressiveness.*] Mama, could I *please* go carry groceries?

RUTH: Honey, it's starting to get so cold evenings.

WALTER: [*Coming in from the bathroom and drawing a make-believe gun from a make-believe holster and shooting at his son.*] What is it he wants to do?

RUTH: Go carry groceries after school at the supermarket.

WALTER: Well, let him go . . .

TRAVIS: [*Quickly, to the ally.*] I *have* to—she won't gimme the fifty cents . . .
WALTER: [*To his wife only.*] Why not?
RUTH: [*Simply, and with flavor.*] 'Cause we don't have it.
WALTER: [*To* RUTH *only.*] What you tell the boy things like that for? [*Reaching down into his pants with a rather important gesture.*] Here, son—

[*He hands the boy the coin, but his eyes are directed to his wife's.* TRAVIS *takes the money happily.*]

TRAVIS: Thanks, Daddy.

[*He starts out.* RUTH *watches both of them with murder in her eyes.* WALTER *stands and stares back at her with defiance, and suddenly reaches into his pocket again on an afterthought.*]

WALTER: [*Without even looking at his son, still staring hard at his wife.*] In fact, here's another fifty cents . . . Buy yourself some fruit today—or take a taxi-cab to school or something!
TRAVIS: Whoopee—

[*He leaps up and clasps his father around the middle with his legs, and they face each other in mutual appreciation; slowly* WALTER LEE *peeks around the boy to catch the violent rays from his wife's eyes and draws his head back as if shot.*]

WALTER: You better get down now—and get to school, man.
TRAVIS: [*At the door.*] O.K. Good-bye.

[*He exits.*]

WALTER: [*After him, pointing with pride.*] That's *my* boy. [*She looks at him in disgust and turns back to her work.*] You know what I was thinking 'bout in the bathroom this morning?
RUTH: No.
WALTER: How come you always try to be so pleasant!
RUTH: What is there to be pleasant 'bout!
WALTER: You want to know what I was thinking 'bout in the bathroom or not!
RUTH: I know what you thinking 'bout.
WALTER: [*Ignoring her.*] 'Bout what me and Willy Harris was talking about last night.
RUTH: [*Immediately—a refrain.*] Willy Harris is a good-for-nothing loud mouth.
WALTER: Anybody who talks to me has got to be a good-for-nothing loud mouth, ain't he? And what you know about who is just a good-for-nothing loud mouth? Charlie Atkins was just a "good-for-nothing loud mouth" too, wasn't he! When he wanted me to go in the dry-cleaning business with him. And now—he's grossing a hundred thousand a year. A hundred thousand dollars a year! You still call *him* a loud mouth!
RUTH: [*Bitterly.*] Oh, Walter Lee . . .

[*She folds her head on her arms over the table.*]

WALTER: [*Rising and coming to her and standing over her.*] You tired, ain't you? Tired of everything. Me, the boy, the way we live—this beat-up hole—everything. Ain't you? [*She doesn't look up, doesn't answer.*] So tired—moaning and groaning all the time, but you wouldn't do nothing to help, would you? You couldn't be on my side that long for nothing, could you?

RUTH: Walter, please leave me alone.

WALTER: A man needs for a woman to back him up . . .

RUTH: Walter—

WALTER: Mama would listen to you. You know she listen to you more than she do me and Bennie. She think more of you. All you have to do is just sit down with her when you drinking your coffee one morning and talking 'bout things like you do and—[*He sits down beside her and demonstrates graphically what he thinks her methods and tone should be.*]—you just sip your coffee, see, and say easy like that you been thinking 'bout that deal Walter Lee is so interested in, 'bout the store and all, and sip some more coffee, like what you saying ain't really that important to you—And the next thing you know, she be listening good and asking you questions and when I come home—I can tell her the details. This ain't no fly-by-night proposition, baby. I mean we figured it out, me and Willy and Bobo.

RUTH: [*With a frown.*] Bobo?

WALTER: Yeah. You see, this little liquor store we got in mind cost seventy-five thousand and we figured the initial investment on the place be 'bout thirty thousand, see. That be ten thousand each. Course, there's a couple of hundred you got to pay so's you don't spend your life just waiting for them clowns to let your license get approved—

RUTH: You mean graft?

WALTER: [*Frowning impatiently.*] Don't call it that. See there, that just goes to show you what women understand about the world. Baby, don't *nothing* happen for you in this world 'less you pay *somebody* off!

RUTH: Walter, leave me alone! [*She raises her head and stares at him vigorously— then says, more quietly.*] Eat your eggs, they gonna be cold.

WALTER: [*Straightening up from her and looking off.*] That's it. There you are. Man say to his woman: I got me a dream. His woman say: Eat your eggs. [*Sadly, but gaining in power.*] Man say: I got to take hold of this here world, baby! And a woman will say: Eat your eggs and go to work. [*Passionately now.*] Man say: I got to change my life, I'm choking to death, baby! And his woman say—[*In utter anguish as he brings his fists down on his thighs.*]—Your eggs is getting cold!

RUTH: [*Softly.*] Walter, that ain't none of our money.

WALTER: [*Not listening at all or even looking at her.*] This morning, I was lookin' in the mirror and thinking about it . . . I'm thirty-five years old; I been married eleven years and I got a boy who sleeps in the living room—[*Very, very quietly.*]—and all I got to give him is stories about how rich white people live . . .

RUTH: Eat your eggs, Walter.

WALTER: *Damn my eggs . . . damn all the eggs that ever was!*

RUTH: Then go to work.

WALTER: [*Looking up at her.*] See—I'm trying to talk to you 'bout myself—[*Shaking his head with the repetition.*]—and all you can say is eat them eggs and go to work.

RUTH: [*Wearily.*] Honey, you never say nothing new. I listen to you every day, every night and every morning, and you never say nothing new. [*Shrugging.*] So you would rather *be* Mr. Arnold than be his chauffeur. So—I would *rather* be living in Buckingham Palace.[3]

WALTER: That is just what is wrong with the colored woman in this world . . . Don't understand about building their men up and making 'em feel like they somebody. Like they can do something.

RUTH: [*Drily, but to hurt.*] There *are* colored men who do things.

WALTER: No thanks to the colored woman.

RUTH: Well, being a colored woman, I guess I can't help myself none.

[*She rises and gets the ironing board and sets it up and attacks a huge pile of rough-dried clothes, sprinkling them in preparation for the ironing and then rolling them into tight fat balls.*]

WALTER: [*Mumbling.*] We one group of men tied to a race of women with small minds.

[*His sister* BENEATHA *enters. She is about twenty, as slim and intense as her brother. She is not as pretty as her sister-in-law, but her lean, almost intellectual face has a handsomeness of its own. She wears a bright-red flannel nightie, and her thick hair stands wildly about her head. Her speech is a mixture of many things; it is different from the rest of the family's insofar as education has permeated her sense of English—and perhaps the Midwest rather than the South has finally—at last—won out in her inflection; but not altogether, because over all of it is a soft slurring and transformed use of vowels which is the decided influence of the Southside. She passes through the room without looking at either* RUTH *or* WALTER *and goes to the outside door and looks, a little blindly, out to the bathroom. She sees that it has been lost to the Johnsons. She closes the door with a sleepy vengeance and crosses to the table and sits down a little defeated.*]

BENEATHA: I am going to start timing those people.

WALTER: You should get up earlier.

BENEATHA: [*Her face in her hands. She is still fighting the urge to go back to bed.*] Really—would you suggest dawn? Where's the paper?

WALTER: [*Pushing the paper across the table to her as he studies her almost clinically, as though he has never seen her before.*] You a horrible-looking chick at this hour.

BENEATHA: [*Drily.*] Good morning, everybody.

WALTER: [*Senselessly.*] How is school coming?

BENEATHA: [*In the same spirit.*] Lovely. Lovely. And you know, biology is the greatest. [*Looking up at him.*] I dissected something that looked just like you yesterday.

WALTER: I just wondered if you've made up your mind and everything.

BENEATHA: [*Gaining in sharpness and impatience.*] And what did I answer yesterday morning—and the day before that?

3. London residence of the queen of the United Kingdom.

RUTH: [*From the ironing board, like someone disinterested and old.*] Don't be so nasty, Bennie.

BENEATHA: [*Still to her brother.*] And the day before that and the day before that!

WALTER: [*Defensively.*] I'm interested in you. Something wrong with that? Ain't many girls who decide—

WALTER AND BENEATHA: [*In unison.*]—"to be a doctor."

[*Silence.*]

WALTER: Have we figured out yet just exactly how much medical school is going to cost?

RUTH: Walter Lee, why don't you leave that girl alone and get out of here to work?

BENEATHA: [*Exits to the bathroom and bangs on the door.*] Come on out of there, please!

[*She comes back into the room.*]

WALTER: [*Looking at his sister intently.*] You know the check is coming tomorrow.

BENEATHA: [*Turning on him with a sharpness all her own.*] That money belongs to Mama, Walter, and it's for her to decide how she wants to use it. I don't care if she wants to buy a house or a rocket ship or just nail it up somewhere and look at it. It's hers. Not ours—*hers.*

WALTER: [*Bitterly.*] Now ain't that fine! You just got your mother's interest at heart, ain't you, girl? You such a nice girl—but if Mama got that money she can always take a few thousand and help you through school too—can't she?

BENEATHA: I have never asked anyone around here to do anything for me.

WALTER: No! And the line between asking and just accepting when the time comes is big and wide—ain't it!

BENEATHA: [*With fury.*] What do you want from me, Brother—that I quit school or just drop dead, which!

WALTER: I don't want nothing but for you to stop acting holy 'round here. Me and Ruth done made some sacrifices for you—why can't you do something for the family?

RUTH: Walter, don't be dragging me in it.

WALTER: You are in it—Don't you get up and go work in somebody's kitchen for the last three years to help put clothes on her back?

RUTH: Oh, Walter—that's not fair . . .

WALTER: It ain't that nobody expects you to get on your knees and say thank you, Brother; thank you, Ruth; thank you, Mama—and thank you, Travis, for wearing the same pair of shoes for two semesters—

BENEATHA: [*Dropping to her knees.*] Well—I *do*—all right?—thank everybody . . . and forgive me for ever wanting to be anything at all . . . forgive me, forgive me!

RUTH: Please stop it! Your mama'll hear you.

WALTER: Who the hell told you you had to be a doctor? If you so crazy 'bout messing 'round with sick people—then go be a nurse like other women—or just get married and be quiet . . .

BENEATHA: Well—you finally got it said . . . it took you three years but you finally got it said. Walter, give up; leave me alone—it's Mama's money.

WALTER: *He was my father, too!*

BENEATHA: So what? He was mine, too—and Travis' grandfather—but the insurance money belongs to Mama. Picking on me is not going to make her give it to you to invest in any liquor stores—[*Underbreath, dropping into a chair.*]—and I for one say, God bless Mama for that!

WALTER: [*To* RUTH.] See—did you hear? Did you hear!

RUTH: Honey, please go to work.

WALTER: Nobody in this house is ever going to understand me.

BENEATHA: Because you're a nut.

WALTER: Who's a nut?

BENEATHA: You—you are a nut. Thee is mad, boy.

WALTER: [*Looking at his wife and his sister from the door, very sadly.*] The world's most backward race of people, and that's a fact.

BENEATHA: [*Turning slowly in her chair.*] And then there are all those prophets who would lead us out of the wilderness—[WALTER *slams out of the house.*]—into the swamps!

RUTH: Bennie, why you always gotta be pickin' on your brother? Can't you be a little sweeter sometimes? [*Door opens.* WALTER *walks in.*]

WALTER: [*To* RUTH.] I need some money for carfare.

RUTH: [*Looks at him, then warms; teasing, but tenderly.*] Fifty cents? [*She goes to her bag and gets money.*] Here, take a taxi.

[WALTER *exits.* MAMA *enters. She is a woman in her early sixties, full-bodied and strong. She is one of those women of a certain grace and beauty who wear it so unobtrusively that it takes a while to notice. Her dark-brown face is surrounded by the total whiteness of her hair, and, being a woman who has adjusted to many things in life and overcome many more, her face is full of strength. She has, we can see, wit and faith of a kind that keep her eyes lit and full of interest and expectancy. She is, in a word, a beautiful woman. Her bearing is perhaps most like the noble bearing of the women of the Hereros of Southwest Africa—rather as if she imagines that as she walks she still bears a basket or a vessel upon her head. Her speech, on the other hand, is as careless as her carriage is precise—she is inclined to slur everything—but her voice is perhaps not so much quiet as simply soft.*]

MAMA: Who that 'round here slamming doors at this hour?

[*She crosses through the room, goes to the window, opens it, and brings in a feeble little plant growing doggedly in a small pot on the window sill. She feels the dirt and puts it back out.*]

RUTH: That was Walter Lee. He and Bennie was at it again.

MAMA: My children and they tempers. Lord, if this little old plant don't get more sun than it's been getting it ain't never going to see spring again. [*She turns from the window.*] What's the matter with you this morning, Ruth? You looks right peaked. You aiming to iron all them things? Leave some for me. I'll get to 'em this afternoon. Bennie honey, it's too drafty for you to be sitting 'round half dressed. Where's your robe?

BENEATHA: In the cleaners.

MAMA: Well, go get mine and put it on.

BENEATHA: I'm not cold, Mama, honest.

MAMA: I know—but you so thin . . .

BENEATHA: [Irritably.] Mama, I'm not cold.

MAMA: [Seeing the make-down bed as TRAVIS has left it.] Lord have mercy, look at that poor bed. Bless his heart—he tries, don't he?

[She moves to the bed TRAVIS has sloppily made up.]

RUTH: No—he don't half try at all 'cause he knows you going to come along behind him and fix everything. That's just how come he don't know how to do nothing right now—you done spoiled that boy so.

MAMA: Well—he's a little boy. Ain't supposed to know 'bout housekeeping. My baby, that's what he is. What you fix for his breakfast this morning?

RUTH: [Angrily.] I feed my son, Lena!

MAMA: I ain't meddling—[Underbreath; busy-bodyish.] I just noticed all last week he had cold cereal, and when it starts getting this chilly in the fall a child ought to have some hot grits or something when he goes out in the cold—

RUTH: [Furious.] I gave him hot oats—is that all right!

MAMA: I ain't meddling. [Pause.] Put a lot of nice butter on it? [RUTH shoots her an angry look and does not reply.] He likes lots of butter.

RUTH: [Exasperated.] Lena—

MAMA: [To BENEATHA. MAMA is inclined to wander conversationally sometimes.] What was you and your brother fussing 'bout this morning?

BENEATHA: It's not important, Mama.

[She gets up and goes to look out at the bathroom, which is apparently free, and she picks up her towels and rushes out.]

MAMA: What was they fighting about?

RUTH: Now you know as well as I do.

MAMA: [Shaking her head.] Brother still worrying hisself sick about that money?

RUTH: You know he is.

MAMA: You had breakfast?

RUTH: Some coffee.

MAMA: Girl, you better start eating and looking after yourself better. You almost thin as Travis.

RUTH: Lena—

MAMA: Un-hunh?

RUTH: What are you going to do with it?

MAMA: Now don't you start, child. It's too early in the morning to be talking about money. It ain't Christian.

RUTH: It's just that he got his heart set on that store—

MAMA: You mean that liquor store that Willy Harris want him to invest in?

RUTH: Yes—

MAMA: We ain't no business people, Ruth. We just plain working folks.

RUTH: Ain't nobody business people till they go into business. Walter Lee say colored people ain't never going to start getting ahead till they start gambling on some different kinds of things in the world—investments and things.

MAMA: What done got into you, girl? Walter Lee done finally sold you on investing.

RUTH: No. Mama, something is happening between Walter and me. I don't know what it is—but he needs something—something I can't give him any- more. He needs this chance, Lena.

MAMA: [*Frowning deeply.*] But liquor, honey—

RUTH: Well—like Walter say—I spec people going to always be drinking them- selves some liquor.

MAMA: Well—whether they drinks it or not ain't none of my business. But whether I go into business selling it to 'em *is*, and I don't want that on my ledger this late in life. [*Stopping suddenly and studying her daughter-in-law.*] Ruth Younger, what's the matter with you today? You look like you could fall over right there.

RUTH: I'm tired.

MAMA: Then you better stay home from work today.

RUTH: I can't stay home. She'd be calling up the agency and screaming at them, "My girl didn't come in today—send me somebody! My girl didn't come in!" Oh, she just have a fit . . .

MAMA: Well, let her have it. I'll just call her up and say you got the flu—

RUTH: [*Laughing.*] Why the flu?

MAMA: 'Cause it sounds respectable to 'em. Something white people get, too. They know 'bout the flu. Otherwise they think you been cut up or something when you tell 'em you sick.

RUTH: I got to go in. We need the money.

MAMA: Somebody would of thought my children done all but starved to death the way they talk about money here late. Child, we got a great big old check coming tomorrow.

RUTH: [*Sincerely, but also self-righteously.*] Now that's your money. It ain't got nothing to do with me. We all feel like that—Walter and Bennie and me— even Travis.

MAMA: [*Thoughtfully, and suddenly very far away.*] Ten thousand dollars—

RUTH: Sure is wonderful.

MAMA: Ten thousand dollars.

RUTH: You know what you should do, Miss Lena? You should take yourself a trip somewhere. To Europe or South America or someplace—

MAMA: [*Throwing up her hands at the thought.*] Oh, child!

RUTH: I'm serious. Just pack up and leave! Go on away and enjoy yourself some. Forget about the family and have yourself a ball for once in your life—

MAMA: [*Drily.*] You sound like I'm just about ready to die. Who'd go with me? What I look like wandering 'round Europe by myself?

RUTH: Shoot—these here rich white women do it all the time. They don't think nothing of packing up they suitcases and piling on one of them big steam- ships and—swoosh!—they gone, child.

MAMA: Something always told me I wasn't no rich white woman.

RUTH: Well—what are you going to do with it then?

MAMA: I ain't rightly decided. [*Thinking. She speaks now with emphasis.*] Some of it got to be put away for Beneatha and her schoolin'—and ain't nothing going to touch that part of it. Nothing. [*She waits several seconds, trying to make up her mind about something, and looks at* RUTH *a little tentatively before going on.*] Been thinking that we maybe could meet the notes on a little old two-story somewhere, with a yard where Travis could play in the summertime, if we use part of the insurance for a down payment and everybody kind of pitch in. I could maybe take on a little day work again, few days a week—

RUTH: [*Studying her mother-in-law furtively and concentrating on her ironing, anxious to encourage without seeming to.*] Well, Lord knows, we've put enough rent into this here rat trap to pay for four houses by now . . .

MAMA: [*Looking up at the words "rat trap" and then looking around and leaning back and sighing—in a suddenly reflective mood—*] "Rat trap"—yes, that's all it is. [*Smiling.*] I remember just as well the day me and Big Walter moved in here. Hadn't been married but two weeks and wasn't planning on living here no more than a year. [*She shakes her head at the dissolved dream.*] We was going to set away, little by little, don't you know, and buy a little place out in Morgan Park. We had even picked out the house. [*Chuckling a little.*] Looks right dumpy today. But Lord, child, you should know all the dreams I had 'bout buying that house and fixing it up and making me a little garden in the back—[*She waits and stops smiling.*] And didn't none of it happen.

[*Dropping her hands in a futile gesture.*]

RUTH: [*Keeps her head down, ironing.*] Yes, life can be a barrel of disappointments, sometimes.

MAMA: Honey, Big Walter would come in here some nights back then and slump down on that couch there and just look at the rug, and look at me and look at the rug and then back at me—and I'd know he was down then . . . . really down. [*After a second very long and thoughtful pause; she is seeing back to times that only she can see.*] And then, Lord, when I lost that baby—little Claude—I almost thought I was going to lose Big Walter too. Oh, that man grieved hisself! He was one man to love his children.

RUTH: Ain't nothin' can tear at you like losin' your baby.

MAMA: I guess that's how come that man finally worked hisself to death like he done. Like he was fighting his own war with this here world that took his baby from him.

RUTH: He sure was a fine man, all right. I always liked Mr. Younger.

MAMA: Crazy 'bout his children! God knows there was plenty wrong with Walter Younger—hard-headed, mean, kind of wild with women—plenty wrong with him. But he sure loved his children. Always wanted them to have something—be something. That's where Brother gets all these notions, I reckon. Big Walter used to say, he'd get right wet in the eyes sometimes, lean his head back with the water standing in his eyes and say, "Seem like God didn't see fit to give the black man nothing but dreams—but He did give us children to make them dreams seem worthwhile." [*She smiles.*] He could talk like that, don't you know.

RUTH: Yes, he sure could. He was a good man, Mr. Younger.

MAMA: Yes, a fine man—just couldn't never catch up with his dreams, that's all.

[BENEATHA *comes in, brushing her hair and looking up to the ceiling, where the sound of a vacuum cleaner has started up.*]

BENEATHA: What could be so dirty on that woman's rugs that she has to vacuum them every single day?

RUTH: I wish certain young women 'round here who I could name would take inspiration about certain rugs in a certain apartment I could also mention.

BENEATHA: [*Shrugging.*] How much cleaning can a house need, for Christ's sakes.

MAMA: [*Not liking the Lord's name used thus.*] Bennie!

RUTH: Just listen to her—just listen!

BENEATHA: Oh, God!

MAMA: If you use the Lord's name just one more time—

BENEATHA: [*A bit of a whine.*] Oh, Mama—

RUTH: Fresh—just fresh as salt, this girl!

BENEATHA: [*Drily.*] Well—if the salt loses its savor[4]—

MAMA: Now that will do. I just ain't going to have you 'round here reciting the scriptures in vain—you hear me?

BENEATHA: How did I manage to get on everybody's wrong side by just walking into a room?

RUTH: If you weren't so fresh—

BENEATHA: Ruth, I'm twenty years old.

MAMA: What time you be home from school today?

BENEATHA: Kind of late. [*With enthusiasm.*] Madeline is going to start my guitar lessons today.

[MAMA *and* RUTH *look up with the same expression.*]

MAMA: Your *what* kind of lessons?

BENEATHA: Guitar.

RUTH: Oh, Father!

MAMA: How come you done taken it in your mind to learn to play the guitar?

BENEATHA: I just want to, that's all.

MAMA: [*Smiling.*] Lord, child, don't you know what to do with yourself? How long it going to be before you get tired of this now—like you got tired of that little play-acting group you joined last year? [*Looking at* RUTH.] And what was it the year before that?

RUTH: The horseback-riding club for which she bought that fifty-five-dollar riding habit that's been hanging in the closet ever since!

MAMA: [*To* BENEATHA.] Why you got to flit so from one thing to another, baby?

BENEATHA: [*Sharply.*] I just want to learn to play the guitar. Is there anything wrong with that?

MAMA: Ain't nobody trying to stop you. I just wonders sometimes why you has to flit so from one thing to another all the time. You ain't never done nothing with all that camera equipment you brought home—

BENEATHA: I don't flit! I—I experiment with different forms of expression—

RUTH: Like riding a horse?

---

4. See Matthew 5.13: "You are the salt of the earth. But if the salt loses its taste, with what can it be seasoned? It is no longer good for anything but to be thrown out and trampled underfoot."

BENEATHA: —People have to express themselves one way or another.

MAMA: What is it you want to express?

BENEATHA: [Angrily.] Me! [MAMA and RUTH look at each other and burst into raucous laughter.] Don't worry—I don't expect you to understand.

MAMA: [To change the subject.] Who you going out with tomorrow night?

BENEATHA: [With displeasure.] George Murchison again.

MAMA: [Pleased.] Oh—you getting a little sweet on him?

RUTH: You ask me, this child ain't sweet on nobody but herself—[Underbreath.]
Express herself!

[They laugh.]

BENEATHA: Oh—I like George all right, Mama. I mean I like him enough to go
out with him and stuff, but—

RUTH: [For devilment.] What does and stuff mean?

BENEATHA: Mind your own business.

MAMA: Stop picking at her now, Ruth. [A thoughtful pause, and then a suspicious
sudden look at her daughter as she turns in her chair for emphasis.] What does
it mean?

BENEATHA: [Wearily.] Oh, I just mean I couldn't ever really be serious about
George. He's—he's so shallow.

RUTH: Shallow—what do you mean he's shallow? He's rich!

MAMA: Hush, Ruth.

BENEATHA: I know he's rich. He knows he's rich, too.

RUTH: Well—what other qualities a man got to have to satisfy you, little girl?

BENEATHA: You wouldn't even begin to understand. Anybody who married Walter could not possibly understand.

MAMA: [Outraged.] What kind of way is that to talk about your brother?

BENEATHA: Brother is a flip—let's face it.

MAMA: [To RUTH, helplessly.] What's a flip?

RUTH: [Glad to add kindling.] She's saying he's crazy.

BENEATHA: Not crazy. Brother isn't really crazy yet—he—he's an elaborate
neurotic.

MAMA: Hush your mouth!

BENEATHA: As for George. Well. George looks good—he's got a beautiful car
and he takes me to nice places and, as my sister-in-law says, he is probably
the richest boy I will ever get to know and I even like him sometimes—but if
the Youngers are sitting around waiting to see if their little Bennie is going to
tie up the family with the Murchisons, they are wasting their time.

RUTH: You mean you wouldn't marry George Murchison if he asked you someday? That pretty, rich thing? Honey, I knew you was odd—

BENEATHA: No I would not marry him if all I felt for him was what I feel now.
Besides, George's family wouldn't really like it.

MAMA: Why not?

BENEATHA: Oh, Mama—The Murchisons are honest-to-God-real-live-rich colored people, and the only people in the world who are more snobbish than
rich white people are rich colored people. I thought everybody knew that.
I've met Mrs. Murchison. She's a scene!

MAMA: You must not dislike people 'cause they well off, honey.

BENEATHA: Why not? It makes just as much sense as disliking people 'cause they are poor, and lots of people do that.

RUTH: [*A wisdom-of-the-ages manner. To* MAMA.] Well, she'll get over some of this—

BENEATHA: Get over it? What are you talking about, Ruth? Listen, I'm going to be a doctor. I'm not worried about who I'm going to marry yet—if I ever get married.

MAMA AND RUTH: *If!*

MAMA: Now, Bennie—

BENEATHA: Oh, I probably will . . . but first I'm going to be a doctor, and George, for one, still thinks that's pretty funny. I couldn't be bothered with that. I am going to be a doctor and everybody around here better understand that!

MAMA: [*Kindly.*] 'Course you going to be a doctor, honey, God willing.

BENEATHA: [*Drily.*] God hasn't got a thing to do with it.

MAMA: Beneatha—that just wasn't necessary.

BENEATHA: Well—neither is God. I get sick of hearing about God.

MAMA: Beneatha!

BENEATHA: I mean it! I'm just tired of hearing about God all the time. What has He got to do with anything? Does He pay tuition?

MAMA: You 'bout to get your fresh little jaw slapped!

RUTH: That's just what she needs, all right!

BENEATHA: Why? Why can't I say what I want to around here, like everybody else?

MAMA: It don't sound nice for a young girl to say things like that—you wasn't brought up that way. Me and your father went to trouble to get you and Brother to church every Sunday.

BENEATHA: Mama, you don't understand. It's all a matter of ideas, and God is just one idea I don't accept. It's not important. I am not going out and be immoral or commit crimes because I don't believe in God. I don't even think about it. It's just that I get tired of Him getting credit for all the things the human race achieves through its own stubborn effort. There simply is no blasted God—there is only man and it is he who makes miracles!

[MAMA *absorbs this speech, studies her daughter and rises slowly and crosses to* BENEATHA *and slaps her powerfully across the face. After, there is only silence and the daughter drops her eyes from her mother's face, and* MAMA *is very tall before her.*]

MAMA: Now—you say after me, in my mother's house there is still God. [*There is a long pause and* BENEATHA *stares at the floor wordlessly.* MAMA *repeats the phrase with precision and cool emotion.*] In my mother's house there is still God.

BENEATHA: In my mother's house there is still God.

[*A long pause.*]

MAMA: [*Walking away from* BENEATHA, *too disturbed for triumphant posture. Stopping and turning back to her daughter.*] There are some ideas we ain't going to have in this house. Not long as I am at the head of this family.

BENEATHA: Yes, ma'am.

[MAMA *walks out of the room.*]

RUTH: [*Almost gently, with profound understanding.*] You think you a woman, Bennie—but you still a little girl. What you did was childish—so you got treated like a child.

BENEATHA: I see. [*Quietly.*] I also see that everybody thinks it's all right for Mama to be a tyrant. But all the tyranny in the world will never put a God in the heavens!

[*She picks up her books and goes out.*]

RUTH: [*Goes to* MAMA's *door.*] She said she was sorry.

MAMA: [*Coming out, going to her plant.*] They frightens me, Ruth. My children.

RUTH: You got good children, Lena. They just a little off sometimes—but they're good.

MAMA: No—there's something come down between me and them that don't let us understand each other and I don't know what it is. One done almost lost his mind thinking 'bout money all the time and the other done commence to talk about things I can't seem to understand in no form or fashion. What is it that's changing, Ruth?

RUTH: [*Soothingly, older than her years.*] Now . . . you taking it all too seriously. You just got strong-willed children and it takes a strong woman like you to keep 'em in hand.

MAMA: [*Looking at her plant and sprinkling a little water on it.*] They spirited all right, my children. Got to admit they got spirit—Bennie and Walter. Like this little old plant that ain't never had enough sunshine or nothing—and look at it . . .

[*She has her back to* RUTH, *who has had to stop ironing and lean against something and put the back of her hand to her forehead.*]

RUTH: [*Trying to keep* MAMA *from noticing.*] You . . . sure . . . loves that little old thing, don't you? . . .

MAMA: Well, I always wanted me a garden like I used to see sometimes at the back of the houses down home. This plant is close as I ever got to having one. [*She looks out of the window as she replaces the plant.*] Lord, ain't nothing as dreary as the view from this window on a dreary day, is there? Why ain't you singing this morning, Ruth? Sing that "No Ways Tired." That song always lifts me up so—[*She turns at last to see that* RUTH *has slipped quietly into a chair, in a state of semiconsciousness.*] Ruth! Ruth honey—what's the matter with you . . . Ruth!

[CURTAIN.]

Scene Two

It is the following morning; a Saturday morning, and house cleaning is in progress at the Youngers. Furniture has been shoved hither and yon and MAMA is giving the kitchen-area walls a washing down. BENEATHA, in dungarees, with a handkerchief tied around her face, is spraying insecticide into the cracks in the walls. As they work, the radio is on and a Southside disk-jockey program is inappropriately filling the house with a rather exotic saxophone blues. TRAVIS, the sole idle one, is leaning on his arms, looking out of the window.

TRAVIS: Grandmama, that stuff Bennie is using smells awful. Can I go down-stairs, please?

MAMA: Did you get all them chores done already? I ain't seen you doing much.

TRAVIS: Yes'm—finished early. Where did Mama go this morning?

MAMA: [Looking at BENEATHA.] She had to go on a little errand.

TRAVIS: Where?

MAMA: To tend to her business.

TRAVIS: Can I go outside then?

MAMA: Oh, I guess so. You better stay right in front of the house, though . . . and keep a good lookout for the postman.

TRAVIS: Yes'm. [He starts out and decides to give his aunt BENEATHA a good swat on the legs as he passes her.] Leave them poor little old cockroaches alone, they ain't bothering you none.

[He runs as she swings the spray gun at him both viciously and playfully. WALTER enters from the bedroom and goes to the phone.]

MAMA: Look out there, girl, before you be spilling some of that stuff on that child!

TRAVIS: [Teasing.] That's right—look out now!

[He exits.]

BENEATHA: [Drily.] I can't imagine that it would hurt him—it has never hurt the roaches.

MAMA: Well, little boys' hides ain't as tough as Southside roaches.

WALTER: [Into phone.] Hello—Let me talk to Willy Harris.

MAMA: You better get over there behind the bureau. I seen one marching out of there like Napoleon yesterday.

WALTER: Hello, Willy? It ain't come yet. It'll be here in a few minutes. Did the lawyer give you the papers?

BENEATHA: There's really only one way to get rid of them, Mama—

MAMA: How?

BENEATHA: Set fire to this building.

WALTER: Good. Good. I'll be right over.

BENEATHA: Where did Ruth go, Walter?

WALTER: I don't know.

[He exits abruptly.]

BENEATHA: Mama, where did Ruth go?

MAMA: [Looking at her with meaning.] To the doctor, I think.

BENEATHA: The doctor? What's the matter? [They exchange glances.] You don't think—

MAMA: [With her sense of drama.] Now I ain't saying what I think. But I ain't never been wrong 'bout a woman neither.

[The phone rings.]

BENEATHA: [At the phone.] Hay-lo . . . [Pause, and a moment of recognition.] Well—when did you get back! . . . And how was it? . . . Of course I've missed you—in my way . . . This morning? No . . . house cleaning and all that and Mama hates it if I let people come over when the house is like this . . . You *have?* Well, that's different . . . What is it—Oh, what the hell, come on over . . . Right, see you then.

[*She hangs up.*]

MAMA: [*Who has listened vigorously, as is her habit.*] Who is that you inviting over here with this house looking like this? You ain't got the pride you was born with!

BENEATHA: Asagai doesn't care how houses look, Mama—he's an intellectual.

MAMA: *Who?*

BENEATHA: Asagai—Joseph Asagai. He's an African boy I met on campus. He's been studying in Canada all summer.

MAMA: What's his name?

BENEATHA: Asagai, Joseph. Ah-sah-guy . . . He's from Nigeria.

MAMA: Oh, that's the little country that was founded by slaves way back . . .

BENEATHA: No, Mama—that's Liberia.

MAMA: I don't think I never met no African before.

BENEATHA: Well, do me a favor and don't ask him a whole lot of ignorant questions about Africans. I mean, do they wear clothes and all that—

MAMA: Well, now, I guess if you think we so ignorant 'round here maybe you shouldn't bring your friends here—

BENEATHA: It's just that people ask such crazy things. All anyone seems to know about when it comes to Africa is Tarzan—

MAMA: [*Indignantly.*] Why should I know anything about Africa?

BENEATHA: Why do you give money at church for the missionary work?

MAMA: Well, that's to help save people.

BENEATHA: You mean save them from *heathenism*—

MAMA: [*Innocently.*] Yes.

BENEATHA: I'm afraid they need more salvation from the British and the French.

[RUTH *comes in forlornly and pulls off her coat with dejection. They both turn to look at her.*]

RUTH: [*Dispiritedly.*] Well, I guess from all the happy faces—everybody knows.

BENEATHA: You pregnant?

MAMA: Lord have mercy, I sure hope it's a little old girl. Travis ought to have a sister.

[BENEATHA *and* RUTH *give her a hopeless look for this grandmotherly enthusiasm.*]

BENEATHA: How far along are you?

RUTH: Two months.

BENEATHA: Did you mean to? I mean did you plan it or was it an accident?

MAMA: What do you know about planning or not planning?

BENEATHA: Oh, Mama.

RUTH: [*Wearily.*] She's twenty years old, Lena.

BENEATHA: Did you plan it, Ruth?

RUTH: Mind your own business.

BENEATHA: It is my business—where is he going to live, on the roof? [*There is silence following the remark as the three women react to the sense of it.*] Gee—I didn't mean that, Ruth, honest. Gee, I don't feel like that at all. I—I think it is wonderful.

RUTH: [*Dully.*] Wonderful.

BENEATHA: Yes—really.

MAMA: [*Looking at* RUTH, *worried.*] Doctor say everything going to be all right?

RUTH: [*Far away.*] Yes—she says everything is going to be fine . . .

MAMA: [*Immediately suspicious.*] "She"—What doctor you went to?

[RUTH *folds over, near hysteria.*]

MAMA: [*Worriedly hovering over* RUTH.] Ruth honey—what's the matter with you—you sick?

[RUTH *has her fists clenched on her thighs and is fighting hard to suppress a scream that seems to be rising in her.*]

BENEATHA: What's the matter with her, Mama?

MAMA: [*Working her fingers in* RUTH's *shoulder to relax her.*] She be all right. Women gets right depressed sometimes when they get her way. [*Speaking softly, expertly, rapidly.*] Now you just relax. That's right . . . just lean back, don't think 'bout nothing at all . . . nothing at all—

RUTH: I'm all right . . .

[*The glassy-eyed look melts and then she collapses into a fit of heavy sobbing. The bell rings.*]

BENEATHA: Oh, my God—that must be Asagai.

MAMA: [*To* RUTH.] Come on now, honey. You need to lie down and rest awhile . . . then have some nice hot food.

[*They exit,* RUTH's *weight on her mother-in-law.* BENEATHA, *herself profoundly disturbed, opens the door to admit a rather dramatic-looking young man with a large package.*]

ASAGAI: Hello, Alaiyo—

BENEATHA: [*Holding the door open and regarding him with pleasure.*] Hello . . . [*Long pause.*] Well—come in. And please excuse everything. My mother was very upset about my letting anyone come here with the place like this.

ASAGAI: [*Coming into the room.*] You look disturbed too . . . Is something wrong?

BENEATHA: [*Still at the door, absently.*] Yes . . . we've all got acute ghetto-itus. [*She smiles and comes toward him, finding a cigarette and sitting.*] So—sit down! How was Canada?

ASAGAI: [*A sophisticate.*] Canadian.

BENEATHA: [*Looking at him.*] I'm very glad you are back.

ASAGAI: [*Looking back at her in turn.*] Are you really?

BENEATHA: Yes—very.

ASAGAI: Why—you were quite glad when I went away. What happened?

BENEATHA: You went away.

ASAGAI: Ahhhhhhhh.

BENEATHA: Before—you wanted to be so serious before there was time.

ASAGAI: How much time must there be before one knows what one feels?

BENEATHA: [*Stalling this particular conversation. Her hands pressed together, in a deliberately childish gesture.*] What did you bring me?

ASAGAI: [*Handing her the package.*] Open it and see.

BENEATHA: [*Eagerly opening the package and drawing out some records and the colorful robes of a Nigerian woman.*] Oh, Asagai! . . . You got them for me! . . . How beautiful . . . and the records too! [*She lifts out the robes and runs to the mirror with them and holds the drapery up in front of herself.*]

ASAGAI: [*Coming to her at the mirror.*] I shall have to teach you how to drape it properly. [*He flings the material about her for the moment and stands back to look at her.*] Ah—Oh-pay-gay-day, oh-gbah-mu-shay. [*A Yoruba exclamation for admiration.*] You wear it well . . . very well . . . mutilated hair and all.

BENEATHA: [*Turning suddenly.*] My hair—what's wrong with my hair?

ASAGAI: [*Shrugging.*] Were you born with it like that?

BENEATHA: [*Reaching up to touch it.*] No . . . of course not.

[*She looks back to the mirror, disturbed.*]

ASAGAI: [*Smiling.*] How then?

BENEATHA: You know perfectly well how . . . as crinkly as yours . . . that's how.

ASAGAI: And it is ugly to you that way?

BENEATHA: [*Quickly.*] Oh, no—not ugly . . . [*More slowly, apologetically.*] But it's so hard to manage when it's, well—raw.

ASAGAI: And so to accommodate that—you mutilate it every week?

BENEATHA: It's not mutilation!

ASAGAI: [*Laughing aloud at her seriousness.*] Oh . . . please! I am only teasing you because you are so very serious about these things. [*He stands back from her and folds his arms across his chest as he watches her pulling at her hair and frowning in the mirror.*] Do you remember the first time you met me at school? . . . [*He laughs.*] You came up to me and you said—and I thought you were the most serious little thing I had ever seen—you said: [*He imitates her.*] "Mr. Asagai—I want very much to talk with you. About Africa. You see, Mr. Asagai, I am looking for my *identity*!"

[*He laughs.*]

BENEATHA: [*Turning to him, not laughing.*] Yes—

[*Her face is quizzical, profoundly disturbed.*]

ASAGAI: [*Still teasing and reaching out and taking her face in his hands and turning her profile to him.*] Well . . . it is true that this is not so much a profile of a Hollywood queen as perhaps a queen of the Nile—[*A mock dismissal of the importance of the question.*] But what does it matter? Assimilationism is so popular in your country.

BENEATHA: [*Wheeling, passionately, sharply.*] I am not an assimilationist!

ASAGAI: [*The protest hangs in the room for a moment and ASAGAI studies her, his laughter fading.*] Such a serious one. [*There is a pause.*] So—you like the robes? You must take excellent care of them—they are from my sister's personal wardrobe.

BENEATHA: [*With incredulity.*] You—you sent all the way home—for me?

ASAGAI: [*With charm.*] For you—I would do much more . . . Well, that is what I came for. I must go.

BENEATHA: Will you call me Monday?

ASAGAI: Yes . . . We have a great deal to talk about. I mean about identity and time and all that.

BENEATHA: Time?

ASAGAI: Yes. About how much time one needs to know what one feels.

BENEATHA: You never understood that there is more than one kind of feeling which can exist between a man and a woman—or, at least, there should be.

ASAGAI: [*Shaking his head negatively but gently.*] No. Between a man and a woman there need be only one kind of feeling. I have that for you . . . Now even . . . right this moment . . .

BENEATHA: I know—and by itself—it won't do. I can find that anywhere.

ASAGAI: For a woman it should be enough.

BENEATHA: I know—because that's what it says in all the novels that men write. But it isn't. Go ahead and laugh—but I'm not interested in being someone's little episode in America or—[*With feminine vengeance.*]—one of them! [ASAGAI *has burst into laughter again.*] That's funny as hell, huh!

ASAGAI: It's just that every American girl I have known has said that to me. White—black—in this you are all the same. And the same speech, too!

BENEATHA: [*Angrily.*] Yuk, yuk, yuk!

ASAGAI: It's how you can be sure that the world's most liberated women are not liberated at all. You all talk about it too much!

[MAMA *enters and is immediately all social charm because of the presence of a guest.*]

BENEATHA: Oh—Mama—this is Mr. Asagai.

MAMA: How do you do?

ASAGAI: [*Total politeness to an elder.*] How do you do, Mrs. Younger. Please forgive me for coming at such an outrageous hour on a Saturday.

MAMA: Well, you are quite welcome. I just hope you understand that our house don't always look like this. [*Chatterish.*] You must come again. I would love to hear all about—[*Not sure of the name.*]—your country. I think it's so sad the way our American Negroes don't know nothing about Africa 'cept Tarzan and all that. And all that money they pour into these churches when they ought to be helping you people over there drive out them French and Englishmen done taken away your land.

[*The mother flashes a slightly superior look at her daughter upon completion of the recitation.*]

ASAGAI: [*Taken aback by this sudden and acutely unrelated expression of sympathy.*] Yes . . . yes . . .

MAMA: [*Smiling at him suddenly and relaxing and looking him over.*] How many miles is it from here to where you come from?

ASAGAI: Many thousands.

MAMA: [*Looking at him as she would* WALTER.] I bet you don't half look after yourself, being away from your mama either. I spec you better come 'round here from time to time and get yourself some decent home-cooked meals . . .

ASAGAI: [*Moved.*] Thank you. Thank you very much. [*They are all quiet, then—*] Well . . . I must go. I will call you Monday, Alaiyo.

MAMA: What's that he call you?

ASAGAI: Oh—"Alaiyo." I hope you don't mind. It is what you would call a nickname, I think. It is a Yoruba word. I am a Yoruba.

MAMA: [*Looking at* BENEATHA.] I—I thought he was from—

ASAGAI: [*Understanding.*] Nigeria is my country. Yoruba is my tribal origin—

BENEATHA: You didn't tell us what Alaiyo means . . . for all I know, you might be calling me Little Idiot or something . . .

ASAGAI: Well . . . let me see . . . I do not know how just to explain it . . . The sense of a thing can be so different when it changes languages.

BENEATHA: You're evading.

ASAGAI: No—really it is difficult . . . [*Thinking.*] It means . . . it means One for Whom Bread—Food—Is Not Enough. [*He looks at her.*] Is that all right?

BENEATHA: [*Understanding, softly.*] Thank you.

MAMA: [*Looking from one to the other and not understanding any of it.*] Well . . . that's nice . . . You must come see us again—Mr.—

ASAGAI: Ah-sah-guy . . .

MAMA: Yes . . . Do come again.

ASAGAI: Good-bye.

[*He exits.*]

MAMA: [*After him.*] Lord, that's a pretty thing just went out here! [*Insinuatingly, to her daughter.*] Yes, I guess I see why we done commence to get so interested in Africa 'round here. Missionaries my aunt Jenny!

[*She exits.*]

BENEATHA: Oh, Mama! . . .

[*She picks up the Nigerian dress and holds it up to her in front of the mirror again. She sets the headdress on haphazardly and then notices her hair again and clutches at it and then replaces the headdress and frowns at herself. Then she starts to wriggle in front of the mirror as she thinks a Nigerian woman might.* TRAVIS *enters and regards her.*]

TRAVIS: You cracking up?

BENEATHA: Shut up.

[*She pulls the headdress off and looks at herself in the mirror and clutches at her hair again and squinches her eyes as if trying to imagine something. Then, suddenly, she gets her raincoat and kerchief and hurriedly prepares for going out.*]

MAMA: [*Coming back into the room.*] She's resting now. Travis, baby, run next door and ask Miss Johnson to please let me have a little kitchen cleanser. This here can is empty as Jacob's kettle.

TRAVIS: I just came in.

MAMA: Do as you told. [*He exits and she looks at her daughter.*] Where you going?

BENEATHA: [*Halting at the door.*] To become a queen of the Nile!

[*She exits in a breathless blaze of glory.* RUTH *appears in the bedroom doorway.*]

MAMA: Who told you to get up?

RUTH: Ain't nothing wrong with me to be lying in no bed for. Where did Bennie go?

MAMA: [*Drumming her fingers.*] Far as I could make out—to Egypt. [RUTH *just looks at her.*] What time is it getting to?

RUTH: Ten twenty. And the mailman going to ring that bell this morning just like he done every morning for the last umpteen years.

[TRAVIS *comes in with the cleanser can.*]

TRAVIS: She say to tell you that she don't have much.

MAMA: [*Angrily.*] Lord, some people I could name sure is tight-fisted! [*Directing her grandson.*] Mark two cans of cleanser down on the list there. If she that hard up for kitchen cleanser, I sure don't want to forget to get her none!

RUTH: Lena—maybe the woman is just short on cleanser—

MAMA: [*Not listening.*]—Much baking powder as she done borrowed from me all these years, she could of done gone into the baking business!

[*The bell sounds suddenly and sharply and all three are stunned—serious and silent—mid-speech. In spite of all the other conversations and distractions of the morning, this is what they have been waiting for, even* TRAVIS, *who looks helplessly from his mother to his grandmother.* RUTH *is the first to come to life again.*]

RUTH: [*To* TRAVIS.] Get down them steps, boy!

[TRAVIS *snaps to life and flies out to get the mail.*]

MAMA: [*Her eyes wide, her hand to her breast.*] You mean it done really come?

RUTH: [*Excited.*] Oh, Miss Lena!

MAMA: [*Collecting herself.*] Well . . . I don't know what we all so excited about 'round here for. We known it was coming for months.

RUTH: That's a whole lot different from having it come and being able to hold it in your hands . . . a piece of paper worth ten thousand dollars . . . [TRAVIS *bursts back into the room. He holds the envelope high above his head, like a little dancer, his face is radiant and he is breathless. He moves to his grandmother with sudden slow ceremony and puts the envelope into her hands. She accepts it, and then merely holds it and looks at it.*] Come on! Open it . . . Lord have mercy, I wish Walter Lee was here!

TRAVIS: Open it, Grandmama!

MAMA: [*Staring at it.*] Now you all be quiet. It's just a check.

RUTH: Open it . . .

MAMA: [*Still staring at it.*] Now don't act silly . . . We ain't never been no people to act silly 'bout no money—

RUTH: [*Swiftly.*] We ain't never had none before—open it!

[MAMA *finally makes a good strong tear and pulls out the thin blue slice of paper and inspects it closely. The boy and his mother study it raptly over* MAMA's *shoulders.*]

MAMA: Travis! [*She is counting off with doubt.*] Is that the right number of zeros.

TRAVIS: Yes'm . . . ten thousand dollars. Gaalee, Grandmama, you rich.

MAMA: [*She holds the check away from her, still looking at it. Slowly her face sobers into a mask of unhappiness.*] Ten thousand dollars. [*She hands it to* RUTH.] Put it away somewhere, Ruth. [*She does not look at* RUTH; *her eyes seem to be seeing something somewhere very far off.*] Ten thousand dollars they give you. Ten thousand dollars.

TRAVIS: [*To his mother, sincerely.*] What's the matter with Grandmama—don't she want to be rich?

RUTH: [*Distractedly.*] You go on out and play now, baby. [TRAVIS *exits.* MAMA *starts wiping dishes absently, humming intently to herself.* RUTH *turns to her, with kind exasperation.*] You've gone and got yourself upset.

MAMA: [*Not looking at her.*] I spec if it wasn't for you all . . . I would just put that money away or give it to the church or something.

RUTH: Now what kind of talk is that. Mr. Younger would just be plain mad if he could hear you talking foolish like that.

MAMA: [*Stopping and staring off.*] Yes . . . he sure would. [*Sighing.*] We got enough to do with that money, all right. [*She halts then, and turns and looks at her daughter-in-law hard;* RUTH *avoids her eyes and* MAMA *wipes her hands with finality and starts to speak firmly to* RUTH.] Where did you go today, girl?

RUTH: To the doctor.

MAMA: [*Impatiently.*] Now, Ruth . . . you know better than that. Old Doctor Jones is strange enough in his way but there ain't nothing 'bout him make somebody slip and call him "she"—like you done this morning.

RUTH: Well, that's what happened—my tongue slipped.

MAMA: You went to see that woman, didn't you?

RUTH: [*Defensively, giving herself away.*] What woman you talking about?

MAMA: [*Angrily.*] That woman who—

[WALTER *enters in great excitement.*]

WALTER: Did it come?

MAMA: [*Quietly.*] Can't you give people a Christian greeting before you start asking about money?

WALTER: [*To* RUTH.] Did it come? [RUTH *unfolds the check and lays it quietly before him, watching him intently with thoughts of her own.* WALTER *sits down and grasps it close and counts off the zeros.*] Ten thousand dollars—[*He turns suddenly, frantically to his mother and draws some papers out of his breast pocket.*] Mama—look. Old Willy Harris put everything on paper—

MAMA: Son—I think you ought to talk to your wife . . . I'll go on out and leave you alone if you want—

WALTER: I can talk to her later—Mama, look—

MAMA: Son—

WALTER: WILL SOMEBODY PLEASE LISTEN TO ME TODAY!

MAMA: [*Quietly.*] I don't 'low no yellin' in this house, Walter Lee, and you know it—[WALTER *stares at them in frustration and starts to speak several times.*] And there ain't going to be no investing in no liquor stores. I don't aim to have to speak on that again.

[*A long pause.*]

WALTER: Oh—so you don't aim to have to speak on that again? So you have decided . . . [*Crumpling his papers.*] Well, *you* tell that to my boy tonight when you put him to sleep on the living-room couch . . . [*Turning to* MAMA *and speaking directly to her.*] Yeah—and tell it to my wife, Mama, tomorrow when she has to go out of here to look after somebody else's kids. And tell it to *me,* Mama, every time we need a new pair of curtains and I have to watch *you* go out and work in somebody's kitchen. Yeah, you tell me then!

[WALTER *starts out.*]

RUTH: Where you going?

WALTER: I'm going out!

RUTH: Where?

WALTER: Just out of this house somewhere—

RUTH: [*Getting her coat.*] I'll come too.

WALTER: I don't want you to come!

RUTH: I got something to talk to you about, Walter.

WALTER: That's too bad.

MAMA: [*Still quietly.*] Walter Lee—[*She waits and he finally turns and looks at her.*] Sit down.

WALTER: I'm a grown man, Mama.

MAMA: Ain't nobody said you wasn't grown. But you still in my house and my presence. And as long as you are—you'll talk to your wife civil. Now sit down.

RUTH: [*Suddenly.*] Oh, let him go on out and drink himself to death! He makes me sick to my stomach! [*She flings her coat against him.*]

WALTER: [*Violently.*] And you turn mine too, baby! [RUTH *goes into their bedroom and slams the door behind her.*] That was my greatest mistake—

MAMA: [*Still quietly.*] Walter, what is the matter with you?

WALTER: Matter with me? Ain't nothing the matter with *me!*

MAMA: Yes there is. Something eating you up like a crazy man. Something more than me not giving you this money. The past few years I been watching it happen to you. You get all nervous acting and kind of wild in the eyes—[WALTER *jumps up impatiently at her words.*] I said sit there now, I'm talking to you!

WALTER: Mama—I don't need no nagging at me today.

MAMA: Seem like you getting to a place where you always tied up in some kind of knot about something. But if anybody ask you 'bout it you just yell at 'em and bust out the house and go out and drink somewheres. Walter Lee, people can't live with that. Ruth's a good, patient girl in her way—but you getting to be too much. Boy, don't make the mistake of driving that girl away from you.

WALTER: Why—what she do for me?

MAMA: She loves you.

WALTER: Mama—I'm going out. I want to go off somewhere and be by myself for a while.

MAMA: I'm sorry 'bout your liquor store, son. It just wasn't the thing for us to do. That's what I want to tell you about—

WALTER: I got to go out, Mama—

[*He rises.*]

MAMA: It's dangerous, son.

WALTER: What's dangerous?

MAMA: When a man goes outside his home to look for peace.

WALTER: [*Beseechingly.*] Then why can't there never be no peace in this house then?

MAMA: You done found it in some other house?

WALTER: No—there ain't no woman! Why do women always think there's a woman somewhere when a man gets restless. [*Coming to her.*] Mama— Mama—I want so many things . . .

MAMA: Yes, son—

WALTER: I want so many things that they are driving me kind of crazy . . . Mama—look at me.

MAMA: I'm looking at you. You a good-looking boy. You got a job, a nice wife, a fine boy and—

WALTER: A job. [*Looks at her.*] Mama, a job? I open and close car doors all day long. I drive a man around in his limousine and I say, "Yes, sir; no, sir; very good, sir; shall I take the Drive, sir?" Mama, that ain't no kind of job . . . that ain't nothing at all. [*Very quietly.*] Mama, I don't know if I can make you understand.

MAMA: Understand what, baby?

WALTER: [*Quietly.*] Sometimes it's like I can see the future stretched out in front of me—just plain as day. The future, Mama. Hanging over there at the edge of my days. Just waiting for me—a big, looming blank space—full of *nothing*. Just waiting for *me*. [*Pause.*] Mama—sometimes when I'm downtown and I pass them cool, quiet-looking restaurants where them white boys are sitting back and talking 'bout things . . . sitting there turning deals worth millions of dollars . . . sometimes I see guys don't look much older than me—

MAMA: Son—how come you talk so much 'bout money?

WALTER: [*With immense passion.*] Because it is life, Mama!

MAMA: [*Quietly.*] Oh—[*Very quietly.*] So now it's life. Money is life. Once upon a time freedom used to be life—now it's money. I guess the world really do change . . .

WALTER: No—it was always money, Mama. We just didn't know about it.

MAMA: No . . . something has changed. [*She looks at him.*] You something new, boy. In my time we was worried about not being lynched and getting to the North if we could and how to stay alive and still have a pinch of dig-nity too . . . Now here come you and Beneatha—talking 'bout things we ain't never even thought about hardly, me and your daddy. You ain't satis-fied or proud of nothing we done. I mean that you had a home; that we kept you out of trouble till you was grown; that you don't have to ride to work on the back of nobody's streetcar—You my children—but how different we done become.

WALTER: You just don't understand, Mama, you just don't understand.

MAMA: Son—do you know your wife is expecting another baby? [WALTER stands, stunned, and absorbs what his mother has said.] That's what she wanted to talk to you about. [WALTER sinks down into a chair.] This ain't for me to be telling—but you ought to know. [She waits.] I think Ruth is thinking 'bout getting rid of that child.[5]

WALTER: [Slowly understanding.] No—no—Ruth wouldn't do that.

MAMA: When the world gets ugly enough—a woman will do anything for her family. The part that's already living.

WALTER: You don't know Ruth, Mama, if you think she would do that.

[RUTH opens the bedroom door and stands there a little limp.]

RUTH: [Beaten.] Yes I would too, Walter. [Pause.] I gave her a five-dollar down payment.

[There is total silence as the man stares at his wife and the mother stares at her son.]

MAMA: [Presently.] Well—[Tightly.] Well—son, I'm waiting to hear you say something . . . I'm waiting to hear how you be your father's son. Be the man he was . . . [Pause.] Your wife say she going to destroy your child. And I'm waiting to hear you talk like him and say we a people who give children life, not who destroys them—[She rises.] I'm waiting to see you stand up and look like your daddy and say we done give up one baby to poverty and that we ain't going to give up nary another one . . . I'm waiting.

WALTER: Ruth—

MAMA: If you a son of mine, tell her! [WALTER turns, looks at her and can say nothing. She continues, bitterly.] You . . . you are a disgrace to your father's memory. Somebody get me my hat.

[CURTAIN.]

ACT II

Scene One

Time: Later the same day.

At rise: RUTH is ironing again. She has the radio going. Presently BENEATHA'S bedroom door opens and RUTH's mouth falls and she puts down the iron in fascination.

RUTH: What have we got on tonight!

BENEATHA: [Emerging grandly from the doorway so that we can see her thoroughly robed in the costume ASAGAI brought.] You are looking at what a well-dressed Nigerian woman wears—[She parades for RUTH, her hair completely hidden

5. Abortions were illegal and dangerous in the United States prior to the 1973 Roe v. Wade Supreme Court decision.

by the headdress; she is coquettishly fanning herself with an ornate oriental fan, mistakenly more like Butterfly[6] than any Nigerian that ever was.] Isn't it beautiful? *[She promenades to the radio and, with an arrogant flourish, turns off the good loud blues that is playing.]* Enough of this assimilationist junk! *[RUTH follows her with her eyes as she goes to the phonograph and puts on a record and turns and waits ceremoniously for the music to come up. Then, with a shout—]* OCOMOGOSIAY!

[RUTH jumps. The music comes up, a lovely Nigerian melody. BENEATHA listens, enraptured, her eyes far away—"back to the past." She begins to dance. RUTH is dumbfounded.]

RUTH: What kind of dance is that?
BENEATHA: A folk dance.
RUTH: *[Pearl Bailey.][7]* What kind of folks do that, honey?
BENEATHA: It's from Nigeria. It's a dance of welcome.
RUTH: Who you welcoming?
BENEATHA: The men back to the village.
RUTH: Where they been?
BENEATHA: How should I know—out hunting or something. Anyway, they are coming back now ....
RUTH: Well, that's good.
BENEATHA: *[With the record.]*

Alundi, alundi
Alundi alunya
Jop pu a jeepua
Ang gu soooooooooo

Ai yai yae . . .
Ayehaye—alundi . . . .

[WALTER comes in during this performance; he has obviously been drinking. He leans against the door heavily and watches his sister, at first with distaste. Then his eyes look off—"back to the past"—as he lifts both his fists to the roof, screaming.]

WALTER: YEAH . . . AND ETHIOPIA STRETCH FORTH HER HANDS AGAIN! . . . [8]
RUTH: *[Drily, looking at him.]* Yes—and Africa sure is claiming her own tonight. *[She gives them both up and starts ironing again.]*
WALTER: *[All in a drunken, dramatic shout.]* Shut up! . . . I'm digging them drums . . . them drums move me! . . . *[He makes his weaving way to his wife's face and leans in close to her.]* In my *heart of hearts—[He thumps his chest.]*—I am much warrior!

6. Madame Butterfly, a Japanese woman married to, and then abandoned by, an American man in the opera *Madama Butterfly* (1904), by Italian composer Giacomo Puccini (1858–1924).
7. That is, in the manner of the popular African American singer and entertainer (1918–90).
8. See Psalms 68.31: "Princes shall come out of Egypt; Ethiopia shall soon stretch out her hands unto God."

RUTH: [*Without even looking up.*] In your heart of hearts you are much drunkard.

WALTER: [*Coming away from her and starting to wander around the room, shouting.*] Me and Jomo . . . [*Intently, in his sister's face. She has stopped dancing to watch him in this unknown mood.*] That's my man, Kenyatta.[9] [*Shouting and thumping his chest.*] FLAMING SPEAR! HOT DAMN! [*He is suddenly in possession of an imaginary spear and actively spearing enemies all over the room.*] OCOMOGOSIAY . . . THE LION IS WAKING . . . OWIMOWEH! [*He pulls his shirt open and leaps up on a table and gestures with his spear. The bell rings. RUTH goes to answer.*]

BENEATHA: [*To encourage WALTER, thoroughly caught up with this side of him.*] OCOMOGOSIAY, FLAMING SPEAR!

WALTER: [*On the table, very far gone, his eyes pure glass sheets. He sees what we cannot, that he is a leader of his people, a great chief, a descendant of Chaka,[1] and that the hour to march has come.*] Listen, my black brothers—

BENEATHA: OCOMOGOSIAY!

WALTER: —Do you hear the waters rushing against the shores of the coastlands—

BENEATHA: OCOMOGOSIAY!

WALTER: —Do you hear the screeching of the cocks in yonder hills beyond where the chiefs meet in council for the coming of the mighty war—

BENEATHA: OCOMOGOSIAY!

WALTER: —Do you hear the beating of the wings of the birds flying low over the mountains and the low places of our land—

[*RUTH opens the door. GEORGE MURCHISON enters.*]

BENEATHA: OCOMOGOSIAY!

WALTER: —Do you hear the singing of the women, singing the war songs of our fathers to the babies in the great houses . . . singing the sweet war songs? OH, DO YOU HEAR, MY BLACK BROTHERS!

BENEATHA: [*Completely gone.*] We hear you, Flaming Spear—

WALTER: Telling us to prepare for the greatness of the time—[*To GEORGE.*] Black Brother!

[*He extends his hand for the fraternal clasp.*]

GEORGE: Black Brother, hell!

RUTH: [*Having had enough, and embarrassed for the family.*] Beneatha, you got company—what's the matter with you? Walter Lee Younger, get down off that table and stop acting like a fool . . .

[*WALTER comes down off the table suddenly and makes a quick exit to the bathroom.*]

RUTH: He's had a little to drink . . . I don't know what her excuse is.

---

9. Jomo Kenyatta (1893?–1978), African political leader and first president of Kenya (1964–78) following its independence from British colonial rule.
1. Zulu chief (1786–1828), also known as "Shaka" and called "the Black Napoleon" for his strategic and organizational genius.

GEORGE: [*To* BENEATHA.] Look honey, we're going *to* the theatre—we're not going to be *in* it . . . so go change, huh?

RUTH: You expect this boy to go out with you looking like that?

BENEATHA: [*Looking at* GEORGE.] That's up to George. If he's ashamed of his heritage—

GEORGE: Oh, don't be so proud of yourself, Bennie—just because you look eccentric.

BENEATHA: How can something that's natural be eccentric?

GEORGE: That's what being eccentric means—being natural. Get dressed.

BENEATHA: I don't like that, George.

RUTH: Why must you and your brother make an argument out of everything people say?

BENEATHA: Because I hate assimilationist Negroes!

RUTH: Will somebody please tell me what assimila-who-ever means!

GEORGE: Oh, it's just a college girl's way of calling people Uncle Toms—but that isn't what it means at all.

RUTH: Well, what does it mean?

BENEATHA: [*Cutting* GEORGE *off and staring at him as she replies to* RUTH.] It means someone who is willing to give up his own culture and submerge himself completely in the dominant, and in this case, *oppressive* culture!

GEORGE: Oh, dear, dear, dear! Here we go! A lecture on the African past! On our Great West African Heritage! In one second we will hear all about the great Ashanti empires; the great Songhay civilizations; and the great sculpture of Bénin—and then some poetry in the Bantu—and the whole monologue will end with the word *heritage*! [*Nastily.*] Let's face it, baby, your heritage is nothing but a bunch of raggedy-assed spirituals and some grass huts!

BENEATHA: *Grass huts!* [RUTH *crosses to her and forcibly pushes her toward the bedroom.*] See there . . . you are standing there in your splendid ignorance talking about people who were the first to smelt iron on the face of the earth! [RUTH *is pushing her through the door.*] The Ashanti were performing surgical operations when the English—[RUTH *pulls the door to, with* BENEATHA *on the other side, and smiles graciously at* GEORGE. BENEATHA *opens the door and shouts the end of the sentence defiantly at* GEORGE.]—were still tattooing themselves with blue dragons . . . [*She goes back inside.*]

RUTH: Have a seat, George. [*They both sit.* RUTH *folds her hands rather primly on her lap, determined to demonstrate the civilization of the family.*] Warm, ain't it? I mean for September. [*Pause.*] Just like they always say about Chicago weather: If it's too hot or cold for you, just wait a minute and it'll change. [*She smiles happily at this cliché of clichés.*] Everybody say it's got to do with them bombs and things they keep setting off.[2] [*Pause.*] Would you like a nice cold beer?

GEORGE: No, thank you. I don't care for beer. [*He looks at his watch.*] I hope she hurries up.

RUTH: What time is the show?

GEORGE: It's an eight-thirty curtain. That's just Chicago, though. In New York standard curtain time is eight forty.

---

2. In the 1950s, people commonly blamed weather fluctuations on atomic testing.

[*He is rather proud of this knowledge.*]

RUTH: [*Properly appreciating it.*] You get to New York a lot?
GEORGE: [*Offhand.*] Few times a year.
RUTH: Oh—that's nice. I've never been to New York.

[WALTER *enters. We feel he has relieved himself, but the edge of unreality is still with him.*]

WALTER: New York ain't got nothing Chicago ain't. Just a bunch of hustling people all squeezed up together—being "Eastern."

[*He turns his face into a screw of displeasure.*]

GEORGE: Oh—you've been?
WALTER: *Plenty* of times.
RUTH: [*Shocked at the lie.*] Walter Lee Younger!
WALTER: [*Staring her down.*] Plenty! [*Pause.*] What we got to drink in this house? Why don't you offer this man some refreshment. [*To* GEORGE.] They don't know how to entertain people in this house, man.
GEORGE: Thank you—I don't really care for anything.
WALTER: [*Feeling his head; sobriety coming.*] Where's Mama?
RUTH: She ain't come back yet.
WALTER: [*Looking* MURCHISON *over from head to toe, scrutinizing his carefully casual tweed sports jacket over cashmere V-neck sweater over soft eyelet shirt and tie, and soft slacks, finished off with white buckskin shoes.*] Why all you college boys wear them fairyish-looking white shoes?
RUTH: Walter Lee!

[GEORGE MURCHISON *ignores the remark.*]

WALTER: [*To* RUTH.] Well, they look crazy as hell—white shoes, cold as it is.
RUTH: [*Crushed.*] You have to excuse him—
WALTER: No he don't! Excuse me for what? What you always excusing me for! I'll excuse myself when I needs to be excused! [*A pause.*] They look as funny as them black knee socks Beneatha wears out of here all the time.
RUTH: It's the college *style*, Walter.
WALTER: Style, hell, She looks like she got burnt legs or something!
RUTH: Oh, Walter—
WALTER: [*An irritable mimic.*] Oh, Walter! Oh, Walter! [*To* MURCHISON.] How's your old man making out? I understand you all going to buy that big hotel on the Drive?[3] [*He finds a beer in the refrigerator, wanders over to* MURCHISON, *sipping and wiping his lips with the back of his hand, and straddling a chair backwards to talk to the other man.*] Shrewd move. Your old man is all right, man. [*Tapping his head and half winking for emphasis.*] I mean he knows how to operate. I mean he thinks *big*, you know what I mean, I mean for a *home*, you know? But I think he's kind of running out of ideas now. I'd like to talk to him. Listen, man, I got some plans that could turn this city upside down. I mean I think like he does. *Big*. Invest big, gamble big, hell, lose *big* if you

3. Lake Shore Drive, a scenic thoroughfare along Lake Michigan.

have to, you know what I mean. It's hard to find a man on this whole South-side who understands my kind of thinking—you dig? [*He scrutinizes* MUR-CHISON *again, drinks his beer, squints his eyes and leans in close, confidential, man to man.*] Me and you ought to sit down and talk sometimes, man. Man, I got me some ideas . . .

GEORGE: [*With boredom.*] Yeah—sometimes we'll have to do that, Walter.

WALTER: [*Understanding the indifference, and offended.*] Yeah—well, when you get the time, man. I know you a busy little boy.

RUTH: Walter, please—

WALTER: [*Bitterly, hurt.*] I know ain't nothing in this world as busy as you colored college boys with your fraternity pins and white shoes . . .

RUTH: [*Covering her face with humiliation.*] Oh, Walter Lee—

WALTER: I see you all the time—with the books tucked under your arms—going to your [*British A—a mimic.*] "clahsses." And for what! What the hell you learning over there? Filling up your heads—[*Counting off on his fingers.*]—with the sociology and the psychology—but they teaching you how to be a man? How to take over and run the world? They teaching you how to run a rubber plantation or a steel mill? Naw—just to talk proper and read books and wear white shoes . . .

GEORGE: [*Looking at him with distaste, a little above it all.*] You're all wacked up with bitterness, man.

WALTER: [*Intently, almost quietly, between the teeth, glaring at the boy.*] And you—ain't you bitter, man? Ain't you just about had it yet? Don't you see no stars gleaming that you can't reach out and grab? You happy?—You contented son-of-a-bitch—you happy? You got it made? Bitter? Man, I'm a volcano. Bitter? Here I am a giant—surrounded by ants! Ants who can't even under-stand what it is the giant is talking about.

RUTH: [*Passionately and suddenly.*] Oh, Walter—ain't you with nobody!

WALTER: [*Violently.*] No! 'Cause ain't nobody with me! Not even my own mother!

RUTH: Walter, that's a terrible thing to say!

[BENEATHA *enters, dressed for the evening in a cocktail dress and earrings.*]

GEORGE: Well—hey, you look great.

BENEATHA: Let's go, George. See you all later.

RUTH: Have a nice time.

GEORGE: Thanks. Good night. [*To* WALTER, *sarcastically.*] Good night, Prometheus.[4]

[BENEATHA *and* GEORGE *exit.*]

WALTER: [*To* RUTH.] Who is Prometheus?

RUTH: I don't know. Don't worry about it.

WALTER: [*In fury, pointing after* GEORGE.] See there—they get to a point where they can't insult you man to man—they got to go talk about something ain't nobody never heard of!

---

4. In Greek mythology, Prometheus represented the bold creative spirit; defying the gods, he stole fire from Olympus (the locale of the gods) and gave it to humankind. Though successful, he was harshly punished by Zeus.

RUTH: How do you know it was an insult? [*To humor him.*] Maybe Prometheus
  is a nice fellow.
WALTER: Prometheus! I bet there ain't even no such thing! I bet that simple-
  minded clown—
RUTH: Walter—

[*She stops what she is doing and looks at him.*]

WALTER: [*Yelling.*] Don't start!
RUTH: Start what?
WALTER: Your nagging! Where was I? Who was I with? How much money did I
  spend?
RUTH: [*Plaintively.*] Walter Lee—why don't we just try to talk about it . . .
WALTER: [*Not listening.*] I been out talking with people who understand me.
  People who care about the things I got on my mind.
RUTH: [*Wearily.*] I guess that means people like Willy Harris.
WALTER: Yes, people like Willy Harris.
RUTH: [*With a sudden flash of impatience.*] Why don't you all just hurry up and
  go into the banking business and stop talking about it!
WALTER: Why? You want to know why? 'Cause we all tied up in a race of people
  that don't know how to do nothing but moan, pray and have babies!

[*The line is too bitter even for him and he looks at her and sits down.*]

RUTH: Oh, Walter . . . [*Softly.*] Honey, why can't you stop fighting me?
WALTER: [*Without thinking.*] Who's fighting you? Who even cares about you?

[*This line begins the retardation of his mood.*]

RUTH: Well—[*She waits a long time, and then with resignation starts to put away
  her things.*] I guess I might as well go on to bed . . . [*More or less to herself.*] I
  don't know where we lost it . . . but we have . . . [*Then, to him.*] I—I'm sorry
  about this new baby, Walter. I guess maybe I better go on and do what I
  started . . . I guess I just didn't realize how bad things was with us . . . I
  guess I just didn't really realize—[*She starts out to the bedroom and stops.*]
  You want some hot milk?
WALTER: Hot milk?
RUTH: Yes—hot milk.
WALTER: Why hot milk?
RUTH: 'Cause after all that liquor you come home with you ought to have some-
  thing hot in your stomach.
WALTER: I don't want no milk.
RUTH: You want some coffee then?
WALTER: No, I don't want no coffee. I don't want nothing hot to drink. [*Almost
  plaintively.*] Why you always trying to give me something to eat?
RUTH: [*Standing and looking at him helplessly.*] What else can I give you, Walter
  Lee Younger?

[*She stands and looks at him and presently turns to go out again. He lifts his
  head and watches her going away from him in a new mood which began to
  emerge when he asked her "Who cares about you?"*]

WALTER: It's been rough, ain't it, baby? [*She hears and stops but does not turn around and he continues to her back.*] I guess between two people there ain't never as much understood as folks generally thinks there is. I mean like between me and you—[*She turns to face him.*] How we gets to the place where we scared to talk softness to each other. [*He waits, thinking hard himself.*] Why you think it got to be like that? [*He is thoughtful, almost as a child would be.*] Ruth, what is it gets into people ought to be close?

RUTH: I don't know, honey. I think about it a lot.

WALTER: On account of you and me, you mean? The way things are with us. The way something done come down between us.

RUTH: There ain't so much between us, Walter . . . Not when you come to me and try to talk to me. Try to be with me . . . a little even.

WALTER: [*Total honesty.*] Sometimes . . . sometimes . . . I don't even know how to try.

RUTH: Walter—

WALTER: Yes?

RUTH: [*Coming to him, gently and with misgiving, but coming to him.*] Honey . . . life don't have to be like this. I mean sometimes people can do things so that things are better . . . You remember how we used to talk when Travis was born . . . about the way we were going to live . . . the kind of house . . . [*She is stroking his head.*] Well, it's all starting to slip away from us . . .

[MAMA *enters, and* WALTER *jumps up and shouts at her.*]

WALTER: Mama, where have you been?

MAMA: My—them steps is longer than they used to be. Whew! [*She sits down and ignores him.*] How you feeling this evening, Ruth?

[RUTH *shrugs, disturbed some at having been prematurely interrupted and watching her husband knowingly.*]

WALTER: Mama, where have you been all day?

MAMA: [*Still ignoring him and leaning on the table and changing to more comfortable shoes.*] Where's Travis?

RUTH: I let him go out earlier and he ain't come back yet. Boy, is he going to get it!

WALTER: Mama!

MAMA: [*As if she has heard him for the first time.*] Yes, son?

WALTER: Where did you go this afternoon?

MAMA: I went downtown to tend to some business that I had to tend to.

WALTER: What kind of business?

MAMA: You know better than to question me like a child, Brother.

WALTER: [*Rising and bending over the table.*] Where were you, Mama? [*Bringing his fists down and shouting.*] Mama, you didn't go do something with that insurance money, something crazy?

[*The front door opens slowly, interrupting him, and* TRAVIS *peeks his head in, less than hopefully.*]

TRAVIS: [*To his mother.*] Mama, I—

RUTH: "Mama" I" nothing! You're going to get it, boy! Get on in that bedroom and get yourself ready!

TRAVIS: But I—

MAMA: Why don't you all never let the child explain hisself.

RUTH: Keep out of it now, Lena.

[MAMA *clamps her lips together, and* RUTH *advances toward her son menacingly.*]

RUTH: A thousand times I have told you not to go off like that—

MAMA: [*Holding out her arms to her grandson.*] Well—at least let me tell him something. I want him to be the first one to hear . . . Come here, Travis. [*The boy obeys, gladly.*] Travis—[*She takes him by the shoulder and looks into his face.*]—you know that money we got in the mail this morning?

TRAVIS: Yes'm—

MAMA: Well—what you think your grandmama gone and done with that money?

TRAVIS: I don't know, Grandmama.

MAMA: [*Putting her finger on his nose for emphasis.*] She went out and she bought you a house! [*The explosion comes from* WALTER *at the end of the revelation and he jumps up and turns away from all of them in a fury.* MAMA *continues, to* TRAVIS.] You glad about the house? It's going to be yours when you get to be a man.

TRAVIS: Yeah—I always wanted to live in a house.

MAMA: All right, gimme some sugar then—[TRAVIS *puts his arms around her neck as she watches her son over the boy's shoulder. Then, to* TRAVIS, *after the embrace.*] Now when you say your prayers tonight, you thank God and your grandfather—'cause it was him who give you the house—in his way.

RUTH: [*Taking the boy from* MAMA *and pushing him toward the bedroom.*] Now you get out of here and get ready for your beating.

TRAVIS: Aw, Mama—

RUTH: Get on in there—[*Closing the door behind him and turning radiantly to her mother-in-law.*] So you went and did it!

MAMA: [*Quietly, looking at her son with pain.*] Yes, I did.

RUTH: [*Raising both arms classically.*] Praise God! [*Looks at* WALTER *a moment, who says nothing. She crosses rapidly to her husband.*] Please, honey—let me be glad . . . you be glad too. [*She has laid her hands on his shoulders, but he shakes himself free of her roughly, without turning to face her.*] Oh, Walter . . . a home . . . a home. [*She comes back to* MAMA.] Well—where is it? How big is it? How much it going to cost?

MAMA: Well—

RUTH: When we moving?

MAMA: [*Smiling at her.*] First of the month.

RUTH: [*Throwing back her head with jubilance.*] Praise God!

MAMA: [*Tentatively, still looking at her son's back turned against her and* RUTH.] It's—it's a nice house too . . . [*She cannot help speaking directly to him. An imploring quality in her voice, her manner, makes her almost like a girl now.*] Three bedrooms—nice big one for you and Ruth . . . Me and Beneatha still have to share our room, but Travis have one of his own—and [*With difficulty.*] I figure if the—new baby—is a boy, we could get one of them double-decker outfits . . . And there's a yard with a little patch of dirt where I could maybe get to grow me a few flowers . . . And a nice big basement . . .

RUTH: Walter honey, be glad—

MAMA: [*Still to his back, fingering things on the table.*] 'Course I don't want to make it sound fancier than it is . . . It's just a plain little old house—but it's made good and solid—and it will be *ours*. Walter Lee—it makes a difference in a man when he can walk on floors that belong to *him* . . .

RUTH: Where is it?

MAMA: [*Frightened at this telling.*] Well—well—it's out there in Clybourne Park[5]—

> [RUTH'S *radiance fades abruptly, and* WALTER *finally turns slowly to face his mother with incredulity and hostility.*]

RUTH: Where?

MAMA: [*Matter-of-factly.*] Four o six Clybourne Street, Clybourne Park.

RUTH: Clybourne Park? Mama, there ain't no colored people living in Clybourne Park.

MAMA: [*Almost idiotically.*] Well, I guess there's going to be some now.

WALTER: [*Bitterly.*] So that's the peace and comfort you went out and bought for us today!

MAMA: [*Raising her eyes to meet his finally.*] Son—I just tried to find the nicest place for the least amount of money for my family.

RUTH: [*Trying to recover from the shock.*] Well—well—'course I ain't one never been 'fraid of no crackers[6] mind you—but—well, wasn't there no other houses nowhere?

MAMA: Them houses they put up for colored in them areas way out all seem to cost twice as much as other houses. I did the best I could.

RUTH: [*Struck senseless with the news, in its various degrees of goodness and trouble, she sits a moment, her fists propping her chin in thought, and then she starts to rise, bringing her fists down with vigor, the radiance spreading from cheek to cheek again.*] Well—well!—All I can say is—if this is my time in life—*my time*—to say good-bye—[*And she builds with momentum as she starts to circle the room with an exuberant, almost tearfully happy release.*]—to these Goddamned cracking walls!—[*She pounds the walls.*]— and these marching roaches!—[*She wipes at an imaginary army of marching roaches.*]—and this cramped little closet which ain't now or never was no kitchen! . . . then I say it loud and good, *Hallelujah! and good-bye misery* . . . I don't never want to see your ugly face again! [*She laughs joyously, having practically destroyed the apartment, and flings her arms up and lets them come down happily, slowly, reflectively, over her abdomen, aware for the first time perhaps that the life therein pulses with happiness and not despair.*] Lena?

MAMA: [*Moved, watching her happiness.*] Yes, honey?

RUTH: [*Looking off.*] Is there—is there a whole lot of sunlight?

MAMA: [*Understanding.*] Yes, child, there's a whole lot of sunlight.

[*Long pause.*]

---

5. On Chicago's Near North Side.
6. Derogatory term for poor Whites.

RUTH: [*Collecting herself and going to the door of the room* TRAVIS *is in.*] Well—I guess I better see 'bout Travis. [*To* MAMA.] Lord, I sure don't feel like whipping nobody today!

[*She exits.*]

MAMA: [*The mother and son are left alone now and the mother waits a long time, considering deeply, before she speaks.*] Son—you—you understand what I done, don't you? [WALTER *is silent and sullen.*] I—I just seen my family falling apart today . . . just falling to pieces in front of my eyes . . . We couldn't of gone on like we was today. We was going backwards 'stead of forwards—talking 'bout killing babies and wishing each other was dead . . . When it gets like that in life—you just got to do something different, push on out and do something bigger . . . [*She waits.*] I wish you say something, son . . . I wish you'd say how deep inside you you think I done the right thing—

WALTER: [*Crossing slowly to his bedroom door and finally turning there and speaking measuredly.*] What you need me to say you done right for? *You* the head of this family. You run our lives like you want to. It was your money and you did what you wanted with it. So what you need for me to say it was all right for? [*Bitterly, to hurt her as deeply as he knows is possible.*] So you butchered up a dream of mine—you—who always talking 'bout your children's dreams . . .

MAMA: Walter Lee—

[*He just closes the door behind him.* MAMA *sits alone, thinking heavily.*]

[CURTAIN.]

Scene Two

Time: Friday night. A few weeks later.

At rise: Packing crates mark the intention of the family to move. BENEATHA *and* GEORGE *come in, presumably from an evening out again.*

GEORGE: O.K. . . . O.K., whatever you say . . . [*They both sit on the couch. He tries to kiss her. She moves away.*] Look, we've had a nice evening; let's not spoil it, huh? . . .

[*He again turns her head and tries to nuzzle in and she turns away from him, not with distaste but with momentary lack of interest; in a mood to pursue what they were talking about.*]

BENEATHA: I'm *trying* to talk to you.

GEORGE: We always talk.

BENEATHA: Yes—and I love to talk.

GEORGE: [*Exasperated; rising.*] I know it and I don't mind it sometimes . . . I want you to cut it out, see—The moody stuff, I mean. I don't like it. You're a nice-looking girl . . . all over. That's all you need, honey, forget the atmosphere. Guys aren't going to go for the atmosphere—they're going to go for what they see. Be glad for that. Drop the Garbo[7] routine. It doesn't go with you. As for myself, I want a nice—[*Groping.*]—simple [*Thoughtfully.*]—sophisticated girl . . . not a poet—O.K.?

[*She rebuffs him again and he starts to leave.*]

BENEATHA: Why are you angry?

GEORGE: Because this is stupid! I don't go out with you to discuss the nature of "quiet desperation"[8] or to hear all about your thoughts—because the world will go on thinking what it thinks regardless—

BENEATHA: Then why read books? Why go to school?

GEORGE: [*With artificial patience, counting on his fingers.*] It's simple. You read books—to learn facts—to get grades—to pass the course—to get a degree. That's all—it has nothing to do with thoughts.

[*A long pause.*]

BENEATHA: I see. [*A longer pause as she looks at him.*] Good night, George.

[GEORGE *looks at her a little oddly, and starts to exit. He meets* MAMA *coming in.*]

GEORGE: Oh—hello, Mrs. Younger.

MAMA: Hello, George, how you feeling?

GEORGE: Fine—fine, how are you?

MAMA: Oh, a little tired. You know them steps can get you after a day's work. You all have a nice time tonight?

GEORGE: Yes—a fine time. Well, good night.

MAMA: Good night. [*He exits.* MAMA *closes the door behind her.*] Hello, honey. What you sitting like that for?

BENEATHA: I'm just sitting.

MAMA: Didn't you have a nice time?

BENEATHA: No.

MAMA: No? What's the matter?

BENEATHA: Mama, George is a fool—honest. [*She rises.*]

MAMA: [*Hustling around unloading the packages she has entered with. She stops.*] Is he, baby?

BENEATHA: Yes.

[BENEATHA *makes up* TRAVIS' *bed as she talks.*]

MAMA: You sure?

BENEATHA: Yes.

MAMA: Well—I guess you better not waste your time with no fools.

[BENEATHA *looks up at her mother, watching her put groceries in the refrigerator. Finally she gathers up her things and starts into the bedroom. At the door she stops and looks back at her mother.*]

---

7. Greta Garbo (1905–90), Swedish-born U.S. film star whose sultry, remote, and European femininity was widely imitated.
8. In *Walden* (1854), Henry David Thoreau asserts that "the mass of men lead lives of quiet desperation."

BENEATHA: Mama—
MAMA: Yes, baby—
BENEATHA: Thank you.
MAMA: For what?
BENEATHA: For understanding me this time.

[*She exits quickly and the mother stands, smiling a little, looking at the place where* BENEATHA *just stood.* RUTH *enters.*]

RUTH: Now don't you fool with any of this stuff, Lena—
MAMA: Oh, I just thought I'd sort a few things out.

[*The phone rings.* RUTH *answers.*]

RUTH: [*At the phone.*] Hello—Just a minute. [*Goes to door.*] Walter, it's Mrs. Arnold. [*Waits. Goes back to the phone. Tense.*] Hello. Yes, this is his wife speaking . . . He's lying down now. Yes . . . well, he'll be in tomorrow. He's been very sick. Yes—I know we should have called, but we were so sure he'd be able to come in today. Yes—yes, I'm very sorry. Yes . . . Thank you very much. [*She hangs up.* WALTER *is standing in the doorway of the bedroom behind her.*] That was Mrs. Arnold.
WALTER: [*Indifferently.*] Was it?
RUTH: She said if you don't come in tomorrow that they are getting a new man . . .
WALTER: Ain't that sad—ain't that crying sad.
RUTH: She said Mr. Arnold has had to take a cab for three days . . . Walter, you ain't been to work for three days! [*This is a revelation to her.*] Where you been, Walter Lee Younger? [WALTER *looks at her and starts to laugh.*] You're going to lose your job.
WALTER: That's right . . .
RUTH: Oh, Walter, and with your mother working like a dog every day—
WALTER: That's sad too—Everything is sad.
MAMA: What you been doing for these three days, son?
WALTER: Mama—you don't know all the things a man what got leisure can find to do in this city . . . What's this—Friday night? Well—Wednesday I borrowed Willy Harris' car and I went for a drive . . . just me and myself and I drove and drove . . . Way out . . . way past South Chicago, and I parked the car and I sat and looked at the steel mills all day long. I just sat in the car and looked at them big black chimneys for hours. Then I drove back and I went to the Green Hat. [*Pause.*] And Thursday—Thursday I borrowed the car again and I got in it and I pointed it the other way and I drove the other way—for hours—way, way up to Wisconsin, and I looked at the farms. I just drove and looked at the farms. Then I drove back and I went to the Green Hat. [*Pause.*] And today—today I didn't get the car. Today I just walked. All over the Southside. And I looked at the Negroes and they looked at me and finally I just sat down on the curb at Thirty-ninth and South Parkway and I just sat there and watched the Negroes go by. And then I went to the Green Hat. You all sad? You all depressed? And you know where I am going right now—

[RUTH *goes out quietly.*]

MAMA: Oh, Big Walter, is this the harvest of our days?

WALTER: You know what I like about the Green Hat? [*He turns the radio on and a steamy, deep blues pours into the room.*] I like this little cat they got there who blows a sax . . . He blows. He talks to me. He ain't but 'bout five feet tall and he's got a conked head[9] and his eyes is always closed and he's all music—

MAMA: [*Rising and getting some papers out of her handbag.*] Walter—

WALTER: And there's this other guy who plays the piano . . . and they got a sound. I mean they can work on some music . . . They got the best little combo in the world in the Green Hat . . . You can just sit there and drink and listen to them three men play and you realize that don't nothing matter worth a damn, but just being there—

MAMA: I've helped do it to you, haven't I, son? Walter, I been wrong.

WALTER: Naw—you ain't never been wrong about nothing, Mama.

MAMA: Listen to me, now. I say I been wrong, son. That I been doing to you what the rest of the world been doing to you. [*She stops and he looks up slowly at her and she meets his eyes pleadingly.*] Walter—what you ain't never understood is that I ain't got nothing, don't own nothing, ain't never really wanted nothing that wasn't for you. There ain't nothing as precious to me . . . There ain't nothing worth holding on to, money, dreams, nothing else—if it means—if it means it's going to destroy my boy. [*She puts her papers in front of him and he watches her without speaking or moving.*] I paid the man thirty-five hundred dollars down on the house. That leaves sixty-five hundred dollars. Monday morning I want you to take this money and take three thousand dollars and put it in a savings account for Beneatha's medical schooling. The rest you put in a checking account—with your name on it. And from now on any penny that come out of it or that go in it is for you to look after. For you to decide. [*She drops her hands a little helplessly.*] It ain't much, but it's all I got in the world and I'm putting it in your hands. I'm telling you to be the head of this family from now on like you supposed to be.

WALTER: [*Stares at the money.*] You trust me like that, Mama?

MAMA: I ain't never stop trusting you. Like I ain't never stop loving you.

[*She goes out, and* WALTER *sits looking at the money on the table as the music continues in its idiom, pulsing in the room. Finally, in a decisive gesture, he gets up, and, in mingled joy and desperation, picks up the money. At the same moment,* TRAVIS *enters for bed.*]

TRAVIS: What's the matter, Daddy? You drunk?

WALTER: [*Sweetly, more sweetly than we have ever known him.*] No, Daddy ain't drunk. Daddy ain't going to never be drunk again. . . .

TRAVIS: Well, good night, Daddy.

[*The father has come from behind the couch and leans over, embracing his son.*]

WALTER: Son, I feel like talking to you tonight.

TRAVIS: About what?

---

9. Straightened hair.

WALTER: Oh, about a lot of things. About you and what kind of man you going to be when you grow up . . . Son—son, what do you want to be when you grow up?

TRAVIS: A bus driver.

WALTER: [*Laughing a little.*] A what? Man, that ain't nothing to want to be!

TRAVIS: Why not?

WALTER: 'Cause, man—it ain't big enough—you know what I mean.

TRAVIS: I don't know then. I can't make up my mind. Sometimes Mama asks me that too. And sometimes when I tell her I just want to be like you—she says she don't want me to be like that and sometimes she says she does . . .

WALTER: [*Gathering him up in his arms.*] You know what, Travis? In seven years you going to be seventeen years old. And things is going to be very different with us in seven years, Travis . . . One day when you are seventeen I'll come home—home from my office downtown somewhere—

TRAVIS: You don't work in no office, Daddy.

WALTER: No—but after tonight. After what your daddy gonna do tonight, there's going to be offices—a whole lot of offices . . .

TRAVIS: What you gonna do tonight, Daddy?

WALTER: You wouldn't understand yet, son, but your daddy's gonna make a transaction . . . a business transaction that's going to change our lives . . . That's how come one day when you 'bout seventeen years old I'll come home and I'll be pretty tired, you know what I mean, after a day of conferences and secretaries getting things wrong the way they do . . . 'cause an executive's life is hell, man—[*The more he talks the farther away he gets.*] And I'll pull the car up on the driveway . . . just a plain black Chrysler, I think, with white walls—no—black tires. More elegant. Rich people don't have to be flashy . . . though I'll have to get something a little sportier for Ruth—maybe a Cadillac convertible to do her shopping in . . . And I'll come up the steps to the house and the gardener will be clipping away at the hedges and he'll say, "Good evening, Mr. Younger." And I'll say, "Hello, Jefferson, how are you this evening?" And I'll go inside and Ruth will come downstairs and meet me at the door and we'll kiss each other and she'll take my arm and we'll go up to your room to see you sitting on the floor with the catalogues of all the great schools in America around you . . . All the great schools in the world. And—and I'll say, all right son—it's your seventeenth birthday, what is it you've decided? . . . Just tell me where you want to go to school and you'll *go.* Just tell me, what it is you want to be— and you'll *be* it . . . Whatever you want to be—Yessir! [*He holds his arms open for* TRAVIS.] You just name it, son . . . [TRAVIS *leaps into them.*] and I hand you the world!

[WALTER's *voice has risen in pitch and hysterical promise and on the last line he lifts* TRAVIS *high.*]

[BLACKOUT.]

Scene Three

Time: Saturday, moving day, one week later.

Before the curtain rises, RUTH's *voice, a strident, dramatic church alto, cuts through the silence.*

It is, in the darkness, a triumphant surge, a penetrating statement of expectation: "Oh, Lord, I don't feel no ways tired! Children, oh, glory hallelujah!"

As the curtain rises we see that RUTH *is alone in the living room, finishing up the family's packing. It is moving day. She is nailing crates and tying cartons.* BENEATHA *enters, carrying a guitar case, and watches her exuberant sister-in-law.*

RUTH: Hey!

BENEATHA: [*Putting away the case.*] Hi.

RUTH: [*Pointing at a package.*] Honey—look in that package there and see what I found on sale this morning at the South Center. [RUTH *gets up and moves to the package and draws out some curtains.*] Lookahere—hand-turned hems!

BENEATHA: How do you know the window size out there?

RUTH: [*Who hadn't thought of that.*] Oh—Well, they bound to fit something in the whole house. Anyhow, they was too good a bargain to pass up. [RUTH *slaps her head, suddenly remembering something.*] Oh, Bennie—I meant to put a special note on that carton over there. That's your mama's good china and she wants 'em to be very careful with it.

BENEATHA: I'll do it.

[BENEATHA *finds a piece of paper and starts to draw large letters on it.*]

RUTH: You know what I'm going to do soon as I get in that new house?

BENEATHA: What?

RUTH: Honey—I'm going to run me a tub of water up to here . . . [*With her fingers practically up to her nostrils.*] And I'm going to get in it—and I am going to sit . . . and sit . . . and sit in that hot water and the first person who knocks to tell *me* to hurry up and come out—

BENEATHA: Gets shot at sunrise.

RUTH: [*Laughing happily.*] You said it, sister! [*Noticing how large* BENEATHA *is absentmindedly making the note.*] Honey, they ain't going to read that from no airplane.

BENEATHA: [*Laughing herself.*] I guess I always think things have more emphasis if they are big, somehow.

RUTH: [*Looking up at her and smiling.*] You and your brother seem to have that as a philosophy of life. Lord, that man—done changed so 'round here. You know—you know what we did last night? Me and Walter Lee?

BENEATHA: What?

RUTH: [*Smiling to herself.*] We went to the movies. [*Looking at* BENEATHA *to see if she understands.*] We went to the movies. You know the last time me and Walter went to the movies together?

BENEATHA: No.

RUTH: Me neither. That's how long it been. [*Smiling again.*] But we went last night. The picture wasn't much good, but that didn't seem to matter. We went—and we held hands.

BENEATHA: Oh, Lord!

RUTH: We held hands—and you know what?

BENEATHA: What?

RUTH: When we come out of the show it was late and dark and all the stores and things was closed up . . . and it was kind of chilly and there wasn't many people on the streets . . . and we was still holding hands, me and Walter.

BENEATHA: You're killing me.

[WALTER *enters with a large package. His happiness is deep in him; he cannot keep still with his new-found exuberance. He is singing and wiggling and snapping his fingers. He puts his package in a corner and puts a phonograph record, which he has brought in with him, on the record player. As the music comes up he dances over to* RUTH *and tries to get her to dance with him. She gives in at last to his raunchiness and in a fit of giggling allows herself to be drawn into his mood and together they deliberately burlesque an old social dance of their youth.*]

BENEATHA: [*Regarding them a long time as they dance, then drawing in her breath for a deeply exaggerated comment which she does not particularly mean.*] Talk about—olddddddddddd-fashionedddddddd—Negroes!

WALTER: [*Stopping momentarily.*] What kind of Negroes?

[*He says this in fun. He is not angry with her today, nor with anyone. He starts to dance with his wife again.*]

BENEATHA: Old-fashioned.

WALTER: [*As he dances with* RUTH.] You know, when these *New Negroes* have their convention—[*Pointing at his sister.*]—that is going to be the chairman of the Committee on Unending Agitation. [*He goes on dancing, then stops.*] Race, race, race! . . . Girl, I do believe you are the first person in the history of the entire human race to successfully brainwash yourself. [BENEATHA *breaks up and he goes on dancing. He stops again, enjoying his tease.*] Damn, even the N double A C P[1] takes a holiday sometimes! [BENEATHA *and* RUTH *laugh. He dances with* RUTH *some more and starts to laugh and stops and pantomimes someone over an operating table.*] I can just see that chick someday looking down at some poor cat on an operating table before she starts to slice him, saying . . . [*Pulling his sleeves back maliciously.*] "By the way, what are your views on civil rights down there? . . ."

[*He laughs at her again and starts to dance happily. The bell sounds.*]

BENEATHA: Sticks and stones may break my bones but . . . words will never hurt me!

[BENEATHA *goes to the door and opens it as* WALTER *and* RUTH *go on with the clowning.* BENEATHA *is somewhat surprised to see a quiet-looking middle-aged white man in a business suit holding his hat and a briefcase in his hand and consulting a small piece of paper.*]

1. National Association for the Advancement of Colored People, civil rights organization founded in 1909.

MAN: Uh—how do you do, miss. I am looking for a Mrs.—[*He looks at the slip of paper.*] Mrs. Lena Younger?

BENEATHA: [*Smoothing her hair with slight embarrassment.*] Oh—yes, that's my mother. Excuse me [*She closes the door and turns to quiet the other two.*] Ruth! Brother! Somebody's here. [*Then she opens the door. The* MAN *casts a curious quick glance at all of them.*] Uh—come in please.

MAN: [*Coming in.*] Thank you.

BENEATHA: My mother isn't here just now. Is it business?

MAN: Yes . . . well, of a sort.

WALTER: [*Freely, the Man of the House.*] Have a seat. I'm Mrs. Younger's son. I look after most of her business matters.

[RUTH *and* BENEATHA *exchange amused glances.*]

MAN: [*Regarding* WALTER, *and sitting.*] Well—My name is Karl Lindner . . .

WALTER: [*Stretching out his hand.*] Walter Younger. This is my wife—[RUTH *nods politely.*]—and my sister.

LINDNER: How do you do.

WALTER: [*Amiably, as he sits himself easily on a chair, leaning with interest forward on his knees and looking expectantly into the newcomer's face.*] What can we do for you, Mr. Lindner!

LINDNER: [*Some minor shuffling of the hat and briefcase on his knees.*] Well—I am a representative of the Clybourne Park Improvement Association—

WALTER: [*Pointing.*] Why don't you sit your things on the floor?

LINDNER: Oh—yes. Thank you. [*He slides the briefcase and hat under the chair.*] And as I was saying—I am from the Clybourne Park Improvement Association and we have had it brought to our attention at the last meeting that you people—or at least your mother—has bought a piece of residential property at—[*He digs for the slip of paper again.*]—four o six Clybourne Street . . .

WALTER: That's right. Care for something to drink? Ruth, get Mr. Lindner a beer.

LINDNER: [*Upset for some reason.*] Oh—no, really. I mean thank you very much, but no thank you.

RUTH: [*Innocently.*] Some coffee?

LINDNER: Thank you, nothing at all.

[BENEATHA *is watching the man carefully.*]

LINDNER: Well, I don't know how much you folks know about our organization. [*He is a gentle man; thoughtful and somewhat labored in his manner.*] It is one of these community organizations set up to look after—oh, you know, things like block upkeep and special projects and we also have what we call our New Neighbors Orientation Committee . . .

BENEATHA: [*Drily.*] Yes—and what do they do?

LINDNER: [*Turning a little to her and then returning the main force to* WALTER.*] Well—it's what you might call a sort of welcoming committee, I guess. I mean they, we, I'm the chairman of the committee—go around and see the new people who move into the neighborhood and sort of give them the low-down on the way we do things out in Clybourne Park.

BENEATHA: [*With appreciation of the two meanings, which escape* RUTH *and* WALTER.] Un-huh.

LINDNER: And we also have the category of what the association calls—[*He looks elsewhere.*]—uh—special community problems . . .

BENEATHA: Yes—and what are some of those?

WALTER: Girl, let the man talk.

LINDNER: [*With understated relief.*] Thank you. I would sort of like to explain this thing in my own way. I mean I want to explain to you in a certain way.

WALTER: Go ahead.

LINDNER: Yes. Well. I'm going to try to get right to the point. I'm sure we'll all appreciate that in the long run.

BENEATHA: Yes.

WALTER: Be still now!

LINDNER: Well—

RUTH: [*Still innocently.*] Would you like another chair—you don't look comfortable.

LINDNER: [*More frustrated than annoyed.*] No, thank you very much. Please. Well—to get right to the point I—[*A great breath, and he is off at last.*] I am sure you people must be aware of some of the incidents which have happened in various parts of the city when colored people have moved into certain areas—[BENEATHA *exhales heavily and starts tossing a piece of fruit up and down in the air.*] Well—because we have what I think is going to be a unique type of organization in American community life—not only do we deplore that kind of thing—but we are trying to do something about it. [BENEATHA *stops tossing and turns with a new and quizzical interest to the man.*] We feel—[*Gaining confidence in his mission because of the interest in the faces of the people he is talking to.*]—we feel that most of the trouble in this world, when you come right down to it—[*He hits his knee for emphasis.*]—most of the trouble exists because people just don't sit down and talk to each other.

RUTH: [*Nodding as she might in church, pleased with the remark.*] You can say that again, mister.

LINDNER: [*More encouraged by such affirmation.*] That we don't try hard enough in this world to understand the other fellow's problem. The other guy's point of view.

RUTH: Now that's right.

[BENEATHA *and* WALTER *merely watch and listen with genuine interest.*]

LINDNER: Yes—that's the way we feel out in Clybourne Park. And that's why I was elected to come here this afternoon and talk to you people. Friendly like, you know, the way people should talk to each other and see if we couldn't find some way to work this thing out. As I say, the whole business is a matter of *caring* about the other fellow. Anybody can see that you are a nice family of folks, hard working and honest I'm sure. [BENEATHA *frowns slightly, quizzically, her head tilted regarding him.*] Today everybody knows what it means to be on the outside of something. And of course, there is always somebody who is out to take the advantage of people who don't always understand.

WALTER: What do you mean?

LINDNER: Well—you see our community is made up of people who've worked hard as the dickens for years to build up that little community. They're not rich and fancy people; just hard-working, honest people who don't really have much but those little homes and a dream of the kind of community they want to raise their children in. Now, I don't say we are perfect and there is a lot wrong in some of the things they want. But you've got to admit that a man, right or wrong, has the right to want to have the neighborhood he lives in a certain kind of way. And at the moment the overwhelming majority of our people out there feel that people get along better, take more of a common interest in the life of the community, when they share a common back-ground. I want you to believe me when I tell you that race prejudice simply doesn't enter into it. It is a matter of the people of Clybourne Park believing, rightly or wrongly, as I say, that for the happiness of all concerned that our Negro families are happier when they live in their *own* communities.

BENEATHA: [*With a grand and bitter gesture.*] This, friends, is the Welcoming Committee!

WALTER: [*Dumfounded, looking at* LINDNER.] Is this what you came marching all the way over here to tell us?

LINDNER: Well, now we've been having a fine conversation. I hope you'll hear me all the way through.

WALTER: [*Tightly.*] Go ahead, man.

LINDNER: You see—in the face of all things I have said, we are prepared to make your family a very generous offer . . .

BENEATHA: Thirty pieces and not a coin less![2]

WALTER: Yeah?

LINDNER: [*Putting on his glasses and drawing a form out of the briefcase.*] Our association is prepared, through the collective effort of our people, to buy the house from you at a financial gain to your family.

RUTH: Lord have mercy, ain't this the living gall!

WALTER: All right, you through?

LINDNER: Well, I want to give you the exact terms of the financial arrangement—

WALTER: We don't want to hear no exact terms of no arrangements. I want to know if you got any more to tell us 'bout getting together?

LINDNER: [*Taking off his glasses.*] Well—I don't suppose that you feel . . .

WALTER: Never mind how I feel—you got any more to say 'bout how people ought to sit down and talk to each other? . . . Get out of my house, man.

[*He turns his back and walks to the door.*]

LINDNER: [*Looking around at the hostile faces and reaching and assembling his hat and briefcase.*] Well—I don't understand why you people are reacting this way. What do you think you are going to gain by moving into a neighborhood where you just aren't wanted and where some elements—well—people can get awful worked up when they feel that their whole way of life and every-thing they've ever worked for is threatened.

WALTER: Get out.

2. See Matthew 26.15, in which Judas Iscariot is paid thirty pieces of silver to betray Jesus.

LINDNER: [*At the door, holding a small card.*] Well—I'm sorry it went like this.

WALTER: Get out.

LINDNER: [*Almost sadly regarding* WALTER.] You just can't force people to change their hearts, son.

[*He turns and puts his card on a table and exits.* WALTER *pushes the door to with stinging hatred, and stands looking at it.* RUTH *just sits and* BENEATHA *just stands. They say nothing.* MAMA *and* TRAVIS *enter.*]

MAMA: Well—this all the packing got done since I left out of here this morning. I testify before God that my children got all the energy of the dead. What time the moving men due?

BENEATHA: Four o'clock. You had a caller, Mama.

[*She is smiling, teasingly.*]

MAMA: Sure enough—who?

BENEATHA: [*Her arms folded saucily.*] The Welcoming Committee.

[WALTER *and* RUTH *giggle.*]

MAMA: [*Innocently.*] Who?

BENEATHA: The Welcoming Committee. They said they're sure going to be glad to see you when you get there.

WALTER: [*Devilishly.*] Yeah, they said they can't hardly wait to see your face.

[*Laughter.*]

MAMA: [*Sensing their facetiousness.*] What's the matter with you all?

WALTER: Ain't nothing the matter with us. We just telling you 'bout the gentleman who came to see you this afternoon. From the Clybourne Park Improvement Association.

MAMA: What he want?

RUTH: [*In the same mood as* BENEATHA *and* WALTER.] To welcome you, honey.

WALTER: He said they can't hardly wait. He said the one thing they don't have, that they just *dying* to have out there is a fine family of colored people! [*To* RUTH *and* BENEATHA.] Ain't that right!

RUTH AND BENEATHA: [*Mockingly.*] Yeah! He left his card in case—

[*They indicate the card, and* MAMA *picks it up and throws it on the floor— understanding and looking off as she draws her chair up to the table on which she has put her plant and some sticks and some cord.*]

MAMA: Father, give us strength. [*Knowingly—and without fun.*] Did he threaten us?

BENEATHA: Oh—Mama—they don't do it like that anymore. He talked Brotherhood. He said everybody ought to learn how to sit down and hate each other with good Christian fellowship.

[*She and* WALTER *shake hands to ridicule the remark.*]

MAMA: [*Sadly.*] Lord, protect us . . .

RUTH: You should hear the money those folks raised to buy the house from us. All we paid and then some.

BENEATHA: What they think we going to do—eat 'em?

RUTH: No, honey, marry 'em.

MAMA: [*Shaking her head.*] Lord, Lord, Lord . . .

RUTH: Well—that's the way the crackers crumble. Joke.

BENEATHA: [*Laughingly noticing what her mother is doing.*] Mama, what are you doing?

MAMA: Fixing my plant so it won't get hurt none on the way . . .

BENEATHA: Mama, you going to take *that* to the new house?

MAMA: Un-huh—

BENEATHA: That raggedy-looking old thing?

MAMA: [*Stopping and looking at her.*] It expresses *me.*

RUTH: [*With delight, to* BENEATHA.] So there, Miss Thing!

> [WALTER *comes to* MAMA *suddenly and bends down behind her and squeezes her in his arms with all his strength. She is overwhelmed by the suddenness of it and, though delighted, her manner is like that of* RUTH *with* TRAVIS.]

MAMA: Look out now, boy! You make me mess up my thing here!

WALTER: [*His face lit, he slips down on his knees beside her, his arms still about her.*] Mama . . . you know what it means to climb up in the chariot?

MAMA: [*Gruffly, very happy.*] Get on away from me now . . . .

RUTH: [*Near the gift-wrapped package, trying to catch* WALTER's *eye.*] Psst—

WALTER: What the old song say, Mama . . .

RUTH: Walter—Now?

> [*She is pointing at the package.*]

WALTER: [*Speaking the lines, sweetly, playfully, in his mother's face.*]

> I got wings . . . you got wings . . .
> All God's Children got wings[3] . . .

MAMA: Boy—get out of my face and do some work . . .

WALTER:

> When I get to heaven gonna put on my wings,
> Gonna fly all over God's heaven . . .

BENEATHA: [*Teasingly, from across the room.*] Everybody talking 'bout heaven ain't going there!

WALTER: [*To* RUTH, *who is carrying the box across to them.*] I don't know, you think we ought to give her that . . . Seems to me she ain't been very appreciative around here.

MAMA: [*Eying the box, which is obviously a gift.*] What is that?

WALTER: [*Taking it from* RUTH *and putting it on the table in front of* MAMA.] Well—what you all think? Should we give it to her?

RUTH: Oh—she was pretty good today.

---

3. Lines from an African American spiritual. Walter's and Beneatha's next lines are also from the song.

MAMA: I'll good you—

[*She turns her eyes to the box again.*]

BENEATHA: Open it, Mama.

[*She stands up, looks at it, turns and looks at all of them, and then presses her hands together and does not open the package.*]

WALTER: [*Sweetly.*] Open it, Mama. It's for you. [MAMA *looks in his eyes. It is the first present in her life without its being Christmas. Slowly she opens her package and lifts out, one by one, a brand-new sparkling set of gardening tools.* WALTER *continues, prodding.*] Ruth made up the note—read it . . .

MAMA: [*Picking up the card and adjusting her glasses.*] "To our own Mrs. Miniver[4]— Love from Brother, Ruth and Beneatha." Ain't that lovely . . .

TRAVIS: [*Tugging at his father's sleeve.*] Daddy, can I give her mine now?

WALTER: All right, son. [TRAVIS *flies to get his gift.*] Travis didn't want to go in with the rest of us, Mama. He got his own. [*Somewhat amused.*] We don't know what it is . . .

TRAVIS: [*Racing back in the room with a large hatbox and putting it in front of his grandmother.*] Here!

MAMA: Lord have mercy, baby. You done gone and bought your grandmother a hat?

TRAVIS: [*Very proud.*] Open it!

[*She does and lifts out an elaborate, but very elaborate, wide gardening hat, and all the adults break up at the sight of it.*]

RUTH: Travis, honey, what is that?

TRAVIS: [*Who thinks it is beautiful and appropriate.*] It's a gardening hat! Like the ladies always have on in the magazines when they work in their gardens.

BENEATHA: [*Giggling fiercely.*] Travis—we were trying to make Mama Mrs. Miniver—not Scarlett O'Hara![5]

MAMA: [*Indignantly.*] What's the matter with you all! This here is a beautiful hat! [*Absurdly.*] I always wanted me one just like it!

[*She pops it on her head to prove it to her grandson, and the hat is ludicrous and considerably oversized.*]

RUTH: Hot dog! Go, Mama!

WALTER: [*Doubled over with laughter.*] I'm sorry, Mama—but you look like you ready to go out and chop you some cotton sure enough!

[*They all laugh except* MAMA, *out of deference to* TRAVIS' *feelings.*]

MAMA: [*Gathering the boy up to her.*] Bless your heart—this is the prettiest hat I ever owned—[WALTER, RUTH *and* BENEATHA *chime in—noisily, festively and insincerely congratulating* TRAVIS *on his gift.*] What are we all standing around here for? We ain't finished packin' yet. Bennie, you ain't packed one book.

4. Courageous, charismatic title character of a 1942 film starring Greer Garson.
5. Glamorous, headstrong heroine of Margaret Mitchell's 1936 novel *Gone with the Wind*, set in antebellum Georgia; Vivien Leigh played Scarlett in the 1939 film adaptation.

[*The bell rings.*]

BENEATHA: That couldn't be the movers . . . it's not hardly two good yet—

[BENEATHA *goes into her room.* MAMA *starts for door.*]

WALTER: [*Turning, stiffening.*] Wait—wait—I'll get it.

[*He stands and looks at the door.*]

MAMA: You expecting company, son?

WALTER: [*Just looking at the door.*] Yeah—yeah . . .

[MAMA *looks at* RUTH, *and they exchange innocent and unfrightened glances.*]

MAMA: [*Not understanding.*] Well, let them in, son.

BENEATHA: [*From her room.*] We need some more string.

MAMA: Travis—you run to the hardware and get me some string cord.

[MAMA *goes out and* WALTER *turns and looks at* RUTH. TRAVIS *goes to a dish for money.*]

RUTH: Why don't you answer the door, man?

WALTER: [*Suddenly bounding across the floor to her.*] 'Cause sometimes it hard to let the future begin! [*Stooping down in her face.*]

I got wings! You got wings!
All God's children got wings!

[*He crosses to the door and throws it open. Standing there is a very slight little man in a not too prosperous business suit and with haunted frightened eyes and a hat pulled down tightly, brim up, around his forehead.* TRAVIS *passes between the men and exits.* WALTER *leans deep in the man's face, still in his jubilance.*]

When I get to heaven gonna put on my wings,
Gonna fly all over God's heaven . . .

[*The little man just stares at him.*]

Heaven—

[*Suddenly he stops and looks past the little man into the empty hallway.*] Where's Willy, man?

BOBO: He ain't with me.

WALTER: [*Not disturbed.*] Oh—come on in. You know my wife.

BOBO: [*Dumbly, taking off his hat.*] Yes—h'you, Miss Ruth.

RUTH: [*Quietly, a mood apart from her husband already, seeing* BOBO.] Hello, Bobo.

WALTER: You right on time today . . . Right on time. That's the way! [*He slaps* BOBO *on his back.*] Sit down . . . lemme hear.

[RUTH *stands stiffly and quietly in back of them, as though somehow she senses death, her eyes fixed on her husband.*]

BOBO: [*His frightened eyes on the floor, his hat in his hands.*] Could I please get a drink of water, before I tell you about it, Walter Lee?

[WALTER *does not take his eyes off the man.* RUTH *goes blindly to the tap and gets a glass of water and brings it to* BOBO.]

WALTER: There ain't nothing wrong, is there?

BOBO: Lemme tell you—

WALTER: Man—didn't nothing go wrong?

BOBO: Lemme tell you—Walter Lee. [*Looking at* RUTH *and talking to her more than to* WALTER.] You know how it was. I got to tell you how it was. I mean first I got to tell you how it was all the way . . . I mean about the money I put in, Walter Lee . . .

WALTER: [*With taut agitation now.*] What about the money you put in?

BOBO: Well—it wasn't much as we told you—me and Willy—[*He stops.*] I'm sorry, Walter. I got a bad feeling about it. I got a real bad feeling about it . . .

WALTER: Man, what you telling me about all this for? . . . Tell me what happened in Springfield . . .

BOBO: Springfield.

RUTH: [*Like a dead woman.*] What was supposed to happen in Springfield?

BOBO: [*To her.*] This deal that me and Walter went into with Willy—Me and Willy was going to go down to Springfield and spread some money 'round so's we wouldn't have to wait so long for the liquor license . . . That's what we were going to do. Everybody said that was the way you had to do, you understand, Miss Ruth?

WALTER: Man—what happened down there?

BOBO: [*A pitiful man, near tears.*] I'm trying to tell you, Walter.

WALTER: [*Screaming at him suddenly.*] THEN TELL ME, GODDAMMIT . . . WHAT'S THE MATTER WITH YOU?

BOBO: Man . . . I didn't go to no Springfield, yesterday.

WALTER: [*Halted, life hanging in the moment.*] Why not?

BOBO: [*The long way, the hard way to tell.*] 'Cause I didn't have no reasons to . . .

WALTER: Man, what are you talking about!

BOBO: I'm talking about the fact that when I got to the train station yesterday morning—eight o'clock like we planned . . . Man—*Willy didn't never show up.*

WALTER: Why . . . where was he . . . where is he?

BOBO: That's what I'm trying to tell you . . . I don't know . . . I waited six hours . . . I called his house . . . and I waited . . . six hours . . . I waited in that train station six hours . . . [*Breaking into tears.*] That was all the extra money I had in the world . . . [*Looking up at* WALTER *with the tears running down his face.*] Man, *Willy is gone.*

WALTER: Gone, what you mean Willy is gone? Gone where? You mean he went by himself. You mean he went off to Springfield by himself—to take care of getting the license—[*Turns and looks anxiously at* RUTH.] You mean maybe he didn't want too many people in on the business down there? [*Looks to* RUTH *again, as before.*] You know Willy got his own ways. [*Looks back to* BOBO.] Maybe you was late yesterday and he just went on down there without you. Maybe—maybe—he's been callin' you at home tryin' to tell you what happened or something. Maybe—maybe—he just got sick. He's somewhere—he's got to be somewhere. We just got to find him—me and you got to find him. [*Grabs* BOBO *senselessly by the collar and starts to shake him.*] We got to!

BOBO: [*In sudden angry, frightened agony.*] What's the matter with you, Walter! *When a cat take off with your money he don't leave you no maps!*

WALTER: [*Turning madly, as though he is looking for* WILLY *in the very room.*] Willy! . . . Willy . . . don't do it . . . Please don't do it . . . Man, not with that money . . . Man, please, not with that money . . . Oh, God . . . Don't let it be true . . . [*He is wandering around, crying out for* WILLY *and looking for him or perhaps for help from God.*] Man . . . I trusted you . . . Man, I put my life in your hands . . . [*He starts to crumple down on the floor as* RUTH *just covers her face in horror.* MAMA *opens the door and comes into the room, with* BENEATHA *behind her.*] Man . . . [*He starts to pound the floor with his fists, sobbing wildly.*] *That money is made out of my father's flesh* . . .

BOBO: [*Standing over him helplessly.*] I'm sorry, Walter . . . [*Only* WALTER'S *sobs reply.* BOBO *puts on his hat.*] I had my life staked on this deal, too . . .

   [*He exits.*]

MAMA: [*To* WALTER.] Son—[*She goes to him, bends down to him, talks to his bent head.*] Son . . . Is it gone? Son, I gave you sixty-five hundred dollars. Is it gone? All of it? Beneatha's money too?

WALTER: [*Lifting his head slowly.*] Mama . . . I never . . . went to the bank at all . . .

MAMA: [*Not wanting to believe him.*] You mean . . . your sister's school money . . . you used that too . . . Walter? . . .

WALTER: Yessss! . . . All of it . . . It's all gone . . . [*There is total silence.* RUTH *stands with her face covered with her hands;* BENEATHA *leans forlornly against a wall, fingering a piece of red ribbon from the mother's gift.* MAMA *stops and looks at her son without recognition and then, quite without thinking about it, starts to beat him senselessly in the face.* BENEATHA *goes to them and stops it.*]

BENEATHA: Mama!

   [MAMA *stops and looks at both of her children and rises slowly and wanders vaguely, aimlessly away from them.*]

MAMA: I seen . . . him . . . night after night . . . come in . . . and look at that rug . . . and then look at me . . . the red showing in his eyes . . . the veins moving in his head . . . I seen him grow thin and old before he was forty . . . working and working and working like somebody's old horse . . . killing himself . . . and you—you give it all away in a day . . .

BENEATHA: Mama—

MAMA: Oh, God . . . [*She looks up to Him.*] Look down here—and show me the strength.

BENEATHA: Mama—

MAMA: [*Folding over.*] Strength . . .

BENEATHA: [*Plaintively.*] Mama . . .

MAMA: Strength!

   [CURTAIN.]

ACT III

An hour later.

At curtain, there is a sullen light of gloom in the living room, gray light not unlike that which began the first scene of Act I. At left we can see WALTER *within his room, alone with himself. He is stretched out on the bed, his shirt out and open, his arms under his head. He does not smoke, he does not cry out, he merely lies there, looking up at the ceiling, much as if he were alone in the world.*

In the living room BENEATHA *sits at the table, still surrounded by the now almost ominous packing crates. She sits looking off. We feel that this is a mood struck perhaps an hour before, and it lingers now, full of the empty sound of profound disappointment. We see on a line from her brother's bedroom the sameness of their attitudes. Presently the bell rings and* BENEATHA *rises without ambition or interest in answering. It is* ASAGAI, *smiling broadly, striding into the room with energy and happy expectation and conversation.*

ASAGAI: I came over . . . I had some free time. I thought I might help with the packing. Ah, I like the look of packing crates! A household in preparation for a journey! It depresses some people . . . but for me . . . it is another feeling. Something full of the flow of life, do you understand? Movement, progress . . . It makes me think of Africa.

BENEATHA: Africa!

ASAGAI: What kind of a mood is this? Have I told you how deeply you move me?

BENEATHA: He gave away the money, Asagai . . .

ASAGAI: Who gave away what money?

BENEATHA: The insurance money. My brother gave it away.

ASAGAI: Gave it away?

BENEATHA: He made an investment! With a man even Travis wouldn't have trusted.

ASAGAI: And it's gone?

BENEATHA: Gone!

ASAGAI: I'm very sorry . . . And you, now?

BENEATHA: Me? . . . Me? . . . Me, I'm nothing . . . Me. When I was very small . . . we used to take our sleds out in the wintertime and the only hills we had were the ice-covered stone steps of some houses down the street. And we used to fill them in with snow and make them smooth and slide down them all day . . . and it was very dangerous you know . . . far too steep . . . and sure enough one day a kid named Rufus came down too fast and hit the sidewalk . . . and we saw his face just split open right there in front of us . . . And I remember standing there looking at his bloody open face thinking that was the end of Rufus. But the ambulance came and they took him to the hospital and they fixed the broken bones and they sewed it all up . . . and the next time I saw Rufus he just had a little line down the middle of his face . . . I never got over that . . .

[WALTER *sits up, listening on the bed. Throughout this scene it is important that we feel his reaction at all times, that he visibly respond to the words of his sister and* ASAGAI.]

ASAGAI: What?

BENEATHA: That that was what one person could do for another, fix him up—sew up the problem, make him all right again. That was the most marvelous thing in the world . . . I wanted to do that. I always thought it was the one concrete thing in the world that a human being could do. Fix up the sick, you know—and make them whole again. This was truly being God . . .

ASAGAI: You wanted to be God?

BENEATHA: No—I wanted to cure. It used to be so important to me. I wanted to cure. It used to matter. I used to care. I mean about people and how their bodies hurt . . .

ASAGAI: And you've stopped caring?

BENEATHA: Yes—I think so.

ASAGAI: Why?

> [WALTER *rises, goes to the door of his room and is about to open it, then stops and stands listening, leaning on the door jamb.*]

BENEATHA: Because it doesn't seem deep enough, close enough to what ails mankind—I mean this thing of sewing up bodies or administering drugs. Don't you understand? It was a child's reaction to the world. I thought that doctors had the secret to all the hurts . . . That's the way a child sees things—or an idealist.

ASAGAI: Children see things very well sometimes—and idealists even better.

BENEATHA: I know that's what you think. Because you are still where I left off—you still care. This is what you see for the world, for Africa. You with the dreams of the future will patch up all Africa—you are going to cure the Great Sore of colonialism with Independence—

ASAGAI: Yes!

BENEATHA: Yes—and you think that one word is the penicillin of the human spirit: "Independence!" But then what?

ASAGAI: That will be the problem for another time. First we must get there.

BENEATHA: And where does it end?

ASAGAI: End? Who even spoke of an end? To life? To living?

BENEATHA: An end to misery!

ASAGAI: [*Smiling.*] You sound like a French intellectual.

BENEATHA: No! I sound like a human being who just had her future taken right out of her hands! While I was sleeping in my bed in there, things were happening in this world that directly concerned me—and nobody asked me, consulted me—they just went out and did things—and changed my life. Don't you see there isn't any real progress, Asagai, there is only one large circle that we march in, around and around, each of us with our own little picture—in front of us—our own little mirage that we think is the future.

ASAGAI: That is the mistake.

BENEATHA: What?

ASAGAI: What you just said—about the circle. It isn't a circle—it is simply a long line—as in geometry, you know, one that reaches into infinity. And because we cannot see the end—we also cannot see how it changes. And it is very odd but those who see the changes are called "idealists"—and those who cannot, or refuse to think, they are the "realists." It is very strange, and amusing too, I think.

BENEATHA: You—you are almost religious.

ASAGAI: Yes . . . I think I have the religion of doing what is necessary in the world—and of worshipping man—because he is so marvelous, you see.

BENEATHA: Man is foul! And the human race deserves its misery!

ASAGAI: You see: *you* have become the religious one in the old sense. Already, and after such a small defeat, you are worshipping despair.

BENEATHA: From now on, I worship the truth—and the truth is that people are puny, small and selfish . . .

ASAGAI: Truth? Why is it that you despairing ones always think that only you have the truth? I never thought to see *you* like that. You! Your brother made a stupid, childish mistake—and you are grateful to him. So that now you can give up the ailing human race on account of it. You talk about what good is struggle; what good is anything? Where are we all going? And why are we bothering?

BENEATHA: *And you cannot answer it!* All your talk and dreams about Africa and Independence. Independence and then what? What about all the crooks and petty thieves and just plain idiots who will come into power to steal and plunder the same as before—only now they will be black and do it in the name of the new Independence—You cannot answer that.

ASAGAI: [*Shouting over her.*] *I live the answer!* [*Pause.*] In my village at home it is the exceptional man who can even read a newspaper . . . or who ever *sees* a book at all. I will go home and much of what I will have to say will seem strange to the people of my village . . . But I will teach and work and things will happen, slowly and swiftly. At times it will seem that nothing changes at all . . . and then again . . . the sudden dramatic events which make history leap into the future. And then quiet again. Retrogression even. Guns, murder, revolution. And I even will have moments when I wonder if the quiet was not better than all that death and hatred. But I will look about my village at the illiteracy and disease and ignorance and I will not wonder long. And perhaps . . . perhaps I will be a great man . . . I mean perhaps I will hold on to the substance of truth and find my way always with the right course . . . and perhaps for it I will be butchered in my bed some night by the servants of empire . . .

BENEATHA: *The martyr!*

ASAGAI: . . . or perhaps I shall live to be a very old man, respected and esteemed in my new nation . . . And perhaps I shall hold office and this is what I'm trying to tell you, Alaiyo; perhaps the things I believe now for my country will be wrong and outmoded, and I will not understand and do terrible things to have things my way or merely to keep my power. Don't you see that there will be young men and women, not British soldiers then, but my own black countrymen . . . to step out of the shadows some evening and slit my then useless throat? Don't you see they have always been there . . . that they always will be. And that such a thing as my own death will be an advance? They who might kill me even . . . actually replenish me!

BENEATHA: Oh, Asagai, I know all that.

ASAGAI: Good! Then stop moaning and groaning and tell me what you plan to do.

BENEATHA: Do?

ASAGAI: I have a bit of a suggestion.

BENEATHA: What?

ASAGAI: [*Rather quietly for him.*] That when it is all over—that you come home with me—

BENEATHA: [*Slapping herself on the forehead with exasperation born of misunderstanding.*] Oh—Asagai—at this moment you decide to be romantic!

ASAGAI: [*Quickly understanding the misunderstanding.*] My dear, young creature of the New World—I do not mean across the city—I mean across the ocean; home—to Africa.

BENEATHA: [*Slowly understanding and turning to him with murmured amazement.*] To—to Nigeria?

ASAGAI: Yes! . . . [*Smiling and lifting his arms playfully.*] Three hundred years later the African Prince rose up out of the seas and swept the maiden back across the middle passage[6] over which her ancestors had come—

BENEATHA: [*Unable to play.*] Nigeria?

ASAGAI: Nigeria. Home. [*Coming to her with genuine romantic flippancy.*] I will show you our mountains and our stars; and give you cool drinks from gourds and teach you the old songs and the ways of our people—and, in time, we will pretend that—[*Very softly.*]—you have only been away for a day—

[*She turns her back to him, thinking. He swings her around and takes her full in his arms in a long embrace which proceeds to passion.*]

BENEATHA: [*Pulling away.*] You're getting me all mixed up—

ASAGAI: Why?

BENEATHA: Too many things—too many things have happened today. I must sit down and think. I don't know what I feel about anything right this minute.

[*She promptly sits down and props her chin on her fist.*]

ASAGAI: [*Charmed.*] All right, I shall leave you. No—don't get up. [*Touching her, gently, sweetly.*] Just sit awhile and think . . . Never be afraid to sit awhile and think. [*He goes to door and looks at her.*] How often I have looked at you and said, "Ah—so this is what the New World hath finally wrought . . ."[7]

[*He exits.* BENEATHA *sits on alone. Presently* WALTER *enters from his room and starts to rummage through things, feverishly looking for something. She looks up and turns in her seat.*]

BENEATHA: [*Hissingly.*] Yes—just look at what the New World hath wrought! . . . Just look! [*She gestures with bitter disgust.*] There he is! *Monsieur le petit bourgeois noir*[8]—himself! There he is—Symbol of a Rising Class! Entrepreneur! Titan of the system! [WALTER *ignores her completely and continues frantically and destructively looking for something and hurling things to the floor and tearing things out of their place in his search.* BENEATHA *ignores the eccentricity of his actions and goes on with the monologue of insult.*] Did you dream of yachts

---

6. Route traveled by slaves trafficked from Africa to the Americas.

7. Allusion to the biblical exclamation "What hath God wrought!" (Num. 23.23).

8. Mister Black Middle Class (French).

on Lake Michigan, Brother? Did you see yourself on that Great Day sitting down at the Conference Table, surrounded by all the mighty bald-headed men in America? All halted, waiting, breathless, waiting for your pronouncements on industry? Waiting for you—Chairman of the Board? [WALTER *finds what he is looking for—a small piece of white paper—and pushes it in his pocket and puts on his coat and rushes out without ever having looked at her. She shouts after him.*] I look at you and I see the final triumph of stupidity in the world!

[*The door slams and she returns to just sitting again.* RUTH *comes quickly out of* MAMA's *room.*]

RUTH: Who was that?

BENEATHA: Your husband.

RUTH: Where did he go?

BENEATHA: Who knows—maybe he has an appointment at U.S. Steel.

RUTH: [*Anxiously, with frightened eyes.*] You didn't say nothing bad to him, did you?

BENEATHA: Bad? Say anything bad to him? No—I told him he was a sweet boy and full of dreams and everything is strictly peachy keen, as the ofay[9] kids say!

[MAMA *enters from her bedroom. She is lost, vague, trying to catch hold, to make some sense of her former command of the world, but it still eludes her. A sense of waste overwhelms her gait; a measure of apology rides on her shoulders. She goes to her plant, which has remained on the table, looks at it, picks it up and takes it to the window sill and sits it outside, and she stands and looks at it a long moment. Then she closes the window, straightens her body with effort and turns around to her children.*]

MAMA: Well—ain't it a mess in here, though? [*A false cheerfulness, a beginning of something.*] I guess we all better stop moping around and get some work done. All this unpacking and everything we got to do. [RUTH *raises her head slowly in response to the sense of the line; and* BENEATHA *in similar manner turns very slowly to look at her mother.*] One of you all better call the moving people and tell 'em not to come.

RUTH: Tell 'em not to come?

MAMA: Of course, baby. Ain't no need in 'em coming all the way here and having to go back. They charges for that too. [*She sits down, fingers to her brow, thinking.*] Lord, ever since I was a little girl, I always remembers people saying, "Lena—Lena Eggleston, you aims too high all the time. You needs to slow down and see life a little more like it is. Just slow down some." That's what they always used to say down home—"Lord, that Lena Eggleston is a high-minded thing. She'll get her due one day!"

RUTH: No, Lena . . .

MAMA: Me and Big Walter just didn't never learn right.

RUTH: Lena, no! We gotta go. Bennie—tell her . . . [*She rises and crosses to* BENEATHA *with her arms outstretched.* BENEATHA *doesn't respond.*] Tell her we

9. White.

can still move . . . the notes ain't but a hundred and twenty-five a month. We got four grown people in this house—we can work . . .

MAMA: [*To herself.*] Just aimed too high all the time—

RUTH: [*Turning and going to* MAMA *fast—the words pouring out with urgency and desperation.*] Lena—I'll work . . . I'll work twenty hours a day in all the kitchens in Chicago . . . I'll strap my baby on my back if I have to and scrub all the floors in America and wash all the sheets in America if I have to—but we got to move . . . We got to get out of here . . .

[MAMA *reaches out absently and pats* RUTH's *hand.*]

MAMA: No—I sees things differently now. Been thinking 'bout some of the things we could do to fix this place up some. I seen a second-hand bureau over on Maxwell Street[1] just the other day that could fit right there. [*She points to where the new furniture might go.* RUTH *wanders away from her.*] Would need some new handles on it and then a little varnish and then it look like something brand-new. And—we can put up them new curtains in the kitchen . . . Why this place be looking fine. Cheer us all up so that we forget trouble ever came . . . [*To* RUTH.] And you could get some nice screens to put up in your room round the baby's bassinet . . . [*She looks at both of them, pleadingly.*] Sometimes you just got to know when to give up some things . . . and hold on to what you got.

[WALTER *enters from the outside, looking spent and leaning against the door, his coat hanging from him.*]

MAMA: Where you been, son?

WALTER: [*Breathing hard.*] Made a call.

MAMA: To who, son?

WALTER: To The Man.

MAMA: What man, baby?

WALTER: The Man, Mama. Don't you know who The Man is?

RUTH: Walter Lee?

WALTER: *The Man.* Like the guys in the streets say—The Man. Captain Boss— Mistuh Charley . . . Old Captain Please Mr. Bossman . . .

BENEATHA: [*Suddenly.*] Lindner!

WALTER: That's right! That's good. I told him to come right over.

BENEATHA: [*Fiercely, understanding.*] For what? What do you want to see him for!

WALTER: [*Looking at his sister.*] We going to do business with him.

MAMA: What you talking 'bout, son?

WALTER: Talking 'bout life, Mama. You all always telling me to see life like it is. Well—I laid in there on my back today . . . and I figured it out. Life just like it is. Who gets and who don't get. [*He sits down with his coat on and laughs.*] Mama, you know it's all divided up. Life is. Sure enough. Between the takers and the "tooken." [*He laughs.*] I've figured it out finally. [*He looks around at them.*] Yeah. Some of us always getting "tooken." [*He laughs.*] People like Willy Harris, they don't never get "tooken." And you know why the rest of us

1. Street market southwest of the Loop.

do? 'Cause we all mixed up. Mixed up bad. We get to looking 'round for the right and the wrong, and we worry about it and cry about it and stay up nights trying to figure out 'bout the wrong and the right of things all the time . . . And all the time, man, them takers is out there operating, just taking and taking. Willy Harris? Shoot—Willy Harris don't even count. He don't even count in the big scheme of things. But I'll say one thing for old Willy Harris . . . he's taught me something. He's taught me to keep my eye on what counts in this world. Yeah—[*Shouting out a little.*] Thanks, Willy!

RUTH: What did you call that man for, Walter Lee?

WALTER: Called him to tell him to come on over to the show. Gonna put on a show for the man. Just what he wants to see. You see, Mama, the man came here today and he told us that them people out there where you want us to move—well they so upset they willing to pay us not to move out there. [*He laughs again.*] And—and oh, Mama—you would of been proud of the way me and Ruth and Bennie acted. We told him to get out . . . Lord have mercy! We told the man to get out. Oh, we was some proud folks this afternoon, yeah. [*He lights a cigarette.*] We were still full of that old-time stuff . . .

RUTH: [*Coming toward him slowly.*] You talking 'bout taking them people's money to keep us from moving in that house?

WALTER: I ain't just talking 'bout it, baby—I'm telling you that's what's going to happen.

BENEATHA: Oh, God! Where is the bottom! Where is the real honest-to-God bottom so he can't go any farther!

WALTER: See—that's the old stuff. You and that boy that was here today. You all want everybody to carry a flag and a spear and sing some marching songs, huh? You wanna spend your life looking into things and trying to find the right and the wrong part, huh? Yeah. You know what's going to happen to that boy someday—he'll find himself sitting in a dungeon, locked in forever—and the takers will have the key! Forget it, baby! There ain't no causes—there ain't nothing but taking in this world, and he who takes most is smartest—and it don't make a damn bit of difference *how.*

MAMA: You making something inside me cry, son. Some awful pain inside me.

WALTER: Don't cry, Mama. Understand. That white man is going to walk in that door able to write checks for more money than we ever had. It's important to him and I'm going to help him . . . I'm going to put on the show, Mama.

MAMA: Son—I come from five generations of people who was slaves and sharecroppers—but ain't nobody in my family never let nobody pay 'em no money that was a way of telling us we wasn't fit to walk the earth. We ain't never been that poor. [*Raising her eyes and looking at him.*] We ain't never been that dead inside.

BENEATHA: Well—we are dead now. All the talk about dreams and sunlight that goes on in this house. All dead.

WALTER: What's the matter with you all! I didn't make this world! It was give to me this way! Hell, yes, I want me some yachts someday! Yes, I want to hang some real pearls 'round my wife's neck. Ain't she supposed to wear no pearls? Somebody tell me—tell me, who decides which women is suppose to wear pearls in this world. I tell you I am a *man*—and I think my wife should wear some pearls in this world!

[*This last line hangs a good while and* WALTER *begins to move about the room. The word "Man" has penetrated his consciousness; he mumbles it to himself repeatedly between strange agitated pauses as he moves about.*]

MAMA: Baby, how you going to feel on the inside?

WALTER: Fine! . . . Going to feel fine . . . a man . . .

MAMA: You won't have nothing left then, Walter Lee.

WALTER: [*Coming to her.*] I'm going to feel fine, Mama. I'm going to look that son-of-a-bitch in the eyes and say—[*He falters.*]—and say, "All right, Mr. Lindner—[*He falters even more.*]—that's your neighborhood out there. You got the right to keep it like you want. You got the right to have it like you want. Just write the check and—the house is yours." And, and I am going to say—[*His voice almost breaks.*] And you—you people just put the money in my hand and you won't have to live next to this bunch of stinking niggers! . . . [*He straightens up and moves away from his mother, walking around the room.*] Maybe—maybe I'll just get down on my black knees . . . [*He does so;* RUTH *and* BENNIE *and* MAMA *watch him in frozen horror.*] Captain, Mistuh, Boss-man. [*He starts crying.*] A-hee-hee-hee! [*Wringing his hands in profoundly anguished imitation.*] Yasssss-suh! Great White Father, just gi' ussen de money, fo' God's sake, and we's ain't gwine come out deh and dirty up yo' white folks neighborhood . . .

[*He breaks down completely, then gets up and goes into the bedroom.*]

BENEATHA: That is not a man. That is nothing but a toothless rat.

MAMA: Yes—death done come in this here house. [*She is nodding, slowly, reflectively.*] Done come walking in my house. On the lips of my children. You what supposed to be my beginning again. You—what supposed to be my harvest. [*To* BENEATHA.] You—you mourning your brother?

BENEATHA: He's no brother of mine.

MAMA: What you say?

BENEATHA: I said that that individual in that room is no brother of mine.

MAMA: That's what I thought you said. You feeling like you better than he is today? [BENEATHA *does not answer.*] Yes? What you tell him a minute ago? That he wasn't a man? Yes? You give him up for me? You done wrote his epitaph too—like the rest of the world? Well, who give you the privilege?

BENEATHA: Be on my side for once! You saw what he just did, Mama! You saw him—down on his knees. Wasn't it you who taught me—to despise any man who would do that. Do what he's going to do.

MAMA: Yes—I taught you that. Me and your daddy. But I thought I taught you something else too . . . I thought I taught you to love him.

BENEATHA: Love him? There is nothing left to love.

MAMA: There is always something left to love. And if you ain't learned that, you ain't learned nothing. [*Looking at her.*] Have you cried for that boy today? I don't mean for yourself and for the family 'cause we lost the money. I mean for him; what he been through and what it done to him. Child, when do you think is the time to love somebody the most; when they done good and made things easy for everybody? Well then, you ain't through learning—because that ain't the time at all. It's when he's at his lowest and can't believe in hisself 'cause the world done whipped him so. When you starts measuring somebody, measure him right, child, measure him right. Make sure you done taken into account what hills and valleys he come through before he got to wherever he is.

[TRAVIS *bursts into the room at the end of the speech, leaving the door open.*]

TRAVIS: Grandmama—the moving men are downstairs! The truck just pulled up.

MAMA: [*Turning and looking at him.*] Are they, baby? They downstairs?

[*She sighs and sits.* LINDNER *appears in the doorway. He peers in and knocks lightly, to gain attention, and comes in. All turn to look at him.*]

LINDNER: [*Hat and briefcase in hand.*] Uh—hello . . . [RUTH *crosses mechanically to the bedroom door and opens it and lets it swing open freely and slowly as the lights come up on* WALTER *within, still in his coat, sitting at the far corner of the room. He looks up and out through the room to* LINDNER.]

RUTH: He's here.

[*A long minute passes and* WALTER *slowly gets up.*]

LINDNER: [*Coming to the table with efficiency, putting his briefcase on the table and starting to unfold papers and unscrew fountain pens.*] Well, I certainly was glad to hear from you people. [WALTER *has begun the trek out of the room, slowly and awkwardly, rather like a small boy, passing the back of his sleeve across his mouth from time to time.*] Life can really be so much simpler than people let it be most of the time. Well—with whom do I negotiate? You, Mrs. Younger, or your son here? [MAMA *sits with her hands folded on her lap and her eyes closed as* WALTER *advances.* TRAVIS *goes close to* LINDNER *and looks at the papers curiously.*] Just some official papers, sonny.

RUTH: Travis, you go downstairs.

MAMA: [*Opening her eyes and looking into* WALTER'S.] No. Travis, you stay right here. And you make him understand what you doing, Walter Lee. You teach him good. Like Willy Harris taught you. You show where our five generations done come to. Go ahead, son—

WALTER: [*Looks down into his boy's eyes.* TRAVIS *grins at him merrily and* WALTER *draws him beside him with his arm lightly around his shoulders.*] Well, Mr. Lindner. [BENEATHA *turns away.*] We called you—[*There is a profound, simple groping quality in his speech.*]—because, well, me and my family [*He looks around and shifts from one foot to the other.*] Well—we are very plain people . . .

LINDNER: Yes—

WALTER: I mean—I have worked as a chauffeur most of my life—and my wife here, she does domestic work in people's kitchens. So does my mother. I mean—we are plain people . . .

LINDNER: Yes, Mr. Younger—

WALTER: [*Really like a small boy, looking down at his shoes and then up at the man.*] And—uh—well, my father, well, he was a laborer most of his life.

LINDNER: [*Absolutely confused.*] Uh, yes—

WALTER: [*Looking down at his toes once again.*] My father almost beat a man to death once because this man called him a bad name or something, you know what I mean?

LINDNER: No, I'm afraid I don't.

WALTER: [*Finally straightening up.*] Well, what I mean is that we come from people who had a lot of pride. I mean—we are very proud people. And that's my sister over there and she's going to be a doctor—and we are very proud—

LINDNER: Well—I am sure that is very nice, but—

WALTER: [*Starting to cry and facing the man eye to eye.*] What I am telling you is that we called you over here to tell you that we are very proud and that this is—this is my son, who makes the sixth generation of our family in this country, and that we have all thought about your offer and we have decided to move into our house because my father—my father—he earned it. [MAMA *has her eyes closed and is rocking back and forth as though she were in church, with her head nodding the amen yes.*] We don't want to make no trouble for nobody or fight no causes—but we will try to be good neighbors. That's all we got to say. [*He looks the man absolutely in the eyes.*] We don't want your money.

[*He turns and walks away from the man.*]

LINDNER: [*Looking around at all of them.*] I take it then that you have decided to occupy.

BENEATHA: That's what the man said.

LINDNER: [*To* MAMA *in her reverie.*] Then I would like to appeal to you, Mrs. Younger. You are older and wiser and understand things better I am sure . . .

MAMA: [*Rising.*] I am afraid you don't understand. My son said we was going to move and there ain't nothing left for me to say. [*Shaking her head with double meaning.*] You know how these young folks is nowadays, mister. Can't do a thing with 'em. Good-bye.

LINDNER: [*Folding up his materials.*] Well—if you are that final about it . . . There is nothing left for me to say. [*He finishes. He is almost ignored by the family, who are concentrating on* WALTER LEE. *At the door* LINDNER *halts and looks around.*] I sure hope you people know what you're doing.

[*He shakes his head and exits.*]

RUTH: [*Looking around and coming to life.*] Well, for God's sake—if the moving men are here—LET'S GET THE HELL OUT OF HERE!

MAMA: [*Into action.*] Ain't it the truth! Look at all this here mess. Ruth, put Travis' good jacket on him . . . Walter Lee, fix your tie and tuck your shirt in, you look just like somebody's hoodlum. Lord have mercy, where is my plant? [*She flies to get it amid the general bustling of the family, who are deliberately trying to ignore the nobility of the past moment.*] You all start on down . . . Travis child, don't go empty-handed . . . Ruth, where did I put that box with my skillets in it? I want to be in charge of it myself . . . I'm going to make us the biggest dinner we ever ate tonight . . . Beneatha, what's the matter with them stockings? Pull them things up, girl . . .

[*The family starts to file out as two moving men appear and begin to carry out the heavier pieces of furniture, bumping into the family as they move about.*]

BENEATHA: Mama, Asagai—asked me to marry him today and go to Africa—

MAMA: [*In the middle of her getting-ready activity.*] He did? You ain't old enough to marry nobody—[*Seeing the moving men lifting one of her chairs precariously.*] Darling, that ain't no bale of cotton, please handle it so we can sit in it again. I had that chair twenty-five years . . .

[*The movers sigh with exasperation and go on with their work.*]

BENEATHA: [*Girlishly and unreasonably trying to pursue the conversation.*] To go to Africa, Mama—be a doctor in Africa . . .

MAMA: [*Distracted.*] Yes, baby—

WALTER: Africa! What he want you to go to Africa for?

BENEATHA: To practice there . . .

WALTER: Girl, if you don't get all them silly ideas out your head! You better marry yourself a man with some loot . . .

BENEATHA: [*Angrily, precisely as in the first scene of the play.*] What have you got to do with who I marry!

WALTER: Plenty. Now I think George Murchison—

[*He and BENEATHA go out yelling at each other vigorously; BENEATHA is heard saying that she would not marry GEORGE MURCHISON if he were Adam and she were Eve, etc. The anger is loud and real till their voices diminish. RUTH stands at the door and turns to MAMA and smiles knowingly.*]

MAMA: [*Fixing her hat at last.*] Yeah—they something all right, my children . . .

RUTH: Yeah—they're something. Let's go, Lena.

MAMA: [*Stalling, starting to look around at the house.*] Yes—I'm coming. Ruth—

RUTH: Yes?

MAMA: [*Quietly, woman to woman.*] He finally come into his manhood today, didn't he? Kind of like a rainbow after the rain . . .

RUTH: [*Biting her lip lest her own pride explode in front of MAMA.*] Yes, Lena.

[*WALTER's voice calls for them raucously.*]

MAMA: [*Waving RUTH out vaguely.*] All right, honey—go on down. I be down directly.

[*RUTH hesitates, then exits. MAMA stands, at last alone in the living room, her plant on the table before her as the lights start to come down. She looks around at all the walls and ceilings and suddenly, despite herself, while the children call below, a great heaving thing rises in her and she puts her fist to her mouth, takes a final desperate look, pulls her coat about her, pats her hat and goes out. The lights dim down. The door opens and she comes back in, grabs her plant, and goes out for the last time.*]

[CURTAIN.]

1959

AUTHORS ON THEIR WORK

LORRAINE HANSBERRY (1930–65)

From "Willie Loman, Walter Younger, and He Who Must Live" (1959)*

Walter Younger is an American more than he is anything else. His ordeal [. . .] is not extraordinary but intensely familiar like Willy [Loman]'s [in Arthur Miller's *Death of a Salesman* (1949)]. The two of them have virtually no values which have not come out of their culture, and to a significant point, no view of the possible solutions to their problems which do not also come out of the selfsame culture. Walter can find no peace with that part of society which seems to permit him no entry into that which has willfully excluded him. He shares with Willy Loman the acute awareness that *something* is obstructing some abstract progress that he feels he *should* be making; that *something* is in the way of his ascendancy. It does not occur to either of them to question the nature of this desired "ascendancy." Walter accepts, he believes in the "world" as it has been presented to him. When we first meet him, he does not wish to alter *it*; merely to change *his* position in it. His mentors and his associates all take the view that the institutions which frustrate him are somehow impeccable, or, at best, "unfortunate." "Things being as they are," he must look to *himself* as the only source of any rewards he may expect. Within himself, he is encouraged to believe, are the only seeds of defeat or victory within the universe. And Walter believes this and when opportunity, haphazard and rooted in death, prevails, he acts.

HUGE OBSTACLES

But the obstacles [. . .] are gigantic; the weight of the loss of the money is in fact, the weight of death. In Walter Lee Younger's life, somebody *has* to die for ten thousand bucks to pile up—if then. Elsewhere in the world, in the face of catastrophe, he might be tempted to don the saffron robes of acceptance and sit on a mountain top all day contemplating the divine justice of his misery. Or, history being what it is turning out to be, he might wander down to his first Communist Party meeting. But here in the dynamic and confusing postwar years on the Southside of Chicago, his choices of action are equal to those gestures only in symbolic terms. The American ghetto hero may give up and contemplate his misery in rose-colored bars to the melodies of hypnotic saxophones, but revolution seems alien to him in his circumstances (America), and it is easier to dream of personal wealth than of a communal state wherein universal dignity is supposed to be a corollary. Yet his position in time and space does allow for one other alternative; he may take his place on any one of a number of frontiers of challenge. Challenges (such as helping to break down restricted neighborhoods) which are admittedly limited because they most certainly do not threaten the basic social order.

NOT SO SMALL

But why is even this final choice possible [. . .]? Well, that is where Walter departs from Willy Loman; there is a second pulse in his still-dual culture. His people have had "somewhere" they have been trying to get for so long that more sophisticated confusions do not yet bind them. [. . .] Walter is, despite his lack of consciousness of it, inextricably as much wedded to his special mass as Willy was to his, and the moods of each are able to decisively determine the dramatic typicality. Furthermore, the very nature of the situation of American Negroes can force their representative hero to recognize that for his *true* ascendancy he must ultimately be at cross-purposes with at least certain of his culture's values. It is to the pathos of Willy Loman that his section of American life seems to have momentarily lost that urgency; that he cannot, like Walter, draw on the strength of an incredible people who, historically, have simply refused to give up.

In other words, the symbolism of moving into the new house is quite as small as it seems and quite as significant. For if there are no waving flags and marching songs at the barricades as Walter marches out with his little battalion, it is not because the battle lacks nobility. On the contrary, he has picked up in his way, still imperfect and wobbly in his small view of human destiny, what I believe Arthur Miller once called "the golden thread of history." He becomes, in spite of those who are too intrigued with despair and hatred of man to see it, King Oedipus refusing to tear out his eyes, but attacking the Oracle instead. He is that last Jewish patriot manning his rifle in the burning ghetto at Warsaw; [. . .] he is the nine small heroes of Little Rock; he is Michelangelo creating David and Beethoven bursting forth with the Ninth Symphony. He is all those things because he has finally reached out in his tiny moment and caught that sweet essence which is human dignity, and it shines like the old star-touched dream that it is in his eyes. We see, in the moment, I think, what becomes, and not for Negroes alone, but for Willy and all of us, entirely an American responsibility.

Out in the darkness where we watch, most of us are not afraid to cry.

*Lorraine Hansberry, "Willie Loman, Walter Younger, and He Who Must Live." *Village Voice*, vol. 4, no. 42, 12 Aug. 1959, pp. 7–8.

Chronology

1938   To challenge restrictive housing convenants, eight-year-old Lorraine Hansberry's family purchases and occupies a house in a White Chicago neighborhood.

1940   The U.S. Supreme Court upholds the Hansberry family's right to remain in their home, but because the court's decision hinges on a technicality, it fails to address the legality of restrictive covenants.

1943   A Detroit, Michigan, race riot kills thirty-four (including twenty-five Blacks), injures almost seven hundred, and ends only after President Roosevelt calls in the National Guard. A race riot in Harlem injures three hundred and kills six African Americans.

1946   A race riot leads Chicago housing authorities to abandon efforts to move Black families into the Airport Homes housing project. Hansberry's father, Carl, dies at age fifty.

1947   A race riot occurs in Chicago when local authorities attempt to move Blacks into the Fernwood Park housing project.

1948   President Truman issues an executive order integrating the armed forces; the U.S. Supreme Court rules restrictive covenants legally unenforceable.

1949   Race riots occur in Chicago's Park Manor when a Black family attempts to move in, and in Englewood Park when a Black man is seen visiting the home of a White union organizer.

1951   The National Guard is called in to quell a riot sparked by a Black family's move into an apartment complex in Cicero, a town bordering Chicago.

1953   Two neighborhood associations lead a nine-month "campaign of terror" after local authorities try to move a Black family into Chicago's Trumbull Park housing project. (See Gruenberg excerpt below.)

1954   In *Brown v. Board of Education*, the U.S. Supreme Court declares school segregation unconstitutional.

1955   A year-long bus boycott begins in Montgomery, Alabama.

1956   The U.S. Supreme Court declares segregation on buses unconstitutional. "[A]fter seeing a play" that made her "disgusted with a whole body of material about Negroes" full of "[c]ardboard characters," Hansberry begins writing *A Raisin in the Sun*.

1957   When Arkansas's governor blocks nine Black students from attending a Little Rock high school, President Eisenhower sends in federal troops to force compliance with court-ordered desegregation.

1959   *A Raisin in the Sun* becomes the first play by an African American woman produced on Broadway; twenty-nine-year-old Hansberry becomes the first African American and the youngest playwright ever to win the Drama Critics' Circle Award for best play.

1960   Refused service at the lunch counter of a Greensboro, North Carolina, Woolworth's, four Black college students stage the first sit-in. SNCC is founded in Raleigh, North Carolina.

1961   Between May and August, approximately one thousand volunteer "freedom riders" take buses to the South in support of integration.

1962   African American James Meredith is denied admission to the University of Mississippi, resulting in race riots that kill two.

1963   Martin Luther King, Jr., jailed in Birmingham, Alabama, for leading civil rights demonstrations, writes "Letter from Birmingham Jail" (excerpted below). President Kennedy forces Governor George Wallace to allow integration of the University of Alabama. Civil rights leader Medgar Evers is assassinated in Mississippi. A quarter of a million people participate in the March on Washington, where King delivers his "I Have a Dream" speech; one month later, a Birmingham, Alabama, church bombing kills four Black girls attending Sunday School and sparks riots in which two African Americans are killed.

1964   Twenty-Fourth Amendment to the U.S. Constitution abolishes the poll tax traditionally used to prevent Blacks from voting. "Freedom Summer" begins with a massive effort to register Black voters throughout the South. Congress passes the Civil Rights Act outlawing employment discrimination and segregation in public facilities. In Mississippi, three people working to register Black voters are murdered, their bodies discovered only after President Johnson sends military personnel to aid in the search. Martin Luther King, Jr., wins the Nobel Peace Prize.

1965   Hansberry dies of cancer at age thirty-five. Malcolm X is assassinated in Harlem. Martin Luther King, Jr., leads a march from Selma to Montgomery, Alabama, to demand protection of voting rights, and, on "Bloody Sunday," fifty marchers are hospitalized after police use tear gas, whips, and clubs against them. The Voting Rights Act makes it easier for southern Blacks to register to vote by outlawing requirements such as literacy tests. Race riots occur in several cities, the worst—in Los Angeles's Watts neighborhood—kills four and injures one thousand.

1966   In Chicago, Martin Luther King, Jr., begins his first northern campaign, leading a series of marches to protest housing conditions and renting an apartment in a South Side slum. Edward Brooke, of Massachusetts, becomes the first African American elected to the U.S. Senate in eighty-five years. As first secretary of the newly created Department of Housing and Urban Development, Robert C. Weaver becomes the first African American to hold a cabinet-level position in the U.S. government (see Weaver excerpt below).

CONTEXTUAL EXCERPTS

THE GREAT MIGRATION AND LIFE IN THE "BLACK METROPOLIS"

RICHARD WRIGHT

From Twelve Million Black Voices: A Folk History of the Negro in the United States (1941)[1]

Perhaps never in history has a more utterly unprepared folk wanted to go to the city; we were barely born as a folk when we headed for the tall and sprawling centers of steel and stone. We, who were landless upon the land; we, who had barely managed to live in family groups; [. . .] we who had never belonged to any organizations except the church and burial societies; we, who had had our personalities blasted with two hundred years of slavery and had been turned loose to shift for ourselves—we were such a folk as this when we moved into a world that was destined to test all we were, that threw us into the scales of competition to weigh our mettle. And how were we to know that, the moment we landless millions of the land—we men who were struggling to be born—set our awkward feet upon the pavements of the city, life would begin to exact of us a heavy toll in death?

We did not know what would happen, what was in store for us. We went innocently, longing and hoping for a life that the Lords of the Land would not let us live. Our hearts were high as we moved northward to the cities. What emotions, fears, what a complex of sensations we felt when, looking out of a train window at the revolving fields, we first glimpsed the sliding waters of the gleaming Ohio! What memories that river evoked in us, memories black and gloomy, yet tinged with the bright border of a wild and desperate hope! The

1. Richard Wright, *Twelve Million Black Voices: A Folk History of the Negro in the United States*. Viking, 1941.

Richard Wright, circa 1945

Ohio is more than a river. It is a symbol, a line that runs through our hearts, dividing hope from despair, just as once it bisected the nation, dividing freedom from slavery.

[Once in the North w]e [. . .] live in the clinging soot just beyond the factory areas, behind the railroad tracks, near the river banks, under the viaducts, by the steel and iron mills, on the edges of the coal and lumber yards. We live in crowded, barn-like rooms, in old rotting buildings where once dwelt rich native whites of a century ago [. . .]. When we return home at night from our jobs, we are afraid to venture into other sections of the city, for we fear that the white boys will gang up and molest us. When we do go out into white neighborhoods, we always go in crowds, for that is the best mode of protection.

White people say that they are afraid of us, and it often makes us laugh. When they see one of us, they either smile with contempt or amusement. [. . .] When they see *six* of us, they become downright apprehensive and alarmed. And because they are afraid of us, we are afraid of them. Especially do we feel fear when we meet the gangs of white boys who have been taught—at home and at school—that we black folk are making their parents lose their homes and life's savings because we have moved into their neighborhoods.

They say our presence in their neighborhoods lowers the value of their property. We do not understand why this should be so. We are poor; but they were once poor, too. They make up their minds, because others tell them to, that they must move at once if we rent an apartment near them. Having been warned against us by the Bosses of the Buildings, having heard tall tales about us, about how "bad" we are, they react emotionally as though we had the plague when we move into their neighborhoods. Is it any wonder, then, that their homes are suddenly and drastically reduced in value? They hastily abandon them, sacrificing them to the Bosses of the Buildings [. . .].

And the Bosses of the Buildings take these old houses and convert them into "kitchenettes," and then rent them to us at rates so high that they make fabulous fortunes before the houses are too old for habitation. What they do is this: they take, say, a seven-room apartment, [. . .] and cut it up into seven small apartments, of one room each; they install one small gas stove and one small sink in each room.

Sometimes five or six of us live in a one-room kitchenette, a place where simple folk such as we should never be held captive. A war sets up in our emotions: one part of our feelings tells us that it is good to be in the city, that we have a chance at life here, that we need but turn a corner to become a stranger, that we no longer need bow and dodge at the sight of the Lords of the Land. Another part of our feelings tells us that, in terms of worry and strain, the cost of living in the kitchenettes is too high, that the city heaps too much responsibility upon us and gives too little security in return.

The kitchenette is the author of the glad tidings that new suckers are in town, ready to be cheated, plundered, and put in their places.

The kitchenette is our prison, our death sentence without a trial, the new form of mob violence that assaults not only the lone individual, but all of us, in its ceaseless attacks.

The kitchenette, with its filth and foul air, with its one toilet for thirty or more tenants, kills our black babies so fast that in many cities twice as many of them die as white babies.

The kitchenette is the seed bed for scarlet fever, dysentery, typhoid, tuberculosis, gonorrhea, syphilis, pneumonia, and malnutrition.

The kitchenette scatters death so widely among us that our death rate exceeds our birth rate, and if it were not for the trains and autos bringing us daily into the city from the plantations, we black folks who dwell in northern cities would die out entirely over the course of a few years.

The kitchenette, with its crowded rooms and incessant bedlam, provides an enticing place for crimes of all sort—crimes against women and children or any stranger who happens to stray into its dark hallways. The noise of our living, boxed in stone and steel, is so loud that even a pistol shot is smothered.

The kitchenette throws desperate and unhappy people into an unbearable closeness of association, thereby increasing latent friction, giving birth to never-ending quarrels of recrimination, accusation, and vindictiveness, producing warped personalities.

The kitchenette injects pressure and tension into our individual personalities, making many of us give up the struggle, walk off and leave wives, husbands, and even children behind to shift as best they can.

The kitchenette creates thousands of one-room homes where our black mothers sit, deserted, with their children about their knees.

The kitchenette blights the personalities of our growing children, disorganizes them, blinds them to hope, creates problems whose effects can be traced in the characters of its child victims for years afterward.

The kitchenette jams our farm girls, while still in their teens, into rooms with men who are restless and stimulated by the noise and lights of the city; and more of our girls have bastard babies than the girls in any other sections of the city.

The kitchenette fills our black boys with longing and restlessness, urging them to run off from home, to join together with other restless black boys in gangs, that brutal form of city courage.

The kitchenette piles up mountains of profits for the Bosses of the Buildings and makes them ever more determined to keep things as they are.

The kitchenette reaches out with fingers full of golden bribes to the officials of the city, persuading them to allow old firetraps to remain standing and occupied long after they should have been torn down.

The kitchenette is the funnel through which our pulverized lives flow to ruin and death on the city pavements, at a profit.

Despite our new worldliness, [. . .] we keep our churches alive. In fact, we have built more of them than ever here on the city pavements, for it is only when we are within the walls of our churches that we are wholly ourselves, that we keep alive a sense of our personalities in relation to the total world in which we live, that we maintain a quiet and constant communion with all that is deepest in us. Our going to church of a Sunday is like placing one's ear to another's chest to hear the unquenchable murmur of the human heart. In our collective outpourings of song and prayer, the fluid emotions of others make us feel the strength in ourselves [. . .]. Our churches are where we dip our tired bodies in cool springs of hope, where we retain our wholeness and humanity [. . .].

Our churches are centers of social and community life, for we have virtually no other mode of communion and we are usually forbidden to worship God in the temples of the Bosses of the Buildings [. . .].

In the Black Belts of the northern cities, our women are the most circumscribed and tragic objects to be found in our lives, and it is to the churches that our black women cling for emotional security and the release of their personalities. Because their orbit of life is narrow—from their kitchenette to the white folk's kitchen and back home again—they love the church more than do our men, who find a large measure of the expression of their lives in the mills and factories. Surrounding our black women are many almost insuperable barriers: they are black, they are women, they are workers; they are triply anchored and restricted in their movements within and without the Black Belts.

So they keep thousands of Little Bethels and Pilgrims and Calvarys and White Rocks and Good Hopes and Mount Olives going with their nickels and dimes [. . .]. Sometimes, even in crowded northern cities, elderly black women, hungry for the South but afraid to return, will cultivate tiny vegetable gardens in the narrow squares of ground in front of their hovels.

Many of our children scorn us; they say that we still wear the red bandanna about our heads, that we are still Uncle Toms. We lean upon our God and scold our children and try to drag them to church with us, but just as we once, years ago, left the plantation to roam the South, so now they leave us for the city pavements. But deep down in us we are glad that our children feel the world hard enough to yearn to wrestle with it. We, the mothers and fathers of the black children, try to hold them back from death, but if we persuade them to stay, or if they come back because we call them, we will pour out our pity upon them. Always our deepest love is toward those children of ours who turn their backs upon our way of life, for our instincts tell us that those brave ones who struggle against death are the ones who bring new life into the world, even though they die to do so, even though our hearts are broken when they die.

We watch strange moods fill our children, and our hearts swell with pain. The streets, with their noise and flaring lights, the taverns, the automobiles, and the poolrooms claim them, and no voice of ours can call them back. They spend their nights away from home; they forget our ways of life, our language, our God. Their swift speech and impatient eyes make us feel weak and foolish. We cannot keep them in school [. . .]. We fall upon our knees and pray for them, but in vain. The city has beaten us, evaded us; but they, with young bodies filled with warm blood, feel bitter and frustrated at the sight of the alluring hopes and prizes denied them. It is not their eagerness to fight that makes us afraid, but that they go to death on the city pavements faster than even disease and starvation can take them [. . .]. The courts and the morgues become crowded with our lost children [. . .].

ROBERT GRUENBERG

From Chicago Fiddles While Trumbull Park Burns (1954)[1]

Chicago
On July 30, 1953, Donald Howard, a war veteran, with his wife and two small children became the first Negro tenants of Trumbull Park Homes, a federal housing project operated by the Chicago Housing Authority in the steel-mill belt of Chicago's South Side. Less than a week later the 462-unit development and surrounding lawns were a fire-gutted, rubble-strewn wasteland. Since then ten other Negro families have moved into the development, and "racial disturbances" ranging from rock-tossing to rioting and arson have become an almost daily occurrence.

Two weeks ago the Howard family, importuned by well-intentioned friends, moved out, in the hope that order would be restored and the other Negro tenants left in peace. But rocks continue to fly and aerial bombs puncture the night. Recently tension rose to such a point that civic, labor, and church leaders, meeting under the sponsorship of the National Association for the Advancement of Colored People, warned Chicago's Mayor Kennelly that unless he took immediate steps to stop the disturbances he would have to face "continuous" mass demonstrations at the City Hall.

In the three months before the Howard family moved into Trumbull Park Homes only three fire alarms were turned in from the area, two of them for minor blazes. Since last summer alarms have averaged two dozen a month, about half of them false. There have been forty-four fires in sheds, garages, and

1. Robert Gruenberg, "Chicago Fiddles While Trumbull Park Burns." *The Nation*, 22 May 1954, pp. 441–43.

barns, eight in the Trumbull Park project itself, and two in liquor stores. A tavern which had served Negroes was completely destroyed.

Many people have dismissed the incidents as either youthful exuberance or genuine expressions of protest by aroused owners of nearby property. Others, however, have been aware for some time that the trouble at Trumbull Park is not altogether spontaneous. All the evidence shows it has been fanned by two small groups, one of them a professional race-baiting outfit.

These are the South Deering Improvement Association, one of scores of "improvement" associations intent on keeping the Negro out of "all white" areas, and the National Citizens' Protective Association, a hate group founded by a former aide of Gerald L. K. Smith, the anti-Semitic race baiter, and boasting among its national officers a former Ku Klux Klan "emperor." The president of the home-grown South Deering association is Louis P. Dinnocenzo, a $6,000-a-year highway engineer on the Cook County pay roll. His organization, he claims, has about 500 members, each of whom pays dues of a dollar a year. They meet once a month in the Trumbull Park fieldhouse.

If you ask Dinnocenzo about the part played by his association in the racial disorders, he answers straightforwardly: "We are requesting our aldermen and our representatives to do everything within their ability to get them [the ten Negro families living in the project] out." What else are you doing? "We're parading around at night—within the law—like we're entitled to do—to picket." Doesn't parading create an atmosphere begetting violence? "Yes, it sometimes does," he admits, "but we don't want the violence. It's the teenagers." Dinnocenzo calls the moving in of Negroes "an encroachment on our right." He explains "While the law is opposed to us, morally we're right."

GOING WITH GOD IN TRUMBULL PARK

> The Trumbull Park housing project is a white housing project. . . . Only the ignoble and shameful and the base can be suppressed, never the heroic truth, for we go with God. If you live like a good American, you don't need the police department and a pressure group to keep you by force in a community where you know you don't belong. Get out, and get off our backs.
> —*From a letter to the editor of the* Daily Calumet *in South Chicago.*

Mayor Kennelly has yet to come out with a strong statement condemning the South Deering lawlessness.

The most outspoken support for the South Deering troublemakers comes from the *Daily Calumet*, a paper published in a neighboring area. Its editor is Colonel Horace F. Wulf, an army-reserve officer. Here is a sample of his writing: "Some white areas may welcome other races with open arms, bless them. But the folks of South Deering have not been sufficiently brainwashed to consent to such practice. Any race mixing must be done with a policeman's nightstick."

Ironically, part of the *Daily Calumet*'s financial support comes from the tax dollars of Chicago's citizens, Negro and white. As a newspaper of "general circulation" it can bid for advertising contracts of the Chicago Sanitary District, and this year it obtained the contract. One of the Republican trustees of the Sanitary District is John Henneberger, for ten years president of United Steelworkers Local 1008 at the Youngstown Sheet and Tube Company's South Chicago plant before he retired in 1951 with a lifetime honorary presidency. On February 1 the *Daily Calumet* reported as follows on Henneberger's talk at a dinner held by the South Deering Improvement Association attended by 500 persons. "He said, 'It is an inspiring sight to see a community fight for what it thinks is right.' He added the Republican Party stands ready to lend its hand to any group of citizens engaged in a struggle for a just cause." Questioned about this, Henneberger denied making the statement.

. . . .

Donald Howard's decision to leave Trumbull Park was sudden and known in advance to only a few police officials and Howard's attorneys. One of Chicago's police captains helped Howard get a new job and a new home. Howard authorized his attorneys to say in his behalf

> Police officials and well-meaning human-relations experts have visited me and they have approached me through well-intentioned persons, all with the view that my continued occupancy of an apartment [. . .] represents a threat to civil peace and tranquility in Trumbull Park Homes. Having in mind the fact that there are ten other Negro families in Trumbull Park Homes and hoping that there is something my family and I can do to contribute to a restoration of order in Trumbull Park I have decided to succumb to the pressures placed on me.

GERTRUDE SAMUELS

From Even More Crucial Than in the South (1963)[1]

A report on the forms the Negro revolution is taking against discrimination, economic and social, in the North.

A policeman tells a street vender to move on and sets off a series of clashes between Negroes and police . . .

A human chain of Negro parents blocks a dozen buses loaded with Negro children going to schools where they will be separated from white children . . .

1. Gertrude Samuels, "Even More Crucial Than in the South." *The New York Times,* 30 June 1963, pp. 143+, timesmachine.nytimes.com/timesmachine/1963/06/30/356941762.html.

A thousand whites gather menacingly at a brick house on an all-white street where a Negro family is attempting to move in . . .

Police rush lines of Negro pickets who are protesting bias in hiring practices. Negroes are beaten and black-jacked; policemen, stabbed . . .

These incidents of recent weeks took place not in the South but in the North. For the past year the attention of the country has been largely concentrated on the racial crisis in the South. Now there is growing awareness that the crisis in the North is boiling, and that it is perhaps more dangerous.

The civil-rights struggle in the South is still largely in its legal, elementary stage: Negro strategy there is to attempt to crumble barriers to school integration, to accommodation at such public facilities as lunch counters, hotels and playgrounds, and in transportation.

But in the North Negroes say the problem revolves around the far more sinister moral questions of private policy—what Negro leaders describe as "the snide, subtle and insidious practice" of economic and social discrimination.

Of the nation's nearly 20,000,000 Negroes—about 10 per cent of the population—some 48 per cent live outside the South. What is the extent of their dissatisfaction?

What is clear from all these reports is that there is an intensification of militancy at the Negro leadership level. [. . .] But there is also a great response at the "followership" level—a willingness to follow, to demonstrate, to be involved in the struggle more decisively than ever before.

The Negro drive in the North is aimed at four main targets: residential segregation, job discrimination, *de facto* school segregation and, above all, affronts to personal dignity.

RESIDENTIAL SEGREGATION

All over the North, but particularly in the giant industrial cities, there are "gentlemen's agreements" to hold the Negro down residentially. How else explain the largest slum area in the country—Negro Harlem in upper Manhattan, with about half a million black persons crowded into its tenements and crumbling brownstones? [. . .]

A few Negro families have escaped—finding enough money, and enough community acceptance to move into integrated neighborhoods in some suburbs—but most are as rigidly held back from living and mixing with whites as in the South. More so in fact, for in many cities of the South—in Little Rock[, Arkansas,] and Vicksburg[, Mississippi,] and Louisville[, Kentucky,]— Negro and white families have lived side by side for years.

* * *

The situation is particularly acute on Chicago's South Side, where half of Illinois' Negro population is segregated. Friction starts when Negroes move— or try to move—into adjoining white neighborhoods.

Recently, a crowd of whites gathered around a two-family brick house in an all-white neighborhood on the South Side when it was rumored that Negroes were about to come. Two Negro men did appear, and some furniture was moved in. Rocks were thrown, the police arrived, according to a well-designed plan, and the situation was brought under control. But the Negro family gave up the idea of "breaking the block," as whites charged they were trying to do.

Horror runs through all white economic levels in the North at the idea of having a Negro family move into the neighborhood—largely because of the belief that their presence will reduce property values. It is a fear seldom substantiated by any person's firsthand knowledge, but Negroes acknowledge its pervasiveness with a bitter saying: "In the South, the whites say, 'I don't care how close you get but don't get too high.' In the North, the whites say, 'I don't care how high you get, but don't get too close.'"

Deerfield, Ill., an upper-income suburb of Chicago, dramatized the extent to which whites will go to avoid having Negro neighbors—even those who can afford $30,000 homes. The village was to have been the site of an interracial real-estate development. The project was killed when the community, encouraged by the Rev. Jack D. Parker of St. Gregory Episcopal Church, condemned the land and floated a bond issue to make a park out of it. Court action up to the Supreme Court resulted in a victory for the village.

JOB DISCRIMINATION

And it is certainly "gentlemen's agreements" or naked prejudice that operate against Northern Negroes in job-hiring practices.

The North has on its books many laws and directives against job discrimination that have meant well. The cause of the seething unrest is that in practice, down at the individual level, the laws don't work. Municipalities and state governments lack the courage to enforce them, and private enterprise is apathetic or worse.

The situation is boiling up because jobs are growing scarcer—twice as many Negroes compared with whites are jobless.

. . . . .

SCHOOL SEGREGATION

But if housing and job discrimination hurt, the greatest outrage that the Northern Negro feels is over the segregation of his children.

. . . .

In Chicago, where only about 10 per cent of pupils go to school with children of another race, "the hottest item for the last two years has been the issue of second-rate education for Negroes." The charge is that the "neighborhood" school-district system [. . .] creates segregation—overcrowding all-Negro schools while white classrooms stand empty. At a recent civil-rights rally, a speaker said school segregation in Chicago and Alabama is as similar as the names [of Chicago School Superintendent Benjamin] Willis and ([Alabama] Governor [George]) Wallace.

Such segregation in the North is, obviously, a direct consequence of residential segregation. John H. Johnson, editor and publisher of the Negro magazine *Ebony*, says bluntly: "If we had integrated housing, the school problem would automatically be solved."

THE PSYCHOLOGICAL FACTOR

Above all these grievances looms the main factor—and that is psychological. Negroes in all walks—from porters and taxi drivers to college professors and political leaders—say that the real drive that is now rising ominously is a demand for personal dignity.

* * *

As Roy Wilkins, executive director of the N.A.A.C.P. puts it: "[. . .] We're making the Constitution and the Declaration of Independence real and alive. We're taking them off parchment and putting them into people's lives, white and black. One of these days, after the fist-shaking is over, the whites are going to understand and to thank us."

THE BLACK MIDDLE CLASS, THE AMERICAN DREAM, AND THE CAMPAIGN FOR CIVIL RIGHTS

WILMA DYKEMAN AND JAMES STOKELY

From New Southerner: The Middle-Class Negro (1959)[1]

His emergence, while its greatest impact is in the South, has meaning for the nation. Paradoxically, the change may mean both a short step back and a leap forward in race relations.

A young Negro father in one of the South's larger cities said recently, "I can't understand why they [certain white politicians in his city] keep shouting that when we try to send our children to the best schools we can, it means we want them to marry whites. What it means is that we want our children to have a chance at owning a station wagon and a ranch-style house and carrying a briefcase instead of a shovel."

If many white Southerners could understand the implications of this man's statement, then the equality which they envision largely as nightmare might be reappraised as closer to the fulfillment of a dream—the American dream. For one of the major forces shaping and energizing the Negro's drive toward full integration into our national life today is a strengthened belief in every man's right to earn his living, own his home and better his place in society, the traditional goals of the white middle class.

1. Wilma Dykeman and James Stokely, "New Southerner: The Middle-Class Negro." *The New York Times*, 9 Aug. 1959, pp. SM11+, timesmachine.nytimes.com/timesmachine/1959/08/09/89230088.html.

And one of the major forces hindering the Negro in this drive, especially in the South, is the white man's persistent image of the Negro as the eternal hewer of wood and drawer of water. One of the matters to which professional segregationist orators have given closest attention is reviving the picture of the "African savage" whom slavery "rescued" from the jungles and brought into beneficent contact with white civilization. Even thus, a century ago, slavery was made to seem the appropriately inferior role of an inferior race.

• • •

There are two points of departure from which to examine the importance of the emerging Southern Negro middle class. It may be compared with its white counterpart and the total American economy—in which case it appears small and severely handicapped. For instance, individual Negro incomes are still only 52 percent as large as white incomes, and two out of every five Negro families still earn less than $2,000 per year.

Or, this middle class may be studied in the light of its own background and recent history—in which case it appears highly significant. For instance, the pre-war percentage difference between Negro and white incomes has been cut by better than 20 per cent and today the total annual cash purchasing power of the Negro population equals the market of the whole of Canada.

Contributing to the growth of this middle class are two basic movements. They can be summarized in two colloquialisms: "going to town" and "heading North."

Both the Negro and white South are "going to town" in a drama of change gripping the entire region. The South is in the process of shifting from a rural, predominantly single-crop economy to urban industrialization. In the brief period between 1940 and 1944, a million Negroes left farming in the South. From 1950 to 1954, the number of Negro farmers in the South declined 17.1 per cent.

Many of these "headed North." Their exodus has meant not only that the South is getting whiter all the time but also that new ways, new standards, new ambitions filter down the family grapevine (as well as the TV serial which sprouts on every roof), replacing the familiar old acceptance of subservience.

As the Southern Negro comes closer to entering the total pattern of American life, he also becomes more aware of those educational and economic opportunities essential to securing and maintaining position in the middle class. His status is still low—but it is changing for the better; it is the combination of these two facts that provides part of the dynamic behind the Negro protest. Because this dynamic is also such a firm part of the American ideal of self-betterment and progress, the protest will neither diminish nor disappear, as so many important white leaders, both North and South, who have not yet understood its full meaning, seem to hope.

The question is frequently asked, and not only in the South, why Negro leadership did not wage to a successful conclusion the fight for full equality in civil rights or the field of health or housing, before tackling the emotion-laden realm of schools. To ask this is to underrate the Negro's powerful push from peasantry, combined with the pull toward the middle class which is one of the real revolutions of our time. One sociologist has observed that "education is a passion with the middle-class Negro." The reasons are obvious.

Education is one of the master keys unlocking the door of opportunity— economic, political, social—into the middle class world [. . .].

[. . .] If the Southern white father could stop seeing the Southern Negro father as a *Negro* and could see him, even for a moment, as another *father,* he might comprehend more clearly some of the determination behind the drive for desegregation.

* * *

When Princeton's Dr. Melvin Tumin and associates published their recent study of a North Carolina county, "Desegregation, Resistance and Readiness," one of their ten major findings included the majority image of the Negro as inferior to the white in morality, intelligence, responsibility and ambition—but with an impressive minority disagreement. "Approximately 27 per cent consider the Negro to be equal or superior to the white in responsibility, 31 per cent in morality, 33 per cent in ambition, and 40 percent in intelligence."

MARTIN LUTHER KING, JR.

From Letter from Birmingham Jail (16 Apr. 1963)[1]

My Dear Fellow Clergymen:

While confined here in the Birmingham city jail, I came across your recent statement calling my present activities "unwise and untimely." Seldom do I pause to answer criticism of my work and ideas. If I sought to answer all the criticisms that cross my desk, my secretaries would have little time for anything other than such correspondence in the course of the day, and I would have no time for constructive work. But since I feel that you are men of genuine good will and that your criticisms are sincerely set forth, I want to try to answer your statement in what I hope will be patient and reasonable terms.

I think I should indicate why I am here in Birmingham, since you have been influenced by the view which argues against "outsiders coming in."

* * *

I am cognizant of the interrelatedness of all communities and states. I cannot sit idly by in Atlanta and not be concerned about what happens in Birmingham. Injustice anywhere is a threat to justice everywhere. We are caught in an inescapable network of mutuality, tied in a single garment of destiny. Whatever affects one directly, affects all indirectly. Never again can we afford to live with the narrow, provincial "outside agitator" idea. Anyone who lives inside the United States can never be considered an outsider anywhere within its bounds.

1. Martin Luther King, Jr., "Letter from Birmingham Jail." *Why We Can't Wait,* Signet Books, 1964, pp. 76–95. Footnote has been added by the editor.

We know through painful experience that freedom is never voluntarily given by the oppressor; it must be demanded by the oppressed. Frankly, I have yet to engage in a direct-action campaign that was "well timed" in the view of those who have not suffered unduly from the disease of segregation. For years now I have heard the word "Wait!" It rings in the ear of every Negro with piercing familiarity. This "Wait" has almost always meant "Never." We must come to see, with one of our distinguished jurists, that "justice too long delayed is justice denied."

We have waited for more than 340 years for our constitutional and God-given rights. The nations of Asia and Africa are moving with jetlike speed toward gaining political independence, but we still creep at horse-and-buggy pace toward gaining a cup of coffee at a lunch counter. Perhaps it is easy for those who have never felt the stinging darts of segregation to say, "Wait." But when you have seen vicious mobs lynch your mothers and fathers at will and drown your sisters and brothers at whim; when you have seen hate-filled police-men curse, kick, and even kill your black brothers and sisters; when you see the vast majority of your twenty million Negro brothers smothering in an airtight cage of poverty in the midst of an affluent society; when you suddenly find your tongue twisted and your speech stammering as you seek to explain to your six-year-old daughter why she can't go to the public amusement park that has just been advertised on television, and see tears welling up in her eyes when she is told that Funtown is closed to colored children, and see ominous clouds of inferiority beginning to form in her little mental sky, and see her beginning to distort her personality by developing an unconscious bitterness toward white people; when you have to concoct an answer for a five-year-old son who is ask-ing, "Daddy, why do white people treat colored people so mean?"; when you take a cross-country drive and find it necessary to sleep night after night in the uncomfortable corners of your automobile because no motel will accept you; when you are humiliated day in and day out by nagging signs reading "white" and "colored"; when your first name becomes "nigger," your middle name becomes "boy" (however old you are) and your last name becomes "John," and your wife and mother are never given the respected title "Mrs."; when you are harried by day and haunted by night by the fact that you are a Negro, living constantly at tiptoe stance, never quite knowing what to expect next, and are plagued with inner fears and outer resentments; when you are forever fighting a degenerating sense of "nobodiness"—then you will understand why we find it difficult to wait. There comes a time when the cup of endurance runs over, and men are no longer willing to be plunged into the abyss of despair. I hope, sirs, you can understand our legitimate and unavoidable impatience.

. . .

Oppressed people cannot remain oppressed forever. The yearning for free-dom eventually manifests itself, and that is what has happened to the American Negro. Something within has reminded him of his birthright of freedom, and something without has reminded him that it can be gained. Consciously or unconsciously, he has been caught up by the *Zeitgeist*,[2] and with his black brothers of Africa and his brown and yellow brothers of Asia, South America,

2. The spirit of the times (German).

and the Caribbean, the United States Negro is moving with a sense of great urgency toward the promised land of racial justice. If one recognizes this vital urge that has engulfed the Negro community, one should readily understand why public demonstrations are taking place. The Negro has many pent-up resentments and latent frustrations, and he must release them. So let him march; let him make prayer pilgrimages to the city hall; let him go on freedom rides—and try to understand why he must do so. If his repressed emotions are not released in nonviolent ways, they will seek expression through violence; this is not a threat but a fact of history. So I have not said to my people, "Get rid of your discontent." Rather, I have tried to say that this normal and healthy discontent can be channeled into the creative outlet of nonviolent direct action. And now this approach is being termed extremist.

But though I was initially disappointed at being categorized as an extremist, as I continued to think about the matter I gradually gained a measure of satisfaction from the label. Was not Jesus an extremist for love: "Love your enemies, bless them that curse you, do good to them that hate you, and pray for them which despitefully use you, and persecute you."[3] Was not Amos an extremist for justice: "Let justice roll down like waters and righteousness like an ever-flowing stream."[4] Was not Paul an extremist for the Christian gospel: "I bear in my body the marks of the Lord Jesus."[5] Was not Martin Luther an extremist: "Here I stand; I cannot do otherwise, so help me God."[6] And John Bunyan: "I will stay in jail to the end of my days before I make a butchery of my conscience."[7] And Abraham Lincoln: "This nation cannot survive half slave and half free." And Thomas Jefferson: "We hold these truths to be self-evident, that all men are created equal. . . ." So the question is not whether we will be extremists, but what kind of extremists we will be. Will we be extremists for hate or for love? Will we be extremists for the preservation of injustice or for the extension of justice?

ROBERT C. WEAVER

From The Negro as an American (1963)[1]

Delivered before the Symposium on Challenges to Democracy of the Fund for the Republic, Chicago, Illinois, June 13, 1963

Most middle-class white Americans frequently ask, "Why do Negroes push so? They have made phenomenal progress in 100 years of freedom, so why don't their leaders do something about the crime rate and illegitimacy?" To them I would reply that when Negroes press for full equality now they are behaving as all other

3. Matthew 5.44.

4. Amos 5.24; Amos was an Old Testament prophet.

5. Galatians 6.17; Paul, a great missionary of the early Christian church, often suffered for his teaching. He wrote some of his own biblical letters from prison.

6. German theologian and leader of the Reformation (1483–1546); the quotation is from Luther's defense of his teaching when he was tried for heresy at the Diet of Worms, 1521.

7. English preacher (1628–88) and author of *Pilgrim's Progress* (1678); this is a paraphrase of a passage in his *Confession of My Faith, and a Reason of My Practice* (1672).

1. Robert C. Weaver, "'The Negro as an American': The Yearning for Human Dignity." *Vital Speeches of the Day*, vol. 29, no. 20, 1963, pp. 625–29.

Americans would under similar circumstances. Every American has the right to be treated as a human being and striving for human dignity is a national characteristic. [. . .]

Negroes who are constantly confronted or threatened by discrimination and inequality articulate a sense of outrage. Many react with hostility, sometimes translating their feelings into overt anti-social actions. In parts of the Negro community a separate culture with deviant values develops. To the members of this subculture I would observe that ours is a middle-class society and those who fail to evidence most of its values and behavior are headed toward difficulties. But I am reminded that the rewards for those who do are often minimal, providing insufficient inducement for large numbers to emulate them.

Robert C. Weaver, 1963. In 1966, Weaver was named the first Secretary of Housing and Urban Development, becoming the first African American to hold a cabinet-level position in the U.S. government.

• • •

The Negro here—as he has so frequently and eloquently demonstrated—is an American. And his status, no less than his aspirations, can be measured meaningfully only in terms of American standards.

Viewed from this point of view what are the facts?

Median family income among non-whites was slightly less than 55 per cent of that for whites in 1959; for individuals the figure was 50 per cent.

Only a third of the Negro families in 1959 earned sufficient to sustain an acceptable American standard of living. [. . .]

Undergirding these overall figures are many paradoxes. Negroes have made striking gains in historical terms, yet their current rate of unemployment is well over double that among whites. Over two-thirds of our colored workers are still concentrated in five major unskilled and semi-skilled occupations, as contrasted to slightly over a third of the white labor force.

In 1959 non-white males who were high school graduates earned, on the average, 32 per cent less than whites; for non-white college graduates the figure was 38 per cent less. Among women a much different situation exists. Non-white women who were high school graduates earned on the average some 24 per cent less than whites. Non-white female college graduates, however, earned but slightly over one per cent less average annual salaries than white women college graduates. Significantly, the median annual income of non-white female college graduates was more than double that of non-white women with only high school education.

Is it any wonder that among non-whites, as contrasted to whites, a larger proportion of women than of men attend and finish college? [. . .]

There is much in these situations that reflects the continuing matriarchal character of Negro society—a situation which had its roots in the family composition under slavery where the father, if identified, had no established role. Subsequent and continuing economic advantages of Negro women who found steady employment as domestics during the post Civil War era and thereafter perpetuated the pattern. This [. . .] served to emasculate many Negro men economically and psychologically. It also explains, in part, the high prevalence of broken homes, illegitimacy, and lack of motivation in the Negro community.

•   •   •

The tragedy of discrimination is that it provides an excuse for failure while erecting barriers to success.

Most colored Americans still are not only outside the mainstream of our society but see no hope of entering it. The lack of motivation and anti-social behavior which result are capitalized upon by the champions of the *status quo*. They say that the average Negro must demonstrate to the average white that the latter's fears are groundless. One proponent of this point of view has stated that Negro crime and illegitimacy must decline and Negro Neighborhoods must stop deteriorating.

In these observations lie a volume on race relations. In the first place, those who articulate this point of view fail to differentiate between acceptance as earned by individual merit and enjoyment of rights guaranteed to everyone. Implicit, also, is the assumption that Negroes can lift themselves by their bootstraps, and that once they become brown counterparts of white middle-class Americans, they will be accepted on the basis of individual merit. Were this true, our race problem would be no more than a most recent phase in the melting pot tradition of the nation.

As compared to the earlier newcomers to our cities from Europe, the later ones who are colored face much greater impediments in moving from the slums or from the bottom of the economic ladder. At the same time, they have less resources to meet the more difficult problems which confront them.

•   •   •

Enforced residential segregation, the most stubborn and universal of the Negro's disadvantages, often leads to exploitation and effects a spatial pattern which facilitates neglect of public services in the well-defined areas where Negroes live. It restricts the opportunities of the more successful as well as the least successful in the group, augmenting artificially the number of non-whites who live in areas of blight and neglect and face impediments to the attainment of values and behavior required for upward social and economic mobility.

The most obvious consequence of involuntary residential segregation is that the housing dollar in a dark hand usually commands less purchasing power than one in a white hand. Clearly, this is a denial of a basic promise of a free economy.

For immigrant groups in the nation, the trend toward improved socioeconomic status has gone hand-and-hand with decreasing residential segregation. The reverse has been true of the Negro.

* * *

I happen to have been born a Negro and to have devoted a large part of my adult energies to the problem of the role of the Negro in America. But I am also a government administrator [. . .].

My responsibilities as a Negro and an American are part of the heritage I received from my parents—a heritage that included a wealth of moral and social values that don't have anything to do with my race. [. . .]

The challenge frequently thrown to me is why I don't go out into the Negro community and exhort Negro youths to prepare themselves for present and future opportunities. [. . .]

Many of the youth which I am urged to exhort come from broken homes. They live in communities where the fellow who stays in school and follows the rules is a "square." They reside in a neighborhood where the most successful are often engaged in shady—if not illegal—activities. They know that the very policeman who may arrest them for violation of the law is sometimes the pay-off man for the racketeers. And they recognize that the majority society, which they frequently believe to be the "enemy," condones this situation. Their experience also leads some of them to believe that getting the kind of job the residents in the neighborhood hold is unrewarding—a commitment to hard work and poverty. For almost all of them, the precepts of Ben Franklin are lily-white in their applicability.

* * *

For many successful older colored Americans, middle-class status has been difficult. Restricted, in large measure, to racial ghettos, they have expended great effort to protect their children from falling back into the dominant values of that environment. And these values are probably more repugnant to them than to most Americans. This is understandable in terms of their social origins. For the most part, they come from lower-middle class families, where industry, good conduct, family ties, and a willingness to postpone immediate rewards for future successes are stressed. Their values and standards of conduct are those of success-oriented middle-class Americans.

These attitudes, too, are shifting. The younger middle-class Negroes are more secure and consequently place less stress upon the quest for respectability. But few Negroes are immune from the toll of upward mobility. Frequently their struggle has been difficult, and the maintenance of their status demands a heavy input. As long as this is true, they will have less energy to devote to the problems of the Negro subculture. It is significant, however, that the sit-ins and Freedom Marches in the South were planned and executed by Negro college students most of whom come from middle-class families.

Middle-class Negroes have long led the fight for civil rights; today its youthful members do not hesitate to resort to direct action, articulating the impatience which is rife throughout the Negro community. In so doing they are forging a new solidarity in the struggle for human dignity.

* * *

The ultimate responsibilities of Negro leadership, however, are to show results and maintain a following. This means that it cannot be so "responsible" that it forgets the trials and tribulations of others who are less fortunate or less recognized than itself. It cannot stress progress—the emphasis which is so palatable to the majority group—without, at the same time, delineating the unsolved business of democracy.

* * *

Most Negroes in leadership capacities have articulated the fact that they and those who follow them are a part of America. They have striven for realization of the American dream. Most recognize their responsibilities as citizens and urge others to follow their example. Sophisticated whites realize that the status of Negroes in our society depends not only upon what the Negro does to achieve his goals and prepare himself for opportunities but, even more, upon what all America does to expand these opportunities. And the quality and nature of future Negro leadership depends upon how effective those leaders who relate to the total society can be in satisfying the yearnings for human dignity which reside in the hearts of all Americans.

AFRICAN AMERICANS AND AFRICA

EARL E. THORPE

From Africa in the Thought of Negro Americans (1959)[1]

The continent of Africa is daily growing in economic, political, and cultural significance. Recently a Negro newspaper in St. Louis, Missouri, contained the statement that the newly independent state of Ghana holds a significance for Negro Americans which is comparable to that which Israel holds for Jewish Americans. How much truth is there in such a statement? Or better still, what does Africa and its history mean to American Negroes? Opinions on this vary greatly, for in an opposite vein from that contained in the St. Louis newspaper, recently the most eminent of all Negro Sociologists[2] stated that most educated Negroes have little but contempt and disdain for Africa and its peoples.

---

1. Earl E. Thorpe, "Africa in the Thought of Negro Americans." *The Negro History Bulletin*, vol. 23, no. 1, Oct. 1959, pp. 5–10. Footnotes have been added by the editor.
2. E. Franklin Frazier (1894–1962), author of several influential sociological studies of African American life and first Black president of the American Sociological Society.

While most Afro-Americans have wished to be a part of the midstream of the national life and culture, not all have wanted this integration. A few, either because they felt that the race actually is inferior and could not compete with whites, or because they went to the opposite extreme and came to believe that Negroes were superior and would lose their distinctive qualities, have desired continued segregation in some form, either here or abroad. Marcus Garvey belonged to the latter group [. . .].

[. . .] Sharing the pessimism and disillusionment, as well as the optimism of the [1920s], Marcus Garvey became convinced that the position of his race within the United States was eternally without hope. Thus he advocated a "back to Africa" movement, and in step with the new appreciation which artists and scholars were beginning to show for African culture, Garvey created a veritable cult of blackness. Reacting against the contempt for dark complexions which many white and Negro Americans held, he proclaimed that black is actually the best and "superior" color. Since it coincided with the efforts of [. . .] scholars in the social sciences, as well as with [. . .] trends in art, music, and creative literature, the movement "put steel into the spine of many Negroes who had previously been ashamed of their color." Especially did Garveyism appeal to lower-class Negroes, and even yet it represents the nearest semblance to a mass movement which has existed among Afro-Americans. Most Negro organizations and intellectuals opposed the movement, however.

⁂

[T]he prominence of the African theatre of battle during the early years of the [second world] war,[3] participation of native African troops in the allied cause, and the possible demise of colonialism as a consequence of the war kept Africa prominent in the thought of Negro Americans. With the return of peace, Afro-American race consciousness and pride were bolstered not only by the phenomenal overthrow of imperialism and colonialism by yellow, brown, and black people in Asia and Africa, but by the dramatic achievements in racial integration within their own country. And just as the personality and efforts of Mahatma Gandhi had inspired Afro-Americans in the twenties and thirties, he, Kwame Nkrumah, Jomo Kenyatta, Gamel Nasser,[4] and other nationalist leaders in Asia and Africa were great sources of inspiration to them in the late forties and fifties.

It seems almost paradoxical that rampant nationalism in Asia and Africa have evoked a greater internationalism in the thought of Afro-Americans.

[. . .] Indeed, a dominant characteristic of the mid-twentieth century Negro vis-à-vis Africa is the greatly increased number who have visited that continent [. . .]. This travel is helping to dispel much of the ignorance about Africa and Africans which has been evident among Negro Americans. Thus many of the old stereotypes once commonly accepted are now rapidly being discarded. [. . .]

3. German forces invaded Libya in 1941; two years later they were driven out of North Africa by Allied forces.
4. Gamel Nasser (1918–70), first president of the republic of Egypt (from 1956–70). Kwame Nkrumah (1909–72), first prime minister, then first president, of Ghana (1957–66). Jomo Kenyatta (1893?–1978), first president of Kenya (from 1964–78).

As a consequence of the degradation of slavery, Negroes have been unique among Americans in the rejection of the land of their fathers. Now a greater maturity and developing race pride are bringing an end to this rejection, and it would not be surprising, to the present writer at least, to see the masses of Afro-Americans soon embrace Africa with a force comparable to that which the Irish and Jewish Americans show for the lands of their fathers.

PHAON GOLDMAN

From The Significance of African Freedom for the Negro American (1960)[1]

With Africa in the headlines every day it behooves us as alert, adult Americans, to know more about Africa and her peoples and the new nations being born almost monthly on this the world's second largest continent. One of my professors used to say that all we know (as Negro Americans) about Africa was that it was shaped like a "po'k chop"—and it is, too, if you'll notice the map. It's a pork chop that's sizzling nowadays.

Africa is significant not only because it's in the news, but also because we have an ancestral connection with the peoples of Africa—a connection we need to review and re-appraise. We have only heard since we were wee tots about Africa in terms of the exotic, the outlandish—land of cannibals, slithering snakes, and people who go around boiling missionaries in a pot. These are the one-sided views of Africa we have been taught; these would furnish material for books and movies that would sell. Seldom, if ever, did we hear the appraisals of Africa made by the most learned scholars of old, such as Ibn Batuda, greatest of the Moslem travelers of the Middle Ages—a man who had traveled throughout most of the then known world, said this of West Africa (in contrast to Spain, Syria, India, China, Turkey, etc.), "Nowhere is there a higher regard for justice or greater security. One can travel throughout the kingdom of the blacks without fear of thieves, robbers, vagabonds, or other evil persons." [. . .]

There is also another instance of our background and connection with Africa which we have come to see only in one light, and that is our outlook on the system of slavery—the instrument that brought us to these shores. When we think of slavery we too often visualize happy-go-lucky slaves captured easily and without a struggle. But the truth of the matter is that the Portuguese, Dutch, and British, fought many a pitched battle to capture most of the Africans that were taken into slavery. Those men, sold into the chains of the European slave-traders by other Africans, were most often warriors who had been captured in inter-village battles. Tens of thousands of these men died by their own hand on the long middle passage rather than submit to that day's form of man's inhumanity to man. So you can see that our ancestors represent not a bunch of cringing cowards but the most valiant of men in body and spirit.

---

1. Phaon Goldman, "The Significance of African Freedom for the Negro American." *The Negro History Bulletin*, vol. 24, no. 1, Oct. 1960, pp. 2, 6.

The valor and sense of justice of the ancient peoples of West Africa can most clearly be seen [. . .] in the determined, forthright, and courageous stand for freedom now being taken by our young Negro youth of the South who in spite of threats, insults, and violence, stand by their right to be accorded the simple human decencies that all other people on earth get in America. The strength of our forefathers is with us still, and make no mistake about it, the students' inspiration came from the fight for freedom now being waged all over the African continent [. . .].

These are sides of our past which have been deliberately buried, for if a man can convince you that you came from nothing, that you are nothing, and that you never will be anything, he doesn't need to worry about you trying to break down segregation barriers, for he has already convinced you that you are different from other human beings and you will be content with your lot.

There are other ways in which we have come to disrespect ourselves too—subtle ways, ways that affect our subconscious mind and blunt our demand for "Freedom Now," and the human dignity accorded all other peoples. [. . .]

[One] subconscious factor causing us to feel we're different from others and therefore perhaps should be treated differently, is the American standard of beauty [. . .]. The faces we see on TV, in the movies and in the magazine ads, reflect the Anglo-Saxon characteristics of the thin nose, a white skin, and straight hair. Being a minority people of physically diametrically opposite characteristics, but set down in the middle of other values, we begin to subconsciously feel that we need to make ourselves over, physically, in order to become acceptable to the majority. So we're told that certain skin preparations will make us "lighter, brighter, and more acceptable" and similar positive attributes are assigned to hair preparations that give us 'straight' hair instead of the curly variety we have.

So to sum up, with Africa in the news every day we must re-view our past concepts of Africa and our relations with the African people, we must view their current battle for "Freedom Now" through the pressures of boycotts, strikes, and mass protests as that stage of man's eternal quest for human dignity that brings the issues out into the open and forces a decision. We must keep ever in mind that the cry of "Freedom Now" is but the present-day application of the ideas of men like Thomas Jefferson and Patrick Henry whose cry of "Give me liberty or give me death" brought freedom to this country and still inspires men to fight for freedom around the world.

Perhaps the greatest significance of African freedom for the Negro American is that it may light the way for those of us of African descent here in America to re-vitalize America's conscience by moving together now for our freedom and force America to solve her moral dilemma of the race question and resume her rightful place as a world leader by showing in deed as well as in preachment that she is truly the land of "liberty and justice for all."

NAACP POLITICAL ACTION COMMITTEE

A RAISIN IN THE SUN REVISITED

Actor-playwright Bruce Norris's *Clybourne Park*, winner of the 2011 Pulitzer Prize for
Drama, consists of two acts, one a prequel, the other a sequel, to *A Raisin in the Sun*.
Set in 1959, Act One depicts a White couple's struggle to deal with the death of their
son and with a neighbor anxious to stop the sale of their home to a Black purchaser.
That neighbor turns out to be Karl Lindner; the Black purchasers, the Youngers. Set in
the same house and featuring the same actors, Act Two takes place fifty years later, in
2009, when the home's new White owners' plan to replace it with a much larger one
brings them into conflict with both city regulations and a neighborhood association
bent on preserving the now mainly Black neighborhood's historic character in the face
of gentrification. The representatives of that neighborhood association are another
young professional couple: Kevin and his wife, Lena, a relative and namesake of Lena
Younger. In the following brief excerpt from Act Two, Kevin and Lena, along with the
neighborhood association lawyer, Tom, battle it out with the new homeowners, Steve
and Lindsey, and their lawyer, Kathy, who happens to be Karl Lindner's daughter.

BRUCE NORRIS

From *Clybourne Park* (2010)

TOM (*holding up a document*): Okay. Here's the wording from the City Council, and I quote: "In recognition of the *historic* status of the Clybourne Park
neighborhood, and its distinctive collection of *low-rise single-family homes*—
(*cont'd.*)

LINDSEY:	KEVIN:	TOM
Aren't *we* a single family?	Hey. Hey. Everything's cool.	(*continuous*): —*intended to house a community of working-class families.*"

LINDSEY: And you know, the thing is? Communities change.
STEVE: They do.
LINDSEY: That's just the reality.
STEVE: It is.
LENA: And some change is inevitable, and we all support that, but it might be
worth asking yourself who exactly is *responsible* for that change?

(*Little pause.*)

LINDSEY:	KEVIN:
I'm not sure what you—?	Wait, what are you trying to—?

LENA: I'm asking you to think about the motivation behind the long-range political initiative to change the face of this neighborhood.

(*Another little pause.*)

Damon Gupton as Kevin, Crystal A. Dickinson as Lena, Annie Parisse as Lindsey, and Jeremy Shamos as Steve in the Playwrights Horizon production of *Clybourne Park*, 2010

LINDSEY:
What does that
mean? I don't know
what that—?

STEVE *(to* LENA*)*:
Wait, say that again?

KEVIN:
The long-range
what?

LENA: I mean that this is a highly desirable area.
STEVE: Well, *we* desire it.
LENA: I know you do.
LINDSEY: Same as you.
LENA: And now the area is *changing.*
KATHY: And for the *better,* right?
LENA: And I'm saying that there are certain economic interests that are being served by those changes and others that are not. That's all.
STEVE *(suspiciously)*: And . . . *which* interests are being—?
LENA *(systematically)*: If you have a residential area, in direct proximity to *downtown*?
STEVE: Right?
LENA: And if that area is occupied by a particular *group*?

STEVE:
Which group?

LINDSEY *(to* LENA*)*:
You know what? We're talking
about *one house.*

LENA *(to* LINDSEY*)*: I understand that.
STEVE: Which group?
LINDSEY: A house for our *family*?
STEVE: Which group?
LENA: That's how it happens.

LINDSEY: In which to raise our *child?*

STEVE: No no. Which group?

LENA: It happens one house at a time.

STEVE: Whoa whoa whoa. Okay. Stop right there.

LINDSEY: What are you doing?

STEVE: No. I'm sorry, but can we just come out and *say* what it is we're actually—? Shouldn't we maybe *do* that? Because if *that's* what this is really about, then . . . jesus, maybe we oughta save ourselves some time and and and and just . . . *say* what it is we're really *saying* instead of doing this elaborate little *dance* around it.

(Dead stop. All stare at STEVE*)*

Never mind.

KATHY: *What* dance?

STEVE: I—I—I—I shouldn't have—whatever.

LENA *(parsing his meaning)*: So . . . you think I haven't been *saying* what I actually—?

STEVE *(laughs)*: Uhhh . . . Not to my way of thinking, no.

LENA: Well, what is it you *think* I'm—?

STEVE: I—I—I . . . *(laughs incredulously)* . . . like we don't all *know?*

LINDSEY: *I* don't.

STEVE: Oh, *yes you do.* Of *course* you do.

KEVIN: Well, maybe you oughta *tell* us what *you* think she was saying.

STEVE: Oh oh, but it has to be *me?*

LENA: Well, you're the one who raised the question as to—*(cont'd.)*

STEVE *(laughs, overlapping)*: Oh, *come on.* It was *blatant.*

LENA *(continuous)*: —the sincerity of my speech.

LINDSEY: What the fuck, Steve?

STEVE: You know what? Forget I said it.

LINDSEY:	LENA:	STEVE:
You didn't *say* anything.	Oh no, I'm *interested.*	Let's forget the whole—

STEVE *(continuous)*: —Okay. Okay. If you really want to—It's . . . *(tries to laugh, then, sotto)* . . . it's *race.* Isn't it? You're trying to tell me that that . . . That implicit in what you *said*—That this entire conversation . . . isn't at least *partly* informed—*am I right? (laughs nervously)* By the issue of . . . *(sotto)* of *racism?*

(Beat, then)

LINDSEY *(to* STEVE*):*	STEVE *(to* LINDSEY*):*
Are you out of your—? (to LENA*)* I have no idea where this is coming from.	And *please* don't do that to me, okay? I've asked you repeatedly.

LENA: Well, the *original* issue was the inappropriately large *house* that—*(cont'd.)*

STEVE *(to* LENA*, overlapping)*: Oh, come *on.*

LENA (*continuous*): —you're planning to build. Only, *now* I'm fairly certain that I've been called a *racist*.

STEVE: But I didn't say that, did I?

LENA: *Sounded* like you did.

STEVE (*to* KEVIN): Did I say that?

KEVIN: Yeah, you kinda did.

STEVE: In what way did I say that?

KEVIN: Uh, *somebody* said racism.

STEVE: -*Cism*! -*Cism*! Not -*cist*!!

KEVIN: Which must originate from *somewhere*.

STEVE: And which we all find totally reprehensi—

KEVIN: So—are *you* the racist?

STEVE: Can I just—?

KEVIN: Is it your wife?

KATHY: Don't look at *me*.

STEVE: Look:

KEVIN: 'Cause, by process of elimination—

STEVE: Here's what I'm saying:

LINDSEY: What *are* you saying?!

STEVE: I'm saying: Was race *not* a factor—

LINDSEY (*re:* STEVE, *exonerating herself*): I don't know this person.

STEVE: Were there *not* these differences—

LINDSEY: *What* differences!!? There's no—

STEVE (*to* LINDSEY *re:* LENA): Okay: She walks in here, from the very beginning, with all these *issues*—(*cont'd.*)

LENA (*overlapping*): About your *house*.

STEVE (*continuous*): —and I'm only asking whether, were we not, shall we say—?

LINDSEY: You're *creating* an issue. *Where none exists.*

STEVE: Oh oh oh you *heard* what she *said*. She as much as claimed that there's some kind of, of, of *secret conspiracy*—

LENA: Oh, it's not a *secret*.

KEVIN (*to* LENA):	LENA (*to* KEVIN):	STEVE:
Ohh, *c'mon.*	Oh, please don't be	*There. Thank you.*
Are you seriously—?	purposely *naive.*	*Now you see what I'm—?*

LENA: This has been under discussion for at least *four decades* now—(*cont'd.*)

KEVIN (*overlapping, to* LENA): *You can't prove that.*

LENA (*continuous*): —at the highest institutional levels of—(to KEVIN—) oh, *don't act like you don't know it's true.*

STEVE (*to* LENA): What, and now we're the evil invaders who are—

LINDSEY (*to* STEVE): *She never said that!!!!*

STEVE: —appropriating your *ancestral homeland*?

LINDSEY (*to* STEVE): This, this, this—No. I'm sorry, this is the most *asinine*—(to LENA and KEVIN) *Half of my friends are black!*

STEVE (*sputtering*): What!!??

LINDSEY (*to* STEVE, *as to a child*): As is true for most *normal* people.

STEVE: Name one.

LINDSEY: *Normal* people? Tend to have *many* friends of a diverse and wide-ranging—

STEVE: You can't name *one*!

LINDSEY: Candace.

STEVE (*beat, then*): Name another.

LINDSEY: *I don't have to stand here compiling a list of*—

STEVE: You said *half*. You *specifically*—

LINDSEY: Theresa.

STEVE: *She works in your office!! She's not your "friend."*

LINDSEY: *She was at the baby shower, Steve! I hope she's not my enemy!!*

TOM: Well, this is all fascinating—

STEVE (*to* LINDSEY): Name another.

TOM: And while I'd love to sit here and review *all* of American History, *maybe* we should concentrate on the plans for your *property*—(*cont'd*)

STEVE (*overlapping*): Yes!! Yes!! (*cont'd*)

TOM (*continuous*): —which *had* been the *original* topic of the convers—

STEVE (*overlapping, continuous*): The history of America *is* the history of private property.

LENA: That may be—

STEVE: Read De Tocqueville.[1]

LENA: —though I rather doubt *your* grandparents were *sold as* private property.

STEVE (*to* KEVIN & LENA): Ohhhhh my *god*. Look. Look. Humans are *territorial*, okay?

LINDSEY (*to* STEVE): Who *are* you?

STEVE: This is why we have *wars*. One group, one *tribe*, tries to usurp some *territory*—and now *you guys* have *this* territory, right? And you don't like having it *stolen away* from you, the way white people stole everything else from black America. *We get it*, okay? And we *apologize*. But what *good* does it do, if we perpetually fall into the same, predictable little euphemistic tap dance around the topic?

KEVIN: You know how to tap dance?

STEVE: *See? See what he's doing?!!*

LINDSEY: Maybe quit while you're ahead.

SUGGESTIONS FOR WRITING

1. Langston Hughes's poem HARLEM poses a question: "What happens to a dream deferred?" Why do you think Lorraine Hansberry chose this poem as the **epigraph** for A RAISIN IN THE SUN? Write an essay in which you discuss the various "dreams" that come into conflict in the play. Which "dream" does the play seem to endorse? Does it ultimately answer Hughes's question?

2. In A RAISIN IN THE SUN's third act, Beneatha asserts that "there isn't any real progress [. . .] there is only one large circle that we march in, around and around, each of us with our own little picture—in front of us—our own little mirage that we think is the future." Asagai replies that progress instead follows "a long line—as in geometry, [. . .] one that reaches into infinity" (1610). Write an essay in which you

---

1. Reference to *Democracy in America* (1835–40), a comprehensive two-volume study of U.S. society by the Frenchman Alexis de Tocqueville (1805–59).

compare these two views of progress as they are depicted in A RAISIN IN THE SUN. Does the play seem to favor one view over the other?

3. In EVEN MORE CRUCIAL THAN IN THE SOUTH, *New York Times* reporter Gertrude Samuels suggests that what African Americans were increasingly demanding in the late 1950s and early 1960s was not only an end to racial discrimination in housing, schooling, and employment, but also and above all "personal dignity" (1630), a point echoed in Martin Luther King, Jr.'s reference, in LETTER FROM BIRMINGHAM JAIL, to "the stinging darts of segregation" (1635). Drawing on these and other contextual excerpts in this chapter, as well as A RAISIN IN THE SUN, write an essay exploring what the play might contribute to our understanding of the psychological and emotional effects of racial discrimination. How does the latter seem to affect the way the characters perceive themselves and each other?

4. A RAISIN IN THE SUN is set in Chicago, but in many ways its heart is in Africa—the Africa of the mythical past, the Africa of the slave trade, and the Africa of the late 1950s, during which the play is set. Write an essay in which you explore the many ways in which both African history and culture and American attitudes toward them inform Hansberry's play. To what extent might *A Raisin in the Sun* illustrate ideas found in Earl E. Thorpe's AFRICA IN THE THOUGHT OF NEGRO AMERICANS and/or Phaon Goldman's THE SIGNIFICANCE OF AFRICAN FREEDOM FOR THE NEGRO AMERICAN?

5. Hansberry's play explores not only the evolving social and economic positions of African Americans in the mid-twentieth century, but also their evolving gender roles, a subject on which Robert C. Weaver also comments briefly in THE NEGRO AS AN AMERICAN. Write an essay in which you discuss the crucial role that gender plays in the action of A RAISIN IN THE SUN. Does the play seem to uphold any particular vision of gender roles, especially within the family? Might it in any way endorse Weaver's provocative claims on the subject?

28 | CRITICAL CONTEXTS: SOPHOCLES'S *ANTIGONE*

Even more than other forms of literature, drama has a relatively stable **canon**, a select group of plays that the theater community thinks of as especially worthy of frequent performance. New plays join this canon, of course, but theater companies worldwide tend to perform the same ones over and over, especially those by Shakespeare, Ibsen, and Sophocles. The reasons are many, involving the plays' themes and continued appeal across times and cultures as well as their formal literary and theatrical features. But their repeated performance means that a relatively small number of plays become much better known than all the others and that there is a tradition of "talk" about those plays. A lot of this talk is informal and local, resulting from the fact that people see plays communally, viewing performances together and often comparing responses afterward. But more permanent and more formal responses also exist; individual productions of plays are often reviewed in newspapers and magazines, on radio and television, online and in podcasts. Such reviews concentrate primarily on evaluating specific productions. But because every production of a play involves a particular interpretation of the text, cumulative accounts of performances add up to a body of interpretive **criticism**—that is, analytical commentary about many aspects of the play as text and as performance. Scholars add to that body of criticism by publishing their own interpretations in academic journals and books.

That body of material is available to you as a way of getting additional perspectives on a play. You don't have to read this accumulated criticism to understand what happens in a text. But reading what others have said can help you—by offering historical information that you hadn't known or hadn't considered relevant, by pointing to problems or possibilities of interpretation you had not yet thought of, or by supporting a reading you had already arrived at. In a sense, reading published criticism is like talking with your fellow students or being involved in a class discussion. In general, you shouldn't read "the critics" until after you have read the play at least once, just as you should read the text in full before you discuss it with others. That way, your initial responses to the play are your own.

Reading criticism can be especially helpful when you have to write an essay. Critics will often guide you to crucial points of debate or to a place in the text that is a crux for deciding on a particular interpretation. You will likely get the most help if you read several critics with different perspectives—not because more is better, but because you will see their differences and, more important, the *grounds* for their differences in the kinds of evidence they use and the various inferences they draw from it. Their disagreements will likely be very useful to you as a new interpreter. But don't regard critics as "authorities": An interpretation is not true simply because it is published or because it is written by somebody famous. Instead, look to critics and their work as a spur to your own thinking.

Often, when you're just starting to think about the essay you want to write, reading criticism can help you see some of the critical issues in the play. Critics frequently disagree on the interpretation of particular issues or passages or even about what the issues really are, but reading their work can make your own thoughts concrete, especially when you're just starting to sort things out. Reacting to someone else's view, especially one that is strongly argued, can help you articulate what you think and can suggest a line of interpretation and argument. Sorting out the important issues can be complicated, and issues do shift from era to era and culture to culture. But often the arguments posed in one era interest subsequent critics in whatever age and from whatever perspective. More generally, studying how professional critics make arguments and what makes some arguments more compelling and effective than others can help you both assess and improve your own.

If you draw on published criticism in your paper, you should acknowledge the critic up front and then work his or her words into your paper the way you have learned to do with lines or phrases from a literary text, though you will often find that summary or paraphrase—stating a source's ideas in your own words—is more effective. Sometimes a particular critic can be especially helpful in focusing your thoughts because you so clearly disagree with what she or he says. In that case, you may well get a good paper out of a rebuttal. Pitting one critic against another— sorting out the issues that interpreters disagree on and showing what their differences consist of—can also be a good way to frame your own contribution. But remember that the point of reading criticism is to *use* it for your own interpretive purposes, to make your responses more sensitive and resonant, to make you a more informed reader of the play, and to make you a better reader and writer in general.

In the critical selections in this chapter, you will find various interpretations of crucial scenes and issues in Sophocles's ANTIGONE. Especially prominent are questions about how to read the opinions of the chorus, how to interpret the character of Antigone, and how to assess both her flaws and Creon's. As you read the critics, pay attention to the way they argue—what kinds of textual evidence they use to back up their claims and how they structure their arguments—as well as the main interpretive claims they make. (Following the chapter is a sample student essay about *Antigone* that draws on critical excerpts in this chapter, as well as other secondary sources.)

Antigone's critical context is an especially rich and interesting one to explore because the play's performance history goes back more than twenty-four centuries, and over that time readers and viewers have recorded many thousands of responses. Sophocles's play attracts attention from a wide variety of scholarly critics—from classicists, who view it in relation to classical myth or ancient Greek language and culture; from philosophers, who may see in it examinations of enduring ideas and ethical problems; from theater historians, who may think about it in relation to traditions of staging and visualization or the particulars of gestures and stage business; from historians and theorists of rhetoric, who may consider the interactions between the chorus and the players or the way characters use or abuse classical rhetorical conventions; and from feminist critics and theorists interested in the questions the play raises about women's position in the state and

Scene from the 2012 National Theatre production of *Antigone* with Christopher Eccleston as Creon and Jodie Whittaker as Antigone

the family and about the relation between family and state. Following the text of the play below, we reprint only a small sample of such work, mostly from the twentieth century. But earlier views are often referred to and debated. The famous comments of the German philosopher G. W. F. Hegel (1770–1831), for example, continue to set the agenda for an astonishing number of interpreters. Many answer him directly; others use him to sharpen, complicate, or flesh out their views or simply to position themselves in some larger debate about specific issues in the play or about literary criticism, ethics, and politics more generally.

Antigone, like virtually any play, certainly invites historicist interpretations. In POLIS AND TRAGEDY IN THE *ANTIGONE*, for example, critic Philip Holt aims to correct what he identifies as modern misreadings of Sophocles's play by attending to the particular fifth-century Greek beliefs, attitudes, and practices that inform it. As classicist Helen Morales's ANTIGONE RISING: THE SUBVERSIVE POWER OF THE ANCIENT MYTHS demonstrates, however, this ancient play's enduring appeal to artists, audiences, and critics, not to mention political commentators and judges, rests equally on its openness to "presentist" interpretations aimed at evoking the play's relevance to contemporary situations and debates. Where German playwright Bertolt Brecht's famous reinterpretation, first staged in 1948, just three years after Germany's defeat in World War II, draws clear parallels between Creon and Hitler, for example, more recent reinterpretations run the gamut and span the globe. Berlin-based Syrian playwright Mohammad al-Attar's *Antigone of Syria* (2014), as produced by award-winning Syrian filmmaker Itab Azaam in Beirut, Lebanon, featured an all-female cast of refugees from the Syrian civil war, one of whom avowed, "I feel that Antigone resembles me a lot." First performed two years later, in Chicago, Caitlin Parrish's *The Burials* unfolds inside a U.S. high school in the aftermath of a mass shooting. Moving from stage to courtroom, when in 2019 activists from No More Deaths/No Más Muertes appealed their conviction for leaving food and water for migrants crossing the Arizona desert, on the grounds that their faith compelled them to do so, U.S. Magistrate Judge Bernardo P. Velasco rejected what he called their "modified Antigone defense"—a decision that unleashed numerous editorials, as well as an amicus brief, challenging the judge's interpretation not only of modern U.S. law but also of Sophocles's ancient yet endlessly resonant, relevant play.

SOPHOCLES

(496?–406? BCE)

Antigone[1]

Sophocles lived at a time when Athens and Greek civilization were at the peak of their power and influence. He served as a general under Pericles, played a prominent role in the city's affairs, and was arguably the greatest of the Greek tragic playwrights, winning the annual dramatic competition about twenty times, a feat unmatched by even his great contemporaries, Aeschylus and Euripides. An innovator, Sophocles fundamentally changed the nature of dramatic performance by adding a third actor, enlarging the chorus, and introducing the use of painted scenery. Aristotle held that Sophocles's *Oedipus the King* (c. 429 BCE) was the perfect tragedy and used it as his model when discussing the nature of tragedy in his *Poetics*. Today only seven of Sophocles's tragedies survive—the Oedipus trilogy (*Oedipus the King, Oedipus at Colonus,* and *Antigone*), *Philoctetes, Ajax, Trachiniae,* and *Electra*—though he is believed to have written as many as 123 plays.

CHARACTERS

ANTIGONE	HAEMON
ISMENE	TEIRESIAS
CHORUS OF THEBAN ELDERS	A MESSENGER
CREON	EURYDICE
A SENTRY	SECOND MESSENGER

The two sisters ANTIGONE *and* ISMENE *meet in front of the palace gates in Thebes.*

ANTIGONE: Ismene, my dear sister,
    whose father was my father, can you think of any
    of all the evils that stem from Oedipus[2]
    that Zeus does not bring to pass for us, while we yet live?

---

1. Translated from the ancient Greek by David Grene.
2. In Greek legend, Oedipus became king of Thebes by inadvertently fulfilling the prophecy that he was destined to kill his father and marry his mother (as depicted in Sophocles's *Oedipus the King*, p. 1840); for these offenses against nature and the gods, Creon sent Oedipus, along with his daughters Antigone and Ismene, into exile at Colonus. Oedipus's sons, Eteocles and Polyneices,

5   No pain, no ruin, no shame, and no dishonor
       but I have seen it in our mischiefs,
       yours and mine.
       And now what is the proclamation that they tell of
       made lately by the commander, publicly,
10   to all the people? Do you know it? Have you heard it?
       Don't you notice when the evils due to enemies
       are headed towards those we love?
   ISMENE: Not a word, Antigone, of those we love,
       either sweet or bitter, has come to me since the moment
15   when we lost our two brothers,
       on one day, by their hands dealing mutual death.
       Since the Argive[3] army fled in this past night,
       I know of nothing further, nothing
       of better fortune or of more destruction.
20 ANTIGONE: *I* knew it well; that is why I sent for you
       to come outside the palace gates
       to listen to me, privately.
   ISMENE: What is it? Certainly your words
       come of dark thoughts.
25 ANTIGONE: Yes, indeed; for those two brothers of ours, in burial
       has not Creon honored the one, dishonored the other?
       Eteocles, they say he has used justly
       with lawful rites and hid him in the earth
       to have his honor among the dead men there.
30   But the unhappy corpse of Polyneices
       he has proclaimed to all the citizens,
       they say, no man may hide
       in a grave nor mourn in funeral,
       but leave unwept, unburied, a dainty treasure
35   for the birds that see him, for their feast's delight.
       That is what, they say, the worthy Creon
       has proclaimed for you and me—for me, I tell you—
       and he comes here to clarify to the unknowing
       his proclamation; he takes it seriously;
40   for whoever breaks the edict death is prescribed,
       and death by stoning publicly.
       There you have it; soon you will show yourself
       as noble both in your nature and your birth,
       or yourself as base, although of noble parents.
45 ISMENE: If things are as you say, poor sister, how
       can I better them? how loose or tie the knot?
   ANTIGONE: Decide if you will share the work, the deed.

---

agreed to take turns ruling Thebes. But when Eteocles refused to give up the throne at the end of his
first allotted year, Polyneices gathered an "Argive army" (line 17) and attacked the city.
3. From Argos, a rival Greek city-state.

ISMENE: What kind of danger is there? How far have your thoughts gone?
ANTIGONE: Here is this hand. Will you help it to lift the dead man?
ISMENE: Would you bury him, when it is forbidden the city? 50
ANTIGONE: At least he is my brother—and yours, too,
    though you deny him. I will not prove false to him.
ISMENE: You are so headstrong. Creon has forbidden it.
ANTIGONE: It is not for him to keep me from my own.
ISMENE: O God! 55
    Consider, sister, how our father died,
    hated and infamous; how he brought to light
    his own offenses; how he himself struck out
    the sight of his two eyes;
    his own hand was their executioner. 60
    Then, mother and wife, two names in one, did shame
    violently on her life, with twisted cords.
    Third, our two brothers, on a single day,
    poor wretches, themselves worked out their mutual doom.
    Each killed the other, hand against brother's hand. 65
    Now there are only the two of us, left behind,
    and see how miserable our end shall be
    if in the teeth of law we shall transgress
    against the sovereign's decree and power.
    You ought to realize we are only women, 70
    not meant in nature to fight against men,
    and that we are ruled, by those who are stronger,
    to obedience in this and even more painful matters.
    I do indeed beg those beneath the earth
    to give me their forgiveness, 75
    since force constrains me,
    that I shall yield in this to the authorities.
    Extravagant action is not sensible.
ANTIGONE: I would not urge you now; nor if you wanted
    to act would I be glad to have you with me. 80
    Be as you choose to be; but for myself
    I myself will bury him. It will be good
    to die, so doing. I shall lie by his side,
    loving him as he loved me; I shall be
    a criminal—but a religious one. 85
    The time in which I must please those that are dead
    is longer than I must please those of this world.
    For there I shall lie forever. You, if you like,
    can cast dishonor on what the gods have honored.
ISMENE: I will not put dishonor on them, but 90
    to act in defiance of the citizenry,
    my nature does not give me means for that.
ANTIGONE: Let that be your excuse. But I will go
    to heap the earth on the grave of my loved brother.

95 ISMENE: How I fear for you, my poor sister!
    ANTIGONE: Do not fear for me. Make straight your own path to destiny.
    ISMENE: At least do not speak of this act to anyone else;
        bury him in secret; I will be silent, too.
    ANTIGONE: Oh, oh, no! shout it out. I will hate you still worse
100   for silence—should you not proclaim it,
        to everyone.
    ISMENE: You have a warm heart for such chilly deeds.
    ANTIGONE: I know I am pleasing those I should please most.
    ISMENE: *If* you can do it. But you are in love
105   with the impossible.
    ANTIGONE: No. When I can no more, then I will stop.
    ISMENE: It is better not to hunt the impossible
        at all.
    ANTIGONE: If you will talk like this I will loathe you,
110   and you will be adjudged an enemy—
        justly—by the dead's decision. Let me alone
        and my folly with me, to endure this terror.
        No suffering of mine will be enough
        to make me die ignobly.
115 ISMENE: Well, if you will, go on.
        Know this; that though you are wrong to go, your friends
        are right to love you.
    CHORUS: Sun's beam, fairest of all
        that ever till now shone
120   on seven-gated Thebes;
        O golden eye of day, you shone
        coming over Dirce's stream;[4]
        You drove in headlong rout
        the whiteshielded man from Argos,
125   complete in arms;
        his bits rang sharper
        under your urging.

        Polyneices brought him here
        against our land, Polyneices,
130   roused by contentious quarrel;
        like an eagle he flew into our country,
        with many men-at-arms,
        with many a helmet crowned with horsehair.

        He stood above the halls, gaping with murderous lances,
135   encompassing the city's
        seven-gated mouth[5]

4. River near Thebes.
5. Thebes was known throughout the ancient world for having seven gateways through the walls protecting the city.

But before his jaws would be sated
with our blood, before the fire,
pine fed, should capture our crown of towers,
he went hence—   140
such clamor of war stretched behind his back,
from his dragon foe, a thing he could not overcome.

For Zeus, who hates the most
the boasts of a great tongue,
saw them coming in a great tide,   145
insolent in the clang of golden armor.
The god struck him down with hurled fire,
as he strove to raise the victory cry,
now at the very winning post.

The earth rose to strike him as he fell swinging.   150
In his frantic onslaught, possessed, he breathed upon us
with blasting winds of hate.
Sometimes the great god of war was on one side,
and sometimes he struck a staggering blow on the other;
the god was a very wheel horse[6] on the right trace.   155

At seven gates stood seven captains,
ranged equals against equals, and there left
their brazen suits of armor
to Zeus, the god of trophies.
Only those two wretches born of one father and mother   160
set their spears to win a victory on both sides;
they worked out their share in a common death.

Now Victory, whose name is great, has come
to Thebes of many chariots
with joy to answer her joy,   165
to bring forgetfulness of these wars;
let us go to all the shrines of the gods
and dance all night long.
Let Bacchus lead the dance,
shaking Thebes to trembling.   170

But here is the king of our land,
Creon,[7] son of Menoeceus;
in our new contingencies with the gods,
he is our new ruler.

6. Strongest and ablest horse in a team pulling a vehicle, harnessed nearest the front wheels "on the right trace."
7. Brother of Jocasta, mother and wife of Oedipus; he became king of Thebes after the deaths of Oedipus's sons.

175   He comes to set in motion some design—
         what design is it? Because he has proposed
         the convocation of the elders.
         He sent a public summons for our discussion.

CREON: Gentlemen: as for our city's fortune,

180   the gods have shaken her, when the great waves broke,
         but the gods have brought her through again to safety.
         For yourselves, I chose you out of all and summoned you
         to come to me, partly because I knew you
         as always loyal to the throne—at first,

185   when Laïus[8] was king, and then again
         when Oedipus saved our city and then again
         when he died and you remained with steadfast truth
         to their descendants,
         until they met their double fate upon one day,

190   striking and stricken, defiled each by a brother's murder.
         Now here I am, holding all authority
         and the throne, in virtue of kinship with the dead.
         It is impossible to know any man—
         I mean his soul, intelligence, and judgment—

195   until he shows his skill in rule and law.
         I think that a man supreme ruler of a whole city,
         if he does not reach for the best counsel for her,
         but through some fear, keeps his tongue under lock and key,
         him I judge the worst of any;

200   I have always judged so; and anyone thinking
         another man more a friend than his own country,
         I rate him nowhere. For my part, God is my witness,
         who sees all, always, I would not be silent
         if I saw ruin, not safety, on the way

205   towards my fellow citizens. I would not count
         any enemy of my country as a friend—
         because of what I know, that she it is
         which gives us our security. If she sails upright
         and we sail on her, friends will be ours for the making.

210   In the light of rules like these, I will make her greater still.

         In consonance with this, I here proclaim
         to the citizens about Oedipus' sons.
         For Eteocles, who died this city's champion,
         showing his valor's supremacy everywhere,

215   he shall be buried in his grave with every rite
         of sanctity given to heroes under earth.
         However, his brother, Polyneices, a returned exile,

---

8. Father of Oedipus.

who sought to burn with fire from top to bottom
his native city, and the gods of his own people;
who sought to taste the blood he shared with us,   220
and lead the rest of us to slavery—
I here proclaim to the city that this man
shall no one honor with a grave and none shall mourn.
You shall leave him without burial; you shall watch him
chewed up by birds and dogs and violated.   225
Such is my mind in the matter; never by me
shall the wicked man have precedence in honor
over the just. But he that is loyal to the state
in death, in life alike, shall have my honor.

CHORUS: Son of Menoeceus, so it is your pleasure   230
    to deal with foe and friend of this our city.
    To use any legal means lies in your power,
    both about the dead and those of us who live.

CREON: I understand, then, you will do my bidding.

CHORUS: Please lay this burden on some younger man.   235

CREON: Oh, watchers of the corpse I have already.

CHORUS: What else, then, do your commands entail?

CREON: That you should not side with those who disagree.

CHORUS: There is none so foolish as to love his own death.

CREON: Yes, indeed those are the wages, but often greed   240
    has with its hopes brought men to ruin.

[*The* SENTRY *whose speeches follow represents a remarkable experiment in Greek tragedy in the direction of naturalism of speech. He speaks with marked clumsiness, partly because he is excited and talks almost colloquially. But also the royal presence makes him think apparently that he should be rather grand in his show of respect. He uses odd bits of archaism or somewhat stale poetical passages, particularly in catch phrases. He sounds something like lower-level Shakespearean characters, e.g. Constable Elbow, with his uncertainty about benefactor and malefactor.*]

SENTRY: My lord, I will never claim my shortness of breath
    is due to hurrying, nor were there wings in my feet.
    I stopped at many a lay-by in my thinking;
    I circled myself till I met myself coming back.   245
    My soul accosted me with different speeches.
    "Poor fool, yourself, why are you going somewhere
    when once you get there you will pay the piper?"
    "Well, aren't you the daring fellow! stopping again?
    and suppose Creon hears the news from someone else—   250
    don't you realize that you will smart for that?"
    I turned the whole matter over. I suppose I may say
    "I made haste slowly" and the short road became long.
    However, at last I came to a resolve:

255   I must go to you; even if what I say
          is nothing, really, still I shall say it.
          I come here, a man with a firm clutch on the hope
          that nothing can betide him save what is fated.
     CREON: What is it then that makes you so afraid?
260 SENTRY: No, I want first of all to tell you my side of it.
          I didn't do the thing; I never saw who did it.
          It would not be fair for me to get into trouble.
     CREON: You hedge, and barricade the thing itself.
          Clearly you have some ugly news for me.
265 SENTRY: Well, you know how disasters make a man
          hesitate to be their messenger.
     CREON: For God's sake, tell me and get out of here!
     SENTRY: Yes, I *will* tell you. Someone just now
          buried the corpse and vanished. He scattered on the skin
270   some thirsty dust; he did the ritual,
          duly, to purge the body of desecration.
     CREON: What! Now who on earth could have done that?
     SENTRY: I do not know. For there was there no mark
          of axe's stroke nor casting up of earth
275   of any mattock; the ground was hard and dry,
          unbroken; there were no signs of wagon wheels.
          The doer of the deed had left no trace.
          But when the first sentry of the day pointed it out,
          there was for all of us a disagreeable
280   wonder. For the body had disappeared;
          not in a grave, of course; but there lay upon him
          a little dust as of a hand avoiding
          the curse of violating the dead body's sanctity.
          There were no signs of any beast nor dog
285   that came there; he had clearly not been torn.
          There was a tide of bad words at one another,
          guard taunting guard, and it might well have ended
          in blows, for there was no one there to stop it.
          Each one of us was the criminal but no one
290   manifestly so; all denied knowledge of it.
          We were ready to take hot bars in our hands
          or walk through fire,[9] and call on the gods with oaths
          that we had neither done it nor were privy
          to a plot with anyone, neither in planning
295   nor yet in execution.
          At last when nothing came of all our searching,
          there was one man who spoke, made every head
          bow to the ground in fear. For we could not
          either contradict him nor yet could we see how

---

9. Ancient legal custom required an accused person to undergo a "trial by ordeal," such as walking
through fire; if the resulting injuries were not serious, the person was considered innocent and therefore divinely protected.

if we did what he said we would come out all right.   300
His word was that we must lay information
about the matter to yourself; we could not cover it.
This view prevailed and the lot of the draw chose me,
unlucky me, to win that prize. So here
I am. I did not want to come,   305
and you don't want to have me. I know that.
For no one likes the messenger of bad news.
CHORUS: My lord: I wonder, could this be God's doing?
This is the thought that keeps on haunting me.
CREON: Stop, before your words fill even me with rage,   310
that you should be exposed as a fool, and you so old.
For what you say is surely insupportable
when you say the gods took forethought for this corpse.
Is it out of excess of honor for the man,
for the favors that he did them, they should cover him?   315
This man who came to burn their pillared temples,
their dedicated offerings—and this land
and laws he would have scattered to the winds?
Or do you see the gods as honoring
criminals? This is not so. But what I am doing   320
now, and other things before this, some men disliked,
within this very city, and muttered against me,
secretly shaking their heads; they would not bow
justly beneath the yoke to submit to me.
I am very sure that these men hired others   325
to do this thing. I tell you the worse currency
that ever grew among mankind is money. This
sacks cities, this drives people from their homes,
this teaches and corrupts the minds of the loyal
to acts of shame. This displays   330
all kinds of evil for the use of men,
instructs in the knowledge of every impious act.
Those that have done this deed have been paid to do it,
but in the end they will pay for what they have done.

It is as sure as I still reverence Zeus—   335
know this right well—and I speak under oath—
if you and your fellows do not find this man
who with his own hand did the burial
and bring him here before me face to face,
your death alone will not be enough for me.   340
You will hang alive till you open up this outrage.
That will teach you in the days to come from what
you may draw profit—safely—from your plundering.
It's not from anything and everything
you can grow rich. You will find out   345
that ill-gotten gains ruin more than they save.

SENTRY: Have I your leave to say something—or should
    I just turn and go?
CREON: Don't you know your talk is painful enough already?
350 SENTRY: Is the ache in your ears or in your mind?
CREON: Why do you dissect the whereabouts of my pain?
SENTRY: Because it is he who did the deed who hurts your
    mind. I only hurt your ears that listen.
CREON: I am sure you have been a chatterbox since you were born.
355 SENTRY: All the same, I did not do this thing.
CREON: You might have done this, too, if you sold your soul.
SENTRY: It's a bad thing if one judges and judges wrongly.
CREON: You may talk as wittily as you like of judgment.
    Only, if you don't bring to light those men
360   who have done this, you will yet come to say
    that your wretched gains have brought bad consequences.
SENTRY: [*Aside.*] It were best that he were found, but whether
    the criminal is taken or he isn't—
    for that chance will decide—one thing is certain,
365   you'll never see me coming here again.
    I never hoped to escape, never thought I could.
    But now I have come off safe, I thank God heartily.
CHORUS: Many are the wonders, none
    is more wonderful than what is man.
370   This it is that crosses the sea
    with the south winds storming and the waves swelling,
    breaking around him in roaring surf.
    He it is again who wears away
    the Earth, oldest of gods, immortal, unwearied,
375   as the ploughs wind across her from year to year
    when he works her with the breed that comes from horses.

    The tribe of the lighthearted birds he snares
    and takes prisoner the races of savage beasts
    and the brood of the fish of the sea,
380   with the close-spun web of nets.
    A cunning fellow is man. His contrivances
    make him master of beasts of the field
    and those that move in the mountains.
    So he brings the horse with the shaggy neck
385   to bend underneath the yoke;
    and also the untamed mountain bull;
    and speech and windswift thought
    and the tempers that go with city living
    he has taught himself, and how to avoid
390   the sharp frost, when lodging is cold
    under the open sky
    and pelting strokes of the rain.
    He has a way against everything,

and he faces nothing that is to come
without contrivance.   395
Only against death
can he call on no means of escape;
but escape from hopeless diseases
he has found in the depths of his mind.
With some sort of cunning, inventive   400
beyond all expectation
he reaches sometimes evil,
and sometimes good.

If he honors the laws of earth,
and the justice of the gods he has confirmed by oath,   405
high is his city; no city
has he with whom dwells dishonor
prompted by recklessness.
He who is so, may he never
share my hearth!   410
may he never think my thoughts!

Is this a portent sent by God?
I cannot tell.
I know her. How can I say
that this is not Antigone?   415
Unhappy girl, child of unhappy Oedipus,
what is this?
Surely it is not you they bring here
as disobedient to the royal edict,
surely not you, taken in such folly.   420

SENTRY: She is the one who did the deed;
    we took her burying him. But where is Creon?
CHORUS: He is just coming from the house, when you most need him.
CREON: What is this? What has happened that I come
    so opportunely?   425
SENTRY: My lord, there is nothing
    that a man should swear he would never do.
    Second thoughts make liars of the first resolution.
    I would have vowed it would be long enough
    before I came again, lashed hence by your threats.   430
    But since the joy that comes past hope, and against all hope,
    is like no other pleasure in extent,
    I have come here, though I break my oath in coming.
    I bring this girl here who has been captured
    giving the grace of burial to the dead man.   435
    This time no lot chose me; this was my jackpot,
    and no one else's. Now, my lord, take her
    and as you please judge her and test her; I

am justly free and clear of all this trouble.

440 CREON: This girl—how did you take her and from where?

SENTRY: She was burying the man. Now you know all.

CREON: Do you know what you are saying? Do you mean it?

SENTRY: She is the one; I saw her burying
　　the dead man you forbade the burial of.

445 　　Now, do I speak plainly and clearly enough?

CREON: How was she seen? How was she caught in the act?

SENTRY: This is how it was. When we came there,
　　with those dreadful threats of yours upon us,
　　we brushed off all the dust that lay upon

450 　　the dead man's body, heedfully
　　leaving it moist and naked.
　　We sat on the brow of the hill, to windward,
　　that we might shun the smell of the corpse upon us.
　　Each of us wakefully urged his fellow

455 　　with torrents of abuse, not to be careless
　　in this work of ours. So it went on,
　　until in the midst of the sky the sun's bright circle
　　stood still; the heat was burning. Suddenly
　　a squall lifted out of the earth a storm of dust,

460 　　a trouble in the sky. It filled the plain,
　　ruining all the foliage of the wood
　　that was around it. The great empty air
　　was filled with it. We closed our eyes, enduring
　　this plague sent by the gods. When at long last

465 　　we were quit of it, why, then we saw the girl.

　　She was crying out with the shrill cry
　　of an embittered bird
　　that sees its nest robbed of its nestlings
　　and the bed empty. So, too, when she saw

470 　　the body stripped of its cover, she burst out in groans,
　　calling terrible curses on those that had done that deed;
　　and with her hands immediately
　　brought thirsty dust to the body; from a shapely brazen
　　urn, held high over it, poured a triple stream

475 　　of funeral offerings; and crowned the corpse.
　　When we saw that, we rushed upon her and
　　caught our quarry then and there, not a bit disturbed.
　　We charged her with what she had done, then and the first time.
　　She did not deny a word of it—to my joy,

480 　　but to my pain as well. It is most pleasant
　　to have escaped oneself out of such troubles
　　but painful to bring into it those whom we love.
　　However, it is but natural for me
　　to count all this less than my own escape.

485 CREON: You there, that turn your eyes upon the ground,

do you confess or deny what you have done?

ANTIGONE: Yes, I confess; I will not deny my deed.

CREON: [*To the* SENTRY.] You take yourself off where you like.
　　You are free of a heavy charge.
　　Now, Antigone, tell me shortly and to the point,　　　　490
　　did you know the proclamation against your action?

ANTIGONE: I knew it; of course I did. For it was public.

CREON: And did you dare to disobey that law?

ANTIGONE: Yes, it was not Zeus that made the proclamation;
　　nor did Justice, which lives with those below, enact　　　495
　　such laws as that, for mankind. I did not believe
　　your proclamation had such power to enable
　　one who will someday die to override
　　God's ordinances, unwritten and secure.
　　They are not of today and yesterday;　　　　　　　　500
　　they live forever; none knows when first they were.
　　These are the laws whose penalties I would not
　　incur from the gods, through fear of any man's temper.

　　I know that I will die—of course I do—
　　even if you had not doomed me by proclamation.　　　505
　　If I shall die before my time, I count that
　　a profit. How can such as I, that live
　　among such troubles, not find a profit in death?
　　So for such as me, to face such a fate as this
　　is pain that does not count. But if I dared to leave　　510
　　the dead man, my mother's son, dead and unburied,
　　that would have been real pain. The other is not.
　　Now, if you think me a fool to act like this,
　　perhaps it is a fool that judges so.

CHORUS: The savage spirit of a savage father　　　　　　515
　　shows itself in this girl. She does not know
　　how to yield to trouble.

CREON: I would have you know the most fanatic spirits
　　fall most of all. It is the toughest iron,
　　baked in the fire to hardness, you may see　　　　　520
　　most shattered, twisted, shivered to fragments.
　　I know hot horses are restrained
　　by a small curb. For he that is his neighbor's slave cannot
　　be high in spirit. This girl had learned her insolence
　　before this, when she broke the established laws.　　525
　　But here is still another insolence
　　in that she boasts of it, laughs at what she did.
　　I swear I am no man and she the man
　　if she can win this and not pay for it.
　　No; though she were my sister's child or closer　　　530
　　in blood than all that my hearth god acknowledges
　　as mine, neither she nor her sister should escape

the utmost sentence—death. For indeed I accuse her,
the sister, equally of plotting the burial.
535 Summon her. I saw her inside, just now,
crazy, distraught. When people plot
mischief in the dark, it is the mind which first
is convicted of deceit. But surely I hate indeed
the one that is caught in evil and then makes
540 that evil look like good.
ANTIGONE: Do you want anything
beyond my taking and my execution?
CREON: Oh, nothing! Once I have that I have everything.
ANTIGONE: Why do you wait, then? Nothing that you say
545 pleases me; God forbid it ever should.
So my words, too, naturally offend you.
Yet how could I win a greater share of glory
than putting my own brother in his grave?
All that are here would surely say that's true,
550 if fear did not lock their tongues up. A prince's power
is blessed in many things, not least in this,
that he can say and do whatever he likes.
CREON: You are alone among the people of Thebes
to see things in that way.
555 ANTIGONE: No, these do, too,
but keep their mouths shut for the fear of you.
CREON: Are you not ashamed to think so differently
from them?
ANTIGONE: There is nothing shameful in honoring my brother.
560 CREON: Was not he that died on the other side your brother?
ANTIGONE: Yes, indeed, of my own blood from father and mother.
CREON: Why then do you show a grace that must be impious
in *his* sight?
ANTIGONE: *That* other dead man
565 would never bear you witness in what you say.
CREON: Yes he would, if you put him only on equality
with one that was a desecrator.
ANTIGONE: It was his brother, not his slave, that died.
CREON: He died destroying the country the other defended.
570 ANTIGONE: The god of death demands these rites for both.
CREON: But the good man does not seek an *equal* share only,
with the bad.
ANTIGONE: Who knows
if in that other world this is true piety?
CREON: My enemy is still my enemy, even in death.
575 ANTIGONE: My nature is to join in love, not hate.
CREON: Go then to the world below, yourself, if you
must love. Love *them*. When I am alive no woman shall rule.
CHORUS: Here before the gates comes Ismene
shedding tears for the love of a brother.

A cloud over her brow casts shame   580
   on her flushed face, as the tears wet
   her fair cheeks.
CREON: You there, who lurked in my house, viper-like—
   secretly drawing its lifeblood; I never thought
   that I was raising two sources of destruction,   585
   two rebels against my throne. Come tell me now,
   will you, too, say you bore a hand in the burial
   or will you swear that you know nothing of it?
ISMENE: I did it, yes—if she will say I did it
   I bear my share in it, bear the guilt, too.   590
ANTIGONE: Justice will not allow you what you refused
   and I will have none of your partnership.
ISMENE: But in your troubles I am not ashamed
   to sail with you the sea of suffering.
ANTIGONE: Where the act was death, the dead are witnesses.   595
   I do not love a friend who loves in words.
ISMENE: Sister, do not dishonor me, denying me
   a common death with you, a common honoring
   of the dead man.
ANTIGONE: Don't die with me, nor make your own   600
   what you have never touched. I that die am enough.
ISMENE: What life is there for me, once I have lost you?
ANTIGONE: Ask Creon; all your care was on his behalf.
ISMENE: Why do you hurt me, when you gain nothing by it?
ANTIGONE: I am hurt by my own mockery—if I mock you.   605
ISMENE: Even now—what can I do to help you still?
ANTIGONE: Save yourself; I do not grudge you your escape.
ISMENE: I cannot bear it! Not even to share your death!
ANTIGONE: Life was your choice, and death was mine.
ISMENE: You cannot say I accepted that choice in silence.   610
ANTIGONE: You were right in the eyes of one party, I in the other.
ISMENE: Well then, the fault is equally between us.
ANTIGONE: Take heart; you are alive, but my life died
   long ago, to serve the dead.
CREON: Here are two girls; I think that one of them   615
   has suddenly lost her wits—the other was always so.
ISMENE: Yes, for, my lord, the wits that they are born with
   do not stay firm for the unfortunate.
   They go astray.
CREON: Certainly yours do,
   when you share troubles with the troublemaker.   620
ISMENE: What life can be mine alone without her?
CREON: Do not
   speak of *her*. *She* isn't, anymore.
ISMENE: Will you kill your son's wife to be?[1]

---

1. Antigone, betrothed to Creon's son Haemon.

CREON: Yes, there are other fields for him to plough.

625 ISMENE: Not with the mutual love of him and her.

CREON: I hate a bad wife for a son of mine.

ANTIGONE: Dear Haemon, how your father dishonors you.

CREON: There is too much of you—and of your marriage!

CHORUS: Will you rob your son of this girl?

630 CREON: Death—it is death that will stop the marriage for me.

CHORUS: Your decision it seems is taken: she shall die.

CREON: Both you and I have decided it. No more delay.

[*He turns to the* SERVANTS.]

Bring her inside, you. From this time forth,
these must be women, and not free to roam.
635 For even the stout of heart shrink when they see
the approach of death close to their lives.

CHORUS: Lucky are those whose lives
know no taste of sorrow.
But for those whose house has been shaken by God
640 there is never cessation of ruin;
it steals on generation after generation
within a breed. Even as the swell
is driven over the dark deep
by the fierce Thracian winds
645 I see the ancient evils of Labdacus' house[2]
are heaped on the evils of the dead.
No generation frees another, some god
strikes them down; there is no deliverance.
Here was the light of hope stretched
650 over the last roots of Oedipus' house,
and the bloody dust due to the gods below
has mowed it down—that and the folly of speech
and ruin's enchantment of the mind.

Your power, O Zeus, what sin of man can limit?
655 All-aging sleep does not overtake it,
nor the unwearied months of the gods; and you,
for whom time brings no age,
you hold the glowing brightness of Olympus.

For the future near and far,
660 and the past, this law holds good:
nothing very great
comes to the life of mortal man
without ruin to accompany it.
For Hope, widely wandering, comes to many of mankind
665 as a blessing,

---

2. Theban royal lineage that included Labdacus; his son, Laïus; and his grandson, Oedipus.

but to many as the deceiver,
using light-minded lusts;
she comes to him that knows nothing
till he burns his foot in the glowing fire.
With wisdom has someone declared   670
a word of distinction:
that evil seems good to one whose mind
the god leads to ruin,
and but for the briefest moment of time
is his life outside of calamity.   675
Here is Haemon, youngest of your sons.
Does he come grieving
for the fate of his bride to be,
in agony at being cheated of his marriage?
CREON: Soon we will know that better than the prophets.   680
My son, can it be that you have not heard
of my final decision on your betrothed?
Can you have come here in your fury against your father?
Or have I your love still, no matter what I do?
HAEMON: Father, I am yours; with your excellent judgment   685
you lay the right before me, and I shall follow it.
No marriage will ever be so valued by me
as to override the goodness of your leadership.
CREON: Yes, my son, this should always be
in your very heart, that everything else   690
shall be second to your father's decision.
It is for this that fathers pray to have
obedient sons begotten in their halls,
that they may requite with ill their father's enemy
and honor his friend no less than he would himself.   695
If a man have sons that are no use to him,
what can one say of him but that he has bred
so many sorrows to himself, laughter to his enemies?
Do not, my son, banish your good sense
through pleasure in a woman, since you know   700
that the embrace grows cold
when an evil woman shares your bed and home.
What greater wound can there be than a false friend?
No. Spit on her, throw her out like an enemy,
this girl, to marry someone in Death's house.   705
I caught her openly in disobedience
alone out of all this city and I shall not make
myself a liar in the city's sight. No, I will kill her.
So let her cry if she will on the Zeus of kinship;
for if I rear those of my race and breeding   710
to be rebels, surely I will do so with those outside it.
For he who is in his household a good man
will be found a just man, too, in the city.
But he that breaches the law or does it violence

715   or thinks to dictate to those who govern him
         shall never have my good word.
         The man the city sets up in authority
         must be obeyed in small things and in just
         but also in their opposites.
720   I am confident such a man of whom I speak
         will be a good ruler, and willing to be well ruled.
         He will stand on his country's side, faithful and just,
         in the storm of battle. There is nothing worse
         than disobedience to authority.
725   It destroys cities, it demolishes homes;
         it breaks and routs one's allies. Of successful lives
         the most of them are saved by discipline.
         So we must stand on the side of what is orderly;
         we cannot give victory to a woman.
730   If we must accept defeat, let it be from a man;
         we must not let people say that a woman beat us.
     CHORUS: We think, if we are not victims of Time the Thief,
         that you speak intelligently of what you speak.
     HAEMON: Father, the natural sense that the gods breed
735   in men is surely the best of their possessions.
         I certainly could not declare you wrong—
         may I never know how to do so!—Still there might
         be something useful that some other than you might think.
         It is natural for me to be watchful on your behalf
740   concerning what all men say or do or find to blame.
         Your face is terrible to a simple citizen;
         it frightens him from words you dislike to hear.
         But what *I* can hear, in the dark, are things like these:
         the city mourns for this girl; they think she is dying
745   most wrongly and most undeservedly
         of all womenkind, for the most glorious acts.
         Here is one who would not leave her brother unburied,
         a brother who had fallen in bloody conflict,
         to meet his end by greedy dogs or by
750   the bird that chanced that way. Surely what she merits
         is golden honor, isn't it? That's the dark rumor
         that spreads in secret. Nothing I own
         I value more highly, father, than your success.
         What greater distinction can a son have than the glory
755   of a successful father, and for a father
         the distinction of successful children?
         Do not bear this single habit of mind, to think
         that what you say and nothing else is true.
         A man who thinks that he alone is right,
760   or what he says, or what he *is* himself,
         unique, such men, when opened up, are seen
         to be quite empty. For a man, though he be wise,

it is no shame to learn—learn many things,
and not maintain his views too rigidly.
You notice how by streams in wintertime   765
the trees that yield preserve their branches safely,
but those that fight the tempest perish utterly.
The man who keeps the sheet[3] of his sail tight
and never slackens capsizes his boat
and makes the rest of his trip keel uppermost.   770
Yield something of your anger, give way a little.
If a much younger man, like me, may have
a judgment, I would say it were far better
to be one altogether wise by nature, but,
as things incline not to be so, then it is good   775
also to learn from those who advise well.
CHORUS: My lord, if he says anything to the point,
you should learn from him, and you, too, Haemon,
learn from your father. Both of you
have spoken well.   780
CREON: Should we that are my age learn wisdom
from young men such as he is?
HAEMON: Not learn injustice, certainly. If I am young,
do not look at my years but what I do.
CREON: Is what you do to have respect for rebels?
HAEMON: I   785
would not urge you to be scrupulous
towards the wicked.
CREON: Is *she* not tainted by the disease of wickedness?
HAEMON: The entire people of Thebes says no to that.
CREON: Should the city tell me how I am to rule them?   790
HAEMON: Do you see what a young man's words these are of yours?
CREON: Must I rule the land by someone else's judgment
rather than my own?
HAEMON: There is no city
possessed by one man only.
CREON: Is not the city thought to be the ruler's?   795
HAEMON: You would be a fine dictator of a desert.
CREON: It seems this boy is on the woman's side.
HAEMON: If you are a woman—my care is all for you.
CREON: You villain, to bandy words with your own father!
HAEMON: I see your acts as mistaken and unjust.   800
CREON: Am I mistaken, reverencing my own office?
HAEMON: There is no reverence in trampling on God's honor.
CREON: Your nature is vile, in yielding to a woman.
HAEMON: You will not find me yield to what is shameful.
CREON: At least, your argument is all for her.   805
HAEMON: Yes, and for you and me—and for the gods below.

---

3. Rope attached to the corner of a sail to hold it at the proper angle to the wind.

CREON: You will never marry her while her life lasts.

HAEMON: Then she must die—and dying destroy another.

CREON: Has your daring gone so far, to threaten me?

810 HAEMON: What threat is it to speak against empty judgments?

CREON: Empty of sense yourself, you will regret
    your schooling of me in sense.

HAEMON: If you were not
    my father, I would say you are insane.

CREON: You woman's slave, do not try to wheedle me.

815 HAEMON: You want to talk but never to hear and listen.

CREON: Is that so? By the heavens above you will not—
    be sure of that—get off scot-free, insulting,
    abusing me.

[*He speaks to the* SERVANTS.]

                 You people bring out this creature,
    this hated creature, that she may die before

820   his very eyes, right now, next her would-be husband.

HAEMON: Not at my side! Never think that! She will not
    die by my side. But you will never again
    set eyes upon my face. Go then and rage
    with such of your friends as are willing to endure it.

825 CHORUS: The man is gone, my lord, quick in his anger.
    A young man's mind is fierce when he is hurt.

CREON: Let him go, and do and think things superhuman.
    But these two girls he shall not save from death.

CHORUS: Both of them? Do you mean to kill them both?

830 CREON: No, not the one that didn't do anything.
    You are quite right there.

CHORUS: And by what form of death do you mean to kill her?

CREON: I will bring her where the path is loneliest,
    and hide her alive in a rocky cavern there.

835   I'll give just enough of food as shall suffice
    for a bare expiation, that the city may avoid pollution.
    In that place she shall call on Hades, god of death,
    in her prayers. That god only she reveres.
    Perhaps she will win from him escape from death

840   or at least in that last moment will recognize
    her honoring of the dead is labor lost.

CHORUS: Love undefeated in the fight,
    Love that makes havoc of possessions,
    Love who lives at night in a young girl's soft cheeks,

845   Who travels over sea, or in huts in the countryside—
    there is no god able to escape you
    nor anyone of men, whose life is a day only,
    and whom you possess is mad.

    You wrench the minds of just men to injustice,

850   to their disgrace; this conflict among kinsmen

it is you who stirred to turmoil.
The winner is desire. She gleaming kindles
from the eyes of the girl good to bed.
Love shares the throne with the great powers that rule.
For the golden Aphrodite[4] holds her play there   855
and then no one can overcome her.

Here I too am borne out of the course of lawfulness
when I see these things, and I cannot control
the springs of my tears
when I see Antigone making her way   860
to her bed—but the bed
that is rest for everyone.

ANTIGONE: You see me, you people of my country,
as I set out on my last road of all,
looking for the last time on this light of this sun—   865
never again. I am alive but Hades who gives sleep to everyone
is leading me to the shores of Acheron,[5]
though I have known nothing of marriage songs
nor the chant that brings the bride to bed.
My husband is to be the Lord of Death.   870

CHORUS: Yes, you go to the place where the dead are hidden,
but you go with distinction and praise.
You have not been stricken by wasting sickness;
you have not earned the wages of the sword;
it was your own choice and alone among mankind   875
you will descend, alive,
to that world of death.

ANTIGONE: But indeed I have heard of the saddest of deaths—
of the Phrygian stranger,[6] daughter of Tantalus,
whom the rocky growth subdued, like clinging ivy.   880
The rains never leave her, the snow never fails,
as she wastes away. That is how men tell the story.
From streaming eyes her tears wet the crags;
most like to her the god brings me to rest.

CHORUS: Yes, but she was a god, and god born,   885
and you are mortal and mortal born.
Surely it is great renown
for a woman that dies, that in life and death
her lot is a lot shared with demigods.

ANTIGONE: You mock me. In the name of our fathers' gods   890
why do you not wait till I am gone to insult me?
Must you do it face to face?
My city! Rich citizens of my city!

4. Goddess of love and beauty.
5. River in Hades, the underworld.
6. Niobe, whose children were slain because of her boastfulness and who was herself turned to stone
on Mount Sipylus. Her tears became the mountain's streams.

You springs of Dirce, you holy groves of Thebes,
895   famed for its chariots! I would still have you as my witnesses,
with what dry-eyed friends, under what laws
I make my way to my prison sealed like a tomb.
Pity me. Neither among the living nor the dead
do I have a home in common—
900   neither with the living nor the dead.

CHORUS: You went to the extreme of daring
and against the high throne of Justice
you fell, my daughter, grievously.
But perhaps it was for some ordeal of your father
905   that you are paying requital.

ANTIGONE: You have touched the most painful of my cares—
the pity for my father, ever reawakened,
and the fate of all of our race, the famous Labdacids;
the doomed self-destruction of my mother's bed
910   when she slept with her own son,
my father.
What parents I was born of, God help me!
To them I am going to share their home,
the curse on me, too, and unmarried.
915   Brother, it was a luckless marriage you made,
and dying killed my life.

CHORUS: There *is* a certain reverence for piety.
But for him in authority,
he cannot see that authority defied;
920   it is your own self-willed temper
that has destroyed you.

ANTIGONE: No tears for me, no friends, no marriage. Brokenhearted
I am led along the road ready before me.
I shall never again be suffered
925   to look on the holy eye of the day.
But my fate claims no tears—
no friend cries for me.

CREON: [*To the* SERVANTS.] Don't you know that weeping and wailing before death
would never stop if one is allowed to weep and wail?
930   Lead her away at once. Enfold her
in that rocky tomb of hers—as I told you to.
There leave her alone, solitary,
to die if she so wishes
or live a buried life in such a home;
935   we are guiltless in respect of her, this girl.
But living above, among the rest of us, this life
she shall certainly lose.

ANTIGONE: Tomb, bridal chamber, prison forever
dug in rock, it is to you I am going
940   to join my people, that great number that have died,

whom in their death Persephone[7] received.
I am the last of them and I go down
in the worst death of all—for I have not lived
the due term of my life. But when I come
to that other world my hope is strong   945
that my coming will be welcome to my father,
and dear to you, my mother, and dear to you,
my brother deeply loved. For when you died,
with my own hands I washed and dressed you all,
and poured the lustral offerings on your graves.   950
And now, Polyneices, it was for such care of your body
that I have earned these wages.
Yet those who think rightly will think I did right
in honoring you. Had I been a mother
of children, and my husband been dead and rotten,   955
I would not have taken this weary task upon me
against the will of the city. What law backs me
when I say this? I will tell you:
If my husband were dead, I might have had another,
and child from another man, if I lost the first.   960
But when father and mother both were hidden in death
no brother's life would bloom for me again.
That is the law under which I gave you precedence,
my dearest brother, and that is why Creon thinks me
wrong, even a criminal, and now takes me   965
by the hand and leads me away,
unbedded, without bridal, without share
in marriage and in nurturing of children;
as lonely as you see me; without friends;
with fate against me I go to the vault of death   970
while still alive. What law of God have I broken?
Why should I still look to the gods in my misery?
Whom should I summon as ally? For indeed
because of piety I was called impious.
If this proceeding is good in the gods' eyes   975
I shall know my sin, once I have suffered.
But if Creon and his people are the wrongdoers
let their suffering be no worse than the injustice
they are meting out to me.

CHORUS: It is the same blasts, the tempests of the soul,   980
    possess her.

CREON: Then for this her guards,
    who are so slow, will find themselves in trouble.

ANTIGONE: [*Cries out.*] Oh, that word has come
    very close to death.

---

7. Abducted by Pluto (known to the Greeks as Hades), god of the underworld, who made her his queen.

985 CREON: I will not comfort you
        with hope that the sentence will not be accomplished.
  ANTIGONE: O my father's city, in Theban land,
        O gods that sired my race,
        I am led away, I have no more stay.
990   Look on me, princes of Thebes,
        the last remnant of the old royal line;
        see what I suffer and who makes me suffer
        because I gave reverence to what claims reverence.
  CHORUS: Danae suffered, too, when, her beauty lost, she gave
995   the light of heaven in exchange for brassbound walls,
        and in the tomb-like cell was she hidden and held;
        yet she was honored in her breeding, child,
        and she kept, as guardian, the seed of Zeus
        that came to her in a golden shower.[8]
1000   But there is some terrible power in destiny
        and neither wealth nor war
        nor tower nor black ships, beaten by the sea,
        can give escape from it.

        The hot-tempered son of Dryas,[9] the Edonian king,
1005   in fury mocked Dionysus,
        who then held him in restraint
        in a rocky dungeon.
        So the terrible force and flower of his madness
        drained away. He came to know the god
1010   whom in frenzy he had touched with his mocking tongue,
        when he would have checked the inspired women
        and the fire of Dionysus,
        when he provoked the Muses[1] that love the lyre.
        By the black rocks, dividing the sea in two,
1015   are the shores of the Bosporus, Thracian Salmydessus.[2]
        There the god of war who lives near the city
        saw the terrible blinding wound
        dealt by his savage wife
        on Phineus' two sons.[3]
1020   She blinded and tore with the points of her shuttle,
        and her bloodied hands, those eyes
        that else would have looked on her vengefully.
        As they wasted away, they lamented

---

8. Danae was locked away because it was prophesized that her son would kill her father. Zeus entered her cell as a shower of gold, impregnated her, and thus fathered Perseus, the child who fulfilled the prophecy.

9. Stricken with madness by Dionysus.

1. Nine sister goddesses of poetry, music, and the arts.

2. City in the land of Thrace, in ancient times erroneously believed to lie on the Bosporus, the strait separating Europe and Asia at the outlet of the Black Sea.

3. King Phineus's second wife blinded the children of his first wife, whom Phineus had imprisoned in a cave.

their unhappy fate that they were doomed
to be born of a mother cursed in her marriage.   1025
She traced her descent from the seed
of the ancient Erechtheidae.
In far-distant caves she was raised
among her father's storms, that child of Boreas[4]
quick as a horse, over the steep hills,   1030
a daughter of the gods.
But, my child, the long-lived Fates[5]
bore hard upon her, too.

[*Enter* TEIRESIAS, *the blind prophet, led by a* BOY.]

TEIRESIAS: My lords of Thebes, we have come here together,
one pair of eyes serving us both. For the blind   1035
such must be the way of going, by a guide's leading.
CREON: What is the news, my old Teiresias?
TEIRESIAS: I will tell you; and you, listen to the prophet.
CREON: Never in the past have I turned from your advice.
TEIRESIAS: And so you have steered well the ship of state.   1040
CREON: I have benefited and can testify to that.
TEIRESIAS: Then realize you are on the razor edge
of danger.
CREON: What can that be? I shudder to hear those words.
TEIRESIAS: When you learn the signs recognized by my art   1045
you will understand.
I sat at my ancient place of divination
for watching the birds, where every bird finds shelter;
and I heard an unwonted voice among them;
they were horribly distressed, and screamed unmeaningly.   1050
I knew they were tearing each other murderously;
the beating of their wings was a clear sign.
I was full of fear; at once on all the altars,
as they were fully kindled, I tasted the offerings,
but the god of fire refused to burn from the sacrifice,   1055
and from the thighbones a dark stream of moisture
oozed from the embers, smoked and sputtered.
The gall bladder burst and scattered to the air
and the streaming thighbones lay exposed
from the fat wrapped round them—   1060
so much I learned from this boy here,
the fading prophecies of a rite that failed.
This boy here is my guide, as I am others'.
This is the city's sickness—and your plans are the cause of it.
For our altars and our sacrificial hearths   1065
are filled with the carrion meat of birds and dogs,

4. God of the cold north wind, who sometimes took the form of a stallion.
5. Supernatural forces, usually represented as three elderly women, who determine the quality and length of life.

torn from the flesh of Oedipus' poor son.
So the gods will not take our prayers or sacrifice
nor yet the flame from the thighbones, and no bird
1070   cries shrill and clear, so glutted
are they with fat of the blood of the killed man.
Reflect on these things, son. All men
can make mistakes; but, once mistaken,
a man is no longer stupid nor accursed
1075   who, having fallen on ill, tries to cure that ill,
not taking a fine undeviating stand.
It is obstinacy that convicts of folly.
Yield to the dead man; do not stab him—
now he is gone—what bravery is this,
1080   to inflict another death upon the dead?
I mean you well and speak well for your good.
It is never sweeter to learn from a good counselor
than when he counsels to your benefit.
CREON: Old man, you are all archers, and I am your mark.
1085   I must be tried by your prophecies as well.
By the breed of you I have been bought and sold
and made a merchandise, for ages now.
But I tell you: make your profit from silver-gold
from Sardis[6] and the gold from India
1090   if you will. But this dead man you shall not hide
in a grave, not though the eagles of Zeus should bear
the carrion, snatching it to the throne of Zeus itself.
Even so, I shall not so tremble at the pollution
to let you bury him.
                     No, I am certain
1095   no human has the power to pollute the gods.
They fall, you old Teiresias, those men,
—so very clever—in a bad fall whenever
they eloquently speak vile words for profit.
TEIRESIAS: I wonder if there's a man who dares consider—
1100 CREON: What do you mean? What sort of generalization
is this talk of yours?
TEIRESIAS: How much the best of possessions is the ability
to listen to wise advice?
CREON: As I should imagine that the worst
1105   injury must be native stupidity.
TEIRESIAS: Now that is exactly where your mind is sick.
CREON: I do not like to answer a seer with insults.
TEIRESIAS: But you do, when you say my prophecies are lies.
CREON: Well,

6. Capital of the ancient kingdom of Lydia, part of modern-day Turkey, and an important trading center, famed for its wealth.

the whole breed of prophets certainly loves money.   1110
TEIRESIAS: And the breed that comes from princes loves to take
    advantage—base advantage.
CREON: Do you realize
    you are speaking in such terms of your own prince?
TEIRESIAS: I know. But it is through me you have saved the city.
CREON: You are a wise prophet, but what you love is wrong.   1115
TEIRESIAS: You will force me to declare what should be hidden
    in my own heart.
CREON: Out with it—
    but only if your words are not for gain.
TEIRESIAS: They won't be for *your* gain—that I am sure of.
CREON: But realize you will not make a merchandise   1120
    of my decisions.
TEIRESIAS: And you must realize
    that you will not outlive many cycles more
    of this swift sun before you give in exchange
    one of your own loins bred, a corpse for a corpse,
    for you have thrust one that belongs above   1125
    below the earth, and bitterly dishonored
    a living soul by lodging her in the grave;
    while one that belonged indeed to the underworld
    gods you have kept on this earth without due share
    of rites of burial, of due funeral offerings,   1130
    a corpse unhallowed. With all of this you, Creon,
    have nothing to do, nor have the gods above.
    These acts of yours are violence, on your part.
    And in requital the avenging Spirits
    of Death itself and the gods' Furies shall   1135
    after *your* deeds, lie in ambush for you, and
    in their hands you shall be taken cruelly.
    Now, look at this and tell me I was bribed
    to say it! The delay will not be long
    before the cries of mourning in your house,   1140
    of men and women. All the cities will stir in hatred
    against you, because their sons in mangled shreds
    received their burial rites from dogs, from wild beasts
    or when some bird of the air brought a vile stink
    to each city that contained the hearths of the dead.   1145
    These are the arrows that archer-like I launched—
    you vexed me so to anger—at your heart.
    You shall not escape their sting. You, boy,
    lead me away to my house, so he may discharge
    his anger on younger men; so may he come to know   1150
    to bear a quieter tongue in his head and a better
    mind than that now he carries in him.
CHORUS: That was a terrible prophecy, my lord.
    The man has gone. Since these hairs of mine grew white

1155   from the black they once were, he has never spoken
   a word of a lie to our city.
  CREON: I know, I know.
   My mind is all bewildered. To yield is terrible.
   But by opposition to destroy my very being
1160   with a self-destructive curse must also be reckoned
   in what is terrible.
  CHORUS: You need good counsel, son of Menoeceus,
   and need to take it.
  CREON: What must I do, then? Tell me; I shall agree.
1165   CHORUS: The girl—go now and bring her up from her cave,
   and for the exposed dead man, give him his burial.
  CREON: That is really your advice? You would have me yield.
  CHORUS: And quickly as you may, my lord. Swift harms
   sent by the gods cut off the paths of the foolish.
1170   CREON: Oh, it is hard; I must give up what my heart
   would have me do. But it is ill to fight
   against what must be.
  CHORUS: Go now, and do this;
   do not give the task to others.
1175   CREON: I will go,
   just as I am. Come, servants, all of you;
   take axes in your hands; away with you
   to the place you see, there.
   For my part, since my intention is so changed,
1180   as I bound her myself, myself will free her.
   I am afraid it may be best, in the end
   of life, to have kept the old accepted laws.
  CHORUS: You of many names,[7] glory of the Cadmeian
   bride, breed of loud thundering Zeus;
1185   you who watch over famous Italy;
   you who rule where all are welcome in Eleusis;
   in the sheltered plains of Deo—
   O Bacchus that dwells in Thebes,
   the mother city of Bacchanals,
1190   by the flowing stream of Ismenus,
   in the ground sown by the fierce dragon's teeth.

   You are he on whom the murky gleam of torches glares,
   above the twin peaks of the crag
   where come the Corycean nymphs
1195   to worship you, the Bacchanals;
   and the stream of Castalia has seen you, too;
   and you are he that the ivy-clad
   slopes of Nisaean hills,
   and the green shore ivy-clustered,

---

7. Refers to Dionysus, known also as Bacchus (especially to the later Romans); son of Zeus and Semele, a mortal princess of Thebes. As god of wine, Dionysus presided over frenzied rites known as Bacchanals.

sent to watch over the roads of Thebes,   1200
where the immortal Evoe chant[8] rings out.

It is Thebes which you honor most of all cities,
you and your mother both,
she who died by the blast of Zeus' thunderbolt.
And now when the city, with all its folk,   1205
is gripped by a violent plague,
come with healing foot, over the slopes of Parnassus,[9]
over the moaning strait.
You lead the dance of the fire-breathing stars,
you are master of the voices of the night.   1210
True-born child of Zeus, appear,
my lord, with your Thyiad attendants,
who in frenzy all night long
dance in your house, Iacchus,
dispenser of gifts.   1215

MESSENGER: You who live by the house of Cadmus and Amphion,[1]
hear me. There is no condition of man's life
that stands secure. As such I would not
praise it or blame. It is chance that sets upright;
it is chance that brings down the lucky and the unlucky,   1220
each in his turn. For men, that belong to death,
there is no prophet of established things.
Once Creon was a man worthy of envy—
of my envy, at least. For he saved this city
of Thebes from her enemies, and attained   1225
the throne of the land, with all a king's power.
He guided it right. His race bloomed
with good children. But when a man forfeits joy
I do not count his life as life, but only
a life trapped in a corpse.   1230
Be rich within your house, yes greatly rich,
if so you will, and live in a prince's style.
If the gladness of these things is gone, I would not
give the shadow of smoke for the rest,
as against joy.   1235

CHORUS: What is the sorrow of our princes
of which you are the messenger?

MESSENGER: Death; and the living are guilty of their deaths.

CHORUS: But who is the murderer? Who the murdered? Tell us.

MESSENGER: Haemon is dead; the hand that shed his blood   1240
was his very own.

CHORUS: Truly his own hand? Or his father's?

---

8. Come forth, come forth!
9. Mountain in central Greece sacred to Apollo, Dionysus, and the Muses; Apollo's shrine, Delphi,
lies at the foot of Parnassus.
1. Alternative name for Thebes.

MESSENGER: His own hand, in his anger
　　　against his father for a murder.
1245 CHORUS: Prophet, how truly you have made good your word!
MESSENGER: These things are so; you may debate the rest.
　　　Here I see Creon's wife Eurydice
　　　approaching. Unhappy woman!
　　　Does she come from the house as hearing about her son
1250　　　or has she come by chance?
EURYDICE: I heard your words, all you men of Thebes, as I
　　　was going out to greet Pallas[2] with my prayers.
　　　I was just drawing back the bolts of the gate
　　　to open it when a cry struck through my ears
1255　　　telling of my household's ruin. I fell backward
　　　in terror into the arms of my servants; I fainted.
　　　But tell me again, what is the story? I
　　　will hear it as one who is no stranger to sorrow.
MESSENGER: Dear mistress, I will tell you, for I was there,
1260　　　and I will leave out no word of the truth.
　　　Why should I comfort you and then tomorrow
　　　be proved a liar? The truth is always best.
　　　I followed your husband, at his heels, to the end of the plain
　　　where Polyneices' body still lay unpitied,
1265　　　and torn by dogs. We prayed to Hecate, goddess
　　　of the crossroads, and also to Pluto[3]
　　　that they might restrain their anger and turn kind.
　　　And him we washed with sacred lustral water
　　　and with fresh-cut boughs we burned what was left of him
1270　　　and raised a high mound of his native earth;
　　　then we set out again for the hollowed rock,
　　　death's stone bridal chamber for the girl.
　　　Someone then heard a voice of bitter weeping
　　　while we were still far off, coming from that unblest room.
1275　　　The man came to tell our master Creon of it.
　　　As the king drew nearer, there swarmed about him
　　　a cry of misery but no clear words.
　　　He groaned and in an anguished mourning voice
　　　cried "Oh, am I a true prophet? Is this the road
1280　　　that I must travel, saddest of all my wayfaring?
　　　It is my son's voice that haunts my ear. Servants,
　　　get closer, quickly. Stand around the tomb
　　　and look. There is a gap there where the stones
　　　have been wrenched away; enter there, by the very mouth,
1285　　　and see whether I recognize the voice of Haemon
　　　or if the gods deceive me." On the command
　　　of our despairing master we went to look.

2. Athena, goddess of wisdom.
3. King of the underworld, known to the Greeks as Hades. *Hecate*: goddess of witchcraft.

In the furthest part of the tomb we saw her, hanging
by her neck. She had tied a noose of muslin on it.
Haemon's hands were about her waist embracing her,   1290
while he cried for the loss of his bride gone to the dead,
and for all his father had done, and his own sad love.
When Creon saw him he gave a bitter cry,
went in and called to him with a groan: "Poor son!
what have you done? What can you have meant?   1295
What happened to destroy you? Come out, I pray you!"
The boy glared at him with savage eyes, and then
spat in his face, without a word of answer.
He drew his double-hilted sword. As his father
ran to escape him, Haemon failed to strike him,   1300
and the poor wretch in anger at himself
leaned on his sword and drove it halfway in,
into his ribs. Then he folded the girl to him,
in his arms, while he was conscious still,
and gasping poured a sharp stream of bloody drops   1305
on her white cheeks. There they lie,
the dead upon the dead. So he has won
the pitiful fulfillment of his marriage
within death's house. In this human world he has shown
how the wrong choice in plans is for a man   1310
his greatest evil.
CHORUS: What do you make of this? My lady is gone,
    without a word of good or bad.
MESSENGER: I, too,
    am lost in wonder. I am inclined to hope
    that hearing of her son's death she could not   1315
    open her sorrow to the city, but chose rather
    within her house to lay upon her maids
    the mourning for the household grief. Her judgment
    is good; she will not make any false step.
CHORUS: I do not know. To me this over-heavy silence   1320
    seems just as dangerous as much empty wailing.
MESSENGER: I will go in and learn if in her passionate
    heart she keeps hidden some secret purpose.
    You are right; there is sometimes danger in too much silence.
CHORUS: Here comes our king himself. He bears in his hands   1325
    a memorial all too clear;
    it is a ruin of none other's making,
    purely his own if one dare to say that.
CREON: The mistakes of a blinded man
    are themselves rigid and laden with death.   1330
    You look at us the killer and the killed
    of the one blood. Oh, the awful blindness
    of those plans of mine. My son, you were so young,
    so young to die. You were freed from the bonds of life

1335   through no folly of your own—only through mine.

CHORUS: I think you have learned justice—but too late.

CREON: Yes, I have learned it to my bitterness. At this moment
      God has sprung on my head with a vast weight
      and struck me down. He shook me in my savage ways;
1340   he has overturned my joy, has trampled it,
      underfoot. The pains men suffer
      are pains indeed.

SECOND MESSENGER: My lord, you have troubles and a store besides;
      some are there in your hands, but there are others
1345   you will surely see when you come to your house.

CREON: What trouble can there be beside these troubles?

SECOND MESSENGER: The queen is dead. She was indeed true mother
      of the dead son. She died, poor lady,
      by recent violence upon herself.

1350 CREON: Haven of death, you can never have enough.
      Why, why do you destroy me?
      You messenger, who have brought me bitter news,
      what is this tale you tell?
      It is a dead man that you kill again—
1355   what new message of yours is this, boy?
      Is this new slaughter of a woman
      a doom to lie on the pile of the dead?

CHORUS: You can see. It is no longer
      hidden in a corner.

[*By some stage device, perhaps the so-called eccyclema,*[4] *the inside of the palace is shown, with the body of the dead* QUEEN.]

1360 CREON: Here is yet another horror
      for my unhappy eyes to see.
      What doom still waits for me?
      I have but now taken in my arms my son,
      and again I look upon another dead face.
1365   Poor mother and poor son!

SECOND MESSENGER: She stood at the altar, and with keen whetted knife
      she suffered her darkening eyes to close.
      First she cried in agony recalling the noble fate of Megareus,[5]
      who died before all this,
1370   and then for the fate of this son; and in the end
      she cursed you for the evil you had done
      in killing her sons.

CREON: I am distracted with fear. Why does not someone
      strike a two-edged sword right through me?
1375   I am dissolved in an agony of misery.

---

4. Wheeled platform rolled forward onto the stage to depict interior scenes; often used in tragedies to reveal dead bodies.

5. Another son of Creon who died defending Thebes.

SECOND MESSENGER: You were indeed accused
    by her that is dead
    of Haemon's and of Megareus' death.
CREON: By what kind of violence did she find her end?
SECOND MESSENGER: Her own hand struck her to the entrails   1380
    when she heard of her son's lamentable death.
CREON: These acts can never be made to fit another
    to free me from the guilt. It was I that killed her.
    Poor wretch that I am, I say it is true!
    Servants, lead me away, quickly, quickly.   1385
    I am no more a live man than one dead.
CHORUS: What you say is for the best—if there be a best
    in evil such as this. For the shortest way
    is best with troubles that lie at our feet.
CREON: O, let it come, let it come,   1390
    that best of fates that waits on my last day.
    Surely best fate of all. Let it come, let it come!
    That I may never see one more day's light!
CHORUS: These things are for the future. We must deal
    with what impends. What in the future is to care for   1395
    rests with those whose duty it is
    to care for them.
CREON: At least, all that *I* want
    is in that prayer of mine.
CHORUS: Pray for no more at all. For what is destined   1400
    for us, men mortal, there is no escape.
CREON: Lead me away, a vain silly man
    who killed you, son, and you, too, lady.
    I did not mean to, but I did.
    I do not know where to turn my eyes   1405
    to look to, for support.
    Everything in my hands is crossed. A most unwelcome fate
    has leaped upon me.
CHORUS: Wisdom is far the chief element in happiness
    and, secondly, no irreverence towards the gods.   1410
    But great words of haughty men exact
    in retribution blows as great
    and in old age teach wisdom.

    THE END

c. 441 BCE

CRITICAL EXCERPTS

RICHARD C. JEBB

From the introduction to The *Antigone* of Sophocles (1902)[1]

The issue defined in the opening scene,—the conflict of divine with human law,—remains the central interest throughout. The action, so simple in plan, is varied by masterly character-drawing, both in the two principal figures, and in those lesser persons who contribute gradations of light and shade to the picture. There is no halting in the march of the drama; at each successive step we become more and more keenly interested to see how this great conflict is to end; and when the tragic climax is reached, it is worthy of such a progress.

The simplicity of the plot is due to the clearness with which two principles are opposed to each other. *Creon represents the duty of obeying the State's laws; Antigone, the duty of listening to the private conscience.* The definiteness and the power with which the play puts the case on each side are conclusive proofs that the question had assumed a distinct shape before the poet's mind. It is the only instance in which a Greek play has for its central theme a practical problem of conduct, involving issues, moral and political, which might be discussed on similar grounds in any age and in any country of the world. Greek tragedy, owing partly to the limitations which it placed on detail, was better suited than modern drama to raise such a question in a general form. The *Antigone*, indeed, raises the question in a form as nearly abstract as is compatible with the nature of drama. The case of Antigone is a thoroughly typical one for the private conscience, because the particular thing which she believes that she ought to do was, in itself, a thing which every Greek of that age recognised as a most sacred duty,—viz.,[2] to render burial rites to kinsfolk. This advantage was not devised by Sophocles; it came to him as part of the story which he was to dramatise; but it forms an additional reason for thinking that, when he dramatised that story in the precise manner which he has chosen, he had a consciously dialectical purpose. Such a purpose was wholly consistent, in this instance, with the artist's first aim,—to produce a work of art. It is because Creon and Antigone are so human that the controversy which they represent becomes so vivid.

But how did Sophocles intend us to view the result? What is the drift of the words at the end, which say that "wisdom is the supreme part of happiness"? If this wisdom, or prudence [. . .], means, generally, the observance of due limit, may not the suggested moral be that both the parties to the conflict were censurable? As Creon overstepped the due limit when, by his edict, he infringed the divine law, so Antigone also overstepped it when she defied the edict. The drama would thus be a conflict between two persons, each of whom defends an intrinsically sound principle, but defends it in a mistaken way; and both persons are therefore punished. This view, of which Boeckh[3] is the chief representative, has found several supporters. Among them is Hegel:—"In the view of the Eter-

---

1. Richard C. Jebb, Introduction. *The* Antigone *of Sophocles*. 1902, abridged by E. S. Shuckburgh. Cambridge UP, 1971, pp. xi–xxx. Unless otherwise indicated, all footnotes have been added by the editor.
2. Namely (abbreviation of the Latin *videlicet*).
3. August Boeckh (1785–1867), German classical scholar.

nal Justice, both were wrong, because they were one-sided, but at the same time both were right."[4]

Or does the poet rather intend us to feel that Antigone is wholly in the right,—*i.e.*, that nothing of which the human lawgiver could complain in her was of a moment's account beside the supreme duty which she was fulfilling;— and that Creon was wholly in the wrong,—*i.e.*, that the intrinsically sound maxims of government on which he relies lose all validity when opposed to the higher law which he was breaking? If that was the poet's meaning, then the "wisdom" taught by the issue of the drama means the sense which duly subordinates human to divine law,—teaching that, if the two come into conflict, human law must yield.

A careful study of the play itself will suffice (I think) to show that the second of these two views is the true one. Sophocles has allowed Creon to put his case ably, and (in a measure from which an inferior artist might have shrunk) he has been content to make Antigone merely a nobly heroic woman, not a being exempt from human passion and human weakness; but none the less does he mean us to feel that, in this controversy, the right is wholly with her, and the wrong wholly with her judge.

MAURICE BOWRA

From Sophoclean Tragedy (1944)[1]

Modern critics who do not share Sophocles' conviction about the paramount duty of burying the dead and who attach more importance than he did to the claims of political authority have tended to underestimate the way in which he justifies Antigone against Creon. To their support they have called in the great name of Hegel, who was fascinated by the play and advanced remarkable views on it.[2] [H]e has been made responsible for the opinion that Sophocles dramatized a conflict not between right and wrong but between right and right, that Antigone and Creon are equally justified in their actions and that the tragedy arises out of this irreconcilable conflict. [. . .] Hegel used the *Antigone* to illustrate his view of tragedy and his view of existence. He drew his own conclusions about the actions portrayed in it, as he was fully entitled to do. But his views are not those of Sophocles, and he should not be thought to maintain that Creon and Antigone were equally right in the eyes of their creator.

Sophocles leaves no doubt what conclusion should be drawn from the *Antigone*. He closes with a moral on the lips of the Chorus which tells the audience what to think:

> Wisdom has first place in happiness,
> And to fail not in reverence to the gods.
> The big words of the arrogant

---

4. *Religionsphilosophie*, II. 114 [Jebb's note].
1. Maurice Bowra, *Sophoclean Tragedy*. Clarendon Press, 1944. Bowra's notes have been edited.
2. *Philosophie der Religion*, xvi, I.133, *Aesthetik*, ii.2, Absch. I. Cf. A. C. Bradley, *Oxford Lectures on Poetry*, pp. 69–92 [Bowra's note].

>Lay big stripes on the boasters' backs.
>They pay the price
>And learn in old age to be wise.[3]

This can refer to no one but Creon, whose lack of wisdom has brought him to misery, who has shown irreverence to the gods in refusing burial to Polynices, been chastened for his proud words, and learned wisdom in his old age. To this lesson the preceding action in which Creon has lost son and wife and happiness has already made its effective contribution. We may be sure that the Chorus speak for the poet. It is as silent about Antigone as it is emphatic about Creon. There is no hint that she has in any way acted wrongly or that her death should be regarded as a righteous punishment. Of course the final words do not sum up everything important in the play, but we may reasonably assume that they pass judgement on its salient events as they appear in retrospect when the action is finished. There is no real problem about the ethical intention of the *Antigone*. It shows the fall of a proud man, and its lesson is that the gods punish pride and irreverence. But what matters much more than the actual conclusion is the means by which it is reached, the presentation of the different parties in the conflict, the view that we take of each, the feelings that are forced on us. The interest and power of the *Antigone* lie in the tangled issues which are unravelled in it.

A conclusion so clear as this is only worth reaching if it has been preceded by a drama in which the issues are violent and complex. The rights and wrongs of the case must not throughout be so obvious as they are at the end; the audience must feel that the issue is difficult, that there is much to be said on both sides, that the ways of the gods are hard to discern. Without this the play will fail in dramatic and human interest. And Sophocles has taken great care to show the issues in their full difficulty before he provides a solution for them. He makes the two protagonists appear in such a light that at intervals we doubt if all the right is really with Antigone and all the wrong with Creon. To Creon, who defies the divine ordinance of burial, he gives arguments and sentiments which sound convincing enough when they are put forward, and many must feel that he has some good reason to act as he does. On the other hand Antigone, who fearlessly vindicates the laws of the gods, is by no means a gentle womanly creature who suffers martyrdom for the right. She may be right, but there are moments when we qualify our approval of her, when she seems proud and forbidding in her determination to do her duty and to do it alone. For these variations in our feelings Sophocles is responsible. He makes us find some right in Creon, some wrong in Antigone, even if we are misled about both. He built his play on a contrast not between obvious wrong and obvious right but between the real arrogance of Creon and the apparent arrogance of Antigone. The first deceives by its fine persuasive sentiments; the second works through Antigone's refusal to offer concessions or to consider any point of view but her own. This contrast runs through much of the play, accounts for misunderstandings of what takes place in it, provides false clues and suggests wrong conclusions, and adds greatly to the intensity of the drama. When a play is written round a moral issue, that issue must be a real problem about which more than one view is tenable until all the relevant facts are known. So the *Antigone* dramatizes a conflict which was familiar

---

3. Bowra's translation of lines 1409–13 [editor's note].

to the Periclean age,[4] would excite divergent judgements and feelings, and make some support Antigone, some Creon, until the end makes all clear.

BERNARD KNOX

From the introduction to Antigone (1982)[1]

The opening scenes show us the conflicting claims and loyalties of the two adversaries, solidly based, in both cases, on opposed political and religious principles. This is of course the basic insight of Hegel's famous analysis of the play: he sees it as "a collision between the two highest moral powers." What is wrong with them, in his view, is that they are both "one-sided." But Hegel goes much further than that. He was writing in the first half of the nineteenth century, a period of fervent German nationalism in which the foundations of the unified German state were laid: his views on loyalty to the state were very much those of Creon. "Creon," he says, "is not a tyrant, he is really a moral power. He is not in the wrong."

However, as the action develops the favorable impression created by Creon's opening speech is quickly dissipated. His announcement of his decision to expose the corpse, the concluding section of his speech, is couched in violent, vindictive terms—"carrion for the birds and dogs to tear" (225)[2]—which stand in shocking contrast to the ethical generalities that precede it. This hint of a cruel disposition underlying the statesmanlike façade is broadened by the threat of torture leveled at the sentry (335–41) and the order to execute Antigone in the presence of Haemon, her betrothed (818–20). And as he meets resistance from a series of opponents—Antigone's contemptuous defiance, the rational, political advice of his son Haemon, the imperious summons to obedience of the gods' spokesman, Tiresias—he swiftly abandons the temperate rhetoric of his inaugural address for increasingly savage invective. Against the two sanctions invoked by Antigone, the demands of blood relationship, the rights and privileges of the gods below, he rages in terms ranging from near-blasphemous defiance to scornful mockery.

> Sister's child or closer in blood
> than all my family clustered at my altar
> worshiping Guardian Zeus—she'll never escape,
> . . . the most barbaric death. (530–33)

He will live to regret this wholesale denial of the family bond, for it is precisely through that family clustered at his altar that his punishment will be administered, in the suicides of his son and his wife, both of whom die cursing him.

---

4. The height of Athenian culture and political power in the time of the Athenian statesman Pericles (c. 495–29 BCE) [editor's note].

1. Bernard Knox, Introduction to *Antigone. The Three Theban Plays: Antigone, Oedipus the King, Oedipus at Colonus*, translated by Robert Fagles, Penguin, 1982, pp. 21–37. All footnotes have been added by the editor.

2. Knox's references are to Robert Fagles's translation, printed in *The Three Theban Plays*. Here and throughout we have substituted for the line numbers in Knox's parenthetical citations numbers for the relevant lines in the translation reprinted in this anthology. The wording varies between translations.

And for Antigone's appeals to Hades, the great god of the underworld to whom the dead belong, Creon has nothing but contempt; for him "Hades" is simply a word meaning "death," a sentence he is prepared to pass on anyone who stands in his way. He threatens the sentry with torture as a prelude: "simple death won't be enough for you" (340). When asked if he really intends to deprive Haemon of his bride he answers sarcastically: "Death will do it for me" (630). He expects to see Antigone and Ismene turn coward "once they see Death coming for their lives" (635–36). With a derisive comment he tells his son to abandon Antigone: "Spit her out, / . . . Let her find a husband down among the dead [in Hades' house]" (704–5). And he dismisses Antigone's reverence for Hades and the rights of the dead with mockery as he condemns her to be buried alive: "There let her pray to the one god she worships: / Death" (837–38). But this Hades is not something to be so lightly referred to, used or mocked. In the great choral ode which celebrated Man's progress and powers this was the one insurmountable obstacle that confronted him:

> ready, resourceful man!
> Never without resources
> never an impasse as he marches on the future—
> only Death, from Death alone he will find no rescue . . . (381, 393–97)

And Creon, in the end, looking at the corpse of his son and hearing the news of his wife's suicide, speaks of Hades for the first time with the fearful respect that is his due, not as an instrument of policy or a subject for sardonic wordplay, but as a divine power, a dreadful presence: "harbor of Death, so choked, so hard to cleanse!—/ why me? why are you killing me?" (1350–51).

Creon is forced at last to recognize the strength of those social and religious imperatives that Antigone obeys, but long before this happens he has abandoned the principles which he had proclaimed as authority for his own actions. His claim to be representative of the whole community is forgotten as he refuses to accept Haemon's report that the citizens, though they dare not speak out, disapprove of his action; he denies the relevance of such a report even if true—"And is Thebes about to tell me how to rule?" (790)—and finally repudiates his principles in specific terms by an assertion that the city belongs to him—"The city *is* the king's— that's the law!" (795). This autocratic phrase puts the finishing touch to the picture Sophocles is drawing for his audience: Creon has now displayed all the characteristics of the "tyrant," a despotic ruler who seizes power and retains it by intimidation and force. Athens had lived under the rule of a "tyrant" before the democracy was established in 508 B.C., and the name and institution were still regarded with abhorrence. Creon goes on to abandon the gods whose temples crown the city's high places, the gods he once claimed as his own, and his language is even more violent. The blind prophet Tiresias tells him that the birds and dogs are fouling the altars of the city's gods with the carrion flesh of Polynices; he must bury the corpse. His furious reply begins with a characteristic accusation that the prophet has been bribed (the sentry had this same accusation flung at him), but what follows is a hideously blasphemous defiance of those gods Creon once claimed to serve:

> You'll never bury that body in the grave,
> not even if Zeus's eagles rip the corpse
> and wing their rotten pickings off to the throne of god! (1090–92)

At this high point in his stubborn rage (he will break by the end of the scene and try, too late, to avoid the divine wrath), he is sustained by nothing except his tyrannical insistence on his own will, come what may, and his outraged refusal to be defeated by a woman. "No woman," he says, "is going to lord it over me" (577). "I'm not the man, not now: she is the man / if this victory goes to her and she goes free" (528–29).

Antigone, on her side, is just as indifferent to Creon's principles of action as he is to hers. She mentions the city only in her last agonized laments before she is led off to her living death:

> O my city, all your fine rich sons!
> . . . springs of the Dirce,
> holy grove of Thebes . . . (893–94)

But here she is appealing for sympathy to the city over the heads of the chorus, the city's symbolic representative on stage. In all her arguments with Creon and Ismene she speaks as one wholly unconscious of the rights and duties membership in the city confers and imposes, as if no unit larger than the family existed. It is a position just as extreme as Creon's insistence that the demands of the city take precedence over all others, for the living and the dead alike.

Like Creon, she acts in the name of gods, but they are different gods. There is more than a little truth in Creon's mocking comment that Hades is "the one god she worships (838)." She is from the beginning "much possessed by death"; together with Ismene she is the last survivor of a doomed family, burdened with such sorrow that she finds life hardly worth living. "Who on earth," she says to Creon, "alive in the midst of so much grief as I, / could fail to find his death a rich reward?" (507–8). She has performed the funeral rites for mother, father and her brother Eteocles:

> I washed you with my hands,
> I dressed you all, I poured the cups
> across your tombs. (948–50)

She now sacrifices her life to perform a symbolic burial, a handful of dust sprinkled on the corpse, for Polynices, the brother left to rot on the battlefield. She looks forward to her reunion with her beloved dead in that dark kingdom where Persephone, the bride of Hades, welcomes the ghosts (939–41). It is in the name of Hades, one of the three great gods who rule the universe, that she defends the right of Polynices and of all human beings to proper burial. "Death [Hades] longs for the same rites for all" (570), she tells Creon—for patriot and traitor alike; she rejects Ismene's plea to be allowed to share her fate with an appeal to the same stern authority: "Who did the work? / Let the dead and the god of death bear witness!" (595). In Creon's gods, the city's patrons and defenders, she shows no interest at all. Zeus she mentions twice: once as the source of all the calamities that have fallen and are still to fall on the house of Oedipus (2–5), and once again at the beginning of her famous speech about the unwritten laws. But the context here suggests strongly that she is thinking about Zeus in his special relationship to the underworld, Zeus *Chthonios* (Underworld Zeus). "It wasn't Zeus," she says,

> who made this proclamation. . . .
> Nor did that Justice, dwelling with the gods
> beneath the earth, ordain such laws for men. (494–96)

From first to last her religious devotion and duty are to the divine powers of the world below, the masters of that world where lie her family dead, to which she herself, reluctant but fascinated, is irresistibly drawn.

But, like Creon, she ends by denying the great sanctions she invoked to justify her action. In his case the process was spread out over the course of several scenes, as he reacted to each fresh pressure that was brought to bear on him; Antigone turns her back on the claims of blood relationship and the nether gods in one sentence: three lines in Greek, no more. They are the emotional high point of the speech she makes just before she is led off to her death.

> Never, I tell you,
> if I had been the mother of children
> or if my husband died, exposed and rotting—
> I'd never have taken this ordeal upon myself,
> never defied our people's will. (954–57)

These unexpected words are part of the long speech that concludes a scene of lyric lamentation and is in effect her farewell to the land of the living. They are certainly a total repudiation of her proud claim that she acted as the champion of the unwritten laws and the infernal gods, for, as she herself told Creon, those laws and those gods have no preferences, they long "for the same rites for all" (570). And her assertion that she would not have done for her children what she has done for Polynices is a spectacular betrayal of that fanatical loyalty to blood relationship which she urged on Ismene and defended against Creon, for there is no closer relationship imaginable than that between the mother and the children of her own body. Creon turned his back on his guiding principles step by step, in reaction to opposition based on those principles; Antigone's rejection of her public values is just as complete, but it is the sudden product of a lonely, brooding introspection, a last-minute assessment of her motives, on which the imminence of death confers a merciless clarity. She did it because Polynices was her brother; she would not have done it for husband or child. She goes on to justify this disturbing statement by an argument which is more disturbing still: husband and children, she says, could be replaced by others but, since her parents are dead, she could never have another brother. It so happens that we can identify the source of this strange piece of reasoning; it is a story in the *Histories* of Sophocles' friend Herodotus (a work from which Sophocles borrowed material more than once). Darius the Great King had condemned to death for treason a Persian noble, Intaphrenes, and all the men of his family. The wife of Intaphrenes begged importunately for their lives; offered one, she chose her brother's. When Darius asked her why, she replied in words that are unmistakably the original of Antigone's lines. But what makes sense in the story makes less in the play. The wife of Intaphrenes saves her brother's life, but Polynices is already dead; Antigone's phrase "no brother could ever spring to light again" (962) would be fully appropriate only if Antigone had managed to save Polynices' life rather than bury his corpse.

For this reason, and also because of some stylistic anomalies in this part of the speech, but most of all because they felt that the words are unworthy of the Antigone who spoke so nobly for the unwritten laws, many great scholars and also a great poet and dramatist, Goethe, have refused to believe that Sophocles wrote them. "I would give a great deal," Goethe told his friend Eckermann in 1827, "if some talented scholar could prove that these lines were interpolated, not genuine." Goethe did not know that the attempt had already been made, six years earlier; many others have tried since—Sir Richard Jebb, the greatest English editor of Sophocles, pronounced against them—and opinion today is still divided. Obviously a decision on this point is of vital significance for the interpretation of the play as a whole: with these lines removed, Antigone goes to her prison-tomb with no flicker of self-doubt, the flawless champion of the family bond and the unwritten laws, "whole as the marble, founded as the rock"[3]—unlike Creon, she is not, in the end, reduced to recognizing that her motive is purely personal.

There is however one objective piece of evidence that speaks volumes for the authenticity of the disputed lines. Aristotle, writing his treatise on rhetoric less than a century after the death of Sophocles, summarizes this part of Antigone's speech and quotes the two lines about the irreplaceability of a brother. He is telling the would-be orator that if, in a law-court speech for the defense, he has to describe an action that seems inappropriate for the character of his client and hard to believe, he must provide an explanation for it "as in the example Sophocles gives, the one from *Antigone*"—the phrasing suggests that the passage was well known to Aristotle's readers. Evidently he does not find the passage as repellent as Goethe and Jebb did; he recognizes that Antigone's initial statement is, in terms of her character, "hard to believe" [. . .], but apparently he finds her explanation rhetorically satisfactory. He does not, however, for one moment suspect the authenticity of the lines. [. . .] His acceptance of Antigone's speech as genuine demands that rather than suppress it we should try to understand it.

This is Antigone's third and last appearance on stage; in the prologue she planned her action, in the confrontation with Creon she defended it, and now, under guard, she is on her way to the prison which is to be her tomb. In lyric meters, the dramatic medium for unbridled emotion, she appeals to the chorus for sympathy and mourns for the marriage hymn she will never hear (this is as close as she ever comes to mentioning Haemon). She gets little comfort from the Theban elders; the only consolation they offer is a reminder that she may be the victim of a family curse—"do you pay for your father's terrible ordeal?" (904–5)—a suggestion that touches her to the quick and provokes a horrorstruck rehearsal of the tormented loves and crimes of the house of Oedipus. There is, as she goes on to say, no one left to mourn her; the lyric lament she sings in this scene is her attempt to provide for herself that funeral dirge which her blood relatives would have wailed over her corpse, if they had not already preceded her into the realm of Hades. This is recognized by Creon, who cuts off the song with a sarcastic comment: "if a man could wail his own dirge *before* he dies, / he'd never finish" (928–29). And he orders the guards to take her away.

3. Shakespeare's *Macbeth* 3.4.22.

Her song cut off, she turns from the lyric medium of emotion to spoken verse, the vehicle of reasoned statement, for her farewell speech. It is not directed at anyone on stage; it resembles a soliloquy, a private meditation. It is an attempt to understand the real reasons for the action that has brought her to the brink of death. After an address to the tomb and prison where she expects to be reunited with her family she speaks to Polynices (Creon is referred to in the third person). It is to Polynices that she is speaking when she says that she would not have given her life for anyone but a brother; it is as if she had already left the world of the living and joined that community of the family dead she speaks of with such love. Now, in the face of death, oblivious of the presence of Creon and the chorus, with no public case to make, no arguments to counter, she can at last identify the driving force behind her action, the private, irrational imperative which was at the root of her championship of the rights of family and the dead against the demands of the state. It is her fanatical devotion to one particular family, her own, the doomed, incestuous, accursed house of Oedipus and especially to its most unfortunate member, the brother whose corpse lay exposed to the birds and dogs. When she tells him that she has done for him what she would not have done for husband or children she is not speaking in wholly hypothetical terms, for in sober fact she has sacrificed, for his sake, her marriage to Haemon and the children that might have issued from it.

And in this moment of self-discovery she realizes that she is absolutely alone, not only rejected by men but also abandoned by gods. "What law of the mighty gods have I transgressed?" (971) she asks—as well she may, for whatever her motive may have been, her action was a blow struck for the rights of Hades and the dead. Unlike Christians whose master told them not to look for signs from heaven (Matthew 16:4),[4] the ancient Greek expected if not direct intervention at least some manifestation of favor or support from his gods when he believed his cause was just—a flight of eagles, the bird of Zeus, or lightning and thunder, the signs which, in the last play,[5] summon Oedipus to his resting place. But Antigone has to renounce this prospect: "Why look to heavens any more . . . ?" (972). She must go to her death as she has lived, alone, without a word of approval or a helping hand from men or gods.

Antigone's discovery that her deepest motives were purely personal has been overinterpreted by those who would suppress the passage on the grounds that, to quote Jebb's eloquent indictment, "she suddenly gives up that which, throughout the drama, has been the immovable basis of her action—the universal and unqualified validity of the divine law." This formulation is too absolute. Before the raw immediacy of death, which, as Doctor Johnson remarked, wonderfully concentrates the mind,[6] she has sounded the depths of her own soul and identified the determinant of those high principles she proclaimed in public. But that does not mean that they were a pretense, still less that she has now abandoned them. She dies for them. In her very last words, as she calls on the chorus to bear witness to her unjust fate, she claims once more and for the last time

---

4. "A wicked and adulterous generation seeketh after a sign; and there shall no sign be given unto it [. . .]."
5. *Oedipus at Colonus.*
6. Samuel Johnson (1709–84), as quoted in James Boswell's *Life of Samuel Johnson* (1791): "[W]hen a man knows he is to be hanged in a fortnight, it concentrates his mind wonderfully."

that she is the champion of divine law—she suffers "all for reverence, my reverence for the gods!" (993).

Unlike Creon, who after proclaiming the predominance of the city's interests rides roughshod over them, speaking and acting like a tyrant, who after extolling the city's gods dismisses Tiresias, their spokesman, with a blasphemous insult, Antigone does not betray the loyalties she spoke for. No word of compromise or surrender comes to her lips, no plea for mercy.

This is a pattern of character and behavior which is found in other Sophoclean dramatic figures also; not only in the Oedipus of the other two plays of this volume but also in the protagonists of *Ajax, Electra* and *Philoctetes.* They are of course very different from each other, but they all have in common the same uncompromising determination, the same high sense of their own worth and a consequent quickness to take offense, the readiness to die rather than surrender—a heroic temper. This figure of the tragic hero [. . .] seems, as far as we can tell from what remains of Attic tragedy, to have been a peculiarly Sophoclean creation. In his plays he explores time and again the destinies of human beings who refuse to recognize the limits imposed on the individual will by men and gods, and go to death or triumph, magnificently defiant to the last.

Antigone is such a heroic figure, and this is another of the ways in which she is different from Creon. Not only does Creon, unlike Antigone, betray in action the principles he claimed to stand for; he also, subjected to pressure that falls short of the death Antigone is faced with, collapses in abject surrender. He was sure Antigone would give way when force was applied; he has seen "the stiffest stubborn wills / fall the hardest; the toughest iron . . . crack and shatter" (518–21)—but he is wrong. He is the one who is shattered. Tiresias tells him that he will lose a child of his own to death in return for the living being he has imprisoned in the tomb and the corpse he has kept in the sunlight. He hesitates: "I'm shaken, torn. / It's a dreadful thing to yield . . ." (1158). But yield he does. "What should I do?" he asks the chorus (1164) and they tell him: release Antigone, bury Polynices. But he arrives too late; Antigone, independent to the last, has chosen her own way to die. [. . .]

[. . .] His savage dismissal of the claims of that blood relationship Antigone stood for has been punished with exquisite appropriateness, in the destruction of his own family, the curses of his son and wife. [. . .] The gods of the city whom he claimed to defend, have, through the medium of the blind seer, denounced his action, and the city he proposed to steer on a firm course is now, as Tiresias told him, threatened by the other cities whose dead were left to rot, like Polynices, outside the walls of Thebes (1141–45). He is revealed as a disastrous failure, both as head of a family and head of state, an offender against heaven and a man without family or friends, without the respect of his fellow-citizens. He may well describe himself as "no one. Nothing" (1386).

Antigone asked the gods to punish Creon if he was wrong [975–79], and they have. They have shown to all the world that her action was right. But she did not live to see her vindication. [. . . T]he will of the gods remains, as in all three of these plays, mysterious; revealed partially, if at all, through prophets rejected and prophecies misunderstood, it is the insoluble riddle at the heart of Sophocles' tragic vision. The gods told Creon he was wrong, but it is noticeable that Tiresias, their spokesman, does not say Antigone was right, he does not praise her—in fact he does not mention her. Antigone was ready to admit, if the gods did not save her and she suffered death, that she was wrong (975–76); these words suggest that she hanged herself not just to cut short the lingering agony of starvation and imprisonment but in a sort of existential despair. [. . .]

The gods do not praise Antigone, nor does anyone else in the play—except the young man who loves her so passionately that he cannot bear to live without her. Haemon tells his father what the Thebans are saying behind his back, the "murmurs in the dark" (743): that Antigone deserves not death but "a glowing crown of gold!" (751). Whether this is a true report (and the chorus does not praise Antigone even when they have been convinced that she was right) or just his own feelings attributed to others for the sake of his argument, it is a timely reminder of Antigone's heroic status. In the somber world of the play, against the background of so many sudden deaths and the dark mystery of the divine dispensation, her courage and steadfastness are a gleam of light; she is the embodiment of the only consolation tragedy can offer—that in certain heroic natures unmerited suffering and death can be met with a greatness of soul which, because it is purely human, brings honor to us all.

MARTHA C. NUSSBAUM

From Sophocles' *Antigone*: Conflict, Vision, and Simplification (1986, 2001)[1]

[A]lmost all interpreters of this play have agreed that the play shows Creon to be morally defective, though they might not agree about the particular nature of his defect. The situation of Antigone is more controversial. Hegel assimilated her defect to Creon's; some more recent writers uncritically hold her up as a blameless heroine. Without entering into an exhaustive study of her role in the tragedy, I should like to claim (with the support of an increasing number of recent critics) that there is at least some justification for the Hegelian assimilation—though the criticism needs to be focused more clearly and specifically than it is in Hegel's brief remarks. I want to suggest that Antigone, like Creon, has engaged in a ruthless simplification of the world of value which effectively eliminates conflicting obligations. Like Creon, she can be blamed for refusal of vision. But there are important differences, as well, between her project and Creon's. When these are seen, it will also emerge that this criticism of Antigone is not incompatible with the judgment that she is morally superior to Creon.

---

1. Martha C. Nussbaum, "Sophocles' *Antigone*: Conflict, Vision, and Simplification." *The Fragility of Goodness: Luck and Ethics in Greek Tragedy and Philosophy.* 1986. Revised ed., Cambridge UP, 2001, pp. 51–84. Unless otherwise indicated, all footnotes are Nussbaum's. Nussbaum's footnotes and parenthetical citations have been edited.

There has been a war. On one side was an army led by Eteocles, brother of Antigone and Ismene. On the other side was an invading army, made up partly of foreigners, but led by a Theban brother, Polynices. This heterogeneity is denied, in different ways, by both Creon and Antigone. Creon's strategy is to draw, in thought, a line between the invading and defending forces. What falls to one side of this line is a foe, bad, unjust; what falls to the other (if loyal to the city's cause) becomes, indiscriminately, friend or loved one. Antigone, on the other hand, denies the relevance of this distinction entirely. She draws, in imagination, a small circle around the members of her family: what is inside (with further restrictions which we shall mention) is family, therefore loved one and friend; what is outside is non-family, therefore, in any conflict with the family, enemy. If one listened only to Antigone, one would not know that a war had taken place or that anything called "city" was ever in danger.[2] To her it is a simple injustice that Polynices should not be treated like a friend.

"Friend" (*philos*) and "enemy," then, are functions solely of family relationship.[3] When Antigone says, "It is my nature to join in loving (*sumphilein*), not to join in hating," she is expressing not a general attachment to love, but a devotion to the *philia* of the family. It is the nature of these *philia* bonds to make claims on one's commitments and actions regardless of one's occurrent desires. This sort of love is not something one decides about; the relationships involved may have little to do with liking or fondness. We might say (to use terminology borrowed from Kant[4]) that Antigone, in speaking of love, means "practical," not "pathological" love (a love that has its source in fondness or inclination). "He is my own brother," she says to Ismene in explanation of her defiance of the city's decree, "and yours too, even if you don't want it. I certainly will never be found a traitor to him" (51–52). Relationship is itself a source of obligation, regardless of the feelings involved. When Antigone speaks of Polynices as "my dearest [. . .] brother" (94), even when she proclaims, "I shall lie with him as a loved one with a loved one [. . .] " (83–84), there is no sense of closeness, no personal memory, no particularity animating her speech.[5] Ismene, the one person who ought, historically, to be close to her, is treated from the beginning with remote coldness; she is even called enemy (110) when she takes the wrong stand on matters of pious obligation. It is Ismene whom we see weeping "sister-loving tears," who acts out of commitment to a felt love. "What life is worth living for me, bereft of you?" (602)

2. Cf. [S. G.] Benardete, "A Reading [of Sophocles' *Antigone*.]" [*Interpretation*, vol. 4, no. 3, 1975, pp. 148–96; vol. 5, no. 1, 1975, pp. 1–55; vol. 5, no. 2, 1975, pp. 148–84] 2.4.

3. [. . .] Cf. Benardete, *op. cit.* 8.6, 9.5, [C.] Segal, *Tragedy [and Civilization: An Interpretation of Sophocles.* Harvard UP, 1981] 189, [R. P.] Winnington-Ingram, *Sophocles[: An Interpretation.* Cambridge UP, 1980] 129ff, [B.] Knox, [*The*] *Heroic Temper[: Studies in Sophoclean Tragedy.* U of California P, 1964] 79–80.

4. Immanuel Kant (1724–1804), German philosopher who uses these terms in his *Critique of Pure Reason* [editor's note].

5. A number of scholars have claimed that Antigone is motivated by deep personal love for Polynices: for example, [M.] Santirocco, "Justice [in Sophocles' *Antigone*.]" [*Phil Lit*, vol. 4, no. 2, 1980, pp. 1880–98] 188, Knox, *Heroic Temper* 107ff., Winnington-Ingram, *op cit.* 130. Contrast the effective negative arguments of [G.] Perrotta, *Sofocle* [Principato, 1935] 112–14, [H.] Lloyd-Jones, [*The Justice of Zeus.* U of California P, 1971] 116, [I. M.] Linforth, "Antigone and Creon" [*University of California Publications in Classical Philology*, vol. 15, no. 5, 1961, pp. 183–260] 250. Perrotta correctly observes that she loves Polynices not *qua* Polynices, but *qua* falling under a family duty. [. . .]

she asks with an intensity of feeling that never animates her sister's piety. To Haemon, the man who passionately loves and desires her, Antigone never addresses a word throughout the entire play.[6] It is Haemon, not Antigone, whom the Chorus views as inspired by *erōs* (842–56). Antigone is as far from *erōs* as Creon.[7] For Antigone, the dead are "those whom it is most important to please" (103). "You have a warm heart for the cold" (102), observes her sister, failing to comprehend this impersonal and single-minded passion.

Duty to the family dead is the supreme law and the supreme passion. And Antigone structures her entire life and her vision of the world in accordance with this simple, self-contained system of duties. Even within this system, should a conflict ever arise, she is ready with a fixed priority ordering that will clearly dictate her choice. The strange speech (954–64) in which she ranks duties to different family dead, placing duty to brother above duties to husband and children, is in this sense (if genuine) highly revealing: it makes us suspect that she is capable of a strangely ruthless simplification of duties, corresponding not so much to any known religious law as to the exigencies of her own practical imagination.[8]

Other values fall into place, confirming these suspicions. Her single-minded identification with duties to the dead (and only some of these) effects a strange reorganization of piety, as well as of honor and justice. She is truly, in her own words, *hosia panourgēsasa*, one who will do anything for the sake of the pious;[9] and her piety takes in only a part of conventional religion.[1] She speaks of her

6. Cf. Perrotta, *op. cit.* 112. We must ascribe "O dearest Haemon, how your father dishonors you," to Ismene as in all the manuscripts. Pearson and other editors have assigned it to Antigone, out of their desire to have Antigone say something affectionate about Haemon. But *philtate*, "dearest," is not unusually strong inside a close family relationship, and it is perfectly appropriate to the affectionate Ismene; it need not, in fact, even designate close affection. Creon's reply that the speaker's continued harping on marriage "irritates" him is appropriate to his relationship with Ismene (who is, in any case, the one who has been "harping" on marriage), but is far too mild to express his deep hatred for and anger against Antigone. See the arguments of Linforth, *op. cit.* 209, Benardete *ad loc.*
7. On Antigone's refusal of *eros*, see [J.-P.] Vernant, "Tensions [et ambiguités dans la tragédie grecque]," in [J-P.] Vernant and [P.] Vidal-Naquet, *Mythe et tragédie en grèce ancienne* (Paris, 1972), 34–5, Benardete, "A reading" 8.6; compare Segal, *Tragedy* §VIII.
8. This speech is notoriously controversial. It would surely have been branded spurious had it not been quoted as genuine by Aristotle in the *Rhetoric*; this dates it so early that, if spurious, it could only be an actor's interpolation. And it is difficult to imagine an actor giving himself such an oddly legalistic and unemotional speech at a climactic moment in the dramatic action. It is, then, [. . .] almost certainly genuine; and it is very difficult to explain as a confused and incoherent outpouring of passionate love—though this approach has indeed been tried (e.g. by Winnington-Ingram, *Sophocles* 145ff., Knox, *Heroic Temper* 144ff.). The best explanation for this coldly determined priority-ordering of duties is that Antigone is not animated by personal love at all, but by a stern determination to have a fixed set of ordered requirements that will dictate her actions without engendering conflict; her refusal of the erotic [. . .] is then sufficient to explain her choice of the brother. For review of the controversy about authenticity and about the relation of the passage to Herodotus III.119, see [D. A.] Hester, "Sophocles the unphilosophical[: A Study in the *Antigone*.]" [*Mnemosyne*, 4th ser., vol. 24, 1971, pp. 11–59] 55–80, [R. C.] Jebb, [*Sophocles: The Antigone*. Cambridge UP, 1900] Appendix, 258–65, [G.] Müller, *Sophokles, Antigone* [winter, 1967] 198ff, 106ff., Knox, *op. cit.* 105–6, Winnington-Ingram, *op. cit.* 145ff. See also D. Page, *Actors' Interpolations in Greek Tragedy* (Oxford, 1934).
9. See Benardete, "A reading" 9.3.
1. See Knox, *Heroic Temper* 94ff., Segal, *Tragedy* §VIII. Winnington-Ingram calls the way in which she denies the hatred of brothers for one another after death a "heroic fiat," "a supreme effort to impose heroic will upon a recalcitrant world" (*Sophocles* 132).

allegiance to Zeus [. . .], but she refuses to recognize his role as guardian of the city and backer of Eteocles. The very expression of her devotion is suspect: "Zeus did not decree this, as far as I am concerned" ([. . .] 494). She sets herself up as the arbiter of what Zeus can and cannot have decreed, just as Creon took it upon himself to say whom the gods could and could not have covered: no other character bears out her view of Zeus as single-mindedly backing the rights of the dead. She speaks, too, of the goddess *Dikē*, Justice; but *Dikē* for her is, simply, "the Justice who lives together with the gods below" (495). The Chorus recognizes another *Dikē*.[2] Later they will say to her, "Having advanced to the utmost limit of boldness, you struck hard against the altar of *Dikē* on high, o child" (901–03). Justice is up here in the city, as well as below the earth. It is not as simple as she says it is. Antigone, accordingly, is seen by them not as a conventionally pious person, but as one who improvised her piety, making her own decisions about what to honor. She is a "maker of her own law [. . .]"; her defiance is "self-invented passion" ([. . .] 920). Finally they tell her unequivocally that her pious respect is incomplete: "[This] reverent action [. . .] is a part of piety [. . .]" (917). Antigone's rigid adherence to a single narrow set of duties has caused her to misinterpret the nature of piety itself, a virtue within which a more comprehensive understanding would see the possibility of conflict.

Creon's strategy of simplification led him to regard others as material for his aggressive exploitation. Antigone's dutiful subservience to the dead leads to an equally strange, though different (and certainly less hideous) result. Her relation to others in the world above is characterized by an odd coldness. "You are alive," she tells her sister, "but my life . . . is long since dead, to the end of serving the dead." The safely dutiful human life requires, or is, life's annihilation.[3] Creon's attitude towards others is like necrophilia: he aspires to possess the inert and unresisting. Antigone's subservience to duty is, finally, the ambition to be a *nekros*, a corpse beloved of corpses. (Her apparent similarity to martyrs in our own tradition, who expect a fully active life after death, should not conceal from us the strangeness of this goal.) In the world below, there are no risks of failure or wrongdoing.

Neither Creon nor Antigone, then, is a loving or passionate being in anything like the usual sense. Not one of the gods, not one human being escapes the power of *erōs*, says the Chorus (842–47); but these two oddly inhuman beings do, it appears, escape. Creon sees loved persons as functions of the civic good, replaceable producers of citizens. For Antigone, they are either dead, fellow servants of the dead, or objects of complete indifference. No living being is loved for his or her personal qualities, loved with the sort of love that Haemon feels and Ismene praises. By altering their beliefs about the nature and value of persons, they have, it seems, altered or restructured the human passions themselves. They achieve harmony in this way; but at a cost. The Chorus speaks of *erōs* as a force as important and obligating as the ancient *thesmoi* or laws of right, a force against which it is both foolish and, apparently, blameworthy to rebel [. . .].

2. On Antigone's conception of *dikē* and its novelty, see R. Hirzel, *Themis, Dike, and Verwandtes* (Leipzig, 1907) 147ff.; also Santirocco, "Justice" 186, Segal, *op. cit.* 170.

3. Segal, *op. cit.* provides an excellent discussion of this aspect of Antigone in several places—esp. 156ff., §VIII, §IV, 196.

Antigone learns too—like Creon, by being forced to recognize a problem that lies at the heart of her single-minded concern. Creon saw that the city itself is pious and loving; that he could not be its champion without valuing what it values, in all its complexity. Antigone comes to see that the service of the dead requires the city, that her own religious aims cannot be fulfilled without civic institutions. By being her own law, she has not only ignored a part of piety, she has also jeopardized the fulfillment of the very pious duties to which she is so attached. Cut off from friends, from the possibility of having children, she cannot keep herself alive in order to do further service to the dead; nor can she guarantee the pious treatment of her own corpse. In her last speeches she laments not so much the fact of imminent death as, repeatedly, her isolation from the continuity of offspring, from friends and mourners. She emphasizes the fact that she will never marry; she will remain childless. Acheron will be her husband, the tomb her bridal chamber. Unless she can successfully appeal to the citizens whose needs as citizens she had refused to consider, she will die without anyone to mourn her death or to replace her as guardian of her family religion. She turns therefore increasingly, in this final scene, to the citizens and the gods of the city [. . .], until her last words closely echo an earlier speech made by Creon [. . .] and blend his concerns with hers:

> O city of my fathers in this land of Thebes. O gods, progenitors of our race.
> I am led away, and wait no longer. Look, leaders of Thebes, the last of your
> royal line. Look what I suffer, at whose hands, for having respect for piety.
> (987–93)

We have, then, two narrowly limited practical worlds, two strategies of avoidance and simplification. In one, a single human value has become *the* final end; in the other, a single set of duties has eclipsed all others. But we can now acknowledge that we admire Antigone, nonetheless, in a way that we do not admire Creon. It seems important to look for the basis of this difference.

First, in the world of the play, it seems clear that Antigone's actual choice is preferable to Creon's. The dishonour to civic values involved in giving pious burial to an enemy's corpse is far less radical than the violation of religion involved in Creon's act. Antigone shows a deeper understanding of the community and its values than Creon does when she argues that the obligation to bury the dead is an unwritten law, which cannot be set aside by the decree of a particular ruler. The belief that not all values are utility-relative, that there are certain claims whose neglect will prove deeply destructive of communal attunement and individual character, is a part of Antigone's position left untouched by the play's implicit criticism of her single-mindedness.

Furthermore, Antigone's pursuit of virtue is her own. It involves nobody else and commits her to abusing no other person. Rulership must be rulership *of* something; Antigone's pious actions are executed alone, out of a solitary commitment. She may be strangely remote from the world; but she does no violence to it.

Finally, and perhaps most important, Antigone remains ready to risk and to sacrifice her ends in a way that is not possible for Creon, given the singleness of his conception of value. There is a complexity in Antigone's virtue that permits genuine sacrifice *within* the defense of piety. She dies recanting nothing; but still she is torn by a conflict. Her virtue is, then, prepared to admit a contingent conflict, at least in the extreme case where its adequate exercise requires the cancellation of the conditions of its exercise. From within her single-minded devotion to the dead, she recognizes the power of these contingent circumstances and yields to them, comparing herself to Niobe wasted away by nature's snow and rain (878–84).[4] (Earlier she had been compared, in her grief, to a mother bird crying out over an empty nest; so she is, while heroically acting, linked with the openness and vulnerability of the female.) The Chorus here briefly tries to console her with the suggestion that her bad luck does not really matter, in view of her future fame; she calls their rationalization a mockery of her loss. This vulnerability in virtue, this ability to acknowledge the world of nature by mourning the constraints that it imposes on virtue, surely contributes to making her the more humanly rational and the richer of the two protagonists: both active and receptive, neither exploiter nor simply victim.

PHILIP HOLT

From Polis and Tragedy in the *Antigone* (1999)[1]

I. INTRODUCTION

Sophokles' *Antigone* is an easy play for moderns, even modern classicists, to get wrong.[2] We are likely to see Antigone as the champion of moral right, or conscience, or religion against the authority of the state, as represented by Kreon. She is then a martyr for a cause, and our age is rather drawn to causes and martyrs. This does much to explain the scholarly predilection for what Hester called "the orthodox view" of the play: Antigone right and noble, Kreon wrong and tyrannical.[3] But these terms for describing the conflict—and even more the ethical weight and emotional coloring these terms carry—are relatively modern. "The state" to us means a nation-state with extensive powers over the lives of its citizens and an extensive apparatus of bureaucrats and police to enforce its dictates. We worry about its powers and want to protect our freedom within

---

4. The importance of this link with the yielding world of nature is seen by Segal, *Tragedy* 154ff.

1. Philip Holt, "*Polis* and Tragedy in the *Antigone*." *Mnemosyne*, 4th ser., vol. 52, no. 6, Dec. 1999, pp. 658–90. *JSTOR*, www.jstor.org/stable/4433045. All footnotes are Holt's, but some have been edited and others omitted.

2. The following works are cited by author's name (and short title where necessary) only: [. . .] Helene Foley, *Tragedy and Democratic Ideology: The Case of Sophocles'* Antigone, in: Barbara Goff (ed.), *History, Tragedy, Theory: Dialogues on Athenian Drama* (Austin 1995), 131–50; Simon Goldhill, *Reading Greek Tragedy* (Cambridge 1986); Bernard M. W. Knox, *The Heroic Temper: Studies in Sophoclean Tragedy* (Berkeley 1964); Christiane Sourvinou-Inwood, *Assumptions and the Creation of Meaning: Reading Sophocles'* Antigone, JHS 109 (1989), 134–48 and (with substantial overlap) *Sophocles' Antigone as a "Bad Woman,"* in: F. Dieteren, E. Kloek (ed.), *Writing Women into History* (Amsterdam 1990), 11–38; and the commentaries of Brown (Warminster 1987) [. . . and] Kamerbeek (Leiden 1978) [. . .]. I have used the text of Lloyd-Jones and Wilson (Oxford 1990).

3. Hester's extensive review of scholarship on the play found this view to be far more popular than what he called the "Hegelian" view, which sees Antigone and Kreon as being more evenly matched with flaws on both sides: D. A. Hester, *Sophocles the Unphilosophical: A Study in the* Antigone, Mnemosyne 24 (1971), 11–59. For a similar tilt in Germany (Schlegel over Hegel), see Erick Eberlein, *Über die verschiedenen Deutungen des tragischen Konflikts in der Tragödie 'Antigone' des Sophokles*, Gymnasium 68 (1961), 16–34 at 16–9.

it, especially after twentieth-century experience with totalitarian regimes. "Conscience" and "morality" to us mean the personal values of an autonomous individual, influenced by society but often at variance with it. "Religion" to us is likely to include notions of divinely revealed truth and an organized body of believers, both of them distinct from, and often at odds with, political authority. For us, then, conscience, morality, and religion set the individual apart from, perhaps even against, the state. It is easy for us to make Antigone into a heroic dissident. She upholds principle against political authority, and she is right.

We must understand fifth-century Athenian beliefs about the state, the role of the individual within it, and its relations to religion, funerals, and related matters—the *"polis"* part of my title—before we can make sense of the *Antigone*. These will be surveyed, with some large debts to previous work, in part II. Here the "orthodox" view is particularly weak, and its weaknesses still need attention. [. . .]

Still, understanding Greek beliefs and attitudes is only a first step towards interpretation. We need to consider not so much what Greeks thought and felt generally as how they are likely to have thought and felt under the conditions of a tragic performance, this tragedy in particular. Hence the "tragedy" part of my title: a discussion of how decent Greek opinion fares over the course of the *Antigone* (part III) and a coda on how it might fare in tragedy generally (part IV). Tragedy is the *polis'* partner in an intricate dialogue. She has her own agenda and her own ways of making her points, some of them quite sly,[4] and she is rather more on Antigone's side than the *polis* is. The main burden of this essay is to understand better her side of the conversation, an area where history-minded critics, straining to catch the voice of the *polis*, often miss things.

II. *POLIS*

*   *   *

Broad construction of the public interest gave the Athenian *polis* considerable power to regulate what its citizens did. Among other things, the *polis* could regulate funerals. A funeral was basically a family function, but the display and ostentation which the family could employ were restricted by the state.[5] The state could also restrict funeral rites for certain classes of people—suicides, for example.[6]

This brings us to a fact which is troublesome for devotees of St. Antigone the Martyr but important for assessing how an Athenian audience would respond to the play: Athenian law forbade the burial of traitors and sacrilegious people

---

4. "Drama . . . unfolds as a complex dialogue that refuses to be bound in any direct fashion by the discourses of the agora" (Foley, 132); it provides a "radical critique" of "the city's discourse" (Goldhill, 78; on how this applies to some particular issues in the *Antigone*, see 104–6, 174–80).

5. Erwin Rohde, *Psyche: The Cult of Souls and Belief in Immortality among the Greeks*, English trans. (London 1925), 164 f.; Robert Garland, *The Greek Way of Death* (Ithaca, N.Y. 1985), 21–3.

6. Thalheim, *Selbstmord*, RE II A.1 (1921), 1134 f.

in Athenian territory. There is abundant evidence of this law, and of similar laws in other states.[7] Now, Polyneikes, who led an army against his homeland, was certainly a traitor, and if Kreon is right that he planned to burn the temples of the gods (*Ant.* 199–201, 284–7), he aspired to sacrilege as well. Hence in refusing him burial, Kreon was imposing a sanction that was recognizable to the audience as part of their law. He had good reasons for it. In a small city-state, defeat in war could mean civic destruction and the loss of everything one had; treason was a serious business, a threat to the survival of the community.

. . . . .

To sum up, in fifth-century terms Kreon is within his rights as the leader of his *polis*, and his ban on burying Polyneikes is a reasonable sanction. In fifth-century terms, Antigone's defiance of that ban is seriously, perhaps even shockingly, out of line: an individual defying due authority in the *polis*, in time of crisis, on behalf of a national enemy, and moreover a woman defying due male authority.

Critics often see Antigone as an isolated figure, willful and obstinate, proud and cold to others, acting from a mixed bag of reasons, both principled and personal.[8] There are good reasons why they should. To a degree which may be hard for us to imagine, she stands alone, forced to rely heavily on her own heroic temper. A modern Antigone comes with some ready-made bases for defying the community, respected and well-articulated values to which she can appeal. The ancient Antigone is not so well equipped. Conscience and religious authority are largely out. "The wide range of ideals, eccentricities and obsessions which we nowadays amalgamate under the name of 'conscience' did not seem to Greeks to be good reasons for defying the law."[9] Religion was focused more on prayer and ritual than on beliefs and ethical demands, more apt to produce traditionalists and conformists than dissidents and martyrs. Far from providing a basis for criticizing the *polis*, religion was an integral part of it. The *polis*, after all, administered, financed, and regulated much of the religious activity within it.[1] It had large scope in making decisions about religious matters.

7. Gustave Glotz, *La solidarité de la famille dans le droit criminel en Grèce* (Paris 1904), 460f. gives an extensive collection of evidence; also basic, and long neglected for bringing the issue into discussion of the *Antigone*, is W. Vischer, *Zu Sophokles Antigone*, RhM 20 (1865), 444–54 at 445–9.

8. So (with considerable variation) Elizabeth Bryson Bongie, *The Daughter of Oedipus*, in: John L. Heller (ed.), *Serta Turyniana* (Urbana 1974), 239–67; Brown, 7–10; Gerald F. Else, *The Madness of Antigone* (Heidelberg 1976); Knox, 62–8, 102–7, 113–6. Two important recent studies have done much to clear Antigone of the charge of inconsistency: Helene P. Foley, *Antigone as Moral Agent*, in: M. S. Silk (ed.), *Tragedy and the Tragic: Greek Theatre and Beyond* (Oxford 1996), 49–73; Matt Neuburg, *How Like a Woman: Antigone's "Inconsistency,"* CQ 40 (1990): 54–76. But her consistent reasons are nevertheless complicated and strongly rooted in the specifics of her unusual situation, dying unmarried (Neuburg, 66–70) and acting on behalf of a brother (Foley, 51–7). Complex situations produce complex motives. It is possible to see her as both consistent and self-willed: Martin Cropp, *Antigone's Final Speech* (Sophocles, Antigone 891–928), G&R 44 (1997), 137–60.

9. [K. J.] Dover[, *Greek Popular Morality in the Time of Plato and Aristotle.* U of California P, 1974], (n.13) 309.

1. Christiane Sourvinou-Inwood, *What Is* Polis *Religion?*, in: Oswyn Murray, Simon Price (ed.), *The Greek City from Homer to Alexander* (Oxford 1990), 295–322 and *Further Aspects of Polis Religion*, AION (archeol) 10 (1988), 259–74.

There remains the family, whose entanglements with the *polis*, interdependent yet often conflicting, were important in Greek history and have been important in *Antigone* criticism at least since Hegel. There is no anachronism in raising family concerns. Antigone does, after all, break Kreon's edict on behalf of her brother, precisely because he is her brother, and she appeals repeatedly to that blood-tie to justify her action.[2] Still, family and *polis* do not meet in the play as an evenly balanced pair of opposites, a thesis and antithesis in search of a synthesis.[3] The *Antigone* presents a situation which the fifth-century *polis* had already decided in its own favor. As we have seen, the *polis* could override the family to regulate funerals, or even ban them for certain classes of people—including traitors like Polyneikes. [. . .]

Sophokles, then, gives Kreon a strong position, far stronger than we moderns are generally prepared or able to recognize. What becomes of that position on the stage, however, is another matter.

III. THE *ANTIGONE*

It should not escape the reader's notice that the discussion so far is aimed at estimating how fifth-century Athenians would react to Antigone's action if it were a real event in civic life—if they were debating it in the assembly or judging it as jurors in a court of law or discussing it as a piece of recent news. [. . .] But of course, Polyneikes' burial is not an event in real life. It is part of a tragic drama, which is to say, it is presented to the audience by the playwright in a certain way and observed by the audience under certain conditions. This complicates the task of interpretation. We may know, more or less, what decent Athenian opinion held; but what does the play do with it?

I shall argue that the structure of Sophokles' drama—his arrangement and presentation of events, the playwright's devices for getting his story across—does much to encourage sympathy for Antigone, undercutting the shock and condemnation that her action would likely arouse in real life. Moreover, this sympathy for a lawbreaker is of a piece with what tragedy does elsewhere: it tests limits, defies norms, gives a certain kind of outlet for antisocial feelings. The audience did not come to a tragedy to vent its orthodoxies upon the characters; it came, I suggest, partly for the more interesting and exciting experience of watching the characters defy the orthodoxies.

We may begin with the premise of Sophokles' drama—Kreon's edict forbidding the burial of Polyneikes. As we have seen, the edict was in keeping with

2. *Ant.* 21 f., 45 f., 80 f., 466–8, 502–4, 511, 517; see also 696–8 (spoken by Haimon), 10, 73, 89 (*philos* and related expressions). Kreon's valuation of kinship ties is considerably lower (486–9, 658 f.). Antigone's notorious declaration that she would not have broken Kreon's edict to bury anyone but her brother (904–20), however odd critics find it, is consistent with her motives as repeatedly stated elsewhere. Antigone's loyalty to Polyneikes may not be simply a matter of blood-ties: Patricia J. Johnson, *Woman's Third Face: A Psycho/Social Reconsideration of Sophocles' Antigone*, Arethusa 30 (1997), 369–98 raises the issue, with a highly speculative answer.
3. One can question more broadly whether Antigone's action really respects proper family loyalties and proper responsibilities in burying dead kin: Sourvinou-Inwood, *Bad Woman*, 17–21 and 29–31. I find some of the arguments too intricate to be helpful in estimating a theatre audience's responses to the play, but the question deserves fuller consideration. I confine my remarks here to narrow grounds involving funerals.

Athenian law; but that does not settle the question of how an Athenian audience would have regarded it. Denying burial to traitors and temple-robbers was, after all, a circumscribed exception to a widely accepted norm, the right to a decent funeral. It was an extreme reprisal, and it may well have occasioned doubts, reservations, and ambivalence in the community that resorted to it.

· · ·

To a large extent, the action of the *Antigone* is taken up with unfolding th[e "heavy unanticipated"] costs [of Kreon's edict]. Kreon's position is repeatedly challenged, he repeatedly resists, but each challenge reveals new weaknesses, and eventually he crumbles. Orthodox critics tend to regard this result as a foregone conclusion: Kreon's position is of course wrong, so he is bound to end badly. This is too harsh: it underestimates the basic reasonableness (in Greek terms) of Kreon's position, and it tends to read the play backwards, interpreting the early scenes out of our advance knowledge of how things will turn out and magnifying small hints in those early scenes accordingly.[4] Historically minded critics, on the other hand, sometimes appear to regard the outcome as a surprise, as though we had to wait for Teiresias to tell us how wrong Kreon is.[5] This is too sanguine: it scants some important signs in the text of the stages by which Kreon's edict is undone. We would do better to see the play as a progression of complications, with Kreon's position undermined bit by bit. The outcome is not clear from the start, but we can see it coming as the play goes on. Tragic complications encroach more and more upon the dictates of the *polis*. Sophokles first deals Kreon a strong hand and then has us watch him lose with it.

· · ·

The play opens towards dawn, with two women in conversation. Kreon, we are told, has already issued his edict but is on his way "to proclaim it clearly to those who do not know" (*Ant.* 31–4).[6] This cusp of time gives Antigone a chance to respond to the edict in advance, after it is formulated but before any other character or the audience hears it. Sophokles uses this bit of timing to let her launch a pre-emptive strike upon it to win the audience's sympathy.

Her strike is an impressive one. The terms of the edict are revealed only after a dramatic buildup. The house of Oidipous has suffered everything imaginable, she says, "for there is nothing painful or destructive or shameful or dishonorable which I have not seen among your sufferings and mine" (*Ant.* 4–6). And now [. . .] on top of it all, this terrible proclamation [. . .]. We have not yet heard what the proclamation says, but by the time Ismene asks [. . .], twenty lines into this scene, we are primed to hear something terrible.

4. A. S. McDevitt, *Sophocles' Praise of Man in the Antigone*, Ramus 1 (1972), 152–64 at 159f. and Sourvinou-Inwood, *Assumptions*, 135 f. both raise some powerful objections to such backward reading.

5. Sourvinou-Inwood waits for Teiresias; Calder [. . .], 401 f. holds out even after that. [William M. Calder III, *Sophokles' Political Tragedy*, Antigone. *GRBS*, vol. 9, no. 4, 1968, pp. 389–407.]

6. [. . .] On the timing, see Brown, *ad* 31–4.

Terrible indeed [. . .]. Eteokles' burial is described simply and approvingly (23–5), but the other brother and his treatment are described more fully, in more emotional terms [. . .] (26–30). Polyneikes is "wretchedly dead," and the consequences of exposing his corpse are graphically depicted: no lamentation, no funeral, only the birds to devour him. [. . .] First impressions are powerful, and our first impression of Kreon's edict comes to us filtered through Antigone's grief and indignation.[7]

We need not wait long for a second impression, even before Kreon's entrance. Ismene elicits gradually, through a series of questions, the details of Antigone's plan to bury Polyneikes (*Ant.* 39–48), and she finds it bold and dangerous. The series of questions brings out Antigone's plan in stages, each more shocking than the last, and we are invited to share Ismene's surprise and alarm [. . .]. Like Antigone, she can rehearse the sad history of the family (49–57), but it affects her differently. It does not sting her to outrage, it urges her to caution: "Consider how we two, left alone, will perish wretchedly if despite the law we transgress the ruler's decision and power" (58–60). Ismene also reminds us that Antigone's plan is illegal. [. . .]

Ismene, notoriously, is no tragic heroine. We could, like many critics, cheer Antigone's heroism and castigate Ismene's cowardice, but the scene is not quite so one-sided. At the very least, Ismene reminds us that more than one reaction to Kreon's edict is possible. [. . .]

Still, Antigone has had the chance to strike the first blow, and she has done it well, passionately, and dramatically. The audience may well sympathize with her, not necessarily because they would agree with her, but because shock and distress seen up close arouse sympathy. Ismene's objections, although often underrated, do not erase this. Kreon comes to the plate with one strike against him.

After the parodos, we move from the private world of Antigone to the public world of Kreon. Despite Antigone's pre-emptive strike, Kreon's opening address to the Chorus gives him every chance to look good in the audience's eyes. The Chorus has just given thanks to the gods for delivering Thebes from great danger, and their song has reminded us vividly of the impiety and violence of Polyneikes' army, the sufferings that awaited the Thebans had they lost the battle.[8] As a new ruler in a difficult time, Kreon has a claim on our sympathy, and for the most part he comes off well. His speech is reasoned, his tone moderate under the circumstances. His heart is clearly in the right place: he seeks good advice in guiding the city (*Ant.* 178–81), he puts the city first, before private connections (182–91), and he is determined to distinguish between the patriotic Eteokles and the treacherous Polyneikes. [. . .]

Still, the question is raised whether Thebes is in good hands, and the answer is not altogether satisfactory.[9] "It is impossible to know any man's soul and thought and mind," Kreon says, "before he is experienced in office and law" (*Ant.* 175–7). This puts us on notice that Kreon is untested at this point in the

7. "Thus we learn of the edict, not from a bald report, but through Antigone's sense of outrage at it" (Brown, 135).
8. McDevitt [. . .] 157–9.
9. R. P. Winnington-Ingram, *Sophocles: An Interpretation* (Cambridge 1980), 123–5 offers a more extensive discussion than mine of "warning signals" in this scene.

play, hence unknown. More telling, his edict forbidding funeral rites for Polyneikes, presented after a slow, careful buildup, gets a remarkably lukewarm reception from the Chorus. [. . .] Indeed, all through the play the merits of Kreon's edict (as distinguished from his authority to impose it) go unsupported by anybody but him. Saying that he has the power or the right to command something is not the same as saying that it is a good idea.

Kreon's position is almost immediately challenged. The Guard enters with news that Polyneikes' corpse has been sprinkled with dust. Kreon, untried in "office and law" (*Ant.* 177), is on trial here, for we will see how he stands up to the first test of his new regime. Our attention begins to shift, and will shift more markedly in the following scene, from the proclamation to the ruler who issues it. The ruler does not come off well, for he meets the challenge with anger, error, and obstinacy.

In the Guard's narrative as in the prologue, Antigone's grief and outrage are given play, stressing the terrible consequences of Kreon's edict. She wails like a bird robbed of its young, laments the corpse "when she saw it bare," and curses those who left it that way (422–8). Kreon does not change his plans when he finds out that the perpetrator of the crime is his own niece and his son's fiancée; he is still determined to put her to death. These developments show Kreon persisting in his intention as the emotional costs mount. Kreon's edict may be based on sound principles, but it takes a tough heart and a strong stomach to maintain his position in the extreme situation which the play presents. Unfortunately, Kreon possesses both these qualities.

By this point in the play, principles have gotten mixed up with personalities. We have come away from the noble abstractions of Kreon's "inaugural address" and gotten a chance to see something of Kreon himself. He is less impressive than his ideals, and he is not doing terribly well on the test he set for himself— how well he performs "in office and law" (*Ant.* 175–7). Still, a Greek audience might well hold back from shifting all its sympathy to Antigone. Her ringing declaration of the unwritten laws, eternal and not to be altered by human decree, makes a fine sound to modern ears, but fifth-century Greeks were not so well primed to hear it. More important, the unwritten laws occupy only half her speech to Kreon (450–60). The other half (460–70) is more specific and personal [. . .]. The Chorus' response to all this is that she is her father's daughter, all right, "raw" and stubborn (471 f.). This is not an endorsement of the unwritten laws, and it is not altogether complimentary to Antigone either. Like Kreon's rule, Antigone's defiance is a complex combination of principle and personality, and she is driven by will, pride, and family honor at least as much as by devotion to the unwritten laws.[1] The conflict is between two characters, Kreon and Antigone, not between the principles of state and family, or

---

1. This deserves fuller discussion, for which I must refer the reader to Bongie [. . .] and Knox, inter alia. Bongie, 252 goes so far as to call the speech on the unwritten laws "a rationalization of the more compelling personal motives."

human and divine law, to which they appeal.[2] It is more personal and thereby more dramatic, and neither comes off unscathed.

Kreon's scene with Haimon shows his weaknesses as a ruler to a higher degree.

Nestled in all Haimon's deference is one piece of information: the people of Thebes pity Antigone and support her (*Ant.* 692–700). [. . . P]opular opinion is beginning to tilt against Kreon.

Kreon, predictably, [. . .] reacts with rage and disbelief. His world is being turned upside down: a younger man is venturing to instruct an elder (*Ant.* 726 f.), Antigone is rebellious (730–2), the city is not submitting to its ruler (734–9). Perhaps worst of all, women are getting the better of men (740, 746, 756; the point has also appeared at 484 f., 525, 677–80). The world thus disturbed is actually that of the *polis* to a large degree; most Greeks in the audience would probably have been quite content with the idea that the young ought to submit to the old, people to authority, women to men.[3] But accepting a principle does not mean that we will automatically agree with everyone who invokes it. Kreon's nervous insistence on these principles begins to look like a sign of weakness, inflexibility, or even tyranny. He does not so much espouse civic norms as hide behind them.

The denouement of the play can be discussed more briefly, at least for the issues that concern us here. Antigone's kommos and final speech draw critical attention mostly for what they tell us about her, about her motives for defying Kreon and her feelings as she faces death. These are important questions, but for this enquiry it is worth stressing a simpler and more obvious point, what Kreon is doing to her. [. . .] Amid the many problems of this scene—whether the Chorus is sympathetic or aloof, what Antigone means in comparing herself to Niobe, why she values her brother over other kin—we are invited to grieve over her. This echoes in a different key something which we encountered in the prologue, when we saw at close range Antigone's grief and outrage over Kreon's edict. In both scenes, whatever we might think of the practice of throwing out traitors unburied, or of Antigone herself, we are invited to pity her.[4] Pity can be potent. The Thebans, Haimon tells us, grieved for Antigone [. . .] and so came to support her. The Chorus grieves in spite of Kreon's rulings[5] and does not break with him openly. We may turn our pity into a political position, like the Thebans, or decide not to, like the Chorus. Either way, we are invited again to contemplate the costs of Kreon's edict, and of his way of running the *polis*.

2. See inter alia Eberlein [. . .], passim; Else [. . .] 42; Hester [. . .] 40; Knox, 102–16.
3. [Vittorio] Citti[, *Strutture e tensioni sociali nell'Antigone di Sofocle. AIV*, no. 134, 1975–76, pp. 477–501] [. . .], 487–92 and [*Sofocle e le strutture di potere nell'Atene del V secolo. BIFG*, no. 3, 1976, pp. 84–120 at 103], passim; Sourvinou-Inwood, *Assumptions*, 138–40, 144 f.
4. Sourvinou-Inwood, *Bad Woman*, 17 notes the shift from portraying Antigone as a threatening rebellious woman earlier in the play to showing her as a pitiable bride of Hades here.
5. The Chorus says that they are "carried outside the *thesmoi*" ([. . .] 801 f.) upon seeing Antigone and are unable to restrain their tears. I take it that the *thesmoi* here are Kreon's (Jebb, Kamerbeek), whether his sentence against Antigone or his royal authority generally.

The costs become far more apparent in the Teiresias scene, when the seer first reports dire omens and disruptions in the kosmos and then announces that it is all because of Kreon. Kreon tries to make amends, but too late: three people die, and Kreon is left ruined.

The verdict of the gods is in at last, but as often, the verdict is plainer than the story leading up to it. We miss much of the story, and much of the achievement of the *Antigone*, if we make Kreon merely impious in issuing his proclamation and Antigone merely noble in defying him. As we have seen, Kreon starts in a stronger position, and one more in keeping with fifth-century values, than we often recognize. Consequently, the play takes on a larger task than we often recognize in making his ruin credible and satisfying. In succeeding, it is a better play than we often recognize—not only a great one, but a deft one as well. [. . .]

[. . . T]he modern picture of Antigone as a heroic dissenter is not altogether wrong. Only we must recognize that the play does not generate sympathy for Antigone by appealing to any widely held notions about martyrs for causes or conscience against tyranny. Rather, it works by the way it arranges events and shades their presentation—perhaps even by manipulation. Antigone's distress and passion are given full play, her opponent is made to appear weak and foolish, and she and her allies get most of the good lines.[6] The play encourages the audience to root for a rebel against the values which they would likely espouse and practice in real life.

IV. TRAGEDY

If this reading of the play is reasonably close to the truth, then the *Antigone* does something which tragedy does generally. Defiance of the norms is part of its stock in trade. Tragedy is a "genre of transgression" and features an "interplay between norm and transgression"—an important part of the current lively discussion of drama in relation to the *polis*.[7] The *Antigone* presents quite a lot of transgression. Antigone's defiance of Kreon involves a degree of self-assertion and boldness which would be hard to find, perhaps even hard to conceive of, in a real-life Greek city, but her play lets the antisocial voice speak on stage and gives the audience reason to root for it in spite of itself.

6. A few "zingers": The doer grieves your mind, I grieve your ears (*Ant.* 319); I would have died even if you hadn't sentenced me (460 f.); if my actions seem foolish, I'm accused of folly by a fool (469 f.); there is no city which belongs to one man (737); you'd rule well over a desert alone (739); I speak for her—and you and me and the gods below (749). Kreon's only approach to pithiness (as distinguished from his usual maxim-spouting) is his declaration that one of his nieces has just lost her mind and the other never had any (561 f.).

7. Quotes from Goldhill, ["The] *Great Dionysia [and Civic Ideology*." *Nothing to Do with Dionysos? Athenian Drama in its Social Context*, edited by John J. Winkler and Froma I. Zeitlin, Princeton UP, 1990] [. . .] 126 and 127, a basic study for delineating the paradox of anticivic discourse in a highly ordered civic setting. For the discussion more generally, a good starter bibliography would include the collections edited by Goff [. . .], [Christopher] Pelling[, *Greek Tragedy and the Historian*. Oxford UP, 1997], and Winkler and Zeitlin. [. . .]

HELEN MORALES

From Antigone Rising (2020)[1]

PREFACE

Clearly the girl has a fierce spirit. . . .
She does not yet know how to submit to bad circumstances.
　　—the old men of Thebes on Antigone in Sophocles's *Antigone*

Some people can let things go. I can't
—GRETA THUNBERG[2]

When I was a girl I was lucky enough to read a book called the *Tales of the Greek Heroes.* I was enthralled. No one does power and rebellion and love and loathing quite like the gods and mortals of ancient mythology. [. . .] I still love the way that myths open up new ways of looking at the world.

What makes a myth a myth, rather than just a story, is that it has been told and retold over the centuries and has become meaningful to a culture or community.[3] The Greek and Roman myths have become embedded in, and an influential part of, our culture. They form the foundations and scaffolding of the beliefs that shape our politics and our lives. These can be limiting and destructive but also inspirational and liberating.

The myth of Antigone, as told by the Greek playwright Sophocles, is one of the most well known of the Greek myths and one of the most meaningful for feminism and for revolutionary politics.[4] She has become an icon of resistance. Of pitting personal conviction against state law. Of speaking truth to power.

Antigone insists on burying her brother Polynices, who has been killed while fighting against her city, Thebes, even though her uncle Creon, who is ruler of Thebes, expressly forbids the burial and will impose the death penalty for her defiance. Antigone, just a child of thirteen or fourteen or fifteen, stands up to a powerful adult, even when her sister won't and when the citizens of Thebes are too afraid to do so. Antigone also challenges male authority, in the face of Creon's insistence that women are inferior to men and that men should rule over them. She is vulnerable and terrorized, but she breaks the law anyway.

Antigone was first performed in Athens in (we think) 442 BCE. Today, it is performed all over the world; since 2016, it has been staged, with a new purpose,

1. Helen Morales, *Antigone Rising: The Subversive Power of the Ancient Myths*. Bold Type Books, 2020, pp. ix–xviii, 145–50. All footnotes are Morales's, though some have been omitted or edited.
2. Sophocles, *Antigone* 471–472; Greta Thunberg quoted in an interview with Jonathan Watts for the *Guardian* (Manchester, UK) newspaper, March 11, 2019.
3. See Helen Morales, *Classical Myth: A Very Short Introduction* ([Oxford UP], 2007).
4. See George Steiner, *Antigones: The Antigone Myth in Western Literature, Art and Thought* ([Oxford UP], 1984); Judith Butler, *Antigone's Claim* ([Columbia UP], 2000); Bonnie Honig, *Antigone, Interrupted* ([Cambridge UP], 2013); the chapters by Miriam Leonard, Simon Goldhill, and Katie Fleming in *Laughing with Medusa: Classical Myth and Feminist Thought*, ed. Vanda Zajko and Miriam Leonard ([Oxford UP], 2006); and Fanny Söderbäck, ed., *Feminist Readings of Antigone* ([State U of New York P], 2010).

in Ferguson, Missouri, and in New York City. *Antigone in Ferguson* was conceived by Bryan Doerries after the killing of eighteen-year-old Michael Brown Jr. by a police officer there in 2014. It presents a rehearsed reading of an adaptation of Sophocles's play, followed by a discussion, with community members, police officers, and activists, about social justice and race.[5]

Why not just write a play about the death of Michael Brown? Why turn to *Antigone* to explore this tragedy? Part of the answer must be that using myth allows us to explore extreme situations without risking the crassness of dramatizing the specific events of a young man's death. This was the reason that the ancient Greeks turned to mythology as the material for their tragedies: when they had staged plays about contemporary events, it had proven too painful for the audience to watch. Greek myths also explore difficult subjects about abuses of power and human weaknesses. Being able to explore questions such as what makes good leadership and how to resist state fascism allows audiences to reflect on those issues in relation to particular, local events, at one remove.

Related to this is what the novelist Ralph Ellison called enlargement: myths enlarge people and literary characters when they overlay them with attributes and accomplishments from the figures in the ancient tales.[6] As scholar Patrice Rankine explains, casting his characters as figures from ancient myth enabled Ellison to construct his characters "from outside of a limited, contemporary framework." This gave them "possibilities [that] transcended the limitations that society placed upon them."[7] Seeing a character or person through a kind of dual vision, as himself and in the role of a figure from myth, gives the reader an enhanced prism through which to understand them.

Antigone's myth does not end well for anyone, but we'll save that problem for the end of this book. For now, I want to dwell on the courage and endurance of Antigone's character. She risks everything for a cause that she believes in and refuses to be cowed either by powerful politicians or by what anyone else thinks. The spirit of Antigone lives on in Ieshia Evans, who was photographed standing firm in her flimsy summer dress while facing a wall of police officers in riot gear in a Black Lives Matter protest in Baton Rouge. It lives on in Malala Yousafzai, who campaigned for the rights of girls in Pakistan to be educated, even though it was dangerous to break the law of the Taliban (who tried, unsuccessfully, to

---

5. Bryan Doerries is artistic director of Theater of War Productions, https://theaterofwar.com/projects/antigone-in-ferguson.

6. Ralph Ellison, "On Initiation Rites and Power: Ralph Ellison Speaks at West Point," in *Going to the Territory* ([. . .] Random House, 1986), 39–63. See also Ellison's essay "Going to the Territory" in the same volume, 300: "It's as though a transparent overlay of archetypal myth is being placed over the life of an individual, and through him we see ourselves." [Patrice D.] Rankine, *Ulysses in Black: Ralph Ellison, Classicism, and African American Literature* ([U of Wisconsin P], 2006).

7. Ellison is especially interested in the construction of black identity. The quotation in fuller context in Rankine, *Ulysses in Black,* 127: "Mythology and folklore, like fiction in the novel form, allowed Ellison, a black writer in pre-Civil Rights, segregated America, to construct black identity from outside of a limited, contemporary framework. Although his approach garnered him much criticism, Ellison, through folklore and fiction, constructed human characters whose possibilities transcended the limitations that society placed upon them."

kill her in 2012). And it lives on in the resolute opposition to climate change shown by Greta Thunberg, who, at sixteen years old, went on strike from school to protest outside the Swedish parliament: once a lone figure with a cardboard sign, now the inspiration for a global movement.

The "girl against the world" scenario has a glamorous appeal; we like it when the underdog triumphs. Sophocles's *Antigone* is frequently taught in high schools in the United States, and whenever I speak about the play in local schools, the students are clearly on the side of Antigone. She is a heroine, they say, and Creon is a total fascist who deserves everything he gets.

It is unlikely that the play's original audience would have been so one-sided in their sympathies. The Greeks would likely have been more critical of Antigone, a girl who spoke and acted out of turn, even as many would have also recognized the failings of the king, Creon.

A medical text from the time called *On the Diseases of Virgins* tells us that girls in Antigone's situation, who were old enough to be married but had not yet taken husbands, were thought to be diseased.[8] They went mad and had visions of death. In *Antigone,* Antigone longs for death; she obsessively imagines her own death and tells us that she welcomes it. Much is also made of the fact that she is unmarried, despite being old enough to be married. Her name is a clue: it can mean against (*anti*) procreation (*gonē*). The medical text gives us a new frame through which to understand Antigone's resolve. Instead of seeing her as a heroine who is determined to do the right thing, even if she risks being put to death, we now see her as showing symptoms of the "disease of young girls," as dysfunctional, unhinged, mad.

Sometimes simply juxtaposing ancient and modern can reveal new and unexpected perspectives. Greta Thunberg's behavior has also been pathologized: she has been criticized and belittled for having Asperger's syndrome. It has made her, critics say, more open to exploitation by others. But Thunberg herself has spoken about how having Asperger's has helped with her activism: it is a gift that "makes her see things outside the box."[9] She has not allowed herself to be defined negatively but has turned the pathology around into something positive. Perhaps we can also take this approach with Antigone. We can understand her madness and dysfunction, as some ancients would have seen it, as giving Antigone a political edge, as enabling her not to fear death, and as fueling her single-mindedness. Through this lens, ancient myths don't just enlarge human stories; modern figures and events can also invite us to see the ancient myths in new ways.

8. We are not certain of the date of the text. It might have been written after the date of Sophocles's *Antigone,* but if so, it still gives us an insight into the kinds of ideas about girls' behavior that were circulating. See Rebecca Flemming and Ann Ellis Hanson, "Hippocrates' 'Peri Parthenión' (Diseases of Young Girls): Text and Translation," *Early Science and Medicine* 3, no. 3 (1998): 241–252.

9. Interview with Greta Thunberg, *CBS This Morning,* CBS News, September 10, 2019, www.cbsnews.com/news/greta-thunberg-climate-change-gift-of-aspergers/. See also Greta Thunberg's speech "Almost Everything Is Black and White," Declaration of Rebellion, Extinction Rebellion, Parliament Square, London, October 31, 2018, the text of which is printed in Greta Thunberg, *No One Is Too Small to Make a Difference* ([. . .] Penguin, 2019), 6–13.

For the ancient Greeks and Romans, the gods were more than just exciting characters. Most worshipped them and took religious rituals very seriously.[1] But, there is a crucial difference between ancient Greek and Roman religious practice and the main religions practiced today. Unlike our monotheistic religions of Christianity, Islam, and Judaism, Greek and Roman religion was polytheistic. Zeus or Jupiter (as the Greeks and Romans called him, respectively) was the most powerful god, and it was sensible not to get on the wrong side of his thunderbolt, but all of the gods demanded worship, and there was no religious text or commandments to follow. (When Antigone appeals to the eternal and unwritten laws, what she means is unclear, which is part of the problem.)

A couple of key things follow from this. The first is that mythological narratives became a way of thinking through complicated moral dilemmas. This makes them useful for us too; we keep returning to Greek and Roman myths precisely because they avoid the simple "good versus evil" stories, from fairy tales to Disney movies, that are such a strong part of our culture. Second, myths, especially those that were told in epic poetry and drama, were widely known and authoritative. All educated, and many uneducated, Greek and Romans would have known their Homer. We don't have anything like this: when I asked my class of seven hundred students, the book that was familiar to most of them was not the Bible or the Koran or Shakespeare or Walt Whitman—but Dr. Seuss.

The cultural authority of epic and tragedy continued through the advent of Christianity as a major religion. Christian texts often rewrote Greek and Roman myths to give them a different message. Greek and Roman mythology, and classical antiquity more broadly, have been enormously influential in Western culture and beyond.[2] By classical antiquity I mean the period when Greek and Roman cultures flourished in the lands that we now call Europe, North Africa, and Western Asia, from the eighth century BCE, when the epic poems of Homer were first sung, to the fifth century CE, when what we now call the Middle Ages began. (I'm all too aware of the fast leaps across time and space and how imprecise a phrase *Greek and Roman* can be.) Intellectual history, by which I mean the major philosophers, novelists, theorists, playwrights, politicians, and other thinkers from antiquity to today, has continually drawn on Greek and Roman myths. That means that for us to enter into conversations—philosophical, historical, artistic, and political—more often than not involves engaging with ideas and arguments from ancient Greece and Rome.

1. See Esther Eidinow and Julia Kindt, eds., "Part III: Myths? Contexts and Representations," in *The Oxford Handbook of Ancient Greek Religion* ([Oxford UP], 2015); and Mary Beard, John North, and Simon Price, *Religions of Rome, Volume 1: A History* ([Cambridge UP], 1998). Not all ancient Greeks and Romans believed in the existence of gods and goddesses: see Tim Whitmarsh, *Battling the Gods: Atheism in the Ancient World* ([. . .] Alfred A. Knopf, 2015).

2. On the reception of Greek tragedy and other aspects of classical antiquity in different parts of the world, see Betine van Zyl Smit, *A Handbook to the Reception of Greek Drama* ([. . .] Wiley-Blackwell, 2019); Zara Martirosova Torlone, Dana Lacourse Munteanu, and Dorota Dutsch, eds., *A Handbook to Classical Reception in Eastern and Central Europe* ([. . .] Wiley-Blackwell, 2001); Almut-Barbara Renger, *Receptions of Greek and Roman Antiquity in East Asia* ([. . .] Brill, 2018); Barbara Goff and Michael Simpson, *Crossroads in the Black Aegean: Oedipus, Antigone, and Dramas of the African Diaspora* ([Oxford UP], 2008); and Kathryn Bosher, Fiona Macintosh, Justine McConnell, and Patrice Rankine, eds., *The Oxford Handbook of Greek Drama in the Americas* ([Oxford UP], 2015).

The ideological purpose of these conversations has varied widely. Classical antiquity has been used to justify fascism, slavery, white supremacy, and misogyny. It has also played a crucial role in political idealism, inspiring, variously, the Founding Fathers (and influencing foundational statements such as the Declaration of Independence and the US Constitution), trades union movements, Marxism, and the gay rights movement.[3] As ancient historian Neville Morley writes of classical antiquity, in his book *Classics: Why It Matters,* "There is always a struggle over its ownership, and who gets to claim and define it."[4] So maybe we're due for a fresh understanding of how ancient Greek and Roman myths, and their characters, can be claimed and defined by all of us who want to resist the current movement toward greater patriarchal control and who are working to make this a more equal, empathetic, and enlightened world.

This book brings together two parts of my life: my professional self and my role as a mother. I have been researching and teaching ancient mythology for over twenty-five years, in universities in England and the United States. It is through teaching the myths to my students that I have seen how powerful these tales are and how reading them critically and creatively can be empowering. Telling new stories is, of course, essential, but viewing our worlds through the lens of the old myths is also meaningful.

I am also the mother of a teenage daughter, Athena. She and her friends have been taught about ancient Greece and its myths and culture but without any understanding that what they were learning had much relevance to their lives today, beyond vague notions of inheriting democracy. This book grew from my attempts to explain to Athena that the things that were preoccupying her and her peer group—girls' safety, school dress codes, and dieting, as well as dealing with a changing political climate in which their freedoms were being curtailed and environmental protections reversed—are all underpinned by cultural narratives. One of the planks in the ideological scaffolding is classical mythology. Part of being empowered and fighting back involves understanding these myths and their cultural impact and turning them to our own advantage.

• • • • •

[R]e-creations of ancient myths ask over and over: Who owns classical antiquity? Who owns culture? The response: We do.

• • • • •

3. See Donna Zuckerberg, *Not All Dead White Men: Classics and Misogyny in the Digital Age* ([Harvard UP], 2018); Alex Scobie, *Hitler's State Architecture: The Impact of Classical Antiquity* ([Penn State UP], 1990); Thomas E. Jenkins, *Antiquity Now: The Classical World in the Contemporary American Imagination* ([Cambridge UP], 2015); Simon Goldhill, *Love, Sex & Tragedy: How the Ancient World Shapes Our Lives* ([. . .] John Murray, 2004); Kostas Vlassopoulos, *Politics: Antiquity and Its Legacy* ([. . .] I. B. Tauris, 2015); Page DuBois, *Slavery: Antiquity and Its Legacy* ([. . .] I. B. Tauris, 2010); Jared Hickman, *Black Prometheus: Race and Radicalism in the Age of Atlantic Slavery* ([Oxford UP], 2017); and Edith Hall and Henry Stead, *A People's History of Classics: Class and Greco-Roman Antiquity in Britain 1689 to 1939.* ([. . .] Routledge, 2020).
4. Neville Morley, *Classics; Why It Matters* ([. . .] Polity Press, 2018), 91.

CODA: *ANTIGONE RISING*

Stories matter. Many stories matter. Stories
have been used to dispossess and to malign.
But stories can also be used to empower and
to humanize. Stories can break the dignity of a
people. But stories can also repair that dignity.

— CHIMAMANDA NGOZI ADICHIE,
   "The Danger of a Single Story," TED Talk

Somos muchos. We are many.

— SARA URIBE, *Antígona González*

The courageous *spirit* of Antigone may live on in Malala Yousafzai [. . .] and Greta Thunberg and in the many young women who stand up to the misuses of power, but the *story* of Antigone, as told by Sophocles in his tragic drama, ends in catastrophe, pain, and ruin.

Antigone breaks the law and defies her uncle Creon, the king of Thebes, when she buries her brother who was an enemy of the state. When she will not back down, Creon orders that she be buried alive in a tomb. (This is a particularly cowardly act: Antigone is left to starve to death, but because Creon has not ordered her immediate death, he hopes to avoid the religious stain that might arise from executing his niece.) Creon has a change of heart after a visit from the blind seer Teiresias who tells him that his actions have been immoral, but it is too late: when his guards go to release Antigone, they find that she has hanged herself inside the cave. Haemon, who is Creon's son and Antigone's fiancé, kills himself, and his death leads to the suicide of Queen Eurydice, his mother. Creon is left a broken man, but at what cost? As a script for successful activism, this story leaves quite a bit to be desired.

Antigone's lack of sisterhood is also a problem.[5] At the very beginning of the play, Antigone asks Ismene to join with her in burying their brother, but when Ismene voices objections to Antigone's plan, Antigone allows for no debate, disagreement, or compromise: "You will be my enemy," she says.[6] When Ismene attempts, later in the play, to share the blame for burying their brother and to be Antigone's ally, Antigone will have none of it. It is striking that in Sophocles's play, Antigone never says *we*. Toward the beginning of the play, she uses the formula *you and I* or *you and me*, and after that, her speech is all about *I* or *me*. Her language of exclusion reflects, and reveals, her politics.

Antigone's certainty and single-mindedness are part of her appeal. But certainty also breeds extremism, which, as Sophocles cautions, can be destructive. Today, Antigone's kind of intolerance and self-righteousness can be seen especially on social media, which tends to aggravate and inflame disagreements. Feminists are primed to call one another out, to punish transgressions, no matter how minor, to lack perspective, and to create a culture of silencing and shame. As Jessa Crispin puts it in her critique of modern feminism: "An environment

---

5. See Simon Goldhill, chapter 9, "Antigone and the Politics of Sisterhood: The Tragic Language of Sharing," in *Sophocles and the Language of Tragedy* ([Oxford UP], 2012), 231–248.
6. Sophocles, *Antigone* 93.

where we strong-arm dissidence and varied opinion is an environment devoid of possibility and dynamism."[7] "Burn it down" is a catchphrase of keyboard warriors; it is easier to castigate and condemn than to persuade, inspire, and do the hard work needed to bring about positive change. There's a strand of nihilism in Sophocles's play *Antigone* that we would do well to reject.

One of the conclusions of this book is that ancient myths (stories) have subversive power precisely because they can be told—and read—in different ways. In the words of novelist Ben Okri, myths "always take wings and soar beyond the place where we can keep them fixed."[8] This can be due to their inherent ambiguities and their ability to reveal a different perspective if we read them with care [. . .]. It is also due to the creative reimagining of myths by modern artists like Ali Smith and Beyoncé and by activists [. . .]. These new adaptations change not only the plots of the ancient tales but also what they have to say about women, about race, and about human relations: in other words, in changing the myths (stories), artists subvert the myths (false ideas and beliefs) too.

The problem is that misogynist myths are more strongly culturally entrenched in our societies than myths that subvert them. The beliefs that women, especially foreign women, are to be controlled, conquered, and even killed, that some women deserve to be raped and will not be believed if they speak the truth about sexual violence are hardwired into our culture. The diet industry and the use of dress codes to control and punish girls and women and to enforce gender and racial norms are global social phenomena that cause immense damage and misery. The paradigms from antiquity that challenge these stories, beliefs, and practices are not as well established or widely implemented.

However, the creative adaptations of myth—the stories, videos, images, and novels that present radically different perspectives—are more than individual contestations: they amount to a formidable cultural trend. This was always the case: rewriting myth from different perspectives goes back to antiquity. [. . .]

The Antigone myth is a good example of this. Euripides's play about Antigone, which no longer survives, almost certainly revised Sophocles's tragedy and allowed Antigone and Haemon to get married and have a baby son! Scholars' educated guesses, based on later summaries of the play, envisage wildly different endings for Antigone and her family. Perhaps Creon tracked them down, recognized them, and had them killed. Perhaps the hero Hercules intervened, and they all lived happily after, an ending that would have allowed Antigone to rebel against Creon's authoritarianism *and* to have a future.[9]

Even more shocking is the likelihood that in Euripides's version of the myth Haemon helped Antigone to bury her brother. She did not act alone. The possibility of Antigone taking collaborative action is also raised in an exquisite modern adaptation of the myth: a book (not exactly poem, play, novel, or newspaper article but containing elements of all these) called *Antígona González,*

---

7. Jessa Crispin, *Why I Am Not a Feminist: A Feminist Manifesto* ([. . .] Melville House, 2017), 102.
8. Ben Okri, *A Way of Being Free* ([. . .] Head of Zeus, 2015), 44.
9. The fragments of Euripides's *Antigone* that have survived are in Christopher Collard and Martin Cropp, eds. and trans., *Euripides Fragments: Aegeus to Meleager* ([Harvard UP], 2008).

written by Sara Uribe and translated by John Pluecker.[1] It contains elements of, and meditates upon, previous Antigones in life, literature, and political theory, as it traces the journey of Antígona González, who searches for the body of her brother who has "disappeared" in Tamaulipas, Mexico, so that she can give him a proper burial. It gives us a sense of the long and rich tradition of using the Antigone myth to articulate abuses of power. Uribe's Antigone quotes a Colombian activist who took her name, even as she harks back to Sophocles:

> : *No quería ser una Antígona*
> *Pero me tocó.*
> : *I didn't want to be an Antigone*
> *But it happened to me.*[2]

She fights a system, not a despot:

> *Supe que Tamaulipas era Tebas y Creonte este silencio*
> *amordazándolo todo.*
> *I realize Tamaulipas was Thebes / and Creon this*
> *silence stifling everything.*

The book draws on a long Latin American tradition that identifies Polynices with the marginalized, the separated, and the lost.[3] It evokes the mothers and fathers whom the US media calls migrants, although the mildness of that word erases their desperation, as they search for the children snatched from them by the country that they hoped would give them sanctuary but took their children instead.

A repeated refrain in *Antígona González* quotes Sophocles: "Will you join me in taking up the body?"[4] But whereas in Sophocles the character Antigone asks the question to her sister Ismene, in Sara Uribe's book, Antigone asks the question to us, the readers. Within this haunted question is a reminder that how the past influences the present and whether it is used to uphold or subvert brutality depends on us. Unlike in Sophocles's tragedy, Sara Uribe's Antigone insists on there being an "us" and an "us" with power.

Antigone is rising. Antigones (and Ismenes and Haemons) are rising.

Somos muchos. We are many.

1. Sara Uribe, *Antígona González*, trans. John Pluecker ([. . .] Les Figues Press, 2016). First published as *Antígona González* by Sur+ Editions, 2012. The 2016 edition is laid out with Uribe's text on the lefthand page and Pluecker's translation on the right. Actor and director Sandra Muñoz commissioned Uribe to write the book in 2011; A-tar Company performed it April 29, 2012, in Tampico, Tamaulipas, Mexico.
2. Uribe, *Antígona González*, 175: "From the journal antigonagomez.blogspot.mx by the Colombian activist Antígona Gómez or Diana Gómez, daughter of Jaime Gómez who was disappeared and later found dead in April 2006, the autobiographical sentence: 'I didn't want to be an Antigone but it happened to me.'"
3. See, for example, Leopoldo Marechal's *Antígona Vélez* (1951), María Zambrano's *La tumba de Antígona* (1967), and Griselda Gambaro's *Antígona Furiosa* (1989). For other playwrights, discussion, and bibliography, see Uribe, *Antígona González*, 172–187. More generally, see Kathryn Bosher, Fiona Macintosh, Justine McConnell, and Patrice Rankine, eds., *The Oxford Handbook of Greek Drama in the Americas* ([Oxford UP], 2015); and Rosa Andújar and Konstantinos P. Nikoloutsos, eds., *Greeks and Romans on the Latin American Stage* ([. . .] Bloomsbury Academic, 2020).
4. The translation used is by H. D. F. Kitto; see Uribe, *Antígona González*, 173.

SUGGESTIONS FOR WRITING

1. The first two scenes or episodes of ANTIGONE introduce us to each of the play's two main characters—first Antigone, then Creon. Write an essay in which you explore what each scene shows us about who these characters are, what motives and values drive them, and why they come into conflict. What does Sophocles achieve by showing us Antigone in conversation with her sister, or Creon with a "convocation of the elders" (line 177)? In terms of characterization and conflict, what is the significance of the choral songs that end each of these two opening episodes?

2. As is conventional in Greek drama, ANTIGONE ends with a final choral song that articulates the theme of the play, while also leaving a great deal of room for interpretation about just what that theme is. Drawing on evidence from the entire play, explain how we should interpret the final song and the play's theme.

3. Write an essay that draws on evidence from this ancient Greek play to explore precisely how and why it remains relevant to the world in which you live, perhaps by also drawing on and developing a specific claim or example from Helen Morales's AN-TIGONE RISING. Does ANTIGONE, for example, depict a type of person, situation, or conflict still common in the twenty-first century, or might it articulate a theme that still applies?

4. Many of the critical excerpts in this chapter focus on the conflict between Antigone and Creon, debating not only how that conflict is ultimately resolved but also what the nature of the conflict is. To take just two examples, Richard C. Jebb takes the conflict to be one between "*the duty of obeying the State's laws*" and "*the duty of listening to the private conscience*" (1688), while Maurice Bowra implies that the conflict is instead between duty to the laws of man versus those of the gods and/or between the human tendency toward "arrogance" versus the need for humility and reverence (1688). Carefully read the other critical excerpts in the chapter, working to understand how each characterizes the conflict between Creon and Antigone. Then, write an essay in which you first describe the views of all the critics and then draw on evidence from the play either to defend one of these views or to offer an alternative interpretation of the play's central conflict.

5. Though he acknowledges that ANTIGONE depicts an external conflict between Antigone and Creon and the views and values each represents, Bernard Knox suggests that the play also presents Creon as internally conflicted. Carefully read the excerpt from Knox's introduction, and write an essay exploring whether the play supports his interpretation of Creon's internal conflict and its resolution.

6. Re-read the critical excerpts in this chapter and then make a list of at least three moments in ANTIGONE or aspects or elements of the play that strike you as important, but that aren't given adequate attention in the critical excerpts. Then write an essay that explains why any one of these moments, aspects, or elements is especially important to the play's effect and meaning.

SAMPLE WRITING: RESEARCH ESSAY

The student essay below was written in response to an assignment that asked students to draw on at least five works of literary criticism, including any relevant excerpts in this chapter and at least one journal article *not* included here, to develop their own interpretations of any aspect of ANTIGONE. Student writer Jackie Izawa decided to explore rival interpretations of Antigone's treatment of her siblings and her fiancé. The resulting essay demonstrates unusual strengths and a few common problems, particularly in the way it uses, presents, and quotes from both primary and secondary sources. The instructor comments that accompany the essay highlight some of those strengths and weaknesses.

Perhaps the weakest moment in the essay is a conclusion that does not fulfill the promise made in the introduction that the essay will ultimately "dra[w] a conclusion" about Antigone's motives. The simplest way to fix that inconsistency would be to change the thesis statement so that it matches up with the conclusion and to devote the conclusion to discussing why it's so "essential that we consider different perspectives" and interpretations rather than simply endorsing one. What might the play itself say about that issue, particularly through Haemon's remarks to his father?

Izawa 1

Jackie Izawa
Dr. Mays
ENG 298X
15 May 2021

The Two Faces of Antigone

Antigone's strong yet harsh nature motivates her to defy Creon's edict, but it also isolates her from those who love her. Throughout the play, Antigone tries to convince Creon that her fallen brother, Polyneices, deserves a proper burial. Her unwavering loyalty to her brother shows she might be capable of love. But if so, why does she only seem to love the person who's dead before the play even begins? She barely shows any affection for her only living sibling, Ismene, and none for her betrothed, Haemon. It is possible that Antigone is so overwhelmed by a desire for justice for her brother that she becomes blinded to every other person. The other possibility is that she is creating the illusion that she does not love Ismene and Haemon because she wants to spare them. "Namely, that

Izawa 2

Margin note (left): Introduce quotations from sources with a signal phrase providing information about the source necessary to understand the quotation and its relationship to your statement. Is Simpson endorsing one of the two possible interpretations you've just described, or does the quotation suggest a third possibility? Also, make sure that the quotation makes sense on its own. The sentence fragment you quote here is confusing.

Margin note (left, lower): You provide good evidence from the play to support your claims about Ismene's reluctance to defy the law, but none to back up your other claim—that her reluctance is also due to her sense of her particular position and duties "as an obedient woman."

although now Antigone does not mean to be stern and hard, as she is simply being herself, yet all the same she *is* stern and hard" (Simpson and Millar 79). Before drawing a conclusion about Antigone's motives, it is important to recognize and acknowledge both positions.

Ismene is Antigone's opposite in every way, in W. H. D. Rouse's words, "a nice girl, soft-hearted and devoted, but a shadow of her strong sister" (41). In the opening scene of *Antigone*, the two sisters have just heard of Creon's edict, and both have different opinions about how to handle it. While Antigone is set on burying her brother, Ismene tries to reason with her. She recalls all the horrible events that happened in their family history. First Oedipus "himself struck out / the sight of his two eyes," and then his wife and mother "did shame / violently on her life, with twisted cords" (lines 58-59, 61-62). Ismene continues talking about the family's tragedies, ending with the deaths of her brothers. Both sisters know that the sentence for burying Polyneices is death. Ismene does not want herself or Antigone to follow in the steps of her deceased family members or to "put dishonor on them" by defying Creon (90). Ismene is timid and fearful of breaking the law. By nature, Ismene is submissive. She views herself as an obedient woman, a compliant citizen. Naturally, when Antigone asks for Ismene's help in burying their brother, Ismene declines. Ismene would like to bury her brother, but she cannot break the law. She tells Antigone, "to act in defiance of the citizenry, / my nature does not give me means for that" (91-92).

In the play's very first line, Antigone calls Ismene "my dear sister." But this is the first and only time that Antigone shows affection for Ismene. Because Ismene is afraid to go against Creon's edict, Antigone regards Ismene as a coward and disowns her. Immediately, Antigone verbally attacks her sister, showing that she is unable to view things as others do: "At least he is my brother—and yours, too, / though you deny him. *I* will not prove false to him" (51-52). The emphasis on the "*I*" shows that Antigone feels a degree of rivalry. It is likely she feels that because *she* is determined to bury Polyneices, she is better than Ismene. This kind of rivalry is common between siblings even today. The idea of proving your superiority is always attractive, especially if you can demonstrate it publicly, to an entire city. Antigone is rather cruel and ruthless to her sister, whether out of pure anger, rivalry, or pain at her betrayal of the family. Towards the end of their first encounter, Ismene promises that she will keep silent, but Antigone retorts, "Oh, oh, no! shout it out. I will hate you still worse / for silence— should you not proclaim it, / to everyone" (lines 99-101). Despite all that both of them have endured because of their shared family history, Antigone is willing to throw it away when Ismene does not help her:

> If you will talk like this I will loathe you,
> and you will be adjudged an enemy—
> justly—by the dead's decision. Let me alone
> and my folly with me, to endure this terror.

Margin note (right): Interesting observation! Does this introduce a third possible interpretation of Antigone (in addition to the two you introduce early on)?

What exactly do you mean to demonstrate with this quotation? Does this provide evidence for your point about Antigone's desire to publicly demonstrate her superiority? or the point about her cruelty? or something else?

Izawa 3

No suffering of mine will be enough
to make me die ignobly. (109-14)

The two sisters are seen together only briefly later in the play, but the dynamic between them is much the same. After Antigone attempts to bury Polyneices and both sisters are brought to Creon, Antigone lashes out at Ismene, effectively severing any ties she has with her sister. As Charles Levy argues, "in [a] . . . tense stichomythic exchange with Ismene" shortly after her argument with Creon, "she reacts with still greater vehemence than during their earlier encounter to what she regards as her sister's irremediable betrayal of her, scorning Ismene" (142). Ismene wants to share the sentence of death with her sister, pleading, "Sister, do not dishonor me, denying me / a common death with you, a common honoring / of the dead man." But Antigone refuses to listen, saying, "Don't die with me, nor make your own / what you have never touched" (lines 597-601). Antigone is consistently cold towards her sister.

Showing the same consistency (in the opposite way), Ismene seems to disregard the ill treatment she receives from her sister, continuing to show love for Antigone though Ismene knows that she is no longer welcome in Antigone's eyes. Being the compassionate and devoted sister that she is, Ismene still does her best to save Antigone. Even after being rejected, Ismene tries to reason with Creon. She pleads again that her life would be incomplete without Antigone. When Creon refuses to change his mind, Ismene brings up Haemon, hoping that Creon is not cruel enough to execute his future daughter-in-law. Unfortunately, even that does not budge Creon. Ismene is loving and caring, showing as much loyalty to her sister as Antigone does for their brother, but Ismene's gesture is never acknowledged.

Or might Antigone in fact be making a gesture of love even greater than her sister's? As A. W. Simpson and C. M. H. Millar argue, Antigone's treatment of Ismene could in fact be viewed as liberating Ismene or saving her from death (79). They believe that Antigone is brutal with Ismene because she is "unwillingly" putting up a façade for Creon (80). One of the main driving factors in their argument is the irony in Antigone's decision: "The *irony* of the situation is brought out, because, from love for Ismene, Antigone alienates herself from her, in order to save her, and goes to her death thinking she has failed; and she never finds out that she succeeded after all" (80).

Likewise, there are also two different ways of interpreting Antigone's interaction with her betrothed. Haemon, from the first moment he is introduced, immediately sides with Antigone and is completely devoted to her. He defends his wife-to-be and defies his father, Creon, ironically with as much passion as Antigone shows. When he first appears in the play, he is naturally dedicated to his father. He shows that he respects his father, but at the same time he also reasons with Creon both about the rule of the city and about the punishment of Antigone:

Margin notes:

This quotation from your secondary source consists mainly of plot summary. It would be more effective to describe the action yourself, while acknowledging that Levy, too, notes its importance.

What evidence from your primary text supports this claim, and what do you think of it? Remember that quoting a critic's claim isn't enough to prove the claim valid.

Izawa 4

Haemon: You will not find me yield to what is shameful.

Creon: At least, your argument is all for her.

Haemon: Yes, and for you and me—and for the gods below.

Creon: You will never marry her while her life lasts.

Haemon: Then she must die—and dying destroy another. (lines 804-08)

Haemon is showing his devotion to Antigone as well as foreshadowing his own fate in the play. Even though Creon tells him he can find another wife, Haemon refuses. His love for Antigone dooms him to his death. All of his actions following his argument with his father are undertaken for Antigone. When Haemon finds Antigone dead in the cave, he is consumed with rage and anger. As Walter H. Johns puts it, because "Haemon hears his father's voice and realizes that the cause of all his grief is close at hand," he "turn[s] his sword against himself and d[ies] with his arms about the body of Antigone" (100). Haemon's rage is likely equivalent to his love for Antigone, and for him to kill himself because of his grief over her death only supports this likelihood.

The reader empathizes with and even pities Haemon because although he speaks of great affection for Antigone, she does not do the same for him. In fact, as Martha Nussbaum points out, "Antigone never [even] addresses a word throughout the entire play" to this "man who passionately loves and desires her" (1698). And Antigone says his name only once in the play when she responds to Creon, "Dear Haemon, how your father dishonors you" (line 627). Though "dear" is usually a term of endearment, the context in which it is used and Antigone's silence about Haemon in the rest of the play suggest that she says it in a pitying manner. Perhaps she felt sympathy for Haemon because he had a father who was willing to kill the love of his life, but that's not the same as loving him as he does her. The relationship is completely one-sided, and Antigone's lack of affection for her betrothed seems to give a new kind of meaning to Ismene's remark much earlier in the play that her sister is "in love / with the impossible" (104-05). Antigone does seem to be more in love with the idea of burying her brother than she is with Haemon.

Again, though, is hard-heartedness or single-heartedness the only explanation for Antigone's behavior? Some critics argue that it isn't, that Antigone's lack of attention to Haemon is inspired by her desire to ensure that he does not share her fate. She could very well love him, but because she is sentenced to death, she breaks off ties with him. Simpson and Millar, for example, conclude that ". . . Antigone has broken the ties between herself and her sister, in order to save her, and is now completely alone in the world. Haemon cannot reach her, as far as she knows, because Creon has just forbidden their marriage" (80). Perhaps Antigone realized that she and Haemon would never have a happy marriage, so she let him go. Unfortunately, Haemon does not realize her intentions.

Again, this section seems a bit light on evidence (versus secondary source material), while the latter consists of plot summary.

Great point! Is it one any other critic makes as well?

Izawa 5

The true motive behind Antigone's actions will always be debated. There are always at least two sides to everything, and it is essential that we consider different perspectives. Antigone can be viewed as hard-hearted and cruel, able to cut herself off from those who love and cherish her. However, she can also be seen as the type of heroine who does everything for the greater good of those she is closest to. In this view, she is compassionate, loyal, and unafraid to make sacrifices. Either way, Antigone remains a heroine who has made a huge impact not only on other characters in the play, but on those who read it as well.

Izawa 6

Works Cited

Johns, Walter H. "Dramatic Effect in Sophocles' *Antigone* 1232." *Classical Journal*, vol. 43, no. 2, 1947, pp. 99-100. *JSTOR*, www.jstor.org/stable/3293075.

Levy, Charles S. "Antigone's Motives: A Suggested Interpretation." *Transactions and Proceedings of the American Philological Association*, no. 94, 1963, pp. 137-44. *JSTOR*, www.jstor.org/stable/283641.

Mays, Kelly J., editor. *The Norton Introduction to Literature*. Shorter 14th ed., W. W. Norton, 2021.

Nussbaum, Martha C. "*From* Sophocles' *Antigone*: Conflict, Vision, and Simplification." Mays, pp. 1696-1701.

Rouse, W. H. D. "The Two Burials in *Antigone*." *Classical Review*, vol. 25, no. 2, 1911, pp. 40-42. *JSTOR*, www.jstor.org/stable/694563.

Simpson, A. W., and C. M. H. Millar. "A Note on Sophocles' *Antigone*, Lines 531-81." *Greece & Rome*, vol. 17, no. 50, 1948, pp. 78-81. *JSTOR*, www.jstor.org/stable/641167.

Sophocles. *Antigone*. Mays, pp. 1653-85.

Reading More Drama

HENRIK IBSEN
(1828–1906)

A Doll House[1]

Born in Skien, Norway, Henrik Ibsen was apprenticed to an apothecary until 1850, when he left for Oslo and published his first play, *Catilina*, a verse tragedy. By 1857 Ibsen was director of Oslo's Norwegian Theater, but his early plays, such as *Love's Comedy* (1862), were poorly received. Disgusted with what he saw as Norway's backwardness, Ibsen left in 1864 for Rome, Italy, where he wrote two more verse plays, *Brand* (1866) and *Peer Gynt* (1867), before turning to the realistic style and harsh criticism of traditional social mores for which he is best known. *The League of Youth* (1869), *Pillars of Society* (1877), *A Doll House* (1879), *Ghosts* (1881), *An Enemy of the People* (1882), *The Wild Duck* (1884), and *Hedda Gabler* (1890) won him a reputation throughout Europe as a controversial and outspoken advocate of moral and social reform. Near the end of his life, Ibsen explored the human condition in the explicitly symbolic terms of *The Master Builder* (1892) and *When We Dead Awaken* (1899). Ibsen's works had enormous influence on twentieth-century drama.

CHARACTERS

TORVALD HELMER, *a lawyer*
NORA, *his wife*
DR. RANK
MRS. LINDE
NILS KROGSTAD, *a bank clerk*

THE HELMERS' THREE SMALL CHILDREN
ANNE-MARIE, *their nurse*
HELENE, *a maid*
A DELIVERY BOY

The action takes place in HELMER's *residence.*

ACT I

A comfortable room, tastefully but not expensively furnished. A door to the right in the back wall leads to the entryway; another to the left leads to HELMER's *study. Between these doors, a piano. Midway in the left-hand wall a door, and further back a window. Near the window a round*

1. Translated from the Danish by Rolf Fjelde.

*table with an armchair and a small sofa. In the right-hand wall, toward the
rear, a door, and nearer the foreground a porcelain stove with two armchairs
and a rocking chair beside it. Between the stove and the side door, a small
table. Engravings on the walls. An etagère with china figures and other small
art objects; a small bookcase with richly bound books; the floor carpeted; a
fire burning in the stove. It is a winter day.*

*A bell rings in the entryway; shortly after we hear the door being unlocked.
NORA comes into the room, humming happily to herself; she is wearing street
clothes and carries an armload of packages, which she puts down on the table
to the right. She has left the hall door open; and through it a DELIVERY BOY is
seen, holding a Christmas tree and a basket, which he gives to the MAID who
let them in.*

NORA: Hide the tree well, Helene. The children mustn't get a glimpse of it till
this evening, after it's trimmed. [*To the* DELIVERY BOY, *taking out her purse.*]
How much?

DELIVERY BOY: Fifty, ma'am.

NORA: There's a crown. No, keep the change. [*The* BOY *thanks her and leaves.*
NORA *shuts the door. She laughs softly to herself while taking off her street
things. Drawing a bag of macaroons from her pocket, she eats a couple, then
steals over and listens at her husband's study door.*] Yes, he's home. [*Hums again
as she moves to the table right.*]

HELMER: [*From the study.*] Is that my little lark twittering out there?

NORA: [*Busy opening some packages.*] Yes, it is.

HELMER: Is that my squirrel rummaging around?

NORA: Yes!

HELMER: When did my squirrel get in?

NORA: Just now. [*Putting the macaroon bag in her pocket and wiping her mouth.*]
Do come in, Torvald, and see what I've bought.

HELMER: Can't be disturbed. [*After a moment he opens the door and peers in,
pen in hand.*] Bought, you say? All that there? Has the little spendthrift been
out throwing money around again?

NORA: Oh, but Torvald, this year we really should let ourselves go a bit. It's the
first Christmas we haven't had to economize.

HELMER: But you know we can't go squandering.

NORA: Oh yes, Torvald, we can squander a little now. Can't we? Just a tiny, wee
bit. Now that you've got a big salary and are going to make piles and piles of
money.

HELMER: Yes—starting New Year's. But then it's a full three months till the
raise comes through.

NORA: Pooh! We can borrow that long.

HELMER: Nora! [*Goes over and playfully takes her by the ear.*] Are your scatter-
brains off again? What if today I borrowed a thousand crowns, and you
squandered them over Christmas week, and then on New Year's Eve a roof
tile fell on my head, and I lay there—

NORA: [*Putting her hand on his mouth.*] Oh! Don't say such things!

HELMER: Yes, but what if it happened—then what?

NORA: If anything so awful happened, then it just wouldn't matter if I had debts or not.

HELMER: Well, but the people I'd borrowed from?

NORA: Them? Who cares about them! They're strangers.

HELMER: Nora, Nora, how like a woman! No, but seriously, Nora, you know what I think about that. No debts! Never borrow! Something of freedom's lost—and something of beauty, too—from a home that's founded on borrowing and debt. We've made a brave stand up to now, the two of us; and we'll go right on like that the little while we have to.

NORA: [*Going toward the stove.*] Yes, whatever you say, Torvald.

HELMER: [*Following her.*] Now, now, the little lark's wings mustn't droop. Come on, don't be a sulky squirrel. [*Taking out his wallet.*] Nora, guess what I have here.

NORA: [*Turning quickly.*] Money!

HELMER: There, see. [*Hands her some notes.*] Good grief, I know how costs go up in a house at Christmastime.

NORA: Ten—twenty—thirty—forty. Oh, thank you, Torvald; I can manage no end on this.

HELMER: You really will have to.

NORA: Oh yes, I promise I will. But come here so I can show you everything I bought. And so cheap! Look, new clothes for Ivar here—and a sword. Here a horse and a trumpet for Bob. And a doll and a doll's bed here for Emmy; they're nothing much, but she'll tear them to bits in no time anyway. And here I have dress material and handkerchiefs for the maids. Old Anne-Marie really deserves something more.

HELMER: And what's in that package there?

NORA: [*With a cry.*] Torvald, no! You can't see that till tonight!

HELMER: I see. But tell me now, you little prodigal, what have you thought of for yourself?

NORA: For myself? Oh, I don't want anything at all.

HELMER: Of course you do. Tell me just what—within reason—you'd most like to have.

NORA: I honestly don't know. Oh, listen, Torvald—

HELMER: Well?

NORA: [*Fumbling at his coat buttons, without looking at him.*] If you want to give me something, then maybe you could—you could—

HELMER: Come, on, out with it.

NORA: [*Hurriedly.*] You could give me money, Torvald. No more than you think you can spare; then one of these days I'll buy something with it.

HELMER: But Nora—

NORA: Oh, please, Torvald darling, do that! I beg you, please. Then I could hang the bills in pretty gilt paper on the Christmas tree. Wouldn't that be fun?

HELMER: What are those little birds called that always fly through their fortunes?

NORA: Oh yes, spendthrifts; I know all that. But let's do as I say, Torvald; then I'll have time to decide what I really need most. That's very sensible, isn't it?

HELMER: [*Smiling.*] Yes, very—that is, if you actually hung onto the money I give you, and you actually used it to buy yourself something. But it goes for the house and for all sorts of foolish things, and then I only have to lay out some more.

NORA: Oh, but Torvald—

HELMER: Don't deny it, my dear little Nora. [*Putting his arm around her waist.*] Spendthrifts are sweet, but they use up a frightful amount of money. It's incredible what it costs a man to feed such birds.

NORA: Oh, how can you say that! Really, I save everything I can.

HELMER: [*Laughing.*] Yes, that's the truth. Everything you can. But that's nothing at all.

NORA: [*Humming, with a smile of quiet satisfaction.*] Hm, if you only knew what expenses we larks and squirrels have, Torvald.

HELMER: You're an odd little one. Exactly the way your father was. You're never at a loss for scaring up money; but the moment you have it, it runs right out through your fingers; you never know what you've done with it. Well, one takes you as you are. It's deep in your blood. Yes, these things are hereditary, Nora.

NORA: Ah, I could wish I'd inherited many of Papa's qualities.

HELMER: And I couldn't wish you anything but just what you are, my sweet little lark. But wait; it seems to me you have a very—what should I call it?—a very suspicious look today—

NORA: I do?

HELMER: You certainly do. Look me straight in the eye.

NORA: [*Looking at him.*] Well?

HELMER: [*Shaking an admonitory finger.*] Surely my sweet tooth hasn't been running riot in town today, has she?

NORA: No. Why do you imagine that?

HELMER: My sweet tooth really didn't make a little detour through the confectioner's?

NORA: No, I assure you, Torvald—

HELMER: Hasn't nibbled some pastry?

NORA: No, not at all.

HELMER: Not even munched a macaroon or two?

NORA: No, Torvald, I assure you, really—

HELMER: There, there now. Of course I'm only joking.

NORA: [*Going to the table, right.*] You know I could never think of going against you.

HELMER: No, I understand that; and you *have* given me your word. [*Going over to her.*] Well, you keep your little Christmas secrets to yourself, Nora darling. I expect they'll come to light this evening, when the tree is lit.

NORA: Did you remember to ask Dr. Rank?

HELMER: No. But there's no need for that; it's assumed he'll be dining with us. All the same, I'll ask him when he stops by here this morning. I've ordered some fine wine. Nora, you can't imagine how I'm looking forward to this evening.

NORA: So am I. And what fun for the children, Torvald!

HELMER: Ah, it's so gratifying to know that one's gotten a safe, secure job, and with a comfortable salary. It's a great satisfaction, isn't it?

NORA: Oh, it's wonderful!

HELMER: Remember last Christmas? Three whole weeks before, you shut your-self in every evening till long after midnight, making flowers for the Christ-mas tree, and all the other decorations to surprise us. Ugh, that was the dullest time I've ever lived through.

NORA: It wasn't at all dull for me.

HELMER: [*Smiling.*] But the outcome *was* pretty sorry, Nora.

NORA: Oh, don't tease me with that again. How could I help it that the cat came in and tore everything to shreds.

HELMER: No, poor thing, you certainly couldn't. You wanted so much to please us all, and that's what counts. But it's just as well that the hard times are past.

NORA: Yes, it's really wonderful.

HELMER: Now I don't have to sit here alone, boring myself, and you don't have to tire your precious eyes and your fair little delicate hands—

NORA: [*Clapping her hands.*] No, is it really true, Torvald, I don't have to? Oh, how wonderfully lovely to hear! [*Taking his arm.*] Now I'll tell you just how I've thought we should plan things. Right after Christmas—[*The doorbell rings.*] Oh, the bell. [*Straightening the room up a bit.*] Somebody would have to come. What a bore!

HELMER: I'm not at home to visitors, don't forget.

MAID: [*From the hall doorway.*] Ma'am, a lady to see you—

NORA: All right, let her come in.

MAID: [*To* HELMER.] And the doctor's just come too.

HELMER: Did he go right to my study?

MAID: Yes, he did.

[HELMER *goes into his room. The* MAID *shows in* MRS. LINDE, *dressed in traveling clothes, and shuts the door after her.*]

MRS. LINDE: [*In a dispirited and somewhat hesitant voice.*] Hello, Nora.

NORA: [*Uncertain.*] Hello—

MRS. LINDE: You don't recognize me.

NORA: No, I don't know—but wait, I think—[*Exclaiming.*] What! Kristine! Is it really you?

MRS. LINDE: Yes, it's me.

NORA: Kristine! To think I didn't recognize you. But then, how could I? [*More quietly.*] How you've changed, Kristine!

MRS. LINDE: Yes, no doubt I have. In nine—ten long years.

NORA: Is it so long since we met! Yes, it's all of that. Oh, these last eight years have been a happy time, believe me. And so now you've come in to town, too. Made the long trip in the winter. That took courage.

MRS. LINDE: I just got here by ship this morning.

NORA: To enjoy yourself over Christmas, of course. Oh, how lovely! Yes, enjoy ourselves, we'll do that. But take your coat off. You're not still cold? [*Helping her.*] There now, let's get cozy here by the stove. No, the easy chair there! I'll take the rocker here. [*Seizing her hands.*] Yes, now you have your old look again; it was only in that first moment. You're a bit more pale, Kristine—and maybe a bit thinner.

MRS. LINDE: And much, much older, Nora.

NORA: Yes, perhaps a bit older; a tiny, tiny bit; not much at all. [*Stopping short; suddenly serious.*] Oh, but thoughtless me, to sit here, chattering away. Sweet, good Kristine, can you forgive me?

MRS. LINDE: What do you mean, Nora?

NORA: [*Softly.*] Poor Kristine, you've become a widow.

MRS. LINDE: Yes, three years ago.

NORA: Oh, I knew it, of course; I read it in the papers. Oh, Kristine, you must believe me; I often thought of writing you then, but I kept postponing it, and something always interfered.

MRS. LINDE: Nora dear, I understand completely.

NORA: No, it was awful of me, Kristine. You poor thing, how much you must have gone through. And he left you nothing?

MRS. LINDE: No.

NORA: And no children?

MRS. LINDE: No.

NORA: Nothing at all, then?

MRS. LINDE: Not even a sense of loss to feed on.

NORA: [*Looking incredulously at her.*] But Kristine, how could that be?

MRS. LINDE: [*Smiling wearily and smoothing her hair.*] Oh, sometimes it happens, Nora.

NORA: So completely alone. How terribly hard that must be for you. I have three lovely children. You can't see them now; they're out with the maid. But now you must tell me everything—

MRS. LINDE: No, no, no, tell me about yourself.

NORA: No, you begin. Today I don't want to be selfish. I want to think only of you today. But there *is* something I must tell you. Did you hear of the wonderful luck we had recently?

MRS. LINDE: No, what's that?

NORA: My husband's been made manager in the bank, just think!

MRS. LINDE: Your husband? How marvelous!

NORA: Isn't it? Being a lawyer is such an uncertain living, you know, especially if one won't touch any cases that aren't clean and decent. And of course Torvald would never do that, and I'm with him completely there. Oh, we're simply delighted, believe me! He'll join the bank right after New Year's and start getting a huge salary and lots of commissions. From now on we can live quite differently—just as we want. Oh, Kristine, I feel so light and happy! Won't it be lovely to have stacks of money and not a care in the world?

MRS. LINDE: Well, anyway, it would be lovely to have enough for necessities.

NORA: No, not just for necessities, but stacks and stacks of money!

MRS. LINDE: [*Smiling.*] Nora, Nora, aren't you sensible yet? Back in school you were such a free spender.

NORA: [*With a quiet laugh.*] Yes, that's what Torvald still says. [*Shaking her finger.*] But "Nora, Nora" isn't as silly as you all think. Really, we've been in no position for me to go squandering. We've had to work, both of us.

MRS. LINDE: You too?

NORA: Yes, at odd jobs—needlework, crocheting, embroidery, and such—[*Casually.*] and other things too. You remember that Torvald left the department when we were married? There was no chance of promotion in his office, and of course he needed to earn more money. But that first year he drove himself terribly. He took on all kinds of extra work that kept him going morning and night. It wore him down, and then he fell deathly ill. The doctors said it was essential for him to travel south.

MRS. LINDE: Yes, didn't you spend a whole year in Italy?

NORA: That's right. It wasn't easy to get away, you know. Ivar had just been born. But of course we had to go. Oh, that was a beautiful trip, and it saved Torvald's life. But it cost a frightful sum, Kristine.

MRS. LINDE: I can well imagine.

NORA: Four thousand, eight hundred crowns it cost. That's really a lot of money.

MRS. LINDE: But it's lucky you had it when you needed it.

NORA: Well, as it was, we got it from Papa.

MRS. LINDE: I see. It was just about the time your father died.

NORA: Yes, just about then. And, you know, I couldn't make that trip out to nurse him. I had to stay here, expecting Ivar any moment, and with my poor sick Torvald to care for. Dearest Papa, I never saw him again, Kristine. Oh, that was the worst time I've known in all my marriage.

MRS. LINDE: I know how you loved him. And then you went off to Italy?

NORA: Yes. We had the means now, and the doctors urged us. So we left a month after.

MRS. LINDE: And your husband came back completely cured?

NORA: Sound as a drum!

MRS. LINDE: But—the doctor?

NORA: Who?

MRS. LINDE: I thought the maid said he was a doctor, the man who came in with me.

NORA: Yes, that was Dr. Rank—but he's not making a sick call. He's our closest friend, and he stops by at least once a day. No, Torvald hasn't had a sick moment since, and the children are fit and strong, and I am, too. [*Jumping up and clapping her hands.*] Oh, dear God, Kristine, what a lovely thing to live and be happy! But how disgusting of me—I'm talking of nothing but my own affairs. [*Sits on a stool close by* KRISTINE, *arms resting across her knees.*] Oh, don't be angry with me! Tell me, is it really true that you weren't in love with your husband? Why did you marry him, then?

MRS. LINDE: My mother was still alive, but bedridden and helpless—and I had my two younger brothers to look after. In all conscience, I didn't think I could turn him down.

NORA: No, you were right there. But was he rich at the time?

MRS. LINDE: He was very well off, I'd say. But the business was shaky, Nora. When he died, it all fell apart, and nothing was left.

NORA: And then—?

MRS. LINDE: Yes, so I had to scrape up a living with a little shop and a little teaching and whatever else I could find. The last three years have been like one endless workday without a rest for me. Now it's over, Nora. My poor mother doesn't need me, for she's passed on. Nor the boys, either; they're working now and can take care of themselves.

NORA: How free you must feel—

MRS. LINDE: No—only unspeakably empty. Nothing to live for now. [*Standing up anxiously.*] That's why I couldn't take it any longer out in that desolate hole. Maybe here it'll be easier to find something to do and keep my mind occupied. If I could only be lucky enough to get a steady job, some office work—

NORA: Oh, but Kristine, that's so dreadfully tiring, and you already look so tired. It would be much better for you if you could go off to a bathing resort.

MRS. LINDE: [*Going toward the window.*] I have no father to give me travel money, Nora.

NORA: [*Rising.*] Oh, don't be angry with me.

MRS. LINDE: [*Going to her.*] Nora dear, don't you be angry with me. The worst of my kind of situation is all the bitterness that's stored away. No one to work for, and yet you're always having to snap up your opportunities. You have to live; and so you grow selfish. When you told me the happy change in your lot, do you know I was delighted less for your sakes than for mine?

NORA: How so? Oh, I see. You think maybe Torvald could do something for you.

MRS. LINDE: Yes, that's what I thought.

NORA: And he will, Kristine! Just leave it to me; I'll bring it up so delicately— find something attractive to humor him with. Oh, I'm so eager to help you.

MRS. LINDE: How very kind of you, Nora, to be so concerned over me—doubly kind, considering you really know so little of life's burdens yourself.

NORA: I—? I know so little—?

MRS. LINDE: [*Smiling.*] Well, my heavens—a little needlework and such—Nora, you're just a child.

NORA: [*Tossing her head and pacing the floor.*] You don't have to act so superior.

MRS. LINDE: Oh?

NORA: You're just like the others. You all think I'm incapable of anything serious—

MRS. LINDE: Come now—

NORA: That I've never had to face the raw world.

MRS. LINDE: Nora dear, you've just been telling me all your troubles.

NORA: Hm! Trivia! [*Quietly.*] I haven't told you the big thing.

MRS. LINDE: Big thing? What do you mean?

NORA: You look down on me so, Kristine, but you shouldn't. You're proud that you worked so long and hard for your mother.

MRS. LINDE: I don't look down on a soul. But it *is* true: I'm proud—and happy, too—to think it was given to me to make my mother's last days almost free of care.

NORA: And you're also proud thinking of what you've done for your brothers.

MRS. LINDE: I feel I've a right to be.

NORA: I agree. But listen to this, Kristine—I've also got something to be proud and happy for.

MRS. LINDE: I don't doubt it. But whatever do you mean?

NORA: Not so loud. What if Torvald heard! He mustn't, not for anything in the world. Nobody must know, Kristine. No one but you.

MRS. LINDE: But what is it, then?

NORA: Come here. [*Drawing her down beside her on the sofa.*] It's true—I've also got something to be proud and happy for. I'm the one who saved Torvald's life.

MRS. LINDE: Saved—? Saved how?

NORA: I told you about the trip to Italy. Torvald never would have lived if he hadn't gone south—

MRS. LINDE: Of course; your father gave you the means—

NORA: [*Smiling.*] That's what Torvald and all the rest think, but—

MRS. LINDE: But—?

NORA: Papa didn't give us a pin. I was the one who raised the money.

MRS. LINDE: You? That whole amount?

NORA: Four thousand, eight hundred crowns. What do you say to that?

MRS. LINDE: But Nora, how was it possible? Did you win the lottery?

NORA: [*Disdainfully.*] The lottery? Pooh! No art to that.

MRS. LINDE: But where did you get it from then?

NORA: [*Humming, with a mysterious smile.*] Hmm, tra-la-la-la.

MRS. LINDE: Because you couldn't have borrowed it.

NORA: No? Why not?

MRS. LINDE: A wife can't borrow without her husband's consent.

NORA: [*Tossing her head.*] Oh, but a wife with a little business sense, a wife who knows how to manage—

MRS. LINDE: Nora, I simply don't understand—

NORA: You don't have to. Whoever said I *borrowed* the money? I could have gotten it other ways. [*Throwing herself back on the sofa.*] I could have gotten it from some admirer or other. After all, a girl with my ravishing appeal—

MRS. LINDE: You lunatic.

NORA: I'll bet you're eaten up with curiosity, Kristine.

MRS. LINDE: Now listen here, Nora—you haven't done something indiscreet?

NORA: [*Sitting up again.*] Is it indiscreet to save your husband's life?

MRS. LINDE: I think it's indiscreet that without his knowledge you—

NORA: But that's the point: he mustn't know! My Lord, can't you understand? He mustn't ever know the close call he had. It was to *me* the doctors came to say his life was in danger—that nothing could save him but a stay in the south. Didn't I try strategy then! I began talking about how lovely it would be for me to travel abroad like other young wives; I begged and I cried; I told him please to remember my condition, to be kind and indulge me; and then I dropped a hint that he could easily take out a loan. But at that, Kristine, he nearly exploded. He said I was frivolous, and it was his duty as man of the house not to indulge me in whims and fancies—as I think he called them. Aha, I thought, now you'll just have to be saved—and that's when I saw my chance.

MRS. LINDE: And your father never told Torvald the money wasn't from him?

NORA: No, never. Papa died right about then. I'd considered bringing him into my secret and begging him never to tell. But he was too sick at the time—and then, sadly, it didn't matter.

MRS. LINDE: And you've never confided in your husband since?

NORA: For heaven's sake, no! Are you serious? He's so strict on that subject. Besides—Torvald, with all his masculine pride—how painfully humiliating for him if he ever found out he was in debt to me. That would just ruin our relationship. Our beautiful, happy home would never be the same.

MRS. LINDE: Won't you ever tell him?

NORA: [*Thoughtfully.*] Yes—maybe sometime years from now, when I'm no longer so attractive. Don't laugh! I only mean when Torvald loves me less than now, when he stops enjoying my dancing and dressing up and reciting for him. Then it might be wise to have something in reserve—[*Breaking off.*] How ridiculous! That'll never happen—Well, Kristine, what do you think of my big secret? I'm capable of something too, hm? You can imagine, of course, how this thing hangs over me. It really hasn't been easy meeting the payments on time. In the business world there's what they call quarterly interest and what they call amortization, and these are always so terribly hard to manage. I've had to skimp a little here and there, wherever I could, you know. I could hardly spare anything from my house allowance, because Torvald has to live well. I couldn't let the children go poorly dressed; whatever I got for them, I felt I had to use up completely—the darlings!

MRS. LINDE: Poor Nora, so it had to come out of your own budget, then?

NORA: Yes, of course. But I was the one most responsible, too. Every time Torvald gave me money for new clothes and such, I never used more than half; always bought the simplest, cheapest outfits. It was a godsend that everything looks so well on me that Torvald never noticed. But it did weigh me down at times, Kristine. It *is* such a joy to wear fine things. You understand.

MRS. LINDE: Oh, of course.

NORA: And then I found other ways of making money. Last winter I was lucky enough to get a lot of copying to do. I locked myself in and sat writing every evening till late in the night. Ah, I was tired so often, dead tired. But still it was wonderful fun, sitting and working like that, earning money. It was almost like being a man.

MRS. LINDE: But how much have you paid off this way so far?

NORA: That's hard to say, exactly. These accounts, you know, aren't easy to figure. I only know that I've paid out all I could scrape together. Time and again I haven't known where to turn. [*Smiling.*] Then I'd sit here dreaming of a rich old gentleman who had fallen in love with me—

MRS. LINDE: What! Who is he?

NORA: Oh, really! And that he'd died, and when his will was opened, there in big letters it said, "All my fortune shall be paid over in cash, immediately, to that enchanting Mrs. Nora Helmer."

MRS. LINDE: But Nora dear—who *was* this gentleman?

NORA: Good grief, can't you understand? The old man never existed; that was only something I'd dream up time and again whenever I was at my wits' end for money. But it makes no difference now; the old fossil can go where he pleases for all I care; I don't need him or his will—because now I'm free. [*Jumping up.*] Oh, how lovely to think of that, Kristine! Carefree! To know you're carefree, utterly carefree; to be able to romp and play with the children, and to keep up a beautiful, charming home—everything just the way Torvald likes it! And think, spring is coming, with big blue skies. Maybe we can travel a little then. Maybe I'll see the ocean again. Oh yes, it *is* so marvelous to live and be happy!

[*The front doorbell rings.*]

MRS. LINDE: [*Rising.*] There's the bell. It's probably best that I go.

NORA: No, stay. No one's expected. It must be for Torvald.

MAID: [*From the hall doorway.*] Excuse me, ma'am—there's a gentleman here to see Mr. Helmer, but I didn't know—since the doctor's with him—

NORA: Who is the gentleman?

KROGSTAD: [*From the doorway.*] It's me, Mrs. Helmer.

[MRS. LINDE *starts and turns away toward the window.*]

NORA: [*Stepping toward him, tense, her voice a whisper.*] You? What is it? Why do you want to speak to my husband?

KROGSTAD: Bank business—after a fashion. I have a small job in the investment bank, and I hear now your husband is going to be our chief—

NORA: In other words, it's—

KROGSTAD: Just dry business, Mrs. Helmer. Nothing but that.

NORA: Yes, then please be good enough to step into the study. [*She nods indifferently as she sees him out by the hall door, then returns and begins stirring up the stove.*]

MRS. LINDE: Nora—who was that man?

NORA: That was a Mr. Krogstad—a lawyer.

MRS. LINDE: Then it really was him.

NORA: Do you know that person?

MRS. LINDE: I did once—many years ago. For a time he was a law clerk in our town.

NORA: Yes, he's been that.

MRS. LINDE: How he's changed.

NORA: I understand he had a very unhappy marriage.

MRS. LINDE: He's a widower now.

NORA: With a number of children. There now, it's burning. [*She closes the stove door and moves the rocker a bit to one side.*]

MRS. LINDE: They say he has a hand in all kinds of business.

NORA: Oh? That may be true; I wouldn't know. But let's not think about business. It's so dull.

[DR. RANK *enters from* HELMER'S *study.*]

RANK: [*Still in the doorway.*] No, no, really—I don't want to intrude, I'd just as soon talk a little while with your wife. [*Shuts the door, then notices* MRS. LINDE.] Oh, beg pardon. I'm intruding here too.

NORA: No, not at all. [*Introducing him.*] Dr. Rank, Mrs. Linde.

RANK: Well now, that's a name much heard in this house. I believe I passed the lady on the stairs as I came.

MRS. LINDE: Yes, I take the stairs very slowly. They're rather hard on me.

RANK: Uh-hm, some touch of internal weakness?

MRS. LINDE: More overexertion, I'd say.

RANK: Nothing else? Then you're probably here in town to rest up in a round of parties?

MRS. LINDE: I'm here to look for work.

RANK: Is that the best cure for overexertion?

MRS. LINDE: One has to live, Doctor.

RANK: Yes, there's a common prejudice to that effect.

NORA: Oh, come on, Dr. Rank—you really do want to live yourself.

RANK: Yes, I really do. Wretched as I am, I'll gladly prolong my torment indef-
    initely. All my patients feel like that. And it's quite the same, too, with the
    morally sick. Right at this moment there's one of those moral invalids in
    there with Helmer—

MRS. LINDE: [Softly.] Ah!

NORA: Who do you mean?

RANK: Oh, it's a lawyer, Krogstad, a type you wouldn't know. His character is
    rotten to the root—but even he began chattering all-importantly about how
    he had to *live*.

NORA: Oh? What did he want to talk to Torvald about?

RANK: I really don't know. I only heard something about the bank.

NORA: I didn't know that Krog—that this man Krogstad had anything to do with
    the bank.

RANK: Yes, he's gotten some kind of berth down there. [To MRS. LINDE.] I don't
    know if you also have, in your neck of the woods, a type of person who
    scuttles about breathlessly, sniffing out hints of moral corruption, and then
    maneuvers his victim into some sort of key position where he can keep an
    eye on him. It's the healthy these days that are out in the cold.

MRS. LINDE: All the same, it's the sick who most need to be taken in.

RANK: [With a shrug.] Yes, there we have it. That's the concept that's turning
    society into a sanatorium.

[NORA, *lost in her thoughts, breaks out into quiet laughter and claps her
hands.*]

RANK: Why do you laugh at that? Do you have any real idea of what society is?

NORA: What do I care about dreary old society? I was laughing at something
    quite different—something terribly funny. Tell me, Doctor—is everyone
    who works in the bank dependent now on Torvald?

RANK: Is that what you find so terribly funny?

NORA: [Smiling and humming.] Never mind, never mind [Pacing the floor.] Yes,
    that's really immensely amusing: that we—that Torvald has so much power
    now over all those people. [Taking the bag out of her pocket.] Dr. Rank, a little
    macaroon on that?

RANK: See here, macaroons! I thought they were contraband here.

NORA: Yes, but these are some that Kristine gave me.

MRS. LINDE: What? I—?

NORA: Now, now, don't be afraid. You couldn't possibly know that Torvald had
    forbidden them. You see, he's worried they'll ruin my teeth. But hmp! Just this
    once! Isn't that so, Dr. Rank? Help yourself! [Puts a macaroon in his mouth.]
    And you too, Kristine. And I'll also have one, only a little one—or two, at the
    most. [Walking about again.] Now I'm really tremendously happy. Now there's
    just one last thing in the world that I have an enormous desire to do.

RANK: Well! And what's that?

NORA: It's something I have such a consuming desire to say so Torvald could hear.

RANK: And why can't you say it?

NORA: I don't dare. It's quite shocking.

MRS. LINDE: Shocking?

RANK: Well, then it isn't advisable. But in front of us you certainly can. What do you have such a desire to say so Torvald could hear?

NORA: I have such a huge desire to say—to hell and be damned!

RANK: Are you crazy?

MRS. LINDE: My goodness, Nora!

RANK: Go on, say it. Here he is.

NORA: [Hiding the macaroon bag.] Shh, shh, shh!

[HELMER comes in from his study, hat in hand, overcoat over his arm.]

NORA: [Going toward him.] Well, Torvald dear, are you through with him?

HELMER: Yes, he just left.

NORA: Let me introduce you—this is Kristine, who's arrived here in town.

HELMER: Kristine—? I'm sorry, but I don't know—

NORA: Mrs. Linde, Torvald dear. Mrs. Kristine Linde.

HELMER: Of course. A childhood friend of my wife's, no doubt?

MRS. LINDE: Yes, we knew each other in those days.

NORA: And just think, she made the long trip down here in order to talk with you.

HELMER: What's this?

MRS. LINDE: Well, not exactly—

NORA: You see, Kristine is remarkably clever in office work, and so she's terribly eager to come under a capable man's supervision and add more to what she already knows—

HELMER: Very wise, Mrs. Linde.

NORA: And then when she heard that you'd become a bank manager—the story was wired out to the papers—then she came in as fast as she could and— Really, Torvald, for my sake you can do a little something for Kristine, can't you?

HELMER: Yes, it's not at all impossible. Mrs. Linde, I suppose you're a widow?

MRS. LINDE: Yes.

HELMER: Any experience in office work?

MRS. LINDE: Yes, a good deal.

HELMER: Well, it's quite likely that I can make an opening for you—

NORA: [Clapping her hands.] You see, you see!

HELMER: You've come at a lucky moment, Mrs. Linde.

MRS. LINDE: Oh, how can I thank you?

HELMER: Not necessary. [Putting his overcoat on.] But today you'll have to excuse me—

RANK: Wait, I'll go with you. [He fetches his coat from the hall and warms it at the stove.]

NORA: Don't stay out long, dear.

HELMER: An hour; no more.

NORA: Are you going too, Kristine?

MRS. LINDE: [*Putting on her winter garments.*] Yes, I have to see about a room now.

HELMER: Then perhaps we can all walk together.

NORA: [*Helping her.*] What a shame we're so cramped here, but it's quite impossible for us to—

MRS. LINDE: Oh, don't even think of it! Good-bye, Nora dear, and thanks for everything.

NORA: Good-bye for now. Of course you'll be back this evening. And you too, Dr. Rank. What? If you're well enough? Oh, you've got to be! Wrap up tight now.

[*In a ripple of small talk the company moves out into the hall; children's voices are heard outside on the steps.*]

NORA: There they are! There they are! [*She runs to open the door. The children come in with their nurse,* ANNE-MARIE.] Come in, come in! [*Bends down and kisses them.*] Oh, you darlings—! Look at them, Kristine. Aren't they lovely!

RANK: No loitering in the draft here.

HELMER: Come, Mrs. Linde—this place is unbearable now for anyone but mothers.

[DR. RANK, HELMER, *and* MRS. LINDE *go down the stairs.* ANNE-MARIE *goes into the living room with the children.* NORA *follows, after closing the hall door.*]

NORA: How fresh and strong you look. Oh, such red cheeks you have! Like apples and roses. [*The children interrupt her throughout the following.*] And it was so much fun? That's wonderful. Really? You pulled both Emmy and Bob on the sled? Imagine, all together! Yes, you're a clever boy, Ivar. Oh, let me hold her a bit, Anne-Marie. My sweet little doll baby! [*Takes the smallest from the nurse and dances with her.*] Yes, yes, Mama will dance with Bob as well. What? Did you throw snowballs? Oh, if I'd only been there! No, don't bother, Anne-Marie—I'll undress them myself. Oh yes, let me. It's such fun. Go in and rest; you look half frozen. There's hot coffee waiting for you on the stove. [*The nurse goes into the room to the left.* NORA *takes the children's winter things off, throwing them about, while the children talk to her all at once.*] Is that so? A big dog chased you? But it didn't bite? No, dogs never bite little, lovely doll babies. Don't peek in the packages, Ivar! What is it? Yes, wouldn't you like to know. No, no, it's an ugly something. Well? Shall we play? What shall we play? Hide-and-seek? Yes, let's play hide-and-seek. Bob must hide first. I must? Yes, let me hide first. [*Laughing and shouting, she and the children play in and out of the living room and the adjoining room to the right. At last* NORA *hides under the table. The children come storming in, search, but cannot find her, then hear her muffled laughter, dash over to the table, lift the cloth up and find her. Wild shouting. She creeps forward as if to scare them. More shouts. Meanwhile, a knock at the hall door; no one has noticed it. Now the door half opens, and* KROGSTAD *appears. He waits a moment; the game goes on.*]

KROGSTAD: Beg pardon, Mrs. Helmer—

NORA: [*With a strangled cry, turning and scrambling to her knees.*] Oh! What do you want?

KROGSTAD: Excuse me. The outer door was ajar; it must be someone forgot to shut it—

NORA: [*Rising.*] My husband isn't home, Mr. Krogstad.

KROGSTAD: I know that.

NORA: Yes—then what do you want here?

KROGSTAD: A word with you.

NORA: With—? [*To the children, quietly.*] Go in to Anne-Marie. What? No, the strange man won't hurt Mama. When he's gone, we'll play some more. [*She leads the children into the room to the left and shuts the door after them. Then, tense and nervous:*] You want to speak to me?

KROGSTAD: Yes, I want to.

NORA: Today? But it's not yet the first of the month—

KROGSTAD: No, it's Christmas Eve. It's going to be up to you how merry a Christmas you have.

NORA: What is it you want? Today I absolutely can't—

KROGSTAD: We won't talk about that till later. This is something else. You do have a moment to spare, I suppose?

NORA: Oh yes, of course—I do, except—

KROGSTAD: Good. I was sitting over at Olsen's Restaurant when I saw your husband go down the street—

NORA: Yes?

KROGSTAD: With a lady.

NORA: Yes. So?

KROGSTAD: If you'll pardon my asking: wasn't that lady a Mrs. Linde?

NORA: Yes.

KROGSTAD: Just now come into town?

NORA: Yes, today.

KROGSTAD: She's a good friend of yours?

NORA: Yes, she is. But I don't see—

KROGSTAD: I also knew her once.

NORA: I'm aware of that.

KROGSTAD: Oh? You know all about it. I thought so. Well, then let me ask you short and sweet: is Mrs. Linde getting a job in the bank?

NORA: What makes you think you can cross-examine me, Mr. Krogstad—you, one of my husband's employees? But since you ask, you might as well know— yes, Mrs. Linde's going to be taken on at the bank. And I'm the one who spoke for her, Mr. Krogstad. Now you know.

KROGSTAD: So I guessed right.

NORA: [*Pacing up and down.*] Oh, one does have a tiny bit of influence, I should hope. Just because I am a woman, don't think it means that—When one has a subordinate position, Mr. Krogstad, one really ought to be careful about pushing somebody who—hm—

KROGSTAD: Who has influence?

NORA: That's right.

KROGSTAD: [*In a different tone.*] Mrs. Helmer, would you be good enough to use your influence on my behalf?

NORA: What? What do you mean?

KROGSTAD: Would you please make sure that I keep my subordinate position in the bank?

NORA: What does that mean? Who's thinking of taking away your position?

KROGSTAD: Oh, don't play the innocent with me. I'm quite aware that your friend would hardly relish the chance of running into me again; and I'm also aware now whom I can thank for being turned out.

NORA: But I promise you—

KROGSTAD: Yes, yes, yes, to the point: there's still time, and I'm advising you to use your influence to prevent it.

NORA: But Mr. Krogstad, I have absolutely no influence.

KROGSTAD: You haven't? I thought you were just saying—

NORA: You shouldn't take me so literally. I! How can you believe that I have any such influence over my husband?

KROGSTAD: Oh, I've known your husband from our student days. I don't think the great bank manager's more steadfast than any other married man.

NORA: You speak insolently about my husband, and I'll show you the door.

KROGSTAD: The lady has spirit.

NORA: I'm not afraid of you any longer. After New Year's, I'll soon be done with the whole business.

KROGSTAD: [Restraining himself.] Now listen to me, Mrs. Helmer. If necessary, I'll fight for my little job in the bank as if it were life itself.

NORA: Yes, so it seems.

KROGSTAD: It's not just a matter of income; that's the least of it. It's something else—All right, out with it! Look, this is the thing. You know, just like all the others, of course, that once, a good many years ago, I did something rather rash.

NORA: I've heard rumors to that effect.

KROGSTAD: The case never got into court; but all the same, every door was closed in my face from then on. So I took up those various activities you know about. I had to grab hold somewhere; and I dare say I haven't been among the worst. But now I want to drop all that. My boys are growing up. For their sakes, I'll have to win back as much respect as possible here in town. That job in the bank was like the first rung in my ladder. And now your husband wants to kick me right back down in the mud again.

NORA: But for heaven's sake, Mr. Krogstad, it's simply not in my power to help you.

KROGSTAD: That's because you haven't the will to—but I have the means to make you.

NORA: You certainly won't tell my husband that I owe you money?

KROGSTAD: Hm—what if I told him that?

NORA: That would be shameful of you. [Nearly in tears.] This secret—my joy and my pride—that he should learn it in such a crude and disgusting way—learn it from you. You'd expose me to the most horrible unpleasantness—

KROGSTAD: Only unpleasantness?

NORA: [Vehemently.] But go on and try. It'll turn out the worse for you, because then my husband will really see what a crook you are, and then you'll never be able to hold your job.

KROGSTAD: I asked if it was just domestic unpleasantness you were afraid of?

NORA: If my husband finds out, then of course he'll pay what I owe at once, and then we'd be through with you for good.

KROGSTAD: [A step closer.] Listen, Mrs. Helmer—you've either got a very bad memory, or else no head at all for business. I'd better put you a little more in touch with the facts.

NORA: What do you mean?

KROGSTAD: When your husband was sick, you came to me for a loan of four thousand, eight hundred crowns.

NORA: Where else could I go?

KROGSTAD: I promised to get you that sum—

NORA: And you got it.

KROGSTAD: I promised to get you that sum, on certain conditions. You were so involved in your husband's illness, and so eager to finance your trip, that I guess you didn't think out all the details. It might just be a good idea to remind you. I promised you the money on the strength of a note I drew up.

NORA: Yes, and that I signed.

KROGSTAD: Right. But at the bottom I added some lines for your father to guarantee the loan. He was supposed to sign down there.

NORA: Supposed to? He did sign.

KROGSTAD: I left the date blank. In other words, your father would have dated his signature himself. Do you remember that?

NORA: Yes, I think—

KROGSTAD: Then I gave you the note for you to mail to your father. Isn't that so?

NORA: Yes.

KROGSTAD: And naturally you sent it at once—because only some five, six days later you brought me the note, properly signed. And with that, the money was yours.

NORA: Well, then; I've made my payments regularly, haven't I?

KROGSTAD: More or less. But—getting back to the point—those were hard times for you then, Mrs. Helmer.

NORA: Yes, they were.

KROGSTAD: Your father was very ill, I believe.

NORA: He was near the end.

KROGSTAD: He died soon after?

NORA: Yes.

KROGSTAD: Tell me, Mrs. Helmer, do you happen to recall the date of your father's death? The day of the month, I mean.

NORA: Papa died the twenty-ninth of September.

KROGSTAD: That's quite correct; I've already looked into that. And now we come to a curious thing—[*Taking out a paper.*] which I simply cannot comprehend.

NORA: Curious thing? I don't know—

KROGSTAD: This is the curious thing: that your father co-signed the note for your loan three days after his death.

NORA: How—? I don't understand.

KROGSTAD: Your father died the twenty-ninth of September. But look. Here your father dated his signature October second. Isn't that curious, Mrs. Helmer? [NORA *is silent.*] Can you explain it to me? [NORA *remains silent.*] It's also remarkable that the words "October second" and the year aren't written in your father's hand, but rather in one that I think I know. Well, it's easy to understand. Your father forgot perhaps to date his signature, and then someone or other added it, a bit sloppily, before anyone knew of his death. There's nothing wrong in that. It all comes down to the signature. And there's no question about *that*, Mrs. Helmer. It really *was* your father who signed his own name here, wasn't it?

NORA: [*After a short silence, throwing her head back and looking squarely at him.*] No, it wasn't. *I* signed papa's name.

KROGSTAD: Wait, now—are you fully aware that this is a dangerous confession?

NORA: Why? You'll soon get your money.

KROGSTAD: Let me ask you a question—why didn't you send the paper to your father?

NORA: That was impossible. Papa was so sick. If I'd asked him for his signature, I also would have had to tell him what the money was for. But I couldn't tell him, sick as he was, that my husband's life was in danger. That was just impossible.

KROGSTAD: Then it would have been better if you'd given up the trip abroad.

NORA: I couldn't possibly. The trip was to save my husband's life. I couldn't give that up.

KROGSTAD: But didn't you ever consider that this was a fraud against me?

NORA: I couldn't let myself be bothered by that. You weren't any concern of mine. I couldn't stand you, with all those cold complications you made, even though you knew how badly off my husband was.

KROGSTAD: Mrs. Helmer, obviously you haven't the vaguest idea of what you've involved yourself in. But I can tell you this: it was nothing more and nothing worse that I once did—and it wrecked my whole reputation.

NORA: You? Do you expect me to believe that you ever acted bravely to save your wife's life?

KROGSTAD: Laws don't inquire into motives.

NORA: Then they must be very poor laws.

KROGSTAD: Poor or not—if I introduce this paper in court, you'll be judged according to law.

NORA: This I refuse to believe. A daughter hasn't a right to protect her dying father from anxiety and care? A wife hasn't a right to save her husband's life? I don't know much about laws, but I'm sure that somewhere in the books these things are allowed. And you don't know anything about it—you who practice the law? You must be an awful lawyer, Mr. Krogstad.

KROGSTAD: Could be. But business—the kind of business we two are mixed up in—don't you think I know about that? All right. Do what you want now. But I'm telling you *this*: if I get shoved down a second time, you're going to keep me company. [*He bows and goes out through the hall.*]

NORA: [*Pensive for a moment, then tossing her head.*] Oh, really! Trying to frighten me! I'm not so silly as all that. [*Begins gathering up the children's clothes, but soon stops.*] But—? No, but that's impossible! I did it out of love.

THE CHILDREN: [*In the doorway, left.*] Mama, that strange man's gone out the door.

NORA: Yes, yes, I know it. But don't tell anyone about the strange man. Do you hear? Not even Papa!

THE CHILDREN: No, Mama. But now will you play again?

NORA: No, not now.

THE CHILDREN: Oh, but Mama, you promised.

NORA: Yes, but I can't now. Go inside; I have too much to do. Go in, go in, my sweet darlings. [*She herds them gently back in the room and shuts the door after them. Settling on the sofa, she takes up a piece of embroidery and makes some stitches, but soon stops abruptly.*] No! [*Throws the work aside, rises, goes to the hall door and calls out.*] Helene! Let me have the tree in here. [*Goes to the table, left, opens the table drawer, and stops again.*] No, but that's utterly impossible!

MAID: [*With the Christmas tree.*] Where should I put it, ma'am?

NORA: There. The middle of the floor.

MAID: Should I bring anything else?

NORA: No, thanks. I have what I need.

[*The* MAID, *who has set the tree down, goes out.*]

NORA: [*Absorbed in trimming the tree.*] Candles here—and flowers here. That terrible creature! Talk, talk, talk! There's nothing to it at all. The tree's going to be lovely. I'll do anything to please you, Torvald. I'll sing for you, dance for you—

[HELMER *comes in from the hall, with a sheaf of papers under his arm.*]

NORA: Oh! You're back so soon?

HELMER: Yes. Has anyone been here?

NORA: Here? No.

HELMER: That's odd. I saw Krogstad leaving the front door.

NORA: So? Oh yes, that's true. Krogstad was here a moment.

HELMER: Nora, I can see by your face that he's been here, begging you to put in a good word for him.

NORA: Yes.

HELMER: And it was supposed to seem like your own idea? You were to hide it from me that he'd been here. He asked you that, too, didn't he?

NORA: Yes, Torvald, but—

HELMER: Nora, Nora, and you could fall for that? Talk with that sort of person and promise him anything? And then in the bargain, tell me an untruth.

NORA: An untruth—?

HELMER: Didn't you say that no one had been here? [*Wagging his finger.*] My little songbird must never do that again. A songbird needs a clean beak to warble with. No false notes. [*Putting his arm about her waist.*] That's the way it should be, isn't it? Yes, I'm sure of it. [*Releasing her.*] And so, enough of that. [*Sitting by the stove.*] Ah, how snug and cozy it is here. [*Leafing among his papers.*]

NORA: [*Busy with the tree, after a short pause.*] Torvald!

HELMER: Yes.

NORA: I'm so much looking forward to the Stenborgs' costume party, day after tomorrow.

HELMER: And I can't wait to see what you'll surprise me with.

NORA: Oh, that stupid business!

HELMER: What?

NORA: I can't find anything that's right. Everything seems so ridiculous, so inane.

HELMER: So my little Nora's come to *that* recognition?

NORA: [*Going behind his chair, her arms resting on its back.*] Are you very busy, Torvald?

HELMER: Oh—

NORA: What papers are those?

HELMER: Bank matters.

NORA: Already?

HELMER: I've gotten full authority from the retiring management to make all necessary changes in personnel and procedure. I'll need Christmas week for that. I want to have everything in order by New Year's.

NORA: So that was the reason this poor Krogstad—

HELMER: Hm.

NORA: [*Still leaning on the chair and slowly stroking the nape of his neck.*] If you weren't so very busy, I would have asked you an enormous favor, Torvald.

HELMER: Let's hear. What is it?

NORA: You know, there isn't anyone who has your good taste—and I want so much to look well at the costume party. Torvald, couldn't you take over and decide what I should be and plan my costume?

HELMER: Ah, is my stubborn little creature calling for a lifeguard?

NORA: Yes, Torvald, I can't get anywhere without your help.

HELMER: All right—I'll think it over. We'll hit on something.

NORA: Oh, how sweet of you. [*Goes to the tree again. Pause.*] Aren't the red flowers pretty—? But tell me, was it really such a crime that this Krogstad committed?

HELMER: Forgery. Do you have any idea what that means?

NORA: Couldn't he have done it out of need?

HELMER: Yes, or thoughtlessness, like so many others. I'm not so heartless that I'd condemn a man categorically for just one mistake.

NORA: No, of course not, Torvald!

HELMER: Plenty of men have redeemed themselves by openly confessing their crimes and taking their punishment.

NORA: Punishment—?

HELMER: But now Krogstad didn't go that way. He got himself out by sharp practices, and that's the real cause of his moral breakdown.

NORA: Do you really think that would—?

HELMER: Just imagine how a man with that sort of guilt in him has to lie and cheat and deceive on all sides, has to wear a mask even with the nearest and dearest he has, even with his own wife and children. And with the children, Nora—that's where it's most horrible.

NORA: Why?

HELMER: Because that kind of atmosphere of lies infects the whole life of a home. Every breath the children take in is filled with the germs of something degenerate.

NORA: [*Coming closer behind him.*] Are you sure of that?

HELMER: Oh, I've seen it often enough as a lawyer. Almost everyone who goes bad early in life has a mother who's a chronic liar.

NORA: Why just—the mother?

HELMER: It's usually the mother's influence that's dominant, but the father's works in the same way, of course. Every lawyer is quite familiar with it. And still this Krogstad's been going home year in, year out, poisoning his own children with lies and pretense; that's why I call him morally lost. [*Reaching his hands out toward her.*] So my sweet little Nora must promise me never to plead his cause.

Your hand on it. Come, come, what's this? Give me your hand. There, now. All settled. I can tell you it'd be impossible for me to work alongside of him. I literally feel physically revolted when I'm anywhere near such a person.

NORA: [*Withdraws her hand and goes to the other side of the Christmas tree.*] How hot it is here! And I've got so much to do.

HELMER: [*Getting up and gathering his papers.*] Yes, and I have to think about getting some of these read through before dinner. I'll think about your costume, too. And something to hang on the tree in gilt paper, I may even see about that. [*Putting his hand on her head.*] Oh you, my darling little songbird. [*He goes into his study and closes the door after him.*]

NORA: [*Softly, after a silence.*] Oh, really! it isn't so. It's impossible. It must be impossible.

ANNE-MARIE: [*In the doorway, left.*] The children are begging so hard to come in to Mama.

NORA: No, no, no, don't let them in to me! You stay with them, Anne-Marie.

ANNE-MARIE: Of course, ma'am. [*Closes the door.*]

NORA: [*Pale with terror*]. Hurt my children—! Poison my home? [*A moment's pause; then she tosses her head.*] That's not true. Never. Never in all the world.

ACT II

Same room. Beside the piano the Christmas tree now stands stripped of ornament, burned-down candle stubs on its ragged branches. NORA's *street clothes lie on the sofa.* NORA, *alone in the room, moves restlessly about; at last she stops at the sofa and picks up her coat.*

NORA: [*Dropping the coat again.*] Someone's coming! [*Goes toward the door, listens.*] No—there's no one. Of course—nobody's coming today, Christmas Day—or tomorrow, either. But maybe—[*Opens the door and looks out.*] No, nothing in the mailbox. Quite empty. [*Coming forward.*] What nonsense! He won't do anything serious. Nothing terrible could happen. It's impossible. Why, I have three small children.

[ANNE-MARIE, *with a large carton, comes in from the room to the left.*]

ANNE-MARIE: Well, at last I found the box with the masquerade clothes.

NORA: Thanks. Put it on the table.

ANNE-MARIE: [*Does so.*] But they're all pretty much of a mess.

NORA: Ahh! I'd love to rip them in a million pieces!

ANNE-MARIE: Oh, mercy, they can be fixed right up. Just a little patience.

NORA: Yes, I'll go get Mrs. Linde to help me.

ANNE-MARIE: Out again now? In this nasty weather? Miss Nora will catch cold—get sick.

NORA: Oh, worse things could happen—How are the children?

ANNE-MARIE: The poor mites are playing with their Christmas presents, but—

NORA: Do they ask for me much?

ANNE-MARIE: They're so used to having Mama around, you know.

NORA: Yes, but Anne-Marie, I *can't* be together with them as much as I was.

ANNE-MARIE: Well, small children get used to anything.

NORA: You think so? Do you think they'd forget their mother if she was gone for good?

ANNE-MARIE: Oh, mercy—gone for good!

NORA: Wait, tell me, Anne-Marie—I've wondered so often—how could you ever have the heart to give your child over to strangers?

ANNE-MARIE: But I had to, you know, to become little Nora's nurse.

NORA: Yes, but how could you *do* it?

ANNE-MARIE: When I could get such a good place? A girl who's poor and who's gotten in trouble is glad enough for that. Because that slippery fish, he didn't do a thing for me, you know.

NORA: But your daughter's surely forgotten you.

ANNE-MARIE: Oh, she certainly has not. She's written to me, both when she was confirmed and when she was married.

NORA: [*Clasping her about the neck.*] You old Anne-Marie, you were a good mother for me when I was little.

ANNE-MARIE: Poor little Nora, with no other mother but me.

NORA: And if the babies didn't have one, then I know that you'd—What silly talk! [*Opening the carton.*] Go in to them. Now I'll have to—Tomorrow you can see how lovely I'll look.

ANNE-MARIE: Oh, there won't be anyone at the party as lovely as Miss Nora. [*She goes off into the room, left.*]

NORA: [*Begins unpacking the box, but soon throws it aside.*] Oh, if I dared to go out. If only nobody would come. If only nothing would happen here while I'm out. What craziness—nobody's coming. Just don't think. This muff—needs a brushing. Beautiful gloves, beautiful gloves. Let it go. Let it go! One, two, three, four, five, six—[*With a cry.*] Oh, there they are! [*Poises to move toward the door, but remains irresolutely standing.* MRS. LINDE *enters from the hall, where she has removed her street clothes.*]

NORA: Oh, it's you, Kristine. There's no one else out there? How good that you've come.

MRS. LINDE: I hear you were up asking for me.

NORA: Yes, I just stopped by. There's something you really can help me with. Let's get settled on the sofa. Look, there's going to be a costume party tomorrow evening at the Stenborgs' right above us, and now Torvald wants me to go as a Neapolitan peasant girl and dance the tarantella[2] that I learned in Capri.

MRS. LINDE: Really, are you giving a whole performance?

NORA: Torvald says yes, I should. See, here's the dress. Torvald had it made for me down there; but now it's all so tattered that I just don't know—

MRS. LINDE: Oh, we'll fix that up in no time. It's nothing more than the trimmings—they're a bit loose here and there. Needle and thread? Good, now we have what we need.

NORA: Oh, how sweet of you!

MRS. LINDE: [*Sewing.*] So you'll be in disguise tomorrow, Nora. You know what? I'll stop by then for a moment and have a look at you all dressed up. But listen, I've absolutely forgotten to thank you for that pleasant evening yesterday.

---

2. Lively folk dance of southern Italy, thought to cure the bite of the tarantula.

NORA: [*Getting up and walking about.*] I don't think it was as pleasant as usual yesterday. You should have come to town a bit sooner, Kristine—Yes, Torvald really knows how to give a home elegance and charm.

MRS. LINDE: And you do, too, if you ask me. You're not your father's daughter for nothing. But tell me, is Dr. Rank always so down in the mouth as yesterday?

NORA: No, that was quite an exception. But he goes around critically ill all the time—tuberculosis of the spine, poor man. You know, his father was a disgusting thing who kept mistresses and so on—and that's why the son's been sickly from birth.

MRS. LINDE: [*Lets her sewing fall to her lap.*] But my dearest Nora, how do you know about such things?

NORA: [*Walking more jauntily.*] Hmp! When you've had three children, then you've had a few visits from—from women who know something of medicine, and they tell you this and that.

MRS. LINDE: [*Resumes sewing; a short pause.*] Does Dr. Rank come here every day?

NORA: Every blessed day. He's Torvald's best friend from childhood, and *my* good friend, too. Dr. Rank almost belongs to this house.

MRS. LINDE: But tell me—is he quite sincere? I mean, doesn't he rather enjoy flattering people?

NORA: Just the opposite. Why do you think that?

MRS. LINDE: When you introduced us yesterday, he was proclaiming that he'd often heard my name in this house; but later I noticed that your husband hadn't the slightest idea who I really was. So how could Dr. Rank—?

NORA: But it's all true, Kristine. You see, Torvald loves me beyond words, and, as he puts it, he'd like to keep me all to himself. For a long time he'd almost be jealous if I even mentioned any of my old friends back home. So of course I dropped that. But with Dr. Rank I talk a lot about such things, because he likes hearing about them.

MRS. LINDE: Now listen, Nora; in many ways you're still like a child. I'm a good deal older than you, with a little more experience. I'll tell you something: you ought to put an end to all this with Dr. Rank.

NORA: What should I put an end to?

MRS. LINDE: Both parts of it, I think. Yesterday you said something about a rich admirer who'd provide you with money—

NORA: Yes, one who doesn't exist—worse luck. So?

MRS. LINDE: Is Dr. Rank well off?

NORA: Yes, he is.

MRS. LINDE: With no dependents?

NORA: No, no one. But—

MRS. LINDE: And he's over here every day?

NORA: Yes, I told you that.

MRS. LINDE: How can a man of such refinement be so grasping?

NORA: I don't follow you at all.

MRS. LINDE: Now don't try to hide it, Nora. You think I can't guess who loaned you the forty-eight hundred crowns?

NORA: Are you out of your mind? How could you think such a thing! A friend of ours, who comes here every single day. What an intolerable situation that would have been!

MRS. LINDE: Then it really wasn't him.

NORA: No, absolutely not. It never even crossed my mind for a moment—And he had nothing to lend in those days; his inheritance came later.

MRS. LINDE: Well, I think that was a stroke of luck for you, Nora dear.

NORA: No, it never would have occurred to me to ask Dr. Rank—Still, I'm quite sure that if I had asked him—

MRS. LINDE: Which you won't, of course.

NORA: No, of course not. I can't see that I'd ever need to. But I'm quite positive that if I talked to Dr. Rank—

MRS. LINDE: Behind your husband's back?

NORA: I've got to clear up this other thing; *that's* also behind his back. I've *got* to clear it all up.

MRS. LINDE: Yes, I was saying that yesterday, but—

NORA: [*Pacing up and down.*] A man handles these problems so much better than a woman—

MRS. LINDE: One's husband does, yes.

NORA: Nonsense. [*Stopping.*] When you pay everything you owe, then you get your note back, right?

MRS. LINDE: Yes, naturally.

NORA: And can rip it into a million pieces and burn it up—that filthy scrap of paper!

MRS. LINDE: [*Looking hard at her, laying her sewing aside, and rising slowly.*] Nora, you're hiding something from me.

NORA: You can see it in my face?

MRS. LINDE: Something's happened to you since yesterday morning. Nora, what is it?

NORA: [*Hurrying toward her.*] Kristine! [*Listening.*] Shh! Torvald's home. Look, go in with the children a while. Torvald can't bear all this snipping and stitching. Let Anne-Marie help you.

MRS. LINDE: [*Gathering up some of the things.*] All right, but I'm not leaving here until we've talked this out. [*She disappears into the room, left, as* TORVALD *enters from the hall.*]

NORA: Oh, how I've been waiting for you, Torvald dear.

HELMER: Was that the dressmaker?

NORA: No, that was Kristine. She's helping me fix up my costume. You know, it's going to be quite attractive.

HELMER: Yes, wasn't that a bright idea I had?

NORA: Brilliant! But then wasn't I good as well to give in to you?

HELMER: Good—because you give in to your husband's judgment? All right, you little goose, I know you didn't mean it like that. But I won't disturb you. You'll want to have a fitting, I suppose.

NORA: And you'll be working?

HELMER: Yes. [*Indicating a bundle of papers.*] See. I've been down to the bank. [*Starts toward his study.*]

NORA: Torvald.

HELMER: [*Stops.*] Yes.

NORA: If your little squirrel begged you, with all her heart and soul, for something—?

HELMER: What's that?

NORA: Then would you do it?

HELMER: First, naturally, I'd have to know what it was.

NORA: Your squirrel would scamper about and do tricks, if you'd only be sweet and give in.

HELMER: Out with it.

NORA: Your lark would be singing high and low in every room—

HELMER: Come on, she does that anyway.

NORA: I'd be a wood nymph and dance for you in the moonlight.

HELMER: Nora—don't tell me it's that same business from this morning?

NORA: [Coming closer.] Yes, Torvald, I beg you, please!

HELMER: And you actually have the nerve to drag that up again?

NORA: Yes, yes, you've got to give in to me; you *have* to let Krogstad keep his job in the bank.

HELMER: My dear Nora, I've slated his job for Mrs. Linde.

NORA: That's awfully kind of you. But you could just fire another clerk instead of Krogstad.

HELMER: This is the most incredible stubbornness! Because you go and give an impulsive promise to speak up for him, I'm expected to—

NORA: That's not the reason, Torvald. It's for your own sake. That man does writing for the worst papers; you said it yourself. He could do you any amount of harm. I'm scared to death of him—

HELMER: Ah, I understand. It's the old memories haunting you.

NORA: What do you mean by that?

HELMER: Of course, you're thinking about your father.

NORA: Yes, all right. Just remember how those nasty gossips wrote in the papers about Papa and slandered him so cruelly. I think they'd have had him dismissed if the department hadn't sent you up to investigate, and if you hadn't been so kind and open-minded toward him.

HELMER: My dear Nora, there's a notable difference between your father and me. Your father's official career was hardly above reproach. But mine is; and I hope it'll stay that way as long as I hold my position.

NORA: Oh, who can ever tell what vicious minds can invent? We could be so snug and happy now in our quiet, carefree home—you and I and the children, Torvald! That's why I'm pleading with you so—

HELMER: And just by pleading for him you make it impossible for me to keep him on. It's already known at the bank that I'm firing Krogstad. What if it's rumored around now that the new bank manager was vetoed by his wife—

NORA: Yes, what then—?

HELMER: Oh yes—as long as our little bundle of stubbornness gets her way—! I should go and make myself ridiculous in front of the whole office—give people the idea I can be swayed by all kinds of outside pressure. Oh, you can bet I'd feel the effects of that soon enough! Besides—there's something that rules Krogstad right out at the bank as long as I'm the manager.

NORA: What's that?

HELMER: His moral failings I could maybe overlook if I had to—

NORA: Yes, Torvald, why not?

HELMER: And I hear he's quite efficient on the job. But he was a crony of mine back in my teens—one of those rash friendships that crop up again and again to embarrass you later in life. Well, I might as well say it straight out: we're on a first-name basis. And that tactless fool makes no effort at all to hide it in front of others. Quite the contrary—he thinks that entitles him to take a familiar air around me, and so every other second he comes booming out with his "Yes, Torvald!" and "Sure thing, Torvald!" I tell you, it's been excruciating for me. He's out to make my place in the bank unbearable.

NORA: Torvald, you can't be serious about all this.

HELMER: Oh no? Why not?

NORA: Because these are such petty considerations.

HELMER: What are you saying? Petty? You think I'm petty!

NORA: No, just the opposite, Torvald dear. That's exactly why—

HELMER: Never mind. You call my motives petty; then I might as well be just that. Petty! All right! We'll put a stop to this for good. [*Goes to the hall door and calls.*] Helene!

NORA: What do you want?

HELMER: [*Searching among his papers.*] A decision. [*The* MAID *comes in.*] Look here; take this letter; go out with it at once. Get hold of a messenger and have him deliver it. Quick now. It's already addressed. Wait, here's some money.

MAID: Yes, sir. [*She leaves with the letter.*]

HELMER: [*Straightening his papers.*] There, now, little Miss Willful.

NORA: [*Breathlessly.*] Torvald, what was that letter?

HELMER: Krogstad's notice.

NORA: Call it back, Torvald! There's still time. Oh, Torvald, call it back! Do it for my sake—for your sake, for the children's sake! Do you hear, Torvald; do it! You don't know how this can harm us.

HELMER: Too late.

NORA: Yes, too late.

HELMER: Nora dear, I can forgive you this panic, even though basically you're insulting me. Yes, you are! Or isn't it an insult to think that *I* should be afraid of a courtroom hack's revenge? But I forgive you anyway, because this shows so beautifully how much you love me. [*Takes her in his arms.*] This is the way it should be, my darling Nora. Whatever comes, you'll see: when it really counts, I have strength and courage enough as a man to take on the whole weight myself.

NORA: [*Terrified.*] What do you mean by that?

HELMER: The whole weight, I said.

NORA: [*Resolutely.*] No, never in all the world.

HELMER: Good. So we'll share it, Nora, as man and wife. That's as it should be. [*Fondling her.*] Are you happy now? There, there, there—not these frightened dove's eyes. It's nothing at all but empty fantasies—Now you should run through your tarantella and practice your tambourine. I'll go to the inner office and shut both doors, so I won't hear a thing; you can make all the noise you like. [*Turning in the doorway.*] And when Rank comes, just tell him where he can find me. [*He nods to her and goes with his papers into the study, closing the door.*]

NORA: [*Standing as though rooted, dazed with fright, in a whisper.*] He really could do it. He will do it. He'll do it in spite of everything. No, not that, never,

never! Anything but that! Escape! A way out—[*The doorbell rings.*] Dr. Rank! Anything but that! *Anything,* whatever it is! [*Her hands pass over her face, smoothing it; she pulls herself together, goes over and opens the hall door.* DR. RANK *stands outside, hanging his fur coat up. During the following scene, it begins getting dark.*]

NORA: Hello, Dr. Rank. I recognized your ring. But you mustn't go in to Torvald yet; I believe he's working.

RANK: And you?

NORA: For you, I always have an hour to spare—you know that. [*He has entered, and she shuts the door after him.*]

RANK: Many thanks. I'll make use of these hours while I can.

NORA: What do you mean by that? While you can?

RANK: Does that disturb you?

NORA: Well, it's such an odd phrase. Is anything going to happen?

RANK: What's going to happen is what I've been expecting so long—but I honestly didn't think it would come so soon.

NORA: [*Gripping his arm.*] What is it you've found out? Dr. Rank, you have to tell me!

RANK: [*Sitting by the stove.*] It's all over with me. There's nothing to be done about it.

NORA: [*Breathing easier.*] Is it you—then—?

RANK: Who else? There's no point in lying to one's self. I'm the most miserable of all my patients, Mrs. Helmer. These past few days I've been auditing my internal accounts. Bankrupt! Within a month I'll probably be laid out and rotting in the churchyard.

NORA: Oh, what a horrible thing to say.

RANK: The thing itself is horrible. But the worst of it is all the other horror before it's over. There's only one final examination left; when I'm finished with that, I'll know about when my disintegration will begin. There's something I want to say. Helmer with his sensitivity has such a sharp distaste for anything ugly. I don't want him near my sickroom.

NORA: Oh, but Dr. Rank—

RANK: I won't have him in there. Under no condition. I'll lock my door to him—As soon as I'm completely sure of the worst, I'll send you my calling card marked with a black cross, and you'll know then the wreck has started to come apart.

NORA: No, today you're completely unreasonable. And I wanted you so much to be in a really good humor.

RANK: With death up my sleeve? And then to suffer this way for somebody else's sins. Is there any justice in that? And in every single family, in some way or another, this inevitable retribution of nature goes on—

NORA: [*Her hands pressed over her ears.*] Oh, stuff! Cheer up! Please—be gay!

RANK: Yes, I'd just as soon laugh at it all. My poor, innocent spine, serving time for my father's gay army days.

NORA: [*By the table, left.*] He was so infatuated with asparagus tips and *pâté de foie gras,* wasn't that it?

RANK: Yes—and with truffles.

NORA: Truffles, yes. And then with oysters, I suppose?

RANK: Yes, tons of oysters, naturally.

NORA: And then the port and champagne to go with it. It's so sad that all these delectable things have to strike at our bones.

RANK: Especially when they strike at the unhappy bones that never shared in the fun.

NORA: Ah, that's the saddest of all.

RANK: [*Looks searchingly at her.*] Hm.

NORA: [*After a moment.*] Why did you smile?

RANK: No, it was you who laughed.

NORA: No, it was you who smiled, Dr. Rank!

RANK: [*Getting up.*] You're even a bigger tease than I'd thought.

NORA: I'm full of wild ideas today.

RANK: That's obvious.

NORA: [*Putting both hands on his shoulders.*] Dear, dear Dr. Rank, you'll never die for Torvald and me.

RANK: Oh, that loss you'll easily get over. Those who go away are soon forgotten.

NORA: [*Looks fearfully at him.*] You believe that?

RANK: One makes new connections, and then—

NORA: Who makes new connections?

RANK: Both you and Torvald will when I'm gone. I'd say you're well under way already. What was that Mrs. Linde doing here last evening?

NORA: Oh, come—you can't be jealous of poor Kristine?

RANK: Oh yes, I am. She'll be my successor here in the house. When I'm down under, that woman will probably—

NORA: Shh! Not so loud. She's right in there.

RANK: Today as well. So you see.

NORA: Only to sew on my dress. Good gracious, how unreasonable you are. [*Sitting on the sofa.*] Be nice now, Dr. Rank. Tomorrow you'll see how beautifully I'll dance; and you can imagine then that I'm dancing only for you—yes, and of course for Torvald, too—that's understood. [*Takes various items out of the carton.*] Dr. Rank, sit over here and I'll show you something.

RANK: [*Sitting.*] What's that?

NORA: Look here. Look.

RANK: Silk stockings.

NORA: Flesh-colored. Aren't they lovely? Now it's so dark here, but tomorrow— No, no, no, just look at the feet. Oh well, you might as well look at the rest.

RANK: Hm—

NORA: Why do you look so critical? Don't you believe they'll fit?

RANK: I've never had any chance to form an opinion on that.

NORA: [*Glancing at him a moment.*] Shame on you. [*Hits him lightly on the ear with the stockings.*] That's for you. [*Puts them away again.*]

RANK: And what other splendors am I going to see now?

NORA: Not the least bit more, because you've been naughty. [*She hums a little and rummages among her things.*]

RANK: [*After a short silence.*] When I sit here together with you like this, completely easy and open, then I don't know—I simply can't imagine—whatever would have become of me if I'd never come into this house.

NORA: [*Smiling.*] Yes, I really think you feel completely at ease with us.

RANK: [*More quietly, staring straight ahead.*] And then to have to go away from it all—

NORA: Nonsense, you're not going away.

RANK: [*His voice unchanged.*]—and not even be able to leave some poor show of gratitude behind, scarcely a fleeting regret—no more than a vacant place that anyone can fill.

NORA: And if I asked you now for—? No—

RANK: For what?

NORA: For a great proof of your friendship—

RANK: Yes, yes?

NORA: No, I mean—for an exceptionally big favor—

RANK: Would you really, for once, make me so happy?

NORA: Oh, you haven't the vaguest idea what it is.

RANK: All right, then tell me.

NORA: No, but I can't, Dr. Rank—it's all out of reason. It's advice and help, too—and a favor—

RANK: So much the better. I can't fathom what you're hinting at. Just speak out. Don't you trust me?

NORA: Of course. More than anyone else. You're my best and truest friend, I'm sure. That's why I want to talk to you. All right, then, Dr. Rank: there's something you can help me prevent. You know how deeply, how inexpressibly dearly Torvald loves me; he'd never hesitate a second to give up his life for me.

RANK: [*Leaning close to her.*] Nora—do you think he's the only one—

NORA: [*With a slight start.*] Who—?

RANK: Who'd gladly give up his life for you.

NORA: [*Heavily.*] I see.

RANK: I swore to myself you should know this before I'm gone. I'll never find a better chance. Yes, Nora, now you know. And also you know now that you can trust me beyond anyone else.

NORA: [*Rising, natural and calm.*] Let me by.

RANK: [*Making room for her, but still sitting.*] Nora—

NORA: [*In the hall doorway.*] Helene, bring the lamp in. [*Goes over to the stove.*] Ah, dear Dr. Rank, that was really mean of you.

RANK: [*Getting up.*] That I've loved you just as deeply as somebody else? Was *that* mean?

NORA: No, but that you came out and told me. That was quite unnecessary—

RANK: What do you mean? Have you known—?

[*The* MAID *comes in with the lamp, sets it on the table, and goes out again.*]

RANK: Nora—Mrs. Helmer—I'm asking you: have you known about it?

NORA: Oh, how can I tell what I know or don't know? Really, I don't know what to say—Why did you have to be so clumsy, Dr. Rank! Everything was so good.

RANK: Well, in any case, you now have the knowledge that my body and soul are at your command. So won't you speak out?

NORA: [*Looking at him.*] After that?

RANK: Please, just let me know what it is.

NORA: You can't know anything now.

RANK: I have to. You mustn't punish me like this. Give me the chance to do whatever is humanly possible for you.

NORA: Now there's nothing you can do for me. Besides, actually, I don't need any help. You'll see—it's only my fantasies. That's what it is. Of course! [*Sits in the rocker, looks at him, and smiles.*] What a nice one you are, Dr. Rank. Aren't you a little bit ashamed, now that the lamp is here?

RANK: No, not exactly. But perhaps I'd better go—for good?

NORA: No, you certainly can't do that. You must come here just as you always have. You know Torvald can't do without you.

RANK: Yes, but *you?*

NORA: You know how much I enjoy it when you're here.

RANK: That's precisely what threw me off. You're a mystery to me. So many times I've felt you'd almost rather be with me than with Helmer.

NORA: Yes—you see, there are some people that one loves most and other people that one would almost prefer being with.

RANK: Yes, there's something to that.

NORA: When I was back home, of course I loved Papa most. But I always thought it was so much fun when I could sneak down to the maids' quarters, because they never tried to improve me, and it was always so amusing, the way they talked to each other.

RANK: Aha, so it's *their* place that I've filled.

NORA: [*Jumping up and going to him.*] Oh, dear, sweet Dr. Rank, that's not what I meant at all. But you can understand that with Torvald it's just the same as with Papa—

[*The* MAID *enters from the hall.*]

MAID: Ma'am—please! [*She whispers to* NORA *and hands her a calling card.*]

NORA: [*Glancing at the card.*] Ah! [*Slips it into her pocket.*]

RANK: Anything wrong?

NORA: No, no, not at all. It's only some—it's my new dress—

RANK: Really? But—there's your dress.

NORA: Oh, that. But this is another one—I ordered it—Torvald mustn't know—

RANK: Ah, now we have the big secret.

NORA: That's right. Just go in with him—he's back in the inner study. Keep him there as long as—

RANK: Don't worry. He won't get away. [*Goes into the study.*]

NORA: [*To the* MAID.] And he's standing waiting in the kitchen?

MAID: Yes, he came up by the back stairs.

NORA: But didn't you tell him somebody was here?

MAID: Yes, but that didn't do any good.

NORA: He won't leave?

MAID: No, he won't go till he's talked with you, ma'am.

NORA: Let him come in, then—but quietly. Helene, don't breathe a word about this. It's a surprise for my husband.

MAID: Yes, yes, I understand—[*Goes out.*]

NORA: This horror—it's going to happen. No, no, no, it can't happen, it mustn't.

[*She goes and bolts* HELMER's *door. The* MAID *opens the hall door for* KROG-STAD *and shuts it behind him. He is dressed for travel in a fur coat, boots, and a fur cap.*]

NORA: [*Going toward him.*] Talk softly. My husband's home.

KROGSTAD: Well, good for him.

NORA: What do you want?

KROGSTAD: Some information.

NORA: Hurry up, then. What is it?

KROGSTAD: You know, of course, that I got my notice.

NORA: I couldn't prevent it, Mr. Krogstad. I fought for you to the bitter end, but nothing worked.

KROGSTAD: Does your husband's love for you run so thin? He knows everything I can expose you to, and all the same he dares to—

NORA: How can you imagine he knows anything about this?

KROGSTAD: Ah, no—I can't imagine it either, now. It's not at all like my fine Torvald Helmer to have so much guts—

NORA: Mr. Krogstad, I demand respect for my husband!

KROGSTAD: Why, of course—all due respect. But since the lady's keeping it so carefully hidden, may I presume to ask if you're also a bit better informed than yesterday about what you've actually done?

NORA: More than you ever could teach me.

KROGSTAD: Yes, I *am* such an awful lawyer.

NORA: What is it you want from me?

KROGSTAD: Just a glimpse of how you are, Mrs. Helmer. I've been thinking about you all day long. A cashier, a night-court scribbler, a—well, a type like me also has a little of what they call a heart, you know.

NORA: Then show it. Think of my children.

KROGSTAD: Did you or your husband ever think of mine? But never mind. I simply wanted to tell you that you don't need to take this thing too seriously. For the present, I'm not proceeding with any action.

NORA: Oh no, really! Well—I knew that.

KROGSTAD: Everything can be settled in a friendly spirit. It doesn't have to get around town at all; it can stay just among us three.

NORA: My husband must never know anything of this.

KROGSTAD: How can you manage that? Perhaps you can pay me the balance?

NORA: No, not right now.

KROGSTAD: Or you know some way of raising the money in a day or two?

NORA: No way that I'm willing to use.

KROGSTAD: Well, it wouldn't have done you any good, anyway. If you stood in front of me with a fistful of bills, you still couldn't buy your signature back.

NORA: Then tell me what you're going to do with it.

KROGSTAD: I'll just hold onto it—keep it on file. There's no outsider who'll even get wind of it. So if you've been thinking of taking some desperate step—

NORA: I have.

KROGSTAD: Been thinking of running away from home—

NORA: I have!

KROGSTAD: Or even of something worse—

NORA: How could you guess that?

KROGSTAD: You can drop those thoughts.

NORA: How could you guess I was thinking of *that*?

KROGSTAD: Most of us think about *that* at first. I thought about it too, but I discovered I hadn't the courage—

NORA: [*Lifelessly.*] I don't either.

KROGSTAD: [*Relieved.*] That's true, you haven't the courage? You too?

NORA: I don't have it—I don't have it.

KROGSTAD: It would be terribly stupid, anyway. After that first storm at home blows out, why, then—I have here in my pocket a letter for your husband—

NORA: Telling everything?

KROGSTAD: As charitably as possible.

NORA: [*Quickly.*] He mustn't ever get that letter. Tear it up. I'll find some way to get money.

KROGSTAD: Beg pardon, Mrs. Helmer, but I think I just told you—

NORA: Oh, I don't mean the money I owe you. Let me know how much you want from my husband, and I'll manage it.

KROGSTAD: I don't want any money from your husband.

NORA: What do you want, then?

KROGSTAD: I'll tell you what. I want to recoup, Mrs. Helmer; I want to get on in the world—and there's where your husband can help me. For a year and a half I've kept myself clean of anything disreputable—all that time struggling with the worst conditions; but I was satisfied, working my way up step by step. Now I've been written right off, and I'm just not in the mood to come crawling back. I tell you, I want to move on. I want to get back in the bank—in a better position. Your husband can set up a job for me—

NORA: He'll never do that!

KROGSTAD: He'll do it. I know him. He won't dare breathe a word of protest. And once I'm in there together with him, you just wait and see! Inside of a year, I'll be the manager's right-hand man. It'll be Nils Krogstad, not Torvald Helmer, who runs the bank.

NORA: You'll never see the day!

KROGSTAD: Maybe you think you can—

NORA: I have the courage now—for *that*.

KROGSTAD: Oh, you don't scare me. A smart, spoiled lady like you—

NORA: You'll see; you'll see!

KROGSTAD: Under the ice, maybe? Down in the freezing, coal-black water? There, till you float up in the spring, ugly, unrecognizable, with your hair falling out—

NORA: You don't frighten me.

KROGSTAD: Nor do you frighten me. One doesn't do these things, Mrs. Helmer. Besides, what good would it be? I'd still have him safe in my pocket.

NORA: Afterwards? When I'm no longer—?

KROGSTAD: Are you forgetting that *I'll* be in control then over your final reputation? [NORA *stands speechless, staring at him.*] Good; now I've warned you. Don't do anything stupid. When Helmer's read my letter, I'll be waiting for his reply. And bear in mind that it's your husband himself who's forced me back to my old ways. I'll never forgive him for that. Good-bye, Mrs. Helmer. [*He goes out through the hall.*]

NORA: [*Goes to the hall door, opens it a crack, and listens.*] He's gone. Didn't leave the letter. Oh no, no, that's impossible too! [*Opening the door more and more.*]

What's that? He's standing outside—not going downstairs. He's thinking it over? Maybe he'll—? [*A letter falls in the mailbox; then* KROGSTAD's *footsteps are heard, dying away down a flight of stairs.* NORA *gives a muffled cry and runs over toward the sofa table. A short pause.*] In the mailbox. [*Slips warily over to the hall door.*] It's lying there. Torvald, Torvald—now we're lost!

MRS. LINDE: [*Entering with the costume from the room, left.*] There now, I can't see anything else to mend. Perhaps you'd like to try—

NORA: [*In a hoarse whisper.*] Kristine, come here.

MRS. LINDE: [*Tossing the dress on the sofa.*] What's wrong? You look upset.

NORA: Come here. See that letter? *There!* Look—through the glass in the mailbox.

MRS. LINDE: Yes, yes, I see it.

NORA: That letter's from Krogstad—

MRS. LINDE: Nora—it's Krogstad who loaned you the money!

NORA: Yes, and now Torvald will find out everything.

MRS. LINDE: Believe me, Nora, it's best for both of you.

NORA: There's more you don't know. I forged a name.

MRS. LINDE: But for heaven's sake—?

NORA: I only want to tell you that, Kristine, so that you can be my witness.

MRS. LINDE: Witness? Why should I—?

NORA: If I should go out of my mind—it could easily happen—

MRS. LINDE: Nora!

NORA: Or anything else occurred—so I couldn't be present here—

MRS. LINDE: Nora, Nora, you aren't yourself at all!

NORA: And someone should try to take on the whole weight, all of the guilt, you follow me—

MRS. LINDE: Yes, of course, but why do you think—?

NORA: Then you're the witness that it isn't true, Kristine. I'm very much myself; my mind right now is perfectly clear; and I'm telling you: nobody else has known about this; I alone did everything. Remember that.

MRS. LINDE: I will. But I don't understand all this.

NORA: Oh, how could you ever understand it? It's the miracle now that's going to take place.

MRS. LINDE: The miracle?

NORA: Yes, the miracle. But it's so awful, Kristine. It mustn't take place, not for anything in the world.

MRS. LINDE: I'm going right over and talk with Krogstad.

NORA: Don't go near him; he'll do you some terrible harm!

MRS. LINDE: There was a time once when he'd gladly have done anything for me.

NORA: He?

MRS. LINDE: Where does he live?

NORA: Oh, how do I know? Yes. [*Searches in her pocket.*] Here's his card. But the letter, the letter—!

HELMER: [*From the study, knocking on the door.*] Nora!

NORA: [*With a cry of fear.*] Oh! What is it? What do you want?

HELMER: Now, now, don't be so frightened. We're not coming in. You locked the door—are you trying on the dress?

NORA: Yes, I'm trying it. I'll look just beautiful, Torvald.

MRS. LINDE: [*Who has read the card.*] He's living right around the corner.

NORA: Yes, but what's the use? We're lost. The letter's in the box.

MRS. LINDE: And your husband has the key?

NORA: Yes, always.

MRS. LINDE: Krogstad can ask for his letter back unread; he can find some excuse—

NORA: But it's just this time that Torvald usually—

MRS. LINDE: Stall him. Keep him in there. I'll be back as quick as I can. [*She hurries out through the hall entrance.*]

NORA: [*Goes to* HELMER's *door, opens it, and peers in.*] Torvald!

HELMER: [*From the inner study.*] Well—does one dare set foot in one's own living room at last? Come on, Rank, now we'll get a look—[*In the doorway.*] But what's this?

NORA: What, Torvald dear?

HELMER: Rank had me expecting some grand masquerade.

RANK: [*In the doorway.*] That was my impression, but I must have been wrong.

NORA: No one can admire me in my splendor—not till tomorrow.

HELMER: But Nora dear, you look so exhausted. Have you practiced too hard?

NORA: No, I haven't practiced at all yet.

HELMER: You know, it's necessary—

NORA: Oh, it's absolutely necessary, Torvald. But I can't get anywhere without your help. I've forgotten the whole thing completely.

HELMER: Ah, we'll soon take care of that.

NORA: Yes, take care of me, Torvald, please! Promise me that? Oh, I'm so nervous. That big party—You must give up everything this evening for me. No business—don't even touch your pen. Yes? Dear Torvald, promise?

HELMER: It's a promise. Tonight I'm totally at your service—you little helpless thing. Hm—but first there's one thing I want to—[*Goes toward the hall door.*]

NORA: What are you looking for?

HELMER: Just to see if there's any mail.

NORA: No, no, don't do that, Torvald!

HELMER: Now what?

NORA: Torvald, please. There isn't any.

HELMER: Let me look, though. [*Starts out.* NORA, *at the piano, strikes the first notes of the tarantella.* HELMER, *at the door, stops.*] Aha!

NORA: I can't dance tomorrow if I don't practice with you.

HELMER: [*Going over to her.*] Nora dear, are you really so frightened?

NORA: Yes, so terribly frightened. Let me practice right now; there's still time before dinner. Oh, sit down and play for me, Torvald. Direct me. Teach me, the way you always have.

HELMER: Gladly, if it's what you want. [*Sits at the piano.*]

NORA: [*Snatches the tambourine up from the box, then a long, varicolored shawl, which she throws around herself, whereupon she springs forward and cries out:*] Play for me now! Now I'll dance!

[HELMER *plays and* NORA *dances.* RANK *stands behind* HELMER *at the piano and looks on.*]

HELMER: [*As he plays.*] Slower. Slow down.

NORA: Can't change it.

HELMER: Not so violent, Nora!

NORA: Has to be just like this.

HELMER: [*Stopping.*] No, no, that won't do at all.

NORA: [*Laughing and swinging her tambourine.*] Isn't that what I told you?

RANK: Let me play for her.

HELMER: [*Getting up.*] Yes, go on. I can teach her more easily then.

[RANK *sits at the piano and plays;* NORA *dances more and more wildly.* HELMER *has stationed himself by the stove and repeatedly gives her directions; she seems not to hear them; her hair loosens and falls over her shoulders; she does not notice, but goes on dancing.* MRS. LINDE *enters.*]

MRS. LINDE: [*Standing dumbfounded at the door.*] Ah—!

NORA: [*Still dancing.*] See what fun, Kristine!

HELMER: But Nora darling, you dance as if your life were at stake.

NORA: And it is.

HELMER: Rank, stop! This is pure madness. Stop it, I say!

[RANK *breaks off playing, and* NORA *halts abruptly.*]

HELMER: [*Going over to her.*] I never would have believed it. You've forgotten everything I taught you.

NORA: [*Throwing away the tambourine.*] You see for yourself.

HELMER: Well, there's certainly room for instruction here.

NORA: Yes, you see how important it is. You've got to teach me to the very last minute. Promise me that, Torvald?

HELMER: You can bet on it.

NORA: You mustn't, either today or tomorrow, think about anything else but me; you mustn't open any letters—or the mailbox—

HELMER: Ah, it's still the fear of that man—

NORA: Oh yes, yes, that too.

HELMER: Nora, it's written all over you—there's already a letter from him out there.

NORA: I don't know. I guess so. But you mustn't read such things now; there mustn't be anything ugly between us before it's all over.

RANK: [*Quietly to* HELMER.] You shouldn't deny her.

HELMER: [*Putting his arm around her.*] The child can have her way. But tomorrow night, after you've danced—

NORA: Then you'll be free.

MAID: [*In the doorway, right.*] Ma'am, dinner is served.

NORA: We'll be wanting champagne, Helene.

MAID: Very good, ma'am. [*Goes out.*]

HELMER: So—a regular banquet, hm?

NORA: Yes, a banquet—champagne till daybreak! [*Calling out.*] And some macaroons, Helene. Heaps of them—just this once.

HELMER: [*Taking her hands.*] Now, now, now—no hysterics. Be my own little lark again.

NORA: Oh, I will soon enough. But go on in—and you, Dr. Rank. Kristine, help me put up my hair.

RANK: [*Whispering, as they go.*] There's nothing wrong—really wrong, is there?

HELMER: Oh, of course not. It's nothing more than this childish anxiety I was telling you about. [*They go out, right.*]

NORA: Well?

MRS. LINDE: Left town.

NORA: I could see by your face.

MRS. LINDE: He'll be home tomorrow evening. I wrote him a note.

NORA: You shouldn't have. Don't try to stop anything now. After all, it's a wonderful joy, this waiting here for the miracle.

MRS. LINDE: What is it you're waiting for?

NORA: Oh, you can't understand that. Go in to them; I'll be along in a moment.

[MRS. LINDE *goes into the dining room.* NORA *stands a short while as if composing herself; then she looks at her watch.*]

NORA: Five. Seven hours to midnight. Twenty-four hours to the midnight after, and then the tarantella's done. Seven and twenty-four? Thirty-one hours to live.

HELMER: [*In the doorway, right.*] What's become of the little lark?

NORA: [*Going toward him with open arms.*] Here's your lark!

ACT III

Same scene. The table, with chairs around it, has been moved to the center of the room. A lamp on the table is lit. The hall door stands open. Dance music drifts down from the floor above. MRS. LINDE *sits at the table, absently paging through a book, trying to read, but apparently unable to focus her thoughts. Once or twice she pauses, tensely listening for a sound at the outer entrance.*

MRS. LINDE: [*Glancing at her watch.*] Not yet—and there's hardly any time left. If only he's not—[*Listening again.*] Ah, there he is. [*She goes out in the hall and cautiously opens the outer door. Quiet footsteps are heard on the stairs. She whispers:*] Come in. Nobody's here.

KROGSTAD: [*In the doorway.*] I found a note from you at home. What's back of all this?

MRS. LINDE: I just *had* to talk to you.

KROGSTAD: Oh? And it just *had* to be here in this house?

MRS. LINDE: At my place it was impossible; my room hasn't a private entrance. Come in; we're all alone. The maid's asleep, and the Helmers are at the dance upstairs.

KROGSTAD: [*Entering the room.*] Well, well, the Helmers are dancing tonight? Really?

MRS. LINDE: Yes, why not?

KROGSTAD: How true—why not?

MRS. LINDE: All right, Krogstad, let's talk.

KROGSTAD: Do we two have anything more to talk about?

MRS. LINDE: We have a great deal to talk about.

KROGSTAD: I wouldn't have thought so.

MRS. LINDE: No, because you've never understood me, really.

KROGSTAD: Was there anything more to understand—except what's all too common in life? A calculating woman throws over a man the moment a better catch comes by.

MRS. LINDE: You think I'm so thoroughly calculating? You think I broke it off lightly?

KROGSTAD: Didn't you?

MRS. LINDE: Nils—is that what you really thought?

KROGSTAD: If you cared, then why did you write me the way you did?

MRS. LINDE: What else could I do? If I had to break off with you, then it was my job as well to root out everything you felt for me.

KROGSTAD: [*Wringing his hands.*] So that was it. And this—all this, simply for money!

MRS. LINDE: Don't forget I had a helpless mother and two small brothers. We couldn't wait for you, Nils; you had such a long road ahead of you then.

KROGSTAD: That may be; but you still hadn't the right to abandon me for somebody else's sake.

MRS. LINDE: Yes—I don't know. So many, many times I've asked myself if I did have that right.

KROGSTAD: [*More softly.*] When I lost you, it was as if all the solid ground dissolved from under my feet. Look at me; I'm a half-drowned man now, hanging onto a wreck.

MRS. LINDE: Help may be near.

KROGSTAD: It was near—but then you came and blocked it off.

MRS. LINDE: Without my knowing it, Nils. Today for the first time I learned that it's you I'm replacing at the bank.

KROGSTAD: All right—I believe you. But now that you know, will you step aside?

MRS. LINDE: No, because that wouldn't benefit you in the slightest.

KROGSTAD: Not "benefit" me, hm! I'd step aside anyway.

MRS. LINDE: I've learned to be realistic. Life and hard, bitter necessity have taught me that.

KROGSTAD: And life's taught me never to trust fine phrases.

MRS. LINDE: Then life's taught you a very sound thing. But you do have to trust in actions, don't you?

KROGSTAD: What does that mean?

MRS. LINDE: You said you were hanging on like a half-drowned man to a wreck.

KROGSTAD: I've good reason to say that.

MRS. LINDE: I'm also like a half-drowned woman on a wreck. No one to suffer with; no one to care for.

KROGSTAD: You made your choice.

MRS. LINDE: There wasn't any choice then.

KROGSTAD: So—what of it?

MRS. LINDE: Nils, if only we two shipwrecked people could reach across to each other.

KROGSTAD: What are you saying?

MRS. LINDE: Two on one wreck are at least better off than each on his own.

KROGSTAD: Kristine!

MRS. LINDE: Why do you think I came into town?

KROGSTAD: Did you really have some thought of me?

MRS. LINDE: I have to work to go on living. All my born days, as long as I can remember, I've worked, and it's been my best and my only joy. But now I'm completely alone in the world; it frightens me to be so empty and lost. To work for yourself—there's no joy in that. Nils, give me something—someone to work for.

KROGSTAD: I don't believe all this. It's just some hysterical feminine urge to go out and make a noble sacrifice.

MRS. LINDE: Have you ever found me to be hysterical?

KROGSTAD: Can you honestly mean this? Tell me—do you know everything about my past?

MRS. LINDE: Yes.

KROGSTAD: And you know what they think I'm worth around here.

MRS. LINDE: From what you were saying before, it would seem that with me you could have been another person.

KROGSTAD: I'm positive of that.

MRS. LINDE: Couldn't it happen still?

KROGSTAD: Kristine—you're saying this in all seriousness? Yes, you are! I can see it in you. And do you really have the courage, then—?

MRS. LINDE: I need to have someone to care for; and your children need a mother. We both need each other. Nils, I have faith that you're good at heart— I'll risk everything together with you.

KROGSTAD: [*Gripping her hands.*] Kristine, thank you, thank you—Now I know I can win back a place in their eyes. Yes—but I forgot—

MRS. LINDE: [*Listening.*] Shh! The tarantella. Go now! Go on!

KROGSTAD: Why? What is it?

MRS. LINDE: Hear the dance up there? When that's over, they'll be coming down.

KROGSTAD: Oh, then I'll go. But—it's all pointless. Of course, you don't know the move I made against the Helmers.

MRS. LINDE: Yes, Nils, I know.

KROGSTAD: And all the same, you have the courage to—?

MRS. LINDE: I know how far despair can drive a man like you.

KROGSTAD: Oh, if I only could take it all back.

MRS. LINDE: You easily could—your letter's still lying in the mailbox.

KROGSTAD: Are you sure of that?

MRS. LINDE: Positive. But—

KROGSTAD: [*Looks at her searchingly.*] Is that the meaning of it, then? You'll save your friend at any price. Tell me straight out. Is that it?

MRS. LINDE: Nils—anyone who's sold herself for somebody else once isn't going to do it again.

KROGSTAD: I'll demand my letter back.

MRS. LINDE: No, no.

KROGSTAD: Yes, of course. I'll stay here till Helmer comes down; I'll tell him to give me my letter again—that it only involves my dismissal—that he shouldn't read it—

MRS. LINDE: No, Nils, don't call the letter back.

KROGSTAD: But wasn't that exactly why you wrote me to come here?

MRS. LINDE: Yes, in that first panic. But it's been a whole day and night since then, and in that time I've seen such incredible things in this house. Helmer's got to learn everything; this dreadful secret has to be aired; those two have to come to a full understanding; all these lies and evasions can't go on.

KROGSTAD: Well, then, if you want to chance it. But at least there's one thing I can do, and do right away—

MRS. LINDE: [*Listening.*] Go now, go, quick! The dance is over. We're not safe another second.

KROGSTAD: I'll wait for you downstairs.

MRS. LINDE: Yes, please do; take me home.

KROGSTAD: I can't believe it; I've never been so happy. [*He leaves by way of the outer door; the door between the room and the hall stays open.*]

MRS. LINDE: [*Straightening up a bit and getting together her street clothes.*] How different now! How different! Someone to work for, to live for—a home to build. Well, it is worth the try! Oh, if they'd only come! [*Listening.*] Ah, there they are. Bundle up. [*She picks up her hat and coat.* NORA's *and* HELMER's *voices can be heard outside; a key turns in the lock, and* HELMER *brings* NORA *into the hall almost by force. She is wearing the Italian costume with a large black shawl about her; he has on evening dress, with a black domino*[3] *open over it.*]

NORA: [*Struggling in the doorway.*] No, no, no, not inside! I'm going up again. I don't want to leave so soon.

HELMER: But Nora dear—

NORA: Oh, I beg you, please, Torvald. From the bottom of my heart, *please*— only an hour more!

HELMER: Not a single minute, Nora darling. You know our agreement. Come on, in we go; you'll catch cold out here. [*In spite of her resistance, he gently draws her into the room.*]

MRS. LINDE: Good evening.

NORA: Kristine!

HELMER: Why, Mrs. Linde—are you here so late?

MRS. LINDE: Yes, I'm sorry, but I did want to see Nora in costume.

NORA: Have you been sitting here, waiting for me?

MRS. LINDE: Yes. I didn't come early enough; you were all upstairs; and then I thought I really couldn't leave without seeing you.

HELMER: [*Removing* NORA's *shawl.*] Yes, take a good look. She's worth looking at, I can tell you that, Mrs. Linde. Isn't she lovely?

MRS. LINDE: Yes, I should say—

HELMER: A dream of loveliness, isn't she? That's what everyone thought at the party, too. But she's horribly stubborn—this sweet little thing. What's to be done with her? Can you imagine, I almost had to use force to pry her away.

NORA: Oh, Torvald, you're going to regret you didn't indulge me, even for just a half hour more.

HELMER: There, you see. She danced her tarantella and got a tumultuous hand— which was well earned, although the performance may have been a bit too naturalistic—I mean it rather overstepped the proprieties of art. But never mind—what's important is, she made a success, an overwhelming success. You think I could let her stay on after that and spoil the effect? Oh no; I took my lovely little Capri girl—my capricious little Capri girl, I should say—took her under my arm; one quick tour of the ballroom, a curtsy to every side, and then—as they say in novels—the beautiful vision disappeared. An exit should

---

3. Hood worn by members of some religious orders.

always be effective, Mrs. Linde, but that's what I can't get Nora to grasp. Phew, it's hot in here. [*Flings the domino on a chair and opens the door to his room.*] Why's it dark in here? Oh yes, of course. Excuse me. [*He goes in and lights a couple of candles.*]

NORA: [*In a sharp, breathless whisper.*] So?

MRS. LINDE: [*Quietly.*] I talked with him.

NORA: And—?

MRS. LINDE: Nora—you must tell your husband everything.

NORA: [*Dully.*] I knew it.

MRS. LINDE: You've got nothing to fear from Krogstad, but you have to speak out.

NORA: I won't tell.

MRS. LINDE: Then the letter will.

NORA: Thanks, Kristine. I know now what's to be done. Shh!

HELMER: [*Reentering.*] Well, then, Mrs. Linde—have you admired her?

MRS. LINDE: Yes, and now I'll say good night.

HELMER: Oh, come, so soon? Is this yours, this knitting?

MRS. LINDE: Yes, thanks. I nearly forgot it.

HELMER: Do you knit, then?

MRS. LINDE: Oh yes.

HELMER: You know what? You should embroider instead.

MRS. LINDE: Really? Why?

HELMER: Yes, because it's a lot prettier. See here, one holds the embroidery so, in the left hand, and then one guides the needle with the right—so—in an easy, sweeping curve—right?

MRS. LINDE: Yes, I guess that's—

HELMER: But, on the other hand, knitting—it can never be anything but ugly. Look, see here, the arms tucked in, the knitting needles going up and down—there's something Chinese about it. Ah, that was really a glorious champagne they served.

MRS. LINDE: Yes, good night, Nora, and don't be stubborn anymore.

HELMER: Well put, Mrs. Linde!

MRS. LINDE: Good night, Mr. Helmer.

HELMER: [*Accompanying her to the door.*] Good night, good night. I hope you get home all right. I'd be very happy to—but you don't have far to go. Good night, good night. [*She leaves. He shuts the door after her and returns.*] There, now, at last we got her out the door. She's a deadly bore, that creature.

NORA: Aren't you pretty tired, Torvald?

HELMER: No, not a bit.

NORA: You're not sleepy?

HELMER: Not at all. On the contrary, I'm feeling quite exhilarated. But you? Yes, you really look tired and sleepy.

NORA: Yes, I'm very tired. Soon now I'll sleep.

HELMER: See! You see! I was right all along that we shouldn't stay longer.

NORA: Whatever you do is always right.

HELMER: [*Kissing her brow.*] Now my little lark talks sense. Say, did you notice what a time Rank was having tonight?

NORA: Oh, was he? I didn't get to speak with him.

HELMER: I scarcely did either, but it's a long time since I've seen him in such high spirits. [*Gazes at her a moment, then comes nearer her.*] Hm—it's marvelous, though, to be back home again—to be completely alone with you. Oh, you bewitchingly lovely young woman!

NORA: Torvald, don't look at me like that!

HELMER: Can't I look at my richest treasure? At all that beauty that's mine, mine alone—completely and utterly.

NORA: [*Moving around to the other side of the table.*] You mustn't talk to me that way tonight.

HELMER: [*Following her.*] The tarantella is still in your blood, I can see—and it makes you even more enticing. Listen. The guests are beginning to go. [*Dropping his voice.*] Nora—it'll soon be quiet through this whole house.

NORA: Yes, I hope so.

HELMER: You do, don't you, my love? Do you realize—when I'm out at a party like this with you—do you know why I talk to you so little, and keep such a distance away; just send you a stolen look now and then—you know why I do it? It's because I'm imagining then that you're my secret darling, my secret young bride-to-be, and that no one suspects there's anything between us.

NORA: Yes, yes; oh, yes, I know you're always thinking of me.

HELMER: And then when we leave and I place the shawl over those fine young rounded shoulders—over that wonderful curving neck—then I pretend that you're my young bride, that we're just coming from the wedding, that for the first time I'm bringing you into my house—that for the first time I'm alone with you—completely alone with you, your trembling young beauty! All this evening I've longed for nothing but you. When I saw you turn and sway in the tarantella—my blood was pounding till I couldn't stand it—that's why I brought you down here so early—

NORA: Go away, Torvald! Leave me alone. I don't want all this.

HELMER: What do you mean? Nora, you're teasing me. You will, won't you? Aren't I your husband—?

[*A knock at the outside door.*]

NORA: [*Startled.*] What's that?

HELMER: [*Going toward the hall.*] Who is it?

RANK: [*Outside.*] It's me. May I come in a moment?

HELMER: [*With quiet irritation.*] Oh, what does he want now? [*Aloud.*] Hold on. [*Goes and opens the door.*] Oh, how nice that you didn't just pass us by!

RANK: I thought I heard your voice, and then I wanted so badly to have a look in. [*Lightly glancing about.*] Ah, me, these old familiar haunts. You have it snug and cozy in here, you two.

HELMER: You seemed to be having it pretty cozy upstairs, too.

RANK: Absolutely. Why shouldn't I? Why not take in everything in life? As much as you can, anyway, and as long as you can. The wine was superb—

HELMER: The champagne especially.

RANK: You noticed that too? It's amazing how much I could guzzle down.

NORA: Torvald also drank a lot of champagne this evening.

RANK: Oh?

NORA: Yes, and that always makes him so entertaining.

RANK: Well, why shouldn't one have a pleasant evening after a well-spent day?

HELMER: Well spent? I'm afraid I can't claim that.

RANK: [*Slapping him on the back.*] But I can, you see!

NORA: Dr. Rank, you must have done some scientific research today.

RANK: Quite so.

HELMER: Come now—little Nora talking about scientific research!

NORA: And can I congratulate you on the results?

RANK: Indeed you may.

NORA: Then they were good?

RANK: The best possible for both doctor and patient—certainty.

NORA: [*Quickly and searchingly.*] Certainty?

RANK: Complete certainty. So don't I owe myself a gay evening afterwards?

NORA: Yes, you're right, Dr. Rank.

HELMER: I'm with you—just so long as you don't have to suffer for it in the morning.

RANK: Well, one never gets something for nothing in life.

NORA: Dr. Rank—are you very fond of masquerade parties?

RANK: Yes, if there's a good array of odd disguises—

NORA: Tell me, what should we two go as at the next masquerade?

HELMER: You little featherhead—already thinking of the next!

RANK: We two? I'll tell you what: you must go as Charmed Life—

HELMER: Yes, but find a costume for *that*!

RANK: Your wife can appear just as she looks every day.

HELMER: That was nicely put. But don't you know what you're going to be?

RANK: Yes, Helmer, I've made up my mind.

HELMER: Well?

RANK: At the next masquerade I'm going to be invisible.

HELMER: That's a funny idea.

RANK: They say there's a hat—black, huge—have you never heard of the hat that makes you invisible? You put it on, and then no one on earth can see you.

HELMER: [*Suppressing a smile.*] Ah, of course.

RANK: But I'm quite forgetting what I came for. Helmer, give me a cigar, one of the dark Havanas.

HELMER: With the greatest pleasure. [*Holds out his case.*]

RANK: Thanks. [*Takes one and cuts off the tip.*]

NORA: [*Striking a match*] Let me give you a light.

RANK: Thank you. [*She holds the match for him; he lights the cigar.*] And now good-bye.

HELMER: Good-bye, good-bye, old friend.

NORA: Sleep well, Doctor.

RANK: Thanks for that wish.

NORA: Wish me the same.

RANK: You? All right, if you like—Sleep well. And thanks for the light. [*He nods to them both and leaves.*]

HELMER: [*His voice subdued.*] He's been drinking heavily.

NORA: [*Absently.*] Could be. [HELMER *takes his keys from his pocket and goes out in the hall.*] Torvald—what are you after?

HELMER: Got to empty the mailbox; it's nearly full. There won't be room for the morning papers.

NORA: Are you working tonight?

HELMER: You know I'm not. Why—what's this? Someone's been at the lock.

NORA: At the lock—?

HELMER: Yes, I'm positive. What do you suppose—? I can't imagine one of the maids—? Here's a broken hairpin. Nora, it's yours—

NORA: [*Quickly.*] Then it must be the children—

HELMER: You'd better break them of that. Hm, hm—well, opened it after all. [*Takes the contents out and calls into the kitchen.*] Helene! Helene, would you put out the lamp in the hall. [*He returns to the room, shutting the hall door, then displays the handful of mail.*] Look how it's piled up. [*Sorting through them.*] Now what's this?

NORA: [*At the window.*] The letter! Oh, Torvald, no!

HELMER: Two calling cards—from Rank.

NORA: From Dr. Rank?

HELMER: [*Examining them.*] "Dr. Rank, Consulting Physician." They were on top. He must have dropped them in as he left.

NORA: Is there anything on them?

HELMER: There's a black cross over the name. See? That's a gruesome notion. He could almost be announcing his own death.

NORA: That's just what he's doing.

HELMER: What! You've heard something? Something he's told you?

NORA: Yes. That when those cards came, he'd be taking his leave of us. He'll shut himself in now and die.

HELMER: Ah, my poor friend! Of course I knew he wouldn't be here much longer. But so soon—And then to hide himself away like a wounded animal.

NORA: If it has to happen, then it's best it happens in silence—don't you think so, Torvald?

HELMER: [*Pacing up and down.*] He'd grown right into our lives. I simply can't imagine him gone. He with his suffering and loneliness—like a dark cloud setting off our sunlit happiness. Well, maybe it's best this way. For him, at least. [*Standing still.*] And maybe for us too, Nora. Now we're thrown back on each other, completely. [*Embracing her.*] Oh you, my darling wife, how can I hold you close enough? You know what, Nora—time and again I've wished you were in some terrible danger, just so I could stake my life and soul and everything, for your sake.

NORA: [*Tearing herself away, her voice firm and decisive.*] Now you must read your mail, Torvald.

HELMER: No, no, not tonight. I want to stay with you, dearest.

NORA: With a dying friend on your mind?

HELMER: You're right. We've both had a shock. There's ugliness between us— these thoughts of death and corruption. We'll have to get free of them first. Until then—we'll stay apart.

NORA: [*Clinging about his neck.*] Torvald—good night! Good night!

HELMER: [*Kissing her on the cheek.*] Good night, little songbird. Sleep well, Nora. I'll be reading my mail now. [*He takes the letters into his room and shuts the door after him.*]

NORA: [*With bewildered glances, groping about, seizing* HELMER's *domino, throwing it around her, and speaking in short, hoarse, broken whispers.*] Never see him again. Never, never. [*Putting her shawl over her head.*] Never see the children either—them, too. Never, never. Oh, the freezing black water! The depths—down—Oh, I wish it were over—He has it now; he's reading it—now. Oh no, no, not yet. Torvald, good-bye, you and the children—[*She starts for the hall; as she does,* HELMER *throws open his door and stands with an open letter in his hand.*]

HELMER: Nora!

NORA: [*Screams.*] Oh—!

HELMER: What is this? You know what's in this letter?

NORA: Yes, I know. Let me go! Let me out!

HELMER: [*Holding her back.*] Where are you going?

NORA: [*Struggling to break loose.*] You can't save me, Torvald!

HELMER: [*Slumping back.*] True! Then it's true what he writes? How horrible! No, no, it's impossible—it can't be true.

NORA: It *is* true. I've loved you more than all this world.

HELMER: Ah, none of your slippery tricks.

NORA: [*Taking one step toward him.*] Torvald—!

HELMER: What *is* this you've blundered into!

NORA: Just let me loose. You're not going to suffer for my sake. You're not going to take on my guilt.

HELMER: No more playacting. [*Locks the hall door.*] You stay right here and give me a reckoning. You understand what you've done? Answer! You understand?

NORA: [*Looking squarely at him, her face hardening.*] Yes. I'm beginning to understand everything now.

HELMER: [*Striding about.*] Oh, what an awful awakening! In all these eight years—she who was my pride and joy—a hypocrite, a liar—worse, worse—a criminal! How infinitely disgusting it all is! The shame! [NORA *says nothing and goes on looking straight at him. He stops in front of her.*] I should have suspected something of the kind. I should have known. All your father's flimsy values—Be still! All your father's flimsy values have come out in you. No religion, no morals, no sense of duty—Oh, how I'm punished for letting him off! I did it for your sake, and you repay me like this.

NORA: Yes, like this.

HELMER: Now you've wrecked all my happiness—ruined my whole future. Oh, it's awful to think of. I'm in a cheap little grafter's hands; he can do anything he wants with me, ask for anything, play with me like a puppet—and I can't breathe a word. I'll be swept down miserably into the depths on account of a featherbrained woman.

NORA: When I'm gone from this world, you'll be free.

HELMER: Oh, quit posing. Your father had a mess of those speeches too. What good would that ever do me if you were gone from this world, as you say? Not the slightest. He can still make the whole thing known; and if he does, I could be falsely suspected as your accomplice. They might even think that I was behind it—that I put you up to it. And all that I can thank you for—you that I've coddled the whole of our marriage. Can you see now what you've done to me?

NORA: [*Icily calm.*] Yes.

HELMER: It's so incredible, I just can't grasp it. But we'll have to patch up whatever we can. Take off the shawl. I said, take it off! I've got to appease him somehow or other. The thing has to be hushed up at any cost. And as for you and me, it's got to seem like everything between us is just as it was—to the outside world, that is. You'll go right on living in this house, of course. But you can't be allowed to bring up the children; I don't dare trust you with them—Oh, to have to say this to someone I've loved so much, and that I still—! Well, that's done with. From now on happiness doesn't matter; all that matters is saving the bits and pieces, the appearance—[*The doorbell rings.* HELMER *starts.*] What's that? And so late. Maybe the worst—? You think he'd—? Hide, Nora! Say you're sick. [NORA *remains standing motionless.* HELMER *goes and opens the door.*]

MAID: [*Half dressed, in the hall.*] A letter for Mrs. Helmer.

HELMER: I'll take it. [*Snatches the letter and shuts the door.*] Yes, it's from him. You don't get it; I'm reading it myself.

NORA: Then read it.

HELMER: [*By the lamp.*] I hardly dare. We may be ruined, you and I. But—I've got to know. [*Rips open the letter, skims through a few lines, glances at an enclosure, then cries out joyfully.*] Nora! [NORA *looks inquiringly at him.*] Nora! Wait—better check it again—Yes, yes, it's true. I'm saved. Nora, I'm saved!

NORA: And I?

HELMER: You too, of course. We're both saved, both of us. Look. He's sent back your note. He says he's sorry and ashamed—that a happy development in his life—oh, who cares what he says! Nora, we're saved! No one can hurt you. Oh, Nora, Nora—but first, this ugliness all has to go. Let me see—[*Takes a look at the note.*] No, I don't want to see it; I want the whole thing to fade like a dream. [*Tears the note and both letters to pieces, throws them into the stove and watches them burn.*] There—now there's nothing left—He wrote that since Christmas Eve you—Oh, they must have been three terrible days for you, Nora.

NORA: I fought a hard fight.

HELMER: And suffered pain and saw no escape but—No, we're not going to dwell on anything unpleasant. We'll just be grateful and keep on repeating: it's over now, it's over! You hear me, Nora? You don't seem to realize—it's over. What's it mean—that frozen look? Oh, poor little Nora, I understand. You can't believe I've forgiven you. But I have, Nora; I swear I have. I know that what you did, you did out of love for me.

NORA: That's true.

HELMER: You loved me the way a wife ought to love her husband. It's simply the means that you couldn't judge. But you think I love you any the less for not knowing how to handle your affairs? No, no—just lean on me; I'll guide you and teach you. I wouldn't be a man if this feminine helplessness didn't make you twice as attractive to me. You mustn't mind those sharp words I said— that was all in the first confusion of thinking my world had collapsed. I've forgiven you, Nora; I swear I've forgiven you.

NORA: My thanks for your forgiveness. [*She goes out through the door, right.*]

HELMER: No, wait—[*Peers in.*] What are you doing in there?

NORA: [*Inside.*] Getting out of my costume.

HELMER: [*By the open door.*] Yes, do that. Try to calm yourself and collect your thoughts again, my frightened little songbird. You can rest easy now; I've got wide wings to shelter you with. [*Walking about close by the door.*] How snug and nice our home is, Nora. You're safe here; I'll keep you like a hunted dove I've rescued out of a hawk's claws. I'll bring peace to your poor, shuddering heart. Gradually it'll happen, Nora; you'll see. Tomorrow all this will look different to you; then everything will be as it was. I won't have to go on repeating I forgive you; you'll feel it for yourself. How can you imagine I'd ever conceivably want to disown you—or even blame you in any way? Ah, you don't know a man's heart, Nora. For a man there's something indescribably sweet and satisfying in knowing he's forgiven his wife—and forgiven her out of a full and open heart. It's as if she belongs to him in two ways now: in a sense he's given her fresh into the world again, and she's become his wife and his child as well. From now on that's what you'll be to me—you little, bewildered, helpless thing. Don't be afraid of anything, Nora; just open your heart to me, and I'll be conscience and will to you both—[NORA *enters in her regular clothes.*] What's this? Not in bed? You've changed your dress?

NORA: Yes, Torvald, I've changed my dress.

HELMER: But why now, so late?

NORA: Tonight I'm not sleeping.

HELMER: But Nora dear—

NORA: [*Looking at her watch.*] It's still not so very late. Sit down, Torvald; we have a lot to talk over. [*She sits at one side of the table.*]

HELMER: Nora—what is this? That hard expression—

NORA: Sit down. This'll take some time. I have a lot to say.

HELMER: [*Sitting at the table directly opposite her.*] You worry me, Nora. And I don't understand you.

NORA: No, that's exactly it. You don't understand me. And I've never understood you either—until tonight. No, don't interrupt. You can just listen to what I say. We're closing out accounts, Torvald.

HELMER: How do you mean that?

NORA: [*After a short pause.*] Doesn't anything strike you about our sitting here like this?

HELMER: What's that?

NORA: We've been married now eight years. Doesn't it occur to you that this is the first time we two, you and I, man and wife, have ever talked seriously together?

HELMER: What do you mean—seriously?

NORA: In eight whole years—longer even—right from our first acquaintance, we've never exchanged a serious word on any serious thing.

HELMER: You mean I should constantly go and involve you in problems you couldn't possibly help me with?

NORA: I'm not talking of problems. I'm saying that we've never sat down seriously together and tried to get to the bottom of anything.

HELMER: But dearest, what good would that ever do you?

NORA: That's the point right there: you've never understood me. I've been wronged greatly, Torvald—first by Papa, and then by you.

HELMER: What! By us—the two people who've loved you more than anyone else?

NORA: [*Shaking her head.*] You never loved me. You've thought it fun to be in love with me, that's all.

HELMER: Nora, what a thing to say!

NORA: Yes, it's true now, Torvald. When I lived at home with Papa, he told me all his opinions, so I had the same ones too; or if they were different I hid them, since he wouldn't have cared for that. He used to call me his doll-child, and he played with me the way I played with my dolls. Then I came into your house—

HELMER: How can you speak of our marriage like that?

NORA: [*Unperturbed.*] I mean, then I went from Papa's hands into yours. You arranged everything to your own taste, and so I got the same taste as you—or I pretended to; I can't remember. I guess a little of both, first one, then the other. Now when I look back, it seems as if I'd lived here like a beggar—just from hand to mouth. I've lived by doing tricks for you, Torvald. But that's the way you wanted it. It's a great sin what you and Papa did to me. You're to blame that nothing's become of me.

HELMER: Nora, how unfair and ungrateful you are! Haven't you been happy here?

NORA: No, never. I thought so—but I never have.

HELMER: Not—not happy!

NORA: No, only lighthearted. And you've always been so kind to me. But our home's been nothing but a playpen. I've been your doll-wife here, just as at home I was Papa's doll-child. And in turn the children have been my dolls. I thought it was fun when you played with me, just as they thought it fun when I played with them. That's been our marriage, Torvald.

HELMER: There's some truth in what you're saying—under all the raving exaggeration. But it'll all be different after this. Playtime's over; now for the schooling.

NORA: Whose schooling—mine or the children's?

HELMER: Both yours and the children's, dearest.

NORA: Oh, Torvald, you're not the man to teach me to be a good wife to you.

HELMER: And you can say that?

NORA: And I—how am I equipped to bring up children?

HELMER: Nora!

NORA: Didn't you say a moment ago that that was no job to trust me with?

HELMER: In a flare of temper! Why fasten on that?

NORA: Yes, but you were so very right. I'm not up to the job. There's another job I have to do first. I have to try to educate myself. You can't help me with that. I've got to do it alone. And that's why I'm leaving you now.

HELMER: [*Jumping up.*] What's that?

NORA: I have to stand completely alone, if I'm ever going to discover myself and the world out there. So I can't go on living with you.

HELMER: Nora, Nora!

NORA: I want to leave right away. Kristine should put me up for the night—

HELMER: You're insane! You've no right! I forbid you!

NORA: From here on, there's no use forbidding me anything. I'll take with me whatever is mine. I don't want a thing from you, either now or later.

HELMER: What kind of madness is this!

NORA: Tomorrow I'm going home—I mean, home where I came from. It'll be easier up there to find something to do.

HELMER: Oh, you blind, incompetent child!

NORA: I must learn to be competent, Torvald.

HELMER: Abandon your home, your husband, your children! And you're not even thinking what people will say.

NORA: I can't be concerned about that. I only know how essential this is.

HELMER: Oh, it's outrageous. So you'll run out like this on your most sacred vows.

NORA: What do you think are my most sacred vows?

HELMER: And I have to tell you that! Aren't they your duties to your husband and children?

NORA: I have other duties equally sacred.

HELMER: That isn't true. What duties are they?

NORA: Duties to myself.

HELMER: Before all else, you're a wife and a mother.

NORA: I don't believe in that anymore. I believe that, before all else, I'm a human being, no less than you—or anyway, I ought to try to become one. I know the majority thinks you're right, Torvald, and plenty of books agree with you, too. But I can't go on believing what the majority says, or what's written in books. I have to think over these things myself and try to understand them.

HELMER: Why can't you understand your place in your own home? On a point like that, isn't there one everlasting guide you can turn to? Where's your religion?

NORA: Oh, Torvald, I'm really not sure what religion is.

HELMER: What—?

NORA: I only know what the minister said when I was confirmed. He told me religion was this thing and that. When I get clear and away by myself, I'll go into that problem too. I'll see if what the minister said was right, or, in any case, if it's right for me.

HELMER: A young woman your age shouldn't talk like that. If religion can't move you, I can try to rouse your conscience. You do have some moral feeling? Or, tell me—has that gone too?

NORA: It's not easy to answer that, Torvald. I simply don't know. I'm all confused about these things. I just know I see them so differently from you. I find out, for one thing, that the law's not at all what I'd thought—but I can't get it through my head that the law is fair. A woman hasn't a right to protect her dying father or save her husband's life! I can't believe that.

HELMER: You talk like a child. You don't know anything of the world you live in.

NORA: No, I don't. But now I'll begin to learn for myself. I'll try to discover who's right, the world or I.

HELMER: Nora, you're sick; you've got a fever. I almost think you're out of your head.

NORA: I've never felt more clearheaded and sure in my life.

HELMER: And—clearheaded and sure—you're leaving your husband and children?

NORA: Yes.

HELMER: Then there's only one possible reason.

NORA: What?

HELMER: You no longer love me.

NORA: No. That's exactly it.

HELMER: Nora! You can't be serious!

NORA: Oh, this is so hard, Torvald—you've been so kind to me always. But I can't help it. I don't love you anymore.

HELMER: [Struggling for composure.] Are you also clearheaded and sure about that?

NORA: Yes, completely. That's why I can't go on staying here.

HELMER: Can you tell me what I did to lose your love?

NORA: Yes, I can tell you. It was this evening when the miraculous thing didn't come—then I knew you weren't the man I'd imagined.

HELMER: Be more explicit; I don't follow you.

NORA: I've waited now so patiently eight long years—for, my Lord, I know miracles don't come every day. Then this crisis broke over me, and such a certainty filled me: *now* the miraculous event would occur. While Krogstad's letter was lying out there, I never for an instant dreamed that you could give in to his terms. I was so utterly sure you'd say to him: go on, tell your tale to the whole wide world. And when he'd done that—

HELMER: Yes, what then? When I'd delivered my own wife into shame and disgrace—!

NORA: When he'd done that, I was so utterly sure that you'd step forward, take the blame on yourself and say: I am the guilty one.

HELMER: Nora—!

NORA: You're thinking I'd never accept such a sacrifice from you? No, of course not. But what good would my protests be against you? That was the miracle I was waiting for, in terror and hope. And to stave that off, I would have taken my life.

HELMER: I'd gladly work for you day and night, Nora—and take on pain and deprivation. But there's no one who gives up honor for love.

NORA: Millions of women have done just that.

HELMER: Oh, you think and talk like a silly child.

NORA: Perhaps. But you neither think nor talk like the man I could join myself to. When your big fright was over—and it wasn't from any threat against me, only for what might damage you—when all the danger was past, for you it was just as if nothing had happened. I was exactly the same, your little lark, your doll, that you'd have to handle with double care now that I'd turned out so brittle and frail. [Gets up.] Torvald—in that instant it dawned on me that for eight years I've been living here with a stranger, and that I'd even conceived three children—oh, I can't stand the thought of it! I could tear myself to bits.

HELMER: [Heavily.] I see. There's a gulf that's opened between us—that's clear. Oh, but Nora, can't we bridge it somehow?

NORA: The way I am now, I'm no wife for you.

HELMER: I have the strength to make myself over.

NORA: Maybe—if your doll gets taken away.

HELMER: But to part! To part from you! No, Nora, no—I can't imagine it.

NORA: [Going out, right.] All the more reason why it has to be. [She reenters with her coat and a small overnight bag, which she puts on a chair by the table.]

HELMER: Nora, Nora, not now! Wait till tomorrow.

NORA: I can't spend the night in a strange man's room.

HELMER: But couldn't we live here like brother and sister—

NORA: You know very well how long that would last. [*Throws her shawl about her.*] Good-bye, Torvald. I won't look in on the children. I know they're in better hands than mine. The way I am now, I'm no use to them.

HELMER: But someday, Nora—someday—?

NORA: How can I tell? I haven't the least idea what'll become of me.

HELMER: But you're my wife, now and wherever you go.

NORA: Listen, Torvald—I've heard that when a wife deserts her husband's house just as I'm doing, then the law frees him from all responsibility. In any case, I'm freeing you from being responsible. Don't feel yourself bound, any more than I will. There has to be absolute freedom for us both. Here, take your ring back. Give me mine.

HELMER: That too?

NORA: That too.

HELMER: There it is.

NORA: Good. Well, now it's all over. I'm putting the keys here. The maids know all about keeping up the house—better than I do. Tomorrow, after I've left town, Kristine will stop by to pack up everything that's mine from home. I'd like those things shipped up to me.

HELMER: Over! All over! Nora, won't you ever think about me?

NORA: I'm sure I'll think of you often, and about the children and the house here.

HELMER: May I write you?

NORA: No—never. You're not to do that.

HELMER: Oh, but let me send you—

NORA: Nothing. Nothing.

HELMER: Or help you if you need it.

NORA: No. I accept nothing from strangers.

HELMER: Nora—can I never be more than a stranger to you?

NORA: [*Picking up the overnight bag.*] Ah, Torvald—it would take the greatest miracle of all—

HELMER: Tell me the greatest miracle!

NORA: You and I both would have to transform ourselves to the point that—Oh, Torvald, I've stopped believing in miracles.

HELMER: But I'll believe. Tell me! Transform ourselves to the point that—?

NORA: That our living together could be a true marriage. [*She goes out down the hall.*]

HELMER: [*Sinks down on a chair by the door, face buried in his hands.*] Nora! Nora! [*Looking about and rising.*] Empty. She's gone. [*A sudden hope leaps in him.*] The greatest miracle—?

[*From below, the sound of a door slamming shut.*]

1879

LYNN NOTTAGE

(b. 1964)

Sweat

One of very few playwrights and the only woman so far awarded the Pulitzer Prize for Drama twice, Lynn Nottage today lives in the same Brooklyn, New York, brownstone in which she grew up, the daughter of a social worker and a schoolteacher. Just down the block lived (future) novelist Jonathan Lethem, with whom Nottage commuted to Manhattan's High School of Music & Art. Inspired by the storytelling of her grandmother and the other gifted female raconteurs who regularly gathered around the family table, Nottage became a professional storyteller herself after taking a few detours: Initially majoring in pre-med at Brown University (BA, 1986), she earned an MFA at the Yale School of Drama (1989) only to sign on as national press officer for the nonprofit human-rights organization Amnesty International. Convinced, in her words, that "[t]here must be a better way of communicating stories" than press releases, Nottage returned to writing for stage and screen, producing a remarkably wide-ranging body of work distinguished (as the *New Yorker*'s Michael Schulman observes) for being at once "vigorously researched," "unapologetic about [its] social concerns," and committed to "making invisible people visible." The diversity and the continuity of Nottage's work are well demonstrated by her three best-known, multi-award-winning plays: *Intimate Apparel* (2003), about an early twentieth-century New York seamstress who (re)claims her independence by crafting lingerie for both wealthy White women and Black prostitutes; and her

Clare Perkins as Cynthia, Martha Plimpton as Tracey, and Leanne Best as Jessie in a staging of *Sweat* directed by Lynette Linton at the Gielgud Theatre, London, 2019

two Pulitzer winners—*Ruined* (2008), set in Mama Nadi's poolroom/bar/brothel in civil war–torn Congo, and *Sweat* (2015). Featuring a multi-racial, multi-generational community of Reading, Pennsylvania, factory workers caught up in that "de-industrial revolution" to which Nottage attributes "the biggest shift in American sensibilities since the nineteen-sixties," *Sweat*—which opened off-Broadway just days before the 2016 presidential election—was famously hailed by Schulman as "the first theatrical landmark of the Trump era: a tough yet empathetic portrait of the America that came undone."

For Wallace Nottage[1]

CHARACTERS

EVAN, *African-American, forties*
JASON, *white American of German descent, twenty-one/twenty-nine*
CHRIS, *African-American, twenty-one/twenty-nine*
STAN, *white American of German descent, fifties*
OSCAR, *Colombian-American, twenty-two/thirty*
TRACEY, *white American of German descent, forty-five/fifty-three*
CYNTHIA, *African-American, forty-five/fifty-three*
JESSIE, *Italian-American, forties*
BRUCIE, *African-American, forties*

All of the characters were born in Berks County, Pennsylvania.

SETTING: Reading, Pennsylvania

TIME: 2000/2008

NOTE: A (///) indicates where overlapping dialogue should begin.

In general the dialogue should have the free-flowing velocity of a bar conversation: people step on each other's thoughts, but also occasionally find moments of silence and introspection.

O, yes,
I say it plain,
America never was America to me,
And yet I swear this oath—
America will be!

Out of the rack and ruin of our gangster death,
The rape and rot of graft, and stealth, and lies,
We, the people, must redeem
The land, the mines, the plants, the rivers.
The mountains and the endless plain—
All, all the stretch of these great green states—
And make America again!

—LANGSTON HUGHES[2]

---

1. Lynn Nottage's father (1928–2017).
2. Concluding lines of Hughes's poem "Let America Be America Again" (1936).

ACT ONE

Scene 1

September 29, 2008

Outside it's 72°F.

> *In the news: The 63rd session of the United Nations General Assembly³ convenes. The Dow Jones Industrial Average falls 778.68 points, marking the largest single-day decline in stock market history. Reading residents sample fresh apple cider at the Annual Fall Festival on Old Dry Road Farm.*
> *Music. Lights up.*
> *Parole office. Spare. Institutional.*
> *Jason (white American, twenty-nine), hair closely shorn. He has a black eye and white supremacist tattoos inked across his face. Evan (African-American, forties), comfortably puffy.*

EVAN: So, you got a job?

JASON: Yeah.

EVAN: I'm not gonna run down everything. You know the drill.

JASON: Yeah.

EVAN: So, you're making pretzels?

JASON: Yeah.

> *(A moment.)*

EVAN: Soft?

JASON: Yeah.

EVAN: Living at the same address?

JASON: Yeah.

EVAN: The mission?

JASON: Yeah, finally got a bed downstairs.

EVAN: That's real good. I hear that shelter's pretty clean.

JASON: Yeah, but fucking guys steal. Can't have nice stuff. But, um, Father Hunt lets me keep my turtles.

> *(Jason fidgets. Evan assesses.)*

EVAN: So. You gonna tell me what happened?

JASON: What?

EVAN: I know you don't wanna be here. I don't wanna be here either.

JASON: Yeah, whatever.

EVAN: Don't whatever me. I'm not one of your stupid friends, let's be clear about that.

JASON: Whatever.

EVAN: Try me! I'm not playing fucking games. I'll knock you clear into tomorrow, understood? But, fortunately for you, I don't have to, you know why? Because I got this pen, and you know what this pen does?

JASON: Yeah—

---

3. Main deliberative, policy-making organ of the UN (founded 1945); including representatives of all 193 member states, it convenes in New York every September.

EVAN: It writes. And, you know what it's gonna write if you don't give me more than one- or two-syllable answers? It's gonna write that you're belligerent, defiant, reluctant to observe protocol. You understand those words, Jason?

JASON: Yeah.

EVAN (*Voice slowly crescendos*): It's gonna write that you have issues with authority that may prove too challenging. This pen could make things very difficult for you, young man. And you know what happens to young men that don't cooperate? . . . Huh? . . . Huh?

JASON: You asking me?

EVAN: Whatcha think I'm asking—myself? Of course I'm asking you, moron! You want me to ask again?

JASON: No. I don't need you to ask again.

EVAN: Very good. A sentence. We're making some progress here. So, what happened?

JASON: I mean . . . I didn't do shit.

EVAN: So you didn't do shit, but someone did . . . do shit.

JASON: Uh—

EVAN: And, you gave yourself a black eye and busted lip?

(*A moment.*)

What happened?

JASON: I got sucker-punched.

EVAN: Cuz—?

JASON: I dunno.

EVAN: Some guy just comes up and hits ya. And you, you didn't do nothing?

JASON: Nah. Not really. I was in the bathroom at Loco's.

EVAN: Loco's?

JASON: Yeah, Loco's.

EVAN: I'm sorry? Loco's?

JASON: I can't go to Loco's?

EVAN: We've talked about Loco's. Go on.

JASON: This big fucking biker dude, I don't know 'em, like steps up behind me. He's like you were looking at my girl. I am so, like, dude, I don't even know who the fuck your girl is. And he's wearing these huge rings, both fucking hands, like medieval biker knight.

EVAN: Hmm.

JASON: And . . . then he hits me hard, so hard that I swear to God I see stars. Like Bam! My whole face goes numb. Sparky had to pull 'em off of me.

EVAN: Just because you looked at his girl.

JASON: I didn't look at his girl, that's why it's so fucked up.

EVAN: And if I ask you to piss in this cup, what's it gonna tell me?

JASON: You don't gotta believe me, but I'm telling ya the // truth.

EVAN: Okay. There's the cup.

JASON: What?

EVAN: What do you mean, what?

JASON: C'mon.

EVAN: The cup, pick it up.

JASON: I just got a job. What do you want?

EVAN: I don't want anything from you, but the state does and it's my unfortunate job to ensure that you comply.

JASON: Are we gonna do this?

EVAN: Pick it up.

JASON: You are a fucking asshole. Fuck you, nigga!

(*A moment. Evan, stone, stares long and hard at Jason.*)

(*Less committed*) Fuck you!

EVAN: Pick it up!

JASON: I got a job. I mean, c'mon, give me a fucking break.

EVAN: Pick . . . it . . . up!

(*Jason makes a show of picking up the cup.*)

Okay. What do you wanna tell me?

(*A moment.*)

JASON: I dunno.

EVAN: I dunno, either.

JASON: Look—

EVAN: What?

JASON: I dunno.

EVAN: Yeah, we covered that fertile territory. What's going on Jason?

JASON: Yo, ease up. I'm doing what I am supposed to be doing.

EVAN: You think so? You looking to get back inside?

JASON: . . . !

EVAN: Might wanna get rid of those tats. We've talked about it. They're gonna cause you trouble out here. Might make you a tough guy inside, out here . . . guess what? Every time I look at them I wanna punch you out. That's me being honest. But, lucky for you I'm here to help.

(*Jason fidgets.*)

What's going on Jason? I shouldn't have to track you down.

(*A moment. Jason rolls his eyes.*)

JASON: Can I go?

EVAN: We don't have to talk. It's no sweat off my back. I'm gonna leave this page blank. How about that? Blank page. You wanna blank page?

JASON: . . .

EVAN: You in trouble?

JASON: No.

EVAN: I could fish all day. I am a fisherman.

(*Jason runs a story through his head, deciding whether to share it.*)

JASON: I—

EVAN: Yeah—

JASON: Ran into Chris.

(*Jason is caught off-guard by his own emotions.*)

EVAN: All right? You okay? We knew this might happen. Yeah?

JASON: Yeah.

EVAN: He's out there. He ain't going nowhere. Whatcha gonna do about it?

JASON: I dunno. I dunno. The whole time inside, I pushed what happened, you know, Chris, all of it, outta my head. Then he was . . . I dunno, it's all I can think, you know—

> (*Evan turns around, and he's now talking to Chris [African-American, twenty-nine]. He is very neatly dressed, but quite fidgety and anxious.*)

EVAN: You okay, man? You seem antsy.

CHRIS: Not gonna lie, it's been tough. Not sleeping so good. Still trying to get used to things.

EVAN: Well, you been away a long time. The river keeps flowing.

CHRIS (*Anxious*): I guess. People. Psh. People, they're a trip. You know? Before it was . . . um . . . it was easy, now every conversation I have, it's like I'm circling in a traffic pattern, just circling. I don't got shit to say to anyone, and nobody got shit to say to me.

EVAN: You find someplace to stay . . . Chris?

CHRIS: Yeah. Reverend Duckett lets me sleep in the rectory. I do some chores. It's all right for now. Quiet. Trying to find my feet.

EVAN: It's gonna be that way for a while.

CHRIS: Yeah, I'm figuring that out quickly!

EVAN: What about work?

CHRIS: Looking.

EVAN: Did you follow up with the leads I gave you?

CHRIS: Yeah, went down there, filled out a few applications, but they ain't offering nothing real, I'm talking bullshit, you know . . . seven, eight dollars an hour.

EVAN: Gotta begin somewhere.

CHRIS: I guess. And I keep hitting up against that box. That damn question's a barbed-wire fence, can't go over it, can't get around it.

EVAN: I know, I know. But, whatcha doing to keep your head?

CHRIS: Going to prayer meetings. Doing it one day at a time. Reverend Duckett has been real cool to me.

EVAN: Good. Good. What about that prison program? How many credits you short?

CHRIS: Eight. But first . . . I gotta throw a little money in my pocket. Get things on track, you know. Then, psh, I can think about finishing up my bachelor's.

EVAN: I'm really glad to hear that.

CHRIS: That was the plan, you know, before the shit went down.

EVAN: You seem a little on edge today.

CHRIS: Yeah, well. Some days are like that. I get real mad at myself.

> (*A moment. Chris, suddenly introspective.*)

EVAN: You okay? You need some air or something?

CHRIS: Nah. I . . . I ran into Jason. Wasn't expecting it.

EVAN: What was that like?

CHRIS: Weird . . . weird. He looked different.

EVAN: Yeah?

CHRIS: He had tats on his face. Big fucking tats. He looked ridiculous. I had to deal with that bullshit inside. You know, Aryan Brotherhood.[4] But, Jason . . . that shit surprised me. He looked old, like a man. Like his dad useta, before he died. It kinda freaked me out.

EVAN: I bet.

CHRIS (*Escalating emotions*): I dunno. A couple minutes, and your whole life changes, that's it. It's gone. Every day I think about what if I hadn't . . . You know . . . I run it and run it, a tape over and over again. What if. What if. What if. All night. In my head. I can't turn it off. Reverend Duckett said, "Lean on God for forgiveness. Lean on God to find your way through the terrible storm." I'm leaning into the wind, I'm fuckin' leaning . . . And.

(*A moment.*)

And then there's Jason. Crossing Penn, you know, and I'm just chilling, looking in the window of Sneaker Villa, not thinking about anything. He sees me. I see him. Neither of us could . . . um, move for a second. We . . . it was . . . I've been thinking about what I would do in that moment. How I would react, what I would say. I mean . . . fuck it. What we did was unforgivable . . .

EVAN: So, what—?

CHRIS: Next thing I know I'm walking fast toward him, I don't know what I'm gonna do. But the emotions are right there in my chest. A fist pressing right there. Pressing. And I keep walking. And I'm expecting him to walk away, do something, but he just stands there like he's been waiting on me all these years. And . . . we come face to face. Like right there. I can smell his breath, that's how close we are. I can see the fucking veins in his eyes. And my fists clench. My fingernails dig into the palms of my hands and then it just happens . . . weird . . . . We're hugging. Hugging. I don't know why. And for the first time in eight years, I feel like I could go home.

(*Tears are close, but they don't come.*
A loud blast of music: Santana's "Smooth."[5] The past rips through 2008.)

Scene 2

January 18, 2000

Eight years earlier.
  Outside it's 19°F.
  In the news: American think tanks report that the booming stock market is widening the income gap between the poorest and richest U.S. families. Reading

4. Infamous White supremacist prison gang and organized crime syndicate believed to have first formed c. 1964, in the wake of prison desegregation.
5. Billboard-topping hit (1999) originally performed by the rock band Santana (fronted by Mexican American guitarist Carlos Santana, b. 1947) and Matchbox Twenty vocalist Rob Thomas (b. 1972). According to Nottage, "From the moment I conceived the play, that's how I heard it starting," with this song combining elements as diverse as her characters: "a little R. & B., a little rock and roll, a little pop, a little Latino flavor."

passes an aggressive dog ordinance to regulate ownership of certain pet breeds including pit bulls.

Santana's "Smooth" plays loudly from a jukebox.

Lights up. Bar. Lived-in and comfortable. End of a raucous celebration. Music blares.

Cynthia (African-American, forty-five) and Tracey (white American, forty-five), just a little too drunk, are dancing. Stan (white American, fifties), the bartender, stands behind the bar, smiling, and enjoying the show. Jessie (Italian-American, forties) is passed out, face planted on the table.

Tracey and Cynthia dance together with the intimacy of close friends who've shared many adventures.

CYNTHIA: C'mon, Stan.

STAN: Nah, don't dance!

CYNTHIA: I don't believe ya!

TRACEY: Stan the man! Don't fail me! I know ya got some moves!

STAN: Nope!

(*Tracey does a sexy, enticing dance.*)

Don't break anything.

(*The music ends.*)

CYNTHIA AND TRACEY: Aww.

(*Cynthia walks over to the jukebox. Tracey flops down next to Jessie and finishes her friend's drink.*)

STAN: Hey. Who's driving her home?

TRACEY: Howard just locks up and leaves her there. Somehow she always manages to punch in to work on time. Right, Cynth?

CYNTHIA: Showered and dressed.

TRACEY: We all got a seven A.M. call and that one's out drinking until two every night.

STAN: Well, someone's gotta drive her.

TRACEY: Not happening. I got the inside of my car cleaned Thursday.

STAN: Hey, Cynthia, can you drive Jessie home?

CYNTHIA: Hell no, she was the designated driver.

(*Tracey laughs and nudges Jessie.*)

TRACEY: Jessie!

(*Jessie rouses.*)

JESSIE: What?!

(*She slumps back onto the table. Laughter.*)

STAN: Well, she can't stay here.

(*Stan, with a pronounced limp, an old bothersome injury, hobbles over, and takes Jessie's keys from her pocket. He throws them into a key jar on the shelf.*)

CYNTHIA: How many keys you collect?
STAN: Didn't fill the jar, but the night's still young.

(*Stan places a bottle of bourbon on the bar.*)

One more drink?

(*He pours Tracey a drink.*)

TRACEY: Now, you're really trying to get over.
STAN (*Seductively*): It's an open invitation.
TRACEY: Yeah? Really?

(*Stan gives her a disarmingly seductive smile and strokes her arm.*)

Nice. Does that work for you? Because, I'm not feeling anything. I mean should I be feeling something?
STAN: I'm definitely reading something.
TRACEY: Get outta here! It was one fucking time, it's definitely not happening again.

(*Stan continues to work his charm.*)

STAN: Two.
TRACEY: Not technically.
STAN: Oh really?
TRACEY: Really!

(*Tracey laughs. She's a laugher, it's her refuge.*
  Oscar, the Colombian-American busboy, twenty-two, hauls in a rack of glasses. He wipes down the bar. He goes about his business, rarely acknowledged by anyone except Stan.)

STAN: Thanks, Oscar.

CYNTHIA: Okay. I love you, but I'm officially drunk-b-dunk, which means I gotta go.

TRACEY: No . . .
CYNTHIA: Got an early shift.
TRACEY: Frank can kiss my ass. Jesus, haven't you done enough overtime?
CYNTHIA: Babe, come hell or high water, I'm taking that cruise through the Panama Canal this summer.
TRACEY: One more drink. One. It's my birthday. C'mon, c'mon. Stan, pour this bitch another drink!
CYNTHIA: Okay. But, if I lose a finger in the mill, it'll be your fault. Remember that. It's her fault!
STAN: It's her fault!

(*Tracey gives Cynthia a hug. Stan chuckles and pours Cynthia's drink.*)

CYNTHIA: You gonna have a drink with us?
TRACEY: One . . .
STAN: Sure. Two pretty ladies. No downside to that.
TRACEY: Watch what he's putting in there. That's how I got into trouble last time.

STAN (*Seductively*): Oh, c'mon, trouble?

What a night! A lot of folks turned out to celebrate.

TRACEY: It was fun, huh? Never thought I'd make it to this age.

STAN: Tell me about it. Hadn't seen some of those guys in ages. And I was kinda hopin' I'd see Brucie.

(*A moment. Tracey looks at Cynthia.*)

CYNTHIA: Well, don't hold your breath. I put his ass out.

STAN: Oh no. What happened?

CYNTHIA: I let him move back in.

TRACEY: // Told ya.

CYNTHIA: You know Brucie, he can be as smooth as satin. Turn that shit on and off at the drop of a dime. Things were going fine, then Christmas Day, we've got this nice bottle of Chablis. He's looking dapper. I'm dressed for danger. We're laughing, chilling and having fun. And . . . we talk. I mean, talk. It's all good. We drink wine, we drink some more wine, then we do what you do after you drink too much wine. Middle of the night—

TRACEY: Listen to this—

CYNTHIA: I go downstairs. My Christmas presents under the tree are gone—

STAN: // Get outta here.

CYNTHIA: AND my fish tank with my expensive new tropical fish, gone.

STAN: Don't tell me—

CYNTHIA: A week later, New Year's Eve, I wake up. And this fool's digging in the refrigerator like he actually put something there. High as a muthafucking kite. Says nothing. No apology. Nada. I damn near lost my mind. Brucie was lucky I wasn't holding a gun, cuz right now he'd be in hell trying to hustle the devil.

STAN: That don't sound like him.

CYNTHIA: The hell it don't, let me tell you something, once he started messing with that dope, I don't recognize the man. I know it's tough out there, I understand. Yeah, yeah, yeah. He went through hell when his plant locked him out,[6] I understand, but I can't have it.

TRACEY: More importantly, you don't // have to.

STAN: So, what—?

CYNTHIA: I tell that joker, it's time to go. Bye-bye. And we get into it. Police come down, chest-pumped, I get cuffed, photographed and fingerprinted for disorderly conduct in my own damn house.

STAN: No way.

CYNTHIA: Yes . . .	TRACEY: Yeah, can you believe it? I had to go down there and bail her out. New Year's Eve. I'm wearing heels and a sequin dress.

6. A lockout is the opposite of a strike, though both are means of applying pressure to the opposing side in a labor dispute: In a strike, a company's employees refuse to work until management meets their demands; in a lockout, a company refuses its employees the right to work or even enter the workplace until they meet management's demands.

STAN: Jesus. What about Brucie?

CYNTHIA: Ask me if I give a goddamn.

STAN: Tough. Sorry to hear it. You two were good together.

CYNTHIA: Yeah, well, not anymore.

STAN: Oh shit, speaking of arrests, did you guys read about Freddy in the paper this morning?

CYNTHIA: No, what was Freddy doing in the paper?

STAN: God, you didn't hear?

TRACEY: Nah. What happened?

STAN: He burned his fucking house down.

CYNTHIA: What?

TRACEY: Was anybody hurt?

STAN: Just the dog.

CYNTHIA: Pepper? Oh my God—

STAN: Yeah, crazy, huh?

CYNTHIA: Oh my // God

TRACEY: What about Maggie?

STAN: I thought you knew, she walked out . . . two weeks ago.

CYNTHIA: What?   TRACEY: What happened?

STAN: Yeah.

> (*Jessie rouses for a second.*)

STAN: Gone.   JESSIE: Yeah!

CYNTHIA: That's some shit.

TRACEY: Our Freddy? Freddy Brunner?

STAN: Freddy—

CYNTHIA: I don't get it. Why would the man burn down his own house?

STAN: // Dunno.   TRACEY: Crazy.
  Three-alarm fire.   That sucks.
  Nothing // left.

STAN: He was in here on Saturday, got shit-faced. Maggie just up and left him—

TRACEY: Where would that bitch go?

STAN: That's what he said. Dunno. The paper says he tried to shoot himself in the head. Can you believe it? But, he was too wasted, and ended up shooting off his right ear.

TRACEY: Ow.   CYNTHIA: Get the hell outta
                                         here.

STAN: They found him lying on his neighbor's lawn, bleeding—

CYNTHIA: Damn. That's all I gotta say. // DAMN!

TRACEY: Freddy Brunner?

STAN: Turns out he was up to his neck in fucking debt.

TRACEY: Terrible—

STAN: And Clarence—

CYNTHIA: Clarence Jones?

STAN: Says he got wind that they were gonna cut back his line[7] at the plant. Couldn't handle the stress.

CYNTHIA: That rumor's been flying around for months. Nobody's going anywhere.

STAN: Okay, you keep telling yourself that, but you saw what happened over at Clemmons Technologies. No one saw that coming. Right? You could wake up tomorrow and all your jobs are in Mexico, whatever, it's this NAFTA[8] bullshit—

TRACEY: What the fuck is NAFTA? Sounds like a laxative. NAFTA.

(Tracey laughs.)

STAN: You don't read the paper?

TRACEY: You read the paper?

STAN: Yes, I do.

TRACEY: Well, I don't read the paper, okay? I'm dyslexic, thank you.

STAN: Eyes open. Not a good philosophy to resist knowledge.

TRACEY: Where'd you read that bullshit?

STAN: I didn't read it, I intuit it.

CYNTHIA: Whatever. It's a rumor. Management // spreads that crap to keep us on edge.

STAN: I'm just saying. But, it ain't my problem // anymore.

TRACEY: Hey, is it against the law to burn down your own house?

STAN: Dunno. I think you need a permit.

(Jessie rouses again.)

JESSIE: Where's the FIRE at?

TRACEY: What?!

STAN: A permit.

TRACEY: Really? For your own damn house?

STAN: Ya can't set a fire that big without a permit.

TRACEY: Wait a minute, you're saying if he got a permit he could legally burn his house down?

JESSIE: Yeah.

CYNTHIA: Shit, I should burn down my house. Crappy little money trap.

TRACEY: To hell with the permit, I'd hire someone else to do it.

CYNTHIA: Shut up, who do you know?

TRACEY: I dunno.

(Tracey laughs, then gestures to Oscar.)

Hey. What about you?

OSCAR: Me? What? Ya need water?

TRACEY: No, but . . . if I wanted to hire someone to burn down my house where would I go?

---

7. That is, reduce the operation of (and thus the number of people employed on) the assembly or production line on which Clarence works at the factory.

8. The North American Free Trade Agreement (acronym), which lowered or eliminated barriers to trade among the United States, Canada, and Mexico (1 Jan. 1994–1 July 2020); its effects, especially on U.S. manufacturing and manufacturing jobs, became a major issue in the 2016 presidential campaign.

OSCAR: I dunno. How would I know?

TRACEY: What do you mean, you don't know? C'mon.

OSCAR: I don't know.

TRACEY: You Puerto Ricans are burning shit down all over Reading, you gotta know.

OSCAR: Well, I'm Colombian. And I don't know.

TRACEY: Yeah, right.

CYNTHIA: Ignore her. She's stupid.

TRACEY: He fucking knows, he's just not saying.

CYNTHIA: Let it go!

TRACEY: He fucking knows.

STAN: Lighten up! Let it go!

OSCAR: Psh.

TRACEY: Psh.

(*Oscar cuts his eyes at Tracey and walks back to the bar. Stan redirects Tracey, defusing the tension.*)

STAN: Hey, you know, Freddy was on the line with my old man. He trained me. Yeah.

CYNTHIA: Really?

STAN: As matter of fact, when I got injured, it was Freddy who shut down the mill.

TRACEY: I didn't know that.

STAN: Yeah. If it wasn't for him. I would have lost my entire leg.

(*Jessie suddenly alert:*)

JESSIE: Hey, Stan, quit yapping, get me another gimlet.[9]

STAN: You're joking. Absolutely not.

JESSIE: What? Are you the bartender on tonight?

STAN: Not giving you another drink.

JESSIE: C'mon! Gimme another drink! You gave her a drink, why can't I have one?

STAN: Because that's how it goes. You've had enough.

JESSIE: You got a fucking problem.

STAN: No, you got a fucking problem.

JESSIE: You can't talk to me that way. My husband—

STAN: You mean your ex.

JESSIE: All I gotta do is make one phone call and he'll wipe that fucking smile off your face.

STAN: Yeah, go ahead. Here, use my phone. Wake up his beautiful young wife, what's her name again, Tiffany?

CYNTHIA: That wasn't // necessary.

JESSIE: You are a asshole!

STAN: Take her home.

TRACEY: C'mon. // Don't start this again—

JESSIE: You fucking cripple.

STAN: Nice language.	CYNTHIA: She's had a little too much to drink.

STAN: And that's why it's time for her to go home. Night-night.

9. Cocktail made of gin or vodka and lime juice.

JESSIE: I'll kick your ass, gimp!

(*Jessie struggles to her feet. She attempts to walk, but is completely wasted.*)

CYNTHIA: Jessie. // C'mon.
JESSIE: Cripple! You fucking warlock!

CYNTHIA: Calm down.   STAN: Relax . . .

CYNTHIA: All right. We're celebrating . . .

JESSIE: Fucker. Fucker!!   STAN: That's nice . . . Nice . . .

CYNTHIA: You've had enough. Okay. Calm the fuck down.
JESSIE (*Snaps*): Don't talk to me!
CYNTHIA: Don't start with me, babe.

(*Cynthia makes an "I mean business" face. Tracey laughs.*)

JESSIE: Oh shit.
CYNTHIA: You okay? You need a hand?

(*Jessie struggles to walk to the bathroom, attempting to maintain her dignity, but it's a herculean task. Finally:*)

STAN: Hey Oscar, give her a hand.
OSCAR: Okay.

(*Jessie leans onto Oscar.*)

Hold onto me. I gotchu.
JESSIE: Are we together?
OSCAR: No!
CYNTHIA: And get her a glass of water.
TRACEY: You mean a gallon.

(*Oscar leads Jessie to the bathroom.*)

OSCAR: Just a couple of steps. Okay. Take your time.
STAN: Jesus. Fucking pathetic.
CYNTHIA (*To Tracey*): I thought you were gonna talk to her! She keeps showing up at work smelling like a bottle of vodka.
TRACEY: No shit, she's been a complete wreck since Dan got remarried.
CYNTHIA: // Talk to her!
TRACEY: My husband died and you don't see me bathing in booze. And I'm sorry, but I just can't hear her go on about him one more time. He was a creep, and it's my fucking birthday, you'd think she'd be able to hold it together.
CYNTHIA: I know, but seriously, talk to her. Someone's gonna get hurt.
TRACEY: You gonna report her?
CYNTHIA: Listen babe, they're always looking for reasons to let us go. 'Specially now, with this damn shake up—
STAN: Then the rumor's true, huh? Butz is getting promoted?
CYNTHIA: Yeah.
TRACEY: He's heading to some plant outta state.

STAN: Who they bringing in?

TRACEY: They're talking about hiring someone from the floor.

STAN: Get outta here. Really? You gonna apply?

TRACEY: Me? No fucking way.

(*Stan glances over at Cynthia.*)

STAN: You're awful quiet, Cynth.

CYNTHIA: Who knows? I might apply.

TRACEY: What?! Get outta here.

CYNTHIA: Why the hell not? I've got twenty-four years on the floor.

TRACEY: Well, I got you beat by two. Started in '74, walked in straight outta high school. First and only job. Management is for them. Not us.

CYNTHIA: More money. More heat. More vacation. Less work. That's all I need to know.

TRACEY: Hey Stan, how many years did you put in before the injury?

STAN: Twenty-eight.

TRACEY: And in those twenty-eight years you ever see anyone move off the floor?

STAN: . . . Um, no . . . wait, wait . . . there was Griff Parker.

TRACEY: Yeah, but he left, went to college came back as management. They didn't pluck him off the line. Doesn't count.

CYNTHIA: Shit, you wanna be fifty and standing on your feet for ten hours a day? Titties sagging into the machines. I got bunions the size of damn apples. // My back—

TRACEY: Bla . . . bla. Write a book.

CYNTHIA: Don't know about you, but I can feel my body slowing down, a little every day. I go home and my hands are frozen, I can't even hold a frying pan. I gotta rub 'em together for an hour before they even move.

TRACEY: But be serious, Butz's job?

CYNTHIA: I know the machines. I know the people.

TRACEY: Hold on, hold on. You're really gonna apply?! No bullshit.

CYNTHIA: All they can do is say no, right Stan?

STAN: That's right.

(*A moment.*)

TRACEY: Well . . . If that's the case, maybe I should throw my name into the mix. Right? I need a vacation. I got the same experience you got. But, I mean none of us girls are gonna get it, right?

CYNTHIA: It's been a helluva lot better since Olstead's grandson took over—

STAN: Gimme a break. That place hasn't changed since I walked in there in '69. Not a lightbulb, not one single nut or bolt. As a matter of fact it hasn't changed much since my grandfather began working there in '22. Good luck, sweetheart. I don't know him, but I can tell you that Olstead's grandson is the same brand of asshole as all of 'em, stuffing his pockets, rather than improving the floor.

CYNTHIA: // Word.

STAN: Now, the old man, he used to be on the floor every single day. I didn't like him, but I respected him for it. You know why?

TRACEY: He was a prick and a perv—

STAN: Because he knew what was going on, and you can only know that by being there. A machine was broken, he knew. A worker was having trouble, he knew. You don't see the young guys out there. They find it offensive to be on the floor with their Wharton MBAs.[1] And the problem is they don't wanna get their feet dirty, their diplomas soiled with sweat . . . or understand the real cost, the human cost of making their shitty product.

CYNTHIA: Amen to that.

JESSIE (*From off*): Oh, shit.

(*From off, a crash and a thud.*)

STAN: Hey, maybe one of you should check on Jessie.

TRACEY: Nah, she's fine.

CYNTHIA: Did you get a load of what she's wearing? Looks like her prom dress.

TRACEY: Probably was.

(*Jessie reenters unseen. Her dress is caught up in the back of her underwear.*)

CYNTHIA: I love that woman, but she's gonna drag us all down with her.

JESSIE: Who?

CYNTHIA: Don't worry about it, babe.

JESSIE: Were you talking about me?

CYNTHIA: We're just talking.

JESSIE: Okay.

(*A moment.*)

Stan, can I get another gim—

STAN: No! N-O.

JESSIE: You're bullshit.

STAN: I can live with that.

JESSIE: Bullshit!

STAN: Enough already. Jesus.

TRACEY: C'mon, Jessie, relax.

CYNTHIA: Get your shit together. Frank's lookin' for reasons—

TRACEY: Can we not have this conversation, it's like seriously cutting into my buzz. We've been having the same conversation for twenty years. So, let's stop complaining and have some fun.

(*Music. Laughter. Celebration.*)

Scene 3

February 10, 2000

Outside it's 44°F.

In the news: *Billionaire Steve Forbes[2] drops out of the Republican Primary after investing $66,000,000 of his own money. Work begins on the Downtown Civic Convention Center in Reading.*

---

1. Masters of Business Administration (acronym). *Wharton*: University of Pennsylvania's prestigious Wharton Business School (founded 1881).
2. Publishing executive (b. 1947), editor in chief of *Forbes* business magazine, the eldest son of its founder, and a presidential candidate in 1996 and 2000.

Lights up. Bar. Chris and Jason, their younger selves, stand at the bar, tipsy. Once again, Oscar is a quiet but visible presence throughout the scene, watching, listening and working.

JASON: I spoke to the owner. It has something like twenty-three-thousand miles on it. Can you believe it? An old man kept it in his garage like a trophy. It's in beautiful condition. Mint.

CHRIS: Phat. You gonna do it?

JASON: Thinking about it.

CHRIS: Dude.

(*Jason proudly displays a picture.*)

JASON: What do you think?

STAN: Nice.

JASON: Right. It's exactly like the one my dad had, but in better condition. Yo, check out the logo on the side. Dooope . . .

STAN: A Harley?[3] What's your mom think?

JASON: So as far as I'm concerned, if she ain't paying for it then she don't got no say. In October, when I turned twenty-one, she made it dead clear that her work was done. She changed the locks on the front door and didn't give me a key. That sends a pretty clear fucking message, huh?

CHRIS: Yo.

STAN: That kinda sounds like Tracey.

JASON: All I can say is that when I saw the bike, my first urge was to fuck it.

(*Jason simulates humping the bike.*)

CHRIS: Get outta here.

(*Throughout the scene, Oscar scrapes gum from the bottom of the tables. It is an unpleasant task, but Oscar is focused and determined.*)

STAN: Yeah? Whatcha waiting on, why don't you buy it?

JASON: I figure I got another (*Calculating*) month and half of saving and it's mine. Fucking union got all our money tied up in benefits and shit, don't have nothing left for fun.

CHRIS: You ain't lying. Between my new lady—

JASON: Monique!

CHRIS: —and Uncle Sam, money got a way of running outcha pocket. Nobody tells you that no matter how hard you work there will never be enough money to rest. It's fact. A fact that should be taught to every child! Look at me. I been trying to save a little something for school, right? But every time I tuck it away, I hear the cry of "Nike Flightposite," "Air Jordan XV," a meal at the Olive Garden, and a movie will set you back two days' work.

JASON: Dude, you got more sneakers than the entire Sixers.[4]

CHRIS: No swagger without the proper kicks. It's how I roll. A man gotta have one vice that keeps him hungry.

STAN: Is that a rule?

3. Motorcycle made by Wisconsin-based Harley-Davidson, Inc. (founded 1903).
4. Philadelphia 76ers, one of the oldest franchises in the NBA (National Basketball Association).

CHRIS: No, no my friend it's a mandate.

JASON: And, wait a minute, did I . . . did I hear you say school?

CHRIS: Yeah. School. S-C-H-O-O-L!

JASON: Thanks for that clarification.

CHRIS: I . . . I got accepted into the teaching program at Albright.[5]

JASON: What? Come again?

CHRIS: Yeah. Starting in September. Yup! Plan on working double shifts. Put away a little something, you know, for tuition.

STAN: Good for you!

JASON: Wait . . . Wait, no way. Dude, what the fuck are you saying? Why didn't you tell me?

CHRIS: Cuz, I knew you'd make fun of me.

JASON: Of course I will. Whatcha gonna do? Teach history at Reading High for the next twenty years?

CHRIS: I might.

JASON: Yeah? You'll fucking suck.

CHRIS: You know what? You need to shut up an' drink your beer. That's exactly why I didn't say anything.

JASON: Whatever. In four years, max, guarantee you'll be back begging for your job at Olstead's. And yo, have you been up to Reading High lately? It's like a prison yard, they got thirty-year-old freshmen. Dude, that don't pay jack-shit, you'll have to take a second job just to keep your lights on.

STAN: He's got a point. Do you know what teachers make these days?

JASON: Tell him.

STAN: Seriously, son, not many people walk away from Olstead's, cuz you're not gonna find better money out there. You leave, it'll be impossible to get back in. They'll be ten guys lining up for your fucking job.

JASON: Yup.

STAN: That's the way it is. And I know a couple of the old guys who are bringing in close to forty-something dollars an hour.

JASON: Listen.

STAN: Teaching, well—

CHRIS: That's cool. Good for them. But, I kinda wanna do something a little different than my moms and pops. Yo, I got aspirations. There it is. And I won't apologize.

JASON: You got aspirations? What is this, Black History Month?[6]

CHRIS: As a matter of fact it is. You got a problem with that?

JASON: If we're being perfectly honest, I get a little tired of the syrupy commercials. Actually, it shouldn't be called Black History Month, it should be called "Make White People Feel Guilty Month." Right, Stan?

STAN: Don't pull me into this.

JASON: And how come there's no White History Month?

---

5. Albright College (founded 1856), private liberal arts college in Reading, Pennsylvania.

6. Since 1976, U.S. presidents have officially designated February Black or African American History Month, "paying tribute to the generations of African Americans who struggled with adversity to achieve full citizenship in American Society."

CHRIS: Psh. I'm gonna let you ponder that question! Which may be a little difficult for you, I know, and I'm sorry.

JASON: Fuck you. You haven't even gone to college and you're already an asshole.

CHRIS: No offense, but I'm fucking sick of jacking.[7] Phomp. Phomp. Phomp. The machines are so fucking loud I can't even think. It's getting harder and harder to pull myself up and go to work every day.

JASON: You're tripping.

STAN: I hear you, but the trick is, you gotta find a rhythm and stay inside of it, that's how you manage.

CHRIS: Well, it ain't a rhythm I wanna learn.

JASON: What the floor, it ain't good enough for you?!

CHRIS: Don't get it twisted, I'm not saying that. But . . .

JASON: What?

CHRIS: You ain't noticed the shit that's been going on.

JASON: What are you talking about?

CHRIS: I dunno. Forget it. But—

JASON: Don't do that! C'mon. What?

CHRIS: Like, last week, remember, they had a couple of them white hats walking the floor.

JASON: Yeah, so? Dude, maybe they're just upgrading the equipment.

CHRIS: Well, they got buttons now, BOOP, that can replace all of us. Boop. Boop.

JASON: C'mon, you're being paranoid.

CHRIS: Man, you ever given any thought to what you might do if this don't work out?

JASON: . . . Nah, not really. Knock on wood. I plan on retiring from the plant when I'm like fifty with a killa pension and money to burn, buy a condo in Myrtle Beach,[8] open a Dunkin' Donuts and live my life. Right, Stan?

STAN: Not a bad plan.

CHRIS: Really? Dunkin' Donuts, that's your vision, huh? Dunkin'-Fuckin'-Donuts?

JASON: Yeah, so?

CHRIS: Punch in, punch out, and at the end of the day you end up with a box of donuts and diabetes. My man, where's your imagination? You need to get on a bus and do some traveling.

JASON: What about our cruise to Jamaica? Quit whining.

(*A moment.*)

But seriously, man, why didn't you tell me?

CHRIS: Cuz—

JASON: Shit, I just kinda thought we'd retire and open a franchise together. We're a team, you can't leave!!

CHRIS: Yeah, I can.

JASON: What about me?

CHRIS: What about you?

---

7. Presumably, operating a jackhammer.
8. City and resort on the South Carolina coast.

JASON: You coulda told me.

CHRIS: Dude, it's just something I gotta do.

JASON: Yeah, right!

CHRIS: What?

JASON: Okay.

CHRIS: What?!

JASON: Whatever. Hey Stan, pour this bitch a shot so he'll shut the fuck up.

Scene 4

March 2, 2000

Outside it's 48°F.

In the news: In the Republican Presidential Debate, Alan Keyes,[9] John McCain and George Bush. In Reading, an overnight fire leaves a mother with five children homeless. Baldwin Hardware Corporation, a brass hardware maker, announces plans to open a new 280,000-square-foot facility in Leesport.[1]

Lights up. Bar. Brucie (African-American, forties) sits at the bar nursing a drink. The Republican Debate (Keyes, McCain, Bush) plays on the television.

STAN: Who are you liking?

BRUCIE: Don't matter. They'll all shit on us in the end.

STAN: What do you think of this Bush guy?

BRUCIE: I dunno. He looks like a little fucking chimp. But, if I gotta go with someone, Bradley's my man. Always liked him, cut through the bullshit, got to the ball, kept it up in the air.

STAN: Yeah, for sure, a real smart player. Like 'im, don't know how good a president he'd be, but I'd want him in a pickup game. You watching this?

BRUCIE: Nah.

(Stan channel-surfs, grows bored, then switches off the television. Oscar enters and begins replenishing the bar. He works silently and methodically, actively listening to the conversation. His quiet but alert presence should be felt throughout the scene.)

You see Garth?

STAN: Nah, what's up?

BRUCIE: He opened a B and B.

STAN: Get outta here, you're the third person to tell me that.

BRUCIE: He always said he was gonna do it. He used to talk about it all of the time. "A bed-and-breakfast in Honduras. It's gonna be dope, y'all." I was, like, "What? Yeah, where the fuck is Honduras?"[2] Garth was a cheap-ass bastard. He would never buy a round. Now, I get it.

9. Conservative African American political activist, pundit, and former ambassador (b. 1950). Like others mentioned below—Arizona senator John McCain (1936–2018), also a Republican, and professional basketball player-turned-Democratic New Jersey senator William Warren ("Bill") Bradley (b. 1943)—Keyes ran in the 2000 presidential race ultimately won by Republican former Texas governor George Walker Bush (b. 1946).

1. Town just north of Reading, Pennsylvania. *Baldwin Hardware Corporation*: brass fixture manufacturer whose production facility operated in Reading 1956–2011, when the company relocated to Nogales, Mexico, after purchase by Stanley Black & Decker, Inc.

2. In Central America, between Guatemala and El Salvador.

STAN: Eyes on the prize.

BRUCIE: Yeah.

STAN: Whatcha up to?

BRUCIE: Shit, you know—

STAN: Yeah—

BRUCIE: Out there. I don't wanna go backwards.

STAN: I hear that, so how many days you guys been locked out?

BRUCIE: Ninety-three weeks.

STAN: That's what I thought. Tough.

BRUCIE: Yup. Didn't wanna take the new contract. Be a fucking slave. That's what they want. We offered to take a fifty-percent pay cut, they won't budge, they want us to give up our retirement. What's the point? Full circle, a life-time, and be the same place I was when I was eighteen. What is that?

STAN: They bring in temps?

BRUCIE: Yeah, mostly Spanish cats, whatever. Cross the line, they work 'em to the bone, then get a fresh batch in three months.

STAN: Fuck 'em, you can do better.

BRUCIE: I know a coupla cats have moved on, but if we win this new contract at the textile mill, there's a big payout. That's why I'm holding out. They're try-ing to break the union.

STAN: Can't be done. I'm proud of you guys.

BRUCIE: It's pointless.

STAN: Don't say that.

BRUCIE: I been on the hustle for how many years? Worked hard. Right? Had the family. Now, I'm forty-nine.

STAN: Get outta here.

BRUCIE: Yeah, forty-fucking-nine, but listen, I was thinking the other day, I gotta do this for the next, what? fifteen-twenty years. You know this! Worry-ing. The hustle, man, my pop didn't go through this shit. I mean, he . . . he clocked in every day until he didn't, and went out with a nice package. He went on an eighteen-day cruise through the Greek Islands last October. Me, shit, I run the full mile, I put in the time, do the right thing, don't get me wrong, I had some good years . . . But, dude, tell me what I did wrong, huh?

STAN: I hear you. Getting injured was the best thing that ever happened to me. Got me out of that vortex. Three generations on the floor. Loyal as hell, I never imagined working anywhere else. I get injured. I'm in the hospital for nearly two months. I can't walk. Can't feel my toes. Not one of those Olstead fuckers called to check on me, to say, "I'm sorry for not fixing the machine." They knew that machine was trouble. Ramsey, Smitz—everyone wrote it up.

BRUCIE: I know how that goes.

STAN: The only time I heard from Olstead is when they sent their hard-ass lawyer to the hospital, 'cause they didn't want me to sue. Fucking pricks. Twenty-eight years. That's when I understood. That's when I knew, I was nobody to them. Nobody! Three generations of loyalty to the same company. This is America, right? You'd think that would mean something. They behave like they're doing you a goddamn favor.

BRUCIE: I hear you.

STAN: Bottom line, they don't understand that human decency is at the core of everything. I been jacking all them years and I can count on my hand the number of times they said thank you. Management: look me in the eye, say "thank you" now and then. "Thanks, Stan, for coming in early and working on the weekend. Good job." I loved my job. I was good at my job. Twenty-eight years jacking. And look at my leg! That's what I get.

BRUCIE: I feel you. But can I be real honest? . . .

STAN: Yeah, of course.

BRUCIE (*Raw and honest*): . . . I don't know what to do.

STAN: Whatcha mean?

BRUCIE: I don't know what to do? (*Meaning: "What's my purpose?"*) You know . . . I don't know anymore. What's the point? You know? I'm being dead serious.

STAN: You can't think that way.

BRUCIE: This is *me* being honest. I mean, what's the fucking point? Huh?

STAN: Things'll pick up.

BRUCIE (*With edge*): Yeah, you think so?!

STAN: I do.

BRUCIE: I'm not receiving that message! Last week, I was at the union office signing up for some bullshit training and this old white cat, whatever, gets in my face, talking about how we took his job. We? I asked him who he was talking about, and he pointed at me. ME? So I said, if you ain't noticed I'm in the same fucking line as you. Hello?! You'd think that would shut him down. But, no. He's a scratch in the vinyl,[3] going on and on about us coming here and ruining everything. Like I'm fresh off the boat or some shit. He don't know my biography. October 2nd, 1952, my father picked his last bale of cotton. He packed his razor and a Bible and headed North. Ten days later he had a job at Dixon's Hosieries. He clawed his way up from the filth of the yard to Union Rep,[4] fighting for fucking assholes just like that cat. So, I don't understand it. This damn blame game, I got enough of that in my marriage.

STAN: Don't worry about it.

(*Cynthia, Tracey and Jessie enter, in the midst of conversation.*)

TRACEY: Fill her up, Stan!

BRUCIE: Cynth.

CYNTHIA: What are you doing here?!

BRUCIE: Same as you, getting a drink.

CYNTHIA: Here?

BRUCIE: Hey Jessie, Tracey.

JESSIE: Brucie.

TRACEY: What's up?

BRUCIE: Not much. You guys look good.

TRACEY: You've always been a sweet liar.

BRUCIE: Hey Cynth, you got a minute?

CYNTHIA: No.

BRUCIE: Just—

CYNTHIA: No!

---

3. That is, a vinyl LP or record album that, when damaged, repeats the same sound over and over again.
4. Employee of an organization or company who represents and defends the interests of fellow employees as a member and official of their trades union; often an elected position.

(*Cynthia plops down with Jessie and Tracey.*)

It's been a long day. I don't wanna start. Let me have a drink. K?

TRACEY: Ignore 'im.

JESSIE: Don't worry about it, we'll get one drink and then go. K?

(*Brucie approaches the women.*)

BRUCIE: C'mon, Cynth—

CYNTHIA: What do you want?

BRUCIE: Can I talk to you?

CYNTHIA: No.

BRUCIE: Can I talk to you?!

CYNTHIA: No!

BRUCIE: CAN I TALK TO YOU?

CYNTHIA: NO!

(*Brucie slams the table. It's jarring. The women stand in unison, a united front.*)

STAN: C'mon, Brucie. Sit down. You want another drink?

TRACEY: She doesn't want to talk to you.

BRUCIE: You stay outta this!

STAN: Hey. Hey. C'mon—

TRACEY: Let's go.

CYNTHIA: I'm not going. This is my place.

JESSIE: That's right.

BRUCIE: Let's just talk.

CYNTHIA: I know what you want. Don't have it.

(*Cynthia turns her pockets inside out.*)

BRUCIE: Nice show. I heard you're—

CYNTHIA: What?

BRUCIE: We gotta do this in front of everyone?

CYNTHIA: We don't gotta do this at all. I don't recall having anything to say to you.

TRACEY: Relax, ignore him.   JESSIE: Don't listen, don't!

STAN: Come on, let me buy you one . . . It's okay. What're you drinking?

(*De-escalating.*)

BRUCIE: Same.

STAN: C'mon, sit. Let it go. Don't worry.

(*Tense. Stan pours Brucie a drink.*)

BRUCIE (*To Stan*): She's playing games.

STAN: Don't worry about it.

CYNTHIA: He's like clockwork. Thursday. Paycheck.

TRACEY: You want me to talk to him?

CYNTHIA: Nah. It'll just make him crazier.

(*Brucie stares at Cynthia.*)

TRACEY: Don't even look at him.

CYNTHIA: He's gonna sit there just to fuck with me.

JESSIE: Stay strong!

(*The women actively ignore Brucie as he tries to get Cynthia's attention. He mouths, "Cynthia." Finally:*)

(*To Brucie*) Why don't you leave her alone?!

BRUCIE: Why don't you relax your mouth?!

CYNTHIA: Don't talk to her that way!

(*Brucie demonstratively places his hands over his heart.*)

BRUCIE: Cynth? Babe?

STAN: Brucie . . .

BRUCIE: You're not being fair.

CYNTHIA: Who's not being fair?! Where are my muthafucking fish, Brucie? Huh?

(*Cynthia suddenly gets up from the table and marches toward Brucie.*)

TRACEY: Don't.   JESSIE (*To Brucie*): You got
                                            some nerve!

BRUCIE: Just wanna talk.

CYNTHIA: Here I am! Talk!

(*Brucie gently takes her hand.*)

TRACEY: Cynthia!

BRUCIE: Hey, mouth, give us a second.

TRACEY: You don't have any respect for women.

BRUCIE: No, I don't have no respect for you. So shut up!

TRACEY: And *you* wonder why your wife won't talk to you.

BRUCIE: . . . Can you just give us some room?

CYNTHIA (*To Tracy*): I got this.

(*A moment.*)

What do you want, Brucie?

BRUCIE: I keep trying to explain.

(*Brucie produces a piece of paper.*)

CYNTHIA: What's that?

(*He hands it to Cynthia. She reads.*)

BRUCIE: I'm in a program.[5]

CYNTHIA: And is having a drink part of that program?

BRUCIE: It's not the same.

CYNTHIA: I beg to differ.

BRUCIE: That's all you gotta say?

CYNTHIA: Whatcha want me to say?

BRUCIE: Just wanna show you I'm trying.

5. That is, an addiction recovery program.

CYNTHIA: K.

BRUCIE: And?

CYNTHIA: We done?

(*Brucie folds the paper and puts it in his pocket.*)

BRUCIE: Yeah.

CYNTHIA: K. Nice piece of paper. Maybe I'd be impressed if it was a pay stub. You call your son?

BRUCIE: How's he doing?

CYNTHIA: Good. Evolution. Chris tell you his news?

BRUCIE: Nah.

CYNTHIA: He got into Albright.

BRUCIE: Psh, for real?

CYNTHIA: That's all you gotta say? You know, he really wants you to . . . Forget it, just call 'im. K. He's starting in September.

BRUCIE: College? Who's paying for it?

CYNTHIA: He is.

BRUCIE: You gonna let him walk away from that steady money at the plant? Ask me, he'd be a damn fool to—

CYNTHIA: Good advice. How's that working out for you?

BRUCIE: . . .

CYNTHIA: Look, if you speak to him, do me a favor, say you're proud of 'im and leave it at that. Don't put any other ideas in his head. Cuz if you do, so help me God . . . This is a good thing. And you should be proud of him.

TRACEY: That's right, he's always been smart, Cynth.

BRUCIE: I'm just saying—

CYNTHIA: Say nothing for a change.

(*A moment.*)

BRUCIE: You doing okay?

CYNTHIA: Yeah. I'm cool.

BRUCIE: Stan says you're being considered for a promotion.

CYNTHIA: Yeah. Warehouse Supervisor. Not just me. Tracey, Clarence and Fat Henry. We're all in the running.

BRUCIE (*To Tracey*):   That true?

TRACEY: Yeah. Deciding soon. But, I'm not holding my breath, they're just blowing smoke up our asses, because some fancy consultant told 'em it would be a good idea to chum the waters.[6]

CYNTHIA: C'mon. You want this as bad as I do. You won't own it, but I know you do.

JESSIE: Of course she does, Tracey likes giving fucking orders.

TRACEY: Get outta here.   CYNTHIA: But, c'mon if one us
                                                      gets this job, how sweet'll
                                                      that be?

(*Cynthia gives Tracey a warm hug.*)

BRUCIE (*Humor with edge*): They must be hard up if they're considering you guys.

---

6. Churn or muddy the waters, as when fishermen throw "chum" (often, chopped fish and fish fluids) into the water to attract other fish.

CYNTHIA: Don't start with me. Listen, I'm glad you're getting things together. But, I got—

BRUCIE: Wait a minute, wait a minute. Don't walk away. Please. I feel bad about what went down in December. It wasn't me . . . I'm sorry. Look, I'm getting clean. Okay? It's not gonna happen again. It's too embarrassing. You know me. Psh. I useta make fun of cats like me.

(*He takes her hand. Smooth. Cynthia is vulnerable to his charm.*)

I'm sorry. K, babe? You look good. You always looked sexy in your work clothing.

JESSIE: Tracey, do something.

BRUCIE: I couldn't help but notice when I was by the house that the gutter needs to be rehung. I can come by and do it. We'll keep things simple, you know, talk. I feel like if things was good with us, it would be easier to get back on my feet.

CYNTHIA: Don't think so. You can call Chris . . . Get off that dope, but don't come by.

BRUCIE: When I get my job back—

CYNTHIA: If. If. I'm all for you guys standing strong, babe, but at some point you gotta think about what this is doing to us.

BRUCIE (*All smoothness*): Can I get a kiss?

CYNTHIA: What?

BRUCIE: Can I at least get a kiss?

(*He goes in for a kiss, Cynthia surrenders. An intimate moment. Then Tracey jumps to attention.*)

TRACEY: I think you better go!

BRUCIE: I'm not talking to you, mouth!

TRACEY: You're talking to her, you're talking to me.

BRUCIE: You got a lotta moxie for a white girl.

TRACEY: I got more than moxie! Try me! Leave her alone. Okay? She's doing really well—

JESSIE: Don't fuck this up for her!

TRACEY: You wanna do something for Cynthia? Get clean or get lost. That's the best thing you can do for her.

BRUCIE: Don't you tell me what I need to do! I know what I need to do!

STAN: Brucie, maybe you better—

(*Brucie is suddenly emotional. He tries to pull it together, but he's battling a tsunami.*)

BRUCIE: Cynthia! Please—

CYNTHIA: No!!

Scene 5

April 17, 2000

Outside it's 60°F.

In the news: Three days after a record 617-point drop in the Dow Jones as the tech bubble bursts. DC protesters disrupt the World Bank and International

Monetary Fund[7] meeting. A 26-year-old man is shot leaving a bar on Woodward Street in Reading.

Bar exterior. Tracey stands outside, smoking a cigarette. Oscar steps outside and stands in the doorway.

OSCAR: Hey.
TRACEY: Hey.
OSCAR: Can I bum a cigarette?
TRACEY *(Dismissive)*: No.
OSCAR: Thank you for nothing.
TRACEY: You're welcome.

(Beat. Oscar is still standing in the doorway.)

Don't you got something to do?
OSCAR: It's my break.

(An awkward moment.)

Did you know they're waiting for you inside?
TRACEY: Yeah, I know.
OSCAR: Do you want me to tell 'em you're out here?
TRACEY: Do I look like I need you to mind my business?
OSCAR: Okay, whatever. Just trying to help.
TRACEY: Can you, like, give me my space?
OSCAR: Technically, this is my space. This is where I chill. This is my spot. But, I'm a gentleman.
TRACEY: Good for you. Now, fuck off.
OSCAR *(Under his breath)*: Bitch.
TRACEY: Asshole.
OSCAR: Fuck you.
TRACEY: No, fuck you!

(A brief standoff, neither will surrender ground.)

. . . What?
OSCAR: What?!

(Finally, Tracey melts and gives him a cigarette.)

TRACEY: Happy?
OSCAR: Thank you.

(She lights his cigarette. They smoke.)

. . . You—
TRACEY: Yeah?
OSCAR: Um. Um, uh, uh—

7. International organization (based in Washington, D.C., and founded 1945) tasked, on behalf of its 189 member-countries, with ensuring the stability of the international monetary system, especially by managing financial crises, exchange rates, and payments between governments. *World Bank*: international financial institution providing loans and grants to developing countries. Both organizations have been a prime target of the anti-globalization movement, which argues that such institutions facilitate the economic and environmental exploitation of developing countries, exacerbating global inequities.

TRACEY: Are you retarded? What?

OSCAR: You work at the plant, right?

TRACEY: Along with everyone else who comes in here. Dah!

OSCAR: It awright?

TRACEY: It's okay, it's a job. Steady. Whatever.

OSCAR: They pay good?

TRACEY: I pay my bills. What's with all the questions?

OSCAR: I'm just asking cuz I saw a posting down at the Centro Hispano.

TRACEY: What the fuck is that?

OSCAR: The Latino Community Center.

TRACEY: What do you mean you saw a posting?

OSCAR: A posting, a job posting. Olstead's? Steel Tubing? That's your place, right?

TRACEY: It's not my place, it's where I work.

OSCAR: Yeah, okay . . . they're looking to hire folks, and I know it gotta pay better than here.

TRACEY: What are you talking about? Olstead's isn't hiring.

OSCAR: That ain't what I heard. They's looking to train packers, shippers . . . I got the info.

(Oscar takes a folded flyer from his pocket.)

TRACEY: Let me see that.

(Tracey takes the flyer.)

All I can read is "Olstead's." The rest is gibberish.

OSCAR: No it's Spanish. See there, it gives times when you go down to the plant to fill out an application for training.

TRACEY: This is a joke. I don't think so. No. No. First off, you gotta be in the union.

OSCAR: Not according to the flyer.

TRACEY: Well, you got it wrong.

OSCAR: Okay.

TRACEY: You got it wrong!

OSCAR: Okay!

TRACEY: *And* that's not how it works. Anyway. You gotta know somebody to get in. My dad worked there, I work there and my son works there. It's that kinda shop. Always been.

OSCAR: I know you.

TRACEY: You don't know me.

OSCAR: How does someone get in?

TRACEY: Enough with the questions. Your mother didn't teach you to respect your elders?

OSCAR: They're getting pretty lit in there.

TRACEY: Yeah?

OSCAR: Sooo, what are they celebrating?

TRACEY: You know Cynthia.

OSCAR: Yeah.

TRACEY: Well, she just got promoted last week. They gave her a frigging cushion of a job. A recliner. And I wish she'd just shut up about it already.

OSCAR: I thought you guys was friends.

TRACEY: Yeah, we're friends. So? You don't get sick of your friends sometimes?

(*Tracey draws on her cigarette.*)

You know how long I been working at the plant? Forget it . . . Never mind, it's not important . . . But, I know the floor as good as Cynthia. I do. You wanna know the truth, the only reason I didn't get the job is because Butz tried to fuck me and I wouldn't let him, and he told everyone in management that I'm unstable. I'm not unstable. I'm like—

OSCAR: That's some shit.

TRACEY: Yeah. It sucks. And, I betcha they wanted a minority. I'm not prejudice, but that's how things are going these days. I got eyes. They get tax breaks or something.

OSCAR: I dunno know about all that.

TRACEY: It's a fact. That's how things are going. And I'm not prejudice, I say, you are who you are, you know? I'm cool with everyone. But, I mean . . . c'mon . . . you guys coming over here, you can get a job faster than—

OSCAR: I was born here.

TRACEY: Still . . . you wasn't born here, Berks.[8]

OSCAR: Yeah, I was.

TRACEY: Yeah? Well, my family's been here a long time. Since the twenties, okay? They built the house that I live in. They built this town. My grand-father was German, and he could build anything. Cabinets, fine furniture, anything. He had these amazing hands. Sturdy. Meaty. Real firm. You couldn't shake his hand without feeling his presence, feeling his power. And those hands, let me tell you, they were solid, worker hands, you know, and they really, really knew how to make things. Beautiful things. I'm not talking about now, how you got these guys who can patch a hole with spackle and think they're the shit. My grandfather was the real thing. A craftsman . . . And I remember when I was a kid, I mean eight or nine, we'd go downtown to Penn with Opa. To walk and look in store windows. Downtown was real nice back then. You'd get dressed up to go shopping. You know, Pomeroy's, Whitner's,[9] whatever. I felt really special, because he was this big, strapping man and people gave him room. But, what I really loved was that he'd take me to office buildings, banks . . . you name it, and he'd point out the woodwork. And if you got really, really close he'd show some detail that he'd carved for me. An apple blossom. Really. That's what I'm talking about. It was back when if you worked with your hands people respected you for it. It was a gift. But now, there's nothing on Penn. You go into the buildings, the walls are covered over with sheetrock, the wood painted gray, or some ungodly color, and it just makes me sad. It makes me . . . Whatever.

OSCAR: You okay?

TRACEY: Listen, that piece of paper that you're holding is an insult, it don't mean anything, Olstead's isn't for you.

---

8. Berks County, Pennsylvania; Reading is its county seat.

9. Like Pomeroy's, a department store (founded 1870s); these downtown stores closed in the 1980s, the buildings demolished in 1995 and 2004, respectively.

Scene 6

May 5, 2000

Outside it's 84°F.

In the news: The U.S. unemployment rate tumbles to a 30-year low, 3.9%. The City of Reading fires a dozen employees, fearing a deficit of $10,000,000. Allen Iverson[1] and the Philadelphia 76ers prepare for Game 1 of the Eastern Conference Semifinals.

Lights up. Bar. Stan prepares a gimlet. Jessie sits at the bar eyeing a birthday cake. Oscar is behind the bar, playing a portable video game.

STAN: A gimlet, shaken but not stirred.

(Stan places the cocktail on the bar.)

JESSIE: Did you actually put some alcohol in it this time?
STAN: Against my better judgment, I did—
JESSIE: Very funny.

(Jessie takes a sip, savoring.)

STAN: You been warming that seat for a long time. Are the ladies coming?
JESSIE: That's what they say, but who knows at this point?
STAN: What time were they supposed to meet ya?
JESSIE: Officially? Over an hour ago.
STAN: Jesus. Is something going on that I should know?
JESSIE: Dunno. Cynthia. The promotion. Whatever. Tracey pretends like it ain't a big deal. But, I can tell she don't like taking orders from Cynthia. And don't spread this, but things haven't been so good between them.
STAN: That's the way people are in this town. Bitch and moan, want something better. But, then the minute someone does well, forget it.
JESSIE: Tell me about it. Tracey's been going around town whispering that the only reason Cynthia got the job is cuz she's black. Two months ago she couldn't give a shit, and suddenly—
STAN: C'mon. Bullshit. Cynthia earned that promotion.
JESSIE: Sure, but I know for a fact that it pissed off a lot of people.
STAN: Gimme a break. People don't like change. I wouldn't lose any sleep over it—
JESSIE: You're right, fuck 'em all, I'm sick of being in the middle. Let's cut the cake.
STAN: You sure?
JESSIE: Yeah!
STAN: Hey, Oscar.
OSCAR: Yeah?
STAN: Will you get me a knife?

(Oscar retrieves a knife from the bar.)

You got any special birthday wishes?

1. Hall-of-Fame basketball player (b. 1975) who began and ended his career with the Philadelphia 76ers (1996–2006, 2009–10); in 2000–2001, he led the team to their first NBA final series since 1983 and earned both NBA Most Valuable Player (MVP) and NBA All-Star Game MVP titles.

JESSIE: Hell yeah. But, you know what would be nice, a kiss. I just wanna be kissed today.

(*Jessie blows out the candles.*)

STAN: Happy birthday, sweetheart.

OSCAR: Happy birthday.

JESSIE: Thank you.

(*Jessie cuts the cake. Cynthia rushes in, winded.*)

CYNTHIA: I'm so sorry, babe.

JESSIE: Here comes the boss!

CYNTHIA: What a headache, I got stuck at a meeting.

JESSIE: Everything okay?

CYNTHIA: Don't worry about it. Today is your day. Here. Happy birthday.

(*Cynthia passes Jessie a Cher CD.*)[2]

(*Singing:*)
Do you believe in life after love?

(*Cynthia hugs Jessie. They both sing:*)

CYNTHIA AND JESSIE:
I can feel something inside me say
I really don't think you're strong enough.

JESSIE: I almost forgive you.

CYNTHIA: There's no way I'd miss this, but I couldn't get out of there. I was trapped in a room of "supervisors," all of 'em had passionate ideas about how the floor could be run more efficiently, yet none of those donkeys have actually operated a machine.

JESSIE: No shit.

CYNTHIA: There's this one idiot who seriously thinks that the plant can be run by five and a half people.

JESSIE: Ha! Where are you going to find half a person?

STAN: Whiskey?

CYNTHIA: Double, babe.

STAN (*Sarcastically*): Jeez, how's the new job?

CYNTHIA: Exhausting.

JESSIE: As long as they fix the air-conditioning this summer, I'm happy.

CYNTHIA: It's number sixteen on my very long list, babe, don't hold your breath.

STAN: Look at you. You got a list?

CYNTHIA: I also got a desk, whoa, and a computer.

STAN: What?!

JESSIE: I seen it, she ain't lying.

STAN: I mean shit, all of them years on the floor. That must taste sweet.

2. Compact disk. *Cher*: American singer-actress (b. Cherilyn Sarkisian, 1946). The title song of her Grammy-winning quadruple platinum dance-pop album, *Believe* (1998), begins with the three lines Cynthia and Jessie sing below.

CYNTHIA: Sweet don't even begin to describe it, babe. First day, I park. Get out, and immediately head for the floor, it's a reflex. I just do it, get to the door, same as usual, I smell the oil and metal dust, I hear the machinery churning and feel the energy of the room. I go to my station, say, "Hey Lance, Becky," get ready, my body knows it's there to pack tubes. That's what I do.

STAN: // That's what you do.

CYNTHIA: I fire up the machine, but everyone is looking at me, and Tracey says, "What the fuck you doing here?" Then I remember. I can go sit down.

JESSIE: // Yes, you can

CYNTHIA: I'm not wearing my Carhartt, not gonna be on my feet for ten hours, I loosen my support belt,[3] I don't have to worry about my fingers cramping or the blood blister on my left foot. I can stop sweating because goddamn the office has air-conditioning. These muthafuckers got air-conditioning.

JESSIE: Of course they do.

CYNTHIA: Twenty-four years, and I can't remember talking to anyone in the office, except to do paperwork. I mean some of these folks been working there as long as us, but they're as unfamiliar as a stranger sitting next to you on a bus.

JESSIE: That's for sure.

STAN: Yeah—

CYNTHIA: It's like looking at a map, and discovering that you're only just a few miles away from the ocean. But you didn't know because it was on the other side of the damn mountains.

JESSIE: I'm so proud of you. You got off the fucking floor.

(*Chris and Jason sweep in with energy and hug Jessie. Suddenly it's a party.*)

CHRIS: WHASSUP?!

JASON: We miss the party?!

JESSIE: Nah. You're just in time, we're cutting the cake.

JASON: Looks good.

(*Jason swipes frosting with his fingers.*)

STAN: Hey, get outta there.

JASON: Happy birthday!

CHRIS (*Singing*): "Happy birthday to ya!"

JESSIE: Thank you!

CYNTHIA: Where you guys coming from?

CHRIS: Just took a spin on Jason's new bike.

STAN: No!

JASON: Yes!

STAN: Congratulations!

CYNTHIA: I hope you were wearing a helmet.

CHRIS (*To Stan*): Whatcha got on tap?

---

3. Lightweight, usually elastic belt worn to support the back and, theoretically, prevent strain or injury. *Carhartt*: work clothes made by U.S.-based apparel maker Carhartt, Inc. (founded 1889).

STAN: You need to ask?

CHRIS: Keep hope alive. That's all I'm saying.

JASON: Dude.

(*Jason scans the room.*)

Where's Ma?

JESSIE: I dunno, you tell me.

JASON: Don't worry. She'll be here. You know her.

JESSIE: Yeah.   CHRIS (*To Cynthia*): You look
                                       all important.

CYNTHIA: Gotta dress the part.

(*Chris gives Cynthia a hug.*)

JESSIE: Betcha proud of your ma?

CHRIS: She's aight.

(*Cynthia gives Chris a playful jab.*)

JESSIE (*To Cynthia*): Hey Cynth, you remember the first day we met? You were
    sporting an afro and platforms and I thought there's no way you were gonna
    make a day on the line.

CYNTHIA: And you looked like fucking Joni Mitchell[4] with a headband and hair
    down to your butt.

JESSIE: Guess how old I was when I started, Stan?

STAN: Nineteen—

JESSIE: Eighteen. Eighteen! Can you believe it? The summer I started, I was a
    couple years younger than you guys!

JASON: Betcha were hot.

JESSIE: You know, I was.

STAN: She was.

JESSIE: God, that was a summer, huh? A lot of fun. Wasn't thinking about any-
    thing, I figured I'd be at Olstead's for six to eight months max. Can you believe
    it? I was collecting Green Stamps[5] the whole year, remember Green Stamps? I
    was gonna trade 'em in for a backpack, a tent. Had like ten thousand of 'em. I
    was going to hitch my way across the country with my boyfriend, Felix.

CYNTHIA: Felix. I remember Felix, he was a musician, right?

JESSIE: He had a harmonica. And we planned to wind up in Alaska where my
    dad worked in a cannery. Kodiak.

STAN: I knew your dad, Phil Lombardi, he looked liked, um—

JESSIE: James Garner.[6]

---

4. Canadian folk singer-songwriter (b. 1943) whose *Blue* (1971) is widely hailed as among the best
albums of the twentieth century.
5. S&H Green Stamps, popular from the 1930s through the late 1970s; earned with purchases at
supermarkets and department stores across the United States, stamps could be redeemed for a range
of products.
6. American actor (1928–2014), handsome star of television series including *The Rockford Files* (1974–80),
in which he played a wrongly imprisoned ex-convict-turned-private detective. *Phil Lombardi*: professional baseball player (1963–2021), mainly for the New York Yankees and New York Mets (1986–89).

STAN: Yeah. That's right.

JESSIE: He split for Alaska when I was thirteen. A lotta folks went up there that summer. Remember?

STAN: Sure.

JESSIE: God. Me. Felix. That was so long ago. We were gonna do Alaska, camp, live clean, you know, and save enough money to get to India. Live in an ashram[7] for a while, then bum along the hippie trail. Istanbul, Tehran, Kandahar, Kabul, Peshawar, Lahore, Kathmandu. Places. Still remember 'em all. I used to say 'em every night like a mantra, a prayer: Istanbul, Tehran, Kandahar, Kabul, Peshawar, Lahore, Kathmandu. I mapped the whole thing out. Yeah, we had this, um, world map, that Felix had ripped outta an atlas in the library. *The World Book.*[8] God . . . That was the plan.

JASON: So, why didn't you go?

JESSIE: Started working, met Dan, I guess I got caught in the riptide, couldn't get back to shore. That's how it is.

CHRIS: You ever sorry?

(The weight of the question lands on Jessie.)

JESSIE: I guess, I wish . . . I had gotten to see the world. You know, left Berks, if only for a year. That's what I regret. Not the work, I regret the fact that for a little while it seemed like, I don't know, there was possibility. I think about that Jessie on the other side of the world and what she woulda seen.

(Surprising emotions.)

Whoa. I'm sorry. I didn't see that coming.

STAN: Look, I got to see a little of the world after 'Nam.[9] Shit follows you everywhere. In some ways you're better off not knowing.

JESSIE: Yeah? You don't know what you don't know, until you wanna know, right? And then it's too late. Istanbul, Tehran, Kandahar, Kabul, Peshawar, Lahore, Kathmandu.

(Tracey enters with a flurry of energy.)

STAN: There she is!

TRACEY: The party can officially begin!

CYNTHIA: Look who finally showed up.

(Tracey and Jessie hug.)

JESSIE *(Smiling)*: Thank you for making room for us.

CYNTHIA *(Offhanded)*: Yeah! You get lost on your way over?

TRACEY: Gimme a break, I'm here. Okay. I'm sorry. Get over it!

(Tracey gives Cynthia a cutting glance.)

JESSIE: C'mon, you guys. We're here to celebrate! Both of you get over it. Okay? Calm down. It's my birthday. I'm just happy my besties are here.

7. Religious retreat, especially in South Asia. All the famous "places" Jessie goes on to list here are (mostly capital) cities in South Asia or the Middle East: Istanbul (Turkey), Tehran (Iran), Kandahar, Kabul, Peshawar (Afghanistan), Lahore (Pakistan), Kathmandu (Nepal).
8. Popular American encyclopedia; it began publication in 1917.
9. Vietnam War (c. 1955–75).

CYNTHIA: She brought the attitude. I was chill—

TRACEY: What's your problem? Relax. Jason, get your ma a beer.

JASON: Ma?!!

TRACEY: C'mon, c'mon.

(She hugs him.)

I love you!!!

(Jason walks over to the bar.)

JASON: A pint.

(Stan pours a beer.)

JESSIE: You okay?

TRACEY: Why wouldn't I be okay?

JESSIE: I don't know, you just—

TRACEY: What? I'm fine. Let's celebrate. Yahoo!

JESSIE: Suddenly, it doesn't feel like a celebration.

(Chris searches for a song on the jukebox. Jason digs into a slice of cake.)

TRACEY: Why are you making such a big deal? I'm late. I'm sorry. I'm here.

(A moment. Jason gives Tracey the beer. Tracey visibly avoids sitting next to Cynthia.)

CYNTHIA: Hey, Tracey. We good? Cuz since all of this went down I definitely feel some tension. Maybe I'm making it up, but . . . We've been friends a long time, you've always been straight with me. You got a problem, tell me.

TRACEY: Yeah?

CYNTHIA: I'm sorry, but I don't know why I'm catching shade? What's up?

TRACEY: Now's not the time for this. K.

CYNTHIA: I took this promotion cuz I thought it would be good for all of us.

TRACEY: Yeah, right?!

CYNTHIA: And I don't deserve the things you've been saying. You've always been cool. Be angry, but don't make it about this . . . (Points to the skin on the back of her hand) Look at me, Tracey. You don't want to go down that road, we've got too much history between us. You got a problem, you tell me to my face.

TRACEY: I just feel like, um . . . I . . . I see you getting pretty chummy with "them" . . . And . . . The other day on the floor I called out to you, but you brushed me off.

CYNTHIA: I gotta look busy, that's half the job, babe.

TRACEY: I know that, but it's the way you did it.

CYNTHIA: Well, I'm sorry! I'm learning. Cut me some slack, okay? There's a lotta pressure on me right now. // They're watching.

TRACEY: Yeah?

CYNTHIA: Yeah!

JESSIE: C'mon guys, let's not do this.

TRACEY: . . . And is there something you aren't telling us?

CYNTHIA: What do you mean?

TRACEY: I dunno.

CYNTHIA: C'mon, don't play games.

TRACEY: Are they gonna be laying people off?

JASON: Whoa!   CHRIS: Come again?

TRACEY: Answer me.
CYNTHIA: Where'd you hear that bullshit?
TRACEY: A little bird.

(*They all look at Cynthia.*)

CYNTHIA: . . .
TRACEY: Are they?
CYNTHIA: Look, there's been a little talk about trimming overhead, but there always is—
STAN: // Talk? We'll see about that.
CYNTHIA: I know what's important, don't think because I went upstairs that I can't see the grit on the floor. I got the same aches and pains as you guys. I wouldn't—
TRACEY: You'd tell us, right?
CYNTHIA: Of course.
TRACEY: Promise?!
CYNTHIA: Yes.

(*Tracey pulls a flyer out of her pocket.*)

TRACEY: Have you guys seen this flyer?
JESSIE: No.

CYNTHIA: No.   JASON: What is it?

TRACEY: When I first saw it I didn't believe it. Then a week ago, I saw a couple of these taped up at the gas station. Do you know what it says?

(*Tracey shows Cynthia the flyer.*)

CYNTHIA: It's in Spanish. I can't read it.
TRACEY: Hey Oscar.
OSCAR: Yeah?

(*Tracey holds up the flyer.*)

TRACEY: Do you wanna read this for Cynthia?

Scene 7

July 4, 2000

Outside it's 84°F.

In the news: Working Woman magazine[1] *reports that the salary gap is narrowing between men and women in some U.S. industries. Reading police crack down on high-crime neighborhoods in response to a recent rise in violent crime.*

1. American monthly (1976–2001).

The City of Reading purchases a number of run-down buildings with plans to demolish them in an effort to combat urban blight.

    Outside the bar. Brucie smokes a cigarette, clearly high. Chris and Jason rush out of the bar, past him. Bottle rockets explode in the distance.

BRUCIE: Chris! Chris! Your mom inside?

CHRIS: No, but give her some space, she don't want to talk to you . . .

BRUCIE: Hold up. You got a minute?

CHRIS: No, gotta run.

BRUCIE: What's the rush?

CHRIS: Something's going on down at the plant.

JASON: C'mon, Chris. // Let's move.

BRUCIE: It'll only take a minute.

JASON: Yo!

CHRIS: Quick—

BRUCIE: I was just wondering whether you could spot me—

CHRIS: Now's not a good time.

JASON: Yo! Let's—

BRUCIE (*Smiling*): Gotcha, but it only takes five seconds to reach into your pocket.

CHRIS: Yeah, and a whole week of work to replace what's in there.

BRUCIE: What about you, Jason?

JASON: Sorry, Brucie.

BRUCIE: I'm getting some benefits next week. The check hasn't come.

JASON: Can't do it.

BRUCIE: All right I hear you. But . . . Wait, wait, wait. Chris? C'mon?

    (*Chris gives Brucie a hug.*)

CHRIS: Ten. That's all I can spare.

BRUCIE: Easy breezy, not complaining, thank you.

CHRIS: Listen, we really gotta go.

BRUCIE: Why are you rushing? What's happening?

JASON: Dunno, but Wilson says they moved three of the mills outta the factory over the long weekend.

BRUCIE: What?

JASON: Don't ask me. All I know is he passed by there about an hour ago to pick up something from his locker, and the machines were gone.

CHRIS: Gone . . .

JASON: Fucking assholes. He's calling everyone.

BRUCIE: What are you talking about?

CHRIS: Gone. Removed. // Gone.

JASON: Like not fucking there.

CHRIS: They posted a sign on the door, nobody was supposed to see it until tomorrow morning.

JASON: A list of names. Me, Chris—our names are on it.

BRUCIE: What do you think it means?

JASON: I don't know, but I'm gonna find out—

BRUCIE: Sly muthafuckas—

CHRIS: Makes you wanna hit somebody.

JASON: We're going by the plant, I wanna see it for myself.

BRUCIE: And your mom? She know about this?

CHRIS: Man, I hope she didn't.

(*Brucie laughs, knowingly.*)

What's funny?

BRUCIE: I'm not laughing at you, shit I'm just sorry to hear it. I know I'm not in the best position to give advice, but this is just the first step. They're gonna come at you. My two cents, take the small concessions.

CHRIS: What are you talkin' about?

BRUCIE: Cuz when we walked out of the textile mill thinking big, they locked us out, beat down our optimism and we couldn't get back in. And nearly two years later there ain't a damn thing we can do about it. Don't let them bring those temps in—fight it. Because once they do, you're out. You hear me? I wouldn't have said that six months ago, but I'm telling you truth.

JASON: Man, I pray it don't come to that.

BRUCIE: Get down on your knees, son . . .

JASON: . . . C'mon, Chris, let's move.

(*Brucie holds out the ten dollars.*)

BRUCIE: Here, I'll make do. Believe me, you're gonna need this. No machines, no jobs. That's pretty simple arithmetic.

JASON: Fuck // that!

CHRIS: Let's move.

ACT TWO

Scene 1

October 13, 2008

Outside it's 79°F.

In the news: The Dow Jones gains 936 points, its largest gain ever, following news that the government-funded bank bailouts[2] were approved around the world. In Berks County, Pennsylvania, power shutoffs for delinquent utility customers rise 111% over the previous year.

TRACEY: You gonna talk or are you waiting for me to dance for you?

JASON: It took a lot of nerve for me to ring the bell.

TRACEY: Ding dong, that's real hard.

JASON: I didn't wanna come, but I thought you might be kinda happy to see me. You got anything to drink?

TRACEY: Who told you, you could sit down?

JASON: I'm sitting cuz I'm tired.

TRACEY: Why the fuck did you do that to your face?

2. Passed at the height of the 2007–8 financial crisis, the Emergency Economic Stabilization Act of 2008 authorized the Treasury Department to spend some $700 billion purchasing toxic assets from distressed U.S. banks.

JASON: They're just tats. Get over it.

TRACEY: Well, it looks stupid.

(*Tracey hands Jason five dollars.*)

JASON: This is all you got?

TRACEY: You know what, leave it there. I don't need this shit right now. You call me up outta the blue: "Ma, I need money!" I almost didn't answer. What if I didn't answer? Huh? What would you do then?

(*Jason examines the bill.*)

JASON: Seriously? Five dollars, what's that, three cigarettes and a Slurpee? When I called you, you said you had money. I traveled all the way here for this? Fucking hell.

TRACEY: Sorry to inconvenience you. I had the money, but—

JASON: Shit. Really?

(*A moment. It becomes evident that Tracey is strung out.*)

How long has that been going on?

TRACEY: How long what?

JASON: Don't fuck with me, you know exactly what I'm talkin' about.

TRACEY: That's very rich coming from you. Gimme back my money, and get the fuck outta here.

JASON: You look like shit.

TRACEY: I look like shit? Have you looked in the mirror lately?

JASON: Is this really all you got?

TRACEY: Yeah. I'm not running a money farm.

JASON: I didn't believe Fat Henry when he said you were strung out.

TRACEY: Fat Henry needs to mind his business. It's for my back pain.

JASON: Aspirin won't do?

TRACEY: Ha, ha. Very funny. You have no idea. You . . . Have . . . No . . . Idea!

JASON: OKAY!

TRACEY: We done?

JASON: . . .

TRACEY: When can I git it back?

JASON: You want this five dollars back?

TRACEY: Yeah. I want it back. Tomorrow?

JASON: You know what, never mind. This is too much trouble.

TRACEY: Fine. Give it here.

(*She grows antsy. She needs a fix. Jason extends the money, and she snatches it from him, desperate.*)

JASON: Jesus, look at you.

TRACEY: What?!

JASON: How the fuck did this happen?

(*Cynthia's sparse apartment. Cynthia, nervous and excited, scrambles into the room. She wears a nursing-home maintenance uniform. She picks up a couple of take-out food containers littering the floor.*)

CHRIS: So. This is where you live?

CYNTHIA: Yeah. It's what I could manage for now. You hungry?

CHRIS: Nah. Where should I put my stuff?

CYNTHIA: Anywhere.

(*Chris looks around. He drops his backpack.*)

CHRIS: You didn't mention you moved.

CYNTHIA: No?

CHRIS: What happened to the house?

CYNTHIA: I got behind . . . You wanna drink or something?

CHRIS: Nah.

CYNTHIA: Why didn't you let me know you got out? I had to hear it from the grapevine.

CHRIS: I just needed some time. Still trying to get adjusted. Get my head back.

CYNTHIA: How long have you been out?

CHRIS: Six weeks?

CYNTHIA: Why didn't you call me? I woulda picked you up.

CHRIS: I dunno, I didn't wanna bother you.

CYNTHIA: Don't get it mixed up. You're staying here.

(*Chris fidgets with the Bible in his hand.*)

What's that?

CHRIS: It's my Bible.

CYNTHIA: A Bible?

CHRIS: Yeah, a Bible.

CYNTHIA: I heard you got all churchy.

CHRIS: I don't know what you heard, but this book saved my life.

CYNTHIA: Why don't you sit down? You're making me nervous just hovering there. Sit. Relax. You're home.

(*Chris sits on the couch. Cynthia smiles, trying to break the ice.*)

You got sorta mannish, huh? Put on weight since my last visit. You look different.

CHRIS: So do you. You okay?

CYNTHIA: Yeah. Yeah.

CHRIS: How are things?

CYNTHIA: Good. Good.

CHRIS: You, um, working?

CYNTHIA: I got some hours over at the university, maintenance. Also working at the nursing home, on weekends. Piecing things together. You know me, I'm a worker. Get restless otherwise.

CHRIS: Yeah. I walked around . . . Saw that Snookie's place closed.

CYNTHIA: Yeah.

CHRIS: Ran into . . . um . . .

CYNTHIA: Who?

CHRIS: Folks.

CYNTHIA: I'm sorry I couldn't get out to see you the last couple months, it got too expensive.

CHRIS: Um.

CYNTHIA: Everybody's been asking me about when you was getting out. But all those damn years you'd just become X's marked off on the calendar and it made me crazy. God . . . You know after everything. I wanna say that . . .

(*Cynthia fights back emotions.*)

I'm sorry.

CHRIS: For what?

CYNTHIA: It's just, I shoulda . . .

(*Chris places his arms around Cynthia.*)

CHRIS: C'mon. C'mon. I don't want this to be a big deal. Tell me about what's been going on. You hear from the old gang? Tracey?

CYNTHIA: Fuck her. After what went down. We don't really—

CHRIS: You hear, Jason's out.

CYNTHIA: Yeah? When did that happen?

CHRIS: Dunno. A couple months ago.

CYNTHIA: That little bastard. What did he have to say? He got you into this shit. If it wasn't for him . . . you'd . . . I coulda killed him.

CHRIS: It's done. I can't stay in that place.

CYNTHIA: Well, I'm still trying to understand what happened, Chris. What happened?

Scene 2

July 17, 2000

Eight years earlier.
    Outside it's 82°F.
    In the news: Federal eligibility guidelines ease, allowing more families in Read-ing public schools to receive free and reduced school lunches. Several U.S. compa-nies, including 3M, Johnson & Johnson, and General Electric, increase leadership development internally, expanding opportunities for minority employees.
    Bar. Loud arguing. Chris, Jason, Jessie, Tracey, Cynthia, Stan and Oscar in the bar.

CYNTHIA: Stop yelling! Stop yelling! // Stop yelling!

TRACEY: Tell us what's going on? // Tell us the truth!

(*Chris, Jason and Jessie raise their voices in agreement. Chaos. They con-tinue to berate Cynthia.*)

CYNTHIA: Stop shouting at me! Stop shouting. Listen. Listen. Listen! I'm tr . . . I'm trying.

TRACEY: What the hell is going on?!

CYNTHIA: I think what they did is bullshit. I promise you. I didn't know. I found out the same time as you guys . . . look . . . I'm in there fighting for us.

TRACEY: Us? You promised!!!

CYNTHIA: . . . If I'd known they were gonna ship out half of the machines, I woulda told you. But I didn't know until I got the call from Wilson.

TRACEY: Then why have you been avoiding us?

JASON: Yeah!

CYNTHIA: I'm not avoiding you! I'm working. And for your information, I'm the only supervisor who's even bothered to give you real face time.

TRACEY: Good for you, but what are we gonna do?! Huh?

CYNTHIA: I'm trying to get answers same as you. I just left the meeting . . .

JESSIE: What meeting?

CYNTHIA: I'm not even supposed to be talking to you guys.

TRACEY: Did they send you here?

CYNTHIA: Don't be an idiot, I'm off the clock, I'd lose my job if they knew I was here talking about this.

TRACEY: But I don't understand what you're telling us.

CYNTHIA: Okay, you're not going to like it, but they're going to use this opportunity to renegotiate your contracts.

TRACEY: What? Since when?   JESSIE: I fucking knew it.

CYNTHIA: And word is they're gonna push for real concessions, and they're prepared to fight.

JASON: Fuck that.

TRACEY: So are we. You tell   CHRIS: Nah.
'em no, they can't do that.

TRACEY: We're not afraid to strike.

CHRIS: Hell no!   JASON: Fuck yeah.

TRACEY: What do they want? Wasn't it enough that they shipped out the machines? And they better not ask us to work longer shifts.

CHRIS: Fuck that shit. I can't.   TRACEY: We're not mules.
No!   We can't . . .

JESSIE: No way.   JASON: No fucking way.

CYNTHIA: I've told 'em there'd be blowback. I've been up three nights thinking about this. About you guys. But, I'm gonna be straight with you. They're eyeing jobs and some of you are making a lot of money.

TRACEY: What are you   CYNTHIA: You've been at
making?   Olstead's a long time and
          they don't want to carry
          the burden anymore.

(Collective response.)

JESSIE: Oh, now we're the burden?

JASON: We're the fucking   CHRIS: Woah! Woah!
burden?

CYNTHIA: With this NAFTA bullshit they can move the whole factory to Mexico tomorrow morning, and a woman like you will stand for sixteen hours and be happy making a fraction of what they're paying you.

TRACEY: Well, they can't do it.

JESSIE: Why now?

JASON: The union won't stand for it.

CHRIS: Lester's on it.

(Collective response.)

CYNTHIA: Guess what, the union don't got a lot to say about it.

JESSIE: What?   CHRIS: How's that possible?

CYNTHIA: Those machines are gone. They're not coming back.

JESSIE: Where are they?   CHRIS: That is fucked up.

(Collective response.)

CYNTHIA: But, if we do this right we can protect the rest of your jobs. That's the point. None of us wanna go anywhere. But be real, you think you're alone? Look at what went down at Clemmons. The union took a hard line, and look what happened to them. You wanna join those folks on unemployment, be my guest. But, listen—

TRACEY: C'mon.   JESSIE: I don't understand why
                                         this is happening!

CYNTHIA: I'm trying—

JESSIE: We work hard, our   JASON: If they got a problem,
  plant is making money.   why won't they be direct!

CHRIS: Let her speak. Let her speak. Ma, are they trying to squeeze us out?

CYNTHIA: You saw how easy it was for them to sneak in and break down those machines while all of us were at home sleeping.

JESSIE: // Where are the machines?

CYNTHIA: I guarantee you   CHRIS: Come the fuck on, man.
  they're in Mexico.

CYNTHIA: Management is saying that it's too expensive for them to operate here. I—

JASON: Why don't they take a pay cut if they wanna save their precious plant?

CHRIS: Exactly!

CYNTHIA: Because they won't, and you know their solution, if you don't meet them halfway, they'll pick up and run. That way they won't even have to see your bodies as they flee.

JASON: That's bullshit.

CYNTHIA: I'm telling you what's going on. Right now, I don't want this fucking job, but if I walk away, then you got nobody. I may not have a lot of say, but I'm on your side.

TRACEY: Then act like it. You're making the same sorry excuses that they do. We're friends!

CYNTHIA: . . . I am doing everything I can, babe. And I don't know what more you want me to do?

TRACEY: Fight for us!

JASON: Yeah!

CYNTHIA: You think it's that easy?

TRACEY: All of us are on that line. Be straight!

CYNTHIA: . . .

CHRIS: Ma?!

TRACEY: Cynthia!

JESSIE: Just tell us the goddamn truth!

CHRIS: Step off and listen.

CYNTHIA: It ain't gonna be easy. I can tell you how it's gonna play out. They're gonna ask for everyone to take a pay cut to save jobs. Sixty percent.

TRACEY: What?

CHRIS: Sixty fucking percent?

JESSIE: Sixty?!

JASON: What the hell?

CYNTHIA: They're gonna ask for concessions on your benefits package next. I'm being straight. No bullshit. They're gonna ask you for more hours. They will give you a little bit of room for negotiation, and then they'll wait until your breaking point, at which time you'll be convinced that you've had a small victory.

TRACEY: What are you talking about?

CYNTHIA: Ask Lester, he's the union rep. He's been talking to them.

(Tracey fights back tears. Jason comforts her.)

JASON: They can't do this!

CHRIS: No!

JASON: And if we say no?

CHRIS: Yeah!

CYNTHIA: You're dealing with vipers. The game's changed! They'll lock you out. And once they get you out, they're not gonna let you back in.

TRACEY: Well, fuck you! Fuck them! I ain't going down without a fight. You can tell those bastards I will burn this factory down before I let them take my life.

JASON: Fuck yeah!

CHRIS: Word.

(A chorus of discontent.)

CYNTHIA: Now you know. The vote's coming! Decide!

(Silence.)

Scene 3

August 4, 2000

Outside it's 80°F. Partly cloudy and pleasant.

In the news: Republican presidential candidate George W. Bush begins a post-convention train blitz across the Midwest.

Bar. Cynthia sits alone at a table. Stan pours her a drink.

CYNTHIA: On a cruise, Panama Canal. That's where I'd like to be right now. Poolside, piña colada in my hand. High and happy.

STAN: A nice breeze blowing off the water. Not a bad way to spend your birthday.

You all right? Hot in here? You want me to crank the air?

CYNTHIA: Nah, I'm okay.

(Cynthia looks around.)

I was kinda hoping they'd show up. It's the one thing we always do together.

STAN: Can you blame 'em?

CYNTHIA: Like I had a choice.

STAN: I'm just saying.

CYNTHIA: C'mon, Don't gimme that look.

STAN: Well, it can't be easy.

CYNTHIA: It isn't . . . You know what's crazy, when I started at the plant it felt like I was invited into an exclusive club. Not many of us folks worked there. Not us. So, when I put on my jacket, I knew I'd accomplished something. I was set. And when I got my union card, you couldn't tell me anything. Sometimes when I was shopping I would let it slip out of my wallet onto the counter just so folks could see it. I was that proud of it.

STAN: I remember the feeling.

(Cynthia smiles.)

CYNTHIA: Right. No one in my family ever made it beyond the floor.

STAN: // Yup . . .

CYNTHIA: And, I wanted this job so bad. Ever since I stepped into the plant, and saw how the white hats left work in clothes as clean as when they walked in. They seemed untouchable.

STAN: How are you holding up?

CYNTHIA: Shit. I locked out my friends, Stan. I explained, I fought, I begged. But those cowards upstairs still had me tape a note to the door telling 'em they weren't welcome. Ninety-five degrees. I'm standing in the door watching some irritable fat guy change the locks. Shut outta the plant. And you know what? I wonder if they gave me this job on purpose. Pin a target on me so they can stay in their air-conditioned offices. Do you know what it feels like, to say to the people you've worked with for years that they're not welcome anymore? I haven't slept in . . . in over a week.

STAN: Well, you're not alone.

CYNTHIA: I'm scared, Stan. I got a mortgage to meet, car payments, and Brucie, you've seen what being outta work has done to him. I'm not going down that way, I've worked too hard. Am I wrong?

STAN: Jesus.

CYNTHIA: I know. I know. But what could I have done? You tell me! The plant offered them a deal. The union voted it down. Not me!

STAN: What do you want me to say, sweetheart? Those are my friends.

CYNTHIA: Our friends.

STAN: Then imagine how they feel. Some folks wouldn't even want me to pour you a drink.

CYNTHIA: I've lived half my life on that floor. My son was practically born in that place. So don't get sanctimonious with me.

STAN: Okay, I'll keep out of it, but you know people will say what they say.

CYNTHIA: I thought they'd take the damn deal. You think I'm happy about this? I locked out my own son. My own son. I saw the hurt on his face. But you wanna know the truth, and this is the truth, maybe it's for the best, right? It'll finally get him out of this sinkhole.

> (*Cynthia doesn't finish her thought, but she's thinking it's all too hard. Stan senses this, and pours Cynthia another drink.*)

STAN: It ain't your fault things shook out the way they did. I've spoken to a half dozen guys in your position. My cousin's over at Clemmons, they laid off four hundred people. Just like that, one day life is good, the next you're treading water. Clemmons! That's not supposed to happen to folks like us, but I'm pouring a lotta drinks these days. Business is good. You ain't the only one.

CYNTHIA: What the hell is going on, Stan?

STAN: Don't know. Don't get it. But, I watch these politicians talking bullshit and I get no sense that they even know what's going on beyond the wind-shield of their cars as they speed past. But, I decided a month ago that I'm not voting, cuz no matter what lever I pull it will lead to disappointment.

CYNTHIA (*Emotionally*): Amen. You remember about seven months ago? Remem-ber when Freddy Brunner burned down his house?

STAN: Of course.

CYNTHIA: We thought he was crazy.

STAN: Yeah.

CYNTHIA: Was he?

> (*Tracey and Jessie enter. They stop short upon seeing Cynthia. The tension is palpable.*)

TRACEY (*Under her breath*): Fucking traitor.

CYNTHIA: What did you say?

TRACEY: I said you fucking traitor.

JESSIE: How does it feel to shit on your friends?

> (*Cynthia stands up.*)

CYNTHIA (*To Stan*): I'm gonna go.

TRACEY: That's right. Walk away.

CYNTHIA: I'm not walking away, I'm leaving. There's a difference, don't get it confused. You know, you coulda taken the deal.

TRACEY: What deal?! I'd rather get locked out, and take handouts from the union than let go of everything I worked for. That's the truth.

JESSIE: What you did wasn't right!

TRACEY: They didn't even give us a fucking choice! After all of those years.

CYNTHIA: I just delivered the news, babe. I didn't make the policy.

JESSIE (*Shouts*): You're supposed to be on our side!

CYNTHIA (*Shouts back*): I am!

TRACEY: Do you know what it felt like to walk up to that plant, and be told after all them years I can't go in? I can't even go into my locker and get my stuff. I have photos of my husband in there. I have my grandfather's toolbox.

CYNTHIA: I'll get it for you, babe.

TRACEY: I don't want you to touch anything in that locker! They didn't even have the decency to let us clear out with dignity. A note taped to the door, what is that? And then to see you just standing there. I thought I was gonna lose my shit.

CYNTHIA: I tried to warn you. I hated it.

TRACEY: I looked for your eyes. Just gimme something, Cynth. A little look, to let me know it's okay, but you wouldn't even fucking look at me.

CYNTHIA: I'm in a tough-ass position, babe. I got enough attitude from folks to give me a heart attack. I'm trying to hold things together as best as I can.

TRACEY: What the fuck am I supposed to do? Huh? You coulda called me. Given me a heads-up. I mean come on. What am I supposed to do? Who's gonna hire me?

CYNTHIA: I know it hurts, babe. Take the deal.

TRACEY: NO! You hear yourself?

JESSIE: Can I have a beer, Stan?

STAN: Sure.

TRACEY: The other day, I walked over to the union office. Do you know what they offered me? A bag of groceries and some vouchers to the supermarket. They asked us to hold out, they're gonna help. Yeah, pay my fucking bills, that's how you can help. But, you know how many people were there for handouts? I looked for your eyes. Gimme something, Cynth. It was fucking humiliating.

CYNTHIA: Look, I'm sorry.

TRACEY: What am I supposed to do with that? Huh? What do you want me to do with that? You know what? This is my first time outta my house in one solid week. Do you know what it's like to get up and have no place to go? I ain't had the feeling ever. I'm a worker. I have worked since I could count money. That's me. And I'm thinking I'm not gonna go out, you know why? Because I don't wanna spend money, because when my unemployment runs out I'll have nothing. So, I don't go anywhere. And if Jessie hadn't called me, I'd still be sitting on my couch feeling sorry for myself, picking at my fucking cuticles. Why'd you come in here? Huh? What do you want?

CYNTHIA: It's my birthday. And this is where we've always celebrated.

(*A moment. Tracey lights a cigarette.*)

TRACEY: Do you remember that time we went to Atlantic City[3] for your twenty-fifth?

CYNTHIA: Yeah, it was before Hank got sick.

TRACEY: The boys, Jason and Chris, were little. It was the four of us. You, Brucie, me and Hank. We splurged, got a suite.

CYNTHIA: Of course I remember . . . It was for the fight. Larry Holmes.[4]

TRACEY: That's right. Hank had a friend, a high roller,[5] and after the fight he invited us to one of those back-room clubs, you know very fancy. Champagne, buffet, seafood fountain, everything, really classy stuff.

---

3. Resort city on the New Jersey coast known for its boardwalk and casinos.
4. Pennsylvania-born professional boxer (b. 1949), holder of major heavyweight titles 1978–85.
5. Someone who gambles or spends large sums.

CYNTHIA: Why are you bringing this up, Tracey?

TRACEY: Brucie was at the craps[6] table rolling like a pro. Drenched in luck. It was just dripping off of him. The chips were leaping into his hands. And if I recall, he was also looking sorta fine that evening.

CYNTHIA: Yes, he was.

TRACEY: And then this chick.

CYNTHIA: C'mon, stop—

TRACEY: Yes. This chick. Legs, ass, boobs, weave.[7] She was giving a full-service vibe, "walks" up and settles in next to Brucie—

JESSIE: "Settles"?

TRACEY: Her breasts were enormous, epic. Her dress, barely visible. I'm not a lesbian, but I couldn't take my eyes off of her boobs.

CYNTHIA: Why are you telling this story?

TRACEY: This chick was in heat, and she ever so gently places her hand on Brucie's shoulder, like this. I look over at Cynthia—

CYNTHIA: Don't—

TRACEY: And—

CYNTHIA: No—

TRACEY: She—

CYNTHIA: Lord, help me—

TRACEY: Is wearing the look: Stone Age. Prehistoric. T-rex. And I know what it means, Brucie knows what it means, but this bitch doesn't. Boobs leans over and whispers something into Brucie's ear. That's it. You just grab this chick's tits, and dig your fingernails in as hard as you can.

CYNTHIA: Yes, I did.

STAN: Whoa.

CYNTHIA: I'd had a couple tequilas. I wanted to deflate those fake tits. Puncture them with my fingernails.

TRACEY: Next thing I know, Cynthia's on the floor rolling around. Two grown women. It was sick. You put up a fight like a pro wrestler.

STAN: Jesus. Atlantic City. That's why I avoid it.

TRACEY: But, I remember thinking: that's my friend. She's tough as hell. Don't mess with her. She'll fight for what she loves, even if it means getting scrappy and looking ugly. That's my friend, and I miss the Cynthia who understood that.

CYNTHIA: What do you want from me, Tracey?

TRACEY: Walk out with us.

JESSIE: Walk with us. C'mon.

CYNTHIA: I can't.

JESSIE: C'mon.

CYNTHIA: I've stood on that line, same line since I was nineteen. I've taken orders from idiots who were dangerous, or even worse, racist. But I stood on line, patiently waiting for a break. I don't think you get it, but if I walk away, I'm giving up more than a job, I'm giving up all that time I spent standing on line waiting for one damn opportunity.

6. Dice-throwing game.
7. Hairstyle created by weaving real or artificial hair into existing hair, usually to increase length or thickness.

TRACEY: You want us to feel sorry for you?

CYNTHIA: . . . I didn't expect you to understand, babe. You don't know what it's been like to walk in my shoes. I've absorbed a lotta shit over the years, but I worked hard to get off that floor. Call me selfish, I don't care, call me whatever you need to call me, but remember, one of us has to be left standing to fight.

Scene 4

September 28, 2000

Outside it's 63°F.

In the news: First Lady Hillary Rodham Clinton posts strong polling numbers in her New York Senate race against Rick Lazio.[8] *Americans Venus and Serena Williams win a gold medal in women's doubles tennis at the Sydney Summer Olympics. Three Mexican migrant farmworkers are killed when their car crashes into trees in Reading.*

Bar. Brucie sits at a table, Stan is at the bar. Brucie is slightly disheveled, strung out. Chris and Jason stumbled in, all energy.

JASON: I don't wanna hear it. I don't care what anybody has to say, rhythmic gymnastics[9] is not a sport!

CHRIS: You try catching a ball with your toes, and then tell me it's not a sport.

STAN: Chris.

(*Stan gestures to Brucie slumped at the table.*)

CHRIS (*Relieved*): Jesus. Look atcha. Where've you been? I mean, I've been calling everyone. Goddamnit, where've you been?

BRUCIE: Chill. I'm here. Whassup?

CHRIS: Yo, J. Order me a beer.

JASON: Okay. (*Concern*) What's up, Brucie? You all right?

BRUCIE: Why wouldn't I be all right?

CHRIS: // Shit.

BRUCIE: You guys hanging tough?

JASON: You know. Miss the grind. Feeling the pinch. But Lester says it'll all work out.

BRUCIE: I've heard that before.

(*Jason moves toward Brucie.*)

JASON: Yo, everyone's been—

BRUCIE: I'm fine. Take a step back.

JASON: All right. All right.

(*Jason moves to the bar.*)

CHRIS: You can't do that. Disappear? Look at me. Where've you been?

BRUCIE: Around.

---

8. Former U.S. congressman from New York (b. 1958) who lost this 2000 senate race to Clinton.

9. Sport in which gymnasts perform on a floor with apparatus such as hoops, balls, and ribbons; at the international level, an exclusively female sport.

CHRIS: Mom won't say it, but she's worried as hell.

BRUCIE: Well, she has a damn funny way of showing it.

CHRIS: Nobody's seen you in a month. What's going on? What the hell? You stopped walking the line?[1]

BRUCIE: . . . Yeah.

CHRIS: Dad! I'm talking to you! Where've you been?!!

BRUCIE: Um, crashing at your Uncle Cliff's crib, for now.

CHRIS: You need to pull yourself together! This bullshit's got to stop.

BRUCIE: I'm trying. Hey, don't give me that look. I'm trying. Okay?

CHRIS: . . .

BRUCIE: I'm *trying*.

CHRIS: You high?

BRUCIE: I'm a grown-ass man, I don't gots to report to nobody. Especially you, boy! So step off.

CHRIS: That's all you got for me? Then go be a zombie, I don't give a shit.

(*Chris goes to sit at the bar.*)

JASON: Leave it.

(*A moment.*)

BRUCIE: C'mon. Chris. I didn't come down here for this. C'mon.

CHRIS: What's going on with you? Earl and Saunders, both of 'em called me.

BRUCIE: I dunno. Can I tell you something that happened a couple of weeks ago?

CHRIS: You know what, I don't wanna // hear your bullshit—

BRUCIE: Chris . . . please! Chris!

(*Chris walks over to Brucie.*)

CHRIS: What?

BRUCIE: I was doing my rotation on the line, same as always. And it began to rain, all at once a downpour, folks fled, but I . . . I just stood there . . . couldn't move. I got soaked through to my skin. I still couldn't move. And . . . and finally someone pulled me into the tent to get dry, but my whole body was shaking, wouldn't stop. It was scary. And I hadn't had that feeling of being outta control since my mother died.

CHRIS: You okay? Don't let 'em do this to you.

BRUCIE: . . .

CHRIS: You hear me?

BRUCIE: Yeah. Yeah. I'm okay. Will you buy me a drink?

CHRIS: . . . Sure.

BRUCIE: Thank you. Thank you.

(*Chris crosses to the bar. Stan pours a beer.*)

And you . . . you guys awright?

CHRIS: It's been rough. Man, they're testing us. Folks are getting real hot.

JASON: Tell me about it!

CHRIS: I see those dudes heading into the plant and I wanna smack 'em—

---

1. Picket line, as in a workers' strike or (as in this case) lockout.

JASON (*Clenching his fist*): Fucking pricks!

BRUCIE: I hear that. But whassup? You start school?

CHRIS: Nah, I didn't enroll this semester.

BRUCIE: Why? What's your mom think about that?

CHRIS: Things have been a little strained between us. So—

BRUCIE: You need to tell her.

CHRIS: Why? I know what she's gonna say. But, you feel me, right?

BRUCIE: . . .

CHRIS: Right? And with the shit that's going down I didn't make tuition. Things are tight. I was counting on those double shifts this summer.

BRUCIE: Look, Chris, I can't help you // I'm—

CHRIS: I'm not looking for your help. Okay? My head's not in it right now.

BRUCIE: You need to get your head in it. I've been out here, and shit's real. You sure this is a good idea?

CHRIS: It's what it is! And you're the one that's always saying—

BRUCIE: Never mind // what—

CHRIS: You taught me how to throw a rock. I remember the first time you walked the line.

BRUCIE: Yeah, we were out almost two months. What about it?

CHRIS: There was this one night you had a big meeting at the house.

BRUCIE: // Yeah—

CHRIS: Like ten–fifteen guys. It was loud, like a street brawl. I was hiding in the doorway, I had no idea what you guys were talking about, but it felt like it was gonna get ugly—

BRUCIE: It was when Bobby Holden lost his hand in the mill.

CHRIS: And you were all shouting about how you were gonna vote if they didn't meet your demands.

BRUCIE: That's right.

CHRIS: And suddenly you stood up, and for like a second you looked like another man, bigger, like a Transformer,[2] and when you spoke everyone got real calm and began nodding. You said, um . . . "We . . . we will not continue to bare our backs for them to strike us down."

BRUCIE: Is that really what I said?

CHRIS: Or something like that. I dunno. But, I remember the fire in your voice and how it made me feel. And after school, me and my friends rode our bikes to the mill and watched you guys picketing. You looked like warriors, arms linked, standing together.

BRUCIE: Fuckin' Bobby Holden—

CHRIS: And you know, yesterday as I was walking the line, and listening to Lester tell us about what we'd have to sacrifice to keep the plant running, all I could think about was your words that evening. You! What it means to stand strong.

BRUCIE: It's tough for me to say, I'm union to the end, but this don't have to be your fight. // You—

---

2. Originally, a series of fierce-looking toy robots that could be reconfigured into vehicles, weapons, and so on; later, the subject of comic books, multiple animated television series, and both animated and live-action films.

CHRIS: But it is. I'm not gonna be a punk-ass bitch! That's what they want.
JASON: That's right!
CHRIS: I don't care what anybody gots to say, we're gonna stand together. And they're not gonna break us!
JASON: Hell, yes!
BRUCIE: You think they give a damn about your black ass?! Let me tell you something, they don't even see you!
CHRIS: I'm gonna make 'em see me.
BRUCIE: You think so?! After that storm hits, and all the dust clears, who's gonna pick you up? Huh?
CHRIS: . . .
BRUCIE: You got options that I didn't. School always scared me, that's the honest-to-God truth. That's all I'm saying.

> (*A moment.*)

> You really wanna know where I been?
CHRIS: . . . No.
BRUCIE: I didn't think so. Don't back away from what you want. That line is gonna thin out, and then what? That's what I'm trying to figure out—and then what?!

Scene 5

October 26, 2000

Outside it's 72°F.

> *In the news: After yet another gun incident at a school, Attorney General Janet Reno[3] reassures the public that "American schools are safe places." 200 people camp overnight at a Reading electronics superstore hoping to be the first to buy the $350 Sony PlayStation 2.*

> *Bar. Television screen. Jessie sits slumped at a table. Stan is checking inventory. Oscar enters. A moment.*

STAN: So, when were you gonna tell me?
OSCAR: What?
STAN: . . . You crossed the line.
OSCAR: Who told you?
STAN: Nelson.
OSCAR: They were hiring part-time temps to replace some of the locked-out workers. I can pick up a couple of hours in the mornings, and maybe get a full shift.
STAN: Be careful.
OSCAR: Why?
STAN: Why?! Emotions are running high. That's why.
OSCAR: Yeah, well, they're offering eleven dollars an hour.
STAN: I know. Looks good from where you're standing, but that eleven dollars is gonna come outta the pockets of a lot of good people. And they ain't gonna like it.

---

3. Florida-born lawyer (1938–2016), the first woman to serve as U.S. Attorney General, under President Bill Clinton (1993–2001); in April 1999, the then-deadliest school shooting in U.S. history occurred at Colorado's Columbine High School.

OSCAR: Well, I'm sorry about that. But it ain't my problem. I been trying to get into that shop for two years. And each time I asked any of 'em, I get nothing but pushback. So now, I'm willing to be a little flexible and they ain't.

STAN: You want my opinion?

OSCAR: Do I have a choice?

STAN: Don't do it.

OSCAR: That's your opinion. You gonna give me a raise? Huh?

STAN: It's not up to me, it's Howard's call. I just put the money in the till, I ain't responsible for taking it out. But, let me ask him.

OSCAR: They're offering me three dollars more per hour than I make here. Three dollars. What they're offering is better than anything I've touched since I got outta high school. So yo, I ain't afraid to cross the line. Let 'em puff up their chest, but it don't scare me no more than walking through my 'hood. I know rough. I ain't afraid to roll in the dirt.

STAN: Fine, tough guy. But, trust me you're gonna make some real enemies. Couple of folks you know.

OSCAR: They ain't my friends. They don't come into my house and water my plants.

STAN: Okay. But for the record, I think it's seriously fucked up. Six months, watch, they're gonna get another set of guys like you who'll cross the line, and guess what? They'll offer them ten dollars. Watch. Then you'll be outta a job, wanting someone to stand by you. But ain't nobody gonna do it. And, let me tell you something. My ol' man—

OSCAR: Yeah, yeah—

STAN: Don't you "yeah, yeah" me. My dad put forty-two years into building that plant, those benefits, those wages, that vacation time you're so hungry for, guess what? He fought for 'em when the going wasn't so great. That's right. And you think you're gonna walk in and tear it all down in a day. There are folks out there that won't go down easy.

OSCAR: Why are you coming at me that way? I'm not disrespectin' you. I'm just trying to get paid, that's all. For three years I've been carrying nothing but crates. I've got twenty-dollar bills taped to my wall, and a drawer full of motivational tapes. Got a jar of buena suerte from the botanica,[4] and a candle that I keep lit 24/7. I keep asking for some good fortune. That's it. A little bit of money. That's it. My father, he swept up the floor in a factory like Olstead's—those fuckas wouldn't even give him a union card. But he woke up every morning at four A.M. because he wanted a job in the steel factory, it was the American way, so he swept fucking floors thinking, "One day they'll let me in." I know how he feels, people come in here every day. They brush by me without seeing me. No: "Hello, Oscar." If they don't see me, I don't need to see them.

STAN: I hear ya. But, c'mon, really? Look elsewhere, not Olstead's. You don't wanna do this.

OSCAR: You know what I don't wanna do? This.

(Oscar makes a show of putting on his apron. He then lifts and carries a crate of beers into the back.
   Tracey stumbles in, untidy. She goes to the end of the bar.)

4. Herbal dispensary (Spanish). *Buena suerte*: literally, "good luck" (Spanish); here, an herbal mixture believed to bring good fortune when mixed in bathwater.

TRACEY: Hey, Stan.

STAN: Look who it is. I been holding a spot, you want me to put you down for fifty dollars for the Series' pool?

TRACEY: Nah. Not this time.

STAN: You sure? You won two years ago.

TRACEY: Not this time. Um, can I have a double vodka on the rocks?

(*Stan pours a drink.*)

STAN: You keeping yourself busy?

TRACEY: Trying. Been walking the line in the mornings. Working the phones in the afternoon. Nothing yet. Union's offering money for folks to go back to school, but I never liked school, so I'm taking what little support they give until I can find something to pay the bills.

STAN: Almost three months. Fuck.

TRACEY: Who woulda thought.

STAN: I still think the way everything went down—

TRACEY: Don't. Stop it. Everyone is treating us like we lost a limb. I'm fine. And the good news is, my back pain is gone.

STAN: Glad to hear it.

TRACEY: Thanks. Put my drink on the tab.

STAN: I can't. Gotta run your card.

TRACEY: Since when?

STAN: Howard. That's what he wants.

TRACEY: Stan! C'mon.

STAN: Sorry.

TRACEY: I don't have a credit card.

STAN: Sorry. Too many folks not paying. Howard's cracking down.

TRACEY: Stan! It's me.

STAN: Can't.

TRACEY (*Pointing to Jessie*): How's she paying?

STAN: She pays.

TRACEY: She's crashing with her sister, betcha she goes into her purse at night.

(*Tracey downs the drink. Then digs into her pocket. She makes a show of counting out loose change on the bar.*)

STAN: Oh, for God's sake. Really?

TRACEY: You changed the rules, not me.

(*Tracey continues to make a show of counting her coins.*)

Fucking Howard. Jesus, I just came down here to get outta the house to relax.

STAN: Awright, awright. You're so dramatic. Today it's on me, but now you know.

TRACEY: I know. I know. God, I know, already. Thank you. I love you.

STAN: Do you?

TRACEY: Not going there.

STAN: I'm just saying. Life might be a little easier if you did.

TRACEY: I'm not sure whether you're being really romantic or a little bit sleazy.

STAN: Whatever turns you on. You know where I stand.

(*Oscar reenters and looks at Tracey, sheepishly.*)

TRACEY: Well, I ain't that desperate. *(To Oscar)* What are you looking at?

OSCAR: Is that how you say hello?

TRACEY: Yeah, to a fuck-face scab[5] like you. You're a piece of shit.

STAN: Hey, c'mon. None of that.

OSCAR: If you wasn't a woman I'd slap you in your mouth. You're lucky I was raised good.

TRACEY: Well, I wasn't.   STAN: Hey, hey hey!

(*Tracey charges toward Oscar. Stan intercepts, and holds her back. Oscar laughs.*)

OSCAR: What are you gonna do?

STAN: Oscar! Take a break.

TRACEY: Let's see if you talk // to me that way when my son is here.

OSCAR: I have no problem with you. This ain't personal.

TRACEY: You better believe it's personal . . . for me.

Scene 6

November 3, 2000

Outside it's 66°F.
    In the news: It's four days before the U.S. election and George Bush and Al Gore[6] are running neck and neck in the polls. The Mayor of Reading proposes a budget to increase earned income tax.
    Bar. Chris and Jason burst in, adrenaline pumping. Jessie sits at a table, shit-faced but content.

CHRIS: They better not come at me again! // Cuz—

JASON: I'm ready! I'm ready for whatever they got!

STAN: What the hell's going on?

JASON (*Amped up*): Aw, some of the guys got into a scrape with the scabs. McManus got cut, he's gonna need ten stitches on the side of his face.

STAN: Yeah?

JASON: Some of the guys feel we shouldn't make it so easy to cross the line.

STAN: Don't like the sound of that.

CHRIS: Some shit, huh?

STAN: Seen it before. It's not gonna help your cause.

(*Jason sneaks a drink from a small bottle of whiskey tucked in his pocket.*)

CHRIS: Same shit, nobody's budging. The workers coming in ain't feeling so temporary.

STAN: Tough. Whatcha gonna do?

JASON: Who the fuck knows? There's a few guys, Stubbs, Godski, talking about taking the deal, but I don't know, seems like a big waste of time if

---

5. Worker who refuses to join a union or, as here, replaces a striking or locked-out union worker, accepting lesser, non-union wages or working conditions.

6. Former Tennessee senator, U.S. vice president, and 2000 Democratic presidential candidate (b. 1948); he won the popular vote but lost the electoral college after a controversial, U.S. Supreme Court–ordered recount of Florida votes.

we give in now. They'll break us, and there's no going back. I figure I can hold out another three months. Push comes to shove, I'll sell the bike. But me, honestly, I think we teach some of those guys a lesson, what do you think?

STAN: Hell, why are you asking me? I dunno. You're young, I mean there are a lotta things you could do. Maybe it's time to move on, this place ain't what it used to be.

JASON: And go where?

STAN: Anywhere. Sometimes I think we forget that we're meant to pick up and go when the well runs dry. Our ancestors knew that. You stay put for too long, you get weighed down by things, things you don't need. It's true. Then your life becomes this pathetic accumulation of stuff. Emotional and physical junk. You gotta ask yourself what you're hanging on to, huh? I knew your dad, he was a good enough guy, but that place took him young. Sure he made decent money, but jacking's hard—

CHRIS: Word.

JASON: Well, if things get too real, I got a buddy who works on a rig in the Gulf,[7] says he can get me something in the spring.

STAN: Yeah? I hear you can make like a grand a week. Work half the year, and then do whatever.

JASON: Yeah. Just gotta get the card, and get down there.

STAN: Why the hell not? Me, if I was thirty years younger, I'd already be down there. Nothing but mildew lingering in these cracks. This place is for shit. Sure, it used to be something. But nostalgia's a disease, I'm not gonna be one of those guys that surrenders to it. What do you get?

CHRIS: I don't wanna think about it. My jaw's tired of the damn chatter. Just wanna get drunk, smoke a blunt[8] and chill for a little while.

JASON: That's an excellent plan.

CHRIS: You know . . . I see my dad and—

STAN: He's going through a rough patch.

CHRIS: That's very polite. Not me, I'll probably ride out unemployment, maybe pick up some heavy lifting, day stuff, then start college next September. The union's offering some financial aid.

JASON: I can tell ya what they're gonna say: "Fuck you, fuck you and—"

(*Jason playfully jumps on Chris's back.*)

CHRIS AND JASON: "Fuck you!"

STAN: All right, all right. Break it up before it gets too kinky.

CHRIS: Whatcha got on tap?

STAN: The usual! C'mon, why do ya gotta ask me that every single time?

CHRIS: Keep hoping for a surprise.

STAN: You're in the fucking wrong town for that. (*Laughs*) How's your girl? I haven't seen her around.

CHRIS: It didn't work out.

JASON: She couldn't fit his big dick in her mouth.

---

7. Of Mexico. *Rig*: offshore oil-drilling platform.
8. Marijuana cigar.

CHRIS: Shut up!

JASON: She was—

CHRIS: Shut up!

JASON: She—

CHRIS: Was sweating me.

STAN: Yeah? How long wuz you together?

CHRIS: Just under a year. She was pushing for more. But, I wasn't feeling it, whatever holds people together, that thing. I didn't feel it. So I guess, it's for the best. No?

STAN: Good for you.

CHRIS: I told my girl that things were gonna be tight for a little while. And she's all like, "What does that mean for us?" I break it down. It's gonna get real. And she's like, "Well, you need to find another job, playa." I tell her that's what I'm trying to do. But she got that old-school mentality, she wants what she wants in the moment, and can't be thinking about tomorrow. Yo, she was too much work for a man outta work. She was plenty happy when I was a paycheck, numbers and pretty things, but the minute I ask her to borrow twenty dollars to put a little gas in the car she treats me like I've broken into her crib. What's that about?

STAN: I remain unattached for those very reasons.

CHRIS: Now is the moment. You're right, Stan. Maybe we should move on. We can complain until kingdom come. Bla, bla, bla. That shit gets old real fast. I'm out there on the picket lines every morning. I shout "fuck you" at a bunch of pathetic hungry guys. I feel good and superior about it all, for like five minutes, and then reality hits. They're inside. And then I think about my pops. Who wants that shit?

JASON: Yo, if I was—

CHRIS: Hey, yo, shut up, man! Don't say nothing, Jason, because I swear I will punch you out. And just let me finish! Okay? I used to worry about what people would think if I didn't want to work in the factory. Now they got us fighting for scraps. But, Stan said it, the writing's on the wall, and we're still out here pretending like we can't read.

JASON: Women cost money. All the shit they want these days, it's too much. You gotta sew your pockets shut.

CHRIS: Wow, really, that's your takeaway from what I just said?

(*Jessie, suddenly:*)

JESSIE: No. You're a cheap-ass bastard.

CHRIS: Go to rehab!

JASON: But, seriously—

(*Tracey comes out of the bathroom.*)

TRACEY: Why don't you ever have paper towels?

STAN: Doing our little bit for the environment.

TRACEY: Hey Jason, buy your mom a drink.

(*Tracey drapes herself around Jason's shoulders and gives him a kiss.*)

JASON: Really? C'mon. That means I won't be able to have another one.

TRACEY: Poor baby, what ever happened to the notion of sacrifice?

STAN: Jason, c'mon.

CHRIS: I got you, Mrs. T.

TRACEY: Is it your mother's money?

CHRIS: . . . No.

TRACEY: Then okay. Stan. Pour!

(*Jessie rouses.*)

JESSIE: Hey, gimme one while the bottle's open.

(*Stan pours Jessie and Tracey drinks.*)

JASON: Jesus, Chris, you're making me look bad.

CHRIS: Don't have to try very hard.

TRACEY: Okay, I got a story for you guys—

JASON: Oh no.

TRACEY: Shut up, you gotta hear it, you guys know Ronnie Golmolka, well he got caught—

(*Oscar walks in. Tracey sees him and stops talking. It's too late for Oscar to retreat.*)

OSCAR: Hey Stan.

STAN: Oscar.

OSCAR: I came to pick up the rest of my stuff. But, if now ain't such a good time . . . I thought . . .

(*Jason and Chris stare down Oscar. Stan breaks the tension.*)

STAN: It's in the back. You want me to get it?

OSCAR: Nah, I'll get it.

JESSIE (*Shouts*): Fucking scab!

(*Oscar goes to the back. Jason stands up.*)

STAN: Don't!

JASON: Don't what?

STAN: You know what. Sit down.

JASON: That fucking spic.

STAN: Hey, hey, c'mon. None of that in here. Oscar's a good guy. Let him get his stuff, okay?

JASON: I don't give a fuck.

TRACEY: Amen. That piece of shit knows what he's doing. I don't care about his sorry story. So what he's got an apartment filled with seventeen relatives that gotta eat. I'm tired of their shit. I worked that line for over twenty years and he thinks he can push in.

STAN: Enough, c'mon. This is neutral territory.

JASON: She's got a point. I'll be damned if I'm gonna let that fucker walk over my toes. It ain't gonna happen.

CHRIS: J, sit the fuck down, you don't got a beef with him. Not here. He's just—

JASON: What?

CHRIS: Trying to make a dollar. Okay? The same as you or me.

JASON: Nah, it ain't the same. We got history here. Us! Me, you, him, her! What the fuck does he have, huh? A green card[9] that gives him the right to shit on everything we worked for?

STAN: Why don't you take a walk around the block?

CHRIS: Yeah, let's go.

(*Chris tries to pull Jason out. Jason wrenches himself away.*)

JASON: Do you hear yourself? I'm the problem? I should sit the fuck down? No way.

CHRIS: Let it alone. Fuck 'em. Now, ain't the moment. That muthafucka ain't worth it. Okay?

TRACEY: Did you see the way he looked at you guys? He's eating your dinner, your steak and potatoes, your fucking dessert.

JESSIE: Yum! Yum!

(*Jessie laughs.*)

STAN: Shut up!

TRACEY: I'm not shutting up!

JESSIE: Tell 'em.

STAN (*To Jason*): You heard, it ain't worth it. Why do you need trouble?

JASON: Just gonna set him straight. Simple talk.

STAN: Don't be an asshole.

JASON: I'm an asshole? What I done? Eleven dollars an hour? No thank you. They'll work us down to nothing if we let 'em. "Jacking ain't for softies!" But they know they can always find somebody willing to get their hands sweaty. And they're right. There will always be someone who'll step in, unless we say NO!

STAN: Look. Olstead is a prick. If he was here I wouldn't stop you. In fact I'd hold him down for you to give him a proper beating, but Oscar . . . he's another story. He's gonna walk outta here, and you, you're gonna keep your mouth shut or I—

JASON: What?! All I'm saying is that he needs to understand the price of that dinner he's putting on his table.

STAN (*Shouts*): What the fuck do you want him to do? Huh? It ain't his fault. Talk to Olstead, his cronies. Fucking Wall Street.[1] Oscar ain't getting rich off your misery.

CHRIS: Jason, he's right. He's hustling. We're all hustling.

JASON: Chris, what's wrong with you? He ain't with us otherwise he'd be walking the line. Am I the only one seeing this clearly?

TRACEY: No, you're not wrong. He's breaking the rules, not us!

STAN: Don't let her get into your head. She's drunk.

TRACEY: So what? It don't change the truth.

JESSIE: // That's for sure.

9. Permit allowing a foreign national to live and work permanently in the United States. (As a natural-born citizen, Oscar would neither have nor need a green card.)

1. Powerful U.S. financial institutions and interests; a metonym, as the New York Stock Exchange is located on Wall Street in Manhattan.

STAN: You can either sit back down or you can leave. I'm dead serious. But, you're not starting trouble in here. Not with Oscar!

JASON: Oh, I see how this is gonna be.

(*Stan slams a bat onto the bar.*)

STAN: SIT DOWN!

(*Jason reluctantly sits, the boy inside prevails.*)

CHRIS: Yo, let's finish up, and drive over to see what Gibney's up to.

JASON (*Moping*): Yeah, maybe.

CHRIS: Play some cards. Win some money off of him. Two drinks and he's sloppy and he'll open up his wallet.

JASON (*Smiling*): Yeah.

CHRIS: Hit up a club in Philly.[2]

JASON: Sounds good.

CHRIS: Cool?

JASON: Cool. I'm all right. I was just, you know—

CHRIS: Okay—

JASON: Whatever. I'm fine.

TRACEY (*To Jason*): That's the problem. We all just roll over, and offer up our ass-holes for anyone who wants to fuck us. We will be fucked. Chris, they fucked your father, and Jason, if your father was here, I'd tell you what he'd do, he'd—

(*Jason balls up his fist.*)

STAN (*To Tracey*): Shut up!

JASON: Hey, watch your mouth. Don't talk to her that way.

(*Oscar reenters with a backpack slung over his shoulder.*)

STAN: Take care.

OSCAR: Thanks for everything.

STAN: And tell your ma, thank you for the aripa.

OSCAR: Arepas.[3] Will do.

STAN: Don't be a stranger.

(*They shake hands. Oscar heads for the door.*)

TRACEY: Hey Jason, he's heading out to cash your check.

STAN: Oh shit.

(*Before Oscar can get to the door Jason pops up and blocks his path. They stand face to face, eye to eye. A game of Chicken.*)

OSCAR: Excuse me.

(*Jason doesn't move.*)

I said, excuse me.

---

2. Philadelphia; Pennsylvania's capital, roughly sixty miles southeast of Reading.

3. Cornmeal cakes, usually grilled and filled with cheese and/or meat; a staple of Colombian cuisine.

(*Jason still doesn't move. Oscar goes to walk around him. Again Jason blocks his path.*)

STAN: Let him pass, Jason.

(*Jason provokes Oscar.*)

OSCAR: I don't have no problem with you.

JASON: Too late for that

(*Chris stands up.*)

CHRIS: Yo J, let's get up from outta here, okay?

(*Stan moves from behind the bar.*)

JASON: I can't. I don't know why, but I can't let him walk outta here.

STAN: Sure you can! Nobody here is gonna think any less of you.

OSCAR: Move!

JASON: Or?

(*A stare-down. Jason shoves Oscar.*
    Stan intervenes, grabbing Jason's arm. Jason shoves him away violently. Stan loses his balance and tumbles to the ground. Oscar goes to aid Stan, but Jason grabs him first.)

JESSIE: Oh shit!

(*A loud and untidy fight ensues. It tumbles across the bar. Oscar manages to hold his own against Jason. Oscar breaks free, and runs for the door.*)

OSCAR: Fuck you!

(*Jason grabs Oscar. They tussle. Tracey picks up a glass to throw. Chris grabs her. Then Jason grabs Oscar. The fight continues. Chris tries to break it up. Oscar head-butts Chris, bloodying his nose.*)

Bitch!

JESSIE: Don't let him go.

(*Chris's anger has been ignited. He puts Oscar in a headlock and punches him several times in the stomach. Oscar drops to his knees.*)

CHRIS: Motherfucker!

(*Chris kicks him in the ribs. Oscar writhes in pain. Jason grabs the bat from the bar.*)

JASON: Hold him!

(*Chris grabs Oscar and yanks him to his feet. Tracey watches the battle, her face contorted with rage.*)

STAN: Let him go!

(*Stan manages to get to his feet, but it's too late. Jason hits Oscar in the stomach with the bat. Oscar crumples to the ground. Jason hits him again. As Jason winds up for another swing, Stan tries to intervene, but the bat hits him hard in the head. Stan falls back, hitting his head on the bar—blood. He slumps to the ground. Jessie gasps. Jason, and then Chris, recognizes the weight of what they've done. They flee.)*

TRACEY: Stan?!

Transition

September 24, 2008

> *In the news: President Bush prepares to present a very dire warning to the American people. He will suggest that unless Congress approves a $700,000,000,000 bailout for Wall Street, and it is approved within a matter of only a few days, there will be ominous consequences for the entire U.S. economy and for millions of Americans.*

Scene 7

October 15, 2008

Outside it's 77°F.

> *In the news: Baghdad and Washington have reached a final agreement on a pact requiring U.S. forces to withdraw from Iraq by 2012.[4] U.S. stocks plunge 733 points, the second biggest point loss in history. John McCain and Barack Obama[5] hold their final televised debate at Hofstra University in Hempstead, New York. Federal prosecutors convict a multimillion-dollar drug ring that converted several Reading houses into indoor marijuana farms.*

> *Evan stands over Chris, who is finishing describing his encounter with Jason.*

EVAN: It's not a big place. You two were bound to run into each other sooner or later. I don't want this to be a problem.

CHRIS: I'd spent so much time being angry at Jason, but standing there I don't even know what I was feeling.

EVAN: That's okay. These things ain't simple. I had a 'banger[6] who was up in here, hard as stone. He got out, made amends, crossed so many bridges he was practically walking on water. He found forgiveness to be the easier of his two paths.

CHRIS: Dunno about all of that. Shit, I remember when I sat down at the bar I knew I didn't want the same flat-ass beer that Stan always poured. I knew I was gonna drive down to Philly that evening and hit a club with some friends. And the next day, I had planned to go over to Albright. I was feeling free, like for the first time I had an option other than jacking and a hangover. And I coulda walked away, and today I'd // be—

EVAN: Don't.

CHRIS: I hate the way people be looking at me now. I feel like they can see what I done. I pray on it. I ask for forgiveness. But every morning I wake up with

---

4. The Iraq War began with the 2003 invasion of Iraq by a U.S.-led coalition of nations aiming to overthrow the government of Saddam Hussein.
5. Illinois senator (b. 1961) and first African American U.S. president (2009–17).
6. "Gangbanger," member of a street gang.

the same panic. All I see is a closed door, and when I finally get the courage to open it, it leads to yet another closed door.

(*Evan shifts. He is now talking to Jason.*)

EVAN: Maybe you two need to sit down and talk?

JASON: . . . Yeah. I hear you. Been thinking.

(*Jason smiles.*)

EVAN: That's new. Look, I know what you're avoiding, and man, I don't blame you, but—

JASON: I ain't thought about that day in the bar in a long time. Now I can't get away from it. Every place I walk in this city reminds me of that day, it's like the whole city was in that bar and got turned upside down in the same way I did.

EVAN: Got a call that you were fighting at the shelter. That true? Where are you sleeping these days?

JASON: My mom's place was too depressing, and a friend of mine gave me a tent and sleeping bag, so I've been camping in the woods with a couple of other guys. It's easy.

EVAN: I'm gonna need an address.

JASON: It don't cost me nothing. It's easier than playing musical beds at the shelter. Nobody calls me out.

EVAN: It's gonna get cold soon.

JASON: Well, I'll cross that bridge when I get there. Ever since I ran into Chris I haven't been able to focus. I'm trying to figure it out, you know? What happened. I just remember the fury. The blind fury. And I ain't been able to shake it. It's like a wool jacket that I wear all of the fucking time. Someone looks at me wrong, I wanna bash them in the face, and I don't know why.

EVAN: Man, you're not gonna like what I have to say. But I'm just gonna say it. Shame.

JASON: What?

EVAN: I've seen enough guys in your situation to know that over time it's . . . it's crippling. I'm not a therapist, I'm not the right dude to talk to about all of this. But what I do know, is that it's not a productive emotion. Most folks think it's the guilt or rage that destroys us in the end, but I know from experience that it's shame that eats us away until we disappear. You put in your time. But look here, we been talking, and we can keep talking—but whatcha gonna do about where you're at right now? You hear me?

(*Light shift. We're back with Chris.*)

JASON: Yeah.

CHRIS: Yeah, I hear you.

Scene 8

October 18, 2008

Outside it's 58°F.

In the news: Thousands of Latin American immigrants are returning home as U.S. jobs dry up in the construction, landscaping and restaurant industries. Pennsylvania's Republican Party sues the community activist group

ACORN,[7] *accusing the group of fostering voter registration fraud. The Philadel-phia Phillies prepare to face off against the Tampa Bay Rays in the 2008 Major League Baseball World Series.*

Bar. It has been refurbished, polished. Oscar, older and more mature, stands behind the bar. Chris enters and reluctantly sits at a table. A moment. Oscar contemplates whether to speak.

OSCAR: You want me to turn on the game?

CHRIS: Nah. You awright?

OSCAR: Yeah. I heard you guys got out.

(*A moment.*)

CHRIS: Oscar, I—

OSCAR: Didn't know you knew my name.

CHRIS: I—

OSCAR: Whatchu drinking?

CHRIS: . . . . Whatcha got on tap?

OSCAR: It's this artisanal[8] stuff. A guy, local, makes it.

CHRIS: You're joking.

OSCAR: Nah. It's good.

CHRIS: Um, okay.

(*Oscar pours a beer.*)

The place looks nice.

OSCAR: New crowd. We get a lot of college kids since the plant closed. I been trying to keep it up, you know—

CHRIS: Yeah. How's, um, Howard?

OSCAR: Retired. Moved to Phoenix. I'm the manager.

CHRIS: Really?

OSCAR: Yeah. Bartend on weekends.

CHRIS: That's real cool.

OSCAR: Thanks.

CHRIS: I . . .

OSCAR: Look. Whatever you gotta say—

CHRIS: Listen—

(*Jason enters. Oscar's surpised, and grows a little on edge.*)

OSCAR: Whoa, what's going on here?

(*Jason stops short, panic, then turns to leave.*)

CHRIS: Jason!

OSCAR: I don't want—

JASON: Yo, I can't do—

CHRIS: Don't walk outta here. I didn't think you'd come. We have—

---

7. Association of Community Organizations for Reform Now (1970–2010), national nonprofit social-justice organization (acronym).

8. Made in a traditional, often non-mechanized manner.

(*A moment. Jason contemplates whether or not to leave. Then Stan, severely crippled, enters. A traumatic brain injury. He moves with extreme difficulty; it is painful to watch. Finally:*)

Hey Stan. Stan.

(*Stan doesn't register their presence.*)

OSCAR: He can't really hear good.
CHRIS: Jesus.

(*Stan goes about wiping tables. They all watch. Stan drops his cloth. He struggles to get it. Jason runs over and picks it up.*)

STAN (*Garbled*): Thank . . . you.
JASON: It's nice that you take care of him.
OSCAR: That's how it oughta be.

(*There's apology in their eyes, but Chris and Jason are unable to conjure words just yet. The four men, uneasy in their bodies, await the next moment in a fractured togetherness. Blackout.*)

END OF PLAY

2015

AUTHORS ON THEIR WORK

LYNN NOTTAGE (b. 1964)

From "Playwright Lynn Nottage: 'We Are a Country That Has Lost Its Narrative'" (2018)*

[INTERVIEWER:] Why did you write *Sweat*?

[NOTTAGE:] I was commissioned by the Oregon Shakespeare festival, which was asking playwrights across the country to write about American revolutions. For a couple of years, I wasn't sure which revolution I wanted to write about—the American civil war? The civil rights movement?

Then one evening I got an email from a friend sharing the fact that for a period of time she had been completely and absolutely broke. She was someone I knew quite well and saw regularly. I felt horrible that I had no idea she was struggling.

The next morning, we had a long conversation that coincided with the beginning of the first week of the Occupy Wall Street protest against economic inequality. So, these two middle-aged women went down there and chanted. [. . .]

To me, Occupy Wall Street raised a lot of questions that were not answered. That put me out on the street to figure out how economic stagnation was shifting the American narrative and how so many people who had so thoroughly invested in the American dream found themselves broadsided.

[INTERVIEWER:] Why did you set *Sweat* in Reading, Pennsylvania?

[NOTTAGE:] [. . .] We ended up with the poorest city in America of its size [. . .].

One of the first questions we asked [people there] was, how do you describe your city? People would respond by saying: "Reading *was* . . ." They were incredibly nostalgic for this glorious imagined past. It nearly broke my heart. I thought this is a city that cannot conceive of itself in the present or future tense. It is a micro-cosm of what is happening in America today. We are a country that has lost our narrative. We can't project our future because we don't know where we are going.

After about a year and a half of research [in Reading], I met the steelworkers who would become the inspiration for the play—middle-aged white men who shared stories that absolutely broke my heart. I hadn't anticipated I would be moved in the way I was. I hadn't anticipated that, sitting with them in a circle, I would feel we had a shared narrative—one of struggle, disillusionment and frustration with our government and our society.

[INTERVIEWER:] How do you transform your research into drama?

[NOTTAGE:] I push the research away and never look at it again until I finish the play. I don't want the research to censor the way I shape my characters. What I create is very much a work of fiction. The characters are constructs of my imagination; they are inspired by some of the conversations I had but I really didn't want them to be facsimiles of the people I spoke to.

[INTERVIEWER:] A lot of American plays are set in a bar. Why did you choose one for your setting?

[NOTTAGE:] Bars are places where a lot of people retreat, a place where people go to unwind and they tell stories in ways they wouldn't otherwise.
  [. . .] People speak candidly once their tongues have been loosened by liquor. A bar is also a space where people can meet across age, race and gender. I was interested in that dynamic [. . .].

*"Playwright Lynn Nottage: 'We Are a Country That Has Lost Its Narrative.'" Interview by Sarah Crompton. *The Guardian* [UK], 2 Dec. 2018, www.theguardian.com/stage/2018/dec/02/lynn-nottage-interview-play-sweat-america.

SOPHOCLES
Oedipus the King[1]
(See Sophocles biography on p. 1653.)

CHARACTERS

OEDIPUS, *King of Thebes*
JOCASTA, *His Wife*
CREON, *His Brother-in-Law*
TEIRESIAS, *an Old Blind Prophet*
A PRIEST

FIRST MESSENGER
SECOND MESSENGER
A HERDSMAN
A CHORUS *of Old Men of Thebes*

SCENE: *In front of the palace of* OEDIPUS *at Thebes. To the right of the stage near the altar stands the* PRIEST *with a crowd of children.* OEDIPUS *emerges from the central door.*

---

1. Translated from the ancient Greek by David Grene.

OEDIPUS: Children, young sons and daughters of old Cadmus,[2]
    why do you sit here with your suppliant crowns?
    The town is heavy with a mingled burden
    of sounds and smells, of groans and hymns and incense;
    I did not think it fit that I should hear   5
    of this from messengers but came myself,—
    I Oedipus whom all men call the Great.

    [*He turns to the* PRIEST.]

    You're old and they are young; come, speak for them.
    What do you fear or want, that you sit here
    suppliant? Indeed I'm willing to give all   10
    that you may need; I would be very hard
    should I not pity suppliants like these.
PRIEST: O ruler of my country, Oedipus,
    you see our company around the altar;
    you see our ages; some of us, like these,   15
    who cannot yet fly far, and some of us
    heavy with age; these children are the chosen
    among the young, and I the priest of Zeus.[3]
    Within the market place sit others crowned
    with suppliant garlands, at the double shrine   20
    of Pallas and the temple where Ismenus
    gives oracles by fire. King, you yourself
    have seen our city reeling like a wreck
    already; it can scarcely lift its prow
    out of the depths, out of the bloody surf.   25
    A blight is on the fruitful plants of the earth,
    a blight is on the cattle in the fields,
    a blight is on our women that no children
    are born to them; a God that carries fire,
    a deadly pestilence, is on our town,   30
    strikes us and spares not, and the house of Cadmus
    is emptied of its people while black Death
    grows rich in groaning and in lamentation.
    We have not come as suppliants to this altar
    because we thought of you as of a God,   35
    but rather judging you the first of men
    in all the chances of this life and when
    we mortals have to do with more than man.
    You came and by your coming saved our city,
    freed us from tribute which we paid of old   40
    to the Sphinx, cruel singer.[4] This you did

---

2. Founder of Thebes.
3. Principal god and father of Athena or "Pallas" (line 21), goddess of wisdom.
4. Thebes was in the thrall of the monstrous Sphinx—part human, part lion, part eagle, part serpent—until Oedipus was able to answer a riddle; freed at last from the monster's cruelty, the grateful citizens of Thebes made Oedipus their king.

in virtue of no knowledge we could give you,
in virtue of no teaching; it was God
that aided you, men say, and you are held
45   with God's assistance to have saved our lives.
Now Oedipus, Greatest in all men's eyes,
here falling at your feet we all entreat you,
find us some strength for rescue.
Perhaps you'll hear a wise word from some God,
50   perhaps you will learn something from a man
(for I have seen that for the skilled of practice
the outcome of their counsels live the most).
Noblest of men, go, and raise up our city,
go,—and give heed. For now this land of ours
55   calls you its savior since you saved it once.
So, let us never speak about your reign
as of a time when first our feet were set
secure on high, but later fell to ruin.
Raise up our city, save it and raise it up.
60   Once you have brought us luck with happy omen;
be no less now in fortune.
If you will rule this land, as now you rule it,
better to rule it full of men than empty.
For neither tower nor ship is anything
65   when empty, and none live in it together.
OEDIPUS: I pity you, children. You have come full of longing,
but I have known the story before you told it
only too well. I know you are all sick,
yet there is not one of you, sick though you are,
70   that is as sick as I myself.
Your several sorrows each have single scope
and touch but one of you. My spirit groans
for city and myself and you at once.
You have not roused me like a man from sleep;
75   know that I have given many tears to this,
gone many ways wandering in thought,
but as I thought I found only one remedy
and that I took. I sent Menoeceus' son
Creon, Jocasta's brother, to Apollo,[5]
80   to his Pythian temple,
that he might learn there by what act or word
I could save this city. As I count the days,
it vexes me what ails him; he is gone
far longer than he needed for the journey.
85   But when he comes, then, may I prove a villain,
if I shall not do all the God commands.

5. God of truth and of light, worshipped at many shrines, most famously that at Pytho (an ancient name for Delphi), where an oracle was believed to speak for the god.

PRIEST: Thanks for your gracious words. Your servants here
　　signal that Creon is this moment coming.
OEDIPUS: His face is bright. O holy Lord Apollo,
　　grant that his news too may be bright for us　　　　　　　　　90
　　and bring us safety.
PRIEST: It is happy news,
　　I think, for else his head would not be crowned
　　with sprigs of fruitful laurel.
OEDIPUS:　　　　　　　　　　　We will know soon,
　　he's within hail. Lord Creon, my good brother,　　　　　　　95
　　what is the word you bring us from the God?

　　[CREON enters.]

CREON: A good word,—for things hard to bear themselves
　　if in the final issue all is well
　　I count complete good fortune.
OEDIPUS:　　　　　　　　　　What do you mean?
　　What you have said so far　　　　　　　　　　　　　　　　100
　　leaves me uncertain whether to trust or fear.
CREON: If you will hear my news before these others
　　I am ready to speak, or else to go within.
　　OEDIPUS: Speak it to all;
　　the grief I bear, I bear it more for these　　　　　　　　　105
　　than for my own heart.
CREON:　　　　　　　　I will tell you, then,
　　what I heard from the God.
　　King Phoebus[6] in plain words commanded us
　　to drive out a pollution from our land,
　　pollution grown ingrained within the land;　　　　　　　110
　　drive it out, said the God, not cherish it,
　　till it's past cure.
OEDIPUS:　　　　　What is the rite
　　of purification? How shall it be done?
CREON: By banishing a man, or expiation
　　of blood by blood, since it is murder guilt　　　　　　　115
　　which holds our city in this destroying storm.
OEDIPUS: Who is this man whose fate the God pronounces?
CREON: My Lord, before you piloted the state
　　we had a king called Laius.
　　OEDIPUS: I know of him by hearsay. I have not seen him.　　　120
　　CREON: The God commanded clearly: let someone
　　punish with force this dead man's murderers.
　　OEDIPUS: Where are they in the world? Where would a trace
　　of this old crime be found? It would be hard
　　to guess where.
CREON:　　　　　　The clue is in this land;　　　　　125

6. Another name for Apollo.

that which is sought is found;
the unheeded thing escapes:
so said the God.

OEDIPUS   Was it at home,
or in the country that death came upon him,
130   or in another country travelling?
CREON: He went, he said himself, upon an embassy,
but never returned when he set out from home.
OEDIPUS: Was there no messenger, no fellow traveller
who knew what happened? Such a one might tell
135   something of use.
CREON: They were all killed save one. He fled in terror
and he could tell us nothing in clear terms
of what he knew, nothing, but one thing only.
OEDIPUS: What was it?
140   If we could even find a slim beginning
in which to hope, we might discover much.
CREON: This man said that the robbers they encountered
were many and the hands that did the murder
were many; it was no man's single power.
145 OEDIPUS: How could a robber dare a deed like this
were he not helped with money from the city,
money and treachery?
CREON: That indeed was thought.
But Laius was dead and in our trouble
there was none to help.
150 OEDIPUS: What trouble was so great to hinder you
inquiring out the murder of your king?
CREON: The riddling Sphinx induced us to neglect
mysterious crimes and rather seek solution
of troubles at our feet.
155 OEDIPUS: I will bring this to light again. King Phoebus
fittingly took this care about the dead,
and you too fittingly.
And justly you will see in me an ally,
a champion of my country and the God.
160   For when I drive pollution from the land
I will not serve a distant friend's advantage,
but act in my own interest. Whoever
he was that killed the king may readily
wish to dispatch me with his murderous hand;
165   so helping the dead king I help myself.

Come, children, take your suppliant boughs and go;
up from the altars now. Call the assembly
and let it meet upon the understanding
that I'll do everything. God will decide
170   whether we prosper or remain in sorrow.

PRIEST: Rise, children—it was this we came to seek,
    which of himself the king now offers us.
    May Phoebus who gave us the oracle
    come to our rescue and stay the plague.

[*Exeunt*[7] *all but the* CHORUS.]

CHORUS: [*Strophe.*][8] What is the sweet spoken word of God from the shrine of 175
        Pytho, rich in gold
    that has come to glorious Thebes?
    I am stretched on the rack of doubt, and terror and trembling hold
    my heart, O Delian Healer,[9] and I worship full of fears
    for what doom you will bring to pass, new or renewed in the revolving
        years.
    Speak to me, immortal voice, 180
    child of golden Hope.

[*Antistrophe.*][1]

    First I call on you, Athene,[2] deathless daughter of Zeus,
    and Artemis,[3] Earth Upholder,
    who sits in the midst of the marketplace in the throne which men call
        Fame,
    and Phoebus, the Far Shooter, three averters of Fate, 185
    come to us now, if ever before, when ruin rushed upon the state,
    you drove destruction's flame away
    out of our land.

[*Strophe.*]

    Our sorrows defy number;
    all the ship's timbers are rotten; 190
    taking of thought is no spear for the driving away of the plague.
    There are no growing children in this famous land;
    there are no women bearing the pangs of childbirth.
    You may see them one with another, like birds swift on the wing,
    quicker than fire unmastered, 195
    speeding away to the coast of the Western God.

[*Antistrophe.*]

    In the unnumbered deaths
    of its people the city dies;
    those children that are born lie dead on the naked earth
    unpitied, spreading contagion of death; and grey haired mothers and wives 200
    everywhere stand at the altar's edge, suppliant, moaning;

7. Exit the stage (Latin for "they go out").
8. In Greek stagecraft, choral song and corresponding dance of the chorus to one side.
9. Apollo was also god of healing; one of his principal shrines was located on the island of Delos.
1. After the strophe, the chorus's answering song and returning dance.
2. Goddess of war and peace, as well as wisdom.
3. Goddess of the earth and the hunt, twin sister of Apollo.

the hymn to the healing God rings out but with it the wailing voices are
    blended.
From these our sufferings grant us, O golden Daughter of Zeus,
glad-faced deliverance.

[*Strophe.*]

205   There is no clash of brazen shields but our fight is with the War God,
    a War God ringed with the cries of men, a savage God who burns us;
    grant that he turn in racing course backwards out of our country's bounds
    to the great palace of Amphitrite[4] or where the waves of the Thracian sea
    deny the stranger safe anchorage.
210   Whatsoever escapes the night
    at last the light of day revisits;
    so smite the War God,[5] Father Zeus,
    beneath your thunderbolt,
    for you are the Lord of the lightning, the lightning that carries fire.

[*Antistrophe.*]

215   And your unconquered arrow shafts, winged by the golden corded bow,
    Lycean King,[6] I beg to be at our side for help;
    and the gleaming torches of Artemis with which she scours the Lycean
        hills,
    and I call on the God with the turban of gold, who gave his name to this
        country of ours,
    the Bacchic God with the wind flushed face,
220   Evian One, who travel
    with the Maenad[7] company,
    combat the God that burns us
    with your torch of pine;
    for the God that is our enemy is a God unhonoured among the Gods.

[OEDIPUS *returns.*]

225 OEDIPUS: For what you ask me—if you will hear my words,
    and hearing welcome them and fight the plague,
    you will find strength and lightening of your load
    Hark to me; what I say to you, I say
    as one that is a stranger to the story
230   as stranger to the deed. For I would not
    be far upon the track if I alone
    were tracing it without a clue. But now,
    since after all was finished, I became
    a citizen among you, citizens—
235   now I proclaim to all the men of Thebes:

4. Queen of the sea and wife of Poseidon, sometimes said to dwell in the Atlantic Ocean.
5. Ares, son of Zeus and half brother to Athena.
6. Apollo, a major shrine to whom was located at Lycia in Anatolia, modern-day Turkey.
7. Female worshippers of Dionysus (Bacchus to the Romans; see line 219), god of fertility and wine.
Evian One: Dionysus (also known as Evius).

who so among you knows the murderer
by whose hand Laius, son of Labdacus,
died—I command him to tell everything
to me,—yes, though he fears himself to take the blame
on his own head; for bitter punishment 240
he shall have none, but leave this land unharmed.
Or if he knows the murderer, another,
a foreigner, still let him speak the truth.
For I will pay him and be grateful, too.
But if you shall keep silence, if perhaps 245
some one of you, to shield a guilty friend,
or for his own sake shall reject my words—
hear what I shall do then:
I forbid that man, whoever he be, my land,
my land where I hold sovereignty and throne; 250
and I forbid any to welcome him
or cry him greeting or make him a sharer
in sacrifice or offering to the gods,
or give him water for his hands to wash.
I command all to drive him from their homes, 255
since he is our pollution, as the oracle
of Pytho's god proclaimed him now to me.
So I stand forth a champion of the god
and of the man who died.
Upon the murderer I invoke this curse— 260
whether he is one man and all unknown,
or one of many—may he wear out his life
in misery to miserable doom!
If with my knowledge he lives at my hearth
I pray that I myself may feel my curse. 265
On you I lay my charge to fulfill all this
for me, for the god, and for this land of ours
destroyed and blighted, by the god forsaken.

Even were this no matter of God's ordinance
it would not fit you so to leave it lie, 270
unpurified, since a good man is dead
and one that was a king. Search it out.
Since I am now the holder of his office,
and have his bed and wife that once was his,
and had his line not been unfortunate 275
we would have common children—(fortune leaped
upon his head)—because of all these things,
I fight in his defence as for my father,
and I shall try all means to take the murderer
of Laius the son of Labdacus 280
the son of Polydorus and before him
of Cadmus and before him of Agenor.

Those who do not obey me, may the Gods
grant no crops springing from the ground they plough
285 nor children to their women! May a fate
like this, or one still worse than this consume them!
For you whom these words please, the other Thebans,
may Justice as your ally and all the Gods
live with you, blessing you now and for ever!
290 CHORUS: As you have held me to my oath, I speak:
I neither killed the king nor can declare
the killer; but since Phoebus set the quest
it is his part to tell who the man is.
OEDIPUS: Right; but to put compulsion on the Gods
295 against their will—no man can do that.
CHORUS: May I then say what I think second best?
OEDIPUS: If there's a third best, too, spare not to tell it.
CHORUS: I know that what the Lord Teiresias
sees, is most often what the Lord Apollo
300 sees. If you should inquire of this from him
you might find out most clearly.
OEDIPUS: Even in this my actions have not been sluggard.
On Creon's word I have sent two messengers
and why the prophet is not here already
I have been wondering.
305 CHORUS: His skill apart
there is besides only an old faint story.
OEDIPUS: What is it?
I look at every story.
CHORUS: It was said
that he was killed by certain wayfarers.
310 OEDIPUS: I heard that, too, but no one saw the killer.
CHORUS: Yet if he has a share of fear at all,
his courage will not stand firm, hearing your curse.
OEDIPUS: The man who in the doing did not shrink
will fear no word.
CHORUS: Here comes his prosecutor:
315 led by your men the godly prophet comes
in whom alone of mankind truth is native.

[*Enter* TEIRESIAS, *led by a* LITTLE BOY.]

OEDIPUS: Teiresias, you are versed in everything,
things teachable and things not to be spoken,
things of the heaven and earth-creeping things.
320 You have no eyes but in your mind you know
with what a plague our city is afflicted.
My lord, in you alone we find a champion,
in you alone one that can rescue us.
Perhaps you have not heard the messengers,
325 but Phoebus sent in answer to our sending

an oracle declaring that our freedom
from this disease would only come when we
should learn the names of those who killed King Laius,
and kill them or expel from our country.
Do not begrudge us oracles from birds,　　　　　　　330
or any other way of prophecy
within your skill; save yourself and the city,
save me; redeem the debt of our pollution
that lies on us because of this dead man.
We are in your hands; pains are most nobly taken　　335
to help another when you have means and power.

TEIRESIAS: Alas, how terrible is wisdom when
　　it brings no profit to the man that's wise!
　　This I knew well, but had forgotten it,
　　else I would not have come here.

OEDIPUS:　　　　　　　　　　What is this?　　　　340
　　How sad you are now you have come!

TEIRESIAS:　　　　　　　　　　Let me
　　go home. It will be easiest for us both
　　to bear our several destinies to the end
　　if you will follow my advice.

OEDIPUS:　　　　　　　　You'd rob us
　　of this your gift of prophecy? You talk　　　　　345
　　as one who had no care for law nor love
　　for Thebes who reared you.

TEIRESIAS: Yes, but I see that even your own words
　　miss the mark; therefore I must fear for mine.

OEDIPUS: For God's sake if you know of anything,　　350
　　do not turn from us; all of us kneel to you,
　　all of us here, your suppliants.

TEIRESIAS: All of you here know nothing. I will not
　　bring to the light of day my troubles, mine—
　　rather than call them yours.

OEDIPUS:　　　　　　　　What do you mean?　　355
　　You know of something but refuse to speak.
　　Would you betray us and destroy the city?

TEIRESIAS: I will not bring this pain upon us both,
　　neither on you nor on myself. Why is it
　　you question me and waste your labour? I　　　360
　　will tell you nothing.

OEDIPUS: You would provoke a stone! Tell us, you villain,
　　tell us, and do not stand there quietly
　　unmoved and balking at the issue.

TEIRESIAS: You blame my temper but you do not see　　365
　　your own that lives within you; it is me
　　you chide.

OEDIPUS: Who would not feel his temper rise
　　at words like these with which you shame our city?

370 TEIRESIAS: Of themselves things will come, although I hide them
and breathe no word of them.

OEDIPUS: Since they will come
tell them to me.

TEIRESIAS: I will say nothing further.
Against this answer let your temper rage
as wildly as you will.

OEDIPUS: Indeed I am
375 so angry I shall not hold back a jot
of what I think. For I would have you know
I think you were complotter of the deed
and doer of the deed save in so far
as for the actual killing. Had you had eyes
380 I would have said alone you murdered him.

TEIRESIAS: Yes? Then I warn you faithfully to keep
the letter of your proclamation and
from this day forth to speak no word of greeting
to these nor me; you are the land's pollution.

385 OEDIPUS: How shamelessly you started up this taunt!
How do you think you will escape?

TEIRESIAS: I have.
I have escaped; the truth is what I cherish
and that's my strength.

OEDIPUS: And who has taught you truth?
Not your profession surely!

TEIRESIAS: You have taught me,
390 for you have made me speak against my will.

OEDIPUS: Speak what? Tell me again that I may learn it better.

TEIRESIAS: Did you not understand before or would you
provoke me into speaking?

OEDIPUS: I did not grasp it,
not so to call it known. Say it again.

395 TEIRESIAS: I say you are the murderer of the king
whose murderer you seek.

OEDIPUS: Not twice you shall
say calumnies like this and stay unpunished.

TEIRESIAS: Shall I say more to tempt your anger more?

OEDIPUS: As much as you desire; it will be said
in vain.

400 TEIRESIAS: I say that with those you love best
you live in foulest shame unconsciously
and do not see where you are in calamity.

OEDIPUS: Do you imagine you can always talk
like this, and live to laugh at it hereafter?

405 TEIRESIAS: Yes, if the truth has anything of strength.

OEDIPUS: It has, but not for you; it has no strength
for you because you are blind in mind and ears
as well as in your eyes.

TEIRESIAS: You are a poor wretch
    to taunt me with the very insults which
    everyone soon will heap upon yourself.   410
OEDIPUS: Your life is one long night so that you cannot
    hurt me or any other who sees the light.
TEIRESIAS: It is not fate that I should be your ruin,
    Apollo is enough; it is his care
    to work this out.
OEDIPUS: Was this your own design   415
    or Creon's?
TEIRESIAS: Creon is no hurt to you,
    but you are to yourself.
OEDIPUS: Wealth, sovereignty and skill outmatching skill
    for the contrivance of an envied life!
    Great store of jealousy fill your treasury chests,   420
    if my friend Creon, friend from the first and loyal,
    thus secretly attacks me, secretly
    desires to drive me out and secretly
    suborns this juggling, trick devising quack,
    this wily beggar who has only eyes   425
    for his own gains, but blindness in his skill.
    For, tell me, where have you seen clear, Teiresias,
    with your prophetic eyes? When the dark singer,
    the Sphinx, was in your country, did you speak
    word of deliverance to its citizens?   430
    And yet the riddle's answer was not the province
    of a chance comer. It was a prophet's task
    and plainly you had no such gift of prophecy
    from birds nor otherwise from any God
    to glean a word of knowledge. But I came,   435
    Oedipus, who knew nothing, and I stopped her.
    I solved the riddle by my wit alone.
    Mine was no knowledge got from birds.[8] And now
    you would expel me,
    because you think that you will find a place   440
    by Creon's throne. I think you will be sorry,
    both you and your accomplice, for your plot
    to drive me out. And did I not regard you
    as an old man, some suffering would have taught you
    that what was in your heart was treason.   445
CHORUS: We look at this man's words and yours, my king,
    and we find both have spoken them in anger.
    We need no angry words but only thought
    how we may best hit the God's meaning for us.
TEIRESIAS: If you are king, at least I have the right   450
    no less to speak in my defence against you.

8. Prophetic knowledge derived from observing the flight of birds or inspecting bird entrails.

Of that much I am master. I am no slave
of yours, but Loxias',[9] and so I shall not
enroll myself with Creon for my patron.
455   Since you have taunted me with being blind,
here is my word for you.
You have your eyes but see not where you are
in sin, nor where you live, nor whom you live with.
Do you know who your parents are? Unknowing
460   you are an enemy to kith and kin
in death, beneath the earth, and in this life.
A deadly footed, double striking curse,
from father and mother both, shall drive you forth
out of this land, with darkness on your eyes,
465   that now have such straight vision. Shall there be
a place will not be harbour to your cries,
a corner of Cithaeron[1] will not ring
in echo to your cries, soon, soon,—
when you shall learn the secret of your marriage,
470   which steered you to a haven in this house,—
haven no haven, after lucky voyage?
And of the multitude of other evils
establishing a grim equality
between you and your children, you know nothing.
475   So, muddy with contempt my words and Creon's!
Misery shall grind no man as it will you.

OEDIPUS: Is it endurable that I should hear
such words from him? Go and a curse go with you!
Quick, home with you! Out of my house at once!

480 TEIRESIAS: I would not have come either had you not called me.

OEDIPUS: I did not know then you would talk like a fool—
or it would have been long before I called you.

TEIRESIAS: I am a fool then, as it seems to you—
but to the parents who have bred you, wise.

485 OEDIPUS: What parents? Stop! Who are they of all the world?

TEIRESIAS: This day will show your birth and will destroy you.

OEDIPUS: How needlessly your riddles darken everything.

TEIRESIAS: But it's in riddle answering you are strongest.

OEDIPUS: Yes. Taunt me where you will find me great.

490 TEIRESIAS: It is this very luck that has destroyed you.

OEDIPUS: I do not care, if it has saved this city.

TEIRESIAS: Well, I will go. Come, boy, lead me away.

OEDIPUS: Yes, lead him off. So long as you are here,
you'll be a stumbling block and a vexation;
once gone, you will not trouble me again.

495 TEIRESIAS: I have said

---

9. Yet another name for Apollo.
1. Mountain where Oedipus was abandoned as a child.

what I came here to say not fearing your
countenance: there is no way you can hurt me.
I tell you, king, this man, this murderer
(whom you have long declared you are in search of,
indicting him in threatening proclamation 500
as murderer of Laius)—he is here.
In name he is a stranger among citizens
but soon he will be shown to be a citizen
true native Theban, and he'll have no joy
of the discovery: blindness for sight 505
and beggary for riches his exchange,
he shall go journeying to a foreign country
tapping his way before him with a stick.
He shall be proved father and brother both
to his own children in his house; to her 510
that gave him birth, a son and husband both;
a fellow sower in his father's bed
with that same father that he murdered.
Go within, reckon that out, and if you find me
mistaken, say I have no skill in prophecy. 515

[*Exeunt separately* TEIRESIAS *and* OEDIPUS.]

CHORUS: [*Strophe.*] Who is the man proclaimed
by Delphi's[2] prophetic rock
as the bloody handed murderer,
the doer of deeds that none dare name?
Now is the time for him to run 520
with a stronger foot
than Pegasus[3]
for the child of Zeus leaps in arms upon him
with fire and the lightning bolt,
and terribly close on his heels 525
are the Fates[4] that never miss.

[*Antistrophe.*]

Lately from snowy Parnassus[5]
clearly the voice flashed forth,
bidding each Theban track him down,
the unknown murderer. 530
In the savage forests he lurks and in
the caverns like
the mountain bull.
He is sad and lonely, and lonely his feet
that carry him far from the navel of earth; 535

2. Location of Greece's most important shrine to Apollo, renowned for its oracle.
3. Winged horse.
4. Goddesses who decide the course of human life.
5. Mountain sacred to Apollo.

but its prophecies, ever living,
flutter around his head.

[*Strophe.*]

The augur has spread confusion,
terrible confusion;
540 I do not approve what was said
nor can I deny it.
I do not know what to say;
I am in a flutter of foreboding;
I never heard in the present
545 nor past of a quarrel between
the sons of Labdacus and Polybus,[6]
that I might bring as proof
in attacking the popular fame
of Oedipus, seeking
550 to take vengeance for undiscovered
death in the line of Labdacus.

[*Antistrophe.*]

Truly Zeus and Apollo are wise
and in human things all knowing;
but amongst men there is no
555 distinct judgment, between the prophet
and me—which of us is right.
One man may pass another in wisdom
but I would never agree
with those that find fault with the king
560 till I should see the word
proved right beyond doubt. For once
in visible form the Sphinx
came on him and all of us
saw his wisdom and in that test
565 he saved the city. So he will not be condemned by my mind.

[*Enter* CREON.]

CREON: Citizens, I have come because I heard
deadly words spread about me, that the king
accuses me. I cannot take that from him.
If he believes that in these present troubles
570 he has been wronged by me in word or deed
I do not want to live on with the burden
of such a scandal on me. The report
injures me doubly and most vitally—
for I'll be called a traitor to my city
575 and traitor also to my friends and you.

6. King who adopted Oedipus.

CHORUS: Perhaps it was a sudden gust of anger
    that forced that insult from him, and no judgment.
CREON: But did he say that it was in compliance
    with schemes of mine that the seer told him lies?
CHORUS: Yes, he said that, but why, I do not know.   580
CREON: Were his eyes straight in his head? Was his mind right
    when he accused me in this fashion?
CHORUS: I do not know; I have no eyes to see
    what princes do. Here comes the king himself.

    [*Enter* OEDIPUS.]

OEDIPUS: You, sir, how is it you come here? Have you so much   585
    brazen-faced daring that you venture in
    my house although you are proved manifestly
    the murderer of that man, and though you tried,
    openly, highway robbery of my crown?
    For God's sake, tell me what you saw in me,   590
    what cowardice or what stupidity,
    that made you lay a plot like this against me?
    Did you imagine I should not observe
    the crafty scheme that stole upon me or
    seeing it, take no means to counter it?   595
    Was it not stupid of you to make the attempt,
    to try to hunt down royal power without
    the people at your back or friends? For only
    with the people at your back or money can
    the hunt end in the capture of a crown.   600
CREON: Do you know what you're doing? Will you listen
    to words to answer yours, and then pass judgment?
OEDIPUS: You're quick to speak, but I am slow to grasp you,
    for I have found you dangerous,—and my foe.
CREON: First of all hear what I shall say to that.   605
OEDIPUS: At least don't tell me that you are not guilty.
CREON: If you think obstinacy without wisdom
    a valuable possession, you are wrong.
OEDIPUS: And you are wrong if you believe that one,
    a criminal, will not be punished only   610
    because he is my kinsman.
CREON: This is but just—
    but tell me, then, of what offense I'm guilty?
OEDIPUS: Did you or did you not urge me to send
    to this prophetic mumbler?
CREON: I did indeed,
    and I shall stand by what I told you.   615
OEDIPUS: How long ago is it since Laius . . .
CREON: What about Laius? I don't understand.
OEDIPUS: Vanished—died—was murdered?
CREON: It is long,

a long, long time to reckon.

OEDIPUS: Was this prophet
in the profession then?

620 CREON: He was, and honoured
as highly as he is today.

OEDIPUS: At that time did he say a word about me?

CREON: Never, at least when I was near him.

OEDIPUS: You never made a search for the dead man?

625 CREON: We searched, indeed, but never learned of anything.

OEDIPUS: Why did our wise old friend not say this then?

CREON: I don't know; and when I know nothing, I
usually hold my tongue.

OEDIPUS: You know this much,
and can declare this much if you are loyal.

630 CREON: What is it? If I know, I'll not deny it.

OEDIPUS: That he would not have said that I killed Laius
had he not met you first.

CREON: You know yourself
whether he said this, but I demand that I
should hear as much from you as you from me.

635 OEDIPUS: Then hear,—I'll not be proved a murderer.

CREON: Well, then. You're married to my sister.

OEDIPUS: Yes,
that I am not disposed to deny.

CREON: You rule
this country giving her an equal share
in the government?

OEDIPUS: Yes, everything she wants
she has from me.

640 CREON: And I, as thirdsman to you,
am rated as the equal of you two?

OEDIPUS: Yes, and it's there you've proved yourself false friend.

CREON: Not if you will reflect on it as I do.
Consider, first, if you think anyone
645   would choose to rule and fear rather than rule
and sleep untroubled by a fear if power
were equal in both cases. I, at least,
I was not born with such a frantic yearning
to be a king—but to do what kings do.
650   And so it is with everyone who has learned
wisdom and self-control. As it stands now,
the prizes are all mine—and without fear.
But if I were the king myself, I must
do much that went against the grain.
655   How should despotic rule seem sweeter to me
than painless power and an assured authority?
I am not so besotted yet that I
want other honours than those that come with profit.

Now every man's my pleasure; every man greets me;
now those who are your suitors fawn on me,— 660
success for them depends upon my favour.
Why should I let all this go to win that?
My mind would not be traitor if it's wise;
I am no treason lover, of my nature,
nor would I ever dare to join a plot. 665
Prove what I say. Go to the oracle
at Pytho and inquire about the answers,
if they are as I told you. For the rest,
if you discover I laid any plot
together with the seer, kill me, I say, 670
not only by your vote but by my own.
But do not charge me on obscure opinion
without some proof to back it. It's not just
lightly to count your knaves as honest men,
nor honest men as knaves. To throw away 675
an honest friend is, as it were, to throw
your life away, which a man loves the best.
In time you will know all with certainty;
time is the only test of honest men,
one day is space enough to know a rogue. 680
CHORUS: His words are wise, king, if one fears to fall.
    Those who are quick of temper are not safe.
OEDIPUS: When he that plots against me secretly
    moves quickly, I must quickly counterplot.
    If I wait taking no decisive measure 685
    his business will be done, and mine be spoiled.
CREON: What do you want to do then? Banish me?
OEDIPUS: No, certainly; kill you, not banish you.[7]
CREON: I do not think that you've your wits about you.
OEDIPUS: For my own interests, yes.
CREON: But for mine, too, 690
    you should think equally.
OEDIPUS: You are a rogue.
CREON: Suppose you do not understand?
OEDIPUS: But yet
    I must be ruler.
CREON: Not if you rule badly.
OEDIPUS: O, city, city!
CREON: I too have some share
    in the city; it is not yours alone. 695
CHORUS: Stop, my lords! Here—and in the nick of time
    I see Jocasta coming from the house;

---

7. *Translator's note:* Two lines omitted here owing to the confusion in the dialogue consequent on the loss of a third line. The lines as they stand in Jebb's edition (1902) are: OED: That you may show what manner of thing is envy. / CREON: You speak as one that will not yield or trust. [OED: *lost line.*]

with her help lay the quarrel that now stirs you.

[*Enter* JOCASTA.]

JOCASTA: For shame! Why have you raised this foolish squabbling
700   brawl? Are you not ashamed to air your private
         griefs when the country's sick? Go in, you, Oedipus,
         and you, too, Creon, into the house. Don't magnify
         your nothing troubles.
CREON: Sister, Oedipus,
         your husband, thinks he has the right to do
705   terrible wrongs—he has but to choose between
         two terrors: banishing or killing me.
OEDIPUS: He's right, Jocasta; for I find him plotting
         with knavish tricks against my person.
CREON: That God may never bless me! May I die
710   accursed, if I have been guilty of
         one tittle of the charge you bring against me!
JOCASTA: I beg you, Oedipus, trust him in this,
         spare him for the sake of this his oath to God,
         for my sake, and the sake of those who stand here.
715 CHORUS: Be gracious, be merciful,
         we beg of you.
OEDIPUS: In what would you have me yield?
CHORUS: He has been no silly child in the past.
         He is strong in his oath now.
720   Spare him.
OEDIPUS: Do you know what you ask?
CHORUS: Yes.
OEDIPUS: Tell me then.
CHORUS: He has been your friend before all men's eyes; do not cast him
725   away dishonoured on an obscure conjecture.
OEDIPUS: I would have you know that this request of yours
         really requests my death or banishment.
CHORUS: May the Sun God,[8] king of Gods, forbid! May I die without God's bless-
         ing, without friends' help, if I had any such thought. But my spirit is broken
730   by my unhappiness for my wasting country; and this would but add troubles
         amongst ourselves to the other troubles.
OEDIPUS: Well, let him go then—if I must die ten times for it,
         or be sent out dishonoured into exile.
         It is your lips that prayed for him I pitied,
735   not his; wherever he is, I shall hate him.
CREON: I see you sulk in yielding and you're dangerous
         when you are out of temper; natures like yours
         are justly heaviest for themselves to bear.
OEDIPUS: Leave me alone! Take yourself off, I tell you.
740 CREON: I'll go, you have not known me, but they have,

8. Helios, closely associated with Apollo, the god of light.

and they have known my innocence.

[*Exit.*]

CHORUS: Won't you take him inside, lady?

JOCASTA: Yes, when I've found out what was the matter.

CHORUS: There was some misconceived suspicion of a story, and on the other
    side the sting of injustice.   745

JOCASTA: So, on both sides?

CHORUS: Yes.

JOCASTA: What was the story?

CHORUS: I think it best, in the interests of the country, to leave it where it ended.

OEDIPUS: You see where you have ended, straight of judgment   750
    although you are, by softening my anger.

CHORUS: Sir, I have said before and I say again—be sure that I would have been
    proved a madman, bankrupt in sane council, if I should put you away, you
    who steered the country I love safely when she was crazed with troubles.
    God grant that now, too, you may prove a fortunate guide for us.   755

JOCASTA: Tell me, my lord, I beg of you, what was it
    that roused your anger so?

OEDIPUS: Yes, I will tell you.
    I honour you more than I honour them.
    It was Creon and the plots he laid against me.

JOCASTA: Tell me—if you can clearly tell the quarrel—

OEDIPUS: Creon says   760
    that I'm the murderer of Laius.

JOCASTA: Of his own knowledge or on information?

OEDIPUS: He sent this rascal prophet to me, since
    he keeps his own mouth clean of any guilt.

JOCASTA: Do not concern yourself about this matter;   765
    listen to me and learn that human beings
    have no part in the craft of prophecy.
    Of that I'll show you a short proof.
    There was an oracle once that came to Laius,—
    I will not say that it was Phoebus' own,   770
    but it was from his servants—and it told him
    that it was fate that he should die a victim
    at the hands of his own son, a son to be born
    of Laius and me. But, see now, he,
    the king, was killed by foreign highway robbers   775
    at a place where three roads meet—so goes the story;
    and for the son—before three days were out
    after his birth King Laius pierced his ankles
    and by the hands of others cast him forth
    upon a pathless hillside. So Apollo   780
    failed to fulfill his oracle to the son,
    that he should kill his father, and to Laius
    also proved false in that the thing he feared,
    death at his son's hands, never came to pass.

785   So clear in this case were the oracles,
         so clear and false. Give them no heed, I say;
         what God discovers need of, easily
         he shows to us himself.
OEDIPUS: O dear Jocasta,
         as I hear this from you, there comes upon me
790   a wandering of the soul—I could run mad.
JOCASTA: What trouble is it, that you turn again
         and speak like this?
OEDIPUS: I thought I heard you say
         that Laius was killed at a crossroads.
JOCASTA: Yes, that was how the story went and still
         that word goes round.
795 OEDIPUS: Where is this place, Jocasta,
         where he was murdered?
JOCASTA: Phocis is the country
         and the road splits there, one of two roads from Delphi,
         another comes from Daulia.
OEDIPUS: How long ago is this?
JOCASTA: The news came to the city just before
800   you became king and all men's eyes looked to you.
         What is it, Oedipus, that's in your mind?
OEDIPUS: What have you designed, O Zeus, to do with me?
JOCASTA: What is the thought that troubles your heart?
OEDIPUS: Don't ask me yet—tell me of Laius—
805   How did he look? How old or young was he?
JOCASTA: He was a tall man and his hair was grizzled
         already—nearly white—and in his form
         not unlike you.
OEDIPUS: O God, I think I have
         called curses on myself in ignorance.
810 JOCASTA: What do you mean? I am terrified
         when I look at you.
OEDIPUS: I have a deadly fear
         that the old seer had eyes. You'll show me more
         if you can tell me one more thing.
JOCASTA: I will.
         I'm frightened,—but if I can understand,
         I'll tell you all you ask.
815 OEDIPUS: How was his company?
         Had he few with him when he went this journey,
         or many servants, as would suit a prince?
JOCASTA: In all there were but five, and among them
         a herald; and one carriage for the king.
820 OEDIPUS: It's plain—it's plain—who was it told you this?
JOCASTA: The only servant that escaped safe home.
OEDIPUS: Is he at home now?
JOCASTA: No, when he came home again

and saw you king and Laius was dead,
he came to me and touched my hand and begged
that I should send him to the fields to be   825
my shepherd and so he might see the city
as far off as he might. So I
sent him away. He was an honest man,
as slaves go, and was worthy of far more
than what he asked of me.   830
OEDIPUS: O, how I wish that he could come back quickly!
JOCASTA: He can. Why is your heart so set on this?
OEDIPUS: O dear Jocasta, I am full of fears
that I have spoken far too much; and therefore
I wish to see this shepherd.
JOCASTA: He will come;   835
but, Oedipus, I think I'm worthy too
to know what it is that disquiets you.
OEDIPUS: It shall not be kept from you, since my mind
has gone so far with its forebodings. Whom
should I confide in rather than you, who is there   840
of more importance to me who have passed
through such a fortune?
Polybus was my father, king of Corinth,
and Merope, the Dorian, my mother.
I was held greatest of the citizens   845
in Corinth till a curious chance befell me
as I shall tell you—curious, indeed,
but hardly worth the store I set upon it.
There was a dinner and at it a man,
a drunken man, accused me in his drink   850
of being bastard. I was furious
but held my temper under for that day.
Next day I went and taxed my parents with it;
they took the insult very ill from him,
the drunken fellow who had uttered it.   855
So I was comforted for their part, but
still this thing rankled always, for the story
crept about widely. And I went at last
to Pytho, though my parents did not know.
But Phoebus sent me home again unhonoured   860
in what I came to learn, but he foretold
other and desperate horrors to befall me,
that I was fated to lie with my mother,
and show to daylight an accursed breed
which men would not endure, and I was doomed   865
to be murderer of the father that begot me.
When I heard this I fled, and in the days
that followed I would measure from the stars
the whereabouts of Corinth—yes, I fled

870   to somewhere where I should not see fulfilled
         the infamies told in that dreadful oracle.
         And as I journeyed I came to the place
         where, as you say, this king met with his death.
         Jocasta, I will tell you the whole truth.
875   When I was near the branching of the crossroads,
         going on foot, I was encountered by
         a herald and a carriage with a man in it,
         just as you tell me. He that led the way
         and the old man himself wanted to thrust me
880   out of the road by force. I became angry
         and struck the coachman who was pushing me.
         When the old man saw this he watched his moment,
         and as I passed he struck me from his carriage,
         full on the head with his two pointed goad.
885   But he was paid in full and presently
         my stick had struck him backwards from the car
         and he rolled out of it. And then I killed them
         all. If it happened there was any tie
         of kinship twixt this man and Laius,
890   who is then now more miserable than I,
         what man on earth so hated by the Gods,
         since neither citizen nor foreigner
         may welcome me at home or even greet me,
         but drive me out of doors? And it is I,
895   I and no other have so cursed myself.
         And I pollute the bed of him I killed
         by the hands that killed him. Was I not born evil?
         Am I not utterly unclean? I had to fly
         and in my banishment not even see
900   my kindred nor set foot in my own country,
         or otherwise my fate was to be yoked
         in marriage with my mother and kill my father,
         Polybus who begot me and had reared me.
         Would not one rightly judge and say that on me
905   these things were sent by some malignant God?
         O no, no, no—O holy majesty
         of God on high, may I not see that day!
         May I be gone out of men's sight before
         I see the deadly taint of this disaster
910   come upon me.
      CHORUS: Sir, we too fear these things. But until you see this man face to face
         and hear his story, hope.
      OEDIPUS: Yes, I have just this much of hope—to wait until the herdsman comes.
      JOCASTA: And when he comes, what do you want with him?
915   OEDIPUS: I'll tell you; if I find that his story is the same as yours, I at least will
         be clear of this guilt.
      JOCASTA: Why what so particularly did you learn from my story?

OEDIPUS: You said that he spoke of highway *robbers* who killed Laius. Now if he
uses the same number, it was not I who killed him. One man cannot be the
same as many. But if he speaks of a man travelling alone, then clearly the 920
burden of the guilt inclines towards me.

JOCASTA: Be sure, at least, that this was how he told the story. He cannot unsay
it now, for everyone in the city heard it—not I alone. But, Oedipus, even if he
diverges from what he said then, he shall never prove that the murder of
Laius squares rightly with the prophecy—for Loxias declared that the king 925
should be killed by his own son. And that poor creature did not kill him
surely,—for he died himself first. So as far as prophecy goes, henceforward I
shall not look to the right hand or the left.

OEDIPUS: Right. But yet, send someone for the peasant to bring him here; do not
neglect it.   930

JOCASTA: I will send quickly. Now let me go indoors. I will do nothing except
what pleases you.

    [*Exeunt.*]

CHORUS: [*Strophe.*] May destiny ever find me
    pious in word and deed
    prescribed by the laws that live on high: 935
    laws begotten in the clear air of heaven,
    whose only father is Olympus;
    no mortal nature brought them to birth,
    no forgetfulness shall lull them to sleep;
    for God is great in them and grows not old.   940

[*Antistrophe.*]

Insolence breeds the tyrant, insolence
if it is glutted with a surfeit, unseasonable, unprofitable,
climbs to the roof-top and plunges
sheer down to the ruin that must be,
and there its feet are no service.   945
But I pray that the God may never
abolish the eager ambition that profits the state.
For I shall never cease to hold the God as our protector.

[*Strophe.*]

If a man walks with haughtiness
of hand or word and gives no heed   950
to Justice and the shrines of Gods
despises—may an evil doom
smite him for his ill-starred pride of heart!—
if he reaps gains without justice
and will not hold from impiety   955
and his fingers itch for untouchable things.
When such things are done, what man shall contrive
to shield his soul from the shafts of the God?
When such deeds are held in honour,

960   why should I honour the Gods in the dance?

[*Antistrophe.*]

No longer to the holy place,
to the navel of earth I'll go
to worship, nor to Abae
nor to Olympia,[9]
965   unless the oracles are proved to fit,
for all men's hands to point at.
O Zeus, if you are rightly called
the sovereign lord, all-mastering,
let this not escape you nor your ever-living power!
970   The oracles concerning Laius
are old and dim and men regard them not.
Apollo is nowhere clear in honour; God's service perishes.

[*Enter* JOCASTA, *carrying garlands.*]

JOCASTA: Princes of the land, I have had the thought to go
to the Gods' temples, bringing in my hand
975   garlands and gifts of incense, as you see.
For Oedipus excites himself too much
at every sort of trouble, not conjecturing,
like a man of sense, what will be from what was,
but he is always at the speaker's mercy,
980   when he speaks terrors. I can do no good
by my advice, and so I came as suppliant
to you, Lycaean Apollo, who are nearest.
These are the symbols of my prayer and this
my prayer: grant us escape free of the curse.
985   Now when we look to him we are all afraid;
he's pilot of our ship and he is frightened.

[*Enter* MESSENGER.]

MESSENGER: Might I learn from you, sirs, where is the house of Oedipus? Or
best of all, if you know, where is the king himself?
CHORUS: This is his house and he is within doors. This lady is his wife and
990   mother of his children.
MESSENGER: God bless you, lady, and God bless your household! God bless
Oedipus' noble wife!
JOCASTA: God bless you, sir, for your kind greeting! What do you want of us that
you have come here? What have you to tell us?
995 MESSENGER: Good news, lady. Good for your house and for your husband.
JOCASTA: What is your news? Who sent you to us?
MESSENGER: I come from Corinth and the news I bring will give you pleasure.
Perhaps a little pain too.

---

9. Mountain in Greece said to be the home of Zeus and the other principal gods. *Abae:* site of one of
Apollo's oracles.

JOCASTA: What is this news of double meaning?

MESSENGER: The people of the Isthmus[1] will choose Oedipus to be their king.   1000
 That is the rumour there.

JOCASTA: But isn't their king still old Polybus?

MESSENGER: No. He is in his grave. Death has got him.

JOCASTA: Is that the truth? Is Oedipus' father dead?

MESSENGER: May I die myself if it be otherwise!   1005

JOCASTA: [To a SERVANT.] Be quick and run to the King with the news! O oracles
 of the Gods, where are you now? It was from this man Oedipus fled, lest he
 should be his murderer! And now he is dead, in the course of nature, and not
 killed by Oedipus.

  [Enter OEDIPUS.]

OEDIPUS: Dearest Jocasta, why have you sent for me?   1010

JOCASTA: Listen to this man and when you hear reflect what is the outcome of
 the holy oracles of the Gods.

OEDIPUS: Who is he? What is his message for me?

JOCASTA: He is from Corinth and he tells us that your father Polybus is dead and
 gone.   1015

OEDIPUS: What's this you say, sir? Tell me yourself.

MESSENGER: Since this is the first matter you want clearly told: Polybus has
 gone down to death. You may be sure of it.

OEDIPUS: By treachery or sickness?

MESSENGER: A small thing will put old bodies asleep.   1020

OEDIPUS: So he died of sickness, it seems,—poor old man!

MESSENGER: Yes, and of age—the long years he had measured.

OEDIPUS: Ha! Ha! O dear Jocasta, why should one
 look to the Pythian hearth?[2] Why should one look
 to the birds screaming overhead? They prophesied   1025
 that I should kill my father! But he's dead,
 and hidden deep in earth, and I stand here
 who never laid a hand on spear against him,—
 unless perhaps he died of longing for me,
 and thus I am his murderer. But they,   1030
 the oracles, as they stand—he's taken them
 away with him, they're dead as he himself is,
 and worthless.

JOCASTA: That I told you before now.

OEDIPUS: You did, but I was misled by my fear.

JOCASTA: Then lay no more of them to heart, not one.   1035

OEDIPUS: But surely I must fear my mother's bed?

JOCASTA: Why should man fear since chance is all in all
 for him, and he can clearly foreknow nothing?
 Best to live lightly, as one can, unthinkingly.

1. That is, Corinth, the city-state located on the isthmus connecting the Peloponnesian peninsula
with mainland Greece.
2. Delphi.

1040   As to your mother's marriage bed,—don't fear it.
       Before this, in dreams too, as well as oracles,
       many a man has lain with his own mother.
       But he to whom such things are nothing bears
       his life most easily.
1045   OEDIPUS: All that you say would be said perfectly
       if she were dead; but since she lives I must
       still fear, although you talk so well, Jocasta.
       JOCASTA: Still in your father's death there's light of comfort?
       OEDIPUS: Great light of comfort; but I fear the living.
1050   MESSENGER: Who is the woman that makes you afraid?
       OEDIPUS: Merope, old man, Polybus' wife.
       MESSENGER: What about her frightens the queen and you?
       OEDIPUS: A terrible oracle, stranger, from the Gods.
       MESSENGER: Can it be told? Or does the sacred law
1055   forbid another to have knowledge of it?
       OEDIPUS: O no! Once on a time Loxias said
       that I should lie with my own mother and
       take on my hands the blood of my own father.
       And so for these long years I've lived away
1060   from Corinth; it has been to my great happiness;
       but yet it's sweet to see the face of parents.
       MESSENGER: This was the fear which drove you out of Corinth?
       OEDIPUS: Old man, I did not wish to kill my father.
       MESSENGER: Why should I not free you from this fear, sir,
1065   since I have come to you in all goodwill?
       OEDIPUS: You would not find me thankless if you did.
       MESSENGER: Why, it was just for this I brought the news,—
       to earn your thanks when you had come safe home.
       OEDIPUS: No, I will never come near my parents.
       MESSENGER: Son,
1070   it's very plain you don't know what you're doing.
       OEDIPUS: What do you mean, old man? For God's sake, tell me.
       MESSENGER: If your homecoming is checked by fears like these.
       OEDIPUS: Yes, I'm afraid that Phoebus may prove right.
       MESSENGER: The murder and the incest?
       OEDIPUS: Yes, old man;
       that is my constant terror.
1075   MESSENGER: Do you know
       that all your fears are empty?
       OEDIPUS: How is that,
       if they are father and mother and I their son?
       MESSENGER: Because Polybus was no kin to you in blood.
       OEDIPUS: What, was not Polybus my father?
       MESSENGER: No more than I but just so much.
1080   OEDIPUS: How can
       my father be my father as much as one
       that's nothing to me?

MESSENGER: Neither he nor I
    begat you.
OEDIPUS: Why then did he call me son?
MESSENGER: A gift he took you from these hands of mine.
OEDIPUS: Did he love so much what he took from another's hand?   1085
MESSENGER: His childlessness before persuaded him.
OEDIPUS: Was I a child you bought or found when I
    was given to him?
MESSENGER: On Cithaeron's slopes
    in the twisting thickets you were found.
OEDIPUS: And why
    were you a traveller in those parts?
MESSENGER: I was   1090
    in charge of mountain flocks.
OEDIPUS: You were a shepherd?
    A hireling vagrant?
MESSENGER: Yes, but at least at that time
    the man that saved your life, son.
OEDIPUS: What ailed me when you took me in your arms?
MESSENGER: In that your ankles should be witnesses.   1095
OEDIPUS: Why do you speak of that old pain?
MESSENGER: I loosed you;
    the tendons of your feet were pierced and fettered,—
OEDIPUS: My swaddling clothes brought me a rare disgrace.
MESSENGER: So that from this you're called your present name.[3]
OEDIPUS: Was this my father's doing or my mother's?   1100
    For God's sake, tell me.
MESSENGER: I don't know, but he
    who gave you to me has more knowledge than I.
OEDIPUS: You yourself did not find me then? You took me
    from someone else?
MESSENGER: Yes, from another shepherd.
OEDIPUS: Who was he? Do you know him well enough   1105
    to tell?
MESSENGER: He was called Laius' man.
OEDIPUS: You mean the king who reigned here in the old days?
MESSENGER: Yes, he was that man's shepherd.
OEDIPUS: Is he alive
    still, so that I could see him?
MESSENGER: You who live here
    would know that best.
OEDIPUS: Do any of you here   1110
    know of this shepherd whom he speaks about
    in town or in the fields? Tell me. It's time
    that this was found out once for all.
CHORUS: I think he is none other than the peasant

---

3. *Oedipus* literally means "swollen foot" (cf. lines 777–80).

1115   whom you have sought to see already; but
             Jocasta here can tell us best of that.
         OEDIPUS: Jocasta, do you know about this man
             whom we have sent for? Is he the man he mentions?
         JOCASTA: Why ask of whom he spoke? Don't give it heed;
1120   nor try to keep in mind what has been said.
             It will be wasted labour.
         OEDIPUS: With such clues
             I could not fail to bring my birth to light.
         JOCASTA: I beg you—do not hunt this out—I beg you,
             if you have any care for your own life.
             What I am suffering is enough.
1125   OEDIPUS: Keep up
             your heart, Jocasta. Though I'm proved a slave,
             thrice slave, and though my mother is thrice slave,
             you'll not be shown to be of lowly lineage.
         JOCASTA: O be persuaded by me, I entreat you;
1130   do not do this.
         OEDIPUS: I will not be persuaded to let be
             the chance of finding out the whole thing clearly.
         JOCASTA: It is because I wish you well that I
             give you this counsel—and it's the best counsel.
1135   OEDIPUS: Then the best counsel vexes me, and has
             for some while since.
         JOCASTA: O Oedipus, God help you!
             God keep you from the knowledge of who you are!
         OEDIPUS: Here, someone, go and fetch the shepherd for me;
             and let her find her joy in her rich family!
1140   JOCASTA: O Oedipus, unhappy Oedipus!
             that is all I can call you, and the last thing
             that I shall ever call you.

             [Exit.]

         CHORUS: Why has the queen gone, Oedipus, in wild
             grief rushing from us? I am afraid that trouble
1145   will break out of this silence.
         OEDIPUS: Break out what will! I at least shall be
             willing to see my ancestry, though humble.
             Perhaps she is ashamed of my low birth,
             for she has all a woman's high-flown pride.
1150   But I account myself a child of Fortune,
             beneficent Fortune, and I shall not be
             dishonoured. She's the mother from whom I spring;
             the months, my brothers, marked me, now as small,
             and now again as mighty. Such is my breeding,
1155   and I shall never prove so false to it,
             as not to find the secret of my birth.

CHORUS: [*Strophe.*] If I am a prophet and wise of heart
    you shall not fail, Cithaeron,
    by the limitless sky, you shall not!—
    to know at tomorrow's full moon   1160
    that Oedipus honours you,
    as native to him and mother and nurse at once;
    and that you are honoured in dancing by us, as finding favour in sight of
      our king.
    Apollo, to whom we cry, find these things pleasing!

    [*Antistrophe.*]

    Who was it bore you, child? One of   1165
    the long-lived nymphs who lay with Pan[4]—
    the father who treads the hills?
    Or was she a bride of Loxias, your mother? The grassy slopes
    are all of them dear to him. Or perhaps Cyllene's[5] king
    or the Bacchants' God[6] that lives on the tops   1170
    of the hills received you a gift from some
    one of the Helicon Nymphs,[7] with whom he mostly plays?

    [*Enter an* OLD MAN, *led by* OEDIPUS' *servants.*]

OEDIPUS: If someone like myself who never met him
    may make a guess,—I think this is the herdsman,
    whom we were seeking. His old age is consonant   1175
    with the other. And besides, the men who bring him
    I recognize as my own servants. You
    perhaps may better me in knowledge since
    you've seen the man before.
CHORUS: You can be sure
    I recognize him. For if Laius   1180
    had ever an honest shepherd, this was he.
OEDIPUS: You, sir, from Corinth, I must ask you first,
    is this the man you spoke of?
MESSENGER: This is he
    before your eyes.
OEDIPUS: Old man, look here at me
    and tell me what I ask you. Were you ever   1185
    a servant of King Laius?
HERDSMAN: I was,—
    no slave he bought but reared in his own house.
OEDIPUS: What did you do as work? How did you live?
HERDSMAN: Most of my life was spent among the flocks.
OEDIPUS: In what part of the country did you live?   1190

4. God of nature; half man, half goat.
5. Mountain reputed to be the birthplace of Hermes, the messenger god.
6. Dionysus.
7. The Muses, nine sister goddesses who presided over poetry, music, and the arts.

HERDSMAN: Cithaeron and the places near to it.

OEDIPUS: And somewhere there perhaps you knew this man?

HERDSMAN: What was his occupation? Who?

OEDIPUS: This man here,
    have you had any dealings with him?

HERDSMAN: No—
1195   not such that I can quickly call to mind.

MESSENGER: That is no wonder, master. But I'll make him remember what he
    does not know. For I know, that he well knows the country of Cithaeron, how
    he with two flocks, I with one kept company for three years—each year half
    a year—from spring till autumn time and then when winter came I drove my
1200   flocks to our fold home again and he to Laius' steadings. Well—am I right or
    not in what I said we did?

HERDSMAN: You're right—although it's a long time ago.

MESSENGER: Do you remember giving me a child
    to bring up as my foster child?

HERDSMAN: What's this?
    Why do you ask this question?

1205 MESSENGER: Look old man,
    here he is—here's the man who was that child!

HERDSMAN: Death take you! Won't you hold your tongue?

OEDIPUS: No, no,
    do not find fault with him, old man. Your words
    are more at fault than his.

HERDSMAN: O best of masters,
    how do I give offense?

1210 OEDIPUS: When you refuse
    to speak about the child of whom he asks you.

HERDSMAN: He speaks out of his ignorance, without meaning.

OEDIPUS: If you'll not talk to gratify me, you
    will talk with pain to urge you.

HERDSMAN: O please, sir,
    don't hurt an old man, sir.

1215 OEDIPUS: [*To the* SERVANTS.]   Here, one of you,
    twist his hands behind him.

HERDSMAN: Why, God help me, why?
    What do you want to know?

OEDIPUS: You gave a child
    to him,—the child he asked you of?

HERDSMAN: I did.
    I wish I'd died the day I did.

OEDIPUS: You will
    unless you tell me truly.

1220 HERDSMAN: And I'll die
    far worse if I should tell you.

OEDIPUS: This fellow
    is bent on more delays, as it would seem.

HERDSMAN: O no, no! I have told you that I gave it.

OEDIPUS: Where did you get this child from? Was it your own or did you get it
    from another?

HERDSMAN: Not   1225
    my own at all; I had it from someone.

OEDIPUS: One of these citizens? or from what house?

HERDSMAN: O master, please—I beg you, master, please
    don't ask me more.

OEDIPUS: You're a dead man if I
    ask you again.

HERDSMAN: It was one of the children   1230
    of Laius.

OEDIPUS: A slave? Or born in wedlock?

HERDSMAN: O God, I am on the brink of frightful speech.

OEDIPUS: And I of frightful hearing. But I must hear.

HERDSMAN: The child was called his child; but she within,
    your wife would tell you best how all this was.   1235

OEDIPUS: *She* gave it to you?

HERDSMAN: Yes, she did, my lord.

OEDIPUS: To do what with it?

HERDSMAN: Make away with it.

OEDIPUS: She was so hard—its mother?

HERDSMAN: Aye, through fear
    of evil oracles.

OEDIPUS: Which?

HERDSMAN: They said that he
    should kill his parents.

OEDIPUS: How was it that you   1240
    gave it away to this old man?

HERDSMAN: O master,
    I pitied it, and thought that I could send it
    off to another country and this man
    was from another country. But he saved it
    for the most terrible troubles. If you are   1245
    the man he says you are, you're bred to misery.

OEDIPUS: O, O, O, they will all come,
    all come out clearly! Light of the sun, let me
    look upon you no more after today!
    I who first saw the light bred of a match   1250
    accursed, and accursed in my living
    with them I lived with, cursed in my killing.

    [*Exeunt all but the* CHORUS.]

CHORUS: [*Strophe.*] O generations of men, how I
    count you as equal with those who live
    not at all!   1255
    What man, what man on earth wins more
    of happiness than a seeming
    and after that turning away?

Oedipus, you are my pattern of this,
1260　Oedipus, you and your fate!
Luckless Oedipus, whom of all men
I envy not at all.

[*Antistrophe.*]

In as much as he shot his bolt
beyond the others and won the prize
1265　of happiness complete—
O Zeus—and killed and reduced to nought
the hooked taloned maid of the riddling speech,[8]
standing a tower against death for my land:
hence he was called my king and hence
1270　was honoured the highest of all
honours; and hence he ruled
in the great city of Thebes.

[*Strophe.*]

But now whose tale is more miserable?
Who is there lives with a savager fate?
1275　Whose troubles so reverse his life as his?
O Oedipus, the famous prince
for whom a great haven
the same both as father and son
sufficed for generation,
1280　how, O how, have the furrows ploughed
by your father endured to bear you, poor wretch,
and hold their peace so long?

[*Antistrophe.*]

Time who sees all has found you out
against your will; judges your marriage accursed,
1285　begetter and begot at one in it.

O child of Laius,
would I had never seen you.
I weep for you and cry
a dirge of lamentation.

1290　To speak directly, I drew my breath
from you at the first and so now I lull
my mouth to sleep with your name.

[*Enter a* SECOND MESSENGER.]

SECOND MESSENGER: O Princes always honoured by our country,
　　what deeds you'll hear of and what horrors see,

8. The Sphinx, who killed herself when Oedipus was the first to give a correct answer to her riddle:
"What walks on four feet in the morning, on two at noon, and on three in the evening?" (cf. line 41n.).

what grief you'll feel, if you as true born Thebans   1295
care for the house of Labdacus' sons.[9]
Phasis nor Ister[1] cannot purge this house,
I think, with all their streams, such things
it hides, such evils shortly will bring forth
into the light, whether they will or not;   1300
and troubles hurt the most
when they prove self-inflicted.
CHORUS: What we had known before did not fall short
of bitter groaning's worth; what's more to tell?
SECOND MESSENGER: Shortest to hear and tell—our glorious queen   1305
Jocasta's dead.
CHORUS: Unhappy woman! How?
SECOND MESSENGER: By her own hand. The worst of what was done
you cannot know. You did not see the sight.
Yet in so far as I remember it
you'll hear the end of our unlucky queen.   1310
When she came raging into the house she went
straight to her marriage bed, tearing her hair
with both her hands, and crying upon Laius
long dead—Do you remember, Laius,
that night long past which bred a child for us   1315
to send you to your death and leave
a mother making children with her son?
And then she groaned and cursed the bed in which
she brought forth husband by her husband, children
by her own child, an infamous double bond.   1320
How after that she died I do not know,—
for Oedipus distracted us from seeing.
He burst upon us shouting and we looked
to him as he paced frantically around,
begging us always: Give me a sword, I say,   1325
to find this wife no wife, this mother's womb,
this field of double sowing whence I sprang
and where I sowed my children! As he raved
some god showed him the way—none of us there.
Bellowing terribly and led by some   1330
invisible guide he rushed on the two doors,—
wrenching the hollow bolts out of their sockets,
he charged inside. There, there, we saw his wife
hanging, the twisted rope around her neck.
When he saw her, he cried out fearfully   1335
and cut the dangling noose. Then, as she lay,
poor woman, on the ground, what happened after,
was terrible to see. He tore the brooches—

9. Labdacus, king of Thebes, was father of Laïus and grandfather of Oedipus.
1. Phasis and Ister are rivers near Thebes.

the gold chased[2] brooches fastening her robe—
1340   away from her and lifting them up high
dashed them on his own eyeballs, shrieking out
such things as: they will never see the crime
I have committed or had done upon me!
Dark eyes, now in the days to come look on
1345   forbidden faces, do not recognize
those whom you long for—with such imprecations
he struck his eyes again and yet again
with the brooches. And the bleeding eyeballs gushed
and stained his beard—no sluggish oozing drops
1350   but a black rain and bloody hail poured down.
So it has broken—and not on one head
but troubles mixed for husband and for wife.
The fortune of the days gone by was true
good fortune—but today groans and destruction
1355   and death and shame—of all ills can be named
not one is missing.
CHORUS: Is he now in any ease from pain?
SECOND MESSENGER: He shouts
for someone to unbar the doors and show him
to all the men of Thebes, his father's killer,
1360   his mother's—no I cannot say the word,
it is unholy—for he'll cast himself,
out of the land, he says, and not remain
to bring a curse upon his house, the curse
he called upon it in his proclamation. But
1365   he wants for strength, aye, and someone to guide him;
his sickness is too great to bear. You, too,
will be shown that. The bolts are opening.
Soon you will see a sight to waken pity
even in the horror of it.

[*Enter the blinded* OEDIPUS.]

1370   CHORUS: This is a terrible sight for men to see!
I never found a worse!
Poor wretch, what madness came upon you!
What evil spirit leaped upon your life
to your ill-luck—a leap beyond man's strength!
1375   Indeed I pity you, but I cannot
look at you, though there's much I want to ask
and much to learn and much to see.
I shudder at the sight of you.
OEDIPUS: O, O,
1380   where am I going? Where is my voice
borne on the wind to and fro?

2. Decorated with ornamental indentations.

Spirit, how far have you sprung?

CHORUS: To a terrible place whereof men's ears
    may not hear, nor their eyes behold it.

OEDIPUS: Darkness!   1385
    Horror of darkness enfolding, resistless, unspeakable visitant sped by an
        ill wind in haste!
    Madness and stabbing pain and memory
    of evil deeds I have done!

CHORUS: In such misfortunes it's no wonder
    if double weighs the burden of your grief.   1390

OEDIPUS: My friend,
    you are the only one steadfast, the only one that attends on me;
    you still stay nursing the blind man.
    Your care is not unnoticed. I can know
    your voice, although this darkness is my world.   1395

CHORUS: Doer of dreadful deeds, how did you dare
    so far to do despite to your own eyes?
    what spirit urged you to it?

OEDIPUS: It was Apollo, friends, Apollo,
    that brought this bitter bitterness, my sorrows to completion.   1400
    But the hand that struck me
    was none but my own.
    Why should I see
    whose vision showed me nothing sweet to see?

CHORUS: These things are as you say.   1405

OEDIPUS: What can I see to love?
    What greeting can touch my ears with joy?
    Take me away, and haste—to a place out of the way!
    Take me away, my friends, the greatly miserable,
    the most accursed, whom God too hates   1410
    above all men on earth!

CHORUS: Unhappy in your mind and your misfortune,
    would I had never known you!

OEDIPUS: Curse on the man who took
    the cruel bonds from off my legs, as I lay in the field.   1415
    He stole me from death and saved me,
    no kindly service.
    Had I died then
    I would not be so burdensome to friends.

CHORUS: I, too, could have wished it had been so.   1420

OEDIPUS: Then I would not have come
    to kill my father and marry my mother infamously.
    Now I am godless and child of impurity,
    begetter in the same seed that created my wretched self.
    If there is any ill worse than ill,   1425
    that is the lot of Oedipus.

CHORUS: I cannot say your remedy was good;
    you would be better dead than blind and living.

OEDIPUS: What I have done here was best done—don't tell me
1430   otherwise, do not give me further counsel.
          I do not know with what eyes I could look
          upon my father when I die and go
          under the earth, nor yet my wretched mother—
          those two to whom I have done things deserving
1435   worse punishment than hanging. Would the sight
          of children, bred as mine are, gladden me?
          No, not these eyes, never. And my city,
          its towers and sacred places of the Gods,
          of these I robbed my miserable self
1440   when I commanded all to drive *him* out,
          the criminal since proved by God impure
          and of the race of Laius.
          To this guilt I bore witness against myself—
          with what eyes shall I look upon my people?
1445   No. If there were a means to choke the fountain
          of hearing I would not have stayed my hand
          from locking up my miserable carcase,
          seeing and hearing nothing; it is sweet
          to keep our thoughts out of the range of hurt.

1450   Cithaeron, why did you receive me? why
          having received me did you not kill me straight?
          And so I had not shown to men my birth.

          O Polybus and Corinth and the house,
          the old house that I used to call my father's—
1455   what fairness you were nurse to, and what foulness
          festered beneath! Now I am found to be
          a sinner and a son of sinners. Crossroads,
          and hidden glade, oak and the narrow way
          at the crossroads, that drank my father's blood
1460   offered you by my hands, do you remember
          still what I did as you looked on, and what
          I did when I came here? O marriage, marriage!
          you bred me and again when you had bred
          bred children of your child and showed to men
1465   brides, wives and mothers and the foulest deeds
          that can be in this world of ours.

          Come—it's unfit to say what is unfit
          to do.—I beg of you in God's name hide me
          somewhere outside your country, yes, or kill me,
1470   or throw me into the sea, to be forever
          out of your sight. Approach and deign to touch me
          for all my wretchedness, and do not fear.
          No man but I can bear my evil doom.
CHORUS: Here Creon comes in fit time to perform
1475   or give advice in what you ask of us.

Creon is left sole ruler in your stead.
OEDIPUS: Creon! Creon! What shall I say to him?
    How can I justly hope that he will trust me?
    In what is past I have been proved towards him
    an utter liar.

[*Enter* CREON.]

CREON: Oedipus, I've come   1480
    not so that I might laugh at you nor taunt you
    with evil of the past. But if you still
    are without shame before the face of men
    reverence at least the flame that gives all life,
    our Lord the Sun, and do not show unveiled   1485
    to him pollution such that neither land
    nor holy rain nor light of day can welcome.

[*To a* SERVANT.]

    Be quick and take him in. It is most decent
    that only kin should see and hear the troubles
    of kin.
OEDIPUS: I beg you, since you've torn me from   1490
    my dreadful expectations and have come
    in a most noble spirit to a man
    that has used you vilely—do a thing for me.
    I shall speak for your own good, not for my own.
CREON: What do you need that you would ask of me?   1495
OEDIPUS: Drive me from here with all the speed you can
    to where I may not hear a human voice.
CREON: Be sure, I would have done this had not I
    wished first of all to learn from the God the course
    of action I should follow.
OEDIPUS: But his word   1500
    has been quite clear to let the parricide,
    the sinner, die.
CREON: Yes, that indeed was said.
    But in the present need we had best discover
    what we should do.
OEDIPUS: And will you ask about
    a man so wretched?
CREON: Now even you will trust   1505
    the God.
OEDIPUS: So. I command you—and will beseech you—
    to her that lies inside that house give burial
    as you would have it; she is yours and rightly
    you will perform the rites for her. For me—
    never let this my father's city have me   1510
    living a dweller in it. Leave me live
    in the mountains where Cithaeron is, that's called
    my mountain, which my mother and my father

while they were living would have made my tomb.
1515 So I may die by their decree who sought
indeed to kill me. Yet I know this much:
no sickness and no other thing will kill me.
I would not have been saved from death if not
for some strange evil fate. Well, let my fate
go where it will.
1520 Creon, you need not care
about my sons; they're men and so wherever
they are, they will not lack a livelihood.
But my two girls—so sad and pitiful—
whose table never stood apart from mine,
1525 and everything I touched they always shared—
O Creon, have a thought for them! And most
I wish that you might suffer me to touch them
and sorrow with them.

[*Enter* ANTIGONE *and* ISMENE, OEDIPUS' *two daughters.*]

O my lord! O true noble Creon! Can I
1530 really be touching them, as when I saw?
What shall I say?
Yes, I can hear them sobbing—my two darlings!
and Creon has had pity and has sent me
what I loved most?
1535 Am I right?
CREON: You're right: it was I gave you this
because I knew from old days how you loved them
as I see now.
OEDIPUS: God bless you for it, Creon,
and may God guard you better on your road
than he did me!
1540 O children,
where are you? Come here, come to my hands,
a brother's hands which turned your father's eyes,
those bright eyes you knew once, to what you see,
a father seeing nothing, knowing nothing,
1545 begetting you from his own source of life.
I weep for you—I cannot see your faces—
I weep when I think of the bitterness
there will be in your lives, how you must live
before the world. At what assemblages
1550 of citizens will you make one? to what
gay company will you go and not come home
in tears instead of sharing in the holiday?
And when you're ripe for marriage, who will he be,
the man who'll risk to take such infamy
1555 as shall cling to my children, to bring hurt
on them and those that marry with them? What
curse is not there? "Your father killed his father

and sowed the seed where he had sprung himself
and begot you out of the womb that held him."
These insults you will hear. Then who will marry you? 1560
No one, my children; clearly you are doomed
to waste away in barrenness unmarried.
Son of Menoeceus,[3] since you are all the father
left these two girls, and we, their parents, both
are dead to them—do not allow them wander 1565
like beggars, poor and husbandless.
They are of your own blood.
And do not make them equal with myself
in wretchedness; for you can see them now
so young, so utterly alone, save for you only. 1570
Touch my hand, noble Creon, and say yes.
If you were older, children, and were wiser,
there's much advice I'd give you. But as it is,
let this be what you pray: give me a life
wherever there is opportunity 1575
to live, and better life than was my father's.

CREON: Your tears have had enough of scope; now go within the house.

OEDIPUS: I must obey, though bitter of heart.

CREON: In season, all is good.

OEDIPUS: Do you know on what conditions I obey?

CREON: You tell me them, 1580
    and I shall know them when I hear.

OEDIPUS: That you shall send me out
    to live away from Thebes.

CREON: That gift you must ask of the Gods.

OEDIPUS: But I'm now hated by the Gods.

CREON: So quickly you'll obtain your prayer.

OEDIPUS: You consent then?

CREON: What I do not mean, I do not use to say.

OEDIPUS: Now lead me away from here.

CREON: Let go the children, then, and come. 1585

OEDIPUS: Do not take them from me.

CREON: Do not seek to be master in everything,
    for the things you mastered did not follow you throughout your life.

[As CREON and OEDIPUS go out.]

CHORUS: You that live in my ancestral Thebes, behold this Oedipus,—
    him who knew the famous riddles and was a man most masterful;
    not a citizen who did not look with envy on his lot— 1590
    see him now and see the breakers of misfortune swallow him!
    Look upon that last day always. Count no mortal happy till
    he has passed the final limit of his life secure from pain.

                                        c. 429 BCE

3. Father of Creon and Jocasta.

OSCAR WILDE

(1854–1900)

The Importance of Being Earnest

Born and raised in Dublin, Ireland, Oscar Wilde studied classical languages at Trinity College and took his degree from the University of Oxford in 1878. While at Oxford, he was captivated by the aesthetic theories of John Ruskin and Walter Pater. Upon graduation, he moved to London to write, soon becoming both a much-quoted wit, famous for his epigrams, and the most visible exponent of the "art for art's sake" movement. Emphasizing aesthetics over social and moral "utility" or usefulness, artistic form over content, and studied artfulness over naturalism, that movement upended conventional Victorian thinking and values. So, too, did Wilde's deliberately outlandish public persona and much of his writing. That writing includes criticism, poetry, and fiction, most notably the novel *The Picture of Dorian Gray* (1891). However, Wilde achieved his greatest success as a comic dramatist, with clever, witty plays such as *Lady Windermere's Fan* (1892), *A Woman of No Importance* (1893), and his masterpiece *The Importance of Being Earnest* (1895). At the height of his career, Wilde was accused of homosexual acts by his lover's father, the marquess of Queensbury; Wilde sued for libel, lost the case, and was imprisoned for two years, a ruinous experience that inspired his best-known poem, *The Ballad of Reading Gaol* (1898). Upon his release, Wilde emigrated to France under an assumed name, dying there three years later. "In this world," he wrote, "there are only two tragedies. One is not getting what one wants, and the other is getting it."

CHARACTERS

ALGERNON MONCRIEFF
LANE
ERNEST WORTHING
LADY AUGUSTA BRACKNELL
GWENDOLEN FAIRFAX

MISS PRISM
CECILY CARDEW
CANON CHASUBLE
MERRIMAN

ACT I

SCENE: *Morning room in* ALGERNON's *flat in Half-Moon Street.*[1]
The room is luxuriously and artistically furnished. The sound of a piano is heard in the adjoining room.

[LANE *is arranging afternoon tea on the table, and after the music has ceased,* ALGERNON *enters.*]

ALGERNON: Did you hear what I was playing, Lane?

---

1. Like many of the addresses in the play, Half-Moon Street is in Mayfair, an exclusive section of London. It runs north from Piccadilly near Hyde Park.

Rupert Everett as Algernon, Judi Dench as Lady Bracknell, and Reese Witherspoon as Cecily in the 2002 film adaptation of *The Importance of Being Earnest*

LANE: I didn't think it polite to listen, sir.

ALGERNON: I'm sorry for that, for your sake. I don't play accurately—anyone can play accurately—but I play with wonderful expression. As far as the piano is concerned, sentiment is my forte. I keep science for Life.

LANE: Yes, sir.

ALGERNON: And, speaking of the science of Life, have you got the cucumber sandwiches cut for Lady Bracknell?

LANE: Yes, sir. [*Hands them on a salver.*]

ALGERNON: [*Inspects them, takes two, and sits down on the sofa.*] Oh! . . . by the way, Lane, I see from your book that on Thursday night, when Lord Shoreham and Mr. Worthing were dining with me, eight bottles of champagne are entered as having been consumed.

LANE: Yes, sir; eight bottles and a pint.

ALGERNON: Why is it that at a bachelor's establishment the servants invariably drink the champagne? I ask merely for information.

LANE: I attribute it to the superior quality of the wine, sir. I have often observed that in married households the champagne is rarely of a first-rate brand.

ALGERNON: Good heavens! Is marriage so demoralizing as that?

LANE: I believe it *is* a very pleasant state, sir. I have had very little experience of it myself up to the present. I have only been married once. That was in consequence of a misunderstanding between myself and a young person.

ALGERNON: [*Languidly.*] I don't know that I am much interested in your family life, Lane.

LANE: No, sir; it is not a very interesting subject. I never think of it myself.

ALGERNON: Very natural, I am sure. That will do, Lane, thank you.

LANE: Thank you, sir. [LANE *goes out.*]

ALGERNON: Lane's views on marriage seem somewhat lax. Really, if the lower orders don't set us a good example, what on earth is the use of them? They seem, as a class, to have absolutely no sense of moral responsibility.

[*Enter* LANE.]

LANE: Mr. Ernest Worthing.

[*Enter* JACK. LANE *goes out.*]

ALGERNON: How are you, my dear Ernest? What brings you up to town?

JACK: Oh, pleasure, pleasure! What else should bring one anywhere? Eating as usual, I see, Algy!

ALGERNON: [*Stiffly.*] I believe it is customary in good society to take some slight refreshment at five o'clock. Where have you been since last Thursday?

JACK: [*Sitting down on the sofa.*] In the country.

ALGERNON: What on earth do you do there?

JACK: [*Pulling off his gloves.*] When one is in town one amuses oneself. When one is in the country one amuses other people. It is excessively boring.

ALGERNON: And who are the people you amuse?

JACK: [*Airily.*] Oh, neighbors, neighbors.

ALGERNON: Got nice neighbors in your part of Shropshire?[2]

JACK: Perfectly horrid! Never speak to one of them.

ALGERNON: How immensely you must amuse them! [*Goes over and takes sandwich.*] By the way, Shropshire is your county, is it not?

JACK: Eh? Shropshire? Yes, of course. Hallo! Why all these cups? Why cucumber sandwiches? Why such reckless extravagance in one so young? Who is coming to tea?

ALGERNON: Oh! merely Aunt Augusta and Gwendolen.

JACK: How perfectly delightful!

ALGERNON: Yes, that is all very well; but I am afraid Aunt Augusta won't quite approve of your being here.

JACK: May I ask why?

ALGERNON: My dear fellow, the way you flirt with Gwendolen is perfectly disgraceful. It is almost as bad as the way Gwendolen flirts with you.

JACK: I am in love with Gwendolen. I have come up to town expressly to propose to her.

ALGERNON: I thought you had come up for pleasure? . . . . I call that business.

JACK: How utterly unromantic you are!

ALGERNON: I really don't see anything romantic in proposing. It is very romantic to be in love. But there is nothing romantic about a definite proposal. Why, one may be accepted. One usually is, I believe. Then the excitement is all over. The very essence of romance is uncertainty. If ever I get married, I'll certainly try to forget the fact.

JACK: I have no doubt about that, dear Algy. The divorce court was specially invented for people whose memories are so curiously constituted.

ALGERNON: Oh! there is no use speculating on that subject. Divorces are made in heaven— [JACK *puts out his hand to take a sandwich.* ALGERNON *at once*

---

2. County on the Welsh border, northwest of London; Jack's country house is actually in Hertfordshire, north of London.

interferes.] Please don't touch the cucumber sandwiches. They are ordered specially for Aunt Augusta. [*Takes one and eats it.*]

JACK: Well, you have been eating them all the time.

ALGERNON: That is quite a different matter. She is my aunt. [*Takes plate from below.*] Have some bread and butter. The bread and butter is for Gwendolen. Gwendolen is devoted to bread and butter.

JACK: [*Advancing to table and helping himself.*] And very good bread and butter it is too.

ALGERNON: Well, my dear fellow, you need not eat as if you were going to eat it all. You behave as if you were married to her already. You are not married to her already, and I don't think you ever will be.

JACK: Why on earth do you say that?

ALGERNON: Well, in the first place, girls never marry the men they flirt with. Girls don't think it right.

JACK: Oh, that is nonsense!

ALGERNON: It isn't. It is a great truth. It accounts for the extraordinary number of bachelors that one sees all over the place. In the second place, I don't give my consent.

JACK: Your consent!

ALGERNON: My dear fellow, Gwendolen is my first cousin. And before I allow you to marry her, you will have to clear up the whole question of Cecily. [*Rings bell.*]

JACK: Cecily! What on earth do you mean? What do you mean, Algy, by Cecily? I don't know anyone of the name of Cecily.

[*Enter* LANE.]

ALGERNON: Bring me that cigarette case Mr. Worthing left in the smoking-room the last time he dined here.

LANE: Yes, sir. [LANE *goes out.*]

JACK: Do you mean to say you have had my cigarette case all this time? I wish to goodness you had let me know. I have been writing frantic letters to Scotland Yard[3] about it. I was very nearly offering a large reward.

ALGERNON: Well, I wish you would offer one. I happen to be more than usually hard up.

JACK: There is no good offering a large reward now that the thing is found.

[*Enter* LANE *with the cigarette case on a salver.* ALGERNON *takes it at once.* LANE *goes out.*]

ALGERNON: I think that is rather mean[4] of you, Ernest, I must say. [*Opens case and examines it.*] However, it makes no matter, for, now that I look at the inscription inside, I find that the thing isn't yours after all.

JACK: Of course it's mine. [*Moving to him.*] You have seen me with it a hundred times, and you have no right whatsoever to read what is written inside. It is a very ungentlemanly thing to read a private cigarette case.

ALGERNON: Oh! it is absurd to have a hard-and-fast rule about what one should read and what one shouldn't. More than half of modern culture depends on what one shouldn't read.

---

3. Famed original headquarters of (and thus also a metonym for) London's Metropolitan Police force.
4. Cheap or stingy.

JACK: I am quite aware of the fact, and I don't propose to discuss modern culture. It isn't the sort of thing one should talk of in private. I simply want my cigarette case back.

ALGERNON: Yes; but this isn't your cigarette case. This cigarette case is a present from someone of the name of Cecily, and you said you didn't know anyone of that name.

JACK: Well, if you want to know, Cecily happens to be my aunt.

ALGERNON: Your aunt!

JACK: Yes. Charming old lady she is, too. Lives at Tunbridge Wells.[5] Just give it back to me, Algy.

ALGERNON: [*Retreating to back of sofa.*] But why does she call herself Cecily if she is your aunt and lives at Tunbridge Wells? [*Reading.*] "From little Cecily with her fondest love."

JACK: [*Moving to sofa and kneeling upon it.*] My dear fellow, what on earth is there in that? Some aunts are tall, some aunts are not tall. That is a matter that surely an aunt may be allowed to decide for herself. You seem to think that every aunt should be exactly like your aunt! That is absurd! For heaven's sake give me back my cigarette case. [*Follows* ALGY *round the room.*]

ALGERNON: Yes. But why does your aunt call you her uncle? "From little Cecily, with her fondest love to her dear Uncle Jack." There is no objection, I admit, to an aunt being a small aunt, but why an aunt, no matter what her size may be, should call her own nephew her uncle, I can't quite make out. Besides, your name isn't Jack at all; it is Ernest.

JACK: It isn't Ernest; it's Jack.

ALGERNON: You have always told me it was Ernest. I have introduced you to everyone as Ernest. You answer to the name of Ernest. You look as if your name was Ernest. You are the most earnest looking person I ever saw in my life. It is perfectly absurd your saying that your name isn't Ernest. It's on your cards. Here is one of them. [*Taking it from case.*] "Mr. Ernest Worthing, B. 4, The Albany."[6] I'll keep this as a proof that your name is Ernest if ever you attempt to deny it to me, or to Gwendolen, or to anyone else. [*Puts the card in his pocket.*]

JACK: Well, my name is Ernest in town and Jack in the country, and the cigarette case was given to me in the country.

ALGERNON: Yes, but that does not account for the fact that your small Aunt Cecily, who lives at Tunbridge Wells, calls you her dear uncle. Come, old boy, you had much better have the thing out at once.

JACK: My dear Algy, you talk exactly as if you were a dentist. It is very vulgar to talk like a dentist when one isn't a dentist. It produces a false impression.

ALGERNON: Well, that is exactly what dentists always do. Now, go on! Tell me the whole thing. I may mention that I have always suspected you of being a confirmed and secret Bunburyist; and I am quite sure of it now.

JACK: Bunburyist? What on earth do you mean by a Bunburyist?

5. Affluent town in Kent, southeast of London, long considered a bastion of middle-class respectability.
6. Apartment building for single gentlemen on Piccadilly, east of Algernon's flat.

ALGERNON: I'll reveal to you the meaning of that incomparable expression as soon as you are kind enough to inform me why you are Ernest in town and Jack in the country.

JACK: Well, produce my cigarette case first.

ALGERNON: Here it is. [*Hands cigarette case.*] Now produce your explanation, and pray make it improbable. [*Sits on sofa.*]

JACK: My dear fellow, there is nothing improbable about my explanation at all. In fact it's perfectly ordinary. Old Mr. Thomas Cardew, who adopted me when I was a little boy, made me in his will guardian to his granddaughter, Miss Cecily Cardew. Cecily, who addresses me as her uncle from motives of respect that you could not possibly appreciate, lives at my place in the country under the charge of her admirable governess, Miss Prism.

ALGERNON: Where is that place in the country, by the way?

JACK: That is nothing to you, dear boy. You are not going to be invited. . . . I may tell you candidly that the place is not in Shropshire.

ALGERNON: I suspected that, my dear fellow! I have Bunburyed all over Shropshire on two separate occasions. Now, go on. Why are you Ernest in town and Jack in the country?

JACK: My dear Algy, I don't know whether you will be able to understand my real motives. You are hardly serious enough. When one is placed in the position of guardian, one has to adopt a very high moral tone on all subjects. It's one's duty to do so. And as a high moral tone can hardly be said to conduce very much to either one's health or one's happiness, in order to get up to town I have always pretended to have a younger brother of the name of Ernest, who lives in the Albany, and gets into the most dreadful scrapes. That, my dear Algy, is the whole truth pure and simple.

ALGERNON: The truth is rarely pure and never simple. Modern life would be very tedious if it were either, and modern literature a complete impossibility!

JACK: That wouldn't be at all a bad thing.

ALGERNON: Literary criticism is not your forte, my dear fellow. Don't try it. You should leave that to people who haven't been at a university. They do it so well in the daily papers. What you really are is a Bunburyist. I was quite right in saying you were a Bunburyist. You are one of the most advanced Bunburyists I know.

JACK: What on earth do you mean?

ALGERNON: You have invented a very useful young brother called Ernest, in order that you may be able to come up to town as often as you like. I have invented an invaluable permanent invalid called Bunbury, in order that I may be able to go down into the country whenever I choose. Bunbury is perfectly invaluable. If it wasn't for Bunbury's extraordinary bad health, for instance, I wouldn't be able to dine with you at Willis's[7] tonight, for I have been really engaged to Aunt Augusta for more than a week.

JACK: I haven't asked you to dine with me anywhere tonight.

ALGERNON: I know. You are absurdly careless about sending out invitations. It is very foolish of you. Nothing annoys people so much as not receiving invitations.

7. Well-known restaurant on King Street, off St. James's Street, near Piccadilly.

JACK: You had much better dine with your Aunt Augusta.

ALGERNON: I haven't the smallest intention of doing anything of the kind. To begin with, I dined there on Monday, and once a week is quite enough to dine with one's own relations. In the second place, whenever I do dine there I am always treated as a member of the family, and sent down[8] with either no woman at all, or two. In the third place, I know perfectly well whom she will place me next to, tonight. She will place me next Mary Farquhar, who always flirts with her own husband across the dinner table. That is not very pleasant. Indeed, it is not even decent . . . and that sort of thing is enormously on the increase. The amount of women in London who flirt with their own husbands is perfectly scandalous. It looks so bad. It is simply washing one's clean linen in public. Besides, now that I know you to be a confirmed Bunburyist, I naturally want to talk to you about Bunburying. I want to tell you the rules.

JACK: I'm not a Bunburyist at all. If Gwendolen accepts me, I am going to kill my brother, indeed I think I'll kill him in any case. Cecily is a little too much interested in him. It is rather a bore. So I am going to get rid of Ernest. And I strongly advise you to do the same with Mr. . . . with your invalid friend who has the absurd name.

ALGERNON: Nothing will induce me to part with Bunbury, and if you ever get married, which seems to me extremely problematic, you will be very glad to know Bunbury. A man who marries without knowing Bunbury has a very tedious time of it.

JACK: That is nonsense. If I marry a charming girl like Gwendolen, and she is the only girl I ever saw in my life that I would marry, I certainly won't want to know Bunbury.

ALGERNON: Then your wife will. You don't seem to realize, that in married life three is company and two is none.

JACK: [Sententiously.] That, my dear young friend, is the theory that the corrupt French drama has been propounding for the last fifty years.[9]

ALGERNON: Yes; and that the happy English home has proved in half the time.

JACK: For heaven's sake, don't try to be cynical. It's perfectly easy to be cynical.

ALGERNON: My dear fellow, it isn't easy to be anything nowadays. There's such a lot of beastly competition about. [The sound of an electric bell is heard.] Ah! that must be Aunt Augusta. Only relatives, or creditors, ever ring in that Wagnerian manner.[1] Now, if I get her out of the way for ten minutes, so that you can have an opportunity for proposing to Gwendolen, may I dine with you tonight at Willis's?

JACK: I suppose so, if you want to.

ALGERNON: Yes, but you must be serious about it. I hate people who are not serious about meals. It is so shallow of them.

[Enter LANE.]

LANE: Lady Bracknell and Miss Fairfax.

---

8. That is, sent into dinner. Traditionally, men escorted women to the table when dinner was served.

9. Starting in the mid-nineteenth century, the French produced plays dealing with such subjects as adultery, prostitution, and illegitimacy. The heavily censored English theater either avoided such subjects or dealt with them more cautiously.

1. Many early listeners found the music of Richard Wagner (1813–83) extremely loud and unpleasantly demanding.

[ALGERNON *goes forward to meet them. Enter* LADY BRACKNELL *and* GWENDOLEN.]

LADY BRACKNELL: Good afternoon, dear Algernon, I hope you are behaving very well.

ALGERNON: I'm feeling very well, Aunt Augusta.

LADY BRACKNELL: That's not quite the same thing. In fact the two things rarely go together. [*Sees* JACK *and bows to him with icy coldness.*]

ALGERNON: [*To* GWENDOLEN.] Dear me, you are smart![2]

GWENDOLEN: I am always smart! Aren't I, Mr. Worthing?

JACK: You're quite perfect, Miss Fairfax.

GWENDOLEN: Oh! I hope I am not that. It would leave no room for developments, and I intend to develop in many directions. [GWENDOLEN *and* JACK *sit down together in the corner.*]

LADY BRACKNELL: I'm sorry if we are a little late, Algernon, but I was obliged to call on dear Lady Harbury. I hadn't been there since her poor husband's death. I never saw a woman so altered; she looks quite twenty years younger. And now I'll have a cup of tea, and one of those nice cucumber sandwiches you promised me.

ALGERNON: Certainly, Aunt Augusta. [*Goes over to teatable.*]

LADY BRACKNELL: Won't you come and sit here, Gwendolen?

GWENDOLEN: Thanks, mamma, I'm quite comfortable where I am.

ALGERNON: [*Picking up empty plate in horror.*] Good heavens! Lane! Why are there no cucumber sandwiches? I ordered them specially.

LANE: [*Gravely.*] There were no cucumbers in the market this morning, sir. I went down twice.

ALGERNON: No cucumbers!

LANE: No, sir. Not even for ready money.

ALGERNON: That will do, Lane, thank you.

LANE: Thank you, sir.

ALGERNON: I am greatly distressed, Aunt Augusta, about there being no cucumbers, not even for ready money.

LADY BRACKNELL: It really makes no matter, Algernon. I had some crumpets[3] with Lady Harbury, who seems to me to be living entirely for pleasure now.

ALGERNON: I hear her hair has turned quite gold from grief.

LADY BRACKNELL: It certainly has changed its color. From what cause I, of course, cannot say. [ALGERNON *crosses and hands tea.*] Thank you. I've quite a treat for you tonight, Algernon. I am going to send you down with Mary Farquhar. She is such a nice woman, and so attentive to her husband. It's delightful to watch them.

ALGERNON: I am afraid, Aunt Augusta, I shall have to give up the pleasure of dining with you tonight after all.

LADY BRACKNELL: [*Frowning.*] I hope not, Algernon. It would put my table completely out.[4] Your uncle would have to dine upstairs. Fortunately he is accustomed to that.

2. Neat and stylish in appearance.
3. Small, round, savory cakes traditionally served with tea.
4. That is, disturb the arrangement of guests at the table.

ALGERNON: It is a great bore, and, I need hardly say, a terrible disappointment to me, but the fact is I have just had a telegram to say that my poor friend Bunbury is very ill again. [*Exchanges glances with* JACK.] They seem to think I should be with him.

LADY BRACKNELL: It is very strange. This Mr. Bunbury seems to suffer from curiously bad health.

ALGERNON: Yes; poor Bunbury is a dreadful invalid.

LADY BRACKNELL: Well, I must say, Algernon, that I think it is high time that Mr. Bunbury made up his mind whether he was going to live or to die. This shilly-shallying with the question is absurd. Nor do I in any way approve of the modern sympathy with invalids. I consider it morbid. Illness of any kind is hardly a thing to be encouraged in others. Health is the primary duty of life. I am always telling that to your poor uncle, but he never seems to take much notice . . . as far as any improvement in his ailments goes. I should be obliged if you would ask Mr. Bunbury, from me, to be kind enough not to have a relapse on Saturday, for I rely on you to arrange my music for me. It is my last reception, and one wants something that will encourage conversation, particularly at the end of the season when everyone has practically said whatever they had to say, which, in most cases, was probably not much.

ALGERNON: I'll speak to Bunbury, Aunt Augusta, if he is still conscious, and I think I can promise you he'll be all right by Saturday. Of course the music is a great difficulty. You see, if one plays good music, people don't listen, and if one plays bad music, people don't talk. But I'll run over the program I've drawn out, if you will kindly come into the next room for a moment.

LADY BRACKNELL: Thank you, Algernon. It is very thoughtful of you. [*Rising, and following* ALGERNON.] I'm sure the program will be delightful, after a few expurgations. French songs I cannot possibly allow. People always seem to think that they are improper, and either look shocked, which is vulgar, or laugh, which is worse. But German sounds a thoroughly respectable language, and indeed, I believe is so. Gwendolen, you will accompany me.

GWENDOLEN: Certainly, mamma.

[LADY BRACKNELL *and* ALGERNON *go into the music room,* GWENDOLEN *remains behind.*]

JACK: Charming day it has been, Miss Fairfax.

GWENDOLEN: Pray don't talk to me about the weather, Mr. Worthing. Whenever people talk to me about the weather, I always feel quite certain that they mean something else. And that makes me so nervous.

JACK: I do mean something else.

GWENDOLWN: I thought so. In fact, I am never wrong.

JACK: And I would like to be allowed to take advantage of Lady Bracknell's temporary absence . . .

GWENDOLEN: I would certainly advise you to do so. Mamma has a way of coming back suddenly into a room that I have often had to speak to her about.

JACK: [*Nervously.*] Miss Fairfax, ever since I met you I have admired you more than any girl . . . I have ever met since . . . I met you.

GWENDOLEN: Yes, I am quite aware of the fact. And I often wish that in public, at any rate, you had been more demonstrative. For me you have always had an irresistible fascination. Even before I met you I was far from indifferent to you. [JACK *looks at her in amazement.*] We live, as I hope you know, Mr. Worthing, in an age of ideals. The fact is constantly mentioned in the more expensive monthly magazines, and has reached the provincial pulpits, I am told: and my ideal has always been to love someone of the name of Ernest. There is something in that name that inspires absolute confidence. The moment Algernon first mentioned to me that he had a friend called Ernest, I knew I was destined to love you.

JACK: You really love me, Gwendolen?

GWENDOLEN: Passionately!

JACK: Darling! You don't know how happy you've made me.

GWENDOLEN: My own Ernest!

JACK: But you don't really mean to say that you couldn't love me if my name wasn't Ernest?

GWENDOLEN: But your name is Ernest.

JACK: Yes, I know it is. But supposing it was something else? Do you mean to say you couldn't love me then?

GWENDOLEN: [*Glibly.*] Ah! that is clearly a metaphysical speculation, and like most metaphysical speculations has very little reference at all to the actual facts of real life, as we know them.

JACK: Personally, darling, to speak quite candidly, I don't much care about the name of Ernest . . . I don't think the name suits me at all.

GWENDOLEN: It suits you perfectly. It is a divine name. It has a music of its own. It produces vibrations.

JACK: Well, really, Gwendolen, I must say that I think there are lots of other much nicer names. I think Jack, for instance, a charming name.

GWENDOLEN: Jack? . . . No, there is very little music in the name Jack, if any at all, indeed. It does not thrill. It produces absolutely no vibrations. . . . I have known several Jacks, and they all, without exception, were more than usually plain. Besides, Jack is a notorious domesticity[5] for John! And I pity any woman who is married to a man called John. She would probably never be allowed to know the entrancing pleasure of a single moment's solitude. The only really safe name is Ernest.

JACK: Gwendolen, I must get christened at once—I mean we must get married at once. There is no time to be lost.

GWENDOLEN: Married, Mr. Worthing?

JACK: [*Astounded.*] Well . . . surely. You know that I love you, and you led me to believe, Miss Fairfax, that you were not absolutely indifferent to me.

GWENDOLEN: I adore you. But you haven't proposed to me yet. Nothing has been said at all about marriage. The subject has not even been touched on.

JACK: Well . . . may I propose to you now?

GWENDOLEN: I think it would be an admirable opportunity. And to spare you any possible disappointment, Mr. Worthing, I think it only fair to tell you quite frankly beforehand that I am fully determined to accept you.

JACK: Gwendolen!

GWENDOLEN: Yes, Mr. Worthing, what have you got to say to me?

---

5. That is, a familiar or familial ("domestic") nickname or abbreviation.

JACK: You know what I have got to say to you.

GWENDOLEN: Yes, but you don't say it.

JACK: Gwendolen, will you marry me? [*Goes on his knees.*]

GWENDOLEN: Of course I will, darling. How long you have been about it! I am afraid you have had very little experience in how to propose.

JACK: My own one, I have never loved anyone in the world but you.

GWENDOLEN: Yes, but men often propose for practice. I know my brother Gerald does. All my girlfriends tell me so. What wonderfully blue eyes you have, Ernest! They are quite, quite blue. I hope you will always look at me just like that, especially when there are other people present.

[*Enter* LADY BRACKNELL.]

LADY BRACKNELL: Mr. Worthing! Rise, sir, from this semi-recumbent posture. It is most indecorous.

GWENDOLEN: Mamma! [*He tries to rise; she restrains him.*] I must beg you to retire. This is no place for you. Besides, Mr. Worthing has not quite finished yet.

LADY BRACKNELL: Finished what, may I ask?

GWENDOLEN: I am engaged to Mr. Worthing, mamma.

[*They rise together.*]

LADY BRACKNELL: Pardon me, you are not engaged to anyone. When you do become engaged to someone, I, or your father, should his health permit him, will inform you of the fact. An engagement should come on a young girl as a surprise, pleasant or unpleasant, as the case may be. It is hardly a matter that she could be allowed to arrange for herself. . . . And now I have a few questions to put to you, Mr. Worthing. While I am making these inquiries, you, Gwendolen, will wait for me below in the carriage.

GWENDOLEN: [*Reproachfully.*] Mamma!

LADY BRACKNELL: In the carriage, Gwendolen! [GWENDOLEN *goes to the door. She and* JACK *blow kisses to each other behind* LADY BRACKNELL's *back.* LADY BRACKNELL *looks vaguely about as if she could not understand what the noise was. Finally turns round.*] Gwendolen, the carriage!

GWENDOLEN: Yes, mamma. [*Goes out, looking back at* JACK.]

LADY BRACKNELL: [*Sitting down.*] You can take a seat, Mr. Worthing.

[*Looks in her pocket for notebook and pencil.*]

JACK: Thank you, Lady Bracknell, I prefer standing.

LADY BRACKNELL: [*Pencil and notebook in hand.*] I feel bound to tell you that you are not down on my list of eligible young men, although I have the same list as the dear Duchess of Bolton has. We work together, in fact. However, I am quite ready to enter your name, should your answers be what a really affectionate mother requires. Do you smoke?

JACK: Well, yes, I must admit I smoke.

LADY BRACKNELL: I am glad to hear it. A man should always have an occupation of some kind. There are far too many idle men in London as it is. How old are you?

JACK: Twenty-nine.

LADY BRACKNELL: A very good age to be married at. I have always been of opinion that a man who desires to get married should know either everything or nothing. Which do you know?

JACK: [*After some hesitation.*] I know nothing, Lady Bracknell.

LADY BRACKNELL: I am pleased to hear it. I do not approve of anything that tampers with natural ignorance. Ignorance is like a delicate exotic fruit; touch it and the bloom is gone. The whole theory of modern education is radically unsound. Fortunately in England, at any rate, education produces no effect whatsoever. If it did, it would prove a serious danger to the upper classes, and probably lead to acts of violence in Grosvenor Square.[6] What is your income?

JACK: Between seven and eight thousand a year.[7]

LADY BRACKNELL: [*Makes a note in her book.*] In land, or in investments?

JACK: In investments, chiefly.

LADY BRACKNELL: That is satisfactory. What between the duties expected of one during one's lifetime, and the duties exacted from one after one's death, land has ceased to be either a profit or a pleasure. It gives one position, and prevents one from keeping it up. That's all that can be said about land.

JACK: I have a country house with some land, of course, attached to it, about fifteen hundred acres, I believe; but I don't depend on that for my real income. In fact, as far as I can make out, the poachers are the only people who make anything out of it.

LADY BRACKNELL: A country house! How many bedrooms? Well, that point can be cleared up afterwards. You have a town house, I hope? A girl with a simple, unspoiled nature, like Gwendolen, could hardly be expected to reside in the country.

JACK: Well, I own a house in Belgrave Square,[8] but it is let by the year to Lady Bloxham. Of course, I can get it back whenever I like, at six months' notice.

LADY BRACKNELL: Lady Bloxham? I don't know her.

JACK: Oh, she goes about very little. She is a lady considerably advanced in years.

LADY BRACKNELL: Ah, nowadays that is no guarantee of respectability of character. What number in Belgrave Square?

JACK: 149.

LADY BRACKNELL: [*Shaking her head.*] The unfashionable side. I thought there was something. However, that could easily be altered.

JACK: Do you mean the fashion, or the side?

LADY BRACKNELL: [*Sternly.*] Both, if necessary, I presume. What are your politics?

JACK: Well, I am afraid I really have none. I am a Liberal Unionist.

LADY BRACKNELL: Oh, they count as Tories.[9] They dine with us. Or come in the evening, at any rate. Now to minor matters. Are your parents living?

JACK: I have lost both my parents.

---

6. Fashionable location in Mayfair.

7. A very large income in the late nineteenth century.

8. Near the southeast corner of Hyde Park in Belgravia, another fashionable London neighborhood.

9. Members of the Conservative party. Opposed to independence (or "home rule") for Ireland, they joined forces with the Liberal Unionists, who had split from the Liberal party over the issue.

LADY BRACKNELL: Both? To lose one parent may be regarded as a misfortune— to lose *both* seems like carelessness. Who was your father? He was evidently a man of some wealth. Was he born in what the Radical papers call the purple[1] of commerce, or did he rise from the ranks of aristocracy?

JACK: I am afraid I really don't know. The fact is, Lady Bracknell, I said I had lost my parents. It would be nearer the truth to say that my parents seem to have lost me. . . . I don't actually know who I am by birth. I was . . . well, I was found.

LADY BRACKNELL: Found!

JACK: The late Mr. Thomas Cardew, an old gentleman of a very charitable and kindly disposition, found me, and gave me the name of Worthing, because he happened to have a first-class ticket for Worthing in his pocket at the time. Worthing is a place in Sussex.[2] It is a seaside resort.

LADY BRACKNELL: Where did the charitable gentleman who had a first-class ticket for this seaside resort find you?

JACK: [*Gravely.*] In a handbag.

LADY BRACKNELL: A handbag?

JACK: [*Very seriously.*] Yes, Lady Bracknell. I was in a handbag—a somewhat large, black leather handbag, with handles to it—an ordinary handbag, in fact.

LADY BRACKNELL: In what locality did this Mr. James, or Thomas, Cardew come across this ordinary handbag?

JACK: In the cloak room at Victoria Station.[3] It was given to him in mistake for his own.

LADY BRACKNELL: The cloak room at Victoria Station?

JACK: Yes. The Brighton line.

LADY BRACKNELL: The line is immaterial. Mr. Worthing, I confess I feel somewhat bewildered by what you have just told me. To be born, or at any rate, bred in a handbag, whether it had handles or not, seems to me to display a contempt for the ordinary decencies of family life that reminds one of the worst excesses of the French Revolution. And I presume you know what that unfortunate movement led to? As for the particular locality in which the handbag was found, a cloak room at a railway station might serve to conceal a social indiscretion—has probably, indeed, been used for that purpose before now—but it could hardly be regarded as an assured basis for a recognized position in good society.

JACK: May I ask you then what you would advise me to do? I need hardly say I would do anything in the world to ensure Gwendolen's happiness.

LADY BRACKNELL: I would strongly advise you, Mr. Worthing, to try and acquire some relations as soon as possible, and to make a definite effort to produce at any rate one parent, of either sex, before the season is quite over.

JACK: Well, I don't see how I could possibly manage to do that. I can produce the handbag at any moment, it is in my dressing room at home. I really think that should satisfy you, Lady Bracknell.

1. Traditionally, the color of royalty or nobility.
2. County in southern England.
3. Major London railway station.

LADY BRACKNELL: Me, sir! What has it to do with me? You can hardly imagine that I and Lord Bracknell would dream of allowing our only daughter—a girl brought up with the utmost care—to marry into a cloak room, and form an alliance with a parcel? Good morning, Mr. Worthing!

[LADY BRACKNELL *sweeps out in majestic indignation.*]

JACK: Good morning! [ALGERNON, *from the other room, strikes up the Wedding March.* JACK *looks perfectly furious, and goes to the door.*] For goodness' sake don't play that ghastly tune, Algy! How idiotic you are!

[*The music stops, and* ALGERNON *enters cheerily.*]

ALGERNON: Didn't it go off all right, old boy? You don't mean to say Gwendolen refused you? I know it is a way she has. She is always refusing people. I think it is most ill-natured of her.

JACK: Oh, Gwendolen is as right as a trivet.[4] As far as she is concerned, we are engaged. Her mother is perfectly unbeatable. Never met such a Gorgon[5] . . . I don't really know what a Gorgon is like, but I am quite sure that Lady Bracknell is one. In any case, she is a monster, without being a myth, which is rather unfair. . . . I beg your pardon, Algy, I suppose I shouldn't talk about your own aunt in that way before you.

ALGERNON: My dear boy, I love hearing my relations abused. It is the only thing that makes me put up with them at all. Relations are simply a tedious pack of people who haven't got the remotest knowledge of how to live, nor the smallest instinct about when to die.

JACK: Oh, that is nonsense!

ALGERNON: It isn't!

JACK: Well, I won't argue about the matter. You always want to argue about things.

ALGERNON: That is exactly what things were originally made for.

JACK: Upon my word, if I thought that, I'd shoot myself. . . . [*A pause.*] You don't think there is any chance of Gwendolen becoming like her mother in about a hundred and fifty years, do you, Algy?

ALGERNON: All women become like their mothers. That is their tragedy. No man does. That's his.

JACK: Is that clever?

ALGERNON: It is perfectly phrased! and quite as true as any observation in civilized life should be.

JACK: I am sick to death of cleverness. Everybody is clever nowadays. You can't go anywhere without meeting clever people. The thing has become an absolute public nuisance. I wish to goodness we had a few fools left.

ALGERNON: We have.

JACK: I should extremely like to meet them. What do they talk about?

ALGERNON: The fools? Oh! about the clever people, of course.

JACK: What fools!

---

4. Proverbial expression, referring to the stability of a tripod on its three legs.
5. Mythological creature with a horrible face and snakes in lieu of hair. According to myth, those who looked at a Gorgon turned to stone.

ALGERNON: By the way, did you tell Gwendolen the truth about your being Ernest in town, and Jack in the country?

JACK: [*In a very patronizing manner.*] My dear fellow, the truth isn't quite the sort of thing one tells to a nice sweet refined girl. What extraordinary ideas you have about the way to behave to a woman!

ALGERNON: The only way to behave to a woman is to make love to her,[6] if she is pretty, and to someone else if she is plain.

JACK: Oh, that is nonsense.

ALGERNON: What about your brother? What about the profligate Ernest?

JACK: Oh, before the end of the week I shall have got rid of him. I'll say he died in Paris of apoplexy. Lots of people die of apoplexy, quite suddenly, don't they?

ALGERNON: Yes, but it's hereditary, my dear fellow. It's a sort of thing that runs in families. You had much better say a severe chill.

JACK: You are sure a severe chill isn't hereditary, or anything of that kind?

ALGERNON: Of course it isn't!

JACK: Very well, then. My poor brother Ernest is carried off suddenly in Paris, by a severe chill. That gets rid of him.

ALGERNON: But I thought you said that . . . Miss Cardew was a little too much interested in your poor brother Ernest? Won't she feel his loss a good deal?

JACK: Oh, that is all right. Cecily is not a silly romantic girl, I am glad to say. She has got a capital appetite, goes on long walks, and pays no attention at all to her lessons.

ALGERNON: I would rather like to see Cecily.

JACK: I will take very good care you never do. She is excessively pretty, and she is only just eighteen.

ALGERNON: Have you told Gwendolen yet that you have an excessively pretty ward who is only just eighteen?

JACK: Oh! one doesn't blurt these things out to people. Cecily and Gwendolen are perfectly certain to be extremely great friends. I'll bet you anything you like that half an hour after they have met, they will be calling each other sister.

ALGERNON: Women only do that when they have called each other a lot of other things first. Now, my dear boy, if we want to get a good table at Willis's, we really must go and dress. Do you know it is nearly seven?

JACK: [*Irritably.*] Oh! it always is nearly seven.

ALGERNON: Well, I'm hungry.

JACK: I never knew you when you weren't. . . .

ALGERNON: What shall we do after dinner? Go to the theater?

JACK: Oh no! I loathe listening.

ALGERNON: Well, let us go to the club?

JACK: Oh, no! I hate talking.

ALGERNON: Well, we might trot around to the Empire[7] at ten?

JACK: Oh no! I can't bear looking at things. It is so silly.

---

6. In the original sense of "woo" or "pay amorous attention to."

7. The Empire Theatre of Varieties, a music hall on Leicester Square.

ALGERNON: Well, what shall we do?

JACK: Nothing!

ALGERNON: It is awfully hard work doing nothing. However, I don't mind hard work where there is no definite object of any kind.

[*Enter* LANE.]

LANE: Miss Fairfax.

[*Enter* GWENDOLEN. LANE *goes out.*]

ALGERNON: Gwendolen, upon my word!

GWENDOLEN: Algy, kindly turn your back. I have something very particular to say to Mr. Worthing.

ALGERNON: Really, Gwendolen, I don't think I can allow this at all.

GWENDOLEN: Algy, you always adopt a strictly immoral attitude towards life. You are not quite old enough to do that.

[ALGERNON *retires to the fireplace.*]

JACK: My own darling!

GWENDOLEN: Ernest, we may never be married. From the expression on mamma's face I fear we never shall. Few parents nowadays pay any regard to what their children say to them. The old-fashioned respect for the young is fast dying out. Whatever influence I ever had over mamma, I lost at the age of three. But although she may prevent us from becoming man and wife, and I may marry someone else, and marry often, nothing that she can possibly do can alter my eternal devotion to you.

JACK: Dear Gwendolen!

GWENDOLEN: The story of your romantic origin, as related to me by mamma, with unpleasing comments, has naturally stirred the deeper fibers of my nature. Your Christian name has an irresistible fascination. The simplicity of your character makes you exquisitely incomprehensible to me. Your town address at the Albany I have. What is your address in the country?

JACK: The Manor House, Woolton, Hertfordshire.

[ALGERNON, *who has been carefully listening, smiles to himself, and writes the address on his shirt-cuff. Then picks up the Railway Guide.*]

GWENDOLEN: There is a good postal service, I suppose? It may be necessary to do something desperate. That of course will require serious consideration. I will communicate with you daily.

JACK: My own one!

GWENDOLEN: How long do you remain in town?

JACK: Till Monday.

GWENDOLEN: Good! Algy, you may turn round now.

ALGERNON: Thanks, I've turned round already.

GWENDOLEN: You may also ring the bell.

JACK: You will let me see you to your carriage, my own darling?

GWENDOLEN: Certainly.

JACK: [*To* LANE, *who now enters.*] I will see Miss Fairfax out.

LANE: Yes, sir.

[JACK *and* GWENDOLEN *go off.* LANE *presents several letters on a salver to* ALGERNON. *It is to be surmised that they are bills, as* ALGERNON, *after looking at the envelopes, tears them up.*]

ALGERNON: A glass of sherry, Lane.

LANE: Yes, sir.

ALGERNON: Tomorrow, Lane, I'm going Bunburying.

LANE: Yes, sir.

ALGERNON: I shall probably not be back till Monday. You can put up my dress clothes, my smoking jacket, and all the Bunbury suits. . . .

LANE: Yes, sir. [*Handing sherry.*]

ALGERNON: I hope tomorrow will be a fine day, Lane.

LANE: It never is, sir.

ALGERNON: Lane, you're a perfect pessimist.

LANE: I do my best to give satisfaction, sir.

[*Enter* JACK. LANE *goes off.*]

JACK: There's a sensible, intellectual girl! the only girl I ever cared for in my life. [ALGERNON *is laughing immoderately.*] What on earth are you so amused at?

ALGERNON: Oh, I'm a little anxious about poor Bunbury, that is all.

JACK: If you don't take care, your friend Bunbury will get you into a serious scrape some day.

ALGERNON: I love scrapes. They are the only things that are never serious.

JACK: Oh, that's nonsense, Algy. You never talk anything but nonsense.

ALGERNON: Nobody ever does.

[JACK *looks indignantly at him, and leaves the room.* ALGERNON *lights a cigarette, reads his shirt-cuff, and smiles.*]

ACT-DROP[8]

ACT II

SCENE: *Garden at the Manor House. A flight of gray stone steps leads up to the house. The garden, an old-fashioned one, full of roses. Time of year, July. Basket chairs, and a table covered with books, are set under a large yew tree.*

[MISS PRISM *discovered seated at the table.* CECILY *is at the back watering flowers.*]

MISS PRISM: [*Calling.*] Cecily, Cecily! Surely such a utilitarian occupation as the watering of flowers is rather Moulton's duty than yours? Especially at a moment when intellectual pleasures await you. Your German grammar[9] is on the table. Pray open it at page fifteen. We will repeat yesterday's lesson.

CECILY: [*Coming over very slowly.*] But I don't like German. It isn't at all a becoming language. I know perfectly well that I look quite plain after my German lesson.

8. Lowering of the curtain to permit a scene change.
9. That is, grammar textbook.

MISS PRISM: Child, you know how anxious your guardian is that you should improve yourself in every way. He laid particular stress on your German, as he was leaving for town yesterday. Indeed, he always lays stress on your German when he is leaving for town.

CECILY: Dear Uncle Jack is so very serious! Sometime he is so serious that I think he cannot be quite well.

MISS PRISM: [*Drawing herself up.*] Your guardian enjoys the best of health, and his gravity of demeanor is especially to be commended in one so comparatively young as he is. I know no one who has a higher sense of duty and responsibility.

CECILY: I suppose that is why he often looks a little bored when we three are together.

MISS PRISM: Cecily! I am surprised at you. Mr. Worthing has many troubles in his life. Idle merriment and triviality would be out of place in his conversation. You must remember his constant anxiety about that unfortunate young man his brother.

CECILY: I wish Uncle Jack would allow that unfortunate young man, his brother, to come down here sometimes. We might have a good influence over him, Miss Prism. I am sure you certainly would. You know German, and geology, and things of that kind influence a man very much. [CECILY *begins to write in her diary.*]

MISS PRISM: [*Shaking her head.*] I do not think that even I could produce any effect on a character that according to his own brother's admission is irretrievably weak and vacillating. Indeed I am not sure that I would desire to reclaim him. I am not in favor of this modern mania for turning bad people into good people at a moment's notice. As a man sows so let him reap. You must put away your diary, Cecily. I really don't see why you should keep a diary at all.

CECILY: I keep a diary in order to enter the wonderful secrets of my life. If I didn't write them down I should probably forget all about them.

MISS PRISM: Memory, my dear Cecily, is the diary that we all carry about with us.

CECILY: Yes, but it usually chronicles the things that have never happened, and couldn't possibly have happened. I believe that memory is responsible for nearly all the three-volume novels that Mudie sends us.[1]

MISS PRISM: Do not speak slightingly of the three-volume novel, Cecily. I wrote one myself in earlier days.

CECILY: Did you really, Miss Prism? How wonderfully clever you are! I hope it did not end happily? I don't like novels that end happily. They depress me so much.

MISS PRISM: The good ended happily, and the bad unhappily. That is what fiction means.

CECILY: I suppose so. But it seems very unfair. And was your novel ever published?

1. From the 1840s to the 1890s, most novels were published in three volumes. Because of the price, most readers could not afford to buy copies and instead borrowed them from subscription lending libraries, of which Mudie's in London was the largest. By the 1890s, three-volume novels and lending libraries were seen by many as old-fashioned. Wilde's own novel, *The Picture of Dorian Gray* (1891), was a single volume.

MISS PRISM: Alas! no. The manuscript unfortunately was abandoned. I use the word in the sense of lost or mislaid. To your work, child—these speculations are profitless.

CECILY: [*Smiling.*] But I see dear Dr. Chasuble coming up through the garden.

MISS PRISM: [*Rising and advancing.*] Dr. Chasuble! This is indeed a pleasure.

[*Enter* CANON CHASUBLE.]

CHASUBLE: And how are we this morning? Miss Prism, you are, I trust, well?

CECILY: Miss Prism has just been complaining of a slight headache. I think it would do her so much good to have a short stroll with you in the park, Dr. Chasuble.

MISS PRISM: Cecily, I have not mentioned anything about a headache.

CECILY: No, dear Miss Prism, I know that, but I felt instinctively that you had a headache. Indeed I was thinking about that, and not about my German lesson, when the Rector came in.

CHASUBLE: I hope, Cecily, you are not inattentive.

CECILY: Oh, I am afraid I am.

CHASUBLE: That is strange. Were I fortunate enough to be Miss Prism's pupil, I would hang upon her lips. [MISS PRISM *glares.*] I spoke metaphorically.—My metaphor was drawn from bees.[2] Ahem! Mr. Worthing, I suppose, has not returned from town yet?

MISS PRISM: We do not expect him till Monday afternoon.

CHASUBLE: Ah yes, he usually likes to spend his Sunday in London. He is not one of those whose sole aim is enjoyment, as, by all accounts, that unfortunate young man his brother seems to be. But I must not disturb Egeria[3] and her pupil any longer.

MISS PRISM: Egeria? My name is Laetitia, Doctor.

CHASUBLE: [*Bowing.*] A classical allusion merely, drawn from the Pagan authors. I shall see you both no doubt at Evensong?[4]

MISS PRISM: I think, dear Doctor, I will have a stroll with you. I find I have a headache after all, and a walk might do it good.

CHASUBLE: With pleasure, Miss Prism, with pleasure. We might go as far as the schools and back.

MISS PRISM: That would be delightful. Cecily, you will read your Political Economy[5] in my absence. The chapter on the Fall of the Rupee you may omit. It is somewhat too sensational. Even these metallic problems have their melodramatic side. [*Goes down the garden with* CANON CHASUBLE.]

CECILY: [*Picks up books and throws them back on table.*] Horrid Political Economy! Horrid Geography! Horrid, horrid German!

[*Enter* MERRIMAN *with a card on a salver.*]

MERRIMAN: Mr. Ernest Worthing has just driven over from the station. He has brought his luggage with him.

CECILY: [*Takes the card and reads it.*] "Mr. Ernest Worthing, B. 4, The Albany, W." Uncle Jack's brother! Did you tell him Mr. Worthing was in town?

2. Reference to the "honey" of Miss Prism's instruction.

3. In classical mythology, a nymph famous as the wise counselor of Numa Pompilius, the second of Rome's legendary kings.

4. Evening church services.

5. That is, book about economics.

MERRIMAN: Yes, Miss. He seemed very much disappointed. I mentioned that you and Miss Prism were in the garden. He said he was anxious to speak to you privately for a moment.

CECILY: Ask Mr. Ernest Worthing to come here. I suppose you had better talk to the housekeeper about a room for him.

MERRIMAN: Yes, Miss. [MERRIMAN *goes off*.]

CECILY: I have never met any really wicked person before. I feel rather frightened. I am so afraid he will look just like everyone else. [*Enter* ALGERNON, *very gay and debonair.*] He does!

ALGERNON: [*Raising his hat.*] You are my little cousin Cecily, I'm sure.

CECILY: You are under some strange mistake. I am not little. In fact, I believe I am more than usually tall for my age. [ALGERNON *is rather taken aback.*] But I am your cousin Cecily. You, I see from your card, are Uncle Jack's brother, my cousin Ernest, my wicked cousin Ernest.

ALGERNON: Oh! I am not really wicked at all, cousin Cecily. You mustn't think that I am wicked.

CECILY: If you are not, then you have certainly been deceiving us all in a very inexcusable manner. I hope you have not been leading a double life, pretending to be wicked and being really good all the time. That would be hypocrisy.

ALGERNON: [*Looks at her in amazement.*] Oh! Of course I have been rather reckless.

CECILY: I am glad to hear it.

ALGERNON: In fact, now you mention the subject, I have been very bad in my own small way.

CECILY: I don't think you should be so proud of that, though I am sure it must have been very pleasant.

ALGERNON: It is much pleasanter being here with you.

CECILY: I can't understand how you are here at all. Uncle Jack won't be back till Monday afternoon.

ALGERNON: That is a great disappointment. I am obliged to go up by the first train on Monday morning. I have a business appointment that I am anxious . . . to miss.

CECILY: Couldn't you miss it anywhere but in London?

ALGERNON: No: the appointment is in London.

CECILY: Well, I know, of course, how important it is not to keep a business engagement, if one wants to retain any sense of the beauty of life, but still I think you had better wait till Uncle Jack arrives. I know he wants to speak to you about your emigrating.

ALGERNON: About my what?

CECILY: Your emigrating. He has gone up to buy your outfit.

ALGERNON: I certainly wouldn't let Jack buy my outfit. He has no taste in neckties at all.

CECILY: I don't think you will require neckties. Uncle Jack is sending you to Australia.[6]

ALGERNON: Australia? I'd sooner die.

---

6. Though no longer a penal colony in Wilde's day, Australia was still a British colony perceived as a place where disreputable family members might be sent.

CECILY: Well, he said at dinner on Wednesday night, that you would have to choose between this world, the next world, and Australia.

ALGERNON: Oh, well! The accounts I have received of Australia and the next world are not particularly encouraging. This world is good enough for me, cousin Cecily.

CECILY: Yes, but are you good enough for it?

ALGERNON: I'm afraid I'm not that. That is why I want you to reform me. You might make that your mission, if you don't mind, cousin Cecily.

CECILY: I'm afraid I've no time, this afternoon.

ALGERNON: Well, would you mind my reforming myself this afternoon?

CECILY: It is rather Quixotic of you. But I think you should try.

ALGERNON: I will. I feel better already.

CECILY: You are looking a little worse.

ALGERNON: That is because I am hungry.

CECILY: How thoughtless of me. I should have remembered that when one is going to lead an entirely new life, one requires regular and wholesome meals. Won't you come in?

ALGERNON: Thank you. Might I have a buttonhole[7] first? I never have any appetite unless I have a buttonhole first.

CECILY: A Maréchal Niel? [Picks up scissors.]

ALGERNON: No, I'd sooner have a pink rose.

CECILY: Why? [Cuts a flower.]

ALGERNON: Because you are like a pink rose, cousin Cecily.

CECILY: I don't think it can be right for you to talk to me like that. Miss Prism never says such things to me.

ALGERNON: Then Miss Prism is a shortsighted old lady. [CECILY puts the rose in his buttonhole.] You are the prettiest girl I ever saw.

CECILY: Miss Prism says that all good looks are a snare.

ALGERNON: They are a snare that every sensible man would like to be caught in.

CECILY: Oh! I don't think I would care to catch a sensible man. I shouldn't know what to talk to him about.

[They pass into the house. MISS PRISM and DR. CHASUBLE return.]

MISS PRISM: You are too much alone, dear Dr. Chasuble. You should get married. A misanthrope I can understand—a womanthrope, never!

CHASUBLE: [With a scholar's shudder.] Believe me, I do not deserve so neologistic a phrase. The precept as well as the practice of the Primitive Church[8] was distinctly against matrimony.

MISS PRISM: [Sententiously.] That is obviously the reason why the Primitive Church has not lasted up to the present day. And you do not seem to realize, dear Doctor, that by persistently remaining single, a man converts himself into a permanent public temptation. Men should be more careful; this very celibacy leads weaker vessels astray.

CHASUBLE: But is a man not equally attractive when married?

MISS PRISM: No married man is ever attractive except to his wife.

7. A flower to be worn on the lapel of a man's coat, in this case the Maréchal Niel, a popular yellow rose of the period.
8. Early Christian Church.

CHASUBLE: And often, I've been told, not even to her.

MISS PRISM: That depends on the intellectual sympathies of the woman. Maturity can always be depended on. Ripeness can be trusted. Young women are green. [DR. CHASUBLE *starts.*] I spoke horticulturally. My metaphor was drawn from fruits. But where is Cecily?

CHASUBLE: Perhaps she followed us to the schools.

> [*Enter* JACK *slowly from the back of the garden. He is dressed in the deepest mourning, with crape hat-band and black gloves.*]

MISS PRISM: Mr. Worthing!

CHASUBLE: Mr. Worthing?

MISS PRISM: This is indeed a surprise. We did not look for you till Monday afternoon.

JACK: [*Shakes* MISS PRISM's *hand in a tragic manner.*] I have returned sooner than I expected. Dr. Chasuble, I hope you are well?

CHASUBLE: Dear Mr. Worthing, I trust this garb of woe does not betoken some terrible calamity?

JACK: My brother.

MISS PRISM: More shameful debts and extravagance?

CHASUBLE: Still leading his life of pleasure?

JACK: [*Shaking his head.*] Dead!

CHASUBLE: Your brother Ernest dead?

JACK: Quite dead.

MISS PRISM: What a lesson for him! I trust he will profit by it.

CHASUBLE: Mr. Worthing, I offer you my sincere condolence. You have at least the consolation of knowing that you were always the most generous and forgiving of brothers.

JACK: Poor Ernest! He had many faults, but it is a sad, sad blow.

CHASUBLE: Very sad indeed. Were you with him at the end?

JACK: No. He died abroad; in Paris, in fact. I had a telegram last night from the manager of the Grand Hotel.

CHASUBLE: Was the cause of death mentioned?

JACK: A severe chill, it seems.

MISS PRISM: As a man sows, so shall he reap.

CHASUBLE: [*Raising his hand.*] Charity, dear Miss Prism, charity! None of us are perfect. I myself am peculiarly susceptible to drafts. Will the interment take place here?

JACK: No. He seemed to have expressed a desire to be buried in Paris.

CHASUBLE: In Paris! [*Shakes his head.*] I fear that hardly points to any very serious state of mind at the last. You would no doubt wish me to make some slight allusion to this tragic domestic affliction next Sunday. [JACK *presses his hand convulsively.*] My sermon on the meaning of the manna in the wilderness can be adapted to almost any occasion, joyful, or, as in the present case, distressing. [*All sigh.*] I have preached it at harvest celebrations, christenings, confirmations, on days of humiliation and festal days. The last time I delivered it was in the Cathedral, as a charity sermon on behalf of the Society for the Prevention of Discontent among the Upper Orders. The Bishop, who was present, was much struck by some of the analogies I drew.

JACK: Ah! That reminds me, you mentioned christenings, I think, Dr. Chasuble? I suppose you know how to christen all right? [DR. CHASUBLE *looks astounded.*] I mean, of course, you are continually christening, aren't you?

MISS PRISM: It is, I regret to say, one of the Rector's most constant duties in this parish. I have often spoken to the poorer classes on the subject. But they don't seem to know what thrift is.

CHASUBLE: But is there any particular infant in whom you are interested, Mr. Worthing? Your brother was, I believe, unmarried, was he not?

JACK: Oh yes.

MISS PRISM: [*Bitterly.*] People who live entirely for pleasure usually are.

JACK: But it is not for any child, dear Doctor. I am very fond of children. No! the fact is, I would like to be christened myself, this afternoon, if you have nothing better to do.

CHASUBLE: But surely, Mr. Worthing, you have been christened already?

JACK: I don't remember anything about it.

CHASUBLE: But have you any grave doubts on the subject?

JACK: I certainly intend to have. Of course I don't know if the thing would bother you in any way, or if you think I am a little too old now.

CHASUBLE: Not at all. The sprinkling, and, indeed, the immersion of adults is a perfectly canonical practice.

JACK: Immersion!

CHASUBLE: You need have no apprehensions. Sprinkling is all that is necessary, or indeed I think advisable. Our weather is so changeable. At what hour would you wish the ceremony performed?

JACK: Oh, I might trot round about five if that would suit you.

CHASUBLE: Perfectly, perfectly! In fact I have two similar ceremonies to perform at that time. A case of twins that occurred recently in one of the outlying cottages on your own estate. Poor Jenkins the carter,[9] a most hard-working man.

JACK: Oh! I don't see much fun in being christened along with other babies. It would be childish. Would half-past five do?

CHASUBLE: Admirably! Admirably! [*Takes out watch.*] And now, dear Mr. Worthing, I will not intrude any longer into a house of sorrow. I would merely beg you not to be too much bowed down by grief. What seem to us bitter trials are often blessings in disguise.

MISS PRISM: This seems to me a blessing of an extremely obvious kind.

[*Enter* CECILY *from the house.*]

CECILY: Uncle Jack! Oh, I am pleased to see you back. But what horrid clothes you have got on! Do go and change them.

MISS PRISM: Cecily!

CHASUBLE: My child! my child!

[CECILY *goes towards* JACK; *he kisses her brow in a melancholy manner.*]

CECILY: What is the matter, Uncle Jack? Do look happy! You look as if you had toothache, and I have got such a surprise for you. Who do you think is in the dining room? Your brother!

9. Cart-driver.

JACK: Who?

CECILY: Your brother Ernest. He arrived about half an hour ago.

JACK: What nonsense! I haven't got a brother!

CECILY: Oh, don't say that. However badly he may have behaved to you in the past he is still your brother. You couldn't be so heartless as to disown him. I'll tell him to come out. And you will shake hands with him, won't you, Uncle Jack? [*Runs back into the house.*]

CHASUBLE: These are very joyful tidings.

MISS PRISM: After we had all been resigned to his loss, his sudden return seems to me peculiarly distressing.

JACK: My brother is in the dining room? I don't know what it all means. I think it is perfectly absurd. [*Enter* ALGERNON *and* CECILY *hand in hand. They come slowly up to* JACK.] Good heavens! [*Motions* ALGERNON *away.*]

ALGERNON: Brother John, I have come down from town to tell you that I am very sorry for all the trouble I have given you, and that I intend to lead a better life in the future. [JACK *glares at him and does not take his hand.*]

CECILY: Uncle Jack, you are not going to refuse your own brother's hand?

JACK: Nothing will induce me to take his hand. I think his coming down here disgraceful. He knows perfectly well why.

CECILY: Uncle Jack, do be nice. There is some good in everyone. Ernest has just been telling me about his poor invalid friend Mr. Bunbury whom he goes to visit so often. And surely there must be much good in one who is kind to an invalid, and leaves the pleasures of London to sit by a bed of pain.

JACK: Oh! he has been talking about Bunbury, has he?

CECILY: Yes, he has told me all about poor Mr. Bunbury, and his terrible state of health.

JACK: Bunbury! Well, I won't have him talk to you about Bunbury or about anything else. It is enough to drive one perfectly frantic.

ALGERNON: Of course I admit that the faults were all on my side. But I must say that I think that Brother John's coldness to me is peculiarly painful. I expected a more enthusiastic welcome, especially considering it is the first time I have come here.

CECILY: Uncle Jack, if you don't shake hands with Ernest, I will never forgive you.

JACK: Never forgive me?

CECILY: Never, never, never!

JACK: Well, this is the last time I shall ever do it. [*Shakes hands with* ALGERNON *and glares.*]

CHASUBLE: It's pleasant, is it not, to see so perfect a reconciliation? I think we might leave the two brothers together.

MISS PRISM: Cecily, you will come with us.

CECILY: Certainly, Miss Prism. My little task of reconciliation is over.

CHASUBLE: You have done a beautiful action today, dear child.

MISS PRISM: We must not be premature in our judgments.

CECILY: I feel very happy.

[*They all go off.*]

JACK: You young scoundrel, Algy, you must get out of this place as soon as possible. I don't allow any Bunburying here.

[*Enter* MERRIMAN.]

MERRIMAN: I have put Mr. Ernest's things in the room next to yours, sir. I suppose that is all right?

JACK: What?

MERRIMAN: Mr. Ernest's luggage, sir. I have unpacked it and put it in the room next to your own.

JACK: His luggage?

MERRIMAN: Yes, sir. Three portmanteaus, a dressing case, two hat-boxes, and a large luncheon basket.

ALGERNON: I am afraid I can't stay more than a week this time.

JACK: Merriman, order the dogcart[1] at once. Mr. Ernest has been suddenly called back to town.

MERRIMAN: Yes, sir. [*Goes back into the house.*]

ALGERNON: What a fearful liar you are, Jack. I have not been called back to town at all.

JACK: Yes, you have.

ALGERNON: I haven't heard anyone call me.

JACK: Your duty as a gentleman calls you back.

ALGERNON: My duty as a gentleman has never interfered with my pleasures in the smallest degree.

JACK: I can quite understand that.

ALGERNON: Well, Cecily is a darling.

JACK: You are not to talk of Miss Cardew like that. I don't like it.

ALGERNON: Well, I don't like your clothes. You look perfectly ridiculous in them. Why on earth don't you go up and change? It is perfectly childish to be in deep mourning for a man who is actually staying for a whole week with you in your house as a guest. I call it grotesque.

JACK: You are certainly not staying with me for a whole week as a guest or anything else. You have got to leave . . . by the four-five train.

ALGERNON: I certainly won't leave you so long as you are in mourning. It would be most unfriendly. If I were in mourning you would stay with me, I suppose. I should think it very unkind if you didn't.

JACK: Well, will you go if I change my clothes?

ALGERNON: Yes, if you are not too long. I never saw anybody take so long to dress, and with such little result.

JACK: Well, at any rate, that is better than being always overdressed as you are.

ALGERNON: If I am occasionally a little overdressed, I make up for it by being always immensely overeducated.

JACK: Your vanity is ridiculous, your conduct an outrage, and your presence in my garden utterly absurd. However, you have got to catch the four-five, and I hope you will have a pleasant journey back to town. This Bunburying, as you call it, has not been a great success for you. [*Goes into the house.*]

ALGERNON: I think it has been a great success. I'm in love with Cecily, and that is everything. [*Enter* CECILY *at the back of the garden. She picks up the can and begins to water the flowers.*] But I must see her before I go, and make arrangements for another Bunbury. Ah, there she is.

---

1. Light, two-wheeled carriage, usually drawn by one horse.

CECILY: Oh, I merely came back to water the roses. I thought you were with Uncle Jack.

ALGERNON: He's gone to order the dogcart for me.

CECILY: Oh, is he going to take you for a nice drive?

ALGERNON: He's going to send me away.

CECILY: Then have we got to part?

ALGERNON: I am afraid so. It's very painful parting.

CECILY: It is always painful to part from people whom one has known for a very brief space of time. The absence of old friends one can endure with equanimity. But even a momentary separation from anyone to whom one has just been introduced is almost unbearable.

ALGERNON: Thank you.

    [*Enter* MERRIMAN.]

MERRIMAN: The dogcart is at the door, sir. [ALGERNON *looks appealingly at* CECILY.]

CECILY: It can wait, Merriman . . . . for . . . five minutes.

MERRIMAN: Yes, Miss. [*Exit* MERRIMAN.]

ALGERNON: I hope, Cecily, I shall not offend you if I state quite frankly and openly that you seem to me to be in every way the visible personification of absolute perfection.

CECILY: I think your frankness does you great credit, Ernest. If you will allow me I will copy your remarks into my diary. [*Goes over to table and begins writing in diary.*]

ALGERNON: Do you really keep a diary? I'd give anything to look at it. May I?

CECILY: Oh no. [*Puts her hand over it.*] You see, it is simply a very young girl's record of her own thoughts and impressions, and consequently meant for publication. When it appears in volume form I hope you will order a copy. But pray, Ernest, don't stop. I delight in taking down from dictation. I have reached "absolute perfection." You can go on. I am quite ready for more.

ALGERNON: [*Somewhat taken aback.*] Ahem! Ahem!

CECILY: Oh, don't cough, Ernest. When one is dictating one should speak fluently and not cough. Besides, I don't know how to spell a cough. [*Writes as* ALGERNON *speaks.*]

ALGERNON: [*Speaking very rapidly.*] Cecily, ever since I first looked upon your wonderful and incomparable beauty, I have dared to love you wildly, passionately, devotedly, hopelessly.

CECILY: I don't think that you should tell me that you love me wildly, passionately, devotedly, hopelessly. Hopelessly doesn't seem to make much sense, does it?

ALGERNON: Cecily!

    [*Enter* MERRIMAN.]

MERRIMAN: The dogcart is waiting, sir.

ALGERNON: Tell it to come round next week, at the same hour.

MERRIMAN: [*Looks at* CECILY, *who makes no sign.*] Yes, sir. [MERRIMAN *retires.*]

CECILY: Uncle Jack would be very much annoyed if he knew you were staying on till next week, at the same hour.

ALGERNON: Oh, I don't care about Jack. I don't care for anybody in the whole world but you. I love you, Cecily. You will marry me, won't you?

CECILY: You silly boy! Of course. Why, we have been engaged for the last three months.

ALGERNON: For the last three months?

CECILY: Yes, it will be exactly three months on Thursday.

ALGERNON: But how did we become engaged?

CECILY: Well, ever since dear Uncle Jack first confessed to us that he had a younger brother who was very wicked and bad, you of course have formed the chief topic of conversation between myself and Miss Prism. And of course a man who is much talked about is always very attractive. One feels there must be something in him after all. I daresay it was foolish of me, but I fell in love with you, Ernest.

ALGERNON: Darling! And when was the engagement actually settled?

CECILY: On the 14th of February last. Worn out by your entire ignorance of my existence, I determined to end the matter one way or the other, and after a long struggle with myself I accepted you under this dear old tree here. The next day I bought this little ring in your name, and this is the little bangle with the true lovers' knot I promised you always to wear.

ALGERNON: Did I give you this? It's very pretty, isn't it?

CECILY: Yes, you've wonderfully good taste, Ernest. It's the excuse I've always given for your leading such a bad life. And this is the box in which I keep all your dear letters. [Kneels at table, opens box, and produces letters tied up with blue ribbon.]

ALGERNON: My letters! But my own sweet Cecily, I have never written you any letters.

CECILY: You need hardly remind me of that, Ernest. I remember only too well that I was forced to write your letters for you. I always wrote three times a week, and sometimes oftener.

ALGERNON: Oh, do let me read them, Cecily?

CECILY: Oh, I couldn't possibly. They would make you far too conceited. [Replaces box.] The three you wrote me after I had broken off the engagement are so beautiful, and so badly spelled, that even now I can hardly read them without crying a little.

ALGERNON: But was our engagement ever broken off?

CECILY: Of course it was. On the 22nd of last March. You can see the entry if you like. [Shows diary.] "Today I broke off my engagement with Ernest. I feel it is better to do so. The weather still continues charming."

ALGERNON: But why on earth did you break it off? What had I done? I had done nothing at all. Cecily, I am very much hurt indeed to hear you broke it off. Particularly when the weather was so charming.

CECILY: It would hardly have been a really serious engagement if it hadn't been broken off at least once. But I forgave you before the week was out.

ALGERNON: [Crossing to her, and kneeling.] What a perfect angel you are, Cecily.

CECILY: You dear romantic boy. [He kisses her, she puts her fingers through his hair.] I hope your hair curls naturally, does it?

ALGERNON: Yes, darling, with a little help from others.

CECILY: I am so glad.

ALGERNON: You'll never break off our engagement again, Cecily?

CECILY: I don't think I could break it off now that I have actually met you. Besides, of course, there is the question of your name.

ALGERNON: Yes, of course. [*Nervously.*]

CECILY: You must not laugh at me, darling, but it had always been a girlish dream of mine to love someone whose name was Ernest. [ALGERNON *rises,* CECILY *also.*] There is something in that name that seems to inspire absolute confidence. I pity any poor married woman whose husband is not called Ernest.

ALGERNON: But, my dear child, do you mean to say you could not love me if I had some other name?

CECILY: But what name?

ALGERNON: Oh, any name you like—Algernon—for instance . . .

CECILY: But I don't like the name of Algernon.

ALGERNON: Well, my own dear, sweet, loving little darling, I really can't see why you should object to the name of Algernon. It is not at all a bad name. In fact, it is rather an aristocratic name. Half of the chaps who get into the Bankruptcy Court are called Algernon. But seriously, Cecily . . . [*Moving to her.*] . . . if my name was Algy, couldn't you love me?

CECILY: [*Rising.*] I might respect you, Ernest, I might admire your character, but I fear that I should not be able to give you my undivided attention.

ALGERNON: Ahem! Cecily! [*Picking up hat.*] Your Rector here is, I suppose, thoroughly experienced in the practice of all the rites and ceremonials of the Church?

CECILY: Oh, yes. Dr. Chasuble is a most learned man. He has never written a single book, so you can imagine how much he knows.

ALGERNON: I must see him at once on a most important christening—I mean on most important business.

CECILY: Oh!

ALGERNON: I shan't be away more than half an hour.

CECILY: Considering that we have been engaged since February the 14th, and that I only met you today for the first time, I think it is rather hard that you should leave me for so long a period as half an hour. Couldn't you make it twenty minutes?

ALGERNON: I'll be back in no time. [*Kisses her and rushes down the garden.*]

CECILY: What an impetuous boy he is! I like his hair so much. I must enter his proposal in my diary.

[*Enter* MERRIMAN.]

MERRIMAN: A Miss Fairfax has just called to see Mr. Worthing. On very important business, Miss Fairfax states.

CECILY: Isn't Mr. Worthing in his library?

MERRIMAN: Mr. Worthing went over in the direction of the rectory some time ago.

CECILY: Pray ask the lady to come out here; Mr. Worthing is sure to be back soon. And you can bring tea.

MERRIMAN: Yes, Miss. [*Goes out.*]

CECILY: Miss Fairfax! I suppose one of the many good elderly women who are associated with Uncle Jack in some of his philanthropic work in London. I don't quite like women who are interested in philanthropic work. I think it is so forward of them.

[*Enter* MERRIMAN.]

MERRIMAN: Miss Fairfax.

[*Enter* GWENDOLEN. *Exit* MERRIMAN.]

CECILY: [*Advancing to meet her.*] Pray let me introduce myself to you. My name is Cecily Cardew.

GWENDOLEN: Cecily Cardew? [*Moving to her and shaking hands.*] What a very sweet name! Something tells me that we are going to be great friends. I like you already more than I can say. My first impressions of people are never wrong.

CECILY: How nice of you to like me so much after we have known each other such a comparatively short time. Pray sit down.

GWENDOLEN: [*Still standing up.*] I may call you Cecily, may I not?

CECILY: With pleasure!

GWENDOLEN: And you will always call me Gwendolen, won't you?

CECILY: If you wish.

GWENDOLEN: Then that is all quite settled, is it not?

CECILY: I hope so. [*A pause. They both sit down together.*]

GWENDOLEN: Perhaps this might be a favorable opportunity for my mentioning who I am. My father is Lord Bracknell. You have never heard of papa, I suppose?

CECILY: I don't think so.

GWENDOLEN: Outside the family circle, papa, I am glad to say, is entirely unknown. I think that is quite as it should be. The home seems to me to be the proper sphere for the man. And certainly once a man begins to neglect his domestic duties he becomes painfully effeminate, does he not? And I don't like that. It makes men so very attractive. Cecily, mamma, whose views on education are remarkably strict, has brought me up to be extremely shortsighted; it is part of her system; so do you mind my looking at you through my glasses?

CECILY: Oh! not at all, Gwendolen. I am very fond of being looked at.

GWENDOLEN: [*After examining* CECILY *carefully through a lorgnette.*][2] You are here on a short visit, I suppose.

CECILY: Oh no! I live here.

GWENDOLEN: [*Severely.*] Really? Your mother, no doubt, or some female relative of advanced years, resides here also?

CECILY: Oh no! I have no mother, nor, in fact, any relations.

GWENDOLEN: Indeed?

CECILY: My dear guardian, with the assistance of Miss Prism, has the arduous task of looking after me.

GWENDOLEN: Your guardian?

CECILY: Yes, I am Mr. Worthing's ward.

GWENDOLEN: Oh! It is strange he never mentioned to me that he had a ward. How secretive of him! He grows more interesting hourly. I am not sure, however, that the news inspires me with feelings of unmixed delight. [*Rising and*

2. Glasses with a long handle; they are held to the eyes rather than worn.

going to her.] I am very fond of you, Cecily; I have liked you ever since I met you! But I am bound to state that now that I know that you are Mr. Worthing's ward, I cannot help expressing a wish you were—well just a little older than you seem to be—and not quite so very alluring in appearance. In fact, if I may speak candidly—

CECILY: Pray do! I think that whenever one has anything unpleasant to say, one should always be quite candid.

GWENDOLEN: Well, to speak with perfect candor, Cecily, I wish that you were fully forty-two, and more than usually plain for your age. Ernest has a strong upright nature. He is the very soul of truth and honor. Disloyalty would be as impossible to him as deception. But even men of the noblest possible moral character are extremely susceptible to the influence of the physical charms of others. Modern, no less than ancient history, supplies us with many most painful examples of what I refer to. If it were not so, indeed, history would be quite unreadable.

CECILY: I beg your pardon, Gwendolen, did you say Ernest?

GWENDOLEN: Yes.

CECILY: Oh, but it is not Mr. Ernest Worthing who is my guardian. It is his brother—his elder brother.

GWENDOLEN: [*Sitting down again.*] Ernest never mentioned to me that he had a brother.

CECILY: I am sorry to say they have not been on good terms for a long time.

GWENDOLEN: Ah! that accounts for it. And now that I think of it I have never heard any man mention his brother. The subject seems distasteful to most men. Cecily, you have lifted a load from my mind. I was growing almost anxious. It would have been terrible if any cloud had come across a friendship like ours, would it not? Of course you are quite, quite sure that it is not Mr. Ernest Worthing who is your guardian?

CECILY: Quite sure. [*A pause.*] In fact, I am going to be his.

GWENDOLEN: [*Inquiringly.*] I beg your pardon?

CECILY: [*Rather shy and confidingly.*] Dearest Gwendolen, there is no reason why I should make a secret of it to you. Our little county newspaper is sure to chronicle the fact next week. Mr. Ernest Worthing and I are engaged to be married.

GWENDOLEN: [*Quite politely, rising.*] My darling Cecily, I think there must be some slight error. Mr. Ernest Worthing is engaged to me. The announcement will appear in the *Morning Post* on Saturday at the latest.

CECILY: [*Very politely, rising.*] I am afraid you must be under some misconception. Ernest proposed to me exactly ten minutes ago. [*Shows diary.*]

GWENDOLEN: [*Examines diary through her lorgnette carefully.*] It is certainly very curious, for he asked me to be his wife yesterday afternoon at 5:30. If you would care to verify the incident, pray do so. [*Produces diary of her own.*] I never travel without my diary. One should always have something sensational to read in the train. I am so sorry, dear Cecily, if it is any disappointment to you, but I am afraid *I* have the prior claim.

CECILY: It would distress me more than I can tell you, dear Gwendolen, if it caused you any mental or physical anguish, but I feel bound to point out that since Ernest proposed to you he clearly has changed his mind.

GWENDOLEN: [*Meditatively.*] If the poor fellow has been entrapped into any foolish promise I shall consider it my duty to rescue him at once, and with a firm hand.

CECILY: [*Thoughtfully and sadly.*] Whatever unfortunate entanglement my dear boy may have got into, I will never reproach him with it after we are married.

GWENDOLEN: Do you allude to me, Miss Cardew, as an entanglement? You are presumptuous. On an occasion of this kind it becomes more than a moral duty to speak one's mind. It becomes a pleasure.

CECILY: Do you suggest, Miss Fairfax, that I entrapped Ernest into an engagement? How dare you? This is no time for wearing the shallow mask of manners. When I see a spade I call it a spade.

GWENDOLEN: [*Satirically.*] I am glad to say that I have never seen a spade. It is obvious that our social spheres have been widely different.

[*Enter* MERRIMAN, *followed by the footman. He carries a salver, tablecloth, and plate stand.* CECILY *is about to retort. The presence of the servants exercises a restraining influence, under which both girls chafe.*]

MERRIMAN: Shall I lay tea here as usual, Miss?

CECILY: [*Sternly, in a calm voice.*] Yes, as usual.

[MERRIMAN *begins to clear table and lay cloth. A long pause.* CECILY *and* GWENDOLEN *glare at each other.*]

GWENDOLEN: Are there many interesting walks in the vicinity, Miss Cardew?

CECILY: Oh! yes! a great many. From the top of one of the hills quite close one can see five counties.

GWENDOLEN: Five counties! I don't think I should like that. I hate crowds.

CECILY: [*Sweetly.*] I suppose that is why you live in town?

[GWENDOLEN *bites her lip, and beats her foot nervously with her parasol.*]

GWENDOLEN: [*Looking round.*] Quite a well-kept garden this is, Miss Cardew.

CECILY: So glad you like it, Miss Fairfax.

GWENDOLEN: I had no idea there were any flowers in the country.

CECILY: Oh, flowers are as common here, Miss Fairfax, as people are in London.

GWENDOLEN: Personally I cannot understand how anybody manages to exist in the country, if anybody who is anybody does. The country always bores me to death.

CECILY: Ah! This is what the newspapers call agricultural depression, is it not? I believe the aristocracy are suffering very much from it just at present. It is almost an epidemic amongst them, I have been told. May I offer you some tea, Miss Fairfax?

GWENDOLEN: [*With elaborate politeness.*] Thank you. [*Aside.*] Detestable girl! But I require tea!

CECILY: [*Sweetly.*] Sugar?

GWENDOLEN: [*Superciliously.*] No, thank you. Sugar is not fashionable anymore.

[CECILY *looks angrily at her, takes up the tongs and puts four lumps of sugar into the cup.*]

CECILY: [*Severely.*] Cake or bread and butter?

GWENDOLEN: [*In a bored manner.*] Bread and butter, please. Cake is rarely seen at the best houses nowadays.

CECILY: [*Cuts a very large slice of cake, and puts it on the tray.*] Hand that to Miss Fairfax.

[MERRIMAN *does so, and goes out with footman.* GWENDOLEN *drinks the tea and makes a grimace. Puts down cup at once, reaches out her hand to the bread and butter, looks at it, and finds it is cake. Rises in indignation.*]

GWENDOLEN: You have filled my tea with lumps of sugar, and though I asked most distinctly for bread and butter, you have given me cake. I am known for the gentleness of my disposition, and the extraordinary sweetness of my nature, but I warn you, Miss Cardew, you may go too far.

CECILY: [*Rising.*] To save my poor, innocent, trusting boy from the machinations of any other girl there are no lengths to which I would not go.

GWENDOLEN: From the moment I saw you I distrusted you. I felt that you were false and deceitful. I am never deceived in such matters. My first impressions of people are invariably right.

CECILY: It seems to me, Miss Fairfax, that I am trespassing on your valuable time. No doubt you have many other calls of a similar character to make in the neighborhood.

[*Enter* JACK.]

GWENDOLEN: [*Catching sight of him.*] Ernest! My own Ernest!

JACK: Gwendolen! Darling! [*Offers to kiss her.*]

GWENDOLEN: [*Drawing back.*] A moment! May I ask if you are engaged to be married to this young lady? [*Points to* CECILY.]

JACK: [*Laughing.*] To dear little Cecily! Of course not! What could have put such an idea into your pretty little head?

GWENDOLEN: Thank you. You may! [*Offers her cheek.*]

CECILY: [*Very sweetly.*] I knew there must be some misunderstanding, Miss Fairfax. The gentleman whose arm is at present round your waist is my dear guardian, Mr. John Worthing.

GWENDOLEN: I beg your pardon?

CECILY: This is Uncle Jack.

GWENDOLEN: [*Receding.*] Jack! Oh!

[*Enter* ALGERNON.]

CECILY: Here is Ernest.

ALGERNON: [*Goes straight over to* CECILY *without noticing anyone else.*] My own love! [*Offers to kiss her.*]

CECILY: [*Drawing back.*] A moment, Ernest! May I ask you—are you engaged to be married to this young lady?

ALGERNON: [*Looking round.*] To what young lady? Good heavens! Gwendolen!

CECILY: Yes! to good heavens, Gwendolen, I mean to Gwendolen.

ALGERNON: [*Laughing.*] Of course not! What could have put such an idea into your pretty little head?

CECILY: Thank you. [*Presenting her cheek to be kissed.*] You may. [ALGERNON *kisses her.*]

GWENDOLEN: I felt there was some slight error, Miss Cardew. The gentleman who is now embracing you is my cousin, Mr. Algernon Moncrieff.

CECILY: [*Breaking away from* ALGERNON.] Algernon Moncrieff! Oh! [*The two girls move towards each other and put their arms round each other's waists as if for protection.*] Are you called Algernon?

ALGERNON: I cannot deny it.

CECILY: Oh!

GWENDOLEN: Is your name really John?

JACK: [*Standing rather proudly.*] I could deny it if I liked, I could deny anything if I liked. But my name certainly is John. It has been John for years.

CECILY: [*To* GWENDOLEN.] A gross deception has been practiced on both of us.

GWENDOLEN: My poor wounded Cecily!

CECILY: My sweet wronged Gwendolen!

GWENDOLEN: [*Slowly and seriously.*] You will call me sister, will you not?

[*They embrace.* JACK *and* ALGERNON *groan and walk up and down.*]

CECILY: [*Rather brightly.*] There is just one question I would like to be allowed to ask my guardian.

GWENDOLEN: An admirable idea! Mr. Worthing, there is just one question I would like to be permitted to put to you. Where is your brother Ernest? We are both engaged to be married to your brother Ernest, so it is a matter of some importance to us to know where your brother Ernest is at present.

JACK: [*Slowly and hesitatingly.*] Gwendolen—Cecily—it is very painful for me to be forced to speak the truth. It is the first time in my life that I have ever been reduced to such a painful position, and I am really quite inexperienced in doing anything of the kind. However I will tell you quite frankly that I have no brother Ernest. I have no brother at all. I never had a brother in my life, and certainly have not the smallest intention of ever having one in the future.

CECILY: [*Surprised.*] No brother at all?

JACK: [*Cheerily.*] None!

GWENDOLEN: [*Severely.*] Had you never a brother of any kind?

JACK: [*Pleasantly.*] Never. Not even of any kind.

GWENDOLEN: I am afraid it is quite clear, Cecily, that neither of us is engaged to be married to anyone.

CECILY: It is not a very pleasant position for a young girl suddenly to find herself in. Is it?

GWENDOLEN: Let us go into the house. They will hardly venture to come after us there.

CECILY: No, men are so cowardly, aren't they?

[*They retire into the house with scornful looks.*]

JACK: This ghastly state of things is what you call Bunburying, I suppose?

ALGERNON: Yes, and a perfectly wonderful Bunbury it is. The most wonderful Bunbury I have ever had in my life.

JACK: Well, you've no right whatsoever to Bunbury here.

ALGERNON: That is absurd. One has a right to Bunbury anywhere one chooses. Every serious Bunburyist knows that.

JACK: Serious Bunburyist! Good heavens!

ALGERNON: Well, one must be serious about something, if one wants to have any amusement in life. I happen to be serious about Bunburying. What on earth you are serious about I haven't got the remotest idea. About everything, I should fancy. You have such an absolutely trivial nature.

JACK: Well, the only small satisfaction I have in the whole of this wretched business is that your friend Bunbury is quite exploded. You won't be able to run down to the country quite so often as you used to do, dear Algy. And a very good thing too.

ALGERNON: Your brother is a little off-color,[3] isn't he, dear Jack? You won't be able to disappear to London quite so frequently as your wicked custom was. And not a bad thing either.

JACK: As for your conduct towards Miss Cardew, I must say that your taking in a sweet, simple, innocent girl like that is quite inexcusable. To say nothing of the fact that she is my ward.

ALGERNON: I can see no possible defense at all for your deceiving a brilliant, clever, thoroughly experienced young lady like Miss Fairfax. To say nothing of the fact that she is my cousin.

JACK: I wanted to be engaged to Gwendolen, that is all. I love her.

ALGERNON: Well, I simply wanted to be engaged to Cecily. I adore her.

JACK: There is certainly no chance of your marrying Miss Cardew.

ALGERNON: I don't think there is much likelihood, Jack, of you and Miss Fairfax being united.

JACK: Well, that is no business of yours.

ALGERNON: If it was my business, I wouldn't talk about it. [*Begins to eat muffins.*] It is very vulgar to talk about one's business. Only people like stockbrokers do that, and then merely at dinner parties.

JACK: How can you sit there, calmly eating muffins when we are in this horrible trouble, I can't make out. You seem to me to be perfectly heartless.

ALGERNON: Well, I can't eat muffins in an agitated manner. The butter would probably get on my cuffs. One should always eat muffins quite calmly. It is the only way to eat them.

JACK: I say it's perfectly heartless your eating muffins at all, under the circumstances.

ALGERNON: When I am in trouble, eating is the only thing that consoles me. Indeed, when I am in really great trouble, as anyone who knows me intimately will tell you, I refuse everything except food and drink. At the present moment I am eating muffins because I am unhappy. Besides, I am particularly fond of muffins. [*Rising.*]

JACK: [*Rising.*] Well, that is no reason why you should eat them all in that greedy way. [*Takes muffins from* ALGERNON.]

ALGERNON: [*Offering tea cake.*] I wish you would have tea cake instead. I don't like tea cake.

JACK: Good heavens! I suppose a man may eat his own muffins in his own garden.

ALGERNON: But you have just said it was perfectly heartless to eat muffins.

3. In poor health.

JACK: I said it was perfectly heartless of you, under the circumstances. That is a very different thing.

ALGERNON: That may be. But the muffins are the same. [*He seizes the muffin dish from* JACK.]

JACK: Algy, I wish to goodness you would go.

ALGERNON: You can't possibly ask me to go without having some dinner. It's absurd. I never go without my dinner. No one ever does, except vegetarians and people like that. Besides I have just made arrangements with Dr. Chasuble to be christened at a quarter to six under the name of Ernest.

JACK: My dear fellow, the sooner you give up that nonsense the better. I made arrangements this morning with Dr. Chasuble to be christened myself at 5:30, and I naturally will take the name of Ernest. Gwendolen would wish it. We can't both be christened Ernest. It's absurd. Besides, I have a perfect right to be christened if I like. There is no evidence at all that I ever have been christened by anybody. I should think it extremely probable I never was, and so does Dr. Chasuble. It is entirely different in your case. You have been christened already.

ALGERNON: Yes, but I have not been christened for years.

JACK: Yes, but you have been christened. That is the important thing.

ALGERNON: Quite so. So I know my constitution can stand it. If you are not quite sure about your ever having been christened, I must say I think it rather dangerous your venturing on it now. It might make you very unwell. You can hardly have forgotten that someone very closely connected with you was very nearly carried off this week in Paris by a severe chill.

JACK: Yes, but you said yourself that a severe chill was not hereditary.

ALGERNON: It usen't to be, I know—but I daresay it is now. Science is always making wonderful improvements in things.

JACK: [*Picking up the muffin dish.*] Oh, that is nonsense; you are always talking nonsense.

ALGERNON: Jack, you are at the muffins again! I wish you wouldn't. There are only two left. [*Takes them.*] I told you I was particularly fond of muffins.

JACK: But I hate tea cake.

ALGERNON: Why on earth then do you allow tea cake to be served up for your guests? What ideas you have of hospitality!

JACK: Algernon! I have already told you to go. I don't want you here. Why don't you go!

ALGERNON: I haven't quite finished my tea yet! and there is still one muffin left.

[JACK *groans, and sinks into a chair.* ALGERNON *still continues eating.*]

ACT-DROP

ACT III

SCENE: *Morning room at the Manor House.*

[GWENDOLEN *and* CECILY *are at the window, looking out into the garden.*]

GWENDOLEN: The fact that they did not follow us at once into the house, as anyone else would have done, seems to me to show that they have some sense of shame left.

CECILY: They have been eating muffins. That looks like repentance.

GWENDOLEN: [*After a pause.*] They don't seem to notice us at all. Couldn't you cough?

CECILY: But I haven't got a cough.

GWENDOLEN: They're looking at us. What effrontery!

CECILY: They're approaching. That's very forward of them.

GWENDOLEN: Let us preserve a dignified silence.

CECILY: Certainly. It's the only thing to do now.

[*Enter* JACK *followed by* ALGERNON. *They whistle some dreadful popular air from a British Opera.*]

GWENDOLEN: This dignified silence seems to produce an unpleasant effect.

CECILY: A most distasteful one.

GWENDOLEN: But we will not be the first to speak.

CECILY: Certainly not.

GWENDOLEN: Mr. Worthing, I have something very particular to ask you. Much depends on your reply.

CECILY: Gwendolen, your common sense is invaluable. Mr. Moncrieff, kindly answer me the following question. Why did you pretend to be my guardian's brother?

ALGERNON: In order that I might have an opportunity of meeting you.

CECILY: [*To* GWENDOLEN.] That certainly seems a satisfactory explanation, does it not?

GWENDOLEN: Yes, dear, if you can believe him.

CECILY: I don't. But that does not affect the wonderful beauty of his answer.

GWENDOLEN: True. In matters of grave importance, style, not sincerity, is the vital thing. Mr. Worthing, what explanation can you offer to me for pretending to have a brother? Was it in order that you might have an opportunity of coming up to town to see me as often as possible?

JACK: Can you doubt it, Miss Fairfax?

GWENDOLEN: I have the gravest doubts upon the subject. But I intend to crush them. This is not the moment for German skepticism.[4] [*Moving to* CECILY.] Their explanations appear to be quite satisfactory, especially Mr. Worthing's. That seems to me to have the stamp of truth upon it.

CECILY: I am more than content with what Mr. Moncrieff said. His voice alone inspires one with absolute credulity.

GWENDOLEN: Then you think we should forgive them?

CECILY: Yes. I mean no.

GWENDOLEN: True! I had forgotten. There are principles at stake that one cannot surrender. Which of us should tell them? The task is not a pleasant one.

CECILY: Could we not both speak at the same time?

GWENDOLEN: An excellent idea! I nearly always speak at the same time as other people. Will you take the time from me?

CECILY: Certainly. [GWENDOLEN *beats time with uplifted finger.*]

---

4. Reference to such philosophical movements as the Materialism of Ludwig Feuerbach (1804–72) and such theological movements as the "Higher Criticism," which promoted studying the Bible in the same way as other literary works.

GWENDOLEN AND CECILY: [*Speaking together.*] Your Christian names are still an insuperable barrier. That is all!

JACK AND ALGERNON: [*Speaking together.*] Our Christian names! Is that all? But we are going to be christened this afternoon.

GWENDOLEN: [*To* JACK.] For my sake you are prepared to do this terrible thing?

JACK: I am.

CECILY: [*To* ALGERNON.] To please me you are ready to face this fearful ordeal?

ALGERNON: I am!

GWENDOLEN: How absurd to talk of the equality of the sexes! Where questions of self-sacrifice are concerned, men are infinitely beyond us.

JACK: We are. [*Clasps hands with* ALGERNON.]

CECILY: They have moments of physical courage of which we women know absolutely nothing.

GWENDOLEN: [*To* JACK.] Darling!

ALGERNON: [*To* CECILY.] Darling. [*They fall into each other's arms.*]

[*Enter* MERRIMAN. *When he enters he coughs loudly, seeing the situation.*]

MERRIMAN: Ahem! Ahem! Lady Bracknell!

JACK: Good heavens!

[*Enter* LADY BRACKNELL. *The couples separate in alarm. Exit* MERRIMAN.]

LADY BRACKNELL: Gwendolen! What does this mean?

GWENDOLEN: Merely that I am engaged to be married to Mr. Worthing, mamma.

LADY BRACKNELL: Come here. Sit down. Sit down immediately. Hesitation of any kind is a sign of mental decay in the young, of physical weakness in the old. [*Turns to* JACK.] Apprised, sir, of my daughter's sudden flight by her trusty maid, whose confidence I purchased by means of a small coin, I followed her at once by a luggage train. Her unhappy father is, I am glad to say, under the impression that she is attending a more than usually lengthy lecture by the University Extension Scheme[5] on the Influence of a Permanent Income on Thought. I do not propose to undeceive him. Indeed I have never undeceived him on any question. I would consider it wrong. But of course, you will clearly understand that all communication between yourself and my daughter must cease immediately from this moment. On this point, as indeed on all points, I am firm.

JACK: I am engaged to be married to Gwendolen, Lady Bracknell!

LADY BRACKNELL: You are nothing of the kind, sir. And now, as regards Algernon! . . . Algernon!

ALGERNON: Yes, Aunt Augusta.

LADY BRACKNELL: May I ask if it is in this house that your invalid friend Mr. Bunbury resides?

ALGERNON: [*Stammering.*] Oh! No! Bunbury doesn't live here. Bunbury is somewhere else at present. In fact, Bunbury is dead.

LADY BRACKNELL: Dead! When did Mr. Bunbury die? His death must have been extremely sudden.

5. Program of public lectures delivered by university professors.

ALGERNON: [*Airily.*] Oh! I killed Bunbury this afternoon. I mean poor Bunbury died this afternoon.

LADY BRACKNELL: What did he die of?

ALGERNON: Bunbury? Oh, he was quite exploded.

LADY BRACKNELL: Exploded! Was he the victim of a revolutionary outrage?[6] I was not aware that Mr. Bunbury was interested in social legislation. If so, he is well punished for his morbidity.

ALGERNON: My dear Aunt Augusta, I mean he was found out! The doctors found out that Bunbury could not live, that is what I mean—so Bunbury died.

LADY BRACKNELL: He seems to have had great confidence in the opinion of his physicians. I am glad, however, that he made up his mind at the last to some definite course of action, and acted under proper medical advice. And now that we have finally got rid of this Mr. Bunbury, may I ask, Mr. Worthing, who is that young person whose hand my nephew Algernon is now holding in what seems to me a peculiarly unnecessary manner?

JACK: That lady is Miss Cecily Cardew, my ward.

[LADY BRACKNELL *bows coldly to* CECILY.]

ALGERNON: I am engaged to be married to Cecily, Aunt Augusta.

LADY BRACKNELL: I beg your pardon?

CECILY: Mr. Moncrieff and I are engaged to be married, Lady Bracknell.

LADY BRACKNELL: [*With a shiver, crossing to the sofa and sitting down.*] I do not know whether there is anything peculiarly exciting in the air of this particular part of Hertfordshire, but the number of engagements that go on seems to me considerably above the proper average that statistics have laid down for our guidance. I think some preliminary inquiry on my part would not be out of place. Mr. Worthing, is Miss Cardew at all connected with any of the larger railway stations in London? I merely desire information. Until yesterday I had no idea that there were any families or persons whose origin was a terminus.

[JACK *looks perfectly furious, but restrains himself.*]

JACK: [*In a clear, cold voice.*] Miss Cardew is the granddaughter of the late Mr. Thomas Cardew of 149, Belgrave Square, S.W.; Gervase Park, Dorking, Surrey; and the Sporran, Fifeshire, N.B.[7]

LADY BRACKNELL: That sounds not unsatisfactory. Three addresses always inspire confidence, even in tradesmen. But what proof have I of their authenticity?

JACK: I have carefully preserved the Court Guides[8] of the period. They are open to your inspection, Lady Bracknell.

LADY BRACKNELL: [*Grimly.*] I have known strange errors in that publication.

JACK: Miss Cardew's family solicitors are Messrs.[9] Markby, Markby, and Markby.

6. That is, of violence committed by revolutionaries or radicals. Bombings, especially by anarchists and Irish radicals, did occur periodically in the 1880s and 1890s.

7. In addition to his London residence in Belgrave Square (referred to in Act I), Mr. Cardew has homes in the south of England (Dorking, Surrey) and in Scotland (Fifeshire; N.B.: North Britain).

8. Directories of names and addresses of the gentry and nobility.

9. Short for "Messieurs" ("Misters" in French). *Solicitors*: lawyers.

LADY BRACKNELL: Markby, Markby, and Markby? A firm of the very highest position in their profession. Indeed I am told that one of the Mr. Markbys is occasionally to be seen at dinner parties. So far I am satisfied.

JACK: [*Very irritably.*] How extremely kind of you, Lady Bracknell! I have also in my possession, you will be pleased to hear, certificates of Miss Cardew's birth, baptism, whooping cough, registration, vaccination, confirmation, and the measles; both the German and the English variety.

LADY BRACKNELL: Ah! A life crowded with incident, I see; though perhaps somewhat too exciting for a young girl. I am not myself in favor of premature experiences. [*Rises, looks at her watch.*] Gwendolen! the time approaches for our departure. We have not a moment to lose. As a matter of form, Mr. Worthing, I had better ask you if Miss Cardew has any little fortune?

JACK: Oh! about a hundred and thirty thousand pounds in the Funds.[1] That is all. Good-bye, Lady Bracknell. So pleased to have seen you.

LADY BRACKNELL: [*Sitting down again.*] A moment, Mr. Worthing. A hundred and thirty thousand pounds! And in the Funds! Miss Cardew seems to me a most attractive young lady, now that I look at her. Few girls of the present day have any really solid qualities, any of the qualities that last, and improve with time. We live, I regret to say, in an age of surfaces. [*To* CECILY.] Come over here, dear. [CECILY *goes across.*] Pretty child! your dress is sadly simple, and your hair seems almost as Nature might have left it. But we can soon alter all that. A thoroughly experienced French maid produces a really marvelous result in a very brief space of time. I remember recommending one to young Lady Lancing, and after three months her own husband did not know her.

JACK: [*Aside.*] And after six months nobody knew her.

LADY BRACKNELL: [*Glares at* JACK *for a few moments. Then bends, with a practiced smile, to* CECILY.] Kindly turn round, sweet child. [CECILY *turns completely round.*] No, the side view is what I want. [CECILY *presents her profile.*] Yes, quite as I expected. There are distinct social possibilities in your profile. The two weak points in our age are its want of principle and its want of profile. The chin a little higher, dear. Style largely depends on the way the chin is worn. They are worn very high, just at present. Algernon!

ALGERNON: Yes, Aunt Augusta!

LADY BRACKNELL: There are distinct social possibilities in Miss Cardew's profile.

ALGERNON: Cecily is the sweetest, dearest, prettiest girl in the whole world. And I don't care twopence[2] about social possibilities.

LADY BRACKNELL: Never speak disrespectfully of Society, Algernon. Only people who can't get into it do that. [*To* CECILY.] Dear child, of course you know that Algernon has nothing but his debts to depend upon. But I do not approve of mercenary marriages. When I married Lord Bracknell I had no fortune of any kind. But I never dreamed for a moment of allowing that to stand in my way. Well, I suppose I must give my consent.

ALGERNON: Thank you, Aunt Augusta.

LADY BRACKNELL: Cecily, you may kiss me!

1. Millions in today's U.S. currency, invested in stock of the British National Debt and thus very secure.
2. That is, two pennies, a trifling amount.

CECILY: [*Kisses her.*] Thank you, Lady Bracknell.

LADY BRACKNELL: You may also address me as Aunt Augusta for the future.

CECILY: Thank you, Aunt Augusta.

LADY BRACKNELL: The marriage, I think, had better take place quite soon.

ALGERNON: Thank you, Aunt Augusta.

CECILY: Thank you, Aunt Augusta.

LADY BRACKNELL: To speak frankly, I am not in favor of long engagements. They give people the opportunity of finding out each other's character before marriage, which I think is never advisable.

JACK: I beg your pardon for interrupting you, Lady Bracknell, but this engagement is quite out of the question. I am Miss Cardew's guardian, and she cannot marry without my consent until she comes of age. That consent I absolutely decline to give.

LADY BRACKNELL: Upon what grounds may I ask? Algernon is an extremely, I may almost say an ostentatiously, eligible young man. He has nothing, but he looks everything. What more can one desire?

JACK: It pains me very much to have to speak frankly to you, Lady Bracknell, about your nephew, but the fact is that I do not approve at all of his moral character. I suspect him of being untruthful.

[ALGERNON *and* CECILY *look at him in indignant amazement.*]

LADY BRACKNELL: Untruthful! My nephew Algernon? Impossible! He is an Oxonian.[3]

JACK: I fear there can be no possible doubt about the matter. This afternoon, during my temporary absence in London on an important question of romance, he obtained admission to my house by means of the false pretense of being my brother. Under an assumed name he drank, I've just been informed by the butler, an entire pint bottle of my Perrier-Jouet, Brut, '89;[4] a wine I was specially reserving for myself. Continuing his disgraceful deception, he succeeded in the course of the afternoon in alienating the affections of my only ward. He subsequently stayed to tea, and devoured every single muffin. And what makes his conduct all the more heartless is, that he was perfectly well aware from the first that I have no brother, that I never had a brother, and that I don't intend to have a brother, not even of any kind. I distinctly told him so myself yesterday afternoon.

LADY BRACKNELL: Ahem! Mr. Worthing, after careful consideration I have decided entirely to overlook my nephew's conduct to you.

JACK: That is very generous of you, Lady Bracknell. My own decision, however, is unalterable. I decline to give my consent.

LADY BRACKNELL: [*To* CECILY.] Come here, sweet child. [CECILY *goes over.*] How old are you, dear?

CECILY: Well, I am really only eighteen, but I always admit to twenty when I go to evening parties.

LADY BRACKNELL: You are perfectly right in making some slight alteration. Indeed, no woman should ever be quite accurate about her age. It looks so

---

3. Graduate of the University of Oxford.
4. Very fine champagne.

calculating. . . . [*In a meditative manner.*] Eighteen, but admitting to twenty at evening parties. Well, it will not be very long before you are of age and free from the restraints of tutelage. So I don't think your guardian's consent is, after all, a matter of any importance.

JACK: Pray excuse me, Lady Bracknell, for interrupting you again, but it is only fair to tell you that according to the terms of her grandfather's will Miss Cardew does not come legally of age till she is thirty-five.

LADY BRACKNELL: That does not seem to me to be a grave objection. Thirty-five is a very attractive age. London society is full of women of the very highest birth who have, of their own free choice, remained thirty-five for years. Lady Dumbleton is an instance in point. To my own knowledge she has been thirty-five ever since she arrived at the age of forty, which was many years ago now. I see no reason why our dear Cecily should not be even still more attractive at the age you mention than she is at present. There will be a large accumulation of property.

CECILY: Algy, could you wait for me till I was thirty-five?

ALGERNON: Of course I could, Cecily. You know I could.

CECILY: Yes, I felt it instinctively, but I couldn't wait all that time. I hate waiting even five minutes for anybody. It always makes me rather cross. I am not punctual myself, I know, but I do like punctuality in others, and waiting, even to be married, is quite out of the question.

ALGERNON: Then what is to be done, Cecily?

CECILY: I don't know, Mr. Moncrieff.

LADY BRACKNELL: My dear Mr. Worthing, as Miss Cardew states positively that she cannot wait till she is thirty-five—a remark which I am bound to say seems to me to show a somewhat impatient nature—I would beg of you to reconsider your decision.

JACK: But my dear Lady Bracknell, the matter is entirely in your own hands. The moment you consent to my marriage with Gwendolen, I will most gladly allow your nephew to form an alliance with my ward.

LADY BRACKNELL: [*Rising and drawing herself up.*] You must be quite aware that what you propose is out of the question.

JACK: Then a passionate celibacy is all that any of us can look forward to.

LADY BRACKNELL: This is not the destiny I propose for Gwendolen. Algernon, of course, can choose for himself. [*Pulls out her watch.*] Come, dear; [GWENDOLEN *rises.*] we have already missed five, if not six, trains. To miss any more might expose us to comment on the platform.

[*Enter* CANON CHASUBLE.]

CHASUBLE: Everything is quite ready for the christenings.

LADY BRACKNELL: The christenings, sir! Is not that somewhat premature!

CHASUBLE: [*Looking rather puzzled, and pointing to* JACK *and* ALGERNON.] Both these gentlemen have expressed a desire for immediate baptism.

LADY BRACKNELL: At their age? The idea is grotesque and irreligious! Algernon, I forbid you to be baptized. I will not hear of such excesses. Lord Bracknell would be highly displeased if he learned that that was the way in which you wasted your time and money.

CHASUBLE: Am I to understand then that there are to be no christenings at all this afternoon?

JACK: I don't think that, as things are now, it would be of much practical value to either of us, Dr. Chasuble.

CHASUBLE: I am grieved to hear such sentiments from you, Mr. Worthing. They savor of the heretical views of the Anabaptists,[5] views that I have completely refuted in four of my unpublished sermons. However, as your present mood seems to be one peculiarly secular, I will return to the church at once. Indeed, I have just been informed by the pew-opener[6] that for the last hour and a half Miss Prism has been waiting for me in the vestry.

LADY BRACKNELL: [*Starting.*] Miss Prism! Did I hear you mention a Miss Prism?

CHASUBLE: Yes, Lady Bracknell. I am on my way to join her.

LADY BRACKNELL: Pray allow me to detain you for a moment. This matter may prove to be one of vital importance to Lord Bracknell and myself. Is this Miss Prism a female of repellent aspect, remotely connected with education?

CHASUBLE: [*Somewhat indignantly.*] She is the most cultivated of ladies, and the very picture of respectability.

LADY BRACKNELL: It is obviously the same person. May I ask what position she holds in your household?

CHASUBLE: [*Severely.*] I am a celibate, madam.

JACK: [*Interposing.*] Miss Prism, Lady Bracknell, has been for the last three years Miss Cardew's esteemed governess and valued companion.

LADY BRACKNELL: In spite of what I hear of her, I must see her at once. Let her be sent for.

CHASUBLE: [*Looking off.*] She approaches; she is nigh.

[*Enter* MISS PRISM *hurriedly.*]

MISS PRISM: I was told you expected me in the vestry, dear Canon. I have been waiting for you there for an hour and three quarters. [*Catches sight of* LADY BRACKNELL, *who has fixed her with a stony glare.* MISS PRISM *grows pale and quails. She looks anxiously round as if desirous to escape.*]

LADY BRACKNELL: [*In a severe, judicial voice.*] Prism! [MISS PRISM *bows her head in shame.*] Come here, Prism! [MISS PRISM *approaches in a humble manner.*] Prism! Where is that baby? [*General consternation.* THE CANON *starts back in horror.* ALGERNON *and* JACK *pretend to be anxious to shield* CECILY *and* GWENDOLEN *from hearing the details of a terrible public scandal.*] Twenty-eight years ago, Prism, you left Lord Bracknell's house, Number 104, Upper Grosvenor Street, in charge of a perambulator that contained a baby, of the male sex. You never returned. A few weeks later, through the elaborate investigations of the Metropolitan police, the perambulator was discovered at midnight, standing by itself in a remote corner of Bayswater.[7] It contained

5. Sixteenth-century religious group, somewhat like contemporary Mennonites. Dr. Chasuble, however, is probably using the term loosely to apply to a group more like contemporary Baptists.
6. Usher. Since most pews were enclosed and rented by specific persons, his duties would have included opening the gate that allowed worshipers to enter and seeing that worshipers were seated in the correct pews.
7. Fashionable residential London neighborhood north of Hyde Park and Kensington Gardens.

the manuscript of a three-volume novel of more than usually revolting sentimentality. [MISS PRISM *starts in involuntary indignation.*] But the baby was not there! [*Everyone looks at* MISS PRISM.] Prism! Where is that baby? [*A pause.*]

MISS PRISM: Lady Bracknell, I admit with shame that I do not know. I only wish I did. The plain facts of the case are these. On the morning of the day you mention, a day that is forever branded on my memory, I prepared as usual to take the baby out in its perambulator. I had also with me a somewhat old, but capacious handbag, in which I had intended to place the manuscript of a work of fiction that I had written during my few unoccupied hours. In a moment of mental abstraction, for which I never can forgive myself, I deposited the manuscript in the bassinette, and placed the baby in the handbag.

JACK: [*Who has been listening attentively.*] But where did you deposit the handbag?

MISS PRISM: Do not ask me, Mr. Worthing.

JACK: Miss Prism, this is a matter of no small importance to me. I insist on knowing where you deposited the handbag that contained that infant.

MISS PRISM: I left it in the cloak room of one of the larger railway stations in London.

JACK: What railway station?

MISS PRISM: [*Quite crushed.*] Victoria. The Brighton line. [*Sinks into a chair.*]

JACK: I must retire to my room for a moment. Gwendolen, wait here for me.

GWENDOLEN: If you are not too long, I will wait here for you all my life.

    [*Exit* JACK *in great excitement.*]

CHASUBLE: What do you think this means, Lady Bracknell?

LADY BRACKNELL: I dare not even suspect, Dr. Chasuble. I need hardly tell you that in families of high position strange coincidences are not supposed to occur. They are hardly considered the thing.

    [*Noises heard overhead as if someone was throwing trunks about. Everyone looks up.*]

CECILY: Uncle Jack seems strangely agitated.

CHASUBLE: Your guardian has a very emotional nature.

LADY BRACKNELL: This noise is extremely unpleasant. It sounds as if he was having an argument. I dislike arguments of any kind. They are always vulgar, and often convincing.

CHASUBLE: [*Looking up.*] It has stopped now. [*The noise is redoubled.*]

LADY BRACKNELL: I wish he would arrive at some conclusion.

GWENDOLEN: This suspense is terrible. I hope it will last.

    [*Enter* JACK *with a handbag of black leather in his hand.*]

JACK: [*Rushing over to* MISS PRISM.] Is this the handbag, Miss Prism? Examine it carefully before you speak. The happiness of more than one life depends on your answer.

MISS PRISM: [*Calmly.*] It seems to be mine. Yes, here is the injury it received through the upsetting of a Gower Street omnibus in younger and happier days. Here is the stain on the lining caused by the explosion of a temperance beverage,[8] an incident that occurred at Leamington. And here, on the lock, are my initials. I had forgotten that in an extravagant mood I had had them placed there. The bag is undoubtedly mine. I am delighted to have it so unexpectedly restored to me. It has been a great inconvenience being without it all these years.

JACK: [*In a pathetic voice.*] Miss Prism, more is restored to you than this handbag. I was the baby you placed in it.

MISS PRISM: [*Amazed.*] You!

JACK: [*Embracing her.*] Yes . . . mother!

MISS PRISM: [*Recoiling in indignant astonishment.*] Mr. Worthing! I am unmarried!

JACK: Unmarried! I do not deny that is a serious blow. But after all, who has the right to cast a stone against one who has suffered? Cannot repentance wipe out an act of folly? Why should there be one law for men, and another for women? Mother, I forgive you. [*Tries to embrace her again.*]

MISS PRISM: [*Still more indignant.*] Mr. Worthing, there is some error. [*Pointing to* LADY BRACKNELL.] There is the lady who can tell you who you really are.

JACK: [*After a pause.*] Lady Bracknell, I hate to seem inquisitive, but would you kindly inform me who I am?

LADY BRACKNELL: I am afraid that the news I have to give you will not altogether please you. You are the son of my poor sister, Mrs. Moncrieff, and consequently Algernon's elder brother.

JACK: Algy's elder brother! Then I have a brother after all. I knew I had a brother! I always said I had a brother! Cecily—how could you have ever doubted that I had a brother? [*Seizes hold of* ALGERNON.] Dr. Chasuble, my unfortunate brother. Miss Prism, my unfortunate brother. Gwendolen, my unfortunate brother. Algy, you young scoundrel, you will have to treat me with more respect in the future. You have never behaved to me like a brother in all your life.

ALGERNON: Well, not till today, old boy, I admit. I did my best, however, though I was out of practice. [*Shakes hands.*]

GWENDOLEN: [*To* JACK.] My own! But what own are you? What is your Christian name, now that you have become someone else?

JACK: Good heavens! . . . I had quite forgotten that point. Your decision on the subject of my name is irrevocable, I suppose?

GWENDOLEN: I never change, except in my affections.

CECILY: What a noble nature you have, Gwendolen!

JACK: Then the question had better be cleared up at once. Aunt Augusta, a moment. At the time when Miss Prism left me in the handbag, had I been christened already?

LADY BRACKNELL: Every luxury that money could buy, including christening, had been lavished on you by your fond and doting parents.

JACK: Then I was christened! That is settled. Now, what name was I given? Let me know the worst.

LADY BRACKNELL: Being the eldest son you were naturally christened after your father.

---

8. Carbonated soda drinks were marketed in the 1890s as "temperance beverages" (healthy alternatives to alcohol).

JACK: [*Irritably.*] Yes, but what was my father's Christian name?

LADY BRACKNELL: [*Meditatively.*] I cannot at the present moment recall what the General's Christian name was. But I have no doubt he had one. He was eccentric, I admit. But only in later years. And that was the result of the Indian climate, and marriage, and indigestion, and other things of that kind.

JACK: Algy! Can't you recollect what our father's Christian name was?

ALGERNON: My dear boy, we were never even on speaking terms. He died before I was a year old.

JACK: His name would appear in the Army Lists of the period, I suppose, Aunt Augusta?

LADY BRACKNELL: The General was essentially a man of peace, except in his domestic life. But I have no doubt his name would appear in any military directory.

JACK: The Army Lists of the last forty years are here. These delightful records should have been my constant study. [*Rushes to bookcase and tears the books out.*] M. Generals . . . Mallam, Maxbohm, Magley, what ghastly names they have—Markby, Migsby, Mobbs, Moncrieff! Lieutenant 1840, Captain, Lieutenant Colonel, Colonel, General 1869, Christian names, Ernest John. [*Puts book very quietly down and speaks quite calmly.*] I always told you, Gwendolen, my name was Ernest, didn't I? Well, it is Ernest after all. I mean it naturally is Ernest.

LADY BRACKNELL: Yes, I remember now that the General was called Ernest. I knew I had some particular reason for disliking the name.

GWENDOLEN: Ernest! My own Ernest! I felt from the first that you could have no other name!

JACK: Gwendolen, it is a terrible thing for a man to find out suddenly that all his life he has been speaking nothing but the truth. Can you forgive me?

GWENDOLEN: I can. For I feel that you are sure to change.

JACK: My own one!

CHASUBLE: [*To* MISS PRISM.] Laetitia! [*Embraces her.*]

MISS PRISM: [*Enthusiastically.*] Frederick! At last!

ALGERNON: Cecily! [*Embraces her.*] At last!

JACK: Gwendolen! [*Embraces her.*] At last!

LADY BRACKNELL: My nephew, you seem to be displaying signs of triviality.

JACK: On the contrary, Aunt Augusta, I've now realized for the first time in my life the vital Importance of Being Earnest.

CURTAIN

1895   1899

TENNESSEE WILLIAMS

(1911–83)

A Streetcar Named Desire

Born in Columbus, Mississippi, Thomas Lanier Williams moved to St. Louis, Missouri, with his family at the age of seven. Williams's father was a violent alcoholic; his mother was ill; and his sister, Rose, suffered from various mental illnesses: Each family member became a model for the domineering men and sensitive women of his plays. He attended the University of Missouri and Washington University in St. Louis, but earned his BA from the University of Iowa. While there, Williams won prizes for his fiction and began to write plays. His extensive body of work, with its explosive dramatic tension and dazzling dialogue, confronts issues of adultery, homosexuality, incest, and mental illness. In 1944, *The Glass Menagerie* won the New York Drama Critics' Circle Award. In 1948, Williams earned his first Pulitzer Prize, for *A Streetcar Named Desire*; in 1955, he won a second Pulitzer for *Cat on a Hot Tin Roof*. His other dramas include *Suddenly Last Summer* (1958) and *The Night of the Iguana* (1961). Williams also wrote screenplays, poetry, and both fiction and nonfiction, including a 1975 memoir and the illuminating reflections on his own and others' work collected in *New Selected Essays: Where I Live* (2009).

And so it was I entered the broken world
To trace the visionary company of love, its voice
An instant in the wind (I know not whither hurled)
But not for long to hold each desperate choice.

—"THE BROKEN TOWER" BY HART CRANE[1]

CHARACTERS

BLANCHE	EUNICE	A DOCTOR
STELLA	STEVE	A NURSE (MATRON)
STANLEY	PABLO	A YOUNG COLLECTOR
MITCH	A NEGRO WOMAN	A MEXICAN WOMAN

Scene 1

The exterior of a two-story corner building on a street in New Orleans which is named Elysian Fields and runs between the L & N tracks and the river.[2] The section is poor but, unlike corresponding sections in other American cities, it has a raffish charm. The houses are mostly white frame, weathered grey, with rickety outside stairs and galleries and quaintly ornamented gables. This building

---

1. American poet (1899–1932).
2. Elysian Fields is a New Orleans street at the northern tip of the French Quarter, between the Louisville & Nashville railroad tracks and the Mississippi River. In Greek mythology, the Elysian Fields are the abode of the blessed in the afterlife; in Paris, the Champs-Élysées ("Elysian Fields") is a grand boulevard.

*contains two flats, upstairs and down. Faded white stairs ascend to the entrances
of both.*

*It is first dark of an evening early in May. The sky that shows around the dim
white building is a peculiarly tender blue, almost a turquoise, which invests the
scene with a kind of lyricism and gracefully attenuates the atmosphere of decay.
You can almost feel the warm breath of the brown river beyond the river warehouses with their faint redolences of bananas and coffee. A corresponding air is
evoked by the music of Negro entertainers at a barroom around the corner. In
this part of New Orleans you are practically always just around the corner, or a
few doors down the street, from a tinny piano being played with the infatuated
fluency of brown fingers. This "Blue Piano" expresses the spirit of the life which
goes on here.*

*Two women, one white and one colored, are taking the air on the steps of the
building. The white woman is* EUNICE, *who occupies the upstairs flat; the*
NEGRO WOMAN, *a neighbor, for New Orleans is a cosmopolitan city where there
is a relatively warm and easy intermingling of races in the old part of town.*

*Above the music of the "Blue Piano" the voices of people on the street can be
heard overlapping.*

[*Two men come around the corner,* STANLEY KOWALSKI *and* MITCH. *They
are about twenty-eight, or thirty years old, roughly dressed in blue denim
work clothes.* STANLEY *carries his bowling jacket and a red-stained package
from a butcher's. They stop at the foot of the steps.*]

STANLEY: [*Bellowing.*] Hey there! Stella, baby!

[STELLA *comes out on the first floor landing, a gentle young woman, about
twenty-five, and of a background obviously quite different from her husband's.*]

STELLA: [*Mildly.*] Don't holler at me like that. Hi, Mitch.
STANLEY: Catch!
STELLA: What?
STANLEY: Meat!

[*He heaves the package at her. She cries out in protest but manages to catch
it: then she laughs breathlessly. Her husband and his companion have already
started back around the corner.*]

STELLA: [*Calling after him.*] Stanley! Where are you going?
STANLEY: Bowling!
STELLA: Can I come watch?
STANLEY: Come on. [*He goes out.*]
STELLA: Be over soon. [*To the* WHITE WOMAN.] Hello, Eunice. How are you?
EUNICE: I'm all right. Tell Steve to get him a poor boy's sandwich[3] 'cause noth-
ing's left here.

[*They all laugh; the* NEGRO WOMAN *does not stop.* STELLA *goes out.*]

NEGRO WOMAN: What was that package he th'ew at 'er? [*She rises from steps, laughing louder.*]

---

3. Usually called just "poor boy" or "po' boy"; similar to a hero or submarine sandwich.

EUNICE: You hush, now!

NEGRO WOMAN: Catch *what*!

[*She continues to laugh.* BLANCHE *comes around the corner, carrying a valise. She looks at a slip of paper, then at the building, then again at the slip and again at the building. Her expression is one of shocked disbelief. Her appearance is incongruous to this setting. She is daintily dressed in a white suit with a fluffy bodice, necklace and earrings of pearl, white gloves and hat, looking as if she were arriving at a summer tea or cocktail party in the garden district.[4] She is about five years older than* STELLA. *Her delicate beauty must avoid a strong light. There is something about her uncertain manner, as well as her white clothes, that suggests a moth.*]

EUNICE: [*Finally.*] What's the matter, honey? Are you lost?

BLANCHE: [*With faintly hysterical humor.*] They told me to take a street-car named Desire, and then transfer to one called Cemeteries[5] and ride six blocks and get off at—Elysian Fields!

EUNICE: That's where you are now.

BLANCHE: At Elysian Fields?

EUNICE: This here is Elysian Fields.

BLANCHE: They mustn't have—understood—what number I wanted. . . .

EUNICE: What number you lookin' for?

[BLANCHE *wearily refers to the slip of paper.*]

BLANCHE: Six thirty-two.

EUNICE: You don't have to look no further.

BLANCHE: [*Uncomprehendingly.*] I'm looking for my sister, Stella DuBois, I mean—Mrs. Stanley Kowalski.

EUNICE: That's the party.—You just did miss her, though.

BLANCHE: This—can this be—her home?

EUNICE: She's got the downstairs here and I got the up.

BLANCHE: Oh. She's—out?

EUNICE: You noticed that bowling alley around the corner?

BLANCHE: I'm—not sure I did.

EUNICE: Well, that's where she's at, watchin' her husband bowl. [*There is a pause.*] You want to leave your suitcase here an' go find her?

BLANCHE: No.

NEGRO WOMAN: I'll go tell her you come.

BLANCHE: Thanks.

NEGRO WOMAN: You welcome. [*She goes out.*]

EUNICE: She wasn't expecting you?

BLANCHE: No. No, not tonight.

EUNICE: Well, why don't you just go in and make yourself at home till they get back.

BLANCHE: How could I—do that?

EUNICE: We own this place so I can let you in.

---

4. Wealthy, fashionable section of New Orleans.

5. End of a streetcar line that stopped at a cemetery. *Desire*: street in New Orleans.

[*She gets up and opens the downstairs door. A light goes on behind the blind, turning it light blue.* BLANCHE *slowly follows her into the downstairs flat. The surrounding areas dim out as the interior is lighted. Two rooms can be seen, not too clearly defined. The one first entered is primarily a kitchen but contains a folding bed to be used by* BLANCHE. *The room beyond this is a bedroom. Off this room is a narrow door to a bathroom.*]

EUNICE: [*Defensively, noticing* BLANCHE's *look.*] It's sort of messed up right now but when it's clean it's real sweet.

BLANCHE: Is it?

EUNICE: Uh-huh, I think so. So you're Stella's sister?

BLANCHE: Yes. [*Wanting to get rid of her.*] Thanks for letting me in.

EUNICE: *Por nada,* as the Mexicans say, *por nada!*[6] Stella spoke of you.

BLANCHE: Yes?

EUNICE: I think she said you taught school.

BLANCHE: Yes.

EUNICE: And you're from Mississippi, huh?

BLANCHE: Yes.

EUNICE: She showed me a picture of your home-place, the plantation.

BLANCHE: Belle Reve?[7]

EUNICE: A great big place with white columns.

BLANCHE: Yes . . .

EUNICE: A place like that must be awful hard to keep up.

BLANCHE: If you will excuse me, I'm just about to drop.

EUNICE: Sure, honey. Why don't you set down?

BLANCHE: What I meant was I'd like to be left alone.

EUNICE: [*Offended.*] Aw. I'll make myself scarce, in that case.

BLANCHE: I didn't mean to be rude, but—

EUNICE: I'll drop by the bowling alley an' hustle her up. [*She goes out the door.*]

[BLANCHE *sits in a chair very stiffly with her shoulders slightly hunched and her legs pressed close together and her hands tightly clutching her purse as if she were quite cold. After a while the blind look goes out of her eyes and she begins to look slowly around. A cat screeches. She catches her breath with a startled gesture. Suddenly she notices something in a half opened closet. She springs up and crosses to it, and removes a whiskey bottle. She pours a half tumbler of whiskey and tosses it down. She carefully replaces the bottle and washes out the tumbler at the sink. Then she resumes her seat in front of the table.*]

BLANCHE: [*Faintly to herself.*] I've got to keep hold of myself!

[STELLA *comes quickly around the corner of the building and runs to the door of the downstairs flat.*]

STELLA: [*Calling out joyfully.*] Blanche!

[*For a moment they stare at each other. Then* BLANCHE *springs up and runs to her with a wild cry.*]

6. It's nothing (Spanish).
7. Beautiful Dream (French).

BLANCHE: Stella, oh, Stella, Stella! Stella for Star![8] [*She begins to speak with feverish vivacity as if she feared for either of them to stop and think. They catch each other in a spasmodic embrace.*] Now, then, let me look at you. But don't you look at me, Stella, no, no, no, not till later, not till I've bathed and rested! And turn that over-light off! Turn that off! I won't be looked at in this merciless glare! [STELLA *laughs and complies.*] Come back here now! Oh, my baby! Stella! Stella for Star! [*She embraces her again.*] I thought you would never come back to this horrible place! What am I saying? I didn't mean to say that. I meant to be nice about it and say—Oh, what a convenient location and such—Ha-a-ha! Precious lamb! You haven't said a *word* to me.

STELLA: You haven't given me a chance to, honey! [*She laughs, but her glance at* BLANCHE *is a little anxious.*]

BLANCHE: Well, now you talk. Open your pretty mouth and talk while I look around for some liquor! I know you must have some liquor on the place! Where could it be, I wonder? Oh, I spy, I spy! [*She rushes to the closet and removes the bottle; she is shaking all over and panting for breath as she tries to laugh. The bottle nearly slips from her grasp.*]

STELLA: [*Noticing.*] Blanche, you sit down and let me pour the drinks. I don't know what we've got to mix with. Maybe a Coke in the icebox. Look'n see, honey, while I'm—

BLANCHE: No Coke, honey, not with my nerves tonight! Where—where—where is—?

STELLA: Stanley? Bowling! He loves it. They're having a—found some soda!—tournament. . . .

BLANCHE: Just water, baby, to chase it! Now don't get worried, your sister hasn't turned into a drunkard, she's just all shaken up and hot and tired and dirty! You sit down, now, and explain this place to me! What are you doing in a place like this?

STELLA: Now, Blanche—

BLANCHE: Oh, I'm not going to be hypocritical, I'm going to be honestly critical about it! Never, never, never in my worst dreams could I picture—Only Poe! Only Mr. Edgar Allan Poe!—could do it justice! Out there I suppose is the ghoul-haunted woodland of Weir![9] [*She laughs.*]

STELLA: No, honey, those are the L & N tracks.

BLANCHE: No, now seriously, putting joking aside. Why didn't you tell me, why didn't you write me, honey, why didn't you let me know?

STELLA: [*Carefully, pouring herself a drink.*] Tell you what, Blanche?

BLANCHE: Why, that you had to live in these conditions!

STELLA: Aren't you being a little intense about it? It's not that bad at all! New Orleans isn't like other cities.

BLANCHE: This has got nothing to do with New Orleans. You might as well say—forgive me, blessed baby! [*She suddenly stops short.*] The subject is closed!

STELLA: [*A little drily.*] Thanks.

8. *Stella* is "star" in Latin.
9. From the refrain of Edgar Allan Poe's gothic ballad "Ulalume" (1847).

[*During the pause,* BLANCHE *stares at her. She smiles at* BLANCHE.]

BLANCHE: [*Looking down at her glass, which shakes in her hand.*] You're all I've got in the world, and you're not glad to see me!

STELLA: [*Sincerely.*] Why, Blanche, you know that's not true.

BLANCHE: No?—I'd forgotten how quiet you were.

STELLA: You never did give me a chance to say much, Blanche. So I just got in the habit of being quiet around you.

BLANCHE: [*Vaguely.*] A good habit to get into . . . [*Then, abruptly.*] You haven't asked me how I happened to get away from the school before the spring term ended.

STELLA: Well, I thought you'd volunteer that information—if you wanted to tell me.

BLANCHE: You thought I'd been fired?

STELLA: No, I—thought you might have—resigned. . . .

BLANCHE: I was so exhausted by all I'd been through my—nerves broke. [*Nervously tamping cigarette.*] I was on the verge of—lunacy, almost! So Mr. Graves—Mr. Graves is the high school superintendent—he suggested I take a leave of absence. I couldn't put all of those details into the wire.[1] . . . [*She drinks quickly.*] Oh, this buzzes right through me and feels so *good*!

STELLA: Won't you have another?

BLANCHE: No, one's my limit.

STELLA: Sure?

BLANCHE: You haven't said a word about my appearance.

STELLA: You look just fine.

BLANCHE: God love you for a liar! Daylight never exposed so total a ruin! But you—you've put on some weight, yes, you're just as plump as a little partridge! And it's so becoming to you!

STELLA: Now, Blanche—

BLANCHE: Yes, it is, it is or I wouldn't say it! You just have to watch around the hips a little. Stand up.

STELLA: Not now.

BLANCHE: You hear me? I said stand up! [STELLA *complies reluctantly.*] You messy child, you, you've spilt something on that pretty white lace collar! About your hair—you ought to have it cut in a feather bob with your dainty features. Stella, you have a maid, don't you?

STELLA: No. With only two rooms it's—

BLANCHE: What? *Two* rooms, did you say?

STELLA: This one and— [*She is embarrassed.*]

BLANCHE: The other one? [*She laughs sharply. There is an embarrassed silence.*] I am going to take just one little tiny nip more, sort of to put the stopper on, so to speak. . . . Then put the bottle away so I won't be tempted. [*She rises.*] I want you to look at *my* figure! [*She turns around.*] You know I haven't put on one ounce in ten years, Stella? I weigh what I weighed the summer you left Belle Reve. The summer Dad died and you left us. . . .

STELLA: [*A little wearily.*] It's just incredible, Blanche, how well you're looking.

---

1. Telegram.

BLANCHE: [*They both laugh uncomfortably.*] But, Stella, there's only two rooms, I don't see where you're going to put me!

STELLA: We're going to put you in here.

BLANCHE: What kind of bed's this—one of those collapsible things? [*She sits on it.*]

STELLA: Does it feel all right?

BLANCHE: [*Dubiously.*] Wonderful, honey. I don't like a bed that gives much. But there's no door between the two rooms, and Stanley—will it be decent?

STELLA: Stanley is Polish, you know.

BLANCHE: Oh, yes. They're something like Irish, aren't they?

STELLA: Well—

BLANCHE: Only not so—highbrow? [*They both laugh again in the same way.*] I brought some nice clothes to meet all your lovely friends in.

STELLA: I'm afraid you won't think they are lovely.

BLANCHE: What are they like?

STELLA: They're Stanley's friends.

BLANCHE: Polacks?

STELLA: They're a mixed lot, Blanche.

BLANCHE: Heterogeneous—types?

STELLA: Oh, yes. Yes, types is right!

BLANCHE: Well—anyhow—I brought nice clothes and I'll wear them. I guess you're hoping I'll say I'll put up at a hotel, but I'm not going to put up at a hotel. I want to be *near* you, got to be *with* somebody, I *can't* be *alone!* Because—as you must have noticed—I'm—*not* very *well.* . . . [*Her voice drops and her look is frightened.*]

STELLA: You seem a little bit nervous or overwrought or something.

BLANCHE: Will Stanley like me, or will I be just a visiting in-law, Stella? I couldn't stand that.

STELLA: You'll get along fine together, if you'll just try not to—well—compare him with men that we went out with at home.

BLANCHE: Is he so—different?

STELLA: Yes. A different species.

BLANCHE: In what way; what's he like?

STELLA: Oh, you can't describe someone you're in love with! Here's a picture of him! [*She hands a photograph to* BLANCHE.]

BLANCHE: An officer?

STELLA: A Master Sergeant in the Engineers' Corps. Those are decorations!

BLANCHE: He had those on when you met him?

STELLA: I assure you I wasn't just blinded by all the brass.

BLANCHE: That's not what I—

STELLA: But of course there were things to adjust myself to later on.

BLANCHE: Such as his civilian background! [STELLA *laughs uncertainly.*] How did he take it when you said I was coming?

STELLA: Oh, Stanley doesn't know yet.

BLANCHE: [*Frightened.*] You—haven't told him?

STELLA: He's on the road a good deal.

BLANCHE: Oh. Travels?

STELLA: Yes.

BLANCHE: Good. I mean—isn't it?

STELLA: [*Half to herself.*] I can hardly stand it when he is away for a night . . .

BLANCHE: Why, Stella!

STELLA: When he's away for a week I nearly go wild!

BLANCHE: Gracious!

STELLA: And when he comes back I cry on his lap like a baby. . . . [*She smiles to herself.*]

BLANCHE: I guess that is what is meant by being in love. . . . [STELLA *looks up with a radiant smile.*] Stella—

STELLA: What?

BLANCHE: [*In an uneasy rush.*] I haven't asked you the things you probably thought I was going to ask. And so I'll expect you to be understanding about what I have to tell *you.*

STELLA: What, Blanche? [*Her face turns anxious.*]

BLANCHE: Well, Stella—you're going to reproach me, I know that you're bound to reproach me—but before you do—take into consideration—you left! I stayed and struggled! You came to New Orleans and looked out for yourself! *I* stayed at Belle Reve and tried to hold it together! I'm not meaning this in any reproachful way, but *all* the burden descended on *my* shoulders.

STELLA: The best I could do was make my own living, Blanche.

[BLANCHE *begins to shake again with intensity.*]

BLANCHE: I know, I know. But you are the one that abandoned Belle Reve, not I! I stayed and fought for it, bled for it, almost died for it!

STELLA: Stop this hysterical outburst and tell me what's happened? What do you mean fought and bled? What kind of—

BLANCHE: I knew you would, Stella. I knew you would take this attitude about it!

STELLA: About—what?—please!

BLANCHE: [*Slowly.*] The loss—the loss . . .

STELLA: Belle Reve? Lost, is it? No!

BLANCHE: Yes, Stella.

[*They stare at each other across the yellow-checked linoleum of the table.* BLANCHE *slowly nods her head and* STELLA *looks slowly down at her hands folded on the table. The music of the "Blue Piano" grows louder.* BLANCHE *touches her handkerchief to her forehead.*]

STELLA: But how did it go? What happened?

BLANCHE: [*Springing up.*] You're a fine one to ask me how it went!

STELLA: Blanche!

BLANCHE: You're a fine one to sit there *accusing me* of it!

STELLA: *Blanche!*

BLANCHE: I, I, *I* took the blows in my face and my body! All of those deaths! The long parade to the graveyard! Father, Mother! Margaret, that dreadful way! So big with it, it couldn't be put in a coffin! But had to be burned like rubbish! You just came home in time for the funerals, Stella. And funerals are pretty compared to deaths. Funerals are quiet, but deaths—not always. Sometimes their breathing is hoarse, and sometimes it rattles, and sometimes they even cry out to you, "Don't let me go!" Even the old, sometimes, say, "Don't let me go." As if you were able to stop them! But funerals are quiet, with pretty flowers. And, oh, what gorgeous boxes they pack them away in! Unless you were there at the bed when they cried out, "Hold me!" you'd never suspect there was the struggle for breath and bleeding. You didn't dream, but I saw! *Saw! Saw!* And now you sit there telling me with your eyes that I let the place go! How in hell do you think all that sickness and dying was paid for? Death is expensive, Miss Stella! And old Cousin Jessie's right after Margaret's, hers! Why, the Grim Reaper[2] had put up his tent on our doorstep! . . . Stella. Belle Reve was his headquarters! Honey—that's how it slipped through my fingers! Which of them left us a fortune? Which of them left a cent of insurance even? Only poor Jessie—one hundred to pay for her coffin. That was all, Stella! And I with my pitiful salary at the school. Yes, accuse me! Sit there and stare at me, thinking I let the place go! *I* let the place go? Where were *you!* In bed with your—Polack!

STELLA: [*Springing.*] Blanche! You be still! That's enough! [*She starts out.*]

BLANCHE: Where are you going?

STELLA: I'm going into the bathroom to wash my face.

BLANCHE: Oh, Stella, Stella, you're crying!

STELLA: Does that surprise you?

BLANCHE: Forgive me—I didn't mean to—

[*The sound of men's voices is heard.* STELLA *goes into the bathroom, closing the door behind her. When the men appear, and* BLANCHE *realizes it must be* STANLEY *returning, she moves uncertainly from the bathroom door to the dressing table, looking apprehensively toward the front door.* STANLEY *enters, followed by* STEVE *and* MITCH. STANLEY *pauses near his door,* STEVE *by the foot of the spiral stair, and* MITCH *is slightly above and to the right of them, about to go out. As the men enter, we hear some of the following dialogue.*]

STANLEY: Is that how he got it?

STEVE: Sure that's how he got it. He hit the old weather-bird for 300 bucks on a six-number-ticket.[3]

MITCH: Don't tell him those things; he'll believe it. [MITCH *starts out.*]

STANLEY: [*Restraining* MITCH.] Hey, Mitch—come back here.

[BLANCHE, *at the sound of voices, retires in the bedroom. She picks up* STAN-LEY'S *photo from dressing table, looks at it, puts it down. When* STANLEY *enters the apartment, she darts and hides behind the screen at the head of bed.*]

STEVE: [*To* STANLEY *and* MITCH.] Hey, are we playin' poker tomorrow?

STANLEY: Sure—at Mitch's.

MITCH: [*Hearing this, returns quickly to the stair rail.*] No—not at my place. My mother's still sick!

STANLEY: Okay, at my place . . . [MITCH *starts out again.*] But you bring the beer!

[MITCH *pretends not to hear—calls out "Good night, all," and goes out, singing.* EUNICE's *voice is heard, above.*]

---

2. Death.

3. That is, he won $300 in a lottery. *Hit the old weather-bird*: in target shooting, to shoot at a barn and hit the ornamental rooster on the weathervane—an extraordinarily lucky shot.

EUNICE: Break it up down there! I made the spaghetti dish and ate it myself.

STEVE: [*Going upstairs.*] I told you and phoned you we was playing. [*To the men.*] Jax[4] beer!

EUNICE: You never phoned me once.

STEVE: I told you at breakfast—and phoned you at lunch. . . .

EUNICE: Well, never mind about that. You just get yourself home here once in a while.

STEVE: You want it in the papers?

[*More laughter and shouts of parting come from the men.* STANLEY *throws the screen door of the kitchen open and comes in. He is of medium height, about five feet eight or nine, and strongly, compactly built. Animal joy in his being is implicit in all his movements and attitudes. Since earliest manhood the center of his life has been pleasure with women, the giving and taking of it, not with weak indulgence, dependently, but with the power and pride of a richly feathered male bird among hens. Branching out from this complete and satisfying center are all the auxiliary channels of his life, such as his heartiness with men, his appreciation of rough humor, his love of good drink and food and games, his car, his radio, everything that is his, that bears his emblem of the gaudy seed-bearer. He sizes women up at a glance, with sexual classifications, crude images flashing into his mind and determining the way he smiles at them.*]

BLANCHE: [*Drawing involuntarily back from his stare.*] You must be Stanley. I'm Blanche.

STANLEY: Stella's sister?

BLANCHE: Yes.

STANLEY: H'lo. Where's the little woman?

BLANCHE: In the bathroom.

STANLEY: Oh. Didn't know you were coming in town.

BLANCHE: I—uh—

STANLEY: Where you from, Blanche?

BLANCHE: Why, I—live in Laurel.

[*He has crossed to the closet and removed the whiskey bottle.*]

STANLEY: In Laurel, huh? Oh, yeah. Yeah, in Laurel, that's right. Not in my territory. Liquor goes fast in hot weather. [*He holds the bottle to the light to observe its depletion.*] Have a shot?

BLANCHE: No, I—rarely touch it.

STANLEY: Some people rarely touch it, but it touches them often.

BLANCHE: [*Faintly.*] Ha-ha.

STANLEY: My clothes're stickin' to me. Do you mind if I make myself comfortable?

[*He starts to remove his shirt.*]

BLANCHE: Please, please do.

STANLEY: Be comfortable is my motto.

---

4. A local brand.

BLANCHE: It's mine, too. It's hard to stay looking fresh. I haven't washed or even powdered my face and—here you are!

STANLEY: You know you can catch cold sitting around in damp things, especially when you been exercising hard like bowling is. You're a teacher, aren't you?

BLANCHE: Yes.

STANLEY: What do you teach, Blanche?

BLANCHE: English.

STANLEY: I never was a very good English student. How long you here for, Blanche?

BLANCHE: I—don't know yet.

STANLEY: You going to shack up here?

BLANCHE: I thought I would if it's not inconvenient for you all.

STANLEY: Good.

BLANCHE: Traveling wears me out.

STANLEY: Well, take it easy.

[*A cat screeches near the window.* BLANCHE *springs up.*]

BLANCHE: What's that?

STANLEY: Cats, . . . Hey, Stella!

STELLA: [*Faintly, from the bathroom.*] Yes, Stanley.

STANLEY: Haven't fallen in, have you? [*He grins at* BLANCHE. *She tries unsuccessfully to smile back. There is a silence.*] I'm afraid I'll strike you as being the unrefined type. Stella's spoke of you a good deal. You were married once, weren't you?

[*The music of the polka rises up, faint in the distance.*]

BLANCHE: Yes. When I was quite young.

STANLEY: What happened?

BLANCHE: The boy—the boy died. [*She sinks back down.*] I'm afraid I'm—going to be sick! [*Her head falls on her arms.*]

Scene 2

It is six o'clock the following evening. BLANCHE *is bathing.* STELLA *is completing her toilette.* BLANCHE's *dress, a flowered print, is laid out on* STELLA's *bed.*

   STANLEY *enters the kitchen from outside, leaving the door open on the perpetual "Blue Piano" around the corner.*

STANLEY: What's all this monkey doings?

STELLA: Oh, Stan! [*She jumps up and kisses him, which he accepts with lordly composure.*] I'm taking Blanche to Galatoire's[5] for supper and then to a show, because it's your poker night.

STANLEY: How about my supper, huh? I'm not going to no Galatoire's for supper!

STELLA: I put you a cold plate on ice.

STANLEY: Well, isn't that just dandy!

5. Famous old restaurant on Bourbon Street, the principal street in the French Quarter.

STELLA: I'm going to try to keep Blanche out till the party breaks up because I don't know how she would take it. So we'll go to one of the little places in the Quarter afterward and you'd better give me some money.

STANLEY: Where is she?

STELLA: She's soaking in a hot tub to quiet her nerves. She's terribly upset.

STANLEY: Over what?

STELLA: She's been through such an ordeal.

STANLEY: Yeah?

STELLA: Stan, we've—lost Belle Reve!

STANLEY: The place in the country?

STELLA: Yes.

STANLEY: How?

STELLA: [*Vaguely.*] Oh, it had to be—sacrificed or something. [*There is a pause while* STANLEY *considers.* STELLA *is changing into her dress.*] When she comes in be sure to say something nice about her appearance. And, oh! Don't mention the baby. I haven't said anything yet, I'm waiting until she gets in a quieter condition.

STANLEY: [*Ominously.*] So?

STELLA: And try to understand her and be nice to her, Stan.

BLANCHE: [*Singing in the bathroom.*] "From the land of the sky blue water, They brought a captive maid!"[6]

STELLA: She wasn't expecting to find us in such a small place. You see I'd tried to gloss things over a little in my letters.

STANLEY: So?

STELLA: And admire her dress and tell her she's looking wonderful. That's important with Blanche. Her little weakness!

STANLEY: Yeah. I get the idea. Now let's skip back a little to where you said the country place was disposed of.

STELLA: Oh!—yes . . .

STANLEY: How about that? Let's have a few more details on that subjeck.

STELLA: It's best not to talk much about it until she's calmed down.

STANLEY: So that's the deal, huh? Sister Blanche cannot be annoyed with business details right now!

STELLA: You saw how she was last night.

STANLEY: Uh-hum, I saw how she was. Now let's have a gander at the bill of sale.

STELLA: I haven't seen any.

STANLEY: She didn't show you no papers, no deed of sale or nothing like that, huh?

STELLA: It seems like it wasn't sold.

STANLEY: Well, what in hell was it then, give away? To charity?

STELLA: Shhh! She'll hear you.

STANLEY: I don't care if she hears me. Let's see the papers!

STELLA: There weren't any papers, she didn't show any papers, I don't care about papers.

STANLEY: Have you ever heard of the Napoleonic code?[7]

6. From the song "From the Land of Sky-Blue Water" (1908), by Nelle Richmond Eberhart and Charles Wakefield Cadman, popularized by the Andrews Sisters in the late 1930s.

7. This codification of French law (1802), made by Napoleon as emperor, is the basis for Louisiana's civil law.

STELLA: No, Stanley, I haven't heard of the Napoleonic code and if I have, I don't see what it—

STANLEY: Let me enlighten you on a point or two, baby.

STELLA: Yes?

STANLEY: In the state of Louisiana we have the Napoleonic code according to which what belongs to the wife belongs to the husband and vice versa. For instance if I had a piece of property, or you had a piece of property—

STELLA: My head is swimming!

STANLEY: All right. I'll wait till she gets through soaking in a hot tub and then I'll inquire if *she* is acquainted with the Napoleonic code. It looks to me like you have been swindled, baby, and when you're swindled under the Napoleonic code I'm swindled *too*. And I don't like to be *swindled*.

STELLA: There's plenty of time to ask her questions later but if you do now she'll go to pieces again. I don't understand what happened to Belle Reve but you don't know how ridiculous you are being when you suggest that my sister or I or anyone of our family could have perpetrated a swindle on anyone else.

STANLEY: Then where's the money if the place was sold?

STELLA: Not sold—*lost, lost!* [*He stalks into bedroom, and she follows him.*] Stanley!

[*He pulls open the wardrobe trunk standing in middle of room and jerks out an armful of dresses.*]

STANLEY: Open your eyes to this stuff! You think she got them out of a teacher's pay?

STELLA: Hush!

STANLEY: Look at these feathers and furs that she come here to preen herself in! What's this here? A solid-gold dress, I believe! And this one! What is these here? Fox-pieces! [*He blows on them.*] Genuine fox fur-pieces, a half a mile long! Where are your fox-pieces, Stella? Bushy snowwhite ones, no less! Where are your white fox-pieces?

STELLA: Those are inexpensive summer furs that Blanche has had a long time.

STANLEY: I got an acquaintance who deals in this sort of merchandise. I'll have him in here to appraise it. I'm willing to bet you there's thousands of dollars invested in this stuff here!

STELLA: Don't be such an idiot, Stanley!

[*He hurls the furs to the day bed. Then he jerks open a small drawer in the trunk and pulls up a fistful of costume jewelry.*]

STANLEY: And what have we here? The treasure chest of a pirate!

STELLA: Oh, Stanley!

STANLEY: Pearls! Ropes of them! What is this sister of yours, a deep-sea diver? Bracelets of solid gold, too! Where are your pearls and gold bracelets?

STELLA: Shhh! Be still, Stanley!

STANLEY: And diamonds! A crown for an empress!

STELLA: A rhinestone tiara she wore to a costume ball.

STANLEY: What's rhinestone?

STELLA: Next door to glass.

STANLEY: Are you kidding? I have an acquaintance that works in a jewelry store. I'll have him in here to make an appraisal of this. Here's your plantation, or what was left of it, here!

STELLA: You have no idea how stupid and horrid you're being! Now close that trunk before she comes out of the bathroom!

[*He kicks the trunk partly closed and sits on the kitchen table.*]

STANLEY: The Kowalskis and the DuBoises have different notions.

STELLA: [*Angrily.*] Indeed they have, thank heavens!—*I'm* going outside. [*She snatches up her white hat and gloves and crosses to the outside door.*] You come out with me while Blanche is getting dressed.

STANLEY: Since when do you give me orders?

STELLA: Are you going to stay here and insult her?

STANLEY: You're damn tootin' I'm going to stay here.

[STELLA *goes out to the porch.* BLANCHE *comes out of the bathroom in a red satin robe.*]

BLANCHE: [*Airily.*] Hello, Stanley! Here I am, all freshly bathed and scented, and feeling like a brand new human being!

[*He lights a cigarette.*]

STANLEY: That's good.

BLANCHE: [*Drawing the curtains at the windows.*] Excuse me while I slip on my pretty new dress!

STANLEY: Go right ahead, Blanche.

[*She closes the drapes between the rooms.*]

BLANCHE: I understand there's to be a little card party to which we ladies are cordially *not* invited!

STANLEY: [*Ominously.*] Yeah?

[BLANCHE *throws off her robe and slips into a flowered print dress.*]

BLANCHE: Where's Stella?

STANLEY: Out on the porch.

BLANCHE: I'm going to ask a favor of you in a moment.

STANLEY: What could that be, I wonder?

BLANCHE: Some buttons in back! You may enter! [*He crosses through the drapes with a smoldering look.*] How do I look?

STANLEY: You look all right.

BLANCHE: Many thanks! Now the buttons!

STANLEY: I can't do nothing with them.

BLANCHE: You men with your big clumsy fingers. May I have a drag on your cig?

STANLEY: Have one for yourself.

BLANCHE: Why, thanks! . . . It looks like my trunk has exploded.

STANLEY: Me an' Stella were helping you unpack.

BLANCHE: Well, you certainly did a fast and thorough job of it!

STANLEY: It looks like you raided some stylish shops in Paris.

BLANCHE: Ha-ha! Yes—clothes are my passion!

STANLEY: What does it cost for a string of fur-pieces like that?

BLANCHE: Why, those were a tribute from an admirer of mine!

STANLEY: He must have had a lot of—admiration!

BLANCHE: Oh, in my youth I excited some admiration. But look at me now! [*She smiles at him radiantly.*] Would you think it possible that I was once considered to be—attractive?

STANLEY: Your looks are okay.

BLANCHE: I was fishing for a compliment, Stanley.

STANLEY: I don't go in for that stuff.

BLANCHE: What—stuff?

STANLEY: Compliments to women about their looks. I never met a woman that didn't know if she was good-looking or not without being told, and some of them give themselves credit for more than they've got. I once went out with a doll who said to me, "I am the glamorous type, I am the glamorous type!" I said, "So what?"

BLANCHE: And what did she say then?

STANLEY: She didn't say nothing. That shut her up like a clam.

BLANCHE: Did it end the romance?

STANLEY: It ended the conversation—that was all. Some men are took in by this Hollywood glamor stuff and some men are not.

BLANCHE: I'm sure you belong in the second category.

STANLEY: That's right.

BLANCHE: I cannot imagine any witch of a woman casting a spell over you.

STANLEY: That's—right.

BLANCHE: You're simple, straightforward and honest, a little bit on the primitive side I should think. To interest you a woman would have to— [*She pauses with an indefinite gesture.*]

STANLEY: [*Slowly.*] Lay . . . her cards on the table.

BLANCHE: [*Smiling.*] Well, I never cared for wishy-washy people. That was why, when you walked in here last night, I said to myself—"My sister has married a man!"—Of course that was all that I could tell about you.

STANLEY: [*Booming.*] Now let's cut the re-bop![8]

BLANCHE: [*Pressing hands to her ears.*] Ouuuuu!

STELLA: [*Calling from the steps.*] Stanley! You come out here and let Blanche finish dressing!

BLANCHE: I'm through dressing, honey.

STELLA: Well, you come out, then.

STANLEY: Your sister and I are having a little talk.

BLANCHE: [*Lightly.*] Honey, do me a favor. Run to the drugstore and get me a lemon Coke with plenty of chipped ice in it!—Will you do that for me, sweetie?

STELLA: [*Uncertainly.*] Yes. [*She goes around the corner of the building.*]

BLANCHE: The poor little thing was out there listening to us, and I have an idea she doesn't understand you as well as I do. . . . All right; now, Mr. Kowalski, let us proceed without any more double-talk. I'm ready to answer all questions. I've nothing to hide. What is it?

---

8. Nonsense (from "bop," a form of jazz).

STANLEY: There is such a thing in this state of Louisiana as the Napoleonic code, according to which whatever belongs to my wife is also mine—and vice versa.

BLANCHE: My, but you have an impressive judicial air!

[*She sprays herself with her atomizer; then playfully sprays him with it. He seizes the atomizer and slams it down on the dresser. She throws back her head and laughs.*]

STANLEY: If I didn't know that you was my wife's sister I'd get ideas about you!

BLANCHE: Such as what!

STANLEY: Don't play so dumb. You know what!

BLANCHE: [*She puts the atomizer on the table.*] All right. Cards on the table. That suits me. [*She turns to* STANLEY.] I know I fib a good deal. After all, a woman's charm is fifty per cent illusion, but when a thing is important I tell the truth, and this is the truth: I haven't cheated my sister or you or anyone else as long as I have lived.

STANLEY: Where's the papers? In the trunk?

BLANCHE: Everything that I own is in that trunk. [STANLEY *crosses to the trunk, shoves it roughly open and begins to open compartments.*] What in the name of heaven are you thinking of! What's in the back of that little boy's mind of yours? That I am absconding with something, attempting some kind of treachery on my sister?—Let me do that! It will be faster and simpler. . . . [*She crosses to the trunk and takes out a box.*] I keep my papers mostly in this tin box. [*She opens it.*]

STANLEY: What's them underneath? [*He indicates another sheaf of paper.*]

BLANCHE: These are love-letters, yellowing with antiquity, all from one boy. [*He snatches them up. She speaks fiercely.*] Give those back to me!

STANLEY: I'll have a look at them first!

BLANCHE: The touch of your hands insults them!

STANLEY: Don't pull that stuff!

[*He rips off the ribbon and starts to examine them.* BLANCHE *snatches them from him, and they cascade to the floor.*]

BLANCHE: Now that you've touched them I'll burn them!

STANLEY: [*Staring, baffled.*] What in hell are they?

BLANCHE: [*On the floor gathering them up.*] Poems a dead boy wrote. I hurt him the way that you would like to hurt me, but you can't! I'm not young and vulnerable any more. But my young husband was and I—never mind about that! Just give them back to me!

STANLEY: What do you mean by saying you'll have to burn them?

BLANCHE: I'm sorry, I must have lost my head for a moment. Everyone has something he won't let others touch because of their—intimate nature. . . . [*She now seems faint with exhaustion and she sits down with the strong box and puts on a pair of glasses and goes methodically through a large stack of papers.*] Ambler & Ambler. Hmmmmm. . . . Crabtree. . . . More Ambler & Ambler.

STANLEY: What is Ambler & Ambler?

BLANCHE: A firm that made loans on the place.

STANLEY: Then it *was* lost on a mortgage?

BLANCHE: [*Touching her forehead.*] That must've been what happened.

STANLEY: I don't want no ifs, ands or buts! What's all the rest of them papers?

[*She hands him the entire box. He carries it to the table and starts to examine the papers.*]

BLANCHE: [*Picking up a large envelope containing more papers.*] There are thousands of papers, stretching back over hundreds of years, affecting Belle Reve as, piece by piece, our improvident grandfathers and father and uncles and brothers exchanged the land for their epic fornications—to put it plainly! [*She removes her glasses with an exhausted laugh.*] The four-letter word deprived us of our plantation, till finally all that was left—and Stella can verify that!—was the house itself and about twenty acres of ground, including a graveyard, to which now all but Stella and I have retreated. [*She pours the contents of the envelope on the table.*] Here all of them are, all papers! I hereby endow you with them! Take them, peruse them—commit them to memory, even! I think it's wonderfully fitting that Belle Reve should finally be this bunch of old papers in your big, capable hands! . . . I wonder if Stella's come back with my lemon Coke. . . . [*She leans back and closes her eyes.*]

STANLEY: I have a lawyer acquaintance who will study these out.

BLANCHE: Present them to him with a box of aspirin tablets.

STANLEY: [*Becoming somewhat sheepish.*] You see, under the Napoleonic code—a man has to take an interest in his wife's affairs—especially now that she's going to have a baby.

[BLANCHE *opens her eyes. The "Blue Piano" sounds louder.*]

BLANCHE: Stella? Stella going to have a baby? [*Dreamily.*] I didn't know she was going to have a baby! [*She gets up and crosses to the outside door.* STELLA *appears around the corner with a carton from the drugstore.* STANLEY *goes into the bedroom with the envelope and the box. The inner rooms fade to darkness and the outside wall of the house is visible.* BLANCHE *meets* STELLA *at the foot of the steps to the sidewalk.*] Stella, Stella for star! How lovely to have a baby! It's all right. Everything's all right.

STELLA: I'm sorry he did that to you.

BLANCHE: Oh, I guess he's just not the type that goes for jasmine perfume, but maybe he's what we need to mix with our blood now that we've lost Belle Reve. We thrashed it out. I feel a bit shaky, but I think I handled it nicely, I laughed and treated it all as a joke. [STEVE *and* PABLO *appear, carrying a case of beer.*] I called him a little boy and laughed and flirted. Yes, I was flirting with your husband! [*As the men approach.*] The guests are gathering for the poker party. [*The two men pass between them, and enter the house.*] Which way do we go now, Stella—this way?

STELLA: No, this way. [*She leads* BLANCHE *away.*]

BLANCHE: [*Laughing.*] The blind are leading the blind!

[*A tamale* VENDOR *is heard calling.*]

VENDOR'S VOICE: Red-hot![9]

---

9. Hot dog! *Blind!*: See Matthew 15.14: "If a blind person leads a blind person, both will fall into a pit."

Scene 3. The Poker Night

*There is a picture of Van Gogh's of a billiard-parlor at night.[1] The kitchen now suggests that sort of lurid nocturnal brilliance, the raw colors of childhood's spectrum. Over the yellow linoleum of the kitchen table hangs an electric bulb with a vivid green glass shade. The poker players—*STANLEY, STEVE, MITCH *and* PABLO—*wear colored shirts, solid blues, a purple, a red-and-white check, a light green, and they are men at the peak of their physical manhood, as coarse and direct and powerful as the primary colors. There are vivid slices of watermelon on the table, whiskey bottles and glasses. The bedroom is relatively dim with only the light that spills between the portieres and through the wide window on the street. For a moment, there is absorbed silence as a hand is dealt.*

STEVE: Anything wild this deal?

PABLO: One-eyed jacks are wild.

STEVE: Give me two cards.

PABLO: You, Mitch?

MITCH: I'm out.

PABLO: One.

MITCH: Anyone want a shot?

STANLEY: Yeah. Me.

PABLO: Why don't somebody go to the Chinaman's and bring back a load of chop suey?

STANLEY: When I'm losing you want to eat! Ante up! Openers? Openers! Get y'r ass off the table, Mitch. Nothing belongs on a poker table but cards, chips and whiskey. [*He lurches up and tosses some watermelon rinds to the floor.*]

MITCH: Kind of on your high horse, ain't you?

STANLEY: How many?

STEVE: Give me three.

STANLEY: One.

MITCH: I'm out again. I oughta go home pretty soon.

STANLEY: Shut up.

MITCH: I gotta sick mother. She don't go to sleep until I come in at night.

STANLEY: Then why don't you stay home with her?

MITCH: She says to go out, so I go, but I don't enjoy it. All the while I keep wondering how she is.

STANLEY: Aw, for the sake of Jesus, go home, then!

PABLO: What've you got?

STEVE: Spade flush.

MITCH: You all are married. But I'll be alone when she goes.—I'm going to the bathroom.

STANLEY: Hurry back and we'll fix you a sugar-tit.[2]

MITCH: Aw, go rut. [*He crosses through the bedroom into the bathroom.*]

STEVE: [*Dealing a hand.*] Seven card stud. [*Telling his joke as he deals.*] This ole farmer is out in back of his house sittin' down th'owing corn to the chickens

---

1. *The Night Café*, by Vincent van Gogh (1853–90), Dutch postimpressionist painter.
2. Baby's pacifier dipped in sugar.

when all at once he hears a loud cackle and this young hen comes lickety split around the side of the house with the rooster right behind her and gaining on her fast.

STANLEY: [*Impatient with the story.*] Deal!

STEVE: But when the rooster catches sight of the farmer th'owing the corn he puts on the brakes and lets the hen get away and starts pecking corn. And the old farmer says, "Lord God, I hopes I never gits *that* hongry!"

[STEVE *and* PABLO *laugh. The sisters appear around the corner of the building.*]

STELLA: The game is still going on.

BLANCHE: How do I look?

STELLA: Lovely, Blanche.

BLANCHE: I feel so hot and frazzled. Wait till I powder before you open the door. Do I look done in?

STELLA: Why no. You are as fresh as a daisy.

BLANCHE: One that's been picked a few days.

[STELLA *opens the door and they enter.*]

STELLA: Well, well, well. I see you boys are still at it?

STANLEY: Where you been?

STELLA: Blanche and I took in a show. Blanche, this is Mr. Gonzales and Mr. Hubbell.

BLANCHE: Please don't get up.

STANLEY: Nobody's going to get up, so don't be worried.

STELLA: How much longer is this game going to continue?

STANLEY: Till we get ready to quit.

BLANCHE: Poker is so fascinating. Could I kibitz?[3]

STANLEY: You could not. Why don't you women go up and sit with Eunice?

STELLA: Because it is nearly two-thirty. [BLANCHE *crosses into the bedroom and partially closes the portieres.*] Couldn't you call it quits after one more hand?

[*A chair scrapes.* STANLEY *gives a loud whack of his hand on her thigh.*]

STELLA: [*Sharply.*] That's not fun, Stanley. [*The men laugh.* STELLA *goes into the bedroom.*] It makes me so mad when he does that in front of people.

BLANCHE: I think I will bathe.

STELLA: Again?

BLANCHE: My nerves are in knots. Is the bathroom occupied?

STELLA: I don't know.

[BLANCHE *knocks.* MITCH *opens the door and comes out, still wiping his hands on a towel.*]

BLANCHE: Oh!—good evening.

MITCH: Hello. [*He stares at her.*]

3. That is, watch a card player from behind and offer advice.

STELLA: Blanche, this is Harold Mitchell. My sister, Blanche DuBois.

MITCH: [*With awkward courtesy.*] How do you do, Miss DuBois.

STELLA: How is your mother now, Mitch?

MITCH: About the same, thanks. She appreciated your sending over that custard.—Excuse me, please.

[*He crosses slowly back into the kitchen, glancing back at* BLANCHE *and coughing a little shyly. He realizes he still has the towel in his hands and with an embarrassed laugh hands it to* STELLA. BLANCHE *looks after him with a certain interest.*]

BLANCHE: That one seems—superior to the others.

STELLA: Yes, he is.

BLANCHE: I thought he had a sort of sensitive look.

STELLA: His mother is sick.

BLANCHE: Is he married?

STELLA: No.

BLANCHE: Is he a wolf?

STELLA: Why, Blanche! [BLANCHE *laughs.*] I don't think he would be.

BLANCHE: What does—what does he do? [*She is unbuttoning her blouse.*]

STELLA: He's on the precision bench in the spare parts department. At the plant Stanley travels for.

BLANCHE: Is that something much?

STELLA: No. Stanley's the only one of his crowd that's likely to get anywhere.

BLANCHE: What makes you think Stanley will?

STELLA: Look at him.

BLANCHE: I've looked at him.

STELLA: Then you should know.

BLANCHE: I'm sorry, but I haven't noticed the stamp of genius even on Stanley's forehead.

[*She takes off the blouse and stands in her pink silk brassiere and white skirt in the light through the portieres. The game has continued in undertones.*]

STELLA: It isn't on his forehead and it isn't genius.

BLANCHE: Oh. Well, what is it, and where? I would like to know.

STELLA: It's a drive that he has. You're standing in the light, Blanche!

BLANCHE: Oh, am I!

[*She moves out of the yellow streak of light.* STELLA *has removed her dress and put on a light blue satin kimona.*[4]]

STELLA: [*With girlish laughter.*] You ought to see their wives.

BLANCHE: [*Laughingly.*] I can imagine. Big, beefy things, I suppose.

STELLA: You know that one upstairs? [*More laughter.*] One time [*Laughing.*] the plaster— [*Laughing.*] cracked—

STANLEY: You hens cut out that conversation in there!

STELLA: You can't hear us.

STANLEY: Well, you can hear me and I said to hush up!

4. Kimono.

STELLA: This is my house and I'll talk as much as I want to!

BLANCHE: Stella, don't start a row.

STELLA: He's half drunk!—I'll be out in a minute.

[*She goes into the bathroom.* BLANCHE *rises and crosses leisurely to a small white radio and turns it on.*]

STANLEY: Awright, Mitch, you in?

MITCH: What? Oh!—No, I'm out!

[BLANCHE *moves back into the streak of light. She raises her arms and stretches, as she moves indolently back to the chair. Rhumba music comes over the radio.* MITCH *rises at the table.*]

STANLEY: Who turned that on in there?

BLANCHE: I did. Do you mind?

STANLEY: Turn it off!

STEVE: Aw, let the girls have their music.

PABLO: Sure, that's good, leave it on!

STEVE: Sounds like Xavier Cugat![5] [STANLEY *jumps up and, crossing to the radio, turns it off. He stops short at the sight of* BLANCHE *in the chair. She returns his look without flinching. Then he sits again at the poker table. Two of the men have started arguing hotly.*] I didn't hear you name it.

PABLO: Didn't I name it, Mitch?

MITCH: I wasn't listenin'.

PABLO: What were you doing, then?

STANLEY: He was looking through them drapes. [*He jumps up and jerks roughly at curtains to close them.*] Now deal the hand over again and let's play cards or quit. Some people get ants when they win.

[MITCH *rises as* STANLEY *returns to his seat.*]

STANLEY: [*Yelling.*] Sit down!

MITCH: I'm going to the "head." Deal me out.

PABLO: Sure he's got ants now. Seven five-dollar bills in his pants pocket folded up tight as spitballs.

STEVE: Tomorrow you'll see him at the cashier's window getting them changed into quarters.

STANLEY: And when he goes home he'll deposit them one by one in a piggy bank his mother give him for Christmas. [*Dealing.*] This game is Spit in the Ocean.

[MITCH *laughs uncomfortably and continues through the portieres. He stops just inside.*]

BLANCHE: [*Softly.*] Hello! The Little Boys' Room is busy right now.

MITCH: We've—been drinking beer.

BLANCHE: I hate beer.

MITCH: It's—a hot weather drink.

BLANCHE: Oh, I don't think so; it always makes me warmer. Have you got any cigs?

5. Spanish-born Cuban bandleader (1900–90), well-known for composing and playing rumbas.

[*She has slipped on the dark red satin wrapper.*]

MITCH: Sure.

BLANCHE: What kind are they?

MITCH: Luckies.

BLANCHE: Oh, good. What a pretty case. Silver?

MITCH: Yes. Yes; read the inscription.

BLANCHE: Oh, is there an inscription? I can't make it out. [*He strikes a match and moves closer.*] Oh! [*Reading with feigned difficulty.*] "And if God choose, / I shall but love thee better—after—death!" Why, that's from my favorite sonnet by Mrs. Browning![6]

MITCH: You know it?

BLANCHE: Certainly I do!

MITCH: There's a story connected with that inscription.

BLANCHE: It sounds like a romance.

MITCH: A pretty sad one.

BLANCHE: Oh?

MITCH: The girl's dead now.

BLANCHE: [*In a tone of deep sympathy.*] Oh!

MITCH: She knew she was dying when she give me this. A very strange girl, very sweet—very!

BLANCHE: She must have been fond of you. Sick people have such deep, sincere attachments.

MITCH: That's right, they certainly do.

BLANCHE: Sorrow makes for sincerity, I think.

MITCH: It sure brings it out in people.

BLANCHE: The little there is belongs to people who have experienced some sorrow.

MITCH: I believe you are right about that.

BLANCHE: I'm positive that I am. Show me a person who hasn't known any sorrow and I'll show you a shuperficial—Listen to me! My tongue is a little—thick! You boys are responsible for it. The show let out at eleven and we couldn't come home on account of the poker game so we had to go somewhere and drink. I'm not accustomed to having more than one drink. Two is the limit—and *three*! [*She laughs.*] Tonight I had three.

STANLEY: Mitch!

MITCH: Deal me out. I'm talking to Miss—

BLANCHE: DuBois.

MITCH: Miss DuBois?

BLANCHE: It's a French name. It means woods and Blanche means white, so the two together mean white woods. Like an orchard in spring! You can remember it by that.

MITCH: You're French?

BLANCHE: We are French by extraction. Our first American ancestors were French Huguenots.[7]

6. Elizabeth Barrett Browning (1806–61), British poet, famous for her sequence of love poems, *Sonnets from the Portuguese*, which includes the poem quoted here, "How do I love thee? Let me count the ways" (p. 995).

7. Protestants who fled persecution in Catholic France after the Edict of Nantes (1685); many settled in the American South.

MITCH: You are Stella's sister, are you not?

BLANCHE: Yes, Stella is my precious little sister. I call her little in spite of the fact she's somewhat older than I. Just slightly. Less than a year. Will you do something for me?

MITCH: Sure. What?

BLANCHE: I bought this adorable little colored paper lantern at a Chinese shop on Bourbon. Put it over the light bulb! Will you, please?

MITCH: Be glad to.

BLANCHE: I can't stand a naked light bulb, any more than I can a rude remark or a vulgar action.

MITCH: [*Adjusting the lantern.*] I guess we strike you as being a pretty rough bunch.

BLANCHE: I'm very adaptable—to circumstances.

MITCH: Well, that's a good thing to be. You are visiting Stanley and Stella?

BLANCHE: Stella hasn't been so well lately, and I came down to help her for a while. She's very run down.

MITCH: You're not—?

BLANCHE: Married? No, no. I'm an old maid schoolteacher!

MITCH: You may teach school but you're certainly not an old maid.

BLANCHE: Thank you, sir! I appreciate your gallantry!

MITCH: So you are in the teaching profession?

BLANCHE: Yes. Ah, yes . . .

MITCH: Grade school or high school or—

STANLEY: [*Bellowing.*] Mitch!

MITCH: Coming!

BLANCHE: Gracious, what lung-power! . . . I teach high school. In Laurel.

MITCH: What do you teach? What subject?

BLANCHE: Guess!

MITCH: I bet you teach art or music? [BLANCHE *laughs delicately.*] Of course I could be wrong. You might teach arithmetic.

BLANCHE: Never arithmetic, sir; never arithmetic! [*With a laugh.*] I don't even know my multiplication tables! No, I have the misfortune of being an English instructor. I attempt to instill a bunch of bobby-soxers and drugstore Romeos with reverence for Hawthorne and Whitman and Poe!

MITCH: I guess that some of them are more interested in other things.

BLANCHE: How very right you are! Their literary heritage is not what most of them treasure above all else! But they're sweet things! And in the spring, it's touching to notice them making their first discovery of love! As if nobody had ever known it before! [*The bathroom door opens and* STELLA *comes out.* BLANCHE *continues talking to* MITCH.] Oh! Have you finished? Wait—I'll turn on the radio.

[*She turns the knobs on the radio and it begins to play "Wien, Wien, nur du allein."*[8] BLANCHE *waltzes to the music with romantic gestures.* MITCH *is delighted and moves in awkward imitation like a dancing bear.* STANLEY *stalks fiercely through the portieres into the bedroom. He crosses to the small white radio and snatches it off the table. With a shouted oath, he tosses the instrument out the window.*]

8. "Vienna, Vienna, you are my only" (German), a waltz from an operetta by Franz Lehár (1870–1948).

STELLA: Drunk—drunk—animal thing, you! [*She rushes through to the poker table.*] All of you—please go home! If any of you have one spark of decency in you—

BLANCHE: [*Wildly.*] Stella, watch out, he's—

[STANLEY *charges after* STELLA.]

MEN: [*Feebly.*] Take it easy, Stanley. Easy, fellow.—Let's all—

STELLA: You lay your hands on me and I'll—

[*She backs out of sight. He advances and disappears. There is the sound of a blow,* STELLA *cries out.* BLANCHE *screams and runs into the kitchen. The men rush forward and there is grappling and cursing. Something is over-turned with a crash.*]

BLANCHE: [*Shrilly.*] My sister is going to have a baby!

MITCH: This is terrible.

BLANCHE: Lunacy, absolute lunacy!

MITCH: Get him in here, men.

[STANLEY *is forced, pinioned by the two men, into the bedroom. He nearly throws them off. Then all at once he subsides and is limp in their grasp. They speak quietly and lovingly to him and he leans his face on one of their shoulders.*]

STELLA: [*In a high, unnatural voice, out of sight.*] I want to go away, I want to go away!

MITCH: Poker shouldn't be played in a house with women.

[BLANCHE *rushes into the bedroom.*]

BLANCHE: I want my sister's clothes! We'll go to that woman's upstairs!

MITCH: Where is the clothes?

BLANCHE: [*Opening the closet.*] I've got them! [*She rushes through to* STELLA.] Stella, Stella, precious! Dear, dear little sister, don't be afraid!

[*With her arm around* STELLA, BLANCHE *guides her to the outside door and upstairs.*]

STANLEY: [*Dully.*] What's the matter; what's happened?

MITCH: You just blew your top, Stan.

PABLO: He's okay, now.

STEVE: Sure, my boy's okay!

MITCH: Put him on the bed and get a wet towel.

PABLO: I think coffee would do him a world of good, now.

STANLEY: [*Thickly.*] I want water.

MITCH: Put him under the shower!

[*The men talk quietly as they lead him to the bathroom.*]

STANLEY: Let the rut go of me, you sons of bitches!

[*Sounds of blows are heard. The water goes on full tilt.*]

STEVE: Let's get quick out of here!

[*They rush to the poker table and sweep up their winnings on their way out.*]

MITCH: [*Sadly but firmly.*] Poker should not be played in a house with women.

[*The door closes on them and the place is still. The Negro entertainers in the bar around the corner play "Paper Doll"*[9] *slow and blue. After a moment* STANLEY *comes out of the bathroom dripping water and still in his clinging wet polka dot drawers.*]

STANLEY: Stella! [*There is a pause.*] My baby doll's left me! [*He breaks into sobs. Then he goes to the phone and dials, still shuddering with sobs.*] Eunice? I want my baby! [*He waits a moment; then he hangs up and dials again.*] Eunice! I'll keep on ringin' until I talk with my baby! [*An indistinguishable shrill voice is heard. He hurls phone to floor. Dissonant brass and piano sounds as the rooms dim out to darkness and the outer walls appear in the night light. The "Blue Piano" plays for a brief interval. Finally,* STANLEY *stumbles half-dressed out to the porch and down the wooden steps to the pavement before the building. There he throws back his head like a baying hound and bellows his wife's name: "Stella! Stella, sweetheart! Stella!"*] Stell-lahhhhh!

EUNICE: [*Calling down from the door of her upper apartment.*] Quit that howling out there an' go back to bed!

STANLEY: I want my baby down here. Stella, Stella!

EUNICE: She ain't comin' down so you quit! Or you'll git th' law on you!

STANLEY: Stella!

EUNICE: You can't beat on a woman an' then call 'er back! She won't come! And her goin' t' have a baby! . . . You stinker! You whelp of a Polack, you! I hope they do haul you in and turn the fire hose on you, same as the last time!

STANLEY: [*Humbly.*] Eunice, I want my girl to come down with me!

EUNICE: Hah! [*She slams her door.*]

STANLEY: [*With heaven-splitting violence.*] STELL-LAHHHHH!

[*The low-tone clarinet moans. The door upstairs opens again.* STELLA *slips down the rickety stairs in her robe. Her eyes are glistening with tears and her hair loose about her throat and shoulders. They stare at each other. Then they come together with low, animal moans. He falls to his knees on the steps and presses his face to her belly, curving a little with maternity. Her eyes go blind with tenderness as she catches his head and raises him level with her. He snatches the screen door open and lifts her off her feet and bears her into the dark flat.* BLANCHE *comes out the upper landing in her robe and slips fearfully down the steps.*]

BLANCHE: Where is my little sister? Stella? Stella?

[*She stops before the dark entrance of her sister's flat. Then catches her breath as if struck. She rushes down to the walk before the house. She looks right and left as if for a sanctuary. The music fades away.* MITCH *appears from around the corner.*]

MITCH: Miss DuBois?

BLANCHE: Oh!

9. Song by Johnny S. Black (1915), popularized by the Mills Brothers in the early 1940s.

MITCH: All quiet on the Potomac now?[1]

BLANCHE: She ran downstairs and went back in there with him.

MITCH: Sure she did.

BLANCHE: I'm terrified!

MITCH: Ho-ho! There's nothing to be scared of. They're crazy about each other.

BLANCHE: I'm not used to such—

MITCH: Naw, it's a shame this had to happen when you just got here. But don't take it serious.

BLANCHE: Violence! Is so—

MITCH: Set down on the steps and have a cigarette with me.

BLANCHE: I'm not properly dressed.

MITCH: That don't make no difference in the Quarter.

BLANCHE: Such a pretty silver case.

MITCH: I showed you the inscription, didn't I?

BLANCHE: Yes. [*During the pause, she looks up at the sky.*] There's so much—so much confusion in the world. . . . [*He coughs diffidently.*] Thank you for being so kind! I need kindness now.

Scene 4

It is early the following morning. There is a confusion of street cries like a choral chant.

STELLA *is lying down in the bedroom. Her face is serene in the early morning sunlight. One hand rests on her belly, rounding slightly with new maternity. From the other dangles a book of colored comics. Her eyes and lips have that almost narcotized tranquility that is in the faces of Eastern idols.*

The table is sloppy with remains of breakfast and the debris of the preceding night, and STANLEY's *gaudy pyjamas lie across the threshold of the bathroom. The outside door is slightly ajar on a sky of summer brilliance.*

BLANCHE *appears at this door. She has spent a sleepless night and her appearance entirely contrasts with* STELLA's. *She presses her knuckles nervously to her lips as she looks through the door, before entering.*

BLANCHE: Stella?

STELLA: [*Stirring lazily.*] Hmmh?

> [BLANCHE *utters a moaning cry and runs into the bedroom, throwing herself down beside* STELLA *in a rush of hysterical tenderness.*]

BLANCHE: Baby, my baby sister!

STELLA: [*Drawing away from her.*] Blanche, what is the matter with you?

> [BLANCHE *straightens up slowly and stands beside the bed looking down at her sister with knuckles pressed to her lips.*]

BLANCHE: He's left?

STELLA: Stan? Yes.

BLANCHE: Will he be back?

1. "All Quiet on the Potomac" was a Civil War catchphrase, attributed to Union general George McClellan, who pushed the Confederate army back over the Potomac River in 1862.

STELLA: He's gone to get the car greased. Why?

BLANCHE: Why! I've been half crazy, Stella! When I found out you'd been insane enough to come back in here after what happened—I started to rush in after you!

STELLA: I'm glad you didn't.

BLANCHE: What were you thinking of? [STELLA *makes an indefinite gesture.*] Answer me! What? What?

STELLA: Please, Blanche! Sit down and stop yelling.

BLANCHE: All right, Stella. I will repeat the question quietly now. How could you come back in this place last night? Why, you must have slept with him!

[STELLA *gets up in a calm and leisurely way.*]

STELLA: Blanche, I'd forgotten how excitable you are. You're making much too much fuss about this.

BLANCHE: Am I?

STELLA: Yes, you are, Blanche. I know how it must have seemed to you and I'm awful sorry it had to happen, but it wasn't anything as serious as you seem to take it. In the first place, when men are drinking and playing poker anything can happen. It's always a powder-keg. He didn't know what he was doing. . . . He was as good as a lamb when I came back and he's really very, very ashamed of himself.

BLANCHE: And that—that makes it all right?

STELLA: No, it isn't all right for anybody to make such a terrible row, but—people do sometimes. Stanley's always smashed things. Why, on our wedding night—soon as we came in here—he snatched off one of my slippers and rushed about the place smashing light bulbs with it.

BLANCHE: He did—*what?*

STELLA: He smashed all the lightbulbs with the heel of my slipper! [*She laughs.*]

BLANCHE: And you—you *let* him? Didn't *run,* didn't *scream?*

STELLA: I was—sort of—thrilled by it. [*She waits for a moment.*] Eunice and you had breakfast?

BLANCHE: Do you suppose I wanted any breakfast?

STELLA: There's some coffee left on the stove.

BLANCHE: You're so—matter-of-fact about it, Stella.

STELLA: What other can I be? He's taken the radio to get it fixed. It didn't land on the pavement so only one tube was smashed.

BLANCHE: And you are standing there smiling!

STELLA: What do you want me to do?

BLANCHE: Pull yourself together and face the facts.

STELLA: What are they, in your opinion?

BLANCHE: In my opinion? You're married to a madman!

STELLA: No!

BLANCHE: Yes, you are, your fix is worse than mine is! Only you're not being sensible about it. I'm going to *do* something. Get hold of myself and make myself a new life!

STELLA: Yes?

BLANCHE: But you've given in. And that isn't right, you're not old! You can get out.

STELLA: [*Slowly and emphatically.*] I'm not in anything I want to get out of.

BLANCHE: [*Incredulously.*] What—Stella?

STELLA: I said I am not in anything that I have a desire to get out of. Look at the mess in this room! And those empty bottles! They went through two cases last night! He promised this morning that he was going to quit having these poker parties, but you know how long such a promise is going to keep. Oh, well, it's his pleasure, like mine is movies and bridge. People have got to tolerate each other's habits, I guess.

BLANCHE: I don't understand you. [STELLA *turns toward her.*] I don't understand your indifference. Is this a Chinese philosophy you've—cultivated?

STELLA: Is what—what?

BLANCHE: This—shuffling about and mumbling—"One tube smashed—beer bottles—mess in the kitchen!"—as if nothing out of the ordinary has happened! [STELLA *laughs uncertainly and picking up the broom, twirls it in her hands.*] Are you deliberately shaking that thing in my face?

STELLA: No.

BLANCHE: Stop it. Let go of that broom. I won't have you cleaning up for him!

STELLA: Then who's going to do it? Are you?

BLANCHE: I? I!

STELLA: No, I didn't think so.

BLANCHE: Oh, let me think, if only my mind would function! We've got to get hold of some money, that's the way out!

STELLA: I guess that money is always nice to get hold of.

BLANCHE: Listen to me. I have an idea of some kind. [*Shakily she twists a cigarette into her holder.*] Do you remember Shep Huntleigh? [STELLA *shakes her head.*] Of course you remember Shep Huntleigh. I went out with him at college and wore his pin for a while. Well—

STELLA: Well?

BLANCHE: I ran into him last winter. You know I went to Miami during the Christmas holidays?

STELLA: No.

BLANCHE: Well, I did. I took the trip as an investment, thinking I'd meet someone with a million dollars.

STELLA: Did you?

BLANCHE: Yes. I ran into Shep Huntleigh—I ran into him on Biscayne Boulevard, on Christmas Eve, about dusk . . . getting into his car—Cadillac convertible; must have been a block long!

STELLA: I should think it would have been—inconvenient in traffic!

BLANCHE: You've heard of oil wells?

STELLA: Yes—remotely.

BLANCHE: He has them, all over Texas. Texas is literally spouting gold in his pockets.

STELLA: My, my.

BLANCHE: Y'know how indifferent I am to money. I think of money in terms of what it does for you. But he could do it, he could certainly do it!

STELLA: Do what, Blanche?

BLANCHE: Why—set us up in a—shop!

STELLA: What kind of shop?

BLANCHE: Oh, a—shop of some kind! He could do it with half what his wife throws away at the races.

STELLA: He's married?

BLANCHE: Honey, would I be here if the man weren't married? [STELLA *laughs a little.* BLANCHE *suddenly springs up and crosses to phone. She speaks shrilly.*] How do I get Western Union?[2]—Operator! Western Union!

STELLA: That's a dial phone, honey.

BLANCHE: I can't dial, I'm too—

STELLA: Just dial O.

BLANCHE: O?

STELLA: Yes, "O" for Operator!

[BLANCHE *considers a moment; then she puts the phone down.*]

BLANCHE: Give me a pencil. Where is a slip of paper? I've got to write it down first—the message, I mean. . . . [*She goes to the dressing table, and grabs up a sheet of Kleenex and an eyebrow pencil for writing equipment.*] Let me see now. . . . [*She bites the pencil.*] "Darling Shep. Sister and I in desperate situation."

STELLA: I beg your pardon!

BLANCHE: "Sister and I in desperate situation. Will explain details later. Would you be interested in—?" [*She bites the pencil again.*] "Would you be—interested—in . . ." [*She smashes the pencil on the table and springs up.*] You never get anywhere with direct appeals!

STELLA: [*With a laugh.*] Don't be so ridiculous, darling!

BLANCHE: But I'll think of something, I've *got* to think of—*something!* Don't laugh at me, Stella! Please, please don't—I—I want you to look at the contents of my purse! Here's what's in it! [*She snatches her purse open.*] Sixty-five measly cents in coin of the realm!

STELLA: [*Crossing to bureau.*] Stanley doesn't give me a regular allowance, he likes to pay bills himself, but—this morning he gave me ten dollars to smooth things over. You take five of it, Blanche, and I'll keep the rest.

BLANCHE: Oh, no. No, Stella.

STELLA: [*Insisting.*] I know how it helps your morale just having a little pocket-money on you.

BLANCHE: No, thank you—I'll take to the streets!

STELLA: Talk sense! How did you happen to get so low on funds?

BLANCHE: Money just goes—it goes places. [*She rubs her forehead.*] Sometime today I've got to get hold of a Bromo![3]

STELLA: I'll fix you one now.

BLANCHE: Not yet—I've got to keep thinking!

STELLA: I wish you'd just let things go, at least for a—while.

BLANCHE: Stella, I can't live with him! You can, he's your husband. But how could I stay here with him, after last night, with just those curtains between us?

STELLA: Blanche, you saw him at his worst last night.

2. America's largest telegraph company for most of the twentieth century.
3. Short for Bromo-Seltzer, a headache remedy.

BLANCHE: On the contrary, I saw him at his best! What such a man has to offer is animal force and he gave a wonderful exhibition of that! But the only way to live with such a man is to—go to bed with him! And that's your job—not mine!

STELLA: After you've rested a little, you'll see it's going to work out. You don't have to worry about anything while you're here. I mean—expenses . . .

BLANCHE: I have to plan for us both, to get us both—out!

STELLA: You take it for granted that I am in something that I want to get out of.

BLANCHE: I take it for granted that you still have sufficient memory of Belle Reve to find this place and these poker players impossible to live with.

STELLA: Well, you're taking entirely too much for granted.

BLANCHE: I can't believe you're in earnest.

STELLA: No?

BLANCHE: I understand how it happened—a little. You saw him in uniform, an officer, not here but—

STELLA: I'm not sure it would have made any difference where I saw him.

BLANCHE: Now don't say it was one of those mysterious electric things between people! If you do I'll laugh in your face.

STELLA: I am not going to say anything more at all about it!

BLANCHE: All right, then, don't!

STELLA: But there are things that happen between a man and a woman in the dark—that sort of make everything else seem—unimportant. [Pause.]

BLANCHE: What you are talking about is brutal desire—just—Desire!—the name of that rattle-trap streetcar that bangs through the Quarter, up one old narrow street and down another. . . .

STELLA: Haven't you ever ridden on that streetcar?

BLANCHE: It brought me here.—Where I'm not wanted and where I'm ashamed to be. . . .

STELLA: Then don't you think your superior attitude is a bit out of place?

BLANCHE: I am not being or feeling at all superior, Stella. Believe me I'm not! It's just this. This is how I look at it. A man like that is someone to go out with—once—twice—three times when the devil is in you. But live with? Have a child by?

STELLA: I have told you I love him.

BLANCHE: Then I *tremble* for you! I just—*tremble* for you. . . .

STELLA: I can't help your trembling if you insist on trembling!

[There is a pause.]

BLANCHE: May I—speak—*plainly*?

STELLA: Yes, do. Go ahead. As plainly as you want to.

[Outside, a train approaches. They are silent till the noise subsides. They are both in the bedroom. Under cover of the train's noise STANLEY enters from outside. He stands unseen by the women, holding some packages in his arms, and overhears their following conversation. He wears an undershirt and grease-stained seersucker pants.]

BLANCHE: Well—if you'll forgive me—he's *common*!

STELLA: Why, yes, I suppose he is.

BLANCHE: Suppose! You can't have forgotten that much of our bringing up, Stella, that you just *suppose* that any part of a gentleman's in his nature! *Not one particle, no!* Oh, if he was just—*ordinary!* Just *plain*—but good and wholesome, but—*no.* There's something downright—*bestial*—about him! You're hating me saying this, aren't you?

STELLA: [*Coldly.*] Go on and say it all, Blanche.

BLANCHE: He acts like an animal, has an animal's habits! Eats like one, moves like one, talks like one! There's even something—sub-human—something not quite to the stage of humanity yet! Yes, something—ape-like about him, like one of those pictures I've seen in—anthropological studies! Thousands and thousands of years have passed him right by, and there he is—Stanley Kowalski—survivor of the Stone Age! Bearing the raw meat home from the kill in the jungle! And you—*you* here—*waiting* for him! Maybe he'll strike you or maybe grunt and kiss you! That is, if kisses have been discovered yet! Night falls and the other apes gather! There in the front of the cave, all grunting like him, and swilling and gnawing and hulking! His poker night! you call it—this party of apes! Somebody growls—some creature snatches at something—the fight is on! *God!* Maybe we are a long way from being made in God's image, but Stella—my sister—there has been *some* progress since then! Such things as art—as poetry and music—such kinds of new light have come into the world since then! In some kinds of people some tenderer feelings have had some little beginning! That we have got to make *grow!* And *cling* to, and hold as our flag! In this dark march toward whatever it is we're approaching. . . . *Don't—don't hang back with the brutes!*

[*Another train passes outside.* STANLEY *hesitates, licking his lips. Then suddenly he turns stealthily about and withdraws through front door. The women are still unaware of his presence. When the train has passed he calls through the closed front door.*]

STANLEY: Hey! Hey, Stella!

STELLA: [*Who has listened gravely to* BLANCHE.] Stanley!

BLANCHE: Stell, I—

[*But* STELLA *has gone to the front door.* STANLEY *enters casually with his packages.*]

STANLEY: Hiyuh, Stella. Blanche back?

STELLA: Yes, she's back.

STANLEY: Hiyuh, Blanche. [*He grins at her.*]

STELLA: You must've got under the car.

STANLEY: Them darn mechanics at Fritz's don't know their ass fr'm—Hey!

[STELLA *has embraced him with both arms, fiercely, and full in the view of* BLANCHE. *He laughs and clasps her head to him. Over her head he grins through the curtains at* BLANCHE. *As the lights fade away, with a lingering brightness on their embrace, the music of the "Blue Piano" and trumpet and drums is heard.*]

Scene 5

BLANCHE *is seated in the bedroom fanning herself with a palm leaf as she reads over a just-completed letter. Suddenly she bursts into a peal of laughter.* STELLA *is dressing in the bedroom.*

STELLA: What are you laughing at, honey?

BLANCHE: Myself, myself, for being such a liar! I'm writing a letter to Shep. [*She picks up the letter.*] "Darling Shep. I am spending the summer on the wing, making flying visits here and there. And who knows, perhaps I shall take a sudden notion to *swoop* down on *Dallas*! How would you feel about that? Ha-ha! [*She laughs nervously and brightly, touching her throat as if actually talking to Shep.*] Forewarned is forearmed, as they say!"—How does that sound?

STELLA: Uh-huh . . .

BLANCHE: [*Going on nervously.*] "Most of my sister's friends go north in the summer but some have homes on the Gulf and there has been a continued round of entertainments, teas, cocktails, and luncheons—"

[*A disturbance is heard upstairs at the Hubbells' apartment.*]

STELLA: Eunice seems to be having some trouble with Steve. [EUNICE's *voice shouts in terrible wrath.*]

EUNICE: I heard about you and that blonde!

STEVE: That's a damn lie!

EUNICE: You ain't pulling the wool over my eyes! I wouldn't mind if you'd stay down at the Four Deuces, but you always going up.

STEVE: Who ever seen me up?

EUNICE: I seen you chasing her 'round the balcony—I'm gonna call the vice squad!

STEVE: Don't you throw that at me!

EUNICE: [*Shrieking.*] You hit me! I'm gonna call the police!

[*A clatter of aluminum striking a wall is heard, followed by a man's angry roar, shouts, and overturned furniture. There is a crash; then a relative hush.*]

BLANCHE: [*Brightly.*] Did he *kill* her?

[EUNICE *appears on the steps in daemonic disorder.*]

STELLA: No! She's coming downstairs.

EUNICE: Call the police, I'm going to call the police! [*She rushes around the corner.*]

[*They laugh lightly.* STANLEY *comes around the corner in his green and scarlet silk bowling shirt. He trots up the steps and bangs into the kitchen.* BLANCHE *registers his entrance with nervous gestures.*]

STANLEY: What's a matter with Eun-uss?

STELLA: She and Steve had a row. Has she got the police?

STANLEY: Naw. She's gettin' a drink.

STELLA: That's much more practical!

[STEVE *comes down nursing a bruise on his forehead and looks in the door.*]

STEVE: She here?

STANLEY: Naw, naw. At the Four Deuces.

STEVE: That rutting hunk! [*He looks around the corner a bit timidly, then turns with affected boldness and runs after her.*]

BLANCHE: I must jot that down in my notebook. Ha-ha! I'm compiling a notebook of quaint little words and phrases I've picked up here.

STANLEY: You won't pick up nothing here you ain't heard before.

BLANCHE: Can I count on that?

STANLEY: You can count on it up to five hundred.

BLANCHE: That's a mighty high number. [*He jerks open the bureau drawer, slams it shut and throws shoes in a corner. At each noise* BLANCHE *winces slightly. Finally she speaks.*] What sign were you born under?

STANLEY: [*While he is dressing.*] Sign?

BLANCHE: Astrological sign. I bet you were born under Aries. Aries people are forceful and dynamic. They dote on noise! They love to bang things around! You must have had lots of banging around in the army and now that you're out, you make up for it by treating inanimate objects with such a fury!

[STELLA *has been going in and out of closet during this scene. Now she pops her head out of the closet.*]

STELLA: Stanley was born just five minutes after Christmas.

BLANCHE: Capricorn—the Goat!

STANLEY: What sign were *you* born under?

BLANCHE: Oh, my birthday's next month, the fifteenth of September; that's under Virgo.

STANLEY: What's Virgo?

BLANCHE: Virgo is the Virgin.

STANLEY: [*Contemptuously.*] Hah! [*He advances a little as he knots his tie.*] Say, do you happen to know somebody named Shaw?

[*Her face expresses a faint shock. She reaches for the cologne bottle and dampens her handkerchief as she answers carefully.*]

BLANCHE: Why, everybody knows somebody named Shaw!

STANLEY: Well, this somebody named Shaw is under the impression he met you in Laurel, but I figure he must have got you mixed up with some other party because this other party is someone he met at a hotel called the Flamingo.

[BLANCHE *laughs breathlessly as she touches the cologne-dampened handkerchief to her temples.*]

BLANCHE: I'm afraid he does have me mixed up with this "other party." The Hotel Flamingo is not the sort of establishment I would dare to be seen in!

STANLEY: You know of it?

BLANCHE: Yes, I've seen it and smelled it.

STANLEY: You must've got pretty close if you could smell it.

BLANCHE: The odor of cheap perfume is penetrating.

STANLEY: That stuff you use is expensive?

BLANCHE: Twenty-five dollars an ounce! I'm nearly out. That's just a hint if you want to remember my birthday! [*She speaks lightly but her voice has a note of fear.*]

STANLEY: Shaw must've got you mixed up. He goes in and out of Laurel all the time so he can check on it and clear up any mistake.

[*He turns away and crosses to the portieres.* BLANCHE *closes her eyes as if faint. Her hand trembles as she lifts the handkerchief again to her forehead.* STEVE *and* EUNICE *come around corner.* STEVE's *arm is around* EUNICE's *shoulder and she is sobbing luxuriously and he is cooing love-words. There is a murmur of thunder as they go slowly upstairs in a tight embrace.*]

STANLEY: [*To* STELLA.] I'll wait for you at the Four Deuces!
STELLA: Hey! Don't I rate one kiss?
STANLEY: Not in front of your sister.

[*He goes out.* BLANCHE *rises from her chair. She seems faint; looks about her with an expression of almost panic.*]

BLANCHE: Stella! What have you heard about me?
STELLA: Huh?
BLANCHE: What have people been telling you about me?
STELLA: Telling?
BLANCHE: You haven't heard any—unkind—gossip about me?
STELLA: Why, no, Blanche, of course not!
BLANCHE: Honey, there was—a good deal of talk in Laurel.
STELLA: About *you*, Blanche?
BLANCHE: I wasn't so good the last two years or so, after Belle Reve had started to slip through my fingers.
STELLA: All of us do things we—
BLANCHE: I never was hard or self-sufficient enough. When people are soft—soft people have got to shimmer and glow—they've got to put on soft colors, the colors of butterfly wings, and put a—paper lantern over the light. . . . It isn't enough to be soft *and attractive*. And I—I'm fading now! I don't know how much longer I can turn the trick. [*The afternoon has faded to dusk.* STELLA *goes into the bedroom and turns on the light under the paper lantern. She holds a bottled soft drink in her hand.*] Have you been listening to me?
STELLA: I don't listen to you when you are being morbid! [*She advances with the bottled Coke.*]
BLANCHE: [*With abrupt change to gaiety.*] Is that Coke for me?
STELLA: Not for anyone else!
BLANCHE: Why, you precious thing, you! Is it just Coke?
STELLA: [*Turning.*] You mean you want a shot in it!
BLANCHE: Well, honey, a shot never does a Coke any harm! Let me! You mustn't wait on me!
STELLA: I like to wait on you, Blanche. It makes it seem more like home. [*She goes into the kitchen, finds a glass and pours a shot of whiskey into it.*]
BLANCHE: I have to admit I love to be waited on . . . [*She rushes into the bedroom.* STELLA *goes to her with the glass.* BLANCHE *suddenly clutches* STELLA's *free hand with a moaning sound and presses the hand to her lips.* STELLA *is embarrassed by her show of emotion.* BLANCHE *speaks in a choked voice.*] You're—you're—so *good* to me! And I—

STELLA: Blanche.

BLANCHE: I know, I won't! You hate me to talk sentimental! But honey, *believe* I feel things more than I *tell* you! I *won't* stay long! I won't, I *promise* I—

STELLA: Blanche!

BLANCHE: [*Hysterically.*] I won't, I promise, *I'll* go! Go *soon*! I will *really*! I *won't* hang around until he—throws me out. . . .

STELLA: Now will you stop talking foolish?

BLANCHE: Yes, honey. Watch how you pour—that fizzy stuff foams over!

[BLANCHE *laughs shrilly and grabs the glass, but her hand shakes so it almost slips from her grasp.* STELLA *pours the Coke into the glass. It foams over and spills.* BLANCHE *gives a piercing cry.*]

STELLA: [*Shocked by the cry.*] Heavens!

BLANCHE: Right on my pretty white skirt!

STELLA: Oh . . . Use my hanky. Blot gently.

BLANCHE: [*Slowly recovering.*] I know—gently—gently . . .

STELLA: Did it stain?

BLANCHE: Not a bit. Ha-ha! Isn't that lucky? [*She sits down shakily, taking a grateful drink. She holds the glass in both hands and continues to laugh a little.*]

STELLA: Why did you scream like that?

BLANCHE: I don't know why I screamed! [*Continuing nervously.*] Mitch—Mitch is coming at seven. I guess I am just feeling nervous about our relations. [*She begins to talk rapidly and breathlessly.*] He hasn't gotten a thing but a good-night kiss, that's all I have given him, Stella. I want his respect. And men don't want anything they get too easy. But on the other hand men lose interest quickly. Especially when the girl is over—thirty. They think a girl over thirty ought to—the vulgar term is—"put out." . . . And I—I'm not "putting out." Of course he—he doesn't know—I mean I haven't informed him—of my real age!

STELLA: Why are you sensitive about your age?

BLANCHE: Because of hard knocks my vanity's been given. What I mean is—he thinks I'm sort of—prim and proper, you know! [*She laughs out sharply.*] I want to *deceive* him enough to make him—want me . . .

STELLA: Blanche, do you want *him*?

BLANCHE: I want to *rest*! I want to breathe quietly again! Yes—I *want* Mitch . . . *very badly*! Just think! If it happens! I can leave here and not be anyone's problem. . . .

[STANLEY *comes around the corner with a drink under his belt.*]

STANLEY: [*Bawling.*] Hey, Steve! Hey, Eunice! Hey, Stella!

[*There are joyous calls from above. Trumpet and drums are heard from around the corner.*]

STELLA: [*Kissing* BLANCHE *impulsively.*] It *will* happen!

BLANCHE: [*Doubtfully.*] It will?

STELLA: It *will*! [*She goes across into the kitchen, looking back at* BLANCHE.] It will, honey, *it will*. . . . But don't take another drink! [*Her voice catches as she goes out the door to meet her husband.*]

[BLANCHE *sinks faintly back in her chair with her drink.* EUNICE *shrieks with laughter and runs down the steps.* STEVE *bounds after her with goat-like screeches and chases her around corner.* STANLEY *and* STELLA *twine arms as they follow, laughing. Dusk settles deeper. The music from the Four Deuces is slow and blue.*]

BLANCHE: Ah, me, ah, me, ah, me . . . [*Her eyes fall shut and the palm leaf fan drops from her fingers. She slaps her hand on the chair arm a couple of times. There is a little glimmer of lightning about the building. A* YOUNG MAN *comes along the street and rings the bell.*] Come in. [*The* YOUNG MAN *appears through the portieres. She regards him with interest.*] Well, well! What can I do for *you*?

YOUNG MAN: I'm collecting for *The Evening Star.*

BLANCHE: I didn't know that stars took up collections.

YOUNG MAN: It's the paper.

BLANCHE: I know, I was joking—feebly! Will you—have a drink?

YOUNG MAN: No, ma'am. No, thank you. I can't drink on the job.

BLANCHE: Oh, well, now, let's see. . . . No, I don't have a dime! I'm not the lady of the house. I'm her sister from Mississippi. I'm one of those poor relations you've heard about.

YOUNG MAN: That's all right. I'll drop by later. [*He starts to go out. She approaches a little.*]

BLANCHE: Hey! [*He turns back shyly. She puts a cigarette in a long holder.*] Could you give me a light? [*She crosses toward him. They meet at the door between the two rooms.*]

YOUNG MAN: Sure. [*He takes out a lighter.*] This doesn't always work.

BLANCHE: It's temperamental? [*It flares.*] Ah!—thank you. [*He starts away again.*] Hey! [*He turns again, still more uncertainly. She goes close to him.*] Uh—what time is it?

YOUNG MAN: Fifteen of seven, ma'am.

BLANCHE: So late? Don't you just love these long rainy afternoons in New Orleans when an hour isn't just an hour—but a little piece of eternity dropped into your hands—and who knows what to do with it? [*She touches his shoulders.*] You—uh—didn't get wet in the rain?

YOUNG MAN: No, ma'am. I stepped inside.

BLANCHE: In a drugstore? And had a soda?

YOUNG MAN: Uh-huh.

BLANCHE: Chocolate?

YOUNG MAN: No, ma'am. Cherry.

BLANCHE: [*Laughing.*] Cherry!

YOUNG MAN: A cherry soda.

BLANCHE: You make my mouth water. [*She touches his cheek lightly, and smiles. Then she goes to the trunk.*]

YOUNG MAN: Well, I'd better be going—

BLANCHE: [*Stopping him.*] Young man! [*He turns. She takes a large, gossamer scarf from the trunk and drapes it about her shoulders. In the ensuing pause, the "Blue Piano" is heard. It continues through the rest of this scene and the opening of the next. The* YOUNG MAN *clears his throat and looks yearningly at the door.*] Young man! Young, young, young man! Has anyone ever told you that you look like a young Prince out of the Arabian Nights?[4] [*The* YOUNG MAN *laughs uncomfortably and stands like a bashful kid.* BLANCHE *speaks softly to him.*] Well, you do, honey lamb! Come here. I want to kiss you, just once, softly and sweetly on your mouth! [*Without waiting for him to accept, she crosses quickly to him and presses her lips to his.*] Now run along, now, quickly! It would be nice to keep you, but I've got to be good—and keep my hands off children.

[*He stares at her a moment. She opens the door for him and blows a kiss at him as he goes down the steps with a dazed look. She stands there a little dreamily after he has disappeared. Then* MITCH *appears around the corner with a bunch of roses.*]

BLANCHE: [*Gaily.*] Look who's coming! My Rosenkavalier! Bow to me first . . . now present them! *Ahhhh—Merciiii!*[5] [*She looks at him over them, coquettishly pressing them to her lips. He beams at her self-consciously.*]

Scene 6

It is about two a.m. on the same evening. The outer wall of the building is visible. BLANCHE *and* MITCH *come in. The utter exhaustion which only a neurasthenic personality*[6] *can know is evident in* BLANCHE's *voice and manner.* MITCH *is stolid but depressed. They have probably been out to the amusement park on Lake Pontchartrain, for* MITCH *is bearing, upside down, a plaster statuette of Mae West,*[7] *the sort of prize won at shooting galleries and carnival games of chance.*

BLANCHE: [*Stopping lifelessly at the steps.*] Well—[MITCH *laughs uneasily.*] Well . . .
MITCH: I guess it must be pretty late—and you're tired.
BLANCHE: Even the hot tamale man has deserted the street, and he hangs on till the end. [MITCH *laughs uneasily again.*] How will you get home?
MITCH: I'll walk over to Bourbon and catch an owl-car.[8]
BLANCHE: [*Laughing grimly.*] Is that street-car named Desire still grinding along the tracks at this hour?
MITCH: [*Heavily.*] I'm afraid you haven't gotten much fun out of this evening, Blanche.
BLANCHE: I spoiled it for *you.*
MITCH: No, you didn't, but I felt all the time that I wasn't giving you much—entertainment.
BLANCHE: I simply couldn't rise to the occasion. That was all. I don't think I've ever tried so hard to be gay and made such a dismal mess of it. I get ten points for trying!—I *did* try.

---

4. *The Arabian Nights* is a collection of Persian, Indian, and Arabic folktales.
5. *Merci*: thank you (French). *Rosenkavalier: Knight of the Rose* (German), title of a romantic opera (1911) by Richard Strauss (1864–1949).
6. Nineteenth-century diagnostic term for a psychological disorder characterized by nervous exhaustion and other physical symptoms.
7. American star of stage and film (1892–1980). *Lake Pontchartrain*: large coastal inlet in southern Louisiana; New Orleans is located on its south shore.
8. All-night streetcar.

MITCH: Why did you try if you didn't feel like it, Blanche?

BLANCHE: I was just obeying the law of nature.

MITCH: Which law is that?

BLANCHE: The one that says the lady must entertain the gentleman—or no dice! See if you can locate my door key in this purse. When I'm so tired my fingers are all thumbs!

MITCH: [*Rooting in her purse.*] This it?

BLANCHE: No, honey, that's the key to my trunk which I must soon be packing.

MITCH: You mean you are leaving here soon?

BLANCHE: I've outstayed my welcome.

MITCH: This it?

[*The music fades away.*]

BLANCHE: Eureka! Honey, you open the door while I take a last look at the sky. [*She leans on the porch rail. He opens the door and stands awkwardly behind her.*] I'm looking for the Pleiades,[9] the Seven Sisters, but these girls are not out tonight. Oh, yes they are, there they are! God bless them! All in a bunch going home from their little bridge party. . . . Y' get the door open? Good boy! I guess you—want to go now. . . .

[*He shuffles and coughs a little.*]

MITCH: Can I—uh—kiss you—good night?

BLANCHE: Why do you always ask me if you may?

MITCH: I don't know whether you want me to or not.

BLANCHE: Why should you be so doubtful?

MITCH: That night when we parked by the lake and I kissed you, you—

BLANCHE: Honey, it wasn't the kiss I objected to. I liked the kiss very much. It was the other little—familiarity—that I—felt obliged to—discourage. . . . I didn't resent it! Not a bit in the world! In fact, I was somewhat flattered that you—desired me! But, honey, you know as well as I do that a single girl, a girl alone in the world, has got to keep a firm hold on her emotions or she'll be lost!

MITCH: [*Solemnly.*] Lost?

BLANCHE: I guess you are used to girls that like to be lost. The kind that get lost immediately, on the first date!

MITCH: I like you to be exactly the way that you are, because in all my—experience—I have never known anyone like you. [BLANCHE *looks at him gravely; then she bursts into laughter and then claps a hand to her mouth.*] Are you laughing at me?

BLANCHE: No, honey. The lord and lady of the house have not yet returned, so come in. We'll have a nightcap. Let's leave the lights off. Shall we?

MITCH: You just—do what you want to.

[BLANCHE *precedes him into the kitchen. The outer wall of the building disappears and the interiors of the two rooms can be dimly seen.*]

BLANCHE: [*Remaining in the first room.*] The other room's more comfortable—go on in. This crashing around in the dark is my search for some liquor.

9. Constellation named for the seven daughters of Atlas who were changed into stars.

MITCH: You want a drink?

BLANCHE: I want *you* to have a drink! You have been so anxious and solemn all evening, and so have I; we have both been anxious and solemn and now for these few last remaining moments of our lives together—I want to create—*joie de vivre*![1] I'm lighting a candle.

MITCH: That's good.

BLANCHE: We are going to be very Bohemian. We are going to pretend that we are sitting in a little artists' cafe on the Left Bank in Paris! [*She lights a candle stub and puts it in a bottle.*] *Je suis la Dame aux Camellias! Vous êtes—Armand!*[2] Understand French?

MITCH: [*Heavily.*] Naw. Naw, I—

BLANCHE: *Voulez-vous couchez avec moi ce soir? Vous ne comprenez pas? Ah, quelle dommage!*[3]—I mean it's a damned good thing. . . . I've found some liquor! Just enough for two shots without any dividends, honey. . . .

MITCH: [*Heavily.*] That's—good.

[*She enters the bedroom with the drinks and the candle.*]

BLANCHE: Sit down! Why don't you take off your coat and loosen your collar?

MITCH: I better leave it on.

BLANCHE: No. I want you to be comfortable.

MITCH: I am ashamed of the way I perspire. My shirt is sticking to me.

BLANCHE: Perspiration is healthy. If people didn't perspire they would die in five minutes. [*She takes his coat from him.*] This is a nice coat. What kind of material is it?

MITCH: They call that stuff alpaca.

BLANCHE: Oh. Alpaca.

MITCH: It's very light-weight alpaca.

BLANCHE: Oh. Light-weight alpaca.

MITCH: I don't like to wear a wash-coat[4] even in summer because I sweat through it.

BLANCHE: Oh.

MITCH: And it don't look neat on me. A man with a heavy build has got to be careful of what he puts on him so he don't look too clumsy.

BLANCHE: You are not too heavy.

MITCH: You don't think I am?

BLANCHE: You are not the delicate type. You have a massive bone-structure and a very imposing physique.

MITCH: Thank you. Last Christmas I was given a membership to the New Orleans Athletic Club.

BLANCHE: Oh, good.

1. Joy of life (French).
2. I am the Lady of the Camellias! You are—Armand! (French). Both are characters in the popular romantic play *La Dame aux Camélias* (1852) by the French author Alexandre Dumas (1824–95); she is a courtesan who gives up her true love, Armand. *Left Bank*: section of Paris on the westward ("left") bank of the river Seine, long associated with students and artists.
3. Would you like to sleep with me this evening? You don't understand? Ah, what a pity! (French).
4. Light washable jacket.

MITCH: It was the finest present I ever was given. I work out there with the weights and I swim and I keep myself fit. When I started there, I was getting soft in the belly but now my belly is hard. It is so hard now that a man can punch me in the belly and it don't hurt me. Punch me! Go on! See? [*She pokes lightly at him.*]

BLANCHE: Gracious. [*Her hand touches her chest.*]

MITCH: Guess how much I weigh, Blanche?

BLANCHE: Oh, I'd say in the vicinity of—one hundred and eighty?

MITCH: Guess again.

BLANCHE: Not that much?

MITCH: No. More.

BLANCHE: Well, you're a tall man and you can carry a good deal of weight without looking awkward.

MITCH: I weigh two hundred and seven pounds and I'm six feet one and one half inches tall in my bare feet—without shoes on. And that is what I weigh stripped.

BLANCHE: Oh, my goodness, me! It's awe-inspiring.

MITCH: [*Embarrassed.*] My weight is not a very interesting subject to talk about. [*He hesitates for a moment.*] What's yours?

BLANCHE: My weight?

MITCH: Yes.

BLANCHE: Guess!

MITCH: Let me lift you.

BLANCHE: Samson![5] Go on, lift me. [*He comes behind her and puts his hands on her waist and raises her lightly off the ground.*] Well?

MITCH: You are light as a feather.

BLANCHE: Ha-ha! [*He lowers her but keeps his hands on her waist.* BLANCHE *speaks with an affectation of demureness.*] You may release me now.

MITCH: Huh?

BLANCHE: [*Gaily.*] I said unhand me, sir. [*He fumblingly embraces her. Her voice sounds gently reproving.*] Now, Mitch. Just because Stanley and Stella aren't at home is no reason why you shouldn't behave like a gentleman.

MITCH: Just give me a slap whenever I step out of bounds.

BLANCHE: That won't be necessary. You're a natural gentleman, one of the very few that are left in the world. I don't want you to think that I am severe and old maid school-teacherish or anything like that. It's just—well—

MITCH: Huh?

BLANCHE: I guess it is just that I have—old-fashioned ideals! [*She rolls her eyes, knowing he cannot see her face.* MITCH *goes to the front door. There is a considerable silence between them.* BLANCHE *sighs and* MITCH *coughs self-consciously.*]

MITCH: [*Finally.*] Where's Stanley and Stella tonight?

BLANCHE: They have gone out. With Mr. and Mrs. Hubbell upstairs.

MITCH: Where did they go?

BLANCHE: I think they were planning to go to a midnight prevue at Loew's State.

MITCH: We should all go out together some night.

BLANCHE: No. That wouldn't be a good plan.

---

5. Legendary strong man, an Israelite in the Old Testament.

MITCH: Why not?

BLANCHE: You are an old friend of Stanley's?

MITCH: We was together in the Two-forty-first.[6]

BLANCHE: I guess he talks to you frankly?

MITCH: Sure.

BLANCHE: Has he talked to you about me?

MITCH: Oh—not very much.

BLANCHE: The way you say that, I suspect that he has.

MITCH: No, he hasn't said much.

BLANCHE: But what he *has* said. What would you say his attitude toward me was?

MITCH: Why do you want to ask that?

BLANCHE: Well—

MITCH: Don't you get along with him?

BLANCHE: What do you think?

MITCH: I don't think he understands you.

BLANCHE: That is putting it mildly. If it weren't for Stella about to have a baby, I wouldn't be able to endure things here.

MITCH: He isn't—nice to you?

BLANCHE: He is insufferably rude. Goes out of his way to offend me.

MITCH: In what way, Blanche?

BLANCHE: Why, in every conceivable way.

MITCH: I'm surprised to hear that.

BLANCHE: Are you?

MITCH: Well, I—don't see how anybody could be rude to you.

BLANCHE: It's really a pretty frightful situation. You see, there's no privacy here. There's just these portieres between the two rooms at night. He stalks through the rooms in his underwear at night. And I have to ask him to close the bathroom door. That sort of commonness isn't necessary. You probably wonder why I don't move out. Well, I'll tell you frankly. A teacher's salary is barely sufficient for her living expenses. I didn't save a penny last year and so I had to come here for the summer. That's why I have to put up with my sister's husband. And he has to put up with me, apparently so much against his wishes. . . . Surely he must have told you how much he hates he!

MITCH: I don't think he hates you.

BLANCHE: He hates me. Or why would he insult me? The first time I laid eyes on him I thought to myself, that man is my executioner! That man will destroy me, unless——

MITCH: Blanche—

BLANCHE: Yes, honey?

MITCH: Can I ask you a question?

BLANCHE: Yes. What?

MITCH: How old are you?

[*She makes a nervous gesture.*]

BLANCHE: Why do you want to know?

6. Battalion of engineers in World War II (1939–45).

MITCH: I talked to my mother about you and she said, "How old is Blanche?" And I wasn't able to tell her. [*There is another pause.*]

BLANCHE: You talked to your mother about me?

MITCH: Yes.

BLANCHE: Why?

MITCH: I told my mother how nice you were, and I liked you.

BLANCHE: Were you sincere about that?

MITCH: You know I was.

BLANCHE: Why did your mother want to know my age?

MITCH: Mother is sick.

BLANCHE: I'm sorry to hear it. Badly?

MITCH: She won't live long. Maybe just a few months.

BLANCHE: Oh.

MITCH: She worries because I'm not settled.

BLANCHE: Oh.

MITCH: She wants me to be settled down before she— [*His voice is hoarse and he clears his throat twice, shuffling nervously around with his hands in and out of his pockets.*]

BLANCHE: You love her very much, don't you?

MITCH: Yes.

BLANCHE: I think you have a great capacity for devotion. You will be lonely when she passes on, won't you? [MITCH *clears his throat and nods.*] I understand what that is.

MITCH: To be lonely?

BLANCHE: I loved someone, too, and the person I loved I lost.

MITCH: Dead? [*She crosses to the window and sits on the sill, looking out. She pours herself another drink.*] A man?

BLANCHE: He was a boy, just a boy, when I was a very young girl. When I was sixteen, I made the discovery—love. All at once and much, much too completely. It was like you suddenly turned a blinding light on something that had always been half in shadow, that's how it struck the world for me. But I was unlucky. Deluded. There was something different about the boy, a nervousness, a softness and tenderness which wasn't like a man's, although he wasn't the least bit effeminate looking—still—that thing was there. . . . He came to me for help. I didn't know that. I didn't find out anything till after our marriage when we'd run away and come back and all I knew was I'd failed him in some mysterious way and wasn't able to give the help he needed but couldn't speak of! He was in the quicksands and clutching at me—but I wasn't holding him out, I was slipping in with him! I didn't know that. I didn't know anything except I loved him unendurably but without being able to help him or help myself. Then I found out. In the worst of all possible ways. By coming suddenly into a room that I thought was empty—which wasn't empty, but had two people in it . . . the boy I had married and an older man who had been his friend for years. . . . [*A locomotive is heard approaching outside. She claps her hands to her ears and crouches over. The headlight of the locomotive glares into the room as it thunders past. As the noise recedes she straightens slowly and continues speaking.*] Afterward we pretended that nothing had been discovered. Yes, the three of us drove out to Moon Lake Casino,[7] very drunk and laughing all the way. [*Polka music sounds, in a minor key faint with distance.*] We danced the "Varsouviana!"[8] Suddenly in the middle of the dance the boy I had married broke away from me and ran out of the casino. A few moments later—a shot! [*The polka stops abruptly.* BLANCHE *rises stiffly. Then, the polka resumes in a major key.*] I ran out—all did!—all ran and gathered about the terrible thing at the edge of the lake! I couldn't get near for the crowding. Then somebody caught my arm. "Don't go any closer! Come back! You don't want to see!" See? See what! Then I heard voices say—Allan! Allan! The Grey boy! He'd stuck the revolver into his mouth, and fired—so that the back of his head had been—blown away! [*She sways and covers her face.*] It was because—on the dance floor—unable to stop myself—I'd suddenly said—"I saw! I know! You disgust me. . . ." And then the searchlight which had been turned on the world was turned off again and never for one moment since has there been any light that's stronger than this—kitchen—candle. . . .

[MITCH *gets up awkwardly and moves toward her a little. The polka music increases.* MITCH *stands beside her.*]

MITCH: [*Drawing her slowly into his arms.*] You need somebody. And I need somebody, too. Could it be—you and me, Blanche?

[*She stares at him vacantly for a moment. Then with a soft cry huddles in his embrace. She makes a sobbing effort to speak but the words won't come. He kisses her forehead and her eyes and finally her lips. The polka tune fades out. Her breath is drawn and released in long, grateful sobs.*]

BLANCHE: Sometimes—there's God—so quickly!

Scene 7

It is late afternoon in mid-September.

The portieres are open and a table is set for a birthday supper, with cake and flowers.

STELLA *is completing the decorations as* STANLEY *comes in.*

STANLEY: What's all this stuff for?
STELLA: Honey, it's Blanche's birthday.
STANLEY: She here?
STELLA: In the bathroom.
STANLEY: [*Mimicking.*] "Washing out some things"?
STELLA: I reckon so.
STANLEY: How long she been in there?
STELLA: All afternoon.
STANLEY: [*Mimicking.*] "Soaking in a hot tub"?
STELLA: Yes.
STANLEY: Temperature 100 on the nose, and she soaks herself in a hot tub.

7. Casino and nightclub in Dundee, Mississippi, popular during the 1940s.
8. Fast Polish dance, similar to the polka.

STELLA: She says it cools her off for the evening.

STANLEY: And you run out an' get her cokes, I suppose? And serve 'em to Her Majesty in the tub? [STELLA *shrugs*.] Set down here a minute.

STELLA: Stanley, I've got things to do.

STANLEY: Set down! I've got th' dope on your big sister, Stella.

STELLA: Stanley, stop picking on Blanche.

STANLEY: That girl calls *me* common!

STELLA: Lately you been doing all you can think of to rub her the wrong way, Stanley, and Blanche is sensitive and you've got to realize that Blanche and I grew up under very different circumstances than you did.

STANLEY: So I been told. And told and told and told! You know she's been feeding us a pack of lies here?

STELLA: No, I don't and—

STANLEY: Well, she has, however. But now the cat's out of the bag! I found out some things!

STELLA: What—things?

STANLEY: Things I already suspected. But now I got proof from the most reliable sources—which I have checked on!

> [BLANCHE *is singing in the bathroom a saccharine popular ballad which is used contrapuntally*[9] *with* STANLEY'S *speech*.]

STELLA: [*To* STANLEY.] Lower your voice!

STANLEY: Some canary bird, huh!

STELLA: Now please tell me quietly what you think you've found out about my sister.

STANLEY: Lie Number One: All this squeamishness she puts on! You should just know the line she's been feeding to Mitch. He thought she had never been more than kissed by a fellow! But Sister Blanche is no lily! Ha-ha! Some lily she is!

STELLA: What have you heard and who from?

STANLEY: Our supply-man down at the plant has been going through Laurel for years and he knows all about her and everybody else in the town of Laurel knows all about her. She is as famous in Laurel as if she was the President of the United States, only she is not respected by any party! This supply-man stops at a hotel called the Flamingo.

BLANCHE: [*Singing blithely.*] "Say, it's only a paper moon, / Sailing over a cardboard sea / —But it wouldn't be make-believe / If you believed in me!"[1]

STELLA: What about the—Flamingo?

STANLEY: She stayed there, too.

STELLA: My sister lived at Belle Reve.

STANLEY: This is after the home-place had slipped through her lily-white fingers! She moved to the Flamingo! A second-class hotel which has the advantage of not interfering in the private social life of the personalities there! The Flamingo is used to all kinds of goings-on. But even the management of the

---

9. Musical term meaning "in an alternating or contrasting manner." *Saccharine*: cloyingly sweet; overly sentimental.

1. From "It's Only a Paper Moon" (1933), a popular song by Harold Arlen (1905–86).

Flamingo was impressed by Dame Blanche! In fact they was so impressed by Dame Blanche that they requested her to turn in her room key—for permanently! This happened a couple of weeks before she showed here.

BLANCHE: [*Singing.*] "It's a Barnum and Bailey[2] world, / Just as phony as it can be— / But it wouldn't be make-believe / If you believed in me!"

STELLA: What—contemptible—lies!

STANLEY: Sure, I can see how you would be upset by this. She pulled the wool over your eyes as much as Mitch's!

STELLA: It's pure invention! There's not a word of truth in it and if I were a man and this creature had dared to invent such things in my presence—

BLANCHE: [*Singing.*] "Without your love, / it's a honky-tonk parade! / Without your love, / It's a melody played / In a penny arcade . . ."

STANLEY: Honey, I told you I thoroughly checked on these stories! Now wait till I finish. The trouble with Dame Blanche was that she couldn't put on her act anymore in Laurel! They got wised up after two or three dates with her and then they quit, and she goes on to another, the same old line, same old act, same old hooey! But the town was too small for this to go on forever! And as time went by she became a town character. Regarded as not just different but downright loco—nuts. [STELLA *draws back.*] And for the last year or two she has been washed up like poison. That's why she's here this summer, visiting royalty, putting on all this act—because she's practically told by the mayor to get out of town! Yes, did you know there was an army camp near Laurel and your sister's was one of the places called "Out-of-Bounds"?

BLANCHE: "It's only a paper moon, / Just as phony as it can be— / But it wouldn't be make-believe / If you believed in me!"

STANLEY: Well, so much for her being such a refined and particular type of girl. Which brings us to Lie Number Two.

STELLA: I don't want to hear any more!

STANLEY: She's not going back to teach school! In fact I am willing to bet you that she never had no idea of returning to Laurel! She didn't resign temporarily from the high school because of her nerves! No, siree, Bob! She didn't. They kicked her out of that high school before the spring term ended—and I hate to tell you the reason that step was taken! A seventeen-year-old boy— she'd gotten mixed up with!

BLANCHE: "It's a Barnum and Bailey world, / Just as phony as it can be—"

[*In the bathroom the water goes on loud; little breathless cries and peals of laughter are heard as if a child were frolicking in the tub.*]

STELLA: This is making me—sick!

STANLEY: The boy's dad learned about it and got in touch with the high school superintendent. Boy, oh, boy, I'd like to have been in that office when Dame Blanche was called on the carpet! I'd like to have seen her trying to squirm out of that one! But they had her on the hook good and proper that time and she knew that the jig was all up! They told her she better move on to some fresh territory. Yep, it was practickly a town ordinance passed against her!

2. P. T. Barnum (1810–91) and James Bailey (1847–1906), circus promoters of "The Greatest Show on Earth."

[*The bathroom door is opened and* BLANCHE *thrusts her head out, holding a towel about her hair.*]

BLANCHE: Stella!

STELLA: [*Faintly.*] Yes, Blanche?

BLANCHE: Give me another bath-towel to dry my hair with. I've just washed it.

STELLA: Yes, Blanche. [*She crosses in a dazed way from the kitchen to the bathroom door with a towel.*]

BLANCHE: What's the matter, honey?

STELLA: Matter? Why?

BLANCHE: You have such a strange expression on your face!

STELLA: Oh—[*She tries to laugh.*] I guess I'm a little tired!

BLANCHE: Why don't you bathe, too, soon as I get out?

STANLEY: [*Calling from the kitchen.*] How soon is that going to be?

BLANCHE: Not so terribly long! Possess your soul in patience![3]

STANLEY: It's not my soul, it's my kidneys I'm worried about! [BLANCHE *slams the door.* STANLEY *laughs harshly.* STELLA *comes slowly back into the kitchen.*] Well, what do you think of it?

STELLA: I don't believe all of those stories and I think your supply-man was mean and rotten to tell them. It's possible that some of the things he said are partly true. There are things about my sister I don't approve of—things that caused sorrow at home. She was always—flighty!

STANLEY: Flighty!

STELLA: But when she was young, very young, she married a boy who wrote poetry. . . . He was extremely good-looking. I think Blanche didn't just love him but worshipped the ground he walked on! Adored him and thought him almost too fine to be human! But then she found out—

STANLEY: What?

STELLA: This beautiful and talented young man was a degenerate. Didn't your supply-man give you that information?

STANLEY: All we discussed was recent history. That must have been a pretty long time ago.

STELLA: Yes, it was—a pretty long time ago. . . .

[STANLEY *comes up and takes her by the shoulders rather gently. She gently withdraws from him. Automatically she starts sticking little pink candles in the birthday cake.*]

STANLEY: How many candles you putting in that cake?

STELLA: I'll stop at twenty-five.

STANLEY: Is company expected?

STELLA: We asked Mitch to come over for cake and ice-cream.

[STANLEY *looks a little uncomfortable. He lights a cigarette from the one he has just finished.*]

STANLEY: I wouldn't be expecting Mitch over tonight.

---

3. "In your patience you will possess your souls" (Luke 21.19).

[STELLA *pauses in her occupation with candles and looks slowly around at* STANLEY.]

STELLA: *Why?*

STANLEY: Mitch is a buddy of mine. We were in the same outfit together—Two-forty-first Engineers. We work in the same plant and now on the same bowling team. You think I could face him if—

STELLA: Stanley Kowalski, did you—did you repeat what that—?

STANLEY: You're goddam right I told him! I'd have that on my conscience the rest of my life if I knew all that stuff and let my best friend get caught!

STELLA: Is Mitch through with her?

STANLEY: Wouldn't you be if—?

STELLA: I said, *Is Mitch through with her?*

[BLANCHE'S *voice is lifted again, serenely as a bell. She sings "But it wouldn't be make-believe / If you believed in me."*]

STANLEY: No, I don't think he's necessarily through with her—just wised up!

STELLA: Stanley, she thought Mitch was—going to—going to marry her. I was hoping so, too.

STANLEY: Well, he's not going to marry her. Maybe he *was*, but he's not going to jump in a tank with a school of sharks—now! [*He rises.*] Blanche! Oh, Blanche! Can I please get in my bathroom? [*There is a pause.*]

BLANCHE: Yes, indeed, sir! Can you wait one second while I dry?

STANLEY: Having waited one hour I guess one second ought to pass in a hurry.

STELLA: And she hasn't got her job? Well, what will she do!

STANLEY: She's not stayin' here after Tuesday. You know that, don't you? Just to make sure I bought her ticket myself. A bus ticket.

STELLA: In the first place, Blanche wouldn't go on a bus.

STANLEY: She'll go on a bus and like it.

STELLA: No, she won't, no, she won't, Stanley!

STANLEY: *She'll go!* Period. P.S. She'll go *Tuesday!*

STELLA: [*Slowly.*] What'll—she—do? What on earth will she—*do!*

STANLEY: Her future is mapped out for her.

STELLA: What do you mean?

[BLANCHE *sings.*]

STANLEY: Hey, canary bird! Toots! Get *OUT* of the *BATHROOM!*

[*The bathroom door flies open and* BLANCHE *emerges with a gay peal of laughter, but as* STANLEY *crosses past her, a frightened look appears in her face, almost a look of panic. He doesn't look at her but slams the bathroom door shut as he goes in.*]

BLANCHE: [*Snatching up a hairbrush.*] Oh, I feel so good after my long, hot bath, I feel so good and cool and—rested!

STELLA: [*Sadly and doubtfully from the kitchen.*] Do you, Blanche?

BLANCHE: [*Snatching up a hairbrush.*] Yes, I do, so refreshed! [*She tinkles her highball glass.*] A hot bath and a long, cold drink always give me a brand new outlook on life! [*She looks through the portieres at* STELLA, *standing between them, and slowly stops brushing.*] Something has happened!—What is it?

STELLA: [*Turning away quickly.*] Why, nothing has happened, Blanche.

BLANCHE: You're lying! Something has! [*She stares fearfully at* STELLA, *who pretends to be busy at the table. The distant piano goes into a hectic breakdown.*]

Scene 8

Three quarters of an hour later.

> *The view through the big windows is fading gradually into a still-golden dusk. A torch of sunlight blazes on the side of a big water-tank or oil-drum across the empty lot toward the business district which is now pierced by pinpoints of lighted windows or windows reflecting the sunset.*
>
> *The three people are completing a dismal birthday supper.* STANLEY *looks sullen.* STELLA *is embarrassed and sad.*
>
> BLANCHE *has a tight, artificial smile on her drawn face. There is a fourth place at the table which is left vacant.*

BLANCHE: [*Suddenly.*] Stanley, tell us a joke, tell us a funny story to make us all laugh. I don't know what's the matter, we're all so solemn. Is it because I've been stood up by my beau? [STELLA *laughs feebly.*] It's the first time in my entire experience with men, and I've had a good deal of all sorts, that I've actually been stood up by anybody! Ha-ha! I don't know how to take it. . . . Tell us a funny little story, Stanley! Something to help us out.

STANLEY: I didn't think you liked my stories, Blanche.

BLANCHE: I like them when they're amusing but not indecent.

STANLEY: I don't know any refined enough for your taste.

BLANCHE: Then let me tell one.

STELLA: Yes, you tell one, Blanche. You used to know lots of good stories.

[*The music fades.*]

BLANCHE: Let me see, now. . . . I must run through my repertoire! Oh, yes—I love parrot stories! Do you all like parrot stories? Well, this one's about the old maid and the parrot. This old maid, she had a parrot that cursed a blue streak and knew more vulgar expressions than Mr. Kowalski!

STANLEY: Huh.

BLANCHE: And the only way to hush the parrot up was to put the cover back on its cage so it would think it was night and go back to sleep. Well, one morning the old maid had just uncovered the parrot for the day—when who should she see coming up the front walk but the preacher! Well, she rushed back to the parrot and slipped the cover back on the cage and then she let in the preacher. And the parrot was perfectly still, just as quiet as a mouse, but just as she was asking the preacher how much sugar he wanted in his coffee— the parrot broke the silence with a loud— [*She whistles.*] —and said—"God *damn,* but that was a short day!" [*She throws back her head and laughs.* STELLA *also makes an ineffectual effort to seem amused.* STANLEY *pays no attention to the story but reaches way over the table to spear his fork into the remaining chop which he eats with his fingers.*] Apparently Mr. Kowalski was not amused.

STELLA: Mr. Kowalski is too busy making a pig of himself to think of anything else!

STANLEY: That's right, baby.

STELLA: Your face and your fingers are disgustingly greasy. Go and wash up and then help me clear the table.

[*He hurls a plate to the floor.*]

STANLEY: That's how I'll clear the table! [*He seizes her arm.*] Don't ever talk that way to me! "Pig—Polack—disgusting—vulgar—greasy!"—them kind of words have been on your tongue and your sister's too much around here! What do you two think you are? A pair of queens? Remember what Huey Long[4] said— "Every Man is a King!" And I am the king around here, so don't forget it! [*He hurls a cup and saucer to the floor.*] My place is cleared! You want me to clear your places?

[STELLA *begins to cry weakly.* STANLEY *stalks out on the porch and lights a cigarette. The Negro entertainers around the corner are heard.*]

BLANCHE: What happened while I was bathing? What did he tell you, Stella?

STELLA: Nothing, nothing, nothing!

BLANCHE: I think he told you something about Mitch and me! You know why Mitch didn't come but you won't tell me! [STELLA *shakes her head helplessly.*] I'm going to call him!

STELLA: I wouldn't call him, Blanche.

BLANCHE: I am, I'm going to call him on the phone.

STELLA: [*Miserably.*] I wish you wouldn't.

BLANCHE: I intend to be given some explanation from someone!

[*She rushes to the phone in the bedroom.* STELLA *goes out on the porch and stares reproachfully at her husband. He grunts and turns away from her.*]

STELLA: I hope you're pleased with your doings. I never had so much trouble swallowing food in my life, looking at that girl's face and the empty chair! [*She cries quietly.*]

BLANCHE: [*At the phone.*] Hello. Mr. Mitchell, please. . . . Oh. . . . I would like to leave a number if I may. Magnolia 9047. And say it's important to call. . . . Yes, very important. . . . Thank you. [*She remains by the phone with a lost, frightened look.*]

[STANLEY *turns slowly back toward his wife and takes her clumsily in his arms.*]

STANLEY: Stell, it's gonna be all right after she goes and after you've had the baby. It's gonna be all right again between you and me the way that it was. You remember the way that it was? Them nights we had together? God, honey, it's gonna be sweet when we can make noise in the night the way that we used to and get the colored lights going with nobody's sister behind the curtains to hear us! [*Their upstairs neighbors are heard in bellowing laughter at something.* STANLEY *chuckles.*] Steve an' Eunice . . .

4. Louisiana political leader, governor, and senator (1893–1935), a fiery, flamboyant populist known as "the Kingfish."

STELLA: Come on back in. [*She returns to the kitchen and starts lighting the candles on the white cake.*] Blanche?

BLANCHE: Yes. [*She returns from the bedroom to the table in the kitchen.*] Oh, those pretty, pretty little candles! Oh, don't burn them, Stella.

STELLA: I certainly will.

[STANLEY *comes back in.*]

BLANCHE: You ought to save them for baby's birthdays. Oh, I hope candles are going to glow in his life and I hope that his eyes are going to be like candles, like two blue candles lighted in a white cake!

STANLEY: [*Sitting down.*] What poetry!

BLANCHE: [*She pauses reflectively for a moment.*] I shouldn't have called him.

STELLA: There's lots of things could have happened.

BLANCHE: There's no excuse for it, Stella. I don't have to put up with insults. I won't be taken for granted.

STANLEY: Goddamn, it's hot in here with the steam from the bathroom.

BLANCHE: I've said I was sorry three times. [*The piano fades out.*] I take hot baths for my nerves. Hydrotherapy, they call it. You healthy Polack, without a nerve in your body, of course you don't know what anxiety feels like!

STANLEY: I am not a Polack. People from Poland are Poles, not Polacks. But what I am is a one-hundred-per-cent American, born and raised in the greatest country on earth and proud as hell of it, so don't ever call me a Polack.

[*The phone rings.* BLANCHE *rises expectantly.*]

BLANCHE: Oh, that's for me, I'm sure.

STANLEY: *I'm* not sure. Keep your seat. [*He crosses leisurely to phone.*] H'lo. Aw, yeh, hello, Mac.

[*He leans against wall, staring insultingly in at* BLANCHE. *She sinks back in her chair with a frightened look.* STELLA *leans over and touches her shoulder.*]

BLANCHE: Oh, keep your hands off me, Stella. What is the matter with you? Why do you look at me with that pitying look?

STANLEY: [*Bawling.*] QUIET IN THERE!—We've got a noisy woman on the place.—Go on, Mac. At Riley's? No, I don't wanta bowl at Riley's. I had a little trouble with Riley last week. I'm the team captain, ain't I? All right, then, we're not gonna bowl at Riley's, we're gonna bowl at the West Side or the Gala! All right, Mac. See you! [*He hangs up and returns to the table.* BLANCHE *fiercely controls herself, drinking quickly from her tumbler of water. He doesn't look at her but reaches in a pocket. Then he speaks slowly and with false amiability.*] Sister Blanche, I've got a little birthday remembrance for you.

BLANCHE: Oh, have you, Stanley? I wasn't expecting any, I—I don't know why Stella wants to observe my birthday! I'd much rather forget it—when you— reach twenty-seven! Well—age is a subject that you'd prefer to—ignore!

STANLEY: Twenty-seven?

BLANCHE: [*Quickly.*] What is it? Is it for *me*?

[*He is holding a little envelope toward her.*]

STANLEY: Yes, I hope you like it!

BLANCHE: Why, why—Why, it's a—

STANLEY: Ticket! Back to Laurel! On the Greyhound![5] Tuesday! [*The "Varsouviana" music steals in softly and continues playing.* STELLA *rises abruptly and turns her back.* BLANCHE *tries to smile. Then she tries to laugh. Then she gives both up and springs from the table and runs into the next room. She clutches her throat and then runs into the bathroom. Coughing, gagging sounds are heard.*] Well!

STELLA: You didn't need to do that.

STANLEY: Don't forget all that I took off her.

STELLA: You needn't have been so cruel to someone alone as she is.

STANLEY: Delicate piece she is.

STELLA: She is. She was. You didn't know Blanche as a girl. Nobody, nobody, was tender and trusting as she was. But people like you abused her, and forced her to change. [*He crosses into the bedroom, ripping off his shirt, and changes into a brilliant silk bowling shirt. She follows him.*] Do you think you're going bowling now?

STANLEY: Sure.

STELLA: You're not going bowling. [*She catches hold of his shirt.*] Why did you do this to her?

STANLEY: I done nothing to no one. Let go of my shirt. You've torn it.

STELLA: I want to know why. Tell me why.

STANLEY: When we first met, me and you, you thought I was common. How right you was, baby. I was common as dirt. You showed me the snapshot of the place with the columns. I pulled you down off them columns and how you loved it, having them colored lights going! And wasn't we happy together, wasn't it all okay till she showed here? [STELLA *makes a slight movement. Her look goes suddenly inward as if some interior voice had called her name. She begins a slow, shuffling progress from the bedroom to the kitchen, leaning and resting on the back of the chair and then on the edge of a table with a blind look and listening expression.* STANLEY, *finishing with his shirt, is unaware of her reaction.*] And wasn't we happy together? Wasn't it all okay? Till she showed here. Hoity-Toity, describing me as an ape. [*He suddenly notices the change in* STELLA.] Hey, what is it, Stell? [*He crosses to her.*]

STELLA: [*Quietly.*] Take me to the hospital.

[*He is with her now, supporting her with his arm, murmuring indistinguishably as they go outside.*]

Scene 9

A while later that evening. BLANCHE *is seated in a tense hunched position in a bedroom chair that she has recovered with diagonal green and white stripes. She has on her scarlet satin robe. On the table beside chair is a bottle of liquor and a glass. The rapid, feverish polka tune, the "Varsouviana," is heard. The music is in her mind; she is drinking to escape it and the sense of disaster closing in on her, and she seems to whisper the words of the song. An electric fan is turning back and forth across her.*

5. Long-distance bus company.

MITCH *comes around the corner in work clothes: blue denim shirt and pants. He is unshaven. He climbs the steps to the door and rings.* BLANCHE *is startled.*

BLANCHE: Who is it, please?
MITCH: [*Hoarsely.*] Me. Mitch.

[*The polka tune stops.*]

BLANCHE: Mitch!—Just a minute. [*She rushes about frantically, hiding the bottle in a closet, crouching at the mirror and dabbing her face with cologne and powder. She is so excited that her breath is audible as she dashes about. At last she rushes to the door in the kitchen and lets him in.*] Mitch!—Y'know, I really shouldn't let you in after the treatment I have received from you this evening! So utterly uncavalier! But hello, beautiful! [*She offers him her lips. He ignores it and pushes past her into the flat. She looks fearfully after him as he stalks into the bedroom.*] My, my, what a cold shoulder! And such uncouth apparel! Why, you haven't even shaved! The unforgivable insult to a lady! But I forgive you. I forgive you because it's such a relief to see you. You've stopped that polka tune that I had caught in my head. Have you ever had anything caught in your head? No, of course you haven't, you dumb angel-puss, you'd never get anything awful caught in your head!

[*He stares at her while she follows him while she talks. It is obvious that he has had a few drinks on the way over.*]

MITCH: Do we have to have that fan on?
BLANCHE: No!
MITCH: I don't like fans.
BLANCHE: Then let's turn it off, honey. I'm not partial to them! [*She presses the switch and the fan nods slowly off. She clears her throat uneasily as* MITCH *plumps himself down on the bed in the bedroom and lights a cigarette.*] I don't know what there is to drink. I—haven't investigated.
MITCH: I don't want Stan's liquor.
BLANCHE: It isn't Stan's. Everything here isn't Stan's. Some things on the premises are actually mine! How is your mother? Isn't your mother well?
MITCH: Why?
BLANCHE: Something's the matter tonight, but never mind. I won't cross-examine the witness. I'll just— [*She touches her forehead vaguely. The polka tune starts up again.*]—pretend I don't notice anything different about you! That—music again . . .
MITCH: What music?
BLANCHE: The "Varsouviana"! The polka tune they were playing when Allan— Wait! [*A distant revolver shot is heard.* BLANCHE *seems relieved.*] There now, the shot! It always stops after that. [*The polka music dies out again.*] Yes, now it's stopped.
MITCH: Are you boxed out of your mind?
BLANCHE: I'll go and see what I can find in the way of—[*She crosses into the closet, pretending to search for the bottle.*] Oh, by the way, excuse me for not being dressed. But I'd practically given you up! Had you forgotten your invitation to supper?

MITCH: I wasn't going to see you anymore.

BLANCHE: Wait a minute. I can't hear what you're saying and you talk so little that when you do say something, I don't want to miss a single syllable of it. . . . What am I looking around here for? Oh, yes—liquor! We've had so much excitement around here this evening that I *am* boxed out of my mind! [*She pretends suddenly to find the bottle. He draws his foot up on the bed and stares at her contemptuously.*] Here's something. Southern Comfort![6] What is that, I wonder?

MITCH: If you don't know, it must belong to Stan.

BLANCHE: Take your foot off the bed. It has a light cover on it. Of course you boys don't notice things like that. I've done so much with this place since I've been here.

MITCH: I bet you have.

BLANCHE: You saw it before I came. Well, look at it now! This room is almost— dainty! I want to keep it that way. I wonder if this stuff ought to be mixed with something? Ummm, it's sweet! It's terribly, terribly sweet! Why, it's a *liqueur*, I believe! Yes, that's what it *is*, a liqueur! [MITCH *grunts.*] I'm afraid you won't like it, but try it, and maybe you will.

MITCH: I told you already I don't want none of his liquor and I mean it. You ought to lay off his liquor. He says you been lapping it up all summer like a wild cat!

BLANCHE: What a fantastic statement! Fantastic of him to say it, fantastic of you to repeat it! I won't descend to the level of such cheap accusations to answer them, even!

MITCH: Huh.

BLANCHE: What's in your mind? I see something in your eyes!

MITCH: [*Getting up.*] It's dark in here.

BLANCHE: I like it dark. The dark is comforting to me.

MITCH: I don't think I ever seen you in the light. [BLANCHE *laughs breathlessly.*] That's a fact!

BLANCHE: Is it?

MITCH: I've never seen you in the afternoon.

BLANCHE: Whose fault is that?

MITCH: You never want to go out in the afternoon.

BLANCHE: Why, Mitch, you're at the plant in the afternoon!

MITCH: Not Sunday afternoon. I've asked you to go out with me sometimes on Sundays but you always make an excuse. You never want to go out till after six and then it's always some place that's not lighted much.

BLANCHE: There is some obscure meaning in this but I fail to catch it.

MITCH: What it means is I've never had a real good look at you, Blanche. Let's turn the light on here.

BLANCHE: [*Fearfully.*] Light? Which light? What for?

MITCH: This one with the paper thing on it.

[*He tears the paper lantern off the light bulb. She utters a frightened gasp.*]

BLANCHE: What did you do that for?

6. Peach-flavored bourbon liqueur.

MITCH: So I can take a look at you good and plain!

BLANCHE: Of course you don't really mean to be insulting!

MITCH: No, just realistic.

BLANCHE: I don't want realism. I want magic! [MITCH *laughs*.] Yes, yes, magic! I try to give that to people. I misrepresent things to them. I don't tell truth, I tell what *ought* to be truth. And if that is sinful, then let me be damned for it!—Don't turn the light on!

[MITCH *crosses to the switch. He turns the light on and stares at her. She cries out and covers her face. He turns the lights off again.*]

MITCH: [*Slowly and bitterly.*] I don't mind you being older than what I thought. But all the rest of it—Christ! That pitch about your ideals being so old-fashioned and all the malarkey that you've dished out all summer. Oh, I knew you weren't sixteen anymore. But I was a fool enough to believe you was straight.

BLANCHE: Who told you I wasn't—"straight"? My loving brother-in-law. And you believed him.

MITCH: I called him a liar at first. And then I checked on the story. First I asked our supply-man who travels through Laurel. And then I talked directly over long-distance to this merchant.

BLANCHE: Who is this merchant?

MITCH: Kiefaber.

BLANCHE: The merchant Kiefaber of Laurel! I know the man. He whistled at me. I put him in his place. So now for revenge he makes up stories about me.

MITCH: Three people, Kiefaber, Stanley, and Shaw, swore to them!

BLANCHE: Rub-a-dub-dub, three men in a tub! And such a filthy tub!

MITCH: Didn't you stay at a hotel called The Flamingo?

BLANCHE: Flamingo? No! Tarantula was the name of it! I stayed at a hotel called The Tarantula Arms!

MITCH: [*Stupidly.*] Tarantula?

BLANCHE: Yes, a big spider! That's where I brought my victims. [*She pours herself another drink.*] Yes, I had many intimacies with strangers. After the death of Allan—intimacies with strangers was all I seemed able to fill my empty heart with. . . . I think it was panic, just panic, that drove me from one to another, hunting for some protection—here and there, in the most—unlikely places— even, at last, in a seventeen-year-old boy but—somebody wrote the superintendent about it—"This woman is morally unfit for her position!" [*She throws back her head with convulsive, sobbing laughter. Then she repeats the statement, gasps, and drinks.*] True? Yes, I suppose—unfit somehow—anyway. . . . So I came here. There was nowhere else I could go. I was played out. You know what played out is? My youth was suddenly gone up the water-spout, and—I met you. You said you needed somebody. Well, I needed somebody, too. I thanked God for you, because you seemed to be gentle—a cleft in the rock of the world that I could hide in! But I guess I was asking, hoping—too much! Kiefaber, Stanley, and Shaw have tied an old tin can to the tail of the kite.

[*There is a pause.* MITCH *stares at her dumbly.*]

MITCH: You lied to me, Blanche.

BLANCHE: Don't say I lied to you.

MITCH: Lies, lies, inside and out, all lies.

BLANCHE: Never inside, I didn't lie in my heart. . . .

[*A vendor comes around the corner. She is a blind* MEXICAN WOMAN *in a dark shawl, carrying bunches of those gaudy tin flowers that lower-class Mexicans display at funerals and other festive occasions. She is calling barely audibly. Her figure is only faintly visible outside the building.*]

MEXICAN WOMAN: *Flores. Flores, Flores para los muertos.*[7] *Flores. Flores.*

BLANCHE: What? Oh! Somebody outside . . . [*She goes to the door, opens it and stares at the* MEXICAN WOMAN.]

MEXICAN WOMAN: [*She is at the door and offers* BLANCHE *some of her flowers.*] *Flores? Flores para los muertos?*

BLANCHE: [*Frightened.*] No, no! Not now! Not now! [*She darts back into the apartment, slamming the door.*]

MEXICAN WOMAN: [*She turns away and starts to move down the street.*] *Flores para los muertos.*

[*The polka tune fades in.*]

BLANCHE: [*As if to herself.*] Crumble and fade and—regrets—recriminations . . . "If you'd done this, it wouldn't've cost me that!"

MEXICAN WOMAN: *Corones*[8] *para los muertos. Corones . . .*

BLANCHE: Legacies! Huh. . . . And other things such as bloodstained pillow-slips—"Her linen needs changing"—"Yes, Mother. But couldn't we get a colored girl to do it?" No, we couldn't of course. Everything gone but the—

MEXICAN WOMAN: *Flores.*

BLANCHE: Death—I used to sit here and she used to sit over there and death was as close as you are. . . . We didn't dare even admit we had ever heard of it!

MEXICAN WOMAN: *Flores para los muertos, flores—flores . . .*

BLANCHE: The opposite is desire. So do you wonder? How could you possibly wonder! Not far from Belle Reve, before we had lost Belle Reve, was a camp where they trained young soldiers. On Sunday nights they would go in town to get drunk—

MEXICAN WOMAN: [*Softly.*] *Corones . . .*

BLANCHE: —and on the way back they would stagger onto my lawn and call—"Blanche! Blanche!"—the deaf old lady remaining suspected nothing. But sometimes I slipped outside to answer their calls. . . . Later the paddy-wagon[9] would gather them up like daisies . . . the long way home. . . . [*The* MEXICAN WOMAN *turns slowly and drifts back off with her soft mournful cries.* BLANCHE *goes to the dresser and leans forward on it. After a moment,* MITCH *rises and follows her purposefully. The polka music fades away. He places his hands on her waist and tries to turn her about.*] What do you want?

MITCH: [*Fumbling to embrace her.*] What I been missing all summer.

7. Flowers for the dead (Spanish).
8. Wreaths (Spanish).
9. Police van.

BLANCHE: Then marry me, Mitch!

MITCH: I don't think I want to marry you anymore.

BLANCHE: No?

MITCH: [*Dropping his hands from her waist.*] You're not clean enough to bring in the house with my mother.

BLANCHE: Go away, then. [*He stares at her.*] Get out of here quick before I start screaming fire! [*Her throat is tightening with hysteria.*] Get out of here quick before I start screaming fire. [*He still remains staring. She suddenly rushes to the big window with its pale blue square of the soft summer light and cries wildly.*] Fire! Fire! Fire!

[*With a startled gasp,* MITCH *turns and goes out the outer door, clatters awkwardly down the steps and around the corner of the building.* BLANCHE *staggers back from the window and falls to her knees. The distant piano is slow and blue.*]

Scene 10

It is a few hours later that night.

BLANCHE *has been drinking fairly steadily since* MITCH *left. She has dragged her wardrobe trunk into the center of the bedroom. It hangs open with flowery dresses thrown across it. As the drinking and packing went on, a mood of hysterical exhilaration came into her and she has decked herself out in a somewhat soiled and crumpled white satin evening gown and a pair of scuffed silver slippers with brilliants[1] set in their heels.*

Now she is placing the rhinestone tiara on her head before the mirror of the dressing-table and murmuring excitedly as if to a group of spectral admirers.

BLANCHE: How about taking a swim, a moonlight swim at the old rock-quarry? If anyone's sober enough to drive a car! Ha-ha! Best way in the world to stop your head buzzing! Only you've got to be careful to dive where the deep pool is—if you hit a rock you don't come up till tomorrow . . . . [*Tremblingly she lifts the hand mirror for a closer inspection. She catches her breath and slams the mirror face down with such violence that the glass cracks. She moans a little and attempts to rise.* STANLEY *appears around the corner of the building. He still has on the vivid green silk bowling shirt. As he rounds the corner the honky-tonk music is heard. It continues softly throughout the scene. He enters the kitchen, slamming the door. As he peers in at* BLANCHE, *he gives a low whistle. He has had a few drinks on the way and has brought some quart beer bottles home with him.*] How is my sister?

STANLEY: She is doing okay.

BLANCHE: And how is the baby?

STANLEY: [*Grinning amiably.*] The baby won't come before morning so they told me to go home and get a little shut-eye.

BLANCHE: Does that mean we are to be alone in here?

STANLEY: Yep. Just me and you, Blanche. Unless you got somebody hid under the bed. What've you got on those fine feathers for?

---

1. Sparkling gems.

BLANCHE: Oh, that's right. You left before my wire came.

STANLEY: You got a wire?

BLANCHE: I received a telegram from an old admirer of mine.

STANLEY: Anything good?

BLANCHE: I think so. An invitation.

STANLEY: What to? A fireman's ball?

BLANCHE: [*Throwing back her head.*] A cruise of the Caribbean on a yacht!

STANLEY: Well, well. What do you know?

BLANCHE: I have never been so surprised in my life.

STANLEY: I guess not.

BLANCHE: It came like a bolt from the blue!

STANLEY: Who did you say it was from?

BLANCHE: An old beau of mine.

STANLEY: The one that give you the white fox-pieces?

BLANCHE: Mr. Shep Huntleigh. I wore his ATO[2] pin my last year at college. I hadn't seen him again until last Christmas. I ran in to him on Biscayne Boulevard. Then—just now—this wire—inviting me on a cruise of the Caribbean! The problem is clothes. I tore into my trunk to see what I have that's suitable for the tropics!

STANLEY: And come up with that—gorgeous—diamond—tiara?

BLANCHE: This old relic? Ha-ha! It's only rhinestones.

STANLEY: Gosh. I thought it was Tiffany diamonds. [*He unbuttons his shirt.*]

BLANCHE: Well, anyhow, I shall be entertained in style.

STANLEY: Uh-huh. It goes to show, you never know what is coming.

BLANCHE: Just when I thought my luck had begun to fail me—

STANLEY: Into the picture pops this Miami millionaire.

BLANCHE: This man is not from Miami. This man is from Dallas.

STANLEY: This man is from Dallas?

BLANCHE: Yes, this man is from Dallas where gold spouts out of the ground!

STANLEY: Well, just so he's from somewhere! [*He starts removing his shirt.*]

BLANCHE: Close the curtains before you undress any further.

STANLEY: [*Amiably.*] This is all I'm going to undress right now. [*He rips the sack off a quart beer bottle.*] Seen a bottle-opener? [*She moves slowly toward the dresser, where she stands with her hands knotted together.*] I used to have a cousin who could open a beer bottle with his teeth. [*Pounding the bottle cap on the corner of table.*] That was his only accomplishment, all he could do— he was just a human bottle-opener. And then one time, at a wedding party, he broke his front teeth off! After that he was so ashamed of himself he used t' sneak out of the house when company came . . . [*The bottle cap pops off and a geyser of foam shoots up.* STANLEY *laughs happily, holding up the bottle over his head.*] Ha-ha! Rain from heaven! [*He extends the bottle toward her.*] Shall we bury the hatchet and make it a loving-cup? Huh?

BLANCHE: No, thank you.

STANLEY: Well, it's a red-letter night for us both. You having an oil millionaire and me having a baby. [*He goes to the bureau in the bedroom and crouches to remove something from the bottom drawer.*]

2. Probably Alpha Tau Omega, a college fraternity.

BLANCHE: [*Drawing back.*] What are you doing in here?

STANLEY: Here's something I always break out on special occasions like this. The silk pyjamas I wore on my wedding night!

BLANCHE: Oh.

STANLEY: When the telephone rings and they say, "You've got a son!" I'll tear this off and wave it like a flag! [*He shakes out a brilliant pyjama coat.*] I guess we are both entitled to put on the dog. [*He goes back to the kitchen with the coat over his arm.*]

BLANCHE: When I think of how divine it is going to be to have such a thing as privacy once more—I could weep with joy!

STANLEY: This millionaire from Dallas is not going to interfere with your privacy any?

BLANCHE: It won't be the sort of thing you have in mind. This man is a gentleman and he respects me. [*Improvising feverishly.*] What he wants is my companionship. Having great wealth sometimes makes people lonely! A cultivated woman, a woman of intelligence and breeding, can enrich a man's life—immeasurably! I have those things to offer, and this doesn't take them away. Physical beauty is passing. A transitory possession. But beauty of the mind and richness of the spirit and tenderness of the heart—and I have all of those things—aren't taken away, but grow! Increase with the years! How strange that I should be called a destitute woman! When I have all of these treasures locked in my heart. [*A choked sob comes from her.*] I think of myself as a very, very rich woman! But I have been foolish—casting my pearls before swine![3]

STANLEY: Swine, huh?

BLANCHE: Yes, swine! Swine! And I'm thinking not only of you but of your friend, Mr. Mitchell. He came to see me tonight. He dared to come here in his work clothes! And to repeat slander to me, vicious stories that he had gotten from you! I gave him his walking papers . . .

STANLEY: You did, huh?

BLANCHE: But then he came back. He returned with a box of roses to beg my forgiveness! He implored my forgiveness. But some things are not forgivable. Deliberate cruelty is not forgivable. It is the one unforgivable thing in my opinion and it is the one thing of which I have never, ever been guilty. And so I told him, I said to him, "Thank you," but it was foolish of me to think that we could ever adapt ourselves to each other. Our ways of life are too different. Our attitudes and our backgrounds are incompatible. We have to be realistic about such things. So farewell, my friend! And let there be no hard feelings. . . .

STANLEY: Was this before or after the telegram came from the Texas oil millionaire?

BLANCHE: What telegram? No! No, after! As a matter of fact, the wire came just as—

STANLEY: As a matter of fact there wasn't no wire at all!

BLANCHE: Oh, oh!

---

3. See Matthew 7.6: "Do not give what is holy to dogs, or throw your pearls before swine, lest they trample them underfoot, and turn and tear you to pieces."

STANLEY: There isn't no millionaire! And Mitch didn't come back with roses
'cause I know where he is—

BLANCHE: Oh!

STANLEY: There isn't a goddam thing but imagination!

BLANCHE: Oh!

STANLEY: And lies and conceit and tricks!

BLANCHE: Oh!

STANLEY: And look at yourself! Take a look at yourself in that worn-out Mardi
Gras[4] outfit, rented for fifty cents from some ragpicker! And with the crazy
crown on! What queen do you think you are?

BLANCHE: Oh—God . . .

STANLEY: I've been on to you from the start! Not once did you pull any wool over
this boy's eyes! You come in here and sprinkle the place with powder and
spray perfume and cover the light-bulb with a paper lantern, and lo and
behold the place has turned into Egypt and you are the Queen of the Nile![5]
Sitting on your throne and swilling down my liquor! I say—Ha!—Ha! Do you
hear me? Ha—ha—ha! [He walks into the bedroom.]

BLANCHE: Don't come in here! [Lurid reflections appear on the walls around
BLANCHE. The shadows are of a grotesque and menacing form. She catches her
breath, crosses to the phone and jiggles the hook. STANLEY goes into the bathroom and closes the door.] Operator, operator! Give me long-distance,
please. . . . I want to get in touch with Mr. Shep Huntleigh of Dallas. He's so
well known he doesn't require any address. Just ask anybody who—
Wait!!—No, I couldn't find it right now. . . . Please understand, I—No! No,
wait! . . . One moment! Someone is—Nothing! Hold on, please! [She sets the
phone down and crosses warily into the kitchen. The night is filled with inhuman
voices like cries in a jungle. The shadows and lurid reflections move sinuously
as flames along the wall spaces. Through the back wall of the rooms, which have
become transparent, can be seen the sidewalk. A prostitute has rolled[6] a drunkard. He pursues her along the walk, overtakes her and there is a struggle. A
policeman's whistle breaks it up. The figures disappear. Some moments later the
NEGRO WOMAN appears around the corner with a sequined bag which the prostitute had dropped on the walk. She is rooting excitedly through it. BLANCHE
presses her knuckles to her lips and returns slowly to the phone. She speaks in a
hoarse whisper.] Operator! Operator! Never mind long-distance. Get Western
Union. There isn't time to be—Western—Western Union! [She waits anxiously.] Western Union? Yes! I—want to—Take down this message! "In desperate, desperate circumstances! Help me! Caught in a trap. Caught in—" Oh!

[The bathroom door is thrown open and STANLEY comes out in the brilliant
silk pyjamas. He grins at her as he knots the tassled sash about his waist. She
gasps and backs away from the phone. He stares at her for a count of ten.
Then a clicking becomes audible from the telephone, steady and rasping.]

4. Literally, "Fat Tuesday" (French), the carnival before Lent, the period of self-denial that begins on
Ash Wednesday.
5. Cleopatra, Queen of Egypt.
6. Robbed.

STANLEY: You left th' phone off th' hook.

[*He crosses to it deliberately and sets it back on the hook. After he has replaced it, he stares at her again, his mouth slowly curving into a grin, as he weaves between* BLANCHE *and the outer door. The barely audible "Blue Piano" begins to drum up louder. The sound of it turns into the roar of an approaching locomotive.* BLANCHE *crouches, pressing her fists to her ears until it has gone by.*]

BLANCHE: [*Finally straightening.*] Let me—let me get by you!

STANLEY: Get by me? Sure. Go ahead. [*He moves back a pace in the doorway.*]

BLANCHE: You—you stand over there! [*She indicates a further position.*]

STANLEY: You got plenty of room to walk by me now.

BLANCHE: Not with you there! But I've got to get out somehow!

STANLEY: You think I'll interfere with you? Ha-ha! [*The "Blue Piano" goes softly. She turns confusedly and makes a faint gesture. The inhuman jungle voices rise up. He takes a step toward her, biting his tongue, which protrudes between his lips. Softly.*] Come to think of it—maybe you wouldn't be bad to—interfere with. . . .

[BLANCHE *moves backward through the door into the bedroom.*]

BLANCHE: Stay back! Don't you come toward me another step or I'll—

STANLEY: What?

BLANCHE: Some awful thing will happen! It will!

STANLEY: What are you putting on now?

[*They are now both inside the bedroom.*]

BLANCHE: I warn you, don't, I'm in danger!

[*He takes another step. She smashes a bottle on the table and faces him, clutching the broken top.*]

STANLEY: What did you do that for?

BLANCHE: So I could twist the broken end in your face!

STANLEY: I bet you would do that!

BLANCHE: I would! I will if you—

STANLEY: Oh! So you want some roughhouse! All right, let's have some roughhouse! [*He springs toward her, overturning the table. She cries out and strikes at him with the bottle top but he catches her wrist.*] Tiger—tiger! Drop the bottle-top! Drop it! We've had this date with each other from the beginning!

[*She moans. The bottle-top falls. She sinks to her knees: He picks up her inert figure and carries her to the bed. The hot trumpet and drums from the Four Deuces sound loudly.*]

Scene 11

It is some weeks later. STELLA *is packing* BLANCHE's *things. Sounds of water can be heard running in the bathroom.*

The portieres are partly open on the poker players— STANLEY, STEVE, MITCH *and* PABLO—*who sit around the table in the kitchen. The atmosphere of the kitchen is now the same raw, lurid one of the disastrous poker night.*

The building is framed by the sky of turquoise. STELLA *has been crying as she arranges the flowery dresses in the open trunk.*

EUNICE *comes down the steps from her flat above and enters the kitchen. There is an outburst from the poker table.*

STANLEY: Drew to an inside straight and made it, by God.

PABLO: *Maldita sea tu suerto!*

STANLEY: Put it in English, greaseball.

PABLO: I am cursing your rutting luck.

STANLEY: [*Prodigiously elated.*] You know what luck is? Luck is believing you're lucky. Take at Salerno.[7] I believed I was lucky. I figured that 4 out of 5 would not come through but I would . . . and I did. I put that down as a rule. To hold front position in this rat-race you've got to believe you are lucky.

MITCH: You . . . you . . . you . . . Brag . . . brag . . . bull . . . bull.

[STELLA *goes into the bedroom and starts folding a dress.*]

STANLEY: What's the matter with him?

EUNICE: [*Walking past the table.*] I always did say that men are callous things with no feelings but this does beat anything. Making pigs of yourselves. [*She comes through the portieres into the bedroom.*]

STANLEY: What's the matter with her?

STELLA: How is my baby?

EUNICE: Sleeping like a little angel. Brought you some grapes. [*She puts them on a stool and lowers her voice.*] Blanche?

STELLA: Bathing.

EUNICE: How is she?

STELLA: She wouldn't eat anything but asked for a drink.

EUNICE: What did you tell her?

STELLA: I—just told her that—we'd made arrangements for her to rest in the country. She's got it mixed in her mind with Shep Huntleigh.

[BLANCHE *opens the bathroom door slightly.*]

BLANCHE: Stella.

STELLA: Yes.

BLANCHE: That cool yellow silk—the bouclé.[8] See if it's crushed. If it's not too crushed I'll wear it and on the lapel that silver and turquoise pin in the shape of a seahorse. You will find them in the heart-shaped box I keep my accessories in. And Stella . . . Try and locate a bunch of artificial violets in that box, too, to pin with the seahorse on the lapel of the jacket.

[*She closes the door.* STELLA *turns to* EUNICE.]

STELLA: I don't know if I did the right thing.

EUNICE: What else could you do?

STELLA: I couldn't believe her story and go on living with Stanley.

7. Important beachhead in the Allied invasion of Italy in World War II.
8. Textile woven with uneven yarn to produce a rough, uneven surface.

EUNICE: Don't ever believe it. Life has got to go on. No matter what happens, you've got to keep on going.

[*The bathroom door opens a little.*]

BLANCHE: [*Looking out.*] Is the coast clear?
STELLA: Yes, Blanche. [*To* EUNICE.] Tell her how well she's looking.
BLANCHE: Please close the curtains before I come out.
STELLA: They're closed.
STANLEY: —How many for you?
PABLO: Two.
STEVE: Three.

[BLANCHE *appears in the amber light of the door. She has a tragic radiance in her red satin robe following the sculptural lines of her body. The "Varsouviana" rises audibly as* BLANCHE *enters the bedroom.*]

BLANCHE: [*With faintly hysterical vivacity.*] I have just washed my hair.
STELLA: Did you?
BLANCHE: I'm not sure I got the soap out.
EUNICE: Such fine hair!
BLANCHE: [*Accepting the compliment.*] It's a problem. Didn't I get a call?
STELLA: Who from, Blanche?
BLANCHE: Shep Huntleigh . . .
STELLA: Why, not yet, honey!
BLANCHE: How strange! I—

[*At the sound of* BLANCHE'S *voice* MITCH'S *arm supporting his cards has sagged and his gaze is dissolved into space.* STANLEY *slaps him on the shoulder.*]

STANLEY: Hey, Mitch, come to!

[*The sound of this new voice shocks* BLANCHE. *She makes a shocked gesture, forming his name with her lips.* STELLA *nods and looks quickly away.* BLANCHE *stands quite still for some moments—the silver-backed mirror in her hand and a look of sorrowful perplexity as though all human experience shows on her face.* BLANCHE *finally speaks but with sudden hysteria.*]

BLANCHE: What's going on here? [*She turns from* STELLA *to* EUNICE *and back to* STELLA. *Her rising voice penetrates the concentration of the game.* MITCH *ducks his head lower but* STANLEY *shoves back his chair as if about to rise.* STEVE *places a restraining hand on his arm. Continuing.*] What's happened here? I want an explanation of what's happened here.
STELLA: [*Agonizingly.*] Hush! Hush!
EUNICE: Hush! Hush! Honey.
STELLA: Please, Blanche.
BLANCHE: Why are you looking at me like that? Is something wrong with me?
EUNICE: You look wonderful, Blanche. Don't she look wonderful?
STELLA: Yes.
EUNICE: I understand you are going on a trip.
STELLA: Yes, Blanche *is*. She's going on a vacation.
EUNICE: I'm green with envy.

BLANCHE: Help me, help me get dressed!

STELLA: [*Handing her dress.*] Is this what you—

BLANCHE: Yes, it will do! I'm anxious to get out of here—this place is a trap!

EUNICE: What a pretty blue jacket.

STELLA: It's lilac colored.

BLANCHE: You're both mistaken. It's Della Robbia blue.[9] The blue of the robe in the old Madonna pictures. Are these grapes washed? [*She fingers the bunch of grapes which* EUNICE *had brought in.*]

EUNICE: Huh?

BLANCHE: Washed, I said. Are they washed?

EUNICE: They're from the French Market.

BLANCHE: That doesn't mean they've been washed. [*The cathedral bells chime.*] Those cathedral bells—they're the only clean thing in the Quarter. Well, I'm going now. I'm ready to go.

EUNICE: [*Whispering.*] She's going to walk out before they get here.

STELLA: Wait, Blanche.

BLANCHE: I don't want to pass in front of those men.

EUNICE: Then wait'll the game breaks up.

STELLA: Sit down and . . .

[BLANCHE *turns weakly, hesitantly about. She lets them push her into a chair.*]

BLANCHE: I can smell the sea air. The rest of my time I'm going to spend on the sea. And when I die, I'm going to die on the sea. You know what I shall die of? [*She plucks a grape.*] I shall die of eating an unwashed grape one day out on the ocean. I will die—with my hand in the hand of some nice-looking ship's doctor, a very young one with a small blond mustache and a big silver watch. "Poor lady," they'll say, "the quinine[1] did her no good. That unwashed grape has transported her soul to heaven." [*The cathedral chimes are heard.*] And I'll be buried at sea sewn up in a clean white sack and dropped overboard—at noon—in the blaze of summer—and into an ocean as blue as [*Chimes again.*] my first lover's eyes!

[A DOCTOR *and a* MATRON[2] *have appeared around the corner of the building and climbed the steps to the porch. The gravity of their profession is exaggerated—the unmistakable aura of the state institution with its cynical detachment. The* DOCTOR *rings the doorbell. The murmur of the game is interrupted.*]

EUNICE: [*Whispering to* STELLA.] That must be them.

[STELLA *presses her fists to her lips.*]

BLANCHE: [*Rising slowly.*] What is it?

EUNICE: [*Affectedly casual.*] Excuse me while I see who's at the door.

STELLA: Yes.

9. Light blue seen in terra-cottas made by the Della Robbia family during the Italian Renaissance.
1. Medicinal salt used to treat malaria.
2. Female supervisor at a hospital or other institution.

[EUNICE *goes into the kitchen.*]

BLANCHE: [*Tensely.*] I wonder if it's for me.

[*A whispered colloquy takes place at the door.*]

EUNICE: [*Returning, brightly.*] Someone is calling for Blanche.

BLANCHE: It *is* for me, then! [*She looks fearfully from one to the other and then to the portieres. The "Varsouviana" faintly plays.*] Is it the gentleman I was expecting from Dallas?

EUNICE: I think it is, Blanche.

BLANCHE: I'm not quite ready.

STELLA: Ask him to wait outside.

BLANCHE: I . . .

[EUNICE *goes back to the portieres. Drums sound very softly.*]

STELLA: Everything packed?

BLANCHE: My silver toilet articles are still out.

STELLA: Ah!

EUNICE: [*Returning.*] They're waiting in front of the house.

BLANCHE: They! Who's "they"?

EUNICE: There's a lady with him.

BLANCHE: I cannot imagine who this "lady" could be! How is she dressed?

EUNICE: Just—just a sort of a—plain-tailored outfit.

BLANCHE: Possibly she's—[*Her voice dies out nervously.*]

STELLA: Shall we go, Blanche?

BLANCHE: Must we go through that room?

STELLA: I will go with you.

BLANCHE: How do I look?

STELLA: Lovely.

EUNICE: [*Echoing.*] Lovely.

[BLANCHE *moves fearfully to the portieres.* EUNICE *draws them open for her.* BLANCHE *goes into the kitchen.*]

BLANCHE: [*To the men.*] Please don't get up. I'm only passing through.

[*She crosses quickly to outside door.* STELLA *and* EUNICE *follow. The poker players stand awkwardly at the table—all except* MITCH, *who remains seated, looking down at the table.* BLANCHE *steps out on a small porch at the side of the door. She stops short and catches her breath.*]

DOCTOR: How do you do?

BLANCHE: You are not the gentleman I was expecting. [*She suddenly gasps and starts back up the steps. She stops by* STELLA, *who stands just outside the door, and speaks in a frightening whisper.*] That man isn't Shep Huntleigh.

[*The "Varsouviana" is playing distantly.* STELLA *stares back at* BLANCHE. EUNICE *is holding* STELLA's *arm. There is a moment of silence—no sound but that of* STANLEY *steadily shuffling the cards.* BLANCHE *catches her breath again and slips back into the flat. She enters the flat with a peculiar smile, her eyes wide and brilliant. As soon as her sister goes past her,* STELLA *closes her eyes and clenches her hands.* EUNICE *throws her arms comfortingly about her. Then she starts up to her flat.* BLANCHE *stops just inside the door.* MITCH *keeps staring down at his hands on the table, but the other men look at her curiously. At last she starts around the table toward the bedroom. As she does,* STANLEY *suddenly pushes back his chair and rises as if to block her way. The* MATRON *follows her into the flat.*]

STANLEY: Did you forget something?
BLANCHE: [*Shrilly.*] Yes! Yes, I forgot something!

[*She rushes past him into the bedroom. Lurid reflections appear on the walls in odd, sinuous shapes. The "Varsouviana" is filtered into a weird distortion, accompanied by the cries and noises of the jungle.* BLANCHE *seizes the back of a chair as if to defend herself.*]

STANLEY: [*Sotto voce.*][3] Doc, you better go in.
DOCTOR: [*Sotto voce, motioning to the* MATRON.] Nurse, bring her out.

[*The* MATRON *advances on one side,* STANLEY *on the other. Divested of all the softer properties of womanhood, the* MATRON *is a peculiarly sinister figure in her severe dress. Her voice is bold and toneless as a firebell.*]

MATRON: Hello, Blanche.

[*The greeting is echoed and re-echoed by other mysterious voices behind the walls, as if reverberated through a canyon of rock.*]

STANLEY: She says that she forgot something.

[*The echo sounds in threatening whispers.*]

MATRON: That's all right.
STANLEY: What did you forget, Blanche?
BLANCHE: I—I—
MATRON: It don't matter. We can pick it up later.
STANLEY: Sure. We can send it along with the trunk.
BLANCHE: [*Retreating in panic.*] I don't know you—I don't know you. I want to be—left alone—please!
MATRON: Now, Blanche!
ECHOES: [*Rising and falling.*] Now, Blanche—now, Blanche—now, Blanche!
STANLEY: You left nothing here but spilt talcum and old empty perfume bottles—unless it's the paper lantern you want to take with you. You want the lantern?

[*He crosses to dressing table and seizes the paper lantern, tearing it off the light bulb, and extends it toward her. She cries out as if the lantern was herself. The* MATRON *steps boldly toward her. She screams and tries to break past the* MATRON. *All the men spring to their feet.* STELLA *runs out to the porch, with* EUNICE *following to comfort her, simultaneously with the confused voices of the men in the kitchen.* STELLA *rushes into* EUNICE's *embrace on the porch.*]

3. In an undertone (Italian).

STELLA: Oh, my God, Eunice help me! Don't let them do that to her, don't let them hurt her! Oh, God, oh, please God, don't hurt her! What are they doing to her? What are they doing? [*She tries to break from* EUNICE's *arms.*]

EUNICE: No, honey, no, no, honey. Stay here. Don't go back in there. Stay with me and don't look.

STELLA: What have I done to my sister? Oh, God, what have I done to my sister?

EUNICE: You done the right thing, the only thing you could do. She couldn't stay here; there wasn't no other place for her to go.

[*While* STELLA *and* EUNICE *are speaking on the porch the voices of the men in the kitchen overlap them.* MITCH *has started toward the bedroom.* STANLEY *crosses to block him.* STANLEY *pushes him aside.* MITCH *lunges and strikes at* STANLEY. STANLEY *pushes* MITCH *back.* MITCH *collapses at the table, sobbing. During the preceding scenes, the* MATRON *catches hold of* BLANCHE's *arm and prevents her flight.* BLANCHE *turns wildly and scratches at the* MATRON. *The heavy woman pinions her arms.* BLANCHE *cries out hoarsely and slips to her knees.*]

MATRON: These fingernails have to be trimmed. [*The* DOCTOR *comes into the room and she looks at him.*] Jacket,[4] Doctor?

DOCTOR: Not unless necessary. [*He takes off his hat and now he becomes personalized. The unhuman quality goes. His voice is gentle and reassuring as he crosses to* BLANCHE *and crouches in front of her. As he speaks her name, her terror subsides a little. The lurid reflections fade from the walls, the inhuman cries and noises die out and her own hoarse crying is calmed.*] Miss DuBois. [*She turns her face to him and stares at him with desperate pleading. He smiles; then he speaks to the* MATRON.] It won't be necessary.

BLANCHE: [*Faintly.*] Ask her to let go of me.

DOCTOR: [*To the* MATRON.] Let go.

[*The* MATRON *releases her.* BLANCHE *extends her hands toward the* DOCTOR. *He draws her up gently and supports her with his arm and leads her through the portieres.*]

BLANCHE: [*Holding tight to his arm.*] Whoever you are—I have always depended on the kindness of strangers.

[*The poker players stand back as* BLANCHE *and the* DOCTOR *cross the kitchen to the front door. She allows him to lead her as if she were blind. As they go out on the porch,* STELLA *cries out her sister's name from where she is crouched a few steps up on the stairs.*]

STELLA: Blanche! Blanche, Blanche!

[BLANCHE *walks on without turning, followed by the* DOCTOR *and the* MATRON. *They go around the corner of the building.* EUNICE *descends to* STELLA *and places the child in her arms. It is wrapped in a pale blue blanket.* STELLA *accepts the child, sobbingly.* EUNICE *continues downstairs and enters the kitchen where the men, except for* STANLEY, *are returning silently*

---

4. That is, straitjacket, used to restrain the mentally ill.

to their places about the table. STANLEY *has gone out on the porch and stands at the foot of the steps looking at* STELLA.]

STANLEY: [*A bit uncertainly.*] Stella? [*She sobs with inhuman abandon. There is something luxurious in her complete surrender to crying now that her sister is gone. Voluptuously, soothingly.*] Now, honey. Now, love. Now, now, love. [*He kneels beside her and his fingers find the opening of her blouse.*] Now, now, love. Now, love. . . .

[*The luxurious sobbing, the sensual murmur fade away under the swelling music of the "Blue Piano" and the muted trumpet.*]

STEVE: This game is seven-card stud.

CURTAIN

1947

Writing
about
PART FOUR Literature

Writing about Literature

In the study of literature, reading and writing are closely interrelated—even mutually dependent—activities. The quality of whatever we write about literature depends on the quality of our work as readers. Conversely, our reading isn't truly complete until we've tried to capture our interpretation in writing so as to make it intelligible, persuasive, and meaningful to other people. We read literature more actively and attentively both when we integrate informal writing into the reading process—pausing periodically to mark important or confusing passages, to jot down significant facts, to describe the impressions and responses the text provokes—and when we envision our reading of literature as preparation for writing about it in a more sustained and formal way. The actual process of writing, in turn, requires re-reading and rethinking, testing our first impressions and initial hypotheses.

As we've suggested from the beginning of this book, literature itself is a vast conversation in which we participate most fully when we engage with other readers. Writing allows us the opportunity—and even imposes on us the obligation—to do just that: In writing we respond not only to what other readers have actually said or written about the work but also to how we imagine other readers *might* realistically see it. By trying to see as other readers see and working to persuade them to accept alternative ways of interpreting a literary work, we ourselves gain new insights.

Writing about literature can take any number of forms, ranging from the informal and personal to the formal and public. Your instructor may well ask you to try your hand at more than one form. However, the essay is by far the most common form that writing about literature—or **literary criticism**—takes. As a result, the following chapters will focus primarily on the essay.

Whether they require an essay, a response paper, or something else, however, assignments in literature courses often include a warning that goes something like this: "DO NOT SIMPLY RESTATE THE FACTS, PARAPHRASE, OR SUMMARIZE." We thus start here with a brief chapter (ch. 29) explaining what paraphrase, summary, and description are and how you can use them to move from response to essay.

Chapter 30, "The Literature Essay," reviews the five basic elements of all literature essays before turning, briefly, to two specific types—the comparative essay and the in-class exam essay. The chapter aims to give you a vivid sense of what you want to end up with at the end of the essay-writing process.

Chapter 31, "The Writing Process," focuses on how you get there, providing tips on every stage of essay development, from interpreting an assignment and generating a thesis to editing, proofreading, and manuscript formatting.

Chapter 32, "The Literature Research Essay," introduces the most common types of literary research and the key steps and strategies involved in writing literature research essays, from identifying and evaluating sources to responsibly and effectively integrating source material into your essay.

Whether they involve research or not, *all* essays about literature require accurate and effective quotation and citation; these are discussed in a separate chapter, "Quotation, Citation, and Documentation" (ch. 33).

Finally, this section concludes with a sample research essay (ch. 34), annotated to highlight some of the features and strategies discussed in earlier chapters.

29 | BASIC MOVES: PARAPHRASE, SUMMARY, AND DESCRIPTION

In literature courses, writing assignments often include a warning that goes something like this: "DO NOT SIMPLY RESTATE THE FACTS, PARAPHRASE, OR SUMMARIZE." It's a warning you ignore at your peril: *Paraphrase, summary,* and *description* are different ways of "simply restating the facts," and a paper for a literature course will rarely pass muster if it does only that. Such papers must make arguments *about* facts and their significance, using statements of fact like those that make up paraphrases, summaries, and descriptions in order to substantiate and develop debatable claims about the literary text. (For more on factual statements versus debatable claims, see 30.1.2.)

As this suggests, however, any literature paper will need to include *some* paraphrase, description, and/or summary, since effective arguments must be based on, supported by, and developed with statements of fact. As important, paraphrase, summary, and description can be effective ways to *start* the writing process, helping you to discover potential topics and debatable claims of the sort that drive literature essays.

Later chapters discuss and demonstrate ways to use paraphrase, summary, and description in literature essays. The rest of this chapter simply defines and models these three basic, nonargumentative forms of writing about literature and discusses how you can use them to move from initial response to more argumentative writing.

29.1 PARAPHRASE

29.1.1 What It Is

To paraphrase a statement is to restate it in your own words. Since the goal of paraphrase is to represent a statement fully and faithfully, a paraphrase tends to be at least as long as the original.

Below are paraphrases of sentences from a work of fiction (Jane Austen's *Pride and Prejudice*), a poem (Li-Young Lee's PERSIMMONS), and an essay of the sort that could be a secondary source in a literature research essay (George L. Dillon's "Styles of Reading").

Three Examples of Paraphrase

ORIGINAL SENTENCES	PARAPHRASE
It is a truth universally acknowledged, that a single man in possession of a good fortune, must be in want of a wife.	Everyone knows that a wealthy bachelor wants to get married.
In sixth grade Mrs. Walker slapped the back of my head and made me stand in the corner for not knowing the difference between *persimmon* and *precision*. How to choose persimmons. This is precision.	My sixth-grade teacher physically punished and publicly humiliated me for confusing the words *persimmon* and *precision*. Because it requires precision, the procedure for choosing the best persimmons demonstrates what *precision* means.
[M]aking order out of Emily's life is a complicated matter, since the narrator recalls the details through a nonlinear filter.	It's difficult to figure out when things happen to Emily because the narrator doesn't relate events in chronological order.

29.1.2 How to Use It

- Paraphrasing ensures and demonstrates that you understand what you've read. It can be especially helpful when an **author**'s diction and syntax or logic seems especially difficult, complex, or "foreign" to you. Paraphrase can thus be especially useful when reading and responding to a poem (see ch. 11) and when taking notes on secondary sources (see 32.3.2).
- Paraphrasing can help you recognize nuances of tone or significant details in any literary text, especially when you pay attention to anything you have difficulty paraphrasing. For example, paraphrasing Austen's sentence (above) might call your attention to the multiple—and thus difficult-to-paraphrase—meanings of phrases such as *a good fortune* and *in want of*.
- By making you aware of such details, paraphrasing may help you generate the kind of interpretive questions an essay might explore. For example, the Austen paraphrase might lead you to ask, *What does* Pride and Prejudice *define as "a good fortune"? Does the novel illustrate different definitions? Does it endorse one definition over another?*

On the use of paraphrase in literature essays, see 30.1.4 (on evidence), 30.2.2 (on in-class exam essays), and 32.4.2 (on incorporating secondary source material into the literature research essay).

29.2 SUMMARY

29.2.1 What It Is

A summary is a fairly succinct restatement or overview—in your own words—of the content of an entire literary text or other source or a significant portion thereof. A summary of a fictional work is generally called a *plot summary* because it focuses on the **action** or **plot**. Though a summary should be significantly shorter than the original, it can be any length you need it to be. (For more on plot summary, see ch. 2.)

Different readers—or even the same reader on different occasions and with different purposes in mind—will summarize the same text or source in different ways. Summarizing entails selection and emphasis. As a result, any summary reflects a particular point of view and may begin to imply a possible interpretation or argument. When writing a summary, you should be as objective as possible. Nevertheless, your summary will reflect a particular understanding and attitude, which is why it's useful.

Here are three quite different one-sentence summaries of *Hamlet.*

1. In the process of avenging his uncle's murder of his father, a young prince kills his uncle, himself, and many others.

2. A young Danish prince avenges the murder of his father, the king, by his uncle, who has usurped the throne, but the prince himself is killed, as are others, and a well-led foreign army has no trouble successfully invading the troubled state.

3. When a young prince hears, from the ghost of his murdered father, that his uncle, who has married the prince's mother, is the father's murderer, the prince devotes himself to learning the truth and avenging the wrong, feigning madness, acting erratically, causing the suicide of his beloved and the deaths of numerous others including, ultimately, himself.

29.2.2 How to Use It

Because even the most objective summary implies a point of view, summarizing a literary work may help you to discover what your particular point of view is or at least what aspects of the work strike you as most important and potentially worthy of analysis, especially if you compare your summary to that of another reader (as in the exercise in ch. 2) or try out different ways of summarizing the same work yourself. The second *Hamlet* summary above, for example, suggests a more political interpretation of the play than either of the other two summaries, by emphasizing the characters' political roles, the political nature of the crimes in the play (usurpation and regicide), and the fact that the play ends with a foreign invasion.

On the use of summary in literature essays, see 30.1.4 (on evidence), 30.1.5 (on introductions), 30.2.2 (on in-class exam essays), and 32.4.2 (on incorporating secondary source material into the literature research essay).

29.3 DESCRIPTION

29.3.1 What It Is

Where both summary and paraphrase focus on content, a description of a literary text focuses more on that text's form, style, or structure, or any particular aspect thereof.

Below are two such descriptions—one of the rhyme scheme of Thomas Hardy's THE RUINED MAID, the other of Sandra Cisneros's MERICANS.

Description of "The Ruined Maid"

A dialogue between "the ruined maid," 'Melia, and another woman from her hometown, Hardy's twenty-four-line poem consists of six four-line stanzas. Each stanza contains two rhyming couplets and ends with the same two words ("said she") and thus with the same (long *e*) rhyme sound. In stanzas 2 through 5, the first couplets each feature different rhymes ("socks/docks," "thou/now," "bleak/cheek," "dream/seem"). But in the first and last stanza they involve the same rhyme and even the same final word ("crown/Town," "gown/Town"). As in these examples, most of the poem's end rhymes involve one-syllable words. But in four out of six stanzas, line 3 instead ends with a polysyllabic word (rhyming with "she") in which the rhyming syllable is set off from the first syllables by a dash: "prosperi-ty" (line 3), "compa-ny" (11), "la-dy" (15), "melancho-ly" (19).

Description of "Mericans"

The short story "Mericans" consists of only twenty-five paragraphs, narrated in English by someone we ultimately learn is a young girl (par. 8) named Micaela (par. 14). But the narration oscillates between first-person singular and plural, and the story includes dialogue in Spanish and translated from Spanish. Though set in Mexico City, Mexico, the story also moves between two settings and the characters associated with each, with Micaela the only character connecting the two. The first five paragraphs, narrated in first-person plural ("We're waiting," par. 1), focus mainly on the "awful grandmother" (par. 1) and the dark church inside which she prays. Here, we also get some of her words, reported in italics, presumably because they are translated (par. 2), and we learn about all that the grandchildren ("we") are *not* supposed to do while they wait for her (par. 3). Paragraphs 6-9 instead focus on the children and the plaza where they wait, "outside in the sun" (par. 6). Now we learn that there are three of them, that two are boys (nick)named Junior and Keeks (par. 6), and that the narrator is a (still unnamed) "*girl*" (par. 8). For the first time, she uses first-person singular ("I"), and we get dialogue in quotation marks (words spoken to her in English by her brothers, par. 7). In paragraphs 10-14 the focus shifts again, as Micaela (still using first-person singular) goes inside the church alone, only for her grandmother to tell her to go back outside (in an italicized/translated sentence of dialogue, from which we first learn both Micaela's name and her brothers' official, Spanish ones, par. 14). Finally, the story's last ten paragraphs are set outside, where the siblings converse with a couple who turn out to be U.S. tourists. This section is thus mostly dialogue (first in italicized Spanish, then in unitalicized English), except for the last sentence/paragraph. Here (as at the beginning) Micaela again uses first-person plural to refer to her brothers and herself, then alludes to the story's other major setting and character: "We're Mericans, we're Mericans, and inside the awful grandmother prays" (par. 25).

29.3.2 How to Use It

Responding actively to a text and preparing to write about it require attending closely to form, style, and structure, as well as content. Describing a text or some aspect of it (its **imagery, rhyme scheme,** or **meter**; plotting or point of view; divisions into **stanzas,** acts and **scenes,** or chapters; and so on) is a useful way to ensure that you are paying that kind of attention, identifying the sort of details whose significance you might explore in an essay. To move from description to argument begins with asking, *How do these details relate to each other? How do they individually and collectively contribute to the text's effect and meaning?*

On the use of description in literature essays, see 30.1.4 (on evidence) and 30.1.5 (on introductions).

30 | THE LITERATURE ESSAY

The literature essay is a distinct subgenre of writing with unique elements and conventions. Just as you come to a poem, play, or short story with specific expectations, so will readers approach your essay *about* a poem, play, or story. They will be looking for particular elements, anticipating that the work will unfold in a certain way. This chapter explains and explores those elements so as to give you a clear sense of what an effective essay about literature looks like and how it works, along with concrete advice about how to craft your own.

A literature essay has particular elements and a particular form because it serves a specific purpose. Like any essay, it is a relatively short written composition that articulates, supports, and develops one major idea or claim. Like any work of expository prose, it aims to explain something complex—in this case, at least one literary work—so that a reader may gain a new and deeper understanding. Explaining here entails both *analysis* (breaking the work down into its constituent parts and showing how they work together to form a meaningful whole) and *argument* (working to convince someone that the analysis is valid). Your essay needs to show your readers a particular way to understand the work, to interpret or read it. That interpretation starts with your own personal response. But your essay also needs to persuade readers that your interpretation is reasonable and enlightening—that though it is distinctive and new, it is more than merely idiosyncratic or subjective.

30.1 ELEMENTS OF THE LITERATURE ESSAY

To achieve its purpose, a literature essay must incorporate five elements: an effective *tone*; a compelling *thesis* and *motive*; ample, appropriate *evidence*; and a coherent *structure*. Though these five elements are essential to essays of any kind, each needs to take a specific shape in literature essays. This section aims to give you a clear sense of that shape.

30.1.1 Tone (and Audience)

Although your reader or audience isn't an element *in* your essay, **tone** is. And tone and audience are closely interrelated. In everyday life, the tone we adopt depends on whom we're talking to and what situation we're in. We talk differently to our parents than to our best friends. And in different situations we talk to the same person differently, depending on the response we want to elicit. What tone do you adopt with your best friend when you need a favor? when you want advice? when you want him to take your advice? In each situation, you act on your knowledge of whom your audience is, what information they already have, and what their response is likely to be. But you also adopt a tone that will encourage your listener to respond in the desired way. In writing, as in life, your sense of audience shapes your tone, even as you use tone to shape your audience's response.

So who is your audience? When you write an essay for class, the obvious answer is your instructor. But in an important sense, that's the wrong answer. Although your instructor could literally be the only person besides you who will ever read your essay, you write about literature to learn how to write for a general audience of peers—people a lot like you who are sensible and educated and appreciate having a literary work explained so that they can understand it more fully. Picture your readers as people with at least the same educational background. Assume they have some experience in reading literature and some familiarity with the basic literary terminology outlined in this book. (You should not feel the need to explain what a stanza is or to define the term *in medias res*.) But assume, too, that your readers have read the specific literary work(s) only once, have not closely analyzed the work(s), and have not been privy to class discussions.

Above all, don't think of yourself as writing for only one reader and especially one reader who already sees the text and the world as you do. Remember that the purpose of your essay is to *persuade* multiple readers with differing outlooks and opinions to see the text your way. That process begins with persuading those readers that you deserve their time, their attention, and their respect. The tone of your paper should be serious and straightforward, respectful toward your readers and the literary work. But its approach and vocabulary, while formal enough for academic writing, should be lively enough to capture and hold the interest of busy, distracted readers. Demonstrate *in* your essay the stance you want readers to take *toward* your essay: Earn careful attention and respect by demonstrating care, attentiveness, and respect; encourage your readers to keep an open mind by doing the same; engage your readers by demonstrating genuine engagement with the text, the topic, and the very enterprise of writing.

WAYS OF SETTING THE RIGHT TONE

- *Write about literature in the present tense.*
  Convincing your readers that you are a knowledgeable student of literature whose ideas they should respect requires not only correctly using—without feeling the need to explain—basic literary terms such as *stanza* and *in medias res* but also following other long-established conventions. Writing in present tense is one such convention, and it has two practical advantages. One, it helps you avoid confusing tense shifts. Simply put, you can more clearly indicate *when* in a text something happens by specifying, "When X first visits Y" or "In the first stanza," and so on, than you can by switching tenses. Two, present tense actually makes logical sense if you think about it: Though each time you pick up a story, poem, or play, your interpretation of the work might be different, the work itself isn't. Similarly, though in reading we experience a text as unfolding in time, it actually doesn't: Everything in the text simply always *is*. Thus, yesterday, today, and tomorrow, Shakespeare's Iago *plots* against Othello, Jamaica Kincaid's "Girl" *asks* what it means to grow up a girl, John Donne *depicts* our relationship with God as a lifelong struggle, **and so on.**

That said, things do get a bit tricky when you write about contexts as well as texts or about *actual authors* versus *implied authors*. Notice, for example, how the following sentence moves from past to present tense as it moves from a statement about the actual author to one about the text: Inspired by these real-life events, as well as her own experiences as a journalist, Allende *wrote* "And of Clay Are We Created," which *explores* mass media coverage of disasters and its effects. Again, this switch (from past to present tense) makes logical sense: The actual author Isabel Allende *wrote* this story in the historical past, even as the story *explores* now what it always has and always will (if we accept this writer's interpretation). By the same logic, the same tenses would be appropriate if we revised the sentence so as to make Isabel Allende, the implied author, rather than her story, the subject of our sentence's second half: Inspired by these real-life events, as well as her own experiences as a journalist, Allende *wrote* "And of Clay Are We Created," the short story in which she *explores* mass media coverage of disasters and its effects.

- *Use the word "I" carefully.*

Many instructors have no problem with your using "I" when context makes that appropriate and effective; and used well, the first person can create a sense of real engagement and of "presence," of a distinctive mind at work. However, some instructors strongly object to any use of the word "I" because inexperienced writers so often use it inappropriately and ineffectively. Since the job of a literature essay is to use evidence to persuade readers to accept an interpretation of the work that is generally and objectively—not just personally or subjectively—valid and meaningful, resorting to "I feel" or "I think" can defeat that purpose. Sometimes such phrases can even signal that you've gotten off track, substituting expressions of feeling for argument or dwelling more on your thoughts about an issue the text explores than on the text and the thoughts *it* communicates about that issue (as in the last example in 30.1.2). Generally speaking, if everything that follows a phrase like *I feel* or *I think* makes sense and has merit and relevance on its own, cut to the chase by cutting the phrase.

30.1.2 Thesis

A **thesis** is to an essay what a **theme** is to a short story, play, or poem: the governing idea or claim. Yet where a literary work implies at least one theme and often more, an essay about a literary work needs to have only one thesis, which is explicitly stated in about one to three sentences somewhere in the introduction, usually at or near its end. Like a theme, as we have defined that term in earlier chapters, your thesis must be debatable—a claim that all readers won't automatically accept. It's a proposition you *can* prove with evidence from the literary text, yet it's one you *have* to prove, that isn't obviously true or merely factual.

Though it's unlikely that any of that is news to you, even experienced writers sometimes feel flummoxed about what makes for a debatable claim about literature. To clarify, we juxtapose below two sets of sentences. On the left are inarguable statements—ones that are merely factual or descriptive and thus might easily find a home in a paraphrase, summary, or description (see ch. 29). On the right are debatable claims about the same topic or fact, each of which might work well as a thesis.

FACTUAL STATEMENT	THESIS
"The Story of an Hour" explores the topic of marriage.	"The Story of an Hour" poses a troubling question: Does marriage inevitably encourage people to "impose [their] private will upon a fellow-creature" (par. 14)?
"Cathedral" features a character with a physical handicap.	By depicting an able-bodied protagonist who discovers his own emotional and spiritual shortcomings through an encounter with a physically handicapped person, "Cathedral" invites us to question traditional definitions of "disability."
"London" has four discrete stanzas, and each ends with a period; two-thirds of the lines are end-stopped.	In "London," William Blake uses various formal devices to suggest the unnatural rigidity of modern urban life.
Creon and Antigone are both similar and different.	Antigone and Creon share the same fatal flaw: Each recognizes only one set of obligations. In the end, however, the play presents Antigone as more admirable.

All of the thesis statements above are arguable because each implicitly answers a compelling interpretive question to which multiple, equally reasonable answers seem possible—for instance, *What is the key similarity between Antigone and Creon? Which character's actions and values does Sophocles's play ultimately champion?* or, *What exactly does Blake demonstrate about modern urban life?* But these thesis statements share other traits as well. All are clear and emphatic. All use *active verbs* to capture what the text or its implied author does (*poses, invites, uses, presents* versus *has, is, tries to*). And each entices us to read further by implying further interpretive questions—*What "set of obligations" do Antigone and Creon each "recognize"? Given how alike they are, what makes Antigone more admirable than Creon?* or, *According to Blake, what specifically is "unnatural" and "rigid" about modern urban life?* (Note, by the way, that the arguable claim in the Blake example *isn't* that he "uses various formal devices to suggest" something: *All* authors do that. Instead, the arguable claim specifies *what* Blake suggests through formal devices.)

An effective thesis enables the reader to enter the essay with a clear sense that its writer has something to prove and what that something is, and it inspires readers with the desire to see the writer's proof. We want to understand how the writer arrived at this view, to test whether it's valid, and to see how the writer will answer the other questions the thesis has generated in our minds. A good thesis captures readers' interest and shapes their expectations. In so doing, it also makes promises that the rest of the essay must fulfill.

Nonetheless, an arguable claim about literature is not one-sided or narrow-minded. A thesis needs to stake out a position, but a position can admit complexity. Literature, after all, tends to focus more on exploring problems, conflicts, and questions than on offering easy solutions, resolutions, and answers. Its goal is to complicate and enrich, not to simplify, our way of looking at the world. The best essays about literature and the theses that drive them often do the same. As some of the sample thesis statements above demonstrate, for example, a good thesis can be a claim about what the key question or conflict explored in a text is rather than about how that question is answered or that conflict resolved. Though an essay with this sort of thesis wouldn't be complete unless it ultimately considered possible answers and resolutions, it need not *start* there.

INTERPRETATION VERSUS EVALUATION
(OR WHY A LITERATURE ESSAY IS *NOT* A REVIEW)

All the sample theses above make *interpretive* claims—claims about how a literary text works, what it says, how one should understand it. Unless your instructor suggests otherwise, this is the kind of claim you need for a thesis in a literature essay.

That said, it's useful to remember that in reading and writing about literature we often make (and debate) a different type of claim—the *evaluative*. Evaluation entails assessment, and evaluative claims about literature tend to be of two kinds. The first involves aesthetic assessment and/or personal preference—whether a text (or a part or element thereof) succeeds, or seems to you "good," in artistic terms or whether you personally "like" it. This kind of claim features prominently in movie and book reviews, but literature essays are not reviews. Where a review of Raymond Carver's CATHEDRAL, for example, might claim that "Carver's story fails as a story because of its lack of action and unlikeable narrator" or that "'Cathedral' does a great job of characterizing its narrator-protagonist," a better thesis for a literature essay might be something like "Through his words even more than his actions, the narrator unwittingly shows us why nothing much happens to him by continually demonstrating his utter inability to connect with others or to understand himself." In other words, where reviewers are mainly concerned with answering the question of *whether* a text "works," literary critics focus primarily on showing *how* it does so and with what effects. Likewise, though personal preferences may well influence your choice of which texts to write about, such preferences shouldn't be the primary focus of your essay—who, after all, can argue with your personal preferences?

The second kind of evaluative claim involves moral, philosophical, social, or political judgment—whether an idea or action is wise or good, valid or admirable, something you "agree with." Both interpretive and evaluative claims involve informed opinion (which is why they are debatable). But whereas interpretive claims of the kind literary critics tend to privilege aim to elucidate the opinions and values expressed or enacted *in* and *by* a text or its characters, evaluative claims of this second type instead assess the validity *of* those opinions and values, often by comparison with one's own. Our sample thesis statement about ANTIGONE, for example, is a claim about which character *the play presents* as more admirable, not about which character the essay writer herself admires more.

The latter kind of claim is far from irrelevant or unimportant. One major reason why we read and write about literature is that literature encourages us to grapple with real moral, social, and political issues of the kind we *should* develop informed opinions about. The question is simply one of emphasis: In a literature essay, the literature itself must be your primary focus, not your personal experience with or opinions about the issues it raises or the situations it explores.

Your primary job in a literature essay is to thoughtfully explore *what* the work communicates and *how* it does so. Making an interpretive claim in your thesis ensures that you keep your priorities straight. Once you have done that job thoroughly and well in the body of your essay, *then* you can consider evaluative questions in your conclusion (see "End: The Conclusion," in 30.1.5).

The poem "Ulysses" demonstrates that traveling and meeting new people are important parts of life. The speaker argues that staying in one place for too long is equivalent to substituting the simple act of breathing for truly living. I very much agree with the speaker's argument because I also believe that travel is one of life's most valuable experiences. Traveling allows you to experience different cultures, different political systems, and different points of view. It may change your way of thinking or make you realize that people all over the world are more similar than they are different.	This paragraph might be the kernel of a good conclusion to an essay that develops the thesis that "'Ulysses' demonstrates that traveling and meeting new people are important parts of life." Unfortunately, however, this paragraph actually appeared at the beginning of a student paper so full of similar paragraphs that it simply never managed to be about Ulysses at all. Unfortunately, too, then, this paragraph demonstrates one of the reasons why some instructors forbid you to use the word "I" in literature essays (see 30.1.1).

30.1.3 Motive ("Although . . . , I Think . . .")

One reason inexperienced writers might be tempted to emphasize evaluation over interpretation is that evaluative claims sometimes *seem* more debatable. It isn't always apparent, in other words, why there is anything useful or revelatory, even arguable or debatable, about a claim like *Antigone* presents Antigone's form of over-simplification as more admirable than Creon's or Emily Dickinson questions traditional Christian doctrines. If you read the critical excerpts scattered throughout this book, however, you may notice something important: In the work of professional literary critics, such claims seem compelling because they are never presented in a vacuum but rather as a response to other actual or potential claims about the text. Such a presentation provides a *motive* for the reader of such an essay just as it does its writer.

Boil any good literature essay down to its essence, in other words, and you'll end up with a sentence that goes something like this (even though such a sentence never appears in the essay):

Although they say/I used to think/someone might reasonably think _____ about this text, I say/now think _____ because _____.

An effective essay doesn't just state a thesis ("I say/now think . . .") and prove it by providing reasons and evidence ("because . . ."); it also interests us in that thesis by framing it as a response to some other actual or potential thesis—something that "they" actually "say" about a text; that you "used to think" about it, perhaps on a first, casual reading; or that some reader *might* reasonably think or say.[1] In a literature research essay, "they" may well be published literary critics. But you don't have to read published work on a literary text to discover alternative readings to which to respond: If you have discussed a text in class, you have heard plenty of statements made and questions raised about it, all of which are fodder for response.

---

1. For a more extensive discussion of this approach to writing, see Gerald Graff and Cathy Birkenstein's *"They Say/I Say": The Moves That Matter in Academic Writing*, 5th ed., W. W. Norton, 2021.

If you've read and re-read a work carefully, your view of it has likely evolved, ensuring that you have a "naive reading" to compare to your more enlightened one. Finally, to write effectively about a text inevitably requires imagining other possible interpretations, and those *potential* readings are also ones you can "take on" in your essay.

Below, an introduction to one student writer's essay on Emily Dickinson appears first, followed by two different paraphrases of the "Although . . . , I think . . . " statement that this introduction implies.

> When cataloguing Christian poets, it might be tempting to place Emily Dickinson between Dante and John Donne. She built many poems around biblical quotations, locations, and characters. She meditated often on the afterlife, prayer, and trust in God. Yet Dickinson was also intensely doubtful of the strand of Christianity that she inherited. In fact, she never became a Christian by the standards of her community in nineteenth-century Amherst, Massachusetts. Rather, like many of her contemporaries in Boston, Dickinson recognized the tension between traditional religious teaching and modern ideas. And these tensions between hope and doubt, between tradition and modernity, animate her poetry. In "Some keep the Sabbath going to church—," "The Brain—is wider than the Sky—," "Because I could not stop for Death—," and "The Bible is an antique Volume," the poet uses traditional religious terms and biblical allusions. But she does so in order both to criticize traditional doctrines and practices and to articulate her own unorthodox beliefs.

> 1. *Although someone might reasonably think* of Emily Dickinson as a conventionally religious poet, *I think* she only uses traditional religious terms and biblical allusions to criticize traditional doctrines and practices and to articulate her own unorthodox beliefs.

> 2. *Although someone might reasonably think* of Emily Dickinson as either a conventionally religious poet or as an intensely doubtful one, *I think* she is both: her poetry enacts a tension between traditional religious teaching and modern doubt.

The introduction above is an especially useful example because it demonstrates three things to keep in mind when articulating motive:

1. *Crafting a strong motive requires giving real substance to the argument you respond to,* taking it seriously enough that your readers do, too. The introduction above does that by listing a few good reasons why it might be entirely reasonable to consider Emily Dickinson either as an exclusively religious poet or as an exclusively skeptical one before making the claim that she is both. Simply put, you lose credibility from the get-go if you seem to be building a "straw man" just so you can knock him down.

2. *Responding to another point of view need not mean disagreeing with it.* Instead, you might

   • agree with, but complicate or qualify, the original claim;

   > Although others might be right to see Sonny as the protagonist of "Sonny's Blues," I think the story is just as much about how the narrator's view of his brother changes.

- present your thesis as a middle way between two extreme alternatives (as in the sample introduction above); or

- as in any conversation, change the subject by turning attention to something previously or easily ignored.

  Though our class discussion about "A Rose for Emily" focused exclusively on Miss Emily, we shouldn't ignore her father, since he makes Miss Emily what she is.

3. *"Although . . . , I think . . . because . . ." is a useful sentence as you plan or summarize an argument, not a sentence that should actually appear in an essay,* in part because it creates problems with tone (see 30.1.1).

30.1.4 Evidence

Showing readers that your interpretation and argument are valid requires ample, appropriate evidence. And the appropriateness of your evidence will depend on how you prepare and present it. Simply speaking, the term *evidence* refers to facts. But a fact by itself isn't really evidence for anything, or rather—as lawyers well know—any one fact can be evidence for many things. Like lawyers, literary critics turn a fact into evidence by interpreting it, drawing an inference from it, giving the reader a vivid sense of why and how the fact demonstrates a specific claim. You need, then, both to present facts and to interpret them. *Show* readers why and how each fact matters.

KINDS OF LITERARY EVIDENCE: QUOTATION, PARAPHRASE, SUMMARY, DESCRIPTION

Quotations are an especially important form of evidence in literature essays. Any essay about literature that contains no quotations will likely be weak. Readers of such an essay may doubt whether its writer has a thorough knowledge of the literary work or has paid adequate attention to details. And certain kinds of claims—about a character's motivations, a speaker's tone, a narrator's attitude toward a character, and so on—can't be adequately substantiated or developed *without* recourse to quotations.

At the same time, inexperienced writers sometimes make the mistake of thinking quotations are the *only* form of evidence in literature essays. They aren't. In fact, because a quotation will lead your reader to expect commentary on its language, you should quote directly from the text only when the actual wording is significant. Otherwise, keep attention on the facts that truly matter by simply paraphrasing, describing, or summarizing. (For a discussion and examples of paraphrase, summary, and description, see ch. 29.)

In this paragraph, note how the student writer simply summarizes and paraphrases (highlighted) when the key facts are what happens (who does what,

At this point in the novel, Tess is so conflicted about what to do that she can't decide or do anything at all. Only after asking her to marry him several times and repeatedly wondering aloud why Tess is hesitating does Angel finally get her to say yes or no. Even after agreeing to be his bride, Tess refuses to set a date, and it is Angel who finally, weeks later, suggests December 31. *Once Tess agrees, the narrator describes this more as a matter of totally letting go than of finally taking charge:* "carried along upon the wings of the hours, without the sense of a will," she simply "drifted into . . . passive responsiveness to all things her lover suggested" (221; ch. 32). *Tess has given up agency and responsibility, letting events take whatever course they will rather than exerting her will,* even though—or maybe because—she is so terrified about the direction they will take.

to whom, when) and what the "gist" of a character's remarks are, but she quotes when the specific wording is the key evidence. Notice, too, how the writer turns the quotation into evidence by both introducing and following it with interpretive commentary (in italics).

Through its form, the poem demonstrates that division can increase instead of lessen meaning, as well as love. On the one hand, just as the poem's content stresses the power of the love among *three people*, so the poem's form also stresses "threeness" as well as "twoness." It is after all divided into *three* distinctly numbered stanzas, and each stanza consists of *three* sentences. On the other hand, every *sentence* is "divided equally twixt two" *lines*, just as the speaker's "passion" is divided equally between two men. Formally, then, the poem mirrors the kinds of division it describes. Sound and especially rhyme reinforce this pattern, since the two lines that make up one sentence usually rhyme with each other to form a couplet. The only lines that don't conform to this pattern come at the beginning of the second stanza, where we instead have alternating rhyme—*is* (line 7) rhymes with *miss* (9), *mourn* (8) rhymes with *scorn* (10). But here, again, form reinforces content, since these lines describe how the speaker "miss[es]" one man when the other is "by," a sensation she arguably reproduces in us as we read by ensuring we twice "miss" the rhyme that the rest of the poem leads us to expect.

Description (highlighted) provides the evidence in this paragraph from the essay on Aphra Behn's ON HER LOVING TWO EQUALLY that appears earlier in this book.

For more on effective quotation, see 33.1–2.

30.1.5 Structure

Like an effective short story, poem, or play, your essay needs a beginning (or introduction), a middle (or body), and an end (or conclusion). Each of these parts plays its own unique role in creating a persuasive and satisfying whole.

BEGINNING: THE INTRODUCTION

Your essay's introduction needs to draw readers in and prepare them for what's to come by articulating your thesis and your motive and providing any basic information—about the author, the topic, the text, or its contexts—readers will need in order to follow and assess your argument. At the very least, you need to specify the title of the work you're writing about and the author's full name. Very short (one-sentence) plot summaries or descriptions of the text can also be useful, but they should be "slanted" so as to emphasize the aspects of the text you'll be most concerned with. (On summary and description, see ch. 29.)

Below are the first few sentences of two different essays on *Hamlet*. Notice how each uses plot summary to establish motive and build toward a thesis. Though we don't yet know what each thesis will be, each summary is slanted to suggest the essay's general topic and the kind of thesis it's heading toward.

1. It would be easy to read William Shakespeare's *Hamlet* as a play dealing with exclusively personal issues and questions—"To be, or not to be"? Am I really crazy? Did Mommy really love Daddy? Do I love Mommy too much? What such a reading ignores is the play's political dimension: Hamlet isn't just any person; he's the Prince of Denmark. The crime he investigates isn't just any old murder or even simple fratricide: by killing his brother, Denmark's rightful king, Claudius commits regicide only in order to usurp the throne that Hamlet is supposed to inherit. Thanks to their actions, the tragedy ends not only with the decimation of Denmark's entire royal family, but also with a successful foreign invasion that we—and all of the characters—have been warned about from the beginning.

2. As everyone knows, William Shakespeare's *Hamlet* depicts a young man's efforts to figure out whether his uncle murdered his father and what to do about it. What everyone may not have thought about is this: does it matter that the young man is a prince? that his uncle is now king? or even that the action takes place in ancient Denmark rather than in modern America? Ultimately, it does not. Though the play's setting and its characters' political roles and responsibilities might add an extra layer of interest, they shouldn't distract us from the universal and deeply personal questions the play explores.

Like the sentences in these partial introductions, every sentence in your introduction should contribute to your effort to spark readers' interest, articulate thesis and motive, or provide necessary background information. Avoid sentences that are only "filler," especially vapid (hence boring and uninformative) generalizations or "truisms" about literature or life such as Throughout human history, people have struggled with the question . . .; Literature often portrays conflicts; This story deals with many relevant issues; or In life, joy and sorrow often go together. To offer up one more truism worth keeping in mind, "you only get one chance to make a first impression," and generalizations, truisms, and clichés seldom make a good one.

MIDDLE: THE BODY

The body of your essay is where you do the essential work of supporting and developing your thesis by presenting and analyzing evidence. Each body paragraph needs to articulate, support, and develop *one* claim—a debatable idea directly related to the thesis, but smaller and more specific. This claim should be stated fairly early in the paragraph in a *topic sentence*. (If your paragraphs open with factual statements, you may have a problem.) And every sentence in the paragraph should help prove and elaborate on that claim. Indeed, each paragraph ideally should build from an initial, general statement of the claim to the more complex form of it that you develop by presenting and analyzing evidence. In this way, each paragraph functions a bit like a miniature essay with its own thesis, body, and conclusion.

Your essay as a whole should develop logically, just as each paragraph does. To ensure that happens, you need to do the following:

- Order your paragraphs so that each builds on the last, with one idea following another in a *logical* sequence. The goal is to lay out a clear path for the reader. Like any path, it should go somewhere. Don't just prove your point; develop it.
- Present each idea/paragraph so that the logic behind the order is clear. Try to start each paragraph with a sentence that functions as a bridge, transporting the reader from one claim to the next. The reader shouldn't have to leap.

The specific sorts of topic and transition sentences you need will depend in part on the kind of essay you're writing. Later in this and other chapters, we'll demonstrate what these sentences tend to look like in comparative essays, for example. But your thesis should always be your main guide.

Below are the thesis and topic sentences from a student essay on Raymond Carver's "Cathedral." Notice that just as the thesis is a claim about the narrator, so, too, are all the topic sentences, and that the writer begins with the "most evident" or obvious claim.

> <u>Thesis</u>: Through his words even more than his actions, the narrator unwittingly demonstrates his utter inability to connect with others or to understand himself.
>
> <u>Topic Sentences</u>:
> 1. The narrator's isolation is most evident in the distanced way he introduces his own story and the people in it.
>
> 2. At least three times the narrator himself notices that this habit of not naming or really acknowledging people is significant.
>
> 3. Also reinforcing the narrator's isolation and dissatisfaction with it are the awkward euphemisms and clichés he uses, which emphasize how disconnected he is from his own feelings and how uncomfortable he is with other people's.
>
> 4. Once the visit actually begins, the narrator's interactions and conversations with the other characters are even more awkward.
>
> 5. Despite Robert's best attempt to make a connection with the narrator, the narrator resorts to labels again.
>
> 6. There is hope for the narrator at the end as he gains some empathy and forges a bond with Robert over the drawing of a cathedral.
>
> 7. However, even at the very end it isn't clear just whether or how the narrator has really changed.

END: THE CONCLUSION

In terms of their purpose (not their content), conclusions are introductions in reverse. Whereas introductions draw readers away from their world and into your essay, conclusions send them back. Introductions work to convince readers that they should read the essay; conclusions tell them why the experience was worthwhile. You should approach conclusions, then, by thinking about what lasting impression you want to create. What can you give readers to take back into the "real world"?

In literature essays, effective conclusions often consider at least one of the following three things:

1. *Implications*—What picture of your author's work or worldview does your argument imply? Alternatively, what might your argument suggest about some real-world issue or situation? Implications don't have to be earth-shattering. It's unlikely that your reading of August Wilson's FENCES will rock your readers' world. But your argument about this play should in some small but worthwhile way change how readers see Wilson's work or provide some new insight into some topic that work explores—how racism is manifested, or how difficult it is for people to adjust to changes in the world around us, or how a parent or spouse might go wrong, and so on. If your essay has not, to this point, dealt with theme, now is the time to do so. If you have not mentioned the author's name since the introduction, do so now; often, making the implied or actual author the subject of at least some of your sentences helps to ensure that you are moving from argument to implications.

2. *Evaluation*—Though literature essays should focus primarily on interpretation, conclusions are a good place to move to evaluation. In a sense, careful interpretation earns you the right to engage in thoughtful evaluation. What might your specific interpretation of the text reveal about its literary quality or effectiveness? Alternatively, to what extent do you agree or disagree with the author's conclusions about a particular issue? How, for example, might your own view of how racism is manifested compare to the view implied in *Fences*? (For more on evaluative and/versus interpretive claims, see 30.1.2.)

3. *Areas of ambiguity or unresolved questions*—Are there any remaining puzzles or questions that your argument or the text itself doesn't resolve or answer? Or might your argument suggest a new question or puzzle worth investigating?

Above all, don't merely repeat what you've already said. If your essay has done its job to this point, and especially if your essay is relatively short, your readers will likely feel bored or even insulted if they get a mere summary. Clarify anything that needs clarifying, but go further. The best essays are rounded wholes in which conclusions do, in a sense, circle back to the place where they started. But the best essays remind readers of where they began only in order to give them a more palpable sense of how far they've come and why it matters. Your conclusion is your chance to ensure that readers *don't* leave your essay wondering, "Okay. So what?"

It's possible that not feeling "inside anything" (par. 135) could be a feeling of freedom from his own habits of guardedness and insensitivity, his emotional "blindness." But even with this final hope for connection, for the majority of the story the narrator is a closed, judgmental man who isolates himself and cannot connect with others. The narrator's view of the world is one filled with misconceptions that the visit from Robert starts to slowly change, yet it is not clear what those changes are, how far they will go, or whether they will last. Living with such a narrator for the length even of a short story and the one night it describes can be a frustrating experience. But in the end, that might be Raymond Carver's goal: by making us temporarily see the world through the eyes of its judgmental narrator, "Cathedral" forces us to do what the narrator himself has a hard time doing. The question is, will that change us?

In its original state, this conclusion to a student essay on Raymond Carver's "Cathedral" might elicit the "So what?" question. Yet notice what happens when we add just three sentences that try to answer that question.

30.2 COMMON ESSAY TYPES

All literature essays have the same basic purpose and the same five elements. Yet they come in infinite varieties, each of which handles those elements somewhat differently and thus also poses somewhat different writing challenges. In the next chapter, for example, we discuss a few literature essay topics so common that they virtually define distinct types or subgenres of the literature essay (31.1.3). The rest of this chapter instead concentrates on two especially common essay types—the comparative essay and the in-class exam essay.

30.2.1 The Comparative Essay

Comparison is a fundamental part of all reading: We develop our expectations about how a poem, play, or story will unfold by consciously or unconsciously comparing it to other poems, plays, and stories we've read; we get a sense of who a character is by comparing her to other characters; and so on. Not surprisingly, then, one of the most common types of essays assigned in literature classes is one that considers similarities and differences within a work, between two works, or among several. You might, for example, write an essay comparing different characters' interpretations of Georgiana's birthmark in Nathaniel Hawthorne's THE BIRTH-MARK or one comparing the use of symbolism in this Hawthorne story to that in Edwidge Danticat's A WALL OF FIRE RISING.

The key challenges involved in writing effective comparison essays are achieving the right balance between comparison and contrast, crafting an appropriate thesis, and effectively structuring the body of the essay.

COMPARISON AND/VERSUS CONTRAST

"Comparison-contrast" is a label commonly applied to comparison essays, but it is somewhat misleading: Though some comparative essays give greater stress to similarities, others to differences (or contrast), *all* comparison has to pay some attention to both. Contrast is *always* part of comparison.

Where the emphasis falls in your essay will depend partly on your assignment, so scrutinize it carefully. An assignment that asks you to "explain how and why children feature prominently in Romantic literature" by "analyzing the work of at least two Romantic poets," for example, encourages you to attend mainly to similarities so as to demonstrate understanding of a single "Romantic" outlook. Conversely, an assignment asking you to "contrast Harlem Renaissance poets Langston Hughes and Claude McKay" and describe "the major differences in their poetry" emphasizes contrast. Again, however, even an assignment stressing differences requires you first to establish some similarities as a ground for contrast, even as an assignment stressing similarities requires you to acknowledge the differences that make the similarities meaningful.

If the assignment gives you leeway, your topic and thesis will determine the relative emphasis you give to similarities and differences. In Out-Sonneting Shakespeare: An Examination of Edna St. Vincent Millay's Use of the Sonnet Form, for example, student writer Melissa Makolin makes her case for the distinctiveness and radicalism of Millay's sonnets both by contrasting them with those of Shakespeare and by demonstrating the similarities among three sonnets by Shakespeare, on the one hand, and two sonnets by Millay, on the other. But one could easily imagine an essay that instead demonstrated Millay's range by exploring the differences between her two sonnets, perhaps by building a thesis out of Makolin's claim that one poem is about "impermanent lust," the other "eternal love."

THE COMPARATIVE ESSAY THESIS

Like any essay, a comparative essay requires a thesis—*one* argumentative claim that embraces all the things (texts, characters, etc.) being compared. If you're like most of us, you may be tempted to fall back on a statement such as "These things are similar but different." Sadly, that won't cut it as a thesis. It isn't arguable (what two or more things *aren't* both similar and different?), nor is it specific enough to give your comparison direction and purpose: What such a thesis promises is less a coherent argument than a series of seemingly random, only loosely related observations about similarities and differences, desperately in search of a point.

At the end of the introduction to his comparative essay (below), student writer Charles Collins first articulates his main claim about each of the two short stories he will compare and then offers *one* overarching thesis statement:

> In "The Birth-Mark," the main character, Aylmer, views his wife's birthmark as a flaw in her beauty, as well as a symbol of human imperfection, and tries to remove it. In "The Thing in the Forest," the protagonists, Penny and Primrose, react to the Thing both as a real thing and as a symbol. The characters' interpretation of these things is what creates conflict, and the stories are both shaped by the symbolic meanings that the characters ascribe to those things.

(You can find the entire essay at the end of ch. 6.)

COMPARATIVE ESSAY STRUCTURES

In structuring the body of a comparative essay, you have two basic options, though it's also possible to combine these two approaches. Choose the option that best suits your texts, topics, and thesis rather than simply falling back on whichever structure feels most familiar or easy to you. Your structure and your thesis should work together to create a coherent essay that illuminates something about the works that can only be seen through comparison.

The Block Method

The first option tends to work best both for shorter essays and for essays, of any length, in which you want to stress differences at least as much as similarities. As its common label, "the block method," implies, this approach entails dividing your essay into "blocks" or sections, each of which lays out your entire argument about one of the things you're comparing. Charles Collins's essay comparing two stories, for example, is divided roughly in half: His first three body paragraphs analyze one story ("The Birth-Mark"), his last four body paragraphs another story (THE THING IN THE FOREST). To knit the two halves of the essay together into one whole, Collins begins the second block with the paragraph below, which discusses both stories. Such transitions are crucial to making the block method work:

> The symbolism in "The Birth-Mark" is fairly straightforward. The characters openly acknowledge the power of the symbol, and the narrator of the story clearly states what meaning Aylmer finds in it. In "The Thing in the Forest" what the Thing represents is not as clear. Penny and Primrose, the story's main characters, do not view the Thing as symbolic, as Aylmer does the birthmark. Neither the narrator nor the characters directly say why the Thing is important to Penny and Primrose or even whether the Thing they see in the forest is the monster, the Loathly Worm, that they later read about in the book at the mansion. . . .

In addition to strong transition paragraphs, effective use of the block method also requires that you

- *make each block or section of your essay match the other* in terms of the issues it takes up or the questions it answers, so as to maintain clear points of comparison. In Collins's essay, for example, each block answers the same questions with regard to each of the two stories and main characters being compared: whether or not the characters in a story see something as a symbol, what it ultimately comes to symbolize to them or to the reader, and how the characters' response to the symbol shapes their behavior.
- *order and present the blocks so that each builds on the last*: Though your blocks should match, their order shouldn't be random; rather, each block should *build* on the one that came before, just as should each paragraph/topic sentence in any essay. In Collins's essay, for example, the discussion of "The Birth-Mark" comes first because his argument is that symbolism here is more "straightforward" or simple than it is in "The Thing in the Forest," and Collins's transition paragraph homes in on that difference. As in many essays, then, the overall movement here is from the most to the least obvious and simple points.

The Point-by-Point or Side-by-Side Method

The second method of structuring a comparative essay requires you to integrate your discussions of the things—texts or characters, for example—that you are comparing. Each section of your essay (which might be one paragraph or two) should begin with a topic sentence that refers to all the things you're comparing rather than exclusively to one.

Below is a paragraph from a student essay comparing Samuel Taylor Coleridge's Frost at Midnight and Matthew Arnold's Dover Beach using this "point-by-point method." Like every body paragraph in this essay, this one discusses both poems.

> Differently but equally disturbed by the thoughts and emotions stirred by the natural scene before them, both speakers turn to the past, without finding much consolation in it. In Coleridge's poem, that past is specific and personal: what the speaker remembers are his school days, a time when he was just as bored and lonely and just as trapped inside his own head as he is now. Then, as now, he "gazed upon the" fire and "watch[ed] that fluttering" ash (lines 26-27), feeling no more connection then to his "stern precepto[r]" than he does now to his sleeping baby (38). In Arnold's poem, the past the speaker thinks of is more distant and historical. What he remembers are lines by Sophocles written thousands of years ago and thousands of miles away. But in his case, too, the past seems to offer only more of the same instead of any comfort or relief. Just as he now—standing by a "distant northern sea" (20)—hears in the waves "[t]he eternal note of sadness" (14), so "Sophocles long ago"— "on the Aegean"—"[h]eard" in them "the turbid ebb and flow / Of human misery" (15-18).

Below are the thesis and outline for another point-by-point comparison essay, this one analyzing Franz Kafka's A Hunger Artist and Flannery O'Connor's Everything That Rises Must Converge. In the essay itself, each numbered section consists of two paragraphs, the first (a) discussing O'Connor's protagonist, the second (b) Kafka's.

Thesis: "A Hunger Artist" and "Everything That Rises Must Converge" depict changing worlds in which the refusal to adapt amounts to a death sentence.

Outline:

1. Both Julian's mother and the hunger artist live in rapidly changing worlds in which they don't enjoy the status they once did.

   a) Julian's mother's world: the civil rights movement and economic change → loss of status

   b) hunger artist's world: declining "interest in professional fasting" → loss of status

2. Rather than embracing such changes, both the artist and the mother resist them.

   a) Julian's mother: verbally expressed nostalgia, refusal to even *see* that things are changing

     b) the hunger artist: nostalgia expressed through behavior, does see that things are changing

  3. Both characters take pride in forms of self-sacrifice that they see as essential to upholding "old-world" standards.

     a) Julian's mother: sacrifices for him, upholding family position and honor

     b) hunger artist: sacrifices for himself, upholding traditions of his art

  4. Both characters nonetheless die as a result of their unwillingness to adapt.

     a) Julian's mother

     b) hunger artist

  5. The endings of both stories create uncertainty about how we are to judge these characters and their attitudes.

     a) Julian's mother: Julian's last words and the story's create more sympathy for the mother

     b) hunger artist: his last words and description of the panther that replaces him make him less sympathetic

30.2.2 The Essay Test

Essays written for in-class exams do not fundamentally differ from those written outside of class. Obviously, however, having to generate an essay on the spot presents peculiar challenges. Below, we offer some general tips before discussing the two basic types of in-class essay exams (open versus closed book).

GENERAL TIPS

- *Carefully review instructions.*

  Though instructors rarely provide exam questions in advance, they usually do indicate how many questions you'll have to answer, what kind of questions they will be, and how much each will count. Whether you get such instructions before or during the exam, consider them carefully before you start writing. Make sure you understand exactly what is expected, and ask your instructor about anything confusing or ambiguous. You don't want to produce a great essay on a Gwendolyn Brooks poem only to discover that your essay was supposed to compare two of her poems. Nor do you want to spend 75 percent of your time on the question worth twenty-five points and 25 percent on the question worth seventy-five points.

- *Glean all the information you can from sample questions.*

  Sometimes instructors will provide sample questions in advance of an exam. Read rightly, such questions can give you a lot of information about what you need to be prepared to do on the exam. If presented with the sample question "What are three characteristic features of short stories by Louise Erdrich, and what is their combined effect?," for example, you should come to the exam prepared to write an essay addressing this specific question; an essay addressing either a different question about the assigned Erdrich stories (i.e., same texts, different topic); or a similar question about other authors that you read multiple works by (i.e., same topic, different texts).

- *Anticipate questions or topics and strategize about how to use what you know.*
Even if an instructor does not provide sample questions, exam questions rarely come out of the blue. Instead they typically emerge directly out of class lectures and discussions. And even questions that ask you to approach a text in what seems like a new way can still be answered effectively by drawing upon the facts and ideas discussed in class. Keeping good notes and reviewing them as you prepare for the exam should thus help you both to anticipate the topics you'll be asked to address and to master the information and ideas well enough so that you can use what you know in responding to unanticipated questions.

- *Review and brainstorm with classmates.*
Just as discussing a work in class can broaden and deepen your understanding of it, so reviewing with classmates can help you see different ways of understanding and organizing the material and the information and ideas discussed in class. Compare notes, certainly, but also discuss and brainstorm. What sorts of questions do your classmates anticipate?

- *Read questions carefully and make sure you answer them.*
Once you have the exam questions, read them carefully before you start writing. Make sure you understand exactly what the question asks you to do, and—again—ask your instructor to clarify anything confusing or ambiguous.

  Don't ignore any part of a question, but do put your emphasis where the question does. Let's suppose your question is "What does Dickinson seem to mean by 'Telling all the truth but telling it slant'? How might she do that in her poetry? How might Dickinson's personal experience or historical milieu have encouraged her to approach things this way?" An essay in response to this question that says nothing about biographical or historical context or that doesn't speculate about how one or the other shaped Dickinson's notion of truth telling would be incomplete. Yet the question allows you to consider only *one* of these two contexts, if you choose. More important, it asks you to devote most of your essay to analyzing *at least two poems* ("poetry") rather than discussing context. A good strategy might thus be to consider context only in your introduction and/or conclusion.

- *Be specific.*
One key difference between good exam essays and so-so or poor ones is the detail they provide: One thing an exam is testing is whether you have read and know the material; another is how well you can draw on facts to make an argument rather than simply regurgitating general ideas expressed in class. In response to the question above, for example, noodling on in a general way about Dickinson's use of dashes or metaphor will only take you so far—and not nearly far enough to score well. In answering this question, you should mention the titles of at least two poems and explain how each of them tells the truth slantwise or helps us understand what Dickinson means by slantwise truth. For example: In the poem that actually begins "Tell all the truth but tell it slant," Dickinson suggests that to successfully convey the truth, you have to do it in a roundabout way. People need to be eased into the truth; if it comes all at once, it's too much. She even compares that kind of direct truth telling to being struck by lightning. (See below for further discussion of specificity and how to achieve it in closed- versus open-book exams.)

• *Allow time to review and reconsider your essays.*

Though you're obviously pressed for time in an exam, leave yourself at least a few minutes to read over your essay before you have to submit it. In addition to correcting mistakes, look for places where you could use more concrete evidence or make clearer connections between one claim and another.

CLOSED- VERSUS OPEN-BOOK EXAMS

How you prepare for exam essays and how those essays will be judged will depend, in part, on whether your exam is "open book" or "closed book"—whether, in other words, you are allowed to consult the literary texts and perhaps even your notes about them during the exam.

At first glance, open-book exams seem much easier. Having the literary text(s) in front of you ensures that you don't have to rely entirely on memory to conjure up factual evidence: You can double-check characters' names, see what a poem's rhyme scheme is, actually quote the text, and so on. The fact that you *can* do all that also means, however, that you need to: Instructors expect more concrete and specific evidence, including quotations, in open-book exam essays. The bar, in short, is higher.

Be wary, however, of spending so much time during the exam looking back through the text that you don't have adequate time to craft your argument about it. Here, good preparation can help. If you know which texts you will likely be asked about on the exam, make sure that you mark them up in advance, highlighting key passages (including those discussed in class), making notations about rhyme scheme and meter, and so on. That way you can marshal your evidence quickly during the exam. Just make sure that you consult with your instructor in advance about what, if any, notes you are allowed to write in the book you bring with you to the exam.

If the exam is closed book, your instructor won't demand quite the same level of detail when it comes to evidence, but that doesn't mean you don't need any. Preparing for a closed-book exam will require some memorizing: Knowing a text word for word is rarely necessary or helpful, but you must master the basic facts about it such as **genre**, title, author, and characters' names. You should have a general sense of its **plot**, structure, and form and be able to recall any facts about context that were stressed in class. In your essay, you will need to make good use of paraphrase, summary, and description (see ch. 29).

Below are two versions of a paragraph from an essay written for a closed-book exam. Without consulting the texts, the essayist cannot quote them. What she can do is paraphrase an important piece of **dialogue** and summarize key episodes. What makes the second version superior is its greater specificity about action, timing, characters, and dialogue—who says and does what to whom, when, and in what story.

1. Sometimes in Erdrich's stories, conventional, biological families don't seem so healthy or happy, like with Mooshum or the adopted protagonist of "The Years of My Birth."

2. Sometimes in Erdrich's stories, conventional, biological families don't seem so healthy or happy. In "The Plague of Doves" Mooshum and his future bride run away together, partly because of their families. His older

brother treats him badly and wants to force him to become a priest just like he is. Her aunt beats her. In the first scene of "The Years of My Birth," a mother tells a doctor not to try to save her newborn daughter because the baby looks deformed. Then, when the baby survives, the mother and father refuse to take her home, the mother not contacting Tuffy (the story's adult narrator) until decades later, after the dad's death, and only because the mom wants Tuffy to donate an organ to save Linden, the "normal" twin brother the mom kept and raised. At least in these two stories, one problem is that the biological families seem to expect children to be like them in their looks or job or religious beliefs.

Finally, we present below a third version of the same paragraph, revised to include the even greater specificity, as well as effective use of direct quotations and citation, expected of essays produced for open-book exams. (Additions and revisions are highlighted.)

3. Sometimes in Erdrich's stories, conventional, biological families don't seem so healthy or happy. In "The Plague of Doves" Mooshum and his future bride, Junesse, run away partly to "escap[e]" their families, "sli[p] their knots, cut the harnesses that their relatives had tightened" around them (par. 15). Mooshum's older brother wants to force him to become a priest just like he is. Junesse's aunt beats her and makes her do "the endless drudgery of caring for six younger cousins" (par. 15). In the first scene of "The Years of My Birth," a mother tells a doctor not to try to save her newborn daughter after the doctor tells her this second twin "has a congenital deformity and may die" anyway (par. 2). Then, when their baby survives, George and Nancy Lasher refuse to take her home, Mrs. Lasher not contacting Tuffy (the story's adult narrator) until decades later, after George's death, and only because Nancy wants Tuffy to donate an organ to save Linden, the "normal" twin brother the Lashers kept and raised, the one who is "nice-looking" and has "the best of his mother's features" (par. 74). At least in these two stories, one problem is that the biological families seem to expect children to be like them in their looks or work or religious beliefs.

31 | THE WRITING PROCESS

Doing anything well requires both knowing what you're trying to achieve and having strategies for how to go about it. Where "The Literature Essay" chapter (ch. 30) focuses mainly on the *what*, this chapter focuses more on the *how*. In practice, of course, the writing process will vary from writer to writer and from assignment to assignment. No one can provide a recipe. What we instead do here is present you with strategies to try out and adapt to your particular tendencies as a writer and to the requirements of specific writing occasions.

As you do so, remember that writing needn't be a solitary enterprise. Ultimately, your essay must be your own work. That is essential; anything else is plagiarism. But most writers—working in every genre and discipline, at every level—get inspiration, guidance, and feedback from others throughout the writing process, and so can you. Use class discussions to generate and test out topics and theses. Ask your instructor to clarify assignments or to discuss your ideas. Have classmates, friends, or roommates critique your drafts. In writing about literature, as in reading it, we get a better sense of what our own ideas are and how best to convey them by considering others' impressions.

31.1 GETTING STARTED

31.1.1 Scrutinizing the Assignment

For student essayists, as for most professional ones, the writing process begins with an assignment. Though assignments vary, all impose restrictions. These are designed not to hinder your creativity but to direct it into productive channels, ensuring you hone particular skills, try different approaches, and avoid common pitfalls.

Your first task as a writer is thus to scrutinize your assignment. Make sure that you fully understand what you are being asked to do (and not do), and ask questions about anything unclear or puzzling.

Most assignments impose word or page limits. Keep those limits in mind as you consider potential topics, choosing a topic you can cover in the space allowed. In three pages, you cannot thoroughly analyze all the characters in August Wilson's FENCES. But you might within that limit say something significant about some specific aspect of a character or of characterization—perhaps how Troy Maxson's approach to parenting relates to the way he was parented or how Wilson's inclusion of the final scene, set after Troy's death, affects our interpretation of his character.

Many assignments impose further restrictions, often indicating the texts and/or topics your essay should explore. As a result, any assignment will shape whether and how you tackle later steps such as "Choosing a Text" or "Identifying Topics."

Below are several representative essay assignments (on the left), each of which imposes a particular set of restrictions (discussed on the right).

Choose any story in this anthology and write an essay analyzing how and why its protagonist changes.	This assignment dictates your topic and main question. It also provides you with the kernel of a thesis: *In [story title], [protagonist's name] goes from being a _____ to a _____.* OR *By the end of [story title], [protagonist's name] has learned that _____.* Though the assignment lets you choose your story, it limits you to those in which the protagonist changes or learns some lesson.
Write an essay analyzing one of the following sonnets: "America," "In an Artist's Studio," or "In the Park." Be sure to consider how the poem's form contributes to its meaning.	This assignment limits your choice of texts to three. It also requires that your essay address the effects of the poet's choice to use the sonnet form. Notice, though, that the assignment doesn't require that this be the main topic of your essay, but instead leaves you free to pursue any topic related to the poem's meaning.
Write an essay exploring the significance of references to eyes and vision in *A Midsummer Night's Dream*. What, through them, does the play suggest about the power and the limitations of human vision?	This assignment is more restrictive, indicating both text and topic. At the same time, it requires you to narrow the topic to formulate a specific thesis.
Write an essay comparing at least two poems by any one author in your anthology.	This assignment specifies the type of essay you must write (a comparison essay) and limits your choice of texts. Yet it leaves you the choice of which author to focus on, how many and which poems to analyze, what topic to explore, and what relative weight to give to similarities and differences.
Explain how and why children feature prominently in Romantic literature by analyzing the work of at least two Romantic poets.	This assignment is more restrictive, specifying the type of essay (comparison), the topic (depictions of children), and the kinds of texts (Romantic poems), while also encouraging you to focus mainly on similarities so as to define a single Romantic outlook on children and childhood.

31.1.2 Choosing a Text

If your assignment allows you to choose which text to write about, try letting your initial impressions or gut reactions guide you. Do that, and your first impulse may be to choose a text that you immediately like or "get." Perhaps its language resembles your own; it depicts speakers, characters, or situations you easily relate to; or it explores issues you care deeply about. Following that first impulse can be a good strategy. Writing an engaging essay requires *being* engaged, and we all find it easier to engage with texts, authors, and characters that we "like" immediately.

Paradoxically, however, writers often discover that they have little interesting or new to say about such a text. Perhaps they're too emotionally invested to analyze it closely or to imagine alternative ways to read it, or maybe its meaning seems so obvious that there's no puzzle or problem to drive an argument. Often, then, it can be more productive to choose a work that provokes the opposite reaction—that initially puzzles or even frustrates or angers you, one whose characters seem alien or whom you don't "like," one that investigates an issue you haven't thought much about, or one that articulates a theme you disagree with. Sometimes negative first reactions can have surprisingly positive results when it comes to writing. When you have to dig deeper, you may discover more. And your own initial response might also provide you with the kernel of a good motive (see 30.1.3).

So, too, might the responses of your classmates. If you are writing about a text you've discussed as a class, in other words, you might instead start with your responses to that discussion. Were you surprised by anything your classmates claimed about the text? Or did you strongly agree or disagree with any of your classmates' interpretations? Especially in hindsight, was anything *not* said or discussed that you think should have been?

31.1.3 Generating Topics

When an assignment allows you to create your own topic, you are more likely to build a lively, engaging essay from a particular insight or question that captures your attention and makes you want to say something, solve a problem, or stake out a position. The best essays originate in an individual response to a text and focus on a genuine question about it. Even when an instructor assigns you a topic, your essay's effectiveness will depend on whether you have made the topic your own, turning it into a real question to which you discover your own answer.

Often we refer to "finding" a topic, as if there are a bevy of topics "out there" just waiting to be plucked like ripe fruit off the topic tree. In at least two ways, that's true. For one thing, as we read a literary work, certain topics often do jump out and say, "Hey, look at me! I'm a topic!" A title alone may have that effect: *What "lesson" seems to be learned in Toni Cade Bambara's "The Lesson"? Why is Keats so fixated on that darn nightingale; what does it symbolize for him? Or what the heck is an "ode" anyway, and how might it matter that Keats's poem is an "Ode to a Nightingale"?*

For another thing, certain general topics can be adapted to fit many different literary works. In fact, that's just another way of saying that there are certain common types (even subgenres) of literary essays, just as there are of short stories, plays, and poems. Here are a few especially common topics:

- the significance of a seemingly insignificant aspect or element of a work— a word or group of related words, an image or image cluster, a minor character, a seemingly small incident or action, and so on. (This topic is appealing in part because it comes with a built-in motive: "Although a casual reader would likely ignore X . . .");

- the outlook or worldview of a single character or **speaker** (or of a group of characters) and its consequences;
- the changes a major character or speaker undergoes over the course of a literary work (What is the change? When, how, and why does it occur?);
- the precise nature and wider significance of an internal or external **conflict** and its ultimate resolution.

Especially when you're utterly befuddled about where to begin, it can be very useful to keep in mind such generic topics or essay types and to use them as starting points. But remember that they are only starting points. You have to adapt and narrow a generic topic such as "imagery" or "character change" in order to produce an effective essay. In practice, then, no writer simply "finds" a topic; she *makes* one.

Here are some other techniques that might help you generate topics. (And generating *topics*, giving yourself a choice, is often a good idea.)

- *Analyze your initial response.*
  If you've chosen a text you feel strongly about, start with those responses. Try to describe your feelings and trace them to their source. Be as specific as possible. What moments, aspects, or elements of the text most affected you? How and why? Try to articulate the question behind your feelings. Often, strong responses result when a work either challenges or affirms an expectation, assumption, or conviction that you bring *to* it. Think about whether and how that's true in your case. Define the specific expectation, assumption, or conviction. How, where, and why does the text challenge it? fulfill or affirm it? Which of your responses and expectations are objectively valid, likely to be shared by other readers?

- *Think through the elements.*
  Start with a list of elements and work your way through them, identifying anything that might be especially unique, interesting, or puzzling about the text in terms of each element. What stands out about the **tone**, the speaker, the **situation**, and so on? Come up with a statement about each. Look for patterns among your statements. Also, think about the questions your statements imply or ignore.

- *Pose motive questions.*
  In articulating a motive in your essay's introduction, your concern is your readers, your goal to give *them* a reason to find your thesis new and interesting and your essay worth reading. But you can also work your way toward a topic and, eventually, a thesis by considering motive-related questions. Keep in mind the basic *"Although they say/I used to think/someone might reasonably think . . . , I say/now think . . ."* statement and turn it into questions:
  —What element(s) or aspect(s) of this work might a casual reader misinterpret? Or which might you have misinterpreted on a first reading? Or which did your classmates seem to misinterpret?
  —What potentially significant element(s) or aspect(s) of this work were ignored entirely in class discussion? Or which did you ignore on a first reading? Or which might any reasonable person ignore?

—What aspect(s) or element(s) of this work have your classmates disagreed about or taken extreme positions on? Or which have you seen in very different ways as you've read and thought about the work?

—What interesting paradox(es), contradiction(s), or tension(s) do you see in the work?

31.1.4 Formulating a Question and a Thesis

Before you begin writing an essay, you need to articulate a thesis or hypothesis—an arguable statement about the topic. Quite often, topic and thesis occur to you simultaneously: You might well decide to write about a topic precisely because you've got something specific to say about it. At other times, that's not the case: The topic comes more easily than the thesis. In this event, it helps to formulate a specific question about the topic and to develop a specific answer. That answer will be your thesis.

Again, your question and thesis should focus on something specific, yet they need to be generally valid, involving more than your personal feelings. One way to move from an initial, subjective response to an arguable thesis is to re-read the text and then freewrite, as in the example below. At this point, don't worry what form your writing takes or how good it is: Just write. Don't pause to look things up in the text: Just draw on what you remember and note things you might need to double-check later.

Okay, this kid in "Araby" bugs me. But I feel sorry for him. He's totally in his own head. Obsessed with Mangan's sister. Does he even know her name? He just looks at her. Scratch that. He *thinks* about looking at her. And then when he does talk to her, I can't remember what they say. Should look again. But it didn't seem that exciting. She didn't seem that exciting. Is she pretty? I'll check, but don't remember her being described that way. So what's the attraction? And then the whole Araby thing; that's the one thing I do remember about their conversation. It turns out to be nothing. But he builds it up in his head. Just like he does with her. And nothing really turns out to be anything. Even he thinks he's an idiot by the end. Why the obsession? If it were just sex, then the whole Araby thing wouldn't make sense, right? It's like he thinks he's on a quest, a knight in shining armor going to some foreign land and bringing some precious object back for his lady love. I think he might even say something like this? Anyway, the fantasy sounds pretty stupid. *He* decides it's stupid once he actually sees Araby. But his real life *is* pretty crappy. Where are his parents? Do we know? He lives with his aunt and uncle. The uncle doesn't seem to be around much. He forgets about him. Doesn't he come home drunk? The aunt does stand up for him. But not much of a home really. It seems pretty lonely. There are kids in the neighborhood. But everything in the whole story seemed brown to me. (Was it?) Blah. Even all the Catholic stuff? Which is funny because I think of Catholicism as sort of colorful compared to my church: you're allowed to drink, priests wear robes. Anyway, here it's all depressing. Ugly. So I did feel sorry for him. Maybe his fantasy is his way of coping with a "blah" world that doesn't seem to offer much excitement or connection to other people, much chance to be a hero, much—I don't know—color or beauty or something?

However you arrive at your thesis or however strongly you believe in it, you should still think of it for now as a working hypothesis—a claim that's provisional, open to rethinking and revision, like the one with which our example ends.

31.2 PLANNING

Once you've formulated a tentative thesis and, ideally, a motive ("Although . . . , I think . . ."), you need to work on the "because" part of the equation, which means both (1) figuring out how to structure your argument, articulating and ordering your claims or sub-ideas; and (2) identifying the evidence you need to prove and develop each of those claims.

Start by studying your thesis. As in almost every phase of writing, it helps to temporarily fill your readers' shoes: Try to see your thesis and the promises it makes from their point of view. What will they need to be shown, and in what order? If a good thesis shapes readers' expectations, it can also guide you as a writer.

A good thesis usually implies not only what the essay's claims should be but also how they should be ordered. For instance, a thesis that focuses on the development of a character implies that the first body paragraphs will explain what that character is initially like and that later paragraphs will explore when, how, and why that character changes.

Working wholly from the thesis and this rough sense of structure, generate an outline, either listing each claim (to create a *sentence outline*) or each topic to be covered (to create a *topic outline*). Though a sentence outline is more helpful, you may find that at this stage you can only identify topics.

Take, for example, the ARABY thesis developed in the last section (31.1.4): Though the protagonist of "Araby" may seem like a silly dreamer, even to himself, his fantasy is his way of coping with a colorless, lonely, unheroic world. From this thesis, we can generate the following outline, which begins with four clear claims/topic sentences, then simply describes a fifth topic that will need to be covered:

1. <u>Claim</u>: The protagonist of "Araby" spins an elaborate quest fantasy around Mangan's sister and the Araby bazaar.
2. <u>Claim</u>: In the end, he recognizes his fantasy for a fantasy, dismissing it and himself as foolish.
3. <u>Claim</u>: But the protagonist's fantasy is his way of trying to find the things his real world lacks, starting with literal color.
4. <u>Claim</u>: The protagonist's world also lacks color in the figurative sense: meaningful human relationships, excitement, or heroism.
5. <u>Topic</u>: role of Catholicism

At this stage, it's clear that our "Araby" essay needs first to show *that* and *how* the protagonist's fantasy develops (claim 1) and then to show *that, how,* and *why* he comes to see himself and his own fantasy as foolish (claim 2). Not only are these the most obvious and least debatable claims, but they also lay the groundwork for the rest: Questions about why the narrator's fantasy might be more than simply foolish, given the world he lives in (claims 3 and 4), only follow logically once you establish that there is a fantasy and show what it looks like. To further refine the first four items on the outline and to draft these parts of the essay, its hypothetical writer need only review the story and her notes about it to identify appropriate evidence. Her discoveries will also determine whether she can fully develop each of these claims in one paragraph or whether she might need more than one.

The shape of the last part of the essay is less clear and will demand more work. In reviewing the story and her notes, the writer would need to come up with claims about what role Catholicism plays in making the protaganist's world so dreary.

As this example demonstrates, just as your thesis can guide you to an outline, so an outline can show you exactly what you need to figure out and what evidence you need to look for as you move toward a draft. The more detailed your outline, the easier drafting tends to be. But sometimes we can only figure out what our claims or ideas are by trying to write them out, which might mean moving straight from a rough outline to a draft rather than further refining the outline before drafting.

As you begin to gather evidence, let the evidence guide you, as well as your outline. As you look back at the text, you may well discover facts that are relevant to the thesis but that don't seem to relate directly to any of the claims or topics you've articulated. In that case, you may need to insert a new claim-topic into your outline. Additionally, you may find (and should actively look for) facts that challenge your argument. Test and reassess your claims against those facts and adjust accordingly. Don't ignore inconvenient truths.

31.3 DRAFTING

If you've put time and care into getting started and planning, you may already be close to a first draft. If you've instead jumped straight into writing, you may have to move back and forth between composing and some of the steps described earlier in this chapter.

Either way, remember that first drafts are called *rough drafts* for a reason. Think of yourself as a painter "roughing out" a sketch in preparation for the more detailed painting to come. At this stage, try not to worry about grammar, punctuation, and mechanics. Concentrate on the argument—articulating your ideas and proving them.

Sometimes the best way to start is to copy your thesis and outline into a new document. Forget about introducing your thesis, and just go right to work on your first body paragraph. Sometimes, however, you'll find that starting with the introduction helps: Having to draw readers in and set up your thesis and motive can give you a clearer sense of where you're going and why.

However you start, you will almost certainly feel frustrated at times. Stick to it. If you hit a roadblock, try explaining your point to another person or getting out a piece of paper and a pen and *writing* for a few minutes before returning to your computer. If all else fails, make a note about what needs to go in the spot you can't get through. Then move on and come back to that spot later. Whatever it takes, stay with your draft until you've at least got a middle, or body, that you're relatively satisfied with. Then take a break.

Later—or, better yet, tomorrow—come back, look at the draft with fresh eyes, and take another shot, attaching a conclusion and (if you don't already have one) an introduction, filling in any gaps, crafting smooth(er) transitions within and between paragraphs, deleting anything that now seems irrelevant. (Better yet, copy it into a separate "outtakes" document just in case you figure out later how to make it relevant.) Do your utmost to create a relatively satisfying whole. Now pat yourself on the back and take another break.

31.4 REVISING

Revision is one of the most important and difficult tasks for any writer. It's a crucial stage in the writing process, yet one that is easy to ignore or mismanage. The difference between a so-so essay and a good one, between a good essay and a great one, often depends entirely on effective revision. Give yourself time to revise more than once. Develop revision strategies that work for you. The investment in time and effort will pay rich dividends on this essay and on future ones.

The essential thing is to not confuse *revising* with *editing and proofreading*. We've devoted separate sections of this chapter to each of these steps because they *are* different processes. Where editing and proofreading focus mainly on sentence-level matters such as grammar and spelling, revision is about the whole essay, "the big picture." Revision entails assessing and improving both (1) the essay's working parts or elements and (2) your overall argument. Doing these two things well requires *not* getting distracted by small grammatical errors, spelling mistakes, and so on.

Before considering in depth what it means to assess the elements and enrich the argument, here are a few general tips about how to approach revision:

- *Think like readers.* Effective revision requires you to temporarily play the role of reader, as well as writer, of your essay. Take a step back from your draft, trying to see it from a more objective, even skeptical standpoint. Revision demands *re-vision*—looking again, seeing anew.
- *Get input from real readers.* This is an especially good time to involve other people in your writing process. Copy the "Assessing the Elements" checklist below and have a friend or classmate use it to critique your draft.
- *Think strengths and weaknesses, not right and wrong.* In critiquing a draft, it helps to think less in absolute terms (right and wrong, good and bad) than in terms of strengths and weaknesses—specific elements and aspects that work well and those that need more work.
- *Work with a hard copy.* Computers are a godsend when it comes to revision. But because they allow us to view only one or two pages of an essay at a time, they make it harder to see the essay as a whole. During the revision process, then, move away from the computer sometimes. Print out hard copies so that you can review your entire essay and mark it up, identifying problems that you can return to the computer to fix.

31.4.1 Assessing the Elements

The first step in revision is to ensure that all the working parts of your essay are, indeed, working. To help with that process, run through the following checklist to identify the strengths and weaknesses of your draft—or ask someone else to do so. Try to answer each question with ruthless honesty.

Whenever you can't justify a check, you and/or your readers need to identify the specific problems in order to solve them—if information is missing from the introduction, *what information?* If every sentence in the introduction isn't serving a clear purpose, *which sentence is the problem?* And so on.

Thesis and Motive

- ☐ Is there *one* claim that effectively controls the essay?
- ☐ Is the claim debatable?
- ☐ Does the claim demonstrate real thought? Does it truly illuminate the text and topic?
- ☐ Does the writer *show* us that (and why) the thesis is new and worthwhile by suggesting an actual or potential alternative view?

Structure

BEGINNING/INTRODUCTION

- ☐ Does the introduction provide readers all—and only—the information they need about the author, text, context, and topic?
- ☐ Does the introduction imply a clear, substantive, debatable but plausible thesis? Is it clear which claim is the thesis?
- ☐ Does every sentence either help to articulate the thesis and motive or to provide essential information?

MIDDLE/BODY

- ☐ Does each paragraph clearly state one debatable claim? Does everything in the paragraph directly relate to, and help support and develop, that claim?
- ☐ Is each of those claims clearly related to (but different from) the thesis?
- ☐ Are the claims logically ordered?
- ☐ Is that logic clear? Is each claim clearly linked to those that come before and after? Are there any logical "leaps" that readers might have trouble following?
- ☐ Does each claim/paragraph build on the last one? Does the argument move forward, or does it seem more like a list or a tour through a museum of interesting but unrelated observations?
- ☐ Do any key claims or logical steps in the argument seem to be missing?

ENDING/CONCLUSION

- ☐ Does the conclusion give readers the sense that they've gotten somewhere and that the journey has been worthwhile?
- ☐ Does it indicate the implications of the argument, consider relevant evaluative questions, or discuss questions that remain unanswered?

Evidence

- ☐ Is there ample, appropriate evidence for each claim?
- ☐ Are the appropriateness and significance of each fact—its relevance to the claim—clear?
- ☐ Are there any weak examples or inferences that aren't reasonable? Are there moments when readers might reasonably ask, "But couldn't that fact instead mean this?"
- ☐ Are all the relevant facts considered? What about facts that might complicate or contradict any of the claims? Are there moments when readers might reasonably think, "But what about X?"
- ☐ Is each piece of evidence clearly presented? Do readers have all the contextual information they need to understand a quotation, for example?
- ☐ Are there any unnecessary or overly long quotations—instances when the writer should instead paraphrase, summarize, or describe or provide more analysis of a long quotation?

Tone

- ☐ Does the writer maintain an effective tone—do any moments in the essay make its writer seem anything other than serious, credible, engaged, and engaging? respectful toward the text(s) and a range of readers?
- ☐ Does the writer correctly and consistently use literary terminology?
- ☐ Does the writer ever assume too much or too little readerly knowledge or interest?

COMMON PROBLEMS AND TIPS

Though you want to consider everything on the checklist above, certain problems are common in early drafts. Here are three:

- *mismatch between thesis or argument or between introduction and body*
  Sometimes an early draft ends up being a means of discovering what you really want to say. As a result, you may find that the thesis of your draft—or even your entire introduction—no longer adequately fits or introduces the argument you've ended up making. If so, you will need to rework the thesis and introduction. Then go back through the essay, making sure that each claim or topic sentence fits the new thesis.

- *the list or "museum tour" structure*
  In a draft, writers sometimes present each claim as if it were merely an item on a list (*First, second,* and so on) or as a stop on a tour of potentially interesting but unrelated topics (*And this is also important . . .*). But presenting your material in this way fails to help you and your readers make logical connections between ideas. It may also prevent your argument from developing. Sometimes it can even signal that you've ceased arguing, falling into mere plot summary or description rather than articulating real *ideas* at all. Check to see if number-like words or phrases appear prominently at the beginning of your paragraphs or if your paragraphs could be reordered without fundamentally changing what you're saying. Sometimes solving this problem will require wholesale rethinking and reorganizing—a process that should probably start with crafting a meatier, more specific thesis. But sometimes all that's required is adding or reworking topic sentences. Again, make sure that there is a clearly stated, *debatable* claim at the beginning of each paragraph; that each claim relates to the thesis but does not simply restate it; and that each claim *builds* logically on the preceding one.

- *missing sub-ideas*
  When you step back from your draft, you may discover that you've skipped a logical step in your argument—that the claim you make in, say, body paragraph 3 actually depends on, or makes sense only in light of, a more basic claim that you neglected to cover. In the second half of an essay about how a character changes, for example, you might suggest that there is something significant about the character being decisive, but decisiveness counts as change—and thus your point about decisiveness relates to your thesis—only if the first part of your essay has demonstrated that the character is initially *indecisive*. Whatever the missing idea is, you'll need to create and insert a new paragraph that articulates, supports, and develops it.

31.4.2 Enriching the Argument

The first step of the revision process is all about ensuring that your essay does the best possible job of making your argument. But revision is also an opportunity to go further—to think about ways in which your overall argument might be made more thorough and complex. In drafting an essay, our attention is often and rightly focused on emphatically staking out a particular position and proving its validity. This is the fundamental task of any essay, and you don't want to do anything at this stage to compromise that. At the same time, you do want to make sure that you haven't purchased clarity at the cost of oversimplification (by, for example, ignoring evidence that might undermine or complicate your claims), of alternative interpretations of the evidence you do present, or of alternative claims or points of view. Remember, you have a better chance of persuading readers to accept your argument if you show them that it's based on a thorough, open-minded exploration of the text and topic. Don't invent unreasonable or irrelevant complications or counterarguments. Do try to assess your argument objectively and honestly, perhaps testing it against the text one more time. Think like a skeptical reader: Are there moments where such a reader might reasonably disagree with your argument? Are there places where *two* interpretations might be equally plausible? Have you ignored or glossed over any questions that a reasonable reader might expect an essay on this topic to address?

Such questions should *always* be asked in revision. But they are especially crucial if you finish your draft only to discover that it is shorter than the assignment requires. Inexperienced writers of literature essays often run out of things to say too quickly because they don't keep asking relevant questions (*How? Why?*) or make enough allowance for alternative answers.

31.5 EDITING AND PROOFREADING

Once you've gotten the overall argument in good shape, *then* it's time to focus on the small but crucial stuff—words and sentences. Your prose should not only convey your ideas to your readers but also demonstrate how much you care about your essay. Flawless prose can't disguise or compensate for a vapid or illogical argument. But faulty, flabby, boring prose can undermine a potentially persuasive and thoughtful one. Don't sabotage all your hard work by failing to correct misspelled words, grammatical problems, misquotations, incorrect citations, and typographical errors. Little oversights make all the difference when it comes to clarity and credibility. Readers care more about careful work. Especially when you are writing about literature, the art of language, *your* language matters.

When it comes to words and sentences, each writer has particular strengths and weaknesses. Likewise, every writer tends to be overly fond of certain phrases and sentence structures, which become monotonous and ineffective if overused. With practice, you will learn to watch out for the particular mistakes and repetitions to which you are most prone. Then you can develop your own personalized editing checklist. Below is one to start with.

Sentences
- [ ] Does each one read clearly and crisply?
- [ ] Are they varied in length, structure, and syntax?
- [ ] Is the phrasing direct rather than roundabout?
- [ ] Are tenses appropriate and consistent?

- Try using the Find function to search for every preposition (especially *of* and *in*) and every *to be* verb. Since these can lead to confusing or roundabout phrasing, weed out as many as you can.
- Try reading your paper aloud or having a friend read it aloud to you. Mark places where you or your friend stumble, and listen for sentences that are hard to get through or understand.

Words
☐ Have you used any words whose meaning you're not sure of?
☐ Is terminology correct and consistent?
☐ Is a "fancy" word or phrase ever used where a simpler one might do?
☐ Are there unnecessary words or phrases?
☐ Do metaphors and other figures of speech make literal sense?
☐ Are verbs active and precise?
☐ Are pronoun references always clear and correct?
☐ Do subjects and verbs always agree?

Punctuation and Mechanics
☐ Are all words spelled correctly? (Double-check your autocorrect and spell-checker: These can create new errors in the process of correcting others.)
☐ Are all titles formatted correctly? (See the section following this checklist.)
☐ Is every quotation accurate and punctuated correctly? (See ch. 33.)

Citation and Documentation (See ch. 33.)
☐ Is the source of each quotation, as well as any fact or idea drawn from sources, clearly indicated through parenthetical citation?
☐ Do parenthetical citations correctly coordinate with the list of works cited?
☐ Are all parenthetical citations and all entries in the list of works cited formatted correctly?

Titles

Formatting titles correctly in both the body of your essay and your list of works cited is essential to your essay's clarity, as well as to your self-presentation as a knowledgeable and careful writer: Othello is a character; *Othello* is a play. "Interpreter of Maladies" is a short story, but *Interpreter of Maladies* is a book (which contains that short story). To make sure you get this right, here is a quick review:

- Italicize the titles of all books and other "stand-alone" works, including
  —novels and novellas (*To Kill a Mockingbird, The House on Mango Street*)
  —collections and anthologies of short stories, essays, or poems (*Interpreter of Maladies, The Norton Introduction to Literature*)
  —long poems that could be or have been published as books (*The Odyssey, Paradise Lost, Goblin Market*)
  —plays (*Fences, Water by the Spoonful*)
  —periodicals, including newspapers, magazines, and scholarly journals (*USA Today, People, College English*)
  —websites, blogs, and databases (*Google Scholar, HuffPo, JSTOR*)
  —movies and television programs or series (*Black Panther, Buffy the Vampire Slayer*).

- Put quotation marks around the titles of works that are part of such "stand-alone" works, including
  —short stories ("Interpreter of Maladies," "Volar")
  —poems ("America," "Ode to a Nightingale")
  —essays and articles in periodicals ("A Narrator's Blindness in Raymond Carver's 'Cathedral'"; "When We Dead Awaken: Writing as Re-Vision"; "Chicago Fiddles While Trumbull Park Burns")
  —parts of websites (e.g., web pages, blog posts)
  —episodes of a television series.

31.6 FINISHING UP

31.6.1 Crafting a Title

Your essay is incomplete without a title. A good title both informs and interests. Inform readers by telling them the work(s) you will analyze ("The Road Not Taken" or "two poems by Robert Frost") and something about your topic ("Symbolism," "Nonconformity"). To interest them, try using one of the following:

- an especially vivid and relevant word or phrase from the literary work ("'They Have Eaten Me Alive': Motherhood in 'In the Park' and 'Daystar'")
- a bit of wordplay ("Wordsworth and the Art of Artlessness")
- a bit of both ("'Nobody's Listening': Learning to Listen and Listening to Learn in 'Sonny's Blues'").

Do not put your own title in quotation marks, but do correctly format any titles that appear within your title.

31.6.2 Formatting Your Essay

Unless your instructor provides specific instructions on how to format your essay, follow these guidelines, adapted from the Modern Language Association's *MLA Style Center* (style.mla.org/formatting-papers) and demonstrated in the sample research essay in chapter 34.

- Choose a readable eleven- or twelve-point font, set your page margins at 1 inch, and double-space throughout. Do not add extra lines between paragraphs or before or after block quotations. Indent the first line of each paragraph ½ inch. An entire block quotation should be indented ½ inch. (For more on formatting quotations, see 33.1.)
- Do not include a title page. Instead, in the top left corner of the first page, type your name, your instructor's name, the course number, and the date, each on a separate line. Center your title on the next line. (Do not enclose your own title in quotation marks.)
- Number every page consecutively, putting your last name and the page number in the upper-right corner ½ inch below the top of the page and aligned with the right margin. (Do not put any punctuation between your name and the page number.)
- Begin your list of works cited on a new page, *after* the last page of your essay. Center the words *Works Cited* at the top of the page. (Do not put quotation marks around or italicize these words.) Indent the second and subsequent lines of each works cited entry ½ inch. (For more on formatting the list of works cited, see 33.3.2.)

32 | THE LITERATURE RESEARCH ESSAY

Whenever we read, discuss, and write about literature, our primary concern is the text. But literature speaks to and about the real world even when it depicts an entirely unreal one. Both texts and our readings of them are inevitably shaped by, and intervene in, particular contexts. Literary research is simply a way to learn more about those contexts. In a literature research essay we bring what we learn to bear in order to illuminate the work in a new way.

On the one hand, writing a research essay may at first seem like a daunting task. Research adds more steps to the writing process, so you must give yourself more time. Those steps also require you to draw on and develop skills somewhat different from those involved in crafting essays that focus exclusively on the literary text. Were this not the case, no one would ask you to write a research essay.

On the other hand, however, a literature research essay is still a literature essay. Its core elements are the same, as is its basic purpose—to articulate and develop a debatable, interpretive claim about at least one literary work. As a result, this kind of essay requires many of the same skills and strategies you've already begun to develop. And though you will need to add a few new steps, the process of writing a literature research essay still involves getting started, planning, drafting, revising, editing, and finishing up—exactly the same dance whose rhythms you've already begun to master.

The only distinctive thing about a research essay is that it requires you to draw on sources in addition to the literary text itself. Though that adds to your burden in some ways, it can lighten it in others. Think of such sources not as another ball you have to juggle but as another tool you add to your tool belt: You're still being asked to build a cabinet, but now you can use a hammer *and* an electric drill. This chapter will help you make the best use of these powerful tools.

One thing to keep in mind from the outset is that this anthology includes excerpts from numerous scholarly articles about literature—each one is a published literature research essay. Some of these excerpts may be appropriate sources for your essay. But even if they aren't, they can still be very helpful to you as examples of how professional literary critics go about doing the same things you need to do in your research essay. What do these critics' theses look like? What are their motives? What kinds of sources do they use, and how do they use them? How do they manage to stay focused on *their* arguments about the literary text? In this chapter, we'll draw on examples from these and other published essays to show you what we mean.

32.1 TYPES OF ESSAYS AND SOURCES

The three most common types of literature research essay are those suggested by the "Contexts" chapters in this anthology. But though we treat these types separately here for clarity's sake, many literature research essays are in fact hybrids of one sort or another. The sample research essay in chapter 34 is a case in point: It analyzes a short story by Alice Munro by drawing on literary criticism; biographical materials; and a study of Canadian farm families, which provides social and historical context. Should your assignment allow, your essay, too, could combine two or more of these approaches. Either way, it's useful to remember that your secondary sources probably will.

32.1.1 Critical Contexts

Whenever we write a literature essay, we engage in conversation with other readers about the meaning and significance of a literary work. Effective argumentation always depends on anticipating how other readers are likely to respond to, and interpret, that work. As the "Critical Contexts" chapters in this anthology demonstrate, most texts and authors are also the subject of actual public conversations, often extending over many years and involving all the numerous scholarly readers who have published their readings of the work. A "critical contexts" research essay is an opportunity both to investigate this conversation and to contribute to it.

For this kind of essay, your secondary sources will be work by literary scholars on the specific text you're writing about; on an author's body of work; or on a relevant genre or body of literature (e.g., *The Development of the Sonnet: An Introduction* or *Movements in Chicano Poetry: Against Myths, Against Margins*). The latter, more general sorts of sources may be especially crucial if you are researching a relatively recent work about which little literary criticism has yet been published. In that case, too, you may want to consult book reviews; just remember that it's reviewers' *interpretive* claims you're most interested in, not their evaluation of the work. (On interpretation versus evaluation, see 30.1.2. For examples of critical context essays by student writers, see chs. 28 and 34. For examples by professional critics, see the excerpts in chs. 10, 23, and 28.)

32.1.2 Biographical Contexts

If literature *only* reflected, and gave us insight into, its author's psyche, it ultimately wouldn't be that interesting: Good poets, fiction writers, and playwrights write about and for others, not just themselves. Nonetheless, authors are real people whose unique experiences and outlooks shape both what they write and how. A "biographical contexts" research essay is a chance to learn more about an author's life, work, and ideas and to explore how these might have shaped or be reflected in the text. Sources for this sort of project will likely include biographies (secondary sources) and essays, letters, and other nonfiction prose by the author (primary sources). (For examples of biographical context essays, see the excerpts from Eileen Pollack's FLANNERY O'CONNOR AND THE NEW CRITICISM and from Steven Gould Axelrod's SYLVIA PLATH: THE WOUND AND THE CURE OF WORDS.)

32.1.3 Historical and Cultural Contexts

Every literary work is both shaped by and speaks to the circumstances, events, and debates peculiar to its historical and cultural context, though some literary works speak of their times by depicting other times. A "cultural and historical contexts" essay explores the interconnections between a text and the context it was either written in or depicts. Sources useful for this sort of essay might include studies of a relevant historical period or literary movement (secondary sources) or documents dating from that period or written by others involved in that movement (primary sources). (For an example of a historical and cultural context essay by a student writer, see ch. 22. For examples by professional critics, see the excerpts from Steven Kaplan's THE UNDYING UNCERTAINTY OF THE NARRATOR IN TIM O'BRIEN'S *THE THINGS THEY CARRIED*, Steven Gould Axelrod's SYLVIA PLATH: THE WOUND AND THE CURE OF WORDS, and Philip Holt's POLIS AND TRAGEDY IN THE *ANTIGONE*.)

32.2 WHAT SOURCES DO

Unless your instructor indicates otherwise, *your* argument about the literary text should be the focus of your essay, and sources should function simply as tools that you use to deepen and enrich your argument about the literary text. They shouldn't substitute for your argument. Your essay should never simply repeat or report on what other people have already said.

Sources, in other words, are *not* the source of your ideas. Instead, to paraphrase writing expert Gordon Harvey's *Writing with Sources* (Hackett, 1998), they are the source of

- *argument* or *debatable claim*—other readers' views and interpretations of a text, author, topic, literary movement, period, and so on, which "you support, criticize, or develop";
- *information*—facts about an author's life; about the work's composition, publication, or reception; about the era during, or about which, the author wrote; about movements in which the author participated; and so on;
- *concept*—general terms or theoretical frameworks that you borrow and apply to your author or text. (In an essay excerpted in ch. 24, for example, Stephen Gould Axelrod uses concepts drawn from Sigmund Freud's theories of psychological development to interpret Sylvia Plath's poem DADDY; in an essay on Tim O'Brien's THE THINGS THEY CARRIED excerpted in ch. 10, Steven Kaplan applies the concepts of literary theorist Wolfgang Iser.)

Any one source will likely offer you more than one of these things. In the Axelrod excerpt mentioned above, for example, you will find *argument* about the poem "Daddy," as well as potentially useful *information* about its author's life and about the domestic poem in the 1950s. Nonetheless, the distinction between argument or debatable claim, on the one hand, and information or factual statement, on the other, is crucial. As you read a source, you must discriminate between the two.

When drawing on sources in your essay, remember, too, that an argument about the text, no matter how well-informed, isn't the same as evidence. Only facts can serve that function. Suppose, for example, you are writing an essay on "Daddy." You claim that the speaker adopts two voices, that of her child self and that of her adult self—a claim Axelrod also makes in his essay. You cannot prove this claim to be true merely by showing that Axelrod makes the same claim. Like any debatable claim, this one must be backed up with evidence from the primary text. In this situation, however, you must indicate that a source has made the same claim that you do in order to accomplish three things:

1. give the source credit for having this idea before you did (to avoid even the appearance of plagiarism; see 32.4.1);

2. encourage readers to see you as a knowledgeable, trustworthy writer who has done your research and taken the time to explore, digest, and fairly represent others' views; and

3. demonstrate that your opinion isn't merely idiosyncratic because another informed, even expert, reader agrees with you.

Were you to disagree with the source's claim, it would be just as important to your argument to acknowledge that disagreement in order to demonstrate the originality of your interpretation, while also, again, encouraging readers to see you as a knowledgeable, careful writer.

You will need to cite sources throughout your essay whenever you make a claim that resembles, complements, or contradicts the claim of another source; rely on information or concepts from a source; or paraphrase, quote, or summarize anything in a source. Especially in a critical contexts essay, you should also at least consider using sources to establish motive (see 32.2.1).

32.2.1 Source-Related Motives

Not all research essays use sources to articulate motive. But doing so is one way both to ensure and to demonstrate that your own ideas are the focus of your essay and that your essay contributes to a literary critical conversation rather than just reporting on it or repeating what others have already said. In these essays, in other words, your "Although . . ." statement (as outlined in 30.1.3) may refer to sources—actual "theys" and what they "say." Indeed, whether you ultimately use sources to articulate a motive or not, keeping motive-related questions in mind as you read sources is a good idea, for reasons we'll detail in the next section of this chapter. Here are the three most common source-related motives:

1. Sources offer different opinions about a particular issue in the text, thus suggesting that there is still a problem or puzzle worth investigating. (Your argument might agree with one side or the other or offer a "third way.")

[A]lmost all interpreters of [*Antigone*] have agreed that the play shows Creon to be morally defective [. . .]. The situation of Antigone is more controversial. Hegel assimilated her defect to Creon's; some more recent writers uncritically hold her up as a blameless heroine. Without entering into an exhaustive study of her role in the tragedy, I should like to claim (with the support of an increasing number of recent critics) that there is at least some justification for the Hegelian assimilation—though the criticism needs to be focused more clearly and specifically than it is in Hegel's brief remarks.

In these sentences from THE FRAGILITY OF GOODNESS, Martha C. Nussbaum summarizes an ongoing debate about ANTIGONE and then positions her argument as contributing to that debate by supporting and developing one of the two usual positions.

2. A source or sources make(s) a faulty claim that needs to be challenged, modified, or clarified.

Modern critics who do not share Sophocles' conviction about the paramount duty of burying the dead and who attach more importance than he did to the claims of political authority have tended to underestimate the way in which he justifies Antigone against Creon.

In this sentence from the introduction to SOPHOCLEAN TRAGEDY, Maurice Bowra makes a generalization about the stance taken by "[m]odern critics" that his essay will challenge. (Subsequent sentences provide more details about that stance.)

While I find Smith's article thoughtful and intriguing, and while I agree with much feminist criticism of Vietnam War literature, this essay proposes that the work of Tim O'Brien, particularly *The Things They Carried*, stands apart from the genre as a whole. O'Brien is much more self-consciously aware of gender issues and critical of traditional gender dichotomies than are the bulk of U.S. writers about the Vietnam War.

In TIM O'BRIEN AND GENDER: A DEFENSE OF THE THINGS THEY CARRIED, Susan Farrell does the opposite of what Bowra does above. Having first summarized the arguments of one specific critic (Smith), she now (in this sentence) articulates her contrary view.

3. Sources either neglect a significant aspect or element of the text, or they make a claim that needs to be further developed or applied in a new way (perhaps to a text other than the one the sources discuss).

Tim O'Brien's 1990 book of interlocked stories, *The Things They Carried*, garnered one rave review after another, reinforcing O'Brien's already established position as one of the most important veteran writers of the Vietnam War. The Penguin paperback edition serves up six pages of superlative blurbs like "consummate artistry," "classic," "the best American writer of his generation," "unique," and "master work." [. . .] Yet, O'Brien—and his reviewers—seem curiously unselfconscious about this book's obsession with and ambivalence about representations of masculinity and femininity, particularly in the five stories originally published during the 1980s in *Esquire*.

Here, in "THE THINGS MEN DO": THE GENDERED SUBTEXT IN TIM O'BRIEN'S ESQUIRE STORIES, Lorrie N. Smith suggests not that others' claims are wrong but that they simply ignore something that her essay will investigate.

(In ch. 34, you'll find a research essay on Alice Munro's BOYS AND GIRLS that combines versions of the first and third kinds of source-related motives described above.)

32.3 THE RESEARCH PROCESS

32.3.1 Finding Authoritative Secondary Sources

Regardless of your author, text, or topic, you will likely find a wealth of sources to consult. The conversation about literature and its contexts occurs online and in print, in periodicals and in books. Your instructor may well give you specific guidance about which sorts of sources to use. If not, it's usually best to consult at least some print sources or sources that appear in both print and digital form (e.g., the scholarly journals housed in databases such as *JSTOR* or *Academic Search Premier*). Citing only one kind of source—books but not articles, online but not print—may cast doubt on the thoroughness of your research; you want your reader to know that you sought out the *best* sources, not just the most easily available ones.

Whatever their form, your secondary sources should be authoritative, since the credibility and persuasiveness of your research essay will depend on that of your sources: At the very least, you do not want to look like someone who doesn't know the difference or care enough to figure it out. Learning how to identify authoritative sources is one of the rationales for research essay assignments. "Evaluating sources" thus initially means evaluating their credibility and importance. At this stage, concentrate on whether the opinions expressed and the information provided are worthy of serious consideration, not on whether you agree with them. Save that question for later.

As a general rule and with the exception of a general dictionary, *you should not rely on or cite any secondary source that is not attributed to a named author*. This includes (but is not limited to) *Wikipedia* and websites such as *Shmoop* and *LitCharts*. Because these will likely be the first things a general *Google* search turns up and because they are probably familiar to you, it's tempting to rely on them. Avoid the temptation. Though much of the information on such sites is correct and useful, much of it isn't. As important, the very virtue of such sites—the fact that they are designed for, and mainly written by, nonexperts—makes them inappropriate as sources for a research essay, since the goal of such an essay is to engage in a conversation among acknowledged experts.

In these terms, the most valuable sources tend to be books published by academic and university presses and articles published in scholarly or professional journals (rather than magazines or newspapers). This isn't mere snobbishness: Such work appears in print or online only after a rigorous peer-review process. As a result, you and your readers can trust that these publications have been judged credible by more than one acknowledged expert.

Rather than heading straight to *Google* and searching the entire Internet, then, try starting instead with your library's website. In addition to the catalog, you will here find a wealth of specialized reference works, bibliographies, and databases. Which of these are available to you will depend on your library. But here are two common and helpful resources to start with:

- *Oxford Encyclopedia of American Literature* and *Oxford Encyclopedia of British Literature*: Both include signed entries by recognized experts on major authors and topics. Each entry ends with a short annotated bibliography. In addition to being a source, such an entry will thus lead you to other authoritative sources. In a sense, the entry's writer has already done some of your research for you.

- *MLA International Bibliography*, the "go-to" source for identifying all scholarly work—books, articles, and book chapters—on any author, work, or topic. The virtue and (for your purposes) potential limitation of this bibliography is its inclusiveness: You can generally trust that sources included in the bibliography are, indeed, scholarly, published mainly by academic presses or in scholarly journals. MLA does not, however, discriminate among those sources in terms of quality, importance, and so on.

Once you have identified potentially useful articles and books, you may be able to access some of them online. Many full-text scholarly articles are accessible via subscription databases such as *JSTOR*, *Project Muse*, and *Academic Search Premier*. Your library may have e-book versions of some of the books you are interested in, while other, especially older books can be found online: In addition to *Google Books*, try *HathiTrust* and *Internet Archive*. Again, however, do not neglect any important source simply because you have to go to the library to look at it; this includes books only *partly* viewable on *Google*.

Look for the most-up-to-date secondary sources, but don't automatically discount older ones. You should consult recent sources in order to get the most-up-to-date information on your topic and a sense of what scholars today consider the most significant, debatable interpretive questions and claims. But be aware that in literary studies (and the humanities generally), newer work doesn't always supersede older work, as it tends to do in the sciences. As the literary criticism excerpted in chapter 28 demonstrates, for example, twenty-first-century scholars still cite and debate the arguments about *Antigone* made well over a hundred years ago by German philosopher Georg Wilhelm Friedrich Hegel (1770–1831).

Once you find an especially good secondary source, its bibliography will lead you to others. Test sources against one another: If multiple reliable sources agree about a given fact, you can probably assume it's accurate. If they all cite a particular article or book, you know it's considered a key contribution to the conversation.

32.3.2 Reading and Taking Notes

Once you've acquired or accessed your secondary sources, it's a good idea to skim each one. (In the case of a book, concentrate on the introduction and on the chapter that seems most relevant.) Focus at this point on assessing the relevance of each source to your topic. Or, if you're working your way toward a topic, look for things that spark your interest. Either way, try to get a rough sense of the overall conversation—of the issues and topics that come up repeatedly across the various sources.

Once you've identified the most pertinent sources, it's time to begin reading more carefully and taking notes. For each source, make sure to note down all the bibliographical information that you will ultimately need to cite the source correctly. (For details, see the guide to citation in ch. 33.) Your notes for each source will likely include four things: summary, paraphrase, quotation, and your own comments and thoughts. To avoid confusion (even plagiarism), it's crucial that you develop a system for clearly differentiating each of these from the other. Whenever you write down, type out, or paste in two or more consecutive words from a source, you should place these words in quotation marks so that you will later recognize them as direct quotations; make sure to quote with absolute accuracy; and record the page where the quotation is found (if the source is paginated) or other location information (if it is not). Keep quotations to a minimum. In lieu of extensive quotations, try to summarize and paraphrase as much as possible. You can't decide how to use the source or whether you agree with its argument unless you've first understood it, and you can usually best test your understanding through summary and paraphrase. You might, for example, either start or conclude your notes with a one- or two-sentence summary of the author's overall argument, perhaps using the "Although . . . , I think . . . because" rubric. Paraphrase especially important points, making sure to note where in the source each appears. (For more on paraphrase, summary, and description, see ch. 29 and 32.4.2 below.)

32.3.3 Synthesizing

It can be very useful to complete the note-taking process by writing a summary that synthesizes all of your secondary sources. Your goal is to show how all the arguments fit together to form one coherent conversation. (Like any conversation, however, a scholarly one usually considers multiple topics.) Doing so will require that you both define the main questions at issue in the conversation and indicate what stance each source takes on each question—where and how their opinions coincide and differ. If you tend to be a visual learner, you might also try diagramming the conversation somehow.

One might say, for example, that the main questions about *Antigone* that preoccupy most of the scholars represented in chapter 28 are (1) *What is the exact nature of the conflict between Antigone and Creon, or what two conflicting worldviews do they represent?* and (2) *How is that conflict resolved? Which, if either, of the two characters and worldviews does the play ultimately endorse?* A synthetic summary of these sources (i.e., one that combines or "synthesizes" them) would explain how each critic answers each of these questions.

This kind of summary can be especially helpful when you haven't yet identified a specific essay topic or crafted a thesis because it may help you to see gaps in the conversation, places where you can enter and contribute. If you have identified a topic or thesis, a synthetic summary is still useful for identifying points of agreement and disagreement and for articulating motive (32.2). Indeed, students required to write a synthetic summary often end up using it as the kernel of their introduction.

32.4 WRITING WITH SOURCES

32.4.1 Using Sources Responsibly and Avoiding Plagiarism

The clarity and credibility of any research essay depend on responsible use of sources. And using secondary sources responsibly entails accurately representing them, clearly discriminating between their ideas and words and your own, giving credit where credit is due. Since ideas, words, information, and concepts not clearly attributed to a source will be taken as your own, any lack of clarity on that score amounts to plagiarism. Representing anyone else's ideas or data as your own, even if you state them in your own words, is plagiarism—whether you do so intentionally or unintentionally; whether the ideas or data come from a published book or article, another student's paper, the Internet, or any other source. Plagiarism is among the most serious of offenses within academe because it amounts both to taking credit for someone else's hard labor and to stealing ideas—the resource most precious to this community and its members. That's why the punishments for plagiarism are severe—including failure, suspension, and expulsion, for students; the loss of a job, for teachers who are also researchers.

To avoid both the offense and its consequences, you must always do the following:

- *put quotation marks around any quotation from a source* (a quotation being any two or more consecutive words or any one especially distinctive word, label, or concept) *or indent it to create a "block quotation"*; and

- *credit a source whenever you take from it any of the following*:
  —*a quotation* (as described above);
  —*a nonfactual or debatable claim* (an idea, opinion, interpretation, evaluation, or conclusion) stated in your own words;
  —*a distinctive concept or term*;
  —*a fact or piece of data that isn't common knowledge*; or
  —*a distinctive way of organizing factual information*.

To clarify, a fact counts as "common knowledge"—and therefore doesn't need to be credited to a source—whenever you can find it in multiple reputable sources, none of which seriously question its validity. It is common knowledge, for instance, that Jorge Luis Borges was born in Buenos Aires, Argentina, in 1899 and that the first English translation of his short-story collection *Ficciones* was published in 1962. No source can "own" or get credit for these facts. However, a source can still "own" a particular way of arranging or presenting such facts. If you begin your essay by stating—in your own words—a series of facts about Borges's life in exactly the same order they appear in a specific source, then you would need to acknowledge that source. When in doubt, cite. (For guidance about *how* to do so, see both 32.4.2 below and ch. 33.)

32.4.2 Integrating Secondary Source Material into Your Essay

The responsible use of sources depends as much on how you integrate ideas, facts, and words from sources into your essay as on how effectively you use a citation and documentation system like that outlined in chapter 33. Indeed, in this (the MLA) system, where a citation belongs and what it looks like depend on what information you provide about the source in your text.

Research essays can refer to secondary sources in various ways. You may

- *briefly allude to them*:

  Many critics, including Maurice Bowra and Bernard Knox, see Creon as morally inferior to Antigone.

- *summarize or paraphrase their contents*:

  According to Maurice Bowra, Creon's arrogance is his downfall. However prideful Antigone may occasionally seem, Bowra insists that Creon is genuinely, deeply, and consistently so (1688).

- *quote them directly*:

  Maurice Bowra reads Creon as the prototypical "proud man"; where Antigone's arrogance is only "apparent," says Bowra, Creon's is all too "real" (1688).

Choose whichever strategy suits your purpose in a particular context. But keep the number and length of quotations from secondary sources to a minimum. This is *your* essay. Your ideas about the text are its primary focus. And you should use your own words whenever possible, even when you are articulating what you must clearly acknowledge to be someone else's ideas or facts.

USING SIGNAL PHRASES

Whether you quote, summarize, or paraphrase a source, always introduce source material with a signal phrase. Usually, this phrase should include the author's name. You might also include the author's title or any information about the author or source that affects its credibility or clarifies the relationship between the source's argument and your own. Titles of sources can be especially helpful when you cite more than one by the same author.

Oyin Ogunba, himself a scholar of Yoruban descent, suggests that many of Wole Soyinka's plays attempt to capture the mood and rhythm of traditional Yoruban festivals (8).	Since most of the authors cited in a literature research essay should be scholars, calling them that is usually redundant and unhelpful. Here, however, the phrase "scholar of Yoruban descent" implies that the author is doubly authoritative, since he writes about a culture he knows through both experience and study.
As historian R. K. Webb observes, "Britain is a country in miniature" (1).	In a literature research essay, most scholars you cite will be literary critics. If they aren't and it matters, identify their discipline.
In his study of the Frankenstein myth, Chris Baldick claims that "[m]ost myths, in literate societies at least, prolong their lives not by being retold at great length, but by being alluded to" (3)—a claim that definitely applies to the Othello myth.	Notice how crucial this signal phrase is to making clear that its author is applying a source's claim about one thing (myths in general and the Frankenstein myth in particular) to another, entirely different thing (the Othello myth). Such clarity is key both to accurately representing the source and to establishing the author's own originality.

If your summary goes on for more than a sentence or two, keep using signal phrases to remind readers that you're still summarizing others' ideas rather than stating your own.

The ways of interpreting Emily's decision to murder Homer are numerous. [. . .] For simple clarification, they can be summarized along two lines. One group finds the murder growing out of Emily's demented attempt to forestall the inevitable passage of time—toward her abandonment by Homer, toward her own death, and toward the steady encroachment of the North and the	In this paragraph from his essay "'We All Said, "She Will Kill Herself"': The Narrator/Detective in William Faulkner's 'A Rose for Emily,'" Lawrence R. Rodgers heads into a general summary of other critics' arguments by announcing that it's coming (*"For simple clarification, they can be summarized . . ."*). Then, as he begins summarizing each view, he reminds us that it is a "view," that

New South on something loosely defined as the "tradition" of the Old South. Another view sees the murder in more psychological terms. It grows out of Emily's complex relationship to her father, who, by elevating her above all of the eligible men of Jefferson, insured that to yield to what one commentator called the "normal emotions" associated with desire, his daughter had to "retreat into a marginal world, into fantasy" (O'Connor 184).

he's still articulating others' ideas, not his own. Notice that he only quotes "one commentator" among the many to whom he refers; the others are indicated in a footnote.

For the sake of interest and clarity, vary the content and placement of signal phrases, and always choose the most accurate verb. (*Says*, for example, implies that words are spoken, not written.) Here is a list of verbs you might find useful to describe what sources do.

acknowledges	considers	explores	maintains	sees
affirms	contends	finds	notes	shows
argues	demonstrates	identifies	observes	speculates
asks	describes	illustrates	points out	states
asserts	discusses	implies	posits	stresses
claims	draws attention to	indicates	remarks	suggests
comments	emphasizes	insists	reminds us	surmises
concludes	explains	investigates	reports	writes

33 | QUOTATION, CITATION, AND DOCUMENTATION

The bulk of any literature essay you write should consist of your own ideas expressed in your own words. Yet you can develop your ideas and persuade readers to accept them only if you present and analyze evidence. In literature essays, quotations are an especially privileged kind of evidence, though paraphrase, summary, and description also play key roles (see ch. 29 and 30.1.4). Likewise, a literature research essay, which must make use of other primary and secondary sources, typically quotes selectively from these as well (see 32.4.2). In all literature essays, then, your clarity, credibility, and persuasiveness greatly depend on two things: (1) how responsibly, effectively, and gracefully you present, differentiate, and move between others' words and ideas and your own; and (2) how careful you are to tell readers exactly where they can find each quotation and each fact or idea that you paraphrase from a source. This chapter addresses the question of *how* to quote, cite, and document sources of all kinds. (For a discussion of *when* to do so, see 30.1.4 and 32.4.1.)

Rules for quoting, citing, and documenting sources can seem daunting, even arcane or trivial. Why the heck should it matter whether you put a word in brackets or parentheses, or where in a sentence your parentheses appear? By demonstrating mastery of such conventions, you assert your credibility as a member of the scholarly community. But such conventions also serve an eminently practical purpose: They provide a system for conveying a wealth of important information clearly, concisely, and unobtrusively, with the least distraction to you and your reader.

As you probably know, there are many such systems. And different disciplines, publications, and individual instructors prefer or require different ones. In English and other humanities disciplines, however, the preferred system is that developed by the Modern Language Association (MLA) and laid out in the *MLA Handbook* (9th ed., 2021) and the *MLA Style Center* (style.mla.org). All the rules presented in this chapter accord with these two sources, which we encourage you to consult for more extensive and detailed guidance than we can provide here.

33.1 THE RULES OF RESPONSIBLE QUOTING

When it comes to quoting, there are rules that you must follow in order to be responsible both to your sources and to the integrity of your own prose. Additionally, there are certain strategies that, though not required, will help make your argument more clear, engaging, and persuasive. The next section of this chapter (33.2) discusses strategies; this one concentrates on the rules, starting with the cardinal principles of responsible quotation before turning first to those rules specific to the genres of prose, poetry, and drama and then to those rules that aren't genre specific.

33.1.1 Cardinal Principles

Three requirements so crucial to your credibility that you should regard them as cardinal principles rather than simple rules are these:

1. *A quotation means any two or more consecutive words or any one especially distinctive word or label that appears in a source.*

Representation as O'Brien practices it in this book is not a mimetic act but a "game," as Iser also calls it in a more recent essay, "The Play of the Text," a process of acting things out. . . .	In this sentence from THE UNDYING UNCERTAINTY OF THE NARRATOR IN TIM O'BRIEN'S *THE THINGS THEY CARRIED*, Steven Kaplan puts the word *game* in quotation marks because it is a key concept defined in distinctive ways in his source.

2. *Except in the few cases and specific ways outlined in the rest of this section, you must reproduce each quotation exactly as it appears in a source*, including every word and preserving original spelling, punctuation, capitalization, italics, spacing, and so on.

ORIGINAL SOURCE	INCORRECT VS. CORRECT QUOTATION
[MRS. PETERS *sits down. The two women sit there not looking at one another, but as if peering into something and at the same time holding back. When they talk now it is in the manner of feeling their way over strange ground, as if afraid of what they are saying, but as if they cannot help saying it.*]	**Incorrect:** After they discover the dead bird and the men leave the room, Mrs. Peters and Mrs. Hale simply "sit there not looking at each other," compelled to speak but also "afraid of what they are saying." **Correct:** After they discover the dead bird and the men leave the room, Mrs. Peters and Mrs. Hale simply *"sit there not looking at one another,"* compelled to speak but also *"afraid of what they are saying."*

3. *No change to a quotation, however much it accords with the rules outlined below, is acceptable if it in any way distorts the original meaning of the quoted passage.*

33.1.2 Genre-Specific Rules

Because prose, poetry, and drama each work somewhat differently, there are special rules governing how to quote texts in each of these genres. This section spells out the rules specific to prose (both fiction and nonfiction), poetry, and drama; the next section covers rules applicable to all genres.

PROSE (FICTION OR NONFICTION)

- When a quotation from a single paragraph of a prose source takes up no more than four lines of your essay, put it in quotation marks.

Georgiana's birthmark becomes "a frightful object" only because "Aylmer's somber imagination" turns it into one, "selecting it as the symbol of his wife's liability to sin, sorrow, decay, and death."

- When a prose quotation takes up more than four lines of your essay or includes a paragraph break, indent it ½ inch from the left margin to create a *block quotation*. Do not enclose the quotation in quotation marks, since these are implied by the formatting. On the rare occasions you quote more than one paragraph, reproduce any paragraph break that occurs within the quotation by indenting the first line an additional ¼ inch.

Georgiana's birthmark becomes "a frightful object" only because "Aylmer's somber imagination" turns it into a "symbol" of

> the fatal flaw of humanity which Nature, in one shape or another, stamps ineffaceably on all her productions, either to imply that they are temporary and finite, or that their perfection must be wrought by toil and pain. The crimson hand expressed the ineludible gripe in which mortality clutches the highest and purest of earthly mould. . . .

POETRY

- When quoting three or fewer **lines** of poetry, put the quotation in quotation marks. Use a slash mark (/) with a space on either side to indicate any line break that occurs in the quotation, and a double slash mark (//) to indicate a stanza break.

Before Milton's speaker can question his "Maker" for allowing him to go blind, "Patience" intervenes "to prevent / That murmur."

- When quoting more than three lines, indent the quotation ½ inch from the left margin to create a *block quotation*. Do not enclose the quotation in quotation marks, since these are implied by the formatting, but do reproduce original line and stanza breaks and the spatial arrangement of the original lines, including indentation.

Midway through the poem, the speaker suddenly shifts to second person, for the first time addressing the drowned girl directly and almost affectionately as he also begins to imagine her as a living person rather than a dead corpse:

> Little adulteress,
> before they punished you
>
> you were flaxen-haired,
> undernourished, and your
> tar-black face was beautiful.

- When a block quotation begins in the middle of a line of verse, indent the partial line as much as necessary in order to approximate its original positioning.

The speaker first demonstrates both his knowledge of persimmons and his understanding of precision by telling us exactly what ripe fruits look and smell like and then, step by careful step,

> How to eat:
> put the knife away, lay down newspaper.
> Peel the skin tenderly, not to tear the meat.
> Chew the skin, suck it,
> and swallow. Now, eat
> the meat of the fruit

- **If you omit one or more lines in the middle of a block quotation, indicate the omission with a line of spaced periods approximately the same length as a complete line of the quoted poem.**

About another image on the urn, the speaker has more questions than answers:

> Who are these coming to the sacrifice?
> To what green altar, O mysterious priest,
> Lead'st thou that heifer lowing at the skies,
> And all her silken flanks with garlands dressed?
> What little town by river or sea shore,
> . . . .
> Is emptied of its folk, this pious morn?

DRAMA

- **With one exception (covered in the next rule), a quotation from a play is governed by the same rules as outlined above under "Prose" if the quotation is in prose, under "Poetry" if in verse.**
- **Regardless of its length, if a quotation from a play includes dialogue between two or more characters, indent it ½ inch from the left margin to create a *block quotation*. Begin each character's speech with the character's name in capital letters followed by a period; indent the second and subsequent lines an additional ¼ inch. If a speech is in verse, you must also follow the applicable rules outlined in the "Poetry" section above, by reproducing original line breaks and so on (as in the second example below).**

1. Everything would be so different if Troy could just express to his son the feelings and motives he expresses in the following exchange with Rose:

> ROSE: Why don't you let the boy go ahead and play football, Troy? . . . He's
> just trying to be like you with the sports.
> TROY: I don't want him to be like me! I want him to move as far away from
> my life as he can get. You the only decent thing that ever happened to me.
> I wish him that. But I don't wish him a thing else from my life.

2. Antigone and Ismene's initial exchange climaxes with Antigone declaring her sister an "enemy," even as Ismene declares herself one of Antigone's loving "friends":

> ANTIGONE. If you will talk like this I will loathe you,
> and you will be adjudged an enemy—
> justly—by the dead's decision. Let me alone
> and my folly with me, to endure this terror.
> No suffering of mine will be enough
> to make me die ignobly.
> ISMENE. Well, if you will, go on.
> Know this; that though you are wrong to go, your friends
> are right to love you.

33.1.3 General Rules and Strategies

Unlike the rules covered in the last section, the ones laid out here apply regardless of whether you are quoting prose, poetry, or drama.

GRAMMAR, SYNTAX, TENSE, AND THE USE OF BRACKETS

- Quotations need not be complete sentences and may go anywhere in your sentence.

  1. The narrator says of Mr. Kapasi, "In his youth he'd been a devoted scholar of foreign languages" who "dreamed of being an interpreter for diplomats and dignitaries."
  2. "In his youth . . . a devoted scholar of foreign languages," says the narrator, Mr. Kapasi once "dreamed of being an interpreter for diplomats and dignitaries."

- Every sentence that includes a quotation and every quotation you present as if it is a sentence must—like every other sentence in your essay— observe all the usual rules of grammar, syntax, and consistency of tense. (In terms of these rules, words inside quotation marks don't operate any differently than do words outside of quotation marks.)

1. The woman in all the portraits is idealized. "Not as she is, but as she fills his dream."	Sentence 1 includes a quotation that is treated as a sentence but isn't one. Sentence 2 corrects that problem by using a colon to make the quoted fragment part of the preceding sentence. Yet the fragment still contains a pronoun (*his*) that lacks any clear referent in the sentence, making sentence 3 a better fix.
2. The woman in all the portraits is idealized: "Not as she is, but as she fills his dream."	
3. The woman in all the paintings is idealized, portrayed by the artist "[n]ot as she is, but as she fills his dream."	

4. As Joy waits for Manley's arrival, "She looked up and down the empty highway and had the furious feeling that she had been tricked, that he had only meant to make her walk to the gate after the idea of him" rather than the reality.	The fact that fiction typically uses past tense, while we write about it in present tense, often creates confusing tense shifts like that in sentence 4. Usually, partial paraphrase is a good solution: As in sentence 5, quote only the most essential words from the passage, remembering that what those words are will depend on the point you want to make.
5. As Joy waits for Manley's arrival, she becomes "furious," convinced that he has "tricked" her and only "meant to make her walk to the gate after the idea of him" rather than the reality.	

- When necessary to the grammar of your sentence or the intelligibility of your quotation, you may add words to the quotation or make minor changes to words within it, but you must enclose your additions or alterations in brackets ([]) to let readers know that they *are* alterations. (In sentence 3 above, for example, the first letter of the word *not* appears in brackets because a capital *N* has been changed to a lowercase *n*.)

1. As Joy waits for Manley's arrival, "She look[s] up and down the empty highway and ha[s] the furious feeling that she ha[s] been tricked, that he had only meant to make her walk to the gate after the idea of him."

This sentence demonstrates how changing verb endings and putting the new ones in brackets can solve tense shift problems of the kind found in example 4 above.

---

2. The woman in all the portraits is idealized, represented "[n]ot as she is, but as she fills his [the painter's] dream."

If a pronoun reference in a quotation is unclear, one solution is to put the noun to which the pronoun refers in brackets after the pronoun, as in this sentence. For an alternative fix, see example 3 above.

---

3. As Kelly J. Mays explains, writers "can assume that their readers will recognize the traditional meanings of these ["traditional"] symbols," but "invented symbols" work differently.

In this sentence, the phrase "these symbols" refers to something outside the quoted sentence. The added and thus bracketed word *traditional* appears in quotation marks because it, too, comes directly from the same source.

> **Tip:** Though such alterations are permissible, they are often so much less effective than other techniques that some of them (including changes to verb endings) are not actually mentioned in the *MLA Handbook*. Used too often, this technique can become distracting and put you at risk of appearing as if you're "fiddling" with sources. To avoid this, look for other fixes whenever possible.

OMISSIONS AND ELLIPSES

- A quotation that is obviously a sentence fragment need not be preceded or followed by an ellipsis (. . .). But you must use an ellipsis whenever
  —your quotation appears to be a complete sentence but actually isn't one in the source (as in the first sentence in the example below),
  —you omit words from the middle of a quoted sentence (as in the second sentence in the example below), or
  —you omit one or more sentences between quoted sentences (as between the second and third sentences in the example below).

When the ellipsis coincides with the end of your sentence, add a period followed by an ellipsis (as in the first sentence below).

The narrator says of Mr. Kapasi,

> In his youth he'd been a devoted scholar of foreign languages. . . . He had dreamed of being an interpreter for diplomats and dignitaries, . . . settling disputes of which he alone could understand both sides. . . . Now only a handful of European phrases remained in his memory, scattered words for things like saucers and chairs.

> **Tip:** If you omit the end of a sentence *and* one or more of the sentences that immediately follow it, the four dots are sufficient; you do not need two ellipses.

- If the quoted source uses an ellipsis, put your ellipsis in brackets to distinguish between the two. [NOTE: Throughout this book, we have instead put *every* added ellipsis in brackets.]

As an excited Ruth explains, the prospect of receiving a check is "a whole lot different from having it come and being able to hold it in your hands . . . a piece of paper worth ten thousand dollars." "[. . .] I wish Walter Lee was here!," she exclaims.	The first (unbracketed) ellipsis here occurs in the original source; the second (bracketed) ellipsis doesn't.

OTHER ACCEPTABLE CHANGES TO QUOTATIONS: *SIC* AND *EMPHASIS*

- If a quotation includes what is or might seem to your reader an error of fact or of grammar, spelling, and so on, you may signal to the reader that you haven't introduced the error yourself by putting the word *sic* (Latin for "thus" or "so") next to the error. Put parentheses around *sic* if it comes *after* the quotation (as in the first example below), brackets if it appears *within* the quotation (as in the second example). Do not use *sic* if context makes it obvious that the error isn't yours or isn't truly an error, as in the case of texts featuring archaic spelling, dialect, and so on.

1. Shaw admitted, "Nothing can extinguish my interest in Shakespear" (sic).	In sentence 1 (from the *MLA Handbook*) parentheses work because nothing has been added *into* the quotation; the second, slightly modified sentence requires brackets. Either way, the word *sic* appears next to the misspelled word and is not italicized.
2. In the preface to *Shakes versus Shav: A Puppet Play* (1949), Shaw avows, "Nothing can extinguish my interest in Shakespear [sic]. It began when I was a small boy. . . ."	
3. Charley gets to the heart of the matter when he asks Willy, "when're you gonna realize that them things don't mean anything?"	*Sic* would be inappropriate here, since it's clear this quotation accurately reproduces the character's speech patterns.
4. The Misfit firmly rejects the idea that he should pray, insisting, "I don't want no hep" (sic), "I'm doing all right by myself."	In this case, though use of the word *hep* (for *help*) is entirely characteristic of the character's speech, it could so easily look like a typo that the word *sic* seems helpful.

- On the rare occasions when you need to emphasize a specific word or phrase within a quotation, you may put it in italics and indicate this change by putting the phrase *emphasis added* or *my emphasis* in parentheses after the quotation, ideally at the end of the clause or sentence.

Avowing that men "must help them [women] to stay in that beautiful world of their own, *lest ours get worse*" (emphasis added), Marlow acknowledges that men have a selfish interest in preserving women's innocence and idealism.

PUNCTUATING QUOTATIONS

• Though you must always reproduce original punctuation *within* a quotation, you may *end* a quotation with whatever punctuation your sentence requires, and this is one change you do not need to indicate with brackets.

1. Whether portrayed as "queen," "saint," or "angel," the same "nameless girl" appears in "all his canvases."	In the poem quoted here, no commas appear after the words *queen* and *angel*, but the syntax of the sentence requires that they be added. Similarly, the comma that appears after the word *canvases* in the poem is here replaced by a period.
2. The narrator tells us that Mr. Kapasi's "job was a sign of his failings," for "[i]n his youth he'd been a devoted scholar of foreign languages" who "dreamed of being an interpreter for diplomats and dignitaries."	Here, a comma replaces the original period after *failings*, and a period replaces the original comma after *dignitaries.*

• Commas and periods belong *inside* the closing quotation mark (as in the above examples). All other punctuation marks belong *outside* the closing quotation mark if they are your additions (as in the first and second examples below), inside if they are not (as in the third example below).

1. Wordsworth calls nature a "homely Nurse"; she has "something of a Mother's mind."
2. What exactly does Lili mean when she tells Guy, "You are here to protect me if anything happens"?
3. Bobby Lee speaks volumes about the grandmother when he says, "She was a talker, wasn't she?"

• When your indented block quotation includes a quotation, put the latter in double quotation marks (" ").

Written just four years after *A Raisin in the Sun*'s debut, Martin Luther King, Jr.'s "Letter from Birmingham Jail" stresses the urgency of the situation of African Americans like the Youngers by comparing it to those of Africans like Joseph Asagai:

> We have waited for more than 340 years for our constitutional and God-given rights. The nations of . . . Africa are moving with jetlike speed toward gaining political independence, but we still creep at horse-and-buggy pace toward gaining a cup of coffee at a lunch counter. Perhaps it is easy for those who have never felt the stinging darts of segregation to say, "Wait."

• When a shorter (non-block) quotation includes a quotation, put the latter in single quotation marks (' ').

1. As Martin Luther King, Jr., insisted in 1963, "it is easy for those who have never felt the stinging darts of segregation," or the "degenerating sense of 'nobodiness'" it instills, "to say, 'Wait,'" be patient, your time will come.
2. In a poem less about Hard Rock himself than about the way he is perceived by his fellow inmates, it makes sense that many words and lines take the form of unattributed quotations, as in the unforgettable opening, "Hard Rock was 'known not to take no shit / From nobody.'"

- When your quotation consists *entirely* of words that appear within quotation marks in the source, use double quotation marks, while introducing the quotation in a way that makes the special status of these words and their provenance clear.

  1. "[K]nown not to take no shit / From nobody," as his fellow inmates put it, Hard Rock initially appears almost superhuman.
  2. The Misfit's response is as shocking as it is simple: "I don't want no hep," "I'm doing all right by myself."
  3. In an introductory note quoted by Alvarez, Plath describes the poem's speaker as "a girl with an Electra complex" whose "father died while she thought he was God."

33.2 STRATEGIES FOR EFFECTIVE QUOTING

- Though it is not a rule that all of your quotations must appear inside one of your sentences, your clarity will be greatly enhanced if you treat it like one, making the connection between quotation and inference as seamless as possible.

  1. Smith is highly critical of O'Brien's portrayal of Martha. "Like other women in the book, she represents all those back home who will never understand the warrior's trauma."

  2. Smith is highly critical of O'Brien's portrayal of Martha: "Like other women in the book, she represents all those back home who will never understand the warrior's trauma."

  3. Smith is highly critical of O'Brien's portrayal of Martha, claiming that, "[l]ike other women in the book," Martha "represents all those back home who will never understand the warrior's trauma."

  Example 1 includes a quotation that isn't part of any sentence. Example 2 corrects that problem with a colon, but the reader still has to pause to figure out that it's Smith who's being quoted here and that the quotation refers to Martha. Sentence 3 thus offers a better solution.

- Avoid drawing attention to your evidence as evidence with "filler" phrases such as *This statement is proof that* . . . ; *This phrase is significant because* . . . ; *This idea is illustrated by* . . . ; *There is good evidence for this.* . . . Explain *how* and *why* facts are meaningful or interesting rather than saying *that* they are.

INEFFECTIVE QUOTATION	EFFECTIVE QUOTATION
Wordsworth calls nature a "homely Nurse" and says that she has "something of a Mother's mind." This diction supports the idea that he sees nature as a healing, maternal force. He is saying that nature heals and cares for us.	Personifying nature as a "homely Nurse" with "something of a Mother's mind," Wordsworth depicts nature as healing and nurturing the humans it also resembles. OR

	A "homely Nurse" with "something of a Mother's mind," nature, implies Wordsworth, both heals and nurtures the humans it also resembles.
Tennyson advocates decisive action, even as he highlights the forces that often prohibited his contemporaries from taking it. This is suggested by the lines "Made weak by time and fate, but strong in will, / To strive, to seek, to find, and not to yield."	Tennyson advocates forceful action, encouraging his contemporaries "To strive, to seek, to find, and not to yield." Yet he recognizes that his generation is more tempted to "yield" than earlier ones because they have been "Made weak by time and fate."

- On the one hand, make sure that you provide readers the information they need to understand a quotation and to appreciate its relevance to your argument. Quite often, contextual information—for instance, about who's speaking to whom and in what situation—is crucial to a quotation's meaning. On the other hand, keep such contextual information to a minimum and put the emphasis on the words that really matter and on your inferences about why and how they matter.

1. Strong as Mama is, she and Walter share a similar, traditional vision of gender roles: "I'm telling you to be the head of this family . . . like you supposed to be"; "the colored woman" should be "building their men up and making 'em feel like they somebody."	
2. Strong as Mama is, she shares Walter's traditional vision of gender roles. When she urges him "to be the head of this family from now on like you supposed to be," she affirms that her son is the family's rightful leader—not her daughter, not her daughter-in-law, not even herself, despite her seniority. Implicitly, she's also doing what Walter elsewhere says "the colored woman" should do—"building their men up and making 'em feel like they somebody."	Example 2 is more effective because it offers crucial information about who is speaking to whom (*"When she urges him," "Walter elsewhere says"*) and includes inferences (*"she affirms that her son is the family's rightful leader . . ."; "Implicitly, she's also doing"*). Purely contextual information is, however, stated briefly and early, in subordinate clauses.

3. Julian expresses disgust for the class distinctions so precious to his mother: "Rolling his eyes upward, he put his tie back on. 'Restored to my class,' he muttered."	
4. Julian professes disgust for the class distinctions so precious to his mother. At her request, he puts back on his tie, but he can't do so without "[r]olling his eyes" and making fun (at least under his breath) of the idea that he is thereby "[r]estored to [his] class."	Again, example 4 improves on example 3 by providing missing information (*"At her request"*), yet paraphrasing and subordinating what is only information (*"he puts back on his tie"*).

- Lead your readers into long quotations—especially block quotations—with a clear sense of just what in the quotation they should be paying attention to and why. Follow it up with at least a sentence or more of analysis/inferences, perhaps repeating especially key words and phrases from the long quotation.

> Whereas the second stanza individualizes the dead martyrs, the third considers the characteristics they shared with each other and with all those who dedicate themselves utterly to one cause:
>> Hearts with one purpose alone
>> Through summer and winter seem
>> Enchanted to a stone
>> To trouble the living stream.
> Whereas all other "living" people and things are caught up in the "stream" of change represented by the shift of seasons, those who fill their "[h]earts with one purpose alone" become as hard, unchanging, and immovable as stone.

- Though long quotations—including block quotations—can be effective, they should be used sparingly and strategically. All too easily, they can create information overload for readers, making it hard to see what is most significant and why. When you quote only individual words or short phrases, weaving them into your sentences in the ways demonstrated earlier in this section, you and your readers can more easily stay focused on what's significant and on *why* and *how* it is.
- Vary the length of quotations and the way you present them. It can be very tempting to fall into a pattern—always, for example, choosing quotations that are at least a sentence long and attaching them to your sentence with a colon. But overusing *any* one technique can easily render your essay monotonous and might even prompt readers to focus more on the (repetitive) way you present evidence than on the evidence and argument themselves. To demonstrate, here are two sets of sentences that present the same material in varying ways.

1. According to Wordsworth, nature is a "homely Nurse" with "something of a Mother's mind"; it heals and nurtures the humans it also resembles.

2. A "homely Nurse" with "something of a Mother's mind," nature, suggests Wordsworth, both heals and nurtures the humans it also resembles.

3. Personifying nature as a "homely Nurse" with "something of a Mother's mind," Wordsworth depicts nature as healing and nurturing the humans it also resembles.

4. Healing and nurturing the humans it also resembles, Wordsworth's nature is a "homely Nurse" with "something of a Mother's mind."

---

1. Howe insists that the poem's "personal-confessional element . . . is simply too obtrusive," "strident and undisciplined," to allow a reader to interpret "Daddy" "as a dramatic presentation, a monologue spoken by a disturbed girl not necessarily to be identified with Sylvia Plath," especially given the resemblances between "events" described in the poem and those that actually occurred in Plath's life.

2. "Daddy," argues Howe, cannot be read "as a dramatic presentation, a monologue spoken by a disturbed girl not necessarily to be identified with Sylvia Plath." Its "personal-confessional element . . . is simply too obtrusive," too

"strident and undisciplined," he reasons, while the "events of the poem" too closely correspond to "the events of her life."

33.3 CITATION AND DOCUMENTATION

In addition to indicating which words, facts, and ideas in your essay derive from sources, you must let your readers know where each can be found. You want to enable readers not only to "check up" on you but also to follow in your footsteps and build on your work. After all, you hope that your analysis of a text will entice readers to re-read certain passages from the text in a different way or to consult other sources that you've made sound interesting. This is another way your essay contributes to keeping the conversation about literature going. And this is where citation and documentation come into play.

In the MLA system, parenthetical citations embedded in your essay are keyed to an alphabetized list of works cited that follows your essay. By virtue of both their content and placement, parenthetical citations help you to quickly, unobtrusively indicate *what* you have derived from *which* source and *where* in that source your readers can find that material. The list of works cited communicates the information about the source that your readers need both to find it themselves and, in the meantime, to begin evaluating its relevance, credibility, currency, and so on *without* having to find it.

To demonstrate how this works, here is a typical sentence with parenthetical citation, followed by the coordinating works-cited entry:

In-Text Citation

In one critic's view, "Freeway 280" "provides an image of 'persistence,' of the continued existence of cultural differences within and despite oppressive and hostile conditions" (Hamilton 46).

Placed at the end of the sentence and beginning with the word *Hamilton* (sans quotation marks or italics) and the number 46, this parenthetical citation tells us that the last name of the "critic" the sentence mentions and quotes is Hamilton, that the source of the quotation is something he or she authored, and that the quotation comes from page 46 of that source. To find out more, we have to turn to the list of works cited and look for an entry, like the following, that begins with the name Hamilton.

Works-Cited Entry

Hamilton, Patrick L. *Of Space and Mind: Cognitive Mappings of Contemporary Chicano/a Fiction.* U of Texas P, 2011.

This coordinating works-cited entry gives us Hamilton's complete name as it appears in the source and indicates the source's title, publisher, and date of publication. By its format, the entry also tells us that the source is a printed book.

That our explanations of this sample parenthetical citation and works-cited entry take up much more space than the citation and entry themselves demonstrates the value of the MLA system. This example also demonstrates the importance of the placement and content of each citation and entry: Where the parenthetical citation falls in a sentence is key to clearly indicating what is being "sourced"; what the parenthetical citation and works-cited entry include and in what order are all key to ensuring that the citation leads us seamlessly to *one* source in the works cited and tells us where to look in that source.

The exact content and placement of each parenthetical citation and works-cited entry will thus depend on a host of factors. The next sections explain how this works.

33.3.1 Parenthetical Citation

THE STANDARD PARENTHETICAL CITATION: CONTENT AND PLACEMENT

Because lists of works cited are organized primarily by author or creator, the standard MLA parenthetical citation looks like, and appears in the same place as, the ones in the sample sentences above and below. It includes an author or creator's name and a page number or numbers with nothing but a space in between. (Do not write *page* or *p.*, for example, or insert a comma.) The citation comes at the end of a sentence—*inside* the period (because it is part of the sentence in which you borrow from a source) and *outside* any quotation marks within the sentence (since it is *not* part of an actual quotation; it is not *in* the source but provides information *about* the source). In keeping with the rules for punctuating quotations laid out earlier in this chapter (33.1.3), you omit any final punctuation mark within your quotation, as in the second example below.

1. Most domestic poems of the 1950s foreground the parent-child relationship (Axelrod 1179).
2. As a character in one of the most famous works of Southern fiction memorably declares of the South, "I dont [sic] hate it" (Faulkner 378).

When citing a work from an anthology, refer to the author of the work, not the anthology editor, and create a corresponding entry in your list of works cited. Below is an example of this kind of citation, followed by the corresponding works-cited entry.

In-Text Citation

The story focuses on what Gan calls his "last night of childhood" (Butler 335).

Works-Cited Entry

Butler, Octavia. "Bloodchild." *The Norton Introduction to Literature*, edited by Kelly J. Mays, shorter 14th ed., W. W. Norton, 2021, pp. 335–49.

The next two sections detail the variations on the standard MLA parenthetical citation format, starting with variations in *where* the citation goes before turning to variations in *what* it includes.

VARIATIONS IN PLACEMENT

- In the case of a block quotation, the parenthetical citation should immediately *follow* (not precede) the punctuation mark that ends the quotation.

According to the narrator,

> The job was a sign of his failings. In his youth he'd been a devoted scholar of foreign languages, the owner of an impressive collection of dictionaries. He had dreamed of being an interpreter for diplomats and dignitaries, resolving conflicts between people and nations, settling disputes of which he alone could understand both sides. (Lahiri 475)

- If a sentence either incorporates material from multiple sources (as in the first example below) or refers both to something from a source and to your own idea (as in the second example), put the appropriate parenthetical citation in midsentence next to the material to which it refers. Ideally, you should insert the citation before a comma or semicolon, since it will be less obtrusive that way. But your first priority should be clarity about which material comes from which source (see the third example below).

1. Critics describe Caliban as a creature with an essentially "unalterable natur[e]" (Garner 458), "incapable of comprehending the good or of learning from the past" (Peterson 442), "impervious to genuine moral improvement" (Wright 451).
2. If Caliban is truly "incapable of . . . learning from the past" (Peterson 442), then how do we explain the changed attitude he demonstrates at play's end?
3. Tanner (7) and Smith (viii) have looked at works from a cultural perspective.

- If, in a single paragraph, you make several *uninterrupted* references to the same source and especially to the same passage in a source, you may save the parenthetical citation until after the last such reference, as in the following sentences from Susan Farrell's TIM O'BRIEN AND GENDER: A DEFENSE OF *THE THINGS THEY CARRIED*.

> Smith connects a 1980s backlash against the feminist movement to the misogyny she reads in Vietnam War literature, a misogyny which she describes as "very visible," as seemingly "natural and expected." In popular representations, Smith argues, the "Vietnam War is being reconstructed as a site where white American manhood—figuratively as well as literally wounded during the war and assaulted by the women's movement for twenty years—can reassert its dominance in the social hierarchy" ("Back" 115).

VARIATIONS IN CONTENT: IDENTIFYING THE SOURCE

The standard MLA parenthetical citation may contain the author's name and the relevant page number(s). But variations are the rule when it comes to content. In this section, we deal with variations in how a citation indicates *which* source you refer to; the next section instead covers variations in how you indicate *where* in the source borrowed material can be found.

Your parenthetical citation should include something instead of or in addition to one author or creator's name whenever you do the following:

- *Name the author(s) or creator(s) in your text.*
  Parenthetical citations should include only information that isn't crucial to the intelligibility and credibility of your argument. Yet in most cases, information about *whose* ideas, data, or words you cite is crucial. As a result, you should try whenever possible to indicate this in your text, usually via a *signal phrase* (as

described in 32.4.2). When you do so, your parenthetical citation usually need only include location information such as page number(s).

1. According to Patrick L. Hamilton, "Freeway 280" is only one of many Chicano/a literary works emphasizing "persistence" over resistance (46).
2. Admitting that he is "out of touch" and "ignorant" about jazz, Baldwin's narrator asks his brother "to be patient" (102).

> **TIP:** In literature essays, parenthetical citations containing the name of the author whose work you are analyzing should be relatively rare. (Notice that there are none, for example, in any of the critical excerpts on Tim O'Brien's THE THINGS THEY CARRIED found in ch. 10.)

- *Cite a source with multiple authors or creators.*
If the source has two authors or creators, and they are not named in your text, the parenthetical citation should include both last names (as in the example below). If the source has three or more authors or creators, include the first author's name followed by the words *et al.* (abbreviated Latin for "and others").

Surprisingly, "it seems not to have been primarily the coarseness and sexuality of *Jane Eyre* which shocked Victorian reviewers" so much as its "rebellious feminism" (Gilbert and Gubar 338).

- *Cite multiple works by the same author/creator or an anonymous work.*
In either of these cases, you will need to indicate the title of your source. If possible, do so in your text, putting only location information in the parenthetical citation (as in the first example below). Otherwise, your parenthetical citation must include a shortened version of the title (as in the second example below). If your parenthetical citation also needs to include the author or creator's name(s), this comes first, followed by a comma, the shortened title, and the location information (as in the third example below).

1. Like Joy in O'Connor's "Good Country People," the protagonist of her story "Everything That Rises Must Converge" takes enormous pride in his intellect, even believing himself "too intelligent to be a success" (527).
2. Many of O'Connor's most faulty characters put enormous stock in their intellects, one even secretly believing himself "too intelligent to be a success" ("Everything" 527).
3. Intellectuals fare poorly in much Southern fiction. When we learn that the protagonist of one short story secretly believes himself "too intelligent to be a success," we can be pretty sure that he's in for a fall (O'Connor, "Everything" 527).

Be sure to format shortened titles just as you do full titles, either putting them in quotation marks or italicizing them, as appropriate (see 31.5).

- *Cite multiple authors or creators with the same last name.*
In this case, you should ideally indicate the author or creator's full name in the text so that your parenthetical citation need only include location information. Otherwise, the parenthetical citation should begin with the author or creator's first initial followed by a period, followed by his or her last name and the location information (as in the first example below). If your authors or creators share the same first initial, however, you will need to include a first name instead (as in the second example).

1. As one of Joyce's fellow writers points out, "To be absolutely faithful to what one sees and hears and not to speculate on what may lie behind it . . . is a creed that produces obvious limitations" (F. O'Connor 188).

2. As one of Flannery O'Connor's fellow short-story writers points out, "To be absolutely faithful to what one sees and hears and not to speculate on what may lie behind it . . . is a creed that produces obvious limitations" (Frank O'Connor 188).

• *Cite multiple authors or creators simultaneously.*
In this case, include all the citations within a single set of parentheses, separating them with semicolons.

Many scholars attribute Caliban's bestiality to a seemingly innate inability to learn or change (Garner 438; Peterson 442; Wright 451).

• *Quote a source quoted in another source.*
You should quote from an original source whenever possible. But on the rare occasions when you quote something quoted in another source, indicate the original source in your text. Then start your parenthetical citation with the abbreviation *qtd. in* followed by the name of the secondhand source's author and the location information.

In an introductory note to "Daddy" that Plath wrote for a radio program, she describes the poem's speaker as "a girl with an Electra complex" (qtd. in Alvarez 1166).

VARIATIONS IN CONTENT: INDICATING A LOCATION WITHIN THE SOURCE

Though page numbers are the usual means by which we indicate where in a source a reader can find the ideas, information, or words we cite, there are exceptions. Indeed, exceptions are unusually frequent in literature essays. The most important reason for this is that literary texts tend to be available in different editions, so it's helpful to give readers the information they need to locate material in the text regardless of the edition they use.

When it comes to the question of how to do so, there is some ambiguity and wiggle room in the MLA guidelines. Thus, as we explain below, different instructors may interpret some of these guidelines differently or simply prefer that you use one method rather than another.

Your parenthetical citation will generally need to include location information other than, or in addition to, a page number whenever you cite any of the following:

• *Poetry*
When citing poetry, it is customary to refer to line (not page) number(s) and to indicate that you are doing so by including the word *line* or *lines*, as appropriate, in your first such parenthetical citation. Though MLA guidelines stipulate that later parenthetical citations may include only the line number (as in the example below), some instructors prefer that the word *line* or *lines* appear in every poem-related parenthetical citation. And this practice can be especially helpful when your sources include prose as well as poetry.

In a poem less about Hard Rock himself than about the way he is perceived by his fellow inmates, it makes sense that many words and lines take the form of unattributed quotations, as in the unforgettable opening, "Hard Rock was 'known not to take no shit / From nobody'" (lines 1-2), or "'Yeah, remember when he / Smacked the captain with his dinner tray?'" (17-18).

• *Play with more than one act or scene*
At least when it comes to canonical plays, MLA guidelines call for omitting page numbers and referring instead to act, scene, and line numbers, as appropriate, always using arabic numerals (*1, 2,* etc.), and separating each with a period (as in the first example below). Some instructors, however, prefer that you use roman numerals (*I, II, i, ii,* etc.) for acts and scenes (as in the second example below).

1. "I know not 'seems,'" Hamlet famously declares (1.2.76).
2. "I know not 'seems,'" Hamlet famously declares (I.ii.76).

• *Commonly studied work of fiction or nonfiction prose*
Parenthetical citations of this kind should always include page numbers unless your instructor indicates otherwise. But you may also need to include additional location information. If so, the page number comes first, followed by a semicolon and the additional information. Use common abbreviations to indicate what this information is (e.g., *vol.* for *volume, bk.* for *book, sec.* for *section*), and use arabic numerals (*1, 2,* etc.), even if the text uses roman numerals (*I, II,* etc.). (The second example below is quoted directly from the *MLA Handbook.*)

1. "I learned," explains Frankenstein's creature, "that the possessions most esteemed by your fellow-creatures were, high and unsullied descent united with riches" (96; vol. 2, ch. 5).
2. In *A Vindication of the Rights of Woman*, Mary Wollstonecraft recollects many "women who, not led by degrees to proper studies, and not permitted to choose for themselves, have indeed been overgrown children" (185; ch. 13, sec. 2).

• *Works in which paragraphs are numbered*
When you cite prose works from an anthology like this one, in which paragraphs are numbered, your instructor may prefer that you cite paragraph numbers, using the appropriate abbreviation (*par.*). If you include both page and paragraph number, insert a semicolon after the page number (as in the first example below). If your parenthetical citations include only paragraph numbers, your instructor may allow you to omit the abbreviation *par.* from the second and subsequent such citations (as in the second example).

1. When they meet years later in the supermarket, Roberta's "lovely and summery and rich" appearance leaves the narrator not only "dying to know" how this transformation came about but also resentful of Roberta and people like her: "Everything is so easy for them," she thinks (224; par. 68).
2. Though "dying to know" just how Roberta came to be so "lovely and summery and rich" since they last met (par. 68), all the narrator initially asks is, "How long have you been here?" (69).

• *Multiple volumes of a multivolume work*
If you cite material from more than one volume of a multivolume work, your parenthetical citation must indicate both volume and page numbers. Put the volume number first, followed by a colon, a space, and the page number(s). Though page numbers should take the same form they do in the source (e.g.,

11 or *xi*), volume numbers should always be in Arabic numerals (*1, 2, 3*). (The following example comes from the *MLA Handbook*.)

"The contributions to criticism of semantics, sociology, psychoanalysis, and anthropology are largely new," writes Wellek, acknowledging that the problems addressed by criticism in the modern era have historical specificity, too (1: 5). Ultimately, he asserts, "An evolutionary history of criticism must fail. I have come to this resigned conclusion" (5: xxii).

If you cite material from only one volume of a multivolume work, omit the volume number from your parenthetical citations, since it will be included in your works-cited entry.

- *Scripture*
When citing scripture such as the Bible or the Quran, indicate either in your text or in your parenthetical citation the title, editor, or translator of the edition you're using on the first occasion you cite it. Then include in your parenthetical citation(s) the book, chapter, and verse (or their equivalent), separated by periods, unless you have indicated these in your text. (Either way, do not include page numbers.) Abbreviate the names of the books of the Bible, but don't put these abbreviations in quotation marks or italicize them. (The second example below is quoted directly from the *MLA Handbook*.)

1. *The New English Bible* version of the verse reads, "In the beginning of creation, when God made heaven and earth, the earth was without form and void, with darkness over the face of the abyss, and a mighty wind that swept over the surface of the waters" (Gen. 1.1-2).
2. In one of the most vivid prophetic visions in the Bible, Ezekiel saw "what seemed to be four living creatures" (*New Jerusalem Bible*, Ezek. 1.5). John of Patmos echoes this passage when describing his vision (Rev. 4.6-8).

- *An entire source, a source without pagination or numbered pages, a source that is only one page long, and some e-books*
When you refer in a blanket way to an entire source rather than to something particular in it, or to a source that lacks numbered pages, your parenthetical citation will include no page numbers. The same is true of one-page sources, since your works-cited entry will include the page number. If you clearly identify such sources in your text, you won't need a parenthetical citation at all (as in the first example below). Otherwise, your citation will include only author or creator's name(s) (as in the second example) and/or a shortened title.

1. Many critics, including Maurice Bowra, see Creon as morally inferior to Antigone.
2. Where some critics see the play as siding unequivocally with Antigone (Bowra), others see it as more ambivalent and/or ambiguous on this score (Nussbaum).

However, if a source lacking numbered pages has other numbered divisions such as sections or paragraphs, your parenthetical citation will need to include these: Use Arabic numerals (e.g., *1, 2, 3*), regardless of what kind the source uses, and introduce them with the appropriate abbreviation (e.g., *sec.* or *secs.*, *par.* or *pars.*, *ch.* or *chs.*). If your parenthetical citation also includes author name(s) and/or short title, use a comma to separate these from your location information.

Because e-books are formatted differently on different devices, chapters or other numbered divisions, where possible, should be used in citations instead of page numbers, as in the following example from the *MLA Handbook*:

"What is it about us human beings that we can't let go of lost things?" asks the author (Silko, ch. 2).

OTHER VARIATIONS IN CONTENT: *SIC* AND *EMPHASIS*

When a parenthetical citation intervenes between the end of a quotation that you need to follow with *sic* or an indication of added emphasis (for the reasons outlined in 33.1.3), it's usually advisable to put *sic* in brackets within the quotation, next to the error to which it applies (as in the first example below), but to put *emphasis added* at the end of the parenthetical citation, preceding it with a semicolon (as in the second example).

1. Shaw admitted, "Nothing can extinguish my interest in Shakespear [sic]" (1).
2. Avowing that men "must help them [women] to stay in that beautiful world of their own, *lest ours get worse*" (1196; emphasis added), Marlow acknowledges that men have a selfish interest in preserving women's innocence and idealism.

33.3.2 The List of Works Cited

Your list of works cited must include all, and only, the sources that you cite in your essay, providing full publication information about each. This section explains both how to format and organize the list and how to assemble each entry in it.

FORMATTING THE LIST

Your list of works cited should begin on a separate page after the conclusion of your essay. Center the heading *Works Cited* (without quotation marks or italics) at the top of the first page, and double-space throughout.

The first line of each entry should begin at the left margin; the second and subsequent lines should be indented ½ inch.

Your list should be alphabetized, ignoring articles (such as *A*, *An*, *The*) in titles when an entry lacks an author and therefore begins with the title.

If your list includes multiple works by the same author, begin the first entry with the author's name, and then begin each subsequent entry with three hyphens followed by a period. Alphabetize these entries by title, again ignoring articles (*A*, *An*, *The*).

Works Cited

Canby, Vincent. "Film: 'Smooth Talk,' from Joyce Carol Oates Tale." *The New York Times*, 28 Feb. 1986, www.nytimes.com/1986/02/28/movies/film-smooth-talk -from-joyce-carol-oates-tale.html.

Daly, Brenda O. "An Unfilmable Conclusion: Joyce Carol Oates at the Movies." *The Journal of Popular Culture*, vol. 23, no. 3, winter 1989, pp. 101-14. *Periodicals Archive Online*, ezproxy.library.unlv.edu/login?url=http://search.proquest.com /docview/1297343870?accountid=3611.

Dylan, Bob. "It's All Over Now, Baby Blue." *Bob Dylan*, Sony Music Entertainment, 1965. bobdylan.com/songs/its-all-over-now-baby-blue/.

Lupack, Barbara Tepa. "Smoothing Out the Rough Spots: The Film Adaptation of 'Where Are You Going, Where Have You Been?'" *Vision/Revision: Adapting Contemporary American Fiction by Women to Film*, edited by Lupack, Bowling Green State U Popular P, 1996, pp. 85-100.

Oates, Joyce Carol. "Where Are You Going, Where Have You Been?" 1966. *The Norton Introduction to Literature,* edited by Kelly J. Mays, shorter 14th ed., W. W. Norton, 2021, pp. 94-106.

---. "'Where Are You Going, Where Have You Been?' and *Smooth Talk*: Short Story into Film." *(Woman) Writer: Occasions and Opportunities,* Dutton, 1988, pp. 316-21.

Smooth Talk. Directed by Joyce Chopra, American Playhouse, 1985.

FORMATTING INDIVIDUAL ENTRIES—GENERAL PRINCIPLES

Though many sources, especially those online, as well as bibliographic programs such as *RefWorks* and *EndNote*, will create or model works-cited entries for you, they can rarely be trusted to get the format exactly right, especially given recent changes to the MLA system. As a result, you should always double-check such entries against the guidelines in this chapter and revise accordingly.

In general, all information in a works-cited entry should come from the source itself. The names of authors or other creators and contributors, for example, should typically appear in your entry just as they do on the title page (if your source is a book); in a byline (if your source is a periodical article or web page); or in the credits (if your source is a film or television series). There are a few exceptions, however— for instance, if you are citing multiple works by the same author, and the author uses different names for those works, you might choose to cite them all under one name for clarity. And if you are citing a work by an author whose name has since changed and the author no longer uses the old name, you should cite the work under the name the author currently uses without reference to the old one. (MLA also gives you the option of providing especially important information missing from a source; on how to do so correctly, see below, "Formatting Individual Entries— Additional Options.")

Many sources do not stand on their own but are instead produced or experienced as part of larger wholes—or what MLA calls *containers.* If you cite an article in a journal or newspaper, for example, the article is your source; the journal or newspaper is its container (as in the first example below). If you cite part of a website, the part is your source; the website is the container (as in the second example below). If you cite a poem, story, or play from this anthology, the poem, story, or play is your source; the anthology is its container (as in the third example below).

In works-cited entries, the title of a container is italicized and followed by a comma and then by all other required pieces of information about that container, separated from each other by commas, with a period following the last piece (to signal that you've gotten to the end of the information about that container). In the following examples from our sample works cited, container titles are highlighted:

Article in an Online Newspaper

Canby, Vincent. "Film: 'Smooth Talk,' from Joyce Carol Oates Tale." *The New York Times,* 28 Feb. 1986, www.nytimes.com/1986/02/28/movies/film-smooth-talk -from-joyce-carol-oates-tale.html.

Part of a Website

Dylan, Bob. "It's All Over Now, Baby Blue." *Bob Dylan,* Sony Music Entertainment, 1965, bobdylan.com/songs/its-all-over-now-baby-blue/.

Short Story in an Anthology

Oates, Joyce Carol. "Where Are You Going, Where Have You Been?" *The Norton Introduction to Literature*, edited by Kelly J. Mays, shorter 14th ed., W. W. Norton, 2021, pp. 94-106.

Any one source may be contained within multiple containers, nested one inside the other. If you access your journal article in an online database such as *JSTOR* or on a website such as *Google Books*, for example, the article has two containers: 1) the journal containing the article and 2) the database or website containing the journal. *Works-cited entries need to include the titles of, and relevant publication and location information for, all containers*, as in the example below (in which container titles are again highlighted):

Article in a Journal Contained in a Database

Daly, Brenda O. "An Unfilmable Conclusion: Joyce Carol Oates at the Movies." *The Journal of Popular Culture*, vol. 23, no. 3, winter 1989, pp. 101-14. *Periodicals Archive Online*, ezproxy.library.unlv.edu/login?url=http://search.proquest.com /docview/1297343870?accountid=3611.

Any one work can potentially be either a source or a container or both, depending on whether you cite the entire work or only part of it. To take a common example, if you cite in your essay both Ralph Ellison's novel *Invisible Man* and an editor's introduction to it, then your works cited should include entries for both: In one, the book *Invisible Man* would be the source (as in the first entry below); in the other, the same book would be the container of the source, which is the editor's introduction (as in the second entry below).

Print Book

Ellison, Ralph. *Invisible Man*. Penguin, 2001.

Untitled Introduction to a Print Book

Callahan, John. Introduction. *Invisible Man*, by Ralph Ellison, Penguin, 2001, pp. ix-xxiv.

FORMATTING INDIVIDUAL ENTRIES—CORE, REQUIRED ELEMENTS

Works-cited entries include up to nine core elements, one of which is the container title. Generally speaking, these appear in the following order:

1 creator(s), usually author(s)
2 source title and/or description of source
3 container title
4 contributor(s)
5 version
6 number
7 publisher
8 publication date
9 location.

These core elements are *required* elements: Each of them *must* be included when it is relevant and available for a given source or container because it is crucial to identifying that source or container. Yet not all core elements will *always* be relevant or available: If a source or container exists in only one version, for example, you need not include the "version" element; if its publication date isn't known, you may omit that element; and so on.

In addition to core, required elements, works-cited entries may include various optional elements. In the next section, we turn to the most important of these, as well as one optional shortcut especially useful in literature essays. In the rest of this section, we introduce the remaining eight core elements by means of the crucial questions they answer rather than in the order they appear in the entry.

WHO made it?

1. **CREATOR(S):** Except in three cases (specified below), all works-cited entries begin with the name of the source's creator, usually its author, followed by a period, as in the following examples:

Source with One Author

> Walker, Alice. *The Color Purple.* Washington Square Press, 1982.
> Yoshida, Atsuhiko. "Epic." *Encyclopedia Britannica,* 19 Mar. 2014, www.britannica
> .com/art/epic.

If a source has multiple creators, list their names in the order the source does, using the following format for two versus three or more creators:

Source with Two Authors

> Gilbert, Sandra M., and Susan Gubar. *The Madwoman in the Attic: The Woman Writer and the Nineteenth-Century Literary Imagination.* Yale UP, 1984.

Source with Three or More Authors

> White, Karen, et al. *The Forgotten Room.* Berkley, 2016.

If your source is an interview, *treat the interviewee as its author,* regardless of who gets credit in the source, as in the following example:

Interview

> Munro, Alice. "Alice Munro, The Art of Fiction No. 137." Interview by Jeanne McCulloch and Mona Simpson. *The Paris Review,* no. 131, summer 1994, www .theparisreview.org/interviews/1791/the-art-of-fiction-no-137-alice-munro.

If a creator is someone other than an author, insert a comma and a descriptor such as *editor* (for one person) or *editors* (for two or more) between the final name and the period, as in the following example:

Sources with Creators Other Than Authors (e.g., Editors)

> Kitchen, Judith, and Mary Paumier Jones, editors. *In Short: A Collection of Brief Creative Nonfiction.* W. W. Norton, 1996.

(Remember that if your works-cited list includes multiple sources by the same creator, the second and subsequent entries will substitute three hyphens for the creator's name: See above, "Formatting the List.")

In the following cases, begin your works-cited entry not with a creator but with a SOURCE TITLE (#3, below):

• the source has no known author;

Anonymous Source

> "The 10 Best Books of 2017." *New York Times Book Review,* 30 Nov. 2017, www .nytimes.com/interactive/2017/books/review/10-best-books-2017.html.

- the source is authored by an organization that is also its publisher, as in the following example (from the *MLA Handbook*):

Source Authored by Its Publisher

> *Report to the Teagle Foundation on the Undergraduate Major in Language and Literature.* Modern Language Association of America, 2009.

- the source is a film or television program, and your essay does not emphasize the work of any particular person, as in the following example:

> *Smooth Talk.* Directed by Joyce Chopra, American Playhouse, 1985.

2. **CONTRIBUTOR(S):** In addition to creators, works-cited entries often must acknowledge other important contributors to a source and/or its container. The entry above, for example, includes a contributor to the film *Smooth Talk*—its director. As this example demonstrates, a contributor's name should generally follow the title of the relevant source or container and is always preceded by a description of the contributor's role (in this case, "directed by").

Other kinds of contributors commonly acknowledged in literature essays include the following:

- INTERVIEWERS (versus interviewees)

> Munro, Alice. "Alice Munro, The Art of Fiction No. 137." Interview by Jeanne McCulloch and Mona Simpson. *The Paris Review*, no. 131, summer 1994, www .theparisreview.org/interviews/1791/the-art-of-fiction-no-137-alice-munro.

- TRANSLATORS of works originally published in another language

> Kafka, Franz. *The Metamorphosis.* Translated by Joyce Crick, e-book ed., Oxford UP, 2009.

- EDITORS of particular editions of a source or of a container such as an anthology

> Kafka, Franz. *The Metamorphosis.* Translated by Joyce Crick, edited by Ritchie Robertson, e-book ed., Oxford UP, 2009.

> Oates, Joyce Carol. "Where Are You Going, Where Have You Been?" *The Norton Introduction to Literature*, edited by Kelly J. Mays, shorter 14th ed., W. W. Norton, 2021, pp. 94-106.

- ILLUSTRATORS

> Pekar, Harvey. *American Splendor: Bob and Harv's Comics.* Illustrated by R. Crumb, Four Walls Eight Windows, 1996.

If a contributor to a source's container is also the source's creator, use only that person's last name in identifying his or her contribution, as in the following example:

Source Whose Contributor Is Also Its Author

> Rowell, Charles Henry. Preface. *Angles of Ascent: A Norton Anthology of Contemporary African American Poetry*, edited by Rowell, W. W. Norton, 2013, pp. xxiii-xxvii.

Sometimes whether a person is treated as a CONTRIBUTOR or a CREATOR will depend on what you emphasize in or about a source in your essay. If what you cite or emphasize is the work of a source's editor(s), translator(s), or illustrator(s), for example, then treat that person as the creator and the work's author as a contributor. In these cases, the author's name is preceded by the word *by*, as in the following examples:

> Crick, Joyce, translator. *The Metamorphosis.* By Franz Kafka, edited by Ritchie Robertson, e-book ed., Oxford UP, 2009.
>
> Crumb, R., illustrator. *American Splendor: Bob and Harv's Comics.* By Harvey Pekar, Four Walls Eight Windows, 1996.

Just remember that your in-text citations for a particular source must always coordinate with your works-cited entry for that source: Both must refer to the same creator(s).

WHAT is it?

3. SOURCE TITLE AND/OR DESCRIPTION: Like the creator's name, the source's title should be taken from the source, reproduced in full, and followed by a period. But the title must be formatted according to the rules explained in 31.5, since this standardized formatting ensures that your reader immediately recognizes the kind of source it is.

For any untitled source, substitute a brief generic description. To indicate that it is not an actual title, capitalize only the first word and proper nouns; do not enclose the description in quotation marks; and italicize *only* titles of other works, if any, that appear in the description, as in the first example below.

In literature essays, especially common types of untitled sources include introductions, prefaces, forewords, afterwords, and reviews. Works-cited entries for these usually need to treat the container's author as a contributor (as with Ralph Ellison in the second example below). In entries for reviews, your description should indicate the work being reviewed and its creator (as in the first example below).

Untitled Review

> Review of *The Bluest Eye*, by Toni Morrison. *Kirkus Reviews*, 1 Oct. 1970.

Untitled Introduction to a Print Book

> Callahan, John. Introduction. *Invisible Man*, by Ralph Ellison, Penguin, 2001, pp. ix–xxiv.

Entries for *titled* prefaces, introductions, forewords, and afterwords should also include the appropriate descriptor *after* the title, with a period separating the two (as in the first example below). Though the *MLA Handbook*, 9th ed., does not require that *titled* reviews be handled the same way (as in the second example below), your instructor may prefer that you do so. Either way, descriptions, like titles, are followed by periods.

Titled Introduction to a Book

> Ozick, Cynthia. "Portrait of the Artist as a Warm Body." Introduction. *The Best American Essays 1998*, edited by Ozick, Houghton Mifflin, 1998, pp. xv-xxi.

Titled Review

> Marks, Peter. "'Water by the Spoonful' Dispenses Measured Fury." Review of *Water by the Spoonful*, by Quiara Alegría Hudes. *The Washington Post*, 10 Mar. 2014, www.washingtonpost.com/entertainment/theater_dance/water-by-the -spoonful-dispenses-measured-fury/2014/03/10/840c1a68-a887-11e3-8a7b -c1c684e2771f_story.html.

4. **VERSION**: If a source or container indicates that it is only one of multiple versions or editions of a work, you must indicate *which* version or edition in order to identify the source or container precisely—or to fully answer the "What is it?" question. Identify the version or edition just as the source or container does, but abbreviate the word *edition* to *ed.* (as in the third and fourth examples below). (The first two examples come directly from the *MLA Handbook*.)

> *The Bible.* Authorized King James Version, Oxford UP, 1998.
>
> *Blade Runner.* 1982. Directed by Ridley Scott, director's cut, Warner Bros., 1992.
>
> Drabble, Margaret, editor. *The Oxford Companion to English Literature.* Revised ed., Oxford UP, 1998.
>
> Oates, Joyce Carol. "Where Are You Going, Where Have You Been?" *The Norton Introduction to Literature,* edited by Kelly J. Mays, shorter 14th ed., W. W. Norton, 2021, pp. 94-106.

Since an e-book is an electronic *version* of a book, it should be cited accordingly, using either the generic descriptor *e-book ed.* (as in the first example below) or a more specific one such as *Kindle ed.*, if available (as in the second example below).

> *E-Book*
>
> Kafka, Franz. *The Metamorphosis.* Translated by Joyce Crick, edited by Ritchie Robertson, e-book ed., Oxford UP, 2009.

> *Kindle Edition of a Book*
>
> *MLA Handbook.* 9th ed., Kindle ed., Modern Language Association of America, 2021.

5. **NUMBER(S)**: If your source or its container is only one of a numbered sequence of items, such as volumes, issues, or—in the case of television—seasons and episodes, then specifying the relevant number(s) is also essential to precisely identifying what it is. Each such number is preceded by the appropriate descriptor and followed by a comma. The most common descriptors—*volume* and *number*—can be abbreviated (as *vol.* or *no.*), but others must be spelled out. (All but one of the following examples come from the *MLA Handbook*.)

> *Journal Articles*
>
> Daly, Brenda O. "An Unfilmable Conclusion: Joyce Carol Oates at the Movies." *The Journal of Popular Culture,* vol. 23, no. 3, winter 1989, pp. 101-14. *Periodicals Archive Online,* ezproxy.library.unlv.edu/login?url=http://search.proquest.com /docview/1297343870?accountid=3611.
>
> Kafka, Ben. "The Demon of Writing: Paperwork, Public Safety, and the Reign of Terror." *Representations,* no. 98, 2007, pp. 1-24.

> *Episode in a Series*
>
> "Hush." *Buffy the Vampire Slayer,* created by Joss Whedon, season 4, episode 10, Mutant Enemy, 1999.

> *One Volume of a Multivolume Book*
>
> Wellek, René. *A History of Modern Criticism, 1750–1950.* Vol. 5, Yale UP, 1986.

NOTE: If you cite multiple volumes of a multivolume work such as the one in the last example above (Wellek's *History of Modern Criticism*), your works-cited entry will omit this element, since your source is considered to be the entire work. (See also "Optional Element: Number of Volumes in a Multivolume Work," below.)

WHO published it?

6. **PUBLISHER:** Shorten publishers' names by omitting initial articles (*The*) and business words and abbreviations such as *Company, Co.,* or *Inc.* If the name of a press does not include the word *University,* spell out *Press,* as in the first example. For academic presses with *University* and *Press* in the name, shorten to the abbreviation *UP* or the equivalent, as in the last two examples below.

Gilman, Charlotte Perkins. *The Yellow Wallpaper.* Feminist Press, 1973.

Lupack, Barbara Tepa. "Smoothing Out the Rough Spots: The Film Adaptation of 'Where Are You Going, Where Have You Been?'" *Vision/Revision: Adapting Contemporary American Fiction by Women to Film,* edited by Lupack, Bowling Green State U Popular P, 1996, pp. 85-100.

Wellek, René. *A History of Modern Criticism, 1750–1950.* Vol. 5, Yale UP, 1986.

Omit publishers' names entirely for the following sorts of sources and containers:

- periodicals (since a periodical retains its identity even when it changes publishers);
- websites whose publishers are the same as their titles (e.g., *The New York Times, Encyclopedia Britannica*); and
- websites, databases, or archives that house sources whose content they have not contributed to producing (e.g., *YouTube, JSTOR, Periodical Archives Online*).

WHEN was it published?

7. **PUBLICATION DATE:** For a book or journal's publication date, use the most recent year on the title or copyright page; for web pages, use the copyright date or the date of most recent update, if available. For entire websites and multi-volume print works developed over time, a date range may be indicated. (The publication date of the online *Blake Archive,* for example, is 1996–2014; that of the eight-volume *History of Modern Criticism, 1750–1950* is 1955–92.) In giving dates, abbreviate the names of all months except May, June, and July. And when including day, month, and year, give the information in that order, as in the first two examples below:

Entry in an Online Encyclopedia

Yoshida, Atsuhiko. "Epic." *Encyclopedia Britannica,* 19 Mar. 2014, www.britannica .com/art/epic.

Newspaper Article

Canby, Vincent. "Film: 'Smooth Talk,' from Joyce Carol Oates Tale." *The New York Times,* 28 Feb. 1986, www.nytimes.com/1986/02/28/movies/film-smooth-talk -from-joyce-carol-oates-tale.html.

Journal Article

Daly, Brenda O. "An Unfilmable Conclusion: Joyce Carol Oates at the Movies." *The Journal of Popular Culture,* vol. 23, no. 3, winter 1989, pp. 101-14. *ProQuest Periodicals Archive Online,* ezproxy.library.unlv.edu/login?url=http://search.proquest .com/docview/1297343870?accountid=3611.

Chapter in a Book

> Lupack, Barbara Tepa. "Smoothing Out the Rough Spots: The Film Adaptation of 'Where Are You Going, Where Have You Been?'" *Vision/Revision: Adapting Contemporary American Fiction by Women to Film*, edited by Lupack, Bowling Green State U Popular P, 1996, pp. 85-100.

WHERE can it be found?

8. **LOCATION INFORMATION:** If a container is paginated, include the page number(s) on which the source appears, preceded by the abbreviation *p.* (for *page*, if the source is only one page long) or *pp.* (for *pages*, if the source is two or more pages). If you cite a periodical article that isn't printed on consecutive pages, include only the first page number followed by a plus sign (e.g., "pp. B1+").

> Alexie, Sherman. "When the Story Stolen Is Your Own." *Time*, 6 Feb. 2006, p. 72.

For an online source or container, MLA requires including a digital object identifier (DOI), if available. If the DOI, a string of numbers and letters, in your source is not preceded by *http://* or *https://*, in your entry precede it with *https://doi.org/*, as in the second example below. If a DOI is not available, MLA recommends instead including a URL or, better, a permalink (a URL intended to remain unchanged), copied in full except for the opener *http://* or *https://*. Omit the URL, however, if your instructor prefers: Because URLs, unlike DOIs, are impermanent and unwieldy, they are recommended rather than required by MLA.

Source with URL

> Alexie, Sherman. "When the Story Stolen Is Your Own." *Time*, 6 Feb. 2006, p. 72. *Academic Search Premier*, connection.ebscohost.com/c/essays/19551314/when -story-stolen-your-own.

Source with DOI

> Marcus, Mordecai. "What Is an Initiation Story?" *Journal of Aesthetics and Art Criticism*, vol. 19, no. 2, winter 1960, pp. 221-28. *JSTOR*, https://doi.org/10.2307/428289.

FORMATTING INDIVIDUAL ENTRIES—ADDITIONAL OPTIONS

The core elements described in the last section are the only ones works-cited entries must include, when those elements are available and relevant. Yet MLA also allows you to include various supplemental elements, at your and your instructor's discretion. It also gives you the possibility of taking a shortcut when you cite multiple sources from a single collection or anthology. Here we describe those options most relevant to undergraduate literature essays.

- *OPTIONAL SHORTCUT: CROSS-REFERENCE ENTRIES FOR MULTIPLE SOURCES CONTAINED IN ONE COLLECTION*
  If you cite multiple sources from a single collection such as an anthology according to the directions we've presented thus far, your list of works cited will include multiple entries like the following that all repeat the same information (here highlighted) about the anthology/container:

  > Dove, Rita. "Heroes." *Angles of Ascent: A Norton Anthology of Contemporary African American Poetry*, edited by Charles Henry Rowell, W. W. Norton, 2013, pp. 215-16.

Sanchez, Sonia. "A Poem for My Father." *Angles of Ascent: A Norton Anthology of Contemporary African American Poetry*, edited by Charles Henry Rowell, W. W. Norton, 2013, p. 70.

Though these entries are perfectly correct, MLA encourages a two-step short-cut. First, create one entry for the anthology that contains all the core elements. Then, for each source you cite from that anthology, create a shortened, "cross-reference" entry that includes only SOURCE CREATOR. SOURCE TITLE. CONTAINER CREATOR(S)'S LAST NAME(S), LOCATION INFORMATION. If we take this shortcut with our two sample entries above, for example, we end up with the three more streamlined ones below:

Dove, Rita. "Heroes." Rowell, pp. 215-16.

Rowell, Charles Henry, editor. *Angles of Ascent: A Norton Anthology of Contemporary African American Poetry.* W. W. Norton, 2013.

Sanchez, Sonia. "A Poem for My Father." Rowell, p. 70.

As our highlighting in the above examples is meant to demonstrate, the end of a cross-reference entry works like an in-text parenthetical citation: Each refers readers to the entry that contains full publication information about the container, while providing source-specific location information.

• OPTIONAL ELEMENT: ORIGINAL PUBLICATION INFORMATION

For a republished source, it's often helpful to include information about when and how the source was originally published. If you include the original publication date, place it immediately after the source title and follow it with a period, as in the examples below:

Gillman, Charlotte Perkins. *The Yellow Wallpaper.* 1892. Feminist Press, 1973.

Oates, Joyce Carol. "Where Are You Going, Where Have You Been?" 1966. *The Norton Introduction to Literature*, edited by Kelly J. Mays, shorter 14th ed., W. W. Norton, 2021, pp. 94-106.

When a source was originally published in a different form or container or under a different title, you may want to give your reader more than its original publication date. If so, *all* this information, including the date, belongs at the end of your citation. Precede it with a period and the phrase *Originally published as* (if the title has changed) or *Originally published in* (if it hasn't). Include all the relevant core elements, ordered and formatted as they would be if they occurred elsewhere in your entry, as in the following examples:

Source Republished with the Same Title

Nischik, Reingard M. "(Un-)Doing Gender: Alice Munro, 'Boys and Girls' (1964)." *Contemporary Literary Criticism*, edited by Lawrence J. Trudeau, vol. 370, Gale, 2015. *Literature Resource Center*, go.galegroup.com/ps/i.do?id=GALE%7CH1100118828&v=2.1&u=unlv_main&it=r&p=LitRC&sw=w&asid=1ec18259fbc8af3aecfc233e918cf0e8. Originally published in *The Canadian Short Story*, edited by Nischik, Camden House, 2007, pp. 203-18.

Source Republished with a Different Title

Strong, Roy. *Painting the Past: The Victorian Painter and British History.* Pimlico, 2004. Originally published as *And When Did You Last See Your Father?: The Victorian Painter and British History*, Thames and Hudson, 1978.

- **OPTIONAL ELEMENT: *ACCESS DATE***

Since an online work can change or disappear more readily than a print one, knowing when you accessed it can be helpful to your reader, especially when the source has no publication date. For this reason, earlier editions of the *MLA Handbook* required that works-cited entries include access dates. This is now an optional element, which we've thus omitted throughout this book. Some instructors may, however, prefer that you include this element. If so, the access date— day, month, and year—comes after the relevant URL or DOI, preceded by a period, a space, and the word *Accessed*, and followed by a period, as in the following example:

> Yoshida, Atsuhiko. "Epic." *Encyclopedia Britannica*, 19 Mar. 2014, www.britannica
> .com/art/epic. Accessed 24 Jan. 2015.

With access dates, as with publication dates, abbreviate the names of all months except May, June, and July.

- **OPTIONAL ELEMENT: *MISSING CORE ELEMENTS FROM AN EXTERNAL SOURCE***

When essential facts about a source (core elements) are not indicated in the source itself, MLA recommends supplying them when you can, based on other reliable sources. If so added, this information—publisher or publication date, for example—should be placed exactly where it would normally go in the entry, but enclosed in brackets to indicate that it does not come from the source. If you are uncertain about the accuracy of this information, follow it with a question mark (e.g., [1950?]); if a date is approximate, introduce it with the word *circa* (e.g., [circa 1950]).

If you cite a newspaper whose title doesn't indicate the city in which it was published, add the city, in brackets, after the title, as in the following example:

> Malvern, Jack. "Globe Offers Shakespeare on Demand." *The Times* [London], 4
> Nov. 2014, p. 3. *EBSCOhost Newspaper Source Plus*, ezproxy.library.unlv.edu
> /login?url=http://search.ebscohost.com/login.aspx?direct=true&db=n5h&AN
> =7EH92164329&site=ehost-live.

- **OPTIONAL ELEMENT: *NUMBER OF VOLUMES IN A MULTIVOLUME WORK***

If you cite more than one volume from a multivolume work, the entire work is your source, and you will need only one entry for it. To make sure that your readers immediately recognize it as a multivolume work and that they know how many volumes it contains, you may end your entry with this information, using the abbreviation *vols.* (for *volumes*), as in the following example:

> Wellek, René. *A History of Modern Criticism, 1750-1950*. Yale UP, 1955-92. 8 vols.

(For instructions on how to format in-text parenthetical citations so that they coordinate with this sort of entry, see 33.3.1, "Variations in Content: Indicating a Location within the Source.")

- **OPTIONAL ELEMENT: *SERIES TITLE AND NUMBER***

If your source is a book in a series, it might be easier for your readers to find the book if you include the series title at the end of your entry. If so, do not italicize the series title, enclose it in quotation marks, or include the word *series*. Individual books in some series are numbered. In that case, put the number right after the title, as in the second example below:

Book in a Series with Unnumbered Volumes

Stabb, Martin S. *Borges Revisited.* Twayne Publishers, 1991. Twayne's World Authors.

Book in a Series with Numbered Volumes

Unruh, Vicky. *Latin American Vanguards: The Art of Contentious Encounters.* U of California P, 1994. Latin American Literature and Culture 11.

33.3.3 Abbreviations Used in Citation and Documentation: A Recap

The following chart lists abbreviations commonly used in the list of works cited and in in-text and parenthetical citations (as explained in sections 33.3.1 and 33.3.2). As the chart suggests, MLA now allows few abbreviations and greatly restricts their use: There is, for example, no acceptable abbreviation for the word *line* or *lines* (in parenthetical citations referring to poetry), and *ed.* is used only to mean *edition*, not *editor* (in works-cited entries).

ABBREVIATION		USED IN . . .
ch.	chapter	parenthetical citations, to indicate location
chs.	chapters	parenthetical citations, to indicate location
doi	digital object identifier	works-cited entries, to indicate location of articles accessed online
ed.	edition	works-cited entries, to indicate version
et al.	and others	signal phrases, parenthetical citations, and works-cited entries, for works (sources or containers) with three or more authors or editors
no.	number	works-cited entries, preceding a journal or magazine's issue number
p.	page	works-cited entries, to indicate location
pp.	pages	works-cited entries, to indicate location
par.	paragraph	parenthetical citations, to indicate location
qtd. in	quoted in	parenthetical citations, for material in a cited source taken from another, uncited source
sec.	section	parenthetical citations, to indicate location
secs.	sections	parenthetical citations, to indicate location
U	University	works-cited entries, in names of university presses (publisher)
UP	University Press	works-cited entries, in names of university presses (publisher)
vol.	volume	parenthetical citations, to indicate location, and works-cited entries, usually preceding a journal or magazine volume number

34 | SAMPLE RESEARCH ESSAY

The following research essay analyzes Alice Munro's short story Boys and Girls. As you will see, the essay gives some consideration to the story's biographical and historical contexts, drawing on interviews with Munro and a sociological study of Canadian farm families. Yet the essay is primarily a critical contexts essay, as we define that term in chapter 32. In addition to considering the critical conversation about "Boys and Girls," however, this essay examines one about the initiation-story genre as well. The essay's literary critical secondary sources thus include three scholarly articles that focus exclusively on Munro's story, as well as two articles that use other stories to make arguments about initiation-story conventions. Diverse as are the sources and contexts this essay considers, however, its thesis is an original, debatable interpretive claim about the literary text which the body of the essay supports and develops by presenting and analyzing textual evidence.

Sarah Roberts
Prof. Jernigan
English 204
7 June 2021

"Only a Girl"? Gendered Initiation in Alice Munro's
"Boys and Girls"

In 1960, an article in the *Journal of Aesthetics and Art Criticism* asked a question still worth asking over sixty years later: "What is an initiation story?" That article, by Mordecai Marcus, points out that literary critics frequently "used the term 'initiation' to describe a theme and a type of story" but that they didn't all use or define it exactly the same way. Marcus defines it as a story that "show[s] its young protagonist experiencing a significant change of knowledge about the world or himself, or a change of character, or of both," which "must point or lead him towards an adult world" (222). For Marcus, the only significant difference between initiation stories has to do with their endings. He divides them into three types, depending on how far and "decisively" into that "adult world" their protagonists travel by the end (223). Published fifteen years after Marcus's essay, however, Elaine Ginsberg's "The Female Initiation

Theme in American Fiction" (1975) suggests that it matters more what gender the story's protagonist is, at least in American fiction. According to her, "the female initiation story is rare in American literature," the first really "legitimat[e]" ones appearing only in the twentieth century (27, 31). Further, she argues those twentieth-century stories follow a pattern that is distinct in at least five ways: (1) "young girls are always introduced to a heterosexual world, in which relationships between men and women . . . are the most important," "a world in which men are always present, always important, and always more free and independent" (31, 37); (2) they "seem to see their future roles as women almost always in relation to men" (31, 36); (3) their "initiation process" involves both "sexual experience" and (4) "dropping" the attributes like boyish "clothing" or "names" that make them "androgynous creatures" at the beginning of the story; and (5) they never seem "to be aided or guided by an older" person of the same sex, as boys in initiation stories are (31). As a result, according to Ginsberg, the "sense of disillusionment, disappointment, and regret is perhaps the most significant characteristic of the female initiate in American literature" (35).

Whether Ginsberg is right about all of American literature, her argument does offer a way to think about a story she doesn't consider, Canadian Nobel Prize winner Alice Munro's "Boys and Girls." Published in 1968, "Boys and Girls" appeared in *Dance of the Happy Shades*, Munro's first book and the event that basically launched her career as an author. "Boys and Girls" is clearly a female initiation story. Its narrator is a woman remembering events that happened around the time she was eleven, and it ends with her admitting that "[m]aybe" she truly is "only a girl" (par. 65, 64). Her initiation mostly does follow the pattern Ginsberg outlines in a way that draws on Munro's personal experience and reflects that of other Canadian farm families. However, Munro's story does all that even better because it also depicts, as Reingard M. Nischik, Marlene Goldman, and Heliane Ventura show, another character and another initiation—that of the protagonist's younger brother, Laird. As Goldman puts it, the story "highlights the almost invisible societal forces which shape children, in this case, *the narrator and her brother Laird*, into gendered adults" (emphasis added). Rather than being either a male or female initiation story, "Boys and Girls" is both.

Roberts establishes a motive for her essay by presenting two competing scholarly arguments about the initiation-story genre (in par. 1), then indicating (in the highlighted sentence) that she will be "siding" with the second of these and expanding on it by considering a story the source does not.

Roberts here prepares readers for the consideration of biographical and historical context later in the essay but makes the story and its critical contexts her main focus.

Here, Roberts briefly alludes to the three contributions to the second critical conversation her essay engages with—that about "Boys and Girls" specifically (rather than the initiation story generally).

Roberts 3

Like the heroines in the female initiation stories that Ginsberg discusses, Munro's protagonist starts out as an "androgynous creatur[e]" (31). But in Munro's story, that androgyny doesn't have anything to do with the protagonist's clothes or her name. In "Boys and Girls," clothes and names aren't very important. On the Ontario fox farm where it is set, horses and "foxes all ha[ve] names" (par. 8), but only two human characters in the story do, Laird and "the hired man," Henry Bailey (par. 2). The only pieces of clothing described are a school dress the protagonist's mother makes for her (par. 17), some dresses her mother once wore and describes to her (par. 10), and the aprons her mother and her father wear when she sees them talking together outside the barn one night (par. 12-13).

Instead of clothes or names, what really makes adult men and women different in the story is, as all the story's critics notice, the kind of work they do, where they do it, and whom they do it with. What makes the outdoor meeting between the parents so "odd" is that the mother does "not often come out of the house" or get much exercise, as the "bumpy" shape and pale color of her legs show. Her workplace is the house and especially the "hot dark kitchen," where she cans and cooks the family's food. The father instead works "out of doors" (par. 13), even if outdoors includes the barn and the fox pens he builds outside it and even if, to the mother's disgust, he has to do the "pelting . . . in the house" in winter (par. 2). Also, the mother performs her work alone and isn't paid for it, but the father gets paid enough for the furs he sells "to the Hudson's Bay Company or the Montreal Fur Traders" to hire Henry Bailey to help him (par. 1).

The narrator's androgyny, then, has to do with two things. One is the way she moves across these male and female places and activities, as Ventura observes, too (83). In the kitchen, she is "given jobs to do" like "peeling peaches . . . or cutting up onions" with her mother (par. 13). Outdoors, her "job" includes getting the foxes water and raking up the grass between their pens after her father cuts it (par. 7, 10). But in terms of her androgyny, the second and just as important thing is how close she is to her brother. The narrator and Laird are so much a unit early on in the story that the narrator slips practically automatically from "I" to "we." After she introduces Laird, Henry Bailey, and her mother in the story's second paragraph, when she says in the next one, "*We* admired him [Henry] for this performance" and "It was . . . always possible that" he "might be [laughing] at *us*," it's not exactly clear who "we" or "us" means until she starts the next paragraph by saying, "After *we* had been sent to bed" (emphasis added). And this

Roberts 4

paragraph is all about the bedroom that she and her brother share, their shared fears about it, and the "rules" they both follow to make themselves feel safe (par. 4). As Goldman argues, this room is the only place in the story that isn't either clearly "male" or "female," its "unfinished state" symbolizing "the undifferentiated consciousness of the children" at this point in the story.

What's strange about this, however, is that even though they share so much, Laird is treated differently. He helps out when it comes to outdoor work like watering the foxes, but there's never any hint that he helps out in the house. There is a difference between boy and girl in terms of the work they do from the very beginning, even if it's not a difference the narrator or the story's critics point out. What two critics (Ventura and Nischik) do point out is another difference, that unlike the narrator, Laird gets a name, and his name is Scottish for "landowner": ". . . Laird is a potential laird, the male heir to the family" (Ventura 82).

In these ways, the story seems to accurately reflect the reality of life on Canadian family farms through the 1950s and 1960s. As Munro, who grew up on one, insists in one interview, because "what's going on" on those farms, "chiefly, is [or was] making enough to live on," "everybody has to work and be useful to the family" ("Interview" 183). Based on her study of ten farm families (in Saskatchewan instead of Ontario), sociologist June Corman describes that work as "distinctly gendered." While men had legal "title to the land" and "retained control of the agricultural income-producing work" in which "women . . . were not extensively involved," women "laboured . . . to make home made essentials instead of buying consumer goods so farm income could be used to pay down . . . debt" (70). Furthermore, she argues, "This structured gendered division of labour had implications for their . . . children": "From childhood onward girls learned" both "the skills required of farm wives" and "at least a minimal amount of skills related to grain and livestock production." But boys worked exclusively with their fathers and learned "agricultural skills . . . not . . . domestic knowledge" (71). Farm families required equal work from all members of the family, but not the same work.

At the same time that she reflects this reality about Canadian farm life, Munro's choice to focus specifically on a fox farm like the one she grew up on takes on importance in terms of how female and male worlds are characterized in the story. It's not entirely clear in the story that men are truly any more "free and independent" than women are, as Ginsberg suggests is true in a lot of female initiation stories (37), since both the mother and the father are "enslaved by the farm, harassed by [their] work" (Ventura 85). But Goldman does seem right to say that

---

Roberts doesn't include a paren-thetical citation here because the source is unpagi-nated and its author's name is mentioned in a signal phrase ("As Goldman argues").

Roberts's signal phrase indicates that two sources make the same observation, even though she only quotes one. To specify which, Roberts repeats its author's name in her parenthetical citation.

Roberts here speci-fies the basis for the source's claims (a "study of ten" Sas-katchewan "farm families") and the author's key creden-tial ("sociologist").

Rather than letting her source get the last word in her paragraph, Roberts summa-rizes the key point in her own words.

Roberts transitions from one para-graph/claim to another by restating the main idea of the last paragraph in the first part of this sentence and then, in the second part, stating the claim developed in this paragraph.

Roberts 5

men's work in this story is all about controlling other wild and dangerous creatures. "Alive, the foxes inhabited a world my father made for them," the narrator explains (par. 7). Here, they "prow[l] up and down" inside "sturdy pens" that are "surrounded by a high guard fence" with a "padlocked" gate that no one but the narrator's father is ever brave enough to go into (par. 9, 7). And, as Goldman points out, the fox pen does sort of resemble "[t]he dark, hot, stifling kitchen [that] imprisons the narrator's mother and threatens to imprison the narrator."

Maybe as a result of his power and bravery, the protagonist—as Nischik, Ventura, and Goldman all notice—clearly sees her father's work and world as superior to her mother's. She "hate[s]" the kitchen, whose "bumpy linoleum" resembles her mother's "lumpy legs," and sees housework as so "endless, dreary and peculiarly depressing" that she runs away as soon as she can (par. 13). But her father's "world," especially the pens he creates, seems to her "tidy and ingenious" (par. 7). And his work seems to her so "tirelessly inventive" (par. 7) and "ritualistically important" (par. 13) that she always helps him "willingly . . . and with a feeling of pride" (par. 10).

The adults around her reinforce that feeling. The only time her father praises her, he does it by calling her a "man" (par. 10), even specifically his "new hired man." In saying that, he compares her to Henry Bailey, which is interesting, but more important, he communicates the same message about the jobs of men and women and their unequal worth that the salesman does when he responds to the father by saying, "I thought it was only a girl." Paired with the word *only*, the word *girl*, as the narrator thinks later, becomes a label "always touched . . . with reproach and disappointment" or even "a joke on [her]" that the real hired man, Henry, especially, finds funny (par. 21). The label also gets associated with prohibitions as much as confinement. When the narrator's grandmother (the last of only three female characters total) arrives on the scene, the only thing we hear from her are commands about the things girls shouldn't do—"slam doors," sit with their knees apart, ask questions (par. 22).

The narrator *is* thus, in a way, "aided or guided by an older" person of the same sex, as boys in initiation stories are, according to Ginsberg (31). But that aid isn't positive. In fact, the girl sees her mother as her "enemy" because she thinks her mother is the one "plotting" to imprison her in the house and the inferior adult role it implies (par. 17). She sees that her mother is "kinder than [her] father" and "love[s] her" enough to stay up all night making the "difficult" dress she wants for school. But she still sides with her father and even likes his dismissive attitude toward her mother when they talk about her in the yard: "I was pleased by the way he stood listening [to her], politely as he would to a salesman or a stranger, but with an air of wanting to get on with his real work" (par. 15), she says: "I did not expect my father to pay any attention to what she said" (par. 18).

Goldman identifies a parallel between the protagonist's attitudes to her mother and the foxes. As Goldman puts it, just as she earlier in the story "does not comprehend that the hostility she sees in the foxes' 'malevolent faces' . . . is a response to their enforced captivity," so she now interprets "her mother's behaviour . . . not as an expression of frustration and disappointment, or loneliness, but as a manifestation of innate wickedness and petty tyranny. . . ." What Goldman doesn't say is that we learn about these other possible interpretations, however, because the adult narrator *does* see them. When the narrator says, "*It did not occur to me* that she could be lonely, or jealous" (par. 17; emphasis added), it's obvious that it *does* occur to her *now*, as an adult.

In this way, too, the story actually seems to reflect and bend reality, but in this case the reality of Munro's personal life instead of Canadian farm families'. Munro biographer Hallvard Dahlie claims that many Munro stories include "unfulfilled and despairing mothers" like Munro's real mother, a former teacher who "expended her energies during the formative years of the three Laidlaw children in the nurturing of a family under conditions of deprivation and hardship" (qtd. in Nischik). In interviews, Munro often mentions her mother in a way that implies her attitude toward her mother changed in the same way her narrator-protagonist's does. She told *The New Yorker* that her "mother . . . is still a main figure in my life because her life was so sad and unfair and she so brave, but also because she was determined to make me into the Sunday-school-recitation little girl I was, from the age of seven or so, fighting not to be" ("On 'Dear'"). She told *The Paris Review*, "The tenderness I feel now for my mother, I didn't feel for a long time" ("Alice"). At the same time, Munro leaves out of "Boys and Girls" one of the things that made her real-life mother's life particularly "sad and unfair," which was the fact that she had Parkinson's disease. By not giving her fictional mother that kind of illness or even a name, for that matter, Munro makes her more like all women, just as she makes her story about boys versus girls (period) by not giving the protagonist what she had in real life—a sister and a brother.

In the story, the protagonist's full initiation into womanhood doesn't really involve a change in her relationship to her mother. (Late in the story she does think about confiding in her, but she doesn't [par. 51].) Instead, it involves changes in the way she relates to her father, animals, and her brother. That change begins with the scene where she and Laird secretly witness their father and Henry shooting the horse, Mack. We can tell that what she sees disturbs her partly

---

Because Roberts found the quotation from one source (Dahlie's biography) in another (Nischik's article), she puts the essential information about the original source in a signal phrase ("Munro biographer Hallvard Dahlie claims..."), then uses the parenthetical citation to tell us which of her sources it was quoted in.

Because Roberts doesn't mention the titles of these sources in a signal phrase, she needs parenthetical citations. The latter don't include page numbers because these sources are unpaginated.

Roberts doesn't cite a source for the fact that Munro's mother had Parkinson's, two daughters, and a son because this is common knowledge.

because her legs shake and partly because she suddenly mentions a memory of Laird that makes her feel "the sadness of unexorcized guilt" (par. 37). But the question is why, since she and her brother have watched their father killing and skinning other animals and, unlike their mother, weren't bothered by that or the gross smells it produced (par. 2)? Or, as she herself explains,

> I did not have any great feeling of horror and opposition, such
> as a city child might have had. I was used to seeing the death
> of animals as a necessity by which we lived. Yet I felt a little
> ashamed, and there was a new wariness, a sense of holding-
> off, in my attitude to my father and his work. (par. 43)

There are many possible reasons for her reaction, but one might be that even before this point the girl begins to identify with the horses in a way she never does with the foxes. It is when—in her life and in the story—she is beginning to feel most pressured about being a girl and first expresses a wish to remain "free" that she remembers to mention how the foxes were fed at all and to describe, in detail, the two particular horses, Mack and Flora, and the different ways they respond to their similarly unfree situation (par. 22). (Mack is "slow and easy to handle"; Flora rears and kicks at people and fences [par. 20, 23].) That identification might explain why she might suddenly have a new "wariness" of her father and his work after seeing one of the horses killed (par. 43).

That feeling might be compounded, too, by the way Henry behaves, especially the fact that he laughs about Mack being shot in the same ways he's already laughed at her more than once in the story (par. 2, 21). But her sense of being "ashamed" about the shooting seems to come from seeing how she in a way acted like him long ago when she endangered her little brother's life just "for excitement" (par. 43, 37). As Goldman argues,

> Bailey's laughter [when "the horse kicks its legs in the air"] is
> particularly unnerving because it fully exposes his delight in
> power based on sheer inequality.
>
> The narrator recognizes this as an abuse of power . . . as a
> result of her own experience. She, too, lorded power over an
> innocent victim. . . .

It doesn't seem surprising, then, that when the narrator has the chance to save Flora ten days later, even just temporarily, she just does it, without "mak[ing] any decision" or even "understand[ing] why" (par. 48, 50). By doing that, in Ventura's words, "the girl vicariously achieves her own temporary liberation" (84), and, in Goldman's words, "she radically breaks from her male-identified position." As the narrator points out, she disobeys her father for the very first time in her

By putting the narrator's character-izations of Mack's and Flora's different reactions to their imprisonment in parentheses, Roberts substanti-ates her claim about the narrator's detailed descrip-tions, while staying focused on this paragraph's main topic—the narra-tor's *feelings about* the horses.

Here, as through-out the essay, Roberts never substitutes the claim of a source for the textual evidence necessary to substantiate and develop it.

life and in a way she knows will change their relationship forever (par. 50). Rather than helping him as she's always wanted to do before, she "make[s] more work for" him by letting Flora go (par. 50). Worse, she knows that once he figures out what she's done he won't "trust me any more," but "would know that I was not entirely on his side. I was on Flora's side . . ." (par. 50). Her change of "side[s]," though, isn't complete or recognized by other people until dinner. When the truth about how she let Flora go is revealed, her father responds in a way that "absolved and dismissed [her] for good" by repeating the words the salesman used earlier, "She's only a girl" (par. 64). More important, the narrator doesn't "protest . . . , even in [her] heart" (par. 65). Like Mack and unlike the foxes and Flora, she now silently accepts her fate.

Just as important, though, is the way she separates herself from her brother. At the exact same time that the narrator permanently separates herself from her father, by letting Flora out, she also separates herself from Laird in a way that seems ironic, given that it was in a way sympathy with Laird or guilt about him that started the change in her in the first place. At any rate, when Henry and her father go off to get Flora, Laird goes with them, but the narrator doesn't. When she says, "I shut the gate after they were all gone," it seems like the first time in the story that Henry, the father, and Laird become a "they" that doesn't include her (par. 49). At least it seems like a far cry from the "we" she and Laird are early in the story. Importantly, though, it isn't really true that, as Ventura claims, the narrator "is not allowed aboard the bouncing truck" because she, unlike Laird, never actually asks to go (86). That change in her relationship to Laird is confirmed by the way, in between Flora's escape and the dinner that ends the story, the narrator mentions their bedroom one more time. In addition to decorating her part of the room, she "planned to put up some kind of barricade between [her] bed and Laird's, to keep my section separate from his" (par. 52).

As Goldman argues, though, Laird's very different initiation and behavior are significant:

> As they lift him into the truck, the little boy becomes a man: he joins the hunting party. Upon his return, he brandishes the streak of blood on his arm. . . . [T]he mark of blood and the domination of the Other continues to function as a cru- cial element in the rites of manhood. The boy cements his alliance with the father on the basis of their mutual triumph over nature.

In fact, that "alliance" isn't "cemented" until that night, when Laird, "look[ing] across the table at" her, "proudly, distinctly" tells her secret to everyone (par. 56). In a weird way, he reverses the roles they each

To reinforce her claim about the narrator's develop- ment over the course of the story and connect the earlier parts of her essay with the later ones, Roberts briefly alludes to evidence and a point she made earlier.

Roberts 9

play in the memory that sparks her change—now he's the powerful one who leaves her figuratively hanging.

Here, though, is where the male and female initiations in this one story differ in a way that totally accords with Ginsberg's argument. Laird becomes a man in relationship to other men, grown-ups of his own gender, but in a way that has nothing to do with actual sex. Like the protagonists of most female initiation stories, according to Ginsberg, however, the protagonist of this one "seem[s] to see [her] future rol[e] as [a] wom[a]n . . . in relation to men" in a way that involves "sexual experience" (31). We see this in the stories she tells herself at night. Where the stories she makes up at the beginning of the story are all adventure stories in which she does things like shoot animals (just as Laird actually ends up doing by the end of this story), the stories she makes up at the end of the story are more like romances featuring boys she knows from school or one of her male teachers (par. 52).

If we go back to Marcus's question, "What is an initiation story?," then, "Boys and Girls" shows us that Ginsberg is right to say that the answer can depend most on whether the story features boys, girls, or "boys and girls." Or at least it once did, because here is where it might matter that Munro's story was published in 1968 and is set much earlier. In interviews, Munro expresses the idea that things were, in real life, changing even in her generation, which is also, as Nischik points out, her protagonist's. "If I had been a farm girl of a former generation," Munro says in one interview, "I wouldn't have had a chance" to go to college or be a writer, for example. Instead, her only option would have been to become a farm wife like her own mother or her protagonist's mother. "But in the generation that I was, there were scholarships. Girls were not encouraged to get them, but you could. I could imagine, from an early age, that I would be a writer" ("Interview" 183). Even if her protagonist never imagines herself someday being a writer, she is writing stories in her head every night. And that doesn't change over the course of the story, even if the kinds of stories she tells do. Even if at the end of the story the protagonist ends up accepting the idea that she is "only a girl" and not saying anything, the fact that she keeps telling herself stories and that she is, in fact, narrating her story to us as an adult suggests that the end of the story *isn't* the end of the story. Girls don't have to grow up to be "only" one thing after all. They can grow up to tell both their stories and their brothers'. They can even win Nobel Prizes for it.

Roberts opens her conclusion by referring us back to the "frame" she established in her introduction—the different views of two sources (Marcus and Ginsberg).

Works Cited

Corman, June. "The 'Good Wife' and Her Farm Husband: Changing Household Practices in Rural Saskatchewan." *Canadian Woman Studies*, vol. 24, no. 4, summer/fall 2005, pp. 69-74, https://cws.journals.yorku.ca/index.php /cws/article/view/6067/5255.

Ginsberg, Elaine. "The Female Initiation Theme in American Fiction." *Studies in American Fiction*, vol. 3, no. 1, spring 1975, pp. 27-37. *Periodicals Archive Online,* ezproxy.library.unlv.edu/login?url=http://search.proquest.com /docview/1297894583?accountid=3611.

Goldman, Marlene. "Penning in the Bodies: The Construction of Gendered Subjects in Alice Munro's 'Boys and Girls.'" *Studies in Canadian Literature*, vol. 15, no. 1, 1990, journals.lib.unb.ca/index.php/SCL/article/view/8112.

Marcus, Mordecai. "What Is an Initiation Story?" *The Journal of Aesthetics and Art Criticism*, vol. 19, no. 2, winter 1960, pp. 221-28. *JSTOR*, https://doi .org/10.2307/428289.

Munro, Alice. "Alice Munro, The Art of Fiction No. 137." Interview by Jeanne McCulloch and Mona Simpson. *The Paris Review*, no. 131, summer 1994, www.theparisreview.org/interviews/1791/the-art-of-fiction-no-137-alice -munro.

---. "Boys and Girls." *The Norton Introduction to Literature*, edited by Kelly J. Mays, shorter 14th ed., W. W. Norton, 2021, pp. 166-76.

---. "An Interview with Alice Munro." Interview by Lisa Dickler Awano. *Virginia Quarterly Review*, vol. 89, no. 2, spring 2013, pp. 180-84, https:// www.vqronline.org/vqr-portfolio/interview-alice-munro.

---. "On 'Dear Life': An Interview with Alice Munro." Interview by Deborah Treisman. *The New Yorker*, 20 Nov. 2012, www.newyorker.com/books/page -turner/on-dear-life-an-interview-with-alice-munro.

Nischik, Reingard M. "(Un-)Doing Gender: Alice Munro, 'Boys and Girls' (1964)." *Contemporary Literary Criticism*, edited by Lawrence J. Trudeau, vol. 370, Gale, 2015. *Literature Resource Center*, go.galegroup.com/ps/i.do?id =GALE%7CH1100118828&v=2.1&u=unlv_main&it=r&p=LitRC&sw=w&asid =1ec18259fbc8af3aecfc233e918cf0e8. Originally published in *The Canadian Short Story*, edited by Nischik, Camden House, 2007, pp. 203-18.

Ventura, Heliane. "Alice Munro's 'Boys and Girls': Mapping out Boundaries." *Commonwealth*, no. 15, autumn 1992, pp. 80-87.

Critical Approaches

F ew human abilities are more remarkable than the ability to read and interpret literature. A computer program or a database can't perform the complex process of reading and interpreting—not to mention writing about—a literary text, although computers can easily exceed human powers of processing codes and information. Readers follow the sequence of printed words and as if by magic re-create a scene between characters in a novel or play, or they respond to the almost inexpressible emotional effect of a poem's figurative language. Experienced readers can pick up on a multitude of literary signals all at once. With re-reading and some research, readers can draw on information about the author's life or the time period when this work and others like it were first published. Varied and complex as the approaches to literary criticism may be, they are not difficult to learn. For the most part, schools of criticism and theory have developed to address questions that any reader can begin to answer.

There are essentially three participants in the literary exchange or interaction: the *text*, the *source* (the *author* and other factors that produce the text), and the *receiver* (the *reader* and other aspects of *reception*). All varieties of literary analysis concern themselves with these aspects of the literary exchange to varying degrees and with varying emphases. Although each of these elements has a role in any form of literary analysis, systematic studies of literature and its history have defined approaches or methods that focus on the different elements and circumstances of the literary interaction. The first three sections below—"Emphasis on the Text," "Emphasis on the Source," and "Emphasis on the Receiver"—describe briefly those schools or modes of literary analysis that have concentrated on one of the three participants while de-emphasizing the others. These different emphases, plainly speaking, are habits of asking different kinds of questions. Answers or interpretations will vary according to the questions we ask of a literary work. In practice the range of questions can be—and to some extent *should* be—combined whenever we develop a literary interpretation. Such questions can always generate the thesis or argument of a critical essay.

Although some approaches to literary analysis treat the literary exchange (text, source, receiver) in isolation from the world surrounding that exchange (the world of economics, politics, religion, cultural tradition, and sexuality—in other words, the world in which we live), most contemporary modes of analysis acknowledge the importance of that world to the literary exchange. These days, even if literary scholars focus primarily on the text or its source or receiver, they nonetheless often incorporate some of the observations and methods developed by theorists and critics who have turned their attention toward the larger world. We describe the work of such theorists and critics in the fourth section below, "Historical and Ideological Criticism."

Before expanding on the kinds of critical approaches within these four categories, let's consider one example in which questions concerning the text, source, and receiver, and a consideration of historical and ideological questions, would contribute to a richer interpretation of a text. To begin as usual with preliminary questions about the *text*: *What* is FIRST FIGHT. THEN FIDDLE.? Printed correctly on a separate piece of paper, the text would tell us at once that it is a poem because of its form: rhythm, repeating word sounds, lines that leave very wide margins on the page. Because you are reading this poem in this book, you know even more about its form. (In this way, the publication *source* gives clues about the *text*.) By putting it in a section with other poetry, we have encouraged you to approach it as a poem worth reading, re-reading, and thinking about. (What other ways do you encounter poems, and what does the medium in which a poem is presented tell you about it?)

You should pursue other questions focused on the text. What *kind* of poem is it? Here we have helped you, especially if you are not already familiar with the sonnet form, by grouping this poem with other sonnets (in "The Sonnet: An Album"). Classifying "First Fight. Then Fiddle." as a sonnet might then prompt you to interpret the ways that this poem is or is not like other sonnets. Well and good: You can check off its fourteen lines of (basically) iambic pentameter and note its somewhat unusual rhyme scheme and meter in relation to the rules of Italian and English sonnets. But *why* does this experiment with the sonnet form matter?

To answer questions about the purpose of form, you need to answer some basic questions about *source*, such as: *When* was this sonnet written and published? *Who* wrote it? *What* do you know about Gwendolyn Brooks, about 1949, about African American women and/or poets in the United States at that time? A short historical and biographical contexts essay answering such questions might help put the "sonnetness" of this poem in context. But assembling all the available information about the source and original context of the poem, even some sort of documented testimony from Brooks about her intentions or interpretation of it, would still leave room for other questions leading to new interpretations.

What about the *receiver* of "First Fight. Then Fiddle."? Even within the poem a kind of audience exists. This sonnet seems to be a set of instructions addressed to "you." (Although many sonnets are addressed by a speaker, "I," to an auditor, "you," such address rarely sounds like a series of military commands, as it does here.) This internal audience is not of course to be confused with real people responding to the poem, and it is the latter who are its *receivers*. How did readers respond to it when it was first published? Can you find any published reviews, or any criticism of this sonnet published in studies of Gwendolyn Brooks?

Questions about the receiver, like those about the author and other sources, readily connect with questions about historical and cultural context. Would a reader or someone hearing this poem read aloud respond differently in the years after World War II than in an age of global terrorism? Does it make a difference whether the audience addressed by the speaker inside the poem is imagined as a group of African American men and women or as a group of European American male commanders? (The latter question could be regarded as an inquiry involving the text and the source as well as the receiver.) Does a reader need to identify with any of the particular groups the poem fictitiously addresses, or would any reader, from any background, respond to it the same way? Even the formal qualities of the text could be examined through historical lenses: The sonnet form has been associated with prestigious European literature and with themes of love and mortality since the Renaissance. It is significant that a twentieth-century African American poet chose *this* traditional form to twist "[t]hreadwise" into a poem about conflict (line 5).

The above are only some of the worthwhile questions that might help illuminate this short, intricate poem. (We will develop a few more thoughts about it in illustrating different approaches to the text and to the source.) Similarly, the complexity of critical approaches far exceeds our four categories. While a great deal of worthwhile scholarship and criticism borrows from a range of theories and methods, below we give necessarily simplified descriptions of various critical approaches that have continuing influence. We cannot trace a history of the issues involved or capture all the complexity of these movements. Instead think of what follows as a road map to the terrain of literary analysis. Many available resources, including the works listed in the bibliography at the end of this overview, describe the entire landscape in more precise detail.

EMPHASIS ON THE TEXT

This broad category encompasses approaches that de-emphasize questions about the author/source or the reader/reception in order to focus on the work itself. In a sense any writing about literature presupposes recognition of form, in that it deems the object of study to *be* a literary work that belongs to a genre or subgenre of literature, as Brooks's poem belongs with sonnets. Moreover, almost all literary criticism notes some details of style or structure, some *intrinsic* features such as the relation between dialogue or narration, or the pattern of rhyme and meter. But *formalist* approaches go further by privileging the design of the text itself above other considerations.

Some formalists, reasonably denying the division of content from form (since the form is an aspect of the content or meaning), have more controversially excluded any discussion of *extrinsic* or contextual matters such as the author's biography or questions of psychology, sociology, or history. This has led to accusations that formalism, in avoiding reference to actual authors and readers or to the world of economic power or social change, also avoids political issues or commitments. Some historical or ideological critics have therefore argued that formalism supports the status quo. Conversely, some formalists charge that any extrinsic—that is, historical, political, ideological, biographical, or psychological—interpretations of literature threaten to reduce the text to propaganda. A formalist might maintain that the inventive wonders of art exceed any practical function it serves. In practice, however, influential formalists have generated modes of *close reading* that balance attention to form and context, with some acknowledgment of the political implications of literature. In the early twenty-first century the formalist methods of close reading remain influential, especially in classrooms. Indeed, *The Norton Introduction to Literature* adheres to these methods in its emphasis on textual elements and interpretation of form.

New Criticism

One strain of formalism, loosely identified as the New Criticism, dominated literary studies from approximately the 1920s to the 1970s. New Critics rejected the two approaches that then prevailed in the relatively new field of English studies: the dry analysis of the development of the English language and the misty-eyed appreciation and evaluation of "Great Works." Generally, New Criticism minimizes consideration of both the source and the receiver, emphasizing instead the intrinsic qualities of a literary work perceived to be unified, coherent, and self-contained. Psychological or historical information about the author, the intentions or feelings of authors and readers, and any philosophical or socially relevant "messages" derived from the work are all out-of-bounds in a strict New Critical reading. The text in a fundamental way refers to itself: Its medium is its message. Although interested in ambiguity and irony as well as figurative language, a New Critical reader considers the organic unity of the unique work. Like an organism, the work develops in a synergetic relation of parts to whole.

A New Critic might, for example, publish an article titled "A Reading of 'First Fight. Then Fiddle.'" (The method works best with **lyric** or other short forms because it requires painstaking attention to details such as metaphors or alliteration.) Little if anything would be said of Gwendolyn Brooks or the poem's relation to Modernist poetry. The critic's task is to give credit to the poem, not the poet or the period, and if it is a good poem, then—implicitly—it can't be merely "about" World War II or civil rights. New Criticism presumes that a good literary work addresses universal human themes and may be interpreted objectively on many levels. These levels may be related more by tension and contradiction than harmony, yet that relation demonstrates the coherence of the whole.

Thus the New Critic's essay might include some of the following observations. The poem's title—which reappears as half of the first line—consists of a pair of two-word imperative sentences, and most statements in the poem paraphrase these two sentences, especially the first of them, "First fight." Thus an alliterative two-word command, "Win war" (line 12), follows a longer version of such a command: "But first to arms, to armor" (9). Echoes of this sort of exhortation appear throughout. We, as audience, begin to feel "[b]ewitch[ed], bewilder[ed]" (4) by a buildup of undesirable urgings, whether at the beginning of a line ("Be deaf," 11) or the end of a line ("Be remote," 7; "Carry hate," 9) or in the middle of a line ("Rise bloody," 12). It's hardly what we would want to do. Yet the speaker makes a strong case for the practical view that a society needs to take care of defense before it can "[d]evote" itself to "silks and honey" (6–7)—in other words, the soft and sweet pleasures of art. But what kind of culture would place "hate / In front of [. . .] harmony" and try to ignore "music" and "beauty" (9–11)? What kind of people are only "remote / A while from malice and from murdering" (7–8)? A society of warlike heroes would rally to this speech. Yet on re-reading, many of the words jar with the tone of heroic battle cry.

The New Critic examines not only the speaker's style and words but also the order of ideas and lines in the poem. Ironically, the poem defies the speaker's command; it fiddles first, and then fights, since the octave (first eight lines) concerns art, and the sestet (last six) concerns war. The New Critic might be delighted by the ironic way that the two segments of the poem in fact unite, in that their topics—octave on how to fiddle, sestet on how to fight—mirror each other. The beginning of the poem plays with metaphors for music and art as means of inflicting "hurting love" (line 3) or emotional conquest, that is, ways to "fight." War and art are both, as far as we know, universal in all human societies. The poem, then, is an organic whole that explores timeless concerns.

Later critics have pointed out that New Criticism, despite its avoidance of extrinsic questions, had a political context of its own. The insistence on the autonomy of the artwork should be regarded as a strategy adopted during the Cold War as a counterbalance to the politicization of art in fascist and communist regimes. New Criticism also provided a program for literary reading accessible to beginners of every social background, which was extremely useful at a time when more women, minorities, and members of the working class than ever before were entering college. By the 1970s these same groups had helped generate two sources of opposition to New Criticism's ostensible neutrality and transparency: (1) critical studies emphasizing the politics of social differences (e.g., feminist criticism and ethnic studies); and (2) theoretical approaches, based on linguistics, philosophy, and political theory, that effectively distanced nonspecialists once more.

Structuralism

Whereas New Criticism was largely a British and American phenomenon, structuralism and its successor, poststructuralism, derive primarily from French theorists. Each of these movements was drawn to scientific objectivity and wary of political commitment. Politics, after all, had inspired the censorship of science, art, and inquiry throughout centuries and in recent memory.

Structuralist philosophy, however, was something rather new. Influenced by the Swiss linguist Ferdinand de Saussure (1857–1913), structuralists sought an objective system for studying the principles of language. Saussure distinguished between individual uses of language, such as the sentences you or I might have just spoken or written (*parole*), and the sets of rules governing English or any language (*langue*). Just as a structuralist linguist would study the interrelations of signs in the *langue* rather than the variations in specific utterances in *parole*, a structuralist literary or cultural critic would study shared systems of meaning, such as genres or myths that pass from one country or period to another, rather than a particular poem in isolation (the favored subject of New Criticism).

Another structuralist principle derived from Saussure is the emphasis on the arbitrary association between a word and what it is said to signify—that is, between the *signifier* and the *signified*. The word *horse*, for example, has no divine, natural, or necessary connection to that four-legged, domesticated mammal, which is named by other combinations of sounds and letters in other languages. Any language is a network of relations among such arbitrary signifiers, just as each word in the dictionary must be defined using other words in that dictionary. Structuralists largely attribute the meanings of words to rules of differentiation from other words. Such differences may be phonetic (as among the words *cat* and *bat* and *hat*), or they may belong to conceptual associations (as among the words *dinky, puny, tiny, small, miniature, petite, compact*). Structuralist thought has directed particular attention to the way that opposites or dualisms such as "night" and "day" or "feminine" and "masculine" define each other through opposition to each other rather than by direct reference to objective reality. For example, the earth's motion around the sun produces changing exposure to sunlight daily and seasonally, but by linguistic convention we call it "night" between, let's say, 8 p.m. and 5 a.m., no matter how light it is. (We may differ in opinions about "evening" or "dawn." But our "day" at work may begin or end in the dark.) The point is that arbitrary labels divide what in fact is continuous, encouraging us to see and think in dualistic or binary terms ("male"/"female").

Structuralism's linguistic insights have greatly influenced literary studies. Like New Critics, structuralist critics show little interest in the creative process or in authors, authorial intentions, or authorial circumstances. Similarly, structuralism discounts the idiosyncrasies of particular readings; it takes texts to represent interactions of words and ideas that stand apart from individual human identities or sociopolitical commitments. Structuralist approaches have applied less to lyric poetry than to myths, narratives, and cultural practices such as sports or fashion. Although structuralism tends to affirm a universal humanity just as New Criticism does, structuralist work in comparative mythology and anthropology challenged the absolute value that New Criticism tended to grant to time-honored canons of great literature.

The structuralist would regard a text not as a self-sufficient icon but as part of a network of conventions. A structuralist essay on "First Fight. Then Fiddle." thus might ask why the string is plied with the "feathery sorcery" (line 2) of the "bow" (7). These words suggest the art of a Native American trickster or primitive sorcerer, while at the same time the instrument is a disguised weapon: a stringed bow with feathered arrows (the term "muzzle" is a similar pun, suggesting an animal's snout and the discharging end of a gun). Or is the fiddle—a violin played in musical forms such as bluegrass—a metaphor for popular art or folk resistance to official culture? In many folktales a hero is taught to play the fiddle by the devil or tricks the devil with a fiddle or similar instrument. Further, a structuralist reading might attach great significance to the sonnet form as a paradigm that has shaped poetic expression for centuries. The classic "turn" or reversal of thought in a sonnet may imitate the form of many narratives of departure and return, separation and reconciliation. Brooks's poem repeats in the numerous short reversing imperatives, as well as in the structure of octave versus sestet, the eternal oscillation between love and death, creation and destruction.

Poststructuralism

By emphasizing the paradoxes of dualisms and the ways that language constructs our awareness, structuralism planted the seeds of its own destruction or, rather, deconstruction. Dualisms (e.g., masculine/feminine, mind/body, culture/nature) cannot be separate but equal; rather, they take effect as differences of power in which one dominates the other. Yet as the German philosopher of history Georg Wilhelm Friedrich Hegel (1770–1831) insisted, the relations of the dominant and subordinate, of master and slave, readily invert themselves. The master is dominated by his need for the slave's subordination; the possession of subordinates defines his mastery. As Brooks's poem implies, each society reflects its own identity through an opposing "they," in a dualism of civilized/barbaric. The instability of the speaker's position in this poem (is he or she among the conquerors or the conquered?) is a model of the instability of roles throughout the human world. There is no transcendent ground—except on another planet, perhaps—from which to measure the relative positions of the polar opposites on earth. French theorist Roland Barthes (1915–80) and others, influenced by the radical movements of the 1960s and the increasing complexity of culture in an era of mass consumerism and global media, extended structuralism into more profoundly relativist perspectives.

Poststructuralism is the broad term used to designate the philosophical position that attacks the objective, universalizing claims central to most fields of knowledge since the eighteenth century or the Enlightenment. Poststructuralists, distrusting the optimism of a positivist philosophy that suggests the world is knowable and explicable, ultimately doubt the possibility of certainties of any kind, since language signifies only through a chain of other words rather than through any fundamental link to reality. This argument derives from structuralism, yet it also criticizes structuralism's tendency both to universalize and to ignore socio-political issues. Ideology is a key conceptual ingredient in the poststructuralist argument against structuralism. *Ideology* is a slippery term that can broadly be defined as a socially shared set of ideas that shape behavior; often it refers to the values that legitimate the ruling interests in a society, and in many accounts it is the hidden code that is officially denied. (We discuss kinds of ideological criticism later.) Poststructuralist theory has influenced a variety of critical schools introduced below, including some that emphasize *source* or *receiver* over *text*. But in literary criticism, poststructuralism has marshaled most forces under the banner of deconstruction.

Deconstruction

Deconstruction insists on the logical impossibility of knowledge that is not influenced or biased by the words used to express it. Deconstruction also claims that language is incapable of representing any sort of reality directly. As practiced by its most famous proponent, French philosopher Jacques Derrida (1930–2004), deconstruction endeavors to trace the way texts imply the contradiction of their explicit meanings. The deconstructionist delights in the sense of dizziness experienced when the grounds of conviction crumble away; *aporia*, or irresolvable doubt, is the desired, if fleeting, end of an encounter with a text. Deconstruction questions *humanism*, or the worldview that is centered on human values and the self-sufficient individual, because deconstruction denies that there is an ultimate, solid reality on which to base truth or the identity of the self. All values and identities, deconstructionists insist, are constructed by competing systems of meaning, or *discourses*. This is a remarkably influential set of ideas that you will meet again as we discuss other approaches.

The traditional concept of the author as creative origin of the text comes under fire in deconstructionist criticism, which emphasizes instead both the creative power of language or the text and the ingenious work of the critic in detecting gaps and contradictions in the text. Thus, like New Criticism, deconstruction disregards the author and concentrates on textual close reading. But unlike New Criticism, deconstruction also emphasizes the role of the reader as well and insists that the text need not be respected as a pure and coherent icon. Deconstructionists might "read" many kinds of writing and representation in other media in much the same way that they might read John Milton's *Paradise Lost*—that is, irreverently. Indeed, when deconstruction erupted in university literature departments traditional critics and scholars feared what they saw as the resulting breakdown of the distinctions between literature and other kinds of texts. Many attacks on literary theory have particularly lambasted deconstructionists for apparently rejecting all the reasons to care about literature in the first place and for writing in a style so flamboyantly obscure that no one but specialists can understand. Yet in practice Derrida and others have carried harmony before them, to paraphrase Brooks; their readings often delight in the play of figurative language, thereby enhancing rather than undermining our sense of literature's value.

A deconstructionist might read "First Fight. Then Fiddle." in a manner somewhat similar to the New Critic's, but with even more focus on puns and paradoxes and on the poem's resistance to organic unity. For instance, the two alliterative commands, "fight" and "fiddle," might be opposites, twins, or inseparable consequences of each other. The word "fiddle" is tricky. Does it suggest that art is trivial? Does it allude to a dictator who "fiddles while Rome burns," as the saying goes? Someone who "fiddles" is not performing a grand, honest, or even competent act: One fiddles with a hobby, with the account books, with car keys in the dark. The artist in this poem defies the orthodoxy of the sonnet form, instead making a kind of harlequin patchwork out of different traditions, breaking the rhythm, intermixing endearments and assaults.

To the deconstructionist the recurring broken antitheses of war and art, art and war cancel each other out. The very metaphors undermine the speaker's summons to war. The command "Be deaf to music and to beauty blind" (line 11), which takes the form of a *chiasmus*, or X-shaped sequence (adjective, noun; noun, adjective), is a kind of miniature version of this chiasmic poem. (We are supposed to follow a sequence, fight then fiddle, but instead reverse that by imagining ways to do violence with art or to create beauty through destruction.) The poem, a lyric written but imagined as spoken or sung, puts the senses and the arts under erasure; we are somehow not to hear music (by definition audible), not to see beauty (here a visual attribute). "[M]aybe not too late" comes rather too late: At the end of the poem it will be too late to start over, although "having first to civilize a space / Wherein to play your violin with grace" comes across as a kind of beginning (12–14). These comforting lines form the only *heroic* **couplet** in the poem, the only two lines that run smoothly from end to end. (All the other lines have **caesuras**, **enjambments**, or balanced pairs of concepts, as in "from malice and from murdering" [8].) But the violence behind "civilize," the switch to the high-art term "violin," and the use of the Christian term "grace" all suggest that the pagan erotic art promised at the outset, the "sorcery" of "hurting love" that can "bewitch," will be suppressed.

Like other formalisms, deconstruction can appear apolitical or conservative because of its skepticism about the referential connection between literature and the larger world. Yet poststructuralist linguistics provides a theory of *difference* that clearly pertains to questions about status and power in society, as in earlier examples of masculine/feminine, master/slave. The *Other*, the negative of the norm, is always less than an equal counterpart. Deconstruction has been a tool for various poststructuralist thinkers including historian Michel Foucault, feminist theorist and psychoanalyst Julia Kristeva, and psychoanalytic theorist Jacques Lacan, while deconstructionist conceptualizations of difference and othering inform much ideological criticism.

Narrative Theory

Before concluding the discussion of text-centered approaches, we should mention the schools of narratology and narrative theory that have shaped study of the novel and other kinds of narrative. Criticism of fiction has been in a boom period since the 1950s, but narrative theory per se has had more limited influence than the approaches discussed above. Since the 1960s different analysts of the forms and techniques of narrative, most notably the Chicago formalists and the structuralist narratologists, have developed terminology for the various interactions of author, implied author, narrator, and characters; of plot and the treatment of time in the selection and sequence of scenes; of voice, point of view, or focus and other aspects of fiction (terminology often referenced in this book). As formalisms, narrative theories tend to ignore the author's biography, individual reader response, and the historical context of the work or its actual reception.

Narratology began by presenting itself as a structuralist science; its branches have grown from psychoanalytic theory or extended to reader-response criticism. In recent decades studies of narrative technique and form have responded to Marxist, feminist, and other ideological criticisms that insist on the political contexts of literature. One important influence on this shift has been the revival of the work of the Russian literary theorist Mikhail Bakhtin (1895–1975), which considers the novel as a *dialogic* form that pulls together the many discourses and voices of a culture and its history. Part of the appeal of Bakhtin's work has been the fusion of textual close reading with attention to material factors such as economics and class and a sense of the open-endedness and contradictoriness of writing (in the spirit of deconstruction more than of New Criticism). Like other Marxist-trained European formalists, Bakhtin sought to understand the complexity of literary modes of communication in the light of politics and history.

EMPHASIS ON THE SOURCE

As the examples above suggest, a great deal can be drawn from a text without referring to its source or author. For millennia many anonymous works were shared in oral or manuscript form, and even after printing spread in Europe few thought it necessary to know the author's name or anything about him or her. Yet criticism from its beginnings in ancient Greece has nonetheless been interested in the designing intention "behind" the text. Even when no evidence remained about the author, a legendary personality has sometimes been invented to satisfy readers' curiosity. From the legend of blind Homer to the latest debates about who "really" wrote "Shakespeare's" plays, literary criticism has been interested in the author.

Biographical Criticism

This approach reached its height in an era when humanism prevailed in literary studies (roughly the 1750s to the 1960s). At this time there was widely shared confidence in the ideas that art and literature were the direct expressions of the artist's or writer's genius and that criticism of great works involved veneration of the great persons who created them. The lives of some famous writers became the models that aspiring writers emulated. Criticism at times was skewed by social judgments, as when John Keats was put down as a "Cockney" poet—that is, London-bred and lower-class. Women and writers from other marginalized groups have at times used pseudonyms or published anonymously to avoid having their work judged only in terms of expectations, negative or positive, of what and how people like them might, should, or even could write. Such writers, in other words, had good reason to be leery of biographical criticism. Others have objected on other grounds to reading literature as a reflection of the author's personality. Such critics have supported the idea that the highest literary art is pure form, untouched by gossip or personal emotion. In this spirit some early twentieth-century critics as well as Modernist writers such as T. S. Eliot, James Joyce, and Virginia Woolf tried to dissociate the text from the personality or political commitments of the author. (The theories of these writers and their actual practices did not always coincide.)

   In the early twentieth century, psychoanalytic criticism interpreted the text in light of the author's emotional conflicts, while other interpretations relied heavily on the author's stated intentions. (Although psychoanalytic criticism entails more than analysis of the author, we will introduce it as an approach that primarily concerns the human source[s] of literature; it usually has less to say about the form and receiver of the text.) Author-based readings can be reductive. All the accessible information about a writer's life cannot definitively explain the writings. As a young man, novelist D. H. Lawrence might have hated his father and loved his mother, but all men who hate their fathers and love their mothers do not write fiction as powerful as Lawrence's. Indeed, Lawrence himself cautioned that we should "trust the tale, not the teller."

Any kind of criticism benefits to some extent, however, from drawing on knowledge of the writer's life and career. Certain critical approaches, devoted to identifying and even honoring distinct literary traditions, make sense only in light of supporting biographical evidence. Studies of Irish literature, Asian American literature, or women's literature require reliable information about the writers' birth and upbringing and even some judgment of the writers' intentions to write *as* members of such groups and traditions. (We discuss feminist, African American, and other studies of distinct literatures in the "Historical and Ideological Criticism" section that follows, although such studies recognize the biographical "source" as a starting point.)

We might read "First Fight. Then Fiddle." rather differently when we know more about Gwendolyn Brooks. An African American, she was raised in Chicago in the 1920s. In the 1940s she began to associate with Harriet Monroe's magazine, *Poetry*, which had been influential in promoting Modernist poetry. Brooks received early acclaim for books of poetry that depict the everyday lives of poor, urban African Americans; in 1950 she was the first African American to win a Pulitzer Prize. In 1967 she became an outspoken advocate for the Black Arts movement, which promoted a separate tradition rather than integration into the aesthetic mainstream. But even before this political commitment, her work never sought to "pass" or to distance itself from the reality of racial difference, nor did it become any less concerned with poetic tradition and form when she published it through small, independent Black presses in her "political" phase.

It is reasonable, then, to read "First Fight. Then Fiddle.," published in 1949, in relation to the role of a racial outsider mastering and adapting the forms of a dominant tradition. Perhaps Brooks's speaker addresses an African American audience in the voice of a revolutionary, calling for violence to gain the right to express African American culture. Perhaps the lines "the music that they wrote / Bewitch, bewilder. Qualify to sing / Threadwise" (lines 3–5) suggest the way that the marginalized may transform the dominant culture's music rather than the other way around. Ten years before the poem was published, a famous African American singer, Marian Anderson, had more than "[q]ualif[ied] to sing" opera and classical concert music, but had still encountered the color barrier in the United States. Honored throughout Europe as the greatest living contralto, Anderson was barred in 1939 from performing at Constitution Hall in Washington, D.C., because of her race. Instead she performed at the Lincoln Memorial on Easter Sunday to an audience of seventy-five thousand people. It was not easy to find a "space" in which to practice her art. Such a contextual reference, whether or not intended, relates biographically to Brooks's role as an African American woman wisely reweaving classical traditions "[t]hreadwise" rather than straining them into "hempen" ropes (5). Beneath the manifest reference to the recent world war, this poem refers to the segregation of the arts in America. (Questions of source and historical context often interrelate.)

Besides readings (like this one) that rely on biographical and historical information, there are still other ways to read aspects of the *source* rather than the *text* or the *receiver*. The source of the work extends beyond the life of the person who wrote it to include not only the writer's other works but also the circumstances of contemporary publishing; contemporary literary movements; the history of the composition, editing, and publication of this particular text, with all the variations; and so on. While entire schools of literary scholarship have been devoted to each of these matters, any analyst of a particular work should bear in mind what is known about the circumstances of writers at a given time and the material conditions of the work's first publication. It makes a difference in our interpretation to know that a certain sonnet circulated in manuscript among a small courtly audience or that a particular novel was serialized in a weekly journal cheap enough for the masses to read it.

Psychoanalytic Criticism

With the development of psychology and psychoanalysis toward the end of the nineteenth century, critics began to apply psychological theories to literary analysis. Symbolism, dreamlike imagery, emotional rather than rational logic, and a pleasure in language all suggested that literature profoundly evoked a mental and emotional landscape, often one of disorder or abnormality. From mad poets to patients speaking in verse, imaginative literature might be regarded as a representation of shared irrational structures within all *psyches* or selves. While psychoanalytic approaches have developed along with structuralism and poststructuralist linguistics and philosophy, they rarely focus on textual form. Rather, they attribute latent or hidden meaning to unacknowledged desires in some person, often the author or source behind the character in a narrative or drama. A psychoanalytic critic can also focus on the response of readers and, in recent decades, usually accepts the influence of changing social history on the structures of sexual desire represented in the work. Nevertheless, psychoanalysis has typically aspired to a universal, unchanging theory of the mind and personality, and criticism that applies it has tended to emphasize the authorial source.

FREUDIAN CRITICISM

For most of the twentieth century, the dominant school of psychoanalytic criticism was the Freudian, based on the work of Austrian neurologist and founder of psychoanalysis Sigmund Freud (1856–1939). Many of its practitioners assert that the meaning of a literary work exists not on its surface but in the psyche (some would even claim in the neuroses) of the author. Classic psychoanalytic criticism read works as though they were the recorded dreams of patients; interpreted the life histories of authors as keys to the works; or analyzed characters as though they, like real people, possess a set of repressed childhood memories. (In fact, many novels and most plays leave out information about characters' development from infancy through adolescence, the period that psychoanalysis especially strives to reconstruct.)

A well-known Freudian reading of *Hamlet*, for example, insists that Hamlet suffers from an Oedipus complex, a Freudian term for a group of repressed desires and memories that corresponds with the Greek myth on which Sophocles's play OEDIPUS THE KING is based. In this view Hamlet envies his uncle because he unconsciously wants to sleep with his mother, who was the first object of his desire as a baby. The ghost of Hamlet, Sr., who appears early in the play and urges his son to avenge his murder, may then be a manifestation of Hamlet's unconscious desire or of his guilt over wanting to kill his father, the person who has a right to the desired mother's body. Hamlet's later madness is not, by this account, a mere pretense, but the result of this frustrated desire; his cruel mistreatment of Ophelia is a deflection of his disgust at his mother's being "unfaithful" to him. Freudian critics who stress the author's psyche might read *Hamlet* as the expression of Shakespeare's own Oedipus complex. Other psychoanalytic critics, reading imaginative literature as symbolic fulfillment of unconscious wishes much as psychoanalysts read dreams, look for objects, spaces, or actions that appear to relate to sexual anatomy or activity. Much as if tracing out the extended metaphors of an erotic poem by John Donne or a blues or Motown lyric, the Freudian reads containers, empty spaces, or bodies of water as female; tools, weapons, towers, trees, trains, or planes as male.

JUNGIAN AND MYTH CRITICISM

Just as a Freudian assumes that all human psyches have similar histories and structures, a Jungian critic assumes that we all share a universal or collective unconscious (just as each of us has an individual unconscious). According to Swiss psychiatrist and psychoanalyst Carl Gustav Jung (1875–1961) and his followers, the unconscious harbors universal patterns and forms of human experiences, or **archetypes**. We can never know these archetypes directly, but they surface in art in an imperfect, shadowy way, taking the form of literary archetypes—the snake with its tail in its mouth, rebirth, the mother, the double or doppelgänger, the descent into hell. In the classic quest narrative, the hero struggles to free himself (the gender of the pronoun is significant) from the Great Mother to become a separate, self-sufficient being (combating a demonic antagonist), surviving trials to gain the reward of union with his ideal other, the feminine anima. In a related school of *archetypal criticism*, influenced by Canadian-born critic Northrop Frye (1912–91), the prevailing myth follows a seasonal cycle of death and rebirth. Frye proposed a system that classified all literary forms according to a cycle of genres associated with the phases of human experience from birth to death and the natural cycle of seasons (e.g., spring/romance).

These approaches have been useful in the study of folklore and early literatures as well as in comparative studies of different national literatures. While most myth critics focus on the hero's quest, there have been forays into feminist archetypal criticism. These emphasize variations on the myths of Isis and Demeter, goddesses of fertility or seasonal renewal, who take different forms to restore either the sacrificed woman (Persephone's season in the underworld) or the sacrificed man (Isis's search for Osiris and her rescue of their son, Horus). Many twentieth-century poets were drawn to the heritage of archetypes and myths. Adrienne Rich's DIVING INTO THE WRECK, for example, self-consciously rewrites a number of gendered archetypes, with a female protagonist on a quest into a submerged world.

Most critics today, influenced by poststructuralism, have become wary of universal patterns. Like structuralists, Jungians and archetypal critics strive to compare and unite the ages and peoples of the world and to reveal fundamental truths. Rich, as a feminist poet, suggests that the "book of myths" is an eclectic anthology that needs to be revised. Claims of universality tend to obscure the detailed differences among cultures and often appeal to some idea of *biological determinism*. Such determinism diminishes the power of individuals to design alternative life patterns and even implies that no literature can really surprise us.

LACANIAN CRITICISM

As it has absorbed the indeterminacies of poststructuralism under the influence of thinkers such as French theorist Jacques Lacan (1901–81) and Franco-Bulgarian psychoanalyst Julia Kristeva (b. 1941), psychological criticism has become increasingly complex. Few critics today are strict Freudian analysts of authors or texts, and few maintain (as would a conventional Jungian) that universal archetypes explain the meaning of a tree or water in a text. Yet psychoanalytic theory continues to inform many varieties of criticism, and most new work in this field is affiliated with Lacanian psychoanalysis. Lacan's theory unites poststructuralist linguistics with Freudian theory. The Lacanian critic, like a deconstructionist, perceives the text as defying conscious authorial control, foregrounding instead the powerful interpretation of the critic. Accepting the Oedipal paradigm and the unconscious as the realm of repressed desire, Lacanian theory aligns the development and structure of the individual human *subject* with the development and structure of language. To simplify a purposefully dense theory: The very young infant inhabits the Imaginary, in a preverbal, undifferentiated phase dominated by a sense of union with the Mother. Recognition of identity begins with the Mirror Stage, ironically with a disruption of a sense of oneness. For when one first looks into a mirror, one begins to recognize a split or difference between one's body and the image in the mirror. This splitting prefigures a sense that the *object* of desire is Other and distinct from the subject. With difference or the splitting of subject and object comes language and entry into the Symbolic Order, since we use words to summon the absent object of desire (as a child would cry "Mama" to bring her back). But what language signifies most is the lack of that object. The imaginary, perfectly nurturing Mother would never need to be called.

As in the biblical Genesis, the Lacanian "genesis" of the human subject tells of a loss of paradise through knowledge of the difference between subject and object or Man and Woman (eating of the Tree of the Knowledge of Good and Evil leads to the sense of shame that teaches Adam and Eve to hide their nakedness). In Lacanian theory the Father governs language or the Symbolic Order; the Word spells the end of a child's sense of oneness with the Mother. Further, the Father's power claims omnipotence, the possession of male prerogative symbolized by the Phallus, which is not the anatomical difference between men and women but the idea or construction of that difference. Thus it is language or culture rather than nature that generates the difference and inequality between the sexes. Some feminist theorists have adopted aspects of Lacanian psychoanalytic theory, particularly the concept of *the gaze*. This concept notes that the subject who looks tends to be figured as masculine, whereas the object to be looked at tends instead to be feminine.

Another influential concept is *abjection*. Kristeva's theory of abjection most simply reimagines the infant's blissful sense of union with the mother and the darker side of that possible union. To return to the mother's body would be death, as metaphorically we are buried in Mother Earth. Yet according to the theory, people both desire and dread such loss of boundaries. A sense of self or *subjectivity* and hence of independence and power depends on resisting abjection. The association of the maternal body with abjection or with the powerlessness symbolized by the female's Lack of the Phallus can help explain negative cultural images of women. Many narrative genres seem to split the images of women between an angelic and a witchlike, even demonic or monstrous type. Lacanian or Kristevan theory has been well adapted to film criticism and to fantasy and other popular forms favored by structuralism or archetypal criticism.

Psychoanalytic literary criticism today—as distinct from specialized discussion of Lacanian theory, for example—treads more lightly than in the past, as we might demonstrate with a look at James Joyce's ARABY. Here, a young Dublin boy, orphaned and raised by an aunt and uncle, likes to haunt a back room in the house, where the "former tenant, [. . .] a priest, had died" (par. 2). (Disused rooms at the margins of houses resemble the unconscious, and a dead celibate "father" suggests a kind of failure of the Law, of conscience, or in Freudian terms, of the superego.) The priest had left behind a "rusty bicycle-pump" in the "wild garden" with "a central apple tree" (these echoes of the garden of Eden suggesting the impotence of Catholic religious symbolism). The boy seems to gain consciousness of a separate self by gazing upon an idealized female object, Mangan's sister, whose "name was like a summons to all my foolish blood" (par. 4). Though he secretly watches and follows her, she is not so much a sexual fantasy as a beautiful art object (par. 9). He retreats to the back room to think of her in a kind of ecstasy that resembles masturbation. Yet it is not masturbation: It is preadolescent, dispersed through all orifices—the rain feels like "incessant needles [. . .] playing in the sodden beds"; and it is sublimated, that is, repressed and redirected into artistic or religious forms rather than directly expressed by bodily pleasure: "All my senses seemed to desire to veil themselves" (par. 6).

It is not in the back room but on the street that the girl finally speaks to the hero, charging him to go on a quest to Araby. After several trials, the hero, carrying the talisman, arrives in a darkened hall "girdled at half its height by a gallery," an underworld or maternal space that also resembles a deserted temple (par. 25). The story ends without his grasping the prize to carry back, the "chalice" or holy grail (symbolic of female sexuality) that he had once thought to bear "safely through a throng of foes" (par. 5).

Such a reading seems likely to raise the objection that it is overreading: *You're seeing too much in it; the author didn't mean that.* This has been a popular reaction to psychoanalysis for over a hundred years, but it is only a heightened version of a response to many kinds of criticism. This sample reading pays close attention to the text, but does not really follow a formal approach because its goal is to explain the psychological implications or resonance of the story's details. We have mentioned nothing about the author, though we could have used this reading to forward a psychoanalytic reading of Joyce's biography.

EMPHASIS ON THE RECEIVER

In some sense critical schools develop in reaction to the perceived excesses of earlier critical schools. By the 1970s, in a time of political upheaval that highly valued individual expression, a number of critics felt that the various routes toward objective criticism had led to dead ends. New Critics, structuralists, and psychoanalytic or myth critics had sought objective, scientific systems that disregarded changing times, political issues, or the reader's personal response. New Critics and other formalists tended to value a literary canon made up of works that were regarded as complete, unchanging objects to be interpreted according to ostensibly timeless standards.

Reader-Response Criticism

Among critics who challenge New Critical assumptions, reader-response critics regard the work not as what is printed on the page but as what is experienced, even created through each act of reading. According to such critics, the reader effectively performs the text into existence the way a musician creates music from a score. Reader-response critics ask not what a work means but what a work does to and through a reader. Literary texts leave gaps that experienced readers fill according to expectations or conventions. Individual readers differ, of course, and gaps in a text provide space for different interpretations. Some of these lacunae are temporary—such as the withholding of the murderer's name until the end of a mystery novel—and are closed by the text sooner or later, though each reader will in the meantime fill them somewhat differently. But other lacunae are permanent and can never be filled with certainty; they result in a degree of indeterminacy in the text.

The reader-response critic observes the expectations aroused by a text; how they are satisfied or modified; and how the reader comprehends the work when all of it has been read, and when it is re-read. Such criticism attends to the reading habits associated with different genres and to the shared assumptions that, in a particular cultural context, help to determine how readers fill in gaps in the text.

The role of the reader or receiver in the literary exchange has also been studied from a political or ideological perspective. Literature helps shape social identity, and social status shapes access to different kinds of literature, as well as ways of reading it (which are thus never entirely or simply individual or "personal"). Studies of African American literature and other ethnic literatures have often featured discussion of literacy and of the obstacles for readers who either cannot find their counterparts within literary texts or there encounter negative stereotypes of their group. Thus, as we will discuss below, most forms of historical and ideological criticism include some consideration of the reader. But they do not treat that reader as passive. Feminist critics adapted reader-response criticism, for example, to note that girls often do not identify with many American literary classics as boys do, and thus girls do not simply accept the stereotype of women as angels, temptresses, or scolds who should be abandoned for the sake of all-male adventures.

Reception Studies

Where reader-response critics tend to analyze the experience of a hypothetical reader of one sort or another, reception studies instead explores how texts have been received by actual readers and how literacy and reading have themselves evolved over time. A critic in this school might examine documents ranging from contemporary reviews to critical essays written across the generations since the work was first published or diaries and other documents in which readers describe their encounters with particular works. Alternatively, they might turn to quantitative measures for reading, from sales and library lending rates to questionnaires. Just as there are histories of publishing and of the book, so there are histories of literacy and reading practices. Poetry, fiction, and drama often directly represent the act of reading as well as writing. Many published works over the centuries have debated the benefits and perils of reading works such as sermons or novels. Particular genres and works construct different classes or kinds of readers in the way they address readers or supply what readers are supposed to want.

HISTORICAL AND IDEOLOGICAL CRITICISM

The approaches to the text, the author, and the reader outlined above may each take some note of historical contexts, including changes in formal conventions, the writer's milieu, or audience expectations. In the nineteenth century, historical criticism took the obvious facts that a work is created in a specific historical and cultural context and that the author is a part of that context as reasons to treat literature as a reflection of society and its history. Twentieth-century formalists rejected this *reflectivist* model of art—that is, the assumption that literature and other arts straightforwardly represent, as in a mirror, the collective spirit of a society at a given time. But as we have remarked, the formalist tendency to isolate the work of art from social and historical context met resistance in the last decades of the twentieth century. The new historical approaches that developed out of that resistance replace the reflectivist model with a *constructivist* model, whereby literature and other cultural discourses are seen to help *construct* social relations and roles rather than merely *reflect* them. A society's ideology, its system of representations (ideas, myths, images), is inscribed in literature and other cultural forms, which in turn help shape identities and social practices.

From the 1980s until quite recently, historical approaches have dominated literary studies. Some such approaches have been insistently *materialist*—that is, seeking causes more in concrete conditions such as technology, modes of production, and distribution of wealth. Such criticism usually owes an acknowledged debt to Marxism, the large and complex body of concepts and theories built on the work of German-born philosopher Karl Marx (1818–83). Other historical approaches have been influenced to a degree by Marxist critics and cultural theorists, but work within the realm of ideology, textual production, and interpretation, using some of the methods and concerns of traditional literary history. Still others emerge from the civil rights movement and the struggles for recognition of marginalized groups including women; Black, Indigenous, and People of Color (BIPOC); and the Lesbian, Gay, Bisexual, Transgender, Queer, and Intersex (LGBTQI) community.

Feminist studies, African American studies, gay and lesbian studies, and studies of the literatures of different immigrant and ethnic populations within and beyond the United States have each developed along similar theoretical lines. These schools, like Marxist criticism, adopt a constructivist position: Literature, they argue, is not simply a reflection of prejudices and norms; it also helps define social norms and identities, such as what it means to be an African American woman. Generally speaking, each of these schools has moved through stages of first claiming *equality* with the literature dominated by White Anglo American men, then affirming the *difference* or distinctiveness of their own separate culture and literature, and then theoretically *questioning the terms and standards* of such comparisons. At a certain point in its development, each group rejects *essentialism*, the notion of innate or biological bases for differentiating sexes, races, or other groups. This rejection of essentialism is usually called the constructivist position, in a somewhat different but related sense to our definition above. Constructivism maintains that identity is socially formed rather than biologically determined. Differences of anatomical sex, skin color, first language, parental ethnicity, and eventual sexual preferences have great impact on how one is classified, brought up, and treated socially, and on one's subjectivity or sense of identity. Constructivists maintain that these differences, however, are constructed more by ideology and the resulting behaviors than by any natural programming.

All of these areas of study have, moreover, been enriched in recent years by embracing the concept of *intersectionality*, first introduced in 1989 by American legal scholar Kimberlé Crenshaw (b. 1959) and coming into widespread use in the 2000s. Rejecting what Crenshaw calls "single-issue analyses" focusing exclusively on gender, sexuality, race, ethnicity, or class, taken in isolation, intersectional analyses instead attend to the sometimes unpredictable ways in which these various factors (and thus related forms of discrimination such as racism and sexism) intersect to redefine one another, ensuring that the identities and experiences of Black women or Latinas, for example, differ not only from each other but also from those of both White women, on the one hand, and Black men or Latinos, on the other, because so, too, does the treatment accorded these different groups—in law, in literature, and in real life.

Marxist Criticism

The most insistent and vigorous historical approach through the twentieth century to the present has been Marxism. With roots in nineteenth-century historicism, Marxist criticism was initially reflectivist. Economics, the underlying cause of history, was thus considered the *base*; and culture, including literature and the other arts, was regarded as the *superstructure*, simultaneously an outcome and a reflection of the base. Viewed from this simple Marxist perspective, the literary works of a period are economically determined; they *reflect* the state of the struggle between classes in a particular place and time. History enacts recurrent three-step cycles, a pattern that Hegel had defined as *dialectic*. (Hegel was cited above on the interdependence of master and slave.) Each socioeconomic phase, or *thesis*, is counteracted by its *antithesis*, and the resulting conflict yields a *synthesis*, which becomes the ensuing *thesis*, and so on. As with early Freudian criticism, early Marxist criticism was often preoccupied with labeling and exposing illusions or deceptions. A novel might be read as a thinly disguised defense of the power of bourgeois industrial capital; its appeal on behalf of the suffering poor might be dismissed as an effort to fend off class rebellion.

As a rationale for state control of the arts, Marxism was abused in the Soviet Union and other totalitarian states in the early- to mid-twentieth century. In the hands of sophisticated critics, however, Marxism as a school of thought has been richly rewarding. Various approaches that unite formal close reading and political analysis developed under Soviet communism and under fascism in Europe, often in covert resistance. These schools in turn have influenced critical movements in North America; New Criticism, structuralist linguistics, deconstruction, and narrative theory have each borrowed from European Marxist critics.

Most recently, a new mode of Marxist theory has developed, largely guided by the thinking of Walter Benjamin (1892–1940) and Theodor Adorno (1903–69) of the Frankfurt School in Germany, Louis Althusser (1918–90) in France, and Raymond Williams in Britain. This work has generally tended to modify the base/ superstructure distinction and to interrelate public and private life, economics and culture. Newer Marxist (or so-called *Marxian*) interpretation assumes that the relation of a literary work to its historical context is *overdetermined*—the relation has multiple determining factors rather than a sole cause or aim. This thinking similarly acknowledges that neither the source nor the receiver of the literary interaction is a mere tool or victim of the ruling powers or state. Representation of all kinds, including literature, always has a political dimension, according to this approach; conversely, political and material conditions such as work, money, or institutions depend on representation.

Showing some influence of psychoanalytic and poststructuralist theories, recent Marxist literary studies examine the effects of ideology by focusing on the works' gaps and silences: Ideology may be conveyed in what is repressed or contradicted. In many ways, such criticism has adapted to the conditions of consumer rather than industrial capitalism and to global rather than national economies. The worldwide revolution to which early Marxists looked forward, when the proletariat or working classes would overthrow the capitalists, has never taken place; in many countries industrial labor has instead been swallowed up by the service sector, and workers reject the political Left that would seem their most likely ally. Increasingly, Marxist criticism has acknowledged that the audience of literature may be active rather than passive, just as the text and source may be more than straightforward instructions for toeing a given political line. Marxist criticism has been especially successful with the novel, since that genre more than drama or short fiction is capable of representing numerous people from different classes as they develop over long periods of time.

Feminist Criticism

Like Marxist criticism and the schools discussed below, feminist criticism derives from a critique of a history of oppression, in this case the history of women's inequality. Feminist criticism has no single founder like Freud or Marx; it has been practiced to some extent since the 1790s, when praise of women's cultural achievements went hand in hand with arguments by Briton Mary Wollstonecraft, among others, that women were rational beings deserving equal rights and education. While paying homage to earlier efforts such as British novelist Virginia Woolf's influential *A Room of One's Own* (1929), modern feminist criticism emerged from a "second wave" of feminist activism, in the 1960s and 1970s, associated with the civil rights and antiwar movements. One of the first disciplines in which women's activism took root was literary studies, but feminist theory and women's studies quickly became recognized methods across the disciplines.

Feminist literary studies began by denouncing the misrepresentation of women in literature and affirming the importance of women's writings, before quickly adopting the insights of poststructuralist theory; yet the early strategies continue to have their use. At first, feminist criticism in the 1970s, like early Marxist criticism, regarded literature as a reflection of patriarchal society's sexist base; the demeaning images of women in literature were symptoms of a system that had to be overthrown. Feminist literary studies soon began, however, to claim the *equal* but distinctive qualities of writings by women. American critics such as Elaine Showalter (b. 1941), Sandra M. Gilbert (b. 1936), and Susan Gubar (b. 1944) explored canonical works by women, relying on close reading with some aid from historicist and psychoanalytic methods.

By the 1980s it was widely recognized that a New Critical method would leave most of the male-dominated canon intact and most women writers still in obscurity, because many women had written in different genres and styles, on different themes, and for different audiences than had male writers. To affirm the *difference* or distinctiveness of female literary traditions, some feminist scholars championed what they hailed as women's innate or universal affinity for fluidity and cycle rather than solidity and linear progress. Others concentrated on the role of the mother in human psychological development, often drawing on the work of American sociologist Nancy Chodorow (b. 1944). According to this argument, girls, not having to adopt a gender role different from that of their first object of desire, the mother, grow up with less rigid boundaries of self and a relational and situational rather than judgmental ethic.

The dangers of such essentialist generalizations soon became apparent. If women's differences from men were biologically determined or due to universal archetypes, there was no solution to women's oppression, which many cultures had justified in terms of biological reproduction or archetypes of nature. At this point in the debate, feminist literary studies intersected with poststructuralist linguistic theory in *questioning the terms and standards* of comparison. French feminist theory, articulated most prominently by Hélène Cixous (b. 1937) and Luce Irigaray (b. 1930), deconstructed the supposed archetypes of gender written into the founding discourses of Western culture. We have seen that deconstruction helps expose the power imbalance in every dualism. Thus man is to woman as culture is to nature or mind is to body, and in each case the second term is held to be inferior or Other. The language and hence the worldview and social formations of our culture, not nature or eternal archetypes, constructed woman as Other. This insight was helpful in challenging essentialism or biological determinism.

Having reached a theoretical criticism of the terms on which women might claim equality or difference from men in the field of literature, feminist studies also confronted other issues in the 1980s. Deconstructionist readings of gender difference in texts by men as well as women could lose sight of the real world, in which women are paid less and are more likely to be victims of sexual and domestic violence. With this in mind, some feminist critics pursued links with Marxist or African American studies; gender roles, like those of class and race, were interdependent systems for registering the material consequences of people's differences. It no longer seemed so easy to say what the term "women" referred to, when the interests of different kinds of women had been opposed to each other. Black women asked if feminism was really their cause, when White women had so long enjoyed power over both men and women of their race and when the early women's movement largely ignored the experience and concerns of women of color. In a classic Marxist view, women allied with men of their class rather than with women of other classes. It became more difficult to make universal claims about women's literature, as the horizon of the college-educated North American feminists expanded to recognize the range of conditions of women and of literature worldwide. Intersectional feminist criticism thus concerns itself with race, class, nationality, and sexuality, as well as gender, and the way these differences shape each other and intersect in the experience and representation of particular individuals and groups.

Gender Studies and Queer Theory

From the 1970s, feminists sought recognition for lesbian writers and lesbian culture, which they felt had been even less visible than male homosexual writers and gay culture. Concurrently, feminist studies abandoned the simple dualism of male/female, part of the very binary logic of patriarchy that seemed to cause the oppression of women. Thus feminists recognized a zone of inquiry, the study of gender, as distinct from historical studies of women, and increasingly they included masculinity as a subject of investigation. As gender studies turned to interpretation of the text in ideological context regardless of the sex or intention of the author, it incorporated the ideas of French philosopher Michel Foucault's *History of Sexuality* (1976). Foucault (1926–84) helped show that there was nothing natural, universal, or timeless in the constructions of sexual difference, sexual identities, or sexual practices. Foucault also historicized the concept of homosexuality, which only in the later nineteenth century came to be defined as a condition associated with a distinctive personality type. Literary scholars began to study the history of sexuality as a key to shifts in modern culture that had also shaped literature.

By the 1980s gender had come to be widely regarded as a discourse that imposed binary social norms on human diversity. American theorists as disparate as biologist Donna Haraway (b. 1944) and philosopher Judith Butler (b. 1956) insisted further that sex and sexuality have no natural basis; even the anatomical differences are representations from the moment the newborn is put in a pink or blue blanket. Moreover, these theorists claimed that gender and sexuality are *performative* and malleable positions, enacted in many more than two varieties. From cross-dressing to surgical sex changes, the alternatives chosen by real people have influenced critical theory and generated both writings and literary criticism about those writings. Perhaps biographical and feminist studies face new challenges when identity seems subject to radical change and it is less easy to determine the sex of an author.

Gay and lesbian literary studies have included practices that parallel those of feminist criticism. At times critics identify oppressive or positive representations of homosexuality in works by men or women, gay, lesbian, or straight. At other times critics seek to establish the equivalent stature of a work by a gay or lesbian writer or, because these identities tended to be hidden in the past, to reveal that a writer *was* gay or lesbian. Again stages of *equality* and *difference* have yielded to a *questioning of the terms of difference*, in this case in what has been called *queer theory*. The field of queer theory hopes to leave everyone guessing rather than to identify gay or lesbian writers, characters, or themes. One of its founding texts, *Between Men* (1985), by American critic Eve Kosofsky Sedgwick (1950–2009), drew on structuralist insight into desire as well as anthropological models of kinship to show that, in canonical works of English literature, male characters form "homosocial" (versus homosexual) bonds through their rivalry for and exchange of a woman. Queer theory, because it rejects the idea of a fixed identity or innate or essential gender, likes to discover resistance to heterosexuality in unexpected places. Queer theorists value gay writers such as Oscar Wilde, but they also find queer implications regardless of the author's acknowledged identity. This approach emphasizes not the surface signals of the text but the subtler meanings an audience or receiver might detect. It encompasses elaborate close reading of many varieties of literary work; characteristically, a leading queer theorist, University of California, Berkeley Professor Emeritus D. A. Miller (b. 1948), has written in loving detail about both Jane Austen and Broadway musicals.

African American and Ethnic Literary Studies

Critics sought to define an African American literary tradition as early as the turn of the twentieth century. The 1920s Harlem Renaissance produced some of the first classic essays on writings by African Americans. Criticism and histories of African American literature tended to ignore and dismiss women writers, while feminist literary histories, guided by Woolf's classic *A Room of One's Own*, neglected women writers of color. Only after feminist critics began to succeed in the academy and African American studies programs were established did the Whiteness of feminist studies and the masculinity of African American studies become glaring; both fields have for some time worked to correct this narrowness of vision, in part by learning from each other.

The study of African American literature followed the general pattern that we have noted, first striving to claim equality, on established aesthetic grounds, of works such as Ralph Ellison's magnificent *Invisible Man* (1952). Then in the 1960s the Black Arts or Black Aesthetic movement emerged. Once launched in the academy, however, African American studies has been devoted less to celebrating an essential racial difference than to tracing the historical construction of a racial Other and a subordinated literature. The field sought to recover neglected genres such as slave narratives and traced common elements in fiction or poetry to the conditions of slavery and segregation. By the 1980s, feminist and poststructuralist theory had an impact in the work of some Black critics such as Henry Louis Gates, Jr. (b. 1950), Houston A. Baker, Jr. (b. 1943), and Hazel V. Carby (b. 1948), while others objected that the doubts raised by "theory" stood in the way of political commitment. African Americans' cultural contributions to America have gained much more recognition than before. New histories of American culture have been written with the view that racism is not an aberration but inherent to the guiding narratives of national identity and progress. Critics now regard race as a discourse with no basis in genetics but with weighty investments in ideology. This poststructuralist position coexists with scholarship that takes into account the race of the author or reader or that focuses on African American characters or themes.

In recent years a series of fields has arisen in recognition of the literatures of other American ethnic groups, large and small: Asian Americans, Native Americans, Latina/os, and Chicana/os. Increasingly, such studies avoid romanticizing an original, pure culture or assuming that these literatures by their very nature undermine the values and power of the dominant culture. Instead, critics emphasize the *hybridity* of all cultures in a global economy. The contact and intermixture of cultures across geographical borders and languages (translations, "creole" speech made up of native and acquired languages, dialects) may be read as enriching literature and art, despite their roots in economic exploitation. In method and in aim these fields have much in common with African American studies, though each cultural and historical context is very different. Each field richly deserves the separate, more detailed and nuanced consideration that we cannot offer here.

All of these fields have, in recent decades, been influenced by and themselves profoundly influenced Critical Race Theory (CRT). Today an international, multidisciplinary, and multifaceted approach and movement made familiar and controversial to a wide audience through best sellers like African Americanist Ibram X. Kendi's *How to Be an Antiracist* and the *New York Times'* Pulitzer Prize–winning "1619 Project" (both 2019), CRT originated in the late 1980s within the field of American legal studies through the work of scholars including Derrick Bell (1930–2011); Kimberlé Crenshaw, who coined the term; and Richard Delgado (b. 1939), coauthor of *Critical Race Theory: An Introduction* (2001). Rooted in the constructionist (versus essentialist) views of race that we have already examined, CRT involves activism as well as analysis. It thus seeks, in Delgado's words, to "transform" society "for the better" by "ascertain[ing] how society organizes itself along racial lines and hierarchies," particularly through the law and other dominant discourses, institutions, and policies rather than simply through the attitudes and behaviors of individuals. Basic tenets of CRT, as outlined by Delgado, include the ideas that (1) racialization and racism are and, in a U.S. context, always have been, "ordinary, not aberrational"— that is, part of the everyday experience "of most people of color" in part because (2) racialization and racism also have "served" and do serve "important purposes, both psychic and material, for the dominant group," giving "large segments of society . . . little incentive to eradicate" them or even to recognize that and how they operate; as a result, (3) members of that dominant group potentially have much to learn from BIPOC, whose "different histories and experiences" ensure them quite different perspectives. As should come as no surprise, however, given that CRT founder Crenshaw also coined the term *intersectionality*, the latter concept is foundational to CRT.

Not so very long ago, critics might have been charged with a fundamental misunderstanding of the nature of literature if they pursued matters considered the business of sociologists, matters—such as class, race, sexuality, and gender—that seemed extrinsic to the text. The rise of the above-noted fields has made it standard practice for critics to address questions about class, race, sexuality, and gender in placing a text, its source, and its reception in historical and ideological context. One brief example might illustrate the way Marxist, feminist, queer, and African American studies' perspectives can contribute to a literary reading.

Tennessee Williams's A STREETCAR NAMED DESIRE was first produced in 1947 and won the Pulitzer Prize in 1948. Its acclaim was partly due to its fashionable blend of naturalism and symbolism: The action takes place in a shabby tenement on an otherworldly street, Elysian Fields—in an "atmosphere of decay" laced with "lyricism," as Williams's stage directions put it (1.1). After the Depression and World War II, U.S. audiences welcomed a turn away from world politics into the psychological core of human sexuality. This turn to ostensibly individual conflict was a kind of alibi for at least two sets of issues that Williams and middle-class theatergoers in New York and elsewhere sought to avoid. First are racial questions that intersect with ones of gender and class: What is the play's attitude to race, and what is Williams's attitude? Biography seems relevant, though not the last word on what the play means. Williams's family had included slaveholding cotton growers, and he chose to spend much of his adult life in the South, which he saw as representing a beautiful but dying way of life. He was deeply attached to women in his family who might be models for the brilliant, fragile, cultivated Southern White woman, Blanche DuBois. Blanche ("white" in French), representative of a genteel, feminine past that has gambled, prostituted, dissipated itself, speaks some of the most eloquent lines in the play when she mourns the faded Delta plantation society. Neither the playwright nor his audience wished to deal with segregation in the South as it existed in their own (Jim Crow) era, a region that since the Civil War had stagnated as a kind of agricultural working class in relation to the dominant North—which had its racism, too.

The play scarcely notices race. The main characters are White. The cast includes a "Negro Woman" as servant and a blind Mexican woman who offers artificial flowers to remember the dead, but these figures seem more like props or symbols than fully developed characters. Instead, racial difference is arguably transposed into ethnic and class difference in the story of a working-class Pole intruding into a family clinging to French gentility. Stella warns Blanche that she lives among "heterogeneous types" and that Stanley is "a different species" (1.1). The play can thus be seen to transfigure contemporary anxieties about miscegenation, as the virile (Black) man dominates the ideal White woman and rapes the spirit of the plantation South. A former soldier who works in a factory, Stanley represents as well the defeat of the old, agricultural economy by industrialization.

The second set of issues that neither the playwright nor his audience confronts directly is the disturbance of sexual and gender roles that would in later decades lead to movements for women's and gay rights. It was well-known in New Orleans at least that Williams was gay. In the 1940s he lived with his Mexican American lover, Pancho Rodriguez y Gonzales, in the French Quarter. Like many homosexual writers in other eras, Williams arguably recasts homosexual desire in heterosexual costume. Blanche, performing femininity with a kind of camp excess, might be a fading queen pursuing and failing to capture younger men. Stanley, hypermasculine, might caricature the (butch) object of desire of both men and women as well as the anti-intellectual brute force in postwar America. His conquest of women (he had "the power and pride of a richly feathered male bird among hens" [1.1]) appears to be biologically determined. By the same token it seems natural that Stanley and his buddies go out to work and that their wives are homemakers in the way now seen as typical of the 1950s. In this world, artists, homosexuals, or unmarried working women like Blanche would be both vulnerable and threatening. Blanche, after all, has secret pleasures— drinking and sex—that Stanley can indulge in openly. Blanche is the one who is taken into custody by the medical establishment, which in this period categorized homosexuality as a form of insanity.

New Historicism

Three interrelated schools of historical and ideological criticism did much to reshape literary studies in the twentieth century's final decades: New Historicism and both cultural and postcolonial studies. These are part of the swing of the pendulum away from formal analysis of the text and toward historical analysis of context.

New historicism has less obvious political commitments than Marxism, feminism, or queer theory, but it shares their interest in the power of discourse to shape ideology. Old historicism, in the 1850s through the 1950s, confidently told a story of civilization's progress from a Western point of view; a historicist critic would offer a close reading of the plays of Shakespeare and then locate them within the prevailing Elizabethan "worldview." "New Historicism," labeled in 1982 by American Shakespeareanist Stephen Greenblatt (b. 1943), rejected the technique of plugging samples of a culture into a history of ideas. Influenced by poststructuralist anthropology, New Historicism instead sought to offer a multilayered impression or "thick description" of a culture at one moment in time, considering popular as well as elite forms of expression. As a method, New Historicism belongs with those that deny the unity of the text, defy the authority of the source, and license the receiver—much like deconstruction. Accordingly, New Historicism doubts the accessibility of the past, insisting that all we have is discourse. One model for New Historicism was the historiography of Michel Foucault, who insisted on the power of discourses—that is, not only writing but all structuring myths or ideologies that underlie and shape social relations. The New Historicist, like Foucault, is interested in the transition from the external powers of the state and church in the feudal order to modern forms of power. The rule of the modern state and middle-class ideology is enforced insidiously by systems of surveillance and by each individual's internalization of discipline.

No longer so "new," New Historicism has helped to produce a more narrative and concrete style of criticism even among those who espouse poststructuralist and Marxian theories. A New Historicist article begins with an anecdote, often a description of a public spectacle, and teases out the many contributing causes that brought disparate social elements together in a particular way. It usually applies techniques of close reading to forms that would not traditionally have received such attention. Although it often concentrates on events several hundred years ago, in some ways it defies historicity, flouting the idea that a complete objective impression of the entire context could ever be achieved.

Cultural Studies

Popular culture often gets major attention in the work of New Historicists. Yet today most studies of popular culture would acknowledge their debt instead to cultural studies, as filtered through the now-defunct Center for Contemporary Cultural Studies, founded in 1964 by Jamaican-born Stuart Hall (1932–2014) and others at the University of Birmingham in England. Method, style, and subject matter may be similar in New Historicism and cultural studies: Both attend to historical context, theoretical method, political commitment, and textual analysis. But whereas the American movement shares Foucault's paranoid view of state domination through discourse, the British school, influenced by Raymond Williams (1921–88) and his concept of "structures of feeling," emphasizes the way that ordinary people, the receivers of cultural forms, can and do resist dominant ideology. The documents examined in a cultural-studies essay may be recent, such as artifacts of tourism at Shakespeare's birthplace, rather than sixteenth-century maps. Cultural studies today influences history, sociology, communications and media, and literature departments; its studies may focus on television, film, romance novels, and advertising, or on museums and the art market, sports and stadiums, New Age religious groups, and other forms and practices.

The questions raised by cultural studies might encourage a critic to place a poem like Marge Piercy's BARBIE DOLL in the context of the history of that toy, a doll whose slender, impossibly long legs, tiptoe feet (not unlike the bound feet of Chinese women of an earlier era), small nose, and torpedo breasts epitomized a 1950s ideal of the female body. A critic influenced by cultural studies might align the poem with other works published around 1973 that express feminist protest concerning cosmetics, body image, consumption, and the objectification of women, while she or he would draw on research into the creation, marketing, and use of Mattel toys. The poem reverses the Sleeping Beauty story: This heroine puts herself into the coffin rather than waking up. The poem omits any hero—Ken?—who would rescue her. "Barbie Doll" protests the pressure a girl feels to fit into a heterosexual plot of romance and marriage; no one will buy her if she is not the right toy or accessory.

Indeed, accessories such as "GE stoves and irons" (line 3) taught girls to plan their lives as domestic consumers, and Barbie's lifestyle is decidedly middle-class and suburban (everyone has a house, car, pool, and lots of handbags). The Whiteness of the typical "girlchild" (1) goes without saying. Although Mattel produced Barbie's African American friend, Christie, in 1968, Piercy's title makes the reader imagine Barbie, not Christie. In 1997 Mattel issued Share a Smile Becky, a friend in a wheelchair, as though in answer to the humiliation of the girl in Piercy's poem, who feels so deformed, in spite of her "strong arms and back, / abundant sexual drive and manual dexterity" (8–9), that she finally cripples herself. The icon, in short, responds to changing ideology. Perhaps responding to generations of objections like Piercy's, Barbies over the years have been given feminist career goals, yet women's lives are still plotted according to physical image.

In this manner a popular product might be "read" alongside a literary work. The approach would be influenced by Marxist, feminist, gender, and ethnic studies, but it would not be driven by a desire to destroy Barbie as sinister, misogynist propaganda. Piercy's kind of protest against indoctrination has gone out of style. As a cultural studies scholar would point out, girls have found ways to respond to such messages and divert them into stories of empowerment. To explore such processes and trends, a researcher could gather data on Barbie sales and could interview girls or videotape their play in order to establish the actual effects of the dolls and the way girls use and transform them. Whereas traditional anthropology examined non-European or preindustrial cultures, cultural studies may direct its fieldwork, or ethnographic research, inward, at home. Nevertheless, many contributions to cultural studies rely on methods of textual close reading or Marxist and Freudian literary criticism developed in the mid-twentieth century.

Postcolonial Criticism and Studies of World Literature

In the middle of the twentieth century, the remaining colonies of the European nations struggled toward independence. French-speaking Frantz Fanon (1925–61) of Martinique was one of the most compelling voices for the point of view of the colonized or exploited countries, which like the feminine Other had been objectified and denied the right to look and talk back. Palestinian American critic Edward Said (1935–2003), in *Orientalism* (1978), brought poststructuralist analysis to bear on the history of colonization, illustrating the ways that Western culture and Western literature feminized and objectified the East. Postcolonial literary studies developed into a distinct field in the 1990s in tandem with globalization and the replacement of direct colonial power with international corporations and NGOs (nongovernmental agencies such as the World Bank). In general this field cannot share the optimism of cultural studies, given the histories of slavery and economic exploitation of colonies and the violence committed in the name of civilization and progress. Studies by Indian-born scholars Gayatri Chakravorty Spivak (b. 1942) and Homi K. Bhabha (b. 1949) have further mingled Marxist, feminist, and poststructuralist theory to re-read both canonical Western works and the writings of marginalized peoples. Colonial or postcolonial literatures may include works set or published in countries during colonial rule or after independence, or they may feature texts produced in the context of international cultural exchange, such as a novel in English by a woman of Chinese descent writing in Malaysia.

Like feminist and queer studies and studies of African American or other ethnic literatures, postcolonial criticism is inspired by recovery of neglected works, redress of a systematic denial of rights and recognition, and increasing realization that the dualisms of opposing groups reveal interdependence. In this field the stage of difference came early, with the celebrations of African heritage known as *Négritude*, but the danger of that essentialist claim was soon apparent: The Dark Continent or wild island might be romanticized and idealized as a source of innate qualities of vitality long repressed in Enlightened Europe. Currently, most critics accept that the context for literature in all countries is hybrid, with immigration and educational intermixing. Close readings of texts are always linked to the author's biography and literary influences and placed within the context of contemporary international politics as well as colonial history. Many fiction writers, from Salman Rushdie (b. 1947) to Jhumpa Lahiri (b. 1967) and Zadie Smith (b. 1975), make the exploration of cultural mixture or hybridity central to their work, whether in a pastiche of Charles Dickens or a story of an Indian family growing up in New Jersey and returning as tourists to their supposed "native" land. Poststructuralist theories of trauma, and theories of the interrelation of narrative and memory, provide explanatory frames for interpreting writings from Afghanistan to Zambia.

Studies of postcolonial culture retain a clear political mission that feminist and Marxist criticism have found difficult to sustain. Perhaps this is because the scale of the power relations is so vast between nations, rather than between the sexes or classes within those nations. Imperialism can be called an absolute evil, and the destruction of local cultures a crime against humanity. Yet today some of the most exciting literature in English emerges from countries once under the British Empire, and all the techniques of criticism will be brought to bear on it.

If history is any guide, in later decades some critical school will attempt to read the diverse literatures of the early twenty-first century in pure isolation from authorship and national origin, as self-enclosed form. The themes of hybridity, indeterminacy, trauma, and memory will be praised as universal. It is even possible that readers' continuing desire to revere authors as creative geniuses in control of their meanings will regain respectability among specialists. The elements of the literary exchange—text, source, and receiver—are always there to provoke questions that generate criticism, which in turn produces articulations of the methods of that criticism. It is an ongoing discussion well worth participating in.

BIBLIOGRAPHY

For good introductions to the issues discussed here, see the following books, from which we have drawn in this overview. Some of these provide bibliographies of the works of critics and schools mentioned above.

Alter, Robert. *The Pleasure of Reading in an Ideological Age*. W. W. Norton, 1996. Originally published as *The Pleasures of Reading: Thinking about Literature in an Ideological Age*, 1989.

Barnet, Sylvan, and William E. Cain. *A Short Guide to Writing about Literature*. 12th ed., Longman, 2012.

Barry, Peter. *Beginning Theory: An Introduction to Literary and Cultural Theory*. 3rd ed., Manchester UP, 2009.

Bressler, Charles E. *Literary Criticism: An Introduction to Theory and Practice*. 5th ed., Pearson, 2011.

Culler, Jonathan. *Literary Theory: A Very Short Introduction*. 2nd ed., Oxford UP, 2011.

Davis, Robert Con, and Ronald Schleifer. *Contemporary Literary Criticism: Literary and Cultural Studies*. 4th ed., Addison Wesley Longman, 1999.

Eagleton, Terry. *Literary Theory: An Introduction*. Anniversary ed., U of Minnesota P, 2008.

Groden, Michael, et al., editors. *The Johns Hopkins Guide to Literary Theory and Criticism*. 2nd ed., Johns Hopkins UP, 2004.

Hawthorn, Jeremy. *A Glossary of Contemporary Literary Theory*. 4th ed., Bloomsbury Academic, 2000.

Leitch, Vincent B. *American Literary Criticism since the 1930s*. 2nd ed., Routledge, 2010.

————, et al., editors. *The Norton Anthology of Theory and Criticism*. 3rd ed., W. W. Norton, 2018.

Lentricchia, Frank. *After the New Criticism*. U of Chicago P, 1980.

Murfin, Ross, and Supryia M. Ray, editors. *The Bedford Glossary of Critical and Literary Terms*. 3rd ed., Bedford/St. Martin's, 2008.

Selden, Raman, and Peter Widdowson. *A Reader's Guide to Contemporary Literary Theory*. 3rd ed., U of Kentucky P, 1993.

Stevens, Anne H. *Literary Theory and Criticism: An Introduction*. Broadview Press, 2015.

Turco, Lewis. *The Book of Literary Terms*. UP of New England, 1999.

Wolfreys, Julian, editor. *Literary Theories: A Reader and Guide*. Edinburgh UP, 1999.

Permissions Acknowledgments

TEXT CREDITS

Introduction

Hai-Dang Phan: "My Father's 'Norton Introduction to Literature,' Third Edition (1981)" first published in *Poetry*, 207.2 (Nov. 2015). Commentary by Hai-Dang Phan from "Contributor's Notes and Comments" was published in THE BEST AMERICAN POETRY 2016, ed. by Edward Hirsch and David Lehman. Reprinted by permission of Hai-Dang Phan.

John Crowe Ransom: "Bells for John Whiteside's Daughter" from SELECTED POEMS.

Fiction

Chimamanda Ngozi Adichie: "Apollo" by Chimamanda Adichie, first printed in *The New Yorker*. Copyright © 2015 by Chimamanda Ngozi Adichie, used by permission of The Wylie Agency LLC.

Isabel Allende: "And of Clay Are We Created," from THE STORIES OF EVA LUNA by Isabel Allende, translated from the Spanish by Margaret Sayers Peden. Copyright © 1989 by Isabel Allende. English translation copyright © 1991 by Macmillan Publishing Company. Reprinted with the permission of Atria Books, a division of Simon & Schuster, Inc. All rights reserved. Excerpts from "An Interview with Isabel Allende" by Farhat Iftekharuddin from SPEAKING OF THE SHORT STORY: INTERVIEWS WITH CONTEMPORARY WRITERS, pp. 3–14. Farhat Iftekharuddin and Mary Rohrberger, eds. Copyright © 1997 by University Press of Mississippi.

Margaret Atwood "Lusus Naturae" from STONE MATTRESS: NINE TALES by Margaret Atwood, compilation copyright © 2014 by O. W. Toad, Ltd. Used by permission of Nan A. Talese, an imprint of the Knopf Doubleday Publishing Group, a division of Penguin Random House LLC. All rights reserved. Rights in Canada by permission of Emblem/McClelland & Stewart, a division of Penguin Random House Canada Limited.

James Baldwin: "Sonny's Blues" copyright © 1957 by James Baldwin. Reprinted with permission from The Estate of James Baldwin.

Toni Cade Bambara: "The Lesson," copyright © 1972 by Toni Cade Bambara; from GORILLA, MY LOVE by Toni Cade Bambara. Used by permission of Random House, an imprint and division of Penguin Random House LLC. All rights reserved.

Jorge Luis Borges: "The House of Asterion," copyright © 1998 by Maria Kodama; translation copyright © 1998 by Penguin Random House LLC; from COLLECTED FICTIONS: VOLUME 3 by Jorge Luis Borges, translated by Andrew Hurley. Used by permission of Viking Books, an imprint of Penguin Publishing Group, a division of Penguin Random House LLC. All rights reserved.

Ray Bradbury: "The Veldt" first published in *The Saturday Evening Post*, Sept. 23, 1950, is reprinted by permission of Don Congdon Associates, Inc. Copyright © 1953 by the Curtis Publishing Company, renewed 1977 by Ray Bradbury. Excerpts from "TANGENT Online Presents: An Interview with Ray Bradbury" by Robert Jacobs, Dave Truesdale, and Bob Wayne. First published in *Tangent #5*, Summer 1976, and *Tangent* online, June 9, 2012. Reprinted by permission of the publisher of *Tangent*, Dave Truesdale, and Robert Jacobs. Copyright © 1976, 2012 by Robert Jacobs and *Tangent*/Tangent Online. All rights reserved.

Linda Brewer: "20/20" from MICRO FICTION: AN ANTHOLOGY OF REALLY SHORT STORIES, ed. by Jerome Stern. Reprinted by permission of the author.

Alissa Nutting: "Model's Assistant [pp. 17–28] from UNCLEAN JOBS FOR WOMEN AND GIRLS. Copyright © 2010 by Alissa Nutting. Reprinted by permission of HarperCollins Publishers.

Joyce Carol Oates: "Where Are You Going, Where Have You Been?" from HIGH LONESOME by Joyce Carol Oates. Copyright © 2006 by The Ontario Review, Inc. Used by permission of HarperCollins Publishers. Excerpt from "'Where Are You Going, Where Have You Been?' and Smooth Talk: Short Story into Film" from WOMAN WRITER: OCCASIONS AND OPPORTUNITIES. Copyright © 1988 by The Ontario Review, Inc. Used by permission John Hawkins and Associates, Inc.

Tim O'Brien: "The Lives of The Dead" and "The Things They Carried" from THE THINGS THEY CARRIED. Copyright © 1990 by Tim O'Brien. Reprinted by permission of Houghton Mifflin Harcourt Publishing Company. All rights reserved.

Flannery O'Connor: Excerpts from THE HABIT OF BEING: LETTERS OF FLANNERY O'CONNOR, ed. by Sally Fitzgerald. Copyright © 1979 by Regina O'Connor. Excerpts from MYSTERY AND MANNERS by Flannery O'Connor. Copyright © 1969 by the Estate of Mary Flannery O'Connor. "Everything That Rises Must Converge" from EVERYTHING THAT RISES MUST CONVERGE. Copyright © 1965 by the Estate of Mary Flannery O'Connor. Copyright renewed 1993 by Regina O'Connor. All reprinted by permission of Farrar, Straus & Giroux. "A Good Man is Hard to Find" and "Good Country People" are reprinted from A GOOD MAN IS HARD TO FIND AND OTHER STORIES by permission of Houghton Mifflin Harcourt Publishing Company. Copyright © 1953 by Flannery O'Connor and renewed 1981 by Regina O'Connor. All rights reserved.

Eileen Pollack: Excerpts from "Flannery O'Connor and the New Criticism" republished with permission of Oxford University Press. From American Literary History 19:2 (2007); permission conveyed through Copyright Clearance Center Inc.

Annie Proulx: "Job History" from CLOSE RANGE: WYOMING STORIES by Annie Proulx. Copyright © 1999 by Dead Line Ltd. Reprinted with the permission of Scribner, a division of Simon & Schuster, Inc. All rights reserved.

Ann E. Reuman: From "Revolting Fictions" by Ann E. Reuman, first published in Papers on Language and Literature vol. 29, # 2, Spring 1993. Copyright © 1993 by The Board of Trustees, Southern Illinois University Edwardsville. Reprinted by permission.

Karen Russell: "St. Lucy's Home for Girls Raised by Wolves" from ST. LUCY'S HOME FOR GIRLS RAISED BY WOLVES: STORIES by Karen Russell, copyright © 2006 by Karen Russell. Used by permission of Alfred A. Knopf, an imprint of the Knopf Doubleday Publishing Group, a division of Penguin Random House LLC. All rights reserved.

George Saunders: "Puppy," first published in The New Yorker, May 28, 2007, is reprinted by permission of the author. Copyright © 2007 by George Saunders. Collected in TENTH OF DECEMBER: STORIES, copyright © 2013 by George Saunders. Used by permission of Random House, an imprint and division of Penguin Random House LLC. All rights reserved. Excerpt from "Knowable in the Smallest Fragment: An Interview with George Saunders" by Matthew Vollmer from Gutcult, online, June 14, 2011. Reprinted by permission of Matthew Vollmer.

David Sedaris: "Jesus Shaves" first published in Esquire, from ME TALK PRETTY ONE DAY by David Sedaris. Copyright © 2000 by David Sedaris. Used by permission of Little, Brown and Company. All rights reserved. Electronic rights by permission of Don Congdon Associates, Inc.

Lorrie N. Smith: Excerpts from "The Things Men Do: The Gendered Subtext in Tim O'Brien's Esquire Stories" republished with permission of Taylor & Francis Ltd. From Critique: Studies in Contemporary Fiction 35.1 (Fall 1993); permission conveyed through Copyright Clearance Center Inc. Taylor & Francis Ltd., http://www.tandfonline.com.

Zadie Smith: "Meet the President!" by Zadie Smith. Published by The New Yorker, 2013. Copyright © Zadie Smith. Reproduced by permission of the author c/o Rogers, Coleridge & White Ltd., 20 Powis Mews, London W11 1JN.

Amy Tan: "A Pair of Tickets" from THE JOY LUCK CLUB by Amy Tan, copyright © 1989 by Amy Tan. Used by permission of G. P. Putnam's Sons, an imprint of Penguin Publishing Group, a division of Penguin Random House LLC. All rights reserved.

Poetry

W. E. B. Du Bois: W. W. Norton wishes to thank the Crisis Publishing Co., Inc., the publisher of the magazine of the National Association for the Advancement of Colored People, for use of the *Crisis* Magazine material, an excerpt from "Two Novels: *Home to Harlem* and *Quicksand*" by W.E. B. Du Bois, first published in *Crisis* Magazine, June 1928 issue.

Denise Duhamel: "Humanity 101" from SCALD by Denise Duhamel, copyright © 2017. Reprinted by permission of the University of Pittsburgh Press.

Bob Dylan: "The Times They Are A-Changin'," words and music by Bob Dylan. Copyright © 1963, 1964 Universal Tunes. Copyright Renewed. All rights reserved. Reprinted by permission of Hal Leonard LLC.

Martín Espada: "Coca-Cola and Coco Frío", from CITY OF COUGHING AND DEAD RADIATORS by Martín Espada. Copyright © 1993 by Martín Espada. Used by permission of W. W. Norton & Company, Inc. "Of the Threads that Connect the Stars" first published in *Ploughshares*, Spring 2013, Vol. 39, # 1, is reprinted by permission of the author. Copyright © 2013 by Martín Espada.

Robert Frost: "Acquainted with the Night," "Fire and Ice," "Stopping by Woods on a Snowy Evening," "The Road Not Taken," and "'Out, Out—'" from the book THE POETRY OF ROBERT FROST, ed. by Edward Connery Lathem. Copyright © 1916, 1923, 1928, 1969 by Henry Holt and Company, copyright © 1944, 1951, 1956 by Robert Frost. Reprinted by permission of Henry Holt and Company. All rights reserved.

Ross Gay: "A Small Needful Fact" from THE QUARRY: A SOCIAL JUSTICE POETRY DATABASE (April 30, 2015). Also published by Split This Rock. Reprinted by permission of Ross Gay.

Allen Ginsberg: "The old pond" and "Looking over my shoulder" from COLLECTED POEMS 1947–1980 by Allen Ginsberg. Copyright © 1984 by Allen Ginsberg. Used by permission of HarperCollins Publishers.

Elisa Gonzalez: "In Quarantine, I Reflect on the Death of Ophelia," originally published in *The New Yorker*. Reprinted by permission of the author.

Angelina Grimké: "Tenebris" and "The Black Finger" from SELECTED WORKS OF ANGELINA GRIMKE, Angelina Grimke Papers, Moorland-Spingarn Research Center, Howard University. Reprinted by permission of Moorland-Spingarn Research Center, Howard University.

Emily Grosholz: "Eden" from THE STARS OF EARTH: NEW AND SELECTED POEMS (2017). Reprinted by permission of Able Muse Press. Print rights by permission of Story Line Press.

Joy Harjo: "By the Way" from *The New Yorker* (Dec. 5, 2016). Copyright © 2016 by Joy Harjo. Reprinted with permission of The Permissions Company, Inc., on behalf of the author, www.joyharjo.com. "The Woman Hanging from The Thirteenth Floor Window" from HOW WE BECOME HUMAN: NEW AND SELECTED POEMS: 1975–2001. Copyright © 1983 by Joy Harjo. Used by permission of W. W. Norton & Company, Inc.

Gwen Harwood: "In the Park" from SELECTED POEMS by Gwen Harwood, ed. by Gregory Kratzmann (2001). Copyright © 2001 by John Harwood. First published by Penguin Books Australia in 2001. Reproduced with permission of Penguin Random House Australia Pty Ltd.

Robert Hayden: "Homage to the Empress of the Blues", "A Letter from Phillis Wheatley". Copyright © 1978 by Robert Hayden, "Those Winter Sundays". Copyright © 1966 by Robert Hayden, from COLLECTED POEMS OF ROBERT HAYDEN by Robert Hayden, edited by Frederick Glaysher. Copyright © 1985 by Emma Hayden. Used by permission of Liveright Publishing Corporation.

Terrance Hayes: "Mr. T—" from HIP LOGIC by Terrance Hayes, copyright © 2002 by Terrance Hayes. Used by permission of Penguin Books, an imprint of Penguin Publishing Group, a division of Penguin Random House LLC. All rights reserved. "Carp Poem," and "The Golden Shovel" from LIGHTHEAD: POEMS by Terrance Hayes, copyright © 2010 by Terrance Hayes. Used by permission of Penguin Books, an imprint of Penguin Publishing Group, a division of Penguin Random House LLC. All rights reserved.

Seamus Heaney: "Digging," and "Punishment" from OPENED GROUND: SELECTED POEMS 1966–1996 by Seamus Heaney. Copyright © 1998 by Seamus Heaney. Reprinted by permission of Farrar, Straus & Giroux and Faber & Faber Ltd.

Bob Hicok: "O my pa-pa" from *Poetry*, May 2007, pp. 87–88. Used by permission of Bob Hicock.

DEAD. Copyright © 2017 by Danez Smith. Reprinted with the permission of The Permissions Company, LLC on behalf of Graywolf Press, Minneapolis, Minnesota, graywolfpress.org.

Patricia Smith: "Sagas of the Accidental Saints" from INCENDIARY ART: POEMS. Copyright © 2017 by Patricia Smith. Published 2017 by TriQuarterly Books/Northwestern University Press. All rights reserved.

Tracy K. Smith: "Ash" from WADE IN THE WATER. Originally from *The New Yorker*, Nov. 23, 2015. Copyright © 2015, 2018 by Tracy K. Smith. "Sci-Fi" from LIFE ON MARS. Copyright © 2011 by Tracy K. Smith. "Unrest in Baton Rouge" from WADE IN THE WATER. Reprinted with the permission of The Permissions Company, Inc. on behalf of Graywolf Press, Minneapolis, Minnesota, www.graywolfpress.org. "Dear Black America: A Letter," © Tracy K. Smith, 2020. Reprinted by permission of Regal Hoffmann & Associates LLC.

Cathy Song: "Heaven", from FRAMELESS WINDOWS, SQUARES OF LIGHT: POEMS by Cathy Song. Copyright © 1988 by Cathy Song. Used by permission of W. W. Norton & Company, Inc.

Bruce Springsteen: "Nebraska" by Bruce Springsteen. Copyright © 1982 by Bruce Springsteen (Global Music Rights). Reprinted by permission. International copyright secured. All rights reserved.

A. E. Stallings: "Sestina: Like" from LIKE: POEMS by A. E. Stallings. Copyright © 2018 by A. E. Stallings. Reprinted by permission of Farrar, Straus and Giroux. "Hades Welcomes His Bride," first published in *Beloit Poetry Journal*, 43 (Summer 1993), reprinted by permission of Alicia E. Stallings.

Sue Standing: "Diamond Haiku" is reprinted from *Ploughshares*, vol. 37.4 (Winter 2011–2012), by permission of the author. Copyright © 2011 by Sue Standing.

George Steiner: "Dying Is an Art" from LANGUAGE AND SILENCE by George Steiner. Copyright © 1967 by George Steiner. Reprinted by permission of Georges Borchardt, Inc. on behalf of the author.

Adrienne Su: "On Writing" from LIVING QUARTERS, copyright © 2015 by Adrienne Su. "Escape from the Old Country" from SANCTUARY, copyright © 2006 by Adrienne Su. Reprinted by permission of Manic D Press, Inc. Commentary by Adrienne Su from THE BEST AMERICAN POETRY 2013, ed. by Denise Duhamel, by permission of Adrienne Su.

Natasha Trethewey: "Pilgrimage" and "Myth" from NATIVE GUARD: POEMS by Natasha Trethewey. Copyright © 2006 by Natasha Trethewey. Reprinted by permission of Houghton Mifflin Harcourt Publishing Company. All rights reserved.

Dylan Thomas: "Do Not Go Gentle into That Good Night" from THE POEMS OF DYLAN THOMAS, copyright © 1952 by Dylan Thomas. Reprinted by permission of New Directions Publishing Corp.

Ellen Bryant Voigt: "My Mother" from HEADWATERS: A POEM, copyright © 2013 by Ellen Bryant Voigt. Used by permission of W. W. Norton & Company, Inc.

David Wagoner: "My Father's Garden" from TRAVELING LIGHT: COLLECTED AND NEW POEMS by David Wagoner. Copyright © 1999 by David Wagoner. Used by permission of the University of Illinois Press.

Stacy Waite: "The Kind of Man I am at the DMV" from BUTCH GEOGRAPHY, published by Tupelo Press. Copyright © 2013 by Stacey Waite. Used with permission of the publisher.

Derek Walcott: "A Far Cry from Africa" from THE POETRY OF DEREK WALCOTT 1948–2013 by Derek Walcott, selected by Glyn Maxwell. Copyright © 2014 by Derek Walcott. Reprinted by permission of Farrar, Straus & Giroux. Excerpts from "An Interview with Derek Walcott" by Edward Hirsch, *Contemporary Literature* vol. 20.3, Summer (1979): pp. 282, 285. © 1979 by the Board of Regents of the University of Wisconsin System. Reprinted courtesy of the University of Wisconsin Press.

Richard Wilbur: "Love Calls Us to the Things of This World" from THINGS OF THIS WORLD, copyright © 1956 and renewed 1984 by Richard Wilbur. "Terza Rima" from ANTEROOMS: NEW POEMS AND TRANSLATIONS by Richard Wilbur. Copyright © 2010 by Richard Wilbur. Reprinted by permission of Houghton Mifflin Harcourt Publishing Company. All rights reserved.

Drama

PHOTO CREDITS

Introduction

Fiction

Poetry

[Rare Book RR]; **p. 784:** Tim Hester/Alamy; **p. 800:** Image Courtesy of The Advertising Archives; **p. 804:** Roger Ressmeyer/Corbis/VCG/Via Getty Images; **p. 813:** Pascal Saez/Sipa USA/Newscom; **p. 816, counterclockwise from top left:** 20th Century Fox/Getty Images, Blank Archives/Getty Images, Tony Korody/Sygma via Getty Images; **p. 839:** AP Photo/Nasser Shiyoukhi; **p. 841:** Lucas Vallecillos/VWPics via AP Photo; **p. 844:** Francois Lo Presti/AFP via Getty Images; **p. 846:** Michael Ochs Archives/Getty Images; **p. 848:** Christopher Felver/ Corbis via Getty Images; **p. 859:** Bettmann/Getty Images; **p. 861:** Courtesy Adrienne Su/ Photo by Guy Freeman; **p. 865:** J. R. Eyerman/The LIFE Picture Collection/Getty Images; **p. 870, top to bottom:** H. Armstrong Roberts/Corbis via Getty Images, Visage/Stockbyte/ Getty Images, Yellow Dog Productions/Getty Images; **p. 876:** Album/British Library/Alamy Stock Photo; **p. 886:** Christopher Felver/Corbis via Getty Images; **p. 889:** Lisa Larsen/The LIFE Picture Collection/Getty Images; **p. 900:** Adrian Pope; **p. 904:** AP Photo/Jason DeCrow; **p. 908:** Popperfoto/Getty Images **p. 944, top to bottom:** Prince Williams/Film-Magic/Getty Images, Pictorial Press Ltd/Alamy Stock Photo, John Cohen/Getty Images; **p. 986:** Justin Phillip Reed; **p. 988:** Ink on paper from 'Black Grey and White: A Book of Visual Sonnets' (Veer Books). © David Miller; **p. 1002:** National Diet Library Digital Collection Site; **p. 1006:** Judy Ray; **p. 1010:** Perry H. Kretz/Keystone Features/Getty Images; **p. 1024, top:** Bettmann/Getty Images, **bottom:** Bettmann/Getty Images; **p. 1025:** David Corio/Michael Ochs Archive/Getty Images; **p. 1031:** Neal Boenzi/New York Times Co./Getty Images; **p. 1056:** IanDagnall Computing/Alamy Stock Photo; **p. 1058:** Bettmann/Getty Images; **p. 1066:** Hulton Archive/Getty Images; **p. 1069:** Bettmann/Corbis/via Getty Images; **p. 1077:** Imagno/Getty Images; **p. 1080:** Cheron Bayna; **p. 1086:** Angela Hampton/Latitud-eStock/Alamy Stock Photo; **p. 1086:** Chris Felver/Getty Images; **p. 1090, top:** Underwood & Underwood/Corbis via Getty Images, **bottom:** Bettmann/Getty Image; **p. 1091:** Library of Congress Prints & Photographs Division Carl Van Vechten Collection LC-USZ62-105919; **p. 1092, top:** Science History Images/Alamy Stock Photo, **bottom:** Library of Congress Prints & Photographs Division Farm Security Administration/ Office of War Information Photograph Collection LC-USW3- 031102-C; **p. 1093:** Bettmann/Corbis via Getty Images; **p. 1094:** Library of Congress Prints & Photographs Division Carl Van Vechten Collection LC-USZ62-100856; **p. 1096:** Courtesy of the Moorland-Spingarn Research Center, Howard University Archives, Howard University, Washington DC; **p. 1097:** Everett Collection; **p. 1098:** The Walter O. Evans Collection, Aaron Douglas, "The Negro Speaks of Rivers (For Langston Hughes)," pen and ink on paper, 5.5″ × 11″, 1941. SCAD Museum of Art Permanent Collection. Gift of Dr. Walter O. Evans and Mrs. Linda J. Evans; **p. 1102:** Corbis via Getty Images; **p. 1113:** HarperCollins Publishers Inc.; **p. 1114:** Library of Congress Prints & Photographs Division Carl Van Vechten Collection LC-DIG-van-5a52142; **p. 1126, clockwise from top left:** Tylonn J. Sawyer, Conde Nast, Oli Scarff/AFP via Getty Images; **p. 1140:** Reuters/Jonathan Bachman/Alamy Stock Photo; **p. 1147:** AP Photo/Chicago Sun-Times; **p. 1161:** Science History Images/Alamy Stock Photo; **p. 1165:** John Bigelow Taylor/Art Resource NY/©ARS NY; **p. 1199:** Two-handled jar with Herakles driving a bull to sacrifice c.525-520 BC (ceramic) Greek (6th century BC)/Museum of Fine Arts Boston Massachusetts USA/Henry Lillie Pierce Fund/Bridgeman Images; **p. 1202:** Andrew Caballero-Reynolds/AFP/Getty Images; **p. 1216:** Pictorial Press Ltd/Alamy Stock Photo; **p. 1228:** (Alvarez): Erika Larsen/Redux, (Angelou): Chris Felver/Getty Images; **p. 1229:** (Bashō): National Diet Library Digital Collection Site, (Betts): Chion Wolf/Connecticut Public Radio, (Bishop): Bettmann/Corbis, (Blake): The Print Collector/Alamy Stock Photo; **p. 1230:** (Blanco): Joyce Tenneson, (Brooks): AP Photos, (Cervantes): Lorna Dee Cervantes; **p. 1231:** (Cofer): Emily Schoone, (Coleridge): Pictorial Press Ltd/Alamy Stock Photo, (Collins): AP Photo/Gino Domenico, (cummings): Bettmann/ Corbis via Getty Images, (Cullen): Science History Images/Alamy Stock Photo; **p. 1232:** (Diaz): Chris Felver/Getty Images, (Dickenson): IanDagnall Computing/Alamy Stock Photo, (Donne): Chronicle/Alamy Stock Photo; **p. 1233:** (Dove): Joey Mcleister/Minneapolis Star Tribune/ ZUMA Wire/Alamy Live News, (Dunbar): Historic Images/Alamy Stock Photo, (Espada): AP Photo/Daily Hampshire Gazette Kevin Gutting; **p. 1234:** (Frost): Library of Congress/Corbis/ VCG via Getty Images, (Ginsberg): AP Photo/Susan Ragan, (Grimke): Courtesy of the Moorland-Spingarn Research Center, Howard University Archives, Howard University,

Drama

Writing about Literature

Index of Authors

Index of Titles and First Lines

Glossary / Index of Literary Terms

Boldface words within definitions are themselves defined in the glossary.

abecedarian, 977 ancient poetic form in which the opening words of each line (or, occasionally, each **stanza**) reproduce the letters of the alphabet (from A to Z).

action, 79, 754, 775, 1997 any event or series of events depicted in a literary work; an event may be verbal as well as physical, so that saying something or telling a story within the story may be an event. *See also* **climax, complication, falling action, inciting incident, plot,** and **rising action.**

allegory, 362 a literary work in which characters, actions, and even settings have two connected levels of meaning. Elements of the literal level signify (or serve as **symbols** for) a figurative level that often imparts a lesson or moral to the reader. One of the most famous English-language allegories is John Bunyan's *Pilgrim's Progress*, in which a character named Christian has to make his way through obstacles such as the Valley of Humiliation to get to the Celestial City.

alliteration, 756, 776, 925, 927, 1286 the repetition of usually initial consonant sounds through a sequence of words—for example, "cease, my song, till fair Aurora rise" (Phillis Wheatley, "An Hymn to the Evening").

allusion, 364, 823, 905, 1162, 1286 brief, often implicit and indirect reference within a literary text to something outside the text, whether another text (e.g., the Bible, a **myth**, another literary work, a painting, or a piece of music) or any imaginary or historical person, place, or thing. Many of the footnotes in this book explain allusions.

amphitheater, 1282 a theater consisting of a stage area surrounded by a semicircle of tiered seats.

analogy, 897, 956 like a **metaphor**, a representation of one thing or idea by something else; in this case, often a simpler explanation that gets at the gist of the more complicated example (e.g., "the brain is like a computer").

anapestic, 777, 932, 934 referring to a metrical form in which each **foot** consists of two unstressed syllables followed by a stressed one—for example, "There are mán- | y who sáy | that a dóg | has his dáy" (Dylan Thomas, "The Song of the Mischievous Dog"). A single foot of this type is called an *anapest*.

anaphora, 927, 1144 **figure of speech** involving the repetition of the same word or phrase in (and especially at the beginning of) successive lines, clauses, or sentences, as in *"We passed* the Fields of Gazing Grain— / *We passed* the Setting Sun—" (Emily Dickinson, "Because I could not stop for Death—").

antagonist, 211, 1278, 1394 a **character** or a nonhuman force that opposes or is in **conflict** with the **protagonist.**

antihero, 212 **protagonist** who is in one way or another the very opposite of a traditional **hero**. Instead of being courageous and determined, for instance, an antihero might be timid, hypersensitive, and indecisive to the point of paralysis. Antiheroes are especially common in modern literary works; examples might include the **speaker** of T. S. Eliot's "The Love Song of J. Alfred Prufrock" or the protagonist of Franz Kafka's *The Metamorphosis*.

apostrophe, 774 **figure of speech** in which a **speaker** or **narrator** addresses an abstraction, an object, or a dead or absent person. An example occurs at the end of Herman Melville's "Bartleby, the Scrivener": "Ah Bartleby! Ah humanity!"

archetype, 213, 362, A12 a **character**, ritual, **symbol**, or **plot** pattern that recurs in the **myth** and literature of many cultures; examples include the **scapegoat** or trickster (character type), the rite of passage (ritual), and the quest or descent into the underworld (plot pattern). The concept derives from the work of psychologist Carl Jung (1875–1961), who argued that archetypes emerge from—and give us a clue to the workings of—the "collective unconscious," a reservoir of memories and impulses that all humans share without being consciously aware of.

arena stage, 1282   stage design in which the audience is seated all the way around the acting area; actors make their entrances and exits through the auditorium.

aside   in **drama**, a brief speech or remark spoken by a **character** either to the audience or, in an undertone, to another character or oneself. Either way, the remark is supposed to be inaudible to other characters on stage.

assonance, 927   repetition of vowel sounds in a sequence of words with different endings—for example, "The death of the poet was kept from his poems" in W. H. Auden's "In Memory of W. B. Yeats."

aubade, 834   poem in which the coming of dawn is either celebrated or denounced as a nuisance, as in John Donne's "The Sun Rising."

auditor, 178, 767, 774, 794, 819   imaginary listener within a literary work, as opposed to the actual reader or audience outside the work.

author, 25, 805, 854, 1279, 1997, 2002   the *actual* or *real author* of a work is the historical person who wrote it and the focus of biographical criticism, which interprets a work by drawing on facts about the author's life and career. The *implied author* is the vision of the author's personality and outlook implied by the work as a whole. Thus when we make a claim about the author that relies solely on evidence from the work rather than from other sources, our subject is the implied author.

author time   *see* **time.**

autobiography   *see* **biography.**

ballad, 759, 777, 945   a verse narrative that is, or originally was, meant to be sung. Ballads were originally a folk creation, transmitted orally from person to person and age to age and characterized by relatively simple **diction, meter, rhyme scheme**; by stock **imagery**; by repetition; and often by a refrain (a recurrent phrase or series of phrases). An example is Dudley Randall's "Ballad of Birmingham."

ballad stanza, 777, 945, 976, 1068   common stanza form, consisting of a **quatrain** that alternates four-**foot** and three-foot lines; lines 1 and 3 are unrhymed **iambic** tetrameter (four feet), and lines 2 and 4 are rhymed iambic trimeter (three feet), as in "Sir Patrick Spens."

bildungsroman, 5   literally, "education novel" (German), a novel that depicts the intellectual, emotional, and moral development of its protagonist from childhood into adulthood; also sometimes called an *apprenticeship novel.* This type of novel tends to envision character as the product of environment, experience, nurture, and education (in the widest sense) rather than of nature, fate, and so on. Charlotte Brontë's *Jane Eyre* is a famous example.

biography, 5   a work of **nonfiction** that recounts the life of a real person. If the person depicted in a biography is also its author, then we instead use the term *autobiography.* An autobiography that focuses only on a specific aspect of, or episode in, its author's life is a *memoir.*

blank verse, 777, 976, 1396   the metrical verse form most like everyday human speech in English; blank verse consists of unrhymed lines in **iambic pentameter.** Many of Shakespeare's plays are partly in blank verse, as are the entirety of John Milton's *Paradise Lost* and Alfred Tennyson's "Ulysses."

caesura, 934, A8   short pause within a line of poetry; often but not always signaled by punctuation. Note the two caesuras in this line from Edgar Allan Poe's "The Raven": "Once upon a midnight dreary, while I pondered, weak and weary."

canon, 1, 621, 1390, 1650   the range of works that a consensus of scholars, teachers, and readers of a particular time and culture consider "great" or "major."

carpe diem, 831, 834   literally, "seize the day" (Latin), a common **theme** of literary works that emphasize the brevity of life and the need to make the most of the present. Andrew Marvell's "To His Coy Mistress" is a well-known example.

central consciousness, 178   **character** whose inner thoughts, perceptions, and feelings are revealed by a *third-person limited* **narrator** who does not reveal the thoughts, perceptions, or feelings of other characters.

character, 6, 211, 754, 774, 1277   imaginary personage who acts, appears, or is referred to in a literary work. *Major* or *main characters* are those that receive most attention, *minor characters* least. *Flat characters* are relatively simple, have a few dominant traits, and tend to be predictable. Conversely, *round characters* are complex and multifaceted and act in a way that readers might not expect but accept as possible. *Static characters* do not change; *dynamic characters* do. *Stock characters* represent familiar types that recur frequently in literary works, especially of a particular **genre** (e.g., the mad scientist of horror fiction and film or the fool in Renaissance, especially Shakespearean, drama).

characterization, 214   the presentation of a fictional personage. A term like "a good character" can, then, be ambiguous—it may mean that the personage is virtuous or that he or she is well presented regardless of his or her characteristics or moral qualities. In fiction, *direct characterization* occurs when a narrator explicitly tells us what a character is like. *Indirect characterization* occurs when a character's traits are revealed implicitly, through his or her speech, behavior, thoughts, appearance, and so on.

chorus, 1279   group of actors in a drama who comment on and describe the **action**. In classical Greek theater, members of the chorus often wore masks and relied on song, dance, and recitation to make their commentary.

classical unities, 1284   as derived from Aristotle's *Poetics*, the three principles of structure that require a play to have one **plot** (*unity of action*) that occurs in one place (*unity of place*) and within one day (*unity of time*); also called the *dramatic unities*. Susan Glaspell's *Trifles* and Sophocles's *Antigone* observe the classical unities.

climax, 83, 1280   the third part of **plot**, the point at which the **action** stops rising and begins falling or reversing; also called *turning point* or (following Aristotle) *peripeteia*. *See also* **crisis**.

closet drama   *see* **drama**.

comedy, 86, 1251, 1392   a broad category of literary, especially dramatic, works intended primarily to entertain and amuse an audience. Comedies take many different forms, but they share three basic characteristics: (1) the values that are expressed and that typically cause **conflict** are determined by the general opinion of society (as opposed to being universal and beyond the control of humankind, as in **tragedy**); (2) **characters** in comedies are often defined primarily in terms of their social identities and roles and tend to be *flat* or *stock characters* rather than highly individualized or *round* ones; (3) comedies conventionally end happily with an act of social reintegration and celebration such as marriage. William Shakespeare's *A Midsummer Night's Dream* is a famous example.

The term *high* or *verbal comedy* may refer either to a particular type of comedy or to a sort of humor found within any literary work that employs subtlety and wit and usually represents high society. Conversely, *low* or *physical comedy* is a type of either comedy or humor that involves burlesque, horseplay, and the representation of unrefined life. *See also* **farce**.

coming-of-age story   *see* **initiation story**.

complication, 83   in plot, an **action** or event that introduces a new **conflict** or intensifies the existing one, especially during the rising action phase of **plot**.

conclusion, 84, 1280   also called *resolution*, the fifth and last phase or part of **plot**, the point at which the situation that was destabilized at the beginning becomes stable once more and the **conflict** is resolved.

concrete poetry, 985   poetry in which the words on the page are arranged to look like an object; also called *shaped verse*. George Herbert's "Easter Wings," for example, is arranged to look like two pairs of wings.

conflict, 80, 755, 860, 1280, 2023   struggle between opposing forces. A conflict is *external* when it pits a character against something or someone outside himself or herself—another **character** or characters or some impersonal force (e.g., nature or society). A conflict is *internal* when the opposing forces are two drives, impulses, or parts of a single character.

connotation, 881   what is suggested by a word, apart from what it literally means or how it is defined in the dictionary. *See also* **denotation**.

consonance, 927   the repetition of certain consonant sounds in close proximity, as in *mishmash*; especially prominent in Middle English poems such as *Beowulf*.

controlling metaphor   *see* **metaphor**.

convention, 6, 85, 759 in literature, a standard or traditional way of presenting or expressing something, or a traditional or characteristic feature of a particular literary **genre** or subgenre. For example, division into lines and **stanzas** is a convention of poetry; conventions of the type of poem known as the **epic** include a plot that begins *in medias res* and frequent use of **epithets** and extended **similes**.

cosmic irony *see* **irony**.

couplet, 777, 926, 976, A8 two consecutive lines of verse linked by **rhyme** and **meter**; the meter of a *heroic couplet* is **iambic pentameter**.

crisis, 83 in plot, the moment when the **conflict** comes to a head, often requiring the **character** to make a decision; sometimes the crisis is equated with the **climax** or *turning point* and sometimes it is treated as a distinct moment that precedes and prepares for the climax.

criticism *see* **literary criticism**.

cycle *see* **sequence**.

dactylic, 932 referring to the metrical pattern in which each **foot** consists of a stressed syllable followed by two unstressed ones—for example, "Fláshed all their / sábres bare" (Alfred Tennyson, "The Charge of the Light Brigade"). A single foot of this type is called a *dactyl*.

denotation, 881, 911 a word's direct and literal meaning, as opposed to its **connotation**.

dénouement, 84 literally, "untying," as of a knot (French); a **plot**-related term used in three ways: (1) as a synonym for **falling action**, (2) as a synonym for **conclusion** or resolution, and (3) as the label for a phase following the conclusion in which any loose ends are tied up.

destabilizing event *see* **inciting incident**.

deus ex machina, 84 literally, "god out of the machine" (Latin); any improbable, unprepared-for **plot** contrivance introduced late in a literary work to resolve the **conflict**. The term derives from the ancient Greek theatrical practice of using a mechanical device to lower a god or gods onto the stage to resolve the conflicts of the human characters.

dialogue, 178, 760, 1250, 2018 (1) usually, words spoken by **characters** in a literary work, especially as opposed to words that come directly from the **narrator** in a work of fiction; (2) more rarely, a literary work that consists mainly or entirely of the speech of two or more characters; examples include Thomas Hardy's poem "The Ruined Maid" and Plato's treatise *Republic*.

diction, 497, 755, 855, 880, 945, 974, 1057 choice of words. Diction is often described as either *informal* or *colloquial* if it resembles everyday speech, or as *formal* if it is instead lofty, impersonal, and dignified. **Tone** is determined largely through diction.

discriminated occasion, 80 a specific, discrete moment portrayed in a fictional work, often signaled by phrases such as "At 5:05 in the morning . . . ," "It was about dusk, one evening during the supreme madness of the carnival season . . . ," or "The day before Maggie fell down . . ."

drama, 5, 1250 literary genre consisting of works in which action is performed and all words are spoken before an audience by an actor or actors impersonating the **characters**. (Drama typically lacks the **narrators** and **narration** found in fiction.) *Closet drama*, however, is a subgenre of drama that has most of these features yet is intended to be read, either silently by a single reader or out loud in a group setting. *Verse drama* is drama written in verse rather than prose. *Ensemble drama* refers to a play, television series, or film or to a subgenre thereof that gives fairly equal attention to an entire ensemble of characters rather than a single **protagonist** or two. Lynn Nottage's *Sweat* is a good example.

dramatic irony *see* **irony**.

dramatic monologue, 767, 794 a type or subgenre of poetry in which a **speaker** addresses a silent **auditor** or auditors in a specific situation and **setting** that is revealed entirely through the speaker's words; this kind of poem's primary aim is the revelation of the speaker's personality, views, and values. For example, Alfred Tennyson's "Ulysses" consists of an aged Ulysses's words to the mariners whom he hopes to convince to return to sea with him; most of Robert Browning's best-known poems are dramatic monologues.

dramatic poem, 758 poem structured so as to present a scene or series of scenes, as in a work of drama. *See also* **dramatic monologue**.

dramatic unities *see* **classical unities**.

dramatis personae literally, "persons of the drama" (Latin); the list of **characters**

that appears either in a play's program or at the top of a written play's first page.

dynamic character   *see* **character**.

elegy, 6, 758   (1) since the Renaissance, usually a formal lament on the death of a particular person, but focusing mainly on the **speaker**'s efforts to come to terms with his or her grief; (2) more broadly, any **lyric** in sorrowful mood that takes death as its primary subject. An example is W. H. Auden's "In Memory of W. B. Yeats."

end-stopped line, 776   line of verse that contains or concludes a complete clause and usually ends with a punctuation mark. *See also* **enjambment**.

English sonnet   *see* **sonnet**.

enjambment, 776, 934, A8   in poetry, the technique of running over from one line to the next without stop, as in the following lines by Pat Mora: "I live in a doorway / between two rooms." The lines themselves would be described as *enjambed*.

ensemble drama   *see* **drama**.

epic, 3, 6, 85, 759, 845   long narrative poem that celebrates the achievements of mighty **heroes** and **heroines**, usually in founding a nation or developing a culture, and uses elevated language and a grand, high style. Other epic **conventions** include a beginning *in medias res*, an invocation of the muse, a journey to the underworld, battle scenes, and a scene in which the hero arms himself for battle. Examples include *Beowulf* and Homer's *Iliad*. A *mock epic* is a form of satire in which epic language and conventions are used to depict **characters**, **actions**, and **settings** utterly unlike those in conventional epics, usually (though not always) with the purpose of ridiculing the social milieu or types of people portrayed in the poem. A famous example is Alexander Pope's *The Rape of the Lock*.

epigram   very short, usually witty verse with a quick turn at the end; not to be confused with **epigraph**.

epigraph, 278, 1648   quotation appearing at the beginning of a literary work or of one section of such a work; not to be confused with **epigram**.

epilogue, 84   (1) in fiction, a short section or chapter that comes after the **conclusion**, tying up loose ends and often describing what happens to the **characters** after the resolution of the **conflict**; (2) in drama, a short speech, often addressed directly to the audience, delivered by a character at the end of a play.

epiphany, 83   sudden revelation of truth, often inspired by a seemingly simple or commonplace event. The term, originally from Christian theology, was first popularized by James Joyce, though he also used the term to describe the individual short stories collected in his book *Dubliners*.

episode, 80   distinct action or series of actions within a **plot**.

epistolary novel   *see* **novel**.

epitaph, 882   inscription on a tombstone or grave marker; not to be confused with **epigram**, **epigraph**, or **epithet**.

epithet, 774, 958   characterizing word or phrase that precedes, follows, or substitutes for the name of a person or thing, such as *slain civil rights leader* Martin Luther King, Jr., or Zeus, *the god of trophies*; not to be confused with **epitaph**. **Epics** conventionally make frequent use of epithets.

eponymous   having a name used in the title of a literary work. For example, Sula Peace is the eponymous **protagonist** of Toni Morrison's *Sula*.

exposition, 83, 1250, 1280   first phase or part of **plot**, which sets the scene, introduces and identifies characters, and establishes the situation at the beginning of a story or play. Additional exposition is often scattered throughout the work.

extended metaphor   *see* **metaphor**.

external conflict   *see* **conflict**.

external narration or narrator   *see* **narrator**.

fable, 2, 424   ancient type of short **fiction**, in verse or prose, illustrating a **moral** or satirizing human beings. **Characters** in a fable are often animals that talk and act like human beings. The fable is sometimes treated as a specific type of **folktale** and sometimes as a fictional subgenre in its own right. An example is Aesop's "The Two Crabs."

fairy tale   *see* **tale**.

falling action, 84, 1280   fourth of the five phases or parts of **plot**, in which the **conflict** or conflicts move toward resolution.

fantasy, 280   **genre** of literary work featuring strange settings and characters and often involving magic or the supernatural; though closely related to horror and science fiction, fantasy is typically less concerned with the macabre or with science and technology. J. R. R. Tolkien's *The Hobbit* is a well-known example.

farce, 1251   literary work, especially drama, characterized by broad humor, wild antics, and often slapstick, pratfalls, or other physical humor. *See also* **comedy**.

fiction, 5, 16   any **narrative**, especially in prose, about invented or imagined **characters** and **action**. Today, we tend to divide fiction into three major subgenres based on length—the **short story**, **novella**, and **novel**. Older, originally oral forms of short fiction include the **fable**, **legend**, **parable**, and **tale**. Fictional works may also be categorized not by their length but by their handling of particular elements such as **plot** and **character**. Detective and science fiction, for example, are subgenres that include both novels and novellas such as Frank Herbert's *Dune* and short stories such as Edgar Allan Poe's "The Murders at the Rue Morgue" or Octavia Butler's "Bloodchild." *See also* **gothic fiction**, **historical fiction**, **nonfiction**, and **romance**.

figurative language, 363   language that uses **figures of speech**.

figure of speech, 363, 497, 755, 882, 1286   any word or phrase that creates a "figure" in the mind of the reader by effecting an obvious change in the usual meaning or order of words, by comparing or identifying one thing with another; also called a *trope*. **Metaphor**, **simile**, **metonymy**, **overstatement**, **oxymoron**, and **understatement** are common figures of speech.

first-person narrator   *see* **narrator**.

flashback, 80   **plot**-structuring device whereby a scene from the fictional past is inserted into the fictional present or is dramatized out of order.

flashforward, 80   **plot**-structuring device whereby a scene from the fictional future is inserted into the fictional present or is dramatized out of order.

flat character   *see* **character**.

focus, 177   visual component of **point of view**, the point from which people, events, and other details in a story are viewed; also called *focalization*. *See also* **voice**.

foil, 212, 1278   **character** that serves as a contrast to another.

folktale   *see* **tale**.

foot, 931   the basic unit of poetic **meter**, consisting of any of various fixed patterns of one to three stressed and unstressed syllables. A foot may contain more than one word or just one syllable of a multisyllabic word. In **scansion**, breaks between feet are usually indicated with a vertical line or slash mark, as in the following example (which contains five feet): "Some viéw | our sá- | ble ráce | with scórn- | ful éye" (Phillis Wheatley, "On Being Brought from Africa to America"). *For specific examples of metrical feet, see* **anapestic**, **dactylic**, **iambic**, **pyrrhic**, **spondee**, and **trochaic**.

foreshadowing, 80   hint or clue to the reader about what will happen at a later moment in the **plot**.

formal diction   *see* **diction**.

frame narrative   *see* **narrative**.

free verse, 757, 925, 977, 1068   poetry characterized by varying line lengths, lack of traditional **meter**, and nonrhyming lines.

Freytag's pyramid, 82   diagram of **plot** structure first created by the German novelist and critic Gustav Freytag (1816–95).

general setting   *see* **setting**.

genre, 1, 1277, 2018   type or category of works sharing particular formal or textual features and **conventions**; especially used to refer to the largest categories for classifying literature—fiction, poetry, drama, and nonfiction. A smaller division within a genre is usually known as a *subgenre*, such as **gothic fiction** or **epic** poetry.

golden shovel, 977, 1011   poem or subgenre thereof in which the end words of each line, read sequentially, reproduce at least one line from a poem or song lyric by another author. Terrance Hayes invented the form with "The Golden Shovel" (2010), a poem inspired by Gwendolyn Brooks's "We Real Cool."

gothic fiction, 6, 311   subgenre of **fiction** conventionally featuring **plots** that involve secrets, mystery, and the supernatural (or the seemingly supernatural) and large, gloomy, and usually antiquated (especially medieval) buildings as settings. Examples include Horace Walpole's *The Castle of Otranto*, Edgar Allan Poe's "The Fall of the House of Usher," and Toni Morrison's *Beloved*.

haiku, 977, 1003   poetic form, Japanese in origin, that in English consists of seventeen syllables arranged in three unrhymed lines of five, seven, and five syllables, respectively.

hero/heroine, 211, 1278 character in a literary work, especially the leading male/female character, who is especially virtuous, usually larger than life, sometimes almost godlike. *See also* **antihero, protagonist,** and **villain**.

heroic couplet *see* **couplet**.

hexameter, 976 line of poetry with six feet: "She comes, | she comes | again, | like ring | dove frayed | and fled" (John Keats, "The Eve of St. Agnes").

high (verbal) comedy *see* **comedy**.

historical fiction, 6, 27, 280, 311 subgenre of **fiction**, of whatever length, in which the temporal setting, or plot time, is significantly earlier than the time in which the work was written (typically, a period before the birth of the author). Conventionally, such works describe the atmosphere and mores of the setting in vivid detail and explore the influence of historical factors on the characters and action; though focusing mainly on invented or imaginary characters and events, historical fiction sometimes includes some characters and action based on actual personages and events. The *historical novel* is a type of historical fiction pioneered by nineteenth-century Scottish writer Walter Scott in works such as *Ivanhoe*.

hyperbole *see* **overstatement**. *See also* **understatement**.

iambic, 932, 934, 975, 989, 1396 referring to a metrical form in which each **foot** consists of an unstressed syllable followed by a stressed one; this type of foot is an *iamb*. The most common poetic meter in English is iambic **pentameter**—a metrical form in which most lines consist of five iambs: "Some view | our sá- | ble ráce | with scórn- | ful éye" (Phillis Wheatley, "On Being Brought from Africa to America").

image/imagery, 363, 497, 974, 1999 broadly defined, any sensory detail or evocation in a work; more narrowly, the use of **figurative language** to evoke a feeling, to call to mind an idea, or to describe an object. Imagery may be described as *auditory, tactile, visual,* or *olfactory* depending on which sense it primarily appeals to—hearing, touch, vision, or smell. An *image* is a particular instance of imagery.

implied author *see* **author**.

inciting incident, 83, 1280 an **action** that sets a **plot** in motion by creating **conflict**; also called *destabilizing event*.

informal diction *see* **diction**.

initiation story, 145 kind of short story in which a **character**—often a child or young person—first learns a significant, usually life-changing truth about the universe, society, people, or himself or herself; also called a *coming-of-age story*. James Joyce's "Araby" is a notable example.

in medias res, **80, 2001** "in the midst of things" (Latin); refers to opening a **plot** in the middle of the action, and then filling in past details by means of **exposition** and/or **flashback**.

interior monologue *see* **monologue**.

internal conflict *see* **conflict**.

internal narration or **narrator** *see* **narrator**.

intrusive narration or **narrator** *see* **narrator**.

inversion, 772 a change in normal **syntax** such as putting a verb before its subject. Common in poetry, the technique is also famously used by *Star Wars*'s Yoda, as in "When nine hundred years old you reach, look as good you will not."

irony, 177, 364, 497, 761, 819 situation or statement characterized by a significant difference between what is expected or understood and what actually happens or is meant. *Verbal irony* occurs when a word or expression in context means something different from, and usually the opposite of, what it appears to mean; when the intended meaning is harshly critical or satiric, verbal irony becomes *sarcasm*. *Situational irony* occurs when a **character** holds a position or has an expectation that is reversed or fulfilled in an unexpected way. When there is instead a gap between what an audience knows and what a character believes or expects, we have *dramatic irony*; when this occurs in a **tragedy**, dramatic irony is sometimes called *tragic irony*. Finally, the terms *cosmic irony* and *irony of fate* are sometimes used to refer to situations in which situational irony is the result of fate, chance, the gods, or some other superhuman force or entity.

Italian sonnet *see* **sonnet**.

legend, 855 type of tale conventionally set in the real world and in either the present or historical past, based on actual people and events and offering an exaggerated or distorted version of the truth about those people and events. American examples might include stories featuring Johnny Appleseed or John Henry. British examples are the legends of King Arthur or Robin Hood.

limerick, 936, 977 light or humorous **poem** or subgenre of poems consisting of mainly **anapestic** lines of which the first, second, and fifth are of three feet; the third and fourth lines are of two feet; and the rhyme scheme is *aabba*.

limited narrator *see* **narrator**.

limited point of view *see* **point of view**.

lines, 4, 756, 2046 in a poem, a discrete organization of words; the length and shape of a line can communicate meaning in a poem, and can be a formal element characterizing a poem, such as the fourteen lines that make up a sonnet.

literary criticism, 5, 1158, 1994 mainly interpretive (versus evaluative) work written by readers of literary texts, especially professional ones (who are thus known as *literary critics*). It is "criticism" not because it is negative or corrective but because those who write criticism ask probing, analytical, "critical" questions about the works they read.

litotes, 497 form of understatement in which one negates the contrary of what one means. Examples from common speech include "not bad" (meaning "good") and "a novelist of no small repute" (meaning "a novelist with a big reputation"), and so on.

low (physical) comedy *see* **comedy**.

lyric, 758, 762, 796, 805, 954, 1025, 1067, 1092 originally, a poem meant to be sung to the accompaniment of a lyre; now, any relatively short poem in which the speaker expresses his or her thoughts and feelings in the first person rather than recounting a narrative or portraying a dramatic situation.

magic realism, 280 type of **fiction** that involves the creation of a fictional world in which the kind of familiar, plausible **action** and **characters** one might find in more straightforwardly realist fiction coexist with utterly fantastic ones straight out of **myths** or dreams. This style of **realism** is associated especially with modern Latin American writers such as Gabriel García Márquez and Jorge Luis Borges. But the label is also sometimes applied to works by other contemporary writers from around the world, including Italo Calvino and Salman Rushdie.

major (main) character *see* **character**.

memoir *see* **biography**.

metafiction, 658 subgenre of works that playfully draw attention to their status as **fiction** in order to explore the nature of fiction and the role of authors and readers.

metaphor, 4, 364, 898, 1162, 1270 **figure of speech** in which two unlike things are compared implicitly—that is, without the use of a signal such as the word *like* or *as*—as in "Love is a rose, but you better not pick it." *See also* **simile**.

An *extended metaphor* is a detailed and complex metaphor that stretches across a long section of a work. If such a metaphor is so extensive that it dominates or organizes an entire literary work, especially a poem, it is called a *controlling metaphor*. A *mixed metaphor* occurs when two or more usually incompatible metaphors are entangled together so as to become unclear and often unintentionally humorous, as in "Her blazing words dripped all over him."

meter, 776, 925, 931, 945, 974, 1057, 1286, 1999 the more or less regular pattern of stressed and unstressed syllables in a line of poetry. This is determined by the kind of **foot** (**iambic** or **dactylic**, for example) and by the number of feet per line (e.g., five feet = **pentameter**, six feet = **hexameter**).

metonymy, 364, 755, 902 **figure of speech** in which the name of one thing is used to refer to another associated thing. When we say, "The White House has promised to veto the bill," for example, we use the White House as a metonym for the president and his administration. **Synecdoche** is a specific type of metonymy.

minor character *see* **character**.

mock epic *see* **epic**.

monologue, 1286 (1) long speech, usually in a play but also in other **genres**, spoken by one person and uninterrupted by the speech of anyone else, or (2) an entire work consisting of this sort of speech. In **fiction**, an *interior monologue* takes place entirely within the mind of a character rather than being spoken aloud. A **soliloquy** is a particular type of monologue occurring in drama, while a **dramatic monologue** is a type of poem.

moral, 426 rule of conduct or maxim for living (that is, a statement about how one should live or behave) communicated in a literary work. Though **fables** often have morals, such as "Don't count your chickens before they hatch," more modern literary works instead tend to have **themes**.

motif, 845 recurrent device, formula, or situation within a literary work.

motive, 621, 2005 animating impulse for an action, the reason why something is done or attempted.

myth, 363, 905 (1) originally and narrowly, **narrative** explaining how the world and humanity developed into their present form and, unlike a **folktale**, generally considered to be true by the people who develop it. Many, though not all, myths feature supernatural beings and have a religious significance or function within their culture of origin. Two especially common types of myth are the *creation myth*, which explains how the world, human beings, a god or gods, or good and evil came to be (e.g., the myth of Adam and Eve), and the *explanatory myth*, which explains features of the natural landscape or natural processes or events (e.g., "How the Leopard Got His Spots"). (2) more broadly and especially in its adjectival form (*mythic*), any narrative that obviously seeks to work like a myth in the first and more narrow sense, especially by portraying experiences or conveying truths that it implies are universally valid regardless of culture or time.

narration, 177 (1) broadly, the act of telling a story or recounting a **narrative**; (2) more narrowly, the portions of a narrative attributable to the **narrator** rather than words spoken by **characters** (that is, **dialogue**).

narrative, 25 story, whether fictional or true and in prose or verse, related by a **narrator** or narrators (rather than acted out onstage, as in drama). A *frame narrative* is a narrative that recounts and thus "frames" the telling of another narrative or story. An example is Samuel Taylor Coleridge's "The Rime of the Ancient Mariner," in which an anonymous third-person narrator recounts how an old sailor comes to tell a young wedding guest the story of his adventures at sea.

narrative poem, 758 poem in which a **narrator** tells a story.

narrator, 20, 177, 754, 792, 1250, 1277 someone who recounts a narrative or tells a story. Though we usually instead use the term **speaker** when referring to poetry as opposed to prose fiction, *narrative poems* include at least one speaker who functions as a narrator. *See also* **narrative**.

A narrator or narration is said to be *internal* when the narrator is a **character** within the work, telling the story to an equally fictional **auditor** or listener; internal narrators are usually first- or second-person narrators (*see below*). A narrator or narration is instead said to be *external* when the narrator is not a character.

A *first-person narrator* is an internal narrator who consistently refers to himself or herself using the first-person pronouns *I* or *we*. A *second-person narrator* consistently uses the second-person pronoun *you* (a very uncommon technique). A *third-person narrator* uses third-person pronouns such as *she, he, they, it,* and so on: third-person narrators are almost always external narrators. Third-person narrators are said to be *omniscient* (literally, "all-knowing," in Latin) when they describe the inner thoughts and feelings of multiple characters; they are said to be *limited* when they relate the thoughts, feelings, and perceptions of only one character (the **central consciousness**). If a work encourages us to view a narrator's account of events with suspicion, the narrator (usually first person) is called *unreliable*. An *intrusive narrator* is a third-person narrator who occasionally disrupts his or her narrative to speak directly to the reader or audience in what is sometimes called *direct address*.

narrator time *see* **time**.

nonfiction, 5, 26 work or genre of prose works that describe actual, as opposed to imaginary or fictional, characters and events. Subgenres of nonfiction include **biography**, memoir, and the essay. *See also* **fiction**.

novel, 5, 26 long work of **fiction** (approximately 40,000+ words), typically published (or at least publishable) as a stand-alone book; though most novels are written in prose, those written as poetry are called *verse novels*. A novel (as opposed to a **short story**) conventionally has a complex **plot** and, often, at least one **subplot**, as well as a fully realized **setting** and a relatively large number of **characters**. One important novelistic subgenre is the *epistolary novel*—a novel composed entirely of letters written by its characters. Another is the **bildungsroman**.

novella, 5, 26 work of prose **fiction** that falls somewhere in between a **short story** and a **novel** in terms of length, scope, and complexity. Novellas can be, and have been, published either as books in their own right or as parts of books that include other works. Kate Chopin's *The Awakening* is an example.

occasional poem, 829 poem written to celebrate or commemorate a specific event such as a birth, marriage, death, coronation, inauguration, or military battle. Examples include Richard Blanco's "One Today" (written for U.S. president Barack Obama's second inauguration) and W. B. Yeats's "Easter 1916" (about the Easter Uprising in Ireland).

octameter, 933 line of poetry with eight **feet**: "Once u- | pon a | midnight | dreary, | while I | pondered, | weak and | weary," (Edgar Allan Poe, "The Raven").

octave, 989 eight lines of verse linked by a pattern of end **rhymes**, especially the first eight lines of an Italian, or Petrarchan, **sonnet**. *See also* **sestet.**

ode, 762, 777 lyric poem characterized by a serious topic and formal **tone** but without a prescribed formal pattern in which the **speaker** talks about, and often to, an especially revered person or thing. Examples include Shelley's "Ode to the West Wind."

oeuvre, 494, 1390 all of the works verifiably written by one author.

omniscient narrator *see* **narrator.**

omniscient point of view *see* **point of view.**

onomatopoeia, 927 word capturing or approximating the sound of what it describes; *buzz* is a good example.

orchestra, 1282 in classical Greek theater, semicircular area used mostly for dancing by the chorus.

ottava rima, 1068 literally, "octave (eighth) rhyme" (Italian); verse form consisting of eight-line **stanzas** with an *ababcc* **rhyme scheme** and iambic meter (usually **pentameter**). W. B. Yeats's "Sailing to Byzantium" is written in ottava rima.

overplot, 1392 especially in Shakespearean drama, subplot that resembles the main plot but stresses the political implications of the depicted **action** and situation.

overstatement, 497 exaggerated language; also called *hyperbole.*

oxymoron, 364 figure of speech that combines two apparently contradictory elements, as in *wise fool.*

palindrome, 977 word, sentence, or poem that reads the same backward and forward. Good examples are *civic* (a word); *Madam, I'm Adam* (a sentence); and Natasha Trethewey's "Myth" (a poem).

parable, 26 short work of **fiction** that illustrates an explicit moral but that, unlike a **fable**, lacks fantastic or anthropomorphic characters. Especially familiar examples are the stories attributed to Jesus in the Bible—about the prodigal son, the good Samaritan, and so on.

parody, 6 any work that imitates or spoofs another work or **genre** for comic effect by exaggerating the style and changing the content of the original; parody is a subgenre of **satire.** Examples include mockumentaries, such as *District 9* (2009), which parody documentaries, and *The Onion,* which spoofs newspapers.

pastoral literature, 6, 827 work or category of works—whether **fiction, poetry, drama,** or **nonfiction**—describing and idealizing the simple life of country folk, usually shepherds who live a painless life in a world full of beauty, music, and love. An example is Christopher Marlowe's "The Passionate Shepherd to His Love."

pentameter, 934, 975, 989, 1396 line of poetry with five **feet:** "Nuns fret | not at | their con- | vent's nar- | row room" (William Wordsworth).

persona, 797, 1057 the voice or figure of the **author** who tells and who may or may not share the values of the actual author. *See also* **author.**

personification, 364, 755, 901, 1286 figure of speech that involves treating something nonhuman, such as an abstraction, as if it were a person by endowing it with humanlike qualities, as in "Death entered the room."

Petrarchan sonnet *see* **sonnet.**

plot, 6, 79, 754, 775, 860, 1272, 1279, 1997, 2018 arrangement of the **action.** The five main parts or phases of plot are **exposition, rising action, climax** or turning point, **falling action,** and **conclusion** or resolution. *See also* **subplot** and **overplot.**

plot summary, 85, 1997 brief recounting of the principal action of a work of **fiction, drama,** or narrative poetry, usually in the same order in which the action is

hero/heroine, 211, 1278 character in a literary work, especially the leading male/female character, who is especially virtuous, usually larger than life, sometimes almost godlike. *See also* **antihero, protagonist**, and **villain**.

heroic couplet *see* **couplet**.

hexameter, 976 line of poetry with six feet: "She comes, | she comes | again, | like ring | dove frayed | and fled" (John Keats, "The Eve of St. Agnes").

high (verbal) comedy *see* **comedy**.

historical fiction, 6, 27, 280, 311 sub-genre of **fiction**, of whatever length, in which the temporal setting, or plot time, is significantly earlier than the time in which the work was written (typically, a period before the birth of the author). Conventionally, such works describe the atmosphere and mores of the setting in vivid detail and explore the influence of historical factors on the characters and action; though focusing mainly on invented or imaginary characters and events, historical fiction sometimes includes some characters and action based on actual personages and events. The *historical novel* is a type of historical fiction pioneered by nineteenth-century Scottish writer Walter Scott in works such as *Ivanhoe*.

hyperbole *see* **overstatement**. *See also* **understatement**.

iambic, 932, 934, 975, 989, 1396 referring to a metrical form in which each **foot** consists of an unstressed syllable followed by a stressed one; this type of foot is an *iamb*. The most common poetic meter in English is iambic **pentameter**—a metrical form in which most lines consist of five iambs: "Some view | our sá- | ble ráce | with scórn- | ful éye" (Phillis Wheatley, "On Being Brought from Africa to America").

image/imagery, 363, 497, 974, 1999 broadly defined, any sensory detail or evocation in a work; more narrowly, the use of **figurative language** to evoke a feeling, to call to mind an idea, or to describe an object. Imagery may be described as *auditory*, *tactile*, *visual*, or *olfactory* depending on which sense it primarily appeals to—hearing, touch, vision, or smell. An *image* is a particular instance of imagery.

implied author *see* **author**.

inciting incident, 83, 1280 an **action** that sets a **plot** in motion by creating **conflict**; also called *destabilizing event*.

informal diction *see* **diction**.

initiation story, 145 kind of short story in which a **character**—often a child or young person—first learns a significant, usually life-changing truth about the universe, society, people, or himself or herself; also called a *coming-of-age story*. James Joyce's "Araby" is a notable example.

in medias res, **80, 2001** "in the midst of things" (Latin); refers to opening a **plot** in the middle of the action, and then filling in past details by means of **exposition** and/or **flashback**.

interior monologue *see* **monologue**.

internal conflict *see* **conflict**.

internal narration or **narrator** *see* **narrator**.

intrusive narration or **narrator** *see* **narrator**.

inversion, 772 a change in normal **syntax** such as putting a verb before its subject. Common in poetry, the technique is also famously used by *Star Wars*'s Yoda, as in "When nine hundred years old you reach, look as good you will not."

irony, 177, 364, 497, 761, 819 situation or statement characterized by a significant difference between what is expected or understood and what actually happens or is meant. *Verbal irony* occurs when a word or expression in context means something different from, and usually the opposite of, what it appears to mean; when the intended meaning is harshly critical or satiric, verbal irony becomes *sarcasm*. *Situational irony* occurs when a **character** holds a position or has an expectation that is reversed or fulfilled in an unexpected way. When there is instead a gap between what an audience knows and what a character believes or expects, we have *dramatic irony*; when this occurs in a **tragedy**, dramatic irony is sometimes called *tragic irony*. Finally, the terms *cosmic irony* and *irony of fate* are sometimes used to refer to situations in which situational irony is the result of fate, chance, the gods, or some other superhuman force or entity.

Italian sonnet *see* **sonnet**.

legend, 855 type of tale conventionally set in the real world and in either the present or historical past, based on actual people and events and offering an exaggerated or distorted version of the truth about those people and events. American examples might include stories featuring Johnny Appleseed or John Henry. British

recounted in the original work rather than in chronological order.

plot time *see* **time**.

poetry, 5 one of the three major **genres** of imaginative literature, which has its origins in music and oral performance and is characterized by controlled patterns of **rhythm** and **syntax** (often using **meter** and **rhyme**); compression and compactness and an allowance for ambiguity; a particularly concentrated emphasis on the sensual, especially visual and aural, qualities and effects of words and word order; and especially vivid, often **figurative language**.

point of view, 177 perspective from which people, events, and other details in a work of fiction are viewed; also called focus, though the term *point of view* usually includes both focus and voice. *See also* **narrator**.

prop, 1284 in drama, an object used on the stage.

proscenium stage, 1281 the most common type of modern theater, in which the stage is clearly demarcated from the auditorium by an arch (or proscenium), which thus "frames" the "picture" that unfolds onstage.

prose, 26 the regular form of spoken and written language, measured in sentences rather than lines, as in poetry.

protagonist, 211, 1278, 1392 most neutral and broadly applicable term for the main **character** in a work, whether male or female, heroic or not heroic. *See also* **antagonist**, **antihero**, and **hero/heroine**.

pyrrhic, 932 rarely used metrical **foot** consisting of two unstressed syllables.

quatrain, 989 four-line unit of verse, whether an entire poem, a **stanza**, or a group of four lines linked by a pattern of rhyme (as in an English or Shakespearean **sonnet**).

reader time *see* **time**.

realism, 1546 (1) generally, the practice in literature, especially fiction and drama, of attempting to describe nature and life as they are without idealization and with attention to detail, especially the everyday life of ordinary people. *See also* **verisimilitude**.

Just as notions of how life and nature differ widely across cultures and time periods, however, so do notions of what is "realistic." Thus, there are many different kinds of realism. *Psychological realism*

refers, broadly, to any literary attempt to accurately represent the workings of the human mind and, more specifically, to the practice of a particular group of late nineteenth- and early twentieth-century writers including Joseph Conrad, Henry James, James Joyce, and Virginia Woolf, who developed the **stream-of-consciousness** technique of depicting the flow of thought. *See also* **magic realism**.

(2) more narrowly and especially when capitalized, a mid- to late nineteenth-century literary and artistic movement, mainly in the United States and Europe, that championed realism in the first, more general sense; rejected what its proponents saw as the elitism and idealism of earlier literature and art; and emphasized **settings**, situations, **action**, and (especially middle- and working-class) **characters** ignored or belittled in earlier literature and art. Writers associated with the movement include Gustave Flaubert and Émile Zola (in France), George Eliot and Thomas Hardy (in Britain), and Theodore Dreiser (in the United States).

resolution *see* **conclusion**.

rhetoric, 363 art and scholarly study of effective communication, whether in writing or speech. Many literary terms, especially those for **figures of speech**, derive from classical and Renaissance rhetoric.

rhyme, 756, 776, 925, 945, 974, 1057, 1396, 1999 repetition or correspondence of the terminal sounds of words ("How now, brown cow?"). The most common type, *end rhyme*, occurs when the last words in two or more lines of a poem rhyme with each other. *Internal rhyme* occurs when a word *within* a line of poetry rhymes with another word in the same or adjacent lines, as in "The *Dews drew* quivering and chill" (Emily Dickinson). *Eye rhyme* or *sight rhyme* involves words that don't rhyme but look like they do because of their similar spelling ("cough" and "bough"). *Off, half, near,* or *slant rhyme* is rhyme that is slightly "off" or only approximate, usually because words' final consonant sounds correspond, but not the vowels that proceed them ("phases" and "houses"). When two syllables rhyme and the last is unstressed or unaccented, they create a *feminine rhyme* ("ocean" and "motion"); *masculine rhyme* involves only a single stressed or accented syllable ("cat" and "hat"). *See also* **rhyme scheme**.

rhyme scheme, 926, 945, 1999 pattern of *end* rhymes in a poem, often noted by lowercase letters, such as *abab* or *abba*.

rhythm, 754, 1396 the modulation of weak and strong (or stressed and unstressed) elements in the flow of speech. In most poetry written before the twentieth century, rhythm was often expressed in meter; in prose and in free verse, rhythm is present but in a much less predictable and regular manner.

rising action, 83, 1280 second of the five phases or parts of **plot**, in which events complicate the situation that existed at the beginning of a work, intensifying the initial **conflict** or introducing a new one.

romance, 6, 759, 845 (1) originally, a long medieval **narrative** in verse or prose written in one of the Romance languages (French, Spanish, Italian, etc.) and depicting the quests of knights and other chivalric **heroes** and the vicissitudes of courtly love; also known as *chivalric romance*; (2) later and more broadly, any literary work, especially a long work of prose **fiction**, characterized by a nonrealistic and idealizing use of the imagination; (3) commonly today, works of prose fiction aimed at a mass, primarily female, audience and focusing on love affairs (as in Harlequin romances).

round character *see* **character**.

sarcasm *see* **irony**.

satire, 6 literary work—whether **fiction, poetry,** or **drama**—that holds up human failings to ridicule and censure. Examples include Jonathan Swift's novel *Gulliver's Travels* and Jordan Peele's film *Get Out* (2017).

scansion, 933 process of analyzing (and sometimes also marking) verse to determine its **meter**, line by line.

scapegoat, 213, 257 in a work of literature, **character** or characters that take the blame for others' actions; usually an innocent party or someone only tangentially responsible, their punishment lets others off the hook and often serves to solidify a community.

scene, 1, 79, 754, 1251, 1999 section or subdivision of a play or **narrative** that presents continuous **action** in one specific **setting**.

second-person narrator *see* **narrator**.

sequence, 79, 806, 1281 (1) the ordering of **action** in a fictional **plot**; (2) a closely linked series or *cycle* of individual literary works, especially short stories or poems, designed to be read or performed together, as in the **sonnet** sequences of William Shakespeare, Edna St. Vincent Millay, and Terrance Hayes.

sestet, 989 six lines of verse linked by a pattern of rhyme, as in the last six lines of the Italian, or Petrarchan, **sonnet**. *See also* **octave**.

sestina, 977 an elaborate verse structure written in **blank verse** that consists of six **stanzas** of six lines each followed by a three-line stanza. The final words of each line in the first stanza appear in variable order in the next five stanzas and are repeated in the middle and at the end of the three lines in the final stanza. Elizabeth Bishop's "Sestina" is an example.

set, 1284 the design, decoration, and scenery of the stage during a play; not to be confused with **setting**.

setting, 6, 280, 495, 758, 774, 819, 855, 974, 1283 time and place of the action in a work of **fiction, poetry,** or **drama**. The *spatial setting* is the place or places in which action unfolds; the *temporal setting* is the time. (Temporal setting is thus the same as *plot time*.) It is sometimes also helpful to distinguish between *general setting*—the general time and place in which all the action unfolds—and *particular settings*—the times and places in which individual **episodes** or scenes take place.

Shakespearean sonnet *see* **sonnet**.

shaped verse *see* **concrete poetry**.

short short story *see* **short story**.

short story, 5, 26 relatively short work of prose **fiction** (approximately 500 to 10,000 words) that, according to Edgar Allan Poe, can be read in a single sitting of two hours or less and works to create "a single effect." Two types of short story are the **initiation story** and the *short short story*. (Also sometimes called *microfiction*, a short short story is, as its name suggests, a short story that is especially brief; examples include Linda Brewer's "20/20" and Jamaica Kincaid's "Girl.")

simile, 4, 364, 897, 956 **figure of speech** involving a direct, explicit comparison of one thing to another, usually using the words *like* or *as* to draw the connection, as in "My love is like a red, red rose." An **analogy** is an extended simile. *See also* **metaphor**.

situation, 758, 775, 819, 855, 974, 2023 basic circumstances depicted in a literary work, especially when the story, play, or poem begins or at a specific later moment in the action. In John Keats's "Ode to a Nightingale," for example, the situation involves a man (the **speaker**) sitting under a tree as he listens to a nightingale's song.

situational irony *see* **irony**.

skene, 1282 low building in the back of the stage area in classical Greek theaters. It represented the palace or temple in front of which the action took place.

soliloquy **monologue** in which the **character** in a play is alone onstage (or believes herself to be) and thinking out loud, as in the famous Hamlet speech that begins "To be, or not to be."

sonnet, 758, 777, 977, 989, 1092 fixed verse form consisting of fourteen lines usually in **iambic pentameter**. An *Italian sonnet* consists of eight rhyme-linked lines (an **octave**) plus six rhyme-linked lines (a **sestet**), often with either an *abbaabba cdecde* or *abbacddc defdef* **rhyme scheme**. This type of sonnet is also called the *Petrarchan sonnet* in honor of the Italian poet Petrarch (1304–74). An *English* or *Shakespearean sonnet* instead consists of three **quatrains** (four-line units) and a **couplet** and often rhymes *abab cdcd efef gg*.

spatial setting *see* **setting**.

speaker, 774, 792, 805, 819, 855, 974, 2023 (1) the person who is the voice of a poem; (2) anyone who speaks dialogue in a work of **fiction**, **poetry**, or **drama**.

Spenserian stanza, 975 stanza consisting of eight lines of **iambic pentameter** (five feet) followed by a ninth line of iambic **hexameter** (six feet). The **rhyme scheme** is *ababbcbcc*. The stanza form takes its name from Edmund Spenser (c. 1552–99), who used it in *The Faerie Queene*.

spondee, 932 metrical **foot** consisting of a pair of stressed syllables ("déad sét").

stage directions, 1250, 1277 words in the printed text of a play that inform the director, crew, actors, and readers how to stage, perform, or imagine the play. Stage directions are not spoken aloud and may appear at the beginning of a play, before any scene, or attached to a line of dialogue; they are often set in italics. The place and time of the **action**, the design of the **set**, and at times the **characters'** actions or **tone** of voice are indicated in stage directions and interpreted by those who put on a performance.

stanza, 756, 955, 974, 1999 section of a poem, marked by extra line spacing before and after, that often has a single pattern of **meter** and/or **rhyme**. Conventional stanza forms include **ballad stanza**, **Spenserian stanza**, **ottava rima**, and **terza rima**. *See also* **verse paragraph**.

static character *see* **character**.

stock character *see* **character**.

stream of consciousness type of third-person narration that replicates the thought processes of a **character** without much or any intervention by a **narrator**. The term was originally coined by the nineteenth-century American psychologist William James (brother of novelist Henry James) to describe the workings of the human mind and only later adopted to describe the type of narration that seeks to replicate this process. The technique is closely associated with twentieth-century fiction writers of psychological **realism** such as Virginia Woolf, James Joyce, and William Faulkner, who were all heavily influenced by early psychologists such as William James and Sigmund Freud.

style, 177, 496 distinctive manner of expression; each author's style is expressed through his or her **diction, rhythm, imagery**, and so on.

subgenre *see* **genre**.

subplot, 80, 1280 secondary **plot** in a work of fiction or drama. *See also* **overplot** and **underplot**.

symbol, 361, 364, 911, 1286 person, place, thing, or event that figuratively represents or stands for something else. Often the thing or idea represented is more abstract and general, and the symbol is more concrete and particular. A *traditional symbol* is one that recurs frequently in (and beyond) literature and is thus immediately recognizable to those who belong to a given culture. In Western literature and culture, for example, the rose and snake traditionally symbolize love and evil, respectively. Other symbols such as the balloon in Edwidge Danticat's "A Wall of Fire Rising" instead accrue their complex meanings only within a particular literary work; these are sometimes called *invented symbols*.

symbolic poem, 916 poem in which the use of symbols is so pervasive and internally consistent that the reference to the outside world being symbolized becomes secondary. William Blake's "The Sick Rose" and W. B. Yeats's "The Second Coming" are examples.

synecdoche, 364, 902   type of **metonymy** in which the part is used to name or stand in for the whole, as when we refer to manual laborers as *hands* or say *wheels* to mean a car.

syntax, 755, 771, 884   word order; the way words are put together to form phrases, clauses, and sentences.

tale, 2, 17, 311   brief narrative with a simple **plot** and characters, an ancient and originally oral form of storytelling. Unlike **fables**, tales typically don't convey or state a simple or single **moral**. An especially common type of tale is the *folktale*, the **conventions** of which include a formulaic beginning and ending ("Once upon a time . . . ," ". . . And so they lived happily ever after."); a **setting** that is not highly particularized in terms of time or place; *flat* and often *stock characters*, animal or human; and fairly simple plots. Though the term *fairy tale* is often used as a synonym for *folktale*, it more narrowly and properly designates a specific type of folktale featuring fairies or other fantastic creatures such as pixies or ogres.

temporal setting   *see* **setting**.

terza rima, 975   literally, "third rhyme" (Italian); a verse form consisting of three-line **stanzas** in which the second line of each stanza rhymes with the first and third of the next. Percy Bysshe Shelley's "Ode to the West Wind" is written in terza rima.

tetrameter, 976   a line of poetry with four feet: "The Grass | divides | as with | a Comb" (Emily Dickinson).

theme, 79, 424, 855, 871, 963, 974, 1286, 2002   (1) broadly and commonly, a topic explored in a literary work (e.g., "the value of all life"); (2) more narrowly and properly, the insight about a topic communicated in a work (e.g., "All living things are equally precious"). Most literary works have multiple themes, though some people reserve the term *theme* for the central or main insight and refer to others as *subthemes*. Usually, a theme is implicitly communicated by the work as a whole rather than explicitly stated in it, though **fables** are an exception. *See also* **moral**.

thesis, 1162, 2002   central debatable claim articulated, supported, and developed in an essay or other work of expository prose.

third-person narrator   *see* **narrator**.

thrust stage, 1282   stage design that allows the audience to sit around three sides of the major acting area.

time, 280, 1545   in literature, at least four potentially quite different time frames are at issue: (1) *author time*, when the author originally created or published a literary text; (2) *narrator time*, when the **narrator** in a work of fiction supposedly narrated the story; (3) *plot time*, when the action depicted in the work supposedly took place (in other words, the work's temporal **setting**); and (4) *reader* (or *audience*) *time*, when an actual reader reads the work or an actual audience sees it performed.

In some cases, author, narrator, plot, and reader time will be roughly the same. But in some cases, some or all of these time frames might differ. Walter Scott's novel *Rob Roy*, for example, was written and published in the early nineteenth century (1817); this is its author time. But the novel (a work of **historical fiction**) is set one hundred years earlier (1715); this is its plot time. The novel's narrator is a **character** supposedly writing down the story of his youthful adventures in his old age and long after the deaths of many of the principal characters; this is the narrator time. Were you to read the novel today, reader time would be roughly two hundred years later than author time and three hundred years later than plot time.

tone, 177, 497, 771, 855, 871, 954, 974, 1057, 1162, 1285, 2000, 2023   attitude a literary work takes toward its subject or that a character in the work conveys, especially as revealed through diction.

traditional symbol   *see* **symbol**.

tragedy, 86, 1251, 1285, 1392   work, especially of drama, in which a **character** (traditionally a good and noble person of high rank) is brought to a disastrous end in his or her confrontation with a superior force (fortune, the gods, human nature, universal values), but also comes to understand the meaning of his or her deeds and to accept an appropriate punishment. In some cases, the **protagonist**'s downfall can be the direct result of a fatal but common character flaw. Examples include

Sophocles's *Antigone* and William Shakespeare's *Othello*.

trimeter, 976   line of poetry with three **feet**: "Little | lamb, who | made thee?" (William Blake, "The Lamb").

trochaic, 932, 934   referring to a metrical form in which the basic **foot** is a *trochee*—a metrical foot consisting of a stressed syllable followed by an unstressed one ("Hómer").

trope   *see* **figure of speech**.

turning point   *see* **climax**.

underplot, 1392   particular type of **subplot**, especially in Shakespeare's plays, that is a parodic or highly romantic version of the main plot. A good example is the subplot in *A Midsummer Night's Dream* that features the character Bottom. *See also* **overplot**.

understatement, 497   language that makes its point by self-consciously downplaying its real emphasis, as in "Final exams aren't exactly a walk in the park"; **litotes** is one form of understatement. *See also* **overstatement**.

unity of action   *see* **classical unities**.

unity of place   *see* **classical unities**.

unity of time   *see* **classical unities**.

unlimited point of view   *see* **point of view**.

unreliable narrator   *see* **narrator**.

verbal irony   *see* **irony**.

verisimilitude   from the Latin phrase *veri similes* ("like the truth"); the internal truthfulness, lifelikeness, and consistency of the world created within any literary work when we judge that world on its own terms rather than in terms of its correspondence to the real world. Thus, even a work that contains utterly fantastic or supernatural **characters** or **actions** (and doesn't aim at **realism**) may achieve a high degree of verisimilitude.

verse drama   *see* **drama**.

verse novel   *see* **novel**.

verse paragraph   though sometimes used as a synonym for **stanza**, this term technically designates passages of verse, often beginning with an indented line, that are unified by topic (as in a prose paragraph) rather than by **rhyme** or **meter**.

villain, 211, 795, 1278   character who opposes the **hero** or **heroine** (and is thus an **antagonist**) and is characterized as an especially evil person or "bad guy."

villanelle, 977   verse form consisting of nineteen lines divided into six **stanzas**—five tercets (three-line stanzas) and one **quatrain** (four-line stanza). The first and third lines of the first tercet rhyme with each other, and this rhyme is repeated through each of the next four tercets and in the last two lines of the concluding quatrain. The villanelle is also known for its repetition of select lines. An example is Dylan Thomas's "Do Not Go Gentle into That Good Night."

voice, 177   verbal aspect of **point of view**, the acknowledged or unacknowledged source of a story's words; the **speaker**; the "person" telling the story and that person's particular qualities of insight, attitude, and verbal style. *See also* **focus**.